The Norton Anthology of World Literature

SHORTER SECOND EDITION

VOLUME 1

The Norton Anthology
of World Literature

SHORTER SECOND EDITION

VOLUME 1

W • W • NORTON & COMPANY • *New York* • *London*

W. W. Norton & Company has been independent since its founding in 1923, when William Warder Norton and Mary D. Herter Norton first published lectures delivered at the People's Institute, the adult education division of New York City's Cooper Union. The firm soon expanded its program beyond the Institute, publishing books by celebrated academics from America and abroad. By mid-century, the two major pillars of Norton's publishing program— trade books and college texts—were firmly established. In the 1950s, the Norton family trans-ferred control of the company to its employees, and today—with a staff of four hundred and a comparable number of trade, college, and professional titles published each year—W. W. Norton & Company stands as the largest and oldest publishing house owned wholly by its employees.

Editor: Peter Simon
Assistant Editor: Conor Sullivan
Marketing Associate: Katie Hannah
Electronic Media Editor: Eileen Connell
Permissions Management: Margaret Gorenstein, Nancy J. Rodwan
Book Design: Antonina Krass
Production Manager: Jane Searle
Managing Editor, College: Marian Johnson

The text of this book is composed in Fairfield Medium with the display set in Bernhard Mod-ern. Composition by Binghamton Valley Composition. Manufacturing by RR Donnelley & Sons.

ISBN 978-0-393-93302-4 (pbk.)

W. W. Norton & Company, Inc. 500 Fifth Avenue, New York NY 10110
wwnorton.com

W. W. Norton & Company Ltd. Castle House, 75/76 Wells Street, London W1T 3QT

5 6 7 8 9 0

Contents

Ancient Greece and the Formation of the Western Mind

Poetry and Thought in Early China   677

India's Heroic Age 715

The Roman Empire 783

From Roman Empire to Christian Europe   883

China's "Middle Period"

T'ANG POETRY

The Rise of Islam and Islamic Literature   1001

The Formation of a Western Literature 1075

Preface

The Norton Anthology of World Literature, Shorter Second Edition, offers many new works from around the world and a fresh new format that responds to contemporary needs. The global reach of this anthology encompasses important works from Asia and Africa, central Asia and India, the Near East, Europe, and North and South America—all presented in the light of their own literary traditions, as a shared heritage of generations of readers in many countries and as part of a network of cultural and literary relationships whose scope is still being discovered. With this edition, we institute a shift in title that reflects the way the anthology has grown. In altering the current title to *The Norton Anthology of World Literature,* we do not abandon the anthology's focus on major works of literature or a belief that these works especially repay close study. It is their consummate artistry, their ability to express complex signifying structures that give access to multiple dimensions of meaning, meanings that are always rooted in a specific setting and cultural tradition but that further constitute, upon comparison, a thought-provoking set of perspectives on the varieties of human experience. Readers familiar with the anthology's one-volume predecessor, whose size reflected the abundance of material contained within it, will welcome the new boxed format, which divides the anthology's contents into two portable and attractive volumes.

For pedagogical reasons, our structure is guided by the broad continuities of different cultural traditions and the literary or artistic periods they recognize for themselves. This means that chronology advises but does not dictate the order in which works appear. If Western tradition names a certain time slot "the Renaissance" or "the Enlightenment" (each term implying a shared set of beliefs), that designation has little relevance in other parts of the globe; similarly, "vernacular literature" does not have the same literary-historical status in all traditions; and "classical" periods come at different times in India, China, and western Europe. We find that it is more useful to start from a tradition's own sense of itself and the specific shape it gives to the community memory embodied as art. Occasionally there are displacements of absolute chronology: Petrarch, for example, belongs chronologically with Boccaccio and Chaucer, and Rousseau is a contemporary of Voltaire. Each can be read as a new and dissonant voice within his own century, a foil and balance for accepted ideas, or he can be considered as part of a powerful new consciousness, along with those indebted to his thought and example. In the first and last sections of the anthology, for different pedagogical purposes, we have chosen to present diverse cultural traditions together. The first section, "The Invention of Writing and the Earliest Literatures," introduces students to the study of world literature with works from three different cultural traditions—Babylonian, Egyptian, Judaic—each among the oldest works that have come down to us in written form, each in its origins reaching well back into a preliterate past, yet directly accessible as an image of human experience and still provocative at the beginning of the twenty-first century. The last section, "The Twentieth Century," reminds us that separation in the modern world is no longer a possibility. Works in the twentieth century are demonstrably part of a new global consciousness, itself fostered by advances in communications, that experiences reality in terms of interrelationships, of boundaries asserted or transgressed, and of the creation of personal and social identity from the interplay of sameness and difference. We have tried to structure an anthology that is usable, accessible, and engaging in the classroom—that clarifies patterns and relationships for your students, while leaving you free to organize selections from this wealth of material into the themes, genres, topics, and special emphases that best fit your needs.

In renewing this edition, we have taken several routes: introducing new authors, choosing an alternate work by the same author when it resonates with material in other sections or speaks strongly to current concerns, and adding small sections to existing larger pieces to fill out a theme or narrative line or to suggest connections with other texts. What follows is an overview of these changes.

Volume 1

Four new pieces, including Akhenaten's "Hymn to the Sun," have been added to our selection of Egyptian poetry. *The Epic of Gilgamesh* is now offered in Benjamin Foster's recent verse translation. The passages from Genesis and Exodus in the Hebrew Bible are newly translated by Robert Alter and now include the stories of Abraham and Sarah and of Moses receiving the Law. Job is newly translated by Raymond Scheindlin. (The familiar and influential cadence of the King James version is retained in our selections from the Psalms and the Song of Songs.) Selections from Homer's *Iliad*—in a dynamic recent translation by Stanley Lombardo—are newly added to the anthology, joining *The Odyssey*, which is now offered in Robert Fagles's widely praised translation. An expanded selection of Sappho's lyrics are now translated by Anne Carson, and Plato's *Apology*, by C. D. Reeve. The selections from the Chinese "Classic of Poetry" are now translated by Stephen Owen. The *Rāmāyaṇa of Vālmīki* is now offered in an increased selection and a new and exceptionally accessible translation by Swami Venkatesananda. Our selection from Barbara Stoler Miller's translation of *The Bhaghavad-Gītā* is also increased. The selections from both Catullus and Ovid have been augmented, and both are newly offered in translations by Charles Martin. Richmond Lattimore translates the selections from the New Testament. The section "India's Classical Age,"—previously consisting of only the Sanskrit drama *Sakuntala*—now contains selections from Viṣṇuśarman's *Pañcatantra*, Bhartṛhari's *Śatakatrayam*, Amaru's *Amaruśataka*, and Somadeva's *Kathāsaritsāgara*, thus providing a more wide-ranging and teachable introduction to this cultural moment. The surah "Jonah" has been added to an already extensive selection from the Koran, and the poet-mystic Jalâloddin Rumi, is newly added to this edition. One of the anthology's new complete texts is *Beowulf*, in Seamas Heaney's celebrated new translation. Marie de France is now represented by two lais—"Lanval" and "Laüstic"—in a translation by Glyn S. Burgess and Keith Busby. Dante's *Inferno* is now offered in Mark Musa's translation, and a new illustration provides students with a "map" of Dante's hell. Boccaccio's *Decameron* is now represented by three newly selected tales: the first tale of the first day (Ser Cepperello), the eighth story of the fifth day (Nastagio), and the tenth story of the tenth day (Griselda), and the entire selection is newly offered in G. H. McWilliams's translation. Nō drama is now represented by two plays by the great theorist of Nō, Zeami Motokiyo: *Atsumori* and *Haku Rakuten*. Montaigne's essay "Of the Powers of the Imagination" has been newly added, as have a few famous episodes (and the important "Prologue" to Part II) from Cervantes's *Don Quixote*.

Volume 2

Our collection of Chinese vernacular literature adds a selection from Wu Ch'eng-en's *Monkey*. Rousseau's *Confessions* is offered in an expanded selection and in a new translation by J. M. Cohen. We are especially pleased to offer Goethe's *Faust*, Part I, in Martin Greenberg's remarkable translation. Newly included lyric poets from the nineteenth century are Friedrich Hölderlin, John Keats, Heinrich Heine, Giacomo Leopardi, Victor Hugo, and Arthur Rimbaud. Our selection of Walt Whitman now adds "Out of the Cradle Endlessly Rocking." Henrik Ibsen's *Hedda Gabler* is now offered in a new translation by Rick Davis and Brian Johnston. The twentieth-century selection begins with another new complete work, Joseph Conrad's *Heart of Darkness*. The poets William Butler Yeats and Federico García Lorca are newly included. Virginia Woolf is now represented by chapters two and three of *A Room of Her Own*. Franz Kafka's *Metamorphosis* is offered in a new translation by Michael Hoffman. Closing out our selection, in addition to Chinua Achebe's *Things Fall Apart*, still offered in its entirety, are newly included short stories by Albert Camus, Tadeusz Borowski, Mahasweta Devi, Gabriel García Márquez, Nawal el Saadawi, and Leslie Marmon Silko.

The Shorter Second Edition contains all of the pedagogical support to which our users are accustomed: maps, time lines, pronunciation glossaries, and, of course, the informative introductions and notes. The thirty-two color plates new to this edition are captioned and broadly coordinated with each period. In addition, *The Norton Anthology of World Literature* now provides free access to Norton Literature Online, Norton's extensive online resource for students of literature. Each section of *The Norton Anthology of World Literature* has added new material to old favorites, allowing the teacher to keep tried-and-true works and also to experiment with different contexts and combinations. Some links are suggested by the organization of the table of contents, but there is no prescribed way of using the anthology, and we are confident that the materials presented here offer a wealth of viable options to support customized syllabi geared to specific student needs. A separate *Instructor's Guide*, with further suggestions and helpful guidance for new and experienced instructors alike, is available from the publisher on request.

Acknowledgments

Among our many critics, advisers, and friends, the following were of special help in providing suggestions and corrections: Joseph Barbarese (Rutgers University); Carol Clover (University of California, Berkeley); Patrick J. Cook (George Washington University); Janine Gerzanics (University of Southern California); Matthew Giancarlo (Yale University); Kevis Goodman (University of California at Berkeley); Roland Greene (University of Oregon); Dmitri Gutas (Yale University); John H. Hayes (Emory University); H. Mack Horton (University of California at Berkeley); Suzanne Keen (Washington and Lee University); Charles S. Kraszewski (King's College); Gregory F. Kuntz; Michelle Latiolais (University of California at Irvine); Sharon L. James (Bryn Mawr College); Ivan Marcus (Yale University); Timothy Martin (Rutgers University, Camden); William Naff, University of Massachusetts; Stanley Radosh Our Lady of the Elms College; Fred C. Robinson (Yale University); John Rogers (Yale University); Robert Rothstein (University of Massachusetts); Lawrence Senelick (Boston University); Jack Shreve (Alleghany Community College); Frank Stringfellow (University of Miami); Nancy Vickers (Bryn Mawr College); and Jack Welch (Abilene Christian University).

We would also like to thank the following people who contributed to the planning of the Second Edition: Charles Adams, University of Arkansas; Dorothy S. Anderson, Salem State College; Roy Anker, Calvin College; John Apwah, County College of Morris; Doris Bargen, University of Massachusetts; Carol Barrett, Austin Community College, Northridge Campus; Michael Beard, University of North Dakota; Lysbeth Em Berkert, Northern State University; Marilyn Booth, University of Illinois; George Byers, Fairmont State College; Shirley Carnahan, University of Colorado; Ngwarsungu Chiwengo, Creighton University; Stephen Cooper, Troy State University; Bonita Cox, San Jose State University; Richard A. Cox, Abilene Christian University; Dorothy Deering, Purdue University; Donald Dickson, Texas A&M University; Alexander Dunlop, Auburn University; Janet Eber, County College of Morris; Angela Esterhammer, University of Western Ontario; Walter Evans, Augusta State University; Fidel Fajardo-Acosta, Creighton University; John C. Freeman, El Paso Community College, Valle Verde Campus; Barbara Gluck, Baruch College; Michael Grimwood, North Carolina State University; Rafey Habib, Rutgers University, Camden; John E. Hallwas, Western Illinois College; Jim Hauser, William Patterson College; Jack Hussey, Fairmont State College; Dane Johnson, San Francisco State University; Andrew Kelley, Jackson State Community College; Jane Kinney, Valdosta State University; Candace Knudson, Truman State University; Jameela Lares, University of Southern Mississippi; Thomas L. Long, Thomas Nelson Community College; Sara MacDonald, Sterling College; Linda Macri, University of Maryland; Rita Mayer, San

Antonio College; Christopher Morris, Norwich University; Deborah Nestor, Fairmont State College; John Netland, Calvin College; Kevin O'Brien, Chapman University; Mariannina Olcott, San Jose State University; Charles W. Pollard, Calvin College; Pilar Rotella, Chapman University; Rhonda Sandford, Fairmont State College; Daniel Schenker, University of Alabama at Huntsville; Robert Scotto, Baruch College; Carl Seiple, Kutztown University; Glenn Simshaw, Chemeketa Community College; Evan Lansing Smith, Midwestern State University; William H. Smith, Piedmont College; Floyd C. Stuart, Norwich University; Cathleen Tarp, Fairmont State College; Diane Thompson, Northern Virginia Community College; Sally Wheeler, Georgia Perimeter College; Jean Wilson, McMaster University; Susan Wood, University of Nevada, Las Vegas; Tom Wymer, Bowling Green State University.

Phonetic Equivalents

For use with the Pronouncing Glossaries preceding most
selections in this volume

a as in *cat*
ah as in *father*
ai as in *light*
aw as in *raw*
ay as in *day*
e as in *pet*
ee as in *street*
ehr as in *air*
er as in *bird*
eu as in *lurk*
g as in *good*
i as in *sit*
j as in *joke*
nh a nasal sound (as in French *vin, vẽ*)
o as in *pot*
oh as in *no*
oo as in *boot*
or as in *bore*
ow as in *now*
oy as in *toy*
s as in *mess*
ts as in *ants*
u as in *us*
zh as in *vision*

The Norton Anthology
of World Literature

SHORTER SECOND EDITION

VOLUME 1

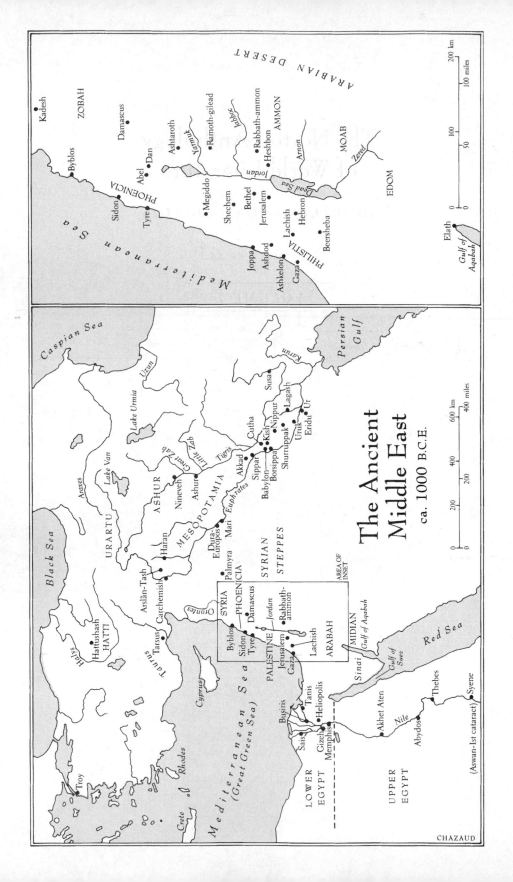

The Ancient
Middle East
ca. 1000 B.C.E.

CHAZAUD

The Invention of Writing
and the Earliest
Literatures

Long before people learned to write, they made up and told stories; they composed and sang songs. Because people who have not learned to write must develop a retentive and accurate memory, such stories and songs could be preserved for generations in something like their original form or could be improved, expanded, or combined with other material to be passed on as, so to speak, another edition. But such oral traditional literature can be irrevocably lost if it is not transferred to a written medium; a sudden catastrophic break in the life of the community—foreign conquest, for example, which was always a present danger in the clash of ancient empires—might easily, through massacre, enslavement, and mass deportation, wipe out the memory of what had been a shared inheritance.

Writing, which has preserved some ancient literatures for us, was not invented for that purpose. The earliest written documents we have contain commercial, administrative, political, and legal information. They are the records of the first advanced, centralized civilizations, those that emerged in the area we know as the Middle East.

Ancient civilization was based on agriculture, and it flourished first in regions where the soil gave rich rewards: in the valley of the Nile, where annual floods left large tracts of land moist and fertile under the Egyptian sun, and in the valleys of the Euphrates and Tigris rivers, which flowed through the Fertile Crescent, a region centered on modern Iraq. Great cities—Thebes and Memphis in Egypt and Babylon and Nineveh in the Fertile Crescent—came into being as centers for the complicated administration of the irrigated fields. Supported by the surplus the land produced, they became centers also for government, religion, and culture. Civilization begins with cities; the word itself is derived from a Latin word that means "citizen." As far back as 3000 B.C.E. the pharaohs of Egypt began to build their splendid temples and gigantic pyramids as well as to record their political acts and religious beliefs in hieroglyphic script. The Sumerians, Babylonians, and Assyrians began to build the palaces and temples of Babylon and record their laws in cuneiform script on clay tablets.

It was in the region of the Tigris and Euphrates rivers that writing was first developed; the earliest texts date from around 3300 to 2990 B.C.E. The characters were inscribed on tablets of wet clay with a pointed stick; the tablets were then left in the sun to bake to hardness. The characters are pictographic: the sign for *ox* looks like an ox head and so on. The bulk of the texts are economic—lists of foodstuffs, textiles, and cattle. But the script is too primitive to handle anything much more complicated than lists, and by 2800 B.C.E. scribes began to use the wedge-shaped end of the stick to make marks rather than the pointed end to draw pictures. The resulting script is known as cuneiform, from the Latin word *cuneus,* "a wedge." By 2500 B.C.E. the texts were no longer confined to lists; they record historical events and even material that can be regarded as literature.

This writing system was not, however, designed for a large reading public. The wedge-shaped signs, grouped in various patterns, denote not letters of an alphabet but syllables—consonants plus a vowel—and this meant that the reader had to be familiar with a very large number of signs. Furthermore, the same sign often represents two or more different sounds, and the same sound can be represented by several different signs. It is a script that could be written and read only by experts—the scribes, who often proudly recorded their own names on the tablets.

It was, however, the most efficient system yet devised, and it stayed in use through all the historical vicissitudes of more than two millennia: the rise and fall of new dynasties and new conquerors, who became in their turn masters of the Fertile Crescent—Akkadians, Babylonians, Hittites, and Assyrians—until the area was incorporated in the Persian empire of Cyrus, who captured Babylon in 539 B.C.E. When in the fourth century B.C.E. the area became part of the Greek kingdom of one of the successors of Alexander the Great, the ancient script gradually fell out of use; the latest specimens to survive come from the first century C.E.

It was on clay tablets and in cuneiform script that the great Sumerian epic poem *Gilgamesh* was written down, in differing versions and in the different languages of the successive conquerors of the fertile river valleys, only to disappear in the ruins of the cities and be totally forgotten until modern excavators discovered the tablets and deciphered the enigmatic script that had preserved the poem through so many centuries.

The writing system invented by the Egyptians was even more esoteric than cuneiform. It is called hieroglyphic, an adjective formed from the Greek words for "sacred" and "carving." Although it appears on many different materials, its most conspicuous and continuous use was for inscriptions carved on the temple walls and public monuments. It was pictographic, like the earliest Sumerian script, but the pictures were more elaborate and artistic. Unlike the Sumerian pictographs, they were not replaced by a more efficient system; the pictures remained in use for the walls of temples and tombs, while more cursive versions of hieroglyphics—the hieratic and demotic scripts—were developed for faster writing. A writing system consisting of logograms (pictures standing for objects) is obviously incapable of communicating anything but the simplest of ideas, and at a very early stage the logograms were used to denote consonantal sounds. The Egyptian word for "house," for example, was *pr,* and its logogram was a rectangle with a gap in one of the long sides to indicate the door. The sign could still mean "house," but it could now also be used, in combination with other logograms indicating sounds, to denote simply the sound *pr.* This was only one of many complications that made even the modified versions of the script a difficult medium of communication for anyone not trained in its intricacies. The fact that only the consonantal sounds were represented (we do not know what vowel was sounded between the *p* and the *r* of *pr*) was one more barrier to easy interpretation. It is no wonder that one of the frequent figures to appear in Egyptian sculpture and painting is the professional scribe, his legs tucked underneath him, his writing material in his lap, and his brush in his hand.

Unlike the cuneiform tablets that remained buried, waiting for the trowel of the excavator, the Egyptian hieroglyphs were carved on the walls of ruined temples and remained open to view but defied interpretation. The key to the solution of the problem came in 1799, when some French soldiers of Napoleon's army, digging the foundation for a redoubt in Egypt, unearthed a large block of basalt, the Rosetta stone, on which was a text inscribed in three different versions. Two were Egyptian, one hieroglyphic and one demotic, and the other was in Greek, which had been the official language of Egypt ever since Ptolemy, one of Alexander's generals, had established himself as pharaoh in Egypt after Alexander died in 323 B.C.E.

There was one ancient writing system that, unlike cuneiform and hieroglyphic, was destined to survive, in modified forms, until the present day. It was a script developed by the Semitic peoples of the area, notably the enterprising Phoenicians, whose seaports on the Palestine coast, Tyre and Sidon, were bases for trading ventures and colonial expeditions to distant seas. The script consisted of twenty-two simple signs for consonantal sounds, an alphabet, to use the later Greek term, that could be easily learned. The Phoenicians have left us no literary texts, but the Hebrews, another Semitic people, used the system to record in a collection of books—part of which became what Christians call the Old Testament—their history; their sorrows and triumphs; and, above all, their concept, unique in the polytheistic ancient world, of a single god.

Unlike the rulers of the Tigris-Euphrates and Nile valleys, the Hebrews, located in Palestine, did not control territory of economic or military importance; their record is not that of an imperial people. In their period of independence, from their beginnings as a pastoral tribe to their high point as a kingdom with a splendid capital in Jerusalem, they accomplished little of note in the political or military spheres. Their later history was a bitter and unsuccessful struggle for freedom against a series of foreign masters—Babylonian, Greek, and Roman.

After the period of expansion and prosperity under the great kings David and Solomon (1005–925 B.C.E.), the kingdom fell apart into warring factions, which called in outside powers. The melancholy end of a long period of internal and external struggle was the destruction of the cities and the deportation of the population to Babylon (586 B.C.E.). This period of exile (which ended in 539 B.C.E. when Cyrus, the Persian conqueror of Babylon, released the Hebrews from bondage) was a formative period for Hebrew religious thought, which was enriched and refined by the teachings of the prophet Ezekiel and the prophet known as the second Isaiah. The return to Palestine was crowned by the rebuilding of the Temple and the creation of the canonical version of the Pentateuch, or Torah—the first five books of the Bible. The religious legacy of the Hebrew people was now codified for future generations.

But the independent state of Israel was not destined to last long. By 300 B.C.E. the Macedonian successors of Alexander the Great had encroached on its borders and prerogatives; in spite of a heroic resistance, the territory eventually became part of a Hellenistic Greek-speaking kingdom and, finally, was absorbed by the Roman empire. A desperate revolt against Rome was crushed in 70 C.E. by the emperor Titus (on the arch of Titus in Rome a relief shows the legionaries carrying a seven-branched menorah, or candlestick, in Titus' triumph). In 131–134 C.E., a second revolt, against the emperor Hadrian, resulted in the final extermination or removal from Palestine of the Hebrew people. Henceforward, they were the people of the *Diaspora,* the "scattering": religious communities in the great cities of the ancient world who maintained local cohesion and universal religious solidarity but who were stateless, as they were to be all through the centuries until the creation, in the mid-twentieth century, of the state of Israel.

The political history of the ancient Hebrews ended in a series of disasters. In the field of the arts they left behind them no painting or sculpture and little or no secular literature—no drama, for example, no epic poetry. What they did leave us is a religious literature, written down probably between the eighth and second centuries B.C.E., which is informed by an attitude different from that of any other nation of the ancient world. It is founded on the idea of one God, the creator of all things, all-powerful and just—a conception of the divine essence and the government of the universe so simple that to those of us who have inherited it, it seems obvious. But in its time it was so revolutionary that it made the Hebrews a nation apart, sometimes laughed at, sometimes feared, but always alien.

The consonantal script in which their literary legacy was handed down to us was a great step forward from the hieroglyphic and cuneiform systems; writing now called for no artistic skills and reading, for no long period of training. But it was still an unsatisfactory medium for mass communication; the absence of notation for the vowels made for ambiguity and possible misreading and, at times, may have called for inspired guesswork. We still do not know, for example, what the vowel sounds were in the sacred name of God, often called the Tetragrammaton, because it consists of four letters; in our alphabet the name is written as YHWH. The usual surmise is Jahweh (*ya'-way*), but for a long time the traditional English-language version was Jehovah.

One thing was needed to make the script fully efficient: signs for the vowels. And this was the contribution of the Greeks, who, in the eighth or possibly the ninth century B.C.E., adopted the Phoenician script for their own language but used for the vowels some Phoenician signs that stood for consonantal combinations not native to Greek. They took over (but soon modified) the Phoenician letter shapes and also their names: *alpha*, a meaningless word in Greek, represents the original *aleph* ("ox"), and *beta* represents the original *beta* ("house"). The Greeks were frank to admit their indebtedness; Greek myths told the story of Cadmus, king of Tyre, who taught the Greeks how to write; and as the historian Herodotus tells us, the letters were called Phoenician. But in fact the Greek creation of signs for the vowels produced the first real alphabet, and the Romans, who adapted it for their own language, carved their inscriptions on stone in the same capital letters that we still use today.

TIME LINE

TEXTS	CONTEXTS
	ca. 3000 B.C.E. Mesopotamia: Sumerian cuneiform writing on clay tablets • Egypt: writing in hieroglyphic script
	2700 Gilgamesh is king in Uruk
	ca. 2575–2130 Old Kingdom (Egypt) • Great Pyramids; Sphinx
	ca. 2130–1540 Middle Kingdom (Egypt)
ca. 2000 B.C.E. Legends about King Gilgamesh appear on clay tablets	
	ca. 1900 Hebrew migration from Mesopotamia begins
	18th century Hammurabi's Code of Law written in Babylon
1600 The epic of *Gilgamesh* begins to take shape	
1500 Egyptian *Book of the Dead*	**ca. 1539–1200** New Kingdom (Egypt)
1375–1358 Akhenaten's "Hymn to the Sun" composed	**1375–1354** King Akhenaten dedicates his capital to Aten, the sun god
1300 The epic of *Gilgamesh* written down	
1300–1100 Love lyrics of the New Kingdom composed	
1238 *The Leiden Hymns* written down	
	ca. 1200 Moses leads the Jews in Exodus from Egypt to Palestine
1000 The Torah text assembled • Psalms	**1000–925** David, then Solomon, king in Israel

Boldface titles indicate works in the anthology.

TIME LINE

TEXTS	CONTEXTS
6th century Aesop's *Fables*	
	586 Jerusalem captured by Babylonian king Nebuchadnezzar; many Jews taken to exile in Babylon
	539 The Persian shah Cyrus the Great conquers Babylon and allows the Jews to return to Israel. He founds the Iranian empire, which later envelops most of the Middle East and Central Asia
	525 Cambyses, king of Persia, conquers Egypt
ca. 450 Herodotus, *History*	
	331–330 Alexander the Great conquers Syria, Mesopotamia, and Iran; defeats the last Persian army at Sungamela and occupies Babylon and Persopolis
	330–323 Alexander conquers Central Asia and the Indus Valley, but dies in Babylon (323). His generals divide up the empire. Seleucus becomes king of Syria, Mesopotamia, and Iran; Ptolemy, of Egypt
	202–198 Palestine falls to Antiochus III, king of a land empire stretching east from Asia Minor • Rome defeats Antiochus III in 190 • Successful Jewish revolt against Antiochus IV between 173 and 167
	40–4 Herod is king of Judaea
	30 Rome conquers Egypt

GILGAMESH

ca. 2500–1500 B.C.E.

Gilgamesh is a poem of unparalleled antiquity, the first great heroic narrative of world literature. Its origins stretch back to the margins of prehistory, and its evolution spans millennia. When it was known, it was widely known. The Tablets containing portions of *Gilgamesh* have been found at sites throughout the Middle East and in all the languages written in cuneiform characters, wedge-shaped characters incised in clay or stone. But then, at a time when the civilizations of the Hebrews, Greeks, and Romans had only just developed beyond their infancy, *Gilgamesh* vanished from memory. For reasons that scholars have not yet fathomed, the literature of the cuneiform languages was not translated into the new alphabets that replaced them. Some portions of this once-famous work survived in subsequent traditions, but they did so as scattered and anonymous fragments. They became a kind of invisible substratum that was buried under what was previously believed to be the earliest level of our common tradition. Until Utnapishtim's "Story of the Flood," a portion of *Gilgamesh,* was accidentally rediscovered and published in 1872, no one suspected that the biblical story of Noah and the great flood was neither original nor unique.

The story of Gilgamesh and his companion, Enkidu, speaks to contemporary readers with astonishing immediacy. Its moving depiction of the bonds of friendship, of the quest for worldly renown, and of the tragic attempt to escape that death which is the common fate of humanity has a timeless resonance and appeal. Yet despite this immediate recognition of something profoundly familiar there is, because of the millennial gap in the history of its transmission, a strangeness and remoteness about the work that strikes us in virtually every line. That strangeness has diminished each year as more tablets have been discovered and translated and as our understanding of the languages and cultures of the ancient Middle East has increased, but what we know is still relatively slight compared with what we know of the cultures that succeeded them. Today the names of Ulysses and Achilles and the gods and goddesses of Mount Olympus are familiar even to many who have not read Homer. The names of Gilgamesh, Enkidu, Utnapishtim, Enlil, and Ea are virtually unknown outside the poem itself.

Gilgamesh developed over a period of nearly a thousand years. The version discovered in the city of Nineveh amid the ruins of the great royal library of Assurbanipal, the last great king of the Assyrian empire—what modern scholars now call the Stan dard Version—circulated widely throughout the ancient Middle East for a millennium or more. While the history of the text is a long and complex one, and is still far from fully understood, it is possible to identify three principal stages in its development. The first begins in roughly 2700 B.C.E. when the historical Gilgamesh ruled in Uruk, a city in ancient Mesopotamia. Tales both mythical and legendary grew up around him and were repeated and copied for centuries. The stories that were later incorporated into the *Gilgamesh* epic existed in this literature, albeit in different form, as well as in other material concerning the historical Gilgamesh that was not included in the epic. The earliest written versions of these stories date from roughly 2000 B.C.E., but oral versions of the stories both preceded them and continued on, parallel to the written tradition. The language of these materials was Sumerian, the earliest written language in Mesopotamia and one that has little if any connection to any other known language.

The history of the epic itself begins sometime before 1600 B.C.E., some eight centuries before Homer, when a Babylonian author (Mesopotamian tradition identifies a priest-exorcist named Sîn-leqi-unninni) assembled free translations of the oral versions of some of these tales into a connected narrative. This new work was not simply a sequence of tales linked by the character of Gilgamesh but a conscious selection and recasting of the Sumerian materials into a new form. Some Gilgamesh tales were ignored, while elements from stories not associated with him in the Sumerian accounts were incorporated. This earliest version of the epic, which exists only in fragmentary form, continued to develop for the next few centuries. However, no comparable recasting of the poem was made. By the time of Assurbanipal (ruled 668–627 B.C.E.) the text was essentially stabilized.

Assurbanipal's synthetic version—the Standard Version—was also the first discovered. It was written on twelve hardened clay tablets in Akkadian, a Semitic language like Hebrew and Arabic and one of the principal languages of Babylonia and Assyria. The first eleven of these tablets make up the story as printed here. The twelfth tells another story of Gilgamesh, "Gilgamesh and the Underworld," and because it is unclear how it is to be incorporated into the preceding tablets, it is usually presented as a kind of appendix to the story.

The tablets of the Standard Version are poorly preserved at a number of points, most notably in the adventure in the Cedar Forest. The translation printed here is a poetic version based on the Standard Version of *Gilgamesh* with some interpolations from older manuscripts. Benjamin R. Foster is a professor and translator of ancient Near Eastern languages and literature, an anthologist of ancient Mesopotamian literature, and a scholar experienced in the verbal intricacies and stylistic peculiarities of Akkadian texts; his aim is to provide, in readable English, a close approximation of the ancient epic. Foster preserves the repetitions that charmed the Babylonian audience, reproduces patterns of diction (e.g., Utanapishtim's elevated, sagelike speech), does not ease the difficulty of problematic passages, and tries whenever possible to re-create the characteristic wordplay—humorous or serious—permeating the text. His text recaptures the pattern of traditional Mesopotamian poetry, in which each line offers a complete sentence or idea. Insofar as it is possible, his translation offers a word-for-word rendition of the Akkadian text. Like other modern editors of ancient manuscripts, he leaves gaps when passages are missing and uses various symbols to identify textual problems. Square brackets enclose important words that are visible in the text and whose meaning seems clear—though that meaning has not been established in other manuscripts. Square brackets enclosing ellipses mark places where the characters are clear but the translator cannot guess their meaning. Question marks within parentheses indicate uncertain restorations, and simple parentheses set off explanatory additions by the translator. Foster's translation presents a *Gilgamesh* of its own time and cultural context, consciously preserving much of its strangeness and mystery for today's readers.

The epic narrates the legendary deeds of Gilgamesh, king of Uruk, but it begins with a prologue that emphasizes not his adventures but the wisdom he acquired and the monuments he constructed at the end of his epic journey. It also tells us that Gilgamesh was endowed by his divine creators with extraordinary strength, courage, and beauty. He is more god than man. His father, however, is mortal, and that fact is decisive in shaping the narrative that follows. The prologue also suggests that Gilgamesh himself has written this account and left the tablets in the foundation of the city wall of Uruk for all to read.

In our first view of him, Gilgamesh is the epitome of a bad ruler: arrogant, oppressive, and brutal. The people of Uruk complain of his oppression to the Sumerian gods, and the gods' response is to create Enkidu as a foil or counterweight to Gilgamesh. Whereas Gilgamesh is a mixture of human and divine, Enkidu, who also appears godlike, is a blend of human and wild animal, with the animal predominating at first. He is raised by wild beasts, lives as they do, and embodies the conflict between animal and human natures that is a recurrent theme in Mesopotamian literature and myth. When he becomes a kind of protector of the animals, breaking the hunters' traps and filling in their pits, Enkidu poses a threat to the human community. This threat is neutralized by civilizing him. First a harlot (prostitute) seduces him across the line separating animal from human and educates him in the elements of human society. Then shepherds teach him to eat prepared food, wear clothing, and anoint himself as humans do. He is weakened somewhat by this transformation and estranged from his animal companions, but he is also glorified and made greater than he was. The prostitute leads him to Uruk and the confrontation with Gilgamesh for which the gods have created him. His coming has been announced to Gilgamesh in one of the many dreams that play such an important role in the poem. Although the two are bent on destroying each other at first, their encounter results, as it was meant to, in a deep bond of friendship. Each finds in the other the true companion he has sought. The consequence of their union is that their prodigious energies are directed outward toward heroic achievements.

Gilgamesh proposes the first of their adventures both to gain them universal renown and to refresh the spirit of Enkidu, who has been weakened and confused by civilization. He suggests that they go to the great Cedar Forest in the Country of the Living and there slay the terrible giant Humbaba. Enkidu is reluctant at first because he knows the danger in this adventure better than Gilgamesh. But the latter prevails, and with the blessing of the sun god, Shamash, they succeed. Their victory is not a simple, glorious triumph, however, and its meaning is unclear. Humbaba poses no apparent threat to Uruk and its people, and he curses them before he dies. Enlil, the god of wind and storm, is enraged by the slaying of his creature, curses the heroes, and gives to others the seven splendors that had been Humbaba's.

Their second adventure is not of their choosing and also leads to another ambiguous success. Gilgamesh's just but harsh rejection of Ishtar's advances provokes her to send the Bull of Heaven against the people of Uruk. The terrible destruction the Bull causes obliges Gilgamesh and Enkidu to destroy it, but that victory brings about the slow and painful death of Enkidu.

The death of his companion reveals to Gilgamesh the hollowness of mortal fame and leads him to undertake a solitary journey in search of immortality. This journey sets *Gilgamesh* apart from more straightforward heroic narratives and gives it a special appeal to modern readers. Gilgamesh's specific goal is to discover the secret of immortality from the one man, Utnapishtim, who has survived the Flood. His journey begins with a conventional challenge, the fierce lions who guard the mountain passes. But the challenges he faces subsequently—the dark tunnel that brings him to a prototypical garden of paradise, the puzzling and perilous voyage to Dilmun—have a different and more magical character. He is discouraged at every step, but Gilgamesh perseveres. Although he at last finds Utnapishtim and hears his story, his goal eludes him. He fails a simple test of his potential for immortality when he cannot remain awake for six days and seven nights. Moreover, he fails a second test as well when he first finds the plant that ensures eternal rejuvenation and then, in a moment of carelessness, loses it to the serpent. Discouraged and defeated, Gilgamesh returns at last to Uruk empty-handed. His consolation is the assurance that his worldly accomplishments will endure beyond his own lifetime.

In long, belated retrospect we can see that *Gilgamesh* explores many of the mysteries of the human condition for the first time in our literature—the complex and perilous relations between gods and mortals and between nature and civilization, the depths of friendship, and the immortality of art. It is both humbling and thrilling to hear so familiar a voice from so vast a distance.

Gilgamesh[1]

Translator's Note

[*Western literary tradition since classical antiquity has transmitted ancient works, such as the epics of Homer or the plays of Sophocles, as single unified texts with only minor "variants." This term refers to changes in wording for the same passage from one manuscript to another, or to important passages omitted in some manuscripts but included in others. For the most part, however, there are no substantive deviations among manuscripts of the same classical work, even those from centuries apart. Furthermore, ancient classical literature that survives only in fragments or quotations, such as the poetry of Sappho, has little chance of ever being pieced together into its original form, because it was written on perishable materials.*

The situation for ancient Mesopotamian texts is quite different. For The Epic of Gilgamesh, there are numerous ancient manuscripts on durable clay tablets, some more than a thousand years older than others, from many places. When these deal with the same episodes, they show fascinating and significant variations in wording and content. This allows us to see what was added, subtracted, changed, and reinterpreted over the centuries, but it complicates presentation of the text to a modern reader. Since no single version of The Epic of Gilgamesh has survived intact from antiquity, any translator has to make difficult decisions about how to treat the material. The method followed here has been to take as the basic text the Standard Version. These are later copies of the eleven-tablet edition associated with Sin-leqe-unninni. Where lines, sections, or episodes are missing or omitted from this version, I have supplied them where possible from other versions, both earlier and later. There is no consistent line numbering for any original text of The Epic of Gilgamesh. The line numbers used here refer to lines of the translation only.

Even when all versions are consulted, there are still major gaps in the narrative, as well as in individual lines or passages. Editors and translators have guessed about what the missing elements might have been; new discoveries often prove these guesses wrong. In this translation, important words or phrases not found in any ancient manuscript and not restorable from surviving traces or parallel passages are enclosed in square brackets, meaning that these are only modern interpretive surmises. Where such inferences are not possible, square brackets enclose ellipses. Question marks within parentheses following words or phrases indicate particularly uncertain restorations that might have a significant impact upon the meaning of the passage. Words or phrases in parentheses indicate explanatory additions by the translator. Ellipses without brackets indicate signs or words of unknown meaning.

It is important to remember that the ancient languages in which The Epic of Gilgamesh was written or translated, including Akkadian, Sumerian, and Hittite, are not so well understood as other ancient languages, such as Greek and Latin. This means that translators frequently disagree among themselves as to what a given word or phrase could mean. While this translation is based on study of the ancient manuscripts, consultation of the extensive scholarly literature about the epic, and comparison with the best modern translations, it remains a more individual product than a translation of a work by Homer or Virgil is likely to be. The goal has been to produce a readable text well grounded in the ancient sources. New discoveries constantly enlarge our understanding of the epic, whose genius and power can still move the modern reader four thousand years after it was written.]

---

1. Translated by Benjamin R. Foster.

Tablet I

[*The prologue introduces Gilgamesh as a man who gained knowledge through exceptional trials. The narrator invites us to read Gilgamesh's account of his hardships and to admire the city walls and treasury for the goddess Ishtar, his architectural legacy in Uruk.*]

He who saw the wellspring, the foundations of the land,
Who knew [. . .], was wise in all things,
Gilgamesh, who saw the wellspring, the foundations of the land,
Who knew [. . .], was wise in all things,
[He . . .] throughout,   5
Full understanding of it all he gained,
He saw what was secret and revealed what was hidden,
He brought back tidings from before the flood,
From a distant journey came home, weary, at peace,
Engraved all his hardships on a monument of stone,   10
He built the walls of ramparted Uruk,
The lustrous treasury of hallowed Eanna![2]
See its upper wall, whose facing gleams like copper,
Gaze at the lower course, which nothing will equal,
Mount the stone stairway, there from days of old,   15
Approach Eanna, the dwelling of Ishtar,[3]
Which no future king, no human being will equal.
Go up, pace out the walls of Uruk,
Study the foundation terrace and examine the brickwork.
Is not its masonry of kiln-fired brick?   20
And did not seven masters lay its foundations?
One square mile of city, one square mile of gardens,
One square mile of clay pits, a half square mile of Ishtar's
    dwelling,
Three and a half square miles is the measure of Uruk!
[Search out] the foundation box of copper,   25
[Release] its lock of bronze,
Raise the lid upon its hidden contents,
Take up and read from the lapis tablet
Of him, Gilgamesh, who underwent many hardships.

[*The narrator tells of the extraordinary characteristics of Gilgamesh. An old version of the epic began here.*]

Surpassing all kings, for his stature renowned,   30
Heroic offspring of Uruk, a charging wild bull,
He leads the way in the vanguard,
He marches at the rear, defender of his comrades.
Mighty floodwall, protector of his troops,
Furious flood-wave smashing walls of stone,   35
Wild calf of Lugalbanda,[3] Gilgamesh is perfect in strength,

2. Eanna: the temple precinct, sacred to the god Anu (father of all other gods) and the goddess Ishtar (goddess of love, fertility, and war), located in the city of Uruk. An important city in southern Babylonia, Uruk was the seat of a dynasty of kings (among whom Gilgamesh was the fifth and most famous) after the great flood.   3. Lugalbanda: third king of Uruk and Gilgamesh's father.

Suckling of the sublime wild cow, the woman Ninsun,[4]
Towering Gilgamesh is uncannily perfect.
Opening passes in the mountains,
Digging wells at the highlands' verge,   40
Traversing the ocean, the vast sea, to the sun's rising,
Exploring the furthest reaches of the earth,
Seeking everywhere for eternal life,
Reaching in his might Utanapishtim the Distant One,[5]
Restorer of holy places that the deluge had destroyed,   45
Founder of rites for the teeming peoples,
Who could be his like for kingly virtue?[6]
And who, like Gilgamesh, can proclaim, "I am king!"
Gilgamesh was singled out from the day of his birth,
Two-thirds of him was divine, one-third of him was human!   50
The Lady of Birth drew his body's image,
The God of Wisdom brought his stature to perfection.[7]

                              [gap]

[. . .] stately in feature,
[. . .] in body, lofty [. . .]
His foot was a triple cubit,[8] his leg six times twelve,   55
His stride was six times twelve cubits,
His thumb was [. . .] cubits.
His cheeks had a beard like [. . .]
The locks of his hair grew thick as a grainfield.
He was perfection in height,   60
Ideally handsome [. . .]

[*Gilgamesh, in his arrogance and superior strength, abuses his subjects, apparently through some strenuous athletic competition at which he excelled. At the complaint of the citizenry, the gods create a wild man, Enkidu, as a fitting rival for Gilgamesh.*]

In the enclosure of Uruk he strode back and forth,
Lording it like a wild bull, his head thrust high.
The onslaught of his weapons had no equal.
His teammates stood forth by his game stick,   65
He was harrying the young men of Uruk beyond reason.
Gilgamesh would leave no son to his father,
Day and night he would rampage fiercely.
Gilgamesh [. . .]
This was the shepherd of ramparted Uruk,   70
This was the people's shepherd,
Bold, superb, accomplished, and mature!

4. Ninsun: Gilgamesh's mother.   **5.** Utnapishtim and his wife were the only humans saved from the great flood, and the only humans given immortality by the gods. Gilgamesh will seek out Utnapishtim (in Tablet 9) in his own quest for eternal life.   **6.** Mesopotamian rulers sometimes boasted of restoring ancient temples that had been destroyed and forgotten long ago. In line 45, the poet suggests that Gilgamesh became a dutiful king of this kind. Mesopotamian rulers also sometimes boasted of endowing temples with new offerings. This pair of lines (45–46) thus sums up religious duties expected of a good king [*Translator's note*].   **7.** According to one Mesopotamian tradition, the first human being was created by Mami, goddess of birth, whom the gods thereupon rewarded with the title "Mistress of All the Gods," and Enki, god of wisdom, working together. Subsequent human beings were born naturally. This passage means that Gilgamesh was physically a perfect human being, so much so that he resembled the first human created by the gods more than the product of a normal birth [*Translator's note*].   **8.** An ancient unit of measure corresponding roughly to the length of an adult-male forearm.

Gilgamesh would leave no girl to her [mother]!
The warrior's daughter, the young man's spouse,
Goddesses kept hearing their plaints.[9]   75
The gods of heaven, the lords who command,
[Said to Anu]:

> You created this headstrong wild bull in ramparted Uruk,
> The onslaught of his weapons has no equal.
> His teammates stand forth by his game stick,   80
> He is harrying the young men of Uruk beyond reason.
> Gilgamesh leaves no son to his father!
> Day and night he rampages fiercely.
> This is the shepherd of ramparted Uruk,
> This is the people's shepherd,   85
> Bold, superb, accomplished, and mature!
> Gilgamesh leaves no girl to her [mother]!

The warrior's daughter, the young man's spouse,
Anu(?) kept hearing their plaints.

[*Anu speaks.*]

> Let them summon [Aruru], the great one,   90
> [She created] the boundless human race.
> [Let her create a partner for Gilgamesh], mighty in strength,
> [Let them contend with each other], that Uruk may have
>   peace.

They summoned the birth goddess, Aruru:

> You, Aruru, created [the boundless human race],   95
> Now, create what Anu commanded,
> To his stormy heart, let that one be equal,
> Let them contend with each other, that Uruk may have
>   peace.

When Aruru heard this,
She conceived within her what Anu commanded.   100
Aruru wet her hands,
She pinched off clay, she tossed it upon the steppe,
She created valiant Enkidu in the steppe,
Offspring of potter's clay(?), with the force of the hero Ninurta.[1]
Shaggy with hair was his whole body,   105
He was made lush with head hair, like a woman,
The locks of his hair grew thick as a grainfield.
He knew neither people nor inhabited land,
He dressed as animals do.
He fed on grass with gazelles,   110

9. Certain goddesses were believed to pay particular attention to prayers of women. In this case, they are moved by the constant complaints of the women of Uruk that Gilgamesh was mistreating the women and men of the city [*Translator's note*].   1. Ninurta: A god, son of Enlil and Ninlil, who is portrayed in some legends as a slayer of monsters.

With beasts he jostled at the water hole,
With wildlife he drank his fill of water.

[A distraught hunter seeks his father's advice as to how to stop Enkidu's interference with his trapping. The father counsels him to go to Gilgamesh, who
will give him a woman to seduce Enkidu from his untamed way of life.]

A hunter, a trapping-man,
Encountered him at the edge of the water hole.
One day, a second, and a third he encountered him at the edge
    of the water hole.   115
When he saw him, the hunter stood stock-still with terror,
As for Enkidu, he went home with his beasts.
Aghast, struck dumb,
His heart in a turmoil, his face drawn,
With woe in his vitals,   120
His face like a traveler's from afar,
The hunter made ready to speak, saying to his father:

    My father, there is a certain fellow who has come
        [from the uplands],
    He is the mightiest in the land, strength is his,
    Like the force of heaven, so mighty is his strength.   125
    He constantly ranges over the uplands,
    Constantly feeding on grass with beasts,
    Constantly making his way to the edge of the water hole.
    I am too frightened to approach him.
    He has filled in the pits I dug,   130
    He has torn out my traps I set,
    He has helped the beasts, wildlife of the steppe, slip
        from my hands,
    He will not let me work the steppe.

His father made ready to speak, saying to the hunter:

    My son, in Uruk [dwells] Gilgamesh,   135
    [There is no one more mighty] than he.
    Like the force of heaven, so mighty is his strength.
    Take the road, set off [towards Uruk],
    [Tell Gilgamesh of] the mightiness-man.
    [He will give you Shamhat the harlot], take her with you,   140
    [Let her prevail over him], instead of a mighty man.
    When the wild beasts draw near the water hole,
    Let her strip off her clothing, laying bare her charms.
    When he sees her, he will approach her.
    His beasts that grew up with him on the steppe will deny
        him.   145

[Giving heed] to the advice of his father,
The hunter went forth [. . .].
He took the road, set off towards Uruk,
To [the king], Gilgamesh, [he said these words]:

There is a certain fellow [who has come from the uplands], 150
He is mightiest in the land, strength is his,
Like the force of heaven, so mighty is his strength.
He constantly ranges over the uplands,
Constantly feeding on grass with his beasts,
Constantly making his way to the edge of the water hole. 155
I am too frightened to approach him.
He has filled in the pits I dug,
He has torn out my traps I set,
He has helped the beasts, wildlife of the steppe, slip
    from my hands,
He will not allow me to work the steppe. 160

Gilgamesh said to him, to the hunter:

    Go, hunter, take with you Shamhat the harlot,
    When the wild beasts draw near the water hole,
    Let her strip off her clothing, laying bare her charms.
    When he sees her, he will approach her, 165
    His beasts that grew up with him on the steppe will deny
      him.

Forth went the hunter, taking with him Shamhat the harlot,
They took the road, going straight on their way.
On the third day they arrived at the appointed place.
Hunter and harlot sat down to wait. 170
One day, a second day, they sat by the edge of the water hole,
The beasts came to the water hole to drink,
The wildlife came to drink their fill of water.
But as for him, Enkidu, born in the uplands,
Who feeds on grass with gazelles, 175
Who drinks at the water hole with beasts,
Who, with wildlife, drinks his fill of water,
Shamhat looked upon him, a human-man,
A barbarous fellow from the midst of the steppe:

    There he is, Shamhat, open your embrace, 180
    Open your embrace, let him take your charms!
    Be not bashful, take his vitality!
    When he sees you, he will approach you,
    Toss aside your clothing, let him lie upon you,
    Treat him, a human, to woman's work! 185
    His wild beasts that grew up with him will deny him,
    As in his ardor he caresses you!

Shamhat loosened her garments,
She exposed her loins, he took her charms.
She was not bashful, she took his vitality. 190
She tossed aside her clothing and he lay upon her,
She treated him, a human, to woman's work,
As in his ardor he caressed her.
Six days, seven nights was Enkidu aroused, flowing into Shamhat.
After he had his fill of her delights, 195

He set off towards his beasts.
When they saw him, Enkidu, the gazelles shied off,
The wild beasts of the steppe shunned his person.
Enkidu had spent himself, his body was limp,
His knees stood still, while his beasts went away.   200
Enkidu was too slow, he could not run as before,
But he had gained [reason] and expanded his understanding.

[*Shamhat urges Enkidu to return with her to Uruk, artfully piquing his interest with tales of the pleasures awaiting him there, then feigning second
thoughts as she describes Gilgamesh.*]

He returned, he sat at the harlot's feet,
The harlot gazed upon his face,
While he listened to what the harlot was saying.   205
The harlot said to him, to Enkidu:

> You are handsome, Enkidu, you are become like a god,
> Why roam the steppe with wild beasts?
> Come, let me lead you to ramparted Uruk,
> To the holy temple, abode of Anu and Ishtar,   210
> The place of Gilgamesh, who is perfect in strength,
> And so, like a wild bull, he lords it over the young men.

As she was speaking to him, her words found favor,
He was yearning for one to know his heart, a friend.
Enkidu said to her, to the harlot: 215

> Come, Shamhat, escort me
> To the lustrous hallowed temple, abode of Anu and Ishtar,
> The place of Gilgamesh, who is perfect in strength,
> And so, like a wild bull, he lords it over the young men.
> I myself will challenge him, [I will speak out] boldly,   220
> [I will] raise a cry in Uruk: I am the mighty one!
> [I am come forward] to alter destinies!
> He who was born in the steppe [is mighty], strength is his!

[*Shamhat speaks.*]

> [Come then], let him see your face,
> [I will show you Gilgamesh], where he is I know full well.   225
> Come then, Enkidu, to ramparted Uruk,
> Where fellows are resplendent in holiday clothing,
> Where every day is set for celebration,
> Where harps and drums are [played].
> And the harlots too, they are fairest of form,   230
> Rich in beauty, full of delights,
> Even the great (gods) are kept from sleeping at night!
> Enkidu, you who [have not] learned to live,
> Oh, let me show you Gilgamesh, the joy-woe man.
> Look at him, gaze upon his face,   235
> He is radiant with virility, manly vigor is his,
> The whole of his body is seductively gorgeous.

Mightier strength has he than you,
Never resting by day or night.
O Enkidu, renounce your audacity!   240
Gilgamesh is beloved of Shamash,
Anu, Enlil, and Ea[2] broadened his wisdom.
Ere you come down from the uplands,
Gilgamesh will dream of you in Uruk.

[*The scene shifts to Uruk, where Gilgamesh is telling his mother, Ninsun, his
dreams. She explains them to him.*]

Gilgamesh went to relate the dreams, saying to his mother: 245

Mother, I had a dream last night:
There were stars of heaven around me,
Like the force of heaven, something kept falling upon me!
I tried to carry it but it was too strong for me,
I tried to move it but I could not budge it.   250
The whole of Uruk was standing by it,
The people formed a crowd around it,
A throng was jostling towards it,
Young men were mobbed around it,
Infantile, they were groveling before it!   255
[I fell in love with it], like a woman I caressed it,
I carried it off and laid it down before you,
Then you were making it my partner.

The mother of Gilgamesh, knowing and wise,
Who understands everything, said to her son,   260
Ninsun [the wild cow], knowing and wise,
Who understands everything, said to Gilgamesh:

The stars of heaven around you,
Like the force of heaven, what kept falling upon you,
Your trying to move it but not being able to budge it,   265
Your laying it down before me,
Then my making it your partner,
Your falling in love with it, your caressing it like a woman,
Means there will come to you a strong one,
A companion who rescues a friend.   270
He will be mighty in the land, strength will be his,
Like the force of heaven, so mighty will be his strength.
You will fall in love with him and caress him like a woman.
He will be mighty and rescue you, time and again.

He had a second dream,   275
He arose and went before the goddess, his mother,
Gilgamesh said to her, to his mother:

Mother, I had a second dream.
An axe was thrown down in a street of ramparted Uruk,

2. Ea: God associated with, among other things, wisdom and craftsmanship.

They were crowding around it, 280
The whole of Uruk was standing by it,
The people formed a crowd around it,
A throng was jostling towards it.
I carried it off and laid it down before you,
I fell in love with it, like a woman I caressed it, 285
Then you were making it my partner.

The mother of Gilgamesh, knowing and wise,
Who understands everything, said to her son,
Ninsun [the wild cow], knowing and wise,
Who understands everything, said to Gilgamesh: 290

My son, the axe you saw is a man.
Your loving it like a woman and caressing it,
And my making it your partner
Means there will come to you a strong one,
A companion who rescues a friend, 295
He will be mighty in the land, strength will be his,
Like the strength of heaven, so mighty will be his strength.

Gilgamesh said to her, to his mother:

Let this befall according to the command of the great
counselor Enlil,
I want a friend for my own counselor, 300
For my own counselor do I want a friend!

Even while he was having his dreams,
Shamhat was telling the dreams of Gilgamesh to Enkidu,
Each was drawn by love to the other.

Tablet II

[*Shamhat begins the process of civilizing Enkidu. She takes him to an encampment of shepherds, where he learns how to eat, drink, dress, and groom himself to human standards. Whereas Gilgamesh keeps his subjects awake at night with his roistering, Enkidu stays up all night to protect the flocks. Most of this tablet is known from older versions, combined here with later ones.*]

While Enkidu was seated before her,
Each was drawn by love to the other.
Enkidu forgot the steppe where he was born,
For six days, seven nights Enkidu was aroused and flowed
into Shamhat.
The harlot said to him, to Enkidu: 5

You are handsome, Enkidu, you are become like a god,
Why roam the steppe with wild beasts?
Come, let me lead you to ramparted Uruk,
To the holy temple, abode of Anu,
Let me lead you to ramparted Uruk, 10

To hallowed Eanna, abode of Ishtar,
The place of Gilgamesh, who is perfect in strength,
And so, like a wild bull, he lords it over the people.
You [are just like him],
You will love him like your own self.   15
Come away from this desolation, bereft even of shepherds.

He heard what she said, accepted her words,
He was yearning for one to know his heart, a friend.
The counsel of Shamhat touched his heart.
She took off her clothing, with one piece she dressed him,   20
The second she herself put on.
Clasping his hand, like a guardian deity she led him,[3]
To the shepherds' huts, where a sheepfold was,
The shepherds crowded around him,
They murmured their opinions among themselves: 25

     This fellow, how like Gilgamesh in stature,
     In stature tall, proud as a battlement.
     No doubt he was born in the steppe,
     Like the force of heaven, mighty is his strength.

They set bread before him,   30
They set beer before him.
He looked uncertainly, then stared,
Enkidu did not know to eat bread,
Nor had he ever learned to drink beer!
The harlot made ready to speak, saying to Enkidu: 35

     Eat the bread, Enkidu, the staff of life,
     Drink the beer, the custom of the land.

Enkidu ate the bread until he was sated,
He drank seven juglets of the beer.
His mood became relaxed, he was singing joyously,   40
He felt lighthearted and his features glowed.
He treated his hairy body with water,
He anointed himself with oil, turned into a man,
He put on clothing, became like a warrior.
He took his weapon, hunted lions,   45
The shepherds lay down to rest at night.
He slew wolves, defeated lions,
The herdsmen, the great gods, lay down to sleep.
Enkidu was their watchman, a wakeful man,
He was [. . .] tall.   50

                              [gap]

[A passerby on his way to a wedding feast tells Enkidu of Gilgamesh's abuse of
marriage: he is the first to have the bride. Enkidu, aghast, strides off to Uruk.

3. In Mesopotamian art, an individual guardian deity, often female, is shown leading a person into the
presence of a great god. [Translator's note].

*Whereas before Shamhat had led him, like a guardian deity, now he walks in
front like a challenger.*]

He was making love with Shamhat.
He lifted his eyes, he saw a man.
He said to the harlot:

> Shamhat, bring that man here!
> Why has he come?   55
> I will ask him to account for himself.

The harlot summoned the man,
He came over, Enkidu said to him:

> Fellow, where are you rushing?
> What is this, your burdensome errand?   60

The man made ready to speak, said to Enkidu:

> They have invited me to a wedding,
> Is it not people's custom to get married?
> I have heaped high on the festival tray
> The fancy dishes for the wedding.   65
> People's loins are open for the taking.
> For Gilgamesh, king of ramparted Uruk,
> People's loins are open for the taking!
> He mates with the lawful wife,
> He first, the groom after.   70
> By divine decree pronounced,
> From the cutting of his umbilical cord, she is his due.[4]

At the man's account, his face went pale.

[gap]

Enkidu was walking in front, with Shamhat behind him.

[*As foretold in Gilgamesh's dream, a crowd gathers around Enkidu as he enters Uruk. He has arrived in time for a wedding ceremony, but this may have
been the yearly religious ritual wherein the king joined with a representative
of a goddess to ensure universal fertility and engender a royal heir, so not in
fact the abuse of power described by the man with the tray, above.*]

When he entered the street of ramparted Uruk,   75
A multitude crowded around him.
He stood there in the street of ramparted Uruk,
With the people crowding around him.
They said about him:

---

4. This means that by his birthright Gilgamesh can take brides first on their wedding nights, then leave
them to their wedded husbands [*Translator's note*].

He is like Gilgamesh in build,   80
Though shorter in stature, he is stronger of frame.
[This man, where] he was born,
[Ate] the springtime [grass],
He must have nursed on the milk of wild beasts.

The whole of Uruk was standing beside him,   85
The people formed a crowd around him,
A throng was jostling towards him,
Young men were mobbed around him,
Infantile, they groveled before him.

In Uruk at this time sacrifices were underway,   90
Young men were celebrating.
The hero stood ready for the upright young man,
For Gilgamesh, as for a god, the partner was ready.
For the goddess of lovemaking, the bed was made,
Gilgamesh was to join with the girl that night.   95

[*Enkidu blocks the king's way to the ceremony. They wrestle in the street. Gilgamesh wins by pinning Enkidu over his shoulders while keeping one foot and
the other knee on the ground. He turns away to indicate cessation of the
match. Enkidu praises his superiority and royal birth.*]

Enkidu approached him,
They met in the public street.
Enkidu blocked the door to the wedding with his foot,
Not allowing Gilgamesh to enter.
They grappled each other, holding fast like wrestlers,   100
They shattered the doorpost, the wall shook.
Gilgamesh and Enkidu grappled each other,
Holding fast like wrestlers,
They shattered the doorpost, the wall shook!
They grappled each other at the door to the wedding,   105
They fought in the street, the public square.
It was Gilgamesh who knelt for the pin, his foot on the ground.
His fury abated, he turned away.
After he turned away,
Enkidu said to him, to Gilgamesh: 110

As one unique did your mother bear you,
The wild cow of the ramparts, Ninsun,
Exalted you above the most valorous of men!
Enlil has granted you kingship over the people.

[*gap*]

They kissed each other and made friends.   115

[*gap*]

[*As foretold in the dream, Gilgamesh goes off to his mother, Ninsun, perhaps
seeking her blessing on his friendship with Enkidu.*]

He is mighty in the land, strength is his,
Like the force of heaven, mighty is his strength.
His tall stature [. . .]

The mother of Gilgamesh made ready to speak,
Said to Gilgamesh,   120
Ninsun, the wild cow made ready to speak,
Said to Gilgamesh:

    My son, [. . .]
    Bitterly [. . .]

                      [*gap*]

[*In a second speech, Gilgamesh describes Enkidu's friendless state.*]

    Enkidu has neither [father nor mother],   125
    His hair was growing freely [. . .]
    He was born in the steppe, no one [. . .]

Enkidu stood still, [listening to what he said],
He shuddered and [sat down . . .]
Tears filled his eyes,   130
He was listless, his strength turned to weakness.
They clasped each other [. . .],
They joined hands like [. . .].

Gilgamesh made ready to speak,
Saying to Enkidu: 135

    Why are your eyes full of tears,
    Why are you listless, your strength turned to weakness?

Enkidu said to him, to Gilgamesh:

    Cries of sorrow, my friend, have cramped my muscles,
    Woe has entered my heart [. . .]   140

[*Gilgamesh proposes a quest to kill a monster named Humbaba, in order to
cut a giant cedar tree in the forest Humbaba guards. Felling evergreen trees on
distant mountains was a well-known demonstration of kingly power in early
Mesopotamia. Enkidu, horrified, tries vainly to dissuade him.*]

Gilgamesh made ready to speak,
Saying to Enkidu:

    There dwells in the forest the fierce monster Humbaba,
    [You and I shall] kill [him]
    [And] wipe out [something evil from the land].   145

                      [*gap*]

Enkidu made ready to speak,
Saying to Gilgamesh:

My friend, I knew that country
When I roamed with the wild beasts.
The forest is . . . sixty double leagues[5] in every direction,   150
Who can go into it?
Humbaba's cry is the roar of a deluge,
His maw is fire, his breath is death.
Why do you want to do this?
The haunt of Humbaba is a hopeless quest.   155

Gilgamesh made ready to speak,
Saying to Enkidu:

> I must go up the mountain [. . .] forest,
> I must cut [a cedar tree . . .]
> That cedar must be [big] enough   160
> [To make] whirlwinds [when it falls]

[gap]

Enkidu made ready to speak,
Saying to Gilgamesh:

> How shall the likes of us go to the forest of cedars, my friend?
> In order to safeguard the forest of cedars,   165
> Enlil has appointed him to terrify the people,
> Enlil has destined him seven fearsome glories.[6]
> That journey is not to be undertaken,
> That creature is not to be looked upon.
> The guardian of [. . .], the forest of cedars,   170
> Humbaba's cry is the roar of a deluge,
> His maw is fire, his breath is death.
> He can hear rustling in the forest for sixty double leagues.
> Who can go into his forest?
> Adad[7] is first and Humbaba is second.   175
> Who, even among the gods, could attack him?
> In order to safeguard the forest of cedars,
> Enlil has appointed him to terrify the people,
> Enlil has destined him seven fearsome glories.
> Besides, whosoever enters his forest is struck down by disease.   180

Gilgamesh made ready to speak,
Saying to Enkidu:

> Why, my friend, do you raise such unworthy objections?
> Who, my friend, can go up to heaven?
> The gods dwell forever in the sun,   185
> People's days are numbered,
> Whatever they attempt is a puff of air.
> Here you are, even you, afraid of death,

---

5. league: the distance a person can walk in an hour—a little over three miles.   6. The Mesopotamians believed that divine beings were surrounded by a blinding, awe-inspiring radiance. In the old versions of *The Epic of Gilgamesh*, this radiance, called here "glories," was considered removable, like garments or jewelry [*Translator's note*].   7. Adad: a storm deity.

What has become of your bravery's might?
I will go before you,   190
You can call out to me, "Go on, be not afraid!"
If I fall on the way, I'll establish my name:
"Gilgamesh, who joined battle with fierce Humbaba"
    (they'll say).
You were born and grew up on the steppe,
When a lion sprang at you, you knew what to do.   195
Young men fled before you

[gap]

You speak unworthily,
How you pule! You make me ill.
I must set [my hand to cutting] a cedar tree,
I must establish eternal fame.   200
Come, my friend, let's both be off to the foundry,
Let them cast axes such as we'll need.

[After supervising the casting of enormous axes and weapons, Gilgamesh informs the citizenry of Uruk of his planned campaign. First he addresses the
elders, speaking of his desire for eternal fame, next the young men, appealing
to their sense of adventure. He promises to return in time to celebrate the
springtime festival of the new year. Enkidu and the elders attempt unsuccessfully to dissuade him.]

Off they went to the craftsmen,
The craftsmen, seated around, discussed the matter.
They cast great axes,   205
Axe blades weighing 180 pounds each they cast.
They cast great daggers,
Their blades were 120 pounds each,
The cross guards of their handles thirty pounds each.
They carried daggers worked with thirty pounds of gold,   210
Gilgamesh and Enkidu bore ten times sixty pounds each.

He bolted the seven gates of Uruk,
[. . .] listened, the multitude convened.
[. . .] turned out in the street of ramparted Uruk,
Gilgamesh [. . .] his throne,   215
[. . . in the street] of ramparted Uruk,
[Enkidu] sat before him.
[Gilgamesh spoke to the elders of ramparted Uruk]:

    [Hear me, O elders of ramparted Uruk],
    The one of whom they speak   220
    I, Gilgamesh, would see!
    The one whose name resounds across the whole world,
    I will hunt him down in the forest of cedars.
    I will make the land hear
    How mighty is the scion of Uruk.   225
    I will set my hand to cutting a cedar,
    An eternal name I will make for myself!

[*Gilgamesh turns to the young men of the city. In an old version of this episode,
the elders respond at this point, see below, lines 257–73: the standard version
apparently expanded this incident to include parallel speeches to both the elders and the young men.*]

> Hear me, O young men [of ramparted Uruk],
> Young men of Uruk who understand this cause!
> I have taken on a noble quest,   230
> I travel a distant road, to where Humbaba is.
> I face a battle unknown,
> I mount a campaign unknown.
> Give me your blessing, that I may go on my journey,
> [That I may indeed see] your faces [safely again],   235
> That I may indeed reenter joyfully the gate of ramparted
>   Uruk,
> That I may indeed return to hold the festival for the new year,
> That I may indeed celebrate the festival for the new year
>   twice over.
> May that festival be held in my presence, the fanfare sound!
> May the drums resound before [you]!   240

Enkidu pressed advice upon the elders,
Upon the young men of Uruk who understood this cause:

> Tell him he must not go to the forest of cedars,
> That journey is not to be undertaken,
> That creature is not to be looked upon.   245
> The guardian of the forest of cedars [. . .]
> Humbaba's cry is the roar of a deluge,
> His maw is fire, his breath is death,
> He can hear rustling in the forest for sixty double leagues.
> Who can go into his forest?   250
> Adad is first and Humbaba is second.
> Who, even among the gods, could attack him?
> In order to safeguard the forest of cedars,
> Enlil has appointed him to terrify the people,
> Enlil has destined him seven fearsome glories.   255
> Besides, whosoever enters his forest is struck down by disease.

The elders of ramparted Uruk arose,
They responded to Gilgamesh with their advice:

> You are young, Gilgamesh, your feelings carry you away,
> You are ignorant of what you speak, flightiness has taken you,   260
> You do not know what you are attempting.
> We have heard of Humbaba, his features are grotesque,
> Who is there who could face his weaponry?
> He can hear rustling in the forest for sixty double leagues.
> Who can go into it?   265
> Humbaba's cry is the roar of a deluge,
> His maw is fire, his breath is death.
> Adad is first and Humbaba is second.
> Who, even among the gods, could attack him?

In order to safeguard the forest of cedars,   270
Enlil has appointed him to terrify the people,
Enlil has destined him seven fearsome glories.
Besides, whosoever enters his forest is struck down by disease.

When Gilgamesh heard the speech of his counselors,
He looked at his friend and laughed: 275

> Now then, my friend, [do you say the same?]:
> "I am afraid [to die]"?

[gap]

Tablet III

[*The elders offer advice to Gilgamesh for the quest. They entrust his safety to Enkidu.*]

The elders spoke to him, saying to Gilgamesh:

> [Come back safely to] Uruk's haven,
> Trust not, Gilgamesh, in your strength alone,
> Let your eyes see all, make your blow strike home.
> He who goes in front saves his companion,   5
> He who knows the path protects his friend.
> Let Enkidu walk before you,
> He knows the way to the forest of cedars,
> He has seen battle, been exposed to combat.
> Enkidu will protect his friend, safeguard his companion,   10
> Let him return, to be a grave husband.
> We in our assembly entrust the king to you,
> On your return, entrust the king again to us.

[*Gilgamesh and Enkidu go off to the temple of Ninsun, to ask her blessing.*]

Gilgamesh made ready to speak,
Saying to Enkidu: 15

> Come, my friend, let us go the sublime temple,
> To go before Ninsun, the great queen.
> Ninsun the wise, who is versed in all knowledge,
> Will send us on our way with good advice.

Clasping each other, hand in hand,   20
Gilgamesh and Enkidu went to the sublime temple,
To go before Ninsun, the great queen.
Gilgamesh came forward and entered before her:

> O Ninsun, I have taken on a noble quest,
> I travel a distant road, to where Humbaba is,   25
> To face a battle unknown,
> To mount a campaign unknown.
> Give me your blessing, that I may go on my journey,

[That I may indeed see] your face [safely again],
That I may indeed reenter joyfully the gate of ramparted Uruk,   30
That I may indeed return to hold the festival for the new year,
That I may indeed celebrate the festival for the new year
   twice over.
May that festival be held in my presence, the fanfare sound!
May their drums resound before [you]!

[*Ninsun prays to Shamash to help her son on his quest.*]

Ninsun the [wild cow] heard them out with sadness,   35
The speeches of Gilgamesh, her son, and Enkidu.
Ninsun entered the bathhouse seven times,
She bathed herself in water with tamarisk and soapwort.[8]
[She put on] a garment as beseemed her body,
[She put on] an ornament as beseemed her breast,   40
She set [. . .] and donned her tiara.
[. . .] harlots [. . .] the ground,
She climbed [the stairs], mounted to the roof terrace,
She set up an incense offering to Shamash.[9]
She made the offering, to Shamash she raised her hands in prayer: 45

   Why did you endow my son Gilgamesh with a restless heart?
   Now you have moved him to travel
   A distant road, to where Humbaba is,
   To face a battle unknown,
   To mount an expedition unknown.   50
   Until he goes and returns,
   Until he reaches the forest of cedars,
   Until he has slain fierce Humbaba,
   And wipes out from the land the evil thing you hate,
   In the day, [when you traverse the sky],   55
   May Aya, your bride, not fear to remind you,
   "Entrust him to the watchmen of the night."

                              [*gap*]

   O [Shamash], you opened [. . .] for the beasts of the steppe,
   You came out for the land to [. . .],
   The mountains [glow], the heavens [brighten],   60
   The beasts of the steppe [behold] your fierce radiance.
   At your light's rising, [. . .] assembles,
   The great gods stand in attendance [upon your glow],
   May [Aya, your bride], not fear to remind you,
   "Entrust him to the watchmen of the night."   65

                              [*gap*]

   While Gilgamesh journeys to the forest of cedars,
   May the days be long, may the nights be short,
   May his loins be girded, his arms [strong]!

8. A medicinal plant used in cleansing and magic [*Translator's note*].   9. Shamash: The Babylonian sungod and god of justice.

At night, let him make a camp for sleeping,
[Let him make a shelter] to fall asleep in.   70
May Aya, your bride, not fear to remind you,
When Gilgamesh, Enkidu, and Humbaba meet,
Raise up for his sake, O Shamash, great winds against
    Humbaba,
South wind, north wind, east wind, west wind, moaning wind,
Blasting wind, lashing wind, contrary wind, dust storm,   75
Demon wind, freezing wind, storm wind, whirlwind:
Raise up thirteen winds to blot out Humbaba's face,
So he cannot charge forward, cannot retreat,
Then let Gilgamesh's weapons defeat Humbaba.
As soon as your own [radiance] flares forth,   80
At that very moment heed the man who reveres you.
May your swift mules [. . .] you,
A comfortable seat, a [. . .] bed is laid for you,
May the gods, your brethren, serve you your [favorite] foods,
May Aya, the great bride, dab your face with the fringe
    of her spotless garment.   85

Ninsun the wild cow made a second plea to Shamash:

O Shamash, will not Gilgamesh [. . .] the gods for you?
Will he not share heaven with you?
Will he not share tiara and scepter with the moon?
Will he not act in wisdom with Ea in the depths?   90
Will he not rule the human race with Irnina?
Will he not dwell with Ningishzida in the Land of No Return?[1]

[gap]

[Ninsun apparently inducts Enkidu into the staff of her temple.]

After Ninsun the wild cow had made her plea,
Ninsun the wild cow, knowing and wise, who understands
    everything,
[. . .] Gilgamesh [. . .].   95
She extinguished the incense, [she came down from the roof
    terrace],
She summoned Enkidu to impart her message:

Mighty Enkidu, though you are no issue of my womb,
Your little ones shall be among the devotees of Gilgamesh,
The priestesses, votaries, cult women of the temple.   100

She placed a token around Enkidu's neck:

As the priestesses take in a foundling,
And the daughters of the gods bring up an adopted child,
I herewith take Enkidu, whom [. . .], as my adopted son,
Enkidu for [. . .], may Gilgamesh treat him well.   105

1. Ningishzida: Mesopotamian god of the underworld.

[*gap*]

While you journey [. . .] to the forest of cedars,
May the days be long, may the nights be short,
May your loins be girded, your arms [strong].
At night make a camp for sleeping,
Let [. . .] watch over [. . .]   110

[*Enkidu promises Ninsun that he will bring Gilgamesh back safely.*]

Until he has gone and returned,
Until he has reached the forest of cedars

[*gap*]

[*The following episodes are taken from an old version, which arranged the
material differently from the standard version. Gilgamesh takes an oracle to
determine the prognosis for his quest. Divination, often by slaughtering a
sheep or goat and looking for certain marks or formations on the liver or entrails, was normal practice in Mesopotamia to predict the outcome of important
undertakings or crises, such as illness. The result of Gilgamesh's divination is
apparently unfavorable, so he tries to change the prognosis by offering various
blandishments to Shamash, god of oracles.*]

Gilgamesh knelt before [Shamash],
The speech he made [. . .]:

I am going, O Shamash, with my hands [raised in prayer],   115
Afar off may my life be safe.
Return me [in safety to ramparted Uruk],
Place your protection [upon me].

Gilgamesh summoned [the diviners],
His oracle [. . .]   120
To the [. . .] temple.
Tears poured down Gilgamesh's [face]:

My god, the road [. . .]
[. . .] and his ways, my god, I do not know.
[If] I come out safely,   125
[I will . . .] you to your heart's content,
[I will build] a house for your delight,
[I will seat you] on thrones.

[*In the large gap in the text that occurs here, Gilgamesh and Enkidu are still
in Uruk, perhaps carrying out various rites and drawing up plans for a great
door to be made from the cedar tree they plan to cut down. Next Gilgamesh
gives instructions for the city in his absence. The town officials wish him well.
The two friends begin final preparations for departure, with the blessing of
the elders and the young men. Enkidu at last gives up his objections.*]

The young men should not form a crowd in the street [. . .],
Judge the lawsuit of the weak, call the strong to account,[2]   130
While in a trice we attain our desire,
And set up our [. . .] at Humbaba's gate.

His dignitaries stood by, wishing him well,
In a crowd, the young men of Uruk ran along behind him,
While his dignitaries made obeisance to him: 135

> Come back safely to Uruk's haven!
> Trust not, Gilgamesh, in your strength alone,
> Let your eyes see all, make your blow strike home.
> He who goes in front saves his companion,
> He who knows the path protects his friend.   140
> Let Enkidu walk before you,
> He knows the way to the forest of cedars.
> He has seen battle, been exposed to combat.
> [. . .] at the mountain passes.
> Enkidu will protect his friend, safeguard his companion,   145
> Let him return, to be a grave husband.
> We in our assembly entrust the king to you,
> On your return, entrust the king again to us.

Enkidu made ready to speak, saying to Gilgamesh:

> Turn back, my friend, [. . .]   150
> You must not [. . .] this journey!

[gap]

[. . .] his equipment,
[. . .] the great daggers,
[The bow] and the quiver
[. . .] in their hands.   155
He took up the axes,
[. . .] his quiver, the Elamite bow,[3]
[He set] his dagger at his belt.
[The elders] made way for him,
[The young men] sent him on his way: 160

> Gilgamesh, [how long] till you return to the city [. . .]?

The elders [hailed him],
Counseled Gilgamesh for the journey:

> Trust not, Gilgamesh, in your own strength,
> Let your vision be clear, take care of yourself.   165
> Let Enkidu go ahead of you,
> He has seen the road, has traveled the way.

---

2. Mesopotamian rulers were supposed to ensure that poor and defenseless people received the same legal process as the rich and powerful [Translator's note].   3. Elam was a country in southwestern Iran, apparently known for its fine bows [Translator's note].

He knows the ways into the forest
And all the tricks of Humbaba.
He who goes first safeguards his companion,   170
His vision is clear, [he protects himself].
May Shamash help you to your goal,
May he disclose to you what your words propose,
May he open for you the barred road,
Make straight the pathway to your tread,   175
Make straight the upland to your feet.
May nightfall bring you good tidings,
May Lugalbanda stand by you in your cause.
In a trice accomplish what you desire,
Wash your feet in the river of Humbaba whom you seek.   180
When you stop for the night, dig a well,
May there always be pure water in your waterskin.
You should libate cool water to Shamash
And be mindful of Lugalbanda.

Enkidu made ready to speak, saying to Gilgamesh: 185

[As] you insist, make the journey.
Do not be afraid, watch me.
[. . .] who made his dwelling in the forest,
The [. . .], where Humbaba goes.

[gap]

[. . .] who goes with me,   190
[I will bring him safe] to you,
[. . .] in joy!

Upon hearing this speech,
The young men acclaimed him:

Go, Gilgamesh, may [. . .]   195
May your god go [by your side],
May he disclose to you [your heart's desire].
May [. . .] advise you,
He who knows [. . .]

[In the gap that follows, the two friends set out on their quest.]

Tablet IV

[Gilgamesh and Enkidu go on their journey. As they camp each night, Enkidu
makes Gilgamesh a shelter and lays out a magic circle for him to sleep in. This
may be a circle of flour as known from Mesopotamian sorcery and oath-
taking. Gilgamesh prays for a dream to portend the outcome of the expedition.
He dreams three times of mountains. The first falls upon him, the second
holds him fast, and the third erupts. In each case, he barely escapes the mountain's fury. Enkidu explains that the mountain is Humbaba, who will make a
terrifying attack but will collapse and die. Next he dreams of a lion-headed
monster-bird and then a bull attacking him. Since the text is very damaged

here and various versions exist, the number, sequence, and contents of the
dreams are most uncertain.]

At twenty double leagues they took a bite to eat,
At thirty double leagues they made their camp,
Fifty double leagues they went in a single day,
A journey of a month and a half in three days.
They approached Mount Lebanon.   5
Towards sunset they dug a well,
Filled [their waterskin with water].
Gilgamesh went up onto the mountain,
He poured out flour for an [offering, saying]:

  O mountain, bring me a propitious dream!   10

Enkidu made Gilgamesh a shelter for receiving dreams,
A gust was blowing, he fastened the door.
He had him lie down in a circle of [flour],
And spreading out like a net, Enkidu lay down in the doorway.
Gilgamesh sat there, chin on his knee.   15
Sleep, which usually steals over people, fell upon him.
In the middle of the night he awoke,
Got up and said to his friend:

  My friend, did you not call me? Why am I awake?
  Did you not touch me? Why am I disturbed?   20
  Did a god not pass by? Why does my flesh tingle?
  My friend, I had a dream,
  And the dream I had was very disturbing.
  [We . . .] on the flanks of a mountain,
  The mountain fell [upon us],   25
  We [. . .] like flies!

The one born in the steppe [. . .],
Enkidu explained the dream to his friend:

  My friend, your dream is favorable,
  The dream is very precious [as an omen].   30
  My friend, the mountain you saw is [Humbaba],
  We will catch Humbaba and [kill him],
  Then we will throw down his corpse on the field of battle.
  Further, at dawn the word of Shamash will be in our favor.

At twenty double leagues they took a bite to eat,   35
At thirty double leagues they made their camp,
Fifty double leagues they went in a single day,
A journey of a month and a half in three days.
They approached Mount Lebanon.
Towards sunset they dug a well,   40
They filled [their waterskin with water].
Gilgamesh went up onto the mountain,
He poured out flour for [an offering, saying]:

O mountain, bring me a propitious dream!

Enkidu made Gilgamesh a shelter for receiving dreams, 45
A gust was blowing, he fastened the door.
He had him lie down in a circle of [flour],
And spreading out like a net, Enkidu lay down in the doorway.
Gilgamesh sat there, chin on his knee.
Sleep, which usually steals over people, fell upon him. 50
In the middle of the night he awoke,
Got up and said to his friend:

> My friend, did you not call me? Why am I awake?
> Did you not touch me? Why am I disturbed?
> Did a god not pass by? Why does my flesh tingle? 55
> My friend, I had a second dream,
> And the dream I had was very disturbing.
> A mountain was in my dream, [. . . an enemy].
> It threw me down, pinning my feet [. . .],
> A fearsome glare grew ever more intense. 60
> A certain young man, handsomest in the world, truly
>   handsome he was,
> He pulled me out from the base of the mountain [. . .],
> He gave me water to drink and eased my fear,
> He set my feet on the ground again.

The one born in the steppe [. . .], 65
Enkidu explained the dream to his friend:

> My friend, your dream is favorable,
> The dream is very precious [as an omen].
> My friend, we will go [. . .]
> The strange thing [was] Humbaba, 70
> Was not the mountain, the strange thing, Humbaba?
> Come then, banish your fear,
> [. . .]
> As for the man you saw [. . .]

[gap]

[*Enkidu's explanation presumably was that the man was Shamash or Lugalbanda coming to help them, but only scattered words of the explanation are
preserved.*]

At twenty double leagues they took a bite to eat, 75
At thirty double leagues they made their camp,
Fifty double leagues they went in a single day,
A journey of a month and a half in three days.
They approached Mount Lebanon.
Towards sunset they dug a well, 80
They filled [their waterskin with water].
Gilgamesh went up onto the mountain,
He poured out flour as [an offering, saying]:

O mountain, bring me a propitious dream!

Enkidu made Gilgamesh a shelter for receiving dreams,   85
A gust was blowing, he fastened the door.
He had him lie down in a circle of [flour],
And spreading out like a net, Enkidu lay down in the doorway.
Gilgamesh sat there, chin on his knee.
Sleep, which usually steals over people, fell upon him.   90
In the middle of the night he awoke,
Got up and said to his friend:

> My friend, did you not call me? Why am I awake?
> Did you not touch me? Why am I disturbed?
> Did a god not pass by? Why does my flesh tingle?   95
> My friend, I had a third dream,
> And the dream I had was very disturbing.
> The heavens cried out, the earth was thundering,
> Daylight faded, darkness fell,
> Lightning flashed, fire shot up,   100
> The [flames] burgeoned, spewing death.
> Then the glow was dimmed, the fire was extinguished,
> The [burning coals] that were falling turned to ashes.
> You who were born in the steppe, let us discuss it.

Enkidu [explained], helped him accept his dream,   105
Saying to Gilgamesh:

[gap]

[*Enkidu's explanation is mostly lost, but perhaps it was that the volcanolike
explosion was Humbaba, who flared up, then died.*]

> Humbaba, like a god [. . .]
> [. . .] the light flaring [. . .]
> We will be [victorious] over him.
> Humbaba aroused our fury [. . .]   110
> [. . .] we will prevail over him.
> Further, at dawn the word of Shamash will be in our favor.

At twenty double leagues they took a bite to eat,
A thirty double leagues they made their camp.
Fifty double leagues they went in a single day,   115
A journey of a month and a half in three days.
They approached Mount Lebanon.
Towards sunset they dug a well,
They filled [their waterskin with water].
Gilgamesh went up onto the mountain,   120
He poured out flour as [an offering, saying]:

> O mountain, bring me a propitious dream!

Enkidu made Gilgamesh a shelter for receiving dreams,
A gust was blowing, he fastened the door.

He had him lie down in a circle of [flour],   125
And spreading out like a net, Enkidu lay down in the doorway.
Gilgamesh sat there, chin on his knee.
Sleep, which usually steals over people, fell upon him.
In the middle of the night he awoke,

> My friend, did you not call me? Why am I awake?   130
> Did you not touch me? Why am I disturbed?
> Did a god not pass by? Why does my flesh tingle?
> My friend, I had a [fourth] dream,
> The dream I had was very disturbing.
> My friend, I saw a fourth dream,   135
> More terrible than the other three.
> I saw the lion-headed monster-bird Anzu in the sky.
> He began to descend upon us, like a cloud.
> He was terrifying, his appearance was horrible!
> His maw was fire, his breath death.   140
> A young man [. . .] a way to go across(?),
> [. . .] he was standing by me in my dream.
> [He . . .] its wings, he seized its arms,
> Then he threw it [to the ground].

[gap]

[*Enkidu explains the fourth dream.*]

> The lion-headed monster-bird Anzu who descended
>   upon us, like a cloud,   145
> Who was terrifying, whose appearance was horrible,
> Whose maw was fire, whose breath was death,
> Whose dreadful aura frightens you,
> I will . . . its foot, I will lift you up(?).
> The young man you saw was mighty Shamash   150

[gap]

At twenty double leagues they took a bite to eat,
At thirty double leagues they made their camp,
Fifty double leagues they went in a single day,
A journey of a month and a half in three days.
They approached Mount Lebanon.   155
Towards sunset they dug a well,
Filled [their waterskin with water].
Gilgamesh went up onto the mountain,
He poured out flour for an [offering, saying]:

> O mountain, bring me a propitious dream!   160

Enkidu made him a shelter for receiving dreams,
A gust was blowing, he fastened the door.
He had him lie down in a circle of [flour],
And spreading out like a net, Enkidu lay down in the doorway.
Gilgamesh sat there, chin on his knee.   165

Sleep, which usually steals over people, fell upon him.
In the middle of the night he awoke,
Got up and said to his friend:

> My friend, did you not call me? Why am I awake?
> Did you not touch me? Why am I disturbed? 170
> Did a god not pass by? Why does my flesh tingle?
> My friend, I had a dream,
> And the dream I had was very disturbing.

[*It is not clear how many dreams there were in all though one version refers to five. A poorly preserved manuscript of an old version includes the following dream that could be inserted here, as portions of it are fulfilled in Tablet VI.*]

> I was grasping a wild bull of the steppe!
> As it bellowed, it split the earth, 175
> It raised clouds of dust, blotting out the sky.
> I crouched down before it,
> It seized my hands [. . .], pinioned my arms.
> (Someone) pulled me out [. . .]
> He stroked my cheeks, he gave me to drink from his waterskin. 180

[*gap*]

[*Enkidu explains the dream.*]

> It is the god, my friend, to whom we go,
> The wild bull was no enemy at all,
> The wild bull you saw is Shamash, the protector,
> He will take our hands in need.
> The one who gave you water to drink from his waterskin 185
> Is your god who proclaims your glory, Lugalbanda.
> We should rely on one another,
> We will accomplish together a deed unheard of in the land.

[*gap*]

[*Something has happened to discourage Gilgamesh, perhaps an unfavorable oracle. Shamash comes to their aid with timely advice, just before they hear Humbaba's cry.*]

[Before Shamash his tears flowed down]:

> [What . . .] said [in Uruk . . .], 190
> Remember, stand by me, hear [my prayer],
> Gilgamesh, scion of [ramparted Uruk]!

Shamash heard what he said,
From afar a warning voice called to him from the sky:

> Hurry, confront him, do not let him go off [into the forest], 195
> Do not let him enter the thicket nor [. . .]!
> He has not donned [all] of his seven fearsome glories,
> One he has on, six he has left off!

They [. . .]
They charged forward like wild bulls. 200
He let out a single bloodcurdling cry,
The guardian of the forest shrieked aloud,
[. . .]
Humbaba was roaring like thunder.

Gilgamesh made ready to speak, 205
Said to Enkidu:

>   Humbaba [. . .]
>   We cannot confront him separately.

[gap]

*[In the broken section here, the two friends, exchanging terms of encourage-
ment, reach the edge of the forest.]*

Gilgamesh spoke to him, said to Enkidu:

>   My friend, why do we raise such unworthy objections? 210
>   Have we not crossed all [the mountains . . .]?
>   [The end of the quest] is before us.
>   Before we [. . .]
>   My friend knows battle,
>   One who [. . .] combat, 215
>   You rubbed on [herbs], you did not fear [death],[4]
>   [. . .], like a street hawker(?),
>   Your battle cry should be dinning like a drum!
>   Let the paralysis leave your arm, let weakness quit your
>   [knees],
>   Take my hand, my friend, let us [walk on] together! 220
>   Your heart should be urging you to battle.
>   Forget about death, [. . .] life!
>   [. . .], the circumspect-man,
>   He who marches [first], protects himself,
>   Let him keep his comrade safe! 225
>   Those two will have established fame down through the ages.

The pair reached [the edge of the forest],
They stopped their talk and stood there.

Tablet V

*[The friends are found admiring the wondrous forest and the paths of Hum-
baba, its guardian.]*

They stood at the edge of the forest,
They gazed at the height of the cedars,
They gazed at the way into the forest.

---

4. The meaning of this line is very uncertain. It may refer to some protective magical procedure. In the
Mesopotamian "Epic of Creation," for example, the hero god carries vegetable antidotes to counteract
magic spells cast by the enemy [*Translator's note*].

Where Humbaba would walk, a path was made,
Straight were the ways and easy the going.   5
They saw the cedar mountain, dwelling of the gods, sacred
    to the goddess Irnina.
On the slopes of that mountain, the cedar bears its abundance,
Agreeable is its shade, full of pleasures.
The undergrowth is tangled, the [thicket] interwoven.
Near the cedar [. . .] the balsam tree   10

                            [gap]

[*Weapons at the ready, the two friends advance, encouraging each other.*]

From afar off the swords [. . .]
And after the scabbards were [. . .]
Axes touched with [the whetstone],
Daggers and swords [. . .]
One by one [. . .]   15
They crept forward [. . .]
Humbaba [. . .]

                            [gap]

Enkidu made ready to speak, saying to Gilgamesh:

    Humbaba [. . .]
    One by one [. . .].   20
    [Two] garments [. . .]
    On the treacherous pathway [we can go together],
    Two [. . .]
    A three-strand rope does not [. . .],
    Two cubs are [stronger] than a mighty lion.   25

                            [gap]

[*In older versions, they begin to cut trees and Humbaba hears the noise. In the standard version, they meet Humbaba first. He proves to be something of a snob, disdaining the steppe-born Enkidu, whom he ridicules as a midget and a reptile. Gilgamesh then has second thoughts.*]

Humbaba made ready to speak, saying to Gilgamesh:

    How well-advised they are, the fool Gilgamesh and the yokel-
        man!
    Why have you come here to me?
    Come now, Enkidu, small-fry, who does not know his father,
    Spawn of a turtle or tortoise, who sucked no mother's milk!   30
    I used to see you when you were younger but would not go
        near you.
    [Had I killed the likes of] you, would I have filled my belly?
    [. . .] you have brought Gilgamesh before me,
    [. . .] you stand there, a barbarian foe!
    I should [cut off your head], Gilgamesh, throat and neck,   35

I should let cawing buzzard, screaming eagle, and vulture
    feed on your flesh.

Gilgamesh made ready to speak, saying to Enkidu:

My friend, Humbaba's features have grown more grotesque,
We strode up like heroes towards [. . .] to vanquish him,
Yet my heart [. . .] right away.   40

[*Enkidu urges him on, quoting his brave words at Uruk and seeking to stiffen
his resolve.*]

Enkidu made ready to speak, saying to Gilgamesh:

Why, my friend, do you raise such unworthy objections?
How you pule! You make me ill.
Now, my friend, this has dragged on long enough.
The time has come to pour the copper into the mold.   45
Will you take another hour to blow the bellows,
An hour more to let it cool?
To launch the flood weapon, to wield the lash,
Retreat not a foot, you must not turn back,
[Let your eyes see all], let your blow strike home!   50

[*gap*]

[*In the combat with Humbaba, the rift valley of Lebanon is formed by their
circling feet.*]

He struck the ground and [. . .] to confront him.
At their heels the earth split apart,
As they circled, the ranges of Lebanon were sundered!
The white clouds turned black,
Death rained down like fog upon them.   55
Shamash raised the great winds against Humbaba,
South wind, north wind, east wind, west wind, moaning wind,
Blasting wind, lashing wind, contrary wind, dust storm,
Demon wind, freezing wind, storm wind, whirlwind:
The thirteen winds blotted out Humbaba's face,   60
He could not charge forward, he could not retreat.
Then Gilgamesh's weapons defeated Humbaba.

[*Humbaba begs for his life. Gilgamesh wavers but Enkidu is adamant. Humbaba calls him a beast and a boor, appealing to Gilgamesh's superior sensibili-
ties. Gilgamesh is willing to spare Humbaba, with no further mention of the
alleged evil that Shamash hates, but Enkidu urges him to the deed.*]

Humbaba begged for life, saying to Gilgamesh:

You were once a child, Gilgamesh, you had a mother who
    bore you,
You are the offspring [of Ninsun the wild cow].   65

[You grew up to fulfill] the oracle of Shamash, lord of the
　　mountain:
"Gilgamesh, scion of Uruk, is to be king."

[gap]

O Gilgamesh, a dead man cannot [. . .],
[. . .] a living being can [. . .] his master.
O Gilgamesh, spare my life!　　　　　　　　　　　　　　　　70
Let me dwell here for you [as your . . .],
Say however many trees you [require . . .],
For you I will guard the myrtle wood [. . .]
Trees, the pride of [your . . .] palace.

Enkidu made ready to speak, saying to Gilgamesh:　　　　　75

My friend! Do not listen to what Humbaba [says],
[Do not heed] his entreaties!

[gap]

[Humbaba is speaking to Enkidu.]

You know the lore of my forest, the lore of [. . .],
And you understand all I have to say.
I might have lifted you up, dangled you from a twig at the
　　entrance to my forest,　　　　　　　　　　　　　　　　80
I might have let cawing buzzard, screaming eagle, and vulture
　　feed on your flesh.
Now then, Enkidu, [mercy] is up to you [. . .],
Tell Gilgamesh to spare my life!

Enkidu made ready to speak, saying to Gilgamesh:

My friend! Humbaba is guardian of the forest [of cedars],　　85
Finish him off for the kill, put him out of existence.
Humbaba is guardian of the forest [of cedars],
Finish him off for the kill, put him out of existence,
Before Enlil the foremost one hears of this!
[The great] gods will become angry with us,　　　　　　　90
Enlil in Nippur, Shamash [in Larsa . . .].
Establish [your reputation] for all time:
"Gilgamesh, who slew Humbaba."

When Humbaba heard [. . .]
Humbaba [raised] his head [. . .]　　　　　　　　　　　95

[gap]

[Humbaba continues to plead with Enkidu.]

You sit like a shepherd before [. . .]
And like a hired man you [. . .]

Now is the time, Enkidu, [. . .]
Tell Gilgamesh to spare my life!

Enkidu made ready to speak, saying to Gilgamesh: 100

My friend, Humbaba is guardian of the forest [of cedars],
Finish him off for the kill, put him out of existence.
Humbaba is guardian of the forest [of cedars],
Finish him off for the kill, put him out of existence,
Before [Enlil] the foremost one hears of this! 105
The great gods will become angry with us,
Enlil in Nippur, Shamash [in Larsa . . .].
Establish your reputation for all time:
"Gilgamesh, who slew Humbaba."

When Humbaba heard [. . .]   110

[gap]

[Realizing he is doomed, Humbaba curses them, concluding with an elaborate wordplay.]

May they never [. . .]
May the pair of them never reach old age!
May Gilgamesh and Enkidu come across no graver friend
    to bank on!

Enkidu made ready to speak, saying to Gilgamesh:

My friend, I speak to you, but you do not heed me [. . .]   115
    Until the curse [. . .]

[gap]

[An old version contains the following exchange between Gilgamesh and Enkidu concerning the seven fearsome glories of Humbaba.]

Gilgamesh said to Enkidu:

Now, [my friend], let us go on to victory!
The glories will be lost in the confusion,
The glories will be lost and the brightness will [. . .].   120

Enkidu said to him, to Gilgamesh:

My friend, catch the bird and where will its chicks go?
Let us search out the glories later,
They will run around in the grass like chicks.
Strike him again, then kill his retinue [. . .]   125

[Gilgamesh kills Humbaba. In some versions he has to strike multiple blows before the monster falls.]

Gilgamesh heeded his friend's command,
He raised the axe at his side,
He drew the sword at his belt.
Gilgamesh struck him on the neck,
Enkidu, his friend, [. . .].   130
They pulled out [. . .] as far as the lungs,
He tore out the [. . .],
He forced the head into a cauldron.
[. . .] in abundance fell on the mountain,
[. . .] in abundance fell on the mountain,   135
[. . .]
He struck him, Humbaba the guardian, down to the ground.
His blood [. . .]
For two leagues the cedars [. . .].
He killed the [glories] with him.   140
The forest [. . .].
He slew the monster, guardian of the forest,
At whose cry the mountains of Lebanon [trembled],
At whose cry all the mountains [quaked].
He slew the monster, guardian of the forest,   145
[He trampled on] the broken [. . .],
He struck down the seven [glories].
The battle net [. . .], the sword weighing eight times sixty
     pounds,
He took the weight of ten times sixty pounds upon him,
He forced his way into the forest,   150
He opened the secret dwelling of the supreme gods.

[gap]

[*They cut cedars, then Enkidu builds a gigantic door that they float down the
Euphrates as a gift to Enlil. Enkidu, not anticipating the consequences, hopes
that Enlil will be grateful to Gilgamesh for the door.*]

[. . .] the cedars that they cut, one after another.
[. . .] the flying chips,
Gilgamesh cut down the trees,
Enkidu chose the timbers.   155
Enkidu made ready to speak, said to Gilgamesh:

     You killed the guardian by your strength,
     Who else could cut through this forest of trees?
     My friend, we have felled the lofty cedar,
     Whose crown once pierced the sky.   160
     I will make a door six times twelve cubits high, two times
          twelve cubits wide,
     One cubit shall be its thickness,
     Its hinge pole, ferrule, and pivot box shall be unique.[5]
     Let no stranger approach it, may only a god go through.

5. Mesopotamian doors did not use hinges but were often made of a panel attached to a post. It was this
post, or "hinge pole," that rotated when the door was opened or closed, sometimes on a piece of metal, or
"ferrule," at the bottom. The top of the post was cased or enclosed so the door post would not slip off its
pivot point [*Translator's note*].

Let the Euphrates bring it to Nippur,   165
Nippur, the sanctuary of Enlil.
May Enlil be delighted with you,
May Enlil rejoice over it!

[. . .]
They lashed together a raft [. . .]   170
Enkidu embarked [. . .]
And Gilgamesh [. . .] the head of Humbaba.

Tablet VI

[Gilgamesh strips to put on fresh garments after the expedition. Ishtar, goddess of love and sex, is attracted to him and proposes marriage, offering him majesty and wealth.]

He washed his matted locks, cleaned his head strap,[6]
He shook his hair down over his shoulders.
He threw off his filthy clothes, he put on clean ones,
Wrapping himself in a cloak, he tied on his sash,
Gilgamesh put on his kingly diadem.   5
The princess Ishtar coveted Gilgamesh's beauty:

Come, Gilgamesh, you shall be my bridegroom!
Give, oh give me of your lusciousness!
You shall be my husband and I shall be your wife.
I will ready for you a chariot of lapis and gold,   10
With golden wheels and fittings of gemstones,
You shall harness storm demons as if they were giant mules.
Enter our house amidst fragrance of cedar,
When you enter our house,
The splendid exotic doorsill shall do you homage,   15
Kings, nobles, and princes shall kneel before you,
They shall bring you gifts of mountain and lowland as tribute,
Your goats shall bear triplets, your ewes twins,
Your pack-laden donkey shall overtake the mule,
Your horses shall run proud before the wagon,   20
Your ox in the yoke shall have none to compare!

[Gilgamesh spurns Ishtar's proposal, heaping scorn upon her. He enumerates her past lovers, all of whom she doomed to a cruel destiny.]

Gilgamesh made ready to speak,
Saying to the princess Ishtar:
[What shall I give you] if I take you to wife?
[Shall I give you] a headdress(?) for your person, or clothing?   25
[Shall I give you] bread or drink?
[Shall I give you] food, worthy of divinity?
[Shall I give you] drink, worthy of queenship?
Shall I bind [. . .]?

6. This may refer to a band of cloth that held up Gilgamesh's long hair. When it was released, the hair fell free over the shoulders, a sign of undress in Mesopotamia [*Translator's note*].

Shall I heap up [. . .]?   30
[. . .] for a garment.
[What would I get] if I marry you?
[You are a brazier that goes out] when it freezes,
A flimsy door that keeps out neither wind nor draught,
A palace [that crushes] a warrior,   35
A mouse(?) that [gnaws through] its housing,
Tar that [smears] its bearer,
Waterskin that [soaks] its bearer,
Weak stone that undermines a wall,
Battering ram that destroys the wall for an enemy,   40
Shoe that pinches its wearer!
Which of your lovers [lasted] forever?
Which of your heroes went up [to heaven]?
Come, I call you to account for your lovers:
He who had [jugs of cream] on his shoulders and [. . .]
     on his arm,   45
For Dumuzi,[7] your girlhood lover,
You ordained year after year of weeping.
You fell in love with the brightly colored roller bird,
Then you struck him and broke his wing.
In the woods he sits crying "My-wing!"   50
You fell in love with the lion, perfect in strength,
Then you dug for him ambush pits, seven times seven.
You fell in love with the wild stallion, eager for the fray,
Whip, goad, and lash you ordained for him,
Seven double leagues of galloping you ordained for him,   55
You ordained that he muddy his water when he drinks,
You ordained perpetual weeping for his mother, divine Silili.[8]
You fell in love with the shepherd, keeper of herds,
Who always set out cakes baked in embers for you,
Slaughtered kids for you every day.   60
You struck him and turned him into a wolf,
His own shepherd boys harry him off,
And his own hounds snap at his heels!
You fell in love with Ishullanu, your father's gardener,
Who always brought you baskets of dates,   65
Who daily made your table splendid.
You wanted him, so you sidled up to him:
"My Ishullanu, let's have a taste of your vigor!

     Bring out your member, touch our sweet spot!"
     Ishullanu said to you,   70
     "Me? What do you want of me?
     Hath my mother not baked? Have I not eaten?
     Shall what I taste for food be insults and curses?
     In the cold, is my cover to be the touch of a reed?"
     When you heard what he said,   75
     You struck him and turned him into a scarecrow(?),
     You left him stuck in his own garden patch,

7. Dumuzi: god of vegetation, fertility, growth, and decay.   8. Silili: a divine mare; mother of all horses.

His well sweep goes up no longer, his bucket does not
    descend.
As for me, now that you've fallen in love with me, you will
    treat me like them!

[*Ishtar rushes off to her parents in a passion and sobs out her indignation.
Her speech is noteworthy for its jarring colloquialisms. Her father, Anu, the
sky god, attempts mildly to pacify her, but Ishtar will have punishment at
any price. She demands her father's bull to let loose against the heroes. She
gets her way after threatening to release the dead. She also promises to gar-
ner food against the seven years of famine that will follow the attack of the
bull.*]

When Ishtar heard this,   80
Ishtar was furious and went up to heaven,
Ishtar went sobbing before Anu, her father,
Before Antum, her mother, her tears flowed down:

    Father, Gilgamesh has said outrageous things about me,
    Gilgamesh's been spouting insults about me,   85
    Insults and curses against me!

Anu made ready to speak,
Saying to the princess Ishtar:

    Well now, did you not provoke the king, Gilgamesh,
    And so Gilgamesh spouted insults about you,   90
    Insults and curses against you?

Ishtar made ready to speak,
Saying to Anu, her father:

    Well then, Father, pretty please, the Bull of Heaven,
    So I can kill Gilgamesh on his home ground   95
    If you don't give me the Bull of Heaven,
    I'll strike [. . .] to its foundation,
    I'll [. . .],
    I'll raise up the dead to devour the living,
    The dead shall outnumber the living!   100

Anu made ready to speak,
Saying to the princess Ishtar:

    If you insist on the Bull of Heaven from me,
    Let the widow of Uruk gather seven years of chaff,
    [Let the farmer of Uruk] raise [seven years of hay].   105

Ishtar made ready to speak,
Saying to Anu, her father:

    [. . .] I stored up,
    [. . .] I provided,
    [The widow of Uruk has] gathered seven years of chaff,   110

The farmer [of Uruk] has raised [seven years of] hay.
[With] the Bull of Heaven's [fury I will kill him]!

When Anu heard what Ishtar said,
He placed the lead rope of the Bull of Heaven in her hand,
Ishtar led the Bull of Heaven away.   115

[*The bull rampages down the Euphrates, lowering its water level with great
gulps and opening up enormous pits in the ground with its snorts. Enkidu pinions the animal, and Gilgamesh stabs it to death.*]

When it reached Uruk,
It dried up the groves, reedbeds, and marshes,
It went down to the river, it lowered the river by seven cubits.
At the bull's snort, a pit opened up,
One hundred young men of Uruk fell into it.   120
At its second snort, a pit opened up,
Two hundred young men of Uruk fell into it.
At its third snort, a pit opened up,
Enkidu fell into it, up to his middle.
Enkidu jumped out and seized the bull by its horns,   125
The bull spewed its foam in his face,
Swished dung at him with the tuft of its tail.
Enkidu made ready to speak,
Saying to Gilgamesh:

    My friend, we boasted of [. . .],   130
    How shall we answer [. . .]?
    I have seen, my friend, the strength of the Bull of
       Heaven . . . ,
    So knowing its strength, [I know] how to deal with it.
    I will get around the strength of the Bull of Heaven,
    I will circle behind the Bull of Heaven,   135
    I will grab it by the tuft of its tail,
    I will set my feet on its [. . .],
    Then you, like a strong, skillful slaughterer,
    Thrust your dagger between neck, horn, and tendon!

Enkidu circled behind the Bull of Heaven,   140
He grabbed it by the tuft of its tail,
He set his feet on its [. . .],
And Gilgamesh, like a strong, skillful slaughterer,
Thrust his dagger between neck, horn, and tendon!

[*Gilgamesh and Enkidu offer the creature's heart to Shamash with a prayer.
Ishtar is distraught, again using colloquial language. Enkidu rips off the bull's
haunch and throws it at her. He insults her, saying he would butcher her too
if he could. Ishtar convenes her cult women and sets up a lament over the
bull's haunch.*]

After they had killed the Bull of Heaven,   145
They ripped out its heart and set it before Shamash.
They stepped back and prostrated themselves before Shamash,

Then the two comrades sat down beside each other.
Ishtar went up on the wall of ramparted Uruk,
She writhed in grief, she let out a wail: 150

> That bully Gilgamesh who demeaned me, he's killed the
>   Bull of Heaven!

When Enkidu heard what Ishtar said,
He tore off the bull's haunch and flung it at her:

> If I could vanquish you, I'd turn you to this,
> I'd drape the guts beside you!   155

Ishtar convened the cult women, prostitutes, harlots,
She set up a lament over the haunch of the bull.

[*The bull's immense horns are marvels of craftsmanship. Gilgamesh hangs
them up in his bedroom as a trophy.*]

Gilgamesh summoned all the expert craftsmen,
The craftsmen marveled at the massiveness of its horns,
They were molded from thirty pounds each of lapis blue,   160
Their outer shell was two thumbs thick!
Six times three hundred quarts of oil, the capacity of both,
He donated to anoint the statue of his god, Lugalbanda.
He brought them inside and hung them up in his master bedroom.

[*Gilgamesh and Enkidu parade in triumph. Gilgamesh makes a short speech,
ending with a final condemnation of Ishtar.*]

They washed their hands in the Euphrates,   165
Clasping each other, they came away,
Paraded through the streets of Uruk.
The people of Uruk crowded to look upon them.
Gilgamesh made a speech
To the servant-women of [his palace]:   170

> Who is the handsomest of young men?
> Who is the most glorious of males?
> Gilgamesh is the handsomest of young men!
> [Gilgamesh] is the most glorious of males!
> [She at whom] we flung [the haunch] in our passion,   175
> [Ishtar], she has no one in the street to satisfy her,
> [. . .]

Gilgamesh held a celebration in his palace.
The young men slept stretched out on the couch of night.
While Enkidu slept, he had a dream.   180
Enkidu went to relate his dream,
Saying to his friend:

Tablet VII

My friend, why were the great gods in council?

[*gap*]

[*According to a Hittite version Enkidu sees the gods Anu, Enlil, Ea, and Shamash in council. Anu decrees that because Enkidu and Gilgamesh killed the bull and cut cedars, one of them must die. Enlil, perhaps grateful for the cedar door, decides that it should be Enkidu. Shamash considers this unfair, but Enlil overrules him. When the standard version resumes, Enkidu is cursing the cedar door. The concluding words of his curse parody traditional Mesopotamian inscriptions affixed to monuments, which called the wrath of the gods upon anyone who damaged, removed, or usurped the monument.*]

Enkidu raised [. . .],
He spoke to the door [as if it were human]:

> O bosky door, insensate,
> Which lends an ear that is not there, 5
> I sought your wood for twenty double leagues,
> Till I beheld a lofty cedar [. . .]
> No rival had your tree [in the forest . . .].
> Six times twelve cubits was your height, two times twelve
>   cubits was your width,
> One cubit was your thickness, 10
> Your hinge pole, ferrule, and pivot box were unique.
> I made you, I brought you to Nippur, I set you up.
> Had I known, O door, how you would [requite me],
> And that this your goodness [towards me . . .],
> I would have raised my axe, I would have chopped you down, 15
> I would have floated you as a raft to the temple of Shamash,
> I would have brought you into the temple of Shamash,
> I would have set up the cedar [. . . in the . . .] of the
>   temple of Shamash,
> I would have set up the lion-headed monster-bird Anzu at
>   its gate,
> [. . .] the way to you [. . .] 20
> I would have [. . .],
> Then in Uruk [. . .] you,
> Because Shamash heard my plea . . .
> He gave me the weapon to [kill Humbaba].
> Now then, O door, it was I who made you, it was I who set
>   you up. 25
> I [. . .], I will tear you out!
> May a king who shall arise after me despise you,
> May [. . .] conceal you,
> May he alter my inscription and put on his own!

He tore out [his hair], threw away [his clothing]. 30

When he heard out this speech, swiftly, quickly his tears flowed
    down,

When Gilgamesh heard out Enkidu's speech, swiftly, quickly,
   his tears flowed down.

*[Gilgamesh comforts Enkidu by suggesting that death may be a greater burden
for those left behind than for the deceased. Gilgamesh promises that he will
make a magnificent funerary statue of his friend. Death is inevitable; it is
foolish to complain.]*

Gilgamesh made ready to speak, saying to Enkidu:

    [. . .] superb,
    My friend, you are rational but [you say] strange things,   35
    Why, my friend, does your heart speak strange things?
    The dream is a most precious omen, though very frightening,
    Your [lips] are buzzing like flies.
    [Though frightening], the dream is a precious omen.
    The [gods] left mourning for the living,   40
    The dream left mourning for the living,
    The dream left woe for the living!
    Now I shall go pray to the great gods,
    I will be assiduous to [my own god], I will pray to yours,
    To [Anu], father of the gods [. . .],   45
    [To] Enlil, counselor of the gods, [. . .],
    [. . .]
    I will make your image of gold beyond measure.
    You can pay no silver, no gold can you [. . .],
    What Enlil commanded is not like the [. . .] of the gods,   50
    What he commanded, he will not retract.
    The verdict he has scrivened, he will not reverse nor erase.
    My friend, he will not [. . .]
    People often die before their time.

*[At dawn, Enkidu prays to Shamash, god of justice and right-dealing. He calls
his curse upon the two human agents whom he blames for his destiny, the
hunter and the harlot. For the hunter he wishes a poor catch, for the harlot
the worst of a whore's life.]*

At the first glimmer of dawn,   55
Enkidu lifted his head, weeping before Shamash,
Before the sun's fiery glare, his tears flowed down:

    I have turned to you, O Shamash, on account of the precious
      days of my life,
    As for that hunter, the entrapping-man,
    Who did not let me get as much life as my friend,   60
    May that hunter not get enough to make him a living.
    Make his profit loss, cut down his take,
    May his income, his portion evaporate before you,
    Any wildlife that enters [his traps], make it go out the window!

When he had cursed the hunter to his heart's content,   65
He resolved to curse the harlot Shamhat:

Come, Shamhat, I will ordain you a destiny,
A destiny that will never end, forever and ever!
I will lay on you the greatest of all curses,
Swiftly, inexorably, may my curse come upon you.   70
May you never make a home that you can enjoy,
May you never caress [a child] of your own,
May you never be received among decent women.
May [beer sludge(?)] impregnate your lap,
May the drunkard bespatter your best clothes with vomit.   75
[May your swain prefer] beauties,
[May he pinch you] like potter's clay.
May you get no [. . .] alabaster,
[May no . . .] table to be proud of be set in your house.
May the nook you enjoy be a doorstep,   80
May the public crossroads be your dwelling,
May vacant lots be your sleeping place,
May the shade of a wall be your place of business.
May brambles and thorns flay your feet,
May toper and sober slap your cheek.⁹   85
May [riffraff] of the street shove each other in your brothel,
May there be a brawl [there . . .].
[When you stroll with your cronies], may they catcall
     after you.
May the builder not keep your roof in repair,
May the screech owl roost [in the ruins of your home].   90
May a feast never be held [where you live].

                    [gap]

May your purple finery be expropriated,
May filthy underwear be what you are given,
Because you diminished me, an innocent,
Yes me, an innocent, you wronged me(?) in my steppe.   95

[Shamash remonstrates, asserting that friendship with Gilgamesh was worth
an untimely death and promising Enkidu a fine funeral. He also tells him that
Gilgamesh will take his place as "wild man" of the steppe, no doubt the fullest
possible observance of the loss of his friend, short of taking his place in the
netherworld.]

When Shamash heard what he said,
From afar a warning voice called to him from the sky:

     O Enkidu, why curse Shamhat the harlot,
     Who fed you bread, fit for a god,
     Who poured you beer, fit for a king,   100
     Who dressed you in a noble garment,
     And gave you handsome Gilgamesh for a comrade?
     Now then, Gilgamesh is your friend and blood brother!
     Won't he lay you down in the ultimate resting place?

9. That is, may anyone hit her, drunk or not [Translator's note].

In a perfect resting place he will surely lay you down!   105
He will settle you in peaceful rest in that dwelling sinister,
Rulers of the netherworld will do you homage.
He will have the people of Uruk shed bitter tears for you,
He will make the [pleasure-loving] people burdened down for
    you,
And, as for him, after your death, he will let his hair grow
    matted,   110
He will put on a lion skin and roam the steppe.

[Enkidu, with bitter humor, immediately reverses the "destiny that will never
end" for the harlot. He now wishes her the best of a whore's life: an eager, generous clientele from all levels of society.]

When Enkidu heard the speech of the valiant Shamash,
His raging heart was calmed,
[. . .] his fury was calmed:

    Come, Shamhat, I will ordain you a destiny,   115
    My mouth that cursed you, let it bless you instead.
    May governors and dignitaries fall in love with you,
    May the man one double league away slap his thighs
      in excitement,
    May the man two double leagues away let down his hair.
    May the subordinate not hold back from you, but open
      his trousers,   120
    May he give you obsidian, lapis, and gold,
    May ear bangles be your gift.
    To the man whose wealth is secure, whose granaries are full,
    May Ishtar, [. . .] of the gods, introduce you,
    For your sake may the wife and mother of seven be
      abandoned.   125

Enkidu was sick at heart,
He lay there lonely.
[He told] his friend what weighed on his mind:

[Enkidu tells Gilgamesh a dream he had the night before. The timing of this
is not clear, suggesting that the text has been assembled from different materials at this point. The dream is of dying and the afterlife. Mesopotamian tradition was unanimous on this grim view of the netherworld, characterized by
darkness, hunger and thirst, dust, and no rewards beyond those provided by
the solicitude of one's surviving kin. A fragment discovered at Megiddo, perhaps dating to the fourteenth century B.C.E. preserves a version of this episode
in which Enkidu may blame Gilgamesh for the killing of Humbaba, but this
is uncertain.]

    My friend, what a dream I had last night!
    Heaven cried out, earth made reply,   130
    I was standing between them.
    There was a certain man, his face was somber,
    His face was like that of the lion-headed monster-bird Anzu,

His hands were the paws of a lion,
His fingernails were the talons of an eagle.   135
He seized me by the hair, he was too strong for me,
I hit him but he sprang back like a swing rope,
He hit me and capsized me like a [raft].
Like a wild bull he trampled me,
He [. . .] my whole body with his slaver,   140
"Save me, my friend!"—[but you did not save me]!
You were afraid and did not [. . .]
You [. . .]

[gap]

[. . .] and turned me into a dove,
He trussed my limbs like a bird's.   145
Holding me fast, he took me down to the house of
    shadows, the dwelling of hell,
To the house whence none who enters comes forth,
On the road from which there is no way back,
To the house whose dwellers are deprived of light,
Where dust is their fare and their food is clay.   150
They are dressed like birds in feather garments,
Yea, they shall see no daylight, for they abide in darkness.
[Dust lies thick] on the door [and bolt],
To the house [. . .].
When I entered that house of dust,   155
I saw crowns in a heap,
There dwelt the kings, the crowned heads who once
    ruled the land,
Who always set out roast meat for Anu and Enlil,
Who always set out baked offerings, libated cool water
    from waterskins.
In that house of dust I entered,   160
Dwelt high priests and acolytes,
Dwelt reciters of spells and ecstatics,[1]
Dwelt the anointers of the great gods,
Dwelt old King Etana and the god of the beasts,
Dwelt the queen of the netherworld, Ereshkigal.   165
Belet-seri, scribe of the netherworld, was kneeling before her,
She was holding [a tablet] and reading to her,
[She lifted] her head, she looked at me:
"Who brought this man?"

[gap]

[Whereas the two friends have interpreted or, one might say, explained away
the grim symbolism of all the dreams they have had since the beginning of

---

1. Mesopotamian poets often used extremes to convey totality: high priests were at the top of the hierarchy, assistants, or "acolytes," at the bottom, so line 161 means that all ranks of the priesthood were in the
netherworld along with other people. Reciters of spells were learned scholars while prophets, or "ecstatics," were people who spoke in a trance without having studied their words. They were sometimes social
outcasts or people without education. Line 162 therefore refers to all who communicated or made use of
the words of the gods [Translator's note].

*their friendship, this dream is so obvious and compelling in its portent that no
interpretation is called for.*]

> I who went with you through all hardships,   170
> Remember me, my friend, do not forget what I have
>   undergone!
> My friend had a dream needing no interpretation.

[*Enkidu's final illness is conveyed by monotonous repetition of the days of its
course. This climaxes in a parting speech, little of which is now preserved.*]

The day he had the dream, [his strength] ran out.
Enkidu lay there one day, [a second day] he was ill,
Enkidu lay in his bed, [his illness grew worse].   175
A third day, a fourth day, [Enkidu's illness grew worse].
A fifth, a sixth, a seventh,
An eighth, a ninth, [a tenth day],
[Enkidu's illness grew worse].
An eleventh, a twelfth day,   180
Enkidu lay in his bed.
He called for Gilgamesh, [roused him with his cry]:

> My friend laid on me [the greatest] curse of all!
> When in battle [. . .]
> I feared the battle [but will die in my bed],   185
> My friend, he who [falls quickly] in battle [is glorious].
> I [. . .] in battle.

[gap]

[*Enkidu dies.*]

Tablet VIII

[*Gilgamesh laments his dead friend, Enkidu.*]

At the first glimmer of dawn,
Gilgamesh [lamented] his friend:

> Enkidu, my friend, your mother the gazelle,
> Your father the wild ass brought you into the world,
> Onagers raised you on their milk,   5
> And the wild beasts taught you all the grazing places.
> The pathways, O Enkidu, to the forest of cedars,
> May they weep for you, without falling silent, night and day.
> May the elders of the teeming city, ramparted Uruk, weep
>   for you,
> May the crowd who blessed our departure weep for you.   10
> May the heights of highland and mountain [weep for you],
> [. . .]
> May the lowlands wail like your mother.
> May [the forest] of balsam and cedar weep for you,
> Which we slashed in our fury.   15

May bear, hyena, panther, leopard, deer, jackal,
Lion, wild bull, gazelle, ibex, the beasts and creatures
   of the steppe, weep for you.
May the sacred Ulaya River weep for you, along whose
   banks we once strode erect,[2]
May the holy Euphrates weep for you,
Whose waters we libated from waterskins.   20
May the young men of ramparted Uruk weep for you,
Who watched us slay the Bull of Heaven in combat.
May the plowman weep for you [at his plow],
Who extolled your name in the sweet song of harvest home.[3]
May they weep for you, [. . .] of the teeming city of Uruk,   25
Who exalted your name at the first [. . .].
May the shepherd and herdsman weep for you,
Who held the milk and buttermilk to your mouth,
May the [nurse] weep for you,
Who treated your rashes(?) with butter.   30
May the [. . .] weep for you,
Who held the ale to your mouth.
May the harlot weep for you,
Who massaged you with sweet-smelling oil.
May the wedding guests weep for you,   35
Who [. . .]
Like brothers may they weep for you,
Like sisters may they tear out their hair for your sake.
[. . .] Enkidu, as your father, your mother,
I weep for you bitterly, [. . .]   40

Hear me, O young men, listen to me,
Hear me, O elders of [Uruk], listen to me!
I mourn my friend Enkidu,
I howl as bitterly as a professional keener.
Oh for the axe at my side, oh for the safeguard by my hand,   45
Oh for the sword at my belt, oh for the shield before me,
Oh for my best garment, oh for the raiment that pleased me
   most!
An ill wind rose against me and snatched it away!
O my friend, swift wild donkey, mountain onager, panther
   of the steppe,
O Enkidu my friend, swift wild donkey, mountain onager,
   panther of the steppe!   50
You who stood by me when we climbed the mountain,
Seized and slew the Bull of Heaven,
Felled Humbaba who [dwelt] in the forest of cedar,
What now is this sleep that has seized you?
Come back to me! You hear me not.   55

But, as for him, he did not raise his head.
He touched his heart but it was not beating.

---

2. ". . . banks we once strode erect": This line refers to an episode that does not appear in the extant portions of the epic [*Translator's note*].   3. Mesopotamian literature referred to work songs sung when the crops were brought in from the harvest as symbols of happiness and prosperity [*Translator's note*].

Then he covered his friend's face, like a bride's.
He hovered round him like an eagle,
Like a lioness whose cubs are in a pitfall, 60
He paced to and fro, back and forth,
Tearing out and hurling away the locks of his hair,
Ripping off and throwing away his fine clothes like something
    foul.

[*Gilgamesh commissions a memorial statue for Enkidu.*]

At the first glimmer of dawn,
Gilgamesh sent out a proclamation to the land: 65

> Hear ye, blacksmith, lapidary, metalworker, goldsmith,
>   jeweler!
> Make [an image] of my friend,
> [Such as no one ever] made of his friend!
> The limbs of my friend [. . .]
> [Your beard] of lapis, your chest of gold, 70
> Your skin of [. . .]

[*gap*]

> I will lay you down in the ultimate resting place,
> In a perfect resting place I will surely lay you down.
> I will settle you in peaceful rest in that dwelling sinister,
> Rulers of the netherworld will do you homage. 75
> I will have the people of Uruk shed bitter tears for you,
> I will make the pleasure-loving people burdened down for
>   you,
> And, as for me, now that you are dead, I will let my hair
>   grow matted,
> I will put on a lion skin and roam the steppe!

[*gap*]

At the first glimmer of dawn, Gilgamesh arose, 80
[He . . . the storehouse],
He broke its seal, he surveyed the treasure,
[He brought out] carnelian,[4] [. . .] alabaster,
He fashioned [. . .]
He set out [. . .] for his friend. 85
[. . .]
[. . . made of] ten pounds of gold,
[. . .] pounds of gold,
[. . .] pounds of gold,
[. . .] pounds of gold, 90
[. . .]
[. . .] between them, mounted in thirty pounds of gold.

---

4. A reddish stone, prized in Mesopotamia for making beads and seals [*Translator's note*].

[*gap*]

[*In the fragmentary lines that follow, there is mention of weapons and ornaments of gold, silver, ivory, and iron.*]

He slaughtered fatted [cattle] and sheep, heaped them high for
   his friend,
[. . .]
They carried off all the meat for the rulers of the netherworld.   95
[. . .] Ishtar, the great queen,
[. . . made of . . .], the sacred wood,
He displayed in the open for Ishtar, the great queen,
Saying: "May Ishtar, the great queen, accept this,
May she welcome my friend and walk at his side."   100
[. . .]
He displayed in the open for Ashimbabbar [. . .],
Saying: "May Ashimbabbar, [. . .], accept this,
May he welcome my friend and walk at his side."
A jar of lapis [. . .],   105
[. . .]
He displayed in the open for Ereshkigal, [queen of the
   netherworld],
Saying: "May Ereshkigal, [queen of the crowded netherworld],
   accept this,
May she welcome my friend and walk at his side."
A flute of carnelian [. . .],   110
He displayed in the open for Dumuzi, the shepherd, beloved of
   [Ishtar],
Saying: "May Dumuzi, the shepherd, beloved of [Ishtar],
   accept this,
May he welcome my friend and walk at his side."
A chair of lapis [. . .]
A staff of lapis [. . .]   115
He displayed in the open for Namtar, [courier of the netherworld],
Saying: "May Namtar, [courier of the crowded netherworld],
   accept this,
May he welcome my friend and walk at his side."

[*gap*]

A bracelet(?) of silver, a ring(?) of [. . .],
He displayed in the open for Qassa-tabat, sweeper(?)
   [of the netherworld],   120
Saying: "May Qassa-tabat, sweeper(?) [of the crowded
   netherworld], accept this,
May he welcome my friend and walk at his side.
May my friend not . . . nor lose courage."
[. . .] of alabaster, the inside inlaid with lapis and carnelian,
[. . .] of the cedar forest,   125
[. . .] inlaid with carnelian,
He displayed in the open for Ninshuluhha, housekeeper
   of the netherworld,

Saying: "May Ninshuluhha, housekeeper of the crowded
   netherworld, accept this,
May she welcome my friend and walk at his side.
May she intercede on behalf of my friend, lest he lose courage."   130
The obsidian knife with lapis fitting,
The sharpening stone pure-whetted with Euphrates water,
He displayed in the open for Bibbu, meat carver of the
   netherworld,
Saying: "May Bibbu, meat carver of the crowded netherworld,
   accept this,
Welcome my friend and walk at his side."   135
[. . .] carnelian and alabaster,
He displayed in the open for [. . .]-absu, blame-bearer
   of the netherworld,
Saying: "May [. . .]-absu, blame-bearer of the crowded
   netherworld, accept this,
Welcome my friend and walk at his side."

[gap]

[*The lying-in-state and obsequies continue.*]

At the first glimmer of dawn, Gilgamesh opened the [. . .],   140
He brought out a great table of precious wood,
He filled a carnelian bowl with honey,
He filled a lapis bowl with butter,
He adorned [. . .] and displayed it in the open.

[gap]

Tablet IX

[*Gilgamesh, distraught, roams the steppe. He then sets forth on a quest to find Utanapishtim, the survivor of the flood.*]

Gilgamesh was weeping bitterly for Enkidu, his friend,
As he roamed the steppe:

    Shall I not die too? Am I not like Enkidu?
    Oh woe has entered my vitals!
    I have grown afraid of death, so I roam the steppe.   5
    Having come this far, I will go on swiftly
    Towards Utanapishtim, son of Ubar-Tutu.
    I have reached mountain passes at night.
    I saw lions, I felt afraid,
    I looked up to pray to the moon,
    To the moon, beacon of the gods, my prayers went forth: 10
    "[. . .] keep me safe!"

[At night] he lay down, then awoke from a dream.
[. . .] moon, he rejoiced to be alive.
He raised the axe at his side,   15

He drew the sword from his belt,
He dropped among them like an arrow,
He struck [the lions], scattered, [and killed them].

[*gap*]

[*The following episode, found in an old version, may be placed here. In an ob-*
scure passage, a god apparently tells Shamash what Gilgamesh is doing.]

He has put on their skins, he eats their flesh.
Gilgamesh [digs] wells where they never were before,   20
[. . .] the water, he pursues the winds.

Shamash was distressed, bending down, he said to Gilgamesh:

Gilgamesh, wherefore do you wander?
The eternal life you are seeking you shall not find.

Gilgamesh spoke to him, the valiant Shamash: 25

After my restless roaming in the steppe,
There will be ample repose, deep in the earth.
I have been asleep all these years!
Now let my eyes see the sun, let me have all the light
    I could wish for,
Darkness is infinite, how little light there is!   30
When may the dead see the radiance of the sun?

[*As the standard version resumes, Gilgamesh approaches in awe the scorpion*
monsters who guard the gateway to the sun's passage through the mountains.
The description of the scorpion monsters is so hyperbolic as to suggest humor-
ous intent, especially when the scorpion monster's wife corrects her husband.]

The twin peaks are called Mashum.
When he arrived at the twin peaks called Mashum,
Which daily watch over the rising [and setting of the sun],
Whose peaks thrust upward to the vault of heaven,   35
Whose flanks reach downward to hell,
Where scorpion monsters guard its gateway,
Whose appearance is dreadful, whose venom is death,
Their fear-inspiring radiance spreads over the mountains,
They watch over the sun at its rising and setting,   40
When Gilgamesh saw their fearsomeness and terror,
He covered his face.
He took hold of himself and approached them.

The scorpion monster called to his wife:

This one who has come to us, his body is flesh of a god!   45

The wife of the scorpion monster answered him:

Two-thirds of him is divine, one-third is human.

The scorpion monster, the male one, called out,
[To Gilgamesh, scion] of the gods, he said these words:

> [Who are you] who have come this long way,   50
> [. . .] before me,
> [. . .] whose crossing is arduous,
> [. . .] I want to know,
> [The goal towards which] you are setting forth,
> [. . .] I want to know.   55

[gap]

[When Gilgamesh explains his quest, the scorpion monster asserts that no one
can traverse the tunnel through mountains. Apparently the sun crosses the sky
during the twelve hours of day and passes through the tunnel during the
twelve hours of night so as to return to its rising point.]

> [. . .] Utanapishtim my forefather [. . .]
> Who took his place in the assembly of the gods [. . .]
> Death and life [. . .]

The scorpion monster made ready to speak, spoke to him,
Saying to Gilgamesh: 60

> There is no [. . .], Gilgamesh,
> No one has ever [. . .] the mountain.
> Its passage is twelve double hours [. . .]
> Dense is the darkness, [no light is there],
> To the rising of the sun [. . .]   65
> To the setting of the sun [. . .]
> To the setting of the sun [. . .]

[gap]

[In the intervening gap, something persuades the scorpion monster to open
the gateway to the tunnel through the mountains. To judge from the analogy
of Utanapishtim and his wife, encountered later in the epic, not to mention
Ninsun and the tavern keeper, also later in the epic, the scorpion monster's
wife intervenes on Gilgamesh's behalf and convinces her husband to admit
him.]

> Woe [in his vitals],
> [His features weathered] by cold [and sun],
> With sighs [. . .],   70
> Now then, [show him the way to Utanapishtim].

[The scorpion monster apparently warns Gilgamesh that he has only twelve
hours to get through the sun's tunnel before the sun enters it at nightfall.]

The scorpion monster made ready to speak, spoke to him,
Said to Gilgamesh, [scion of the gods]:

Go, Gilgamesh, [. . .]
Mount Mashum [. . .]   75
The mountain ranges [. . .]
Safely [. . .].

[He opened to him] the gateway of the mountain,
Gilgamesh [entered the mountain . . .]
[He heeded] the words of the [scorpion monster],   80
[He set out on] the way of the sun.

[*Gilgamesh races through the tunnel, a heroic run equal to the sun's journey
across the sky. It is so dark that he cannot reassure himself by looking back to
the light from the entrance behind him to know that the sun is still in the
heavens. At the same time, he knows that if he sees light ahead of him, he is
doomed.*]

When he had gone one double hour,
Dense was the darkness, no light was there,
It would not let him look behind him.
When he had gone two double hours,   85
Dense was the darkness, no light was there,
It would not let him look behind him.
When he had gone three double hours,
Dense was the darkness, no light was there,
It would not let him look behind him.   90
When he had gone four double hours,
Dense was the darkness, no light was there,
It would not let him look behind him.
When he had gone five double hours,
Dense was the darkness, no light was there,   95
It would not let him look behind him.
When he had gone six double hours,
Dense was the darkness, no light was there,
It would not let him look behind him.
When he had gone seven double hours,   100
Dense was the darkness, there was no light,
It would not let him look behind him.
When he had gone eight double hours, he rushed ahead,
Dense was the darkness, there was no light,
It would not let him look behind him.   105
When he had gone nine double hours, he felt the north wind,
[. . .] his face,
Dense was the darkness, there was no light,
It would not let him look behind him.
When he had gone ten double hours,   110
[The time for the sun's entry] was drawing near.
[When he had gone eleven double hours], just one double hour
    [was left],
[When he had gone twelve double hours], he came out ahead of
    the sun!
[He had run twelve double hours], bright light still reigned!
He went forward, seeing [. . .], the trees of the gods.   115

The carnelian bore its fruit,
Like bunches of grapes dangling, lovely to see,
The lapis bore foliage,
Fruit it bore, a delight to behold.

[*The fragmentary lines that remain continue the description of the wonderful grove. Identification of most of the stones is conjectural.*]

[. . .] balsam [. . .],   120
[. . .] cedar [. . .].
Its fronds were green chlorite, [. . .] sweet dates,
Coral(?), [. . .], rubies(?),
Instead of thorns and brambles, there were [. . .] of red stone,
He took up a carob, it was [. . .] of green stone!   125
Agates, hematite, [. . .], amber(?),
Instead of [. . .] and cucumbers, there were [. . .] of yellow
    stone,
Instead of [. . .] there were [. . .] of turquoise,
The [. . .] cowrie shells.[5]
It had water to make the [. . .] delightful.   130
Gilgamesh [. . .] as he walked along,
He looked up and gazed at it.

Tablet X

[*Gilgamesh approaches the tavern of Siduri, a female tavern keeper who lives at the end of the earth. This interesting personage is unknown outside this poem, nor is it clear who her clientele might be in such a remote spot. Alarmed by Gilgamesh's appearance, she locks her door. In contrast to his deference to the scorpion monster, Gilgamesh is aggressive. When he identifies himself, the tavern keeper is skeptical and wants to know why anyone so splendid as Gilgamesh appears in such condition.*]

Siduri the tavern keeper, who dwells at the edge of the sea,
She sits on a [stool of . . .]
For her was wrought the cuprack,[6] for her the [brewing vat of gold],
It(?) is covered with a lid(?) [of . . .].
Gilgamesh made his way towards her [. . .],   5
He was clad in a skin, fearsomeness [. . .]
He had flesh of gods in [his body].
Woe was in his vitals,
His face was like a traveler's from afar.
The tavern keeper eyed him from a distance,   10
Speaking to herself, she said these words,
She [debated] with herself:

---

5. Chlorite (line 122), a soft stone, was prized in Mesopotamia for making bowls and small containers. Carob (line 125) was a common seedpod eaten or made into juice; hence, the most ordinary-looking fruit turned out to be a precious stone in this garden. Cowries (line 129), or small imported seashells, were prized for making jewelry and were sometimes used in burial rites [*Translator's note*].   6. Some Mesopotamian drinking cups were conical, with pointed bottoms, so they were set in a wooden rack to hold them up when they were full of liquid [*Translator's note*].

This no doubt is a slaughterer of wild bulls!
Why would he make straight for my door?

At the sight of him the tavern keeper barred her door,   15
She barred her door and mounted to the roof terrace.
But he, Gilgamesh, put his ear to the [door . . .],
He lifted his chin and [. . .].

Gilgamesh said to her, to the tavern keeper:

Tavern keeper, when you saw me why did you bar your door,   20
Bar your door and mount to the roof terrace?
I will strike down your door, I will shatter [your doorbolt],
[. . .] my [. . .]
[. . .] in the steppe.

[The tavern keeper said to him, to] Gilgamesh: 25

[. . .] I barred my door,
[. . . I mounted to] the roof terrace.
[. . .] I want to know.

Gilgamesh said to her, to the tavern keeper:

[. . .]   30
[I am Gilgamesh . . .], who killed the guardian,
Who seized and killed the bull that came down from heaven,
Who felled Humbaba who dwelt in the forest of cedars,
Who killed lions at the mountain passes.

The tavern keeper said to him, to Gilgamesh: 35

[If you are indeed Gilgamesh], who killed the guardian,
Who felled Humbaba who dwelt in the forest of cedars,
Who killed lions at the mountain passes,
Who seized and killed the bull that came down from heaven,
Why are your cheeks emaciated, your face cast down,   40
Your heart wretched, your features wasted,
Woe in your vitals,
Your face like a traveler's from afar,
Your features weathered by cold and sun,
Why are you clad in a lion skin, roaming the steppe?   45

Gilgamesh said to her, to the tavern keeper:

My cheeks would not be emaciated, nor my face cast down,
Nor my heart wretched nor my features wasted,
Nor would there be woe in my vitals,
Nor would my face be like a traveler's from afar,   50
Nor would my features be weathered by cold and sun,
Nor would I be clad in a lion skin, roaming the steppe,
But for my friend, swift wild donkey, mountain onager,
    panther of the steppe,

But for Enkidu, swift wild donkey, mountain onager,
    panther of the steppe,
My friend whom I so loved, who went with me
    through every hardship,   55
Enkidu, whom I so loved, who went with me
    through every hardship,
The fate of mankind has overtaken him.
Six days and seven nights I wept for him,
I would not give him up for burial,
Until a worm fell out of his nose.   60
I was frightened [. . .]
I have grown afraid of death, so I roam the steppe,
My friend's case weighs heavy upon me.
A distant road I roam over the steppe,
My friend Enkidu's case weighs heavy upon me!   65
A distant road I roam over the steppe,
How can I be silent? How can I hold my peace?
My friend whom I loved is turned into clay,
Enkidu, my friend whom I loved, is turned into clay!
Shall I too not lie down like him,   70
And never get up forever and ever?

[*An old version adds the following episode.*]

After his death I could find no life,
Back and forth I prowled like a bandit in the steppe.
Now that I have seen your face, tavern keeper,
May I not see that death I constantly fear!   75

The tavern keeper said to him, to Gilgamesh:

Gilgamesh, wherefore do you wander?
The eternal life you are seeking you shall not find.
When the gods created mankind,
They established death for mankind,   80
And withheld eternal life for themselves.
As for you, Gilgamesh, let your stomach be full,
Always be happy, night and day.
Make every day a delight,
Night and day play and dance.   85
Your clothes should be clean,
Your head should be washed,
You should bathe in water,
Look proudly on the little one holding your hand,
Let your mate be always blissful in your loins,   90
This, then, is the work of mankind.

[*gap*]

Gilgamesh said to her, to the tavern keeper:

What are you saying, tavern keeper?
I am heartsick for my friend.

What are you saying, tavern keeper? 95
I am heartsick for Enkidu!

[*gap*]

[*The standard version resumes.*]

Gilgamesh said to her, to the tavern keeper:

Now then, tavern keeper, what is the way to Utanapishtim?
What are its signs? Give them to me.
Give, oh give me its signs! 100
If need be, I'll cross the sea,
If not, I'll roam the steppe.

The tavern keeper said to him, to Gilgamesh:

Gilgamesh, there has never been a place to cross,
There has been no one from the dawn of time who could
   ever cross this sea. 105
The valiant Shamash alone can cross this sea,
Save for the sun, who could cross this sea?
The crossing is perilous, highly perilous the course,
And midway lie the waters of death, whose surface is
   impassable.
Suppose, Gilgamesh, you do cross the sea, 110
When you reach the waters of death, what will you do?
Yet, Gilgamesh, there is Ur-Shanabi, Utanapishtim's boatman,
He has the Stone Charms with him as he trims pine trees
   in the forest.
Go, show yourself to him,
If possible, cross with him, if not, then turn back. 115

[*Gilgamesh advances and without preamble attacks Ur-Shanabi and smashes
the Stone Charms. Ur-Shanabi tells Gilgamesh that the Stone Charms were
needed to cross the waters of death. The nature of these objects has never been
satisfactorily explained. Although some scholars suggest that they were anchors
or counterweights, the Hittite version calls them "images," so they may have
been magic amulets that warded off the waters of death.*]

When Gilgamesh heard this,
He raised the axe at his side,
He drew the sword at his belt,
He crept forward, went down towards them,
Like an arrow he dropped among them, 120
His battle cry resounded in the forest.
When Ur-Shanabi saw the shining [. . .],
He raised his axe, he [trembled(?)] before him,
But he, for his part, struck his head [. . .] Gilgamesh,
He seized his arm [. . .] his chest. 125
And the Stone Charms, the [protection . . . (?)] of the boat,
Without which no one [crosses the waters] of death,

He smashed them [and threw them into] the broad sea,
Into the channel [he threw them, his own hands] foiled him,
He smashed them [and threw them] into the channel!   130
[. . .] the boat,
And he [. . .] to the bank.

[*An old version preserves the following, in which Sur-Sunabu is another form
of the name Ur-Shanabi.*]

He turned back and stood before him.
Sur-Sunabu stared at him,
Sur-Sunabu said to him, to Gilgamesh: 135

> What is your name, pray tell?
> I am Sur-Sunabu, servant of Utanapishtim the Distant One.

Gilgamesh said to him, to Sur-Sunabu:

> Gilgamesh is my name.
> I am he who came from [Uruk], the abode of Anu,   140
> Who traveled here around the mountains,
> A distant road where the sun comes forth.
> Now that I have see your face, Sur-Sunabu,
> Show me Utanapishtim the Distant One.

[*The standard version resumes.*]

Ur-Shanabi said to him, to Gilgamesh: 145

> Why are your cheeks emaciated, your face cast down,
> Your heart wretched, your features wasted,
> Woe in your vitals,
> Your face like a traveler's from afar,
> Your features weathered by cold and sun,   150
> Why are you clad in a lion skin, roaming the steppe?

Gilgamesh said to him, to Ur-Shanabi:

> My cheeks would not be emaciated, nor my face cast down,
> Nor my heart wretched, nor my features wasted,
> Nor would there be woe in my vitals,   155
> Nor would my face be like a traveler's from afar,
> Nor would my features be weathered by cold and sun,
> Nor would I be clad in a lion skin, roaming the steppe,
> But for my friend, swift wild donkey, mountain onager,
>   panther of the steppe,
> But for Enkidu, my friend, swift wild donkey, mountain
>   onager, panther of the steppe,   160
> He who stood by me as we ascended the mountain,
> Seized and killed the bull that came down from heaven,
> Felled Humbaba who dwelt in the forest of cedars,
> Killed lions at the mountain passes,

My friend whom I so loved, who went with me through
    every hardship,   165
Enkidu, whom I so loved, who went with me through
    every hardship,
The fate of mankind has overtaken him.
Six days and seven nights I wept for him,
I would not give him up for burial,
Until a worm fell out of his nose.   170
I was frightened [. . .]
I have grown afraid of death, so I roam the steppe,
My friend's case weighs heavy upon me.
A distant road I roam over the steppe,
My friend Enkidu's case weighs heavy upon me!   175
A distant road I roam over the steppe,
How can I be silent? How can I hold my peace?
My friend whom I loved is turned into clay,
Enkidu, my friend whom I loved, is turned into clay!
Shall I too not lie down like him,   180
And never get up forever and ever?

Gilgamesh said to him, to Ur-Shanabi:

Now then, Ur-Shanabi, what is the way to Utanapishtim?
What are its signs? Give them to me,
Give, oh give me its signs!   185
If need be, I'll cross the sea,
If not, I'll roam the steppe.

Ur-Shanabi said to him, to Gilgamesh:

Your own hands have foiled you, Gilgamesh,
You have smashed the Stone Charms, you have [thrown them
    into the channel],   190
The Stone Charms are smashed [. . .]

[gap]

[An old version has the following here.]

The Stone Charms, Gilgamesh, are what carry me,
Lest I touch the waters of death.
In your fury you have smashed them,
The Stone Charms, they are what I had with me to make
    the crossing!   195

[As the standard version resumes, Gilgamesh cuts punting poles. Then they set
out across the sea. When they reach the waters of death, Gilgamesh pushes
once with each punting pole, then lets it go, lest he touch the waters of death.
For the last part of the journey, beyond the waters of death, Gilgamesh desperately holds up his clothing as an improvised sail. The numbers and distances in this passage have not been convincingly explained.]

Gilgamesh, raise the axe in your hand,
Go down into the forest, [cut twice sixty] poles each
 five times twelve cubits long,
Dress them, set on handguards(?),
Bring them to me.

When Gilgamesh heard this,   200
He raised the axe at his side,
He drew the sword at his belt,
He went down into the forest, cut [twice sixty] poles each
 five times twelve cubits long,
He dressed them, set on handguards(?),
He brought them to him.   205
Gilgamesh and Ur-Shanabi embarked [in the boat],
They launched the boat, they [embarked] upon it.
A journey of a month and a half they made in three days!
Ur-Shanabi reached the waters of death,
Ur-Shanabi said to him, to Gilgamesh: 210

 Stand back, Gilgamesh! Take the first [pole],
 Your hand must not touch the waters of death [. . .],
 Take the second, the third, the fourth pole, Gilgamesh,
 Take the fifth, sixth, and seventh pole, Gilgamesh,
 Take the eight, ninth, and tenth pole, Gilgamesh,   215
 Take the eleventh and twelfth pole, Gilgamesh.

With twice sixty Gilgamesh had used up the poles.
Then he, for his part, took off his belt [. . .],
Gilgamesh tore off his clothes from his body,
Held high his arms for a mast.   220
Utanapishtim was watching him from a distance,
Speaking to himself, he said these words,
He debated to himself:

 Why have [the Stone Charms], belonging to the boat,
 been smashed,
 And one not its master embarked [thereon]?   225
 He who comes here is no man of mine,
 And at his right [. . .]?
 I look but he is no [man] of mine,
 I look but he is [. . .]
 I look but he is [. . .]   230

[gap]

[*In the fragmentary lines that follow, Gilgamesh lands at Utanapishtim's wharf and questions him.*]

Utanapishtim said to him, to Gilgamesh:

 Why are your cheeks emaciated, your face cast down,
 Your heart wretched, your features wasted,

Woe in your vitals,
Your face like a traveler's from afar,   235
Your features weathered by cold and sun,
Why are you clad in a lion skin, roaming the steppe?

[*Gilgamesh tells Utanapishtim his mission, wallowing in the luxury of self-pity on the difficulties of his quest.*]

Gilgamesh said to him, to Utanapishtim:

My cheeks would not be emaciated, nor my face cast down,
Nor my heart wretched, nor my features wasted,   240
Nor would there be woe in my vitals,
Nor would my face be like a traveler's from afar,
Nor would my features be weathered by cold and sun,
Nor would I be clad in a lion skin, roaming the steppe,
But for my friend, swift wild donkey, mountain onager,
   panther of the steppe,   245
But for Enkidu, my friend, swift wild donkey, mountain
   onager, panther of the steppe,
He who stood by me as we ascended the mountain,
Seized and killed the bull that came down from heaven,
Felled Humbaba who dwelt in the forest of cedars,
Killed lions at the mountain passes,   250
My friend whom I so loved, who went with me through
   every hardship,
Enkidu, whom I so loved, who went with me through
   every hardship,
The fate of mankind has overtaken him.
Six days and seven nights I wept for him,
I would not give him up for burial,   255
Until a worm fell out of his nose.
I was frightened [. . .]
I have grown afraid of death, so I roam the steppe,
My friend's case weighs heavy upon me.
A distant road I roam over the steppe,   260
My friend Enkidu's case weighs heavy upon me!
A distant path I roam over the steppe,
How can I be silent? How can I hold my peace?
My friend whom I loved is turned into clay,
Enkidu, my friend whom I loved, is turned into clay!   265
Shall I too not lie down like him,
And never get up, forever and ever?

Gilgamesh said to him, to Utanapishtim:

So it is to go find Utanapishtim, whom they call the
   "Distant One,"
I traversed all lands,   270
I came over, one after another, wearisome mountains,
Then I crossed, one after another, all the seas.
Too little sweet sleep has smoothed my countenance,

I have worn myself out in sleeplessness,
My muscles ache for misery,   275
What have I gained for my trials?
I had not reached the tavern keeper when my clothes
   were worn out,
I killed bear, hyena, lion, panther, leopard, deer, ibex,
   wild beasts of the steppe,
I ate their meat, I [. . .] their skins.
Let them close behind me the doors of woe,   280
[Let them seal them] with pitch and tar,
For my part, I [. . .] no amusement,
For me, [. . .]

[*Utanapishtim responds in a long speech, poorly known because of damage to
the manuscripts. He chides Gilgamesh for his self-pity and ostentatious mourning, all the more unseemly because the gods had favored him. The village idiot, he points out, wears rags and eats bad food, but no one accords him merit
for that. After a gap in the text, Utanapishtim is found discoursing on the nature of death.*]

Utanapishtim said to him, to Gilgamesh:

   Why, O Gilgamesh, did you prolong woe,   285
   You who are [formed] of the flesh of gods and mankind,
   You for whom [the gods] acted like fathers and mothers?
   When was it, Gilgamesh, you [. . .] to a fool?
   They set a throne for you in the assembly of elders [. . .]
   While the fool is given beer dregs instead of butter,   290
   Bran and coarse flour instead of [. . .].
   He wears sacking instead of a [. . .],
   But he ties it round himself like a sash of honor,
   Because he has no sense [nor reason],
   He has no good advice [. . .].   295
   Think on him, Gilgamesh, [. . .]

[gap]

   You strive ceaselessly, what do you gain?
   When you wear out your strength in ceaseless striving,
   When you torture your limbs with pain,
   You hasten the distant end of your days.   300
   Mankind, whose descendants are snapped off like reeds
      in a canebrake,
   The handsome young man, the lovely young woman,
      death [. . .]
   No one sees death,
   No one sees the face of death,
   No one [hears] the voice of death,   305
   But cruel death cuts off mankind.
   Do we build a house forever?
   Do we make a home forever?
   Do brothers divide an inheritance forever?

Do disputes prevail [in the land] forever?   310
Do rivers rise in flood forever?
Dragonflies drift downstream on a river,
Their faces staring at the sun,
Then, suddenly, there is nothing.
The sleeper and the dead, how alike they are!   315
They limn not death's image,
No one dead has ever greeted a human in this world.
The supreme gods, the great gods, being convened,
Mammetum, she who creates destinies, ordaining destinies
     with them,
They established death and life,   320
They did not reveal the time of death.

Tablet XI

[*Gilgamesh, whose search for Utanapishtin has been characterized by increasing violence, now finds to his astonishment that there is no battle to be fought; heroics will bring him no further. Now he needs knowledge. He asks Utanapishtim, the wisest man who ever lived, his great question: how did he alone escape the universal fate of the human race?*]

Gilgamesh said to him, to Utanapishtim the Distant One:

As I look upon you, Utanapishtim,
Your limbs are not different, you are just as I am.
Indeed, you are not different at all, you are just as I am!
Yet your heart is drained of battle spirit,   5
You lie flat on your back, your arm [idle].
You then, how did you join the ranks of the gods and find
     eternal life?

[*In answer, Utanapishtim relates the story of the flood. According to Tablet I, among Gilgamesh's main achievements was bringing back to the human race this hitherto unknown history. The story as told here is abbreviated. In the fuller account, preserved in a Babylonian narrative poem called "Atrahasis," the gods sent the flood because the human race had multiplied to such an extent that their clamor was unbearable to Enlil, the chief god living on earth. After various attempts to reduce the population of the earth were thwarted by Enki (Ea), the god of wisdom and fresh water, Enlil ordered a deluge to obliterate the entire human race. At this point, Utanapishtim takes up the story. He lived at the long-vanished city of Shuruppak and was a favorite of the god Ea, who warned him of the flood, despite his oath not to reveal it. Ea circumvented this by addressing the wall of a reed enclosure Utanapishtim had built near water, perhaps as a place to receive dreams and commands from his god. Utanapishtim is ordered to build a boat. When his fellow citizens ask him what he is about, he is to reply in ambiguous language, foretelling a "shower of abundance" soon.*]

Utanapishtim said to him, to Gilgamesh:

I will reveal to you, O Gilgamesh, a secret matter,
And a mystery of the gods I will tell you.   10

The city Shuruppak, a city you yourself have knowledge of,
Which once was set on the [bank] of the Euphrates,
That aforesaid city was ancient and gods once were within it.
The great gods resolved to send the deluge,
Their father Anu was sworn,   15
The counselor the valiant Enlil,
Their throne-bearer Ninurta,
Their canal-officer Ennugi,
Their leader Ea was sworn with them.
He repeated their plans to the reed fence: 20
"Reed fence, reed fence, wall, wall!
Listen, O reed fence! Pay attention, O wall!
O Man of Shuruppak, son of Ubar-Tutu,
Wreck house, build boat,
Forsake possessions and seek life,   25
Belongings reject and life save!
Take aboard the boat seed of all living things.
The boat you shall build,
Let her dimensions be measured out:
Let her width and length be equal,   30
Roof her over like the watery depths."
I understood full well, I said to Ea, my lord:
"Your command, my lord, exactly as you said it,
I shall faithfully execute.
What shall I answer the city, the populace, and the elders?"   35
Ea made ready to speak,
Saying to me, his servant:
"So, you shall speak to them thus:
'No doubt Enlil dislikes me,
I shall not dwell in your city.   40
I shall not set my foot on the dry land of Enlil,
I shall descend to the watery depths and dwell with my
    lord Ea.
Upon you he shall shower down in abundance,
A windfall of birds, a surprise of fishes,
He shall pour upon you a harvest of riches,   45
In the morning cakes in spates,
In the evening grains in rains.'"

[*The entire community helps to build the boat. The hull is constructed before
the interior framing, as was customary in the ancient world, with cordage
used to sew the planks together and to truss the hull for strength. The boat is
an enormous cube. Utanapishtim, here referred to as "Atrahasis," loads on his
family, his possessions, and every type of animal, as well as skilled individuals
to keep alive knowledge of arts and crafts.*]

At the first glimmer of dawn,
The land was assembling at the gate of Atrahasis:
The carpenter carried his axe,   50
The reed cutter carried his stone,
The old men brought cordage(?),
The young men ran around [. . .],

The wealthy carried the pitch,
The poor brought what was needed of [. . .].   55
In five days I had planked her hull:
One full acre was her deck space,
Ten dozen cubits, the height of each of her sides,
Ten dozen cubits square, her outer dimensions.
I laid out her structure, I planned her design: 60
I decked her in six,
I divided her in seven,
Her interior I divided in nine.
I drove the water plugs into her,
I saw to the spars and laid in what was needful.   65
Thrice thirty-six hundred measures of pitch I poured
    in the oven,
Thrice thirty-six hundred measures of tar [I poured out]
    inside her.
Thrice thirty-six hundred measures basket-bearers brought
    aboard for oil,
Not counting the thirty-six hundred measures of oil that the
    offering consumed,
And the twice thirty-six hundred measures of oil that the
    boatbuilders made off with.   70
For the [builders] I slaughtered bullocks,
I killed sheep upon sheep every day,
Beer, ale, oil, and wine
[I gave out] to the workers like river water,
They made a feast as on New Year's Day,   75
[. . .] I dispensed ointment with my own hand.
By the setting of Shamash,[7] the ship was completed.
[Since boarding was(?)] very difficult,
They brought up gangplanks(?), fore and aft,
They came up her sides(?) two-thirds (of her height).   80
[Whatever I had] I loaded upon her:
What silver I had I loaded upon her,
What gold I had I loaded upon her,
What living creatures I had I loaded upon her,
I sent up on board all my family and kin,   85
Beasts of the steppe, wild animals of the steppe, all types
    of skilled craftsmen I sent up on board.
Shamash set for me the appointed time:
"In the morning, cakes in spates,
In the evening, grains in rains,
Go into your boat and caulk the door!"   90
That appointed time arrived,
In the morning cakes in spates,
In the evening grains in rains,
I gazed upon the face of the storm,

7. The references to Shamash here and in line 87 suggest that in some version of this story, now lost, Shamash, rather than Enki, warned Utanapishtim of the flood and told him how much time he had to build his ship. This substitution of the one god for the other may have been suggested by Shamash's role as protector of Gilgamesh in the epic. In the oldest account of the Babylonian story of the flood, Enki sets a timing device, apparently a water clock, to tell Utanapishtim how much time he has before the coming of the deluge [Translator's note].

The weather was dreadful to behold!   95
I went into the boat and caulked the door.
To the caulker of the boat, to Puzur-Amurri the boatman,
I gave over the edifice, with all it contained.

[*The flood, accompanied by thunder and a fiery glow, overwhelms the earth.
The gods are terrified by its violence and what they have done.*]

At the first glimmer of dawn,
A black cloud rose above the horizon.   100
Inside it Adad was thundering,
While the destroying gods Shullat and Hanish went in front,
Moving as an advance force over hill and plain.
Errakal tore out the mooring posts (of the world),
Ninurta came and made the dikes overflow.   105
The supreme gods held torches aloft,
Setting the land ablaze with their glow.
Adad's awesome power passed over the heavens,
Whatever was light was turned into darkness,
[He flooded] the land, he smashed it like a [clay pot]!   110
For one day the storm wind [blew],
Swiftly it blew, [the flood came forth],
It passed over the people like a battle,
No one could see the one next to him,
The people could not recognize one another in the
     downpour.   115
The gods became frightened of the deluge,
They shrank back, went up to Anu's highest heaven.
The gods cowered like dogs, crouching outside.
Ishtar screamed like a woman in childbirth,
And sweet-voiced Belet-ili wailed aloud: 120
"Would that day had come to naught,
When I spoke up for evil in the assembly of the gods!
How could I have spoken up for evil in the assembly
     of the gods,
And spoken up for battle to destroy my people?
It was I myself who brought my people into the world,   125
Now, like a school of fish, they choke up the sea!"
The supreme gods were weeping with her,
The gods sat where they were, weeping,
Their lips were parched, taking on a crust.
Six days and seven nights   130
The wind continued, the deluge and windstorm leveled
     the land.
When the seventh day arrived,
The windstorm and deluge left off their battle,
Which had struggled, like a woman in labor.
The sea grew calm, the tempest stilled, the deluge ceased.   135

[*As the floodwaters recede, Utanapishtim can see land at the far horizon. The
boat is caught on a mountain.*]

I looked at the weather, stillness reigned,
And the whole human race had turned into clay.
The landscape was flat as a rooftop.
I opened the hatch, sunlight fell upon my face.
Falling to my knees, I sat down weeping,   140
Tears running down my face.
I looked at the edges of the world, the borders of the sea,
At twelve times sixty double leagues the periphery emerged.
The boat had come to rest on Mount Nimush,
Mount Nimush held the boat fast, not letting it move.   145
One day, a second day Mount Nimush held the boat fast,
    not letting it move.
A third day, a fourth day Mount Nimush held the boat fast,
    not letting it move.
A fifth day, a sixth day Mount Nimush held the boat fast,
    not letting it move.

[*Utanapishtim sends out three birds to see if land has emerged near the boat.
He then quits the boat and makes an offering to the gods, who crowd around
it, famished.*]

When the seventh day arrived,
I brought out a dove and set it free.   150
The dove went off and returned,
No landing place came to its view, so it turned back.
I brought out a swallow and set it free,
The swallow went off and returned,
No landing place came to its view, so it turned back.   155
I brought out a raven and set it free,
The raven went off and saw the ebbing of the waters.
It ate, preened, left droppings, did not turn back.
I released all to the four directions,
I brought out an offering and offered it to the four directions.   160
I set up an incense offering on the summit of the mountain,
I arranged seven and seven cult vessels,
I heaped reeds, cedar, and myrtle in their bowls.[8]
The gods smelled the savor,
The gods smelled the sweet savor,   165
The gods crowded round the sacrificer like flies.

[*The mother goddess blames Enlil for the flood, saying her glittering necklace
of fly-shaped beads, which may stand for the rainbow, will memorialize the
human race drowned in the flood.*]

As soon as Belet-ili arrived,
She held up the great fly-ornaments that Anu had made
    in his ardor:
"O gods, these shall be my lapis necklace, lest I forget,
I shall be mindful of these days and not forget, not ever!   170

---

8. The Mesopotamians sometimes burned various plants and branches in order to produce an attractive
odor when making offerings to the gods [*Translator's note*].

The gods should come to the incense offering,
But Enlil should not come to the incense offering,
For he, irrationally, brought on the flood,
And marked my people for destruction!"
As soon as Enlil arrived,   175
He saw the boat, Enlil flew into a rage,
He was filled with fury at the gods:
"Who came through alive? No man was to survive destruction!"
Ninurta made ready to speak,
Said to the valiant Enlil: 180
"Who but Ea could contrive such a thing?
For Ea alone knows every artifice."

[*Ea's speech urges future limits. Punish but do not kill; diminish but do not annihilate. He suggests that in the future less drastic means than a flood be used to
reduce the human population. He refers to Utanapishtim as Atrahasis, his name
in the independent Babylonian flood story. Enlil grants Utanapishtim and his
wife eternal life but removes them far away from the rest of the human race.*]

Ea made ready to speak,
Said to the valiant Enlil:
"You, O valiant one, are the wisest of the gods,   185
How could you, irrationally, have brought on the flood?
Punish the wrongdoer for his wrongdoing,
Punish the transgressor for his transgression,
But be lenient, lest he be cut off,
Bear with him, lest he [. . .].   190
Instead of your bringing on a flood,
Let the lion rise up to diminish the human race!
Instead of your bringing on a flood,
Let the wolf rise up to diminish the human race!
Instead of your bringing on a flood,   195
Let famine rise up to wreak havoc in the land!
Instead of your bringing on a flood,
Let pestilence rise up to wreak havoc in the land!
It was not I who disclosed the secret of the great gods,
I made Atrahasis have a dream and so he heard the secret
   of the gods.   200
Now then, make some plan for him."
Then Enlil came up into the boat,
Leading me by the hand, he brought me up too.
He brought my wife up and had her kneel beside me.
He touched our brows, stood between us to bless us: 205
"Hitherto Utanapishtim has been a human being,
Now Utanapishtim and his wife shall become like us gods.
Utanapishtim shall dwell far distant at the source
   of the rivers."
Thus it was that they took me far distant and had me dwell
   at the source of the rivers.
Now then, who will convene the gods for your sake,   210
That you may find the eternal life you seek?
Come, come, try not to sleep for six days and seven nights.

[*Utanapishtim has challenged Gilgamesh to go without sleep for a week; if he fails this test, how could he expect to live forever? Even as he speaks, Gilgamesh drifts off to sleep.*]

As he sat there on his haunches,
Sleep was swirling over him like a mist.
Utanapishtim said to her, to his wife: 215

> Behold this fellow who seeks eternal life!
> Sleep swirls over him like a mist.

[*Utanapishtim's wife, taking pity on Gilgamesh, urges her husband to awaken him and let him go home. Utanapishtim insists on a proof of how long he slept, lest Gilgamesh claim that he had only dozed. She is to bake him fresh bread every day and set it beside him, marking the wall for the day. The bread spoils progressively as Gilgamesh sleeps for seven days.*]

His wife said to him, to Utanapishtim the Distant One:

> Do touch him that the man may wake up,
> That he may return safe on the way whence he came,   220
> That through the gate he came forth he may return
>   to his land.

Utanapishtim said to her, to his wife:

> Since the human race is duplicitous, he'll endeavor
>   to dupe you.
> Come, come, bake his daily loaves, put them one after another
>   by his head,
> Then mark the wall for each day he has slept.   225

She baked his daily loaves for him, put them one after another
    by his head,
Then dated the wall for each day he slept.
The first loaf was dried hard,
The second was leathery, the third soggy,
The crust of the fourth turned white,   230
The fifth was gray with mold, the sixth was fresh,
The seventh was still on the coals when he touched him, the man
    woke up.

[*Gilgamesh wakes at last. Claiming at first that he has scarcely dozed a moment, he sees the bread and realizes that he has slept for the entire time he was supposed to remain awake for the test. He gives up in despair. What course is left for him? Utanapishtim does not answer directly but orders the boatman to take him home. Further, the boatman himself is never to return. Thus access to Utanapishtim is denied the human race forever. Gilgamesh is bathed and given clothing that will stay magically fresh until his return to Uruk.*]

Gilgamesh said to him, to Utanapishtim the Distant One:

> Scarcely had sleep stolen over me,
> When straightaway you touched me and roused me.   235

Utanapishtim said to him, to Gilgamesh:

> [Up with you], Gilgamesh, count your daily loaves,
> [That the days you have slept] may be known to you.
> The first loaf is dried hard,
> The second is leathery, the third soggy,   240
> The crust of the fourth has turned white,
> The fifth is gray with mold,
> The sixth is fresh,
> The seventh was still in the coals when I touched you and
>   you woke up.

Gilgamesh said to him, to Utanapishtim the Distant One: 245

> What then should I do, Utanapishtim, whither should I go,
> Now that the Bereaver has seized my [flesh]?[9]
> Death lurks in my bedchamber,
> And wherever I turn, there is death!

Utanapishtim said to him, to Ur-Shanabi the boatman: 250

> Ur-Shanabi, may the harbor [offer] you no [haven],
> May the crossing point reject you,
> Be banished from the shore you shuttled to.
> The man you brought here,
> His body is matted with filthy hair,   255
> Hides have marred the beauty of his flesh.
> Take him away, Ur-Shanabi, bring him to the washing place.
> Have him wash out his filthy hair with water, clean as snow,
> Have him throw away his hides, let the sea carry them off,
> Let his body be rinsed clean.   260
> Let his headband be new,
> Have him put on raiment worthy of him.
> Until he reaches his city,
> Until he completes his journey,
> Let his garments stay spotless, fresh and new.   265

Ur-Shanabi took him away and brought him to the washing place.
He washed out his filthy hair with water, clean as snow,
He threw away his hides, the sea carried them off,
His body was rinsed clean.
He renewed his headband,   270
He put on raiment worthy of him.
Until he reached his city,
Until he completed his journey,
His garments would stay spotless, fresh and new.

9. "The Bereaver" is an epithet of death. It could also mean something like "kidnappe." [*Translator's note*].

[*Gilgamesh and Ur-Shanabi embark on their journey to Uruk. As they push off from the shore, Utanapishtim's wife intervenes, asking her husband to give the hero something to show for his quest. Gilgamesh brings the boat back to shore and waits expectantly. Utanapishtim tells him of a plant of rejuvenation. Gilgamesh dives for the plant by opening a shaft through the earth's surface to the water below. He ties stones to his feet, a technique used in traditional pearl diving in the Gulf. When he comes up from securing the plant, he is on the opposite side of the ocean, where he started from.*]

Gilgamesh and Ur-Shanabi embarked on the boat,   275
They launched the boat, they embarked upon it.
His wife said to him, to Utanapishtim the Distant One:

>   Gilgamesh has come here, spent with exertion,
>   What will you give him for his homeward journey?

At that he, Gilgamesh, lifted the pole,   280
Bringing the boat back by the shore.
Utanapishtim said to him, to Gilgamesh:

>   Gilgamesh, you have come here, spent with exertion,
>   What shall I give you for your homeward journey?
>   I will reveal to you, O Gilgamesh, a secret matter,   285
>   And a mystery of the gods I will tell you.
>   There is a certain plant, its stem is like a thornbush,
>   Its thorns, like the wild rose, will prick [your hand].
>   If you can secure this plant, [. . .]
>   [. . .]   290

No sooner had Gilgamesh heard this,
He opened a shaft, [flung away his tools].
He tied heavy stones [to his feet],
They pulled him down into the watery depths [. . .].
He took the plant though it pricked [his hand].   295
He cut the heavy stones [from his feet],
The sea cast him up on his home shore.

[*Gilgamesh resolves to take the plant to Uruk to experiment on an old man. While Gilgamesh is bathing on the homeward journey, a snake eats the plant and rejuvenates itself by shedding its skin. Gilgamesh gives up. Immense quantities of water have flooded up through the shaft he dug and covered the place. He has left behind his tools so cannot dig another shaft. He has also lost the boat, so there is no going back.*]

Gilgamesh said to him, to Ur-Shanabi the boatman:

>   Ur-Shanabi, this plant is cure for heartache,
>   Whereby a man will regain his stamina.   300
>   I will take it to ramparted Uruk,
>   I will have an old man eat some and so test the plant.
>   His name shall be "Old Man Has Become Young-Again-Man."
>   I myself will eat it and so return to my carefree youth.

At twenty double leagues they took a bite to eat,   305
At thirty double leagues they made their camp.

Gilgamesh saw a pond whose water was cool,
He went down into it to bathe in the water.
A snake caught the scent of the plant,
[Stealthily] it came up and carried the plant away,   310
On its way back it shed its skin.

Thereupon Gilgamesh sat down weeping,
His tears flowed down his face,
He said to Ur-Shanabi the boatman:

> For whom, Ur-Shanabi, have my hands been toiling?   315
> For whom has my heart's blood been poured out?
> For myself I have obtained no benefit,
> I have done a good deed for a reptile!
> Now, floodwaters rise against me for twenty double leagues,
> When I opened the shaft, I flung away the tools.   320
> How shall I find my bearings?
> I have come much too far to go back, and I abandoned
>   the boat on the shore.

[*Upon completing his journey, Gilgamesh invites Ur-Shanabi to inspect the
walls of Uruk, using the same words used by the narrator in Tablet I.*]

At twenty double leagues they took a bite to eat,
At thirty double leagues they made their camp.
When they arrived in ramparted Uruk,   325
Gilgamesh said to him, to Ur-Shanabi the boatman:

> Go up, Ur-Shanabi, pace out the walls of Uruk.
> Study the foundation terrace and examine the brickwork.
> Is not its masonry of kiln-fired brick?
> And did not seven masters lay its foundations?   330
> One square mile of city, one square mile of gardens,
> One square mile of clay pits, a half square mile of Ishtar's
>   dwelling,
> Three and a half square miles is the measure of Uruk!

ANCIENT EGYPTIAN POETRY
ca. 1500–ca. 1200 B.C.E.

The architecture of the ancient Egyptians is well known to us by reason of the vast
tombs, temples, and pyramids they built for their pharaohs and gods. Their art is also
available to us, both because they left many bas reliefs and paintings on the walls of
these temples and tombs and because they filled the burial chambers of their noble and

royal dead with a rich variety of objects that were to accompany the dead into the next world. By contrast, the literature of ancient Egypt has survived to us only in scattered fragments, and because of the difficulty of the Egyptian language and writing system (a complex system of stylized pictographs called hieroglyphics), it is far less well known than either the art or the architecture. Yet even that small sample is enough to show that the ancient Egyptians possessed a poetry that was rich and varied in both its subjects and its forms. The largest and earliest group of poems comes from the pyramids that were constructed in the period of the Old Kingdom (ca. 2575–2130 B.C.E.). They include narratives, incantations, and invocations designed to help the pharaoh's soul on its journey to the other world. Despite their value in illuminating early Egyptian religious beliefs, the poems are prosaic and repetitive. Of far greater appeal are the lyrics, narratives, and devotional poems that were composed during the millennium that includes all the dynasties of the Middle and New Kingdoms (ca. 2130–1200 B.C.E.).

AKHENATEN'S "HYMN TO THE SUN"

During the reign of Amun-hotep IV—Pharaoh Akhenaten of the Eighteenth Dynasty, who reigned from 1375 to 1358 B.C.E.—the royal family elevated worship of the sun disc, Aten, above that of other deities and of Amun-Re, the imperial and universal god of the New Kingdom, in particular. Akhenaten built a royal city called Heliopolis (the city of the sun), named it Akhet-Aten in honor of the god, and caused the names of the older gods to be hacked out of inscriptions wherever they appeared throughout the land. Akhenaten emphasized the universal supremacy of the sun, and the images he uses to evoke the scope and depth of Aten's powers suggest an emerging monotheism. At the time, however, the movement was viewed as a return to the royal sun cult of the pyramid builders and was later abandoned as heretical. In the hymn printed here, Akhenaten presents himself as the son of the sun god and the sole interpreter between him and the people of Egypt.

THE LEIDEN HYMNS

The Leiden Hymns cycle of poems appears on a papyrus dated to the fifty-second regnal year of Ramesses II (ca. 1238 B.C.E.) and so may be dated from this period or somewhat earlier. In The Leiden Hymns the poet evokes the image of the sun god—called Horus, Amun, and Amun-Re—as the one preeminent god, master of all creation, and the father of all other gods. Amun appears in a multitude of forms or incarnations, including those of the other gods: source of the Nile, inseminator of the earth, fashioner of day and night. The poem cycle is in large part built up by the repetition of titles such as these that are associated with individual gods. The effect, however, is to create the image of a god who is greater and more powerful than all individual gods. As the translator of these poems puts it, "He moves in unfathomable ways and takes many forms to human comprehension—as the various poems demonstrate; but though He is hidden from human sight, He is indeed the ultimate godhead, God alone." The poet-theologian who composed these poems uses all these metaphors to evoke the being who created all. One seems to hear in these poems echoes of the language of the Old and New Testaments, although, of course, these poems precede them. Like later Jewish and Christian poets, the author of The Leiden Hymns drew on the common stock of human experience to express the inexpressible.

LOVE SONGS

Love songs are the most immediately appealing of all ancient Egyptian poems and need the least explanation. In them one finds the entire range of love's possibilities. The moods and attitudes vary from chaste and idyllic to passionately erotic. Both males and females speak, and thus one sees both sides of love. These pieces all come from the Ramesside period (ca. 1300–1100 B.C.E.) and derive from small collections or anthologies on papyri, bits of smoothed limestone, and pottery (now in London, Turin, and Cairo). Reading these poems one feels that love has hardly altered at all over the intervening centuries.

PRONOUNCING GLOSSARY

The following list uses common English syllables and stress accents to provide rough equivalents of selected words whose pronunciation may be unfamiliar to the general reader.

Akhenaten: *ah-ke-nah'-ten*   Hapy: *hah'-pee*

Amun-hotpe: *ah'-mun—*hot'*-pay*   Ramesses: *ra'-me-seez*

Amun-Re: *ah-mun—ray'*

Akhenaten's "Hymn to the Sun"[1]

I

When in splendor you first took your throne
        high in the precinct of heaven,
   O living God,
        life truly began!
Now from eastern horizon risen and streaming,   5
    you have flooded the world with your beauty.
You are majestic, awesome, bedazzling, exalted,
        overlord over all earth,
   yet your rays, they touch lightly, compass the lands
      to the limits of all your creation.   10
There in the Sun, you reach to the farthest of those
    you would gather in for your Son,[2]
        whom you love;
Though you are far, your light is wide upon earth;
    and you shine in the faces of all   15
        who turn to follow your journeying.

II

When you sink to rest below western horizon
    earth lies in darkness like death,
Sleepers are still in bedchambers, heads veiled,
        eye cannot spy a companion;   20
All their goods could be stolen away,
        heads heavy there, and they never knowing!
Lions come out from the deeps of their caves,
        snakes bite and sting;
Darkness muffles, and earth is silent: 25
        he who created all things lies low in his tomb.

III

Earth-dawning mounts the horizon,
    glows in the sun-disk as day:

---

1. All selections translated by John L. Foster.　　2. Pharoah Akhenaten.

You drive away darkness, offer your arrows of shining,
        and the Two Lands[3] are lively with morningsong.   30
Sun's children awaken and stand,
        for you, golden light, have upraised the sleepers;
Bathed are their bodies, who dress in clean linen,
        their arms held high to praise your Return.
Across the face of the earth   35
        they go to their crafts and professions.

IV

The herds are at peace in their pastures,
        trees and the vegetation grow green;
Birds start from their nests,
        wings wide spread to worship your Person;   40
Small beasts frisk and gambol, and all
        who mount into flight or settle to rest
            live, once you have shone upon them;
Ships float downstream or sail for the south,
        each path lies open because of your rising;   45
Fish in the River leap in your sight,
        and your rays strike deep in the Great Green Sea.[4]

V

It is *you* create the new creature in Woman,
        shape the life-giving drops into Man,
Foster the son in the womb of his mother,   50
        soothe him, ending his tears;
Nurse through the long generations of women
        to those given Air,[5]
        you ensure that your handiwork prosper.
When the new one descends from the womb   55
        to draw breath the day of its birth,
You open his mouth,
        make him aware of life newly given,
        for you determine his destiny.

VI

Hark to the chick in the egg,   60
        he who speaks in the shell!
You give him air within
        to save and prosper him;
And you have allotted to him his set time
        before the shell shall be broken;   65
Then out from the egg he comes,
        from the egg to peep at his natal hour!
        and up on his own two feet goes he
        when at last he struts forth therefrom.

---

3. Upper and Lower Egypt.   4. The Mediterranean.   5. That is, life.

VII

How various is the world you have created,   70
    each thing mysterious, sacred to sight,
O sole God,
    beside whom is no other!
You fashioned earth to your heart's desire,
    while you were still alone,   75
Filled it with man and the family of creatures,
    each kind on the ground, those who go upon feet,
        he on high soaring on wings,
The far lands of Khor and Kush,[6]
    and the rich Black Land of Egypt.   80

VIII

And you place each one in his proper station,
    where you minister to his needs;
Each has his portion of food,
    and the years of life are reckoned him.
Tongues are divided by words,   85
    natures made diverse as well,
Even men's skins are different
    that you might distinguish the nations.

IX

You make Hapy,[7] the Nile, stream through the underworld,
    and bring him, with whatever fullness you will,   90
To preserve and nourish the People
    in the same skilled way you fashion them.
You are Lord of each one,
    who wearies himself in their service,
Yet Lord of all earth, who shines for them all,   95
    Sun-disk of day, Great Lightener!
All of the far foreign countries—
    you are the cause they live,
For you have put a Nile in the sky
    that he might descend upon them in rain—   100
He makes waves on the very mountains
        like waves on the Great Green Sea
    to water their fields and their villages.

X

How splendidly ordered are they,
        your purposes for this world,   105
    O Lord of eternity, Hapy in heaven!
Although you belong to the distant peoples,
    to the small shy beasts
        who travel the deserts and uplands,

---

6. In the Nubian region in the Sudan, which is to the south. Khor is Syro-Palestine in the northeast.
7. God of the annual flooding of the Nile.

Yet Hapy, he comes from Below   110
        for the dear Land of Egypt as well.
And your Sunlight nurses each field and meadow:
        when you shine, they live,
                they grow sturdy and prosper through you.
You set seasons to let the world flower and flourish—   115
        winter to rest and refresh it,
                the hot blast of summer to ripen;
And you have made heaven far off
        in order to shine down therefrom,
                in order to watch over all your creation.   120

XI

You are the one God,
        shining forth from your possible incarnations
                as Aten, the Living Sun,
Revealed like a king in glory, risen in light,
        now distant, now bending nearby.   125
You create the numberless things of this world
              from yourself, who are One alone—
        cities, towns, fields, the roadway, the River;
And each eye looks back and beholds you
        to learn from the day's light perfection.   130
O God, you are in the Sun-disk of Day,
        Over-Seer of all creation
              —your legacy
                passed on to all who shall ever be;
For you fashioned their sight, who perceive your universe,   135
        that they praise with one voice
                all your labors.

XII

And you are in my heart;
        there is no other who truly knows you
                but for your son, Akhenaten.   140
May you make him wise with your inmost counsels,
              wise with your power,
        that earth may aspire to your godhead,
            its creatures fine as the day you made
                them.
Once you rose into shining, they lived;   145
        when you sink to rest, they shall die.
For it is you who are Time itself,
        the span of the world;
              life is by means of you.

Eyes are filled with Beauty   150
            until you go to your rest;
All work is laid aside
            as you sink down the western horizon.
Then, Shine reborn!   Rise splendidly!

my Lord, let life thrive for the King!   155
For I have kept pace with your every footstep
      since you first measured ground for the world.
Lift up the creatures of earth for your Son
      who came forth from your Body of Fire!

The Leiden Hymns

[How splendid you ferry the skyways]

How splendid you ferry the skyways,
      Horus of Twin Horizons,[1]
The needs of each new day
      firm in your timeless pattern,
Who fashion the years,   5
      weave months into order—
Days, nights, and the very hours
      move to the gait of your striding.

Refreshed by your diurnal shining, you quicken,
      bright above yesterday,   10
Making the zone of night sparkle
      although you belong to the light,
Sole one awake there
      —sleep is for mortals,
Who go to rest grateful: 15
      your eyes oversee.
And theirs by the millions you open
      when your face new-rises, beautiful;
Not a bypath escapes your affection
      during your season on earth.   20

Stepping swift over stars,
      riding the lightning flash,
You circle the earth in an instant,
      with a god's ease crossing heaven,
Treading dark paths of the underworld,   25
      yet, sun on each roadway,
You deign to walk daily with men.

      The faces of all are upturned to you,
As mankind and gods
      alike lift their morningsong: 30
"Lord of the daybreak,
      Welcome!"

---

1. Dawn and dusk. Horus is the hawk-headed sun god.

[God is a master craftsman]

God is a master craftsman;
        yet none can draw the lines of his Person.
Fair features first came into being
        in the hushed dark where he mused alone;
He forged his own figure there,   5
        hammered his likeness out of himself—
All powerful one (yet kindly,
        whose heart would lie open to men).

He mingled his heavenly god-seed
        with the inmost parts of his being.   10
Planting his image there
        in the unknown depths of his mystery.
He cared, and the sacred form
        took shape and contour, splendid at birth!
God, skilled in the intricate ways of the craftsman,   15
        first fashioned Himself to perfection.

[When Being began back in the days of the genesis]

When Being began back in days of the genesis,
        it was Amun appeared first of all,
                unknown his mode of inflowing;
There was no god come before him,
        nor was other god with him there   5
                when he uttered himself into visible form;
There was no mother to him, that she might have borne him his name,
        there was no father to father the one
                who first spoke the words, "I Am!"
Who fashioned the seed of him all on his own,   10
        sacred first cause, whose birth lay in mystery,
                who crafted and carved his own splendor—
He is God the Creator, self-created, the Holy;
        all other gods came after;
                with Himself he began the world.   15

[The mind of God is perfect knowing]

The mind of God is perfect knowing,
        his lips its flawless expression,
    all that exists is his spirit,
        by his tongue named into being;
He strides, and hollows under his feet become Nile-heads—   5
        Hapy[1] wells from the hidden grotto into his footprints.
His soul is all space,

---

1. God of the annual flooding of the Nile.

     his heart the lifegiving moisture,
   he is falcon of twin horizons,
      sky god skimming heaven,   10
His right eye the day,
     while his left is the night,
   and he guides human seeing down every way.
His body is Nun, the swirling original waters;
       within it the Nile   15
   shaping, bringing to birth,
       fostering all creation;
His burning breath is the breeze,
      gift offered every nostril,
   from him too the destiny fallen to each;   20
His consort the fertile field,
      he shoots his seed into her,
   and new vegetation, and grain,
      growing strong as his children.
Fruitful One, Eldest,   25
      he fathered gods in those first days,
   whose faces turn to him
      daily and everywhere.
That countenance still shines on mankind and deities,
     and it mirrors the sum of the world.   30

Love Songs

[My love is one and only, without peer]

My love is one and only, without peer,
   lovely above all Egypt's lovely girls.
On the horizon of my seeing,
   see her, rising,
Glistening goddess of the sunrise star   5
   bright in the forehead of a lucky year.
So there she stands, epitome
   of shining, shedding light,
Her eyebrows, gleaming darkly, marking
   eyes which dance and wander.   10
Sweet are those lips, which chatter
   (but never a word too much),
And the line of the long neck lovely, dropping
   (since song's notes slide that way)
To young breasts firm in the bouncing light   15
   which shimmers that blueshadowed sidefall of hair.
And slim are those arms, overtoned with gold,
   those fingers which touch like a brush of lotus.
And (ah) how the curve of her back slips gently
   by a whisper of waist to god's plenty below.   20

(Such thighs as hers pass knowledge
        of loveliness known in the old days.)
Dressed in the perfect flesh of woman
        (heart would run captive to such slim arms),
                she ladies it over the earth,   25
Schooling the neck of each schoolboy male
        to swing on a swivel to see her move.
(He who could hold that body tight
        would know at last
              perfection of delight—   30
Best of the bullyboys,
        first among lovers.)
Look you, all men, at that golden going,
        like Our Lady of Love,
             without peer.   35

[I wish I were her Nubian girl]

I wish I were her Nubian[1] girl,
        one to attend her (bosom companion),
Confidante, and a child of discretion:
        Close hidden at nightfall we whisper
As (modest by day) she offers   5
        breasts like ripe berries to evening—
Her long gown settles, then, bodiless,
        hangs from my helping hand.
O she'll give pleasure! in future
        no grown man will deny it!   10
But tonight, to me, this chaste girl
        bares unthinking the delicate blush
Of a most secret landscape,
        her woman's body.

[Love, how I'd love to slip down to the pond]

Love, how I'd love to slip down to the pond,
        bathe with you close by on the bank.
Just for you I'd wear my new Memphis swimsuit,
        made of sheer linen, fit for a queen—
Come see how it looks in the water!   5

Couldn't I coax you to wade in with me?
        Let the cool creep slowly around us?
Then I'd dive deep down
        and come up for you dripping,
Let you fill your eyes   10
        with the little red fish that I'd catch.

---

1. In ancient Egypt, Nubians were commonly servants.

And I'd say, standing there tall in the shallows:
Look at my fish, love,
        how it lies in my hand,
How my fingers caress it,   15
           slip down its sides . . .
But then I'd say softer,
           eyes bright with your seeing:
               A gift, love. No words.
Come closer and   20
           look, it's all me.

[Why, just now, must you question your heart?]

Why, just now, must you question your heart?
           Is it really the time for discussion?
To her, say I,
           take her tight in your arms!
For god's sake, sweet man,   5
           it's me coming at you,
My tunic
           loose at the shoulder!

[I was simply off to see Nefrus my friend]

I was simply off to see Nefrus my friend,
Just to sit and chat at her place
                (about men),
When there, hot on his horses, comes Mehy
           (oh god, I said to myself, it's Mehy!)   5
Right over the crest of the road
           wheeling along with the boys.

Oh Mother Hathor, what shall I do?
           Don't let him see me!
                    Where can I hide?   10
Make me a small creeping thing
           to slip by his eye
               (sharp as Horus')
                   unseen.

Oh, look at you, feet—   15
           (this road is a river!)
               you walk me right out of my depth!
Someone, silly heart, is exceedingly ignorant here—
           aren't you a little too easy near Mehy?
If he sees that I see him, I know   20
           he will know how my heart flutters (Oh, Mehy!)

I know I will blurt out,
        "Please take me!"
                (I mustn't!)

No, all he would do is brag out my name,   25
      just one of the many . . . (I know) . . .
Mehy would make me just one of the girls
      for all of the boys in the palace.
                (Oh Mehy)

[I think I'll go home and lie very still]

I think I'll go home and lie very still,
      feigning terminal illness.
Then the neighbors will all troop over to stare,
      my love, perhaps, among them.
How she'll smile while the specialists   5
      snarl in their teeth!—
      she perfectly well knows what ails me.

[Love of you is mixed deep in my vitals]

Love of you is mixed deep in my vitals,
      like water stirred into flour for bread,
Like simples compound in a sweet-tasting drug,
      like pastry and honey mixed to perfection.
Oh, hurry to look at your love!   5
      Be like horses charging in battle,
Like a gardener up with the sun
      burning to watch his prize bud open.
High heaven causes a girl's lovelonging.
      It is like being too far from the light,   10
Far from the hearth of familiar arms.
      It is this being so tangled in you.

THE HEBREW BIBLE
ca. 1000–300 B.C.E.

The sacred writings of the Jews encompass a rich variety of texts from different periods composed in poetry and prose, and sometimes in a mixture of both. They represent a striking mixture of literary types; a partial list is historical narrative, short story, genealogy, proverbs, laws, visionary narrative (prophecy), and many kinds of lyric poetry. Together they tell the story of the Jewish people in different modes and from various perspectives. This history is filled with risks and trials, but it is given meaning by the Jews' relation to their god, who rewards righteousness and punishes wrongdoing and who, it is believed, works through that history to fulfill his covenant, or agreement, with the people he has chosen.

GENESIS

The book of Genesis forms the first part of an interconnected group of writings that are central to Jewish belief and are known collectively in Hebrew as the Torah (a word meaning "instruction" or "guidance" but also with the specific sense of "law"); they are also often called the Pentateuch ("five scrolls"), a name derived from Greek. The division into five books was artificial and probably was determined by how much would fit on individual papyrus rolls. The narrative parts of the Torah told a continuous story, from the creation of the world to the sojourn in Egypt, the Israelites' exodus from Egypt, their subsequent wandering led by Moses, and finally Moses' death just before the entry into the Promised Land. Embedded within this narrative, however, and occupying a considerable amount of the Torah, are laws given by God to Moses, and passed on by Moses to his people. The core experience of the exodus was the interlude at Mount Sinai, which occupies Exodus from chapter 19 on, the whole book of Leviticus, and the first part of Numbers (to 10.11). Here God reveals to Moses laws of various kinds, especially those, including the Ten Commandments, meant to guide individual life (Exodus) and those concerned with cult and ritual (all of Leviticus). The selection from Exodus printed here describes Moses receiving the Ten Commandments. Much of the final book of the Torah, Deuteronomy, consists of Moses' address to his people on the last day of his life, in which (among other things) he partly repeats and partly elaborates on the laws delivered at Sinai to give guidance for life in Canaan, which the Israelites are about to enter. Just as the story of the exodus is essential to Jewish faith because it tells of God's deliverance of his people in the execution of his plan for them, so the law is central because it defines the Jews' relation to God; and Moses dominates the Torah and Jewish tradition as the intermediary through whom God gave the law to his people.

The narratives in Genesis give background to these later events, not just by telling what happened before them but also by providing a framework through which to understand their importance and by characterizing the relation between God and his people through a series of exemplary stories. The book falls into two distinct parts. The first (chapters 1–11) recounts "creation history"—God's creation of the world and of humankind—and the evolution of early human society. Human beings occupy center stage in this account of the world's origin, as they do not in, for example, Mesopotamian and Greek creation stories. This early age is marked especially by human wrongdoing and God's punishment, from the disobedience of Adam and Eve and their expulsion from Eden to the construction of the Tower of Babel, which results in God scattering human beings and dividing their single language into many languages. Because this view of the world is human centered (when God blesses man and woman after he creates them in chapter 1, he gives them all the plants and animals that fill the world), it is fitting that when God decides to destroy humanity he reverses his original act of creation. The flood mixes together again the waters that were separated on the second day of creation, and it destroys all the different kinds of animal created on the fifth and sixth days, together with all humans.

Not quite all, of course. The world is not destroyed. Noah and his family, and the pairs of animals taken onto the ark, are spared, because Noah is righteous and has found favor in God's eyes. With this dramatic demonstration of God's justice, and its pendant in the story of the Tower of Babel, there is a new beginning. In this second part of Genesis (chapters 12–50) the focus shifts from humanity in general to four generations of ancestors of the people of Israel: Abraham and Sarah; Isaac and Rebekah; Jacob and his wives, Leah and Rachel; and Joseph and his brothers. In the transition between the two sections, a passage at the beginning of chapter 12 plays a pivotal role. When God tells Noah's descendant Abram (who will be renamed Abraham) to leave his home in Mesopotamia, he says, "Go forth from your land and your birthplace and your father's house to the land I will show you. And I will make you a great nation and I will bless you and make your name great, and you shall be a blessing. And I will bless those who bless you, and those who damn you I will curse, and all the clans of the earth through you shall be blessed." This is the first statement of God's covenant with Israel, which is repeated a number of times throughout the Torah. After the flood God made a covenant with humanity in general, but it was essentially negative: he would never again destroy the world by flood (chapter 9). This new covenant implies a positive purpose in history: other peoples will be blessed through the people of Israel, who are chosen for a particularly close relation with God. This destiny, viewed as the ultimate goal of history, gives that history meaning. But two other pledges made as part of that destiny are more immediately relevant to the narrative of Genesis: a land to dwell in and a multitude of descendants (implied here in the phrase "a great nation" and made more explicit in God's subsequent promises to Abraham in chapters 17 and 22 and to Jacob in chapter 35).

The emphasis on posterity as part of God's covenant gives significance to the genealogical lists that are scattered throughout Genesis as well as to the generational structure of the main story, and the Promised Land figures not just in the story of Moses but in the narrative of every generation of the ancestors. But complications arise in respect to both the family and the land that seem to threaten the fulfillment of the covenant. Abraham's wife, Sarah, is barren, and they are childless into their nineties. Though both understandably laugh when God promises them a son, Isaac is born to them. God then demands, but at the last moment forestalls, Abraham's sacrifice of Isaac. Jacob and Esau, Isaac's sons, are rivals and struggle with each other even in the womb. When Jacob tricks Esau out of his patrimony, Esau intends to kill him, and their mother, Rebekah, saves him by sending him to live with her brother Laban. Jacob's sons renew the pattern: their jealous resentment of their brother Joseph leads to Joseph's being sold into slavery in Egypt after their plot to kill him is frustrated. This strife among brothers, with the threat of fratricide, recalls the story of Cain and Abel. The land is involved in these tensions because as a result of them Jacob as a young man and later Joseph, followed eventually by his brothers and the aged Jacob, leave it and go to live somewhere else. In the first generation too Abraham leaves the land to which God has led him and goes to Egypt to avoid a famine, in a clear anticipation of the story of Joseph (chapter 12). In Genesis, this land is left again and again, and the attainment of a settled home in it is deferred beyond the end of the Torah.

In the end, God fulfills his purpose and shapes events according to his covenant, and he does so in unexpected ways. Aged parents beget a son, and in the next two generations it is the younger branch of the family (Jacob, Joseph) that serves as the vehicle for carrying out God's purpose (according to the rule of primogeniture in Hebrew society, primacy would be given to the oldest son). In addition, fraternal strife and exile, which at first seem to derail God's plan, turn out to be the means for carrying it out. Jacob brings back from refuge with his uncle Laban the latter's two daughters, Leah and Rachel, as his wives, and the line is perpetuated through them. Joseph's servitude in Egypt becomes the means of preserving his father and brothers from famine in Canaan and leads, generations later, to the exodus from Egypt and the giving of the law to Moses. This pattern of near-disaster turned to a positive outcome reveals God's power and his surpassing of merely human expectations. It is also excellent narrative technique.

JOB

Genesis depicts a world in which people get exactly what they deserve: goodness is rewarded and sin is punished. This is a world that makes sense. All one has to do to live well is to obey God and conform to his law. It is in this sense that the stories in Genesis and the law of Moses in the rest of the Torah give guidance on how to live. Even apparently arbitrary events, such as the younger brother being favored over the elder (Jacob and Esau), can be referred to God's plan.

The book of Job challenges this sense of coherence and intelligibility because it

shows a good and upright man who nevertheless suffers horribly—who even is selected for suffering *because* of his goodness. It raises the question not only of why
the innocent suffer but more generally of why there is misfortune and unhappiness
in the world. "Have you taken note of my servant Job," God asks the Accuser, "for
there is no one like him on earth: innocent, upright, and God-fearing, and keeping
himself apart from evil." But Job loses his family and wealth in a series of calamities
that strike one on the other like hammer blows and is then plagued with a loathsome
disease. In a series of magnificent speeches, he expresses his sense of his own innocence and demands one thing: to understand the reason for his suffering.

From the beginning, we can see a little farther into the problem than Job. The
verse speeches of Job and his comforters, which fill most of the book, are framed by
a prologue and epilogue in prose. In the prologue, the Accuser challenges God's
praise of Job by pointing out that Job's goodness has never been tested; it is easy to be
righteous in prosperity. Because we see that Job's afflictions originate in a test, we
know that there is a reason for his suffering. We may think it not much of a reason,
and feel that Job is the object of sport for higher powers. If so, what we know from
the prologue only makes the problem of innocent suffering worse. We may, however,
want to take the explanation more seriously. In his wager with the Adversary, God is
putting his trust in Job, and trust is a very important and wonderful aspect of his relation with humankind. In some ways too it seems to be not just Job who is being
tested but humanity through him, and the question is whether people can have and
retain their faith in God, and remain good, independently of circumstances. Should
we expect to be rewarded for goodness with material and physical well-being, and are
we good only because of these rewards? These are not trivial questions.

This line of thought puts the problem in some perspective but does not solve it. The
fact remains that Job is innocent, and he still suffers. What kind of order can we find
in a world where that can happen? The prologue in no way cancels the profundity with
which Job seeks to probe the reasons for his suffering, or his need for understanding.

For Job's comforters, there is no problem. They are anchored solidly within the
world of goodness rewarded and wickedness punished. They can account for suffering easily. If Job is suffering, he must have done something wrong. All he has to do,
then, is to repent his sin and be reconciled with God. All their speeches essentially
express and elaborate this one thought. Their pious formula, however, will not cover
Job's situation. As we know from the prologue, their mistake is to confuse moral
goodness with outward circumstance. Despite or because of their conventional piety,
they do not understand Job's suffering, and they get God wrong. In the epilogue,
God says to Eliphaz, "I am very angry at you and your two friends, for you have not
spoken rightly about me as did my servant Job." Job has spoken rightly by insisting on
his innocence and not reducing God's ways to a formula. He also avoids identifying
goodness with his fortune in life; it is their disparity, in fact, that appalls him. But he
fulfills God's expectations because he does not curse or in any way repudiate him. Instead, Job wants God to meet him on his own terms and explain:

> You can call, and I will answer,
> or I will speak and You can answer me.
> How many are my sins and my offenses?
> Advise me of my crimes and sins.
> Why do You hide Your face,
> regard me as Your enemy?

Far from cursing God, he is speaking from within an assumed relationship with
him. But he is mistaken to think that he and God can meet on such equal terms that
he merits an explanation. In the end, God does speak to him; he gets that much. But
God addresses him with a series of questions, not answers:

> Cinch your waist like a fighter.
> I will put questions, and you will inform me:

Where were you when I founded the earth?
Speak, if you have any wisdom:
Who set its measurements, if you know,
　　laid out the building lot, stretching the plumb line?
Where was the ground where He sank its foundations?

There is no reciprocal conversation; Job has no answers, and is silent except to confess his error.

God's magnificent speech from the storm ranges over all of creation and its animal life. The contrast with the account of creation in the first chapter of Genesis, which puts human beings at the center, is dramatic. Here there are beasts whose might far surpasses that of humans, who seem just a part of the created world, and the poetry of this speech conveys the awe and mystery that are attributes of God. The book of Job does not succeed in explaining innocent suffering, if that is its purpose, but it does leave us with a sense of what we cannot understand.

THE SONG OF SONGS

In this great dialogue between lovers, a man and a woman, frankly and in detail, express their appreciation of each other's bodies. The Song of Songs (or Song of Solomon) celebrates human sexuality and love in all their sensual splendor, as well as human life itself: "for love," it says, "is strong as death." Each of the lovers, again and again, takes inventory of the other's body, describing each part and comparing it to an animal, some feature of the natural landscape, or an aspect of the built human environment, so that we not only feel the power of physical desire but also appreciate the human body and love as harmonious parts of the world. Some of these comparisons are of great natural beauty ("thy belly is like a heap of wheat set about with lilies"); others are extravagant, fantastic ("thy hair is as a flock of goats," "thy teeth are like a flock of sheep," "thy neck is like the tower of David," "thy nose is as the tower of Lebanon"). The concreteness of the imagery and the piling of image upon image make the pair of bodies a figure of the world itself, to be contemplated in wonder.

But the incorporation of this poem in sacred scripture raises the possibility of further meanings, although what these might be is an open question. This challenging and beautiful text has had a long history of divergent interpretations; a medieval Jewish commentator described it as "locks to which the key has been lost." Is it an allegory, and if so, is it religious or is it historical? If the former, does the allegory concern the love between God and his chosen people? Christians later understood the poem to describe the love between Christ and his church, or between God or Christ and the individual soul. The question of allegory is complicated by other uncertainties. Is the text as we have it a single composition, or is it a collection of poems? How are passages to be divided between the pair of lovers? Are there other speakers as well? In addition, many words and phrases in the Hebrew text are ambiguous and obscure. For this reason, English translations differ markedly. The King James version is given here because of its beauty as an English poem and because of its influence on Anglophone literature and music, but readers should be aware that it is less accurate than modern translations.

Many scholars today consider the Song of Songs to be one or several love poems, similar in important ways to Middle Eastern marriage songs that were collected early in the twentieth century, and perhaps rooted in ancient fertility rituals of the great pagan religions of Asia Minor. But we may want to ask if there are not also aspects of this text that invite an allegorical reading and if we must choose between sensual and more abstract meanings. Where do we draw the line between the literal and figurative meanings of words? Would we always want to? If the Song of Songs is an allegory, it is one that is wonderfully in touch with the world of the senses, as Dante's *Divine Comedy*, another great allegorical poem, is in a different way.

A NOTE ON THESE TRANSLATIONS

Genesis and Job are given here in clear, readable modern English translations to make the narrative of the former and the arguments of the latter accessible to contemporary readers. The other selections from the Hebrew Bible are from the King James or authorized version of 1611, so called because it was the work of a team of fifty-four scholars named by King James I of England to produce a new translation "appointed to be read in churches." Since that time advances in biblical scholarship have corrected some of the translators' mistakes and substituted clearer versions where their prose is obscure. Yet the King James version remains one of the greatest literary texts in the history of the English language. The echoes of its magnificent rhythms and cadences can be heard in the verse of English poets from John Milton to T.S. Eliot, in the prose of John Bunyan, and in the speeches of Abraham Lincoln.

PRONOUNCING GLOSSARY

The following list uses common English syllables and stress accents to provide rough equivalents of selected words whose pronunciation may be unfamiliar to the general reader.

Baalhamon: *bahl-ha'-mon*
Canaan: *kay'-nuhn*
Esau: *ee'-saw*

Euphrates: *yoo-fray'-teez*
Job: *johb*
Tirzah: *teer'-zah*

THE HEBREW BIBLE

From Genesis[1]

GENESIS 1–3

[*The Creation—The Fall*]

1. When God[2] began to create heaven and earth, and the earth then was welter and waste and darkness over the deep and God's breath hovering over the waters, God said, "Let there be light." And there was light. And God saw the light, that it was good, and God divided the light from the darkness. And God called the light Day, and the darkness He called Night. And it was evening and it was morning, first day. And God said, "Let there be a vault in the midst of the waters,[3] and let it divide water from water." And God made the vault and it divided the water beneath the vault from the water above the vault, and so it was. And God called the vault Heavens, and it was evening and it was morning, second day. And God said, "Let the waters under the heavens be gathered in one place so that the dry land will appear," and so it was. And God called the dry land Earth and the gathering of waters He called Seas, and God saw that it was good. And God said, "Let the earth grow grass, plants yielding seed of each kind and trees bearing fruit of each kind, that has its seed within it." And so it

---

1. Translated by Robert Alter.   2. This translates *Elohim*, one of the two most common names for God in the Torah. The other is YHWH, probably pronounced *Yahweh*; it is used, for example, in the story of Adam and Eve in chapter 2 of Genesis (signified in the translation by "LORD").   3. Those that come down in the form of rain. "Vault": the sky, which seen from below has the appearance of a ceiling.

was. And the earth put forth grass, plants yielding seed of each kind, and trees bearing fruit that has its seed within it of each kind, and God saw that it was good. And it was evening and it was morning, third day. And God said, "Let there be lights in the vault of the heavens to divide the day from the night, and they shall be signs for the fixed times[4] and for days and years, and they shall be lights in the vault of the heavens to light up the earth." And so it was. And God made the two great lights, the great light for dominion of day and the small light for dominion of night, and the stars. And God placed them in the vault of the heavens to light up the earth and to have dominion over day and night and to divide the light from the darkness. And God saw that it was good. And it was evening and it was morning, fourth day. And God said, "Let the waters swarm with the swarm of living creatures and let fowl fly over the earth across the vault of the heavens." And God created the great sea monsters and every living creature that crawls, which the water had swarmed forth of each kind, and the winged fowl of each kind, and God saw that it was good. And God blessed them, saying, "Be fruitful and multiply and fill the water in the seas and let the fowl multiply in the earth." And it was evening and it was morning, fifth day. And God said, "Let the earth bring forth living creatures of each kind, cattle and crawling things and wild beasts of each kind. And so it was. And God made wild beasts of each kind and cattle of every kind and crawling things on the ground of each kind, and God saw that it was good.

And God said, "Let us make a human in our image, by our likeness, to hold sway over the fish of the sea and the fowl of the heavens and the cattle and the wild beasts and all the crawling things that crawl upon the earth."

> And God created the human in his image,
> in the image of God He created him,
> male and female He created them.

And God blessed them, and God said to them, "Be fruitful and multiply and fill the earth and conquer it, and hold sway over the fish of the sea and the fowl of the heavens and every beast that crawls upon the earth." And God said, "Look, I have given you every seed-bearing plant on the face of all the earth and every tree that has fruit bearing seed, yours they will be for food. And to all the beasts of the earth and to all the fowl of the heavens and to all that crawls on the earth, which has the breath of life within it, the green plants for food." And so it was. And God saw all that He had done, and, look, it was very good. And it was evening and it was morning, the sixth day.

2. Then the heavens and the earth were completed, and all their array. And God completed on the seventh day the work He had done, and He ceased on the seventh day from all the work He had done. And God blessed the seventh day and hallowed it, for on it He had ceased from all His work that He had done. This is the tale of the heavens and the earth when they were created.

On the day the LORD God made earth and heavens,[5] no shrub of the field being yet on the earth and no plant of the field yet sprouted, for the LORD God had not caused rain to fall on the earth and there was no human to till the soil, and wetness would well from the earth to water all the surface of

---

4. Probably the seasons, but possibly the days and years that follow (the word translated by "and" would then mean "that is").   5. A very different account of the creation begins here.

the soil, then the Lord God fashioned the human, humus[6] from the soil, and blew into his nostrils the breath of life, and the human became a living creature. And the Lord God planted a garden in Eden, to the east, and He placed there the human He had fashioned. And the Lord God caused to sprout from the soil every tree lovely to look at and good for food, and the tree of life was in the midst of the garden, and the tree of knowledge, good and evil. Now a river runs out of Eden to water the garden and from there splits off into four streams. The name of the first is Pishon, the one that winds through the whole land of Havilah, where there is gold. And the gold of that land is goodly, bdellium is there, and lapis lazuli. And the name of the second river is Gihon, the one that winds through all the land of Cush. And the name of the third river is Tigris, the one that goes to the east of Ashur. And the fourth river is Euphrates. And the Lord God took the human and set him down in the garden of Eden to till it and watch it. And the Lord God commanded the human, saying, "From every fruit of the garden you may surely eat. But from the tree of knowledge, good and evil, you shall not eat, for on the day you eat from it, you are doomed to die."

And the Lord God said, "It is not good for the human to be alone, I shall make him a sustainer beside him." And the Lord God fashioned from the soil each beast of the field and each fowl of the heavens and brought each to the human to see what he would call it, and whatever the human called a living creature, that was its name. And the human called names to all the cattle and to the fowl of the heavens and to all the beasts of the field, but for the human no sustainer beside him was found. And the Lord God cast a deep slumber on the human, and he slept, and He took one of his ribs and closed over the flesh where it had been, and the Lord God built the rib He had taken from the human into a woman and He brought her to the human. And the human said:

> This one at last, bone of my bones
> and flesh of my flesh,
> This one shall be called Woman,
> for from man was this one taken.

Therefore does a man leave his father and his mother and cling to his wife and they become one flesh. And the two of them were naked, the human and his woman, and they were not ashamed.

3. Now the serpent was most cunning of all the beasts of the field that the Lord God had made. And he said to the woman, "Though God said, you shall not eat from any tree of the garden—" And the woman said to the serpent, "From the fruit of the garden's trees we may eat, but from the fruit of the tree in the midst of the garden God has said, 'You shall not eat from it and you shall not touch it, lest you die.'" And the serpent said to the woman, "You shall not be doomed to die. For God knows that on the day you eat of it your eyes will be opened and you will become as gods knowing good and evil." And the woman saw that the tree was good for eating and that it was lust to the eyes and the tree was lovely to look at,[7] and she took of its fruit and ate, and

---

6. The Hebrew text makes a pun on the words for *human* and *soil*, which are similar in sound.   7. The Hebrew verb translated "to look at" may also imply gaining wisdom.

she also gave to her man, and he ate. And the eyes of the two were opened, and they knew they were naked, and they sewed fig leaves and made themselves loincloths.

And they heard the sound of the LORD God walking about in the garden in the evening breeze, and the human and his woman hid from the LORD God in the midst of the trees of the garden. And the LORD God called to the human and said to him, "Where are you?" And he said, "I heard your sound in the garden and I was afraid, for I was naked, and I hid." And He said, "Who told you that you were naked? From the tree I commanded you not to eat have you eaten?" And the human said, "The woman whom you gave by me, she gave me from the tree, and I ate." And the LORD God said to the woman, "What is this you have done?" And the woman said, "The serpent beguiled me and I ate." And the LORD God said to the serpent, "Because you have done this,

> Cursed be you
>   of all cattle and all beasts of the field.
> On your belly shall you go
>   and dust shall you eat all the days of your life.
> Enmity will I set between you and the woman,
>   between your seed and hers.
> He will boot[8] your head
>   and you will bite his heel."

To the woman He said,

> "I will terribly sharpen your birth pangs,
>   in pain shall you bear children.
> And for your man shall be your longing,
>   and he shall rule over you."

And to the human he said, "Because you listened to the voice of your wife and ate from the tree that I commanded you, 'You shall not eat from it,'

> Cursed be the soil for your sake,
>   with pangs shall you eat from it all the days of your life.
> Thorn and thistle shall it sprout for you
>   and you shall eat the plants of the field.
> By the sweat of your brow shall you eat bread
>   till you return to the soil,
>   for from there were you taken,
> for dust you are
>   and to dust shall you return."

And the human called his woman's name Eve,[9] for she was the mother of all that lives. And the LORD God made skin coats for the human and his woman, and He clothed them. And the LORD God said, "Now that the human has become like one of us, knowing good and evil, he may reach out and take as well from the tree of life and live forever." And the LORD God

---

8. Trample. The translation reproduces the pun in Hebrew between this word and the word for "bite" in the next line.   9. The name Eve resembles the word for "to live" in Hebrew.

sent him from the garden of Eden to till the soil from which he had been taken. And he drove out the human and set up east of the garden of Eden the cherubim and the flame of the whirling sword to guard the way to the tree of life.

FROM GENESIS 4

[The First Murder]

4. And the human knew Eve his woman and she conceived and bore Cain, and she said, "I have got me a man with the LORD." And she bore as well his brother, Abel, and Abel became a herder of sheep while Cain was a tiller of the soil. And it happened in the course of time that Cain brought from the fruit of the soil an offering to the LORD. And Abel too had brought from the choice firstlings of his flock, and the LORD regarded Abel and his offering but He did not regard Cain and his offering, and Cain was very incensed, and his face fell. And the LORD said to Cain.

> "Why are you incensed,
> and why is your face fallen?
> For whether you offer well,
> or whether you do not,
> at the tent flap sin crouches
> and for you is its longing
> but you will rule over it."

And Cain said to Abel his brother, "Let us go out to the field." And when they were in the field, Cain rose against Abel his brother and killed him. And the LORD said to Cain, "Where is Abel your brother?" And he said, "I do not know. Am I my brother's keeper?" And He said, "What have you done? Listen! your brother's blood cries out to me from the soil. And so, cursed shall you be by the soil that gaped with its mouth to take your brother's blood from your hand. If you till the soil, it will no longer give you its strength. A restless wanderer shall you be on the earth." And Cain said to the LORD, "My punishment is too great to bear. Now that You have driven me this day from the soil and I must hide from Your presence, I shall be a restless wanderer on the earth and whoever finds me will kill me." And the LORD said to him, "Therefore whoever kills Cain shall suffer sevenfold vengeance." And the LORD set a mark upon Cain so that whoever found him would not slay him.

* * *

FROM GENESIS 6–9

[The Flood]

6. * * * And the LORD saw that the evil of the human creature was great on the earth and that every scheme of his heart's devising was only perpetually evil. And the LORD regretted having made the human on earth and was grieved to the heart. And the LORD said, "I will wipe out the human race I created from the face of the earth, from human to cattle to crawling thing to the fowl of the heavens, for I regret that I have made them." But Noah found favor in the eyes of the LORD. This is the lineage of Noah—Noah was a righteous man, he was blameless in his time, Noah walked with God—and Noah

begot three sons, Shem and Ham and Japheth. And the earth was corrupt before God and the earth was filled with outrage. And God saw the earth and, look, it was corrupt, for all flesh had corrupted its ways on the earth. And God said to Noah, "The end of all flesh is come before me, for the earth is filled with outrage by them, and I am now about to destroy them, with the earth. Make yourself an ark of cypress wood, with cells you shall make the ark, and caulk it inside and out with pitch. This is how you shall make it: three hundred cubits,[1] the ark's length; fifty cubits, its width; thirty cubits, its height. Make a skylight in the ark, within a cubit of the top you shall finish it, and put an entrance in the ark on one side. With lower and middle and upper decks you shall make it. As for me, I am about to bring the Flood, water upon the earth, to destroy all flesh that has within it the breath of life from under the heavens, everything on the earth shall perish. And I will set up my covenant with you, and you shall enter the ark, you and your sons and your wife and the wives of your sons, with you. And from all that lives, from all flesh, two of each thing you shall bring to the ark to keep alive with you, male and female they shall be. From the fowl of each kind and from the cattle of each kind and from all that crawls on the earth of each kind, two of each thing shall come to you to be kept alive. As for you, take you from every food that is eaten and store it by you, to serve for you and for them as food." And this Noah did; as all that God commanded him, so he did.

7. * * * Noah was six hundred years old when the Flood came, water over the earth. And Noah and his sons and his wife and his sons' wives came into the ark because of the waters of the Flood. Of the clean[2] animals and of the animals that were not clean and of the fowl and of all that crawls upon the ground two each came to Noah into the ark, male and female, as God had commanded Noah. And it happened after seven days, that the waters of the Flood were over the earth. In the six hundredth year of Noah's life, in the second month, on the seventeenth day of the month, on that day,

> All the wellsprings of the great deep burst
> and the casements of the heavens were opened.

And the rain was over the earth forty days and forty nights. That very day, Noah and Shem and Ham and Japheth, the sons of Noah, and Noah's wife, and the three wives of his sons together with them, came into the ark, they as well as beasts of each kind and cattle of each kind and each kind of crawling thing that crawls on the earth and each kind of bird, each winged thing. They came to Noah into the ark, two by two of all flesh that has the breath of life within it. And those that came in, male and female of all flesh they came, as God had commanded him, and the LORD shut him in. And the Flood was forty days over the earth, and the waters multiplied and bore the ark upward and it rose above the earth. And the waters surged and multiplied mightily over the earth, and the ark went on the surface of the water. And the waters surged most mightily over the earth, and all the high mountains under the heavens were covered. Fifteen cubits above them the waters surged as the mountains were covered. And all flesh that stirs on the earth

---

1. That is, about 450 feet (a cubit was about 18 inches).   2. Ritually pure and probably thus fit for sacrifice.

perished, the fowl and the cattle and the beasts and all swarming things that swarm upon the earth, and all humankind. All that had the quickening breath of life in its nostrils, of all that was on dry land, died. And He wiped out all existing things from the face of the earth, from humans to cattle to crawling things to the fowl of the heavens, they were wiped out from the earth. And Noah alone remained, and those with him in the ark. And the waters surged over the earth one hundred and fifty days.

8. And God remembered Noah and all the beasts and all the cattle that were with him in the ark. And God sent a wind over the earth and the waters subsided. And the wellsprings of the deep were dammed up, and the casements of the heavens, the rain from the heavens held back. And the waters receded from the earth little by little, and the waters ebbed. At the end of a hundred and fifty days the ark came to rest, on the seventeenth day of the seventh month, on the mountains of Ararat. The waters continued to ebb, until the tenth month, on the first day of the tenth month, the mountaintops appeared. And it happened, at the end of forty days, that Noah opened the window of the ark he had made. And he let out the raven and it went forth to and fro until the waters should dry up from the earth. And he let out the dove to see whether the waters had abated from the surface of the ground. But the dove found no resting place for its foot and it returned to him to the ark, for the waters were over all the earth. And he reached out and took it and brought it back to him into the ark. Then he waited another seven days and again let the dove out of the ark. And the dove came back to him at eventide and, look, a plucked olive leaf was in its bill, and Noah knew that the waters had abated from the earth. Then he waited still another seven days and let out the dove, and it did not return to him again. And it happened in the six hundred and first year, in the first month, on the first day of the month, the waters dried up from the earth, and Noah took off the covering of the ark and he saw and, look, the surface of the ground was dry. And in the second month, on the twenty-seventh day of the month, the earth was completely dry. And God spoke to Noah, saying, "Go out of the ark, you and your wife and your sons and your sons' wives, with you. All the animals that are with you of all flesh, fowl and cattle and every crawling thing that crawls on the earth, take out with you, and let them swarm through the earth and be fruitful and multiply on the earth." And Noah went out, his sons and his wife and his sons' wives with him. Every beast, every crawling thing, and every fowl, everything that stirs on the earth, by families, came out of the ark. And Noah built an altar to the LORD and he took from every clean cattle and every clean fowl and offered burnt offerings on the altar. And the LORD smelled the fragrant odor and the LORD said in His heart, "I will not again damn the soil on humankind's score. For the devisings of the human heart are evil from youth. And I will not again strike down all living things as I did. As long as all the days of the earth—

> seedtime and harvest
> and cold and heat
> and summer and winter
> and day and night
> shall not cease."

9. And God blessed Noah and his sons and He said to them, "Be fruitful and multiply and fill the earth. And the dread and fear of you shall be upon all the beasts of the field and all the fowl of the heavens, in all that crawls on the ground and in all the fish of the sea. In your hand they are given. All stirring things that are alive, yours shall be for food, like the green plants, I have given all to you. But flesh with its lifeblood still in it you shall not eat.[3] And just so, your lifeblood I will requite, from every beast I will requite it, and from humankind, from every man's brother, I will requite human life.

> He who sheds human blood
>   by humans his blood shall be shed,
> for in the image of God
>   He made humankind.
> As for you, be fruitful and multiply,
>   swarm through the earth, and hold sway over it."

And God said to Noah and to his sons with him, "And I, I am about to establish My covenant with you and with your seed after you, and with every living creature that is with you, the fowl and the cattle and every beast of the earth with you, all that have come out of the ark, every beast of the earth. And I will establish My covenant with you, that never again shall all flesh be cut off by the waters of the Flood, and never again shall there be a Flood to destroy the earth." And God said, "This is the sign of the covenant that I set between Me and you and every living creature that is with you, for everlasting generations: My bow[4] I have set in the clouds to be a sign of the covenant between Me and the earth, and so, when I send clouds over the earth, the bow will appear in the cloud. Then I will remember My covenant, between Me and you and every living creature of all flesh, and the waters will no more become a Flood to destroy all flesh. And the bow shall be in the cloud and I will see it, to remember the everlasting covenant between God and all living creatures, all flesh that is on the earth." And God said to Noah, "This is the sign of the covenant I have established between Me and all flesh that is on the earth."

* * *

FROM GENESIS 11

[The Origin of Languages]

11. And all the earth was one language, one set of words. And it happened as they journeyed from the east that they found a valley in the land of Shinar[5] and settled there. And they said to each other, "Come, let us bake bricks and burn them hard." And the brick served them as stone and bitumen served them as mortar. And they said, "Come, let us build us a city and a tower[6] with its top in the heavens, that we may make us a name, lest we be scattered over all the earth." And the LORD came down to see the city and the tower that the human creatures had built. And the LORD said, "As one

---

3. A reference to the biblical dietary laws: blood was supposed to be drained from a slaughtered animal.
4. The rainbow.   5. In Mesopotamia. *They:* humankind.   6. This story is based on the Babylonian practice of building temples in the form of terraced pyramids (ziggurats).

people with one language for all, if this is what they have begun to do, nothing they plot will elude them. Come, let us go down and baffle their language there so that they will not understand each other's language." And the LORD scattered them from there over all the earth and they left off building the city. Therefore it is called Babel, for there the LORD made the language of all the earth babble. And from there the LORD scattered them over all the earth.

* * *

FROM GENESIS 17–19

[Abraham and Sarah]

17. And Abram[7] was ninety-nine years old and the LORD appeared to Abram and said to him, "I am El Shaddai.[8] Walk with Me and be blameless, and I will grant My covenant between Me and you and I will multiply you very greatly." And Abram flung himself on his face, and God spoke to him, saying, "As for Me, this is My covenant with you: you shall be father to a multitude of nations. And no longer shall your name be called Abram but your name shall be Abraham,[9] for I have made you father to a multitude of nations. And I will make you most abundantly fruitful and turn you into nations, and kings shall come forth from you. And I will establish My covenant between Me and you and your seed after you through their generations as an everlasting covenant to be God to you and to your seed after you. And I will give unto you and your seed after you the land in which you sojourn, the whole land of Canaan, as an everlasting holding, and I will be their God."

And God said to Abraham, "As for you, you shall keep My commandment, you and your seed after you through their generations. This is My covenant which you shall keep, between Me and you and your seed after you: every male among you must be circumcised. You shall circumcise the flesh of your foreskin and it shall be the sign of the covenant between Me and you. Eight days old every male among you shall be circumcised through your generations, even slaves born in the household and those purchased with silver from any foreigner who is not of your seed. Those born in your household and those purchased with silver must be circumcised, and My covenant in your flesh shall be an everlasting covenant. And a male with a foreskin, who has not circumcised the flesh of his foreskin, that person shall be cut off from his folk. My covenant he has broken." And God said to Abraham, "Sarai your wife shall no longer call her name Sarai, for Sarah is her name." And I will bless her and I will also give you from her a son and I will bless him, and she shall become nations, kings of peoples shall issue from her." And Abraham flung himself on his face and he laughed, saying to himself,

> "To a hundred-year-old will a child be born,
> will ninety-nine-year-old Sarah give birth?"

---

7. Soon to be renamed Abraham: a descendant, in the tenth generation, of Noah's son Shem, and the first great patriarch.   8. Another name for God.   9. Both names mean "exalted father," and there is little difference between them. Abraham undergoes a change of name to indicate his new status under the covenant that God now announces. The same holds for the change of his wife's name from Sarai to Sarah (both mean "princess").

And Abraham said to God, "Would that Ishmael[1] might live in Your favor!" And God said, "Yet Sarah your wife is to bear you a son and you shall call his name Isaac[2] and I will establish My covenant with him as an everlasting covenant, for his seed after him. As for Ishmael, I have heard you. Look, I will bless him and make him fruitful and will multiply him most abundantly, twelve chieftains he shall beget, and I will make him a great nation. But My covenant I will establish with Isaac whom Sarah will bear you by this season next year." And He finished speaking with him, and God ascended from Abraham.

And Abraham took Ishmael his son and all the slaves born in his household and those purchased with silver, every male among the people of Abraham's household, and he circumcised the flesh of their foreskin on that very day as God had spoken to him. And Abraham was ninety-nine years old when the flesh of his foreskin was circumcised. And Ishmael was thirteen years old when the flesh of his foreskin was circumcised. On that very day Abraham was circumcised, and Ishmael his son, and all the men of his household, those born in the household and those purchased with silver from the foreigners, were circumcised with him.

18. And the LORD appeared to him in the Terebinths of Mamre when he was sitting by the tent flap in the heat of the day. And he raised his eyes and saw, and, look, three men were standing before him. He saw, and he ran toward them from the tent flap and bowed to the ground. And he said, "My lord, if I have found favor in your eyes, please do not go on past your servant. Let a little water be fetched and bathe your feet and stretch out under the tree, and let me fetch a morsel of bread, and refresh yourselves. Then you may go on, for have you not come by your servant?" And they said, "Do as you have spoken." And Abraham hurried to the tent to Sarah and he said, "Hurry! Knead three *seahs*[3] of choice flour and make loaves." And to the herd Abraham ran and fetched a tender and goodly calf and gave it to the lad, who hurried to prepare it. And he fetched curds and milk and the calf that had been prepared and he set these before them, he standing over them under the tree, and they ate. And they said to him, "Where is Sarah your wife?" And he said, "There, in the tent." And he[4] said, "I will surely return to you at this very season and, look, a son shall Sarah your wife have," and Sarah was listening at the tent flap, which was behind him. And Abraham and Sarah were old, advanced in years, Sarah no longer had her woman's flow. And Sarah laughed inwardly, saying, "After being shriveled, shall I have pleasure, and my husband is old?" And the LORD said to Abraham, "Why is it that Sarah laughed, saying, 'Shall I really give birth, old as I am?' Is anything beyond the LORD? In due time I will return to you, at this very season, and Sarah shall have a son." And Sarah dissembled, saying, "I did not laugh," for she was afraid. And He said, "Yes, you did laugh."

And the men arose from there and looked out over Sodom, Abraham walking along with them to see them off. And the LORD had thought, "Shall I conceal from Abraham what I am about to do? For Abraham will surely be a

---

1. The son Abraham has had with the slave woman Hagar.   2. The name plays on the word translated "he laughed" above.   3. A dry measure; estimates of its size vary, but this was a very generous amount.
4. One of the visitors.

great and mighty nation, and all the nations of the earth will be blessed through him. For I have embraced him so that he will charge his sons and his household after him to keep the way of the LORD to do righteousness and justice, that the LORD may bring upon Abraham all that He spoke concerning him." And the LORD said,

> "The outcry of Sodom and Gomorrah, how great!
> Their offense is very grave.

Let Me go down and see whether as the outcry that has come to me they have dealt destruction, and if not, I shall know." And the men turned from there and went on toward Sodom while the LORD was still standing before Abraham. And Abraham stepped forward and said, "Will you really wipe out the innocent with the guilty? Perhaps there may be fifty innocent within the city. Will you really really wipe out the place and not spare it for the sake of the fifty innocent within it? Far be it from You to do such a thing, to put to death the innocent with the guilty, making innocent and guilty the same. Far be it from You! Will not the Judge of all the earth do justice?" And the LORD said, "Should I find in Sodom fifty innocent within the city, I will forgive the whole place for their sake." And Abraham spoke up and said, "Here, pray, I have presumed to speak to my Lord when I am but dust and ashes. Perhaps the fifty innocent will lack five. Would you destroy the whole city for the five?" And He said, "I will not destroy if I find there forty-five." And he spoke to Him still again and he said, "Perhaps there will be found forty." And He said, "I will not do it on account of the forty." And he said, "Please, let not my Lord be incensed and let me speak, perhaps there will be found thirty." And He said, "I will not do it if I find there thirty." And he said, "Here, pray, I have presumed to speak to my Lord. Perhaps there will be found twenty." And He said, "I will not destroy for the sake of the twenty." And he said, "Please, let not my Lord be incensed and let me speak just this time. Perhaps there will be found ten." And He said, "I will not destroy for the sake of the ten." And the LORD went off when He finished speaking with Abraham, and Abraham returned to his place.

19. And the two messengers came into Sodom at evening, when Lot[5] was sitting in the gate of Sodom. And Lot saw, and he rose to greet them and bowed, with his face to the ground. And he said, "O please, my lords, turn aside to your servant's house to spend the night, and bathe your feet, and you can set off early on your way." And they said, "No. We will spend the night in the square." And he pressed them hard, and they turned aside to him and came into his house, and he prepared them a feast and baked flat bread, and they ate. They had not yet lain down when the men of the city, the men of Sodom, surrounded the house, from lads to elders, every last man of them. And they called out to Lot and said, "Where are the men who came to you tonight? Bring them out to us so that we may know them!" And Lot went out to them at the entrance, closing the door behind him, and he said, "Please, my brothers, do no harm. Look, I have two daughters who have known no man. Let me bring them out to you and do to them whatever

5. Abraham's nephew.

you want.[6] Only to these men do nothing, for have they not come under the shadow of my roof-beam?" And they said, "Step aside." And they said, "This person came as a sojourner and he sets himself up to judge! Now we'll do more harm to you than to them," and they pressed hard against the man Lot and moved forward to break down the door. And the men[7] reached out their hands and drew Lot to them into the house and closed the door. And the men at the entrance of the house they struck with blinding light, from the smallest to the biggest, and they could not find the entrance. And the men said to Lot, "Whom do you still have here? Your sons and your daughters and whomever you have in the city take out of the place. For we are about to destroy this place because the outcry against them has grown great before the Lord and the Lord has sent us to destroy it."

And Lot went out and spoke to his sons-in-law who had married his daughters and he said, "Rise, get out of this place, for the Lord is about to destroy the city." And he seemed to be joking to his sons-in-law. And as dawn was breaking the messengers urged Lot, saying, "Rise, take your wife and your two daughters who remain with you, lest you be wiped out in the punishment of the city." And he lingered, and the men seized his hand and his wife's hand and the hands of his two daughters in the Lord's compassion for him and led them outside the city. And as they were bringing them out, he said, "Flee for your life. Don't look behind you and don't stop anywhere on the plain. Flee to the high country lest you be wiped out." And Lot said to them, "Oh, no, my lord. Look, pray, your servant has found favor in your eyes, and you have shown such great kindness in what you have done for me in saving my life, but I cannot flee to the high country, lest evil overtake me and I die. Here, pray, this town is nearby to escape there, and it is a small place. Let me flee there, for it is but a small place, and my life will be saved." And he said, "I grant you a favor in this matter as well, and I will not overthrow the town of which you spoke. Hurry, flee there, for I can do nothing before you arrive there." Thus is the name of the town called Zoar. The sun had just come out over the earth when Lot arrived at Zoar. And the Lord rained upon Sodom and Gomorrah brimstone and fire from the Lord from the heavens. And He overthrew all those cities and all the plain and all the inhabitants of the cities and what grew in the soil. And his wife looked back and she became a pillar of salt. And Abraham hastened early in the morning to the place where he had stood in the presence of the Lord. And he looked out over Sodom and Gomorrah and over all the land of the plain, and he saw and, look, smoke was rising like the smoke from a kiln.

* * *

FROM GENESIS 22

[Abraham and Isaac]

22. And it happened after these things that God tested Abraham. And He said to him, "Abraham!" and he said, "Here I am." And He said, "Take, pray, your son, your only one, whom you love, Isaac, and go forth to the land of Moriah and offer him up as a burnt offering on one of the mountains which I

---

6. One possible explanation for this extraordinary offer is that the code of hospitality prevalent in the Near East and elsewhere required Lot to protect his guests at all costs.　　7. Lot's guests.

shall say to you." And Abraham rose early in the morning and saddled his donkey and took his two lads with him, and Isaac his son, and he split wood for the offering, and rose and went to the place that God had said to him. On the third day Abraham raised his eyes and saw the place from afar. And Abraham said to his lads, "Sit you here with the donkey and let me and the lad walk ahead and let us worship and return to you." And Abraham took the wood for the offering and put it on Isaac his son and he took in his hand the fire and the cleaver, and the two of them went together. And Isaac said to Abraham his father, "Father!" and he said, "Here I am, my son." And he said, "Here is the fire and the wood but where is the sheep for the offering?" And Abraham said, "God will see to the sheep for the offering, my son." And the two of them went together. And they came to the place that God had said to him, and Abraham built there an altar and laid out the wood and bound Isaac his son and placed him on the altar on top of the wood. And Abraham reached out his hand and took the cleaver to slaughter his son. And the LORD's messenger called out to him from the heavens and said, "Abraham, Abraham!" and he said, "Here I am." And he said, "Do not reach out your hand against the lad, and do nothing to him, for now I know that you fear God and you have not held back your son, your only one, from Me." And Abraham raised his eyes and saw and, look, a ram was caught in the thicket by its horns, and Abraham went and took the ram and offered him up as a burnt offering instead of his son. And Abraham called the name of that place YHWH-yireh, as is said to this day, "On the mount of the LORD there is sight."[8] And the LORD's messenger called out to Abraham once again from the heavens, and He said, "By my own Self I swear, declares the LORD, that because you have done this thing and have not held back your son, your only one, I will greatly bless you and will greatly multiply your seed, as the stars in the heavens and as the sand on the shore of the sea, and your seed shall take hold of its enemies' gate. And all the nations of the earth will be blessed through your seed because you have listened to my voice." And Abraham returned to his lads, and they rose and went together to Beer-sheba, and Abraham dwelled in Beer-sheba.

* * *

FROM GENESIS 25, 27

[Jacob and Esau]

25. * * * And Isaac pleaded with the LORD on behalf of his wife, for she was barren, and the LORD granted his plea, and Rebekah his wife conceived. And the children clashed together within her, and she said, "Then why me?" and she went to inquire of the LORD. And the LORD said to her:

> "Two nations—in your womb,
>   two peoples from your loins shall issue.
> People over people shall prevail,
>   the elder, the younger's slave."

And when her time was come to give birth, look, there were twins in her womb. And the first one came out ruddy, like a hairy mantle all over, and

---

8. Either "he sees" or "he is seen (appears)."

they called his name Esau. Then his brother came out, his hand grasping Esau's heel, and they called his name Jacob. And Isaac was sixty years old when they were born.

And the lads grew up, and Esau was a man skilled in hunting, a man of the field, and Jacob was a simple man, a dweller in tents. And Isaac loved Esau for the game that he brought him, but Rebekah loved Jacob. And Jacob prepared a stew and Esau came from the field, and he was famished. And Esau said to Jacob, "Let me gulp down some of this red red stuff, for I am famished." Therefore is his name called Edom.[9] And Jacob said, "Sell now your birthright to me." And Esau said, "Look, I am at the point of death, so why do I need a birthright?"

And Jacob said, "Swear to me now," and he swore to him, and he sold his birthright to Jacob. Then Jacob gave Esau bread and lentil stew, and he ate and he drank and he rose and he went off, and Esau spurned the birthright.

27. And it happened when Isaac was old, that his eyes grew too bleary to see, and he called to Esau his elder son and said to him, "My son!" and he said, "Here I am." And he said, "Look, I have grown old; I know not how soon I shall die. So now, take up, pray, your gear, your quiver and your bow, and go out to the field, and hunt me some game, and make me a dish of the kind that I love and bring it to me that I may eat, so that I may solemnly bless you before I die." And Rebekah was listening as Isaac spoke to Esau his son, and Esau went off to the field to hunt game to bring.

And Rebekah said to Jacob her son, "Look, I have heard your father speaking to Esau your brother, saying, 'Bring me some game and make me a dish that I may eat, and I shall bless you in the LORD's presence before I die.' So now, my son, listen to my voice, to what I command you. Go, pray, to the flock, and fetch me from there two choice kids that I may make them into a dish for your father of the kind he loves. And you shall bring it to your father and he shall eat, so that he may bless you before he dies." And Jacob said to Rebekah his mother, "Look, Esau my brother is a hairy man and I am a smooth-skinned man. What if my father feels me and I seem a cheat to him and bring on myself a curse and not a blessing?" And his mother said, "Upon me your curse, my son. Just listen to my voice and go, fetch them for me." And he went and he fetched and he brought to his mother, and his mother made a dish of the kind his father loved. And Rebekah took the garments of Esau her elder son, the finery that was with her in the house, and put them on Jacob her younger son, and the skins of the kids she put on his hands and on the smooth part of his neck. And she placed the dish, and the bread she had made, in the hand of Jacob her son. And he came to his father and said, "Father!" And he said, "Here I am. Who are you, my son?" And Jacob said to his father, "I am Esau your first-born. I have done as you have spoken to me. Rise, pray, sit up, and eat of my game so that you may solemnly bless me." And Isaac said to his son, "How is it you found it this soon, my son?" And he said, "Because the LORD your God gave me good luck." And Isaac said to Jacob, "Come close, pray, that I may feel you, my son, whether you are my son Esau or not." And Jacob came close to Isaac his father and he felt him and he said, "The voice is the voice of Jacob and the hands are Esau's hands." But he did not recognize him for his hands

9. From a semitic root meaning "red."

were, like Esau's hands, hairy, and he blessed him. And he said, "Are you my son Esau? "And he said, "I am." And he said, "Serve me, that I may eat of the game of my son, so that I may solemnly bless you." And he served him and he ate, and he brought him wine and he drank. And Isaac his father said to him, "Come close, pray, and kiss me, my son." And he came close and kissed him, and he smelled his garments and he blessed him and he said, "See, the smell of my son is like the smell of the field that the LORD has blessed.

> May God grant you
>> from the dew of the heavens and the fat of the earth.
> May peoples serve you,
>> and nations bow before you.
> Be overlord to your brothers,
>> may your mother's sons bow before you.
> Those who curse you be cursed,
>> and those who bless you, blessed."

And it happened as soon as Isaac finished blessing Jacob, and Jacob barely had left the presence of Isaac his father, that Esau his brother came back from the hunt. And he, too, made a dish and brought it to his father and he said to his father, "Let my father rise and eat of the game of his son so that you may solemnly bless me." And his father Isaac said, "Who are you?" And he said, "I am your son, your firstborn, Esau." And Isaac was seized with a very great trembling and he said, "Who is it, then, who caught game and brought it to me and I ate everything before you came and blessed him? Now blessed he stays." When Esau heard his father's words, he cried out with a great and very bitter outcry and he said to his father, "Bless me, too, Father!" And he said, "Your brother has come in deceit and has taken your blessing." And he said,

> "Was his name called Jacob
>> that he should trip me now twice by the heels?[1]
> My birthright he took,
>> and look, now, he's taken my blessing."

And he said, "Have you not kept back a blessing for me?"

And Isaac answered and said to Esau, "Look, I made him overlord to you, and all his brothers I gave him as slaves, and with grain and wine I endowed him. For you, then, what can I do, my son?" And Esau said to his father, "Do you have but one blessing, my father? Bless me, too, Father." And Esau raised his voice and he wept. And Isaac his father answered and said to him,

> "Look, from the fat of the earth be your dwelling
>> and from the dew of the heavens above.
> By your sword shall you live
>> and your brother you'll serve.
> And when you rebel
>> you shall break off his yoke from your neck."

* * *

---

1. There is a pun on the name Jacob (which means something like "God protects") and the word for "heel," which is set up earlier when Jacob grasps Esau's heel at birth.

GENESIS 37, 39–46

[The Story of Joseph]

37. And Jacob dwelled in the land of his father's sojournings, in the land of Canaan. This is the lineage of Jacob—Joseph, seventeen years old, was tending the flock with his brothers, assisting the sons of Bilhah and the sons of Zilpah, the wives of his father. And Joseph brought ill report of them to their father. And Israel loved Joseph more than all his sons, for he was the child of his old age, and he made him an ornamented tunic.[2] And his brothers saw it was he their father loved more than all his brothers, and they hated him and could not speak a kind word to him. And Joseph dreamed a dream and told it to his brothers and they hated him all the more. And he said to them, "Listen, pray, to this dream that I dreamed. And, look, we were binding sheaves in the field, and, look, my sheaf arose and actually stood up, and, look, your sheaves drew round and bowed to my sheaf." And his brothers said to him, "Do you mean to reign over us, do you mean to rule us?" And they hated him all the more, for his dreams and for his words. And he dreamed yet another dream and recounted it to his brothers, and he said, "Look, I dreamed a dream again, and, look, the sun and the moon and eleven stars were bowing to me." And he recounted it to his father and to his brothers, and his father rebuked him and said to him, "What is this dream that you have dreamed? Shall we really come, I and your mother and your brothers, to bow before you to the ground?" And his brothers were jealous of him, while his father kept the thing in mind.

And his brothers went to graze their father's flock at Shechem. And Israel said to Joseph, "You know, your brothers are pasturing at Shechem. Come, let me send you to them," and he said to him, "Here I am." And he said to him, "Go, pray, to see how your brothers fare, and how the flock fares, and bring me back word." And he sent him from the valley of Hebron and he came to Shechem. And a man found him and, look, he was wandering in the field, and the man asked him, saying, "What is it you seek?" And he said, "My brothers I seek. Tell me, pray, where are they pasturing?" And the man said, "They have journeyed on from here, for I heard them say, 'Let us go to Dothan.'" And Joseph went after his brothers and found them at Dothan. And they saw him from afar before he drew near them and they plotted against him to put him to death. And they said to each other, "Here comes that dream-master! And so now, let us kill him and fling him into one of the pits and we can say, a vicious beast has devoured him, and we shall see what will come of his dreams." And Reuben heard and came to his rescue and said, "We must not take his life." And Reuben said to them, "Shed no blood! Fling him into this pit in the wilderness and do not raise a hand against him"—that he might rescue him from their hands to bring him back to his father. And it happened when Joseph came to his brothers that they stripped Joseph of his tunic, the ornamented tunic that he had on him. And they took him and flung him into the pit, and the pit was empty, there was no water in it. And they sat down to eat bread, and they raised their eyes and saw and, look, a caravan of Ishmaelites was coming from Gilead, their camels bearing

---

2. This is the "coat of many colors" made famous by the King James translation. A parallel in a cuneiform text suggests a garment with ornaments sewn on.

gum and balm and ladanum on their way to take down to Egypt. And Judah
said to his brothers, "What gain is there if we kill our brother and cover up
his blood?³ Come, let us sell him to the Ishmaelites and our hand will not be
against him, for he is our brother, our own flesh." And his brothers agreed.
And Midianite merchantmen passed by and pulled Joseph up out of the pit
and sold Joseph to the Ishmaelites for twenty pieces of silver.⁴ And Reuben
came back to the pit and, look, Joseph was not in the pit, and he rent his
garments, and he came back to his brothers, and he said, "The boy is gone,
and I, where can I turn?" And they took Joseph's tunic and slaughtered a kid
and dipped the tunic in the blood, and they sent the ornamented tunic and
had it brought to their father, and they said, "Recognize, pray, is it your son's
tunic or not?" And he recognized it, and he said, "It is my son's tunic.

> A vicious beast has devoured him,
> Joseph's been torn to shreds!"

And Jacob rent his clothes and put sackcloth round his waist and mourned
for his son many days. And all his sons and all his daughters rose to console
him and he refused to be consoled and he said, "Rather I will go down to my
son in Sheol⁵ mourning," and his father bewailed him.

But the Midianites had sold him into Egypt to Potiphar, Pharoah's
courtier, the high chamberlain.

39. And Joseph was brought down to Egypt, and Potiphar, courtier of Pharaoh, the high chamberlain, an Egyptian man, bought him from the hands
of the Ishmaelites who had brought him down there. And the LORD was with
Joseph and he was a successful man, and he was in the house of his Egyptian master. And his master saw that the LORD was with him, and all that he
did the LORD made succeed in his hand, and Joseph found favor in his eyes
and he ministered to him, and he put him in charge of his house, and all
that he had he placed in his hands. And it happened from the time he put
him in charge of his house that the LORD blessed the Egyptian's house for
Joseph's sake and the LORD's blessing was on all that he had in house and
field. And he left all that he had in Joseph's hands, and he gave no thought
to anything with him there save the bread he ate. And Joseph was comely in
features and comely to look at.

And it happened after these things that his master's wife raised her eyes to
Joseph and said, "Lie with me." And he refused. And he said to his master's
wife, "Look, my master has given no thought with me here to what is in the
house, and all that he has he has placed in my hands. He is not greater in
this house than I, and he has held back nothing from me except you, as you
are his wife, and how could I do this great evil and give offense to God?" And
so she spoke to Joseph day after day, and he would not listen to her, to lie by
her, to be with her. And it happened, on one such day, that he came into the
house to perform his task, and there was no man of the men of the house
there in the house. And she seized him by his garment, saying, "Lie with
me." And he left his garment in her hand and he fled and went out. And so,

3. That is, the fact that we have killed him. 4. The text at this point seems to combine two different
versions of the story: (1) Joseph's brothers took him out of the pit and sold him to the Ishmaelites; (2) Midianite merchants passing by discovered Joseph in the pit and sold him to the Ishmaelites. Reuben then returned to the pit and discovered that Joseph was gone. 5. The dwelling place of the dead.

when she saw that he had left his garment in her hand and fled outside, she called out to the people of the house and said to them, "See, he has brought us a Hebrew man to play with us. He came into me to lie with me and I called out in a loud voice, and so, when he heard me raise my voice and call out, he left his garment by me and fled and went out." And she laid out his garment by her until his master returned to his house. And she spoke to him things of this sort, saying, "The Hebrew slave came into me, whom you brought us, to play with me. And so, when I raised my voice and called out, he left his garment by me and fled outside." And it happened, when his master heard his wife's words which she spoke to him, saying, "Things of this sort your slave has done to me," he became incensed. And Joseph's master took him and placed him in the prison-house, the place where the king's prisoners were held.

And he was there in the prison-house, and God was with Joseph and extended kindness to him, and granted him favor in the eyes of the prison-house warden. And the prison-house warden placed in Joseph's hands all the prisoners who were in the prison-house, and all that they were to do there, it was he who did it. The prison-house warden had to see to nothing that was in his hands, as the LORD was with him, and whatever he did, the LORD made succeed.

40. And it happened after these things that the cupbearer of the king of Egypt and his baker gave offense to their lord, the king of Egypt. And Pharaoh was furious with his two courtiers, the chief cupbearer and the chief baker. And he put them under guard in the house of the high chamberlain, the prison-house, the place where Joseph was held. And the high chamberlain assigned Joseph to them and he ministered to them, and they stayed a good while under guard.

And the two of them dreamed a dream, each his own dream, on a single night, each a dream with its own solution—the cupbearer and the baker to the king of Egypt who were held in the prison-house. And Joseph came to them in the morning and saw them and, look, they were frowning. And he asked Pharaoh's courtiers who were with him under guard in his lord's house, saying, "Why are your faces downcast today?" And they said to him, "We dreamed a dream and there is no one to solve it." And Joseph said to them, "Are not solutions from God? Pray, recount them to me." And the chief cupbearer recounted his dream to Joseph and said to him, "In my dream—and look, a vine was before me. And on the vine were three tendrils, and as it was budding, its blossom shot up, its clusters ripened to grapes. And Pharaoh's cup was in my hand. And I took the grapes and crushed them into Pharaoh's cup and I placed the cup in Pharaoh's palm." And Joseph said, "This is its solution. The three tendrils are three days. Three days hence Pharaoh will lift up your head and restore you to your place, and you will put Pharaoh's cup in his hand, as you used to do when you were his cupbearer. But if you remember I was with you once it goes well for you, do me the kindness, pray, to mention me to Pharaoh and bring me out of this house. For indeed I was stolen from the land of the Hebrews, and here, too, I have done nothing that I should have been put in the pit." And the chief baker saw that he had solved well, and he said to Joseph, "I, too, in my dream—and look, there were three openwork baskets on my head, and in the topmost were all sorts of food for Pharaoh, baker's ware, and birds were eating from the basket over my head." And Joseph answered and said, "This is its solution. The three baskets are three days. Three days hence Pharaoh will lift up your head from upon you and impale you on a pole and the birds will eat your flesh from upon you."

And it happened on the third day, Pharaoh's birthday, that he made a feast for all his servants, and he lifted up the head of the chief cupbearer and the head of the chief baker in the midst of his servants. And he restored the chief cupbearer to his cupbearing, and he put the cup in Pharaoh's hand; and the chief baker he impaled—just as Joseph had solved it for them. But the chief cupbearer did not remember Joseph, no, he forgot him.

41. And it happened at the end of two full years that Pharaoh dreamed, and, look, he was standing by the Nile. And, look, out of the Nile came up seven cows, fair to look at and fat in flesh, and they grazed in the rushes. And, look, another seven cows came up after them out of the Nile, foul to look at and meager in flesh, and stood by the cows on the bank of the Nile. And the foul-looking meager-fleshed cows ate up the seven fair-looking fat cows, and Pharaoh awoke. And he slept and dreamed a second time, and, look, seven ears of grain came up on a single stalk, fat and goodly. And, look, seven meager ears, blasted by the east wind, sprouted after them. And the meager ears swallowed the fat and full ears, and Pharaoh awoke, and, look, it was a dream. And it happened in the morning that his heart pounded, and he sent and called in all the soothsayers of Egypt and all its wise men, and Pharaoh recounted to them his dreams, but none could solve them for Pharaoh. And the chief cupbearer spoke to Pharaoh, saying, "My offenses I recall today. Pharaoh had been furious with his servants and he placed me under guard in the house of the high chamberlain—me and the chief baker. And we dreamed a dream on the same night, he and I, each of us dreamed a dream with its own solution.

And there with us was a Hebrew lad, a slave of the high chamberlain, and we recounted to him and he solved our dreams, each of us according to his dream he solved it. And it happened just as he had solved it for us, so it came about—me he restored to my post and him he impaled."

And Pharaoh sent and called for Joseph, and they hurried him from the pit, and he shaved and changed his garments and came before Pharaoh. And Pharaoh said to Joseph, "I dreamed a dream and none can solve it, and I have heard about you that you can understand a dream to solve it." And Joseph answered Pharaoh, saying, "Not I! God will answer for Pharaoh's well-being." And Pharaoh spoke to Joseph: "In my dream, here I was standing on the bank of the Nile, and, look, out of the Nile came up seven cows fat in flesh and fair in feature, and they grazed in the rushes. And, look, another seven cows came up after them, gaunt and very foul-featured and meager in flesh, I had not seen their like in all the land of Egypt for foulness. And the meager, foul cows ate up the first seven fat cows, and they were taken into their bellies and you could not tell that they had come into their bellies, for their looks were as foul as before, and I woke. And I saw in my dream, and, look, seven ears of grain came up on a single stalk, full and goodly. And, look, seven shriveled, meager ears, blasted by the east wind, sprouted after them. And the meager ears swallowed the seven goodly ears, and I spoke to my soothsayers and none could tell me the meaning." And Joseph said to Pharaoh, "Pharaoh's dream is one.

What God is about to do He has told Pharaoh. The seven goodly cows are seven years, and the seven ears of grain are seven years. The dream is one. And the seven meager and foul cows who came up after them are seven years, and the seven meager ears of grain, blasted by the east wind, will be seven years of famine. It is just as I said to Pharaoh: what God is about to do He has shown Pharaoh. Look, seven years are coming of great plenty through all the land of Egypt. And seven years of famine will arise after them and all the plenty will be forgotten in the land of Egypt, and the famine will ravage the land, and you will not be able to tell there was plenty in the land because of that famine afterward, for it will be very grave. And the repeating of the dream to Pharaoh two times, this means that the thing has been fixed by God and God is hastening to do it. And so, let Pharaoh look out for a discerning, wise man and set him over the land of Egypt. Let Pharaoh do this: appoint overseers for the land and muster the land of Egypt in the seven years of plenty. And let them collect all the food of these good years that are coming and let them pile up grain under Pharaoh's hand; food in the cities, to keep under guard. And the food will be a reserve for the land for the seven years of famine which will be in the land of Egypt, that the land may not perish in the famine." And the thing seemed good in Pharaoh's eyes and in the eyes of his servants. And Pharaoh said to his servants, "Could we find a man like him, in whom is the spirit of God?" And Pharaoh said to Joseph, "After God has made known to you all this, there is none as discerning and wise as you. You shall be over my house, and by your lips all my folk shall be guided. By the throne alone shall I be greater than you." And Pharaoh said to Joseph, "See, I have set you over all the land of Egypt." And Pharaoh took off his ring from his hand and put it on Joseph's hand and had him clothed in fine linen clothes and placed the golden collar round his neck. And he had him ride in the chariot of his viceroy, and they called out before him *Abrekh*,[6] setting him over all the land of Egypt. And Pharaoh said to Joseph, "I am Pharaoh! Without you no man shall raise hand or foot in all the land of Egypt." And Pharaoh called Joseph's name Zaphenath-paneah, and he gave him Asenath daughter of Poti-phera, priest of On, as wife, and Joseph went out over the land of Egypt.

And Joseph was thirty years old when he stood before Pharaoh king of Egypt, and Joseph went out from Pharaoh's presence and passed through all the land of Egypt. And the land in the seven years of plenty made gatherings. And he collected all the food of the seven years that were in the land of Egypt and he placed food in the cities, the food from the fields round each city he placed within it. And Joseph piled up grain like the sand of the sea, very much, until he ceased counting, for it was beyond count.

And to Joseph two sons were born before the coming of the year of famine, whom Asenath daughter of Poti-phera priest of On bore him. And Joseph called the name of the firstborn Manasseh, meaning, God has released me from all the debt of my hardship, and of all my father's house. And the name of the second he called Ephraim, meaning, God has made me fruitful in the land of my affliction.

And the seven years of the plenty that had been in the land of Egypt came to an end. And the seven years of famine began to come, as Joseph had said, and there was famine in all the lands, but in the land of Egypt there was

---

6. Probably "Make way!" (evidently an Egyptian word).

bread. And all the land of Egypt was hungry and the people cried out to Pharaoh for bread, and Pharaoh said to all of Egypt, "Go to Joseph. What he says to you, you must do." And the famine was over all the land. And Joseph laid open whatever had grain within and sold provisions to Egypt. And the famine grew harsh in the land of Egypt. And all the earth came to Egypt, to Joseph, to get provisions, for the famine had grown harsh in all the earth.

42. And Jacob saw that there were provisions in Egypt, and Jacob said to his sons, "Why are you fearful?" And he said, "Look, I have heard that there are provisions in Egypt. Go down there, and get us provisions from there that we may live and not die." And the ten brothers of Joseph went down to buy grain from Egypt. But Benjamin, Joseph's brother,[7] Jacob did not send with his brothers, for he thought, Lest harm befall him.

And the sons of Israel came to buy provisions among those who came, for there was famine in the land of Canaan. As for Joseph, he was the regent of the land, he was the provider to all the people of the land. And Joseph's brothers came and bowed down to him, their faces to the ground. And Joseph saw his brothers and recognized them, and he played the stranger to them and spoke harshly to them, and said to them, "Where have you come from?" And they said, "From the land of Canaan, to buy food." And Joseph recognized his brothers but they did not recognize him. And Joseph remembered the dreams he had dreamed about them, and he said to them, "You are spies! To see the land's nakedness you have come." And they said to him, "No, my lord, for your servants have come to buy food. We are all the sons of one man. We are honest. Your servants would never be spies." He said to them, "No! For the land's nakedness you have come to see." And they said, "Your twelve servants are brothers, we are the sons of one man in the land of Canaan, and, look, the youngest is now with our father, and one is no more." And Joseph said to them, "That's just what I told you, you are spies. In this shall you be tested—by Pharaoh! You shall not leave this place unless your youngest brother comes here. Send one of you to bring your brother, and as for the rest of you, you will be detained, and your words will be tested as to whether the truth is with you, and if not, by Pharaoh, you must be spies!" And he put them under guard for three days. And Joseph said to them on the third day, "Do this and live, for I fear God. If you are honest, let one of your brothers be detained in this very guardhouse, and the rest of you go forth and bring back provisions to stave off the famine in your homes. And your youngest brother you shall bring to me, that your words may be confirmed and you need not die." And so they did. And they said each to his brother, "Alas, we are guilty for our brother, whose mortal distress we saw when he pleaded with us and we did not listen. That is why this distress has overtaken us." Then Reuben spoke out to them in these words: "Didn't I say to you, 'Do not sin against the boy,' and you would not listen? And now, look, his blood is requited." And they did not know that Joseph understood, for there was an interpreter between them. And he turned away from them and wept and returned to them and spoke to them, and he took Simeon from them and placed him in fetters before their eyes.

7. Only Benjamin is Joseph's full brother; both are sons of Jacob and Rachel. The other ten are his half-brothers, sons of Jacob by other women.

And Joseph gave orders to fill their baggage with grain and to put back their silver into each one's pack and to give them supplies for the way, and so he did for them. And they loaded their provisions on their donkeys and they set out. Then one of them opened his pack to give provender to his donkey at the encampment, and he saw his silver and, look, it was in the mouth of his bag. And he said to his brothers, "My silver has been put back and, look, it's actually in my bag." And they were dumbfounded and trembled each before his brother, saying, "What is this that God has done to us?" And they came to Jacob their father, to the land of Canaan, and they told him all that had befallen them, saying, "The man who is lord of the land spoke harshly to us and made us out to be spies in the land. And we said to him, 'We are honest. We would never be spies. Twelve brothers we are, the sons of our father. One is no more and the youngest is now with our father in the land of Canaan.' And the man who is lord of the land said to us, 'By this shall I know if you are honest: one of your brothers leave with me and provisions against the famine in your homes take, and go. And bring your youngest brother to me that I may know you are not spies but are honest. I shall give you back your brother and you can trade in the land.'" And just as they were emptying their packs, look, each one's bundle of silver was in his pack. And they saw their bundles, both they and their father, and were afraid. And Jacob their father said to them, "Me you have bereaved. Joseph is no more and Simeon is no more, and Benjamin you would take! It is I who bear it all." And Reuben spoke to his father, saying, "My two sons you may put to death if I do not bring him back to you. Place him in my hands and I will return him to you." And he said, "My son shall not go down with you, for his brother is dead, and he alone remains, and should harm befall him on the way you are going, you would bring down my gray head in sorrow to Sheol."

43. And the famine grew grave in the land. And it happened when they had eaten up the provisions they had brought from Egypt, that their father said to them, "Go back, buy us some food." And Judah said to him, saying, "The man firmly warned us, saying, 'You shall not see my face unless your brother is with you.' If you are going to send our brother with us, we may go down and buy you food, but if you are not going to send him, we will not go down, for the man said to us, 'You shall not see my face unless your brother is with you.'" And Israel said, "Why have you done me this harm to tell the man you had another brother?" And they said, "The man firmly asked us about ourselves and our kindred, saying, "Is your father still living? Do you have a brother?' And we told him, in response to these words. Could we know he would say, 'Bring down your brother?'" And Judah said to Israel his father, "Send the lad with me, and let us rise and go, that we may live and not die, neither we, nor you, nor our little ones. I will be his pledge, from my hand you may seek him: if I do not bring him to you and set him before you, I will bear the blame to you for all time. For had we not tarried, by now we could have come back twice." And Israel their father said to them, "If it must be so, do this: take of the best yield of the land in your baggage and bring down to the man as tribute, some balm and some honey, gum and ladanum, pistachio nuts and almonds. And double the silver take in your hand, and the silver that was put back in the mouths of your bags bring back in your hand. Perhaps it was a mistake. And your brother take, and rise and go back

to the man. And may El Shaddai grant you mercy before the man, that he discharge to you your other brother, and Benjamin. As for me, if I must be bereaved, I will be bereaved."

And the men took this tribute and double the silver they took in their hand, and Benjamin, and they rose and went down to Egypt and stood in Joseph's presence. And Joseph saw Benjamin with them and he said to the one who was over his house, "Bring the men into the house, and slaughter an animal and prepare it, for with me the men shall eat at noon." And the man did as Joseph had said, and the man brought the men to Joseph's house. And the men were afraid at being brought to Joseph's house, and they said, "Because of the silver put back in our bags the first time we've been brought, in order to fall upon us, to attack us, and to take us as slaves, and our donkeys." And they approached the man who was over Joseph's house, and they spoke to him by the entrance of the house. And they said, "Please, my lord, we indeed came down the first time to buy food, and it happened when we came to the encampment that we opened our bags and, look, each man's silver was in the mouth of his bag, our silver in full weight, and we have brought it back in our hand, and we have brought down more silver to buy food. We do not know who put our silver in our bags." And he said, "All is well with you, do not fear. Your God and the God of your father has placed treasure for you in your bags. Your silver has come to me."[8] And he brought Simeon out to them. And the man brought the men into Joseph's house, and he gave them water and they bathed their feet, and he gave provender to their donkeys. And they prepared the tribute against Joseph's arrival at noon, for they had heard that there they would eat bread. And Joseph came into the house, and they brought him the tribute that was in their hand, into the house, and they bowed down to him to the ground. And he asked how they were, and he said, "Is all well with your aged father of whom you spoke? Is he still alive?" And they said, "All is well with your servant, our father. He is still alive." And they did obeisance and bowed down. And he raised his eyes and saw Benjamin his brother, his mother's son, and he said, "Is this your youngest brother of whom you spoke to me?" And he said, "God be gracious to you, my son." And Joseph hurried out, for his feelings for his brother overwhelmed him and he wanted to weep, and he went into the chamber and wept there. And he bathed his face and came out and held himself in check and said, "Serve bread." And they served him and them separately and the Egyptians that were eating with him separately, for the Egyptians would not eat bread with the Hebrews, as it was abhorrent to Egypt. And they were seated before him, the firstborn according to his birthright, the youngest according to his youth, and the men marvelled to each other. And he had portions passed to them from before him, and Benjamin's portion was five times more than the portion of all the rest, and they drank, and they got drunk with him.

44. And he commanded the one who was over his house, saying, "Fill the men's bags with as much food as they can carry, and put each man's silver in the mouth of his bag. And my goblet, the silver goblet, put in the mouth of the bag of the youngest, with the silver for his provisions." And he did as Joseph had spoken. The morning had just brightened when the men were sent off, they and their donkeys. They had come out of the city, they were not

8. That is, "I have been paid."

far off, when Joseph said to the one who was over his house, "Rise, pursue the men, and when you overtake them, say to them, 'Why have you paid back evil for good? Is not this the one from which my lord drinks, and in which he always divines?[9] You have wrought evil in what you did.'" And he overtook them and spoke to them these words. And they said to him, "Why should our lord speak words like these? Far be it from your servants to do such a thing! Why, the silver we found in the mouth of our bags we brought back to you from the land of Canaan. How then could we steal from your master's house silver or gold? He of your servants with whom it be found shall die, and, what's more, we shall become slaves to our lord." And he said, "Even so, as by your words, let it be: he with whom it be found shall become a slave to me, and you shall be clear." And they hurried and each man set down his bag on the ground and each opened his bag. And he searched, beginning with the oldest and ending with the youngest, and he found the goblet in Benjamin's bag. And they rent their garments, and each loaded his donkey and they returned to the city.

And Judah with his brothers came into Joseph's house, for he was still there, and they threw themselves before him to the ground. And Joseph said to them, "What is this deed you have done? Did you not know that a man like me would surely divine?" And Judah said, "What shall we say to my lord? What shall we speak and how shall we prove ourselves right? God has found out your servants' crime. Here we are, slaves to my lord, both we and the one in whose hand the goblet was found." And he said, "Far be it from me to do this! The man in whose hand the goblet was found, he shall become my slave, and you, go up in peace to your father." And Judah approached him and said, "Please, my lord, let your servant speak a word in my lord's hearing and let your wrath not kindle against your servant, for you are like Pharaoh. My lord had asked his servants, saying, 'Do you have a father or brother?' And we said to my lord, 'We have an aged father and a young child of his old age, and his brother being dead, he alone is left of his mother, and his father loves him.' And you said to your servants, 'Bring him down to me, that I may set my eyes on him.' And we said to my lord, 'The lad cannot leave his father. Should he leave his father, he would die.' And you said to your servants, 'If your youngest brother does not come down with you, you shall not see my face again.' And it happened when we went up to your servant, my father, that we told him the words of my lord. And our father said, 'Go back, buy us some food.' And we said, 'We cannot go down. If our youngest brother is with us, we shall go down. For we cannot see the face of the man if our youngest brother is not with us.' And your servant, our father, said to us, 'You know that two did my wife bear me.[1] And one went out from me and I thought, O, he's been torn to shreds, and I have not seen him since. And should you take this one, too, from my presence and harm befall him, you would bring down my gray head in evil to Sheol.' And so, should I come to your servant, my father, and the lad be not with us, for his life is bound to the lad's, when he saw the lad was not with us, he would die, and your servants would bring down the gray head of your servant, our father, in sorrow to Sheol. For your servant became pledge for the lad to my father, saying, 'If I do not bring him to you, I will

---

9. Predicts the future from the appearance of a liquid in the cup.   1. Rachel. His other wife was Rachel's sister, Leah, who bore him six sons. Jacob also had two sons each by two slave girls (one of Rachel, the other of Leah).

bear the blame to my father for all time.' And so, let your servant, pray, stay instead of the lad as a slave to my lord, and let the lad go up with his brothers. For how shall I go up to my father, if the lad be not with us? Let me see not the evil that would find out my father!"

45. And Joseph could no longer hold himself in check before all who stood attendance upon him, and he cried, "Clear out everyone around me!" And no man stood with him when Joseph made himself known to his brothers. And he wept aloud and the Egyptians heard and the house of Pharaoh heard. And Joseph said to his brothers, "I am Joseph. Is my father still alive?" But his brothers could not answer him, for they were dismayed before him. And Joseph said to his brothers, "Come close to me, pray," and they came close, and he said, "I am Joseph your brother whom you sold into Egypt. And now, do not be pained and do not be incensed with yourselves that you sold me down here, because for sustenance God has sent me before you. Two years now there has been famine in the heart of the land, and there are yet five years without plowing and harvest. And God has sent me before you to make you a remnant on earth[2] and to preserve life, for you to be a great surviving group. And so, it is not you who sent me here but God, and he has made me father to Pharaoh and lord to all his house and ruler over all the land of Egypt. Hurry and go up to my father and say to him, 'Thus says your son Joseph: God has made me lord to all Egypt. Come down to me, do not delay. And you shall dwell in the land of Goshen[3] and shall be close to me, you and your sons and the sons of your sons and your flocks and your cattle and all that is yours. And I will sustain you there, for yet five years of famine remain—lest you lose all, you and your household and all that is yours.' And, look, your own eyes can see, and the eyes of my brother Benjamin, that it is my very mouth that speaks to you. And you must tell my father all my glory in Egypt and all that you have seen, and hurry and bring down my father here." And he fell upon the neck of his brother Benjamin and he wept, and Benjamin wept on his neck. And he kissed all his brothers and wept over them. And after that, his brothers spoke with him.

And the news was heard in the house of Pharaoh, saying, "Joseph's brothers have come." And it was good in Pharaoh's eyes and in his servants' eyes. And Pharaoh said to Joseph, "Say to your brothers: This now do. Load up your beasts and go, return to the land of Canaan. And take your father and your households and come back to me, that I may give you the best of the land of Egypt, and you shall live off the fat of the land.' And you, command them: 'This now do. Take you from the land of Egypt wagons for your little ones and for your wives, and convey your father, and come. And regret not your belongings, for the best of all the land of Egypt is yours.'"

And so the sons of Israel did, and Joseph gave them wagons, as Pharaoh had ordered, and he gave them supplies for the journey. To all of them, each one, he gave changes of garments, and to Benjamin he gave three hundred pieces of silver and five changes of garments. And to his father he sent as follows: ten donkeys conveying from the best of Egypt, and ten she-asses conveying grain and bread and food for his father for the journey. And he

---

2. That is, "to ensure a posterity for you."   3. Probably the Nile Delta.

sent off his brothers and they went, and he said to them, "Do not be perturbed on the journey."

And they went up from Egypt and they came to the land of Canaan to Jacob their father. And they told him, saying, "Joseph is still alive," and that he was ruler in all the land of Egypt. And his heart stopped, for he did not believe them. And they spoke to him all the words of Joseph that he had spoken to them, and he saw the wagons that Joseph had sent to convey him, and the spirit of Jacob their father revived. And Israel said, "Enough! Joseph my son is still alive. Let me go see him before I die."

46. And Israel journeyed onward, with all that was his, and he came to Beer-sheba, and he offered sacrifices to the God of his father Isaac. And God said to Israel through visions of the night, "Jacob, Jacob," and he said, "Here I am." And He said, "I am the god, God of your father. Fear not to go down to Egypt, for a great nation I will make you there. I Myself will go down with you to Egypt and I Myself will surely bring you back up as well, and Joseph shall lay his hand on your eyes." And Jacob arose from Beer-sheba, and the sons of Israel conveyed Jacob their father and their little ones and their wives in the wagons Pharaoh had sent to convey him. And they took their cattle and their substance that they had got in the land of Canaan and they came to Egypt, Jacob and all his seed with him. His sons, and the sons of his sons with him, his daughters and the daughters of his sons, and all his seed, he brought with him to Egypt.

* * *

From Exodus[1]

FROM EXODUS 19–20

[*Moses Receives the Law*]

19. On the third new moon of the Israelites' going out from Egypt, on this day did they come to the Wilderness of Sinai.[2] And they journeyed onward from Rephidim and they came to the Wilderness of Sinai, and Israel camped there over against the mountain. And Moses had gone up to God, and the LORD called out to him from the mountain, saying, "Thus shall you say to the house of Jacob, and shall you tell to the Israelites: 'You yourselves saw what I did to Egypt, and I bore you on the wings of eagles[3] and I brought you to Me. And now, if you will truly heed My voice and keep My covenant, you will become for Me a treasure among all the peoples, for Mine is all the earth. And as for you, you will become for Me a kingdom of priests and a holy nation.' These are the words that you shall speak to the Israelites."

And Moses came and he called to the elders of the people, and he set before them all these words that the LORD had charged him. And all the people an-

---

1. Translated by Robert Alter, to whose notes some of the following annotations are indebted.   2. The peninsula, shaped like an inverted triangle, that lies between Egypt and Palestine. The mountain was called either Sinai or Horeb.   3. A metaphor for salvation. "What I did to Egypt": a reference to the plagues that afflicted Egypt and to the destruction of the Egyptian army, as it pursued the departing Israelites, at the Red Sea.

swered together and said, "Everything that the LORD has spoken we shall do."
And Moses brought back the people's words to the LORD. And the LORD said
to Moses, "Look, I am about to come to you in the utmost cloud, so that the
people may hear as I speak to you, and you as well they will trust for all time."
And Moses told the people's words to the LORD. And the LORD said to Moses,
"Go to the people and consecrate them today and tomorrow, and they shall
wash their cloaks. And they shall ready themselves for the third day, for on the
third day the LORD will come down before the eyes of all the people on Mount
Sinai. And you shall set bounds for the people all around, saying, 'Watch yourselves not to go up on the mountain or to touch its edge. Whosoever touches
the mountain is doomed to die. No hand shall touch him,[4] but He shall surely
be stoned or be shot, whether beast or man, he shall not live. When the ram's
horn blasts long, they[5] it is who will go up the mountain.'" And Moses came
down from the mountain to the people, and he consecrated the people, and they
washed their cloaks. And he said to the people, "Ready yourselves for three
days. Do not go near a woman."[6] And it happened on the third day as it turned
morning, that there was thunder and lightning and a heavy cloud on the
mountain and the sound of the ram's horn, very strong, and all the people who
were in the camp trembled. And Moses brought out the people toward God
from the camp and they stationed themselves at the bottom of the mountain.
And Mount Sinai was all in smoke because the LORD had come down on it in
fire, and its smoke went up like the smoke from a kiln, and the whole mountain trembled greatly. And the sound of the ram's horn grew stronger and
stronger. Moses would speak, and God would answer him with voice.[7] And the
LORD came down on Mount Sinai, to the mountaintop, and the LORD called
Moses to the mountaintop, and Moses went up. And the LORD said to Moses,
"Go down, warn the people, lest they break through to the LORD to see and
many of them perish.[8] And the priests, too, who come near to the LORD, shall
consecrate themselves,[9] lest the LORD burst forth against them." And Moses
said to the Lord, "The people will not be able to come up to Mount Sinai, for
You Yourself warned us, saying, 'Set bounds to the mountain and consecrate
it.'" And the LORD said to him, "Go down, and you shall come up, you and
Aaron[1] with you, and the priests and the people shall not break through to go
up to the LORD, lest He burst forth against them." And Moses went down to
the people and said it to them.

20. And God spoke all these words, saying: "I am the LORD your God Who
brought you out of the land of Egypt, out of the house of slaves. You[2] shall have
no other gods beside Me. You shall make you no carved likeness and no image
of what is in the heavens above or what is on the earth below or what is in the
waters beneath the earth.[3] You shall not bow to them and you shall not worship

---

4. Whoever violates the ban on touching the mountain will be impure and an outcast from the community.
Therefore he has to be killed at a distance, with stones or arrows.   5. That is, Moses and Aaron, as the
end of chapter 19 shows.   6. Sexual abstinence and the washing of clothes were methods of ritual purification.   7. That is, with words, as two mortals might communicate with one another.   8. Moses
has already delivered this warning. The repetition emphasizes both the solemnity of the ban and Moses'
role as intermediary between God and the people of Israel.   9. That is, they are to purify themselves and
remain at the bottom of the mountain as the rest of the people do.   1. Moses' closest companion and in
an early tradition his brother; Aaron was Israel's first High Priest.   2. Here and throughout this passage,
the Hebrew text uses the singular of *you* (formulations of law elsewhere in the Hebrew Bible use the plural). The commandments are thus addressed to each person individually.   3. In ancient polytheistic religions, statues of gods and of personified natural powers were worshiped.

them, for I am the LORD your God, a jealous god, reckoning the crime of fathers with sons, with the third generation and with the fourth, for My foes,[4] and doing kindness to the thousandth generation for My friends and for those who keep My commands. You shall not take the name of the LORD your God in vain,[5] for the LORD will not acquit whosoever takes His name in vain. Remember the sabbath day to hallow it. Six days you shall work and you shall do your tasks, but the seventh day is a sabbath to the LORD your God. You shall do no task, you and your son and your daughter, your male slave and your slavegirl and your beast and your sojourner who is within your gates. For six days did the LORD make the heavens and the earth, the sea and all that is in it, and He rested on the seventh day.[6] Therefore did the LORD bless the sabbath day and hallow it. Honor your father and your mother, so that your days may be long on the soil that the LORD your God has given you. You shall not murder. You shall not commit adultery. You shall not steal. You shall not bear false witness against your fellow man.[7] You shall not covet your fellow man's wife, or his male slave, or his slavegirl, or his ox, or his donkey, or anything that your fellow man has."

And all the people were seeing the thunder and the flashes and the sound of the ram's horn and the mountain in smoke, and the people saw and they drew back and stood at a distance. And they said to Moses, "Speak you with us that we may hear, and let not God speak with us lest we die." And Moses said to the people, "Do not fear, for in order to test you God has come and in order that His fear be upon you, so that you do not offend." And the people stood at a distance, and Moses drew near the thick cloud where God was.

* * *

From Job[1]

1. A man once lived in the land of Utz. His name was Job. This man was innocent, upright, and God-fearing, and kept himself apart from evil. Seven sons and three daughters were born to him. His flock consisted of seven thousand sheep, three thousand camels, five hundred yoke of oxen, five hundred female donkeys, and a large staff of servants. He was the greatest of the men of the East.

His sons would make a feast each year, each one in his own house by turns, and they would invite their three sisters to eat and drink with them. When the days of the feast would come round, Job would send to purify them, rising early in the morning to offer wholeburnt offerings, one for each. For Job thought, "Perhaps my sons have sinned by cursing God in their hearts." Job did this every year.

One day, the lesser gods came to attend upon Yahweh, and the Accuser[2] came among them. Yahweh said to the Accuser, "Where are you coming

---

4. This can be read in at least two ways. (1) Limiting vengeance to the fourth generation of the transgressor's family may be a sign of mercy (by contrast with extending blessings on the righteous to the thousandth generation). (2) Or it may be a statement of the severity of God's punishment and, in particular, a reference to the common belief that if someone did wrong and seemed to go unpunished, vengeance would fall on his or her posterity.   5. That is, falsely—in the taking of oaths, for example.   6. See Genesis 2. 7. Testify falsely in a lawsuit.   1. Translated by Raymond P. Scheindlin.   2. "The Satan" in the original. But here he is not the principle of evil that the name conjures up for us. He is a member of Yahweh's court and seems to have the job of roaming the world to keep watch on humankind for Yahweh (his name sounds like the Hebrew word for "roam").

from?" and the Accuser answered Yahweh, "From roving and roaming about the world." Yahweh said to the Accuser, "Have you taken note of my servant Job, for there is no one like him on earth: innocent, upright, and God-fearing, and keeping himself apart from evil." The Accuser answered Yahweh, "Is Job God-fearing for nothing? Look how You have sheltered him on all sides, him and his household and everything he has, and have blessed everything he does, so that his cattle have spread out all over the land. But reach out with Your hand and strike his property, and watch him curse You to Your face!"

Yahweh said to the Accuser, "Everything he has is in your power, but do not harm his person."

The Accuser took his leave of Yahweh.

One day, when his sons and daughters were feasting and drinking wine in the house of the eldest brother, a messenger came to Job and said, "The cattle were plowing and the donkeys were grazing by their side and Sabeans fell on them and seized them and killed the servants with their swords, and only I got away to tell you!"

While he was speaking, another came and said, "A fearful fire fell from heaven and burned up the sheep and the servants and consumed them, and only I got away to tell you!"

While he was speaking, another came and said, "The Chaldeans formed into three companies and came at the camels from all directions and took them and killed the servants with their swords, and only I got away to tell you!"

While he was speaking, another came and said, "Your sons and daughters were eating and drinking wine in the house of the eldest brother and a great wind came from across the desert and struck the four corners of the house and it fell on the young people and they died, and only I got away to tell you!"

Job got up and tore his robe and shaved his head and flung himself to the ground and lay there prostrate and said,

> "Naked I came from my mother's womb
> and naked I return there.
> Yahweh has given and Yahweh has taken.
> Blessed be the name of Yahweh."

In spite of everything, Job did not sin and did not attach blame to God.

2. One day, the lesser gods came to attend upon Yahweh, and among them came the Accuser to attend upon Yahweh. Yahweh said to the Accuser, "Where are you coming from?" and the Accuser answered Yahweh, "From roving and roaming about the world." Yahweh said to the Accuser, "Have you taken note of my servant Job, for there is no one like him on earth: innocent, upright, and God-fearing, and keeping himself apart from evil; he even persists in his innocence, though you prevailed upon me to ruin him for no reason!" The Accuser answered Yahweh,

"Skin protecting skin![3] A man will give whatever he has for the sake of his own life. But reach out with Your hand and strike his person, his flesh, and watch him curse You to Your face!"

Yahweh said to the Accuser, "He is in your power, but see that you preserve his life."

---

3. Perhaps "Job's wounds are only superficial" (an outer layer of skin protects the inner layers). Job has not yet been injured in his own person, or had his life threatened.

The Accuser took his leave of Yahweh and smote Job with sickening eruptions from the soles of his feet to the crown of his head. Job took a shard to
scrape himself with and sat down in ashes.[4] His wife said to him, "Are you
still persisting in your innocence? Curse God and die!"

He said to her, "You are speaking like a disgraceful woman! Should we accept the good from God and not accept the bad?" In spite of everything, Job
did not sin with his lips.

Job's three friends heard about all the trouble that had come upon him,
and each one came from his own place: Eliphaz the Temanite, Bildad the
Shuhite, and Zophar the Naamatite. They agreed to meet to go and to
mourn with him and comfort him. Peering from the distance, they could not
recognize him. They raised their voices and wept, and each tore his robe,
and all put dirt on their heads, throwing it heavenward. Seven days and
seven nights they sat with him on the ground, none saying a word to him, for
they saw that his pain was very great.

3. Then Job spoke and cursed his day and raised his voice and said:

Blot out the day when I was born
 and the night that said, "A male has been conceived!"
Make that day dark!
 No god look after it from above,
 no light flood it.
Foul it, darkness, deathgloom;
 rain-clouds settle on it;
 heat-winds turn it to horror.
Black take that night!
 May it not count in the days of the year,
 may it not come in the round of the months.
That night be barren! That night!
 No joy ever come in it!
Curse it, men who spell the day,[5]
 men skilled to stir Leviathan.[6]
May its morning stars stay dark,
 may it wait for light in vain,
 never look on the eyelids of dawn—
because it did not lock the belly's gates[7]
 and curtain off my eyes from suffering.

Why did I not die inside the womb,
 or, having left it, give up breath at once?
Why did knees advance to greet me,
 or breasts, for me to suck?
Now I would be lying quietly;
 I would be sleeping then, at rest,
with kings and counselors of the earth,
 men who build rubble heaps for themselves,
or with princes, men with gold,
 men who fill their tombs with silver.
Why was I not like a stillbirth, hidden,

4. Gestures of mourning.   5. Sorcerers. "Spell": cast spells on.   6. A sea monster, the embodiment of
the forces of chaos. "Stir": summon forth.   7. That is, prevent my birth.

like infants who never saw the light?
There the wicked cease their troubling,
    there the weary are at rest,
where the captives have repose,
    and need not heed the foreman's voice;
where the humble and the great are,
    the slave, now free, beside his lord.

Why is the sufferer given light?
    Why life, to men who gag on bile,
who wait for a death that never comes,
    though they would rather dig for it than gold;
whose joy exceeds mere happiness,
    thrill to find the grave?
Why, to a man whose way is hidden,
    because a god has blocked his path?
For my sighs are brought to me for bread,
    and my cries poured out for water.
One thing I feared, and it befell,
    and what I dreaded came to me.
No peace had I, nor calm, nor rest;
    but torment came.

4. Eliphaz the Temanite then took up the argument and said:

Might one try a word with you, or would you tire?—
    But who could hold back words now?
You were always the one to instruct the many,
    to strengthen failing hands;
your words would pick up men who had fallen
    and firm up buckling knees;
yet now it is your turn, and you go faint;
    it has reached you, and you are undone.
Isn't your innocence some reassurance?
    Doesn't your righteousness offer you hope?
Think: What really guiltless man has gone under?
    Where have the upright perished?
I see men plowing wickedness,
    seeding, harvesting trouble—
one breath from God and they perish;
    one snort from Him and they're gone.
The lion roars! Listen! The lion!—
    The lion's teeth are cracked.
    The lion wanders, finds no prey.
    Young lions scatter.

Now, word has reached me in stealth—
    my ear caught only a snatch of it—
in wisps of thought, night visions,
    when slumber drifts down upon men.
Fear came over me, fear and a shudder,
    every bone in me shook.

Then—a gust crossing my face,
bristling the hairs on my skin,
and there he was standing—I could not make him out—
a shape before my eyes—
Hush! I hear his voice:
    "Can man be more righteous than God,
        or purer than He who made him?
    God does not trust His own courtiers,
        sees folly in His own angels;
    what then of dwellers in houses of clay,
        their foundations sunk in the dirt,
    that crumble before the moth,
            crack into shards between morning and evening,
                perish forever, not even aware of their fate?
    See how their wealth wanders away with them,
    how they die without wisdom.

5.   Go, cry out your rage—but who will answer?

        Which of the angels would you implore?
    Remember: Only fools are killed by anger,
        only simpletons by jealous fury.

    I have seen a fool strike roots;
    snap! I cursed his house:
    Now his sons are far from help,
        crushed in the public square;
        no one came to their rescue.
    Now the hungry dine on his harvest,
    while he has to scrabble for it among thorns,
    and thirsty men gulp his wealth.
    Remember: Evil does not emerge from the soil,
        or trouble sprout from the ground.
    Man was born to trouble
    as sparks dart to the sky."

No, I look to El,[8]
    entrust my affairs to the care of a god
who makes things great beyond man's grasp,
    and wonders beyond any numbering;
who puts the rain on the face of the earth,
    sends water to the countryside;
raises the humble to the heights,
    lifts gloomy men to rescue;
spoils the plans of cunning men,
    so their hands can do nothing clever;
traps the shrewd in their own cunning,
    makes the schemer's plotting seem like rashness
(by day they stumble against the darkness,
    grope in midday as if it were night);

8. God.

who saves the poor from the knife,
  from the maw, from the mighty,
so that the humble have hope,
  and evil has to shut its mouth.

Yes, happy the man whom God reproves!
Do not reject Shaddai's[9] correction.
  He may give pain, but He binds the wound;
  He strikes, but His hands bring healing.
In six-times-trouble He will save you;
in seven, no harm will touch you.
  He will rescue you from death in dearth,
  from sword in war.
When the tongue's lash snaps, you will be well hidden,
have nothing to fear when raiders arrive.
  Raiders and famine will make you smile,
  wild beasts give you nothing to fear.
The stones in the field will be your allies;
predators will yield to you.
  You will be sure of peace in your household;
  visit it when you like—you will not fail!
Then, be assured of plentiful seed,
of offspring like the earth's green shoots.
  Still robust you will reach the grave,
  like sheaves heaped high in their season.
All this we have studied and know it is so.
Think it over; take it to heart!

6. Job answered:

If there were some way to weigh my rage,
  if my disaster would fit in a balance,
they would drag down the ocean's sands;
that is why my speech is clumsy.
For Shaddai's arrows are all around me—
  my breath absorbs their venom—
  terror of the god invests me.

Is that a wild ass braying over his grass?—
an ox bellowing over his feed?[1]
Who can eat unsalted food?[2]
What flavor is there in the drool of mallows?
I have no appetite to touch them;
they are as nauseous as my flesh!

If only what I ask would happen—
if some god would grant my hope—
if that god would consent to crush me,
loose his hand and crack me open—

9. Another name for God.   1. Animals do not complain without reason; therefore, when a rational person complains, he or she must have some justification for it.   2. This and the next sentence may either refer to Job's situation or express his opinion of Eliphaz's arguments.

even that would comfort me
(though I writhed in pain unsparing),
for never have I suppressed the Holy One's commands.

What strength have I to go on hoping?
How far off is my end,
even if I live long?
Have I the bearing-strength of rock? Is my flesh bronze?
Is there no help within myself?
Has common sense been driven from me
to one who holds back kindnesses from friends,
to one who has lost the fear of Shaddai?

As for my friends—
they failed me like a riverbed,
wandered off, like water in a wadi.[3]
    Gloomy on an icy day,
    covered up with snow;
    they flow one moment, then are gone;
    when it is hot, they flicker away.
    Their dry courses twist,
    wander into wasteland, vanish.
        Caravans from Tema peer;
            Sebean trains move toward them, hoping:[4]
        Disappointment for their trust—
            they reach them, find frustration.
    That is how you are to me:
    You see terror, take fright yourselves.

When have I said to you, "Give me, give"?
"Bribe someone for me with your wealth"?
"Save me from my enemy"?
"Pay my ransom to some tyrant"?
All I ask is that you teach me—
I will listen quietly:
Tell me what I have done wrong!
    How eloquent are honest words—
    How then can you teach effectively?
    Do you think you can teach me with words?
    Is a speech of despair just wind?
    Would you also divide an orphan's goods by lot
    and haggle over your neighbor's property?

And now, be good enough to turn toward me—
    See if I lie to your faces.
Come back! You'll find no evil here—
    Come back!—only my vindication.
Is there error on my tongue?
    What am I speaking of except disaster?

---

3. A streambed in the desert. Because it cheats the traveler's longing for water by being dry for most of the year or by emptying itself quickly of the water that flows through it, it can serve as an image for treachery.
4. That is, for water, as the caravans from Tema also look for it.

7.   Man's life on earth is a term of indenture;
        his days are like a laborer's,
a slave, who pants for a little shade,
        a day laborer, who only wants his wages.
I too am granted blank moons;[5]
        troubled nights have been my lot.
When I lie down, I say,
        "How soon can I get up?"
            The night time stretches,
and I have tossing and turning enough to last till dawn.
My flesh is covered with worms and dirty scabs;
        my skin is cracked and oozing.
My days are swifter than a weaver's shuttle;
        they end when the thread of hope gives out.
Remember: My life is just a breath;
my eye will never again see pleasure.
The questing eye will not detect me;
Your eye will catch me—just!—
        and I'll be gone.

A cloud dissipates, vanishes,
and once below the ground
no man comes up again;
he never goes back to his home;
        his place no longer knows him.

Why should I restrain my mouth?—
        I speak from a dejected spirit,
        complain out of sheer bitterness:
Am I Yamm-ocean or the Serpent,[6]
that You post a guard over me?
I tell myself, "My couch will comfort me,
        my bed will bear a part of my complaint,"
only to have You frighten me with nightmares,
        panic me with visions of the night;
            I'd rather choke—
        death is better than this misery.
I've had enough! I will not live forever!
Let me alone; my life is just a breath.
What is man that You make so much of him,
        and think about him so,
examine him each morning,
        appraise him every moment?
How long till You turn away from me
long enough for me to swallow my own spit?[7]
I have sinned: But what have I done to You,
keeper, jailer of men?

---

5. Empty (that is, morally and materially unprofitable) months.   **6.** Job, now addressing God directly, compares his situation with that of the sea monster whom the weather god Baal fought against in Babylonian myth. He reproves God for exerting his power against anything as small as Job himself.   **7.** That is, even for a moment.

Why should You make me Your target,
    a burden to myself?
Why not forgive my crimes,
    and pardon me my sin?
In no time, I'll be lying in the earth;
    when You come looking for me, I'll be gone.

8. Bildad the Shuhite then took up the argument and said:

How long will you go on like this?
    What a great wind are the words from your mouth!
Would El pervert judgment?
    Would Shaddai pervert what is right?
Your sons have sinned against Him, that is all,
       and He got rid of them
       on account of their own crimes.
If you would now seek out the god,
       beseech Shaddai,
       be pure and true—
       He would rouse Himself for you,
       restore your righteous home.
Your former life will seem a paltry thing,
    so greatly will you prosper in the end.

Just ask the older generation,
    and set your mind to questioning *their* fathers
(for we are no older than yesterday
    and do not really know;
    our days on earth are only shadows):
They will teach you,
    they will tell you,
       they will bring words up from memory.
Can papyrus grow tall without a marsh
    or reeds flourish without water?
    Still in flower,
    not yet cut,
    even before the grass,
    it withers.
Such is the fate of all who put God out of mind;
    thus the hope of the wicked man fades,
    whatever he trusts in fails.
He puts his trust in a spider's web,
    leans on his house, but it does not stand;
    grasps at it, but it does not hold.

Juicy green before the sun,
his suckers creep over his planting bed,
his roots tangle-twist a rock heap,
he clutches a house of stones.
But let him be snatched from his place,
    and his place denies him: "I know you not!"
Such is his happy lot—

others sprout from that dirt. . . .
No, God would not reject the innocent,
    would not take hold of a bad man's hand.
He will yet fill your mouth with laughter,
    fill your lips with cries of joy.
Your foe will yet be clothed in shame,
    the wicked untented.

9. Job answered:

True, I know that this is so;
but can a mortal beat a god at law?
If someone chose to challenge Him,
He would not answer even the thousandth part!
Shrewd or powerful one may be,
but who has faced Him hard and come out whole?
He moves the mountains and they are unaware,
    overturns them in His rage.
He shakes the earth from its place;
    its pillars totter.
He orders the sun not to rise,
    seals up the stars.
He stretches out the heavens all alone,
    and treads Yamm's back.
He makes the Pleiades, Orion, and the Bear,
    the South Wind's chambers.
He makes things great beyond man's grasp,
    and wonders beyond any numbering.
Yet when He comes my way, I do not notice;
    He passes on, and I am unaware.

If He should seize a thing, who could restore it?
    Who could say to Him, "What are You doing?"
A god could not avert His anger—
    Rahab's[8] cohorts bent beneath Him—
how then could I raise my voice at Him,
    or choose to match my words with His?
Even if I were right, I could not answer,
    could only plead with my opponent;
and if I summoned Him, and if He answered me,
    I doubt that He would listen to my voice,
since He crushes me for just a hair,
    and bruises me for nothing,
will not let me catch my breath,
    feeds me full of poison.
Is it power? He is mighty!
Is it judgment? Who can summon Him?
I may be righteous, but my mouth convicts me;
    innocent, yet it makes me seem corrupt.
I *am* good.

8. Another name for the sea monster conquered by the god in Near Eastern myth.

I do not know myself.
I hate my life.
It is all one; and so I say,
"The good and the guilty He destroys alike."
If some scourge brings sudden death,
   He mocks the guiltless for their melting hearts;
some land falls under a tyrant's sway—
   He veils its judges' faces;
if not He, then who?

But I—
my days are lighter than a courier's feet;
they flee and never see a moment's joy;
they dart away as if on skiffs of reed,[9]
swift as a vulture swooping to his food.

I tell myself to give up my complaining,
   put aside my sullenness and breathe a while;
but still I fear my suffering,
knowing You will never count me innocent.
I am always the one in the wrong—
why should I struggle in vain?
Even if I bathed in liquid snow
   and purified my palms with lye,
You would just dip me in a ditch—
   my very clothes would find me sickening.

For a man like me cannot just challenge Him,
"Let's go to court together!"
Now if there were an arbiter between us
to lay his hand on both of us,
   to make Him take His rod away,
   so that His terror would not cow me,
then I could speak without this fear of Him;
   for now I am not steady in His presence.

10. I am fed up with my life;
   I might as well complain with all abandon,
   and put my bitter spirit into words.
So to the god I say, "Do not condemn me!
Just tell me what the accusation is!
Do You get pleasure from harassing,
   spurning what You wore Yourself out making,
   shining on the councils of the wicked?
Do You have eyes of flesh?
   Do You see as mortals do?
Is Your life span the same as any human's,
   Your years like those of ordinary men,
that You come seeking out my every sin
   and leave no fault of mine unpunished—

9. Papyrus. Boats made from it were fast.

knowing I've done nothing truly wicked,
    that nothing can be rescued from Your hands?

Your hands shaped me, kneaded me
together, round about—
    and now would You devour me?
Remember, You kneaded me like clay;
    will You turn me back to dirt?
Just look:
You poured me out like milk,
    You curdled me like cheese;
You covered me with flesh and skin,
    wove me a tangle of sinews and bones,
gave me life, a gift,
    sustained my breath with Your command.
Yet all these things You stored up in Your heart—
I know how Your mind works!
When I do sin, You keep Your eye on me,
and You would never clear me of my guilt.
If I do wrong, too bad for me!
But even when I'm good I cannot raise my head,
so filled with shame,
    so drenched with my own misery.
Proud as a lion You stalk me
and then withdraw,
pleased with Yourself for what You've done to me.
You keep Your enmity toward me fresh,
    work up Your anger at me;
so my travail is constantly renewed.

Why did You ever take me from the womb?
I could have died, and no eye had to see.
I could have been as if I never were,
hauled from belly to grave.
But as it is, my days are few, so stop!
Let me alone so I can catch my breath
before I go my way, not to return,
into a land of dark and deathgloom,
land obscure as any darkness,
land of deathgloom, land of chaos,
where You blaze forth in rays of black!"

11. Zophar the Naamatite then took up the argument and said:

Should a speech go unanswered just because it is long?
    Is someone with ready lips always right?
You want to silence people with your bluster,
    cow them with sarcasm, no one restrains you.
You say, "My teaching's perfect," "I was pious"—
Yes, in *your* eyes.
But how I wish the god would speak,
    open His lips when you are present,

tell you some of wisdom's mysteries
(for wisdom comes wrapped up in double folds)—
then you would realize:
The god is punishing you less than you deserve.

Can you find out God's depths,
    or find the outer limits of Shaddai?
What can you do at the heavens' height?
    What can you know that is deeper than Sheol,[1]
    greater than the earth's extension, wider than the sea?
Should He pass by, confine, or confiscate,
who could restore?
He knows which men are false;
could He see wrong and look the other way?
Yet hollow-core man thinks he has some wisdom—
man, born no better than a saddle-ass or onager.[2]

If you would only set your mind,
    stretch out your hands to Him,
get rid of anything you own through crime,
    and harbor nothing wrongly gotten in your home—
then you could hold your head up, blameless,
    be rock-solid, fearing nothing.
Then you would put your troubles out of mind,
    remember them no more than water
    vanished from a wadi.
Your earthbound days would rise as high as noon,
    and darkness turn to morning.
You'd live in confidence, with hope,
    dig your burrow, lie secure,
    crouch there, fearing no one.
Multitudes would seek your favor,
while the wicked gaze with longing eyes,
all refuge lost to them,
    their hopes all spent in sighs.

12. Job answered:

What a distinguished tribe you are!
    All wisdom dies with you!
But I too have a mind.
I am no less a man than you;
    and who does *not* have such ideas as these?
I am one who gives his neighbors cause to smile:
    "He calls to God and He answers him!"—
    a laughingstock—righteous, innocent.
Smug men's minds hold scorn for disaster,
    ready for anyone who stumbles.
Highway robbers' families lie tranquil;
    men who anger El are confident
    of what the god has brought into their hands.

---

1. The dwelling place of the dead.   2. A wild ass.

But just ask the animals—they will instruct you;
    the birds of heaven—they will tell.
Or speak to the earth and it will instruct you,
    the fish of the ocean will tell you the tale:
Who of all these is not aware
that Yahweh's hand has done all this,[3]
the hand that controls every living soul,
    the breath of every man made of flesh?

"The ear," they say, "is the best judge of speech,
    the palate knows what food is tasty."
    "Wisdom," they say, "belongs to elders;
    length of years makes a man perspicacious."
He has wisdom and power;
    He has counsel and insight.
If He tears down, there is no rebuilding;
    if He confines, there is no release.
If He blocks the water, the water dries up;
    but if He lets it loose,
    if overturns the earth.
Both skill and might are with Him;
    He owns both those who do wrong
    and those who lead others astray.
He makes counselors go mad and judges rave,
    unties the bonds of kings,
    (though He Himself had bound the sash about their waists).
He makes the priests go mad,
    and gives eternal truths the lie.
He strips the ready counselors of speech,
    makes off with the elders' reason,
heaps scorn on nobles,
    weakens the pride of the mighty.
He discloses deep things out of darkness,
    brings deathdark to the light.
He elevates some nations, then destroys them,
    spreads traps for other nations,
    but guides them safely through.
He strips the peoples' leaders of their judgment,
    sends them off-course in a trackless wasteland,
    groping in the darkness, lightless,
    wandering crazily like drunken men.

13. Look, there is nothing my eye hasn't seen,

    nothing my ear hasn't heard and taken in,
    nothing that you know that I do not.
    I am no less a man than you.
But I would speak to Shaddai,
    I want to dispute with El,

---

3. If *this* refers to Job's suffering, the meaning is that even animals know that God acts arbitrarily, whereas "smug men" (previous stanza) think that if a man suffers he has done something to deserve it.

while you are merely smearers, liars,
　　mountebanks, every one of you.
If only you would just be quiet!—
　　In you, that would be wisdom!

Listen to my accusation,
　　pay heed to my lips' complaint.
Will you speak falsehood for the sake of El,
　　and speak deceit on His account?
Will you show partiality to Him,
　　argue on El's behalf?
How would it be if He questioned you?
　　Could you play Him for a fool, as you do with people?
He is sure to reprimand you,
　　if you behave with secret partiality.
Think how you would panic if He were to loom,
　　and all His fearsomeness came down on you:
　　Your memory would turn to ashes,
　　your bodies, into lumps of clay.

Be silent in my presence! I will speak,
　　and let whatever happens to me happen.
Why am I carrying my body in my teeth,
　　my life-breath in my hands?[4]
Let Him kill me!—I will never flinch,
　　but will protest His conduct to His face,
and He Himself will be my vindication,
　　for flatterers can never come before Him.

Listen, all who hear me, to my speech,
　　my declaration in your ears:
I am laying out my case,
knowing I am in the right.
Who would contend with me?—
I will shut my mouth at once and die.
Only two things do not do to me,
and then I will not hide from You:
Take Your palm away from me,
　　and do not cow me with the fear of You.
Then You can call, and I will answer,
or I will speak and You can answer me.
How many are my sins and my offenses?
　　Advise me of my crimes and sins.
Why do You hide Your face,
　　regard me as Your enemy?
Would You tyrannize a driven leaf
　　or hound a shriveled straw,
that You record my every bitter deed,
　　charge me with my boyhood sins?

---

4. Like a wild beast at bay, defending its life with its teeth.

    Is that why You put my feet in stocks,
        watch my every step,
        mark the roots of my feet?[5]

14. Man born of woman:
    His days are few, his belly full of rage.
    He blooms and withers like a blossom,
        flees, unlingering, like a shadow,
        wears out like a rotten thing,
        a cloth moth-eaten.
    Do You really keep a watch on such a thing?
        Do You call a man like me
        to judgement against You?

    Who can purify a thing impure?
    No one!
    If his years are predetermined,
        and You control the number of his months,
        and You have set him bounds he cannot cross—
    just turn away from him and let him be!
    Let him work off his contract,
    day laborer that he is.

    Even a tree has hope:
    If you cut it, it sprouts again.
    Its suckers never fail.
    Its roots may grow old in the earth,
        its stumps may die in the ground,
    but just the smell of water makes it bud
    and put out branches like a sapling.
    But man, when he wearies and dies,
        when a human gives out—where is he then?
    Water vanishes from a lake,
        rivers dry up parched,
    and man lies down and does not rise;
    they will not wake till the skies disappear;
        they will not rise from their sleep.

    If You would only hide me in Sheol,
        conceal me till Your anger passes,
        set me a term and then remember me
        (but if a person dies, how can he live?),
    I could endure my term in hope,
    until my time came round to sprout again.
    Then You would call, and I would answer,
        when You longed to see Your handiwork.
    But as it is, You count my every step,
        see nothing but my sins.
    My sin is sealed up in a bundle,
        and You attached the seal.

5. The meaning here is obscure.

Yes, the mountain collapses and wears away;
    the cliff is dislodged from its place;
stones are scoured by water into dust,
    torrents wash away earth's soil—
    and You destroy man's hopes.
You assault him and he vanishes forever;
    You turn his face dark and send him away.
His sons become great and he never knows,
    or else they fail, and he never finds out.
All he knows is his own body's ache;
he mourns himself alone.

*   *   *

29. Job went on with his poem:

If only I could be under the moons of old again,
back in the days when the god watched over me!
When He held His lamp so it shone above my head,
and I could walk by the light in darkness.
If I could be again as I was in my daring days,
with the god above my tent, protecting;
when Shaddai was still with me—
    my men around me too!—
my feet washed with butter,
    the rocks pouring oil out for me in streams!

When I would stride out to the gate of the town,
    and take my place in the city square,[6]
young men would see me and hide in the crowd,
    elders would rise and stand still in their places;
chieftains would dam their words' flow,
    putting their hands to their lips;
commanders' voices were muffled;
    tongues stuck to the roofs of mouths;
but ears would hear and admire;
    eyes would see and bear witness to me:
how I rescued poor men when they cried,
    and orphans, people none would help.

Desperate, ruined men would bless me,
    and I brought song to the widow's heart.
I put on justice and it suited me;
    my decree was my turban and robe.
I was the blind man's eyes;
I was feet for the lame;
I was father to the poor.
I studied the stranger's complaint.
I cracked the fangs of villains,
    ripped the prey from their teeth.

---

6. Towns were walled, and the town's meeting place and law court were just inside the gate.

So I said:
I will die in my nest,
    live as long as the phoenix,[7]
my roots open to water,
    my shoots night-moistened by dew.
My pride constantly renewed for me,
    my bow blooming in my hand. . . .

They would listen to me, waiting
silently for my advice;
when I had spoken they would not ask again,
once my word had dripped over them.
They would look to me as if for rain,
    their mouths wide to the spring showers.
When I smiled at them, they were uneasy;
    they took care not to make my face fall.
I chose their paths;
I sat at their head;
I dwelt among them like a king with his troops,
    or like one who comforts men who mourn.

30. And now I find myself mocked by men younger than myself, men
whose fathers I rejected from working alongside my sheepdogs!

Even their manual labor, what good was it to me?
Their vigor was long gone
in dearth and famine, barren,
fleeing to the wilderness,
a horror-night of ruin;
plucking saltwort from scrub-brush,
burning broom-root to get warm,
driven from society,
shouted at like thieves;
squatting in the wadi-channels,
dust-caves, cliff-hollows;
braying in the bushes,
keeping company among thorns;
louts' brood, no one's children,
ousted from the world of men—
now I am their mocking song,
    the topic of their gossip!
They scorn me, they shun me,
    they spare my face no spit.

For He undid my cord, tormented me,
and they shake loose my reins.
Young bullies crop up on my right,
range anywhere they like,

---

7. The King James version's "multiply my days as the sand" is more literal (sand is a common biblical image for a quantity past counting). The phoenix was a fabulous bird that lived for several hundred years and
then burned to death in its nest. A young phoenix arose from the ashes.

pave right up to me their highways of destruction,
ruin my own paths.
They work effectively to bring me down,
   they need no help.
They come on like a wide rush of water,
   downward, ravaging, rolling.

Horror has rolled over me,
and driven off my dignity like wind;
my wealth has vanished like a cloud,
and now my life is spilling out of me.
Days of suffering have seized me;
   by night my bones are hacked from me,
   my sinews cannot rest.
Just to dress takes all my strength;
my collar fits my waist.

He conceived me as clay,
and I have come to be like dust and ashes.

I cry to You—no answer;
   I stand—You stare at me,
You harden Yourself to me,
   spurn me with Your mighty hand.
You lift me up and mount me on a wind,
   dissolve my cunning,
and I know that You will send me back to death,
   to the house awaiting every living creature.
But why this violence to a pile of rubble?
   In his disaster is there some salvation?
Did I not weep for the hapless?
   Did my soul not grieve for the poor?
Yes—
I hoped for good, got only wrong;
   I hoped for light, got only darkness.
My insides seethe and never stop,
   I face days of suffering,
I go about in sunless gloom.
In assembly I stand up and wail,
changed to a jackal's brother,
   fellow to the ostrich.[8]
My skin has blackened on my body,
   my bones are charred with fever.
My lyre has gone to mourning,
   my pipe to the sound of sobs.

31. Then what does the god above have in store,
    what lot from Shaddai in the heavens?
  Only disaster for doers of evil,
    estrangement for men who do wrong.

---

8. Both animals are known for their loud, mournful cries.

Does He not see my ways,
    count all my steps?
Have I walked the way of falsehood?
    Was my foot fleet to deceit?
Let God weigh me in an honest balance—
    He will have to see my innocence.

If my step has left the path,
if my heart has obeyed my eye,
if anyone's goods have stuck to my palms,
    may I sow for another to eat;
    may my offspring be uprooted.
If I have let a woman beguile me,
if I have lurked at my neighbor's door,
    may my own wife grind for another,
    may other men crouch over her;
    for that would be indecent, foul,
    that would be a crime for the judges.
    For it is fire
    raging down to Abaddon[9]
    and would uproot my increase.
    I have made a pact with my eyes
    never to gaze at young women.
If I deny my men-slaves or women-slaves justice
when they raise complaints to me,
    what will I do when God comes forward,
    to demand accounting?
    What will I answer Him?
    Did not my maker make him[1] in the selfsame belly,
    form us in a single womb?
If I have refused the poor their wants,
    or made the eyes of widows languish,
if I have eaten my bread alone,
without an orphan sharing it
    (for since I was a boy, I raised him[2] like a father,
    and from my mother's womb I guided her)[3]—
If ever I saw someone dying naked,
or a poor man with no clothing,
    I swear, his very loins would bless me,
    as he warmed himself in the wool of my sheep.
If ever I raised my hand to an orphan,
seeing I had support in the gate,[4]
    may my shoulder fall out of its socket,
    and my forearm break off at the elbow;
    for disaster from El is terror to me;
    I cannot bear His awesome looming.
If ever I put my hope in gold,
    or thought to place my trust in it;
if I was smug because my wealth was great,
    because my hand had acquired so much—

9. The underworld.   1. The slave.   2. The orphan.   3. The widow.   4. That is, when I had influence in the court and other public places.

If I have ever looked at the sun as it beamed,
or at the moon coming on in splendor,
and my heart was secretly beguiled,
and my hand crept up to touch my mouth,[5]
　　that too would be a crime for judges,
　　for it would mean denying God on high.
If ever I rejoiced in my enemy's downfall,
or felt a rush of joy when trouble found him,
　　never did I let my mouth taste sin,
　　asking for his life by execration.[6]
If the men of my household ever failed to say,
"Why did we consume his flesh?"—
　　No stranger ever spent the night in the street;
　　for I would open my doors to the wanderer.
If, as men will, I hid my crimes,
　　concealed my sin inside me,
　　fearing public scandal,
　　frightened by the scorn of clans,
　　kept silent, never setting foot outdoors—
If my land cries out because of me,
　　and its furrows weep together,
if I consumed its produce without paying,
　　made its workers sigh their souls out,
may it sprout up thorns instead of wheat,
　　stinkweed instead of barley.

If only I had someone to hear me!

Here is my desire: that Shaddai answer me,
　　that my opponent write a brief;
I swear that I would wear it on my shoulder,
　　bind it on me like a crown.
I would tell my steps to Him by number,
　　come before Him as before a prince.

Here Job's speeches ended.

❊　　❊　　❊

38. Yahweh answered Job from the storm:

Who dares speak darkly words with no sense?

Cinch your waist like a fighter.
I will put questions, and you will inform me:
Where were you when I founded the earth?
Speak, if you have any wisdom:
Who set its measurements, if you know,
　　laid out the building lot, stretching the plumb line?
Where was the ground where He sank its foundations?

5. Idolatrous acts of worship of the sun and moon.　　6. A formal curse.

Who was setting the cornerstone
when the morning stars were all singing,
    when the gods were all shouting, triumphant?
Who barred the sea behind double gates
as it was gushing out of the womb?
When I made the clouds its covering, fog its swaddling,
broke its will with my decree,
set bar and double gate,
and said, "This far, no farther!
    Here stops your breakers' surge."
When did you ever give dawn his orders,
    assign the rising sun his post,
to grasp the corners of the world
    and shake the wicked out of it,[7]
make the world heave, break like a seal of clay:
    They stand up naked.
The wicked are denied their light,
    the haughty arm is broken.

Have you ever reached the depths of the sea
    and walked around there, exploring the abyss?
Have you been shown behind the Gates of Death,
    or seen the Gates of Deathdark?
Have you beheld the earth's expanses?
Tell me, if you know everything!—
Where is the path to where light dwells,
    and darkness, where does it belong?
Can you conduct them to their regions,
    or even imagine their homeward paths?
You must know, you were born long ago!
    So many years you have counted!

Have you reached the stores of snow,
    or seen the stock of hailstones
that I have laid up for times of trouble,
    days of battle, days of war?

Where is the path to where lightning forks,
    when an east wind scatters it over the ground?
Who cracked open a channel for the torrent,
    clove the path for the thundershower,
to rain on lands where no man lives,
    on wildernesses uninhabited,
to feed a wasteland, fill a desolation,
    make it flower, sprout grass?
Does the shower have a father?
    Who begot the drops of dew?
From whose womb did the ice come forth?
Who gave birth to the sky-frost—
    water clotting as to stone,
        the abyss congeals.

---

7. That is, the sun exposes the wicked, who commit their crimes in the darkness of night.

Do you tie the Sky-Sisters[8] with ropes
    or undo Orion's bonds?
Do you bring out the stars as they are due,
    guide the Great Bear and her young?
Do you know the laws that rule the sky,
    and can you make it control the earth?
Can you thunder at the clouds
    so that a flood of water covers you?
Can you loose the lightning,
    and have it say, as it goes, "Your servant!"?
Who gave wisdom to the ibis,
    gave the cock its knowledge?
Who is wise enough to count the clouds,
    pour out the jars of heaven,
when the soil is fused solid
    and clods stick thickly?

Do you hunt prey for the lioness?
    Do you satisfy her young,
when they are crouching in their lair,
    sitting in ambush in the covert?
Who puts prey in the raven's way,
    when her fledglings cry to God,
        wandering, aimless, without food?

39. Do you know when the antelope gives birth,
    watch for the calving of the deer?
Do you count the months they have to pass,
    know how, when their time has come,
    they crouch, split open for their young,
    release their newborns?
The calves thrive, grow in the wild,
    then leave them, never return.

Who gave the wild ass his freedom,
    undid his bonds—
the beast I made to live in wasteland,
    gave the salt flat as a home,
so that he might laugh at crowded cities
    and never hear the driver's call,
but scour the hills for pasturage,
    hunting for any bit of green?

Does the buffalo deign to serve you?
    Will he sleep by your feeding trough?
Can you tie him to a furrow with a rope?
    Will he harrow the plain behind you?
Can you rely on him, for all his power,
    and leave your work to him?
Can you trust him to bring in your produce

8. The Pleiades.

and heap it up for threshing?
Delightful is the ostrich wing—
 but is it a pinion, like stork or vulture?
Does the eagle soar at your bidding,
 building his nest up high?—
He dwells, shelters on cliffs,
 on rock crags and fastnesses.
From there he seeks food,
 and his eyes peer far;
 his chicks lap gore.
Where there's a corpse you will find him.

40. Yahweh turned back to Job:

One who brings Shaddai to court should fight!
 He who charges a god should speak.

But Job answered Yahweh:

I see how little I am.
I will not answer You.
I am putting my hand to my lips:
 One time I spoke;
  I will not speak again;
 two times I spoke,
  and I will not go on.

Yahweh answered Job from the storm:

Cinch your waist like a fighter.
 I will put questions, and you will inform me.
Would you really annul my judgment,
 make me out to be guilty, and put yourself in the right?
Is your arm as mighty as God's?
 Does your voice thunder like His?
Just dress up in majesty, greatness!
 Try wearing splendor and glory!
Snort rage in every direction!
 Seek out the proud, bring him down!
Seek out the proud man, subdue him,
 crush cruel men where they stand,
hide them together in dirt,
 bind them in the Hidden Place:
Then even I would concede to you,
 when your right hand had gained you a triumph.

Just look at the River Beast[9] that I put alongside you:
He eats grass like cattle.
Look at his thighs: What power!
 The might in his belly muscles!

9. The Hebrew word is *behemot* (rendered in English as "behemoth"), a general term for animals; but the description seems to be modeled on the hippopotamus.

He wills his tail into cedar—
    his thigh-thews twist tight.
His bones are unyielding bronze,
    his limbs are like iron bars.
He is the first of God's ways.
    Let none but his maker bring forth his sword![1]

For the hills bring their yield, their tribute to him,
    the hills where the wild beasts play—
to him, who lies under the lotus,
    in a marsh, in a covert of reeds.

Sheltered, shaded by lotus,
    surrounded by droop-leaf willows.
Look: He gulps a whole river, but languidly,
    calm, as the Jordan surges into his mouth!

    Can you catch him by the eye?
    Can you pierce his nose with thorns?

Can you draw the River Coiler[2] with a hook?
    Bind down his tongue with a rope?
String him through the nose with a reed?
    Bore his cheek with a thistle?
Would he beg you for mercy,
    gentle you with words?
Would he deign to be your ally?
    Could you make him a slave for life?
Could you pet him like a bird,
    leash him for your girls to play with?
Will partners haggle over him
    or cut him into lots for mongers?
Can you fill his skin with darts,
    get his head into a fishnet?
Just put your hand on him—
you will remember the battle, you will not do it again!

41. Look: Hope of him is delusion;
    even to glance at him is to fall.
        Is he not fierce when aroused?
Who could stand ground in his presence?
    Who could address him unscathed?
Under all the heavens, that man would be mine!
    I would not silence his boasting,
    his talk of feats,
        his grace in battle.
Who could strip away the surface that covers him,
    get him into the folds of his bridle?
Who could throw open the gates of his countenance?—
    his teeth cast terror all round.
Haughty, his mighty shields,[3]

---

1. That is, to kill him.   2. Leviathan (see n. 6, p.126). The description here seems modeled on the crocodile.   3. That is, scales.

shut, sealed tight;
each comes right up to the other,
    no air gets between them;
each clings to each,
    untied, unparting.

His sneezes make the light shimmer;
    his eyes are like the eyelids of dawn.
From his mouth come torches,
    fire-sparks fleeting.

His nostrils smoke
    like a pot that seethes over reeds.
His throat blazes like coals;
    his mouth emits flame.

Might resides in his neck;
    misery dances before him.
The cascades of his flesh cling,
    like cast metal on him, immovable.
Solid as rock is his heart,
    millstone-solid.
When he erupts, the gods cower,
    shrink from the waves.

Reach him with a sword and it fails,
    far-traveling spear or arrow.
Iron to him is straw;
    bronze, a rotten tree.
Arrows cannot repel him,
    fling-stones he turns to chaff;
    stubble to him, the shaft.
        He laughs at the lances' whir.

His underside is sharp shards;
    he drags a threshing sledge on the mud.
He makes the deep boil,
    the sea like soup.
Behind him gleams his wake,
    the abyss, white as an old man's head.

Nothing on dusty earth is like him,
    made not to fear.
He gazes at lofty creatures,
    king of the haughtiest beings!

42. Job answered Yahweh:

I know that You are all-powerful,
and that no plan is beyond You.
"Who dares to speak hidden words with no sense?"[4]

---

4. Here and in the next quotation, Job repeats Yahweh's words from the beginning of his first speech and responds to them from the perspective of his new understanding.

I see that I spoke with no wisdom
  of things beyond me I did not know.

"Listen now and I will speak,
  I will put questions, and you will inform me. . . ."

I knew You, but only by rumor;
  my eye has beheld You today.
I retract. I even take comfort
  for dust and ashes.[5]

After Yahweh had said these things to Job, He said to Eliphaz the Temanite, "I am very angry at you and your two friends, for you have not spoken rightly about me as did my servant Job. So take seven bulls and seven rams and go to my servant Job and offer them as wholeburnt offerings for yourselves. And make sure that Job my servant prays for you; for only him will I heed not to treat you with the disgrace you deserve for not speaking rightly of me as did my servant Job." Eliphaz the Temanite and Bildad the Shuhite and Zophar the Naamatite went and did exactly what Yahweh told them to do, and Yahweh accepted Job's prayer.

Yahweh restored Job's fortunes after he prayed for his friends, doubling everything Job had.

All his brothers and sisters and all his former acquaintances came and ate bread with him in his house and mourned with him and comforted him for all the harm that Yahweh had brought upon him. Each one gave him a qesita coin[6] and a gold ring.

Yahweh made Job more prosperous in the latter part of his life than in the former. He had fourteen thousand sheep, six thousand camels, a thousand yoke of cattle, and a thousand female donkeys, besides seven sons and three daughters. He named the first daughter Dove, and the second daughter Cinnamon, and the third daughter Horn-of-Kohl[7]—there were no women as beautiful as Job's daughters in all the land—and he gave them an inheritance alongside their brothers.

Afterward, Job lived one hundred forty years; he lived to see his sons and grandsons to the fourth generation and died in old age after a full life span.

From Psalms[1]

Psalm 8

1. O Lord our Lord, how excellent is thy name in all the earth! who hast set thy glory above the heavens.

2. Out of the mouth of babes and sucklings hast thou ordained strength because of thine enemies, that thou mightest still the enemy and the avenger.

---

5. Mortality. 6. Value unknown. 7. Kohl is a powdered cosmetic often stored in animal horns. The name thus suggests feminine beauty. 1. The text of Psalms and the Song of Songs is that of the King James version (see "A Note on These Translations," on p. 97).

3. When I consider thy heavens, the work of thy fingers, the moon and the stars, which thou hast ordained;

4. What is man, that thou art mindful of him? and the son of man, that thou visitest him?

5. For thou hast made him a little lower than the angels, and hast crowned him with glory and honour.

6. Thou madest him to have dominion over the works of thy hands; thou hast put all things under his feet:

7. All sheep and oxen, yea, and the beasts of the field;

8. The fowl of the air, and the fish of the sea, and whatsoever passeth through the paths of the seas.

9. O Lord our Lord, how excellent is thy name in all the earth!

Psalm 19

1. The heavens declare the glory of God; and the firmament sheweth his handywork.

2. Day unto day uttereth speech, and night unto night sheweth knowledge.

3. There is no speech nor language, where their voice is not heard.

4. Their line is gone out through all the earth, and their words to the end of the world. In them hath he set a tabernacle for the sun,

5. Which is as a bridegroom coming out of his chamber, and rejoiceth as a strong man to run a race.

6. His going forth is from the end of the heaven, and his circuit unto the ends of it: and there is nothing hid from the heat thereof.

7. The law of the Lord is perfect, converting the soul: the testimony of the Lord is sure, making wise the simple.

8. The statutes of the Lord are right, rejoicing the heart: the command-ment of the Lord is pure, enlightening the eyes.

9. The fear of the Lord is clean, enduring for ever: the judgments of the Lord are true and righteous altogether.

10. More to be desired are they than gold, yea, than much fine gold: sweeter also than honey and the honeycomb.

11. Moreover by them is thy servant warned: and in keeping of them there is great reward.

12. Who can understand his errors? cleanse thou me from secret faults.

13. Keep back thy servant also from presumptuous sins; let them not have dominion over me: then shall I be upright, and I shall be innocent from the great transgression.

14. Let the words of my mouth, and the meditation of my heart, be ac-ceptable in thy sight, O Lord, my strength, and my redeemer.

Psalm 23

1. The Lord is my shepherd; I shall not want.

2. He maketh me to lie down in green pastures: he leadeth me beside the still waters.

3. He restoreth my soul: he leadeth me in the paths of righteousness for his name's sake.

4. Yea, though I walk through the valley of the shadow of death, I will fear no evil: for thou art with me; thy rod and thy staff they comfort me.

5. Thou preparest a table before me in the presence of mine enemies: thou anointest my head with oil; my cup runneth over.

6. Surely goodness and mercy shall follow me all the days of my life: and I will dwell in the house of the Lord for ever.

Psalm 104

1. Bless the Lord, O my soul. O Lord my God, thou art very great; thou art clothed with honour and majesty.

2. Who coverest thyself with light as with a garment: who stretchest out the heavens like a curtain:

3. Who layeth the beams of his chambers in the waters: who maketh the clouds his chariot: who walketh upon the wings of the wind:

4. Who maketh his angels spirits; his ministers a flaming fire:

5. Who laid the foundations of the earth, that it should not be removed for ever.

6. Thou coveredst it with the deep as with a garment: the waters stood above the mountains.

7. At thy rebuke they fled; at the voice of thy thunder they hasted away.

8. They go up by the mountains; they go down by the valleys unto the place which thou hast founded for them.

9. Thou hast set a bound that they may not pass over; that they turn not again to cover the earth.

10. He sendeth the springs into the valleys, which run among the hills.

11. They give drink to every beast of the field: the wild asses quench their thirst.

12. By them shall the fowls of the heaven have their habitation, which sing among the branches.

13. He watereth the hills from his chambers: the earth is satisfied with the fruit of thy works.

14. He causeth the grass to grow for the cattle, and herb for the service of man: that he may bring forth food out of the earth;

15. And wine that maketh glad the heart of man, and oil to make his face to shine, and bread which strengtheneth man's heart.

16. The trees of the Lord are full of sap; the cedars of Lebanon, which he hath planted;

17. Where the birds make their nests: as for the stork, the fir trees are her house.

18. The high hills are a refuge for the wild goats; and the rocks for the conies.

19. He appointed the moon for seasons: the sun knoweth his going down.

20. Thou makest darkness, and it is night: wherein all the beasts of the forest do creep forth.

21. The young lions roar after their prey, and seek their meat from God.

22. The sun ariseth, they gather themselves together, and lay them down in their dens.

23. Man goeth forth unto his work and to his labour until the evening.

24. O Lord, how manifold are thy works! in wisdom hast thou made them all: the earth is full of thy riches.

25. So is this great and wide sea, wherein are things creeping innumerable, both small and great beasts.

26. There go the ships: there is that leviathan, whom thou hast made to play therein.

27. These wait all upon thee; that thou mayest give them their meat in due season.

28. That thou givest them they gather: thou openest thine hand, they are filled with good.

29. Thou hidest thy face, they are troubled: thou takest away their breath, they die, and return to their dust.

30. Thou sendest forth thy spirit, they are created: and thou renewest the face of the earth.

31. The glory of the Lord shall endure for ever: the Lord shall rejoice in his works.

32. He looketh on the earth, and it trembleth: he toucheth the hills, and they smoke.

33. I will sing unto the Lord as long as I live: I will sing praise to my God while I have my being.

34. My meditation of him shall be sweet: I will be glad in the Lord.

35. Let the sinners be consumed out of the earth, and let the wicked be no more. Bless thou the Lord, O my soul. Praise ye the Lord.

Psalm 137

1. By the rivers of Babylon,[2] there we sat down, yea, we wept, when we remembered Zion.

2. We hanged our harps upon the willows in the midst thereof.

3. For there they that carried us away captive required of us a song; and they that wasted us required of us mirth, saying, Sing us one of the songs of Zion.

4. How shall we sing the Lord's song in a strange land?

5. If I forget thee, O Jerusalem, let my right hand forget her cunning.

6. If I do not remember thee, let my tongue cleave to the roof of my mouth; if I prefer not Jerusalem above my chief joy.

7. Remember, O Lord, the children of Edom[3] in the day of Jerusalem; who said, Rase it, rase it, even to the foundation thereof.

8. O daughter of Babylon, who art to be destroyed; happy shall he be, that rewardeth thee as thou hast served us.

9. Happy shall he be, that taketh and dasheth thy little ones against the stones.

---

2. On the Euphrates River. Jerusalem was captured and sacked by the Babylonians in 586 B.C.E. The Hebrews were taken away into captivity in Babylon.   3. The Edomites helped the Babylonians capture Jerusalem.

The Song of Songs

1. The song of songs, which is Solomon's.

Let him kiss me with the kisses of his mouth: for thy love is better than wine. Because of the savor of thy good ointments thy name is as ointment poured forth, therefore do the virgins love thee. Draw me, we will run after thee: the King hath brought me into his chambers: we will be glad and rejoice in thee, we will remember thy love more than wine: the upright love thee. I am black,[1] but comely, O ye daughters of Jerusalem, as the tents of Kedar,[2] as the curtains of Solomon. Look[3] not upon me, because I am black, because the sun hath looked upon me: my mother's children were angry with me; they made me the keeper of the vineyards; but mine own vineyard have I not kept. Tell me, O thou whom my soul loveth, where thou feedest, where thou makest thy flock to rest at noon: for why should I be as one that turneth aside by the flocks of thy companions?

If thou know not, O thou fairest among women, go thy way forth by the footsteps of the flock, and feed thy kids beside the shepherds' tents. I have compared thee, O my love, to a company of horses in Pharaoh's chariots. Thy cheeks are comely with rows of jewels, thy neck with chains of gold. We will make thee borders of gold with studs of silver.

While the King sitteth at his table, my spikenard[4] sendeth forth the smell thereof. A bundle of myrrh is my well-beloved unto me; he shall lie all night betwixt my breasts. My beloved is unto me as a cluster of camphire in the vineyards of En-gedi.[5] Behold, thou art fair, my love; behold, thou art fair; thou hast doves' eyes. Behold, thou art fair, my beloved, yea, pleasant: also our bed is green. The beams of our house are cedar, and our rafters of fir.

2. I am the rose of Sharon,[6] and the lily of the valleys. As the lily among thorns, so is my love among the daughters. As the apple tree among the trees of the wood, so is my beloved among the sons. I sat down under his shadow with great delight, and his fruit was sweet to my taste. He brought me to the banqueting house, and his banner over me was love. Stay me with flagons, comfort me with apples: for I am sick of love. His left hand is under my head, and his right hand doth embrace me. I charge you, O ye daughters of Jerusalem, by the roes, and by the hinds of the field, that ye stir not up, nor awake my love, till he please. The voice of my beloved! behold he cometh leaping upon the mountains skipping upon the hills. My beloved is like a roe or a young hart: behold, he standeth behind our wall, he looketh forth at the windows, showing himself through the lattice. My beloved spake, and said unto me, Rise up, my love, my fair one, and come away. For, lo, the winter is past, the rain is over and gone; the flowers appear on the earth; the time of the singing of birds is come, and the voice of the turtle[7] is heard in our land; the fig tree putteth forth her green figs, and the vines with the tender grape give a good smell. Arise, my love, my fair one, and come away.

1. Tanned from sun and weather; feminine beauty required a protected and fair skin.   2. A nomadic people of northern Arabia, living east of Palestine.   3. Better, *gaze* or *stare* (with fascination).   4. Fragrant oil made from an Indian plant.   5. An oasis on the western shore of the Dead Sea, a source of fragrant oil made from the camphire (henna) plant.   6. A plain on the coast of Palestine, notable for its wildflowers. 7. The turtledove.

O my dove, that art in the clefts of the rock, in the secret places of the stairs, let me see thy countenance, let me hear thy voice; for sweet is thy voice, and thy countenance is comely. Take us the foxes, the little foxes, that spoil the vines: for our vines have tender grapes.

My beloved is mine, and I am his: he feedeth among the lilies. Until the day break, and the shadows flee away, turn, my beloved, and be thou like a roe or a young hart upon the mountains of Bether.[8]

3. By night on my bed I sought him whom my soul loveth: I sought him, but I found him not. I will rise now, and go about the city in the streets, and in the broad ways I will seek him whom my soul loveth: I sought him, but I found him not. The watchmen that go about the city found me: to whom I said, Saw ye him whom my soul loveth? It was but a little that I passed from them, but I found him whom my soul loveth: I held him, and would not let him go, until I had brought him into my mother's house, and into the chamber of her that conceived me. I charge you, O ye daughters of Jerusalem, by the roes, and by the hinds of the field, that ye stir not up, nor wake my love, till he please.

Who is this that cometh out of the wilderness like pillars of smoke, perfumed with myrrh and frankincense, with all powders of the merchant? Behold his bed, which is Solomon's; threescore valiant men are about it, of the valiant of Israel. They all hold swords, being expert in war: every man hath his sword upon his thigh because of fear in the night. King Solomon made himself a chariot of the wood of Lebanon. He made the pillars thereof of silver, the bottom thereof of gold, the covering of it of purple, the midst thereof being paved with love, for the daughters of Jerusalem. Go forth, O ye daughters of Zion, and behold king Solomon with the crown wherewith his mother crowned him in the day of his espousals, and in the day of the gladness of his heart.

4. Behold, thou art fair, my love; behold, thou art fair; thou hast doves' eyes within thy locks: thy hair is as a flock of goats, that appear from mount Gilead.[9] Thy teeth are like a flock of sheep that are even shorn, which came up from the washing; whereof every one bear twins, and none is barren among them. Thy lips are like a thread of scarlet, and thy speech is comely: thy temples are like a piece of a pomegranate within thy locks. Thy neck is like the tower of David builded for an armory, whereon there hang a thousand bucklers, all shields of mighty men. Thy two breasts are like two young roes that are twins, which feed among the lilies. Until the day break, and the shadows flee away, I will get me to the mountain of myrrh, and to the hill of frankincense. Thou art all fair, my love; there is no spot in thee.

Come with me from Lebanon, my spouse, with me from Lebanon: look from the top of Amana, from the top of Shenir and Hermon,[1] from the lions' dens, from the mountains of the leopards. Thou hast ravished my heart, my sister, my spouse; thou hast ravished my heart with one of thine eyes, with one chain of thy neck. How fair is thy love, my sister, my spouse! how much

8. Name of a city of Judah, southwest of Jerusalem. The phrase may also mean "the cleft mountains" (a reference to female breasts or genitals). 9. Location uncertain; perhaps a high inland plateau. 1. Mountains in the Antilebanon range of Syria.

better is thy love than wine! and the smell of thine ointments than all spices!
Thy lips, O my spouse, drop as the honeycomb: honey and milk are under
thy tongue; and the smell of thy garments is like the smell of Lebanon. A
garden inclosed is my sister, my spouse; a spring shut up, a fountain sealed.
Thy plants are an orchard of pomegranates, with pleasant fruits; camphire,
with spikenard, spikenard and saffron; calamus[2] and cinnamon, with all
trees of frankincense; myrrh and aloes, with all the chief spices: a fountain
of gardens, a well of living waters, and streams from Lebanon.

Awake, O north wind; and come, thou south; blow upon my garden, that
the spices thereof may flow out. Let my beloved come into his garden, and eat
his pleasant fruits.

5. I am come into my garden, my sister, my spouse: I have gathered my
myrrh with my spice; I have eaten my honeycomb with my honey; I have
drunk my wine with my milk: eat, O friends; drink, yea, drink abundantly, O
beloved.

I sleep, but my heart waketh: it is the voice of my beloved that knocketh,
saying, Open to me, my sister, my love, my dove, my undefiled: for my head
is filled with dew, and my locks with the drops of the night. I have put off my
coat; how shall I put it on? I have washed my feet; how shall I defile them?
My beloved put in his hand by the hole of the door, and my bowels[3] were
moved for him. I rose up to open to my beloved; and my hands dropped with
myrrh, and my fingers with sweet smelling myrrh, upon the handles of the
lock. I opened to my beloved; but my beloved had withdrawn himself, and
was gone: my soul failed when he spake: I sought him, but I could not find
him; I called him, but he gave me no answer. The watchmen that went about
the city found me, they smote me, they wounded me; the keepers of the
walls took away my veil from me. I charge you, O daughters of Jerusalem, if
ye find my beloved, that ye tell him, that I am sick of love. What is thy
beloved more than another beloved, O thou fairest among women? what is
thy beloved more than another beloved, that thou dost so charge us? My
beloved is white and ruddy, the chiefest among ten thousand. His head is as
the most fine gold; his locks are bushy, and black as a raven: his eyes are as
the eyes of doves by the rivers of waters, washed with milk, and fitly set: his
cheeks are as a bed of spices, as sweet flowers: his lips like lilies, dropping
sweet smelling myrrh: his hands are as gold rings set with the beryl: his belly
is as bright ivory overlaid with sapphires: his legs are as pillars of marble, set
upon sockets of fine gold: his countenance is as Lebanon, excellent as the
cedars: his mouth is most sweet: yea, he is altogether lovely. This is my
beloved, and this is my friend, O daughters of Jerusalem.

6. Whither is thy beloved gone, O thou fairest among women? whither is
thy beloved turned aside? that we may seek him with thee. My beloved is
gone down into his garden, to the beds of spices, to feed in the gardens, and
to gather lilies. I am my beloved's, and my beloved is mine: he feedeth
among the lilies.

---

2. Cane, an aromatic spice.   3. Entrails, considered the seat of tender emotions. "Hand": possibly a eu-
phemism for *phallus*.

Thou art beautiful, O my love, as Tirzah,[4] comely as Jerusalem, terrible as an army with banners. Turn away thine eyes from me, for they have overcome me: thy hair is as a flock of goats that appear from Gilead: thy teeth are as a flock of sheep which go up from the washing, whereof every one beareth twins, and there is not one barren among them. As a piece of a pomegranate are thy temples within thy locks. There are threescore queens, and fourscore concubines, and virgins without number. My dove, my undefiled, is but one; she is the only one of her mother, she is the choice one of her that bare her. The daughters saw her, and blessed her; yea, the queens and the concubines, and they praised her. Who is she that looketh forth as the morning, fair as the moon, clear as the sun, and terrible as an army with banners? I went down into the garden of nuts to see the fruits of the valley, and to see whether the vine flourished, and the pomegranates budded. Or ever I was aware, my soul made me like the chariots of Amminadib. Return, return, O Shulamite;[5] return, return, that we may look upon thee. What will ye see in the Shulamite? As it were the company of two armies.

7. How beautiful are thy feet with shoes, O prince's daughter! the joints of thy thighs are like jewels, the work of the hands of a cunning workman. Thy navel is like a round goblet, which wanteth not liquor: thy belly is like a heap of wheat set about with lilies. Thy two breasts are like two young roes that are twins. Thy neck is as a tower of ivory; thine eyes like the fishpools in Heshbon, by the gate of Bathrabbim:[6] thy nose is as the tower of Lebanon which looketh toward Damascus. Thine head upon thee is like Carmel,[7] and the hair of thine head like purple; the King is held in the galleries. How fair and how pleasant art thou, O love, for delights! This thy stature is like to a palm tree, and thy breasts to clusters of grapes. I said, I will go up to the palm tree, I will take hold of the boughs thereof: now also thy breasts shall be as clusters of the vine, and the smell of thy nose like apples: and the roof of thy mouth like the best wine for my beloved, that goeth down sweetly, causing the lips of those that are asleep to speak.

I am my beloved's, and his desire is toward me. Come, my beloved, let us go forth into the field; let us lodge in the villages. Let us get up early to the vineyards; let us see if the vine flourish, whether the tender grape appear, and the pomegranates bud forth: there will I give thee my loves. The mandrakes[8] give a smell, and at our gates are all manner of pleasant fruits, new and old, which I have laid up for thee, O my beloved.

8. O that thou wert as my brother, that sucked the breasts of my mother! when I should find thee without, I would kiss thee; yea, I should not be despised. I would lead thee, and bring thee into my mother's house, who would instruct me: I would cause thee to drink of spiced wine of the juice of my pomegranate. His left hand should be under my head, and his right hand should embrace me. I charge you, O daughters of Jerusalem, that ye stir not up, nor awake my love, until he please. Who is this that cometh up from the

---

4. A Canaanite city.   5. The name, often taken as the feminine counterpart to Solomon, may also be the name or epithet of a Near Eastern goddess or a reference to the town Shunem.   6. Another name for Heshbon, a city east of the northern end of the Dead Sea; or one of its gates.   7. A high promontory on the seacoast of Palestine.   8. A common plant in Palestine, known for its narcotic or aphrodisiac effect, whose root was thought to look like the male genitalia.

wilderness, leaning upon her beloved? I raised thee up under the apple tree: there thy mother brought thee forth; there she brought thee forth that bare thee. Set me as a seal upon thine heart, as a seal upon thine arm: for love is strong as death; jealousy is cruel as the grave: the coals thereof are coals of fire, which hath a most vehement flame. Many waters cannot quench love, neither can the floods drown it: if a man would give all the substance of his house for love, it would utterly be contemned.

We have a little sister, and she hath no breasts: what shall we do for our sister in the day when she shall be spoken for? If she be a wall, we will build upon her a palace of silver: and if she be a door, we will inclose her with boards of cedar. I am a wall, and my breasts like towers: then was I in his eyes as one that found favor. Solomon had a vineyard at Baalhamon;[9] he let out the vineyard unto keepers; every one for the fruit thereof was to bring a thousand pieces of silver. My vineyard, which is mine, is before me: thou, O Solomon, must have a thousand, and those that keep the fruit thereof two hundred. Thou that dwellest in the gardens, the companions hearken to thy voice: cause me to hear it. Make haste, my beloved, and be thou like to a roe or to a young hart upon the mountains of spices.

9. Otherwise unknown. The name means "lord of a crowd."

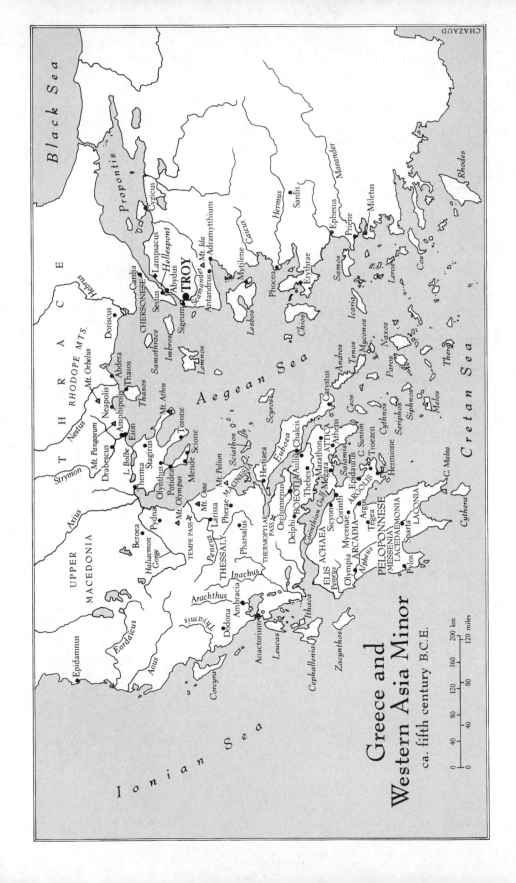

Greece and Western Asia Minor

ca. fifth century B.C.E.

CHAZAUD

Black Sea

Propontis

Ionian Sea

Aegean Sea

Cretan Sea

THRACE

RHODOPE MTS.

UPPER MACEDONIA

THESSALY

MAGNESIA

BOEOTIA

ATTICA

ARGOLIS

ARCADIA

LACEDAEMONIA

LACONIA

MESSENIA

PELOPONNESE

ACHAEA

ELIS

TROY

Black Sea

Hebrus

Hebrus

Mt. Orbelus

Doriscus

Abdera

Neapolis

Mt. Pangaeum

Amphipolis

Eion

Thasos

Mt. Athos

Torone

Mende   Scione

Olynthus

Potidea

Stagirus

Therma

L. Bolbe

Drabescus

Beroea

Pydna

Mt. Olympus

Haliacmon Gorge

Mt. Ossa

Larissa

Peneus

Pherae

Pharsalus

TEMPE PASS

Mt. Pelion

Inachus

Scyros

Sc=iathos

Hestiaea

Euboea

Chalcis

Aulis

Thebes

Orchomenus

Marathon

Megara

Athens

Salamis

Epidaurus

Troezen

Hermione

Mycenae

Corinth

Sicyon

Argos

Tegea

Olympia

Sparta

Pylos

Alpheus

Peneus

Corinthian Gulf

Delphi

THERMOPYLAE PASS

Strymon

Nestus

Axius

Eordaicus

Thyamis

Dodona

Ambracia

Arachthus

Anactorium

Leucas

Corcyra

Cephallenia

Zacynthos

Ithaca

Aous

Epidamnus

C. Malea

Cythera

C. Sunium

Seriphos

Siphnos

Cythnos

Ceos

Carystus

Andros

Tenos

Mycanos

Naxos

Paros

Melos

Thera

Siphnos

Delos

Scione

Cardia

CHERSONESE

Sestus

Abydus

Sigeum

Antandrus

Lampsacus

Cyzicus

Hellespont

Scamander   Mt. Ida

Adramythium

Caicus

Mytilene

Phocea

Erythrae

Lesbos

Chios

Samos

Icaria

Leros

Cos

Rhodes

Ephesus

Priene

Miletus

Maeander

Hermus

Sardis

Imbros

Lemnos

Samothrace

200 km

120 miles

Ancient Greece
and the Formation
of the Western Mind

The origin of the peoples who eventually called themselves Hellenes is still a mystery. The language they spoke belongs clearly to the great Indo-European family (which includes the Germanic, Celtic, Italic, and Sanskrit language groups), but many of the ancient Greek words and place-names have terminations that are definitely not Indo-European—the word for sea (*thalassa*), for example. The Greeks of historic times were presumably a blend of the native tribes and the Indo-European invaders, en route from the European landmass.

In the last hundred years archaeology has given us a clearer picture than our fore-bears had of the level of civilization in early Greece. The second millennium B.C.E. saw a brilliant culture, called Minoan after the mythical king Minos, flourishing on the large island of Crete; and the citadel of Mycenae and the palace at Pylos show that mainland Greece, in that same period, had centers of wealth and power unsuspected before the excavators discovered the gold masks of the buried kings and clay tablets covered with strange signs. The decipherment of these signs (published in 1953) revealed that the language of these Myceneans was an early form of Greek. It must have been the memory of these rich kingdoms that inspired Homer's vision of "Mycenae rich in gold" and the splendid armed hosts that assembled for the attack on Troy.

It was a blurred memory (Homer does not remember the writing, for example, or the detailed bureaucratic accounting recorded on the tablets) and this is easy to understand: some time in the last century of the millennium the great palaces were destroyed by fire. With them disappeared not only the arts and skills that had created Mycenean wealth but even the system of writing. For the next few hundred years the Greeks were illiterate and so no written evidence survives for what, in view of our ignorance about so many aspects of it, we call the Dark Age of Greece.

One thing we do know about it: it produced a body of oral epic poetry that was the raw material Homer shaped into the two great poems, the *Iliad* and *Odyssey*. These Homeric poems seem from internal evidence to date from the eighth century B.C.E.—which is incidentally, or perhaps not incidentally, the century in which the Greeks learned how to write again. They played in the subsequent development of Greek civilization the same role that the Torah had played in Palestine: they became the basis of an education and therefore of a whole culture. Not only did the great characters of the epic serve as models of conduct for later generations of Greeks but the figures of the Olympian gods retained, in the prayers, poems, and sculpture of the succeeding centuries, the shapes and attributes set down by Homer. The difference between the Greek and the Hebrew hero, between Achilles and Joseph, for example, is remarkable, but the difference between "the God of Abraham and of Isaac" and the Olympians who interfere capriciously in the lives of Hector or Achilles

161

or Helen is an unbridgeable chasm. The two conceptions of the power that governs the universe are irreconcilable; and in fact the struggle between them ended, not in synthesis but in the complete victory of the one and the disappearance of the other. The Greek conception of the nature of the gods and of their relation to humanity is so alien to us that it is difficult for the modern reader to take it seriously. The Hebrew basis of European religious thought has made it almost impossible for us to imagine a god who can be feared and laughed at, blamed and admired, and still sincerely worshiped. Yet all these are proper attitudes toward the gods on Olympus; they are all implicit in Homer's poems.

The Hebrew conception of God emphasizes those aspects of the universe that imply a harmonious order. The elements of disorder in the universe are, in the story of Creation, blamed on humankind, and in all Hebrew literature the evidences of disorder are something the writer tries to reconcile with an assumption of an all-powerful, just God. Just as clearly, the Greeks conceived their gods as an expression of the disorder of the world in which they lived. The Olympian gods, like the natural forces of sea and sky, follow their own will even to the extreme of conflict with each other, and always with a sublime disregard for the human beings who may be affected by the results of their actions. It is true that they are all subjects of a single more powerful god, Zeus. But his authority over them is based only on superior strength; though he cannot be openly resisted, he can be temporarily deceived by his fellow Olympians. And Zeus, although by virtue of his superior power his will is finally accomplished in the matter of Achilles' wrath, knows limits to his power too. He cannot save the life of his son the Lycian hero Sarpedon. Behind Zeus stands the mysterious power of Fate, to which even he must bow.

Such gods as these, representing as they do the blind forces of the universe that humans cannot control, are not always thought of as connected with morality. Morality is a human creation, and though the gods may approve of it, they are not bound by it. And violent as they are, they cannot feel the ultimate consequence of violence: death is a human fear, just as the courage to face it is a human quality. There is a double standard, one for gods, one for mortals, and the inevitable consequence is that our real admiration and sympathy are directed not toward the gods but toward the mortals. With Hector and Andromache, and even with Achilles at his worst, we can sympathize; but the gods, though they may excite terror or laughter, can never have our sympathy. We could as easily sympathize with a blizzard or the force of gravity. Homer imposed on Greek literature the anthropocentric emphasis that is its distinguishing mark and its great contribution to the Western mind. Though the gods are ever-present characters in the incidents of his poems, his true concern, first and last, is with men and women.

THE CITY-STATES OF GREECE

The stories told in the Homeric poems are set in the age of the Trojan War, which archaeologists (those who believe that it happened at all) date to the twelfth century B.C.E. Though the poems do preserve some faded memories of the Mycenaean Age, as we have them they are probably the creation of later centuries, the tenth to the eighth B.C.E., the so-called Dark Age that succeeded the collapse (or destruction) of Mycenaean civilization. This was the time of the final settlement of the Greek peoples, an age of invasion perhaps and migration certainly, which saw the foundation and growth of many small independent cities. The geography of Greece—a land of mountain barriers and scattered islands—encouraged this fragmentation. The Greek cities never lost sight of their common Hellenic heritage, but it was not enough to unite them except in the face of unmistakable and overwhelming danger, and even then only partially and for a short time. They differed from each other in custom, political constitution, and even dialect: their relations with each other were those of rivals and fierce competitors.

These cities, constantly at war in the pursuit of more productive land for growing populations, were dominated from the late eighth century B.C.E. by aristocratic oligarchies, which maintained a stranglehold on the land and the economy of which it was the base. An important safety valve was colonization. In the eighth and seventh centuries B.C.E. landless Greeks founded new cities (always near the sea and generally owing little or no allegiance to the home base) all over the Mediterranean coast— in Spain, southern France (Marseilles, Nice, and Antibes were all Greek cities), in south Italy (Naples), Sicily (Syracuse), North Africa (Cyrene), all along the coast of Asia Minor (Smyrna, Miletus), and even on the Black Sea as far as Russian Crimea. Many of these new outposts of Greek civilization experienced a faster economic and cultural development than the older cities of the mainland. It was in the cities founded on the Asian coast that the Greeks adapted to their own language the Phoenician system of writing, adding signs for the vowels to create their alphabet, the forerunner of the Roman alphabet and of our own. Its first use was probably for commercial records and transactions; but as literacy became a general condition all over the Greek world in the course of the seventh century B.C.E., treaties and political decrees were inscribed on stone and literary works written on rolls of paper made from the Egyptian papyrus plant.

ATHENS AND SPARTA

By the beginning of the fifth century B.C.E. the two most prominent city-states were Athens and Sparta. These two cities led the combined Greek resistance to the Persian invasion of Europe in the years 490 to 479 B.C.E. The defeat of the solid Persian power by the divided and insignificant Greek cities surprised the world and inspired in Greece, and particularly in Athens, a confidence that knew no bounds.

Athens was at this time a democracy, the first in Western history. It was a direct, not a representative, democracy, for the number of free citizens was small enough to permit the exercise of power by a meeting of the citizens as a body in assembly. Athens's power lay in the fleet with which it had played its decisive part in the struggle against Persia, and with this fleet Athens rapidly became the leader of a naval alliance that included most of the islands of the Aegean Sea and many Greek cities on the coast of Asia Minor. Sparta, on the other hand, was rigidly conservative in government and policy. Because the individual citizen was reared and trained by the state for the state's business, war, the Spartan land army was superior to any other in Greece, and the Spartans controlled, by direct rule or by alliance, a majority of the city-states of the Peloponnese.

These two cities, allies for the war of liberation against Persia, became enemies when the external danger was eliminated. The middle years of the fifth century were disturbed by indecisive hostilities between them and haunted by the probability of full-scale war to come. As the years went by, this war came to be accepted as "inevitable" by both sides, and in 431 B.C.E. it began. It was to end in 404 B.C.E. with the total defeat of Athens.

Before the beginning of this disastrous war, known as the Peloponnesian War, Athenian democracy provided its citizens with a cultural and political environment that was without precedent in the ancient world. The institutions of Athens encouraged the maximum development of the individual's capacities and at the same time inspired the maximum devotion to the interests of the community. It was a moment in history of delicate and precarious balance between the freedom of the individual and the demands of the state. It was the proud boast of the Athenians that without sacrificing the cultural amenities of civilized life they could yet when called upon surpass in policy and war their adversary, Sparta, whose citizen body was an army in constant training. The Athenians were, in this respect as in others, a nation of amateurs. "The individual Athenian," said Pericles, Athens's great statesman at this time, "in his own person seems to have the power of adapting himself to the most varied forms of action with the utmost versatility and grace." But the freedom of the individual did not, in Athens's great days, produce anarchy. "While we are . . . unconstrained in our private intercourse," Pericles had observed earlier in his speech, "a spirit of reverence pervades our public acts."

There were limits on who could participate in the democracy. The "individual Athenian" of whom Pericles spoke was the adult male citizen. In his speech, he mentioned women only once, to tell them that the way for them to obtain glory was not to be worse than their nature made them and to be least talked of among males for either praise or blame. Women could not own property, hold office, or vote. Peasant women may have had to work in the fields with their husbands, but affluent women were expected to remain inside the house except for funerals and religious festivals, rarely seen by men other than their husbands or male relatives. Their reputations for sexual chastity were fiercely protected; no suspicion of illegitimacy must fall on the sons they were expected to produce: future Athenian citizens, heirs to the family property, and continuators of the family line (which was traced through the male side). There were, in addition, a number of men from other cities who settled in Athens, often for business reasons—*metics*, or "resident aliens." They could not own land or take part in civic affairs. A great deal of labor—in the houses and fields, in craftsmen's shops, in the silver mines that underlay Athens's wealth—was performed by slaves, who of course had no rights at all. And finally, even among citizens who participated in civic life on a footing of equality, there were marked divisions between the elite and the poorer classes and tensions between them existed. Still, although it was exclusionary in all these ways, and although it pursued a ruthless imperialist policy abroad, Athenian democracy represented a bold achievement of civic equality for those who belonged.

This democracy came under strain as the Peloponnesian War progressed. Under the mounting pressure of the long conflict, the Athenians lost the "spirit of reverence" that Pericles saw as the stabilizing factor in Athenian democracy. They subordinated all considerations to the immediate interest of the city and surpassed their enemy in the logical ferocity of their actions. They finally fell victim to leaders who carried the process one step further and subordinated all considerations to their own private interest. The war years saw the decay of that freedom in unity that is celebrated in Pericles' speech. By the end of the fifth century Athens was divided internally as well as defeated externally. The individual citizen no longer thought of himself and Athens as one and the same; the balance was gone forever.

One of the solvents of traditional values was an intellectual revolution that was taking place in the advanced Athenian democracy of the last half of the fifth century, a critical reevaluation of accepted ideas in every sphere of thought and action. It stemmed from innovations in education. Democratic institutions had created a demand for an education that would prepare men for public life, especially by training them in the art of public speaking. The demand was met by the appearance of the professional teacher, the Sophist, as he was called, who taught, for a handsome fee, not only the techniques of public speaking but also the subjects that gave a man something to talk about—government, ethics, literary criticism, even astronomy. The curriculum of the Sophists, in fact, marks the first appearance in European civilization of liberal education (for affluent males), just as they themselves were the first professors.

The Sophists were great teachers, but like most teachers they had little or no control over the results of their teaching. Their methods placed an inevitable emphasis on effective presentation of a point of view, to the detriment, and if necessary the exclusion, of anything that might make it less convincing. They produced a generation that had been trained to see both sides of any question and to argue the weaker side as effectively as the stronger, the false as effectively as the true. They taught how to argue inferentially from probability in the absence of concrete evidence; to appeal to the audience's sense of its own advantage rather than to accepted moral standards; and to justify individual defiance of general prejudice and even of law by making a distinction between "nature" and "convention." These methods dominated the thinking of the Athenians of the late fifth and fourth centuries B.C.E. Emphasis on the technique of effective presentation of both sides of any case encouraged a relativistic point of view. The canon of probability (which implies an appeal to human reason as the supreme authority) became a critical weapon for an attack on myth and on traditional conceptions of the gods; though it had its constructive side, too, for it was the base for historical reconstruction of the unrecorded past and of the stages of human progress from savagery to civilization. The rhetorical appeal to the self-interest of the audience, to expediency, became the method of the political leaders of the wartime democracy and the fundamental doctrine of new theories of power politics. These theories served to justify the increasing severity of the measures Athens took to terrorize her rebellious subjects. The new spirit in Athens had magnificent achievements to its credit, but it undermined traditional moral convictions. At its roots was a supreme confidence in the human intelligence and a secular view of humanity's position in the universe that is best expressed in the statement of Protagoras, the most famous of the Sophists: "Man is the measure of all things." These shifts in worldview and moral beliefs led to new forms of creativity in art, literature, and thought, although they also caused bitter debates, and sometimes conflicts, between traditionalists and proponents of the new ideas.

THE DECLINE OF THE CITY-STATE

In the last quarter of the fifth century the whole traditional basis of individual conduct, which had been concern for the unity and cohesion of the city-state, was undermined—gradually at first by the critical approach of the Sophists and their pupils, and then rapidly, as the war accelerated the loosening of the old standards. "In peace and prosperity," says Thucydides, "both states and individuals are actuated by higher motives . . . but war, which takes away the comfortable provision of daily life, is a hard master, and tends to assimilate men's characters to their conditions." The war brought to Athens the rule of new politicians who were schooled in the doctrine of power politics and initiated savage reprisals against Athens's rebellious subject allies, launching the city on an expansionist course that ended in disaster in Sicily (413 B.C.E.) and a short-lived oligarchic revolution (411 B.C.E.). Seven years later Athens, her last fleet gone, surrendered to the Spartans. A pro-Spartan antidemocratic regime, the Thirty Tyrants, was installed, but soon overthrown. Athens became a democracy again, but the confidence and unity of its great age were gone forever. Community and individual were no longer one. Yet despite a perceptible retreat into privacy, Athenian democracy continued to work through most of the fourth century, until the conquest of Philip. That same century witnessed, in addition to continued creativity in poetry, painting, and sculpture, two new developments. It saw the flowering of Athenian rhetoric, a legacy of the Sophists and one of Greek culture's greatest contributions to Rome in turn. During the same time, Plato and Aristotle revolutionized philosophy and laid the foundations for later ancient and European philosophical thought. But they had a predecessor in Plato's great teacher, Socrates.

In the wake of their defeat by Sparta, Athenians began to feel more and more exasperation with a voice they had been listening to for many years. This was the voice of

Socrates, a stonemason who for most of his adult life had made it his business to discuss with his fellow citizens such great issues as the nature of justice, of truth, of piety. Unlike the Sophists, he did not lecture nor did he charge a fee: his method was dialectic, a search for truth through questions and answers, and his dedication to his mission had kept him poor. But the initial results of his discussions were often infuriatingly like the results of sophistic teaching. By questions and answers he exposed the illogicality of his opponent's position, but did not often provide a substitute for the belief he had destroyed. Yet it is clear that he did believe in absolute standards and, what is more, believed they could be discovered by a process of logical inquiry and supported by logical proof. His ethics rested on an intellectual basis. The resentment against him, which came to a head in 399 B.C.E., is partly explained by his questioning of the old standards to establish new and by his refusal to let the Athenians live in peace, for he preached that it was every person's duty to think through to the truth. In this last respect he was the prophet of the new age. For him, the city and the accepted code were no substitute for the task of self-examination that each individual must carry through to a conclusion. The characteristic statement of the old Athens was public, in the assembly or the theater; Socrates proclaimed the responsibility of each individual to work out a means to fulfillment and happiness and made clear his distrust of public life: "he who will fight for the right . . . must have a private station and not a public one."

The Athenians sentenced him to death on a charge of impiety. They hoped, no doubt, that he would go into exile to escape execution, but he remained, as he put it himself, at his post, and they were forced to have the sentence carried out. If they thought they were finished with him, they were sadly mistaken. In the next century Athens became the center for a large group of philosophical schools, all of them claiming to develop and interpret the ideas of Socrates.

The century that followed his death saw the exhaustion of the Greek city-states in constant internecine warfare. Politically and economically bankrupt, they fell under the power of Macedon in the north, whose king, Philip, combined a ferocious energy with a cynicism that enabled him to take full advantage of the disunity of the city-states. Greek liberty ended at the battle of Chaeronea in 338 B.C.E., and Philip's son Alexander inherited a powerful army and the political control of all Greece. He led his Macedonian and Greek armies against Persia and, in a few brilliant campaigns became master of an empire that extended into Egypt in the south and to the borders of India in the east. He died at Babylon in 323 B.C.E., and his empire broke up into a number of independent kingdoms ruled by his generals. One of these generals, Ptolemy, founded a Greek dynasty that ruled Egypt until after the Roman conquest and ended only with the death of the famous Cleopatra. The results of Alexander's fantastic achievements were more durable than might have been expected. Into the newly conquered territories came thousands of Greeks who wished to escape from the political futility and economic crisis of the homeland. Wherever they went they took with them their language, their culture, and their typical buildings, the gymnasium and the theater. At Alexandria in Egypt, for example, the Ptolemies formed a Greek library to preserve the texts of Greek literature for the scholars who edited them, a school of Greek poetry flourished, and Greek mathematicians and geographers made new advances in science. The Middle East became, as far as the cities were concerned, a Greek-speaking area; and when, some two or three centuries later, the first accounts of the life and teaching of Jesus of Nazareth were written down, they were written in Greek, the language on which the cultural homogeneity of the whole area was based.

TIME LINE

TEXTS	CONTEXTS
	2200–1450 B.C.E. Minoan civilization flourishes on Crete
	ca. 1450 Mycenaeans from mainland Greece occupy Crete
	ca. 1150 Troy destroyed by the Achaeans
	776 Olympic Games founded in Greece
late 8th century B.C.E. Greek alphabetic scripts	
ca. 700 Homer, *The Iliad, The Odyssey*	
600 Sappho writing her **lyrics** on the island of Lesbos	
	594 Solon reforms laws at Athens, which becomes the world's first democracy (508), and defeats a Persian invasion at Marathon (490)
	490–479 Greece turns back a massive Persian invasion by sea at Salamis and by land at Plataea
458 Aeschylus's dramatic trilogy, *The Oresteia,* produced in Athens	
ca. 441 Sophocles, *Antigone*	
431 Euripides, **Medea**	431–404 Peloponnesian War between Athens and Sparta; Athens surrenders (404)
429–347 Plato, author of **The Apology of Socrates** and *Phaedo*	
426? Sophocles, **Oedipus the King**	
411 Aristophanes, *Lysistrata*	
	399 Trial and execution of Socrates
384–322 Aristotle, author of **Poetics**	
	ca. 385 Plato founds the Academy

Boldface titles indicate works in the anthology.

TIME LINE

TEXTS	CONTEXTS
	ca. 350 Beginnings of Indian epic, *Mahaābhārata* • Shuang-tse founds monist religious philosophy in China • Greek amphitheater built at Epidauros
	338 United Greeks defeated by Philip II of Macedon at Chaeronea
	335 Aristotle founds Peripatetic school of philosophy and lectures in the Lyceum
	334 Alexander of Macedon, Philip's son, conquers Persian empire
	323 Euclid writes *Elements,* the first work of geometry
	307 Library and museum established at Alexandria, Egypt
	148 Macedonia becomes a Roman province
	31 At Actium, Octavian Augustus Caesar defeats Antony and Cleopatra
	ca. 6 Birth of Jesus
	26–36 C.E. Pontius Pilate, Roman governor
	ca. 33 Crucifixion of Jesus
	ca. 35 Conversion of Paul
	47–58 Paul's missionary journeys
	66–70 Jewish revolt against Roman rule; Roman emperor Titus captures Jerusalem
ca. 75 C.E. Luke, Gospels, and Acts of the Apostles	
ca. 80 Matthew, Gospels	

HOMER
eighth century B.C.E.

Greek literature begins with two masterpieces, the *Iliad* and *Odyssey*, which cannot be accurately dated (the conjectural dates range over three centuries) and which are attributed to the poet Homer, about whom nothing is known except his name. The Greeks believed that he was blind, perhaps because the bard Demodocus in the *Odyssey* was blind. Seven different cities put forward claims to be his birthplace. They are all in what the Greeks called Ionia, the western coast of Asia Minor, which was heavily settled by Greek colonists. It does seem likely that he came from this area; the *Iliad* contains several accurate descriptions of natural features of the Ionian landscape, but Homer's grasp of the geography of mainland, especially western, Greece is unsure. But even this is a guess, and all the other stories the Greeks told about him are obvious inventions.

The two great epics that have made his name supreme among poets may have been fixed in something like their present form before the art of writing was in general use in Greece; it is certain that they were intended not for reading but for oral recitation. The earliest stages of their composition date from around the beginnings of Greek literacy—the late eighth century B.C.E. The poems exhibit the unmistakable characteristics of oral composition.

The oral poet had at his disposal not reading and writing but a vast and intricate system of metrical formulas—phrases that would fit in at different places in the line—and a repertoire of standard scenes (the arming of the warrior, the battle of two champions), as well as the known outline of the story. Of course he could and did invent new phrases and scenes as he recited—but his base was the immense poetic reserve created by many generations of singers who lived before him. When he told again for his hearers the old story of Achilles and his wrath, he was re-creating a traditional story that had been recited, with variations, additions, and improvements, by a long line of predecessors. The poem was not, in the modern sense, the poet's creation, still less an expression of his personality. Consequently, there is no trace of individual identity to be found in it; the poet remains as hidden behind the action and speech of his characters as if he were a dramatist.

The *Iliad* and *Odyssey* as we have them, however, are unlike most of the oral literature we know from other times and places. The poetic organization of each of these two epics—the subtle interrelationship of the parts, which creates their structural and emotional unity—has suggested to many that they owe their present form to the shaping hand of a single poet, the architect who selected from the enormous wealth of the oral tradition and fused what he took with original material to create, perhaps with the aid of the new medium of writing, the two magnificently ordered poems known as the *Iliad* and *Odyssey*. Others imagine the texts becoming more and more fixed over centuries of oral performance.

THE ILIAD

Of the two poems the *Iliad* is perhaps the earlier. Its subject is war; its characters are men in battle and women whose fate depends on the outcome. The war is fought by the Achaeans against the Trojans for the recovery of Helen, the wife of the Achaean chieftain Menelaus; the combatants are heroes who engage in individual duels before the supporting lines of infantry and archers. There is no sentimentality in Homer's descriptions of these battles.

> Patrolcus eased up
> Alongside him and shattered his right jaw
> With his spear, driving the point through his teeth,

> Then, gripping the shaft, levered him up
> And over his chariot rail, the way a man
> Sitting on a jutting rock with a fishing rod
> Flips a flounder he has hooked out of the sea.
> So Thestor was prised gaping from his chariot
> And left flat on his face. His soul crawled off.

This is meticulously accurate; there is no attempt to suppress the ugliness of Thestor's death. The bare, careful description creates the true nightmare quality of battle, in which men perform monstrous actions with the same matter-of-fact efficiency they display in their normal occupations, and the simile reproduces the grotesque appearance of violent death—the simple spear thrust takes away Thestor's dignity as a human being even before it takes his life. He is gaping, like a fish on the hook.

The simile also does something else. It glorifies Patroclus. He skewers Thestor and flips him from the chariot as easily as a fisherman lands a fish. Thestor is simply no match for him; his ignominy is Patroclus's honor. This function of the simile is important because, shortly afterward and in the same battle, Patroclus himself will die, killed by Hector (who will later be killed in revenge by Achilles). Patroclus will fall at the height of his exploits and abilities as a warrior; that is how he will be remembered and commemorated in epic poetry like the *Iliad*. This simile, like so many other passages in the poem, displays the two aspects of war: it is destructive but it also calls forth the warriors' highest efforts and achievements. The *Iliad* shows us people constantly faced with death and yet managing to find meaning in that death: their survival in the memory of future generations for what they did. More generally, we see men and women placed in a situation in which violence always threatens to spiral out of control and not only destroy them but also force them to act in ways that de-humanize them. They have to find ways to claim their humanity. The *Iliad* raises profound questions about violence but also faces it directly, without sentimentality, as a basic aspect of human life. After three thousand years, Homer is still one of war's greatest interpreters.

The story of Achilles greatly complicates these issues. The *Iliad* describes the events of a few weeks near the end of the ten-year siege of Troy. The particular subject of the poem, as its first line announces, is the anger of Achilles, the bravest of the Achaean chieftains encamped outside the city. Achilles is a man who comes to live by and for violence. His anger cuts him off from his commander and his fellow princes; to spite them he withdraws from the fighting. He is brought back into it at last by the death of his closest friend, Patroclus; the consequences of his wrath and withdrawal fall heavily on the Achaeans but most heavily on himself.

The great champion of the Trojans, Hector, fights bravely but reluctantly. War, for him, is a necessary evil, and he thinks nostalgically of the peaceful past, though he has little hope of peace to come. His preeminence in peace is emphasized by the tenderness of his relations with his wife and child and also by his kindness to Helen, the cause of the war that he knows in his heart will bring his city to destruction. We see Hector, as we do not see Achilles, against the background of the patterns of civilized life—the rich city with its temples and palaces, the continuity of the family. The duel between these two men is the inevitable crisis of the poem, and just as inevitable is Hector's defeat and death.

At the climactic moment of Hector's death, as everywhere in the poem, Homer's firm control of his material preserves the balance in which our contrary emotions are held; pity for Hector does not entirely rob us of sympathy for Achilles. His brutal words to the dying Hector and the insults he inflicts on Hector's corpse are truly savage, but we are never allowed to forget that this inflexible hatred is the expression of his love for Patroclus. And the final book of the poem shows us an Achilles whose iron heart is moved at last; he is touched by the sight of Hector's father clasping in supplication the terrible hands that have killed so many of his sons. He remembers that he has a father and that he will never see him again; Achilles and Priam, the slayer and the father of the slain, weep together. Achilles gives Hector's body to Priam for honorable burial. His anger has run its full course and been appeased. It has brought death, first to the Achaeans and then to the Trojans, to Patroclus and to Hector, and so to Achilles himself, for his death is fated to come soon after Hector's.

This tragic action is the center of the poem, but it is surrounded by scenes that remind us that the organized destruction of war, though an integral part of human life, is still only a part of it. The yearning for peace and its creative possibilities is never far below the surface. This is most poignantly expressed by the scenes that take place in Troy, especially the farewell between Hector and Andromache, but it is made clear that the Achaeans too are conscious of what they have sacrificed. Early in the poem, when Agamemnon, the Achaean commander, tests the morale of his troops by suggesting that the war be abandoned, they rush for the ships so eagerly and with such heartfelt relief that their commanders are hard put to stop them. These two poles of the human condition—war and peace, with their corresponding aspects of human nature, the destructive and the creative—are implicit in every situation and statement of the poem, and they are put before us, in symbolic form, in the shield that the god Hephaestus makes for Achilles, with its scenes of human life in both peace and war. Whether these two sides of life can ever be integrated, or even reconciled, is a question that the *Iliad* raises but cannot answer.

Yet the poem leaves us with a vision that is not entirely bleak. War puts human values under stress but it also clarifies them, a point made clear especially in the final book. Achilles has killed Priam's son Hector, but because of the grief he feels for Patroclus, he understands and shares Priam's grief. And it is because he knows that he himself will soon die that he can see his father, Peleus, in the aged king of Troy, his enemy.

THE ODYSSEY

The other Homeric epic, the *Odyssey*, is concerned with the peace that followed the war and in particular with the return of the heroes who survived. Its subject is the long, drawn-out return of one of the heroes, Odysseus of Ithaca, who was destined to spend ten years wandering in unknown seas before he returned to his rocky kingdom. When Odysseus' wanderings began, Achilles had already received, at the hands of Apollo, the death that he had chosen. Odysseus struggles for life, and his outstanding quality is a probing and versatile intelligence that, combined with long experience, keeps him safe and alive through the trials and dangers of twenty years of war and seafaring. To stay alive he has to do things that Achilles would never have done and use an ingenuity and experience that Achilles did not possess, but his life is just as much a struggle.

Although Odysseus has become for us the archetypal adventurer, the *Odyssey* gives us a hero whose one goal is to get home. He struggles not simply for his own and his shipmates' personal survival but also to preserve and complete the heroic reputation that he won in war at Troy. It may seem ironic that Odysseus succeeds by concealing his name, as when he tricks the Cyclops by presenting himself as "Nobody," or when, at home on Ithaca, he tricks his wife's suitors by disguising himself as a beggar. But Odysseus's shiftiness, his talent for disguise, deception, and plain lying, is part of his versatility. It complements his strength and courage in battle—qualities he demonstrated at Troy as he will do again when he fights the suitors in his own hall. It makes this complex hero dangerous to his enemies, and sometimes to his friends, as the Phaeacians discover when Poseidon punishes them for helping him.

The adventures on the voyage home test these mental qualities, as well as Odysseus's physical endurance, by tempting him to lapse from the struggle homeward. The Lotus flower offers forgetfulness of home and family. Circe gives him a life of ease and self-indulgence on an enchanted island. In Phaeacia, Odysseus is offered the love of a young princess and her hand in marriage. The Sirens tempt him to live in the memory of the glorious past. Calypso, the goddess with whom he spends seven years, offers him the greatest temptation of all: immortality. In refusing, Odysseus chooses the human condition, with all its struggle, its disappointments, and its inevitable end. And the end, death, is ever-present. But he hangs on tenaciously and, in the midst of his ordeals, he is sent living to the world of the dead to see for himself what death means. Dark and comfortless, Homer's land of the dead is the most frightening picture of the afterlife in European literature. Odysseus talks to the dead, and when he consoles the shade of Achilles with talk of everlasting glory Achilles replies that it is better to be the most insignificant person on Earth than lord of the dead. Here the heroes of the two great epics confront one another over the chasm of death. Through them, the *Odyssey* defines its values by contrast with those of the *Iliad*. Against the dark background of Achilles' regret for life, Odysseus's dedication to life— his acceptance of its limitations and his ability to seize its possibilities—shines out. His death, Tiresias assures him in this same episode, will come late and gently. Odysseus gets both long life and glory; Achilles could have only either one.

The *Odyssey* celebrates return to ordinary life and makes it seem a worthy prize after excitement, toil, and danger. The adventures occupy only four of twenty-four books (or eight if we include Calypso and the Phaeacians). For the entire second half of the poem, Odysseus is back on Ithaca, winning his way, by deceit that only paves the way for force, from the swineherd Eumaeus's hut to the center of his own house. There, and in books I through IV, we see the social disorder on Ithaca that Odysseus's return is to set right. We also see Telemachus, his son, emerging from adolescence and impatient with all that keeps him from assuming a man's role (his mother as well as her suitors). In his aspirations a foil to Odysseus's mature wisdom, he is his father's potential rival, though in the end his willing subordinate. And we see Penelope's dealings with her son, with her suitors, and with the beggar who is really her husband in disguise. Penelope is a challenging figure, because the narrative does not give us full access to her thoughts and motives. But she seems, with a cunning that matches Odysseus's, to keep in balance two contradictory requirements of her situation. First, she has a duty to herself. If Odysseus, absent twenty years now, is lost for good, then she ought to remarry instead of devoting herself to a house without a head (and in Homeric and later Greek culture, a woman as head of a household was unthinkable). More immediately, she seems to take a natural pleasure in being wooed. On the other hand, she has a duty to her former marriage. If she remarries and Odysseus then returns, she will seem to have betrayed him and, in his and society's eyes, she will be classed with those other adulterers Helen and Clytemnestra. In its ambivalence, Penelope's trick of the web (she promised the suitors to choose one of them when she had finished a shroud for Odysseus's father, Laertes, and for three years she unwove each night what she had woven by day) perfectly encapsulates the way she is forced to play loyal wife and available bride at the same time; it is both a delaying tactic and a way of stringing the suitors along. Odysseus evidently interprets the trick simply as an expression of Penelope's faithfulness to him, and so have readers over the ages. But that shows only how Penelope's interests are folded into his at the end, how his restoration to home and authority retrospectively arranges potentially disorderly elements within a patriarchal order. That is not to say that Penelope lacks autonomy or initiative, at least in the shorter term. To a large extent she controls the timing and means of Odysseus's final homecoming (and therefore she controls key stages in the plot of the poem), not only by her famous trick of the marriage bed in book XXIII but also by deciding in book XIX to set the contest of the bow, which will ultimately get a weapon into the beggar's hands (book XXII). Why she does so, after the beggar has assured her that Odysseus is about to return, is one of the poem's mysteries. Has she recognized this beggar as her husband, consciously or not, so that she helps him against the suitors? Does she neither recognize nor believe the beggar, so that she acts in despair? Or is she again calculating probabilities to her best advantage?

The period in which the *Iliad* and the *Odyssey* probably took shape, 750–700 B.C.E. or a little after, saw enormous cultural, political, and social developments in Greece, especially the formation, in many areas, of the *polis,* or "city-state." As often happens, these changes occurred amid sharp conflicts and debates, in which the Homeric epics, publicly performed as they were, must have taken part. Along with the issue of peace and war, for instance, a central conflict of the *Iliad* concerns the nature of political authority. Which has the stronger claim, acknowledged position (Agamemnon) or merit (Achilles)? It is difficult to tell which side wins in the end, if either does, but the poem examines the ramifications of this debate, even while showing, paradoxically, the Greeks maintaining enough unity to destroy a tightly knit and orderly city. The problems of violence and order in this poem are as much political as individual. They involve profound questions about the nature of a political community.

The *Odyssey* offers a more positive meditation on the nature of civilization and of the structures of daily political life as the Greeks experienced it. It does so by showing what a community has to lose by the absence of those structures and to gain by their affirmation, as we see in the contrast between the disorder created by the suitors and Odysseus's restoration of hierarchical and patriarchal order in house and polity. In addition, Odysseus's adventures explore alternatives to "ordinary" (that is, Greek) civilization. Odysseus experiences nature itself as the threatening antithesis to human culture, and he encounters other cultural forms that seem defective or excessive when measured against Ithaca. The richest contrast is provided by the Cyclopes, who lack many of the features of the evolving Greek civilization: houses (they live in caves), agriculture (they are herders), ships for trade and colonization, political integration (their highest political unit is the family), and the key institution of hospitality. (This episode is complex, however, since the Cyclopes enjoy a golden-age existence on which Odysseus intrudes, and Polyphemus has the last word, his curse on Odysseus.) The Laestrygonians are organized as a community and not just by families—they have a ruler and an assembly place—but they share the Cyclopes' unfortunate habit of eating guests. Aeolus, like the Phaeacians, offers Odysseus flawless hospitality, but he lives isolated with his family and marries his daughters to his sons (in contrast to the Greek practice of knitting households together by exchanging women in marriage). Calypso lives in a cave, Circe in a house (she weaves like Penelope), but both live alone. Both are heads of households without husbands, and this, besides the fact that they are sexually threatening to males, makes them "strong" female figures intended to show the need for women's subordination. The Phaeacians, on the other hand, represent an idealized form of "normal" culture but are isolated from other communities and excessively civilized, with no opportunity for heroic achievement. When Odysseus finally is restored to Ithaca, he, and his Greek audience, can appreciate the familiar for having explored alternatives to it in these and many other ways. This self-fashioning by reference to the foreign, which was to have a long history among the Greeks, must have been especially important during this formative period of their culture.

But the *Odyssey* is a much more complex poem than this account suggests, its resolution of issues anything but tidy. One enormous contradiction underlies the final books: Odysseus restores order by killing men from his own community, within his house, and he is prepared to prolong internal warfare by killing the suitors' relatives in the final book. In fact, this struggle recapitulates the Trojan War and resembles the dispute between Achilles and Agamemnon in book I of the *Iliad.* In all three cases, men compete for honor over a woman. What is more, Odysseus kills the suitors within his own house, which should be exempt from competition and conflict, as the

Odyssey's many scenes of feasting in this same hall show. The *Odyssey* is no more successful than the *Iliad*, then, in resolving the problem of violence. Both poems leave us with questions. How can human aggression be controlled, if not eliminated? Can violence within the community be channeled into safe, perhaps even socially creative, forms? Can it be successfully controlled by being turned outward, against other communities? If so, does that justify the human suffering and waste that external wars cause? And what about the more refined forms of violence at the heart of social hierarchies that create asymmetries of gender and class? Such are the issues raised by the epics amid the formation of the polis, which was to lead, through a long process, to the modern state. Thousands of years later, we cannot claim to have solved them.

NOTE ON THESE TRANSLATIONS

By re-creating the *Iliad* as a war poem in English, Stanley Lombardo has been faithful to what the *Iliad* essentially is. Using a spare language that attempts to reproduce the rhythms and idioms of ordinary spoken English, he gets the essential meanings of the Greek into a flexible line of four or five beats. In this way, he conveys Homer's rapidity and flow, as well as the range of his narrative: the anger of the quarrel between Achilles and Agamemnon (book I), the excitement and pathos of the battle scenes, the tenderness of Hector's scene with Andromache (book VI), the savagery of Hector's death (book XXII), and the sorrowing pity that Achilles and Priam feel in the poem's final book. His language shows a corresponding wide variety of registers, from the fairly standard and perhaps somewhat literary diction at moments of high intensity to informal, and even occasionally colloquial, English in circumstances that seem to call for plain speaking (for example, the speech of soldiers on the battlefield). He takes an equally flexible approach to Homer's highly formulaic language; whereas Homer repeats phrases, lines, and groups of lines with few or no changes, Lombardo usually varies his translations of them to bring out different meanings according to context. But whenever it matters that the same formula is used in different places, the reader can rely on him to convey that faithfully. Lombardo has also found a unique way to convey the effect of one of Homer's most wonderful devices, his many similes—for example, extended comparisons of warriors in battle to animals (for example, lions) stalking and killing their prey. These similes can do many things, but what they have in common is that they interrupt the action, drawing the reader or listener out of the immediate situation and relating it to typical events in the world beyond the battlefield. Lombardo reproduces this effect of interruption, of fading out from and back into the action of the poem, by printing the similes in italics. In all these ways, Lombardo gives us an *Iliad* that is immediately accessible to modern readers *and* puts them firmly in touch with Homer's world and his poetry.

Robert Fagles's *Odyssey* in its own way creates for English readers the excitement, suspense, and deep emotion of this poem about a homecoming and its difficulties. Fagles translates into an English that is recognizably literary: a little more formal than day-to-day language but always as readable and clear in its meanings. He uses a somewhat longer line than Lombardo (five or six beats), occasionally with longer lines to slow the pace for emphasis or weight, and a shorter line here and there for particular emphasis. Like Lombardo, he varies his translations of formulas according to context. He uses this method especially with epithets and lines introducing speeches; by contrast, there is little variation in his translation of typical scenes (such as feasting, setting sail, going to bed), so that the reader gets a full sense of recurring action. Fagles's style of translating is an excellent match for the depth and sophistication of the *Odyssey*'s narrative.

Both of these translations succeed as English poems and as versions of Homer. They superbly meet the challenge of rendering poetry that was orally performed (if not orally composed) into a written medium. To see how good they are, read them— not just silently, but out loud.

PRONOUNCING GLOSSARY

The following list uses common English syllables and stress accents to provide rough equivalents of selected words whose pronunciation may be unfamiliar to the general reader.

Achaeans: *a-kee'-anz / a-kai'-ans*

Achelous: *a-ke-loh'-us*

Achilles: *a-kil'-eez*

Aeantes: *ee-an'-teez / ai-an'-teez*

Aepea: *ee-pee'-a / ai-pay'-a*

Alcinous: *al-sin'-oh-uhs / al-kin'-oh-uhs*

Andromache: *an-dro'-ma-kee*

Atreus: *ay'-tree-uhs / ay'-troos*

Atrides: *a-trai'-deez / ah'-tri-deez*

Caeneus: *seen'-yoos / cai'-nyoos*

Chiron: *kai'-ron / ki'-ron*

Chryseis *krai-se'-is / kri-say'-is*

Chryses: *krai'-seez / Kri'-seez*

Circe: *ser'-see / keer-kay*

Danaans: *da'-nay-unz*

Deiphobus: *dee-i'-foh-bus / day-i'-foh-bus*

Demodocus: *de-mo'-do-kuhs*

Eetion: *ee-e'-tee-on*

Eurystheus: *yoo-ris'-thyoos*

Glaucus: *glow'-kus*

Helios: *hee'-lee-os / hay'-lee-os*

Hephaestus: *he-fess'-tus / hay-fais'-tus*

Hermes: *her'-meez*

Idaeus: *ai-dee'-us / i-dai'us*

Scyros: *skai'-ros / ski'-ros*

Smintheus: *smin'-thyoos*

Telemachus: *te-le'-ma-kus*

Idomeneus: *i-do'-men-yoos*

Laertes: *lay-er'-teez*

Laodice: *lay-o'-di-see / lay-o'-di-kay*

Laothoë: *lay-o'-thoh-ee*

Menelaus: *me-ne-lay'-us / me-ne-lah'-us*

Myrmidons: *mer'-mi-donz*

Mysians: *mee'-shunz / mi'-see-unz*

Nausicaa: *naw-si'-kay-ah / now-si'-ka-ah*

Odysseus: *oh-dis'-yoos*

Oeneus: *een'-yoos / oi'-nyoos*

Orestes: *o-res'-teez*

Panthous: *pan'-tho-us*

Patroclus: *pa-troh'-klus*

Peleus: *peel'-yoos*

Phaeacians: *fee-ay'-shunz / fai-ah'-ki-ans*

Pherae: *fee'-ree / fay'-rai*

Phoebus: *fee'-bus / foy'-bus*

Phthia: *fthai'-uh / fthee'-uh*

Polyphemus: *po-li-fee'-mus*

Pirithous: *pai-ri'-tho-us / pi-ri'-thoh-us*

Priam: *prai'-am*

Sarpedon: *sar-pee'-don*

Scaean: *see'-an / skai'-an*

Scylla: *si'-lah / skil'-ah*

Theseus: *thee'-see-uhs/thee'-syoos*

Xanthus: *zan'-thus/ksan'-thus*

The Iliad[1]

BOOK I

[The Rage of Achilles]

Rage:
        Sing; Goddess,[2] Achilles' rage,
Black and murderous, that cost the Greeks
Incalculable pain, pitched countless souls
Of heroes into Hades' dark,
And left their bodies to rot as feasts   5
For dogs and birds, as Zeus' will was done.
    Begin with the clash between Agamemnon—
The Greek warlord—and godlike Achilles.

Which of the immortals set these two
At each other's throats?
                     Apollo,   10
Zeus' son and Leto's, offended
By the warlord. Agamemnon had dishonored
Chryses,[3] Apollo's priest, so the god
Struck the Greek camp with plague,
And the soldiers were dying of it.
                        Chryses   15
Had come to the Greek beachhead camp
Hauling a fortune for his daughter's ransom.
Displaying Apollo's sacral ribbons
On a golden staff, he made a formal plea
To the entire Greek army, but especially   20
The commanders, Atreus' two sons:

"Sons of Atreus and Greek heroes all:
May the gods on Olympus grant you plunder
Of Priam's city[4] and a safe return home.
But give me my daughter back and accept   25
This ransom out of respect for Zeus' son,
Lord Apollo, who deals death from afar."

A murmur rippled through the ranks:
"Respect the priest and take the ransom."
But Agamemnon was not pleased   30
And dismissed Chryses with a rough speech:

"Don't let me ever catch you, old man, by these ships again,
Skulking around now or sneaking back later.
The god's staff and ribbons won't save you next time.
The girl is mine, and she'll be an old woman in Argos[5]   35

---

1. Translated by Stanley Lombardo.   2. The Muse, inspiration for epic poetry.   3. Chryses is from the town of Chryse near Troy. The Greeks had captured his daughter when they sacked Thebes (see line 17) and had given her to Agamemnon as his share of the booty.   4. Troy; Priam is its king. Olympus is the mountain in northern Greece that was supposed to be the home of the gods.   5. Agamemnon's home in the northeastern Peloponnesus, the southern part of mainland Greece.

Before I let her go, working the loom in my house
And coming to my bed, far from her homeland.
Now clear out of here before you make me angry!"

The old man was afraid and did as he was told.
He walked in silence along the whispering surf line,   40
And when he had gone some distance the priest
Prayed to Lord Apollo, son of silken-haired Leto:

"Hear me, Silverbow, Protector of Chryse,
Lord of Holy Cilla, Master of Tenedos,[6]
And Sminthian[7] God of Plague!   45
If ever I've built a temple that pleased you
Or burnt fat thighbones of bulls and goats[8]—
    Grant me this prayer:
Let the Danaans[9] pay for my tears with your arrows!"

Apollo heard his prayer and descended Olympus' crags   50
Pulsing with fury, bow slung over one shoulder,
The arrows rattling in their case on his back
As the angry god moved like night down the mountain.

He settled near the ships and let loose an arrow.
Reverberation from his silver bow hung in the air.   55
He picked off the pack animals first, and the lean hounds,
But then aimed his needle-tipped arrows at the men
And shot until the death-fires crowded the beach.

    Nine days the god's arrows rained death on the camp.
On the tenth day Achilles called an assembly.   60
Hera,[1] the white-armed goddess, planted the thought in him
Because she cared for the Greeks and it pained her
To see them dying. When the troops had all mustered,
Up stood the great runner Achilles, and said:

"Well, Agamemnon, it looks as if we'd better give up   65
And sail home—assuming any of us are left alive—
If we have to fight both the war and this plague.
But why not consult some prophet or priest
Or a dream interpreter, since dreams too come from Zeus,
Who could tell us why Apollo is so angry,   70
If it's for a vow or a sacrifice he holds us at fault.
Maybe he'd be willing to lift this plague from us
If he savored the smoke from lambs and prime goats."

Achilles had his say and sat down. Then up rose
Calchas, son of Thestor, bird-reader supreme,   75
Who knew what is, what will be, and what has been.

6. An island off the Trojan coast. Like Chryse, Cilla is a town near Troy.   7. A cult epithet of Apollo,
probably a reference to his role as the destroyer of field mice (the Greek *sminthos* means "mouse").   8.
In sacrifice to Apollo.   9. The Greeks. Homer also calls them Achaeans and Argives.   1. Sister and
wife of Zeus; she was hostile to the Trojans and therefore favored the Greeks.

He had guided the Greek ships to Troy
Through the prophetic power Apollo
Had given him, and he spoke out now:

"Achilles, beloved of Zeus, you want me to tell you   80
About the rage of Lord Apollo, the Arch-Destroyer.
And I will tell you. But you have to promise me and swear
You will support me and protect me in word and deed.
I have a feeling I might offend a person of some authority
Among the Greeks, and you know how it is when a king   85
Is angry with an underling. He might swallow his temper
For a day, but he holds it in his heart until later
And it all comes out. Will you guarantee my security?"

Achilles, the great runner, responded:

"Don't worry. Prophesy to the best of your knowledge.   90
I swear by Apollo, to whom you pray when you reveal
The gods' secrets to the Greeks, Calchas, that while I live
And look upon this earth, no one will lay a hand
On you here beside these hollow ships, no, not even
Agamemnon, who boasts he is the best of the Achaeans."   95

And Calchas, the perfect prophet, taking courage:

"The god finds no fault with vow or sacrifice.
It is for his priest, whom Agamemnon dishonored
And would not allow to ransom his daughter,
That Apollo deals and will deal death from afar.   100
He will not lift this foul plague from the Greeks
Until we return the dancing-eyed girl to her father
Unransomed, unbought, and make formal sacrifice
On Chryse. Only then might we appease the god."

He finished speaking and sat down. Then up rose   105
Atreus' son, the warlord Agamemnon,
Furious, anger like twin black thunderheads seething
In his lungs, and his eyes flickered with fire
As he looked Calchas up and down, and said:

                                        "You damn soothsayer!   110
You've never given me a good omen yet.
You take some kind of perverse pleasure in prophesying
Doom, don't you? Not a single favorable omen ever!
Nothing good ever happens! And now you stand here
Uttering oracles before the Greeks, telling us   115
That your great ballistic god is giving us all this trouble
Because I was unwilling to accept the ransom
For Chryses' daughter but preferred instead to keep her
In my tent! And why shouldn't I? I like her better than
My wife Clytemnestra. She's no worse than her   120
When it comes to looks, body, mind, or ability.

Still, I'll give her back, if that's what's best.
I don't want to see the army destroyed like this.
But I want another prize ready for me right away.
I'm not going to be the only Greek without a prize,   125
It wouldn't be right. And you all see where mine is going."

And Achilles, strong, swift, and godlike:

"And where do you think, son of Atreus,
You greedy glory-hound, the magnanimous Greeks
Are going to get another prize for you?   130
Do you think we have some kind of stockpile in reserve?
Every town in the area has been sacked and the stuff all divided.
You want the men to count it all back and redistribute it?
All right, you give the girl back to the god. The army
Will repay you three and four times over—when and if   135
Zeus allows us to rip Troy down to its foundations."

The warlord Agamemnon responded:

"You may be a good man in a fight, Achilles,
And look like a god, but don't try to put one over on me—
It won't work. So while you have your prize,   140
You want me to sit tight and do without?
Give the girl back, just like that? Now maybe
If the army, in a generous spirit, voted me
Some suitable prize of their own choice, something fair—
But if it doesn't, I'll just go take something myself,   145
Your prize perhaps, or Ajax's, or Odysseus',[2]
And whoever she belongs to, it'll stick in his throat.

But we can think about that later.
                                    Right now we launch
A black ship on the bright salt water, get a crew aboard,
Load on a hundred bulls, and have Chryseis[3] board her too,   150
My girl with her lovely cheeks. And we'll want a good man
For captain, Ajax or Idomeneus[4] or godlike Odysseus—
Or maybe you, son of Peleus, our most formidable hero—
To offer sacrifice and appease the Arch-Destroyer for us."

Achilles looked him up and down and said: 155

"You shameless, profiteering excuse for a commander!
How are you going to get any Greek warrior
To follow you into battle again? You know,
I don't have any quarrel with the Trojans,
They didn't do anything to *me* to make me   160
Come over here and fight, didn't run off *my* cattle or horses
Or ruin *my* farmland back home in Phthia,[5] not with all

2. Odysseus was the most crafty of the Greeks. Ajax, son of Telamon, was the bravest of the Greeks after
Achilles.   3. Daughter of Chryses.   4. King of Crete and a prominent leader on the Greek side.
5. Achilles' home in northern Greece.

The shadowy mountains and moaning seas between.
It's for *you*, dogface, for your precious pleasure—
And Menelaus'[6] honor—that we came here,   165
A fact you don't have the decency even to mention!
And now you're threatening to take away the prize
That I sweated for and the Greeks gave me.
I never get a prize equal to yours when the army
Captures one of the Trojan strongholds.   170
No, I do all the dirty work with my own hands,
And when the battle's over and we divide the loot
You get the lion's share and I go back to the ships
With some pitiful little thing, so worn out from fighting
I don't have the strength left even to complain.   175
Well, I'm going back to Phthia now. Far better
To head home with my curved ships than stay here,
Unhonored myself and piling up a fortune for you."

The warlord Agamemnon responded:

"Go ahead and desert, if that's what you want!   180
I'm not going to beg you to stay. There are plenty of others
Who will honor me, not least of all Zeus the Counselor.
To me, you're the most hateful king under heaven,
A born troublemaker. You actually *like* fighting and war.
If you're all that strong, it's just a gift from some god.   185
So why don't you go home with your ships and lord it over
Your precious Myrmidons.[7] I couldn't care less about you
Or your famous temper. But I'll tell you this:
Since Phoebus Apollo is taking away my Chryseis,
Whom I'm sending back aboard ship with my friends,   190
I'm coming to your hut and taking Briseis,[8]
Your own beautiful prize, so that you will see just how much
Stronger I am than you, and the next person will wince
At the thought of opposing me as an equal."

Achilles' chest was a rough knot of pain   195
Twisting around his heart: should he
Draw the sharp sword that hung by his thigh,
Scatter the ranks and gut Agamemnon,
Or control his temper, repress his rage?
He was mulling it over, inching the great sword   200
From its sheath, when out of the blue
Athena[9] came, sent by the white-armed goddess
Hera, who loved and watched over both men.
She stood behind Achilles and grabbed his sandy hair,
Visible only to him: not another soul saw her.   205
Awestruck, Achilles turned around, recognizing

6. Agamemnon's brother. The aim of the expedition against Troy was to recover his wife, Helen, who had run off with Paris, a son of Priam.   7. The contingent led by Achilles.   8. A captive woman who had been awarded to Achilles.   9. A goddess, daughter of Zeus, and a patron of human ingenuity and resourcefulness, whether exemplified by handicrafts (such as carpentry or weaving) or cunning in dealing with others. One of her epithets is Pallas. Like Hera, she sided with the Greeks in the war.

Pallas Athena at once—it was her eyes—
And words flew from his mouth like winging birds:

"Daughter of Zeus! Why have you come here?
To see Agamemnon's arrogance, no doubt.   210
I'll tell you where I place my bets, Goddess:
Sudden death for this outrageous behavior."

Athena's eyes glared through the sea's salt haze.

"I came to see if I could check this temper of yours,
Sent from heaven by the white-armed goddess   215
Hera, who loves and watches over both of you men.
Now come on, drop this quarrel, don't draw your sword.
Tell him off instead. And I'll tell you,
Achilles, how things will be: You're going to get
Three times as many magnificent gifts   220
Because of his arrogance. Just listen to us and be patient."

Achilles, the great runner, responded:

"When you two speak, Goddess, a man has to listen
No matter how angry. It's better that way.
Obey the gods and they hear you when you pray."   225

With that he ground his heavy hand
Onto the silver hilt and pushed the great sword
Back into its sheath. Athena's speech
Had been well-timed. She was on her way
To Olympus by now, to the halls of Zeus   230
And the other immortals, while Achilles
Tore into Agamemnon again:

                    "You bloated drunk,
With a dog's eyes and a rabbit's heart!
You've never had the guts to buckle on armor in battle
Or come out with the best fighting Greeks   235
On any campaign! Afraid to look Death in the eye,
Agamemnon? It's far more profitable
To hang back in the army's rear—isn't it?—
Confiscating prizes from any Greek who talks back
And bleeding your people dry. There's not a real man   240
Under your command, or this latest atrocity
Would be your last, son of Atreus.
Now get this straight. I swear a formal oath:
   By this scepter,[1] which will never sprout leaf
Or branch again since it was cut from its stock   245
In the mountains, which will bloom no more
Now that bronze has pared off leaf and bark,

---

1. A wooden staff that symbolized authority. It was handed by a herald to whichever leader rose to speak
in an assembly as a sign of his authority to speak.

And which now the sons of the Greeks hold in their hands
At council, upholding Zeus' laws—
                  By this scepter I swear:
When every last Greek desperately misses Achilles,   250
Your remorse won't do any good then,
When Hector[2] the man-killer swats you down like flies.
And you will eat your heart out
Because you failed to honor the best Greek of all."

Those were his words, and he slammed the scepter,   255
Studded with gold, to the ground and sat down.

Opposite him, Agamemnon fumed.
                    Then Nestor
Stood up, sweet-worded Nestor, the orator from Pylos[3]
With a voice high-toned and liquid as honey.
He had seen two generations of men pass away   260
In sandy Pylos and was now king in the third.
He was full of good will in the speech he made:

"It's a sad day for Greece, a sad day.
Priam and Priam's sons would be happy indeed,
And the rest of the Trojans too, glad in their hearts,   265
If they learned all this about you two fighting,
Our two best men in council and in battle.
Now you listen to me, both of you. You are both
Younger than I am, and I've associated with men
Better than you, and they didn't treat me lightly.   270
I've never seen men like those, and never will,
The likes of Peirithous and Dryas, a shepherd to his people,
Caineus and Exadius and godlike Polyphemus,
And Aegeus' son, Theseus,[4] who could have passed for a god,
The strongest men who ever lived on earth, the strongest,   275
And they fought with the strongest, with wild things
From the mountains, and beat the daylights out of them.
I was their companion, although I came from Pylos,
From the ends of the earth—they sent for me themselves.
And I held my own fighting with them. You couldn't find   280
A mortal on earth who could fight with them now.
And when I talked in council, they took my advice.
So should you two now: taking advice is a good thing.
    Agamemnon, for all your nobility, don't take his girl.
Leave her be: the army originally gave her to him as a prize.   285
Nor should you, son of Peleus, want to lock horns with a king.
A scepter-holding king has honor beyond the rest of men,
Power and glory given by Zeus himself.
You are stronger, and it is a goddess[5] who bore you.

2. Son of Priam; he was the foremost warrior among the Trojans.   3. A territory on the western shore of
the Peloponnesus.   4. Heroes of an earlier generation. Except for the Athenian Theseus, these are the
Lapiths from Thessaly in northern Greece. At the wedding of Peirithous, the mountain-dwelling centaurs
(half human, half horse) got drunk and tried to rape the women who were present. The Lapiths killed them
after a fierce fight.   5. The sea nymph Thetis, who was married to the mortal Peleus (Achilles' father).
She later left him and went to live with her father, Nereus, in the depths of the Aegean Sea.

But he is more powerful, since he rules over more.   290
Son of Atreus, cease your anger. And I appeal
Personally to Achilles to control his temper, since he is,
For all Greeks, a mighty bulwark in this evil war."

And Agamemnon, the warlord:

"Yes, old man, everything you've said is absolutely right.   295
But this man wants to be ahead of everyone else,
He wants to rule everyone, give orders to everyone,
Lord it over everyone, and he's not going to get away with it.
If the gods eternal made him a spearman, does that mean
They gave him permission to be insolent as well?"   300

And Achilles, breaking in on him:

"Ha, and think of the names people would call me
If I bowed and scraped every time you opened your mouth.
Try that on somebody else, but not on me.
I'll tell you this, and you can stick it in your gut: 305
I'm not going to put up a fight on account of the girl.
You, all of you, gave her and you can all take her back.
But anything else of mine in my black sailing ship
You keep your goddamn hands off, you hear?
Try it. Let everybody here see how fast   310
Your black blood boils up around my spear."

     So it was a stand-off, their battle of words,
And the assembly beside the Greek ships dissolved.
Achilles went back to the huts by his ships
With Patroclus[6] and his men. Agamemnon had a fast ship   315
Hauled down to the sea, picked twenty oarsmen,
Loaded on a hundred bulls due to the god, and had Chryses' daughter,
His fair-cheeked girl, go aboard also. Odysseus captained,
And when they were all on board, the ship headed out to sea.

Onshore, Agamemnon ordered a purification.   320
The troops scrubbed down and poured the filth
Into the sea. Then they sacrificed to Apollo
Oxen and goats by the hundreds on the barren shore.
The smoky savor swirled up to the sky.

That was the order of the day. But Agamemnon   325
Did not forget his spiteful threat against Achilles.
He summoned Talthybius and Eurybates,
Faithful retainers who served as his heralds:

"Go to the hut of Achilles, son of Peleus;
Bring back the girl, fair-cheeked Briseis.   330
If he won't give her up, I'll come myself
With my men and take her—and freeze his heart cold."

6. Achilles' closest friend.

It was not the sort of mission a herald would relish.
The pair trailed along the barren seashore
Until they came to the Myrmidons' ships and encampment.   335
They found Achilles sitting outside his hut
Beside his black ship. He was not glad to see them.
They stood respectfully silent, in awe of this king,
And it was Achilles who was moved to address them first:

"Welcome, heralds, the gods' messengers and men's.   340
Come closer. You're not to blame, Agamemnon is,
Who sent you here for the girl, Briseis.
                                        Patroclus,
Bring the girl out and give her to these gentlemen.
You two are witnesses before the blessed gods,
Before mortal men and that hard-hearted king,   345
If ever I'm needed to protect the others
From being hacked to bits. His mind is murky with anger,
And he doesn't have the sense to look ahead and behind
To see how the Greeks might defend their ships."

Thus Achilles.
                    Patroclus obeyed his beloved friend   350
And brought Briseis, cheeks flushed, out of the tent
And gave her to the heralds, who led her away.
She went unwillingly.
                        Then Achilles, in tears,
Withdrew from his friends and sat down far away
On the foaming white seashore, staring out   355
At the endless sea. Stretching out his hands,
He prayed over and over to his beloved mother:

"Mother, since you bore me for a short life only,
Olympian Zeus was supposed to grant me honor.
Well, he hasn't given me any at all. Agamemnon   360
Has taken away my prize and dishonored me."

His voice, choked with tears, was heard by his mother
As she sat in the sea-depths beside her old father.
She rose up from the white-capped sea like a mist,
And settling herself beside her weeping child   365
She stroked him with her hand and talked to him:

"Why are you crying, son? What's wrong?
Don't keep it inside. Tell me so we'll both know."

And Achilles, with a deep groan:

"You already know. Why do I have to tell you?
We went after Thebes, Eëtion's[7] sacred town,
Sacked it and brought the plunder back here.   370
The army divided everything up and chose

---

7. King of the Cilicians in Asia Minor and father of Hector's wife, Andromache. Thebes (or Thebe) was
the Cilicians' capital city, not the Greek or Egyptian city of the same name.

For Agamemnon fair-cheeked Chryseis.
Then her father, Chryses, a priest of Apollo,
Came to our army's ships on the beachhead,
Hauling a fortune for his daughter's ransom.   375
He displayed Apollo's sacral ribbons
On a golden staff and made a formal plea
To the entire Greek army, but especially
The commanders, Atreus' two sons.
You could hear the troops murmuring,   380
'Respect the priest and take the ransom.'
But Agamemnon wouldn't hear of it
And dismissed Chryses with a rough speech.
The old man went back angry, and Apollo
Heard his beloved priest's prayer.   385
He hit the Greeks hard, and the troops
Were falling over dead, the god's arrows
Raining down all through the Greek camp.
A prophet told us the Arch-Destroyer's will,
And I demanded the god be appeased.   390
Agamemnon got angry, stood up
And threatened me, and made good his threat.
The high command sent the girl on a fast ship
Back to Chryse with gifts for Apollo,
And heralds led away my girl, Briseis,   395
Whom the army had given to me.
Now you have to help me, if you can.
   Go to Olympus
And call in the debt that Zeus owes you.
I remember often hearing you tell   400
In my father's house how you alone managed,
Of all the immortals, to save Zeus' neck
When the other Olympians wanted to bind him—
Hera and Poseidon[8] and Pallas Athena.
You came and loosened him from his chains,   405
And you lured to Olympus' summit the giant
With a hundred hands whom the gods call
Briareus but men call Aegaeon, stronger
Even than his own father Uranus,[9] and he
Sat hulking in front of cloud-black Zeus,   410
Proud of his prowess, and scared all the gods
Who were trying to put the son of Cronus in chains.
   Remind Zeus of this, sit holding his knees,
See if he is willing to help the Trojans
Hem the Greeks in between the fleet and the sea.   420
Once they start being killed, the Greeks may
Appreciate Agamemnon for what he is,
And the wide-ruling son of Atreus will see
What a fool he's been because he did not honor
The best of all the fighting Achaeans."   425

And Thetis, now weeping herself:

8. Brother of Zeus and god of the sea.   9. The Sky, husband of Earth and the first divine ruler. He was
overthrown by his son Cronus, who in turn was overthrown by his son Zeus.

"O my poor child. I bore you for sorrow,
Nursed you for grief. Why? You should be
Spending your time here by your ships
Happily and untroubled by tears,   430
Since life is short for you, all too brief.
Now you're destined for both an early death
And misery beyond compare. It was for this
I gave birth to you in your father's palace
Under an evil star.

                I'll go to snow-bound Olympus   435
And tell all this to the Lord of Lightning.
I hope he listens. You stay here, though,
Beside your ships and let the Greeks feel
Your spite; withdraw completely from the war.
Zeus left yesterday for the River Ocean   440
On his way to a feast with the Ethiopians.[1]
All the gods went with him. He'll return
To Olympus twelve days from now,
And I'll go then to his bronze threshold
And plead with him. I think I'll persuade him."

And she left him there, angry and heartsick   445
At being forced to give up the silken-waisted girl.

    Meanwhile, Odysseus was putting in
At Chryse with his sacred cargo on board.
When they were well within the deepwater harbor
They furled the sail and stowed it in the ship's hold,   450
Slackened the forestays and lowered the mast,
Working quickly, then rowed her to a mooring, where
They dropped anchor and made the stern cables fast.
The crew disembarked on the seabeach
And unloaded the bulls for Apollo the Archer.   455
Then Chryses' daughter stepped off the seagoing vessel,
And Odysseus led her to an altar
And placed her in her father's hands, saying:

"Chryses, King Agamemnon has sent me here
To return your child and offer to Phoebus   460
Formal sacrifice on behalf of the Greeks.
So may we appease Lord Apollo, and may he
Lift the afflictions he has sent upon us."

Chryses received his daughter tenderly.

Moving quickly, they lined the hundred oxen   465
Round the massive altar, a glorious offering,
Washed their hands and sprinkled on the victims
Sacrificial barley. On behalf of the Greeks
Chryses lifted his hands and prayed aloud:

---

1. A people believed to live at the extreme edges of the world. The ocean was thought of as a river that
encircled the earth.

"Hear me, Silverbow, Protector of Chryse,   470
Lord of Holy Cilla, Master of Tenedos,
As once before you heard my prayer,
Did me honor, and smote the Greeks mightily,
So now also grant me this prayer:
                              Lift the plague
From the Greeks and save them from death."   475

Thus the old priest, and Apollo heard him.

After the prayers and the strewing of barley
They slaughtered and flayed the oxen,
Jointed the thighbones and wrapped them
In a layer of fat with cuts of meat on top.
The old man roasted them over charcoal   480
And doused them with wine. Younger men
Stood by with five-tined forks in their hands.
When the thigh pieces were charred and they had
Tasted the tripe, they cut the rest into strips,   485
Skewered it on spits and roasted it skillfully.
When they were done and the feast was ready,
Feast they did, and no one lacked an equal share.
When they had all had enough to eat and drink,
The young men topped off mixing bowls with wine   490
And served it in goblets to all the guests.
All day long these young Greeks propitiated
The god with dancing, singing to Apollo
A paean[2] as they danced, and the god was pleased.
When the sun went down and darkness came on,   495
They went to sleep by the ship's stern-cables.

Dawn came early, a palmetto of rose,
Time to make sail for the wide beachhead camp.
They set up mast and spread the white canvas,
And the following wind, sent by Apollo,   500
Boomed in the mainsail. An indigo wave
Hissed off the bow as the ship surged on,
Leaving a wake as she held on course through the billows.
When they reached the beachhead they hauled the black ship
High on the sand and jammed in the long chocks;   505
Then the crew scattered to their own huts and ships.

All this time Achilles, the son of Peleus in the line of Zeus,[3]
Nursed his anger, the great runner idle by his fleet's fast hulls.
He was not to be seen in council, that arena for glory,
Nor in combat. He sat tight in camp consumed with grief,   510
His great heart yearning for the battle cry and war.

   Twelve days went by. Dawn.
The gods returned to Olympus,
Zeus at their head.

2. A song of praise to Apollo.   3. Peleus was the son of Aeacus, son of Zeus.

Thetis did not forget
Her son's requests. She rose from the sea   515
And up through the air to the great sky
And found Cronus' wide-seeing son
Sitting in isolation on the highest peak
Of the rugged Olympic massif.
She settled beside him, and touched his knees   520
With her left hand, his beard with her right,[4]
And made her plea to the Lord of Sky:

"Father Zeus, if I have ever helped you
In word or deed among the immortals,
    Grant me this prayer: 525
Honor my son, doomed to die young
And yet dishonored by King Agamemnon,
Who stole his prize, a personal affront.
Do justice by him, Lord of Olympus.
Give the Trojans the upper hand until the Greeks   530
Grant my son the honor he deserves."

Zeus made no reply but sat a long time
In silence, clouds scudding around him.
Thetis held fast to his knees and asked again:

"Give me a clear yes or no. Either nod in assent   535
Or refuse me. Why should you care if I know
How negligible a goddess I am in your eyes."

This provoked a troubled, gloomy response:

"This is disastrous. You're going to force me
Into conflict with Hera. I can just hear her now,   540
Cursing me and bawling me out. As it is,
She already accuses me of favoring the Trojans.
Please go back the way you came. Maybe
Hera won't notice. I'll take care of this.
And so you can have some peace of mind,   545
I'll say yes to you by nodding my head,
The ultimate pledge. Unambiguous,
Irreversible, and absolutely fulfilled,
Whatever I say yes to with a nod of my head."

And the Son of Cronus nodded. Black brows   550
Lowered, a glory of hair cascaded down from the Lord's
Immortal head, and the holy mountain trembled.

    Their conference over, the two parted. The goddess
Dove into the deep sea from Olympus' snow-glare
And Zeus went to his home. The gods all   555

---

4. She takes on the posture of the suppliant, which physically emphasizes the desperation and urgency of
her request. Zeus was, above all other gods, the protector of suppliants.

Rose from their seats at their father's entrance. Not one
Dared watch him enter without standing to greet him.
And so the god entered and took his high seat.
                                          But Hera
Had noticed his private conversation with Thetis,
The silver-footed daughter of the Old Man of the Sea,   560
And flew at him with cutting words:

"Who was that you were scheming with just now?
You just love devising secret plots behind my back,
Don't you? You can't bear to tell me what you're thinking,
Or you don't dare. Never have and never will."   565

The Father of Gods and Men answered:

"Hera, don't hope to know all my secret thoughts.
It would strain your mind even though you are my wife.
What it is proper to hear, no one, human or divine,
Will hear before you. But what I wish to conceive   570
Apart from the other gods, don't pry into that."

And Lady Hera, with her oxen eyes wide:

"Oh my. The awesome son of Cronus has spoken.
Pry? You know that I never pry. And you always
Cheerfully volunteer—whatever information you please.   575
It's just that I have this feeling that somehow
The silver-footed daughter of the Old Man of the Sea
May have won you over. She *was* sitting beside you
Up there in the mists, and she did touch your knees.
And I'm pretty sure that you agreed to honor Achilles   580
And destroy Greeks by the thousands beside their ships."

And Zeus, the master of cloud and storm:

"You witch! Your intuitions are always right.
But what does it get you? Nothing, except that
I like you less than ever. And so you're worse off.   585
If it's as you think it is, it's my business, not yours.
So sit down and shut up and do as I say.
You see these hands? All the gods on Olympus
Won't be able to help you if I ever lay them on you."

Hera lost her nerve when she heard this.   590
She sat down in silence, fear cramping her heart,
And gloom settled over the gods in Zeus' hall.
Hephaestus,[5] the master artisan, broke the silence,
Out of concern for his ivory-armed mother:

---

5. The lame god of fire and the patron of craftspeople, especially metalworkers.

"This is terrible; it's going to ruin us all.   595
If you two quarrel like this over mortals
It's bound to affect us gods. There'll be no more
Pleasure in our feasts if we let things turn ugly.
Mother, please, I don't have to tell you,
You have to be pleasant to our father Zeus   600
So he won't be angry and ruin our feast.
If the Lord of Lightning want to blast us from our seats,
He can—that's how much stronger he is.
So apologize to him with silken-soft words,
And the Olympian in turn will be gracious to us."   605

He whisked up a two-handled cup, offered it
To his dear mother, and said to her:

"I know it's hard, mother, but you have to endure it.
I don't want to see you getting beat up, and me
Unable to help you. The Olympian can be rough.   610
Once before when I tried to rescue you
He flipped me by my foot off our balcony.
I fell all day and came down when the sun did
On the island of Lemnos⁶ scarcely alive.
The Sintians had to nurse me back to health."   615

By the time he finished, the ivory-armed goddess
Was smiling at her son. She accepted the cup from him.
Then the lame god turned serving boy, siphoning nectar⁷
From the mixing bowl and pouring the sweet liquor
For all of the gods, who couldn't stop laughing   620
At the sight of Hephaestus hustling through the halls.

And so all day long until the sun went down
They feasted to their hearts' content,
Apollo playing beautiful melodies on the lyre,
The Muses singing responsively in lovely voices.   625
And when the last gleams of sunset had faded,
They turned in for the night, each to a house
Built by Hephaestus, the renowned master craftsman,
The burly blacksmith with the soul of an artist.
And the Lord of Lightning, Olympian Zeus, went to his bed, 630
The bed he always slept in when sweet sleep overcame him.
He climbed in and slept, next to golden-throned Hera.

[The Greeks, in spite of Achilles' withdrawal, continued to fight. They did not suffer immoderately from Achilles' absence; on the contrary, they pressed the Trojans so hard that Hector, the Trojan leader, after rallying his men, returned to the city to urge the Trojans to offer special prayers and sacrifices to the gods.]

---

6. An island in the Aegean Sea, inhabited by the Sintians.   7. The drink of the gods.

FROM BOOK VI

[Hector Returns to Troy]

And Hector left, helmet collecting light
Above the black-hide shield whose rim tapped
His ankles and neck with each step he took.

Then Glaucus, son of Hippolochus,   120
Met Diomedes[8] in no-man's-land.
Both were eager to fight, but first Tydeus' son
Made his voice heard above the battle noise:

"And which mortal hero are you? I've never seen you
Out here before on the fields of glory,   125
And now here you are ahead of everyone,
Ready to face my spear. Pretty bold.
I feel sorry for your parents. Of course,
You may be an immortal, down from heaven.
Far be it from me to fight an immortal god.   130
Not even mighty Lycurgus[9] lived long
After he tangled with the immortals,
Driving the nurses of Dionysus[1]
Down over the Mountain of Nysa
And making them drop their wands   135
As he beat them with an ox-goad. Dionysus
Was terrified and plunged into the sea,
Where Thetis received him into her bosom,
Trembling with fear at the human's threats.
Then the gods, who live easy, grew angry   140
With Lycurgus, and the Son of Cronus
Made him go blind, and he did not live long,
Hated as he was by the immortal gods.
No, I wouldn't want to fight an immortal.
But if you are human, and shed blood,   145
Step right up for a quick end to your life."

And Glaucus, Hippolochus' son:

"Great son of Tydeus, why ask about my lineage?
Human generations are like leaves in their seasons.
The wind blows them to the ground, but the tree   150
Sprouts new ones when spring comes again.
Men too. Their generations come and go.
But if you really do want to hear my story,
You're welcome to listen. Many men know it.
    Ephyra,[2] in the heart of Argive horse country,   155
Was home to Sisyphus, the shrewdest man alive,
Sisyphus son of Aeolus. He had a son, Glaucus,
Who was the father of faultless Bellerophon,

8. One of the foremost Greek leaders, son of Tydeus. Glaucus was a Trojan ally, from Lycia in Asia Minor.
9. King of Thrace, a half-wild region along the north shore of the Aegean Sea.   1. God of the vine.
2. An old name for Corinth, a city in the northeast Peloponnesus.

A man of grace and courage by gift of the gods.
But Proetus, whom Zeus had made king of Argos,   160
Came to hate Bellerophon
And drove him out. It happened this way.
Proetus' wife, the beautiful Anteia,
Was madly in love with Bellerophon
And wanted to have him in her bed.   165
But she couldn't persuade him, not at all,
Because he was so virtuous and wise.
So she made up lies and spoke to the king:
'Either die yourself, Proetus, or kill Bellerophon.
He wanted to sleep with me against my will.'   170
The king was furious when he heard her say this.
He did not kill him—he had scruples about that—
But he sent him to Lycia with a folding tablet
On which he had scratched many evil signs,
And told him to give it to Anteia's father,   175
To get him killed. So off he went to Lycia,
With an immortal escort, and when he reached
The river Xanthus,³ the king there welcomed him
And honored him with entertainment
For nine solid days, killing an ox each day.   180
But when the tenth dawn spread her rosy light,
He questioned him and asked to see the tokens
He brought from Proetus, his daughter's husband.
And when he saw the evil tokens from Proetus,
He ordered him, first, to kill the Chimaera,   185
A raging monster, divine, inhuman—
A lion in the front, a serpent in the rear,
In the middle a goat—and breathing fire.
Bellerophon killed her, trusting signs from the gods.
Next he had to fight the glorious Solymi,   190
The hardest battle, he said, he ever fought,
And, third, the Amazons, women the peers of men.
As he journeyed back the king wove another wile.
He chose the best men in all wide Lycia
And laid an ambush. Not one returned home;   195
Blameless Bellerophon killed them all.
When the king realized his guest had divine blood,
He kept him there and gave him his daughter
And half of all his royal honor. Moreover,
The Lycians cut out for him a superb   200
Tract of land, plow-land and orchard.
His wife, the princess, bore him three children,
Isander, Hippolochus, and Laodameia.
Zeus in his wisdom slept with Laodameia,
And she bore him the godlike warrior Sarpedon.   205
But even Bellerophon lost the gods' favor
And went wandering alone over the Aleian plain.
His son Isander was slain by Ares
As he fought against the glorious Solymi,

3. A river in Lycia.

And his daughter was killed by Artemis.   210
Of the golden reins. But Hippolochus
Bore me, and I am proud he is my father.
He sent me to Troy with strict instructions
To be the best ever, better than all the rest,
And not to bring shame on the race of my fathers,   215
The noblest men in Ephyra and Lycia.
This, I am proud to say, is my lineage."

Diomedes grinned when he heard all this.
He planted his spear in the bounteous earth
And spoke gently to the Lycian prince: 220

"We have old ties of hospitality!
My grandfather Oeneus long ago
Entertained Bellerophon in his halls
For twenty days, and they gave each other
Gifts of friendship.⁴ Oeneus gave   225
A belt bright with scarlet, and Bellerophon
A golden cup, which I left at home.
I don't remember my father Tydeus,
Since I was very small when he left for Thebes
In the war that killed so many Achaeans.⁵   230
But that makes me your friend and you my guest
If ever you come to Argos, as you are my friend
And I your guest whenever I travel to Lycia.
So we can't cross spears with each other
Even in the thick of battle. There are enough   235
Trojans and allies for me to kill, whomever
A god gives me and I can run down myself.
And enough Greeks for you to kill as you can.
And let's exchange armor, so everyone will know
That we are friends from our fathers' days."   240

With this said, they vaulted from their chariots,
Clasped hands, and pledged their friendship.
But Zeus took away Glaucus' good sense,
For he exchanged his golden armor for bronze,
The worth of one hundred oxen for nine.   245
    When Hector reached the oak tree by the Western Gate,
Trojan wives and daughters ran up to him,
Asking about their children, their brothers,
Their kinsmen, their husbands. He told them all,
Each woman in turn, to pray to the gods.   250
Sorrow clung to their heads like mist.

Then he came to Priam's palace, a beautiful
Building made of polished stone with a central courtyard
Flanked by porticoes, upon which opened fifty

4. It was customary for guest-friends to exchange gifts.   5. Tydeus was one of the seven heroes who attacked Thebes. They were led by Oedipus's son Polynices, who was attempting to dislodge his brother, Eteocles, from the kingship. The brothers killed each other, and the rest of the seven also perished. Diomedes, along with the sons of the other champions, later sacked Thebes.

Adjoining rooms, where Priam's sons   255
Slept with their wives. Across the court
A suite of twelve more bedrooms housed
His modest daughters and their husbands.
It was here that Hector's mother[6] met him,
A gracious woman, with Laodice,   260
Her most beautiful daughter, in tow.
Hecuba took his hand in hers and said:

"Hector, my son, why have you left the war
And come here? Are those abominable Greeks
Wearing you down in the fighting outside,   265
And does your heart lead you to our acropolis
To stretch your hands upward to Zeus?
But stay here while I get you
Some honey-sweet wine, so you can pour a libation
To Father Zeus first and the other immortals,   270
Then enjoy some yourself, if you will drink.
Wine greatly bolsters a weary man's spirits,
And you are weary from defending your kinsmen."

Sunlight shimmered on great Hector's helmet.

"Mother, don't offer me any wine.   275
It would drain the power out of my limbs.
I have too much reverence to pour a libation
With unwashed hands to Zeus almighty,
Or to pray to Cronion[7] in the black cloudbanks
Spattered with blood and the filth of battle.   280
But you must go to the War Goddess's[8] temple
To make sacrifice with a band of old women.
Choose the largest and loveliest robe in the house,
The one that is dearest of all to you,
And place it on the knees of braided Athena.   285
And promise twelve heifers to her in her temple,
Unblemished yearlings, if she will pity
The town of Troy, its wives, and its children,
And if she will keep from holy Ilion[9]
Wild Diomedes, who's raging with his spear.   290
Go then to the temple of Athena the War Goddess,
And I will go over to summon Paris,[1]
If he will listen to what I have to say.
I wish the earth would gape open beneath him.
Olympian Zeus has bred him as a curse   295
To Troy, to Priam, and all Priam's children.
If I could see him dead and gone to Hades,
I think my heart might be eased of its sorrow."

Thus Hector. Hecuba went to the great hall
And called to her handmaidens, and they   300

6. Hecuba.   7. The son of Cronus (that is, Zeus).   8. Athena.   9. Another name for Troy.
1. Hector's brother, whose seduction and abduction of Helen, the wife of Menelaus, caused the war.

Gathered together the city's old women.
She went herself to a fragrant storeroom
Which held her robes, the exquisite work
Of Sidonian[2] women whom godlike Paris
Brought from Phoenicia when he sailed the sea   305
On the voyage he made for high-born Helen.
Hecuba chose the robe that lay at the bottom,
The most beautiful of all, woven of starlight,
And bore it away as a gift for Athena.
A stream of old women followed behind.   310

They came to the temple of Pallas Athena
On the city's high rock, and the doors were opened
By fair-cheeked Theano, daughter of Cisseus
And wife of Antenor, breaker of horses.
The Trojans had made her Athena's priestess.   315
With ritual cries they all lifted their hands
To Pallas Athena. Theano took the robe
And laid it on the knees of the rich-haired goddess,
Then prayed in supplication to Zeus' daughter:

"Lady Athena who defends our city,   320
Brightest of goddesses, hear our prayer.
Break now the spear of Diomedes
And grant that he fall before the Western Gate,
That we may now offer twelve heifers in this temple,
Unblemished yearlings. Only do thou pity   325
The town of Troy, its wives and its children."

But Pallas Athena denied her prayer.

   While they prayed to great Zeus' daughter,
Hector came to Paris' beautiful house,
Which he had built himself with the aid   330
Of the best craftsmen in all wide Troy:
Sleeping quarters, a hall, and a central courtyard
Near to Priam's and Hector's on the city's high rock.
Hector entered, Zeus' light upon him,
A spear sixteen feet long cradled in his hand,   335
The bronze point gleaming, and the ferrule gold.
He found Paris in the bedroom, busy with his weapons,
Fondling his curved bow, his fine shield, and breastplate.
Helen of Argos sat with her household women
Directing their exquisite handicraft.   340

Hector meant to shame Paris and provoke him:[3]

"This is a fine time to be nursing your anger,
You idiot! We're dying out there defending the walls.

---

2. From the Phoenician city Sidon, on the coast of what is now Lebanon.   3. In book III Paris fought with Menelaus in single combat to settle the war. He was about to lose when Aphrodite spirited him off to his house in Troy, where she then persuaded Helen to join him. In book IV fighting broke out again when the Trojan archer Pandarus, on Athena's advice, wounded Menelaus.

It's because of you the city is in this hellish war.
If you saw someone else holding back from combat   345
You'd pick a fight with him yourself. Now get up
Before the whole city goes up in flames!"

And Paris, handsome as a god:

"That's no more than just, Hector,
But listen now to what I have to say.   350
It's not out of anger or spite toward the Trojans
I've been here in my room. I only wanted
To recover from my pain. My wife was just now
Encouraging me to get up and fight,
And that seems the better thing to do.   355
Victory takes turns with men. Wait for me
While I put on my armor, or go on ahead—
I'm pretty sure I'll catch up with you."

To which Hector said nothing.

But Helen said to him softly:
                              "Brother-in-law   360
Of a scheming, cold-blooded bitch,
I wish that on the day my mother bore me
A windstorm had swept me away to a mountain
Or into the waves of the restless sea,
Swept me away before all this could happen.   365
But since the gods have ordained these evils,
Why couldn't I be the wife of a better man,
One sensitive at least to repeated reproaches?
Paris has never had an ounce of good sense
And never will. He'll pay for it someday.   370
But come inside and sit down on this chair,
Dear brother-in-law. You bear such a burden
For my wanton ways and Paris' witlessness.
Zeus has placed this evil fate on us so that
In time to come poets will sing of us."   375

And Hector, in his burnished helmet:

"Don't ask me to sit, Helen, even though
You love me. You will never persuade me.
My heart is out there with our fighting men.
They already feel my absence from battle.   380
Just get Paris moving, and have him hurry
So he can catch up with me while I'm still
Inside the city. I'm going to my house now
To see my family, my wife and my boy. I don't know
Whether I'll ever be back to see them again, or if   385
The gods will destroy me at the hands of the Greeks."

And Hector turned and left. He came to his house
But did not find white-armed Andromache there.

She had taken the child and a robed attendant
And stood on the tower, lamenting and weeping—   390
His blameless wife. When Hector didn't find her inside,
He paused on his way out and called to the servants:

"Can any of you women tell me exactly
Where Andromache went when she left the house?
To one of my sisters or one of my brothers' wives?   395
Or to the temple of Athena along with the other
Trojan women to beseech the dread goddess?"

The spry old housekeeper answered him:

"Hector, if you want the exact truth, she didn't go
To any of your sisters, or any of your brothers' wives,   400
Or to the temple of Athena along with the other
Trojan women to beseech the dread goddess.
She went to Ilion's great tower, because she heard
The Trojans were pressed and the Greeks were strong.
She ran off to the wall like a madwoman,   405
And the nurse went with her, carrying the child."

Thus the housekeeper, but Hector was gone,
Retracing his steps through the stone and tile streets
Of the great city, until he came to the Western Gate.
He was passing through it out onto the plain   410
When his wife came running up to meet him,
His beautiful wife, Andromache,
A gracious woman, daughter of great Eëtion,
Eëtion, who lived in the forests of Plakos
And ruled the Cilicians from Thebes-under-Plakos—   415
His daughter was wed to bronze-helmeted Hector.
She came up to him now, and the nurse with her
Held to her bosom their baby boy,
Hector's beloved son, beautiful as starlight,
Whom Hector had named Scamandrius[4]   420
But everyone else called Astyanax, Lord of the City,
For Hector alone could save Ilion now.
He looked at his son and smiled in silence.
Andromache stood close to him, shedding tears,
Clinging to his arm as she spoke these words: 425

"Possessed is what you are, Hector. Your courage
Is going to kill you, and you have no feeling left
For your little boy or for me, the luckless woman
Who will soon be your widow. It won't be long
Before the whole Greek army swarms and kills you.   430
And when they do, it will be better for me
To sink into the earth. When I lose you, Hector,
There will be nothing left, no one to turn to,
Only pain. My father and mother are dead.

4. After the Trojan river Scamander.

Achilles killed my father when he destroyed   435
Our city, Thebes with its high gates,
But had too much respect to despoil his body.
He burned it instead with all his armor
And heaped up a barrow. And the spirit women⁵
Came down from the mountain, daughters   440
Of the storm god, and planted elm trees around it.
I had seven brothers once in that great house.
All seven went down to Hades on a single day,
Cut down by Achilles in one blinding sprint
Through their shambling cattle and silver sheep.   445
Mother, who was queen in the forests of Plakos,
He took back as prisoner, with all her possessions,
Then released her for a fortune in ransom.
She died in our house, shot by Artemis'⁶ arrows.
Hector, you are my father, you are my mother,   450
You are my brother and my blossoming husband.
But show some pity and stay here by the tower,
Don't make your child an orphan, your wife a widow.
Station your men here by the fig tree, where the city
Is weakest because the wall can be scaled.   455
Three times their elite have tried an attack here
Rallying around Ajax or glorious Idomeneus
Or Atreus' sons or mighty Diomedes,
Whether someone in on the prophecy told them
Or they are driven here by something in their heart."   460

And great Hector, helmet shining, answered her:

"Yes, Andromache, I worry about all this myself,
But my shame before the Trojans and their wives,
With their long robes trailing, would be too terrible
If I hung back from battle like a coward.   465
And my heart won't let me. I have learned to be
One of the best, to fight in Troy's first ranks,
Defending my father's honor and my own.
Deep in my heart I know too well
There will come a day when holy Ilion will perish,   470
And Priam and the people under Priam's ash spear.
But the pain I will feel for the Trojans then,
For Hecuba herself and for Priam king,
For my many fine brothers who will have by then
Fallen in the dust behind enemy lines—   475
All that pain is nothing to what I will feel
For you, when some bronze-armored Greek
Leads you away in tears, on your first day of slavery.
And you will work some other woman's loom
In Argos or carry water from a Spartan spring,   480
All against your will, under great duress.

5. Mountain nymphs.   6. The virgin goddess of the hunt, dispenser of natural and painless death to women.

And someone, seeing you crying, will say,
'That is the wife of Hector, the best of all
The Trojans when they fought around Ilion.'
Someday someone will say that, renewing your pain   485
At having lost such a man to fight off the day
Of your enslavement. But may I be dead
And the earth heaped up above me
Before I hear your cry as you are dragged away."

With these words, resplendent Hector   490
Reached for his child, who shrank back screaming
Into his nurse's bosom, terrified of his father's
Bronze-encased face and the horsehair plume
He saw nodding down from the helmet's crest.
This forced a laugh from his father and mother,   495
And Hector removed the helmet from his head
And set it on the ground all shimmering with light.
Then he kissed his dear son and swung him up gently
And said a prayer to Zeus and the other immortals:

"Zeus and all gods: grant that this my son   500
Become, as I am, foremost among Trojans,
Brave and strong, and ruling Ilion with might.
And may men say he is far better than his father
When he returns from war, bearing bloody spoils,
Having killed his man. And may his mother rejoice."   505

And he put his son in the arms of his wife,
And she enfolded him in her fragrant bosom
Laughing through her tears. Hector pitied her
And stroked her with his hand and said to her:

"You worry too much about me, Andromache.   510
No one is going to send me to Hades before my time,
And no man has ever escaped his fate, rich or poor,
Coward or hero, once born into this world.
Go back to the house now and take care of your work,
The loom and the shuttle, and tell the servants   515
To get on with their jobs. War is the work of men,
Of all the Trojan men, and mine especially."

With these words, Hector picked up
His plumed helmet, and his wife went back home,
Turning around often, her cheeks flowered with tears.   520
When she came to the house of man-slaying Hector,
She found a throng of servants inside,
And raised among these women the ritual lament.
And so they mourned for Hector in his house
Although he was still alive, for they did not think   525
He would ever again come back from the war,
Or escape the murderous hands of the Greeks.

Paris meanwhile
Did not dally long in his high halls.
He put on his magnificent bronze-inlaid gear   530
And sprinted with assurance out through the city.

> Picture a horse that has fed on barley in his stall
> Breaking his halter and galloping across the plain,
> Making for his accustomed swim in the river,
> A glorious animal, head held high, mane streaming   535
> Like wind on his shoulders. Sure of his splendor
> He prances by the horse-runs and the mares in pasture.

That was how Paris, son of Priam, came down
From the high rock of Pergamum,[7]
Gleaming like amber and laughing in his armor,   540
And his feet were fast.
                                   He caught up quickly
With Hector just as he turned from the spot
Where he'd talked with his wife, and called out:

"Well, dear brother, have I delayed you too much?
Am I not here in time, just as you asked?"   545

Hector turned, his helmet flashing light:

"I don't understand you, Paris.
No one could slight your work in battle.
You're a strong fighter, but you slack off—
You don't have the will. It breaks my heart   550
To hear what the Trojans say about you.
It's on your account they have all this trouble.
Come on, let's go. We can settle this later,
If Zeus ever allows us to offer in our halls
The wine bowl of freedom to the gods above,   555
After we drive these bronze-kneed[8] Greeks from Troy."

[The Trojans rallied successfully and went over to the offensive. They drove the
Greeks back to the light fortifications they had built around their beached ships. The
Trojans lit their watchfires on the plain, ready to deliver the attack in the morning.]

FROM BOOK VIII

[The Tide of Battle Turns]

But the Trojans had great notions that night,
Sitting on the bridge of war by their watchfires.

> Stars: crowds of them in the sky, sharp   565
> In the moonglow when the wind falls
> And all the cliffs and hills and peaks
> Stand out and the air shears down

---

7. The citadel of Troy.   8. That is, with bronze greaves (the shin protectors of Homeric warriors).

From heaven, and all the stars are visible
And the watching shepherd smiles.   570

So the bonfires between the Greek ships
And the banks of the Xanthus,[9] burning
On the plain before Ilion.
                    And fifty men
Warmed their hands by the flames of each fire.

And the horses champed white barley,   575
Standing by their chariots, waiting for Dawn
To take her seat on brocaded cushions.

BOOK IX

[The Embassy to Achilles]

So the Trojans kept watch. But Panic,
Fear's sister, had wrapped her icy fingers
Around the Greeks, and all their best
Were stricken with unendurable grief.

When two winds rise on the swarming deep,   5
Boreas and Zephyr,[1] blowing from Thrace
In a sudden squall, the startled black waves
Will crest and tangle the surf with seaweed.

The Greeks felt like that, pummeled and torn.

Agamemnon's heart was bruised with pain   10
As he went around to the clear-toned criers
Ordering them to call each man to assembly,
But not to shout. He pitched in himself.
It was a dispirited assembly. Agamemnon
Stood up, weeping, his face like a sheer cliff   15
With dark springwater washing down the stone.
Groaning heavily he addressed the troops:
"Friends, Argive commanders and counsellors:
Great Zeus, son of Cronus,
Is a hard god, friends. He's kept me in the dark   20
After all his promises, all his nods my way
That I'd raze Ilion's walls before sailing home.
It was all a lie, and I see now that his orders
Are for me to return to Argos in disgrace,
And this after all the armies I've destroyed.   25
I have no doubt that this is the high will
Of the god who has toppled so many cities
And will in the future, all glory to his power.
So this is my command for the entire army:
Clear out with our ships and head for home.   30
There's no hope we will take Troy's tall town."

---

9. One of the rivers of the Trojan plain.   1. The north and west winds, respectively.

He spoke, and they were all stunned to silence,
The silence of an army too grieved to speak,
Until at last Diomedes' voice boomed out:

"I'm going to oppose you if you talk foolishness—   35
As is my right in assembly, lord. Keep your temper.
First of all, you insulted me, saying in public
I was unwarlike and weak.[2] Every Greek here,
Young and old alike, knows all about this.
The son of crooked Cronus split the difference   40
When he gave you gifts. He gave you a scepter
And honor with it, but he didn't give you
Strength to stand in battle, which is real power.
Are you out of your mind? Do you really think
The sons of the Achaeans are unwarlike and weak?   45
If you yourself are anxious to go home.
Then go. You know the way. Your ships are here
Right by the sea, and a whole fleet will follow you
Back to Mycenae.[3] But many a long-haired Achaean
Will stay, too, until we conquer Troy. And if they won't—   50
Well, let them all sail back to their own native land.
The two of us, Sthenelus[4] and I, will fight on
Until we take Ilion. We came here with Zeus."

He spoke, and all the Greeks cheered
The speech of Diomedes, breaker of horses.   55
Then up stood Nestor, the old charioteer:

"Son of Tydeus, you are our mainstay in battle
And the best of your age in council as well.
No Greek will find fault with your speech
Or contradict it. But it is not the whole story.   60
You are still young. You might be my son,
My youngest. Yet you have given prudent advice
To the Argive kings, since you have spoken aright.
But I, who am privileged to be your senior,
Will speak to all points. Nor will anyone   65
Scorn my words, not even King Agamemnon.
Only outlaws and exiles favor civil strife.
For the present, however, let us yield to night
And have our dinner. Guards should be posted
Outside the wall along the trench. I leave   70
This assignment to the younger men. But you,
Son of Atreus, take charge. You are King.
Serve the elders a feast. It is not unseemly.
Your huts are filled with wine which our ships
Transport daily over the sea from Thrace.   75
You have the means to entertain us and the men.
Then choose the best counsel your assembled guests

---

2. This insult was voiced during Agamemnon's review of his forces before the battle (book IV).   3. The
city near Argos that Agamemnon ruled.   4. Diomedes' companion.

Can offer. The Achaeans are in great need
Of good counsel. The enemies' campfires
Are close to our ships. Can this gladden any heart?   80
This night will either destroy the army or save it."

They all heard him out and did as he said.
The guard details got their gear and filed out
On the double under their commanders:
Thrasymedes, Nestor's son; Ascalaphus   85
And Ialmenus, sons of Ares; Meriones,
Aphareus, and Diphyrus; and Creion,
The son of Lycomedes. Each of these seven
Had a hundred men under his command.
Spears in hand, they took up their positions   90
In a long line between the wall and the trench,[5]
Where they lit fires and prepared their supper.

Agamemnon meanwhile gathered the elders
Into his hut and served them a hearty meal.
They helped themselves to the dishes before them,   95
And when they had enough of food and drink,
The first to spin out his plan for them was Nestor,
Whose advice had always seemed best before,
And who spoke with their best interests at heart:

"Son of Atreus, most glorious lord,   100
I begin and end with you, since you are
King of a great people, with authority
To rule and right of judgment from Zeus.
It is yours to speak as well as to listen,
And to stand behind others whenever they speak   105
To our good. The final word is yours.
But I will speak as seems best to me.
No one will have a better idea
Than I have now, nor has anyone ever,
From the time, divine prince, you wrested away   110
The girl Briseis from Achilles' shelter,
Defying his anger and my opposition.
I tried to dissuade you, but you gave in
To your pride and dishonored a great man
Whom the immortals esteem. You took his prize   115
And keep it still. But it is not too late. Even now
We must think of how to win him back
With appeasing gifts and soothing words."

And the warlord Agamemnon responded:

"Yes, old man, you were right on the mark   120
When you said I was mad. I will not deny it.
Zeus' favor multiplies a man's worth,

---

5. In book VII, the Greeks built a wall and dug the trench in front of it to protect their ships, which were
threatened by the Trojans.

As it has here, and the army has suffered for it.
But since I did succumb to a fit of madness,
I want to make substantial amends. 125
I hereby announce my reparations:
Seven unfired tripods,[6] ten gold bars,
Twenty burnished cauldrons, a dozen horses—
Solid, prizewinning racehorses
Who have won me a small fortune— 130
And seven women who do impeccable work,
Surpassingly beautiful women from Lesbos[7]
I chose for myself when Achilles captured the town.
And with them will be the woman I took,
Briseus's daughter, and I will solemnly swear 135
I never went to her bed and lay with her
Or did what is natural between women and men.
All this he may have at once. And if it happens
That the gods allow us to sack Priam's city,
He may when the Greeks are dividing the spoils 140
Load a ship to the brim with gold and bronze,
And choose for himself the twenty Trojan women
Who are next in beauty to Argive Helen.
And if we return to the rich land of Argos,
He will marry my daughter, and I will honor him 145
As I do Orestes,[8] who is being reared in luxury.
I have three daughters in my fortress palace,
Chrysothemis, Laodice, and Iphianassa.
He may lead whichever he likes as his bride
Back to Peleus' house, without paying anything, 150
And I will give her a dowry richer than any
A father has ever given his daughter.
And I will give him seven populous cities,
Cardamyle, Enope, grassy Hire,
Sacred Pherae, Antheia with its meadowlands, 155
Beautiful Aepeia, and Pedasus, wine country.
They are all near the sea, on sandy Pylos' frontier,
And cattlemen live there, rich in herds and flocks,
Who will pay him tribute as if he were a god
And fulfill the shining decrees of his scepter. 160
I will do all this if he will give up his grudge.
And he should. Only Hades cannot be appeased,
Which is why of all gods mortals hate him most.
And he should submit to me, inasmuch as I
Am more of a king and can claim to be elder." 165

And then spoke Nestor, the Gerenian rider:

"Son of Atreus, most glorious Agamemnon,
Your gifts for Achilles are beyond reproach.
But come, we must dispatch envoys
As soon as possible to Achilles' tent, 170

6. Three-footed kettles. Such metal equipment was rare and highly valued.   7. A large island off the coast of present-day Turkey.   8. Agamemnon's son.

And I see before me who should volunteer.
Phoenix,[9] dear to Zeus, should lead the way,
Followed by Ajax and brilliant Odysseus.
Odius and Eurybates can attend them as heralds.
Now bring water for our hands and observe silence,   175
That we may beseech Zeus to have mercy on us."

Nestor spoke, and his speech pleased them all.
Heralds poured water over their hands,
And then youths filled bowls to the brim with drink
And served it all around, first tipping the cups.   180
Having made their libations and drunk their fill,
They went out in a body from Agamemnon's hut.
Gerenian Nestor filled their ears with advice,
Glancing at each, but especially at Odysseus,
On how to persuade Peleus' peerless son.   185

They went in tandem along the seething shore,
Praying over and over to the god in the surf[1]
For an easy time in convincing Achilles.
They came to the Myrmidons' ships and huts
And found him plucking clear notes on a lyre—   190
A beautiful instrument with a silver bridge
He had taken when he ransacked Eëtion's[2] town—
Accompanying himself as he sang the glories
Of heroes in war. He was alone with Patroclus,
Who sat in silence waiting for him to finish.   195
His visitors came forward, Odysseus first,
And stood before him. Surprised, Achilles
Rose from his chair still holding his lyre.
Patroclus, when he saw them, also rose,
And Achilles, swift and sure, received them: 200

"Welcome. Things must be bad to bring you here,
The Greeks I love best, even in my rage."

With these words Achilles led them in
And had them sit on couches and rugs
Dyed purple, and he called to Patroclus: 205

"A larger bowl, son of Menoetius,
And stronger wine, and cups all around.
My dearest friends are beneath my roof."

Patroclus obliged his beloved companion.
Then he cast a carving block down in the firelight   210
And set on it a sheep's back and a goat's,
And a hog chine too, marbled with fat.
Automedon[3] held the meat while Achilles

9. He is especially suited for this embassy because he was tutor to the young Achilles.   1. Poseidon, god
of the sea.   2. Andromache's father. In book VI, she recalls his death at Achilles' hands.   3. Achilles'
charioteer.

Carved it carefully and spitted the pieces.
Patroclus, godlike in the fire's glare,   215
Fed the blaze. When the flames died down
He laid the spits over the scattered embers,
Resting them on stones, and sprinkled the morsels
With holy salt. When the meat was roasted
He laid it on platters and set out bread   220
In exquisite baskets. Achilles served the meat,
Then sat down by the wall opposite Odysseus
And asked Patroclus to offer sacrifice.
After he threw the offerings[4] in the fire,
They helped themselves to the meal before them,   225
And when they had enough of food and drink,
Ajax nodded to Phoenix. Odysseus saw this,
And filling a cup he lifted it to Achilles:

"To your health, Achilles, for a generous feast.
There is no shortage in Agamemnon's hut,   230
Or now here in yours, of satisfying food.
But the pleasures of the table are not on our minds.
We fear the worst. It is doubtful
That we can save the ships without your strength.
The Trojans and their allies are encamped   235
Close to the wall that surrounds our black ships
And are betting that we can't keep them
From breaking through. They may be right.
Zeus has been encouraging them with signs,
Lightning on the right. Hector trusts this—   240
And his own strength—and has been raging
Recklessly, like a man possessed.
He is praying for dawn to come early
So he can fulfill his threat to lop the horns
From the ships' sterns, burn the hulls to ash,   245
And slaughter the Achaeans dazed in the smoke.
This is my great fear, that the gods make good
Hector's threats, dooming us to die in Troy
Far from the fields of home. Up with you, then,
If you intend at all, even at this late hour,   250
To save our army from these howling Trojans.
Think of yourself, of the regret you will feel
For harm that will prove irreparable.
This is the last chance to save your countrymen.
Is it not true, my friend, that your father Peleus   255
Told you as he sent you off with Agamemnon:
'My son, as for strength, Hera and Athena
Will bless you if they wish, but it is up to you
To control your proud spirit. A friendly heart
Is far better. Steer clear of scheming strife,   260
So that Greeks young and old will honor you.'
You have forgotten what the old man said,
But you can still let go of your anger, right now.

4. The portion of meat reserved for the gods.

Agamemnon is offering you worthy gifts
If you will give up your grudge. Hear me   265
While I list the gifts he proposed in his hut:
Seven unfired tripods, ten gold bars,
Twenty burnished cauldrons, a dozen horses—
Solid, prizewinning racehorses
Who have won him a small fortune—   270
And seven women who do impeccable work,
Surpassingly beautiful women from Lesbos
He chose for himself when you captured the town.
And with them will be the woman he took from you,
Briseus' daughter, and he will solemnly swear   275
He never went to her bed and lay with her
Or did what is natural between women and men.
All this you may have at once. And if it happens
That the gods allow us to sack Priam's city,
You may when the Greeks are dividing the spoils   280
Load a ship to the brim with gold and bronze,
And choose for yourself the twenty Trojan women
Who are next in beauty to Argive Helen.
And if we return to the rich land of Argos,
You would marry his daughter, and he would honor you   285
As he does Orestes, who is being reared in luxury.
He has three daughters in his fortress palace,
Chrysothemis, Laodice, and Iphianassa.
You may lead whichever you like as your bride
Back to Peleus' house, without paying anything,   290
And he would give her a dowry richer than any
A father has ever given his daughter.
And he will give you seven populous cities,
Cardamyle, Enope, grassy Hire,
Sacred Pherae, Antheia with its meadowlands,   295
Beautiful Aepeia, and Pedasus, wine country.
They are all near the sea, on sandy Pylos' frontier,
And cattlemen live there, rich in herds and flocks,
Who will pay you tribute as if you were a god
And fulfill the shining decrees of your scepter.   300
All this he will do if you give up your grudge.
But if Agamemnon is too hateful to you,
Himself and his gifts, think of all the others
Suffering up and down the line, and of the glory
You will win from them. They will honor you   305
Like a god.
                   And don't forget Hector.
You just might get him now. He's coming in close,
Deluded into thinking that he has no match
In the Greek army that has landed on his beach."

And Achilles, strong, swift, and godlike: 310

"Son of Laertes in the line of Zeus,
Odysseus the strategist—I can see

That I have no choice but to speak my mind
And tell you exactly how things are going to be.
Either that or sit through endless sessions   315
Of people whining at me. I hate like hell
The man who says one thing and thinks another.
So this is how I see it.
I cannot imagine Agamemnon,
Or any other Greek, persuading me,   320
Not after the thanks I got for fighting this war,
Going up against the enemy day after day.
It doesn't matter if you stay in camp or fight—
In the end, everybody comes out the same.
Coward and hero get the same reward: 325
You die whether you slack off or work.
And what do I have for all my suffering,
Constantly putting my life on the line?
Like a bird who feeds her chicks
Whatever she finds, and goes without herself,   330
That's what I've been like, lying awake
Through sleepless nights, in battle for days
Soaked in blood, fighting men for their wives.
I've raided twelve cities with our ships
And eleven on foot in the fertile Troad,   335
Looted them all, brought back heirlooms
By the ton, and handed it all over
To Atreus' son, who hung back in camp
Raking it in and distributing damn little.
What the others did get they at least got to keep.   340
They all have their prizes, everyone but me—
I'm the only Greek from whom he took something back.
He should be happy with the woman he has.
Why do the Greeks have to fight the Trojans?
Why did Agamemnon lead the army to Troy   345
If not for the sake of fair-haired Helen?
Do you have to be descended from Atreus
To love your mate? Every decent, sane man
Loves his woman and cares for her, as I did,
Loved her from my heart. It doesn't matter   350
That I won her with my spear. He took her,
Took her right out of my hands, cheated me,
And now he thinks he's going to win me back?
He can forget it. I know how things stand.
It's up to you, Odysseus, and the other kings   355
To find a way to keep the fire from the ships.
He's been pretty busy without me, hasn't he,
Building a wall, digging a moat around it,
Pounding in stakes for a palisade.
None of that stuff will hold Hector back.   360
When I used to fight for the Greeks,
Hector wouldn't come out farther from his wall
Than the oak tree by the Western Gate.
He waited for me there once, and barely escaped.

Now that I don't want to fight him anymore,   365
I will sacrifice to Zeus and all gods tomorrow,
Load my ships, and launch them on the sea.
Take a look if you want, if you give a damn,
And you'll see my fleet on the Hellespont
In the early light, my men rowing hard.   370
With good weather from the sea god,
I'll reach Phthia after a three-day sail.
I left a lot behind when I hauled myself here,
And I'll bring back more, gold and bronze,
Silken-waisted women, grey iron—   375
Everything except the prize of honor
The warlord Agamemnon gave me
And in his insulting arrogance took back.
So report back to him everything I say,
And report it publicly—get the Greeks angry,   380
In case the shameless bastard still thinks
He can steal us blind. He doesn't dare
Show his dogface here. Fine. I don't want
To have anything to do with him either.
He cheated me, wronged me. Never again.   385
He's had it. He can go to hell in peace,
The half-wit that Zeus has made him.
His gifts? His gifts mean nothing to me.
Not even if he offered me ten or twenty times
His present gross worth and added to it   390
All the trade Orchomenus[5] does in a year,
All the wealth laid up in Egyptian Thebes,
The wealthiest city in all the world,
Where they drive two hundred teams of horses
Out through each of its hundred gates.   395
Not even if Agamemnon gave me gifts
As numberless as grains of sand or dust,
Would he persuade me or touch my heart—
Not until he's paid in full for all my grief.
His daughter? I would not marry   400
The daughter of Agamemnon son of Atreus
If she were as lovely as golden Aphrodite
Or could weave like owl-eyed Athena.
Let him choose some other Achaean
More to his lordly taste. If the gods   405
Preserve me and I get home safe
Peleus will find me a wife himself.
There are many Greek girls in Hellas[6] and Phthia,
Daughters of chieftains who rule the cities.
I can have my pick of any of them.   410
I've always wanted to take a wife there,
A woman to have and to hold, someone with whom
I can enjoy all the goods old Peleus has won.

5. A city in central Greece, northwest of Thebes: it was one of the most important Greek cities from the
Bronze Age onward.   6. Although Hellas later became the name for all of Greece, in Homer it refers to
a region next to Achilles' home district of Phthia. Both are in northern Greece.

Nothing is worth my life, not all the riches
They say Troy held before the Greeks came,   415
Not all the wealth in Phoebus Apollo's
Marble shrine up in craggy Pytho.[7]
Cattle and flocks are there for the taking;
You can always get tripods and chestnut horses.
But a man's life cannot be won back   420
Once his breath has passed beyond his clenched teeth.
My mother Thetis, a moving silver grace,
Tells me two fates sweep me on to my death.
If I stay here and fight, I'll never return home,
But my glory will be undying forever.   425
If I return home to my dear fatherland
My glory is lost but my life will be long,
And death that ends all will not catch me soon.
As for the rest of you, I would advise you too
To sail back home, since there's no chance now   430
Of storming Ilion's height. Zeus has stretched
His hand above her, making her people bold.
What's left for you now is to go back to the council
And announce my message. It's up to them
To come up with another plan to save the ships   435
And the army with them, since this one,
Based on appeasing my anger, won't work.
Phoenix can spend the night here. Tomorrow
He sails with me on our voyage home,
If he wants to, that is. I won't force him to come."   440

He spoke, and they were hushed in silence,
Shocked by his speech and his stark refusal.
Finally the old horseman Phoenix spoke,
Bursting into tears. He felt the ships were lost.

"If you have set your mind on going home,   445
Achilles, and will do nothing to save the ships
From being burnt, if your heart is that angry,
How could I stay here without you, my boy,
All by myself? Peleus sent me with you
On that day you left Phthia to go to Agamemnon,   450
A child still, knowing nothing of warfare
Or assemblies where men distinguish themselves.
He sent me to you to teach you this—
To be a speaker of words and a doer of deeds.
I could not bear to be left behind now   455
Apart from you, child, not even if a god
Promised to smooth my wrinkles and make me
As young and strong as I was when I first left
The land of Hellas and its beautiful women.
I was running away from a quarrel with Amyntor,   460
My father, who was angry with me

7. Apollo's oracular shrine at Delphi. Its wealth consisted of offerings made to the god by grateful worshipers.

Over his concubine, a fair-haired woman
Whom he loved as much as he scorned his wife,
My mother. She implored me constantly
To make love to his concubine so that this woman   465
Would learn to hate the old man. I did as she asked.
My father found out and cursed me roundly,
Calling on the Furies[8] to ensure that never
Would a child of mine sit on his knees.
The gods answered his prayers, Underworld Zeus   470
And dread Persephone.[9] I decided to kill him
With a sharp sword, but some god calmed me down—
Putting in my mind what people would say,
The names they would call me—so that in fact
I would not be known as a parricide.   475
From then on I could not bear to linger
In my father's house, although my friends
And my family tried to get me to stay,
Entreating me, slaughtering sheep and cattle,
Roasting whole pigs on spits, and drinking   480
Jar after jar of the old man's wine.
For nine solid days they kept watch on me,
Working in shifts, staying up all night.
The fires stayed lit, one under the portico
Of the main courtyard, one on the porch   485
In front of my bedroom door. On the tenth night,
When it got dark, I broke through the latches
And vaulted over the courtyard fence,
Eluding the watchmen and servant women.
I was on the run through wide Hellas   490
And made it to Phthia's black soil, her flocks,
And to Lord Peleus. He welcomed me kindly
And loved me as a father loves his only son,
A grown son who will inherit great wealth.
He made me rich and settled me on the border,   495
Where I lived as king of the Dolopians.
I made you what you are, my godlike Achilles,
And loved you from my heart. You wouldn't eat,
Whether it was at a feast or a meal in the house,
Unless I set you on my lap and cut your food up   500
And fed it to you and held the wine to your lips.
Many a time you wet the tunic on my chest,
Burping up wine when you were colicky.
I went through a lot for you, because I knew
The gods would never let me have a child   505
Of my own. No, I tried to make you my child,
Achilles, so you would save me from ruin.
But you have to master your proud spirit.
It's not right for you to have a pitiless heart.
Even the gods can bend. Superior as they are   510
In honor, power, and every excellence,

8. Avenging spirits, particularly concerned with crimes committed by kin against kin.   9. Wife of Hades
(the "Underworld Zeus").

They can be turned aside from wrath
When humans who have transgressed
Supplicate them with incense and prayers,
With libations and savor of sacrifice.   515
Yes, for Prayers are daughters of great Zeus.
Lame and wrinkled and with eyes averted,
They are careful to follow in Folly's footsteps,
But Folly is strong and fleet, and outruns them all,
Beating them everywhere and plaguing humans,   520
Who are cured by the Prayers when they come behind.
Revere the daughters of Zeus when they come,
And they will bless you and hear your cry.
Reject them and refuse them stubbornly,
And they will ask Zeus, Cronus' son, to have   525
Folly plague you,[1] so you will pay in pain.
No, Achilles, grant these daughters of Zeus
The respect that bends all upright men's minds.
If the son of Atreus were not offering gifts
And promising more, if he were still raging mad,   530
I would not ask you to shrug off your grudge
And help the Greeks, no matter how sore their need.
But he is offering gifts and promising more,
And he has sent to you a delegation
Of the best men in the army, your dearest friends.   535
Don't scorn their words or their mission here.
    No one could blame you for being angry before.
We all know stories about heroes of old,
How they were furiously angry, but later on
Were won over with gifts or appeased with words.   540
I remember a very old story like this, and since
We are all friends here, I will tell it to you now.
    The Curetes were fighting the Aetolians
In a bloody war around Calydon town.[2]
The Aetolians were defending their city   545
And the Curetes meant to burn it down.
This was all because gold-throned Artemis
Had cursed the Curetes,[3] angry that Oeneus
Had not offered her his orchard's first fruits.
The other gods feasted on bulls by the hundred,   550
But Oeneus forgot somehow or other
Only the sacrifice to great Zeus' daughter.
So the Archer Goddess, angry at heart,
Roused a savage boar, with gleaming white tusks,
And sent him to destroy Oeneus' orchard.   555
The boar did a good job, uprooting trees
And littering the ground with apples and blossoms.
But Oeneus' son, Meleager, killed it
After getting up a party of hunters and hounds
From many towns: it took more than a few men   560

---

1. A serious curse, since the Greek word for "folly" can also mean "destruction."   2. A city in
northwestern Greece. The Curetes and Aetolians were the local tribes, once allied but at odds in this story.
3. The Greek says, ambiguously, "had cursed them." Possibly Artemis cursed both Aetolians and Curetes
because Oeneus was king of the Aetolian city Calydon.

To kill this huge boar, and not before
It set many a hunter on the funeral pyre.
But the goddess caused a bitter argument
About the boar's head and shaggy hide
Between the Curetes and Aetolians.   565
They went to war. While Meleager still fought
The Curetes had the worst of it
And could not remain outside Calydon's wall.[4]
But when wrath swelled Meleager's heart,
As it swells even the hearts of the wise,   570
And his anger rose against Althaea his mother,
He lay in bed with his wife, Cleopatra,
Child of Marpessa and the warrior Idas.
Idas once took up his bow against Apollo
To win lissome Marpessa. Her parents   575
Called the girl Halcyone back then
Because her mother wept like a halcyon,
The bird of sorrows, because the Archer God,
Phoebus Apollo, had stolen her daughter.
Meleager nursed his anger at Cleopatra's side,   580
Furious because his mother had cursed him,
Cursed him to the gods for murdering his uncle,[5]
Her brother, that is, and she beat the earth,
The nurturing earth, with her hands, and called
Upon Hades and Persephone the dread,   585
As she knelt and wet her bosom with tears,
To bring death to her son. And the Fury
Who walks in darkness heard her
From the pit of Erebus,[6] and her heart was iron.
Soon the enemy was heard at the walls again,   590
Battering the gates. The Aetolian elders
Sent the city's high priests to pray to Meleager
To come out and defend them, offering him
Fifty acres of Calydon's richest land
Wherever he chose, half in vineyard,   595
Half in clear plowland, to be cut from the plain.
And the old horseman Oeneus shook his doors,
Standing on the threshold of his gabled room,
And recited a litany of prayers to his son,
As did his sisters and his queenly mother.   600
He refused them all, and refused his friends,
His very best friends and boon companions.
No one could move his heart or persuade him
Until the Curetes, having scaled the walls
Were burning the city and beating down   605
His bedroom door. Then his wife wailed
And listed for him all the woes that befall
A captured people—the men killed,
The town itself burnt, the women and children

---

4. The Greek text says only "the wall"—probably not Calydon's wall because the Curetes should be attacking that city. It may be the wall of Pleuron, the Curetes' city. Or, as one commentator has suggested, the wall could be one built by the besieging Curetes around their encampment outside Calydon, as the Greeks have done at Troy.   5. In the course of the battles Meleager had killed one of his mother's brothers.   6. The underworld.

Led into slavery. This roused his spirit.   610
He clapped on armor and went out to fight.
And so he saved the Aetolians from doom
Of his own accord, and they paid him none
Of those lovely gifts, savior or not.
    Don't be like that. Don't think that way,   615
And don't let your spirit turn that way.
The ships will be harder to save when they're burning.
Come while there are gifts, while the Achaeans
Will still honor you as if you were a god.
But if you go into battle without any gifts,   620
Your honor will be less, save us or not."

And strong, swift-footed Achilles answered:

"I don't need that kind of honor, Phoenix.
My honor comes from Zeus, and I will have it
Among these beaked ships as long as my breath   625
Still remains and my knees still move.
Now listen to this. You're listening? Good.
Don't try to confuse me with your pleading
On Agamemnon's behalf. If you're his friend
You're no longer mine, although I love you.   630
Hate him because I hate him. It's as simple as that.
You're like a second father to me. Stay here,
Be king with me and share half the honor.
These others can take my message. Lie down
And spend the night on a soft couch. At daybreak   635
We will decide whether to set sail or stay."

And he made a silent nod to Patroclus
To spread a thick bed for Phoenix. It was time
For the others to think about leaving. Big Ajax,
Telamon's godlike son, said as much: 640

"Son of Laertes in the line of Zeus,
Resourceful Odysseus—it's time we go.
I do not think we will accomplish
What we were sent here to do. Our job now
Is to report this news quickly, bad as it is.   645
They will be waiting to hear. Achilles
Has made his great heart savage.
He is a cruel man, and has no regard
For the love that his friends honored him with,
Beyond anyone else who camps with the ships.   650
Pitiless. A man accepts compensation
For a murdered brother, a dead son.
The killer goes on living in the same town
After paying blood money, and the bereaved
Restrains his proud spirit and broken heart   655
Because he has received payment. But you,
The gods have replaced your heart

With flint and malice, because of one girl,
One single girl, while we are offering you
Seven of the finest women to be found   660
And many other gifts. Show some generosity
And some respect. We have come under your roof,
We few out of the entire army, trying hard
To be the friends you care for most of all."

And Achilles, the great runner, answered him: 665

"Ajax, son of Telamon in the line of Zeus,
Everything you say is after my own heart.
But I swell with rage when I think of how
The son of Atreus treated me like dirt
In public, as if I were some worthless tramp.   670
Now go, and take back this message:
I won't lift a finger in this bloody war
Until Priam's illustrious son Hector
Comes to the Myrmidons' ships and huts
Killing Greeks as he goes and torching the fleet.   675
But when he comes to my hut and my black ship
I think Hector will stop, for all his battle lust."

He spoke. They poured their libations
And headed for the ships, Odysseus leading.
Patroclus ordered a bed made ready   680
For Phoenix, and the old man lay down
On fleeces and rugs covered with linen
And waited for bright dawn. Achilles slept
In an inner alcove, and by his side
Lay a woman he had brought from Lesbos   685
With high, lovely cheekbones, Diomede her name,
Phorbas' daughter. Patroclus lay down
In the opposite corner, and with him lay Iphis,
A silken girl Achilles had given him
When he took steep Scyrus, Enyeus' city.   690

By now Odysseus and Ajax
Were in Agamemnon's quarters,
Surrounded by officers drinking their health
From gold cups and shouting questions.
Agamemnon, the warlord, had priority: 695

"Odysseus, pride of the Achaeans, tell me,
Is he willing to repel the enemy fire
And save the ships, or does he refuse,
His great heart still in the grip of wrath?"

Odysseus, who endured all, answered: 700

"Son of Atreus, most glorious Agamemnon,
Far from quenching his wrath, Achilles

Is filled with even more. He spurns you
And your gifts, and suggests that you
Think of a way to save the ships and the army.   705
He himself threatens, at dawn's first light,
To get his own ships onto the water,
And he said he would advise the others as well
To sail for home, since there is no chance now
You will storm Ilion's height. Zeus has stretched   710
His hand above her, making her people bold.
This is what he said, as these men here
Who came with me will tell you, Ajax
And the two heralds, prudent men both.
Phoenix will spend the night there. Tomorrow   715
He sails with Achilles on his voyage home,
If he wants to. He will not be forced to go."

They were stunned by the force of his words
And fell silent for a long time, hushed in grief,
Until at last Diomedes said in his booming voice: 720

"Son of Atreus, glorious Agamemnon,
You should never have pleaded with him
Or offered all those gifts. Achilles
Was arrogant enough without your help.
Let him do what he wants, stay here   725
Or get the hell out. He'll fight later, all right,
When he is ready or a god tells him to.
Now I want everyone to do as I say.
Enjoy some food and wine to keep up
Your strength, and then get some sleep.   730
When the rosy light first streaks the sky
Get your troops and horses into formation
Before the ships. Fight in the front yourselves."

The warlords assented, taken aback
By the authority of Diomedes' speech.   735
Each man poured libation and went to his hut,
Where he lay down and took the gift of sleep.

[After Achilles' refusal, the situation of the Greeks worsened rapidly. Agamemnon,
Diomedes, and Odysseus were all wounded. The Trojans breached the stockade and
fought beside the ships. Patroclus tried to bring Achilles to the aid of the Greeks, but
the most he could obtain was permission for himself to fight, clad in Achilles' armor, at
the head of the Myrmidons.]

FROM BOOK XVI

[Patroclus Fights and Dies]

Sarpedon[7] saw his comrades running   455
With their tunics flapping loose around their waists

---

7. King of Lycia in Asia Minor, son of Zeus and a mortal woman; he is a Trojan ally. (For his genealogy, see
his cousin Glaucus's account in his speech to Diomedes in book VI, esp. line 205.)

And being swatted down like flies by Patroclus.
He called out, appealing to their sense of shame:

"Why this sudden burst of speed, Lycian heroes?
Slow down a little, while I make the acquaintance   460
Of this nuisance of a Greek[8] who seems by now
To have hamstrung half the Trojan army."

And he stepped down from his chariot in his bronze
As Patroclus, seeing him, stepped down from his.

> High above a cliff vultures are screaming   465
> In the air as they savage each other's craws
> With their hooked beaks and talons.

And higher still,
Zeus watched with pity as the two heroes closed
And said to his wife Hera, who is his sister too: 470

"Fate has it that Sarpedon, whom I love more
Than any man, is to be killed by Patroclus.
Shall I take him out of battle while he still lives
And set him down in the rich land of Lycia,
Or shall I let him die under Patroclus' hands?"   475

And Hera, his lady, her eyes soft and wide:

"Son of Cronus, what a thing to say!
A mortal man, whose fate has long been fixed,
And you want to save him from rattling death?
Do it. But don't expect all of us to approve.   480
Listen to me. If you send Sarpedon home alive,
You will have to expect other gods to do the same
And save their own sons—and there are many of them
In this war around Priam's great city.
Think of the resentment you will create.   485
But if you love him and are filled with grief,
Let him fall in battle at Patroclus' hands,
And when his soul and life have left him,
Send Sleep[9] and Death to bear him away
To Lycia, where his people will give him burial   490
With mound and stone, as befits the dead."

The Father of Gods and Men agreed
Reluctantly, but shed drops of blood as rain
Upon the earth in honor of his own dear son
Whom Patroclus was about to kill   495
On Ilion's rich soil, far from his native land.

---

8. He is referring to Patroclus, who has returned to the battle wearing Achilles' armor.   9. The brother
of Death, according to the Greeks.

When they were close, Patroclus cast, and hit
Not Prince Sarpedon, but his lieutenant
Thrasymelus, a good man—a hard throw
Into the pit of his belly. He collapsed in a heap.   500
Sarpedon countered and missed. His bright spear
Sliced instead through the right shoulder
Of Pedasus,[1] who gave one pained, rasping whinny,
Then fell in the dust. His spirit fluttered off.
With the trace horse down, the remaining two   505
Struggled in the creaking yoke, tangling the reins.
Automedon[2] remedied this by drawing his sword
And cutting loose the trace horse. The other two
Righted themselves and pulled hard at the reins,
And the two warriors closed again in mortal combat.   510
Sarpedon cast again. Another miss. The spearpoint
Glinted as it sailed over Patroclus' left shoulder
Without touching him at all. Patroclus came back,
Leaning into his throw, and the bronze point
Caught Sarpedon just below the rib cage   515
Where it protects the beating heart. Sarpedon fell

> As a tree falls, oak, or poplar, or spreading pine,
> When carpenters cut it down in the forest
> With their bright axes, to be the beam of a ship,

And he lay before his horses and chariot,   520
Groaning heavily and clawing the bloody dust,

> Like some tawny, spirited bull a lion has killed
> In the middle of the shambling herd, groaning
> As it dies beneath the predator's jaws.

Thus beneath Patroclus the Lycian commander   525
Struggled in death. And he called his friend:

"Glaucus, it's time to show what you're made of
And be the warrior you've always been,
Heart set on evil war—if you're fast enough.
Hurry, rally our best to fight for my body,   530
All the Lycian leaders. Shame on you,
Glaucus, until your dying day, if the Greeks
Strip my body bare beside their ships.
Be strong and keep the others going."

The end came as he spoke, and death settled   535
On his nostrils and eyes. Patroclus put his heel
On Sarpedon's chest and pulled out his spear.
The lungs came out with it, and Sarpedon's life.

---

1. The third or trace horse that ran alongside the pair pulling Patroclus's chariot to help it maneuver. The other two horses are immortal, given by the gods to Achilles' father, Peleus. In the next lines, they shy away from contact with Death.   2. Patroclus's charioteer.

The Myrmidons steadied his snorting horses.
They did not want to leave their master's chariot.   540

Glaucus could hardly bear to hear Sarpedon's voice,
He was so grieved that he could not save him.
He pressed his arm with his hand. His wound
Tormented him, the wound he got when Teucer
Shot him with an arrow as he attacked the wall.[3]   545
He prayed to Apollo, lord of bright distances:

"Hear me, O Lord, wherever you are
In Lycia or Troy, for everywhere you hear
Men in their grief, and grief has come to me.
I am wounded, Lord, my arm is on fire,   550
And the blood can't be staunched. My shoulder
Is so sore I cannot hold a steady spear
And fight the enemy. Sarpedon is dead,
My Lord, and Zeus will not save his own son.
Heal my wound and deaden my pain,[4]   555
And give me the strength to call the Lycians
And urge them on to fight, and do battle myself
About the body of my fallen comrade."

Thus Glaucus' prayer, and Apollo heard him.
He stilled his pain and staunched the dark blood   560
That flowed from his wound. Glaucus felt
The god's strength pulsing through him,
Glad that his prayers were so quickly answered.
He rounded up the Lycian leaders
And urged them to fight for Sarpedon's body,   565
Then went with long strides to the Trojans,
To Polydamas, Agenor, Aeneas,
And then saw Hector's bronze-strapped face,
Went up to him and said levelly:

"Hector, you have abandoned your allies.   570
We have been putting our lives on the line for you
Far from our homes and loved ones,
And you don't care enough to lend us aid.
Sarpedon is down, our great warlord,
Whose word in Lycia was Lycia's law,   575
Killed by Patroclus under Ares' prodding.
Show some pride and fight for his body,
Or the Myrmidons will strip off the armor
And defile his corpse, in recompense
For all the Greeks we have killed by the ships."   580

This was almost too much for the Trojans.
Sarpedon, though a foreigner, had been

---

3. The wall erected by the Greeks to protect their ships, which was breached by the Trojans. "Teucer": an archer on the Greek side, half-brother of Ajax. 4. Apollo, who inflicted the plague in book I, is also the god of healing.

A mainstay of their city, the leader
Of a large force and its best fighter.
Hector led them straight at the Greeks, "For Sarpedon!"   585
And Patroclus, seeing them coming,
Urged on the already eager two Ajaxes:[5]

"Let me see you push these Trojans back
With everything you've ever had and more.
Sarpedon is down, first to breach our wall.   590
He's ours, to carve up his body and strip
The armor off. And all his little saviors
Are ours to massacre with cold bronze."

They heard this as if hearing their own words.
The lines on both sides hardened to steel.   595
Then Trojans and Lycians, Myrmidons and Greeks
Began fighting for the corpse, howling and cursing
As they threw themselves into the grinding battle.
And Zeus stretched hellish night over the armies
So they might do their lethal work over his son.   600

The Trojans at first pushed back the Greeks
When Epeigeus was hit, Agacles' son.
This man was far from the worst of the Myrmidons.
He once lived in Boudeum, but having killed
A cousin of his, came as a suppliant   605
To Peleus and silver-footed Thetis,
Who sent him with Achilles to fight at Troy.
He had his hand on the corpse when Hector
Brought down a stone on his head, splitting his skull
In two inside his heavy helmet. He collapsed   610
On Sarpedon's body, and death drifted over him.
Patroclus ached for his friend and swooped
Into the front like a hawk after sparrows—
Yes, my Patroclus—and they scattered like birds
Before your anger for your fallen comrade.   615
Sthenelaos, Ithaemenes' beloved son,
Never knew what hit him. The stone Patroclus threw
Severed the tendons at the nape of his neck.
The Trojan champions, including Hector,
Now withdrew, about as far as a javelin flies   620
When a man who knows how throws it hard
In competition or in mortal combat.

The Greeks pressed after them, and Glaucus,
The Lycian commander now, wheeled around
And killed Bathycles, a native of Hellas   625
And the wealthiest of the Myrmidons.
He was just catching up with Glaucus

5. Of the two Greek warriors with this name, the son of Telamon was among the most outstanding fighters
at Troy; the less distinguished son of Oïleus still played a prominent role in battle (and, according to poetry
outside the *Iliad*, in the sack of Troy). They are sometimes found fighting together.

When the Lycian suddenly pivoted on his heel
And put his spear straight into Bathycles' chest.
He fell hard, and the Greeks winced.   630
A good man was down, much to the pleasure
Of the Trojans, who thronged around his body.

But the Greeks took the offensive again,
And Meriones[6] killed Laogonus,
A priest of Idaean[7] Zeus who was himself   635
Honored as a god. Meriones thrust hard
Into his jaw, just beneath the ear,
And he was dead, in the hated dark.
Aeneas launched his spear at Meriones,
Hoping to hit him as he advanced   640
Under cover of his shield, but Meriones
Saw the spear coming and ducked forward,
Leaving it to punch into the ground and stand there
Quivering, as if Ares had twanged it
So it could spend its fury. Aeneas fumed: 645

"That would have been your last dance,[8] Meriones,
Your last dance, if only my spear had hit you!"

And Meriones, himself famed for his spear:

"Do you think you can kill everyone
Who comes up against you, Aeneas,   650
And defends himself? You're mortal stuff too.
If I got a solid hit on you with my spear
You'd be down in no time, for all your strength.
You'd give me the glory, and your life to Hades."
Patroclus would have none of this, and yelled: 655

"Cut the chatter, Meriones. You're a good man,
But don't think the Trojans are going to retreat
From the corpse because you make fun of them.
Use hands in war, words in council.

Save your big speeches; we've got fighting to do."   660

And he moved ahead, with Meriones,
Who himself moved like a god, in his wake.

    Woodcutters are working in a distant valley,
    But the sound of their axes, and of trees falling,
    Can be heard for miles around in the mountains.   665

The plain of Troy thrummed with the sound
Of bronze and hide stretched into shields,
And of swords and spears knifing into these.

6. A warrior from Crete on the Greek side.   7. Of Ida, a high mountain near Troy where Zeus had a cult
(and from which he watches the fighting on the plain).   8. In Homer, the opposite of warfare.

Sarpedon's body was indistinguishable
From the blood and grime and splintered spears   670
That littered his body from head to foot.

    But if you have ever seen how flies
    Cluster about the brimming milk pails
    On a dairy farm in early summer,

You will have some idea of the throng   675
Around Sarpedon's corpse.
                  And not once did Zeus
Avert his luminous eyes from the combatants.
All this time he looked down at them and pondered
When Patroclus should die, whether
Shining Hector should kill him then and there   680
In the conflict over godlike Sarpedon
And strip the armor from his body, or whether
He should live to destroy even more Trojans.
And as he pondered it seemed preferable
That Achilles' splendid surrogate should once more   685
Drive the Trojans and bronze-helmed Hector
Back to the city, and take many lives.
And Hector felt it, felt his blood turn milky,
And mounted his chariot, calling to the others
To begin the retreat, that Zeus' scales were tipping.   690
Not even the Lycians stayed, not with Sarpedon
Lying at the bottom of a pile of bodies
That had fallen upon him in this node of war.

The Greek stripped at last the glowing bronze
From Sarpedon's shoulders, and Patroclus gave it   695
To some of his comrades to take back to the ships.

Then Zeus turned to Apollo and said:

"Sun God, take our Sarpedon out of range.
Cleanse his wounds of all the clotted blood,
And wash him in the river far away   700
And anoint him with our holy chrism
And wrap the body in a deathless shroud
And give him over to be taken swiftly
By Sleep and Death to Lycia,
Where his people shall give him burial   705
With mound and stone, as befits the dead."

And Apollo went down from Ida
Into the howling dust of war,
And cleansed Sarpedon's wounds of all the blood,
And washed him in the river far away   710
And anointed him with holy chrism
And wrapped the body in a deathless shroud
And gave him over to be taken swiftly
By Sleep and Death to Lycia.

Patroclus called to his horses and charioteer   715
And pressed on after the Trojans and Lycians,
Forgetting everything Achilles had said[9]
And mindless of the black fates gathering above.
Even then you might have escaped them,
Patroclus, but Zeus' mind is stronger than men's,   720
And Zeus now put fury in your heart.

Do you remember it, Patroclus, all the Trojans
You killed as the gods called you to your death?
Adrastus was first, then Autonous, and Echeclus,
Perimas, son of Megas, Epistor, Melanippus,   725
Elasus, Mulius, and last, Pylartes,
And it would have been more, but the others ran,
Back to Troy, which would have fallen that day
By Patroclus' hands.

                But Phoebus Apollo
Had taken his stand on top of Troy's wall.   730

              Three times Patroclus
Reached the parapet, and three times
Apollo's fingers flicked against the human's shield
And pushed him off. But when he came back
A fourth time, like a spirit from beyond,   735
Apollo's voice split the daylight in two:

"Get back, Patroclus, back where you belong.
Troy is fated to fall, but not to you,
Nor even to Achilles, a better man by far."

And Patroclus was off, putting distance   740
Between himself and that wrathful voice.

   Hector had halted his horses at the Western Gate
And was deciding whether to drive back into battle
Or call for a retreat to within the walls.
While he pondered this, Phoebus Apollo   745
Came up to him in the guise of Asius.
This man was Hector's uncle on his mother's side,
And Apollo looked just like him as he spoke:

"Why are you out of action, Hector? It's not right.
If I were as much stronger than you as I am weaker,   750
You'd pay dearly for withdrawing from battle.
Get in that chariot and go after Patroclus.
Who knows? Apollo may give you the glory."

Hector commanded Cebriones, his charioteer,
To whip the horses into battle. Apollo melted   755

---

9. In sending Patroclus into battle, Achilles told him only to chase the Trojans from the Greek ships and not to pursue them all the way back to Troy.

Into the throng, a god into the toil of men.
The Greeks felt a sudden chill,
While Hector and the Trojans felt their spirits lift.
Hector was not interested in the other Greeks.
He drove through them and straight for Patroclus,   760
Who leapt down from his own chariot
With a spear in one hand and in the other
A jagged piece of granite he had scooped up
And now cupped in his palm. He got set,
And without more than a moment of awe   765
For who his opponent was, hurled the stone.
The throw was not wasted. He hit Hector's
Charioteer, Cebriones, Priam's bastard son,
As he stood there holding the reins. The sharp stone
Caught him right in the forehead, smashing   770
His brows together and shattering the skull.
So that his eyeballs spurted out and dropped
Into the dirt before his feet. He flipped backward
From the chariot like a diver, and his soul
Dribbled away from his bones. And you,   775
Patroclus, you, my horseman, mocked him:

"What a spring the man has! Nice dive!
Think of the oysters he could come up with
If he were out at sea, jumping off the boat
In all sorts of weather, to judge by the dive   780
He just took from his chariot onto the plain."

And with that he rushed at the fallen warrior

   Like a lion who has been wounded in the chest
   As he ravages a farmstead, and his own valor
   Destroys him.

                    Yes, Patroclus, that is how you leapt   785
Upon Cebriones.
                    Hector vaulted from his chariot,
And the two of them fought over Cebriones

   Like a pair of lions fighting over a slain deer
   In the high mountains, both of them ravenous,
   Both high of heart,

                              very much like these two   790
Human heroes hacking at each other with bronze.
Hector held Cebriones' head and would not let go.
Patroclus had hold of a foot, and around them
Greeks and Trojans squared off and fought.

   Winds sometimes rise in a deep mountain wood   795
   From different directions, and the trees—
   Beech, ash, and cornelian cherry—

Batter each other with their long, tapered branches,
And you can hear the sound from a long way off,
The unnerving splintering of hardwood limbs.   800

The Trojans and Greeks collided in battle,
And neither side thought of yielding ground.

Around Cebriones many spears were stuck,
Many arrows flew singing from the string,
And many stones thudded onto the shields   805
Of men fighting around him. But there he lay
In the whirling dust, one of the great,
    Forgetful of his horsemanship.

    While the sun still straddled heaven's meridian,
Soldiers on both sides were hit and fell.   810
But when the sun moved down the sky and men
All over earth were unyoking their oxen,
The Greeks' success exceeded their destiny.
They pulled Cebriones from the Trojan lines
And out of range, and stripped his armor.   815

And then Patroclus unleashed himself.

Three times he charged into the Trojan ranks
With the raw power of Ares, yelling coldly,
And on each charge he killed nine men.
But when you made your fourth, demonic charge,   820
Then—did you feel it, Patroclus?—out of the mist,
Your death coming to meet you. It was
Apollo, whom you did not see in the thick of battle,
Standing behind you, and the flat of his hand
Found the space between your shoulder blades.   825
The sky's blue disk went spinning in your eyes
As Achilles' helmet rang beneath the horses' hooves,
And rolled in the dust—no, that couldn't be right[1]—
Those handsome horsehair plumes grimed with blood,
The gods would never let that happen to the helmet   830
That had protected the head and graceful brow
Of divine Achilles. But the gods did
Let it happen, and Zeus would now give the helmet
To Hector, whose own death was not far off.

Nothing was left of Patroclus' heavy battle spear   835
But splintered wood, his tasselled shield and baldric
Fell to the ground, and Apollo, Prince of the Sky,
Split loose his breastplate. And he stood there, naked,
Astounded, his silvery limbs floating away,
Until one of the Trojans slipped up behind him   840
And put his spear through, a boy named Euphorbus,

---

1. Because it was divinely made, part of the armor given by the gods to Peleus on his marriage to Thetis.

The best his age with a spear, mounted or on foot.
He had already distinguished himself in this war
By knocking twenty warriors out of their cars
The first time he went out for chariot lessons.   845
It was this boy who took his chance at you,
Patroclus, but instead of finishing you off,
He pulled his spear out and ran back where he belonged,
Unwilling to face even an unarmed Patroclus,
Who staggered back toward his comrades, still alive,   850
But overcome by the god's stroke, and the spear.

Hector was watching this, and when he saw
Patroclus withdrawing with a wound, he muscled
His way through to him and rammed his spearhead
Into the pit of his belly and all the way through.   855
Patroclus fell heavily. You could hear the Greeks wince.

>   *A boar does not wear out easily, but a lion*
>   *Will overpower it when the two face off*
>   *Over a trickling spring up in the mountains*
>   *They both want to drink from. The boar*   860
>   *Pants hard, but the lion comes out on top.*

So too did Hector, whose spear was draining the life
From Menoetius' son, who had himself killed many.

His words beat down on Patroclus like dark wings:

"So, Patroclus, you thought you could ransack my city   865
And ship our women back to Greece to be your slaves.
You little fool. They are defended by me,
By Hector, by my horses and my spear. I am the one,
Troy's best, who keeps their doom at bay. But you,
Patroclus, the vultures will eat you   870
On this very spot. Your marvelous Achilles.
Has done you no good at all. I can just see it,
Him sitting in his tent and telling you as you left:
'Don't bother coming back to the ships,
Patroclus, until you have ripped Hector's heart out   875
Through his bloody shirt.[2] That's what he said,
Isn't it? And you were stupid enough to listen.'"

And Patroclus, barely able to shake the words out:

"Brag while you can, Hector. Zeus and Apollo
Have given you an easy victory this time.   880
If they hadn't knocked off my armor,
I could have made mincemeat of twenty like you.
It was Fate, and Leto's son, who killed me.
Of men, Euphorbus. You came in third at best.

---

2. Hector is, of course, wrong.

And one more thing for you to think over.   885
You're not going to live long. I see Death
Standing at your shoulder, and you going down
Under the hands of Peleus' perfect son."

Death's veil covered him as he said these things;
And his soul, bound for Hades, fluttered out   890
Resentfully, forsaking manhood's bloom.
He was dead when Hector said to him:

"Why prophesy my death, Patroclus?
Who knows? Achilles, son of Thetis,
May go down first under my spear."   895

And propping his heel against the body,
He extracted his bronze spear and took off
After Automedon. But Automedon was gone,
Pulled by immortal horses, the splendid gifts
   The gods once gave to Peleus.   900

[Hector stripped Achilles' divine armor from Patroclus's corpse. A fierce fight for the body itself ended in partial success for the Greeks; they took Patroclus's body but had to retreat to their camp, with the Trojans at their heels.]

BOOK XVIII

[*The Shield of Achilles*]

   The fight went on, like wildfire burning.
Antilochus,[3] running hard like a herald,
Found Achilles close to his upswept hulls,
His great heart brooding with premonitions
Of what had indeed already happened.   5

   "This looks bad,
All these Greeks with their hair in the wind
Stampeding off the plain and back to the ships.
God forbid that what my mother told me
Has now come true, that while I'm still alive   10
Trojan hands would steal the sunlight
From the best of all the Myrmidons.
Patroclus, Menoetius' brave son, is dead.
Damn him! I told him only to repel
The enemy fire from our ships,   15
And not to take on Hector in a fight."

Antilochus was in tears when he reached him
And delivered his unendurable message:

"Son of wise Peleus, this is painful news
For you to hear, and I wish it were not true.   20

---

3. A son of Nestor. He has been sent to tell Achilles that Patroclus is dead.

Patroclus is down, and they are fighting
For his naked corpse. Hector has the armor."

A mist of black grief enveloped Achilles.
He scooped up fistfuls of sunburnt dust
And poured it on his head, fouling   25
His beautiful face. Black ash grimed
His fine-spun cloak as he stretched his huge body
Out in the dust and lay there,
Tearing out his hair with his hands.
The women, whom Achilles and Patroclus   30
Had taken in raids, ran shrieking out of the tent
To be with Achilles, and they beat their breasts
Until their knees gave out beneath them.
Antilochus, sobbing himself, stayed with Achilles
And held his hands—he was groaning   35
From the depths of his soul—for fear
He would lay open his own throat with steel.

The sound of Achilles' grief stung the air.

Down in the water his mother heard him,
Sitting in the sea depths beside her old father,   40
And she began to wail.
                        And the saltwater women
Gathered around her, all the deep-sea Nereids,
Glaucē and Thaleia and Cymodocē,
Neseia and Speio, Thoē and ox-eyed Haliē,
Cymothoē, Actaeē, and Limnoeira,   45
Melitē and Iaera, Amphithoē and Agauē,
Doris, Panopē, and milk-white Galateia,
Nemertes, Apseudes, and Callianassa,
Clymenē, Ianeira, Ianassa, and Maera,
Oreithyia and Amatheia, hair streaming behind her,   50
And all of the other deep-sea Nereids.
They filled the silver, shimmering cave,
And they all beat their breasts.

                        Thetis led the lament:

"Hear me, sisters, hear the pain in my heart.
I gave birth to a son, and that is my sorrow,   55
My perfect son, the best of heroes.
He grew like a sapling, and I nursed him
As I would a plant on the hill in my garden,
And I sent him to Ilion on a sailing ship
To fight the Trojans. And now I will never   60
Welcome him home again to Peleus' house.
As long as he lives and sees the sunlight
He will be in pain, and I cannot help him.
But I'll go now to see and hear my dear son,
Since he is suffering while he waits out the war."   65

She left the cave, and they went with her,
Weeping, and around them a wave
Broke through the sea, and they came to Troy.
They emerged on the beach where the Myrmidons' ships
Formed an encampment around Achilles.   70
He was groaning deeply, and his mother
Stood next to him and held her son's head.
Her lamentation hung sharp in the air,
And then she spoke in low, sorrowful tones:

"Child, why are you crying? What pain   75
Has come to your heart? Speak, don't hide it.
Zeus has granted your prayer. The Greeks
Have all been beaten back to their ships
And suffered horribly. They can't do without you."

Achilles answered her: 80

"Mother, Zeus may have done all this for me,
But how can I rejoice? My friend is dead,
Patroclus, my dearest friend of all. I loved him,
And I killed him. And the armor—
Hector cut him down and took off his body   85
The heavy, splendid armor, beautiful to see,
That the gods gave to Peleus as a gift
On the day they put you to bed with a mortal.
You should have stayed with the saltwater women,
And Peleus should have married a mortal.   90
But now—it was all so you would suffer pain
For your ravaged son. You will never again
Welcome me home, since I no longer have the will
To remain alive among men, not unless Hector
Loses his life on the point of my spear   95
And pays for despoiling Menoetius' son."

And Thetis, in tears, said to him:

"I won't have you with me for long, my child,
If you say such things. Hector's death means yours."

From under a great weight, Achilles answered: 100

"Then let me die now. I was no help
To him when he was killed out there. He died
Far from home, and he needed me to protect him.
But now, since I'm not going home, and wasn't
A light for Patroclus or any of the rest   105
Of my friends who have been beaten by Hector,
But just squatted by my ships, a dead weight on the earth . . .
I stand alone in the whole Greek army
When it comes to war—though some do speak better.
I wish all strife could stop, among gods   110

And among men, and anger too—it sends
Sensible men into fits of temper,
It drips down our throats sweeter than honey
And mushrooms up in our bellies like smoke.
Yes, the warlord Agamemnon angered me.   115
But we'll let that be, no matter how it hurts,
And conquer our pride, because we must.
But I'm going now to find the man who destroyed
My beloved—Hector.
                    As for my own fate,
I'll accept it whenever it pleases Zeus   120
And the other immortal gods to send it.
Not even Heracles[4] could escape his doom.
He was dearest of all to Lord Zeus, but fate
And Hera's hard anger destroyed him.
If it is true that I have a fate like his, then I too   125
Will lie down in death.
                    But now to win glory
And make some Trojan woman or deep-breasted
Dardanian[5] matron wipe the tears
From her soft cheeks, make her sob and groan.
Let them feel how long I've been out of the war.   130
Don't try, out of love, to stop me. I won't listen."

And Thetis, her feet silver on the sand:

"Yes, child. It's not wrong to save your friends
When they are beaten to the brink of death.
But your beautiful armor is in the hands of the Trojans,   135
The mirrored bronze. Hector himself
Has it on his shoulders. He glories in it.
Not for long, though. I see his death is near.
But you, don't dive into the red dust of war
Until with your own eyes you see me returning.   140
Tomorrow I will come with the rising sun
Bearing beautiful armor from Lord Hephaestus."

Thetis spoke, turned away
From her son, and said to her saltwater sisters:

"Sink now into the sea's wide lap   145
And go down to our old father's house
And tell him all this. I am on my way
Up to Olympus to visit Hephaestus,
The glorious smith, to see if for my sake
He will give my son glorious armor."   150

As she spoke they dove into the waves,
And the silver-footed goddess was gone
Off to Olympus to fetch arms for her child.

4. The greatest of Greek hereos, the son of Zeus by a mortal woman; pursued by the jealousy of Hera, he
was forced to undertake twelve great labors and finally died in agony from the effects of a poisoned garment.   5. Trojan.

And while her feet carried her off to Olympus,
Hector yelled, a yell so bloodcurdling and loud   155
It stampeded the Greeks all the way back
To their ships beached on the Hellespont's shore.
They could not pull the body of Patroclus
Out of javelin range, and soon Hector,
With his horses and men, stood over it again.   160
Three times Priam's resplendent son
Took hold of the corpse's heels and tried
To drag it off, bawling commands to his men.
Three times the two Ajaxes put their heads down,
Charged, and beat him back. Unshaken, Hector   165
Sidestepped, cut ahead, or held his ground
With a shout, but never yielded an inch.

    It was like shepherds against a starving lion,
    Helpless to beat it back from a carcass,

The two Ajaxes unable to rout   170
The son of Priam from Patroclus' corpse.
And Hector would have, to his eternal glory,
Dragged the body off, had not Iris[6] stormed
Down from Olympus with a message for Achilles,
Unbeknownst to Zeus and the other gods.   175
Hera had sent her, and this was her message:

"Rise, son of Peleus, most formidable of men.
Rescue Patroclus, for whom a terrible battle
Is pitched by the ships, men killing each other,
Some fighting to save the dead man's body,   180
The Trojans trying to drag it back
To windy Ilion. Hector's mind especially
Is bent on this. He means to impale the head
On Troy's palisade after he strips off its skin.
And you just lie there? Think of Patroclus   185
Becoming a ragbone for Trojan dogs. Shame
To your dying day if his corpse is defiled."

The shining sprinter Achilles answered her:

"Iris, which god sent you here?"

And Iris, whose feet are wind, responded: 190

"None other than Hera, Zeus' glorious wife.
But Zeus on high does not know this, nor do
Any of the immortals on snow-capped Olympus."

And Achilles, the great runner:

---

6. Goddess of the rainbow and the usual messenger of the gods in the *Iliad*.

"How can I go to war? They have my armor.   195
And my mother told me not to arm myself
Until with my own eyes I see her come back
With fine weapons from Hephaestus.
I don't know any other armor that would fit,
Unless maybe the shield of Telamonian Ajax.[7]   200
But he's out there in the front ranks, I hope,
Fighting with his spear over Patroclus dead."

Windfoot Iris responded:

"We know very well that they have your armor.
Just go to the trench and let the Trojans see you.   205
One look will be enough. The Trojans will back off
Out of fear of you, and this will give the Greeks
Some breathing space, what little there is in war."

Iris spoke and was gone. And Achilles,
Whom the gods loved, rose. Around   210
His mighty shoulders Athena threw
Her tasselled aegis,[8] and the shining goddess
Haloed his head with a golden cloud
That shot flames from its incandescent glow.

Smoke is rising through the pure upper air   215
From a besieged city on a distant island.
Its soldiers have fought hard all day,
But at sunset they light innumerable fires
So that their neighbors in other cities
Might see the glare reflected off the sky   220
And sail to their help as allies in war.

So too the radiance that flared
From Achilles' head and up to the sky.
He went to the trench—away from the wall
And the other Greeks, out of respect   225
For his mother's tense command. Standing there,
He yelled, and behind him Pallas Athena
Amplified his voice, and shock waves
Reverberated through the Trojan ranks.

You have heard the piercing sound of horns   230
When squadrons come to destroy a city.

The Greek's voice was like that,
Speaking bronze that made each Trojan heart
Wince with pain.
              And the combed horses
Shied from their chariots, eyes wide with fear,   235

---

7. The son of Telemon, the more famous of the two heroes named Ajax. His distinctive attribute in the *Iliad* is a huge shield that covers his whole body.   8. A tasseled garment or piece of armor that belonged to Zeus but was often carried by Athena in poetry and art. It induced panic when shaken at an enemy.

And their drivers went numb when they saw
The fire above Achilles' head
Burned into the sky by the Grey-Eyed One.[9]
Three times Achilles shouted from the trench;
Three times the Trojans and their confederates   240
Staggered and reeled, twelve of their best
Lost in the crush of chariots and spears.
But the Greeks were glad to pull Patroclus' body
Out of range and placed it on a litter. His comrades
Gathered around, weeping, and with them Achilles,   245
Shedding hot tears when he saw his loyal friend
Stretched out on the litter, cut with sharp bronze.
He had sent him off to war with horses and chariot,
But he never welcomed him back home again.

And now the ox-eyed Lady Hera   250
Sent the tireless, reluctant sun
Under the horizon into Ocean's streams,
Its last rays touching the departing Greeks with gold.
It had been a day of brutal warfare.

   After the Trojans withdrew from battle,   255
They unhitched their horses from the chariots
And held an assembly before thinking of supper.
They remained on their feet, too agitated to sit,
Terrified, in fact, that Achilles,
After a long absence, was back.   260
Polydamas was the first to speak, prudent
Son of Panthous, the only Trojan who looked
Both ahead and behind.[1] This man was born
The same night as Hector, and was his comrade,
As good with words as Hector was with a spear.   265
He had their best interests at heart when he spoke:

"Take a good look around, my friends. My advice
Is to return to the city and not wait for daylight
On the plain by the ships. We are far from our wall.
As long as this man raged against Agamemnon,   270
The Greeks were easier to fight against.
I too was glad when I spent the night by the ships,
Hoping we would capture their upswept hulls.
That hope has given way to a terrible fear
Of Peleus' swift son. He is a violent man   275
And will not be content to fight on the plain
Where Greeks and Trojans engage in combat.
It is for our city he will fight, and our wives.
We must go back. Trust me, this is how it will be:
Night is holding him back now, immortal night.   280
But if he finds us here tomorrow
When he comes out in his armor in daylight,

9. Athena.   1. That is, he was a prophet; he knew the past and foresaw the future.

Then you will know what Achilles is,
And you will be glad to be back in sacred Ilion—
If you make it back, and are not one   285
Of the many Trojans the dogs and vultures
Will feast upon. I hope I'm not within earshot.
But if we trust my words, as much as it may gall,
We will camp tonight in the marketplace, where
The city is protected by its towers, walls,   290
And high gates closed with bolted, polished doors.
At dawn we take our positions on the wall
In full armor, and so much the worse for him
If he wants to come out from the ships and fight us
For our wall. He will go back to the ships   295
After he has had enough of parading
His high-necked prancers in front of the city.
He will not have the will to force his way in.
Dogs will eat him before he takes our town."

And Hector, glaring at him under his helmet: 300

"Polydamas, I don't like this talk
About a retreat and holing up in the city.
Aren't you sick of being penned inside our walls?
People everywhere used to talk about how rich
Priam's city was, all the gold, all the bronze.   305
Now the great houses are empty, their heirlooms
Sold away to Phrygia, to Maeonia,² since Zeus
Has turned wrathful. But now—when the great god,
Son of Cronus, has vouchsafed me the glory
Of hemming the Greeks in beside the sea—   310
Now is no time for you to talk like a fool.
Not a Trojan here will listen. I won't let them.
   Now hear this! All troops will mess tonight
With guards posted and on general alert.
If any of you are worried about your effects,   315
You can hand them over for distribution!
Better our men should have them than the Greeks.
At first light we strap on our armor
And start fighting hard by the ships.
If Achilles really has risen up again   320
And wants to come out, he'll find it tough going,
For I will be there. I, for one,
Am not retreating. Maybe he'll win, maybe I will.
The War God doesn't care which one he kills."

Thus Hector, and the Trojans cheered,   325
The fools, their wits dulled by Pallas Athena.
Hector's poor counsel won all the applause,
And not a man praised Polydamas' good sense.
Then the troops started supper.

---

2. Countries in Asia Minor allied with Troy.

But the Greeks
Mourned Patroclus the whole night through.   330
Achilles began the incessant lamentation,
Laying his man-slaying hands on Patroclus' chest
And groaning over and over like a bearded lion

    Whose cubs some deer hunter has smuggled out
    Of the dense woods. When the lion returns,   335
    It tracks the human from valley to valley,
    Growling low the whole time. Sometimes it finds him.

Achilles' deep voice sounded among the Myrmidons:

"It was all for nothing, what I said that day
When I tried to hearten the hero Menoetius,   340
Telling him I would bring his glorious son
Home to Opoeis[3] with his share of the spoils
After I had sacked Ilion. Zeus does not fulfill
A man's every thought. We two are fated
To redden the selfsame earth with our blood,   345
Right here in Troy. I will never return home
To be welcomed by my old father, Peleus,
Or Thetis, my mother. The earth here will hold me.
And since I will pass under the earth after you,
Patroclus, I will not bury you until   350
I have brought here the armor and head of Hector,
Who killed you, great soul. And I will cut
The throats of twelve Trojan princes
Before your pyre in my wrath. Until then,
You will lie here beside our upswept hulls   355
Just as you are, and round about you
Deep-bosomed Trojan and Dardanian women
Will lament you day and night, weeping,
Women we won with blood, sweat and tears,
Women we cut through rich cities to get."   360

With that, he ordered his companions
To put a great cauldron on the fire,
So they could wash the gore
From Patroclus' body without further delay.
They put a cauldron used for heating baths   365
Over a blazing fire and poured in the water,
Then stoked the fire with extra wood.
The flames licked the cauldron's belly
And the water grew warm. When it was boiling
In the glowing bronze, they washed the body,   370
Anointed it with rich olive oil,
And filled the wounds with a seasoned ointment.
Then they laid him on his bed, covered him
From head to foot with a soft linen cloth,

---

3. An ancient city near the eastern coast of the central Greek mainland and home of Menoetius, father of
Patroclus.

And spread a white mantle above it.   375
Then the whole night through the Myrmidons
Stood with Achilles, mourning Patroclus.

Zeus said to Hera, his wife and sister:

"So you have had your way, my ox-eyed lady.
You have roused Achilles, swift of foot. Truly,   380
The long-haired Greeks must be from your womb."

And the ox-eyed lady Hera replied:

"Awesome son of Cronus, what a thing to say!
Even a mortal man, without my wisdom,
Will succeed in his efforts for another man.   385
How then was I—the highest of goddesses
Both by my own birth and by marriage to you,
The lord and ruler of all the immortals—
Not to cobble up evil for Troy in my wrath?"

   While they spoke to each other this way,   390
Thetis' silver feet took her to Hephaestus' house,
A mansion the lame god had built himself
Out of starlight and bronze, and beyond all time.
She found him at his bellows, glazed with sweat
As he hurried to complete his latest project,   395
Twenty cauldrons on tripods to line his hall,
With golden wheels at the base of each tripod
So they could move by themselves to the gods' parties
And return to his house—a wonder to see.
They were almost done. The intricate handles   400
Still had to be attached. He was getting these ready,
Forging the rivets with inspired artistry,
When the silver-footed goddess came up to him.
And Charis,[4] Hephaestus' wife, lovely
In her shimmering veil, saw her, and running up,   405
She clasped her hand and said to her:

"My dear Thetis, so grave in your long, robe,
What brings you here now? You almost never visit.
Do come inside so I can offer you something."

And the shining goddess led her along   410
And had her sit down in a graceful
Silver-studded chair with a footstool.
Then she called to Hephaestus, and said:

"Hephaestus, come here.
Thetis needs you for something."   415

---

4. Literally, "grace" or "beauty."

And the renowned smith called back:

"Thetis? Then the dread goddess I revere
Is inside. She saved me when I lay suffering
From my long fall, after my shameless mother
Threw me out, wanting to hide my infirmity.   420
And I really would have suffered, had not Thetis
And Eurynome, a daughter of Ocean Stream,
Taken me into their bosom. I stayed with them
Nine years, forging all kinds of jewelry,
Brooches and bracelets and necklaces and pins,   425
In their hollow cave, while the Ocean's tides,
Murmuring with foam, flowed endlessly around.
No one knew I was there, neither god nor mortal,
Except my rescuers, Eurynome and Thetis.
Now the goddess has come to our house.   430
I owe her my life and would repay her in full.
Set out our finest for her, Charis,
While I put away my bellows and tools."

He spoke and raised his panting bulk
Up from his anvil, limping along quickly   435
On his spindly shanks. He set the bellows
Away from the fire, gathered up the tools
He had been using, and put them away
In a silver chest. Then he took a sponge
And wiped his face and hands, his thick neck,   440
And his shaggy chest. He put on a tunic,
Grabbed a stout staff, and as he went out
Limping, attendants rushed up to support him,
Attendants made of gold who looked like real girls,
With a mind within, and a voice, and strength,   445
And knowledge of crafts from the immortal gods.
These busily moved to support their lord,
And he came hobbling up to where Thetis was,
Sat himself down on a polished chair,
And clasping her hand in his, he said: 450

"My dear Thetis, so grave in your long robe,
What brings you here now? You almost never visit.
Tell me what you have in mind, and I will do it
If it is anything that is at all possible to do."

And Thetis, shedding tears as she spoke: 455

"Hephaestus, is there a goddess on Olympus
Who has suffered as I have? Zeus son of Cronus
Has given me suffering beyond all the others.
Of all the saltwater women he singled me out
To be subject to a man, Aeacus' son Peleus.   460
I endured a man's bed, much against my will.
He lies in his halls forspent with old age,

But I have other griefs now. He gave me a son
To bear and to rear, the finest of heroes.
He grew like a sapling, and I nursed him   465
As I would nurse a plant in my hillside garden,
And I sent him to Ilion on a sailing ship
To fight the Trojans. And now I will never
Welcome him home again to Peleus' house.
As long as he lives and sees the sunlight   470
He will be in pain, and I cannot help him.
The girl that the army chose as his prize
Lord Agamemnon took out of his arms.
He was wasting his heart out of grief for her,
But now the Trojans have penned the Greeks   475
In their beachhead camp, and the Argive elders
Have petitioned him with a long list of gifts.
He refused to beat off the enemy himself,
But he let Patroclus wear his armor,
And sent him into battle with many men.   480
All day long they fought by the Scaean Gates
And would have sacked the city that very day,
But after Menoetius' valiant son
Had done much harm, Apollo killed him
In the front ranks and gave Hector the glory.   485
So I have come to your knees, to see if you
Will give my son, doomed to die young,
A shield and helmet, a fine set of greaves,
And a corselet too. His old armor was lost
When the Trojans killed his faithful companion,   490
And now he lies on the ground in anguish."

And the renowned smith answered her:

"Take heart, Thetis, and do not be distressed.
I only regret I do not have the power
To hide your son from death when it comes.   495
But armor he will have, forged to a wonder,
And its terrible beauty will be a marvel to men."

Hephaestus left her there and went to his bellows,
Turned them toward the fire and ordered them to work.
And the bellows, all twenty, blew on the crucibles,   500
Blasting out waves of heat in whatever direction
Hephaestus wanted as he hustled here and there
Around his forge and the work progressed.
He cast durable bronze onto the fire, and tin,
Precious gold and silver. Then he positioned   505
His enormous anvil up on its block
And grasped his mighty hammer
In one hand, and in the other his tongs.

He made a shield first, heavy and huge,
Every inch of it intricately designed.   510

He threw a triple rim around it, glittering
Like lightning, and he made the strap silver.
The shield itself was five layers thick, and he
Crafted its surface with all of his genius.

On it he made the earth, the sky, the sea,   515
The unwearied sun, and the moon near full,
And all the signs that garland the sky,
Pleiades, Hyades, mighty Orion,
And the Bear[5] they also call the Wagon,
Which pivots in place and looks back at Orion   520
    And alone is aloof from the wash of Ocean.

On it he made two cities, peopled
And beautiful. Weddings in one, festivals,
Brides led from their rooms by torchlight
Up through the town, bridal song rising,   525
Young men reeling in dance to the tune
Of lyres and flutes, and the women
Standing in their doorways admiring them.
There was a crowd in the market-place
And a quarrel arising between two men   530
Over blood money for a murder,
One claiming the right to make restitution,
The other refusing to accept any terms.
They were heading for an arbitrator
And the people were shouting, taking sides,   535
But heralds restrained them. The elders sat
On polished stone seats in the sacred circle
And held in their hands the staves of heralds.
The pair rushed up and pleaded their cases,
And between them lay two ingots of gold   540
    For whoever spoke straightest in judgment.

Around the other city two armies
Of glittering soldiery were encamped.
Their leaders were at odds—should they
Move in for the kill or settle for a division   545
Of all the lovely wealth the citadel held fast?
The citizens wouldn't surrender, and armed
For an ambush. Their wives and little children
Were stationed on the wall, and with the old men
Held it against attack. The citizens moved out,   550
Led by Ares and Pallas Athena,
Both of them gold, and their clothing was gold,
Beautiful and larger than life in their armor, as befits
Gods in their glory, and all the people were smaller.
They came to a position perfect for an ambush,   555
A spot on the river where stock came to water,

---

5. Ursa Major, or the Big Dipper, which never descends below the horizon (that is, into Ocean). The Pleiades, Hyades, and Orion are all clusters of stars or constellations. Orion was a giant hunter of Greek mythology.

And took their places, concealed by fiery bronze.
Farther up they had two lookouts posted
Waiting to sight shambling cattle and sheep,
Which soon came along, trailed by two herdsmen   560
Playing their panpipes, completely unsuspecting.
When the townsmen lying in ambush saw this
They ran up, cut off the herds of cattle and fleecy
Silver sheep, and killed the two herdsmen.
When the armies sitting in council got wind   565
Of the ruckus with the cattle, they mounted
Their high-stepping horses and galloped to the scene.
They took their stand and fought along the river banks,
Throwing bronze-tipped javelins against each other.
Among them were Hate and Din and the Angel of Death,   570
Holding a man just wounded, another unwounded,
And dragging one dead by his heels from the fray,
And the cloak on her shoulders was red with human blood.
They swayed in battle and fought like living men,
    And each side salvaged the bodies of their dead.   575

    On it he put a soft field, rich farmland
Wide and thrice-tilled, with many plowmen
Driving their teams up and down rows.
Whenever they came to the end of the field
And turned, a man would run up and hand them   580
A cup of sweet wine. Then they turned again
Back up the furrow pushing on through deep soil
To reach the other end. The field was black
Behind them, just as if plowed, and yet
    It was gold, all gold, forged to a wonder.   585

    On it he put land sectioned off for a king,
Where reapers with sharp sickles were working.
Cut grain lay deep where it fell in the furrow,
And binders made sheaves bound with straw bands.
Three sheaf-binders stood by, and behind them children   590
Gathered up armfuls and kept passing them on.
The king stood in silence near the line of reapers,
Holding his staff, and his heart was happy.
Under an oaktree nearby heralds were busy
Preparing a feast from an ox they had slaughtered   595
In sacrifice, and women were sprinkling it
    With abundant white barley for the reapers' dinner.

    On it he put a vineyard loaded with grapes,
Beautiful in gold. The clusters were dark,
And the vines were set everywhere on silver poles.   600
Around he inlaid a blue enamel ditch
And a fence of tin. A solitary path led to it,
And vintagers filed along it to harvest the grapes.
Girls, all grown up, and light-hearted boys
Carried the honey-sweet fruit in wicker baskets.   605

Among them a boy picked out on a lyre
A beguiling tune and sang the Linos song[6]
In a low, light voice, and the harvesters
    Skipped in time and shouted the refrain.

On it he made a herd of straight-horn cattle.   610
The cows were wrought of gold and tin
And rushed out mooing from the farmyard dung
To a pasture by the banks of a roaring river,
Making their way through swaying reeds.
Four golden herdsmen tended the cattle,   615
And nine nimble dogs followed along.
Two terrifying lions at the front of the herd
Were pulling down an ox. Its long bellows alerted
The dogs and the lads, who were running on up,
But the two lions had ripped the bull's hide apart   620
And were gulping down the guts and black blood.
The shepherds kept trying to set on the dogs,
But they shied away from biting the lions
    And stood there barking just out of harm's way.

On it the renowned lame god made a pasture   625
In a lovely valley, wide, with silvery sheep in it,
    And stables, roofed huts, and stone animal pens.

On it the renowned lame god embellished
A dancing ground, like the one Daedalus
Made for ringleted Ariadne in wide Cnossus.[7]   630
Young men and girls in the prime of their beauty
Were dancing there, hands clasped around wrists.
The girls wore delicate linens, and the men
Finespun tunics glistening softly with oil.
Flowers crowned the girls' heads, and the men   635
Had golden knives hung from silver straps.
They ran on feet that knew how to run
With the greatest ease, like a potter's wheel
When he stoops to cup it in the palms of his hands
And gives it a spin to see how it runs. Then they   640
Would run in lines that weaved in and out.
A large crowd stood round the beguiling dance,
Enjoying themselves, and two acrobats
    Somersaulted among them on cue to the music.

On it he put the great strength of the River Ocean,   645
Lapping the outermost rim of the massive shield.

And when he had wrought the shield, huge and heavy,
He made a breastplate gleaming brighter than fire

---

6. That is, a dirge for Linos, a fabled musician. It may originally have been associated in Near Eastern cult with the annual "death" of vegetation.   7. The site of the great palace of Minos, king of Crete. Daedalus was the prototypical craftsman who built the labyrinth to house the Minotaur and who escaped from Crete on wings with his son Icarus. Ariadne was Minos's daughter.

And a durable helmet that fit close at the temples,
Lovely and intricate, and crested with gold.   650
And he wrought leg-armor out of pliant tin.
And when the renowned lame god had finished this gear,
He set it down before Achilles' mother,
And she took off like a hawk from snow-capped Olympus,
Carrying armor through the sky like summer lightning.   655

[Achilles finally accepted gifts of restitution from Agamemnon, as he had refused to
do earlier. His return to the fighting brought terror to the Trojans and turned the battle into a rout in which Achilles killed every Trojan that crossed his path. As he pursued Agenor, Apollo tricked him by rescuing his intended victim (he spirited him
away in a mist) and assumed Agenor's shape to lead Achilles away from the walls of
Troy. The Trojans took refuge in the city, all except Hector.]

BOOK XXII

[The Death of Hector]

Everywhere you looked in Troy, exhausted
Soldiers, glazed with sweat like winded deer,
Leaned on the walls, cooling down
And slaking their thirst.
                        Outside, the Greeks
Formed up close to the wall, locking their shields.   5
In the dead air between the Greeks
And Troy's Western Gate, Destiny
Had Hector pinned, waiting for death.

Then Apollo called back to Achilles:

"Son of Peleus, you're fast on your feet,   10
But you'll never catch me, man chasing god.
Or are you too raging mad to notice
I'm a god? Don't you care about fighting
The Trojans anymore? You've chased them back
Into their town, but now you've veered off here.   15
You'll never kill me. You don't hold my doom."

And the shining sprinter, Achilles:

"That was a dirty trick, Apollo,
Turning me away from the wall like that!
I could have ground half of Troy face down   20
In the dirt! Now you've robbed me
Of my glory and saved them easily
Because you have no retribution to fear.
I swear, I'd make you pay if I could!"

His mind opened to the clear space before him,   25
And he was off toward the town, moving

Like a thoroughbred stretching it out
Over the plain for the final sprint home—

Achilles, lifting his knees as he lengthened his stride.

Priam saw him first, with his old man's eyes,   30
A single point of light on Troy's dusty plain.

   Sirius[8] *rises late in the dark, liquid sky*
   On summer nights, star of stars,
   Orion's Dog they call it, brightest
   Of all, but an evil portent, bringing heat   35
   And fevers to suffering humanity.

Achilles' bronze gleamed like this as he ran.

And the old man groaned, and beat his head
With his hands, and stretched out his arms
To his beloved son, Hector, who had   40
Taken his stand before the Western Gate,
Determined to meet Achilles in combat.

Priam's voice cracked as he pleaded:

"Hector, my boy, you can't face Achilles
Alone like that, without any support—   45
You'll go down in a minute. He's too much
For you, son, he won't stop at anything!
O, if only the gods loved him as I do:
Vultures and dogs would be gnawing his corpse.
Then some grief might pass from my heart.   50
So many fine sons he's taken from me,
Killed or sold them as slaves in the islands.
Two of them now, Lycaon and Polydorus,
I can't see with the Trojans safe in town,
Laothoë's boys.[9] If the Greeks have them   55
We'll ransom them with the gold and silver
Old Altes gave us.[1] But if they're dead
And gone down to Hades, there will be grief
For myself and the mother who bore them.
The rest of the people won't mourn so much   60
Unless *you* go down at Achilles' hands.
So come inside the wall, my boy.
Live to save the men and women of Troy.
Don't just hand Achilles the glory
And throw your life away. Show some pity for me   65
Before I go out of my mind with grief
And Zeus finally destroys me in my old age,
After I have seen all the horrors of war—
My sons butchered, my daughters dragged off,
Raped, bedchambers plundered, infants   70
Dashed to the ground in this terrible war,

---

8. The Dog Star, the brightest star in the constellation Canis Major. In Greece it rises in late summer, the hottest time of the year.   9. Priam had more than one wife. Achilles killed Polydorus and Lycaon in the fighting outside the city (books XX and XXI).   1. The dowry of Laothoë, Altes' daughter.

My sons' wives abused by murderous Greeks.
And one day some Greek soldier will stick me
With cold bronze and draw the life from my limbs,
And the dogs that I fed at my table, 75
My watchdogs, will drag me outside and eat
My flesh raw, crouched in my doorway, lapping
My blood.
            When a young man is killed in war,
Even though his body is slashed with bronze,
He lies there beautiful in death, noble. 80
But when the dogs maraud an old man's head,
Griming his white hair and beard and private parts,
There's no human fate more pitiable."

And the old man pulled the white hair from his head,
But did not persuade Hector.
                    His mother then, 85
Wailing, sobbing, laid open her bosom
And holding out a breast spoke through her tears:

"Hector, my child, if ever I've soothed you
With this breast, remember it now, son, and
Have pity on me. Don't pit yourself 90
Against that madman. Come inside the wall.
If Achilles kills you I will never
Get to mourn you laid out on a bier, O
My sweet blossom, nor will Andromache,
Your beautiful wife, but far from us both 95
Dogs will eat your body by the Greek ships."

So the two of them pleaded with their son,
But did not persuade him or touch his heart.
Hector held his ground as Achilles' bulk
Loomed larger. He waited as a snake waits, 100

    Tense and coiled
    As a man approaches
    Its lair in the mountains,
    Venom in its fangs
    And poison in its heart, 105
    Glittering eyes
    Glaring from the rocks:

So Hector waited, leaning his polished shield
Against one of the towers in Troy's bulging wall,
But his heart was troubled with brooding thoughts: 110

"Now what? If I take cover inside,
Polydamas will be the first to reproach me.
He begged me to lead the Trojans back
To the city on that black night when Achilles rose.
But I wouldn't listen, and now I've destroyed 115

Half the army through my recklessness.
I can't face the Trojan men and women now,
Can't bear to hear some lesser man say,
'Hector trusted his strength and lost the army.'
That's what they'll say. I'll be much better off   120
Facing Achilles, either killing him
Or dying honorably before the city.
     But what if I lay down all my weapons,
Bossed shield, heavy helmet, prop my spear
Against the wall, and go meet Achilles,   125
Promise him we'll surrender Helen
And everything Paris brought back with her
In his ships' holds to Troy—that was the beginning
Of this war—give all of it back
To the sons of Atreus and divide   130
Everything else in the town with the Greeks,
And swear a great oath not to hold
Anything back, but share it all equally,
All the treasure in Troy's citadel.
     But why am I talking to myself like this?   135
I can't go out there unarmed. Achilles
Will cut me down in cold blood if I take off
My armor and go out to meet him
Naked like a woman. This is no time
For talking, the way a boy and a girl   140
Whisper to each other from oak tree or rock,
A boy and a girl with all their sweet talk.
Better to lock up in mortal combat
As soon as possible and see to whom
God on Olympus grants the victory."   145

Thus spoke Hector.
                And Achilles closed in
Like the helmeted God of War himself,
The ash-wood spear above his right shoulder
Rocking in the light that played from his bronze
In gleams of fire and the rising sun.   150
And when Hector saw it he lost his nerve,
Panicked, and ran, leaving the gates behind,
With Achilles on his tail, confident in his speed.

     You have seen a falcon
     In a long, smooth dive   155
     Attack a fluttering dove
     Far below in the hills.
     The falcon screams,
     Swoops, and plunges
     In its lust for prey.   160

So Achilles swooped and Hector trembled
In the shadow of Troy's wall.
                Running hard,

They passed Lookout Rock and the windy fig tree,
Following the loop of the wagon road.
They came to the wellsprings of eddying   165
Scamander,[2] two beautiful pools, one
Boiling hot with steam rising up,
The other flowing cold even in summer,
Cold as freezing sleet, cold as tundra snow.
There were broad basins there, lined with stone,   170
Where the Trojan women used to wash their silky clothes
In the days of peace, before the Greeks came.

They ran by these springs, pursuer and pursued—
A great man out front, a far greater behind—
And they ran all out. This was not a race   175
For such a prize as athletes compete for,
An oxhide or animal for sacrifice, but a race
For the lifeblood of Hector, breaker of horses.

    But champion horses wheeling round the course,
    Hooves flying, pouring it on in a race for a prize   180
    A woman or tripod—at a hero's funeral games

Will give you some idea of how these heroes looked
As they circled Priam's town three times running
    While all the gods looked on.

Zeus, the gods' father and ours, spoke: 185

"I do not like what I see, a man close
To my heart chased down around Troy's wall.
Hector has burned many an ox's thigh
To me, both on Ida's peaks and in the city's
High holy places, and now Achilles   190
Is running him down around Priam's town.
Think you now, gods, and take counsel whether
We should save him from death or deliver him
Into Achilles' hands, good man though he be."

The grey-eyed goddess Athena answered: 195

    "O Father,
You may be the Lord of Lightning and the Dark Cloud,
But what a thing to say, to save a mortal man,
With his fate already fixed, from rattling death!
Do it. But don't expect us all to approve."   200

Zeus loomed like a thunderhead, but answered gently:

"There, there, daughter, my heart wasn't in it.
I did not mean to displease you, my child. Go now,
Do what you have in mind without delay."

2. One of the two rivers in the plain of Troy.

Athena had been longing for action   205
And at his word shot down from Olympus,

As Achilles bore down on Hector.

> *A hunting hound starts a fawn in the hills,*
> *Follows it through brakes and hollows,*
> *And if it hides in a thicket, circles,*   210
> *Picks up the trail, and renews the chase.*

No more could Hector elude Achilles.
Every time Hector surged for the Western Gate
Under the massive towers, hoping for
Trojan archers to give him some cover,   215
Achilles cut him off and turned him back
Toward the plain, keeping the inside track.

> *Running in a dream, you can't catch up,*
> *You can't catch up and you can't get away.*

No more could Achilles catch Hector   220
Or Hector escape.
                              And how could Hector
Have ever escaped death's black birds
If Apollo had not stood by his side
This one last time and put life in his knees?
Achilles shook his head at his soldiers: 225
He would not allow anyone to shoot
At Hector and win glory with a hit,
Leaving him only to finish him off.

But when they reached the springs the fourth time,
Father Zeus stretched out his golden scales   230
And placed on them two agonizing deaths,
One for Achilles and one for Hector.
When he held the beam, Hector's doom sank down
Toward Hades. And Phoebus Apollo left him.

By now the grey-eyed goddess Athena   235
Was at Achilles' side, and her words flew fast:

"There's nothing but glory on the beachhead
For us now, my splendid Achilles,
Once we take Hector out of action, and
There's no way he can escape us now,   240
Not even if my brother Apollo has a fit
And rolls on the ground before the Almighty.
You stay here and catch your breath while I go
To persuade the man to put up a fight."

Welcome words for Achilles. He rested,   245
Leaning on his heavy ash and bronze spear,

While the goddess made her way to Hector,
The spitting image of Deïphobus.[3]
And her voice sounded like his as she said:

"Achilles is pushing you hard, brother,   250
In this long footrace around Priam's town.
Why don't we stand here and give him a fight?"

Hector's helmet flashed as he turned and said:

"Deïphobus, you've always been my favorite
Brother, and again you've shown me why,   255
Having the courage to come out for me,
Leaving the safety of the wall, while all
Priam's other sons are cowering inside."

And Athena, her eyes as grey as winter moons:

"Mother and father begged me by my knees   260
To stay inside, and so did all my friends.
That's how frightened they are, Hector. But I
Could not bear the pain in my heart, brother.
Now let's get tough and fight and not spare
Any spears. Either Achilles kills us both   265
And drags our blood-soaked gear to the ships,
Or he goes down with your spear in his guts."

That's how Athena led him on, with guile.
And when the two heroes faced each other,
Great Hector, helmet shining, spoke first: 270

"I'm not running any more, Achilles.
Three times around the city was enough.
I've got my nerve back. It's me or you now.
But first we should swear a solemn oath.
With all the gods as witnesses, I swear: 275
If Zeus gives me the victory over you,
I will not dishonor your corpse, only
Strip the armor and give the body back
To the Greeks. Promise you'll do the same."

And Achilles, fixing his eyes on him: 280

"Don't try to cut any deals with me, Hector.
Do lions make peace treaties with men?
Do wolves and lambs agree to get along?
No, they hate each other to the core,
And that's how it is between you and me,   285
No talk of agreements until one of us

3. Hector's brother.

Falls and gluts Ares with his blood.
By God, you'd better remember everything
You ever knew about fighting with spears.
But you're as good as dead. Pallas Athena   290
And my spear will make you pay in a lump
For the agony you've caused by killing my friends."

With that he pumped his spear arm and let fly.
Hector saw the long flare the javelin made, and ducked.
The bronze point sheared the air over his head   295
And rammed into the earth. But Athena
Pulled it out and gave it back to Achilles
Without Hector noticing. And Hector,
Prince of Troy, taunted Achilles:

"Ha! You missed! Godlike Achilles! It looks like   300
You didn't have my number after all.
You said you did, but you were just trying
To scare me with big words and empty talk.
Did you think I'd run and you'd plant a spear
In my back? It'll take a direct hit in my chest,   305
Coming right at you, that and a god's help too.
Now see if you can dodge this piece of bronze.
Swallow it whole! The war will be much easier
On the Trojans with you dead and gone."

And Hector let his heavy javelin fly,   310
A good throw, too, hitting Achilles' shield
Dead center, but it only rebounded away.
Angry that his throw was wasted, Hector
Fumbled about for a moment, reaching
For another spear. He shouted to Deïphobus,   315
But Deïphobus was nowhere in sight.
It was then that Hector knew in his heart
What had happened, and said to himself:

"I hear the gods calling me to my death.
I thought I had a good man here with me,   320
Deïphobus, but he's still on the wall.
Athena tricked me. Death is closing in
And there's no escape. Zeus and Apollo
Must have chosen this long ago, even though
They used to be on my side. My fate is here,   325
But I will not perish without some great deed
That future generations will remember."

And he drew the sharp broadsword that hung
By his side and gathered himself for a charge.

A high-flying eagle dives   330
Through ebony clouds down

> *To the sun-scutched[4] plain to claw*
> *A lamb or a quivering hare*

Thus Hector's charge, and the light
That played from his blade's honed edge.   335

Opposite him, Achilles exploded forward, fury
Incarnate behind the curve of his shield,
A glory of metalwork, and the plumes
Nodded and rippled on his helmet's crest,
Thick golden horsehair set by Hephaestus,   340
And his spearpoint glinted like the Evening Star

> *In the gloom of night*
> *Star of perfect splendor,*

A gleam in the air as Achilles poised
His spear with murderous aim at Hector,   345
Eyes boring into the beautiful skin,
Searching for the weak spot. Hector's body
Was encased in the glowing bronze armor
He had stripped from the fallen Patroclus,
But where the collarbones join at the neck   350
The gullet offered swift and certain death.
It was there Achilles drove his spear through
As Hector charged. The heavy bronze apex
Pierced the soft neck but did not slit the windpipe,
So that Hector could speak still.   355

He fell back in the dust.

                    And Achilles exulted:

"So you thought you could get away with it
Didn't you, Hector? Killing Patroclus
And ripping off his armor, *my* armor,
Thinking I was too far away to matter.   360
You fool. His avenger was far greater—
And far closer—than you could imagine,
Biding his time back in our beachhead camp.
And now I have laid you out on the ground.
Dogs and birds are going to draw out your guts   365
While the Greeks give Patroclus burial."

And Hector, barely able to shake the words out:

"I beg you, Achilles, by your own soul
And by your parents, do not
Allow the dogs to mutilate my body   370

---

4. Sun-beaten.

By the Greek ships. Accept the gold and bronze
Ransom my father and mother will give you
And send my body back home to be burned
In honor by the Trojans and their wives."

And Achilles, fixing him with a stare: 375

"Don't whine to me about my parents,
You dog! I wish my stomach would let me
Cut off your flesh in strips and eat it raw
For what you've done to me. There is no one
And no way to keep the dogs off your head,   380
Not even if they bring ten or twenty
Ransoms, pile them up here and promise more,
Not even if Dardanian Priam weighs your body
Out in gold, not even then will your mother
Ever get to mourn you laid out on a bier.   385
No, dogs and birds will eat every last scrap."

Helmet shining, Hector spoke his last words:

"So this is Achilles. There was no way
To persuade you. Your heart is a lump
Of iron. But the gods will not forget this,   390
And I will have my vengeance on that day
When Paris and Apollo destroy you
In the long shadow of Troy's Western Gate."

Death's veil covered him as he said these things,
And his soul, bound for Hades, fluttered out   395
Resentfully, forsaking manhood's bloom.

He was dead when Achilles spoke to him:

"Die and be done with it. As for my fate,
I'll accept it whenever Zeus sends it."

And he drew the bronze spear out of the corpse,   400
Laid it aside, then stripped off the blood-stained armor.
The other Greeks crowded around
And could not help but admire Hector's
Beautiful body, but still they stood there
Stabbing their spears into him, smirking.   405

"Hector's a lot softer to the touch now
Than he was when he was burning our ships,"

One of them would say, pulling out his spear.

After Achilles had stripped the body
He rose like a god and addressed the Greeks: 410

"Friends, Argive commanders and councillors,
The gods have granted us this man's defeat,
Who did us more harm than all the rest
Put together. What do you say we try
Laying a close siege on the city now   415
So we can see what the Trojans intend—
Whether they will give up the citadel
With Hector dead, or resolve to fight on?
　　But what am I thinking of? Patroclus' body
Still lies by the ships, unmourned, unburied,   420
Patroclus, whom I will never forget
As long as I am among the living,
Until I rise no more; and even if
In Hades the dead do not remember,
Even there I will remember my dear friend.   425
　　Now let us chant the victory paean, sons
Of the Achaeans, and march back to our ships
With this hero in tow. The power and the glory
Are ours. We have killed great Hector,
Whom all the Trojans honored as a god."   430

But it was shame and defilement Achilles
Had in mind for Hector. He pierced the tendons
Above the heels and cinched them with leather thongs
To his chariot, letting Hector's head drag.
He mounted, hoisted up the prize armor,   435
And whipped his team to a willing gallop
Across the plain. A cloud of dust rose
Where Hector was hauled, and the long black hair
Fanned out from his head, so beautiful once,
As it trailed in the dust. In this way Zeus   440
Delivered Hector into his enemies' hands
To be defiled in his own native land.

Watching this from the wall, Hector's mother
Tore off her shining veil and screamed,
And his old father groaned pitifully,   445
And all through town the people were convulsed
With lamentation, as if Troy itself,
The whole towering city, were in flames.
They were barely able to restrain
The old man, frantic to run through the gates,   450
Imploring them all, rolling in the dung,
And finally making this desperate appeal:

"Please let me go, alone, to the Greek ships.
I don't care if you're worried. I want to see
If that monster will respect my age, pity me   455
For the sake of his own father, Peleus,
Who is about my age, old Peleus
Who bore him and bred him to be a curse
For the Trojans, but he's caused me more pain
Than anyone, so many of my sons,   460

Beautiful boys, he's killed. I miss them all,
But I miss Hector more than all of them.
My grief for him will lay me in the earth.
Hector! You should have died in my arms, son!
Then we could have satisfied our sorrow,   465
Mourning and weeping, your mother and I."

The townsmen moaned as Priam was speaking.
Then Hecuba raised the women's lament:

"Hector, my son, I am desolate!
How can I live with suffering like this,   470
With you dead? You were the only comfort
I had, day and night, wherever you were
In the town, and you were the only hope
For Troy's men and women. They honored you
As a god when you were alive, Hector.   475
Now death and doom have overtaken you."

    And all this time Andromache had heard
Nothing about Hector—news had not reached her
That her husband was caught outside the walls.
She was working the loom in an alcove   480
Of the great hall, embroidering flowers
Into a purple cloak, and had just called
To her serving women, ordering them
To put a large cauldron on the fire, so
A steaming bath would be ready for Hector   485
When he came home from battle. Poor woman,
She had little idea how far from warm baths
Hector was, undone by the Grey-Eyed One
And delivered into the hands of the Greeks.

Then she heard the lamentation from the tower.   490

She trembled, and the shuttle fell
To the floor. Again she called her women:

"Two of you come with me. I must see
What has happened. That was Hecuba's voice.
My heart is in my throat, my knees are like ice.   495
Something terrible has happened to one
Of Priam's sons. O God, I'm afraid
Achilles has cut off my brave Hector
Alone on the plain outside the city
And has put an end to my husband's   500
Cruel courage. Hector never held back
Safe in the ranks; he always charged ahead,
Second to no one in fighting spirit."

With these words on her lips Andromache
Ran outdoors like a madwoman, heart racing,   505
Her two waiting-women following behind.

She reached the tower, pushed through the crowd,
And looking out from the wall saw her husband
As the horses dragged him disdainfully
Away from the city to the hollow Greek ships.   510

Black night swept over her eyes.
She reeled backward, gasping, and her veil
And glittering headbands flew off,
And the diadem golden Aphrodite
Gave her on that day when tall-helmed Hector   515
Led her from her father's house in marriage.
And now her womenfolk were around her,
Hector's sisters and his brother's wives,
Holding her as she raved madly for death,
Until she caught her breath and her distraught   520
Spirit returned to her breast. She moaned then
And, surrounded by Trojan women, spoke:

"Hector, you and I have come to the grief
We were both born for, you in Priam's Troy
And I in Thebes in the house of Eëtion   525
Who raised me there beneath wooded Plakos
Under an evil star. Better never to have been born.
And now you are going to Hades' dark world,
Underground, leaving me in sorrow,
A widow in the halls, with an infant,   530
The son you and I bore but cannot bless.
You can't help him now you are dead, Hector,
And he can never help you. Even if
He lives through this unbearable war,
There's nothing left for him in life but pain   535
And deprivation, all his property
Lost to others. An orphan has no friends.
He hangs his head, his cheeks are wet with tears.
He has to beg from his dead father's friends,
Tugging on one man's cloak, another's tunic,   540
And if they pity him he gets to sip
From someone's cup, just enough to moisten
His lips but not enough to quench his thirst.
Or a child with both parents still alive
Will push him away from a feast, taunting him,   545
'Go away, your father doesn't eat with us.'
And the boy will go to his widowed mother
In tears, Astyanax, who used to sit
In his father's lap and eat nothing, but
Mutton and marrow. When he got sleepy   550
And tired of playing he would take a nap
In a soft bed nestled in his nurse's arms
His dreaming head filled with blossoming joy.
But now he'll suffer, now he's lost his father.
The Trojans called him Astyanax   555
Because you alone were Troy's defender,

You alone protected their walls and gates.
Now you lie by the curved prows of the ships,
Far from your parents. The dogs will glut
On your naked body, and shiny maggots   560
Will eat what's left.
               Your clothes are stored away,
Beautiful, fine clothes made by women's hands—
I'll burn them all now in a blazing fire.
They're no use to you, you'll never lie
On the pyre in them. Burning them will be   565
Your glory before Trojan men and women."

And the women's moans came in over her lament.

[Achilles buried Patroclus, and the Greeks celebrated the dead hero's fame with athletic games, for which Achilles gave the prizes.]

BOOK XXIV

[*Achilles and Priam*]

   The funeral games were over.
The troops dispersed and went to their ships,
Where they turned their attention to supper
And a good night's sleep. But sleep
That masters all had no hold on Achilles.   5
Tears wet his face as he remembered his friend.
He tossed and turned, yearning for Patroclus,
For his manhood and his noble heart,
And all they had done together, the shared pain,
The battles fought, the hard times at sea.   10
Thinking on all this, he would weep softly,
Lying now on his side, now on his back,
And now face down. Then he would rise
To his feet and wander in a daze along the shore.
Dawn never escaped him. As soon as she appeared   15
Over the sea and the dunes, he would hitch
Horses to his chariot and drag Hector behind.
When he had hauled him three times around
Patroclus' tomb, he would rest again in his hut,
Leaving Hector stretched face down in the dust.   20
But Apollo kept Hector's flesh undefiled,
Pitying the man even in death. He kept him
Wrapped in his golden aegis, so that Achilles
Would not scour the skin as he dragged him.

So Achilles defiled Hector in his rage.   25
The gods, looking on, pitied Hector,
And urged Hermes to steal the body,
A plan that pleased all but Hera,
Poseidon, and the Grey-Eyed One,
Who were steady in their hatred   30
For sacred Ilion and Priam's people

Ever since Paris in his blindness
Offended these two goddesses
And honored the one who fed his fatal lust.[5]

    Twelve days went by. Dawn.   35
Phoebus Apollo addressed the immortals:

"How callous can you get? Has Hector
Never burned for you thighs of bulls and goats?
Of course he has. But now you cannot
Bring yourselves to save even his bare corpse   40
For his wife to look upon, and his mother,
And child, and Priam, and his people, who would
Burn him in fire and perform his funeral rites.
No, it's the dread Achilles that you prefer.
His twisted mind is set on what he wants,   45
As savage as a lion bristling with pride,
Attacking men's flocks to make himself a feast.
Achilles has lost all pity and has no shame left.
Shame sometimes hurts men, but it helps them too.
A man may lose someone dearer than Achilles has,   50
A brother from the same womb, or a son,
But when he has wept and mourned, he lets go.
The Fates have given men an enduring heart.
But this man? After he kills Hector,
He ties him behind his chariot   55
And drags him around his dear friend's tomb.
Does this make him a better or nobler man?
He should fear our wrath, good as he may be,
For he defiles the dumb earth in his rage."

This provoked an angry response from Hera: 60

"What you say might be true, Silverbow,
If we valued Achilles and Hector equally.
But Hector is mortal and suckled at a woman's breast,
While Achilles is born of a goddess whom I
Nourished and reared myself, and gave to a man,   65
Peleus, beloved of the gods, to be his wife.
All of you gods came to her wedding,
And you too were at the feast, lyre in hand,
Our forever faithless and fair-weather friend."

And Zeus, who masses the thunderheads: 70

"Calm down, Hera, and don't be so indignant.
Their honor will not be the same. But Hector
Was dearest to the gods of all in Ilion,
At least to me. He never failed to offer

5. Aphrodite, whom Paris judged more beautiful than Athena and Hera because he found the bribe that she offered him—Helen—the most attractive.

A pleasing sacrifice. My altar never lacked   75
Libation or burnt savor, our worship due.
But we will not allow his body to be stolen—
Achilles would notice in any case. His mother
Visits him continually night and day.
But I would have one of you summon Thetis   80
So that I might have a word with her. Achilles
Must agree to let Priam ransom Hector."

    Thus spoke Zeus,
And Iris stormed down to deliver his message.
Midway between Samos[6] and rocky Imbros,   85
She dove into the dark sea. The water moaned
As it closed above her, and she sank into the deep

    Like a lead sinker on a line
    That takes a hook of sharpened horn
    Down to deal death to nibbling fish.   90

She found Thetis in a cave's hollow, surrounded
By her saltwater women and wailing
The fate of her faultless son, who would die
On Trojan soil, far from his homeland.
Iris, whose feet are like wind, stood near her: 95

"Rise, Thetis. Zeus in his wisdom commands you."

And the silver-footed goddess answered her:

"Why would the great god want me? I am ashamed
To mingle with the immortals, distraught as I am.
But I will go, and he will not speak in vain."   100

And she veiled her brightness in a shawl
Of midnight blue and set out with Iris before her.
The sea parted around them in waves.
They stepped forth on the beach
And sped up the sky, and found themselves   105
Before the face of Zeus. Around him
Were seated all the gods, blessed, eternal.
Thetis sat next to him, and Athena gave place.
Hera put in her hand a fine golden cup
And said some comforting words. Thetis drank   110
And handed the cup back. Then Zeus,
The father of gods and men, began to speak:

"You have come to Olympus, Thetis,
For all your incurable sorrow. I know.
Even so, I will tell you why I have called you.   115
For nine days the gods have argued

6. That is, Samothrace. It and Imbros are islands in the northeast Aegean Sea.

About Hector's corpse and about Achilles.
Some want Hermes to steal the body away,
But I accord Achilles the honor in this, hoping
To retain your friendship along with your respect.   120
Go quickly now and tell your son our will.
The gods are indignant, and I, above all,
Am angry that in his heart's fury
He holds Hector by the beaked ships
And will not give him up. He may perhaps fear me   125
And so release the body. Meanwhile,
I will send Iris to great-souled Priam
To have him ransom his son, going to the ships
With gifts that will warm Achilles' heart."

Zeus had spoken, and the silver-footed goddess   130
Streaked down from the peaks of Olympus
And came to her son's hut. She found him there
Lost in grief. His friends were all around,
Busily preparing their morning meal,
For which a great, shaggy ram had been slaughtered.   135
Settling herself beside her weeping child,
She stroked him with her hand and talked to him:

"My son, how long will you let this grief
Eat at your heart, mindless of food and rest?
It would be good to make love to a woman.   140
It hurts me to say it, but you will not live
Much longer. Death and Doom are beside you.
Listen now, I have a message from Zeus.
The gods are indignant, and he, above all,
Is angry that in your heart's fury   145
You hold Hector by these beaked ships
And will not give him up. Come now,
Release the body and take ransom for the dead."

And Achilles, swift of foot, answered her:

"So be it. Let them ransom the dead,   150
If the god on Olympus wills it so."

So mother and son spoke many words
To each other, with the Greek ships all around.

Meanwhile, Zeus dispatched Iris to Troy:

"Up now, swift Iris, leave Olympus   155
For sacred Ilion and tell Priam
He must go to the Greek ships to ransom his son
With gifts that will soften Achilles' heart.
Alone he must go, with only one attendant,
An elder, to drive the mule cart and bear the man   160
Slain by Achilles back to the city.
He need have no fear. We will send

As his guide and escort Hermes himself,
Who will lead him all the way to Achilles.
And when he is inside Achilles' hut,   165
Achilles will not kill him, but will protect him
From all the rest, for he is not a fool,
Nor hardened, nor past awe for the gods.[7]
He will in kindness spare a suppliant."

Iris stormed down to deliver this message.   170
She came to the house of Priam and found there
Mourning and lamentation. Priam's sons
Sat in the courtyard around their father,
Fouling their clothes with tears. The old man,
Wrapped in his mantle, sat like graven stone.   175
His head and neck were covered with dung
He had rolled in and scraped up with his hands.
His daughters and sons' wives were wailing
Throughout the house, remembering their men,
So many and fine, dead by Greek hands.   180
Zeus' messenger stood near Priam,
Who trembled all over as she whispered:

"Courage, Priam, son of Dardanus,
And have no fear. I have come to you
Not to announce evil, but good.   185
I am a messenger from Zeus, who
Cares for you greatly and pities you.
You must go to the Greek ships to ransom Hector
With gifts that will soften Achilles' heart.
You must go alone, with only one attendant,   190
An elder, to drive the mule cart and bear the man
Slain by Achilles back to the city.
You need have no fear. We will send
As your guide and escort Hermes himself,
Who will lead you all the way to Achilles.   195
And when you are inside Achilles' hut,
Achilles will not kill you, but will protect you
From all the rest, for he is not a fool,
Nor hardened, nor past awe for the gods.
He will in kindness spare a suppliant."   200

Iris spoke and was gone, a blur in the air.
Priam ordered his sons to ready the mule cart
And fasten onto it the wicker trunk.
He himself went down to a high-vaulted chamber,
Fragrant with cedar, that glittered with jewels.   205
And he called to Hecuba, his wife, and said:

"A messenger has come from Olympian Zeus.
I am to go to the ships to ransom our son

---

7. Suppliants were under the protection of the gods, especially of Zeus.

And bring gifts that will soften Achilles' heart.
What do you make of this, Lady? For myself,   210
I have a strange compulsion to go over there,
Into the wide camp of the Achaean ships."

Her first response was a shrill cry, and then:

"This is madness. Where is the wisdom
You were once respected for at home and abroad?   215
How can you want to go to the Greek ships alone
And look into the eyes of the man who has killed
So many of your fine sons? Your heart is iron.
If he catches you, or even sees you,
He will not pity you or respect you,   220
Savage and faithless as he is. No, we must mourn
From afar, sitting in our hall. This is how Fate
Spun her stern thread[8] for him in my womb,
That he would glut lean hounds far from his parents,
With that violent man close by. I could rip   225
His liver bleeding from his guts and eat it whole.
That would be at least some vengeance
For my son. He was no coward, but died
Protecting the men and women of Troy
Without a thought of shelter or flight."   230

And the old man, godlike Priam:

"Don't hold me back when I want to go,
And don't be a bird of ill omen
In my halls. You will not persuade me!
If anyone else on earth told me to do this,   235
A seer, diviner, or priest, we would
Set it aside and count it false.
But I heard the goddess myself and saw her face.
I will go, and her word will not be in vain.
If I am fated to die by the Achaean ships,   240
It must be so. Let Achilles cut me down
As soon as I have taken my son in my arms
And have satisfied my desire for grief."

He began to lift up the lids of chests
And took out a dozen beautiful robes,   245
A dozen single-fold cloaks, as many rugs,
And added as many white mantles and tunics.
He weighed and brought out ten talents of gold,
Two glowing tripods and four cauldrons with them,
And an exquisite cup, a state gift from the Thracians   250
And a great treasure. The old man spared nothing
In his house, not even this, in his passion
To ransom his son. Once out in the portico,
He drove off the men there with bitter words:

8. Fate or the Fates were often pictured as spinning the thread of a person's life.

"Get out, you sorry excuses for Trojans!   255
Don't you have enough grief at home that you
Have to come here and plague me? Isn't it enough
That Zeus has given me the pain and sorrow
Of losing my finest son? You'll feel it yourselves
Soon enough. With him dead you'll be much easier   260
For the Greeks to pick off. But may I be dead and gone
Before I see my city plundered and destroyed."

And he waded through them, scattering them
With his staff. Then he called to his sons
In a harsh voice—Helenus and Paris,   265
Agathon, Pammon, Antiphonus, Polites,
Deïphobus, Hippothous, and noble Dius—
These nine, and shouted at them:

"Come here, you miserable brats. I wish
All of you had been killed by the ships   270
Instead of Hector. I have no luck at all.
I have fathered the best sons in all wide Troy,
And not one, not one I say, is left. Not Mestor,
Godlike Mestor, not Troilus, the charioteer,
Not Hector, who was like a god among men,   275
Like the son of a god, not of a mortal.
Ares killed them, and now all I have left
Are these petty delinquents, pretty boys, and cheats,
These dancers, toe-tapping champions,
Renowned throughout the neighborhood for filching goats!   280
Now will you please get the wagon ready
And load all this on, so I can leave?"

They cringed under their father's rebuke
And brought out the smooth-rolling wagon,
A beauty, just joinered,⁹ and clamped on   285
The wicker trunk. They took the mule yoke
Down from its peg, a knobbed boxwood yoke
Fitted with guide rings, and the yoke-band with it,
A rope fifteen feet long. They set the yoke with care
Upon the upturned end of the polished pole,   290
Placing the ring on the thole-pin, and lashed it
Tight to the knob with three turns each way,
Then tied the ends to the hitch under the hook.
This done, they brought from the treasure chamber
The lavish ransom for Hector's head and heaped it   295
On the hand-rubbed wagon. Then they yoked the mules,
Strong-hooved animals that pull in harness,
Splendid gifts of the Mysians¹ to Priam.
And for Priam they yoked to a chariot horses
Reared by the king's hand at their polished stall.   300

9. That is, new-made.   1. A people of central Asia Minor.

So Priam and his herald, their minds racing,
Were having their rigs yoked in the high palace
When Hecuba approached them sorrowfully.
She held in her right hand a golden cup
Of honeyed wine for them to pour libation   305
Before they went. Standing by the horses she said:

"Here, pour libation to Father Zeus, and pray
For your safe return from the enemy camp,
Since you are set on going there against my will.
Pray to Cronion, the Dark Cloud of Ida,   310
Who watches over the whole land of Troy,
And ask for an omen, that swiftest of birds
That is his messenger, the king of birds,
To appear on the right before your own eyes,
Something to trust in as you go to the ships.   315
But if Zeus will not grant his own messenger,
I would not advise or encourage you
To go to the ships, however eager you are."

And Priam, with grave dignity:

"I will not disregard your advice, my wife.   320
It is good to lift hands to Zeus for mercy."

And he nodded to the handmaid to pour
Pure water over his hands, and she came up
With basin and pitcher. Hands washed,
He took the cup from his wife and prayed,   325
Standing in the middle of the courtyard
And pouring out wine as he looked up to heaven:

"Father Zeus, who rules from Ida,
Most glorious, most great,
Send me to Achilles welcome and pitied.   330
And send me an omen, that swiftest of birds
That is your messenger, the king of birds,
To appear on the right before my own eyes,
That I may trust it as I go to the ships."

Zeus heard his prayer and sent an eagle,   335
The surest omen in the sky, a dusky hunter
Men call the dark eagle, a bird as large
As a doorway, with a wingspan as wide
As the folding doors to a vaulted chamber
In a rich man's house. It flashed on the right   340
As it soared through the city, and when they saw it
Their mood brightened.

                              Hurrying now, the old man
Stepped into his chariot and drove off
From the gateway and echoing portico.
In front of him the mules pulled the wagon   345

With Idaeus at the reins. Priam
Kept urging his horses with the lash
As they drove quickly through the city.
His kinsmen trailed behind, all of them
Wailing as if he were going to his death.   350
When they had gone down from the city
And onto the plain, his sons and sons-in-law
Turned back to Troy. But Zeus saw them
As they entered the plain, and he pitied
The old man, and said to his son, Hermes: 355

"Hermes, there's nothing you like more
Than being a companion to men,[2] and you do obey—
When you have a mind to. So go now
And lead Priam to the Achaean ships, unseen
And unnoticed, until he comes to Achilles."   360

Thus Zeus, and the quicksilver courier complied,
Lacing on his feet the beautiful sandals,
Immortal and golden, that carry him over
Landscape and seascape in a rush of wind.
And he took the wand he uses to charm   365
Mortal eyes asleep and make sleepers awake.
Holding this wand, the tough quicksilver god
Flew down to Troy on the Hellespont,
And walked off as a young prince whose beard
Was just darkening, youth at its loveliest.   370

Priam and Idaeus had just driven past
The barrow of Ilus[3] and had halted
The mules and horses in the river to drink.
By now it was dusk. Idaeus looked up
And was aware of Hermes close by.   375
He turned to Priam and said:

"Beware, son of Dardanus, there's someone here,
And if we're not careful we'll be cut to bits.
Should we escape in the chariot
Or clasp his knees and see if he will pity us?"   380

But the old man's mind had melted with fear.
The hair bristled on his gnarled limbs,
And he stood frozen with fear. But the Helper came up
And took the old man's hand and said to him:

"Sir, where are you driving your horses and mules   385
At this hour of the night, when all else is asleep?
Don't you fear the fury of the Achaeans,
Your ruthless enemies, who are close at hand?

2. Among his many functions, Hermes is an escort to travelers (in particular, he guides the souls of the dead to the underworld). He is also a trickster and will put the guards at the Greek wall to sleep so that Priam can pass through.   3. Priam's grandfather. The tomb ("barrow") was a landmark on the Trojan plain.

If one of them should see you bearing such treasure
Through the black night, what would you do? 390
You are not young, sir, and your companion is old,
Unable to defend you if someone starts a fight.
But I will do you no harm and will protect you
From others. You remind me of my own dear father."

And the old man, godlike Priam, answered: 395

"Yes, dear son, it is just as you say.
But some god has stretched out his hand
And sent an auspicious wayfarer to meet me.
You have an impressive build, good looks,
And intelligence. Blessed are your parents." 400

And the Guide, limned in silver light:

"A very good way to put it, old sir.
But tell me this now, and tell me the truth:
Are you taking all of this valuable treasure
For safekeeping abroad or are you 405
All forsaking sacred Ilion in fear?
You have lost such a great warrior, the noblest,
Your son. He never let up against the Achaeans."

And the old man, godlike Priam, answered:

"Who are you, and from what parents born, 410
That you speak so well about my ill-fated son?"

And Hermes, limned in silver, answered:

"Ah, a test! And a question about Hector.
I have often seen him win glory in battle
He would drive the Argives back to their ships 415
And carve them to pieces with his bronze blade.
And we stood there and marvelled, for Achilles,
Angry with Agamemnon, would not let us fight.
I am his comrade in arms, from the same ship,
A Myrmidon. My father is Polyctor, 420
A wealthy man, and about as old as you.
He has six other sons, seven, counting me.
We cast lots, and I was chosen to come here.
Now I have come out to the plain from the ships
Because at dawn the Achaeans 425
Will lay siege to the city. They are restless,
And their lords cannot restrain them from battle."

And the old man, godlike Priam, answered him:

"If you really are one of Achilles' men,
Tell me this, and I want the whole truth. 430

Is my son still by the ships, or has Achilles
Cut him up by now and thrown him to the dogs?"

And Hermes, limned in silver light:

"Not yet, old sir. The dogs and birds have not
Devoured him. He lies beside Achilles' ship   435
Amid the huts just as he was at first. This is now
The twelfth day he has been lying there,
But his flesh has not decayed at all, nor is it
Consumed by worms that eat the battle-slain.
Achilles does drag him around his dear friend's tomb,   440
And ruthlessly, every morning at dawn,
But he stays unmarred. You would marvel, if you came,
To see him lie as fresh as dew, washed clean of blood,
And uncorrupted. All the wounds he had are closed,
And there were many who drove their bronze in him.   445
This is how the blessed gods care for your son,
Corpse though he be, for he was dear to their hearts."

And the old man was glad, and answered:

"Yes, my boy. It is good to offer
The immortals their due. If ever   450
There was anyone in my house
Who never forgot the Olympian gods,
It was my son. And so now they have
Remembered him, even in death.
But come, accept from me this fine cup,   455
And give me safe escort with the gods
Until I come to the hut of Peleus' son."

And Hermes, glimmering in the dark:

"Ah, an old man testing a young one.
But you will not get me to take gifts from you   460
Without Achilles' knowledge. I respect him
And fear him too much to defraud him.
I shudder to think of the consequences.
But I would escort you all the way to Argos,
With attentive care, by ship or on foot,   465
And no one would fight you for scorn of your escort."

And he leapt onto the chariot,
Took the reins and whip, and breathed
Great power into the horses and mules.
When they came to the palisade and trench   470
Surrounding the ships, the guards were at supper.
Hermes sprinkled them with drowsiness,
Then opened the gates, pushed back the bars,
And led in Priam and the cart piled with ransom.
They came to the hut of the son of Peleus   475

That the Myrmidons had built for their lord.
They built it high, out of hewn fir beams,
And roofed it with thatch reaped from the meadows.
Around it they made him a great courtyard
With thick-set staves. A single bar of fir   480
Held the gate shut. It took three men
To drive this bar home and three to pull it back,
But Achilles could work it easily alone.
Hermes opened the gate for Priam
And brought in the gifts for Peleus' swift son.   485
As he stepped to the ground he said:

"I am one of the immortals, old sir—the god
Hermes. My father sent me to escort you here.
I will go back now and not come before
Achilles' eyes. It would be offensive   490
For a god to greet a mortal face to face.
You go in, though, and clasp the knees
Of the son of Peleus, and entreat him
By his father and rich-haired mother
And by his son, so you will stir his soul."   495

And with that Hermes left and returned
To high Olympus. Priam jumped down
And left Idaeus to hold the horses and mules.
The old man went straight to the house
Where Achilles, dear to Zeus, sat and waited.   500

   He found him inside. His companions sat
Apart from him, and a solitary pair,
Automedon and Alcimus, warriors both,
Were busy at his side. He had just finished
His evening meal. The table was still set up.   505
Great Priam entered unnoticed. He stood
Close to Achilles, and touching his knees,
He kissed the dread and murderous hands
That had killed so many of his sons.

   Passion sometimes blinds a man so completely   510
   That he kills one of his own countrymen.
   In exile, he comes into a wealthy house,
   And everyone stares at him with wonder.

So Achilles stared in wonder at Priam.
Was he a god?
               And the others there stared   515
And wondered and looked at each other.
But Priam spoke, a prayer of entreaty:

"Remember your father, godlike Achilles.
He and I both are on the doorstep
Of old age. He may well be now   520

Surrounded by enemies wearing him down
And have no one to protect him from harm.
But then he hears that you are still alive
And his heart rejoices, and he hopes all his days
To see his dear son come back from Troy.   525
But what is left for me? I had the finest sons
In all wide Troy, and not one of them is left.
Fifty I had when the Greeks came over,
Nineteen out of one belly, and the rest
The women in my house bore to me.   530
It doesn't matter how many they were,
The god of war has cut them down at the knees.
And the only one who could save the city
You've just now killed as he fought for his country,
My Hector. It is for him I have come to the Greek ships,   535
To get him back from you. I've brought
A fortune in ransom. Respect the gods, Achilles.
Think of your own father, and pity me.
I am more pitiable. I have borne what no man
Who has walked this earth has ever yet borne.   540
I have kissed the hand of the man who killed my son."

He spoke, and sorrow for his own father
Welled up in Achilles. He took Priam's hand
And gently pushed the old man away.
The two of them remembered. Priam,   545
Huddled in grief at Achilles' feet, cried
And moaned softly for his man-slaying Hector.
And Achilles cried for his father and
For Patroclus. The sound filled the room.

When Achilles had his fill of grief   550
And the aching sorrow left his heart,
He rose from his chair and lifted the old man
By his hand, pitying his white hair and beard.
And his words enfolded him like wings:

"Ah, the suffering you've had, and the courage.   555
To come here alone to the Greek ships
And meet my eye, the man who slaughtered
Your many fine sons! You have a heart of iron.
But come, sit on this chair. Let our pain
Lie at rest a while, no matter how much we hurt.   560
There's nothing to be gained from cold grief.
Yes, the gods have woven pain into mortal lives,
While they are free from care.
                            Two jars
Sit at the doorstep of Zeus, filled with gifts
That he gives, one full of good things,   565
The other of evil. If Zeus gives a man
A mixture from both jars, sometimes

Life is good for him, sometimes not.
But if all he gives you is from the jar of woe,
You become a pariah, and hunger drives you   570
Over the bright earth, dishonored by gods and men.
Now take Peleus. The gods gave him splendid gifts
From the day he was born. He was the happiest
And richest man on earth, king of the Myrmidons,
And although he was a mortal, the gods gave him   575
An immortal goddess to be his wife.
But even to Peleus the god gave some evil:
He would not leave offspring to succeed him in power,
Just one child, all out of season. I can't be with him
To take care of him now that he's old, since I'm far   580
From my fatherland, squatting here in Troy,
Tormenting you and your children. And you, old sir,
We hear that you were prosperous once.
From Lesbos down south clear over to Phrygia
And up to the Hellespont's boundary,   585
No one could match you in wealth or in sons.
But then the gods have brought you trouble,
This constant fighting and killing around your town.
You must endure this grief and not constantly grieve.
You will not gain anything by torturing yourself   590
Over the good son you lost, not bring him back.
Sooner you will suffer some other sorrow."

And Priam, old and godlike, answered him:

"Don't sit me in a chair, prince, while Hector
Lies uncared for in your hut. Deliver him now   595
So I can see him with my own eyes, and you—
Take all this ransom we bring, take pleasure in it,
And go back home to your own fatherland,
Since you've taken this first step and allowed me
To live and see the light of day."   600

Achilles glowered at him and said:

"Don't provoke me, old man. It's my own decision
To release Hector to you. A messenger came to me
From Zeus—my own natural mother,
Daughter of the old sea god. And I know you,   605
Priam, inside out. You don't fool me one bit.
Some god escorted you to the Greek ships.
No mortal would have dared come into our camp,
Not even your best young hero. He couldn't have
Gotten past the guards or muscled open the gate.   610
So just stop stirring up grief in my heart,
Or I might not let you out of here alive, old man—
Suppliant though you are—and sin against Zeus."

The old man was afraid and did as he was told.

The son of Peleus leapt out the door like a lion,   615
Followed by Automedon and Alcimus, whom Achilles
Honored most now that Patroclus was dead.
They unyoked the horses and mules, and led
The old man's herald inside and seated him on a chair.
Then they unloaded from the strong-wheeled cart   620
The endless ransom that was Hector's blood price,
Leaving behind two robes and a fine-spun tunic
For the body to be wrapped in and brought inside.
Achilles called the women and ordered them
To wash the body well and anoint it with oil,   625
Removing it first for fear that Priam might see his son
And in his grief be unable to control his anger
At the sight of his child, and that this would arouse
Achilles' passion and he would kill the old man
And so sin against the commandments of Zeus.   630

After the female slaves had bathed Hector's body
And anointed it with olive, they wrapped it 'round
With a beautiful robe and tunic, and Achilles himself
Lifted him up and placed him on a pallet
And with his friends raised it onto the polished cart.   635
Then he groaned and called out to Patroclus:

"Don't be angry with me, dear friend, if somehow
You find out, even in Hades, that I have released
Hector to his father. He paid a handsome price,
And I will share it with you, as much as is right."   640

Achilles reentered his hut and sat down again
In his ornately decorated chair
Across the room from Priam, and said to him:

"Your son is released, sir, as you ordered.
He is lying on a pallet. At dawn's first light   645
You will go see him yourself.
   Now let's think about supper.
Even Niobe[4] remembered to eat
Although her twelve children were dead in her house,
Six daughters and six sturdy sons.   650
Apollo killed them with his silver bow,
And Artemis, showering arrows, angry with Niobe
Because she compared herself to beautiful Leto.
Leto, she said, had borne only two, while she
Had borne many. Well, these two killed them all.   655
Nine days they lay in their gore, with no one
To bury them, because Zeus had turned
The people to stone. On the tenth day
The gods buried them. But Niobe remembered
She had to eat, exhausted from weeping.   660

4. Wife of Amphion, one of the two founders of the great Greek city of Thebes.

Now she is one of the rocks in the lonely hills
Somewhere in Sipylos, a place they say is haunted
By nymphs who dance on the Achelous' banks,
And although she is stone she broods on the sorrows
The gods gave her.[5]

                Well, so should we, old sir,   665
Remember to eat. You can mourn your son later
When you bring him to Troy. You owe him many tears."

A moment later Achilles was up and had slain
A silvery sheep. His companions flayed it
And prepared it for a meal, sliced it, spitted it,   670
Roasted the morsels and drew them off the spits.
Automedon set out bread in exquisite baskets
While Achilles served the meat. They helped themselves
And satisfied their desire for food and drink.
Then Priam, son of Dardanus, gazed for a while   675
At Achilles, so big, so much like one of the gods,
And Achilles returned his gaze, admiring
Priam's face, his words echoing in his mind.
When they had their fill of gazing at each other,
Priam, old and godlike, broke the silence: 680

"Show me to my bed now, prince, and quickly,
So that at long last I can have the pleasure of sleep.
My eyes have not closed since my son lost his life
Under your hands. I have done nothing but groan
And brood over my countless sorrows,   685
Rolling in the dung of my courtyard stables.
Finally I have tasted food and let flaming wine
Pass down my throat. I had eaten nothing till now."

Achilles ordered his companions and women
To set bedsteads on the porch and pad them   690
With fine, dyed rugs, spread blankets on top,
And cover them over with fleecy cloaks.
The women went out with torches in their hands
And quickly made up two beds. And Achilles,
The great sprinter, said in a bitter tone: 695

"You will have to sleep outside, dear Priam.
One of the Achaean counselors may come in,
As they always do, to sit and talk with me,
As well they should. If one of them saw you here
In the dead of night, he would tell Agamemnon,   700
And that would delay releasing the body.
But tell me this, as precisely as you can.
How many days do you need for the funeral?
I will wait that long and hold back the army."

---

5. The legend of Niobe being turned into stone is thought to have had its origin in a rock face of Mount Sipylus (in Asia Minor) that resembled a woman who wept inconsolably for the loss of her children. The Achelous River runs near Mount Sipylus.

And the old man, godlike Priam, answered: 705

"If you really want me to bury my Hector,
Then you could do this for me, Achilles.
You know how we are penned in the city,
Far from any timber, and the Trojans are afraid.
We would mourn him for nine days in our halls,   710
And bury him on the tenth, and feast the people.
On the eleventh we would heap a barrow over him,
And on the twelfth day fight, if fight we must."

And Achilles, strong, swift, and godlike:

"You will have your armistice."   715

And he clasped the old man's wrist
So he would not be afraid.
                        And so they slept,
Priam and his herald, in the covered courtyard,
Each with a wealth of thoughts in his breast.
But Achilles slept inside his well-built hut,   720
And by his side lay lovely Briseis.

Gods and heroes slept the night through,
Wrapped in soft slumber. Only Hermes
Lay awake in the dark, pondering how
To spirit King Priam away from the ships   725
And elude the strong watchmen at the camp's gates.
He hovered above Priam's head and spoke:

"Well, old man, you seem to think it's safe
To sleep on and on in the enemy camp
Since Achilles spared you. Think what it cost you   730
To ransom your son. Your own life will cost
Three times that much to the sons you have left
If Agamemnon and the Greeks know you are here."

Suddenly the old man was afraid. He woke up the herald.
Hermes harnessed the horses and mules   735
And drove them through the camp. No one noticed.
And when they reached the ford of the Xanthus,
The beautiful, swirling river that Zeus begot,
Hermes left for the long peaks of Olympus.

    Dawn spread her saffron light over earth,   740
And they drove the horses into the city
With great lamentation. The mules pulled the corpse.
No one in Troy, man or woman, saw them before
Cassandra, who stood like golden Aphrodite
On Pergamon's height. Looking out she saw   745
Her dear father standing in the chariot
With the herald, and then she saw Hector

Lying on the stretcher in the mule cart.
And her cry went out through all the city:

"Come look upon Hector, Trojan men and women,   750
If ever you rejoiced when he came home alive
From battle, a joy to the city and all its people."

She spoke. And there was not a man or woman
Left in the city, for an unbearable sorrow
Had come upon them. They met Priam by the gates   755
As he brought the body through, and in the front
Hector's dear wife and queenly mother threw themselves
On the rolling cart and pulled out their hair
As they clasped his head amid the grieving crowd.
They would have mourned Hector outside the gates   760
All the long day until the sun went down,
Had not the old man spoken from his chariot:

"Let the mules come through. Later you will have
Your fill of grieving, after I have brought him home."

He spoke, and the crowd made way for the cart.   765
And they brought him home and laid him
On a corded bed, and set around him singers
To lead the dirge and chant the death song.
They chanted the dirge, and the women with them.
White-armed Andromache led the lamentation   770
As she cradled the head of her man-slaying Hector:

"You have died young, husband, and left me
A widow in the halls. Our son is still an infant,
Doomed when we bore him. I do not think
He will ever reach manhood. No, this city   775
Will topple and fall first. You were its savior,
And now you are lost. All the solemn wives
And children you guarded will go off soon
In the hollow ships, and I will go with them.
And you, my son, you will either come with me   780
And do menial labor for a cruel master,
Or some Greek will lead you by the hand
And throw you from the tower, a hideous death,[6]
Angry because Hector killed his brother,
Or his father, or son. Many, many Greeks   785
Fell in battle under Hector's hands.
Your father was never gentle in combat.
And so all the townspeople mourn for him,
And you have caused your parents unspeakable
Sorrow, Hector, and left me endless pain.   790
You did not stretch your hand out to me
As you lay dying in bed, nor did you whisper

6. Astyanax was, in fact, hurled from Troy's walls after the city fell.

A final word I could remember as I weep
All the days and nights of my life."

The women's moans washed over her lament,   795
And from the sobbing came Hecuba's voice:

"Hector, my heart, dearest of all my children,
The gods loved you when you were alive for me,
And they have cared for you also in death.
My other children Achilles sold as slaves   800
When he captured them, shipped them overseas
To Samos, Imbros, and barren Lemnos.
After he took your life with tapered bronze
He dragged you around Patroclus' tomb, his friend
Whom you killed, but still could not bring him back.   805
And now you lie here for me as fresh as dew,
Although you have been slain, like one whom Apollo
Has killed softly with his silver arrows."

The third woman to lament was Helen.

"Oh, Hector, you were the dearest to me by far   810
Of all my husband's brothers. Yes, Paris
Is my husband, the godlike prince
Who led me to Troy. I should have died first.
This is now the twentieth year
Since I went away and left my home,   815
And I have never had an unkind word from you.
If anyone in the house ever taunted me,
Any of my husband's brothers or sisters,
Or his mother—my father-in-law was kind always—
You would draw them aside and calm them   820
With your gentle heart and gentle words.
And so I weep for you and for myself,
And my heart is heavy, because there is no one left
In all wide Troy who will pity me
Or be my friend. Everyone shudders at me."   825

And the people's moan came in over her voice.

Then the old man, Priam, spoke to his people:

"Men of Troy, start bringing wood to the city,
And have no fear of an Argive ambush.
When Achilles sent me from the black ships,   830
He gave his word he would not trouble us
Until the twelfth day should dawn."

He spoke, and they yoked oxen and mules
To wagons, and gathered outside the city.
For nine days they hauled in loads of timber.   835
When the tenth dawn showed her mortal light,

They brought out their brave Hector
And all in tears lifted the body high
Onto the bier, and threw on the fire.

Light blossomed like roses in the eastern sky.   840

The people gathered around Hector's pyre,
And when all of Troy was assembled there
They drowned the last flames with glinting wine.
Hector's brothers and friends collected
His white bones, their cheeks flowered with tears.   845
They wrapped the bones in soft purple robes
And placed them in a golden casket, and laid it
In the hollow of the grave, and heaped above it
A mantle of stones. They built the tomb
Quickly, with lookouts posted all around   850
In case the Greeks should attack early.
When the tomb was built, they all returned
To the city and assembled for a glorious feast
In the house of Priam, Zeus' cherished king.

That was the funeral of Hector, breaker of horses.   855

The Odyssey[1]

BOOK I

[Athena Inspires the Prince]

Sing to me of the man, Muse, the man of twists and turns
driven time and again off course, once he had plundered
the hallowed heights of Troy.
Many cities of men he saw and learned their minds,
many pains he suffered, heartsick on the open sea,   5
fighting to save his life and bring his comrades home.
But he could not save them from disaster, hard as he strove—
the recklessness of their own ways destroyed them all,
the blind fools, they devoured the cattle of the Sun
and the Sungod blotted out the day of their return.   10
Launch out on his story, Muse, daughter of Zeus,
start from where you will—sing for our time too.
                                                    By now,
all the survivors, all who avoided headlong death
were safe at home, escaped the wars and waves.
But one man alone . . .   15
his heart set on his wife and his return—Calypso,[2]
the bewitching nymph, the lustrous goddess, held him back,
deep in her arching caverns, craving him for a husband.
But then, when the wheeling seasons brought the year around,

---

1. Translated by Robert Fagles.   2. Her name suggests the Greek verb that means "cover, hide."

that year spun out by the gods when he should reach his home,   20
Ithaca[3]—though not even there would he be free of trials,
even among his loved ones—then every god took pity,
all except Poseidon.[4] He raged on, seething against
the great Odysseus till he reached his native land.

                                          But now
Poseidon had gone to visit the Ethiopians worlds away,   25
Ethiopians off at the farthest limits of mankind,
a people split in two, one part where the Sungod sets
and part where the Sungod rises. There Poseidon went
to receive an offering, bulls and rams by the hundred—
far away at the feast the Sea-lord sat and took his pleasure.   30
But the other gods, at home in Olympian Zeus's halls,
met for full assembly there, and among them now
the father of men and gods was first to speak,
sorely troubled, remembering handsome Aegisthus,[5]
the man Agamemnon's son, renowned Orestes, killed.   35
Recalling Aegisthus, Zeus harangued the immortal powers:
"Ah how shameless—the way these mortals blame the gods.
From us alone, they say, come all their miseries, yes,
but they themselves, with their own reckless ways,
compound their pains beyond their proper share.   40
Look at Aegisthus now . . .
above and beyond *his* share he stole Atrides'[6] wife,
he murdered the warlord coming home from Troy
though he knew it meant his own total ruin.
Far in advance we told him so ourselves,   45
dispatching the guide, the giant-killer Hermes.
'Don't murder the man,' he said, 'don't court his wife.
Beware, revenge will come from Orestes, Agamemnon's son,
that day he comes of age and longs for his native land.'
So Hermes warned, with all the good will in the world,   50
but would Aegisthus' hardened heart give way?
Now he pays the price—all at a single stroke."

    And sparkling-eyed Athena[7] drove the matter home:
"Father, son of Cronus, our high and mighty king,
surely he goes down to a death he earned in full!   55
Let them all die so, all who do such things.
But my heart breaks for Odysseus,
that seasoned veteran cursed by fate so long—
far from his loved ones still, he suffers torments
off on a wave-washed island rising at the center of the seas.   60
A dark wooded island, and there a goddess makes her home,
a daughter of Atlas, wicked Titan[8] who sounds the deep

---

3. An island off the northwest coast of Greece.   4. God of the sea.   5. The cousin of Agamemnon.
While Agamennon was away at Troy, Aegisthus seduced his wife. Clytemnestra; the two of them murdered
Agamemnon when he returned. Orestes, Agamemnon's son, later avenged his father. The story is told or
alluded to several times in the *Odyssey*, notably in books III and XI.   6. The son of Atreus (that is,
Agamemnon).   7. The warrior goddess, also patroness of handicrafts and intelligence. She is often given
the epithet "Pallas."   8. The Titans were the generation of gods ruled by Cronus, who were deposed by
Zeus and the other Olympians. One of them, Atlas, was condemned to hold up the sky on his shoulders,
perhaps in punishment for his part in their war against Zeus.

in all its depths, whose shoulders lift on high
the colossal pillars thrusting earth and sky apart.
Atlas' daughter it is who holds Odysseus captive,   65
luckless man—despite his tears, forever trying
to spellbind his heart with suave, seductive words
and wipe all thought of Ithaca from his mind.
But he, straining for no more than a glimpse
of hearth-smoke drifting up from his own land,   70
Odysseus longs to die . . .
                          Olympian Zeus,
have you no care for *him* in your lofty heart?
Did he never win your favor with sacrifices
burned beside the ships on the broad plain of Troy?
Why, Zeus, why so dead set against Odysseus?"   75

   "My child," Zeus who marshals the thunderheads replied,
"what nonsense you let slip through your teeth. Now,
how on earth could I forget Odysseus? Great Odysseus
who excels all men in wisdom, excels in offerings too
he gives the immortal gods who rule the vaulting skies?   80
No, it's the Earth-Shaker, Poseidon, unappeased,
forever fuming against him for the Cyclops
whose giant eye he blinded: godlike Polyphemus,
towering over all the Cyclops' clans in power.
The nymph Thoosa bore him, daughter of Phorcys,   85
lord of the barren salt sea—she met Poseidon
once in his vaulted caves and they made love.
And now for his blinded son the earthquake god—
though he won't quite kill Odysseus—
drives him far off course from native land.   90
But come, all of us here put heads together now,
work out his journey home so Odysseus can return.
Lord Poseidon, I trust, will let his anger go.
How can he stand his ground against the will
of all the gods at once—one god alone?"   95

   Athena, her eyes flashing bright, exulted,
"Father, son of Cronus, our high and mighty king!
If now it really pleases the blissful gods
that wise Odysseus shall return—home at last—
let us dispatch the guide and giant-killer Hermes   100
down to Ogygia Island,[9] down to announce at once
to the nymph with lovely braids our fixed decree:
Odysseus journeys home—the exile must return!
While I myself go down to Ithaca, rouse his son
to a braver pitch, inspire his heart with courage   105
to summon the flowing-haired Achaeans[1] to full assembly,
speak his mind to all those suitors, slaughtering on and on
his droves of sheep and shambling longhorn cattle.

9. Calypso's home.   1. Greeks (who have a number of collective names in Homer).

Next I will send him off to Sparta and sandy Pylos,[2]
there to learn of his dear father's journey home.   110
Perhaps he will hear some news and make his name
throughout the mortal world."
                  So Athena vowed
and under her feet she fastened the supple sandals,
ever-glowing gold, that wing her over the waves
and boundless earth with the rush of gusting winds.   115
She seized the rugged spear tipped with a bronze point—
weighted, heavy, the massive shaft she wields to break the lines
of heroes the mighty Father's daughter storms against.
And down she swept from Olympus' craggy peaks
and lit on Ithaca, standing tall at Odysseus' gates,   120
the threshold of his court. Gripping her bronze spear,
she looked for all the world like a stranger now,
like Mentes, lord of the Taphians.[3]
There she found the swaggering suitors, just then
amusing themselves with rolling dice before the doors,   125
lounging on hides of oxen they had killed themselves.
While heralds and brisk attendants bustled round them,
some at the mixing-bowls, mulling wine and water,
others wiping the tables down with sopping sponges,
setting them out in place, still other servants   130
jointed and carved the great sides of meat.

    First by far to see her was Prince Telemachus,
sitting among the suitors, heart obsessed with grief.
He could almost see his magnificent father, here . . .
in the mind's eye—if only *he* might drop from the clouds   135
and drive these suitors all in a rout throughout the halls
and regain his pride of place and rule his own domains!
Daydreaming so as he sat among the suitors,
he glimpsed Athena now
and straight to the porch he went, mortified   140
that a guest might still be standing at the doors.
Pausing beside her there, he clasped her right hand
and relieving her at once of her long bronze spear,
met her with winged words: "Greetings, stranger!
Here in our house you'll find a royal welcome.   145
Have supper first, then tell us what you need."

    He led the way and Pallas Athena followed.
Once in the high-roofed hall, he took her lance
and fixed it firm in a burnished rack against
a sturdy pillar, there where row on row of spears,   150
embattled Odysseus' spears, stood stacked and waiting.
Then he escorted her to a high, elaborate chair of honor,
over it draped a cloth, and here he placed his guest

---

2. Either in the northwest Peloponnesus, as some hints in the *Odyssey* seem to suggest, or a region in the southwest Peloponnesus later known as Pylos, where a great Mycenaean palace has been excavated. Sparta is in the south-central Peloponnesus.   3. A nearby seafaring people.

with a stool to rest her feet. But for himself
he drew up a low reclining chair beside her,   155
richly painted, clear of the press of suitors,
concerned his guest, offended by their uproar,
might shrink from food in the midst of such a mob.
He hoped, what's more, to ask him about his long-lost father.
A maid brought water soon in a graceful golden pitcher   160
and over a silver basin tipped it out
so they might rinse their hands,
then pulled a gleaming table to their side.
A staid housekeeper brought on bread to serve them,
appetizers aplenty too, lavish with her bounty.   165
A carver lifted platters of meat toward them,
meats of every sort, and set beside them golden cups
and time and again a page came round and poured them wine.

But now the suitors trooped in with all their swagger
and took their seats on low and high-backed chairs.   170
Heralds poured water over their hands for rinsing,
serving maids brought bread heaped high in trays
and the young men brimmed the mixing-bowls with wine.
They reached out for the good things that lay at hand,
and when they'd put aside desire for food and drink   175
the suitors set their minds on other pleasures,
song and dancing, all that crowns a feast.
A herald placed an ornate lyre in Phemius'[4] hands,
the bard who always performed among them there;
they forced the man to sing.
                       A rippling prelude—   180
and no sooner had he struck up his rousing song
than Telemachus, head close to Athena's sparkling eyes,
spoke low to his guest so no one else could hear:
"Dear stranger, would you be shocked by what I say?
Look at them over there. Not a care in the world,   185
just lyres and tunes! It's easy for them, all right,
they feed on another's goods and go scot-free—
a man whose white bones lie strewn in the rain somewhere,
rotting away on land or rolling down the ocean's salty swells.
But that man—if they caught sight of him home in Ithaca,   190
by god, they'd all pray to be faster on their feet
than richer in bars of gold and heavy robes.
But now, no use, he's died a wretched death.
No comfort's left for us . . . not even if
someone, somewhere, says he's coming home.   195
The day of his return will never dawn.
                         Enough.
Tell me about yourself now, clearly, point by point.

---

4. Literally, "One Who Spreads Fame." Phemius is a poet-singer who seems to have some kind of association with Odysseus's household. In Homer, poetry (including epic poetry) is always referred to as song, and
it is performed to the accompaniment of a four-stringed instrument (the forerunner of the later seven-
stringed lyre).

Who are you? where are you from? your city? your parents?
What sort of vessel brought you? Why did the sailors
land you here in Ithaca? Who did they say they are?   200
I hardly think you came this way on foot!
And tell me this for a fact—I need to know—
is this your first time here? Or are you a friend of father's,
a guest from the old days? Once, crowds of other men
would come to our house on visits—visitor that he was,   205
when he walked among the living."
                              Her eyes glinting,
goddess Athena answered, "My whole story, of course,
I'll tell it point by point. Wise old Anchialus
was my father. My own name is Mentes,
lord of the Taphian men who love their oars.   210
And here I've come, just now, with ship and crew,
sailing the wine-dark sea to foreign ports of call,
to Temese, out for bronze—our cargo gleaming iron.
Our ship lies moored off farmlands far from town,
riding in Rithron Cove, beneath Mount Nion's woods.   215
As for the ties between your father and myself,
we've been friends forever, I'm proud to say,
and he would bear me out
if you went and questioned old lord Laertes.[5]
He, I gather, no longer ventures into town   220
but lives a life of hardship, all to himself,
off on his farmstead with an aged serving-woman
who tends him well, who gives him food and drink
when weariness has taken hold of his withered limbs
from hauling himself along his vineyard's steep slopes.   225
And now I've come—and why? I heard that he was back . . .
your father, that is. But no, the gods thwart his passage.
Yet I tell you great Odysseus is not dead. He's still alive,
somewhere in this wide world, held captive, out at sea
on a wave-washed island, and hard men, savages,   230
somehow hold him back against his will.
                                        Wait,
I'll make you a prophecy, one the immortal gods
have planted in my mind—it will come true, I think,
though I am hardly a seer or know the flights of birds.
He won't be gone long from the native land he loves,   235
not even if iron shackles bind your father down.
He's plotting a way to journey home at last;
he's never at a loss.
                        But come, please,
tell me about yourself now, point by point.
You're truly Odysseus' son? You've sprung up so!   240
Uncanny resemblance . . . the head, and the fine eyes—
I see him now. How often we used to meet in the old days
before he embarked for Troy, where other Argive[6] captains,

5. Odysseus's father.   6. Greek.

all the best men, sailed in the long curved ships.
From then to this very day   245
I've not set eyes on Odysseus or he on me."

And young Telemachus cautiously replied,
"I'll try, my friend, to give you a frank answer.
Mother has always told me I'm his son, it's true,
but I am not so certain. Who, on his own,   250
has ever really known who gave him life?
Would to god I'd been the son of a happy man
whom old age overtook in the midst of his possessions!
Now, think of the most unlucky mortal ever born—
since you ask me, yes, they say I am his son."   255

    "Still," the clear-eyed goddess reassured him,
"trust me, the gods have not marked out your house
for such an unsung future,
not if Penelope has borne a son like you.
But tell me about all this and spare me nothing.   260
What's this banqueting, this crowd carousing here?
And what part do you play yourself? Some wedding-feast,
some festival? Hardly a potluck supper, I would say.
How obscenely they lounge and swagger here, look,
gorging in your house. Why, any man of sense   265
who chanced among them would be outraged,
seeing such behavior."
                          Ready Telemachus
took her up at once: "Well, my friend,
seeing you want to probe and press the question,
once this house was rich, no doubt, beyond reproach   270
when the man you mentioned still lived here, at home.
Now the gods have reversed our fortunes with a vengeance—
wiped that man from the earth like no one else before.
I would never have grieved so much about his death
if he'd gone down with comrades off in Troy   275
or died in the arms of loved ones,
once he had wound down the long coil of war.
Then all united Achaea would have raised his tomb
and he'd have won his son great fame for years to come.
But now the whirlwinds have ripped him away, no fame for him!   280
He's lost and gone now—out of sight, out of mind—and I . . .
he's left me tears and grief. Nor do I rack my heart
and grieve for him alone. No longer. Now the gods
have invented other miseries to plague me.
                          Listen.
All the nobles who rule the islands round about,   285
Dulichion, and Same, and wooded Zacynthus too,
and all who lord it in rocky Ithaca as well—
down to the last man they court my mother,
they lay waste my house! And mother . . .
she neither rejects a marriage she despises   290
nor can she bear to bring the courting to an end—

while they continue to bleed my household white.
Soon—you wait—they'll grind *me* down as well."
                                        "Shameful!"—
brimming with indignation, Pallas Athena broke out.
"Oh how much you need Odysseus, gone so long—   295
how *he'd* lay hands on all these brazen suitors!
If only he would appear, now,
at his house's outer gates and take his stand,
armed with his helmet, shield and pair of spears,
as strong as the man I glimpsed that first time   300
in our own house, drinking wine and reveling there . . .
just come in from Ephyra,[7] visiting Ilus, Mermerus' son.
Odysseus sailed that way, you see, in his swift trim ship,
hunting deadly poison to smear on his arrows' bronze heads.
Ilus refused—he feared the wrath of the everlasting gods—   305
but father, so fond of him, gave him all he wanted.
If only *that* Odysseus sported with these suitors,
a blood wedding, a quick death would take the lot!
True, but all lies in the lap of the great gods,
whether or not he'll come and pay them back,   310
here, in his own house.
                        But you, I urge you,
think how to drive these suitors from your halls.
Come now, listen closely. Take my words to heart.
At daybreak summon the island's lords to full assembly,
give your orders to all and call the gods to witness: 315
tell the suitors to scatter, each to his own place.
As for your mother, if the spirit moves her to marry,
let her go back to her father's house, a man of power.
Her kin will arrange the wedding, provide the gifts,
the array that goes with a daughter dearly loved.
                                        For you,   320
I have some good advice, if only you will accept it.
Fit out a ship with twenty oars, the best in sight,
sail in quest of news of your long-lost father.
Someone may tell you something
or you may catch a rumor straight from Zeus,   325
rumor that carries news to men like nothing else.
First go down to Pylos, question old King Nestor,
then cross over to Sparta, to red-haired Menelaus,
of all the bronze-armored Achaeans the last man back.
Now, if you hear your father's alive and heading home,   330
hard-pressed as you are, brave out one more year.
If you hear he's dead, no longer among the living,
then back you come to the native land you love,
raise his grave-mound, build his honors high
with the full funeral rites that he deserves—   335
and give your mother to another husband.
                                        Then,
once you've sealed those matters, seen them through,

7. Probably a town on the northwest coast of mainland Greece.

think hard, reach down deep in your heart and soul
for a way to kill these suitors in your house,
by stealth or in open combat.   340
You must not cling to your boyhood any longer—
it's time you were a man. Haven't you heard
what glory Prince Orestes won throughout the world
when he killed that cunning, murderous Aegisthus,
who'd killed his famous father?
                And you, my friend—   345
how tall and handsome I see you now—be brave, you too,
so men to come will sing your praises down the years.
But now I must go back to my swift trim ship
and all my shipmates, chafing there, I'm sure,
waiting for my return. It all rests with you.   350
Take my words to heart."
                "Oh stranger,"
heedful Telemachus replied, "indeed I will.
You've counseled me with so much kindness now,
like a father to a son. I won't forget a word.
But come, stay longer, keen as you are to sail,   355
so you can bathe and rest and lift your spirits,
then go back to your ship, delighted with a gift,
a prize of honor, something rare and fine
as a keepsake from myself. The kind of gift
a host will give a stranger, friend to friend."   360

    Her eyes glinting, Pallas declined in haste:
"Not now. Don't hold me here. I long to be on my way.
As for the gift—whatever you'd give in kindness—
save it for my return so I can take it home.
Choose something rare and fine, and a good reward   365
that gift is going to bring you."
                  With that promise,
off and away Athena the bright-eyed goddess flew
like a bird in soaring flight
but left his spirit filled with nerve and courage,
charged with his father's memory more than ever now.   370
He felt his senses quicken, overwhelmed with wonder—
this was a god, he knew it well and made at once
for the suitors, a man like a god himself.
                     Amidst them still
the famous bard sang on, and they sat in silence, listening
as he performed The Achaeans' Journey Home from Troy: 375
all the blows Athena doomed them to endure.
                     And now,
from high above in her room and deep in thought,
she caught his inspired strains . . .
Icarius' daughter Penelope, wary and reserved,
and down the steep stair from her chamber she descended,   380
not alone: two of her women followed close behind.
That radiant woman, once she reached her suitors,
drawing her glistening veil across her cheeks,

paused now where a column propped the sturdy roof,
with one of her loyal handmaids stationed either side.   385
Suddenly, dissolving in tears and bursting through
the bard's inspired voice, she cried out, "Phemius!
So many other songs you know to hold us spellbound,
works of the gods and men that singers celebrate.
Sing one of those as you sit beside them here   390
and they drink their wine in silence.
                              But break off this song—
the unendurable song that always rends the heart inside me . . .
the unforgettable grief, it wounds me most of all!
How I long for my husband—alive in memory, always,
that great man whose fame resounds through Hellas   395
right to the depths of Argos!"
                              "Why, mother,"
poised Telemachus put in sharply, "why deny
our devoted bard the chance to entertain us
any way the spirit stirs him on?
Bards are not to blame—   400
Zeus is to blame. He deals to each and every
laborer on this earth whatever doom he pleases.
Why fault the bard if he sings the Argives' harsh fate?
It's always the latest song, the one that echoes last
in the listeners' ears, that people praise the most.   405
Courage, mother. Harden your heart, and listen.
Odysseus was scarcely the only one, you know,
whose journey home was blotted out at Troy.
Others, so many others, died there too.
                              So, mother,
go back to your quarters. Tend to your own tasks,   410
the distaff and the loom, and keep the women
working hard as well. As for giving orders,
men will see to that, but I most of all:
I hold the reins of power in this house."
                              Astonished,
she withdrew to her own room. She took to heart   415
the clear good sense in what her son had said.
Climbing up to the lofty chamber with her women,
she fell to weeping for Odysseus, her beloved husband,
till watchful Athena sealed her eyes with welcome sleep.

    But the suitors broke into uproar through the shadowed halls,   420
all of them lifting prayers to lie beside her, share her bed,
until discreet Telemachus took command: "You suitors
who plague my mother, you, you insolent, overweening . . .
for this evening let us dine and take our pleasure,
no more shouting now. What a fine thing it is   425
to listen to such a bard as we have here—
the man sings like a god.
                              But at first light
we all march forth to assembly, take our seats
so I can give my orders and say to you straight out:

You must leave my palace! See to your feasting elsewhere,   430
devour your own possessions, house to house by turns.
But if you decide the fare is better, richer here,
destroying one man's goods and going scot-free,
all right then, carve away!
But I'll cry out to the everlasting gods in hopes   435
that Zeus will pay you back with a vengeance—all of you
destroyed in0 my house while I go scot-free myself!"

    So Telemachus declared. And they all bit their lips,
amazed the prince could speak with so much daring.

    Eupithes' son Antinous broke their silence: 440
"Well, Telemachus, only the gods could teach you
to sound so high and mighty! Such brave talk.
I pray that Zeus will never make *you* king of Ithaca,
though your father's crown is no doubt yours by birth."

    But cool-headed Telemachus countered firmly: 445
"Antinous, even though my words may offend you,
I'd be happy to take the crown if Zeus presents it.
You think that nothing worse could befall a man?
It's really not so bad to be a king. All at once
your palace grows in wealth, your honors grow as well.   450
But there are hosts of other Achaean princes, look—
young and old, crowds of them on our island here—
and any one of the lot might hold the throne,
now great Odysseus is dead . . .
But I'll be lord of my own house and servants,   455
all that King Odysseus won for me by force."

    And now Eurymachus, Polybus' son, stepped in:
"Surely this must lie in the gods' lap, Telemachus—
which Achaean will lord it over seagirt Ithaca.
Do hold on to your own possessions, rule your house.   460
God forbid that anyone tear your holdings from your hands
while men still live in Ithaca.
                      But about your guest,
dear boy, I have some questions. Where does he come from?
Where's his country, his birth, his father's old estates?
Did he bring some news of your father, his return?   465
Or did he come on business of his own?
How he leapt to his feet and off he went!
No waiting around for proper introductions.
And no mean man, not by the looks of him, I'd say."

    "Eurymachus," Telemachus answered shrewdly,   470
"clearly my father's journey home is lost forever.
I no longer trust in rumors—rumors from the blue—
nor bother with any prophecy, when mother calls
some wizard into the house to ask him questions.
As for the stranger though,   475

the man's an old family friend, from Taphos,
wise Anchialus' son. He says his name is Mentes,
lord of the Taphian men who love their oars."
                                        So he said
but deep in his mind he knew the immortal goddess.
Now the suitors turned to dance and song,   480
to the lovely beat and sway,
waiting for dusk to come upon them there . . .
and the dark night came upon them, lost in pleasure.
Finally, to bed. Each to his own house.
                                        Telemachus,
off to his bedroom built in the fine courtyard—   485
a commanding, lofty room set well apart—
retired too, his spirit swarming with misgivings.
His devoted nurse attended him, bearing a glowing torch,
Eurycleia the daughter of Ops, Pisenor's son.
Laertes had paid a price for the woman years ago,   490
still in the bloom of youth. He traded twenty oxen,
honored her on a par with his own loyal wife at home
but fearing the queen's anger, never shared her bed.
She was his grandson's escort now and bore a torch,
for she was the one of all the maids who loved   495
the prince the most—she'd nursed him as a baby.
He spread the doors of his snug, well-made room,
sat down on the bed and pulled his soft shirt off,
tossed it into the old woman's conscientious hands,
and after folding it neatly, patting it smooth,   500
she hung it up on a peg beside his corded bed,
then padded from the bedroom,
drawing the door shut with the silver hook,
sliding the doorbolt home with its rawhide strap.
There all night long, wrapped in a sheep's warm fleece,   505
he weighed in his mind the course Athena charted.

BOOK II

[Telemachus Sets Sail]

When young Dawn with her rose-red fingers shone once more
the true son of Odysseus sprang from bed and dressed,
over his shoulder he slung his well-honed sword,
fastened rawhide sandals under his smooth feet
and stepped from his bedroom, handsome as a god.   5
At once he ordered heralds to cry out loud and clear
and summon the flowing-haired Achaeans to full assembly.
Their cries rang out. The people filed in quickly.
When they'd grouped, crowding the meeting grounds,
Telemachus strode in too, a bronze spear in his grip   10
and not alone: two sleek hounds went trotting at his heels.
And Athena lavished a marvelous splendor on the prince
so the people all gazed in wonder as he came forward,
the elders making way as he took his father's seat.
The first to speak was an old lord, Aegyptius,   15

stooped with age, who knew the world by heart.
For one dear son had sailed with King Odysseus,
bound in the hollow ships to the stallion-land of Troy—
the spearman Antiphus—but the brutal Cyclops killed him,
trapped in his vaulted cave, the last man the monster ate.   20
Three other sons he had: one who mixed with the suitors,
Eurynomus, and two kept working their father's farms.
Still, he never forgot the soldier, desolate in his grief.
In tears for the son he lost, he rose and said among them,
"Hear me, men of Ithaca. Hear what I have to say.   25
Not once have we held assembly, met in session
since King Odysseus sailed away in the hollow ships.
Who has summoned us now—one of the young men,
one of the old-timers? What crisis spurs him on?
Some news he's heard of an army on the march,   30
word he's caught firsthand so he can warn us now?
Or some other public matter he'll disclose and argue?
He's a brave man, I'd say. God be with him, too!
May Zeus speed him on to a happy end,
whatever his heart desires!"   35
                              Winning words
with a lucky ring. Odysseus' son rejoiced;
the boy could sit no longer—fired up to speak,
he took his stand among the gathered men.
The herald Pisenor, skilled in custom's ways,
put the staff in his hand,[8] and then the prince,   40
addressing old Aegyptius first, led off with, "Sir,
that man is not far off—you'll soon see for yourself—
I was the one who called us all together.
Something wounds me deeply . . .
not news I've heard of an army on the march,   45
word I've caught firsthand so I can warn you now,
or some other public matter I'll disclose and argue.
No, the crisis is my own. Trouble has struck my house—
a double blow. First, I have lost my noble father
who ruled among you years ago, each of you here,   50
and kindly as a father to his children.
                            But now this,
a worse disaster that soon will grind my house down,
ruin it all, and all my worldly goods in the bargain.
Suitors plague my mother—against her will—
sons of the very men who are your finest here!   55
They'd sooner die than approach her father's house
so Icarius himself might see to his daughter's bridal,
hand her to whom he likes, whoever meets his fancy.
Not they—they infest our palace day and night,
they butcher our cattle, our sheep, our fat goats,   60
feasting themselves sick, swilling our glowing wine
as if there's no tomorrow—all of it, squandered.

8. As in the assembly in book I of the *Iliad*, the herald hands the person who is given the floor a staff, the symbol of authority.

Now we have no man like Odysseus in command
to drive this curse from the house. We ourselves?
We're hardly the ones to fight them off. All we'd do   65
is parade our wretched weakness. A boy inept at battle.
Oh I'd swing to attack if I had the power in me.
By god, it's intolerable, what they do—disgrace,
my house a shambles!
                You should be ashamed yourselves,
mortified in the face of neighbors living round about!   70
Fear the gods' wrath—before they wheel in outrage
and make these crimes recoil on your heads.
I beg you by Olympian Zeus, by Themis[9] too,
who sets assemblies free and calls us into session—
stop, my friends! Leave me alone to pine away in anguish . . .   75
Unless, of course, you think my noble father Odysseus
did the Achaean army damage, deliberate harm,
and to pay me back you'd do me harm, deliberately
setting these parasites against me. Better for me
if *you* were devouring all my treasure, all my cattle—   80
if you were the ones, we'd make amends in no time.
We'd approach you for reparations round the town,
demanding our goods till you'd returned the lot.
But now, look, you load my heart with grief—
there's nothing I can do!"
                Filled with anger,   85
down on the ground he dashed the speaker's scepter—
bursting into tears. Pity seized the assembly.
All just sat there, silent . . .
no one had the heart to reply with harshness.
Only Antinous, who found it in himself to say,   90
"So high and mighty, Telemachus—such unbridled rage!
Well now, fling your accusations at *us*?
Think to pin the blame on *us*? You think again.
It's not the suitors here who deserve the blame,
it's your own dear mother, the matchless queen of cunning.   95
Look here. For three years now, getting on to four,
she's played it fast and loose with all our hearts,
building each man's hopes—
dangling promises, dropping hints to each—
but all the while with something else in mind.   100
This was her latest masterpiece of guile:
she set up a great loom in the royal halls
and she began to weave, and the weaving finespun,
the yarns endless, and she would lead us on: 'Young men,
my suitors, now that King Odysseus is no more,   105
go slowly, keen as you are to marry me, until
I can finish off this web . . .
so my weaving won't all fray and come to nothing.
This is a shroud for old lord Laertes, for that day

9. A daughter of Zeus. She embodies the principle of what is right and proper, both in the natural world
and in human society.

when the deadly fate that lays us out at last will take him down.   110
I dread the shame my countrywomen would heap upon me,
yes, if a man of such wealth should lie in state
without a shroud for cover.'
                         Her very words,
and despite our pride and passion we believed her.
So by day she'd weave at her great and growing web—   115
by night, by the light of torches set beside her,
she would unravel all she'd done. Three whole years
she deceived us blind, seduced us with this scheme . . .
Then, when the wheeling seasons brought the fourth year on,
one of her women, in on the queen's secret, told the truth   120
and we caught her in the act—unweaving her gorgeous web.
So she finished it off. Against her will. We forced her.

    Now Telemachus, here is how the suitors answer *you*—
you burn it in your mind, you and all our people:
send your mother back! Direct her to marry   125
whomever her father picks, whoever pleases her.
So long as she persists in tormenting us,
quick to exploit the gifts Athena gave her—
a skilled hand for elegant work, a fine mind
and subtle wiles too—we've never heard the like,   130
not even in old stories sung of all Achaea's
well-coifed queens who graced the years gone by:
Mycenae crowned with garlands, Tyro and Alcmena[1] . . .
Not one could equal Penelope for intrigue
but in this case she intrigued beyond all limits.   135
So, we will devour your worldly goods and wealth
as long as *she* holds out, holds to that course
the gods have charted deep inside her heart.
Great renown she wins for herself, no doubt,
great loss for you in treasure. We'll not go back   140
to our old estates or leave for other parts,
not till she weds the Argive man she fancies."

    But with calm good sense Telemachus replied:
"Antinous, how can I drive my mother from our house
against her will, the one who bore me, reared me too?   145
My father is worlds away, dead or alive, who knows?
Imagine the high price I'd have to pay Icarius
if all on my own I send my mother home.
Oh what I would suffer from her father—
and some dark god would hurt me even more   150
when mother, leaving her own house behind,
calls down her withering Furies[2] on my head,
and our people's cries of shame would hound my heels.
I will never issue that ultimatum to my mother.
And you, if you have any shame in your own hearts,   155

---

1. Famous heroines of earlier legend who bore heroes to gods. Alcmena was the mother of Heracles.
Odysseus sees the ghosts of Tyro and Alcmena in book XI.   2. Avenging spirits, particularly concerned
with crimes committed by kin against kin.

you must leave my palace! See to your feasting elsewhere,
devour your own possessions, house to house by turns.
But if you decide the fare is better, richer here,
destroying one man's goods and going scot-free,
all right then, carve away!   160
But I'll cry out to the everlasting gods in hopes
that Zeus will pay you back with a vengeance—all of you
destroyed in my house while I go scot-free myself!"

    And to seal his prayer, farseeing Zeus sent down a sign.
He launched two eagles[3] soaring high from a mountain ridge   165
and down they glided, borne on the wind's draft a moment,
wing to wingtip, pinions straining taut till just
above the assembly's throbbing hum they whirled,
suddenly, wings thrashing, wild onslaught of wings
and banking down at the crowd's heads—a glaring, fatal sign—   170
talons slashing each other, tearing cheeks and throats
they swooped away on the right through homes and city.
All were dumbstruck, watching the eagles trail from sight,
people brooding, deeply, what might come to pass . . .
Until the old warrior Halitherses,   175
Mastor's son, broke the silence for them—
the one who outperformed all men of his time
at reading bird-signs, sounding out the omens,
rose and spoke, distraught for each man there:
"Hear me, men of Ithaca! Hear what I have to say,   180
though my revelations strike the suitors first of all—
a great disaster is rolling like a breaker toward their heads.
Clearly Odysseus won't be far from loved ones any longer—
now, right now, he's somewhere near, I tell you,
breeding bloody death for all these suitors here,   185
pains aplenty too for the rest of us who live
in Ithaca's sunlit air.
                        Long before that,
we must put heads together, find some way
to stop these men, or let them stop themselves.
Better for them that way, by far, I myself   190
am no stranger to prophecy—I can see it now!
Odysseus . . . all is working out for him, I say,
just as I said it would that day the Argives sailed
for Troy and the mastermind of battle boarded with them.
I said then: after many blows, and all his shipmates lost,   195
after twenty years had wheeled by, he would come home,
unrecognized by all . . .
and now, look, it all comes to pass!"
                                    "Stop, old man!"
Eurymachus, Polybus' son, rose up to take him on.
"Go home and babble your omens to your children—   200
save *them* from some catastrophe coming soon.
I'm a better hand than you at reading portents.

3. The royal bird, emblem of Zeus.

Flocks of birds go fluttering under the sun's rays,
not all are fraught with meaning. Odysseus?
He's dead now, far from home—   205
would to god that you'd died with him too.
We'd have escaped your droning prophecies then
and the way you've loosed the dogs of this boy's anger—
your eyes peeled for a house-gift he might give you.
Here's *my* prophecy, bound to come to pass.   210
If you, you old codger, wise as the ages,
talk him round, incite the boy to riot,
he'll be the first to suffer, let me tell you.
And you, old man, we'll clap some fine on you
you'll weep to pay, a fine to crush your spirit!
                                    Telemachus?   215
Here in front of you all, here's my advice for him.
Let him urge his mother back to her father's house—
her kin will arrange the wedding, provide the gifts,
the array that goes with a daughter dearly loved.[4]
Not till then, I'd say, will the island princes quit   220
their taxing courtship. Who's there to fear? I ask you.
Surely not Telemachus, with all his tiresome threats.
Nor do we balk, old man, at the prophecies you mouth—
they'll come to grief, they'll make us hate you more.
The prince's wealth will be devoured as always,   225
mercilessly—no reparations, ever . . . not
while the queen drags out our hopes to wed her,
waiting, day after day, all of us striving hard
to win one matchless beauty. Never courting others,
bevies of brides who'd suit each noble here."   230

    Telemachus answered, firm in his resolve:
"Eurymachus—the rest of you fine, brazen suitors—
I have done with appeals to you about these matters.
I'll say no more. The gods know how things stand
and so do all the Achaeans. And now all I ask   235
is a good swift ship and a crew of twenty men
to speed me through my passage out and back.
I'm sailing off to Sparta, sandy Pylos too,
for news of my long-lost father's journey home.
Someone may tell me something   240
or I may catch a rumor straight from Zeus,
rumor that carries news to men like nothing else.
Now, if I hear my father's alive and heading home,
hard-pressed as I am, I'll brave out one more year.
If I hear he's dead, no longer among the living,   245
then back I'll come to the native land I love,
raise his grave-mound, build his honors high
with the full funeral rites that he deserves—
and give my mother to another husband."

4. A dowry. In other passages, it is the suitors who offer gifts to the bride's father. Such mixing of customs
from different periods or places is characteristic of oral epic traditions.

A declaration,
and the prince sat down as Mentor took the floor,   250
Odysseus' friend-in-arms to whom the king,
sailing off to Troy, committed his household,
ordering one and all to obey the old man
and he would keep things steadfast and secure.
With deep concern for the realm, he rose and warned,   255
"Hear me, men of Ithaca. Hear what I have to say.
Never let any sceptered king be kind and gentle now,
not with all his heart, or set his mind on justice—
no, let him be cruel and always practice outrage.
Think: not one of the people whom he ruled   260
remembers Odysseus now, that godlike man,
and kindly as a father to his children!
I don't grudge these arrogant suitors for a moment,
weaving their violent work with all their wicked hearts—
they lay their lives on the line when they consume   265
Odysseus' worldly goods, blind in their violence,
telling themselves that he'll come home no more.
But all the rest of you, how you rouse my fury!
Sitting here in silence . . .
never a word put forth to curb these suitors,   270
paltry few as they are and you so many."

                              "Mentor!"
Euenor's son Leocritus rounded on him, shouting,
"Rabble-rousing fool, now what's this talk?
Goading them on to try and hold us back!
It's uphill work, I warn you,   275
fighting a force like ours—for just a meal.
Even if Odysseus of Ithaca did arrive in person,
to find us well-bred suitors feasting in his halls,
and the man were hell-bent on routing us from the palace—
little joy would his wife derive from his return,   280
for all her yearning. Here on the spot he'd meet
a humiliating end if he fought against such odds.
You're talking nonsense—idiocy.
                              No more. Come,
dissolve the assembly. Each man return to his holdings.
Mentor and Halitherses can speed our young prince on,   285
his father's doddering friends since time began.
He'll sit tight a good long while, I trust,
scrabbling for news right here in Ithaca—
he'll never make that trip."

     This broke up the assembly, keen to leave.   290
The people scattered quickly, each to his own house,
while the suitors strolled back to King Odysseus' palace.

     Telemachus, walking the beach now, far from others,
washed his hands in the foaming surf and prayed to Pallas:
"Dear god, hear me! Yesterday you came to my house,   295
you told me to ship out on the misty sea and learn

if father, gone so long, is ever coming home . . .
Look how my countrymen—the suitors most of all,
the pernicious bullies—foil each move I make."

Athena came to his prayer from close at hand,   300
for all the world with Mentor's build and voice,
and she urged him on with winging words: "Telemachus,
you'll lack neither courage nor sense from this day on,
not if your father's spirit courses through your veins—
now there was a man, I'd say, in words and action both!   305
So how can your journey end in shipwreck or defeat?
Only if you were not his stock, Penelope's too,
then I'd fear your hopes might come to grief.
Few sons are the equals of their fathers;
most fall short, all too few surpass them.   310
But you, brave and adept from this day on—
Odysseus' cunning has hardly given out in you—
there's every hope that you will reach your goal.
Put them out of your mind, these suitors' schemes and plots.
They're madmen. Not a shred of sense or decency in the crowd.   315
Nor can they glimpse the death and black doom hovering
just at their heads to crush them all in one short day.
But you, the journey that stirs you now is not far off,
not with the likes of me, your father's friend and yours,
to rig you a swift ship and be your shipmate too.   320
Now home you go and mix with the suitors there.
But get your rations ready,
pack them all in vessels, the wine in jars,
and barley-meal—the marrow of men's bones—
in durable skins, while I make rounds in town   325
and quickly enlist your crew of volunteers.
Lots of ships in seagirt Ithaca, old and new.
I'll look them over, choose the best in sight,
we'll fit her out and launch her into the sea at once!"

And so Athena, daughter of Zeus, assured him.   330
No lingering now—he heard the goddess voice—
but back he went to his house with aching heart
and there at the palace found the brazen suitors
skinning goats in the courtyard, singeing pigs for roasting.
Antinous, smiling warmly, sauntered up to the prince,   335
grasped his hand and coaxed him, savoring his name:
"Telemachus, my high and mighty, fierce young friend,
no more nursing those violent words and actions now.
Come, eat and drink with us, just like the old days.
Whatever you want our people will provide. A ship   340
and a picked crew to speed you to holy Pylos,
out for the news about your noble father."

But self-possessed Telemachus drew the line:
"Antinous, now how could I dine with you in peace
and take my pleasure? You ruffians carousing here!   345

Isn't it quite enough that you, my mother's suitors,
have ravaged it all, my very best, these many years,
while I was still a boy? But now that I'm full-grown
and can hear the truth from others, absorb it too—
now, yes, that the anger seethes inside me . . .   350
I'll stop at nothing to hurl destruction at your heads,
whether I go to Pylos or sit tight here at home.
But the trip I speak of will not end in failure.
Go I will, as a passenger, nothing more,
since I don't seem to command my own crew.   355
That, I'm sure, is the way that suits you best."
                                              With this
he nonchalantly drew his hand from Antinous' hand
while the suitors, busy feasting in the halls,
mocked and taunted him, flinging insults now.
"God help us," one young buck kept shouting,   360
"he wants to slaughter us all!
He's off to sandy Pylos to hire cutthroats,
even Sparta perhaps, so hot to have our heads.
Why, he'd rove as far as Ephyra's dark rich soil
and run back home with lethal poison, slip it   365
into the bowl and wipe us out with drink!"

   "Who knows?" another young blade up and ventured.
"Off in that hollow ship of his, he just might drown,
far from his friends, a drifter like his father.
What a bore! He'd double our work for us,   370
splitting up his goods, parceling out his house
to his mother and the man who weds the queen."
                                         So they scoffed
but Telemachus headed down to his father's storeroom,
broad and vaulted, piled high with gold and bronze,
chests packed with clothing, vats of redolent oil.   375
And there, standing in close ranks against the wall,
were jars of seasoned, mellow wine, holding the drink
unmixed inside them, fit for a god, waiting the day
Odysseus, worn by hardship, might come home again.
Doors, snugly fitted, doubly hung, were bolted shut   380
and a housekeeper was in charge by night and day—
her care, her vigilance, guarding all those treasures—
Eurycleia the daughter of Ops, Pisenor's son.
Telemachus called her into the storeroom: "Come, nurse,
draw me off some wine in smaller traveling jars,   385
mellow, the finest vintage you've been keeping,
next to what you reserve for our unlucky king—
in case Odysseus might drop in from the blue
and cheat the deadly spirits, make it home.
Fill me an even dozen, seal them tightly.   390
Pour me barley in well-stitched leather bags,
twenty measures of meal, your stone-ground best.
But no one else must know. These rations now,
put them all together. I'll pick them up myself,

toward evening, just about the time that mother   395
climbs to her room and thinks of turning in.
I'm sailing off to Sparta, sandy Pylos too,
for news of my dear father's journey home.
Perhaps I'll catch some rumor."
                            A wail of grief—
and his fond old nurse burst out in protest, sobbing: 400
"Why, dear child, what craziness got into your head?
Why bent on rambling over the face of the earth?—
a darling only son! Your father's worlds away,
god's own Odysseus, dead in some strange land.
And these brutes here, just wait, the moment you're gone   405
they'll all be scheming against you. Kill you by guile,
they will, and carve your birthright up in pieces.
No, sit tight here, guard your own things here.
Don't go roving over the barren salt sea—
no need to suffer so!"
                    "Courage, old woman,"   410
thoughtful Telemachus tried to reassure her,
"there's a god who made this plan.
But swear you won't say anything to my mother.
Not till ten or a dozen days have passed
or she misses me herself and learns I'm gone.   415
She mustn't mar her lovely face with tears."

    The old one swore a solemn oath to the gods
and vowing she would never breathe a word,
quickly drew off wine in two-eared jars
and poured barley in well-stitched leather bags.   420
Telemachus returned to the hall and joined the suitors.

    Then bright-eyed Pallas thought of one more step.
Disguised as the prince, the goddess roamed through town,
pausing beside each likely crewman, giving orders:
"Gather beside our ship at nightfall—be there."   425
She asked Noëmon, Phronius' generous son,
to lend her a swift ship. He gladly volunteered.

    The sun sank and the roads of the world grew dark.
Now the goddess hauled the swift ship down to the water,
stowed in her all the tackle well-rigged vessels carry,   430
moored her well away at the harbor's very mouth
and once the crew had gathered, rallying round,
she heartened every man.

    Then bright-eyed Pallas thought of one last thing.
Back she went to King Odysseus' halls and there   435
she showered sweet oblivion over the suitors,
dazing them as they drank, knocking cups from hands.
No more loitering now, their eyes weighed down with sleep,
they rose and groped through town to find their beds.
But calling the prince outside his timbered halls,   440

taking the build and voice of Mentor once again,
flashing-eyed Athena urged him on: "Telemachus,
your comrades-at-arms are ready at the oars,
waiting for your command to launch. So come,
on with our voyage now, we're wasting time." 445

And Pallas Athena sped away in the lead
as he followed in her footsteps, man and goddess.
Once they reached the ship at the water's edge
they found their long-haired shipmates on the beach.
The prince, inspired, gave his first commands: 450
"Come, friends, get the rations aboard!
They're piled in the palace now.
My mother knows nothing of this. No servants either.
Only one has heard our plan."
                         He led them back
and the men fell in and fetched down all the stores 455
and stowed them briskly, deep in the well-ribbed holds
as Odysseus' son directed. Telemachus climbed aboard.
Athena led the way, assuming the pilot's seat
reserved astern, and he sat close beside her.
Cables cast off, the crew swung to the oarlocks. 460
Bright-eyed Athena sent them a stiff following wind
rippling out of the west, ruffling over the wine-dark sea
as Telemachus shouted out commands to all his shipmates:
"All lay hands to tackle!" They sprang to orders,
hoisting the pinewood mast, they stepped it firm 465
in its block amidships, lashed it fast with stays
and with braided rawhide halyards hauled the white sail high.
Suddenly wind hit full and the canvas bellied out
and a dark blue wave, foaming up at the bow,
sang out loud and strong as the ship made way, 470
skimming the whitecaps, cutting toward her goal.
All running gear secure in the swift black craft,
they set up bowls and brimmed them high with wine
and poured libations out to the everlasting gods
who never die—to Athena first of all, 475
the daughter of Zeus with flashing sea-gray eyes—
and the ship went plunging all night long and through the dawn.

BOOK III

[King Nestor Remembers]

As the sun sprang up, leaving the brilliant waters in its wake,
climbing the bronze sky to shower light on immortal gods
and mortal men across the plowlands ripe with grain—
the ship pulled into Pylos, Neleus'[5] storied citadel,
where the people lined the beaches, 5
sacrificing sleek black bulls to Poseidon,
god of the sea-blue mane who shakes the earth.

---

5. Father of Nestor and mortal son of Poseidon.

They sat in nine divisions, each five hundred strong,
each division offering up nine bulls, and while the people
tasted the innards, burned the thighbones for the god,   10
the craft and crew came heading straight to shore.
Striking sail, furling it in the balanced ship,
they moored her well and men swung down on land.
Telemachus climbed out last, with Athena far in front
and the bright-eyed goddess urged the prince along: 15
"Telemachus, no more shyness, this is not the time!
We sailed the seas for this, for news of your father—
where does he lie buried? what fate did he meet?
So go right up to Nestor,[6] breaker of horses.
We'll make him yield the secrets of his heart.   20
Press him yourself to tell the whole truth:
he'll never lie—the man is far too wise."

       The prince replied, wise in his own way too,
"How can I greet him, Mentor, even approach the king?
I'm hardly adept at subtle conversation.   25
Someone my age *might* feel shy, what's more.
interrogating an older man."
                              "Telemachus,"
the bright-eyed goddess Athena reassured him,
"some of the words you'll find within yourself,
the rest some power will inspire you to say.   30
You least of all—I know—
were born and reared without the gods' good will."

     And Pallas Athena sped away in the lead
as he followed in her footsteps—man and goddess
gained the place where the Pylians met and massed.   35
There sat Nestor among his sons as friends around them
decked the banquet, roasted meats and skewered strips for broiling.
As soon as they saw the strangers, all came crowding down,
waving them on in welcome, urging them to sit.
Nestor's son Pisistratus, first to reach them,   40
grasped their hands and sat them down at the feast
on fleecy throws spread out along the sandbanks,
flanking his brother Thrasymedes and his father.
He gave them a share of innards, poured some wine
in a golden cup and, lifting it warmly toward Athena,   45
daughter of Zeus whose shield is storm and thunder,
greeted the goddess now with an invitation:
"Say a prayer to lord Poseidon, stranger,
his is the feast you've found on your arrival.
But once you've made your libation and your prayer—   50
all according to ancient custom—hand this cup
of hearty, seasoned wine to your comrade here
so he can pour forth too. He too, I think,
should pray to the deathless ones himself.

6. The oldest of the warriors at the siege of Troy.

All men need the gods . . . 55
but the man is younger, just about my age.
That's why I give the gold cup first to you."
                                    With that
Pisistratus placed in her hand the cup of mellow wine
and Pallas rejoiced at the prince's sense of tact
in giving the golden winecup first to her. 60
At once she prayed intensely to Poseidon:
"Hear me, Sea-lord, you who embrace the earth—
don't deny our wishes, bring our prayers to pass!
First, then, to Nestor and all his sons grant glory.
Then to all these Pylians, for their splendid rites 65
grant a reward that warms their gracious hearts.
And last, Poseidon, grant Telemachus and myself
safe passage home, the mission accomplished
that sped us here in our rapid black ship."

    So she prayed, and brought it all to pass. 70
She offered the rich two-handled cup to Telemachus,
Odysseus' son, who echoed back her prayer word for word.
They roasted the prime cuts, pulled them off the spits
and sharing out the portions, fell to the royal feast.
Once they'd put aside desire for food and drink, 75
old Nestor the noble charioteer began, at last:
"Now's the time, now they've enjoyed their meal,
to probe our guests and find out who they are.
Strangers—friends, who are you?
Where did you sail from, over the running sea-lanes? 80
Out on a trading spree or roving the waves like pirates,
sea-wolves raiding at will, who risk their lives
to plunder other men?"
                        Poised Telemachus answered,
filled with heart, the heart Athena herself inspired,
to ask for the news about his father, gone so long, 85
and make his name throughout the mortal world.
"Nestor, son of Neleus, Achaea's pride and glory—
where are we from, you ask? I will tell you all.
We hail from Ithaca, under the heights of Nion.
Our mission here is personal, nothing public now. 90
I am on the trail of my father's widespread fame,
you see, searching the earth to catch some news
of great-hearted King Odysseus who, they say,
fought with you to demolish Troy some years ago.
About all the rest who fought the Trojans there, 95
we know where each one died his wretched death,
but father . . . even his death—
the son of Cronus shrouds it all in mystery.
No one can say for certain where he died,
whether he went down on land at enemy hands 100
or out on the open sea in Amphitrite's[7] breakers.

7. A sea nymph; here she personifies the sea.

That's why I've come to plead before you now,
if you can tell me about his cruel death:
perhaps you saw him die with your own eyes
or heard the wanderer's end from someone else.   105
More than all other men, that man was born for pain.
Don't soften a thing, from pity, respect for me—
tell me, clearly, all your eyes have witnessed.
I beg you—if ever my father, lord Odysseus,
pledged you his word and made it good in action   110
once on the fields of Troy where you Achaeans suffered,
remember his story now, tell *me* the truth."

    Nestor the noble charioteer replied at length:
"Ah dear boy, since you call back such memories,
such living hell we endured in distant Troy—   115
we headstrong fighting forces of Achaea—
so many raids from shipboard down the foggy sea,
cruising for plunder, wherever Achilles led the way;
so many battles round King Priam's walls we fought,
so many gone, our best and bravest fell.   120
There Ajax lies, the great man of war.
There lies Achilles too.
There Patroclus, skilled as the gods in counsel.[8]
And there my own dear son, both strong and staunch,
Antilochus—lightning on his feet and every inch a fighter!   125
But so many other things we suffered, past that count—
what mortal in this wide world could tell it all?
Not if you sat and probed his memory, five, six years,
delving for all the pains our brave Achaeans bore there.
Your patience would fray, you'd soon head for home . . .   130

    Nine years we wove a web of disaster for those Trojans,
pressing them hard with every tactic known to man,
and only after we slaved did Zeus award us victory.
And no one there could hope to rival Odysseus,
not for sheer cunning—   135
at every twist of strategy he excelled us all.
Your father, yes, if you are in fact his son . . .
I look at you and a sense of wonder takes me.
Your way with words—it's just like his—I'd swear
no youngster could ever speak like you, so apt, so telling.   140
As long as I and great Odysseus soldiered there,
why, never once did we speak out at odds,
neither in open muster nor in royal council:
forever one in mind, in judgment balanced, shrewd,
we mapped our armies' plans so things might turn out best.   145
But then, once we'd sacked King Priam's craggy city,

---

8. Nestor lists the great Greek heroes who fell at Troy. Achilles was the bravest of the Greeks and the central hero of the *Iliad*. Priam, king of Troy, was killed when the city fell. Ajax committed suicide when the dead Achilles' armor, which was to go to the best warrior after Achilles, was awarded to Odysseus. Patroclus was Achilles' closest friend. Odysseus will meet the ghosts of Achilles and Ajax when he visits the land of the dead in book XI.

Zeus contrived in his heart a fatal homeward run
for all the Achaeans who were fools, at least,
dishonest too, so many met a disastrous end,
thanks to the lethal rage   150
of the mighty Father's daughter.[9] Eye afire,
Athena set them feuding, Atreus' two sons[1] . . .
They summoned all the Achaean ranks to muster,
rashly, just at sunset—no hour to rally troops—
and in they straggled, sodden with wine, our heroes.   155
The brothers harangued them, told them why they'd met:
a crisis—Menelaus urging the men to fix their minds
on the voyage home across the sea's broad back,
but it brought no joy to Agamemnon, not at all.
He meant to detain us there and offer victims,   160
anything to appease Athena's dreadful wrath—
poor fool, he never dreamed Athena would not comply.
The minds of the everlasting gods don't change so quickly.
So the two of them stood there, wrangling, back and forth
till the armies sprang up, their armor clashing, ungodly uproar—   165
the two plans split the ranks. That night we barely slept,
seething with hard feelings against our own comrades,
for Zeus was brooding over us, poised to seal our doom . . .
At dawn, half of us hauled our vessels down to sea,
we stowed our plunder, our sashed and lovely women.   170
But half the men held back, camped on the beach,
waiting it out for Agamemnon's next commands
while our contingent embarked—
we pushed off and sailed at a fast clip
as a god smoothed out the huge troughing swells.   175
We reached Tenedos[2] quickly, sacrificed to the gods,
the crews keen for home, but a quick return was not
in Zeus's plans, not yet: that cruel power
loosed a cursed feud on us once again.
Some swung their rolling warships hard about—   180
Odysseus sailed them back, the flexible, wily king,
veering over to Agamemnon now to shore his fortunes up.
But not I. Massing the ships that came in my flotilla,
I sped away as the god's mischief kept on brewing,
dawning on me now. And Tydeus' fighting son   185
Diomedes[3] fled too, rousing all his comrades.
Late in the day the red-haired Menelaus joined us,
overtook us at Lesbos,[4] debating the long route home:
whether to head north, over the top of rocky Chios,
skirting Psyrie, keeping that island off to port   190
or run south of Chios, by Mimas' gusty cape.
We asked the god for a sign. He showed us one,

9. Athena. She was on the Greeks' side in the war, but her wrath was aroused when Ajax, son of Oïleus, raped the Trojan princess Cassandra, who had taken refuge in Athena's temple during the sack of Troy. Athena's anger included the whole Greek army because they did not punish Ajax.   1. Agamemnon and Menelaus, the leaders of the Greeks.   2. An island off the coast of present-day Turkey, southwest of Troy. 3. One of the greatest Greek warriors at Troy; his home was Argos.   4. A large island off the coast of Asia Minor, south of Troy and Tenedos.

he urged us to cut out on the middle passage,
straight to Euboea now,
escape a catastrophe, fast as we could sail!   195
A shrilling wind came up, stiff, driving us on
and on we raced, over the sea-lanes rife with fish
and we made Geraestus Point in the dead of night.[5]
Many thighs of bulls we offered Poseidon there—
thank god we'd crossed that endless reach of sea.   200
Then on the fourth day out the crews of Diomedes,
breaker of horses, moored their balanced ships
at Argos port, but I held course for Pylos, yes,
and never once did the good strong wind go limp
from the first day the good unleashed its blast.   205

       And so, dear boy, I made it home from Troy,
in total ignorance, knowing nothing of their fates,
the ones who stayed behind:
who escaped with their lives and who went down.
But still, all I've gathered by hearsay, sitting here   210
in my own house—that you'll learn, it's only right,
I'll hide nothing now.
                    They say the Myrmidons,[6]
those savage spearmen led by the shining son
of lionhearted Achilles, traveled home unharmed.
Philoctetes[7] the gallant son of Poias, safe as well.   215
Idomeneus[8] brought his whole contingent back to Crete,
all who'd escaped the war—the sea snatched none from him.
But Atreus' son Agamemnon . . . you yourselves, even
in far-off Ithaca, must have heard how he returned,
how Aegisthus hatched the king's horrendous death.   220
But what a price he paid, in blood, in suffering.
Ah how fine it is, when a man is brought down,
to leave a son behind! Orestes took revenge,
he killed that cunning, murderous Aegisthus,
who'd killed his famous father.
                          And you, my friend—   225
how tall and handsome I see you now—be brave, you too,
so men to come will sing your praises down the years."

       Telemachus, weighing the challenge closely, answered,
"Oh Nestor, son of Neleus, Achaea's pride and glory,
what a stroke of revenge that was! All Achaeans   230
will spread Orestes' fame across the world,
a song for those to come.

---

5. Sailing frail ships and lacking compasses, Greek sailors preferred to hug the shore. The normal route
would have been east and then south of the island of Chios, past the headland of Mimas on the shore of
Asia Minor, and across the Aegean Sea along the island chain of the Cyclades. But Nestor, in a hurry, went
north of Chios and directly across the northern Aegean to Cape Geraistos, on the tip of the long island of
Euboea, which hugs the eastern coast of the Greek mainland.   6. The contingent led by Achilles. His
son, Neoptolemus, came to Troy to avenge his father; he killed the Trojan king Priam on the altar in his
house.   7. A great archer, abandoned on a desert island by the Greeks on their way to Troy because he
fell sick as a result of a snake bite. Because it was prophesied that the city could be captured only with his
bow, he was brought to Troy for the final assault.   8. Leader of the Greek troops from Crete.

If only the gods would arm me in such power
I'd take revenge on the lawless, brazen suitors
riding roughshod over me, plotting reckless outrage.   235
But for me the gods have spun out no such joy,
for my father or myself. I must bear up,
that's all."
                    And the old charioteer replied,
"Now that you mention it, dear boy, I do recall
a mob of suitors, they say, besets your mother   240
there in your own house, against your will,
and plots your ruin. Tell me, though, do you
let yourself be so abused, or do people round about,
stirred up by the prompting of some god, despise you now?
Who knows if he will return someday to take revenge   245
on all their violence? Single-handed perhaps
or with an Argive army at his back? If only
the bright-eyed goddess chose to love you just
as she lavished care on brave Odysseus, years ago
in the land of Troy where we Achaeans struggled!   250
I've never seen the immortals show so much affection
as Pallas openly showed *him*, standing by your father—
if only she'd favor you, tend you with all her heart,
many a suitor then would lose all thought of marriage,
blotted out forever."
                        "Never, your majesty,"   255
Telemachus countered gravely, "that will never
come to pass, I know. What you say dumbfounds me,
staggers imagination! Hope, hope as I will
that day will never dawn . . .
not even if the gods should will it so."
                                    "Telemachus!"   260
Pallas Athena broke in sharply, her eyes afire—
"What's this nonsense slipping through your teeth?
It's light work for a willing god to save a mortal
even half the world away. Myself, I'd rather
sail through years of trouble and labor home   265
and see that blessed day, than hurry home
to die at my own hearth like Agamemnon,
killed by Aegisthus' cunning—by his own wife.
But the great leveler, Death: not even the gods
can defend a man, not even one they love, that day   270
when fate takes hold and lays him out at last."
                                            "Mentor,"
wise Telemachus said, "distraught as we are for him,
let's speak of this no more. My father's return?
It's inconceivable now. Long ago the undying gods
have sealed his death, his black doom. But now   275
there's another question I would put to Nestor:
Nestor excels all men for sense and justice,
his knowledge of the world.
Three generations he has ruled, they say,
and to my young eyes he seems a deathless god!   280

Nestor, son of Neleus, tell me the whole story—
how did the great king Agamemnon meet his death?
Where was Menelaus? What fatal trap did he set,
that treacherous Aegisthus, to bring down a man
far stronger than himself? Was Menelaus gone   285
from Achaean Argos,[9] roving the world somewhere,
so the coward found the nerve to kill the king?"

    And old Nestor the noble charioteer replied:
"Gladly, my boy, I'll tell you the story first to last . . .
Right you are, you guess what would have happened   290
if red-haired Menelaus, arriving back from Troy,
had found Aegisthus alive in Agamemnon's palace.
No barrow piled high on the earth for *his* dead body,
no, the dogs and birds would have feasted on his corpse,
sprawled on the plain outside the city gates, and no one,   295
no woman in all Achaea, would have wept a moment,
such a monstrous crime the man contrived!
But there we were, camped at Troy, battling out
the long hard campaign while he at his ease at home,
in the depths of Argos, stallion-country—he lay siege   300
to the wife of Agamemnon, luring, enticing her with talk.
At first, true, she spurned the idea of such an outrage,
Clytemnestra the queen, her will was faithful still.
And there was a man, what's more, a bard close by,
to whom Agamemnon, setting sail for Troy,   305
gave strict commands to guard his wife. But then,
that day the doom of the gods had bound her to surrender,
Aegisthus shipped the bard away to a desert island,
marooned him there, sweet prize for the birds of prey,
and swept her off to his own house, lover lusting for lover.   310
And many thighbones he burned on the gods' holy altars,
many gifts he hung on the temple walls—gold, brocades—
in thanks for a conquest past his maddest hopes.
                                        Now we,
you see, were sailing home from Troy in the same squadron,
Menelaus and I, comrades-in-arms from years of war.   315
But as we rounded holy Sounion, Athens' headland,
lord Apollo attacked Atrides' helmsman, aye,
with his gentle shafts he shot the man to death[1]—
an iron grip on the tiller, the craft scudding fast—
Phrontis, Onetor's son, who excelled all men alive   320
at steering ships when gales bore down in fury.
So Menelaus, straining to sail on, was held back
till he could bury his mate with fitting rites.
But once he'd got off too, plowing the wine-dark sea
in his ribbed ships, and made a run to Malea's beetling cape,[2]   325
farseeing Zeus decided to give the man rough sailing,

---

9. In a broad sense, the realm of Agamemnon, who ruled Mycenae.   1. A formula for a sudden death that
has no obvious explanation; for women the arrows come from Artemis, Apollo's sister.   2. The eastern-
most of the three capes in which the Peloponnesus ends, still a place of storms. Menelaus would have to
round it to reach a harbor for Sparta.

poured a hurricane down upon him, shrilling winds,
giant, rearing whitecaps, monstrous, mountains high.
There at a stroke he cut the fleet in half and drove
one wing to Crete, where Cydonians make their homes   330
along the Iardanus River. Now, there's a sheer cliff
plunging steep to the surf at the farthest edge of Gortyn,
out on the mist-bound sea, where the South Wind piles breakers,
huge breakers, left of the headland's horn, toward Phaestos,[3]
with only a low reef to block the crushing tides.   335
In they sailed, and barely escaped their death—
the ships' crews, that is—
the rollers smashed their hulls against the rocks.
But as for the other five[4] with pitch-black prows,
the wind and current swept them on toward Egypt.   340

    So Menelaus, amassing a hoard of stores and gold,
was off cruising his ships to foreign ports of call
while Aegisthus hatched his vicious work at home.
Seven years he lorded over Mycenae rich in gold,
once he'd killed Agamemnon—he ground the people down.   345
But the eighth year ushered in his ruin, Prince Orestes
home from Athens, yes, he cut him down, that cunning,
murderous Aegisthus, who'd killed his famous father.
Vengeance done, he held a feast for the Argives,
to bury his hated mother, craven Aegisthus too,   350
the very day Menelaus arrived, lord of the warcry,
freighted with all the wealth his ships could carry.
                                        So you,
dear boy, take care. Don't rove from home too long,
too far, leaving your own holdings unprotected—
crowds in your palace so brazen   355
they'll carve up all your wealth, devour it all,
and then your journey here will come to nothing.
Still I advise you, urge you to visit Menelaus.
He's back from abroad at last, from people so removed
you might abandon hope of ever returning home,   360
once the winds had driven you that far off course,
into a sea so vast not even cranes could wing their way
in one year's flight—so vast it is, so awesome . . .

    So, off you go with your ships and shipmates now.
Or if you'd rather go by land, there's team and chariot,   365
my sons at your service too, and they'll escort you
to sunny Lacedaemon,[5] home of the red-haired king.
Press him yourself to tell the whole truth:
he'll never lie—the man is far too wise."
                                        So he closed
as the sun set and darkness swept across the earth   370
and the bright-eyed goddess Pallas spoke for all:

---

3. Gortyn and Phaestos are inland from the south coast of Crete.   4. Including Menelaus's ship.
5. Sparta, Menelaus's home.

"There was a tale, old soldier, so well told.
Come, cut out the victims' tongues[6] and mix the wine,
so once we've poured libations out to the Sea-lord
and every other god, we'll think of sleep. High time—   375
the light's already sunk in the western shadows.
It's wrong to linger long at the gods' feast;
we must be on our way."
                                    Zeus's daughter—
they all hung closely on every word she said.
Heralds sprinkled water over their hands for rinsing,   380
the young men brimmed the mixing bowls with wine,
they tipped first drops for the god in every cup
then poured full rounds for all. They rose and flung
the victims' tongues on the fire and poured libations out.
When they'd poured, and drunk to their hearts' content,   385
Athena and Prince Telemachus both started up
to head for their ship at once.
But Nestor held them there, objecting strongly:
"Zeus forbid—and the other deathless gods as well—
that you resort to your ship and put my house behind   390
like a rank pauper's without a stitch of clothing,
no piles of rugs, no blankets in his place
for host and guests to slumber soft in comfort.
Why, I've plenty of fine rugs and blankets here.
No, by god, the true son of my good friend Odysseus   395
won't bed down on a ship's deck, not while I'm alive
or my sons are left at home to host our guests,
whoever comes to our palace, newfound friends."
                                    "Dear old man,
you're right," Athena exclaimed, her eyes brightening now.
"Telemachus should oblige you. Much the better way.   400
Let him follow you now, sleep in your halls,
but I'll go back to our trim black ship,
hearten the crew and give each man his orders.
I'm the only veteran in their ranks, I tell you.
All the rest, of an age with brave Telemachus,   405
are younger men who sailed with him as friends.
I'll bed down there by the dark hull tonight,
at dawn push off for the proud Cauconians.[7]
Those people owe me a debt long overdue,
and no mean sum, believe me.   410
But you, seeing my friend is now your guest,
speed him on his way with a chariot and your son
and give him the finest horses that you have,
bred for stamina, trained to race the wind."

    With that the bright-eyed goddess winged away   415
in an eagle's form and flight.
Amazement fell on all the Achaeans there.

---

6. The tongue was one of the parts of the meat reserved for the gods; it was thrown on the fire.   7. A
people in the western Peloponnesus.

The old king, astonished by what he'd seen,
grasped Telemachus' hand and cried out to the prince,
"Dear boy—never fear you'll be a coward or defenseless,   420
not if at your young age the gods will guard you so.
Of all who dwell on Olympus, this was none but she,
Zeus's daughter, the glorious one, his third born,
who prized your gallant father among the Argives.
Now, O Queen, be gracious! Give us high renown,   425
myself, my children, my loyal wife and queen.
And I will make you a sacrifice, a yearling heifer
broad in the brow, unbroken, never yoked by men.
I'll offer it up to you—I'll sheathe its horns in gold."

   So he prayed, and Pallas Athena heard his prayer.   430
And Nestor the noble chariot-driver led them on,
his sons and sons-in-law, back to his regal palace.
Once they reached the storied halls of the aged king
they sat on rows of low and high-backed chairs.
As they arrived the old man mixed them all a bowl,   435
stirring the hearty wine, seasoned eleven years
before a servant broached it, loosed its seal.
Mulling it in the bowl, old Nestor poured
a libation out, praying hard to Pallas Athena,
daughter of Zeus whose shield is storm and thunder.   440

   Once they had poured their offerings, drunk their fill,
the Pylians went to rest, each in his own house.
But the noble chariot-driver let Telemachus,
King Odysseus' son, sleep at the palace now,
on a corded bed inside the echoing colonnade,   445
with Prince Pisistratus close beside him there,
the young spearman, already captain of armies,
though the last son still unwed within the halls.
The king retired to chambers deep in his lofty house
where the queen his wife arranged and shared their bed.   450

   When young Dawn with her rose-red fingers shone once more
old Nestor the noble chariot-driver climbed from bed,
went out and took his seat on the polished stones,
a bench glistening white, rubbed with glossy oil,
placed for the king before his looming doors.   455
There Neleus held his sessions years ago,
a match for the gods in counsel,
but his fate had long since forced him down to Death.
Now royal Nestor in turn, Achaea's watch and ward,
sat there holding the scepter while his sons,   460
coming out of their chambers, clustered round him,
hovering near: Echephron, Stratius, Perseus
and Aretus, Thrasymedes like a god, and sixth,
young lord Pisistratus came to join their ranks.
They escorted Prince Telemachus in to sit beside them.   465
Nestor, noble charioteer, began the celebration:

"Quickly, my children, carry out my wishes now
so I may please the gods, Athena first of all—
she came to me at Poseidon's flowing feast,
Athena in all her glory!   470
Now someone go to the fields to fetch a heifer,
lead her here at once—a herdsman drive her in.
Someone hurry down to Prince Telemachus' black ship
and bring up all his crewmen, leave just two behind.
And another tell our goldsmith, skilled Laerces,   475
to come and sheathe the heifer's horns in gold.
The rest stay here together. Tell the maids
inside the hall to prepare a sumptuous feast—
bring seats and firewood, bring pure water too."

    They all pitched in to carry out his orders.   480
The heifer came from the fields, the crewmen came
from brave Telemachus' ship, and the smith came in
with all his gear in hand, the tools of his trade,
the anvil, hammer and well-wrought tongs he used
for working gold. And Athena came as well   485
to attend her sacred rites.
The old horseman passed the gold to the smith,
and twining the foil, he sheathed the heifer's horns
so the goddess' eyes might dazzle, delighted with the gift.
Next Stratius and Echephron led the beast by the horns.   490
Aretus, coming up from the storeroom, brought them
lustral water filling a flower-braided bowl,
in his other hand, the barley in a basket.[8]
Thrasymedes, staunch in combat, stood ready,
whetted ax in his grasp to cut the heifer down,   495
and Perseus held the basin for the blood.
Now Nestor the old charioteer began the rite.
Pouring the lustral water, scattering barley-meal,
he lifted up his ardent prayers to Pallas Athena,
launching the sacrifice, flinging onto the fire   500
the first tufts of hair from the victim's head.

    Prayers said, the scattering barley strewn,
suddenly Nestor's son impetuous Thrasymedes
strode up close and struck—the ax chopped
the neck tendons through—
                            and the blow stunned   505
the heifer's strength—
                        The women shrilled their cry,[9]
Nestor's daughters, sons' wives and his own loyal wife
Eurydice, Clymenus' eldest daughter. Then, hoisting up
the victim's head from the trampled earth, they held her fast
as the captain of men Pisistratus slashed her throat.   510
Dark blood gushed forth, life ebbed from her limbs—
they quartered her quickly, cut the thighbones out

8. Barley was sprinkled on the sacrificial victim.   9. The ritual cry uttered at the moment of sacrifice.

and all according to custom wrapped them round in fat,
a double fold sliced clean and topped with strips of flesh.[1]
And the old king burned these over dried split wood   515
and over the fire poured out glistening wine
while young men at his side held five-pronged forks.
Once they'd burned the bones and tasted the organs,
they sliced the rest into pieces, spitted them on skewers
and raising points to the fire, broiled all the meats.   520

    During the ritual lovely Polycaste, youngest daughter
of Nestor, Neleus' son, had bathed Telemachus.
Rinsing him off now, rubbing him down with oil,
she drew a shirt and handsome cape around him.
Out of his bath he stepped, glistening like a god,   525
strode in and sat by the old commander Nestor.

    They roasted the prime cuts, pulled them off the spits
and sat down to the feast while ready stewards saw
to rounds of wine and kept the gold cups flowing.
When they'd put aside desire for food and drink,   530
Nestor the noble chariot-driver issued orders:
"Hurry, my boys! Bring Telemachus horses,
a good full-maned team—
hitch them to a chariot—he must be off at once."

    They listened closely, snapped to his commands   535
and hitched a rapid team to a chariot's yoke in haste.
A housekeeper stowed some bread and wine aboard
and meats too, food fit for the sons of kings.
Telemachus vaulted onto the splendid chariot—
right beside him Nestor's son Pisistratus,   540
captain of armies, boarded, seized the reins,
whipped the team to a run and on the horses flew,
holding nothing back, out into open country,
leaving the heights of Pylos fading in their trail,
shaking the yoke across their shoulders all day long.   545

    The sun sank and the roads of the world grew dark
as they reached Phera, pulling up to Diocles' halls,
the son of Ortilochus, son of the Alpheus River.
He gave them a royal welcome; there they slept the night.

    When young Dawn with her rose-red fingers shone once more   550
they yoked their pair again, mounted the blazoned car
and out through the gates and echoing colonnade
they whipped the team to a run and on they flew,
holding nothing back—and the princes reached
the wheatlands, straining now for journey's end,   555
so fast those purebred stallions raced them on
as the sun sank and the roads of the world grew dark.

---

1. The bones wrapped in fat are burned as the gods' portion of the sacrificial meal; the humans roast and
eat the meat.

BOOK IV

[The King and Queen of Sparta]

At last they gained the ravines of Lacedaemon ringed by hills
and drove up to the halls of Menelaus in his glory.
They found the king inside his palace, celebrating
with throngs of kinsmen a double wedding-feast
for his son and lovely daughter. The princess   5
he was sending on to the son of great Achilles,[2]
breaker of armies. Years ago Menelaus vowed,
he nodded assent at Troy and pledged her hand
and now the gods were sealing firm the marriage.
So he was sending her on her way with team and chariot,   10
north to the Myrmidons' famous city governed by her groom.
From Sparta he brought Alector's daughter as the bride
for his own full-grown son, the hardy Megapenthes,[3]
born to him by a slave. To Helen the gods had granted
no more offspring once she had borne her first child,   15
the breathtaking Hermione,
a luminous beauty gold as Aphrodite.
                    So now
they feasted within the grand, high-roofed palace,
all the kin and clansmen of Menelaus in his glory,
reveling warmly here as in their midst   20
an inspired bard sang out and struck his lyre—
and through them a pair of tumblers dashed and sprang,
whirling in leaping handsprings, leading on the dance.

    The travelers, Nestor's shining son and Prince Telemachus,
had brought themselves and their horses to a standstill   25
just outside the court when good lord Eteoneus,
passing through the gates now, saw them there,
and the ready aide-in-arms of Menelaus
took the message through his sovereign's halls
and stepping close to his master broke the news: 30
"Strangers have just arrived, your majesty, Menelaus.
Two men, but they look like kin of mighty Zeus himself.
Tell me, should we unhitch their team for them
or send them to someone free to host them well?"

    The red-haired king took great offense at that: 35
"Never a fool before, Eteoneus, son of Boëthous,
now I see you're babbling like a child!
Just think of all the hospitality *we* enjoyed
at the hands of other men before we made it home,
and god save us from such hard treks in years to come.   40
Quick, unhitch their team. And bring them in,
strangers, guests, to share our flowing feast."

---

2. Neoptolemus.   3. Literally, "Great Grief." In Homer, sons are often named for characteristics of their fathers. Compare Telemachus: either "One Who Fights Far Away" or "Fighter from Afar" (that is, with the bow).

    Back through the halls he hurried, calling out
to other brisk attendants to follow quickly.
They loosed the sweating team from under the yoke,   45
tethered them fast by reins inside the horse-stalls,
tossing feed at their hoofs, white barley mixed with wheat,
and canted the chariot up against the polished walls,
shimmering in the sun, then ushered in their guests,
into that magnificent place. Both struck by the sight,   50
they marveled up and down the house of the warlord dear to Zeus—
a radiance strong as the moon or rising sun came flooding
through the high-roofed halls of illustrious Menelaus.
Once they'd feasted their eyes with gazing at it all,
into the burnished tubs they climbed and bathed.   55
When women had washed them, rubbed them down with oil
and drawn warm fleece and shirts around their shoulders,
they took up seats of honor next to Atrides Menelaus.
A maid brought water soon in a graceful golden pitcher
and over a silver basin tipped it out   60
so they might rinse their hands,
then pulled a gleaming table to their side.
A staid housekeeper brought on bread to serve them,
appetizers aplenty too, lavish with her bounty.
As a carver lifted platters of meat toward them,   65
meats of every sort, and set before them golden cups,
the red-haired king Menelaus greeted both guests warmly:
"Help yourselves to food, and welcome! Once you've dined
we'll ask you who you are. But your parents' blood
is hardly lost in you. You must be born of kings,   70
bred by the gods to wield the royal scepter.
No mean men could sire sons like you."
                          With those words
he passed them a fat rich loin with his own hands,
the choicest part, that he'd been served himself.
They reached for the good things that lay outspread   75
and when they'd put aside desire for food and drink,
Telemachus, leaning his head close to Nestor's son,
spoke low to the prince so no one else could hear:
"Look, Pisistratus—joy of my heart, my friend—
the sheen of bronze, the blaze of gold and amber,   80
silver, ivory too, through all this echoing mansion!
Surely Zeus's court on Olympus must be just like this,
the boundless glory of all this wealth inside!
My eyes dazzle . . . I am struck with wonder."

    But the red-haired warlord overheard his guest   85
and cut in quickly with winged words for both:
"No man alive could rival Zeus, dear boys,
with his everlasting palace and possessions.
But among men, I must say, few if any
could rival me in riches. Believe me,   90
much I suffered, many a mile I roved to haul
such treasures home in my ships. Eight years out,

wandering off as far as Cyprus, Phoenicia, even Egypt,
I reached the Ethiopians, Sidonians, Erembians—Libya too,
where lambs no sooner spring from the womb than they grow horns.   95
Three times in the circling year the ewes give birth.
So no one, neither king nor shepherd could want
for cheese or mutton, or sweet milk either,
udders swell for the sucklings round the year.

But while I roamed those lands, amassing a fortune,   100
a stranger killed my brother, blind to the danger, duped blind—
thanks to the cunning of his cursed, murderous queen!
So I rule all this wealth with no great joy.
You must have heard my story from your fathers,
whoever they are—what hardships I endured,   105
how I lost this handsome palace built for the ages,
filled to its depths with hoards of gorgeous things.
Well, would to god I'd stayed right here in my own house
with a third of all that wealth and they were still alive,
all who died on the wide plain of Troy those years ago,   110
far from the stallion-land of Argos.
                                    And still,
much as I weep for all my men, grieving sorely,
time and again, sitting here in the royal halls,
now indulging myself in tears, now brushing tears away—
the grief that numbs the spirit gluts us quickly—   115
for none of all those comrades, pained as I am,
do I grieve as much for one . . .
that man who makes sleep hateful, even food,
as I pore over his memory. No one, no Achaean
labored hard as Odysseus labored or achieved so much.   120
And how did his struggles end? In suffering for that man;
for me, in relentless, heartbreaking grief for him,
lost and gone so long now—dead or alive, who knows?
How they must mourn him too, Laertes, the old man,
and self-possessed Penelope. Telemachus as well,   125
the boy he left a babe in arms at home."
                                    Such memories
stirred in the young prince a deep desire to grieve
for Odysseus. Tears streamed down his cheeks
and wet the ground when he heard his father's name,
both hands clutching his purple robe before his eyes.   130
Menelaus recognized him at once but pondered
whether to let him state his father's name
or probe him first and prompt him step by step.

While he debated all this now within himself,
Helen emerged from her scented, lofty chamber—   135
striking as Artemis[4] with her golden shafts—
and a train of women followed . . .
Adreste drew up her carved reclining-chair,

4. A virgin goddess, Apollo's sister, she is associated with wild animals and childbirth. Helen, Menelaus's wife, was the daughter of Leda and Zeus. Her elopement with Paris was the cause of the Trojan War.

Alcippe brought a carpet of soft-piled fleece,
Phylo carried her silver basket given by Alcandre,   140
King Polybus' wife, who made his home in Egyptian Thebes
where the houses overflow with the greatest troves of treasure.
The king gave Menelaus a pair of bathing-tubs in silver,
two tripods, ten bars of gold, and apart from these
his wife presented Helen her own precious gifts: 145
a golden spindle, a basket that ran on casters,
solid silver polished off with rims of gold.
Now Phylo her servant rolled it in beside her,
heaped to the brim with yarn prepared for weaving;
the spindle swathed in violet wool lay tipped across it.   150
Helen leaned back in her chair, a stool beneath her feet,
and pressed her husband at once for each detail:
"Do we know, my lord Menelaus, who our visitors
claim to be, our welcome new arrivals?
Right or wrong, what can I say? My heart tells me   155
to come right out and say I've never seen such a likeness,
neither in man nor woman—I'm amazed at the sight.
To the life he's like the son of great Odysseus,
surely he's Telemachus! The boy that hero left
a babe in arms at home when all you Achaeans   160
fought at Troy, launching your headlong battles
just for *my* sake, shameless whore that I was."

    "My dear, my dear," the red-haired king assured her,
"now that you mention it, I see the likeness too . . .
Odysseus' feet were like the boy's, his hands as well,   165
his glancing eyes, his head, and the fine shock of hair.
Yes, and just now, as I was talking about Odysseus,
remembering how he struggled, suffered, all for me,
a flood of tears came streaming down his face
and he clutched his purple robe before his eyes."   170

    "Right you are"—Pisistratus stepped in quickly—
"son of Atreus, King Menelaus, captain of armies:
here is the son of that great hero, as you say.
But the man is modest, he would be ashamed
to make a show of himself, his first time here,   175
and interrupt you. We delight in your voice
as if some god were speaking!
The noble horseman Nestor sent me along
to be his escort. Telemachus yearned to see you,
so you could give him some advice or urge some action.   180
When a father's gone, his son takes much abuse
in a house where no one comes to his defense.
So with Telemachus now. His father's gone.
No men at home will shield him from the worst."

    "Wonderful!" the red-haired king cried out.   185
"The son of my dearest friend, here in my own house!
That man who performed a hundred feats of arms for me.

And I swore that when he came I'd give him a hero's welcome,
him above all my comrades—if only Olympian Zeus,
farseeing Zeus, had granted us both safe passage   190
home across the sea in our swift trim ships.
Why, I'd have settled a city in Argos for him,
built him a palace, shipped him over from Ithaca,
him and all his wealth, his son, his people too—
emptied one of the cities nestling round about us,   195
one I rule myself. Both fellow-countrymen then,
how often we'd have mingled side-by-side!
Nothing could have parted us,
bound by love for each other, mutual delight . . .
till death's dark cloud came shrouding round us both.   200
But god himself, jealous of all this, no doubt,
robbed that unlucky man, him and him alone,
of the day of his return."
                            So Menelaus mused
and stirred in them all a deep desire to grieve.
Helen of Argos, daughter of Zeus, dissolved in tears,   205
Telemachus wept too, and so did Atreus' son Menelaus.
Nor could Nestor's son Pisistratus stay dry-eyed,
remembering now his gallant brother Antilochus,
cut down by Memnon[5] splendid son of the Morning.
Thinking of him, the young prince broke out: 210
"Old Nestor always spoke of you, son of Atreus,
as the wisest man of all the men he knew,
whenever we talked about you there at home,
questioning back and forth. So now, please,
if it isn't out of place, indulge me, won't you?   215
Myself, I take no joy in weeping over supper.
Morning will soon bring time enough for that.
Not that I'd grudge a tear
for any man gone down to meet his fate.
What other tribute can we pay to wretched men   220
than to cut a lock,[6] let tears roll down our cheeks?
And I have a brother of my own among the dead,
and hardly the poorest soldier in our ranks.
You probably knew him. I never met him, never
saw him myself. But they say he outdid our best,   225
Antilochus—lightning on his feet and every inch a fighter!"

    "Well said, my friend," the red-haired king replied.
"Not even an older man could speak and do as well.
Your father's son you are—your words have all his wisdom.
It's easy to spot the breed of a man whom Zeus   230
has marked for joy in birth and marriage both.
Take great King Nestor now:
Zeus has blessed him, all his livelong days,

---

5. The son of the goddess Dawn. After the events recounted in the *Iliad*, Memnon arrived as an ally of Troy and killed Nestor's son Antilochus in battle. Achilles took his life in revenge, drove the Trojans back to the city, and was then killed himself by Paris and Apollo.   6. Dedicating a lock of hair at the tomb was a gesture to mourn and commemorate the dead.

growing rich and sleek in his old age at home,
his sons expert with spears and full of sense.   235
Well, so much for the tears that caught us just now;
let's think again of supper. Come, rinse our hands.
Tomorrow, at dawn, will offer me and Telemachus
time to talk and trade our thoughts in full."

Asphalion quickly rinsed their hands with water,   240
another of King Menelaus' ready aides-in-arms.
Again they reached for the good things set before them.

Then Zeus's daughter Helen thought of something else.
Into the mixing-bowl from which they drank their wine
she slipped a drug, heart's-ease, dissolving anger,   245
magic to make us all forget our pains . . .
No one who drank it deeply, mulled in wine,
could let a tear roll down his cheeks that day,
not even if his mother should die, his father die,
not even if right before his eyes some enemy brought down   250
a brother or darling son with a sharp bronze blade.
So cunning the drugs that Zeus's daughter plied,
potent gifts from Polydamna the wife of Thon,
a woman of Egypt,[7] land where the teeming soil
bears the richest yield of herbs in all the world: 255
many health itself when mixed in the wine,
and many deadly poison.
Every man is a healer there, more skilled
than any other men on earth—Egyptians born
of the healing god himself. So now Helen, once   260
she had drugged the wine and ordered winecups filled,
resuming the conversation, entertained the group:
"My royal king Menelaus—welcome guests here,
sons of the great as well! Zeus can present us
times of joy and times of grief in turn: 265
all lies within his power.
So come, let's sit back in the palace now,
dine and warm our hearts with the old stories.
I will tell something perfect for the occasion.
Surely I can't describe or even list them all,   270
the exploits crowding fearless Odysseus' record,
but what a feat that hero dared and carried off
in the land of Troy where you Achaeans suffered!
Scarring his own body with mortifying strokes,
throwing filthy rags on his back like any slave,   275
he slipped into the enemy's city, roamed its streets—
all disguised, a totally different man, a beggar,
hardly the figure he cut among Achaea's ships.
That's how Odysseus infiltrated Troy,
and no one knew him at all . . .   280

7. The Greeks had great respect for Egyptian doctors; surviving papyri document their skill as surgeons and their expertise with drugs.

I alone, I spotted him for the man he was,
kept questioning him—the crafty one kept dodging.
But after I'd bathed him, rubbed him down with oil,
given him clothes to wear and sworn a binding oath
not to reveal him as Odysseus to the Trojans, not   285
till he was back at his swift ships and shelters,
then at last he revealed to me, step by step,
the whole Achaean strategy. And once he'd cut
a troop of Trojans down with his long bronze sword,
back he went to his comrades, filled with information.   290
The rest of the Trojan women shrilled their grief. Not I:
my heart leapt up—
                    my heart had changed by now—
                                        I yearned
to sail back home again! I grieved too late for the madness
Aphrodite sent me,[8] luring me there, far from my dear land,
forsaking my own child, my bridal bed, my husband too,   295
a man who lacked for neither brains nor beauty."

     And the red-haired Menelaus answered Helen:
"There was a tale, my lady. So well told.
Now then, I have studied, in my time,
the plans and minds of great ones by the score.   300
And I have traveled over a good part of the world
but never once have I laid eyes on a man like him—
what a heart that fearless Odysseus had inside him!
What a piece of work the hero dared and carried off
in the wooden horse where all our best encamped,   305
our champions armed with bloody death for Troy . . .
when along you came, Helen—roused, no doubt,
by a dark power bent on giving Troy some glory,
and dashing Prince Deiphobus[9] squired your every step.
Three times you sauntered round our hollow ambush,   310
feeling, stroking its flanks,
challenging all our fighters, calling each by name—
yours was the voice of all our long-lost wives!
And Diomedes and I, crouched tight in the midst
with great Odysseus, hearing you singing out,   315
were both keen to spring up and sally forth
or give you a sudden answer from inside,
but Odysseus damped our ardor, reined us back.
Then all the rest of the troops kept stock-still,
all but Anticlus. He was hot to salute you now   320
but Odysseus clamped his great hands on the man's mouth
and shut it, brutally—yes, he saved us all,
holding on grim-set till Pallas Athena
lured you off at last."

8. By promising him Helen's love, Aphrodite bribed Paris to judge her more beautiful than Hera or Athena. Her flight with Paris from Menelaus's house ignited the Trojan War.   9. A son of Priam and thus brother of Hector and Paris. Helen married him after Paris's death.

But clear-sighted Telemachus ventured, 325
"Son of Atreus, King Menelaus, captain of armies,
so much the worse, for not one bit of that
saved *him* from grisly death . . .
not even a heart of iron could have helped.
But come, send us off to bed. It's time to rest, 330
time to enjoy the sweet relief of sleep."

And Helen briskly told her serving-women
to make beds in the porch's shelter, lay down
some heavy purple throws for the beds themselves,
and over them spread some blankets, thick woolly robes, 335
a warm covering laid on top. Torches in hand,
they left the hall and made up beds at once.
The herald led the two guests on and so they slept
outside the palace under the forecourt's colonnade,
young Prince Telemachus and Nestor's shining son. 340
Menelaus retired to chambers deep in his lofty house
with Helen the pearl of women loosely gowned beside him.

When young Dawn with her rose-red fingers shone once more
the lord of the warcry climbed from bed and dressed,
over his shoulder he slung his well-honed sword, 345
fastened rawhide sandals under his smooth feet,
stepped from his bedroom, handsome as a god,
and sat beside Telemachus, asking, kindly,
"Now, my young prince, tell me what brings you here
to sunny Lacedaemon, sailing over the sea's broad back. 350
A public matter or private? Tell me the truth now."

And with all the poise he had, Telemachus replied,
"Son of Atreus, King Menelaus, captain of armies,
I came in the hope that you can tell me now
some news about my father. 355
My house is being devoured, my rich farms destroyed,
my palace crammed with enemies, slaughtering on and on
my droves of sheep and shambling longhorn cattle.
Suitors plague my mother—the insolent, overweening . . .
That's why I've come to plead before you now, 360
if you can tell me about his cruel death:
perhaps you saw him die with your own eyes
or heard the wanderer's end from someone else.
More than all other men, that man was born for pain.
Don't soften a thing, from pity, respect for me— 365
tell me, clearly, all your eyes have witnessed.
I beg you—if ever my father, lord Odysseus,
I pledged you his word and made it good in action
once on the fields of Troy where you Achaeans suffered,
remember his story now, tell *me* the truth."

                                  "How shameful!" 370
the red-haired king burst out in anger. "That's the bed
of a brave man of war they'd like to crawl inside,

those spineless, craven cowards!
Weak as the doe that beds down her fawns
in a mighty lion's den—her newborn sucklings— 375
then trails off to the mountain spurs and grassy bends
to graze her fill, but back the lion comes to his own lair
and the master deals both fawns a ghastly bloody death,
just what Odysseus will deal that mob—ghastly death.
Ah if only—Father Zeus, Athena and lord Apollo— 380
that man who years ago in the games at Lesbos
rose to Philomelides'[1] challenge, wrestled him,
pinned him down with one tremendous throw
and the Argives roared with joy . . .
if only *that* Odysseus sported with those suitors, 385
a blood wedding, a quick death would take the lot!
But about the things you've asked me, so intently,
I'll skew and sidestep nothing, not deceive you, ever.
Of all he told me—the Old Man of the Sea who never lies—
I'll hide or hold back nothing, not a single word. 390

It was in Egypt, where the gods still marooned me,[2]
eager as I was to voyage home . . . I'd failed,
you see, to render them full, flawless victims,
and gods are always keen to see their rules obeyed.
Now, there's an island out in the ocean's heavy surge, 395
well off the Egyptian coast—they call it Pharos—
far as a deep-sea ship can go in one day's sail
with a whistling wind astern to drive her on.
There's a snug harbor there, good landing beach
where crews pull in, draw water up from the dark wells 400
then push their vessels off for passage out.
But here the gods becalmed me twenty days . . .
not a breath of the breezes ruffling out to sea
that speed a ship across the ocean's broad back.
Now our rations would all have been consumed, 405
our crews' stamina too, if one of the gods
had not felt sorry for me, shown me mercy,
Eidothea, a daughter of Proteus,
that great power, the Old Man of the Sea.
My troubles must have moved her to the heart 410
when she met me trudging by myself without my men.
They kept roaming around the beach, day in, day out,
fishing with twisted hooks, their bellies racked by hunger.
Well, she came right up to me, filled with questions:
'Are you a fool, stranger—soft in the head and lazy too? 415
Or do you let things slide because you *like* your pain?
Here you are, cooped up on an island far too long,
with no way out of it, none that you can find,
while all your shipmates' spirit ebbs away.'

1. A king of Lesbos who challenged all comers to wrestle with him.   2. On the way home from Troy, Menelaus had been blown off course and ended up in Egypt, as Nestor tells Telemachus in book III.

So she prodded and I replied at once,   420
'Let me tell you, goddess—whoever you are—
I'm hardly landlocked here of my own free will.
So I must have angered one of the deathless gods
who rule the skies up there. But you tell *me*—
you immortals know it all—which one of you   425
blocks my way here, keeps me from my voyage?
How can I cross the swarming sea and reach home at last?'

    And the glistening goddess reassured me warmly,
'Of course, my friend, I'll answer all your questions.
Who haunts these parts? Proteus of Egypt does,   430
the immortal Old Man of the Sea who never lies,
who sounds the deep in all its depths, Poseidon's servant.
He's my father, they say, he gave me life. And he,
if only you ambush him somehow and pin him down,
will tell you the way to go, the stages of your voyage,   435
how you can cross the swarming sea and reach home at last.
And he can tell you too, if you want to press him—
you are a king, it seems—
all that's occurred within your palace, good and bad,
while you've been gone your long and painful way.'   440

    'Then you are the one'—I quickly took her up.
'Show me the trick to trap this ancient power,
or he'll see or sense me first and slip away.
It's hard for a mortal man to force a god.'

    'True, my friend,' the glistening one agreed,   445
'and again I'll tell you all you need to know.
When the sun stands striding at high noon,
then up from the waves he comes—
the Old Man of the Sea who never lies—
under a West Wind's gust that shrouds him round   450
in shuddering dark swells, and once he's out on land
he heads for his bed of rest in deep hollow caves
and around him droves of seals—sleek pups bred
by his lovely ocean-lady—bed down too
in a huddle, flopping up from the gray surf,   455
giving off the sour reek of the salty ocean depths.
I'll lead you there myself at the break of day
and couch you all for attack, side-by-side.
Choose three men from your crew, choose well,
the best you've got aboard the good decked hulls.   460
Now I will tell you all the old wizard's tricks . . .
First he will make his rounds and count the seals
and once he's checked their number, reviewed them all,
down in their midst he'll lie, like a shepherd with his flock.
That's your moment. Soon as you see him bedded down,   465
muster your heart and strength and hold him fast,
wildly as he writhes and fights you to escape.
He'll try all kinds of escape—twist and turn

into every beast that moves across the earth,
transforming himself into water, superhuman fire,   470
but you hold on for dear life, hug him all the harder!
And when, at last, he begins to ask you questions—
back in the shape you saw him sleep at first—
relax your grip and set the old god free
and ask him outright, hero,   475
which of the gods is up in arms against you?
How can you cross the swarming sea and reach home at last?'

    So she urged and under the breaking surf she dove
as I went back to our squadron beached in sand,
my heart a heaving storm at every step . . .   480
Once I reached my ship hauled up on shore
we made our meal and the godsent night came down
and then we slept at the sea's smooth shelving edge.
When young Dawn with her rose-red fingers shone once more
I set out down the coast of the wide-ranging sea,   485
praying hard to the gods for all their help,
taking with me the three men I trusted most
on every kind of mission.
                       Eidothea, now,
had slipped beneath the sea's engulfing folds
but back from the waves she came with four sealskins,   490
all freshly stripped, to deceive her father blind.
She scooped out lurking-places deep in the sand
and sat there waiting as we approached her post,
then couching us side-by-side she flung a sealskin
over each man's back. Now there was an ambush   495
that would have overpowered us all—overpowering,
true, the awful reek of all those sea-fed brutes!
Who'd dream of bedding down with a monster of the deep?
But the goddess sped to our rescue, found the cure
with ambrosia, daubing it under each man's nose—   500
that lovely scent, it drowned the creatures' stench.
So all morning we lay there waiting, spirits steeled,
while seals came crowding, jostling out of the sea
and flopped down in rows, basking along the surf.
At high noon the old man emerged from the waves   505
and found his fat-fed seals and made his rounds,
counting them off, counting *us* the first four,
but he had no inkling of all the fraud afoot.
Then down he lay and slept, but we with a battle-cry,
we rushed him, flung our arms around him—he'd lost nothing,   510
the old rascal, none of his cunning quick techniques!
First he shifted into a great bearded lion
and then a serpent—
                a panther—
                       a ramping wild boar—
a torrent of water—
                a tree with soaring branchtops—

but we held on for dear life, braving it out   515
until, at last, that quick-change artist,
the old wizard, began to weary of all this
and burst out into rapid-fire questions:
'Which god, Menelaus, conspired with you
to trap me in ambush? seize me against my will?   520
What on earth do you want?'
                       'You know, old man,'
I countered now. 'Why put me off with questions?
Here I am, cooped up on an island far too long,
with no way out of it, none that I can find,
while my spirit ebbs away. But you tell *me*—   525
you immortals know it all—which one of you
blocks my way here, keeps me from my voyage?
How can I cross the swarming sea and reach home at last?'

   'How wrong you were!' the seer shot back at once.
'You should have offered Zeus and the other gods   530
a handsome sacrifice, *then* embarked, if you ever hoped
for a rapid journey home across the wine-dark sea.
It's not your destiny yet to see your loved ones,
reach your own grand house, your native land at last,
not till you sail back through Egyptian waters—   535
the great Nile swelled by the rains of Zeus—
and make a splendid rite to the deathless gods
who rule the vaulting skies. Then, only then
will the gods grant you the voyage you desire.'

   So he urged, and broke the heart inside me,   540
having to double back on the mist-bound seas,
back to Egypt, that, that long and painful way . . .
Nevertheless I caught my breath and answered,
'That I will do, old man, as you command.
But tell me this as well, and leave out nothing: 545
Did all the Achaeans reach home in the ships unharmed,
all we left behind, Nestor and I, en route from Troy?
Or did any die some cruel death by shipwreck
or die in the arms of loved ones,
once they'd wound down the long coil of war?'   550

   And he lost no time in saying, 'Son of Atreus,
why do you ask me that? Why do you need to know?
Why probe my mind? You won't stay dry-eyed long,
I warn you, once you have heard the whole story.
Many of them were killed, many survived as well,   555
but only two who captained your bronze-armored units
died on the way home—you know who died in the fighting,
you were there yourself.
                And one is still alive,
held captive, somewhere, off in the endless seas . . .

Ajax,[3] now, went down with his long-oared fleet.   560
First Poseidon drove him onto the cliffs of Gyrae,[4]
looming cliffs, then saved him from the breakers—
he'd have escaped his doom, too, despite Athena's hate,
if he hadn't flung that brazen boast, the mad blind fool.
"In the teeth of the gods," he bragged, "I have escaped   565
the ocean's sheer abyss!" Poseidon heard that frantic vaunt
and the god grasped his trident in both his massive hands
and struck the Gyraean headland, hacked the rock in two,
and the giant stump stood fast but the jagged spur
where Ajax perched at first, the raving madman—   570
toppling into the sea, it plunged him down, down
in the vast, seething depths. And so he died,
having drunk his fill of brine.
                                        Your brother?
He somehow escaped that fate; Agamemnon got away
in his beaked ships. Queen Hera[5] pulled him through.   575
But just as he came abreast of Malea's beetling cape
a hurricane snatched him up and swept him way off course—
groaning, desperate—driving him over the fish-infested sea
to the wild borderland where Thyestes[6] made his home
in the days of old and his son Aegisthus lived now.   580
But even from there a safe return seemed likely,
yes, the immortals swung the wind around to fair
and the victors sailed home. How he rejoiced,
Atrides setting foot on his fatherland once more—
he took that native earth in his hands and kissed it,   585
hot tears flooding his eyes, so thrilled to see his land!
But a watchman saw him too—from a lookout high above—
a spy that cunning Aegisthus stationed there,
luring the man with two gold bars in payment.
One whole year he'd watched . . .   590
so the great king would not get past unseen,
his fighting power intact for self-defense.
The spy ran the news to his master's halls
and Aegisthus quickly set his stealthy trap.
Picking the twenty best recruits from town   595
he packed them in ambush at one end of the house,
at the other he ordered a banquet dressed and spread
and went to welcome the conquering hero, Agamemnon,
went with team and chariot, and a mind aswarm with evil.
Up from the shore he led the king, he ushered him in—   600
suspecting nothing of all his doom—he feasted him well
then cut him down as a man cuts down some ox at the trough!
Not one of your brother's men-at-arms was left alive,
none of Aegisthus' either. All, killed in the palace.'

---

3. The lesser of the two heroes named Ajax, who had enraged Athena by raping Cassandra in the goddess's temple.   4. Located by ancient writers on Tenos or Mykonos (both islands in the Cyclades group) or at the western tip of Euboea, the long island that stretches along the north coast of Attica.   5. Wife of Zeus and a partisan of the Greeks in the Trojan War.   6. Brother of Atreus, Agamemnon's father. In a tradition drawn on by Aeschylus's *Oresteia* but ignored by or unknown to Homer, the brothers were bitter rivals over the kingship of Argos.

So Proteus said, and his story crushed my heart.   605
I knelt down in the sand and wept. I'd no desire
to go on living and see the rising light of day.
But once I'd had my fill of tears and writhing there,
the Old Man of the Sea who never lies continued,
'No more now, Menelaus. How long must you weep?   610
Withering tears, what good can come of tears?
None I know of. Strive instead to return
to your native country—hurry home at once!
Either you'll find the murderer still alive
or Orestes will have beaten you to the kill.   615
You'll be in time to share the funeral feast.'

    So he pressed, and I felt my heart, my old pride,
for all my grieving, glow once more in my chest
and I asked the seer in a rush of winging words,
'Those two I know now. Tell me the third man's name.   620
Who is still alive, held captive off in the endless seas?
Unless he's dead by now. I want to know the truth
though it grieves me all the more.'
                                                    'Odysseus'—
the old prophet named the third at once—
'Laertes' son, who makes his home in Ithaca . . .   625
I saw him once on an island, weeping live warm tears
in the nymph Calypso's house—she holds him there by force.
He has no way to voyage home to his own native land,
no trim ships in reach, no crew to ply the oars
and send him scudding over the sea's broad back.   630
But about your own destiny, Menelaus,
dear to Zeus, it's not for you to die
and meet your fate in the stallion-land of Argos,
no, the deathless ones will sweep you off to the world's end,
the Elysian Fields, where gold-haired Rhadamanthys[7] waits,   635
where life glides on in immortal ease for mortal man;
no snow, no winter onslaught, never a downpour there
but night and day the Ocean River sends up breezes,
singing winds of the West refreshing all mankind.
All this because you are Helen's husband now—   640
the gods count *you* the son-in-law of Zeus.'

    So he divined and down the breaking surf he dove
as I went back to the ships with my brave men,
my heart a rising tide at every step.
Once I reached my craft hauled up on shore   645
we made our meal and the godsent night came down
and then we slept at the sea's smooth shelving edge.
When young Dawn with her rose-red fingers shone once more
we hauled the vessels down to the sunlit breakers first
then stepped the masts amidships, canvas brailed—   650

---

7. A son of Zeus by the mortal Europa, and brother to King Minos of Crete. Elysium is the paradise
reserved for a few mortal relatives of the gods.

the crews swung aboard, they sat to the oars in ranks
and in rhythm churned the water white with stroke on stroke.
Back we went to the Nile swelled by the rains of Zeus,
I moored the ships and sacrificed in a splendid rite,
and once I'd slaked the wrath of the everlasting gods   655
I raised a mound for Agamemnon, his undying glory.
All this done, I set sail and the gods sent me
a stiff following wind that sped me home,
home to the native land I love.
                                        But come,
my boy, stay on in my palace now with me,   660
at least till ten or a dozen days have passed.
Then I'll give you a princely send-off—shining gifts,
three stallions and a chariot burnished bright—
and I'll add a gorgeous cup so you can pour
libations out to the deathless gods on high   665
and remember Menelaus all your days."
                                        Telemachus,
summoning up his newfound tact, replied,
"Please, Menelaus, don't keep me quite so long.
True, I'd gladly sit beside you one whole year
without a twinge of longing for home or parents.   670
It's wonderful how you tell your stories, all you say—
I delight to listen! Yes, but now, I'm afraid,
my comrades must be restless in sacred Pylos,
and here you'd hold me just a little longer.
As for the gift you give me, let it be a keepsake.   675
Those horses I really cannot take to Ithaca;
better to leave them here to be your glory.
You rule a wide level plain
where the fields of clover roll and galingale
and wheat and oats and glistening full-grain barley.   680
No running-room for mares in Ithaca though, no meadows.
Goat, not stallion, land, yet it means the world to me.
None of the rugged islands slanting down to sea
is good for pasture or good for bridle paths,
but Ithaca, best of islands, crowns them all!"   685

   So he declared. The lord of the warcry smiled,
patted him with his hand and praised his guest, concluding,
"Good blood runs in you, dear boy, your words are proof.
Certainly I'll exchange the gifts. The power's mine.
Of all the treasures lying heaped in my palace   690
you shall have the finest, most esteemed. Why,
I'll give you a mixing-bowl, forged to perfection—
it's solid silver finished off with a lip of gold.
Hephaestus[8] made it himself. And a royal friend,
Phaedimus, king of Sidon,[9] lavished it on me   695

8. God of the forge and patron of metal workers, married to the goddess Aphrodite; in the *Iliad* (book XVIII) he made Achilles' armor.   9. A wealthy and powerful city on the coast of Phoenicia (present-day Lebanon).

when his palace welcomed me on passage home.
How pleased I'd be if you took it as a gift!"

    And now as the two confided in each other,
banqueters arrived at the great king's palace,
leading their own sheep, bearing their hearty wine,   700
and their wives in lovely headbands sent along the food.
And so they bustled about the halls preparing dinner . . .
But all the while the suitors, before Odysseus' palace,
amused themselves with discus and long throwing spears,
out on the leveled grounds, free and easy as always,   705
full of swagger. But lord Antinous sat apart,
dashing Eurymachus beside him, ringleaders,
head and shoulders the strongest of the lot.
Phronius' son Noëmon approached them now,
quick to press Antinous with a question: 710
"Antinous, have we any notion or not
when Telemachus will return from sandy Pylos?
He sailed in a ship of mine and now I need her back
to cross over to Elis[1] Plain where I keep a dozen horses,
brood-mares suckling some heavy-duty mules, unbroken.   715
I'd like to drive one home and break him in."

    That dumbfounded them both. They never dreamed
the prince had gone to Pylos, Neleus' city—
certain the boy was still nearby somewhere,
out on his farm with flocks or with the swineherd.   720

    "Tell me the truth!" Antinous wheeled on Noëmon.
"When did he go? And what young crew went with him?
Ithaca's best? Or his own slaves and servants?
Surely he has enough to man a ship.
Tell me this—be clear—I've got to know: 725
did he commandeer your ship against your will
or did you volunteer it once he'd won you over?"

    "I volunteered it, of course," Noëmon said.
"What else could anyone do, when such a man,
a prince weighed down with troubles,   730
asked a favor? Hard to deny him anything.
And the young crew that formed his escort? Well,
they're the finest men on the island, next to us.
And Mentor took command—I saw him climb aboard—
or a god who looked like Mentor head to foot,   735
and that's what I find strange. I saw good Mentor
yesterday, just at sunup, here. But clearly
he boarded ship for Pylos days ago."

    With that he headed back to his father's house,
leaving the two lords stiff with indignation.   740

---

1. A region in the northwestern Peloponnesus, slightly southeast of Ithaca.

They made the suitors sit down in a group
and stop their games at once. Eupithes' son
Antinous rose up in their midst to speak,
his dark heart filled with fury,
blazing with anger—eyes like searing fire: 745
"By god, what a fine piece of work he's carried off!
Telemachus—what insolence—and we thought his little jaunt
would come to grief. But in spite of us all, look,
the young cub slips away, just like that—
picks the best crew in the land and off he sails.   750
And this is just the start of the trouble he can make.
Zeus kill that brazen boy before he hits his prime!
Quick, fetch me a swift ship and twenty men—
I'll waylay him from ambush, board him coming back
in the straits between Ithaca and rocky Same.[2]   755
This gallant voyage of his to find his father
will find *him* wrecked at last!"

       They all roared approval, urged him on,
rose at once and retired to Odysseus' palace.

      But not for long was Penelope unaware   760
of the grim plots her suitors planned in secret.
The herald Medon told her. He'd overheard their schemes,
listening in outside the court while they wove on within.
He rushed the news through the halls to tell the queen
who greeted him as he crossed her chamber's threshold: 765
"Herald, why have the young blades sent you now?
To order King Odysseus' serving-women
to stop their work and slave to fix their feast?
I hate their courting, their running riot here—
would to god that this meal, here and now,   770
were their last meal on earth!
               Day after day,
all of you swarming, draining our life's blood,
my wary son's estate. What, didn't you listen
to your fathers—when you were children, years ago—
telling you how Odysseus treated them, your parents?   775
Never an unfair word, never an unfair action
among his people here, though that's the way
of our god-appointed kings,
hating one man, loving the next, with luck.
Not Odysseus. Never an outrage done to any man alive.   780
But you, you and your ugly outbursts, shameful acts,
they're plain to see. Look at the thanks he gets
for all past acts of kindness!"
               Medon replied,
sure of his own discretion, "Ah my queen,
if only *that* were the worst of all you face.   785

---

2. An island close to Ithaca (probably the modern Cephallenia).

Now your suitors are plotting something worse,
harsher, crueler. God forbid they bring it off!
They're poised to cut Telemachus down with bronze swords
on his way back home. He's sailed off, you see . . .
for news of his father—to sacred Pylos first,   790
then out to the sunny hills of Lacedaemon."

    Her knees gave way on the spot, her heart too.
She stood there speechless a while, struck dumb,
tears filling her eyes, her warm voice choked.
At last she found some words to make reply: 795
"Oh herald, why has my child gone and left me?
No need in the world for him to board the ships,
those chariots of the sea that sweep men on,
driving across the ocean's endless wastes . . .
Does he want his very name wiped off the earth?"   800

    Medon, the soul of thoughtfulness, responded,
"I don't know if a god inspired your son
or the boy's own impulse led him down to Pylos,
but he went to learn of his father's journey home,
or whatever fate he's met."   805

    Back through King Odysseus' house he went
but a cloud of heartbreak overwhelmed the queen.
She could bear no longer sitting on a chair
though her room had chairs aplenty.
Down she sank on her well-built chamber's floor,   810
weeping, pitifully, as the women whimpered round her,
all the women, young and old, who served her house.
Penelope, sobbing uncontrollably, cried out to them,
"Hear me, dear ones! Zeus has given me torment—
me above all the others born and bred in *my* day.   815
My lionhearted husband, lost, long years ago,
who excelled the Argives all in every strength—
that great man whose fame resounds through Hellas
right to the depths of Argos!
               But now my son,
my darling boy—the whirlwinds have ripped him   820
out of the halls without a trace! I never heard
he'd gone—not even from you, you hard, heartless . . .
not one of you even thought to rouse me from my bed,
though well you knew when he boarded that black ship.
Oh if only I had learned he was planning such a journey,   825
he would have stayed, by god, keen as he was to sail—
or left me dead right here within our palace.
Go, someone, quickly! Call old Dolius now,
the servant my father gave me when I came,
the man who tends my orchard green with trees,   830
so he can run to Laertes, sit beside him,
tell him the whole story, point by point.

Perhaps—who knows?—he'll weave some plan,
he'll come out of hiding, plead with all these people
mad to destroy his line, his son's line of kings!"   835

        "Oh dear girl," Eurycleia the fond old nurse replied,
"kill me then with a bronze knife—no mercy—or let me live,
here in the palace—I'll hide nothing from you now!
I knew it all, I gave him all he asked for,
bread and mellow wine, but he made me take   840
a binding oath that I, I wouldn't tell you,
no, not till ten or a dozen days had passed
or you missed the lad yourself and learned he'd gone,
so tears would never mar your lovely face . . .
Come, bathe now, put on some fresh clothes,   845
climb to the upper rooms with all your women
and pray to Pallas, daughter of storming Zeus—
she may save Telemachus yet, even at death's door.
Don't worry an old man, worried enough by now.
I can't believe the blessed gods so hate   850
the heirs of King Arcesius,[3] through and through.
One will still live on—I know it—born to rule
this lofty house and the green fields far and wide."
                                        With that
she lulled Penelope's grief and dried her eyes of tears.
And the queen bathed and put fresh clothing on,   855
climbed to the upper rooms with all her women
and sifting barley into a basket, prayed to Pallas,
"Hear me, daughter of Zeus whose shield is thunder—
tireless one, Athena! If ever, here in his halls,
resourceful King Odysseus   860
burned rich thighs of sheep or oxen in your honor,
oh remember it now for *my* sake, save my darling son,
defend him from these outrageous, overbearing suitors!"

        She shrilled a high cry and the goddess heard her prayer
as the suitors burst into uproar through the shadowed halls 865
and one of the lusty young men began to brag, "Listen,
our long-courted queen's preparing us all a marriage—
with no glimmer at all
how the murder of her son has been decreed."
                                        Boasting so,
with no glimmer at all of what had been decreed.   870
But Antinous took the floor and issued orders:
"Stupid fools! Muzzle your bragging now—
before someone slips inside and reports us.
Up now, not a sound, drive home our plan—
it suits us well, we approved it one and all."   875

        With that he picked out twenty first-rate men
and down they went to the swift ship at the sea's edge.

---

3. Laertes' father (thus Odysseus's grandfather).

First they hauled the craft into deeper water,
stepped the mast amidships, canvas brailed,
made oars fast in the leather oarlock straps   880
while zealous aides-in-arms brought weapons on.
They moored her well out in the channel, disembarked
and took their meal on shore, waiting for dusk to fall.

    But there in her upper rooms she lay, Penelope
lost in thought, fasting, shunning food and drink,   885
brooding now . . . would her fine son escape his death
or go down at her overweening suitors' hands?
Her mind in torment, wheeling
like some lion at bay, dreading gangs of hunters
closing their cunning ring around him for the finish.   890
Harried so she was, when a deep kind sleep overcame her,
back she sank and slept, her limbs fell limp and still.

    And again the bright-eyed goddess Pallas thought
of one more way to help. She made a phantom now,
its build like a woman's build, Iphthime's,[4] yes,   895
another daughter of generous Lord Icarius,
Eumelus' bride, who made her home in Pherae.[5]
Athena sped her on to King Odysseus' house
to spare Penelope, worn with pain and sobbing,
further spells of grief and storms of tears.   900
The phantom entered her bedroom,
passing quickly in through the doorbolt slit[6]
and hovering at her head she rose and spoke now:
"Sleeping, Penelope, your heart so wrung with sorrow?
No need, I tell you, no, the gods who live at ease   905
can't bear to let you weep and rack your spirit.
Your son will still come home—it is decreed.
He's never wronged the gods in any way."

    And Penelope murmured back, still cautious,
drifting softly now at the gate of dreams,   910
"Why have you come, my sister?
Your visits all too rare in the past,
for you make your home so very far away.
You tell me to lay to rest the grief and tears
that overwhelm me now, torment me, heart and soul?   915
With my lionhearted husband lost long years ago,
who excelled the Argives all in every strength?
That great man whose fame resounds through Hellas
right to the depths of Argos . . .
                And now my darling boy,
he's off and gone in a hollow ship! Just a youngster,   920
still untrained for war or stiff debate.
Him I mourn even more than I do my husband—

---

4. Penelope's sister.   5. A town in Thessaly, far from Ithaca in north-central Greece. Eumelus, who has
a minor role in the *Iliad*, was of very distinguished ancestry.   6. We would say "through the keyhole."
The inside bolt could be closed from outside by means of a strap that came through a slit in the door.

I quake in terror for all that he might suffer
either on open sea or shores he goes to visit.
Hordes of enemies scheme against him now,   925
keen to kill him off
before he can reach his native land again."

  "Courage!" the shadowy phantom reassured her.
"Don't be overwhelmed by all your direst fears.
He travels with such an escort, one that others   930
would pray to stand beside them. She has power—
Pallas Athena. She pities you in your tears.
She wings me here to tell you all these things."

  But the circumspect Penelope replied,
"If you *are* a god and have heard a god's own voice,   935
come, tell me about that luckless man as well.
Is he still alive? does he see the light of day?
Or is he dead already, lost in the House of Death?"

  "About that man," the shadowy phantom answered,
"I cannot tell you the story start to finish,   940
whether he's dead or alive.
It's wrong to lead you on with idle words."
                                         At that
she glided off by the doorpost past the bolt—
gone on a lifting breeze. Icarius' daughter
started up from sleep, her spirit warmed now   945
that a dream so clear had come to her in darkest night.

  But the suitors boarded now and sailed the sea-lanes,
plotting in their hearts Telemachus' plunge to death.
Off in the middle channel lies a rocky island,
just between Ithaca and Same's rugged cliffs—   950
Asteris—not large, but it has a cove,
a harbor with two mouths where ships can hide.
Here the Achaeans lurked in ambush for the prince.

                        BOOK V

                [*Odysseus—Nymph and Shipwreck*]

As Dawn rose up from bed by her lordly mate Tithonus,[7]
bringing light to immortal gods and mortal men,
the gods sat down in council, circling Zeus
the thunder king whose power rules the world.
Athena began, recalling Odysseus to their thoughts,   5
the goddess deeply moved by the man's long ordeal,
held captive still in the nymph Calypso's house:
"Father Zeus—you other happy gods who never die—
never let any sceptered king be kind and gentle now,
not with all his heart, or set his mind on justice—   10

---

7. A mortal man, given immortality (but not youth) by Zeus at the request of Dawn (Eos).

no, let him be cruel and always practice outrage.
Think: not one of the people whom he ruled
remembers Odysseus now, that godlike man,
and kindly as a father to his children.
                                                Now
he's left to pine on an island, racked with grief   15
in the nymph Calypso's house—she holds him there by force.
He has no way to voyage home to his own native land,
no trim ships in reach, no crew to ply the oars
and send him scudding over the sea's broad back.
And now his dear son . . . they plot to kill the boy   20
on his way back home. Yes, he has sailed off
for news of his father, to holy Pylos first,
then out to the sunny hills of Lacedaemon."

    "My child," Zeus who marshals the thunderheads replied,
"what nonsense you let slip through your teeth. Come now,   25
wasn't the plan your own? You conceived it yourself:
Odysseus shall return and pay the traitors back.
Telemachus? Sail him home with all your skill—
the power is yours, no doubt—
home to his native country all unharmed   30
while the suitors limp to port, defeated, baffled men."

    With those words, Zeus turned to his own son Hermes.
"You are our messenger, Hermes, sent on all our missions.
Announce to the nymph with lovely braids our fixed decree:
Odysseus journeys home—the exile must return.   35
But not in the convoy of the gods or mortal men.
No, on a lashed, makeshift raft and wrung with pains,
on the twentieth day he will make his landfall, fertile Scheria,
the land of Phaeacians, close kin to the gods themselves,
who with all their hearts will prize him like a god   40
and send him off in a ship to his own beloved land,
giving him bronze and hoards of gold and robes—
more plunder than he could ever have won from Troy
if Odysseus had returned intact with his fair share.
So his destiny ordains. He shall see his loved ones,   45
reach his high-roofed house, his native land at last."

    So Zeus decreed and the giant-killing guide obeyed at once.
Quickly under his feet he fastened the supple sandals,
ever-glowing gold, that wing him over the waves
and boundless earth with the rush of gusting winds.   50
He seized the wand that enchants the eyes of men
whenever Hermes wants, or wakes us up from sleep.
That wand in his grip, the powerful giant-killer,
swooping down from Pieria,[8] down the high clear air,
plunged to the sea and skimmed the waves like a tern   55
that down the deadly gulfs of the barren salt swells

---

8. Region in northern Greece, just north of the gods' home on Mount Olympus.

glides and dives for fish,
dipping its beating wings in bursts of spray—
so Hermes skimmed the crests on endless crests.
But once he gained that island worlds apart,   60
up from the deep-blue sea he climbed to dry land
and strode on till he reached the spacious cave
where the nymph with lovely braids had made her home,
and he found her there inside . . .
                 A great fire
blazed on the hearth and the smell of cedar   65
cleanly split and sweetwood burning bright
wafted a cloud of fragrance down the island.
Deep inside she sang, the goddess Calypso, lifting
her breathtaking voice as she glided back and forth
before her loom, her golden shuttle weaving.   70
Thick, luxuriant woods grew round the cave,
alders and black poplars, pungent cypress too,
and there birds roosted, folding their long wings,
owls and hawks and the spread-beaked ravens of the sea,
black skimmers who make their living off the waves.   75
And round the mouth of the cavern trailed a vine
laden with clusters, bursting with ripe grapes.
Four springs in a row, bubbling clear and cold,
running side-by-side, took channels left and right.
Soft meadows spreading round were starred with violets,   80
lush with beds of parsley. Why, even a deathless god
who came upon that place would gaze in wonder,
heart entranced with pleasure. Hermes the guide,
the mighty giant-killer, stood there, spellbound . . .
But once he'd had his fill of marveling at it all   85
he briskly entered the deep vaulted cavern.
Calypso, lustrous goddess, knew him at once,
as soon as she saw his features face-to-face.
Immortals are never strangers to each other,
no matter how distant one may make her home.   90
But as for great Odysseus—
Hermes could not find him within the cave.
Off he sat on a headland, weeping there as always,
wrenching his heart with sobs and groans and anguish,
gazing out over the barren sea through blinding tears.   95
But Calypso, lustrous goddess, questioned Hermes,
seating him on a glistening, polished chair.
"God of the golden wand, why have you come?
A beloved, honored friend,
but it's been so long, your visits much too rare.   100
Tell me what's on your mind. I'm eager to do it,
whatever I *can* do . . . whatever can be done."

     And the goddess drew a table up beside him,
heaped with ambrosia, mixed him deep-red nectar.[9]

---

9. Ambrosia (which literally means "immortality") and nectar are the food and drink of the gods.

Hermes the guide and giant-killer ate and drank. 105
Once he had dined and fortified himself with food
he launched right in, replying to her questions:
"As one god to another, you ask me why I've come.
I'll tell you the whole story, mince no words—
your wish is my command. 110
It was Zeus who made me come, no choice of mine.
Who would willingly roam across a salty waste so vast,
so endless? Think: no city of men in sight, and not a soul
to offer the gods a sacrifice and burn the fattest victims.
But there is no way, you know, for another god to thwart 115
the will of storming Zeus and make it come to nothing.
Zeus claims you keep beside you a most unlucky man,
most harried of all who fought for Priam's Troy
nine years, sacking the city in the tenth,
and then set sail for home. 120
But voyaging back they outraged Queen Athena
who loosed the gales and pounding seas against them.
There all the rest of his loyal shipmates died
but the wind drove him on, the current bore him here.
Now Zeus commands you to send him off with all good speed: 125
it is not his fate to die here, far from his own people.
Destiny still ordains that he shall see his loved ones,
reach his high-roofed house, his native land at last."

    But lustrous Calypso shuddered at those words
and burst into a flight of indignation. "Hard-hearted 130
you are, you gods! You unrivaled lords of jealousy—
scandalized when goddesses sleep with mortals,
openly, even when one has made the man her husband.
So when Dawn with her rose-red fingers took Orion,[1]
you gods in your everlasting ease were horrified 135
till chaste Artemis throned in gold attacked him,
out on Delos,[2] shot him to death with gentle shafts.
And so when Demeter[3] the graceful one with lovely braids
gave way to her passion and made love with Iasion,[4]
bedding down in a furrow plowed three times— 140
Zeus got wind of it soon enough, I'd say,
and blasted the man to death with flashing bolts.
So now at last, you gods, you train your spite on *me*
for keeping a mortal man beside me. The man I saved,
riding astride his keel-board, all alone, when Zeus 145
with one hurl of a white-hot bolt had crushed
his racing warship down the wine-dark sea.
There all the rest of his loyal shipmates died
but the wind drove him on, the current bore him here.
And I welcomed him warmly, cherished him, even vowed 150

---

1. A legendary mighty hunter; after death, he became a constellation.   2. A small island in the middle of the Aegean Sea, the birthplace of Apollo and Artemis and a center of their worship.   3. Goddess associated with the growth of crops, especially wheat.   4. He was evidently a vegetation god, and his intercourse with Demeter "in a furrow plowed three times" (line 140) seems to allude to a fertility ritual.

to make the man immortal, ageless, all his days . . .
But since there is no way for another god to thwart
the will of storming Zeus and make it come to nothing,
let the man go—if the Almighty insists, commands—
and destroy himself on the barren salt sea! 155
I'll send him off, but not with any escort.
I have no ships in reach, no crew to ply the oars
and send him scudding over the sea's broad back.
But I will gladly advise him—I'll hide nothing—
so he can reach his native country all unharmed." 160

    And the guide and giant-killer reinforced her words:
"Release him at once, just so. Steer clear of the rage of Zeus!
Or down the years he'll fume and make your life a hell."

    With that the powerful giant-killer sped away.
The queenly nymph sought out the great Odysseus— 165
the commands of Zeus still ringing in her ears—
and found him there on the headland, sitting, still,
weeping, his eyes never dry, his sweet life flowing away
with the tears he wept for his foiled journey home,
since the nymph no longer pleased. In the nights, true, 170
he'd sleep with her in the arching cave—he had no choice—
unwilling lover alongside lover all too willing . . .
But all his days he'd sit on the rocks and beaches,
wrenching his heart with sobs and groans and anguish,
gazing out over the barren sea through blinding tears. 175
So coming up to him now, the lustrous goddess ventured,
"No need, my unlucky one, to grieve here any longer,
no, don't waste your life away. Now I am willing,
heart and soul, to send you off at last. Come,
take bronze tools, cut your lengthy timbers, 180
make them into a broad-beamed raft
and top it off with a half-deck high enough
to sweep you free and clear on the misty seas.
And I myself will stock her with food and water,
ruddy wine to your taste—all to stave off hunger— 185
give you clothing, send you a stiff following wind
so you can reach your native country all unharmed.
If only the gods are willing. They rule the vaulting skies.
They're stronger than I to plan and drive things home."

    Long-enduring Odysseus shuddered at that 190
and broke out in a sharp flight of protest.
"Passage home? Never. Surely you're plotting
something else, goddess, urging me—in a raft—
to cross the ocean's mighty gulfs. So vast, so full
of danger not even deep-sea ships can make it through, 195
swift as they are and buoyed up by the winds of Zeus himself.
I won't set foot on a raft until you show good faith,
until you consent to swear, goddess, a binding oath
you'll never plot some new intrigue to harm me!"

He was so intense the lustrous goddess smiled,   200
stroked him with her hand, savored his name and chided,
"Ah what a wicked man you are, and never at a loss.
What a thing to imagine, what a thing to say!
Earth be my witness now, the vaulting Sky above
and the dark cascading waters of the Styx[5]—I swear   205
by the greatest, grimmest oath that binds the happy gods:
I will never plot some new intrigue to harm you.
Never. All I have in mind and devise for *you*
are the very plans I'd fashion for myself
if I were in your straits. My every impulse   210
bends to what is right. Not iron, trust me,
the heart within *my* breast. I am all compassion."

    And lustrous Calypso quickly led the way
as he followed in the footsteps of the goddess.
They reached the arching cavern, man and god as one,   215
and Odysseus took the seat that Hermes just left,
while the nymph set out before him every kind
of food and drink that mortal men will take.
Calypso sat down face-to-face with the king
and the women served her nectar and ambrosia.   220
They reached out for the good things that lay at hand
and when they'd had their fill of food and drink
the lustrous one took up a new approach. "So then,
royal son of Laertes, Odysseus, man of exploits,
still eager to leave at once and hurry back   225
to your own home, your beloved native land?
Good luck to you, even so. Farewell!
But if you only knew, down deep, what pains
are fated to fill your cup before you reach that shore,
you'd stay right here, preside in our house with me   230
and be immortal. Much as you long to see your wife,
the one you pine for all your days . . . and yet
I just might claim to be nothing less than she,
neither in face nor figure. Hardly right, is it,
for mortal woman to rival immortal goddess?   235
How, in build? in beauty?"
                                          "Ah great goddess,"
worldly Odysseus answered, "don't be angry with me,
please. All that you say is true, how well I know.
Look at my wise Penelope. She falls far short of you,
your beauty, stature. She is mortal after all   240
and you, you never age or die . . .
Nevertheless I long—I pine, all my days—
to travel home and see the dawn of my return.
And if a god will wreck me yet again on the wine-dark sea,
I can bear that too, with a spirit tempered to endure.   245
Much have I suffered, labored long and hard by now
in the waves and wars. Add this to the total—

---

5. One of the rivers of the underworld, by which gods regularly swore oaths.

bring the trial on!"
                    Even as he spoke
the sun set and the darkness swept the earth.
And now, withdrawing into the cavern's deep recesses,   250
long in each other's arms they lost themselves in love.

   When young Dawn with her rose-red fingers shone once more
Odysseus quickly dressed himself in cloak and shirt
while the nymph slipped on a loose, glistening robe,
filmy, a joy to the eye, and round her waist   255
she ran a brocaded golden belt
and over her head a scarf to shield her brow,
then turned to plan the great man's voyage home.
She gave him a heavy bronze ax that fit his grip,
both blades well-honed, with a fine olive haft   260
lashed firm to its head. She gave him a polished
smoothing-adze as well and then she led the way
to the island's outer edge where trees grew tall,
alders, black poplars and firs that shot sky-high,
seasoned, drying for years, ideal for easy floating.   265
Once she'd shown her guest where the tall timber stood,
Calypso the lustrous goddess headed home again.
He set to cutting trunks—the work was done in no time.
Twenty in all he felled, he trimmed them clean with his ax
and split them deftly, trued them straight to the line.   270
Meanwhile the radiant goddess brought him drills—
he bored through all his planks and wedged them snugly,
knocking them home together, locked with pegs and joints.
Broad in the beam and bottom flat as a merchantman
when a master shipwright turns out her hull,   275
so broad the craft Odysseus made himself.
Working away at speed
he put up half-decks pinned to close-set ribs
and a sweep of gunwales rounded off the sides.
He fashioned the mast next and sank its yard in deep   280
and added a steering-oar to hold her right on course,
then he fenced her stem to stern with twigs and wicker,
bulwark against the sea-surge, floored with heaps of brush.
And lustrous Calypso came again, now with bolts of cloth
to make the sail, and he finished that off too, expertly.   285
Braces, sheets and brails—he rigged all fast on board,
then eased her down with levers into the sunlit sea.

   That was the fourth day and all his work was done.
On the fifth, the lovely goddess launched him from her island,
once she had bathed and decked him out in fragrant clothes.   290
And Calypso stowed two skins aboard—dark wine in one,
the larger one held water—added a sack of rations,
filled with her choicest meats to build his strength,
and summoned a wind to bear him onward, fair and warm.
The wind lifting his spirits high, royal Odysseus   295
spread sail—gripping the tiller, seated astern—

and now the master mariner steered his craft,
sleep never closing his eyes, forever scanning
the stars, the Pleiades and the Plowman[6] late to set
and the Great Bear that mankind also calls the Wagon:[7]   300
she wheels on her axis always fixed, watching the Hunter,
and she alone is denied a plunge in the Ocean's baths.[8]
Hers were the stars the lustrous goddess told him
to keep hard to port as he cut across the sea.
And seventeen days he sailed, making headway well;   305
on the eighteenth, shadowy mountains slowly loomed . . .
the Phaeacians' island[9] reaching toward him now,
over the misty breakers, rising like a shield.

    But now Poseidon, god of the earthquake, saw him—
just returning home from his Ethiopian friends,   310
from miles away on the Solymi mountain-range[1]
he spied Odysseus sailing down the sea
and it made his fury boil even more.
He shook his head and rumbled to himself,
"Outrageous! Look how the gods have changed their minds   315
about Odysseus—while I was off with my Ethiopians.
Just look at him there, nearing Phaeacia's shores
where he's fated to escape his noose of pain
that's held him until now. Still my hopes ride high—
I'll give that man his swamping fill of trouble!"   320

    With that he rammed the clouds together—both hands
clutching his trident—churned the waves into chaos, whipping
all the gales from every quarter, shrouding over in thunderheads
the earth and sea at once—and night swept down from the sky—
East and South Winds clashed and the raging West and North,   325
sprung from the heavens, roiled heaving breakers up—
and Odysseus' knees quaked, his spirit too;
numb with fear he spoke to his own great heart:
"Wretched man—what becomes of me now, at last?
I fear the nymph foretold it all too well—   330
on the high seas, she said, before I can reach
my native land I'll fill my cup of pain! And now,
look, it all comes to pass. What monstrous clouds—
King Zeus crowning the whole wide heaven black—
churning the seas in chaos, gales blasting,   335
raging around my head from every quarter—
my death-plunge in a flash, it's certain now!
Three, four times blessed, my friends-in-arms
who died on the plains of Troy those years ago,
serving the sons of Atreus to the end. Would to god   340
I'd died there too and met my fate that day the Trojans,

6. Another name for the constellation Boötes. The Pleiades are a cluster of stars in the constellation
Taurus.   7. The Big Dipper.   8. That is, it never sets. The Hunter, or Orion, is also a constellation.
9. Identified by later Greeks with Corcyra (modern Corfu), an island off the northwest coast of mainland
Greece.   1. In Lycia in Asia Minor—a very long distance from Odysseus, sailing far to the west of
Greece.

swarms of them, hurled at *me* with bronze spears,
fighting over the corpse of proud Achilles!
A hero's funeral then, my glory spread by comrades—
now what a wretched death I'm doomed to die!"   345

    At that a massive wave came crashing down on his head,
a terrific onslaught spinning his craft round and round—
he was thrown clear of the decks—
                                        the steering-oar wrenched
from his grasp—
                    and in one lightning attack the brawling
galewinds struck full-force, snapping the mast mid-shaft   350
and hurling the sail and sailyard far across the sea.
He went under a good long while, no fast way out,
no struggling up from under the giant wave's assault,
his clothing dragged him down—divine Calypso's gifts—
but at last he fought his way to the surface spewing   355
bitter brine, streams of it pouring down his head.
But half-drowned as he was, he'd not forget his craft—
he lunged after her through the breakers, laying hold
and huddling amidships, fled the stroke of death.
Pell-mell the rollers tossed her along down-current,   360
wild as the North Wind tossing thistle along the fields
at high harvest—dry stalks clutching each other tightly—
so the galewinds tumbled her down the sea, this way, that way,
now the South Wind flinging her over to North to sport with,
now the East Wind giving her up to West to harry on and on.   365

    But someone saw him—Cadmus' daughter with lovely ankles,
Ino,[2] a mortal woman once with human voice and called
Leucothea now she lives in the sea's salt depths,
esteemed by all the gods as she deserves.
She pitied Odysseus, tossed, tormented so—   370
she broke from the waves like a shearwater on the wing,
lit on the wreck and asked him kindly, "Ah poor man,
why is the god of earthquakes so dead set against you?
Strewing your way with such a crop of troubles!
But he can't destroy you, not for all his anger.   375
Just do as I say. You seem no fool to me.
Strip off those clothes and leave your craft
for the winds to hurl, and swim for it now, you must,
strike out with your arms for landfall there,
Phaeacian land where destined safety waits.   380
Here, take this scarf,
tie it around your waist—it is immortal.
Nothing to fear now, neither pain nor death.
But once you grasp the mainland with your hands
untie it quickly, throw it into the wine-dark sea,   385
far from the shore, but you, you turn your head away!"

---

2. Pursued by her insane husband, she leaped into the sea with her infant son and was made immortal.
Cadmus was founder and king of Thebes.

With that the goddess handed him the scarf
and slipped back in the heavy breaking seas
like a shearwater once again
and a dark heaving billow closed above her.   390
But battle-weary Odysseus weighed two courses,
deeply torn, probing his fighting spirit: "Oh no—
I fear another immortal weaves a snare to trap me,
urging me to abandon ship! I won't. Not yet.
That shore's too far away—   395
I glimpsed it myself—where she says refuge waits.
No, here's what I'll do, it's what seems best to *me*.
As long as the timbers cling and joints stand fast,
I'll hold out aboard her and take a whipping—
once the breakers smash my craft to pieces,   400
then I'll swim—no better plan for now."

    But just as great Odysseus thrashed things out,
Poseidon god of the earthquake launched a colossal wave,
terrible, murderous, arching over him, pounding down on him,
hard as a windstorm blasting piles of dry parched chaff,   405
scattering flying husks—so the long planks of his boat
were scattered far and wide. But Odysseus leapt aboard
one timber and riding it like a plunging racehorse
stripped away his clothes, divine Calypso's gifts,
and quickly tying the scarf around his waist   410
he dove headfirst in the sea,
stretched his arms and stroked for life itself.
But again the mighty god of earthquakes spied him,
shook his head and grumbled deep in his spirit, "Go, go,
after all you've suffered—rove your miles of sea—   415
till you fall in the arms of people loved by Zeus.³
Even so I can hardly think you'll find
your punishments too light!"
                            With that threat
he lashed his team with their long flowing manes,
gaining Aegae⁴ port where his famous palace stands.   420

    But Zeus's daughter Athena countered him at once.
The rest of the winds she stopped right in their tracks,
commanding them all to hush now, go to sleep.
All but the boisterous North—she whipped him up
and the goddess beat the breakers flat before Odysseus,   425
dear to Zeus, so he could reach the Phaeacians,
mingle with men who love their long oars
and escape his death at last.
                            Yes, but now,
adrift on the heaving swells two nights, two days—
quite lost—again and again the man foresaw his death.   430
Then when Dawn with her lovely locks brought on

---

3. That is, the Phaeacians.   4. Several places share this name. Homer mentions Poseidon's cult at
Aegae several times.

the third day, the wind fell in an instant,
all glazed to a dead calm, and Odysseus,
scanning sharply, raised high by a groundswell,
looked up and saw it—landfall, just ahead.   435
Joy . . . warm as the joy that children feel
when they see their father's life dawn again,
one who's lain on a sickbed racked with torment,
wasting away, slowly, under some angry power's onslaught—
then what joy when the gods deliver him from his pains!   440
So warm, Odysseus' joy when he saw that shore, those trees,
as he swam on, anxious to plant his feet on solid ground again.
But just offshore, as far as a man's shout can carry,
he caught the boom of a heavy surf on jagged reefs—
roaring breakers crashing down on an ironbound coast,   445
exploding in fury—
                        the whole sea shrouded—
                                        sheets of spray—
no harbors to hold ships, no roadstead where they'd ride,
nothing but jutting headlands, riptooth reefs, cliffs.
Odysseus' knees quaked and the heart inside him sank;
he spoke to his fighting spirit, desperate: "Worse and worse!   450
Now that Zeus has granted a glimpse of land beyond my hopes,
now I've crossed this waste of water, the end in sight,
there's no way out of the boiling surf—I see no way!
Rugged reefs offshore, around them breakers roaring,
above them a smooth rock face, rising steeply, look,   455
and the surge too deep inshore, no spot to stand
on my own two legs and battle free of death.
If I clamber out, some big comber will hoist me,
dash me against that cliff—my struggles all a waste!
If I keep on swimming down the coast, trying to find   460
a seabeach shelving against the waves, a sheltered cove—
I dread it—another gale will snatch me up and haul me
back to the fish-infested sea, retching in despair.
Or a dark power will loose some monster at me,
rearing out of the waves—one of the thousands   465
Amphitrite's breakers teem with. Well I know
the famous god of earthquakes hates my very name!"

     Just as that fear went churning through his mind
a tremendous roller swept him toward the rocky coast
where he'd have been flayed alive, his bones crushed   470
if the bright-eyed goddess Pallas had not inspired him now.
He lunged for a reef, he seized it with both hands and clung
for dear life, groaning until the giant wave surged past
and so he escaped its force, but the breaker's backwash
charged into him full fury and hurled him out to sea.   475
Like pebbles stuck in the suckers of some octopus
dragged from its lair—so strips of skin torn
from his clawing hands stuck to the rock face.
A heavy sea covered him over, then and there
unlucky Odysseus would have met his death—   480

against the will of Fate—
but the bright-eyed one inspired him yet again.
Fighting out from the breakers pounding toward the coast,
out of danger he swam on, scanning the land, trying to find
a seabeach shelving against the waves, a sheltered cove,   485
and stroking hard he came abreast of a river's mouth,
running calmly, the perfect spot, he thought . . .
free of rocks, with a windbreak from the gales.
As the current flowed he felt the river's god and
prayed to him in spirit: "Hear me, lord, whoever you are,   490
I've come to you, the answer to all my prayers—
rescue me from the sea, the Sea-lord's curse!
Even immortal gods will show a man respect,
whatever wanderer seeks their help—like me—
I throw myself on your mercy, on your current now—   495
I have suffered greatly. Pity me, lord,
your suppliant cries for help!"
                    So the man prayed
and the god stemmed his current, held his surge at once
and smoothing out the swells before Odysseus now,
drew him safe to shore at the river's mouth.   500
His knees buckled, massive arms fell limp,
the sea had beaten down his striving heart.
His whole body swollen, brine aplenty gushing
out of his mouth and nostrils—breathless, speechless,
there he lay, with only a little strength left in him,   505
deathly waves of exhaustion overwhelmed him now . . .
But once he regained his breath and rallied back to life,
at last he loosed the goddess' scarf from his body,
dropped it into the river flowing out to sea
and a swift current bore it far downstream   510
and suddenly Ino caught it in her hands.
Struggling up from the banks, he flung himself
in the deep reeds, he kissed the good green earth
and addressed his fighting spirit, desperate still:
"Man of misery, what next? Is this the end?   515
If I wait out a long tense night by the banks,
I fear the sharp frost and the soaking dew together
will do me in—I'm bone-weary, about to breathe my last,
and a cold wind blows from a river on toward morning.
But what if I climb that slope, go for the dark woods   520
and bed down in the thick brush? What if I'm spared
the chill, fatigue, and a sweet sleep comes my way?
I fear wild beasts will drag me off as quarry."

    But this was the better course, it struck him now.
He set out for the woods and not far from the water   525
found a grove with a clearing all around and crawled
beneath two bushy olives sprung from the same root,
one olive wild, the other well-bred stock.
No sodden gusty winds could ever pierce them,
nor could the sun's sharp rays invade their depths,   530

nor could a downpour drench them through and through,
so dense they grew together, tangling side-by-side.
Odysseus crept beneath them, scraping up at once
a good wide bed for himself with both hands.
A fine litter of dead leaves had drifted in,   535
enough to cover two men over, even three,
in the wildest kind of winter known to man.
Long-enduring great Odysseus, overjoyed at the sight,
bedded down in the midst and heaped the leaves around him.
As a man will bury his glowing brand in black ashes,   540
off on a lonely farmstead, no neighbors near,
to keep a spark alive—no need to kindle fire
from somewhere else—so great Odysseus buried
himself in leaves and Athena showered sleep
upon his eyes . . . sleep in a swift wave   545
delivering him from all his pains and labors,
blessed sleep that sealed his eyes at last.

BOOK VI

[The Princess and the Stranger]

So there he lay at rest, the storm-tossed great Odysseus,
borne down by his hard labors first and now deep sleep
as Athena traveled through the countryside
and reached the Phaeacians' city. Years ago
they lived in a land of spacious dancing-circles,   5
Hyperia,[5] all too close to the overbearing Cyclops,
stronger, violent brutes who harried them without end.
So their godlike king, Nausithous, led the people off
in a vast migration, settled them in Scheria,
far from the men who toil on this earth—   10
he flung up walls around the city, built the houses,
raised the gods' temples and shared the land for plowing.
But his fate had long since forced him down to Death
and now Alcinous ruled, and the gods made him wise.
Straight to his house the clear-eyed Pallas went,   15
full of plans for great Odysseus' journey home.
She made her way to the gaily painted room
where a young girl lay asleep . . .
a match for the deathless gods in build and beauty,
Nausicaa, the daughter of generous King Alcinous.   20
Two handmaids fair as the Graces[6] slept beside her,
flanking the two posts, with the gleaming doors closed.
But the goddess drifted through like a breath of fresh air,
rushed to the girl's bed and hovering close she spoke,
in face and form like the shipman Dymas' daughter,   25
a girl the princess' age, and dearest to her heart.
Disguised, the bright-eyed goddess chided, "Nausicaa,
how could your mother bear a careless girl like you?

---

5. Probably an imaginary place; however, the description of migration under pressure and the founding of a new city suggests the atmosphere of the great age of Greek colonization (8th century B.C.E.).   6. Goddesses (usually three) personifying charm and beauty.

Look at your fine clothes, lying here neglected—
with your marriage not far off,   30
the day you should be decked in all your glory
and offer elegant dress to those who form your escort.
That's how a bride's good name goes out across the world
and it brings her father and queenly mother joy. Come,
let's go wash these clothes at the break of day—   35
I'll help you, lend a hand, and the work will fly!
You won't stay unwed long. The noblest men
in the country court you now, all Phaeacians
just like you, Phaeacia-born and raised. So come,
the first thing in the morning press your kingly father   40
to harness the mules and wagon for you, all to carry
your sashes, dresses, glossy spreads for your bed.
It's so much nicer for you to ride than go on foot.
The washing-pools are just too far from town."
                                          With that
the bright-eyed goddess sped away to Olympus, where,   45
they say, the gods' eternal mansion stands unmoved,
never rocked by galewinds, never drenched by rains,
nor do the drifting snows assail it, no, the clear air
stretches away without a cloud, and a great radiance
plays across that world where the blithe gods   50
live all their days in bliss. There Athena went,
once the bright-eyed one had urged the princess on.

　　Dawn soon rose on her splendid throne and woke
Nausicaa finely gowned. Still beguiled by her dream,
down she went through the house to tell her parents now,   65
her beloved father and mother. She found them both inside.
Her mother sat at the hearth with several waiting-women,
spinning yarn on a spindle, lustrous sea-blue wool.
Her father she met as he left to join the lords
at a council island nobles asked him to attend.   60
She stepped up close to him, confiding, "Daddy dear,
I wonder, won't you have them harness a wagon for me,
the tall one with the good smooth wheels . . . so I
can take our clothes to the river for a washing?
Lovely things, but lying before me all soiled.   65
And you yourself, sitting among the princes,
debating points at your council,
you really should be wearing spotless linen.
Then you have five sons, full-grown in the palace,
two of them married, but three are lusty bachelors   70
always demanding crisp shirts fresh from the wash
when they go out to dance. Look at my duties—
that all rests on me."
                      So she coaxed, too shy
to touch on her hopes for marriage, young warm hopes,
in her father's presence. But he saw through it all   75
and answered quickly, "I won't deny you the mules,
my darling girl . . . I won't deny you anything.

Off you go, and the men will harness a wagon,
the tall one with the good smooth wheels,
fitted out with a cradle on the top."
                                        With that   80
he called to the stablemen and they complied.
They trundled the wagon out now, rolling smoothly,
backed the mule-team into the traces, hitched them up,
while the princess brought her finery from the room
and piled it into the wagon's polished cradle.   85
Her mother packed a hamper—treats of all kinds,
favorite things to refresh her daughter's spirits—
poured wine in a skin, and as Nausicaa climbed aboard,
the queen gave her a golden flask of suppling olive oil
for her and her maids to smooth on after bathing.   90
Then, taking the whip in hand and glistening reins,
she touched the mules to a start and out they clattered,
trotting on at a clip, bearing the princess and her clothes
and not alone: her maids went with her, stepping briskly too.

     Once they reached the banks of the river flowing strong   95
where the pools would never fail, with plenty of water
cool and clear, bubbling up and rushing through
to scour the darkest stains—they loosed the mules,
out from under the wagon yoke, and chased them down
the river's rippling banks to graze on luscious clover.   100
Down from the cradle they lifted clothes by the armload,
plunged them into the dark pools and stamped them down
in the hollows, one girl racing the next to finish first
until they'd scoured and rinsed off all the grime,
then they spread them out in a line along the beach   105
where the surf had washed a pebbly scree ashore.
And once they'd bathed and smoothed their skin with oil,
they took their picnic, sitting along the river's banks
and waiting for all the clothes to dry in the hot noon sun.
Now fed to their hearts' content, the princess and her retinue   110
threw their veils to the wind, struck up a game of ball.
White-armed Nausicaa led their singing, dancing beat . . .
as lithe as Artemis with her arrows striding down
from a high peak—Taygetus' towering ridge or Erymanthus[7]—
thrilled to race with the wild boar or bounding deer,   115
and nymphs of the hills race with her,
daughters of Zeus whose shield is storm and thunder,
ranging the hills in sport, and Leto's[8] heart exults
as head and shoulders over the rest her daughter rises,
unmistakable—she outshines them all, though all are lovely.   120
So Nausicaa shone among her maids, a virgin, still unwed.

     But now, as she was about to fold her clothes
and yoke the mules and turn for home again,

7. A mountain in Arcadia. Taygetus is the mountain range west of Sparta.   8. Mother of Artemis and
Apollo.

now clear-eyed Pallas thought of what came next,
to make Odysseus wake and see this young beauty   125
and she would lead him to the Phaeacians' town.
The ball—
                    the princess suddenly tossed it to a maid
but it missed the girl, splashed in a deep swirling pool
and they all shouted out—
                                and that woke great Odysseus.
He sat up with a start, puzzling, his heart pounding: 130
"Man of misery, whose land have I lit on now?
What *are* they here—violent, savage, lawless?
or friendly to strangers, god-fearing men?
Listen: shouting, echoing round me—women, girls—
or the nymphs who haunt the rugged mountaintops   135
and the river springs and meadows lush with grass!
Or am I really close to people who speak my language?
Up with you, see how the land lies, see for yourself now . . ."

      Muttering so, great Odysseus crept out of the bushes,
stripping off with his massive hand a leafy branch   140
from the tangled olive growth to shield his body,
hide his private parts. And out he stalked
as a mountain lion exultant in his power
strides through wind and rain and his eyes blaze
and he charges sheep or oxen or chases wild deer   145
but his hunger drives him on to go for flocks,
even to raid the best-defended homestead.
So Odysseus moved out . . .
about to mingle with all those lovely girls,
naked now as he was, for the need drove him on,   150
a terrible sight, all crusted, caked with brine—
they scattered in panic down the jutting beaches.
Only Alcinous' daughter held fast, for Athena planted
courage within her heart, dissolved the trembling in her limbs,
and she firmly stood her ground and faced Odysseus, torn now—   155
Should he fling his arms around her knees,[9] the young beauty,
plead for help, or stand back, plead with a winning word,
beg her to lead him to the town and lend him clothing?
This was the better way, he thought. Plead now
with a subtle, winning word and stand well back,   160
don't clasp her knees, the girl might bridle, yes.
He launched in at once, endearing, sly and suave:
"Here I am at your mercy, princess—
are you a goddess or a mortal? If one of the gods
who rule the skies up there, you're Artemis to the life,   165
the daughter of mighty Zeus—I see her now—just look
at your build, your bearing, your lithe flowing grace . . .
But if you're one of the mortals living here on earth,
three times blest are your father, your queenly mother,

9. In the typical suppliant's posture.

three times over your brothers too. How often their hearts   170
must warm with joy to see you striding into the dances—
such a bloom of beauty. True, but he is the one
more blest than all other men alive, that man
who sways you with gifts and leads you home, his bride!
I have never laid eyes on anyone like you,   175
neither man nor woman . . .
I look at you and a sense of wonder takes me.
                           Wait,
once I saw the like—in Delos, beside Apollo's altar—
the young slip of a palm-tree springing into the light.
There I'd sailed, you see, with a great army in my wake,   180
out on the long campaign that doomed my life to hardship.
That vision! Just as I stood there gazing, rapt, for hours . . .
no shaft like that had ever risen up from the earth—
so now I marvel at *you*, my lady: rapt, enthralled,
too struck with awe to grasp you by the knees   185
though pain has ground me down.
                         Only yesterday,
the twentieth day, did I escape the wine-dark sea.
Till then the waves and the rushing gales had swept me on
from the island of Ogygia. Now some power has tossed me here,
doubtless to suffer still more torments on your shores.   190
I can't believe they'll stop. Long before that
the gods will give me more, still more.
                         Compassion—
princess, please! You, after all that I have suffered,
you are the first I've come to. I know no one else,
none in your city, no one in your land.   195
Show me the way to town, give me a rag for cover,
just some cloth, some wrapper you carried with you here.
And may the good gods give you all your heart desires:
husband, and house, and lasting harmony too.
No finer, greater gift in the world than that . . .   200
when man and woman possess their home, two minds,
two hearts that work as one. Despair to their enemies,
a joy to all their friends. Their own best claim to glory."

   "Stranger," the white-armed princess answered staunchly,
"friend, you're hardly a wicked man, and no fool, I'd say—   205
it's Olympian Zeus himself who hands our fortunes out,
to each of us in turn, to the good and bad,
however Zeus prefers . . .
He gave you pain, it seems. You simply have to bear it.
But now, seeing you've reached our city and our land,   210
you'll never lack for clothing or any other gift,
the right of worn-out suppliants come our way.
I'll show you our town, tell you our people's name.
Phaeacians we are, who hold this city and this land,
and I am the daughter of generous King Alcinous.   215
All our people's power stems from him."

She called out to her girls with lovely braids:
"Stop, my friends! Why run when you see a man?
Surely you don't think *him* an enemy, do you?
There's no one alive, there never will be one,   220
who'd reach Phaeacian soil and lay it waste.
The immortals love us far too much for that.
We live too far apart, out in the surging sea,
off at the world's end—
no other mortals come to mingle with us.   225
But here's an unlucky wanderer strayed our way
and we must tend him well. Every stranger and beggar
comes from Zeus, and whatever scrap we give him
he'll be glad to get. So, quick, my girls,
give our newfound friend some food and drink   230
and bathe the man in the river,
wherever you find some shelter from the wind."
                                                        At that
they came to a halt and teased each other on
and led Odysseus down to a sheltered spot
where he could find a seat,   235
just as great Alcinous' daughter told them.
They laid out cloak and shirt for him to wear,
they gave him the golden flask of suppling olive oil
and pressed him to bathe himself in the river's stream.
Then thoughtful Odysseus reassured the handmaids,   240
"Stand where you are, dear girls, a good way off,
so I can rinse the brine from my shoulders now
and rub myself with oil . . .
how long it's been since oil touched my skin!
But I won't bathe in front of you. I would be embarrassed—   245
stark naked before young girls with lovely braids."

     The handmaids scurried off to tell their mistress.
Great Odysseus bathed in the river, scrubbed his body
clean of brine that clung to his back and broad shoulders,
scoured away the brackish scurf that caked his head.   250
And then, once he had bathed all over, rubbed in oil
and donned the clothes the virgin princess gave him,
Zeus's daughter Athena made him taller to all eyes,
his build more massive now, and down from his brow
she ran his curls like thick hyacinth clusters   255
full of blooms. As a master craftsman washes
gold over beaten silver—a man the god of fire[1]
and Queen Athena trained in every fine technique—
and finishes off his latest effort, handsome work,
so she lavished splendor over his head and shoulders now.   260
And down to the beach he walked and sat apart,
glistening in his glory, breathtaking, yes,
and the princess gazed in wonder . . .

1. Hephaestus.

then turned to her maids with lovely braided hair:
"Listen, my white-armed girls, to what I tell you.   265
The gods of Olympus can't be all against this man
who's come to mingle among our noble people.
At first he seemed appalling, I must say—
now he seems like a god who rules the skies up there!
Ah, if only a man like *that* were called my husband,   270
lived right here, pleased to stay forever . . .
                                    Enough.
Give the stranger food and drink, my girls."

    They hung on her words and did her will at once,
set before Odysseus food and drink, and he ate and drank,
the great Odysseus, long deprived, so ravenous now—   275
it seemed like years since he had tasted food.

    The white-armed princess thought of one last thing.
Folding the clothes, she packed them into her painted wagon,
hitched the sharp-hoofed mules, and climbing up herself,
Nausicaa urged Odysseus, warmly urged her guest,   280
"Up with you now, my friend, and off to town we go.
I'll see you into my wise father's palace where,
I promise you, you'll meet all the best Phaeacians.
Wait, let's do it this way. You seem no fool to me.
While we're passing along the fields and plowlands,   285
you follow the mules and wagon, stepping briskly
with all my maids. I'll lead the way myself.
But once we reach our city, ringed by walls
and strong high towers too, with a fine harbor either side . . .
and the causeway in is narrow; along the road the rolling ships 290
are all hauled up, with a slipway cleared for every vessel.
There's our assembly, round Poseidon's royal precinct,
built of quarried slabs planted deep in the earth.
Here the sailors tend their black ships' tackle,
cables and sails, and plane their oarblades down.   295
Phaeacians, you see, care nothing for bow or quiver,
only for masts and oars and good trim ships themselves—
we glory in our ships, crossing the foaming seas!
But I shrink from all our sea-dogs' nasty gossip.
Some old salt might mock us behind our backs—   300
we have our share of insolent types in town
and one of the coarser sort, spying us, might say,
'Now who's that tall, handsome stranger Nausicaa has in tow?
Where'd she light on *him?* Her husband-to-be, just wait!
But who—some shipwrecked stray she's taken up with,   305
some alien from abroad? Since nobody lives nearby.
Unless it's really a god come down from the blue
to answer all her prayers, and to have her all his days.
Good riddance! Let the girl go roving to find herself
a man from foreign parts. She only spurns her own—   310
countless Phaeacians round about who court her,

nothing but our best.'
              So they'll scoff . . .
just think of the scandal that would face me then.
I'd find fault with a girl who carried on that way,
flouting her parents' wishes—father, mother, still alive— 315
consorting with men before she'd tied the knot in public.
No, stranger, listen closely to what I say, the sooner
to win your swift voyage home at my father's hands.
Now, you'll find a splendid grove along the road—
poplars, sacred to Pallas— 320
a bubbling spring's inside and meadows run around it.
There lies my father's estate, his blossoming orchard too,
as far from town as a man's strong shout can carry.
Take a seat there, wait a while, and give us time
to make it into town and reach my father's house. 325
Then, when you think we're home, walk on yourself
to the city, ask the way to my father's palace,
generous King Alcinous. You cannot miss it,
even an innocent child could guide you there.
No other Phaeacian's house is built like that: 330
so grand, the palace of Alcinous, our great hero.
Once the mansion and courtyard have enclosed you, go,
quickly, across the hall until you reach my mother.
Beside the hearth she sits in the fire's glare,
spinning yarn on a spindle, sea-blue wool— 335
a stirring sight, you'll see . . .
she leans against a pillar, her ladies sit behind.
And my father's throne is drawn up close beside her;
there he sits and takes his wine, a mortal like a god.
Go past him, grasp my mother's knees—if you want 340
to see the day of your return, rejoicing, soon,
even if your home's a world away.
If only the queen will take you to her heart,
then there's hope that you will see your loved ones,
reach your own grand house, your native land at last." 345

   At that she touched the mules with her shining whip
and they quickly left the running stream behind.
The team trotted on, their hoofs wove in and out.
She drove them back with care so all the rest,
maids and Odysseus, could keep the pace on foot, 350
and she used the whip discreetly.
The sun sank as they reached the hallowed grove,
sacred to Athena, where Odysseus stopped and sat
and said a prayer at once to mighty Zeus's daughter:
"Hear me, daughter of Zeus whose shield is thunder— 355
tireless one, Athena! Now hear my prayer at last,
for you never heard me then, when I was shattered,
when the famous god of earthquakes wrecked my craft.
Grant that here among the Phaeacian people
I may find some mercy and some love!" 360

So he prayed and Athena heard his prayer
but would not yet appear to him undisguised.
She stood in awe of her Father's brother, lord of the sea
who still seethed on, still churning with rage against
the great Odysseus till he reached his native land.   365

BOOK VII

[Phaeacia's Halls and Gardens]

Now as Odysseus, long an exile, prayed in Athena's grove,
the hardy mule-team drew the princess toward the city.
Reaching her father's splendid halls, she reined in,
just at the gates—her brothers clustering round her,
men like gods, released the mules from the yoke   5
and brought the clothes indoors
as Nausicaa made her way toward her bedroom.
There her chambermaid lit a fire for her—
Eurymedusa, the old woman who'd come from Apiraea
years ago, when the rolling ships had sailed her in   10
and the country picked her out as King Alcinous' prize,
for he ruled all the Phaeacians, they obeyed him like a god.
Once, she had nursed the white-armed princess in the palace.
Now she lit a fire and made her supper in the room.

    At the same time, Odysseus set off toward the city.   15
Pallas Athena, harboring kindness for the hero,
drifted a heavy mist around him, shielding him
from any swaggering islander who'd cross his path,
provoke him with taunts and search out who he was.
Instead, as he was about to enter the welcome city,   20
the bright-eyed goddess herself came up to greet him there,
for all the world like a young girl, holding a pitcher,
standing face-to-face with the visitor, who asked,
"Little girl, now wouldn't you be my guide
to the palace of the one they call Alcinous?   25
The king who rules the people of these parts.
I am a stranger, you see, weighed down with troubles,
come this way from a distant, far-off shore.
So I know no one here, none at all
in your city and the farmlands round about."
                                        "Oh yes, sir,   30
good old stranger," the bright-eyed goddess said,
"I'll show you the very palace that you're after—
the king lives right beside my noble father.
Come, quietly too, and I will lead the way.
Now not a glance at anyone, not a question.   35
The men here never suffer strangers gladly,
have no love for hosting a man from foreign lands.
All they really trust are their fast, flying ships
that cross the mighty ocean. Gifts of Poseidon,
ah what ships they are—   40
quick as a bird, quick as a darting thought!"

   And Pallas Athena sped away in the lead
as he followed in her footsteps, man and goddess.
But the famed Phaeacian sailors never saw him,
right in their midst, striding down their streets.   45
Athena the one with lovely braids would not permit it,
the awesome goddess poured an enchanted mist around him,
harboring kindness for Odysseus in her heart.
And he marveled now at the balanced ships and havens,
the meeting grounds of the great lords and the long ramparts   50
looming, coped and crowned with palisades of stakes—
an amazing sight to see . . .
And once they reached the king's resplendent halls
the bright-eyed goddess cried out, "Good old stranger,
here, here is the very palace that you're after—   55
I've guided you all the way. Here you'll find
our princes dear to the gods, busy feasting.
You go on inside. Be bold, nothing to fear.
In every venture the bold man comes off best,
even the wanderer, bound from distant shores.   60
The queen is the first you'll light on in the halls.
Arete, she is called, and earns the name:
she answers all our prayers:[2] She comes, in fact,
from the same stock that bred our King Alcinous.
First came Nausithous, son of the earthquake god   65
Poseidon and Periboea, the lovely, matchless beauty,
the youngest daughter of iron-willed Eurymedon,
king of the overweening Giants[3] years ago.
He led that reckless clan to its own ruin,
killed himself in the bargain, but the Sea-lord   70
lay in love with Periboea and she produced a son,
Nausithous, that lionheart who ruled Phaeacia well.
Now, Nausithous had two sons, Rhexenor and Alcinous,
but the lord of the silver bow, Apollo, shot Rhexenor down—
married, true, yet still without a son in the halls,   75
he left one child behind, a daughter named Arete.
Alcinous made the girl his wife and honors her
as no woman is honored on this earth, of all the wives
now keeping households under their husbands' sway.
Such is her pride of place, and always will be so: 80
dear to her loving children, to Alcinous himself
and all our people. They gaze on her as a god,
saluting her warmly on her walks through town.
She lacks nothing in good sense and judgment—
she can dissolve quarrels, even among men,   85
whoever wins her sympathies.
If only our queen will take you to her heart,
then there's hope that you will see your loved ones,
reach your high-roofed house, your native land at last."

2. Her name is related to Greek *araomai*, "pray."   3. A monstrous race, born of Earth; they were
defeated in battle by the Olympian gods.

And with that vow the bright-eyed goddess sped away,   90
over the barren sea, leaving welcome Scheria far behind,
and reaching Marathon and the spacious streets of Athens,
entered Erechtheus[4] sturdy halls, Athena's stronghold.
Now as Odysseus approached Alcinous' famous house
a rush of feelings stirred within his heart,   95
bringing him to a standstill,
even before he crossed the bronze threshold . . .
A radiance strong as the moon or rising sun came flooding
through the high-roofed halls of generous King Alcinous.
Walls plated in bronze, crowned with a circling frieze   100
glazed as blue as lapis, ran to left and right
from outer gates to the deepest court recess
And solid golden doors enclosed the palace.
Up from the bronze threshold silver doorposts rose
with silver lintel above, and golden handle hooks.   105
And dogs of gold and silver were stationed either side,
forged by the god of fire with all his cunning craft
to keep watch on generous King Alcinous' palace,
his immortal guard-dogs, ageless, all their days.
Inside to left and right, in a long unbroken row   110
from farthest outer gate to the inmost chamber,
thrones stood backed against the wall, each draped
with a finely spun brocade, women's handsome work.
Here the Phaeacian lords would sit enthroned,
dining, drinking—the feast flowed on forever.   115
And young boys, molded of gold, set on pedestals
standing firm, were lifting torches high in their hands
to flare through the nights and light the feasters down the hall.
And Alcinous has some fifty serving-women in his house:
some, turning the handmill, grind the apple-yellow grain,   120
some weave at their webs or sit and spin their yarn,
fingers flickering quick as aspen leaves in the wind
and the densely woven woolens dripping oil droplets.
Just as Phaeacian men excel the world at sailing,
driving their swift ships on the open seas,   125
so the women excel at all the arts of weaving.
That is Athena's gift to them beyond all others—
a genius for lovely work, and a fine mind too.

Outside the courtyard, fronting the high gates,
a magnificent orchard stretches four acres deep   130
with a strong fence running round it side-to-side.
Here luxuriant trees are always in their prime,
pomegranates and pears, and apples glowing red,
succulent figs and olives swelling sleek and dark.
And the yield of all these trees will never flag or die,   135
neither in winter nor in summer, a harvest all year round
for the West Wind always breathing through will bring
some fruits to the bud and others warm to ripeness—

---

4. Legendary king of Athens. Marathon is a village north of Athens on the coast of Attica.

pear mellowing ripe on pear, apple on apple,
cluster of grapes on cluster, fig crowding fig.   140
And here is a teeming vineyard planted for the kings,
beyond it an open level bank where the vintage grapes
lie baking to raisins in the sun while pickers gather others;
some they trample down in vats, and here in the front rows
bunches of unripe grapes have hardly shed their blooms   145
while others under the sunlight slowly darken purple.
And there by the last rows are beds of greens,
bordered and plotted, greens of every kind,
glistening fresh, year in, year out. And last,
there are two springs, one rippling in channels   150
over the whole orchard—the other, flanking it,
rushes under the palace gates
to bubble up in front of the lofty roofs
where the city people come and draw their water.
                                                        Such
were the gifts, the glories showered down by the gods   155
on King Alcinous' realm.
                              And there Odysseus stood,
gazing at all this bounty, a man who'd borne so much . . .
Once he'd had his fill of marveling at it all,
he crossed the threshold quickly,
strode inside the palace. Here he found   160
the Phaeacian lords and captains tipping out
libations now to the guide and giant-killer Hermes,
the god to whom they would always pour the final cup
before they sought their beds. Odysseus went on
striding down the hall, the man of many struggles   165
shrouded still in the mist Athena drifted round him,
till he reached Arete and Alcinous the king. And then,
the moment he flung his arms around Arete's knees,
the godsent mist rolled back to reveal the great man.
And silence seized the feasters all along the hall—   170
seeing him right before their eyes, they marveled,
gazing on him now as Odysseus pleaded, "Queen,
Arete, daughter of godlike King Rhexenor!
Here after many trials I come to beg for mercy,
your husband's, yours, and all these feasters' here.   175
May the gods endow them with fortune all their lives,
may each hand down to his sons the riches in his house
and the pride of place the realm has granted *him*.
But as for myself, grant me a rapid convoy home
to my own native land. How far away I've been   180
from all my loved ones—how long I have suffered!"

   Pleading so, the man sank down in the ashes,
just at the hearth beside the blazing fire,[5]
while all the rest stayed hushed, stock-still.

5. The fire, or hearth, was the sacred center of the home; the suppliant who sat there could not be forcibly
removed without offending the gods.

At last the old revered Echeneus broke the spell,   185
the eldest lord in Phaeacia, finest speaker too,
a past master at all the island's ancient ways.
Impelled by kindness now, he rose and said,
"This is no way, Alcinous. How indecent, look,
our guest on the ground, in the ashes by the fire!   190
Your people are holding back, waiting for your signal.
Come, raise him up and seat the stranger now,
in a silver-studded chair,
and tell the heralds to mix more wine for all
so we can pour out cups to Zeus who loves the lightning,   195
champion of suppliants—suppliants' rights are sacred.
And let the housekeeper give our guest his supper,
unstinting with her stores."
                              Hearing that,
Alcinous, poised in all his majesty, took the hand
of the seasoned, worldly-wise Odysseus, raised him up   200
from the hearth and sat him down in a burnished chair,
displacing his own son, the courtly Lord Laodamas
who had sat beside him, the son he loved the most.
A maid brought water soon in a graceful golden pitcher
and over a silver basin tipped it out   205
so the guest might rinse his hands,
then pulled a gleaming table to his side.
A staid housekeeper brought on bread to serve him,
appetizers aplenty too, lavish with her bounty.
As long-suffering great Odysseus ate and drank,   210
the hallowed King Alcinous called his herald:
"Come, Pontonous! Mix the wine in the bowl,
pour rounds to all our banqueters in the house
so we can pour out cups to Zeus who loves the lightning,
champion of suppliants—suppliants' rights are sacred."   215

    At that Pontonous mixed the heady, honeyed wine
and tipped first drops for the god in every cup,
then poured full rounds for all. And once they'd poured
libations out and drunk to their hearts' content,
Alcinous rose and addressed his island people: 220
"Hear me, lords and captains of Phaeacia,
hear what the heart inside me has to say.
Now, our feast finished, home you go to sleep.
But at dawn we call the elders in to full assembly,
host our guest in the palace, sacrifice to the gods   225
and then we turn our minds to his passage home,
so under our convoy our new friend can travel back
to his own land—no toil, no troubles—soon,
rejoicing, even if his home's a world away.
And on the way no pain or hardship suffered,   230
not till he sets foot on native ground again.
There in the future he must suffer all that Fate
and the overbearing Spinners spun out on his life line
the very day his mother gave him birth . . . But if

he's one of the deathless powers, out of the blue,   235
the gods are working now in strange, new ways.
Always, up to now, they came to us face-to-face
whenever we'd give them grand, glorious sacrifices—
they always sat beside us here and shared our feasts.
Even when some lonely traveler meets them on the roads,   240
they never disguise themselves. We're too close kin for that,
close as the wild Giants are, the Cyclops too."
                                         "Alcinous!"
wary Odysseus countered, "cross that thought from your mind.
I'm nothing like the immortal gods who rule the skies,
either in build or breeding. I'm just a mortal man.   245
Whom do you know most saddled down with sorrow?
They are the ones I'd equal, grief for grief.
And I could tell a tale of still more hardship,
all I've suffered, thanks to the gods' will.
But despite my misery, let me finish dinner.   250
The belly's a shameless dog, there's nothing worse.
Always insisting, pressing, it never lets us forget—
destroyed as I am, my heart racked with sadness,
sick with anguish, still it keeps demanding,
'Eat, drink!' It blots out all the memory   255
of my pain, commanding, 'Fill me up!'
                                        But you,
at the first light of day, hurry, please,
to set your unlucky guest on his own home soil.
How much I have suffered . . . Oh just let me see
my lands, my serving-men and the grand high-roofed house—   260
then I can die in peace."
                           All burst into applause,
urging passage home for their newfound friend,
his pleading rang so true. And once they'd poured
libations out and drunk to their hearts' content,
each one made his way to rest in his own house.   265
But King Odysseus still remained at hall,
seated beside the royal Alcinous and Arete
as servants cleared the cups and plates away.
The white-armed Queen Arete took the lead;
she'd spotted the cape and shirt Odysseus wore,   270
fine clothes she'd made herself with all her women,
so now her words flew brusquely, sharply: "Stranger,
I'll be the first to question you—myself.
Who are you? Where are you from?
Who gave you the clothes you're wearing now?   275
Didn't you say you reached us roving on the sea?"

  "What hard labor, queen," the man of craft replied,
"to tell you the story of my troubles start to finish.
The gods on high have given me my share.
Still, this much I will tell you . . .   280
seeing you probe and press me so intently.
There is an island, Ogygia, lying far at sea,

where the daughter of Atlas, Calypso, has her home,
the seductive nymph with lovely braids—a danger too,
and no one, god or mortal, dares approach her there. But I,   285
cursed as I am, some power brought me to her hearth,
alone, when Zeus with a white-hot bolt had crushed
my racing warship down the wine-dark sea.
There all the rest of my loyal shipmates died
but I, locking my arms around my good ship's keel,   290
drifted along nine days. On the tenth, at dead of night,
the gods cast me up on Ogygia, Calypso's island,
home of the dangerous nymph with glossy braids,
and the goddess took me in in all her kindness,
welcomed me warmly, cherished me, even vowed   295
to make me immortal, ageless, all my days—
but she never won the heart inside me, never.
Seven endless years I remained there, always drenching
with my tears the immortal clothes Calypso gave me.
Then, at last, when the eighth came wheeling round,   300
she insisted that I sail—inspired by warnings sent
from Zeus, perhaps, or her own mind had changed.
She saw me on my way in a solid craft.
tight and trim, and gave me full provisions,
food and mellow wine, immortal clothes to wear   305
and summoned a wind to bear me onward, fair and warm.
And seventeen days I sailed, making headway well;
on the eighteenth, shadowy mountains slowly loomed . . .
your land! My heart leapt up, unlucky as I am,
doomed to be comrade still to many hardships.   310
Many pains the god of earthquakes piled upon me,
loosing the winds against me, blocking passage through,
heaving up a terrific sea, beyond belief—nor did the whitecaps
let me cling to my craft, for all my desperate groaning.
No, the squalls shattered her stem to stern, but I,   315
I swam hard, I plowed my way through those dark gulfs
till at last the wind and current bore me to your shores.
But here, had I tried to land, the breakers would have hurled me,
smashed me against the jagged cliffs of that grim coast,
so I pulled away, swam back till I reached a river,   320
the perfect spot at last, or so it struck me,
free of rocks, with a windbreak from the gales.
So, fighting for life, I flung myself ashore
and the godsent, bracing night came on at once.
Clambering up from the river, big with Zeus's rains,   325
I bedded down in the brush, my body heaped with leaves,
and a god poured down a boundless sleep upon me, yes,
and there in the leaves, exhausted, sick at heart,
I slept the whole night through
and on to the break of day and on into high noon   330
and the sun was wheeling down when sweet sleep set me free.
And I looked up, and there were your daughter's maids
at play on the beach, and she, she moved among them
like a deathless goddess! I begged her for help

and not once did her sense of tact desert her;   335
she behaved as you'd never hope to find
in one so young, not in a random meeting—
time and again the youngsters prove so flighty.
Not she. She gave me food aplenty and shining wine,
a bath in the river too, and gave me all this clothing.   340
That's my whole story. Wrenching to tell, but true."

   "Ah, but in one regard, my friend," the king replied,
"her good sense missed the mark, this daughter of mine.
She never escorted you to our house with all her maids
but she was the first you asked for care and shelter."   345

   "Your majesty," diplomatic Odysseus answered,
"don't find fault with a flawless daughter now,
not for my sake, please.
She urged me herself to follow with her maids.
I chose not to, fearing embarrassment in fact—   350
what if you took offense, seeing us both together?
Suspicious we are, we men who walk the earth."

   "Oh no, my friend," Alcinous stated flatly,
"I'm hardly a man for reckless, idle anger.
Balance is best in all things.   355
Father Zeus, Athena and lord Apollo! if only—
seeing the man you are, seeing we think as one—
you could wed my daughter and be my son-in-law
and stay right here with us. I'd give you a house
and great wealth—if you chose to stay, that is.   360
No Phaeacian would hold you back by force.
The curse of Father Zeus on such a thing!
And about your convoy home, you rest assured:
I have chosen the day and I decree it is tomorrow.
And all that voyage long you'll lie in a deep sleep   365
while my people sail you on through calm and gentle tides
till you reach your land and house, or any place you please.
True, even if landfall lies more distant than Euboea,[6]
off at the edge of the world . . .
So say our crews, at least, who saw it once,   370
that time they carried the gold-haired Rhadamanthys
out to visit Tityus,[7] son of Mother Earth. Imagine,
there they sailed and back they came in the same day,
they finished the homeward run with no strain at all.
You'll see for yourself how far they top the best—   375
my ships and their young shipmates
tossing up the whitecaps with their oars!"   So he vowed
and the long-enduring great Odysseus glowed with joy

---

6. For many in the *Odyssey*'s Greek audiences, this large island, which stretches along the northern coast of Attica, would have been close by and familiar.   7. A giant who tried to rape Leto. In book XI Odysseus sees him in the underworld, eternally punished for his crime. Why Rhadymanthus—renowned for justice and in later tradition one of the judges in the underworld—went to visit Tityus we have no idea.

and raised a prayer and called the god by name:
"Father Zeus on high—   380
may the king fulfill his promises one and all!
Then his fame would ring through the fertile earth
and never die—and I should reach my native land at last!"

And now as the two men exchanged their hopes,
the white-armed queen instructed her palace maids   385
to make a bed in the porch's shelter, lay down
some heavy purple throws for the bed itself,
and over it spread some blankets, thick woolly robes,
a warm covering laid on top. Torches in hand,
they left the hall and fell to work at once,   390
briskly prepared a good snug resting-place
and then returned to Odysseus, urged the guest,
"Up, friend, time for sleep. Your bed is made."
How welcome the thought of sleep to that man now . . .
So there after many trials Odysseus lay at rest   395
on a corded bed inside the echoing colonnade.
Alcinous slept in chambers deep in his lofty house
where the queen his wife arranged and shared their bed.

BOOK VIII

[A Day for Songs and Contests]

When young Dawn with her rose-red fingers shone once more
royal Alcinous, hallowed island king, rose from bed
and great Odysseus, raider of cities, rose too.
Poised in his majesty, Alcinous led the way
to Phaeacia's meeting grounds, built for all   5
beside the harbored ships. Both men sat down
on the polished stone benches side-by-side
as Athena started roaming up and down the town,
in build and voice the wise Alcinous' herald,
furthering plans for Odysseus' journey home,   10
and stopped beside each citizen, urged them all,
"Come this way, you lords and captains of Phaeacia,
come to the meeting grounds and learn about the stranger!
A new arrival! Here at our wise king's palace now,
he's here from roving the ocean, driven far off course—   15
he looks like a deathless god!"
                                   Rousing their zeal,
their curiosity, each and every man, and soon enough
the assembly seats were filled with people thronging,
gazing in wonder at the seasoned man of war . . .
Over Odysseus' head and shoulders now   20
Athena lavished a marvelous splendor, yes,
making him taller, more massive to all eyes,
so Phaeacians might regard the man with kindness,
awe and respect as well, and he might win through
the many trials they'd pose to test the hero's strength.   25
Once they'd grouped, crowding the meeting grounds,

Alcinous rose and addressed his island people:
"Hear me, lords and captains of Phaeacia,
hear what the heart inside me has to say.
This stranger here, our guest—   30
I don't know who he is, or whether he comes
from sunrise lands or the western lands of evening,
but he has come in his wanderings to my palace;
he pleads for passage, he begs we guarantee it.
So now, as in years gone by, let us press on   35
and grant him escort. No one, I tell you, no one
who comes to *my* house will languish long here,
heartsick for convoy home.
                          Come, my people!
Haul a black ship down to the bright sea,
rigged for her maiden voyage—   40
enlist a crew of fifty-two young sailors,
the best in town, who've proved their strength before.
Let all hands lash their oars to the thwarts then disembark,
come to my house and fall in for a banquet, quickly.
I'll lay on a princely feast for all. So then,   45
these are the orders I issue to our crews.
For the rest, you sceptered princes here,
you come to my royal halls so we can give
this stranger a hero's welcome in our palace—
no one here refuse. Call in the inspired bard   50
Demodocus. God has given the man the gift of song,
to him beyond all others, the power to please,
however the spirit stirs him on to sing."

    With those commands Alcinous led the way
and a file of sceptered princes took his lead   55
while the herald went to find the gifted bard.
And the fifty-two young sailors, duly chosen,
briskly following orders,
went down to the shore of the barren salt sea.
And once they reached the ship at the surf's edge,   60
first they hauled the craft into deeper water,
stepped the mast amidships, canvas brailed,
they made oars fast in the leather oarlock straps,
moored her riding high on the swell, then disembarked
and made their way to wise Alcinous' high-roofed halls.   65
There colonnades and courts and rooms were overflowing
with crowds, a mounting host of people young and old.
The king slaughtered a dozen sheep to feed his guests,
eight boars with shining tusks and a pair of shambling oxen.
These they skinned and dressed, and then laid out a feast   70
to fill the heart with savor.
                          In came the herald now,
leading along the faithful bard the Muse adored
above all others, true, but her gifts were mixed
with good and evil both: she stripped him of sight
but gave the man the power of stirring, rapturous song.   75

Pontonous brought the bard a silver-studded chair,
right amid the feasters, leaning it up against
a central column—hung his high clear lyre
on a peg above his head and showed him how
to reach up with his hands and lift it down.   80
And the herald placed a table by his side
with a basket full of bread and cup of wine
for him to sip when his spirit craved refreshment.
All reached out for the good things that lay at hand
and when they'd put aside desire for food and drink,   85
the Muse inspired the bard
to sing the famous deeds of fighting heroes—
the song whose fame had reached the skies those days:
The Strife Between Odysseus and Achilles, Peleus' Son . . .
how once at the gods' flowing feast the captains clashed   90
in a savage war of words, while Agamemnon, lord of armies,
rejoiced at heart that Achaea's bravest men were battling so.
For this was the victory sign that Apollo prophesied
at his shrine in Pytho[8] when Agamemnon strode across
the rocky threshold, asking the oracle for advice—   95
the start of the tidal waves of ruin tumbling down
on Troy's and Achaea's forces, both at once,
thanks to the will of Zeus who rules the world.

    That was the song the famous harper sang
but Odysseus, clutching his flaring sea-blue cape   100
in both powerful hands, drew it over his head
and buried his handsome face,
ashamed his hosts might see him shedding tears.
Whenever the rapt bard would pause in the song,
he'd lift the cape from his head, wipe off his tears   105
and hoisting his double-handled cup, pour it out to the gods.
But soon as the bard would start again, impelled to sing
by Phaeacia's lords, who reveled in his tale,
again Odysseus hid his face and wept.
His weeping went unmarked by all the others;   110
only Alcinous, sitting close beside him,
noticed his guest's tears,
heard the groan in the man's labored breathing
and said at once to the master mariners around him,
"Hear me, my lords and captains of Phaeacia!   115
By now we've had our fill of food well-shared
and the lyre too, our loyal friend at banquets.
Now out we go again and test ourselves in contests,
games of every kind—so our guest can tell his friends,
when he reaches home, how far we excel the world   120
at boxing, wrestling, jumping, speed of foot."

    He forged ahead and the rest fell in behind.
The herald hung the ringing lyre back on its peg

---

8. Delphi, on the southern slopes of Mount Parnassus, on the Greek mainland.

and taking Demodocus by the hand, led him from the palace,
guiding him down the same path the island lords   125
had just pursued, keen to watch the contests.
They reached the meeting grounds
with throngs of people streaming in their trail
as a press of young champions rose for competition.
Topsail and Riptide rose, the helmsman Rowhard too   130
and Seaman and Sternman, Surf-at-the-Beach and Stroke-Oar,
Breaker and Bowsprit, Racing-the-Wind and Swing-Aboard
and Seagirt the son of Greatfleet, Shipwrightson
and the son of Launcher, Broadsea, rose up too,
a match for murderous Ares,[9] death to men—   135
in looks and build the best of all Phaeacians
after gallant Laodamas, the Captain of the People.
Laodamas rose with two more sons of great Alcinous,
Halius bred to the sea and Clytoneus famed for ships.
And now the games began, the first event a footrace . . .   140
They toed the line—
                    and broke flat out from the start
with a fast pack flying down the field in a whirl of dust
and Clytoneus the prince outstripped them all by far,
flashing ahead the length two mules will plow a furrow
before he turned for home, leaving the pack behind   145
and raced to reach the crowds.
                              Next the wrestling,
grueling sport. They grappled, locked, and Broadsea,
pinning the strongest champions, won the bouts.
Next, in the jumping, Seagirt leapt and beat the field.
In the discus Rowhard up and outhurled them all by far.   150
And the king's good son Laodamas boxed them to their knees.
When all had enjoyed the games to their hearts' content
Alcinous' son Laodamas spurred them: "Come, my friends,
let's ask our guest if he knows the ropes of any sport.
He's no mean man, not with a build like that . . .   155
Look at his thighs, his legs, and what a pair of arms—
his massive neck, his big, rippling strength!
Nor is he past his prime,
just beaten down by one too many blows.
Nothing worse than the sea, I always say,   160
to crush a man, the strongest man alive."

   And Broadsea put in quickly,
"Well said, Laodamas, right to the point.
Go up to the fellow, challenge him yourself."

   On that cue, the noble prince strode up   165
before Odysseus, front and center, asking,
"Come, stranger, sir, won't you try your hand
at our contests now? If you have skill in any.
It's fit and proper for you to know your sports.

9. God of war.

What greater glory attends a man, while he's alive,   170
than what he wins with his racing feet and striving hands?
Come and compete then, throw your cares to the wind!
It won't be long, your journey's not far off—
your ship's already hauled down to the sea,
your crew is set to sail."
                    "Laodamas,"   175
quick to the mark Odysseus countered sharply,
"why do you taunt me so with such a challenge?
Pains weigh on my spirit now, not your sports—
I've suffered much already, struggled hard.
But here I sit amid your assembly still,   180
starved for passage home, begging your king,
begging all your people."
                 "Oh I knew it!"
Broadsea broke in, mocking him to his face.
"I never took you for someone skilled in games,
the kind that real men play throughout the world.   185
Not a chance. You're some skipper of profiteers,
roving the high seas in his scudding craft,
reckoning up his freight with a keen eye out
for home-cargo, grabbing the gold he can!
You're no athlete. I see that."
                   With a dark glance   190
wily Odysseus shot back, "Indecent talk, my friend.
You, you're a reckless fool—I see *that.* So,
the gods don't hand out all their gifts at once,
not build and brains and flowing speech to all.
One man may fail to impress us with his looks   195
but a god can crown his words with beauty, charm,
and men look on with delight when he speaks out.
Never faltering, filled with winning self-control,
he shines forth at assembly grounds and people gaze
at him like a god when he walks through the streets.   200
Another man may look like a deathless one on high
but there's not a bit of grace to crown his words.
Just like you, my fine, handsome friend. Not even
a god could improve those lovely looks of yours
but the mind inside is worthless.   205
Your slander fans the anger in my heart!
I'm no stranger to sports—for all your taunts—
I've held my place in the front ranks, I tell you,
long as I could trust to my youth and striving hands.
But now I'm wrestled down by pain and hardship, look,   210
I've borne my share of struggles, cleaving my way
through wars of men and pounding waves at sea.
Nevertheless, despite so many blows,
I'll compete in your games, just watch. Your insults
cut to the quick—you rouse my fighting blood!"   215

   Up he sprang, cloak and all, and seized a discus,
huge and heavy, more weighty by far than those

the Phaeacians used to hurl and test each other.
Wheeling round, he let loose with his great hand
and the stone whirred on—and down to ground they went,   220
those lords of the long oars and master mariners cringing
under the rock's onrush, soaring lightly out of his grip,
flying away past all the other marks, and Queen Athena,
built like a man, staked out the spot and cried
with a voice of triumph, "Even a blind man,   225
friend, could find your mark by groping round—
it's not mixed up in the crowd, it's far in front!
There's nothing to fear in *this* event—
no one can touch you, much less beat your distance!"

      At that the heart of the long-suffering hero laughed,   230
so glad to find a ready friend in the crowd that,
lighter in mood, he challenged all Phaeacia's best:
"Now go match *that*, you young pups, and straightaway
I'll hurl you another just as far, I swear, or even farther!
All the rest of you, anyone with the spine and spirit,   235
step right up and try me—you've incensed me so—
at boxing, wrestling, racing; nothing daunts me.
Any Phaeacian here except Laodamas himself.
The man's my host. Who would fight his friend?
He'd have to be good-for-nothing, senseless, yes,   240
to challenge his host and come to grips in games,
in a far-off land at that. He'd cut his own legs short.
But there are no others I'd deny or think beneath me—
I'll take on all contenders, gladly, test them head-to-head!
I'm no disgrace in the world of games where men compete.   245
Well I know how to handle a fine polished bow,
the first to hit my man in a mass of enemies,
even with rows of comrades pressing near me,
taking aim with our shafts to hit our targets.
Philoctetes[1] alone outshot me there at Troy   250
when ranks of Achaean archers bent their bows.
Of the rest I'd say that I outclass them all—
men still alive, who eat their bread on earth.
But I'd never vie with the men of days gone by,
not Heracles, not Eurytus[2] of Oechalia—archers   255
who rivaled immortal powers with their bows.
That's why noble Eurytus died a sudden death:
no old age, creeping upon him in his halls . . .
Apollo shot him down, enraged that the man
had challenged *him*, the Archer God.
                              As for spears,   260
I can fling a spear as far as the next man wings an arrow!
Only at sprinting I fear you'd leave me in the dust.

1. Inheritor of the bow of Heracles, which never missed its mark.   2. King of Oechalia (several towns had this name, and it is uncertain which is his). Eurytus's bow was given by his son Iphitus to Odysseus, and it is with this bow that Odysseus will kill the suitors in book XXII. The bow's history is given at the beginning of book XXI.

I've taken a shameful beating out on heavy seas,
no conditioning there on shipboard day by day.
My legs have lost their spring."   265

    He finished. All stood silent, hushed.
Only Alcinous found a way to answer. "Stranger,
friend—nothing you say among us seems ungracious.
You simply want to display the gifts you're born with,
stung that a youngster marched up to you in the games,   270
mocking, ridiculing your prowess as no one would
who had some sense of fit and proper speech.
But come now, hear me out,
so you can tell our story to other lords
as you sit and feast in your own halls someday,   275
your own wife and your children by your side,
remembering there our island prowess here:
what skills great Zeus has given *us* as well,
down all the years from our fathers' days till now.
We're hardly world-class boxers or wrestlers, I admit,   280
but we can race like the wind, we're champion sailors too,
and always dear to our hearts, the feast, the lyre and dance
and changes of fresh clothes, our warm baths and beds.
So come—all you Phaeacian masters of the dance—
now dance away! So our guest can tell his friends,   285
when he reaches home, how far we excel the world
in sailing, nimble footwork, dance and song.
                              Go, someone,
quickly, fetch Demodocus now his ringing lyre.
It must be hanging somewhere in the palace."

    At the king's word the herald sprang to his feet   290
and ran to fetch the ringing lyre from the house.
And stewards rose, nine in all, picked from the realm
to set the stage for contests: masters-at-arms who
leveled the dancing-floor to make a fine broad ring.
The herald returned and placed the vibrant lyre now   295
in Demodocus' hands, and the bard moved toward the center,
flanked by boys in the flush of youth, skilled dancers
who stamped the ground with marvelous pulsing steps
as Odysseus gazed at their flying, flashing feet,
his heart aglow with wonder.
                       A rippling prelude—   300
now the bard struck up an irresistible song:
The Love of Ares and Aphrodite Crowned with Flowers . . .
how the two had first made love in Hephaestus' mansion,
all in secret. Ares had showered her with gifts
and showered Hephaestus' marriage bed with shame   305
but a messenger ran to tell the god of fire—
Helios, lord of the sun,[3] who'd spied the couple
lost in each other's arms and making love.

---

3. As the sun, Helios sees everything.

Hephaestus, hearing the heart-wounding story,
bustled toward his forge, brooding on his revenge—   310
planted the huge anvil on its block and beat out chains,
not to be slipped or broken, all to pin the lovers on the spot.
This snare the Firegod forged, ablaze with his rage at War,
then limped to the room where the bed of love stood firm
and round the posts he poured the chains in a sweeping net   315
with streams of others flowing down from the roofbeam,
gossamer-fine as spider webs no man could see,
not even a blissful god—
the Smith had forged a masterwork of guile.
Once he'd spun that cunning trap around his bed   320
he feigned a trip to the well-built town of Lemnos,[4]
dearest to him by far of all the towns on earth.
But the god of battle kept no blind man's watch.
As soon as he saw the Master Craftsman leave
he plied his golden reins and arrived at once   325
and entered the famous god of fire's mansion,
chafing with lust for Aphrodite crowned with flowers.
She'd just returned from her father's palace, mighty Zeus,
and now she sat in her rooms as Ares strode right in
and grasped her hand with a warm, seductive urging: 330
"Quick, my darling, come, let's go to bed
and lose ourselves in love! Your husband's away—
by now he must be off in the wilds of Lemnos,
consorting with his raucous Sintian friends."
                                    So he pressed
and her heart raced with joy to sleep with War   335
and off they went to bed and down they lay—
and down around them came those cunning chains
of the crafty god of fire, showering down now
till the couple could not move a limb or lift a finger—
then they knew at last: there was no way out, not now.   340
But now the glorious crippled Smith was drawing near . . .
he'd turned around, miles short of the Lemnos coast,
for the Sungod kept *his* watch and told Hephaestus all,
so back he rushed to his house, his heart consumed with anguish.
Halting there at the gates, seized with savage rage   345
he howled a terrible cry, imploring all the gods,
"Father Zeus, look here—
the rest of you happy gods who live forever—
here is a sight to make you laugh, revolt you too!
Just because I am crippled, Zeus's daughter Aphrodite   350
will always spurn me and love that devastating Ares,
just because of his stunning looks and racer's legs
while I am a weakling, lame from birth, and who's to blame?
Both my parents—who else? If only they'd never bred me!
Just look at the two lovers . . . crawled inside my bed,   355
locked in each other's arms—the sight makes me burn!

---

4. Island in the northeastern Aegean, where there was a cult of Hephaestus. When Zeus in anger threw him off Olympus, Hephaestus landed on Lemnos and was cared for by its inhabitants, the Sintians (*Iliad* 1.622–26).

But I doubt they'll want to lie that way much longer,
not a moment more—mad as they are for each other.
No, they'll soon tire of bedding down together,
but then my cunning chains will bind them fast   360
till our Father pays my bride-gifts back in full,
all I handed *him* for that shameless bitch his daughter,
irresistible beauty—all unbridled too!"

                So Hephaestus wailed
as the gods came crowding up to his bronze-floored house.
Poseidon god of the earthquake came, and Hermes came,   365
the running god of luck, and the Archer, lord Apollo,
while modesty kept each goddess to her mansion.
The immortals, givers of all good things, stood at the gates,
and uncontrollable laughter burst from the happy gods
when they saw the god of fire's subtle, cunning work.   370
One would glance at his neighbor, laughing out,
"A bad day for adultery! Slow outstrips the Swift."

    "Look how limping Hephaestus conquers War,
the quickest of all the gods who rule Olympus!"

    "The cripple wins by craft."
                            "The adulterer,   375
he will pay the price!"
                    So the gods would banter
among themselves but lord Apollo goaded Hermes on:
"Tell me, Quicksilver, giver of all good things—
even with those unwieldy shackles wrapped around you,
how would you like to bed the golden Aphrodite?"   380

    "Oh Apollo, if only!" the giant-killer cried.
"Archer, bind me down with triple those endless chains!
Let all you gods look on, and all you goddesses too—
how I'd love to bed that golden Aphrodite!"

    A peal of laughter broke from the deathless ones   385
but not Poseidon, not a smile from him; he kept on
begging the famous Smith to loose the god of war,
pleading, his words flying, "Let him go!
I guarantee you Ares will pay the price,
whatever you ask, Hephaestus,   390
whatever's right in the eyes of all the gods."

    But the famous crippled Smith appealed in turn,
"God of the earthquake, please don't urge this on me.
A pledge for a worthless man is a worthless pledge indeed.
What if he slips out of his chains—his debts as well?   395
How could I shackle *you* while all the gods look on?"

    But the god of earthquakes reassured the Smith,
"Look, Hephaestus, if Ares scuttles off and away,
squirming out of his debt, I'll pay the fine myself."

And the famous crippled Smith complied at last: 400
"Now *there*'s an offer I really can't refuse!"

With all his force the god of fire loosed the chains
and the two lovers, free of the bonds that overwhelmed them so,
sprang up and away at once, and the Wargod sped to Thrace[5]
while Love with her telltale laughter sped to Paphos,[6]   405
Cyprus Isle, where her grove and scented altar stand.
There the Graces bathed and anointed her with oil,
ambrosial oil, the bloom that clings to the gods
who never die, and swathed her round in gowns
to stop the heart . . . an ecstasy—a vision.   410

That was the song the famous harper sang
and Odysseus relished every note as the islanders,
the lords of the long oars and master mariners rejoiced.

Next the king asked Halius and Laodamas to dance,
the two alone, since none could match that pair.   415
So taking in hand a gleaming sea-blue ball,
made by the craftsman Polybus—arching back,
one prince would hurl it toward the shadowy clouds
as the other leaping high into the air would catch it
quickly, nimbly, before his feet hit ground again.   420
Once they'd vied at throwing the ball straight up,
they tossed it back and forth in a blur of hands
as they danced across the earth that feeds us all,
while boys around the ring stamped out the beat
and a splendid rhythmic drumming sound arose   425
and good Odysseus looked at his host, exclaiming,
"King Alcinous, shining among your island people,
you boasted Phaeacia's dancers are the best—
they prove your point—I watch and I'm amazed!"

His praises cheered the hallowed island king   430
who spoke at once to the master mariners around him:
"Hear me, my lords and captains of Phaeacia,
our guest is a man of real taste, I'd say. Come,
let's give him the parting gifts a guest deserves.
There are twelve peers of the realm who rule our land,   435
thirteen, counting myself. Let each of us contribute
a fresh cloak and shirt and a bar of precious gold.
Gather the gifts together, hurry, so our guest
can have them all in hand when he goes to dine,
his spirit filled with joy.   440
As for Broadsea, let him make amends,
man-to-man, with his words as well as gifts.
His first remarks were hardly fit to hear."

---

5. Non-Greek territory to the north; it was thought to be Ares' home.   6. A town on the island of Cyprus (in the eastern Mediterranean, opposite Syria), where an important cult of Aphrodite was located.

All assented and gave their own commands,
each noble sent a page to fetch his gifts.   445
And Broadsea volunteered in turn, obliging:
"Great Alcinous, shining among our island people,
of course I'll make amends to our newfound friend
as you request. I'll give the man this sword.
It's solid bronze and the hilt has silver studs,   450
the sheath around it ivory freshly carved.
Here's a gift our guest will value highly."

He placed the silver-studded sword in Odysseus' hands
with a burst of warm words: "Farewell, stranger, sir—
if any remark of mine gave you offense,   455
may stormwinds snatch it up and sweep it off!
May the gods grant *you* safe passage home to see your wife—
you've been so far from loved ones, suffered so!"

Tactful Odysseus answered him in kind:
"And a warm farewell to you, too, my friend.   460
May the gods grant *you* good fortune—
may you never miss this sword, this gift you give
with such salutes. You've made amends in full."

                                                              With that
he slung the silver-studded sword across his shoulder.
As the sun sank, his glittering gifts arrived   465
and proud heralds bore them into the hall
where sons of King Alcinous took them over,
spread them out before their noble mother's feet—
a grand array of gifts. The king in all his majesty
led the rest of his peers inside, following in a file   470
and down they sat on rows of high-backed chairs.
The king turned to the queen and urged her, "Come,
my dear, bring in an elegant chest, the best you have,
and lay inside it a fresh cloak and shirt, your own gifts.
Then heat a bronze cauldron over the fire, boil water,   475
so once our guest has bathed and reviewed his gifts—
all neatly stacked for sailing,
gifts our Phaeacian lords have brought him now—
he'll feast in peace and hear the harper's songs.
And I will give him this gorgeous golden cup of mine,   480
so he'll remember Alcinous all his days to come
when he pours libations out in his own house
to Father Zeus and the other gods on high."

And at that Arete told her serving-women,
"Set a great three-legged cauldron over the fire—   485
do it right away!"
                              And hoisting over the blaze
a cauldron, filling it brimful with bathing water,
they piled fresh logs beneath and lit them quickly.
The fire lapped at the vessel's belly, the water warmed.
Meanwhile the queen had a polished chest brought forth   490

from an inner room and laid the priceless gifts inside,
the clothes and gold the Phaeacian lords had brought,
and added her own gifts, a cloak and a fine shirt,
and gave her guest instructions quick and clear:
"Now look to the lid yourself and bind it fast   495
with a good tight knot, so no one can rob you
on your voyage—drifting into a sweet sleep
as the black ship sails you home."
                                        Hearing that,
the storm-tossed man secured the lid straightway,
he battened it fast with a swift, intricate knot   500
the lady Circe[7] had taught him long ago.
And the housekeeper invited him at once
to climb into a waiting tub and bathe—
a hot, steaming bath . . .
what a welcome sight to Odysseus' eyes!   505
He'd been a stranger to comforts such as these
since he left the lovely-haired Calypso's house,
yet all those years he enjoyed such comforts there,
never-ending, as if he were a god . . . And now,
when maids had washed him, rubbed him down with oil   510
and drawn warm fleece and a shirt around his shoulders,
he stepped from the bath to join the nobles at their wine.
And there stood Nausicaa as he passed. Beside a column
that propped the sturdy roof she paused, endowed
by the gods with all her beauty, gazing at   515
Odysseus right before her eyes. Wonderstruck,
she hailed her guest with a winning flight of words:
"Farewell, my friend! And when you are at home,
home in your own land, remember me at times.
Mainly to me you owe the gift of life."   520

   Odysseus rose to the moment deftly, gently:
"Nausicaa, daughter of generous King Alcinous,
may Zeus the Thunderer, Hera's husband, grant it so—
that I travel home and see the dawn of my return.
Even at home I'll pray to you as a deathless goddess   525
all my days to come. You saved my life, dear girl."

   And he went and took his seat beside the king.
By now they were serving out the portions, mixing wine,
and the herald soon approached, leading the faithful bard
Demodocus, prized by all the people—seated him in a chair   530
amid the feasters, leaning it against a central column.
At once alert Odysseus carved a strip of loin,
rich and crisp with fat, from the white-tusked boar
that still had much meat left, and called the herald over:
"Here, herald, take this choice cut to Demodocus   535
so he can eat his fill—with warm regards
from a man who knows what suffering is . . .

---

7. A divine sorceress. Odysseus stayed for a year on her island as her lover (book X).

From all who walk the earth our bards deserve
esteem and awe, for the Muse herself has taught them
paths of song. She loves the breed of harpers."   540

    The herald placed the gift in Demodocus' hands
and the famous blind bard received it, overjoyed.
They reached for the good things that lay outspread
and when they'd put aside desire for food and drink,
Odysseus, master of many exploits, praised the singer: 545
"I respect you, Demodocus, more than any man alive—
surely the Muse has taught you, Zeus's daughter,
or god Apollo himself. How true to life,
all too true . . . you sing the Achaeans' fate,
all they did and suffered, all they soldiered through,   550
as if you were there yourself or heard from one who was.
But come now, shift your ground. Sing of the wooden horse
Epeus built with Athena's help, the cunning trap that
good Odysseus brought one day to the heights of Troy,
filled with fighting men who laid the city waste.   555
Sing that for me—true to life as it deserves—
and I will tell the world at once how freely
the Muse gave *you* the gods' own gift of song."

    Stirred now by the Muse, the bard launched out
in a fine blaze of song, starting at just the point   560
where the main Achaean force, setting their camps afire,
had boarded the oarswept ships and sailed for home
but famed Odysseus' men already crouched in hiding—
in the heart of Troy's assembly—dark in that horse
the Trojans dragged themselves to the city heights.   565
Now it stood there, looming . . .
and round its bulk the Trojans sat debating,
clashing, days on end. Three plans split their ranks:
either to hack open the hollow vault with ruthless bronze
or haul it up to the highest ridge and pitch it down the cliffs   570
or let it stand—a glorious offering made to pacify the gods—
and that, that final plan, was bound to win the day.
For Troy was fated to perish once the city lodged
inside her walls the monstrous wooden horse
where the prime of Argive power lay in wait   575
with death and slaughter bearing down on Troy.
And he sang how troops of Achaeans broke from cover,
streaming out of the horse's hollow flanks to plunder Troy—
he sang how left and right they ravaged the steep city,
sang how Odysseus marched right up to Deiphobus' house   580
like the god of war on attack with diehard Menelaus.
There, he sang, Odysseus fought the grimmest fight
he had ever braved but he won through at last,
thanks to Athena's superhuman power.

    That was the song the famous harper sang   585
but great Odysseus melted into tears,

running down from his eyes to wet his cheeks . . .
as a woman weeps, her arms flung round her darling husband,
a man who fell in battle, fighting for town and townsmen,
trying to beat the day of doom from home and children.   590
Seeing the man go down, dying, gasping for breath,
she clings for dear life, screams and shrills—
but the victors, just behind her,
digging spear-butts into her back and shoulders,
drag her off in bondage, yoked to hard labor, pain,   595
and the most heartbreaking torment wastes her cheeks.
So from Odysseus' eyes ran tears of heartbreak now.
But his weeping went unmarked by all the others;
only Alcinous, sitting close beside him,
noticed his guest's tears,   600
heard the groan in the man's labored breathing
and said at once to the master mariners around him,
"Hear me, my lords and captains of Phaeacia!
Let Demodocus rest his ringing lyre now—
this song he sings can hardly please us all.   605
Ever since our meal began and the stirring bard
launched his song, our guest has never paused
in his tears and throbbing sorrow.
Clearly grief has overpowered his heart.
Break off this song! Let us all enjoy ourselves,   610
the hosts and guest together. Much the warmer way.
All these things are performed for him, our honored guest,
the royal send-off here and gifts we give in love.
Treat your guest and suppliant like a brother:
anyone with a touch of sense knows that.   615
So don't be crafty now, my friend, don't hide
the truth I'm after. Fair is fair, speak out!
Come, tell us the name they call you there at home—
your mother, father, townsmen, neighbors round about.
Surely no man in the world is nameless, all told.   620
Born high, born low, as soon as he sees the light
his parents always name him, once he's born.
And tell me your land, your people, your city too,
so our ships can sail you home—their wits will speed them there.
For we have no steersmen here among Phaeacia's crews   625
or steering-oars that guide your common craft.
Our ships know in a flash their mates' intentions,
know all ports of call and all the rich green fields.
With wings of the wind they cross the sea's huge gulfs,
shrouded in mist and cloud—no fear in the world of foundering, 630
fatal shipwreck.
                    True, there's an old tale I heard
my father telling once. Nausithous used to say
that lord Poseidon was vexed with us because
we escorted all mankind and never came to grief.
He said that one day, as a well-built ship of ours   635
sailed home on the misty sea from such a convoy,
the god would crush it, yes,

and pile a huge mountain round about our port.
So the old king foretold . . . And as for the god, well,
he can do his worst or leave it quite undone,   640
whatever warms his heart.
                                   But come, my friend,
tell us your own story now, and tell it truly.
Where have your rovings forced you?
What lands of men have you seen, what sturdy towns,
what men themselves? Who were wild, savage, lawless?   645
Who were friendly to strangers, god-fearing men? Tell me,
why do you weep and grieve so sorely when you hear
the fate of the Argives, hear the fall of Troy?
That is the gods' work, spinning threads of death
through the lives of mortal men,   650
and all to make a song for those to come . . .
Did one of your kinsmen die before the walls of Troy,
some brave man—a son by marriage? father by marriage?
Next to our own blood kin, our nearest, dearest ties.
Or a friend perhaps, someone close to your heart,   655
staunch and loyal? No less dear than a brother,
the brother-in-arms who shares our inmost thoughts."

BOOK IX

[In the One-Eyed Giant's Cave]

Odysseus, the great teller of tales, launched out on his story:
"Alcinous, majesty, shining among your island people,
what a fine thing it is to listen to such a bard
as we have here—the man sings like a god.
The crown of life, I'd say. There's nothing better   5
than when deep joy holds sway throughout the realm
and banqueters up and down the palace sit in ranks,
enthralled to hear the bard, and before them all, the tables
heaped with bread and meats, and drawing wine from a mixing-bowl
the steward makes his rounds and keeps the winecups flowing.   10
This, to my mind, is the best that life can offer.
                                   But now
you're set on probing the bitter pains I've borne,
so I'm to weep and grieve, it seems, still more.
Well then, what shall I go through first,
what shall I save for last?   15
What pains—the gods have given me my share.
Now let me begin by telling you my name . . .
so you may know it well and I in times to come,
if I can escape the fatal day, will be your host,
your sworn friend, though my home is far from here.   20
I am Odysseus, son of Laertes, known to the world
for every kind of craft—my fame has reached the skies.
Sunny Ithaca is my home. Atop her stands our seamark,
Mount Neriton's leafy ridges shimmering in the wind.
Around her a ring of islands circle side-by-side,   25
Dulichion, Same, wooded Zacynthus too, but mine

lies low and away, the farthest out to sea,
rearing into the western dusk
while the others face the east and breaking day.
Mine is a rugged land but good for raising sons—   30
and I myself, I know no sweeter sight on earth
than a man's own native country.
                    True enough,
Calypso the lustrous goddess tried to hold me back,
deep in her arching caverns, craving me for a husband.
So did Circe, holding me just as warmly in her halls,   35
the bewitching queen of Aeaea keen to have me too.
But they never won the heart inside me, never.
So nothing is as sweet as a man's own country,
his own parents, even though he's settled down
in some luxurious house, off in a foreign land   40
and far from those who bore him.
                  No more. Come,
let me tell you about the voyage fraught with hardship
Zeus inflicted on me, homeward bound from Troy . . .

    The wind drove me out of Ilium on to Ismarus,[8]
the Cicones' stronghold. There I sacked the city,   45
killed the men, but as for the wives and plunder,
that rich haul we dragged away from the place—
we shared it round so no one, not on my account,
would go deprived of his fair share of spoils.
Then I urged them to cut and run, set sail,   50
but would they listen? Not those mutinous fools;
there was too much wine to swill, too many sheep to slaughter
down along the beach, and shambling longhorn cattle.
And all the while the Cicones sought out other Cicones,
called for help from their neighbors living inland: 55
a larger force, and stronger soldiers too,
skilled hands at fighting men from chariots,
skilled, when a crisis broke, to fight on foot.
Out of the morning mist they came against us—
packed as the leaves and spears that flower forth in spring—   60
and Zeus presented us with disaster, me and my comrades
doomed to suffer blow on mortal blow. Lining up,
both armies battled it out against our swift ships,
both raked each other with hurtling bronze lances.
Long as morning rose and the blessed day grew stronger   65
we stood and fought them off, massed as they were, but then,
when the sun wheeled past the hour for unyoking oxen,
the Cicones broke our lines and beat us down at last.
Out of each ship, six men-at-arms were killed;
the rest of us rowed away from certain doom.   70

---

8. In Thrace, on the north of the Aegean Sea. This alone of Odysseus's adventures in books IX to XII is set in the known world. The Cicones were allies of Troy, but Odysseus evidently does not think any justification of the piratical raid is necessary. Ilium is Troy.

From there we sailed on, glad to escape our death
yet sick at heart for the dear companions we had lost.
But I would not let our rolling ships set sail until the crews
had raised the triple cry, saluting each poor comrade
cut down by the fierce Cicones on that plain.   75
Now Zeus who masses the stormclouds hit the fleet
with the North Wind—
                          a howling, demonic gale, shrouding over
in thunderheads the earth and sea at once—
                                       and night swept down
from the sky and the ships went plunging headlong on,
our sails slashed to rags by the hurricane's blast!   80
We struck them—cringing at death we rowed our ships
to the nearest shoreline, pulled with all our power.
There, for two nights, two days, we lay by, no letup,
eating our hearts out, bent with pain and bone-tired.
When Dawn with her lovely locks brought on the third day,   85
then stepping the masts and hoisting white sails high,
we lounged at the oarlocks, letting wind and helmsmen
keep us true on course . . .
                          And now, at long last,
I might have reached my native land unscathed,
but just as I doubled Malea's cape, a tide-rip   90
and the North Wind drove me way off course
careering past Cythera.[9]
                          Nine whole days
I was borne along by rough, deadly winds
on the fish-infested sea. Then on the tenth
our squadron reached the land of the Lotus-eaters,[1]   95
people who eat the lotus, mellow fruit and flower.
We disembarked on the coast, drew water there
and crewmen snatched a meal by the swift ships.
Once we'd had our fill of food and drink I sent
a detail ahead, two picked men and a third, a runner,   100
to scout out who might live there—men like us perhaps,
who live on bread? So off they went and soon enough
they mingled among the natives, Lotus-eaters, Lotus-eaters
who had no notion of killing my companions, not at all,
they simply gave them the lotus to taste instead . . .   105
Any crewmen who ate the lotus, the honey-sweet fruit,
lost all desire to send a message back, much less return,
their only wish to linger there with the Lotus-eaters,
grazing on lotus, all memory of the journey home
dissolved forever. But *I* brought them back, back   110
to the hollow ships, and streaming tears—I forced them,
hauled them under the rowing benches, lashed them fast
and shouted out commands to my other, steady comrades:
'Quick, no time to lose, embark in the racing ships!'—

9. A large island off Malea, the southeastern tip of the Peloponnesus.   1. It is generally thought that
this story contains some memory of early Greek contact with North Africa. The north wind Odysseus
describes would have taken him to the area of Cyrenaica, or modern Libya. The lotus has been variously
identified (suggestions range from dates to hashish).

so none could eat the lotus, forget the voyage home.   115
They swung aboard at once, they sat to the oars in ranks
and in rhythm churned the water white with stroke on stroke.

    From there we sailed on, our spirits now at a low ebb,
and reached the land of the high and mighty Cyclops,[2]
lawless brutes, who trust so to the everlasting gods   120
they never plant with their own hands or plow the soil.
Unsown, unplowed, the earth teems with all they need,
wheat, barley and vines, swelled by the rains of Zeus
to yield a big full-bodied wine from clustered grapes.
They have no meeting place for council, no laws either,   125
no, up on the mountain peaks they live in arching caverns—
each a law to himself, ruling his wives and children,
not a care in the world for any neighbor.
                                        Now,
a level island stretches flat across the harbor,
not close inshore to the Cyclops' coast, not too far out,   130
thick with woods where the wild goats breed by hundreds.
No trampling of men to start them from their lairs,
no hunters roughing it out on the woody ridges,
stalking quarry, ever raid their haven.
No flocks browse, no plowlands roll with wheat;   135
unplowed, unsown forever—empty of humankind—
the island just feeds droves of bleating goats.
For the Cyclops have no ships with crimson prows,[3]
no shipwrights there to build them good trim craft
that could sail them out to foreign ports of call   140
as most men risk the seas to trade with other men.
Such artisans would have made this island too
a decent place to live in . . . No mean spot,
it could bear you any crop you like in season.
The water-meadows along the low foaming shore   145
run soft and moist, and your vines would never flag.
The land's clear for plowing. Harvest on harvest,
a man could reap a healthy stand of grain—
the subsoil's dark and rich.
There's a snug deep-water harbor there, what's more,   150
no need for mooring-gear, no anchor-stones to heave,
no cables to make fast. Just beach your keels, ride out
the days till your shipmates' spirit stirs for open sea
and a fair wind blows. And last, at the harbor's head
there's a spring that rushes fresh from beneath a cave   155
and black poplars flourish round its mouth.
                                        Well,
here we landed, and surely a god steered us in
through the pitch-black night.
Not that he ever showed himself, with thick fog
swirling around the ships, the moon wrapped in clouds   160

---

2. Sicily, according to post-Homeric tradition.   3. Greek ships were painted red on the bows and could be decorated with an emblem (often shown on vase paintings as a huge eye).

and not a glimmer stealing through that gloom.
Not one of us glimpsed the island—scanning hard—
or the long combers rolling us slowly toward the coast,
not till our ships had run their keels ashore.
Beaching our vessels smoothly, striking sail,   165
the crews swung out on the low shelving sand
and there we fell asleep, awaiting Dawn's first light.

When young Dawn with her rose-red fingers shone once more
we all turned out, intrigued to tour the island.
The local nymphs, the daughters of Zeus himself,   170
flushed mountain-goats so the crews could make their meal.
Quickly we fetched our curved bows and hunting spears
from the ships and, splitting up into three bands,
we started shooting, and soon enough some god
had sent us bags of game to warm our hearts.   175
A dozen vessels sailed in my command
and to each crew nine goats were shared out
and mine alone took ten. Then all day long
till the sun went down we sat and feasted well
on sides of meat and rounds of heady wine.   180
The good red stock in our vessels' holds
had not run out, there was still plenty left;
the men had carried off a generous store in jars
when we stormed and sacked the Cicones' holy city.
Now we stared across at the Cyclops' shore, so near   185
we could even see their smoke, hear their voices,
their bleating sheep and goats . . .
And then when the sun had set and night came on
we lay down and slept at the water's shelving edge.
When young Dawn with her rose-red fingers shone once more   190
I called a muster briskly, commanding all the hands,
'The rest of you stay here, my friends-in-arms.
I'll go across with my own ship and crew
and probe the natives living over there.
What *are* they—violent, savage, lawless?   195
or friendly to strangers, god-fearing men?'

With that I boarded ship and told the crew
to embark at once and cast off cables quickly.
They swung aboard, they sat to the oars in ranks
and in rhythm churned the water white with stroke on stroke.   200
But as soon as we reached the coast I mentioned—no long trip—
we spied a cavern just at the shore, gaping above the surf,
towering, overgrown with laurel. And here big flocks,
sheep and goats, were stalled to spend the nights,
and around its mouth a yard was walled up   205
with quarried boulders sunk deep in the earth
and enormous pines and oak-trees looming darkly . . .
Here was a giant's lair, in fact, who always pastured
his sheepflocks far afield and never mixed with others.
A grim loner, dead set in his own lawless ways.   210

Here was a piece of work, by god, a monster
built like no mortal who ever supped on bread,
no, like a shaggy peak, I'd say—a man-mountain
rearing head and shoulders over the world.
                                        Now then,
I told most of my good trusty crew to wait,   215
to sit tight by the ship and guard her well
while I picked out my dozen finest fighters
and off I went. But I took a skin of wine along,
the ruddy, irresistible wine that Maron gave me once,
Euanthes' son, a priest of Apollo, lord of Ismarus,   220
because we'd rescued him, his wife and children,
reverent as we were;
he lived, you see, in Apollo's holy grove.
And so in return he gave me splendid gifts,
he handed me seven bars of well-wrought gold,   225
a mixing-bowl of solid silver, then this wine . . .
He drew it off in generous wine-jars, twelve in all,
all unmixed—and such a bouquet, a drink fit for the gods!
No maid or man of his household knew that secret store,
only himself, his loving wife and a single servant.   230
Whenever they'd drink the deep-red mellow vintage,
twenty cups of water he'd stir in one of wine[4]
and what an aroma wafted from the bowl—
what magic, what a godsend—
no joy in holding back when *that* was poured!   235
Filling a great goatskin now, I took this wine,
provisions too in a leather sack. A sudden foreboding
told my fighting spirit I'd soon come up against
some giant clad in power like armor-plate—
a savage deaf to justice, blind to law.   240

    Our party quickly made its way to his cave
but we failed to find our host himself inside;
he was off in his pasture, ranging his sleek flocks.
So we explored his den, gazing wide-eyed at it all,
the large flat racks loaded with drying cheeses,   245
the folds crowded with young lambs and kids,
split into three groups—here the spring-born,
here mid-yearlings, here the fresh sucklings
off to the side—each sort was penned apart.
And all his vessels, pails and hammered buckets   250
he used for milking, were brimming full with whey.
From the start my comrades pressed me, pleading hard,
'Let's make away with the cheeses, then come back—
hurry, drive the lambs and kids from the pens
to our swift ship, put out to sea at once!'   255
But I would not give way—
and how much better it would have been—

4. The Greeks regularly mixed water with their wine, but the extraordinarily high ratio of water to wine mentioned here (twenty to one) shows how strong this wine is.

not till I saw him, saw what gifts he'd give.
But he proved no lovely sight to my companions.

    There we built a fire, set our hands on the cheeses,   260
offered some to the gods and ate the bulk ourselves
and settled down inside, awaiting his return . . .
And back he came from pasture, late in the day,
herding his flocks home, and lugging a huge load
of good dry logs to fuel his fire at supper.   265
He flung them down in the cave—a jolting crash—
we scuttled in panic into the deepest dark recess.
And next he drove his sleek flocks into the open vault,
all he'd milk at least, but he left the males outside,
rams and billy goats out in the high-walled yard.   270
Then to close his door he hoisted overhead
a tremendous, massive slab—
no twenty-two wagons, rugged and four-wheeled,
could budge that boulder off the ground, I tell you,
such an immense stone the monster wedged to block his cave!   275
Then down he squatted to milk his sheep and bleating goats,
each in order, and put a suckling underneath each dam.
And half of the fresh white milk he curdled quickly,
set it aside in wicker racks to press for cheese,
the other half let stand in pails and buckets,   280
ready at hand to wash his supper down.
As soon as he'd briskly finished all his chores
he lit his fire and spied us in the blaze and
'Strangers!' he thundered out, 'now who are you?
Where did you sail from, over the running sea-lanes?   285
Out on a trading spree or roving the waves like pirates,
sea-wolves raiding at will, who risk their lives
to plunder other men?'
                      The hearts inside us shook,
terrified by his rumbling voice and monstrous hulk.
Nevertheless I found the nerve to answer, firmly,   290
'Men of Achaea we are and bound now from Troy!
Driven far off course by the warring winds,
over the vast gulf of the sea—battling home
on a strange tack, a route that's off the map,
and so we've come to you . . .   295
so it must please King Zeus's plotting heart.
We're glad to say we're men of Atrides Agamemnon,
whose fame is the proudest thing on earth these days,
so great a city he sacked, such multitudes he killed!
But since we've chanced on you, we're at your knees   300
in hopes of a warm welcome, even a guest-gift,
the sort that hosts give strangers. That's the custom.
Respect the gods, my friend. We're suppliants—at your mercy!'[5]

---

5. In the *Odyssey*, the civilized (such as Menelaus and Alcinous) welcome strangers and send them on their way with gifts. In fact, as Odysseus says to the Cyclops, hospitality is a religious duty.

Zeus of the Strangers guards all guests and suppliants:
strangers are sacred—Zeus will avenge their rights!'   305

    'Stranger,' he grumbled back from his brutal heart,
'you must be a fool, stranger, or come from nowhere,
telling *me* to fear the gods or avoid their wrath!
We Cyclops never blink at Zeus and Zeus's shield
of storm and thunder, or any other blessed god—   310
we've got more force by far.
I'd never spare you in fear of Zeus's hatred,
you or your comrades here, unless I had the urge.
But tell me, where did you moor your sturdy ship
when you arrived? Up the coast or close in?   315
I'd just like to know.'
                        So he laid his trap
but he never caught me, no, wise to the world
I shot back in my crafty way, 'My ship?
Poseidon god of the earthquake smashed my ship,
he drove it against the rocks at your island's far cape,   320
he dashed it against a cliff as the winds rode us in.
I and the men you see escaped a sudden death.'

    Not a word in reply to that, the ruthless brute.
Lurching up, he lunged out with his hands toward my men
and snatching two at once, rapping them on the ground   325
he knocked them dead like pups—
their brains gushed out all over, soaked the floor—
and ripping them limb from limb to fix his meal
he bolted them down like a mountain-lion, left no scrap,
devoured entrails, flesh and bones, marrow and all!   330
We flung our arms to Zeus, we wept and cried aloud,
looking on at his grisly work—paralyzed, appalled.
But once the Cyclops had stuffed his enormous gut
with human flesh, washing it down with raw milk,
he slept in his cave, stretched out along his flocks.   335
And I with my fighting heart, I thought at first
to steal up to him, draw the sharp sword at my hip
and stab his chest where the midriff packs the liver—
I groped for the fatal spot but a fresh thought held me back.
There at a stroke we'd finish off ourselves as well—   340
how could *we* with our bare hands heave back
that slab he set to block his cavern's gaping maw?
So we lay there groaning, waiting Dawn's first light.

    When young Dawn with her rose-red fingers shone once more
the monster relit his fire and milked his handsome ewes,   345
each in order, putting a suckling underneath each dam,
and as soon as he'd briskly finished all his chores
he snatched up two more men and fixed his meal.
Well-fed, he drove his fat sheep from the cave,
lightly lifting the huge doorslab up and away,   350
then slipped it back in place

as a hunter flips the lid of his quiver shut.
Piercing whistles—turning his flocks to the hills
he left me there, the heart inside me brooding on revenge:
how could I pay him back? would Athena give me glory?   355
Here was the plan that struck my mind as best . . .
the Cyclops' great club: there it lay by the pens,
olivewood, full of sap. He'd lopped it off to brandish
once it dried. Looking it over, we judged it big enough
to be the mast of a pitch-black ship with her twenty oars,   360
a freighter broad in the beam that plows through miles of sea—
so long, so thick it bulked before our eyes. Well,
flanking it now, I chopped off a fathom's length,
rolled it to comrades, told them to plane it down,
and they made the club smooth as I bent and shaved   365
the tip to a stabbing point. I turned it over
the blazing fire to char it good and hard,
then hid it well, buried deep under the dung
that littered the cavern's floor in thick wet clumps.
And now I ordered my shipmates all to cast lots—   370
who'd brave it out with me
to hoist our stake and grind it into his eye
when sleep had overcome him? Luck of the draw:
I got the very ones I would have picked myself,
four good men, and I in the lead made five . . .   375

    Nightfall brought him back, herding his woolly sheep
and he quickly drove the sleek flock into the vaulted cavern,
rams and all—none left outside in the walled yard—
his own idea, perhaps, or a god led him on.
Then he hoisted the huge slab to block the door   380
and squatted to milk his sheep and bleating goats,
each in order, putting a suckling underneath each dam,
and as soon as he'd briskly finished all his chores
he snatched up two more men and fixed his meal.
But this time I lifted a carved wooden bowl,   385
brimful of my ruddy wine,
and went right up to the Cyclops, enticing,
'Here, Cyclops, try this wine—to top off
the banquet of human flesh you've bolted down!
Judge for yourself what stock our ship had stored.   390
I brought it here to make you a fine libation,
hoping you would pity me, Cyclops, send me home,
but your rages are insufferable. You barbarian—
how can any man on earth come visit you after *this*?
What you've done outrages all that's right!'   395

    At that he seized the bowl and tossed it off[6]
and the heady wine pleased him immensely—'More'—
he demanded a second bowl—'a hearty helping!'

6. That the Cyclops drinks this strong wine neat both conveniently gets him drunk and marks him as a
savage (in the Greek view, drinking undiluted wine demonstrated a lack of the self-restraint they prized).

And tell me your name now, quickly,
so I can hand my guest a gift to warm *his* heart.   400
Our soil yields the Cyclops powerful, full-bodied wine
and the rains from Zeus build its strength. But this,
this is nectar, ambrosia—this flows from heaven!'

    So he declared. I poured him another fiery bowl—
three bowls I brimmed and three he drank to the last drop,   405
the fool, and then, when the wine was swirling round his brain,
I approached my host with a cordial, winning word:
'So, you ask me the name I'm known by, Cyclops?
I will tell you. But you must give me a guest-gift
as you've promised. Nobody—that's my name. Nobody—   410
so my mother and father call me all, my friends.'

    But he boomed back at me from his ruthless heart,
'Nobody? I'll eat Nobody last of all his friends—
I'll eat the others first! That's my gift to *you!*'

                                With that
he toppled over, sprawled full-length, flat on his back   415
and lay there, his massive neck slumping to one side,
and sleep that conquers all overwhelmed him now
as wine came spurting, flooding up from his gullet
with chunks of human flesh—he vomited, blind drunk.
Now, at last, I thrust our stake in a bed of embers   420
to get it red-hot and rallied all my comrades:
'Courage—no panic, no one hang back now!'
And green as it was, just as the olive stake
was about to catch fire—the glow terrific, yes—
I dragged it from the flames, my men clustering round   425
as some god breathed enormous courage through us all.
Hoisting high that olive stake with its stabbing point,
straight into the monster's eye they rammed it hard—
I drove my weight on it from above and bored it home
as a shipwright bores his beam with a shipwright's drill   430
that men below, whipping the strap back and forth, whirl
and the drill keeps twisting faster, never stopping—
So we seized our stake with its fiery tip
and bored it round and round in the giant's eye
till blood came boiling up around that smoking shaft   435
and the hot blast singed his brow and eyelids round the core
and the broiling eyeball burst—
                      its crackling roots blazed
and hissed—
            as a blacksmith plunges a glowing ax or adze
in an ice-cold bath and the metal screeches steam
and its temper hardens—that's the iron's strength—   440
so the eye of the Cyclops sizzled round that stake!
He loosed a hideous roar, the rock walls echoed round
and we scuttled back in terror. The monster wrenched the spike
from his eye and out it came with a red geyser of blood—
he flung it aside with frantic hands, and mad with pain   445

he bellowed out for help from his neighbor Cyclops
living round about in caves on windswept crags.
Hearing his cries, they lumbered up from every side
and hulking round his cavern, asked what ailed him:
'What, Polyphemus, what in the world's the trouble?   450
Roaring out in the godsent night to rob us of our sleep.
Surely no one's rustling your flocks against your will—
surely no one's trying to kill you now by fraud or force!'

   '*Nobody*, friends'—Polyphemus bellowed back from his cave—
'*Nobody's* killing me now by fraud and not by force!'   455

   'If you're alone,' his friends boomed back at once,
'and nobody's trying to overpower you now—look,
it must be a plague sent here by mighty Zeus
and there's no escape from *that*.
You'd better pray to your father, Lord Poseidon.'   460

   They lumbered off, but laughter filled my heart
to think how nobody's name—my great cunning stroke—
had duped them one and all.[7] But the Cyclops there,
still groaning, racked with agony, groped around
for the huge slab, and heaving it from the doorway,   465
down he sat in the cave's mouth, his arms spread wide,
hoping to catch a comrade stealing out with sheep—
such a blithering fool he took me for!
But I was already plotting . . .
what was the best way out? how could I find   470
escape from death for my crew, myself as well?
My wits kept weaving, weaving cunning schemes—
life at stake, monstrous death staring us in the face—
till this plan struck my mind as best. That flock,
those well-fed rams with their splendid thick fleece,   475
sturdy, handsome beasts sporting their dark weight of wool:
I lashed them abreast, quietly, twisting the willow-twigs
the Cyclops slept on—giant, lawless brute—I took them
three by three; each ram in the middle bore a man
while the two rams either side would shield him well.   480
So three beasts to bear each man, but as for myself?
There was one bellwether ram, the prize of all the flock,
and clutching him by his back, tucked up under
his shaggy belly, there I hung, face upward,
both hands locked in his marvelous deep fleece,   485
clinging for dear life, my spirit steeled, enduring . . .
So we held on, desperate, waiting Dawn's first light.
                        As soon
as young Dawn with her rose-red fingers shone once more

---

7. In the Greek, an elaborate pun comes to fruition here. Odysseus has told the Cyclops that his name is
Outis, identical to the word for "nobody" except for a difference in the pitch at which the first syllable was
pronounced. The other Cyclops, misunderstanding, reply to Polyphemus using another term for "nobody,"
mē tis, which Odysseus echoes in referring to his "great cunning stroke," or *mētis* (again, differing only in
the pitch of the first syllable). This word, which means "craft" in senses that range from guile to skill at
craftsmanship, is persistently associated with Odysseus.

the rams went rumbling out of the cave toward pasture,
the ewes kept bleating round the pens, unmilked, 490
their udders about to burst. Their master now,
heaving in torment, felt the back of each animal
halting before him here, but the idiot never sensed
my men were trussed up under their thick fleecy ribs.
And last of them all came my great ram now, striding out, 495
weighed down with his dense wool and my deep plots.
Stroking him gently, powerful Polyphemus murmured,
'Dear old ram, why last of the flock to quit the cave?
In the good old days you'd never lag behind the rest—
you with your long marching strides, first by far 500
of the flock to graze the fresh young grasses,
first by far to reach the rippling streams,
first to turn back home, keen for your fold
when night comes on—but now you're last of all.
And why? Sick at heart for your master's eye 505
that coward gouged out with his wicked crew?—
only after he'd stunned my wits with wine—
that, that Nobody . . .
who's not escaped his death, I swear, not yet.
Oh if only you thought like *me*, had words like *me* 510
to tell me where that scoundrel is cringing from my rage!
I'd smash him against the ground, I'd spill his brains—
flooding across my cave—and that would ease my heart
of the pains that good-for-nothing Nobody made me suffer!'

     And with that threat he let my ram go free outside. 515
But soon as we'd got one foot past cave and courtyard,
first I loosed myself from the ram, then loosed my men,
then quickly, glancing back again and again we drove
our flock, good plump beasts with their long shanks,
straight to the ship, and a welcome sight we were 520
to loyal comrades—we who'd escaped our deaths—
but for all the rest they broke down and wailed.
I cut it short, I stopped each shipmate's cries,
my head tossing, brows frowning, silent signals
to hurry, tumble our fleecy herd on board, 525
launch out on the open sea!
They swung aboard, they sat to the oars in ranks
and in rhythm churned the water white with stroke on stroke.
But once offshore as far as a man's shout can carry,
I called back to the Cyclops, stinging taunts: 530
'So, Cyclops, no weak coward it was whose crew
you bent to devour there in your vaulted cave—
you with your brute force! Your filthy crimes
came down on your own head, you shameless cannibal,
daring to eat your guests in your own house— 535
so Zeus and the other gods have paid you back!'

     That made the rage of the monster boil over.
Ripping off the peak of a towering crag, he heaved it

so hard the boulder landed just in front of our dark prow
and a huge swell reared up as the rock went plunging under—   540
a tidal wave from the open sea. The sudden backwash
drove us landward again, forcing us close inshore
but grabbing a long pole, I thrust us off and away,
tossing my head for dear life, signaling crews
to put their backs in the oars, escape grim death.   545
They threw themselves in the labor, rowed on fast
but once we'd plowed the breakers twice as far,
again I began to taunt the Cyclops—men around me
trying to check me, calm me, left and right:
'So headstrong—why? Why rile the beast again?'   550

    'That rock he flung in the sea just now, hurling our ship
to shore once more—we thought we'd die on the spot!'

    'If he'd caught a sound from one of us, just a moan,
he would have crushed our heads and ship timbers
with one heave of another flashing, jagged rock!'   555

    'Good god, the brute can throw!'
                              So they begged
but they could not bring my fighting spirit round.
I called back with another burst of anger, 'Cyclops—
if any man on the face of the earth should ask you
who blinded you, shamed you so—say Odysseus,   560
raider of cities, *he* gouged out your eye,
Laertes' son who makes his home in Ithaca!'

    So I vaunted and he groaned back in answer,
'Oh no, no—that prophecy years ago . . .
it all comes home to me with a vengeance now!   565
We once had a prophet here, a great tall man,
Telemus, Eurymus' son, a master at reading signs,
who grew old in his trade among his fellow-Cyclops.
All this, he warned me, would come to pass someday—
that I'd be blinded here at the hands of one Odysseus.   570
But I always looked for a handsome giant man to cross my path,
some fighter clad in power like armor-plate, but now,
look what a dwarf, a spineless good-for-nothing,
stuns me with wine, then gouges out my eye!
Come here, Odysseus, let me give you a guest-gift   575
and urge Poseidon the earthquake god to speed you home.
I am his son and he claims to be my father, true,
and he himself will heal me if he pleases—
no other blessed god, no man can do the work!'
                                    'Heal you!'—
here was my parting shot—'Would to god I could strip you   580
of life and breath and ship you down to the House of Death
as surely as no one will ever heal your eye,
not even your earthquake god himself!'

But at that he bellowed out to lord Poseidon,
thrusting his arms to the starry skies, and prayed, 'Hear me—   585
Poseidon, god of the sea-blue mane who rocks the earth!
If I really am your son and you claim to be my father—
come, grant that Odysseus, raider of cities,
Laertes' son who makes his home in Ithaca,
never reaches home. Or if he's fated to see   590
his people once again and reach his well-built house
and his own native country, let him come home late
and come a broken man—all shipmates lost,
alone in a stranger's ship—
and let him find a world of pain at home!'
                  So he prayed   595
and the god of the sea-blue mane Poseidon heard his prayer.
The monster suddenly hoisted a boulder—far larger—
wheeled and heaved it, putting his weight behind it,
massive strength, and the boulder crashed close,
landing just in the wake of our dark stern,   600
just failing to graze the rudder's bladed edge.
A huge swell reared up as the rock went plunging under,
yes, and the tidal breaker drove us out to our island's
far shore where all my well-decked ships lay moored,
clustered, waiting, and huddled round them, crewmen   605
sat in anguish, waiting, chafing for our return.
We beached our vessel hard ashore on the sand,
we swung out in the frothing surf ourselves,
and herding Cyclops' sheep from our deep holds
we shared them round so no one, not on my account,   610
would go deprived of his fair share of spoils.
But the splendid ram—as we meted out the flocks
my friends-in-arms made him my prize of honor,
mine alone, and I slaughtered him on the beach
and burnt his thighs to Cronus' mighty son,   615
Zeus of the thundercloud who rules the world.
But my sacrifices failed to move the god:
Zeus was still obsessed with plans to destroy
my entire oarswept fleet and loyal crew of comrades.
Now all day long till the sun went down we sat   620
and feasted on sides of meat and heady wine.
Then when the sun had set and night came on
we lay down and slept at the water's shelving edge.
When young Dawn with her rose-red fingers shone once more
I roused the men straightway, ordering all crews   625
to man the ships and cast off cables quickly.
They swung aboard at once, they sat to the oars in ranks
and in rhythm churned the water white with stroke on stroke.
And from there we sailed on, glad to escape our death
yet sick at heart for the comrades we had lost."   630

BOOK X

[*The Bewitching Queen of Aeaea*]

"We reached the Aeolian island next, the home of Aeolus,[8]
Hippotas' son, beloved by the gods who never die—
a great floating island it was, and round it all
huge ramparts rise of indestructible bronze
and sheer rock cliffs shoot up from sea to sky.   5
The king had sired twelve children within his halls,
six daughters and six sons in the lusty prime of youth,
so he gave his daughters as wives to his six sons.
Seated beside their dear father and doting mother,
with delicacies aplenty spread before them,   10
they feast on forever . . . All day long
the halls breathe the savor of roasted meats
and echo round to the low moan of blowing pipes,
and all night long, each one by his faithful mate,
they sleep under soft-piled rugs on corded bedsteads.   15
To this city of theirs we came, their splendid palace,
and Aeolus hosted me one entire month, he pressed me for news
of Troy and the Argive ships and how we sailed for home,
and I told him the whole long story, first to last.
And then, when I begged him to send me on my way,   20
he denied me nothing, he went about my passage.
He gave me a sack, the skin of a full-grown ox,
binding inside the winds that howl from every quarter,
for Zeus had made that king the master of all the winds,
with power to calm them down or rouse them as he pleased.   25
Aeolus stowed the sack inside my holds, lashed so fast
with a burnished silver cord
not even a slight puff could slip past that knot.
Yet he set the West Wind free to blow us on our way
and waft our squadron home. But his plan was bound to fail,   30
yes, our own reckless folly swept us on to ruin . . .

    Nine whole days we sailed, nine nights, nonstop.
On the tenth our own land hove into sight at last—
we were so close we could see men tending fires.
But now an enticing sleep came on me, bone-weary   35
from working the vessel's sheet myself, no letup,
never trusting the ropes to any other mate,
the faster to journey back to native land.
But the crews began to mutter among themselves,
sure I was hauling troves of gold and silver home,   40
the gifts of open-hearted Aeolus, Hippotas' son.
'The old story!' One man glanced at another, grumbling.
'Look at our captain's luck—so loved by the world,
so prized at every landfall, every port of call.'

---

8. King of the winds; his name in Greek means "Shifting, Changeable." Aeolia has been placed by modern geographers in the Lipari Islands off the Sicilian coast, but the great ancient geographer Eratosthenes observed that we would know exactly where Odysseus wandered after we had traced the leatherworker who made the bag in which the winds were contained.

'Heaps of lovely plunder he hauls home from Troy,   45
while we who went through slogging just as hard,
we go home empty-handed.'
                                   'Now this Aeolus loads him
down with treasure. Favoritism, friend to friend!'

    'Hurry, let's see what loot is in that sack,
how much gold and silver. Break it open—now!'   50

    A fatal plan, but it won my shipmates over.
They loosed the sack and all the winds burst out
and a sudden squall struck and swept us back to sea,
wailing, in tears, far from our own native land.
And I woke up with a start, my spirit churning—   55
should I leap over the side and drown at once or
grit my teeth and bear it, stay among the living?
I bore it all, held firm, hiding my face,
clinging tight to the decks
while heavy squalls blasted our squadron back   60
again to Aeolus' island, shipmates groaning hard.

    We disembarked on the coast, drew water there
and crewmen snatched a meal by the swift ships.
Once we'd had our fill of food and drink
I took a shipmate along with me, a herald too,   65
and approached King Aeolus' famous halls and here
we found him feasting beside his wife and many children.
Reaching the doorposts at the threshold, down we sat
but our hosts, amazed to see us, only shouted questions:
'Back again, Odysseus—why? Some blustering god attacked you?   70
Surely we launched you well, we sped you on your way
to your own land and house, or any place you pleased.'

    So they taunted, and I replied in deep despair,
'A mutinous crew undid me—that and a cruel sleep.
Set it to rights, my friends. You have the power!'   75

    So I pleaded—gentle, humble appeals—
but our hosts turned silent, hushed . . .
and the father broke forth with an ultimatum:
'Away from my island—fast—most cursed man alive!
It's a crime to host a man or speed him on his way   80
when the blessed deathless gods despise him so.
Crawling back like this—
it proves the immortals hate you! Out—get out!'

    Groan as I did, his curses drove me from his halls
and from there we pulled away with heavy hearts,   85
with the crews' spirit broken under the oars' labor,
thanks to our own folly . . . no favoring wind in sight.

    Six whole days we rowed, six nights, nonstop.
On the seventh day we raised the Laestrygonian land,

Telepylus heights where the craggy fort of Lamus[9] rises.   90
Where shepherd calls to shepherd as one drives in his flocks
and the other drives his out and he calls back in answer,
where a man who never sleeps could rake in double wages,
one for herding cattle, one for pasturing fleecy sheep,
the nightfall and the sunrise march so close together.[1]   95
We entered a fine harbor there, all walled around
by a great unbroken sweep of sky-scraping cliff
and two steep headlands, fronting each other, close
around the mouth so the passage in is cramped.
Here the rest of my rolling squadron steered,   100
right into the gaping cove and moored tightly,
prow by prow. Never a swell there, big or small;
a milk-white calm spreads all around the place.
But I alone anchored my black ship outside,
well clear of the harbor's jaws   105
I tied her fast to a cliffside with a cable.
I scaled its rock face to a lookout on its crest
but glimpsed no trace of the work of man or beast from there;
all I spied was a plume of smoke, drifting off the land.
So I sent some crew ahead to learn who lived there—   110
men like us perhaps, who live on bread?
Two good mates I chose and a third to run the news.
They disembarked and set out on a beaten trail
the wagons used for hauling timber down to town
from the mountain heights above . . .   115
and before the walls they met a girl, drawing water,
Antiphates' strapping daughter—king of the Laestrygonians.
She'd come down to a clear running spring, Artacia,
where the local people came to fill their pails.
My shipmates clustered round her, asking questions: 120
who was king of the realm? who ruled the natives here?
She waved at once to her father's high-roofed halls.
They entered the sumptuous palace, found his wife inside—
a woman huge as a mountain crag who filled them all with horror.
Straightaway she summoned royal Antiphates from assembly,   125
her husband, who prepared my crew a barbarous welcome.
Snatching one of my men, he tore him up for dinner—
the other two sprang free and reached the ships.
But the king let loose a howling through the town
that brought tremendous Laestrygonians swarming up   130
from every side—hundreds, not like men, like Giants!
Down from the cliffs they flung great rocks a man could hardly hoist
and a ghastly shattering din rose up from all the ships—
men in their death-cries, hulls smashed to splinters—
They speared the crews like fish   135
and whisked them home to make their grisly meal.
But while they killed them off in the harbor depths
I pulled the sword from beside my hip and hacked away

9. Presumably the founder of the city of the Laestrygonians.   1. Generally thought to be a confused
reference to the short summer nights of the far north.

at the ropes that moored my blue-prowed ship of war
and shouted rapid orders at my shipmates: 140
'Put your backs in the oars—now row or die!'
In terror of death they ripped the swells—all as one—
and what a joy as we darted out toward open sea,
clear of those beetling cliffs . . . my ship alone.
But the rest went down en masse. Our squadron sank.   145

    From there we sailed on, glad to escape our death
yet sick at heart for the dear companions we had lost.
We reached the Aeaean island next, the home of Circe
the nymph with lovely braids, an awesome power too
who can speak with human voice,   150
the true sister of murderous-minded Aeetes.[2]
Both were bred by the Sun who lights our lives;
their mother was Perse, a child the Ocean bore.
We brought our ship to port without a sound
as a god eased her into a harbor safe and snug,   155
and for two days and two nights we lay by there,
eating our hearts out, bent with pain and bone-tired.
When Dawn with her lovely locks brought on the third day,
at last I took my spear and my sharp sword again,
rushed up from the ship to find a lookout point,   160
hoping to glimpse some sign of human labor,
catch some human voices . . .
I scaled a commanding crag and, scanning hard,
I could just make out some smoke from Circe's halls,
drifting up from the broad terrain through brush and woods.   165
Mulling it over, I thought I'd scout the ground—
that fire aglow in the smoke, I saw it, true,
but soon enough this seemed the better plan:
I'd go back to shore and the swift ship first,
feed the men, then send *them* out for scouting.   170
I was well on my way down, nearing our ship
when a god took pity on me, wandering all alone;
he sent me a big stag with high branching antlers,
right across my path—the sun's heat forced him down
from his forest range to drink at a river's banks—   175
just bounding out of the timber when I hit him
square in the backbone, halfway down the spine
and my bronze spear went punching clean through—
he dropped in the dust, groaning, gasping out his breath.
Treading on him, I wrenched my bronze spear from the wound,   180
left it there on the ground, and snapping off some twigs
and creepers, twisted a rope about a fathom long,
I braided it tight, hand over hand, then lashed
the four hocks of that magnificent beast.
Loaded round my neck I lugged him toward the ship,   185

---

2. King of Colchis, on the Black Sea, and owner of the Golden Fleece. It is widely believed that
Odysseus's wanderings in the *Odyssey* were patterned after the voyage of Jason and the Argonauts, heroes
of an earlier generation, in quest of the fleece.

trudging, propped on my spear—no way to sling him
over a shoulder, steadying him with one free arm—
the kill was so immense!
I flung him down by the hull and roused the men,
going up to them all with a word to lift their spirits: 190
'Listen to me, my comrades, brothers in hardship—
we won't go down to the House of Death, not yet,
not till our day arrives. Up with you, look,
there's still some meat and drink in our good ship.
Put our minds on food—why die of hunger here?'   195

    My hardy urging brought them round at once.
Heads came up from cloaks and there by the barren sea
they gazed at the stag, their eyes wide—my noble trophy.
But once they'd looked their fill and warmed their hearts,
they washed their hands and prepared a splendid meal.   200
Now all day long till the sun went down we sat
and feasted on sides of meat and seasoned wine.
Then when the sun had set and night came on
we lay down and slept at the water's shelving edge.
When young Dawn with her rose-red fingers shone once more   205
I called a muster quickly, informing all the crew,
'Listen to me, my comrades, brothers in hardship,
we can't tell east from west, the dawn from the dusk,
nor where the sun that lights our lives goes under earth
nor where it rises. We must think of a plan at once,   210
some cunning stroke. I doubt there's one still left.
I scaled a commanding crag and from that height
surveyed an entire island
ringed like a crown by endless wastes of sea.
But the land itself lies low, and I did see smoke   215
drifting up from its heart through thick brush and woods.'

    My message broke their spirit as they recalled
the gruesome work of the Laestrygonian king Antiphates
and the hearty cannibal Cyclops thirsting for our blood.
They burst into cries, wailing, streaming live tears   220
that gained us nothing—what good can come of grief?

    And so, numbering off my band of men-at-arms
into two platoons, I assigned them each a leader:
I took one and lord Eurylochus the other.
We quickly shook lots in a bronze helmet—   225
the lot of brave Eurylochus leapt out first.
So he moved off with his two and twenty comrades,
weeping, leaving us behind in tears as well . . .
Deep in the wooded glens they came on Circe's palace
built of dressed stone on a cleared rise of land.   230
Mountain wolves and lions were roaming round the grounds—
she'd bewitched them herself, she gave them magic drugs.
But they wouldn't attack my men; they just came pawing
up around them, fawning, swishing their long tails—

eager as hounds that fawn around their master,   235
coming home from a feast,
who always brings back scraps to calm them down.
So they came nuzzling round my men—lions, wolves
with big powerful claws—and the men cringed in fear
at the sight of those strange, ferocious beasts . . . But still   240
they paused at her doors, the nymph with lovely braids,
Circe—and deep inside they heard her singing, lifting
her spellbinding voice as she glided back and forth
at her great immortal loom, her enchanting web
a shimmering glory only goddesses can weave.   245
Polites, captain of armies, took command,
the closest, most devoted man I had: 'Friends,
there's someone inside, plying a great loom,
and how she sings—enthralling!
The whole house is echoing to her song.   250
Goddess or woman—let's call out to her now!'

    So he urged and the men called out and hailed her.
She opened her gleaming doors at once and stepped forth,
inviting them all in, and in they went, all innocence.
Only Eurylochus stayed behind—he sensed a trap . . .   255
She ushered them in to sit on high-backed chairs,
then she mixed them a potion—cheese, barley
and pale honey mulled in Pramnian wine[3]—
but into the brew she stirred her wicked drugs
to wipe from their memories any thought of home.   260
Once they'd drained the bowls she filled, suddenly
she struck with her wand, drove them into her pigsties,
all of them bristling into swine—with grunts,
snouts—even their bodies, yes, and only
the men's minds stayed steadfast as before.   265
So off they went to their pens, sobbing, squealing
as Circe flung them acorns, cornel nuts and mast,
common fodder for hogs that root and roll in mud.

    Back Eurylochus ran to our swift black ship
to tell the disaster our poor friends had faced.   270
But try as he might, he couldn't get a word out.
Numbing sorrow had stunned the man to silence—
tears welled in his eyes, his heart possessed by grief.
We assailed him with questions—all at our wits' end—
till at last he could recount the fate our friends had met: 275
'Off we went through the brush, captain, as you commanded.
Deep in the wooded glens we came on Circe's palace
built of dressed stone on a cleared rise of land.
Someone inside was plying a great loom,
and how she sang—in a high clear voice!   280
Goddess or woman—we called out and hailed her . . .
She opened her gleaming doors at once and stepped forth,

3. A wine also mentioned by later writers; one of then calls it harsh and dark.

inviting us all in, and in we went, all innocence.
But *I* stayed behind—I sensed a trap. Suddenly
all vanished—blotted out—not one face showed again,   285
though I sat there keeping watch a good long time.'

    At that report I slung the hefty bronze blade
of my silver-studded sword around my shoulder,
slung my bow on too and told our comrade,
'Lead me back by the same way that you came.'   290
But he flung both arms around my knees and pleaded,
begging me with his tears and winging words:
'Don't force me back there, captain, king—
leave me here on the spot.
You will never return yourself, I swear,   295
you'll never bring back a single man alive.
Quick, cut and run with the rest of us here—
we can still escape the fatal day!'

But I shot back, 'Eurylochus, stay right here,
eating, drinking, safe by the black ship.   300
I must be off. Necessity drives me on.'

    Leaving the ship and shore, I headed inland,
clambering up through hushed, entrancing glades until,
as I was nearing the halls of Circe skilled in spells,
approaching her palace—Hermes god of the golden wand   305
crossed my path, and he looked for all the world
like a young man sporting his first beard,
just in the prime and warm pride of youth,
and grasped me by the hand and asked me kindly,
'Where are you going now, my unlucky friend—   310
trekking over the hills alone in unfamiliar country?
And your men are all in there, in Circe's palace,
cooped like swine, hock by jowl in the sties.
Have you come to set them free?
Well, I warn you, you won't get home yourself,   315
you'll stay right there, trapped with all the rest.
But wait, I can save you, free you from that great danger.
Look, here is a potent drug. Take it to Circe's halls—
its power alone will shield you from the fatal day.
Let me tell you of all the witch's subtle craft . . .   320
She'll mix you a potion, lace the brew with drugs
but she'll be powerless to bewitch you, even so—
this magic herb I give will fight her spells.
Now here's your plan of action, step by step.
The moment Circe strikes with her long thin wand,   325
you draw your sharp sword sheathed at your hip
and rush her fast as if to run her through!
She'll cower in fear and coax you to her bed—
but don't refuse the goddess' bed, not then, not if
she's to release your friends and treat you well yourself.   330
But have her swear the binding oath of the blessed gods

she'll never plot some new intrigue to harm you,
once you lie there naked—
never unman you, strip away your courage!'
                                    With that
the giant-killer handed over the magic herb,   335
pulling it from the earth,
and Hermes showed me all its name and nature.
Its root is black and its flower white as milk
and the gods call it moly. Dangerous for a mortal man
to pluck from the soil but not for deathless gods.   340
All lies within their power.
                              Now Hermes went his way
to the steep heights of Olympus, over the island's woods
while I, just approaching the halls of Circe,
my heart a heaving storm at every step,
paused at her doors, the nymph with lovely braids—   345
I stood and shouted to her there. She heard my voice,
she opened her gleaming doors at once and stepped forth,
inviting me in, and in I went, all anguish now . . .
She led me in to sit on a silver-studded chair,
ornately carved, with a stool to rest my feet.   350
In a golden bowl she mixed a potion for me to drink,
stirring her poison in, her heart aswirl with evil.
And then she passed it on, I drank it down
but it never worked its spell—
she struck with her wand and 'Now,' she cried,   355
'off to your sty, you swine, and wallow with your friends!'
But I, I drew my sharp sword sheathed at my hip
and rushed her fast as if to run her through—
She screamed, slid under my blade, hugged my knees
with a flood of warm tears and a burst of winging words: 360
'Who are you? where are you from? your city? your parents?
I'm wonderstruck—you drank my drugs, you're not bewitched!
Never has any other man withstood my potion, never,
once it's past his lips and he has drunk it down.
You have a mind in *you* no magic can enchant!   365
You must be Odysseus, man of twists and turns—
Hermes the giant-killer, god of the golden wand,
he always said you'd come,
homeward bound from Troy in your swift black ship.
Come, sheathe your sword, let's go to bed together,   370
mount my bed and mix in the magic work of love—
we'll breed deep trust between us.'
                                    So she enticed
but I fought back, still wary. 'Circe, Circe,
how dare you tell me to treat you with any warmth?
You who turned my men to swine in your own house and now   375
you hold me here as well—teeming with treachery
you lure me to your room to mount your bed,
so once I lie there naked
you'll unman me, strip away my courage!
Mount your bed? Not for all the world. Not   380

until you consent to swear, goddess, a binding oath
you'll never plot some new intrigue to harm me!'
                                                          Straightaway
she began to swear the oath that I required—never,
she'd never do me harm—and when she'd finished,
then, at last, I mounted Circe's gorgeous bed . . .   385

    At the same time her handmaids bustled through the halls,
four in all who perform the goddess' household tasks:
nymphs, daughters born of the springs and groves
and the sacred rivers running down to open sea.
One draped the chairs with fine crimson covers   390
over the seats she'd spread with linen cloths below.
A second drew up silver tables before the chairs
and laid out golden trays to hold the bread.
A third mulled heady, heart-warming wine
in a silver bowl and set out golden cups.   395
A fourth brought water and lit a blazing fire
beneath a massive cauldron. The water heated soon,
and once it reached the boil in the glowing bronze
she eased me into a tub and bathed me from the cauldron,
mixing the hot and cold to suit my taste, showering   400
head and shoulders down until she'd washed away
the spirit-numbing exhaustion from my body.
The bathing finished, rubbing me sleek with oil,
throwing warm fleece and a shirt around my shoulders,
she led me in to sit on a silver-studded chair,   405
ornately carved, with a stool to rest my feet.
A maid brought water soon in a graceful golden pitcher
and over a silver basin tipped it out
so I might rinse my hands,
then pulled a gleaming table to my side.   410
A staid housekeeper brought on bread to serve me,
appetizers aplenty too, lavish with her bounty.
She pressed me to eat. I had no taste for food.
I just sat there, mind wandering, far away . . .
lost in grim forebodings.
                              As soon as Circe saw me,   415
huddled, not touching my food, immersed in sorrow,
she sidled near with a coaxing, winged word:
'Odysseus, why just sit there, struck dumb,
eating your heart out, not touching food or drink?
Suspect me of still more treachery? Nothing to fear.   420
Haven't I just sworn my solemn, binding oath?'

    So she asked, but I protested, 'Circe—
how could any man in his right mind endure
the taste of food and drink before he'd freed
his comrades-in-arms and looked them in the eyes?   425
If you, you really want me to eat and drink,
set them free, all my beloved comrades—
let me feast my eyes.'

So I demanded.
Circe strode on through the halls and out,
her wand held high in hand and, flinging open the pens,   430
drove forth my men, who looked like full-grown swine.
Facing her, there they stood as she went along the ranks,
anointing them one by one with some new magic oil—
and look, the bristles grown by the first wicked drug
that Circe gave them slipped away from their limbs   435
and they turned men again: younger than ever,
taller by far, more handsome to the eye, and yes,
they knew me at once and each man grasped my hands
and a painful longing for tears overcame us all,
a terrible sobbing echoed through the house . . .   440
The goddess herself was moved and, standing by me,
warmly urged me on—a lustrous goddess now:
'Royal son of Laertes, Odysseus, tried and true,
go at once to your ship at the water's edge,
haul her straight up on the shore first   445
and stow your cargo and running gear in caves,
then back you come and bring your trusty crew.'

     Her urging won my stubborn spirit over.
Down I went to the swift ship at the water's edge,
and there on the decks I found my loyal crew   450
consumed with grief and weeping live warm tears.
But now, as calves in stalls when cows come home,
droves of them herded back from field to farmyard
once they've grazed their fill—as all their young calves
come frisking out to meet them, bucking out of their pens,   455
lowing nonstop, jostling, rushing round their mothers—
so my shipmates there at the sight of my return
came pressing round me now, streaming tears,
so deeply moved in their hearts they felt as if
they'd made it back to their own land, their city,   460
Ithaca's rocky soil where they were bred and reared.
And through their tears their words went winging home:
'You're back again, my king! How thrilled we are—
as if we'd reached our country, Ithaca, at last!
But come, tell us about the fate our comrades met.'   465
Still I replied with a timely word of comfort:
'Let's haul our ship straight up on the shore first
and stow our cargo and running gear in caves.
Then hurry, all of you, come along with me
to see our friends in the magic halls of Circe,   470
eating and drinking—the feast flows on forever.'

     So I said and they jumped to do my bidding.
Only Eurylochus tried to hold my shipmates back,
his mutinous outburst aimed at one and all:
'Poor fools, where are we running now?   475
Why are we tempting fate?—
why stumble blindly down to Circe's halls?

She'll turn us all into pigs or wolves or lions
made to guard that palace of hers—by force, I tell you—
just as the Cyclops trapped our comrades in his lair   480
with hotheaded Odysseus right beside them all—
thanks to this man's rashness they died too!'

So he declared and I had half a mind
to draw the sharp sword from beside my hip
and slice his head off, tumbling down in the dust,   485
close kin[4] that he was. But comrades checked me,
each man trying to calm me, left and right:
'Captain, we'll leave him here if you command,
just where he is, to sit and guard the ship.
Lead us on to the magic halls of Circe.'
                                With that,   490
up from the ship and shore they headed inland.
Nor did Eurylochus malinger by the hull;
he straggled behind the rest,
dreading the sharp blast of my rebuke.
                                All the while
Circe had bathed my other comrades in her palace,   495
caring and kindly, rubbed them sleek with oil
and decked them out in fleecy cloaks and shirts.
We found them all together, feasting in her halls.
Once we had recognized each other, gazing face-to-face,
we all broke down and wept—and the house resounded now   500
and Circe the lustrous one came toward me, pleading,
'Royal son of Laertes, Odysseus, man of action,
no more tears now, calm these tides of sorrow.
Well I know what pains you bore on the swarming sea,
what punishment you endured from hostile men on land.   505
But come now, eat your food and drink your wine
till the same courage fills your chests, now as then,
when you first set sail from native land, from rocky Ithaca!
Now you are burnt-out husks, your spirits haggard, sere,
always brooding over your wanderings long and hard,   510
your hearts never lifting with any joy—
you've suffered far too much.'
                                So she enticed
and won our battle-hardened spirits over.
And there we sat at ease,
day in, day out, till a year had run its course,   515
feasting on sides of meat and drafts of heady wine . . .
But then, when the year was through and the seasons wheeled by
and the months waned and the long days came round again,
my loyal comrades took me aside and prodded,
'Captain, this is madness!   520
High time you thought of your own home at last,

---

4. The Greek word suggests a relation by marriage. This is the only mention in the poem of such a tie
between Odysseus and Eurylochus, who opposes Odysseus here and in the episode of the Sun's cattle in
book XII.

if it really is your fate to make it back alive
and reach your well-built house and native land.'

   Their urging brought my stubborn spirit round.
So all that day till the sun went down we sat   525
and feasted on sides of meat and heady wine.
Then when the sun had set and night came on
the men lay down to sleep in the shadowed halls
but I went up to that luxurious bed of Circe's,
hugged her by the knees   530
and the goddess heard my winging supplication:
'Circe, now make good a promise you gave me once—
it's time to help me home. My heart longs to be home,
my comrades' hearts as well. They wear me down,
pleading with me whenever you're away.'
                     So I pressed   535
and the lustrous goddess answered me in turn:
'Royal son of Laertes, Odysseus, old campaigner,
stay on no more in my house against your will.
But first another journey calls. You must travel down
to the House of Death and the awesome one, Persephone,   540
there to consult the ghost of Tiresias,[5] seer of Thebes,
the great blind prophet whose mind remains unshaken.
Even in death—Persephone has given him wisdom,
everlasting vision to him and him alone . . .
the rest of the dead are empty, flitting shades.'   545

   So she said and crushed the heart inside me.
I knelt in her bed and wept. I'd no desire
to go on living and see the rising light of day.
But once I'd had my fill of tears and writhing there,
at last I found the words to venture, 'Circe, Circe,   550
who can pilot us on that journey? Who has ever
reached the House of Death in a black ship?'

The lustrous goddess answered, never pausing,
'Royal son of Laertes, Odysseus, born for exploits,
let no lack of a pilot at the helm concern you, no,   555
just step your mast and spread your white sail wide—
sit back and the North Wind will speed you on your way.
But once your vessel has cut across the Ocean River
you will raise a desolate coast and Persephone's Grove,
her tall black poplars, willows whose fruit dies young.   560
Beach your vessel hard by the Ocean's churning shore
and make your own way down to the moldering House of Death.
And there into Acheron, the Flood of Grief, two rivers flow,
the torrent River of Fire, the wailing River of Tears
that branches off from Styx, the Stream of Hate,   565
and a stark crag looms
where the two rivers thunder down and meet.

5. A blind prophet who figures prominently in the legends of Thebes (he is a character in Sophocles' *Oedipus the King* and *Antigone*). Persephone was queen of the dead.

Once there, go forward, hero. Do as I say now.
Dig a trench of about a forearm's depth and length
and around it pour libations out to all the dead—   570
first with milk and honey, and then with mellow wine,
then water third and last, and sprinkle glistening barley
over it all, and vow again and again to all the dead,
to the drifting, listless spirits of their ghosts,
that once you return to Ithaca you will slaughter   575
a barren heifer in your halls, the best you have,
and load a pyre with treasures—and to Tiresias,
alone, apart, you will offer a sleek black ram,
the pride of all your herds. And once your prayers
have invoked the nations of the dead in their dim glory,   580
slaughter a ram and a black ewe, turning both their heads
toward Erebus,[6] but turn your head away, looking toward
the Ocean River. Suddenly then the countless shades
of the dead and gone will surge around you there.
But order your men at once to flay the sheep   585
that lie before you, killed by your ruthless blade,
and burn them both, and then say prayers to the gods,
to the almighty god of death and dread Persephone.
But you—draw your sharp sword from beside your hip,
sit down on alert there, and never let the ghosts   590
of the shambling, shiftless dead come near that blood
till you have questioned Tiresias yourself. Soon, soon
the great seer will appear before you, captain of armies:
he will tell you the way to go, the stages of your voyage,
how you can cross the swarming sea and reach home at last.'   595

     And with those words Dawn rose on her golden throne
and Circe dressed me quickly in sea-cloak and shirt
while the queen slipped on a loose, glistening robe,
filmy, a joy to the eye, and round her waist
she ran a brocaded golden belt   600
and over her head a scarf to shield her brow.
And I strode on through the halls to stir my men,
hovering over each with a winning word: 'Up now!
No more lazing away in sleep, we must set sail—
Queen Circe has shown the way.'
                                       I brought them round,   605
my hardy friends-in-arms, but not even from there
could I get them safely off without a loss . . .
There was a man, Elpenor, the youngest in our ranks,
none too brave in battle, none too sound in mind.
He'd strayed from his mates in Circe's magic halls   610
and keen for the cool night air,
sodden with wine he'd bedded down on her roofs.[7]
But roused by the shouts and tread of marching men,
he leapt up with a start at dawn but still so dazed

6. Here the innermost and darkest region of the land of the dead.   7. The flat roof was the coolest place
to sleep.

he forgot to climb back down again by the long ladder—   615
headfirst from the roof he plunged, his neck snapped
from the backbone, his soul flew down to Death.

    Once on our way, I gave the men their orders:
'You think we are headed home, our own dear land?
Well, Circe sets us a rather different course . . .   620
down to the House of Death and the awesome one, Persephone,
there to consult the ghost of Tiresias, seer of Thebes.'

    So I said, and it broke my shipmates' hearts.
They sank down on the ground, moaning, tore their hair.
But it gained us nothing—what good can come of grief?   625

    Back to the swift ship at the water's edge we went,
our spirits deep in anguish, faces wet with tears.
But Circe got to the dark hull before us,
tethered a ram and black ewe close by—
slipping past unseen. Who can glimpse a god   630
who wants to be invisible gliding here and there?"

BOOK XI

[The Kingdom of the Dead]

"Now down we came to the ship at the water's edge,
we hauled and launched her into the sunlit breakers first,
stepped the mast in the black craft and set our sail
and loaded the sheep aboard, the ram and ewe,
then we ourselves embarked, streaming tears,   5
our hearts weighed down with anguish . . .
But Circe the awesome nymph with lovely braids
who speaks with human voice, sent us a hardy shipmate,
yes, a fresh following wind ruffling up in our wake,
bellying out our sail to drive our blue prow on as we,   10
securing the running gear from stem to stern, sat back
while the wind and helmsman kept her true on course.
The sail stretched taut as she cut the sea all day
and the sun sank and the roads of the world grew dark.

    And she made the outer limits, the Ocean River's bounds   15
where Cimmerian people have their homes—their realm and city
shrouded in mist and cloud.[8] The eye of the Sun can never
flash his rays through the dark and bring them light,
not when he climbs the starry skies or when he wheels
back down from the heights to touch the earth once more—   20
an endless, deadly night overhangs those wretched men.
There, gaining that point, we beached our craft
and herding out the sheep, we picked our way
by the Ocean's banks until we gained the place

---

8. Although Homer usually places the land of the dead below the earth, here it is across a great expanse of sea—apparently in the far west (some think north), on the shore of Ocean, the great river that encircles the earth. Homer's Cimmerians are probably a mythical people.

that Circe made our goal.
                  Here at the spot   25
Perimedes and Eurylochus held the victims fast,
and I, drawing my sharp sword from beside my hip,
dug a trench of about a forearm's depth and length
and around it poured libations out to all the dead,
first with milk and honey, and then with mellow wine,   30
then water third and last, and sprinkled glistening barley
over it all, and time and again I vowed to all the dead,
to the drifting, listless spirits of their ghosts,
that once I returned to Ithaca I would slaughter
a barren heifer in my halls, the best I had,   35
and load a pyre with treasures—and to Tiresias,
alone, apart, I would offer a sleek black ram,
the pride of all my herds. And once my vows
and prayers had invoked the nations of the dead,
I took the victims, over the trench I cut their throats   40
and the dark blood flowed in—and up out of Erebus they came,
flocking toward me now, the ghosts of the dead and gone . . .
Brides and unwed youths and old men who had suffered much
and girls with their tender hearts freshly scarred by sorrow
and great armies of battle dead, stabbed by bronze spears,   45
men of war still wrapped in bloody armor—thousands
swarming around the trench from every side—
unearthly cries—blanching terror gripped me!
I ordered the men at once to flay the sheep
that lay before us, killed by my ruthless blade,   50
and burn them both, and then say prayers to the gods,
to the almighty god of death and dread Persephone.
But I, the sharp sword drawn from beside my hip,
sat down on alert there and never let the ghosts
of the shambling, shiftless dead come near that blood   55
till I had questioned Tiresias myself.
                       But first
the ghost of Elpenor, my companion, came toward me.
He'd not been buried under the wide ways of earth,
not yet, we'd left his body in Circe's house,
unwept, unburied—this other labor pressed us.   60
But I wept to see him now, pity touched my heart
and I called out a winged word to him there: 'Elpenor,
how did you travel down to the world of darkness?
Faster on foot, I see, than I in my black ship.'

My comrade groaned as he offered me an answer: 65
'Royal son of Laertes, Odysseus, old campaigner,
the doom of an angry god, and god knows how much wine—
they were my ruin, captain . . . I'd bedded down
on the roof of Circe's house but never thought
to climb back down again by the long ladder—   70
headfirst from the roof I plunged, my neck snapped
from the backbone, my soul flew down to Death. Now,
I beg you by those you left behind, so far from here,

your wife, your father who bred and reared you as a boy,
and Telemachus, left at home in your halls, your only son.   75
Well I know when you leave this lodging of the dead
that you and your ship will put ashore again
at the island of Aeaea—then and there,
my lord, remember me, I beg you! Don't sail off
and desert me, left behind unwept, unburied, don't,   80
or my curse may draw god's fury on your head.
No, burn me in full armor, all my harness,
heap my mound by the churning gray surf—
a man whose luck ran out—
so even men to come will learn my story.   85
Perform my rites, and plant on my tomb that oar
I swung with mates when I rowed among the living.'

　　'All this, my unlucky friend,' I reassured him,
'I will do for you. I won't forget a thing.'
　　　　　　　　　　　　So we sat
and faced each other, trading our bleak parting words,   90
I on my side, holding my sword above the blood,
he across from me there, my comrade's phantom
dragging out his story.
　　　　　　　　　But look, the ghost
of my mother came! My mother, dead and gone now . . .
Anticlcia—daughter of that great heart Autolycus—   95
whom I had left alive when I sailed for sacred Troy.
I broke into tears to see her here, but filled with pity,
even throbbing with grief, I would not let her ghost
approach the blood till I had questioned Tiresias myself.

　　At last he came. The shade of the famous Theban prophet,   100
holding a golden scepter, knew me at once and hailed me:
'Royal son of Laertes, Odysseus, master of exploits,
man of pain, what now, what brings you here,
forsaking the light of day
to see this joyless kingdom of the dead?   105
Stand back from the trench—put up your sharp sword
so I can drink the blood and tell you all the truth.'

　　Moving back, I thrust my silver-studded sword
deep in its sheath, and once he had drunk the dark blood
the words came ringing from the prophet in his power:[9]   110
'A sweet smooth journey home, renowned Odysseus,
that is what you seek
but a god will make it hard for you—I know—
you will never escape the one who shakes the earth,
quaking with anger at you still, still enraged   115
because you blinded the Cyclops, his dear son.
Even so, you and your crew may still reach home,
suffering all the way, if you only have the power

9. Tiresias here predicts the future of Odysseus. Like many Greek prophecies, this one contains alternatives: leave the cattle of the Sun alone or harm them.

to curb their wild desire and curb your own, what's more,
from the day your good trim vessel first puts in   120
at Thrinacia Island, flees the cruel blue sea.
There you will find them grazing,
herds and fat flocks, the cattle of Helios,
god of the sun who sees all, hears all things.
Leave the beasts unharmed, your mind set on home,   125
and you all may still reach Ithaca—bent with hardship,
true—but harm them in any way, and I can see it now:
your ship destroyed, your men destroyed as well.
And even if *you* escape, you'll come home late
and come a broken man—all shipmates lost,   130
alone in a stranger's ship—
and you will find a world of pain at home,
crude, arrogant men devouring all your goods,
courting your noble wife, offering gifts to win her.
No doubt you will pay them back in blood when you come home!   135
But once you have killed those suitors in your halls—
by stealth or in open fight with slashing bronze—
go forth once more, you must . . .
carry your well-planed oar until you come
to a race of people who know nothing of the sea,   140
whose food is never seasoned with salt, strangers all
to ships with their crimson prows and long slim oars,
wings that make ships fly. And here is your sign—
unmistakable, clear, so clear you cannot miss it:
When another traveler falls in with you and calls   145
that weight across your shoulder a fan to winnow grain,[1]
then plant your bladed, balanced oar in the earth
and sacrifice fine beasts to the lord god of the sea,
Poseidon—a ram, a bull and a ramping wild boar—
then journey home and render noble offerings up   150
to the deathless gods who rule the vaulting skies,
to all the gods in order.
And at last your own death will steal upon you . . .
a gentle, painless death, far from the sea it comes
to take you down, borne down with the years in ripe old age   155
with all your people there in blessed peace around you.
All that I have told you will come true.'
                                        'Oh Tiresias,'
I replied as the prophet finished, 'surely the gods
have spun this out as fate, the gods themselves.
But tell me one thing more, and tell me clearly.   160
I see the ghost of my long-lost mother here before me.
Dead, crouching close to the blood in silence,
she cannot bear to look me in the eyes—
her own son—or speak a word to me. How,
lord, can I make her know me for the man I am?'   165

---

1. A pole with a broad blade at the end, used to scoop up ears of wheat and toss them in the air so that the wind can separate the lighter chaff from the heavy kernels. People who mistake an oar for a winnowing fan have never seen the sea, and evidently Odysseus will appease the sea god Poseidon by spreading his cult to those who do not know him.

'One rule there is,' the famous seer explained,
'and simple for me to say and you to learn.
Any one of the ghosts you let approach the blood
will speak the truth to you. Anyone you refuse
will turn and fade away.'
               And with those words,   170
now that his prophecies had closed, the awesome shade
of lord Tiresias strode back to the House of Death.
But I kept watch there, steadfast till my mother
approached and drank the dark, clouding blood.
She knew me at once and wailed out in grief   175
and her words came winging toward me, flying home:
'Oh my son—what brings you down to the world
of death and darkness? You are still alive!
It's hard for the living to catch a glimpse of this . . .
Great rivers flow between us, terrible waters,   180
the Ocean first of all—no one could ever ford
that stream on foot, only aboard some sturdy craft.
Have you just come from Troy, wandering long years
with your men and ship? Not yet returned to Ithaca?
You've still not seen your wife inside your halls?'
                                  'Mother,'   185
I replied, 'I had to venture down to the House of Death,
to consult the shade of Tiresias, seer of Thebes.
Never yet have I neared Achaea, never once
set foot on native ground,
always wandering—endless hardship from that day   190
I first set sail with King Agamemnon bound for Troy,
the stallion-land, to fight the Trojans there.
But tell me about yourself and spare me nothing.
What form of death overcame you, what laid you low,
some long slow illness? Or did Artemis showering arrows   195
come with her painless shafts and bring you down?
Tell me of father, tell of the son I left behind:
do my royal rights still lie in their safekeeping?
Or does some stranger hold the throne by now
because men think that I'll come home no more?   200
Please, tell me about my wife, her turn of mind,
her thoughts . . . still standing fast beside our son,
still guarding our great estates, secure as ever now?
Or has she wed some other countryman at last,
the finest prince among them?'
                          'Surely, surely,'   205
my noble mother answered quickly, 'she's still waiting
there in your halls, poor woman, suffering so,
her life an endless hardship like your own . . .
wasting away the nights, weeping away the days.
No one has taken over your royal rights, not yet.   210
Telemachus still holds your great estates in peace,
he attends the public banquets shared with all,
the feasts a man of justice should enjoy,
for every lord invites him. As for your father,

he keeps to his own farm—he never goes to town— 215
with no bed for him there, no blankets, glossy throws;
all winter long he sleeps in the lodge with servants,
in the ashes by the fire, his body wrapped in rags.
But when summer comes and the bumper crops of harvest,
any spot on the rising ground of his vineyard rows 220
he makes his bed, heaped high with fallen leaves,
and there he lies in anguish . . .
with his old age bearing hard upon him, too,
and his grief grows as he longs for your return.
And I with the same grief I died and met my fate. 225
No sharp-eyed Huntress[2] showering arrows through the halls
approached and brought me down with painless shafts,
nor did some hateful illness strike me, that so often
devastates the body, drains our limbs of power.
No, it was my longing for *you*, my shining Odysseus— 230
you and your quickness, you and your gentle ways—
that tore away my life that had been sweet.'

    And I, my mind in turmoil, how I longed
to embrace my mother's spirit, dead as she was!
Three times I rushed toward her, desperate to hold her, 235
three times she fluttered through my fingers, sifting away
like a shadow, dissolving like a dream, and each time
the grief cut to the heart, sharper, yes, and I,
I cried out to her, words winging into the darkness:
'Mother—why not wait for me? How I long to hold you!— 240
so even here, in the House of Death, we can fling
our loving arms around each other, take some joy
in the tears that numb the heart. Or is this just
some wraith that great Persephone sends my way
to make me ache with sorrow all the more?' 245

    My noble mother answered me at once:
'My son, my son, the unluckiest man alive!
This is no deception sent by Queen Persephone,
this is just the way of mortals when we die.
Sinews no longer bind the flesh and bones together— 250
the fire in all its fury burns the body down to ashes
once life slips from the white bones, and the spirit,
rustling, flitters away . . . flown like a dream.
But you must long for the daylight. Go, quickly.
Remember all these things 255
so one day you can tell them to your wife.'

    And so we both confided, trading parting words,
and there slowly came a grand array of women,
all sent before me now by august Persephone,
and all were wives and daughters once of princes.[3] 260

---

2. Artemis. 3. The famous and beautiful legendary women who follow helped establish some of the
most important lineages in Greek legend through the sons they bore.

They swarmed in a flock around the dark blood
while I searched for a way to question each alone,
and the more I thought, the more this seemed the best:
Drawing forth the long sharp sword from beside my hip,
I would not let them drink the dark blood, all in a rush,   265
and so they waited, coming forward one after another.
Each declared her lineage, and I explored them all.

    And the first I saw there? Tyro, born of kings,
who said her father was that great lord Salmoneus,
said that she was the wife of Cretheus, Aeolus' son.   270
And once she fell in love with the river god, Enipeus,
far the clearest river flowing across the earth,
and so she'd haunt Enipeus' glinting streams,
till taking his shape one day
the god who girds the earth and makes it tremble   275
bedded her where the swirling river rushes out to sea,
and a surging wave reared up, high as a mountain, dark,
arching over to hide the god and mortal girl together.
Loosing her virgin belt, he lapped her round in sleep
and when the god had consummated his work of love   280
he took her by the hand and hailed her warmly:
'Rejoice in our love, my lady! And when this year
has run its course you will give birth to glorious children—
bedding down with the gods is never barren, futile—
and you must tend them, breed and rear them well.   285
Now home you go, and restrain yourself, I say,
never breathe your lover's name but know—
I am Poseidon, god who rocks the earth!'

    With that he dove back in the heaving waves
and she conceived for the god and bore him Pelias, Neleus,[4]   290
and both grew up to be stalwart aides of Zeus almighty,
both men alike. Pelias lived on the plains of Iolcos,
rich in sheepflocks, Neleus lived in sandy Pylos.
And the noble queen bore sons to Cretheus too:
Aeson[5] Pheres and Amythaon, exultant charioteer.   295

    And after Tyro I saw Asopus'[6] daughter Antiope,
proud she'd spent a night in the arms of Zeus himself
and borne the god twin sons, Amphion and Zethus,
the first to build the footings of seven-gated Thebes,
her bastions too, for lacking ramparts none could live   300
in a place so vast, so open—strong as both men were.

    And I saw Alcmena next, Amphitryon's wife,
who slept in the clasp of Zeus and merged in love
and brought forth Heracles, rugged will and lion heart.
And I saw Megara too, magnanimous Creon's daughter   305
wed to the stalwart Heracles, the hero never daunted.

---

4. Father of Nestor of Pylos (book III). Pelias was Jason's uncle, who sent him on the quest for the Golden
Fleece.   5. Father of Jason the Argonaut.   6. A river in Boeotia, the region in which Thebes is located.

And I saw the mother of Oedipus, beautiful Epicaste.[7]
What a monstrous thing she did, in all innocence—
she married her own son . . .
who'd killed his father, then he married *her*!   310
But the gods soon made it known to all mankind.
So he in growing pain ruled on in beloved Thebes,
lording Cadmus' people—thanks to the gods' brutal plan—
while she went down to Death who guards the massive gates.
Lashing a noose to a steep rafter, there she hanged aloft,   315
strangling in all her anguish, leaving her son to bear
the world of horror a mother's Furies bring to life.

    And I saw magnificent Chloris, the one whom Neleus
wooed and won with a hoard of splendid gifts,
so dazzled by her beauty years ago . . .   320
the youngest daughter of Iasus' son Amphion,
the great Minyan king who ruled Orchomenos[8] once.
She was his queen in Pylos, she bore him shining sons,
Nestor and Chromius, Periclymenus too, good prince.
And after her sons she bore a daughter, majestic Pero,   325
the marvel of her time, courted by all the young lords
round about. But Neleus would not give her to any suitor,
none but the man who might drive home the herds
that powerful Iphiclus had stolen. Lurching,
broad in the brow, those longhorned beasts,   330
and no small task to round them up from Phylace.
Only the valiant seer Melampus volunteered—
he would drive them home—
but a god's iron sentence bound him fast:
barbarous herdsmen dragged him off in chains.   335
Yet when the months and days had run their course
and the year wheeled round and the seasons came again,
then mighty Iphiclus loosed the prophet's shackles,
once he had told him all the gods' decrees.
And so the will of Zeus was done at last.   340

    And I saw Leda next, Tyndareus' wife,
who'd borne the king two sons, intrepid twins,[9]
Castor, breaker of horses, and the hardy boxer Polydeuces,
both buried now in the life-giving earth though still alive.
Even under the earth Zeus grants them that distinction: 345
one day alive, the next day dead, each twin by turns,
they both hold honors equal to the gods'.

    And I saw Iphimedeia next, Aloeus' wife,
who claimed she lay in the Sea-lord's loving waves
and gave the god two sons, but they did not live long,   350
Otus staunch as a god and far-famed Ephialtes.

---

7. More often known as Jocasta.   8. A very ancient city in Boeotia, northwest of Thebes. This is not the same Amphion who built the walls of Thebes (line 298).   9. She also bore him Clytemnestra, wife of Agamemnon, and she bore Helen, wife of Menelaus, to Zeus. Tyndareus was king of Sparta.

They were the tallest men the fertile earth has borne,
the handsomest too, by far, aside from renowned Orion.
Nine yards across they measured, even at nine years old,
nine fathoms tall they towered. They even threatened   355
the deathless gods they'd storm Olympus' heights
with the pounding rush and grinding shock of battle.
They were wild to pile Ossa upon Olympus, then on Ossa
Pelion dense with timber—their toeholds up the heavens.[1]
And they'd have won the day if they had reached peak strength   360
but Apollo the son of Zeus, whom sleek-haired Leto bore,
laid both giants low before their beards had sprouted,
covering cheek and chin with a fresh crop of down.

    Phaedra and Procris too I saw, and lovely Ariadne,
daughter of Minos,[2] that harsh king. One day Theseus tried   365
to spirit her off from Crete to Athens' sacred heights
but he got no joy from her. Artemis killed her first
on wave-washed Dia's shores, accused by Dionysus.[3]

    And I saw Clymene, Maera and loathsome Eriphyle[4]—   370
bribed with a golden necklace
to lure her lawful husband to his death . . .
But the whole cortege I could never tally, never name,
not all the daughters and wives of great men I saw there.
Long before that, the godsent night would ebb away.
But the time has come for sleep, either with friends   375
aboard your swift ship or here in your own house.
My passage home will rest with the gods and you."

    Odysseus paused . . . They all fell silent, hushed,
his story holding them spellbound down the shadowed halls
till the white-armed queen Arete suddenly burst out,   380
"Phaeacians! How does this man impress you now,
his looks, his build, the balanced mind inside him?
The stranger is my guest
but each of you princes shares the honor here.
So let's not be too hasty to send him on his way,   385
and don't scrimp on his gifts. His need is great,
great as the riches piled up in your houses,
thanks to the gods' good will."
                       Following her,
the old revered Echeneus added his support,
the eldest lord on the island of Phaeacia: 390
"Friends, the words of our considerate queen—

---

1. Two mountains in Thessaly, near Olympus.   2. King of Crete and father of Phaedra and Ariadne,
who helped Theseus of Athens kill the Minotaur and left Crete with him. Phaedra, who married Theseus,
fell in love with her stepson Hippolytus; when he rejected her advances, she killed herself and contrived his
death. Procris was the unfaithful wife of Cephalus, king of Athens.   3. God of the vine. His motive is
unknown. In the usual later version of this story, Dionysus carried Ariadne off to be his bride after Theseus
abandoned her on the island of Dia (or Naxos).   4. Bribed by Polynices, son of Oedipus, she persuaded
her husband, Amphiaraus, to take part in the attack on Thebes in which he was killed. There were several
legendary women named Clymene; perhaps Homer is referring to the mother of Iphiclus (line 329). Maera
(or Maira) was a nymph of Artemis who broke her vow of chastity and was killed by the goddess.

they never miss the mark or fail our expectations.
So do as Arete says, though on Alcinous here
depend all words and action."
                            "And so it will be"—
Alcinous stepped in grandly—"sure as I am alive   395
and rule our island men who love their oars!
Our guest, much as he longs for passage home,
must stay and wait it out here till tomorrow,
till I can collect his whole array of parting gifts.
His send-off rests with every noble here   400
but with me most of all:
I hold the reins of power in the realm."

    Odysseus, deft and tactful, echoed back,
"Alcinous, majesty, shining among your island people,
if you would urge me now to stay here one whole year   405
then speed me home weighed down with lordly gifts,
I'd gladly have it so. Better by far, that way.
The fuller my arms on landing there at home,
the more respected, well received I'd be
by all who saw me sailing back to Ithaca."   410

    "Ah Odysseus," Alcinous replied, "one look at you
and we know that you are no one who would cheat us—
no fraud, such as the dark soil breeds and spreads
across the face of the earth these days. Crowds of vagabonds
frame their lies so tightly none can test them. But you,   415
what grace you give your words, and what good sense within!
You have told your story with all a singer's skill,
the miseries you endured, your great Achaeans too.
But come now, tell me truly: your godlike comrades—
did you see any heroes down in the House of Death,   420
any who sailed with you and met their doom at Troy?
The night's still young, I'd say the night is endless.
For us in the palace now, it's hardly time for sleep.
Keep telling us your adventures—they are wonderful.
I could hold out here till Dawn's first light   425
if only you could bear, here in our halls,
to tell the tale of all the pains you suffered."

    So the man of countless exploits carried on:
"Alcinous, majesty, shining among your island people,
there is a time for many words, a time for sleep as well.   430
But if you insist on hearing more, I'd never stint
on telling my own tale and those more painful still,
the griefs of my comrades, dead in the war's wake,
who escaped the battle-cries of Trojan armies
only to die in blood at journey's end—   435
thanks to a vicious woman's will.
                            Now then,
no sooner had Queen Persephone driven off
the ghosts of lovely women, scattering left and right,

than forward marched the shade of Atreus' son Agamemnon,
fraught with grief and flanked by all his comrades,　　　　　440
troops of his men-at-arms who died beside him,
who met their fate in lord Aegisthus' halls.
He knew me at once, as soon as he drank the blood,
and wailed out, shrilly; tears sprang to his eyes,
he thrust his arms toward me, keen to embrace me there—　　445
no use—the great force was gone, the strength lost forever,
now, that filled his rippling limbs in the old days.
I wept at the sight, my heart went out to the man,
my words too, in a winging flight of pity:
'Famous Atrides, lord of men Agamemnon!　　　　　450
What fatal stroke of destiny brought you down?
Wrecked in the ships when lord Poseidon roused
some punishing blast of stormwinds, gust on gust?
Or did ranks of enemies mow you down on land
as you tried to raid and cut off herds and flocks　　　　455
or fought to win their city, take their women?'

　　The field marshal's ghost replied at once:
'Royal son of Laertes, Odysseus, mastermind of war,
I was not wrecked in the ships when lord Poseidon
roused some punishing blast of stormwinds gust on gust,　　　460
nor did ranks of enemies mow me down on land—
Aegisthus hatched my doom and my destruction,
he killed me, he with my own accursed wife . . .
he invited me to his palace, sat me down to feast
then cut me down as a man cuts down some ox at the trough!　　465
So I died—a wretched, ignominious death—and round me
all my comrades killed, no mercy, one after another,
just like white-tusked boars
butchered in some rich lord of power's halls
for a wedding, banquet or groaning public feast.　　　　470
You in your day have witnessed hundreds slaughtered,
killed in single combat or killed in pitched battle, true,
but if you'd laid eyes on this it would have wrenched your heart—
how we sprawled by the mixing-bowl and loaded tables there,
throughout the palace, the whole floor awash with blood.　　475
But the death-cry of Cassandra, Priam's daughter[5]—
the most pitiful thing I heard! My treacherous queen,
Clytemnestra, killed her over my body, yes, and I,
lifting my fists, beat them down on the ground,
dying, dying, writhing around the sword.　　　　480
But she, that whore, she turned her back on me,
well on my way to Death—she even lacked the heart
to seal my eyes with her hand or close my jaws.[6]
　　　　　　　　　　　　So
there's nothing more deadly, bestial than a woman
set on works like these—what a monstrous thing　　　485
she plotted, slaughtered her own lawful husband!

---

5. Part of Agamemnon's share of the booty at Troy.　　**6.** That is, to give him a proper burial.

Why, I expected, at least, some welcome home
from all my children, all my household slaves
when I came sailing back again . . . But she—
the queen hell-bent on outrage—bathes in shame   490
not only herself but the whole breed of womankind,
even the honest ones to come, forever down the years!'

So he declared and I cried out, 'How terrible!
Zeus from the very start, the thunder king
has hated the race of Atreus with a vengeance—   495
his trustiest weapon women's twisted wiles.
What armies of us died for the sake of Helen . . .
Clytemnestra schemed your death while you were worlds away!'

'True, true,' Agamemnon's ghost kept pressing on,
'so even your own wife—never indulge her too far.   500
Never reveal the whole truth, whatever you may know;
just tell her a part of it, be sure to hide the rest.
Not that you, Odysseus, will be murdered by your wife.
She's much too steady, her feelings run too deep,
Icarius' daughter Penelope, that wise woman.   505
She was a young bride, I well remember . . .
we left her behind when we went off to war,
with an infant boy she nestled at her breast.
That boy must sit and be counted with the men now—
happy man! His beloved father will come sailing home   510
and see his son, and he will embrace his father,
that is only right. But *my* wife—she never
even let me feast my eyes on my own son;
she killed me first, his father!
I tell you this—bear it in mind, you must—   515
when you reach your homeland steer your ship
into port in secret, never out in the open . . .
the time for trusting women's gone forever!

Enough. Come, tell me this, and be precise.
Have you heard news of my son? Where's he living now?   520
Perhaps in Orchomenos, perhaps in sandy Pylos
or off in the Spartan plains with Menelaus?
He's not dead yet, my Prince Orestes, no,
he's somewhere on the earth.'
                    So he probed
but I cut it short: 'Atrides, why ask me that?   525
I know nothing, whether he's dead or alive.
It's wrong to lead you on with idle words.'

So we stood there, trading heartsick stories,
deep in grief, as the tears streamed down our faces.
But now there came the ghosts of Peleus' son Achilles,   530
Patroclus, fearless Antilochus[7]—and Great Ajax too,

---

7. Nestor's son; he was Achilles' closest friend after Patroclus.

the first in stature, first in build and bearing
of all the Argives after Peleus' matchless son.
The ghost of the splendid runner knew me at once
and hailed me with a flight of mournful questions: 535
'Royal son of Laertes, Odysseus, man of tactics,
reckless friend, what next?
What greater feat can that cunning head contrive?
What daring brought you down to the House of Death?—
where the senseless, burnt-out wraiths of mortals make their home.'   540

    The voice of his spirit paused, and I was quick to answer:
'Achilles, son of Peleus, greatest of the Achaeans,
I had to consult Tiresias, driven here by hopes
he would help me journey home to rocky Ithaca.
Never yet have I neared Achaea, never once   545
set foot on native ground . . .
my life is endless trouble.
                  But you, Achilles,
there's not a man in the world more blest than you—
there never has been, never will be one.
Time was, when you were alive, we Argives   550
honored you as a god, and now down here, I see,
you lord it over the dead in all your power.
So grieve no more at dying, great Achilles.'

I reassured the ghost, but he broke out, protesting,
'No winning words about death to *me*, shining Odysseus!   555
By god, I'd rather slave on earth for another man—
some dirt-poor tenant farmer who scrapes to keep alive—
than rule down here over all the breathless dead.
But come, tell me the news about my gallant son.
Did he make his way to the wars,   560
did the boy become a champion—yes or no?
Tell me of noble Peleus, any word you've heard—
still holding pride of place among his Myrmidon hordes,
or do they despise the man in Hellas and in Phthia
because old age has lamed his arms and legs?   565
For I no longer stand in the light of day—
the man I was—comrade-in-arms to help my father
as once I helped our armies, killing the best fighters
Troy could field in the wide world up there . . .
Oh to arrive at father's house—the man I was,   570
for one brief day—I'd make my fury and my hands,
invincible hands, a thing of terror to all those men
who abuse the king with force and wrest away his honor!'

    So he grieved but I tried to lend him heart:
'About noble Peleus I can tell you nothing,   575
but about your own dear son, Neoptolemus,
I can report the whole story, as you wish.
I myself, in my trim ship, I brought him

out of Scyros to join the Argives under arms.[8]
And dug in around Troy, debating battle-tactics,   580
he always spoke up first, and always on the mark—
godlike Nestor and I alone excelled the boy. Yes,
and when our armies fought on the plain of Troy
he'd never hang back with the main force of men—
he'd always charge ahead,   585
giving ground to no one in his fury,
and scores of men he killed in bloody combat.
How could I list them all, name them all, now,
the fighting ranks he leveled, battling for the Argives?
But what a soldier he laid low with a bronze sword: 590
the hero Eurypylus, Telephus' son, and round him
troops of his own Cetean comrades[9] slaughtered,
lured to war by the bribe his mother took.
The only man I saw to put Eurypylus
in the shade was Memnon,[1] son of the Morning.   595
Again, when our champions climbed inside the horse
that Epeus built with labor, and I held full command
to spring our packed ambush open or keep it sealed,
all our lords and captains were wiping off their tears,
knees shaking beneath each man—but not your son.   600
Never once did I see his glowing skin go pale;
he never flicked a tear from his cheeks, no,
he kept on begging me there to let him burst
from the horse, kept gripping his hilted sword,
his heavy bronze-tipped javelin, keen to loose   605
his fighting fury against the Trojans. Then,
once we'd sacked King Priam's craggy city,
laden with his fair share and princely prize
he boarded his own ship, his body all unscarred.
Not a wound from a flying spear or a sharp sword,   610
cut-and-thrust close up—the common marks of war.
Random, raging Ares plays no favorites.'
                                             So I said and
off he went, the ghost of the great runner, Aeacus'[2] grandson
loping with long strides across the fields of asphodel,
triumphant in all I had told him of his son,   615
his gallant, glorious son.

     Now the rest of the ghosts, the dead and gone
came swarming up around me—deep in sorrow there,
each asking about the grief that touched him most.
Only the ghost of Great Ajax, son of Telamon,   620
kept his distance, blazing with anger at me still
for the victory I had won by the ships that time
I pressed my claim for the arms of Prince Achilles.
His queenly mother[3] had set them up as prizes,

8. The Greeks were told by a prophet that Troy would fall only to Achilles' son Neoptolemus, who was living on the island of Scyros.   9. Eurypylus's people (from Asia Minor), who came to the aid of the Trojans.   1. King of the Ethiopians, a Trojan ally; his mother was the goddess Dawn.   2. A son of Zeus.
3. Thetis

Pallas and captive Trojans served as judges.   625
Would to god I'd never won such trophies!
All for them the earth closed over Ajax,
that proud hero Ajax . . .
greatest in build, greatest in works of war
of all the Argives after Peleus' matchless son.   630
I cried out to him now, I tried to win him over:
'Ajax, son of noble Telamon, still determined,
even in death, not once to forget that rage
you train on me for those accursed arms?
The gods set up that prize to plague the Achaeans—   635
so great a tower of strength we lost when you went down!
For *your* death we grieved as we did for Achilles' death—
we grieved incessantly, true, and none's to blame
but Zeus, who hated Achaea's fighting spearmen
so intensely, Zeus sealed your doom.   640
Come closer, king, and listen to my story.
Conquer your rage, your blazing, headstrong pride!'

So I cried out but Ajax answered not a word.
He stalked off toward Erebus, into the dark
to join the other lost, departed dead.   645
Yet now, despite his anger,
he might have spoken to me, or I to him,
but the heart inside me stirred with some desire
to see the ghosts of others dead and gone.

And I saw Minos there, illustrious son of Zeus,   650
firmly enthroned, holding his golden scepter,
judging all the dead . . .
Some on their feet, some seated, all clustering
round the king of justice, pleading for his verdicts
reached in the House of Death with its all-embracing gates. 655

I next caught sight of Orion,[4] that huge hunter,
rounding up on the fields of asphodel those wild beasts
the man in life cut down on the lonely mountain-slopes,
brandishing in his hands the bronze-studded club
that time can never shatter.
                          I saw Tityus too,   660
son of the mighty goddess Earth—sprawling there
on the ground, spread over nine acres—two vultures
hunched on either side of him, digging into his liver,
beaking deep in the blood-sac, and he with his frantic hands
could never beat them off, for he had once dragged off   665
the famous consort of Zeus in all her glory,
Leto, threading her way toward Pytho's ridge,
over the lovely dancing-rings of Panopeus.

And I saw Tantalus[5] too, bearing endless torture.

---

4. In other legends, transformed after death into a constellation.   5. A king in Asia Minor, a confidant
of the gods who ate at their table but abused their hospitality (accounts differ as to how).

He stood erect in a pool as the water lapped his chin— 670
parched, he tried to drink, but he could not reach the surface,
no, time and again the old man stooped, craving a sip,
time and again the water vanished, swallowed down,
laying bare the caked black earth at his feet—
some spirit drank it dry. And over his head 675
leafy trees dangled their fruit from high aloft,
pomegranates and pears, and apples glowing red,
succulent figs and olives swelling sleek and dark,
but as soon as the old man would strain to clutch them fast
a gust would toss them up to the lowering dark clouds. 680

And I saw Sisyphus[6] too, bound to his own torture,
grappling his monstrous boulder with both arms working,
heaving, hands struggling, legs driving, he kept on
thrusting the rock uphill toward the brink, but just
as it teetered, set to topple over—
                                        time and again 685
the immense weight of the thing would wheel it back and
the ruthless boulder would bound and tumble down to the plain again—
so once again he would heave, would struggle to thrust it up,
sweat drenching his body, dust swirling above his head.

And next I caught a glimpse of powerful Heracles— 690
his ghost, I mean: the man himself delights
in the grand feasts of the deathless gods on high,
wed to Hebe,[7] famed for her lithe, alluring ankles,
the daughter of mighty Zeus and Hera shod in gold.
Around him cries of the dead rang out like cries of birds, 695
scattering left and right in horror as on he came like night,
naked bow in his grip, an arrow grooved on the bowstring,
glaring round him fiercely, forever poised to shoot.
A terror too, that sword-belt sweeping across his chest,
a baldric of solid gold emblazoned with awesome work . . . 700
bears and ramping boars and lions with wild, fiery eyes,
and wars, routs and battles, massacres, butchered men.
May the craftsman who forged that masterpiece—
whose skills could conjure up a belt like that—
never forge another! 705
Heracles knew me at once, at first glance,
and hailed me with a winging burst of pity:
'Royal son of Laertes, Odysseus famed for exploits,
luckless man, you too? Braving out a fate as harsh
as the fate I bore, alive in the light of day? 710
Son of Zeus that I was, my torments never ended,
forced to slave for a man not half the man I was:
he saddled me with the worst heartbreaking labors.[8]

---

6. King of Corinth, the archetype of the liar and trickster; we do not know what crime he is being punished for in this passage. 7. Literally, "Youth." Heracles was made immortal after his death, and so he lives among the gods while only his image remains with the dead (the word translated here as "ghost" literally means "likeness"). 8. Because of Hera's enmity, Heracles was forced to obey Eurystheus of Argos, who ordered him to perform his twelve famous labors.

Why, he sent me down here once, to retrieve the hound
that guards the dead[9]—no harder task for me, he thought—
but I dragged the great beast up from the underworld to earth
and Hermes and gleaming-eyed Athena blazed the way!'

715

    With that he turned and back he went to the House of Death
but I held fast in place, hoping that others might still come,
shades of famous heroes, men who died in the old days
and ghosts of an even older age I longed to see,
Theseus and Pirithous,[1] the gods' own radiant sons.
But before I could, the dead came surging round me,
hordes of them, thousands raising unearthly cries,
and blanching terror gripped me—panicked now
that Queen Persephone might send up from Death
some monstrous head, some Gorgon's staring face![2]
I rushed back to my ship, commanded all hands
to take to the decks and cast off cables quickly.
They swung aboard at once, they sat to the oars in ranks
and a strong tide of the Ocean River swept her on downstream,
sped by our rowing first, then by a fresh fair wind."

720

725

730

BOOK XII

[The Cattle of the Sun]

"Now when our ship had left the Ocean River rolling in her wake
and launched out into open sea with its long swells to reach
the island of Aeaea—east where the Dawn forever young
has home and dancing-rings and the Sun his risings[3]—
heading in we beached our craft on the sands,
the crews swung out on the low sloping shore
and there we fell asleep, awaiting Dawn's first light.

5

    As soon as Dawn with her rose-red fingers shone again
I dispatched some men to Circe's halls to bring
the dead Elpenor's body. We cut logs in haste
and out on the island's sharpest jutting headland
held his funeral rites in sorrow, streaming tears.
Once we'd burned the dead man and the dead man's armor,
heaping his grave-mound, hauling a stone that coped it well,
we planted his balanced oar aloft to crown his tomb.

10

15

    And so we saw to his rites, each step in turn.
Nor did our coming back from Death escape Circe—
she hurried toward us, decked in rich regalia,
handmaids following close with trays of bread
and meats galore and glinting ruddy wine.
And the lustrous goddess, standing in our midst,
hailed us warmly: 'Ah my daring, reckless friends!

20

9. Cerberus.   1. After his adventures in Crete, Theseus went with his friend Pirithous to Hades to kidnap Persephone. The venture failed, and the two heroes, imprisoned in Hades, were rescued by Heracles.
2. Looking at the face of a Gorgon, a female snake-headed monster, turned the viewer to stone.   3. This description places Circe's island to the east of Greece, though Odysseus's ship, when it was blown past Cape Malea, was headed west (one more indication that Odyssean geography is highly imaginative).

You who ventured down to the House of Death alive,
doomed to die twice over—others die just once.
Come, take some food and drink some wine,   25
rest here the livelong day
and then, tomorrow at daybreak, you must sail.
But I will set you a course and chart each seamark,
so neither on sea nor land will some new trap
ensnare you in trouble, make you suffer more.'   30

    Her foresight won our fighting spirits over.
So all that day till the sun went down we sat
and feasted on sides of meat and heady wine,
and then when the sun had set and night came on
the men lay down to sleep by the ship's stern-cables.   35
But Circe, taking me by the hand, drew me away
from all my shipmates there and sat me down
and lying beside me probed me for details.
I told her the whole story, start to finish,
then the queenly goddess laid my course: 40
'Your descent to the dead is over, true,
but listen closely to what I tell you now
and god himself will bring it back to mind.
First you will raise the island of the Sirens,
those creatures who spellbind any man alive,   45
whoever comes their way. Whoever draws too close,
off guard, and catches the Sirens' voices in the air—
no sailing home for him, no wife rising to meet him,
no happy children beaming up at their father's face.
The high, thrilling song of the Sirens will transfix him,   50
lolling there in their meadow, round them heaps of corpses
rotting away, rags of skin shriveling on their bones . . .
Race straight past that coast! Soften some beeswax
and stop your shipmates' ears so none can hear,
none of the crew, but if *you* are bent on hearing,   55
have them tie you hand and foot in the swift ship,
erect at the mast-block, lashed by ropes to the mast
so you can hear the Sirens' song to your heart's content.
But if you plead, commanding your men to set you free,
then they must lash you faster, rope on rope.   60

    But once your crew has rowed you past the Sirens
a choice of routes is yours. I cannot advise you
which to take, or lead you through it all—
you must decide for yourself—
but I can tell you the ways of either course.   65
On one side beetling cliffs shoot up, and against them
pound the huge roaring breakers of blue-eyed Amphitrite—
the Clashing Rocks[4] they're called by all the blissful gods.

4. These Wandering Rocks (*Planctae*) may or may not be the Symplegades, the Clashing Rocks (thought
to be located at the entrance to the Black Sea) that came together to crush whatever tried to pass between
them. Homer puts them near Scylla and Charybdis, which later tradition placed in the strait between Italy
and Sicily. Once again the text seems to be creating imaginative geography that fuses landmarks of the east
and west.

Not even birds can escape them, no, not even the doves
that veer and fly ambrosia home to Father Zeus: 70
even of those the sheer Rocks always pick off one
and Father wings one more to keep the number up.
No ship of men has ever approached and slipped past—
always some disaster—big timbers and sailors' corpses
whirled away by the waves and lethal blasts of fire.   75
One ship alone, one deep-sea craft sailed clear,
the *Argo*,[5] sung by the world, when heading home
from Aeetes' shores. And *she* would have crashed
against those giant rocks and sunk at once if Hera,
for love of Jason, had not sped her through.   80

        On the other side loom two enormous crags . . .
One thrusts into the vaulting sky its jagged peak,
hooded round with a dark cloud that never leaves—
no clear bright air can ever bathe its crown,
not even in summer's heat or harvest-time.   85
No man on earth could scale it, mount its crest,
not even with twenty hands and twenty feet for climbing,
the rock's so smooth, like dressed and burnished stone.
And halfway up that cliffside stands a fog-bound cavern
gaping west toward Erebus, realm of death and darkness—   90
past it, great Odysseus, you should steer your ship.
No rugged young archer could hit that yawning cave
with a winged arrow shot from off the decks.
Scylla lurks inside it—the yelping horror,
yelping, no louder than any suckling pup   95
but she's a grisly monster, I assure you.
No one could look on her with any joy,
not even a god who meets her face-to-face . . .
She has twelve legs, all writhing, dangling down
and six long swaying necks, a hideous head on each,   100
each head barbed with a triple row of fangs, thickset,
packed tight—and armed to the hilt with black death!
Holed up in the cavern's bowels from her waist down
she shoots out her heads, out of that terrifying pit,
angling right from her nest, wildly sweeping the reefs   105
for dolphins, dogfish or any bigger quarry she can drag
from the thousands Amphitrite spawns in groaning seas.
No mariners yet can boast they've raced their ship
past Scylla's lair without some mortal blow—
with each of her six heads she snatches up   110
a man from the dark-prowed craft and whisks him off.

        The other crag is lower—you will see, Odysseus—
though both lie side-by-side, an arrow-shot apart.
Atop it a great fig-tree rises, shaggy with leaves,
beneath it awesome Charybdis gulps the dark water down.   115

5. The ship of the Argonauts, who brought the Golden Fleece back to Greece from King Aeetes. This line
suggests that epic poetry about the Argonauts' voyage preceded the *Odyssey* and may have provided the
model for some of Odysseus's wanderings.

Three times a day she vomits it up, three times she gulps it down,
that terror! Don't be there when the whirlpool swallows down—
not even the earthquake god could save you from disaster.
No, hug Scylla's crag—sail on past her—top speed!
Better by far to lose six men and keep your ship   120
than lose your entire crew.'
                              'Yes, yes,
but tell me the truth now, goddess,' I protested.
'Deadly Charybdis—can't I possibly cut and run from *her*
and still fight Scylla off when Scylla strikes my men?'

    'So stubborn!' the lovely goddess countered.   125
'Hell-bent yet again on battle and feats of arms?
Can't you bow to the deathless gods themselves?
Scylla's no mortal, she's an immortal devastation,
terrible, savage, wild, no fighting her, no defense—
just flee the creature, that's the only way.   130
Waste any time, arming for battle beside her rock,
I fear she'll lunge out again with all of her six heads
and seize as many men. No, row for your lives,
invoke Brute Force, I tell you, Scylla's mother—
she spawned her to scourge mankind,   135
she can stop the monster's next attack!

    Then you will make the island of Thrinacia[6] . . .
where herds of the Sungod's cattle graze, and fat sheep
and seven herds of oxen, as many sheepflocks, rich and woolly,
fifty head in each. No breeding swells their number,   140
nor do they ever die. And goddesses herd them on,
nymphs with glinting hair, Phaëthousa, Lampetie,
born to the Sungod Helios by radiant Neaera.
Their queenly mother bred and reared them both
then settled them on the island of Thrinacia—   145
their homeland seas away—
to guard their father's sheep and longhorn cattle.
Leave the beasts unharmed, your mind set on home,
and you all may still reach Ithaca—bent with hardship,
true—but harm them in any way, and I can see it now: 150
your ship destroyed, your men destroyed as well!
And even if *you* escape, you'll come home late,
all shipmates lost, and come a broken man.'

    At those words Dawn rose on her golden throne
and lustrous Circe made her way back up the island.   155
I went straight to my ship, commanding all hands
to take to the decks and cast off cables quickly.
They swung aboard at once, they sat to the oars in ranks
and in rhythm churned the water white with stroke on stroke.
And Circe the nymph with glossy braids, the awesome one   160
who speaks with human voice, sent us a hardy shipmate,

6. Later Greeks identified this island as Sicily.

yes, a fresh following wind ruffling up in our wake,
bellying out our sail to drive our blue prow on as we,
securing the running gear from stem to stern, sat back
while the wind and helmsman kept her true on course.   165
At last, and sore at heart, I told my shipmates,
'Friends . . . it's wrong for only one or two
to know the revelations that lovely Circe
made to me alone. I'll tell you all,
so we can die with our eyes wide open now   170
or escape our fate and certain death together.
First, she warns, we must steer clear of the Sirens,
their enchanting song, their meadow starred with flowers.
I alone was to hear their voices, so she said,
but you must bind me with tight chafing ropes   175
so I cannot move a muscle, bound to the spot,
erect at the mast-block, lashed by ropes to the mast.
And if I plead, commanding you to set me free,
then lash me faster, rope on pressing rope.'

    So I informed my shipmates point by point,   180
all the while our trim ship was speeding toward
the Sirens' island, driven on by the brisk wind.
But then—the wind fell in an instant,
all glazed to a dead calm . . .
a mysterious power hushed the heaving swells.   185
The oarsmen leapt to their feet, struck the sail,
stowed it deep in the hold and sat to the oarlocks,
thrashing with polished oars, frothing the water white.
Now with a sharp sword I sliced an ample wheel of beeswax
down into pieces, kneaded them in my two strong hands   190
and the wax soon grew soft, worked by my strength
and Helios' burning rays, the sun at high noon,
and I stopped the ears of my comrades one by one.
They bound me hand and foot in the tight ship—
erect at the mast-block, lashed by ropes to the mast—   195
and rowed and churned the whitecaps stroke on stroke.
We were just offshore as far as a man's shout can carry,
scudding close, when the Sirens sensed at once a ship
was racing past and burst into their high, thrilling song:
'Come closer, famous Odysseus—Achaea's pride and glory—   200
moor your ship on our coast so you can hear our song!
Never has any sailor passed our shores in his black craft
until he has heard the honeyed voices pouring from our lips,
and once he hears to his heart's content sails on, a wiser man.
We know all the pains that the Greeks and Trojans once endured   205
on the spreading plain of Troy when the gods willed it so—
all that comes to pass on the fertile earth, we know it all!'

    So they sent their ravishing voices out across the air
and the heart inside me throbbed to listen longer.
I signaled the crew with frowns to set me free—   210
they flung themselves at the oars and rowed on harder,

Perimedes and Eurylochus springing up at once
to bind me faster with rope on chafing rope.
But once we'd left the Sirens fading in our wake,
once we could hear their song no more, their urgent call—   215
my steadfast crew was quick to remove the wax I'd used
to seal their ears and loosed the bonds that lashed me.

   We'd scarcely put that island astern when suddenly
I saw smoke and heavy breakers, heard their booming thunder.
The men were terrified—oarblades flew from their grip,   220
clattering down to splash in the vessel's wash.
She lay there, dead in the water . . .
no hands to tug the blades that drove her on.
But I strode down the decks to rouse my crewmen,
halting beside each one with a bracing, winning word: 225
'Friends, we're hardly strangers at meeting danger—
and this danger is no worse than what we faced
when Cyclops penned us up in his vaulted cave
with crushing force! But even from there my courage,
my presence of mind and tactics saved us all,   230
and we will live to remember *this* someday,
I have no doubt. Up now, follow my orders,
all of us work as one! You men at the thwarts—
lay on with your oars and strike the heaving swells,
trusting that Zeus will pull us through these straits alive.   235
You, helmsman, here's your order—burn it in your mind—
the steering-oar of our rolling ship is in your hands.
Keep her clear of that smoke and surging breakers,
head for those crags or she'll catch you off guard,
she'll yaw over there—you'll plunge us all in ruin!'   240

   So I shouted. They snapped to each command.
No mention of Scylla—how to fight that nightmare?—
for fear the men would panic, desert their oars
and huddle down and stow themselves away.
But now I cleared my mind of Circe's orders—   245
cramping my style, urging me not to arm at all.
I donned my heroic armor, seized long spears
in both my hands and marched out on the half-deck,
forward, hoping from there to catch the first glimpse
of Scylla, ghoul of the cliffs, swooping to kill my men.   250
But nowhere could I make her out—and my eyes ached,
scanning that mist-bound rock face top to bottom.

   Now wailing in fear, we rowed on up those straits,
Scylla to starboard, dreaded Charybdis off to port,
her horrible whirlpool gulping the sea-surge down, down   255
but when she spewed it up—like a cauldron over a raging fire—
all her churning depths would seethe and heave—exploding spray
showering down to splatter the peaks of both crags at once!
But when she swallowed the sea-surge down her gaping maw
the whole abyss lay bare and the rocks around her roared,   260

terrible, deafening—
                    bedrock showed down deep, boiling
black with sand—
                    and ashen terror gripped the men.
But now, fearing death, all eyes fixed on Charybdis—
now Scylla snatched six men from our hollow ship,
the toughest, strongest hands I had, and glancing   265
backward over the decks, searching for my crew
I could see their hands and feet already hoisted,
flailing, high, higher, over my head, look—
wailing down at me, comrades riven in agony,
shrieking out my name for one last time!   270
Just as an angler poised on a jutting rock
flings his treacherous bait in the offshore swell,
whips his long rod—hook sheathed in an oxhorn lure—
and whisks up little fish he flips on the beach-break,
writhing, gasping out their lives . . . so now they writhed,   275
gasping as Scylla swung them up her cliff and there
at her cavern's mouth she bolted them down raw—
screaming out, flinging their arms toward me,
lost in that mortal struggle . . .
Of all the pitiful things I've had to witness,   280
suffering, searching out the pathways of the sea,
this wrenched my heart the most.
                              But now, at last,
putting the Rocks, Scylla and dread Charybdis far astern,
we quickly reached the good green island of the Sun
where Helios, lord Hyperion, keeps his fine cattle,   285
broad in the brow, and flocks of purebred sheep.
Still aboard my black ship in the open sea
I could hear the lowing cattle driven home,
the bleating sheep. And I was struck once more
by the words of the blind Theban prophet, Tiresias,   290
and Aeaean Circe too: time and again they told me
to shun this island of the Sun, the joy of man.
So I warned my shipmates gravely, sick at heart,
'Listen to me, my comrades, brothers in hardship,
let me tell you the dire prophecies of Tiresias   295
and Aeaean Circe too: time and again they told me
to shun this island of the Sun, the joy of man.
Here, they warned, the worst disaster awaits us.
Row straight past these shores—race our black ship on!'

    So I said, and the warnings broke their hearts.   300
But Eurylochus waded in at once—with mutiny on his mind:
'You're a hard man, Odysseus. Your fighting spirit's
stronger than ours, your stamina never fails.
You must be made of iron head to foot. Look,
your crew's half-dead with labor, starved for sleep,   305
and you forbid us to set foot on land, this island here,
washed by the waves, where we might catch a decent meal again.
Drained as we are, night falling fast, you'd have us desert

this haven and blunder off, into the mist-bound seas?
Out of the night come winds that shatter vessels—   310
how can a man escape his headlong death
if suddenly, out of nowhere, a cyclone hits,
bred by the South or stormy West Wind? They're the gales
that tear a ship to splinters—the gods, our masters,
willing or not, it seems. No, let's give way   315
to the dark night, set out our supper here.
Sit tight by our swift ship and then at daybreak
board and launch her, make for open sea!'

    So Eurylochus urged, and shipmates cheered.
Then I knew some power was brewing trouble for us,   320
so I let fly with an anxious plea: 'Eurylochus,
I'm one against all—the upper hand is yours.
But swear me a binding oath, all here, that if
we come on a herd of cattle or fine flock of sheep,
not one man among us—blind in his reckless ways—   325
will slaughter an ox or ram. Just eat in peace,
content with the food immortal Circe gave us.'

    They quickly swore the oath that I required
and once they had vowed they'd never harm the herds,
they moored our sturdy ship in the deep narrow harbor,   330
close to a fresh spring, and all hands disembarked
and adeptly set about the evening meal.
Once they'd put aside desire for food and drink,
they recalled our dear companions, wept for the men
that Scylla plucked from the hollow ship and ate alive,   335
and a welcome sleep came on them in their tears.
                                                    But then,
at the night's third watch, the stars just wheeling down,
Zeus who marshals the stormclouds loosed a ripping wind,
a howling, demonic gale, shrouding over in thunderheads
the earth and sea at once—and night swept down from the sky.   340
When young Dawn with her rose-red fingers shone once more
we hauled our craft ashore, securing her in a vaulted cave
where nymphs have lovely dancing-rings and hold their sessions.
There I called a muster, warning my shipmates yet again,
'Friends, we've food and drink aplenty aboard the ship—   345
keep your hands off all these herds or we will pay the price!
The cattle, the sleek flocks, belong to an awesome master,
Helios, god of the sun who sees all, hears all things.'

    So I warned, and my headstrong men complied.
But for one whole month the South Wind blew nonstop,   350
no other wind came up, none but the South, Southeast.
As long as our food and ruddy wine held out, the crew,
eager to save their lives, kept hands off the herds.
But then, when supplies aboard had all run dry,
when the men turned to hunting, forced to range   355
for quarry with twisted hooks: for fish, birds,

anything they could lay their hands on—
hunger racked their bellies—I struck inland,
up the island, there to pray to the gods.
If only one might show me some way home!   360
Crossing into the heartland, clear of the crew,
I rinsed my hands in a sheltered spot, a windbreak,
but soon as I'd prayed to all the gods who rule Olympus,
down on my eyes they poured a sweet, sound sleep . . .
as Eurylochus opened up his fatal plan to friends: 365
'Listen to me, my comrades, brothers in hardship.
All ways of dying are hateful to us poor mortals,
true, but to die of hunger, starve to death—
that's the worst of all. So up with you now,
let's drive off the pick of Helios' sleek herds,   370
slaughter them to the gods who rule the skies up there.
If we ever make it home to Ithaca, native ground,
erect at once a glorious temple to the Sungod,
line the walls with hoards of dazzling gifts!
But if the Sun, inflamed for his longhorn cattle,   375
means to wreck our ship and the other gods pitch in—
I'd rather die at sea, with one deep gulp of death,
than die by inches on this desolate island here!'

   So he urged, and shipmates cheered again.
At once they drove off the Sungod's finest cattle—   380
close at hand, not far from the blue-prowed ship they grazed,
those splendid beasts with their broad brows and curving horns.
Surrounding them in a ring, they lifted prayers to the gods,
plucking fresh green leaves from a tall oak for the rite,
since white strewing-barley was long gone in the ship.   385
Once they'd prayed, slaughtered and skinned the cattle,
they cut the thighbones out, they wrapped them round in fat,
a double fold sliced clean and topped with strips of flesh.
And since they had no wine to anoint the glowing victims,
they made libations with water, broiling all the innards,   390
and once they'd burned the bones and tasted the organs—
hacked the rest into pieces, piercing them with spits.[7]

   That moment soothing slumber fell from my eyes
and down I went to our ship at the water's edge
but on my way, nearing the long beaked craft,   395
the smoky savor of roasts came floating up around me . . .
I groaned in anguish, crying out to the deathless gods:
'Father Zeus! the rest of you blissful gods who never die—
you with your fatal sleep, you lulled me into disaster.
Left on their own, look what a monstrous thing   400
my crew concocted!'

---

7. The killing and cooking of the victims follow the usual Homeric pattern of sacrifice, with two exceptions that are conspicuous because sacrifice scenes in Homer are formulaic: the sailors sprinkle the victims
with leaves instead of barley, and they pour libations with water instead of wine. These departures from the
usual ritual make the sacrifice defective, with ominous implications for Odysseus's companions.

Quick as a flash
with her flaring robes Lampetie sped the news
to the Sun on high that we had killed his herds
and Helios burst out in rage to all the immortals:
'Father Zeus! the rest of you blissful gods who never die—   405
punish them all, that crew of Laertes' son Odysseus—
what an outrage! They, they killed my cattle,
the great joy of my heart . . . day in, day out,
when I climbed the starry skies and when I wheeled
back down from the heights to touch the earth once more.   410
Unless they pay me back in blood for the butchery of my herds,
down I go to the House of Death and blaze among the dead!'

But Zeus who marshals the thunderheads insisted,
'Sun, you keep on shining among the deathless gods
and mortal men across the good green earth.   415
And as for the guilty ones, why, soon enough
on the wine-dark sea I'll hit their racing ship
with a white-hot bolt, I'll tear it into splinters.'

—Or so I heard from the lovely nymph Calypso,
who heard it herself, she said, from Hermes, god of guides.   420

As soon as I reached our ship at the water's edge
I took the men to task, upbraiding each in turn,
but how to set things right? We couldn't find a way.
The cattle were dead already . . .
and the gods soon showed us all some fateful signs—   425
the hides began to crawl, the meat, both raw and roasted,
bellowed out on the spits, and we heard a noise
like the moan of lowing oxen.
                              Yet six more days
my eager companions feasted on the cattle of the Sun,
the pick of the herds they'd driven off, but then,   430
when Cronian Zeus brought on the seventh day,
the wind in its ceaseless raging dropped at last,
and stepping the mast at once, hoisting the white sail
we boarded ship and launched her, made for open sea.

But once we'd left that island in our wake—   435
no land at all in sight, nothing but sea and sky—
then Zeus the son of Cronus mounted a thunderhead
above our hollow ship and the deep went black beneath it.
Nor did the craft scud on much longer. All of a sudden
killer-squalls attacked us, screaming out of the west,   440
a murderous blast shearing the two forestays off
so the mast toppled backward, its running tackle spilling
into the bilge. The mast itself went crashing into the stern,
it struck the helmsman's head and crushed his skull to pulp
and down from his deck the man flipped like a diver—   445
his hardy life spirit left his bones behind.
Then, then in the same breath Zeus hit the craft

with a lightning-bolt and thunder. Round she spun,
reeling under the impact, filled with reeking brimstone,
shipmates pitching out of her, bobbing round like seahawks   450
swept along by the whitecaps past the trim black hull—
and the god cut short their journey home forever.

   But I went lurching along our battered hulk
till the sea-surge ripped the plankings from the keel
and the waves swirled it away, stripped bare, and snapped   455
the mast from the decks—but a backstay[8] made of bull's-hide
still held fast, and with this I lashed the mast and keel
together, made them one, riding my makeshift raft
as the wretched galewinds bore me on and on.

   At last the West Wind quit its wild rage   460
but the South came on at once to hound me even more,
making me double back my route toward cruel Charybdis.
All night long I was rushed back and then at break of day
I reached the crag of Scylla and dire Charybdis' vortex
right when the dreadful whirlpool gulped the salt sea down.   465
But heaving myself aloft to clutch at the fig-tree's height,
like a bat I clung to its trunk for dear life—not a chance
for a good firm foothold there, no clambering up it either,
the roots too far to reach, the boughs too high overhead,
huge swaying branches that overshadowed Charybdis.   470
But I held on, dead set . . . waiting for her
to vomit my mast and keel back up again—
Oh how I ached for both! and back they came,
late but at last, at just the hour a judge at court,
who's settled the countless suits of brash young claimants,   475
rises, the day's work done, and turns home for supper—
that's when the timbers reared back up from Charybdis.
I let go—I plunged with my hands and feet flailing,
crashing into the waves beside those great beams
and scrambling aboard them fast   480
I rowed hard with my hands right through the straits . . .
And the father of men and gods did not let Scylla see me,
else I'd have died on the spot—no escape from death.

   I drifted along nine days. On the tenth, at night,
the gods cast me up on Ogygia, Calypso's island,   485
home of the dangerous nymph with glossy braids
who speaks with human voice, and she took me in,
she loved me . . . Why cover the same ground again?
Just yesterday, here at hall, I told you all the rest,
you and your gracious wife. It goes against my grain   490
to repeat a tale told once, and told so clearly."

---

8. A rope stretched from the top of the mast to a side or the stern of a ship that, with other ropes fastened
fore and aft, supports the mast.

BOOK XIII

[Ithaca at Last]

His tale was over now. The Phaeacians all fell silent, hushed,
his story holding them spellbound down the shadowed halls
until Alcinous found the poise to say, "Odysseus,
now that you have come to my bronze-floored house,
my vaulted roofs, I know you won't be driven   5
off your course, nothing can hold you back—
however much you've suffered, you'll sail home.
Here, friends, here's a command for one and all,
you who frequent my palace day and night and drink
the shining wine of kings and enjoy the harper's songs.   10
The robes and hammered gold and a haul of other gifts
you lords of our island council brought our guest—
all lie packed in his polished sea-chest now. Come,
each of us add a sumptuous tripod, add a cauldron!
Then recover our costs with levies on the people: 15
it's hard to afford such bounty man by man."

    The king's instructions met with warm applause
and home they went to sleep, each in his own house.
When young Dawn with her rose-red fingers shone once more
they hurried down to the ship with handsome bronze gifts,   20
and striding along the decks, the ardent King Alcinous
stowed them under the benches, shipshape, so nothing
could foul the crewmen tugging at their oars.
Then back the party went to Alcinous' house
and shared a royal feast.
               The majestic king   25
slaughtered an ox for them to Cronus' mighty son,
Zeus of the thundercloud, whose power rules the world.
They burned the thighs and fell to the lordly banquet,
reveling there, while in their midst the inspired bard
struck up a song, Demodocus, prized by all the people.   30
True, but time and again Odysseus turned his face
toward the radiant sun, anxious for it to set,
yearning now to be gone and home once more . . .
As a man aches for his evening meal when all day long
his brace of wine-dark oxen have dragged the bolted plowshare   35
down a fallow field—how welcome the setting sun to him,
the going home to supper, yes, though his knees buckle,
struggling home at last. So welcome now to Odysseus
the setting light of day, and he lost no time
as he pressed Phaeacia's men who love their oars,   40
addressing his host, Alcinous, first and foremost:
"Alcinous, majesty, shining among your island people,
make your libations, launch me safely on my way—
to one and all, farewell!
All is now made good, my heart's desire,   45
your convoy home, your precious, loving gifts,
and may the gods of Olympus bless them for me!

May I find an unswerving wife when I reach home,
and loved ones hale, unharmed! And you, my friends
remaining here in your kingdom now, may you delight   50
in your loyal wives and children! May the gods
rain down all kinds of fortune on your lives,
misfortune never harbor in your homeland!"

All burst into applause, urging passage home
for their parting guest, his farewell rang so true.   55
Hallowed King Alcinous briskly called his herald:
"Come, Pontonous! Mix the wine in the bowl,
pour rounds to all our banqueters in the house,
so we, with a prayer to mighty Zeus the Father,
can sail our new friend home to native land."   60

Pontonous mixed the heady, honeyed wine
and hovering closely, poured full rounds for all.
And from where they sat they tipped libations out
to the happy gods who rule the vaulting skies.
Then King Odysseus rose up from his seat   65
and placing his two-eared cup in Arete's hands,
addressed the queen with parting wishes on the wing:
"Your health, my queen, through all your days to come—
until old age and death, that visit all mankind,
pay you a visit too. Now I am on my way   70
but you, may you take joy in this house of yours,
in your children, your people, in Alcinous the king!"

With that the great Odysseus strode across the threshold.
And King Alcinous sent the herald off with the guest
to lead him down to the swift ship and foaming surf.   75
And Arete sent her serving-women, one to carry
a sea-cloak, washed and fresh, a shirt as well,
another assigned to bear the sturdy chest
and a third to take the bread and ruddy wine.

When they reached the ship at the water's edge   80
the royal escorts took charge of the gifts at once
and stores of food and wine, stowed them deep in the holds,
and then for their guest they spread out rug and sheets
on the half-deck, clear astern on the ship's hull
so he might sleep there soundly, undisturbed.   85
And last, Odysseus climbed aboard himself
and down he lay, all quiet
as crewmen sat to the oarlocks, each in line.
They slipped the cable free of the drilled stone post
and soon as they swung back and the blades tossed up the spray   90
an irresistible sleep fell deeply on his eyes, the sweetest,
soundest oblivion, still as the sleep of death itself . . .
And the ship like a four-horse team careering down the plain,
all breaking as one with the whiplash cracking smartly,
leaping with hoofs high to run the course in no time—   95

so the stern hove high and plunged with the seething rollers
crashing dark in her wake as on she surged unwavering,
never flagging, no, not even a darting hawk,
the quickest thing on wings, could keep her pace
as on she ran, cutting the swells at top speed,   100
bearing a man endowed with the gods' own wisdom,
one who had suffered twenty years of torment, sick at heart,
cleaving his way through wars of men and pounding waves at sea
but now he slept in peace, the memory of his struggles
laid to rest.
    And then, that hour the star rose up,   105
the clearest, brightest star, that always heralds
the newborn light of day, the deep-sea-going ship
made landfall on the island . . . Ithaca, at last.

There on the coast a haven lies, named for Phorcys,
the old god of the deep—with two jutting headlands,   110
sheared off at the seaward side but shelving toward the bay,
that break the great waves whipped by the gales outside
so within the harbor ships can ride unmoored
whenever they come in mooring range of shore.
At the harbor's head a branching olive stands   115
with a welcome cave nearby it, dank with sea-mist,
sacred to nymphs of the springs we call the Naiads.
There are mixing-bowls inside and double-handled jars,
crafted of stone, and bees store up their honey in the hollows.
There are long stone looms as well, where the nymphs weave out   120
their webs from clouds of sea-blue wool—a marvelous sight—
and a wellspring flows forever. The cave has two ways in,
one facing the North Wind, a pathway down for mortals;
the other, facing the South, belongs to the gods,
no man may go that way . . .   125
it is the path for all the deathless powers.

Here at this bay the Phaeacian crew put in—
they'd known it long before—driving the ship so hard
she ran up onto the beach for a good half her length,
such way the oarsmen's brawny arms had made.   130
Up from the benches, swinging down to land,
first they lifted Odysseus off the decks—
linen and lustrous carpet too—and laid him
down on the sand asleep, still dead to the world,
then hoisted out the treasures proud Phaeacians,   135
urged by open-hearted Pallas, had lavished on him,
setting out for home. They heaped them all
by the olive's trunk, in a neat pile, clear
of the road for fear some passerby might spot
and steal Odysseus' hoard before he could awaken.   140
Then pushing off, they pulled for home themselves.

But now Poseidon, god of the earthquake, never once
forgetting the first threats he leveled at the hero,

probed almighty Zeus to learn his plans in full:
"Zeus, Father, I will lose all my honor now   145
among the immortals, now there are mortal men
who show me no respect—Phaeacians, too,
born of my own loins! I said myself
that Odysseus would suffer long and hard
before he made it home, but I never dreamed   150
of blocking his return, not absolutely at least,
once *you* had pledged your word and bowed your head.
But now they've swept him across the sea in their swift ship,
they've set him down in Ithaca, sound asleep, and loaded the man
with boundless gifts—bronze and hoards of gold and robes—   155
aye, more plunder than he could ever have won from Troy
if Odysseus had returned intact with his fair share!"

     "Incredible," Zeus who marshals the thunderheads replied.
"Earth-shaker, you with your massive power, why moaning so?
The gods don't disrespect you. What a stir there'd be   160
if they flung abuse at the oldest, noblest of them all.
Those mortals? If any man, so lost in his strength
and prowess, pays you no respect—just pay him back.
The power is always yours.
Do what you like. Whatever warms your heart."   165

     "King of the dark cloud," the earthquake god agreed,
"I'd like to avenge myself at once, as you advise,
but I've always feared your wrath and shied away.
But now I'll crush that fine Phaeacian cutter
out on the misty sea, now on her homeward run   170
from the latest convoy. They will learn at last
to cease and desist from escorting every man alive—
I'll pile a huge mountain round about their port!"

     "Wait, dear brother," Zeus who collects the clouds
had second thoughts. "Here's what seems best to *me*.   175
As the people all lean down from the city heights
to watch her speeding home, strike her into a rock
that looks like a racing vessel, just offshore—
amaze all men with a marvel for the ages.
Then pile your huge mountain round about their port."[9]   180

     Hearing that from Zeus, the god of the earthquake
sped to Scheria now, the Phaeacians' island home,
and waited there till the ship came sweeping in,
scudding lightly along—and surging close abreast,
the earthquake god with one flat stroke of his hand   185
struck her to stone, rooted her to the ocean floor

9. In the manuscripts, as translated here, Zeus agrees with Poseidon's intention to cut the Phaeacians off from the sea altogether by surrounding their city with a mountain but suggests that instead of wrecking the returning ship he turn it into a rock. But already in antiquity the great Alexandrian scholar Aristophanes of Byzantium (ca. 257–180 B.C.E.) proposed emending the text to read "but *do not* pile your huge mountain around their port." The Phaeacians' ultimate fate is not revealed, and the line has been much discussed since antiquity, because questions of divine justice seem to be at stake.

and made for open sea.
                                        The Phaeacians, aghast,
those lords of the long oars, the master mariners
traded startled glances, sudden outcries:
"Look—who's pinned our swift ship to the sea?"   190

    "Just racing for home!"
                                        "Just hove into plain view!"

    They might well wonder, blind to what had happened,
till Alcinous rose and made things all too clear:
"Oh no—my father's prophecy years ago . . .
it all comes home to me with a vengeance now!   195
He used to say Poseidon was vexed with us because
we escorted all mankind and never came to grief.
He said that one day, as a well-built ship of ours
sailed home on the misty sea from such a convoy,
the god would crush it, yes,   200
and pile a huge mountain round about our port.
So the old king foretold. Now, look, it all comes true!
Hurry, friends, do as I say, let us all comply:
stop our convoys home for every castaway
chancing on our city! As for Poseidon,   205
sacrifice twelve bulls to the god at once—
the pick of the herds. Perhaps he'll pity us,
pile no looming mountain ridge around our port."

    The people, terrified, prepared the bulls at once.
So all of Phaeacia's island lords and captains,   210
milling round the altar, lifted prayers
to Poseidon, master of the sea . . .
                                        That very moment
great Odysseus woke from sleep on native ground at last—
he'd been away for years—but failed to know the land
for the goddess Pallas Athena, Zeus's daughter,   215
showered mist over all, so under cover
she might change his appearance head to foot
as she told him every peril he'd meet at home—
keep him from being known by wife, townsmen, friends,
till the suitors paid the price for all their outrage.   220
And so to the king himself all Ithaca looked strange . . .
the winding beaten paths, the coves where ships can ride,
the steep rock face of the cliffs and the tall leafy trees.
He sprang to his feet and, scanning his own native country,
groaned, slapped his thighs with his flat palms   225
and Odysseus cried in anguish:
"Man of misery, whose land have I lit on now?
What *are* they here—violent, savage, lawless?
or friendly to strangers, god-fearing men?
Where can I take this heap of treasure now   230
and where in the world do I wander off myself?
If only the trove had stayed among the Phaeacians there

and I had made my way to some other mighty king
who would have hosted me well and sent me home!
But now I don't know where to stow all this,   235
and I can't leave it here, inviting any bandit
to rob me blind.
          So damn those lords and captains,
those Phaeacians! Not entirely honest or upright, were they?
Sweeping me off to this, this no-man's-land, and they,
they swore they'd sail me home to sunny Ithaca—well,   240
they never kept their word. Zeus of the Suppliants
pay them back—he keeps an eye on the world of men
and punishes all transgressors!
                Come, quickly,
I'll inspect my treasure and count it up myself.
Did they make off with anything in their ship?"   245

   With that he counted up the gorgeous tripods,
cauldrons, bars of gold and the lovely woven robes.
Not a stitch was missing from the lot. But still
he wept for his native country, trailing down the shore
where the wash of sea on shingle ebbs and flows,   250
his homesick heart in turmoil.
But now Athena appeared and came toward him.
She looked like a young man . . . a shepherd boy
yet elegant too, with all the gifts that grace the sons of kings,
with a well-cut cloak falling in folds across her shoulders,   255
sandals under her shining feet, a hunting spear in hand.
Odysseus, overjoyed at the sight, went up to meet her,
joining her now with salutations on the wing:
"Greetings, friend! Since you are the first
I've come on in this harbor, treat me kindly—   260
no cruelty, please. Save these treasures,
save me too. I pray to you like a god,
I fall before your knees and ask your mercy!
And tell me this for a fact—I need to know—
where on earth am I? what land? who lives here?   265
Is it one of the sunny islands or some jutting shore
of the good green mainland slanting down to sea?"

   Athena answered, her eyes brightening now,
"You must be a fool, stranger, or come from nowhere,
if you really have to ask what land this is.   270
Trust me, it's not so nameless after all.
It's known the world around,
to all who live to the east and rising sun
and to all who face the western mists and darkness.
It's a rugged land, too cramped for driving horses,   275
but though it's far from broad, it's hardly poor.
There's plenty of grain for bread, grapes for wine,
the rains never fail and the dewfall's healthy.
Good country for goats, good for cattle too—
there's stand on stand of timber   280

and water runs in streambeds through the year.
So,
stranger, the name of Ithaca's reached as far as Troy,
and Troy, they say, is a long hard sail from Greece."

    Ithaca . . . Heart racing, Odysseus that great exile
filled with joy to hear Athena, daughter of storming Zeus,   285
pronounce that name. He stood on native ground at last
and he replied with a winging word to Pallas,
not with a word of truth—he choked it back,
always invoking the cunning in his heart:
"Ithaca . . . yes, I seem to have heard of Ithaca,   290
even on Crete's broad island far across the sea,
and now I've reached it myself, with all this loot,
but I left behind an equal measure for my children.
I'm a fugitive now, you see. I killed Idomeneus'[1] son,
Orsilochus, lightning on his legs, a man who beat   295
all runners alive on that long island—what a racer!
He tried to rob me of all the spoil I'd won at Troy,
the plunder I went to hell and back to capture, true,
cleaving my way through wars of men and waves at sea—
and just because I refused to please his father,   300
serve under *him* at Troy. I led my own command.
So now with a friend I lay in wait by the road,
I killed him just loping in from the fields—
with one quick stroke of my bronze spear
in the dead of night, the heavens pitch-black . . .   305
no one could see us, spot me tearing out his life
with a weapon honed for action. Once I'd cut him down
I made for a ship and begged the Phoenician crew[2] for mercy,
paying those decent hands a hearty share of plunder—
asked them to take me on and land me down in Pylos,   310
there or lovely Elis, where Epeans rule in power.
But a heavy galewind blew them way off course,
much against their will—
they'd no desire to cheat me. Driven afar,
we reached this island here at the midnight hour,   315
rowing for dear life, we made it into your harbor—
not a thought of supper, much as we all craved food,
we dropped from the decks and lay down, just like that!
A welcome sleep came over my weary bones at once,
while the crew hoisted up my loot from the holds   320
and set it down on the sand near where I slept.
They reembarked, now homeward bound for Sidon,
their own noble city, leaving me here behind,
homesick in my heart . . ."
                            As his story ended,
goddess Athena, gray eyes gleaming, broke into a smile   325
and stroked him with her hand, and now she appeared a woman,

---

1. A prominent Greek warrior in the *Iliad* and king of Crete (the "long island" of line 296).   **2.** The Phoenicians figure as (sometimes unreliable) traders in several stories told in the second half of the *Odyssey*. Their trading ships in fact reached many parts of the Mediterranean in Homer's time.

beautiful, tall and skilled at weaving lovely things.
Her words went flying straight toward Odysseus:
"Any man—any god who met you—would have to be
some champion lying cheat to get past *you*   330
for all-round craft and guile! You terrible man,
foxy, ingenious, never tired of twists and tricks—
so, not even here, on native soil, would you give up
those wily tales that warm the cockles of your heart!
Come, enough of this now. We're both old hands   335
at the arts of intrigue. Here among mortal men
you're far the best at tactics, spinning yarns,
and I am famous among the gods for wisdom,
cunning wiles, too.
Ah, but you never recognized me, did you?   340
Pallas Athena, daughter of Zeus—who always
stands beside you, shields you in every exploit:
thanks to me the Phaeacians all embraced you warmly.
And now I am here once more, to weave a scheme with you
and to hide the treasure-trove Phaeacia's nobles   345
lavished on you then—I willed it, planned it so
when you set out for home—and to tell you all
the trials you must suffer in your palace . . .
Endure them all. You must. You have no choice.
And to no one—no man, no woman, not a soul—   350
reveal that you are the wanderer home at last.
No, in silence you must bear a world of pain,
subject yourself to the cruel abuse of men."

    "Ah goddess," the cool tactician countered,
"you're so hard for a mortal man to know on sight,   355
however shrewd he is—the shapes you take are endless!
But I do know this: you were kind to me in the war years,
so long as we men of Achaea soldiered on at Troy.
But once we'd sacked King Priam's craggy city,
boarded ship, and a god dispersed the fleet,   360
from then on, daughter of Zeus, I never saw you,
never glimpsed you striding along my decks
to ward off some disaster. No, I wandered on,
my heart forever torn to pieces inside my chest
till the gods released me from my miseries at last,   365
that day in the fertile kingdom of Phaeacia when
you cheered me with words, in person, led me to their city.
But now I beg you by your almighty Father's name . . .
for I can't believe I've reached my sunny Ithaca,
I must be roaming around one more exotic land—   370
you're mocking me, I know it, telling me tales
to make me lose my way. Tell me the truth now,
have I really reached the land I love?"

    "Always the same, your wary turn of mind,"
Athena exclaimed, her glances flashing warmly.   375
"That's why I can't forsake you in your troubles—

you are so winning, so worldly-wise, so self-possessed!
Anyone else, come back from wandering long and hard,
would have hurried home at once, delighted to see
his children and his wife. Oh, but not you,   380
it's not your pleasure to probe for news of them—
you must put your wife to the proof yourself!
But she, she waits in your halls, as always,
her life an endless hardship . . .
wasting away the nights, weeping away the days.   385
I never had doubts myself, no, I knew down deep
that you would return at last, with all your shipmates lost.
But I could not bring myself to fight my Father's brother,
Poseidon, quaking with anger at you, still enraged
because you blinded the Cyclops, his dear son.   390
But come, let me show you Ithaca's setting,
I'll convince you. This haven—look around—
it's named for Phorcys, the old god of the deep,
and here at the harbor's head the branching olive stands
with the welcome cave nearby it, dank with sea-mist,   395
sacred to nymphs of the springs we call the Naiads.
Here, under its arching vault, time and again
you'd offer the nymphs a generous sacrifice
to bring success! And the slopes above you, look,
Mount Neriton decked in forests!"   400
                          At those words
the goddess scattered the mist and the country stood out clear
and the great man who had borne so much rejoiced at last,
thrilled to see his Ithaca—he kissed the good green earth
and raised his hands to the nymphs and prayed at once,
"Nymphs of the springs, Naiads, daughters of Zeus,   405
I never dreamed I would see you yet again . . .
Now rejoice in my loving prayers—and later,
just like the old days, I will give you gifts
if Athena, Zeus's daughter, Queen of Armies
comes to my rescue, grants this fighter life   410
and brings my son to manhood!"
                          "Courage!"—
goddess Athena answered, eyes afire—
"Free your mind of all that anguish now.
Come, quick, let's bury your treasures here
in some recess of this haunted hallowed cave   415
where they'll be safe and sound,
then we'll make plans so we can win the day."
                          With that
the goddess swept into the cavern's shadowed vault,
searching for hiding-places far inside its depths
while Odysseus hauled his treasures closer up,   420
the gold, durable bronze and finespun robes,
the Phaeacians' parting gifts.
Once he'd stowed them well away, the goddess,
Pallas Athena, daughter of storming Zeus,
sealed the mouth of the cavern with a stone.   425

Then down they sat by the sacred olive's trunk
to plot the death of the high and mighty suitors.
The bright-eyed goddess Athena led the way:
"Royal son of Laertes, Odysseus, old campaigner,
think how to lay your hands on all those brazen suitors,   430
lording it over your house now, three whole years,
courting your noble wife, offering gifts to win her.
But she, forever broken-hearted for your return,
builds up each man's hopes—
dangling promises, dropping hints to each—   435
but all the while with something else in mind."

   "God help me!" the man of intrigue broke out:
"Clearly I might have died the same ignoble death
as Agamemnon, bled white in my own house too,
if you had never revealed this to me now,   440
goddess, point by point.
Come, weave us a scheme so I can pay them back!
Stand beside me, Athena, fire me with daring, fierce
as the day we ripped Troy's glittering crown of towers down.
Stand by me—furious now as then, my bright-eyed one—   445
and I would fight three hundred men, great goddess,
with you to brace me, comrade-in-arms in battle!"

   Gray eyes ablaze, the goddess urged him on:
"Surely I'll stand beside you, not forget you,
not when the day arrives for us to do our work.   450
Those men who court your wife and waste your goods?
I have a feeling some will splatter your ample floors
with all their blood and brains. Up now, quickly.
First I will transform you—no one must know you.
I will shrivel the supple skin on your lithe limbs,   455
strip the russet curls from your head and deck you out
in rags you'd hate to see some other mortal wear;
I'll dim the fire in your eyes, so shining once—
until you seem appalling to all those suitors,
even your wife and son you left behind at home.   460
But you, you make your way to the swineherd first,
in charge of your pigs, and true to you as always,
loyal friend to your son, to Penelope, so self-possessed.
You'll find him posted beside his swine, grubbing round
by Raven's Rock and the spring called Arethusa,   465
rooting for feed that makes pigs sleek and fat,
the nuts they love, the dark pools they drink.
Wait there, sit with him, ask him all he knows.
I'm off to Sparta, where the women are a wonder,
to call Telemachus home, your own dear son, Odysseus.   470
He's journeyed to Lacedaemon's rolling hills
to see Menelaus, searching for news of you,
hoping to learn if you are still alive."

Shrewd Odysseus answered her at once:
"Why not tell him the truth? You know it all.   475
Or is *he* too—like father, like son—condemned
to hardship, roving over the barren salt sea
while strangers devour our livelihood right here?"

But the bright-eyed goddess reassured him firmly:
"No need for anguish, trust me, not for him—   480
I escorted your son myself
so he might make his name by sailing there.
Nor is he saddled down with any troubles now.
He sits at ease in the halls of Menelaus,
bathed in endless bounty . . . True enough,   485
some young lords in a black cutter lurk in ambush,
poised to kill the prince before he reaches home,
but I have my doubts they will. Sooner the earth
will swallow down a few of those young gallants
who eat you out of house and home these days!"   490

No more words, not now—
Athena stroked Odysseus with her wand.
She shriveled the supple skin on his lithe limbs,
stripped the russet curls from his head, covered his body
top to toe with the wrinkled hide of an old man   495
and dimmed the fire in his eyes, so shining once.
She turned his shirt and cloak into squalid rags,
ripped and filthy, smeared with grime and soot.
She flung over this the long pelt of a bounding deer,
rubbed bare, and gave him a staff and beggar's sack,   500
torn and tattered, slung from a fraying rope.
                                        All plans made,
they went their separate ways—Athena setting off
to bring Telemachus home from hallowed Lacedaemon.

BOOK XIV

[The Loyal Swineherd]

So up from the haven now Odysseus climbed a rugged path
through timber along high ground—Athena had shown the way—
to reach the swineherd's place, that fine loyal man
who of all the household hands Odysseus ever had
cared the most for his master's worldly goods.   5

Sitting at the door of his lodge he found him,
there in his farmstead, high-walled, broad and large,
with its long view on its cleared rise of ground . . .
The swineherd made those walls with his own hands
to enclose the pigs of his master gone for years.   10
Alone, apart from his queen or old Laertes,
he'd built them up of quarried blocks of stone
and coped them well with a fence of wild pear.
Outside he'd driven stakes in a long-line stockade,

a ring of thickset palings split from an oak's dark heart.   15
Within the yard he'd built twelve sties, side-by-side,
to bed his pigs, and in each one fifty brood-sows
slept aground, penned and kept for breeding.
The boars slept outside, but far fewer of them,
thanks to the lordly suitors' feasts that kept on   20
thinning the herd and kept the swineherd stepping,
sending to town each day the best fat hog in sight.
By now they were down to three hundred and sixty head.
But guarding them all the time were dogs like savage beasts,
a pack of four, reared by the swineherd, foreman of men.   25
The man himself was fitting sandals to his feet,
carving away at an oxhide, dark and supple.
As for his men, three were off with their pigs,
herding them here or there. Under orders he'd sent
a fourth to town, with hog in tow for the gorging suitors   30
to slaughter off and glut themselves with pork.

    Suddenly—those snarling dogs spotted Odysseus,
charged him fast—a shatter of barks—but Odysseus
sank to the ground at once, he knew the trick:
the staff dropped from his hand but here and now,   35
on his own farm, he might have taken a shameful mauling.
Yes, but the swineherd, quick to move, dashed for the gate,
flinging his oxhide down, rushed the dogs with curses,
scattered them left and right with flying rocks
and warned his master, "Lucky to be alive, old man—   40
a moment more, my pack would have torn you limb from limb!
Then you'd have covered me with shame. As if the gods
had never given me blows and groans aplenty . . .
Here I sit, my heart aching, broken for *him*,
my master, my great king—fattening up   45
his own hogs for other men to eat, while he,
starving for food, I wager, wanders the earth,
a beggar adrift in strangers' cities, foreign-speaking lands,
if he's still alive, that is, still sees the rising sun.
Come, follow me into my place, old man, so you,   50
at least, can eat your fill of bread and wine.
Then you can tell me where you're from
and all the pains you've weathered."
                          On that note
the loyal swineherd led the way to his shelter,
showed his guest inside and sat Odysseus down   55
on brush and twigs he piled up for the visitor,
flinging over these the skin of a shaggy wild goat,
broad and soft, the swineherd's own good bedding.
The king, delighted to be so well received,
thanked the man at once: "My host—may Zeus   60
and the other gods give *you* your heart's desire
for the royal welcome you have shown me here!"

And you[3] replied, Eumaeus, loyal swineherd,
"It's wrong, my friend, to send any stranger packing—
even one who arrives in worse shape than you.   65
Every stranger and beggar comes from Zeus
and whatever scrap they get from the likes of us,
they'll find it welcome. That's the best we can do,
we servants, always cowed by our high and mighty masters,
especially our young lords . . . But my old king?   70
The gods, they must have blocked his journey home.
He'd have treated me well, he would, with a house,
a plot of land and a wife you'd gladly prize.
Goods that a kind lord will give a household hand
who labors for him, hard, whose work the gods have sped,   75
just as they speed the work I labor at all day.
My master, I tell you, would have repaid me well
if he'd grown old right here. But now he's dead . . .
If only Helen and all her kind had died out too,
brought to her knees, just as she cut the legs   80
from under troops of men! My king among them,
he went off to the stallion-land of Troy
to fight the Trojans, save Agamemnon's honor!"
                                         Enough—
he brusquely cinched his belt around his shirt,
strode out to the pens, crammed with droves of pigs,   85
picked out two, bundled them in and slaughtered both,
singed them, sliced them down, skewered them through
and roasting all to a turn, set them before Odysseus,
sizzling hot on the spits.
Then coating the meat with white barley groats   90
and mixing honeyed wine in a carved wooden bowl,
he sat down across from his guest, inviting warmly,
"Eat up now, my friend. It's all we slaves have got,
scrawny pork, while the suitors eat the fatted hogs—
no fear of the gods in their hard hearts, no mercy!   95
Trust me, the blessed gods have no love for crime.
They honor justice, honor the decent acts of men.
Even cutthroat bandits who raid foreign parts—
and Zeus grants them a healthy share of plunder,
ships filled to the brim, and back they head for home—   100
even their dark hearts are stalked by the dread of vengeance.
But the suitors know, they've caught some godsent rumor
of master's grisly death! That's why they have no mind
to do their courting fairly or go back home in peace.
No, at their royal ease they devour all his goods,   105
those brazen rascals never spare a scrap!
Not a day or a night goes by, sent down by Zeus,
but they butcher victims, never stopping at one or two,
and drain his wine as if there's no tomorrow—

---

3. This form of direct address by poet to character is confined to Eumaeus in the *Odyssey,* but in the *Iliad* it is used with five different characters (among them the god Apollo and the obscure Melanippus). What special effect was intended, if any, is unknown.

swilling the last drop . . .   110
Believe me, my master's wealth was vast!
No other prince on earth could match his riches,
not on the loamy mainland or here at home in Ithaca—
no twenty men in the world could equal his great treasures!
Let me count them off for you. A dozen herds of cattle   115
back on the mainland, just as many head of sheep,
as many droves of pigs and goatflocks ranging free;
hired hands or his own herdsmen keep them grazing there.
Here in Ithaca, goatflocks, eleven in all, scatter
to graze the island, out at the wild end,   120
and trusty goatherds watch their every move.
And each herdsman, day after day, it never ends,
drives in a beast for the suitors—best in sight,
a sheep or well-fed goat. While I tend to these pigs,
I guard them, pick the best for those carousers   125
and send it to the slaughter!"
                              His voice rose
while the stranger ate his meat and drank his wine,
ravenous, bolting it all down in silence . . .
brooding on ways to serve the suitors right.
But once he'd supped and refreshed himself with food,   130
he filled the wooden bowl he'd been drinking from,
brimmed it with wine and passed it to his host
who received the offer gladly, spirit cheered
as the stranger probed him now with winging words:
"Friend, who was the man who bought you with his goods,   135
the master of such vast riches, powerful as you say?
You tell me he died defending Agamemnon's honor?
What's his name? I just might know such a man . . .
Zeus would know, and the other deathless gods,
if I ever saw him, if I bring you any news.   140
I've roamed the whole earth over."

     And the good swineherd answered, foreman of men,
"Old friend, no wanderer landing here with news of *him*
is likely to win his wife and dear son over.
Random drifters, hungry for bed and board,   145
lie through their teeth and swallow back the truth.
Why, any tramp washed up on Ithaca's shores
scurries right to my mistress, babbling lies,
and she ushers him in, kindly, pressing for details,
and the warm tears of grief come trickling down her cheeks,   150
the loyal wife's way when her husband's died abroad.
Even you, old codger, could rig up some fine tale—
and soon enough, I'd say,
if they gave you shirt and clothing for your pains.
My master? Well, no doubt the dogs and wheeling birds   155
have ripped the skin from his ribs by now, his life is through—
or fish have picked him clean at sea, and the man's bones
lie piled up on the mainland, buried deep in sand . . .
he's dead and gone. Aye, leaving a broken heart

for loved ones left behind, for *me* most of all.   160
Never another master kind as he!
I'll never find one—no matter where I go,
not even if I went back to mother and father,
the house where I was born and my parents reared me once.
Ah, but much as I grieve for them, much as I long   165
to lay my eyes on them, set foot on the old soil,
it's longing for him, him that wrings my heart—
Odysseus, lost and gone!
That man, old friend, far away as he is . . .
I can scarcely bear to say his name aloud,   170
so deeply he loved me, cared for me, so deeply.
Worlds away as he is, I call him Master, Brother!"

    "My friend," the great Odysseus, long in exile, answered,
"since you are dead certain, since you still insist
he's never coming back, still the soul of denial,   175
I won't simply say it—on my oath I swear
Odysseus is on his way!
Reward for such good news? Let me have it
the moment he sets foot in his own house,
dress me in shirt and cloak, in handsome clothes.   180
Before then, poor as I am, I wouldn't take a thing.
I hate that man like the very Gates of Death who,
ground down by poverty, stoops to peddling lies.
I swear by Zeus, the first of all the gods,
by this table of hospitality here, my host,   185
by Odysseus' hearth where I have come for help:
all will come to pass, I swear, exactly as I say.
True, this very month—just as the old moon dies
and the new moon rises into life—Odysseus will return!
He will come home and take revenge on any man   190
who offends his wedded wife and princely son!"

    "Good news," you replied, Eumaeus, loyal swineherd,
"but I will never pay a reward for *that*, old friend—
Odysseus, he'll never come home again. Never . . .
Drink your wine, sit back, let's talk of other things.   195
Don't remind me of all this. The heart inside me
breaks when anyone mentions my dear master.
That oath of yours, we'll let it pass—
                            Odysseus,
oh come back!—
                    Just as *I* wish, I and Penelope,
old Laertes too, Telemachus too, the godlike boy.   200
How I grieve for *him* now, I can't stop—Odysseus' son,
Telemachus. The gods reared him up like a fine young tree
and I often said, 'In the ranks of men he'll match his father,
his own dear father—amazing in build and looks, that boy!'
But all of a sudden a god wrecks his sense of balance—   205
god or man, no matter—off he's gone to catch
some news of his father, down to holy Pylos.

And now those gallant suitors lie in wait for him,
sailing home, to tear the royal line of Arcesius
out of Ithaca, root and branch, good name and all!   210
Enough. Let *him* pass too—whether he's trapped
or the hand of Zeus will pull him through alive.
                                        Come,
old soldier, tell me the story of your troubles,
tell me truly, too, I'd like to know it well . . .
Who are you? where are you from? your city? your parents?   215
What sort of vessel brought you? Why did the sailors
land you here in Ithaca? Who did they say they are?
I hardly think you came this way on foot."

    The great teller of tales returned at length,
"My story—the whole truth—I'm glad to tell it all.   220
If only the two of us had food and mellow wine
to last us long, here in your shelter now,
for us to sup on, undisturbed,
while others take the work of the world in hand,
I could easily spend all year and never reach the end   225
of my endless story, all the heartbreaking trials
I struggled through. The gods willed it so . . .

    I hail from Crete's broad land, I'm proud to say,
and I am a rich man's son. And many other sons
he brought up in his palace, born in wedlock,   230
sprung of his lawful wife. Unlike my mother.
She was a slave, a concubine he'd purchased, yes,
but he treated me on a par with all his true-born sons—
Castor, Hylax' son. I'm proud to boast his blood, that man
revered like a god throughout all Crete those days,   235
for wealth, power and all his glorious offspring.
But the deadly spirits soon swept him down
to the House of Death, and his high and mighty sons
carved up his lands and then cast lots for the parts
and gave me just a pittance, a paltry house as well.   240
But I won myself a wife from wealthy, landed people,
thanks to my own strong points. I was no fool
and never shirked a fight.
                           But now my heyday's gone—
I've had my share of blows. Yet look hard at the husk
and you'll still see, I think, the grain that gave it life.   245
By heaven, Ares gave me courage, Athena too, to break
the ranks of men wide open, once, in the old days,
whenever I picked my troops and formed an ambush,
plotting attacks to spring against our foes—
no hint of death could daunt my fighting spirit!   250
Far out of the front I'd charge and spear my man,
I'd cut down any enemy soldier backing off.
Such was I in battle, true, but I had no love
for working the land, the chores of households either,
the labor that raises crops of shining children. No,   255

it was always oarswept ships that thrilled my heart,
and wars, and the long polished spears and arrows,
dreadful gear that makes the next man cringe.
I loved them all—god planted that love inside me.
Each man delights in the work that suits him best.   260
Why, long before we Achaeans ever camped at Troy,
nine commands I led in our deep-sea-going ships,
raiding foreign men, and a fine haul reached my hands.
I helped myself to the lion's share and still more spoils
came by lot. And my house grew by leaps and bounds,   265
I walked among the Cretans, honored, feared as well.

　　But then, when thundering Zeus contrived that expedition—
that disaster that brought so many fighters to their knees—
and men kept pressing me and renowned Idomeneus
to head a fleet to Troy,   270
there was no way out, no denying them then,
the voice of the people bore down much too hard.
So nine whole years we Achaeans soldiered on at Troy,
in the tenth we sacked King Priam's city, then embarked
for home in the long ships, and a god dispersed the fleet.   275
Unlucky me. Shrewd old Zeus was plotting still more pain.
No more than a month I stayed at home, taking joy
in my children, loyal wife and lovely plunder.
But a spirit in me urged, 'Set sail for Egypt—
fit out ships, take crews of seasoned heroes!'   280
Nine I fitted out, the men joined up at once
and then six days my shipmates feasted well,
while I provided a flock of sheep to offer up
to the gods and keep the feasters' table groaning.
On the seventh we launched out from the plains of Crete   285
with a stiff North Wind fair astern—smooth sailing,
aye, like coasting on downstream . . .
And not one craft in our squadron foundered;
all shipshape, and all hands sound, we sat back
while the wind and helmsmen kept us true on course.   290

　　Five days out and we raised the great river Nile
and there in the Nile delta moored our ships of war.
God knows I ordered my trusty crews to stand by,
just where they were, and guard the anchored fleet
and I sent a patrol to scout things out from higher ground.   295
But swept away by their own reckless fury, the crew went berserk—
they promptly began to plunder the lush Egyptian farms,
dragged off the women and children, killed the men.
Outcries reached the city in no time—stirred by shouts
the entire town came streaming down at the break of day,   300
filling the river plain with chariots, ranks of infantry
and the gleam of bronze. Zeus who loves the lightning
flung down murderous panic on all my men-at-arms—
no one dared to stand his ground and fight,
disaster ringed us round from every quarter.   305

Droves of my men they hacked down with swords,
led off the rest alive, to labor for them as slaves.
And I? Zeus flashed an inspiration through my mind,
though I wish I'd died a soldier down in Egypt then!
A world of pain, you see, still lay in wait for me . . .   310
Quickly I wrenched the skullcap helmet off my head,
I tore the shield from my back and dropped my spear
and ran right into the path of the king's chariot,
hugged and kissed his knees. He pitied me, spared me,
hoisted me onto his war-car, took me home in tears.   315
Troops of his men came rushing after, shaking javelins,
mad to kill me—their fighting blood at the boil—
but their master drove them off.
He feared the wrath of Zeus, the god of guests,
the first of the gods to pay back acts of outrage.
                                                              So,   320
there I lingered for seven years, amassing a fortune
from all the Egyptian people loading me with gifts.
Then, at last, when the eighth had come full turn,
along comes this Phoenician one fine day . . .
a scoundrel, swindler, an old hand at lies   325
who'd already done the world a lot of damage.
Well, he smoothly talked me round and off we sailed,
Phoenicia-bound, where his house and holdings lay.
There in his care I stayed till the year was out.
Then, when the months and days had run their course   330
and the year wheeled round and the seasons came again,
he conned me aboard his freighter bound for Libya,
pretending I'd help him ship a cargo there for sale
but in fact he'd sell *me* there and make a killing!
I suspected as much, of course, but had no choice,   335
so I boarded with him, yes, and the ship ran on
with a good strong North Wind gusting—
fast on the middle passage clear of Crete—
but Zeus was brewing mischief for that crew . . .
Once we'd left the island in our wake—   340
no land at all in sight, nothing but sea and sky—
then Zeus the son of Cronus mounted a thunderhead
above our hollow ship and the deep went black beneath it.
Then, then in the same breath Zeus hit the craft
with a lightning-bolt and thunder. Round she spun,   345
reeling under the impact, filled with reeking brimstone,
shipmates pitching out of her, bobbing round like seahawks
swept along by the breakers past the trim black hull—
and the god cut short their journey home forever.
                                                      Not mine.
Zeus himself—when I was just at the final gasp—   350
thrust the huge mast of my dark-prowed vessel
right into my arms so I might flee disaster
one more time. Wrapping myself around it,
I was borne along by the wretched galewinds,
rushed along nine days—on the tenth, at dead of night,   355

a shouldering breaker rolled me up along Thesprotia's beaches
There the king of Thesprotia, Phidon,[4] my salvation,
treated me kindly, asked for no reward at all.
His own good son had found me, half-dead
from exhaustion and the cold. He raised me up   360
by the hand and led me home to his father's house
and dressed me in cloak and shirt and decent clothes.
That's where I first got wind of *him*—Odysseus . . .
The king told me he'd hosted the man in style,
befriended him on his way home to native land,   365
and showed me all the treasure Odysseus had amassed.
Bronze and gold and plenty of hard wrought iron,
enough to last a man and ten generations of his heirs—
so great the wealth stored up for *him* in the king's vaults!
But Odysseus, he made clear, was off at Dodona[5] then   370
to hear the will of Zeus that rustles forth
from the god's tall leafy oak: how should he return,
after all the years away, to his own green land of Ithaca—
openly or in secret? Phidon swore to me, what's more,
as the princely man poured out libations in his house,   375
'The ship's hauled down and the crew set to sail,
to take Odysseus home to native land.'
                              But I . . .
he shipped me off before. A Thesprotian cutter
chanced to be heading for Dulichion[6] rich in wheat,
so he told the crew to take me to the king, Acastus,   380
treat me kindly, too, but it pleased them more
to scheme foul play against me,
sink me into the very depths of pain. As soon
as the ship was far off land, scudding in mid-sea,
they sprang their trap—my day of slavery then and there!   385
They stripped from my back the shirt and cloak I wore,
decked me out in a new suit of clothes, all rags,
ripped and filthy—the rags you see right now.
But then, once they'd gained the fields of Ithaca,
still clear in the evening light, they lashed me fast   390
to the rowing-benches, twisting a cable round me;
all hands went ashore
and rushed to catch their supper on the beach.
But the gods themselves unhitched my knots at once
with the gods' own ease. I wrapped my head in rags,   395
slid down the gangplank polished smooth, slipped my body
into the water, not a splash, chest-high, then quick,
launched out with both my arms and swam away—
out of the surf in no time, clear of the crew.
I clambered upland, into a flowery, fragrant brush   400
and crouched there, huddling low. They raised a hue and cry,
wildly beat the bushes, but when it seemed no use

4. "He Who Spares" or "Saves." Thesprotio is a region on the west coast of the Greek mainland, north of
Ithaca.   5. Site of an oracle of Zeus in the northwest of the Greek mainland. The god's message was
supposed to come from a sacred oak in the sanctuary, perhaps from the rustling of leaves in the wind.
6. An island evidently near Ithaca (its exact location is unknown)

to pursue the hunt, back they trudged again and
boarded their empty ship.
                              The gods hid me themselves—
it's light work for them—and brought me here,   405
the homestead of a man who knows the world.
So it seems to be my lot that I'll live on."

   And you replied, Eumaeus, loyal swineherd,
"So much misery, friend! You've moved my heart,
deeply, with your long tale . . . such blows, such roving.   410
But one part's off the mark, I know—you'll never persuade me—
what you say about Odysseus. A man in your condition,
who are *you*, I ask you, to lie for no good reason?
Well I know the truth of my good lord's return,
how the gods detested him, with a vengeance—   415
never letting him go under, fighting Trojans,
or die in the arms of loved ones,
once he'd wound down the long coil of war.
Then all united Achaea would have raised his tomb
and he'd have won his son great fame for years to come.   420
But now the whirlwinds have ripped him away—no fame for him!
And I live here, cut off from the world, with all my pigs.
I never go into town unless, perhaps, wise Penelope
calls me back, when news drops in from nowhere.
There they crowd the messenger, cross-examine him,   425
heartsick for their long-lost lord or all too glad
to eat him out of house and home, scot-free.
But I've no love for all that probing, prying,
not since some Aetolian[7] fooled me with his yarn.
He'd killed a man, wandered over the face of the earth,   430
stumbled onto my hut, and I received him warmly.
He told me he'd seen Odysseus
lodged with King Idomeneus down in Crete—
refitting his ships, hard-hit by the gales,
but he'd be home, he said, by summer or harvest-time,   435
his hulls freighted with treasure, manned by fighting crews.
So you, old misery, seeing a god has led you here to me,
don't try to charm me now, don't spellbind me with lies!
Never for *that* will I respect you, treat you kindly;
no, it's my fear of Zeus, the god of guests,   440
and because I pity you . . ."

   "Good god," the crafty man pressed on,
"what a dark, suspicious heart you have inside you!
Not even my oath can win you over, make you see the light.
Come, strike a bargain—all the gods of Olympus   445
witness now our pact!
If your master returns, here to your house,
dress me in shirt and cloak and send me off
to Dulichion at once, the place I long to be.

7. Aetolia is on the mainland, east of Ithaca.

and a shining waist-guard . . . But then at last,
the night's third watch, the stars just wheeling down—
I muttered into his ear, Odysseus, right beside me,   550
nudging him with an elbow—he perked up at once—
'Royal son of Laertes, Odysseus, full of tactics,
I'm not long for the living. The cold will do me in.
See, I've got no cloak. Some spirit's fooled me—
I came out half-dressed. Now there's no escape!'   555
I hadn't finished—a thought flashed in his mind;
no one could touch the man at plots or battles.
'Shhh!' he hissed back—Odysseus had a plan—
'One of our fighters over there might hear you.'
Then he propped his head on his forearm, calling out,   560
'Friends, wake up. I slept and a god sent down a dream.
It warned that we're too far from the ships, exposed.
Go, someone, tell Agamemnon, our field marshal—
he might rush reinforcements from the beach.'
Thoas, son of Andraemon, sprang up at once,   565
flung off his purple cloak and ran to the ships
while I, bundling into his wrap, was glad at heart
till Dawn rose on her golden throne once more.
Oh make me young again
and the strength inside me steady as a rock!   570
One of the swineherds here would lend a wrap
for love of a good soldier, respect as well.
Now they spurn me, dressed in filthy rags."

    And you replied, Eumaeus, loyal swineherd,
"Now that was a fine yarn you told, old-timer,   575
not without point, not without profit either.
You won't want for clothes or whatever else
is due a worn-out traveler come for help—
not for tonight at least. Tomorrow morning
you'll have to flap around in rags again.   580
Here we've got no store of shirts and cloaks,
no changes. Just one wrap per man, that's all.
But just you wait till Odysseus' dear son comes back—
that boy will deck you out in a cloak and shirt
and send you off, wherever your heart desires!"
                                        With that   585
he rose to his feet and laid out a bed by the fire,
throwing over it skins of sheep and goats and
down Odysseus lay. Eumaeus flung on his guest
the heavy flaring cloak he kept in reserve
to wear when winter brought some wild storm.
                                        So here   590
Odysseus slept and the young hands slept beside him.
Not the swineherd. Not his style to bed indoors,
apart from his pigs. He geared up to go outside
and it warmed Odysseus' heart,
Eumaeus cared so much for his absent master's goods.   595
First, over his broad shoulders he slung a whetted sword,

wrapped himself in a cloak stitched tight to block the wind,
and adding a cape, the pelt of a shaggy well-fed goat,
he took a good sharp lance to fight off men and dogs.
Then out he went to sleep where his white-tusked boars   600
had settled down for the night . . . just under
a jutting crag that broke the North Wind's blast.

BOOK XV

[The Prince Sets Sail for Home]

Now south through the spacious dancing-rings of Lacedaemon
Athena went to remind the hero's princely son
of his journey home and spur him on his way.
She found him there with Nestor's gallant son,
bedded down in the porch of illustrious Menelaus—   5
Pisistratus, at least, overcome with deep sound sleep,
but not Telemachus. Welcome sleep could not hold him.
All through the godsent night he lay awake . . .
tossing with anxious thoughts about his father.
Hovering over him, eyes ablaze, Athena said,   10
"It's wrong, Telemachus, wrong to rove so far,
so long from home, leaving your own holdings
unprotected—crowds in your palace so brazen
they'll carve up all your wealth, devour it all,
and then your journey here will come to nothing.   15
Quickly, press Menelaus, lord of the warcry,
to speed you home at once, if you want to find
your irreproachable mother still inside your house.
Even now her father and brothers urge Penelope
to marry Eurymachus, who excels all other suitors   20
at giving gifts and drives the bride-price higher.
She must not carry anything off against your will!
You know how the heart of a woman always works:
she likes to build the wealth of her new groom—
of the sons she bore, of her dear, departed husband,   25
not a memory of the dead, no questions asked.
So sail for home, I say!
With your own hands turn over all your goods
to the one serving-woman you can trust the most,
till the gods bring to light your own noble bride.   30

    And another thing. Take it to heart, I tell you.
Picked men of the suitors lie in ambush, grim-set
in the straits between Ithaca and rocky Same,
poised to kill you before you can reach home,
but I have my doubts they will. Sooner the earth   35
will swallow down a few of those young gallants
who eat you out of house and home these days!
Just give the channel islands a wide berth,
push on in your trim ship, sail night and day,
and the deathless god who guards and pulls you through   40
will send you a fresh fair wind from hard astern.

At your first landfall, Ithaca's outer banks,
speed ship and shipmates round to the city side.
But you—you make your way to the swineherd first,
in charge of your pigs, and true to you as always.   45
Sleep the night there, send him to town at once
to tell the news to your mother, wise Penelope—
you've made it back from Pylos safe and sound."

    Mission accomplished, back she went to Olympus' heights
as Telemachus woke Nestor's son from his sweet sleep;   50
he dug a heel in his ribs and roused him briskly:
"Up, Pisistratus. Hitch the team to the chariot—
let's head for home at once!"
                "No, Telemachus,"
Nestor's son objected, "much as we long to go,
we cannot drive a team in the dead of night.   55
Morning will soon be here. So wait, I say,
wait till he loads our chariot down with gifts—
the hero Atrides, Menelaus, the great spearman—
and gives us warm salutes and sees us off like princes.
That's the man a guest will remember all his days: 60
the lavish host who showers him with kindness."

    At those words Dawn rose on her golden throne
and Menelaus, lord of the warcry, rising up from bed
by the side of Helen with her loose and lovely hair,
walked toward his guests. As soon as he saw him,   65
Telemachus rushed to pull a shimmering tunic on,
over his broad shoulders threw his flaring cape
and the young prince, son of King Odysseus,
strode out to meet his host: "Menelaus,
royal son of Atreus, captain of armies,   70
let me go back to my own country now.
The heart inside me longs for home at last."

    The lord of the warcry reassured the prince,
"I'd never detain you here too long, Telemachus,
not if your heart is set on going home.   75
I'd find fault with another host, I'm sure,
too warm to his guests, too pressing or too cold.
Balance is best in all things. It's bad either way,
spurring the stranger home who wants to linger,
holding the one who longs to leave—you know,   80
'Welcome the coming, speed the parting guest!'
But wait till I load your chariot down with gifts—
fine ones, too, you'll see with your own eyes—
and tell the maids to serve a meal at hall.
We have god's plenty here.   85
It's honor and glory to us, a help to you as well
if you dine in style first, then leave to see the world.
And if you're keen for the grand tour of all Hellas,
right to the depths of Argos, I'll escort you myself,

harness the horses, guide you through the towns. 90
And no host will turn us away with empty hands,
each will give us at least one gift to prize—
a handsome tripod, cauldron forged in bronze,
a brace of mules or a solid golden cup."

Firmly resolved, Telemachus replied, 95
"Menelaus, royal Atrides, captain of armies,
I must go back to my own home at once.
When I started out I left no one behind
to guard my own possessions. God forbid,
searching for my great father, I lose my life 100
or lose some priceless treasure from my house!"

As soon as the lord of the warcry heard *that*,
he told his wife and serving-women to lay out a meal
in the hall at once. They'd stores aplenty there.
Eteoneus, son of Boëthous, came to join them— 105
fresh from bed, he lived close by the palace.
The warlord Menelaus told him to build a fire
and broil some meat. He quickly did his bidding.
Down Atrides walked to a storeroom filled with scent,
and not alone: Helen and Megapenthes went along. 110
Reaching the spot where all the heirlooms lay,
Menelaus chose a generous two-handled cup;
he told his son Megapenthes to take a mixing-bowl,
solid silver, while Helen lingered beside the chests,
and there they were, brocaded, beautiful robes 115
her own hands hand woven. Queenly Helen,
radiance of women, lifted one from the lot,
the largest, loveliest robe, and richly worked
and like a star it glistened, deep beneath the others.
Then all three went up and on through the halls until 120
they found Telemachus. The red-haired king spoke out:
"Oh my boy, may Zeus the Thunderer, Hera's lord,
grant you the journey home your heart desires!
Of all the treasures lying heaped in my palace
you shall have the finest, most esteemed. Look, 125
I'll give you this mixing-bowl, forged to perfection—
it's solid silver finished off with a lip of gold.
Hephaestus made it himself. And a royal friend,
Phaedimus, king of Sidon, lavished it on *me*
when his palace welcomed me on passage home. 130
How pleased I'd be if you took it as a gift!"

And the warlord placed the two-eared cup
in his hands while stalwart Megapenthes carried in
the glittering silver bowl and set it down before him.
Helen, her cheeks flushed with beauty, moved beside him, 135
holding the robe in her arms, and offered, warmly,
"Here, dear boy, I too have a gift to give you,
a keepsake of Helen—I wove it with my hands—

for your own bride to wear
when the blissful day of marriage dawns . . .   140
Until then, let it rest in your mother's room.
And may you return in joy—my parting wish—
to your own grand house, your native land at last."

                                                    With that
she laid the robe in his arms, and he received it gladly.
Prince Pisistratus, taking the gifts, stowed them deep   145
in the chariot cradle, viewed them all with wonder.
The red-haired warlord led them back to his house
and the guests took seats on low and high-backed chairs.
A maid brought water soon in a graceful golden pitcher
and over a silver basin tipped it out   150
so they might rinse their hands,
then pulled a gleaming table to their side.
A staid housekeeper brought on bread to serve them,
appetizers aplenty too, lavish with her bounty.
Ready Eteoneus carved and passed the meat,   155
the son of illustrious Menelaus poured their wine.
They reached out for the good things that lay at hand
and once they'd put aside desire for food and drink,
Prince Telemachus and the gallant son of Nestor
yoked their team, mounted the blazoned car   160
and drove through the gates and echoing colonnade.
The red-haired King Menelaus followed both boys out,
his right hand holding a golden cup of honeyed wine
so the two might pour libations forth at parting.
Just in front of the straining team he strode,   165
lifting his cup and pledging both his guests:
"Farewell, my princes! Give my warm greetings
to Nestor, the great commander,
always kind to me as a father, long ago
when we young men of Achaea fought at Troy."   170

    And tactful Telemachus replied at once,
"Surely, my royal host, we'll tell him all,
as soon as we reach old Nestor—all you say.
I wish I were just as sure I'd find Odysseus
waiting there at home when I reach Ithaca.   175
I'd tell him I come from you,
treated with so much kindness at your hands,
loaded down with all these priceless gifts!"

    At his last words a bird flew past on the right,
an eagle clutching a huge white goose in its talons,   180
plucked from the household yards. And all rushed after,
shouting, men and women, and swooping toward the chariot now
the bird veered off to the right again before the horses.
All looked up, overjoyed—people's spirits lifted.
Nestor's son Pisistratus spoke out first: 185
"Look there! King Menelaus, captain of armies,
what, did the god send down that sign for you

or the two of us?"
         The warlord fell to thinking—
how to read the omen rightly, how to reply? . . .
But long-robed Helen stepped in well before him: 190
"Listen to me and I will be your prophet,
sure as the gods have flashed it in my mind
and it will come to pass, I know it will.
Just as the eagle swooped down from the crags
where it was born and bred, just as it snatched   195
that goose fattened up for the kill inside the house,
just so, after many trials and roving long and hard,
Odysseus will descend on his house and take revenge—
unless he's home already, sowing seeds of ruin
for that whole crowd of suitors!"
                  "Oh if only,"   200
pensive Telemachus burst out in thanks to Helen,
"Zeus the thundering lord of Hera makes it so—
even at home I'll pray to you as a deathless goddess!"

   He cracked the lash and the horses broke quickly,
careering through the city out into open country,   205
shaking the yoke across their shoulders all day long.

   The sun sank and the roads of the world grew dark
as they reached Phera, pulling up to Diocles' halls,
the son of Ortilochus, son of the Alpheus River.
He gave them a royal welcome; there they slept the night.   210

   When young Dawn with her rose-red fingers shone once more
they yoked their pair again, mounted the blazoned car
and out through the gates and echoing colonnade
they whipped the team to a run and on they flew,
holding nothing back, approaching Pylos soon,   215
the craggy citadel. That was when Telemachus
turned to Pisistratus, saying, "Son of Nestor,
won't you do as I ask you, see it through?
We're friends for all our days now, so we claim,
thanks to our fathers' friendship. We're the same age as well   220
and this tour of ours has made us more like brothers.
Prince, don't drive me past my vessel, drop me there.
Your father's old, in love with his hospitality;
I fear he'll hold me, chafing in his palace—
I must hurry home!"
            The son of Nestor pondered . . .   225
how to do it properly, see it through?
Pausing a moment, then this way seemed best.
Swerving his team, he drove down to the ship
tied up on shore and loaded into her stern
the splendid gifts, the robes and gold Menelaus gave,   230
and sped his friend with a flight of winging words:
"Climb aboard now—fast! Muster all your men
before I get home and break the news to father.

With that man's overbearing spirit—I know it,
know it all too well—he'll never let you go,   235
he'll come down here and summon you himself.
He won't return without you, believe me—
in any case he'll fly into a rage."

    With that warning he whipped his sleek horses
back to Pylos city and reached his house in no time.   240
Telemachus shouted out commands to all his shipmates:
"Stow our gear, my comrades, deep in the holds
and board at once—we must be on our way!"

    His shipmates snapped to orders,
swung aboard and sat to the oars in ranks.   245
But just as Telemachus prepared to launch,
praying, sacrificing to Pallas by the stern,
a man from a far-off country came toward him now,
a fugitive out of Argos: he had killed a man . . .
He was a prophet, sprung of Melampus' line of seers,[8]   250
Melampus who lived in Pylos, mother of flocks, some years ago,
rich among his Pylians, at home in his great high house.
But then he was made to go abroad to foreign parts,
fleeing his native land and hot-blooded Neleus—
most imperious man alive—who'd commandeered   255
his vast estate and held it down by force
for one entire year. That year Melampus,
bound by cruel chains in the halls of Phylacus,
suffered agonies—all for Neleus' daughter Pero,
that and the mad spell a Fury, murderous spirit,   260
cast upon his mind. But the seer worked free of death
and drove the lusty, bellowing cattle out of Phylace,
back to Pylos. There he avenged himself on Neleus
for the shameful thing the king had done to him,
and escorted Pero home as his brother's bride.   265
But he himself went off to a distant country,
Argos, land of stallions—his destined home
where he would live and rule the Argive nation.
Here he married a wife and built a high-roofed house
and sired Antiphates and Mantius, two staunch sons.   270
Antiphates fathered Oicles, gallant heart,
Oicles fathered Amphiaraus, driver of armies,
whom storming Zeus and Apollo loved intensely,
showering him with every form of kindness.
But he never reached the threshold of old age,   275

---

8. Melampus's brother (who lived in Pylos under King Neleus, Nestor's father) asked for the hand of
Neleus's daughter Pero (whose shade Odysseus sees in the land of the dead in book XI). Neleus demanded
as bride-price the herds of cattle of a neighboring lord, Phylacus. Attempting to steal the cattle for his
brother, Melampus was caught and imprisoned. In prison he heard the worms in the roof beams announce
that the wood was almost eaten through, and he predicted the collapse of the roof. Phylacus, impressed,
released him and gave him the cattle; his brother was given the bride. Melampus then settled in Argos and
prospered. The prophet Amphiaraus, one of Melampus's great-grandsons, foresaw that if he joined the
champions who went to besiege Thebes he would lose his life. Melampus's son Mantius had a son named
Polyphides, and it is his son Theoclymenus who now begs Telemachus for a place in his ship.

he died at Thebes—undone by a bribe his wife[9] accepted—
leaving behind his two sons, Alcmaeon and Amphilochus.
On his side Mantius sired Polyphides and Clitus both
but Dawn of the golden throne whisked Clitus away,
overwhelmed by his beauty,   280
so the boy would live among the deathless gods.
Yet Apollo made magnanimous Polyphides a prophet—
after Amphiaraus' death—the greatest seer on earth.
But a feud with his father drove him off to Hyperesia[1]
where he made his home and prophesied to the world . . .   285

    This prophet's son it was—Theoclymenus his name—
who approached Telemachus now and found him pouring
wine to a god and saying prayers beside his ship.
"Friend," he said in a winging supplication,
"since I find you burning offerings here,   290
I beg you by these rites and the god you pray to,
then by your own life and the lives of all the men
who travel with you—tell me truly, don't hold back,
who are you? where are you from? your city? your parents?"

    "Of course, stranger," the forthright prince responded,   295
"I will tell you everything, clearly as I can.
Ithaca is my country. Odysseus is my father—
there was a man, or was he all a dream? . . .
but he's surely died a wretched death by now.
Yet here I've come with my crew and black ship,   300
out for news of my father, lost and gone so long."

    And the godlike seer Theoclymenus replied,
Just like you, I too have left my land—
I because I killed a man of my own tribe.
But he has many brothers and kin in Argos,   305
stallion-land, who rule the plains in force.
Fleeing death at their hands, a dismal fate,
I am a fugitive now,
doomed to wander across this mortal world.
So take me aboard, hear a fugitive's prayer: 310
don't let them kill me—they're after me, well I know!"

    "So desperate!" thoughtful Telemachus exclaimed.
"How could I drive you from my ship? Come sail with us,
we'll tend you at home, with all we can provide."

    And he took the prophet's honed bronze spear,   315
laid it down full-length on the rolling deck,
swung aboard the deep-sea craft himself,
assuming the pilot's seat reserved astern
and put the seer beside him. Cables cast off,

9. Eriphyle, whose shade Odysseus sees in book XI.   1. Near Argos.

Telemachus shouted out commands to all his shipmates: 320
"All lay hands to tackle!" They sprang to orders,
hoisting the pinewood mast, they stepped it firm
in its block amidships, lashed it fast with stays
and with braided rawhide halyards hauled the white sail high.
Now bright-eyed Athena sent them a stiff following wind   325
blustering out of a clear sky, gusting on so the ship
might run its course through the salt sea at top speed—
and past the Springs she raced and the Chalcis' rushing stream
as the sun sank and the roads of the world grew dark and
on she pressed for Pheae, driven on by a wind from Zeus   330
and flew past lovely Elis, where Epeans rule in power,
and then Telemachus veered for the Jagged Islands,[2]
wondering all the way—
would he sweep clear of death or be cut down?

    The King and loyal swineherd, just that night,   335
were supping with other fieldhands in the lodge.
And once they'd put aside desire for food and drink,
Odysseus spoke up, eager to test the swineherd,
see if he'd stretch out his warm welcome now,
invite him to stay on in the farmstead here   340
or send him off to town. "Listen, Eumaeus,
all you comrades here—at the crack of dawn
I mean to go to town and do my begging,
not be a drain on you and all your men.
But advise me well, give me a trusty guide   345
to see me there. And then I'm on my own
to roam the streets—I must, I have no choice—
hoping to find a handout, just a crust or cupful.
I'd really like to go to the house of King Odysseus
and give my news to his cautious queen, Penelope.   350
Why, I'd even mix with those overweening suitors—
would they spare me a plateful? Look at all they have!
I'd do good work for them, promptly, anything they want.
Let me tell you, listen closely, catch my drift . . .
Thanks to Hermes the guide, who gives all work   355
of our hands the grace and fame that it deserves,
no one alive can match me at household chores:
building a good fire, splitting kindling neatly,
carving, roasting meat and pouring rounds of wine . . .
anything menials do to serve their noble masters."   360

    "God's sake, my friend!" you broke in now,
Eumaeus, loyal swineherd, deeply troubled.
"What's got into your head, what crazy plan?
You must be hell-bent on destruction, on the spot,
if you're keen to mingle with that mob of suitors—   365
their pride and violence hit the iron skies!
They're a far cry from you,

2. The precise location of these places is uncertain, but the mention of Elis in line 331 suggests that all are on the west coast of the Peloponnesus, south of the Gulf of Corinth.

the men who do their bidding. Young bucks,
all rigged out in their fine robes and shirts,
hair sleeked down with oil, faces always beaming,   370
the ones who slave for *them!* The tables polished,
sagging under the bread and meat and wine.
No, stay here. No one finds you a burden,
surely not I, not any comrade here.
You wait till Odysseus' dear son comes back—   375
that boy will deck you out in a cloak and shirt
and send you off, wherever your heart desires!"

   "If only, Eumaeus," the wayworn exile said,
"you were as dear to Father Zeus as you are to me!
You who stopped my pain, my endless, homesick roving.   380
Tramping about the world—there's nothing worse for a man.
But the fact is that men put up with misery
to stuff their cursed bellies.
But seeing you hold me here, urging me now
to wait for *him*, the prince who's on his way,   385
tell me about the mother of King Odysseus, please,
the father he left as well—on the threshold of old age—
when he sailed off to war. Are they still alive,
perhaps, still looking into the light of day?
Or dead by now, and down in Death's long house?"

                                                      "Friend,"   390
the swineherd, foreman of men, assured his guest,
"I'll tell you the whole story, point by point.
Laertes is still alive, but night and day
he prays to Zeus, waiting there in his house,
for the life breath to slip away and leave his body.   395
His heart's so racked for his son, lost and gone these years,
for his wife so fine, so wise—*her* death is the worst blow
he's had to suffer—it made him old before his time.
She died of grief for her boy, her glorious boy,
it wore her down, a wretched way to go.   400
I pray that no one I love dies such a death,
no island neighbor of mine who treats me kindly!
While she was still alive, heartsick as she was,
it always moved me to ask about her, learn the news.
She'd reared me herself, and right beside her daughter,   405
Ctimene, graceful girl with her long light gown,
the youngest one she'd borne . . .
Just the two of us, growing up together,
the woman tending me almost like her child,
till we both reached the lovely flush of youth   410
and then her parents gave her away in marriage, yes,
to a Samian[3] man, and a haul of gifts they got.
But her mother decked me out in cloak and shirt,
good clothing she wrapped about me—gave me sandals,
sent me here, this farm. She loved me from the heart.   415

---

3. From Same, a nearby island or town.

Oh how I miss her kindness now! The happy gods
speed the work that I labor at, that gives me
food and drink to spare for the ones I value.
But from Queen Penelope I never get a thing,
never a winning word, no friendly gesture,   420
not since this, this plague has hit the house—
these high and mighty suitors. Servants miss it,
terribly, gossiping back and forth with the mistress,
gathering scraps of news, a snack and a cup or two,
then taking home to the fields some little gift.   425
It never fails to cheer a servant's heart."

   "Imagine that," his canny master said,
"you must have been just a little fellow, Eumaeus,
when you were swept so far from home and parents.
Come, tell me the whole story, truly too.   430
Was your city sacked?—
some city filled with people and wide streets
where your father and your mother made their home?
Or were you all alone, herding your sheep and cattle,
when pirates kidnapped, shipped and sold you off   435
to this man's house, who paid a healthy price?"

   "My friend," the swineherd answered, foreman of men,
"you really want my story? So many questions—well,
listen in quiet, then, and take your ease, sit back
and drink your wine. The nights are endless now.   440
We've plenty of time to sleep or savor a long tale.
No need, you know, to turn in before the hour.
Even too much sleep can be a bore.
But anyone else who feels the urge
can go to bed and then, at the crack of dawn,   445
break bread, turn out and tend our master's pigs.
We two will keep to the shelter here, eat and drink
and take some joy in each other's heartbreaking sorrows,
sharing each other's memories. Over the years, you know,
a man finds solace even in old sorrows, true, a man   450
who's weathered many blows and wandered many miles.
My own story? This will answer all your questions . . .

   There's an island, Syrie—you may have heard of it—
off above Ortygia,[4] out where the sun wheels around.
Not so packed with people, still a good place, though,   455
fine for sheep and cattle, rich in wine and wheat.
Hunger never attacks the land, no sickness either,
that always stalks the lives of us poor men.
No, as each generation grows old on the island,
down Apollo comes with his silver bow, with Artemis,   460
and they shoot them all to death with gentle arrows.

---

4. The Greeks knew several islands named Ortygia, but the absence of disease and hunger suggests that
this one, like Phaeacia, is in fantasyland.

Two cities there are, that split the land in half,
and over them both my father ruled in force—
Ormenus' son Ctesius, a man like a deathless god.
                                                     One day
a band of Phoenicians landed there. The famous sea-dogs,   465
sharp bargainers too, the holds of their black ship
brimful with a hoard of flashy baubles. Now,
my father kept a Phoenician woman in his house,
beautiful, tall and skilled at weaving lovely things,
and her rascal countrymen lusted to seduce her, yes,   470
and lost no time—she was washing clothes when one of them
waylaid her beside their ship, in a long deep embrace
that can break a woman's will, even the best alive.
And then he asked her questions . . .
her name, who was she, where did she come from?   475
She waved at once to my father's high-roofed house—
'But I'm proud to hail from Sidon paved in bronze,' she said,
'and Arybas was my father, a man who rolled in wealth.
I was heading home from the fields when Taphian pirates
snatched me away, and they shipped and sold me here   480
to this man's house. He paid a good stiff price!'

     The sailor, her secret lover, lured her on:
'Well then, why don't you sail back home with us?—
see your own high house, your father and mother there.
They're still alive, and people say they're rich!'   485

     'Now there's a tempting offer,' she said in haste,
'if only you sailors here would swear an oath
you'll land me safe at home without a scratch.'

     Those were her terms, and once they vowed to keep them,
swore their oaths they'd never do her harm,   490
the woman hatched a plan: 'Now not a word!
Let none of your shipmates say a thing to me,
meeting me on the street or at the springs.
Someone might go running off to the house
and tell the old king—he'd think the worst,   495
clap me in cruel chains and find a way to kill you.
So keep it a secret, down deep, get on with buying
your home cargo, quickly. But once your holds
are loaded up with goods, then fast as you can
you send the word to me over there at the palace.   500
I'll bring you all the gold I can lay my hands on
and something else I'll give you in the bargain,
fare for passage home . . .
I'm nurse to my master's son in the palace now—
such a precious toddler, scampering round outside,   505
always at my heels. I'll bring him aboard as well.
Wherever you sell him off, whatever foreign parts,
he'll fetch you quite a price!'
                                    Bargain struck,

back the woman went to our lofty halls
and the rovers stayed on with us one whole year,   510
bartering, piling up big hoards in their hollow ship,
and once their holds were loaded full for sailing
they sent a messenger, fast, to alert the woman.
This crafty bandit came to my father's house,
dangling a golden choker linked with amber beads,   515
and while the maids at hall and my noble mother
kept on fondling it—dazzled, feasting their eyes
and making bids—he gave a quiet nod to my nurse,
he gave her the nod and slunk back to his ship.
Grabbing my hand, she swept me through the house   520
and there in the porch she came on cups and tables
left by the latest feasters, father's men of council
just gone off to the meeting grounds for full debate—
and quick as a flash she snatched up three goblets,
tucked them into her bosom, whisked them off   525
and I tagged along, lost in all my innocence!
The sun sank, the roads of the world grew dark
and both on the run, we reached the bay at once
where the swift Phoenician ship lay set to sail.
Handing us up on board, the crewmen launched out   530
on the foaming lanes and Zeus sent wind astern.
Six whole days we sailed, six nights, nonstop
and then, when the god brought on the seventh day,
Artemis showering arrows came and shot the woman—
headfirst into the bilge she splashed like a diving tern   535
and the crewmen heaved her body over, a nice treat
for the seals and fish, but left me all alone,
cowering, sick at heart . . .
                              Until, at last,
the wind and current bore us on to Ithaca,
here where Laertes bought me with his wealth.   540
And so I first laid eyes on this good land."

    And royal King Odysseus answered warmly,
"Eumaeus, so much misery! You've moved my heart,
deeply, with your long tale—such pain, such sorrow.
True, but look at the good fortune Zeus sends you,   545
hand-in-hand with the bad. After all your toil
you reached the house of a decent, kindly man
who gives you all you need in meat and drink—
he's seen to that, I'd say—
it's a fine life you lead! Better than mine . . .   550
I've been drifting through cities up and down the earth
and now I've landed here."
                              So guest and host
confided through the night until they slept,
a little at least, not long.
Dawn soon rose and took her golden throne.
                              That hour   555
Telemachus and his shipmates raised the coasts of home,

they struck sail and lowered the mast, smartly,
rowed her into a mooring under oars.
Out went the bow-stones, cables fast astern,
the crew themselves swung out in the breaking surf,   560
they got a meal together and mixed some ruddy wine.
And once they'd put aside desire for food and drink,
clear-headed Telemachus gave the men commands:
"Pull our black ship round to the city now—
I'm off to my herdsmen and my farms. By nightfall,   565
once I've seen to my holdings, I'll be down in town.
In the morning I'll give you wages for the voyage,
a handsome feast of meat and hearty wine."

    The seer Theoclymenus broke in quickly,
"Where shall I go, dear boy? Of all the lords   570
in rocky Ithaca, whose house shall I head for now?
Or do I go straight to your mother's house and yours?"

    "Surely in better times," discreet Telemachus replied,
"I would invite you home. Our hospitality never fails
but now, I fear, it could only serve you poorly.   575
I'll be away, and mother would never see you.
She rarely appears these days,
what with those suitors milling in the hall;
she keeps to her upper story, weaving at her loom.
But I'll mention someone else you might just visit: 580
Eurymachus, wise Polybus' fine, upstanding son.
He's the man of the hour! Our island people
look on him like a god—the prince of suitors,
hottest to wed my mother, seize my father's powers.
But god knows—Zeus up there in his bright Olympus—   585
whether or not before that wedding day arrives
he'll bring the day of death on all their heads!"

    At his last words a bird flew past on the right,
a hawk, Apollo's wind-swift herald—tight in his claws
a struggling dove, and he ripped its feathers out   590
and they drifted down to earth between the ship
and the young prince himself . . .
The prophet called him aside, clear of his men,
and grasped his hand, exclaiming, "Look, Telemachus,
the will of god just winged that bird on your right!   595
Why, the moment I saw it, here before my eyes,
I knew it was a sign. No line more kingly than yours
in all of Ithaca—yours will reign forever!"
                              "If only, friend,"
alert Telemachus answered, "all you say comes true!
You'd soon know my affection, know my gifts.   600
Any man you meet would call you blest."

    He turned to a trusted friend and said, "Piraeus,
son of Clytius, you are the one who's done my bidding,

more than all other friends who sailed with me to Pylos.
Please, take this guest of mine to your own house,   605
treat him kindly, host him with all good will
till I can come myself."
                           "Of course, Telemachus,"
Piraeus the gallant spearman offered warmly:
"Stay up-country just as long as you like.
I'll tend the man, he'll never lack a lodging."   610

        Piraeus boarded ship and told the crew
to embark at once and cast off cables quickly—
they swung aboard and sat to the oars in ranks.
Telemachus fastened rawhide sandals on his feet
and took from the decks his rugged bronze-tipped spear.   615
The men cast off, pushed out and pulled for town
as Telemachus ordered, King Odysseus' son.
The prince strode out briskly,
legs speeding him on till he reached the farm
where his great droves of pigs crowded their pens   620
and the loyal swineherd often slept beside them,
always the man to serve his masters well.

BOOK XVI

[Father and Son]

As dawn came into the lodge, the king and loyal swineherd
set out breakfast, once they had raked the fire up
and got the herdsmen off with droves of pigs.
And now Telemachus . . .
the howling dogs went nuzzling up around him,   5
not a growl as he approached. From inside
Odysseus noticed the pack's quiet welcome,
noticed the light tread of footsteps too
and turned to Eumaeus quickly, winged a word:
"Eumaeus, here comes a friend of yours, I'd say.   10
Someone you know, at least. The pack's not barking,
must be fawning around him. I can hear his footfall."

        The words were still on his lips when his own son
stood in the doorway, there. The swineherd started up,
amazed, he dropped the bowls with a clatter—he'd been busy   15
mixing ruddy wine. Straight to the prince he rushed
and kissed his face and kissed his shining eyes,
both hands, as the tears rolled down his cheeks.
As a father, brimming with love, welcomes home
his darling only son in a warm embrace—   20
what pain he's borne for him and him alone!—
home now, in the tenth year from far abroad,
so the loyal swineherd hugged the beaming prince,
he clung for dear life, covering him with kisses, yes,
like one escaped from death. Eumaeus wept and sobbed,   25
his words flew from the heart: "You're home, Telemachus,

sweet light of my eyes! I never thought I'd see you again,
once you'd shipped to Pylos! Quick, dear boy, come in,
let me look at you, look to my heart's content—
under my own roof, the rover home at last.   30
You rarely visit the farm and men these days,
always keeping to town, as if it *cheered* you
to see them there, that infernal crowd of suitors!"

    "Have it your way," thoughtful Telemachus replied.
"Dear old man, it's all for you that I've come,   35
to see you for myself and learn the news—
whether mother still holds out in the halls
or some other man has married her at last,
and Odysseus' bed, I suppose, is lying empty,
blanketed now with filthy cobwebs."
                              "Surely,"   40
the foreman of men responded, "she's still waiting
there in your halls, poor woman, suffering so,
her life an endless hardship . . .
wasting away the nights, weeping away the days."
                                          With that
he took the bronze spear from the boy, and Telemachus,   45
crossing the stone doorsill, went inside the lodge.
As he approached, his father, Odysseus, rose
to yield his seat, but the son on his part
waved him back: "Stay where you are, stranger.
I know we can find another seat somewhere,   50
here on our farm, and here's the man to fetch it."

    So Odysseus, moving back, sat down once more,
and now for the prince the swineherd strewed a bundle
of fresh green brushwood, topped it off with sheepskin
and there the true son of Odysseus took his place.   55
Eumaeus set before them platters of roast meat
left from the meal he'd had the day before;
he promptly served them bread, heaped in baskets,
mixed their hearty wine in a wooden bowl
and then sat down himself to face the king.   60
They reached for the good things that lay at hand,
and when they'd put aside desire for food and drink
Telemachus asked his loyal serving-man at last,
"Old friend, where does this stranger come from?
Why did the sailors land him here in Ithaca?   65
Who did they say they are?
I hardly think he came this way on foot."

    You answered him, Eumaeus, loyal swineherd,
"Here, my boy, I'll tell you the whole true story.
He hails from Crete's broad land, he's proud to say,   70
but he claims he's drifted round through countless towns of men,
roaming the earth . . . and so a god's spun out his fate.
He just now broke away from some Thesprotian ship

and came to my farm. I'll put him in *your* hands,
you tend to him as you like.   75
He counts on you, he says, for care and shelter."

    "Shelter? Oh Eumaeus," Telemachus replied,
"that word of yours, it cuts me to the quick!
How can I lend the stranger refuge in my house?
I'm young myself. I can hardly trust my hands   80
to fight off any man who rises up against me.
Then my mother's wavering, always torn two ways:
whether to stay with me and care for the household,
true to her husband's bed, the people's voice as well,
or leave at long last with the best man in Achaea   85
who courts her in the halls, who offers her the most.
But our new guest, since he's arrived at your house,
I'll give him a shirt and cloak to wear, good clothing,
give him a two-edged sword and sandals for his feet
and send him off, wherever his heart desires.   90
Or if you'd rather, keep him here at the farmstead,
tend to him here, and I'll send up the clothes
and full rations to keep the man in food;
he'll be no drain on you and all your men.
But I can't let him go down and join the suitors.   95
They're far too abusive, reckless, know no limits:
they'll make a mockery of him—that would break my heart.
It's hard for a man to win his way against a mob,
even a man of iron. They are much too strong."

    "Friend"—the long-enduring Odysseus stepped in—   100
"surely it's right for *me* to say a word at this point.
My heart, by god, is torn to pieces hearing this,
both of you telling how these reckless suitors,
there in your own house, against your will,
plot your ruin—a fine young prince like you.   105
Tell me, though, do you let yourself be so abused
or do people round about, stirred up by the prompting
of some god, despise you? Or are your brothers at fault?
Brothers a man can trust to fight beside him, true,
no matter what deadly blood-feud rages on.   110
Would I were young as you, to match my spirit now,
or I were the son of great Odysseus, or the king himself
returned from all his roving—there's still room for hope!
Then let some foreigner lop my head off if I failed
to march right into Odysseus' royal halls   115
and kill them all. And what if I went down,
crushed by their numbers—I, fighting alone?
I'd rather die, cut down in my own house
than have to look on at their outrage day by day.
Guests treated to blows, men dragging the serving-women   120
through the noble house, exploiting them all, no shame,
and the gushing wine swilled, the food squandered—
gorging for gorging's sake—
and the courting game goes on, no end in sight!"

"You're right, my friend," sober Telemachus agreed.   ₁₂₅
"Now let me tell you the whole story, first to last.
It's not that all our people have turned against me,
keen for a showdown. Nor have I any brothers at fault,
brothers a man can trust to fight beside him, true,
no matter what deadly blood-feud rages on . . .   ₁₃₀
Zeus made our line a line of only sons.
Arcesius had only one son, Laertes,
and Laertes had only one son, Odysseus,
and I am Odysseus' only son. He fathered me,
he left me behind at home, and from me he got no joy.   ₁₃₅
So now our house is plagued by swarms of enemies.
All the nobles who rule the islands round about,
Dulichion, and Same, and wooded Zacynthus too,
and all who lord it in rocky Ithaca as well—
down to the last man they court my mother,   ₁₄₀
they lay waste my house! And mother . . .
she neither rejects a marriage she despises
nor can she bear to bring the courting to an end—
while they continue to bleed my household white.
Soon—you wait—they'll grind *me* down as well!   ₁₄₅
But all lies in the lap of the great gods.
                               Eumaeus,
good old friend, go, quickly, to wise Penelope.
Tell her I'm home from Pylos safe and sound.
I'll stay on right here. But you come back
as soon as you've told the news to her alone.   ₁₅₀
No other Achaean must hear—
all too many plot to take my life."
                                   "I know."
you assured your prince, Eumaeus, loyal swineherd.
"I see your point—there's sense in this old head.
One thing more, and make your orders clear.   ₁₅₅
On the same trip do I go and give the news
to King Laertes too? For many years, poor man,
heartsick for his son, he'd always keep an eye
on the farm and take his meals with the hired hands
whenever he felt the urge to. Now, from the day   ₁₆₀
you sailed away to Pylos, not a sip or a bite
he's touched, they say, not as he did before,
and his eyes are shut to all the farmyard labors.
Huddled over, groaning in grief and tears,
he wastes away—the man's all skin and bones."   ₁₆₅

"So much the worse," Telemachus answered firmly.
"Leave him alone; though it hurts us now, we must.
If men could have all they want, free for the taking,
I'd take first my father's journey home. So,
you go and give the message, then come back,   ₁₇₀
no roaming over the fields to find Laertes.
Tell my mother to send her housekeeper,
fast as she can, in secret—
she can give the poor old man the news."

That roused Eumaeus. The swineherd grasped his sandals,   175
strapped them onto his feet and made for town.
His exit did not escape Athena's notice . . .
Approaching, closer, now she appeared a woman,
beautiful, tall and skilled at weaving lovely things.
Just at the shelter's door she stopped, visible to Odysseus   180
but Telemachus could not see her, sense her there—
the gods don't show themselves to every man alive.
Odysseus saw her, so did the dogs; no barking now,
they whimpered, cringing away in terror through the yard.
She gave a sign with her brows, Odysseus caught it,   185
out of the lodge he went and past the high stockade
and stood before the goddess. Athena urged him on:
"Royal son of Laertes, Odysseus, old campaigner,
now is the time, now tell your son the truth.
Hold nothing back, so the two of you can plot   190
the suitors' doom and then set out for town.
I myself won't lag behind you long—
I'm blazing for a battle!"

    Athena stroked him with her golden wand.
First she made the cloak and shirt on his body   195
fresh and clean, then made him him taller, supple, young,
his ruddy tan came back, the cut of his jawline firmed
and the dark beard clustered black around his chin.
Her work complete, she went her way once more
and Odysseus returned to the lodge. His own son   200
gazed at him, wonderstruck, terrified too, turning
his eyes away, suddenly—
                this must be some god—
and he let fly with a burst of exclamations:
"Friend, you're a new man—not what I saw before!
Your clothes, they've changed, even your skin has changed—   205
surely you are some god who rules the vaulting skies!
Oh be kind, and we will give you offerings,
gifts of hammered gold to warm your heart—
spare us, please, I beg you!"
                   "No, I am not a god,"
the long-enduring, great Odysseus returned.   210
"Why confuse me with one who never dies?
No, I am your father—
the Odysseus you wept for all your days,
you bore a world of pain, the cruel abuse of men."

    And with those words Odysseus kissed his son   215
and the tears streamed down his cheeks and wet the ground,
though before he'd always reined his emotions back.
But still not convinced that it was his father,
Telemachus broke out, wild with disbelief,
"No, you're not Odysseus! Not my father!   220
Just some spirit spellbinding me now—
to make me ache with sorrow all the more.

Impossible for a mortal to work such marvels,
not with his own devices, not unless some god
comes down in person, eager to make that mortal   225
young or old—like that! Why, just now
you were old, and wrapped in rags, but *now*, look,
you seem like a god who rules the skies up there!"

    "Telemachus," Odysseus, man of exploits, urged his son,
"It's wrong to marvel, carried away in wonder so   230
to see your father here before your eyes.
No other Odysseus will ever return to you.
That man and I are one, the man you see . . .
here after many hardships,
endless wanderings, after twenty years   235
I have come home to native ground at last.
My changing so? Athena's work, the Fighter's Queen[5]—
she has that power, she makes me look as she likes,
now like a beggar, the next moment a young man,
decked out in handsome clothes about my body.   240
It's light work for the gods who rule the skies
to exalt a mortal man or bring him low."
                                        At that
Odysseus sat down again, and Telemachus threw his arms
around his great father, sobbing uncontrollably
as the deep desire for tears welled up in both.   245
They cried out, shrilling cries, pulsing sharper
than birds of prey—eagles, vultures with hooked claws—
when farmers plunder their nest of young too young to fly.
Both men so filled with compassion, eyes streaming tears,
that now the sunlight would have set upon their cries   250
if Telemachus had not asked his father, all at once,
"What sort of ship, dear father, brought you here?—
Ithaca, at last. Who did the sailors say they are?
I hardly think you came back home on foot!"

    So long an exile, great Odysseus replied,   255
"Surely, my son, I'll tell you the whole story now.
Phaeacians brought me here, the famous sailors
who ferry home all men who reach their shores.
They sailed me across the sea in their swift ship,
they set me down in Ithaca, sound asleep, and gave me   260
glittering gifts—bronze and hoards of gold and robes.
All lie stowed in a cave, thanks to the gods' help,
and Athena's inspiration spurred me here, now,
so we could plan the slaughter of our foes.
Come, give me the full tally of these suitors—   265
I must know their numbers, gauge their strength.
Then I'll deploy this old tactician's wits,
decide if the two of us can take them on,
alone, without allies,

5. Athena was a warrior goddess.

or we should hunt reserves to back us up."
                                    "Father," 270
clear-headed Telemachus countered quickly,
"all my life I've heard of your great fame—
a brave man in war and a deep mind in counsel—
but what you say dumbfounds me, staggers imagination!
How on earth could two men fight so many and so strong? 275
These suitors are not just ten or twenty, they're far more—
you count them up for yourself now, take a moment . . .
From Dulichion, fifty-two of them, picked young men,
six servants in their troop; from Same, twenty-four,
from Zacynthus, twenty Achaeans, nobles all, 280
and the twelve best lords from Ithaca itself.
Medon the herald's with them, a gifted bard,
and two henchmen, skilled to carve their meat.
If we pit ourselves against all these in the house,
I fear the revenge you come back home to take 285
will recoil on our heads—a bitter, deadly blow.
Think: can you come up with a friend-in-arms?
Some man to fight beside us, some brave heart?"

      "Let me tell you," the old soldier said,
"bear it in mind now, listen to me closely. 290
Think: will Athena flanked by Father Zeus
do for the two of us?
Or shall I rack my brains for another champion?"

      Telemachus answered shrewdly, full of poise,
"Two great champions, those you name, it's true. 295
Off in the clouds they sit
and they lord it over gods and mortal men."

      "Trust me," his seasoned father reassured him,
"they won't hold off long from the cries and clash of battle,
not when we and the suitors put our fighting strength 300
to proof in my own halls! But now, with daybreak,
home you go and mix with that overbearing crowd.
The swineherd will lead me into the city later,
looking old and broken, a beggar once again.
If they abuse me in the palace, steel yourself, 305
no matter what outrage I must suffer, even
if they drag me through our house by the heels
and throw me out or pelt me with things they hurl—
you just look on, endure it. Prompt them to quit
their wild reckless ways, try to win them over 310
with friendly words. Those men will never listen,
now the day of doom is hovering at their heads.
One more thing. Take it to heart, I urge you.
When Athena, Queen of Tactics, tells me it is time,
I'll give you a nod, and when you catch that signal 315
round up all the deadly weapons kept in the hall,
stow them away upstairs in a storeroom's deep recess—

all the arms and armor—and when the suitors miss them
and ask you questions, put them off with a winning story:
'I stowed them away, clear of the smoke. A far cry   320
from the arms Odysseus left when he went to Troy,
fire-damaged equipment, black with reeking fumes.
And a god reminded me of something darker too.
When you're in your cups a quarrel might break out,
you'd wound each other, shame your feasting here   325
and cast a pall on your courting.
Iron has powers to draw a man to ruin.'
                                        Just you leave
a pair of swords for the two of us, a pair of spears
and a pair of oxhide bucklers, right at hand so we
can break for the weapons, seize them! Then Athena,   330
Zeus in his wisdom—they will daze the suitors' wits.
Now one last thing. Bear it in mind. You must.
If you are my own true son, born of my blood,
let no one hear that Odysseus has come home.
Don't let Laertes know, not Eumaeus either,   335
none in the household, not Penelope herself.
You and I alone will assess the women's mood
and we might test a few of the serving-men as well:
where are the ones who still respect us both,
who hold us in awe? And who shirk their duties?—   340
slighting you because you are so young."

    "Soon enough, father," his gallant son replied,
"you'll sense the courage inside me, that I know—
I'm hardly a flighty, weak-willed boy these days.
But I think your last plan would gain us nothing.   345
Reconsider, I urge you.
You'll waste time, roaming around our holdings,
probing the fieldhands man by man, while the suitors
sit at ease in our house, devouring all our goods—
those brazen rascals never spare a scrap!   350
But I do advise you to sound the women out:
who are disloyal to you, who are guiltless?
The men—I say no to testing them farm by farm.
That's work for later, if you have really seen
a sign from Zeus whose shield is storm and thunder."   355

    Now as father and son conspired, shaping plans,
the ship that brought the prince and shipmates back
from Pylos was just approaching Ithaca, home port.
As soon as they put in to the harbor's deep bay
they hauled the black vessel up onto dry land   360
and eager deckhands bore away their gear
and rushed the priceless gifts to Clytius'[6] house.
But they sent a herald on to Odysseus' halls at once
to give the news to thoughtful, cautious Penelope

6. The father of Piraeus, to whom Telemachus entrusted Theoclymenus (XV.602–7).

that Telemachus was home—just up-country now   365
but he'd told his mates to sail across to port—
so the noble queen would not be seized with fright
and break down in tears. And now those two men met,
herald and swineherd, both out on the same errand,
to give the queen the news. But once they reached   370
the house of the royal king the herald strode up,
into the serving-women's midst, and burst out,
"Your beloved son, my queen, is home at last!"
Eumaeus though, bending close to Penelope,
whispered every word that her dear son   375
entrusted him to say. Message told in full,
he left the halls and precincts, heading for his pigs.

   But the news shook the suitors, dashed their spirits.
Out of the halls they crowded, past the high-walled court
and there before the gates they sat in council.   380
Polybus' son Eurymachus opened up among them:
"Friends, what a fine piece of work he's carried off!
Telemachus—what insolence—and we thought his little jaunt
would come to grief! Up now, launch a black ship,
the best we can find—muster a crew of oarsmen,   385
row the news to our friends in ambush, fast,
bring them back at once."
                         And just then—
he'd not quite finished when Amphinomus,
wheeling round in his seat,
saw their vessel moored in the deep harbor,   390
their comrades striking sail and hoisting oars.
He broke into heady laughter, called his friends:
"No need for a message now. They're home, look there!
Some god gave them the news, or they saw the prince's ship
go sailing past and failed to overtake her."   395

   Rising, all trooped down to the water's edge
as the crew hauled the vessel up onto dry land
and the hot-blooded hands bore off their gear.
Then in a pack they went to the meeting grounds,
suffering no one else, young or old, to sit among them.   400
Eupithes' son Antinous rose and harangued them all:
"What a blow! See how the gods have saved this boy
from bloody death? And our lookouts all day long,
stationed atop the windy heights, kept watch,
shift on shift; and once the sun went down   405
we'd never sleep the night ashore, never,
always aboard our swift ship, cruising till dawn,
patrolling to catch Telemachus, kill him on the spot,
and all the while some spirit whisked him home!
So here at home we'll plot his certain death: 410
he must never slip through our hands again,
that boy—while he still lives,
I swear we'll never bring our venture off.

The clever little schemer, he does have his skills,
and the crowds no longer show us favor, not at all.   415
So act! before he can gather his people in assembly.
He'll never give in an inch, I know, he'll rise
and rage away, shouting out to them all how we,
we schemed his sudden death but never caught him.
Hearing of our foul play, they'll hardly sing our praises.   420
Why, they might do us damage, run us off our lands,
drive us abroad to hunt for strangers' shores.
Strike first, I say, and kill him!—
clear of town, in the fields or on the road.
Then we'll seize his estates and worldly goods,   425
carve them up between us, share and share alike.
But as for his palace, let his mother keep it,
she and the man she weds.
                              There's my plan.
If you find it offensive, if you want him
living on—in full command of his patrimony—   430
gather here no more then, living the life of kings,
consuming all his wealth. Each from his own house
must try to win her, showering her with gifts.
Then she can marry the one who offers most,
the man marked out by fate to be her husband."   435

    That brought them all to a hushed, stunned silence
till Amphinomus rose to have his say among them—
the noted son of Nisus, King Aretias' grandson,
the chief who led the suitors from Dulichion,
land of grass and grains,   440
and the man who pleased Penelope the most,
thanks to his timely words and good clear sense.
Concerned for their welfare now, he stood and argued:
"Friends, I've no desire to kill Telemachus, not I—
it's a terrible thing to shed the blood of kings.   445
Wait, sound out the will of the gods—that first.
If the decrees of mighty Zeus commend the work,
I'll kill the prince myself and spur on all the rest.
If the gods are against it, then I say hold back!"

    So Amphinomus urged, and won them over.   450
They rose at once, returned to Odysseus' palace,
entered and took their seats on burnished chairs.

    But now an inspiration took the discreet Penelope
to face her suitors, brutal, reckless men.
The queen had heard it all . . .   455
how they plotted inside the house to kill her son.
The herald Medon told her—he'd overheard their schemes.
And so, flanked by her ladies, she descended to the hall.
That luster of women, once she reached her suitors,
drawing her glistening veil across her cheeks,   460
paused now where a column propped the sturdy roof

and wheeling on Antinous, cried out against him:
"You Antinous! Violent, vicious, scheming—
you, they say, are the best man your age in Ithaca,
best for eloquence, counsel. You're nothing of the sort!   465
Madman, why do you weave destruction for Telemachus?—
show no pity to those who need it?—those over whom
almighty Zeus stands guard. It's wrong, unholy, yes,
weaving death for those who deserve your mercy!
Don't you know how your father fled here once?   470
A fugitive, terrified of the people, up in arms
against him because he'd joined some Taphian pirates
out to attack Thesprotians, sworn allies of ours.
The mobs were set to destroy him, rip his life out,
devour his vast wealth to their heart's content,   475
but Odysseus held them back, he kept their fury down.
And this is the man whose house you waste, scot-free,
whose wife you court, whose son you mean to kill—
you make my life an agony! Stop, I tell you,
stop all this, and make the rest stop too!"   480

     But Polybus' son Eurymachus tried to calm her:
"Wise Penelope, daughter of Icarius, courage!
Disabuse yourself of all these worries now.
That man is not alive—
he never will be, he never can be born—   485
who'll lift a hand against Telemachus, your son,
not while *I* walk the land and I can see the light.
I tell you this—so help me, it will all come true—
in an instant that man's blood will spurt around my spear!
My spear, since time and again Odysseus dandled me   490
on his knees, the great raider of cities fed me
roasted meat and held the red wine to my lips.
So to *me* your son is the dearest man alive,
and I urge the boy to have no fear of death,
not from the suitors at least.   495
What comes from the gods—there's no escaping that."

     Encouraging, all the way, but all the while
plotting the prince's murder in his mind . . .
The queen, going up to her lofty well-lit room,
fell to weeping for Odysseus, her beloved husband,   500
till watchful Athena sealed her eyes with welcome sleep.

     Returning just at dusk to Odysseus and his son,
the loyal swineherd found they'd killed a yearling pig
and standing over it now were busy fixing supper.
But Athena had approached Laertes' son Odysseus,   505
tapped him with her wand and made him old again.
She dressed him in filthy rags too, for fear Eumaeus,
recognizing his master face-to-face, might hurry
back to shrewd Penelope, blurting out the news
and never hide the secret in his heart.   510

Telemachus was the first to greet the swineherd:
"Welcome home, my friend! What's the talk in town?
Are the swaggering suitors back from ambush yet—
or still waiting to catch me coming home?"

You answered the prince, Eumaeus, loyal swineherd,   515
"I had no time to go roaming all through town,
digging round for that. My heart raced me on
to get my message told and rush back here.
But I met up with a fast runner there,
sent by your crew, a herald,   520
first to tell your mother all the news.
And this I know, I saw with my own eyes—
I was just above the city, heading home,
clambering over Hermes' Ridge, when I caught sight
of a trim ship pulling into the harbor, loaded down   525
with a crowd aboard her, shields and two-edged spears.
I *think* they're the men you're after—I'm not sure."

At that the young prince Telemachus smiled,
glancing toward his father, avoiding Eumaeus' eyes.
                                              And now,
with the roasting done, the meal set out, they ate well   530
and no one's hunger lacked a proper share of supper.
When they'd put aside desire for food and drink,
they remembered bed and took the gift of sleep.

BOOK XVII

[Stranger at the Gates]

When young Dawn with her rose-red fingers shone once more
Telemachus strapped his rawhide sandals to his feet
and the young prince, the son of King Odysseus,
picked up the rugged spear that fit his grip
and striking out for the city, told his swineherd,   5
"I'm off to town, old friend, to present myself to mother.
She'll never stop her bitter tears and mourning,
well I know, till she sees me face-to-face.
And for you I have some orders—
take this luckless stranger to town, so he can beg   10
his supper there, and whoever wants can give the man
some crumbs and a cup to drink. How can *I* put up with
every passerby? My mind's weighed down with troubles.
If the stranger resents it, all the worse for him.
I like to tell the truth and tell it straight."
                                          "My friend,   15
subtle Odysseus broke in, "I've no desire, myself,
to linger here. Better that beggars cadge their meals
in town than in the fields. Some willing soul
will see to my needs. I'm hardly fit, at my age,
to keep to a farm and jump to a foreman's every order.   20
Go on then. This man will take me, as you've told him,

once I'm warm from the fire and the sun's good and strong.
Look at the clothing on my back—all rags and tatters.
I'm afraid the frost at dawn could do me in,
and town, you say, is a long hard way from here."   25

    At that Telemachus strode down through the farm
in quick, firm strides, brooding death for the suitors.
And once he reached his well-constructed palace,
propping his spear against a sturdy pillar
and crossing the stone threshold, in he went.   30

    His old nurse was the first to see him, Eurycleia,
just spreading fleeces over the carved, inlaid chairs.
Tears sprang to her eyes, she rushed straight to the prince
as the other maids of great Odysseus flocked around him,
hugged him warmly, kissed his head and shoulders.   35

    Now down from her chamber came discreet Penelope,
looking for all the world like Artemis or golden Aphrodite—
bursting into tears as she flung her arms around her darling son
and kissed his face and kissed his shining eyes and sobbed,
"You're home, Telemachus!"—words flew from her heart—   40
"sweet light of my eyes! I never thought I'd see you again,
once you shipped to Pylos—against my will, so secret,
out for news of your dear father. Quick tell me,
did you catch sight of the man—meet him—what?"

    "Please, mother," steady Telemachus replied,   45
"don't move me to tears, don't stir the heart inside me.
I've just escaped from death. Sudden death.
No. Bathe now, put on some fresh clothes,
go up to your own room with your serving-women,
pray, and promise the gods a generous sacrifice   50
to bring success, if Zeus will ever grant us
the hour of our revenge. I myself am off
to the meeting grounds to summon up a guest
who came with me from abroad when I sailed home.
I sent him on ahead with my trusted crew.   55
I told Piraeus to take him to his house,
treat him well, host him with all good will
till I could come myself."
                         Words to the mark
that left his mother silent . . .
She bathed now, put on some fresh clothes,   60
prayed, and promised the gods a generous sacrifice
to bring success, if Zeus would ever grant
the hour of their revenge.
                         Spear in hand,
Telemachus strode on through the hall and out,
and a pair of sleek hounds went trotting at his heels.   65
And Athena lavished a marvelous splendor on the prince
so the people all gazed in wonder as he came forward.

The swaggering suitors clustered, milling round him,
welcome words on their lips, and murder in their hearts.
But he gave them a wide berth as they came crowding in   70
and there where Mentor sat, Antiphus, Halitherses too—
his father's loyal friends from days gone by—
he took his seat as they pressed him with their questions.
And just then Piraeus the gallant spearman approached,
leading the stranger through the town and out onto   75
the meeting grounds. Telemachus, not hanging back,
went right up to greet Theoclymenus, his guest,
but Piraeus spoke out first: "Quickly now,
Telemachus, send some women to my house
to retrieve the gifts that Menelaus gave you."   80

    "Wait, Piraeus," wary Telemachus cautioned,
"we've no idea how all of this will go.
If the brazen suitors cut me down in the palace—
off guard—and carve apart my father's whole estate,
I'd rather you yourself, or one of his friends here,   85
keep those gifts and get some pleasure from them.
But if I can bring down slaughter on that crew,
you send the gifts to my house—we'll share the joy."

    Their plans made, he led the wayworn stranger home
and once they reached the well-constructed palace,   90
spreading out their cloaks on a chair or bench,
into the burnished tubs they climbed and bathed.
When women had washed them, rubbed them down with oil
and drawn warm fleece and shirts around their shoulders,
out of the baths they stepped and sat on high-backed chairs.   95
A maid brought water soon in a graceful golden pitcher
and over a silver basin tipped it out
so they might rinse their hands,
then pulled a gleaming table to their side.
A staid housekeeper brought on bread to serve them,   100
appetizers aplenty too, lavish with her bounty.
Penelope sat across from her son, beside a pillar,
leaning back on a low chair and winding finespun yarn.
They reached out for the good things that lay at hand
and when they'd put aside desire for food and drink,   105
the queen, for all her composure, said at last,
"Telemachus, I'm going back to my room upstairs
and lie down on my bed . . .
that bed of pain my tears have streaked, year in,
year out, from the day Odysseus sailed away to Troy   110
with Atreus' two sons.[7]
                        But you, you never had the heart—
before those insolent suitors crowd back to the house—
to tell me clearly about your father's journey home,
if you've heard any news."

7. Agamemnon and Menelaus.

                    "Of course, mother,"
thoughtful Telemachus reassured her quickly,   115
"I will tell you the whole true story now.
We sailed to Pylos, to Nestor, the great king,
and he received me there in his lofty palace,
treated me well and warmly, yes, as a father treats
a long-lost son just home from voyaging, years abroad: 120
such care he showered on me, he and his noble sons.
But of strong, enduring Odysseus, dead or alive,
he's heard no news, he said, from any man on earth.
He sent me on to the famous spearman Atrides Menelaus,
on with a team of horses drawing a bolted chariot.   125
And there I saw her, Helen of Argos—all for her
Achaeans and Trojans suffered so much hardship,
thanks to the gods' decree . . .
The lord of the warcry, Menelaus, asked at once
what pressing need had brought me to lovely Lacedaemon,   130
and when I told him the whole story, first to last,
the king burst out, 'How shameful! That's the bed
of a brave man of war they'd like to crawl inside,
those spineless, craven cowards!
Weak as the doe that beds down her fawns   135
in a mighty lion's den—her newborn sucklings—
then trails off to the mountain spurs and grassy bends
to graze her fill, but back the lion comes to his own lair
and the master deals both fawns a ghastly bloody death,
just what Odysseus will deal that mob—ghastly death.   140
Ah if only—Father Zeus, Athena and lord Apollo—
that man who years ago in the games at Lesbos
rose to Philomelides' challenge, wrestled him,
pinned him down with one tremendous throw
and the Argives roared with joy . . .   145
if only *that* Odysseus sported with those suitors,
a blood wedding, a quick death would take the lot!
But about the things you've asked me, so intently,
I'll skew and sidestep nothing, not deceive you, ever.
Of all he told me—the Old Man of the Sea who never lies—   150
I'll hide or hold back nothing, not a single word.
He said he'd seen Odysseus on an island,
ground down in misery, off in a goddess' house,
the nymph Calypso, who holds him there by force.
He has no way to voyage home to his own native land,   155
no trim ships in reach, no crew to ply the oars
and send him scudding over the sea's broad back.'

    So Menelaus, the famous spearman, told me.
My mission accomplished, back I came at once,
and the gods sent me a stiff following wind   160
that sped me home to the native land I love."

    His reassurance stirred the queen to her depths
and the godlike seer Theoclymenus added firmly,

"Noble lady, wife of Laertes' son, Odysseus,
Menelaus can have no perfect revelations;   165
mark *my* words—I will make you a prophecy,
quite precise, and *I'll* hold nothing back.
I swear by Zeus, the first of all the gods,
by this table of hospitality here, my host,
by Odysseus' hearth where I have come for help—   170
I swear Odysseus *is* on native soil, here and now!
Poised or on the prowl, learning of these rank crimes
he's sowing seeds of ruin for all your suitors.
So clear, so true, that bird-sign I saw
as I sat on the benched ship   175
and sounded out the future to the prince!"

    "If only, my friend," reserved Penelope exclaimed,
"everything you say would come to pass!
You'd soon know my affection, know my gifts.
Any man you meet would call you blest."   180

    And so the three confided in the halls
while all the suitors, before Odysseus' palace,
amused themselves with discus and long throwing spears,
out on the leveled grounds, free and easy as always,
full of swagger. When the dinner-hour approached   185
and sheep came home from pastures near and far,
driven in by familiar drovers,
Medon called them all, their favorite herald,
always present at their meals: "My young lords,
now you've played your games to your hearts' content,   190
come back to the halls so we can fix your supper.
Nothing's better than dining well on time!"

    They came at his summons, rising from the games
and now, hustling into the well-constructed palace,
flinging down their cloaks on a chair or bench,   195
they butchered hulking sheep and fatted goats,
full-grown hogs and a young cow from the herd,
preparing for their feast.
             At the same time
the king and his loyal swineherd geared to leave
the country for the town. Eumaeus, foreman of men,   200
set things in motion: "Friend, I know you're keen
on going down to town today, just as my master bid,
though I'd rather you stay here to guard the farm.
But I prize the boy, I fear he'll blame me later—
a dressing-down from your master's hard to bear.   205
So off we go now. The shank of the day is past.[8]
You'll find it colder with nightfall coming on."

8. That is, much of the day is gone.

and urged him, "Go now, gather crusts from all the suitors,
test them, so we can tell the innocent from the guilty."
But not even so would Athena save one man from death.
Still, off he went, begging from each in turn,⁣ 400
circling left to right, reaching out his hand
like a beggar from the day that he was born.
They pitied him, gave him scraps, were puzzled too,
asking each other, "Who is this?" "Where's he from?"
Till the goatherd Melanthius shouted out in their midst, 405
"Listen to me, you lords who court our noble queen—
I'll tell you about the stranger. I've seen him before.
I know for a fact the swineherd led him in,
though I have no idea who the fellow is
or where he thinks he comes from."
                 At that 410
Antinous wheeled on Eumaeus, lashing out at him:
"Your highness, swineherd—why drag *this* to town?
Haven't we got our share of vagabonds to deal with,
disgusting beggars who lick the feasters' plates?
Isn't it quite enough, these swarming crowds 415
consuming your master's bounty—
must you invite this rascal in the bargain?"
                    "Antinous,
highborn as you are," you told the man, Eumaeus,
"that was a mean low speech!
Now who'd go out, who on his own hook— 420
not I—and ask a stranger in from nowhere
unless he had some skills to serve the house?
A prophet, a healer who cures disease, a worker in wood
or even a god-inspired bard whose singing warms the heart—
they're the ones asked in around the world. A beggar? 425
Who'd invite a beggar to bleed his household white?
You, you of all the suitors are always roughest
on the servants of our king, on me most of all.
Not that I care, no, so long as his queen,
his wise queen, is still alive in the palace, 430
Prince Telemachus too."
                 "Stop, Eumaeus,"
poised Telemachus broke in quickly now,
"don't waste so much breath on Antinous here.
It's just his habit to bait a man with abuse
and spur the rest as well."
                He wheeled on the suitor, 435
letting loose: "How kind you are to me, Antinous,
kind as a father to his son! Encouraging me
to send this stranger packing from my house
with a harsh command! I'd never do it. God forbid.
Take and give to the beggar. I don't grudge it— 440
I'd even urge you on. No scruples now,
never fear your gifts will upset my mother
or any servant in King Odysseus' royal house.
But no such qualm could enter that head of yours,
bent on feeding your own face, not feeding strangers!" 445

Antinous countered the young prince in kind:
"So high and mighty, Telemachus—such unbridled rage!
If all the suitors gave him the sort of gift I'll give,
the house would be rid of *him* for three whole months!"
With that, from under his table he seized the stool   450
that propped his smooth feet as he reveled on—
just lifting it into view . . .
                                        But as for the rest,
all gave to the beggar, filled his sack with handouts,
bread and meat. And Odysseus seemed at the point
of getting back to his doorsill,   455
done with testing suitors, home free himself
when he stopped beside Antinous, begging face-to-face:
"Give me a morsel, friend. You're hardly the worst
Achaean here, it seems. The noblest one, in fact.
You look like a king to me!   460
So you should give a bigger crust than the rest
and I will sing your praises all across the earth.
I too once lived in a lofty house that men admired;
rolling in wealth, I'd often give to a vagabond like myself,
whoever he was, whatever need had brought him to my door.   465
And crowds of servants I had, and lots of all it takes
to live the life of ease, to make men call you rich.
But Zeus ruined it all—god's will, no doubt—
when he shipped me off with a roving band of pirates
bound for Egypt, a long hard sail, to wreck my life.   470
There in the Nile delta I moored our ships of war.
God knows I ordered my trusty crews to stand by,
just where they were, and guard the anchored fleet
and I sent a patrol to scout things out from higher ground.
But swept away by their own reckless fury, the crew went berserk—   475
they promptly began to plunder the lush Egyptian farms,
dragged off the women and children, killed the men.
Outcries reached the city in no time—stirred by shouts
the entire town came streaming down at the break of day,
filling the river plain with chariots, ranks of infantry   480
and the gleam of bronze. Zeus who loves the lightning
flung down murderous panic on all my men-at-arms—
no one dared to stand his ground and fight,
disaster ringed us round from every quarter.
Droves of my men they hacked down with swords,   485
led off the rest alive, to labor for them as slaves.
Myself? They passed me on to a stranger come their way,
to ship me to Cyprus—Iasus' son Dmetor it was,
who ruled Cyprus then with an iron fist.
And from there I sailed to Ithaca,   490
just as you see me now, ground down by pain and sorrow—"

    "Good god almighty!" Antinous cut the beggar short.
"What spirit brought this pest to plague our feast?
Back off! Into the open, clear of my table, or you,
you'll soon land in an Egypt, Cyprus, to break your heart!   495
What a brazen, shameless beggar! Scrounging food

from each man in turn, and look at their handouts,
reckless, never a qualm, no holding back, not
when making free with the next man's goods—
each one's got plenty here."
                              "Pity, pity,"   500
the wry Odysseus countered, drawing away.
"No sense in your head to match your handsome looks.
You'd grudge your servant a pinch of salt from your own larder,
you who lounge at the next man's board but lack the heart
to tear a crust of bread and hand it on to me,   505
though there's god's plenty here."
                              Boiling over
Antinous gave him a scathing look and let fly,
"*Now* you won't get out of the hall unscarred, I swear,
not after such a filthy string of insults!"
                              With that
he seized the stool and hurled it—
                              Square in the back   510
it struck Odysseus, just under the right shoulder
but he stood up against it—steady as a rock,
unstaggered by Antinous' blow—just shook his head,
silent, his mind churning with thoughts of bloody work.
Back he went to the doorsill, crouched, and setting down   515
his sack about to burst, he faced the suitors, saying,
"Hear me out, you lords who court the noble queen,
I must say what the heart inside me urges.
There's nothing to groan about, no hurt, when a man
takes a blow as he fights to save his own possessions,   520
cattle or shining flocks. But Antinous struck me
all because of my good-for-nothing belly—that,
that curse that makes such pain for us poor men.
But if beggars have their gods and Furies too,
let Antinous meet his death before he meets his bride!"   525

    "Enough, stranger!" Antinous volleyed back.
"Sit there and eat in peace—or go get lost! Or else,
for the way you talk, these young men will hale you
up and down the halls by your hands or feet
until you're skinned alive!"
                              Naked threats—   530
but the rest were outraged, even those brash suitors.
One would say to another, "Look, Antinous,
that was a crime, to strike the luckless beggar!"

    "Your fate is sealed if he's some god from the blue."

    "And the gods do take on the look of strangers   535
dropping in from abroad—"
                              "Disguised in every way
as they roam and haunt our cities, watching over us—"

    "All our foul play, all our fair play too!"

So they warned, but Antinous paid no heed.
And the anguish welled up in Telemachus' breast   540
for the blow his father took, yet he let no tears
go rolling down his face—he just shook his head,
silent, his mind churning with thoughts of bloody work.

But then, when cautious Queen Penelope heard
how Antinous struck the stranger, there in the halls,   545
she cried out, with her serving-women round her,
"May Apollo the Archer strike you just as hard!"
And her housekeeper Eurynome added quickly,
"If only our prayers were granted—
then not one of the lot would live to see   550
Dawn climb her throne tomorrow!"
                                        "Dear old woman,"
alert Penelope replied, "they're all hateful,
plotting their vicious plots. But Antinous
is the worst of all—he's black death itself.
Here's this luckless stranger, wandering down   555
the halls and begging scraps—hard-pressed by need—
and the rest all give the man his fill of food
but that one gives him a footstool
hurled at his right shoulder, hits his back!"

While she exclaimed among her household women,   560
sitting there in her room, Odysseus bent to supper.
Penelope called the swineherd in and gave instructions:
"Go, good Eumaeus, tell the stranger to come at once.
I'd like to give him a warm welcome, ask the man
if he's heard some news about my gallant husband   565
or seen him in the flesh . . .
He seems like one who's roved around the world."

"My queen," you answered, Eumaeus, loyal swineherd,
"if only the lords would hold their peace a moment!
Such stories he tells—he'd charm you to your depths.   570
Three nights, three days I kept him in my shelter;
I was the first the fellow stumbled onto,
fleeing from some ship. But not even so
could he bring his tale of troubles to an end.
You know how you can stare at a bard in wonder—   575
trained by the gods to sing and hold men spellbound—
how you can long to sit there, listening, all your life
when the man begins to sing. So he charmed my heart,
I tell you, huddling there beside me at my fire.
He and Odysseus' father go way back, he says,   580
sworn friends, and the stranger hails from Crete
where the stock of old King Minos still lives on,
and from Crete he made his way, racked by hardship,
tumbling on like a rolling stone until he turned up here.
He swears he's heard of Odysseus—just in reach,   585
in rich Thesprotian country—still alive,

laden with treasure, heading home at last!"
        "Go,"
the cautious queen responded, "call him here
so he can tell me his own tale face-to-face.
Our friends can sit at the gates or down the halls   590
and play their games, debauched to their hearts' content.
Why not? Their own stores, their bread and seasoned wine,
lie intact at home; food for their serving-men alone.
But they, they infest our palace day and night,
they butcher our cattle, our sheep, our fat goats,   595
feasting themselves sick, swilling our glowing wine
as if there's no tomorrow—all of it, squandered.
No, there is no man like Odysseus in command
to drive this curse from the house. Dear god,
if only Odysseus came back home to native soil now,   600
he and his son would avenge the outrage of these men—like that!"

  At her last words Telemachus shook with a lusty sneeze
and the sudden outburst echoed up and down the halls.
The queen was seized with laughter, calling out
to Eumaeus winged words: "Quickly, go!   605
Bring me this stranger now, face-to-face!
You hear how my son sealed all I said with a sneeze?[1]
So let death come down with grim finality on these suitors—
one and all—not a single man escape his sudden doom!
And another thing. Mark my words, I tell you.   610
If I'm convinced that all he says is true,
I'll dress him in shirt and cloak, in handsome clothes."

  Off the swineherd went, following her instructions,
made his way to the stranger's side and winged a word:
"Old friend—our queen, wise Penelope, summons you,   615
the prince's mother! The spirit moves her now,
heartsick as she is,
to ask a question or two about her husband.
And if she's convinced that all you say is true,
she'll dress you in shirt and cloak. That's what you need,   620
that most of all now. Bread you can always beg
around the country, fill your belly well—
they'll give you food, whoever has a mind to."

  "Gladly, Eumaeus," the patient man replied,
"I'll tell her the whole truth and nothing but,   625
Icarius' daughter, your wise queen Penelope.
I know all about that man . . .
it's been my lot to suffer what he's suffered.
But I fear the mob's abuse, those rough young bucks,
their pride and violence hit the iron skies!   630
Just now that scoundrel—as I went down the halls,
harming no one—up and dealt me a jolting blow,

---

1. A sneeze was considered an omen that words just uttered would be fulfilled.

and who would raise a hand to save me? Telemachus?
Anyone else? No one. So tell Penelope now,
anxious as she may be, to wait in the halls   635
until the sun goes down. Then she can ask me
all she likes about her husband's journey home.
But let her give me a seat close by the fire.
The clothes on my back are tatters. Well you know—
you are the first I begged for care and shelter."   640

Back the swineherd went, following his instructions.
Penelope, just as he crossed her threshold, broke out,
"Didn't you bring him? What's in the vagrant's mind?
Fear of someone? Embarrassed by something else,
here in the house? Is the fellow bashful?   645
A bashful man will make a sorry beggar."

You answered your queen, Eumaeus, loyal swineherd,
"He talks to the point—he thinks as the next man would
who wants to dodge their blows, that brutal crew.
He tells you to wait here till the sun goes down.   650
It's better for you, my queen. Then you can talk
with the man in private, hear the stranger's news."

"Nobody's fool, that stranger," wise Penelope said,
"he sees how things could go. Surely no men on earth
can match that gang for reckless, deadly schemes."   655

So she agreed, and now, mission accomplished,
back the loyal swineherd went to mix with the suitors.
Moving next to the prince, he whispered a parting word,
their heads close together so no one else could hear.
"Dear boy, I must be off, to see to the pigs   660
and the whole farm—your living, mine as well.
You're the one to tend to all things here.
Look out for your own skin first,
do take care, you mustn't come to grief.
Crowds of your own countrymen plot your death—   665
let Zeus wipe out the lot before they kill us all!"

"Right you are, old friend," the canny prince replied.
"Now off you go, once you've had your supper.
But come back bright and early,
bring some good sound boars for slaughter. Yes,   670
I'll tend to all things here, I and the deathless gods."

And the swineherd sat down again on his polished stool
and once he'd supped and drunk to his heart's content,
back he went to his pigs, leaving the royal precincts
still filled with feasters, all indulging now   675
in the joys of dance and song.
The day was over. Dusk was falling fast.

BOOK XVIII

[The Beggar-King of Ithaca]

Now along came this tramp, this public nuisance
who used to scrounge a living round the streets of Ithaca—
notorious for his belly, a ravenous, bottomless pit
for food and drink, but he had no pith, no brawn,
despite the looming hulk that met your eyes.   5
Arnaeus was his name,
so his worthy mother called him at birth,
but all the young men called him Irus[2] for short
because he'd hustle messages at any beck and call.
Well *he* came by to rout the king from his own house   10
and met Odysseus now with a rough, abusive burst:
"Get off the porch, you old goat, before I haul you
off by the leg! Can't you see them give me the wink,
all of them here, to drag you out—and so I would
but I've got some pangs of conscience. Up with you, man,   15
or before you know it, we'll be trading blows!"

                                     A killing look,
and the wily old soldier countered, "Out of your mind?
What damage have I done *you*? What have I said?
I don't grudge you anything,
not if the next man up and gives you plenty.   20
This doorsill is big enough for the both of us—
you've got no call to grudge me what's not yours.
You're another vagrant, just like me, I'd say,
and it lies with the gods to make us rich or poor. So,
keep your fists to yourself, don't press your luck, don't rile me,   25
or old as I am, I'll bloody your lip, splatter your chest
and buy myself some peace and quiet for tomorrow.
I doubt you'll ever come lumbering back again
to the halls of Laertes' royal son Odysseus."

    "Look who's talking!" the beggar rumbled in anger.   30
"How this pot-bellied pig runs off at the mouth—
like an old crone at her oven!
Well *I've* got a knock-out blow in store for *him*—
I'll batter the tramp with both fists, crack every tooth
from his jaws, I'll litter the ground with teeth   35
like a rogue sow's, punished for rooting corn!
Belt up—so the lords can see us fight it out.
How can you beat a champion half your age?"

    Tongue-lashing each other, tempers flaring,
there on the polished sill before the lofty doors.   40
And Antinous, that grand prince, hearing them wrangle,
broke into gloating laughter, calling out to the suitors,
"Friends, nothing like this has come our way before—
what sport some god has brought the palace now!

2. A pun on *Iris,* the name of the goddess who often served as the gods' messenger.

The stranger and Irus, look, 45
they'd battle it out together, fists flying.
Come, let's pit them against each other—fast!"

    All leapt from their seats with whoops of laughter,
clustering round the pair of ragged beggars there
as Eupithes' son Antinous planned the contest. 50
"Quiet, my fine friends. Here's what I propose.
These goat sausages[3] sizzling here in the fire—
we packed them with fat and blood to have for supper.
Now, whoever wins this bout and proves the stronger,
let that man step up and take his pick of the lot! 55
What's more, from this day on he feasts among us—
no other beggar will we allow inside
to cadge his meals from us!"
                They all cheered
but Odysseus, foxy veteran, plotted on . . .
"Friends, how can an old man, worn down with pain, 60
stand up to a young buck? It's just this belly of mine,
this trouble-maker, tempts me to take a licking.
So first, all of you swear me a binding oath:
come, not one of you steps in for Irus here,
strikes me a foul blow to pull him through 65
and lays me in the dust."
             And at that
they all mouthed the oath that he required,
and once they vowed they'd never interfere,
Prince Telemachus drove the matter home:
"Stranger, if your spine and fighting pride 70
prompt you to go against this fellow now,
have no fear of any suitor in the pack—
whoever fouls you will have to face a crowd.
Count on *me*, your host. And two lords back me up,
Antinous and Eurymachus—both are men of sense." 75

    They all shouted approval of the prince
as Odysseus belted up, roping his rags around his loins,
baring his big rippling thighs—his boxer's broad shoulders,
his massive chest and burly arms on full display
as Athena stood beside him, 80
fleshing out the limbs of the great commander . . .
Despite their swagger, the suitors were amazed,
gaping at one another, trading forecasts:
"Irus will soon be ironed out for good!"

    "He's in for the beating he begged for all along." 85

    "Look at the hams on that old-timer—"
                    "Just under his rags!"

---

3. In Greek these are literally "bellies"—that is, the stomach or intestine used as the membrane for the sausage. As Odysseus says in lines 61–62 (and has said several times before), the belly is what drives beggars and outcasts. The two beggars, under the belly's compulsion, thus compete for a belly as prize.

Each outcry jolted Irus to the core—too late.
The servants trussed his clothes up, dragged him on,
the flesh on his body quaking now with terror.
Antinous rounded on him, flinging insults: 90
"You, you clumsy ox, you're better off dead
or never born at all, if you cringe at *him*,
paralyzed with fear of an old, broken hulk,
ground down by the pains that hound his steps.
Mark my word—so help me I'll make it good—   95
if that old relic whips you and wins the day,
I'll toss you into a black ship and sail you off
to Echetus,[4] the mainland king who wrecks all men alive!
He'll lop your nose and ears with his ruthless blade,
he'll rip your privates out by the roots, he will,   100
and serve them up to his dogs to bolt down raw!"

    That threat shook his knees with a stronger fit
but they hauled him into the ring. Both men put up their fists—
with the seasoned fighter Odysseus deeply torn now . . .
should he knock him senseless, leave him dead where he dropped   105
or just stretch him out on the ground with a light jab?
As he mulled things over, that way seemed the best:
a glancing blow, the suitors would not detect him.
The two men squared off—

                        and Irus hurled a fist
at Odysseus' right shoulder as *he* came through   110
with a hook below the ear, pounding Irus' neck,
smashing the bones inside—

                        Suddenly red blood
came spurting out of his mouth, and headlong down
he pitched in the dust, howling, teeth locked in a grin,
feet beating the ground—

                        And the princely suitors,   115
flinging their hands in the air, died laughing.
Grabbing him by the leg, Odysseus hauled him
through the porch, across the yard to the outer gate,
heaped him against the courtyard wall, sitting slumped,
stuck his stick in his hand and gave him a parting shot: 120
"Now hold your post—play the scarecrow to all the pigs and dogs!
But no more lording it over strangers, no more playing
the beggar-king for you, you loathsome fool,
or you'll bring down something worse around your neck!"

    He threw his beggar's sack across his shoulders—   125
torn and tattered, slung from a fraying rope—
then back he went to the sill and took his seat.
The suitors ambled back as well, laughing jauntily,
toasting the beggar warmly now, those proud young blades,
one man egging the other on: "Stranger, friend, may Zeus   130
and the other deathless gods fill up your sack with blessings!"

---

4. Probably imaginary; at least, we know nothing more of him than Homer tells us here.

"All your heart desires!"

        "You've knocked him out of action,
that insatiable tramp—"

          "That parasite on the land!"

"Ship him off to Echetus, fast—the mainland king
who wrecks all men alive!"

        Welcome words   135
and a lucky omen too—Odysseus' heart leapt up.
Antinous laid before him a generous goat sausage,
bubbling fat and blood. Amphinomus took two loaves
from the wicker tray and set them down beside him,
drank his health in a golden cup and said,   140
"Cheers, old friend, old father,
saddled now as you are with so much trouble—
here's to your luck, great days from this day on!"

    And the one who knew the world replied at length,
"Amphinomus, you seem like a man of good sense to me.   145
Just like your father—at least I've heard his praises,
Nisus of Dulichion, a righteous man, and rich.
You're his son, they say, you seem well-spoken, too.
So I will tell you something. Listen. Listen closely.
Of all that breathes and crawls across the earth,   150
our mother earth breeds nothing feebler than a man.
So long as the gods grant him power, spring in his knees,
he thinks he will never suffer affliction down the years.
But then, when the happy gods bring on the long hard times,
bear them he must, against his will, and steel his heart.   155
Our lives, our mood and mind as we pass across the earth,
turn as the days turn . . .
as the father of men and gods makes each day dawn.
I too seemed destined to be a man of fortune once
and a wild wicked swath I cut, indulged my lust for violence,   160
staking all on my father and my brothers.
                       Look at me now.
And so, I say, let no man ever be lawless all his life,
just take in peace what gifts the gods will send.
                              True,
but here I see you suitors plotting your reckless work,
carving away at the wealth, affronting the loyal wife   165
of a man who won't be gone from kin and country long.
I say he's right at hand—and may some power save you,
spirit you home before you meet him face-to-face
the moment he returns to native ground!
Once under his own roof, he and your friends,   170
believe you me, won't part till blood has flowed."
                         With that
he poured out honeyed wine to the gods and drank deeply,
then restored the cup to the young prince's hands.
Amphinomus made his way back through the hall,
his heart sick with anguish, shaking his head,   175

fraught with grave forebodings . . .
but not even so could he escape his fate.
Even then Athena had bound him fast to death
at the hands of Prince Telemachus and his spear.
Now back he went to the seat that he'd left empty.   180

But now the goddess Athena with her glinting eyes
inspired Penelope, Icarius' daughter, wary, poised,
to display herself to her suitors, fan their hearts,
inflame them more, and make her even more esteemed
by her husband and her son than she had been before.   185
Forcing a laugh, she called her maid: "Eurynome,
my spirit longs—though it never did till now—
to appear before my suitors, loathe them as I do.
I'd say a word to my son too, for his own good,
not to mix so much with that pernicious crowd,   190
so glib with their friendly talk
but plotting wicked plots they'll hatch tomorrow."

"Well said, my child," the old woman answered,
"all to the point. Go to the boy and warn him now,
hold nothing back. But first you should bathe yourself,   195
give a gloss to your face. Don't go down like that—
your eyes dimmed, your cheeks streaked with tears.
It makes things worse, this grieving on and on.
Your son's now come of age—your fondest prayer
to the deathless gods, to see him wear a beard."   200

"Eurynome," discreet Penelope objected,
"don't try to coax me, care for me as you do,
to bathe myself, refresh my face with oils.
Whatever glow I had died long ago . . .
the gods of Olympus snuffed it out that day   205
my husband sailed away in the hollow ships.
But please, have Autonoë and Hippodamia come
and support me in the hall. I'll never brave
those men alone. I'd be too embarrassed."

Now as the old nurse bustled through the house   210
to give the women orders, call them to the queen,
the bright-eyed goddess thought of one more thing.
She drifted a sound slumber over Icarius' daughter,
back she sank and slept, her limbs fell limp and still,
reclining there on her couch, all the while Athena,   215
luminous goddess, lavished immortal gifts on her
to make her suitors lose themselves in wonder . . .
The divine unguent first. She cleansed her cheeks,
her brow and fine eyes with ambrosia smooth as the oils
the goddess Love[5] applies, donning her crown of flowers   220
whenever she joins the Graces' captivating dances.

5. Aphrodite.

She made her taller, fuller in form to all men's eyes,
her skin whiter than ivory freshly carved, and now,
Athena's mission accomplished, off the bright one went
as bare-armed maids came in from their own quarters,   225
chattering all the way, and sleep released the queen.
She woke, touched her cheek with a hand, and mused,
"Ah, what a marvelous gentle sleep, enfolding me
in the midst of all my anguish! Now if only
blessed Artemis sent me a death as gentle, now,   230
this instant—no more wasting away my life,
my heart broken in longing for my husband . . .
He had every strength,
rising over his countrymen, head and shoulders."

    Then, leaving her well-lit chamber, she descended,   235
not alone: two of her women followed close behind.
That radiant woman, once she reached her suitors,
drawing her glistening veil across her cheeks,
paused now where a column propped the sturdy roof,
with one of her loyal handmaids stationed either side.   240
The suitors' knees went slack, their hearts dissolved in lust—
all of them lifted prayers to lie beside her, share her bed.
But turning toward her son, she warned, "Telemachus,
your sense of balance is not what it used to be.
When you were a boy you had much better judgment.   245
Now that you've grown and reached your young prime
and any stranger, seeing how tall and handsome you are,
would think you the son of some great man of wealth—
now your sense of fairness seems to fail you.
Consider the dreadful thing just done in our halls—   250
how you let the stranger be so abused! Why,
suppose our guest, sitting here at peace,
here in our own house,
were hauled and badly hurt by such cruel treatment?
You'd be shamed, disgraced in all men's eyes!"   255

    "Mother . . ." Telemachus paused, then answered.
"I cannot fault your anger at all this.
My heart takes note of everything, feels it, too,
both the good and the bad—the boy you knew is gone.
But how can I plan my world in a sane, thoughtful way?   260
These men drive me mad, hedging me round, right and left,
plotting their lethal plots, and no one takes my side.
Still, this battle between the stranger and Irus
hardly went as the suitors might have hoped:
the stranger beat him down!   265
If only—Father Zeus, Athena and lord Apollo—
these gallants, now, this moment, here in our house,
were battered senseless, heads lolling, knees unstrung,
some sprawled in the courtyard, some sprawled outside!
Slumped like Irus down at the front gates now,   270
whipped, and his head rolling like some drunk.

He can't stand up on his feet and stagger home,
whatever home he's got—the man's demolished."

    So Penelope and her son exchanged their hopes
as Eurymachus stepped in to praise the queen.   275
"Ah, daughter of Icarius, wise Penelope,
if all the princes in Ionian Argos saw you now!
What a troop of suitors would banquet in your halls
tomorrow at sunrise! You surpass all women
in build and beauty, refined and steady mind."   280

    "Oh no, Eurymachus," wise Penelope demurred,
"whatever form and feature I had, what praise I'd won,
the deathless gods destroyed that day the Achaeans
sailed away to Troy, my husband in their ships,
Odysseus—if *he* could return to tend my life   285
the renown I had would only grow in glory.
Now my life is torment . . .
look at the griefs some god has loosed against me!
I'll never forget the day he left this land of ours;
he caught my right hand by the wrist and said, gently,   290
'Dear woman, I doubt that every Achaean under arms
will make it home from Troy, all safe and sound.
The Trojans, they say, are fine soldiers too,
hurling javelins, shooting flights of arrows,
charioteers who can turn the tide—like that!—   295
when the great leveler, War, brings on some deadlock.
So I cannot tell if the gods will sail me home again
or I'll go down out there, on the fields of Troy,
but all things here must rest in your control.
Watch over my father and mother in the palace,   300
just as now, or perhaps a little more,
when I am far from home.
But once you see the beard on the boy's cheek,
you wed the man you like, and leave your house behind.'
So my husband advised me then. Now it all comes true . . .   305
a night will come when a hateful marriage falls my lot—
this cursed life of mine! Zeus has torn away my joy.
But there's something else that mortifies me now.
Your way is a far cry from the time-honored way
of suitors locked in rivalry, striving to win   310
some noble woman, a wealthy man's daughter.
They bring in their own calves and lambs
to feast the friends of the bride-to-be, yes,
and shower her with gleaming gifts as well.
They don't devour the woman's goods scot-free."   315

    Staunch Odysseus glowed with joy to hear all this—
his wife's trickery luring gifts from her suitors now,
enchanting their hearts with suave seductive words
but all the while with something else in mind.
Eupithes' son Antinous took her point at once.   320

"Daughter of Icarius, sensible Penelope,
whatever gifts your suitors would like to bring,
accept them. How ungracious to turn those gifts away!
We won't go back to our own estates, or anywhere else,
till you have wed the man you find the best."   325

    So he proposed, and all the rest agreed.
Each suitor sent a page to go and get a gift.
Antinous' man brought in a grand, resplendent robe,
stiff with embroidery, clasped with twelve gold brooches,
long pins that clipped into sheathing loops with ease.   330
Eurymachus' man brought in a necklace richly wrought,
gilded, strung with amber and glowing like the sun.
Eurydamas' two men came with a pair of earrings,
mulberry clusters dangling in triple drops
with a glint to catch the heart.   335
From the halls of lord Pisander, Polyctor's son,
a servant brought a choker, a fine, gleaming treasure.
And so each suitor in turn laid on a handsome gift.
Then the noble queen withdrew to her upper room,
her file of waiting ladies close behind her,   340
bearing the gorgeous presents in their arms.

    Now the suitors turned to dance and song,
to the lovely beat and sway,
waiting for dusk to come upon them there . . .
and the dark night came upon them, lost in pleasure.   345
They rushed to set up three braziers along the walls
to give them light, piled them high with kindling,
sere, well-seasoned, just split with an ax,
and mixed in chips to keep the torches flaring.
The maids of Odysseus, steady man, took turns   350
to keep the fires up, but the king himself,
dear to the gods and cunning to the core,
gave them orders brusquely: "Maids of Odysseus,
your master gone so long—quick now, off you go
to the room where your queen and mistress waits.   355
Sit with her there and try to lift her spirits,
combing wool in your hands or spinning yarn.
But I will trim the torches for all her suitors,
even if they would like to revel on till Morning
mounts her throne. They'll never wear me down.   360
I have a name for lasting out the worst."
                                    At that
the women burst into laughter, glancing back and forth.
Flushed with beauty, Melantho[6] mocked him shamelessly—
Dolius was her father but Penelope brought her up;
she treated her like her own child and gave her toys   365
to cheer her heart. But despite that, her heart

6. The sister of Melanthius, the goatherd who abuses Odysseus in book XVII.

felt nothing for all her mistress' anguish now.
She was Eurymachus' lover, always slept with him.
She was the one who mocked her king and taunted,
"Cock of the walk, did someone beat your brains out?   370
Why not go bed down at the blacksmith's cozy forge?
Or a public place where tramps collect? Why here—
blithering on, nonstop,
bold as brass in the face of all these lords?
No fear in your heart? Wine's got to your wits?—   375
or do you always play the fool and babble nonsense?
Lost your head, have you, because you drubbed that hobo Irus?
You wait—a better man than Irus will take you on,
he'll box both sides of your skull with heavy fists
and cart you out the palace gushing blood!"

                                                   "*You* wait,   380
you bitch"—the hardened veteran flashed a killing look.
"I'll go straight to the prince with your foul talk.
The prince will chop you to pieces here and now!"

    His fury sent the women fluttering off, scattering
down the hall with panic shaking every limb—   385
they knew he spoke the truth.
But he took up his post by the flaring braziers,
tending the fires closely, looking after them all,
though the heart inside him stirred with other things,
ranging ahead, now, to all that must be done . . .   390

    But Athena had no mind to let the brazen suitors
hold back now from their heart-rending insults—
she meant to make the anguish cut still deeper
into the core of Laertes' son Odysseus.
Polybus' son Eurymachus launched in first,   395
baiting the king to give his friends a laugh:
"Listen to me, you lords who court our noble queen!
I simply have to say what's on my mind. Look,
surely the gods have fetched this beggar here
to Odysseus' house. At least our torchlight *seems*   400
to come from the sheen of the man's own head—
there's not a hair on his bald pate, not a wisp!"

    Then he wheeled on Odysseus, raider of cities:
"Stranger, how would you like to work for me
if I took you on—I'd give you decent wages—   405
picking the stones to lay a tight dry wall
or planting tall trees on the edge of my estate?
I'd give you rations to last you year-round,
clothes for your body, sandals for your feet.
Oh no, you've learned your lazy ways too well,   410
you've got no itch to stick to good hard work,
you'd rather go scrounging round the countryside,
begging for crusts to stuff your greedy gut!"

"Ah, Eurymachus," Odysseus, master of many exploits,
answered firmly, "if only the two of us *could* go   415
man-to-man in the labors of the field . . .
In the late spring, when the long days come round,
out in the meadow, I swinging a well-curved scythe
and you swinging yours—we'd test our strength for work,
fasting right till dusk with lots of hay to mow.   420
Or give us a team of oxen to drive, purebreds,
hulking, ruddy beasts, both lusty with fodder,
paired for age and pulling-power that never flags—
with four acres to work, the loam churning under the plow—
you'd see what a straight unbroken furrow I could cut you then.   425
Or if Zeus would bring some battle on—out of the blue,
this very day—and give me a shield and two spears
and a bronze helmet to fit this soldier's temples,
then you'd see me fight where front ranks clash—
no more mocking this belly of mine, not then.   430
Enough. You're sick with pride, you brutal fool.
No doubt you count yourself a great, powerful man
because you sport with a puny crowd, ill-bred to boot.
If only Odysseus came back home and stood right here,
in a flash you'd find those doors—broad as they are—   435
too cramped for your race to safety through the porch!"

      That made Eurymachus' fury seethe and burst—
he gave the beggar a dark look and let fly, "You,
you odious—I'll make you pay for your ugly rant!
Bold as brass in the face of all these lords?   440
No fear in your heart? Wine's got to your wits?—
or do you always play the fool and babble nonsense?
Lost your head, have you, because you drubbed that hobo Irus?"

      As he shouted out he seized a stool, but Odysseus,
fearing the blow, crouched at Amphinomus' knees   445
as Eurymachus hurled and hit the wine-steward,
clipping his right hand—
his cup dropped, clattered along the floor
and flat on his back he went, groaning in the dust.
The suitors broke into uproar through the shadowed halls,   450
glancing at one another, trading angry outcries:
"Would to god this drifter had dropped dead—"

      "Anywhere else before he landed here!"

      "Then he'd never have loosed such pandemonium."

      "Now we're squabbling over *beggars*!"
                                          "No more joy   455
in the sumptuous feast . . ."
                              "Now riot rules the day!"

But now Prince Telemachus dressed them down:
"Fools, you're out of your minds! No hiding it,
food and wine have gone to your heads. Some god
has got your blood up. Come, now you've eaten well   460
go home to bed—when the spirit moves, that is.
I, for one, I'll drive no guest away."

　　So he declared. And they all bit their lips,
amazed the prince could speak with so much daring.
At last Amphinomus rose to take the floor,   465
the noted son of Nisus, King Aretias' grandson.
"Fair enough, my friends; when a man speaks well
we have no grounds for wrangling, no cause for abuse.
Hands off the stranger! And any other servant
in King Odysseus' palace. Come, steward,   470
pour first drops for the god in every cup;
let's make libations, then go home to bed.
The stranger? Leave him here in Odysseus' halls
and have his host, Telemachus, tend him well—
it's the prince's royal house the man has reached."   475

　　So he said. His proposal pleased them all.
And gallant Mulius, a herald of Dulichion,
a friend-in-arms of lord Amphinomus too,
mixed the men a bowl and, hovering closely,
poured full rounds for all. They tipped cups   480
to the blissful gods and then, libations made,
they drank the heady wine to their hearts' content
and went their ways to bed, each suitor to his house.

BOOK XIX

[Penelope and Her Guest]

That left the great Odysseus waiting in his hall
as Athena helped him plot the slaughter of the suitors.
He turned at once to Telemachus, brisk with orders:
"Now we must stow the weapons out of reach, my boy,
all the arms and armor—and when the suitors miss them   5
and ask you questions, put them off with a winning story:
'I stowed them away, clear of the smoke. A far cry
from the arms Odysseus left when he went to Troy,
fire-damaged equipment, black with reeking fumes.
And a god reminded me of something darker too.   10
When you're in your cups a quarrel might break out,
you'd wound each other, shame your feasting here
and cast a pall on your courting.
Iron has powers to draw a man to ruin.'"

　　Telemachus did his father's will at once,   15
calling out to his old nurse Eurycleia: "Quick,
dear one, close the women up in their own quarters,
till I can stow my father's weapons in the storeroom.
Splendid gear, lying about, neglected, black with soot

since father sailed away. I was only a boy then.   20
Now I must safeguard them from the smoke."

    "High time, child," the loving nurse replied.
"If only you'd bother to tend your whole house
and safeguard *all* your treasures. Tell me,
who's to fetch and carry the torch for you?   25
You won't let out the maids who'd light your way."

    "Our friend here will," Telemachus answered coolly.
"I won't put up with a man who shirks his work,
not if he takes his ration from my stores,
even if he's miles away from home."   30

    That silenced the old nurse.
She barred the doors that led from the long hall—
and up they sprang, Odysseus and his princely son,
and began to carry off the helmets, studded shields
and pointed spears, and Pallas Athena strode before them,   35
lifting a golden lamp that cast a dazzling radiance round about.
"Father," Telemachus suddenly burst out to Odysseus,
"oh what a marvel fills my eyes! Look, look there—
all the sides of the hall, the handsome crossbeams,
pinewood rafters, the tall columns towering—   40
all glow in my eyes like flaming fire!
Surely a god is here—
one of those who rule the vaulting skies!"

    "Quiet," his father, the old soldier, warned him.
"Get a grip on yourself. No more questions now.   45
It's just the way of the gods who rule Olympus.
Off you go to bed. I'll stay here behind
to test the women, test your mother too.
She in her grief will ask me everything I know."

    Under the flaring torchlight, through the hall   50
Telemachus made his way to his own bedroom now,
where he always went when welcome sleep came on him.
There he lay tonight as well, till Dawn's first light.
That left the great king still waiting in his hall
as Athena helped him plot the slaughter of the suitors . . .   55

    Now down from her chamber came reserved Penelope,
looking for all the world like Artemis or golden Aphrodite.
Close to the fire her women drew her favorite chair
with its whorls of silver and ivory, inlaid rings.
The craftsman who made it years ago, Icmalius,   60
added a footrest under the seat itself,
mortised into the frame,
and over it all was draped a heavy fleece.
Here Penelope took her place, discreet, observant.
The women, arms bared, pressing in from their quarters,   65

cleared away the tables, the heaped remains of the feast
and the cups from which the raucous lords had drunk.
Raking embers from the braziers onto the ground,
they piled them high again with seasoned wood,
providing light and warmth.
              And yet again   70
Melantho lashed out at Odysseus: "You still here?—
you pest, slinking around the house all night,
leering up at the women?
Get out, you tramp—be glad of the food you got—
or we'll sling a torch at you, rout you out at once!"   75

    A killing glance, and the old trooper countered,
"What's possessed you, woman? Why lay into me? Such abuse!
Just because I'm filthy, because I wear such rags,
roving round the country, living hand-to-mouth.
But it's fate that drives me on: 80
that's the lot of beggars, homeless drifters.
I too once lived in a lofty house that men admired;
rolling in wealth, I'd often give to a vagabond like myself,
whoever he was, whatever need had brought him to my door.
And crowds of servants I had, and lots of all it takes   85
to live the life of ease, to make men call you rich.
But Zeus ruined it all—god's will, no doubt.
So beware, woman, or one day you may lose it all,
all your glitter that puts your work-mates in the shade.
Or your mistress may just fly in a rage and dress you down   90
or Odysseus may return—there's still room for hope!
Or if he's dead as you think and never coming home,
well there's his son, Telemachus . . .
like father, like son—thanks to god Apollo.
No women's wildness here in the house escapes   95
the prince's eye. He's come of age at last."

    So he warned, and alert Penelope heard him,
wheeled on the maid and tongue-lashed her smartly:
"Make no mistake, you brazen, shameless bitch,
none of your ugly work escapes me either—   100
you will pay for it with your life, you will!
How well you knew—you heard from my own lips—
that I meant to probe this stranger in our house
and ask about my husband . . . my heart breaks for him."

    She turned to her housekeeper Eurynome and said,   105
"Now bring us a chair and spread it soft with fleece,
so our guest can sit and tell me his whole story
and hear me out as well.
I'd like to ask him questions, point by point."

    Eurynome bustled off to fetch a polished chair   110
and set it down and spread it soft with fleece.
Here Odysseus sat, the man of many trials,

as cautious Penelope began the conversation:
"Stranger, let me start our questioning myself. . . .
Who are you? where are you from? your city? your parents?"   115

  "My good woman," Odysseus, master of craft, replied,
"no man on the face of the earth could find fault with *you*.
Your fame, believe me, has reached the vaulting skies.
Fame like a flawless king's who dreads the gods,
who governs a kingdom vast, proud and strong—   120
who upholds justice, true, and the black earth
bears wheat and barley, trees bow down with fruit
and the sheep drop lambs and never fail and the sea
teems with fish—thanks to his decent, upright rule,
and under his sovereign sway the people flourish.   125
So then, here in your house, ask me anything else
but don't, please, search out my birth, my land,
or you'll fill my heart to overflowing even more
as I bring back the past . . .
I am a man who's had his share of sorrows.   130
It's wrong for me, in someone else's house,
to sit here moaning and groaning, sobbing so—
it makes things worse, this grieving on and on.
One of your maids, or you yourself, might scold me,
think it's just the wine that had doused my wits   135
and made me drown in tears."

  "No, no, stranger," wise Penelope demurred,
"whatever form and feature I had, what praise I'd won,
the deathless gods destroyed that day the Achaeans
sailed away to Troy, my husband in their ships,   140
Odysseus—if *he* could return to tend my life
the renown I had would only grow in glory.
Now my life is torment . . .
look at the griefs some god has loosed against me!
All the nobles who rule the islands round about,   145
Dulichion, Same, and wooded Zacynthus too,
and all who lord it in sunny Ithaca itself—
they court me against my will, they lay waste my house.
So I pay no heed to strangers, suppliants at my door,
not even heralds out on their public errands here—   150
I yearn for Odysseus, always, my heart pines away.
They rush the marriage on, and I spin out my wiles.
A god from the blue it was inspired me first
to set up a great loom in our royal halls
and I began to weave, and the weaving finespun,   155
the yarns endless, and I would lead them on: 'Young men,
my suitors, now that King Odysseus is no more,
go slowly, keen as you are to marry me, until
I can finish off this web . . .
so my weaving won't all fray and come to nothing.   160
This is a shroud for old lord Laertes, for that day
when the deadly fate that lays us out at last will take him down.

I dread the shame my countrywomen would heap upon me,
yes, if a man of such wealth should lie in state
without a shroud for cover.'
                              My very words,   165
and despite their pride and passion they believed me.
So by day I'd weave at my great and growing web—
by night, by the light of torches set beside me,
I would unravel all I'd done. Three whole years
I deceived them blind, seduced them with this scheme.   170
Then, when the wheeling seasons brought the fourth year on
and the months waned and the long days came round once more,
then, thanks to my maids—the shameless, reckless creatures—
the suitors caught me in the act, denounced me harshly.
So I finished it off. Against my will. They forced me.   175
And now I cannot escape a marriage, nor can I contrive
a deft way out. My parents urge me to tie the knot
and my son is galled as they squander his estate—
he sees it all. He's a grown man by now, equipped
to tend to his own royal house and tend it well: 180
Zeus grants my son that honor . . .
But for all that—now tell me who you are.
Where do you come from? You've hardly sprung
from a rock or oak like some old man of legend."

    The master improviser answered, slowly,   185
"My lady . . . wife of Laertes' son, Odysseus,
will your questions about my family never end?
All right then. Here's my story. Even though
it plunges me into deeper grief than I feel now.
But that's the way of the world, when one has been   190
so far from home, so long away as I, roving over
many cities of men, enduring many hardships.
                              Still,
my story will tell you all you need to know.

    There is a land called Crete[7] . . .
ringed by the wine-dark sea with rolling whitecaps—   195
handsome country, fertile, thronged with people
well past counting—boasting ninety cities,
language mixing with language side-by-side.
First come the Achaeans, then the native Cretans,
hardy, gallant in action, then Cydonian clansmen,   200
Dorians living in three tribes, and proud Pelasgians last.
Central to all their cities is magnificent Cnossos,
the site where Minos ruled and each ninth year
conferred with almighty Zeus himself. Minos,
father of my father, Deucalion, that bold heart.   205

7. It is impossible to extract historical fact from the following confused account of Crete. Cydonians may
be the inhabitants of the western end of the island. Dorians were the people who, according to Greek
belief (debated by modern scholars), invaded Greece and destroyed the Mycenaean civilization of the second millennium B.C.E. Pelasgians were what Greeks often called the pre-Hellenic inhabitants of the area.
Cnossos is the site of a Bronze Age palace.

Besides myself Deucalion sired Prince Idomeneus,
who set sail for Troy in his beaked ships of war,
escorting Atreus' sons. My own name is Aethon.
I am the younger-born;
my older brother's a better man than I am.   210
Now, it was there in Cnossos that I saw him . . .
Odysseus—and we traded gifts of friendship.
A heavy gale had landed him on our coast,
driven him way off course, rounding Malea's cape
when he was bound for Troy. He anchored in Amnisus,   215
hard by the goddess'[8] cave of childbirth and labor,
that rough harbor—barely riding out the storm.
He came into town at once, asking for Idomeneus,
claiming to be my brother's close, respected friend.
Too late. Ten or eleven days had already passed   220
since he set sail for Troy in his beaked ships.
So I took Odysseus back to my own house,
gave him a hero's welcome, treated him in style—
stores in our palace made for princely entertainment.
As for his comrades, all who'd shipped with him,   225
I dipped into public stock to give them barley,
ruddy wine and fine cattle for slaughter,
beef to their hearts' content. A dozen days
they stayed with me there, those brave Achaeans,
penned up by a North Wind so stiff that a man,   230
even on dry land, could never keep his feet—
some angry spirit raised that blast, I'd say.
Then on the thirteenth day the wind died down
and they set sail for Troy."
                                Falsehoods all,
but he gave his falsehoods all the ring of truth.   235
As she listened on, her tears flowed and soaked her cheeks
as the heavy snow melts down from the high mountain ridges,
snow the West Wind piles there and the warm East Wind thaws
and the snow, melting, swells the rivers to overflow their banks—
so she dissolved in tears, streaming down her lovely cheeks,   240
weeping for him, her husband, sitting there beside her.
Odysseus' heart went out to his grief-stricken wife
but under his lids his eyes remained stock-still—
they might have been horn or iron—
his guile fought back his tears. And she,   245
once she'd had her fill of grief and weeping,
turned again to her guest with this reply:
"Now, stranger, I think I'll test you, just to see
if there in your house, with all his friends-in-arms,
you actually entertained my husband as you say.   250
Come, tell me what sort of clothing he wore,
what cut of man was he?
What of the men who followed in his train?"
                                                "Ah good woman,"

8. Eileithyia's. The cave where she was worshiped from very early times has been excavated at Amnisus,
which is on the coast near Cnossos.

Odysseus, the great master of subtlety, returned,
"how hard it is to speak, after so much time   255
apart . . . why, some twenty years have passed
since he left my house and put my land behind him.
Even so, imagine the man as I portray him—
I can see him now.
                         King Odysseus . . .
he was wearing a heavy woolen cape, sea-purple   260
in double folds, with a golden brooch to clasp it,
twin sheaths for the pins, on the face a work of art:
a hound clenching a dappled fawn in its front paws,
slashing it as it writhed. All marveled to see it,
solid gold as it was, the hound slashing, throttling   265
the fawn in its death-throes, hoofs flailing to break free.
I noticed his glossy tunic too, clinging to his skin
like the thin glistening skin of a dried onion,
silky, soft, the glint of the sun itself.
Women galore would gaze on it with relish.   270
And this too. Bear it in mind, won't you?
I've no idea if Odysseus wore these things at home
or a comrade gave him them as he boarded ship,
or a host perhaps—the man was loved by many.
There were few Achaeans to equal him . . . and I?   275
I gave him a bronze sword myself, a lined cloak,
elegant, deep red, and a fringed shirt as well,
and I saw him off in his long benched ship of war
in lordly style.
                        Something else. He kept a herald
beside him, a man a little older than himself.   280
I'll try to describe him to you, best I can.
Round-shouldered he was, swarthy, curly-haired.
His name? Eurybates. And Odysseus prized him
most of all his men. Their minds worked as one."

His words renewed her deep desire to weep,   285
recognizing the strong clear signs Odysseus offered.
But as soon as she'd had her fill of tears and grief,
Penelope turned again to her guest and said,
"Now, stranger, much as I pitied you before,
now in my house you'll be my special friend,   290
my honored guest. I am the one, myself,
who gave him the very clothes that you describe.
I brought them up from the storeroom, folded them neatly,
fastened the golden brooch to adorn my husband,
Odysseus—never again will I embrace him,   295
striding home to his own native land.
A black day it was
when he took ship to see that cursed city . . .
Destroy,[9] I call it—I hate to say its name!"

9. Literally, "Evil-Ilium."

"Ah my queen," the man of craft assured her,   300
"noble wife of Laertes' son, Odysseus,
ravage no more your lovely face with tears
or consume your heart with grieving for your husband.
Not that I'd blame you, ever. Any woman will mourn
the bridegroom she has lost, lain with in love   305
and borne his children too. Even though he
was no Odysseus—a man like a god, they say.
But dry your tears and take my words to heart.
I will tell you the whole truth and hide nothing:
I have heard that Odysseus now, at last, is on his way,   310
he's just in reach, in rich Thesprotian country—
the man is still alive
and he's bringing home a royal hoard of treasure,
gifts he won from the people of those parts.
His crew? He's lost his crew and hollow ship   315
on the wine-dark waters off Thrinacia Island.
Zeus and Helios raged, dead set against Odysseus
for his men-at-arms had killed the cattle of the Sun,
so down to the last hand they drowned in crashing seas.
But not Odysseus, clinging tight to his ship's keel—   320
the breakers flung him out onto dry land, on Scheria,
the land of Phaeacians, close kin to the gods themselves,
and with all their hearts they prized him like a god,
showered the man with gifts, and they'd have gladly
sailed him home unscathed. In fact Odysseus   325
would have been here beside you long ago
but he thought it the better, shrewder course
to recoup his fortunes roving through the world.
At sly profit-turning there's not a man alive
to touch Odysseus. He's got no rival there.   330
So I learned from Phidon, king of Thesprotia,
who swore to me as he poured libations in his house,
'The ship's hauled down and the shipmates set to sail,
to take Odysseus home to native land.'
                    But I . . .
he shipped me off before. A Thesprotian cutter   335
chanced to be heading for Dulichion rich in wheat.
But he showed me all the treasure Odysseus had amassed,
enough to last a man and ten generations of his heirs—
so great the wealth stored up for *him* in the king's vaults!
But Odysseus, he made clear, was off at Dodona then   340
to hear the will of Zeus that rustles forth
from the god's tall leafy oak: how should he return,
after all the years away, to his own beloved Ithaca,
openly or in secret?
                    And so the man is safe,
as you can see, and he's coming home, soon,   345
he's close, close at hand—
he won't be severed long from kin and country,
no, not now. I give you my solemn, binding oath.
I swear by Zeus, the first, the greatest god—

by Odysseus' hearth, where I have come for help: 350
all will come to pass, I swear, exactly as I say.
True, this very month—just as the old moon dies
and the new moon rises into life—Odysseus will return!"

    "If only, my friend," reserved Penelope exclaimed,
"everything you say would come to pass!   355
You'd soon know my affection, know my gifts.
Any man you meet would call you blest.
But my heart can sense the way it all will go.
Odysseus, I tell you, is never coming back,
nor will you ever gain your passage home,   360
for we have no masters in our house like him
at welcoming in or sending off an honored guest.
Odysseus. There was a man, or was he all a dream?
But come, women, wash the stranger and make his bed,
with bedding, blankets and lustrous spreads to keep him warm   365
till Dawn comes up and takes her golden throne.
Then, tomorrow at daybreak, bathe him well
and rub him down with oil, so he can sit beside
Telemachus in the hall, enjoy his breakfast there.
And anyone who offends our guest beyond endurance—   370
he defeats himself; he's doomed to failure here,
no matter how raucously he raves and blusters on.
For how can you know, my friend, if I surpass
all women in thoughtfulness and shrewd good sense,
if I'd allow you to take your meals at hall   375
so weatherbeaten, clad in rags and tatters?
Our lives are much too brief . . .
If a man is cruel by nature, cruel in action,
the mortal world will call down curses on his head
while he is alive, and all will mock his memory after death.   380
But then if a man is kind by nature, kind in action,
his guests will carry his fame across the earth
and people all will praise him from the heart."

    "Wait, my queen," the crafty man objected,
"noble wife of Laertes' son, Odysseus—   385
blankets and glossy spreads? They're not my style.
Not from the day I launched out in my long-oared ship
and the snowy peaks of Crete went fading far astern.
I'll lie as I've done through sleepless nights before.
Many a night I've spent on rugged beds afield,   390
waiting for Dawn to mount her lovely throne.
Nor do I pine for any footbaths either.
Of all the women who serve your household here,
not one will touch my feet. Unless, perhaps,
there is some old retainer, the soul of trust,   395
someone who's borne as much as I have borne . . .
I wouldn't mind if she would touch my feet."
                                        "Dear friend,"
the discreet Penelope replied, "never has any man

so thoughtful—of all the guests in my palace
come from foreign parts—been as welcome as you . . .   400
so sensible, so apt, is every word you say.
I have just such an old woman, seasoned, wise,
who carefully tended my unlucky husband, reared him,
took him into her arms the day his mother bore him—
frail as the woman is, she'll wash your feet.   405
Up with you now, my good old Eurycleia,
come and wash your master's . . . equal in years.
Odysseus must have feet and hands like his by now—
hardship can age a person overnight."
                                        At that name
the old retainer buried her face in both hands,   410
burst into warm tears and wailed out in grief,
"Oh my child, how helpless I am to help you now!
How Zeus despised you, more than all other men,
god-fearing man that you were . . .
Never did any mortal burn the Old Thunderer   415
such rich thighbones—offerings charred and choice—
never as many as *you* did, praying always to reach
a ripe old age and raise a son to glory. Now,
you alone he's robbed of your home-coming day!
Just so, the women must have mocked my king,   420
far away, when he'd stopped at some fine house—
just as all these bitches, stranger, mock you here.
And because you shrink from their taunts, their wicked barbs,
you will not let them wash you. The work is mine—
Icarius' daughter, wise Penelope, bids me now   425
and I am all too glad. I will wash your feet,
both for my own dear queen and for yourself—
your sorrows wring my heart . . . and why?
Listen to me closely, mark my words.
Many a wayworn guest has landed here   430
but never, I swear, has one so struck my eyes—
your build, your voice, your feet—you're like Odysseus . . .
to the life!"
                "Old woman," wily Odysseus countered,
"that's what they all say who've seen us both.
We bear a striking resemblance to each other,   435
as you have had the wit to say yourself."

    The old woman took up a burnished basin
she used for washing feet and poured in bowls
of fresh cold water before she stirred in hot.
Odysseus, sitting full in the firelight, suddenly   440
swerved round to the dark, gripped by a quick misgiving—
soon as she touched him she might spot the scar!
The truth would all come out.
                            Bending closer
she started to bathe her master . . . then,
in a flash, she knew the scar—
                        that old wound   445

made years ago by a boar's white tusk when Odysseus
went to Parnassus,[1] out to see Autolycus and his sons.
The man was his mother's noble father, one who excelled
the world at thievery, that and subtle, shifty oaths.
Hermes[2] gave him the gift, overjoyed by the thighs   450
of lambs and kids he burned in the god's honor—
Hermes the ready partner in his crimes. Now,
Autolycus once visited Ithaca's fertile land,
to find his daughter's son had just been born.
Eurycleia set him down on the old man's knees   455
as he finished dinner, urging him, "Autolycus,
you must find a name for your daughter's darling son.
The baby comes as the answer to her prayers."

                       "You,
my daughter, and you, my son-in-law," Autolycus replied,
"give the boy the name I tell you now. Just as I   460
have come from afar, creating pain[3] for many—
men and women across the good green earth—
so let his name be *Odysseus* . . .
the Son of Pain, a name he'll earn in full.
And when he has come of age and pays his visit   465
to Parnassus—the great estate of his mother's line
where all my treasures lie—I will give him enough
to cheer his heart, then speed him home to you."

                            And so,
in time, Odysseus went to collect the splendid gifts.
Autolycus and the sons of Autolycus warmed him in   470
with eager handclasps, hearty words of welcome.
His mother's mother, Amphithea, hugged the boy
and kissed his face and kissed his shining eyes.
Autolycus told his well-bred sons to prepare
a princely feast. They followed orders gladly,   475
herded an ox inside at once, five years old,
skinned it and split the carcass into quarters,
deftly cut it in pieces, skewered these on spits,
roasted all to a turn and served the portions out.
So all day long till the sun went down they feasted,   480
consuming equal shares to their hearts' content.
Then when the sun had set and night came on
they turned to bed and took the gift of sleep.

                           As soon
as young Dawn with her rose-red fingers shone once more
they all moved out for the hunt, hounds in the lead,   485
Autolycus' sons and Prince Odysseus in their ranks.
Climbing Parnassus' ridges, thick with timber,
they quickly reached the mountain's windy folds
and just as the sun began to strike the plowlands,

---

1. The mountain range above Apollo's oracular shrine at Delphi, on the Greek mainland.   2. Not only
the messenger of the gods and the god who guided the dead down to the lower world but also the god of
the marketplace and so of trickery and swindling.   3. In Greek, *odyssamenos* (one who is angry and gives
cause for anger), close in sound to the name Odysseus. In line I.75 Athena uses a different form of the
same word when she asks Zeus why he is so hostile to Odysseus. Giving and receiving anger, and therefore
pain, is thus one of Odysseus's essential qualities.

rising out of the deep calm flow of the Ocean River,   490
the beaters came to a wooded glen, the hounds broke,
hot on a trail, and right behind the pack they came,
Autolycus' sons—Odysseus out in front now,
pressing the dogs, brandishing high his spear
with its long shadow waving. Then and there   495
a great boar lay in wait, in a thicket lair so dense
that the sodden gusty winds could never pierce it,
nor could the sun's sharp rays invade its depths
nor a downpour drench it through and through,
so dense, so dark, and piled with fallen leaves.   500
Here, as the hunters closed in for the kill,
crowding the hounds, the tramp of men and dogs
came drumming round the boar—he crashed from his lair,
his razor back bristling, his eyes flashing fire
and charging up to the hunt he stopped, at bay—   505
and Odysseus rushed him first,
shaking his long spear in a sturdy hand,
wild to strike but the boar struck faster,
lunging in on the slant, a tusk thrusting up
over the boy's knee, gouging a deep strip of flesh   510
but it never hit the bone—
                              Odysseus thrust and struck,
stabbing the beast's right shoulder—
                                    a glint of bronze—
the point ripped clean through and down in the dust he dropped,
grunting out his breath as his life winged away.
The sons of Autolycus, working over Odysseus,   515
skillfully binding up his open wound—
the gallant, godlike prince—
chanted an old spell that stanched the blood
and quickly bore him home to their father's palace.
There, in no time, Autolycus and the sons of Autolycus   520
healed him well and, showering him with splendid gifts,
sped Odysseus back to his native land, to Ithaca,
a young man filled with joy. His happy parents,
his father and noble mother, welcomed him home
and asked him of all his exploits, blow-by-blow: 525
how did he get that wound? He told his tale with style,
how the white tusk of a wild boar had gashed his leg,
hunting on Parnassus with Autolycus and his sons[4] . . .
                                                   That scar—
as the old nurse cradled his leg and her hands passed down
she felt it, knew it, suddenly let his foot fall—   530
down it dropped in the basin—the bronze clanged,
tipping over, spilling water across the floor.
Joy and torment gripped her heart at once,
tears rushed to her eyes—voice choked in her throat
she reached for Odysseus' chin and whispered quickly,   535

4. Leaving human society for nature, hunting and killing a fierce animal, and receiving a wound conform
to the pattern of male initiation rituals that helped boys make the transition to adulthood. Odysseus's scar
seems to commemorate his surmounting of such an initiatory ordeal.

"Ah my friend," seasoned Penelope dissented,   630
"dreams are hard to unravel, wayward, drifting things—
not all we glimpse in them will come to pass . . .
Two gates there are for our evanescent dreams,
one is made of ivory, the other made of horn.
Those that pass through the ivory cleanly carved   635
are will-o'-the-wisps, their message bears no fruit.
The dreams that pass through the gates of polished horn
are fraught with truth, for the dreamer who can see them.
But I can't believe my strange dream has come that way,
much as my son and I would love to have it so.   640
One more thing I'll tell you—weigh it well.
The day that dawns today, this cursed day,
will cut me off from Odysseus' house. Now,
I mean to announce a contest with those axes,
the ones he would often line up here inside the hall,   645
twelve in a straight unbroken row like blocks to shore a keel,
then stand well back and whip an arrow through the lot.[6]
Now I will bring them on as a trial for my suitors.
The hand that can string the bow with greatest ease,
that shoots an arrow clean through all twelve axes—   650
he's the man I follow, yes, forsaking this house
where I was once a bride, this gracious house
so filled with the best that life can offer—
I shall always remember it, that I know . . .
even in my dreams."
                    "Oh my queen,"   655
Odysseus, man of exploits, urged her on,
"royal wife of Laertes' son, Odysseus, now,
don't put off this test in the halls a moment.
Before that crew can handle the polished bow,
string it taut and shoot through all those axes—   660
Odysseus, man of exploits, will be home with you!"

    "If only, my friend," the wise Penelope replied,
"you were willing to sit beside me in the house,
indulging me in the comfort of your presence,
sleep would never drift across my eyes.   665
But one can't go without his sleep forever.
The immortals give each thing its proper place
in our mortal lives throughout the good green earth.
So now I'm going back to my room upstairs
and lie down on my bed,   670
that bed of pain my tears have streaked, year in,
year out, from the day Odysseus sailed away to see . . .
Destroy, I call it—I hate to say its name!
There I'll rest, while you lie here in the hall,

---

6. The nature of this archery contest has never been satisfactorily explained. The axes were probably
double-headed; the aperture through which the arrow passed must have been the socket in which the wood
handle fit. If the twelve ax heads were fixed in the ground (Telemachus later digs a trench for them) so that
the empty sockets were perfectly aligned, an arrow might pass through them—although it would take an
extremely powerful shot to make an arrow fly in such a perfectly horizontal line.

spreading your blankets somewhere on the floor,   675
or the women will prepare a decent bed."
                              With that
the queen went up to her lofty well-lit room
and not alone: her women followed close behind.
Penelope, once they reached the upper story,
fell to weeping for Odysseus, her beloved husband,   680
till watchful Athena sealed her eyes with welcome sleep.

                              BOOK XX

                        [Portents Gather]

Off in the entrance-hall the great king made his bed,
spreading out on the ground the raw hide of an ox,
heaping over it fleece from sheep the suitors
butchered day and night, then Eurynome threw
a blanket over him, once he'd nestled down.   5
And there Odysseus lay . . .
plotting within himself the suitors' death—
awake, alert, as the women slipped from the house,
the maids who whored in the suitors' beds each night,
tittering, linking arms and frisking as before.   10
The master's anger rose inside his chest,
torn in thought, debating, head and heart—
should he up and rush them, kill them one and all
or let them rut with their lovers one last time?
The heart inside him growled low with rage,   15
as a bitch mounting over her weak, defenseless puppies
growls, facing a stranger, bristling for a showdown—
so he growled from his depths, hackles rising at their outrage.
But he struck his chest and curbed his fighting heart:
"Bear up, old heart! You've borne worse, far worse,   20
that day when the Cyclops, man-mountain, bolted
your hardy comrades down. But you held fast—
Nobody but your cunning pulled you through
the monster's cave you thought would be your death."

   So he forced his spirit into submission,   25
the rage in his breast reined back—unswerving,
all endurance. But he himself kept tossing, turning,
intent as a cook before some white-hot blazing fire
who rolls his sizzling sausage back and forth,
packed with fat and blood—keen to broil it quickly,   30
tossing, turning it, this way, that way—so he cast about:
how could he get these shameless suitors in his clutches,
one man facing a mob? . . . when close to his side she came,
Athena sweeping down from the sky in a woman's build
and hovering at his head, the goddess spoke: 35
"Why still awake? The unluckiest man alive!
Here is your house, your wife at home, your son,
as fine a boy as one could hope to have."
                              "True,"

the wily fighter replied, "how right you are, goddess,
but still this worry haunts me, heart and soul—   40
how can I get these shameless suitors in my clutches?
Single-handed, braving an army always camped inside.
There's another worry, that haunts me even more.
What if I kill them—thanks to you and Zeus—
how do I run from under their avengers?   45
Show me the way, I ask you."
                                    "Impossible man!"
Athena bantered, the goddess' eyes ablaze.
"Others are quick to trust a weaker comrade,
some poor mortal, far less cunning than I.
But I am a goddess, look, the very one who   50
guards you in all your trials to the last.
I tell you this straight out:
even if fifty bands of mortal fighters
closed around us, hot to kill us off in battle,
still you could drive away their herds and sleek flocks!   55
So, surrender to sleep at last. What a misery,
keeping watch through the night, wide awake—
you'll soon come up from under all your troubles."

    With that she showered sleep across his eyes
and back to Olympus went the lustrous goddess.   60
As soon as sleep came on him, loosing his limbs,
slipping the toils of anguish from his mind,
his devoted wife awoke and,
sitting up in her soft bed, returned to tears.
When the queen had wept to her heart's content   65
she prayed to the Huntress, Artemis, first of all:
"Artemis—goddess, noble daughter of Zeus, if only
you'd whip an arrow through my breast and tear my life out,
now, at once! Or let some whirlwind pluck me up
and sweep me away along those murky paths and   70
fling me down where the Ocean River running
round the world rolls back upon itself!
                                    Quick
as the whirlwinds swept away Pandareus' daughters[7]
years ago, when the gods destroyed their parents,
leaving the young girls orphans in their house.   75
But radiant Aphrodite nursed them well
on cheese and luscious honey and heady wine,
and Hera gave them beauty and sound good sense,
more than all other women—virgin Artemis made them tall
and Athena honed their skills to fashion lovely work.   80
But then, when Aphrodite approached Olympus' peaks
to ask for the girls their crowning day as brides

---

7. The fate of these daughters of Pandareus was different from that of the one who married Zethus and
became a nightingale (alluded to in book XIX). They paid for the wrongdoing of their father, who stole a
golden image from the temple of Hephaestus. Though the gods showered gifts on them, in the end they
were swept away to their deaths by the storm winds.

from Zeus who loves the lightning—Zeus who knows all,
all that's fated, all not fated, for mortal man—
then the storm spirits snatched them away   85
and passed them on to the hateful Furies,
yes, for all their loving care.
                                   Just so
may the gods who rule Olympus blot me out!
Artemis with your glossy braids, come shoot me dead—
so I can plunge beneath this loathsome earth   90
with the image of Odysseus vivid in my mind.
Never let me warm the heart of a weaker man!
Even grief is bearable, true, when someone weeps
through the days, sobbing, heart convulsed with pain
yet embraced by sleep all night—sweet oblivion, sleep   95
dissolving all, the good and the bad, once it seals our eyes—
but even my dreams torment me, sent by wicked spirits.
Again—just this night—someone lay beside me . . .
like Odysseus to the life, when he embarked
with his men-at-arms. My heart raced with joy.   100
No dream, I thought, the waking truth at last!"
                                          At those words
Dawn rose on her golden throne in a sudden gleam of light.
And great Odysseus caught the sound of his wife's cry
and began to daydream—deep in his heart it seemed
she stood beside him, knew him, now, at last . . .   105
Gathering up the fleece and blankets where he'd slept,
he laid them on a chair in the hall, he took the oxhide out
and spread it down, lifted his hands and prayed to Zeus:
"Father Zeus, if you really willed it so—to bring me
home over land and sea-lanes, home to native ground   110
after all the pain you brought me—show me a sign,
a good omen voiced by someone awake indoors,
another sign, outside, from Zeus himself!"

    And Zeus in all his wisdom heard that prayer.
He thundered at once, out of his clear blue heavens   115
high above the clouds, and Odysseus' spirit lifted.
Then from within the halls a woman grinding grain
let fly a lucky word. Close at hand she was,
where the good commander set the handmills once
and now twelve women in all performed their tasks,   120
grinding the wheat and barley, marrow of men's bones.
The rest were abed by now—they'd milled their stint—
this one alone, the frailest of all, kept working on.
Stopping her mill, she spoke an omen for her master:
"Zeus, Father! King of gods and men, now *there*   125
was a crack of thunder out of the starry sky—
and not a cloud in sight!
Sure it's a sign you're showing someone now.
So, poor as I am, grant *me* my prayer as well:
let this day be the last, the last these suitors   130
bolt their groaning feasts in King Odysseus' house!

These brutes who break my knees—heart-wrenching labor,
grinding their grain—now let them eat their last!"

    A lucky omen, linked with Zeus's thunder.
Odysseus' heart leapt up, the man convinced   135
he'd grind the scoundrels' lives out in revenge.
                   By now
the other maids were gathering in Odysseus' royal palace,
raking up on the hearth the fire still going strong.
Telemachus climbed from bed and dressed at once,
brisk as a young god—   140
over his shoulder he slung his well-honed sword,
he fastened rawhide sandals under his smooth feet,
he seized his tough spear tipped with a bronze point
and took his stand at the threshold, calling Eurycleia:
"Dear nurse, how did you treat the stranger in our house?   145
With bed and board? Or leave him to lie untended?
That would be mother's way—sensible as she is—
all impulse, doting over some worthless stranger,
turning a good man out to face the worst."

    "Please, child," his calm old nurse replied,   150
"don't blame *her*—your mother's blameless this time.
He sat and drank his wine till he'd had his fill.
Food? He'd lost his hunger. But she asked him.
And when it was time to think of turning in,
she told the maids to spread a decent bed, but he—   155
so down-and-out, poor soul, so dogged by fate—
said no to snuggling into a bed, between covers.
No sir, the man lay down in the entrance-hall,
on the raw hide of an ox and sheep's fleece,
and we threw a blanket over him, so we did."
                   Hearing that,   160
Telemachus strode out through the palace, spear in hand,
and a pair of sleek hounds went trotting at his heels.
He made for the meeting grounds to join the island lords
while Eurycleia the daughter of Ops, Pisenor's son,
that best of women, gave the maids their orders: 165
"Quick now, look alive, sweep out the house,
wet down the floors!
            You, those purple coverlets,
fling them over the fancy chairs!
                All those tables,
sponge them down—scour the winebowls, burnished cups!
The rest—now off you go to the spring and fetch some water,   170
fast as your legs can run!
Our young gallants won't be long from the palace,
they'll be bright and early—today's a public feast."

    They hung on her words and ran to do her bidding.
Full twenty scurried off to the spring's dark water,   175
others bent to the housework, all good hands.

Then in they trooped, the strutting serving-men,
who split the firewood cleanly now as the women
bustled in from the spring, the swineherd at their heels,
driving three fat porkers, the best of all his herds.   180
And leaving them to root in the broad courtyard,
up he went to Odysseus, hailed him warmly:
"Friend, do the suitors show you more respect
or treat you like the dregs of the earth as always?"

    "Good Eumaeus," the crafty man replied,   185
"if only the gods would pay back their outrage!
Wild and reckless young cubs, conniving here
in another's house. They've got no sense of shame."

    And now as the two confided in each other,
the goatherd Melanthius sauntered toward them,   190
herding his goats with a pair of drovers' help,
the pick of his flocks to make the suitors' meal.
Under the echoing porch he tethered these, then turned
on Odysseus once again with cutting insults: "Still alive?
Still hounding your betters, begging round the house?   195
Why don't you cart yourself away? Get out!
We'll never part, I swear,
till we taste each other's fists. Riffraff,
you and your begging make us sick! Get out—
we're hardly the only banquet on the island."   200

    No reply. The wily one just shook his head,
silent, his mind churning with thoughts of bloody work . . .

    Third to arrive was Philoetius, that good cowherd,
prodding in for the crowd a heifer and fat goats.
Boatmen had brought them over from the mainland,   205
crews who ferry across all travelers too,
whoever comes for passage.
Under the echoing porch he tethered all heads well
and then approached the swineherd, full of questions:
"Who's this stranger, Eumaeus, just come to the house?   210
What roots does the man claim—who are his people?
Where are his blood kin? his father's fields?
Poor beggar. But what a build—a royal king's!
Ah, once the gods weave trouble into our lives
they drive us across the earth, they drown us all in pain,   215
even kings of the realm."
                    And with that thought
he walked up to Odysseus, gave him his right hand
and winged a greeting: "Cheers, old friend, old father,
here's to your luck, great days from this day on—
saddled now as you are with so much trouble.   220
Father Zeus, no god's more deadly than you!
No mercy for men, you give them life yourself
then plunge them into misery, brutal hardship.

I broke into sweat, my friend, when I first saw you—
see, my eyes still brim with tears, remembering *him*,   225
Odysseus . . . He must wear such rags, I know it,
knocking about, drifting through the world
if he's still alive and sees the light of day.
If he's dead already, lost in the House of Death,
my heart aches for Odysseus, my great lord and master.   230
He set me in charge of his herds, in Cephallenian country,
when I was just a youngster. How they've grown by now,
past counting! No mortal on earth could breed
a finer stock of oxen—broad in the brow,
they thrive like ears of corn. But just look,   235
these interlopers tell me to drive them in
for their own private feasts. Not a thought
for the young prince in the house, they never flinch—
no regard for the gods' wrath—in their mad rush
to carve up his goods, my master gone so long!   240
I'm tossed from horn to horn in my own mind . . .
What a traitor I'd be, with the prince still alive,
if I'd run off to some other country, herds and all,
to a new set of strangers. Ah, but isn't it worse
to hold out here, tending the herds for upstarts,   245
not their owners—suffering all the pains of hell?
I could have fled, ages ago, to some great king
who'd give me shelter. It's unbearable here.
True, but I still dream of my old master,
unlucky man—if only *he*'d drop in from the blue   250
and drive these suitors all in a rout throughout the halls!"

    "Cowherd," the cool tactician Odysseus answered,
"you're no coward, and nobody's fool, I'd say.
Even I can see there's sense in that old head.
So I tell you this on my solemn, binding oath: 255
I swear by Zeus, the first of all the gods—
by the table of hospitality waiting for us,
by Odysseus' hearth where I have come for help,
Odysseus will come home while you're still here.
You'll see with your own eyes, if you have the heart,   260
these suitors who lord it here cut down in blood."

    "Stranger, if only," the cowherd cried aloud,
"if only Zeus would make that oath come true—
you'd see my power, my fighting arms in action!"

    Eumaeus echoed his prayer to all the gods   265
that their wise king would soon come home again.

    Now as they spoke and urged each other on,
and once more the suitors were plotting certain doom
for the young prince—suddenly, banking high on the left
an omen flew past, an eagle clutching a trembling dove.   270

And Amphinomus rose in haste to warn them all,
"My friends, we'll never carry off this plot
to kill the prince. Let's concentrate on feasting."

His timely invitation pleased them all.
The suitors ambled into Odysseus' royal house   275
and flinging down their cloaks on a chair or bench,
they butchered hulking sheep and fatted goats,
full-grown hogs and a young cow from the herd.
They roasted all the innards, served them round
and filled the bowls with wine and mixed it well.   280
Eumaeus passed out cups; Philoetius, trusty herdsman,
brought on loaves of bread in ample wicker trays;
Melanthius poured the wine. The whole company
reached out for the good things that lay at hand.

Telemachus, maneuvering shrewdly, sat his father down 285
on the stone threshold, just inside the timbered hall,
and set a rickety stool and cramped table there.
He gave him a share of innards, poured his wine
in a golden cup and added a bracing invitation:
"Now sit right there. Drink your wine with the crowd. 290
I'll defend you from all their taunts and blows,
these young bucks. This is no public place,
this is *Odysseus'* house—
my father won it for me, so it's mine.
You suitors, control yourselves. No insults now,   295
no brawling, no, or it's war between us all."

So he declared. And they all bit their lips,
amazed the prince could speak with so much daring.
Only Eupithes' son Antinous ventured,
"Fighting words, but do let's knuckle under—   300
to our *prince*. Such abuse, such naked threats!
But clearly Zeus had foiled us. Or long before
we would have shut his mouth for him in the halls,
fluent and flowing as he is."
                               So he mocked.
Telemachus paid no heed.
                          And now through the streets   305
the heralds passed, leading the beasts marked out
for sacrifice on Apollo's grand festal day,
and the islanders with their long hair were filing
into the god's shady grove—the distant deadly Archer.

Those in the palace, once they'd roasted the prime cuts, 310
pulled them off the spits and, sharing out the portions,
fell to the royal feast . . .
The men who served them gave Odysseus his share,
as fair as the helping they received themselves.
So Telemachus ordered, the king's own son.   315

But Athena had no mind to let the brazen suitors
hold back now from their heart-rending insults—
she meant to make the anguish cut still deeper
into the core of Laertes' son Odysseus.
There was one among them, a lawless boor—   320
Ctesippus was his name, he made his home in Same,
a fellow so impressed with his own astounding wealth
he courted the wife of Odysseus, gone for years.
Now the man harangued his swaggering comrades:
"Listen to me, my fine friends, here's what I say!   325
From the start our guest has had his fair share—
it's only right, you know.
How impolite it would be, how wrong to scant
whatever guest Telemachus welcomes to his house.
Look here, I'll give him a proper guest-gift too,   330
a prize he can hand the crone who bathes his feet
or a tip for another slave who haunts the halls
of our great king Odysseus!"
                              On that note,
grabbing an oxhoof out of a basket where it lay,
with a brawny hand he flung it straight at the king—   335
but Odysseus ducked his head a little, dodging the blow,
and seething just as the oxhoof hit the solid wall
he clenched his teeth in a wry sardonic grin.
Telemachus dressed Ctesippus down at once:
"Ctesippus, you can thank your lucky stars   340
you missed our guest—he ducked your blow, by god!
Else I would have planted my sharp spear in your bowels—
your father would have been busy with your funeral,
not your wedding here. Enough.
Don't let me see more offenses in my house,   345
not from anyone! I'm alive to it all, now,
the good and the bad—the boy you knew is gone.
But I still must bear with this, this lovely sight . . .
sheepflocks butchered, wine swilled, food squandered—
how can a man fight off so many single-handed?   350
But no more of your crimes against me, please!
Unless you're bent on cutting me down, now,
and I'd rather die, yes, better that by far
than have to look on at your outrage day by day:
guests treated to blows, men dragging the serving-women   355
through our noble house, exploiting them all, no shame!"

    Dead quiet. The suitors all fell silent, hushed.
At last Damastor's son Agelaus rose and said,
"Fair enough, my friends; when a man speaks well
we have no grounds for wrangling, no cause for abuse.   360
Hands off this stranger! Or any other servant
in King Odysseus' palace. But now a word
of friendly advice for Telemachus and his mother—
here's hoping it proves congenial to them both.
So long as your hearts still kept a spark alive   365

that Odysseus would return—that great, deep man—
who could blame you, playing the waiting game at home
and holding off the suitors? The better course, it's true.
What if Odysseus had returned, had made it home at last?
But now it's clear as day—the man will come no more.   370
So go, Telemachus, sit with your mother, coax her
to wed the best man here, the one who offers most,
so you can have and hold your father's estate,
eating and drinking here, your mind at peace
while mother plays the wife in another's house."   375

    The young prince, keeping his poise, replied,
"I swear by Zeus, Agelaus, by all my father suffered—
dead, no doubt, or wandering far from Ithaca these days—
I don't delay my mother's marriage, not a moment,
I press her to wed the man who takes her heart.   380
I'll shower her myself with boundless gifts.
But I shrink from driving mother from our house,
issuing harsh commands against her will.
God forbid it ever comes to that!"
                                    So he vowed
and Athena set off uncontrollable laughter in the suitors,   385
crazed them out of their minds—mad, hysterical laughter
seemed to break from the jaws of strangers, not their own,
and the meat they were eating oozed red with blood—
tears flooded their eyes, hearts possessed by grief.
The inspired seer Theoclymenus wailed out in their midst,   390
"Poor men, what terror is this that overwhelms you so?
Night shrouds your heads, your faces, down to your knees—
cries of mourning are bursting into fire—cheeks rivering tears—
the walls and the handsome crossbeams dripping dank with blood!
Ghosts, look, thronging the entrance, thronging the court,   395
go trooping down to the world of death and darkness!
The sun is blotted out of the sky—look there—
a lethal mist spreads all across the earth!"
                                    At that
they all broke into peals of laughter aimed at the seer—
Polybus' son Eurymachus braying first and foremost,   400
"Our guest just in from abroad, the man is raving!
Quick, my boys, hustle him out of the house,
into the meeting grounds, the light of day—
everything *here* he thinks is dark as night!"

    "Eurymachus," the inspired prophet countered,   405
"when I want your escort, I'll ask for it myself.
I have eyes and ears, and both my feet, still,
and a head that's fairly sound,
nothing to be ashamed of. These will do
to take me past those doors . . .
                                    Oh I can see it now—   410
the disaster closing on you all! There's no escaping it,
no way out—not for a single one of you suitors,

wild reckless fools, plotting outrage here,
the halls of Odysseus, great and strong as a god!"

With that he marched out of the sturdy house   415
and went home to Piraeus, the host who warmed him in.
Now all the suitors, trading their snide glances, started
heckling Telemachus, made a mockery of his guests.
One or another brash young gallant sooffed,
"Telemachus, no one's more unlucky with his guests!"   420

"Look what your man dragged in—this mangy tramp
scraping for bread and wine!"
                                   "Not fit for good hard work,
the bag of bones—"
                                   "A useless dead weight on the land!"

"And then this charlatan up and apes the prophet."

"Take it from me—you'll be better off by far—   425
toss your friends in a slave-ship—"
                                   "Pack them off
to Sicily, fast—they'll fetch you one sweet price!"

So they jeered, but the prince paid no attention . . .
silent, eyes riveted on his father, always waiting
the moment he'd lay hands on that outrageous mob.   430

And all the while Icarius' daughter, wise Penelope,
had placed her carved chair within earshot, at the door,
so she could catch each word they uttered in the hall.
Laughing rowdily, men prepared their noonday meal,
succulent, rich—they'd butchered quite a herd.   435
But as for supper, what could be less enticing
than what a goddess and a powerful man
would spread before them soon? A groaning feast—
for they'd been first to plot their vicious crimes.

BOOK XXI

[Odysseus Strings His Bow]

The time had come. The goddess Athena with her blazing eyes
inspired Penelope, Icarius' daughter, wary, poised,
to set the bow and the gleaming iron axes out
before her suitors waiting in Odysseus' hall—
to test their skill and bring their slaughter on.   5
Up the steep stairs to her room she climbed
and grasped in a steady hand the curved key—
fine bronze, with ivory haft attached—
and then with her chamber-women made her way
to a hidden storeroom, far in the palace depths,   10
and there they lay, the royal master's treasures:
bronze, gold and a wealth of hard wrought iron

and there it lay as well . . . his backsprung bow
with its quiver bristling arrows, shafts of pain.
Gifts from the old days, from a friend he'd met 15
in Lacedaemon—Iphitus, Eurytus'[8] gallant son.
Once in Messene the two struck up together,
in sly Ortilochus'[9] house, that time Odysseus
went to collect a debt the whole realm owed him,
for Messenian raiders had lifted flocks from Ithaca, 20
three hundred head in their oarswept ships, the herdsmen too.
So his father and island elders sent Odysseus off,
a young boy on a mission,
a distant embassy made to right that wrong.
Iphitus went there hunting the stock that *he* had lost, 25
a dozen mares still nursing their hardy suckling mules.
The same mares that would prove his certain death
when he reached the son of Zeus, that iron heart,
Heracles—the past master of monstrous works—
who killed the man, a guest in his own house. 30
Brutal. Not a care for the wrathful eyes of god
or rites of hospitality he had spread before him,
no, he dined him, then he murdered him, commandeered
those hard-hoofed mares for the hero's own grange.
Still on the trail of these when he met Odysseus, 35
Iphitus gave him the bow his father, mighty Eurytus,
used to wield as a young man, but when he died
in his lofty house he left it to his son.
In turn, Odysseus gave his friend a sharp sword
and a rugged spear to mark the start of friendship, 40
treasured ties that bind. But before they got to know
the warmth of each other's board, the son of Zeus
had murdered Iphitus, Eurytus' magnificent son
who gave the prince the bow.
                              That great weapon—
King Odysseus never took it abroad with him 45
when he sailed off to war in his long black ships.
He kept it stored away in his stately house,
guarding the memory of a cherished friend,
and only took that bow on hunts at home.
                                          Now,
the lustrous queen soon reached the hidden vault 50
and stopped at the oaken doorsill, work an expert
sanded smooth and trued to the line some years ago,
planting the doorjambs snugly, hanging shining doors.
At once she loosed the thong from around its hook,
inserted the key and aiming straight and true, 55
shot back the bolts—and the rasping doors groaned
as loud as a bull will bellow, champing grass at pasture.
So as the key went home those handsome double doors
rang out now and sprang wide before her.

8. King of Oechalia, a city in Thessaly. According to another story, Heracles sacked his city, killed him, and took his daughter Iole captive.   9. King of Pherae in the southern Peloponnesus.

She stepped onto a plank where chests stood tall, 60
brimming with clothing scented sweet with cedar.
Reaching, tiptoe, lifting the bow down off its peg,
still secure in the burnished case that held it,
down she sank, laying the case across her knees,
and dissolved in tears with a high thin wail 65
as she drew her husband's weapon from its sheath . . .
Then, having wept and sobbed to her heart's content,
off she went to the hall to meet her proud admirers,
cradling her husband's backsprung bow in her arms,
its quiver bristling arrows, shafts of pain. 70
Her women followed, bringing a chest that held
the bronze and the iron axes, trophies won by the master.
That radiant woman, once she reached her suitors,
drawing her glistening veil across her cheeks,
paused now where a column propped the sturdy roof, 75
with one of her loyal handmaids stationed either side,
and delivered an ultimatum to her suitors:
"Listen to me, my overbearing friends!
You who plague this palace night and day,
drinking, eating us out of house and home 80
with the lord and master absent, gone so long—
the only excuse that you can offer is your zest
to win me as your bride. So, to arms, my gallants!
Here is the prize at issue, right before you, look—
I set before you the great bow of King Odysseus now! 85
The hand that can string this bow with greatest ease,
that shoots an arrow clean through all twelve axes—
he is the man I follow, yes, forsaking this house
where I was once a bride, this gracious house
so filled with the best that life can offer— 90
I shall always remember it, that I know . . .
even in my dreams."
                         She turned to Eumaeus,
ordered the good swineherd now to set the bow
and the gleaming iron axes out before the suitors.
He broke into tears as he received them, laid them down. 95
The cowherd wept too, when he saw his master's bow.
But Antinous wheeled on both and let them have it:
"Yokels, fools—you can't tell night from day!
You mawkish idiots, why are you sniveling here?
You're stirring up your mistress! Isn't she drowned 100
in grief already? She's lost her darling husband.
Sit down. Eat in peace, or take your snuffling
out of doors! But leave that bow right here—
our crucial test that makes or breaks us all.
No easy game, I wager, to string *his* polished bow. 105
Not a soul in the crowd can match Odysseus—
what a man he was . . .
I saw him once, remember him to this day,
though I was young and foolish way back then."
                                        Smooth talk,

but deep in the suitor's heart his hopes were bent   110
on stringing the bow and shooting through the axes.
Antinous—fated to be the first man to taste
an arrow whipped from great Odysseus' hands,
the king he mocked, at ease in the king's house,
egging comrades on to mock him too.
                                        "Amazing!"   115
Prince Telemachus waded in with a laugh:
"Zeus up there has robbed me of my wits.
My own dear mother, sensible as she is,
says she'll marry again, forsake our house,
and look at *me*—laughing for all I'm worth,   120
giggling like some fool. Step up, my friends!
Here is the prize at issue, right before you, look—
a woman who has no equal now in all Achaean country,
neither in holy Pylos, nor in Argos or Mycenae,
not even Ithaca itself or the loamy mainland.   125
You know it well. Why sing my mother's praises?
Come, let the games begin! No dodges, no delays,
no turning back from the stringing of the bow—
we'll see who wins, we will.
I'd even take a crack at the bow myself . . .   130
If I string it and shoot through all the axes,
I'd worry less if my noble mother left our house
with another man and left me here behind—man enough
at last to win my father's splendid prizes!"
                                        With that   135
he leapt to his feet and dropped his bright red cloak,
slipping the sword and sword-belt off his shoulders.
First he planted the axes, digging a long trench,
one for all, and trued them all to a line
then tamped the earth to bed them. Wonder took   140
the revelers looking on: his work so firm, precise,
though he'd never seen the axes ranged before.
He stood at the threshold, poised to try the bow . . .
Three times he made it shudder, straining to bend it,
three times his power flagged—but his hopes ran high
he'd string his father's bow and shoot through every iron   145
and now, struggling with all his might for the fourth time,
he would have strung the bow, but Odysseus shook his head
and stopped him short despite his tensing zeal.
"God help me," the inspired prince cried out,
"must I be a weakling, a failure all my life?   150
Unless I'm just too young to trust my hands
to fight off any man who rises up against me.
Come, my betters, so much stronger than I am—
try the bow and finish off the contest."

    He propped his father's weapon on the ground,   155
tilting it up against the polished well-hung doors
and resting a shaft aslant the bow's fine horn,
then back he went to the seat that he had left.

"Up, friends!" Antinous called, taking over.
"One man after another, left to right,   160
starting from where the steward pours the wine."

    So Antinous urged and all agreed.
The first man up was Leodes, Oenops' son,
a seer who could see their futures in the smoke,
who always sat by the glowing winebowl, well back,   165
the one man in the group who loathed their reckless ways,
appalled by all their outrage. His turn first . . .
Picking up the weapon now and the swift arrow,
he stood at the threshold, poised to try the bow
but failed to bend it. As soon as he tugged the string   170
his hands went slack, his soft, uncallused hands,
and he called back to the suitors, "Friends,
I can't bend it. Take it, someone—try.
Here is a bow to rob our best of life and breath,
all our best contenders! Still, better be dead   175
than live on here, never winning the prize
that tempts us all—forever in pursuit,
burning with expectation every day.
If there's still a suitor here who hopes,
who aches to marry Penelope, Odysseus' wife,   180
just let him try the bow; he'll see the truth!
He'll soon lay siege to another Argive woman
trailing her long robes, and shower her with gifts—
and then our queen can marry the one who offers most,
the man marked out by fate to be her husband."   185

    With those words he thrust the bow aside,
tilting it up against the polished well-hung doors
and resting a shaft aslant the bow's fine horn,
then back he went to the seat that he had left.
But Antinous turned on the seer, abuses flying: 190
"Leodes! what are you saying? what's got past your lips?
What awful, grisly nonsense—it shocks me to hear it—
'here is a bow to rob our best of life and breath!'
Just because _you_ can't string it, you're so weak?
Clearly your genteel mother never bred her boy   195
for the work of bending bows and shooting arrows.
We have champions in our ranks to string it quickly.
Hop to it, Melanthius!"—he barked at the goatherd—
"Rake the fire in the hall, pull up a big stool,
heap it with fleece and fetch that hefty ball   200
of lard from the stores inside. So we young lords
can heat and limber the bow and rub it down with grease
before we try again and finish off the contest!"

    The goatherd bustled about to rake the fire
still going strong. He pulled up a big stool,   205
heaped it with fleece and fetched the hefty ball
of lard from the stores inside. And the young men

limbered the bow, rubbing it down with hot grease,
then struggled to bend it back but failed. No use—
they fell far short of the strength the bow required.   210
Antinous still held off, dashing Eurymachus too,
the ringleaders of all the suitors,
head and shoulders the strongest of the lot.
                                    But now
the king's two men, the cowherd and the swineherd,
had slipped out of the palace side-by-side   215
and great Odysseus left the house to join them.
Once they were past the courtyard and the gates
he probed them deftly, surely: "Cowherd, swineherd,
what, shall I blurt this out or keep it to myself?
No, speak out. The heart inside me says so.   220
How far would you go to fight beside Odysseus?
Say he dropped like *that* from a clear blue sky
and a god brought him back—
would you fight for the suitors or your king?
Tell me how you feel inside your hearts."   225

      "Father Zeus," the trusty cowherd shouted,
"bring my prayer to pass! Let the master come—
some god guide him now! You'd see my power,
my fighting arms in action!"

      Eumaeus echoed his prayer to all the gods   230
that their wise king would soon come home again.
Certain at least these two were loyal to the death,
Odysseus reassured them quickly: "I'm right here,
here in the flesh—myself—and home at last,
after bearing twenty years of brutal hardship.   235
Now I know that of all my men you two alone
longed for my return. From the rest I've heard
not one real prayer that I come back again.
So now I'll tell you what's in store for *you.*
If a god beats down the lofty suitors at my hands,   240
I'll find you wives, both of you, grant you property,
sturdy houses beside my own, and in my eyes you'll be
comrades to Prince Telemachus, brothers from then on.
Come, I'll show you something—living proof—
know me for certain, put your minds at rest.
                                    This scar,   245
look, where a boar's white tusk gored me, years ago,
hunting on Parnassus, Autolycus' sons and I."
                                    With that,
pushing back his rags, he revealed the great scar . . .
And the men gazed at it, scanned it, knew it well,
broke into tears and threw their arms around their master—   250
lost in affection, kissing his head and shoulders,
and so Odysseus kissed their heads and hands.
Now the sun would have set upon their tears
if Odysseus had not called a halt himself.

"No more weeping. Coming out of the house   255
a man might see us, tell the men inside.
Let's slip back in—singly, not in a pack.
I'll go first. You're next. Here's our signal.
When all the rest in there, our lordly friends,
are dead against my having the bow and quiver,   260
good Eumaeus, carry the weapon down the hall
and put it in my hands. Then tell the serving-women
to lock the snugly fitted doors to their own rooms.
If anyone hears from there the jolting blows
and groans of men, caught in our huge net,   265
not one of them show her face—
sit tight, keep to her weaving, not a sound.
You, my good Philoetius, here are your orders.
Shoot the bolt of the courtyard's outer gate,
lock it, lash it fast."
                              With that command   270
the master entered his well-constructed house
and back he went to the stool that he had left.
The king's two men, in turn, slipped in as well.

    Just now Eurymachus held the bow in his hands,
turning it over, tip to tip, before the blazing fire   275
to heat the weapon. But he failed to bend it even so
and the suitor's high heart groaned to bursting.
"A black day," he exclaimed in wounded pride,
"a blow to myself, a blow to each man here!
It's less the marriage that mortifies me now—   280
that's galling too, but lots of women are left,
some in seagirt Ithaca, some in other cities.
What breaks my heart is the fact we fall so short
of great Odysseus' strength we cannot string his bow.
A disgrace to ring in the ears of men to come."   285

    "Eurymachus," Eupithes' son Antinous countered,
"it will never come to that, as you well know.
Today is a feast-day up and down the island
in honor of the Archer God. Who flexes bows today?
Set it aside. Rest easy now. And all the axes,   290
let's just leave them planted where they are.
Trust me, no one's about to crash the gates
of Laertes' son and carry off these trophies.
Steward, pour some drops for the god in every cup,
we'll tip the wine, then put the bow to bed.   295
And first thing in the morning have Melanthius
bring the pick of his goats from all his herds
so we can burn the thighs to Apollo, god of archers—
then try the bow and finish off the contest."

    Welcome advice. And again they all agreed.   300
Heralds sprinkled water over their hands for rinsing,
the young men brimmed the mixing bowls with wine,

they tipped first drops for the god in every cup,
then poured full rounds for all. And now, once
they'd tipped libations out and drunk their fill,   305
the king of craft, Odysseus, said with all his cunning,
"Listen to me, you lords who court the noble queen.
I have to say what the heart inside me urges.
I appeal especially to Eurymachus, and you,
brilliant Antinous, who spoke so shrewdly now.   310
Give the bow a rest for today, leave it to the gods—
at dawn the Archer God will grant a victory
to the man he favors most.
          For the moment,
give me the polished bow now, won't you? So,
to amuse you all, I can try my hand, my strength . . .   315
is the old force still alive inside these gnarled limbs?
Or has a life of roaming, years of rough neglect,
destroyed it long ago?"
          Modest words
that sent them all into hot, indignant rage,
fearing he just might string the polished bow.   320
So Antinous rounded on him, dressed him down:
"Not a shred of sense in your head, you filthy drifter!
Not content to feast at your ease with us, the island's pride?
Never denied your full share of the banquet, never,
you can listen in on our secrets. No one else   325
can eavesdrop on our talk, no tramp, no beggar.
The wine has overpowered you, heady wine—
the ruin of many another man, whoever
gulps it down and drinks beyond his limit.
Wine—it drove the Centaur,[1] famous Eurytion,   330
mad in the halls of lionhearted Pirithous.
There to visit the Lapiths, crazed with wine
the headlong Centaur bent to his ugly work
in the prince's own house! His hosts sprang up,
seized with fury, dragged him across the forecourt,   335
flung him out of doors, hacking his nose and ears off
with their knives, no mercy. The creature reeled away,
still blind with drink, his heart like a wild storm,
loaded with all the frenzy in his mind!
          And so
the feud between mortal men and Centaurs had its start.   340
But the drunk was first to bring disaster on himself
by drowning in his cups. You too, I promise you
no end of trouble if you should string that bow.
You'll meet no kindness in our part of the world—
we'll sail you off in a black ship to Echetus,   345
the mainland king who wrecks all men alive.
Nothing can save you from his royal grip!

---

1. Half horse, half human. At the wedding of Pirithous, king of the Lapiths (their human neighbors), the centaurs got drunk and tried to rape the women who were present. The Lapiths killed them after a fierce fight.

So drink, but hold your peace,
don't take on the younger, stronger men."

"Antinous," watchful Penelope stepped in,   350
"how impolite it would be, how wrong, to scant
whatever guest Telemachus welcomes to his house.
You really think—if the stranger trusts so to his hands
and strength that he strings Odysseus' great bow—
he'll take me home and claim me as his bride?   355
He never dreamed of such a thing, I'm sure.
Don't let that ruin the feast for any reveler here.
Unthinkable—nothing, nothing could be worse."

Polybus' son Eurymachus had an answer:
"Wise Penelope, daughter of Icarius, do we really   360
expect the man to wed you? Unthinkable, I know.
But we do recoil at the talk of men and women.
One of the island's meaner sort will mutter,
'Look at the riffraff courting a king's wife.
Weaklings, look, they can't even string his bow.   365
But along came this beggar, drifting out of the blue—
strung his bow with ease and shot through all the axes!'
Gossip will fly. We'll hang our heads in shame."

"Shame?" alert Penelope protested—
"How can you hope for any public fame at all?   370
You who disgrace, devour a great man's house and home!
Why hang your heads in shame over next to nothing?
Our friend here is a strapping, well-built man
and claims to be the son of a noble father.
Come, hand him the bow now, let's just see . . .   375
I tell you this—and I'll make good my word—
if he strings the bow and Apollo grants him glory,
I'll dress him in shirt and cloak, in handsome clothes,
I'll give him a good sharp lance to fight off men and dogs,
give him a two-edged sword and sandals for his feet   380
and send him off, wherever his heart desires."

                                                   "Mother,"
poised Telemachus broke in now, "my father's bow—
no Achaean on earth has more right than I
to give it or withhold it, as I please.
Of all the lords in Ithaca's rocky heights   385
or the islands facing Elis grazed by horses,
not a single one will force or thwart my will,
even if I decide to give our guest this bow—
a gift outright—to carry off himself.
                          So, mother,
go back to your quarters. Tend to your own tasks,   390
the distaff and the loom, and keep the women
working hard as well. As for the bow now,
men will see to that, but I most of all:
I hold the reins of power in this house."
                                            Astonished,

she withdrew to her own room. She took to heart   395
the clear good sense in what her son had said.
Climbing up to the lofty chamber with her women,
she fell to weeping for Odysseus, her beloved husband,
till watchful Athena sealed her eyes with welcome sleep.

And now the loyal swineherd had lifted up the bow,   400
was taking it toward the king, when all the suitors
burst out in an ugly uproar through the palace—
brash young bullies, this or that one heckling,
"Where on earth are you going with that bow?"

"You, you grubby swineherd, are you crazy?"   405

"The speedy dogs you reared will eat your corpse—"

"Out there with your pigs, out in the cold, alone!"

"If only Apollo and all the gods shine down on us!"

Eumaeus froze in his tracks, put down the bow,
panicked by every outcry in the hall.   410
Telemachus shouted too, from the other side,
and full of threats: "Carry on with the bow, old boy!
If you serve too many masters, you'll soon suffer.
Look sharp, or I'll pelt you back to your farm
with flying rocks. I may be younger than you   415
but I'm much stronger. If only I had that edge
in fists and brawn over all this courting crowd,
I'd soon dispatch them—licking their wounds at last—
clear of our palace where they plot their vicious plots!"

His outburst sent them all into gales of laughter,   420
blithe and oblivious, that dissolved their pique
against the prince. The swineherd took the bow,
carried it down the hall to his ready, waiting king
and standing by him, placed it in his hands,
then he called the nurse aside and whispered,   425
"Good Eurycleia—Telemachus commands you now
to lock the snugly fitted doors to your own rooms.
If anyone hears from there the jolting blows
and groans of men, caught in our huge net,
not one of you show your face—   430
sit tight, keep to your weaving, not a sound."

That silenced the old nurse—
she barred the doors that led from the long hall.
The cowherd quietly bounded out of the house
to lock the gates of the high-stockaded court.   435
Under the portico lay a cable, ship's tough gear:
he lashed the gates with this, then slipped back in
and ran and sat on the stool that he'd just left,
eyes riveted on Odysseus.

Now *he* held the bow
in his own hands, turning it over, tip to tip,   440
testing it, this way, that way . . . fearing worms
had bored through the weapon's horn with the master gone abroad.
A suitor would glance at his neighbor, jeering, taunting,
"Look at our connoisseur of bows!"   "Sly old fox—
maybe he's got bows like it, stored in *his* house."   445

"That or he's bent on making one himself."

"Look how he twists and turns it in his hands!"

"The clever tramp means trouble—"

"I wish him luck," some cocksure lord chimed in,
"as good as his luck in bending back that weapon!"   450

So they mocked, but Odysseus, mastermind in action,
once he'd handled the great bow and scanned every inch,
then, like an expert singer skilled at lyre and song—
who strains a string to a new peg with ease,
making the pliant sheep-gut fast at either end—   455
so with his virtuoso ease Odysseus strung his mighty bow.
Quickly his right hand plucked the string to test its pitch
and under his touch it sang out clear and sharp as a swallow's cry.
Horror swept through the suitors, faces blanching white,
and Zeus cracked the sky with a bolt, his blazing sign,   460
and the great man who had borne so much rejoiced at last
that the son of cunning Cronus flung that omen down for *him*.
He snatched a winged arrow lying bare on the board—
the rest still bristled deep inside the quiver,
soon to be tasted by all the feasters there.   465
Setting shaft on the handgrip, drawing the notch
and bowstring back, back . . . right from his stool,
just as he sat but aiming straight and true, he let fly—
and never missing an ax from the first ax-handle
clean on through to the last and out   470
the shaft with its weighted brazen head shot free!
                                        "My son,"
Odysseus looked to Telemachus and said, "your guest,
sitting here in your house, has not disgraced you.
No missing the mark, look, and no long labor spent
to string the bow. My strength's not broken yet,   475
not quite so frail as the mocking suitors thought.
But the hour has come to serve our masters right—
supper in broad daylight—then to other revels,
song and dancing, all that crowns a feast."

He paused with a warning nod, and at that sign   480
Prince Telemachus, son of King Odysseus,
girding his sharp sword on, clamping hand to spear,

took his stand by a chair that flanked his father—
his bronze spearpoint glinting now like fire . . .

BOOK XXII

[Slaughter in the Hall]

Now stripping back his rags Odysseus master of craft and battle
vaulted onto the great threshold, gripping his bow and quiver
bristling arrows, and poured his flashing shafts before him,
loose at his feet, and thundered out to all the suitors:
"Look—your crucial test is finished, now, at last!   5
But another target's left that no one's hit before—
we'll see if *I* can hit it—Apollo give me glory!"

    With that he trained a stabbing arrow on Antinous . . .
just lifting a gorgeous golden loving-cup in his hands,
just tilting the two-handled goblet back to his lips,   10
about to drain the wine—and slaughter the last thing
on the suitor's mind: who could dream that one foe
in that crowd of feasters, however great his power,
would bring down death on himself, and black doom?
But Odysseus aimed and shot Antinous square in the throat   15
and the point went stabbing clean through the soft neck and out—
and off to the side he pitched, the cup dropped from his grasp
as the shaft sank home, and the man's life-blood came spurting
out his nostrils—
                thick red jets—
                                a sudden thrust of his foot—
he kicked away the table—
                            food showered across the floor,   20
the bread and meats soaked in a swirl of bloody filth.
The suitors burst into uproar all throughout the house
when they saw their leader down. They leapt from their seats,
milling about, desperate, scanning the stone walls—
not a shield in sight, no rugged spear to seize.   25
They wheeled on Odysseus, lashing out in fury:
"Stranger, shooting at men will cost your life!"

    "Your game is over—you, you've shot your last!"

    "You'll never escape your own headlong death!"

    "You killed the best in Ithaca—our fine prince!"   30

    "Vultures will eat your corpse!"
                            Groping, frantic—
each one persuading himself the guest had killed
the man by chance. Poor fools, blind to the fact
that all their necks were in the noose, their doom sealed.
With a dark look, the wily fighter Odysseus shouted back,   35
"You dogs! you never imagined I'd return from Troy—
so cocksure that you bled my house to death,

ravished my serving-women—wooed my wife
behind my back while I was still alive!
No fear of the gods who rule the skies up there,   40
no fear that men's revenge might arrive someday—
now all your necks are in the noose—your doom is sealed!"

    Terror gripped them all, blanched their faces white,
each man glancing wildly—how to escape his instant death?
Only Eurymachus had the breath to venture, "If you,   45
you're truly Odysseus of Ithaca, home at last,
you're right to accuse these men of what they've done—
so much reckless outrage here in your palace,
so much on your lands. But here he lies,
quite dead, and he incited it all—Antinous—   50
look, the man who drove us all to crime!
Not that he needed marriage, craved it so;
he'd bigger game in mind—though Zeus barred his way—
he'd lord it over Ithaca's handsome country, king himself,
once he'd lain in wait for your son and cut him down!   55
But now he's received the death that he deserved.
So spare your own people! Later we'll recoup
your costs with a tax laid down upon the land,
covering all we ate and drank inside your halls,
and each of us here will pay full measure too—   60
twenty oxen in value, bronze and gold we'll give
until we melt your heart. Before we've settled,
who on earth could blame you for your rage?"

    But the battle-master kept on glaring, seething.
"No, Eurymachus! Not if you paid me all your father's wealth—   65
all you possess now, and all that could pour in from the world's end—
no, not even then would I stay my hands from slaughter
till all you suitors had paid for all your crimes!
Now life or death—your choice—fight me or flee
if you hope to escape your sudden bloody doom!   70
I doubt one man in the lot will save his skin!"

    His menace shook their knees, their hearts too
but Eurymachus spoke again, now to the suitors: "Friends!
This man will never restrain his hands, invincible hands—
now that he's seized that polished bow and quiver, look,   75
he'll shoot from the sill until he's killed us all!
So fight—call up the joy of battle! Swords out!
Tables lifted—block his arrows winging death!
Charge him, charge in a pack—
try to rout the man from the sill, the doors,   80
race through town and sound an alarm at once—
our friend would soon see he's shot his bolt!"
                                          Brave talk—
he drew his two-edged sword, bronze, honed for the kill
and hurled himself at the king with a raw savage cry
in the same breath that Odysseus loosed an arrow   85

ripping his breast beside the nipple so hard
it lodged in the man's liver—
Out of his grasp the sword dropped to the ground—
over his table, head over heels he tumbled, doubled up,
flinging his food and his two-handled cup across the floor—   90
he smashed the ground with his forehead, writhing in pain,
both feet flailing out, and his high seat tottered—
the mist of death came swirling down his eyes.

    Amphinomus rushed the king in all his glory,
charging him face-to-face, a slashing sword drawn—   95
if only he could force him clear of the doorway, now,
but Telemachus—too quick—stabbed the man from behind,
plunging his bronze spear between the suitor's shoulders
and straight on through his chest the point came jutting out—
down he went with a thud, his forehead slammed the ground.   100
Telemachus swerved aside, leaving his long spearshaft
lodged in Amphinomus—fearing some suitor just might
lunge in from behind as he tugged the shaft,
impale him with a sword or hack him down,
crouching over the corpse.   105
He went on the run, reached his father at once
and halting right beside him, let fly, "Father—
now I'll get you a shield and a pair of spears,
a helmet of solid bronze to fit your temples!
I'll arm myself on the way back and hand out   110
arms to the swineherd, arm the cowherd too—
we'd better fight equipped!"
                      "Run, fetch them,"
the wily captain urged, "while I've got arrows left
to defend me—or they'll force me from the doors
while I fight on alone!"   115

    Telemachus moved to his father's orders smartly.
Off he ran to the room where the famous arms lay stored,
took up four shields, eight spears, four bronze helmets
ridged with horsehair crests and, loaded with these,
ran back to reach his father's side in no time.   120
The prince was first to case himself in bronze
and his servants followed suit—both harnessed up
and all three flanked Odysseus, mastermind of war,
and he, as long as he'd arrows left to defend himself,
kept picking suitors off in the palace, one by one   125
and down they went, corpse on corpse in droves.
Then, when the royal archer's shafts ran out,
he leaned his bow on a post of the massive doors—
where walls of the hallway catch the light—and armed:
across his shoulder he slung a buckler four plies thick,   130
over his powerful head he set a well-forged helmet,
the horsehair crest atop it tossing, bristling terror,
and grasped two rugged lances tipped with fiery bronze.

Now a side-door was fitted into the main wall—
right at the edge of the great hall's stone sill—   135
and led to a passage always shut by good tight boards.
But Odysseus gave the swineherd strict commands
to stand hard by the side-door, guard it well—
the only way the suitors might break out.
Agelaus called to his comrades with a plan: 140
"Friends, can't someone climb through the hatch?—
tell men outside to sound the alarm, be quick—
our guest would soon see he'd shot his last!"

    The goatherd Melanthius answered, "Not a chance,
my lord—the door to the courtyard's much too near,   145
dangerous too, the mouth of the passage cramped.
One strong man could block us, one and all!
No, I'll fetch you some armor to harness on,
out of the storeroom—there, nowhere else, I'm sure,
the king and his gallant son have stowed their arms!"   150

    With that the goatherd clambered up through smoke-ducts
high on the wall and scurried into Odysseus' storeroom,
bundled a dozen shields, as many spears and helmets
ridged with horsehair crests and, loaded with these,
rushed back down to the suitors, quickly issued arms.   155
Odysseus' knees shook, his heart too, when he saw them
buckling on their armor, brandishing long spears—
here was a battle looming, well he knew.
He turned at once to Telemachus, warnings flying:
"A bad break in the fight, my boy! One of the women's   160
tipped the odds against us—or could it be the goatherd?"

    "My fault, father," the cool clear prince replied,
"the blame's all mine. That snug door to the vault,
I left it ajar—they've kept a better watch than I.
Go, Eumaeus, shut the door to the storeroom,   165
check and see if it's one of the women's tricks
or Dolius' son Melanthius. He's our man, I'd say."

    And even as they conspired, back the goatherd
climbed to the room to fetch more burnished arms,
but Eumaeus spotted him, quickly told his king   170
who stood close by: "Odysseus, wily captain,
there he goes again, the infernal nuisance—
just as we suspected—back to the storeroom.
Give me a clear command!
Do I kill the man—if I can take him down—   175
or drag him back to you, here, to pay in full
for the vicious work he's plotted in your house?"

    Odysseus, master of tactics, answered briskly,
"I and the prince will keep these brazen suitors
crammed in the hall, for all their battle-fury.   180

You two wrench Melanthius' arms and legs behind him,
fling him down in the storeroom—lash his back to a plank
and strap a twisted cable fast to the scoundrel's body,
hoist him up a column until he hits the rafters—
let him dangle in agony, still alive,   185
for a good long time!"

　　They hung on his orders, keen to do his will.
Off they ran to the storeroom, unseen by him inside—
Melanthius, rummaging after arms, deep in a dark recess
as the two men took their stand, either side the doorposts,   190
poised till the goatherd tried to cross the doorsill . . .
one hand clutching a crested helmet, the other
an ample old buckler blotched with mildew,
the shield Laertes bore as a young soldier once
but there it lay for ages, seams on the handstraps split—   195
Quick, they rushed him, seized him, haled him back by the hair,
flung him down on the floor, writhing with terror, bound him
hand and foot with a chafing cord, wrenched his limbs
back, back till the joints locked tight—
just as Laertes' cunning son commanded—   200
they strapped a twisted cable round his body,
hoisted him up a column until he hit the rafters,
then you mocked him, Eumaeus, my good swineherd:
"Now stand guard through the whole night, Melanthius—
stretched out on a soft bed fit for *you*, your highness!   205
You're bound to see the Morning rising up from the Ocean,
mounting her golden throne—at just the hour you always
drive in goats to feast the suitors in the hall!"

　　So they left him, trussed in his agonizing sling;
they clapped on armor again, shut the gleaming doors   210
and ran to rejoin Odysseus, mastermind of war.
And now as the ranks squared off, breathing fury—
four at the sill confronting a larger, stronger force
arrayed inside the hall—now Zeus's daughter Athena,
taking the build and voice of Mentor, swept in   215
and Odysseus, thrilled to see her, cried out,
"Rescue us, Mentor, now it's life or death!
Remember your old comrade—all the service
I offered you! We were boys together!"
　　　　　　　　　　　　　　　So he cried
yet knew in his bones it was Athena, Driver of Armies.   220
But across the hall the suitors brayed against her,
Agelaus first, his outburst full of threats:
"Mentor, never let Odysseus trick you into
siding with *him* to fight against the suitors.
Here's our plan of action, and we will see it through!   225
Once we've killed them both, the father and the son,
we'll kill you too, for all you're bent on doing
here in the halls—you'll pay with your own head!
And once our swords have stopped your violence cold—

all your property, all in your house, your fields,   230
we'll lump it all with Odysseus' rich estate
and never let your sons live on in your halls
or free your wife and daughters to walk through town!"

    Naked threats—and Athena hit new heights of rage,
she lashed out at Odysseus now with blazing accusations: 235
"Where's it gone, Odysseus—your power, your fighting heart?
The great soldier who fought for famous white-armed Helen,
battling Trojans nine long years—nonstop, no mercy,
mowing their armies down in grueling battle—
you who seized the broad streets of Troy   240
with your fine strategic stroke! How can you—
now you've returned to your own house, your own wealth—
bewail the loss of your combat strength in a war with *suitors*?
Come, old friend, stand by me! You'll see action now,
see how Mentor the son of Alcimus, that brave fighter,   245
kills your enemies, pays you back for service!"
                                                        Rousing words—
but she gave no all-out turning of the tide, not yet,
she kept on testing Odysseus and his gallant son,
putting their force and fighting heart to proof.
For all the world like a swallow in their sight   250
she flew on high to perch
on the great hall's central roofbeam black with smoke.

    But the suitors closed ranks, commanded now by Damastor's son
Agelaus, flanked by Eurynomus, Demoptolemus and Amphimedon,
Pisander, Polyctor's son, and Polybus ready, waiting—   255
head and shoulders the best and bravest of the lot
still left to fight for their lives,
now that the pelting shafts had killed the rest.
Agelaus spurred his comrades on with battle-plans:
"Friends, at last the man's invincible hands are useless!   260
Mentor has mouthed some empty boasts and flitted off—
just four are left to fight at the front doors. So now,
no wasting your long spears—all at a single hurl,
just six of us launch out in the first wave!
If Zeus is willing, we may hit Odysseus,   265
carry off the glory! The rest are nothing
once the captain's down!"
                            At his command,
concentrating their shots, all six hurled as one
but Athena sent the whole salvo wide of the mark—
one of them hit the jamb of the great hall's doors,   270
another the massive door itself, and the heavy bronze point
of a third ashen javelin crashed against the wall.
Seeing his men untouched by the suitors' flurry,
steady Odysseus leapt to take command:
"Friends! now it's for *us* to hurl at them, I say,   275
into this ruck of suitors! Topping all their crimes
they're mad to strip the armor off our bodies!"

Taking aim at the ranks, all four let fly as one
and the lances struck home—Odysseus killed Demoptolemus,
Telemachus killed Euryades—the swineherd, Elatus—   280
and the cowherd cut Pisander down in blood.
They bit the dust of the broad floor, all as one.
Back to the great hall's far recess the others shrank
as the four rushed in and plucked up spears from corpses.

And again the suitors hurled their whetted shafts   285
but Athena sent the better part of the salvo wide—
one of them hit the jamb of the great hall's doors,
another the massive door itself, and the heavy bronze point
of a third ashen javelin crashed against the wall.
True, Amphimedon nicked Telemachus on the wrist—   290
the glancing blade just barely broke his skin.
Ctesippus sent a long spear sailing over
Eumaeus' buckler, grazing his shoulder blade
but the weapon skittered off and hit the ground.
And again those led by the brilliant battle-master   295
hurled their razor spears at the suitors' ranks—
and now Odysseus raider of cities hit Eurydamas,
Telemachus hit Amphimedon—Eumaeus, Polybus—
and the cowherd stabbed Ctesippus
right in the man's chest and triumphed over his body: 300
"Love your mockery, do you? Son of that blowhard Polytherses!
No more shooting off your mouth, you idiot, such big talk—
leave the last word to the gods—they're much stronger!
Take this spear, this guest-gift, for the cow's hoof
you once gave King Odysseus begging in his house!"   305

So the master of longhorn cattle had his say—
as Odysseus, fighting at close quarters, ran Agelaus
through with a long lance—Telemachus speared Leocritus
so deep in the groin the bronze came punching out his back
and the man crashed headfirst, slamming the ground full-face.   310
And now Athena, looming out of the rafters high above them,
brandished her man-destroying shield of thunder, terrifying
the suitors out of their minds, and down the hall they panicked—
wild, like herds stampeding, driven mad as the darting gadfly
strikes in the late spring when the long days come round.   315
The attackers struck like eagles, crook-clawed, hook-beaked,
swooping down from a mountain ridge to harry smaller birds
that skim across the flatland, cringing under the clouds
but the eagles plunge in fury, rip their lives out—hopeless,
never a chance of flight or rescue—and people love the sport—   320
so the attackers routed suitors headlong down the hall,
wheeling into the slaughter, slashing left and right
and grisly screams broke from skulls cracked open—
the whole floor awash with blood.
                              Leodes now—
he flung himself at Odysseus, clutched his knees,   325
crying out to the king with a sudden, winging prayer:

"I hug your knees, Odysseus—mercy! spare my life!
Never, I swear, did I harass any woman in your house—
never a word, a gesture—nothing, no, I tried
to restrain the suitors, whoever did such things.   330
They wouldn't listen, keep their hands to themselves—
so reckless, so they earn their shameful fate.
But I was just their prophet—
my hands are clean—and I'm to die their death!
Look at the thanks I get for years of service!"   335

    A killing look, and the wry soldier answered,
"Only a priest, a prophet for this mob, you say?
How hard you must have prayed in my own house
that the heady day of my return would never dawn—
my dear wife would be yours, would bear your children!   340
For that there's no escape from grueling death—you die!"

    And snatching up in one powerful hand a sword
left on the ground—Agelaus dropped it when he fell—
Odysseus hacked the prophet square across the neck
and the praying head went tumbling in the dust.
                           Now one was left,   345
trying still to escape black death. Phemius, Terpis' son,
the bard who always performed among the suitors—
they forced the man to sing . . .
There he stood, backing into the side-door,
still clutching his ringing lyre in his hands,   350
his mind in turmoil, torn—what should he do?
Steal from the hall and crouch at the altar-stone
of Zeus who Guards the Court,[2] where time and again
Odysseus and Laertes burned the long thighs of oxen?
Or throw himself on the master's mercy, clasp his knees?   355
That was the better way—or so it struck him, yes,
grasp the knees of Laertes' royal son. And so,
cradling his hollow lyre, he laid it on the ground
between the mixing-bowl and the silver-studded throne,
then rushed up to Odysseus, yes, and clutched his knees,   360
singing out to his king with a stirring, winged prayer:
"I hug your knees, Odysseus—mercy! spare my life!
What a grief it will be to you for all the years to come
if you kill the singer now, who sings for gods and men.
I taught myself the craft, but a god has planted   365
deep in my spirit all the paths of song—
songs I'm fit to sing for you as for a god.
Calm your bloodlust now—don't take my head!
He'd bear me out, your own dear son Telemachus—
never of *my* own will, never for any gain did I   370
perform in your house, singing after the suitors
had their feasts. They were too strong, too many—
they forced me to come and sing—I had no choice!"

2. Zeus Herkeios, who had an altar in the courtyard of the house.

The inspired Prince Telemachus heard his pleas
and quickly said to his father close beside him,   375
"Stop, don't cut him down! This one's innocent.
So is the herald Medon—the one who always
tended me in the house when I was little—
spare him too. Unless he's dead by now,
killed by Philoetius or Eumaeus here—   380
or ran into *you* rampaging through the halls."

The herald pricked up his anxious ears at that . . .
cautious soul, he cowered, trembling, under a chair—
wrapped in an oxhide freshly stripped—to dodge black death.
He jumped in a flash from there, threw off the smelly hide   385
and scuttling up to Telemachus, clutching his knees,
the herald begged for life in words that fluttered:
"Here I am, dear boy—spare me! Tell your father,
flushed with victory, not to kill me with his sword—
enraged as he is with these young lords who bled   390
his palace white and showed you no respect,
the reckless fools!"
                        Breaking into a smile
the canny Odysseus reassured him, "Courage!
The prince has pulled you through, he's saved you now
so you can take it to heart and tell the next man too: 395
clearly doing good puts doing bad to shame.
Now leave the palace, go and sit outside—
out in the courtyard, clear of the slaughter—
you and the bard with all his many songs.
Wait till I've done some household chores   400
that call for my attention."

The two men scurried out of the house at once
and crouched at the altar-stone of mighty Zeus—
glancing left and right,
fearing death would strike at any moment.   405

Odysseus scanned his house to see if any man
still skulked alive, still hoped to avoid black death.
But he found them one and all in blood and dust . . .
great hauls of them down and out like fish that fishermen
drag from the churning gray surf in looped and coiling nets   410
and fling ashore on a sweeping hook of beach—some noble catch
heaped on the sand, twitching, lusting for fresh salt sea
but the Sungod hammers down and burns their lives out . . .
so the suitors lay in heaps, corpse covering corpse.
At last the seasoned fighter turned to his son: 415
"Telemachus, go, call the old nurse here—
I must tell her all that's on my mind."

Telemachus ran to do his father's bidding,
shook the women's doors, calling Eurycleia:
"Come out now! Up with you, good old woman!   420

You who watch over all the household hands—
quick, my father wants you, needs to have a word!"

    Crisp command that left the old nurse hushed—
she spread the doors to the well-constructed hall,
slipped out in haste, and the prince led her on . . .   425
She found Odysseus in the thick of slaughtered corpses,
splattered with bloody filth like a lion that's devoured
some ox of the field and lopes home, covered with blood,
his chest streaked, both jaws glistening, dripping red—
a sight to strike terror. So Odysseus looked now,   430
splattered with gore, his thighs, his fighting hands,
and she, when she saw the corpses, all the pooling blood,
was about to lift a cry of triumph—here was a great exploit,
look—but the soldier held her back and checked her zeal
with warnings winging home: "Rejoice in your heart,   435
old woman—peace! No cries of triumph now.
It's unholy to glory over the bodies of the dead.
These men the doom of the gods has brought low,
and their own indecent acts. They'd no regard
for any man on earth—good or bad—   440
who chanced to come their way. And so, thanks
to their reckless work, they met this shameful fate.
Quick, report in full on the women in my halls—
who are disloyal to me, who are guiltless?"

                                        "Surely, child,"
his fond old nurse replied, "now here's the truth.   445
Fifty women you have inside your house,
women we've trained to do their duties well,
to card the wool and bear the yoke of service.
Some dozen in all went tramping to their shame,
thumbing their noses at me, at the queen herself!   450
And Telemachus, just now come of age—his mother
would never let the boy take charge of the maids.
But let me climb to her well-lit room upstairs
and tell your wife the news—
some god has put the woman fast asleep."   455

    "Don't wake her yet," the crafty man returned,
"you tell those women to hurry here at once—
just the ones who've shamed us all along."

    Away the old nurse bustled through the house
to give the women orders, rush them to the king.   460
Odysseus called Telemachus over, both herdsmen too,
with strict commands: "Start clearing away the bodies.
Make the women pitch in too. Chairs and tables—
scrub them down with sponges, rinse them clean.
And once you've put the entire house in order,   465
march the women out of the great hall—between
the roundhouse and the courtyard's strong stockade—
and hack them with your swords, slash out all their lives—

blot out of their minds the joys of love they relished
under the suitors' bodies, rutting on the sly!"   470

    The women crowded in, huddling all together . . .
wailing convulsively, streaming live warm tears.
First they carried out the bodies of the dead
and propped them under the courtyard colonnade,
standing them one against another. Odysseus   475
shouted commands himself, moving things along
and they kept bearing out the bodies—they were forced.
Next they scrubbed down the elegant chairs and tables,
washed them with sopping sponges, rinsed them clean.
Then Telemachus and the herdsmen scraped smooth   480
the packed earth floor of the royal house with spades
as the women gathered up the filth and piled it outside.
And then, at last, once the entire house was put in order,
they marched the women out of the great hall—between
the roundhouse and the courtyard's strong stockade—   485
crammed them into a dead end, no way out from there,
and stern Telemachus gave the men their orders:
"No clean death[3] for the likes of them, by god!
Not from me—they showered abuse on my head,
my mother's too!
             You sluts—the suitors' whores!"   490

    With that, taking a cable used on a dark-prowed ship
he coiled it over the roundhouse, lashed it fast to a tall column,
hoisting it up so high no toes could touch the ground.
Then, as doves or thrushes beating their spread wings
against some snare rigged up in thickets—flying in   495
for a cozy nest but a grisly bed receives them—
so the women's heads were trapped in a line,
nooses yanking their necks up, one by one
so all might die a pitiful, ghastly death . . .
they kicked up heels for a little—not for long.
                      Melanthius?   500
They hauled him out through the doorway, into the court,
lopped his nose and ears with a ruthless knife,
tore his genitals out for the dogs to eat raw
and in manic fury hacked off hands and feet.
                       Then,
once they'd washed their own hands and feet,   505
they went inside again to join Odysseus.
Their work was done with now.
But the king turned to devoted Eurycleia, saying,
"Bring sulfur, nurse, to scour all this pollution—
bring me fire too, so I can fumigate the house.   510
And call Penelope here with all her women—
tell all the maids to come back in at once."

3. That is, by sword or spear. Hanging was considered an ignominious way to die.

"Well said, my boy," his old nurse replied,
"right to the point. But wait,
let me fetch you a shirt and cloak to wrap you.   515
No more dawdling round the palace, nothing but rags
to cover those broad shoulders—it's a scandal!"

"Fire first," the good soldier answered.
"Light me a fire to purify this house."

The devoted nurse snapped to his command,   520
brought her master fire and brimstone. Odysseus
purged his palace, halls and court, with cleansing fumes.

Then back through the royal house the old nurse went
to tell the women the news and bring them in at once.
They came crowding out of their quarters, torch in hand,   525
flung their arms around Odysseus, hugged him, home at last,
and kissed his head and shoulders, seized his hands, and he,
overcome by a lovely longing, broke down and wept . . .
deep in his heart he knew them one and all.

BOOK XXIII

[The Great Rooted Bed]

Up to the rooms the old nurse clambered, chuckling all the way,
to tell the queen her husband was here now, home at last.
Her knees bustling, feet shuffling over each other,
till hovering at her mistress' head she spoke:
"Penelope—child—wake up and see for yourself,   5
with your own eyes, all you dreamed of, all your days!
He's here—Odysseus—he's come home, at long last!
He's killed the suitors, swaggering young brutes
who plagued his house, wolfed his cattle down,
rode roughshod over his son!"   10

"Dear old nurse," wary Penelope replied,
"the gods have made you mad. They have that power,
putting lunacy into the clearest head around
or setting a half-wit on the path to sense.
They've unhinged you, and you were once so sane.   15
Why do you mock me?—haven't I wept enough?—
telling such wild stories, interrupting my sleep,
sweet sleep that held me, sealed my eyes just now.
Not once have I slept so soundly since the day
Odysseus sailed away to see that cursed city . . .   20
Destroy, I call it—I hate to say its name!
Now down you go. Back to your own quarters.
If any other woman of mine had come to me,
rousing me out of sleep with such a tale,
I'd have her bundled back to her room in pain.   25
It's only your old gray head that spares you that!"

"Never"—the fond old nurse kept pressing on—
"dear child, I'd never mock you! No, it's all true,
he's here—Odysseus—he's come home, just as I tell you!
He's the stranger they all manhandled in the hall.   30
Telemachus knew he was here, for days and days,
but he knew enough to hide his father's plans
so *he* could pay those vipers back in kind!"

Penelope's heart burst in joy, she leapt from bed,
her eyes streaming tears, she hugged the old nurse   35
and cried out with an eager, winging word,
"Please, dear one, give me the whole story.
If he's really home again, just as you tell me,
how did he get those shameless suitors in his clutches?—
single-handed, braving an army always camped inside."   40

"I have no idea," the devoted nurse replied.
"I didn't see it, I didn't ask—all I heard
was the choking groans of men cut down in blood.
We crouched in terror—a dark nook of our quarters—
all of us locked tight behind those snug doors   45
till your boy Telemachus came and called me out—
his father rushed him there to do just that. And then
I found Odysseus in the thick of slaughtered corpses;
there he stood and all around him, over the beaten floor,
the bodies sprawled in heaps, lying one on another . . .   50
How it would have thrilled your heart to see him—
splattered with bloody filth, a lion with his kill!
And now they're all stacked at the courtyard gates—
he's lit a roaring fire,
he's purifying the house with cleansing fumes   55
and he's sent me here to bring you back to him.
Follow me down! So now, after all the years of grief,
you two can embark, loving hearts, along the road to joy.
Look, your dreams, put off so long, come true at last—
he's back alive, home at his hearth, and found you,   60
found his son still here. And all those suitors
who did him wrong, he's paid them back, he has,
right in his own house!"
                              "Hush, dear woman,"
guarded Penelope cautioned her at once.
"Don't laugh, don't cry in triumph—not yet.   65
You know how welcome the sight of him would be
to all in the house, and to me most of all
and the son we bore together.
But the story can't be true, not as you tell it,
no, it must be a god who's killed our brazen friends—   70
up in arms at their outrage, heartbreaking crimes.
They'd no regard for any man on earth—
good or bad—who chanced to come their way. So,
thanks to their reckless work they die their deaths.

Odysseus? Far from Achaea now, he's lost all hope   75
of coming home . . . he's lost and gone himself."

   "Child," the devoted old nurse protested,
"what nonsense you let slip through your teeth.
Here's your husband, warming his hands at his own hearth,
here—and you, you say he'll never come home again,   80
always the soul of trust! All right, this too—
I'll give you a sign, a proof that's plain as day.
That scar, made years ago by a boar's white tusk—
I spotted the scar myself, when I washed his feet,
and I tried to tell you, ah, but he, the crafty rascal,   85
clamped his hand on my mouth—I couldn't say a word.
Follow me down now. I'll stake my life on it:
if I am lying to *you*—
kill me with a thousand knives of pain!"

   "Dear old nurse," composed Penelope responded,   90
"deep as you are, my friend, you'll find it hard
to plumb the plans of the everlasting gods.
All the same, let's go and join my son
so I can see the suitors lying dead
and see . . . the one who killed them."   95
                                  With that thought
Penelope started down from her lofty room, her heart
in turmoil, torn . . . should she keep her distance,
probe her husband? Or rush up to the man at once
and kiss his head and cling to both his hands?
As soon as she stepped across the stone threshold,   100
slipping in, she took a seat at the closest wall
and radiant in the firelight, faced Odysseus now.
There he sat, leaning against the great central column,
eyes fixed on the ground, waiting, poised for whatever words
his hardy wife might say when she caught sight of him.   105
A long while she sat in silence . . . numbing wonder
filled her heart as her eyes explored his face.
One moment he seemed . . . Odysseus, to the life—
the next, no, he was not the man she knew,
a huddled mass of rags was all she saw.   110

   "Oh mother," Telemachus reproached her,
"cruel mother, you with your hard heart!
Why do you spurn my father so—why don't you
sit beside him, engage him, ask him questions?
What other wife could have a spirit so unbending?   115
Holding back from her husband, home at last for *her*
after bearing twenty years of brutal struggle—
your heart was always harder than a rock!"
                                "My child,"
Penelope, well-aware, explained, "I'm stunned with wonder,
powerless. Cannot speak to him ask him questions,   120
look him in the eyes . . . But if he is truly

Odysseus, home at last, make no mistake:
we two will know each other, even better—
we two have secret signs,
known to us both but hidden from the world."   125

    Odysseus, long-enduring, broke into a smile
and turned to his son with pointed, winging words:
"Leave your mother here in the hall to test me
as she will. She soon will know me better.
Now because I am filthy, wear such grimy rags,   130
she spurns me—your mother still can't bring herself
to believe I am her husband.
                        But you and I,
put heads together. What's our best defense?
When someone kills a lone man in the realm
who leaves behind him no great band of avengers,   135
still the killer flees, goodbye to kin and country.
But *we* brought down the best of the island's princes,
the pillars of Ithaca. Weigh it well, I urge you."

    "Look to it all yourself now, father," his son
deferred at once. "You are the best on earth,   140
they say, when it comes to mapping tactics.
No one, no mortal man, can touch you there.
But we're behind you, hearts intent on battle,
nor do I think you'll find us short on courage,
long as our strength will last."
                      "Then here's our plan,"   145
the master of tactics said. "I think it's best.
First go and wash, and pull fresh tunics on
and tell the maids in the hall to dress well too.
And let the inspired bard take up his ringing lyre
and lead off for us all a dance so full of heart   150
that whoever hears the strains outside the gates—
a passerby on the road, a neighbor round about—
will think it's a wedding-feast that's under way.
No news of the suitors' death must spread through town
till we have slipped away to our own estates,   155
our orchard green with trees. There we'll see
what winning strategy Zeus will hand us then."

    They hung on his words and moved to orders smartly.
First they washed and pulled fresh tunics on,
the women arrayed themselves—the inspired bard   160
struck up his resounding lyre and stirred in all
a desire for dance and song, the lovely lilting beat,
till the great house echoed round to the measured tread
of dancing men in motion, women sashed and lithe.
And whoever heard the strains outside would say,   165
"A miracle—someone's married the queen at last!"

"One of her hundred suitors."

"That callous woman,
too faithless to keep her lord and master's house
to the bitter end—"

"Till he came sailing home."

So they'd say, blind to what had happened: 170
the great-hearted Odysseus was home again at last.
The maid Eurynome bathed him, rubbed him down with oil
and drew around him a royal cape and choice tunic too.
And Athena crowned the man with beauty, head to foot,
made him taller to all eyes, his build more massive,   175
yes, and down from his brow the great goddess
ran his curls like thick hyacinth clusters
full of blooms. As a master craftsman washes
gold over beaten silver—a man the god of fire
and Queen Athena trained in every fine technique—   180
and finishes off his latest effort, handsome work . . .
so she lavished splendor over his head and shoulders now.
He stepped from his bath, glistening like a god,
and back he went to the seat that he had left
and facing his wife, declared,   185
"Strange woman! So hard—the gods of Olympus
made you harder than any other woman in the world!
What other wife could have a spirit so unbending?
Holding back from her husband, home at last for *her*
after bearing twenty years of brutal struggle.   190
Come, nurse, make me a bed, I'll sleep alone.
She has a heart of iron in her breast."

"Strange *man*,"
wary Penelope said. "I'm not so proud, so scornful,
nor am I overwhelmed by your quick change . . .
You look—how well I know—the way he looked,   195
setting sail from Ithaca years ago
aboard the long-oared ship.

Come, Eurycleia,
move the sturdy bedstead out of our bridal chamber—
that room the master built with his own hands.
Take it out now, sturdy bed that it is,   200
and spread it deep with fleece,
blankets and lustrous throws to keep him warm."

Putting her husband to the proof—but Odysseus
blazed up in fury, lashing out at his loyal wife:
"Woman—your words, they cut me to the core!   205
Who could move my bed? Impossible task,
even for some skilled craftsman—unless a god
came down in person, quick to lend a hand,
lifted it out with ease and moved it elsewhere.
Not a man on earth, not even at peak strength,   210
would find it easy to prise it up and shift it, no,
a great sign, a hallmark lies in its construction.
I know, I built it myself—no one else . . .

There was a branching olive-tree inside our court,
grown to its full prime, the bole like a column, thickset.   215
Around it I built my bedroom, finished off the walls
with good tight stonework, roofed it over soundly
and added doors, hung well and snugly wedged.
Then I lopped the leafy crown of the olive,
clean-cutting the stump bare from roots up,   220
planing it round with a bronze smoothing-adze—
I had the skill—I shaped it plumb to the line to make
my bedpost, bored the holes it needed with an auger.
Working from there I built my bed, start to finish,
I gave it ivory inlays, gold and silver fittings,   225
wove the straps across it, oxhide gleaming red.
There's our secret sign, I tell you, our life story!
Does the bed, my lady, still stand planted firm?—
I don't know—or has someone chopped away
that olive-trunk and hauled our bedstead off?"
                                        Living proof—   230
Penelope felt her knees go slack, her heart surrender,
recognizing the strong clear signs Odysseus offered.
She dissolved in tears, rushed to Odysseus, flung her arms
around his neck and kissed his head and cried out,
"Odysseus—don't flare up at me now, not you,   235
always the most understanding man alive!
The gods, it was the gods who sent us sorrow—
they grudged us both a life in each other's arms
from the heady zest of youth to the stoop of old age.
But don't fault me, angry with me now because I failed,   240
at the first glimpse, to greet you, hold you, so . . .
In my heart of hearts I always cringed with fear
some fraud might come, beguile me with his talk;
the world is full of the sort,
cunning ones who plot their own dark ends.   245
Remember Helen of Argos, Zeus's daughter—
would *she* have sported so in a stranger's bed
if she had dreamed that Achaea's sons were doomed
to fight and die to bring her home again?
Some god spurred her to do her shameless work.   250
Not till then did her mind conceive that madness,
blinding madness that caused her anguish, ours as well.
But now, since you have revealed such overwhelming proof—
the secret sign of our bed, which no one's ever seen
but you and I and a single handmaid, Actoris,   255
the servant my father gave me when I came,
who kept the doors of our room you built so well . . .
you've conquered my heart, my hard heart, at last!"

    The more she spoke, the more a deep desire for tears
welled up inside his breast—he wept as he held the wife   260
he loved, the soul of loyalty, in his arms at last.
Joy, warm as the joy that shipwrecked sailors feel
when they catch sight of land—Poseidon has struck

their well-rigged ship on the open sea with gale winds
and crushing walls of waves, and only a few escape, swimming,   265
struggling out of the frothing surf to reach the shore,
their bodies crusted with salt but buoyed up with joy
as they plant their feet on solid ground again,
spared a deadly fate. So joyous now to her
the sight of her husband, vivid in her gaze,   270
that her white arms, embracing his neck
would never for a moment let him go . . .
Dawn with her rose-red fingers might have shone
upon their tears, if with her glinting eyes
Athena had not thought of one more thing.   275
She held back the night, and night lingered long
at the western edge of the earth, while in the east
she reined in Dawn of the golden throne at Ocean's banks,
commanding her not to yoke the windswift team that brings men
       light,
Blaze and Aurora, the young colts that race the Morning on.   280
Yet now Odysseus, seasoned veteran, said to his wife,
"Dear woman . . . we have still not reached the end
of all our trials. One more labor lies in store—
boundless, laden with danger, great and long,
and I must brave it out from start to finish.   285
So the ghost of Tiresias prophesied to me,
the day that I went down to the House of Death
to learn our best route home, my comrades' and my own.
But come, let's go to bed, dear woman—at long last
delight in sleep, delight in each other, come!"   290

   "If it's bed you want," reserved Penelope replied,
"it's bed you'll have, whenever the spirit moves,
now that the gods have brought you home again
to native land, your grand and gracious house.
But since you've alluded to it,   295
since a god has put it in your mind,
please, tell me about this trial still to come.
I'm bound to learn of it later, I am sure—
what's the harm if I hear of it tonight?"

                                    "Still so strange,"
Odysseus, the old master of stories, answered.   300
"Why again, why force me to tell you all?
Well, tell I shall. I'll hide nothing now.
But little joy it will bring you, I'm afraid,
as little joy for me.
             The prophet said
that I must rove through towns on towns of men,   305
that I must carry a well-planed oar until
I come to a people who know nothing of the sea,
whose food is never seasoned with salt, strangers all
to ships with their crimson prows and long slim oars,
wings that make ships fly. And here is my sign,   310
he told me, clear, so clear I cannot miss it,

and I will share it with you now . . .
When another traveler falls in with me and calls
that weight across my shoulder a fan to winnow grain,
then, he told me, I must plant my oar in the earth   315
and sacrifice fine beasts to the lord god of the sea,
Poseidon—a ram, a bull and a ramping wild boar—
then journey home and render noble offerings up
to the deathless gods who rule the vaulting skies,
to all the gods in order.   320
And at last my own death will steal upon me . . .
a gentle, painless death, far from the sea it comes
to take me down, borne down with the years in ripe old age
with all my people here in blessed peace around me.
All this, the prophet said, will come to pass."   325
"And so," Penelope said, in her great wisdom,
"if the gods will really grant a happier old age,
there's hope that we'll escape our trials at last."

    So husband and wife confided in each other,
while nurse and Eurynome, under the flaring brands,   330
were making up the bed with coverings deep and soft.
And working briskly, soon as they'd made it snug,
back to her room the old nurse went to sleep
as Eurynome, their attendant, torch in hand,
lighted the royal couple's way to bed and,   335
leading them to their chamber, slipped away.
Rejoicing in each other, they returned to their bed,
the old familiar place they loved so well.[4]

    Now Telemachus, the cowherd and the swineherd
rested their dancing feet and had the women do the same,   340
and across the shadowed hall the men lay down to sleep.

    But the royal couple, once they'd reveled in all
the longed-for joys of love, reveled in each other's stories,
the radiant woman telling of all she'd borne at home,
watching them there, the infernal crowd of suitors   345
slaughtering herds of cattle and good fat sheep—
while keen to win her hand—
draining the broached vats dry of vintage wine.
And great Odysseus told his wife of all the pains
he had dealt out to other men and all the hardships   350
he'd endured himself—his story first to last—
and she listened on, enchanted . . .
Sleep never sealed her eyes till all was told.

    He launched in with how he fought the Cicones down,
then how he came to the Lotus-eaters' lush green land.   355

4. Two great Alexandrian critics said that this line was the "end" of the *Odyssey* (though one of the words
they are said to have used could mean simply "culmination"). Modern critics are divided; some find the rest
of the poem banal, unartistic, full of linguistic anomalies, and so on. But if the poem stops here we are left
in suspense about many important themes that have been developed—notably, the question of reprisals for
the slaughter in the hall.

Then all the crimes of the Cyclops and how he paid him back
for the gallant men the monster ate without a qualm—
then how he visited Aeolus, who gave him a hero's welcome
then he sent him off, but the homeward run was not his fate,
not yet—some sudden squalls snatched him away once more   360
and drove him over the swarming sea, groaning in despair.
Then how he moored at Telepylus, where Laestrygonians
wrecked his fleet and killed his men-at-arms.
He told her of Circe's cunning magic wiles
and how he voyaged down in his long benched ship   365
to the moldering House of Death, to consult Tiresias,
ghostly seer of Thebes, and he saw old comrades there
and he saw his mother, who bore and reared him as a child.
He told how he caught the Sirens' voices throbbing in the wind
and how he had scudded past the Clashing Rocks, past grim
      Charybdis,   370
past Scylla—whom no rover had ever coasted by, home free—
and how his shipmates slaughtered the cattle of the Sun
and Zeus the king of thunder split his racing ship
with a reeking bolt and killed his hardy comrades,
all his fighting men at a stroke, but he alone   375
escaped their death at sea. He told how he reached
Ogygia's shores and the nymph Calypso held him back,
deep in her arching caverns, craving him for a husband—
cherished him, vowed to make him immortal, ageless, all his days,
yes, but she never won the heart inside him, never . . .   380
then how he reached the Phaeacians—heavy sailing there—
who with all their hearts had prized him like a god
and sent him off in a ship to his own beloved land,
giving him bronze and hoards of gold and robes . . .
and that was the last he told her, just as sleep   385
overcame him . . . sleep loosing his limbs,
slipping the toils of anguish from his mind.

    Athena, her eyes afire, had fresh plans.
Once she thought he'd had his heart's content
of love and sleep at his wife's side, straightaway   390
she roused young Dawn from Ocean's banks to her golden throne
to bring men light and roused Odysseus too, who rose
from his soft bed and advised his wife in parting,
"Dear woman, we both have had our fill of trials.
You in our house, weeping over my journey home,   395
fraught with storms and torment, true, and I,
pinned down in pain by Zeus and other gods,
for all my desire, blocked from reaching home.
But now that we've arrived at our bed together—
the reunion that we yearned for all those years—   400
look after the things still left me in our house.
But as for the flocks those brazen suitors plundered,
much I'll recoup myself, making many raids;
the rest our fellow-Ithacans will supply
till all my folds are full of sheep again.   405

But now I must be off to the upland farm,
our orchard green with trees, to see my father,
good old man weighed down with so much grief for me.
And you, dear woman, sensible as you are,
I would advise you, still . . .   410
quick as the rising sun the news will spread
of the suitors that I killed inside the house.
So climb to your lofty chamber with your women.
Sit tight there. See no one. Question no one."

  He strapped his burnished armor round his shoulders,   415
roused Telemachus, the cowherd and the swineherd,
and told them to take up weapons honed for battle.
They snapped to commands, harnessed up in bronze,
opened the doors and strode out, Odysseus in the lead.
By now the daylight covered the land, but Pallas,   420
shrouding them all in darkness,
quickly led the four men out of town.

BOOK XXIV

[Peace]

Now Cyllenian[5] Hermes called away the suitors' ghosts,
holding firm in his hand the wand of fine pure gold
that enchants the eyes of men whenever Hermes wants
or wakes us up from sleep.
With a wave of this he stirred and led them on[6]   5
and the ghosts trailed after with high thin cries
as bats cry in the depths of a dark haunted cavern,
shrilling, flittering, wild when one drops from the chain—
slipped from the rock face, while the rest cling tight . . .
So with their high thin cries the ghosts flocked now   10
and Hermes the Healer led them on, and down the dank
moldering paths and past the Ocean's streams they went
and past the White Rock and the Sun's Western Gates and past
the Land of Dreams, and they soon reached the fields of asphodel
where the dead, the burnt-out wraiths of mortals, make their home.   15

  There they found the ghosts of Peleus' son Achilles,
Patroclus, fearless Antilochus—and Great Ajax too,
the first in stature, first in build and bearing
of all the Argives after Peleus' matchless son.
They had grouped around Achilles' ghost, and now   20
the shade of Atreus' son Agamemnon marched toward them—
fraught with grief and flanked by all his comrades,
troops of his men-at-arms who died beside him,
who met their fate in lord Aegisthus' halls.
Achilles' ghost was first to greet him: "Agamemnon,   25
you were the one, we thought, of all our fighting princes
Zeus who loves the lightning favored most, all your days,

5. Cyllene, a mountain in Arcadia (near the center of the Peloponnesus), was Hermes' birthplace.
6. One of Hermes' many functions is to guide the souls of the dead to the underworld.

because you commanded such a powerful host of men
on the fields of Troy where we Achaeans suffered.
But you were doomed to encounter fate so early,   30
you too, yet no one born escapes its deadly force.
If only you had died your death in the full flush
of the glory you had mastered—died on Trojan soil!
Then all united Achaea would have raised your tomb
and you'd have won your son great fame for years to come.   35
Not so. You were fated to die a wretched death."

        And the ghost of Atrides Agamemnon answered,
"Son of Peleus, great godlike Achilles! Happy man,
you died on the fields of Troy, a world away from home,
and the best of Trojan and Argive champions died around you,   40
fighting for your corpse. And you . . . there you lay
in the whirling dust, overpowered in all your power
and wiped from memory all your horseman's skills.
That whole day we fought, we'd never have stopped
if Zeus had not stopped us with sudden gales.   45
Then we bore you out of the fighting, onto the ships,
we laid you down on a litter, cleansed your handsome flesh
with warm water and soothing oils, and round your body
troops of Danaans wept hot tears and cut their locks.
Hearing the news, your mother, Thetis, rose from the sea,   50
immortal sea-nymphs in her wake, and a strange unearthly cry
came throbbing over the ocean. Terror gripped Achaea's armies,
they would have leapt in panic, boarded the long hollow ships
if one man, deep in his age-old wisdom, had not checked them:
Nestor—from the first his counsel always seemed the best,   55
and now, concerned for the ranks, he rose and shouted,
'Hold fast, Argives! Sons of Achaea, don't run now!
This is Achilles' mother rising from the sea
with all her immortal sea-nymphs—
she longs to join her son who died in battle!'   60
That stopped our panicked forces in their tracks
as the Old Man of the Sea's daughters gathered round you—
wailing, heartsick—dressed you in ambrosial, deathless robes
and the Muses, nine in all, voice-to-voice in choirs,
their vibrant music rising, raised your dirge.   65
Not one soldier would you have seen dry-eyed,
the Muses' song so pierced us to the heart.
For seventeen days unbroken, days and nights
we mourned you—immortal gods and mortal men.
At the eighteenth dawn we gave you to the flames   70
and slaughtered around your body droves of fat sheep
and shambling longhorn cattle, and you were burned
in the garments of the gods and laved with soothing oils
and honey running sweet, and a long cortege of Argive heroes
paraded in review, in battle armor round your blazing pyre,   75
men in chariots, men on foot—a resounding roar went up.
And once the god of fire had burned your corpse to ash,
at first light we gathered your white bones, Achilles,

cured them in strong neat wine and seasoned oils.
Your mother gave us a gold two-handled urn,   80
a gift from Dionysus, she said,
a masterwork of the famous Smith, the god of fire.
Your white bones rest in that, my brilliant Achilles,
mixed with the bones of dead Patroclus, Menoetius' son,
apart from those of Antilochus, whom you treasured   85
more than all other comrades once Patroclus died.
Over your bones we reared a grand, noble tomb—
devoted veterans all, Achaea's combat forces—
high on its jutting headland over the Hellespont's[7]
broad reach, a landmark glimpsed from far out at sea   90
by men of our own day and men of days to come.
                                            And then
your mother, begging the gods for priceless trophies,
set them out in the ring for all our champions.
You in your day have witnessed funeral games
for many heroes, games to honor the death of kings,   95
when young men cinch their belts, tense to win some prize—
but if you'd laid eyes on these it would have thrilled your heart,
magnificent trophies the goddess, glistening-footed Thetis,
held out in your honor. You were dear to the gods,
so even in death your name will never die . . .   100
Great glory is yours, Achilles,
for all time, in the eyes of all mankind!
                                            But I?
What joy for *me* when the coil of war had wound down?
For my return Zeus hatched a pitiful death
at the hands of Aegisthus—and my accursed wife."   105

    As they exchanged the stories of their fates,
Hermes the guide and giant-killer drew up close to both,
leading down the ghosts of the suitors King Odysseus killed.
Struck by the sight, the two went up to them right away
and the ghost of Atreus' son Agamemnon recognized   110
the noted prince Amphimedon, Melaneus' dear son
who received him once in Ithaca, at his home,
and Atrides' ghost called out to his old friend now,
"Amphimedon, what disaster brings you down to the dark world?
All of you, good picked men, and all in your prime—   115
no captain out to recruit the best in any city
could have chosen better. What laid you low?
Wrecked in the ships when lord Poseidon roused
some punishing blast of gales and heavy breakers?
Or did ranks of enemies mow you down on land   120
as you tried to raid and cut off herds and flocks
or fought to win their city, take their women?
Answer me, tell me. I was once your guest.
Don't you recall the day I came to visit
your house in Ithaca—King Menelaus came too—   125
to urge Odysseus to sail with us in the ships

7. The strait separating Asia Minor from Europe, visible from Troy.

on our campaign to Troy? And the long slow voyage,
crossing wastes of ocean, cost us one whole month.
That's how hard it was to bring him round,
Odysseus, raider of cities."
                         "Famous Atrides!"   130
Amphimedon's ghost called back. "Lord of men, Agamemnon,
I remember it all, your majesty, as you say,
and I will tell you, start to finish now,
the story of our death,
the brutal end contrived to take us off.   135
We were courting the wife of Odysseus, gone so long.
She neither spurned nor embraced a marriage she despised,
no, she simply planned our death, our black doom!
This was her latest masterpiece of guile:
she set up a great loom in the royal halls   140
and she began to weave, and the weaving finespun,
the yarns endless, and she would lead us on: 'Young men,
my suitors, now that King Odysseus is no more,
go slowly, keen as you are to marry me, until
I can finish off this web . . .   145
so my weaving won't all fray and come to nothing.
This is a shroud for old lord Laertes, for that day
when the deadly fate that lays us out at last will take him down.
I dread the shame my countrywomen would heap upon me,
yes, if a man of such wealth should lie in state   150
without a shroud for cover.'
                   Her very words,
and despite our pride and passion we believed her.
So by day she'd weave at her great and growing web—
by night, by the light of torches set beside her,
she would unravel all she'd done. Three whole years   155
she deceived us blind, seduced us with this scheme . . .
Then, when the wheeling seasons brought the fourth year on
and the months waned and the long days came round once more,
one of her women, in on the queen's secret, told the truth
and we caught her in the act—unweaving her gorgeous web.   160
So she finished it off. Against her will. We forced her.
But just as she bound off that great shroud and washed it,
spread it out—glistening like the sunlight or the moon—
just then some wicked spirit brought Odysseus back,
from god knows where, to the edge of his estate   165
where the swineherd kept his pigs. And back too,
to the same place, came Odysseus' own dear son,
scudding home in his black ship from sandy Pylos.
The pair of them schemed our doom, our deathtrap,
then lit out for town—   170
Telemachus first in fact, Odysseus followed,
later, led by the swineherd, and clad in tatters,
looking for all the world like an old and broken beggar
hunched on a stick, his body wrapped in shameful rags.
Disguised so none of us, not even the older ones,   175
could spot that tramp for the man he really was,

bursting in on us there, out of the blue. No,
we attacked him, blows and insults flying fast,
and he took it all for a time, in his own house,
all the taunts and blows—he had a heart of iron.   180
But once the will of thundering Zeus had roused his blood,
he and Telemachus bore the burnished weapons off
and stowed them deep in a storeroom, shot the bolts
and he—the soul of cunning—told his wife to set
the great bow and the gleaming iron axes out   185
before the suitors—all of us doomed now—
to test our skill and bring our slaughter on . . .
Not one of us had the strength to string that powerful weapon,
all of us fell far short of what it took. But then,
when the bow was coming round to Odysseus' hands,   190
we raised a hue and cry—he must not have it,
no matter how he begged! Only Telemachus
urged him to take it up, and once he got it
in his clutches, long-suffering great Odysseus
strung his bow with ease and shot through all the axes,   195
then, vaulting onto the threshold, stood there poised, and pouring
his flashing arrows out before him, glaring for the kill,
he cut Antinous down, then shot his painful arrows
into the rest of us, aiming straight and true,
and down we went, corpse on corpse in droves.   200
Clearly a god was driving him and all his henchmen,
routing us headlong in their fury down the hall,
wheeling into the slaughter, slashing left and right
and grisly screams broke from skulls cracked open—
the whole floor awash with blood.

                 So we died,   205
Agamemnon . . . our bodies lie untended even now,
strewn in Odysseus' palace. They know nothing yet,
the kin in our houses who might wash our wounds
of clotted gore and lay us out and mourn us.
These are the solemn honors owed the dead."

                             "Happy Odysseus!"   210
Agamemnon's ghost cried out. "Son of old Laertes—
mastermind—what a fine, faithful wife you won!
What good sense resided in your Penelope—
how well Icarius' daughter remembered you,
Odysseus, the man she married once!   215
The fame of her great virtue will never die.
The immortal gods will lift a song for all mankind,
a glorious song in praise of self-possessed Penelope.
A far cry from the daughter of Tyndareus, Clytemnestra—
what outrage she committed, killing the man *she* married once!—   220
yes, and the song men sing of her will ring with loathing.
She brands with a foul name the breed of womankind,
even the honest ones to come!"

                        So they traded stories,
the two ghosts standing there in the House of Death,
far in the hidden depths below the earth.   225

Odysseus and his men had stridden down from town
and quickly reached Laertes' large, well-tended farm
that the old king himself had wrested from the wilds,
years ago, laboring long and hard. His lodge was here
and around it stretched a row of sheds where fieldhands,   230
bondsmen who did his bidding, sat and ate and slept.
And an old Sicilian woman was in charge,
who faithfully looked after her aged master
out on his good estate remote from town.
Odysseus told his servants and his son,   235
"Into the timbered lodge now, go, quickly,
kill us the fattest porker, fix our meal.
And I will put my father to the test,
see if the old man knows me now, on sight,
or fails to, after twenty years apart."   240

    With that he passed his armor to his men
and in they went at once, his son as well. Odysseus
wandered off, approaching the thriving vineyard, searching,
picking his way down to the great orchard, searching,
but found neither Dolius nor his sons nor any hand.   245
They'd just gone off, old Dolius in the lead,
to gather stones for a dry retaining wall
to shore the vineyard up. But he did find
his father, alone, on that well-worked plot,
spading round a sapling—clad in filthy rags,   250
in a patched, unseemly shirt, and round his shins
he had some oxhide leggings strapped, patched too,
to keep from getting scraped, and gloves on his hands
to fight against the thorns, and on his head
he wore a goatskin skullcap   255
to cultivate his misery that much more . . .
Long-enduring Odysseus, catching sight of him now—
a man worn down with years, his heart racked with sorrow—
halted under a branching pear-tree, paused and wept.
Debating, head and heart, what should he do now?   260
Kiss and embrace his father, pour out the long tale—
how he had made the journey home to native land—
or probe him first and test him every way?
Torn, mulling it over, this seemed better:
test the old man first,   265
reproach him with words that cut him to the core.
Convinced, Odysseus went right up to his father.
Laertes was digging round the sapling, head bent low
as his famous offspring hovered over him and began,
"You want no skill, old man, at tending a garden.   270
All's well-kept here; not one thing in the plot,
no plant, no fig, no pear, no olive, no vine,
not a vegetable, lacks your tender, loving care.
But I must say—and don't be offended now—
your plants are doing better than yourself.   275
Enough to be stooped with age

but look how squalid you are, those shabby rags.
Surely it's not for sloth your master lets you go to seed.
There's nothing of slave about your build or bearing.
I have eyes: you look like a king to me. The sort   280
entitled to bathe, sup well, then sleep in a soft bed.
That's the right and pride of you old-timers.
Come now, tell me—in no uncertain terms—
whose slave are you? whose orchard are you tending?
And tell me this—I must be absolutely sure—   285
this place I've reached, is it truly Ithaca?
Just as that fellow told me, just now . . .
I fell in with him on the road here. Clumsy,
none too friendly, couldn't trouble himself
to hear me out or give me a decent answer   290
when I asked about a long-lost friend of mine,
whether he's still alive, somewhere in Ithaca,
or dead and gone already, lost in the House of Death.
Do you want to hear his story? Listen. Catch my drift.
I once played host to a man in my own country;   295
he'd come to my door, the most welcome guest
from foreign parts I ever entertained.
He claimed he came of good Ithacan stock,
said his father was Arcesius' son, Laertes.
So I took the new arrival under my own roof,   300
I gave him a hero's welcome, treated him in style—
stores in our palace made for princely entertainment.
And I gave my friend some gifts to fit his station,
handed him seven bars of well-wrought gold,
a mixing-bowl of solid silver, etched with flowers,   305
a dozen cloaks, unlined and light, a dozen rugs
and as many full-cut capes and shirts as well,
and to top it off, four women, perfect beauties
skilled in crafts—he could pick them out himself."

    "Stranger," his father answered, weeping softly,   310
"the land you've reached is the very one you're after,
true, but it's in the grip of reckless, lawless men.
And as for the gifts you showered on your guest,
you gave them all for nothing.
But if you'd found him alive, here in Ithaca,   315
he would have replied in kind, with gift for gift,
and entertained you warmly before he sent you off.
That's the old custom, when one has led the way.
But tell me, please—in no uncertain terms—
how many years ago did you host the man,   320
that unfortunate guest of yours, my son . . .
there was a son, or was he all a dream?
That most unlucky man, whom now, I fear,
far from his own soil and those he loves,
the fish have swallowed down on the high seas   325
or birds and beasts on land have made their meal.
Nor could the ones who bore him—mother, father—

wrap his corpse in a shroud and mourn him deeply.
Nor could his warm, generous wife, so self-possessed,
Penelope, ever keen for her husband on his deathbed, 330
the fit and proper way, or close his eyes at last.
These are the solemn honors owed the dead.
But tell me your own story—that I'd like to know:
Who are you? where are you from? your city? your parents?
Where does the ship lie moored that brought you here, 335
your hardy shipmates too? Or did you arrive
as a passenger aboard some stranger's craft
and men who put you ashore have pulled away?"
                                        "The whole tale,"
his crafty son replied, "I'll tell you start to finish.
I come from Roamer-Town, my home's a famous place, 340
my father's Unsparing, son of old King Pain,
and my name's Man of Strife . . .
I sailed from Sicily, aye, but some ill wind
blew me here, off course—much against my will—
and my ship lies moored off farmlands far from town. 345
As for Odysseus, well, five years have passed
since he left my house and put my land behind him,
luckless man! But the birds were good as he launched out,
all on the right, and I rejoiced as I sent him off
and he rejoiced in sailing. We had high hopes 350
we'd meet again as guests, as old friends,
and trade some shining gifts."
                        At those words
a black cloud of grief came shrouding over Laertes.
Both hands clawing the ground for dirt and grime,
he poured it over his grizzled head, sobbing, in spasms. 355
Odysseus' heart shuddered, a sudden twinge went shooting up
through his nostrils, watching his dear father struggle . . .
He sprang toward him, kissed him, hugged him, crying,
"Father—I am your son—myself, the man you're seeking,
home after twenty years, on native ground at last! 360
Hold back your tears, your grief.
Let me tell you the news, but we must hurry—
I've cut the suitors down in our own house,
I've paid them back their outrage, vicious crimes!"
                                        "Odysseus . . ."
Laertes, catching his breath, found words to answer. 365
"You—you're truly my son, Odysseus, home at last?
Give me a sign, some proof—I must be sure."
                                "This scar first,"
quick to the mark, his son said, "look at this—
the wound I took from the boar's white tusk
on Mount Parnassus. There you'd sent me, you 370
and mother, to see her fond old father, Autolycus,
and collect the gifts he vowed to give me, once,
when he came to see us here.
                Or these, these trees—
let me tell you the trees you gave me years ago,

here on this well-worked plot . . .   375
I begged you for everything I saw, a little boy
trailing you through the orchard, picking our way
among these trees, and you named them one by one.
You gave me thirteen pear, ten apple trees
and forty figs—and promised to give me, look,   380
fifty vinerows, bearing hard on each other's heels,
clusters of grapes year-round at every grade of ripeness,
mellowed as Zeus's seasons weigh them down."
                                        Living proof—
and Laertes' knees went slack, his heart surrendered,
recognizing the strong clear signs Odysseus offered.   385
He threw his arms around his own dear son, fainting
as hardy great Odysseus hugged him to his heart
until he regained his breath, came back to life
and cried out, "Father Zeus—
you gods of Olympus, you still rule on high   390
if those suitors have truly paid in blood
for all their reckless outrage! Oh, but now
my heart quakes with fear that all the Ithacans
will come down on us in a pack, at any time,
and rush the alarm through every island town!"   395

    "There's nothing to fear," his canny son replied,
"put it from your mind. Let's make for your lodge
beside the orchard here. I sent Telemachus on ahead,
the cowherd, swineherd too, to fix a hasty meal."

    So the two went home, confiding all the way   400
and arriving at the ample, timbered lodge,
they found Telemachus with the two herdsmen
carving sides of meat and mixing ruddy wine.
Before they ate, the Sicilian serving-woman
bathed her master, Laertes—his spirits high   405
in his own room—and rubbed him down with oil
and round his shoulders drew a fresh new cloak.
And Athena stood beside him, fleshing out the limbs
of the old commander, made him taller to all eyes,
his build more massive, stepping from his bath,   410
so his own son gazed at him, wonderstruck—
face-to-face he seemed a deathless god . . .
"Father"—Odysseus' words had wings—"surely
one of the everlasting gods has made you
taller, stronger, shining in my eyes!"   415

    Facing his son, the wise old man returned,
"If only—Father Zeus, Athena and lord Apollo—
I were the man I was, king of the Cephallenians
when I sacked the city of Nericus[8] sturdy fortress
out on its jutting cape! If I'd been young in arms   420

---

8. On the mainland. Its exact location is unknown.

last night in our house with harness on my back,
standing beside you, fighting off the suitors,
how many I would have cut the knees from under—
the heart inside you would have leapt for joy!"

So father and son confirmed each other's spirits.   425
And then, with the roasting done, the meal set out,
the others took their seats on chairs and stools,
were just putting their hands to bread and meat
when old Dolius trudged in with his sons,
worn out from the fieldwork.   430
The old Sicilian had gone and fetched them home,
the mother who reared the boys and tended Dolius well,
now that the years had ground the old man down . . .
When they saw Odysseus—knew him in their bones—
they stopped in their tracks, staring, struck dumb,   435
but the king waved them on with a warm and easy air:
"Sit down to your food, old friend. Snap out of your wonder.
We've been cooling our heels here long enough,
eager to get our hands on all this pork,
hoping you'd all troop in at any moment."   440

Spreading his arms, Dolius rushed up to him,
clutched Odysseus by the wrist and kissed his hand,
greeting his king now with a burst of winging words:
"Dear master, you're back—the answer to our prayers!
We'd lost all hope but the gods have brought you home!   445
Welcome—health! The skies rain blessings on you!
But tell me the truth now—this I'd like to know—
shrewd Penelope, has she heard you're home?
Or should we send a messenger?"
                                        "She knows by now,
old man," his wily master answered brusquely.   450
"Why busy yourself with that?"

So Dolius went back to his sanded stool.
His sons too, pressing around the famous king,
greeted Odysseus warmly, grasped him by the hand
then took their seats in order by their father.   455

But now, as they fell to supper in the lodge,
Rumor the herald sped like wildfire through the city,
crying out the news of the suitors' bloody death and doom,
and massing from every quarter as they listened, kinsmen milled
with wails and moans of grief before Odysseus' palace.   460
And then they carried out the bodies, every family
buried their own, and the dead from other towns
they loaded onto the rapid ships for crews
to ferry back again, each to his own home . . .
Then in a long, mourning file they moved to assembly   465
where, once they'd grouped, crowding the meeting grounds,
old lord Eupithes rose in their midst to speak out.

Unforgettable sorrow wrung his heart for his son,
Antinous, the first that great Odysseus killed.
In tears for the one he lost, he stood and cried, 470
"My friends, what a mortal blow this man has dealt
to all our island people! Those fighters, many and brave,
he led away in his curved ships—he lost the ships
and he lost the men and back he comes again
to kill the best of our Cephallenian princes. 475
Quick, after him! Before he flees to Pylos
or holy Elis, where Epeans rule in power—
up, attack! Or we'll hang our heads forever,
all disgraced, even by generations down the years,
if we don't punish the murderers of our brothers and our sons! 480
Why, life would lose its relish—for me, at least—
I'd rather die at once and go among the dead.
Attack!—before the assassins cross the sea
and leave us in their wake."
                              He closed in tears
and compassion ran through every Achaean there. 485
Suddenly Medon and the inspired bard approached them,
fresh from Odysseus' house, where they had just awakened.
They strode into the crowds; amazement took each man
but the herald Medon spoke in all his wisdom:
"Hear me, men of Ithaca. Not without the hand 490
of the deathless gods did Odysseus do these things!
Myself, I saw an immortal fighting at his side—
like Mentor to the life. I saw the same god,
now in front of Odysseus, spurring him on,
now stampeding the suitors through the hall, 495
crazed with fear, and down they went in droves!"

Terror gripped them all, their faces ashen white.
At last the old warrior Halitherses, Mastor's son—
who alone could see the days behind and days ahead—
rose up and spoke, distraught for each man there: 500
"Hear me, men of Ithaca. Hear what I have to say.
Thanks to your own craven hearts these things were done!
You never listened to me or the good commander Mentor,
you never put a stop to your sons' senseless folly.
What fine work they did, so blind, so reckless, 505
carving away the wealth, affronting the wife
of a great and famous man, telling themselves
that he'd return no more! So let things rest now.
Listen to me for once—I say don't attack!
Else some will draw the lightning on their necks."
                                    So he urged 510
and some held fast to their seats, but more than half
sprang up with warcries now. They had no taste
for the prophet's sane plan—winning Eupithes[9]
quickly won them over. They ran for armor

9. Literally, "Good at Persuading."

and once they'd harnessed up in burnished bronze   515
they grouped in ranks before the terraced city.
Eupithes led them on in their foolish, mad campaign,
certain he would avenge the slaughter of his son
but the father was not destined to return—
he'd meet his death in battle then and there.   520

    Athena at this point made appeals to Zeus:
"Father, son of Cronus, our high and mighty king,
now let me ask you a question . . .
tell me the secrets hidden in your mind.
Will you prolong the pain, the cruel fighting here   425
or hand down pacts of peace between both sides?"

    "My child," Zeus who marshals the thunderheads replied,
"why do you pry and probe me so intently? Come now,
wasn't the plan your own? You conceived it yourself:
Odysseus should return and pay the traitors back.   530
Do as your heart desires—
but let me tell you how it should be done.
Now that royal Odysseus has taken his revenge,
let both sides seal their pacts that he shall reign for life,
and let us purge their memories of the bloody slaughter   535
of their brothers and their sons. Let them be friends,
devoted as in the old days. Let peace and wealth
come cresting through the land."
                  So Zeus decreed
and launched Athena already poised for action—
down she swept from Olympus' craggy peaks.   540

    By then Odysseus' men had had their fill
of hearty fare, and the seasoned captain said,
"One of you go outside—see if they're closing in."
A son of Dolius snapped to his command,
ran to the door and saw them all too close   545
and shouted back to Odysseus,
"They're on top of us! To arms—and fast!"
Up they sprang and strapped themselves in armor,
the three men with Odysseus, Dolius' six sons
and Dolius and Laertes clapped on armor too,   550
gray as they were, but they would fight if forced.
Once they had all harnessed up in burnished bronze
they opened the doors and strode out, Odysseus in the lead.

    And now, taking the build and voice of Mentor,
Zeus's daughter Athena marched right in.   555
The good soldier Odysseus thrilled to see her,
turned to his son and said in haste, "Telemachus,
you'll learn soon enough—as you move up to fight
where champions strive to prove themselves the best—
not to disgrace your father's line a moment.   560
In battle prowess we've excelled for ages

all across the world."
                        Telemachus reassured him,
"Now you'll see, if you care to watch, father,
now I'm fired up. Disgrace, you say?
I won't disgrace your line!"   565

    Laertes called out in deep delight,
"What a day for me, dear gods! What joy—
my son and my grandson vying over courage!"
                                        "Laertes!"
Goddess Athena rushed beside him, eyes ablaze:
"Son of Arcesius, dearest of all my comrades,   570
say a prayer to the bright-eyed girl and Father Zeus,
then brandish your long spear and wing it fast!"

    Athena breathed enormous strength in the old man.
He lifted a prayer to mighty Zeus's daughter,
brandished his spear a moment, winged it fast   575
and hit Eupithes, pierced his bronze-sided helmet
that failed to block the bronze point tearing through—
down Eupithes crashed, his armor clanging against his chest.
Odysseus and his gallant son charged straight at the front lines,
slashing away with swords, with two-edged spears and now   580
they would have killed them all, cut them off from home
if Athena, daughter of storming Zeus, had not cried out
in a piercing voice that stopped all fighters cold,
"Hold back, you men of Ithaca, back from brutal war!
Break off—shed no more blood—make peace at once!"   585

    So Athena commanded. Terror blanched their faces,
they went limp with fear, weapons slipped from their hands
and strewed the ground at the goddess' ringing voice.
They spun in flight to the city, wild to save their lives,
but loosing a savage cry, the long-enduring great Odysseus,   590
gathering all his force, swooped like a soaring eagle—
just as the son of Cronus hurled a reeking bolt
that fell at her feet, the mighty Father's daughter,
and blazing-eyed Athena wheeled on Odysseus, crying,
"Royal son of Laertes, Odysseus, master of exploits,   595
hold back now! Call a halt to the great leveler, War—
don't court the rage of Zeus who rules the world!"

    So she commanded. He obeyed her, glad at heart.
And Athena handed down her pacts of peace
between both sides for all the years to come—   600
the daughter of Zeus whose shield is storm and thunder,
yes, but the goddess still kept Mentor's build and voice.

SAPPHO OF LESBOS
born ca. 630 B.C.E.

About Sappho's life we know very little: she was born about 630 B.C.E. on the fertile island of Lesbos off the coast of Asia Minor and spent most of her life there; she was married and had a daughter. Her lyric poems (poems sung to the accompaniment of the lyre) were so admired in the ancient world that a later poet called her the tenth Muse. In the third century B.C.E. scholars at the great library in Alexandria arranged her poems in nine books, of which the first contained more than a thousand lines. But what we have now is a pitiful remnant: one (or possibly two) complete short poems, and a collection of quotations from her work by ancient writers, supplemented by bits and pieces written on ancient scraps of papyrus found in excavations in Egypt. Yet these remnants fully justify the enthusiasm of the ancient critics; Sappho's poems (insofar as we can guess at their nature from the fragments) give us the most vivid evocation of the joys and sorrows of love in all Greek literature.

Her themes are those of a Greek woman's world—girlhood, marriage, and love, especially the love of young women for each other and the poignancy of their parting as they leave to assume the responsibilities of a wife. About the social context of these songs we can only guess; all that can be said is that they reflect a world in which women, at least women of the aristocracy, lived an intense communal life of their own, one of female occasions, functions, and festivities, in which they were fully engaged with each other; to most of them, presumably, this was a stage preliminary to their later career in that world as wife and mother.

The first two poems printed here were quoted in their entirety by ancient critics (though it is possible that there was another stanza at the end of the second); their text is not a problem. But the important recent additions to our knowledge of Sappho's poetry, the pieces of ancient books found in Egypt, are difficult to read and usually full of gaps. Our third selection, in fact, comes from the municipal rubbish heap of the Egyptian village Oxyrhyncus, and several other poems also survive only on papyrus. Most of the gaps in these texts are due to holes or tears in the papyrus and can often be filled in from our knowledge of Sappho's dialect and the strict meter in which she wrote. In "Some Men Say an Army of Horse," for instance, at the end of the third stanza and the beginning of the fourth, the mutilated papyrus tells us that someone or something led Helen astray, and there are traces of a word that seems to have described Helen. The name Cypris (the Cyprian One, the love goddess Aphrodite) and phrases like "against her will" or "as soon as she saw him [Paris]" to refer to Helen would fit the spaces and the meter. Uncertain as these supplements are, they could help determine our understanding of the poem. Rather than give possibly misleading reconstructions here and in similar cases, the translator, Anne Carson, has marked gaps in the text with square brackets, so that the reader can decide what Sappho might have meant.

PRONOUNCING GLOSSARY

The following list uses common English syllables and stress accents to provide rough equivalents of selected words whose pronunciation may be unfamiliar to the general reader.

Anaktoria: *an-a-k-toh'-ree-ah*
Aphrodite: *a-froh-dai'-teeh*
Eros: *ay'-rohs*

Geraistion: *gay-rai'-stee-on*
Pleiades: *plee'-a-deez / play'-a-deez*
Sappho: *saf'-foh*

[Deathless Aphrodite of the spangled mind][1]

Deathless Aphrodite of the spangled mind,[2]
child of Zeus, who twists lures, I beg you
do not break with hard pains,
    O lady, my heart

but come here if ever before   5
you caught my voice far off
and listening left your father's
    golden house and came,

yoking your car. And fine birds brought you,
quick sparrows[3] over the black earth   10
whipping their wings down the sky
    through midair—

they arrived. But you. O blessed one,
smiled in your deathless face
and asked what (now again) I have suffered and why   15
    (now again) I am calling out

and what I want to happen most of all
in my crazy heart. Whom should I persuade (now again)
to lead you back into her love? Who, O
    Sappho, is wronging you?   20

For if she flees, soon she will pursue.
If she refuses gifts, rather will she give them.
If she does not love, soon she will love
    even unwilling.

Come to me now: loose me from hard   25
care and all my heart longs
to accomplish, accomplish. You
    be my ally.

[Some men say an army of horse]

Some men say an army of horse and some men say an army on foot
and some men say an army of ships is the most beautiful thing
on the black earth. But I say it is
    what you love.

---

1. All selections translated by Anne Carson.   2. Or "of the spangled throne"; the manuscripts preserve both readings (in the Greek there is a single letter's difference between them). The word translated here as "spangled" usually refers to a surface shimmering with bright contrasting colors. The reader should choose whether to imagine a goddess seated in splendor on a highly wrought throne or a love goddess whose mind is shifting and fickle.   3. Aphrodite's sacred birds.

Easy to make this understood by all.   5
For she who overcame everyone
in beauty (Helen)
    left her fine husband

behind and went sailing to Troy.
Not for her children nor her dear parents   10
had she a thought, no—
    ]¹led her astray

      ]for
      ]lightly
]reminded me now of Anaktoria   15
who is gone.

I would rather see her lovely step
and the motion of light on her face
than chariots of Lydians² or ranks
    of footsoldiers in arms.³   20

[He seems to me equal to gods]

He seems to me equal to gods that man
whoever he is who opposite you
sits and listens close
    to your sweet speaking

and lovely laughing—oh it   5
puts the heart in my chest on wings
for when I look at you, even a moment, no speaking
    is left in me

no: tongue breaks and thin
fire is racing under skin   10
and in eyes no sight and drumming
    fills ears

and cold sweat holds me and shaking
grips me all, greener than grass
I am and dead—or almost   15
    I seem to me.

But all is to be dared, because even a person of poverty

---

1. Square brackets indicate where the papyrus on which the poem is preserved is torn and words or whole lines are missing.   2. A wealthy and powerful non-Greek people in Asia Minor, with whom Sappho, living on Lesbos just off the coast, shows herself familiar. A generation or so later the Lydians would be absorbed into the expanding Persian empire, but in Sappho's time they were near the height of their prosperity.   3. The poem may have ended here. The papyrus preserves scraps of three more stanzas that may have belonged either to this or to a different poem.

[Stars around the beautiful moon]

stars around the beautiful moon
hide back their luminous form
whenever all full she shines
     on the earth

         silvery   5

[Eros shook my mind]

                    Eros[1] shook my
mind like a mountain wind falling on oak trees

[You came and I was crazy for you]

you came and I was crazy for you
and you cooled my mind that burned with longing

[I simply want to be dead]

I simply want to be dead.[1]
Weeping she left me

with many tears and said this:
Oh how badly things have turned out for us.
Sappho, I swear, against my will I leave you.   5

And I answered her:
Rejoice, go and
remember me. For you know how we cherished you.

But if not, I want
to remind you   10
         ]and beautiful times we had.

For many crowns of violets
and roses
         ]at my side you put on

and many woven garlands   15
made of flowers
around your soft throat.

---

1. God of love.   1. What we have of this poem (on papyrus) begins here, with the last line of a speech
addressed to Sappho or spoken by her.

And with sweet oil
costly
you anointed yourself   20

and on a soft bed
delicate
you would let loose your longing

and neither any[   ]nor any
holy place nor   25
was there from which we were absent

no grove[   ]no dance
                 ]no sound
          [

[Often turning her thoughts here]

]Sardis[1]
often turning her thoughts here

]
you like a goddess
    and in your song most of all she rejoiced.   5

But now she is conspicuous among Lydian women
    as sometimes at sunset
        the rosyfingered moon

surpasses all the stars. And her light
    stretches over salt sea   10
        equally and flowerdeep fields.

And the beautiful dew is poured out
    and roses bloom and frail
        chervil and flowering sweetclover.

But she goes back and forth remembering   15
    gentle Atthis and in longing
        she bites her tender mind

But to go there
    ]much
        talks[20

---

1. The capital city of Lydia. This poem too has survived as a fragment on papyrus, and we do not have the
beginning or the end. Most or all of the fragment seems to be part of a speech addressed by one woman to
another about a third woman who is absent in Lydia.

                Not easy for us
                        to equal goddesses in lovely form
                ]

                ]
                        ]desire   25
                        and[   ]Aphrodite

                ]nectar poured from
                        gold
                        ]with hands Persuasion

                ]   30
                        ]
                                ]

                ]into the Geraistion[2]
                ]beloveds
                        ]of none   35

                ]into desire I shall come

[As the sweetapple reddens on a high branch]

        as the sweetapple reddens on a high branch[1]
                high on the highest branch and the applepickers forgot—
        no, not forgot: were unable to reach

[Like the hyacinth in the mountains]

        like the hyacinth in the mountains that shepherd men[1]
        with their feet trample down and on the ground the purple
                flower

[Moon has set]

        Moon has set[1]
        and Pleiades: middle
        night, the hour goes by,
        alone[2] I lie.

---

2. The reference is uncertain.   1. This fragment may be from an epithalamium, or wedding song. If so, it is probably the bride, who was virgin and inaccessible to men until marriage and who is compared to the sweetapple.   1. Possibly also from an epithalamium.   1. It is not certain that this fragment is by Sappho.   2. In the Greek, the form for this word shows that the speaker is female.

SOPHOCLES

ca. 496–406 B.C.E.

Sophocles lived to see Athens advance in power and prosperity far beyond the city that he was born into. The league of free Greek cities against Persia that Athens had led to victory in the Aegean had become an empire, in which Athens taxed and coerced the subject cities that had once been its free allies. Sophocles, born around 496 B.C.E. , played his part—a prominent one—in the city's affairs. In 443 B.C.E. he served as one of the treasurers of the imperial league and, with Pericles, as one of the ten generals elected for the war against the island of Samos, which tried to secede from the Athenian league a few years later. When the Athenian expedition to Sicily ended in disaster, Sophocles was appointed to a special committee set up in 411 B.C.E. to deal with the emergency. He died two years before Athens surrendered to Sparta.

His career as a brilliantly successful dramatist began in 468; in that year he won first prize at the Dionysia, competing against his older contemporary, Aeschylus. Over the next sixty-two years he produced more than 120 plays. He won first prize no fewer than twenty-four times, and when he was not first, he came in second, never third.

Aeschylus had been an actor as well as a playwright and director, but Sophocles, early in his career, gave up acting. It was he who added a third actor to the team; the early Aeschylean plays (*Persians, Seven against Thebes,* and *Suppliants*) can be played by two actors (who of course can change masks to extend the range of dramatis personae). In the *Oresteia,* Aeschylus has taken advantage of the Sophoclean third actor; this makes possible the role of Cassandra, the one three-line speech of Pylades in *The Libation Bearers,* and the trial scene in *The Eumenides.* But Sophocles used his third actor to create complex triangular scenes like the dialogue between Oedipus and the Corinthian messenger, which reveals to a listening Jocasta the ghastly truth that Oedipus will not discover until the next scene.

We have only seven of his plays, and not many of them can be accurately dated. *Ajax* (which deals with the suicide of the hero whose shade turns silently away from Odysseus in *Odyssey* book XI) and *Trachiniae* (the story of the death of Heracles) are both generally thought to be early productions. *Antigone* is fairly securely fixed in the late 440s, and *Oedipus the King* was probably staged during the early years of the Peloponnesian War (431–404 B.C.E.). For *Electra* we have no date, but it is probably later than *Oedipus the King. Philoctetes,* a tale of the Trojan War, was staged in 409 B.C.E. and *Oedipus at Colonus,* which presents Oedipus's strangely triumphant death on Athenian soil, was produced after Sophocles' death.

Most of these plays date from the last half of the fifth century B.C.E.; they were written in and for an Athens that, since the days of Aeschylus, had undergone an intellectual revolution. It was in a time of critical reevaluation of accepted standards and traditions that Sophocles produced his masterpiece, *Oedipus the King,* and the problems of the time are reflected in the play.

Oedipus the King, which deals with a man of high principles and probing intelligence who follows the prompting of that intelligence to the final consequence of true self-knowledge, was as full of significance for Sophocles' contemporaries as it is for us. Unlike a modern dramatist, Sophocles used for his tragedy a story well known to the audience and as old as their own history, a legend told by parent to child, handed down from generation to generation because of its implicit wealth of meaning, learned in childhood, and rooted deep in the consciousness of every member of the community. Such a story the Greeks called a *myth;* the use of it presented Sophocles with material that, apart from its great inherent dramatic potential, already possessed the significance and authority that modern dramatists must create for themselves. It had the authority of history, for the history of ages that leave no records is myth—that is to say, the significant event of the past, stripped of irrelevancies and imaginatively shaped by the oral tradition. It had a religious authority, for the Oedipus story is concerned with the relation between humanity and gods. Last, and this is especially true of the Oedipus myth, it had the power, because of its subject matter, to arouse the irrational hopes and fears that lie deep and secret in the human consciousness.

The use of the familiar myth enabled the dramatist to draw on all its wealth of unformulated meaning, but it did not prevent him from striking a contemporary note. Oedipus, in Sophocles' play, is at one and the same time the mysterious figure of the past who broke the most fundamental human taboos and a typical fifth-century Athenian. His character contains all the virtues for which the Athenians were famous and the vices for which they were notorious. The best commentary on Oedipus's character is the speech that Thucydides, the contemporary historian of the Peloponnesian War, attributed to a Corinthian spokesman at Sparta; it is a hostile but admiring assessment of the Athenian genius. "Athenians . . . [are] equally quick in the conception and in the execution of every new plan"—so Oedipus has already sent to Delphi when the priest advises him to do so and has already sent for Tiresias when the chorus suggests this course of action. "They are bold beyond their strength; they run risks that prudence would condemn"—as Oedipus risked his life to answer the riddle of the Sphinx and later, in spite of the oracle about his marriage, accepted the hand of the queen. "In the midst of misfortune they are full of hope"— so Oedipus, when he is told that he is not the son of Polybus and Merope, and Jocasta has already realized whose son he is, claims that he is the "child of Fortune." "When they do not carry out an intention that they have formed, they seem to have sustained a personal bereavement"—so Oedipus, shamed by Jocasta and the chorus into sparing Creon's life, yields sullenly and petulantly.

The Athenian devotion to the city, which received the main emphasis in Pericles' praise of Athens, is strong in Oedipus; his answer to the priest at the beginning of the play shows that he is a conscientious and patriotic ruler. His quick rage is the characteristic fault of Athenian democracy, which in 406 B.C.E., to give only one instance, condemned and executed the generals who had failed, in the stress of weather and battle, to pick up the drowned bodies of their own men killed in the naval engagement at Arginusae. Oedipus is like the fifth-century Athenian most of all in his confidence in the human intelligence, especially his own. This confidence takes him in the play through the whole cycle of the critical, rationalist movement of the century— from the piety and orthodoxy he displays in the opening scene, through his taunts at oracles when he hears that Polybus is dead, to the despairing courage with which he accepts the consequences when he sees the abyss opening at his feet. "I'm right at the edge, the horrible truth—I've got to say it!" says the herdsman from whom he is dragging the truth. "And I'm at the edge of hearing horrors, yes," Oedipus replies, "but I must hear!" And hear he does. He learns that the oracle he had first fought against and then laughed at has been fulfilled, that every step his intelligence prompted took him one step nearer to disaster, that his knowledge was ignorance and his clear vision blindness. Faced with the reality that his determined probing finally reveals, he puts out his eyes.

The relation of Oedipus's character to the development of the action is the basis of the most famous attempt to define the nature of the tragic process. Aristotle, writing his *Poetics* in the next century, developed the theory that pity and terror are aroused most effectively by the spectacle of a man who is "not pre-eminent in virtue and justice, and yet on the other hand does not fall into misfortune through vice or depravity, but falls because of some mistake; one among the number of the highly renowned and prosperous, such as Oedipus." Other references by Aristotle to this play make it clear that this influential doctrine of the fall of the tragic hero was based particularly on Sophocles' masterpiece, and it has been universally applied to the play. But the great influence (and validity) of the Aristotelian theory should not be allowed to obscure the fact that Sophocles' *Oedipus the King* is more highly organized and economical than Aristotle implies. The fact that the critics have differed about the nature of Oedipus's mistake or frailty (his errors are many, and his frailties include anger, impiety, and self-confidence) is a clue to the real situation. Oedipus falls not through "some vicious mole of nature" or some "particular fault" (to use Hamlet's terms) but because he is the man he is, because of all aspects of his character, good and bad alike; and the development of the action right through to the catastrophe shows us every aspect of his character at work in the process of self-revelation and self-destruction. His first decision in the play, to hear Creon's message from Delphi in public rather than, as Creon suggests, in private, is evidence of his kingly solicitude for his people and his trust in them, but it makes certain the full publication of the truth. His proclamation of a curse on the murderer of Laius, although prompted by his civic zeal, makes his final situation worse than it otherwise would have been. His anger at Tiresias forces a revelation that drives him on to accuse Creon; this in turn provokes Jocasta's revelations. And throughout the play his confidence in the efficacy of his own action, his hopefulness as the situation darkens, and his passion for discovering the truth guide the steps of the investigation that is to reveal the detective as the criminal. All aspects of his character, good and bad alike, are equally involved; it is no frailty or error that leads him to the terrible truth, but his total personality.

The character of Oedipus as revealed in the play does something more than explain the present action; it also explains his past. In Oedipus's speeches and actions on stage we can see the man who, given the circumstances in which Oedipus was involved, would inevitably do just what Oedipus has done. Each action on stage shows us the mood in which he committed some action in the past; his angry death sentence on Creon reveals the man who killed Laius because of an insult on the highway; his proclamation of total excommunication for the unknown murderer shows us the man who, without forethought, accepted the hand of Jocasta; his intelligent, persistent search for the truth shows us the brain and the courage that solved the riddle of the Sphinx. The revelation of his character in the play is at once a re-creation of his past and an interpretation of the oracle that predicted his future.

This organization of the material is what makes it possible for us to accept the story as tragedy at all, for it emphasizes Oedipus's independence of the oracle. When we first see Oedipus, he has already committed the actions for which he is to suffer—actions prophesied, before his birth, by Apollo. But the dramatist's emphasis on Oedipus's character suggests that although Apollo has predicted what Oedipus will do, he does not determine it; Oedipus determines his own conduct, by being the man he is. The relationship between Apollo's prophecy and Oedipus's actions is not that of cause and effect. It is the relationship of two independent entities that are equated.

This correspondence between his character and his fate removes the obstacle to our full acceptance of the play that an external fate governing his action would set up. Nevertheless, we feel that he suffers more than he deserves. He has served as an example of the inadequacy of the human intellect and a warning that there is a power in the universe that humanity cannot control or even fully understand, but Oedipus the man still has our sympathy. Sophocles felt this too, and in his last play, *Oedipus at Colonus,* he dealt with the reward that finally balanced Oedipus's suffering. In *Oedipus the King* itself there is a foreshadowing of this final development: the last scene shows us a man already beginning to recover from the shock of the catastrophe and reasserting a natural superiority.

"I am going—you know on what condition?" he says to Creon when ordered back into the house, and a few lines later Creon has to say bluntly to him: "Still the king, the master of all things? / No more: here your power ends." This renewed imperious-ness is the first expression of a feeling on his part that he is not entirely guilty, a beginning of the reconstitution of the magnificent man of the opening scenes.

PRONOUNCING GLOSSARY

The following list uses common English syllables and stress accents to provide rough equiva-lents of selected words whose pronunciation may be unfamiliar to the general reader.

Antigone: *an-ti'-go-nee*　　　　　　　Laius: *lay'-us / lai-us*

Cithaeron: *ki-thai'-ron*　　　　　　　Oedipus: *ee'-di-pus* or *e'-di-pus*

Ismene: *iz-mee'-nee*　　　　　　　　Tiresias: *tai-ree'-see-uhs / ti-ray'-see-uhs*

Oedipus the King[1]

CHARACTERS

OEDIPUS, *king of Thebes*
A PRIEST *of Zeus*
CREON, *brother of Jocasta*
A CHORUS *of Theban citizens*
　　and their LEADER
TIRESIAS, *a blind prophet*
JOCASTA, *the queen, wife of Oedipus*

A MESSENGER *from Corinth*
A SHEPHERD
A MESSENGER *from inside the palace*
ANTIGONE, ISMENE, *daughters of*
　　Oedipus and Jocasta
GUARDS *and attendants*
PRIESTS *of Thebes*

[TIME AND SCENE: *The royal house of Thebes. Double doors dominate the façade; a stone altar stands at the center of the stage.*

Many years have passed since OEDIPUS *solved the riddle of the Sphinx and ascended the throne of Thebes, and now a plague has struck the city. A pro-cession of priests enters; suppliants, broken and despondent, they carry branches wound in wool and lay them on the altar.*

The doors open. Guards assemble. OEDIPUS *comes forward, majestic but for a telltale limp, and slowly views the condition of his people.*]

OEDIPUS　Oh my children, the new blood of ancient Thebes,
　why are you here? Huddling at my altar,
　praying before me, your branches wound in wool.[2]
　Our city reeks with the smoke of burning incense,
　rings with cries for the Healer[3] and wailing for the dead.　　　　5
　I thought it wrong, my children, to hear the truth
　from others, messengers. Here I am myself—
　you all know me, the world knows my fame:
　I am Oedipus.
　　　　[*Helping a* PRIEST *to his feet.*]
　　　　　　　Speak up, old man. Your years,
　your dignity—you should speak for the others.　　　　　　　10

---

1. Translated by Robert Fagles.　　2. The insignia of suppliants, laid on the altar and left there until the suppliant's request was granted. At the end of the scene, when Oedipus promises action, he will tell them to take the branches away.　　3. Apollo.

Why here and kneeling, what preys upon you so?
Some sudden fear? some strong desire?
You can trust me. I am ready to help,
I'll do anything. I would be blind to misery
not to pity my people kneeling at my feet.   15

PRIEST   Oh Oedipus, king of the land, our greatest power!
You see us before you now, men of all ages
clinging to your altars. Here are boys,
still too weak to fly from the nest,
and here the old, bowed down with the years,   20
the holy ones—a priest of Zeus myself—and here
the picked, unmarried men, the young hope of Thebes.
And all the rest, your great family gathers now,
branches wreathed, massing in the squares,
kneeling before the two temples of queen Athena   25
or the river-shrine where the embers glow and die
and Apollo sees the future in the ashes.[4]
                                        Our city—
look around you, see with your own eyes—
our ship pitches wildly, cannot lift her head
from the depths, the red waves of death . . .   30
Thebes is dying. A blight on the fresh crops
and the rich pastures, cattle sicken and die,
and the women die in labor, children stillborn,
and the plague, the fiery god of fever hurls down
on the city, his lightning slashing through us—   35
raging plague in all its vengeance, devastating
the house of Cadmus![5] And black Death luxuriates
in the raw, wailing miseries of Thebes.
Now we pray to you. You cannot equal the gods,
your children know that, bending at your altar.   40
But we do rate you first of men,
both in the common crises of our lives
and face-to-face encounters with the gods.
You freed us from the Sphinx,[6] you came to Thebes
and cut us loose from the bloody tribute we had paid   45
that harsh, brutal singer. We taught you nothing,
no skill, no extra knowledge, still you triumphed.
A god was with you, so they say, and we believe it—
you lifted up our lives.
                          So now again,
Oedipus, king, we bend to you, your power—   50
we implore you, all of us on our knees:

---

4. At a temple of Apollo in Thebes the priests foretold the future according to patterns they saw in the ashes of the burned flesh of sacrificial victims.   5. Mythical founder of Thebes and its first king.
6. The winged female monster that terrorized the city of Thebes until her riddle was finally answered by Oedipus. The riddle was "What is it that walks on four feet and two feet and three feet and has only one voice; when it walks on most feet, it is weakest?" Oedipus's answer was "Man." (We have four feet as children crawling on all fours and three feet in old age when we walk with the aid of a stick.) Many young men of Thebes had tried to answer the riddle, failed, and been killed.

find us strength, rescue! Perhaps you've heard
the voice of a god or something from other men,
Oedipus . . . what do you know?
The man of experience—you see it every day— 55
his plans will work in a crisis, his first of all.

Act now—we beg you, best of men, raise up our city!
Act, defend yourself, your former glory!
Your country calls you savior now
for your zeal, your action years ago. 60
Never let us remember of your reign:
you helped us stand, only to fall once more.
Oh raise up our city, set us on our feet.
The omens were good that day you brought us joy—
be the same man today! 65
Rule our land, you know you have the power,
but rule a land of the living, not a wasteland.
Ship and towered city are nothing, stripped of men
alive within it, living all as one.

OEDIPUS   My children,
I pity you. I see—how could I fail to see 70
what longings bring you here? Well I know
you are sick to death, all of you,
but sick as you are, not one is sick as I.
Your pain strikes each of you alone, each
in the confines of himself, no other. But my spirit 75
grieves for the city, for myself and all of you.
I wasn't asleep, dreaming. You haven't wakened me—
I've wept through the nights, you must know that,
groping, laboring over many paths of thought.
After a painful search I found one cure: 80
I acted at once. I sent Creon,
my wife's own brother, to Delphi—
Apollo the Prophet's oracle[7]—to learn
what I might do or say to save our city.

Today's the day. When I count the days gone by 85
it torments me . . . what is he doing?
Strange, he's late, he's gone too long.
But once he returns, then, then I'll be a traitor
if I do not do all the god makes clear.

PRIEST   Timely words. The men over there 90
are signaling—Creon's just arriving.

OEDIPUS   [Sighting CREON, then turning to the altar.]
                              Lord Apollo,
let him come with a lucky word of rescue,
shining like his eyes!

---

7. On the southern slopes of Mount Parnassus in central Greece.

PRIEST   Welcome news, I think—he's crowned, look,
  and the laurel wreath is bright with berries.[8]   95
OEDIPUS   We'll soon see. He's close enough to hear—
      [*Enter* CREON *from the side; his face is shaded with a wreath.*]
  Creon, prince, my kinsman, what do you bring us?
  What message from the god?
CREON   Good news.
  I tell you even the hardest things to bear,
  if they should turn out well, all would be well.   100
OEDIPUS   Of course, but what were the god's *words?* There's no hope
  and nothing to fear in what you've said so far.
CREON   If you want my report in the presence of these . . .
      [*Pointing to the priests while drawing* OEDIPUS *toward the palace.*]
  I'm ready now, or we might go inside.
OEDIPUS   Speak out,
  speak to us all. I grieve for these, my people,   105
  far more than I fear for my own life.
CREON   Very well,
  I will tell you what I heard from the god.
  Apollo commands us—he was quite clear—
  "Drive the corruption from the land,
  don't harbor it any longer, past all cure,   110
  don't nurse it in your soil—root it out!"
OEDIPUS   How can we cleanse ourselves—what rites?
  What's the source of the trouble?
CREON   Banish the man, or pay back blood with blood.
  Murder sets the plague-storm on the city.
OEDIPUS   Whose murder?   115
  Whose fate does Apollo bring to light?
CREON   Our leader,
  my lord, was once a man named Laius,
  before you came and put us straight on course.
OEDIPUS   I know—
  or so I've heard. I never saw the man myself.
CREON   Well, he was killed, and Apollo commands us now—   120
  he could not be more clear,
  "Pay the killers back—whoever is responsible."
OEDIPUS   Where on earth are they? Where to find it now,
  the trail of the ancient guilt so hard to trace?
CREON   "Here in Thebes," he said.   125
  Whatever is sought for can be caught, you know,
  whatever is neglected slips away.
OEDIPUS   But where,
  in the palace, the fields or foreign soil,
  where did Laius meet his bloody death?
CREON   He went to consult an oracle, Apollo said,   130
  and he set out and never came home again.
OEDIPUS   No messenger, no fellow-traveler saw what happened?

---

8. Creon is wearing a crown of laurel as a sign that he brings good news.

Someone to cross-examine?
CREON   No,
   they were all killed but one. He escaped,
   terrified, he could tell us nothing clearly,   135
   nothing of what he saw—just one thing.
OEDIPUS   What's that?
   one thing could hold the key to it all,
   a small beginning give us grounds for hope.
CREON   He said thieves attacked them—a whole band,
   not single-handed, cut King Laius down.
OEDIPUS   A thief,   140
   so daring, so wild, he'd kill a king? Impossible,
   unless conspirators paid him off in Thebes.
CREON   We suspected as much. But with Laius dead
   no leader appeared to help us in our troubles.
OEDIPUS   Trouble? Your *king* was murdered—royal blood!   145
   What stopped you from tracking down the killer
   then and there?
CREON   The singing, riddling Sphinx.
   She . . . persuaded us to let the mystery go
   and concentrate on what lay at our feet.
OEDIPUS   No,
   I'll start again—I'll bring it all to light myself!   150
   Apollo is right, and so are you, Creon,
   to turn our attention back to the murdered man.
   Now you have *me* to fight for you, you'll see:
   I am the land's avenger by all rights,
   and Apollo's champion too.   155
   But not to assist some distant kinsman, no,
   for my own sake I'll rid us of this corruption.
   Whoever killed the king may decide to kill me too,
   with the same violent hand—by avenging Laius
   I defend myself.
      [*To the priests.*]
                        Quickly, my children.   160
   Up from the steps, take up your branches now.
      [*To the guards.*]
   One of you summon the city⁹ here before us,
   tell them I'll do everything. God help us,
   we will see our triumph—or our fall.
      [OEDIPUS *and* CREON *enter the palace, followed by the guards.*]
PRIEST   Rise, my sons. The kindness we came for   165
   Oedipus volunteers himself.
   Apollo has sent his word, his oracle—
   Come down, Apollo, save us, stop the plague.
      [*The priests rise, remove their branches and exit to the side. Enter a*
      CHORUS, *the citizens of Thebes, who have not heard the news that*
      CREON *brings. They march around the altar, chanting.*]

9. Represented by the chorus, which comes onto the circular dancing floor immediately after this scene.

CHORUS   Zeus!
  Great welcome voice of Zeus,[1] what do you bring?
  What word from the gold vaults of Delphi   170
  comes to brilliant Thebes? Racked with terror—
      terror shakes my heart
  and I cry your wild cries, Apollo, Healer of Delos[2]
  I worship you in dread . . . what now, what is your price?
  some new sacrifice? some ancient rite from the past   175
  come round again each spring?—
      what will you bring to birth?
  Tell me, child of golden Hope
      warm voice that never dies!

  You are the first I call, daughter of Zeus   180
  deathless Athena—I call your sister Artemis,[3]
  heart of the market place enthroned in glory,
          guardian of our earth—
  I call Apollo, Archer astride the thunderheads of heaven—
  O triple shield against death, shine before me now!   185
  If ever, once in the past, you stopped some ruin
  launched against our walls
      you hurled the flame of pain
  far, far from Thebes—you gods
      come now, come down once more!
                              No, no   190
  the miseries numberless, grief on grief, no end—
  too much to bear, we are all dying
  O my people . . .
      Thebes like a great army dying
  and there is no sword of thought to save us, no   195
  and the fruits of our famous earth, they will not ripen
  no and the women cannot scream their pangs to birth—
  screams for the Healer, children dead in the womb
      and life on life goes down
          you can watch them go   200
  like seabirds winging west, outracing the day's fire
  down the horizon, irresistibly
      streaking on to the shores of Evening
                                      Death
  so many deaths, numberless deaths on deaths, no end—
  Thebes is dying, look, her children   205
  stripped of pity . . .
      generations strewn on the ground
  unburied, unwept, the dead spreading death
  and the young wives and gray-haired mothers with them
  cling to the altars, trailing in from all over the city—   210

---

1. Apollo was his son and spoke for him.   2. A sacred island, Apollo's birthplace.   3. Apollo's sister,
a goddess associated with hunting and also a protector of women in childbirth.

Thebes, city of death, one long cortege
      and the suffering rises
          wails for mercy rise
  and the wild hymn for the Healer blazes out
clashing with our sobs our cries of mourning—   215
  O golden daughter of god,[4] send rescue
  radiant as the kindness in your eyes!

Drive him back!—the fever, the god of death
      that raging god of war
not armored in bronze, not shielded now, he burns me,[5]   220
battle cries in the onslaught burning on—
O rout him from our borders!
Sail him, blast him out to the Sea-queen's[6] chamber
      the black Atlantic gulfs
    or the northern harbor, death to all   225
where the Thracian[7] surf comes crashing.
Now what the night spares he comes by day and kills—
the god of death.

                    O lord of the stormcloud,
you who twirl the lightning, Zeus, Father,
thunder Death to nothing!   230

Apollo, lord of the light, I beg you—
      whip your longbow's golden cord
showering arrows on our enemies—shafts of power
champions strong before us rushing on!

Artemis, Huntress,   235
torches flaring over the eastern ridges—
      ride Death down in pain!

God of the headdress gleaming gold, I cry to you—
your name and ours are one, Dionysus—
    come with your face aflame with wine   240
        your raving women's[8] cries
    your army on the march! Come with the lightning
come with torches blazing, eyes ablaze with glory!
Burn that god of death that all gods hate!
      [OEDIPUS *enters from the palace to address the* CHORUS, *as if addressing
      the entire city of Thebes.*]
OEDIPUS   You pray to the gods? Let me grant your prayers.   245
  Come, listen to me—do what the plague demands:

---

4. Athena, daughter of Zeus.   5. The plague is identified with Ares, the war god, though he comes now
without armor and shield. Ares is not elsewhere connected with plague; this passage may be an allusion to
the early years of the Peloponnesian War, when Spartan troops threatened the city from outside and the
plague raged inside the walls.   6. Amphitrite, consort of the sea god Poseidon.   7. Ares was thought
to be at home among the savages of Thrace, to the northeast of Greece proper.   8. The Bacchantes,
nymphs or human female votaries of the god Dionysus (Bacchus) who celebrated him with wild dancing
rites.

you'll find relief and lift your head from the depths.
I will speak out now as a stranger to the story,
a stranger to the crime. If I'd been present then,
there would have been no mystery, no long hunt   250
without a clue in hand. So now, counted
a native Theban years after the murder,
to all of Thebes I make this proclamation:
if any one of you knows who murdered Laius,
the son of Labdacus, I order him to reveal   255
the whole truth to me. Nothing to fear,
even if he must denounce himself,
let him speak up
and so escape the brunt of the charge—
he will suffer no unbearable punishment,   260
nothing worse than exile, totally unharmed.
　　[OEDIPUS *pauses, waiting for a reply.*]
　　　　　　　　　　　　　　　　　Next,
if anyone knows the murderer is a stranger,
a man from alien soil, come, speak up.
I will give him a handsome reward, and lay up
gratitude in my heart for him besides.   265
　　[*Silence again, no reply.*]
But if you keep silent, if anyone panicking,
trying to shield himself or friend or kin,
rejects my offer, then hear what I will do.
I order you, every citizen of the state
where I hold throne and power: banish this man—   270
whoever he may be—never shelter him, never
speak a word to him, never make him partner
to your prayers, your victims burned to the gods.
Never let the holy water touch his hands
Drive him out, each of you, from every home.   275
He is the plague, the heart of our corruption,
as Apollo's oracle has just revealed to me.
So I honor my obligations:
I fight for the god and for the murdered man.

Now my curse on the murderer. Whoever he is,   280
a lone man unknown in his crime
or one among many, let that man drag out
his life in agony, step by painful step—
I curse myself as well . . . if by any chance
he proves to be an intimate of our house,   285
here at my hearth, with my full knowledge,
may the curse I just called down on him strike me!

These are your orders: perform them to the last.
I command you, for my sake, for Apollo's, for this country
blasted root and branch by the angry heavens.   290
Even if god had never urged you on to act,

how could you leave the crime uncleansed so long?
A man so noble—your king, brought down in blood—
you should have searched. But I am the king now,
I hold the throne that he held then, possess his bed   295
and a wife who shares our seed . . . why, our seed
might be the same, children born of the same mother
might have created blood-bonds between us
if his hope of offspring hadn't met disaster—
but fate swooped at his head and cut him short.   300
So I will fight for him as if he were my father,
stop at nothing, search the world
to lay my hands on the man who shed his blood,
the son of Labdacus descended of Polydorus,
Cadmus of old and Agenor, founder of the line: 305
their power and mine are one.
                                        Oh dear gods,
my curse on those who disobey these orders!
Let no crops grow out of the earth for them—
shrivel their women, kill their sons,
burn them to nothing in this plague   310
that hits us now, or something even worse.
But you, loyal men of Thebes who approve my actions,
may our champion, Justice, may all the gods
be with us, fight beside us to the end!

LEADER   In the grip of your curse, my king, I swear   315
I'm not the murderer, I cannot point him out.
As for the search, Apollo pressed it on us—
he should name the killer.

OEDIPUS   Quite right,
but to force the gods to act against their will—
no man has the power.

LEADER   Then if I might mention   320
the next best thing . . .

OEDIPUS   The third best too—
don't hold back, say it.

LEADER   I still believe . . .
Lord Tiresias[9] sees with the eyes of Lord Apollo.
Anyone searching for the truth, my king,
might learn it from the prophet, clear as day.   325

OEDIPUS   I've not been slow with that. On Creon's cue
I sent the escorts, twice, within the hour.
I'm surprised he isn't here.

LEADER   We need him—
without him we have nothing but old, useless rumors.

OEDIPUS   Which rumors? I'll search out every word.   330

LEADER   Laius was killed, they say, by certain travelers.

OEDIPUS   I know—but no one can find the murderer.

---

9. The blind prophet of Thebes (whose ghost Odysseus goes to Hades to consult in *Odyssey* book XI).

LEADER   If the man has a trace of fear in him
    he won't stay silent long,
    not with your curses ringing in his ears.   335

OEDIPUS   He didn't flinch at murder,
    he'll never flinch at words.

        [*Enter* TIRESIAS, *the blind prophet, led by a boy with escorts in atten-*
        dance. He remains at a distance.]

LEADER   Here is the one who will convict him, look,
    they bring him on at last, the seer, the man of god.
    The truth lives inside him, him alone.

OEDIPUS   O Tiresias,   340
    master of all the mysteries of our life,
    all you teach and all you dare not tell,
    signs in the heavens, signs that walk the earth!
    Blind as you are, you can feel all the more
    what sickness haunts our city. You, my lord,   345
    are the one shield, the one savior we can find.

    We asked Apollo—perhaps the messengers
    haven't told you—he sent his answer back:
    "Relief from the plague can only come one way.
    Uncover the murderers of Laius,   350
    put them to death or drive them into exile."
    So I beg you, grudge us nothing now, no voice,
    no message plucked from the birds, the embers
    or the other mantic ways within your grasp.
    Rescue yourself, your city, rescue me—   355
    rescue everything infected by the dead.
    We are in your hands. For a man to help others
    with all his gifts and native strength:
    that is the noblest work.

TIRESIAS   How terrible—to see the truth
    when the truth is only pain to him who sees!   360
    I knew it well, but I put it from my mind,
    else I never would have come.

OEDIPUS   What's this? Why so grim, so dire?

TIRESIAS   Just send me home. You bear your burdens,
    I'll bear mine. It's better that way,   365
    please believe me.

OEDIPUS   Strange response . . . unlawful,
    unfriendly too to the state that bred and reared you—
    you withhold the word of god.

TIRESIAS   I fail to see
    that your own words are so well-timed.
    I'd rather not have the same thing said of me . . .   370

OEDIPUS   For the love of god, don't turn away,
    not if you know something. We beg you,
    all of us on our knees.

TIRESIAS   None of you knows—
    and I will never reveal my dreadful secrets,
    not to say your own.   375

OEDIPUS   What? You know and you won't tell?
  You're bent on betraying us, destroying Thebes?
TIRESIAS   I'd rather not cause pain for you or me.
  So why this . . . useless interrogation?
  You'll get nothing from me.
OEDIPUS   Nothing! You,   380
  you scum of the earth, you'd enrage a heart of stone!
  You won't talk? Nothing moves you?
  Out with it, once and for all!
TIRESIAS   You criticize my temper . . . unaware
  of the one[1] *you* live with, you revile me.   385
OEDIPUS   Who could restrain his anger hearing you?
  What outrage—you spurn the city!
TIRESIAS   What will come will come.
  Even if I shroud it all in silence.
OEDIPUS   What will come? You're bound to *tell* me that.   390
TIRESIAS   I'll say no more. Do as you like, build your anger
  to whatever pitch you please, rage your worst—
OEDIPUS   Oh I'll let loose, I have such fury in me—
  now I see it all. You helped hatch the plot,
  you did the work, yes, short of killing him   395
  with your own hands—and given eyes I'd say
  you did the killing single-handed!
TIRESIAS   Is that so!
  I charge you, then, submit to that decree
  you just laid down: from this day onward
  speak to no one, not these citizens, not myself.   400
  You are the curse, the corruption of the land!
OEDIPUS   You, shameless—
  aren't you appalled to start up such a story?
  You think you can get away with this?
TIRESIAS   I have already.
  The truth with all its power lives inside me.   405
OEDIPUS   Who primed you for this? Not your prophet's trade.
TIRESIAS   You did, you forced me, twisted it out of me.
OEDIPUS   What? Say it again—I'll understand it better.
TIRESIAS   Didn't you understand, just now?
  Or are you tempting me to talk?   410
OEDIPUS   No, I can't say I grasped your meaning.
  Out with it, again!
TIRESIAS   I say you are the murderer you hunt.
OEDIPUS   That obscenity, twice—by god, you'll pay.
TIRESIAS   Shall I say more, so you can really rage?   415
OEDIPUS   Much as you want. Your words are nothing—futile.
TIRESIAS   You cannot imagine . . . I tell you,
  you and your loved ones live together in infamy,
  you cannot see how far you've gone in guilt.
OEDIPUS   You think you can keep this up and never suffer?   420

---

1. In the Greek the veiled reference to Jocasta is more forceful, because the word translated "the one" has a feminine ending (agreeing with the feminine noun *orgē*, "temper").

TIRESIAS   Indeed, if the truth has any power.
OEDIPUS   It does
   but not for you, old man. You've lost your power,
   stone-blind, stone-deaf—senses, eyes blind as stone!
TIRESIAS   I pity you, flinging at me the very insults
   each man here will fling at you so soon.
OEDIPUS   Blind,   425
   lost in the night, endless night that cursed you!
   You can't hurt me or anyone else who sees the light—
   you can never touch me.
TIRESIAS   True, it is not your fate
   to fall at my hands. Apollo is quite enough,
   and he will take some pains to work this out.   430
OEDIPUS   Creon! Is this conspiracy his or yours?
TIRESIAS   Creon is not your downfall, no, you are your own.
OEDIPUS   O power—
   wealth and empire, skill outstripping skill
   in the heady rivalries of life,
   what envy lurks inside you! Just for this,   435
   the crown the city gave me—I never sought it,
   they laid it in my hands—for this alone, Creon,
   the soul of trust, my loyal friend from the start
   steals against me . . . so hungry to overthrow me
   he sets this wizard on me, this scheming quack,   440
   this fortune-teller peddling lies, eyes peeled
   for his own profit—seer blind in his craft!

   Come here, you pious fraud. Tell me,
   when did you ever prove yourself a prophet?
   When the Sphinx, that chanting Fury kept her deathwatch here,   445
   why silent then, not a word to set our people free?
   There was a riddle, not for some passer-by to solve—
   it cried out for a prophet. Where were you?
   Did you rise to the crisis? Not a word,
   you and your birds, your gods—nothing.   450
   No, but I came by, Oedipus the ignorant,
   I stopped the Sphinx! With no help from the birds,
   the flight of my own intelligence hit the mark.

   And this is the man you'd try to overthrow?
   You think you'll stand by Creon when he's king?   455
   You and the great mastermind—
   you'll pay in tears, I promise you, for this,
   this witch-hunt. If you didn't look so senile
   the lash would teach you what your scheming means!
LEADER   I would suggest his words were spoken in anger,   460
   Oedipus . . . yours too, and it isn't what we need.
   The best solution to the oracle, the riddle
   posed by god—we should look for that.
TIRESIAS   You are the king no doubt, but in one respect,

at least, I am your equal: the right to reply. 465
I claim that privilege too.
I am not your slave. I serve Apollo.
I don't need Creon to speak for me in public.
                                        So,
you mock my blindness? Let me tell you this.
You with your precious eyes, 470
you're blind to the corruption of your life,
to the house you live in, those you live with—
who *are* your parents? Do you know? All unknowing
you are the scourge of your own flesh and blood,
the dead below the earth and the living here above, 475
and the double lash of your mother and your father's curse
will whip you from this land one day, their footfall
treading you down in terror, darkness shrouding
your eyes that now can see the light!
                          Soon, soon
you'll scream aloud—what haven won't reverberate? 480
What rock of Cithaeron² won't scream back in echo?
That day you learn the truth about your marriage,
the wedding-march that sang you into your halls,
the lusty voyage home to the fatal harbor!
And a crowd of other horrors you'd never dream 485
will level you with yourself and all your children.

There. Now smear us with insults—Creon, myself,
and every word I've said. No man will ever
be rooted from the earth as brutally as you.

OEDIPUS   Enough! Such filth from him? Insufferable— 490
what, still alive? Get out—
faster, back where you came from—vanish!

TIRESIAS   I would never have come if you hadn't called me here.

OEDIPUS   If I thought you would blurt out such absurdities,
you'd have died waiting before I'd had you summoned. 495

TIRESIAS   Absurd, am I! To you, not to your parents:
the ones who bore you found me sane enough.

OEDIPUS   Parents—who? Wait . . . who is my father?

TIRESIAS   This day will bring your birth and your destruction.

OEDIPUS   Riddles—all you can say are riddles, murk and darkness. 500

TIRESIAS   Ah, but aren't you the best man alive at solving riddles?

OEDIPUS   Mock me for that, go on, and you'll reveal my greatness.

TIRESIAS   Your great good fortune, true, it was your ruin.

OEDIPUS   Not if I saved the city—what do I care?

TIRESIAS   Well then, I'll be going.
           [*To his attendant.*]
                          Take me home, boy. 505

OEDIPUS   Yes, take him away. You're a nuisance here.
Out of the way, the irritation's gone.

2. The mountain range near Thebes, on which Oedipus was left to die when an infant.

[*Turning his back on* TIRESIAS, *moving toward the palace.*][3]

TIRESIAS   I will go,
once I have said what I came here to say.
I'll never shrink from the anger in your eyes—
you can't destroy me. Listen to me closely: 510
the man you've sought so long, proclaiming,
cursing up and down, the murderer of Laius—
he is here. A stranger,
you may think, who lives among you,
he soon will be revealed a native Theban   515
but he will take no joy in the revelation.
Blind who now has eyes, beggar who now is rich,
he will grope his way toward a foreign soil,
a stick tapping before him step by step.

            [OEDIPUS *enters the palace.*]

Revealed at last, brother and father both   520
to the children he embraces, to his mother
son and husband both—he sowed the loins
his father sowed, he spilled his father's blood!
Go in and reflect on that, solve that.
And if you find I've lied   525
from this day onward call the prophet blind.

            [TIRESIAS *and the boy exit to the side.*]

CHORUS   Who—
who is the man the voice of god denounces
resounding out of the rocky gorge of Delphi?
    The horror too dark to tell,
whose ruthless bloody hands have done the work?   530
His time has come to fly
    to outrace the stallions of the storm
        his feet a streak of speed—
Cased in armor, Apollo son of the Father
lunges on him, lightning-bolts afire!   535
And the grim unerring Furies[4]
        closing for the kill.
                        Look,
the word of god has just come blazing
flashing off Parnassus' snowy heights!
    That man who left no trace—   540
after him, hunt him down with all our strength!
Now under bristling timber
    up through rocks and caves he stalks
        like the wild mountain bull—
cut off from men, each step an agony, frenzied, racing blind   545
but he cannot outrace the dread voices of Delphi
ringing out of the heart of Earth,

---

3. There are no stage directions in the texts. It is suggested here that Oedipus moves offstage and does not hear the critical section of Tiresias's speech (lines 520 ff.), which he could hardly fail to connect with the prophecy made to him by Apollo many years ago.   4. Avenging spirits who pursued a murderer when no earthly avenger was at hand.

    the dark wings beating around him shrieking doom
        the doom that never dies, the terror—
The skilled prophet scans the birds and shatters me with terror!   550
I can't accept him, can't deny him, don't know what to say,
I'm lost, and the wings of dark foreboding beating—
I cannot see what's come, what's still to come . . .
and what could breed a blood feud between
        Laius' house and the son of Polybus?[5]   555
I know of nothing, not in the past and not now,
no charge to bring against our king, no cause
to attack his fame that rings throughout Thebes—
    not without proof—not for the ghost of Laius,
    not to avenge a murder gone without a trace.   560

    Zeus and Apollo know, they know, the great masters
        of all the dark and depth of human life.
But whether a mere man can know the truth,
whether a seer can fathom more than I—
there is no test, no certain proof   565
        though matching skill for skill
a man can outstrip a rival. No, not till I see
these charges proved will I side with his accusers.
We saw him then, when the she-hawk[6] swept against him,
saw with our own eyes his skill, his brilliant triumph—   570
    there was the test—he was the joy of Thebes!
    Never will I convict my king, never in my heart.
        [*Enter* CREON *from the side.*]
CREON   My fellow-citizens, I hear King Oedipus
levels terrible charges at me. I had to come.
I resent it deeply. If, in the present crisis   575
he thinks he suffers any abuse from me,
anything I've done or said that offers him
the slightest injury, why, I've no desire
to linger out this life, my reputation in ruins.
The damage I'd face from such an accusation   580
is nothing simple. No, there's nothing worse:
branded a traitor in the city, a traitor
to all of you and my good friends.
LEADER   True,
but a slur might have been forced out of him,
by anger perhaps, not any firm conviction.   585
CREON   The charge was made in public, wasn't it?
  I put the prophet up to spreading lies?
LEADER   Such things were said . . .
  I don't know with what intent, if any.
CREON   Was his glance steady, his mind right   590
  when the charge was brought against me?

---

5. King of Corinth and, so far as anyone except Tiresias knows, the father of Oedipus   6. The Sphinx.

LEADER   I really couldn't say. I never look
   to judge the ones in power.
       [*The doors open.* OEDIPUS *enters.*]
                               Wait,
here's Oedipus now.
OEDIPUS   You—here? You have the gall
   to show your face before the palace gates?   595
   You, plotting to kill me, kill the king—
   I see it all, the marauding thief himself
   scheming to steal my crown and power!
                              Tell me,
   in god's name, what did you take me for,
   coward or fool, when you spun out your plot?   600
   Your treachery—you think I'd never detect it
   creeping against me in the dark? Or sensing it,
   not defend myself? Aren't you the fool,
   you and your high adventure. Lacking numbers,
   powerful friends, out for the big game of empire— 605
   you need riches, armies to bring that quarry down!
CREON   Are you quite finished? It's your turn to listen
   for just as long as you've . . . instructed me.
   Hear me out, then judge me on the facts.
OEDIPUS   You've a wicked way with words, Creon,   610
   but I'll be slow to learn—from you.
   I find you a menace, a great burden to me.
CREON   Just one thing, hear me out in this.
OEDIPUS   Just one thing,
   don't tell *me* you're not the enemy, the traitor.
CREON   Look, if you think crude, mindless stubbornness 615
   such a gift, you've lost your sense of balance.
OEDIPUS   If you think you can abuse a kinsman,
   then escape the penalty, you're insane.
CREON   Fair enough, I grant you. But this injury
   you say I've done you, what is it?   620
OEDIPUS   Did you induce me, yes or no,
   to send for that sanctimonious prophet?
CREON   I did. And I'd do the same again.
OEDIPUS   All right then, tell me, how long is it now
   since Laius . . .
CREON   Laius—what did *he* do?
OEDIPUS   Vanished,   625
   swept from sight, murdered in his tracks.
CREON   The count of the years would run you far back . . .
OEDIPUS   And that far back, was the prophet at his trade?
CREON   Skilled as he is today, and just as honored.
OEDIPUS   Did he ever refer to me then, at that time?
CREON   No,   630
   never, at least, when I was in his presence.
OEDIPUS   But you did investigate the murder, didn't you?
CREON   We did our best, of course, discovered nothing.

OEDIPUS   But the great seer never accused me then—why not?
CREON   I don't know. And when I don't, I keep quiet.   635
OEDIPUS   You do know this, you'd tell it too—
   if you had a shred of decency.
CREON   What?
   If I know, I won't hold back.
OEDIPUS   Simply this:
   if the two of you had never put heads together,
   we would never have heard about *my* killing Laius.   640
CREON   If that's what he says . . . well, you know best.
   But now I have a right to learn from you
   as you just learned from me.
OEDIPUS   Learn your fill,
   you never will convict me of the murder.
CREON   Tell me, you're married to my sister, aren't you?   645
OEDIPUS   A genuine discovery—there's no denying that.
CREON   And you rule the land with her, with equal power?
OEDIPUS   She receives from me whatever she desires.
CREON   And I am the third, all of us are equals?
OEDIPUS   Yes, and it's there you show your stripes—   650
   you betray a kinsman.
CREON   Not at all.
   Not if you see things calmly, rationally,
   as I do. Look at it this way first:
   who in his right mind would rather rule
   and live in anxiety than sleep in peace?   655
   Particularly if he enjoys the same authority.
   Not I, I'm not the man to yearn for kingship,
   not with a king's power in my hands. Who would?
   No one with any sense of self-control.
   Now, as it is, you offer me all I need,   660
   not a fear in the world. But if I wore the crown . . .
   there'd be many painful duties to perform,
   hardly to my taste.
            How could kingship
   please me more than influence, power
   without a qualm? I'm not that deluded yet,   665
   to reach for anything but privilege outright,
   profit free and clear.
   Now all men sing my praises, all salute me,
   now all who request your favors curry mine.
   I am their best hope: success rests in me.   670
   Why give up that, I ask you, and borrow trouble?
   A man of sense, someone who sees things clearly
   would never resort to treason.
   No, I've no lust for conspiracy in me,
   nor could I ever suffer one who does.   675

   Do you want proof? Go to Delphi yourself,
   examine the oracle and see if I've reported

the message word-for-word. This too:
if you detect that I and the clairvoyant
have plotted anything in common, arrest me,   680
execute me. Not on the strength of one vote,
two in this case, mine as well as yours.
But don't convict me on sheer unverified surmise.
How wrong it is to take the good for bad,
purely at random, or take the bad for good.   685
But reject a friend, a kinsman? I would as soon
tear out the life within us, priceless life itself.
You'll learn this well, without fail, in time.
Time alone can bring the just man to light—
the criminal you can spot in one short day.

LEADER   Good advice,   690
my lord, for anyone who wants to avoid disaster.
Those who jump to conclusions may go wrong.

OEDIPUS   When my enemy moves against me quickly,
plots in secret, I move quickly too, I must,
I plot and pay him back. Relax my guard a moment,   695
waiting his next move—he wins his objective,
I lose mine.

CREON   What do you want?
You want me banished?

OEDIPUS   No, I want you dead.

CREON   Just to show how ugly a grudge can . . .

OEDIPUS   So,
still stubborn? you don't think I'm serious?   700

CREON   I think you're insane.

OEDIPUS   Quite sane—in my behalf.

CREON   Not just as much in mine?

OEDIPUS   You—my mortal enemy?

CREON   What if you're wholly wrong?

OEDIPUS   No matter—I must rule.

CREON   Not if you rule unjustly.

OEDIPUS   Hear him, Thebes, my city!

CREON   My city too, not yours alone!   705

LEADER   Please, my lords.
        [Enter JOCASTA from the palace.]
                          Look, Jocasta's coming,
and just in time too. With her help
you must put this fighting of yours to rest.

JOCASTA   Have you no sense? Poor misguided men,
such shouting—why this public outburst?   710
Aren't you ashamed, with the land so sick,
to stir up private quarrels?
        [To OEDIPUS.]
Into the palace now. And Creon, you go home.
Why make such a furor over nothing?

CREON   My sister, it's dreadful . . . Oedipus, your husband,   715
he's bent on a choice of punishments for me,

banishment from the fatherland or death.

OEDIPUS   Precisely. I caught him in the act, Jocasta,
plotting, about to stab me in the back.

CREON   Never—curse me, let me die and be damned   720
if I've done you any wrong you charge me with.

JOCASTA   Oh god, believe it, Oedipus,
honor the solemn oath he swears to heaven.
Do it for me, for the sake of all your people.
        [*The* CHORUS *begins to chant.*]

CHORUS   Believe it, be sensible   725
give way, my king, I beg you!

OEDIPUS   What do you want from me, concessions?

CHORUS   Respect him—he's been no fool in the past
and now he's strong with the oath he swears to god.

OEDIPUS   You know what you're asking?

CHORUS   I do.

OEDIPUS   Then out with it!   730

CHORUS   The man's your friend, your kin, he's under oath—
don't cast him out, disgraced
branded with guilt on the strength of hearsay only.

OEDIPUS   Know full well, if that is what you want
you want me dead or banished from the land.

CHORUS   Never—   735
no, by the blazing Sun, first god of the heavens!
    Stripped of the gods, stripped of loved ones,
let me die by inches if that ever crossed my mind.
But the heart inside me sickens, dies as the land dies
and now on top of the old griefs you pile this,   740
your fury—both of you!

OEDIPUS   Then let him go,
even if it does lead to my ruin, my death
or my disgrace, driven from Thebes for life.
It's you, not him I pity—your words move me.
He, wherever he goes, my hate goes with him.   745

CREON   Look at you, sullen in yielding, brutal in your rage—
you'll go too far. It's perfect justice:
natures like yours are hardest on themselves.

OEDIPUS   Then leave me alone—get out!

CREON   I'm going.
You're wrong, so wrong. These men know I'm right.   750
        [*Exit to the side. The* CHORUS *turns to* JOCASTA.]

CHORUS   Why do you hesitate, my lady
why not help him in?

JOCASTA   Tell me what's happened first.

CHORUS   Loose, ignorant talk started dark suspicions
and a sense of injustice cut deeply too.   755

JOCASTA   On both sides?

CHORUS   Oh yes.

JOCASTA   What did they say?

CHORUS   Enough, please, enough! The land's so racked already

or so it seems to me . . .
End the trouble here, just where they left it.

OEDIPUS   You see what comes of your good intentions now?   760
And all because you tried to blunt my anger.

CHORUS   My king,
I've said it once, I'll say it time and again—
    I'd be insane, you know it,
senseless, ever to turn my back on you.
You who set our beloved land—storm-tossed, shattered—   765
straight on course. Now again, good helmsman,
steer us through the storm!

        [*The* CHORUS *draws away, leaving* OEDIPUS *and* JOCASTA *side by side.*]

JOCASTA   For the love of god,
Oedipus, tell me too, what is it?
Why this rage? You're so unbending.

OEDIPUS   I will tell you. I respect you, Jocasta,   770
much more than these . . .

        [*Glancing at the* CHORUS.]
Creon's to blame, Creon schemes against me.

JOCASTA   Tell me clearly, how did the quarrel start?

OEDIPUS   He says I murdered Laius—I am guilty.

JOCASTA   How does he know? Some secret knowledge   775
or simple hearsay?

OEDIPUS   Oh, he sent his prophet in
to do his dirty work. You know Creon,
Creon keeps his own lips clean.

JOCASTA   A prophet?
Well then, free yourself of every charge!
Listen to me and learn some peace of mind: 780
no skill in the world,
nothing human can penetrate the future.
Here is proof, quick and to the point.

An oracle came to Laius one fine day
(I won't say from Apollo himself   785
but his underlings, his priests) and it said
that doom would strike him down at the hands of a son,
our son, to be born of our own flesh and blood. But Laius,
so the report goes at least, was killed by strangers,
thieves, at a place where three roads meet . . . my son—   790
he wasn't three days old and the boy's father
fastened his ankles, had a henchman fling him away
on a barren, trackless mountain.
                              There, you see?
Apollo brought neither thing to pass. My baby
no more murdered his father than Laius suffered—   795
his wildest fear—death at his own son's hands.
That's how the seers and all their revelations
mapped out the future. Brush them from your mind.
Whatever the god needs and seeks

he'll bring to light himself, with ease.

OEDIPUS   Strange,   800
hearing you just now . . . my mind wandered,
my thoughts racing back and forth.

JOCASTA   What do you mean? Why so anxious, startled?

OEDIPUS   I thought I heard you say that Laius
was cut down at a place where three roads meet.   805

JOCASTA   That was the story. It hasn't died out yet.

OEDIPUS   Where did this thing happen? Be precise.

JOCASTA   A place called Phocis, where two branching roads,
one from Daulia, one from Delphi,
come together—a crossroads.   810

OEDIPUS   When? How long ago?

JOCASTA   The heralds no sooner reported Laius dead
than you appeared and they hailed you king of Thebes.

OEDIPUS   My god, my god—what have you planned to do to me?

JOCASTA   What, Oedipus? What haunts you so?

OEDIPUS   Not yet.   815
Laius—how did he look? Describe him.
Had he reached his prime?

JOCASTA   He was swarthy,
and the gray had just begun to streak his temples,
and his build . . . wasn't far from yours.

OEDIPUS   Oh no no,
I think I've just called down a dreadful curse   820
upon myself—I simply didn't know!

JOCASTA   What are you saying? I shudder to look at you.

OEDIPUS   I have a terrible fear the blind seer can see.
I'll know in a moment. One thing more—

JOCASTA   Anything,
afraid as I am—ask, I'll answer, all I can.   825

OEDIPUS   Did he go with a light or heavy escort,
several men-at-arms, like a lord, a king?

JOCASTA   There were five in the party, a herald among them,
and a single wagon carrying Laius.

OEDIPUS   Ai—
now I can see it all, clear as day.   830
Who told you all this at the time, Jocasta?

JOCASTA   A servant who reached home, the lone survivor.

OEDIPUS   So, could he still be in the palace—even now?

JOCASTA   No indeed. Soon as he returned from the scene
and saw you on the throne with Laius dead and gone,   835
he knelt and clutched my hand, pleading with me
to send him into the hinterlands, to pasture,
far as possible, out of sight of Thebes.
I sent him away. Slave though he was,
he'd earned that favor—and much more.   840

OEDIPUS   Can we bring him back, quickly?

JOCASTA   Easily. Why do you want him so?

OEDIPUS   I'm afraid,

Jocasta, I have said too much already.
That man—I've got to see him.
JOCASTA   Then he'll come.
But even I have a right, I'd like to think,   845
to know what's torturing you, my lord.
OEDIPUS   And so you shall—I can hold nothing back from you,
now I've reached this pitch of dark foreboding.
Who means more to me than you? Tell me,
whom would I turn toward but you   850
as I go through all this?

My father was Polybus, king of Corinth.
My mother, a Dorian, Merope. And I was held
the prince of the realm among the people there,
till something struck me out of nowhere,   855
something strange . . . worth remarking perhaps,
hardly worth the anxiety I gave it.
Some man at a banquet who had drunk too much
shouted out—he was far gone, mind you—
that I am not my father's son. Fighting words!   860
I barely restrained myself that day
but early the next I went to mother and father,
questioned them closely, and they were enraged
at the accusation and the fool who let it fly.
So as for my parents I was satisfied,   865
but still this thing kept gnawing at me,
the slander spread—I had to make my move.
                                        And so,
unknown to mother and father I set out for Delphi,
and the god Apollo spurned me, sent me away
denied the facts I came for,   870
but first he flashed before my eyes a future
great with pain, terror, disaster—I can hear him cry,
"You are fated to couple with your mother, you will bring
a breed of children into the light no man can bear to see—
you will kill your father, the one who gave you life!"   875
I heard all that and ran. I abandoned Corinth,
from that day on I gauged its landfall only
by the stars, running, always running
toward some place where I would never see
the shame of all those oracles come true.   880
And as I fled I reached that very spot
where the great king, you say, met his death.

Now, Jocasta, I will tell you all.
Making my way toward this triple crossroad
I began to see a herald, then a brace of colts   885
drawing a wagon, and mounted on the bench . . . a man,
just as you've described him, coming face-to-face,
and the one in the lead and the old man himself

were about to thrust me off the road—brute force—
and the one shouldering me aside, the driver, 890
I strike him in anger!—and the old man, watching me
coming up along his wheels—he brings down
his prod, two prongs straight at my head!
I paid him back with interest!
Short work, by god—with one blow of the staff 895
in this right hand I knock him out of his high seat,
roll him out of the wagon, sprawling headlong—
I killed them all—every mother's son!

Oh, but if there is any blood-tie
between Laius and this stranger . . . 900
what man alive more miserable than I?
More hated by the gods? *I* am the man
no alien, no citizen welcomes to his house,
law forbids it—not a word to me in public,
driven out of every hearth and home. 905
And all these curses I—no one but I
brought down these piling curses on myself!
And you, his wife, I've touched your body with these,
the hands that killed your husband cover you with blood.
Wasn't I born for torment? Look me in the eyes! 910
I am abomination—heart and soul!
I must be exiled, and even in exile
never see my parents, never set foot
on native ground again. Else I am doomed
to couple with my mother and cut my father down . . . 915
Polybus who reared me, gave me life.
                              But why, why?
Wouldn't a man of judgment say—and wouldn't he be right—
some savage power has brought this down upon my head?

Oh no, not that, you pure and awesome gods,
never let me see that day! Let me slip 920
from the world of men, vanish without a trace
before I see myself stained with such corruption,
stained to the heart.
LEADER   My lord, you fill our hearts with fear.
But at least until you question the witness, 925
do take hope.
OEDIPUS   Exactly. He is my last hope—
I am waiting for the shepherd. He is crucial.
JOCASTA   And once he appears, what then? Why so urgent?
OEDIPUS   I will tell you. If it turns out that his story
matches yours, I've escaped the worst. 930
JOCASTA   What did I say? What struck you so?
OEDIPUS   You said *thieves*—
he told you a whole band of them murdered Laius.
So, if he still holds to the same number,

I cannot be the killer. One can't equal many.
But if he refers to one man, one alone,   935
clearly the scales come down on me:
I am guilty.
JOCASTA   Impossible. Trust me,
I told you precisely what he said,
and he can't retract it now;
the whole city heard it, not just I.   940
And even if he should vary his first report
by one man more or less, still, my lord,
he could never make the murder of Laius
truly fit the prophecy. Apollo was explicit:
my son was doomed to kill my husband . . . my son,   945
poor defenseless thing, he never had a chance
to kill his father. They destroyed him first.

So much for prophecy. It's neither here nor there.
From this day on, I wouldn't look right or left.
OEDIPUS   True, true. Still, that shepherd,   950
someone fetch him—now!
JOCASTA   I'll send at once. But do let's go inside.
I'd never displease you, least of all in this.
          [OEDIPUS and JOCASTA enter the palace.]
CHORUS   Destiny guide me always
Destiny find me filled with reverence   955
     pure in word and deed.
Great laws tower above us, reared on high
born for the brilliant vault of heaven—
     Olympian Sky their only father,
nothing mortal, no man gave them birth,   960
their memory deathless, never lost in sleep:
within them lives a mighty god, the god does not grow old.

Pride breeds the tyrant
violent pride, gorging, crammed to bursting
     with all that is overripe and rich with ruin—   965
clawing up to the heights, headlong pride
crashes down the abyss—sheer doom!
     No footing helps, all foothold lost and gone.
But the healthy strife that makes the city strong—
I pray that god will never end that wrestling: 970
god, my champion, I will never let you go.

But if any man comes striding, high and mighty
     in all he says and does,
no fear of justice, no reverence
for the temples of the gods—   975
     let a rough doom tear him down,
repay his pride, breakneck, ruinous pride!
If he cannot reap his profits fairly

cannot restrain himself from outrage—
mad, laying hands on the holy things untouchable!   980

    Can such a man, so desperate, still boast
    he can save his life from the flashing bolts of god?
      If all such violence goes with honor now
        why join the sacred dance?

Never again will I go reverent to Delphi,   985
    the inviolate heart of Earth
or Apollo's ancient oracle at Abae
or Olympia[7] of the fires—
    unless these prophecies all come true
for all mankind to point toward in wonder.   990
King of kings, if you deserve your titles
    Zeus, remember, never forget!
You and your deathless, everlasting reign.

    They are dying, the old oracles sent to Laius,
    now our masters strike them off the rolls.   995
      Nowhere Apollo's golden glory now—
        the gods, the gods go down.
    [*Enter* JOCASTA *from the palace, carrying a suppliant's branch wound in
    wool.*]
JOCASTA   Lords of the realm,[8] it occurred to me,
just now, to visit the temples of the gods,
so I have my branch in hand and incense too.   1000

Oedipus is beside himself. Racked with anguish,
no longer a man of sense, he won't admit
the latest prophecies are hollow as the old—
he's at the mercy of every passing voice
if the voice tells of terror.   1005
I urge him gently, nothing seems to help,
so I turn to you, Apollo, you are nearest.
    [*Placing her branch on the altar, while an old herdsman enters from the
    side, not the one just summoned by the King but an unexpected* MES-
    SENGER *from Corinth.*]
I come with prayers and offerings . . . I beg you,
cleanse us, set us free of defilement!
Look at us, passengers in the grip of fear,   1010
watching the pilot of the vessel go to pieces.
MESSENGER   [*Approaching* JOCASTA *and the* CHORUS.]
Strangers, please, I wonder if you could lead us
to the palace of the king . . . I think it's Oedipus.
Better, the man himself—you know where he is?
LEADER   This is his palace, stranger. He's inside.   1015

---

7. Site of a sanctuary of Zeus in the western Peloponnesus. Divination by means of burnt offerings was
practiced there. Abae is a city in central Greece.   8. The chorus.

But here is his queen, his wife and mother
of his children.
MESSENGER   Blessings on you, noble queen,
queen of Oedipus crowned with all your family—
blessings on you always!
JOCASTA   And the same to you, stranger, you deserve it . . .   1020
such a greeting. But what have you come for?
Have you brought us news?
MESSENGER   Wonderful news—
for the house, my lady, for your husband too.
JOCASTA   Really, what? Who sent you?
MESSENGER   Corinth.
I'll give you the message in a moment.   1025
You'll be glad of it—how could you help it?—
though it costs a little sorrow in the bargain.
JOCASTA   What can it be, with such a double edge?
MESSENGER   The people there, they want to make your Oedipus
king of Corinth, so they're saying now.   1030
JOCASTA   Why? Isn't old Polybus still in power?
MESSENGER   No more. Death has got him in the tomb.
JOCASTA   What are you saying? Polybus, dead?—dead?
MESSENGER   If not,
if I'm not telling the truth, strike me dead too.
JOCASTA   [*To a servant.*] Quickly, go to your master, tell him this!   1035
You prophecies of the gods, where are you now?
This is the man that Oedipus feared for years,
he fled him, not to kill him—and now he's dead,
quite by chance, a normal, natural death,
not murdered by his son.
OEDIPUS   [*Emerging from the palace.*]
                              Dearest,   1040
what now? Why call me from the palace?
JOCASTA   [*Bringing the* MESSENGER *closer.*]
Listen to *him,* see for yourself what all
those awful prophecies of god have come to.
OEDIPUS   And who is he? What can he have for me?
JOCASTA   He's from Corinth, he's come to tell you   1045
your father is no more—Polybus—he's dead!
OEDIPUS   [*Wheeling on the* MESSENGER.]
What? Let me have it from your lips.
MESSENGER   Well,
if that's what you want first, then here it is:
Abae is a city in central Greece.
make no mistake, Polybus is dead and gone.   1050
OEDIPUS   How—murder? sickness?—what? what killed him?
MESSENGER   A light tip of the scales can put old bones to rest.
OEDIPUS   Sickness then—poor man, it wore him down.
MESSENGER   That,
and the long count of years he'd measured out.
OEDIPUS   So!

Jocasta, why, why look to the Prophet's hearth,   1055
the fires of the future? Why scan the birds
that scream above our heads? They winged me on
to the murder of my father, did they? That was my doom?
Well look, he's dead and buried, hidden under the earth,
and here I am in Thebes, I never put hand to sword—   1060
unless some longing for me wasted him away,
then in a sense you'd say I caused his death.
But now, all those prophecies I feared—Polybus
packs them off to sleep with him in hell!
They're nothing, worthless.   1065

JOCASTA   There.
   Didn't I tell you from the start?

OEDIPUS   So you did. I was lost in fear.

JOCASTA   No more, sweep it from your mind forever.

OEDIPUS   But my mother's bed, surely I must fear—

JOCASTA   Fear?
   What should a man fear? It's all chance,   1070
   chance rules our lives. Not a man on earth
   can see a day ahead, groping through the dark.
   Better to live at random, best we can.
   And as for this marriage with your mother—
   have no fear. Many a man before you,   1075
   in his dreams, has shared his mother's bed.
   Take such things for shadows, nothing at all—
   Live, Oedipus,
   as if there's no tomorrow!

OEDIPUS   Brave words,
   and you'd persuade me if mother weren't alive.   1080
   But mother lives, so for all your reassurances
   I live in fear, I must.

JOCASTA   But your father's death,
   that, at least, is a great blessing, joy to the eyes!

OEDIPUS   Great, I know . . . but I fear *her*—she's still alive.

MESSENGER   Wait, who is this woman, makes you so afraid?   1085

OEDIPUS   Merope, old man. The wife of Polybus.

MESSENGER   The queen? What's there to fear in her?

OEDIPUS   A dreadful prophecy, stranger, sent by the gods.

MESSENGER   Tell me, could you? Unless it's forbidden
   other ears to hear.

OEDIPUS   Not at all.   1090
   Apollo told me once—it is my fate—
   I must make love with my own mother,
   shed my father's blood with my own hands.
   So for years I've given Corinth a wide berth,
   and it's been my good fortune too. But still,   1095
   to see one's parents and look into their eyes
   is the greatest joy I know.

MESSENGER   You're afraid of that?
   That kept you out of Corinth?

OEDIPUS   My *father*, old man—
so I wouldn't kill my father.
MESSENGER   So that's it.
Well then, seeing I came with such good will, my king,   1100
why don't I rid you of that old worry now?
OEDIPUS   What a rich reward you'd have for that!
MESSENGER   What do you think I came for, majesty?
So you'd come home and I'd be better off.
OEDIPUS   Never, I will never go near my parents.   1105
MESSENGER   My boy, it's clear, you don't know what you're doing.
OEDIPUS   What do you mean, old man? For god's sake, explain.
MESSENGER   If you ran from *them*, always dodging home . . .
OEDIPUS   Always, terrified Apollo's oracle might come true—
MESSENGER   And you'd be covered with guilt, from both your parents.   1110
OEDIPUS   That's right, old man, that fear is always with me.
MESSENGER   Don't you know? You've really nothing to fear.
OEDIPUS   But why? If I'm their son—Merope, Polybus?
MESSENGER   Polybus was nothing to you, that's why, not in blood.
OEDIPUS   What are you saying—Polybus was not my father?   1115
MESSENGER   No more than I am. He and I are equals.
OEDIPUS   My father—
how can my father equal nothing? You're nothing to me!
MESSENGER   Neither was he, no more your father than I am.
OEDIPUS   Then why did he call me his son?
MESSENGER   You were a gift,
years ago—know for a fact he took you   1120
from my hands.
OEDIPUS   No, from another's hands?
Then how could he love me so? He loved me, deeply . . .
MESSENGER   True, and his early years without a child
made him love you all the more.
OEDIPUS   And you, did you . . .
buy me? find me by accident?
MESSENGER   I stumbled on you,   1125
down the woody flanks of Mount Cithaeron.
OEDIPUS   So close,
what were you doing here, just passing through?
MESSENGER   Watching over my flocks, grazing them on the slopes.
OEDIPUS   A herdsman, were you? A vagabond, scraping for wages?
MESSENGER   Your savior too, my son, in your worst hour.
OEDIPUS   Oh—   1130
when you picked me up, was I in pain? What exactly?
MESSENGER   Your ankles . . . they tell the story. Look at them.
OEDIPUS   Why remind me of that, that old affliction?
MESSENGER   Your ankles were pinned together. I set you free.
OEDIPUS   That dreadful mark—I've had it from the cradle.   1135
MESSENGER   And you got your name[9] from that misfortune too,

---

9. In Greek the name *Oidipous* suggests "swollen foot."

the name's still with you.

OEDIPUS   Dear god, who did it?—
mother? father? Tell me.

MESSENGER   I don't know.
The one who gave you to me, he'd know more.

OEDIPUS   What? You took me from someone else?   1140
You didn't find me yourself?

MESSENGER   No sir,
another shepherd passed you on to me.

OEDIPUS   Who? Do you know? Describe him.

MESSENGER   He called himself a servant of . . .
if I remember rightly—Laius.   1145
        [JOCASTA *turns sharply.*]

OEDIPUS   The king of the land who ruled here long ago?

MESSENGER   That's the one. That herdsman was *his* man.

OEDIPUS   Is he still alive? Can I see him?

MESSENGER   They'd know best, the people of these parts.
        [OEDIPUS *and the* MESSENGER *turn to the* CHORUS.]

OEDIPUS   Does anyone know that herdsman,   1150
the one he mentioned? Anyone seen him
in the fields, in the city? Out with it!
The time has come to reveal this once for all.

LEADER   I think he's the very shepherd you wanted to see,
a moment ago. But the queen, Jocasta,   1155
she's the one to say.

OEDIPUS   Jocasta,
you remember the man we just sent for?
Is *that* the one he means?

JOCASTA   That man . . .
why ask? Old shepherd, talk, empty nonsense,
don't give it another thought, don't even think—   1160

OEDIPUS   What—give up now, with a clue like this?
Fail to solve the mystery of my birth?
Not for all the world!

JOCASTA   Stop—in the name of god,
if you love your own life, call off this search!
My suffering is enough.

OEDIPUS   Courage!   1165
Even if my mother turns out to be a slave,
and I a slave, three generations back,
you would not seem common.

JOCASTA   Oh no,
listen to me, I beg you, don't do this.

OEDIPUS   Listen to you? No more. I must know it all,   1170
must see the truth at last.

JOCASTA   No, please—
for your sake—I want the best for you!

OEDIPUS   Your best is more than I can bear.

JOCASTA   You're doomed—
may you never fathom who you are!

OEDIPUS   [*To a servant.*] Hurry, fetch me the herdsman, now!   1175
Leave her to glory in her royal birth.
JOCASTA   Aieeeeee—
                    man of agony—
that is the only name I have for you,
that, no other—ever, ever, ever!
   [*Flinging through the palace doors. A long, tense silence follows.*]
LEADER   Where's she gone, Oedipus?   1180
Rushing off, such wild grief . . .
I'm afraid that from this silence
something monstrous may come bursting forth.
OEDIPUS   Let it burst! Whatever will, whatever must!
I must know my birth, no matter how common   1185
it may be—I must see my origins face-to-face.
She perhaps, she with her woman's pride
may well be mortified by my birth,
but I, I count myself the son of Chance,
the great goddess, giver of all good things—   1190
I'll never see myself disgraced. She is my mother!
And the moons have marked me out, my blood-brothers,
one moon on the wane, the next moon great with power.
That is my blood, my nature—I will never betray it,
never fail to search and learn my birth!   1195
CHORUS   Yes—if I am a true prophet
        if I can grasp the truth,
    by the boundless skies of Olympus,
at the full moon of tomorrow, Mount Cithaeron
you will know how Oedipus glories in you—   1200
you, his birthplace, nurse, his mountain-mother!
And we will sing you, dancing out your praise—
you lift our monarch's heart!
        Apollo, Apollo, god of the wild cry
        may our dancing please you!
                        Oedipus—   1205
        son, dear child, who bore you?
Who of the nymphs who seem to live forever
mated with Pan,[1] the mountain-striding Father?
Who was your mother? who, some bride of Apollo
the god who loves the pastures spreading toward the sun?   1210
    Or was it Hermes, king of the lightning ridges?
Or Dionysus,[2] lord of frenzy, lord of the barren peaks—
did he seize you in his hands, dearest of all his lucky finds?—
    found by the nymphs, their warm eyes dancing, gift
to the lord who loves them dancing out his joy!   1215
        [OEDIPUS *strains to see a figure coming from the distance. Attended by*
        palace guards, an old SHEPHERD *enters slowly, reluctant to approach the*
        king.]

1. A woodland god, patron of shepherds and flocks. Though nymphs, unlike the gods, were not immortal, they lived much longer than mortals.   2. Dionysus, like Pan and Hermes, haunted the wild country, woods, and mountains. Hermes was born on Mount Kyllene in Arcadia.

OEDIPUS   I never met the man, my friends . . . still,
if I had to guess, I'd say that's the shepherd,
the very one we've looked for all along.
Brothers in old age, two of a kind,
he and our guest here. At any rate   1220
the ones who bring him in are my own men,
I recognize them.
              [*Turning to the* LEADER.]
                              But you know more than I,
you should, you've seen the man before.
LEADER   I know him, definitely. One of Laius' men,
a trusty shepherd, if there ever was one.   1225
OEDIPUS   You, I ask you first, stranger,
you from Corinth—is this the one you mean?
MESSENGER   You're looking at him. He's your man.
OEDIPUS   [*To the* SHEPHERD.] You, old man, come over here—
look at me. Answer all my questions.   1230
Did you ever serve King Laius?
SHEPHERD   So I did . . .
a slave, not bought on the block though,
born and reared in the palace.
OEDIPUS   Your duties, your kind of work?
SHEPHERD   Herding the flocks, the better part of my life.   1235
OEDIPUS   Where, mostly? Where did you do your grazing?
SHEPHERD   Well,
Cithaeron sometimes, or the foothills round about.
OEDIPUS   This man—you know him? ever see him there?
SHEPHERD   [*Confused, glancing from the* MESSENGER *to the King.*]
Doing what?—what man do you mean?
OEDIPUS   [*Pointing to the* MESSENGER.]
This one here—ever have dealings with him?   1240
SHEPHERD   Not so I could say, but give me a chance,
my memory's bad . . .
MESSENGER   No wonder he doesn't know me, master.
But let me refresh his memory for him.
I'm sure he recalls old times we had   1245
on the slopes of Mount Cithaeron;
he and I, grazing our flocks, he with two
and I with one—we both struck up together,
three whole seasons, six months at a stretch
from spring to the rising of Arcturus[3] in the fall,   1250
then with winter coming on I'd drive my herds
to my own pens, and back he'd go with his
to Laius' folds.
              [*To the* SHEPHERD.]
                              Now that's how it was,
wasn't it—yes or no?

3. The principal star in the constellation Boötes; its appearance in the sky ("rising") just before dawn in
September signals the end of summer.

SHEPHERD   Yes, I suppose . . .
   it's all so long ago.
MESSENGER   Come, tell me,   1255
   you gave me a child back then, a boy, remember?
   A little fellow to rear, my very own.
SHEPHERD   What? Why rake up that again?
MESSENGER   Look, here he is, my fine old friend—
   the same man who was just a baby then.   1260
SHEPHERD   Damn you, shut your mouth—quiet!
OEDIPUS   Don't lash out at him, old man—
   you need lashing more than he does.
SHEPHERD   Why,
   master, majesty—what have I done wrong?
OEDIPUS   You won't answer his question about the boy.   1265
SHEPHERD   He's talking nonsense, wasting his breath.
OEDIPUS   So, you won't talk willingly—
   then you'll talk with pain.
      [*The guards seize the* SHEPHERD.]
SHEPHERD   No, dear god, don't torture an old man!
OEDIPUS   Twist his arms back, quickly!
SHEPHERD   God help us, why?—   1270
   what more do you need to know?
OEDIPUS   Did you give him that child? He's asking.
SHEPHERD   I did . . . I wish to god I'd died that day.
OEDIPUS   You've got your wish if you don't tell the truth.
SHEPHERD   The more I tell, the worse the death I'll die.   1275
OEDIPUS   Our friend here wants to stretch things out, does he?
      [*Motioning to his men for torture.*]
SHEPHERD   No, no, I gave it to him—I just said so.
OEDIPUS   Where did you get it? Your house? Someone else's?
SHEPHERD   It wasn't mine, no, I got it from . . . someone.
OEDIPUS   Which one of them?
      [*Looking at the citizens.*]
OEDIPUS   Whose house?
SHEPHERD   No—   1280
   god's sake, master, no more questions!
OEDIPUS   You're a dead man if I have to ask again.
SHEPHERD   Then—the child came from the house . . . of Laius.
OEDIPUS   A slave? or born of his own blood?
SHEPHERD   Oh no,
   I'm right at the edge, the horrible truth—I've got to say it!   1285
OEDIPUS   And I'm at the edge of hearing horrors, yes, but I must
     hear!
SHEPHERD   All right! His son, they said it was—his son!
   But the one inside, your wife,
   she'd tell it best.
OEDIPUS   My wife—   1290
   she gave it to you?
SHEPHERD   Yes, yes, my king.
OEDIPUS   Why, what for?

SHEPHERD   To kill it.

OEDIPUS   Her own child,   1295
how could she?

SHEPHERD   She was afraid—
frightening prophecies.

OEDIPUS   What?

SHEPHERD   They said—   1300
he'd kill his parents.

OEDIPUS   But you gave him to this old man—why?

SHEPHERD   I pitied the little baby, master,
hoped he'd take him off to his own country,
far away, but he saved him for this, this fate.   1305
If you are the man he says you are, believe me,
you were born for pain.

OEDIPUS   O god—
all come true, all burst to light!
O light—now let me look my last on you!
I stand revealed at last—   1310
cursed in my birth, cursed in marriage,
cursed in the lives I cut down with these hands!

> [Rushing through the doors with a great cry. The Corinthian MESSENGER,
> the SHEPHERD and attendants exit slowly to the side.]

CHORUS   O the generations of men
the dying generations—adding the total
of all your lives I find they come to nothing . . .   1315
        does there exist, is there a man on earth
who seizes more joy than just a dream, a vision?
And the vision no sooner dawns than dies
blazing into oblivion.
You are my great example, you, your life   1320
your destiny, Oedipus, man of misery—
I count no man blest.

You outranged all men!
Bending your bow to the breaking-point
you captured priceless glory, O dear god,
and the Sphinx came crashing down,   1325
        the virgin, claws hooked
like a bird of omen singing, shrieking death—
like a fortress reared in the face of death
you rose and saved our land.

From that day on we called you king   1330
we crowned you with honors, Oedipus, towering over all—
mighty king of the seven gates of Thebes.

But now to hear your story—is there a man more agonized?
More wed to pain and frenzy? Not a man on earth,
the joy of your life ground down to nothing   1335
O Oedipus, name for the ages—

one and the same wide harbor served you
    son and father both
son and father came to rest in the same bridal chamber.
How, how could the furrows your father plowed   1340
bear you, your agony, harrowing on
in silence O so long?

                  But now for all your power
Time, all-seeing Time has dragged you to the light,
judged your marriage monstrous from the start—
the son and the father tangling, both one—   1345
O child of Laius, would to god
    I'd never seen you, never never!
      Now I weep like a man who wails the dead
and the dirge comes pouring forth with all my heart!
I tell you the truth, you gave me life   1350
my breath leapt up in you
and now you bring down night upon my eyes.

[*Enter a* MESSENGER *from the palace.*]

MESSENGER: Men of Thebes, always first in honor,
    what horrors you will hear, what you will see,
    what a heavy weight of sorrow you will shoulder . . .   1355
    if you are true to your birth, if you still have
    some feeling for the royal house of Thebes.
    I tell you neither the waters of the Danube
    nor the Nile[4] can wash this palace clean.
    Such things it hides, it soon will bring to light—   1360
    terrible things, and none done blindly now,
    all done with a will. The pains
    we inflict upon ourselves hurt most of all.

LEADER   God knows we have pains enough already.
    What can you add to them?   1365

MESSENGER   The queen is dead.

LEADER   Poor lady—how?

MESSENGER   By her own hand. But you are spared the worst,
    you never had to watch . . . I saw it all,
    and with all the memory that's in me
    you will learn what that poor woman suffered.   1370

Once she'd broken in through the gates,
dashing past us, frantic, whipped to fury,
ripping her hair out with both hands—
straight to her rooms she rushed, flinging herself
across the bridal-bed, doors slamming behind her—   1375
once inside, she wailed for Laius, dead so long,
remembering how she bore his child long ago,
the life that rose up to destroy him, leaving

---

4. The Greek reads "Phasis," a river in Asia Minor. The translator has substituted a big river more familiar to modern readers.

its mother to mother living creatures
with the very son she'd borne.   1380
Oh how she wept, mourning the marriage-bed
where she let loose that double brood—monsters—
husband by her husband, children by her child.

                                And then—
but how she died is more than I can say. Suddenly
Oedipus burst in, screaming, he stunned us so   1385
we couldn't watch her agony to the end,
our eyes were fixed on him. Circling
like a maddened beast, stalking, here, there,
crying out to us—
                    Give him a sword![5] His wife,
no wife, his mother, where can he find the mother earth   1390
that cropped two crops at once, himself and all his children?
He was raging—one of the dark powers pointing the way,
none of us mortals crowding around him, no,
with a great shattering cry—someone, something leading him on—
he hurled at the twin doors and bending the bolts back   1395
out of their sockets, crashed through the chamber.
And there we saw the woman hanging by the neck,
cradled high in a woven noose, spinning,
swinging back and forth. And when he saw her,
giving a low, wrenching sob that broke our hearts,   1400
slipping the halter from her throat, he eased her down,
in a slow embrace he laid her down, poor thing . . .
then, what came next, what horror we beheld!

He rips off her brooches, the long gold pins
holding her robes—and lifting them high,   1405
looking straight up into the points,
he digs them down the sockets of his eyes, crying, "You,
you'll see no more the pain I suffered, all the pain I caused!
Too long you looked on the ones you never should have seen,
blind to the ones you longed to see, to know! Blind   1410
from this hour on! Blind in the darkness—blind!"
His voice like a dirge, rising, over and over
raising the pins, raking them down his eyes.
And at each stroke blood spurts from the roots,
splashing his beard, a swirl of it, nerves and clots—   1415
black hail of blood pulsing, gushing down.

These are the griefs that burst upon them both,
coupling man and woman. The joy they had so lately,
the fortune of their old ancestral house
was deep joy indeed. Now, in this one day,   1420
wailing, madness and doom, death, disgrace

---

5. Presumably so that he could kill himself.

all the griefs in the world that you can name,
all are theirs forever.
LEADER   Oh poor man, the misery—
has he any rest from pain now?
        [*A voice within, in torment.*]
MESSENGER   He's shouting,
"Loose the bolts, someone, show me to all of Thebes!   1425
My father's murderer, my mother's—"
No, I can't repeat it, it's unholy.
Now he'll tear himself from his native earth,
not linger, curse the house with his own curse.
But he needs strength, and a guide to lead him on.   1430
This is sickness more than he can bear.
        [*The palace doors open.*]
                                               Look,
he'll show you himself. The great doors are opening—
you are about to see a sight, a horror
even his mortal enemy would pity.
        [*Enter* OEDIPUS, *blinded, led by a boy. He stands at the palace steps, as
        if surveying his people once again.*]
CHORUS   O the terror—
the suffering, for all the world to see,   1435
the worst terror that ever met my eyes.
What madness swept over you? What god,
what dark power leapt beyond all bounds,
beyond belief, to crush your wretched life?—
godforsaken, cursed by the gods!   1440
I pity you but I can't bear to look.
I've much to ask, so much to learn,
so much fascinates my eyes,
but you . . . I shudder at the sight.
OEDIPUS   Oh, Ohh—
the agony! I am agony—   1445
where am I going? where on earth?
        where does all this agony hurl me?
where's my voice?—
        winging, swept away on a dark tide—
My destiny, my dark power, what a leap you made!   1450
CHORUS   To the depths of terror, too dark to hear, to see.
OEDIPUS   Dark, horror of darkness
        my darkness, drowning, swirling around me
        crashing wave on wave—unspeakable, irresistible
                headwind, fatal harbor! Oh again,   1455
        the misery, all at once, over and over
        the stabbing daggers, stab of memory
raking me insane.
CHORUS   No wonder you suffer
        twice over, the pain of your wounds,
        the lasting grief of pain.
OEDIPUS   Dear friend, still here?   1460

Standing by me, still with a care for me,
the blind man? Such compassion,
   loyal to the last. Oh it's you,
I know you're here, dark as it is
   I'd know you anywhere, your voice—   1465
it's yours, clearly yours.

CHORUS   Dreadful, what you've done . . .
   how could you bear it, gouging out your eyes?
   What superhuman power drove you on?

OEDIPUS   Apollo, friends, Apollo—
   he ordained my agonies—these, my pains on pains!   1470
   But the hand that struck my eyes was mine,
   mine alone—no one else—
      I did it all myself!
   What good were eyes to me?
   Nothing I could see could bring me joy.   1475

CHORUS   No, no, exactly as you say.

OEDIPUS   What can I ever see?
   What love, what call of the heart
   can touch my ears with joy? Nothing, friends.
   Take me away, far, far from Thebes,
   quickly, cast me away, my friends—   1480
this great murderous ruin, this man cursed to heaven,
the man the deathless gods hate most of all!

CHORUS   Pitiful, you suffer so, you understand so much . . .
   I wish you'd never known.

OEDIPUS   Die, die—
   whoever he was that day in the wilds   1485
who cut my ankles free of the ruthless pins,
   he pulled me clear of death, he saved my life
   for this, this kindness—
      Curse him, kill him!
   If I'd died then, I'd never have dragged myself,   1490
   my loved ones through such hell.

CHORUS   Oh if only . . . would to god.

OEDIPUS   I'd never have come to this,
   my father's murderer—never been branded
   mother's husband, all men see me now! Now,
   loathed by the gods, son of the mother I defiled   1495
   coupling in my father's bed, spawning lives in the loins
that spawned my wretched life. What grief can crown this grief?
   It's mine alone, my destiny—I am Oedipus!

CHORUS   How can I say you've chosen for the best?
   Better to die than be alive and blind.   1500

OEDIPUS   What I did was best—don't lecture me,
   no more advice. I, with *my* eyes,
   how could I look my father in the eyes
   when I go down to death? Or mother, so abused . . .
   I have done such things to the two of them,   1505
   crimes too huge for hanging.

Worse yet,
the sight of my children, born as they were born,
how could I long to look into their eyes?
No, not with these eyes of mine, never.
Not this city either, her high towers,   1510
the sacred glittering images of her gods—
I am misery! I, her best son, reared
as no other son of Thebes was ever reared,
I've stripped myself, I gave the command myself.
All men must cast away the great blasphemer,   1515
the curse now brought to light by the gods,
the son of Laius—I, my father's son!

Now I've exposed my guilt, horrendous guilt,
could I train a level glance on you, my countrymen?
Impossible! No, if I could just block off my ears,   1520
the springs of hearing, I would stop at nothing—
I'd wall up my loathsome body like a prison,
blind to the sound of life, not just the sight.
Oblivion—what a blessing . . .
for the mind to dwell a world away from pain.   1525

O Cithaeron, why did you give me shelter?
Why didn't you take me, crush my life out on the spot?
I'd never have revealed my birth to all mankind.
O Polybus, Corinth, the old house of my fathers,
so I believed—what a handsome prince you raised—   1530
under the skin, what sickness to the core.
Look at me! Born of outrage, outrage to the core.
O triple roads—it all comes back, the secret,
dark ravine, and the oaks closing in
where the three roads join . . .   1535
You drank my father's blood, my own blood
spilled by my own hands—you still remember me?
What things you saw me do? Then I came here
and did them all once more!
                    Marriages! O marriage,
you gave me birth, and once you brought me into the world   1540
you brought my sperm rising back, springing to light
fathers, brothers, sons—one murderous breed—
brides, wives, mothers. The blackest things
a man can do, I have done them all!
                              No more—
it's wrong to name what's wrong to do. Quickly,   1545
for the love of god, hide me somewhere,
kill me, hurl me into the sea
where you can never look on me again.
          [Beckoning to the CHORUS as they shrink away.]
                              Closer,
it's all right. Touch the man of grief.

Do. Don't be afraid. My troubles are mine   1550
and I am the only man alive who can sustain them.
  [*Enter* CREON *from the palace, attended by palace guards.*]
LEADER Put your requests to Creon. Here he is,
 just when we need him. He'll have a plan, he'll act.
 Now that he's the sole defense of the country
 in your place.
OEDIPUS   Oh no, what can I say to him?   1555
How can I ever hope to win his trust?
 I wronged him so, just now, in every way.
 You must see that—I was so wrong, so wrong.
CREON I haven't come to mock you, Oedipus,
 or to criticize your former failings.
  [*Turning to the guards.*]
         You there,   1560
 have you lost all respect for human feelings?
 At least revere the Sun, the holy fire
 that keeps us all alive. Never expose a thing
 of guilt and holy dread so great it appalls
 the earth, the rain from heaven, the light of day!   1565
 Get him into the halls—quickly as you can.
 Piety demands no less. Kindred alone
 should see a kinsman's shame. This is obscene.
OEDIPUS Please, in god's name . . . you wipe my fears away,
 coming so generously to me, the worst of men.   1570
 Do one thing more, for your sake, not mine.
CREON What do you want? Why so insistent?
OEDIPUS Drive me out of the land at once, far from sight,
 where I can never hear a human voice.
CREON I'd have done that already, I promise you.   1575
 First I wanted the god to clarify my duties.
OEDIPUS The god? His command was clear, every word:
 death for the father-killer, the curse—
 he said destroy me!
CREON So he did. Still, in such a crisis   1580
 it's better to ask precisely what to do.
OEDIPUS   So miserable—
 you'd consult the god about a man like me?
CREON By all means. And this time, I assume,
 even you will obey the god's decrees.
OEDIPUS   I will,
 I will. And you, I command you—I beg you . . .   1585
 the woman inside, bury her as you see fit.
 It's the only decent thing,
 to give your own the last rites. As for me,
 never condemn the city of my fathers
 to house my body, not while I'm alive, no,   1590
 let me live on the mountains, on Cithaeron,
 my favorite haunt, I have made it famous.
 Mother and father marked out that rock

to be my everlasting tomb—buried alive.
Let me die there, where they tried to kill me.   1595

Oh but this I know: no sickness can destroy me,
nothing can. I would never have been saved
from death—I have been saved
for something great and terrible, something strange.
Well let my destiny come and take me on its way!   1600
About my children, Creon, the boys at least,
don't burden yourself. They're men,
wherever they go, they'll find the means to live.
But my two daughters, my poor helpless girls,
clustering at our table, never without me   1605
hovering near them . . . whatever I touched,
they always had their share. Take care of them,
I beg you. Wait, better—permit me, would you?
Just to touch them with my hands and take
our fill of tears. Please . . . my king.   1610
Grant it, with all your noble heart.
If I could hold them, just once, I'd think
I had them with me, like the early days
when I could see their eyes.
            [ANTIGONE and ISMENE, two small children, are led in from the palace
            by a nurse.]
                              What's that
O god! Do I really hear you sobbing?—   1615
my two children. Creon, you've pitied me?
Sent me my darling girls, my own flesh and blood!
Am I right?
CREON   Yes, it's my doing.
I know the joy they gave you all these years,
the joy you must feel now.
OEDIPUS   Bless you, Creon!   1620
May god watch over you for this kindness,
better than he ever guarded me.
                              Children, where are you?
Here, come quickly—
            [Groping for ANTIGONE and ISMENE, who approach their father cau-
            tiously, then embrace him.]
                              Come to these hands of mine,
your brother's hands, your own father's hands
that served his once bright eyes so well—   1625
that made them blind. Seeing nothing, children,
knowing nothing, I became your father,
I fathered you in the soil that gave me life.
How I weep for you—I cannot see you now . . .
just thinking of all your days to come, the bitterness,   1630
the life that rough mankind will thrust upon you.
Where are the public gatherings you can join,
the banquets of the clans? Home you'll come,

in tears, cut off from the sight of it all,
the brilliant rites unfinished.   1635
And when you reach perfection, ripe for marriage,
who will he be, my dear ones? Risking all
to shoulder the curse that weighs down my parents,
yes and you too—that wounds us all together.
What more misery could you want?   1640
Your father killed his father, sowed his mother,
one, one and the selfsame womb sprang you—
he cropped the very roots of his existence.

Such disgrace, and you must bear it all!
Who will marry you then? Not a man on earth.   1645
Your doom is clear: you'll wither away to nothing,
single, without a child.
            [*Turning to* CREON.]
                              Oh Creon,
you are the only father they have now . . .
we who brought them into the world
are gone, both gone at a stroke—   1650
Don't let them go begging, abandoned,
men without men. Your own flesh and blood!
Never bring them down to the level of my pains.
Pity them. Look at them, so young, so vulnerable,
shorn of everything—you're their only hope.   1655
Promise me, noble Creon, touch my hand!
            [*Reaching toward* CREON, *who draws back.*]
You, little ones, if you were old enough
to understand, there is much I'd tell you.
Now, as it is, I'd have you say a prayer.
Pray for life, my children,   1660
live where you are free to grow and season.
Pray god you find a better life than mine,
the father who begot you.
CREON   Enough.
You've wept enough. Into the palace now.
OEDIPUS   I must, but I find it very hard.   1665
CREON   Time is the great healer, you will see.
OEDIPUS   I am going—you know on what condition?
CREON   Tell me. I'm listening.
OEDIPUS   Drive me out of Thebes, in exile.
CREON   Not I. Only the gods can give you that.   1670
OEDIPUS   Surely the gods hate me so much—
CREON   You'll get your wish at once.
OEDIPUS   You consent?
CREON   I try to say what I mean; it's my habit.
OEDIPUS   Then take me away. It's time.
CREON   Come along, let go of the children.
OEDIPUS   No—   1675
don't take them away from me, not now! No no no!

[*Clutching his daughters as the guards wrench them loose and take them through the palace doors.*]

CREON   Still the king, the master of all things?
No more: here your power ends.
None of your power follows you through life.
[*Exit* OEDIPUS *and* CREON *to the palace. The* CHORUS *comes forward to address the audience directly.*]

CHORUS   People of Thebes, my countrymen, look on Oedipus.   1680
He solved the famous riddle with his brilliance,
he rose to power, a man beyond all power.
Who could behold his greatness without envy?
Now what a black sea of terror has overwhelmed him.
Now as we keep our watch and wait the final day,   1685
count no man happy till he dies, free of pain at last.
[*Exit in procession.*]

EURIPIDES
480–406 B.C.E.

Euripides' *Medea*, produced in 431 B.C.E., the year that brought the beginning of the Peloponnesian War, appeared earlier than Sophocles' *Oedipus the King*, but it has a bitterness that is more in keeping with the spirit of a later age. If *Oedipus* is, in one sense, a warning to a generation that has embarked on an intellectual revolution, *Medea* is the ironic expression of the disillusion that comes after the shipwreck. In this play we are conscious for the first time of an attitude characteristic of modern literature, the artist's feeling of separation from the audience, the isolation of the poet. "Often previously," says Medea to the king,

> Through being considered clever I have suffered much. . . .
> If you put new ideas before the eyes of fools
> They'll think you foolish and worthless into the bargain;
> And if you are thought superior to those who have
> Some reputation for learning, you will become hated.

The common background of audience and poet is disappearing, the old certainties are being undermined, the city divided. Euripides is the first Greek poet to suffer the fate of so many of the great modern writers: rejected by most of his contemporaries (he rarely won first prize and was the favorite target for the scurrilous humor of the comic poets), he was universally admired and revered by the Greeks of the centuries that followed his death.

It is significant that what little biographical information we have for Euripides makes no mention of military service or political office; unlike Sophocles, who took an active part in public affairs from youth to advanced old age, Euripides seems to have lived a private, an intellectual life. Younger than Sophocles (though they died in the same year), he was more receptive to the critical theories and the rhetorical techniques offered by the Sophist teachers; his plays often subject received ideas to fundamental questioning, expressed in vivid dramatic debate. His *Medea* is typical of his iconoclastic approach; his choice of theme and central characters is in itself a challenge to established canons. He still dramatizes myth, but the myth he chooses is exotic and disturbing, and the protagonist is not a man but a woman. Medea is both woman and foreigner—that is, in terms of the audience's prejudice and practice she is a representative of the two freeborn groups in Athenian society that had almost no rights at all (though the male foreign resident had more rights than the native woman). The tragic hero is no longer a king, "one among the . . . highly renowned and prosperous, such as Oedipus," but a woman who, because she finds no redress for her wrongs in society, is driven by her passion to violate that society's most sacred laws in a rebellion against its typical representative, Jason, her husband. She is not just a woman and a foreigner, she is also a person of great intellectual power. Compared with her the credulous king and her complacent husband are children; and once her mind is made up, she moves them like pawns to their proper places in her barbaric game. The myth is used for new purposes, to shock the members of the audience, attack their deepest prejudices, and shake them out of their complacent pride in the superiority of Greek masculinity.

But the play is more compelling than that. Before it is over, our sympathies have come full circle; the contempt with which we regard the Jason of the opening scenes turns to pity as we feel the measure of his loss and the ferocity of Medea's revenge. Medea's passion has carried her too far; the death of Kreon (Creon) and his daughter we might have accepted, but the murder of the children is too much. It was, of course, meant to be. Euripides' theme, like Homer's, is violence, but this is the unspeakable violence of the oppressed, which is greater than the violence of the oppressor and which, because it has been long pent up, cannot be controlled.

In this, as in the other Greek plays, the gods have their place. In the *Oresteia* the will of Zeus is manifested in every action and implied in every word. In *Oedipus the King* the gods bide their time and watch Oedipus fulfill the truth of their prophecy; but in *Medea*, the divine will, which is revealed at the end, is enigmatic and, far from bringing harmony, concludes the play with a terrifying discord. All through *Medea* the human beings involved call on the gods, and two especially are singled out for attention: Earth and Sun. It is by these two gods that Medea makes Aegeus swear to give her refuge in Athens, the chorus invokes them to prevent Medea's violence against her sons, and Jason wonders how Medea can look on Earth and Sun after she has killed her own children. These emphatic appeals clearly raise the question of the attitude of the gods, and the answer to the question is a shock. We are not told what Earth does, but Sun sends the magic chariot on which Medea makes her escape. His reason, too, is stated: it is not any concern for justice but the fact that Medea is his granddaughter. Euripides is here using the letter of the myth for his own purposes. This jarring detail emphasizes the significance of the whole. The play creates a world in which there is no relation whatsoever between the powers that rule the universe and the fundamental laws of human morality. It dramatizes disorder, not just the disorder of the family of Jason and Medea but the disorder of the universe as a whole. It is the nightmare in which the dream of the fifth century B.C.E. was to end, the senseless fury and degradation of permanent violence. "Flow backward to your sources, sacred rivers," the chorus sings. "And let the world's great order be reversed."

PRONOUNCING GLOSSARY

The following list uses common English syllables and stress accents to provide rough equivalents of selected words whose pronunciation may be unfamiliar to the general reader.

Aigeus: *ai'-jioos / ai-gyoos*

Aphrodite: *a-froh-dai'-tee*

Cypris: *sai'-pris / koo'-pris*

Erechtheus: *e-rek'-thee-us / e-rek-thyoos*

Medea: *me-dee'-uh*

Hecate: *he'-kah-tee*

Helios: *hee-lee-os / hay-lee-os*

Iolcos: *yol'-kuhs / ee-ol'-kuhs*

Orpheus: *or'-fee-us* / *or'-fyoos*   Pittheus: *pit'-thee-us* / *pit'-thyoos*

Pelias: *pee'-lee-as*   Scylla: *si'-lah* / *ski'-lah*

Pieria: *pai-ee'-ree-uh* / *pee-ehr'-ee-uh*   Troezen: *troy'-zen*

Medea[1]

CHARACTERS

MEDEA, *princess of Colchis and wife*   AIGEUS, *king of Athens*
of Jason   NURSE *to Medea*
JASON, *son of Aeson, king of Iolcos*   TUTOR *to Medea's children*
Two CHILDREN *of Medea and Jason*   MESSENGER
KREON, *king of Corinth*   CHORUS *of Corinthian women*

[SCENE—*In front of* MEDEA'S *house in Corinth. Enter from the house* MEDEA'S
NURSE.]

NURSE   How I wish the Argo[2] never had reached the land
   Of Colchis, skimming through the blue Symplegades,
   Nor ever had fallen in the glades of Pelion[3]
   The smitten fir-tree to furnish oars for the hands
   Of heroes who in Pelias'[4] name attempted   5
   The Golden Fleece! For then my mistress Medea[5]
   Would not have sailed for the towers of the land of Iolcos,
   Her heart on fire with passionate love for Jason;
   Nor would she have persuaded the daughters of Pelias
   To kill their father,[6] and now be living here   10
   In Corinth[7] with her husband and children. She gave
   Pleasure to the people of her land of exile,
   And she herself helped Jason in every way.
   This is indeed the greatest salvation of all,—
   For the wife not to stand apart from the husband.   15
   But now there's hatred everywhere. Love is diseased.
   For, deserting his own children and my mistress,
   Jason has taken a royal wife to his bed,
   The daughter of the ruler of this land, Kreon.
   And poor Medea is slighted, and cries aloud on the   20

---

1. Translated by Rex Warner.   2. The ship in which Jason and his companions sailed on the quest for
the Golden Fleece.   3. A mountain in northern Greece near Iolcos, the place from which Jason sailed.
The Symplegades were clashing rocks that crushed ships endeavoring to pass between them. They were
supposed to be located at the Hellespont, the passage between the Mediterranean and Black seas.
4. He seized the kingdom of Iolcos, expelling Aeson, Jason's father. When Jason came to claim his rights,
Pelias sent him to get the Golden Fleece.   5. Daughter of the king of Colchis who fell in love with Jason
and helped him take the Golden Fleece away from her own country.   6. After Jason and Medea returned
to Iolcos, Medea (who had a reputation as a sorceress) persuaded Pelias's daughters to cut Pelias up and
boil the pieces, which would restore him to youth. The experiment was, of course, unsuccessful, and
Pelias's son banished Jason and Medea from the kingdom.   7. On the isthmus between the Peloponnesus and Attica, where they took refuge. In Euripides' time it was a wealthy trading city, a commercial
rival of Athens.

Vows they made to each other, the right hands clasped
In eternal promise. She calls upon the gods to witness
What sort of return Jason has made to her love.
She lies without food and gives herself up to suffering,
Wasting away every moment of the day in tears.   25
So it has gone since she knew herself slighted by him.
Not stirring an eye, not moving her face from the ground,
No more than either a rock or surging sea water
She listens when she is given friendly advice.
Except that sometimes she twists back her white neck and   30
Moans to herself, calling out on her father's name,
And her land, and her home betrayed when she came away with
A man who now is determined to dishonor her.
Poor creature, she has discovered by her sufferings
What it means to one not to have lost one's own country.   35
She has turned from the children and does not like to see them.
I am afraid she may think of some dreadful thing,
For her heart is violent. She will never put up with
The treatment she is getting. I know and fear her
Lest she may sharpen a sword and thrust to the heart,   40
Stealing into the palace where the bed is made,
Or even kill the king and the new-wedded groom,
And thus bring a greater misfortune on herself.
She's a strange woman. I know it won't be easy
To make an enemy of her and come off best.   45
But here the children come. They have finished playing.
They have no thought at all of their mother's trouble.
Indeed it is not usual for the young to grieve.
    [*Enter from the right the slave who is the* TUTOR *to* MEDEA's *two small*
    CHILDREN. *The* CHILDREN *follow him.*]
TUTOR   You old retainer of my mistress's household,
   Why are you standing here all alone in front of the   50
   Gates and moaning to yourself over your misfortune?
   Medea could not wish you to leave her alone.
NURSE   Old man, and guardian of the children of Jason,
   If one is a good servant, it's a terrible thing
   When one's master's luck is out; it goes to one's heart.   55
   So I myself have got into such a state of grief
   That a longing stole over me to come outside here
   And tell the earth and air of my mistress's sorrows.
TUTOR   Has the poor lady not yet given up her crying?
NURSE   Given up? She's at the start, not halfway through her tears.   60
TUTOR   Poor fool,—if I may call my mistress such a name,—
   How ignorant she is of trouble more to come.
NURSE   What do you mean, old man? You needn't fear to speak.
TUTOR   Nothing. I take back the words which I used just now.
NURSE   Don't, by your beard, hide this from me, your fellow-servant.   65
   If need be, I'll keep quiet about what you tell me.
TUTOR   I heard a person saying, while I myself seemed
   Not to be paying attention, when I was at the place

Where the old draught-players[8] sit, by the holy fountain,
That Kreon, ruler of the land, intends to drive   70
These children and their mother in exile from Corinth.
But whether what he said is really true or not
I do not know. I pray that it may not be true.
NURSE   And will Jason put up with it that his children
Should suffer so, though he's no friend to their mother?   75
TUTOR   Old ties give place to new ones. As for Jason, he
No longer has a feeling for this house of ours.
NURSE   It's black indeed for us, when we add new to old
Sorrows before even the present sky has cleared.
TUTOR   But you be silent, and keep all this to yourself.   80
It is not the right time to tell our mistress of it.
NURSE   Do you hear, children, what a father he is to you?
I wish he were dead,—but no, he is still my master.
Yet certainly he has proved unkind to his dear ones.
TUTOR   What's strange in that? Have you only just discovered   85
That everyone loves himself more than his neighbor?
Some have good reason, others get something out of it.
So Jason neglects his children for the new bride.
NURSE   Go indoors, children. That will be the best thing.
And you, keep them to themselves as much as possible.   90
Don't bring them near their mother in her angry mood.
For I've seen her already blazing her eyes at them
As though she meant some mischief and I am sure that
She'll not stop raging until she has struck at someone.
May it be an enemy and not a friend she hurts!   95
       [MEDEA *is heard inside the house.*]
MEDEA   Ah, wretch! Ah, lost in my sufferings,
I wish, I wish I might die.
NURSE   What did I say, dear children? Your mother
Frets her heart and frets it to anger.
Run away quickly into the house,   100
And keep well out of her sight.
Don't go anywhere near, but be careful
Of the wildness and bitter nature
Of that proud mind.
Go now! Run quickly indoors.   105
It is clear that she soon will put lightning
In that cloud of her cries that is rising
With a passion increasing. Oh, what will she do,
Proud-hearted and not to be checked on her course,
A soul bitten into with wrong?   110
       [*The* TUTOR *takes the* CHILDREN *into the house.*]
MEDEA   Ah, I have suffered
What should be wept for bitterly. I hate you,
Children of a hateful mother. I curse you
And your father. Let the whole house crash.

8. Checkers players.

NURSE   Ah, I pity you, you poor creature.   115
  How can your children share in their father's
  Wickedness? Why do you hate them? Oh children,
  How much I fear that something may happen!
  Great people's tempers are terrible, always
  Having their own way, seldom checked,   120
  Dangerous they shift from mood to mood.
  How much better to have been accustomed
  To live on equal terms with one's neighbors.
  I would like to be safe and grow old in a
  Humble way. What is moderate sounds best,   125
  Also in practice *is* best for everyone.
  Greatness brings no profit to people.
  God indeed, when in anger, brings
  Greater ruin to great men's houses.
        [*Enter, on the right, a* CHORUS *of Corinthian women. They have come*
        to inquire about MEDEA *and to attempt to console her.*]
CHORUS   I heard the voice, I heard the cry   130
  Of Colchis' wretched daughter.
  Tell me, mother, is she not yet
  At rest? Within the double gates
  Of the court I heard her cry. I am sorry
  For the sorrow of this home. O, say, what has happened?   135
NURSE   There is no home. It's over and done with.
  Her husband holds fast to his royal wedding,
  While she, my mistress, cries out her eyes
  There in her room, and takes no warmth from
  Any word of any friend.   140
MEDEA   Oh, I wish
  That lightning from heaven would split my head open.
  Oh, what use have I now for life?
  I would find my release in death
  And leave hateful existence behind me.   145
CHORUS   O God and Earth and Heaven!
  Did you hear what a cry was that
  Which the sad wife sings?
  Poor foolish one, why should you long
  For that appalling rest?   150
  The final end of death comes fast.
  No need to pray for that.
  Suppose your man gives honor
  To another woman's bed.
  It often happens. Don't be hurt.   155
  God will be your friend in this.
  You must not waste away
  Grieving too much for him who shared your bed.
MEDEA   Great Themis, lady Artemis,[9] behold
  The things I suffer, though I made him promise,   160

9. The protector of women in pain and distress. Themis, a Titan, was justice personified.

My hateful husband. I pray that I may see him,
Him and his bride and all their palace shattered
For the wrong they dare to do me without cause.
Oh, my father! Oh, my country! In what dishonor
I left you, killing my own brother for it.[1]   165

NURSE   Do you hear what she says, and how she cries
On Themis, the goddess of Promises, and on Zeus,
Whom we believe to be the Keeper of Oaths?
Of this I am sure, that no small thing
Will appease my mistress's anger.   170

CHORUS   Will she come into our presence?
Will she listen when we are speaking
To the words we say?
I wish she might relax her rage
And temper of her heart.   175
My willingness to help will never
Be wanting to my friends.
But go inside and bring her
Out of the house to us,
And speak kindly to her: hurry,   180
Before she wrongs her own.
This passion of hers moves to something great.

NURSE   I will, but I doubt if I'll manage
To win my mistress over.
But still I'll attempt it to please you.   185
Such a look she will flash on her servants
If any comes near with a message,
Like a lioness guarding her cubs.
It is right, I think, to consider
Both stupid and lacking in foresight   190
Those poets of old who wrote songs
For revels and dinners and banquets,
Pleasant sounds for men living at ease;
But none of them all has discovered
How to put an end with their singing   195
Or musical instruments grief,
Bitter grief, from which death and disaster
Cheat the hopes of a house. Yet how good
If music could cure men of this! But why raise
To no purpose the voice at a banquet? For *there* is   200
Already abundance of pleasure for men
With a joy of its own.

[*The* NURSE *goes into the house.*]

CHORUS   I heard a shriek that is laden with sorrow.
Shrilling out her hard grief she cries out
Upon him who betrayed both her bed and her marriage.   205
Wronged, she calls on the gods,
On the justice of Zeus, the oath sworn,

---

1. Medea killed him to delay the pursuit when she escaped with Jason.

Which brought her away
To the opposite shore of the Greeks
Through the gloomy salt straits to the gateway   210
Of the salty unlimited sea.

[MEDEA, *attended by servants, comes out of the house.*]

MEDEA   Women of Corinth, I have come outside to you
Lest you should be indignant with me; for I know
That many people are overproud, some when alone,
And others when in company. And those who live   215
Quietly, as I do, get a bad reputation.
For a just judgment is not evident in the eyes
When a man at first sight hates another, before
Learning his character, being in no way injured;
And a foreigner[2] especially must adapt himself.   220
I'd not approve of even a fellow-countryman
Who by pride and want of manners offends his neighbors.
But on me this thing has fallen so unexpectedly,
It has broken my heart. I am finished. I let go
All my life's joy. My friends, I only want to die.   225
It was everything to me to think well of one man,
And he, my own husband, has turned out wholly vile.
Of all things which are living and can form a judgment
We women are the most unfortunate creatures.[3]
Firstly, with an excess of wealth it is required   230
For us to buy a husband and take for our bodies[4]
A master; for not to take one is even worse.
And now the question is serious whether we take
A good or bad one; for there is no easy escape
For a woman, nor can she say no to her marriage.   235
She arrives among new modes of behavior and manners,
And needs prophetic power, unless she has learnt at home,
How best to manage him who shares the bed with her.
And if we work out all this well and carefully,
And the husband lives with us and lightly bears his yoke,   240
Then life is enviable. If not, I'd rather die.
A man, when he's tired of the company in his home,
Goes out of the house and puts an end to his boredom
And turns to a friend or companion of his own age.
But we are forced to keep our eyes on one alone.   245
What they say of us is that we have a peaceful time
Living at home, while they do the fighting in war.
How wrong they are! I would very much rather stand
Three times in the front of battle than bear one child.
Yet what applies to me does not apply to you.   250
You have a country. Your family home is here.
You enjoy life and the company of your friends.

2. Foreign residents were encouraged to come to Athens but were rarely admitted to the rights of full citizenship, which was a jealously guarded privilege.   3. Athenian rights and institutions were made for men; women had few privileges and almost no legal rights.   4. These lines refer to the dowry that the bride's family had to provide.

But I am deserted, a refugee, thought nothing of
By my husband,—something he won in a foreign land.
I have no mother or brother, nor any relation   255
With whom I can take refuge in this sea of woe.
This much then is the service I would beg from you:
If I can find the means or devise any scheme
To pay my husband back for what he has done to me,—
Him and his father-in-law and the girl who married him,—   260
Just to keep silent. For in other ways a woman
Is full of fear, defenseless, dreads the sight of cold
Steel; but, when once she is wronged in the matter of love,
No other soul can hold so many thoughts of blood.

CHORUS   This I will promise. You are in the right, Medea,   265
In paying your husband back. I am not surprised at you
For being sad. But look! I see our king Kreon
Approaching. He will tell us of some new plan.

      [*Enter, from the right,* KREON, *with attendants.*]

KREON   You, with that angry look, so set against your husband,
Medea, I order you to leave my territories   270
An exile, and take along with you your two children,
And not to waste time doing it. It is my decree,
And I will see it done. I will not return home
Until you are cast from the boundaries of my land.

MEDEA   Oh, this is the end for me. I am utterly lost.   275
Now I am in the full force of the storm of hate
And have no harbor from ruin to reach easily.
Yet still, in spite of it all, I'll ask the question:
What is your reason, Kreon, for banishing me?

KREON   I am afraid of you,—why should I dissemble it?—   280
Afraid that you may injure my daughter mortally.
Many things accumulate to support my feeling.
You are a clever woman, versed in evil arts,
And are angry at having lost your husband's love.
I hear that you are threatening, so they tell me,   285
To do something against my daughter and Jason
And me, too. I shall take my precautions first.
I tell you, I prefer to earn your hatred now
Than to be soft-hearted and afterwards regret it.

MEDEA   This is not the first time, Kreon. Often previously   290
Through being considered clever I have suffered much.
A person of sense ought never to have his children
Brought up to be more clever than the average.
For, apart from cleverness bringing them no profit,
It will make them objects of envy and ill-will.   295
If you put new ideas before the eyes of fools
They'll think you foolish and worthless into the bargain;
And if you are thought superior to those who have
Some reputation for learning, you will become hated.
I have some knowledge myself of how this happens;   300
For being clever, I find that some will envy me,

Others object to me. Yet all my cleverness
Is not so much. Well, then, are you frightened, Kreon,
That I should harm you? There is no need. It is not
My way to transgress the authority of a king.   305
How have you injured me? You gave your daughter away
To the man you wanted. O, certainly I hate
My husband, but you, I think, have acted wisely;
Nor do I grudge it you that your affairs go well.
May the marriage be a lucky one! Only let me   310
Live in this land. For even though I have been wronged,
I will not raise my voice, but submit to my betters.

KREON   What you say sounds gentle enough. Still in my heart
I greatly dread that you are plotting some evil,
And therefore I trust you even less than before.   315
A sharp-tempered woman, or for that matter a man,
Is easier to deal with than the clever type
Who holds her tongue. No. You must go. No need for more
Speeches. The thing is fixed. By no manner of means
Shall you, an enemy of mine, stay in my country.   320

MEDEA   I beg you. By your knees, by your new-wedded girl.

KREON   Your words are wasted. You will never persuade me.

MEDEA   Will you drive me out, and give no heed to my prayers?

KREON   I will, for I love my family more than you.

MEDEA   O my country! How bitterly now I remember you!   325

KREON   I love my country too,—next after my children.

MEDEA   O what an evil to men is passionate love!

KREON   That would depend on the luck that goes along with it.

MEDEA   O God, do not forget who is the cause of this!

KREON   Go. It is no use. Spare me the pain of forcing you.   330

MEDEA   I'm spared no pain. I lack no pain to be spared me.

KREON   Then you'll be removed by force by one of my men.

MEDEA   No, Kreon, not that! But do listen, I beg you.

KREON   Woman, you seem to want to create a disturbance.

MEDEA   I *will* go into exile. *This* is not what I beg for.   335

KREON   Why then this violence and clinging to my hand?

MEDEA   Allow me to remain here just for this one day,
So I may consider where to live in my exile,
And look for support for my children, since their father
Chooses to make no kind of provision for them.   340
Have pity on them! You have children of your own.
It is natural for you to look kindly on them.
For myself I do not mind if I go into exile.
It is the children being in trouble that I mind.

KREON   There is nothing tyrannical about my nature,   345
And by showing mercy I have often been the loser.
Even now I know that I am making a mistake.
All the same you shall have your will. But this I tell you,
That if the light of heaven tomorrow shall see you,
You and your children in the confines of my land,   350
You die. This word I have spoken is firmly fixed.

But now, if you must stay, stay for this day alone.
For in it you can do none of the things I fear.
          [*Exit* KREON *with his attendants.*]
CHORUS   Oh, unfortunate one! Oh, cruel!
  Where will you turn? Who will help you?   355
  What house or what land to preserve you
  From ill can you find?
  Medea, a god has thrown suffering
  Upon you in waves of despair.
MEDEA   Things have gone badly every way. No doubt of that.   360
  But not these things this far, and don't imagine so.
  There are still trials to come for the new-wedded pair,
  And for their relations pain that will mean something.
  Do you think that I would ever have fawned on that man
  Unless I had some end to gain or profit in it?   365
  I would not even have spoken or touched him with my hands.
  But he has got to such a pitch of foolishness
  That, though he could have made nothing of all my plans
  By exiling me, he has given me this one day
  To stay here, and in this I will make dead bodies   370
  Of three of my enemies,—father, the girl and my husband.
  I have many ways of death which I might suit to them,
  And do not know, friends, which one to take in hand;
  Whether to set fire underneath their bridal mansion,
  Or sharpen a sword and thrust it to the heart,   375
  Stealing into the palace where the bed is made.
  There is just one obstacle to this. If I am caught
  Breaking into the house and scheming against it,
  I shall die, and give my enemies cause for laughter.
  It is best to go by the straight road, the one in which   380
  I am most skilled, and make away with them by poison.
  So be it then.
  And now suppose them dead. What town will receive me?
  What friend will offer me a refuge in his land,
  Or the guarantee of his house and save my own life?   385
  There is none. So I must wait a little time yet,
  And if some sure defense should then appear for me,
  In craft and silence I will set about this murder.
  But if my fate should drive me on without help,
  Even though death is certain, I will take the sword   390
  Myself and kill, and steadfastly advance to crime.
  It shall not be,—I swear it by her, my mistress,
  Whom most I honor and have chosen as partner,
  Hecate,[5] who dwells in the recesses of my hearth,—
  That any man shall be glad to have injured me.   395
  Bitter I will make their marriage for them and mournful,
  Bitter the alliance and the driving me out of the land.

5. The patron of witchcraft, sometimes identified with Artemis. Medea has a statue and shrine of her in
the house.

Ah, come, Medea, in your plotting and scheming
Leave nothing untried of all those things which you know.
Go forward to the dreadful act. The test has come   400
For resolution. You see how you are treated. Never
Shall you be mocked by Jason's Corinthian wedding,
Whose father was noble, whose grandfather Helios.[6]
You have the skill. What is more, you were born a woman,
And women, though most helpless in doing good deeds,   405
Are of every evil the cleverest of contrivers.

CHORUS   Flow backward to your sources, sacred rivers,
And let the world's great order be reversed.
It is the thoughts of *men* that are deceitful,
Their pledges that are loose.   410
Story shall now turn my condition to a fair one,
Women are paid their due.
No more shall evil-sounding fame be theirs.

Cease now, you muses of the ancient singers,
To tell the tale of my unfaithfulness;   415
For not on us did Phoebus,[7] lord of music,
Bestow the lyre's divine
Power, for otherwise I should have sung an answer
To the other sex. Long time
Has much to tell of us, and much of them.   420

You sailed away from your father's home,
With a heart on fire you passed
The double rocks of the sea.
And now in a foreign country
You have lost your rest in a widowed bed,   425
And are driven forth, a refugee
In dishonor from the land.

Good faith has gone, and no more remains
In great Greece a sense of shame.
It has flown away to the sky.   430
No father's house for a haven
Is at hand for you now, and another queen
Of your bed has dispossessed you and
Is mistress of your home.
          [*Enter* JASON, *with attendants.*]

JASON   This is not the first occasion that I have noticed   435
How hopeless it is to deal with a stubborn temper.
For, with reasonable submission to our ruler's will,
You might have lived in this land and kept your home.
As it is you are going to be exiled for your loose speaking.
Not that I mind myself. You are free to continue   440

6. The Sun, father of Medea's father, Aeëtes.   7. Apollo.

Telling everyone that Jason is a worthless man.
But as to your talk about the king, consider
Yourself most lucky that exile is your punishment.
I, for my part, have always tried to calm down
The anger of the king, and wished you to remain.   445
But you will not give up your folly, continually
Speaking ill of him, and so you are going to be banished.
All the same, and in spite of your conduct, I'll not desert
My friends, but have come to make some provision for you,
So that you and the children may not be penniless   450
Or in need of anything in exile. Certainly
Exile brings many troubles with it. And even
If you hate me, I cannot think badly of you.

MEDEA   O coward in every way,—that is what I call you,
With bitterest reproach for your lack of manliness,   455
You have come, you, my worst enemy, have come to me!
It is not an example of over-confidence
Or of boldness thus to look your friends in the face,
Friends you have injured,—no, it is the worst of all
Human diseases, shamelessness. But you did well   460
To come, for I can speak ill of you and lighten
My heart, and you will suffer while you are listening.
And first I will begin from what happened first.
I saved your life, and every Greek knows I saved it
Who was a ship-mate of yours aboard the Argo,   465
When you were sent to control the bulls that breathed fire
And yoke them, and when you would sow that deadly field.
Also that snake, who encircled with his many folds
The Golden Fleece and guarded it and never slept,[8]
I killed, and so gave you the safety of the light.   470
And I myself betrayed my father and my home,
And came with you to Pelias' land of Iolcos.
And then, showing more willingness to help than wisdom,
I killed him, Pelias, with a most dreadful death
At his own daughters' hands, and took away your fear.   475
This is how I behaved to you, you wretched man,
And you forsook me, took another bride to bed
Though you had children; for, if that had not been,
You would have had an excuse for another wedding.
Faith in your word has gone. Indeed I cannot tell   480
Whether you think the gods whose names you swore by then
Have ceased to rule and that new standards are set up,
Since you must know you have broken your word to me.
O my right hand, and the knees which you often clasped
In supplication, how senselessly I am treated   485
By this bad man, and how my hopes have missed their mark!

8. These lines refer to ordeals through which Jason had to pass to win the fleece and in which Medea
helped him. He had to yoke a team of fire-breathing bulls, then sow a field that immediately sprouted
armed warriors, and then deal with the snake that guarded the fleece.

Come, I will share my thoughts as though you were a friend,—
You! Can I think that you would ever treat me well?
But I will do it, and these questions will make you
Appear the baser. Where am I to go? To my father's?   490
Him I betrayed and his land when I came with you.
To Pelias' wretched daughters? What a fine welcome
They would prepare for me who murdered their father!
For this is my position,—hated by my friends
At home, I have, in kindness to you, made enemies   495
Of others whom there was no need to have injured.
And how happy among Greek women you have made me
On your side for all this! A distinguished husband
I have,—for breaking promises. When in misery
I am cast out of the land and go into exile,   500
Quite without friends and all alone with my children,
That will be a fine shame for the new-wedded groom,
For his children to wander as beggars and she who saved him.
O God, you have given to mortals a sure method
Of telling the gold that is pure from the counterfeit;   505
Why is there no mark engraved upon men's bodies,
By which we could know the true ones from the false ones?

CHORUS It is a strange form of anger, difficult to cure
When two friends turn upon each other in hatred.

JASON As for me, it seems I must be no bad speaker.   510
But, like a man who has a good grip of the tiller,
Reef up his sail, and so run away from under
This mouthing tempest, woman, of your bitter tongue.
Since you insist on building up your kindness to me,
My view is that Cypris[9] was alone responsible   515
Of men and gods for the preserving of my life.
You are clever enough,—but really I need not enter
Into the story of how it was love's inescapable
Power that compelled you to keep my person safe.
On this I will not go into too much detail.   520
In so far as you helped me, you did well enough.
But on this question of saving me, I can prove
You have certainly got from me more than you gave.
Firstly, instead of living among barbarians,
You inhabit a Greek land and understand our ways,   525
How to live by law instead of the sweet will of force.
And all the Greeks considered you a clever woman.
You were honored for it; while, if you were living at
The ends of the earth, nobody would have heard of you.
For my part, rather than stores of gold in my house   530
Or power to sing even sweeter songs than Orpheus,[1]
I'd choose the fate that made me a distinguished man.
There is my reply to your story of my labors.

9. Aphrodite, goddess of love.   1. Legendary musician whose songs charmed animals and made trees
and rocks leave their places to come and listen.

Remember it was you who started the argument.
Next for your attack on my wedding with the princess: 535
Here I will prove that, first, it was a clever move,
Secondly, a wise one, and, finally, that I made it
In your best interests and the children's. Please keep calm.
When I arrived here from the land of Iolcos,
Involved, as I was, in every kind of difficulty, 540
What luckier chance could I have come across than this,
An exile to marry the daughter of the king?
It was not,—the point that seems to upset you—that I
Grew tired of your bed and felt the need of a new bride;
Nor with any wish to outdo your number of children. 545
We have enough already. I am quite content.
But,—this was the main reason—that we might live well,
And not be short of anything. I know that all
A man's friends leave him stone-cold if he becomes poor.
Also that I might bring my children up worthy 550
Of my position, and, by producing more of them
To be brothers of yours, we would draw the families
Together and all be happy. You need no children.
And it pays me to do good to those I have now
By having others. Do you think this a bad plan? 555
You wouldn't if the love question hadn't upset you.
But you women have got into such a state of mind
That, if your life at night is good, you think you have
Everything; but, if in that quarter things go wrong,
You will consider your best and truest interests 560
Most hateful. It would have been better far for men
To have got their children in some other way, and women
Not to have existed. Then life would have been good.
CHORUS   Jason, though you have made this speech of yours look well,
Still I think, even though others do not agree, 565
You have betrayed your wife and are acting badly.
MEDEA   Surely in many ways I hold different views
From others, for I think that the plausible speaker
Who is a villain deserves the greatest punishment.
Confident in his tongue's power to adorn evil, 570
He stops at nothing. Yet he is not really wise.
As in your case. There is no need to put on the airs
Of a clever speaker, for one word will lay you flat.
If you were not a coward, you would not have married
Behind my back, but discussed it with me first. 575
JASON   And you, no doubt, would have furthered the proposal,
If I had told you of it, you who even now
Are incapable of controlling your bitter temper.
MEDEA   It was not that. No, you thought it was not respectable
As you got on in years to have a foreign wife. 580
JASON   Make sure of this: it was not because of a woman
I made the royal alliance in which I now live,
But, as I said before, I wished to preserve you

And breed a royal progeny to be brothers
To the children I have now, a sure defense to us.   585
MEDEA   Let me have no happy fortune that brings pain with it,
Or prosperity which is upsetting to the mind!
JASON   Change your ideas of what you want, and show more sense.
Do not consider painful what is good for you,
Nor, when you are lucky, think yourself unfortunate.   590
MEDEA   You can insult me. You have somewhere to turn to.
But I shall go from this land into exile, friendless.
JASON   It was what you chose yourself. Don't blame others for it.
MEDEA   And how did I choose it? Did I betray my husband?
JASON   You called down wicked curses on the king's family.   595
MEDEA   A curse, that is what I am become to your house too.
JASON   I do not propose to go into all the rest of it;
But, if you wish for the children or for yourself
In exile to have some of my money to help you,
Say so, for I am prepared to give with open hand,   600
Or to provide you with introductions to my friends
Who will treat you well. You are a fool if you do not
Accept this. Cease your anger and you will profit.
MEDEA   I shall never accept the favors of friends of yours,
Nor take a thing from you, so you need not offer it.   605
There is no benefit in the gifts of a bad man.
JASON   Then, in any case, I call the gods to witness that
I wish to help you and the children in every way,
But you refuse what is good for you. Obstinately
You push away your friends. You are sure to suffer for it.   610
MEDEA   Go! No doubt you hanker for your virginal bride,
And are guilty of lingering too long out of her house.
Enjoy your wedding. But perhaps,—with the help of God—
You will make the kind of marriage that you will regret.
            [JASON *goes out with his attendants.*]
CHORUS   When love is in excess   615
It brings a man no honor
Nor any worthiness.
But if in moderation Cypris comes,
There is no other power at all so gracious.
O goddess, never on me let loose the unerring   620
Shaft of your bow in the poison of desire.

Let my heart be wise.
It is the gods' best gift.
On me let mighty Cypris
Inflict no wordy wars or restless anger   625
To urge my passion to a different love.
But with discernment may she guide women's weddings,
Honoring most what is peaceful in the bed.
O country and home,
Never, never may I be without you,   630
Living the hopeless life,

Hard to pass through and painful,
Most pitiable of all.
Let death first lay me low and death
Free me from this daylight.   635
There is no sorrow above
The loss of a native land.

I have seen it myself,
Do not tell of a secondhand story.
Neither city nor friend   640
Pitied you when you suffered
The worst of sufferings.
O let him die ungraced whose heart
Will not reward his friends,
Who cannot open an honest mind   645
No friend will he be of mine.

[Enter AIGEUS, king of Athens, an old friend of MEDEA.]

AIGEUS   Medea, greeting! This is the best introduction
   Of which men know for conversation between friends.
MEDEA   Greeting to you too, Aigeus, son of King Pandion,
   Where have you come from to visit this country's soil?   650
AIGEUS   I have just left the ancient oracle of Phoebus.[2]
MEDEA   And why did you go to earth's prophetic center?
AIGEUS   I went to inquire how children might be born to me.
MEDEA   Is it so? Your life still up to this point childless?
AIGEUS   Yes. By the fate of some power we have no children.   655
MEDEA   Have you a wife, or is there none to share your bed?
AIGEUS   There is. Yes, I am joined to my wife in marriage.
MEDEA   And what did Phoebus say to you about children?
AIGEUS   Words too wise for a mere man to guess their meaning.
MEDEA   Is it proper for me to be told the God's reply?   660
AIGEUS   It is. For sure what is needed is cleverness.
MEDEA   Then what was his message? Tell me, if I may hear.
AIGEUS   I am not to loosen the hanging foot of the wine-skin[3] . . .
MEDEA   Until you have done something, or reached some country?
AIGEUS   Until I return again to my hearth and house.   665
MEDEA   And for what purpose have you journeyed to this land?
AIGEUS   There is a man called Pittheus, king of Troezen.[4]
MEDEA   A son of Pelops, they say, a most righteous man.
AIGEUS   With him I wish to discuss the reply of the god.
MEDEA   Yes. He is wise and experienced in such matters.   670
AIGEUS   And to me also the dearest of all my spear-friends.[5]
MEDEA   Well, I hope you have good luck, and achieve your will.
AIGEUS   But why this downcast eye of yours, and this pale cheek?
MEDEA   O Aigeus, my husband has been the worst of all to me.
AIGEUS   What do you mean? Say clearly what has caused this grief. 675

---

2. Apollo. Delphi, the site of his oracle on the southern slopes of Mount Parnassus, was thought to be the center or "navel" of the earth.   3. Cryptic; probably not to have intercourse.   4. In the Peloponnesus. Pittheus was Aigeus's father-in-law. Corinth was on the way from Delphi to Troezen.   5. Allies in war, companions in fighting.

MEDEA   Jason wrongs me, though I have never injured him.

AIGEUS   What has he done? Tell me about it in clearer words.

MEDEA   He has taken a wife to his house, supplanting me.

AIGEUS   Surely he would not dare to do a thing like that.

MEDEA   Be sure he has. Once dear, I now am slighted by him.   680

AIGEUS   Did he fall in love? Or is he tired of your love?

MEDEA   He was greatly in love, this traitor to his friends.

AIGEUS   Then let him go, if, as you say, he is so bad.

MEDEA   A passionate love,—for an alliance with the king.

AIGEUS   And who gave him his wife? Tell me the rest of it.   685

MEDEA   It was Kreon, he who rules this land of Corinth.

AIGEUS   Indeed, Medea, your grief was understandable.

MEDEA   I am ruined. And there is more to come: I am banished.

AIGEUS   Banished? By whom? Here you tell me of a new wrong.

MEDEA   Kreon drives me an exile from the land of Corinth.   690

AIGEUS   Does Jason consent? I cannot approve of this.

MEDEA   He pretends not to, but he will put up with it.
    Ah, Aigeus, I beg and beseech you, by your beard
    And by your knees I am making myself your suppliant,
    Have pity on me, have pity on your poor friend,   695
    And do not let me go into exile desolate,
    But receive me in your land and at your very hearth.
    So may your love, with God's help, lead to the bearing
    Of children, and so may you yourself die happy.
    You do not know what a chance you have come on here.   700
    I will end your childlessness, and I will make you able
    To beget children. The drugs I know can do this.

AIGEUS   For many reasons, woman, I am anxious to do
    This favor for you. First, for the sake of the gods,
    And then for the birth of children which you promise,   705
    For in that respect I am entirely at my wits' end.
    But this is my position: if you reach my land,
    I, being in my rights, will try to befriend you.
    But this much I must warn you of beforehand:
    I shall not agree to take you out of this country;   710
    But if you by yourself can reach my house, then you
    Shall stay there safely. To none will I give you up.
    But from this land you must make your escape yourself,
    For I do not wish to incur blame from my friends.

MEDEA   It shall be so. But, if I might have a pledge from you   715
    For this, then I would have from you all I desire.

AIGEUS   Do you not trust me? What is it rankles with you?

MEDEA   I trust you, yes. But the house of Pelias hates me,
    And so does Kreon. If you are bound by this oath,
    When they try to drag me from your land, you will not   720
    Abandon me; but if our pact is only words,
    With no oath to the gods, you will be lightly armed,
    Unable to resist their summons. I am weak,
    While they have wealth to help them and a royal house.

AIGEUS   You show much foresight for such negotiations.   725

Well, if you will have it so, I will not refuse.
For, both on my side this will be the safest way
To have some excuse to put forward to your enemies,
And for you it is more certain. You may name the gods.

MEDEA   Swear by the plain of Earth, and Helios, father   730
Of my father, and name together all the gods . . .

AIGEUS   That I will act or not act in what way? Speak.

MEDEA   That you yourself will never cast me from your land,
Nor, if any of my enemies should demand me,
Will you, in your life, willingly hand me over.   735

AIGEUS   I swear by the Earth, by the holy light of Helios,
By all the gods, I will abide by this you say.

MEDEA   Enough. And, if you fail, what shall happen to you?

AIGEUS   What comes to those who have no regard for heaven.

MEDEA   Go on your way. Farewell. For I am satisfied,   740
And I will reach your city as soon as I can,
Having done the deed I have to do and gained my end.

　　　[AIGEUS goes out.]

CHORUS   May Hermes, god of travelers,
Escort you, Aigeus, to your home!
And may you have the things you wish   745
So eagerly; for you
Appear to me to be a generous man.

MEDEA   God, and God's daughter, justice, and light of Helios!
Now, friends, has come the time of my triumph over
My enemies, and now my foot is on the road.   750
Now I am confident they will pay the penalty.
For this man, Aigeus, has been like a harbor to me
In all my plans just where I was most distressed.
To him I can fasten the cable of my safety
When I have reached the town and fortress of Pallas.[6]   755
And now I shall tell to you the whole of my plan.
Listen to these words that are not spoken idly.
I shall send one of my servants to find Jason
And request him to come once more into my sight.
And when he comes, the words I'll say will be soft ones.   760
I'll say that I agree with him, that I approve
The royal wedding he has made, betraying me.
I'll say it was profitable, an excellent idea.
But I shall beg that my children may remain here:
Not that I would leave in a country that hates me   765
Children of mine to feel their enemies' insults,
But that by a trick I may kill the king's daughter.
For I will send the children with gifts in their hands
To carry to the bride, so as not to be banished,—
A finely woven dress and a golden diadem.   770
And if she takes them and wears them upon her skin
She and all who touch the girl will die in agony;

6. Athens, city of Pallas Athena.

Such poison will I lay upon the gifts I send.
But there, however, I must leave that account paid.
I weep to think of what a deed I have to do   775
Next after that; for I shall kill my own children.
My children, there is none who can give them safety.
And when I have ruined the whole of Jason's house,
I shall leave the land and flee from the murder of my
Dear children, and I shall have done a dreadful deed.   780
For it is not bearable to be mocked by enemies.
So it must happen. What profit have I in life?
I have no land, no home, no refuge from my pain.
My mistake was made the time I left behind me
My father's house, and trusted the words of a Greek,   785
Who, with heaven's help, will pay me the price for that.
For those children he had from me he will never
See alive again, nor will he on his new bride
Beget another child, for she is to be forced
To die a most terrible death by these my poisons.   790
Let no one think me a weak one, feeble-spirited,
A stay-at-home, but rather just the opposite,
One who can hurt my enemies and help my friends;
For the lives of such persons are most remembered.
CHORUS   Since you have shared the knowledge of your plan with us,   795
I both wish to help you and support the normal
Ways of mankind, and tell you not to do this thing.
MEDEA   I can do no other thing. It is understandable
For you to speak thus. You have not suffered as I have.
CHORUS   But can you have the heart to kill your flesh and blood?   800
MEDEA   Yes, for this is the best way to wound my husband.
CHORUS   And you too. Of women you will be most unhappy.
MEDEA   So it must be. No compromise is possible.
        [*She turns to the* NURSE.]
    Go, you, at once, and tell Jason to come to me.
    You I employ on all affairs of greatest trust.   805
    Say nothing of these decisions which I have made,
    If you love your mistress, if you were born a woman.
CHORUS   From of old the children of Erechtheus[7] are
    Splendid, the sons of blessed gods. They dwell
    In Athens' holy and unconquered land,[8]   810
    Where famous Wisdom feeds them and they pass gaily
    Always through that most brilliant air where once, they say,
    That golden Harmony gave birth to the nine
    Pure Muses of Pieria.[9]

7. An early king of Athens, a son of Hephaestus.   8. It was the Athenians' boast that their descent from the original settlers was uninterrupted by an invasion. There is a topical reference here, for the play was produced in 431 B.C.E., in a time of imminent war.   9. A fountain in Boeotia where the Muses were supposed to live. The sentence means that the fortunate balance ("Harmony") of the elements and the genius of the people produced the cultivation of the arts ("the nine Pure Muses").

And beside the sweet flow of Cephisos' stream,   815
Where Cypris[1] sailed, they say, to draw the water,
And mild soft breezes breathed along her path,
And on her hair were flung the sweet-smelling garlands
Of flowers of roses by the Lovers, the companions
Of Wisdom, her escort, the helpers of men   820
In every kind of excellence.

How then can these holy rivers
Or this holy land love you,
Or the city find you a home,
You, who will kill your children,   825
You, not pure with the rest?
O think of the blow at your children
And think of the blood that you shed.
O, over and over I beg you,
By your knees[2] I beg you do not   830
Be the murderess of your babes!
O where will you find the courage
Or the skill of hand and heart,
When you set yourself to attempt
A deed so dreadful to do?   835
How, when you look upon them,
Can you tearlessly hold the decision
For murder? You will not be able,
When your children fall down and implore you,
You will not be able to dip   840
Steadfast your hand in their blood.
        [Enter JASON with attendants.]
JASON   I have come at your request. Indeed, although you are
Bitter against me, this you shall have: I will listen
To what new thing you want, woman, to get from me.
MEDEA   Jason, I beg you to be forgiving towards me   845
For what I said. It is natural for you to bear with
My temper, since we have had much love together.
I have talked with myself about this and I have
Reproached myself. "Fool" I said, "why am I so mad?
Why am I set against those who have planned wisely?   850
Why make myself an enemy of the authorities
And of my husband, who does the best thing for me
By marrying royalty and having children who
Will be as brothers to my own? What is wrong with me?
Let me give up anger, for the gods are kind to me.   855
Have I not children, and do I not know that we
In exile from our country must be short of friends?"
When I considered this I saw that I had shown

1. The goddess of love and, therefore, of the principle of fertility. Cephisos is an Athenian river.   2.
Because clasping the other person's knees was a formal gesture of supplication, the knees could be invoked
to add force to entreaties.

Great lack of sense, and that my anger was foolish.
Now I agree with you. I think that you are wise   860
In having this other wife as well as me, and I
Was mad. I should have helped you in these plans of yours,
Have joined in the wedding, stood by the marriage bed,
Have taken pleasure in attendance on your bride.
But we women are what we are,—perhaps a little   865
Worthless; and you men must not be like us in this,
Nor be foolish in return when we are foolish.
Now I give in, and admit that then I was wrong.
I have come to a better understanding now.
　　　[*She turns towards the house.*]
Children, come here, my children, come outdoors to us!   870
Welcome your father with me, and say goodbye to him,
And with your mother, who just now was his enemy,
Join again in making friends with him who loves us.
　　　[*Enter the* CHILDREN, *attended by the* TUTOR.]
We have made peace, and all our anger is over.
Take hold of his right hand,—O God, I am thinking   875
Of something which may happen in the secret future.
O children, will you just so, after a long life,
Hold out your loving arms at the grave? O children,
How ready to cry I am, how full of foreboding!
I am ending at last this quarrel with your father,   880
And, look, my soft eyes have suddenly filled with tears.
CHORUS　　And the pale tears have started also in my eyes.
O may the trouble not grow worse than now it is!
JASON　　I approve of what you say. And I cannot blame you
Even for what you said before. It is natural   885
For a woman to be wild with her husband when he
Goes in for secret love. But now your mind has turned
To better reasoning. In the end you have come to
The right decision, like the clever woman you are.
And of you, children, your father is taking care.   890
He has made, with God's help, ample provision for you.
For I think that a time will come when you will be
The leading people in Corinth with your brothers.
You must grow up. As to the future, your father
And those of the gods who love him will deal with that.   895
I want to see you, when you have become young men,
Healthy and strong, better men than my enemies.
Medea, why are your eyes all wet with pale tears?
Why is your cheek so white and turned away from me?
Are not these words of mine pleasing for you to hear?   900
MEDEA　　It is nothing. I was thinking about these children.
JASON　　You must be cheerful. I shall look after them well.
MEDEA　　I will be. It is not that I distrust your words,
　　But a woman is a frail thing, prone to crying.
JASON　　But why then should you grieve so much for these children?   905
MEDEA　　I am their mother. When you prayed that they might live

I felt unhappy to think that these things will be.
But come, I have said something of the things I meant
To say to you, and now I will tell you the rest.
Since it is the king's will to banish me from here,—   910
And for me too I know that this is the best thing,
Not to be in your way by living here or in
The king's way, since they think me ill-disposed to them,—
I then am going into exile from this land;
But do you, so that you may have the care of them,   915
Beg Kreon that the children may not be banished.
JASON   I doubt if I'll succeed, but still I'll attempt it.
MEDEA   Then you must tell your wife to beg from her father
That the children may be reprieved from banishment.
JASON   I will, and with her I shall certainly succeed.   920
MEDEA   If she is like the rest of us women, you will.
And I too will take a hand with you in this business,
For I will send her some gifts which are far fairer,
I am sure of it, than those which now are in fashion,
A finely-woven dress and a golden diadem,   925
And the children shall present them. Quick, let one of you
Servants bring here to me that beautiful dress.
    [*One of her attendants goes into the house.*]
She will be happy not in one way, but in a hundred,
Having so fine a man as you to share her bed,
And with this beautiful dress which Helios of old,   930
My father's father, bestowed on his descendants.
    [*Enter attendant carrying the poisoned dress and diadem.*]
There, children, take these wedding presents in your hands.
Take them to the royal princess, the happy bride,
And give them to her. She will not think little of them.
JASON   No, don't be foolish, and empty your hands of these.   935
Do you think the palace is short of dresses to wear?
Do you think there is no gold there? Keep them, don't give them
Away. If my wife considers me of any value,
She will think more of me than money, I am sure of it.
MEDEA   No, let me have my way. They say the gods themselves   940
Are moved by gifts, and gold does more with men than words.
Hers is the luck, her fortune that which god blesses;
She is young and a princess; but for my children's reprieve
I would give my very life, and not gold only.
Go children, go together to that rich palace,   945
Be suppliants to the new wife of your father,
My lady, beg her not to let you be banished.
And give her the dress,—for this is of great importance,
That she should take the gift into her hand from yours.
Go, quick as you can. And bring your mother good news   950
By your success of those things which she longs to gain.
    [JASON *goes out with his attendants, followed by the* TUTOR *and the* CHIL-
    DREN *carrying the poisoned gifts.*]
CHORUS   Now there is no hope left for the children's lives.

Now there is none. They are walking already to murder.
The bride, poor bride, will accept the curse of the gold,
Will accept the bright diadem. 955
Around her yellow hair she will set that dress
Of death with her own hands.
The grace and the perfume and glow of the golden robe
Will charm her to put them upon her and wear the wreath,
And now her wedding will be with the dead below, 960
Into such a trap she will fall,
Poor thing, into such a fate of death and never
Escape from under that curse.
You too, O wretched bridegroom, making your match with kings,
You do not see that you bring 965
Destruction on your children and on her,
Your wife, a fearful death.
Poor soul, what a fall is yours!

In your grief too I weep, mother of little children,
You who will murder your own, 970
In vengeance for the loss of married love
Which Jason has betrayed
As he lives with another wife.
    [*Enter the* TUTOR *with the* CHILDREN.]
TUTOR   Mistress, I tell you that these children are reprieved,
And the royal bride has been pleased to take in her hands 975
Your gifts. In that quarter the children are secure.
But come,
Why do you stand confused when you are fortunate?
Why have you turned round with your cheek away from me?
Are not these words of mine pleasing for you to hear? 980
MEDEA   Oh! I am lost!
TUTOR   That word is not in harmony with my tidings.
MEDEA   I am lost, I am lost!
TUTOR   Am I in ignorance telling you
Of some disaster, and not the good news I thought?
MEDEA   You have told what you have told. I do not blame you. 985
TUTOR   Why then this downcast eye, and this weeping of tears?
MEDEA   Oh, I am forced to weep, old man. The gods and I,
I in a kind of madness have contrived all this.
TUTOR   Courage! You too will be brought home by your children.
MEDEA   Ah, before that happens I shall bring others home. 990
TUTOR   Others before you have been parted from their children.
Mortals must bear in resignation their ill luck.
MEDEA   That is what I shall do. But go inside the house,
And do for the children your usual daily work.
    [*The* TUTOR *goes into the house.* MEDEA *turns to her* CHILDREN.]
O children, O my children, you have a city, 995
You have a home, and you can leave me behind you,
And without your mother you may live there for ever.
But I am going in exile to another land

Before I have seen you happy and taken pleasure in you,
Before I have dressed your brides and made your marriage beds   1000
And held up the torch at the ceremony of wedding.
Oh, what a wretch I am in this my self-willed thought!
What was the purpose, children, for which I reared you?
For all my travail and wearing myself away?
They were sterile, those pains I had in the bearing of you.   1005
O surely once the hopes in you I had, poor me,
Were high ones: you would look after me in old age,
And when I died would deck me well with your own hands;
A thing which all would have done. O but now it is gone,
That lovely thought. For, once I am left without you,   1010
Sad will be the life I'll lead and sorrowful for me.
And you will never see your mother again with
Your dear eyes, gone to another mode of living.
Why, children, do you look upon me with your eyes?
Why do you smile so sweetly that last smile of all?   1015
Oh, Oh, what can I do? My spirit has gone from me,
Friends, when I saw that bright look in the children's eyes.
I cannot bear to do it. I renounce my plans
I had before. I'll take my children away from
This land. Why should I hurt their father with the pain   1020
They feel, and suffer twice as much of pain myself?
No, no, I will not do it. I renounce my plans.
Ah, what is wrong with me? Do I want to let go
My enemies unhurt and be laughed at for it?
I must face this thing. Oh, but what a weak woman   1025
Even to admit to my mind these soft arguments.
Children, go into the house. And he whom law forbids
To stand in attendance at my sacrifices,
Let him see to it. I shall not mar my handiwork.
Oh! Oh!   1030
Do not, O my heart, you must not do these things!
Poor heart, let them go, have pity upon the children.
If they live with you in Athens they will cheer you.
No! By Hell's avenging furies it shall not be,—
This shall never be, that I should suffer my children   1035
To be the prey of my enemies' insolence.
Every way is it fixed. The bride will not escape.
No, the diadem is now upon her head, and she,
The royal princess, is dying in the dress, I know it.
But,—for it is the most dreadful of roads for me   1040
To tread, and them I shall send on a more dreadful still—
I wish to speak to the children.
    [*She calls the* CHILDREN *to her.*]
                        Come, children, give
Me your hands, give your mother your hands to kiss them.
O the dear hands, and O how dear are these lips to me,
And the generous eyes and the bearing of my children!   1045
I wish you happiness, but not here in this world.

What is here your father took. O how good to hold you!
How delicate the skin, how sweet the breath of children!
Go, go! I am no longer able, no longer
To look upon you. I am overcome by sorrow.   1050
    [*The* CHILDREN *go into the house.*]
I know indeed what evil I intend to do,
But stronger than all my afterthoughts is my fury,
Fury that brings upon mortals the greatest evils.
    [*She goes out to the right, towards the royal palace.*]
CHORUS   Often before
   I have gone through more subtle reasons,   1055
   And have come upon questionings greater
   Than a woman should strive to search out.
   But we too have a goddess to help us
   And accompany us into wisdom.
   Not all of us. Still you will find   1060
   Among many women a few,
   And our sex is not without learning.
This I say, that those who have never
Had children, who know nothing of it,
In happiness have the advantage   1065
Over those who are parents.
The childless, who never discover
Whether children turn out as a good thing
Or as something to cause pain, are spared
Many troubles in lacking this knowledge.   1070
And those who have in their homes
The sweet presence of children, I see that their lives
Are all wasted away by their worries.
First they must think how to bring them up well and
How to leave them something to live on.   1075
And then after this whether all their toil
Is for those who will turn out good or bad,
Is still an unanswered question.
And of one more trouble, the last of all,
That is common to mortals I tell.   1080
For suppose you have found them enough for their living,
Suppose that the children have grown into youth
And have turned out good, still, if God so wills it,
Death will away with your children's bodies,
And carry them off into Hades.   1085
What is our profit, then, that for the sake of
Children the gods should pile upon mortals
After all else
This most terrible grief of all?
    [*Enter* MEDEA, *from the spectators' right.*]
MEDEA   Friends, I can tell you that for long I have waited   1090
For the event. I stare towards the place from where
The news will come. And now, see one of Jason's servants
Is on his way here, and that labored breath of his

Shows he has tidings for us, and evil tidings.

[*Enter, also from the right, the* MESSENGER.]

MESSENGER Medea, you who have done such a dreadful thing,   1095
So outrageous, run for your life, take what you can,
A ship to bear you hence or chariot on land.

MEDEA And what is the reason deserves such flight as this?

MESSENGER She is dead, only just now, the royal princess,
And Kreon dead too, her father, by your poisons.   1100

MEDEA The finest words you have spoken. Now and hereafter
I shall count you among my benefactors and friends.

MESSENGER What! Are you right in the mind? Are you not mad,
Woman? The house of the king is outraged by you.
Do you enjoy it? Not afraid of such doings?   1105

MEDEA To what you say I on my side have something too
To say in answer. Do not be in a hurry, friend,
But speak. How did they die? You will delight me twice
As much again if you say they died in agony.

MESSENGER When those two children, born of you, had entered in,   1110
Their father with them, and passed into the bride's house,
We were pleased, we slaves who were distressed by your wrongs.
All through the house we were talking of but one thing,
How you and your husband had made up your quarrel.
Some kissed the children's hands and some their yellow hair,   1115
And I myself was so full of my joy that I
Followed the children into the women's quarters.
Our mistress, whom we honor now instead of you,
Before she noticed that your two children were there,
Was keeping her eye fixed eagerly on Jason.   1120
Afterwards however she covered up her eyes,
Her cheek paled and she turned herself away from him,
So disgusted was she at the children's coming there.
But your husband tried to end the girl's bad temper,
And said "You must not look unkindly on your friends.   1125
Cease to be angry. Turn your head to me again.
Have as your friends the same ones as your husband has.
And take these gifts, and beg your father to reprieve
These children from their exile. Do it for my sake."
She, when she saw the dress, could not restrain herself.   1130
She agreed with all her husband said, and before
He and the children had gone far from the palace,
She took the gorgeous robe and dressed herself in it,
And put the golden crown around her curly locks,
And arranged the set of the hair in a shining mirror,   1135
And smiled at the lifeless image of herself in it.
Then she rose from her chair and walked about the room,
With her gleaming feet stepping most soft and delicate,
All overjoyed with the present. Often and often
She would stretch her foot out straight and look along it.   1140
But after that it was a fearful thing to see.
The color of her face changed, and she staggered back,

She ran, and her legs trembled, and she only just
Managed to reach a chair without falling flat down.
An aged woman servant who, I take it, thought   1145
This was some seizure of Pan[3] or another god,
Cried out "God bless us," but that was before she saw
The white foam breaking through her lips and her rolling
The pupils of her eyes and her face all bloodless.
Then she raised a different cry from that "God bless us,"   1150
A huge shriek, and the women ran, one to the king,
One to the newly wedded husband to tell him
What had happened to his bride; and with frequent sound
The whole of the palace rang as they went running.
One walking quickly round the course of a race-track   1155
Would now have turned the bend and be close to the goal,
When she, poor girl, opened her shut and speechless eye,
And with a terrible groan she came to herself.
For a two-fold pain was moving up against her.
The wreath of gold that was resting around her head,   1160
Let forth a fearful stream of all-devouring fire,
And the finely-woven dress your children gave to her,
Was fastening on the unhappy girl's fine flesh.
She leapt up from the chair, and all on fire she ran,
Shaking her hair now this way and now that, trying   1165
To hurl the diadem away; but fixedly
The gold preserved its grip, and, when she shook her hair,
Then more and twice as fiercely the fire blazed out.
Till, beaten by her fate, she fell down to the ground,
Hard to be recognized except by a parent.   1170
Neither the setting of her eyes was plain to see,
Nor the shapeliness of her face. From the top of
Her head there oozed out blood and fire mixed together.
Like the drops on pine-bark, so the flesh from her bones
Dropped away, torn by the hidden fang of the poison.   1175
It was a fearful sight; and terror held us all
From touching the corpse. We had learned from what had happened.
But her wretched father, knowing nothing of the event,
Came suddenly to the house, and fell upon the corpse,
And at once cried out and folded his arms about her,   1180
And kissed her and spoke to her, saying, "O my poor child,
What heavenly power has so shamefully destroyed you?
And who has set me here like an ancient sepulchre,
Deprived of you? O let me die with you, my child!"
And when he had made an end of his wailing and crying,   1185
Then the old man wished to raise himself to his feet;
But, as the ivy clings to the twigs of the laurel,
So he stuck to the fine dress, and he struggled fearfully.

---

3. As the god of wild nature he was supposed to be the source of the sudden, apparently causeless terror that solitude in wild surroundings may produce and hence of all kinds of sudden madness (compare the English word *panic*).

For he was trying to lift himself to his knee,
And she was pulling him down, and when he tugged hard   1190
He would be ripping his aged flesh from his bones.
At last his life was quenched and the unhappy man
Gave up the ghost, no longer could hold up his head.
There they lie close, the daughter and the old father,
Dead bodies, an event he prayed for in his tears.   1195
As for your interests, I will say nothing of them,
For you will find your own escape from punishment.
Our human life I think and have thought a shadow,
And I do not fear to say that those who are held
Wise amongst men and who search the reasons of things   1200
Are those who bring the most sorrow on themselves.
For of mortals there is no one who is happy.
If wealth flows in upon one, one may be perhaps
Luckier than one's neighbor, but still not happy.
      [*Exit.*]
CHORUS   Heaven, it seems, on this day has fastened many   1205
   Evils on Jason, and Jason has deserved them.
   Poor girl, the daughter of Kreon, how I pity you
   And your misfortunes, you who have gone quite away
   To the house of Hades because of marrying Jason.
MEDEA   Women, my task is fixed: as quickly as I may   1210
   To kill my children, and start away from this land,
   And not, by wasting time, to suffer my children
   To be slain by another hand less kindly to them.
   Force every way will have it they must die, and since
   This must be so, then I, their mother, shall kill them.   1215
   O arm yourself in steel, my heart! Do not hang back
   From doing this fearful and necessary wrong.
   O come, my hand, poor wretched hand, and take the sword,
   Take it, step forward to this bitter starting point,
   And do not be a coward, do not think of them,   1220
   How sweet they are, and how you are their mother. Just for
   This one short day be forgetful of your children,
   Afterwards weep; for even though you will kill them,
   They were very dear,—O, I am an unhappy woman!
      [*With a cry she rushes into the house.*]
CHORUS   O Earth, and the far shining   1225
   Ray of the sun, look down, look down upon
   This poor lost woman, look, before she raises
   The hand of murder against her flesh and blood.
   Yours was the golden birth from which
   She sprang, and now I fear divine   1230
   Blood may be shed by men.
   O heavenly light, hold back her hand,
   Check her, and drive from out the house
   The bloody Fury raised by fiends of Hell.
   Vain waste, your care of children;   1235
   Was it in vain you bore the babes you loved,

After you passed the inhospitable strait
Between the dark blue rocks, Symplegades?
O wretched one, how has it come,
This heavy anger on your heart,   1240
This cruel bloody mind?
For God from mortals asks a stern
Price for the stain of kindred blood
In like disaster falling on their homes.
      [*A cry from one of the* CHILDREN *is heard.*]
CHORUS   Do you hear the cry, do you hear the children's cry?   1245
O you hard heart, O woman fated for evil!
ONE OF THE CHILDREN   [*From within.*]   What can I do and how escape
    my mother's hands?
ONE OF THE CHILDREN   [*From within.*]   O my dear brother, I cannot tell.
    We are lost.
CHORUS   Shall I enter the house? O surely I should   1250
    Defend the children from murder.
A CHILD   [*From within.*]   O help us, in God's name, for now we need
    your help.
    Now, now we are close to it. We are trapped by the sword.
CHORUS   O your heart must have been made of rock or steel,
You who can kill   1255
With your own hand the fruit of your own womb.
Of one alone I have heard, one woman alone
Of those of old who laid her hands on her children,
Ino, sent mad by heaven when the wife of Zeus
Drove her out from her home and made her wander;   1260
And because of the wicked shedding of blood
Of her own children she threw
Herself, poor wretch, into the sea and stepped away
Over the sea-cliff to die with her two children.
What horror more can be? O women's love,   1265
So full of trouble,
How many evils have you caused already!
      [*Enter* JASON, *with attendants.*]
JASON   You women, standing close in front of this dwelling,
Is she, Medea, she who did this dreadful deed,
Still in the house, or has she run away in flight?   1270
For she will have to hide herself beneath the earth,
Or raise herself on wings into the height of air,
If she wishes to escape the royal vengeance.
Does she imagine that, having killed our rulers,
She will herself escape uninjured from this house?   1275
But I am thinking not so much of her as for
The children,—her the king's friends will make to suffer
For what she did. So I have come to save the lives
Of my boys, in case the royal house should harm them
While taking vengeance for their mother's wicked deed.   1280
CHORUS   Jason, if you but knew how deeply you are
Involved in sorrow, you would not have spoken so.

JASON   What is it? That she is planning to kill me also?
CHORUS   Your children are dead, and by their own mother's hand.
JASON   What! This is it? O woman, you have destroyed me.   1285
CHORUS   You must make up your mind your children are no more.
JASON   Where did she kill them? Was it here or in the house?
CHORUS   Open the gates and there you will see them murdered.
JASON   Quick as you can unlock the doors, men, and undo
    The fastenings and let me see this double evil,   1290
    My children dead and her,—O her I will repay.
        [*His attendants rush to the door.* MEDEA *appears above the house in a*
        chariot drawn by dragons. She has the dead bodies of the CHILDREN *with*
        her.]
MEDEA   Why do you batter these gates and try to unbar them,
    Seeking the corpses and for me who did the deed?
    You may cease your trouble, and, if you have need of me,
    Speak, if you wish. You will never touch me with your hand,   1295
    Such a chariot has Helios, my father's father,
    Given me to defend me from my enemies.
JASON   You hateful thing, you woman most utterly loathed
    By the gods and me and by all the race of mankind,
    You who have had the heart to raise a sword against   1300
    Your children, you, their mother, and left me childless,—
    You have done this, and do you still look at the sun
    And at the earth, after these most fearful doings?
    I wish you dead. Now I see it plain, though at that time
    I did not, when I took you from your foreign home   1305
    And brought you to a Greek house, you, an evil thing,
    A traitress to your father and your native land.
    The gods hurled the avenging curse of yours on me.
    For your own brother you slew at your own hearthside,
    And then came aboard that beautiful ship, the Argo.   1310
    And that was your beginning. When you were married
    To me, your husband, and had borne children to me,
    For the sake of pleasure in the bed you killed them.
    There is no Greek woman who would have dared such deeds,
    Out of all those whom I passed over and chose you   1315
    To marry instead, a bitter destructive match,
    A monster not a woman, having a nature
    Wilder than that of Scylla[4] in the Tuscan sea.
    Ah! no, not if I had ten thousand words of shame
    Could I sting you. You are naturally so brazen.   1320
    Go, worker in evil, stained with your children's blood.
    For me remains to cry aloud upon my fate,
    Who will get no pleasure from my newly-wedded love,
    And the boys whom I begot and brought up, never
    Shall I speak to them alive. Oh, my life is over!   1325
MEDEA   Long would be the answer which I might have made to

---

4. A monster located in the strait between Italy and Sicily, who snatched sailors off passing ships and devoured them. See *Odyssey* book XII.

These words of yours, if Zeus the father did not know
How I have treated you and what you did to me.
No, it was not to be that you should scorn my love,
And pleasantly live your life through, laughing at me;   1330
Nor would the princess, nor he who offered the match,
Kreon, drive me away without paying for it.
So now you may call me a monster, if you wish,
Or Scylla housed in the caves of the Tuscan sea
I too, as I had to, have taken hold of your heart.   1335

JASON   You feel the pain yourself. You share in my sorrow.
MEDEA   Yes, and my grief is gain when you cannot mock it.
JASON   O children, what a wicked mother she was to you!
MEDEA   They died from a disease they caught from their father.
JASON   I tell you it was not my hand that destroyed them.   1340
MEDEA   But it was your insolence, and your virgin wedding.
JASON   And just for the sake of that you chose to kill them.
MEDEA   Is love so small a pain, do you think, for a woman?
JASON   For a wise one, certainly. But you are wholly evil.
MEDEA   The children are dead. I say this to make you suffer.   1345
JASON   The children, I think, will bring down curses on you.
MEDEA   The gods know who was the author of this sorrow.
JASON   Yes, the gods know indeed, they know your loathsome heart.
MEDEA   Hate me. But I tire of your barking bitterness.
JASON   And I of yours. It is easier to leave you.   1350
MEDEA   How then? What shall I do? I long to leave you too.
JASON   Give me the bodies to bury and to mourn them.
MEDEA   No, that I will not. I will bury them myself,
    Bearing them to Hera's temple on the promontory;
    So that no enemy may evilly treat them   1355
    By tearing up their grave. In this land of Corinth
    I shall establish a holy feast and sacrifice[5]
    Each year for ever to atone for the blood guilt.
    And I myself go to the land of Erechtheus
    To dwell in Aigeus' house, the son of Pandion.   1360
    While you, as is right, will die without distinction,
    Struck on the head by a piece of the Argo's timber,
    And you will have seen the bitter end of my love.
JASON   May a Fury for the children's sake destroy you,
    And justice, requitor of blood.   1365
MEDEA   What heavenly power lends an ear
    To a breaker of oaths, a deceiver?
JASON   O, I hate you, murderess of children.
MEDEA   Go to your palace. Bury your bride.
JASON   I go, with two children to mourn for.   1370
MEDEA   Not yet do you feel it. Wait for the future.
JASON   Oh, children I loved!
MEDEA   I loved them, you did not.

---

5. Some such ceremony was still performed at Corinth in Euripides' time.

JASON   You loved them, and killed them.
MEDEA   To make you feel pain.
JASON   Oh, wretch that I am, how I long
    To kiss the dear lips of my children!   1375
MEDEA   Now you would speak to them, now you would kiss them.
    Then you rejected them.
JASON   Let me, I beg you,
    Touch my boys' delicate flesh.
MEDEA   I will not. Your words are all wasted.
JASON   O God, do you hear it, this persecution,   1380
    These my sufferings from this hateful
    Woman, this monster, murderess of children?
    Still what I can do that I will do:
    I will lament and cry upon heaven,
    Calling the gods to bear me witness   1385
    How you have killed my boys and prevent me from
    Touching their bodies or giving them burial.
    I wish I had never begot them to see them
    Afterwards slaughtered by you.
CHORUS   Zeus in Olympus is the overseer   1390
    Of many doings. Many things the gods
    Achieve beyond our judgment. What we thought
    Is not confirmed and what we thought not god
    Contrives. And so it happens in this story.

PLATO

429–347 B.C.E.

Socrates began a revolution in Western thought and laid the foundations for philosophy as we know it, but he wrote nothing. We know what we do about him mainly from the writings of his pupil Plato, a philosophical and literary genius of the first rank. It is very difficult to distinguish between what Socrates actually said and what Plato put into his mouth, but there is general agreement that the *Apology* is the clearest picture we have of the historical Socrates. In 399 B.C.E., Socrates was put on trial for impiety and "corrupting the youth" of Athens. The *Apology*—the Greek word means "defense speech" and unlike the English word carries no admission of wrongdoing—is Plato's version of the speech Socrates gave at his trial. In it, Socrates does what he so often challenged others to do: he gives an account of himself and of the questioning, thought, and conversation to which he devoted his life. More than a simple rebuttal of the charges, the speech is an eloquent statement of the value of the life of philosophy (literally, "love of wisdom"), and of why the most important thing we can do with our lives is the care of the soul.

Only five years before Socrates' trial, the Peloponnesian War ended in Athens' defeat. The victorious Spartans abolished the democracy and installed a repressive dictatorial regime dominated by thirty Athenians of oligarchic sympathies. "The Thirty," as they came to be known, were overthrown eight months later and a democratic constitution was reinstituted. Some members of the Thirty, as well as other prominent Athenians who had or were suspected of antidemocratic leanings, were associates of Socrates. His trial may well have been part of the reaction against the Thirty, especially since one of his main accusers, Anytus, was a leader of the restored democracy.

If there was a political motive in the background, the reason for his trial given by Socrates in the *Apology* is also surely right: he unsettled and angered a lot of people. He would approach them with deceptively simple questions to which they thought they knew the answers. "What is piety?" "What is rhetoric, and is it an art?" "Can goodness be taught, or is it something we are just born with?" Through a process of question and answer that is still known as the Socratic method, he would get them to admit that they were wrong, that their certainties did not stand up to scrutiny, and that they did not know what they thought they knew. To have one's ignorance exposed and one's assumptions about the world shaken can provide a profoundly educational shock. It can also be infuriating. Many people probably found it easier to silence Socrates than to rethink their values and ideas.

The *Apology* shows why Socrates had to die and why that death was unjust. It is a defiant speech; Socrates rides roughshod over legal forms and seems to neglect no opportunity of outraging his listeners. But this defiance is not stupidity (as he hints himself, he could, if he had wished, have made a speech to please the court), nor is it a deliberate courting of martyrdom. It is the only course possible for him in the circumstances if he is not to betray his life's work, for Socrates knows as well as his accusers that what the Athenians really want is to silence him without having to take his life. What Socrates is making clear is that there is no such easy way out; he will have no part of any compromise that would restrict his freedom of speech or undermine his moral position. The speech is a sample of what the Athenians will have to put up with if they allow him to live; he will continue to be the gadfly that stings the sluggish horse. He will go on persuading them not to be concerned for their persons or their property but first and chiefly to care about the improvement of the soul. He has spent his life denying the validity of worldly standards, and he will not accept them now. To do so would be, as he says, to allow his enemies to harm him.

He was declared guilty and condemned to death. Though influential friends offered means of escape (and there is reason to think the Athenians would have been glad to see him go), Socrates refused to disobey the laws; in any case he had already, in his court speech, rejected the possibility of living in some foreign city.

The sentence was duly carried out. And in Plato's account of the execution in the *Phaedo*, we can see the calmness and kindness of a man who has led a useful life and who is secure in his faith that, contrary to appearances, "no evil can happen to a good man, either in life or after death."

The form of the *Apology* is dramatic: Plato re-creates the personality of his beloved teacher by presenting him as speaking directly to the reader. In most of the many books that he wrote in the course of a long life, Plato continued to feature Socrates as the principal speaker in philosophical dialogues that explored the ethical and political problems of the age. These dialogues (the *Republic* the most famous) were preserved in their entirety and have exerted an enormous influence on Western thought ever since. Plato also founded a philosophical school, the Academy, in 385 B.C.E., and it remained active as a center of philosophical training and research until it was suppressed by the Roman emperor Justinian in 529 C.E. Plato came from an aristocratic Athenian family and as a young man thought of a political career; the execution of Socrates by the courts of democratic Athens disgusted him with politics and prompted his famous remark that there was no hope for the cities until the rulers became philosophers or the philosophers, rulers. His own attempts to influence real rulers—the tyrant Dionysius of Syracuse in Sicily and, later, his son—ended in failure, however.

restoration. You remember, then, what sort of man Chaerephon was, how intense he was in whatever he set out to do. Well, on one occasion in particular he went to Delphi and dared to ask the oracle—as I said, please don't create an uproar, gentlemen—he asked, exactly as I'm telling you, whether anyone was wiser than myself. The Pythia[5] drew forth the response that no one is wiser. His brother here will testify to you about it, since Chaerephon himself is dead.

Please consider my purpose in telling you this, since I'm about to explain to you where the slander against me has come from. You see, when I heard these things, I thought to myself as follows: "What can the god be saying? What does his riddle mean? For I'm only too aware that I've no claim to being wise in anything either great or small. What can he mean, then, by saying that I'm wisest? Surely he can't be lying: that isn't lawful[6] for him."

For a long time I was perplexed about what he meant. Then, very reluctantly, I proceeded to examine it in the following sort of way. I approached one of the people thought to be wise, assuming that in his company, if anywhere, I could refute the pronouncement and say to the oracle, "Here's someone wiser than I, yet you said I was wisest."

Then I examined this person—there's no need for me to mention him by name; he was one of our politicians. And when I examined him and talked with him, men of Athens, my experience was something like this: I thought this man seemed wise to many people, and especially to himself, but wasn't. Then I tried to show him that he thought himself wise, but wasn't. As a result, he came to dislike me, and so did many of the people present. For my part, I thought to myself as I left, "I'm wiser than that person. For it's likely that neither of us knows anything fine and good, but he thinks he knows something he doesn't know, whereas I, since I don't in fact know, don't think that I do either. At any rate, it seems that I'm wiser than he in just this one small way: that what I don't know, I don't think I know." Next, I approached another man, one of those thought to be wiser than the first, and it seemed to me that the same thing occurred, and so I came to be disliked by that man too, as well as by many others.

After that, then, I kept approaching one person after another. I realized, with distress and alarm, that I was arousing hostility. Nevertheless, I thought I must attach the greatest importance to what pertained to the god. So, in seeking what the oracle meant, I had to go to all those with any reputation for knowledge. And, by the dog,[7] men of Athens—for I'm obliged to tell the truth before you—I really did experience something like this: in my investigation in response to the god, I found that, where wisdom is concerned, those who had the best reputations were practically the most deficient, whereas men who were thought to be their inferiors were much better off. Accordingly, I must present all my wanderings to you as if they were labors of some sort that I undertook in order to prove the oracle utterly irrefutable.

---

5. The priestess in Apollo's temple at Delphi who uttered the god's prophecies.　6. That is, according to the order of the world and the gods' nature. One way Apollo avoided lying was to give notoriously obscure or ambiguous oracles.　7. A euphemistic oath (compare "by George").

You see, after the politicians, I approached the poets—tragic, dithyrambic,[8] and the rest—thinking that in their company I'd catch myself in the very act of being more ignorant than they. So I examined the poems with which they seemed to me to have taken the most trouble and questioned them about what they meant, in order that I might also learn something from them at the same time.

Well, I'm embarrassed to tell you the truth, gentlemen, but nevertheless it must be told. In a word, almost all the people present could have discussed these poems better than their authors themselves. And so, in the case of the poets as well, I soon realized it wasn't wisdom that enabled them to compose their poems, but some sort of natural inspiration, of just the sort you find in seers and soothsayers.[9] For these people, too, say many fine things, but know nothing of what they speak about. The poets also seemed to me to be in this sort of situation. At the same time, I realized that, because of their poetry, they thought themselves to be the wisest of people about the other things as well when they weren't. So I left their company, too, thinking that I had gotten the better of them in the very same way as of the politicians.

Finally, I approached the craftsmen. You see, I was conscious of knowing practically nothing myself, but I knew I'd discover that they, at least, would know many fine things. And I wasn't wrong about this. On the contrary, they did know things that I didn't know, and in that respect they were wiser than I. But, men of Athens, the good craftsmen also seemed to me to have the very same flaw as the poets: because he performed his own craft well, each of them also thought himself to be wisest about the other things, the most important ones; and this error of theirs seemed to overshadow their wisdom. So I asked myself on behalf of the oracle whether I'd prefer to be as I am, not in any way wise with their wisdom nor ignorant with their ignorance, or to have both qualities as they did. And the answer I gave to myself, and to the oracle, was that it profited me more to be just the way I was.

From this examination, men of Athens, much hostility has arisen against me of a sort that is harshest and most onerous. This has resulted in many slanders, including that reputation I mentioned of being "wise." You see, the people present on each occasion think that I'm wise about the subjects on which I examine others. But in fact, gentlemen, it's pretty certainly the god who is really wise, and by his oracle he meant that human wisdom is worth little or nothing. And it seems that when he refers to the Socrates here before you and uses my name, he makes me an example, as if he were to say, "That one among you is wisest, mortals, who, like Socrates, has recognized that he's truly worthless where wisdom's concerned."

So even now I continue to investigate these things and to examine, in response to the god, any person, citizen, or foreigner I believe to be wise. Whenever he seems not to be so to me, I come to the assistance of the god and show him that he's not wise. Because of this occupation. I've had no leisure worth talking about for either the city's affairs or my own domestic ones; rather, I live in extreme poverty because of my service to the god.

---

8. The dithyramb was a short performance by a chorus at a public festival, produced, like tragedy, at state expense.   9. For a fuller exposition of this famous theory of poetic inspiration, see Plato's *Ion*.

In addition to these factors, the young people who follow me around of their own accord, those who have the most leisure, the sons of the very rich, enjoy listening to people being cross-examined. They often imitate me themselves and in turn attempt to cross-examine others. Next, I imagine they find an abundance of people who think they possess some knowledge, but in fact know little or nothing. The result is that those they question are angry not at themselves, but at me, and say that Socrates is a thoroughly pestilential fellow who corrupts the young. Then, when they're asked what he's doing or teaching, they've nothing to say, as they don't know. Yet, so as not to appear at a loss, they utter the stock phrases used against all who philosophize: "things in the sky and beneath the earth," and "not acknowledging the gods," and "making the weaker argument the stronger." For they wouldn't be willing to tell the truth, I imagine: that it has become manifest they pretend to know, but know nothing. So, seeing that these people are, I imagine, ambitious, vehement, and numerous, and have been speaking earnestly and persuasively about me, they've long been filling your ears with vehement slanders. On the basis of these slanders, Meletus has brought his charges against me, and Anytus and Lycon along with him: Meletus is aggrieved on behalf of the poets, Anytus on behalf of the artisans and politicians, and Lycon on behalf of the orators. So, as I began by saying, I'd be amazed if I could rid your minds of this slander in the brief time available, when there's so much of it in them.

There, men of Athens, is the truth for you. I've spoken it without concealing or glossing over anything, whether great or small. And yet I pretty much know that I make enemies by doing these very thing. And that's further evidence that I'm right—that this is the prejudice against me and these its causes. Whether you investigate these matters now or later, you'll find it to be so.

Enough, then, for my defense before you against the charges brought by my first accusers. Next, I'll try to defend myself against Meletus—who is, he claims, both good and patriotic—and against my later accusers. Once again, then, just as if they were really a different set of accusers, their affidavit must be examined in turn. It goes something like this:

> Socrates is guilty of corrupting the young, and of not acknowledging the gods the city acknowledges, but new daimonic activities[1] instead.

Such, then, is the charge. Let us examine each point in this charge.

Meletus says, then, that I commit injustice by corrupting the young. But I, men of Athens, reply that it's Meletus who is guilty of playing around with serious matters, of lightly bringing people to trial, and of professing to be seriously concerned about things he has never cared about at all—and I'll try to prove this.

Step forward, Meletus, and answer me.[2] You regard it as most important, do you not, that our young people be as good as possible?

1. The precise meaning of the charge is not clear. The Greek words may mean "new divinities," with a reference to Socrates' famous inner voice, which on occasion warned him against action on which he had decided and which he describes later in the speech. Or the words may mean "practicing strange rites." In any case, because the phrase implies religious belief of some sort, it can later be used against Meletus when he loses his head and accuses Socrates of atheism.   2. In Athens there was no office similar to that of our district attorney. Because the accuser also acted as prosecutor, Socrates can examine him as though he were a witness.

I certainly do.

Come, then, and tell these jurors who improves them. Clearly you know, since you care. For having discovered, as you assert, the one who corrupts them—namely, myself—you bring him before these jurors and accuse him. Come, then, speak up, tell the jurors who it is that improves them. Do you see, Meletus, that you remain silent and have nothing to say? Yet don't you think that's shameful and sufficient evidence of exactly what I say, that you care nothing at all? Speak up, my good man. Who improves them?

The laws.

But that's not what I'm asking, my most excellent fellow, but rather which *person*, who knows the laws themselves in the first place, does this?

These gentlemen, Socrates, the jurors.

What are you saying, Meletus? Are they able to educate and improve the young?

Most certainly.

All of them, or some but not others?

All of them.

That's good news, by Hera, and a great abundance of benefactors[3] that you speak of! What, then, about the audience present here? Do they improve the young or not?

Yes, they do so too.

And what about the members of the Council?[4]

Yes, the councilors too.

But, if that's so, Meletus, surely those in the Assembly, the assemblymen, won't corrupt the young, will they? Won't they all improve them too?

Yes, they will too.

But then it seems that all the Athenians except for me make young people fine and good, whereas I alone corrupt them. Is that what you're saying?

Most emphatically, that's what I'm saying.

I find myself, if you're right, in a most unfortunate situation. Now answer me this. Do you think that the same holds of horses? Do people in general improve them, whereas one particular person corrupts them or makes them worse? Or isn't it wholly the opposite: one particular person—or the very few who are horse trainers—is able to improve them, whereas the majority of people, if they have to do with horses and make use of them, make them worse? Isn't that true, Meletus, both of horses and of all other animals? Of course it is, whether you and Anytus say so or not. Indeed, our young people are surely in a very happy situation if only one person corrupts them, whereas all the rest benefit them.

Well then, Meletus, it has been adequately established that you've never given any thought to young people—you've plainly revealed your indifference—and that you care nothing about the issues on which you bring me to trial.

Next, Meletus, tell us, in the name of Zeus, whether it's better to live among good citizens or bad ones. Answer me, sir. Surely, I'm not asking you

3. Probably about five hundred, all male citizens selected by lot. There was no judge in the Athenian law court. Hera was the wife and sister of Zeus, the ruler of the gods. 4. The executive council of the Assembly, comprising five hundred members chosen by lot. The Assembly was the sovereign body under the Athenian constitution; it consisted, at least in theory, of all male Athenian citizens.

anything difficult. Don't bad people do something bad to [whoever's][5] closest to them at the given moment, whereas good people do something good?

Certainly.

Now is there anyone who wishes to be harmed rather than benefited by those around him? Keep answering, my good fellow. For the law requires you to answer. Is there anyone who wishes to be harmed?

Of course not.

Well, then, when you summon me here for corrupting the young and making them worse, do you mean that I do so intentionally or unintentionally?

Intentionally, I say.

What's that, Meletus? Are you so much wiser at your age than I at mine, that you know bad people do something bad to [whoever's] closest to them at the given moment, and good people something good? Am I, by contrast, so very ignorant that I don't know even this: that if I do something bad to an associate, I risk getting back something bad from him in return? And is the result, as you claim, that I do so very bad a thing intentionally?

I'm not convinced by you of that, Meletus, and neither, I think, is anyone else. No, either I'm not corrupting the young or, if I am corrupting them, it's *un*intentionally, so that in either case what you say is false. But if I'm corrupting them unintentionally, the law doesn't require that I be brought to court for such mistakes—that is, unintentional ones—but that I be taken aside for private instruction and admonishment. For it's clear that if I'm instructed, I'll stop doing what I do unintentionally. You, however, avoided associating with me and were unwilling to instruct me. Instead, you bring me here, where the law requires you to bring those in need of punishment, not instruction.

Well, men of Athens, what I said before is absolutely clear by this point, namely, that Meletus has never cared about these matters to any extent, great or small. Nevertheless, please tell us now, Meletus, how is it you say I corrupt the young? Or is it absolutely clear, from the indictment you wrote, that it's by teaching them not to acknowledge the gods the city acknowledges, but new daimonic activities instead? Isn't that what you say I corrupt them by teaching?

I most emphatically do say that.

Then, in the name of those very gods we're now discussing, Meletus, speak yet more clearly, both for my sake and for that of these gentlemen. You see, I'm unable to tell what you mean. Is it that I teach people to acknowledge that some gods exist—so that I, then, acknowledge their existence myself and am not an out-and-out atheist and am not guilty of that—yet not, of course, the very ones acknowledged by the city, but different ones? Is that what you're charging me with, that they're different ones? Or are you saying that I myself don't acknowledge any gods at all, and that that's what I teach to others?

That's what I mean, that you don't acknowledge any gods at all.

You're a strange fellow, Meletus! Why [do] you say that? Do I not even acknowledge that the sun and the moon are gods, then, as other men do?

No, by Zeus, gentlemen of the jury, he doesn't, since he says that the sun's a stone and the moon earth.

---

5. Bracketed words correct the translation, here and throughout.

My dear Meletus, do you think it's Anaxagoras[6] you're accusing? Are you that contemptuous of the jury? Do you think they're so illiterate that they don't know that the books of Anaxagoras of Clazomenae are full of such arguments? And, in particular, do young people learn these views from me, views they can occasionally acquire in the Orchestra[7] for a drachma at most and that they'd ridicule Socrates for pretending were his own—especially as they're so strange? In the name of Zeus, is that really how I seem to you? Do I acknowledge the existence of no god at all?

No indeed, by Zeus, none at all.

You aren't at all convincing, Meletus, not even, it seems to me, to yourself. You see, men of Athens, this fellow seems very arrogant and intemperate to me and to have written this indictment simply out of some sort of arrogance, intemperance, and youthful rashness. Indeed, he seems to have composed a sort of riddle in order to test me: "Will the so-called wise Socrates recognize that I'm playing around and contradicting myself? Or will I fool him along with the other listeners?" You see, he seems to me to be contradicting himself in his indictment, as if he were to say, "Socrates is guilty of not acknowledging gods, but of acknowledging gods." And that's just childish playing around, isn't it?

Please examine with me, gentlemen, why it seems to me that this is what he's saying. And you, Meletus, answer us. But you, gentlemen, please remember what I asked of you at the beginning: don't create an uproar if I make my arguments in my accustomed manner.

Is there anyone, Meletus, who acknowledges that human activities exist but doesn't acknowledge human beings? Make him answer, gentlemen, and don't let him make one protest after another. Is there anyone who doesn't acknowledge horses but does acknowledge equine activities? Or who doesn't acknowledge that musicians exist but does acknowledge musical activities? There's no one, best of men—if you don't want to answer, I must answer for you and for the others here. But at least answer my next question. Is there anyone who acknowledges the existence of daimonic activities but doesn't acknowledge daimons?

No, there isn't.

How good of you to answer, if reluctantly and when compelled to by these gentlemen. Well then, you say that I acknowledge daimonic activities, whether new or familiar, and teach about them. But then, on your account, I do at any rate acknowledge daimonic activities, and to this you've sworn in your indictment against me. However, if I acknowledge daimonic activities, surely it's absolutely necessary that I acknowledge daimons. Isn't that so? Yes, it is—I assume you agree, since you don't answer. But don't we believe that daimons are either gods or, at any rate, children of gods?[8] Yes or no?

Of course.

---

6. Philosopher (ca. 500–428 B.C.E.), born in Asia Minor, and an intimate friend of Pericles who was forced to leave Athens to escape an indictment for impiety. He is famous for his doctrine that matter was set in motion and ordered by Intelligence, which, however, did not create it. In Plato's *Phaedo*, Socrates says that he was attracted to this doctrine in his youth but criticizes Anaxagoras's views.   7. Evidently part of the *agora*, or marketplace. This passage is usually taken as one of the earliest references to a book trade in ancient Greece.   8. *Daimones* in Greek could range from lesser divinities outside the pantheon of Olympian gods to heroic mortals divinized after death to the general "divinity" when one felt the agency of some unidentified god behind an event. All these senses seem to underlie Socrates' words.

Then, if indeed I do believe in daimons, as you're saying, and if daimons are gods of some sort, that's precisely what I meant when I said that you're presenting us with a riddle and playing around: you're saying that I don't believe in gods and, on the contrary, that I do believe in gods, since in fact I do at least believe in daimons. But if, on the other hand, daimons are children of gods, some sort of bastard offspring of a nymph, or of whomever else tradition says each one is the child, what man could possibly believe that children of gods exist, but not gods? That would be just as unreasonable as believing in the children of horses and asses—namely, mules—while not believing in the existence of horses and asses.

Well then, Meletus, you must have written these things to test us or because you were at a loss about what genuine injustice to charge me with. There's no conceivable way you could persuade any man with even the slightest intelligence that the same person believes in both daimonic activities and gods, and, on the contrary, that this same person believes neither in daimons, nor in gods, nor in heroes.

In fact, then, men of Athens, it doesn't seem to me to require a long defense to show that I'm not guilty of the charges in Meletus' indictment, but what I've said is sufficient. But what I was also saying earlier, that much hostility has arisen against me and among many people—you may be sure that's true. And *it's* what will convict me, if I am convicted: not Meletus or Anytus, but the slander and malice of many people. It has certainly convicted many other good men as well, and I imagine it will do so again. There's no danger it will stop with me.

But perhaps someone may say, "Aren't you ashamed, Socrates, to have engaged in the sort of occupation that has now put you at risk of death?" I, however, would be right to reply to him, "You're not thinking straight, sir, if you think that a man who's any use at all should give any opposing weight to the risk of living or dying, instead of looking to this alone whenever he does anything: whether his actions are just or unjust, the deeds of a good or bad man. You see, on your account, all those demigods who died on the plain of Troy were inferior people, especially the son of Thetis,[9] who was so contemptuous of danger when the alternative was something shameful. When he was eager to kill Hector,[1] his mother, since she was a goddess, spoke to him, I think, in some such words as these: 'My child, if you avenge the death of your friend Patroclus and slay Hector, you will die yourself immediately,' so the poem goes, 'as your death is fated to follow next after Hector's.' But though he heard that, he was contemptuous of death and danger, for he was far more afraid of living as a bad man and of failing to avenge his friends: 'Let me die immediately, then,' it continues, 'once I've given the wrongdoer his just deserts, so that I do not remain here by the curved ships, a laughingstock and a burden upon the earth.' Do you really suppose he gave a thought to death or danger?"

You see, men of Athens, this is the truth of the matter: Wherever someone has stationed himself because he thinks it best, or wherever he's been stationed by his commander, there, it seems to me, he should remain, steadfast in danger, taking no account at all of death or of anything else, in compari-

---

9. Achilles. Thetis was a sea nymph. See *Iliad* XVIII.100 ff.   1. The greatest of the Trojan warriors and eldest son of the king of Troy.

son to what's shameful. I'd therefore have been acting scandalously, men of Athens, if, when I'd been stationed in Potidea, Amphipolis, or Delium[2] by the leaders you had elected to lead me, I had, like many another, remained where they'd stationed me and run the risk of death. But if, when the god stationed me here, as I became thoroughly convinced he did, to live practicing philosophy, examining myself and others, I had—for fear of death or anything else—abandoned my station.

That would have been scandalous, and someone might have rightly and justly brought me to court for not acknowledging that gods exist, by disobeying the oracle, fearing death, and thinking I was wise when I wasn't. You see, fearing death, gentlemen, is nothing other than thinking one is wise when one isn't, since it's thinking one knows what one doesn't know. I mean, no one knows whether death may not be the greatest of all goods for people, but they fear it as if they knew for certain that it's the worst thing of all. Yet surely this is the most blameworthy ignorance of thinking one knows what one doesn't know. But I, gentlemen, may perhaps differ from most people by just this much in this matter too. And if I really were to claim to be wiser than anyone in any way, it would be in this: that as I don't have adequate knowledge about things in Hades, so too I don't think that I have knowledge. To act unjustly, on the other hand, to disobey someone better than oneself, whether god or man, that I do know to be bad and shameful. In any case, I'll never fear or avoid things that may for all I know be good more than things I know are bad.

Suppose, then, you're prepared to let me go now and to disobey Anytus, who said I shouldn't have been brought to court at all but that since I had been brought to court, you had no alternative but to put me to death[3] because, as he stated before you, if I were acquitted, soon your sons would all be entirely corrupted by following Socrates' teachings. Suppose, confronted with that claim, you were to say to me, "Socrates, we will not obey Anytus this time. Instead, we are prepared to let you go. But on the following condition: that you spend no more time on this investigation and don't practice philosophy, and if you're caught doing so, you'll die." Well, as I just said, if you were to let me go on these terms, I'd reply to you, "I've the utmost respect and affection for you, men of Athens, but I'll obey the god rather than you, and as long as I draw breath and am able, I won't give up practicing philosophy, exhorting you and also showing the way to any of you I ever happen to meet, saying just the sorts of things I'm accustomed to say:

> My excellent man, you're an Athenian, you belong to the greatest city, renowned for its wisdom and strength; are you not ashamed that you take care to acquire as much wealth as possible—and reputation and honor—but that about wisdom and truth, about how your soul may be in the best possible condition, you take neither care nor thought?

2. Three battles of the Peloponnesian War in which Socrates had fought as an infantryman—at Potidaea (in northern Greece), in 432 B.C.E.; at Amphipolis (in northern Greece), of uncertain date; and at Delium (in central Greece), in 424 B.C.E. For a fuller account of Socrates' conduct at Potidaea and Delium, see Plato's *Symposium.*   3. The translator (in a note) suggests that Anytus assumed that Socrates would go into exile to avoid trial. Another way to understand the passage (which is perhaps more consistent with the Greek) is that Anytus argued against acquittal and implied that death was the only possible penalty upon conviction (a good rhetorical tactic).

against you. And though the orators were ready to lay information against me and have me summarily arrested, and you were shouting and urging them on. I thought that I should face danger on the side of law and justice, rather than go along with you for fear of imprisonment or death when your proposals were unjust.

This happened when the city was still under democratic rule. But later, when the oligarchy[7] had come to power, it happened once more. The Thirty summoned me and four others to the Tholus and ordered us to arrest Leon of Salamis[8] and bring him from Salamis to die. They gave many such orders to many other people too, of course, since they wanted to implicate as many as possible in their crimes. On *that* occasion, however, I showed once again not by words but by deeds that I couldn't care less about death—if that isn't putting it too bluntly—but that all I care about is not doing anything unjust or impious. You see, that government, powerful though it was, didn't frighten me into unjust action: when we came out of the Tholus, the other four went to Salamis and arrested Leon, whereas I left and went home. I might have died for that if the government hadn't fallen shortly afterward.

There are many witnesses who will testify before you about these events.

Do you imagine, then, that I'd have survived all these years if I'd been regularly active in public affairs, and had come to the aid of justice like a good man, and regarded that as most important, as one should? Far from it, men of Athens, and neither would any other man. But throughout my entire life, in any public activities I may have engaged in, it was evident I was the sort of person—and in private life I was the same—who never agreed to anything with anyone contrary to justice, whether with others or with those whom my slanderers say are my students. In fact, I've never been anyone's teacher at any time. But if anyone, whether young or old, wanted to listen to me while I was talking and performing my own task, I never begrudged that to him. Neither do I engage in conversation only when I receive a fee and not when I don't. Rather, I offer myself for questioning to rich and poor alike, or, if someone prefers, he may listen to me and answer my questions. And if any one of these turned out well, or did not do so, I can't justly be held responsible, since I never at any time promised any of them that they'd learn anything from me or that I'd teach them. And if anyone says that he learned something from me or heard something in private that all the others didn't also hear, you may be sure he isn't telling the truth.

Why, then, you may ask, do some people enjoy spending so much time with me? You've heard the answer, men of Athens. I told you the whole truth: it's because they enjoy listening to people being examined who think they're wise but aren't. For it's not unpleasant. In my case, however, it's something, you may take it from me, I've been ordered to do by the god, both in oracles and dreams, and in every other way that divine providence ever ordered any man to do anything at all.

---

7. The Thirty, who came to power in 404 B.C.E. with Spartan backing and ruled for eight months. They included some men who had been associated with Socrates and influenced by him (especially Critias, a relative of Plato). Socrates is careful to give an instance of his opposition to the oligarchy to balance that of his opposition to an action by the democracy.   8. An island off the Piraeus (Athens' harbor), Athenian territory. The Tholus was a circular building in the *agora* in which the Prytaneis held their meetings and ate their meals. Leon is otherwise unknown; the Thirty arrested a number of affluent citizens, whose property they confiscated.

All these things, men of Athens, are both true and easily tested. I mean, if I really do corrupt the young or have corrupted them in the past, surely if any of them had recognized when they became older that I'd given them bad advice at some point in their youth, they'd now have come forward themselves to accuse me and seek redress. Or else, if they weren't willing to come themselves, some of their family members—fathers, brothers, or other relatives—if indeed their kinsmen had suffered any harm from me—would remember it now and seek redress.

In any case, I see many of these people present here: first of all, there's Crito, my contemporary and fellow demesman,[9] the father of Critobulus here; then there's Lysanius of Sphettus, father of Aeschines here; next, there's Epigenes' father, Antiphon of Cephisia here. Then there are others whose brothers have spent time in this way: Nicostratus, son of Theozotides, Brother of Theodotus—by the way, Theodotus is dead, so that Nicostratus is at any rate not being held back by him; and Paralius here, son of Demodocus, whose brother was Theages; and there's Adeimantus, the son of Ariston, whose brother is Plato here,[1] and Aeantodorus, whose brother here is Apollodorus. And there are many others I could mention, some of whom Meletus most certainly ought to have called as witnesses in the course of his own speech. If he forgot to do so, let him call them now—I yield time to him. Let him tell us if he has any such witness. No, it's entirely the opposite, gentlemen. You'll find that they're all prepared to come to my aid, their corruptor, the one who, Meletus and Anytus claim, is doing harm to their families. Of course, the corrupted ones themselves might indeed have reason to come to my aid. But the *uncorrupted* ones, their relatives, who are older men now, what reason could they possibly have to support me, other than the right and just one: that they know perfectly well that Meletus is lying, whereas I am telling the truth?

Well then, gentlemen, those, and perhaps other similar things, are pretty much all I have to say in my defense. But perhaps one of you might be resentful when he recalls his own behavior. Perhaps when he was contesting even a lesser charge than this charge, he positively entreated the jurors with copious tears, bringing forward his children and many other relatives and friends as well, in order to arouse as much pity as possible. And then he finds that I'll do none of these things, not even when I'm facing what might be considered the ultimate danger. Perhaps someone with these thoughts might feel more willful where I'm concerned and, made angry by these very same thoughts, cast his vote in anger.[2] Well, if there's someone like that among you—of course, I don't expect there to be, but *if* there is—I think it appropriate for me to answer him as follows: "I do indeed have relatives, my excellent man. As Homer puts it, I too 'wasn't born from oak or from rock'[3] but from human parents. And so I do have relatives, sons too, men of Athens, three of them, one already a young man while two are still children.

9. Resident of the same deme, a precinct of Attica (Athens' territory) and the local unit of government. Crito was a friend of Socrates who later tried to persuade him to escape from prison. 1. Plato is subtly claiming eyewitness authority for the version of Socrates' speech he gives in the *Apology*. 2. The accepted ending of the speech for the defense was an unrestrained appeal to the pity of the jury. Socrates' refusal to make it is another shock to the prejudices of the audience. 3. Penelope says to her husband, Odysseus (who is disguised as a beggar), "Tell me who you are. Where do you come from? You've hardly sprung from a rock or oak like some old man of legend" (*Odyssey* XIX.183–84).

Nonetheless, I won't bring any of them forward here and then entreat you to vote for my acquittal."

Why, you may ask, will I do none of these things? Not because I'm willful, men of Athens or want to dishonor you—whether I'm boldly facing death or not is a separate story. The point has to do with reputation—yours and mine and that of the entire city: it doesn't seem noble to me to do these things, especially at my age and with my reputation—for whether truly or falsely, it's firmly believed in any case that Socrates is superior to the majority of people in some way. Therefore, if those of *you* who are believed to be superior—either in wisdom or courage or any other virtue whatever—behave like that, it would be shameful.

I've often seen people of this sort when they're on trial: they're thought to be someone, yet they do astonishing things—as if they imagined they'd suffer something terrible if they died and would be immortal if only you didn't kill them. People like that seem to me to bring such shame to the city that any foreigner might well suppose that those among the Athenians who are superior in virtue—the ones they select from among themselves for political office and other positions of honor—are no better than women. I say this, men of Athens, because none of us who are in any way whatever thought to be someone should behave like that, nor, if we attempt to do so, should you allow it. On the contrary, you should make it clear you're far more likely to convict someone who makes the city despicable by staging these pathetic scenes than someone who minds his behavior.

Reputation aside, gentlemen, it doesn't seem just to me to entreat the jury—nor to be acquitted by entreating it—but rather to inform it and persuade it. After all, a juror doesn't sit in order to grant justice as a favor, but to decide where justice lies. And he has sworn on oath not that he'll favor whomever he pleases, but that he'll judge according to law. We shouldn't accustom you to breaking your oath, then, nor should you become accustomed to doing so—neither of us would be doing something holy if we did. Hence don't expect me, men of Athens, to act toward you in ways I consider to be neither noble, nor just, nor pious—most especially, by Zeus, when I'm being prosecuted for *impiety* by Meletus here. You see, if I tried to persuade and to force you by entreaties, after you've sworn an oath, I clearly would be teaching you not to believe in the existence of gods, and my defense would literally convict me of not acknowledging gods. But that's far from being the case: I do acknowledge them, men of Athens, as none of my accusers does. I turn it over to you and to the god to judge me in whatever way will be best for me and for yourselves.[4]

There are many reasons, men of Athens, why I'm not resentful at this outcome—that you voted to convict me—and this outcome wasn't unexpected by me. I'm much more surprised at the number of votes cast on each side: I didn't think that the decision would be by so few votes but by a great many. Yet now, it seems, that if a mere thirty votes had been cast differently,

4. This is the end of the defense speech proper. It appears from what Socrates says later that the jury was split, 280 to 220, in reaching a verdict of guilty. The jury must now choose between the penalty proposed by the prosecution and the one offered by the defense. Socrates must propose the lightest sentence he thinks he can get away with, but one heavy enough to satisfy the majority of the jury who voted to convict him. The prosecution probably expects him to propose exile from Athens, but Socrates surprises them.

I'd have been acquitted. Or rather, it seems to me that where Meletus is concerned I've been acquitted even as things stand. And not merely acquitted. On the contrary, one thing at least is clear to everyone: if Anytus had not come forward with Lycon to accuse me, Meletus would have been fined a thousand drachmas, since he wouldn't have received a fifth of the votes.[5]

But be that as it may, the man demands the death penalty for me. Well then, what counterpenalty should I now propose to you, men of Athens? Or is it clear that it's whatever I deserve? What then should it be? What do I deserve to suffer or pay just because I didn't mind my own business throughout my life? Because I didn't care about the things most people care about—making money, managing an estate, or being a general, a popular leader, or holding some other political office, or joining the cabals and factions that come to exist in a city—but thought myself too honest, in truth, to engage in these things and survive? Because I didn't engage in things, if engaging in them was going to benefit neither you nor myself, but instead went to each of you privately and tried to perform what I claim is the greatest benefaction? That was what I did. I tried to persuade each of you to care first not about any of his possessions, but about himself and how he'll become best and wisest; and not primarily about the city's possessions, but about the city itself; and to care about all other things in the same way.

What, then, do I deserve to suffer for being such a man? Something good, men of Athens, if I'm indeed to propose a penalty that I truly deserve. Yes, and the sort of good thing, too, that would be appropriate for me. What, then, is appropriate for a poor man who is a public benefactor and needs to have the leisure to exhort you? Nothing could be more appropriate, men of Athens, than for such a man to be given free meals in the Prytaneum[6]—much more so for him, at any rate, than for anyone of you who has won a victory at Olympia, whether with a single horse or with a pair or a team of four. You see, he makes you think you're happy, whereas I make you actually happy. Besides, he doesn't need to be sustained in that way, but I do need it. So if, as justice demands, I must propose a penalty I deserve, that's the penalty I propose: free meals in the Prytaneum.

Now perhaps when I say this, you may think I'm speaking in a quite willful manner—just as when I talked about appeals to pity and supplications. That's not so, men of Athens, rather it's something like this: I'm convinced that I never intentionally do injustice to any man—but I can't get you to share my conviction, because we've talked together a short time. I say this, because if you had a law, as other men in fact do, not to try a capital charge in a single day, but over several,[7] I think you'd be convinced. But as things stand, it isn't easy to clear myself of huge slanders in a short time.

Since I'm convinced that I've done injustice to no one, however, I'm certainly not likely to do myself injustice, to announce that I deserve something bad and to propose a penalty of that sort for myself. Why should I do that? In order not to suffer what Meletus proposes as a penalty for me when I say

5. Socrates jokingly divides the votes against him into three parts, one for each of his three accusers, and suggests that Meletus's votes fall below the minimum needed to justify the trial. To discourage frivolous lawsuits, in such cases the accuser was fined.   6. A building near the *agora* that housed the city's communal hearth; there the Prytaneis, as representatives of the city, entertained distinguished visitors, winners in the athletic contests at Olympia, and those who had done exceptional service to Athens (or in some cases their descendants). To be given free meals in the Prytaneum for life was an enormous honor.   7. There was such a law in Sparta.

that I don't know whether it's a good or a bad thing? As an alternative to that, am I then to choose one of the things I know very well to be bad and propose it? Imprisonment, for example? And why should I live in prison, enslaved to the regularly appointed officers, the Eleven?[8] All right, a fine with imprisonment until I pay? But in my case the effect would be precisely the one I just now described, since I haven't the means to pay.

Well then, should I propose exile? Perhaps that's what *you'd* propose for me. But I'd certainly have to have an excessive love of life, men of Athens, to be so irrational as to do that. I see that you, my fellow citizens, were unable to tolerate my discourses and discussions but came to find them so burdensome and odious that you're now seeking to get rid of them. Is it likely, then, that I'll infer that others will find them easy to bear? Far from it, men of Athens. It would be a fine life for me, indeed, a man of my age,[9] to go into exile and spend his life exchanging one city for another, because he's always being expelled. You see, I well know that wherever I go, the young will come to hear me speaking, just as they do here. And if I drive them away, they will themselves persuade their elders to expel me; whereas if I don't drive them away, their fathers and relatives will expel me because of these same young people.

Now perhaps someone may say, "But by keeping quiet and minding your own business, Socrates, wouldn't it be possible for you to live in exile for us?" This is the very hardest point on which to convince some of you. You see, if I say that to do *that* would be to disobey the god, and that this is why I can't mind my own business you won't believe me, since you'll suppose I'm being ironical. But again, if I say it's the greatest good for a man to discuss virtue every day, and the other things you've heard me discussing and examining myself and others about, on the grounds that the unexamined life isn't worth living for a human being, you'll believe me even less when I say that. But in fact, things are just as I claim them to be, men of Athens, though it isn't easy to convince you of them. At the same time, I'm not accustomed to thinking that I deserve anything bad. If I had the means, I'd have proposed a fine of as much as I could afford to pay, since that would have done me no harm at all. But as things stand, I don't have them—unless you want me to propose as much as I'm in fact able to pay. Perhaps I could pay you about a mina of silver.[1] So I propose a fine of that amount.

One moment, men of Athens. Plato here, and Crito, Critobulus, and Apollodorus as well, are urging me to propose thirty minas and saying that they themselves will guarantee it. I propose a fine of that amount, therefore, and these men will be sufficient guarantors to you of the silver.[2]

For the sake of a little time, men of Athens, you're going to earn from those who wish to denigrate our city both the reputation and the blame for having killed Socrates—that wise man. For those who wish to reproach you will, of course, claim that I'm wise, even if I'm not. In any case, if you'd waited a short time, this would have happened of its own accord. You, of course, see

---

8. A committee that had charge of prisons and public executions.   9. Seventy years old.   1. No. small sum. In Aristotle's time (4th century B.C.E.), one mina was recognized as a fair ransom for a prisoner of war.   2. The jury decides for death. In the following section, Socrates makes a final statement to the court.

my age, you see that I'm already far along in life and close to death. I'm saying this not to all of you, but to those who voted for the death penalty. And to those same people I also say this: Perhaps you imagine, gentlemen, that I was convicted for lack of the sort of arguments I could have used to convince you, if I'd thought I should do or say anything to escape the penalty. Far from it. I *have* been convicted for a lack—not of arguments, however, but of boldfaced shamelessness and for being unwilling to say the sorts of things to you you'd have been most pleased to hear, with me weeping and wailing, and doing and saying many other things I claim are unworthy of me, but that are the very sorts of things you're used to hearing from everyone else. No, I didn't think then that I should do anything servile because of the danger I faced, and so I don't regret now that I defended myself as I did. I'd far rather die after such a defense than live like that.

You see, whether in a trial or in a war, neither I nor anyone else should contrive to escape death at all costs. In battle, too, it often becomes clear that one might escape death by throwing down one's weapons and turning to supplicate one's pursuers. And in each sort of danger there are many other ways one can contrive to escape death, if one is shameless enough to do or say anything. The difficult thing, gentlemen, isn't escaping death; escaping villainy is much more difficult, since it runs faster than death. And now I, slow and old as I am, have been overtaken by the slower runner while my accusers, clever and sharp-witted as they are, have been overtaken by the faster one—vice. And now I take my leave, convicted by you of a capital crime, whereas they stand forever convicted by the truth of wickedness and injustice. And just as I accept my penalty, so must they. Perhaps, things *had* to turn out this way, and I suppose it's good they have.

Next, I want to make a prophecy to those who convicted me. Indeed, I'm now at the point at which men prophesy most—when they're about to die. I say to you men who condemned me to death that as soon as I'm dead vengeance will come upon you, and it will be much harsher, by Zeus, than the vengeance you take in killing me. You did this now in the belief that you'll escape giving an account of your lives. But I say that quite the opposite will happen to you. There will be more people to test you, whom I now restrain, though you didn't notice my doing so. And they'll be all the harsher on you, since they're younger, and you'll resent it all the more. You see, if you imagine that by killing people you'll prevent anyone from reproaching you for not living in the right way, you're not thinking straight. In fact, to escape is neither possible nor noble. On the contrary, what's best and easiest isn't to put down other people, but to prepare oneself to be the best one can. With that prophecy to those of you who voted to convict me, I take my leave.

However, I'd gladly discuss this result with those who voted for my acquittal while the officers of the court are busy and I'm not yet on my way to the place where I must die. Please stay with me, gentlemen, just for that short time. After all, there's nothing to prevent us from having a talk with one another while it's still in our power. To you whom I regard as friends I'm willing to show the meaning of what has just now happened to me. You see, gentlemen of the jury—for in calling *you* "jurors" I no doubt use the term correctly—an amazing thing has happened to me. In previous times, the usual prophecies of my daimonic sign were always very frequent, opposing

lished the world's first research library. At the Lyceum he and his pupils carried on research in zoology, botany, biology, physics, political science, ethics, logic, music, and mathematics. He left Athens when Alexander died in Babylon (323 B.C.E.) and the Athenians, for a while, were able to demonstrate their hatred of Macedon and everything connected with it; he died a year later.

The scope of his written work, philosophical and scientific, is immense. Even more than Plato, Aristotle has exerted a decisive influence on the Western philosophical and intellectual traditions. He is represented here by some excerpts from the *Poetics*, the first systematic work of literary criticism in the West, and one that has played a central role in shaping the theory and production of literature there.

From Poetics[1]

* * * Thus, Tragedy is an imitation of an action that is serious, complete, and possessing magnitude; in embellished language, each kind of which is used separately in the different parts; in the mode of action and not narrated; and effecting through pity and fear [what we call] the *catharsis*[2] of such emotions. By "embellished language" I mean language having rhythm and melody, and by "separately in different parts" I mean that some parts of a play are carried on solely in metrical speech while others again are sung.

The Constituent Parts of Tragedy

Since the imitation is carried out in the dramatic mode by the personages themselves, it necessarily follows, first, that the arrangement of Spectacle will be a part of tragedy, and next, that Melody and Language will be parts, since these are the media in which they effect the imitation. By "language" I mean precisely the composition of the verses, by "melody" only that which is perfectly obvious. And since tragedy is the imitation of an action and is enacted by men in action, these persons must necessarily possess certain qualities of Character and Thought, since these are the basis for our ascribing qualities to the actions themselves—character and thought are two natural causes of actions—and it is in their actions that men universally meet with success or failure. The imitation of the action is the Plot. By plot I here mean the combination of the events; Character is that in virtue of which we say that the personages are of such and such a quality; and Thought is present in everything in their utterances that aims to prove a point or that expresses an opinion. Necessarily, therefore, there are in tragedy as a whole, considered as a special form, six constituent elements, viz. Plot, Character, Language, Thought, Spectacle, and Melody. Of these elements, two [Language

---

1. Translated by James Hutton, who has added for clarity.   2. This is probably the most disputed passage in the Western critical tradition. There are two main schools of interpretation, which differ in their understanding of the bracketed text word *catharsis*. Some critics take it to mean "purification," implying a metaphor from the religious process of purification from guilt; the passions are "purified" by the tragic performance because the excitement of these passions by the performance weakens them and reduces them to just proportions in the individual. This theory was supported by the German critic G. E. Lessing. Others take the metaphor to be medical, reading the word as "purging" and interpreting the phrase to mean that the tragic performance excites the emotions only to allay them, thereby ridding the spectator of the disquieting emotions from which he or she suffers in everyday life. Tragedy thus has a therapeutic effect.

and Melody] are the *media* in which they effect the imitation, one [Specta-cle] is the *manner,* and three [Plot, Character, Thought] are the *objects* they imitate; and besides these there are no other parts. So then they employ these six forms, not just some of them so to speak; for every drama has spec-tacle, character, plot, language, melody, and thought in the same sense, but the most important of them is the organization of the events [the plot].

Plot and Character

For tragedy is not an imitation of men but of actions and of life. It is in action that happiness and unhappiness are found, and the end[3] we aim at is a kind of activity, not a quality; in accordance with their characters men are of such and such a quality, in accordance with their actions they are fortu-nate or the reverse. Consequently, it is not for the purpose of presenting their characters that the agents engage in action, but rather it is for the sake of their actions that they take on the characters they have. Thus, what happens—that is, the plot—is the end for which a tragedy exists, and the end or purpose is the most important thing of all. What is more, without action there could not be a tragedy, but there could be without characteriza-tion. * * *

Now that the parts are established, let us next discuss what qualities the plot should have, since plot is the primary and most important part of tragedy. I have posited that tragedy is an imitation of an action that is a whole and complete in itself and of a certain magnitude—for a thing may be a whole, and yet have no magnitude to speak of. Now a thing is a whole if it has a beginning, a middle, and an end. A beginning is that which does not come necessarily after something else, but after which it is natural for another thing to exist or come to be. An end, on the contrary, is that which naturally comes after something else, either as its necessary sequel or as its usual [and hence probable] sequel, but itself has nothing after it. A middle is that which both comes after something else and has another thing following it. A well-constructed plot, therefore, will neither begin at some chance point nor end at some chance point, but will observe the principles here stated. * * *

Contrary to what some people think, a plot is not ipso facto a unity if it revolves about one man. Many things, indeed an endless number of things, happen to any one man some of which do not go together to form a unity, and similarly among the actions one man performs there are many that do not go together to produce a single unified action. Those poets seem all to have erred, therefore, who have composed a *Heracleid,* a *Theseid,* and other such poems, it being their idea evidently that since Heracles was one man, their plot was bound to be unified. * * *

From what has already been said, it will be evident that the poet's function is not to report things that have happened, but rather to tell of such things as might happen, things that are possibilities by virtue of being in them-selves inevitable or probable. Thus the difference between the historian and the poet is not that the historian employs prose and the poet verse—the work of Herodotus[4] could be put into verse, and it would be no less a history

3. Purpose.   4. Historian of the Persian Wars (ca. 480–430/425? B.C.E.).

with verses than without them; rather the difference is that the one tells of things that have been and the other of such things as might be. Poetry, therefore, is a more philosophical and a higher thing than history, in that poetry tends rather to express the universal, history rather the particular fact. A universal is: The sort of thing that (in the circumstances) a certain kind of person will say or do either probably or necessarily, which in fact is the universal that poetry aims for (with the addition of names for the persons); a particular, on the other hand is: What Alcibiades[5] did or had done to him. * * *

Among plots and actions of the simple type, the episodic form is the worst. I call episodic a plot in which the episodes follow one another in no probable or inevitable sequence. Plots of this kind are constructed by bad poets on their own account, and by good poets on account of the actors; since they are composing entries for a competitive exhibition, they stretch the plot beyond what it can bear and are often compelled, therefore, to dislocate the natural order. * * *

Some plots are simple, others complex; indeed the actions of which the plots are imitation are at once so differentiated to begin with. Assuming the action to be continuous and unified, as already defined, I call that action simple in which the change of fortune takes place without a reversal or recognition, and that action complex in which the change of fortune involves a recognition or a reversal or both. These events [recognitions and reversals] ought to be so rooted in the very structure of the plot that they follow from the preceding events as their inevitable or probable outcome; for there is a vast difference between following from and merely following after. * * *

Reversal (Peripety) is, as aforesaid, a change from one state of affairs to its exact opposite, and this, too, as I say, should be in conformance with probability or necessity. For example, in *Oedipus,* the messenger[6] comes to cheer Oedipus by relieving him of fear with regard to his mother, but by revealing his true identity, does just the opposite of this. * * *

Recognition, as the word itself indicates, is a change from ignorance to knowledge, leading either to friendship or to hostility on the part of those persons who are marked for good fortune or bad. The best form of recognition is that which is accompanied by a reversal, as in the example from *Oedipus.* * * *

Next in order after the points I have just dealt with, it would seem necessary to specify what one should aim at and what avoid in the construction of plots, and what it is that will produce the effect proper to tragedy.

Now since in the finest kind of tragedy the structure should be complex and not simple, and since it should also be a representation of terrible and piteous events (that being the special mark of this type of imitation), in the first place, it is evident that good men ought not to be shown passing from prosperity to misfortune, for this does not inspire either pity or fear, but only revulsion; nor evil men rising from ill fortune to prosperity, for this is the most untragic plot of all—it lacks every requirement, in that it neither elicits human sympathy nor stirs pity or fear. And again, neither should an

---

5. A brilliant but unscrupulous Athenian statesman (ca. 450–404 B.C.E.).   6. The Corinthian herdsman, in Sophocles' *Oedipus the King.*

extremely wicked man be seen falling from prosperity into misfortune, for a plot so constructed might indeed call forth human sympathy, but would not excite pity or fear, since the first is felt for a person whose misfortune is undeserved and the second for someone like ourselves—pity for the man suffering undeservedly, fear for the man like ourselves—and hence neither pity nor fear would be aroused in this case. We are left with the man whose place is between these extremes. Such is the man who on the one hand is not pre-eminent in virtue and justice, and yet on the other hand does not fall into misfortune through vice or depravity, but falls because of some mistake;[7] one among the number of the highly renowned and prosperous, such as Oedipus and Thyestes[8] and other famous men from families like theirs.

It follows that the plot which achieves excellence will necessarily be single in outcome and not, as some contend, double, and will consist in a change of fortune, not from misfortune to prosperity, but the opposite from prosperity to misfortune, occasioned not by depravity, but by some great mistake on the part of one who is either such as I have described or better than this rather than worse. (What actually has taken place confirms this; for though at first the poets accepted whatever myths came to hand, today the finest tragedies are founded upon the stories of only a few houses, being concerned, for example, with Alcmeon, Oedipus, Orestes, Meleager, Thyestes, Telephus, and such others as have chanced to suffer terrible things or to do them.) So, then, tragedy having this construction is the finest kind of tragedy from an artistic point of view. And consequently, those persons fall into the same error who bring it as a charge against Euripides that this is what he does in his tragedies and that most of his plays have unhappy endings. For this is in fact the right procedure, as I have said; and the best proof is that on the stage and in the dramatic contests, plays of this kind seem the most tragic, provided they are successfully worked out, and Euripides, even if in everything else his management is faulty, seems at any rate the most tragic of the poets. * * *

In the characters and the plot construction alike, one must strive for that which is either necessary or probable, so that whatever a character of any kind says or does may be the sort of thing such a character will inevitably or probably say or do and the events of the plot may follow one after another either inevitably or with probability. (Obviously, then, the denouement of the plot should arise from the plot itself and not be brought about "from the machine,' as it is in *Medea* and in the embarkation scene in the *Iliad*.[9] The machine is to be used for matters lying outside the drama, either antecedents of the action which a human being cannot know, or things subsequent to the action that have to be prophesied and announced; for we accept it that the gods see everything. Within the events of the plot itself,

---

7. The Greek word is *hamartia*. It has sometimes been translated as "flaw" (hence the expression "tragic flaw") and thought of as a moral defect, but comparison with Aristotle's use of the word in other contexts suggests strongly that he means by it "mistake" or "error" (of judgment).   8. Brother of Atreus and his rival over the kingship of Argos. Pretending to be reconciled, Atreus gave a feast at which he served Thyestes' own sons to their father. Thyestes' only surviving son, Aegisthus, later helped murder Atreus's son Agamemnon.   9. The reference is to an incident in book II of the *Iliad*: an attempt of the Greek rank and file to return home and abandon the siege is arrested by the intervention of Athena. If it were a drama, she would appear on the *deus es machina* ("god from the machine"), the machine that was employed in the theater to show the gods flying in space. It has come to mean any implausible way of solving complications of the plot. In Euripides' play Medea escapes from Corinth "on the machine" in her magic chariot.

however, there should be nothing unreasonable, or if there is, it should be kept outside the play proper, as is done in the *Oedipus* of Sophocles.) * * *

The chorus in tragedy. The chorus ought to be regarded as one of the actors, and as being part of the whole and integrated into performance, not in Euripides' way but in that of Sophocles. In the other poets, the choral songs have no more relevance to the plot than if they belonged to some other play. And so nowadays, following the practice introduced by Agathon,[1] the chorus merely sings interludes. But what difference is there between the singing of interludes and taking a speech or even an entire episode from one play and inserting it into another?

* * *

---

1. A younger contemporary of Euripides; most of his plays were produced in the 4th century B.C.E.

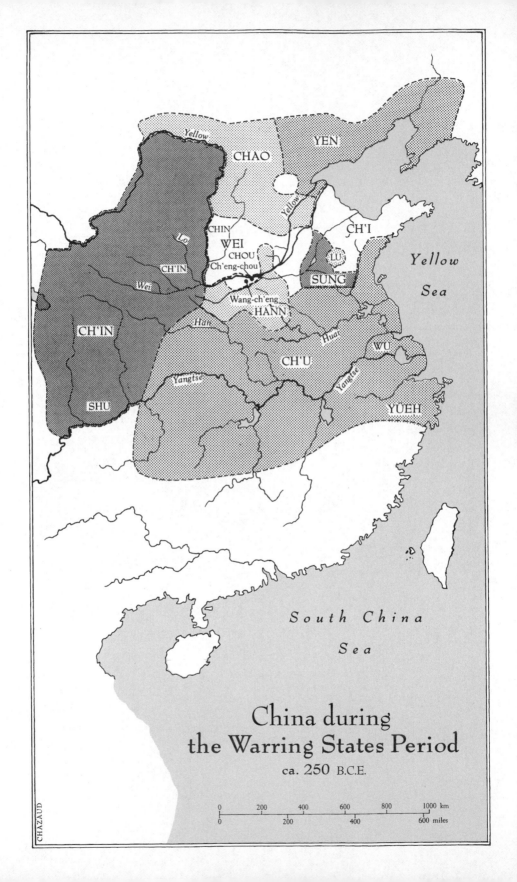

China during
the Warring States Period
ca. 250 B.C.E.

Poetry and Thought
in Early China

Many great civilizations have perished without consequence; they have left vast ruins in deserts and jungles. What we know of them comes from the imaginative reconstructions of scholars, from inscriptions, and from the accounts of early travelers. Other civilizations, like those of ancient Egypt and Mesopotamia, left extensive written records only to be at last swallowed up by other civilizations; the very names by which we refer to them—*Egypt* and *Mesopotamia*—are Greek.

Still other ancient civilizations began long histories that continue to the present; they set patterns and posed questions that shaped the actions and values of their descendants for thousands of years. The writings they produced—continuously read and reinterpreted—served as the binding that gave these civilizations a sense of their unity and continuity. Early in the third century C.E., Ts'ao P'i, the first emperor of the short Wei Dynasty, observed that literary works were "the greatest legacy in governing the kingdom." A writer himself, Ts'ao P'i understood the transience of power, even power well exercised, and he understood that the image of the period preserved in literary works would eventually become—far more than his substantial accomplishments—the "reality" of his age for the future.

In many ways, then, "China" is a literary fiction of cultural and historical unity that eventually became reality by being generally accepted as true. Ancient China covered a vast territory that was inhabited by a diverse people, who spoke a language divided by widely divergent dialects, as well as by many tribes, who spoke their own languages. It might easily have been fragmented, like Europe, by regional interests and linguistic differences. By accepting the writings of ancient China as their own, peoples on the expanding margins of the ancient heartland became "Chinese." Rome was truly an empire, a political center that ruled over many peoples, each with its own sense of distinct identity as a people. Although traditional China is called an empire, regional identity gave way to a belief in cultural unity, a cultural unity that has always sought expression in political unity.

ARCHAIC CHINA

Chinese civilization developed independently from that of the West in the Yellow River basin. Although scholars have noted the possibility of contact with central Asia in the development of its early civilization, China was geographically separated from the earlier Mesopotamian and Indus valley city civilizations and followed its own course. The first historical dynasty was the Shang (ca. 1750–1020 B.C.E.). Although traditional Chinese historians have treated it as a dynasty in the later sense, the Shang seems to have been a loose confederation of city-states ruled by princes who had (or claimed) a common ancestry, one of whom was acknowledged as king. It was during the Shang Dynasty that Chinese writing first developed, and from this period we have inscriptions on tortoiseshells that were used in divination. Throughout its history China retained the use of "characters," rather than changing to an alphabet or syllabary. Some written characters are pictograms (for example, *jih* 日, meaning "sun," from ☉ and some are ideograms (for example, *shang* 上, signifying "above"), but most characters combine an element that indicates the sound and an element, called a "radical," that indicates a conceptual category (for example, *chao* 昭, "shining," consists of the sound element 召 and the radical 日, for "sun"). The fact that written characters remained the same, though they were pronounced differently at different times and in different regions, contributed significantly to the coherence of Chinese civilization.

The end of the second millennium B.C.E. saw the migration of the Chou peoples from the west into the Yellow River heartland and their conquest of the Shang. The Chou were an agrarian people, who traced their descent from Hou Chi, or Lord Millet. The Chou's justification of its conquest set the model for a Chinese polity that was to last for three thousand years. The last rulers of the Shang Dynasty were accused of misrule, of causing such hardship that Heaven grew angry and transferred its "mandate" to the Chou king Wen, whose son, King Wu, completed the overthrow. Such at least were the stories told in the courts of the Chou princes, who were given feudal domains throughout the territory that had once belonged to the Shang Dynasty. They ruled as stewards, responsible to the Chou king, who was in turn only a steward for Heaven.

The idea of Heaven changed through the centuries, and it was never a clearly defined deity: sometimes it was an anthropomorphic divinity, sometimes a natural and moral force, and in this early period, sometimes a collective of ancestral spirits. Power depended on virtuous rule, which in large measure meant holding to the statutes and models of the former kings. These models were preserved in a body of unwritten ritual practice and in a group of early texts: the *Book of Documents,* a collection of royal statements and proclamations from the early Chou; the *Book of Changes,* used for divination; and the *Classic of Poetry,* containing, among other things, hymns to the Chou ancestors and ballads recounting the history of the Chou people. These works, which became the core of the Confucian classics, were attributed to various ancient sages; most modern scholars take them as anonymous.

The belief that virtuous government would ensure continuous power proved tenacious even in the face of political realities that undermined it. After a few prosperous reigns, the Chou Dynasty grew increasingly weak. In 770 B.C.E., under pressure from new warlike tribes pressing in from the north and west, the capital was shifted east, marking the beginning of the period known as the Eastern Chou. A half century later saw the beginning of a court chronicle, called the *Spring and Autumn Annals,* from the feudal state of Lu in east China. The period it covers, from 722 to 466 B.C.E., is thus known as the Spring and Autumn Annals Period.

THE SPRING AND AUTUMN ANNALS AND WARRING STATES PERIODS

The Chou Dynasty proved far more influential in its dissolution than at the height of its dominion. Politically, it was reduced to a tiny sphere surrounded by vigorous states that were still, nominally, its feudal domains. The princes of these states plotted and warred with one another, struggling to reconcile political realities with a nostalgic sense of ceremony and custom. Meanwhile, on the southern and western borders of the old Chou domain, powerful new kingdoms were rising: Ch'u, Wu, and Yüeh in the south and Ch'in in the west. Although many of these new kingdoms developed from autonomous traditions, they gradually absorbed Chou culture, and their rulers often sought to trace their descent either from the Chou royal house or from more ancient north Chinese ancestors (much as European royal families in the Middle Ages and Renaissance often claimed Greek or Trojan ancestry).

The state that most saw itself as the preserver of Chou traditions was the eastern duchy of Lu, the home of Confucius (551–479 B.C.E.). In his collected sayings, the *Analects* (*Lun-yü*), Confucius created a remarkable fusion of ethics and idealized Chou traditions. Although later Confucians credited him with the editorship of the Confucian classics, modern scholars doubt this. Rather he was a teacher of traditional learning, around whom gathered a large group of disciples; the lineages of those disciples preserved through the difficult centuries that followed a version of Chou traditions that lasted until the Han Dynasty, when they were institutionalized.

Although the philosophers that followed Confucius offered compelling alternatives, his union of idealized history and social thought finally won out in the Chinese tradition. The small details of ceremony and decorum were accepted as outer forms of a social order in which respect for others came naturally. In the context of the times, it was a heroic position: it promised a dignity in one's actions that could stubbornly resist a world in which expediency increasingly ruled. One story tells of a disciple of Confucius who, about to be executed, asked the archers to wait a moment so that he could straighten his cap.

The early wars between the feudal domains were ceremonious affairs. The nobility rode in chariots and engaged in single combat. Battles seem to have involved more display than bloodshed, and often one side, recognizing the superior force of the enemy, would simply withdraw. As technology improved and allegiance to Chou traditions declined, wars among the domains became increasingly destructive. Early in the Spring and Autumn Annals Period small regions were ruled by aristocratic families, and their officers were chosen from lesser clans. By the fifth century B.C.E. these domains were evolving into centralized states, with bureaucracies whose primary loyalty was not to their families but to the prince. Chinese historians have called this period the Warring States.

Political upheaval precipitated intellectual upheaval. Various rival schools of thought appeared, most offering a political program meant to appeal to competing princes. The followers of the philosopher Mo-tzu (second half of the fifth century B.C.E.) preached an austere utilitarianism. Seeing that warfare, like Confucian ceremony, was wasteful, they became inventive technicians, developing means of defense against military aggression.

The overriding Confucian concern with government and social life inevitably produced extreme reactions. Some schools were interested more in the individual than in the polity. The most remarkable figure among such thinkers was Chuang Chou (fourth century B.C.E.), who was concerned almost exclusively with the life of the mind, and his writings return to the theme of the relativity of perception and value. Chuang Chou is often grouped with the shadowy figure Lao-tzu as an ancestor of Taoism. Lao-tzu's name is attached to a collection of poems from the late Warring States Period that advocate passivity and following the Way, the natural course of things.

In that same century the Confucian tradition was eloquently represented by Mencius. He held that the innate goodness of human nature was warped only by circumstance and that good government would permit the natural goodness of men and women to show itself once again. But the age clearly favored those who believed not in moral influence and self-cultivation but in increasing outward control. Arguing against Mencius, Hsün-tzu (third century B.C.E.) chose to view learning and Confucian ethics as a means to govern the human creature, otherwise driven by passions and appetites.

Hsün-tzu's vision of human nature and his fascination with control influenced the writings of Han Fei (died 233 B.C.E.). Han Fei, who belonged to a long Chinese tradition of writers on statecraft, composed treatises outlining a policy of rigid state control to strengthen his own tiny state of Han. The treatises did little for his own realm but found particular favor in the western kingdom of Ch'in, which already had a long tradition of authoritarian control. Those who followed the teachings of Han Fei's school came to be known as Legalists for their belief that the state depended on its subjects' absolute adherence to its laws and policies. Among the other states, Ch'in had a reputation for ruthlessness and untrustworthiness, but Ch'in's armies— well disciplined, well equipped, and well supplied—had steadily increased the size of the kingdom and, by the middle of the third century B.C.E., were driving west and south, overwhelming all rivals.

CH'IN AND HAN

As the ancient Mediterranean world is brought to a symbolic close by the fall of Rome, ancient China may be said to end in 221 B.C.E., with the establishment of a unified empire under Emperor Ch'in Shih-huang. Ch'in Shih-huang's draconian megalomania became legendary in later Chinese history, exerting as much fascination as horror. Though much of his statecraft was subtle, many of his most famous policies had a chilling simplicity. Some, such as unifying the currency and the script, deserve credit. But his solution to intellectual disagreement was to burn the books of all schools but those of the Legalists, whom he favored, and his solution to regional loyalties toward the old states was massive deportation. The final victory of Confucian traditionalism in the Han Dynasty was, in no small part, a reaction against Ch'in Shih-huang's disregard for all traditions and norms of humane behavior.

Ch'in's greatest enemy had been the large southern state of Ch'u. Like Ch'in, it had been steadily expanding at the expense of its neighbors and had spread along both sides of the Yangtse River. Though long within the north Chinese cultural sphere, Ch'u had rather different traditions from its neighbors, and it also had the strongest regional consciousness of any of the states. After its conquest by Ch'in, a folk rhyme circulated in Ch'u: "Though only three households be left in Ch'u, / The destroyer of Ch'in will surely be Ch'u." After Ch'in Shih-huang's death, rebellions broke out everywhere, and the Ch'u rebel Hsiang Yü defeated the major Ch'in armies. The last decade of the third century B.C.E. saw not only the destruction of Ch'in but also Hsiang Yü's struggle with a rival Ch'u army led by Liu Pang. Ultimately, Liu Pang was victorious and founded a new dynasty, the Han.

Ch'in survived less than twenty years; the Han Dynasty lasted more than four hundred. The imperial house of Liu (in Chinese the surname comes first), having inherited a unified empire and benefited from Ch'in's destruction of the old aristocracy, learned the lesson of flexibility. Some emperors tightened central control and others loosened it, but none attempted the absolute exercise of imperial will that Ch'in Shih-huang had assumed. The Liu patronized Taoism, shamanistic cults, and Confucianism, freely mixing adherence to traditions with policies that served state interest. With an eye to the reigning emperor and to the example of Ch'in, the Confucians liked to invoke the model of Chou, of rule that depends on the goodwill of those ruled. The Western term *China* names the civilization after Ch'in, but ever thereafter the Chinese have referred to themselves as the "people of Han."

PRONOUNCING GLOSSARY

The following list uses common English syllables to provide rough equivalents of selected words whose pronunciation may be unfamiliar to the general reader.

Ch'in: *chin*

Ch'in Shih-huang: *chin sherr–h-ang*

Chou: *joh*

Ch'u: *choo*

Chuang Chou: *jwahng joh*

Han Fei: *hahn fay*

Hou Chi: *hoh jee*

Hsiang Yü: *shyang yoo*

Hsün-tzu: *shyun–dzuh*

Lao-tzu: *lau–dzuh*

Liu Pang: *lyoo bahng*

Lun-yu: *lwun–yoo*

Mo-tzu: *mwo–dzuh*

Ts'ao P'i: *tsaw pee*

Wei: *way*

Wen: *wun*

Yüeh: *yoo-eh*

TIME LINE

TEXTS	CONTEXTS
ca. 1700–1020 B.C.E. Writing used on tortoiseshells for divination and in inscriptions on bronze vessels	ca. 1700–1020 B.C.E. Shang Dynasty
	1020 Chou Dynasty overthrows the Shang Dynasty
ca. 1000 Earliest portions of *The Classic of Poetry*. • Earliest parts of the *Book of Changes*, the *Yi Ching*	
	ca. 820 Reign of King Hsüan and the expansion of the Chou kingdom south toward the Yangtse River
	770–256 Steady decline of the power of the Chou royal house and the rise of feudal states
	722 Beginning of the Spring and Autumn Annals period
ca. 600 *The Classic of Poetry* reaches its final form	
551–479 Confucius and the *Analects*	
	403 Warring States period begins
	400–250 Period of the "hundred schools" of Chinese thought
	ca. 390–305 Confucian philosopher Mencius, who taught the inherent goodness of human nature
ca. 369–286 Taoist philosopher Chuang Chou and the early chapters of the *Chuang Tzu*	
	350–221 Rise of the state of Ch'in in western China under the influence of a totalitarian political philosophy known as Legalism
340?–278 Ch'ü Yüan, poet of the southern state of Ch'u, to whom was attributed the composition of *The Nine Songs*	
	256 Ch'in dethrones the last Chou ruler

Boldface titles indicate works in the anthology.

TIME LINE

TEXTS	CONTEXTS
	221–206 Under influence of Ch'in Legalism, Confucianism and other schools of thought suppressed
	221 Ch'in Dynasty unifies China under Ch'in Shih-huang, the "First Emperor" • Great Wall extended
	206 Fall of Ch'in and the founding of the Han Dynasty; Han sponsors Confucianism
179–117 Ssu-ma Hsiang-ju, the greatest court poet of the Han and master of a form of long verse known as *fu* or "rhapsody"	
	140–86 Reign of Emperor Wu of the Han, with Chinese military conquests in Central Asia
	120 The Han court establishes a "Music Bureau," one of whose functions is to collect popular songs. Some of these lyrics survive
97 Ssu-ma Ch'ien completes the *Shih-chi*, the Historical Records, a comprehensive history of China up to the reign of Emperor Wu	
32–92 C.E. Pan Ku, author of the *Han History* and of many rhapsodies	
	57 C.E. Japan sends envoys to the Han court
100–200 The rise of anonymous poetry in the five-character line, which would be the most common poetic form for the rest of the premodern period	**ca. 100** Earliest introduction of Buddhism into China
	105 Earliest paper made
	196–220 The breakup of the Han into competing regions dominated by warlords • Ts'ao Ts'ao (155–220) is warlord of north China (200–220) and gathers the most eminent writers of the day to his court

CLASSIC OF POETRY
ca. 1000–600 B.C.E.

In contrast to other ancient literary cultures, which begin with epics, prose legends, or hymns to the gods, the Chinese tradition begins with lyric poetry. The *Classic of Poetry* (also known as *Book of Songs*) is a collection of 305 songs representing the heritage of the Chou people. The earliest in the collection are believed to date from around 1000 B.C.E. and the latest from around 600 B.C.E., at which time it seems to have reached something like its present form.

Although the collection circulated among the Chou aristocracy, it obviously drew from a wide variety of sources, and its diversity represents many levels of Chou society. There are temple hymns to the ancestors of the Chou ruling house, narrative ballads on the foundation and history of the dynasty, royal laments, songs of soldiers glorifying war and deploring war, love songs, marriage songs, hunting songs, songs of women whose husbands had deserted them, banquet songs, poems of mourning, and others. Many seem to have originated as folk songs, but these are mixed together with poems from the Chou aristocracy.

Down through the fifth century B.C.E. the *Classic of Poetry* served as the basic educational text of the Chou upper class. As the various Chou domains gradually evolved into independent states, the *Classic of Poetry* represented their common Chou heritage. The philosopher Confucius (551–479 B.C.E.) advised his disciples:

> By the *Poems* you can stir people and you can observe things through them; you can express your resentment in them and you can show sociable feelings. Close to home you can use them to serve your father, and on a larger scale you can use them to serve your ruler. Moreover, you can learn to recognize many names of birds, beasts, plants, and trees.*

By *observe* Confucius meant something like discovering universal precepts in the *Poems*. But that was not the only way in which the *Poems* were used. The power of the *Classic of Poetry* to "stir people" probably refers to their frequent use in conversation and diplomacy. Citation of one of the poems was often used to clinch a point in an argument or, more subtly, to express an opinion that one would rather not say openly. As with Homer's epics in early Greece, knowledge of the *Classic of Poetry* was considered an essential part of cultural education in early China.

Gradually, the transmission of the *Classic of Poetry* passed into the hands of the Confucian school, and by the fourth century B.C.E. it had become one of the texts in the canon of Confucian classics. Confucius was presumed to have been the editor of the collection, choosing and arranging these particular poems to show implicitly the glory and decline of Chou society. As a Confucian classic, the *Classic of Poetry* remained an essential part of Chinese education up to the twentieth century.

The great epics of early civilizations hold up an image of the values of those civilizations. The heroic values of the Homeric epics and their transformation in the *Aeneid* tell us much about how those civilizations wished to see themselves. Ancient China produced no epic; it left instead the *Classic of Poetry*. In place of the relatively homogeneous point of view of the ancient epics, the *Classic of Poetry* is a collection of many voices; there are the voices of kings, aristocrats, peasants, soldiers, men, and women. The Chou Dynasty's sense of its own authority depended on Heaven's charge to rule, which was contingent on ruling well and receiving the support of the common people. As the ballad that tells of Chou's rise to power says, "Heaven cannot be trusted; / Kingship is easily lost." This same law, by which the Chou Dynasty destroyed the Shang Dynasty, applied no less to the Chou itself. Because the dynasty

*Translated by Steven Owen.

depended on the common people, their concerns were considered an essential part of the polity. Voices of protest are mingled with voices of celebration. And the great influence of the *Classic of Poetry* in later ages was as a continual reminder that society contains many legitimate voices.

Confucius is said to have once told his son that if he did not learn the *Classic of Poetry* he would have no way to speak. The *Poems* gave words to feelings that would otherwise be hard or uncomfortable to articulate. One famous story of a slightly later period tells of a ruler who, on discovering that his people were criticizing him, sent out spies to inform on anyone who spoke against him. His adviser was horrified and warned the ruler strongly against taking such an action, but the ruler ignored his advice. Eventually, the people became frightened and kept their silence, with the result that the ruler was finally overthrown. Traditional Chinese interpretations of the *Classic of Poetry* have always stressed the role of the *Poems* as vehicles for political and social protest. But in a broader sense, the diversity of the *Poems* acknowledged that the contrary forces in individual hearts could still, when given utterance, contribute to a society that would ultimately prove more durable than one dominated by social authority and ideology. The immense cultural authority of the *Classic of Poetry* made it a means to say what one truly thought, rather than silently submitting to social authority. This principle is often found as a theme within the *Poems* themselves, as in these lines of a young woman being pressed to marry against her will: "This heart of mine is no mirror / it cannot take in all."

Even the most pious Confucian moralists always stressed that the voices in the *Classic of Poetry* came naturally and spontaneously from human feeling. The way in which students were taught to read the *Classic of Poetry* had a profound influence on the future development of Chinese literature. It encouraged poets and readers alike to assume that a poem revealed the state of mind of the writer, the writer's nature, and the writer's circumstances. And this led to a notion of literature, particularly poetry, as a form of interior history, revealing in an intensely direct way both the person and the age.

However simple the poems of the *Classic of Poetry* may appear on the surface, they embody the central values (if not the realities) of early Chinese civilization. Again and again the poems return to a fascination with timely action, to the need to speak out, to balances and exchanges, and to acts of explanation. These are the values of an antiheroic world, in which domination and absolute superiority threaten the social fabric. Its gods, the collective ancestors or Heaven, function as numinous mechanisms, holy enforcers of the natural and moral order; unlike the Greek or Mesopotamian gods, they almost never have favorites or act on whim. These values of natural balance can appear in the humblest forms. A young woman tosses a man a piece of fruit as a love gift, and the young man answers with an exchange:

> She cast a quince to me,
> a costly garnet I returned;
> it was no equal return,
> but by this love will last.

The exchange is economically unequal, a jewel returned for fruit. But the young man acts at once to restore the exchange to balance, explaining that the jewel was not given as an object of value, but as a token and message, just as the fruit she threw had been a message.

The poem itself can be an exchange of sorts. In poem LXXVI, when the lover Chung-tzu shows his rashly masculine daring by breaking into the girl's homestead, the poem serves to block his advances; it is a force of words to counterbalance his physical force. Through the words she can tell him that she loves him but also remind him of her family and others in the village, whose opinions should be taken into consideration and weighed against his desires.

PRONOUNCING GLOSSARY

The following list uses common English syllables to provide rough equivalents of selected words whose pronunciation may be unfamiliar to the general reader.

Chiang: *jyahng*   Chung-tzu: *joong–dzuh*

CLASSIC OF POETRY[1]

I. Fishhawk

The fishhawks sing *gwan gwan*
on sandbars of the stream.
Gentle maiden, pure and fair,
fit pair for a prince.

Watercress grows here and there,   5
right and left we gather it.
Gentle maiden, pure and fair,
wanted waking and asleep.

Wanting, sought her, had her not,
waking, sleeping, thought of her,   10
on and on he thought of her,
he tossed from one side to another.

Watercress grows here and there,
right and left we pull it.
Gentle maiden, pure and fair,   15
with harps we bring her company.

Watercress grows here and there,
right and left we pick it out.
Gentle maiden, pure and fair,
with bells and drums do her delight.   20

XX. Plums Are Falling

Plums are falling,
seven are the fruits;
many men want me,
let me have a fine one.

Plums are falling,   5
three are the fruits;

1. Translated by Steven Owen.

many men want me,
let me have a steady one.

Plums are falling,
catch them in the basket;   10
many men want me,
let me be bride of one.

XXIII. Dead Roe Deer

A roe deer dead in the meadow,
all wrapped in white rushes.
The maiden's heart was filled with spring;
a gentleman led her astray.

Undergrowth in forest,   5
dead deer in the meadow,
all wound with white rushes,
a maiden white as marble.

Softly now, and gently, gently,
do not touch my apron, sir,   10
and don't set the cur to barking.

XXVI. Boat of Cypress

That boat of cypress drifts along,
it drifts upon the stream.
Restless am I, I cannot sleep,
as though in torment and troubled.
Nor am I lacking wine   5
to ease my mind and let me roam.

This heart of mine is no mirror,
it cannot take in all.
Yes, I do have brothers,
but brothers will not be my stay.   10
I went and told them of my grief
and met only with their rage.

This heart of mine is no stone;
you cannot turn it where you will.
This heart of mine is no mat;   15
I cannot roll it up within.
I have behaved with dignity,
in this no man can fault me.

My heart is uneasy and restless,
I am reproached by little men.   20

Many are the woes I've met,
and taken slights more than a few.
I think on it in the quiet,
and waking pound my breast.

Oh Sun! and you Moon!   25
Why do you each grow dim in turn?
These troubles of the heart
are like unwashed clothes.
I think on it in the quiet,
I cannot spread wings to fly away.   30

XLII. Gentle Girl

A gentle girl and fair
awaits by the crook of the wall;
in shadows I don't see her;
I pace and scratch my hair.

A gentle girl and comely   5
gave me a scarlet pipe;
scarlet pipe that gleams—
in your beauty I find delight.

Then she brought me a reed from the pastures,
it was truly beautiful and rare.   10
Reed—the beauty is not yours—
you are but beauty's gift.

LXIV. Quince

She cast a quince to me,
a costly garnet I returned;
it was no equal return,
but by this love will last.

She cast a peach to me,   5
costly opal I returned;
it was no equal return,
but by this love will last.

She cast a plum to me,
a costly ruby I returned;   10
it was no equal return,
but by this love will last.

LXXVI. Chung-tzu, Please

Chung-tzu, please
don't cross my village wall,
don't break the willows planted there.
It's not that I care so much for them,
but I dread my father and mother;   5
Chung-tzu may be in my thoughts,
but what my father and mother said—
that too may be held in dread.

Chung-tzu, please
don't cross my fence,   10
don't break the mulberries planted there.
It's not that I care so much for them,
but I dread my brothers;
Chung-tzu may be in my thoughts,
but what my brothers said—   15
that too may be held in dread.

Chung-tzu, please
don't cross into my garden,
don't break the sandalwood planted there.
It's not that I care so much for them,   20
but I dread others will talk much;
Chung-tzu may be in my thoughts,
but when people talk too much—
that too may be held in dread.

LXXXI. I Went along the Broad Road

I went along the broad road
and took you by the sleeve—
do not hate me,
never spurn old friends.

I went along the broad road   5
and took you by the hand—
do not scorn me,
never spurn a love.

LXXXII. Rooster Crows

The woman said, "The rooster crows."
The man said, "Still the dark before dawn."
"Get you up, man—look at the night!—
the morning star is sparkling;

go roving and go roaming,   5
shoot the wild goose and the teal.

When your arrows hit them,
I will dress them just for you;
when they're dressed, we'll drink the wine,
and I will grow old with you.   10
There will be harps to attend us,
and all will be easy and good.

If I know that you will come,
I'll make a gift of many jewels;
if I know you will accept,   15
I'll show my care with many jewels;
if I know you will love me,
I'll answer you with many jewels."

CXL. Willows by the Eastern Gate

Willows by the Eastern Gate,
their leaves so thick and close.
Dusk had been the time set,
and now the morning star glows bright.

Willows by the Eastern Gate,   5
their leaves so dense and full.
Dusk had been the time set,
and now the morning star shines pale.

CCXLV. She Bore the Folk

She who first bore the folk—
Chiang it was, First Parent.
How was it she bore the folk?—
she knew the rite and sacrifice.
To rid herself of sonlessness   5
she trod the god's toeprint
    and she was glad.
She was made great, on her luck settled,
the seed stirred, it was quick.
She gave birth, she gave suck,   10
and this was Lord Millet.

When her months had come to term,
her firstborn sprang up.
Not splitting, not rending,
working no hurt, no harm.   15
He showed his godhead glorious,

the high god was greatly soothed.
He took great joy in those rites
and easily she bore her son.

She set him in a narrow lane,   20
but sheep and cattle warded him.
She set him in the wooded plain,
he met with those who logged the plain.
She set him on cold ice,
birds sheltered him with wings.   25
Then the birds left him
and Lord Millet wailed.
This was long and this was loud;
his voice was a mighty one.

And then he crept and crawled,   30
he stood upright, he stood straight.
He sought to feed his mouth,
and planted there the great beans.
The great beans' leaves were fluttering,
the rows of grain were bristling.   35
Hemp and barley dense and dark,
the melons, plump and round.

Lord Millet in his farming
had a way to help things grow:
He rid the land of thick grass,   40
he planted there a glorious growth.
It was in squares, it was leafy,
it was planted, it grew tall.
It came forth, it formed ears,
it was hard, it was good.   45
Its tassels bent, it was full,
he had his household there in Tai.

He passed us down these wondrous grains:
our black millets, of one and two kernels,
Millets whose leaves sprout red or white,   50
he spread the whole land with black millet,
And reaped it and counted the acres,
spread it with millet sprouting red or white,
hefted on shoulders, loaded on backs,
he took it home and began this rite.   55

And how goes this rite we have?—
at times we hull, at times we scoop,
at times we winnow, at times we stomp,
we hear it slosh as we wash it,
we hear it puff as we steam it.   60
Then we reckon, then we consider,
take artemisia, offer fat.
We take a ram for the flaying,

> then we roast it, then we sear it,
> to rouse up the following year. 65
>
> We heap the wooden trenchers full,
> wooden trenchers, earthenware platters.
> And as the scent first rises
> the high god is peaceful and glad.
> This great odor is good indeed, 70
> for Lord Millet began the rite,
> and hopefully free from failing or fault,
> it has lasted until now.

CONFUCIUS
551–479 B.C.E.

The *Analects* of Confucius (a title more lucidly translated as "Sayings") is the only work that we can confidently connect with the teacher Confucius, who gives his name to the secular social philosophy known as Confucianism. Confucius lived in a period when the unified Chou kingdom had split into a number of feudal states, most supposedly ruled by descendants of the Chou royal house. The period saw even that fragmented vestige of Chou legitimacy threatened by the rise of powerful families within the states.

Confucius himself was a native of Lu in eastern China, a state that prided itself on the preservation of Chou royal traditions but whose dukes were often at the mercy of the powerful Chi clan. Apparently because of a political conflict, Confucius left Lu in 497 B.C.E. and spent the next thirteen years wandering from regional court to regional court, gaining disciples and unsuccessfully seeking a prince who would try to implement his vision of traditional Chou values. At last he returned to Lu and lived out the rest of his life as a teacher, gathering a considerable following.

The *Analects* represents the memory of Confucius's teachings on the part of his disciples and was probably not written down until many centuries after his death. In its present form the *Analects* consists of twenty "books" or chapters, of which modern scholars consider the first fifteen to be authentic (we include passages from two of the last five books because they were considered just as authoritative as the first fifteen well into modern times). Although we can occasionally detect groupings of sayings, in general passages in the *Analects* are put together randomly.

To be a Confucian (the Chinese term is *Ju,* meaning roughly "traditionalist scholar") has meant many things during the nearly twenty-five hundred years since Confucius's death. These various meanings shifted and overlapped from age to age. For some scholars Confucianism was the study of ancient texts that embodied rituals and norms of behavior, for others it was a political philosophy, a social philosophy of the family, or the moral order of nature.

In the centuries that followed Confucius's death his teachings were absorbed into a growing interest in statecraft, and during the Han Dynasty, Confucian values became interwoven with the ideology of the imperial state. In later periods Chinese emperors may have supported Buddhism or religious Taoism out of personal devotion or political expediency, but Confucian learning and values were the very basis of the imperial state, by which the emperor held his office.

Confucius's reverence for antiquity centered on received texts and bodies of learning; these were the *Classic of Poetry,* the *Book of Documents* (*Shang shu*), the *Book of Changes* (*Yi ching*), the rituals (later written down in different texts), and a body of musical practice that accompanied the rituals and the *Classic of Poetry* (the music was lost after Confucius's time). In the third century B.C.E. these texts and traditions, along with a chronicle known as the *Ch'un-ch'iu,* became the core of what would be known as the Confucian classics. Other works came to be added to this core, including the *Analects* itself in the ninth century.

Before commenting on some of the central concerns of the *Analects,* we should consider its peculiar form and the significance of that form. In contrast to the imaginative sweep of works that founded other religious and philosophical traditions (and to the imaginative range of the *Chuang-Tzu* within the Chinese tradition), the *Analects* is a collection of terse and sometimes apparently innocuous sayings as well as a few longer anecdotes. The unity of the *Analects* resides not in an argument or a unified philosophy but rather in a person, Confucius. Instead of writing a treatise explaining his thoughts, the Confucius of the *Analects* responds to people and situations. The words are never thought of as the final and adequate statement of doctrine but as the circumstantial evidence of deeper wisdom. Confucianism is a philosophy of the relations among human beings, and its persuasive force rests not on a claim of transcendental truth but on the wisdom embodied in a person. Thus Confucius's terseness is read as a pregnant terseness, the utterances of someone who knew more and might have said more. The ideal here is captured in the disciple Tzu-kung's praise of Yen Hui, the most brilliant of Confucius's disciples: "When he is told one thing he understands ten." Throughout the *Analects* the reader is reminded that wisdom comes in fragments and fractions; the burden of full understanding is placed on the reader.

The moral philosophy of the *Analects* presupposes an idealized vision of the Chou past and its norms of behavior, which Confucius felt had been lost in his own age. The historically specific aspects of Confucius's values, such as his devotion to ancient rituals, make those values seem alien to a modern age; and indeed the modern reader may wonder why Confucianism remained so persuasive as a social philosophy, revived even in modern times.

The answer lies in looking beneath what is historically specific in the *Analects* to the hope of a perfect unity of social norm and natural behavior. This is succinctly expressed in Confucius's account of his spiritual development, culminating in the following: "At seventy I followed my heart's desire without overstepping the line." By study and self-cultivation, individuals can join their instinctive being and their social being. The hope is for a society whose members behave with a natural decency toward one another, respecting age and hierarchy and adapting to their changing roles. If the Confucianism of the *Analects* has a repugnance for anarchy and struggle, it has an equal repugnance for order achieved by coercion.

In one of the few extended passages in the *Analects,* Confucius asks a group of his disciples about their ambitions. Tzu-lu begins with a grand vision of restoring a state to power and morality. Sensing the master's disapproval, each of the subsequent disciples restricts his ambitions to an ever-narrower scope. At last the master comes to Tseng Hsi, who speaks of the joy in returning home from a festival with a group of friends. "The Master sighed and said, 'I am all in favour of Tien [Tseng Hsi].'" This is a touchstone text of Confucianism: what moves Confucius is the immediacy of Tseng Hsi's prospective joy in ritual and moral action. As Confucius says elsewhere, to delight in the Way is better than merely to understand it.

Confucius generally confined his interests to the human world and, as the *Analects* itself observes, did not speak about Heaven or the supernatural. This was not disbelief in transcendent being, but a remarkable desire to keep it out of human affairs, an ancient separation of church and state: "To keep one's distance from the gods and spirits while showing them reverence can be called wisdom."

The Confucian Way was one of social roles. These usually involved hierarchies of relations, but to Confucius social hierarchy was valid only if it came naturally and spontaneously. The only hierarchical relation that was above judgment was the relation between parent and child, and that natural relation of mutual but differing qualities of affection was the model to which all other social relations aspired.

No contemporary account of Confucianism can be complete without acknowledging the deep hostility it often inspires in modern China and Taiwan. Later, Confucianism became a tool of social coercion, and its demand that social norms of behavior be experienced as "natural" was an invitation to hypocrisy. But as with all religions and cultural philosophies, its historical failures do not entirely discredit the vision and hopes that first made it compelling.

Like other Chinese philosophers, Confucius speaks of the "Way." Each of the ancient Chinese philosophical schools used the term and interpreted the attributes of the Way differently. One should not grant too much value to the term itself; its importance lies in conceptualizing values and truth as process, a natural course of events and a natural course of action.

PRONOUNCING GLOSSARY

The following list uses common English syllables to provide rough equivalents of selected words whose pronunciation may be unfamiliar to the general reader.

Ch'ang Chu: *chahng–joo*

Chi: *jee*

Ch'i: *chee*

Chieh Ni: *jyeh nee*

Ch'ih: *cherr*

Chi K'ang Tzu: *jee kahng dzuh*

Chi-lu: *jee–loo*

Ching: *jing*

Ch'iu: *chyoh*

Chi Wen Tzu: *jee wun dzuh*

Ch'u: *choo*

Ch'un-ch'iu: *choo-en–chyoh*

Chung-kung: *jong–goong*

Ch'u Po-yu: *choo bwoh–yoo*

Fan Ch'ih: *fahn cherr*

Jan Ch'iu: *rahn chyoh*

Jan Yu: *rahn yoh*

K'uang: *kwahng*

K'ung: *koong*

Kung-hsi Hua: *goong–shee hwah*

Meng Ching Tzu: *mung jing dzuh*

Shang shu: *shahng shoo*

Shih Yu: *sherr yoo*

Shun: *shoo-un*

t'ai tsai: *tai dzai*

Tien: *dyen*

Tsai Yu: *dzai yoo*

Tseng Hsi: *dzung shee*

Tseng Tzu: *dzung dzuh*

Tzu-chang: *dzuh–jahng*

Tzu-hsia: *dzuh–shyah*

Tzu-kung: *dzuh–goong*

Tzu-lu: *dzuh–loo*

Wu Ch'eng: *woo chung*

Yen Hui: *yen hway*

Yen Yuan: *yen yoo-en*

Yi ching: *ee jing*

Yuan Jang: *yoo-en rahng*

From Analects[1]

BOOK I

1. The Master said, "Is it not a pleasure, having learned something, to try it out at due intervals? Is it not a joy to have friends come from afar? Is it not gentlemanly not to take offence when others fail to appreciate your abilities?"

11. The Master said, "Observe what a man has in mind to do when his father is living, and then observe what he does when his father is dead. If, for three years, he makes no changes to his father's ways, he can be said to be a good son."

BOOK II

1. The Master said, "The rule of virtue can be compared to the Pole Star which commands the homage of the multitude of stars without leaving its place."

2. The Master said, "The *Odes*[2] are three hundred in number. They can be summed up in one phrase,

Swerving not from the right path."

3. The Master said, "Guide them by edicts, keep them in line with punishments, and the common people will stay out of trouble but will have no sense of shame. Guide them by virtue, keep them in line with the rites, and they will, besides having a sense of shame, reform themselves."

4. The Master said, "At fifteen I set my heart on learning; at thirty I took my stand; at forty I came to be free from doubts; at fifty I understood the Decree of Heaven; at sixty my ear was atuned; at seventy I followed my heart's desire without overstepping the line."

7. The Master said, "There is no contention between gentlemen. The nearest to it is, perhaps, archery. In archery they bow and make way for one another as they go up and on coming down they drink together. Even the way they contend is gentlemanly."

19. Duke Ai asked "What must I do before the common people will look up to me?"

Confucius answered, "Raise the straight and set them over the crooked and the common people will look up to you. Raise the crooked and set them over the straight and the common people will not look up to you."

21. Duke Ai asked Tsai Wo about the altar to the god of earth. Tsai Wo replied, "The Hsia used the pine, the Yin used the cedar, and the men of Chou used the chestnut *(li)*, saying that it made the common people tremble *(li)*."

The Master, on hearing of this reply, commented, "One does not explain away what is already done, one does not argue against what is already accomplished, and one does not condemn what has already gone by."

---

1. Translated by D. C. Lau.   2. An alternative rendering of the poems of the *Classic of Poetry*.

destroyed, those who come after me will not be able to have any part of it. If Heaven does not intend this culture to be destroyed, then what can the men of K'uang do to me?"

6. The t'ai tsai[5] asked Tzu-kung, "Surely the Master is a sage, is he not? Otherwise why should he be skilled in so many things?" Tzu-kung said, "It is true. Heaven set him on the path of sagehood. However, he is skilled in many things besides."

The Master, on hearing of this, said, "How well the t'ai tsai knows me! I was of humble station when young. That is why I am skilled in many menial things. Should a gentleman be skilled in many things? No, not at all."

12. The Master was seriously ill. Tzu-lu told his disciples to act as retainers. During a period when his condition had improved, the Master said, "Yu has long been practising deception. In pretending that I had retainers when I had none, who would we be deceiving? Would we be deceiving Heaven? Moreover, would I not rather die in your hands, my friends, than in the hands of retainers? And even if I were not given an elaborate funeral, it is not as if I was dying by the wayside."

13. Tzu-kung said, "If you had a piece of beautiful jade here, would you put it away safely in a box or would you try to sell it for a good price?" The Master said, "Of course I would sell it. Of course I would sell it. All I am waiting for is the right offer."

14. The Master wanted to settle amongst the Nine Barbarian Tribes of the east. Someone said, "But could you put up with their uncouth ways?" The Master said, "Once a gentleman settles amongst them, what uncouthness will there be?"

22. The Master said, "There are, are there not, young plants that fail to produce blossoms, and blossoms that fail to produce fruit?"

23. The Master said, "It is fitting that we should hold the young in awe. How do we know that the generations to come will not be the equal of the present? Only when a man reaches the age of forty or fifty without distinguishing himself in any way can one say, I suppose, that he does not deserve to be held in awe."

28. The Master said, "Only when the cold season comes is the point brought home that the pine and the cypress are the last to lose their leaves."

BOOK XI

10. When Yen Yüan died, in weeping for him, the Master showed undue sorrow. His followers said, "You are showing undue sorrow." "Am I? Yet if not for him, for whom should I show undue sorrow?"

26. When Tzu-lu, Tseng Hsi, Jan Yu and Kung-hsi Hua were seated in attendance, the Master said, "Do not feel constrained simply because I am a little older than you are. Now you are in the habit of saying, 'My abilities are not appreciated,' but if someone did appreciate your abilities, do tell me how you would go about things."

5. A title of high office. This person has not been identified.

Tzu-lu promptly answered, "If I were to administer a state of a thousand chariots, situated between powerful neighbours, troubled by armed invasions and by repeated famines, I could, within three years, give the people courage and a sense of direction."

The Master smiled at him.

"Ch'iu, what about you?"

"If I were to administer an area measuring sixty or seventy li^6 square, or even fifty or sixty li square, I could, within three years, bring the size of the population up to an adequate level. As to the rites and music, I would leave that to abler gentlemen."

"Ch'ih, how about you?"

"I do not say that I already have the ability, but I am ready to learn. On ceremonial occasions in the ancestral temple or in diplomatic gatherings, I should like to assist as a minor official in charge of protocol, properly dressed in my ceremonial cap and robes."

"Tien, how about you?"

After a few dying notes came the final chord, and then he stood up from his lute. "I differ from the other three in my choice."

The Master said, "What harm is there in that? After all each man is stating what he has set his heart upon."

"In late spring, after the spring clothes have been newly made, I should like, together with five or six adults and six or seven boys, to go bathing in the River Yi and enjoy the breeze on the Rain Altar, and then to go home chanting poetry."

The Master sighed and said, "I am all in favour of Tien."

When the three left, Tseng Hsi stayed behind. He said, "What do you think of what the other three said?"

"They were only stating what they had set their hearts upon."

"Why did you smile at Yu?"

"It is by the rites that a state is administered, but in the way he spoke Yu showed a lack of modesty. That is why I smiled at him."

"In the case of Ch'iu, was he not concerned with a state?"

"What can justify one in saying that sixty or seventy li square or indeed fifty or sixty li square do not deserve the name of 'state'?"

"In the case of Ch'ih, was he not concerned with a state?"

"What are ceremonial occasions in the ancestral temple and diplomatic gatherings if not matters which concern rulers of feudal states? If Ch'iu plays only a minor part, who would be able to play a major role?"

BOOK XII

2. Chung-kung asked about benevolence. The Master said, "When abroad behave as though you were receiving an important guest. When employing the services of the common people behave as though you were officiating at an important sacrifice. Do not impose on others what you yourself do not desire. In this way you will be free from ill will whether in a state or in a noble family."

Chung-kung said, "Though I am not quick, I shall direct my efforts towards what you have said."

6. A unit of distance, about one quarter of a mile.

5. The Master said, "If there was a ruler who achieved order without taking any action, it was, perhaps, Shun. There was nothing for him to do but to hold himself in a respectful posture and to face due south."[9]

7. The Master said, "How straight Shih Yü is! When the Way prevails in the state he is as straight as an arrow, yet when the Way falls into disuse in the state he is still as straight as an arrow.

"How gentlemanly Ch'ü Po-yü is! When the Way prevails in the state he takes office, but when the Way falls into disuse in the state he allows himself to be furled and put away safely."

31. The Master said, "I once spent all day thinking without taking food and all night thinking without going to bed, but I found that I gained nothing from it. It would have been better for me to have spent the time in learning.

BOOK XVII

4. The Master went to Wu Ch'eng. There he heard the sound of stringed instruments and singing. The Master broke into a smile and said, "Surely you don't need to use an ox-knife to kill a chicken."

Tzu-yu answered, "Some time ago I heard it from you, Master, that the gentleman instructed in the Way loves his fellow men and that the small man instructed in the Way is easy to command."

The Master said, "My friends, what Yen says is right. My remark a moment ago was only made in jest."

9. The Master said, "Why is it none of you, my young friends, study the *Odes*? An apt quotation from the *Odes* may serve to stimulate the imagination, to show one's breeding, to smooth over difficulties in a group and to give expression to complaints.

"Inside the family there is the serving of one's father; outside, there is the serving of one's lord; there is also the acquiring of a wide knowledge of the names of birds and beasts, plants and trees."

BOOK XVIII

5. Chieh Yü, the Madman of Ch'u, went past Confucius, singing,

> Phoenix, oh phoenix!
> How thy virtue has declined!
> What is past is beyond help,
> What is to come is not yet lost.
> Give up, give up!
> Perilous is the lot of those in office today.

Confucius got down from his carriage with the intention of speaking with him, but the Madman avoided him by hurrying off, and in the end Confucius was unable to speak with him.

6. Ch'ang Chü and Chieh Ni were ploughing together yoked as a team. Confucius went past them and sent Tzu-lu to ask them where the ford was.

---

9. The direction the emperor's seat faces.

Ch'ang Chü said, "Who is that taking charge of the carriage?" Tzu-lu said, "It is K'ung Ch'iu." "Then, he must be the K'ung Ch'iu of Lu." "He is." "Then, he doesn't have to ask where the ford is."

Tzu-lu asked Chieh Ni. Chieh Ni said, "Who are you?" "I am Chung Yu." "Then, you must be the disciple of K'ung Ch'iu of Lu?" Tzu-lu answered, "I am." "Throughout the Empire men are all the same. Who is there for you to change places with? Moreover, for your own sake, would it not be better if, instead of following a Gentleman who keeps running away from men, you followed one who runs away from the world altogether?" All this while he carried on harrowing without interruption.

Tzu-lu went and reported what was said to Confucius.

The Master was lost in thought for a while and said, "One cannot associate with birds and beasts. Am I not a member of this human race? Who, then, is there for me to associate with? While the Way is to be found in the Empire, I will not change places with him."

CHUANG CHOU
ca. 369–286 B.C.E.

The period known as the Warring States, from 403 B.C.E. until the unification of China by the kingdom of Ch'in in 221 B.C.E., saw an intellectual diversity and vigor of philosophical debate unparalleled in later Chinese history. As the old Chou domains were gradually transforming themselves into contentious independent states, so the map of Chinese thought contained numerous schools and philosophical positions, and these also waged wars for hegemony. The relation between the political and philosophical maps was more than metaphorical; many of the philosophical schools dealt entirely or largely with political philosophy, and thinkers would travel from state to state, arguing with one another and competing for the patronage of princes.

There were, however, some philosophers who sought neither disciples nor patronage, who founded no school, and who were content to write. Such was the fourth-century philosopher Chuang Chou, to whom is attributed the first seven chapters of a work now called the *Chuang Tzu* (Master Chuang). Apart from the evidence of the *Chuang Tzu* itself, we know little about Chuang Chou as a historical person. Yet the first chapters of the *Chuang Tzu* show a remarkable mind at work.

The *Chuang Tzu* is often linked with the *Lao Tzu* as constituting the two primary texts of philosophical Taoism. The two works are quite different, both in style of writing and in style of thought. The *Lao Tzu* is largely in verse and repeats its pithy paradoxes over and over again. The *Chuang Tzu* is in a prose of constantly changing styles, with embedded verse passages. It moves from wise jokes and funny parables to moments of passionate seriousness, to tight philosophical arguments that turn imperceptibly into parodies of tight philosophical arguments. The structure of the first seven chapters is intricate: what seems at first to be a discontinuous series of parables gradually reveals itself as an echoing interplay of themes, sometimes taking the train of thought off in another direction, sometimes standing an earlier argument on its head.

Chuang Chou uses rapid shifts in scale and perspective to remind his readers that proportions, like values, are relative to a particular viewpoint. In *Free and Easy Wandering*, he begins with a monstrous sea creature, whose name is K'un (Fish Eggs). The K'un is transformed into the P'eng bird, which is so large that its wings hang over the sky to both horizons. The P'eng flies so high that when it looks down all it sees is blue. All of a sudden the passage shifts to a hollow in a floor that, if filled with water, floats scraps. On a tiny scale this becomes the analogy of the huge P'eng requiring an amplitude of air to bear up its mighty wings. In dizzying sequence Chuang Chou constantly shifts scales, exercising the reader's imagination to break down his or her habitual perspective, which is based on human magnitude.

As he shifts physical perspective, Chuang Chou also shifts his own standpoint, undermining the authority of what he has previously written. Readers are often uncertain whether he is serious or putting them on, or serious in his putting them on. In chapter 2 he moves into a logical argument on the relativity of the concepts *this* and *that* as well as *right* and *wrong*. The argument is intricate and stylized, and at some point readers begin to suspect that they are reading the parody of an argument, a suspicion confirmed when Chuang Chou reaches his grand summation in a joke. But then readers realize that this was the only proper conclusion for an argument against the absolute validity of arguments.

In the present version of the *Chuang Tzu*, twenty-six additional chapters follow the first seven. These are a miscellaneous gathering of Taoist works and works from related schools. Although none can match the first seven chapters as unified wholes, they contain many smaller sections as good as anything found earlier. Here we find an endless parade of crazy sages, wise peasants, and craftsmen, with all the commonplaces of habitual authority and conventional morality held up for ridicule.

The *Chuang Tzu* is the most inventive and diverse writing in early China, yet throughout the book we find doubts about the capacity of language, and particularly of written language, to convey truth. We read of a duke reading; his wheelwright comes in and asks him what he is reading. When the duke says that he is reading the words of the sages, the wheelwright asks if they are dead. And when the duke says that they are indeed, the wheelwright tells him that he is reading only the "chaff and dregs," that what they really knew could not be passed on by words. Yet the *Chuang Tzu* rarely loses sight of the fact that it too is words, and it solves the problem by laughing at itself, stepping out from behind its own statements with a wink. This happens in the following famous passage from the later chapters, put in the mouth of Chuang Chou:

> The fish trap exists because of the fish; once you've gotten the fish, you can forget the trap. The rabbit snare exists because of the rabbit; once you've gotten the rabbit, you can forget the snare. Words exist because of the meaning; once you've gotten the meaning, you can forget the words. Where can I find a man who has forgotten the words so I can have a word with him?

The term *Tao* (Way) was used by the Confucians and other thinkers as well as by the Taoists. The Way is simply the natural course of things. For the Confucians the Way is moral and potentially to be realized within society; in the *Chuang Tzu* the Way is amoral and escapes conventional human categories. Oppositions such as *up and down*, *right and wrong*, *this and that* all presume a limited perspective from which such distinctions can occur. The Way, in contrast, is everywhere and has no perspective whatsoever. Knowing that the words used to speak of such a Way are precisely the categories he is trying to get beyond, Chuang Chou can only use language against itself.

PRONOUNCING GLOSSARY

The following list uses common English syllables to provide rough equivalents of selected words whose pronunciation may be unfamiliar to the general reader.

Chang Wu-tzu: *jang woo–dzuh*   Mao-ch'iang: *mow–jyahng*

Chao: *jow*   Nieh Ch'üeh: *nyeh choo-eh*

Chü Ch'üeh-tzu: *joo choo-eh–dzuh*   P'eng-tsu: *puhng–dzuh*

Hsi-shih: *shee–sher*   Tzu-ch'i: *dzuh–chee*

Hui Tzu: *hway dzuh*

Chuang Tzu[1]

CHAPTER 2

Discussion on Making All Things Equal

Tzu-ch'i of south wall sat leaning on his armrest, staring up at the sky and breathing—vacant and far away, as though he'd lost his companion.[2] Yen Ch'eng Tzu-yu, who was standing by his side in attendance, said, "What is this? Can you really make the body like a withered tree and the mind like dead ashes? The man leaning on the armrest now is not the one who leaned on it before!"

Tzu-ch'i said, "You do well to ask the question, Yen. Now I have lost myself. Do you understand that? You hear the piping of men, but you haven't heard the piping of earth. Or if you've heard the piping of earth, you haven't heard the piping of Heaven!"

Tzu-yu said, "May I venture to ask what this means?"

Tzu-ch'i said, "The Great Clod[3] belches out breath and its name is wind. So long as it doesn't come forth, nothing happens. But when it does, then ten thousand hollows begin crying wildly. Can't you hear them, long drawn out? In the mountain forests that lash and sway, there are huge trees a hundred spans around with hollows and openings like noses, like mouths, like ears, like jugs, like cups, like mortars, like rifts, like ruts. They roar like waves, whistle like arrows, screech, gasp, cry, wail, moan, and howl, those in the lead calling out *yeee!*, those behind calling out *yuuu!* In a gentle breeze they answer faintly, but in a full gale the chorus is gigantic. And when the fierce wind has passed on, then all the hollows are empty again. Have you never seen the tossing and trembling that goes on?"

Tzu-yu said, "By the piping of earth, then, you mean simply [the sound of] these hollows, and by the piping of man [the sound of] flutes and whistles. But may I ask about the piping of Heaven?"

Tzu-ch'i said, "Blowing on the ten thousand things in a different way, so that each can be itself—all take what they want for themselves, but who does the sounding?"

Great understanding is broad and unhurried; little understanding is cramped and busy. Great words are clear and limpid; little words are shrill

---

1. Translated by Burton Watson.   2. The word "companion" is interpreted variously to mean his associates, his wife, or his own body [translator's note].   3. The earth.

and quarrelsome. In sleep, men's spirits go visiting; in waking hours, their bodies hustle. With everything they meet they become entangled. Day after day they use their minds in strife, sometimes grandiose, sometimes sly, sometimes petty. Their little fears are mean and trembly; their great fears are stunned and overwhelming. They bound off like an arrow or a crossbow pellet, certain that they are the arbiters of right and wrong. They cling to their position as though they had sworn before the gods, sure that they are holding on to victory. They fade like fall and winter—such is the way they dwindle day by day. They drown in what they do—you cannot make them turn back. They grow dark, as though sealed with seals—such are the excesses of their old age. And when their minds draw near to death, nothing can restore them to the light.

Joy, anger, grief, delight, worry, regret, fickleness, inflexibility, modesty, willfulness, candor, insolence—music from empty holes, mushrooms springing up in dampness, day and night replacing each other before us, and no one knows where they sprout from. Let it be! Let it be! [It is enough that] morning and evening we have them, and they are the means by which we live. Without them we would not exist; without us they would have nothing to take hold of. This comes close to the matter. But I do not know what makes them the way they are. It would seem as though they have some True Master, and yet I find no trace of him. He can act—that is certain. Yet I cannot see his form. He has identity but no form.

The hundred joints, the nine openings, the six organs, all come together and exist here [as my body]. But which part should I feel closest to? I should delight in all parts, you say? But there must be one I ought to favor more. If not, are they all of them mere servants? But if they are all servants, then how can they keep order among themselves? Or do they take turns being lord and servant? It would seem as though there must be some True Lord among them. But whether I succeed in discovering his identity or not, it neither adds to nor detracts from his Truth.

Once a man receives this fixed bodily form, he holds on to it, waiting for the end. Sometimes clashing with things, sometimes bending before them, he runs his course like a galloping steed, and nothing can stop him. Is he not pathetic? Sweating and laboring to the end of his days and never seeing his accomplishment, utterly exhausting himself and never knowing where to look for rest—can you help pitying him? I'm not dead yet! he says, but what good is that? His body decays, his mind follows it—can you deny that this is a great sorrow? Man's life has always been a muddle like this. How could I be the only muddled one, and other men not muddled?

If a man follows the mind given him and makes it his teacher, then who can be without a teacher? Why must you comprehend the process of change and form your mind on that basis before you can have a teacher? Even an idiot has his teacher. But to fail to abide by this mind and still insist upon your rights and wrongs—this is like saying that you set off for Yüeh today and got there yesterday.[4] This is to claim that what doesn't exist exists. If you claim that what doesn't exist exists, then even the holy sage Yü couldn't understand you, much less a person like me!

---

4. This was one of the paradoxes of the logician Hui Tzu [translator's note].

Words are not just wind. Words have something to say. But if what they have to say is not fixed, then do they really say something? Or do they say nothing? People suppose that words are different from the peeps of baby birds, but is there any difference, or isn't there? What does the Way rely upon, that we have true and false? What do words rely upon, that we have right and wrong? How can the Way go away and not exist? How can words exist and not be acceptable? When the Way relies on little accomplishments and words rely on vain show, then we have the rights and wrongs of the Confucians and the Mo-ists.[5] What one calls right the other calls wrong; what one calls wrong the other calls right. But if we want to right their wrongs and wrong their rights, then the best thing to use is clarity.

Everything has its "that," everything has its "this." From the point of view of "that" you cannot see it, but through understanding you can know it. So I say, "that" comes out of "this" and "this" depends on "that"—which is to say that "this" and "that" give birth to each other. But where there is birth there must be death; where there is death there must be birth. Where there is acceptability there must be unacceptability; where there is unacceptability there must be acceptability. Where there is recognition of right there must be recognition of wrong; where there is recognition of wrong there must be recognition of right. Therefore the sage does not proceed in such a way, but illuminates all in the light of Heaven.[6] He too recognizes a "this," but a "this" which is also "that," a "that" which is also "this." His "that" has both a right and a wrong in it; his "this" too has both a right and a wrong in it. So, in fact, does he still have a "this" and "that"? Or does he in fact no longer have a "this" and "that"? A state in which "this" and "that" no longer find their opposites is called the hinge of the Way. When the hinge is fitted into the socket, it can respond endlessly. Its right then is a single endlessness and its wrong too is a single endlessness. So, I say, the best thing to use is clarity.

To use an attribute to show that attributes are not attributes is not as good as using a nonattribute to show that attributes are not attributes. To use a horse to show that a horse is not a horse is not as good as using a non-horse to show that a horse is not a horse,[7] Heaven and earth are one attribute; the ten thousand things are one horse.

What is acceptable we call acceptable; what is unacceptable we call unacceptable. A road is made by people walking on it; things are so because they are called so. What makes them so? Making them so makes them so. What makes them not so? Making them not so makes them not so. Things all must have that which is so; things all must have that which is acceptable. There is nothing that is not so, nothing that is not acceptable.

For this reason, whether you point to a little stalk or a great pillar, a leper or the beautiful Hsi-shih, things ribald and shady or things grotesque and strange, the Way makes them all into one. Their dividedness is their completeness; their completeness is their impairment. No thing is either complete or impaired, but all are made into one again. Only the man of far-reaching vision knows how to make them into one. So he has no use [for

---

5. Followers of a utilitarian philosophical school who opposed the traditional ceremonies that the Confucians saw as essential to a good society. 6. Nature or the Way. 7. A reference to the statements of the logician Kung-sun Lung, "A white horse is not a horse" and "Attributes are not attributes in and of themselves" [translator's note].

categories], but relegates all to the constant. The constant is the useful; the useful is the passable; the passable is the successful; and with success, all is accomplished. He relies upon this alone, relies upon it and does not know he is doing so. This is called the Way.

But to wear out your brain trying to make things into one without realizing that they are all the same—this is called "three in the morning." What do I mean by "three in the morning"? When the monkey trainer was handing out acorns, he said, "You get three in the morning and four at night." This made all the monkeys furious. "Well, then," he said, "you get four in the morning and three at night." The monkeys were all delighted. There was no change in the reality behind the words, and yet the monkeys responded with joy and anger. Let them, if they want to. So the sage harmonizes with both right and wrong and rests in Heaven the Equalizer. This is called walking two roads.

The understanding of the men of ancient times went a long way. How far did it go? To the point where some of them believed that things have never existed—so far, to the end, where nothing can be added. Those at the next stage thought that things exist but recognized no boundaries among them. Those at the next stage thought there were boundaries but recognized no right and wrong. Because right and wrong appeared, the Way was injured, and because the Way was injured, love became complete. But do such things as completion and injury really exist, or do they not?

There is such a thing as completion and injury—Mr. Chao playing the lute is an example. There is such a thing as no completion and no injury— Mr. Chao not playing the lute is an example.[8] Chao Wen played the lute; Music Master K'uang waved his baton; Hui Tzu leaned on his desk. The knowledge of these three was close to perfection. All were masters, and therefore their names have been handed down to later ages. Only in their likes they were different from him [the true sage]. What they liked, they tried to make clear. What he is not clear about, they tried to make clear, and so they ended in the foolishness of "hard" and "white."[9] Their sons, too, devoted all their lives to their fathers' theories, but till their death never reached any completion. Can these men be said to have attained completion? If so, then so have all the rest of us. Or can they not be said to have attained completion? If so, then neither we nor anything else have ever attained it.

The torch of chaos and doubt—this is what the sage steers by. So he does not use things but relegates all to the constant. This is what it means to use clarity.

Now I am going to make a statement here. I don't know whether it fits into the category of other people's statements or not. But whether it fits into their category or whether it doesn't, it obviously fits into some category. So in that respect it is no different from their statements. However, let me try making my statement.

---

8. Chao Wen was a famous lute (*ch'in*) player. But the best music he could play (i.e., complete) was only a pale and partial reflection of the ideal music, which was thereby injured and impaired, just as the unity of the Way was injured by the appearance of love—i.e., man's likes and dislikes. Hence, when Mr. Chao refrained from playing the lute, there was neither completion nor injury [translator's note].   9. The logicians Hui Tzu and Kung-sun Lung spent much time discussing the relationship between attributes such as "hard" and "white" and the thing to which they pertain [translator's note].

There is a beginning. There is not yet beginning to be a beginning. There is a not yet beginning to be a not yet beginning to be a beginning. There is being. There is nonbeing. There is a not yet beginning to be nonbeing. There is a not yet beginning to be a not yet beginning to be nonbeing. Suddenly there is nonbeing. But I do not know, when it comes to nonbeing, which is really being and which is nonbeing. Now I have just said something. But I don't know whether what I have said has really said something or whether it hasn't said something.

There is nothing in the world bigger than the tip of an autumn hair,[1] and Mount T'ai is tiny. No one has lived longer than a dead child, and P'eng-tsu died young. Heaven and earth were born at the same time I was, and the ten thousand things are one with me.

We have already become one, so how can I say anything? But I have just said that we are one, so how can I not be saying something? The one and what I said about it make two, and two and the original one make three. If we go on this way, then even the cleverest mathematician can't tell where we'll end, much less an ordinary man. If by moving from nonbeing to being we get to three, how far will we get if we move from being to being? Better not to move, but to let things be!

The Way has never known boundaries; speech has no constancy. But because of [the recognition of a] "this," there came to be boundaries. Let me tell you what the boundaries are. There is left, there is right, there are theories, there are debates, there are divisions, there are discriminations, there are emulations, and there are contentions. These are called the Eight Virtues. As to what is beyond the Six Realms,[2] the sage admits its existence but does not theorize. As to what is within the Six Realms, he theorizes but does not debate. In the case of the *Spring and Autumn*,[3] the record of the former kings of past ages, the sage debates but does not discriminate. So [I say,] those who divide fail to divide; those who discriminate fail to discriminate. What does this mean, you ask? The sage embraces things. Ordinary men discriminate among them and parade their discriminations before others. So I say, those who discriminate fail to see.

The Great Way is not named; Great Discriminations are not spoken; Great Benevolence is not benevolent; Great Modesty is not humble; Great Daring does not attack. If the Way is made clear, it is not the Way. If discriminations are put into words, they do not suffice. If benevolence has a constant object, it cannot be universal. If modesty is fastidious, it cannot be trusted. If daring attacks, it cannot be complete. These five are all round, but they tend toward the square.[4]

Therefore understanding that rests in what it does not understand is the finest. Who can understand discriminations that are not spoken, the Way that is not a way? If he can understand this, he may be called the Reservoir of Heaven. Pour into it and it is never full, dip from it and it never runs dry, and yet it does not know where the supply comes from. This is called the Shaded Light.

1. The strands of animal fur were believed to grow particularly fine in autumn; hence "the tip of an autumn hair" is a cliché for something extremely tiny [translator's note].   **2.** Heaven, earth, and the four directions, i.e., the universe [translator's note].   **3.** Perhaps a reference to the *Spring and Autumn Annals*, a history of the state of Lu said to have been compiled by Confucius. But it may be a generic term referring to the chronicles of the various feudal states [translator's note].   **4.** All are originally perfect, but may become "squared," i.e., impaired by the misuses mentioned [translator's note].

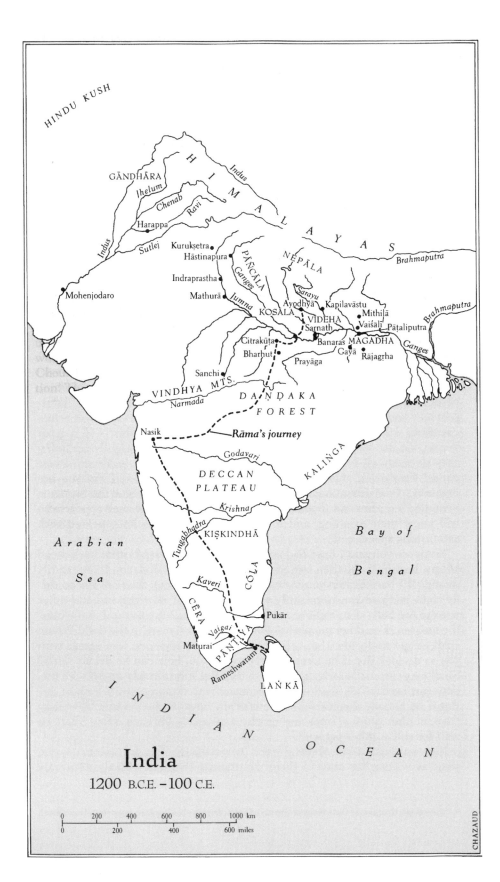

HINDU KUSH

GĀNDHĀRA

Indus

Jhelum

Chenab

Ravi

Harappa

Sutlej

Indus

Mohenjodaro

H I M A L A Y A S

Indus

Kurukṣetra

Hāstinapura

PĀÑCĀLA

NĒPĀLA

Brahmaputra

Indraprastha

Ganges

Mathurā

Jumna

Sarayu

Ayodhyā

Kapilavāstu

KOSALA

VIDEHA

Mithilā

Brahmaputra

Sarnath

Vaiśālī

Pāṭaliputra

Citrakūṭa

Banaras

MAGADHA

Ganges

Bharhut

Prayāga

Gayā

Rājagṛha

Sanchi

VINDHYA MTS.

D A Ṇ Ḍ A K A

Narmada

F O R E S T

Nasik

Rāma's journey

KALIṄGA

Godāvari

D E C C A N

P L A T E A U

Krishna

Bay of

Tungabhadra

KIṢKINDHĀ

A r a b i a n

Bengal

S e a

Kaveri

CŌLA

CĒRA

Pukār

Vaigai

Maturai

PĀṆṬIYA

Rameshwaram

LAṄKĀ

I N D I A N   O C E A N

India
1200 B.C.E.–100 C.E.

| 0 | 200 | 400 | 600 | 800 | 1000 km |
| 0 | | 200 | | 400 | 600 miles |

CHAZAUD

India's Heroic Age

Modern India, with a population of 1.1 billion, has remained remarkably in touch with its ancient roots in the face of centuries of change. The dominant pattern of Indian cultural history is a many-layered pluralism in which numerous subcultures defined by ethnic, religious, and linguistic differences coexist and relate with each other in complex yet coherent ways. This pluralism pervades and colors the vast body of oral and written literature that India has produced over thirty-five hundred years, in more than twenty languages and innumerable local dialects.

The Aryans, a group of nomadic tribes who apparently originated in central Asia and entered India around 1500 B.C.E., brought with them an early form of Sanskrit, a language that, along with nearly all the major languages of Europe and many in Asia, belongs to the Indo-European family. In India, Sanskrit became the principal language of classical literature, administration, and all forms of intellectual endeavor, maintaining this role almost up to the nineteenth century. Sanskrit's primary cultural association is with Hinduism, India's dominant religious tradition, a direct descendant of the Vedic religion of the Aryans. Gautama Buddha (563–483 B.C.E.) and Mahāvīra (died 468 B.C.E.), noblemen of Aryan clans who founded the Buddhist and Jain religious paths as radical alternatives to the Vedic religion, preached their messages in Pali and Prakrit, popular dialects related to Sanskrit. Hindi and the other modern languages of north India descended from the various Prakrit dialects. Sanskrit and its related languages and dialects are known as the Indo-Aryan languages.

Classical Tamil, the language of the ancient literature (first through third centuries C.E.) of south India, is the oldest example of Dravidian, a family of languages to which all the modern languages in south India belong. In later times, the literatures and cultures of both north and south India developed through continuous and fruitful interchange. From the twelfth century onward, various conquering Muslim dynasties—the Mughals (or Moguls) were the latest of these—brought to Indian literature and civilization not only the sensibility of Islam but also the heritage of the Arabic and Persian languages and literatures. Beginning in the seventeenth century, the activities of the British East India Company laid the foundation for British colonial rule and led to the establishment of Western-style education. Though British rule lasted only until India's independence in 1947, the English language and Western ideas have become a permanent piece of India's cultural mosaic.

THE LEGACY OF THE *VEDAS* AND *UPANIṢADS*

As in China, Egypt, and the Near East, civilization in India appears to have begun in a river valley. Of the Indus Valley civilization that flourished in great cities such as Mohenjo Daro and Harappa (ca. 3000–1500 B.C.E.) in northwestern India (now largely in Pakistan) we have only archaeological remains, which include writing in a script that has not yet been deciphered. Thus it is with the Aryans that the continuous history of Indian civilization and religion begins together with the history of Indian literature. Cattle breeders who eventually developed an agriculture, the Aryans settled in the Indus Valley and left as their legacy the *Vedas*, four books of sacred hymns that accompanied the worship of gods who were personifications of nature and the powers of the cosmos. The following verses—from a hymn in the *Rig Veda* to Sūrya, the sun god—epitomize the spirit and imagery of Vedic myth and poetry:

> His brilliant banners draw upwards the god who knows all
> creatures, so that everyone may see the sun.
> The constellations, along with the nights, steal away like
> thieves, making way for the sun who gazes on everyone . . .
> He is the eye with which, O Purifying Varuṇa [god of law], you
> look upon the busy one among men.
> You cross heaven and the vast realm of space, O sun, measuring
> days by nights, looking upon the generations.
> Seven bay mares carry you in the chariot, O sun god with hair
> of flame, gazing from afar.
> We have come up out of darkness, seeing the higher light
> around us, going to the sun, the god among the gods, the highest
> light.*

Preserved in what appears to be an unbroken oral tradition of memorization and recitation, the *Vedas* are Hinduism's primary scripture. For thousands of years priests have chanted Vedic hymns at the major sacramental rites of naming, initiation, marriage, and death; and Hindu rituals are modeled on the Vedic fire sacrifice. Hindus regard the hymns as divine revelation: poet-seers called *ṛṣi* saw the verses in their mind's eye and spontaneously recited them in the form of sacred utterance (*mantra*). Tracing their ancestry to the ancient *ṛṣi*, the brahmans, priestly transmitters of the Vedic hymns and rites, have traditionally commanded the highest status in the Hindu class hierarchy.

The last hymns of the *Rig Veda* (ca. 1000 B.C.E.), reflect a change in the Aryan worldview. The concluding verses of the creation hymn called *Nāsadīya* (The hymn of nonexistence) capture the skeptical spirit that signaled the end of the Vedic age and the beginning of an age of spiritual quest and philosophical speculation:

> Who really knows? Who will here proclaim it? Whence was it
> produced? Whence is this creation? The gods came afterwards,
> with the creation of this universe. Who then knows whence it
> has arisen?
> Whence this creation has arisen—perhaps it formed itself, or
> perhaps it did not—the one who looks down on it, in the
> highest heaven, only he knows—or perhaps he does not know.†

The *Vedas* were followed by the *Upaniṣads* (Mystic doctrines), a genre of philosophical texts containing the mystical and philosophical speculations of thinkers who rejected the ritualistic religion of the *Vedas* in favor of a quest for ultimate wisdom. The prose dialogues of the oldest of these works, the *Bṛhadārakyaka* Upaniṣad (The great mystic doctrine of the forest) and *Chāndogya Upaniṣad* (The mystic doctrine of the *Sāma Veda*), written around 900 to 800 B.C.E., take place between eager pupils—men and women from diverse social classes—and wise teachers, among whom are warriors and artisans as well as brahmans and hermits. The sages of the early *Upaniṣads* teach that a single divine essence (Brahman, different from brahman, the priestly class) pervades the universe, that the human soul is a manifestation of this divine essence, and that spiritual emancipation consists in mystically knowing the essential unity between self and universe. The teachings of the sages did not in effect undermine the authority of the *Vedas,* nor did they result in significant social upheaval. On the other hand, the concepts of the personal spiritual quest, the wise teacher (*guru*), and the transforming power of knowledge remain enduring motifs in Indian civilization.

---

*Translated by Wendy Doniger O'Flaherty.   †Translated by Wendy Doniger O'Flaherty.

THOUGHT AND LITERATURE OF THE HEROIC AGE

The literature of India's heroic age, produced between 550 B.C.E. and 100 C.E., reflects the spread of Aryan civilization over much of north India. It records the development of the Buddhist and Hindu religions from the Vedic civilization and provides a window into the non-Aryan civilization of the Tamil-speaking peoples of south India. The Sanskrit poems *Rāmāyaṇa* (ca. 550 B.C.E.) and *Mahābhārata* (the main portions of which date back in their present form at least to the fourth century B.C.E.) are India's earliest epics and express seminal Hindu values in the making.

Composed and edited over a period of nine hundred years (roughly 550 B.C.E. –400 C.E.), the epics are heroic narratives of an earlier time, originally recited by bards on the battlefield and at royal rituals, preserved in a fluid oral tradition, and finally reworked (like much of the Old Testament of the Bible) by priestly elites. Although the poems contain much mythic and legendary material and each is attributed to a legendary author who, like the Vedic poets, is called a seer (*ṛṣi*), there is reason to believe that they are grounded in actual events that took place between the ninth and seventh centuries B.C.E., when carriers of the Vedic culture spread eastward in north India. The *Mahābhārata*, attributed to Vyāsa, tells the story of a great civil war among Aryan clans, while the *Rāmāyaṇa* of Vālmīki narrates the exile and adventures of Prince Rāma of Kosala. Together the two epics present a poetic history of the north Indian royal houses and the foundations of Aryan rule in the valley of the river Ganges. Hence their traditional Indian classification as *itihāsa* ("historical narrative," literally "thus it was").

Despite similarities with the *Iliad* and *Odyssey*, the flavor of the *Rāmāyaṇa* and *Mahābhārata* is unmistakably Indian, and Hindus have valued the epics above all as sacred narratives that embody religious and ethical teachings. Included among the Hindu scriptures (in a class of texts known as "tradition"), the two epics have served, and continue to serve, as living cultural forces with deep personal meaning for Hindus from all walks of life. The Sanskrit versions of Vālmīki and Vyāsa have given rise to innumerable subsequent retellings in the major Indian languages, while the epic narratives have provided the themes for much of Indian art and literature over the last two thousand years. And their universal dimensions have allowed the Indianized cultures of Southeast Asia—Java, Thailand, and Malaysia, for instance—to "translate" them into their own cultural idioms and so to embrace them as beloved epics of their own.

Not only Hindus but most Indians grow up hearing the *Rāmāyaṇa* and *Mahābhārata*, as told by members of the family or professional storytellers, and seeing them enacted in diverse forms of theater and dance. And it is here that young Hindus first encounter *dharma*, held to be the guiding principle of proper human conduct, and the doctrine of *karma*. In traditional Hindu thought *dharma* (literally, "that which holds") is the force that supports the universe—that is, "holds" it together. It is the underlying principle of the social, moral, and cosmic orders, which are described and classified in hierarchically ordered, interlinked sets of four categories. There are four cyclic ages of the cosmos (*yuga*). There are four "classes" (*varṇa*) in society: the learned or priestly brahman, the *kṣatriya* (warrior and administrator), the *vaiśya* (merchant, farmer, or other member of the productive community), and the *śūdra* (laborer). Likewise, there are four stages of life: celibate student, householder, forest dweller, and wandering ascetic. Although the progression of *yugas* from one to four records a process of decay (somewhat analogous to the decline from golden to iron ages in traditional Western thought) and the four classes are organized from high to low, the stages of life reverse the progression, moving from lower to higher on the spiritual plane.

The dynamic center of all these schemes is the scheme of the four spheres, or goals, that should, ideally, govern life. This set of categories begins with *dharma* (here used in a second, somewhat narrower, sense to mean the sphere of sacred duty, righteousness, and moral law); followed by *artha,* the sphere of worldly profit, wealth, and political power; *kāma,* the sphere of pleasure and love; and *mokṣa,* the ultimate goal of life, the sphere in which one seeks liberation from the constraints of worldly existence. All men, including *śūdras,* are bound by a prescribed program of sacred duty (*dharma*) that is appropriate to their class (*varṇa*), but only men of the three upper classes, known as the "twice born" classes (initiation into the rites and texts of the *Veda* is considered to be a second birth), may work their way through the stages of life toward *mokṣa.* Women form a class in themselves, for a woman's *dharma* is defined as that of a wife, allowing women no identities or aspirations apart from their allegience to their husbands.

The four classes are concerned only with determining one's place in the cosmic scheme of things. The Hindu man's actual status is determined by his being born into one of the innumerable castes (*jāti,* literally, "birth"), which, defined by occupation, kinship, marriage practices, and other factors, make up a minutely stratified society with rigid divisions among groups and individuals. Although the epics and later Hindu texts reflect a constantly shifting balance of power among the brahman, warrior, and merchant classes, the religious basis of the caste system guarantees the subordination of a large number of "service" castes to a small number of elite groups. Furthermore, the idea of sacred duty combines with the doctrine of *karma* to form a powerful rationale for the perpetuation of social hierarchy.

Karma is the premise on which all three ancient religions of India build their doctrines of the ultimate goal of religion. According to the theory of *karma,* all creatures are ultimately responsible for their own existential conditions, and existence is invariably bound up with suffering. To exist is to be perpetually engaged in action (the basic meaning of the word *karma* is "a deed, that which is done"). All deeds, good and bad, have inevitable results, which must be borne by the doer in an existential state, so that the soul is trapped in an endless cycle of birth and death (known as *saṃsāra,* "going round and round").

The earliest descriptions of the theory of *karma,* implying the entire sequence described above, are found in the *Upaniṣads,* whose authors were engaged in contemplating ways to transcend the limitations of the human condition. The thinkers of the *Upaniṣads* put forward the theory that the soul or self is a pure and immutable entity, untouched by *karma,* and that liberation from the cycle of rebirth can be achieved by identifying oneself with this pure self. Gautama Buddha rejected the concept of an immortal soul, concentrating instead on the suffering that was thought to result from *karma* and on the urgent need of all creatures to be freed from this burden of suffering. In the form of animal fables and popular tales, the *Jātaka* stories illustrate the Buddha's teaching regarding the path to liberation from rebirth, a unique combination of radical detachment from desire, the root cause of *karma,* and an ethic of action directed only toward the welfare of one's fellow creatures. Every person, regardless of caste, gender, or social status, could follow the Buddha's path (the *Dharma*) with the ultimate aim of becoming liberated from *karma* rebirth by becoming a *buddha,* or "an enlightened one."

Buddhism arose from social and political contexts that were very different from those of the Hindu epics. Gautama Buddha was a prince of the Śākyas, an Aryan republican tribe on the Nepal border in the Himalayas. It was among the many tribal oligarchies and republics that flourished in northeastern India in the sixth century that he found his largest following, constituted especially of merchants, artisans, women, and others to whom the ritual religion and social hierarchies of early Hinduism had little to offer. Buddhist literature vividly reflects the cosmopolitan atmosphere and urban, mercantile civilization of the Mauryan empire (322–186 B.C.E.), India's first major empire, established by kings of an eastern Indian dynasty who, in the wake of Alexander of Macedon's invasion (326 B.C.E.), conquered most of India.

A Buddhist canonical text records the conversion of Menander, a Greek king of northwestern India; and under the enthusiastic patronage of Aśoka (269–232 B.C.E.)—the greatest of the Mauryan emperors—Buddhism spread as far south as the island of Sri Lanka and traveled, along with textiles and spices, to lands to the north and west of India.

The populist, egalitarian religions preached by Gautama Buddha and his near-contemporary Mahāvīra presented a formidable challenge to the elaborate socioreligious system engineered by the Hindu elites. The god Kṛṣṇa's teachings to the hero Arjuna in the *Bhagavad-Gītā* represent, among other things, a synthesis of the attempts of Hindu thinkers to come to grips with the need of all Hindus, men and women alike, for a nonhierarchical and more personal path to the distant goal of liberation from *karma* rebirth. The eventual triumph of the Hindu religion in India is based, however, not on the greater appeal of its philosophical tenets over those of the rival religions but on its ability to synthesize and absorb features from those very rivals and, above all, on its molding of the cults of charismatic popular gods such as Kṛṣṇa (or Krishna) into a religion of salvation and grace, which attracted even the Greco-Bactrians, Śakas, and others who ruled in north India from the dissolution of the Mauryan empire to the fourth century C.E.

For Hindus the terror of rebirth is mitigated by belief in a triad of great gods who are the highest manifestations of the divine principle underlying the universe. Brahmā, Viṣṇu, and Śiva respectively create, preserve, and destroy the universe and all creatures through the *yuga* cycles of cosmic time. Although there are many gods, Viṣṇu, the preserver, and Śiva, the destroyer, stand out as supreme deities, for Hindus worship one or the other as God, whose grace will help deliver them from the bonds of *karma* rebirth. Kṛṣṇa, the teacher of the *Bhagavad-Gītā*, is an incarnation of Viṣṇu, and his revelation of his divine identity to his devotee Arjuna constitutes the supreme mystery of this mystical text. For the heroes of the epics the belief in God and gods offers an alternative to the mechanistic view of *karma* and suffering. In explaining actions and events, they refer as often to the deeds of the gods and to fate (by which they mean the collective will of the gods as opposed to the will of the individual) as to *karma*.

Although the ancient Tamil poems included here reveal an intimate knowledge of Aryan civilization and religion, everything about them—from the society they portray to the metaphors they employ—is permeated with a Tamil warrior ethos that is completely different from the values embodied in the texts in the north Indian languages. These poems, which give supreme value to love and war and to the lives of men and women in this world, perhaps come closest to Western ideals of the literature of a "heroic age." For most Hindus, however, Rāma and Arjuna are heroes precisely because they are able to temper the inherent violence of the warrior's way of life with compassion and ascetic self-control, thereby lifting their acts to a higher moral plane. In the Buddhist tradition, Gautama Buddha is a superhuman hero-king, one who was destined to become a "world conqueror" (*cakravartin*) with his teaching of spiritual perfection, and a little more than two hundred years after the Buddha's death, Emperor Aśoka affirmed the power of this heroic ideal by laying down his weapons and proclaiming, by public edicts carved on rock, his preference for the "conquest of righteousness" to conquest by the sword.

PRONOUNCING GLOSSARY

The following list uses common English syllables and stress accents to provide rough equivalents of selected words whose pronunciation may be unfamiliar to the general reader.

Arjuna: *uhr'-joo-nuh*

artha: *uhr'-tuh*

Aśoka: *uh-shoh'-kuh*

Bhagavad-Gītā: *buh'-guh-vuhd–gee'-tah*

Bṛhadāraṇyaka Upaniṣad: *bree-huhd-ah'-ruhn-yuh-kuh oo-puh'-nee-shuhd*

cakravartin: *chuh'-kruh-vuhr-ten*

kāma: *kah'-muh*

Kṛṣṇa: *krish'-nuh*

kṣatriya: *kshuh-tree-yuh*

Mahābhārata: *muh-hah-bah'-ruh-tah*

mokṣa: *mohk'-shuh*

Rāmāyaṇa: *rah-mah'-yuh-nuh*

ṛṣi: *ri'-shee*

Śākya: *shahk'-yuh*

saṃsāra: *suhm-sah'-ruh*

Śiva: *shee'-vuh*

śūdra: *shoo'-druh*

Sūrya: *soor'-yuh*

Upaniṣad: *oo-puh'-nee-shuhd*

vaiśya: *vai'-shyuh*

Viṣṇu: *vish'-noo*

Vyāsa: *vee-yah'-suh*

yuga: *yoo'-guh*

TIME LINE

TEXTS	CONTEXTS
	ca. 3000–1500 B.C.E. Indus Valley civilization flourishes in urban centers • Writing in use
ca. 1500–1200 B.C.E. Composition of the *Rig Veda,* oldest of the four Vedas, texts of hymns and chants in an archaic form of the Sanskrit language, for the fire sacrifice of the Aryan Vedic religion	ca. 1500 Aryan tribes speaking Sanskrit, an Indo-European language, enter India via the northwest and settle in the Indus Valley
ca. 900 The Sanskrit *Upaniṣads,* dialogues and meditations of philosophers on the nature of existence, the soul, and the universe	
ca. 700 Homer's *Iliad* and *Odyssey*	ca. 700 Emergence of kingdoms and republics in northern India
	563–483 Gautama Buddha, founder of Buddhism, preaches in Pāli, a dialect related to Sanskrit. He establishes an order of monks and nuns and spreads his new religion in the Ganges River valley in north India • Mahāvīra, Buddha's contemporary, founds Jainism, a religion emphasizing nonviolence and asceticism
ca. 550 Vālmīki's Sanskrit poem *The Rāmāyaṇa,* a heroic epic recounting the deeds of the north Indian prince Rāma	
480–400 Aeschylus, Sophocles, and Euripides	
ca. 400 B.C.E.–400 C.E. The Sanskrit epic *The Mahābhārata,* the narrative of a great war among north Indian clansmen, takes shape	
ca. 400 B.C.E. Pāṇini writes the *Aṣṭādhyāyī* (Eight chapters), the authoritative grammar of the Sanskrit language and a model for modern linguistic science	

Boldface titles indicate works in the anthology.

TIME LINE

TEXTS	CONTEXTS
4th century B.C.E. Early version of *The Jātaka,* a collection of stories about the Buddha in the spoken dialect known as Pali	**ca. 326** Alexander of Macedon invades India **269–232** Asóka Maurya, emperor of India, spreads Buddhism in Sri Lanka, patronizes Buddhist art, and issues royal edicts in praise of Buddhist ethics in Prakrit, spoken dialects related to Sanskrit
200–100 The Sanskrit text *Saddharmapuṇḍarīka* (The lotus of the good law), expounding the doctrines of Mahayana (later) Buddhism, is written	**ca. 200** Beginning of Buddhist cave sanctuaries and art at Ajanta in western India, and of the Hindu Bhagavata cult of devotion to a personal God
100 B.C.E.**–250** C.E. Under the patronage of south Indian kings, anthologies of lyric poems of love and war are produced in Tamil, a language unrelated to Sanskrit and the north Indian languages	
1st century B.C.E. ***The Bhagavad-Gītā,*** the mystical teaching of the god Kṛṣṇa to the hero Arjuna, is added to *The Mahābhārata*	**ca. 90** The Śakas, a Scythian tribe from Bactria (to the northwest of modern Afghanistan), invade India **50** B.C.E.**– 250** C.E. The Sātavāhana kings of central India patronize lyric poetry and narrative literature in Prakrit dialects
ca. 100 C.E. Aśvaghoṣa writes *Buddhacarita* (Acts of the Buddha), a Sanskrit epic poem in the courtly style, on the life of the Buddha • The early Buddhist canonical texts in the Pali language, including the *Jātaka* stories, are written down in Sri Lanka	**1st–2nd centuries** C.E. Buddhism spreads to China
100–200 The *Dharma Śāstra* of Manu (The laws of Manu), the authoritative treatise on laws and codes of conduct according to the Hindu religion, is completed	

THE RĀMĀYAṆA OF VĀLMĪKI
ca. 550 B.C.E.

The Sanskrit epic poem *Rāmāyaṇa* (The Way of Rāma) by Vālmīki is the oldest literary version (ca. 550 B.C.E.) of the tale of the exile and adventures of Prince Rāma, a story that was known from Indian folk traditions as early as the seventh century B.C.E. Because ancient tradition the world over placed little value on the identity of authors or artists, all we know about Vālmīki is gleaned from legends about the circumstances that led him to compose the *Rāmāyaṇa*, work of twenty-four thousand verses, divided into seven "books," called *kāṇḍa*. It is probable that, like Homer, he gathered and shaped the scattered material of many oral traditions into the poetic whole that we read today.

Vālmīki's *Rāmāyaṇa* became the source for a multitude of versions composed in all the major Indian languages over several centuries. The story has also been preserved in oral traditions by storytellers and continues to be enacted in countless regional folk theaters in India. It would be no exaggeration to say that the Rāma story is *the* great story of Indian civilization, the one narrative that all Indians have known and loved through the ages and whose popularity remains undiminished to this day.

In the Indian tradition, Vālmīki is celebrated as the "first poet," his *Rāmāyaṇa* the "original poem." The poem itself begins with the tale of the sage Vālmīki's invention of metrical verse. Responding to Vālmīki's question about who in the world is a perfect man, the sage Nārada outlines the story of the hero Rāma, whose wife was abducted by a demon-king. Brooding on the sad tale, Vālmīki goes for a walk along the banks of the Tamasā River, where he sees a pair of mating herons. Suddenly, a hunter shoots the male bird, and the female cries in anguish as she sees her mate's body writhing on the ground. Moved to intense compassion by her grief, Vālmīki utters inspired words in lyric verse in the form of a couplet. Thus was born, Vālmīki tells us, the *śloka,* the meter of the epics and of many other works in Sanskrit. The legend reflects the classical Indian ideal of the poet as one who transforms the raw emotion and chaos of real life into an ordered work of art. In point of fact, Vālmīki's style is only a crude forerunner of the later *kāvya* style of classical Sanskrit poetry, which abounds in complex meters, figures of speech, and descriptions. On the other hand, the epic retains many of the formulaic devices of oral poetry that we have already met in Homer, such as ready-made epithets that can slip easily into convenient slots in the metrical line—for instance, the formula "Rāma, devoted to righteousness" (*rāmo dharmabhṛtāṃ varaḥ*), which occupies exactly one-quarter of the *śloka* verse.

The *Rāmāyaṇa* blends historical saga, nature myth, morality tale, and religious mythology. Rāma is associated with the line of Ikṣvāku kings who ruled the kingdom of Kosala in the Ganges River valley of north India from their capital in Ayodhyā in the sixth and fifth centuries B.C.E. Legends surrounding the Ikṣvāku royal house and the adventures of Rāma form the core of the epic, books 2 to 6. Book 1, *Bāla* (Childhood), and book 7, *Uttara* (The last book), generally agreed to be additions to the original Vālmīki text, form a frame for the central narrative, introducing and completing the story of Rāma as a divine incarnation (*avatāra*).

In the core story, Rāvaṇa, a powerful king of the *rākṣasas*—evil demons who continually threaten social and moral order (*dharma*) in the world—has obtained a boon (gift) of invulnerability to gods and other superhuman beings who combat him. The gods persuade Viṣṇu, the great god whose function it is to preserve *dharma* in the universe, to incarnate himself as a man in order to destroy Rāvaṇa. Viṣṇu is thus born as Rāma, the son of Daśaratha, king of Kosala, by his senior queen, Kausalyā. Sons born at the same time to Daśaratha's two younger queens—Kaikeyī bore Bharata, and Sumitrā bore the twins Lakṣmaṇa and Śatrughna—share in Viṣṇu's divine essence. All four princes are noble heroes, but Rāma is a paragon of princely virtues. As youths, Rāma and Lakṣmaṇa go to the forest retreat of the hermit Viś-vāmitra to guard his sacrificial rites from hostile demons. They then travel to Mith-ilā, the capital of Videha in eastern India, where Rāma wins the princess Sītā by besting other suitors in a contest to bend a magical bow, a motif we have already met in the *Odyssey*. Sītā, whose name means "furrow," is in reality the daughter of goddess Earth, but has been brought up by King Janaka.

Book 2, *Ayodhyā*, centers on prince Rāma's disinheritance. When King Daśaratha proclaims Rāma as his heir apparent, the whole capital city of Ayodhyā rejoices. Queen Kaikeyī, her jealousy roused by the counsel of a hunchback maidservant, decides to place her own son, Bharata, on the throne. She demands that Rāma be exiled to a life of hardship in the forest for fourteen years and that Bharata—who is absent from the court at this time—be made heir to the kingdom. She reminds the king that, according to a promise he had made her in the past, he owes her two favors of her choice. Bound by his word, Daśaratha has no alternative but to comply. Rāma accepts his exile, and Sītā and Lakṣmaṇa voluntarily join him. When the three have departed, Ayodhyā is left desolate, and the king dies of a broken heart. Upon his return, Bharata is horrified at the events that have taken place in his name. He chas-tises Kaikeyī and tries to hand over the kingdom to Rāma, but Rāma, wishing to honor his father's word, will serve out his exile, and Bharata agrees to rule as regent until his return.

A very different atmosphere dominates books 3 to 6—*Āraṇya* (The forest), *Kiṣkindhā* (The kingdom of the monkeys), *Sundara* (The beautiful), and *Yuddha* (The war). Here, as in Odysseus's stories in Phaeacia, characters and events represent types traceable to older myths and folktales. "The Forest Book" narrates the adven-tures of Rāma, Sītā, and Lakṣmaṇa in the wildernesses of central and western India. Here the trio meets gentle hermits and ascetic sages, but also shape-shifting demons who attack the hermitages and devour their inhabitants. In several episodes Rāma puts to rout the *rākṣasas*, who infest the forest, and Rāvaṇa, the ten-headed king of demons, vows revenge. Using a magic deer to lure Rāma and Lakṣmaṇa away from their forest home, he kidnaps Sītā in his flying chariot. Rāma and Lakṣmaṇa set out in search of Sītā. Their southward journey brings them to Kiṣkindhā, kingdom of the monkeys (*vānaras*), and Rāma strikes up an alliance with the monkey chief Sugrīva. In return for Rāma's help in killing his powerful brother Vāli, who has unfairly seized his kingdom, Sugrīva sends out a horde of monkeys to locate Sītā.

"The Beautiful Book," book 5, so called because of its fine descriptive passages, is devoted to the exploits of the powerful monkey Hanumān, who emerges as a hero in his own right. Searching in the southern direction, Hanumān, whose father is the wind god himself, leaps the ocean in a single bound and searches for Rāma's wife in the *rākṣasas*' fabulous island kingdom of Laṅkā (identified with modern Sri Lanka). He finds Sītā a prisoner in Rāvaṇa's pleasure grove, still rejecting his suit (like Pene-lope in the *Odyssey*) and despairing of Rāma's ever coming to rescue her. Hanumān consoles her, wreaks havoc in Laṅkā, and returns to report to Rāma. In the sixth book, the monkeys build a fabulous bridge and Rāma leads a monkey army to attack Rāvaṇa's rich city. The demons are routed; Rāma kills the *rākṣasa* king and liberates Sītā. After Sītā proves her chastity in an ordeal by fire, the hero returns with her and Lakṣmaṇa to Ayodhyā, where he is crowned.

Tragedy pervades book 7, *Uttara*. Public scandal concerning Sītā's chastity during her captivity in Rāvaṇa's palace forces King Rāma to abandon her to life in the forest. She takes refuge in the hermitage of the poet-sage Vālmīki on a bank of the Ganges River and there gives birth to Rāma's twin sons. From Vālmīki the twins Lava and Kuśa learn the saga of Rāma, which they later sing in their father's court. On hear-ing the story, Rāma asks Sītā to come back to him, but Sītā declares that the purpose of her life has been fulfilled and cries out to her mother, the goddess Earth, who opens up to receive her. Rāma continues his rule until it is time for him to end his incarnation as a mortal.

The later literary versions of the *Rāmāyaṇa* have become classics in their own right. Kampaṉ's *Irāmāvatāram* (The incarnation of rāma, twelfth century) is celebrated as the greatest poem in the Tamil language. Tulsīdās's Hindi *Rāmcaritmānas* (Sacred lake of the acts of Rāma, sixteenth century), which celebrates Rāma's divinity, is a major work in the mystical literary tradition of *bhakti*. Most post-Vālmīki versions of the Rāmāyaṇa end with Rāma's return to Ayodhyā and his coronation, choosing the positive connotations and narrative closure of this ending over the troubling complexities of the events of Vālmīki's last Book.

Vālmīki's *Rāmāyaṇa* and its later adaptations have been enjoyed by Indian audiences in forms as vastly different as religious plays, bedtime stories, and, most recently, "classic" comics and a television serial. Every year, all over India, millions of readers, listeners, and viewers weep at Rāma's exile and the death of Daśaratha, cheer as the monkey Hanumān leaps the sea to Laṅkā, share in Sītā's anguish as she climbs the pyre for her trial by fire, and rejoice at the death of Rāvaṇa. For them, the poem's mythic, political, and social dimensions are of a piece, and the deeds of a warrior-prince of ancient Kosala seem as relevant today as in India's heroic age. Rāma and Sītā are worshiped as deities in temples all over India. Nevertheless, the Rāma story's enduring appeal for Indians, especially as Vālmīki presents it, lies in the affinities people continue to feel with its moral and psychological world.

Character and situation particularly occupy *Ayodhyā*, perhaps the most dramatic of the epic's books. Rāma's character remains the focal point throughout, as he responds to the arguments of various members of his family at a time of personal crisis. At stake are issues of political importance, like succession to the throne, but also significant are the complex relationships within a large patriarchal family. Through the drama of *Ayodhyā*, Rāma teaches the ways of right action according to *dharma*, or sacred duty, the principle on which the hierarchical relationships of the Indian family and society are based.

Faced with disinheritance, Rāma sees clearly that a son's highest duty is to honor his father's word, even if this means giving up the kingdom. His position does not go unchallenged: his mother protests against the exile; his brother is angered and recommends rising against the unjust king; the helpless Daśaratha himself begs Rāma to foil his wicked stepmother and take power. Rāma rejects all these arguments, considering them tainted by self-interest, whereas the actions of the ideal man and perfect king are governed by *dharma*, conceived to be the transcendent ethical basis of the entire social order. In accepting his exile, Rāma points out, he is not merely obeying his father's command, but upholding the integrity of the king's word. The prince's deference to father and king is not simple filial subservience, or "duty" in any narrow sense, but an act honoring *dharma* and, therefore, of cosmic significance, requiring the highest moral courage. It is precisely Rāma's act of renunciation that makes him fit for kingship. On the other hand, where injustice unambiguously demands aggressive action, as when Sītā is abducted, he acts in the manner of the conventional warrior-king, although even here he is guided by his sense of cosmic rather than merely personal responsibility.

For Indians, Rāma's heroism lies in his attitude as well as in his acts. He gives up the kingdom with a generous spirit, cheerfully undertakes the exile imposed on him, treats with kindness and courtesy even those who would harm him, and faces adversity with stoic courage. A slayer of demons, he is equally able to subordinate all personal interest to the universally applicable value of *dharma*. In this he differs from the heroes of Homeric epic and Greek tragedy, whose nobility centers in the passionate intensity with which they illuminate particular heroic virtues. Virgil's "virtuous Aeneas" perhaps comes closest to Vālmīki's Rāma in his dedication to founding Rome, a mandate for the sake of which he gives up his love for Dido; but Rāma embodies a unique blend of virtues, one not expressed even in the characters of the heroes of the *Mahābhārata*, the other Indian epic. In the broader context of Indian civilization, only Rāma's heroism combines the strong sense of duty and dedication to social responsibility demanded of the ideal king and the ideal member of the structured Hindu social order with the ascetic qualities of such figures as the Buddha, who renounces the world to seek perfection on the spiritual plane. It was this combination of qualities that moved India's great leader of the twentieth century, Mahatma Gandhi, to admire Rāma as his personal hero and the personification of the ideal man.

In Vālmīki the portraits of Rāma and Sītā as models of behavior for Indian men and women take on depth and color through contrast with other figures who act in less than perfect ways. Rāma's brothers Bharata and Lakṣmaṇa are clearly idealized in their unswerving devotion to their elder brother; yet both are capable of rebelling at the unjust behavior of their elders. Daśaratha is portrayed as a venial old man; Rāvaṇa's intelligence is clouded by lust. If Rāma is both the ideal man and king, Sītā's role as the exemplar for women is focused solely on her conduct as a wife; not only does she voluntarily accompany her husband in exile but she obeys and honors him during the public trial that he makes her undergo, even though she knows that she does not deserve this humiliation. Measured against this paragon of wifely devotion, not only Kaikeyī but Rāma's own mother, the benign Kausalyā, emerges as a flawed woman: if Kaikeyī's selfishness leads her to inflict great suffering upon her husband, Kausalyā needs to be reminded by Rāma that it is her duty to stand by her husband in adversity.

Not perfect conduct alone, but the capacity to suffer deeply endears Rāma and Sītā to traditional Indian audiences. Although he is an incarnation, throughout the epic Rāma is painfully aware of his own—and others'—suffering, and his awareness of the absolute, transcendent nature of *dharma* in no way prevents him from being compassionate to those who are less perfect than he. The hero's compassion, coupled with the solitude of his burden of duty and knowledge, renders him a lonely yet sympathetic figure. As the eternally self-sacrificing wife, Sītā, on the other hand, embodies the suffering of the Hindu Everywoman. These very qualities have been passionately criticized by some modern Indian readers, who see in the idealization of Rāma and Sītā the perpetuation of patriarchal and hierarchical values that go against the spirit of modern India's striving toward an egalitarian society.

But even critics of the epic's social teachings acknowledge the emotional power of Vālmīki's treatment of the story of Rāma. Despite its stress on absolute standards of morality, and despite the fairy tale–like quality of the hero's conflict with demons, Vālmīki's *Rāmāyaṇa* is sensitive to the complexity of human character. Although the moral standards of Ayodhyā are superior to those of the monkey kingdom and Rāvaṇa's kingdom, even these lesser realms are redeemed by inhabitants who perform acts of goodness, piety, and love. The hunchback Mantharā and the weak-willed Kaikeyī are able to generate evil in Ayodhyā itself, while in Laṅkā Rāvaṇa's wife, Maṇḍodarī, is as devoted to him as Sītā is to Rāma. The greatest appeal of the ape Hanumān, perhaps the most beloved and popular character in the *Rāmāyaṇa*, is his childlike innocence and his supreme devotion to Rāma, which moves him to risk his life for his lord. Rāvaṇa himself exhibits humanity in his love for his sister, brothers, and sons, while his two *rākṣasa* brothers follow contrasting codes, both virtuous; Kumbhakarṇa remains loyal to his elder brother Rāvaṇa to the end, while the pious Vibhīṣ aṇa, measuring *dharma* by a more abstract standard than simple loyalty, abandons the evil Rāvaṇa for Rāma. Much as it is a poem about *dharma*, Vālmīki's *Rāmāyaṇa* is also about human emotion and the redemptive power of love.

PRONOUNCING GLOSSARY

The following list uses common English syllables and stress accents to provide rough equivalents of selected words whose pronunciation may be unfamiliar to the general reader.

Aditi: *uh'-dee-tee*

Agastya: *uh-guhs'-tya*

Aṅgada: *uhn'-guh-duh*

Āraṇya: *ah-ruhn'-yuh*

Aśoka: *uh-shoh'-kuh*

Ayodhyā: *uh-yoh'-dhyah*

Bāla: *bah'-luh*

Bharata: *bhuh'-ruh-ta*

Brahmā: *bruh'-mah*

Citrakūṭa: *chee-trah-koo'-tuh*

Daṇḍaka: *dahn'-duh-kuh*

Daśaratha: *dah'-shuh-ruh'-tha*

dharma: *dhahr'-muh*

gandharva: *guhn-dhuhr'-vuh*

Godāvarī: *goh-dah'-vuh-ree*

Hanumān: *huh'-noo-mahn*

Ikṣvāku: *iksh-vah'-koo*

Indra: *in'-drah*

Indrajit: *in'-drah-jit*

Jāmbavān: *jahm'-buh-vahn*

Janaka: *jah'-nah-kah*

Janasthāna: *jah-nah-stah'-nuh*

Jaṭāyu: *jah-tah'-yoo*

Kaikeyī: *kai-kay'-yee*

Kailāsa: *kai-lah'-suh*

Kāṇḍa: *kahn'-da*

Kaśyapa: *kuhsh'-yuh-puh*

Kausalyā: *kow'-suhl-yah*

Khara: *khuh'-ruh*

Kiṣkindhā: *keesh'-keen-dah*

Kumbhakarṇa: *koom'-bhuh-kuhr-nuh*

Kuśa: *koo'-shuh*

Lakṣmaṇa: *luhksh'-muh-nuh*

Lakṣmī: *luhksh'-mee*

Laṅkā: *luhn'-kah*

Lava: *luh'-vuh*

Maināka: *mai-nah'-kuh*

Mantharā: *muhn'-thuh-rah*

Mārīca: *mah-ree'-chuh*

Mātali: *mah'-tuh-lee*

Nāga: *nah'-guh*

Nahuṣa: *nuh'-hoo-shuh*

Nārāyaṇa: *nah-rah'-yuh-nuh*

Pañcavaṭī: *puhn'-chuh-vuh-tee*

Puṣpaka: *poosh'-puh-kuh*

rākṣasa: *rah'-kshuh-suh*

Rāma: *rah'-muh*

Rāmāyaṇa: *rah-mah'-yuh-nuh*

Rāvaṇa: *rah'-vuh-nuh*

Sagara: *suh'-guh-ruh*

Sāgara: *sah'-guh-ruh*

Sampāti: *suhm-pah'-tee*

Śatrughna: *shuh-troo'-gnuh*

Simhikā: *seeh'-mee-kah*

Siṃśapā: *sheem'-shuh-puh*

Sītā: *see'-tah*

Śiva: *shi'-vuh*

śloka: *shloh'-kuh*

Sugrīva: *soo-gree'-vuh*

Sumantra: *soo-muhn'-truh*

Sumitrā: *soo-mee'-trah*

Sundara: *soon'-duh-ruh*

Surasā: *soo'-ruh-sah*

Śūrpaṇakhā: *shoor'-puh-nuh-khah*

Trijaṭā: *tree'-juh-tah'*

Uttara: *oot'-tuh-ruh*

Vāli: *vah'-lee*

Vālmīki: *vahl-mee'-kee*

vānara: *vah'-nuh-ruh*

Vasiṣṭha: *vuh-see'-shta*

Veda: *vay'-duh*

Vibhīṣaṇa: *vee-bhee'-shuh-nuh*

The vulture said: "You know that Dakṣa Prajāpati[2] had sixty daughters and the sage Kaśyapa married eight of them. One day Kaśyapa said to his wives: 'You will give birth to offspring who will be foremost in the three worlds.' Aditi, Diti, Danu and Kālaka listened attentively; the others were indifferent. As a result, the former four gave birth to powerful offspring who were superhuman. Aditi gave birth to thirty-three gods. Diti gave birth to demons. Danu gave birth to Aśvagrīva. And, Kālaka had Naraka and Kālikā. Of the others, men were born of Manu, and the sub-human species from the other wives of Kaśyapa. Tāmra's daughter was Sukī whose granddaughter was Vinatā who had two sons, Garuḍa and Aruṇa. My brother Sampāti and I are the sons of Aruṇa. I offer my services to you, O Rāma. If you will be pleased to accept them, I shall guard Sītā when you and Lakṣmaṇa may be away from your hermitage. As you have seen, this formidable forest is full of wild animals and demons, too."

Rāma accepted this new friendship. All of them now proceeded towards Pañcavaṭī in search of a suitable place for building a hermitage. Having arrived at Pañcavaṭī, identified by Rāma by the description which the sage Agastya had given, Rāma said to Lakṣmaṇa: "Pray, select a suitable place here for building the hermitage. It should have a charming forest, good water, firewood, flowers and holy grass." Lakṣmaṇa submitted: "Even if we live together for a hundred years, I shall continue to be your servant. Hence, Lord, you select the place and I shall do the needful." Rejoicing at Lakṣmaṇa's attitude, Rāma pointed to a suitable place, which satisfied all the requisites of a hermitage. Rāma said: "This is holy ground; this is charming; it is frequented by beasts and birds. We shall dwell here." Immediately Lakṣmaṇa set about building a hermitage for all of them to live in.

Rāma warmly embraced Lakṣmaṇa and said: "I am delighted by your good work and devoted service: and I embrace you in token of such admiration. Brother, you divine the wish of my heart, you are full of gratitude, you know dharma; with such a man as his son, father is not dead but is eternally alive."

Entering that hermitage, Rāma, Lakṣmaṇa and Sītā dwelt in it with great joy and happiness.

ĀRAṆYA 16

Time rolled on. One day Lakṣmaṇa sought the presence of Rāma early in the morning and described what he had seen outside the hermitage. He said: "Winter, the season which you love most, has arrived, O Rāma. There is dry cold everywhere; the earth is covered with foodgrains. Water is uninviting; and fire is pleasant. The first fruits of the harvest have been brought in; and the agriculturists have duly offered some of it to the gods and the manes, and thus reaffirmed their indebtedness to them. The farmer who thus offers the first fruits to gods and manes is freed from sin.

"The sun moves in the southern hemisphere; and the north looks lusterless. Himālaya, the abode of snow, looks even more so! It is pleasant to take a walk even at noon. The shade of a tree which we loved in summer is unpleasant now. Early in the morning the earth, with its rich wheat and bar-

2. A progenitor god in ancient Hindu mythology.

ley fields, is enveloped by mist. Even so, the rice crop. The sun, even when it rises, looks soft and cool like the moon. Even the elephants which approach the water, touch it with their trunk but pull the trunk quickly away on account of the coldness of the water.

"Rāma, my mind naturally thinks of our beloved brother Bharata. Even in this cold winter, he who could command the luxury of a king, prefers to sleep on the floor and live an ascetic life. Surely, he, too, would have got up early in the morning and has perhaps had a cold bath in the river Sarayū. What a noble man! I can even now picture him in front of me: with eyes like the petals of a lotus, dark brown in color, slim and without an abdomen, as it were. He knows what dharma is. He speaks the truth. He is modest and self-controlled, always speaks pleasantly, is sweet-natured, with long arms and with all his enemies fully subdued.[3] That noble Bharata has given up all his pleasures and is devoted to you. He has already won his place in heaven, Rāma. Though he lives in the city; yet, he has adopted the ascetic mode of life and follows you in spirit.

"We have heard it said that a son takes after his mother in nature: but in the case of Bharata this has proved false. I wonder how Kaikeyī, in spite of having our father as her husband, and Bharata as her son, has turned out to be so cruel."

When Lakṣmaṇa said this, Rāma stopped him, saying: "Do not speak ill of our mother Kaikeyī, Lakṣmaṇa. Talk only of our beloved Bharata. Even though I try not to think of Ayodhyā and our people there, when I think of Bharata, I wish to see him."

ĀRAṆYA 17–18

After their bath and morning prayers, Rāma, Lakṣmaṇa and Sītā returned to their hermitage. As they were seated in their hut, there arrived upon the scene a dreadful demoness. She looked at Rāma and immediately fell in love with him! He had a handsome face; she had an ugly face. He had a slender waist; she had a huge abdomen. He had lovely large eyes; she had hideous eyes. He had lovely soft hair; she had red hair. He had a lovable form; she had a terrible form. He had a sweet voice; hers resembled the barking of a dog. He was young; she was haughty. He was able; her speech was crooked. He was of noble conduct; she was of evil conduct. He was beloved; she had a forbidding appearance. Such a demoness spoke to Rāma: "Who are you, young men; and what are both of you doing in this forest, with this lady?"

Rāma told her the whole truth about himself, Lakṣmaṇa and Sītā, about his banishment from the kingdom, etc. Then Rāma asked her: "O charming lady,[4] now tell me who you are." At once the demoness replied: "Ah, Rāma! I shall tell you all about myself immediately. I am Śūrpaṇakhā, the sister of Rāvaṇa. I am sure you have heard of him. He has two other brothers, Kumbhakarṇa and Vibhīṣaṇa.[5] Two other brothers Khara and Dūṣaṇa live in the neighborhood here. The moment I saw you, I fell in love with you. What have you to do with this ugly, emaciated Sītā? Marry me. Both of us shall roam about this forest. Do not worry about Sītā or Lakṣmaṇa: I shall swallow

---

3. A list of the conventional attributes of a handsome, brave, and virtuous warrior.   4. This formulaic phrase used in addressing a lady is meant ironically here.   5. The names of the demons are suggestive: Śūrpaṇakhā (Woman with Nails as Large as Winnowing Baskets) and Kumbhakarṇa (Pot Ear).

Rāvaṇa crossed the ocean in his flying chariot and reached the hermitage where Mārīca[9] was living in ascetic garb, subsisting on a disciplined diet. Mārīca welcomed Rāvaṇa and questioned him about the purpose of his visit.

ĀRAṆYA 36–37

Rāvaṇa said to Mārīca: "Listen, Mārīca. You know that fourteen thousand demons, including my brother Khara and the great warrior Triśira have been mercilessly killed by Rāma and Lakṣmaṇa who have now promised their protection to the ascetics of Daṇḍlaka forest, thus flouting our authority. Driven out of his country by his angry father, obviously for a disgraceful action, this unrighteous and hard-hearted prince Rāma has killed the demons without any justification. And, they have even dared to disfigure my beloved sister Śūrpaṇakhā. I must immediately take some action to avenge the death of my brother and to restore our prestige and our authority. I need your help; kindly do not refuse this time.

"Disguising yourself as a golden deer of great beauty, roam near the hermitage of Rāma. Sītā would surely be attracted, and she would ask Rāma and Lakṣmaṇa to capture you. When they go after you, leaving Sītā alone in the hermitage, I shall easily abduct Sītā." Even as Rāvaṇa was unfolding this plot, Mārīca's mouth became dry and parched with fear. Trembling with fear, Mārīca said to Rāvaṇa:

"O king, one can easily get in this world a counselor who tells you what is pleasing to you; but hard it is to find a wise counselor who tells you the unpleasant truth which is good for you—and harder it is to find one who heeds such advice. Surely, your intelligence machine is faulty and therefore you have no idea of the prowess of Rāma. Else, you would not talk of abducting Sītā. I wonder: perhaps Sītā has come into this world to end your life, or perhaps there is to be great sorrow on account of Sītā, or perhaps maddened by lust, you are going to destroy yourself and the demons and Laṅkā itself. Oh, no, you were wrong in your estimation of Rāma. He is not wicked; he is righteousness incarnate. He is not cruel hearted; he is generous to a fault. He has not been disgraced and exiled from the kingdom. He is here to honor the promise his father had given his mother Kaikeyī, after joyously renouncing his kingdom.

"O king, when you entertain ideas of abducting Sītā you are surely playing with fire. Please remember: when you stand facing Rāma, you are standing face to face with your own death. Sītā is the beloved wife of Rāma, who is extremely powerful. Nay, give up this foolish idea. What will you gain by thus gambling with your sovereignty over the demons, and with your life itself? Please consult the noble Vibhīṣaṇa and your virtuous ministers before embarking upon such unwise projects. They will surely advise you against them."

* * *

ĀRAṆYA 42

Rāvaṇa was determined, and Mārīca knew that there was no use arguing with him. Hence, after the last-minute attempt to avert the catastrophe, Mārīca said to Rāvaṇa: "What can I do when you are so wicked? I am ready

---

9. An uncle of Rāvaṇa, expert in sorcery.

to go to Rāma's āśrama.[1] God help you!" Not minding the taunt, Rāvaṇa expressed his unabashed delight at Mārīca's consent. He applauded Mārīca and said: "That is the spirit, my friend: you are now the same old Mārīca that I knew. I guess you had been possessed by some evil spirit a few minutes ago, on account of which you had begun to preach a different gospel. Let us swiftly get into this vehicle and proceed to our destination. As soon as you have accomplished the purpose, you are free to go and to do what you please!"

Both of them got into the flying chariot and quickly left the hermitage of Mārīca. Once again they passed forests, hills, rivers and cities: and soon they reached the neighborhood of the hermitage of Rāma. They got down from that chariot which had been embellished with gold. Holding Mārīca by the hand, Rāvaṇa said to him: "Over there is the hermitage of Rāma, surrounded by banana plantations. Well, now, get going with the work for which we have come here." Immediately Mārīca transformed himself into an attractive deer. It was extraordinary, totally unlike any deer that inhabited the forest. It was unique. It dazzled like a huge gem stone. Each part of its body had a different color. The colors had an unearthly brilliance and charm. Thus embellished by the colors of all the precious stones, the deer which was the demon Mārīca in disguise, roamed about near the hermitage of Rāma, nibbling at the grass now and then. At one time it came close to Sītā; then it ran away and joined the other deer grazing at a distance. It was very playful, jumping about and chasing its tail and spinning around. Sītā went out to gather flowers. She cast a glance at that extraordinary and unusual deer. As she did so, the deer too, sensing the accomplishment of the mission, came closer to her. Then it ran away, pretending to be afraid. Sītā marveled at the very appearance of this unusual deer the like of which she had not seen before and which had the hue of jewels.

ĀRAṆYA 43

From where she was gathering flowers, Sītā, filled with wonder to see that unusual deer, called out to Rāma: "Come quick and see, O Lord; come with your brother. Look at this extraordinary creature. I have never seen such a beautiful deer before." Rāma and Lakṣmaṇa looked at the deer, and Lakṣmaṇa's suspicions were aroused: "I am suspicious; I think it is the same demon Mārīca in disguise. I have heard that Mārīca could assume any form at will, and through such tricks he had brought death and destruction to many ascetics in this forest. Surely, this deer is not real: no one has heard of a deer with rainbow colors, each one of its limbs shining resplendent with the color of a different gem! That itself should enable us to understand that it is a demon, not an animal."

Sītā interrupted Lakṣmaṇa's talk, and said: "Never mind, one thing is certain; this deer has captivated my mind. It is such a dear. I have not seen such an animal near our hermitage! There are many types of deer which roam about near the hermitage; this is just an extraordinary and unusual deer. It is superlative in all respects: its color is lovely, its texture is lovely, and even its voice sounds delightful. It would be a wonderful feat if it could

1. Hermitage.

ĀRAṆYA 64

Lakṣmaṇa, too, saw the animals' behavior as sure signs indicating that Sītā had been borne away in a southerly direction, and suggested to Rāma that they should also proceed in that direction. As they were thus proceeding, they saw petals of flowers fallen on the ground. Rāma recognized them and said to Lakṣmaṇa: "Look here, Lakṣmaṇa, these are petals from the flowers that I had given to Sītā. Surely, in their eagerness to please me, the sun, the wind and the earth, have contrived to keep these flowers fresh."

They walked further on. Rāma saw footprints on the ground. Two of them he immediately recognized as those of Sītā. The other two were big— obviously the footprints of a demon. Bits and pieces of gold were strewn on the ground. Lo and behold, Rāma also saw blood which he concluded was Sītā's blood: he wailed again: "Alas, at this spot, the demon killed Sītā to eat her flesh." He also saw evidence of a fight: and he said: "Perhaps there were two demons fighting for the flesh of Sītā."

Rāma saw on the ground pieces of a broken weapon, an armor of gold, a broken canopy, and the propellers and other parts of a flying chariot. He also saw lying dead, one who had the appearance of the pilot of the craft. From these he concluded that two demons had fought for the flesh of Sītā, before one carried her away. He said to Lakṣmaṇa: "The demons have earned my unquenchable hate and wrath. I shall destroy all of them. Nay, I shall destroy all the powers that be who refuse to return Sītā to me. Look at the irony of fate, Lakṣmaṇa: we adhere to dharma, but dharma could not protect Sītā who has been abducted in this forest! When these powers that govern the universe witness Sītā being eaten by the demons, without doing anything to stop it, who is there to do what is pleasing to us? I think our meekness is misunderstood to be weakness. We are full of self-control, compassion and devoted to the welfare of all beings: and yet these virtues have become as good as vices in us now. I shall set aside all these virtues and the universe shall witness my supreme glory which will bring about the destruction of all creatures, including the demons. If Sītā is not immediately brought back to me, I shall destroy the three worlds—the gods, the demons and other creatures will perish, becoming targets of my most powerful missiles. When I take up my weapon in anger, O Lakṣmaṇa, no one can confront me, even as no one can evade old age and death."

ĀRAṆYA 65–66

Seeing the world-destroying mood of Rāma, Lakṣmaṇa endeavored to console him. He said to Rāma:

"Rāma, pray, do not go against your nature. Charm in the moon, brilliance in the sun, motion in the air, and endurance in the earth—these are their essential nature: in you all these are found and in addition, eternal glory. Your nature cannot desert you; even the sun, the moon and the earth cannot abandon their nature! Moreover, being king, you cannot punish all the created beings for the sin of one person. Gentle and peaceful monarchs match punishment to crime: and, over and above this, you are the refuge of all beings and their goal. I shall without fail find out the real criminal who has abducted Sītā; I shall find out whose armor and weapons these are. And you shall mete out just punishment to the sinner. Oh, no, no god will seek to displease you, O Rāma: Nor these trees, mountains and rivers. I am sure they will all eagerly aid us in our search for Sītā. Of course, if Sītā cannot be recovered through peaceful means, we shall consider other means.

"Whom does not misfortune visit in this world, O Rāma? And, misfortune departs from man as quickly as it visits him. Hence, pray, regain your composure. If you who are endowed with divine intelligence betray lack of endurance in the face of this misfortune, what will others do in similar circumstances?

"King Nahuṣa, who was as powerful as Indra, was beset with misfortune.[7] The sage Vasiṣṭha, our family preceptor, had a hundred sons and lost all of them on one day! Earth is tormented by volcanic eruptions, and earthquakes. The sun and the moon are afflicted by eclipses. Misfortune strikes the great ones and even the gods.

"For, in this world people perform actions whose results are not obvious; and these actions which may be good or evil, bear their own fruits. Of course, these fruits are evanescent. People who are endowed with enlightened intelligence know what is good and what is not good. People like you do not grieve over misfortunes and do not get deluded by them.

"Why am I telling you all this, O Rāma? Who in this world is wiser than you? However, since, as is natural, grief seems to veil wisdom, I am saying all this. All this I learnt only from you: I am only repeating what you yourself taught me earlier. Therefore, O Rāma, know your enemy and fight him."

ĀRAṆYA 67–68

Rāma then asked Lakṣmaṇa: "O Lakṣmaṇa, tell me, what should we do now?" Lakṣmaṇa replied: "Surely, we should search this forest for Sītā."

This advice appealed to Rāma. Immediately he fixed the bayonet to his weapon and with a look of anger on his face, set out to search for Sītā. Within a very short time and distance, both Rāma and Lakṣmaṇa chanced upon Jaṭāyu, seriously and mortally wounded and heavily bleeding. Seeing that enormous vulture lying on the ground, Rāma's first thought was: "Surely, this is the one that has swallowed Sītā." He rushed forward with fixed bayonet.

Looking at Rāma thus rushing towards him, and rightly inferring Rāma's mood, Jaṭāyu said in a feeble voice: "Sītā has been taken away by Rāvaṇa. I tried to intervene. I battled with the mighty Rāvaṇa. I broke his armor, his canopy, the propellers and some parts of his chariot. I killed his pilot. I even inflicted injuries on his person. But he cut off my wings and thus grounded me." When Rāma heard that the vulture had news of Sītā, he threw his weapon away and kneeling down near the vulture embraced it.

Rāma said to Lakṣmaṇa: "An additional calamity to endure, O Lakṣmaṇa. Is there really no end to my misfortune? My misfortune plagues even this noble creature, a friend of my father's." Rāma requested more information from Jaṭāyu concerning Sītā, and also concerning Rāvaṇa. Jaṭāyu replied: "Taking Sītā with him, the demon flew away in his craft, leaving a mysterious storm and cloud behind him. I was mortally wounded by him. Ah, my senses are growing dim. I feel life ebbing away, Rāma. Yet, I assure you, you

---

7. King Nahuṣa, an ancestor of Rāma, became so powerful that he claimed the throne of Indra, king of gods, but an arrogant act soon effected his fall from his exalted position.

will recover Sītā." Soon Jaṭāyu lay lifeless. Nay, it was his body, for he himself ascended to heaven. Grief-stricken afresh, Rāma said to Lakṣmaṇa:
"Jaṭāyu lived a very long life; and yet has had to lay down his life today.
Death, no one in this world can escape. And what a noble end! What a great
service this noble vulture has rendered to me! Pious and noble souls are
found even amongst subhuman creatures, O Lakṣmaṇa. Today I have forgotten all my previous misfortunes: I am extremely tormented by the loss of this
dear friend who has sacrificed his life for my sake. I shall myself cremate it,
so that it may reach the highest realms."

Rāma himself performed the funeral rites, reciting those Vedic mantras[8]
which one recites during the cremation of one's own close relations. After
this, Rāma and Lakṣmaṇa proceeded on their journey in search of Sītā.

* * *

From *Book 6*

Yuddha

YUDDHA 109, 110, 111

When Rāma and Rāvaṇa began to fight, their armies stood stupefied,
watching them! Rāma was determined to win; Rāvaṇa was sure he would
die: knowing this, they fought with all their might. Rāvaṇa attacked the
standard on Rāma's car; and Rāma similarly shot the standard on Rāvaṇa's
car. While Rāvaṇa's standard fell; Rāma's did not. Rāvaṇa next aimed at the
"horses" of Rāma's car: even though he attacked them with all his might,
they remained unaffected.

Both of them discharged thousands of missiles: these illumined the skies
and created a new heaven, as it were! They were accurate in their aim and their
missiles unfailingly hit the target. With unflagging zeal they fought each other,
without the least trace of fatigue. What one did the other did in retaliation.

Rāvaṇa shot at Mātali[1] who remained unaffected by it. Then Rāvaṇa sent
a shower of maces and mallets at Rāma. Their very sound agitated the
oceans and tormented the aquatic creatures. The celestials and the holy
brāhmaṇas witnessing the scene prayed: "May auspiciousness attend to all
the living beings, and may the worlds endure forever. May Rāma conquer
Rāvaṇa." Astounded at the way in which Rāma and Rāvaṇa fought with each
other, the sages said to one another: "Sky is like sky, ocean is like ocean; the
fight between Rāma and Rāvaṇa is like Rāma and Rāvaṇa—incomparable."

Taking up a powerful missile, Rāma correctly aimed at the head of
Rāvaṇa; it fell. But another head appeared in its place. Every time Rāma cut
off Rāvaṇa's head, another appeared! Rāma was puzzled. Mātali, Rāma's
driver, said to Rāma: "Why do you fight like an ordinary warrior, O Rāma?
Use the Brahmā-missile; the hour of the demon's death is at hand."

Rāma remembered the Brahmā-missile which the sage Agastya had given
him. It had the power of the wind-god for its "feathers"; the power of fire
and sun at its head; the whole space was its body; and it had the weight of a
mountain. It shone like the sun or the fire of nemesis. As Rāma took it in his

---

8. Sacred chants, usually from the scriptures.   1. Indra, king of the gods, has sent his own charioteer,
Mātali, to drive Rāma's chariot in battle.

hands, the earth shook and all living beings were terrified. Infallible in its destructive power, this ultimate weapon of destruction shattered the chest of Rāvaṇa, and entered deep into the earth.

Rāvaṇa fell dead. And the surviving demons fled, pursued by the vānaras. The vānaras shouted in great jubilation. The air resounded with the drums of the celestials. The gods praised Rāma. The earth became steady, the wind blew softly and the sun was resplendent as before. Rāma was surrounded by mighty heroes and gods who were all joyously felicitating him on the victory.

YUDDHA 112, 113

Seeing Rāvaṇa lying dead on the battlefield, Vibhīṣaṇa burst into tears. Overcome by brotherly affection, he lamented thus: "Alas, what I had predicted has come true: and my advice was not relished by you, overcome as you were by lust and delusion. Now that you have departed, the glory of Laṅkā has departed. You were like a tree firmly established in heroism with asceticism for its strength, spreading out firmness in all aspects of your life: yet you have been cut down. You were like an elephant with splendor, noble ancestry, indignation, and pleasant nature for parts: yet you have been killed. You, who were like blazing fire have been extinguished by Rāma."

Rāma approached the grief-stricken Vibhīṣaṇa and gently and lovingly said to him: "It is not right that you should thus grieve, O Vibhīṣaṇa, for a mighty warrior fallen on the battlefield. Victory is the monopoly of none: a hero is either slain in battle or he kills his opponent. Hence our ancients decreed that the warrior who is killed in combat should not be mourned. Get up and consider what should be done next."

Vibhīṣaṇa regained his composure and said to Rāma: "This Rāvaṇa used to give a lot in charity to ascetics; he enjoyed life; he maintained his servants well; he shared his wealth with his friends, and he destroyed his enemies. He was regular in his religious observances; learned he was in the scriptures. By your grace, O Rāma, I wish to perform his funeral in accordance with the scriptures, for his welfare in the other world." Rāma was delighted and said to Vibhīṣaṇa: "Hostility ends at death. Take steps for the due performance of the funeral rites. He is your brother as he is mine, too."

The womenfolk of Rāvaṇa's court, and his wives, hearing of his end, rushed out of the palace, and, arriving at the battlefield, rolled on the ground in sheer anguish. Overcome by grief they gave vent to their feelings in diverse heart-rending ways. They wailed: "Alas, he who could not be killed by the gods and demons, has been killed in battle by a man standing on earth. Our beloved lord! Surely when you abducted Sītā and brought her to Laṅkā, you invited your own death! Surely it was because death was close at hand that you did not listen to the wise counsel of your own brother Vibhī-ṣaṇa, and you ill-treated him and exiled him. Even later if you had restored Sītā to Rāma, this evil fate would not have overtaken you. However, it is surely not because you did what you liked, because you were driven by lust, that you lie dead now: God's will makes people do diverse deeds. He who is killed by the divine will dies. No one can flout the divine will, and no one can buy the divine will nor bribe it."

* * *

THE BHAGAVAD-GĪTĀ
first century B.C.E.

The Sanskrit poem *Bhagavad-Gītā* (Song of the lord) has been for centuries the great scripture of the Hindus and the Indian text most familiar to the West. The American writer Henry David Thoreau (1817–1862) took the *Gītā* with him to his retreat on Walden Pond, and the *Gītā* was the inspiring force in the life and thought of the eminent modern Indian leader Mahatma Gandhi (1869–1948). The enduring and seemingly universal appeal of this philosophical poem written in India two thousand years ago derives from the powerful, immediate way in which it addresses fundamental human concerns.

The *Bhagavad-Gītā* is a poem in eighteen chapters (and seven hundred verses), forming part of the sixth book of the Sanskrit epic the *Mahābhārata*, which narrates the story of a great war between the virtuous Pāṇḍavas and their evil cousins, the Kauravas, sons of King Dhṛtarāṣṭra of Hāstinapura. The *Gītā* opens at a dramatic moment in the epic narrative, with the blind Kaurava king asking the bard Sanjaya to describe to him what his sons and their enemies did after gathering at the battlefield of Kurukṣetra. The bard reports the reactions of Arjuna, champion among the Pāṇḍava heroes, and the ensuing dialogue between him and his charioteer Krishna (or Kṛṣṇa). Arriving at the battlefield, Arjuna sees cousins, teachers, uncles, and kinsmen standing ready to fight against each other. Horrified at the prospect of killing his kin and overcome by dejection, he lays down his weapons and refuses to fight. But Krishna, who is in reality an incarnation of Viṣṇu (the preserver god), tells Arjuna that his sacred duty (*dharma*) requires him to fight and explains to him how, far from miring him in the dreaded cycle of *karma* and rebirth, action performed in the spirit of sacred duty will advance him on the path to emancipation of the spirit, the Hindu's ultimate religious goal. Krishna's discourse, punctuated by Arjuna's questions, becomes *The Song of the Lord* (*Bhagavad-Gītā*).

There is reason to believe that the *Gītā*, originally an independent philosophical dialogue similar to earlier and contemporary texts such as the *Upaniṣads* and the Buddhist scriptures, was deliberately placed in the popular *Mahābhārata* epic at the beginning of the tale of the great war to give dramatic force to its teachings and underscore its relevance to the lives of common people. Although also an exalted hero, at this point in the narrative Arjuna is a vulnerable human being caught in a very human dilemma. Krishna, on the other hand, is no ordinary teacher, but God, come to instruct his human friend. This new configuration of elements fortified a view that was at once revolutionary for its time and designed to preserve the Hindu social hierarchy.

By the end of the first century B.C.E. the Buddhist and Jain religions had gained a considerable following among the Indian masses and among kings and merchants as well. Focusing on the problem of *karma*—the belief that all actions involve inevitable consequences that must be suffered through many lives—Buddhism in particular offered men and women from all walks of life a religious path on which ethical action could be combined with contemplative spiritual practices, eventually leading to liberation from the burden of *karma*. In the Hindu social order, on the other hand, rigid and hierarchical correlations between birth and occupation locked people into existential situations that held no such prospect of ultimate freedom.

Arjuna's dilemma is a dramatic illustration of the problem: how can a Hindu warrior (*kṣatriya*), whose sacred duty (*dharma*) involves the taking of life (which, by an absolute standard, would entail evil *karma*), ever be liberated from rebirth, which is the ultimate goal of the religious person? The *Gītā* appears to have been the response of brahman thinkers who stood to lose the most from the potential disintegration of the Hindu social system. Through Krishna's teachings, the anonymous author of the

Gītā articulates a new doctrine that will justify the hierarchies of class and social duty (he uses the word *lokasaṃgraha*, "social solidarity") at the same time that it offers universal access to the ultimate goal of the emancipation of the soul from suffering and rebirth, thus answering the personal spiritual needs of Hindus from resistant and disenfranchised groups.

The *Gītā* owes its success to the attractive and ingenious way in which it harmonizes widely differing strands of ancient Indian religious thought and practice. The text synthesizes the contemplative vision of the Buddhists and the sages of the *Upaniṣads* with a philosophy of active engagement in worldly life. Krishna's teachings allow each Hindu to venture on a personal spiritual quest without abandoning social responsibility and its attendant security. Drawing on all of the older religious sects and schools of philosophy, the *Gītā* has accommodated radically different interpretations through the centuries. But the author's stroke of genius is without question his integration of a new teaching of salvation through divine grace, linked to the cult of a popular god, with the older theory of *karma.*

The *Gītā* is a complex text, weaving together as it does ancient, often contradictory ideas regarding existential questions that have preoccupied Indians for centuries. The poet uses the rhetorical device of Arjuna's doubts to repeat and consolidate previous arguments or to reject them as no longer useful, in what is essentially a technique of progressive illumination. In response to Arjuna's anguish at being unable to reconcile the conflict between sacred duty and the personal desire for liberation, Krishna explains to him the real nature of the soul and of action in the universe. He tells the hero that the soul (*ātman*, "the individual self") is not simply the ego but is in reality identical with Brahman, the immortal spirit underlying the entire universe. The knowledge of the soul's immortality, says Krishna, will dispel Arjuna's fear that he is personally responsible for particular actions. For the philosopher-teachers of the *Upaniṣads*, who propounded the theory of an immortal soul, this knowledge (*jñāna*) is the highest end of religious life, but for Krishna it is only a discipline (*yoga*), the first step toward liberation from birth and death.

If the soul is immortal, then Arjuna wants to know why it is involved in action, which inevitably causes rebirth. Adapting aspects of the doctrine of the Sāṃkhya philosophy, Krishna explains the riddle of an immortal soul's engagement in worldly action and a material universe. The perpetual action of all things with and on each other that constitutes the world process is an aspect of the union between God, who is the supreme embodiment of the immortal soul, and material nature, which is the substance of the universe. Action or change is an inescapable reality of living in the world; although the soul is immortal, in its embodied condition it is inevitably involved in deeds. God is himself engaged in the perpetual process of the world on which depend the cosmic, moral, and social orders, constituting *dharma* in its broadest sense. To withdraw from action, says Krishna, is thus an act of self-delusion and the abdication of moral and social responsibility.

This explanation only increases Arjuna's perplexity. If action is inevitable, how can the soul ever cease to be embodied (reborn)? Here Krishna turns to the Yoga philosophy, which propounds the doctrine of *yoga* ("a yoking"), the disciplining of the senses and the mind as the soul's path to transcendence over matter. Moving beyond the thought of traditional Yoga philosophers, he offers the new teaching of *karma yoga* (the "discipline of action") as the solution to Arjuna's problem. It is not action itself but desire for the fruit (profit or reward) of action that results in rebirth. If a person were to discipline his (the *Gītā*'s descriptions are all in the masculine gender) senses and mind to act with no desire whatsoever for the gains that will result, *karma* would not affect his soul. A person who acts in this disciplined way is the perfected *yogi* ("man of discipline"), and his soul is certain to be liberated from birth and death.

But how, then, does one know right action from wrong? The Hindu social order of *dharma*, based on cosmic and moral principles, relieves individuals of the responsibility of determining the content of action: right, or good, action is simply the sacred duty that has been prescribed for one's class, caste, and stage of life. In short, social and moral law takes care of the content of action, but the individual has control over the spirit in which he performs action and, therefore, over how his deeds will affect his soul. When acting in the world is transformed into *yoga*, a key concept in the *Gītā*, it becomes the very means for the soul's liberation from worldly existence.

Intriguing as Krishna's teachings are, they are still philosophical discourses whose greatest appeal is to the intellect. What drives the doctrine home for the majority of Hindus is the emotional power of Arjuna's vision of Krishna's omnipotent form as God, the theophany with which the teaching is clinched. At Arjuna's request, Krishna reveals to him his infinite form, showing himself as the source and refuge of all creatures and the entire universe and, as "time grown old," their destroyer as well. Profoundly moved, Arjuna sings a hymn to Krishna, but he is eventually overcome by terror and awe and begs Krishna to resume his familiar, gentle form once more.

In chapter 11 and elsewhere, the *Gītā* draws on the theology of the Bhagavatas—a group who worshiped Krishna as God and an incarnation of Viṣṇu—and develops the doctrine of *bhakti yoga,* the discipline of devotion. Recognizing God's grace and love in Krishna's earlier discourse as much as in the cosmic vision, Arjuna is at last ready to accept this final teaching, according to which the best way to overcome worldly desire is to make of all one's deeds a loving sacrifice to God. Krishna asserts that love of God will annul the power of desire and, therefore, of *karma,* but what is equally important is that the discipline of sacred duty will become a joyous, transfiguring experience. In his revelation of himself as God, Krishna declares, "If they rely on me, Arjuna, / women, commoners, men of low rank, / even men born in the womb of evil, / reach the highest way." And as if to illustrate this transition from duty to joy, the author of the *Bhagavad-Gītā* gives his auditors and readers not a dry philosophical tract but a poem in which the simple epic stanzas acquire an elegant, epigrammatic quality rendered memorable by vivid metaphors such as the one of the yogi who "does not waver, / like a lamp sheltered from the wind" and the likening of the brilliance of Krishna's divine epiphany to "the light of a thousand suns" rising in the sky at once.

Thoreau is only one among many Western thinkers who have found the *Gītā* ideal of the man of spiritual discipline (*yogi*) attractive. For Indian intellectuals in the late nineteenth century the work had an additional dimension. It was in response to Western education and Western critiques of Hinduism and Indian civilization under British colonial rule that Indian leaders from a very wide range of philosophies— from Swami Vivekananda (1863–1902) to Mahatma Gandhi—found the ideal text for India and the twentieth century in the *Bhagavad-Gītā.*

Much Western writing of the nineteenth century depicts Indians as a passive people with no social consciousness, attributing these shortcomings in part to the lack of a universal scripture and ethical code in Hinduism. Modern Indian leaders have found in the moral teaching of the *Gītā* and its spirit of pluralism and synthesis their greatest inspiration for political and social activism, for service to the Indian people, and for the creation of a modern democratic nation. Most have interpreted the text's spiritual egalitarianism in social terms, arguing that the *Gītā* teachings support, indeed demand, the abolition of traditional social hierarchies such as caste. For Swami Vivekananda, the twentieth-century Indian philosopher Sarvepalli Radhakrishnan (1888–1975), and others, the *Gītā* represents not a scripture for Hindus alone but a universal ethic for the modern world. In our own time, its vision of Krishna as God has flowered anew in the International Krishna Consciousness movement initiated by Swami A. C. Bhaktivedanta (1896–1977). The most remarkable reading of the *Gītā*'s teachings, however, is the one offered by Mahatma Gandhi, who argued that absolute nonviolence is the only logical culmination of Krishna's doctrine of "desireless action." That this ancient text continues to capture the imagination of so many modern thinkers is eloquent testimony to its vitality.

PRONOUNCING GLOSSARY

The following list uses common English syllables and stress accents to provide rough equivalents of selected words whose pronunciation may be unfamiliar to the general reader.

Bhagavad-Gītā: *buh'-guh-vuhd–gee'-tah*

Bhagavān: *buh'-guh-vahn*

Dhṛtarāṣṭra: *dree'-tuh-rahsh-truh*

Jñāna: *gyah'-nuh*

Krishna (Kṛṣṇa): *krish'-nuh*

kṣatriya: *kshuh'-tree-yuh*

Kurukṣetra: *koo-roo-kshay'-truh*

lokasaṃgraha: *loh'-kuh-suhn'-gruh-huh*

Mahābhārata: *muh-hah-bah'-ruh-tuh*

Sāṃkhya: *sahn'-kyuh*

śloka: *shloh'-kuh*

triṣṭubh: *tree'-shtoobh*

Upaniṣad: *oo-puh'-nee-shuhd*

The Bhagavad-Gītā[1]

From *The First Teaching*

[ARJUNA'S[2] DEJECTION]

20 Arjuna, his war flag a rampant monkey,
   saw Dhritarashtra's[3] sons assembled
   as weapons were ready to clash,
   and he lifted his bow.

21 He told his charioteer:
   "Krishna,[4]
   halt my chariot
   between the armies!

22 Far enough for me to see
   these men who lust for war,
   ready to fight with me
   in the strain of battle.

23 I see men gathered here,
   eager to fight,
   bent on serving the folly
   of Dhritarashtra's son."[5]

24 When Arjuna had spoken,
   Krishna halted
   their splendid chariot
   between the armies.

25 Facing Bhishma and Drona[6]
   and all the great kings,
   he said, "Arjuna, see
   the Kuru men[7] assembled here!"

---

1. Translated by Barbara Stoler Miller. Verse numbers run to the left of the text.   2. The third of the five Pāṇḍava brothers.   3. The blind king of the Hastinapura and father of the Kauravas.   4. Incarnation of Viṣṇu, the preserver god.   5. Here Duryodhana.   6. Preceptor of the Kauravas and the Pāṇḍavas. Bhishma is their granduncle.   7. The Kauravas.

26   Arjuna saw them standing there:
      fathers, grandfathers, teachers,
      uncles, brothers, sons,
      grandsons, and friends.

27   He surveyed his elders
      and companions in both armies,
      all his kinsmen
      assembled together.

28   Dejected, filled with strange pity,
      he said this:
          "Krishna, I see my kinsmen
          gathered here, wanting war.

29   My limbs sink,
          my mouth is parched,
          my body trembles,
          the hair bristles on my flesh.

30   The magic bow[8] slips
      from my hand, my skin burns,
      I cannot stand still,
      my mind reels.

31   I see omens of chaos,
      Krishna; I see no good
      in killing my kinsmen
      in battle.

32   Krishna, I see no victory,
      or kingship or pleasures.
      What use to us are kingship,
      delights, or life itself?

33   We sought kingship, delights,
      and pleasures for the sake of those
      assembled to abandon their lives
      and fortunes in battle.

34   They are teachers, fathers, sons,
      and grandfathers, uncles, grandsons,
      fathers and brothers of wives,
      and other men of our family.

35   I do not want to kill them
      even if I am killed, Krishna;
      not for kingship of all three worlds,
      much less for the earth!

36   What joy is there for us, Krishna,
      in killing Dhritarashtra's sons?
          Evil will haunt us if we kill them,
          though their bows are drawn to kill.

---

8. Gāṇḍīva, which he won from the fire god.

37　Honor forbids us to kill
　　our cousins, Dhritarashtra's sons;
　　how can we know happiness
　　if we kill our own kinsmen?

38　The greed that distorts their reason
　　blinds them to the sin they commit
　　in ruining the family, blinds them
　　to the crime of betraying friends.

39　How can we ignore the wisdom
　　of turning from this evil
　　when we see the sin
　　of family destruction, Krishna?

40　When the family is ruined,
　　the timeless laws of family duty
　　perish; and when duty is lost,
　　chaos overwhelms the family.

41　In overwhelming chaos, Krishna,
　　women of the family are corrupted;
　　and when women are corrupted,
　　disorder[9] is born in society.

42　This discord drags the violators
　　and the family itself to hell;
　　for ancestors fall when rites
　　of offering rice and water lapse.[1]

43　The sins of men who violate
　　the family create disorder in society
　　that undermines the constant laws
　　of caste and family duty.

44　Krishna, we have heard
　　that a place in hell
　　is reserved for men
　　who undermine family duties.

45　I lament the great sin
　　we commit when our greed
　　for kingship and pleasures
　　drives us to kill our kinsmen.

46　　　If Dhritarashtra's armed sons
　　　　kill me in battle when I am unarmed
　　　　and offer no resistance,
　　　　it will be my reward."

47　Saying this in the time of war,
　　Arjuna slumped into the chariot
　　and laid down his bow and arrows,
　　his mind tormented by grief.

---

9. Specifically, disruption of the proper ordering of the four principal social classes: brahman, warrior, merchant, and laborer.　1. Hindus are required to make these ritual offerings to their ancestors.

30   The self embodied in the body
of every being is indestructible;
you have no cause to grieve
for all these creatures, Arjuna!

31   Look to your own duty;[3]
do not tremble before it;
nothing is better for a warrior
than a battle of sacred duty.

32   The doors of heaven open
for warriors who rejoice
to have a battle like this
thrust on them by chance.

33   If you fail to wage this war
of sacred duty,
you will abandon your own duty
and fame only to gain evil.

34   People will tell
of your undying shame,
and for a man of honor
shame is worse than death.

*   *   *

47   Be intent on action,
not on the fruits of action;
avoid attraction to the fruits
and attachment to inaction!

48   Perform actions, firm in discipline,
relinquishing attachment;
be impartial to failure and success—
this equanimity is called discipline.

49   Arjuna, action is far inferior
to the discipline of understanding;[4]
so seek refuge in understanding—pitiful
are men drawn by fruits of action.

50   Disciplined by understanding,
one abandons both good and evil deeds;
so arm yourself for discipline—
discipline is skill in actions.

51   Wise men disciplined by understanding
relinquish the fruit born of action;
freed from these bonds of rebirth,
they reach a place beyond decay.

52   When your understanding passes beyond
the swamp of delusion,

---

3. *Dharma,* which for Arjuna is that of his class (warrior) and stage of life (householder).   4. The rational facilities, including intuitive intelligence, in contrast to the mind, or discursive intellect.

you will be indifferent to all
that is heard in sacred lore.[5]

53   When your understanding turns
from sacred lore to stand fixed,
immovable in contemplation,
then you will reach discipline.[6]

54   ARJUNA:
Krishna, what defines a man
deep in contemplation whose insight
and thought are sure? How would he speak?
How would he sit? How would he move?

55   LORD KRISHNA:
When he gives up desires in his mind,
is content with the self within himself,[7]
then he is said to be a man
whose insight is sure, Arjuna.

56   When suffering does not disturb his mind,
when his craving for pleasures has vanished,
when attraction, fear, and anger are gone,
he is called a sage whose thought is sure.

57   When he shows no preference
in fortune or misfortune
and neither exults nor hates,
his insight is sure.

58   When, like a tortoise retracting
its limbs, he withdraws his senses
completely from sensuous objects,
his insight is sure.

From *The Third Teaching*
[DISCIPLINE OF ACTION]

ARJUNA:

1   If you think understanding
is more powerful than action,
why, Krishna, do you urge me
to this horrific act?

2   You confuse my understanding
with a maze of words;
speak one certain truth
so I may achieve what is good.

---

5. The *Vedas* and their ritualistic doctrine. Krishna says that the older ritualistic learning is useless for the emancipation of the soul from *karma*.   6. Used in its broadest sense.   7. A play on the word *ātman*, which means both "the self" (soul) and "oneself." Only one who has realized the true (immutable) nature of the self can be "content with the self within himself." Krishna now begins to describe the techniques and effects of withdrawing one's senses from the outside and focusing them on the interior self, the infinite soul.

LORD KRISHNA:

3   Earlier I taught the twofold
    basis of good in this world—
    for philosophers, disciplined knowledge;
    for men of discipline, action.

4   A man cannot escape the force
    of action by abstaining from actions;
    he does not attain success
    just by renunciation.

5   No one exists for even an instant
    without performing action;
    however unwilling, every being is forced
    to act by the qualities of nature.[8]

6   When his senses are controlled
    but he keeps recalling
    sense objects with his mind,
    he is a self-deluded hypocrite.

7   When he controls his senses
    with his mind and engages in the discipline
    of action with his faculties of action,
    detachment sets him apart.

8   Perform necessary action;
    it is more powerful than inaction;
    without action you even fail
    to sustain your own body.

9   Action imprisons the world
    unless it is done as sacrifice;
    freed from attachment, Arjuna,
    perform action as sacrifice!

10 When creating living beings and sacrifice,
    Prajapati, the primordial creator, said:
        "By sacrifice will you procreate!
        Let it be your wish-granting cow![9]

11   Foster the gods with this,
        and may they foster you;
        by enriching one another,
        you will achieve a higher good.

12   Enriched by sacrifice, the gods
        will give you the delights you desire;
        he is a thief who enjoys their gifts
        without giving to them in return."

13 Good men eating the remnants
    of sacrifice are free of any guilt,

---

8. That is, sublimity, dynamism (passion), and inertia.   9. This image derives from the importance of cattle in Vedic society and religion. Prajapati is a god of the *Vedas*. In the Vedic worldview the preservation of the universe depended on sacrifices made to the gods, and such ritual was at the center of the religion.

but evil men who cook for themselves
eat the food of sin.

14   Creatures depend on food,
food comes from rain,
rain depends on sacrifice,
and sacrifice comes from action.

15   Action comes from the spirit of prayer,
whose source is OM,[1] sound of the imperishable;
so the pervading infinite spirit
is ever present in rites of sacrifice.

16   He who fails to keep turning
the wheel here set in motion
wastes his life in sin,
addicted to the senses, Arjuna.

17   But when a man finds delight
within himself and feels inner joy
and pure contentment in himself,
there is nothing more to be done.

18   He has no stake here
in deeds done or undone,
nor does his purpose
depend on other creatures.

19   Always perform with detachment
any action you must do;
performing action with detachment,
one achieves supreme good.

20   Janaka[2] and other ancient kings
attained perfection by action alone;
seeing the way to preserve
the world, you should act.

21   Whatever a leader does,
the ordinary people also do.
He sets the standard
for the world to follow.

22   In the three worlds,[3]
there is nothing I must do,
nothing unattained to be attained,
yet I engage in action.

23   What if I did not engage
relentlessly in action?
Men retrace my path
at every turn, Arjuna.

---

1. Beginning with the Upaniṣads, the primeval sound, representing the infinite spirit that underlies the universe.   2. Celebrated character in the dialogues of the Bṛhadāraṇyaka Upaniṣad; an exemplar of the warrior-king who is also a man of discipline (a yogi).   3. Heaven, earth, and the underworld.

20   When his thought ceases,
     checked by the exercise of discipline,
     he is content within the self,
     seeing the self through himself.

21   Absolute joy beyond the senses
     can only be grasped by understanding;
     when one knows it, he abides there
     and never wanders from this reality.

22   Obtaining it, he thinks
     there is no greater gain;
     abiding there, he is unmoved,
     even by deep suffering.

23   Since he knows that discipline
     means unbinding the bonds of suffering,
     he should practice discipline resolutely,
     without despair dulling his reason.

24   He should entirely relinquish
     desires aroused by willful intent;
     he should entirely control
     his senses with his mind.

25   He should gradually become tranquil,
     firmly controlling his understanding;
     focusing his mind on the self,
     he should think nothing.

26   Wherever his faltering mind
     unsteadily wanders,
     he should restrain it
     and bring it under self-control.

27   When his mind is tranquil, perfect joy
     comes to the man of discipline;
     his passion is calmed, he is without sin,
     being one with the infinite spirit.

28   Constantly disciplining himself,
     free from sin, the man of discipline
     easily achieves perfect joy
     in harmony with the infinite spirit.

29   Arming himself with discipline,
     seeing everything with an equal eye,
     he sees the self in all creatures
     and all creatures in the self.

30   He who sees me everywhere
     and sees everything in me
     will not be lost to me,
     and I will not be lost to him.

31   I exist in all creatures,
     so the disciplined man devoted to me

grasps the oneness of life;
wherever he is, he is in me.

32   When he sees identity in everything,
whether joy or suffering,
through analogy with the self,
he is deemed a man of pure discipline.

Summary   In the Seventh to Tenth Teachings Krishna explains diverse aspects of
the nature of the infinite spirit, gradually unveiling the mystery of his own identity as
the highest manifestation of that universal spirit and thus leading up to the revelation
of his cosmic form in the Eleventh Teaching.

From *The Eleventh Teaching*

[THE VISION OF KRISHNA'S TOTALITY]

ARJUNA:

1   To favor me you revealed
the deepest mystery of the self,
and by your words
my delusion is dispelled.

2   I heard from you in detail
how creatures come to be and die,
Krishna, and about the self
in its immutable greatness.

3   Just as you have described
yourself, I wish to see your form
in all its majesty,
Krishna, Supreme among Men.

4   If you think I can see it,
reveal to me
your immutable self.
Krishna, Lord of Discipline.

LORD KRISHNA:

5   Arjuna, see my forms
in hundreds and thousands;
diverse, divine,
of many colors and shapes.

6   See the sun gods, gods of light,
howling storm gods, twin gods of dawn,
and gods of wind, Arjuna,
wondrous forms not seen before.

7   Arjuna, see all the universe,
animate and inanimate,
and whatever else you wish to see;
all stands here as one in my body.

8   But you cannot see me
with your own eye;

I will give you a divine eye to see
the majesty of my discipline.

SANJAYA:[5]

9   O King, saying this, Krishna,
the great lord of discipline,
revealed to Arjuna
the true majesty of his form.

10   It was a multiform, wondrous vision,
with countless mouths and eyes[6]
and celestial ornaments,
brandishing many divine weapons.

11   Everywhere was boundless divinity
containing all astonishing things,
wearing divine garlands and garments,
anointed with divine perfume.

12   If the light of a thousand suns
were to rise in the sky at once,
it would be like the light
of that great spirit.

13   Arjuna saw all the universe
in its many ways and parts,
standing as one in the body
of the god of gods.

* * *

44   I bow to you,
I prostrate my body,
I beg you to be gracious,
Worshipful Lord—
as a father to a son,
a friend to a friend,
a lover to a beloved,
O God, bear with me.[7]

45   I am thrilled,
and yet my mind
trembles with fear
at seeing
what has not been seen before.
Show me, God, the form I know—
be gracious, Lord of Gods,
Shelter of the World.

46   I want to see you
as before,

---

5. The bard who is retelling the events of the battle to King Dhṛtarāṣṭra.   6. Standard elements of icons of the Hindu gods, which are worshiped as manifestations of the gods themselves. In most icons, the Hindu gods have four or more arms.   7. The tradition of worshiping God in the intimate relational modes described here became the staple of a popular Hindu religious practice called *bhakti* ("loving devotion to God").

with your crown and mace,
and the discus in your hand.
O Thousand-Armed God,[8]
assume the four-armed form
embodied
in your totality.

LORD KRISHNA:

47 To grace you, Arjuna,
I revealed
through self-discipline
my higher form,
which no one but you
has ever beheld—
brilliant, total,
boundless, primal.

48 Not through sacred lore
or sacrificial ritual
or study or charity,
not by rites
or by terrible penances
can I be seen in this form
in the world of men
by anyone but you, Great Hero.

49 Do not tremble
or suffer confusion
from seeing
my horrific form;
your fear dispelled,
your mind full of love,
see my form again
as it was.

SANJAYA:

50 Saying this to Arjuna,
Krishna once more
revealed
his intimate form;
resuming his gentle body,
the great spirit
let the terrified hero
regain his breath.

ARJUNA:

51 Seeing your gentle human form,
Krishna, I recover
my own nature,
and my reason is restored.

---

8. In this form Viṣṇu-Krishna represents Puruṣa, the cosmic man of the *Rig Veda*. The mace and discus are emblems of Viṣṇu's four-armed form.

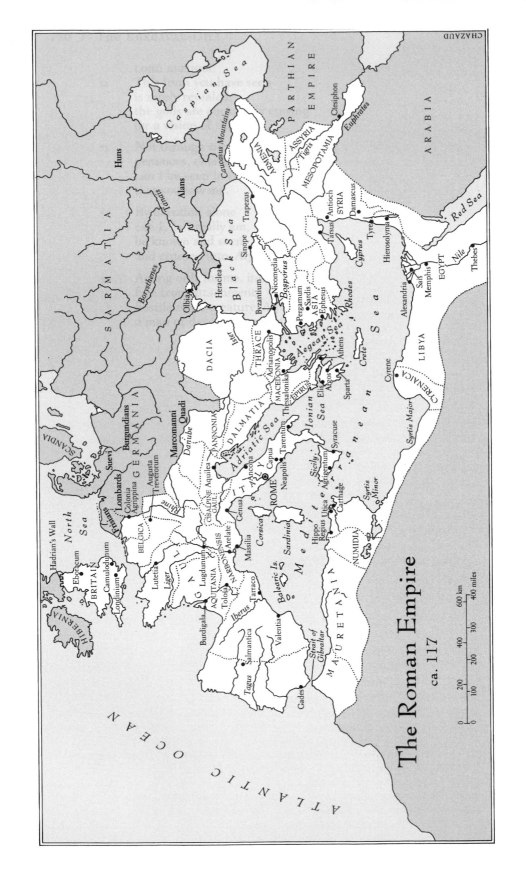

The Roman Empire

ca. 117

The Roman Empire

When Alexander died in 323 B.C.E., the city of Rome, situated on the Tiber in the western coastal plain of Italy, was engaged in a struggle for the control of the surrounding areas. By the middle of the third century B.C.E., it dominated most of the Italian peninsula. Expansion southward brought Rome into collision with Carthage, a city in North Africa that was then the greatest power in the western Mediterranean. Two protracted wars resulted (264–241 and 218–201 B.C.E.), and it was only at the end of a third, shorter war (149–146 B.C.E.) that the Romans destroyed their great rival. The second Carthaginian (or Punic) War was particularly hard fought, both in Spain and in Italy itself, where the Carthaginian general Hannibal, having made a spectacular crossing of the Alps, operated for years, and where Rome's southern Italian allies defected to Carthage and had to be slowly rewon. Rome, however, emerged from this war in 201 B.C.E. not merely victorious but a world power. The next two decades saw frequent wars—in Spain, in Greece, and in Asia Minor—that laid the foundations of the Roman empire. These successes changed Roman social, cultural, and economic life profoundly.

From early on, the Romans had come into contact with Greek culture through the sophisticated Greek cities of southern Italy and Sicily; now, with their involvement in affairs in mainland Greece, this contact intensified. Greek culture began to permeate Roman; the comedies of Plautus and his younger contemporary Terence are just one manifestation of this influence (and of the Roman transformation of Greek tradition). Economic changes were just as far-reaching. The military victories brought in huge numbers of enslaved war captives, and in parts of the Italian countryside wealthy men, mainly aristocrats, accumulated large landholdings that were systematically worked by slaves. With the waning in number of small farmers came an increase in the urban-poor population. Trade and crafts were on the rise, and newly wealthy businessmen were in a position to challenge the power of the senatorial class, whose wealth was based in land and who had long exerted de facto control over the government. These developments laid the groundwork for the sharp conflicts that plagued Rome later in the second century B.C.E. and that led in the next century to civil war and eventually the demise of the Republic and its replacement by imperial rule. For now, general prosperity masked these potential conflicts, especially the growing gulf between the wealthy classes and the poor, but the new wealth itself strained the traditional fabric of Roman society.

These were the changes and the tensions that accompanied the transformation of Rome from city-state on the traditional model to world imperial power. By the end of the first century B.C.E., Rome was the capital of an empire that stretched from the Strait of Gibraltar to the frontiers of Palestine. This empire gave peace and orderly government to the Mediterranean area for the next two centuries, and for two centuries after that it maintained a desperate but losing battle against the invading tribes moving in from the north and east. When it finally went down, the empire left behind it the ideal of the world-state, an ideal that was to be taken over by the medieval church, which ruled from the same center, Rome, and which claimed a spiritual authority as great as the secular authority it replaced.

The achievements of the Romans, not only their conquests but also their success in consolidating the conquests and organizing the conquered, were due in large part to their talent for practical affairs. They might have had no aptitude for pure mathematics, but they could build an aqueduct to last two thousand years. Though they were not notable as political theorists, they organized a complicated yet stable federation that held Italy loyal to them in the presence of invading armies. Romans were conservative to the core; their strongest authority was *mos maiorum*, the custom of predecessors. A monument of this conservatism, the great body of Roman law, is one of their greatest contributions to Western civilization. The quality Romans most admired was *gravitas*, seriousness of attitude and purpose, and their highest words of commendation were *manliness, industry, discipline*. Pericles, in his funeral speech, praised Athenian adaptability, versatility, and grace. This would have seemed strange praise to a Roman, whose idea of personal and civic virtue was different. "By her ancient customs and her men the Roman state stands," says Ennius the Roman poet, in a line that by its metrical heaviness emphasizes the stability implied in the key word "stands": *moribus antiquis res stat Romana virisque*.

Greek history begins not with a king, a battle, or the founding of a city, but with an epic poem. The Romans, on the other hand, had conquered half the world before they began to write. The stimulus to the creation of Latin literature was the Greek literature that the Romans discovered when, in the second century B.C.E., they assumed political responsibility for Greece and the Near East. Latin literature began with a translation of the *Odyssey*, made by a Greek prisoner of war, and with the exception of satire, until Latin literature became Christian, the model was always Greek. The Latin writer (especially the poet) borrowed wholesale from his Greek original, not furtively, but openly and proudly, as a tribute to the master from whom he had learned. But this frank acknowledgment of indebtedness should not blind us to the fact that Latin literature is original, and sometimes profoundly so. This is true above all of Virgil, who based his epic on Homer but chose as his theme the coming of the Trojan prince Aeneas to Italy, where he was to found a city from which, in the fullness of time, would come "the Latin race . . . and the high walls of Rome."

When Virgil was born in 70 B.C.E. the Roman Republic, which had conquered and now governed the Mediterranean world, had barely recovered from one civil war and was drifting inexorably toward another. The institutions of the city-state proved inadequate for world government. The civil conflict that had disrupted the Republic for more than a hundred years ended finally in the establishment of a powerful executive. Although the Senate, which had been the controlling body of the Republic, retained an impressive share of the power, the new arrangement developed inevitably toward autocracy, the rule of the executive, the emperor, as he was called once the system was stabilized. The first of the long line of Roman emperors who gave stable government to the Roman world during the first two centuries C.E. was Octavius, known generally by his title, Augustus. He had made his way cautiously through the intrigues and bloodshed that followed the murder of his uncle Julius Caesar in 44 B.C.E. until by 31 B.C.E. he controlled the western half of the empire. In that year he fought a decisive battle with the ruler of the eastern half of the empire, Mark Antony, who was supported by Cleopatra, queen of Egypt. Octavius's victory at Actium united the empire under one authority and ushered in an age of peace and reconstruction.

For the next two hundred years the successors of Augustus, the Roman emperors, ruled the ancient world with only occasional disturbances, most of them confined to Rome, where emperors who flagrantly abused their immense power—Nero, for example—were overthrown by force. The second half of this period was described by Gibbon, the great historian of imperial Rome, as the period "in the history of the world during which the condition of the human race was most happy and prosperous." The years. 96–180 C.E., those of the "five good emperors," were in fact remarkable: this was the longest period of peace that has ever been enjoyed by the inhabitants of an area that included Britain, France, all southern Europe, the Middle East, and the whole of North Africa. Trade and agriculture flourished, and the cities with their public baths, theaters, and libraries offered all the amenities of civilized life. Yet there was apparent, especially in the literature of the second century, a spiritual emptiness. The old religion offered no comfort to those who looked beyond mere material ends; it had been too closely knit into the fabric of the independent city-state and was inadequate for a time in which men were citizens of the world. New religions arose or were imported from the East, universal religions that made their appeal to all nations and classes: the worship of the Egyptian goddess Isis, of the Persian god Mithras, who offered bliss in the life to come, and of the Hebrew prophet Jesus, crucified in Jerusalem and believed risen from the dead. This was the religion that, working underground and often suppressed (there was a persecution of the christians under Nero in the first century, another under the last of the "good emperors" Marcus Aurelius in the second), finally triumphed and became the official and later the exclusive religion of the Roman world. As the empire in the third and fourth centuries disintegrated under the never-ending invasions by peoples from the north, the church, with its center and spiritual head in Rome, converted the new inhabitants and so made possible the preservation of much of that Latin and Greek literature that was to serve the European Middle Ages and, later, the Renaissance, as a model and a basis for their own great achievements in the arts and letters.

TIME LINE

TEXTS	CONTEXTS
	753 B.C.E. Traditional date of the foundation of Rome
	ca. 750 Foundation of Carthage (North Africa)
	735 Greek colony at Syracuse (Sicily)
	7th century Greek colonies at Marseilles (France) and Cyrene (North Africa)
	509 Expulsion of the king; Rome becomes a republic
	451 Roman law codified—the Twelve Tablets
	264 Rome controls Italy south of the river Po; defeats Carthage at sea
	227 Sicily becomes the first Roman province
	218–202 Hannibal of Carthage invades Italy, fails to capture Rome, defeated at Zama near Carthage in 202
	197 Spain becomes a Roman province
	91–89 Social war in Italy; Italians gain Roman citizenship
	87–81 Civil war ending in dictatorship of Sulla
ca. 84?–54? B.C.E. Catullus	
	74 Cyrene becomes a Roman province
70–19 Virgil, author of *The Aeneid*	
	58–50 Julius Caesar conquers Gaul
	47 Julius Caesar dictator; murdered in 44
43 B.C.E. 17 C.E. Ovid, author of *Metamorphoses*	

Boldface titles indicate works in the anthology.

TIME LINE

TEXTS	CONTEXTS
	27–23 Octavian (now Augustus) establishes imperial regime
	ca. 6 Birth of Jesus
ca. 10–66 C.E. Petronius, author of *The Satyricon*	
	14–37 C.E. Tiberius emperor
	37–41 Caligula emperor
	41–54 Claudius emperor
	54–68 Nero emperor
	64 Persecution of Christians under Nero

VIRGIL

70–19 B.C.E.

Publius Virgilius Maro was born in northern Italy, and very little is known about his life. The earliest work that is certainly his is the *Bucolics*, a collection of poems in the pastoral genre that have had enormous influence. These were followed by the *Georgics*, a didactic poem on farming, in four books, which many critics consider his finest work. The *Aeneid*, the Roman epic, was left unfinished at his death.

Like all the Latin poets, Virgil built on the solid foundations of his Greek predecessors. The story of Aeneas, the Trojan prince who came to Italy and whose descendants founded Rome, combines the themes of the *Odyssey* (the wanderer in search of home) and the *Iliad* (the hero in battle). Virgil borrows Homeric turns of phrase, similes, sentiments, and whole incidents; his Aeneas, like Achilles, sacrifices prisoners to the shade of a friend and, like Odysseus, descends alive to the world of the dead. But unlike Achilles, Aeneas does not satisfy the great passion of his life, nor, like Odysseus, does he find a home and peace. The personal objectives of both of Homer's heroes are sacrificed by Aeneas for a greater objective. His mission, imposed on him by the gods, is to found a city, from which, in the fullness of time, will spring the Roman state.

Homer presents us in the *Iliad* with the tragic pattern of the individual will, Achilles' wrath. But Aeneas is more than an individual. He is the prototype of the ideal Roman ruler; his qualities are the devotion to duty and the seriousness of purpose that were to give the Mediterranean world two centuries of ordered government after Augustus. Aeneas's mission begins in disorder in the burning city of Troy, but he leaves it, carrying his father on his shoulders and leading his little son by the hand. This famous picture emphasizes the fact that, unlike Achilles, he is securely set in a continuity of generations, the immortality of the family group, just as his mission to found a city, a home for the gods of Troy whose statues he carries with him, places him in a political and religious continuity. Achilles has no future. When he mentions his father and son, neither of whom he will see again, he emphasizes for us the loneliness of his short career. Odysseus has a father, wife, and son, and his heroic efforts are directed toward reestablishing himself in his proper context, that home in which he will be no longer a man in a world of magic and terror but a man in an organized and continuous community. But he fights for himself. Aeneas, on the other hand, suffers and fights, not for himself, but for the future; his own life is unhappy, and his death miserable. Yet he can console himself with the glory of his sons to come, the pageant of Roman achievement that he is shown by his father in the world below and that he carries on his shield. Aeneas's future is Virgil's present; the consolidation of the Roman peace under Augustus is the reward of Aeneas's unhappy life of effort and suffering.

Summarized like this, the *Aeneid* sounds like propaganda, which, in one sense of the word, it is. What saves it from the besetting fault of even the best propaganda— the partial concealment of the truth—is the fact that Virgil maintains an independence of the power that he is celebrating and sees his hero in the round. He knows that the Roman ideal of devotion to duty has another side, the suppression of many aspects of the personality, and that the man who wins and uses power must sacrifice much of himself, must live a life that, compared with that of Achilles or Odysseus, is constricted. In Virgil's poem Aeneas betrays the great passion of his life, his love for Dido, queen of Carthage. He does it reluctantly, but nevertheless he leaves her, and the full realization of what he has lost comes to him only when he meets her ghost in the world below. He weeps (as he did not at Carthage) and he pleads, in stronger terms than he did then, the overriding power that forced him to depart: "I left your land against my will, my queen." She leaves him without a word, her silence as impervious to pleas and tears as his was once at Carthage, and she goes back to join her first love, her husband, Sychaeus. Aeneas has sacrificed his love to something greater, but this does not insulate him from unhappiness. The limitations on the dedicated individual are emphasized by the contrasting figure of Dido, who follows her own impulse always, even in death. By her death, Virgil tells us expressly, she forestalls fate, breaks loose from the pattern in which Aeneas remains to the bitter end.

The angry reactions that this part of the poem has produced in many critics are the true measure of Virgil's success. Aeneas does act in such a way that he forfeits much of our sympathy, but this is surely exactly what Virgil intended. The Dido episode is not, as many critics have supposed, a flaw in the great design, a case of Virgil's sympathy outrunning his admiration for Aeneas; it is Virgil's emphatic statement of the sacrifice that the Roman ideal of duty demands. Aeneas's sacrifice is so great that few of us could make it ourselves, and none of us can contemplate it in another without a feeling of loss. It is an expression of the famous Virgilian sadness that informs every line of the *Aeneid* and that makes a poem that was in its historical context a command performance into the great epic that has dominated Western literature ever since.

PRONOUNCING GLOSSARY

The following list uses common English syllables and stress accents to provide rough equivalents of selected words whose pronunciation may be unfamiliar to the general reader.

Aeneas: *i-nee'-uhs*

Aeneid: *i-nee'-id*

Anchises: *an-kai'-seez*

Andromache: *an-dro'-ma-kee*

Aurora: *aw-roh'-rah / ow-roh'-rah*

Automedon: *aw-to'-me-don / ow-to'-me-don*

Charon: *kah'-ron*

Chimaera: *kai-meer'-uh / ki-mai'-ruh*

Cyllene: *si-lee'-nee / ki-lay'-nay*

Cytherëa: *si-the-ree'-uh / si-ther-ai'-uh*

Danaans: *da'-nay-unz / dan'-a-ans*

Deiphobus: *day-i'-fo-bus*

Dido: *dai'-doh*

Dionysus: *dai-oh-nai'-sus*

Eumenidës: *yoo-me'-ni-deez*

Hecate: *he'-kat-ee*

Lethe: *lee'-thee*

Musaeus: *moo-see'-us / moo-sai'-us*

Peneleus: *pee-ne'-lyoos*

Phrygian: *fri'-jun*

Scaean: *see'-an / skai'-an*

Teucer: *tyoo'-ser*

Thymoetes: *thee-moy'-teez*

Xanthus: *zan'-thus / ksan'-thus*

The Aeneid[1]

FROM BOOK I

[Prologue]

I sing of warfare and a man at war.[2]
From the sea-coast of Troy in early days
He came to Italy by destiny,

---

1. Translated by Robert Fitzgerald.　　2. Aeneas, a Trojan champion in the fight for Troy, son of Venus (or Aphrodite, the goddess of love) and Anchises, and a member of the royal house of Troy.

To our Lavinian[3] western shore,
A fugitive, this captain, buffeted   5
Cruelly on land as on the sea
By blows from powers of the air—behind them
Baleful Juno[4] in her sleepless rage.
And cruel losses were his lot in war,
Till he could found a city and bring home   10
His gods to Latium, land of the Latin race,
The Alban[5] lords, and the high walls of Rome.
Tell me the causes now, O Muse, how galled
In her divine pride, and how sore at heart
From her old wound, the queen of gods compelled him—   15
A man apart, devoted to his mission—
To undergo so many perilous days
And enter on so many trials. Can anger
Black as this prey on the minds of heaven?
Tyrian[6] settlers in that ancient time   20
Held Carthage,[7] on the far shore of the sea,
Set against Italy and Tiber's[8] mouth,
A rich new town, warlike and trained for war.
And Juno, we are told, cared more for Carthage
Than for any walled city of the earth,   25
More than for Samos,[9] even. There her armor
And chariot were kept, and, fate permitting,
Carthage would be the ruler of the world.
So she intended, and so nursed that power.
But she had heard long since   30
That generations born of Trojan blood
Would one day overthrow her Tyrian walls,
And from that blood a race would come in time
With ample kingdoms, arrogant in war,
For Libya's ruin: so the Parcae[1] spun.   35
In fear of this, and holding in memory
The old war she had carried on at Troy
For Argos'[2] sake (the origins of that anger,
That suffering, still rankled: deep within her,
Hidden away, the judgment Paris[3] gave,   40
Snubbing her loveliness; the race she hated;
The honors given ravished Ganymede),
Saturnian Juno,[4] burning for it all,

---

3. Near Rome, named after the city of Lavinium. After the fall of Troy, Aeneas went in search of a new home, eventually settling here.   4. Wife of the ruler of the gods (Hera in Greek). As in the *Iliad*, she is a bitter enemy of the Trojans.   5. The city of Alba Longa was founded by Aeneas's son Ascanius. Romulus and Remus, the builders of Rome, were also from Alba. Latium is the coastal plain on which Rome is situated.   6. From Tyre, on the coast of Palestine, the principal city of the Phoenicians, a seafaring people. 7. On the coast of North Africa, opposite Sicily. Originally a Tyrian colony, it became a rich commercial center, controlling traffic in the western Mediterranean.   8. The river that flows through Rome.   9. A large island off the coast of Asia Minor, famous for its cult of Hera (Juno).   1. The Fates, who were imagined as female divinities who spun human destinies. Rome captured and destroyed Carthage in 146 B.C.E. Libya is used as an inclusive name for the North African coast.   2. Home city of the Achaean (Greek) kings Agamemnon and Menelaus. Juno was on their side when they went to Troy to retrieve Helen, Menelaus's wife.   3. Son of King Priam of Troy. He was asked to judge which goddess—Venus, Juno, or Minerva (Athena)—was most beautiful. All three offered bribes, but Venus's promise (of Helen's love) prevailed, and Paris awarded her the prize.   4. Her father was Saturn, a Titan. Ganymede was a Trojan boy of extreme beauty who was taken up into heaven by Jupiter (Zeus), ruler of the gods.

Buffeted on the waste of sea those Trojans
Left by the Greeks and pitiless Achilles,   45
Keeping them far from Latium. For years
They wandered as their destiny drove them on
From one sea to the next: so hard and huge
A task it was to found the Roman people.

[Aeneas Arrives in Carthage]

Summary   The story opens with a storm, provoked by Juno's agency, which scatters Aeneas's fleet off Sicily and separates him from his companions. He lands on the African coast near Carthage. Setting out with his friend Achatës to explore the country, he meets his mother, Venus (Aphrodite), who tells him that the rest of his ships are safe and directs him to the city just founded by Dido, the queen of Carthage. Venus surrounds Aeneas and Achatës with a cloud so that they can see without being seen.

Meanwhile
The two men pressed on where the pathway led,
Soon climbing a long ridge that gave a view
Down over the city and facing towers.
Aeneas found, where lately huts had been,   5
Marvelous buildings, gateways, cobbled ways,
And din of wagons. There the Tyrians
Were hard at work: laying courses for walls,
Rolling up stones to build the citadel,
While others picked out building sites and plowed   10
A boundary furrow. Laws were being enacted,
Magistrates and a sacred senate chosen.
Here men were dredging harbors, there they laid
The deep foundation of a theater,
And quarried massive pillars to enhance   15
The future stage—as bees in early summer
In sunlight in the flowering fields
Hum at their work, and bring along the young
Full-grown to beehood; as they cram their combs
With honey, brimming all the cells with nectar,   20
Or take newcomers' plunder, or like troops
Alerted, drive away the lazy drones,
And labor thrives and sweet thyme scents the honey.
Aeneas said: "How fortunate these are
Whose city walls are rising here and now!"   25

He looked up at the roofs, for he had entered,
Swathed in cloud—strange to relate—among them,
Mingling with men, yet visible to none.
In mid-town stood a grove that cast sweet shade
Where the Phoenicians, shaken by wind and sea,   30
Had first dug up that symbol Juno showed them,
A proud warhorse's head: this meant for Carthage
Prowess in war and ease of life[5] through ages.

---

5. Because they would have a land fertile enough to support horses.

Here being built by the Sidonian[6] queen
Was a great temple planned in Juno's honor,   35
Rich in offerings and the godhead there.
Steps led up to a sill of bronze, with brazen
Lintel, and bronze doors on groaning pins.
Here in this grove new things that met his eyes
Calmed Aeneas' fear for the first time.   40
Here for the first time he took heart to hope
For safety, and to trust his destiny more
Even in affliction. It was while he walked
From one to another wall of the great temple
And waited for the queen, staring amazed   45
At Carthaginian promise, at the handiwork
Of artificers and the toil they spent upon it:
He found before his eyes the Trojan battles
In the old war, now known throughout the world—
The great Atridae, Priam, and Achilles,   50
Fierce in his rage at both sides.[7] Here Aeneas
Halted, and tears came.
                              "What spot on earth,"
He said, "what region of the earth, Achatës,
Is not full of the story of our sorrow?
Look, here is Priam. Even so far away   55
Great valor has due honor; they weep here
For how the world goes, and our life that passes
Touches their hearts. Throw off your fear. This fame
Insures some kind of refuge."
                              He broke off
To feast his eyes and mind on a mere image,   60
Sighing often, cheeks grown wet with tears,
To see again how, fighting around Troy,
The Greeks broke here, and ran before the Trojans,
And there the Phrygians[8] ran, as plumed Achilles
Harried them in his warcar. Nearby, then,   65
He recognized the snowy canvas tents
Of Rhesus,[9] and more tears came: these, betrayed
In first sleep, Diomedes devastated,
Swording many, till he reeked with blood,
Then turned the mettlesome horses toward the beachhead   70
Before they tasted Trojan grass or drank
At Xanthus ford.[1]
                   And on another panel
Troilus,[2] without his armor, luckless boy,
No match for his antagonist, Achilles,
Appeared pulled onward by his team: he clung   75
To his warcar, though fallen backward, hanging

---

6. From Sidon, a Phoenician city.   7. Because Achilles, the greatest warrior on the Achaean side, quarreled with Agamemnon. The Atridae were sons of Atreus—Agamemnon and Menelaus.   8. Trojans. 9. King of Thrace, who came to the aid of Troy just before the end of the war.   1. An oracle proclaimed that if Rhesus's horses ate Trojan grass and drank the water of the river Xanthus, Troy would not fall. Odysseus and Diomedes went into the Trojan lines at night, killed the king, and stole the horses.   2. A young son of Priam.

On to the reins still, head dragged on the ground,
His javelin scribbling S's in the dust.
Meanwhile to hostile Pallas'[3] shrine
The Trojan women walked with hair unbound,   80
Bearing the robe of offering, in sorrow,
Entreating her, beating their breasts. But she,
Her face averted, would not raise her eyes.
And there was Hector, dragged around Troy walls
Three times, and there for gold Achilles sold him,   85
Bloodless and lifeless. Now indeed Aeneas
Heaved a mighty sigh from deep within him,
Seeing the spoils, the chariot, and the corpse
Of his great friend, and Priam, all unarmed,
Stretching his hands out.
                        He himself he saw   90
In combat with the first of the Achaeans,
And saw the ranks of Dawn, black Memnon's[4] arms;
Then, leading the battalion of Amazons
With half-moon shields, he saw Penthesilëa[5]
Fiery amid her host, buckling a golden   95
Girdle beneath her bare and arrogant breast,
A girl who dared fight men, a warrior queen.
Now, while these wonders were being surveyed
By Aeneas of Dardania,[6] while he stood
Enthralled, devouring all in one long gaze,   100
The queen paced toward the temple in her beauty,
Dido, with a throng of men behind.

As on Eurotas bank or Cynthus ridge
Diana[7] trains her dancers, and behind her
On every hand the mountain nymphs appear,   105
A myriad converging; with her quiver
Slung on her shoulders, in her stride she seems
The tallest, taller by a head than any,
And joy pervades Latona's[8] quiet heart:
So Dido seemed, in such delight she moved   110
Amid her people, cheering on the toil
Of a kingdom in the making. At the door
Of the goddess' shrine, under the temple dome,
All hedged about with guards on her high throne,
She took her seat. Then she began to give them   115
Judgments and rulings, to apportion work
With fairness, or assign some tasks by lot,
When suddenly Aeneas saw approaching,
Accompanied by a crowd, Antheus and Sergestus
And brave Cloanthus,[9] with a few companions,   120
Whom the black hurricane had driven far

---

3. Athena (see *Iliad* v1.297ff.).   4. King of the Ethipians, who fought on the Trojan side.   5. Queen
of the Amazons, killed by Achilles.   6. The kingdom of Troy.   7. Virgin goddess of the hunt (Artemis
in Greek). Eurotas is a river near Sparta where Diana was worshiped. Cynthus is a mountain on the island
of Delos, Diana's birthplace.   8. Diana's mother (Leto in Greek).   9. Ship captains of Aeneas's fleet,
from whom he has been separated in the storm.

Over the sea and brought to other coasts.
He was astounded, and Achatës too
Felt thrilled by joy and fear: both of them longed
To take their friends' hands, but uncertainty   125
Hampered them. So, in their cloudy mantle,
They hid their eagerness, waiting to learn
What luck these men had had, where on the coast
They left their ships, and why they came. It seemed
Spokesmen for all the ships were now arriving,   130
Entering the hall, calling for leave to speak.
When all were in, and full permission given
To make their plea before the queen, their eldest,
Ilioneus, with composure said:
                        "Your majesty,
Granted by great Jupiter freedom to found   135
Your new town here and govern fighting tribes
With justice—we poor Trojans, worn by winds
On every sea, entreat you: keep away
Calamity of fire from our ships!
Let a godfearing people live, and look   140
More closely at our troubles. Not to ravage
Libyan hearths or turn with plunder seaward
Have we come; that force and that audacity
Are not for beaten men.
                    There is a country
Called by the Greeks Hesperia,[1] very old,   145
Potent in warfare and in wealth of earth;
Oenotrians farmed it; younger settlers now,
The tale goes, call it by their chief's[2] name, Italy.
We laid our course for this.
But stormy Orion[3] and a high sea rising   150
Deflected us on shoals and drove us far,
With winds against us, into whelming waters,
Unchanneled reefs. We kept afloat, we few,
To reach your coast. What race of men is this?
What primitive state could sanction this behavior?   155
Even on beaches we are denied a landing,
Harried by outcry and attack, forbidden
To set foot on the outskirts of your country.
If you care nothing for humanity
And merely mortal arms, respect the gods   160
Who are mindful of good actions and of evil!

We had a king, Aeneas—none more just,
More zealous, greater in warfare and in arms.
If fate preserves him, if he does not yet
Lie spent amid the insensible shades but still   165
Takes nourishment of air, we need fear nothing;

---

1. The western country. 2. Italus. The Oenotrians were the original inhabitants of Italy. 3. The setting of this constellation in November signaled the onset of stormy weather at sea.

Neither need you repent of being first
In courtesy, to outdo us. Sicily too
Has towns and plowlands and a famous king
Of Trojan blood, Acestës.[4] May we be   170
Permitted here to beach our damaged ships,
Hew timbers in your forest, cut new oars,
And either sail again for Latium, happily,
If we recover shipmates and our king,
Or else, if that security is lost,   175
If Libyan waters hold you, Lord Aeneas,
Best of Trojans, hope of Iulus[5] gone,
We may at least cross over to Sicily
From which we came, to homesteads ready there,
And take Acestës for our king."
                                Ilioneus   180
Finished, and all the sons of Dardanus[6]
Murmured assent. Dido with eyes downcast
Replied in a brief speech:
                           "Cast off your fear,
You Teucrians, put anxiety aside.
Severe conditions and the kingdom's youth   185
Constrain me to these measures, to protect
Our long frontiers with guards.
                        Who has not heard
Of the people of Aeneas, of Troy city,
Her valors and her heroes, and the fires
Of the great war? We are not so oblivious,   190
We Phoenicians. The sun yokes his team
Within our range[7] at Carthage. Whether you choose
Hesperia Magna and the land of Saturn
Or Eryx[8] in the west and King Acestës,
I shall dispatch you safely with an escort,   195
Provisioned from my stores. Or would you care
To join us in this realm on equal terms?
The city I build is yours; haul up your ships;
Trojan and Tyrian will be all one to me.
If only he were here, your king himself,   200
Caught by the same easterly, Aeneas!
Indeed, let me send out trustworthy men
Along the coast, with orders to comb it all
From one end of Libya to the other,
In case the sea cast the man up and now   205
He wanders lost, in town or wilderness."

Elated at Dido's words, both staunch Achatës
And father Aeneas had by this time longed
To break out of the cloud. Achatës spoke
With urgency:

---

4. His mother was Trojan; he had offered Aeneas and his people a home in his dominions. 5. Ascanius, Aeneas's son. 6. Ancestor of the Trojans. 7. That is, we are not outside the circuit of the sun; we are part of the civilized world and hear the news. 8. On the west coast of Sicily. "Land of Saturn": an old legend connected Italy with Saturn, the father of Jupiter.

"My lord, born to the goddess,   210
What do you feel, what is your judgment now?
You see all safe, our ships and friends recovered.
One is lost;[9] we saw that one go down
Ourselves, amid the waves. Everything else
Bears out your mother's own account of it."   215

He barely finished when the cloud around them
Parted suddenly and thinned away
Into transparent air. Princely Aeneas
Stood and shone in the bright light, head and shoulders
Noble as a god's. For she who bore him[1]   220
Breathed upon him beauty of hair and bloom
Of youth and kindled brilliance in his eyes,
As an artist's hand gives style to ivory,
Or sets pure silver, or white stone of Paros,[2]
In framing yellow gold. Then to the queen   225
He spoke as suddenly as, to them all,
He had just appeared:
        "Before your eyes I stand,
Aeneas the Trojan, that same one you look for,
Saved from the sea off Libya.
        You alone,
Moved by the untold ordeals of old Troy,   230
Seeing us few whom the Greeks left alive,
Worn out by faring ill on land and sea,
Needy of everything—you'd give these few
A home and city, allied with yourselves.
Fit thanks for this are not within our power,   235
Not to be had from Trojans anywhere
Dispersed in the great world.
        May the gods—
And surely there are powers that care for goodness,
Surely somewhere justice counts—may they
And your own consciousness of acting well   240
Reward you as they should. What age so happy
Brought you to birth? How splendid were your parents
To have conceived a being like yourself!
So long as brooks flow seaward, and the shadows
Play over mountain slopes, and highest heaven   245
Feeds the stars, your name and your distinction
Go with me, whatever lands may call me."

With this he gave his right hand to his friend
Ilioneus, greeting Serestus with his left,
Then took the hands of those brave men, Cloanthus,   250
Gyas, and the rest.
        Sidonian Dido

---

9. One ship, captained by Orontes, sank in the storm.   1. Venus.   2. The marble of the island of Paros was famous.

Stood in astonishment, first at the sight
Of such a captain, then at his misfortune,
Presently saying:
    "Born of an immortal
Mother though you are, what adverse destiny   255
Dogs you through these many kinds of danger?
What rough power brings you from sea to land
In savage places? Are you truly he,
Aeneas, whom kind Venus bore
To the Dardanian, the young Anchisës,   260
Near to the stream of Phrygian Simoïs?
I remember the Greek, Teucer,[3] came to Sidon,
Exiled, and in search of a new kingdom.
Belus, my father, helped him. In those days
Belus campaigned with fire and sword on Cyprus 265
And won that island's wealth. Since then, the fall
Of Troy, your name, and the Pelasgian kings
Have been familiar to me. Teucer, your enemy,
Spoke often with admiration of the Tyrians
And traced his own descent from Tyrian stock.   270
Come, then, soldiers, be our guests. My life
Was one of hardship and forced wandering
Like your own, till in this land at length
Fortune would have me rest. Through pain I've learned
To comfort suffering men."
        She led Aeneas   275
Into the royal house, but not before
Declaring a festal day in the gods' temples.
As for the ships' companies, she sent
Twenty bulls to the shore, a hundred swine,
Huge ones, with bristling backs, and fatted lambs, 280
A hundred of them, and their mother ewes—
All gifts for happy feasting on that day.

Now the queen's household made her great hall glow
As they prepared a banquet in the kitchens.
Embroidered table cloths, proud crimson-dyed,   285
Were spread, and set with massive silver plate,
Or gold, engraved with brave deeds of her fathers,
A sequence carried down through many captains
In a long line from the founding of the race.

Summary At the banquet, Aeneas, at Dido's request, tells the story of the fall of Troy and of his wanderings in search of a new home. By the end of the evening, Dido, who began to fall in love with him before the banquet (through the intervention of Venus and Juno, who both promote the affair, each for different reasons), now feels the full force of her passion for Aeneas.

---

3. A warrior who fought at Troy and was later exiled from his home. He founded a city on the island of Cyprus. He is not the Trojan king Teucer.

BOOK IV

[The Passion of the Queen]

The queen, for her part, all that evening ached
With longing that her heart's blood fed, a wound
Or inward fire eating her away.
The manhood of the man, his pride of birth,
Came home to her time and again; his looks,⁵
His words remained with her to haunt her mind,
And desire for him gave her no rest.

                          When Dawn
Swept earth with Phoebus' torch and burned away
Night-gloom and damp, this queen, far gone and ill,
Confided to the sister of her heart: 10
"My sister Anna, quandaries and dreams
Have come to frighten me—such dreams!

                         Think what a stranger
Yesterday found lodging in our house:
How princely, how courageous, what a soldier.
I can believe him in the line of gods,   15
And this is no delusion. Tell-tale fear
Betrays inferior souls. What scenes of war
Fought to the bitter end he pictured for us!
What buffetings awaited him at sea!
Had I not set my face against remarriage   20
After my first love died and failed me, left me
Barren and bereaved—and sick to death
At the mere thought of torch and bridal bed—
I could perhaps give way in this one case
To frailty. I shall say it: since that time   25
Sychaeus, my poor husband, met his fate,
And blood my brother⁴ shed stained our hearth gods,
This man alone has wrought upon me so
And moved my soul to yield. I recognize
The signs of the old flame, of old desire.   30
But O chaste life, before I break your laws,
I pray that Earth may open, gape for me
Down to its depth, or the omnipotent
With one stroke blast me to the shades, pale shades
Of Erebus⁵ and the deep world of night!   35
That man who took me to himself in youth
Has taken all my love; may that man keep it,
Hold it forever with him in the tomb."

At this she wept and wet her breast with tears.
But Anna answered:
                  "Dearer to your sister   40
Than daylight is, will you wear out your life,
Young as you are, in solitary mourning,
Never to know sweet children, or the crown

4. Pygmalion, king of Tyre who killed Sychaeus, Dido's "first love" (line 21). Sychaeus's ghost warned her in a dream to leave Tyre and seek a new home.   5. The lower depths of Hades, the underworld.

Of joy that Venus brings? Do you believe
This matters to the dust, to ghosts in tombs?   45
Granted no suitors up to now have moved you,
Neither in Libya nor before, in Tyre—
Iarbas[6] you rejected, and the others,
Chieftains bred by the land of Africa
Their triumphs have enriched—will you contend   50
Even against a welcome love? Have you
Considered in whose lands you settled here?
On one frontier the Gaetulans, their cities,
People invincible in war—with wild
Numidian horsemen, and the offshore banks,   55
The Syrtës; on the other, desert sands,
Bone-dry, where fierce Barcaean[7] nomads range.
Or need I speak of future wars brought on
From Tyre, and the menace of your brother?
Surely by dispensation of the gods   60
And backed by Juno's will, the ships from Ilium
Held their course this way on the wind.
                          Sister,
What a great city you'll see rising here,
And what a kingdom, from this royal match!
With Trojan soldiers as companions in arms   65
By what exploits will Punic[8] glory grow!
Only ask the indulgence of the gods,
Win them with offerings, give your guests ease,
And contrive reasons for delay, while winter
Gales rage, drenched Orion storms at sea,   70
And their ships, damaged still, face iron skies."

This counsel fanned the flame, already kindled,
Giving her hesitant sister hope, and set her
Free of scruple. Visiting the shrines
They begged for grace at every altar first,   75
Then put choice rams and ewes to ritual death
For Ceres Giver of Laws, Father Lyaeus,
Phoebus, and for Juno most of all
Who has the bonds of marriage in her keeping.[9]
Dido herself, splendidly beautiful,   80
Holding a shallow cup, tips out the wine
On a white shining heifer, between the horns,
Or gravely in the shadow of the gods
Approaches opulent altars. Through the day
She brings new gifts, and when the breasts are opened   85

---

6. The most prominent of Dido's African suitors.   7. African groups that lived near Carthage. The Gaetulans, a savage people, lived to the southwest. The Numidians were the most powerful group. The Bar-
caeans lived to the east.   8. Carthaginian.   9. Ceres, the goddess who guarantees the growth of crops;
Lyaeus (Dionysus or Bacchus), the wine god; and Phoebus (Apollo) are selected as deities especially connected with the founding of cities. One of Apollo's titles is "founder," and Ceres and Lyaeus control the
essential crops that will enable the colonists to live. Dido prays to these gods at the moment when she is
about to abandon her responsibilities as founder of a city. A similar irony is present in her prayer to Juno,
who oversees the marriage bond, at the moment when she is about to break her long fidelity to the memory
of Sychaeus.

Pores over organs, living still, for signs.[1]
Alas, what darkened minds have soothsayers!
What good are shrines and vows to maddened lovers?
The inward fire eats the soft marrow away,
And the internal wound bleeds on in silence.   90

Unlucky Dido, burning, in her madness
Roamed through all the city, like a doe
Hit by an arrow shot from far away
By a shepherd hunting in the Cretan woods—
Hit by surprise, nor could the hunter see   95
His flying steel had fixed itself in her;
But though she runs for life through copse and glade
The fatal shaft clings to her side.
                              Now Dido
Took Aeneas with her among her buildings,
Showed her Sidonian wealth, her walls prepared,   100
And tried to speak, but in mid-speech grew still.
When the day waned she wanted to repeat
The banquet as before, to hear once more
In her wild need the throes of Ilium,
And once more hung on the narrator's words.   105
Afterward, when all the guests were gone,
And the dim moon in turn had quenched her light,
And setting stars weighed weariness to sleep,
Alone she mourned in the great empty hall
And pressed her body on the couch he left: 110
She heard him still, though absent—heard and saw him.
Or she would hold Ascanius in her lap,
Enthralled by him, the image of his father,
As though by this ruse to appease a love
Beyond all telling.
                      Towers, half-built, rose   115
No farther; men no longer trained in arms
Or toiled to make harbors and battlements
Impregnable. Projects were broken off,
Laid over, and the menacing huge walls
With cranes unmoving stood against the sky.   120

As soon as Jove's[2] dear consort saw the lady
Prey to such illness, and her reputation
Standing no longer in the way of passion,
Saturn's daughter said to Venus:
                              "Wondrous!
Covered yourself with glory, have you not,   125
You and your boy, and won such prizes, too.
Divine power is something to remember
If by collusion of two gods one mortal
Woman is brought low.

---

1. An Etruscan and Roman practice was to inspect the entrails of the sacrificial victim and interpret irregular or unusual features as signs of the future.   2. Jupiter's.

I am not blind.
Your fear of our new walls has not escaped me,   130
Fear and mistrust of Carthage at her height.
But how far will it go? What do you hope for,
Being so contentious? Why do we not
Arrange eternal peace and formal marriage?
You have your heart's desire: Dido in love,   135
Dido consumed with passion to her core.
Why not, then, rule this people side by side
With equal authority? And let the queen
Wait on her Phrygian lord, let her consign
Into your hand her Tyrians as a dowry."   140

Now Venus knew this talk was all pretence,
All to divert the future power from Italy
To Libya; and she answered:
                              "Who would be
So mad, so foolish as to shun that prospect
Or prefer war with you? That is, provided   145
Fortune is on the side of your proposal.
The fates here are perplexing: would one city
Satisfy Jupiter's will for Tyrians
And Trojan exiles? Does he approve
A union and a mingling of these races?   150
You are his consort: you have every right
To sound him out. Go on, and I'll come, too."

But regal Juno pointedly replied:
"That task will rest with me. Just now, as to
The need of the moment and the way to meet it,   155
Listen, and I'll explain in a few words.
Aeneas and Dido in her misery
Plan hunting in the forest, when the Titan
Sun comes up with rays to light the world.
While beaters in excitement ring the glens   160
My gift will be a black raincloud, and hail,
A downpour, and I'll shake heaven with thunder.
The company will scatter, lost in gloom,
As Dido and the Trojan captain come
To one same cavern. I shall be on hand,   165
And if I can be certain you are willing,
There I shall marry them and call her his.
A wedding, this will be."
                              Then Cytherëa,[3]
Not disinclined, nodded to Juno's plea,
And smiled at the stratagem now given away.   170

Dawn came up meanwhile from the Ocean stream,
And in the early sunshine from the gates
Picked huntsmen issued: wide-meshed nets and snares,

3. Venus.

Broad spearheads for big game, Massylian[4] horsemen
Trooping with hounds in packs keen on the scent.   175
But Dido lingered in her hall, as Punic
Nobles waited, and her mettlesome hunter
Stood nearby, cavorting in gold and scarlet,
Champing his foam-flecked bridle. At long last
The queen appeared with courtiers in a crowd,   180
A short Sidonian cloak edged in embroidery
Caught about her, at her back a quiver
Sheathed in gold, her hair tied up in gold,
And a brooch of gold pinning her scarlet dress.
Phrygians came in her company as well,   185
And Iulus, joyous at the scene. Resplendent
Above the rest, Aeneas walked to meet her,
To join his retinue with hers. He seemed—
Think of the lord Apollo in the spring
When he leaves wintering in Lycia   190
By Xanthus torrent, for his mother's isle
Of Delos, to renew the festival;
Around his altars Cretans, Dryopës,
And painted Agathyrsans[5] raise a shout,
But the god walks the Cynthian ridge alone   195
And smooths his hair, binds it in fronded laurel,
Braids it in gold; and shafts ring on his shoulders.
So elated and swift, Aeneas walked
With sunlit grace upon him.
                              Soon the hunters,
Riding in company to high pathless hills,   200
Saw mountain goats shoot down from a rocky peak
And scamper on the ridges; toward the plain
Deer left the slopes, herding in clouds of dust
In flight across the open lands. Alone,
The boy Ascanius, delightedly riding   205
His eager horse amid the lowland vales,
Outran both goats and deer. Could he only meet
Amid the harmless game some foaming boar,
Or a tawny lion down from the mountainside!

Meanwhile in heaven began a rolling thunder,   210
And soon the storm broke, pouring rain and hail.
Then Tyrians and Trojans in alarm—
With Venus' Dardan grandson[6]—ran for cover
Here and there in the wilderness, as freshets
Coursed from the high hills.
                              Now to the self-same cave   215
Came Dido and the captain of the Trojans.
Primal Earth herself and Nuptial Juno
Opened the ritual, torches of lightning blazed,
High Heaven became witness to the marriage,
And nymphs cried out wild hymns from a mountain top.   220

4. After Massilia (Marseilles), in southern France.   5. Pilgrims from various regions.   6. Ascanius.

That day was the first cause of death, and first
Of sorrow. Dido had no further qualms
As to impressions given and set abroad;
She thought no longer of a secret love
But called it marriage. Thus, under that name,   225
She hid her fault.
            Now in no time at all
Through all the African cities Rumor goes—
Nimble as quicksilver among evils. Rumor
Thrives on motion, stronger for the running,
Lowly at first through fear, then rearing high,   230
She treads the land and hides her head in cloud.
As people fable it, the Earth, her mother,
Furious against the gods, bore a late sister
To the giants Coeus and Enceladus,
Giving her speed on foot and on the wing: 235
Monstrous, deformed, titanic. Pinioned, with
An eye beneath for every body feather,
And, strange to say, as many tongues and buzzing
Mouths as eyes, as many pricked-up ears,
By night she flies between the earth and heaven   240
Shrieking through darkness, and she never turns
Her eye-lids down to sleep. By day she broods,
On the alert, on rooftops or on towers,
Bringing great cities fear, harping on lies
And slander evenhandedly with truth.   245
In those days Rumor took an evil joy
At filling countrysides with whispers, whispers,
Gossip of what was done, and never done:
How this Aeneas landed, Trojan born,
How Dido in her beauty graced his company,   250
Then how they reveled all the winter long
Unmindful of the realm, prisoners of lust.

These tales the scabrous goddess put about
On men's lips everywhere. Her twisting course
Took her to King Iarbas, whom she set   255
Ablaze with anger piled on top of anger.
Son of Jupiter Hammon by a nymph,
A ravished Garamantean, this prince
Had built the god a hundred giant shrines,
A hundred altars, each with holy fires.   260
Alight by night and day, sentries on watch,
The ground enriched by victims' blood, the doors
Festooned with flowering wreaths. Before his altars
King Iarbas, crazed by the raw story,
Stood, they say, amid the Presences,   265
With supplicating hands, pouring out prayer:

"All powerful Jove, to whom the feasting Moors
At ease on colored couches tip their wine,
Do you see this? Are we then fools to fear you

Throwing down your bolts? Those dazzling fires 270
Of lightning, are they aimless in the clouds
And rumbling thunder meaningless? This woman
Who turned up in our country and laid down
A tiny city at a price, to whom
I gave a beach to plow—and on my terms— 275
After refusing to marry me has taken
Aeneas to be master in her realm.
And now Sir Paris with his men, half-men,
His chin and perfumed hair tied up
In a Maeonian bonnet, takes possession. 280
As for ourselves, here we are bringing gifts
Into these shrines—supposedly your shrines—
Hugging that empty fable."
                Pleas like this
From the man clinging to his altars reached
The ears of the Almighty. Now he turned 285
His eyes upon the queen's town and the lovers
Careless of their good name; then spoke to Mercury,[7]
Assigning him a mission:
                "Son, bestir yourself,
Call up the Zephyrs,[8] take to your wings and glide.
Approach the Dardan captain where he tarries 290
Rapt in Tyrian Carthage, losing sight
Of future towns the fates ordain. Correct him,
Carry my speech to him on the running winds:
No son like this did his enchanting mother
Promise to us, nor such did she deliver 295
Twice from peril at the hands of Greeks.
He was to be the ruler of Italy,
Potential empire, armorer of war;
To father men from Teucer's[9] noble blood
And bring the whole world under law's dominion. 300
If glories to be won by deeds like these
Cannot arouse him, if he will not strive
For his own honor, does he begrudge his son,
Ascanius, the high strongholds of Rome?
What has he in mind? What hope, to make him stay 305
Amid a hostile race, and lose from view
Ausonian progeny, Lavinian lands?[1]
The man should sail: that is the whole point.
Let this be what you tell him, as from me."

He finished and fell silent. Mercury 310
Made ready to obey the great command
Of his great father, and he first tied on
The golden sandals, winged, that high in air
Transport him over seas or over land
Abreast of gale winds; then he took the wand 315

---

7. The messenger god; Hermes in Greek. 8. The west winds. 9. The first Trojan king. 1. The dowry of Lavinia, daughter of Latinus, whom Aeneas marries. "Ausonian": Italian.

With which he summons pale souls out of Orcus
And ushers others to the undergloom,
Lulls men to slumber or awakens them,
And opens dead men's eyes. This wand in hand,
He can drive winds before him, swimming down   320
Along the stormcloud. Now aloft, he saw
The craggy flanks and crown of patient Atlas,
Giant Atlas, balancing the sky
Upon his peak[2]—his pine-forested head
In vapor cowled, beaten by wind and rain.   325
Snow lay upon his shoulders, rills cascaded
Down his ancient chin and beard a-bristle,
Caked with ice. Here Mercury of Cyllenë[3]
Hovered first on even wings, then down
He plummeted to sea-level and flew on   330
Like a low-flying gull that skims the shallows
And rocky coasts where fish ply close inshore.
So, like a gull between the earth and sky,
The progeny of Cyllenë, on the wing
From his maternal grandsire, split the winds   335
To the sand bars of Libya.
                         Alighting tiptoe
On the first hutments, there he found Aeneas
Laying foundations for new towers and homes.
He noted well the swordhilt the man wore,
Adorned with yellow jasper; and the cloak   340
Aglow with Tyrian dye upon his shoulders—
Gifts of the wealthy queen, who had inwoven
Gold thread in the fabric. Mercury
Took him to task at once:
                      "Is it for you
To lay the stones for Carthage's high walls,   345
Tame husband that you are, and build their city?
Oblivious of your own world, your own kingdom!
From bright Olympus he that rules the gods
And turns the earth and heaven by his power—
He and no other sent me to you, told me   350
To bring this message on the running winds:
What have you in mind? What hope, wasting your days
In Libya? If future history's glories
Do not affect you, if you will not strive
For your own honor, think of Ascanius,   355
Think of the expectations of your heir,
Iulus, to whom the Italian realm, the land
Of Rome, are due."
                    And Mercury, as he spoke,
Departed from the visual field of mortals
To a great distance, ebbed in subtle air.   360

2. The Atlas Mountains are in western North Africa. The reference here is also to the Titan Atlas, who, as punishment for his part in the revolt against Jupiter, must hold up the heavens on his shoulders.   3. A mountain in Arcadia and Mercury's birthplace.

Amazed, and shocked to the bottom of his soul
By what his eyes had seen, Aeneas felt
His hackles rise, his voice choke in his throat.
As the sharp admonition and command
From heaven had shaken him awake, he now   365
Burned only to be gone, to leave that land
Of the sweet life behind. What can he do? How tell
The impassioned queen and hope to win her over?
What opening shall he choose? This way and that
He let his mind dart, testing alternatives,   370
Running through every one. And as he pondered
This seemed the better tactic: he called in
Mnestheus, Sergestus and stalwart Serestus,
Telling them:
                "Get the fleet ready for sea,
But quietly, and collect the men on shore.   375
Lay in ship stores and gear."
                            As to the cause
For a change of plan, they were to keep it secret,
Seeing the excellent Dido had no notion,
No warning that such love could be cut short;
He would himself look for the right occasion,   380
The easiest time to speak, the way to do it.
The Trojans to a man gladly obeyed.

The queen, for her part, felt some plot afoot
Quite soon—for who deceives a woman in love?
She caught wind of a change, being in fear   385
Of what had seemed her safety. Evil Rumor,
Shameless as before,[4] brought word to her
In her distracted state of ships being rigged
In trim for sailing. Furious, at her wits' end,
She traversed the whole city, all aflame   390
With rage, like a Bacchanté[5] driven wild
By emblems shaken, when the mountain revels
Of the odd year possess her, when the cry
Of Bacchus rises and Cithaeron[6] calls
All through the shouting night. Thus it turned out   395
She was the first to speak and charge Aeneas:

"You even hoped to keep me in the dark
As to this outrage, did you, two-faced man,
And slip away in silence? Can our love
Not hold you, can the pledge we gave not hold you,   400
Can Dido not, now sure to die in pain?
Even in winter weather must you toil
With ships, and fret to launch against high winds
For the open sea? Oh, heartless!

4. Earlier, Rumor (a semidivine being) had spread the report of Dido's "marriage," which had incited Iarbas to make his indignant prayer to Jupiter.   5. A female devotee of the god Bacchus, in an ecstatic
trance at the festival held every other year in the god's honor.   6. Mountain near Thebes, sacred to Bacchus.

Tell me now,
If you were not in search of alien lands   405
And new strange homes, if ancient Troy remained,
Would ships put out for Troy on these big seas?
Do you go to get away from me? I beg you,
By these tears, by your own right hand,[7] since I
Have left my wretched self nothing but that—   410
Yes, by the marriage that we entered on,
If ever I did well and you were grateful
Or found some sweetness in a gift from me,
Have pity now on a declining house!
Put this plan by, I beg you, if a prayer   415
Is not yet out of place.
Because of you, Libyans and nomad kings
Detest me, my own Tyrians are hostile;
Because of you, I lost my integrity
And that admired name by which alone   420
I made my way once toward the stars.
                              To whom
Do you abandon me, a dying woman,
Guest that you are—the only name now left
From that of husband? Why do I live on?
Shall I, until my brother Pygmalion comes   425
To pull my walls down? Or the Gaetulan
Iarbas leads me captive? If at least
There were a child by you for me to care for,
A little one to play in my courtyard
And give me back Aeneas, in spite of all,   430
I should not feel so utterly defeated,
Utterly bereft."
               She ended there.
The man by Jove's command held fast his eyes
And fought down the emotion in his heart.
At length he answered:
                      "As for myself, be sure   435
I never shall deny all you can say,
Your majesty, of what you meant to me.
Never will the memory of Elissa[8]
Stale for me, while I can still remember
My own life, and the spirit rules my body.   440
As to the event, a few words. Do not think
I meant to be deceitful and slip away.
I never held the torches of a bridegroom,
Never entered upon the pact of marriage.
If Fate permitted me to spend my days   445
By my own lights, and make the best of things
According to my wishes, first of all
I should look after Troy and the loved relics
Left me of my people. Priam's great hall
Should stand again; I should have restored the tower 450

7. The handclasp with which he pledged his love and that Dido took as an earnest of marriage.   8. Dido.

Of Pergamum for Trojans in defeat.
But now it is the rich Italian land
Apollo tells me I must make for: Italy,
Named by his oracles. There is my love;
There is my country. If, as a Phoenician,   455
You are so given to the charms of Carthage,
Libyan city that it is, then tell me,
Why begrudge the Teucrian new lands
For homesteads in Ausonia? Are we not
Entitled, too, to look for realms abroad?   460
Night never veils the earth in damp and darkness,
Fiery stars never ascend the east,
But in my dreams my father's troubled ghost[9]
Admonishes and frightens me. Then, too,
Each night thoughts come of young Ascanius,   465
My dear boy wronged, defrauded of his kingdom,
Hesperian lands of destiny. And now
The gods' interpreter, sent by Jove himself—
I swear it by your head and mine—has brought
Commands down through the racing winds! I say   470
With my own eyes in full daylight I saw him
Entering the building! With my very ears
I drank his message in! So please, no more
Of these appeals that set us both afire.
I sail for Italy not of my own free will."   475

During all this she had been watching him
With face averted, looking him up and down
In silence, and she burst out raging now:

"No goddess was your mother. Dardanus
Was not the founder of your family.   480
Liar and cheat! Some rough Caucasian cliff
Begot you on flint. Hyrcanian[1] tigresses
Tendered their teats to you. Why should I palter?
Why still hold back for more indignity?
Sigh, did he, while I wept? Or look at me?   485
Or yield a tear, or pity her who loved him?
What shall I say first, with so much to say?
The time is past when either supreme Juno
Or the Saturnian father[2] viewed these things
With justice. Faith can never be secure.   490
I took the man in, thrown up on this coast
In dire need, and in my madness then
Contrived a place for him in my domain,
Rescued his lost fleet, saved his shipmates' lives.
Oh, I am swept away burning by furies!   495
Now the prophet Apollo, now his oracles,

9. Anchisēs had died in Sicily just before Aeneas, leaving for Italy, was blown by the storm winds to
Carthage.   1. Near the Caspian Sea. "Caucasian": after Caucasus Mountains also near the Caspian
Sea. The adjective connoted outlandishness and cruelty.   2. Jupiter.

Now the gods' interpreter, if you please,
Sent down by Jove himself, brings through the air
His formidable commands! What fit employment
For heaven's high powers! What anxieties   500
To plague serene immortals![3] I shall not
Detain you or dispute your story. Go,
Go after Italy on the sailing winds,
Look for your kingdom, cross the deepsea swell!
If divine justice counts for anything,   505
I hope and pray that on some grinding reef
Midway at sea you'll drink your punishment
And call and call on Dido's name!
From far away I shall come after you
With my black fires, and when cold death has parted   510
Body from soul I shall be everywhere
A shade to haunt you! You will pay for this,
Unconscionable! I shall hear! The news will reach me
Even among the lowest of the dead!"
At this abruptly she broke off and ran   515
In sickness from his sight and the light of day,
Leaving him at a loss, alarmed, and mute
With all he meant to say. The maids in waiting
Caught her as she swooned and carried her
To bed in her marble chamber.
                            Duty-bound,   520
Aeneas, though he struggled with desire
To calm and comfort her in all her pain,
To speak to her and turn her mind from grief,
And though he sighed his heart out, shaken still
With love of her, yet took the course heaven gave him   525
And went back to the fleet. Then with a will
The Teucrians fell to work and launched ships
Along the whole shore: slick with tar each hull
Took to the water. Eager to get away,
The sailors brought oar-boughs out of the woods   530
With leaves still on, and oaken logs unhewn.
Now you could see them issuing from the town
To the water's edge in streams, as when, aware
Of winter, ants will pillage a mound of spelt
To store it in their granary; over fields   535
The black battalion moves, and through the grass
On a narrow trail they carry off the spoil;
Some put their shoulders to the enormous weight
Of a trundled grain, while some pull stragglers in
And castigate delay; their to-and-fro   540
Of labor makes the whole track come alive.
At that sight, what were your emotions, Dido?
Sighing how deeply, looking out and down
From your high tower on the seething shore

---

3. A reference to the Epicurean idea that the gods are unaffected by human events.

With a calm look, a clear and hopeful brow.

"Sister, be glad for me! I've found a way   635
To bring him back or free me of desire.
Near to the Ocean boundary, near sundown,
The Aethiops' farthest territory lies,
Where giant Atlas turns the sphere of heaven
Studded with burning stars. From there   640
A priestess of Massylian[7] stock has come;
She had been pointed out to me: custodian
Of that shrine named for daughters of the west,
Hesperidës;[8] and it is she who fed
The dragon, guarding well the holy boughs   645
With honey dripping slow and drowsy poppy.
Chanting her spells she undertakes to free
What hearts she wills, but to inflict on others
Duress of sad desires; to arrest
The flow of rivers, make the stars move backward,   650
Call up the spirits of deep Night. You'll see
Earth shift and rumble underfoot and ash trees
Walk down mountainsides. Dearest, I swear
Before the gods and by your own sweet self,
It is against my will that I resort   655
For weaponry to magic powers. In secret
Build up a pyre in the inner court
Under the open sky, and place upon it
The arms that faithless man left in my chamber,
All his clothing, and the marriage bed   660
On which I came to grief—solace for me
To annihilate all vestige of the man,
Vile as he is: my priestess shows me this."

While she was speaking, cheek and brow grew pale.
But Anna could not think her sister cloaked   665
A suicide in these unheard-of rites;
She failed to see how great her madness was
And feared no consequence more grave
Than at Sychaeus' death. So, as commanded,
She made the preparations. For her part,   670
The queen, seeing the pyre in her inmost court
Erected huge with pitch-pine and sawn ilex,
Hung all the place under the sky with wreaths
And crowned it with funereal cypress boughs.
On the pyre's top she put a sword he left   675
With clothing, and an effigy on a couch,
Her mind fixed now ahead on what would come.
Around the pyre stood altars, and the priestess,
Hair unbound, called in a voice of thunder
Upon three hundred gods, on Erebus,   680

---

7. From the African tribe.   8. The daughters of Hesperus, who lived in a garden that contained golden apples, guarded by a dragon.

On Chaos, and on triple Hecatë,[9]
Three-faced Diana. Then she sprinkled drops
Purportedly from the fountain of Avernus.[1]
Rare herbs were brought out, reaped at the new moon
By scythes of bronze, and juicy with a milk   685
Of dusky venom; then the rare love-charm
Or caul torn from the brow of a birthing foal
And snatched away before the mother found it.
Dido herself with consecrated grain
In her pure hands, as she went near the altars,   690
Freed one foot from sandal straps, let fall
Her dress ungirdled, and, now sworn to death,
Called on the gods and stars that knew her fate.
She prayed then to whatever power may care
In comprehending justice for the grief   695
Of lovers bound unequally by love.

The night had come, and weary in every land
Men's bodies took the boon of peaceful sleep.
The woods and the wild seas had quieted
At that hour when the stars are in mid-course   700
And every field is still; cattle and birds
With vivid wings that haunt the limpid lakes
Or nest in thickets in the country places
All were asleep under the silent night.
Not, though, the agonized Phoenician queen: 705
She never slackened into sleep and never
Allowed the tranquil night to rest
Upon her eyelids or within her heart.
Her pain redoubled; love came on again,
Devouring her, and on her bed she tossed   710
In a great surge of anger.
                            So awake,
She pressed these questions, musing to herself:

"Look now, what can I do? Turn once again
To the old suitors, only to be laughed at—
Begging a marriage with Numidians   715
Whom I disdained so often? Then what? Trail
The Ilian ships and follow like a slave
Commands of Trojans? Seeing them so agreeable,
In view of past assistance and relief,
So thoughtful their unshaken gratitude?   720
Suppose I wished it, who permits or takes
Aboard their proud ships one they so dislike?
Poor lost soul, do you not yet grasp or feel

---

9. Diana as goddess of sorcery and the moon. Chaos was the Greek personification of the disorder that preceded the creation of the universe.   1. A lake in southern Italy that was supposed to be the entrance to the lower world.

The treachery of the line of Laömedon?[2]   725
What then? Am I to go alone, companion
Of the exultant sailors in their flight?
Or shall I set out in their wake, with Tyrians,
With all my crew close at my side, and send
The men I barely tore away from Tyre
To sea again, making them hoist their sails   730
To more sea-winds? No: die as you deserve,
Give pain quietus with a steel blade.
                        Sister,
You are the one who gave way to my tears
In the beginning, burdened a mad queen
With sufferings, and thrust me on my enemy.   735
It was not given me to lead my life
Without new passion, innocently, the way
Wild creatures live, and not to touch these depths.
The vow I took to the ashes of Sychaeus
Was not kept."
               So she broke out afresh   740
In bitter mourning. On his high stern deck
Aeneas, now quite certain of departure,
Everything ready, took the boon of sleep.
In dream the figure of the god returned
With looks reproachful as before: he seemed   745
Again to warn him, being like Mercury
In every way, in voice, in golden hair,
And in the bloom of youth.
                    "Son of the goddess,
Sleep away this crisis, can you still?
Do you not see the dangers growing round you,   750
Madman, from now on? Can you not hear
The offshore westwind blow? The woman hatches
Plots and drastic actions in her heart,
Resolved on death now, whipping herself on
To heights of anger. Will you not be gone   755
In flight, while flight is still within your power?
Soon you will see the offing boil with ships
And glare with torches; soon again
The waterfront will be alive with fires,
If Dawn comes while you linger in this country.   760
Ha! Come, break the spell! Woman's a thing
Forever fitful and forever changing."

At this he merged into the darkness. Then
As the abrupt phantom filled him with fear,
Aeneas broke from sleep and roused his crewmen: 765
"Up, turn out now! Oarsmen, take your thwarts!
Shake out sail! Look here, for the second time
A god from heaven's high air is goading me
To hasten our break away, to cut the cables.

---

2. A king of Troy who twice broke his promise, once to Heracles and once to Apollo and Poseidon.

Holy one, whatever god you are,   770
We go with you, we act on your command
Most happily! Be near, graciously help us,
Make the stars in heaven propitious ones!"

He pulled his sword aflash out of its sheath
And struck at the stern hawser. All the men   775
Were gripped by his excitement to be gone,
And hauled and hustled. Ships cast off their moorings,
And an array of hulls hid inshore water
As oarsmen churned up foam and swept to sea.

Soon early Dawn, quitting the saffron bed   780
Of old Tithonus,[3] cast new light on earth,
And as air grew transparent, from her tower
The queen caught sight of ships on the seaward reach
With sails full and the wind astern. She knew
The waterfront now empty, bare of oarsmen.   785
Beating her lovely breast three times, four times,
And tearing her golden hair,
                    "O Jupiter,"
She said, "will this man go, will he have mocked
My kingdom, stranger that he was and is?
Will they not snatch up arms and follow him   790
From every quarter of the town? and dockhands
Tear our ships from moorings? On! Be quick
With torches! Give out arms! Unship the oars!
What am I saying? Where am I? What madness
Takes me out of myself? Dido, poor soul,   795
Your evil doing has come home to you.
Then was the right time, when you offered him
A royal scepter. See the good faith and honor
Of one they say bears with him everywhere
The hearthgods of his country! One who bore   800
His father, spent with age, upon his shoulders!
Could I not then have torn him limb from limb
And flung the pieces on the sea? His company,
Even Ascanius could I not have minced
And served up to his father at a feast?   805
The luck of battle might have been in doubt—
So let it have been! Whom had I to fear,
Being sure to die? I could have carried torches
Into his camp, filled passage ways with flame,
Annihilated father and son and followers   810
And given my own life on top of all!
O Sun, scanning with flame all works of earth,
And thou, O Juno, witness and go-between
Of my long miseries; and Hecatë,

---

3. Human consort of Aurora (Eos in Greek), the dawn goddess. He is old because, although she made him immortal when she took him to her bed, she forgot to obtain for him the gift of eternal youth.

Screeched for at night at crossroads in the cities;   815
And thou, avenging Furies, and all gods
On whom Elissa dying may call: take notice,
Overshadow this hell with your high power,
As I deserve, and hear my prayer!
If by necessity that impious wretch   820
Must find his haven and come safe to land,
If so Jove's destinies require, and this,
His end in view, must stand, yet all the same
When hard beset in war by a brave people,
Forced to go outside his boundaries   825
And torn from Iulus, let him beg assistance,
Let him see the unmerited deaths of those
Around and with him, and accepting peace
On unjust terms, let him not, even so,
Enjoy his kingdom or the life he longs for,   830
But fall in battle before his time and lie
Unburied on the sand![4] This I implore,
This is my last cry, as my last blood flows.
Then, O my Tyrians, besiege with hate
His progeny and all his race to come: 835
Make this your offering to my dust. No love,
No pact must be between our peoples; No,
But rise up from my bones, avenging spirit!
Harry with fire and sword the Dardan countrymen
Now, or hereafter, at whatever time   840
The strength will be afforded. Coast with coast
In conflict, I implore, and sea with sea,
And arms with arms: may they contend in war,
Themselves and all the children of their children!"[5]

Now she took thought of one way or another,   845
At the first chance, to end her hated life,
And briefly spoke to Barcë, who had been
Sychaeus' nurse; her own an urn of ash
Long held in her ancient fatherland.
                              "Dear nurse,
Tell Sister Anna to come here, and have her   850
Quickly bedew herself with running water
Before she brings out victims for atonement.
Let her come that way. And you, too, put on
Pure wool around your brows. I have a mind
To carry out that rite to Stygian[6] Jove   855
That I have readied here, and put an end

---

4. Dido's prophecy-wish does come true. Aeneas meets resistance in Italy, and at one point in the war he must leave Ascanius behind and beg aid from King Evander. One of the conditions of peace is that his people call themselves Latins (not Trojans). He is eventually drowned in an Italian river, never to see the glory of his descendants.   5. These prophecies also come true. The Romans and Carthaginians fought three wars (the Punic Wars); Rome won them all, razing Carthage after the third. In the 3rd century b.c.e. Hannibal invaded Italy, winning many battles, although he failed to take Rome.   6. The king of the underworld, Pluto (Hades in Greek). The Styx is one of the rivers of the underworld.

To my distress, committing to the flames
The pyre of that miserable Dardan."

At this with an old woman's eagerness
Barce hurried away. And Dido's heart   860
Beat wildly at the enormous thing afoot.
She rolled her bloodshot eyes, her quivering cheeks
Were flecked with red as her sick pallor grew
Before her coming death. Into the court
She burst her way, then at her passion's height   865
She climbed the pyre and bared the Dardan sword—
A gift desired once, for no such need.
Her eyes now on the Trojan clothing there
And the familiar bed, she paused a little,
Weeping a little, mindful, then lay down   870
And spoke her last words:
                                "Remnants dear to me
While god and fate allowed it, take this breath
And give me respite from these agonies.
I lived my life out to the very end   875
And passed the stages Fortune had appointed.
Now my tall shade goes to the under world.
I built a famous town, saw my great walls,
Avenged my husband, made my hostile brother
Pay for his crime. Happy, alas, too happy,   880
If only the Dardanian keels had never
Beached on our coast." And here she kissed the bed.
"I die unavenged," she said, "but let me die.
This way, this way,[7] a blessed relief to go
Into the undergloom. Let the cold Trojan,   885
Far at sea, drink in this conflagration
And take with him the omen of my death!"

Amid these words her household people saw her
Crumpled over the steel blade, and the blade
Aflush with red blood, drenched her hands. A scream   890
Pierced the high chambers. Now through the shocked city
Rumor went rioting, as wails and sobs
With women's outcry echoed in the palace
And heaven's high air gave back the beating din,
As though all Carthage or old Tyre fell   895
To storming enemies, and, out of hand,
Flames billowed on the roofs of men and gods.
Her sister heard the trembling, faint with terror,
Lacerating her face, beating her breast,
Ran through the crowd to call the dying queen: 900

"It came to this, then, sister? You deceived me?
The pyre meant this, altars and fires meant this?
What shall I mourn first, being abandoned? Did you

---

7. In Latin sic, sic; the repetition represents two thrusts of the sword.

Were those sad souls, benighted, who contrived
Their own destruction, and as they hated daylight,
Cast their lives away. How they would wish
In the upper air now to endure the pain   215
Of poverty and toil! But iron law
Stands in the way, since the drear hateful swamp
Has pinned them down here, and the Styx that winds
Nine times around exerts imprisoning power.
Not far away, spreading on every side,   220
The Fields of Mourning came in view, so called
Since here are those whom pitiless love consumed
With cruel wasting, hidden on paths apart
By myrtle woodland growing overhead.
In death itself, pain will not let them be.   225
He saw here Phaedra, Procris, Eriphylë
Sadly showing the wounds her hard son gave;
Evadnë and Pasiphaë, at whose side
Laodamia walked, and Caeneus,[5]
A young man once, a woman now, and turned   230
Again by fate into the older form.
Among them, with her fatal wound still fresh,
Phoenician Dido wandered the deep wood.
The Trojan captain paused nearby and knew
Her dim form in the dark, as one who sees,   235
Early in the month, or thinks to have seen, the moon
Rising through cloud, all dim. He wept and spoke
Tenderly to her:
                  "Dido, so forlorn,
The story then that came to me was true,
That you were out of life, had met your end   240
By your own hand. Was I, was I the cause?
I swear by heaven's stars, by the high gods,
By any certainty below the earth,
I left your land against my will, my queen.
The gods' commands drove me to do their will,   245
As now they drive me through this world of shades,
These mouldy waste lands and these depths of night.
And I could not believe that I would hurt you
So terribly by going. Wait a little.
Do not leave my sight.   250
Am I someone to flee from? The last word
Destiny lets me say to you is this."

5. Virgil's words in the original are ambiguous (perhaps to reflect the ambiguity of the sex of Caeneus).
The usual explanation of the passage is that Caenis (a woman) was changed by Neptune into a man
(Caeneus) but returned to her original sex after death. Because the name occurs here in a list of women,
this seems the most likely explanation. Phaedra was the wife of Theseus, king of Athens, who fell in love
with Hippolytus, her husband's son by another woman; the result was her death by suicide and Hippolytus's death through his father's curse. Procris was killed by her husband in an accident that was brought
about by her own jealousy. Eriphyle betrayed her husband for gold and was killed by her own son. Evadnë
threw herself on the pyre of her husband, who was killed by Jupiter for impiety. Pasiphaë was the wife of
Minos; she was made to fall in love with a bull, and their union produced the Minotaur. Laodamia begged
to be allowed to talk with her dead husband; the request was granted by the gods, and when his time came
to return she went with him to the underworld.

Aeneas with such pleas tried to placate
The burning soul, savagely glaring back,
And tears came to his eyes. But she had turned   255
With gaze fixed on the ground as he spoke on,
Her face no more affected than if she were
Immobile granite or Marpesian[6] stone.
At length she flung away from him and fled,
His enemy still, into the shadowy grove   260
Where he whose bride she once had been, Sychaeus,
Joined in her sorrows and returned her love.
Aeneas still gazed after her in tears,
Shaken by her ill fate and pitying her.

Summary   After being shown a pageant of the great Romans who will make Rome
mistress of the world, Aeneas returns to the upper air and begins his settlement in
Italy. He is offered the hand of the princess Lavinia by her father Latinus, but this provokes a war against the Trojans, led by King Turnus of Laurentum, in the course of
which Aeneas is wounded and stops by a stream to rest. At this point his mother,
Venus, comes to him with the armor made for him by Vulcan (Hephaestus in Greek),
her husband and guardian of fire. On the shield is carved a representation of the
future glories of Rome.

FROM BOOK VIII

[The Shield of Aeneas]

Venus the gleaming goddess,
Bearing her gifts, came down amid high clouds
And far away still, in a vale apart,
Sighted her son beside the ice-cold stream.
Then making her appearance as she willed   5
She said to him:
                    "Here are the gifts I promised,
Forged to perfection by my husband's craft,
So that you need not hesitate to challenge
Arrogant Laurentines or savage Turnus,
However soon, in battle."
                             As she spoke   10
Cytherëa[7] swept to her son's embrace
And placed the shining arms before his eyes
Under an oak tree. Now the man in joy
At a goddess' gifts, at being so greatly honored,
Could not be satisfied, but scanned each piece   15
In wonder and turned over in his hands
The helmet with its terrifying plumes
And gushing flames, the sword-blade edged with fate,
The cuirass of hard bronze, blood-red and huge—
Like a dark cloud burning with sunset light   20
That sends a glow for miles—the polished greaves[8]
Of gold and silver alloy, the great spear,

6. From the island of Paros.   7. So-called because she was born from the sea foam off the Greek island
Cythera.   8. Leg pieces.

And finally the fabric of the shield
Beyond description.
                There the Lord of Fire,
Knowing the prophets, knowing the age to come,   25
Had wrought the future story of Italy,
The triumphs of the Romans: there one found
The generations of Ascanius' heirs,
The wars they fought, each one. Vulcan had made
The mother wolf, lying in Mars' green grotto;   30
Made the twin boys at play about her teats,[9]
Nursing the mother without fear, while she
Bent round her smooth neck fondling them in turn
And shaped their bodies with her tongue.
                             Nearby,
Rome had been added by the artisan,   35
And Sabine women roughly carried off
Out of the audience at the Circus games;
Then suddenly a new war coming on
To pit the sons of Romulus against
Old Tatius[1] and his austere town of Curës.   40
Later the same kings, warfare laid aside,
In arms before Jove's altar stood and held
Libation dishes as they made a pact
With offering of wine. Not far from this
Two four-horse war-cars, whipped on, back to back,   45
Had torn Mettus apart (still, man of Alba,
You should have kept your word) and Roman Tullus[2]
Dragged the liar's rags of flesh away
Through woods where brambles dripped a bloody dew.
There, too, Porsenna stood, ordering Rome   50
To take the exiled Tarquin back,[3] then bringing
The whole city under massive siege.
There for their liberty Aeneas' sons
Threw themselves forward on the enemy spears.
You might have seen Porsenna imaged there   55
To the life, a menacing man, a man in anger
At Roman daring: Cocles who downed the bridge,
Cloelia[4] who broke her bonds and swam the river.

On the shield's upper quarter Manlius,
guard of the Tarpeian Rock, stood fast   60
Before the temple and held the Capitol,[5]

---

9. The twins who were to build Rome, Romulus and Remus, sons of Mars the war god, were cast out into the woods and there suckled by a she-wolf.   1. A Sabine king. Because the new city of Rome consisted mostly of men, the Romans decided to steal women from the Sabines. The Romans invited them to an athletic festival, and at a given signal every Roman carried off a Sabine bride. The war that followed ended in the amalgamation of the Roman and Sabine peoples.   2. The king who punished Mettus for breaking an agreement made during the early wars of Rome. Mettus was torn apart by two chariots moving in opposite directions.   3. The Etruscan king Porsenna attempted to restore Tarquin, the last of the Roman kings, to the throne from which he had been expelled.   4. A Roman hostage held by Porsenna. Horatius Cocles, with two companions, defended the bridge across the Tiber to give the Romans time to destroy it. 5. In 392 B.C.E. Manlius was in charge of the citadel (*Tarpeian Rock*) at a time when the Gauls from the north held all the rest of the city. They made a night attack on the citadel, but Manlius, awakened by the cackling of the sacred geese, beat it off, and saved Rome.

Where Romulus' house[6] was newly thatched and rough.
Here fluttering through gilded porticos
At night, the silvery goose warned of the Gauls
Approaching: under cover of the darkness   65
Gauls amid the bushes had crept near
And now lay hold upon the citadel.
Golden locks they had and golden dress,
Glimmering with striped cloaks, their milky necks
Entwined with gold. They hefted Alpine spears,   70
Two each, and had long body shields for cover.
Vulcan had fashioned naked Luperci
And Salii[7] leaping there with woolen caps
And fallen-from-heaven shields, and put chaste ladies
Riding in cushioned carriages through Rome   75
With sacred images. At a distance then
He pictured the deep hell of Tartarus,
Dis's high gate, crime's punishments, and, yes,
You, Catiline,[8] on a precarious cliff
Hanging and trembling at the Furies' glare.   80
Then, far away from this, were virtuous souls
And Cato[9] giving laws to them. Mid-shield,
The pictured sea flowed surging, all of gold,
As whitecaps foamed on the blue waves, and dolphins
Shining in silver round and round the scene   85
Propelled themselves with flukes and cut through billows.
Vivid in the center were the bronze-beaked
Ships and the fight at sea off Actium.
Here you could see Leucata[1] all alive
With ships maneuvering, sea glowing gold,   90
Augustus Caesar leading into battle
Italians, with both senators and people,
Household gods and great gods: there he stood
High on the stern, and from his blessed brow
Twin flames gushed upward, while his crest revealed   95
His father's star. Apart from him, Agrippa,[2]
Favored by winds and gods, led ships in column,
A towering figure, wearing on his brows
The coronet adorned with warships' beaks,
Highest distinction for command at sea.   100
Then came Antonius with barbaric wealth
And a diversity of arms, victorious

---

6. In Virgil's time there was still preserved at Rome a rustic building that was supposed to have been the dwelling place of Romulus.   7. The twelve priests of Mars, who danced in his honor carrying shields that had fallen from heaven. The Luperci were priests of Lupercus, a Roman god corresponding to the Greek Pan.   8. Leader of a conspiracy to overthrow the republic; it was halted mainly through the efforts of Cicero, consul in 63 B.C.E. Catiline connotes the type of discord, represented by the civil war that almost destroyed the Roman state, to which Augustus later put an end.   9. The noblest of the republicans who had fought Julius Caesar; he stood for honesty and the seriousness that the Romans most admired. He committed suicide in 47 B.C.E. after Caesar's victory in Africa. Before taking his life he read through Plato's *Phaedo*, a dialogue concerned with the immortality of the soul, which ends with an account of the death of Socrates.   1. A promontory near Actium, on the west coast of Greece, which had a temple of Apollo on it. The naval battle fought here in 31 B.C.E. was the decisive engagement of the civil war. Augustus, the master of the western half of the empire, defeated Antony, who held the eastern half and was supported by Cleopatra, queen of Egypt.   2. Augustus's admiral at Actium.

What do you plan? What are you hoping for,
Keeping your seat apart in the cold clouds?
Fitting, was it, that a mortal archer   10
Wound an immortal? That a blade let slip
Should be restored to Turnus, and new force
Accrue to a beaten man? Without your help
What could Juturna do? Come now, at last
Have done, and heed our pleading, and give way.   15
Let yourself no longer be consumed
Without relief by all that inward burning;
Let care and trouble not forever come to me
From your sweet lips. The finish is at hand.
You had the power to harry men of Troy   20
By land and sea, to light the fires of war
Beyond belief, to scar a family
With mourning before marriage.[7] I forbid
Your going further."
                        So spoke Jupiter,
And with a downcast look Juno replied: 25

"Because I know that is your will indeed,
Great Jupiter, I left the earth below,
Though sore at heart, and left the side of Turnus.
Were it not so, you would not see me here
Suffering all that passes, here alone,   30
Resting on air. I should be armed in flames
At the very battle-line, dragging the Trojans
Into a deadly action. I persuaded
Juturna—I confess—to help her brother
In his hard lot, and I approved her daring   35
Greater difficulties to save his life,
But not that she should fight with bow and arrow.
This I swear by Styx' great fountainhead
Inexorable, which high gods hold in awe.
I yield now and for all my hatred leave   40
This battlefield. But one thing not retained
By fate I beg for Latium, for the future
Greatness of your kin: when presently
They crown peace with a happy wedding day—
So let it be—and merge their laws and treaties,   45
Never command the land's own Latin folk
To change their old name, to become new Trojans,
Known as Teucrians; never make them alter
Dialect or dress. Let Latium be.
Let there be Alban kings for generations,   50
And let Italian valor be the strength
Of Rome in after times. Once and for all
Troy fell, and with her name let her lie fallen."

7. A reference not only to the Italian losses but also to the suicide of Amata, wife of King Latinus, who
hanged herself when the Trojans assaulted the city just before the duel between Aeneas and Turnus began.

The author of men and of the world replied
With a half-smile:
            "Sister of Jupiter[8]   55
Indeed you are, and Saturn's other child,
To feel such anger, stormy in your breast.
But come, no need; put down this fit of rage.
I grant your wish. I yield, I am won over
Willingly. Ausonian folk will keep   60
Their fathers' language and their way of life,
And, that being so, their name. The Teucrians
Will mingle and be submerged, incorporated.
Rituals and observances of theirs
I'll add, but make them Latin, one in speech.   65
The race to come, mixed with Ausonian blood,
Will outdo men and gods in its devotion,
You shall see—and no nation on earth
Will honor and worship you so faithfully."

To all this Juno nodded in assent   70
And, gladdened by his promise, changed her mind.
Then she withdrew from sky and cloud.
                               That done,
The Father set about a second plan—
To take Juturna from her warring brother.
Stories are told of twin fiends, called the Dirae,   75
Whom, with Hell's Megaera,[9] deep Night bore
In one birth. She entwined their heads with coils
Of snakes and gave them wings to race the wind.
Before Jove's throne, a step from the cruel king,
These twins attend him and give piercing fear   80
To ill mankind, when he who rules the gods
Deals out appalling death and pestilence,
Or war to terrify our wicked cities.
Jove now dispatched one of these, swift from heaven,
Bidding her be an omen to Juturna.   85
Down she flew, in a whirlwind borne to earth,
Just like an arrow driven through a cloud
From a taut string, an arrow armed with gall
Of deadly poison, shot by a Parthian[1]—
A Parthian or a Cretan[2]—for a wound   90
Immedicable; whizzing unforeseen
It goes through racing shadows: so the spawn
Of Night went diving downward to the earth.

On seeing Trojan troops drawn up in face
Of Turnus' army, she took on at once   95

---

8. Jupiter and Juno (like the Greek Zeus and Hera) are brother and sister as well as husband and wife.
9. One of the Dirae, literally "dreadful Ones."   1. Parthia was the most dangerous neighbor of the Roman empire in the east.   2. Parthian mounted archers were famous, as were Cretan archers.

The shape of that small bird[3] that perches late
At night on tombs or desolate roof-tops
And troubles darkness with a gruesome song.
Shrunk to that form, the fiend in Turnus' face
Went screeching, flitting, flitting to and fro   100
And beating with her wings against his shield.
Unstrung by numbness, faint and strange, he felt
His hackles rise, his voice choke in his throat.
As for Juturna, when she knew the wings,
The shriek to be the fiend's, she tore her hair,   105
Despairing, then she fell upon her cheeks
With nails, upon her breast with clenched hands.

"Turnus, how can your sister help you now?
What action is still open to me, soldierly
Though I have been? Can I by any skill   110
Hold daylight for you? Can I meet and turn
This deathliness away? Now I withdraw,
Now leave this war. Indecent birds, I fear you;
Spare me your terror. Whip-lash of your wings
I recognize, that ghastly sound, and guess   115
Great-hearted Jupiter's high cruel commands.
Returns for my virginity, are they?
He gave me life eternal[4]—to what end?
Why has mortality been taken from me?
Now beyond question I could put a term   120
To all my pain, and go with my poor brother
Into the darkness, his companion there.
Never to die? Will any brook of mine
Without you, brother, still be sweet to me?
If only earth's abyss were wide enough   125
To take me downward, goddess though I am,
To join the shades below!"
                        So she lamented,
Then with a long sigh, covering up her head
In her grey mantle, sank to the river's depth.

Aeneas moved against his enemy   130
And shook his heavy pine-tree spear. He called
From his hot heart:
                    "Rearmed now, why so slow?
Why, even now, fall back? The contest here
Is not a race, but fighting to the death
With spear and sword. Take on all shapes there are,   135
Summon up all your nerve and skill, choose any
Footing, fly among the stars, or hide
In caverned earth—"
                    The other shook his head,

---

3. The owl.   4. Jupiter had been the lover of Juturna and had rewarded her with immortality.

Saying:
     "I do not fear your taunting fury,
Arrogant prince. It is the gods I fear   140
And Jove my enemy."
                    He said no more,
But looked around him. Then he saw a stone,
Enormous, ancient, set up there to prevent
Landowners' quarrels. Even a dozen picked men
Such as the earth produces in our day   145
Could barely lift and shoulder it. He swooped
And wrenched it free, in one hand, then rose up
To his heroic height, ran a few steps,
And tried to hurl the stone against his foe—
But as he bent and as he ran   150
And as he hefted and propelled the weight
He did not know himself. His knees gave way,
His blood ran cold and froze. The stone itself,
Tumbling through space, fell short and had no impact.

Just as in dreams when the night-swoon of sleep   155
Weighs on our eyes, it seems we try in vain
To keep on running, try with all our might,
But in the midst of effort faint and fail;
Our tongue is powerless, familiar strength
Will not hold up our body, not a sound   160
Or word will come: just so with Turnus now:
However bravely he made shift to fight
The immortal fiend blocked and frustrated him.
Flurrying images passed through his mind.
He gazed at the Rutulians,[5] and beyond them,   165
Gazed at the city, hesitant, in dread.
He trembled now before the poised spear-shaft
And saw no way to escape; he had no force
With which to close, or reach his foe, no chariot
And no sign of the charioteer, his sister.   170
At a dead loss he stood. Aeneas made
His deadly spear flash in the sun and aimed it,
Narrowing his eyes for a lucky hit.
Then, distant still, he put his body's might
Into the cast. Never a stone that soared   175
From a wall-battering catapult went humming
Loud as this, nor with so great a crack
Burst ever a bolt of lightning. It flew on
Like a black whirlwind bringing devastation,
Pierced with a crash the rim of sevenfold shield,   180
Cleared the cuirass' edge, and passed clean through
The middle of Turnus' thigh. Force of the blow
Brought the huge man to earth, his knees buckling,
And a groan swept the Rutulians as they rose,
A groan heard echoing on all sides from all   185

5. The Italian troops watching the combat between Turnus and Aeneas.

The mountain range, and echoed by the forests.
The man brought down, brought low, lifted his eyes
And held his right hand out to make his plea:

"Clearly I earned this, and I ask no quarter.
Make the most of your good fortune here.   190
If you can feel a father's grief—and you, too,
Had such a father in Anchisës—then
Let me bespeak your mercy for old age
In Daunus,[6] and return me, or my body,
Stripped, if you will, of life, to my own kin.   195
You have defeated me. The Ausonians
Have seen me in defeat, spreading my hands.
Lavinia is your bride. But go no further
Out of hatred."
                    Fierce under arms, Aeneas
Looked to and fro, and towered, and stayed his hand   200
Upon the sword-hilt. Moment by moment now
What Turnus said began to bring him round
From indecision. Then to his glance appeared
The accurst swordbelt surmounting Turnus' shoulder,
Shining with its familiar studs—the strap   205
Young Pallas wore when Turnus wounded him
And left him dead upon the field; now Turnus
Bore that enemy token on his shoulder—
Enemy still. For when the sight came home to him,
Aeneas raged at the relic of his anguish   210
Worn by this man as trophy. Blazing up
And terrible in his anger, he called out:

"You in your plunder, torn from one of mine,
Shall I be robbed of you? This wound will come
From Pallas: Pallas makes this offering   215
And from your criminal blood exacts his due."

He sank his blade in fury in Turnus' chest.
Then all the body slackened in death's chill,
And with a groan for that indignity
His spirit fled into the gloom below.   220

6. Father of Turnus.

OVID
43 B.C.E.–17 C.E.

Born in the year after Julius Caesar's assassination, Publius Ovidius Naso did not
know the time of civil war, when no one's property, or life, was safe. He was twenty-
four when Virgil died, and he turned to different themes: the sophisticated and

somewhat racy life of the urban elite in Rome, love in its manifold social and psychological guises, Greco-Roman myth and local Italian legend. Like Catullus and Virgil, he was profoundly influenced by the learned and polished works of the Greek Alexandrian period, but like his predecessors he translated their example into his personal idiom and used it for his own purposes. He was a versifier of genius. "Whatever I tried to say," he wrote, "came out in verse," and Alexander Pope adapted the line for his own case: "I lisped in numbers for the numbers came." Elegance, wit, and precision remained the hallmarks of Ovid's poetry throughout his long and productive career, and his way of telling stories was extraordinary for its subtlety and its depth of psychological understanding. His influence on the poets and artists of the Middle Ages, the Renaissance, and beyond was massive, second only, if at all, to Virgil's.

The early years of Ovid's manhood were marked by rapid literary and social success in the brilliant society of a capital intent on enjoying the peace and prosperity inaugurated by Augustus. The *Amores*, or "Love Affairs," unabashed chronicles of a Roman Don Juan, was his first publication. It was soon followed by the *Art of Love*, a handbook of seduction (originally circulated as books 1 and 2, for men; book 3, for women, was added by popular request). Not content with teaching his readers how to start a love affair, Ovid then advised them how to end it, in the *Remedies of Love*. At some point he wrote a poem on women's cosmetics; another, the *Fasti* (never finished), on the Roman calendar; and a collection of poetic letters, the *Heroides*, purporting to have been written by heroines of legend, such as Helen, to their lovers. In 8 C.E. Ovid was banished by imperial decree to the town of Tomi, in what is now Romania. It was on the fringe of the empire, and to a devotee of Roman high life it seemed a grim place indeed. He remained there until his death, sending back to Rome poetic epistles, collected as the *Sorrows* and the *Letters from Pontus*, that asked for pardon—to no effect. The reason for his banishment is not known. Involvement in some scandal concerning Augustus's daughter Julia is a possibility, but the ultimate cause was probably the love poetry, which ran afoul of Augustus's political and social program. Augustus was trying hard, by propaganda and legislation, to revive old Roman standards of morality and cannot have found Ovid's *Art of Love*, with its suggestion that Rome was a prime location for seduction, amusing. He correctly read the poem as political critique, a mode of resistance to the authoritarian imposition of moral reform. Ovid's greatest work, the *Metamorphoses*, suggests a similar critique. It was still unfinished at the time of his exile.

THE METAMORPHOSES

Virgil had written what Augustus wanted to be the "official" epic of the new order, which was to be seen as the fulfillment of a history that began with Aeneas's journey from Troy to Italy. The *Aeneid*, for all its innovations, was an epic in the traditional style: it focused on the deeds of a single hero, and it exemplified and transmitted its culture's dominant values. The *Metamorphoses* is recognizably epic; it is the only poem Ovid wrote in the epic meter, dactylic hexameter. But it can be seen as a critical response to Virgil, even an anti-*Aeneid*. Ovid produced a series of stories using the Alexandrian form of the *epyllion*, or "miniature epic," and he strung these together into a long narrative of fifteen books. The transitions between them, and the connections drawn by the narrator, are often transparently contrived—perhaps in mockery of the idea of narrative unity. There is no single hero, and one would have to seek hard for representative national values presented without irony. There is, however, a common element to these stories: all in one way or another involve changes of shape. And despite its leisurely and roundabout course, the narrative has a discernible direction— as Ovid says in his introduction, "from the world's beginning to the present day." Starting with the creation of the world, the transformation of matter into living bodies (the first great metamorphosis), Ovid regales his readers with tales of human beings changed into animals, flowers, and trees. He proceeds through Greek myth to

From Metamorphoses[1]

FROM BOOK I

[*Proem*]

My mind leads me to speak now of forms changed
into new bodies: O gods above, inspire
this undertaking (which you've changed as well)
and guide my poem in its epic sweep
from the world's beginning to the present day.   5

[*The Creation*]

Before the seas and lands had been created,
before the sky that covers everything,
Nature displayed a single aspect only
throughout the cosmos; Chaos was its name,
a shapeless, unwrought mass of inert bulk   10
and nothing more, with the discordant seeds
of disconnected elements all heaped
together in anarchic disarray.
    The sun as yet did not light up the earth,
nor did the crescent moon renew her horns,   15
nor was the earth suspended in midair,
balanced by her own weight, nor did the ocean
extend her arms to the margins of the land.
    Although the land and sea and air were present,
land was unstable, the sea unfit for swimming,   20
and air lacked light; shapes shifted constantly,
and all things were at odds with one another,
for in a single mass cold strove with warm,
wet was opposed to dry and soft to hard,
and weightlessness to matter having weight.   25
    Some god (or kinder nature) settled this
dispute by separating earth from heaven,
and then by separating sea from earth
and fluid aether[2] from the denser air;
and after these were separated out   30
and liberated from the primal heap,
he bound the disentangled elements
each in its place and all in harmony.
    The fiery and weightless aether leapt
to heaven's vault and claimed its citadel;   35
the next in lightness to be placed was air;
the denser earth drew down gross elements
and was compressed by its own gravity;
encircling water lastly found its place,
encompassing the solid earth entire.[3]   40

---

1. Translated by Charles Martin.   2. A region of refined air, fiery in nature, believed to be above the
"denser air" that was closer to the earth and composed the breathable atmosphere.   3. From Homer on,
the ancients conceived of Ocean as a stream that surrounded the earth. See the very end of the description
of Achilles' shield in book XVIII of Homer's *Iliad*.

Now when that god (whichever one it was)
had given Chaos form, dividing it
in parts which he arranged, he molded earth
into the shape of an enormous globe,
so that it should be uniform throughout.   45
　　And afterward he sent the waters streaming
in all directions, ordered waves to swell
under the sweeping winds, and sent the flood
to form new shores on the surrounded earth;
he added springs, great standing swamps and lakes,   50
as well as sloping rivers fixed between
their narrow banks, whose plunging waters (all
in varied places, each in its own channel)
are partly taken back into the earth
and in part flow until they reach the sea,   55
when they—received into the larger field
of a freer flood—beat against shores, not banks.
He ordered open plains to spread themselves,
valleys to sink, the stony peaks to rise,
and forests to put on their coats of green.   60
　　And as the vault of heaven is divided
by two zones on the right and two on the left,
with a central zone, much hotter, in between,
so, by the care of this creator god,
the mass that was enclosed now by the sky   65
was zoned in the same way, with the same lines
inscribed upon the surface of the earth.
Heat makes the middle zone unlivable,
and the two outer zones are deep in snow;
between these two extremes, he placed two others   70
of temperate climate, blending cold and warmth.[4]
　　Air was suspended over all of this,
proportionately heavier than aether,
as earth is heavier than water is.
He ordered mists and clouds into position,   75
and thunder, to make test of our resolve,[5]
and winds creating thunderbolts and lightning.
　　Nor did that world-creating god permit
the winds to roam ungoverned through the air;
for even now, with each of them in charge   80
of his own kingdom, and their blasts controlled,
they scarcely can be kept from shattering
the world, such is the discord between brothers.
　　Eurus[6] went eastward, to the lands of Dawn,
the kingdoms of Arabia and Persia,   85
and to the mountain peaks that lie below

---

4. The sky, that is, is divided into five horizontal zones and, therefore, so is the earth beneath it. On either side of the earth's uninhabitable torrid region, over which the sun passes, lies a temperate zone, and the northern one contains the inhabited, civilized lands on earth (ancient writers were vague about what the southern temperate zone contained). The two outermost zones, farthest from the sun, were too cold to live in.　5. Thunder was considered an omen.　6. The east wind. Zephyr, Boreas, and Auster were the west, north, and south winds, respectively.

the morning's rays; and Zephyr took his place
on the western shores warmed by the setting sun.
The frozen north and Scythia were seized
by bristling Boreas; the lands opposite,   90
continually drenched by fog and rain,
are where the south wind, known as Auster, dwells.
Above these winds, he set the weightless aether,
a liquid free of every earthly toxin.
No sooner had he separated all   95
within defining limits, when the stars,
which formerly had been concealed in darkness,
began to blaze up all throughout the heavens;
and so that every region of the world
should have its own distinctive forms of life,   100
the constellations and the shapes of gods
occupied the lower part of heaven;
the seas gave shelter to the shining fishes,
earth received beasts, and flighty air, the birds.
An animal more like the gods than these,   105
more intellectually capable
and able to control the other beasts,
had not as yet appeared: now man was born,
either because the framer of all things,
the fabricator of this better world,   110
created man out of his own divine
substance—or else because Prometheus[7]
took up a clod (so lately broken off
from lofty aether that it still contained
some elements in common with its kin),   115
and mixing it with water, molded it
into the shape of gods, who govern all.
And even though all other animals
lean forward and look down toward the ground,
he gave to man a face that is uplifted,   120
and ordered him to stand erect and look
directly up into the vaulted heavens
and turn his countenance to meet the stars;
the earth, that was so lately rude and formless,
was changed by taking on the shapes of men.   125

*　*　*

[Apollo and Daphne]

Daphne,[8] the daughter of the river god
Peneus, was the first love of Apollo;
this happened not by chance, but by the cruel   630
outrage of Cupid; Phoebus, in the triumph
of his great victory against the Python,[9]

---

7. A god best known for stealing fire from the gods and giving it to mortals. In some stories he also created humans out of clay.　8. Literally, "Laurel" (Greek).　9. The enormous snake that Apollo (Phoebus) had to kill in order to found his oracle at Delphi. Cupid was the god of sexual desire.

observed him bending back his bow and said,
    "What are *you* doing with such manly arms,
lascivious boy? That bow[1] befits *our* brawn, 635
wherewith we deal out wounds to savage beasts
and other mortal foes, unerringly:
just now with our innumerable arrows
we managed to lay low the mighty Python,
whose pestilential belly covered acres! 640
Content yourself with kindling love affairs
with your wee torch—and don't claim *our* glory!"
    The son of Venus[2] answered him with this:
"Your arrow, Phoebus, may strike everything:
mine will strike you: as animals to gods, 645
your glory is so much the less than mine!"
    He spoke, and soaring upward through the air
on wings that thundered, in no time at all
had landed on Parnassus'[3] shaded height;
and from his quiver drew two arrows out 650
which operated at cross-purposes,
for one engendered flight, the other, love;
the latter has a polished tip of gold,
the former has a tip of dull, blunt lead;
with this one, Cupid struck Peneus' daughter, 655
while the other pierced Apollo to his marrow.
    One is in love now, and the other one
won't hear of it, for Daphne calls it joy
to roam within the forest's deep seclusion,
where she, in emulation of the chaste 660
goddess Phoebe,[4] devotes herself to hunting;
one ribbon only bound her straying tresses.
    Many men sought her, but she spurned her suitors,
loath to have anything to do with men,
and rambled through the wild and trackless groves 665
untroubled by a thought for love or marriage.
    Often her father said, "You owe it to me,
child, to provide me with a son-in-law
and grandchildren!"
              "Let me remain a virgin,
father most dear," she said, "as once before 670
Diana's father, Jove, gave her that gift."
    Although Peneus yielded to you, Daphne,
your beauty kept your wish from coming true,
your comeliness conflicting with your vow:
at first sight, Phoebus loves her and desires 675
to sleep with her; desire turns to hope,
and his own prophecy deceives the god.
    Now just as in a field the harvest stubble
is all burned off, or as hedges are set ablaze
when, if by chance, some careless traveler 680

---

1. One of Apollo's attributes.   2. Goddess of love (Aphrodite in Greek).   3. Mountain in central Greece, near Delphi.   4. Diana (Artemis in Greek), Apollo's sister, virgin goddess of the hunt.

should brush one with his torch or toss away
the still-smoldering brand at break of day—
just so the smitten god went up in flames
until his heart was utterly afire,
and hope sustained his unrequited passion.   685

He gazes on her hair without adornment:
"What if it were done up a bit?" he asks,
and gazes on her eyes, as bright as stars,
and on that darling little mouth of hers,
though sight is not enough to satisfy;   690
he praises everything that he can see—
her fingers, hands, and arms, bare to her shoulders—
and what is hidden prizes even more.

She flees more swiftly than the lightest breeze,
nor will she halt when he calls out to her: 695
"Daughter of Peneus, I pray, hold still,
hold still! I'm not a foe in grim pursuit!
Thus lamb flees wolf, thus dove from eagle flies
on trembling wings, thus deer from lioness,
thus any creature flees its enemy,   700
but I am stalking you because of love!

"Wretch that I am: I'm fearful that you'll fall,
brambles will tear your flesh because of me!
The ground you're racing over's very rocky,
slow down, I beg you, restrain yourself in flight,   705
and I will follow at a lesser speed.

"Just ask yourself who finds you so attractive!
I'm not a caveman, not some shepherd boy,
no shaggy guardian of flocks and herds—
you've no idea, rash girl, you've no idea   710
whom you are fleeing, that is why you flee!

"Delphi, Claros, Tenedos are all mine,
I'm worshiped in the city of Patara![5]
Jove is my father, I alone reveal
what was, what is, and what will come to be!   715
The plucked strings answer my demand with song!

"Although my aim is sure, another's arrow
proved even more so, and my careless heart
was badly wounded—the art of medicine
is my invention, by the way, the source   720
of my worldwide fame as a practitioner
of healing through the natural strength of herbs.

"Alas, there is no herbal remedy
for the love that I must suffer, and the arts
that heal all others cannot heal their lord—"   725

He had much more to say to her, but Daphne
pursued her fearful course and left him speechless,
though no less lovely fleeing him; indeed,
disheveled by the wind that bared her limbs
and pressed the blown robes to her straining body   730

---

5. All centers of Apollo's cult.

even as it whipped up her hair behind her,
the maiden was more beautiful in flight!
   But the young god had no further interest
in wasting his fine words on her; admonished
by his own passion, he accelerates,   735
and runs as swiftly as a Gallic hound[6]
chasing a rabbit through an open field;
the one seeks shelter and the other, prey—
he clings to her, is just about to spring,
with his long muzzle straining at her heels,   740
while she, not knowing whether she's been caught,
in one swift burst, eludes those snapping jaws,
no longer the anticipated feast;
so he in hope and she in terror race.
   But her pursuer, driven by his passion,   745
outspeeds the girl, giving her no pause,
one step behind her, breathing down her neck;
her strength is gone; she blanches at the thought
of the effort of her swift flight overcome,
but at the sight of Peneus, she cries,   750
"Help me, dear father! If your waters hold
divinity, transform me and destroy
that beauty by which I have too well pleased!"
   Her prayer was scarcely finished when she feels
a torpor take possession of her limbs—   755
her supple trunk is girdled with a thin
layer of fine bark over her smooth skin;
her hair turns into foliage, her arms
grow into branches, sluggish roots adhere
to feet that were so recently so swift,   760
her head becomes the summit of a tree;
all that remains of her is a warm glow.
   Loving her still, the god puts his right hand
against the trunk, and even now can feel
her heart as it beats under the new bark;   765
he hugs her limbs as if they were still human,
and then he puts his lips against the wood,
which, even now, is adverse to his kiss.
   "Although you cannot be my bride," he says,
"you will assuredly be my own tree,   770
O Laurel,[7] and will always find yourself
girding my locks, my lyre, and my quiver too—
you will adorn great Roman generals
when every voice cries out in joyful triumph
along the route up to the Capitol;   775
you will protect the portals of Augustus,
guarding, on either side, his crown of oak;[8]
and as I am—perpetually youthful,

---

6. A hunting breed famous for speed.   7. The laurel tree, sacred to Apollo, was the symbol of victory not only in athletic contests but also in war; victorious Roman generals honored with a triumphal procession through the city to the capitol wore a laurel wreath.   8. The tree sacred to Jupiter.

"Wearing his crown of sharp pine needles, Pan
saw her returning once from Mount Lycaeus,[1]
and began to say. . . ."
                  There remained to tell
of how the maiden, having spurned his pleas,   970
fled through the trackless wilds until she came
to where the gently flowing Ladon stopped
her in her flight; how she begged the water nymphs
to change her shape, and how the god, assuming
that he had captured Syrinx, grasped instead   975
a handful of marsh reeds! And while he sighed,
the reeds in his hands, stirred by his own breath,
gave forth a similar, low-pitched complaint!
    The god, much taken by the sweet new voice
of an unprecedented instrument,   980
said this to her: "At least we may converse
with one another—I can have that much."
    That pipe of reeds, unequal in their lengths,
and joined together one-on-one with wax,
took the girl's name, and bears it to this day.   985
    Now Mercury was ready to continue
until he saw that Argus had succumbed,
for all his eyes had been closed down by sleep.
He silences himself and waves his wand
above those languid orbs to fix the spell.   990
    Without delay he grasps the nodding head
and where it joins the neck, he severs it
with his curved blade and flings it bleeding down
the steep rock face, staining it with gore.
O Argus, you are fallen, and the light   995
in all your lamps is utterly put out:
one hundred eyes, one darkness all the same!
    But Saturn's daughter[2] rescued them and set
those eyes upon the feathers of her bird,[3]
filling his tail with constellated gems.   1000
    Her rage demanded satisfaction, *now*:
the goddess set a horrifying Fury
before the eyes and the imagination
of her Grecian rival; and in her heart
she fixed a prod that goaded Io on,   1005
driving her in terror through the world
until at last, O Nile, you let her rest
from endless labor; having reached your banks,
she went down awkwardly upon her knees,
and with her neck bent backward, raised her face   1010
as only she could do it, to the stars;
and with her groans and tears and mournful mooing,
entreated Jove, it seemed, to put an end
to her great suffering.

---

1. A high mountain in Arcadia. Pan was a god of the wild mountain pastures and woods, with goat's feet and horns. He was particularly associated with Arcadia.   **2.** Juno.   **3.** The peacock.

Jove threw his arms   1015
around the neck of Juno in embrace,
imploring her to end this punishment:
"In future," he said, "put your fears aside:
never again will you have cause to worry—
about *this* one." And swore upon the Styx.[4]

The goddess was now pacified, and Io   1020
at once began regaining her lost looks,
till she became what she had been before;
her body lost all of its bristling hair,
her horns shrank down, her eyes grew narrower,
her jaws contracted, arms and hands returned,   1025
and hooves divided themselves into nails;
nothing remained of her bovine nature,
unless it was the whiteness of her body.
She had some trouble getting her legs back,
and for a time feared speaking, lest she moo,   1030
and so quite timidly regained her speech.

She is a celebrated goddess now,
and worshiped by the linen-clad Egyptians.[5]
Her son, Epaphus, is believed to be
sprung from the potent seed of mighty Jove,   1035
and temples may be found in every city
wherein the boy is honored with his parent.

* * *

FROM BOOK II

[*Jove and Europa*]

When Mercury had punished her for these
impieties of thought and word,[6] he left
Athena's city, and on beating wings   1145
returned to heaven where his father Jove
took him aside and (without telling him
that his new passion was the reason) said:
"Dear son, who does my bidding faithfully,
do not delay, but with your usual   1150
swiftness fly down to earth and find the land
that looks up to your mother[7] on the left,
called Sidon[8] by the natives; there you will see
a herd of royal cattle some way off
upon a mountain; drive them down to shore."   1155
He spoke and it was done as he had ordered:
the cattle were immediately driven
down to a certain place along the shore

---

4. One of the rivers of the underworld; the gods swore solemn oaths by it.   5. Io was identified with Isis, at least by the Greeks and Romans.   6. Mercury has been in Athens, where he tried to have a love affair with Herse, daughter of King Cecrops. Promised help and then betrayed by her sister Aglauros, he took his revenge on Aglauros by turning her into a statue.   7. See n. 5, p. 853.   8. One of the principal cities of Phoenicia (in modern Lebanon).

where the daughter of a great king used to play,
accompanied by maidens all of Tyre.[9]   1160
    Majestic power and erotic love
do not get on together very well,
nor do they linger long in the same place:
the father and the ruler of all gods,
who holds the lightning bolt in his right hand   1165
and shakes the world when he but nods his head,
now relinquishes authority and power,
assuming the appearance of a bull
to mingle with the other cattle, lowing
as gorgeously he strolls in the new grass.   1170
    He is as white as the untrampled snow
before the south wind turns it into slush.
The muscles stand out bulging on his neck,
and the dewlap[1] dangles on his ample chest;
his horns are crooked, but appear handmade,   1175
and flawless as a pair of matching gems.
His brow is quite unthreatening, his eye
excites no terror, and his countenance
is calm.
        The daughter of King Agenor[2]
admires him, astonished by the presence   1180
of peacefulness and beauty in the beast;
yet even though he seems a gentle creature,
at first she fears to get too close to him,
but soon approaching, reaches out her hand
and pushes flowers into his white mouth.   1185
    The lover, quite beside himself, rejoices,
and as a preview of delights to come,
kisses her fingers, getting so excited
that he can scarcely keep from doing it!
    Now he disports himself upon the grass,   1190
and lays his whiteness on the yellow sands;
and as she slowly overcomes her fear
he offers up his breast for her caresses
and lets her decorate his horns with flowers;
the princess dares to sit upon his back   1195
not knowing who it is that she has mounted,
and he begins to set out from dry land,
a few steps on false feet into the shallows,
then further out and further to the middle
of the great sea he carries off his booty;   1200
she trembles as she sees the shore receding
and holds the creature's horn in her right hand
and with the other clings to his broad back,
her garments streaming in the wind behind her.

---

9. Another city of Phoenicia, but here used of Phoenicia itself.   1. A fold of loose skin hanging from the
neck.   2. Europa. Agenor was the Phoenician king.

FROM BOOK V

[Ceres and Proserpina]

As the Muse spoke,[3] Minerva could hear wings
beating on air, and cries of greeting came
from high in the trees. She peered into the foliage,   430
attempting to discover where those sounds,
the speech of human beings to be sure,
were emanating from: why, from some birds!
Bewailing their sad fate, a flock of nine
magpies (which mimic anyone they wish to)   435
had settled in the branches overhead.
    Minerva having shown astonishment,
the Muse gave her a little goddess-chat:
"This lot has only recently been added
to the throngs of birds. Why? They lost a contest!   440
Their father was Pierus, lord of Pella,
their mother was Evippe of Paeonia;[4]
nine times she called upon Lucina's[5] aid
and nine times she delivered. Swollen up
with foolish pride because they were so many,   445
that crowd of simpleminded sisters went
through all Haemonia and through Achaea[6] too,
arriving here to challenge us in song:
    " 'We'll show you girls just what real class is[7]
Give up tryin' to deceive the masses   450
Your rhymes are fake: accept our wager
Learn which of us is minor and which is major
There's nine of us here and there's nine of you
And you'll be nowhere long before we're through
Nothin's gonna save you 'cuz your songs are lame   455
And the way you sing 'em is really a shame
So stop with, "Well I *never*!" and "This *can't* be real!"
We're the newest New Thing and here is our deal
If we beat you, obsolete you, then you just get gone
From these classy haunts on Mount Helicon   460
We give you Macedonia—*if* we lose
An' that's an offer you just can't refuse
So take the wings off, sisters, get down and jam
And let the nymphs be the judges of our poetry slam!'
    "Shameful it was to strive against such creatures;   465
more shameful not to. Nymphs were picked as judges,
sworn into service on their river banks,
and took their seats on benches made of tufa.

---

3. Minerva (Athena in Greek) has come to Mount Helicon in central Greece, the home of the nine Muses (daughters of Zeus and Memory, they are patronesses of poetry and the other arts). One of the Muses has told her of an attempt recently made to trap and rape them by the wicked Pyreneus.   4. A tribe living north of Macedonia. Pella was a city of Macedonia, in northern Greece.   5. Goddess of childbirth.   6. Regions of central Greece (*Haemonia* is another name for Thessaly). The sisters are traveling south toward Helicon.   7. Although there is no basis for it in the Latin text, the translator uses dialect and rhyme in the speeches and song of Pierus's daughters to show how they challenge, and partially deflate, the "high-culture" assumptions and language of the Muses.

"And then—not even drawing lots!—the one
who claimed to be their champion commenced;   470
she sang of war between the gods and Giants,
giving the latter credit more than due
and deprecating all that the great gods did;
how Typhoeus,[8] from earth's lowest depths,
struck fear in every celestial heart,   475
so that they all turned tail and fled, until,
exhausted, they found refuge down in Egypt,
where the Nile flows from seven distinct mouths;
she sang of how earthborn Typhoeus
pursued them even here and forced the gods   480
to hide themselves by taking fictive shapes:[9]
   "'In Libya the Giants told the gods to scram
The boss god they worship there has horns like a ram[1]
'Cuz Jupiter laid low as the leader of a flock
And Delius[2] his homey really got a shock   485
When the Giants left him with no place to go:
"Fuggedabout Apollo—make me a crow!"
And if you believe that Phoebus was a wuss
His sister Phoebe turned into a puss
Bacchus takes refuge in the skin of a goat   490
And Juno as a cow with a snow-white coat
Venus the queen of the downtown scene, yuh know what her wish is?
"Gimme a body just like a fish's"
Mercury takes on an ibis's shape
And that's how the mighty (cheep cheep) gods escape'   495
   "And then her song, accompanied on the lute,
came to an end, and it was our turn—
but possibly you haven't got the time
to listen to our song?"
                              "Oh, don't think that,"
Minerva said. "I want it word for word: 500
sing it for me just as you sang it then."
   The Muse replied: "We turned the contest over
to one of us, Calliope,[3] who rose,
and after binding up her hair in ivy
and lightly strumming a few plaintive chords,   505
she vigorously launched into her song:

   "'Ceres[4] was first to break up the soil with a curved plowshare,
the first to give us the earth's fruits and to nourish us gently,
and the first to give laws: every gift comes from Ceres.
The goddess must now be my subject. Would that I could sing   510
a hymn that is worthy of her, for she surely deserves it.
   "'Vigorous Sicily sprawled across the gigantic body

---

8. Monstrous son of Earth. Like the Earth-born Giants, he challenged Jupiter and the Olympian gods and
was defeated.   9. An "explanation" of the Egyptian gods' animal forms.   1. Ammon, the chief Egyptian god, identified by the Greeks and Romans with Zeus/Jupiter. He had an important oracular cult in the
Libyan desert (west of the Nile Valley and part of Egypt under Roman rule).   2. Apollo, who was born on
the island of Delos.   3. "Lovely Voice," the Muse of epic poetry.   4. Goddess of grain (Demeter).

of one who had dared aspire to rule in the heavens;
the island's weight held Typhoeus firmly beneath it.
Often exerting himself, he strives yet again to rise up,   515
but there in the north, his right hand is held down by Pelorus,
his left hand by you, Pachynus; off in the west, Lilybaeum[5]
weighs on his legs, while Mount Etna[6] presses his head, as
under it, raging Typhoeus coughs ashes and vomits up fire.
Often he struggles, attempting to shake off the earth's weight   520
and roll its cities and mountains away from his body.
   "'This causes tremors and panics the Lord of the Silent,[7]
who fears that the earth's crust will crack and break open,
and daylight, let in, will frighten the trembling phantoms;
dreading disaster, the tyrant left his tenebrous kingdom;   525
borne in his chariot drawn by its team of black horses,
he crisscrossed Sicily, checking the island's foundation.
   "'After his explorations had left him persuaded
that none of its parts were in imminent danger of falling,
his fears were forgotten, and Venus, there on Mount Eryx,[8]   530
observed him relaxing, and said, as she drew Cupid near her,
"My son, my sword, my strong right arm and source of my power,
take up that weapon by which all your victims are vanquished
and send your swift arrows into the breast of the deity
to whom the last part of the threefold realm[9] was allotted.   535
   "'"You govern the gods and their ruler; you rule the defeated
gods of the ocean and govern the one who rules them, too;
why give up on the dead, when we can extend our empire
into their realm? A third part of the world is involved here!
And yet the celestial gods spurn our forbearance,   540
and the prestige of Love is diminished, even as mine is.
Do you not see how Athena and huntress Diana
have both taken leave of me?[1] The virgin daughter of Ceres
desires to do likewise—and will, if we let her!
But if you take pride in our alliance, advance it   545
by joining her to her uncle!"[2]
                        "'Venus ceased speaking and Cupid
loosened his quiver, and, just as his mother had ordered,
selected, from thousands of missiles, the one that was sharpest
and surest and paid his bow the closest attention,
and using one knee to bend its horn back almost double,   550
he pierces the heart of Dis with his barb-tipped arrow.
   "'Near Henna's[3] walls stands a deep pool of water, called Pergus:
not even the river Cayster,[4] flowing serenely,
hears more songs from its swans; this pool is completely surrounded
by a ring of tall trees, whose foliage, just like an awning,   555
keeps out the sun and preserves the water's refreshing coolness;

5. Mountains on the northeast, southeast, and western promontories of Sicily, respectively.   6. The
large (and still active) volcano near the center of the east coast of Sicily.   7. Pluto or Hades, king of the
dead.   8. Mountain in western Sicily with an important cult of Venus.   9. The underworld, ruled by
Pluto. The other parts of the "threefold realm" are the sea (ruled by Neptune) and the sky or Mount Olympus (Jupiter).   1. Both were perpetually virgin.   2. Pluto (also called Dis) was the brother of Jupiter,
the father by Ceres of Proserpina.   3. A city in central Sicily.   4. River in Lydia in Asia Minor, famous
for its many swans.

the moist ground is covered with flowers of Tyrian purple;
here it is springtime forever. And here Proserpina
was playfully picking its white lilies and violets,
and, while competing to gather up more than her playmates,   560
filling her basket and stuffing the rest in her bosom,
Dis saw her, was smitten, seized her and carried her off;
his love was that hasty. The terrified goddess cried out
for her mother, her playmates—but for her mother most often,
since she had torn the uppermost seam of her garment,   565
and the gathered flowers rained down from her negligent tunic;
because of her tender years and her childish simplicity,
even this loss could move her to maidenly sorrow.

   "'Her abductor rushed off in his chariot, urging his horses,
calling each one by its name and flicking the somber,   570
rust-colored reins over their backs as they galloped
through the deep lakes and the sulphurous pools of Palike
that boil up through the ruptured earth, and where the Bacchiadae,
a race sprung from Corinth, that city between the two seas,
had raised their own walls between two unequal harbors.[5]   575

   "'There is a bay that is landlocked almost completely
between the two pools of Cyane and Pisaean Arethusa,
the residence of the most famous nymph in all Sicily,
Cyane, who gave her very own name to the fountain.
She showed herself now, emerged from her pool at waist level,   580
and recognizing the goddess, told Dis, "Go no further!
You cannot become the son-in-law of great Ceres
against her will: you should have asked and not taken!
If it is right for me to compare lesser with greater,
I accepted Anapis[6] when he desired to have me,   585
yielding to pleas and not—as in this case—to terror."
She spoke, and stretching her arms out in either direction,
kept him from passing. That son of Saturn could scarcely
hold back his anger; he urged on his frightening horses,
and then, with his strong right arm, he hurled his scepter   590
directly into the very base of the fountain;
the stricken earth opened a path to the underworld
and took in the chariot rushing down into its crater.

   "'Cyane, lamenting not just the goddess abducted,
but also the disrespect shown for her rights as a fountain,   595
tacitly nursed in her heart an inconsolable sorrow;
and she who had once been its presiding spirit,
reduced to tears, dissolved right into its substance.
You would have seen her members beginning to soften,
her bones and her fingertips starting to lose their old firmness; 600
her slenderest parts were the first to be turned into fluid:
her feet, her legs, her sea-dark tresses, her fingers
(for the parts with least flesh turn into liquid most quickly);
and after these, her shoulders and back and her bosom

---

5. Syracuse, on the southeastern coast of Sicily, founded by Corinthian colonists in the 8th century B.C.E.
The Bacchiadae were a leading family who then ruled Corinth.   6. A river that empties into the sea near
Syracuse.

and flanks completely vanished in trickling liquid;   605
and lastly the living blood in her veins is replaced by
springwater, and nothing remains that you could have seized on.
    "'Meanwhile, the terrified mother was pointlessly seeking
her daughter all over the earth and deep in the ocean.
Neither Aurora, appearing with dew-dampened tresses,   610
nor Hesperus[7] knew her to quit; igniting two torches
of pine from the fires of Etna, the care-ridden goddess
used them to illumine the wintery shadows of nighttime;
and when the dear day had once more dimmed out the bright stars,
she searched again for her daughter from sunrise to sunset.   615

    "'Worn out by her labors and suffering thirst, with no fountain
to wet her lips at, she happened upon a thatched hovel
and knocked at its humble door, from which there came forth
a crone who looked at the goddess, and, when asked for water,
gave her a sweet drink, sprinkled with toasted barley.   620
And, as she drank it, a boy with a sharp face and bold manner
stood right before her and mocked her and said she was greedy.
Angered by what he was saying, the goddess drenched him
with all she had not yet drunk of the barley mixture.
The boy's face thirstily drank up the spots as his arms were   625
turned into legs, and a tail was joined to his changed limbs;
so that he should now be harmless, the boy was diminished,
and he was transformed into a very small lizard.
Astonished, the old woman wept and reached out to touch him,
but the marvelous creature fled her, seeking a hideout.   630
He now has a name appropriate to his complexion,
Stellio, from the constellations spotting his body.
    "'To speak of the lands and seas the goddess mistakenly searched
would take far too long; the earth exhausted her seeking;
she came back to Sicily; and, as she once more traversed it,   635
arrived at Cyane, who would have told her the story
had she not herself been changed; but, though willing in spirit,
her mouth, tongue, and vocal apparatus were absent;
nevertheless, she gave proof that was clear to the mother:
Persephone's girdle (which happened by chance to have fallen   640
into the fountain) now lay exposed on its surface.
    "'Once recognizing it, the goddess knew that her daughter
had been taken, and tore her hair into utter disorder,
and repeatedly struck her breasts with the palms of both hands.
With her daughter's location a mystery still, she reproaches   645
the whole earth as ungrateful, unworthy her gift of grain crops,
and Sicily more than the others, where she has discovered
the proof of her loss; and so it was here that her fierce hand
shattered the earth-turning plows, here that the farmers and cattle
perished alike, and here that she bade the plowed fields   650
default on their trust by blighting the seeds in their keeping.
Sicilian fertility, which had been everywhere famous,
was given the lie when the crops died as they sprouted,

7. The evening star. Aurora was the goddess of the dawn.

now ruined by too much heat, and now by too heavy a rainfall;
stars and winds harmed them, and the greedy birds devoured   655
the seed as it was sown; the harvest of wheat was defeated
by thorns and darnels and unappeasable grasses.

    " 'Then Arethusa[8] lifted her head from the Elean waters
and swept her dripping hair back away from her forehead,
saying, "O Mother of Grain—and mother, too, of that virgin   660
sought through the whole world—here end your incessant labors,
lest your great anger should injure the earth you once trusted,
and which, unwillingly pillaged, has done nothing ignoble;
nor do I plead for my nation, since I am a guest here:
my nation is Pisa, I am descended from Elis,   665
and live as a stranger in Sicily—this land that delights me
more than all others on earth; here Arethusa
dwells with her household gods. Spare it, merciful goddess,
and when your cares and countenance both have been lightened,
there will come an opportune time to tell you the reason   670
why I was taken from home and borne off to Ortygia[9]
over a waste of waters. The earth gave me access,
showed me a path, and, swept on through underground caverns,
I raised my head here to an unfamiliar night sky.
But while gliding under the earth on a Stygian river,   675
I saw with my very own eyes your dear Proserpina;
grief and terror were still to be seen in her features,
yet she was nonetheless queen of that shadowy kingdom,
the all-powerful consort of the underworld's ruler." '

    " 'The mother was petrified by the speech of the fountain,   680
and stood for a very long time as though she were senseless,
until her madness had been driven off by her outrage,
and then she set out in her chariot for the ethereal regions;
once there, with her face clouded over and hair all disheveled,
she planted herself before Jove and fiercely addressed him: 685
"Jupiter, I have come here as a suppliant, speaking
for my child—and yours: if you have no regard for her mother,
relent as her father—don't hold her unworthy, I beg you,
simply because *I* am the child's other parent!
The daughter I sought for so long is at last recovered,   690
if to recover means only to lose much more surely,
or if to recover means just to learn her location!
Her theft could be borne—if only he would return her!
Then let him do it, for surely *Jove's* daughter is worthy
of a mate who's no brigand, even if *my* daughter isn't." '   695

    " 'Jupiter answered her, "She is indeed *our* daughter,
the pledge of our love and our common concern,
but if you will kindly agree to give things their right names,
this is not an injury requiring my retribution,
but an act of love by a son-in-law who won't shame you,   700
goddess, if you give approval; though much were lacking,

---

8. A spring in Syracuse. Its waters are "Elean" because they were believed to originate in the district of
Pisa in Elis, a region of the western Peloponnesus in mainland Greece.   9. The island on which Syracuse was originally built and on which the Arethusan spring was located.

how much it is to be Jove's brother! But he lacks nothing,
and only yields to me that which the Fates have allotted.
Still, if you're so keen on parting them, your Proserpina
may come back to heaven—but only on one condition: 705
that she has not touched food, for so the Fates have required."

"'He spoke and Ceres was sure she would get back her daughter,
though the Fates were not, for the girl had already placated
her hunger while guilelessly roaming death's formal gardens,
where, from a low-hanging branch, she had plucked without thinking   710
a pomegranate, and peeling its pale bark off, devoured
seven of its seeds. No one saw her but Ascalaphus
(whom it is said that Orphne, a not undistinguished
nymph among those of Avernus, pregnant by Acheron,[1]
gave birth to there in the underworld's dark-shadowed forest);   715
he saw, and by his disclosure, kept her from returning.

"'Raging, the Queen of the Underworld turned that informer
into a bird of ill omen: sprinkling the waters
of Phlegethon[2] into the face of Ascalaphus,
she gave him a beak and plumage and eyes quite enormous.   720
Lost to himself, he is clad now in yellow-brown pinions,
his head increases in size and his nails turn to talons,
but the feathers that spring from his motionless arms scarcely flutter;
a filthy bird he's become, the grim announcer of mourning,
a slothful portent of evil to mortals—the owl.   725

"'That one, because of his tattling tongue, seems quite worthy
of punishment,—but you, daughters of Acheloüs,[3]
why do you have the plumage of birds and the faces of virgins?
Is it because while Proserpina gathered her flowers,
you, artful Sirens, were numbered among her companions?   730
No sooner had you scoured the whole earth in vain for her
than you desired the vast seas to feel your devotion,
and prayed to the gods, whom you found willing to help you,
that you might skim over the flood upon oars that were pinions,
then saw your limbs turn suddenly golden with plumage.   735
And so that your tunefulness, which the ear finds so pleasing,
should not be lost, nor your gifts of vocal expression,
your maidenly faces remain, along with your voices.

"'But poised between his sorrowing sister and brother,
great Jove divided the year into two equal portions,   740
so now in two realms the shared goddess holds sway,
and as many months spent with her mother are spent with her husband.
She changed her mind then, and changed her expression to match it,
and now her fair face, which even Dis found depressing,
beams as the sun does, when, after having been hidden   745
before in dark clouds, at last it emerges in triumph.

1. "Woe," one of the rivers, and Avernus a lake, in the underworld. Orphne means "Darkness" in Greek.
2. Fiery river of the underworld.   3. The Sirens, familiar from book XII of the *Odyssey* and often associated with death in post-Homeric literature and art. Acheloüs is a large river in northwest Greece.

"'This the barbarian heard with great envy, and wishing 840
that he himself might be perceived as the donor,
took him in as a guest, and while the young man was sleeping,
approached with a sword, and as he attempted to stab him,
Ceres changed *Lyncus* to *lynx*, and ordered Triptolemus
to drive her sacred team through the air back to Athens.' 845

"When our eldest sister had concluded
her superb performance, with one voice
the nymphs awarded victory to . . . the Muses!
"And when the others, in defeat, reviled us,
I answered them: 'Since you display such nerve 850
in challenging the Muses, you deserve
chastisement—even more so since you've added
insult to outrage: our wise forbearance
is not without its limits, as you'll learn
when we get to the penalties, and vent 855
our righteous anger on your worthless selves.'
"Then the Pierides[1] mock our threats,
and as they try to answer us by shouting
vulgarities and giving us the finger,
their fingers take on feathers and their arms 860
turn into pinions! Each one sees a beak
replace a sister's face, as a new bird
is added to the species of the forest;
and as they try to beat upon their breasts,
bewailing their new situation, they 865
all hang suspended, flapping in the air,
the forest's scandal—the P-Airides![2]
"And even though they are all feathered now,
their speech remains as fluent as it was,
and they are famous for their noisiness 870
as well as for their love of argument."

FROM BOOK IX

[Iphis and Isis]

Rumor might very well have spread the news 960
of this unprecedented transformation[3]
throughout the hundred towns of Crete, if they
had not just had a wonder of their own
to talk about—the change that came to Iphis.
For, once upon a time, there lived in Phaestus, 965
not far from the royal capital at Cnossus,
a freeborn plebeian named Ligdus, who
was otherwise unknown and undistinguished,
with no more property than fame or status,
and yet devout, and blameless in his life. 970
His wife was pregnant. When her time had come,

---

1. That is, the daughters of Pierus.   2. The translator's pun on the name Pierides.   3. The transformation of Byblis, who loved her brother Caunus, into a fountain.

he gave her his instructions with these words:
"There are two things I pray to heaven for
on your account: an easy birth and a son.
The other fate is much too burdensome,   975
for daughters need what Fortune has denied us:
a dowry.
     "Therefore—and may God prevent
this happening, but if, by chance, it does
and you should be delivered of a girl,
unwillingly I order this, and beg   980
pardon for my impiety—*But let it die!*"
    He spoke, and tears profusely bathed the cheeks
of the instructor and instructed both.
Telethusa continued to implore
her husband, praying him not to confine   985
their hopes so narrowly—to no avail,
for he would not be moved from his decision.
    Now scarcely able to endure the weight
of her womb's burden, as she lay in bed
at midnight, a dream-vision came to her: 990
the goddess Io[4] stood (or seemed to stand)
before her troubled bed, accompanied
with solemn pomp by all her mysteries.
    She wore her crescent horns upon her brow
and a garland made of gleaming sheaves of wheat,   995
and a queenly diadem; behind her stood
the dog-faced god Anubis, and divine
Bubastis (who defends the lives of cats),
and Apis as a bull clothed in a hide
of varied colors, with Harpocrates,   1000
the god whose fingers, pressed against his lips,
command our silence; and one often sought
by his devoted worshipers—Osiris;[5]
and the asp, so rich in sleep-inducing drops.
She seemed to wake, and saw them all quite clearly.   1005
    These were the words the goddess spoke to her:
"O Telethusa, faithful devotee,
put off your heavy cares! Disobey your spouse,
and do not hesitate, when Lucina
has lightened the burden of your labor,   1010
to raise this child, whatever it will be,
I am that goddess who, when asked, delivers,
and you will have no reason to complain
that honors you have paid me were in vain."
After instructing her, the goddess left.   1015
    The Cretan woman rose up joyfully,
lifted her hands up to the stars, and prayed
that her dream-vision would be ratified.

---

4. Identified with the Egyptian Isis, goddess of fertility, marriage, and maternity, whose cult was widespread in the Roman world. See also "[Jove and Io]," p. 850.   **5.** Husband of Isis, killed by his brother Set and restored to life by Isis; he is thus a figure of rebirth.

Then going into labor, she brought forth
a daughter—though her husband did not know it.   1020
The mother (with intention to deceive)
told them *to feed the boy.* Deception prospered,
since no one knew the truth except the nurse.
    The father thanked the gods and named the child
for its grandfather, Iphis; since this name   1025
was given men and women both, his mother
was pleased, for she could use it honestly.
So from her pious lie, deception grew.
She dressed it as a boy—its face was such
that whether boy or girl, it was a beauty.   1030
    Meanwhile, the years went by, thirteen of them:
your father, Iphis, has arranged for you
a marriage to the golden-haired Ianthe,
the daughter of a Cretan named Telestes,
the maid most praised in Phaestus[6] for her beauty.   1035
The two were similar in age and looks,
and had been taught together from the first.
    First love came unexpected to both hearts
and wounded them both equally—and yet
their expectations were quite different: 1040
Ianthe can look forward to a time
of wedding torches and of wedding vows,
and trusts that one whom she believes a man
will be *her* man. Iphis, however, loves
with hopeless desperation, which increases   1045
in strict proportion to its hopelessness,
and burns—a maiden—for another maid!
    And scarcely holding back her tears, she cries,
"Oh, what will be the end reserved for Iphis,
gripped by a strange and monstrous passion known   1050
to no one else? If the gods had wished to spare me,
they should have; if they wanted to destroy me,
they should have given me a natural affliction.
    "Cows do not burn for cows, nor mares for mares;
the ram will have his sheep, the stag his does,   1055
and birds will do the same when they assemble;
there are no animals whose females lust
for other females! I wish that I were dead!
    "That Crete might bring forth monsters of all kinds.
Queen Pasiphaë[7] was taken by a bull,   1060
yet even *that* was male-and-female passion!
My love is much less rational than hers,
to tell the truth. At least she had the hope
of satisfaction, taking in the bull
through guile, and in the image of a cow,   1065
thereby deceiving the adulterer!
    "If every form of ingenuity
were gathered here from all around the world,

6. A city in Crete.   7. Wife of King Minos of Crete, and mother by a bull of the Minotaur.

if Daedalus[8] flew back on waxen wings,
what could he do? Could all his learnèd arts   1070
transform me from a girl into a boy?
Or could *you* change into a boy, Ianthe?
    "But really, Iphis, pull yourself together,
be firm, cast off this stultifying passion:
accept your birth—unless you would deceive   1075
yourself as well as others—look for love
where it is proper to, as a woman should!
Hope both creates and nourishes such love;
reality deprives you of all hope.
    "No watchman keeps you from her dear embrace,   1080
no husband's ever-vigilant concern,
no father's fierceness, nor does she herself
deny the gifts that you would have from her.
And yet you are denied all happiness,
nor could it have been otherwise if all   1085
the gods and men had labored in your cause.
    "But the gods have not denied me anything;
agreeably, they've given what they could;
my father wishes for me what *I* wish,
she and her father both would have it be;   1090
but Nature, much more powerful than they are,
wishes it not—sole source of all my woe!
    "But look—the sun has risen and the day
of our longed-for nuptials dawns at last!
Ianthe will be mine—and yet not mine: 1095
we die of thirst here at the fountainside.
    "Why do you, Juno, guardian of brides,
and you, O Hymen, god of marriage, come
to these rites, which cannot be rites at all,
for no one takes the bride, and both are veiled?"   1100
    She said no more. Nor did her chosen burn
less fiercely as she prayed you swiftly come,
O god of marriage.
               Fearing what you sought,
Telethusa postponed the marriage day
with one concocted pretext and another,   1105
a fictive illness or an evil omen.
But now she had no more excuses left,
and the wedding day was only one day off.
    She tears the hair bands from her daughter's head
and from her own, and thus unbound, she prayed   1110
while desperately clinging to the altar:
"O holy Isis, who art pleased to dwell
and be worshiped at Paraetonium,
at Pharos, in the Mareotic fields,
and where the Nile splits into seven branches;   1115
deliver us, I pray you, from our fear!

---

8. Fabled craftsman, who devised the heifer disguise that enabled Pasiphaë to seduce the bull and, later, built the labyrinth for the Minotaur. Forced to flee Crete, he made wings of feathers held together by wax for himself and his son Icarus.

in the next chamber arose and entered her bedroom:
at sight of the grim preparations, she screams out, and striking
her breasts and tearing her garments, removes the noose from
around the girl's neck, and then, only then she collapses,
and weeping, embraces her, asking her why she would do it.   470
    "Myrrha remained silent, expressionless, with her eyes downcast,
sorrowing only because her attempt was detected.
But the woman persists, baring her flat breasts and white hair,
and by the milk given when she was a babe in the cradle
beseeches her to entrust her old nurse with the cause of her sorrow.   475
The girl turns away with a groan; the nurse is determined
to learn her secret, and promises not just to keep it:
    "'Speak and allow me to aid you,' she says, 'for in my old age,
I am not utterly useless: if you are dying of passion,
my charms and herbs will restore you; if someone wishes you evil,   480
my rites will break whatever spell you are under;
is some god wrathful? A sacrifice placates his anger.
What else could it be? I can't think of anything—Fortune
favors your family, everything's going quite smoothly,
both of your parents are living, your mother, your father—'   485
Myrrha sighed deeply, hearing her father referred to,
but not even then did the nurse grasp the terrible evil
in the girl's heart, although she felt that her darling
suffered a passion of some kind for some kind of lover.
    "Nurse was unyielding and begged her to make known her secret.   490
whatever it was, pressing the tearful girl to her bosom;
and clasping her in an embrace that old age had enfeebled,
she said, 'You're in love—I am certain! I will be zealous
in aiding your cause, never you fear—and your father
will be none the wiser!'
                                    "Myrrha in frenzy leapt up   495
and threw herself onto the bed, pressing her face in the pillows:
'Leave me, I beg you,' she said. 'Avoid my wretched dishonor;
leave me or cease to ask me the cause of my sorrow:
what you attempt to uncover is sinful and wicked!'
    "The old woman shuddered: extending the hands that now trembled   500
with fear and old age, she fell at the feet of her darling,
a suppliant, coaxing her now, and now attempting to scare her;
threatening now to disclose her attempted self-murder,
but pledging to aid her if she confesses her passion.
    "She lifted her head with her eyes full of tears spilling over   505
onto the breast of her nurse and repeatedly tried to
speak out, but repeatedly stopped herself short of confession,
hiding her shame-colored face in the folds of her garments,
until she finally yielded, blurting her secret:
'O mother,' she cried, 'so fortunate you with your husband!'   510
and said no more but groaned.
                            "The nurse, who now understood it,
felt a chill run through her veins, and her bones shook with tremor,
and her white hair stood up in stiff bristles. She said whatever
she could to dissuade the girl from her horrible passion,
and even though Myrrha knew the truth of her warning,   515

she had decided to die if she could not possess him.
'Live, then,' the other replied, 'and possess your—' Not daring
to use the word 'father,' she left her sentence unfinished,
but called upon heaven to stand by her earlier promise.

    "Now it was time for the annual feast days of Ceres; 520
the pious, and married women clad in white vestments,
thronged to the celebration, offering garlands
of wheat as firstfruits of the season; now for nine nights
the intimate touch of their men is considered forbidden.
Among these matrons was Cenchreïs, wife of Cinyras, 525
for her attendance during these rites was required.
And so, while the queen's place in his bed was left vacant,
the overly diligent nurse came to Cinyras,
finding him drunk, and spoke to him of a maiden
whose passion for him was real (although her name wasn't) 530
and praising her beauty; when asked the age of this virgin,
she said, 'the same age as Myrrha.' Commanded to fetch her,
nurse hastened home, and entering, cried to her darling,
'Rejoice, my dear, we have won!' The unlucky maiden
could not feel joy in her heart, but only grim sorrow, 535
yet still she rejoiced, so distorted were her emotions.

    "Now it is midnight, when all of creation is silent;
high in the heavens, between the two Bears, Boötes[1]
had turned his wagon so that its shaft pointed downward;
Myrrha approaches her crime, which is fled by chaste Luna,[2] 540
while under black clouds the stars hide their scandalized faces;
Night lacks its usual fires; you, Icarus,[3] covered
your face and were followed at once by Erigone,
whose pious love of her father merited heaven.

    "Thrice Myrrha stumbles and stops each time at the omen, 545
and thrice the funereal owl sings her his poem of endings;
nevertheless she continues, her shame lessened by shadows.
She holds the left hand of her nurse, and gropes with the other
blindly in darkness: now at the bedchamber's threshold,
and now she opens the door: and now she is led within, 550
where her knees fail her; she falters, nearly collapsing,
her color, her blood, her spirit all flee together.

    "As she approaches the crime, her horror increases;
regretting her boldness, she wishes to turn back, unnoticed,
but even as she holds back, the old woman leads her 555
by the hand to the high bed, where she delivers her, saying,
'Take her, Cinyras—she's yours,' and unites the doomed couple.
The father accepts his own offspring in his indecent
bed and attempts to dispel the girl's apprehensions,
encouraging her not to be frightened of him, and 560
addressing her, as it happened, with a name befitting

---

1. The Ox-herder, a constellation that was thought to drive Ursa Major, the Great Bear. 2. The Moon, often associated with Diana, one of whose attributes was chastity. 3. More properly Icarius, a mythic Athenian. He received Dionysus into the city, and the god rewarded him with wine, which he shared with his countrymen. Feeling its effect, they thought they had been poisoned and killed him. His daughter Erigone hanged herself in grief, and both were changed into stars.

her years: he called her 'daughter' while she called him 'father,'
so the right names were attached to their impious actions.

"Filled with the seed of her father, she left his bedchamber,
having already conceived, in a crime against nature   565
which she repeated the following night and thereafter,
until Cinyras, impatient to see his new lover
after so many encounters, brought a light in,
and in the same moment discovered his crime and his daughter;
grief left him speechless; he tore out his sword from the scabbard;   570
Myrrha sped off, and, thanks to night's shadowy darkness,
escaped from her death. She wandered the wide-open spaces,
leaving Arabia, so rich in palms, and Panchaea,
and after nine months, she came at last to Sabaea,[4]
where she found rest from the weariness that she suffered,   575
for she could scarcely carry her womb's heavy burden.

"Uncertain of what she should wish for, tired of living
but frightened of dying, she summed up her state in this prayer:
'O gods, if there should be any who hear my confession,
I do not turn away from the terrible sentence   580
that my misbehavior deserves; but lest I should outrage
the living by my survival, or the dead by my dying,
drive me from both of these kingdoms, transform me
wholly, so that both life and death are denied me.'

"Some god *did* hear her confession, and heaven answered   585
her final prayer, for, even as she was still speaking,
the earth rose up over her legs, and from her toes burst
roots that spread widely to hold the tall trunk in position;
her bones put forth wood, and even though they were still hollow,
they now ran with sap and not blood; her arms became branches,   590
and those were now twigs that used to be called her fingers,
while her skin turned to hard bark. The tree kept on growing,
over her swollen belly, wrapping it tightly,
and growing over her breast and up to her neck; she
could bear no further delay, and, as the wood rose,   595
plunged her face down into the bark and was swallowed.

"Loss of her body has meant the loss of all feeling;
and yet she weeps, and the warm drops spill from her tree trunk;
those tears bring her honor: the distillate myrrh preserves and
will keep the name of its mistress down through the ages.   600

"But under the bark, the infant conceived in such baseness
continued to grow and now sought a way out of Myrrha;
the pregnant trunk bulged in the middle and its weighty burden
pressed on the mother, who could not cry out in her sorrow
nor summon Lucina with charms to aid those in childbirth.   605
So, like a woman exerting herself to deliver,
the tree groaned and bent over double, wet from its weeping.
Gentle Lucina stood by the sorrowing branches,
laid her hands onto the bark and recited the charms that
aid in delivery; the bark split open; a fissure   610
ran down the trunk of the tree and its burden spilled out,

---

4. Arabia Felix, the southern tip of the Arabian Peninsula.

a bawling boychild, whom naiads placed in soft grasses
and bathed in the tears of its mother. Not even Envy
could have found fault with his beauty, for he resembled
one of the naked cherubs depicted by artists,   615
and would have been taken as one, if you had provided
him with a quiver or else removed one from those others.

[Venus and Adonis]

"Time swiftly glides by in secret, escaping our notice,
and nothing goes faster than years do: the son of his sister
by his grandfather, the one so recently hidden   620
within a tree, so recently born, a most beautiful infant,
now is an adolescent and now a young man
even more beautiful than he was as a baby,
pleasing now even to Venus and soon the avenger
of passionate fires that brought his mother to ruin.   625
    "For while her fond Cupid was giving a kiss to his mother,
he pricked her unwittingly, right in the breast, with an arrow
projecting out of his quiver; annoyed, the great goddess
swatted him off, but the wound had gone in more deeply
than it appeared to, and at the beginning deceived her.   630
    "Under the spell of this fellow's beauty, the goddess
no longer takes any interest now in Cythera,[5]
nor does she return to her haunts on the island of Paphon,
or to fish-wealthy Cnidus or to ore-bearing Amathus;[6]
she avoids heaven as well, now—preferring Adonis,   635
and clings to him, his constant companion, ignoring
her former mode of unstrenuous self-indulgence,
when she shunned natural light for the parlors of beauty;
now she goes roaming with him through woods and up mountains
and over the scrubby rocks with her garments hitched up   640
and girded around her waist like a nymph of Diana,[7]
urging the hounds to pursue unendangering species,
hoppety hares or stags with wide-branching antlers,
or terrified does; but she avoids the fierce wild boars and
rapacious wolves and bears armed with sharp claws,   645
and shuns the lions, sated with slaughter of cattle.
    "And she warns you also to fear the wild beasts, Adonis,
if only her warning were heeded. 'Be bold with the timid,'
she said, 'but against the daring, daring is reckless.
Spare me, dear boy, the risk involved in your courage;   650
don't rile the beasts that Nature has armed with sharp weapons,
lest I should find the glory you gain much too costly!
For lions and bristling boars and other fierce creatures
look with indifferent eyes and minds upon beauty
and youth and other qualities Venus is moved by;   655
pitiless boars deal out thunderbolts with their curved tusks,
and none may withstand the frenzied assault of the lions,

---

5. Island south of the Peloponnesus, and like Cyprus sacred to Venus.   6. All three were important centers of Venus's cult. Paphos and Amathus were cities on the island of Cyprus, and Cnidus was a city in Asia
Minor.   7. As a virgin and huntress, the antithesis of Venus.

whom I despise altogether.'
                    "And when he asked why,
she said, 'I will tell you this story which will amaze you,
with its retribution delivered for ancient wrongdoing.   660
  "'But this unaccustomed labor has left me exhausted—
look, though—a poplar entices with opportune shade, and
offers a soft bed of turf we may rest on together,
as I would like to.' And so she lay down on the grasses
and on her Adonis, and using his breast as a pillow,   665
she told this story, mixing her words with sweet kisses:

  "'Perhaps you'll have heard of a maiden able to vanquish
the swiftest of men in a footrace; this wasn't a fiction,
for she overcame all contestants; nor could you say whether
she deserved praise more for her speed or her beauty.   670
She asked some god about husbands. "A husband," he answered,
"is not for you, Atalanta: flee from a husband!
But you will not flee—and losing yourself, will live on!"
  "'Frightened by his grim prediction, she went to the forest
and lived there unmarried, escaping the large and persistent   675
throng of her suitors by setting out cruel conditions;
"You cannot have me," she said, "unless you outrun me;
come race against me! A bride and a bed for the winner,
death to the losers. Those are the rules of the contest."
  "'Cruel? Indeed—but such was this young maiden's beauty   680
that a foolhardy throng of admirers took up the wager.
As a spectator, Hippomenes sat in the grandstand,
asking why anyone ever would risk such a danger,
just for a bride, and disparaging their headstrong passion.
However, as soon as he caught a glimpse of her beauty,   685
like mine or like yours would be if you were a woman,'
said Venus, 'her face and her body, both bared for the contest,
he threw up both hands and cried out, "I beg your pardons,
who only a moment ago disparaged your efforts,
but truly I had no idea of the trophy you strive for!"   690
  "'Praises ignited the fires of passion and made him
hope that no young man proved to be faster than she was
and fear that one would be. Jealous, he asked himself why he
was leaving the outcome of this competition unventured:
"God helps those who improve their condition by daring,"   695
he said, addressing himself as the maiden flew by him.
Though she seemed no less swift than a Scythian arrow,
nevertheless, he more greatly admired her beauty,
and the grace of her running made her seem even more lovely;
the breezes blew back the wings attached to her ankles   700
while her loose hair streamed over her ivory shoulders
and her brightly edged knee straps fluttered lightly; a russet
glow fanned out evenly over her pale, girlish body,
as when a purple awning covers a white marble surface,
staining its artless candor with counterfeit shadow.   705
  "'She crossed the finish line while he was taking it in, and
Atalanta, victorious, was given a crown and the glory;

the groaning losers were taken off: end of *their* story.
But the youth, undeterred by what had become of the vanquished,
stood on the track and fixed his gaze on the maiden: 710
"Why seek such an easy victory over these sluggards?
Contend with me," he said, "and if Fortune makes me the winner,
you will at least have been beaten by one not unworthy:
I am the son of Megareus, grandson of Neptune,
my great-grandfather; my valor is no less impressive   715
than is my descent; if you should happen to triumph,
you would be famous for having beaten Hippomenes."
    " 'And as he spoke, Atalanta's countenance softened:
she wondered whether she wished to win or to *be* won,
and asked herself which god, jealous of her suitor's beauty,   720
sought to destroy him by forcing him into this marriage:
"If *I* were judging, I wouldn't think I was worth it!
Nor am I moved by his beauty," she said, "though I could be,
but I *am* moved by his youth: his boyishness stirs me—
but what of his valor? His mind so utterly fearless?   725
What of his watery origins? His relation to Neptune?
What of the fact that he loves me and wishes to wed me,
and is willing to die if bitter Fortune denies him?
    " ' "Oh, flee from a bed that still reeks with the gore of past victims,
while you are able to, stranger; marrying *me* is   730
certain destruction! No one would wish to reject you,
and you may be chosen by a much wiser young lady!
    " ' "But why should I care for you—after so many have perished?
Now *he* will learn! Let him die then, since the great slaughter
of suitors has taught him nothing! He must be weary of living!   735
So—must he die then, because he wishes to wed me,
and is willing to pay the ultimate price for his passion?
He shouldn't have to! And even though it won't be *my* fault,
my victory surely will turn the people against me!
    " ' "If only you would just give it up, or if only,   740
since you're obsessed with it, you were a little bit faster!
How very girlish is the boy's facial expression!
O poor Hippomenes! I wish you never had seen me!
You're worthy of life, and if only *my* life had been better,
or if the harsh Fates had not prevented my marriage,   745
you would have been the one I'd have chosen to marry!"
    " 'She spoke, and, moved by desire that struck without warning,
loved without knowing what she was doing or feeling.
Her father and people were clamoring down at the racecourse,
when Neptune's descendent Hippomenes anxiously begged me: 750
"Cytherian Venus, I pray you preside at my venture,
aiding the fires that you yourself have ignited."
A well-meaning breeze brought me this prayer, so appealing
that, I confess, it aroused me and stirred me to action,
though I had scant time enough to bring off his rescue.   755
    " 'There is a field upon Cyprus, known as Tamasus,
famed for its wealth; in olden days it was given
to me and provides an endowment now for my temples;
and there in this field is a tree; its leaves and its branches

glisten and shimmer, reflecting the gold they are made of;   760
now, as it happened, I'd just gotten back from a visit,
carrying three golden apples that I had selected:
and showing myself there to Hippomenes only,
approached him and showed him how to use them to advantage.

   "'Both of them crouched for the start; when horns gave the signal,   765
they took off together, their feet barely brushing the surface;
you would have thought they were able to keep their toes dry
while skimming over the waves, and could touch on the ripened
heads of wheat in the field without bending them under.

   "'Cries of support and encouragement cheered on the young man;   770
"Now is the time," they screamed, "go for it, go for it, hurry,
Hippomenes, give it everything that you've got now!
Don't hold back! Victory!" And I am uncertain whether
these words were more pleasing to him or to his Atalanta,
for often, when she could have very easily passed him,   775
she lingered beside, her gaze full of desperate longing,
until she reluctantly sped ahead of his features.

   "'And now Hippomenes, dry-mouthed, was breathlessly gasping,
the finish line far in the distance; he threw out an apple,
and the sight of that radiant fruit astounded the maiden,   780
who turned from her course and retrieved the glittering missile;
Hippomenes passed her: the crowd roared its approval.

   "'A burst of speed now and Atalanta makes up for lost time:
once more overtaking the lad, she puts him behind her!
A second apple: again she falls back, but recovers,   785
now she's beside him, now passing him, only the finish
remains: "Now, O goddess," he cries, "my inspiration, be with me!"

   "'With all the strength of his youth he flings the last apple
to the far side of the field: *this* will really delay her!
The maiden looked doubtful about its retrieval: I forced her   790
to get it and add on its weight to the burden she carried:
time lost and weight gained were equal obstructions: the maiden
(lest my account should prove longer than even the race was)
took second place: the trophy bride left with the victor.

   "'But really, Adonis, wasn't I worthy of being   795
thanked for my troubles? Offered a gift of sweet incense?
Heedless of all I had done, he offered me neither!
Immediate outrage was followed by keen indignation;
and firmly resolving not to be spurned in the future,
I guarded against it by making this pair an example.   800

   "'Now they were passing a temple deep in the forest,
built long ago by Echion to honor Cybele,[8]
Mother of Gods, and now the length of their journey
urged them to rest here, where unbridled desire
possessed Hippomenes, moved by the strength of my godhead.   805
There was a dim and cave-like recess near the temple,
hewn out of pumice, a shrine to the ancient religion,
wherein a priest of these old rites had set a great many
carved wooden idols. Hippomenes entered that place, and

---

8. A fertility goddess of Asia Minor known as the Great Mother. She was often pictured wearing a crown that resembled a city wall with towers, and flanked by lions or riding in a cart drawn by them.

by his forbidden behavior defiled it;[9] in horror,   810
the sacred images turned away from the act, and Cybele
prepared to plunge the guilty pair in Stygian waters,
but that seemed too easy; so now their elegant pale necks
are cloaked in tawny manes; curved claws are their fingers;
arms are now forelegs, and all the weight of their bodies   815
shifts to their torsos; and now their tails sweep the arena;
fierce now, their faces; growls supplant verbal expression;
the forest now is their bedroom; a terror to others,
meekly these lions champ at the bit of the harness
on either side of the yoke of Cybele's chariot.   820
    " 'My darling, you must avoid these and all other wild beasts,
who will not turn tail, but show off their boldness in battle;
flee them or else your courage will prove our ruin!'

    "And after warning him, she went off on her journey,
carried aloft by her swans; but his courage resisted   825
her admonitions. It happened that as his dogs followed
a boar they were tracking, they roused it from where it was hidden,
and when it attempted to rush from the forest, Adonis
pierced it, but lightly, casting his spear from an angle;
with its long snout, it turned and knocked loose the weapon   830
stained with its own blood, then bore down upon our hero,
and, as he attempted to flee for his life in sheer terror,
it sank its tusks deep into the young fellow's privates,
and stretched him out on the yellow sands, where he lay dying.
    "Aloft in her light, swan-driven chariot, Venus   835
had not yet gotten to Cyprus; from a great distance
she recognized the dying groans of Adonis
and turned her birds back to him; when she saw from midair
his body lying there, lifeless, stained with its own blood,
she beat her breasts and tore at her hair and her garments,   840
and leapt from her chariot, raging, to argue with grim Fate:
    " 'It will not be altogether as you would have it,'
she said. 'My grief for Adonis will be remembered
forever, and every year will see, reenacted
in ritual form, his death and my lamentation;   845
and the blood of the hero will be transformed to a flower.
Or were *you* not once allowed to change a young woman[1]
to fragrant mint, Persephone? Do you begrudge me
the transformation of my beloved Adonis?'
    "And as she spoke, she sprinkled his blood with sweet nectar,   850
which made it swell up, like a transparent bubble
that rises from muck; and in no more than an hour
a flower sprang out of that soil, blood red in its color,
just like the flesh that lies underneath the tough rind
of the seed-hiding pomegranate. Brief is its season,   855
for the winds from which it takes its name, the anemone,
shake off those petals so lightly clinging and fated to perish."

9. It was considered sacrilege to have sexual intercourse in the precinct of a temple.   1. Mentha,
Hades' mistress, trampled by the jealous Proserpina and transformed into the mint (the meaning of her
name).

and equip the armies, and inflation caused by government debasement of the gold and silver currency undermined the economic system. Under Diocletian (ruled 284–305) there was an ineffectual attempt to fix the maximum price of all goods and a successful consolidation of the emperor's powers as the rule of a semidivine despotic monarch.

Through all the years of turmoil the Christian church, often persecuted by the imperial authorities—by Nero in the first century, by Marcus Aurelius and, more severely, by Diocletian in the third—was growing in numbers and influence, its network of religious communities organized by bishops. After Diocletian's retirement from power in 305 a new civil war began; the victor, Constantine, declared himself a Christian and enlisted the support of the church in his reorganization of the empire.

In the course of the long series of defensive wars on the frontiers it had become clear that Rome could no longer serve as the strategic center of the empire; it was too far away from the endangered areas on the northern and eastern frontiers. It had also become clear that the western and eastern halves of the empire needed separate administrative and military organization, and under Diocletian such a system was established. The two halves of the empire were in any case distinct cultural and linguistic entities: Latin and Greek. This was also true of the Christian church. Constantine established a new capital for his reign on the site of the Greek city Byzantium and renamed it Constantinople. By the time one of his successors, Theodosius, made Christianity the official religion of the Roman empire in 391, the two halves of the empire were to all intents and purposes separate states.

They were to have separate destinies. In the east the imperial power based on the capital founded by Constantine maintained a Greek-speaking Christian empire for many centuries until, after fighting a long losing battle against the advance of Islam, the city fell to the Ottoman Turks in 1453. But in the west, collapse came much sooner. In 410 Rome fell to Alaric at the head of an army of Visigoths; many of the western provinces had already been overrun by new peoples moving south. But the church survived, to convert the conquerors to the Christian religion and establish the cultural and religious foundations of the European Middle Ages.

TIME LINE

TEXTS	CONTEXTS
100 The four **Gospels** of the life and sayings of Jesus and the Acts of the Apostles are complete	
	117–138 Hadrian emperor
	131–134 Jewish revolt against Roman rule; Jews expelled from Palestine in 134
	138–161 Antoninus Pius emperor
	161–180 Marcus Aurelius emperor
	ca. 200–300 Systematic effort by the Roman empire to destroy Christianity fails
	284–305 Diocletian emperor
	303–311 Last persecution of Christians
	312–337 Constantine I emperor
	313 Constantine issues Edict of Milan, declaring toleration of all religions
	330 Constantine moves capital of the Roman empire to Byzantium, renaming the city Constantinople
367 Final canon of the **New Testament of the Bible** is established	
387 Augustine baptized as a Christian	
	391 Christianity becomes official religion of the Roman empire; pagan religions outlawed
ca. 393–405 Jerome translates the Bible into Latin	
	395 The Roman empire is permanently divided into the Eastern empire, based in Constantinople, and the Western empire, based in Rome

Boldface titles indicate works in the anthology.

here) were clearly designed with an eye to different readerships. The Gospel according to Matthew, for example, has a Jewish public in mind; one of its main concerns is to convince its readers not only that Jesus was the legitimate heir to the throne of the royal house of David but also that Jesus was the king, the Messiah, announced by the Hebrew prophets. Mark, on the other hand, is clearly written with a Gentile audience in mind and pays particular attention to the needs of the Roman reader, translating Aramaic words and even explaining that the courtyard into which the Roman soldiers took Jesus after he was condemned was the place the Romans called the *praetorium*. And the Gospel according to Luke is obviously addressed to cultured Greek readers; it makes very few references to the Hebrew prophecies and is in fact dedicated to a Greek named Theophilos.

These three Gospels contain a central core of identical material that must come from an earlier source now lost (it is known as the Q document). The fourth Gospel, that of John, draws on different sources and also has greater theological density than the other three. The collection known to Christians as the New Testament was formed by combining the four Gospels with another book by Luke, the Acts of the Apostles, which is an account of Paul's missionary journeys to the cities of Greece and Asia Minor. Added to this were letters of Paul and others to the Christian communities in such cities as Corinth, Thessalonica, and Rome and the book called Revelation, a vision of the end of the world and the second coming of Jesus.

There were, of course, many other documents that gave accounts of the life and teaching of Jesus, but this particular collection contained those judged most reliable by the church authorities and was declared canonical some time in the third century. Latin translations of the Greek texts were made for the use of the churches of the Western Roman empire, but there was no official version until in 382 Pope Damasus commissioned a scholar called Jerome to produce a correct translation. It soon became known as the Vulgate—the "common" or "popular" version. This was the text used and quoted by Augustine, and with some revisions over the centuries, the one that remained in use in the Christian churches of the West through the Middle Ages.

The Christian Bible: The New Testament[1]

Luke 2

[The Birth and Youth of Jesus]

It happened in those days that a decree went forth from Augustus Caesar that all the world[2] should be enrolled in a census. This was the first census, when Quirinius was governor of Syria. And all went to be enrolled, each to his own city. And Joseph also went up from Galilee, from the city of Nazareth, to Judaea, to the city of David which is called Bethlehem, because he was of the house and family of David, to be enrolled with Mary his promised wife, who was pregnant. And it happened that while they were there her time was completed, and she bore a son, her first-born, and she wrapped him in swaddling clothes and laid him in a manger, because there was no room for them in the inn. And there were shepherds in that region, camping

---

1. All selections translated by Richmond Lattimore. 2. The Roman empire. Augustus Caesar (63 B.C.E.–14 C.E.), first Roman emperor.

out at night and keeping guard over their flock. And an angel of the Lord stood before them, and the glory of the Lord shone about them, and they were afraid with a great fear. The angel said to them: Do not be afraid; behold, I tell you good news, great joy which shall be for all the people; because this day there has been born for you in the city of David a savior who is Christ[3] the Lord. And here is a sign for you; you will find a baby wrapped in swaddling clothes and lying in a manger. And suddenly with the angel there was a multitude of the heavenly host, praising God and saying: Glory to God in the highest and peace on earth among men of good will. And it happened that after the angels had gone off from them into the sky, the shepherds began saying to each other: Let us go to Bethlehem and see this thing which has happened, which the Lord made known to us; and they went, hastening, and found Mary and Joseph, and the baby lying in the manger; and when they had seen, they spread the news about what had been told them concerning this baby. And all who heard wondered at what had been told them by the shepherds; and Mary kept in mind all these sayings as she pondered them in her heart. And the shepherds returned, glorifying and praising God over all they had heard and seen, as it had been told them.

And when eight days were past, for his circumcision, his name was called Jesus, as it was named by the angel[4] before he was conceived in the womb.

And when the days for their purification according to the Law of Moses had been completed, they took him up to Jerusalem to set him before the Lord, as it has been written in the Law of the Lord: Every male child who opens the womb shall be called sacred to the Lord;[5] and to give sacrifice as it is stated in the Law of the Lord, a pair of turtle doves or two young pigeons. And behold, there was a man in Jerusalem whose name was Simeon, and this man was righteous and virtuous and looked forward to the consolation of Israel, and the Holy Spirit was upon him; and it had been prophesied to him by the Holy Spirit that he should not look upon his death until he had looked on the Lord's Anointed. And in the spirit he went into the temple; and as his parents brought in the child Jesus so that they could do for him what was customary according to the law, Simeon himself took him in his arms and blessed God and said: Now, Lord, you release your slave, in peace, according to your word; because my eyes have looked on your salvation, what you made ready in the presence of all the peoples; a light for the revelation to the Gentiles,[6] and the glory of your people, Israel. And his father and his mother were in wonder at what was being said about him. And Simeon blessed them and said to Mary his mother: Behold, he is appointed for the fall and the rise[7] of many in Israel; and as a sign which is disputed; and through your soul also will pass the sword; so that the reasonings of many hearts may be revealed. And there was Anna, a prophetess, the daughter of Phanuel, of the tribe of Asher. And she was well advanced in years, having lived with her husband seven years from the time of her maidenhood, and now she was eighty-four years a widow. And she did not leave

3. Greek word for "anointed." The adjective is used of kings, priests, and the deliverer promised by the prophets. 4. In the Annunciation (Luke 1.31); *Jesus* is a form of the name *Joshua*, which means "he shall save." 5. The firstborn son is believed to belong to God (Exodus 13.2). The purification laws are given in Leviticus 12. 6. Non-Jews. 7. The Greek word is the one always used of the resurrection of the dead.

the temple, serving night and day with fastings and prayers. And at this same time she came near and gave thanks to God and spoke of the child to those who looked forward to the deliverance of Jerusalem.

And when they had done everything according to the Law of the Lord, they went back to Galilee, to their own city, Nazareth.

And the child grew in stature and strength as he was filled with wisdom, and the grace of God was upon him.

Now his parents used to journey every year to Jerusalem for the feast of the Passover. And when he was twelve years old, when they went up according to their custom for the festival and had completed their days there, on their return the boy Jesus stayed behind in Jerusalem, and his parents did not know it. And supposing that he was in their company they went a day's journey and then looked for him among their relatives and friends, and when they did not find him they turned back to Jerusalem in search of him. And it happened that after three days they found him in the temple sitting in the midst of the masters,[8] listening to them and asking them questions. And all who heard him were amazed at his intelligence and his answers. And they were astonished at seeing him, and his mother said to him: Child, why did you do this to us? See, your father and I have been looking for you, in distress. He said to them: But why were you looking for me? Did you not know that I must be in my father's house? And they did not understand what he had said to them. And he returned with them and came to Nazareth, and was in their charge. And his mother kept all his sayings in her heart. And Jesus advanced in wisdom and stature, and in the favor of God and men.

Matthew 5–7

[*The Teaching of Jesus; The Sermon on the Mount*]

And seeing the multitudes he went up onto the mountain, and when he was seated, his disciples came to him, and he opened his mouth and taught them, saying:

Blessed are the poor in spirit, because theirs is the Kingdom of Heaven.

Blessed are they who sorrow, because they shall be comforted.

Blessed are the gentle, because they shall inherit the earth.

Blessed are they who are hungry and thirsty for righteousness, because they shall be fed.

Blessed are they who have pity, because they shall be pitied.

Blessed are the pure in heart, because they shall see God.

Blessed are the peacemakers, because they shall be called the sons of God.

Blessed are they who are persecuted for their righteousness, because theirs is the Kingdom of Heaven.

Blessed are you when they shall revile you and persecute you and speak every evil thing of you, lying, because of me. Rejoice and be glad, because your reward in heaven is great; for thus did they persecute the prophets before you.

8. Teachers, rabbis.

You are the salt of the earth; but if the salt loses its power, with what shall it be salted?[1] It is good for nothing but to be thrown away and trampled by men. You are the light of the world. A city cannot be hidden when it is set on top of a hill. Nor do men light a lamp and set it under a basket, but they set it on a stand, and it gives its light to all in the house. So let your light shine before men, so that they may see your good works and glorify your father in heaven.

Do not think that I have come to destroy the law and the prophets. I have not come to destroy but to complete. Indeed, I say to you, until the sky and the earth are gone, not one iota[2] or one end of a letter must go from the law, until all is done. He who breaks one of the least of these commandments and teaches men accordingly shall be called the least in the Kingdom of Heaven; he who performs and teaches these commandments shall be called great in the Kingdom of Heaven. For I tell you, if your righteousness is not more abundant than that of the scribes and the Pharisees,[3] you may not enter the Kingdom of Heaven.

You have heard that it was said to the ancients: You shall not murder. He who murders shall be liable to judgment. I say to you that any man who is angry with his brother shall be liable to judgment; and he who says to his brother, fool, shall be liable before the council; and he who says to his brother, sinner, shall be liable to Gehenna.[4] If then you bring your gift to the altar, and there remember that your brother has some grievance against you, leave your gift before the altar, and go first and be reconciled with your brother, and then go and offer your gift. Be quick to be conciliatory with your adversary at law when you are in the street with him, for fear your adversary may turn you over to the judge, and the judge to the officer, and you be thrown into prison. Truly I tell you, you cannot come out of there until you pay the last penny.

You have heard that it has been said: You shall not commit adultery. I tell you that any man who looks at a woman so as to desire her has already committed adultery with her in his heart. If your right eye makes you go amiss, take it out and cast it from you; it is better that one part of you should be lost instead of your whole body being cast into Gehenna. And if your right hand makes you go amiss, cut it off and cast it from you; it is better that one part of you should be lost instead of your whole body going to Gehenna. It has been said: If a man puts away his wife, let him give her a contract of divorce. I tell you that any man who puts away his wife, except for the reason of harlotry, is making her the victim of adultery; and any man who marries a wife who has been divorced is committing adultery. Again, you have heard that it has been said to the ancients: You shall not swear falsely, but you shall make good your oaths to the Lord. I tell you not to swear at all: not by heaven, because it is the throne of God; not by the earth, because it is the footstool for his feet; not by Jerusalem, because it is the city of the great king; not by

1. That is, how can it regain its savor? 2. The smallest letter in the Greek alphabet, because it is the only letter made with a single stroke. 3. A sect that insisted on strict observance of the Mosaic law. "Scribes": official interpreters of the sacred scriptures. 4. Jesus compares the different degrees of punishment (administered by God) for the new sins listed here with the degrees of punishment recognized by Jewish law. The penalties that might be inflicted for murder were death by the sword (a sentence of a local court, "the judgment"), death by stoning (the sentence of a higher court, "the council"), and the burning of the criminal's body in the place where refuse was thrown, Gehenna, which is hence used as a name for hell.

tree that does not produce good fruit is cut out and thrown in the fire. So from their fruits you will know them. Not everyone who says to me Lord Lord will come into the Kingdom of Heaven, but he who does the will of my father in heaven. Many will say to me on that day: Lord, Lord, did we not prophesy in your name, and in your name did we not cast out demons, and in your name did we not assume great powers? And then I shall admit to them: I never knew you. Go from me, for you do what is against the law.

Every man who hears what I say and does what I say shall be like the prudent man who built his house upon the rock. And the rain fell and the rivers came and the winds blew and dashed against that house, and it did not fall, for it was founded upon the rock. And every man who hears what I say and does not do what I say will be like the reckless man who built his house on the sand. And the rain fell and the rivers came and the winds blew and battered that house, and it fell, and that was a great fall.

And it happened that when Jesus had ended these words, the multitudes were astonished at his teaching, for he taught them as one who has authority, and not like their own scribes.

Luke 15

[The Teaching of Jesus; Parables]

All the tax collectors and the sinners kept coming around him, to listen to him. And the Pharisees and the scribes muttered, saying: This man receives sinners and eats with them. But he told them this parable, saying: Which man among you who has a hundred sheep and has lost one of them will not leave the ninety-nine in the wilds and go after the lost one until he finds it? And when he does find it, he sets it on his shoulders, rejoicing, and goes to his house and invites in his friends and his neighbors, saying to them: Rejoice with me, because I found my sheep which was lost. I tell you that thus there will be joy in heaven over one sinner who repents, rather than over ninety-nine righteous ones who have no need of repentance. Or what woman who has ten drachmas, if she loses one drachma, does not light the lamp and sweep the house and search diligently until she finds it? And finding it she invites in her friends and neighbors, saying: Rejoice with me, because I found the drachma I lost. Such, I tell you, is the joy among the angels of God over one sinner who repents.

And he said: There was a man who had two sons. And the younger of them said to his father: Father, give me my appropriate share of the property. And the father divided his substance between them. And not many days afterward the younger son gathered everything together and left the country for a distant land, and there he squandered his substance in riotous living. And after he had spent everything, there was a severe famine in that country, and he began to be in need. And he went and attached himself to one of the citizens of that country, who sent him out into the fields to feed the pigs. And he longed to be nourished on the nuts that the pigs ate, and no one would give to him. And he went and said to himself: How many hired servants of my father have plenty of bread while I am dying of hunger here. I will rise up and go to my father and say to him: Father, I have sinned against heaven and in your sight, I am no longer worthy to be called your son. Make me like one of your hired servants. And he rose up and went to his father. And when he was still a long way off, his father saw him and was moved and ran and fell on his neck and kissed him. The son said to him: Father, I have sinned against heaven and in your sight, I am no longer worthy to be called your son. But his father said to his slaves: Quick, bring the best clothing and put it on him, and have a ring for his hand and shoes for his feet, and bring the fatted calf, slaughter him, and let us eat and make merry because this man, my son, was a dead man and came to life. He was lost and he has been found. And they began to make merry. His older son was out on the estate, and as he came nearer to the house he heard music and dancing, and he called over one of the servants and asked what was going on. He told him: Your brother is here, and your father slaughtered the fatted calf, because he got him back in good health. He was angry and did not want to go in. But his father came out and entreated him. But he answered and said to his father: Look, all these years I have been your slave and never neglected an order of yours, but you never gave me a kid so that I could make merry with my friends. But when this son of yours comes back, the one who ate up your livelihood in the company of whores, you slaughtered the fatted calf for him. But he said to him: My child, you are always with me, and all that is mine is yours; but we had to make merry and rejoice, because your brother was a dead man and came to life. He was lost and has been found.

From Matthew 13

[Why Jesus Teaches in Parables]

On that day Jesus went out of the house and sat beside the sea; and a great multitude gathered before him, so that he went aboard a ship and sat there, and all the multitude stood on the shore. And he talked to them, speaking mostly in parables: Behold, a sower went out to sow. And as he sowed, some of the grain fell beside the way, and birds came and ate it. Some fell on stony ground where there was not much soil, and it shot up quickly because there was no depth of soil, but when the sun came up it was parched, and because it had no roots it dried away. Some fell among thorns, and the thorns grew up and stifled it. But some fell upon the good soil and bore fruit, some a hundredfold, some sixtyfold, some thirtyfold. He who has ears, let him hear. Then his disciples came to him and said: Why do you talk to them in parables? He answered them and said: Because it is given to you to understand the secrets of the Kingdom of Heaven, but to them it is not given. When a man has, he shall be given, and it will be more than he needs; but when he has not, even what he has shall be taken away from him. Therefore I talk to them in parables, because they have sight but do not see, and hearing but do not hear or understand. And for them is fulfilled the prophecy of Isaiah,[1] saying: With your hearing you shall hear and not understand, and you shall

1. See Isaiah 6.9–10.

use your sight and look but not see. For the heart of this people is stiffened, and they hear with difficulty, and they have closed their eyes, so that they may never see with their eyes, or hear with their ears and with their hearts understand and turn back, so that I can heal them.

Blessed are your eyes because they see, and your ears because they hear. Truly I tell you that many prophets and good men have longed to see what you see, and not seen it, and to hear what you hear, and not heard it. Hear, then, the parable of the sower. To every man who hears the word of the Kingdom and does not understand it, the evil one comes and seizes what has been sown in his heart. This is the seed sown by the way. The seed sown on the stony ground is the man who hears the word and immediately accepts it with joy; but he has no root in himself, and he is a man of the moment, and when there comes affliction and persecution, because of the word, he does not stand fast. The seed sown among thorns is the man who hears the word, and concern for the world and the beguilement of riches stifle the word, and he bears no fruit. And the seed sown on the good soil is the man who hears the word and understands it, who bears fruit and makes it, one a hundred-fold, one sixtyfold, and one thirtyfold.

He set before them another parable, saying: The Kingdom of Heaven is like a man who sowed good seed in his field. And while the people were asleep, his enemy came and sowed darnel[2] in with the grain, and went away. When the plants grew and produced a crop, the darnel was seen. Then the slaves of the master came to him and said: Master, did you not sow good grain in your field? Where does the darnel come from? He said to them: A man who is my enemy did it. His slaves said: Do you wish us to go out and gather it? But he said: No, for fear that when you gather the darnel you may pull up the grain with it. Let them both grow until harvest time, and in the time of harvest I shall say to the harvesters: First gather the darnel, and bind it in sheaves for burning, but store the grain in my granary.

He set before them another parable, saying: The Kingdom of Heaven is like a grain of mustard, which a man took and sowed in his field; which is the smallest of all seeds, but when it grows, it is the largest of the greens and grows into a tree, so that the birds of the air come and nest in its branches.

He told them another parable: The Kingdom of Heaven is like leaven, which a woman took and buried in three measures of dough, so that it all rose.

All this Jesus told the multitudes in parables, and he did not talk to them except in parables; so as to fulfill the word spoken by the prophet, saying: I will open my mouth in parables, and pour out what has been hidden since the creation.

* * *

2. A grassy kind of weed.

From Matthew 26

[*The Betrayal of Jesus*]

And at that time one of the twelve, he who was called Judas Iscariot, went to the high priests and said: What are you willing to give me if I betray him to you? And they paid him thirty pieces of silver. And from that time he looked for an opportunity to betray him.

On the first day of the feast of unleavened bread,[1] his disciples came to Jesus and said: Where do you wish us to make preparations for you to eat the feast of the Passover? He said: Go to the city, to the house of a certain man, and say to him: The teacher says: My time is near. I shall keep the Passover at your house, with my disciples. And his disciples did as Jesus instructed them, and made ready the Passover. When it was evening, he took his place at dinner with the twelve disciples. And as they were eating he said: Truly I tell you that one of you will betray me. They were bitterly hurt and began each one to say: Surely it is not I, Lord? He answered and said: The one who dips his hand in the dish with me, he is the one who will betray me. The son of man goes his way as it has been written for him to do, but woe to that man through whom the son of man is betrayed. It would have been well for that man if he had never been born. Judas, who had betrayed him, answered and said: Master, it is not I? Jesus said to him: It is you who said it. As they ate, Jesus took a loaf of bread, and blessed it, and broke it, and gave it to his disciples, and said: Take it; eat it; this is my body. And he took a cup and gave thanks and gave it to them, saying: Drink from it, all; for this is my blood, of the covenant,[2] which is shed for the sake of many, for the remission of sins. But I tell you, from now on I shall not drink of this produce of the vine, until that day when I drink it with you, new wine, in the kingdom of my father.

And they sang the hymn and went out to the Mount of Olives. Then Jesus said to them: All of you will be made to fail me in the course of this night. For it is written:[3] I will strike the shepherd, and the sheep of his flock will be scattered. But after my resurrection I will lead the way for you into Galilee. Peter spoke forth and said: Though all the others fail you, I will never fail you. Jesus said to him: Truly I tell you that on this night before the cock crows you will disown me three times. Peter said to him: Even if I must die with you, I will never disown you. And so spoke all the disciples.

Then Jesus went with them to a place called Gethsemane; and he said to his disciples: Sit down here, while I go over there and pray. He took with him Peter and the two sons of Zebedee;[4] and then he was in pain and distress. And he said to them: My soul is in anguish to the point of death. Stay here and keep watch with me. Then he went a little farther, and threw himself down on his face, and said in prayer: Father, if it is possible, let this cup pass me by; except only, let it be not as I wish, but as you wish. Then he went back to his disciples and found them asleep, and said to Peter: Are you not

1. Passover, held in remembrance of the delivery of the Jews from captivity in Egypt (Exodus 1–12). 2. The Greek word can mean either "agreement, arrangement" (covenant) or "will" (hence "the new testament" in the King James translation). Jesus compares himself to the lamb that was killed at Passover as a sign of the covenant between God and the Jews. He thus places himself within the Jewish historical tradition even as he depicts the legacy of his sacrifice as the renewal and completion of that tradition. 3. In Zechariah 13.7. 4. James and John.

away while we were sleeping. And if this is heard in the house of the governor, we shall reason with him, and make it so that you have nothing to fear. And they took the money and did as they were instructed. And this is the story that has been spread about among the Jews, to this day.

Then the eleven disciples went on into Galilee, to the mountain where Jesus had given them instructions to go; and when they saw him, they worshipped him; but some doubted. And Jesus came up to them and talked with them, saying: All authority has been given to me, in heaven and on earth. Go out, therefore, and instruct all the nations, baptizing them in the name of the Father and the Son and the Holy Spirit, teaching them to observe all that I have taught you. And behold, I am with you, all the days until the end of the world.

AUGUSTINE
354–430

Aurelius Augustine was born in 354 in Tagaste, in North Africa. He was baptized as a Christian in 387 and ordained bishop of Hippo, in North Africa, in 395. When he died there in 430, the city was besieged by Gothic invaders. Besides the *Confessions* (begun in 397) he wrote *The City of God* (finished in 426) and many polemical works against schismatics and heretics.

He was born into a world that no longer enjoyed the "Roman peace." Invading barbarians had pierced the empire's defenses and were increasing their pressure every year. The economic basis of the empire was cracking under the strain of the enormous taxation needed to support the army; the land was exhausted. The empire was Christian, but the church was split, beset by heresies and organized heretical sects. The empire was on the verge of ruin, and there was every prospect that the church would go down with it.

Augustine, one of the men responsible for the consolidation of the church in the West, especially for the systematization of its doctrine and policy, did not convert to Christianity until he had reached middle life. "Late have I loved Thee, O Beauty so ancient and so new," he says in his *Confessions*, written long after his conversion. The lateness of his conversion and his regret for his wasted youth were among the sources of the energy that drove him to assume the intellectual leadership of the Western church and to guarantee, by combating heresy on the one hand and laying new ideological foundations for Christianity on the other, the church's survival through the dark centuries to come. Augustine had been brought up in the literary and philosophical tradition of the classical world, and it is partly because of his assimilation of classical literature and method to Christian training and teaching that the literature of the ancient world survived at all when Roman power collapsed in a welter of bloodshed and destruction that lasted for generations.

In his *Confessions* he set down, for the benefit of others, the story of his early life and his conversion to Christianity. This is, as far as we know, the first authentic ancient autobiography, and that fact itself is a significant expression of the Christian spirit, which proclaims the value of the individual soul and the importance of its relation with God. Throughout the *Confessions* Augustine talks directly to God, in humility, yet conscious that God is concerned for him personally. At the same time he comes to an understanding of his own feelings and development as a human being which marks his *Confessions* as one of the great literary documents of the Western world. His description of his childhood is the only detailed account of the childhood of a great man that antiquity has left us, and his accurate observation and keen perception are informed by the Hebrew and Christian idea of the sense of sin. "So small a boy and so great a sinner"—from the beginning of his narrative to the end Augustine sees individuals not as the Greeks at their most optimistic tended to see humanity, the center and potential masters of the universe, but as children, wandering in ignorance, capable of reclamation only through the divine mercy that waits eternally for them to turn to it.

In Augustine are combined the intellectual tradition of the ancient world and the religious feeling that was characteristic of the Middle Ages. The transition from the old world to the new can be seen in his pages; his analytical intellect pursues its odyssey through strange and scattered islands—the mysticism of the Manichees, the skepticism of the academic philosophers, the fatalism of the astrologers—until he finds his home in the church, to which he was to render such great service. His account of his conversion in the garden at Milan records the true moment of transition from the ancient to the medieval world. The innumerable defeats and victories, the burning towns and ravaged farms, the bloodshed, dates, and statistics of the end of an era are all illuminated and ordered by this moment in the history of the human spirit. Here is the point of change itself.

From Confessions[1]

FROM BOOK I

[Childhood]

What have I to say to Thee, God, save that I know not where I came from, when I came into this life-in-death—or should I call it death-in-life? I do not know. I only know that the gifts Your mercy had provided sustained me from the first moment: not that I remember it but so I have heard from the parents of my flesh, the father from whom, and the mother in whom, You fashioned me in time.

Thus for my sustenance and my delight I had woman's milk: yet it was not my mother or my nurses who stored their breasts for me: it was Yourself, using them to give me the food of my infancy, according to Your ordinance and the riches set by You at every level of creation. It was by Your gift that I desired what You gave and no more, by Your gift that those who suckled me willed to give me what You had given them: for it was by the love implanted in them by You that they gave so willingly that milk which by Your gift flowed in the breasts. It was a good for them that I received good from them, though I received it not *from* them but only through them: since all good things are from You, O God, and *from God is all my health.*[2] But this I have learnt since: You have made it abundantly clear by all that I have seen You give, within me and about me. For at that time I knew how to suck, to lie quiet when I was content, to cry when I was in pain: and that was all I knew.

Later I added smiling to the things I could do, first in sleep, then awake. This again I have on the word of others, for naturally I do not remember; in

1. Translated by F. J. Sheed.   2. Throughout the *Confessions* Augustine quotes liberally from the Bible; the quotations are set off in italics. When a quotation bears on Augustine's situation, it is annotated.

any event, I believe it, for I have seen other infants do the same. And gradually I began to notice where I was, and the will grew in me to make my wants known to those who might satisfy them; but I could not, for my wants were within me and those others were outside: nor had they any faculty enabling them to enter into my mind. So I would fling my arms and legs about and utter sounds, making the few gestures in my power—these being as apt to express my wishes as I could make them: but they were not very apt. And when I did not get what I wanted, either because my wishes were not clear or the things not good for me, I was in a rage—with my parents as though I had a right to their submission, with free human beings as though they had been bound to serve me; and I took my revenge in screams. That infants are like this, I have learnt from watching other infants; and that I was like it myself I have learnt more clearly from these other infants, who did not know me, than from my nurses who did.

* * *

From infancy I came to boyhood, or rather it came to me, taking the place of infancy. Yet infancy did not go: for where was it to go to? Simply it was no longer there. For now I was not an infant, without speech, but a boy, speaking. This I remember; and I have since discovered by observation how I learned to speak. I did not learn by elders teaching me words in any systematic way, as I was soon after taught to read and write. But of my own motion, using the mind which You, my God, gave me, I strove with cries and various sounds and much moving of my limbs to utter the feelings of my heart—all this in order to get my own way. Now I did not always manage to express the right meanings to the right people. So I began to reflect [I observed that][3] my elders would make some particular sound, and as they made it would point at or move towards some particular thing: and from this I came to realize that the thing was called by the sound they made when they wished to draw my attention to it. That they intended this was clear from the motions of their body, by a kind of natural language common to all races which consists in facial expressions, glances of the eye, gestures, and the tones by which the voice expresses the mind's state—for example whether things are to be sought, kept, thrown away, or avoided. So, as I heard the same words again and again properly used in different phrases, I came gradually to grasp what things they signified; and forcing my mouth to the same sounds, I began to use them to express my own wishes. Thus I learnt to convey what I meant to those about me; and so took another long step along the stormy way of human life in society, while I was still subject to the authority of my parents and at the beck and call of my elders.

O God, my God, what emptiness and mockeries did I now experience: for it was impressed upon me as right and proper in a boy to obey those who taught me, that I might get on in the world and excel in the handling of words[4] to gain honor among men and deceitful riches. I, poor wretch, could not see the use of the things I was sent to school to learn; but if I proved idle in learning, I was soundly beaten. For this procedure seemed wise to our

3. Words in brackets are the translator's.   4. The study of rhetoric, which was the passport to eminence in public life.

ancestors: and many, passing the same way in days past, had built a sorrowful road by which we too must go, with multiplication of grief and toil upon the sons of Adam.

Yet, Lord, I observed men praying to You: and I learnt to do likewise, thinking of You (to the best of my understanding) as some great being who, though unseen, could hear and help me. As a boy I fell into the way of calling upon You, my Help and my Refuge; and in those prayers I broke the strings of my tongue—praying to You, small as I was but with no small energy, that I might not be beaten at school.[5] And when You did not hear me (*not as giving me over to folly*), my elders and even my parents, who certainly wished me no harm, treated my stripes as a huge joke, which they were very far from being to me. Surely, Lord, there is no one so steeled in mind or cleaving to You so close—or even so insensitive, for that might have the same effect—as to make light of the racks and hooks and other torture instruments[6] (from which in all lands men pray so fervently to be saved) while truly loving those who are in such bitter fear of them. Yet my parents seemed to be amused at the torments inflicted upon me as a boy by my masters, though I was no less afraid of my punishments or zealous in my prayers to You for deliverance. But in spite of my terrors I still did wrong, by writing or reading or studying less than my set tasks. It was not, Lord, that I lacked mind or memory, for You had given me as much of these as my age required; but the one thing I revelled in was play; and for this I was punished by men who after all were doing exactly the same things themselves. But the idling of men is called business; the idling of boys, though exactly like, is punished by those same men: and no one pities either boys or men. Perhaps an unbiased observer would hold that I was rightly punished as a boy for playing with a ball: because this hindered my progress in studies—studies which would give me the opportunity as a man to play at things more degraded. And what difference was there between me and the master who flogged me? For if on some trifling point he had the worst of the argument with some fellow-master, he was more torn with angry vanity than I when I was beaten in a game of ball.

* * *

But to continue with my boyhood, which was in less peril of sin than my adolescence. I disliked learning and hated to be forced to it. But I *was* forced to it, so that good was done to me though it was not my doing. Short of being driven to it, I certainly would not have learned. But no one does well against his will, even if the thing he does is a good thing to do. Nor did those who forced me do well: it was by You, O God, that well was done. Those others had no deeper vision of the use to which I might put all they forced me to learn, but to sate the insatiable desire of man for wealth that is but penury and glory that is but shame. But You, Lord, *by Whom the very hairs of our head are numbered*,[7] used for my good the error of those who urged me to study; but my own error, in that I had no will to learn, you used for my

---

5. Augustine recognizes the necessity of this rigorous training; that he never forgot its harshness is clear from his remark in the *City of God* (XXI.14): "If a choice were given him between suffering death and living his early years over again, who would not shudder and choose death?"   6. The instruments of public execution.   7. Who knows and attends to the smallest detail of each life (compare Matthew 10.30).

My one delight was to love and to be loved. But in this I did not keep the measure of mind to mind, which is the luminous line of friendship; but from the muddy concupiscence of the flesh and the hot imagination of puberty mists steamed up to becloud and darken my heart so that I could not distinguish the white light of love from the fog of lust. Both love and lust boiled within me, and swept my youthful immaturity over the precipice of evil desires to leave me half drowned in a whirlpool of abominable sins. Your wrath had grown mighty against me and I knew it not. I had grown deaf from the clanking of the chain of my mortality, the punishment for the pride of my soul: and I departed further from You, and You left me to myself: and I was tossed about and wasted and poured out and boiling over in my fornications: and You were silent, O my late-won Joy. You were silent, and I, arrogant and depressed, weary and restless, wandered further and further from You into more and more sins which could bear no fruit save sorrows.

* * *

Where then was I, and how far from the delights of Your house, in that sixteenth year of my life in this world, when the madness of lust—needing no licence from human shamelessness, receiving no licence from Your laws—took complete control of me, and I surrendered wholly to it? My family took no care to save me from this moral destruction by marriage: their only concern was that I should learn to make as fine and persuasive speeches as possible.

* * *

Your law, O Lord, punishes theft; and this law is so written in the hearts of men that not even the breaking of it blots it out: for no thief bears calmly being stolen from—not even if he is rich and the other steals through want. Yet I chose to steal, and not because want drove me to it—unless a want of justice and contempt for it and an excess for iniquity. For I stole things which I already had in plenty and of better quality. Nor had I any desire to enjoy the things I stole, but only the stealing of them and the sin. There was a pear tree near our vineyard, heavy with fruit, but fruit that was not particularly tempting either to look at or to taste. A group of young blackguards, and I among them, went out to knock down the pears and carry them off late one night, for it was our bad habit to carry on our games in the streets till very late. We carried off an immense load of pears, not to eat—for we barely tasted them before throwing them to the hogs. Our only pleasure in doing it was that it was forbidden. Such was my heart, O God, such was my heart: yet in the depth of the abyss You had pity on it. Let that heart now tell You what it sought when I was thus evil for no object, having no cause for wrongdoing save my wrongness. The malice of the act was base and I loved it—that is to say I loved my own undoing, I loved the evil in me—not the thing for which I did the evil, simply the evil: my soul was depraved, and hurled itself down from security in You into utter destruction, seeking no profit from wickedness but only to be wicked. * * *

FROM BOOK III

[*Student at Carthage*]

I came to Carthage[6] where a cauldron of illicit loves leapt and boiled about me. I was not yet in love, but I was in love with love, and from the very depth of my need hated myself for not more keenly feeling the need. I sought some object to love, since I was thus in love with loving; and I hated security and a life with no snares for my feet. For within I was hungry, all for the want of that spiritual food which is Thyself, my God; yet [though I was hungry for want of it] I did not hunger for it: I had no desire whatever for incorruptible food, not because I had it in abundance but the emptier I was, the more I hated the thought of it. Because of all this my soul was sick, and broke out in sores, whose itch I agonized to scratch with the rub of carnal things—carnal, yet if there were no soul in them, they would not be objects of love. My longing then was to love and to be loved, but most when I obtained the enjoyment of the body of the person who loved me.

Thus I polluted the stream of friendship with the filth of unclean desire and sullied its limpidity with the hell of lust. And vile and unclean as I was, so great was my vanity that I was bent upon passing for clean and courtly. And I did fall in love, simply from wanting to. O my God, my Mercy, with how much bitterness didst Thou in Thy goodness sprinkle the delights of that time! I was loved, and our love came to the bond of consummation: I wore my chains with bliss but with torment too, for I was scourged with the red hot rods of jealousy, with suspicions and fears and tempers and quarrels.

I developed a passion for stage plays, with the mirror they held up to my own miseries and the fuel they poured on my flame. How is it that a man wants to be made sad by the sight of tragic sufferings that he could not bear in his own person? Yet the spectator does want to feel sorrow, and it is actually his feeling of sorrow that he enjoys. Surely this is the most wretched lunacy? For the more a man feels such sufferings in himself, the more he is moved by the sight of them on the stage. Now when a man suffers himself, it is called misery; when he suffers in the suffering of another, it is called pity. But how can the unreal sufferings of the stage possibly move pity? The spectator is not moved to aid the sufferer but merely to be sorry for him; and the more the author of these fictions makes the audience grieve, the better they like him. If the tragic sorrows of the characters—whether historical or entirely fictitious—be so poorly represented that the spectator is not moved to tears, he leaves the theatre unsatisfied and full of complaints; if he *is* moved to tears, he stays to the end, fascinated and revelling in it.

* * *

Those of my occupations at that time which were held as reputable[7] were directed towards the study of the law, in which I meant to excel—and the less honest I was, the more famous I should be. The very limit of human blindness is to glory in being blind. By this time I was a leader in the School of Rhetoric and I enjoyed this high station and was arrogant and swollen with importance: though You know, O Lord, that I was far quieter in my behavior

6. The capital city of the province, where Augustine went to study rhetoric.   7. That is, his rhetorical studies.

and had no share in the riotousness of the *eversores*—the Overturners[8]—for this blackguardly diabolical name they wore as the very badge of sophistication. Yet I was much in their company and much ashamed of the sense of shame that kept me from being like them. I was with them and I did for the most part enjoy their companionship, though I abominated the acts that were their specialty—as when they made a butt of some hapless newcomer, assailing him with really cruel mockery for no reason whatever, save the malicious pleasure they got from it. There was something very like the action of devils in their behavior. They were rightly called Overturners, since they had themselves been first overturned and perverted, tricked by those same devils who were secretly mocking them in the very acts by which they amused themselves in mocking and making fools of others.

With these men as companions of my immaturity, I was studying the books of eloquence; for in eloquence it was my ambition to shine, all from a damnable vaingloriousness and for the satisfaction of human vanity. Following the normal order of study I had come to a book of one Cicero, whose tongue[9] practically everyone admires, though not his heart. That particular book is called *Hortensius*[1] and contains an exhortation to philosophy. Quite definitely it changed the direction of my mind, altered my prayers to You, O Lord, and gave me a new purpose and ambition. Suddenly all the vanity I had hoped in I saw as worthless, and with an incredible intensity of desire I longed after immortal wisdom. I had begun that journey upwards by which I was to return to You. My father was now dead two years; I was eighteen and was receiving money from my mother for the continuance of my study of eloquence. But I used that book not for the sharpening of my tongue; what won me in it was what it said, not the excellence of its phrasing.

* * *

So I resolved to make some study of the Sacred Scriptures and find what kind of books they were. But what I came upon was something not grasped by the proud, not revealed either to children, something utterly humble in the hearing but sublime in the doing, and shrouded deep in mystery. And I was not of the nature to enter into it or bend my neck to follow it. When I first read those Scriptures, I did not feel in the least what I have just said; they seemed to me unworthy to be compared with the majesty of Cicero. My conceit was repelled by their simplicity, and I had not the mind to penetrate into their depths. They were indeed of a nature to grow in Your little ones.[2] But I could not bear to be a little one; I was only swollen with pride, but to myself I seemed a very big man. * * *

FROM BOOK VI

[Worldly Ambitions]

By this time my mother had come to me, following me over sea and land with the courage of piety and relying upon You in all perils. For they were in danger from a storm, and she reassured even the sailors—by whom travelers

---

8. Or *eversores* (Latin), a group of students who prided themselves on their wild actions and lack of discipline.   9. Style.   1. Only fragments of this dialogue remain. In it Cicero replies to an opponent of philosophy with an impassioned defense of the intellectual life.   2. Refers not only to the rhetorical simplicity of Jesus' teachings but also to his interest in teaching children; compare Matthew 19.14: "For of such is the kingdom of heaven."

newly ventured upon the deep are ordinarily reassured—promising them safe arrival because thus You had promised her in a vision. She found me in a perilous state through my deep despair of ever discovering the truth. But even when I told her that if I was not yet a Catholic Christian, I was no longer a Manichean,[3] she was not greatly exultant as at some unlooked-for good news, because she had already received assurance upon that part of my misery; she bewailed me as one dead certainly, but certainly to be raised again by You, offering me in her mind as one stretched out dead, that You might say to the widow's son: *"Young man, I say to thee arise"*:[4] and he should sit up and begin to speak and You should give him to his mother.

*   *   *

Nor did I then groan in prayer for Your help. My mind was intent upon inquiry and unquiet for argumentation. I regarded Ambrose[5] as a lucky man by worldly standards to be held in honor by such important people: only his celibacy seemed to me a heavy burden. I had no means of guessing, and no experience of my own to learn from, what hope he bore within him, what struggles he might have against the temptations that went with his high place, what was his consolation in adversity, and on what joys of Your bread the hidden mouth of his heart fed. Nor did he know how I was inflamed nor the depth of my peril. I could not ask of him what I wished as I wished, for I was kept from any face to face conversation with him by the throng of men with their own troubles, whose infirmities he served. The very little time he was not with these he was refreshing either his body with necessary food or his mind with reading. When he read, his eyes traveled across the page and his heart sought into the sense, but voice and tongue were silent. No one was forbidden to approach him nor was it his custom to require that visitors should be announced: but when we came into him we often saw him reading and always to himself; and after we had sat long in silence, unwilling to interrupt a work on which he was so intent, we would depart again. We guessed that in the small time he could find for the refreshment of his mind, he would wish to be free from the distraction of other men's affairs and not called away from what he was doing. Perhaps he was on his guard lest [if he read aloud] someone listening should be troubled and want an explanation if the author he was reading expressed some idea over-obscurely, and it might be necessary to expound or discuss some of the more difficult questions. And if he had to spend time on this, he would get through less reading than he wished. Or it may be that his real reason for reading to himself was to preserve his voice, which did in fact readily grow tired. But whatever his reason for doing it, that man certainly had a good reason.

*   *   *

3. Augustine had for nine years been a member of this religious sect, which followed the teaching of the Babylonian mystic Mani (216–277). The Manicheans believed that the world was a battleground for the forces of good and evil; redemption in a future life would come to the elect, who renounced worldly occupations and possessions and practiced a severe asceticism (including abstention from meat). Augustine's mother, Monica, was a Christian, and lamented her son's Manichean beliefs.   **4.** Luke 7.14, recounting one of Christ's miracles.   **5.** The leading personality among the Christians of the West; not many years after this he defied the power of Emperor Theodosius and forced him to beg for God's pardon in the church at Milan for having put the inhabitants of Thessalonica to the sword.

I was all hot for honors, money, marriage: and You made mock of my hotness. In my pursuit of these, I suffered most bitter disappointments, but in this You were good to me since I was thus prevented from taking delight in anything not Yourself. Look now into my heart, Lord, by whose will I remember all this and confess it to You. Let my soul cleave to You now that You have freed it from the tenacious hold of death. At that time my soul was in misery, and You pricked the soreness of its wound, that leaving all things it might turn to You, who are over all and without whom all would return to nothing, that it might turn to You and be healed. I was in utter misery and there was one day especially on which You acted to bring home to me the realization of my misery. I was preparing an oration in praise of the Emperor[6] in which I was to utter any number of lies to win the applause of people who knew they were lies. My heart was much wrought upon by the shame of this and inflamed with the fever of the thoughts that consumed it. I was passing along a certain street in Milan when I noticed a beggar. He was jesting and laughing and I imagine more than a little drunk. I fell into gloom and spoke to the friends who were with me about the endless sorrows that our own insanity brings us: for here was I striving away, dragging the load of my unhappiness under the spurring of my desires, and making it worse by dragging it: and with all our striving, our one aim was to arrive at some sort of happiness without care: the beggar had reached the same goal before us, and we might quite well never reach it at all. The very thing that he had attained by means of a few pennies begged from passers-by—namely the pleasure of a temporary happiness—I was plotting for with so many a weary twist and turn.

Certainly his joy was no true joy; but the joy I sought in my ambition was emptier still. In any event he was cheerful and I worried, he had no cares and I nothing but cares. Now if anyone had asked me whether I would rather be cheerful or fearful, I would answer: "Cheerful"; but if he had gone on to ask whether I would rather be like that beggar or as I actually was, I would certainly have chosen my own state though so troubled and anxious. Now this was surely absurd. It could not be for any true reason. I ought not to have preferred my own state rather than his merely because I was the more learned, since I got no joy from my learning, but sought only to please men by it—not even to teach them, only to please them. Therefore did You break my bones with the rod of Your discipline.

* * *

Great effort was made to get me married. I proposed, the girl was promised me. My mother played a great part in the matter for she wanted to have me married and then cleansed with the saving waters of baptism,[7] rejoicing to see me grow every day more fitted for baptism and feeling that her prayers and Your promises were to be fulfilled in my faith. By my request and her own desire she begged You daily with the uttermost intensity of her heart to show her in a vision something of my future marriage, but You would never do it. She did indeed see certain vain fantasies, under the pressure of her mind's preoccupation with the matter; and she told them to me, not, how-

6. Probably the young Valentinian, whose court was at Milan.   7. He could not be baptized while living in sin with his mistress, a liaison that resulted in the birth of a son, Adeodatus, who later accompanied Augustine to Italy.

ever, with the confidence she always had when You had shown things to her, but as if she set small store by them; for she said that there was a certain unanalyzable savor, not to be expressed in words, by which she could distinguish between what You revealed and the dreams of her own spirit. Still she pushed on with the matter of my marriage, and the girl was asked for. She was still two years short of the age for marriage[8] but I liked her and agreed to wait.

There was a group of us friends who had much serious discussion together, concerning the cares and troubles of human life which we found so hard to endure. We had almost decided to seek a life of peace, away from the throng of men. This peace we hoped to attain by putting together whatever we could manage to get, and making one common household for all of us: so that in the clear trust of friendship, things should not belong to this or that individual, but one thing should be made of all our possessions, and belong wholly to each one of us, and everybody own everything. It seemed that there might be perhaps ten men in this fellowship. Among us there were some very rich men, especially Romanianus, our fellow townsman, who had been a close friend of mine from childhood and had been brought to the court in Milan by the press of some very urgent business. He was strongest of all for the idea and he had considerable influence in persuasion because his wealth was much greater than anyone else's. We agreed that two officers should be chosen every year to handle the details of our life together, leaving the rest undisturbed. But then we began to wonder whether our wives would agree, for some of us already had wives and I meant to have one. So the whole plan, which we had built up so neatly, fell to pieces in our hands and was simply dropped. We returned to our old sighing and groaning and treading of this world's broad and beaten ways:[9] for many thoughts were in our hearts, but *Thy counsel standeth forever.* And out of Thy counsel didst Thou deride ours and didst prepare Thine own things for us, meaning to *give us meat in due season and to open Thy hands and fill our souls with Thy blessing.*

Meanwhile my sins were multiplied. She with whom I had lived so long was torn from my side as a hindrance to my forthcoming marriage. My heart which had held her very dear was broken and wounded and shed blood. She went back to Africa, swearing that she would never know another man, and left with me the natural son I had had of her. But I in my unhappiness could not, for all my manhood, imitate her resolve. I was unable to bear the delay of two years which must pass before I was to get the girl I had asked for in marriage. In fact it was not really marriage that I wanted. I was simply a slave to lust. So I took another woman, not of course as a wife; and thus my soul's disease was nourished and kept alive as vigorously as ever, indeed worse than ever, that it might reach the realm of matrimony in the company of its ancient habit. Nor was the wound healed that had been made by the cutting off of my former mistress. For there was first burning and bitter grief; and after that it festered, and as the pain grew duller it only grew more hopeless. * * *

---

8. The legal age was twelve years; Augustine was in his early thirties.   9. Compare Matthew 7.13: "Broad is the way that leadeth to destruction," that is, to damnation.

FROM BOOK VIII

[*Conversion*]

* * * Thus I was sick at heart and in torment, accusing myself with a new intensity of bitterness, twisting and turning in my chain in the hope that it might be utterly broken, for what held me was so small a thing! But it still held me. And You stood in the secret places of my soul, O Lord, in the harshness of Your mercy redoubling the scourges of fear and shame lest I should give way again and that small slight tie which remained should not be broken but should grow again to full strength and bind me closer even than before. For I kept saying within myself: "Let it be now, let it be now," and by the mere words I had begun to move toward the resolution. I almost made it, yet I did not quite make it. But I did not fall back into my original state, but as it were stood near to get my breath. And I tried again and I was almost there, and now I could all but touch it and hold it: yet I was not quite there, I did not touch it or hold it. I still shrank from dying unto death and living unto life. The lower condition which had grown habitual was more powerful than the better condition which I had not tried. The nearer the point of time came in which I was to become different, the more it struck me with horror; but it did not force me utterly back nor turn me utterly away, but held me there between the two.

Those trifles of all trifles, and vanities of vanities, my one-time mistresses, held me back, plucking at my garment of flesh and murmuring softly: "Are you sending us away?" And "From this moment shall we not be with you, now or forever?" And "From this moment shall this or that not be allowed you, now or forever?" What were they suggesting to me in the phrase I have written "this or that," what were they suggesting to me, O my God? Do you in your mercy keep from the soul of Your servant the vileness and uncleanness they were suggesting. And now I began to hear them not half so loud; they no longer stood against me face to face, but were softly muttering behind my back and, as I tried to depart, plucking stealthily at me to make me look behind. Yet even that was enough, so hesitating was I, to keep me from snatching myself free, from shaking them off and leaping upwards on the way I was called: for the strong force of habit said to me: "Do you think you can live without them?"

But by this time its voice was growing fainter. In the direction toward which I had turned my face and was quivering in fear of going, I could see the austere beauty of Continence, serene and indeed joyous but not evilly, honorably soliciting me to come to her and not linger, stretching forth loving hands to receive and embrace me, hands full of multitudes of good examples. With her I saw such hosts of young men and maidens, a multitude of youth and of every age, gray widows and women grown old in virginity, and in them all Continence herself, not barren but the fruitful mother of children, her joys, by You, Lord, her Spouse. And she smiled upon me and her smile gave courage as if she were saying: "Can you not do what these men have done, what these women have done? Or could men or women have done such in themselves, and not in the Lord their God? The Lord their God gave me to them. Why do you stand upon yourself and so not stand at all? Cast yourself upon Him and be not afraid; He will not draw away and let you fall. Cast yourself without fear, He will receive you and heal you."

Yet I was still ashamed, for I could still hear the murmuring of those vanities, and I still hung hesitant. And again it was as if she said: "Stop your ears against your unclean members, that they may be mortified. They tell you of delights, but not of such delights as the law of the Lord your God tells." This was the controversy raging in my heart, a controversy about myself against myself. And Alypius[1] stayed by my side and awaited in silence the issue of such agitation as he had never seen in me.

When my most searching scrutiny had drawn up all my vileness from the secret depths of my soul and heaped it in my heart's sight, a mighty storm arose in me, bringing a mighty rain of tears. That I might give way to my tears and lamentations, I rose from Alypius: for it struck me that solitude was more suited to the business of weeping. I went far enough from him to prevent his presence from being an embarrassment to me. So I felt, and he realized it. I suppose I had said something and the sound of my voice was heavy with tears. I arose, but he remained where we had been sitting, still in utter amazement. I flung myself down somehow under a certain fig tree and no longer tried to check my tears, which poured forth from my eyes in a flood, *an acceptable sacrifice to Thee.* And much I said not in these words but to this effect: *"And Thou, O Lord, how long? How long, Lord; wilt Thou be angry forever? Remember not our former iniquities."*[2] For I felt that I was still bound by them. And I continued my miserable complaining: "How long, how long shall I go on saying tomorrow and again tomorrow? Why not now, why not have an end to my uncleanness this very hour?"

Such things I said, weeping in the most bitter sorrow of my heart. And suddenly I heard a voice from some nearby house, a boy's voice or a girl's voice, I do not know: but it was a sort of singsong, repeated again and again. "Take and read, take and read." I ceased weeping and immediately began to search my mind most carefully as to whether children were accustomed to chant these words in any kind of game, and I could not remember that I had ever heard any such thing. Damming back the flood of my tears I arose, interpreting the incident as quite certainly a divine command to open my book of Scripture and read the passage at which I should open. For it was part of what I had been told about Anthony,[3] that from the Gospel which he happened to be reading he had felt that he was being admonished as though what he read was spoken directly to himself: *Go, sell what thou hast and give to the poor and thou shalt have treasure in heaven; and come follow Me.*[4] By this experience he had been in that instant converted to You. So I was moved to return to the place where Alypius was sitting, for I had put down the Apostle's[5] book there when I arose. I snatched it up, opened it and in silence read the passage upon which my eyes first fell: *Not in rioting and drunkenness, not in chambering and impurities, not in contention and envy, but put ye on the Lord Jesus Christ and make not provision for the flesh in its concupiscences.* [Romans 13.13.] I had no wish to read further, and no need. For in that instant, with the very ending of the sentence, it was as though a light of utter confidence shone in all my heart, and all the darkness of uncertainty

---

1. A student of Augustine's at Carthage; he had joined the Manichees with Augustine, followed him to Rome and Milan, and now shared his desires and doubts. Alypius finally became a bishop in North Africa. 2. Compare Psalm 7.5–8; Augustine compares his spiritual despair with that of captive and subjected Israel.   3. The Egyptian saint whose abstinence and self-control are still proverbial; he was one of the founders of the system of monastic life.   4. Luke 18.22.   5. Paul.

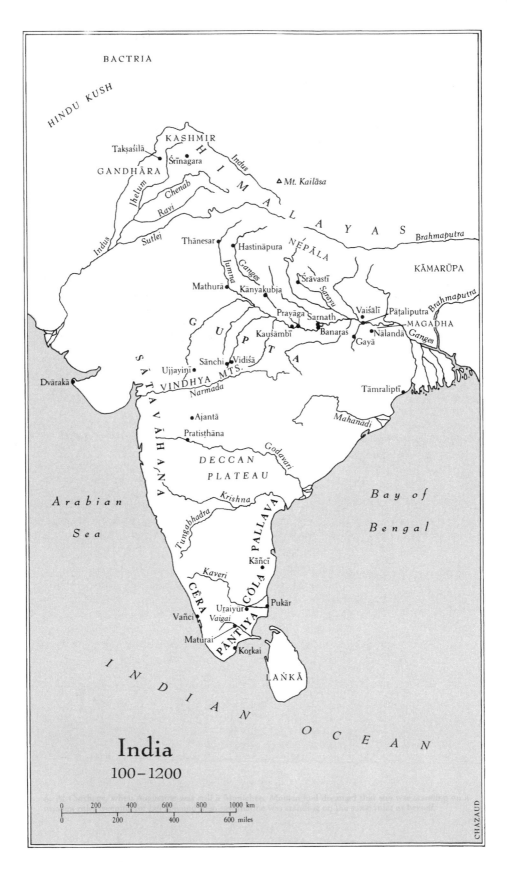

BACTRIA

HINDU KUSH

KASHMIR

Takṣaśilā
GANDHĀRA
Śrīnagara

HIMALAYAS

Indus
△ Mt. Kailāsa

Jhelum
Chenab
Ravi

Indus

Sutlej

Thānesar
Hastināpura
NĒPĀLA
Brahmaputra

KĀMARŪPA

Jumna
Ganges
Śrāvastī

Mathurā
Kānyakubja
Sarayu

Prayāga Sarnath
Vaiśālī
Pāṭaliputra
Brahmaputra

G
Kauśāmbī
Banaras
MAGADHA

U
Gayā
Nālanda
Ganges

P

Sānchi
Vidiśā
Ujjayinī

T

Dvārakā

S
Ā
T
A
V
Ā
H
A
N
A

VINDHYA MTS.
Narmada

A

Tāmraliptī

Ajantā

Pratiṣṭhāna

Mahanadi

DECCAN
PLATEAU

Godavari

Arabian

Sea

Krishna

Tungabhadra

PALLAVA

Bay of

Bengal

Kāñcī

Kaveri
CŌLA

CĒRA
Uraiyūr
Pukār

Vañci
Vaigai

Maturai
PĀNTIYA
Korkai

LAŃKĀ

INDIAN

OCEAN

India
100–1200

0   200   400   600   800   1000 km
0   200   400   600 miles

CHAZAUD

India's Classical Age

The classical literature of India had its great flowering under the Guptas, who ruled over much of India from their north Indian capitals in Pāṭaliputra (modern Patna) and Ujjayinī (modern Ujjain) between 335 and 470. During the Gupta era Ujjayinī in the west and the seaport Tāmraliptī in the east were centers of a flourishing trade with Rome, China, and Southeast Asia. While Indian merchants voyaged on the seas to Java and other islands in the Indonesian archipelago, Chinese pilgrims traveled to the holy sites of Buddhism in the land of its birth. Ancient India's greatest achievements in mathematics, logic, and astronomy as well as in literature and the fine arts were made in this prosperous, cosmopolitan milieu, and the classical ideals expressed in the masterworks of the Gupta period continued to be influential well into the twelfth century and later.

Gupta classicism was closely connected with the development of Sanskrit as a literary language. *Saṃskṛta*, the very name of the language, means "perfected, classified, refined." Already by the end of the heroic age the veneration of the Vedic hymns had led to the ideal of Sanskrit as "correct speech," a speech that was fully codified and frozen in the *Aṣṭādhyāyī* (The book of eight chapters [of the rules of grammar]) of Pāṇini, a pioneer in the science of linguistics. In the Indian view, Sanskrit's nature as a code and construct made it the ideal language for the classics, in contrast to the Prakrit (*prākṛta*, meaning "original" or "natural") dialects that were allowed to change and develop in the manner of "natural," spoken languages.

The Prakrit literature that developed around the second century was soon absorbed into the Sanskrit classical tradition. Until the development of the south Indian regional languages in the tenth and eleventh centuries, Tamil alone continued to nourish a classical tradition that was distinct from that of Sanskrit, in spite of the many features absorbed into Tamil civilization from centuries of interaction with Indo-Aryan culture and literature. The fifth-century *Cilappatikāram* (The poem of the anklet) is the oldest extant epic in Tamil. This classical poem, written at the court of a Cēra king, bears no resemblance whatsoever to the Indo-Aryan epics, although its author, Iḷaṅkōvaṭikaḷ, was a Jaina monk and the Tamil folk narrative on which the epic is based is heavily overlaid with Jaina doctrine.

Classical Sanskrit literature is permeated with the culture of the courts of ancient India. Learned poets (*kavi*) wrote poetry under the patronage of kings and recited their works at court for audiences of connoisseurs, known as *sahṛdaya* ("with heart," or responsive) or *rasika* ("enjoyer of aesthetic mood"). Whatever their specific subject matter, only works whose primary aim was to evoke an aesthetic response were admitted into the classical literary canon, and such works were called *kāvya*, "poetry" in the broadest sense of the word—that is, literature as art. *Kāvya* literature is governed by meticulously formulated norms and conventions that circumscribe the poet's freedom, at the same time putting at his or her disposal a rich array of traditional poetic means, along with the opportunity to refine on the achievements of the past.

The court epic, drama, short lyric, and narrative are the major genres of *kāvya*. The first of these, the *mahākāvya* ("great poem," or court epic), grew out of the older epics and bardic praise poems and treats the martial exploits of kings, warriors, and gods. Unlike the older narrative epics, however, the *kāvya* epics are made up of lyric stanzas, with elaborate figures of speech and a descriptive emphasis. The drama, or *nāṭya* (exemplified in plays: *rūpaka*, "representation"), is a more heterogeneous genre, employing prose and verse, in Sanskrit and Prakrit, and a somewhat wider range of characters than the court epic. In classical plays the warrior-king is portrayed as a romantic hero, and here, too, lyrical description dominates over dramatic action.

The short lyric poem (*muktaka*, "detached verse") is the quintessential genre of classical Sanskrit poetry. Sanskrit poets achieved their finest and most characteristic effects in poems of a single stanza divided into "quarters" (*pāda*), normally of equal length. The brevity of the form (the longest *kāvya* meter has only twenty-one syllables per verse quarter) combined with the complexities of the Sanskrit language and the rules of *kāvya* poetry results in miniature poems that are at once complex and extraordinarily compact, similar in effect to the miniature paintings produced at Indian courts in the seventeenth and eighteenth centuries. The *muktaka* genre encompasses the trenchant epigrams of Bhartṛhari as well as the erotic vignettes of Amaru. Designated *subhāṣita* ("well-wrought verse"), the best stanzas of the classical poets—both men and women—were anthologized in such collections as the eleventh-century *Subhāṣitaratnakoṣa* (A treasury of well-wrought verse), to be memorized, recited, and savored by connoisseurs. Such poets as Bhartṛhari and Amaru, who specialized in particular themes, earned their own anthologies, organized into "centuries [of stanzas]," or *śataka*, perhaps on the model of earlier anthologies of Tamil and Prakrit lyric poetry.

From the earliest times India has been a vast storehouse of tales, many of which have traveled all over the world. Among the most widely known works in the narrative genre known as *kathā* or *ākhyāyikā* ("story") is the *Pañcatantra*, a Gupta-period collection of animal fables. The most popular of the later *kāvya* tale collections, however, is the Kashmirian poet Somadeva's eleventh-century *Kathāsaritsāgara* (Ocean to the rivers of story), a compendium in narrative verse of picaresque tales, tales of the marvelous, and romances. With its gentle but pointed satire of ancient Indian society and manners and its array of vivid, earthy characters, Sanskrit story literature presents a marked contrast to the sober elegance of the other *kāvya* genres.

The practice of *kāvya* literature seems always to have been correlated with an influential body of works on poetics. The first major work devoted solely to poetic theory is the seventh-century *Kāvyādarśa* (Mirror for poetry), in which the south Indian writer on poetic theory Daṇḍin systematically discusses the figures of speech (*alaṃkāra*, literally "ornament") that differentiate poetry from ordinary discourse. An earlier concept, *rasa* or "aesthetic mood," remained the dominant theoretical framework for the aesthetics of drama and also influenced the criticism of the other *kāvya* genres. Finally, in the ninth century, the master critic Ānandavardhana expounded in his *Dhvanyāloka* (Light of suggestion) the aesthetic ideal of *dhvani* ("poetic suggestion"; literally, "resonance") as the measure of the best kind of poetry in all the forms of *kāvya*. Besides poetic theory *kāvya* texts are keyed to technical treatises (*śāstra* or *sūtra*) in every branch of classical learning, ranging from Pāṇini's grammar and Vātsyāyana's *Kāmasūtra* (Treatise on erotics) to the *Dharmaśāstrara* of Manu (Manu's treatise on the religious law) and the *Arthaśāstra,* Kauṭilya's influential text on politics.

Reflecting the conservative values of courtly and learned elites, the masterworks of *kāvya* carry forward the idealization of *dharma* (religious duty), the first of the four aims of human endeavor enjoined for Hindu men and a seminal theme in the major texts of the heroic age, such as the *Rāmāyaṇa* and the *Bhagavad-Gītā*. In the classical texts, however, the concern with religious duty is offset by a more direct preoccupation with *artha* (wealth, politics, public life) and *kāma* (the realm of erotic pleasure and the emotions), the second and third aims, and their vision is of a life in which all four goals of action are harmoniously balanced. Like earlier epic heroes such as Arjuna and Rāma, the exemplary warriors and kings of the courtly literature combine sagelike self-control with more active, worldly, heroic traits, for in Hindu belief austerity is an essential means by which a person may attain the ultimate goal of life—liberation (*mokṣa*) from the chain of birth and death in which souls are trapped because of the results of good and bad action (*karma*).

The philosophy of *karma*-rebirth implies fluid relationships among the human, animal, and divine worlds. In a universe where a king might be a divine incarnation, a god come down to earth (*avatāra*, "descent"), sages and holy people, who have amassed superhuman powers by exercising extraordinary self-control, represent the possibility of the ascent of human beings to godlike states; hence the great respect given to these gods-on-earth. As keepers of both sacred and secular learning, members of the brahman class, the highest of the four classes of Hindu society and the class to which most of the classical poets belonged, are naturally portrayed in a most favorable light in the works of the classical era. Certain genres, however, were allowed the privilege of satire and critique. The "Fool" of the Sanskrit drama is a dull-witted, gluttonous brahman; the story literature is full of corrupt monks and less-than-perfect religious figures; and the animal fables of the *Pañcatantra* offer an unvarnished picture of courtly intrigue.

Śakuntalā, the heroine of Kālidāsa's celebrated play *Śakuntala* (fourth century), a representative *kāvya* classic, reinforces the image of the ideal Hindu wife, a role already exemplified in the personality of the long-suffering Sītā in the *Rāmāyaṇa*. The indispensability of marriage for women in Hindu society, and their near-total dependence on the will of their husbands, dominates even this work with its explicit focus on the erotic aspect of gender relations. In the course of the play, Śakuntalā matures from a naive girl into the ideal wife: chaste, loyal, submissive, and willing to bear suffering patiently. However, the classical literature offers very different images of women as well. The Tamil epic *Cilappatikāram* portrays Kaṇṇaki as a woman whose chastity endows her with independent agency and superhuman power. Chaste though they may be, there is nothing submissive about the women of the Sanskrit story literature, a literature of the merchant-class milieu. Women are as often likely to be the protagonists of these stories as men, and they surpass men—very often, their own husbands—in wit, wisdom, resourcefulness, and the ability to act.

The hierarchy of gender roles is often reversed in the Sanskrit erotic lyrics, which also challenge the normative emphasis on female chastity by their sympathetic treatment of extramarital love. In the spectrum of female figures in classical literature, the courtesan, whose skill in the arts enables her to earn her own living and dispense with marriage, stands at the opposite end from the chaste wife. The courtesans of Sanskrit and Tamil literature are beautiful, intelligent, ruthless, and rapacious women; but there are also sympathetic potraits. Finally, in such characters as the female hermit Gautamī in *Śakuntala*, we have exemplars of women who, as religious contemplatives, are figures of authority and free agents on a par with their male counterparts.

The lives of many *kāvya* poets are shrouded in myth and legend. Likewise, the identities of the royal patrons of early *kāvya*, except in the odd case, remain a matter for speculation. *Kāvya* is a poetry of universals and ideals, and its heroes and heroines are, by and large, types, not individuals. The early epic poetry, too, idealized and universalized its heroes. Whether the hero is a king, merchant, or brahman, and regardless of his distinctive virtues, the ideal personage of the classical literature must possess—to a greater or lesser degree—the generalized qualities of a *nāgaraka*, "citizen" or "courtier," the cultivated person of the courtly civilization. So, too, must the ideal *kāvya* heroine—whether she is a courtesan or a chaste wife—be beautiful and refined in the courtly manner.

Vātsyāyana devotes the opening section of the *Kāmasūtra* to the qualifications of the *nāgaraka* and his female counterpart. The gentleman is enjoined to equip

TIME LINE

TEXTS	CONTEXTS
ca. 2nd century The Sanskrit *Nāṭyaśāstra* of Bharata, the authoritative work on drama, poetry, and aesthetics, is completed	
2nd or 3rd century Viṣṇuśarman completes the Sanskrit animal tale collection **Pañcatantra**	
	335–470 The reign of the Gupta emperors in north India, an age of great achievement in arts, letters, science, international trade, and conquest • Indian civilization spreads to Southeast Asia
ca. 375–425 Kālidāsa, preeminent poet of the Gupta age, writes the play *Śākuntala* and other works in Sanskrit	
5th century The Sanskrit epigrams of Bhartṛhari are collected in the *śatakatrayam* (The anthology of three centuries)	
ca. 400–500 Tiruvaḷḷuvar composes the Tamil *Tirukkuṟaḷ*, a collection of ethical aphorisms • Vātsyāyana writes the Sanskrit *Kāmasūtra*, the authoritative treatise on the science of erotics	**ca. 400–500** A great Buddhist monastery and university are founded in Nālandā in eastern India
	454 The Huns invade India
late 5th century The Jaina monk Iḷaṅkōvaṭikaḷ writes the *Cilappatikāram* (The poem of the anklet), an epic poem in Tamil concerning the heroic deeds and apotheosis of the chaste wife Kaṇṇaki	
7th century *Amaruśataka*	
600–700 The poet-leaders of the south Indian devotional (*bhakti*) movements dedicated to the god Śiva compose Tamil hymns praising the god	**ca. 600–800** Pallava rulers of Kanchipuram in south India patronize populist religious movements and poetry in the Tamil language
	629–645 Chinese Buddhist pilgrim Hsuan-tsang visits India

Boldface titles indicate works in the anthology.

TIME LINE

TEXTS	CONTEXTS
	ca. 711–715 Arabs conquer the province of Sind in western India, bringing Islam to the region
ca. 800 Hindu philosopher Śaṅkara writes commentaries on the *Upaniṣads* and the ***Bhagavad-Gītā***	
900–1000 Māṇikkavācakar, preeminent devotional poet of south India, writes the *Tiruvācakam* (Sacred utterance), a sequence of hymns to the Hindu god Śiva, in Tamil • The *Bhāgavata Purāṇa*, the Sanskrit sacred narrative (*purāṇa*) of the life and deeds of the god Krishna, is completed	
11th century Somadeva writes the Sanskrit compendium of stories called ***Kathāsaritsāgara*** (Ocean to the rivers of story) for Queen Sūryamatī of Kashmir	**1000** The Cōḻa king Rajaraja I builds a great temple for the Hindu god Śiva at Tanjore in south India
12th century Kampaṉ authors the *Irāmāvatāram*, a version of the ***Rāmāyaṇa*** epic in Tamil • The Buddhist monk Vidyākara of Bengal (in eastern India) compiles the *Subhāṣitaratnakoṣa* (Treasury of well-turned verse), an anthology of Sanskrit lyric poems • Cēkkiḻār completes the *Periyapurāṇam* (The great sacred history), a long poem on the lives of the Tamil saints who are devotees of Śiva • Jayadeva composes the Sanskrit lyric-dramatic poem *Gītagovinda* in Bengal, on Krishna's love for the herdswoman Rādhā, the central theme of later poetry about Krishna	**ca. 1100–1200** Buddhist monuments are built at Angkor Wat in Cambodia
	ca. 1193 Turkish warrior Qutb-ud-din Aibak captures the city of Delhi, initiating a period of several centuries of rule in north India by Delhi-based Muslim kings

VIṢṆUŚARMAN
second or third century

The *Pañcatantra* (The five books *or* The five strategies), attributed to Viṣṇuśarman, is the best-known collection of folktales and animal fables in Indian literature. A Gupta-period work in the ornate classical *kāvya* style, the *Pañcatantra* went through many subsequent revisions. Translated into old Persian as early as the mid-seventh century and brought by the Arabs to Europe in the eighth, it is also the source of some of the best-known tales in Middle Eastern and European collections such as the *Thousand and One Nights*, the *Decameron*, the *Canterbury Tales*, Grimm's *Fairy Tales*, and the fables of La Fontaine and Aesop.

The *Pañcatantra*'s central concern is *nīti* ("conduct"), a term connoting a range of explicitly worldly values, most important among which are political expediency and social advantage. The work's prologue, in which we are told that the brahman scholar Viṣṇuśarman used the fables as a strategy to teach the science of politics to three dull-witted princes, affirms its affiliation with the world of kings and policymakers.

Each of the five books of the *Pañcatantra* begins with a frame story, whose characters tell each other stories illustrating the conduct appropriate to diverse social and political situations. The characters within these illustrative tales tell each other stories as well, and so on, until the nested tales eventually lead back to the frame story. The *Pañcatantra* is most probably the source from which the author of the *Thousand and One Nights* adopted the device of the emboxed story, which was eventually incorporated into the European tale collections, although it is in the *Pañcatantra*—and in classical Indian narrative literature in general—that the technique is found at its most complex. As in the Buddhist *Jātaka* tales, each tale in the *Pañcatantra* begins with a narrator reciting an epigrammatic verse that at once summarizes the tale's lesson and points to its subject matter, thus arousing the listener's curiosity. Stylistically, however, the ornate classical prose and elegant *kāvya* stanzas of the *Pañcatantra* are a far cry from the simpler Pali *Jātakas*.

While it is not certain that the *Pañcatantra*'s author intended it, the word *tantra* in the work's title can mean "strategy" as well as "book." The main themes of the *Pañcatantra* are reflected in the titles of its five books; and at least in the case of the first four books, the book's main topic corresponds to one of the topics in the *Arthaśāstra* (Manual of political theory), the preeminent Gupta period treatise on political science. The frame narrative of Book I (*The Loss of Friends*) traces the sowing of dissension between the lion Rusty (Piṅgalaka), king of the beasts, and the mighty bull Lively (Saṃjīvaka), by the former's crafty counselors, the jackals Cheek (Karaṭaka) and Victor (Damanaka). Book II (*The Winning of Friends*) concerns the successful course of friendship among four animals of the forest. Book III (*Crows and Owls*) treats the war between the owls and crows, sworn enemies of each other. The processes by which the animals in these books make friends (*mitra*) and enemies (*para*) closely resemble the strategies of alliance and war Kauṭilya delineates for ancient Indian kings. Books IV and V (*Loss of Gains* and *Ill-Considered Action*) are more broadly concerned with strategies for worldly success.

Among the most appealing features of the *Pañcatantra* is its humorous and faithful portrayal of human nature in all its variety. As in other cultures, the animals of village and forest are assigned stereotypical human traits. Thus the lion, king of animals, is powerful and proud but easily duped; the jackal, like the European fox, is cunning and deceitful; the cat is a hypocrite. Charmingly appropriate names alert the reader to the salient traits of each animal character: the bull of the frame story of Book I is called Lively; the sage of the mouse-maid tale is Godly; and three temperamentally differentiated fish are Forethought, Readywit, and Fatalist.

The *Pañcatantra* bases its counsel on the premises that social life is both necessary and inevitable and that we must make the best of our condition as social beings. Unlike the epics, the animal stories teach not the Hindu ideals of behavior according to the code of *dharma,* but *nīti,* which, as noted earlier, broadly connotes worldly wisdom and the art of living in the world. The *Pañcatantra* views friendship properly contracted, maintained, and used as the sine qua non of social life, but it does not idealize friendship. The world of these stories is a cruel place in which the strong oppress those weaker than themselves, and yet the weak not only survive but triumph over adversity, provided they are intelligent, find the right allies, and have the will and ability to act.

The *Pañcatantra* stories do not offer simple solutions to life's dilemmas. To act wisely, one must exercise discrimination and judgment. Treachery awaits the unwary at every turn, and those who are gullible perish, but paranoia is equally dangerous, as the brahman's wife learns after she has killed the innocent mongoose (in "The Loyal Mungoose"). In her decision to stick to her own kind Mouse-Maid (in "Mouse-Maid Made Mouse") is motivated by a desire for emotional as well as social security in a hierarchically organized, minutely differentiated society. On the other hand, Creep the louse's friendship with Leap the flea ("Leap and Creep") is doomed to disaster as much because of Creep's trusting a fool as her stepping over social boundaries. Indeed, the frame story of Book II, featuring the felicitous friendship of four such unlikely animals as a deer, a turtle, a mouse, and a crow, demonstrates that some difference is essential to really fruitful alliances. Then again, the whole of Book III (*Crows and Owls*) is devoted to the theme of unending strife between those who are "natural" enemies, such as owls and crows and the snake and the mongoose. The enduring popularity of the *Pañcatantra* animal stories—at home and abroad—is due at least in part to their complex mix of realism and optimism and their essentially pluralistic vision of social relations.

PRONOUNCING GLOSSARY

The following list uses common English syllables and stress accents to provide rough equivalents of selected words whose pronunciation may be unfamiliar to the general reader.

Arthaśāstra: *uhrt-huh-shahs'-truh*

Bṛhatkathā: *bree-huht'-kuht-hah*

Damanaka: *duh-muh'-nuh-kuh*

Hitopadeśa: *hee-toh-puh-day'-shuh*

Jātaka: *jah'-tuh-kuh*

Karaṭaka: *kuh-ruh'-tuh-kuh*

Kathāsaritsāgara: *kuht-hah'-suh-reet-sah'-guh-ruh*

Kauṭilya: *kow-teel'-yuh*

Mūladeva: *moo'-luh-day'-vuh*

Nārāyaṇa: *nah-rah'-yuh-nuh*

Pañcatantra: *puhn'-chuh-tuhn'-truh*

Piṅgalaka: *peen'-guh-luh-kuh*

Saṃjīvaka: *suhn-jee'-vuh-kuh*

Viṣṇuśarman: *veesh'-noo-shuhr'-muhn*

Yājñavalkya: *yahg-nyuh-vuhl'-kyuh*

FROM PAÑCATANTRA[1]

From *Book I*

The Loss of Friends

* * *

"With no stranger share your house;
Leap, the flea, killed Creep, the louse."

"How was that?" asked Rusty. And Victor[2] told the story of

LEAP AND CREEP

In the palace of a certain king stood an incomparable bed, blessed with every cubiculary virtue. In a corner of its coverlet lived a female louse named Creep. Surrounded by a thriving family of sons and daughters, with the sons and daughters of sons and daughters, and with more remote descendants, she drank the king's blood as he slept. On this diet she grew plump and handsome.

While she was living there in this manner, a flea named Leap drifted in on the wind and dropped on the bed. This flea felt supreme satisfaction on examining the bed—the wonderful delicacy of its coverlet, its double pillow, its exceptional softness like that of a broad, Gangetic sand-bank, its delicious perfume.[3] Charmed by the sheer delight of touching it, he hopped this way and that until—fate willed it so—he chanced to meet Creep, who said to him: "Where do *you* come from? This is a dwelling fit for a king. Begone, and lose no time about it." "Madam," said he, "you should not say such things. For

The Brahman reverences fire,[4]
Himself the lower castes' desire;
The wife reveres her husband dear;
But all the world must guests revere.

Now I am your guest. I have of late sampled the various blood of Brahmans, warriors, business men, and serfs, but found it acid, slimy, quite unwholesome. On the contrary, he who reposes on this bed must have a delightful vital fluid, just like nectar. It must be free from morbidity, since wind, bile, and phlegm are kept in harmony by constant and heedful use of potions prepared by physicians. It must be enriched by viands unctuous, tender, melting in the mouth; viands prepared from the flesh of the choicest creatures of land, water, and air, seasoned furthermore with sugar, pomegranate, ginger, and pepper. To me it seems an elixir of life. Therefore, with your kind permission, I plan to taste this sweet and fragrant substance, thus combining pleasure and profit."

"No," said she. "For fiery-mouthed stingers like you, it is out of the question. Leave this bed. You know the proverb:

---

1. Translated by Arthur W. Ryder. 2. In the principal frame narrative of Book I, Victor the jackal tells this story to Rusty the lion. 3. This is a parody of the involved style of description found in the more ornate classical *kāvya* poems. "Gangetic": of the Ganges River. 4. Refers to the sacred fire of Hindu ritual.

> The fool who does not know
> His own resource, his foe,
> His duty, time, and place,
> Who sets a reckless pace,
> Will by the wayside fall,
> Will reap no fruit at all."

Thereupon he fell at her feet, repeating his request. And she agreed, since courtesy was her hobby, and since, when the story of that prince of sharpers, Muladeva,[5] was being repeated to the king while she lay on a corner of the coverlet, she had heard how Muladeva quoted this verse in answer to the question of a certain damsel:

> Whoever, angry though he be,
> Has spurned a suppliant enemy,
> In Shiva, Vishnu, Brahma,[6] he
> Has scorned the Holy Trinity.

Recalling this, she agreed, but added: "However, you must not come to dinner at a wrong place or time." "What is the right place and what is the right time?" he asked. "Being a newcomer, I am not *au courant*." And she replied: "When the king's body is mastered by wine, fatigue, or sleep, then you may quietly bite him on the feet. This is the right place and the right time." To these conditions he gave his assent.

In spite of this arrangement, the famished bungler, when the king had just dozed off in the early evening, bit him on the back. And the poor king, as if burned by a firebrand, as if stung by a scorpion, as if touched by a torch, bounded to his feet, scratched his back, and cried to a servant: "Rascal! Somebody bit me. You must hunt through this bed until you find the insect."

Now Leap heard the king's command and in terrified haste crept into a crevice in the bed. Then the king's servants entered, and following their master's orders, brought a lamp and made a minute inspection. As fate would have it, they came upon Creep as she crouched in the nap of the fabric, and killed her with her family.

> "And that is why I say:"
> With no stranger share your house, ...

and the rest of it. And another thing. My lord and king does wrong in neglecting the servants who are his by inheritance. For

> Whoever leaves his friends,
> Strange folk to cherish,
> Like foolish Fierce-Howl, will
> Untimely perish."

"How was that?" asked Rusty. And Victor told the story of

THE BLUE JACKAL

There was once a jackal named Fierce-Howl, who lived in a cave near the suburbs of a city. One day he was hunting for food, his throat pinched with

---

5. A hero in the well-known Sanskrit romance *Bṛhatkathā* (The great romance). See also *Kathāsaritsāgara*.
6. Gods of the Hindu triad. Shiva (Śiva) is the destroyer god. Vishnu (Viṣṇu) is the preserver god. Brahma is the creator god.

hunger, and wandered into the city after nightfall. There the city dogs snapped at his limbs with their sharp-pointed teeth, and terrified his heart with their dreadful barking, so that he stumbled this way and that in his efforts to escape and happened into the house of a dyer. There he tumbled into a tremendous indigo vat, and all the dogs went home.

Presently the jackal—further life being predestined—managed to crawl out of the indigo vat and escaped into the forest. There all the thronging animals in his vicinity caught a glimpse of his body dyed with the juice of indigo, and crying out: "What is this creature enriched with that unprecedented color?" they fled, their eyes dancing with terror, and spread the report: "Oh, oh! Here is an exotic creature that has dropped from somewhere. Nobody knows what his conduct might be, or his energy. We are going to vamoose. For the proverb says:

> Where you do not know
>   Conduct, stock, and pluck,
> 'Tis not wise to trust,
>   If you wish for luck."

Now Fierce-Howl perceived their dismay, and called to them: "Come, come, you wild things! Why do you flee in terror at sight of me? For Indra,[7] realizing that the forest creatures have no monarch, anointed me—my name is Fierce-Howl—as your king. Rest in safety within the cage formed by my resistless paws."

On hearing this, the lions, tigers, leopards, monkeys, rabbits, gazelles, jackals, and other species of wild life bowed humbly, saying: "Master, prescribe to us our duties." Thereupon he appointed the lion prime minister and the tiger lord of the bedchamber, while the leopard was made custodian of the king's betel,[8] the elephant doorkeeper, and the monkey the bearer of the royal parasol. But to all the jackals, his own kindred, he administered a cuffing, and drove them away. Thus he enjoyed the kingly glory, while lions and others killed food-animals and laid them before him. These he divided and distributed to all after the manner of kings.

While time passed in this fashion, he was sitting one day in his court when he heard the sound made by a pack of jackals howling near by. At this his body thrilled, his eyes filled with tears of joy, he leaped to his feet, and began to howl in a piercing tone. When the lions and others heard this, they perceived that he was a jackal, and stood for a moment shamefaced and downcast, then they said: "Look! We have been deceived by this jackal. Let the fellow be killed." And when he heard this, he endeavored to flee, but was torn to bits by a tiger and died.

> "And that is why I say:
>   Whoever leaves his friends, ...

and the rest of it."

* * *

---

7. The king of the gods.   8. The leaves of this plant are chewed as a digestive and stimulant in India.

FORETHOUGHT, READYWIT, AND FATALIST[9]

In a great lake lived three full-grown fishes, whose names were Forethought, Readywit, and Fatalist. Now one day the fish named Forethought overheard passers-by on the bank and fishermen saying: "There are plenty of fish in this pond. Tomorrow we go fishing."

On hearing this, Forethought reflected: "This looks bad. Tomorrow or the day after they will be sure to come here. I will take Readywit and Fatalist and move to another lake whose waters are not troubled." So he called them and put the question.

Thereupon Readywit said: "I have lived long in this lake and cannot move in such a hurry. If fishermen come here, then I will protect myself by some means devised for the occasion."

But poor, doomed Fatalist said: "There are sizable lakes elsewhere. Who knows whether they will come here or not? One should not abandon the lake of his birth merely because of such small gossip. And the proverb says:

> Since scamp and sneak and snake
>   So often undertake
> A plan that does not thrive,
>   The world wags on, alive.

Therefore I am determined not to go." And when Forethought realized that their minds were made up, he went to another body of water.

On the next day, when he had gone, the fishermen with their boys beset the inner pool, cast a net, and caught all the fish without exception. Under these circumstances Readywit, while still in the water, played dead. And since they thought: "This big fellow died without help," they drew him from the net and laid him on the bank, from which he wriggled back to safety in the water. But Fatalist stuck his nose into the meshes of the net, struggling until they pounded him repeatedly with clubs and so killed him.

"And that is why I say:

> Forethought and Readywit thrive;
>   Fatalist can't keep alive."

* * *

From *Book III*

Crows and Owls

* * *

> "Though mountain, sun, and cloud, and wind
>   Were suitors at her feet,
> The mouse-maid turned a mouse again—
>   Nature is hard to beat."

"How was that?" asked Live-Strong. And Red-Eye told the story of

9. In the frame story Constance the plover tells this story to her mate, Sprawl.

MOUSE-MAID MADE MOUSE[1]

The billows of the Ganges were dotted with pearly foam born of the leaping of fishes frightened at hearing the roar of the waters that broke on the rugged, rocky shore. On the bank was a hermitage crowded with holy men devoting their time to the performance of sacred rites—chanting, self-denial, self-torture, study, fasting, and sacrifice. They would take purified water only, and that in measured sips. Their bodies wasted under a diet of bulbs, roots, fruits, and moss. A loin-cloth made of bark formed their scanty raiment.

The father of the hermitage was named Yajnavalkya. After he had bathed in the sacred stream and had begun to rinse his mouth, a little female mouse dropped from a hawk's beak and fell into his hand. When he saw what she was, he laid her on a banyan leaf, repeated his bath and mouth-rinsing, and performed a ceremony of purification. Then through the magic power of his holiness, he changed her into a girl, and took her with him to his hermitage.

As his wife was childless, he said to her: "Take her, my dear wife. She has come into life as your daughter, and you must rear her carefully." So the wife reared her and spoiled her with petting. As soon as the girl reached the age of twelve, the mother saw that she was ready for marriage, and said to her husband: "My dear husband, how can you fail to see that the time is passing when your daughter should marry?"

And he replied: "You are quite right, my dear. The saying goes:

> Before a man is gratified,
> These gods must treat her as a bride—
> The fire, the moon, the choir of heaven;
> In this way, no offense is given.
>
> Holiness is the gift of fire;   5
> A sweet voice, of the heavenly choir;
> The moon gives purity within:
> So is a woman free from sin.
>
> Before nubility, 'tis said
> That she is white; but after, red;   10
> Before her womanhood is plain,
> She is, though naked, free from stain.
>
> The moon, in mystic fashion, weds
> A maiden when her beauty spreads;
> The heavenly choir, when bosoms grow;   15
> The fire, upon the monthly flow.
>
> To wed a maid is therefore good
> Before developed womanhood;
> Nor need the loving parents wait
> Beyond the early age of eight.[2]   20
>
> The early signs one kinsman slay;
> The bosom takes the next away;

---

1. In the frame story of Book III, Red-Eye, the counselor of the king of the owls, tells this story to Live-Strong, the counsel of the king of the crows.   2. Eight indeed was considered a good age for marriage.

> Friends die for passion gratified;
> The father, if she ne'er be bride.

> For if she bides a maiden still, 25
> She gives herself to whom she will;
> Then marry her in tender age:
> So warns the heaven-begotten sage.

> If she, unwed, unpurified,
> Too long within the home abide, 30
> She may no longer married be:
> A miserable spinster, she.

> A father then, avoiding sin,
> Weds her,[3] the appointed time within
> (Where'er a husband may be had) 35
> To good, indifferent, or bad.

Now I will try to give her to one of her own station. You know the saying:

> Where wealth is very much the same,
> And similar the family fame,
> Marriage (or friendship) is secure;
> But not between the rich and poor.

And finally:

> Aim at seven things in marriage;
> All the rest you may disparage:

But

> Get money, good looks,
> And knowledge of books,
> Good family, youth,
> Position, and truth.

"So, if she is willing, I will summon the blessèd sun, and give her to him." "I see no harm in that," said his wife. "Let it be done."

The holy man therefore summoned the sun, who appeared without delay, and said: "Holy sir, why am I summoned?" The father said: "Here is a daughter of mine. Be kind enough to marry her." Then, turning to his daughter, he said: "Little girl, how do you like him, this blessèd lamp of the three worlds?"[4] "No, father," said the girl. "He is too burning hot. I could not like him. Please summon another one, more excellent than he is."

Upon hearing this, the holy man said to the sun: "Blessèd one, is there any superior to you?" And the sun replied: "Yes, the cloud is superior even to me. When he covers me, I disappear."

So the holy man summoned the cloud next, and said to the maiden: "Little girl, I will give you to him." "No," said she. "This one is black and frigid. Give me to someone finer than he."

---

3. Following the Indian tradition of arranged marriages, the father finds a suitable bridegroom for his daughter.   4. That is, heaven, earth, and the underworld.

Then the holy man asked: "O cloud, is there anyone superior to you?" And the cloud replied: "The wind is superior even to me."

So he summoned the wind, and said: "Little girl, I give you to him." "Father," said she, "this one is too fidgety. Please invite somebody superior even to him." So the holy man said: "O wind, is there anyone superior to you?" "Yes," said the wind. "The mountain is superior to me."

So he summoned the mountain and said to the maiden: "Little girl, I give you to him." "Oh, father," said she. "He is rough all over, and stiff. Please give me somebody else."

So the holy man asked: "O kingly mountain, is there anyone superior even to you?" "Yes," said the mountain. "Mice are superior to me."

Then the holy man summoned a mouse, and presented him to the girl, saying: "Little girl, do you like this mouse?"

The moment she saw him, she felt: "My own kind, my own kind," and her body thrilled and quivered, and she said: "Father dear, turn me into a mouse, and give me to him. Then I can keep house as my kind of people ought to do."

And her father, through the magic power of his holiness, turned her into a mouse, and gave her to him.

* * *

From *Book V*

Ill-Considered Action

* * *

Let the well-advised be done;
Ill-advised leave unbegun:
Else, remorse will be let loose,
As with lady and mungoose.

"How was that?" asked Jewel. And they told the story of

THE LOYAL MUNGOOSE[1]

There was once a Brahman named Godly in a certain town. His wife mothered a single son and a mungoose. And as she loved little ones, she cared for the mungoose also like a son, giving him milk from her breast, and salves, and baths, and so on. But she did not trust him, for she thought: "A mungoose is a nasty kind of creature. He might hurt my boy." Yes, there is sense in the proverb:

A son will ever bring delight,
Though bent on folly, passion, spite,
Though shabby, naughty, and a fright.[2]

---

1. A band of judges tells this story to Jewel the merchant. A mungoose (mongoose) is a small mammal and a natural enemy of snakes, which it can kill and eat without harm to itself.   2. A great value is placed on sons in the Indian family.

One day she tucked her son in bed, took a water-jar, and said to her husband: "Now, Professor,[3] I am going for water. You must protect the boy from the mungoose." But when she was gone, the Brahman went off somewhere himself to beg food,[4] leaving the house empty.

While he was gone, a black snake issued from his hole and, as fate would have it, crawled toward the baby's cradle. But the mungoose, feeling him to be a natural enemy, and fearing for the life of his baby brother, fell upon the vicious serpent halfway, joined battle with him, tore him to bits, and tossed the pieces far and wide. Then, delighted with his own heroism, he ran, blood trickling from his mouth, to meet the mother; for he wished to show what he had done.

But when the mother saw him coming, saw his bloody mouth and his excitement, she feared that the villain must have eaten her baby boy, and without thinking twice, she angrily dropped the water-jar upon him, which killed him the moment that it struck. There she left him without a second thought, and hurried home, where she found the baby safe and sound, and near the cradle a great black snake, torn to bits. Then, overwhelmed with sorrow because she had thoughtlessly killed her benefactor, her son, she beat her head and breast.

At this moment the Brahman came home with a dish of rice gruel which he had got from someone in his begging tour, and saw his wife bitterly lamenting her son, the mungoose. "Greedy! Greedy!" she cried. "Because you did not do as I told you, you must now taste the bitterness of a son's death, the fruit of the tree of your own wickedness. Yes, this is what happens to those blinded by greed. For the proverb says:

> Indulge in no excessive greed
> (A little helps in time of need)—
> A greedy fellow in the world
> Found on his head a wheel that whirled."[5]

* * *

3. Priestly brahmans study the *Vedas* and other ritual texts.   4. Brahmans are entitled to live on alms; those priests without ritual commissions are obliged to live by begging.   5. This verse is the come-on for the next story.

BHARTṚHARI
fifth century

The *Śatakatrayam* (The anthology of three centuries—that is, of three hundred poems) of Bhartṛhari contains some of the most celebrated short lyric poems (*muktaka*) in classical Sanskrit literature. Although each of the three sections of the anthology is devoted to a different subject—political wisdom (*nīti*), erotic passion (*śṛṅgāra*), and world renunciation (*vairāgya*)—its epigrammatic stanzas are permeated by a perspective of wise counsel. Perhaps it is the philosophical tone of the poems that led to the identification of their author with the philosopher Bhartṛhari, who wrote the *Vākyapadīya,* an original treatise on metaphysics and the philosophy of language. All that can be said with certainty about the poet of the *Śatakatrayam,* however, is that he lived during the Gupta era, most likely in the fifth century, and that he was already a legend by the seventh century, when he is mentioned by the Chinese Buddhist pilgrim I-ching in his memoir of his travels in India.

The themes of the poems suggest that, like Kālidāsa, Bhartṛhari was a court poet, but there the similarity ends. Bhartṛhari's mordant lyrics reflect a sensibility very different from that of the greatest spokesman for the harmonious vision of the classical culture. The voice that comes across in these poems is that of a proud and bitter man who is painfully aware of life's indignities and of his vulnerability to the very things he despises. Although wise men are infinitely superior to kings, says Bhartṛhari, they are forced to depend on kings for their survival. The poet responds with withering sarcasm to the greed and sycophancy that he witnesses in the courts of the rich. But even a man who has mastered the desire for gold has no defense against the charm of beautiful women, which Bhartṛhari depicts as the most powerful obstacle standing between the wise man and the calm joy that characterizes liberation from *karma* and rebirth, the ultimate goal in the ancient Indian religions.

The wise man's dream in these poems is to find peace in a life of renunciation, to retire "to a sylvan silence, / o the forest where no echo sounds / of wicked men whose muddled minds / show their confusion—/ vile lords whose tongues stammer folly aloud, / confounded by disease of wealth." But no such peace is in store for the poet, who is deeply attracted by the very diversity of human experience: "In life as transient as a flashing glance, / I can choose no single course." The language, imagery, and structural strategies in the philosopher-poet's stanza poems mirror the deep conflicts and tensions in his personality, and his unique personal vision informs them, making them instantly recognizable as his.

Bhartṛhari's poems became the model for epigrammatic poetry, not only in Sanskrit but also in the classical traditions that developed from the tenth century onward in the regional languages of India. No later poet, however, has been able to match them in passion, ironic perspective, or eloquence.

PRONOUNCING GLOSSARY

The following list uses common English syllables and stress accents to provide rough equivalents of selected words whose pronunciation may be unfamiliar to the general reader.

alaṃkāra: *uhl-uhng-kah'-ruh*

Bhartṛhari: *buhr'-tree-huh-ree*

dīpaka: *dee'-puh-kuh*

Kālidāsa: *kah-lee-dah'-suh*

mokṣa: *mohk'-shuh*

saṃskṛta: *suhms'-kri-tuh*

Śatakatrayam: *shu'-tuh-kuh-truh-yuhm*

Śíva: *shi'-vuh*

sragdharā: *sruhg'-duh-rah*

śṛṅgāra: *shreen-gah'-ruh*

subhāṣita: *soo-bah'-shee-tuh*

Vākyapadīya: *vahk'-yuh-puh-dee'-yuh*

This terra-cotta fragment dating from the fifteenth century B.C.E. represents a portion of the Babylonian epic of *Gilgamesh*. Many such tablets have been discovered in modern-day Turkey, Syria, Israel (where this particular fragment was discovered), and—not surprisingly—Iraq, where the epic originated. The cuneiform (wedge-shaped) markings on the surface of this tablet were made by pressing the edge of a reed stylus into the soft clay in different combinations and at different angles. The clay tablet was then baked in order to harden the surface and preserve the markings.

Cuneiform writing first appeared as simple pictograms that were used by the ancient Sumerians for business and administrative records. These pictograms were later transformed into an ideographic (and even later, a syllabic) writing system by the Babylonians, Assyrians, and Persians and employed to record a wide variety of literary texts in several languages, and in stone as well as clay tablets.

The so-called Mask of Agamemnon was discovered by the German archaeologist Heinrich Schliemann (1822–1890) in one of the royal shaft graves at Mycenae in the northern Peloponnesus of Greece. The site of a great palace complex excavated by Schliemann after his excavation at Hissarlik (Troy) in Turkey, Mycenae was the stronghold of Agamemnon in Homer. Schliemann believed that the grave from which this funeral mask was taken contained the remains (and the buried treasure) of Agamemnon, Cassandra, and his companions, killed at a banquet on their return from Troy by Clytemnestra and her lover Aegisthus. The mask is now believed to be the likeness of an Achaean king from the sixteenth century B.C.E.—much earlier than the assumed era of the Trojan War.

The theater of the sanctuary of Asklepios in Epidaurus, Greece, is the finest surviving example of ancient Greek theatrical architecture. Built in two stages from the fourth through the second centuries B.C.E., the theater was partially restored in the 1950s and 1960s to accommodate theatrical performances. Despite its size (it can seat nearly twelve thousand spectators), the theater's acoustics are exceptional: performers' voices are audible from the furthest reaches of the cavea (the seating area), even when the performers are speaking in a whisper.

Behind the round orchestra (stage area) are remnants of a number of structures that were not restored in the twentieth century, including the skene, a small building that served as a backdrop to the play's action. Scenery would have included movable screens for backdrops, a wheeled wooden platform to provide "interior" scenes, and a crane to bring in the gods from heaven.

The European Middle Ages saw the development of a technology (and cultural object) that today we take for granted: the bound book. For most of the period, the mode of book production was slow and painstaking because each copy of any one text had to be rendered by hand by a scribe (the mechanical process of printing wouldn't arise until 1455 with Gutenberg's Bible), and most books were religious in nature, produced to accompany the devotions of the wealthy and the powerful. Inspired by religious feeling and the luxurious tastes of the ultimate recipients of the books, monastic scribes devoted considerable energy and talent to surrounding the religious texts with didactic and sumptuous illustrations.

[1]

By the late thirteenth century, illuminated manuscripts of secular texts were quite common. In addition to classical texts, homegrown literary treasures written in vernacular languages, such as Dante's *Inferno* [1] and Chaucer's *Canterbury Tales* [2], received lush treatment. The illustration from a fourteenth-century manuscript of *Inferno* [1] shows Dante (on the far left) and Virgil talking with two plague-stricken "Falsifiers"—Griffolino and Cappochio—in the eighth circle of hell (canto 29.73–139). The second image is a detail of the opening page of the "Wife of Bath's Tale" from the Ellesmere manuscript of the *Canterbury Tales*. The Ellesmere manuscript, produced very soon after Chaucer's death (ca. 1410), is lavishly illuminated throughout, offering not only individual illustrations of the various pilgrims (all of them, like the Wife of Bath here, on horseback), but also the first known portrait of Chaucer himself.

[2]

Almost immediately on its introduction in the sixth century C.E., Buddhism was enormously successful and influential in Japan. In a country where earthquakes and typhoons were (and are) common occurrences and where people lived close to nature in all its changing aspects, the doctrine of universal impermanence spoke to the realities of Japanese experience. Buddhism quickly took root as the inspiration for a great literature, sprouting in Japan as luxuriantly as anywhere Buddhism ever touched.

Built two centuries after Buddhism was first brought to Japan from China, the Todaiji temple complex in Nara (the capital of Japan during its first great intellectual and cultural flowering) is a visual testament to the religion's monumental impact upon Japanese culture. The colossal seated Buddha statue shown here looms just under fifty feet tall; it is the largest gilded-bronze statue of the Buddha in the world.

The rise of the ancient Mali empire in the thirteenth century was closely associated with the spread of Islam into West Africa—a process that had begun as early as the seventh century. The founding figure of the Mali empire is Son-Jara (also known as Sundiata) Keita, a warrior of the Manding people. In 1235, Sundiata defeated Samanguru, whose policies toward the Manding after his conquest of large portions of West Africa were hostile and oppressive. Sundiata assumed kingship of the new empire and reputedly ruled for twenty-five years from the capital city of Niani, close to his ancestral home. Although he was a convert to Islam, Sundiata tolerated (and perhaps himself retained) the practices of traditional West African religion.

The figure shown here, a terra-cotta warrior wearing a decorative military garment, helmet, and a sheathed dagger on his left arm, dates from the thirteenth century and was excavated in the area around Djenne, a city that is approximately five hundred miles northeast of Niani. Scholars believe that this partial figure was originally on horseback. Its connection to Sundiata's own military forces has not been established, but it is a significant (and evocative) glimpse, however limited, of West African warrior culture.

Born in Crete and trained in Venice, El Greco ("the Greek") is associated with the spirit and character of sixteenth-century Spain, his home from 1577 until his death in 1614. He was especially attuned to the fervent religiosity of his adopted countrymen, producing emotionally vivid pictures for Catholic patrons and the Church itself.

El Greco was a contemporary of Miguel de Cervantes, whose novel, *Don Quixote,* takes a parodic stab at both the image of the Spanish nobleman and the long literary tradition of the chivalric romance. The portrait above, in contrast, is an earnest attempt to capture the appearance and character of a real, not imagined, sixteenth-century Spanish nobleman on the occasion of his knighthood. Pictured here is Don Juan de Silva, Notary Mayor of Toledo in the late 1570s, in a pose and manner that clearly signals his piety, relative austerity, and moral seriousness.

34

She's just a kid,[1]
    but I'm the one who's fainthearted.
She's the woman,
    but I'm the coward.
She bears that high, swollen set of breasts,   5
    but I'm the one who's burdened.
The heavy hips are hers,
    but I'm unable to move.

It's a wonder
how clumsy I've become   10
because of flaws
that shelter themselves
in another.

38

When anger
    was a crease in the brow
and silence
    a catastrophe,

When making up   5
    was a mutual smile
and a glance
    a gift,

now just look at this mess
that you've made of that love.   10

You grovel at my feet
and I berate you
and can't let my anger go.

57

My girl.
    Yes, lord?
Get rid of your anger, proud one.
    What have I done out of anger?
This is tiresome to me.   5
    You haven't offended me.
    All offenses are mine.
So why are you crying yourself hoarse?
    In front of whom am I crying?
In front of me.   10
    So what am I to you?
You're my darling.
    No, I'm not.
    That's why I'm crying.

---

1. *Bālā*, a realistic epithet, because the inexperienced heroines of Sanskrit poems were teenage girls, generally several years younger than their lovers.

69

At first,
our bodies were as one.

Then
you were unloving,
but I still played the wretched mistress.   5

Now
you're the master
and I'm the wife.

What's next?

This is the fruit I reap   10
from our lives
as hard as diamond.

101

When my lover came to bed,
the knot[1] came untied
all by itself.

My dress,
held up by the strings of a loosened belt,   5
barely stayed on my hips.

Friend,
that's as much as I know now.

When he touched my body,
I couldn't at all remember   10
who he was,
who I was,
or how It was.

102

She's in the house.
She's at turn after turn.
She's behind me.
She's in front of me.

She's in my bed.   5
She's on path after path,
and I'm weak from want of her.

O heart,
there is no reality for me
other than she she   10

---

1. That is, of her garment, at the waist.

she she she she[1]
in the whole of the reeling world.

And philosophers talk about Oneness.[2]

1. The repetition of *sā* ("she") in the original is meant to create the effect of a sacred litany; a repeated sacred chant (*mantra*).   2. The poet plays on the doctrine of the Vedanta philosophy, based on the *Upaniṣads*, that the universe if pervaded by the "One," a single divine reality—which obviously, for this lover, "she" is. Cf. John Donne's "The Sun Rising": "She's all states, and all princes I, / Nothing else is."

SOMADEVA
eleventh century

Somadeva tells us that he wrote the *Kathāsaritsāgara* (Ocean to the rivers of story) for the benefit of his patroness, Queen Sūryamatī of Kashmir, "to divert Her Majesty for a while when her mind has been wearied by the continuous study of the sciences." A Sanskrit *kāvya* work in narrative verse (*śloka*), the *Kathāsaritsāgara* is based on a much older tale collection called *The Great Romance* (*Bṛhatkathā*), attributed to Guṇ- āḍhya. Guṇīāḍlhya's Bṛhatkathā has not survived, but the authors of Sanskrit story literature from the seventh century onward acknowledge their debt to the lost work, and the *Kathāsaritsāgara* was preceded by at least two north Indian versions of *The Great Romance* in Sanskrit verse. True to its name, Somadeva's version has been the preeminent repository of tales in Sanskrit literature, containing among its more than 350 stories not only individual tales but originally independent story collections, such as *The Twenty-five Stories of the Ghoul* (*Vetālapañcaviṃśatikā*),   and *The Seventy Tales of the Parrot* (*Śukasaptati*). The charm of the *Kathāsaritsāgara's* stories, enhanced by Somadeva's elegant verse, has delighted generations of Indian readers.

Like most Indian narratives, the *Kathāsaritsāgara* uses the device of nested tales. The main frame story traces the adventures of Naravāhanadatta, son of the legendary King Udayana, relating how he became king of the Vidyādharas (aerial spirits). This central narrative is itself emboxed in a "tale about a tale," which tells how *The Great Romance* came to be written. According to Somadeva, it all began when the goddess Pārvatī cursed Puṣpadanta, a goblin attendant of her husband (the great god Śiva). Puṣlpadanta had overheard and broadcast the tales with which Śiva had been entertaining his wife in their celestial abode. The goblin Mālyavān, who interceded for his friend, was similarly cursed. Both goblins would be reborn on earth, and the curse of exile from heaven would be lifted only when each had retold Śiva's stories to others on earth. All came about as predicted. Puṣpadanta told the stories to a troll (*piśāca*) in the Vindhya forest. Mālyavān, born as Guṇāḍhya, the court poet of King Sātavāhana, heard them from that troll, and related them to the world in his *Bṛhatkathā*.

The Guṇāḍhya story is pervaded by Indian folklore and occult beliefs concerning northwestern India and the Vindhya mountains in central India. In Somadeva's version, Guṇāḍhya wrote *The Great Romance* in the forest, with his own blood, in the Paiśācī language ("trolls' tongue," identified as a northwestern Indo-Aryan dialect) and presented the work to his king, only to have it scorned and rejected on account of the barbarity of its language. The heartbroken Guṇāḍhya returned to the forest, where, weeping, he burned his manuscript, page by page, but only after reciting the contents of each page to the birds and beasts, who listened, enraptured. When this news was brought to the king, he relented, and ordered that the remainder of the manuscript be rescued and preserved in Sanskrit. His task on earth completed, Guṇ- āḍhya regained his celestial identity.

The main themes of the story of Prince Naravāhanadatta are the hero's acquisition of wealth and magical powers and his amorous adventures with a number of princesses and beautiful women, including his great love, the courtesan Madanamañcukā (Seat of the Love God). The many tales embedded in this frame story are told by the characters in the narrative to entertain their friends, lovers, and spouses, replicating the model provided by Śiva and the goddess as well as the goblins of the Guṇāḍhya story. In the *Kathāsaritsāgara* the fairy tale–like quality of the stories is balanced by the witty social commentary and the vivid pictures that are painted of Indian society in the classical period.

Like the *Pañcatantra*, the stories of the *Kathāsaritsāgara* are concerned with *artha*, the second of the four major human pursuits, as the most important value in the context of social life. However, these tales focus on *artha* quite literally and specifically in the sense of "wealth," "profit," and "the success that wealth brings," rather than on political power and the means for acquiring such power. The majority of the heroes of the stories are merchants, bankers, and other experts in acquiring and keeping wealth, a category that includes rogues and thieves. The focus on the merchant class and on sea voyages in search of gold undoubtedly reflects the flourishing overseas commerce of Gupta and post-Gupta India as well as the worldly values cultivated in its prosperous, cosmopolitan cities. Although Naravāhanadatta is a prince, he is very different from the warrior heroes of the epics, and his very name, Gift of the God of Riches, is a name typical of the merchant community.

The tale included here, "The Red Lotus of Chastity," is a microcosm of the Sanskrit story literature and its motifs and values. The story, which is similar to other tales about a test of conjugal fidelity in world literature (Shakespeare's *Cymbeline*, for instance), relates how the heroine Devasmitā secures the lasting love and admiration of her husband, Guhasena, by thwarting a plot hatched by some merchants (who receive help from two procuresses) to seduce her and humiliate her husband. Some of the favorite characters of the story literature are featured here: the adventurous young merchant, the beautiful and clever heroine, the corrupt nun-procuress and her crafty agent, the playboys who lust after an innocent man's wife. While virtue is rewarded and vice punished, the story revolves around the quest for gold and a woman's resourceful action in the face of a dilemma.

Guhasena is a typical hero of story literature: he knows the value of wealth and will travel to the ends of the earth to acquire it, but he is not greedy or crooked, rather, just the sort of man who is likely to be duped by scheming crooks in a foreign land. But the real hero of the story is Devasmitā. The combination of virtue, intelligence, courage, and wit in her character makes her the ideal woman of story literature, refreshingly different from women in the courtly and traditional genres. A woman who does not hesitate to elope with the man she loves, Devasmitā demands that her husband be faithful to her, even as she is to him. She immediately sees through the absurd stories cooked up by the procuresses, and the scheme whereby she gets her own back with the tricksters is testimony as much to her sense of humor as to her genius.

The stories in the *Kathāsaritsāgara* teem with colorful, earthy characters. In the Buddhist nun Yogakaraṇḍikā we have a distant forerunner of the hypocritical Tartuffe in Molière's play, and in the corrupt "holy" men and women we have early versions of the satirical portraits of monks and nuns in Chaucer. Both the nun and her helpmate Siddhikarī embody the qualities usually assigned to the courtesan and bawd in story literature—greed, rapacity, and hearts of stone. "Good" courtesans, such as Naravāhanadatta's lover Madanamañcukā, are considered to be admirable precisely because they defy the stereotype.

Storytelling ranks high among the pleasures depicted in Somadeva's stories, which brim with the enjoyment of life. Yet the recurrent theme of curses, rebirth, and the remembrance of past lives in these stories indicates that in Indian culture telling a tale is more than a pastime; it has, in fact, deep metaphysical implications. In India the gods themselves tell stories—and it is by telling and hearing stories that the sailors, goblins, and women of these stories overcome the curses that blind them to their own inner selves and thus gain access to memory, joy, and liberation at last from *karma*.

PRONOUNCING GLOSSARY

The following list uses common English syllables and stress accents to provide rough equivalents of selected words whose pronunciation may be unfamiliar to the general reader.

Avīcī: *uh-vee'-chee*

Bṛlhatkathā: *bree-huht'-kuh-thah*

Devasmitā: *day'-vuh-smee-tah*

Dhanadatta: *dhuh'-nuh-duht-tuh*

Dharmagupta: *dhuhr'-muh-goop-tuh*

Digambara: *deeg-uhm'-buh-ruh*

Guṇāḍhya: *goo-nah'-dh-yuh*

Kathāsaritsāgara: *kuh-thah'-suh-reet-sah'-guh-ruh*

Madanamañcukā: *muh-duh-nuh-muhn'-choo-kah*

Mālyavān: *mahl'-yuh-vahn*

Maṇibhadra: *muh'-neeb-huhd-ruh*

Naravāhanadatta: *nuh-ruh-vah'-huh_nuh-duht'-tuh*

Paiśācī: *pye'-shah-chee*

Pārvatī: *pahr'-vuh-tee*

piśāca: *pee-shah'-chuh*

Puṣpadanta: *poosh-puh-duhn'-tuh*

Śaktimatī: *shuhk'-tee-muh-tee*

Samudradatta: *suh-moo'-druh-duht-tuh*

Sātavāhana: *sah-tuh-vah'-huh-nuh*

Siddhikarī: *seed'-dhee-kuh-ree*

Śiva: *shee'-vuh*

Somadeva: *soh'-muh-day'-vuh*

Śukasaptati: *shoo-kuh-suhp'-tuh-tee*

Sūryamatī: *soor'-yuh-muh-tee*

Udayana: *oo-duh'-yuh-nuh*

Vetālapañcaviṃśatikā: *vay'-tah-luh-puhn'-chuh-veem-shuh-tee-kah*

Vidyādhara: *veed-yah'-dhuh-ruh*

Vindhya: *veen'-dh-yuh*

Yakṣa: *yuhk'-shuh*

YogakaraṇIḍlikā: *yoh'-guh-kuh-ruhn'-dee-kah*

From Kathāsaritsāgara[1]

The Red Lotus of Chastity

In this world is a famous port, Tāmraliptī,[2] and there lived a rich merchant whose name was Dhanadatta. He had no sons, so he assembled many brahmins, prostrated himself before them, and requested: "See to it that I get a son!"

"That is not at all difficult," said the priests, "for the brahmins can bring about everything on earth by means of the scriptural sacrifices.[3]

"For example," they continued, "long ago there was a king who had no sons, though he had one hundred and five women in his seraglio. He caused

1. Translated by J. A. B. van Buitenen.   2. During the Gupta era, an important port on the Bay of Bengal, a center for north India's trade with south India and Southeast Asia.   3. That is, those described in the Vedas.

a special sacrifice for a son to be performed, and a son was born to him. The boy's name was Jantu, and in the eyes of all the king's wives he was the rising new moon. Once when he was crawling about on all fours, an ant bit him on the thigh, and the frightened child cried out. The incident caused a terrific disturbance in the seraglio, and the king himself lamented—'My son! O my son!'—like a commoner. After a while, when the ant had been removed and the child comforted, the king blamed his own anxiety on the fact that he had only one son.

" 'There must be a way to have more sons,' he thought, and in his grief he consulted the brahmins. They replied: 'Indeed, Your Majesty, there is one way by which you can have more sons. Kill the son you have and sacrifice all his flesh in the sacred fire. When the royal wives smell the burning flesh, they will all bear sons.' The king had everything done as they said and got as many sons as he had wives.

"Thus with the help of a sacrifice," concluded the brahmins, "we can bring you, too, a son."

So at the advice of the brahmins, merchant Dhanadatta settled on a stipend for their sacerdotal services, and the priests performed the sacrifice for him. Subsequently a son was born to the merchant. The boy, who was given the name Guhasena, grew up in due time, and his father Dhanadatta was seeking a wife for him. And the merchant voyaged with his son to the Archipelago[4] to find a bride, though he pretended that it was just a business expedition. In the Archipelago he asked the daughter of a prominent merchant, Dharmagupta, a girl named Devasmitā, On-Whom-the-Gods-Have-Smiled, in marriage for his son Guhasena. Dharmagupta, however, did not favor the alliance, for he loved his daughter very much and thought that Tāmraliptī was too far away. But Devasmitā herself, as soon as she had set eyes on Guhasena, was so carried away by his qualities that she decided to desert her parents. Through a companion of hers she arranged a meeting with the man she loved and sailed off from the island at night with him and his father. On their arrival in Tāmraliptī they were married; and the hearts of husband and wife were caught in the noose of love.

Then father Dhanadatta died, and, urged by his relatives to continue his father's business, Guhasena made plans for a voyage to the island of Cathay.[5] Devasmitā, however, did not approve of his going, for she was a jealous wife and naturally suspected that he would love another woman. So with his relatives urging him on and his wife opposing, Guhasena was caught in the middle and could not get on with his business.

Thereupon he went to a temple and took a vow of fasting. "Let God in this temple show me a way out," he thought. Devasmitā came along, and she took the same vow. God Śiva[6] appeared to both of them in a dream. He gave them two red lotuses and spoke: "Each of you must keep this lotus in his hand. If one of you commits adultery while the other is far away, the lotus in the other's hand will wither away. So be it!" The couple woke up, and each saw in the other's hand the red lotus which was an image of the lover's heart.

---

4. Islands of Southeast Asia and Indonesia.   5. Not China but an island in Southeast Asia or Indonesia.
6. Śiva, the destroyer god, one of the two great gods of Hinduism.

Devasmitā went to the local king and announced: "I have a message. Assemble all your people." Curious, the king summoned all citizens and asked Devasmitā, who still wore her merchant's disguise, "What is your message?"

"Among these people here," said Devasmitā, "are four runaway slaves of mine. May it please Your Majesty to surrender them."

"All the people of this town are assembled here," replied the king. "Look them over, and when you recognize your slaves, take them back."

Thereupon she arrested on their own threshold the four merchant's sons, whom she had manhandled before. They still wore her mark on their foreheads.

"But these are the sons of a caravan trader," protested the merchants who were present. "How can they be your slaves?"

"If you do not believe me," she retorted, "have a look at their foreheads. I have branded them with a dog's paw."

"So we shall," they said. They unwound the turbans of the four men, and they all saw the dog's paw on their foreheads. The merchants' guild was ashamed, and the king surprised.

"What is behind this?" the king asked, questioning Devasmitā in person, and she told the story, and they all burst out laughing.

"By rights they are your slaves, my lady," said the king, whereupon the other merchants paid the king a fine and the virtuous woman a large ransom to free the four from bondage. Honored by all upright people, Devasmitā, with the ransom she had received and the husband she had rejoined, returned to their city Tāmraliptī and never again was she separated from the husband she loved.

T'AO CH'IEN
365–427

In the second decade of the fourth century, non-Chinese invaders from the north conquered north China and took the reigning Chin emperor captive. In the ensuing turmoil many of the great families and their retainers emigrated to the region south of the Yangtse River, where one of the Chin imperial princes had established his own branch of the dynasty. This was an unprecedented situation, in which "China" became a purely cultural tradition, no longer tied to the traditional heartland.

The great families from the north considered themselves an aristocracy, as compared with the local population. Buddhism established itself as a major force and received lavish patronage from the court and aristocracy. Monasteries supported schools and housed non-Chinese monks, who joined their Chinese counterparts in translating the Buddhist scriptures into Chinese. The Taoist "church" (an organized religion to be distinguished from the philosophical Taoism of early China) grew in importance and attracted distinguished followers. While society since the Han empire had always offered many alternatives to a Confucian dedication to political life, in the southern dynasties such alternatives became more and more prominent.

Individualism and eccentricity were much admired in this period, both within the aristocracy and by those who scorned social life altogether and went to live as recluses among the beautiful mountain regions south of the Yangtse. T'ao Ch'ien, who finally came to be seen as the outstanding writer of the age, was very much an individualist, and his courage of conviction was undoubtedly strengthened by the intellectual currents of the time. Despite a claim to at least one illustrious ancestor, T'ao's immediate family consisted of poor provincial gentry. He prided himself on bumbling naïveté rather than aristocratic sophistication, and instead of opulent leisure, he saw pleasure in the simple life of a rural community, offering contentment in the rhythms of farm labor.

An old strain in the Chinese tradition idealized and even sentimentalized the peasant farmer. T'ao Ch'ien stands out from earlier writers by choosing such a life as his own and finding contentment in it. Celebration of this decision and his subsequent life can be found throughout his poetry. T'ao Ch'ien's family background made him a good candidate for minor provincial posts or a place in the entourage of one of the powerful aristocrats who had usurped the political power of the eastern Chin ruler, and he did indeed serve in both capacities. Each time, however, something happened that led him to resign his post: sometimes a death in the family, sometimes sheer dissatisfaction with a career whose formalities and burdens he loathed. His final post was as magistrate of P'eng-tse, a county seat not far from his hometown. After only a little more than two months in office, he quit his post and went home, where he quietly spent the last twenty-two years of his life. It was on this occasion that he wrote his long poem "The Return," in which he states the problem eloquently: "Whenever I have been involved in official life I was mortgaging myself to my mouth and belly."

In his own distinctive way, T'ao Ch'ien shared with other Chin intellectuals a fascination with freedom and the idea of leading a natural life. It was thought that what individuals felt was "natural" and was distinct from their will and bodily desires. Thus T'ao could will himself to serve, even wish to serve, and could satisfy his "mouth and belly," yet still be going against his nature. A joke of the same period clarifies the issue. A poor scholar once visited the house of a wealthy aristocrat. He had to use the toilet and came to a room so lavishly decorated that he thought he had stumbled into the women's quarters by mistake. He made a hasty retreat and apologized to the aristocrat, who told him that it had, indeed, been the toilet. So informed, he returned, but on trying to use the room as it was intended, he found that he could not relieve himself. He returned, said good-bye, and as the anecdote ends, "went to somebody else's toilet." Beneath the joke lies a recognition that we each have a nature in which we feel at ease; that nature can be compelled neither by will (the intention to use the opulent toilet) nor by the body's demands (which sent the scholar to the toilet in the first place). Happiness is possible only in circumstances in which one's nature is not violated.

Throughout his work T'ao returns again and again to defining what is natural to him as an individual, discovering how to live so that his nature will be content, and observing how few needs he actually has. When a fire burns down his house, he looks around and concludes that he still has enough, though the danger of hunger and want is always there, threatening to drive him forth into the world, as it does on several occasions.

The good society, then, is the small world of the farming community, supplying human needs adequately but without excess. The unpleasant alternative is the empire and its government, with its false hierarchies and continual threat of violence. His most famous image of the happy life is based on a legend then current about Peach Blossom Spring, a farming community hidden deep in the mountains, whose inhabitants were the descendants of people who had fled the Chinese heartland during wars some five centuries earlier. A fisherman, following a trail of peach blossoms in the water, stumbles on this village and gives the curious villagers a summary of the wartorn preceding half millennium of Chinese history. On leaving to go home, he pays careful attention to the route, but no one is ever able to find the place again.

In many ways the fisherman is the emblem of T'ao Ch'ien's poetry and prose. He moves from the public world to an enclosed private world, safely cut off from the outside. For the sake of the story he must go back to the public world to tell about Peach Blossom Spring, even though no one will ever be able to get there. In the same way T'ao Ch'ien's poetry and prose writings are sent out from his village to the larger world, to be read by the literate officials who serve in the imperial government. These poems tell them of a possibility of contentment that eludes them and will be hard to find even if they go looking for it.

PRONOUNCING GLOSSARY

The following list uses common English syllables to provide rough equivalents of selected words whose pronunciation may be unfamiliar to the general reader.

Ch'ien-lou: *chyen–loh*

Han Hsin: *hahn shin*

Huan T'ui: *hwahn tway*

Ko-t'ien: *guh–tyen*

Liu Pang: *lyoh bahng*

Liu Tzu-chi: *lyoh dzuh–jee*

P'eng-tse: *puhng–dzuh*

T'ai-yüan: *tay–yooan*

T'ao Ch'ien: *tau chyen*

The Peach Blossom Spring[1]

During the T'ai-yüan period[2] of the Chin dynasty a fisherman of Wu-ling once rowed upstream unmindful of the distance he had gone, when he suddenly came to a grove of peach trees in bloom. For several hundred paces on both banks of the stream there was no other kind of tree. The wild flowers growing under them were fresh and lovely, and fallen petals covered the

---

1. All selections translated by James Robert Hightower except "Biography of Master Five Willows," translated by Stephen Owen.   2. From 376 to 396 C.E.

ground—it made a great impression on the fisherman. He went on for a way with the idea of finding out how far the grove extended. It came to an end at the foot of a mountain whence issued the spring that supplied the stream. There was a small opening in the mountain and it seemed as though light was coming through it. The fisherman left his boat and entered the cave, which at first was extremely narrow, barely admitting his body; after a few dozen steps it suddenly opened out onto a broad and level plain where well-built houses were surrounded by rich fields and pretty ponds. Mulberry, bamboo and other trees and plants grew there, and criss-cross paths skirted the fields. The sounds of cocks crowing and dogs barking could be heard from one courtyard to the next. Men and women were coming and going about their work in the fields. The clothes they wore were like those of ordinary people. Old men and boys were carefree and happy.

When they caught sight of the fisherman, they asked in surprise how he had got there. The fisherman told the whole story, and was invited to go to their house, where he was served wine while they killed a chicken for a feast. When the other villagers heard about the fisherman's arrival they all came to pay him a visit. They told him that their ancestors had fled the disorders of Ch'in times[3] and, having taken refuge here with wives and children and neighbors, had never ventured out again; consequently they had lost all contact with the outside world. They asked what the present ruling dynasty was, for they had never heard of the Han, let alone the Wei and the Chin. They sighed unhappily as the fisherman enumerated the dynasties one by one and recounted the vicissitudes of each. The visitors all asked him to come to their houses in turn, and at every house he had wine and food. He stayed several days. As he was about to go away, the people said, 'There's no need to mention our existence to outsiders.'

After the fisherman had gone out and recovered his boat, he carefully marked the route. On reaching the city, he reported what he had found to the magistrate, who at once sent a man to follow him back to the place. They proceeded according to the marks he had made, but went astray and were unable to find the cave again.

A high-minded gentleman of Nan-yang named Liu Tzu-chi heard the story and happily made preparations to go there, but before he could leave he fell sick and died. Since then there has been no one interested in trying to find such a place.

The Return

I was poor, and what I got from farming was not enough to support my family. The house was full of children, the rice-jar was empty, and I could not see any way to supply the necessities of life. Friends and relatives kept urging me to become a magistrate, and I had at last come to think I should do it, but there was no way for me to get such a position. At the time I happened to have business abroad and made a good impression on the grandees as a conciliatory and humane sort of person. Because of my poverty an uncle

---

3. From 221 to 207 B.C.E.

offered me a job in a small town, but the region was still unquiet and I trembled at the thought of going away from home. However, P'eng-tse was only thirty miles from my native place, and the yield of the fields assigned the magistrate was sufficient to keep me in wine, so I applied for the office. Before many days had passed, I longed to give it up and go back home. Why, you may ask. Because my instinct is all for freedom, and will not brook discipline or restraint. Hunger and cold may be sharp, but this going against myself really sickens me. Whenever I have been involved in official life I was mortgaging myself to my mouth and belly, and the realization of this greatly upset me. I was deeply ashamed that I had so compromised my principles, but I was still going to wait out the year, after which I might pack up my clothes and slip away at night. Then my sister who had married into the Ch'eng family died in Wu-ch'ang, and my only desire was to go there as quickly as possible. I gave up my office and left of my own accord. From mid-autumn to winter I was altogether some eighty days in office, when events made it possible for me to do what I wished. I have entitled my piece 'The Return'; my preface is dated the eleventh moon of the year *i-ssu*.[1]

To get out of this and go back home!
My fields and garden will be overgrown with weeds—I must go back.
It was my own doing that made my mind my body's slave
Why should I go on in melancholy and lonely grief?
I realize that there's no remedying the past   5
But I know that there's hope in the future.
After all I have not gone far on the wrong road
And I am aware that what I do today is right, yesterday wrong.
My boat rocks in the gentle breeze
Flap, flap, the wind blows my gown;   10
I ask a passerby about the road ahead,
Grudging the dimness of the light at dawn.
Then I catch sight of my cottage—
    Filled with joy I run.
The servant boy comes to welcome me   15
    My little son waits at the door.
The three paths are almost obliterated
    But pines and chrysanthemums are still here.
Leading the children by the hand I enter my house
    Where there is a bottle filled with wine.   20
I draw the bottle to me and pour myself a cup;
Seeing the trees in the courtyard brings joy to my face.
I lean on the south window and let my pride expand,
I consider how easy it is to be content with a little space.
Every day I stroll in the garden for pleasure,   25
There is a gate there, but it is always shut.
Cane in hand I walk and rest
Occasionally raising my head to gaze into the distance.
The clouds aimlessly rise from the peaks,
The birds, weary of flying, know it is time to come home.   30

---

1. A cyclical date name. China used a lunar calendar in which the first month began in late January or early February. The eleventh moon or month was probably December.

As the sun's rays grow dim and disappear from view
I walk around a lonely pine tree, stroking it.
Back home again!
May my friendships be broken off and my wanderings come to an end.
The world and I shall have nothing more to do with one another.   35
If I were again to go abroad, what should I seek?
Here I enjoy honest conversation with my family
And take pleasure in books and zither to dispel my worries.
The farmers tell me that now spring is here
There will be work to do in the west fields.   40
Sometimes I call for a covered cart
Sometimes I row a lonely boat
Following a deep gully through the still water
Or crossing the hill on a rugged path.
The trees put forth luxuriant foliage,   45
The spring begins to flow in a trickle.
I admire the seasonableness of nature
And am moved to think that my life will come to its close.
      It is all over—
So little time are we granted human form in the world!   50
Let us then follow the inclinations of the heart:
Where would we go that we are so agitated?
I have no desire for riches
And no expectation of Heaven.
Rather on some fine morning to walk alone   55
Now planting my staff to take up a hoe,
Or climbing the east hill and whistling long
Or composing verses beside the clear stream:
So I manage to accept my lot until the ultimate homecoming.
Rejoicing in Heaven's command, what is there to doubt?   60

Biography of Master Five Willows[1]

We don't know what age the master lived in, and we aren't certain about his
real name. Beside his cottage were five willow trees, so he took his name
from them. He lived in perfect peace, a man of few words, with no desire for
glory or gain. He liked to read but didn't try too hard to understand. Yet
whenever there was something that caught his fancy, he would be so happy
he would forget to eat. He had a wine-loving nature, but his household was
so poor he couldn't always obtain wine. His friends, knowing how he was,
would invite him to drink. And whenever he drank, he finished what he had
right away, hoping to get very drunk. When drunk, he would withdraw, not
really caring whether he went or stayed. His dwelling was a shambles, providing no protection against wind and sun. His coarse clothes were full of
holes and patches; his plate and pitcher always empty; he was at peace. He
forgot all about gain and loss and in this way lived out his life.

---

1. Master Five Willows is T'ao Ch'ien's image of himself.

Ch'ien-lou's[2] wife once said, "Feel no anxiety about loss or low station; don't be too eager for wealth and honor." When we reflect on her words, we suspect that Five Willows may have been such a man—swigging wine and writing poems to satisfy his inclinations. Was he a person of the age of Lord No-Cares? Was he a person of the age of Ko-t'ien?[3]

Returning to the Farm to Dwell

I

From early days I have been at odds with the world;
My instinctive love is hills and mountains.
By mischance I fell into the dusty net
And was thirteen years away from home.
The migrant bird longs for its native grove.   5
The fish in the pond recalls the former depths.
Now I have cleared some land to the south of town,
Simplicity intact, I have returned to farm.
The land I own amounts to a couple of acres
The thatched-roof house has four or five rooms.   10
Elms and willows shade the eaves in back,
Peach and plum stretch out before the hall.
Distant villages are lost in haze,
Above the houses smoke hangs in the air.
A dog is barking somewhere in a hidden lane,   15
A cock crows from the top of a mulberry tree.
My home remains unsoiled by worldly dust
Within bare rooms I have my peace of mind.
For long I was a prisoner in a cage
And now I have my freedom back again.   20

II

Here in the country human contacts are few
On this narrow lane carriages seldom come.
In broad daylight I keep my rustic gate closed,
From the bare rooms all dusty thoughts are banned.
From time to time through the tall grass   5
Like me, village farmers come and go;
When we meet we talk of nothing else
Than how the hemp and mulberry are growing.
Hemp and mulberry grow longer every day
Every day the fields I have plowed are wider;   10
My constant worry is that frost may come
And my crops will wither with the weeds.

---

2. A figure of antiquity who preferred a life of poverty to serving in office.   3. Both are mythical emperors of earliest antiquity, before there were troubles in the world.

Begging for Food

Hunger came and drove me out
To go I had no notion where.
I walked until I reached this town,
Knocked at a door and fumbled for words
The owner guessed what I was after   5
And gave it, but not just the gift alone.
We talked together all day long,
And drained our cups as the bottle passed.
Happy in our new acquaintance
We sang old songs and wrote new poems.   10
You are as kind as the washerwoman,
But to my shame I lack Han's talent.
I have no way to show my thanks[1]
And must repay you from the grave.[2]

On Moving House

I

For long I yearned to live in Southtown—
Not that a diviner told me to—
Where many simple-hearted people live
With whom I would rejoice to pass my days.
This I have had in mind for several years   5
And now at last have carried out my plan.
A modest cottage does not need be large
To give us shelter where we sit and sleep.
From time to time my neighbors come
And we discuss affairs of long ago.   10
A good poem excites our admiration
Together we expound the doubtful points.

II

In spring and fall are many perfect days
For climbing high to write new poetry.
As we pass the doors, we hail each other,
And anyone with wine will pour us some.
When the farm work is done, we all go home   5
And then have time to think of one another—
So thinking, we at once throw on a coat
And visit, never tired of talk and jokês.
There is no better way of life than this,
No need to be in a hurry to go away.   10

1. When Han Hsin was a young man, he found himself in hard straits; a washerwoman pitied him and fed him. Later he became a general of Liu Pang, the founder of the Han Dynasty, and was made a nobleman, able to repay the kindness he had received long before.   2. This echoes a story of a ghost who, out of gratitude, tripped the enemy of Lord Huan of Wei at a crucial moment.

Since food and clothing have to be provided,
If I do the plowing, it will not cheat me.

In the Sixth Month of 408, Fire

I built my thatched hut in a narrow lane,
Glad to renounce the carriages of the great.
In midsummer, while the wind blew long and sharp,
Of a sudden grove and house caught fire and burned.
In all the place not a roof was left to us   5
And we took shelter in the boat by the gate.

Space is vast this early autumn evening,
The moon, nearly full, rides high above.
The vegetables begin to grow again
But the frightened birds still have not returned.   10
Tonight I stand a long time lost in thought;
A glance encompasses the Nine Heavens.[1]
Since youth I've held my solitary course
Until all at once forty years have passed.
My outward form follows the way of change   15
But my heart remains untrammelled still.
Firm and true, it keeps its constant nature,
No jadestone is as strong, adamantine.
I think back to the time when East-Gate[2] ruled
When there was grain left out in the fields   20
And people, free of care, drummed full bellies,
Rising mornings and coming home to sleep.
Since I was not born in such a time,
Let me just go on watering my garden.

From Twenty Poems after Drinking Wine

Preface

Living in retirement here I have few pleasures, and now the nights are
growing longer; so, as I happen to have some excellent wine, not an evening
passes without a drink. All alone with my shadow I empty a bottle until suddenly I find myself drunk. And once I am drunk I write a few verses for my
own amusement. In the course of time the pages have multiplied, but there
is no particular sequence in what I have written. I have had a friend make a
copy, with no more in mind than to provide a diversion.

---

1. Heaven was described as having nine levels; here, simply the whole sky.   2. One of the mythical
rulers of high antiquity when there was such plenty that no one bothered to steal.

V

I built my hut beside a traveled road
Yet here no noise of passing carts and horses.
You would like to know how it is done?
With the mind detached, one's place becomes remote.
Picking chrysanthemums by the eastern hedge   5
I catch sight of the distant southern hills:
The mountain air is lovely as the sun sets
And flocks of flying birds return together.
In these things is a fundamental truth
I would like to tell, but lack the words.   10

IX

I heard a knock this morning at my door
In haste I pulled my gown on wrongside out
And went to ask the caller, Who is there?
It was a well-intentioned farmer, come
With a jug of wine to pay a distant call.   5
Suspecting me to be at odds with the times:
'Dressed in rags beneath a roof of thatch
Is not the way a gentleman should live.
All the world agrees on what to do—
I hope that you will join the muddy game.'   10
'My sincere thanks for your advice, old man.
It's my nature keeps me out of tune.
Though one can learn of course to pull the reins,
To go against oneself is a real mistake.
So let's just have a drink of this together—   15
There's no turning back my carriage now.'[1]

X

Once I made a distant trip
Right to the shore of the Eastern Sea
The road I went was long and far,
The way beset by wind and waves.
Who was it made me take this trip?   5
It seems that I was forced by hunger.
I gave my all to eat my fill
When just a bit was more than enough.
Since this was not a famous plan
I stopped my cart and came back home.   10

---

1. That is, from following the course of life he has chosen.

From On Reading the *Seas and Mountains Classic*[1]

I

In early summer when the grasses grow
And trees surround my house with greenery,
The birds rejoice to have a refuge there
And I too love my home.
The fields are plowed and the new seed planted   5
And now is time again to read my books.
This out-of-the-way lane has no deep-worn ruts
And tends to turn my friends' carts away.
With happy face I pour the spring-brewed wine
And in the garden pick some greens to cook.   10
A gentle shower approaches from the east
Accompanied by a temperate breeze.
I skim through the *Story of King Mu*[2]
And view the pictures in the *Seas and Mountains Classic*.
A glance encompasses the ends of the universe—   15
Where is there any joy, if not in these?

1. A fabulous geography of the countries surrounding China, inhabited by strange creatures and oddly shaped human beings.   2. This is a travel narrative of the Chou king Mu's visits to fantastic places beyond China.

T'ANG POETRY

Lyric poetry has generally been considered China's most important traditional literary form, and in the two millennia during which classical poetry played a powerful role in the culture, no period ever quite seemed to equal the T'ang Dynasty (618–907). The role of lyric poetry in traditional China was very different from that of lyric poetry in the West. By the T'ang Dynasty lyric poems had come to be used in a wide range of situations in both private and social life—in letters to friends, as contributions to a party, or as commemorations of visits to famous places. An educated person visiting the home of a friend might leave a poem if the host was not at home. On returning the host might reply by sending a poem to express regret at having missed the visit. Officials traveling on imperial business would write poems about their journeys on the white plaster walls of government post houses, sometimes responding to other poems on the wall left by previous visitors. In addition to the wide range of social situations that called for or invited the composition of poetry, poems were also written for the more private occasions that are familiar subjects of Western poetry: finding words for the difficult moments of life, communicating love, and simply evoking imaginary scenes and old legends.

In such a world few people defined themselves exclusively as "poets." To write poetry with grace (or at least technical competence) was expected of an educated person. During much of the T'ang period, poetic composition made part of the *chin-shih* examination, by which a candidate qualified for a government appointment. Thus poetic skill touched career, social life, and private life. Although in later centuries women's circles engaged widely in poetic composition, in the T'ang period composition of poetry by women was most common at the top and on the margins of

The following list uses common English syllables and stress accents to provide rough equivalents of selected words whose pronunciation may be unfamiliar to the general reader.

Ch'ang-an: *chahng–ahn*

Ching-t'ing: *jing–ting*

Hsi-ho: *shee–huh*

Jo-yeh: *rwoh–ye*

Li Po: *lee bwoh*

Lu-yang: *loo–yahng*

P'ing-lo: *ping–luh*

Tan-ch'iu: *dahn–chyoh*

Ts'ao Chih: *tsau jerr*

Ts'en: *tsuhn*

Yüeh: *yooeh*

The Sun Rises and Sets[1]

The sun comes up from its nook in the east,
Seems to rise from beneath the earth,
Passes on through Heaven,
    sets once again in the western sea,
And where, oh, where, can its team of six dragons   5
    ever find any rest?
Its daily beginnings and endings,
    since ancient times never resting.
And man is not made of its Primal Stuff—
    how can he linger beside it long?   10
Plants feel no thanks for their flowering in spring's wind,
Nor do trees hate losing their leaves
    under autumn skies:
Who wields the whip that drives along
    four seasons of changes—   15
The rise and the ending of all things
    is just the way things are.

Hsi-ho![2] Hsi-ho!
Why must you always drown yourself
    in those wild and reckless waves?   20
What power had Lu-yang[3]
That he halted your course by shaking his spear?
This perverts the Path of things,
    errs from Heaven's will—
So many lies and deceits!   25
I'll wrap this Mighty Mudball of a world
    all up in a bag
And be wild and free like Chaos itself!

1. All selections translated by Stephen Owen.   2. Goddess who drove the sun's carriage.   3. Reference to the legend that the lord of Lu-yang, engaged in combat, made the sun stop in its course so that the fight could continue.

Bring in the Wine

Look there!
  The waters of the Yellow River,
  coming down from Heaven,
  rush in their flow to the sea,   5
  never turn back again
Look there!
  Bright in the mirrors of mighty halls
  a grieving for white hair,
  this morning blue-black strands of silk,   10
  now turned to snow with evening.
For satisfaction in this life
  taste pleasure to the limit,
And never let a goblet of gold
  face the bright moon empty.   15
Heaven bred in me talents,
  and they must be put to use.
I toss away a thousand in gold,
  it comes right back to me.
So boil a sheep,   20
  butcher an ox,
    make merry for a while,
And when you sit yourself to drink, always
  down three hundred cups.
  Hey, Master Ts'en,   25
  Ho, Tan-ch'iu,[1]
  Bring in the wine!
  Keep the cups coming!
And I, I'll sing you a song,
You bend me your ears and listen—   30
The bells and the drums, the tastiest morsels,
  it's not these that I love—
All I want is to stay dead drunk
  and never sober up.
The sages and worthies of ancient days   35
  now lie silent forever,
And only the greatest drinkers
  have a fame that lingers on!
Once long ago
  the prince of Ch'en[2]
    held a party at P'ing-lo Lodge.[3]   40
A gallon of wine cost ten thousand cash,
  all the joy and laughter they pleased.
    So you, my host,
How can you tell me you're short on cash?   45
Go right out!
  Buy us some wine!
    And I'll do the pouring for you!

---

1. Master Ts'en and Tan-ch'iu are Li Po's friends.   2. The poet Ts'ao Chih (192–232).   3. Reference to a party described in one of Ts'ao Chih's poems.

Then take my dappled horse,
    Take my furs worth a fortune,
Just call the boy to get them,   50
    and trade them for lovely wine,
And here together we'll melt the sorrows
    of all eternity!

Yearning

    Endless yearning
    Here in Ch'ang-an,[1]
Where the cricket spinners cry autumn
    by the rail of the golden well,   5
Where flecks of frost blow chill,
    and the bedmat's color, cold.
No light from the lonely lantern,
    the longing almost broken—
Then roll up the curtain, gaze on the moon,
    heave the sigh that does no good.   10
A lady lovely like the flowers,
    beyond that wall of clouds,
And above, the blue dark of heavens high,
And below, the waves of pale waters.
Endless the sky, far the journey,   15
    the fleet soul suffers in flight,
And in its dreams can't touch its goal
    through the fastness of barrier mountains—
    Then endless yearning
    Crushes a man's heart.   20

Ballad of Youth

A young man of Five Barrows suburb
    east of the Golden Market,[1]
Silver saddle and white horse
    cross through wind of spring.
When fallen flowers are trampled all under,   5
    where is it he will roam?
With a laugh he enters the tavern
    of a lovely Turkish wench.

1. The T'ang Dynasty's capital.   1. In Ch'ang-an.

The Girls of Yüeh

A girl picking lotus on Jo-yeh Creek[1]
Sees the boatman return, singing a rowing song.
With a giggle she hides in the lotus flowers
And, pretending shyness, won't come out.

Dialogue in the Mountains

You ask me why I lodge in these emerald hills;
I laugh, don't answer—my heart is at peace.
Peach blossoms and flowing waters
   go off to mysterious dark,
And there is another world,[1]   5
   not of mortal men.

Summer Day in the Mountains

Lazily waving a fan of white feathers,
Stripped naked here in the green woods,
I take off my headband, hang it on a cliff,
My bare head splattered by wind through pines.

My Feelings

Facing my wine, unaware of darkness growing,
Falling flowers cover my robes.
Drunk I rise, step on the moon in the creek—
Birds are turning back now,
   men too are growing fewer.   5

Drinking Alone by Moonlight

Here among flowers a single jug of wine,
No close friends here, I pour alone
And lift cup to bright moon, ask it to join me,
Then face my shadow and we become three.
The moon never has known how to drink,   5
All my shadow does is follow my body,
But with moon and shadow as companions a while,
This joy I find must catch spring while it's here.
I sing, the moon just lingers on,

---

1. In southeastern China in a region famous for its beautiful women.   1. The image suggests the Peach Blossom Spring described by T'ao Ch'ien, a place removed from the troubles of this world.

I dance, and my shadow scatters wildly.   10
When still sober we share friendship and pleasure,
Then entirely drunk each goes his own way—
Let us join in travels beyond human feelings
And plan to meet far in the river of stars.

Sitting Alone by Ching-t'ing Mountain

The flocks of birds have flown high and away,
A solitary cloud goes off calmly alone.
We look at each other and never get bored—
Just me and Ching-t'ing Mountain.

TU FU
712–770

If Li Po was associated with Taoism and the free, uncaring immortals, Tu Fu has always been strongly associated with Confucian virtues, embodied in his political commitment, his social concerns, and his love of family. A consensus of readers considers Tu Fu to be China's greatest poet, with each successive age finding in Tu Fu's work its own sense of what constitutes greatness. That very ability to satisfy changing values is a tribute to the diversity of his work. Yet he was esteemed in every age of Chinese poetry but his own.

During his lifetime Tu Fu was eminently unsuccessful, both as political figure and as poet. The grandson of one of the most famous court poets of the early eighth century, the young Tu Fu sought political office with no success. When the great rebellion of 755 took the capital by surprise and the emperor fled west, Tu Fu was trapped behind enemy lines. Some of his finest early poems were written at this period, as he heard of the defeat of one imperial army after another. Eventually he slipped through the lines and made his way to the court of the new emperor, who was directing military operations against the rebels. There he briefly held one of those court posts he had so much desired, but following the recapture of the capital, he was exiled to a minor provincial post, a job he came to detest. He quit this post in disgust and took up a life of wandering, first to the northwest, then west to Ch'eng-tu, the capital of Szechwan, then down the Yangtse River, coming in his last year to the lakes region in central China. It was during these last years of his life that Tu Fu wrote most of his poetry.

Because Chinese poetry treats both the minor details and the major crises of a person's life, a poet's work as a whole can be seen as autobiography or even diary. The culture valued poetry as a key to the historical person. One reason for Tu Fu's appeal may be the way he documents his life, from the smallest details to the largest dimensions of social context. Traditional critics often refer to him as the poet historian, in whose work incidents from that important moment in Chinese history come alive. He was also a meticulous craftsman, constantly revising his poems. In that process, like Li Po, he created the personality later readers so admire. But unlike Li Po, he presents himself as a character who has suffered, endured much, and changed.

PRONOUNCING GLOSSARY

The following list uses common English syllables and strees accents to provide rough equivalents of selected words whose pronunciation may be unfamiliar to the general reader.

An Lu-shan: *ahn loo–shahn*

Ch'ang-an: *chahng–ahn*

Ch'eng-tu: *chuhng–doo*

Chiang: *jyahng*

Fu-chou: *foo–joe*

Lu-tzu: *loo–dzuh*

P'eng-ya: *puhng–yah*

Sun Tsai: *swun dzai*

T'ung-chia: *toohng–jyah*

Song of P'eng-ya[1]

I remember when first we fled the rebellion,[2]
Hurrying north, we passed through hardship and danger.
The night was deep on the P'eng-ya Road,
And the moon was shining on Whitewater Mountain.
The whole family had been traveling long on foot—   5
Most whom we met seemed to have no shame.
Here and there birds of the valley sang,
We saw no travelers going the other way.
My baby girl gnawed at me in her hunger,
And I feared wild beasts would hear her cries: 10
I held her to my chest, covered her mouth,
But she twisted and turned crying louder in rage.
My little son did his best to take care of things,
With purpose went off and got sour plums to eat.
It had thundered and rained half the past week,   15
We clung together, pulling through mud and mire,
And having made no provision against the rain,
The paths were slippery, our clothes were cold.
At times we went through great agony
Making only a few miles in an entire day.   20
Fruits of the wilds served as our provisions,
Low-hanging branches became our roof.
Then early in mornings we went through the runoff,
To spend the evening at homestead smoke on horizon.
We stayed a while in T'ung-chia Swamp   25
And were about to go out Lu-tzu Pass,
When an old friend of mine, Sun Tsai by name—
His great goodness reached the tiers of cloud—
Welcomed us as night's blackness was falling,
Hung out lanterns, opened his many gates,   30
With warm water had us wash our feet,
Cut paper flags to summon our souls,
Then afterward brought in his wife and children,
Whose eyes, seeing us, streamed with tears.

1. All selections translated by Stephen Owen.   2. That is, the time Tu Fu took his family out of the path of An Lu-shan's rebel army.

As if unconscious, my brood was sleeping;   35
He woke them kindly and gave them plates of food.
And I make this vow to you,
That forever I will be your brother, your kin.
Then he emptied the hall where we sat,
I rested peacefully—he offered what gave me joy.   40
Who else would be willing in times of such trouble
To show his good heart so openly?
Since we have parted, a year has run its course,
And still the barbarian weaves his calamities.
When shall I ever have the wings   45
To fly off and alight before your eyes?

Moonlit Night[1]

The moon tonight in Fu-chou
She[2] watches alone from her chamber,
While faraway I think lovingly on daughters and sons,
Who do not yet know how to remember Ch'ang-an.[3]
In scented fog, her cloudlike hairdo moist,   5
In its clear beams, her jade-white arms are cold.
When shall we lean in the empty window,
Moonlit together, its light drying traces of tears.

Chiang Village[1]

From west of the towering ochre clouds
    the sun's rays descend to the level earth.

Birds raise a racket in the brushwood gate
    as the traveler comes home from a thousand miles.

Wife and children are amazed I survived,   5
    when surprise settles, they wipe away tears.

I was swept along in the turmoil of the times,
    by chance I managed to make it back alive.

Our neighbors are filling the wall,[2]
    so deeply moved they're sobbing too.   10

Toward night's end I take another candle,
    and face you, as if it still is a dream.

---

1. Tu Fu is trapped behind rebel lines in the capital Ch'ang-an.   2. His wife.   1. Written after Tu Fu
finally rejoined his wife after escaping through rebel lines.   3. That is, the person in the capital, Tu Fu
himself.   2. In other words, all the neighbors are gathering to witness the reunion. Even modest houses
had low walls around the yard.

Thousand League Pool

The blue creek fuses dark mystery within,
A holy creature, sometimes appearing, sometimes concealed—
A dragon resting in massed waters coiled,
His lair sunken under a thousand leagues.
Pace each step with care, pass over cliff rim,   5
Bent for balance go down into mist and haze,
Look out over a stretch of mighty waves,
Then stand back on a greatness of gray stone.
The mountain is steep, the one path here now ends
Where sheer banks form two facing walls: 10
Thus were they hewn, rooted in nothingness,
Their inverted reflections hung in shaking waters.
The black tells of the vortex's bottom,
The clear parts display a shattered sparkling.
Deep within it a lone cloud comes,   15
And the birds in flight are not outside.
High-hung vines for its battle tents,
The winter trees rank its legions' standards.
Streams from afar twist their flows to reach here,
Caves give subterranean vent to swift scouring.   20
I have come to a place hidden, a realm without men,
The response it stirs is all our own.
Now, asking my leave, unwillingness hangs strongly on,
As old age approaches, this visit, the finest.

Hiding himself away, he sleeps in long scales;   25
The mighty stone blocks his going and his coming—
Oh, when shall the blazing skies of summer pass,
That his will may exult in the meeting of wind and rain.

My Thatched Roof Is Ruined by the Autumn Wind

In the high autumn skies of September
    the wind cried out in rage,
Tearing off in whirls from my rooftop
    three plies of thatch.
The thatch flew across the river,   5
    was strewn on the floodplain,
The high stalks tangled in tips
    of tall forest trees,
The low ones swirled in gusts across ground
    and sank into mud puddles.   10
The children from the village to the south
    made a fool of me, impotent with age,
Without compunction plundered what was mine
    before my very eyes,
Brazenly took armfuls of thatch,   15
    ran off into the bamboo,

And I screamed lips dry and throat raw,
    but no use.
Then I made my way home, learning on staff,
    sighing to myself.   20
A moment later the wind calmed down,
    clouds turned dark as ink,
The autumn sky rolling and overcast,
    blacker towards sunset,
And our cotton quilts were years old   25
    and cold as iron,
My little boy slept poorly,
    kicked rips in them.
Above the bed the roof leaked,
    no place was dry,   30
And the raindrops ran down like strings,
    without a break.
I have lived through upheavals and ruin
    and have seldom slept very well,
But have no idea how I shall pass   35
    this night of soaking.
Oh, to own a mighty mansion
    of a hundred thousand rooms,
A great roof for the poorest gentlemen
    of all this world,   40
    a place to make them smile,
A building unshaken by wind or rain,
    as solid as a mountain,
Oh, when shall I see before my eyes
    a towering roof such as this?   45
Then I'd accept the ruin of my own little hut
    and death by freezing.

A Guest Comes

North of my cottage, south of my cottage,
    spring waters everywhere,
And all that I see are the flocks of gulls
    coming here day after day,
My path through the flowers has never yet   5
    been swept for a visitor,
But today this wicker gate of mine
    stands open just for you.
The market is far, so for dinner
    there'll be no wide range of tastes,   10
Our home is poor, and for wine
    we have only an older vintage.
Are you willing to sit here and drink
    with the old man who lives next door?
I'll call to him over the hedge,   15
    and we'll finish the last of the cups.

Spending the Night in a Tower by the River

A visible darkness grows up mountain paths,
I lodge by river gate high in a study,
Frail cloud on cliff edge passing the night,
The lonely moon topples amid the waves.
Steady, one after another, a line of cranes in flight;   5
Howling over the kill, wild dogs and wolves.
No sleep for me. I worry over battles.
I have no strength to right the universe.

Writing of My Feelings Traveling by Night

Slender grasses, breeze faint on the shore;
here, the looming mast, the lonely night boat.

Stars hang down on the breadth of the plain,
the moon gushes in the great river's current.   5

My name shall not be known from my writing,
sick, growing old, I must yield up my post.

Wind-tossed, fluttering—what is my likeness?
in Heaven and Earth, a single gull of the sands.

YÜAN CHEN
779–831

Long fiction was a relatively late development in China. Some elements of a tradition of historical saga survive from the ancient period, but early Chinese literature showed its considerable narrative genius primarily in the anecdote and parable. During the early middle period, between the third and seventh centuries, the anecdotal tradition was further developed in accounts of eccentric or exemplary behavior and witty dialogues. At the same time we begin to find collections of short tales about ghosts, fox spirits, and assorted demons, a genre that remained very popular up to the present century. During the T'ang period (618–907), writers began to expand on the skeletal narrative style of the earlier period.

There are two distinct groups of T'ang stories: one written in classical Chinese and the other in early vernacular Chinese. The vernacular narratives, elaborating known stories from the Buddhist tradition and Chinese history, were discovered early in the twentieth century in a sealed Buddhist repository at Tun-huang, an outpost of the caravan route in northwest China. Most of the tales in classical Chinese, a far larger corpus, were printed in a large collection in 981 and have been known throughout the tradition. The classical tales, known as *ch'uan-ch'i* ("accounts of remarkable things"), are still comparatively short by Western standards, but they show a true delight in the craft of telling—in atmosphere, characterization, and detail. Unlike

vulgar lines to make sure you would come here. It was an improper thing to do, and of course I feel ashamed. But I hope that you will keep within the bounds of decency and commit no outrage."

As she finished speaking, she turned on her heel and left him. For some time Chang stood, dumbfounded. Then he went back over the wall to his quarters, all hope gone.

A few nights later Chang was sleeping alone by the veranda when someone shook him awake. Startled, he rose up, to see Hung-niang standing there, a coverlet and pillow in her arms. She patted him and said, "She is coming! She is coming! Why are you sleeping?" And she spread the quilt and put the pillow beside his. As she left, Chang sat up straight and rubbed his eyes. For some time it seemed as though he were still dreaming, but nonetheless he waited dutifully. Then there was Hung-niang again, with Miss Ts'ui leaning on her arm. She was shy and yielding, and appeared almost not to have the strength to move her limbs. The contrast with her stiff formality at their last encounter was complete.

This evening was the night of the eighteenth, and the slanting rays of the moon cast a soft light over half the bed. Chang felt a kind of floating lightness and wondered whether this was an immortal who visited him, not someone from the world of men. After a while the temple bell sounded. Daybreak was near. As Hung-niang urged her to leave, she wept softly and clung to him. Hung-niang helped her up, and they left. The whole time she had not spoken a single word. With the first light of dawn Chang got up, wondering, was it a dream? But the perfume still lingered, and as it got lighter he could see on his arm traces of her makeup and the teardrops sparkling still on the mat.

For some ten days afterward there was no word from her. Chang composed a poem of sixty lines on "An Encounter with an Immortal" which he had not yet completed when Hung-niang happened by, and he gave it to her for her mistress. After that she let him see her again, and for nearly a month he would join her in what her poem called the "western chamber," slipping out at dawn and returning stealthily at night. Chang once asked what her mother thought about the situation. She said, "She knows there is nothing she can do about it, and so she hopes you will regularize things."

Before long Chang was about to go to Ch'ang-an, and he let her know his intentions in a poem. Miss Ts'ui made no objections at all, but the look of pain on her face was very touching. On the eve of his departure he was unable to see her again. Then Chang went off to the west. A few months later he again made a trip to P'u and stayed several months with Miss Ts'ui.

She was a very good calligrapher and wrote poetry, but for all that he kept begging to see her work, she would never show it. Chang wrote poems for her, challenging her to match them, but she paid them little attention. The thing that made her unusual was that, while she excelled in the arts, she always acted as though she were ignorant, and although she was quick and clever in speaking, she would seldom indulge in repartee. She loved Chang very much, but would never say so in words. At the time she was subject to moods of profound melancholy, but she never let on. She seldom showed on her face the emotions she felt. On one occasion she was playing her zither alone at night. She did not know Chang was listening, and the music was full of sadness. As soon as he spoke, she stopped and would play no more. This made him all the more infatuated with her.

Some time later Chang had to go west again for the scheduled examinations. It was the eve of his departure, and though he had said nothing about what it involved, he sat sighing unhappily at her side. Miss Ts'ui had guessed that he was going to leave for good. Her manner was respectful, but she spoke deliberately and in a low voice. "To seduce someone and then abandon her is perfectly natural, and it would be presumptuous of me to resent it. It would be an act of charity on your part if, having first seduced me, you were to go through with it and fulfill your oath of lifelong devotion. But in either case, what is there to be so upset about in this trip? However, I see you are not happy and I have no way to cheer you up. You have praised my zither playing, and in the past I have been embarrassed to play for you. Now that you are going away, I shall do what you so often requested."

She had them prepare her zither and started to play the prelude to the "Rainbow Robe and Feather Skirt." After a few notes, her playing grew wild with grief until the piece was no longer recognizable. Everyone was reduced to tears, and Miss Ts'ui abruptly stopped playing, put down the zither, and ran back to her mother's room with tears streaming down her face. She did not come back.

The next morning Chang went away. The following year he stayed on in the capital, having failed the examinations. He wrote a letter to Miss Ts'ui to reassure her, and her reply read roughly as follows:

> I have read your letter with its message of consolation, and it filled my childish heart with mingled grief and joy. In addition you sent me a box of ornaments to adorn my hair and a stick of pomade to make my lips smooth. It was most kind of you; but for whom am I to make myself attractive? As I look at these presents my breast is filled with sorrow.
>
> Your letter said that you will stay on in the capital to pursue your studies, and of course you need quiet and the facilities there to make progress. Still it is hard on the person left alone in this far-off place. But such is my fate, and I should not complain. Since last fall I have been listless and without hope. In company I can force myself to talk and smile, but come evening I always shed tears in the solitude of my own room. Even in my sleep I often sob, yearning for the absent one. Or I am in your arms for a moment as it used to be, but before the secret meeting is done I am awake and heartbroken. The bed seems still warm beside me, but the one I love is far away.
>
> Since you said good-bye the new year has come. Ch'ang-an is a city of pleasure with chances for love everywhere. I am truly fortunate that you have not forgotten me and that your affection is not worn out. Loving you as I do, I have no way of repaying you, except to be true to our vow of lifelong fidelity.
>
> Our first meeting was at the banquet, as cousins. Then you persuaded my maid to inform me of your love; and I was unable to keep my childish heart firm. You made advances, like that other poet, Ssuma Hsiang-ju.[9] I failed to repulse them as the girl did who threw her shuttle.[1] When I offered myself in your bed, you treated me with the greatest kindness, and I supposed, in my innocence, that I could always depend on you. How could I have foreseen that our encounter could not possibly lead to something definite, that having disgraced myself by coming to you, there was no further chance of serving you openly as a wife? To the end of my days this will be a lasting regret—I must hide my sighs and be silent. If you, out of kindness, would condescend to fulfill my selfish

9. An allusion to the story of the Han poet, Ssu-ma Hsiang-ju (179–117 B.C.), who enticed the young widow Cho Wen-chün to elope by his zither playing.   1. A neighboring girl, named Kao, repulsed Hsieh K'un's (280–322) advances by throwing her shuttle in his face. He lost two teeth.

wish, though it came on my dying day it would seem to be a new lease on life. But if, as a man of the world, you curtail your feelings, sacrificing the lesser to the more important, and look on this connection as shameful, so that your solemn vow can be dispensed with, still my true love will not vanish though my bones decay and my frame dissolve; in wind and dew it will seek out the ground you walk on. My love in life and death is told in this. I weep as I write, for feelings I cannot express. Take care of yourself; a thousand times over, take care of your dear self.

This bracelet of jade is something I wore as a child; I send it to serve as a gentleman's belt pendant. Like jade may you be invariably firm and tender; like a bracelet may there be no break between what came before and what is to follow. Here are also a skein of multicolored thread and a tea roller of mottled bamboo. These things have no intrinsic value, but they are to signify that I want you to be true as jade, and your love to endure unbroken as a bracelet. The spots on the bamboo are like the marks of my tears,[2] and my unhappy thoughts are as tangled as the thread: these objects are symbols of my feelings and tokens for all time of my love. Our hearts are close, though our bodies are far apart and there is no time I can expect to see you. But where the hidden desires are strong enough, there will be a meeting of spirits. Take care of yourself, a thousand times over. The springtime wind is often chill; eat well for your health's sake. Be circumspect and careful, and do not think too often of my unworthy person.

Chang showed her letter to his friends, and in this way word of the affair got around. One of them, Yang Chü-yüan, a skillful poet, wrote a quatrain on "Young Miss Ts'ui":

> For clear purity jade cannot equal his complexion;
> On the iris in the inner court snow begins to melt.
> A romantic young man filled with thoughts of love.
> A letter from the Hsiao girl,[3] brokenhearted.

Yüan Chen[4] of Ho-nan wrote a continuation of Chang's poem "Encounter with an Immortal," also in thirty couplets:

> Faint moonbeams pierce the curtained window;
> Fireflies glimmer across the blue sky.
> The far horizon begins now to pale;
> Dwarf trees gradually turn darker green.
> A dragon song crosses the court bamboo; 5
> A phoenix air brushes the wellside tree.
> The silken robe trails through the thin mist;
> The pendant circles tinkle in the light breeze.
> The accredited envoy accompanies Hsi wang-mu;[5]
> From the cloud's center comes Jade Boy.[6] 10
> Late at night everyone is quiet;
> At daybreak the rain drizzles.
> Pearl radiance shines on her decorated sandals;

---

2. Alluding to the legend of the two wives of the sage ruler Shun, who stained the bamboo with their tears.
3. In T'ang times the term "Hsiao-niang" referred to young women in general. Here it means Ying-ying.
4. Yüan Chen (775–831) was a key literary figure in the middle of the T'ang period.   5. Hsi wang-mu, the Queen Mother of the West, is a mythological figure supposedly dwelling in the K'un-lun Mountains in China's far west. In early accounts she is sometimes described as part human and part beast, but since early post-Han times she has usually been described as a beautiful immortal. Her huge palace is inhabited by other immortals. Within its precincts grow the magic peach trees which bear the fruits of immortality once every three thousand years. This might be an allusion to Ying-ying's mother.   6. The Jade Boy might allude to Ying-ying's brother.

Flower glow shows off the embroidered skirt.
Jasper hairpin: a walking colored phoenix;   15
Gauze shawl: embracing vermilion rainbow.
She says she comes from Jasper Flower Bank
And is going to pay court at Green Jade Palace.
On an outing north of Lo-yang's[7] wall,
By chance he came to the house east of Sung Yü's.[8]   20
His dalliance she rejects a bit at first,
But her yielding love already is disclosed.
Lowered locks put in motion cicada shadows;[9]
Returning steps raise jade dust.
Her face turns to let flow flower snow   25
As she climbs into bed, silk covers in her arms.
Love birds in a neck-entwining dance;
Kingfishers in a conjugal cage.
Eyebrows, out of shyness, contracted;
Lip rouge, from the warmth, melted.   30
Her breath is pure: fragrance of orchid buds;
Her skin is smooth: richness of jade flesh.
No strength, too limp to lift a wrist;
Many charms, she likes to draw herself together.
Sweat runs: pearls drop by drop;   35
Hair in disorder: black luxuriance.
Just as they rejoice in the meeting of a lifetime
They suddenly hear the night is over.
There is no time for lingering;
It is hard to give up the wish to embrace.   40
Her comely face shows the sorrow she feels;
With fragrant words they swear eternal love.
She gives him a bracelet to plight their troth;
He ties a lovers' knot as sign their hearts are one.
Tear-borne powder runs before the clear mirror;   45
Around the flickering lamp are nighttime insects.
Moonlight is still softly shining
As the rising sun gradually dawns.
Riding on a wild goose she returns to the Lo River.
Blowing a flute he ascends Mount Sung.[1]   50
His clothes are fragrant still with musk perfume;
The pillow is slippery yet with red traces.
Thick, thick, the grass grows on the dyke;
Floating, floating, the tumbleweed yearns for the isle.
Her plain zither plays the "Resentful Crane Song";   55
In the clear Milky Way she looks for the returning wild goose.[2]
The sea is broad and truly hard to cross;
The sky is high and not easy to traverse.
The moving cloud is nowhere to be found—
Hsiao Shih[3] stays in his chamber.   60

---

7. Possibly a reference to the goddess of the Lo River.   8. In "The Lechery of Master Teng-t'u," Sung Yü
tells about the beautiful girl next door to the east who climbed up on the wall to flirt with him.   9. Referring to her hairdo in the cicada style.   1. This is also known as the Central Mountain. . . . Here the one
ascending the mountain may refer to Chang.   2. Which might be carrying a message.   3. Hsiao Shih
was a well-known flute-playing immortal of the Spring and Autumn period.

All of Chang's friends who heard of the affair marveled at it, but Chang had determined on his own course of action. Yüan Chen was especially close to him and so was in a position to ask him for an explanation. Chang said, "It is a general rule that those women endowed by Heaven with great beauty invariably either destroy themselves or destroy someone else. If this Ts'ui woman were to meet someone with wealth and position, she would use the favor her charms gain her to be cloud and rain or dragon or monster—I can't imagine what she might turn into. Of old, King Hsin of the Shang and King Yu of the Chou[4] were brought low by women, in spite of the size of their kingdoms and the extent of their power; their armies were scattered, their persons butchered, and down to the present day their names are objects of ridicule. I have no inner strength to withstand this evil influence. That is why I have resolutely suppressed my love."

At this statement everyone present sighed deeply.

Over a year later Ts'ui was married, and Chang for his part had taken a wife. Happening to pass through the town where she was living, he asked permission of her husband to see her, as a cousin. The husband spoke to her, but Ts'ui refused to appear. Chang's feelings of hurt showed on his face, and she was told about it. She secretly sent him a poem:

> Emaciated, I have lost my looks,
> Tossing and turning, too weary to leave my bed.
> It's not because of others I am ashamed to rise;
> For you I am haggard and before you ashamed.

She never did appear. Some days later when Chang was about to leave, she sent another poem of farewell:

> Cast off and abandoned, what can I say now,
> Whom you loved so briefly long ago?
> Any love you had then for me
> Will do for the one you have now.

After this he never heard any more about her. His contemporaries for the most part conceded that Chang had done well to rectify his mistake. I have often mentioned this among friends so that, forewarned, they might avoid doing such a thing, or if they did, that they might not be led astray by it. In the ninth month of a year in the Chen-yüan period, when an official, Li Kung-ch'ui, was passing the night in my house at the Pacification Quarter, the conversation touched on the subject. He found it most extraordinary and composed a "Song of Ying-ying" to commemorate the affair. Ts'ui's child-name was Ying-ying, and Kung-ch'ui used it for his poem.

---

4. Hsin (Chou) was the familiar last ruler of the Shang Dynasty, whose misrule and fall are attributed to the influence of his favorite Ta-chi. King Yu (ruled 781–771 B.C.), last ruler of the Western Chou, was misled by his consort Pao-ssu. The behavior of both rulers is traditionally attributed to their infatuation with the wicked women they loved.

LI CH'ING-CHAO
1084–ca. 1151

There is no better introduction to Li Ch'ing-chao's life than her "Afterword" to her husband's study of early inscriptions, the *Records on Metal and Stone*. Prefaces and afterwords were usually stylized, scholarly, and relatively impersonal; but in Li Ch'ing-chao's hands the form became the means to show the relation between a work of scholarship and a pair of lives. The "Afterword" tells first of the idyllic early years of marriage while her husband, Chao Te-fu, was a student in the Imperial Academy and of their shared passion for books and learning. Their fate as a couple was somehow mirrored in the fate of their collection of books and antiques: begun for their joint pleasure, it increasingly grew into an obsession that dominated her husband's life, until at last both the collection and her husband's scholarly work came to reveal only the differences between them.

The fate of both the marriage and the collection are set within the larger context of the fate of the Sung Dynasty, which in 1126 and 1127 lost its capital, its emperor, and north China to the invading Chin Tartars. The captured Sung emperor, whose extravagance and inattention to political matters were blamed for the loss of the north, happened himself to be an obsessive connoisseur of artworks. As Li Ch'ing-chao hastily fled south, the huge collection was gradually scattered and lost. Soon after they escaped the north, her husband died. Thereafter the residue of the collection represented many things to Li Ch'ing-chao. At one point it seemed to be the means to purchase her husband's posthumous honor after he was falsely accused of treason; the books were also her companions in her constant flight from place to place, and the few pieces that finally remained became cherished mementos of her former life. Throughout this short work Li Ch'ing-chao returns again and again to the relation between people and their possessions, to their role in human relationships, and to the way in which such objects gain value and meaning.

Li Ch'ing-chao is considered one of the finest writers of traditional song lyric. There was a long and complex relation between poetry and song in traditional China. The works of poets were often set to music and were sometimes modified to answer musical needs. During the T'ang period, however, an entirely new kind of music became popular, stanzaic melodies with musical lines of unequal length. In a language where the pitch of a word (or "tone") is essential to understanding its meaning, Chinese song lyrics had to pay careful attention to the requirements of a particular melody to be comprehensible: the pitch of the word had to match the pitch of the music. T'ang poets began the practice of composing new lyrics for these popular irregular melodies, and this new poetic form came to be known as *tz'u*, best translated as "song lyrics." These often concerned love and were performed in the entertainment quarters of the great cities and at parties. By the early Sung Dynasty (960–1279) the song lyric had evolved into a verse form with a very different character from that of classical poetry. It was primarily associated with delicate sensibility, and it sought to evoke the mood of moments.

The relatively few of Li Ch'ing-chao's song lyrics that survive are among the finest examples of the form. In the lyrics to the melody "Every Note Slow" she takes up the essential concerns of the form and one of the oldest questions in the Chinese tradition, which is the capacity of language to express adequately what occurs in the mind and heart. The lyric attempts to evoke the mood of the moment and closes by comparing the emotion she has evoked to the simple word *sorrow*, which is true, yet too broad to convey what she feels. Li Ch'ing-chao had a genius for scenes that could evoke feeling, as in the lyrics to "Southern Song," in which she changes from her light summer clothes to a warmer autumn dress, decorated with scenes of a lotus pond. But the dress is old and its gilt lotus leaves are flaking off, making it look like the dying vegetation of a real lotus pond, which becomes both the physical evidence and the symbol of her own aging. It is at such moments that she solves in her own way the ancient problem of how words can express the feeling of the moment.

PRONOUNCING GLOSSARY

The following list uses common English syllables to provide rough equivalents of selected words whose pronunciation may be unfamiliar to the general reader.

ch'ai-hu: *chai–hoo*

Chang Fei-ch'ing: *jahng fay–ching*

Chao Te-fu: *jau duh–foo*

Chiang-tu: *jyahng–doo*

Chien-chung: *jyen–juhng*

Ch'ih-yang: *chur–yahng*

Ch'ing-chou: *ching–joh*

chüan: *jooan*

Ch'u-chou: *choo–joh*

Chung Fu-hao: *juhng foo–hau*

Ch'ung-ning: *chuhng–ning*

Hsiang-kuo: *shyahng–gwoh*

Hsiao Yi: *shyau ee*

Hsü Hsi: *shoo shee*

Ko-t'ien: *guh–tyen*

Lai-chou: *lai–joh*

Li Ch'ing-chao: *lee ching–jau*

Liu Tsung-yüan: *lyoh dzuhng–yooan*

P'eng: *puhng*

Shao-hsing: *shau–shing*

Sui: *sway*

Tse-ch'uan: *dzuh–chooahn*

Tso-chuan: *dzwoh–jooahn*

tz'u: *tsuh*

Yüan Tsai: *yooan dzai*

Yüeh-chou: *yooeh–joh*

Afterword to Records on Metal and Stone[1]

What are the preceding chapters of *Records on Metal and Stone?*—the work of the governor, Chao Te-fu. In it he took inscriptions on bells, tripods, steamers, kettles, washbasins, ladles, goblets, and bowls from the Three Dynasties of high antiquity all the way down to the Five Dynasties (immediately preceding our Sung); here also he took the surviving traces of acts by eminent men and obscure scholars inscribed on large steles and stone disks. In all there were two thousand sections of what appeared on metal and stone. Through all these inscriptions, one might be able to correct historical errors, make historical judgements, and mete out praise and blame. It contains things which, on the highest level, correspond to the Way of the Sages, and on a lower level, supplement the omissions of historians. It is a great amount indeed. Yet catastrophe fell on Wang Ya and Yüan Tsai alike: what did it matter that the one hoarded books and paintings while the other merely hoarded pepper? Ch'ang-yu and Yüan-k'ai both had a disease—it made no difference that the disease of one was a passion for money, and of the other, a passion for transmission of knowledge and commentary. Although their reputations differed, they were the same in being deluded.

In 1101, in the first year of the Chien-chung Reign, I came as a bride to the Chao household. At that time my father was a division head in the Ministry of Rites, and my father-in-law, later Grand Councilor, was an executive in the Ministry of Personnel. My husband was then twenty-one and a stu-

1. All selections translated by Stephen Owen.

dent in the Imperial Academy. In those days both families, the Chaos and the Lis, were not well-to-do and were always frugal. On the first and fifteenth day of every month, my husband would get a short vacation from the Academy: he would "pawn some clothes"[2] for five hundred cash and go to the market at Hsiang-kuo Temple, where he would buy fruit and rubbings of inscriptions. When he brought these home, we would sit facing one another, rolling them out before us, examining and munching. And we thought ourselves persons of the age of Ko-t'ien.[3]

When, two years later, he went to take up a post, we lived on rice and vegetables, dressed in common cloth; but he would search out the most remote spots and out-of-the-way places to fulfill his interest in the world's most ancient writings and unusual characters. When his father, the Grand Councilor, was in office, various friends and relations held positions in the Imperial Libraries; there one might find many ancient poems omitted from the *Book of Songs*, unofficial histories, and writings never before seen, works hidden in walls and recovered from tombs. He would work hard at copying such things, drawing ever more pleasure from the activity, until he was unable to stop himself. Later, if he happened to see a work of painting or calligraphy by some person of ancient or modern times, or unusual vessels of the Three Dynasties of high antiquity, he would still pawn our clothes to buy them. I recall that in the Ch'ung-ning Reign[4] a man came with a painting of peonies by Hsü Hsi and asked twenty thousand cash for it. In those days twenty thousand cash was a hard sum to raise, even for children of nobility. We kept it with us a few days, and having thought of no plan by which we could purchase it, we returned it. For several days afterward husband and wife faced one another in deep depression.

Later we lived privately at home for ten years, gathering what we could here and there to have enough for food and clothing. Afterward, my husband governed two provinces in succession, and he used up all his salary on "lead and wooden tablets" [for scholarly work]. Whenever he got a book, we would collate it with other editions and make corrections together, repair it, and label it with the correct title. When he got hold of a piece of calligraphy, a painting, a goblet, or a tripod, we would go over it at our leisure, pointing out faults and flaws, setting for our nightly limit the time it took one candle to burn down. Thus our collection came to surpass all others in fineness of paper and the perfection of the characters.

I happen to have an excellent memory, and every evening after we finished eating, we would sit in the hall called "Return Home" and make tea. Pointing to the heaps of books and histories, we would guess on which line of which page in which chapter of which book a certain passage could be found. Success in guessing determined who got to drink his or her tea first. Whenever I got it right, I would raise the teacup, laughing so hard that the tea would spill in my lap, and I would get up, not having been able to drink anything at all. I would have been glad to grow old in such a world. Thus, even though we were living in anxiety, hardship, and poverty, our wills were not broken.

When the book collection was complete, we set up a library in "Return Home" hall, with huge bookcases where the books were catalogued in

---

2. Refers to the allowance for students at the Imperial Academy.   3. A mythical emperor of earliest antiquity, when all the world was at peace.   4. From 1102 to 1106.

sequence. There we put the books. Whenever I wanted to read, I would ask for the key, make a note in the ledger, then take out the books. If one of them was a bit damaged or soiled, it would be our responsibility to repair the spot and copy it out in a neat hand. There was no longer the same ease and casualness as before. This was an attempt to gain convenience which led instead to nervousness and anxiety. I couldn't bear it. And I began to plan how to do away with more than one meat in our meals, how to do away with all finery in my dress; for my hair there were no ornaments of bright pearls or kingfisher feathers; the household had no implements for gilding or embroidery. Whenever we would come upon a history or the work of a major writer, if there was nothing wrong with the printing and no errors in the edition, we would buy it on the spot to have as a second copy. His family had always specialized in *The Book of Changes* and the *Tso chuan*,[5] so the collection of works in those two traditions was most perfect and complete. Books lay ranged on tables and desks, scattered on top of one another on pillows and bedding. This was what took our fancy and what occupied our minds, what drew our eyes and what our spirits inclined to; and our joy was greater than the pleasure others had in dancing girls, dogs, and horses.

In 1126, the first year of the Ching-k'ang Reign, my husband was governing Tse-ch'uan when we heard that the Chin Tartars were moving against the capital. He was in a daze, realizing that all those full trunks and overflowing chests, which he regarded so lovingly and mournfully, would surely soon be his possessions no longer. In the third month of spring in 1127, the first year of the Chien-yen Reign, we hurried south for the funeral of his mother. Since we could not take the overabundance of our possessions with us, we first gave up the bulky printed volumes, the albums of paintings, and the most cumbersome of the vessels. Thus we reduced the size of the collection several times, and still we had fifteen cartloads of books. When we reached Tung-hai, it took a string of boats to ferry them all across the Huai, and again across the Yangtse to Chien-k'ang. In our old mansion in Ch'ing-chou we still had more than ten rooms of books and various items locked away, and we planned to have them all brought by boat the next year. But in the twelfth month Chin forces sacked Ch'ing-chou, and those ten or so rooms I spoke of were all reduced to ashes.

The next autumn, the ninth month of 1128, my husband took charge of Chien-k'ang Prefecture but relinquished the position in the spring of the following year. Again we put everything in boats and went up to Wu-hu and Ku-shu, intending to take up lodging on the River Kan. That summer in the fifth month we had reached Ch'ih-yang. At that point an imperial decree arrived, ordering my husband to take charge of Hu-chou, and before he assumed that office, to proceed to an audience with the Emperor. Therefore he had the household stop at Ch'ih-yang from which he would go off alone to answer the summons. On the thirteenth day of the sixth month he set off to carry out his duty. He had the boats pulled up onto the shore, and he sat there on the bank, in summer clothes with his headband set high on his forehead, his spirit like a tiger's, his eyes gleaming as though they would shoot into a person, while he gazed toward the boats and took his leave. I was in a terrible state of mind. I shouted to him, "If I hear the city is in dan-

---

5. Confucian classics teaching divination and early history, respectively.

ger, what should I do?" He answered from afar, his hands on his hips: "Follow the crowd. If you can't do otherwise, abandon the household goods first, then the clothes, then the books and scrolls, then the old bronzes—but carry the sacrificial vessels for the ancestral temple yourself; live or die with them; don't give *them* up." With this he galloped off on his horse.

As he was hurrying on his journey, he suffered sunstroke from the intense heat, and by the time he reached imperial headquarters, he had contracted a malarial fever. At the end of the seventh month I received a letter that he was lying sick. I was much alarmed, considering my husband's excitable nature and how nothing had been able to prevent the illness deteriorating into fever; his temperature might rise even higher, and in that case he would have to take chilled medicines; then the sickness would really be something to be worried about. Thereupon I set out by boat and in one day and night traveled three hundred leagues. At the point when I arrived he was taking large doses of *ch'ai-hu* and yellow *ch'in;*[6] he had a recurring fever with dysentery, and the illness appeared terminal. I was weeping, and in such a desperate situation I could not bring myself to ask him what was to be done after his death. On the eighteenth day of the eighth month he could no longer get up; he took his brush and wrote a poem; when he finished, he passed away, with no thought at all for the future provision of his family.

When the funeral was over I had nowhere to go. His Majesty had already sent the palace ladies elsewhere, and I heard that crossings of the Yangtse were to be prohibited. At the time I still had twenty thousand *chüan* of books, two thousand copies of inscriptions on metal and stone with colophons,[7] table service and mats enough to entertain a hundred guests, along with other possessions equaling those already mentioned. I also grew very sick, to the point that my only vital sign was a rasping breath. The situation was getting more serious every day. I thought of my husband's brother-in-law, an executive in the Ministry of War on garrison duty in Hung-chou, and I dispatched two former employees of my husband to go ahead to my brother-in-law, taking the baggage. That winter in the twelfth month Chin invaders sacked Hung-chou and all was lost. Those books which, as I said, took a string of boats to ferry across the Yangtse were scattered into clouds of smoke. What remained were a few light scrolls and calligraphy pieces; manuscript copies of the collections of Li Po, Tu Fu, Han Yü, and Liu Tsung-yüan;[8] a copy of *A New Account of Tales of the World;* a copy of *Discourses on Salt and Iron;* a few dozen rubbings of stone inscriptions from the Han and T'ang; ten or so ancient tripods and cauldrons; a few boxes of Southern T'ang manuscript editions—all of which I happened to have had removed to my chambers to pass the time during my illness—now a solitary pile of leftovers.

Since I could no longer go upriver, and since the movements of the invaders were unfathomable, I went to stay with my younger brother Li Hang, a reviser of edicts. By the time I reached T'ai-chou, the governor of the place had already fled. Proceeding on to Shan through Mu-chou, we left the clothing and linen behind. Hurrying to Yellow Cliff, we hired a boat to take us toward the sea, following the fleeing court. The court halted a while

---

6. Knowledge of herbal lore was expected of wives.   7. Short prose works giving the essential scholarly information on the inscriptions. These were Chao Te-fu's copies and rubbings of early inscriptions. "*Chüan*": like a chapter and the measure used to count the size of a library.   8. T'ang poets and prose writers.

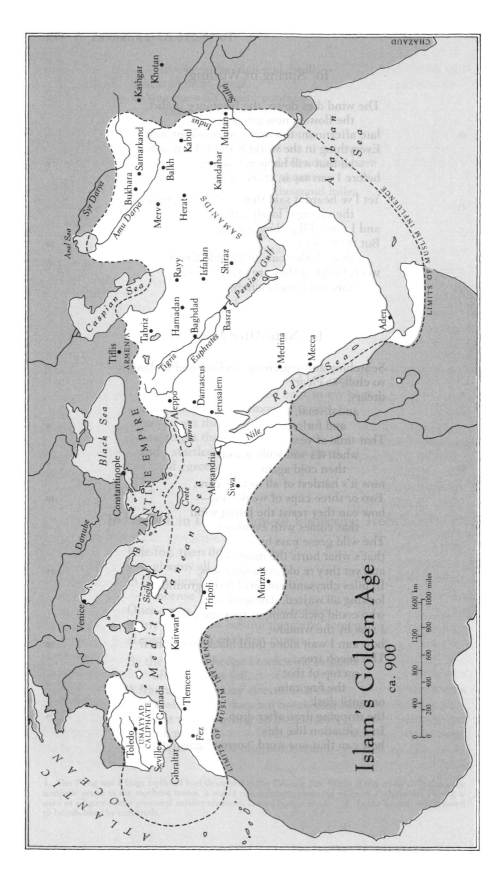

Islam's Golden Age

ca. 900

The Rise of Islam and
Islamic Literature

In the early seventh century the prophet Muhammad received revelations in the Arabic language that his followers gathered together after his death into a book known as the Koran. That book, together with his teachings, became the basis of a new religion and community that we know as Islam. Under Muhammad's leadership, the Muslim community quickly expanded until it included the whole of Arabia, uniting all its many tribes for the first time in their history. After Muhammad's death, these tribes, now united and inspired by the faith of Islam, swept out of Arabia to conquer the Persian and Byzantine empires to the east and west of them. In so doing they radically altered the history of the world.

Charles Martel defeated a Muslim invading force at Tours in 732, an event celebrated in *The Song of Roland*, and so checked the Muslim advance into western Europe; Byzantium also halted the invading armies in central Anatolia, but elsewhere the forces of Islam advanced with miraculous invincibility. Within a century the new empire stretched from southern Spain to northern India and from the Caucasus to the Indian Ocean. Iberia, North Africa, Arabia, Syria, eastern Anatolia and the Caucasus, Mesopotamia, Iran, central Asia and the Indus Valley were all governed by Muslims. This vast empire was ruled by a succession of caliphs (vicars) drawn from the prophet's family. They continued his political and religious leadership of the Islamic community but not his prophetic office. Factional strife, regional loyalties, and personal ambition combined to fragment and weaken the political integrity of the Islamic empire at times, but the primacy of the Islamic religion throughout the region remained constant, and the caliph retained great spiritual authority even when his political authority was challenged. The Islamic civilization that grew up in the wake of the great conquests was a synthesis of the religion and culture of Arabia with the great imperial traditions of the eastern Mediterranean and the Persian empire of the Sassanians. This synthesis molded the politics, science, literature, and arts of the diverse peoples who adopted Islam and, as the dominant culture of the region, had a shaping influence on such non-Islamic peoples as the Armenians and the Jews. In almost every arena of human endeavor, Islamic norms prevailed.

Although the Koran explicitly prohibits forcible conversion to Islam, the spread of the Islamic faith was inevitably linked to the expansion of Islamic rule. Muslim rulers were tolerant of those religions whose faith was based on revelation, such as Judaism and Christianity, but strictly forbade them to increase their numbers by conversion. Islam checked the growth of these religions throughout its empire and within two centuries had virtually eliminated Zoroastrianism as a significant presence in Iran. After the period of the great conquests, the borders of Islam were extended into sub-Saharan Africa, southern India and Ceylon, and throughout Southeast Asia as far as the Philippine Islands. This further expansion was not the result of a single concerted effort but carried out over several centuries by merchants and traders as much as by military conquest.

The history of Islam in its early centuries was both turbulent and violent. The earliest dynasty of caliphs, the Umayyads, was overthrown in a long and bloody revolution from which they retained only their hold over the western-most province of

Islam, al-Andalus (Spain). Their successors, the Abbasids, ruled Islam for five centuries (750–1258) and presided over its fortunes at their height. They founded Islam's great imperial city, Baghdad, in the mid-eighth century, and it became the center of a rich, cosmopolitan culture that was nourished by the ablest minds and greatest talents of every community within the empire. But after the first two centuries of their rule, the Abbasid caliphate's hold on the empire became increasingly tenuous as nominally subordinate dynasties in both the east and the west came to exercise virtually independent rule.

Religious factionalism also threatened the caliphate itself in the tenth century. Muhammad had not designated a successor before his death, and the Muslim community quickly divided between those who believed that the caliphate should remain in the prophet's bloodlines (shi'ites) and those who insisted only that it remain within his clan, the Quraysh (sunnis). Shi'ites were instrumental in the overthrow of the Umayyads, but the Abbasids betrayed their shi'ite followers almost at once, and they became an enduring opposition. In the tenth century, a shi'ite dynasty (the Fatimids) conquered Egypt and established their own caliph there, and a second shi'ite dynasty, the Buyids, gained control of the orthodox sunni caliph in Baghdad. In the eleventh century, the Saljuqs, a Turkoman tribal federation that had only recently been converted to Islam, defeated the established rulers of central Asia and Iran and established themselves as the effective rulers of the lands between Damascus and Bukhara. Despite this turbulence, throughout the Abbasid caliphate Islam enjoyed a long period of relative prosperity and surprising cultural growth.

This long, sunny day of the Islamic empire was shattered in the east by an invasion from outside. In 1219–1220 the Mongol Chinghis Khan's armies, which had already subjugated all of China, swept through central Asia, northern Iran, and Iraq, leveling cities and annihilating whole populations as they advanced. This first incursion was essentially a long, punitive raid, and the Mongols did not establish effective rule over the region in the wake of their devastating conquest. In 1253 they began a new campaign under the leadership of Hulegu Khan, with the intention of adding the Middle East to their empire. They retook the cities of central Asia and northern Iran and extended their conquests into Iraq and Syria. No Muslim army could halt them until the Mamluk rulers of Egypt defeated the Mongols at Ayn Jalut in Palestine in 1260 and ended the myth of their invincibility. However, Hulegu had already dealt the Islamic empire a blow from which it never fully recovered. In 1258 he defeated the caliphal army defending Baghdad, abandoned the city to seven days of looting and burning, and had the caliph al-Musta'sim trampled to death. Hundreds of thousands were killed in the Mongol attack on Baghdad; libraries were burned and the riches that had accumulated there during five centuries of Abbasid rule were looted or destroyed. Successors to the Abbasid caliphate of Baghdad were established in Cairo by the Mamluks, who ruled in Egypt and Syria until 1517, and later in Istanbul, by the Ottomans who dominated the whole Mediterranean region from the fifteenth century to modern times. But these caliphs never became the independent political force that the original dynasty had been, and their spiritual leadership was diminished as well. Nor did Baghdad ever regain its eminence as the chief city of Islam.

The Mongol dynasties that succeeded to rule in the eastern Islamic world converted to Islam, and within a generation they accommodated themselves to Islamic norms of rule. In the fourteenth century Tamerlane (*Timur Lang*; 1336–1405), who claimed the descent from the Mongol great khans, emulated their example and led his armies from his capital at Samarkand in central Asia in successive campaigns of conquest into Iran, Turkey, and Russia. He died as he was planning further campaigns into China. The dynasty Tamerlane founded ruled in central Asia, Iran, and Iraq until the late fifteenth century, but his successors, happily, are remembered now principally for their patronage of the arts, letters, and architecture and for the promotion of Turkish as a literary language. The Timurids were the last powerful dynasty to originate in the steppes. After them, the world of Islam came to be divided between the Ottomans in the west, the Safavids in Iran, and the Moghuls in India. The Ottomans launched the last great movement of conquest, begun in the fourteenth century, when they expanded across the Bosphorus into the Balkans, eventually threatening Vienna itself (1683). The Ottomans and the Moghuls, who came to power as the impact of Columbus's discoveries was beginning to be felt, were also the first dynasties to confront the imperial ambitions of European colonial powers.

ISLAMIC LITERATURE

Before the advent of Islam, Arabia was a small state on the margin of the "civilized" world, and Arabic was the vehicle for a great but little known poetry. Islam established Arabic as the dominant language of religion, trade, and learning throughout a vast empire. The third Abbasid caliph, al-Ma'mun (died 813), established a center of translation in Baghdad in the early ninth century, and Greek science and philosophy, Indian mathematics, Chinese medicine, and Persian literature and natural history were all translated into Arabic, vastly enriching the language. By the latter half of the eighth century Arabic had ceased to be the exclusive property of the Arabs and had become instead the lingua franca of all the many communities that made up Islam, and Arabic literature had extended its horizons beyond tribal Arabia to reflect the international, cosmopolitan culture that Islam had become. Prose, which had next to no role in the pre-Islamic literature of Arabia, came to enjoy exceptional currency because it was a better vehicle than poetry both for the religious learning that was being generated by Islamic religious scholars and for the new secular and humanistic learning that was flooding into Islam from all sides. The literary aesthetic that developed in this period—a synthesis, again, of the language and poetics of pre-Islamic Arabian poetry—provided the foundation for all the literary languages of Islam that developed in subsequent centuries.

Pre-Islamic Arabic poetry was orally composed and performed. Its two principal forms were the short poem, or "fragment" (qit'a), on a single theme—the description and celebration of a raid, a hunt, or a romantic adventure; lament for the departure of a friend; or elegy—and the long poem, or qasida, that linked a number of these themes together. The themes were prescribed by convention, and the language was rhetorically complex, metaphorically dense, and enriched by the close and acute observation of nature. The dominant style of this poetry was heroic, emphasizing the virtues of bravery, loyalty, and generosity. The poetry of pre-Islamic Arabia set standards for manly behavior and for correct use of the language throughout the first two centuries of Islam.

In Baghdad, the poets of the new empire became impatient with the limits of the older poetry and created an urban, cosmopolitan style that reflected the new world of Islam. The only poetry in pre-Islamic Arabia was a highly democratic form, since the best poetry was available to anyone who understood Arabic and was able to memorize a few lines. But as the scope of imaginative writing expanded beyond poetry in Abbasid Baghdad, a new term, adab, was used to describe it. Adab means "polite learning" and implies wealth and leisure enough to devote years of one's life to the formal study of written literature. Adab included not only an extensive knowledge of poetry, both classical and modern, but a familiarity with important writing on virtually every subject from theology to agronomy. The adab style, emphasizing elegance, decorum, and wide learning, was aristocratic and antidemocratic, a fortress that set difficult meters and learned allusions as "gatemen to keep the rabble out," as one poet put it. The natural home of such a tradition was, of course, the court, and royal or aristocratic patronage was the chief prop and support of poets as well as scholars.

Though poetry enjoyed precedence over prose in the classical period, as it continued to do in all the languages of Islamic literature until virtually the present day,

THE KORAN
610–632

For Muslims the Koran is something greater than prophetic revelation. It is an earthly duplicate of a divine Koran that exists in paradise engraved in figures of gold on tablets of marble. Like God, it was not created but exists for all eternity—a complete and sufficient guide to our conduct on earth. It is God's final revelation to humanity and was sent by him to complete and correct all prior revelations. In its divinity it is greater than any prophet or any prophecy. It stands to Muslims as Christ does to Christians. To the glory of Muhammad's community, God chose to make this, his final revelation, in Arabic and through an Arab prophet. Because the Koran is, literally, God's word and is, like him, miraculous and eternal, it cannot be translated. Interpretive renderings into other languages have been made and used for teaching purposes since the earliest period of Islam, but Muslims do not accept them as the Koran in the sense that Christians accept the Bible in English, or any of the other languages into which it has been translated, as still the Bible.

The Koran's revelations were received by Muhammad, known to Muslims as the Prophet of God, during the last two decades of his life—from roughly 610, when the angel Gabriel first appeared to him, to his death on June 8, 632. During his lifetime these revelations were recorded by various of his followers, but they were gathered together into a comprehensive volume only after his death. The title given this collection is the Koran (*al-qur'ân*), or the Recitation, and, as its title suggests, the Koran is a work to be heard and recited, an oral work with a music and rhythm of its own that does not appear to best advantage on the printed page. The text itself is far more dialogic than narrative. God speaks with Muhammad, or instructs him to give his community a particular message, or to "Recite!" Muhammad and other earlier prophets carry on frustrated dialogues with their doubting communities on the one hand and, on the other, with a demanding God. Only rarely does narrative replace the intermingling of voices in dialogue.

The revelations came to Muhammad in verses (*âya*) of varying length and number. These were gathered into larger divisions (Suras) that were organized roughly by subject. These gatherings often appear arbitrary, and there are abrupt transitions from subject in the longer Suras. Only the shortest are thematically unified and only Sura 12, Yusuf, tells a complete narrative. The Suras were then arranged by length, with the longer Suras preceding the shorter. Each Sura was given a name taken from some striking image or theme that appears in it. They are also identified as having been received in either Mecca or Medina, the two communities in which Muhammad lived. It is an article of faith with Muslims that the Koran we now have is a complete and accurate record of God's revelations to Muhammad and an exact copy of the divine Koran that exists in the seventh heaven.

Although the Koran was revealed over a relatively brief period, its style varies enormously. The earliest and shortest Suras sound like charms or incantations, evoking the wonder and glory of God:

> In the Name of God, the Compassionate, the Merciful
> Say: "I seek refuge in the Lord of men, the King of men, the God of men, from the mischief of the slinking prompter who whispers in the hearts of men; from jinn and men" (Men [entire] 114.1–6).

The later and longer ones are filled with legal prescriptions:

> Do not give the feeble-minded the property with which God has entrusted you for their support; but maintain and clothe them with its proceeds, and give them good advice (Women 4.6).

And many, perhaps most, of the Suras have the quality of sermons delivered in a highly charged and poetic language, often enriched by parables and brief narratives that exhort us to remember God and live pious lives. The earlier and longer Suras, like sermons, are mixtures of various styles—exhortation, evocation, legal prescription, and sage counsel.

The style of the individual Suras reflects in general terms the moments in Muhammad's life when they were revealed. In the early Meccan period of his mission, his concerns were those of an embattled prophet exhorting his community to believe in God and fear Him and defending himself against the hostility and skepticism of those who doubted both him and his God. The Suras from this period are filled with fierce and eloquent exhortations promising paradise to those who believe in God and eternal damnation to those who deny Him. These Suras are also marked by calls for social justice, expressed principally in concern for the plight of widows and orphans. It was in Mecca, too, that the accounts of earlier prophets from Noah (Nuh) to Jesus (Isâ)—who, like Muhammad, had to defend themselves against a hostile and unbelieving community—were revealed to him.

Eventually, Muhammad's success in creating a community of believers made him so unwelcome in his home that the Meccans forced him and his followers to emigrate to the nearby oasis of Medina. There he established his community among the tribes already settled around the oasis. While Muhammad continued to be the Prophet of Islam, the legal and political demands of his community now occupied most of his attention. He also had to cope with the growing number of believers who flocked to him and, eventually, to manage a war with the Meccans. The Suras revealed in Medina reflect these concerns in setting forth an extensive and detailed legal code that addresses the demands of the day-to-day life of the community as well as its spiritual needs.

These stylistic differences point out an obvious distinction between the Koran and the Bible. The essence of the Koran is admonition and guidance. No narrative thread runs through it, nor is it embedded in the history of a single people. The Koran's coherence is a product of the themes that are reiterated throughout its many Suras. For all the importance it gives to one language, Arabic, its message is a more general one. The many allusions to Moses (Musa), for example, stress that God may choose even an ordinary, flawed man to be His prophet and say nothing of Moses' role as the leader of his people. The meaning of the Koran, as it often asserts, is for all humanity.

The Exordium, the opening Sura of the Koran, has an exceptional resonance in the life of Muslims. They recite it at the beginning of every formal address and inscribe it at the head of every written document from works of scholarship to the stones that mark a grave. It begins every prayer.

Joseph (Sura 12) is, of course, not a prophet in Judaism or Christianity, but he is in Islam. He is also the only one whose tale is told continuously, and the only one to be mentioned exclusively in a single Sura. The Koranic version of this story includes most of the key events of Genesis 36–38 but excludes virtually everything that links Joseph to the Hebrews. In Genesis, Joseph is a divinely guided young man who is first tested severely and then becomes the leader of his people, guiding them to prosperity in Egypt. In the Koran he is a divinely guided young man but not the leader of any nation. Although God tests Joseph, it is to prove that only those who follow divine guidance prosper. In the most famous scene, the temptation by his master's wife, he is not more righteous than she, but God gives him a sign that he should not succumb. Islam does not believe in original sin and is more accepting of human error than Genesis. Joseph's innocence in this encounter is also explicitly established in Sura 12, while in Genesis only we and God see that Joseph is blameless. His master's wife, identified as Zuleikha in the commentaries, is also treated in a more tolerant fashion than Potiphar's wife. In a remarkable scene she shows the women of the city that they, too, would have been seduced by Joseph's angelic beauty. In the Koran, in short, the story of Joseph has nothing of the epic dimensions it has in Genesis but focuses instead on the more general theme of the importance of trusting in divine guidance.

Sura 19 contains the only allusion to Mary in the Koran, although Jesus appears repeatedly. The miracles surrounding the birth of Jesus do occur here but in a very different form from that in the New Testament. Islam does not accept that Jesus was the son of God. For Muslims such a mixture of divine and human attributes is unthinkable. Jesus they account a great prophet but no more, and, again, one who has no allegiance to a particular community. There is also nothing of the story of his conflicts with the Jews or his execution by the Romans. Muslims do not accept the martyrdom of Jesus but believe that at the crucial moment God placed a substitute in Jesus' place.

In the Koran, Noah (Sura 71) is the first of the major prophets, a step well above his position in the Bible. He establishes the pattern for the role of the prophet in his community. It is a disheartening one and probably reflects Muhammad's view of his relations with his fellow Meccans. The emphasis is on his prophetic role rather than on the details of the ark and the salvation of the animals. Like Muhammad, he is a warner who comes to call his people to submit to God and to threaten them with torment if they do not. His people revile and reject him for years. At last, when it is abundantly clear that their hearts are so hardened that they will never heed him, he calls down God's wrath on his tormentors. His story is alluded to in a great many Suras. One detail found only in the Koran (11.42–46) points out God's concern to give faith priority over blood. Noah has a son who refuses to enter the ark, effectively denying his father's prophecy. The rising waters kill him along with the rest of humanity. When Noah asks God why he has done this, because he promised that Noah's family would be spared, God replies, "Noah, he was no kinsman of yours: he had acted unjustly." That is, shared belief replaces blood as the strongest bond uniting people.

PRONOUNCING GLOSSARY

The following list uses common English syllables and stress accents to provide rough equivalents of selected words whose pronunciation may be unfamiliar to the general reader.

al-qur'ân: *al-ko-ran'*

âya: *eye'-yuh*

bahirah: *buh-hee'-ruh*

Idris: *ee-drees'*

Isâ: *ee'-suh*

Ka'ba: *ka'-buh*

Nuh: *nooh*

Potiphar: *poh'*-tee-far

saibah: *saw'-ee-buh*

Suwâ: *soo-wah'*

wasilah: *wuh-see'-luh*

Ya'uq: *yah-ook'*

Yaghuth: *yah-gooth'*

Yusuf: *you'-suff*

Zuleikha: *zoo-lay'-kuh*

FROM THE KORAN[1]

1. The Exordium

[MECCA]

In the Name of God the Compassionate the Merciful[2]
Praise be to God, Lord of the Creation,
The Compassionate, the Merciful,
King of the Last Judgement!
You alone we worship, and to You alone
we pray for help.
Guide us to the straight path,
The path of those whom You have favoured,
Not of those who have incurred Your wrath,
Nor of those who have gone astray.

From 4. Women

[MEDINA]

In the Name of God, the Compassionate, the Merciful

Men, have fear of your Lord, who created you from a single soul. From that soul He created its mate, and through them He bestrewed the earth with countless men and women.

Fear God, in whose name you plead with one another, and honour the mothers who bore you. God is ever watching over you.

Give orphans[1] the property which belongs to them. Do not exchange their valuables for worthless things or cheat them of their possessions; for this would surely be a great sin. If you fear that you cannot treat orphans with fairness, then you may marry other women who seem good to you: two, three, or four of them. But if you fear that you cannot maintain equality among them, marry one only or any slavegirls you may own. This will make it easier for you to avoid injustice.

Give women their dowry as a free gift; but if they choose to make over to you a part of it, you may regard it as lawfully yours.

Do not give the feeble-minded the property with which God has entrusted you for their support; but maintain and clothe them with its proceeds, and give them good advice.

Put orphans to the test until they reach a marriageable age. If you find them capable of sound judgement, hand over to them their property, and do not deprive them of it by squandering it before they come of age.

Let not the rich guardian touch the property of his orphan ward; and let him who is poor use no more than a fair portion of it for his own advantage.

When you hand over to them their property, call in some witnesses; sufficient is God's accounting of your actions.

1. Translated by N. J. Dawood.   2. According to Islamic law, this phrase, spoken or written, must precede all written work; it is also used by Muslims at the beginning of most formal tasks.   1. Orphan girls.

Men shall have a share in what their parents and kinsmen leave; and women shall have a share in what their parents and kinsmen leave: whether it be little or much, they shall be legally entitled to their share.

If relatives, orphans, or needy men are present at the division of an inheritance, give them, too, a share of it, and speak to them kind words.

Let those who are solicitous about the welfare of their young children after their own death take care not to wrong orphans. Let them fear God and speak for justice.

Those that devour the property of orphans unjustly, swallow fire into their bellies; they shall burn in a mighty conflagration.

God has thus enjoined you concerning your children:

A male shall inherit twice as much as a female. If there be more than two girls, they shall have two-thirds of the inheritance; but if there be one only, she shall inherit the half. Parents shall inherit a sixth each, if the deceased have a child; but if he leave no child and his parents be his heirs, his mother shall have a third. If he have brothers, his mother shall have a sixth after payment of any legacy he may have bequeathed or any debt he may have owed.

You may wonder whether your parents or your children are more beneficial to you. But this is the law of God; God is all-knowing and wise.

You shall inherit the half of your wives' estate if they die childless. If they leave children, a quarter of their estate shall be yours after payment of any legacies they may have bequeathed or any debt they may have owed.

Your wives shall inherit one quarter of your estate if you die childless. If you leave children, they shall inherit one-eighth, after payment of any legacies you may have bequeathed or any debts you may have owed.

If a man or a woman leave neither children nor parents and have a brother or a sister, they shall each inherit one-sixth. If there be more, they shall equally share the third of the estate, after payment of any legacy that he may have bequeathed or any debt he may have owed, without prejudice to the rights of the heirs. That is a commandment from God. God is all-knowing and gracious.

Such are the bounds set by God. He that obeys God and His apostle shall dwell for ever in gardens watered by running streams. That is the supreme triumph. But he that defies God and His apostle and transgresses His bounds, shall be cast into a fire wherein he will abide for ever. A shameful punishment awaits him.

If any of your women commit fornication, call in four witnesses from among yourselves against them; if they testify to their guilt confine them to their houses till death overtakes them or till God finds another way for them.

If two men among you commit indecency punish them both. If they repent and mend their ways, let them be. God is forgiving and merciful.

God forgives those who commit evil in ignorance and then quickly turn to Him in repentance. God will pardon them. God is wise and all-knowing. But He will not forgive those who do evil and, when death comes to them, say: 'Now we repent!' Nor those who die unbelievers: for them We have prepared a woeful scourge.

Believers, it is unlawful for you to inherit the women of your deceased kinsmen against their will, or to bar them from re-marrying, in order that you may force them to give up a part of what you have given them, unless they be guilty of a proven crime. Treat them with kindness; for even if you dislike them, it may well be that you may dislike a thing which God has meant for your own abundant good.

If you wish to (replace a wife with) another, do not take from her the dowry you have given her even if it be a talent of gold. That would be improper and grossly unjust; for how can you take it back when you have lain with each other and entered into a firm contract?

You shall not marry the women whom your fathers married. That was an evil practice, indecent and abominable.

Forbidden to you are your mothers, your daughters, your sisters, your paternal and maternal aunts, the daughters of your brothers and sisters, your foster-mothers, your foster sisters, the mothers of your wives, your step-daughters who are in your charge, born of the wives with whom you have lain (it is no offence for you to marry your step-daughters if you have not consummated your marriage with their mothers), and the wives of your own begotten sons. You are also forbidden to take in marriage two sisters at one and the same time: all previous such marriages excepted. God is forgiving and merciful.

Also married women, except those whom you own as slaves. Such is the decree of God. All women other than these are lawful to you, provided you seek them with your wealth in modest conduct, not in fornication. Give them their dowry for the enjoyment you have had of them as a duty; but it shall be no offence for you to make any other agreement among yourselves after you have fulfilled your duty. God is all-knowing and wise.

If any one of you cannot afford to marry a free believing woman, let him marry a slave-girl who is a believer (God best knows your faith: you are born one of another). Marry them with the permission of their masters and give them their dowry in all justice, provided they are honourable and chaste and have not entertained other men. If after marriage they commit adultery, they shall suffer half the penalty inflicted upon free adulteresses. Such is the law for those of you who fear to commit sin: but if you abstain, it will be better for you. God is forgiving and merciful.

God desires to make this known to you and to guide you along the paths of those who have gone before you, and to turn to you in mercy. God is all-knowing and wise.

God wishes to forgive you, but those who follow their own appetites wish to see you far astray. God wishes to lighten your burdens, for man was created weak.

Believers, do not consume your wealth among yourselves in vanity, but rather trade with it by mutual consent.

Do not destroy yourselves. God is merciful to you, but he that does that through wickedness and injustice shall be burned in fire. That is easy enough for God.

If you avoid the enormities you are forbidden, We shall pardon your misdeeds and usher you in with all honour. Do not covet the favours by which God has exalted some of you above others. Men shall be rewarded according to their deeds, and women shall be rewarded according to their deeds. Rather implore God to bestow on you His gifts. God has knowledge of all things.

To every parent and kinsman We have appointed heirs who will inherit from him. As for those with whom you have entered into agreements, let them, too, have their due. God bears witness to all things.

Men have authority over women because God has made the one superior to the other, and because they spend their wealth to maintain them. Good women are obedient. They guard their unseen parts because God has guarded them. As for those from whom you fear disobedience, admonish them and send them to beds apart and beat them. Then if they obey you, take no further action against them. God is high, supreme.

If you fear a breach between a man and his wife, appoint an arbiter from his people and another from hers. If they wish to be reconciled God will bring them together again. God is all-knowing and wise.

Serve God and associate none with Him. Show kindness to your parents and your kindred, to orphans and to the helpless, to near and distant neighbours, to those that keep company with you, to the traveller in need, and to the slaves whom you own. God does not love arrogant and boastful men, who are themselves niggardly and enjoin others to be niggardly; who conceal the riches which God of His bounty has bestowed upon them (We have prepared a shameful punishment for the unbelievers); and who spend their wealth for the sake of ostentation, believing neither in God nor in the Last Day. He that chooses Satan for his friend, an evil friend has he.

* * *

5. The Table

[MEDINA]

In the Name of God, the Compassionate, the Merciful

Believers, be true to your obligations. It is lawful for you to eat the flesh of all beasts other than that which is hereby announced to you. Game is forbidden while you are on pilgrimage. God decrees what He will.

Believers, do not violate the rites of God, or the sacred month, or the offerings or their ornaments, or those that repair to the Sacred House seeking God's grace and pleasure. Once your pilgrimage is ended, you shall be free to go hunting.

Do not allow your hatred for those who would debar you from the Holy Mosque to lead you into sin. Help one another in what is good and pious, not in what is wicked and sinful. Have fear of God, for He is stern in retribution.

You are forbidden carrion, blood, and the flesh of swine; also any flesh dedicated to any other than God. You are forbidden the flesh of strangled animals and of those beaten or gored to death; of those killed by a fall or mangled by beasts of prey (unless you make it clean by giving the death-stroke yourselves); also of animals sacrificed to idols.

You are forbidden to settle disputes by consulting the Arrows.[1] That is a pernicious practice.

---

1. A form of casting lots.

The unbelievers have this day abandoned all hope of vanquishing your religion. Have no fear of them: fear Me.

This day I have perfected your religion for you and completed My favour to you. I have chosen Islam to be your faith.

He that is constrained by hunger to eat of what is forbidden, not intending to commit sin, will find God forgiving and merciful.

They ask you what is lawful to them. Say: "All good things are lawful to you, as well as that which you have taught the birds and beasts of prey to catch, training them as God has taught you. Eat of what they catch for you, pronouncing upon it the name of God. And have fear of God: swift is God's reckoning."

All good things have this day been made lawful to you. The food of those to whom the Book was given[2] is lawful to you, and yours to them.

Lawful to you are the believing women and the free women from among those who were given the Book before you, provided that you give them their dowries and live in honour with them, neither committing fornication nor taking them as mistresses.

He that denies the Faith shall gain nothing from his labours. In the world to come he shall have much to lose.

Believers, when you rise to pray wash your faces and your hands as far as the elbow, and wipe your heads and your feet to the ankle. If you are polluted cleanse yourselves. But if you are sick or travelling the road; or if, when you have just relieved yourselves or had intercourse with women, you can find no water, take some clean sand and rub your hands and faces with it. God does not wish to burden you; He seeks only to purify you and to perfect His favour to you, so that you may give thanks.

Remember God's favour to you, and the covenant with which He bound you when you said: "We hear and obey." Have fear of God. God knows the innermost thoughts of men.

Believers, fulfil your duties to God and bear true witness. Do not allow your hatred for other men to turn you away from justice. Deal justly; that is nearer to true piety. Have fear of God; God is cognizant of all your actions.

God has promised those that have faith and do good works forgiveness and a rich reward. As for those who disbelieve and deny Our revelations, they are the heirs of Hell.

Believers, remember the favour which God bestowed upon you when He restrained the hands of those who sought to harm you. Have fear of God. In God let the faithful put their trust.

God made a covenant with the Israelites and raised among them twelve chieftains. God said: "I shall be with you. If you attend to your prayers and render the alms levy; if you believe in My apostles and assist them and give God a generous loan, I shall forgive you your sins and admit you to gardens watered by running streams. But he that hereafter denies Me shall stray from the right path."

But because they broke their covenant We laid on them Our curse and hardened their hearts. They have tampered with words out of their context and forgotten much of what they were enjoined. You will ever find them

2. The Jews.

deceitful, except for a few of them. But pardon them and bear with them. God loves those who do good.

With those who said they were Christians We made a covenant also, but they too have forgotten much of what they were enjoined. Therefore We stirred among them enmity and hatred, which shall endure till the Day of Resurrection, when God will declare to them all that they have done.

People of the Book![3] Our aspostle has come to reveal to you much of what you have hidden of the Scriptures, and to forgive you much. A light has come to you from God and a glorious Book, with which God will guide to the paths of peace those that seek to please Him; He will lead them by His will from darkness to the light; He will guide them to a straight path.

Unbelievers are those who declare: "God is the Messiah, the son of Mary." Say: "Who could prevent God, if He so willed, from destroying the Messiah, the son of Mary, his mother, and all the people of the earth? God has sovereignty over the heavens and the earth and all that lies between them. He creates what He will and God has power over all things."

The Jews and the Christians say: "We are the children of God and His loved ones." Say: "Why then does He punish you for your sins? Surely you are mortals of His own creation. He forgives whom He will and punishes whom He pleases. God has sovereignty over the heavens and the earth and all that lies between them. All shall return to Him."

People of the Book! Our apostle has come to you with revelations after an interval during which there were no apostles, lest you say: "No one has come to give us good news or to warn us." Now someone has come to give you good news and to warn you. God has power over all things.

Bear in mind the words of Moses to his people. He said: "Remember, my people, the favours which God has bestowed upon you. He has raised up prophets among you, made you kings, and given you that which He has given to no other nation. Enter, my people, the holy land which God has assigned for you. Do not turn back, or you shall be ruined."

"Moses," they replied, "a race of giants dwells in this land. We will not set foot in it till they are gone. As soon as they are gone we will enter."

Thereupon two God-fearing men whom God had favoured, said: "Go in to them through the gates, and when you have entered you shall surely be victorious. In God put your trust, if you are true believers."

But they replied: "Moses, we will not go in so long as *they* are in it. Go, you and your Lord, and fight. Here we will stay."

"Lord," cried Moses, "I have none but myself and my brother. Do not confound us with these wicked people."

He replied: "They shall be forbidden this land for forty years, during which time they shall wander homeless on the earth. Do not grieve for these wicked people."

Recount to them in all truth the story of Adam's two sons: how they each made an offering, and how the offering of the one was accepted while that of the other was not. One said: "I will surely kill you." The other replied: "God accepts offerings only from the righteous. If you stretch your hand to kill me, I shall not lift mine to slay you; for I fear God, Lord of the Universe.

---

3. Here, Jews and Christians.

I would rather you should add your sin against me to your other sins and thus become an inmate of the Fire. Such is the reward of the wicked."

His soul prompted him to slay his brother; he slew him and thus became one of the lost. Then God sent down a raven, which dug the earth to show him how to bury the naked corpse of his brother. "Alas!" he cried. "Have I not strength enough to do as this raven has done and so bury my brother's naked corpse?" And he repented.

That was why We laid it down for the Israelites that whoever killed a human being, except as a punishment for murder or other villainy in the land, shall be looked upon as though he had killed all mankind; and that whoever saved a human life should be regarded as though he had saved all mankind.

Our apostles brought them veritable proofs: yet it was not long before many of them committed great evils in the land.

Those that make war against God and His apostle and spread disorder in the land shall be put to death or crucified or have their hands and feet cut off on alternate sides, or be banished from the country. They shall be held up to shame in this world and sternly punished in the hereafter: except those that repent before you reduce them. For you must know that God is forgiving and merciful.

Believers, have fear of God and seek the right path to Him. Fight valiantly for His cause, so that you may triumph.

As for the unbelievers, if they offered all that the earth contains and as much besides to redeem themselves from the torment of the Day of Resurrection, it shall not be accepted from them. Theirs shall be a woeful punishment.

They will strive to get out of Hell, but they shall not: theirs shall be a lasting punishment.

As for the man or woman who is guilty of theft, cut off their hands to punish them for their crimes. That is the punishment enjoined by God. God is mighty and wise. But whoever repents after committing evil, and mends his ways, shall be pardoned by God. God is forgiving and merciful.

Do you not know that God has sovereignty over the heavens and the earth? He punishes whom He will and forgives whom He pleases. God has power over all things.

Apostle, do not grieve for those who plunge headlong into unbelief; those who say with their tongues: "We believe," but have no faith in their hearts, and those Jews who listen to the lies of others and pay no heed to you. They tamper with the words out of their context and say: "If this be given you, accept it; if not, then beware!"

You cannot help a man if God seeks to confound him. Those whose hearts He does not please to purify shall be rewarded with disgrace in this world and a grievous punishment in the hereafter.

They listen to falsehoods and practise what is unlawful. If they come to you, give them your judgement or avoid them. If you avoid them they can in no way harm you; but if you do act as their judge, judge them with fairness. God loves those that deal justly.

But how will they come to you for judgement, when they already have the Torah which enshrines God's own judgement? Soon after, they will turn their backs: they are no true believers.

We have revealed the Torah, in which there is guidance and light. By it the

Unbelievers are those that say: "God is one of three." There is but one God. If they do not desist from so saying, those of them that disbelieve shall be sternly punished.

Will they not turn to God in repentance and seek forgiveness of Him? He is forgiving and merciful.

The Messiah, the son of Mary, was no more than an apostle: other apostles passed away before him. His mother was a saintly woman. They both ate earthly food.

See how We make plain to them Our revelations. See how they ignore the truth.

Say: "Will you serve instead of God that which can neither harm nor help you? God hears all and knows all."

Say: "People of the Book! Do not transgress the bounds of truth in your religion. Do not yield to the desires of those who have erred before; who have led many astray and have themselves strayed from the even path."

Those of the Israelites who disbelieved were cursed by David and Jesus, the son of Mary: they cursed them because they rebelled and committed evil. Nor did they censure themselves for any wrong they did. Evil were their deeds.

You see many of them making friends with unbelievers. Evil is that to which their souls prompt them. They have incurred the wrath of God and shall endure eternal torment. Had they believed in God and the Prophet and that which is revealed to him, they would not have befriended them. But many of them are evil-doers.

You will find that the most implacable of men in their enmity to the faithful are the Jews and the pagans, and that the nearest in affection to them are those who say: "We are Christians." That is because there are priests and monks among them; and because they are free from pride.

When they listen to that which was revealed to the Apostle, you will see their eyes fill with tears as they recognize its truth. They say: "Lord, we believe. Count us among Your witnesses. Why should we not believe in God and in the truth that has come down to us? Why should we not hope our Lord will admit us among the righteous?" And for their words God has rewarded them with gardens watered by running streams, where they shall dwell for ever. Such is the recompense of the righteous. But those that disbelieve and deny Our revelations shall be the inmates of Hell.

Believers, do not forbid the wholesome things which God has made lawful to you. Do not transgress; God does not love the transgressors. Eat of the lawful and wholesome things which God has given you. Have fear of God, in whom you believe.

God will not punish you for that which is inadvertent in your oaths. But He will take you to task for the oaths which you solemnly swear. The penalty for a broken oath is the feeding of ten needy men with such food as you normally offer to your own people; or the clothing of ten needy men; or the freeing of one slave. He that cannot afford any of these must fast three days. In this way you shall expiate your broken oaths. Therefore be true to that which you have sworn. Thus God makes plain to you His revelations, so that you may give thanks.

Believers, wine and games of chance, idols and divining arrows, are abominations devised by Satan. Avoid them, so that you may prosper. Satan seeks to stir up enmity and hatred among you by means of wine and gambling, and to keep you from the remembrance of God and from your prayers. Will you not abstain from them?

Obey God, and obey the Apostle. Beware; if you give no heed, know that Our apostle's duty is only to give plain warning.

No blame shall be attached to those that have embraced the faith and done good works in regard to any food they may have eaten, so long as they fear God and believe in Him and do good works; so long as they fear God and believe in Him; so long as they fear God and do good works. God loves the charitable.

Believers, God will put you to the proof by means of the game which you can catch with your hands or with your spears, so that He may know those who fear Him in their hearts. He that transgresses hereafter shall be sternly punished.

Believers, kill no game whilst on pilgrimage. He that kills game by design, shall present, as an offering to the Ka'ba, an animal equivalent to that which he has killed, to be determined by two just men among you; or he shall, in expiation, either feed the poor or fast, so that he may taste the evil consequences of his deed. God has forgiven what is past; but if any one relapses into wrongdoing He will avenge Himself on him: He is mighty and capable of revenge.

Lawful to you is what you catch from the sea and the sustenance it provides; a wholesome food for you and for the seafarer. But you are forbidden the game of the land while you are on pilgrimage. Have fear of God, before whom you shall all be assembled.

God has made the Ka'ba, the Sacred House, the sacred month, and the sacrificial offerings with their ornaments, eternal values for mankind; so that you may know that God has knowledge of all that the heavens and the earth contain; that God has knowledge of all things.

Know that God is stern in retribution, and that God is forgiving and merciful.

The duty of the Apostle is only to give warning. God knows all that you hide and all that you reveal.

Say: "Good and evil are not alike, even though the abundance of evil may tempt you. Have fear of God, you men of understanding, so that you may triumph."

Believers, do not ask questions about things which, if made known to you, would only pain you; but if you ask them when the Koran is being revealed, they shall be made plain to you. God will pardon you for this; God is forgiving and gracious. Other men inquired about them before you, only to disbelieve them afterwards.

God demands neither a *bahirah,* nor a *saibah,* nor a *wasilah,* nor a *hami.*[4] The unbelievers invent falsehoods about God. Most of them are lacking in judgement.

When it is said to them: "Come to that which God has revealed, and to the Apostle," they reply: "Sufficient for us is the faith we have inherited from our fathers," even though their fathers knew nothing and were not rightly guided.

4. Names given by pagan Arabs to sacred animals offered at the Ka'bah.

Believers, you are accountable for none but yourselves; he that goes astray cannot harm you if you are on the right path. To God you shall all return, and He will declare to you what you have done.

Believers, when death approaches you, let two just men from among you act as witnesses when you make your testaments; or two men from another tribe if the calamity of death overtakes you while you are travelling the land. Detain them after prayers, and if you doubt their honesty ask them to swear by God: "We will not sell our testimony for any price even to a kinsman. We will not hide the testimony of God; for we should then be evil-doers." If both prove dishonest, replace them by another pair from among those immediately concerned, and let them both swear by God, saying: "Our testimony is truer than theirs. We have told no lies, for we should then be wrongdoers." Thus they will be more likely to bear true witness or to fear that the oaths of others may contradict theirs. Have fear of God and be obedient. God does not guide the evil-doers.

One day God will gather all the apostles and ask them: "How were you received?" They will reply: "We have no knowledge. You alone know what is hidden." God will say: "Jesus, son of Mary, remember the favour I have bestowed on you and on your mother: how I strengthened you with the Holy Spirit, so that you preached to men in your cradle and in the prime of manhood; how I instructed you in the Book and in wisdom, in the Torah and in the Gospel; how by My leave you fashioned from clay the likeness of a bird and breathed into it so that, by My leave, it became a living bird; how, by My leave, you healed the blind man and the leper, and by My leave restored the dead to life; how I protected you from the Israelites when you had come to them with clear signs: when those of them who disbelieved declared: 'This is but plain sorcery'; how when I enjoined the disciples to believe in Me and in My apostle they replied: 'We believe; bear witness that we submit.'"

"Jesus, son of Mary," said the disciples, "can your Lord send down to us from heaven a table spread with food?"

He replied: "Have fear of God, if you are true believers."

"We wish to eat of it," they said, "so that we may reassure our hearts and know that what you said to us is true, and that we may be witnesses of it."

"Lord," said Jesus, the son of Mary, "send to us from heaven a table spread with food, that it may mark a feast for us and for those that will come after us: a sign from You. Give us our sustenance; You are the best Giver."

God replied: "I am sending one to you. But whoever of you disbelieves hereafter shall be punished as no man has ever been punished."

Then God will say: "Jesus, son of Mary, did you ever say to mankind: 'Worship me and my mother as gods beside God?'"

"Glory to You," he will answer, "how could I ever say that to which I have no right? If I had ever said so, You would have surely known it. You know what is in my mind, but I know not what is in Yours. You alone know what is hidden. I told them only what You bade me. I said: 'Serve God, my Lord and your Lord.' I watched over them while living in their midst, and ever since You took me to Yourself, You have been watching over them. You are the witness of all things. If You punish them, they surely are Your servants; and if You forgive them, surely You are mighty and wise."

God will say: "This is the day when their truthfulness will benefit the truthful. They shall for ever dwell in gardens watered by running streams.

God is pleased with them and they are pleased with Him. That is the supreme triumph."

God has sovereignty over the heavens and the earth and all that they contain. He has power over all things.

10. Jonah

[MECCA]

In the Name of God, the Compassionate, the Merciful

Alif lām rā.[1] These are the verses of the Wise Book: Does it seem strange to mankind that We revealed Our will to a mortal from among themselves, saying: "Give warning to mankind, and tell the faithful their endeavours shall be rewarded by their Lord?"

The unbelievers say: "This man[2] is a skilled enchanter." Yet your Lord is God, who in six days created the heavens and the earth and then ascended His throne, ordaining all things. None has power to intercede for you except him who has received His sanction. Such is God, your Lord: therefore serve Him. Will you not take heed?

To Him you shall all return: God's promise shall be fulfilled. He gives being to all His creatures, and in the end He will bring them back to life, so that He may justly reward those who have believed in Him and done good works. As for the unbelievers, they shall drink scalding water and be sternly punished for their unbelief.

It was He that gave the sun his brightness and the moon her light, ordaining her phases that you may learn to compute the seasons and the years. God created them only to manifest the truth. He makes plain His revelations to men of understanding.

In the alternation of night and day, and in all that God has created in the heavens and the earth, there are signs for righteous men.

Those who entertain no hope of meeting Us, being pleased and contented with the life of this world, and those who give no heed to Our revelations, shall have the Fire as their home in requital for their deeds.

As for those that believe and do good works, God will guide them through their faith. Rivers will run at their feet in the Gardens of Delight. Their prayer will be: "Glory to You, Lord!" and their greeting: "Peace!" "Praise be to God, Lord of the Universe," will be the burthen of their plea.

Had God hastened the punishment of men as they would hasten their reward, their fate would have been sealed. Therefore We let those who entertain no hope of meeting Us blunder about in their wrongdoing.

When misfortune befalls man, he prays to Us lying on his side, standing, or sitting down. But as soon as We relieve his affliction he pursues his former ways, as though he never prayed for Our help. Thus their foul deeds seem fair to the transgressors.

We destroyed generations before your time on account of the wrongs they did; their apostles came to them with veritable signs, but they would not

---

1. A number of Suras begin with several letters of the Arabic alphabet, the meaning of which is unclear.
2. Muhammad.

believe. Thus shall the guilty be rewarded. Then We made you their successors in the land, so that We might observe how you would conduct yourselves.

When Our clear revelations are recited to them, those who entertain no hope of meeting Us say to you: "Give us a different Koran, or make some changes in it."

Say:[3] "It is not for me to change it. I follow only what is revealed to me. I cannot disobey my Lord, for I fear the punishment of a fateful day."

Say: "Had God pleased, I would never have recited it to you, nor would He have given you any knowledge of it. A whole life-time I dwelt amongst you before it was revealed. Will you not understand?"

Who is more wicked than the man who invents a falsehood about God or denies His revelations? Truly, the evil-doers shall not triumph.

They worship idols that can neither harm nor help them, and say: "These will intercede for us with God."

Say: "Do you presume to tell God of what He knows to be neither in the heavens nor in the earth? Glory to Him! Exalted be He above the gods they serve beside Him!"

There was a time when men followed but one religion. Then they disagreed among themselves: and but for a word from your Lord, long since decreed, their differences would have been firmly resolved.

And they ask: "Why has no sign been given him by his Lord?"

Say: "God alone has knowledge of what is hidden. Wait if you will: I too am waiting!"

No sooner do We show mercy to a people after some misfortune has afflicted them than they begin to scheme against Our revelations. Say: "More swift is God's scheming. Our angels are recording your intrigues."

It is He who guides them by land and sea. They embark: and as the ships set sail, rejoicing in a favouring wind, a raging tempest overtakes them. Billows surge upon them from every side and they fear that they are encompassed by death. They pray to God with all fervour, saying: "Deliver us from this peril and we will be truly thankful."

Yet when He does deliver them, they commit evil in the land and act unjustly.

Men, it is your own souls that you are corrupting. Take your enjoyment in this life: to Us you shall in the end return, and We will declare to you all that you have done.

This present life is like the rich garment with which the earth adorns itself when watered by the rain We send down from the sky. Crops, sustaining man and beast, grow luxuriantly: but as its hopeful tenants prepare themselves for the rich harvest, down comes Our scourge upon it, by night or in broad day, laying it waste, even though it did not blossom but yesterday. Thus do We make plain Our revelations to thoughtful men.

God invites you to the Home of Peace. He guides whom He will to a straight path. Those that do good works shall have a good reward and more besides. Neither blackness nor misery shall overcast their faces. They are the heirs of Paradise: in it they shall abide for ever.

As for those that have earned evil, evil shall be rewarded with like evil. Misery will oppress them (they shall have none to defend them from God),

---

3. God's instruction to Muhammad.

as though patches of the night's own darkness veiled their faces. They are the heirs of Hell: in it they shall abide for ever.

On the day when We assemble them all together, We shall say to the idolaters: "Keep to your places, you and your idols!" We will separate them one from another, and then their idols will say to them: "It was not us that you worshipped, God is our all-sufficient witness. Nor were we aware of your worship."

Thereupon each soul will know what it has done. They shall be sent back to God, their true Lord, and the idols they invented will forsake them.

Say: "Who provides for you from heaven and earth? Who has endowed you with sight and hearing? Who brings forth the living from the dead, and the dead from the living? Who ordains all things?"

They will reply: "God."

Say: "Will you not take heed, then? Such is God, your true Lord. That which is not true must needs be false. How then can you turn away from Him?"

Thus is the word of your Lord made good. The evil-doers have no faith.

Say: "Can any of your idols conceive Creation, then renew it? God conceives Creation, then renews it. How is it that you are so misled?"

Say: "Can any of your idols guide you to the truth? God can guide you to the truth. Who is more worthy to be followed: He that can guide to the truth or he that cannot and is himself in need of guidance? What has come over you that you so judge?"

Most of them follow nothing but mere conjecture. But conjecture is in no way a substitute for Truth. God is cognizant of all their actions.

This Koran could not have been devised by any but God. It confirms what was revealed before it and fully explains the Scriptures. It is beyond doubt from the Lord of the Universe.

If they say: "He invented it himself," say: "Bring me one chapter like it. Call on whom you may besides God to help you, if what you say be true!"

Indeed, they disbelieve what they cannot grasp, for they have not yet seen its prophecy fulfilled. Likewise did those who passed before them disbelieve. But see what was the end of the wrong-doers.

Some believe in it, while others do not. But your Lord best knows the evil-doers.

If they disbelieve you, say: "My deeds are mine and your deeds are yours. You are not accountable for my actions, nor am I accountable for what you do."

Some of them listen to you. But can you make the deaf hear you, incapable as they are of understanding?

Some of them look upon you. But can you show the way to the blind, bereft as they are of sight?

Indeed, in no way does God wrong mankind, but men wrong themselves.

The day will come when He will gather them all together, as though they had sojourned in this world but for an hour. They will acquaint themselves with each other. Lost shall be those that disbelieved in meeting and did not follow the right path.

Whether We let you glimpse in some measure the scourge with which We threaten them, or cause you to die before we smite them, to Us they shall return. God is searching over all their actions.

An apostle is sent to every nation. When their apostle comes, justice is done among them; they are not wronged.

They ask: "When will this promise be fulfilled, if what you say be true?"

Say: "I have no control over any harm or benefit to myself, except by the will of God. A space of time is fixed for every nation; when their hour is come, not for one hour shall they delay: nor can they go before it."

Say: "Do but consider. Should His scourge fall upon you by night or by the light of day, what punishment would the guilty hasten? Will you believe in it when it does overtake you, although it was your wish to hurry it on?"

Then it shall be said to the wrongdoers: "Feel the everlasting torment! Shall you not be rewarded according to your deeds?"

They ask you if it is true. Say: "Yes, by the Lord, it is true! And you shall not be immune."

To redeem himself then, each sinner would gladly give all that the earth contains if he possessed it. When they behold the scourge, they will repent in secret. But judgement shall be fairly passed upon them; they shall not be wronged.

To God belongs all that the heavens and the earth contain. The promise of God is true, though most of them may not know it. It is He who ordains life and death, and to Him you shall all return.

Men, an admonition has come to you from your Lord, a cure for the mind, a guide and a blessing to true believers.

Say: "In the grace and mercy of God let them rejoice, for these are better than the worldly riches they amass."

Say: "Do but consider the things that God has given you. Some you pronounced unlawful and others lawful." Say: "Was it God who gave you His leave, or do you invent falsehoods about God?"

What will they think, those who invent falsehoods about God, on the Day of Resurrection? God is bountiful to men: yet most of them do not give thanks.

You shall engage in no affair, you shall recite no verse from the Koran, you shall commit no act, but We will witness it. Not an atom's weight in earth or heaven escapes your Lord, nor is there any object smaller or greater, but is recorded in a glorious book.

The servants of God have nothing to fear or to regret. Those that have faith and keep from evil shall rejoice both in this world and in the hereafter: the word of God shall never change. That is the supreme triumph.

Let their words not grieve you. All glory belongs to God. He alone hears all and knows all.

To God belong all who dwell on earth and in heaven. Those that worship gods beside God follow nothing but idle fancies and preach nothing but falsehoods.

He it is who has ordained the night for your rest and given the day its light. Surely in this there are signs for prudent men.

They say: "God has begotten a son." God forbid! Self-sufficient is He. His is all that the heavens and the earth contain. Surely for this you have no sanction. Would you say of God what you do not know?

Say: "Those that invent falsehoods about God shall not prosper. They may take their ease in this life, but to Us they shall in the end return, and We shall make them taste a grievous torment for their unbelief."

Recount to them the tale of Noah. He said to his people: "If it offends you that I should dwell in your midst and preach to you God's revelations (for in Him I have put my trust), muster all your idols and decide your course of action. Do not intrigue in secret. Execute your judgement and give me no respite. If you turn away from me, remember I demand of you no recompense. Only God will reward me. I am commanded to be one of those who shall submit to Him."

But they disbelieved him. Therefore We saved Noah and those who were with him in the Ark, so that they survived, and drowned the others who denied Our revelations. Consider the fate of those who were forewarned.

After that we sent apostles to their descendants. They showed them veritable signs, but they persisted in their unbelief. Thus do We seal up the hearts of the transgressors.

Then We sent forth Moses and Aaron with Our signs to Pharaoh and his nobles. But they rejected them with scorn, for they were wicked men. When the truth had come to them from Us, they declared: "This is but plain sorcery."

Moses replied: "Is this what you say of the Truth when it has come to you? Is this sorcery? Sorcerers shall never prosper."

They said: "Have you come to turn us away from the faith of our fathers, so that you two may lord it over the land? We will never believe in you."

Then Pharaoh said: "Bring every learned sorcerer to my presence."

And when the sorcerers attended Moses said to them: "Cast down what you wish to cast." And when they had thrown, he said: "The sorcery that you have wrought God will surely bring to nothing. He does not bless the work of those who do evil. By His words He vindicates the truth, much as the guilty may dislike it."

Few of his[4] people believed in Moses, for they feared the persecution of Pharaoh and his nobles. Pharaoh was a tyrant in the land, an evildoer.

Moses said: "If you believe in God, my people, and have surrendered yourselves to Him, in Him alone then put your trust."

They replied: "In God we have put our trust. Lord, do not let us suffer at the hands of wicked men. Deliver us, through Your mercy, from the unbelievers."

We revealed Our will to Moses and his brother, saying: "Build houses in Egypt for your people and make your homes places of worship. Conduct prayers and give good news to the faithful."

"Lord," said Moses. "You have bestowed on Pharaoh and his princes splendour and riches in this life, so that they might stray from your path. Lord, destroy their riches and harden their hearts, so that they shall persist in unbelief until they face the woeful scourge."

God replied: "Your prayer shall be answered. Follow the right path and do not walk in the footsteps of ignorant men."

We led the Israelites across the sea, and Pharaoh and his legions pursued them with wickedness and hate. But as he was drowning, Pharaoh cried: "Now I believe no god exists except the God in whom the Israelites believe. To Him I give up myself."

4. Pharaoh's.

Such was Jesus, the son of Mary. That is the whole truth, which they still doubt. God forbid that He Himself should beget a son! When He decrees a thing He need only say: "Be," and it is.

God is my Lord and your Lord: therefore serve Him. That is the right path.

Yet the Sects are divided concerning Jesus. But when the fateful day arrives, woe to the unbelievers! Their sight and being shall be sharpened on the day when they appear before Us. Truly, the unbelievers are in the grossest error.

Forewarn them of that woeful day, when Our decrees shall be fulfilled whilst they heedlessly persist in unbelief. For We shall inherit the earth and all who dwell upon it. To Us they shall return.

You shall also recount in the Book the story of Abraham:

He was a saintly man and a prophet. He said to his father: "How can you serve a worthless idol, a thing that can neither see nor hear?

"Father, things you know nothing of have come to my knowledge: therefore follow me, that I may guide you along an even path.

"Father, do not worship Satan; for he has rebelled against the Lord of Mercy.

"Father, I fear that a scourge will fall upon you from the Merciful, and you will become one of Satan's minions."

He replied: "Do you dare renounce my gods, Abraham? Desist from this folly or I shall stone you. Begone from my house this instant!"

"Peace be with you," said Abraham. "I shall implore my Lord to forgive you: for to me He has been gracious. But I will not live with you or with your idols. I will call on my Lord, and trust that my prayers will not be ignored."

And when Abraham had cast off his people and the idols which they worshipped, We gave him Isaac and Jacob. Each of them We made a prophet, and We bestowed on them gracious gifts and high renown.

In the Book tell also of Moses, who was a chosen man, an apostle, and a prophet.

We called out to him from the right side of the Mountain, and when he came near We communed with him in secret. We gave him, of Our mercy, his brother Aaron, himself a prophet.

And in the Book you shall tell of Ishmael: he, too, was a man of his word, an apostle, and a prophet.

He enjoined prayer and almsgiving on his people, and his Lord was pleased with him.

And of Idris:[2] he, too, was a saint and a prophet, whom We honoured and exalted.

These are the men to whom God has been gracious: the prophets from among the descendants of Adam and of those whom We carried in the Ark with Noah; the descendants of Abraham, of Israel, and of those whom We have guided and chosen. For when the revelations of the Merciful were recited to them they fell down on their knees in tears and adoration.

But the generations who succeeded them neglected their prayers and succumbed to their desires. These shall assuredly be lost. But those that repent and embrace the Faith and do what is right shall be admitted to Paradise and shall in no way be wronged. They shall enter the gardens of Eden, which the

2. Enoch.

Merciful has promised His servants in reward for their faith. His promise shall be fulfilled.

There they shall hear no idle talk, but only the voice of peace. And their sustenance shall be given them morning and evening. Such is the Paradise which We shall give the righteous to inherit.

We do not descend from Heaven save at the bidding of your Lord.[3] To Him belongs what is before us and behind us, and all that lies between.

Your Lord does not forget. He is the Lord of the heavens and the earth and all that is between them. Worship Him, then, and be patient in His service; for do you know any other worthy of His name?

"What!" says man. "When I am once dead, shall I be raised to life?"

Does man forget that We created him out of the void? By the Lord, We will call them to account in company with all the devils and set them on their knees around the fire of Hell: from every sect We will carry off its stoutest rebels against the Lord of Mercy. We know best who deserves most to be burnt therein.

There is not one of you who shall not pass through it: such is the absolute decree of your Lord. We will deliver those who fear Us, but the wrongdoers shall be left there on their knees.

When Our clear revelations are recited to them the unbelievers say to the faithful: "Which of us two will have a finer dwelling and better companions?"

How many generations have We destroyed before them, far greater in riches and in splendour!

Say: "The Merciful will bear long with those in error, until they witness the fulfilment of His threats: be it a worldly scourge or the Hour of Doom. Then shall they know whose is the worse plight and whose the smaller following."

God will add guidance to those that are rightly guided. Deeds of lasting merit shall earn you a better reward in His sight and a more auspicious end.

Mark the words of him who denies Our signs and who yet boasts: "I shall surely be given wealth and children!" he boasts.

Has the future been revealed to him? Or has the Merciful made him such a promise?

By no means! We will record his words and make his punishment long and terrible. All he speaks of he shall leave behind and come before Us all alone.

They have chosen other gods to help them. But in the end they will renounce their worship and turn against them.

Know that We send down to the unbelievers devils who incite them to evil. Therefore have patience: their days are numbered. The day will surely come when We will gather the righteous in multitudes before the Lord of Mercy, and drive the sinful in great hordes into Hell. None has power to intercede for them save him who has received the sanction of the Merciful.

Those who say: "The Lord of Mercy has begotten a son," preach a monstrous falsehood, at which the very heavens might crack, the earth break asunder, and the mountains crumble to dust. That they should ascribe a son to the Merciful, when it does not become the Lord of Mercy to beget one!

---

3. Commentators say that these are the words of the angel Gabriel, in reply to Muhammad's complaint of long intervals elapsing between periods of revelation.

There is none in the heavens or the earth but shall return to the Merciful in utter submission. He has kept strict count of all His creatures, and one by one they shall approach Him on the Day of Resurrection. He will cherish those who accepted the true faith and were charitable in their lifetime.

We have revealed to you the Koran in your own tongue that you may thereby proclaim good tidings to the upright and give warning to a contentious nation.

How many generations have We destroyed before them! Can you find one of them still alive, or hear so much as a whisper from them?

55. The Merciful[1]

[MECCA]

In the Name of God, the Compassionate, the Merciful

It is the Merciful who has taught the Koran.

He created man and taught him articulate speech. The sun and the moon pursue their ordered course. The plants and the trees bow down in adoration.

He raised the heaven on high and set the balance of all things, that you might not transgress that balance. Give just weight and full measure.

He laid the earth for His creatures, with all its fruits and blossom-bearing palm, chaff-covered grain and scented herbs. Which of your Lord's blessings would you deny?

He created man from potter's clay and the jinn[2] from smokeless fire. Which of your Lord's blessings would you deny?

The Lord of the two easts[3] is He, and the Lord of the two wests. Which of your Lord's blessings would you deny?

He has let loose the two oceans:[4] they meet one another. Yet between them stands a barrier which they cannot overrun. Which of your Lord's blessings would you deny?

Pearls and corals come from both. Which of your Lord's blessings would you deny?

His are the ships that sail like mountains upon the ocean. Which of your Lord's blessings would you deny?

All that lives on earth is doomed to die. But the face of your Lord will abide for ever, in all its majesty and glory. Which of your Lord's blessings would you deny?

All who dwell in heaven and earth entreat Him. Each day some mighty task engages Him. Which of your Lord's blessings would you deny?

Mankind and jinn, We shall surely find the time to judge you! Which of your Lord's blessings would you deny?

Mankind and jinn, if you have power to penetrate the confines of heaven and earth, then penetrate them! But this you shall not do except with Our own authority. Which of your Lord's blessings would you deny?

---

1. Compare this Sura with Psalm 136.　　2. A separate order of creation from humans. The question that follows is addressed to both beings.　　3. The points at which the sun rises in summer and winter. 4. Saltwater and freshwater; more specifically, a reference to freshwater springs in the ocean floor.

Flames of fire shall be lashed at you, and molten brass. There shall be none to help you. Which of your Lord's blessings would you deny?

When the sky splits asunder and reddens like a rose or stainéd leather (which of your Lord's blessings would you deny?), on that day neither man nor jinnee shall be asked about his sins. Which of your Lord's blessings would you deny?

The wrongdoers shall be known by their looks; they shall be seized by their forelocks and their feet. Which of your Lord's blessings would you deny?

That is the Hell which the sinners deny. They shall wander between fire and water fiercely seething. Which of your Lord's blessings would you deny?

But for those that fear the majesty of their Lord there are two gardens (which of your Lord's blessings would you deny?) planted with shady trees. Which of your Lord's blessings would you deny?

Each is watered by a flowing spring. Which of your Lord's blessings would you deny?

Each bears every kind of fruit in pairs. Which of your Lord's blessings would you deny?

They shall recline on couches lined with thick brocade, and within their reach will hang the fruits of both gardens. Which of your Lord's blessings would you deny?

They shall dwell with bashful virgins whom neither man nor jinnee will have touched before. Which of your Lord's blessings would you deny?

Virgins as fair as corals and rubies. Which of your Lord's blessings would you deny?

Shall the reward of goodness be anything but good? Which of your Lord's blessings would you deny?

And beside these there shall be two other gardens (which of your Lord's blessings would you deny?) of darkest green. Which of your Lord's blessings would you deny?

A gushing fountain shall flow in each. Which of your Lord's blessings would you deny?

Each planted with fruit-trees, the palm and the pomegranate. Which of your Lord's blessings would you deny?

In each there shall be virgins chaste and fair. Which of your Lord's blessings would you deny?

Dark-eyed virgins sheltered in their tents (which of your Lord's blessings would you deny?) whom neither man nor jinnee will have touched before. Which of your Lord's blessings would you deny?

They shall recline on green cushions and rich carpets. Which of your Lord's blessings would you deny?

Blessed be the name of your Lord, the lord of majesty and glory!

62. Friday, or the Day of Congregation

[MEDINA]

In the Name of God, the Compassionate, the Merciful

All that is in heaven and earth gives glory to God, the Sovereign Lord, the Holy One, the Almighty, the Wise One.

It is He that has sent forth among the gentiles an apostle of their own to recite to them His revelations, to purify them, and to instruct them in the Book and in wisdom though they have hitherto been in gross error, together with others of their own kin who have not yet followed them. He is the Mighty, the Wise One.

Such is the grace of God: He bestows it on whom He will. His grace is infinite.

Those to whom the burden of the Torah was entrusted and yet refused to bear it are like a donkey laden with books. Wretched is the example of those who deny God's revelations. God does not guide the wrongdoers.

Say to the Jews: "If your claim be true that of all men you alone are God's friends, then you should wish for death, if what you say be true!" But, because of what their hands have done, they will never wish for death. God knows the wrongdoers.

Say: "The death from which you shrink is sure to overtake you. Then you shall be sent back to Him who knows the unknown and the manifest, and He will declare to you all that you have done."

Believers, when you are summoned to Friday prayers hasten to the remembrance of God and cease your trading. That would be best for you, if you but knew it. Then, when the prayers are ended, disperse and go in quest of God's bounty. Remember God always, so that you may prosper.

Yet no sooner do they see some commerce or merriment than they flock to it eagerly, leaving you standing all alone.

Say: "That which God has in store is far better than any commerce or merriment. God is the Most Munificent Giver."

71. Noah

[MECCA]

In the Name of God, the Compassionate, the Merciful

We sent forth Noah to his people, saying: "Give warning to your people before a woeful scourge overtakes them."

He said: "My people, I come to warn you plainly. Serve God and fear Him, and obey me. He will forgive you your sins and give you respite for an appointed time. When God's time arrives, none shall put it back. Would that you understood this!"

"Lord," said Noah, "day and night I have pleaded with my people, but my pleas have only added to their aversion. Each time I call on them to seek Your pardon, they thrust their fingers in their ears and draw their cloaks over their heads, persisting in sin and bearing themselves with insolent pride. I called out loud to them, and appealed to them in public and in private. 'Seek forgiveness of your Lord,' I said. 'He is ever ready to forgive you. He sends down for you abundant rain from heaven and bestows upon you wealth and children. He has provided you with gardens and with running brooks. Why do you deny the greatness of God when He has made you in gradual stages? Can you not see how He created the seven heavens one above the other, placing in them the moon for a light and the sun for a lantern? God has brought you forth from the earth like a plant, and to the earth He will restore you. Then He will bring you back afresh. He has made the earth a vast expanse for you, so that you may roam in spacious paths.'"

And Noah said: "Lord, my people disobey me and follow those whose wealth and offspring will only hasten their perdition. They have devised an outrageous plot, and said to each other: 'Do not renounce your gods. Do not forsake Wadd or Suwā' or Yaghuth or Ya'uq or Nasr.'[1] They have led numerous men astray. You surely drive the wrongdoers to further error."

And because of their sins they were overwhelmed by the Flood and cast into the Fire. They found none besides God to help them.

And Noah said: "Lord, do not leave a single unbeliever in the land. If you spare them they will mislead Your servants and beget none but sinners and unbelievers. Forgive me, Lord, and forgive my parents and every true believer who seeks refuge in my house. Forgive all the faithful, men and women, and hasten the destruction of the wrongdoers."

76. Man

[MECCA]

In the Name of God, the Compassionate, the Merciful

Does there not pass over man a space of time when his life is a blank?[1]

We have created man from the union of the two sexes so that We may put him to the proof. We have endowed him with hearing and sight and, be he thankful or oblivious of Our favours, We have shown him the right path.

For the unbelievers We have prepared fetters and chains, and a blazing Fire. But the righteous shall drink of a cup tempered at the Camphor Fountain, a gushing spring at which the servants of God will refresh themselves: they who keep their vows and dread the far-spread terrors of Judgement-day; who, though they hold it dear, give sustenance to the poor man, the orphan, and the captive, saying: "We feed you for God's sake only; we seek of you neither recompense nor thanks: for we fear from God a day of anguish and of woe."

God will deliver them from the evil of that day and make their faces shine with joy. He will reward them for their steadfastness with robes of silk and the delights of Paradise. Reclining there upon soft couches, they shall feel neither the scorching heat nor the biting cold. Trees will spread their shade around them, and fruits will hang in clusters over them.

They shall be served with silver dishes, and beakers as large as goblets; silver goblets which they themselves shall measure: and cups brim-full with ginger-flavoured water from the Fount of Salsabīl. They shall be attended by boys graced with eternal youth, who to the beholder's eyes will seem like sprinkled pearls. When you gaze upon that scene you will behold a kingdom blissful and glorious.

They shall be arrayed in garments of fine green silk and rich brocade, and adorned with bracelets of silver. Their Lord will give them pure nectar to drink.

Thus you shall be rewarded; your high endeavours are gratifying to God.

---

1. Names of idols that were worshiped in Mecca before Muhammad had them destroyed.   1. In the womb.

We have made known to you the Koran by gradual revelation; therefore wait with patience the judgement of your Lord and do not yield to the wicked and the unbelieving. Remember the name of your Lord morning and evening; in the nighttime worship Him: praise Him all night long.

The unbelievers love this fleeting life too well, and thus prepare for themselves a heavy day of doom. We created them, and endowed their limbs and joints with strength; but if We please We can replace them by other men.

This is indeed an admonition. Let him that will, take the right path to his Lord. Yet you cannot will, except by the will of God. God is wise and all-knowing.

He is merciful to whom He will: but for the wrongdoers He has prepared a woeful punishment.

JALÂLODDIN RUMI
1207–1283

To understand Jalâloddin Rumi and his works, one first needs some understanding of the mystical dimension—sufism—of Islamic religious belief. In place of the conventional modes of worship—prayer, public worship, alms, fasting, and pilgrimage to the holy cities of Mecca and Medina—sufism emphasizes withdrawal from the world into progressively deeper levels of meditation. It has as its goal direct union or communion with the ultimate reality of God. Sufis believe that the world we perceive through our senses is a very seductive illusion that distracts us from the true and eternal reality that lies beyond it. We cannot grasp that transcendent reality directly, but only through metaphor. Reason is a poor guide through the mystical realm, and sufis rely instead on nonrational means of knowing like intuition and the trance states induced by rhythmic movement or the chanting of verses from the Koran and other sacred phrases.

Sufis commonly use the metaphor of the journey to describe their movement toward divinity, but their journeying is all within themselves. For sufis, God lies within all of us, and the journey toward God begins with a stripping away of our worldly self. The purpose of sufi practices, including sufi poetry, is to strengthen and guide us in our progress on that journey. To lessen their attachment to the world, some sufis, known as dervishes, practice a radical asceticism, owning nothing and traveling from city to city as mendicant preachers. They abandon all social conventions along with other worldly concerns and express themselves with a fierce and uncompromising directness. A dervish's authority comes from his indifference to worldly rank and station, and this makes him the natural opponent of kings and princes whose authority rests on their mastery of the world. Many sufi tales, including Sa'di's, play on this opposition.

Although orthodox Muslim teachers rejected the earliest sufis as heretics and saw sufism as hostile to orthodox worship, by the eleventh century they accepted it not as an alternative to conventional forms of worship but as a complement to them. Sufi orders formed around exemplary guides and spread throughout the Islamic world, achieving great influence in many countries and at different times. Many of these orders continue to flourish today, and since early in the twentieth century, offshoots of the most prominent of these orders have taken root in Europe and the United States as well.

Jalâloddin Rumi is without question the greatest mystical poet in Persian and possibly the greatest in the Islamic tradition. In the more than seven centuries since his death, Rumi's poetry has exerted a profound influence on the spiritual life of Muslims living in the Arab world, Turkey, Iran, central Asia, and India and has also gained a wide readership in Europe and America. Rumi also founded a mystical brotherhood, the Mevlevi Order, that was influential in Turkey for many years and has survived to the present day.

Rumi was born in September 1207 in the city of Balkh in northern Afghanistan. His father, a learned theologian known as Bahâ-ye Walad, taught there and in Samarqand, until his disputes with the ruler of the region and with other theologians led him to emigrate to western Anatolia—present-day Turkey. The incursions of the Mongols almost surely contributed to his decision to move so far to the west. The family eventually settled in Konya, where they remained after the death of Bahâ-ye Walad in 1231. After his father's death, Rumi continued his education both in Islamic law, jurisprudence, and traditions as well as in Islamic mysticism, or sufism. Although he received most of his education in Konya at the hands of former students of his father, he also lived and studied in Damascus and Aleppo for several years. On the completion of his studies he became, like his father before him, a teacher in the Muslim religious college in Konya.

At this point Rumi seemed destined to follow closely in his father's footsteps as a scholar and teacher. What transformed him into a great mystical poet and sustained him in that role throughout the remainder of his life was a series of three spiritual friendships. The first and most formative of these was with Shams-e Tabrizi, a dervish who came to Konya late in 1244. We know virtually nothing about Shams, but his presence had an immediate and electrifying effect on Rumi, transforming him from an able but unexceptional teacher into a brilliant and extraordinarily fluent poet. Rumi claims never to have written a line before he encountered Shams, but by the time Rumi died in 1283 he had composed the six thousand lyrics in forty thousand double lines that make up the *Divân-e Shams-e Tabrizi*, a work that honored his teacher, and the *Masnavi-ye Ma'navi* (Spiritual couplets), which contains more than twenty-five thousand couplets. If Rumi did indeed write all of his poetry after his meeting with Shams-e Tabrizi, he must have produced the equivalent of a sonnet virtually every day for the rest of his life, an astonishing performance considering the generally high standard of his work.

Rumi brought Shams into his own home, arranged for him to marry a young woman who was his ward, and gave him his whole and undivided attention for many months. He became so absorbed in Shams and his teaching that he neglected his own students, and they responded with a jealous intensity that eventually drove the dervish away—first for some months in 1246 and then permanently in 1247. Many modern students of Rumi's life and work believe that his students connived with Rumi's second son to murder Shams. However disturbing Rumi's love of Shams was for his students, for him it opened the wellspring of a great and unsuspected poetic talent. In response to the stimulus of Shams's presence Rumi began to compose ecstatic mystical lyrics in a continual, rushing abundance. After the disappearance of Shams, Rumi said that he had re-created him within himself and that he composed his lyrics with his voice. When these lyrics were gathered together in a single volume he called it the *Divân-e* (Collected poems of) *Shams-e Tabrizi*.

The spring of Rumi's talent seems to have required the presence of an intimate, spiritual friend to flow freely. The second person to fill this role was Salâhoddin Zarkub, an illiterate goldsmith who had, nonetheless, pursued spiritual learning with great diligence and had been, like Rumi, a student of Borhanoddin Mohaqqeq, who had been in turn a student of Rumi's own father. Rumi's disciples were again fiercely resentful of Salâhoddin, but he was able to compel their acceptance of him. Salâhoddin remained Rumi's companion and inspiration for the rest of his life. Rumi's third spiritual friend was Chelebi Husamoddin Hasan, who lived with him for the last ten years of his life. Husamoddin inspired Rumi to begin the composition of the *Spiritual Couplets*, the long narrative, didactic poem in rhyming couplets that has an importance for sufis that is second only to the Koran. Husamoddin served as successor to Rumi as sheikh of the mystical brotherhood that took its name from Rumi's spiritual title, Mowlavi ("my master"). After Rumi's death, leadership of the order fell to his son Soltan Walad, who strove successfully during his long life (died 1312) to gain respect for the order and to extend its influence.

Rumi's poetry is divided between two quite different genres: mystical lyric (*ghazal* and *robai*) and didactic narrative (*masnavi*). In each he achieved a level of excellence that has never been surpassed and rarely equaled. In Persian, the worldly erotic lyric relies heavily on exquisite descriptions of a nature that is both sumptuous and highly conventional—a paradise of the senses. It is the same world one finds in Persian miniatures. By contrast, Rumi's references to nature in his mystical lyrics are made in the service of the soul's perception of what lies beyond it. In some an ordinary event or typical scene becomes a parable, as in the poem that begins "You miss the garden, / because you want a small fig from a random tree." In others only the context tells us that what is intended is not worldly but spiritual love.

> Come to the orchard in Spring.
> There is light and wine, and sweethearts in the pomegranate flowers.
> If you do not come, these do not matter.
> If you do come, these do not matter.

Erotic lyrics invite one to romantic love and evoke the pleasures of sensuality. Mystical lyrics, by contrast, invite one to the love of God and evoke the mixed pain and pleasure of spiritual yearning.

While the *Spiritual Couplets* retains some of Rumi's lyric fluency, it is a learned work, rich with references to the Koran and the traditions of Muhammad. It is a didactic narrative in the tradition of Sana'i and Attar. In it Rumi presents anecdotes or parables whose spiritual meaning he then explores. He wrote it at the end of his life, and in it he makes available the fruits of his long scholarly preparation and his many years as a teacher.

PRONOUNCING GLOSSARY

The following list uses common English syllables and stress accents to provide rough equivalents of selected words whose pronunciation may be unfamiliar to the general reader.

Bahâ-ye Walad: *bu-haw'-ye wuh-lad'*

Borhanoddin Mohaqqeq: *bor-hah'-no-deen' mo-hak'-kek*

Chelebi Husamoddin Hasan: *che'-le-bee hoo-saw'-mo-deen ha'-san*

Masnavi-ye Ma'navi: *mas-na-vee'-yay ma-na-vee'*

Jalâloddin Rumi: *juh-lahl'-od-deen roo-mee'*

Salâhoddin Zarkub: *su-lah'-ho-deen' zar-koob'*

Shams-e Tabrizi: *sham'-say tab-ree-zee'*

ROBAIS[1]

[Listen, if you can stand to]

Listen, if you can stand to.
Union with the Friend means not being who you've been,
being instead silence: A place: A view
where language is inside seeing.

[What I most want]

What I most want
is to spring out of this personality,
then to sit apart from that leaping.
I've lived too long where I can be reached.

[Don't come to us without bringing music]

Don't come to us without bringing music.
We celebrate with drum and flute,
with wine not made from grapes,
in a place you cannot imagine.

[Sometimes visible, sometimes not, sometimes]

Sometimes visible, sometimes not, sometimes
devout Christians, sometimes staunchly Jewish.
Until our inner love fits into everyone,
all we can do is take daily these different shapes.

25

Friend, our closeness is this:
Anywhere you put your foot, feel me
in the firmness under you.

How is it with this love,
I see your world and not you?

5

---

1. All selections translated by Coleman Barks.

82

Today, like every other day, we wake up empty
and frightened. Don't open the door to the study
and begin reading. Take down a musical instrument.

Let the beauty we love be what we do.
There are hundreds of ways to kneel and kiss the ground.   5

158

Out beyond ideas of wrongdoing and rightdoing,
there is a field. I'll meet you there.

When the soul lies down in that grass,
the world is too full to talk about.
Ideas, language, even the phrase *each other*   5
doesn't make any sense.

GHAZALS

An Empty Garlic

You miss the garden,
because you want a small fig from a random tree.
You don't meet the beautiful woman.
You're joking with an old crone.
It makes me want to cry how she detains you,
stinking-mouthed, with a hundred talons,   5
putting her head over the roofedge to call down,
tasteless fig, fold over fold, empty
as dry-rotten garlic.

She has you tight by the belt,   10
even though there's no flower and no milk
inside her body.
Death will open your eyes
to what her face is: Leather spine
of a black lizard. No more advice.   15

Let yourself be silently drawn
by the stronger pull of what you really love.

Dissolver of Sugar

Dissolver of sugar, dissolve me,
if this is the time.
Do it gently with a touch of hand, or a look.
Every morning I wait at dawn. That's when it's happened before.
Or do it suddenly like an execution. How else 5
can I get ready for death?

You breathe without a body like a spark.
You grieve, and I begin to feel lighter.
You keep me away with your arm,
but the keeping away is pulling me in. 10

From Spiritual Couplets

[A chickpea leaps almost over the rim of the pot]

A chickpea leaps almost over the rim of the pot
where it's being boiled.

"Why are you doing this to me?"

The cook knocks it down with the ladle.

"Don't you try to jump out. 5
You think I'm torturing you,
I'm giving you flavor,
so you can mix with spices and rice
and be the lovely vitality of a human being.

Remember when you drank rain in the garden. 10
That was for this."

Grace first. Sexual pleasure,
then a boiling new life begins,
and the Friend has something good to eat.

Why Wine Is Forbidden

When the Prophet's ray of Intelligence
struck the dimwitted man he was with,
the man got very happy, and talkative.
Soon, he began unmannerly raving.
This is the problem with a selflessness 5
that comes quickly,
                as with wine.
If the wine-drinker
has a deep gentleness in him,

he will show that,
               when drunk.
But if he has hidden anger and arrogance,   10
those appear,
               and since most people do,
wine is forbidden to everyone.

The Question

One dervish to another, *What was your vision of God's presence?*
I haven't seen anything.
But for the sake of conversation, I'll tell you a story.

God's presence is there in front of me, a fire on the left,
a lovely stream on the right.   5
One group walks toward the fire, *into* the fire, another
toward the sweet flowing water.
No one knows which are blessed and which not.
Whoever walks into the fire appears suddenly in the stream.
A head goes under on the water surface, that head   10
pokes out of the fire.
Most people guard against going into the fire,
and so end up in it.
Those who love the water of pleasure and make it their devotion
are cheated with this reversal.   15
The trickery goes further.
The voice of the fire tells the *truth*, saying *I am not fire.*
I am fountainhead. Come into me and don't mind the sparks.
If you are a friend of God, fire is your water.
You should wish to have a hundred thousand sets of mothwings, 20
so you could burn them away, one set a night.
The moth sees light and goes into fire. You should see fire
and go toward light. Fire is what of God is world-consuming.
Water, world-protecting.
Somehow each gives the appearance of the other. To these eyes you
      have now   25
what looks like water burns. What looks like
fire is a great relief to be inside.
You've seen a magician make a bowl of rice
seem a dish full of tiny, live worms.
Before an assembly with one breath he made the floor swarm   30
with scorpions that weren't there.
How much more amazing God's tricks.
Generation after generation lies down, defeated, they think,
but they're like a woman underneath a man, circling him.
One molecule-mote-second thinking of God's reversal of comfort and
      pain   35
is better than any attending ritual. That splinter
of intelligence is substance.
The fire and water themselves:
Accidental, done with mirrors.

FROM BIRDSONG

[Lovers in their brief delight]

Lovers in their brief delight
gamble both worlds away,
a century's worth of work
for one chance to surrender.

Many slow growth-stages build   5
to quick bursts of blossom.

A thousand half-loves
must be forsaken to take
one whole heart home.

FROM THE GLANCE

Silkworms

The hurt you embrace becomes joy.
Call it to your arms where it can

change. A silkworm eating leaves
makes a cocoon. Each of us weaves

a chamber of leaves and sticks.   5
Silkworms begin to truly exist

as they disappear inside that room.
Without legs, we fly. When I stop

speaking, this poem will close,
and open its silent wings . . .   10

THE THOUSAND AND ONE NIGHTS
fourteenth century

The Thousand and One Nights is rich in paradoxes. An anonymous work, it is nevertheless more widely known in the Arab world than any other work of Arabic literature. It is almost as well known in Europe, and so far is the only work of Arabic letters to become a permanent part of European and, indeed, of world literature. Despite this great popularity, and despite its shaping influence on modern literature, traditional Arabic literary scholars have never recognized it as a work of serious literature, and it is still occasionally banned as immoral by Arab governments.

his brother; then he invited him to see him and said, "Brother, I would like you to know that I intend to go hunting and pursue the roaming deer, for ten days. Then I shall return to prepare you for your journey home. Would you like to go hunting with me?" Shahzaman replied, "Brother, I feel distracted and depressed. Leave me here and go with God's blessing and help." When Shahrayar heard his brother, he thought that his dejection was because of his homesickness for his country. Not wishing to coerce him, he left him behind, and set out with his retainers and men. When they entered the wilderness, he deployed his men in a circle to begin trapping and hunting.

After his brother's departure, Shahzaman stayed in the palace and, from the window overlooking the garden, watched the birds and trees as he thought of his wife and what she had done to him, and sighed in sorrow. While he agonized over his misfortune, gazing at the heavens and turning a distracted eye on the garden, the private gate of his brother's palace opened, and there emerged, strutting like a dark-eyed deer, the lady, his brother's wife, with twenty slave-girls, ten white and ten black. While Shahzaman looked at them, without being seen, they continued to walk until they stopped below his window, without looking in his direction, thinking that he had gone to the hunt with his brother. Then they sat down, took off their clothes, and suddenly there were ten slave-girls and ten black slaves dressed in the same clothes as the girls. Then the ten black slaves mounted the ten girls, while the lady called, "Mas'ud, Mas'ud!" and a black slave jumped from the tree to the ground, rushed to her, and, raising her legs, went between her thighs and made love to her. Mas'ud topped the lady, while the ten slaves topped the ten girls, and they carried on till noon. When they were done with their business, they got up and washed themselves. Then the ten slaves put on the same clothes again, mingled with the girls, and once more there appeared to be twenty slave-girls. Mas'ud himself jumped over the garden wall and disappeared, while the slave-girls and the lady sauntered to the private gate, went in and, locking the gate behind them, went their way.

All of this happened under King Shahzaman's eyes. When he saw this spectacle of the wife and the women of his brother the great king—how ten slaves put on women's clothes and slept with his brother's paramours and concubines and what Mas'ud did with his brother's wife, in his very palace—and pondered over this calamity and great misfortune, his care and sorrow left him and he said to himself, "This is our common lot. Even though my brother is king and master of the whole world, he cannot protect what is his, his wife and his concubines, and suffers misfortune in his very home. What happened to me is little by comparison. I used to think that I was the only one who has suffered, but from what I have seen, everyone suffers. By God, my misfortune is lighter than that of my brother." He kept marveling and blaming life, whose trials none can escape, and he began to find consolation in his own affliction and forget his grief. When supper came, he ate and drank with relish and zest and, feeling better, kept eating and drinking, enjoying himself and feeling happy. He thought to himself, "I am no longer alone in my misery; I am well."

For ten days, he continued to enjoy his food and drink, and when his brother, King Shahrayar, came back from the hunt, he met him happily, treated him attentively, and greeted him cheerfully. His brother, King

Shahrayar, who had missed him, said, "By God, brother, I missed you on this trip and wished you were with me." Shahzaman thanked him and sat down to carouse with him, and when night fell, and food was brought before them, the two ate and drank, and again Shahzaman ate and drank with zest. As time went by, he continued to eat and drink with appetite, and became lighthearted and carefree. His face regained color and became ruddy, and his body gained weight, as his blood circulated and he regained his energy; he was himself again, or even better. King Shahrayar noticed his brother's condition, how he used to be and how he had improved, but kept it to himself until he took him aside one day and said, "My brother Shahzaman, I would like you to do something for me, to satisfy a wish, to answer a question truthfully." Shahzaman asked, "What is it, brother?" He replied, "When you first came to stay with me, I noticed that you kept losing weight, day after day, until your looks changed, your health deteriorated, and your energy sagged. As you continued like this, I thought that what ailed you was your homesickness for your family and your country, but even though I kept noticing that you were wasting away and looking ill, I refrained from questioning you and hid my feelings from you. Then I went hunting, and when I came back, I found that you had recovered and had regained your health. Now I want you to tell me everything and to explain the cause of your deterioration and the cause of your subsequent recovery, without hiding anything from me." When Shahzaman heard what King Shahrayar said, he bowed his head, then said, "As for the cause of my recovery, that I cannot tell you, and I wish that you would excuse me from telling you." The king was greatly astonished at his brother's reply and, burning with curiosity, said, "You must tell me. For now, at least, explain the first cause."

Then Shahzaman related to his brother what happened to him with his own wife, on the night of his departure, from beginning to end, and concluded, "Thus all the while I was with you, great King, whenever I thought of the event and the misfortune that had befallen me, I felt troubled, careworn, and unhappy, and my health deteriorated. This then is the cause." Then he grew silent. When King Shahrayar heard his brother's explanation, he shook his head, greatly amazed at the deceit of women, and prayed to God to protect him from their wickedness, saying, "Brother, you were fortunate in killing your wife and her lover, who gave you good reason to feel troubled, careworn, and ill. In my opinion, what happened to you has never happened to anyone else. By God, had I been in your place, I would have killed at least a hundred or even a thousand women. I would have been furious; I would have gone mad. Now praise be to God who has delivered you from sorrow and distress. But tell me what has caused you to forget your sorrow and regain your health?" Shahzaman replied, "King, I wish that for God's sake you would excuse me from telling you." Shahrayar said, "You must." Shahzaman replied, "I fear that you will feel even more troubled and careworn than I." Shahrayar asked, "How could that be, brother? I insist on hearing your explanation."

Shahzaman then told him about what he had seen from the palace window and the calamity in his very home—how ten slaves, dressed like women, were sleeping with his women and concubines, day and night. He told him everything from beginning to end (but there is no point in repeating that). Then he concluded, "When I saw your own misfortune, I felt better—and said to myself, 'My brother is king of the world, yet such a misfortune has happened to him, and in his very home.' As a result I forgot my care and sorrow, relaxed, and began to eat and drink. This is the cause of my cheer and good spirits."

When King Shahrayar heard what his brother said and found out what had happened to him, he was furious and his blood boiled. He said, "Brother, I can't believe what you say unless I see it with my own eyes." When Shahzaman saw that his brother was in a rage, he said to him, "If you do not believe me, unless you see your misfortune with your own eyes, announce that you plan to go hunting. Then you and I shall set out with your troops, and when we get outside the city, we shall leave our tents and camp with the men behind, enter the city secretly, and go together to your palace. Then the next morning you can see with your own eyes."

King Shahrayar realized that his brother had a good plan and ordered his army to prepare for the trip. He spent the night with his brother, and when God's morning broke, the two rode out of the city with their army, preceded by the camp attendants, who had gone to drive the poles and pitch the tents where the king and his army were to camp. At nightfall King Shahrayar summoned his chief chamberlain and bade him take his place. He entrusted him with the army and ordered that for three days no one was to enter the city. Then he and his brother disguised themselves and entered the city in the dark. They went directly to the palace where Shahzaman resided and slept there till the morning. When they awoke, they sat at the palace window, watching the garden and chatting, until the light broke, the day dawned, and the sun rose. As they watched, the private gate opened, and there emerged as usual the wife of King Shahrayar, walking among twenty slave-girls. They made their way under the trees until they stood below the palace window where the two kings sat. Then they took off their women's clothes, and suddenly there were ten slaves, who mounted the ten girls and made love to them. As for the lady, she called, "Mas'ud, Mas'ud," and a black slave jumped from the tree to the ground, came to her, and said, "What do you want, you slut? Here is Sa'ad al-Din Mas'ud." She laughed and fell on her back, while the slave mounted her and like the others did his business with her. Then the black slaves got up, washed themselves, and, putting on the same clothes, mingled with the girls. Then they walked away, entered the palace, and locked the gate behind them. As for Mas'ud, he jumped over the fence to the road and went on his way.

When King Shahrayar saw the spectacle of his wife and the slave-girls, he went out of his mind, and when he and his brother came down from upstairs, he said, "No one is safe in this world. Such doings are going on in my kingdom, and in my very palace. Perish the world and perish life! This is a great calamity, indeed." Then he turned to his brother and asked, "Would you like to follow me in what I shall do?" Shahzaman answered, "Yes. I will." Shahrayar said, "Let us leave our royal state and roam the world for the love of the Supreme Lord. If we should find one whose misfortune is greater than ours, we shall return. Otherwise, we shall continue to journey through the land, without need for the trappings of royalty." Shahzaman replied, "This is an excellent idea. I shall follow you."

Then they left by the private gate, took a side road, and departed, journeying till nightfall. They slept over their sorrows, and in the morning resumed their day journey until they came to a meadow by the seashore. While they sat in the meadow amid the thick plants and trees, discussing their misfortunes and the recent events, they suddenly heard a shout and a great cry coming from the middle of the sea. They trembled with fear, thinking that the sky had fallen on the earth. Then the sea parted, and there emerged a black pillar that, as it swayed forward, got taller and taller, until it touched the clouds. Shahrayar and Shahzaman were petrified; then they ran in terror and, climbing a very tall tree, sat hiding in its foliage. When they looked again, they saw that the black pillar was cleaving the sea, wading in the water toward the green meadow, until it touched the shore. When they looked again, they saw that it was a black demon, carrying on his head a large glass chest with four steel locks. He came out, walked into the meadow, and where should he stop but under the very tree where the two kings were hiding. The demon sat down and placed the glass chest on the ground. He took out four keys and, opening the locks of the chest, pulled out a full-grown woman. She had a beautiful figure, and a face like the full moon, and a lovely smile. He took her out, laid her under the tree, and looked at her, saying, "Mistress of all noble women, you whom I carried away on your wedding night, I would like to sleep a little." Then he placed his head on the young woman's lap, stretched his legs to the sea, sank into sleep, and began to snore.

Meanwhile, the woman looked up at the tree and, turning her head by chance, saw King Shahrayar and King Shahzaman. She lifted the demon's head from her lap and placed it on the ground. Then she came and stood under the tree and motioned to them with her hand, as if to say, "Come down slowly to me." When they realized that she had seen them, they were frightened, and they begged her and implored her, in the name of the Creator of the heavens, to excuse them from climbing down. She replied, "You must come down to me." They motioned to her, saying, "This sleeping demon is the enemy of mankind. For God's sake, leave us alone." She replied, "You must come down, and if you don't, I shall wake the demon and have him kill you." She kept gesturing and pressing, until they climbed down very slowly and stood before her. Then she lay on her back, raised her legs, and said, "Make love to me and satisfy my need, or else I shall wake the demon, and he will kill you." They replied, "For God's sake, mistress, don't do this to us, for at this moment we feel nothing but dismay and fear of this demon. Please, excuse us." She replied, "You must," and insisted, swearing, "By God who created the heavens, if you don't do it, I shall wake my husband the demon and ask him to kill you and throw you into the sea." As she persisted, they could no longer resist and they made love to her, first the older brother, then the younger. When they were done and withdrew from her, she said to them, "Give me your rings," and, pulling out from the folds of her dress a small purse, opened it, and shook out ninety-eight rings of different fashions and colors. Then she asked them, "Do you know what these rings are?" They answered, "No." She said, "All the owners of these rings slept with me, for whenever one of them made love to me, I took a ring from him. Since you two have slept with me, give me your rings, so that I may add them to the rest, and make a full hundred. A hundred men have known me under the very horns of this filthy, monstrous cuckold, who has imprisoned me in this chest, locked it with four locks, and kept me in the middle of this raging, roaring sea. He has guarded me and tried to keep me pure and

meanness. Being sincere, you exert and exhaust yourself to comfort others. Have you not heard the saying 'Out of bad luck, they hastened on the road'? You go into the field from early morning to endure your torture at the plow to the point of exhaustion. When the plowman takes you back and ties you to the trough, you go on butting and beating with your horns, kicking with your hoofs, and bellowing for the beans, until they toss them to you; then you begin to eat. Next time, when they bring them to you, don't eat or even touch them, but smell them, then draw back and lie down on the hay and straw. If you do this, life will be better and kinder to you, and you will find relief."

As the ox listened, he was sure that the donkey had given him good advice. He thanked him, commended him to God, and invoked His blessing on him, and said, "May you stay safe from harm, watchful one." All of this conversation took place, daughter, while the merchant listened and understood. On the following day, the plowman came to the merchant's house and, taking the ox, placed the yoke upon his neck and worked him at the plow, but the ox lagged behind. The plowman hit him, but following the donkey's advice, the ox, dissembling, fell on his belly, and the plowman hit him again. Thus the ox kept getting up and falling until nightfall, when the plowman took him home and tied him to the trough. But this time the ox did not bellow or kick the ground with his hoofs. Instead, he withdrew, away from the trough. Astonished, the plowman brought him his beans and fodder, but the ox only smelled the fodder and pulled back and lay down at a distance with the hay and straw, complaining till the morning. When the plowman arrived, he found the trough as he had left it, full of beans and fodder, and saw the ox lying on his back, hardly breathing, his belly puffed, and his legs raised in the air. The plowman felt sorry for him and said to himself, "By God, he did seem weak and unable to work." Then he went to the merchant and said, "Master, last night, the ox refused to eat or touch his fodder."

The merchant, who knew what was going on, said to the plowman, "Go to the wily donkey, put him to the plow, and work him hard until he finishes the ox's task." The plowman left, took the donkey, and placed the yoke upon his neck. Then he took him out to the field and drove him with blows until he finished the ox's work, all the while driving him with blows and beating him until his sides were lacerated and his neck was flayed. At nightfall he took him home, barely able to drag his legs under his tired body and his drooping ears. Meanwhile the ox spent his day resting. He ate all his food, drank his water, and lay quietly, chewing his cud in comfort. All day long he kept praising the donkey's advice and invoking God's blessing on him. When the donkey came back at night, the ox stood up to greet him saying, "Good evening, watchful one! You have done me a favor beyond description, for I have been sitting in comfort. God bless you for my sake." Seething with anger, the donkey did not reply, but said to himself, "All this happened to me because of my miscalculation. 'I would be sitting pretty, but for my curiosity.' If I don't find a way to return this ox to his former situation, I will perish." Then he went to his trough and lay down, while the ox continued to chew his cud and invoke God's blessing on him.

"You, my daughter, will likewise perish because of your miscalculation. Desist, sit quietly, and don't expose yourself to peril. I advise you out of compassion for you." She replied, "Father, I must go to the king, and you must give me to him." He said, "Don't do it." She insisted, "I must." He replied, "If you don't desist, I will do to you what the merchant did to his wife." She asked, "Father, what did the merchant do to his wife?" He said:

[The Tale of the Merchant and His Wife]

After what had happened to the donkey and the ox, the merchant and his wife went out in the moonlight to the stable, and he heard the donkey ask the ox in his own language, "Listen, ox, what are you going to do tomorrow morning, and what will you do when the plowman brings you your fodder?" The ox replied, "What shall I do but follow your advice and stick to it? If he brings me my fodder, I will pretend to be ill, lie down, and puff my belly." The donkey shook his head, and said, "Don't do it. Do you know what I heard our master the merchant say to the plowman?" The ox asked, "What?" The donkey replied, "He said that if the ox failed to get up and eat his fodder, he would call the butcher to slaughter him and skin him and would distribute the meat for alms and use the skin for a mat. I am afraid for you, but good advice is a matter of faith; therefore, if he brings you your fodder, eat it and look alert lest they cut your throat and skin you." The ox farted and bellowed.

The merchant got up and laughed loudly at the conversation between the donkey and the ox, and his wife asked him, "What are you laughing at? Are you making fun of me?" He said, "No." She said, "Tell me what made you laugh." He replied, "I cannot tell you. I am afraid to disclose the secret conversation of the animals." She asked, "And what prevents you from telling me?" He answered, "The fear of death." His wife said, "By God, you are lying. This is nothing but an excuse. I swear by God, the Lord of heaven, that if you don't tell me and explain the cause of your laughter, I will leave you. You must tell me." Then she went back to the house crying, and she continued to cry till the morning. The merchant said, "Damn it! Tell me why you are crying. Ask for God's forgiveness, and stop questioning and leave me in peace." She said, "I insist and will not desist." Amazed at her, he replied, "You insist! If I tell you what the donkey said to the ox, which made me laugh, I shall die." She said, "Yes, I insist, even if you have to die." He replied, "Then call your family," and she called their two daughters, her parents and relatives, and some neighbors. The merchant told them that he was about to die, and everyone, young and old, his children, the farmhands, and the servants began to cry until the house became a place of mourning. Then he summoned legal witnesses, wrote a will, leaving his wife and children their due portions, freed his slave-girls, and bid his family good-bye, while everybody, even the witnesses, wept. Then the wife's parents approached her and said, "Desist, for if your husband had not known for certain that he would die if he revealed his secret, he wouldn't have gone through all this." She replied, "I will not change my mind," and everybody cried and prepared to mourn his death.

Well, my daughter Shahrazad, it happened that the farmer kept fifty hens and a rooster at home, and while he felt sad to depart this world and leave his children and relatives behind, pondering and about to reveal and utter his secret, he overheard a dog of his say something in dog language to the rooster, who, beating and clapping his wings, had jumped on a hen and, finishing with her, jumped down and jumped on another. The merchant heard and understood what the dog said in his own language to the rooster, "Shameless, no-good rooster. Aren't you ashamed to do such a thing on a day like this?" The rooster asked, "What is special about this day?" The dog replied, "Don't you know that our master and friend is in mourning today? His wife is demanding that he disclose his secret, and when he discloses it, he will surely die. He is in this predicament, about to interpret to her the language of the animals, and all of us are mourning for him, while you clap your wings and get off one hen and jump on another. Aren't you ashamed?" The merchant heard the rooster reply, "You fool, you lunatic! Our master and friend claims to be wise, but he is foolish, for he has only one wife, yet he does not know how to manage her." The dog asked, "What should he do with her?"

The rooster replied, "He should take an oak branch, push her into a room, lock the door, and fall on her with the stick, beating her mercilessly until he breaks her arms and legs and she cries out, 'I no longer want you to tell me or explain anything.' He should go on beating her until he cures her for life, and she will never oppose him in anything. If he does this, he will live, and live in peace, and there will be no more grief, but he does not know how to manage." Well, my daughter Shahrazad, when the merchant heard the conversation between the dog and the rooster, he jumped up and, taking an oak branch, pushed his wife into a room, got in with her, and locked the door. Then he began to beat her mercilessly on her chest and shoulders and kept beating her until she cried for mercy, screaming, "No, no, I don't want to know anything. Leave me alone, leave me alone. I don't want to know anything," until he got tired of hitting her and opened the door. The wife emerged penitent, the husband learned good management, and everybody was happy, and the mourning turned into a celebration.

"If you don't relent, I shall do to you what the merchant did to his wife." She said, "Such tales don't deter me from my request. If you wish, I can tell you many such tales. In the end, if you don't take me to King Shahrayar, I shall go to him by myself behind your back and tell him that you have refused to give me to one like him and that you have begrudged your master one like me." The vizier asked, "Must you really do this?" She replied, "Yes, I must."

Tired and exhausted, the vizier went to King Shahrayar and, kissing the ground before him, told him about his daughter, adding that he would give her to him that very night. The king was astonished and said to him, "Vizier, how is it that you have found it possible to give me your daughter, knowing that I will, by God, the Creator of heaven, ask you to put her to death the next morning and that if you refuse, I will have you put to death too?" He replied, "My King and Lord, I have told her everything and explained all this to her, but she refuses and insists on being with you tonight." The king was delighted and said, "Go to her, prepare her, and bring her to me early in the evening."

The vizier went down, repeated the king's message to his daughter, and said, "May God not deprive me of you." She was very happy and, after preparing herself and packing what she needed, went to her younger sister, Dinarzad, and said, "Sister, listen well to what I am telling you. When I go to the king, I will send for you, and when you come and see that the king has finished with me, say, 'Sister, if you are not sleepy, tell us a story.' Then I will begin to tell a story, and it will cause the king to stop his practice, save myself, and deliver the people." Dinarzad replied, "Very well."

At nightfall the vizier took Shahrazad and went with her to the great King Shahrayar. But when Shahrayar took her to bed and began to fondle her, she wept, and when he asked her, "Why are you crying?" she replied, "I have a sister, and I wish to bid her good-bye before daybreak." Then the king sent for the sister, who came and went to sleep under the bed. When the night wore on, she woke up and waited until the king had satisfied himself with her sister Shahrazad and they were by now all fully awake. Then Dinarzad cleared her throat and said, "Sister, if you are not sleepy, tell us one of your lovely little tales to while away the night, before I bid you good-bye at daybreak, for I don't know what will happen to you tomorrow." Shahrazad turned to King Shahrayar and said, "May I have your permission to tell a story?" He replied, "Yes," and Shahrazad was very happy and said, "Listen":

[The Story of the Merchant and the Demon]

THE FIRST NIGHT

It is said, O wise and happy King, that once there was a prosperous merchant who had abundant wealth and investments and commitments in every country. He had many women and children and kept many servants and slaves. One day, having resolved to visit another country, he took provisions, filling his saddlebag with loaves of bread and with dates, mounted his horse, and set out on his journey. For many days and nights, he journeyed under God's care until he reached his destination. When he finished his business, he turned back to his home and family. He journeyed for three days, and on the fourth day, chancing to come to an orchard, went in to avoid the heat and shade himself from the sun of the open country. He came to a spring under a walnut tree and, tying his horse, sat by the spring, pulled out from the saddlebag some loaves of bread and a handful of dates, and began to eat, throwing the date pits right and left until he had had enough. Then he got up, performed his ablutions, and performed his prayers.

But hardly had he finished when he saw an old demon, with sword in hand, standing with his feet on the ground and his head in the clouds. The demon approached until he stood before him and screamed, saying, "Get up, so that I may kill you with this sword, just as you have killed my son." When the merchant saw and heard the demon, he was terrified and awestricken. He asked, "Master, for what crime do you wish to kill me?" The demon replied, "I wish to kill you because you have killed my son." The merchant asked, "Who has killed your son?" The demon replied, "You have killed my son." The merchant said, "By God, I did not kill your son. When and how could that have been?" The demon said, "Didn't you sit down, take out some dates from your saddlebag, and eat, throwing the pits right and left?" The merchant replied, "Yes, I did." The demon said, "You killed my son, for as you were throwing the stones right and left, my son happened to be walking by and was struck and killed by one of them, and I must now kill you." The merchant said, "O my lord, please don't kill me." The demon replied, "I must kill you as you killed him—blood for blood." The merchant said, "To God we belong and to God we turn. There is no power or strength, save in God the Almighty, the Magnificent. If I killed him, I did it by mistake. Please forgive me." The demon replied, "By God, I must kill you, as you killed my son." Then he seized him, and throwing him to the ground, raised the sword to strike him. The merchant began to weep and mourn his family and his wife and children. Again, the demon raised his sword to strike, while the merchant cried until he was drenched with tears, saying, "There is no power or strength, save in God the Almighty, the Magnificent." Then he began to recite the following verses:

> Life has two days: one peace, one wariness,
> And has two sides: worry and happiness.
> Ask him who taunts us with adversity,
> "Does fate, save those worthy of note, oppress?
> Don't you see that the blowing, raging storms   5
> Only the tallest of the trees beset,
> And of earth's many green and barren lots,
> Only the ones with fruits with stones are hit,
> And of the countless stars in heaven's vault
> None is eclipsed except the moon and sun?   10
> You thought well of the days, when they were good,
> Oblivious to the ills destined for one.
> You were deluded by the peaceful nights,
> Yet in the peace of night does sorrow stun."

When the merchant finished and stopped weeping, the demon said, "By God, I must kill you, as you killed my son, even if you weep blood." The merchant asked, "Must you?" The demon replied, "I must," and raised his sword to strike.

But morning overtook Shahrazad, and she lapsed into silence, leaving King Shahrayar burning with curiosity to hear the rest of the story. Then Dinarzad said to her sister Shahrazad, "What a strange and lovely story!" Shahrazad replied, "What is this compared with what I shall tell you tomorrow night if the king spares me and lets me live? It will be even better and more entertaining." The king thought to himself, "I will spare her until I hear the rest of the story; then I will have her put to death the next day." When morning broke, the day dawned, and the sun rose; the king left to attend to the affairs of the kingdom, and the vizier, Shahrazad's father, was amazed and delighted. King Shahrayar governed all day and returned home at night to his quarters and got into bed with Shahrazad. Then Dinarzad said to her sister Shahrazad, "Please, sister, if you are not sleepy, tell us one of your lovely little tales to while away the night." The king added, "Let it be the conclusion of the story of the demon and the merchant, for I would like to hear it." Shahrazad replied, "With the greatest pleasure, dear, happy King":

THE SECOND NIGHT

It is related, O wise and happy King, that when the demon raised his sword, the merchant asked the demon again, "Must you kill me?" and the demon replied, "Yes." Then the merchant said, "Please give me time to say good-bye to my family and my wife and children, divide my property among them, and appoint guardians. Then I shall come back, so that you may kill me." The demon replied, "I am afraid that if I release you and grant you time, you will go and do what you wish, but will not come back." The merchant said, "I swear to keep my pledge to come back, as the God of Heaven and earth is my witness." The demon asked, "How much time do you need?" The merchant replied, "One year, so that I may see enough of my children, bid my wife good-bye, discharge my obligations to people, and come back on New Year's Day." The demon asked, "Do you swear to God that if I let you go, you will come back on New Year's Day?" The merchant replied, "Yes, I swear to God."

After the merchant swore, the demon released him, and he mounted his horse sadly and went on his way. He journeyed until he reached his home and came to his wife and children. When he saw them, he wept bitterly, and when his family saw his sorrow and grief, they began to reproach him for his behavior, and his wife said, "Husband, what is the matter with you? Why do you mourn, when we are happy, celebrating your return?" He replied, "Why not mourn when I have only one year to live?" Then he told her of his encounter with the demon and informed her that he had sworn to return on New Year's Day, so that the demon might kill him.

When they heard what he said, everyone began to cry. His wife struck her face in lamentation and cut her hair, his daughters wailed, and his little children cried. It was a day of mourning, as all the children gathered around their father to weep and exchange good-byes. The next day he wrote his will, dividing his property, discharged his obligations to people, left bequests and gifts, distributed alms, and engaged reciters to read portions of the Quran in his house. Then he summoned legal witnesses and in their presence freed his slaves and slave-girls, divided among his elder children their shares of the property, appointed guardians for his little ones, and gave his wife her share, according to her marriage contract. He spent the rest of the time with his family, and when the year came to an end, save for the time needed for the journey, he performed his ablutions, performed his prayers, and, carrying his burial shroud, began to bid his family good-bye. His sons hung around his neck, his daughters wept, and his wife wailed. Their mourning scared him, and he began to weep, as he embraced and kissed his children good-bye. He said to them, "Children, this is God's will and decree, for man was created to die." Then he turned away and, mounting his horse, journeyed day and night until he reached the orchard on New Year's Day.

He sat at the place where he had eaten the dates, waiting for the demon, with a heavy heart and tearful eyes. As he waited, an old man, leading a deer on a leash, approached and greeted him, and he returned the greeting. The old man inquired, "Friend, why do you sit here in this place of demons and devils? For in this haunted orchard none come to good." The merchant replied by telling him what had happened to him and the demon, from beginning to end. The old man was amazed at the merchant's fidelity and said, "Yours is a magnificent pledge," adding, "By God, I shall not leave until I see what will happen to you with the demon." Then he sat down beside him and chatted with him. As they talked . . .

But morning overtook Shahrazad, and she lapsed into silence. As the day dawned, and it was light, her sister Dinarzad said, "What a strange and won-

Then he brought me my son, my heartblood, in the guise of a fat young bull. Then my son saw me, he shook his head loose from the rope, ran toward me, and, throwing himself at my feet, kept rubbing his head against me. I was astonished and touched with sympathy, pity, and mercy, for the blood hearkened to the blood and the divine bond, and my heart throbbed within me when I saw the tears coursing over the cheeks of my son the young bull, as he dug the earth with his hoofs. I turned away and said to the shepherd, "Let him go with the rest of the flock, and be kind to him, for I have decided to spare him. Bring me another one instead of him." My wife, this very deer, shouted, "You shall sacrifice none but this bull." I got angry and replied, "I listened to you and butchered the cow uselessly. I will not listen to you and kill this bull, for I have decided to spare him." But she pressed me, saying, "You must butcher this bull," and I bound him and took the knife . . .

But dawn broke, and morning overtook Shahrazad, and she lapsed into silence, leaving the king all curiosity for the rest of the story. Then her sister Dinarzad said, "What an entertaining story!" Shahrazad replied, "Tomorrow night I shall tell you something even stranger, more wonderful, and more entertaining if the king spares me and lets me live."

THE FIFTH NIGHT

The following night, Dinarzad said to her sister Shahrazad, "Please, sister, if you are not sleepy, tell us one of your little tales." Shahrazad replied, "With the greatest pleasure":

I heard, dear King, that the old man with the deer said to the demon and to his companions:

I took the knife and as I turned to slaughter my son, he wept, bellowed, rolled at my feet, and motioned toward me with his tongue. I suspected something, began to waver with trepidation and pity, and finally released him, saying to my wife, "I have decided to spare him, and I commit him to your care." Then I tried to appease and please my wife, this very deer, by slaughtering another bull, promising her to slaughter this one next season. We slept that night, and when God's dawn broke, the shepherd came to me without letting my wife know, and said, "Give me credit for bringing you good news." I replied, "Tell me, and the credit is yours." He said, "Master, I have a daughter who is fond of soothsaying and magic and who is adept at the art of oaths and spells. Yesterday I took home with me the bull you had spared, to let him graze with the cattle, and when my daughter saw him, she laughed and cried at the same time. When I asked her why she laughed and cried, she answered that she laughed because the bull was in reality the son of our master the cattle owner, put under a spell by his stepmother, and that she cried because his father had slaughtered the son's mother. I could hardly wait till daybreak to bring you the good news about your son."

Demon, when I heard that, I uttered a cry and fainted, and when I came to myself, I accompanied the shepherd to his home, went to my son, and threw myself at him, kissing him and crying. He turned his head toward me, his tears coursing over his cheeks, and dangled his tongue, as if to say, "Look at my plight." Then I turned to the shepherd's daughter and asked, "Can you release him from the spell? If you do, I will give you all my cattle and all my possessions." She smiled and replied, "Master, I have no desire for your wealth, cattle, or possessions. I will deliver him, but on two conditions: first, that you let me marry him; second, that you let me cast a spell on her who had cast a spell on him, in order to control her and guard against her evil power." I replied, "Do whatever you wish and more. My possessions are for you and my son. As for my wife, who has done this to my son and made me slaughter his mother, her life is forfeit to you." She said, "No, but I will let her taste what she has inflicted on others." Then the shepherd's daughter filled a bowl of water, uttered an incantation and an oath, and said to my son, "Bull, if you have been created in this image by the All-Conquering, Almighty Lord, stay as you are, but if you have been treacherously put under a spell, change back to your human form, by the will of God, Creator of the wide world." Then she sprinkled him with the water, and he shook himself and changed from a bull back to his human form.

As I rushed to him, I fainted, and when I came to myself, he told me what my wife, this very deer, had done to him and to his mother. I said to him, "Son, God has sent us someone who will pay her back for what you and your mother and I have suffered at her hands." Then, O demon, I gave my son in marriage to the shepherd's daughter, who turned my wife into this very deer, saying to me, "To me this is a pretty form, for she will be with us day and night, and it is better to turn her into a pretty deer than to suffer her sinister looks." Thus she stayed with us, while the days and nights followed one another, and the months and years went by. Then one day the shepherd's daughter died, and my son went to the country of this very man with whom you have had your encounter. Some time later I took my wife, this very deer, with me, set out to find out what had happened to my son, and chanced to stop here. This is my story, my strange and amazing story.

The demon assented, saying, "I grant you one-third of this man's life."

Then, O King Shahrayar, the second old man with the two black dogs approached the demon and said, "I too shall tell you what happened to me and to these two dogs, and if I tell it to you and you find it stranger and more amazing than this man's story will you grant me one-third of this man's life?" The demon replied, "I will." Then the old man began to tell his story, saying . . .

But dawn broke, and morning overtook Shahrazad, and she lapsed into silence. Then Dinarzad said, "This is an amazing story," and Shahrazad replied, "What is this compared with what I shall tell you tomorrow night if the king spares me and lets me live!" The king said to himself, "By God, I will not have her put to death until I find out what happened to the man with the two black dogs. Then I will have her put to death, God the Almighty willing."

THE SIXTH NIGHT

When the following night arrived and Shahrazad was in bed with King Shahrayar, her sister Dinarzad said, "Sister, if you are not sleepy, tell us a little

to you in the guise in which you saw me, and when I expressed my love for you, you accepted me. Now I must kill your brothers." When I heard what she said, I was amazed and I thanked her and said, "As for destroying my brothers, this I do not wish, for I will not behave like them." Then I related to her what had happened to me and them, from beginning to end. When she heard my story, she got very angry at them, and said, "I shall fly to them now, drown their boat, and let them all perish." I entreated her, saying, "For God's sake, don't. The proverb advises 'Be kind to those who hurt you.' No matter what, they are my brothers after all." In this manner, I entreated her and pacified her. Afterward, she took me and flew away with me until she brought me home and put me down on the roof of my house. I climbed down, threw the doors open, and dug up the money I had buried. Then I went out and, greeting the people in the market, reopened my shop. When I came home in the evening, I found these two dogs tied up, and when they saw me, they came to me, wept, and rubbed themselves against me. I started, when I suddenly heard my wife say, "O my lord, these are your brothers." I asked, "Who has done this to them?" She replied, "I sent to my sister and asked her to do it. They will stay in this condition for ten years, after which they may be delivered." Then she told me where to find her and departed. The ten years have passed, and I was with my brothers on my way to her to have the spell lifted, when I met this man, together with this old man with the deer. When I asked him about himself, he told me about his encounter with you, and I resolved not to leave until I found out what would happen between you and him. This is my story. Isn't it amazing?

The demon replied, "By God, it is strange and amazing. I grant you one-third of my claim on him for his crime."

Then the third old man said, "Demon, don't disappoint me. If I told you a story that is stranger and more amazing than the first two would you grant me one-third of your claim on him for his crime?" The demon replied, "I will." Then the old man said, "Demon, listen":

But morning overtook Shahrazad, and she lapsed into silence. Then her sister said, "What an amazing story!" Shahrazad replied, "The rest is even more amazing." The king said to himself, "I will not have her put to death until I hear what happened to the old man and the demon; then I will have her put to death, as is my custom with the others."

THE EIGHTH NIGHT

The following night Dinarzad said to her sister Shahrazad, "For God's sake, sister, if you are not sleepy, tell us one of your lovely little tales to while away the night." Shahrazad replied, "With the greatest pleasure":

[The Third Old Man's Tale]⁹

The demon said, "This is a wonderful story, and I grant you a third of my claim on the merchant's life."

---

9. Because the earliest manuscript does not include a story for the third sheikh, later narrators supplied one. This brief anecdote comes from a manuscript found in the library of the Royal Academy in Madrid.

The third sheikh approached and said to the demon, "I will tell you a story more wonderful than these two if you will grant me a third of your claim on his life, O demon!"

To which the demon agreed.

So the sheikh began:

O sultan and chief of the demons, this mule was my wife. I had gone off on a journey and was absent from her for a whole year. At last I came to the end of my journey and returned home late one night. When I entered the house I saw a black slave lying in bed with her. They were chatting and dallying and laughing and kissing and quarreling together. When she saw me my wife leaped out of bed, ran to the water jug, recited a spell over it, then splashed me with some of the water and said, "Leave this form for the form of a dog."

Immediately I became a dog and she chased me out of the house. I ran out of the gate and didn't stop running until I reached a butcher's shop. I entered it and fell to eating the bones lying about. When the owner of the shop saw me, he grabbed me and carried me into his house. When his daughter saw me, she hid her face and said, "Why are you bringing this strange man in with you?"

"What man?" her father asked.

"This dog is a man whose wife has put a spell on him," she said, "but I can set him free again." She took a jug of water, recited a spell over it, then splashed a little water from it on me, and said, "Leave this shape for your original one."

And I became myself again. I kissed her hand and said, "I want to cast a spell on my wife as she did on me. Please give me a little of that water."

"Gladly," she said, "if you find her asleep, sprinkle a few drops on her and she will become whatever you wish."

Well, I did find her asleep, and I sprinkled some water on her and said, "Leave this shape for the shape of a she mule." She at once became the very mule you see here, oh sultan and chief of the demons."

The demon then turned to him and asked, "Is this really true?"

"Yes," he answered, nodding his head vigorously, "it's all true."

When the sheikh had finished his story, the demon shook with laughter and granted him a third of his claim on the merchant's blood.

Then the demon released the merchant and departed. The merchant turned to the three old men and thanked them, and they congratulated him on his deliverance and bade him good-bye. Then they separated, and each of them went on his way. The merchant himself went back home to his family, his wife, and his children, and he lived with them until the day he died.

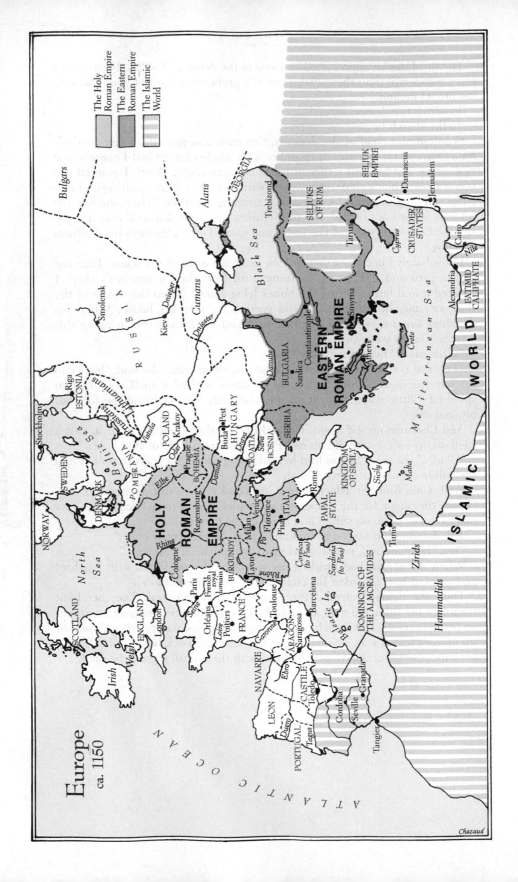

Europe
ca. 1150

The Holy
Roman Empire
The Eastern
Roman Empire
The Islamic
World

NORWAY

SWEDEN

Stockholm

North Sea

SCOTLAND

Irish

Welsh

ENGLAND

London

DENMARK

Baltic Sea

POMERANIA

ESTONIA

Riga

Curonians

Prussians

Lithuanians

RUSSIA

Smolensk

Kiev

Dnieper

Dniester

Bulgars

Alans

GEORGIA

Cumans

Black Sea

Trebizond

SELJUKS
OF RUM

SELJUK
EMPIRE

Damascus

Jerusalem

Tarsus

Smyrna

CRUSADER
STATES

Cyprus

Cairo

Nile

Alexandria

FATIMID
CALIPHATE

Mediterranean Sea

Crete

Athens

Constantinople

EASTERN
ROMAN EMPIRE

BULGARIA

Sardica

SERBIA

BOSNIA

CROATIA

Sava

Drava

HUNGARY

Buda

Pest

Danube

Vistula

POLAND

Krakow

Oder

BOHEMIA

Prague

Elbe

Regensburg

HOLY

ROMAN

EMPIRE

Cologne

Rhine

BURGUNDY

Lyon

Rhône

Venice

Milan

Po

Florence

Pisa

ITALY

Rome

PAPAL
STATE

KINGDOM
OF SICILY

Sicily

Malta

Tunis

Zirids

Hammadids

ISLAMIC WORLD

Corsica
(to Pisa)

Sardinia
(to Pisa)

Balearic Is.

Barcelona

ARAGON

Saragossa

Ebro

NAVARRE

CASTILE

Toledo

LEON

Duero

PORTUGAL

Tagus

Cordoba

Seville

Granada

Tangier

DOMINIONS OF
THE ALMORAVIDES

Toulouse

Garonne

FRANCE

Poitiers

Loire

Orléans

French
royal
domain

Paris

Seine

ATLANTIC OCEAN

Chazaud

The Formation of a Western Literature

The Middle Ages—approximately the thousand years from 500 to 1500—saw the classical civilization of Greece and Rome transformed by contact with three very different cultures. One was the Germanic culture of the tribes who invaded and, by the fifth century, had effectively conquered the western half of the Roman empire. The second was the Christianity that began in Palestine and then quickly spread throughout the empire until almost all of western Europe was thoroughly Christianized by the eleventh century (as early as 325 the emperor Constantine had established Christianity as virtually the official religion of the empire). The third influence—less pronounced but still important—was Islam, which arose in the Arabian peninsula in the seventh century and quickly spread throughout North Africa and into the Iberian peninsula, where it remained a powerful force until the fifteenth century. Because it was an amalgam of these vastly different cultural forces, medieval Europe displayed an unusually wide range of values, ideas, and social forms. But for all this variety there emerged at the end of the process a recognizable culture. In the year 500 "the West" could hardly be characterized either politically or culturally, but by 1500 the map of Europe looked very much as it does today, and many of the values we think of as characteristically Western—individualism, consensual government, a recognition of religious difference, even the idea of Europe itself—were emergent realities. Another central event within Western culture during this period was the emergence of vernacular literatures. The great national literatures of Europe took form during the Middle Ages, and here we find both individual literary masterpieces and traditions of writing that have continued to define what counts as literature.

Because it is the period during which the cultural identities of the European nations took shape, the Middle Ages has always generated both fascination and controversy. Take, for example, its distinctly odd name: the *middle* of what? The answer is that the period was named by the people who came immediately after it, who called their own age the Renaissance because they saw it as the time in which the cultural achievements of antiquity were being reborn. For them the immediately preceding period was a time of middleness, a space of cultural emptiness that separated them from the classical past they so admired: hence, the Middle Ages (or, in Latin, *medium aevum,* from which we get our term *medieval*). That this narrow view of cultural history is still in force today is shown by the way in which "medieval" continues to be used to mean antiquated, or quaint, or barbaric. It is also evident in the widespread notion that the Middle Ages was unusually homogeneous, a time in which all men and women thought and felt more or less the same things and behaved in much the same way. Yet in fact this period contains not one but many different kinds of people with many different cultures.

These cultures were oral and literate; Germanic and Latin; Arabic, Jewish, and Christian; secular and religious; tolerant and repressive; vernacular and learned; rural and urban; skeptical and pious; popular and aristocratic. For every example of one kind of cultural product we can find an example of another, and most significant literary works incorporated elements and values drawn from different and often conflicting traditions. *The Song of Roland,* for instance, composed in the eleventh century, promotes with unabashed enthusiasm the superiority of Christianity to Islam. Yet already in the ninth century, Islamic scholars had translated much of Greek science and philosophy into Arabic, preserving and enriching this tradition at the very time it was in decline in Western Europe. And beginning in the twelfth century, Muslim centers of learning in Spain, Sicily, and southern Italy made it possible for European scholars to regain access to these Greek originals and to study their Muslim commentators. Similarly complex is the way *The Song of Roland* struggles with internal contradictions of its own. A poem that exalts a great warrior according to Germanic traditions of military heroism, it also affirms the necessity of subordinating individual accomplishment to the needs of a unified Christian community. Another example of the clash of competing interests can be found in the work of Geoffrey Chaucer, the founding poet of English literature. For the first two thirds of his career he was a court poet who catered almost exclusively to the narrow tastes of an aristocratic readership, and yet in *The Canterbury Tales* he recorded with remarkable sensitivity the discontents and desires of men and women from almost every social class. These complexities and contradictions are everywhere in medieval writing, and if they frustrate modern attempts to define the period in simple terms they also make reading its literature a process of continuing surprise.

The most familiar description of the Middle Ages is as "an age of faith," by which is meant the notion that medieval people shared a uniform commitment to Catholic Christianity. The Roman empire had provided political unity, law, and order, but beyond that it had pretty much left moral and spiritual issues to be handled by the individual, either singly or in voluntary or ethnic groups. As the Middle Ages developed, however, the church gradually extended its spiritual and institutional authority across most of Europe. By 1200, with the exception of beleaguered Jewish communities, the area of the Iberian peninsula under Muslim control, and frontier lands in the Slavic east, Europe had become virtually identical with Christendom. But this acknowledgment of the primacy of Christian doctrine and the ritual practices that went with it (such as baptism, communion, and confession) meant neither that religious values were universally recognized as primary nor that one single form of Christianity was placidly accepted by all medieval people. On the contrary, as the literature of the period makes clear, many people took the central doctrines of Christianity so much for granted that their daily lives seem largely untroubled by the moral and spiritual demands of religion. In the *Lais* of Marie de France, for example, and the vernacular love lyrics, men and women lead their romantic lives without giving much if any thought to Christian standards of behavior. In a more satiric vein, the tales from Boccaccio's *Decameron* provide an often acerbic and always witty puncturing of the pretensions of individual churchmen. The lecherous priest and the greedy friar are stock characters of medieval satire, as are the wayward nun and the gluttonous monk. Another pressure point at which Christian doctrine is tested is the Germanic epic *Beowulf,* a poem written by a believer who nonetheless deeply admires the pagan past that he knows must be left behind. Even in *The Divine Comedy,* the work that seems most securely and unproblematically located within the Christian worldview, Dante is poignantly aware of the gulf that separates him from the classical past, represented in the *Inferno* and *Purgatorio* by the man he calls "my author and my father," the pagan poet Virgil. The Middle Ages *is* an age of faith, but one that at its best is alert to the complexities and dilemmas that any faith poses to its adherents.

Another familiar description of the Middle Ages is as "an age of chivalry." Medieval literature for the most part expresses the values of the most powerful members of society, the aristocracy. These people achieved their domination through military might, both by imposing their will upon their neighbors and, more benevolently, by providing them with protection from invaders like the Vikings from the north, the

Magyars and Mongols from the east, and the various Islamic peoples from the south. At times, indeed, they became themselves the invaders, most notably in the various crusading expeditions that began in the eleventh century against Islam in the Iberian peninsula and the Levant and, later, against the Slavs in what is now Eastern Europe. Not surprisingly, throughout its medieval history, from the time of *Beowulf* (about the ninth century) to the late fifteenth century, the European nobility—and the writers they supported—celebrated the values that sustained these military practices. These values included unwavering valor in the face of danger, loyalty to one's leader and companions, and an intense concern with personal honor. They also came to include a more or less explicit code of chivalry that stressed gentility of demeanor, generosity of both spirit and material goods, concern for the well-being of the powerless, and— above all—a capacity for experiencing a romantic love that was at once selfless and passionate. Whether or not medieval men actually lived up to these chivalric ideals is impossible to say, but that many believed in them—and believed that they achieved them—is undeniable. Yet many other members of medieval society, especially non- nobles like churchmen, urban dwellers, and peasants, were more likely than not to think that chivalry was just a fancy name for the heavy-handed imposition of force upon those least able to resist. More important for the writing of the time is the fact that chivalric values are never entirely consistent with each other. Where does per- sonal bravery give way to the needs of the group?—this is a question at the heart of both *Beowulf* and *The Song of Roland*. Can one be both a full-hearted lover and a loyal warrior? And can the same people perform both the deeds of war and those of civilization?—this is a question central to Western literature since the time of Homer and still challenging to us today.

The busy millennium we call, in the absence of a more precise term, the Middle Ages is thus dominated by certain leading concerns—the demands of religious faith and the appropriate use of physical force—that remain current. What continues to make its literature compelling to us is the skill with which individual writers dealt with these themes through the creation of unforgettable literary characters. For all its accomplishments in the arts of governing and the skills of commerce, in philoso- phy and theology, and in art and architecture, the most vivid legacy of the Middle Ages is the roster of characters it has contributed to world literature. Roland and Charlemagne, Robin Hood, and Beowulf, the pilgrims of *The Canterbury Tales* and the lost souls of the *Inferno*: whether searching for the road to salvation or killing monsters, whether battling pagan enemies or hoodwinking unwary dupes, the pro- tagonists of medieval literature continue to intrigue readers and inspire writers. In the last analysis the central concern of medieval literature is neither religious truth nor codes of conduct, important as these may be, but individual human beings work- ing out their individual destinies.

TIME LINE

TEXTS	CONTEXTS
	529 Foundation of Monte Cassino, the first Benedictine monastery
9th century *Beowulf* • Latin lyrics, saints' lives, and histories	**8th–10th centuries** Invasions of western Europe by Arabs, Norsemen, and Magyars
	800 Charlemagne crowned Holy Roman emperor
	899 Alfred the Great, king of Wessex in England, dies
11th century Hispano-Arabic and Provençal lyrics	**11th century** Consolidation of feudal social structure
	1066 Norman invasion of England
	1099 Knights of the First Crusade capture Jerusalem
12th century *The Song of Roland* • Marie de France, *Lais* • Arthurian romances • *Romance of Renard*	**12th century** Establishment of the universities of Paris, Oxford, and Bologna • Recovery of Aristotelian philosophy • Period of religious reform
	1187 Arabs recover Jerusalem permanently
13th century Fabliaux • *Romance of the Rose* • *Thorstein the Staff-Struck*	**13th century** Age of the great cathedrals and of scholastic philosophy
	1226 Francis of Assisi, founder of the first order of friars, dies
	1274 Thomas Aquinas, leading scholastic philosopher, dies
1301–1321 Dante, *The Divine Comedy*	**1337** War begins between France and England (the Hundred Years' War), ending only in 1453
	1348–50 Bubonic plague sweeps through Europe, killing almost half the population
1353 Boccaccio, *The Decameron*	
1380? *Sir Gawain and the Green Knight*	
1390–1400 Chaucer, *The Canterbury Tales*	**1384** John Wyclif, promoter of religious views that prepare for the Reformation, dies
	14th century Peasant risings in England, France, Flanders, and Italy

Boldface titles indicate works in the anthology.

TIME LINE

TEXTS	CONTEXTS
	15th century Growing centralization of state power throughout Europe
	1453 Fall of Constantinople to the Muslim Turks
	1455 Gutenberg prints the Bible, the first printed book
ca. 1470 Villon, *The Testament*	
	1492 Christopher Columbus's first voyage to the Western Hemisphere
1495? *Everyman*	

BEOWULF

ca. ninth century

Beowulf, composed perhaps (but not certainly) about 850 in the Anglo-Saxon language then current in England, is both a heroic poem of dark magnificence and the most vivid account left to us of the social world and life experiences of the Germanic and Scandinavian peoples who overran the Roman empire. In its bare narrative outline the poem is a fairy-tale story of how the hero, Beowulf, conquered three monsters: first a man-eating, troll-like creature named Grendel, then Grendel's vengeance-seeking mother, and finally—when Beowulf has become an old man—a fire-breathing dragon. From these unlikely events the poet has fashioned a poem that represents with great power and specificity not merely the details of the warrior life of the Germanic tribes but its meaning to the people who lived it. Although himself a Christian, the poet provides us with a unique insight into a pagan world that had passed away by the time he was writing, but one whose legends and values he knows well. Like those of the Homeric poems and *The Song of Roland,* the historical period of the action of *Beowulf* is many centuries prior to the poem's date of composition: the one event in the poem that can be dated—the death of Beowulf's lord, Hygelac, in a raid on the Franks—occurred around 520. The protagonists of the poem are not the English who were its audience but two of their forebears, the Germanic tribes of the South Danes, who lived in Denmark, and their neighbors to the east, the Geats, who lived in southern Sweden. In addition to these two groups the poem alludes to the history of other northern European peoples, especially the Swedes, the Frisians, and the Franks, and it mentions as well more obscure tribal groupings like the Heatho-Bards, the Wulfings, and the Waegmundings. In reading the poem, we enter into a pre-Christian Germanic world that is both mysterious and fascinating. And that world is also, as Beowulf himself comes to understand, doomed.

The most important fact about Germanic tribal society is its violence, which is why the poet describes that society by means of a narrative of monster-killing. Each of the various tribes is in competition with the others for land and plunder, and even within tribes there are constant struggles for power. The central bond that holds the society together is the loyalty between a lord and his warriors, or thanes. The lord is a "ring-giver," which means that he distributes to his thanes objects of value that include bracelets and necklaces ("rings"), armor and weapons, and even land and political authority. In return the thane is expected to provide unswerving loyalty on the battlefield and good counsel during times of peace. More important, this bond of loyalty establishes the community within which individuals find meaning.

In the Germanic world the worst condition into which a man can fall is to be an outlaw or wanderer, someone who has no home. This is, in fact, the situation of the monster Grendel, described in the poem as a "grim demon / haunting the marches, marauding round the heath / and the desolate fens" (lines 102–4). The Christian poet interprets Grendel and his mother as deriving from the race of Cain, who was condemned by God to wander the earth after his murder of Abel. The poem begins with Grendel's attack upon the great hall Heorot, built as a place to celebrate community solidarity and the beneficence of the deity by Hrothgar, the old Danish king. What motivates Grendel's attack is his sense of exclusion and singularity: in this world, to be an independent individual is to be isolated and rejected. Appropriately, Grendel's slayer, Beowulf, is himself something of an individual, who, by this act, achieves inclusion within his own social world. Almost two thirds of the way through the poem we learn that Beowulf "had been poorly regarded / for a long time" by his people, the Geats: "They firmly believed that he lacked force, / that the prince was a weakling" (lines 2183–88). But the victory over Grendel and his mother, and the gifts he receives from the Danes and gives in turn to his own lord, Hygelac, change all that. Hygelac gives him a sword that had belonged to his own father, Hrethel, and grants him land and lordship: "a hall and a throne." After the deaths of Hygelac and his son Heardred, the Geats then turn to Beowulf to become their king, and he rules for fifty years until his fatal battle with a dragon.

Given that martial prowess is the primary means by which a man earns the respect of his fellows—Beowulf is recognized as worthy not because he is thoughtful or self-controlled (although he is both) but because he is fierce in battle—we should not be surprised that the poet presents a tribal world constantly engulfed in violence. The monster-killing that constitutes the main action of the poem is located within a dense historical context of tribal feuding. These feuds are mentioned so allusively and indirectly that we can assume the poet's English audience was fully informed about the early history of their Germanic ancestors. But the modern reader does not know this history, and it will be helpful to outline it here. (The genealogical table will help to keep the characters straight.)

The poem tells us of five primary feuds. The most important, which we learn about only toward the end of the poem (lines 2379–96, 2472–89, 2922–98), is between the Geats and the Swedes, and takes place in two phases. The first phase begins when the Swedes, under their king Ongentheow, defeat the Geats in a battle at Hreosnahill (or Sorrow Hill) in which great slaughter is committed by Ongentheow's sons, Ohthere and Onela. This slaughter is then avenged by the killing of Ongentheow by the Geat Eofer in the battle of Ravenswood, in which the Geatish king Haethcyn also dies. The second phase of the Swedish-Geatish feud is initiated by a civil war within the Swedish royal family. After the death of his elder brother Ohthere, Onela seizes the throne and drives out the rightful heirs, Ohthere's sons Eanmund and Eadgils. They find refuge with the Geats, then being led by Hygelac's son Heardred. Onela attacks the Geats, killing both Heardred and one of the brothers, Eanmund. (The warrior who actually kills Eanmund is named Weohstan and is the father of Wiglaf, who at the end of the poem is the only one of Beowulf's thanes to stand by him in the attack on the dragon. How Wiglaf—who like Beowulf is referred to as a Waegmunding—came to be accepted among the Geats is never explained.) Heardred's death leaves Beowulf king of the Geats, and he later supports Eadgils, who kills Onela and regains the Swedish throne. Yet despite this apparent alliance, after the death of Beowulf we are told that "this vicious feud" (line 3000) between the Swedes and Geats will now lead to renewed Swedish attacks on the leaderless Geats (possibly because Wiglaf, the presumptive heir to the Geatish throne, is the son of the slayer of Eadgil's brother).

The second feud mentioned in the poem is that between the Heatho-Bards and the Danes. While Beowulf is visiting Hrothgar in order to deal with the monsters, there are several cryptic references to a deadly fire that awaits the great hall Heorot. When Beowulf returns from his adventure and describes the trip to Hygelac, he explains that Hrothgar's daughter Freawaru is promised to Ingeld, the son of the murdered Heatho-Bard king Froda. Yet Beowulf predicts, in a sinister description of the way that enmity will be stirred up when a Heatho-Bard warrior sees a Dane wearing Froda's armor, that the peace will not hold: "But generally the spear / is prompt to retaliate when a prince is killed, / no matter how admirable the bride may be" (lines 2029–31).

The third feud, predicted but not described, is within the Danish royal house. The old king Hrothgar has two young sons, Hrethric and Hrothmund, and his queen, Wealhtheow, asks Beowulf to protect them from their uncle Hrothulf after the death of Hrothgar—protection Beowulf will be unable to provide.

As to the fourth feud, Hrothgar tells Beowulf that Beowulf's father, Ecgtheow, started a feud with the Wulfings by killing a man called Heatholaf, and that the Geats exiled him in order to protect themselves from retaliation. Hrothgar, however, not only provided Ecgtheow with asylum but also settled the feud by paying compensation to the Wulfings for Heatholaf, a compensation known among the Germanic tribes as *wergild*, or "man-money."

The fifth feud is that between the Geats and three tribes to the south of them, the Frisians, the Hetware, and the Franks. This feud started when the Geatish king

Hygelac raided the other tribes' territory—as mentioned, there is an independent record of this raid, which took place about 520—and was killed in the process. As he prepares to fight the dragon, Beowulf tells us that he avenged Hygelac's death: "I killed / Dayraven the Frank in front of the two armies" (lines 2501–2). After Beowulf's death the Geats are told that they face harsh battle at the hands of the Franks.

In addition to these feuds, which occur within the historical world of the poem, one other is mentioned in detail in a song sung by a *scop*, or bard, during the celebrations after the death of Grendel. This is known as the fight at Finnsburg. A Dane named Hnaef and his entourage of warriors, while visiting the Jute Finn at the fortress of Finnsburg, are attacked by the Jutes despite the fact that Finn is married to Hnaef's sister Hildeburh (doubtless as part of an effort to patch up a previous feud). Hnaef is killed, along with the son of Finn and Hildeburh. Neither party is powerful enough to finish off the other, and they agree to a truce: they will winter together in Finnsburg, and the Danes will sail home in the spring. It is not surprising that the coming of spring also awakens "longing . . . for vengeance" (lines 1138–40), and the Danes slaughter Finn and the other Jutes in their hall, returning home with plunder and with the bereft Hildeburh, whose son and husband are now dead.

The poet makes clear that the awful cost of their violence is not lost on these people. The description of the future that awaits the leaderless Geats now that Beowulf is dead—delivered to the waiting people by a messenger sent from the battle with the dragon—is only one of several chilling passages that acknowledge the effect of tribal warfare:

> . . . Many a spear,
> dawn-cold to the touch will be taken down
> and waved on high; the swept harp
> won't waken warriors, but the raven winging
> darkly over the doomed will have news,
> tidings for the eagle of how he hoked and ate,
> how the wolf and he made short work of the dead. (lines 3021–27)

Nor will things go better for the women of the tribe:

> . . . often, repeatedly, in the path of exile
> they shall walk bereft, bowed under woe,
> now that [Beowulf's] laugh is silenced. (lines 3018–20)

Yet the poem also argues that it is only by violence that civilization can be maintained. The attacks by both Grendel and his mother are themselves a feud, in the first instance against God (hence the monsters' descent from the race of Cain), more immediately against the peaceful society that Hrothgar has established in Heorot. As Wealhtheow says of Heorot,

> "Here each comrade is true to the other,
> loyal to lord, loving in spirit.
> The thanes have one purpose, the people are ready:
> having drunk and pledged, the ranks do as I bid." (lines 1228–31)

Grendel wants to destroy this social harmony, and his mother is an avenging spirit who seeks retaliation for the death of her offspring. Similarly, the dragon is roused to rage by the need to avenge the theft of a drinking cup from the hoard he guards: "he worked himself up / by imagining battle" (lines 2298–99). Thus the monsters can be understood, at least in part, as embodiments of the feuding principle that is inevitably destroying Germanic society. Yet in killing them Beowulf is involved in a paradox: violence can be controlled only by violence, a circle from which no one in the poem is able to escape.

Violence is thus part and parcel of this civilization. After Grendel's mother has killed one of Hrothgar's men, Beowulf advises the Danish king, in a succinct sentence that could stand as a motto for the poem, "It is always better / to avenge dear ones than to indulge in mourning" (lines 1384–85). The miserable condition of the man who cannot avenge the death of a kinsman is vividly described in the story Beowulf tells about Hygelac's father, Hrethel. Hrethel had three sons, Herebeald, Haethcyn, and Hygelac. In an accident, Haethcyn killed Herebeald; because it was an accident, and because the perpetrator was his own son, Hrethel could not compensate himself for his loss with either *wergild* or vengeance. As Beowulf arms himself for the battle with the dragon he tells this grim story, and he draws a parallel between Hrethel's unassuageable grief and the sorrow of the father who sees his son die on the gallows as an outlaw. The grieving father looks at his son's empty dwelling-place, the silent winehall, and he goes then to his bed, chanting grief-songs: "everything seems too large, / the steadings and the fields" (lines 2461–62). This sense of emptiness is an effect of more than simply the technical problem of how to find satisfaction for certain kinds of injury. By having Beowulf tell this story as he prepares for what he knows will be his final battle, the poet shows us that the hero understands at some level the futility of the entire world of Germanic heroism that he himself so fully represents. Trolls and dragons can be killed, but how does one eradicate the violence that serves to constitute society itself? The monsters are, finally, instances of a social sickness that infects the culture as a whole: they may be killed, but the violence they represent will continue unabated. Perhaps Beowulf's greatest act of heroism is found not in the physical courage he displays in his battles against human and superhuman foes but in his spiritual capacity to persevere despite his dark realization of the futility of his efforts.

The poem survives in only a single manuscript written about 1000, but it was composed earlier, probably over a period of many years. Like the Homeric poems and *The Song of Roland, Beowulf* emerged from an oral tradition of composition. It was put into its final form by a Christian, but one who is both careful to preserve the distinction between his Christian present and the pagan past and unusually tolerant of the culture of his forebears. For one thing, he avoids putting Christian sentiments in the mouths of pre-Christian characters. The terms with which the characters refer to the deity—God, the Lord, Heavenly Powers, Almighty God, Lord of Ages, Heavenly Shepherd, King of Heaven, and so forth— are, in their original Anglo-Saxon forms, the same terms as appear in explicitly non-Christian writings. We should also remember that the habit of capitalizing sacred names is a modern convention: in the manuscript they are, like all proper names, lowercase. For example, when the Geats arrive in Denmark they are described in the translation as having "thanked God" (line 227) that the trip was successful. But the Anglo-Saxon could just as accurately be translated "thanked a god," which has a very different implication. Another example is the way in which the translator has Hrothgar say that Beowulf was sent to the Danes by "Holy God . . . in His goodness" (lines 381–82); again, one could just as accurately, and more consistently, translate this as "by a divine god of his kindness." Hrothgar's speech of advice to Beowulf is certainly consistent with Christianity, but it contains nothing out of character with the values of the Germanic, pagan world in which Hrothgar and Beowulf live. Perhaps most important, the poet refrains from criticizing his pagan characters for their paganism. While he makes it clear that the Danes are wrong to offer sacrifices to their heathen gods in an effort to fend off Grendels' attacks, he is more sorrowful than judgmental or moralistic (lines 175–88). They commit this error because they do not yet know of the true, Christian God whom the poet himself worships, just as they cannot know that the monsters are of the race of Cain. They do indeed live in a world ruled over by the Christian God: as the poet says, "Past and present, God's will prevails" (lines

There was Shield Sheafson,[2] scourge of many tribes,
a wrecker of mead-benches, rampaging among foes.   5
This terror of the hall-troops had come far.
A foundling to start with, he would flourish later on
as his powers waxed and his worth was proved.
In the end each clan on the outlying coasts
beyond the whale-road had to yield to him   10
and begin to pay tribute. That was one good king.
    Afterward a boy-child was born to Shield,
a cub in the yard, a comfort sent
by God to that nation. He knew what they had tholed,[3]
the long times and troubles they'd come through   15
without a leader; so the Lord of Life,
the glorious Almighty, made this man renowned.
Shield had fathered a famous son:
Beow's name was known through the north.
And a young prince must be prudent like that,   20
giving freely while his father lives
so that afterward in age when fighting starts
steadfast companions will stand by him
and hold the line. Behavior that's admired
is the path to power among people everywhere.   25
    Shield was still thriving when his time came
and he crossed over into the Lord's keeping.
His warrior band did what he bade them
when he laid down the law among the Danes:
they shouldered him out to the sea's flood,   30
the chief they revered who had long ruled them.
A ring-whorled prow rode in the harbor,
ice-clad, outbound, a craft for a prince.
They stretched their beloved lord in his boat,
laid out by the mast, amidships,   35
the great ring-giver. Far-fetched treasures
were piled upon him, and precious gear.
I never heard before of a ship so well furbished
with battle-tackle, bladed weapons
and coats of mail. The massed treasure   40
was loaded on top of him: it would travel far
on out into the ocean's sway.
They decked his body no less bountifully
with offerings than those first ones did
who cast him away when he was a child   45
and launched him alone out over the waves.[4]
And they set a gold standard up
high above his head and let him drift
to wind and tide, bewailing him
and mourning their loss. No man can tell,   50

---

2. Translates Scyld Scefing, which probably means "son of Sheaf." Scyld's origins are mysterious.   3. An Anglo-Saxon word that means "suffered, endured" and that survives in the translator's native land of Northern Ireland. In using this word, he also maintains an alliterative pattern similar to the original ("that . . . they . . . tholed").   4. Because Shield arrived with nothing, this sentence is a litotes or understatement, a characteristic of the laconic style of old Germanic poetry.

no wise man in hall or weathered veteran
knows for certain who salvaged that load.
　　Then it fell to Beow to keep the forts.
He was well regarded and ruled the Danes
for a long time after his father took leave　　　　　　　55
of his life on earth. And then his heir,
the great Halfdane,[5] held sway
for as long as he lived, their elder and warlord.
He was four times a father, this fighter prince:
one by one they entered the world,　　　　　　　　　60
Heorogar, Hrothgar, the good Halga,
and a daughter,[6] I have heard, who was Onela's queen,
a balm in bed to the battle-scarred Swede.
　　The fortunes of war favored Hrothgar.
Friends and kinsmen flocked to his ranks,　　　　　65
young followers, a force that grew
to be a mighty army. So his mind turned
to hall-building: he handed down orders
for men to work on a great mead-hall
meant to be a wonder of the world forever;　　　　70
it would be his throne-room and there he would dispense
his God-given goods to young and old—
but not the common land or people's lives.[7]
Far and wide through the world, I have heard,
orders for work to adorn that wallstead　　　　　　75
were sent to many peoples. And soon it stood there
finished and ready, in full view,
the hall of halls. Heorot[8] was the name
he had settled on it, whose utterance was law.
Nor did he renege, but doled out rings　　　　　　　80
and torques[9] at the table. The hall towered,
its gables wide and high and awaiting
a barbarous burning.[1] That doom abided,
but in time it would come: the killer instinct
unleashed among in-laws, the blood-lust rampant.　　85

[HEOROT IS ATTACKED]

　　Then a powerful demon, a prowler through the dark,
nursed a hard grievance. It harrowed him
to hear the din of the loud banquet
every day in the hall, the harp being struck
and the clear song of a skilled poet　　　　　　　　90
telling with mastery of man's beginnings,
how the Almighty had made the earth
a gleaming plain girdled with waters;
in His splendor He set the sun and the moon

5. According to another source, Halfdane's mother was Swedish; hence his name. 　6. The text is faulty here, so that the name of Halfdane's daughter has been lost. 　7. Apparently, slaves, along with pasture-land used by all, were not in the king's power to give away. 　8. That is, "hart," a symbol of royalty. 9. Golden bands worn around the neck. 　1. The destruction by fire of Heorot occurred at a later time than that of the poem's action, when the Heatho-Bard Ingeld attacked his father-in-law, Hrothgar. For a more detailed account of this feud and of Hrothgar's hope that it could be settled by the marriage of his daughter to Ingeld, see lines 2020–69.

to be earth's lamplight, lanterns for men,   95
and filled the broad lap of the world
with branches and leaves; and quickened life
in every other thing that moved.
　　So times were pleasant for the people there
until finally one, a fiend out of hell,   100
began to work his evil in the world.
Grendel was the name of this grim demon
haunting the marches, marauding round the heath
and the desolate fens; he had dwelt for a time
in misery among the banished monsters,   105
Cain's clan, whom the Creator had outlawed
and condemned as outcasts.[2] For the killing of Abel
the Eternal Lord had exacted a price:
Cain got no good from committing that murder
because the Almighty made him anathema   110
and out of the curse of his exile there sprang
ogres and elves and evil phantoms
and the giants too who strove with God
time and again until He gave them their reward.[3]
　　So, after nightfall, Grendel set out   115
for the lofty house, to see how the Ring-Danes
were settling into it after their drink,
and there he came upon them, a company of the best
asleep from their feasting, insensible to pain
and human sorrow. Suddenly then   120
the God-cursed brute was creating havoc:
greedy and grim, he grabbed thirty men
from their resting places and rushed to his lair,
flushed up and inflamed from the raid,
blundering back with the butchered corpses.   125
　　Then as dawn brightened and the day broke,
Grendel's powers of destruction were plain:
their wassail was over, they wept to heaven
and mourned under morning. Their mighty prince,
the storied leader, sat stricken and helpless,   130
humiliated by the loss of his guard,
bewildered and stunned, staring aghast
at the demon's trail, in deep distress.
He was numb with grief, but got no respite
for one night later merciless Grendel   135
struck again with more gruesome murders.
Malignant by nature, he never showed remorse.
It was easy then to meet with a man
shifting himself to a safer distance
to bed in the bothies,[4] for who could be blind   140
to the evidence of his eyes, the obviousness
of the hall-watcher's hate? Whoever escaped

---

2. Genesis 4.9–12.　　3. The poet is thinking here of Genesis 6.2–8, where the Latin Bible in use at the time refers to giants mating with women who were understood to be the descendents of Cain, and thus creating the wicked race that God destroyed with the flood.　　4. Outlying buildings; the word is current in Northern Ireland.

kept a weather-eye open and moved away.
　　So Grendel ruled in defiance of right,
one against all, until the greatest house　　　　　　　　　　145
in the world stood empty, a deserted wallstead.
For twelve winters, seasons of woe,
the lord of the Shieldings[5] suffered under
his load of sorrow; and so, before long,
the news was known over the whole world.　　　　　　　　150
Sad lays were sung about the beset king,
the vicious raids and ravages of Grendel,
his long and unrelenting feud,
nothing but war; how he would never
parley or make peace with any Dane　　　　　　　　　　155
nor stop his death-dealing nor pay the death-price.[6]
No counselor could ever expect
fair reparation from those rabid hands.
All were endangered; young and old
were hunted down by that dark death-shadow　　　　　　160
who lurked and swooped in the long nights
on the misty moors; nobody knows
where these reavers from hell roam on their errands.
　　So Grendel waged his lonely war,
inflicting constant cruelties on the people,　　　　　　　165
atrocious hurt. He took over Heorot,
haunted the glittering hall after dark,
but the throne itself, the treasure-seat,
he was kept from approaching; he was the Lord's outcast.
　　These were hard times, heartbreaking　　　　　　　　170
for the prince of the Shieldings; powerful counselors,
the highest in the land, would lend advice,
plotting how best the bold defenders
might resist and beat off sudden attacks.
Sometimes at pagan shrines they vowed　　　　　　　　175
offerings to idols, swore oaths
that the killer of souls might come to their aid
and save the people.[7] That was their way,
their heathenish hope; deep in their hearts
they remembered hell. The Almighty Judge　　　　　　　180
of good deeds and bad, the Lord God,
Head of the Heavens and High King of the World,
was unknown to them. Oh, cursed is he
who in time of trouble has to thrust his soul
in the fire's embrace, forfeiting help;　　　　　　　　185
he has nowhere to turn. But blessed is he
who after death can approach the Lord
and find friendship in the Father's embrace.

---

5. That is, Hrothgar; as descendents of Shield, the Danes are called Shieldings.　　6. According to Germanic law, a slayer could achieve peace with his victim's kinsmen only by paying them *wergild* ("man-price") as compensation for the slain man.　　7. The poet interprets the heathen gods to whom the Danes make offerings as different incarnations of Satan. Naturally, the pagan Danes do not think of their gods in these biblical terms, but as the poet makes clear in the following lines, they have no other recourse.

and a sharp mind will take the measure
of two things: what's said and what's done.
I believe what you have told me, that you are a troop   290
loyal to our king. So come ahead
with your arms and your gear, and I will guide you.
What's more, I'll order my own comrades
on their word of honor to watch your boat
down there on the strand—keep her safe   295
in her fresh tar, until the time comes
for her curved prow to preen on the waves
and bear this hero back to Geatland.
May one so valiant and venturesome
come unharmed through the clash of battle."   300
    So they went on their way. The ship rode the water,
broad-beamed, bound by its hawser
and anchored fast. Boar-shapes[9] flashed
above their cheek-guards, the brightly forged
work of goldsmiths, watching over   305
those stern-faced men. They marched in step,
hurrying on till the timbered hall
rose before them, radiant with gold.
Nobody on earth knew of another
building like it. Majesty lodged there,   310
its light shone over many lands.
So their gallant escort guided them
to that dazzling stronghold and indicated
the shortest way to it; then the noble warrior
wheeled on his horse and spoke these words: 315
"It is time for me to go. May the Almighty
Father keep you and in His kindness
watch over your exploits. I'm away to the sea,
back on alert against enemy raiders."
    It was a paved track, a path that kept them   320
in marching order. Their mail-shirts glinted,
hard and hand-linked; the high-gloss iron
of their armor rang. So they duly arrived
in their grim war-graith[1] and gear at the hall,
and, weary from the sea, stacked wide shields   325
of the toughest hardwood against the wall,
then collapsed on the benches; battle-dress
and weapons clashed. They collected their spears
in a seafarers' stook,[2] a stand of grayish
tapering ash. And the troops themselves   330
were as good as their weapons.
                  Then a proud warrior
questioned the men concerning their origins:
"Where do you come from, carrying these
decorated shields and shirts of mail,
these cheek-hinged helmets and javelins?"   335

---

9. Images of boars—a cult animal among the Germanic tribes and sacred to the god Freyr—were fixed
atop helmets in the belief that they would provide protection from enemy blows.
1. Equipment or armor (archaic).   2. A pile or mass (archaic).

I am Hrothgar's herald and officer.
I have never seen so impressive or large
an assembly of strangers. Stoutness of heart,
bravery not banishment, must have brought you to Hrothgar."
The man whose name was known for courage,   340
the Geat leader, resolute in his helmet,
answered in return: "We are retainers
from Hygelac's band. Beowulf is my name.
If your lord and master, the most renowned
son of Halfdane, will hear me out   345
and graciously allow me to greet him in person,
I am ready and willing to report my errand."
Wulfgar replied, a Wendel[3] chief
renowned as a warrior, well known for his wisdom
and the temper of his mind: "I will take this message,   350
in accordance with your wish, to our noble king,
our dear lord, friend of the Danes,
the giver of rings. I will go and ask him
about your coming here, then hurry back
with whatever reply it pleases him to give."   355
With that he turned to where Hrothgar sat,
an old man among retainers;
the valiant follower stood foursquare
in front of his king: he knew the courtesies.
Wulfgar addressed his dear lord: 360
"People from Geatland have put ashore.
They have sailed far over the wide sea.
They call the chief in charge of their band
by the name of Beowulf. They beg, my lord,
an audience with you, exchange of words   365
and formal greeting. Most gracious Hrothgar,
do not refuse them, but grant them a reply.
From their arms and appointment, they appear well born
and worthy of respect, especially the one
who has led them this far: he is formidable indeed."   370
Hrothgar, protector of Shieldings, replied:
"I used to know him when he was a young boy.
His father before him was called Ecgtheow.
Hrethel the Geat[4] gave Ecgtheow
his daughter in marriage. This man is their son,   375
here to follow up an old friendship.
A crew of seamen who sailed for me once
with a gift-cargo across to Geatland
returned with marvelous tales about him:
a thane,[5] they declared, with the strength of thirty   380
in the grip of each hand. Now Holy God
has, in His goodness, guided him here

---

3. The Wendels or Vandals are another Germanic nation; it is not unusual for a person to be a member of a nation different from the one in which he resides. Hence Beowulf himself is both a Geat and a Waegmunding.   4. The leader of the Geats before his son Hygelac, who is the current leader. Note that Ecgtheow's marriage to Hrethel's daughter makes Beowulf part of the royal line.   5. That is, a warrior in the service of a lord like Hrethel or Hrothgar himself.

But worn out as I was, I survived,
came through with my life. The ocean lifted
and laid me ashore, I landed safe   580
on the coast of Finland.
                     Now I cannot recall
any fight you entered, Unferth,
that bears comparison. I don't boast when I say
that neither you nor Breca were ever much
celebrated for swordsmanship   585
or for facing danger on the field of battle.
You killed your own kith and kin,
so for all your cleverness and quick tongue,
you will suffer damnation in the depths of hell.[4]
The fact is, Unferth, if you were truly   590
as keen or courageous as you claim to be
Grendel would never have got away with
such unchecked atrocity, attacks on your king,
havoc in Heorot and horrors everywhere.
But he knows he need never be in dread   595
of your blade making a mizzle[5] of his blood
or of vengeance arriving ever from this quarter—
from the Victory-Shieldings, the shoulderers of the spear.
He knows he can trample down you Danes
to his heart's content, humiliate and murder   600
without fear of reprisal. But he will find me different.
I will show him how Geats shape to kill
in the heat of battle. Then whoever wants to
may go bravely to mead,[6] when the morning light,
scarfed in sun-dazzle, shines forth from the south   605
and brings another daybreak to the world."
    Then the gray-haired treasure-giver was glad;
far-famed in battle, the prince of Bright-Danes
and keeper of his people counted on Beowulf,
on the warrior's steadfastness and his word.   610
So the laughter started, the din got louder
and the crowd was happy. Wealhtheow came in,
Hrothgar's queen, observing the courtesies.
Adorned in her gold, she graciously saluted
the men in the hall, then handed the cup   615
first to Hrothgar, their homeland's guardian,
urging him to drink deep and enjoy it
because he was dear to them. And he drank it down
like the warlord he was, with festive cheer.
So the Helming woman went on her rounds,   620
queenly and dignified, decked out in rings,
offering the goblet to all ranks,
treating the household and the assembled troop,
until it was Beowulf's turn to take it from her hand.
With measured words she welcomed the Geat   625

---

4. The manuscript is damaged here, and the word may well be *hall*. "You will suffer condemnation in the hall" is an acceptable translation of the line.   5. That is, drizzle.   6. An alcoholic drink made by fermenting honey and adding water.

and thanked God for granting her wish
that a deliverer she could believe in would arrive
to ease their afflictions. He accepted the cup,
a daunting man, dangerous in action
and eager for it always. He addressed Wealhtheow; 630
Beowulf, son of Ecgtheow, said:
"I had a fixed purpose when I put to sea.
As I sat in the boat with my band of men,
I meant to perform to the uttermost
what your people wanted or perish in the attempt, 635
in the fiend's clutches. And I shall fulfill that purpose,
prove myself with a proud deed
or meet my death here in the mead-hall."
This formal boast by Beowulf the Geat
pleased the lady well and she went to sit 640
by Hrothgar, regal and arrayed with gold.
    Then it was like old times in the echoing hall,
proud talk and the people happy,
loud and excited; until soon enough
Halfdane's heir had to be away 645
to his night's rest. He realized
that the demon was going to descend on the hall,
that he had plotted all day, from dawn-light
until darkness gathered again over the world
and stealthy night-shapes came stealing forth 650
under the cloud-murk. The company stood
as the two leaders took leave of each other:
Hrothgar wished Beowulf health and good luck,
named him hall-warden and announced as follows:
"Never, since my hand could hold a shield 655
have I entrusted or given control
of the Danes' hall to anyone but you.
Ward and guard it, for it is the greatest of houses.
Be on your mettle now, keep in mind your fame,
beware of the enemy. There's nothing you wish for 660
that won't be yours if you win through alive."

[THE FIGHT WITH GRENDEL]

    Hrothgar departed then with his house-guard.
The lord of the Shieldings, their shelter in war,
left the mead-hall to lie with Wealhtheow,
his queen and bedmate. The King of Glory 665
(as people learned) had posted a lookout
who was a match for Grendel, a guard against monsters,
special protection to the Danish prince.
And the Geat placed complete trust
in his strength of limb and the Lord's favor. 670
    He began to remove his iron breast-mail,
took off the helmet and handed his attendant
the patterned sword, a smith's masterpiece,
ordering him to keep the equipment guarded.
And before he bedded down, Beowulf, 675

that as the pair struggled, mead-benches were smashed   775
and sprung off the floor, gold fittings and all.
Before then, no Shielding elder would believe
there was any power or person upon earth
capable of wrecking their horn-rigged hall
unless the burning embrace of a fire   780
engulf it in flame. Then an extraordinary
wail arose, and bewildering fear
came over the Danes. Everyone felt it
who heard that cry as it echoed off the wall,
a God-cursed scream and strain of catastrophe,   785
the howl of the loser, the lament of the hell-serf
keening his wound. He was overwhelmed,
manacled tight by the man who of all men
was foremost and strongest in the days of this life.

But the earl-troop's leader was not inclined   790
to allow his caller to depart alive:
he did not consider that life of much account
to anyone anywhere. Time and again,
Beowulf's warriors worked to defend
their lord's life, laying about them   795
as best they could, with their ancestral blades.
Stalwart in action, they kept striking out
on every side, seeking to cut
straight to the soul. When they joined the struggle
there was something they could not have known at the time,   800
that no blade on earth, no blacksmith's art
could ever damage their demon opponent.
He had conjured the harm from the cutting edge
of every weapon.[9] But his going away
out of this world and the days of his life   805
would be agony to him, and his alien spirit
would travel far into fiends' keeping.

Then he who had harrowed the hearts of men
with pain and affliction in former times
and had given offense also to God   810
found that his bodily powers failed him.
Hygelac's kinsman kept him helplessly
locked in a handgrip. As long as either lived,
he was hateful to the other. The monster's whole
body was in pain; a tremendous wound   815
appeared on his shoulder. Sinews split
and the bone-lappings burst. Beowulf was granted
the glory of winning; Grendel was driven
under the fen-banks, fatally hurt,
to his desolate lair. His days were numbered,   820
the end of his life was coming over him,
he knew it for certain; and one bloody clash
had fulfilled the dearest wishes of the Danes.
The man who had lately landed among them,

---

9. Grendel is magically protected from weapons.

proud and sure, had purged the hall,   825
kept it from harm; he was happy with his nightwork
and the courage he had shown. The Geat captain
had boldly fulfilled his boast to the Danes:
he had healed and relieved a huge distress,
unremitting humiliations,   830
the hard fate they'd been forced to undergo,
no small affliction. Clear proof of this
could be seen in the hand the hero displayed
high up near the roof: the whole of Grendel's
shoulder and arm, his awesome grasp.   835

[CELEBRATION AT HEOROT]

   Then morning came and many a warrior
gathered, as I've heard, around the gift-hall,
clan-chiefs flocking from far and near
down wide-ranging roads, wondering greatly
at the monster's footprints. His fatal departure   840
was regretted by no one who witnessed his trail,
the ignominious marks of his flight
where he'd skulked away, exhausted in spirit
and beaten in battle, bloodying the path,
hauling his doom to the demons' mere.[1]   845
The bloodshot water wallowed and surged,
there were loathsome upthrows and overturnings
of waves and gore and wound-slurry.
With his death upon him, he had dived deep
into his marsh-den, drowned out his life   850
and his heathen soul: hell claimed him there.
   Then away they rode, the old retainers
with many a young man following after,
a troop on horseback, in high spirits
on their bay steeds. Beowulf's doings   855
were praised over and over again.
Nowhere, they said, north or south
between the two seas or under the tall sky
on the broad earth was there anyone better
to raise a shield or to rule a kingdom.   860
Yet there was no laying of blame on their lord,
the noble Hrothgar; he was a good king.
   At times the war-band broke into a gallop,
letting their chestnut horses race
wherever they found the going good   865
on those well-known tracks. Meanwhile, a thane
of the king's household, a carrier of tales,
a traditional singer deeply schooled
in the lore of the past, linked a new theme
to a strict meter.[2] The man started   870
to recite with skill, rehearsing Beowulf's
triumphs and feats in well-fashioned lines,

1. A lake or pool.   2. The singer or *scop* composes extemporaneously in alliterative verse.

entwining his words.
           He told what he'd heard
repeated in songs about Sigemund's exploits,[3]
all of those many feats and marvels,   875
the struggles and wanderings of Waels's son,
things unknown to anyone
except to Fitela, feuds and foul doings
confided by uncle to nephew when he felt
the urge to speak of them: always they had been   880
partners in the fight, friends in need.
They killed giants, their conquering swords
had brought them down.
                After his death
Sigemund's glory   grew and grew
because of his courage   when he killed the dragon,   885
the guardian of the hoard.   Under gray stone
he had dared to enter   all by himself
to face the worst   without Fitela.
But it came to pass   that his sword plunged
right through   those radiant scales   890
and drove into the wall.   The dragon died of it.
His daring had given him   total possession
of the treasure-hoard,   his to dispose of
however he liked.   He loaded a boat:
Waels's son   weighted her hold   895
with dazzling spoils.   The hot dragon melted.
   Sigemund's name   was known everywhere.
He was utterly valiant   and venturesome,
a fence round his fighters   and flourished therefore
after King Heremod's   prowess declined   900
and his campaigns slowed down.   The king was betrayed,
ambushed in Jutland,   overpowered
and done away with.   The waves of his grief
had beaten him down,   made him a burden,
a source of anxiety   to his own nobles: 905
that expedition   was often condemned
in those earlier times   by experienced men,
men who relied   on his lordship for redress,
who presumed that the part   of a prince was to thrive
on his father's throne   and defend the nation,   910
the Shielding land   where they lived and belonged,
its holdings and strongholds.   Such was Beowulf
in the affection of his friends   and of everyone alive.
But evil entered   into Heremod.
   Meanwhile, the Danes kept racing their mounts   915
down sandy lanes. The light of day
broke and kept brightening. Bands of retainers
galloped in excitement to the gabled hall

---

3. According to Norse legend, Sigemund, the son of Waels (or Volsung, as he is known in Norse), slept with his sister Sigurth, who bore a son named Fitela; Fietla was thus also Sigemund's nephew, as he is described here. The singer here contrasts Sigemund's bravery in killing a dragon with the defeat of the Danish king heremod, who could not protect his people. For more on Heremod as a bad king, see lines 1709–22.

to see the marvel; and the king himself,
guardian of the ring-hoard, goodness in person,   920
walked in majesty from the women's quarters
with a numerous train, attended by his queen
and her crowd of maidens, across to the mead-hall.
    When Hrothgar arrived at the hall, he spoke,
standing on the steps, under the steep eaves,   925
gazing toward the roofwork and Grendel's talon:
"First and foremost, let the Almighty Father
be thanked for this sight. I suffered a long
harrowing by Grendel. But the Heavenly Shepherd
can work His wonders always and everywhere.   930
Not long since, it seemed I would never
be granted the slightest solace or relief
from any of my burdens: the best of houses
glittered and reeked and ran with blood.
This one worry outweighed all others—   935
a constant distress to counselors entrusted
with defending the people's forts from assault
by monsters and demons. But now a man,
with the Lord's assistance, has accomplished something
none of us could manage before now   940
for all our efforts. Whoever she was
who brought forth this flower of manhood,
if she is still alive, that woman can say
that in her labor the Lord of Ages
bestowed a grace on her. So now, Beowulf,   945
I adopt you in my heart as a dear son.
Nourish and maintain this new connection,
you noblest of men; there'll be nothing you'll want for,
no worldly goods that won't be yours.
I have often honored smaller achievements,   950
recognized warriors not nearly as worthy,
lavished rewards on the less deserving.
But you have made yourself immortal
by your glorious action. May the God of Ages
continue to keep and requite you well."   955
    Beowulf, son of Ecgtheow, spoke:
"We have gone through with a glorious endeavor
and been much favored in this fight we dared
against the unknown. Nevertheless,
if you could have seen the monster himself   960
where he lay beaten, I would have been better pleased.
My plan was to pounce, pin him down
in a tight grip and grapple him to death—
have him panting for life, powerless and clasped
in my bare hands, his body in thrall.   965
But I couldn't stop him from slipping my hold.
The Lord allowed it, my lock on him
wasn't strong enough; he struggled fiercely
and broke and ran. Yet he bought his freedom
at a high price, for he left his hand   970

and arm and shoulder to show he had been here,
a cold comfort for having come among us.
And now he won't be long for this world.
He has done his worst but the wound will end him.
He is hasped and hooped and hirpling[4] with pain,   975
limping and looped in it. Like a man outlawed
for wickedness, he must await
the mighty judgment of God in majesty."
　　　There was less tampering and big talk then
from Unferth the boaster, less of his blather   980
as the hall-thanes eyed the awful proof
of the hero's prowess, the splayed hand
up under the eaves. Every nail,
claw-scale and spur, every spike
and welt on the hand of that heathen brute   985
was like barbed steel. Everybody said
there was no honed iron hard enough
to pierce him through, no time-proofed blade
that could cut his brutal, blood-caked claw.
　　　Then the order was given for all hands   990
to help to refurbish Heorot immediately:
men and women thronging the wine-hall,
getting it ready. Gold thread shone
in the wall-hangings, woven scenes
that attracted and held the eye's attention.   995
But iron-braced as the inside of it had been,
that bright room lay in ruins now.
The very doors had been dragged from their hinges.
Only the roof remained unscathed
by the time the guilt-fouled fiend turned tail   1000
in despair of his life. But death is not easily
escaped from by anyone:
all of us with souls, earth-dwellers
and children of men, must make our way
to a destination already ordained   1005
where the body, after the banqueting,
sleeps on its deathbed.
　　　　　　　　　Then the due time arrived
for Halfdane's son to proceed to the hall.
The king himself would sit down to feast.
No group ever gathered in greater numbers   1010
or better order around their ring-giver.
The benches filled with famous men
who fell to with relish; round upon round
of mead was passed; those powerful kinsmen,
Hrothgar and Hrothulf, were in high spirits   1015
in the raftered hall. Inside Heorot
there was nothing but friendship. The Shielding nation
was not yet familiar with feud and betrayal.[5]

---

4. That is, limping.　5. The poet here refers to the later history of the Danes, when after Hrothgar's
death his nephew Hrothulf drove his son Hrethric from the throne. For Wealhtheow's fear that this
betrayal will indeed come to pass; see lines 1168–90.

Then Halfdane's son presented Beowulf
with a gold standard as a victory gift,   1020
an embroidered banner; also breast-mail
and a helmet; and a sword carried high,
that was both precious object and token of honor.
So Beowulf drank his drink, at ease;
it was hardly a shame to be showered with such gifts   1025
in front of the hall-troops. There haven't been many
moments, I am sure, when men exchanged
four such treasures at so friendly a sitting.
An embossed ridge, a band lapped with wire
arched over the helmet: head-protection   1030
to keep the keen-ground cutting edge
from damaging it when danger threatened
and the man was battling behind his shield.
Next the king ordered eight horses
with gold bridles to be brought through the yard   1035
into the hall. The harness of one
included a saddle of sumptuous design,
the battle-seat where the son of Halfdane
rode when he wished to join the sword-play:
wherever the killing and carnage were the worst,   1040
he would be to the fore, fighting hard.
Then the Danish prince, descendant of Ing,[6]
handed over both the arms and the horses,
urging Beowulf to use them well.
And so their leader, the lord and guard   1045
of coffer and strongroom, with customary grace
bestowed upon Beowulf both sets of gifts.
A fair witness can see how well each one behaved.
    The chieftain went on to reward the others:
each man on the bench who had sailed with Beowulf   1050
and risked the voyage received a bounty,
some treasured possession. And compensation,
a price in gold, was settled for the Geat
Grendel had cruelly killed earlier—
as he would have killed more, had not mindful God   1055
and one man's daring prevented that doom.
Past and present, God's will prevails.
Hence, understanding is always best
and a prudent mind. Whoever remains
for long here in this earthly life   1060
will enjoy and endure more than enough.
    They sang then and played to please the hero,
words and music for their warrior prince,
harp tunes and tales of adventure:
there were high times on the hall benches,   1065
and the king's poet performed his part
with the saga of Finn and his sons, unfolding
the tale of the fierce attack in Friesland

6. A Germanic deity and the protector of the Danes.

where Hnaef, king of the Danes, met death.[7]

Hildeburh

        had little cause   1070

to credit the Jutes:

        son and brother,

she lost them both

        on the battlefield.

She, bereft

        and blameless, they

foredoomed, cut down

        and spear-gored. She,

the woman in shock,

        waylaid by grief,   1075

Hoc's daughter—

        how could she not

lament her fate

        when morning came

and the light broke

        on her murdered dears?

And so farewell

        delight on earth,

war carried away

        Finn's troop of thanes   1080

all but a few.

        How then could Finn

hold the line

        or fight on

to the end with Hengest,

        how save

the rump of his force

        from that enemy chief?

So a truce was offered

        as follows: first   1085

separate quarters

        to be cleared for the Danes,

hall and throne

        to be shared with the Frisians.

Then, second:

        every day

at the dole-out of gifts

        Finn, son of Focwald,

should honor the Danes,

        bestow with an even   1090

hand to Hengest

        and Hengest's men

---

7. This song recounts the fight at Finnsburg, described in the headnote, between the Dane Hengest and the Jute (or Frisian) Finn. The poet begins with the bereft Hildeburh, daughter of the Danish king Hoc and wife of the Jute Finn, whose unnamed son and brother Hnaef have already been killed in the first battle with Finn. He then tells how Hengest, the new leader of the Danes, is offered a truce by the weakened Finn, how together they cremate their dead, and then how Hengest and the remaining Danes spend the winter with Finn and the Jutes. But with the coming of spring, the feud breaks out again and Finn and the Jutes are slaughtered by Hengest with the help of two other Danes, Guthlaf and Oslaf.

the wrought-gold rings,
          bounty to match
the measure he gave
          his own Frisians—
to keep morale
          in the beer-hall high.
Both sides then
          sealed their agreement.   1095
With oaths to Hengest
          Finn swore
openly, solemnly,
          that the battle survivors
would be guaranteed
          honor and status.
No infringement
          by word or deed,
no provocation
          would be permitted.   1100
Their own ring-giver
          after all
was dead and gone,
          they were leaderless,
in forced allegiance
          to his murderer.
So if any Frisian
          stirred up bad blood
with insinuations
          or taunts about this,   1105
the blade of the sword
          would arbitrate it.
A funeral pyre
          was then prepared,
effulgent gold
          brought out from the hoard.
The pride and prince
          of the Shieldings lay
awaiting the flame.
          Everywhere   1110
there were blood-plastered
          coats of mail.
The pyre was heaped
          with boar-shaped helmets
forged in gold,
          with the gashed corpses
of wellborn Danes—
          many had fallen.
Then Hildeburh
          ordered her own   1115
son's body
          be burnt with Hnaef's
the flesh on his bones
          to sputter and blaze

beside his uncle's.
              The woman wailed
and sang keens,
              the warrior went up.[8]
Carcass flame
              swirled and fumed,   1120
they stood round the burial
                  mound and howled
as heads melted,
              crusted gashes
spattered and ran
              bloody matter.
The glutton element
              flamed and consumed
the dead of both sides.
              Their great days were gone.   1125
Warriors scattered
              to homes and forts
all over Friesland,
              fewer now, feeling
loss of friends.
              Hengest stayed,
lived out that whole
              resentful, blood-sullen
winter with Finn,
              homesick and helpless.   1130
No ring-whorled prow
                could up then
and away on the sea.
              Wind and water
raged with storms,
              wave and shingle
were shackled in ice
              until another year
appeared in the yard
              as it does to this day,   1135
the seasons constant,
              the wonder of light
coming over us.
              Then winter was gone,
earth's lap grew lovely,
              longing woke
in the cooped-up exile
              for a voyage home—
but more for vengeance,
              some way of bringing   1140
things to a head:
              his sword arm hankered
to greet the Jutes.
              So he did not balk

---

8. The warrior (Hildeburh's son) either goes up on the pyre or up in smoke. "Keens": funeral laments (Irish).

once Hunlafing[9]

    placed on his lap

Dazzle-the-Duel,

    the best sword of all,

whose edges Jutes

    knew only too well.   1145

Thus blood was spilled,

    the gallant Finn

slain in his home

    after Guthlaf and Oslaf[1]

back from their voyage

    made old accusation:

the brutal ambush,

    the fate they had suffered,

all blamed on Finn.

    The wildness in them   1150

had to brim over.

    The hall ran red

with blood of enemies.

    Finn was cut down,

the queen brought away

    and everything

the Shieldings could find

    inside Finn's walls—

the Frisian king's

    gold collars and gemstones—   1155

swept off to the ship.

    Over sea-lanes then

back to Daneland

    the warrior troop

bore that lady home.

     The poem was over,
the poet had performed, a pleasant murmur
started on the benches, stewards did the rounds   1160
with wine in splendid jugs, and Wealhtheow came to sit
in her gold crown between two good men,
uncle and nephew, each one of whom
still trusted the other; and the forthright Unferth,[2]
admired by all for his mind and courage   1165
although under a cloud for killing his brothers,
reclined near the king.   The queen spoke:
"Enjoy this drink, my most generous lord;
raise up your goblet, entertain the Geats
duly and gently, discourse with them,   1170
be open-handed, happy and fond.
Relish their company, but recollect as well
all of the boons that have been bestowed on you.

9. A Danish follower of Hengest. **1.** Danes who seem to have gone home in order to bring reinforcements to Hengest. But it is possible that these two have been with Hengest all along and that "their voyage" is an unrelated journey. **2.** See n. 5, p. 1106.

the wondrous gifts God had showered on him:
he relied for help on the Lord of All,
on His care and favor. So he overcame the foe,
brought down the hell-brute. Broken and bowed,
outcast from all sweetness, the enemy of mankind   1275
made for his death-den. But now his mother
had sallied forth on a savage journey,
grief-racked and ravenous, desperate for revenge.
    She came to Heorot. There, inside the hall,
Danes lay asleep, earls who would soon endure   1280
a great reversal, once Grendel's mother
attacked and entered. Her onslaught was less
only by as much as an amazon warrior's
strength is less than an armed man's
when the hefted sword, its hammered edge   1285
and gleaming blade slathered in blood,
razes the sturdy boar-ridge off a helmet.
Then in the hall, hard-honed swords
were grabbed from the bench, many a broad shield
lifted and braced; there was little thought of helmets   1290
or woven mail when they woke in terror.
    The hell-dam was in panic, desperate to get out,
in mortal terror the moment she was found.
She had pounced and taken one of the retainers
in a tight hold, then headed for the fen.   1295
To Hrothgar, this man was the most beloved
of the friends he trusted between the two seas.
She had done away with a great warrior,
ambushed him at rest.
               Beowulf was elsewhere.
Earlier, after the award of the treasure,   1300
the Geat had been given another lodging.
    There was uproar in Heorot. She had snatched their trophy,
Grendel's bloodied hand. It was a fresh blow
to the afflicted bawn. The bargain was hard,
both parties having to pay   1305
with the lives of friends. And the old lord,
the gray-haired warrior, was heartsore and weary
when he heard the news: his highest-placed adviser,
his dearest companion, was dead and gone.
    Beowulf was quickly brought to the chamber: 1310
the winner of fights, the arch-warrior,
came first-footing in with his fellow troops
to where the king in his wisdom waited,
still wondering whether Almighty God
would ever turn the tide of his misfortunes.   1315
So Beowulf entered with his band in attendance
and the wooden floorboards banged and rang
as he advanced, hurrying to address
the prince of the Ingwins,[5] asking if he'd rested
since the urgent summons had come as a surprise.   1320

5. The friends of the god Ing—that is, the Danes (see n. 6, p. 1107).

Then Hrothgar, the Shieldings' helmet, spoke:
"Rest? What is rest? Sorrow has returned.
Alas for the Danes! Aeschere is dead.
He was Yrmenlaf's elder brother
and a soul-mate to me, a true mentor,   1325
my right-hand man when the ranks clashed
and our boar-crests had to take a battering
in the line of action. Aeschere was everything
the world admires in a wise man and a friend.
Then this roaming killer came in a fury   1330
and slaughtered him in Heorot. Where she is hiding,
glutting on the corpse and glorying in her escape,
I cannot tell; she has taken up the feud
because of last night, when you killed Grendel,
wrestled and racked him in ruinous combat   1335
since for too long he had terrorized us
with his depredations. He died in battle,
paid with his life; and now this powerful
other one arrives, this force for evil
driven to avenge her kinsman's death.   1340
Or so it seems to thanes in their grief,
in the anguish every thane endures
at the loss of a ring-giver, now that the hand
that bestowed so richly has been stilled in death.
    "I have heard it said by my people in hall,   1345
counselors who live in the upland country,
that they have seen two such creatures
prowling the moors, huge marauders
from some other world. One of these things,
as far as anyone ever can discern,   1350
looks like a woman; the other, warped
in the shape of a man, moves beyond the pale
bigger than any man, an unnatural birth
called Grendel by the country people
in former days. They are fatherless creatures,   1355
and their whole ancestry is hidden in a past
of demons and ghosts.[6] They dwell apart
among wolves on the hills, on windswept crags
and treacherous keshes, where cold streams
pour down the mountain and disappear   1360
under mist and moorland.
                            A few miles from here
a frost-stiffened wood waits and keeps watch
above a mere; the overhanging bank
is a maze of tree-roots mirrored in its surface.
At night there, something uncanny happens: 1365
the water burns. And the mere bottom
has never been sounded by the sons of men.
On its bank, the heather-stepper halts:
the hart in flight from pursuing hounds
will turn to face them with firm-set horns   1370

6. Note that Hrothgar doesn't know of the biblical genealogy of Grendel and his mother that the poet has given us in lines 102–14.

and the risk to his life. So there he lost   1470
fame and repute. It was different for the other
rigged out in his gear, ready to do battle.
    Beowulf, son of Ecgtheow, spoke:
"Wisest of kings, now that I have come
to the point of action, I ask you to recall   1475
what we said earlier: that you, son of Halfdane
and gold-friend to retainers, that you, if I should fall
and suffer death while serving your cause,
would act like a father to me afterward.
If this combat kills me, take care   1480
of my young company, my comrades in arms.
And be sure also, my beloved Hrothgar,
to send Hygelac the treasures I received.
Let the lord of the Geats gaze on that gold,
let Hrethel's son take note of it and see   1485
that I found a ring-giver of rare magnificence
and enjoyed the good of his generosity.
And Unferth is to have what I inherited:
to that far-famed man I bequeath my own
sharp-honed, wave-sheened wonder-blade.   1490
With Hrunting I shall gain glory or die."
    After these words, the prince of the Weather-Geats
was impatient to be away and plunged suddenly:
without more ado, he dived into the heaving
depths of the lake. It was the best part of a day   1495
before he could see the solid bottom.
    Quickly the one who haunted those waters,
who had scavenged and gone her gluttonous rounds
for a hundred seasons, sensed a human
observing her outlandish lair from above.   1500
So she lunged and clutched and managed to catch him
in her brutal grip; but his body, for all that,
remained unscathed: the mesh of the chain-mail
saved him on the outside. Her savage talons
failed to rip the web of his war-shirt.   1505
Then once she touched bottom, that wolfish swimmer
carried the ring-mailed prince to her court
so that for all his courage he could never use
the weapons he carried; and a bewildering horde
came at him from the depths, droves of sea-beasts   1510
who attacked with tusks and tore at his chain-mail
in a ghastly onslaught. The gallant man
could see he had entered some hellish turn-hole
and yet the water there did not work against him
because the hall-roofing held off   1515
the force of the current; then he saw firelight,
a gleam and flare-up, a glimmer of brightness.
    The hero observed that swamp-thing from hell,
the tarn[8]-hag in all her terrible strength,

---

8. A small lake.

then heaved his war-sword and swung his arm: 1520
the decorated blade came down ringing
and singing on her head. But he soon found
his battle-torch extinguished; the shining blade
refused to bite. It spared her and failed
the man in his need. It had gone through many   1525
hand-to-hand fight, had hewed the armor
and helmets of the doomed, but here at last
the fabulous powers of that heirloom failed.

    Hygelac's kinsman kept thinking about
his name and fame: he never lost heart.   1530
Then, in a fury, he flung his sword away.
The keen, inlaid, worm-loop-patterned steel
was hurled to the ground: he would have to rely
on the might of his arm. So must a man do
who intends to gain enduring glory   1535
in a combat. Life doesn't cost him a thought.
Then the prince of War-Geats, warming to this fight
with Grendel's mother, gripped her shoulder
and laid about him in a battle frenzy:
he pitched his killer opponent to the floor   1540
but she rose quickly and retaliated,
grappled him tightly in her grim embrace.
The sure-footed fighter felt daunted,
the strongest of warriors stumbled and fell.
So she pounced upon him and pulled out   1545
a broad, whetted knife: now she would avenge
her only child. But the mesh of chain-mail
on Beowulf's shoulder shielded his life,
turned the edge and tip of the blade.
The son of Ecgtheow would have surely perished   1550
and the Geats lost their warrior under the wide earth
had the strong links and locks of his war-gear
not helped to save him: holy God
decided the victory. It was easy for the Lord,
the Ruler of Heaven, to redress the balance   1555
once Beowulf got back up on his feet.

    Then he saw a blade that boded well,
a sword in her armory, an ancient heirloom
from the days of the giants, an ideal weapon,
one that any warrior would envy,   1560
but so huge and heavy of itself
only Beowulf could wield it in a battle.
So the Shieldings' hero hard-pressed and enraged,
took a firm hold of the hilt and swung
the blade in an arc, a resolute blow   1565
that bit deep into her neck-bone
and severed it entirely, toppling the doomed
house of her flesh; she fell to the floor.
The sword dripped blood, the swordsman was elated.

    A light appeared and the place brightened   1570
the way the sky does when heaven's candle

is shining clearly. He inspected the vault:
with sword held high, its hilt raised
to guard and threaten, Hygelac's thane
scouted by the wall in Grendel's wake.   1575
Now the weapon was to prove its worth.
The warrior determined to take revenge
for every gross act Grendel had committed—
and not only for that one occasion
when he'd come to slaughter the sleeping troops,   1580
fifteen of Hrothgar's house-guards
surprised on their benches and ruthlessly devoured,
and as many again carried away,
a brutal plunder. Beowulf in his fury
now settled that score: he saw the monster   1585
in his resting place, war-weary and wrecked,
a lifeless corpse, a casualty
of the battle in Heorot. The body gaped
at the stroke dealt to it after death:
Beowulf cut the corpse's head off.   1590
     Immediately the counselors keeping a lookout
with Hrothgar, watching the lake water,
saw a heave-up and surge of waves
and blood in the backwash. They bowed gray heads,
spoke in their sage, experienced way   1595
about the good warrior, how they never again
expected to see that prince returning
in triumph to their king. It was clear to many
that the wolf of the deep had destroyed him forever.
     The ninth hour of the day arrived.   1600
The brave Shieldings abandoned the cliff-top
and the king went home; but sick at heart,
staring at the mere, the strangers held on.
They wished, without hope, to behold their lord,
Beowulf himself.   1605
                    Meanwhile, the sword
began to wilt into gory icicles
to slather and thaw. It was a wonderful thing,
the way it all melted as ice melts
when the Father eases the fetters off the frost
and unravels the water-ropes, He who wields power   1610
over time and tide: He is the true Lord.
     The Geat captain saw treasure in abundance
but carried no spoils from those quarters
except for the head and the inlaid hilt
embossed with jewels; its blade had melted   1615
and the scrollwork on it burned, so scalding was the blood
of the poisonous fiend who had perished there.
Then away he swam, the one who had survived
the fall of his enemies, flailing to the surface.
The wide water, the waves and pools,   1620
were no longer infested once the wandering fiend
let go of her life and this unreliable world.

The seafarers' leader made for land,
resolutely swimming, delighted with his prize,
the mighty load he was lugging to the surface.   1625
His thanes advanced in a troop to meet him,
thanking God and taking great delight
in seeing their prince back safe and sound.
Quickly the hero's helmet and mail-shirt
were loosed and unlaced. The lake settled,   1630
clouds darkened above the bloodshot depths.

    With high hearts they headed away
along footpaths and trails through the fields,
roads that they knew, each of them wrestling
with the head they were carrying from the lakeside cliff,   1635
men kingly in their courage and capable
of difficult work. It was a task for four
to hoist Grendel's head on a spear
and bear it under strain to the bright hall.
But soon enough they neared the place,   1640
fourteen Geats in fine fettle,
striding across the outlying ground
in a delighted throng around their leader.

    In he came then, the thanes' commander,
the arch-warrior, to address Hrothgar: 1645
his courage was proven, his glory was secure.
Grendel's head was hauled by the hair,
dragged across the floor where the people were drinking,
a horror for both queen and company to behold.
They stared in awe. It was an astonishing sight.   1650

[ANOTHER CELEBRATION AT HEOROT]

    Beowulf, son of Ecgtheow, spoke:
"So, son of Halfdane, prince of the Shieldings,
we are glad to bring this booty from the lake.
It is a token of triumph and we tender it to you.
I barely survived the battle under water.   1655
It was hard-fought, a desperate affair
that could have gone badly; if God had not helped me,
the outcome would have been quick and fatal.
Although Hrunting is hard-edged,
I could never bring it to bear in battle.   1660
But the Lord of Men allowed me to behold—
for He often helps the unbefriended—
an ancient sword shining on the wall,
a weapon made for giants, there for the wielding.
Then my moment came in the combat and I struck   1665
the dwellers in that den. Next thing the damascened[9]
sword blade melted; it bloated and it burned
in their rushing blood. I have wrested the hilt
from the enemies' hand, avenged the evil
done to the Danes; it is what was due.   1670

9. Ornamented with inlaid designs.

And this I pledge, O prince of the Shieldings:
you can sleep secure with your company of troops
in Heorot Hall. Never need you fear
for a single thane of your sept[1] or nation,
young warriors or old, that laying waste of life   1675
that you and your people endured of yore."
   Then the gold hilt was handed over
to the old lord, a relic from long ago
for the venerable ruler. That rare smithwork
was passed on to the prince of the Danes   1680
when those devils perished; once death removed
that murdering, guilt-steeped, God-cursed fiend,
eliminating his unholy life
and his mother's as well, it was willed to that king
who of all the lavish gift-lords of the north   1685
was the best regarded between the two seas.
   Hrothgar spoke; he examined the hilt,
that relic of old times. It was engraved all over
and showed how war first came into the world
and the flood destroyed the tribe of giants.   1690
They suffered a terrible severance from the Lord;
the Almighty made the waters rise,
drowned them in the deluge for retribution.
In pure gold inlay on the sword-guards
there were rune-markings correctly incised,   1695
stating and recording for whom the sword
had been first made and ornamented
with its scrollworked hilt. Then everyone hushed
as the son of Halfdane spoke this wisdom:
"A protector of his people, pledged to uphold   1700
truth and justice and to respect tradition,
is entitled to affirm that this man
was born to distinction. Beowulf, my friend,
your fame has gone far and wide,
you are known everywhere. In all things you are even-tempered,   1705
prudent and resolute. So I stand firm by the promise of friendship
we exchanged before. Forever you will be
your people's mainstay and your own warriors'
helping hand.
        Heremod was different,
the way he behaved to Ecgwela's sons.[2]   1710
His rise in the world brought little joy
to the Danish people, only death and destruction.
He vented his rage on men he caroused with,
killed his own comrades, a pariah king
who cut himself off from his own kind,   1715
even though Almighty God had made him
eminent and powerful and marked him from the start
for a happy life. But a change happened,
he grew bloodthirsty, gave no more rings

1. A clan or division of a tribe (Irish).   2. That is, the Danes. He was evidently a former king of the Danes.

to honor the Danes. He suffered in the end   1720
for having plagued his people for so long:
his life lost happiness.
              So learn from this
and understand true values. I who tell you
have wintered into wisdom.
                 It is a great wonder
how Almighty God in His magnificence   1725
favors our race with rank and scope
and the gift of wisdom; His sway is wide.
Sometimes He allows the mind of a man
of distinguished birth to follow its bent,
grants him fulfillment and felicity on earth   1730
and forts to command in his own country.
He permits him to lord it in many lands
until the man in his unthinkingness
forgets that it will ever end for him.
He indulges his desires; illness and old age   1735
mean nothing to him; his mind is untroubled
by envy or malice or the thought of enemies
with their hate-honed swords. The whole world
conforms to his will, he is kept from the worst
until an element of overweening   1740
enters him and takes hold
while the soul's guard, its sentry, drowses,
grown too distracted. A killer stalks him,
an archer who draws a deadly bow.
And then the man is hit in the heart,   1745
the arrow flies beneath his defenses,
the devious promptings of the demon start.
His old possessions seem paltry to him now.
He covets and resents; dishonors custom
and bestows no gold; and because of good things   1750
that the Heavenly Powers gave him in the past
he ignores the shape of things to come.
Then finally the end arrives
when the body he was lent collapses and falls
prey to its death; ancestral possessions   1755
and the goods he hoarded are inherited by another
who lets them go with a liberal hand.
  "O flower of warriors, beware of that trap.
Choose, dear Beowulf, the better part,
eternal rewards. Do not give way to pride.   1760
For a brief while your strength is in bloom
but it fades quickly; and soon there will follow
illness or the sword to lay you low,
or a sudden fire or surge of water
or jabbing blade or javelin from the air   1765
or repellent age. Your piercing eye
will dim and darken; and death will arrive,
dear warrior, to sweep you away.
  "Just so I ruled the Ring-Danes' country

for fifty years, defended them in wartime   1770
with spear and sword against constant assaults
by many tribes: I came to believe
my enemies had faded from the face of the earth.
Still, what happened was a hard reversal
from bliss to grief. Grendel struck   1775
after lying in wait. He laid waste to the land
and from that moment my mind was in dread
of his depredations. So I praise God
in His heavenly glory that I lived to behold
this head dripping blood and that after such harrowing   1780
I can look upon it in triumph at last.
Take your place, then, with pride and pleasure,
and move to the feast. Tomorrow morning
our treasure will be shared and showered upon you."
    The Geat was elated and gladly obeyed   1785
the old man's bidding; he sat on the bench.
And soon all was restored, the same as before.
Happiness came back, the hall was thronged,
and a banquet set forth; black night fell
and covered them in darkness.
                 Then the company rose   1790
for the old campaigner: the gray-haired prince
was ready for bed. And a need for rest
came over the brave shield-bearing Geat.
He was a weary seafarer, far from home,
so immediately a house-guard guided him out,   1795
one whose office entailed looking after
whatever a thane on the road in those days
might need or require. It was noble courtesy.

[BEOWULF RETURNS HOME]

    That great heart rested. The hall towered,
gold-shingled and gabled, and the guest slept in it   1800
until the black raven with raucous glee
announced heaven's joy, and a hurry of brightness
overran the shadows. Warriors rose quickly,
impatient to be off: their own country
was beckoning the nobles; and the bold voyager   1805
longed to be aboard his distant boat.
Then that stalwart fighter ordered Hrunting
to be brought to Unferth, and bade Unferth
take the sword and thanked him for lending it.
He said he had found it a friend in battle   1810
and a powerful help; he put no blame
on the blade's cutting edge. He was a considerate man.
    And there the warriors stood in their war-gear,
eager to go, while their honored lord
approached the platform where the other sat.   1815
The undaunted hero addressed Hrothgar.
Beowulf, son of Ecgtheow, spoke:
"Now we who crossed the wide sea

have to inform you that we feel a desire
to return to Hygelac. Here we have been welcomed   1820
and thoroughly entertained. You have treated us well.
If there is any favor on earth I can perform
beyond deeds of arms I have done already,
anything that would merit your affections more,
I shall act, my lord, with alacrity.   1825
If ever I hear from across the ocean
that people on your borders are threatening battle
as attackers have done from time to time,
I shall land with a thousand thanes at my back
to help your cause. Hygelac may be young   1830
to rule a nation, but this much I know
about the king of the Geats: he will come to my aid
and want to support me by word and action
in your hour of need, when honor dictates
that I raise a hedge of spears around you.   1835
Then if Hrethric should think about traveling
as a king's son to the court of the Geats,
he will find many friends. Foreign places
yield more to one who is himself worth meeting."
    Hrothgar spoke and answered him: 1840
"The Lord in his wisdom sent you those words
and they came from the heart. I have never heard
so young a man make truer observations.
You are strong in body and mature in mind,
impressive in speech. If it should come to pass   1845
that Hrethel's descendant dies beneath a spear,
if deadly battle or the sword blade or disease
fells the prince who guards your people
and you are still alive, then I firmly believe
the seafaring Geats won't find a man   1850
worthier of acclaim as their king and defender
than you, if only you would undertake
the lordship of your homeland. My liking for you
deepens with time, dear Beowulf.
What you have done is to draw two peoples,   1855
the Geat nation and us neighboring Danes,
into shared peace and a pact of friendship
in spite of hatreds we have harbored in the past.
For as long as I rule this far-flung land
treasures will change hands and each side will treat   1860
the other with gifts; across the gannet's bath,
over the broad sea, whorled prows will bring
presents and tokens. I know your people
are beyond reproach in every respect,
steadfast in the old way with friend or foe."   1865
    Then the earls' defender furnished the hero
with twelve treasures and told him to set out,
sail with those gifts safely home
to the people he loved, but to return promptly.
And so the good and gray-haired Dane,   1870

on his father's account.[4] The killer knows
the lie of the land and escapes with his life.
Then on both sides the oath-bound lords
will break the peace, a passionate hate
will build up in Ingeld, and love for his bride   2065
will falter in him as the feud rankles.
I therefore suspect the good faith of the Heatho-Bards,
the truth of their friendship and the trustworthiness
of their alliance with the Danes.
                            But now, my lord,
I shall carry on with my account of Grendel,   2070
the whole story of everything that happened
in the hand-to-hand fight.
                            After heaven's gem
had gone mildly to earth, that maddened spirit,
the terror of those twilights, came to attack us
where we stood guard, still safe inside the hall.   2075
There deadly violence came down on Hondscio[5]
and he fell as fate ordained, the first to perish,
rigged out for the combat. A comrade from our ranks
had come to grief in Grendel's maw:
he ate up the entire body.   2080
There was blood on his teeth, he was bloated and dangerous,
all roused up, yet still unready
to leave the hall empty-handed;
renowned for his might, he matched himself against me,
wildly reaching. He had this roomy pouch,[6]   2085
a strange accoutrement, intricately strung
and hung at the ready, a rare patchwork
of devilishly fitted dragon-skins.
I had done him no wrong, yet the raging demon
wanted to cram me and many another   2090
into this bag—but it was not to be
once I got to my feet in a blind fury.
It would take too long to tell how I repaid
the terror of the land for every life he took
and so won credit for you, my king,   2095
and for all your people. And although he got away
to enjoy life's sweetness for a while longer,
his right hand stayed behind him in Heorot,
evidence of his miserable overthrow
as he dived into murk on the mere bottom.   2100
    "I got lavish rewards from the lord of the Danes
for my part in the battle, beaten gold
and much else, once morning came
and we took our places at the banquet table.
There was singing and excitement: an old reciter,   2105
a carrier of stories, recalled the early days.
At times some hero made the timbered harp

---

4. A Danish attendant to Freawaru, whose father killed a Heatho-Bard in the original battle; this action is
envisioned as taking place at Ingeld's court after the marriage.   5. A Geat who was accompanying
Beowulf; his name means "Glove."   6. Glove (literal trans., Anglo-Saxon).

tremble with sweetness, or related true
and tragic happenings; at times the king
gave the proper turn to some fantastic tale, 2110
or a battle-scarred veteran, bowed with age,
would begin to remember the martial deeds
of his youth and prime and be overcome
as the past welled up in his wintry heart.
   "We were happy there the whole day long 2115
and enjoyed our time until another night
descended upon us. Then suddenly
the vehement mother avenged her son
and wreaked destruction. Death had robbed her,
Geats had slain Grendel, so his ghastly dam 2120
struck back and with bare-faced defiance
laid a man low. Thus life departed
from the sage Aeschere, an elder wise in counsel.
But afterward, on the morning following,
the Danes could not burn the dead body 2125
nor lay the remains of the man they loved
on his funeral pyre. She had fled with the corpse
and taken refuge beneath torrents on the mountain.
It was a hard blow for Hrothgar to bear,
harder than any he had undergone before. 2130
And so the heartsore king beseeched me
in your royal name to take my chances
underwater, to win glory
and prove my worth. He promised me rewards.
Hence, as is well known, I went to my encounter 2135
with the terror-monger at the bottom of the tarn.
For a while it was hand-to-hand between us,
then blood went curling along the currents
and I beheaded Grendel's mother in the hall
with a mighty sword. I barely managed 2140
to escape with my life; my time had not yet come.
But Halfdane's heir, the shelter of those earls,
again endowed me with gifts in abundance.
   "Thus the king acted with due custom.
I was paid and recompensed completely, 2145
given full measure and the freedom to choose
from Hrothgar's treasures by Hrothgar himself.
These, King Hygelac, I am happy to present
to you as gifts. It is still upon your grace
that all favor depends. I have few kinsmen 2150
who are close, my king, except for your kind self."
Then he ordered the boar-framed standard to be brought,
the battle-topping helmet, the mail-shirt gray as hoar-frost,
and the precious war-sword; and proceeded with his speech:
"When Hrothgar presented this war-gear to me 2155
he instructed me, my lord, to give you some account
of why it signifies his special favor.
He said it had belonged to his older brother,
King Heorogar, who had long kept it,

but that Heorogar had never bequeathed it   2160
to his son Heoroward, that worthy scion,
loyal as he was.
               Enjoy it well."
    I heard four horses were handed over next.
Beowulf bestowed four bay steeds
to go with the armor, swift gallopers,   2165
all alike. So ought a kinsman act,
instead of plotting and planning in secret
to bring people to grief, or conspiring to arrange
the death of comrades. The warrior king
was uncle to Beowulf and honored by his nephew: 2170
each was concerned for the other's good.
    I heard he presented Hygd with a gorget,
the priceless torque that the prince's daughter,
Wealhtheow, had given him; and three horses,
supple creatures brilliantly saddled.   2175
The bright necklace would be luminous on Hygd's breast.
    Thus Beowulf bore himself with valor;
he was formidable in battle yet behaved with honor
and took no advantage; never cut down
a comrade who was drunk, kept his temper   2180
and, warrior that he was, watched and controlled
his God-sent strength and his outstanding
natural powers. He had been poorly regarded
for a long time, was taken by the Geats
for less than he was worth: and their lord too   2185
had never much esteemed him in the mead-hall.
They firmly believed that he lacked force,
that the prince was a weakling; but presently
every affront to his deserving was reversed.
    The battle-famed king, bulwark of his earls,   2190
ordered a gold-chased heirloom of Hrethel's[7]
to be brought in; it was the best example
of a gem-studded sword in the Geat treasury.
This he laid on Beowulf's lap
and then rewarded him with land as well,   2195
seven thousand hides;[8] and a hall and a throne.
Both owned land by birth in that country,
ancestral grounds; but the greater right
and sway were inherited by the higher born.

[THE DRAGON WAKES]

A lot was to happen in later days   2200
in the fury of battle. Hygelac fell
and the shelter of Heardred's shield proved useless
against the fierce aggression of the Shylfings:[9]
ruthless swordsmen, seasoned campaigners,

---

7. Hygelac's father and, through his daughter, Beowulf's grandfather.   8. A measure that varied in size but was considered to be sufficient land to support a peasant and his family.   9. That is, the long feud against the Swedes or Shylfings described in the headnote. For Hygelac's death, see n. 4, p. 1112.

they came against him and his conquering nation,   2205
and with cruel force cut him down
so that afterwards
      the wide kingdom
reverted to Beowulf. He ruled it well
for fifty winters, grew old and wise
as warden of the land
      until one began   2210
to dominate the dark, a dragon on the prowl
from the steep vaults of a stone-roofed barrow[1]
where he guarded a hoard; there was a hidden passage,
unknown to men, but someone managed[2]
to enter by it and interfere   2215
with the heathen trove. He had handled and removed
a gem-studded goblet; it gained him nothing,
though with a thief's wiles he had outwitted
the sleeping dragon. That drove him into rage,
as the people of that country would soon discover.   2220
  The intruder who broached the dragon's treasure
and moved him to wrath had never meant to.
It was desperation on the part of a slave
fleeing the heavy hand of some master,
guilt-ridden and on the run,   2225
going to ground. But he soon began
to shake with terror; . . . . . . in shock
the wretch . . . .
. . . . panicked and ran
away with the precious   2230
metalwork. There were many other
heirlooms heaped inside the earth-house,
because long ago, with deliberate care,
somebody now forgotten
had buried the riches of a highborn race   2235
in this ancient cache. Death had come
and taken them all in times gone by
and the only one left to tell their tale,
the last of their line, could look forward to nothing
but the same fate for himself: he foresaw that his joy   2240
in the treasure would be brief.
      A newly constructed
barrow stood waiting, on a wide headland
close to the waves, its entryway secured.
Into it the keeper of the hoard had carried
all the goods and golden ware   2245
worth preserving. His words were few:
"Now, earth, hold what earls once held
and heroes can no more; it was mined from you first
by honorable men. My own people
have been ruined in war; one by one   2250

---

1. A Burial mound. 2. In the single manuscript of *Beowulf*, the page containing lines 2215–31 is badly damaged, and the translation is therefore conjectural. The ellipses in lines 2227–30 indicate text that cannot be reconstructed at all.

of every sort, after he had purged
Hrothgar's hall, triumphed in Heorot
and beaten Grendel. He outgrappled the monster
and his evil kin.

     One of his cruelest
hand-to-hand encounters had happened   2355
when Hygelac, king of the Geats, was killed
in Friesland: the people's friend and lord,
Hrethel's son, slaked a sword blade's
thirst for blood. But Beowulf's prodigious
gifts as a swimmer guaranteed his safety: 2360
he arrived at the shore, shouldering thirty
battle-dresses, the booty he had won.
There was little for the Hetware[4] to be happy about
as they shielded their faces and fighting on the ground
began in earnest. With Beowulf against them,   2365
few could hope to return home.

  Across the wide sea, desolate and alone,
the son of Ecgtheow swam back to his people.
There Hygd offered him throne and authority
as lord of the ring-hoard: with Hygelac dead,   2370
she had no belief in her son's ability
to defend their homeland against foreign invaders.
Yet there was no way the weakened nation
could get Beowulf to give in and agree
to be elevated over Heardred as his lord   2375
or to undertake the office of kingship.
But he did provide support for the prince,
honored and minded him until he matured
as the ruler of Geatland.

       Then over sea-roads
exiles arrived, sons of Ohthere.[5]   2380
They had rebelled against the best of all
the sea-kings in Sweden, the one who held sway
in the Shylfing nation, their renowned prince,
lord of the mead-hall. That marked the end
for Hygelac's son: his hospitality   2385
was mortally rewarded with wounds from a sword.
Heardred lay slaughtered and Onela returned
to the land of Sweden, leaving Beowulf
to ascend the throne, to sit in majesty
and rule over the Geats. He was a good king.   2390

  In days to come, he contrived to avenge
the fall of his prince; he befriended Eadgils
when Eadgils was friendless, aiding his cause
with weapons and warriors over the wide sea,
sending him men. The feud was settled   2395
on a comfortless campaign when he killed Onela.

---

4. A Frankish tribe. 5. Eanmund and Eadgils. After Ohthere, king of the Swedes or Shylfings, died, his
sons were driven out by their uncle Onela. They were taken in by Heardred, Hygelac's son, who was then
king of the Geats, who was then in turn attacked and killed (along with Eanmund) by Onela. At this point
Beowulf became king of the Geats and supported Eadgils in his successful attack on Onela.

And so the son of Ecgtheow had survived
every extreme, excelling himself
in daring and in danger, until the day arrived
when he had to come face to face with the dragon.   2400
The lord of the Geats took eleven comrades
and went in a rage to reconnoiter.
By then he had discovered the cause of the affliction
being visited on the people. The precious cup
had come to him from the hand of the finder,   2405
the one who had started all this strife
and was now added as a thirteenth to their number.
They press-ganged and compelled this poor creature
to be their guide. Against his will
he led them to the earth-vault he alone knew,   2410
an underground barrow near the sea-billows
and heaving waves, heaped inside
with exquisite metalwork. The one who stood guard
was dangerous and watchful, warden of the trove
buried under earth: no easy bargain   2415
would be made in that place by any man.
　　The veteran king sat down on the cliff-top.
He wished good luck to the Geats who had shared
his hearth and his gold. He was sad at heart,
unsettled yet ready, sensing his death.   2420
His fate hovered near, unknowable but certain:
it would soon claim his coffered soul,
part life from limb. Before long
the prince's spirit would spin free from his body.
　　Beowulf, son of Ecgtheow, spoke: 2425
"Many a skirmish I survived when I was young
and many times of war: I remember them well.
At seven, I was fostered out by my father,
left in the charge of my people's lord.
King Hrethel kept me and took care of me,   2430
was openhanded, behaved like a kinsman.
While I was his ward, he treated me no worse
as a wean[6] about the place than one of his own boys,
Herebeald and Haethcyn, or my own Hygelac.
For the eldest, Herebeald, an unexpected   2435
deathbed was laid out, through a brother's doing,
when Haethcyn bent his horn-tipped bow
and loosed the arrow that destroyed his life.
He shot wide and buried a shaft
in the flesh and blood of his own brother.   2440
That offense was beyond redress, a wrongfooting
of the heart's affections; for who could avenge
the prince's life or pay his death-price?
It was like the misery felt by an old man
who has lived to see his son's body   2445
swing on the gallows. He begins to keen

---

6. "A young child" [translator's note]. A Northern Irish word.

and weep for his boy, watching the raven
gloat where he hangs: he can be of no help.
The wisdom of age is worthless to him.
Morning after morning, he wakes to remember   2450
that his child is gone; he has no interest
in living on until another heir
is born in the hall, now that his first-born
has entered death's dominion forever.
He gazes sorrowfully at his son's dwelling,   2455
the banquet hall bereft of all delight,
the windswept hearthstone; the horsemen are sleeping,
the warriors under ground; what was is no more.
No tunes from the harp, no cheer raised in the yard.
Alone with his longing, he lies down on his bed   2460
and sings a lament; everything seems too large,
the steadings and the fields.
                              Such was the feeling
of loss endured by the lord of the Geats
after Herebeald's death. He was helplessly placed
to set to rights the wrong committed,   2465
could not punish the killer in accordance with the law
of the blood-feud, although he felt no love for him.
Heartsore, wearied, he turned away
from life's joys, chose God's light
and departed, leaving buildings and lands   2470
to his sons, as a man of substance will.
    "Then over the wide sea Swedes and Geats
battled and feuded and fought without quarter.
Hostilities broke out when Hrethel died.
Ongentheow's sons[7] were unrelenting,   2475
refusing to make peace, campaigning violently
from coast to coast, constantly setting up
terrible ambushes around Hreosnahill.[8]
My own kith and kin avenged
these evil events, as everybody knows,   2480
but the price was high: one of them paid
with his life. Haethcyn, lord of the Geats,
met his fate there and fell in the battle.
Then, as I have heard, Hygelac's sword
was raised in the morning against Ongentheow,   2485
his brother's killer. When Eofor cleft
the old Swede's helmet, halved it open,
he fell, death-pale: his feud-calloused hand
could not stave off the fatal stroke.
    "The treasures that Hygelac lavished on me   2490
I paid for when I fought, as fortune allowed me,
with my glittering sword. He gave me land
and the security land brings, so he had no call

---

7. Ohthere and Onela, who attacked the Geats and killed Haethcyn. Haethcyn was then avenged by his
brother Hygelac, whose attack on the Swedes resulted in the death of Ongentheow at the hands of the
Geat Eofor (described in lines 2922–98). These events took place before those of lines 2379–96, which
describe the Geats' role in the struggle between Onela and Ohthere's two sons after Ongentheow's death.
8. "Sorrow Hill."

to go looking for some lesser champion,
some mercenary from among the Gifthas[9]   2495
or the Spear-Danes or the men of Sweden.
I marched ahead of him, always there
at the front of the line; and I shall fight like that
for as long as I live, as long as this sword
shall last, which has stood me in good stead   2500
late and soon, ever since I killed
Dayraven the Frank in front of the two armies.
He brought back no looted breastplate
to the Frisian king but fell in battle,
their standard-bearer, highborn and brave.   2505
No sword blade sent him to his death:
my bare hands stilled his heartbeats
and wrecked the bone-house. Now blade and hand,
sword and sword-stroke, will assay the hoard."

[BEOWULF ATTACKS THE DRAGON]

    Beowulf spoke, made a formal boast   2510
for the last time: "I risked my life
often when I was young. Now I am old,
but as king of the people I shall pursue this fight
for the glory of winning, if the evil one will only
abandon his earth-fort and face me in the open."   2515
    Then he addressed each dear companion
one final time, those fighters in their helmets,
resolute and highborn: "I would rather not
use a weapon if I knew another way
to grapple with the dragon and make good my boast   2520
as I did against Grendel in days gone by.
But I shall be meeting molten venom
in the fire he breathes, so I go forth
in mail-shirt and shield. I won't shift a foot
when I meet the cave-guard: what occurs on the wall   2525
between the two of us will turn out as fate,
overseer of men, decides. I am resolved.
I scorn further words against this sky-borne foe.
    "Men-at-arms, remain here on the barrow,
safe in your armor, to see which one of us   2530
is better in the end at bearing wounds
in a deadly fray. This fight is not yours,
nor is it up to any man except me
to measure his strength against the monster
or to prove his worth. I shall win the gold   2535
by my courage, or else mortal combat,
doom of battle, will bear your lord away."
    Then he drew himself up beside his shield.
The fabled warrior in his war-shirt and helmet
trusted in his own strength entirely   2540
and went under the crag. No coward path.

---

9. A tribe related to the Goths.

Hard by the rock-face that hale veteran,
a good man who had gone repeatedly
into combat and danger and come through,
saw a stone arch and a gushing stream   2545
that burst from the barrow, blazing and wafting
a deadly heat. It would be hard to survive
unscathed near the hoard, to hold firm
against the dragon in those flaming depths.
Then he gave a shout. The lord of the Geats   2550
unburdened his breast and broke out
in a storm of anger. Under gray stone
his voice challenged and resounded clearly.
Hate was ignited. The hoard-guard recognized
a human voice, the time was over   2555
for peace and parleying. Pouring forth
in a hot battle-fume, the breath of the monster
burst from the rock. There was a rumble under ground.
Down there in the barrow, Beowulf the warrior
lifted his shield: the outlandish thing   2560
writhed and convulsed and viciously
turned on the king, whose keen-edged sword,
an heirloom inherited by ancient right,
was already in his hand. Roused to a fury,
each antagonist struck terror in the other.   2565
Unyielding, the lord of his people loomed
by his tall shield, sure of his ground,
while the serpent looped and unleashed itself.
Swaddled in flames, it came gliding and flexing
and racing toward its fate. Yet his shield defended   2570
the renowned leader's life and limb
for a shorter time than he meant it to:
that final day was the first time
when Beowulf fought and fate denied him
glory in battle. So the king of the Geats   2575
raised his hand and struck hard
at the enameled scales, but scarcely cut through:
the blade flashed and slashed yet the blow
was far less powerful than the hard-pressed king
had need of at that moment. The mound-keeper   2580
went into a spasm and spouted deadly flames:
when he felt the stroke, battle-fire
billowed and spewed. Beowulf was foiled
of a glorious victory. The glittering sword,
infallible before that day,   2585
failed when he unsheathed it, as it never should have.
For the son of Ecgtheow, it was no easy thing
to have to give ground like that and go
unwillingly to inhabit another home
in a place beyond; so every man must yield   2590
the leasehold of his days.
                              Before long
the fierce contenders clashed again.

The hoard-guard took heart, inhaled and swelled up
and got a new wind; he who had once ruled
was furled in fire and had to face the worst.   2595
No help or backing was to be had then
from his highborn comrades; that hand-picked troop
broke ranks and ran for their lives
to the safety of the wood. But within one heart
sorrow welled up: in a man of worth   2600
the claims of kinship cannot be denied.
    His name was Wiglaf,[1] a son of Weohstan's,
a well-regarded Shylfing warrior
related to Aelfhere.[2] When he saw his lord
tormented by the heat of his scalding helmet,   2605
he remembered the bountiful gifts bestowed on him,
how well he lived among the Waegmundings,
the freehold he inherited from his father[3] before him.
He could not hold back: one hand brandished
the yellow-timbered shield, the other drew his sword—   2610
an ancient blade that was said to have belonged
to Eanmund, the son of Ohthere, the one
Weohstan had slain when he was an exile without friends.
He carried the arms to the victim's kinfolk,
the burnished helmet, the webbed chain-mail   2615
and that relic of the giants. But Onela returned
the weapons to him, rewarded Weohstan
with Eanmund's war-gear. He ignored the blood-feud,
the fact that Eanmund was his brother's son.[4]
Weohstan kept that war-gear for a lifetime,   2620
the sword and the mail-shirt, until it was the son's turn
to follow his father and perform his part.
Then, in old age, at the end of his days
among the Weather-Geats, he bequeathed to Wiglaf
innumerable weapons.
                And now the youth   2625
was to enter the line of battle with his lord,
his first time to be tested as a fighter.
His spirit did not break and the ancestral blade
would keep its edge, as the dragon discovered
as soon as they came together in the combat.   2630
    Sad at heart, addressing his companions,
Wiglaf spoke wise and fluent words:
"I remember that time when mead was flowing,
how we pledged loyalty to our lord in the hall,
promised our ring-giver we would be worth our price,   2635
make good the gift of the war-gear,
those swords and helmets, as and when

---

1. Like Beowulf, a member of the clan of the Waegmundings (see lines 2813–14), although both consider themselves Geats as well (see n. 3, p. 1093).   2. Nothing is known of him.   3. Wiglaf's father is Weohstan, who, as we learn shortly, was the man who killed Eanmund, Ohthere's son, when he had taken refuge among the Geats (lines 2379–84). How Wiglaf then became a Geat is not clear, although it may have been when Beowulf helped Eanmund's brother Eadgils avenge himself on Onela, who had usurped the throne of the Swedes; Eadgils then became king.   4. That is, Onela ignored the fact that Weohstan had killed his nephew Eanmund since he in fact wanted Eanmund dead.

his need required it. He picked us out
from the army deliberately, honored us and judged us
fit for this action, made me these lavish gifts— 2640
and all because he considered us the best
of his arms-bearing thanes. And now, although
he wanted this challenge to be one he'd face
by himself alone—the shepherd of our land,
a man unequaled in the quest for glory 2645
and a name for daring—now the day has come
when this lord we serve needs sound men
to give him their support. Let us go to him,
help our leader through the hot flame
and dread of the fire. As God is my witness, 2650
I would rather my body were robed in the same
burning blaze as my gold-giver's body
than go back home bearing arms.
That is unthinkable, unless we have first
slain the foe and defended the life 2655
of the prince of the Weather-Geats. I well know
the things he has done for us deserve better.
Should he alone be left exposed
to fall in battle? We must bond together,
shield and helmet, mail-shirt and sword." 2660
Then he waded the dangerous reek and went
under arms to his lord, saying only:
"Go on, dear Beowulf, do everything
you said you would when you were still young
and vowed you would never let your name and fame 2665
be dimmed while you lived. Your deeds are famous,
so stay resolute, my lord, defend your life now
with the whole of your strength. I shall stand by you."
     After those words, a wildness rose
in the dragon again and drove it to attack, 2670
heaving up fire, hunting for enemies,
the humans it loathed. Flames lapped the shield,
charred it to the boss, and the body armor
on the young warrior was useless to him.
But Wiglaf did well under the wide rim 2675
Beowulf shared with him once his own had shattered
in sparks and ashes.
                    Inspired again
by the thought of glory, the war-king threw
his whole strength behind a sword stroke
and connected with the skull. And Naegling snapped. 2680
Beowulf's ancient iron-gray sword
let him down in the fight. It was never his fortune
to be helped in combat by the cutting edge
of weapons made of iron. When he wielded a sword,
no matter how blooded and hard-edged the blade, 2685
his hand was too strong, the stroke he dealt
(I have heard) would ruin it. He could reap no advantage.
     Then the bane of that people, the fire-breathing dragon,

was mad to attack for a third time.
When a chance came, he caught the hero   2690
in a rush of flame and clamped sharp fangs
into his neck. Beowulf's body
ran wet with his life-blood: it came welling out.
   Next thing, they say, the noble son of Weohstan
saw the king in danger at his side   2695
and displayed his inborn bravery and strength.
He left the head alone,[5] but his fighting hand
was burned when he came to his kinsman's aid.
He lunged at the enemy lower down
so that his decorated sword sank into its belly   2700
and the flames grew weaker.
                         Once again the king
gathered his strength and drew a stabbing knife
he carried on his belt, sharpened for battle.
He stuck it deep in the dragon's flank.
Beowulf dealt it a deadly wound.   2705
They had killed the enemy, courage quelled his life;
that pair of kinsmen, partners in nobility,
had destroyed the foe. So every man should act,
be at hand when needed; but now, for the king,
this would be the last of his many labors   2710
and triumphs in the world.
                    Then the wound
dealt by the ground-burner earlier began
to scald and swell; Beowulf discovered
deadly poison suppurating inside him,
surges of nausea, and so, in his wisdom,   2715
the prince realized his state and struggled
toward a seat on the rampart. He steadied his gaze
on those gigantic stones, saw how the earthwork
was braced with arches built over columns.
And now that thane unequaled for goodness   2720
with his own hands washed his lord's wounds,
swabbed the weary prince with water,
bathed him clean, unbuckled his helmet.
   Beowulf spoke: in spite of his wounds,
mortal wounds, he still spoke   2725
for he well knew his days in the world
had been lived out to the end—his allotted time
was drawing to a close, death was very near.
   "Now is the time when I would have wanted
to bestow this armor on my own son,   2730
had it been my fortune to have fathered an heir
and live on in his flesh. For fifty years
I ruled this nation. No king
of any neighboring clan would dare
face me with troops, none had the power   2735
to intimidate me. I took what came,

5. That is, the dragon's flame-breathing head.

exulting in his riches: he fell to earth
through the battle-strength in Beowulf's arm.   2835
There were few, indeed, as far as I have heard,
big and brave as they may have been,
few who would have held out if they had had to face
the outpourings of that poison-breather
or gone foraging on the ring-hall floor   2840
and found the deep barrow-dweller
on guard and awake.
                The treasure had been won,
bought and paid for by Beowulf's death.
Both had reached the end of the road
through the life they had been lent.
                      Before long   2845
the battle-dodgers abandoned the wood,
the ones who had let down their lord earlier,
the tail-turners, ten of them together.
When he needed them most, they had made off.
Now they were ashamed and came behind shields,   2850
in their battle-outfits, to where the old man lay.
They watched Wiglaf, sitting worn out,
a comrade shoulder to shoulder with his lord,
trying in vain to bring him round with water.
Much as he wanted to, there was no way   2855
he could preserve his lord's life on earth
or alter in the least the Almighty's will.
What God judged right would rule what happened
to every man, as it does to this day.
    Then a stern rebuke was bound to come   2860
from the young warrior to the ones who had been cowards.
Wiglaf, son of Weohstan, spoke
disdainfully and in disappointment:
"Anyone ready to admit the truth
will surely realize that the lord of men   2865
who showered you with gifts and gave you the armor
you are standing in—when he would distribute
helmets and mail-shirts to men on the mead-benches,
a prince treating his thanes in hall
to the best he could find, far or near—   2870
was throwing weapons uselessly away.
It would be a sad waste when the war broke out.
Beowulf had little cause to brag
about his armed guard; yet God who ordains
who wins or loses allowed him to strike   2875
with his own blade when bravery was needed.
There was little I could do to protect his life
in the heat of the fray, but I found new strength
welling up when I went to help him.
Then my sword connected and the deadly assaults   2880
of our foe grew weaker, the fire coursed
less strongly from his head. But when the worst happened
too few rallied around the prince.

"So it is good-bye now to all you know and love
on your home ground, the open-handedness,   2885
the giving of war-swords. Every one of you
with freeholds of land, our whole nation,
will be dispossessed, once princes from beyond
get tidings of how you turned and fled
and disgraced yourselves. A warrior will sooner   2890
die than live a life of shame."
    Then he ordered the outcome of the fight to be reported
to those camped on the ridge, that crowd of retainers
who had sat all morning, sad at heart,
shield-bearers wondering about   2895
the man they loved: would this day be his last
or would he return? He told the truth
and did not balk, the rider who bore
news to the cliff-top. He addressed them all:
"Now the people's pride and love,   2900
the lord of the Geats, is laid on his deathbed,
brought down by the dragon's attack.
Beside him lies the bane of his life,
dead from knife-wounds. There was no way
Beowulf could manage to get the better   2905
of the monster with his sword. Wiglaf sits
at Beowulf's side, the son of Weohstan,
the living warrior watching by the dead,
keeping weary vigil, holding a wake
for the loved and the loathed.
                        Now war is looming   2910
over our nation, soon it will be known
to Franks and Frisians, far and wide,
that the king is gone. Hostility has been great
among the Franks since Hygelac sailed forth
at the head of a war-fleet into Friesland: 2915
there the Hetware harried and attacked
and overwhelmed him with great odds.
The leader in his war-gear was laid low,
fell among followers: that lord did not favor
his company with spoils. The Merovingian king   2920
has been an enemy to us ever since.
    "Nor do I expect peace or pact-keeping
of any sort from the Swedes. Remember:
at Ravenswood, Ongentheow
slaughtered Haethcyn, Hrethel's son,   2925
when the Geat people in their arrogance
first attacked the fierce Shylfings.
The return blow was quickly struck
by Ohthere's father.[9] Old and terrible,
he felled the sea-king and saved his own   2930
aged wife, the mother of Onela
and of Ohthere, bereft of her gold rings.

9. Ongentheow.

rose in tears, then took their way
to the uncanny scene under Earnaness.[4]
There, on the sand, where his soul had left him,
they found him at rest, their ring-giver
from days gone by. The great man   3035
had breathed his last. Beowulf the king
had indeed met with a marvelous death.
    But what they saw first was far stranger:
the serpent on the ground, gruesome and vile,
lying facing him. The fire-dragon   3040
was scaresomely burned, scorched all colors.
From head to tail, his entire length
was fifty feet. He had shimmered forth
on the night air once, then winged back
down to his den; but death owned him now,   3045
he would never enter his earth-gallery again.
Beside him stood pitchers and piled-up dishes,
silent flagons, precious swords
eaten through with rust, ranged as they had been
while they waited their thousand winters under ground.   3050
That huge cache, gold inherited
from an ancient race, was under a spell—
which meant no one was ever permitted
to enter the ring-hall unless God Himself,
mankind's Keeper, True King of Triumphs,   3055
allowed some person pleasing to Him—
and in His eyes worthy—to open the hoard.
    What came about brought to nothing
the hopes of the one who had wrongly hidden
riches under the rock-face. First the dragon slew   3060
that man among men, who in turn made fierce amends
and settled the feud. Famous for his deeds
a warrior may be, but it remains a mystery
where his life will end, when he may no longer
dwell in the mead-hall among his own.   3065
So it was with Beowulf, when he faced the cruelty
and cunning of the mound-guard. He himself was ignorant
of how his departure from the world would happen.
The highborn chiefs who had buried the treasure
declared it until doomsday so accursed   3070
that whoever robbed it would be guilty of wrong
and grimly punished for their transgression,
hasped in hell-bonds in heathen shrines.
Yet Beowulf's gaze at the gold treasure
when he first saw it had not been selfish.   3075
    Wiglaf, son of Weohstan, spoke:
"Often when one man follows his own will
many are hurt. This happened to us.
Nothing we advised could ever convince
the prince we loved, our land's guardian,   3080

---

4. "Eagleness," the place where Beowulf fought the dragon.

not to vex the custodian of the gold,
let him lie where he was long accustomed,
lurk there under earth until the end of the world.
He held to his high destiny. The hoard is laid bare,
but at a grave cost; it was too cruel a fate   3085
that forced the king to that encounter.
I have been inside and seen everything
amassed in the vault. I managed to enter
although no great welcome awaited me
under the earthwall. I quickly gathered up   3090
a huge pile of the priceless treasures
handpicked from the hoard and carried them here
where the king could see them. He was still himself,
alive, aware, and in spite of his weakness
he had many requests. He wanted me to greet you   3095
and order the building of a barrow that would crown
the site of his pyre, serve as his memorial,
in a commanding position, since of all men
to have lived and thrived and lorded it on earth
his worth and due as a warrior were the greatest.   3100
Now let us again go quickly
and feast our eyes on that amazing fortune
heaped under the wall. I will show the way
and take you close to those coffers packed with rings
and bars of gold. Let a bier be made   3105
and got ready quickly when we come out
and then let us bring the body of our lord,
the man we loved, to where he will lodge
for a long time in the care of the Almighty."
    Then Weohstan's son, stalwart to the end,   3110
had orders given to owners of dwellings,
many people of importance in the land,
to fetch wood from far and wide
for the good man's pyre:
                    "Now shall flame consume
our leader in battle, the blaze darken   3115
round him who stood his ground in the steel-hail,
when the arrow-storm shot from bowstrings
pelted the shield-wall. The shaft hit home.
Feather-fledged, it finned the barb in flight."
    Next the wise son of Weohstan   3120
called from among the king's thanes
a group of seven: he selected the best
and entered with them, the eighth of their number,
under the God-cursed roof; one raised
a lighted torch and led the way.   3125
No lots were cast for who should loot the hoard
for it was obvious to them that every bit of it
lay unprotected within the vault,
there for the taking. It was no trouble
to hurry to work and haul out   3130
the priceless store. They pitched the dragon

over the cliff-top, let tide's flow
and backwash take the treasure-minder.
Then coiled gold was loaded on a cart
in great abundance, and the gray-haired leader,   3135
the prince on his bier, borne to Hronesness.
    The Geat people built a pyre for Beowulf,
stacked and decked it until it stood foursquare,
hung with helmets, heavy war-shields
and shining armor, just as he had ordered.   3140
Then his warriors laid him in the middle of it,
mourning a lord far-famed and beloved.
On a height they kindled the hugest of all
funeral fires; fumes of woodsmoke
billowed darkly up, the blaze roared   3145
and drowned out their weeping, wind died down
and flames wrought havoc in the hot bone-house,
burning it to the core. They were disconsolate
and wailed aloud for their lord's decease.
A Geat woman too sang out in grief;   3150
with hair bound up, she unburdened herself
of her worst fears, a wild litany
of nightmare and lament: her nation invaded,
enemies on the rampage, bodies in piles,
slavery and abasement. Heaven swallowed the smoke.   3155
    Then the Geat people began to construct
a mound on a headland, high and imposing,
a marker that sailors could see from far away,
and in ten days they had done the work.
It was their hero's memorial; what remained from the fire   3160
they housed inside it, behind a wall
as worthy of him as their workmanship could make it.
And they buried torques in the barrow, and jewels
and a trove of such things as trespassing men
had once dared to drag from the hoard.   3165
They let the ground keep that ancestral treasure,
gold under gravel, gone to earth,
as useless to men now as it ever was.
Then twelve warriors rode around the tomb,
chieftains' sons, champions in battle,   3170
all of them distraught, chanting in dirges,
mourning his loss as a man and a king.
They extolled his heroic nature and exploits
and gave thanks for his greatness; which was the proper thing,
for a man should praise a prince whom he holds dear   3175
and cherish his memory when that moment comes
when he has to be convoyed from his bodily home.
So the Geat people, his hearth-companions,
sorrowed for the lord who had been laid low.
They said that of all the kings upon earth   3180
he was the man most gracious and fair-minded,
kindest to his people and keenest to win fame.

THE SONG OF ROLAND

ca. 1100

The Song of Roland is the foundation of the French literary tradition. One of the earliest poems written in French, it describes the process by which France left behind its Germanic past as a loose confederation of powerful families and accepted its future as a Christian nation united by loyalties to king and country. This story is told as a clash of powerful personalities who are together engaged in a holy war against the Muslims in Spain. The central protagonist is the great warrior Roland, who embodies in a pure form the spirit of feudal loyalty to one's overlord. The emperor Charlemagne is the object of this loyalty, but his commitments are split: he owes to Roland a reciprocal loyalty, but he is also the head of the Holy Roman empire, the institutional heir to classical Rome that is endowed with the mission not merely to defend but to expand Christendom. Opposed to Roland is his stepfather, Ganelon, a member of Charlemagne's Frankish nobility who believes he can pursue a feud with Roland without compromising his loyalty to the king. And surrounding these three main characters are men who provide further perspectives on the central issue of what kind of loyalty is valid. Oliver, Roland's closest companion in arms, criticizes Roland's narrow conception of his duty; Turpin, a warrior archbishop, provides justifications for Roland's actions that may be merely rationalizations; Pinabel, one of Ganelon's kinsmen, comes to his defense when he is charged with treason for his part in Roland's death; and Tierri, a warrior, challenges Pinabel not merely to defend Roland or even Charlemagne but to promote national and supranational loyalties that transcend Ganelon's tribal conception.

Many modern readers have been tempted to read the poem as a kind of medieval *Iliad*, with the heroic yet arrogantly intransigent Roland as a French Achilles. Yet in the manuscript the poem is untitled, Roland dies less than two thirds of the way through, and the beginning and ending of the poem focus on "Charles the King, our Emperor, the Great." The poem could with equal justice be titled—as indeed it was in some of its medieval versions—*The Song of Charlemagne*. In fact, the relation of Roland's story to Charles's—the relation, that is, of the heroic acts of one man to the historically transcendent mission of establishing a universal Christian empire—is the poem's overriding theme. Roland embodies the unswerving and reciprocal allegiance that bound together lord and vassal into a stable unit, a relationship that made possible the establishment of the feudal system that, from the tenth through twelfth centuries, came to dominate Europe. From his first appearance in the poem, at the council scene in which the Franks debate whether to accept the offer of the Saracen leader Marsilion to submit to Charles if the Franks will leave Spain, Roland both promotes and himself displays this fidelity. He argues against accepting the offer for three reasons, all of them having to do with loyalty. First, Marsilion has already been proven untrustworthy in fulfilling his sworn oath; second, Basan and Basile, the ambassadors whom Marsilion killed during the previous negotiations, must be avenged (they were, Roland reminds Charles, "*your* men"); and third, Charles must also be true to his commitment to conquer Spain ("Fight the war you came to fight!"), an obligation he owes to God, who has sanctioned this holy war. Again, the poem's climactic scene, in which the members of the rear guard are ambushed and Roland refuses to blow his horn to call back the army to help them, has often been read as expressing Roland's intemperate and unjustified reliance on his own prowess. Yet another interpretation, centered on loyalty, is also possible. As the leader of the rear guard, Roland has sworn to protect the army: to call it back now, in the face of overwhelming enemy forces, would be to place it in danger and to betray his commitment. Indeed, when he accepted this dangerous assignment—dangerous because everyone, including Roland, suspected that Ganelon had conspired with the Saracens to set a

as the army made its way through the narrow valleys of the Pyrenees, the rear guard protecting its retreat was annihilated in an ambush set by the native Basques. Among those killed was one Hruodlandus, governor of the marches (or borders) of Brittany. About 350 years later, between 1125 and 1150, someone wrote out the manuscript that contains the poem that we now call *The Song of Roland*. This manuscript was written in the French spoken at the time in England, a dialect known as Anglo-Norman, but the poem itself was composed in continental French around the year 1100. This date fits well with two contemporary conditions. One is the struggle then under way between the French king Philip I and the powerful barons who were technically subordinate to him but controlled much of what now constitutes France—a struggle that finds a parallel in the poem in the confrontation between Charles and Ganelon. The other is the growing interest in crusading. Throughout the eleventh century French knights fought against the Arab rulers of Spain, and in 1095 Pope Urban urged the nobility of Europe, and especially of France, to direct their martial energies away from their internal wrangling and toward the Holy Land, at the time governed by Muslim "infidels" (although governed in fact in a spirit of religious tolerance). The result was the First Crusade, which succeeded in capturing Jerusalem in 1099, in massacring most of the non-Christian population, and in establishing the French-controlled kingdom of Jerusalem. *The Song of Roland* is steeped in this crusading spirit: as Roland says, and as the poem continually insists, "Pagans are wrong and Christians are right!"

Although there have been a number of theories, no one really knows how—or why—the story of the ill-fated Hruodlandus survived. It was a traditional story by at least the eleventh century: one later medieval chronicler even tells us that a minstrel called Taillefer sang about Roland to the Norman army of William the Conqueror before the battle of Hastings in 1066. The poem shows unmistakable signs of having emerged from a period of oral composition. As in the Homeric poems and *Beowulf*, many of its phrases are metrical formulas originally combined by an oral poet into complete lines and then larger passages as he re-created the poem anew at each performance. Even when written, the poem was almost certainly presented orally by a minstrel, or *jongleur* (like Taillefer), who would accompany himself with a simple stringed instrument. Like *Beowulf*, the poem would be chanted rather than sung, producing an effect of cadenced, ritualistic ceremony. This effect was doubtless enhanced by the so-called *laisses similaires*, groups of *laisses* that repeat, with variations, an especially significant scene or act. These groups of *laisses* endow such moments with a powerful sense of solemnity and consequence.

PRONOUNCING GLOSSARY

The following list uses common English syllables to provide rough equivalents of selected words whose pronunciation may be unfamiliar to the general reader.

Aquitaine: *ah-kee-ten*

Blancandrin: *blanh-cahn-drinh*

Durendal: *dur-ahn-dahl*

Gerer: *zhehr-air*

Gerin: *zhehr-anh'*

Halteclere: *ahl-te-clehr'*

Haltille: *ahl-tee*

Malduit: *mahl-dwee*

Marsilion: *mahr-see-lyonh'*

Munjoie: *munh-zhwah*

Ogier: *oh-zhyay*

Rencesvals: *ren-ses-vahls*

Roland: *roh-lanh*

Rousillon: *roo-see-yonh*

Veillantif: *ve-yanh-teef*

From The Song of Roland[1]

1

Charles the King, our Emperor, the Great,
has been in Spain for seven full years,
has conquered the high land down to the sea.
There is no castle that stands against him now,
no wall, no citadel left to break down— 5
except Saragossa, high on a mountain.[2]
King Marsilion holds it, who does not love God,
who serves Mahumet and prays to Apollin.[3]
He cannot save himself: his ruin will find him there. AOI.[4]

2

King Marsilion was in Saragossa. 10
He has gone forth into a grove, beneath its shade,
and he lies down on a block of blue marble,
twenty thousand men, and more, all around him.
He calls aloud to his dukes and his counts:
"Listen, my lords, to the troubles we have. 15
The Emperor Charles of the sweet land of France
has come into this country to destroy us.
I have no army able to give him battle,
I do not have the force to break his force.
Now act like my wise men: give me counsel, 20
save me, save me from death, save me from shame!"
No pagan there has one word to say to him
except Blancandrin, of the castle of Valfunde.

3

One of the wisest pagans was Blancandrin,
brave and loyal, a great mounted warrior, 25
a useful man, the man to aid his lord;
said to the King: "Do not give way to panic.
Do this: send Charles, that wild, terrible man,
tokens of loyal service and great friendship:
you will give him bears and lions and dogs, 30
seven hundred camels, a thousand molted hawks,
four hundred mules weighed down with gold and silver,
and fifty carts, to cart it all away:
he'll have good wages for his men who fight for pay.
Say he's made war long enough in this land: 35
let him go home, to France, to Aix, at last—
come Michaelmas[5] you will follow him there,

---

1. Translated by Frederick Goldin. Many of Goldin's notes have been adapted for use here.
2. Saragossa, in northeastern Spain, is not actually on a mountaintop. The poet's geography is not always accurate.   3. The Greek god Apollo. The poet is mistaken, for these people worship only one god, Allah. Mahumet, or Muhammed, founder of the Islamic religion.   4. These three mysterious letters appear at certain moments throughout the text, 180 times in all. No one has ever adequately explained them, though every reader feels their effect.   5. The feast of St. Michael, September 29. Aix is Aix-la-Chapelle, or Aachen, the capital of Charlemagne's empire.

You have stayed long—long enough!—in this land,
it is time to go home, to France, to Aix.   135
My master swears he will follow you there."
The Emperor holds out his hands toward God,
bows down his head, begins to meditate. AOI.

10

The Emperor held his head bowed down;
never was he too hasty with his words: 140
his custom is to speak in his good time.
When his head rises, how fierce the look of him;
he said to them: "You have spoken quite well.
King Marsilion is my great enemy.
Now all these words that you have spoken here—   145
how far can I trust them? How can I be sure?"
The Saracen:[9] "He wants to give you hostages.
How many will you want? ten? fifteen? twenty?
I'll put my son with the others named to die.[1]
You will get some, I think, still better born.   150
When you are at home in your high royal palace,
at the great feast of Saint Michael-in-Peril,[2]
the lord who nurtures me will follow you,
and in those baths[3]—the baths God made for you—
my lord will come and want to be made Christian."   155
King Charles replies: "He may yet save his soul." AOI.

11

Late in the day it was fair, the sun was bright.
Charles has them put the ten mules into stables.
The King commands a tent pitched in the broad grove,
and there he has the ten messengers lodged;   160
twelve serving men took splendid care of them.
There they remained that night till the bright day.
The Emperor rose early in the morning,
the King of France, and heard the mass and matins.
And then the King went forth beneath a pine,   165
calls for his barons to complete his council:
he will proceed only with the men of France. AOI.

* * *

13

"Barons, my lords," said Charles the Emperor,   180
"King Marsilion has sent me messengers,
wants to give me a great mass of his wealth,

---

9. The usual term for the enemy.   1. That is, if the promise is broken.   2. The epithet "in peril of the sea" was applied to the famous sanctuary Mont-St.-Michel off the Normandy coast because it could be reached on foot only at low tide, and pilgrims were endangered by the incoming tide. Eventually, the phrase was applied to the saint himself.   3. Famous healing springs at Aix-la-Chapelle.

bears and lions and hunting dogs on chains,
seven hundred camels, a thousand molting hawks,
four hundred mules packed with gold of Araby,   185
and with all that, more than fifty great carts;
but also asks that I go back to France:
he'll follow me to Aix, my residence,
and take our faith, the one redeeming faith,
become a Christian, hold his march lands[4] from me.   190
But what lies in his heart? I do not know."
And the French say: "We must be on our guard!" AOI.

14

The Emperor has told them what was proposed.
Roland the Count will never assent to that,
gets to his feet, comes forth to speak against it;   195
says to the King: "Trust Marsilion—and suffer!
We came to Spain seven long years ago,
I won Noples for you, I won Commibles,
I took Valterne and all the land of Pine,
and Balaguer and Tudela and Seville.   200
And then this king, Marsilion, played the traitor:
he sent you men, fifteen of his pagans—
and sure enough, each held an olive branch;
and they recited just these same words to you.
You took counsel with all your men of France;   205
they counseled you to a bit of madness:
you sent two Counts across to the Pagans,
one was Basan, the other was Basile.
On the hills below Haltille, he took their heads.
They were your men. Fight the war you came to fight!   210
Lead the army you summoned on to Saragossa!
Lay siege to it all the rest of your life!
Avenge the men that this criminal murdered!" AOI.

15

The Emperor held his head bowed down with this,
and stroked his beard, and smoothed his mustache down,   215
and speaks no word, good or bad, to his nephew.
The French keep still, all except Ganelon:
he gets to his feet and, come before King Charles,
how fierce he is as he begins his speech;
said to the King: "Believe a fool—me or   220
another—and suffer! Protect your interest!
When Marsilion the King sends you his word
that he will join his hands[5] and be your man,
and hold all Spain as a gift from your hands
and then receive the faith that we uphold—   225

---

4. A frontier province or territory.   5. Part of the gesture of homage; the lord enclosed the joined hands of his vassal with his own.

give him your aid, and hold him as your lord."
And he starts down the road; he is on his way. AOI.   365

28

Ganelon rides to a tall olive tree,
there he has joined the pagan messengers.
And here is Blancandrin, who slows down for him:
and what great art they speak to one another.
Said Blancandrin: "An amazing man, Charles!   370
conquered Apulia, conquered all of Calabria,
crossed the salt sea on his way into England,
won its tribute, got Peter's pence[7] for Rome:
what does he want from us here in our march?"
Ganelon answers: "That is the heart in him.   375
There'll never be a man the like of him." AOI.

29

Said Blancandrin: "The Franks are a great people.
Now what great harm all those dukes and counts do
to their own lord when they give him such counsel:
they torment him, they'll destroy him, and others."   380
Ganelon answers: "Well, now, I know no such man
except Roland, who'll suffer for it yet.
One day the Emperor was sitting in the shade:
his nephew came, still wearing his hauberk,
he had gone plundering near Carcassonne;   385
and in his hand he held a bright red apple:
'Dear Lord, here, take,' said Roland to his uncle;
'I offer you the crowns of all earth's kings.'
Yes, Lord, that pride of his will destroy him,
for every day he goes riding at death.   390
And *should* someone kill him, we would have peace." AOI.

30

Said Blancandrin: "A wild man, this Roland!
wants to make every nation beg for his mercy
and claims a right to every land on earth!
But what men support him, if that is his aim?"   395
Ganelon answers: "Why, Lord, the men of France.
They love him so, they will never fail him.
He gives them gifts, masses of gold and silver,
mules, battle horses, brocaded silks, supplies.
And it is all as the Emperor desires: 400
he'll win the lands from here to the Orient." AOI.

---

7. A tribute of one penny per house "for the use of Saint Peter"—that is, for the pope in Rome. Although begun perhaps as early as the 8th century, the tribute was not the result of any effort of Charlemagne, who did not in fact visit England.

31

Ganelon and Blancandrin rode on until
each pledged his faith to the other and swore
they'd find a way to have Count Roland killed.

* * *

32

Blancandrin came before Marsilion,
his hand around the fist of Ganelon,   415
said to the King: "May Mahumet save you,
and Apollin, whose sacred laws we keep!
We delivered your message to Charlemagne:
when we finished, he raised up both his hands
and praised his god. He made no other answer.   420
Here he sends you one of his noble barons,
a man of France, and very powerful.
You'll learn from him whether or not you'll have peace."
"Let him speak, we shall hear him," Marsilion answers. AOI.

33

But Ganelon had it all well thought out.   425
With what great art he commences his speech,
a man who knows his way about these things;
said to the King: "May the Lord God save you,
that glorious God, whom we must all adore.
Here is the word of Charlemagne the King: 430
you are to take the holy Christian faith;
he will give you one half of Spain in fief.
If you refuse, if you reject this peace,
you will be taken by force, put into chains,
and then led forth to the King's seat at Aix;   435
you will be tried; you will be put to death:
you will die there, in shame, vilely, degraded."
King Marsilion, hearing this, was much shaken.
In his hand was a spear, with golden feathers.
He would have struck, had they not held him back. AOI.   440

* * *

36

Now Ganelon drew closer to the King
and said to him: "You are wrong to get angry,
for Charles, who rules all France, sends you this word: 470
you are to take the Christian people's faith;
he will give you one half of Spain in fief,
the other half goes to his nephew: Roland—
quite a partner you will be getting there!
If you refuse, if you reject this peace,   475
he will come and lay siege to Saragossa;

52

Marsilion took Ganelon by the shoulder
and said to him: "You're a brave man, a wise man.
Now by that faith you think will save your soul,
take care you do not turn your heart from us.   650
I will give you a great mass of my wealth,
ten mules weighed down with fine Arabian gold;
and come each year, I'll do the same again.
Now you take these, the keys to this vast city:
present King Charles with all of its great treasure;   655
then get me Roland picked for the rear-guard.
Let me find him in some defile or pass,
I will fight him, a battle to the death."
Ganelon answers: "It's high time that I go."
Now he is mounted, and he is on his way. AOI.   660

* * *

54

The Emperor rose early in the morning,
the King of France, and has heard mass and matins.   670
On the green grass he stood before his tent.
Roland was there, and Oliver, brave man,
Naimon the Duke, and many other knights.
Ganelon came, the traitor, the foresworn.
With what great cunning he commences his speech;   675
said to the King: "May the Lord God save you!
Here I bring you the keys to Saragossa.
And I bring you great treasure from that city,
and twenty hostages, have them well guarded.
And good King Marsilion sends you this word: 680
Do not blame him concerning the Algalife:
I saw it all myself, with my own eyes:
        four hundred thousand men, and all in arms,
their hauberks on, some with their helms laced on,
swords on their belts, the hilts enameled gold,
who went with him to the edge of the sea.   685
They are in flight: it is the Christian faith—
they do not want it, they will not keep its law.
They had not sailed four full leagues out to sea
when a high wind, a tempest swept them up.
They were all drowned; you will never see them;   690
if he were still alive, I'd have brought him.
As for the pagan King, Lord, believe this:
before you see one month from this day pass,
he'll follow you to the Kingdom of France
and take the faith—he will take your faith, Lord,   695
and join his hands and become your vassal.
He will hold Spain as a fief from your hand."
Then the King said: "May God be thanked for this.
You have done well, you will be well rewarded."
Throughout the host they sound a thousand trumpets. 700

The French break camp, strap their gear on their pack-horses.
They take the road to the sweet land of France. AOI.

55

King Charlemagne laid waste the land of Spain,
stormed its castles, ravaged its citadels.
The King declares his war is at an end.
The Emperor rides toward the land of sweet France.   705
Roland the Count affixed the gonfanon,[2]
raised it toward heaven on the height of a hill;
the men of France make camp across that country.
Pagans are riding up through these great valleys,   710
their hauberks on, their tunics of double mail,
their helms laced on, their swords fixed on their belts,
shields on their necks, lances trimmed with their banners.
In a forest high in the hills they gathered:
four hundred thousand men waiting for dawn.   715
God, the pity of it! the French do not know! AOI.

* * *

58

The day goes by, and the bright dawn arises.
Throughout that host. . . .[3]
The Emperor rides forth with such fierce pride.
"Barons, my lords," said the Emperor Charles,   740
"look at those passes, at those narrow defiles—
pick me a man to command the rear-guard."
Ganelon answers: "Roland, here, my stepson.
You have no baron as great and brave as Roland."
When he hears that, the King stares at him in fury;   745
and said to him: "You are the living devil,
a mad dog—the murderous rage in you!
And who will precede me, in the vanguard?"
Ganelon answers, "Why, Ogier of Denmark,
you have no baron who could lead it so well."   750

59

Roland the Count, when he heard himself named,
knew what to say, and spoke as a knight must speak:
"Lord Stepfather, I have to cherish you!
You have had the rear-guard assigned to me.
Charles will not lose, this great King who rules France,   755
I swear it now, one palfrey, one war horse—
    while I'm alive and know what's happening—
one he-mule, one she-mule that he might ride,
Charles will not lose one sumpter, not one pack horse
that has not first been bought and paid for with swords."
Ganelon answers: "You speak the truth, I know." AOI.   760

* * *

2. Pennant.   3. Rest of line unintelligible in the manuscript.

61

"Just Emperor," said Roland, that great man,
"give me the bow that you hold in your hand.
And no man here, I think, will say in reproach
I let it drop, as Ganelon let the staff drop[4]
from his right hand, when he should have taken it."   770
The Emperor bowed down his head with this,
he pulled his beard, he twisted his mustache,
cannot hold back, tears fill his eyes, he weeps.

62

And after that there came Naimon the Duke,
no greater vassal in the court than Naimon,   775
said to the King: "You've heard it clearly now:
it is Count Roland. How furious he is.
He is the one to whom the rear-guard falls,
no baron here can ever change that now.
Give him the bow that you have stretched and bent,   780
and then find him good men to stand with him."
The King gives him the bow; Roland has it now.

63

The Emperor calls forth Roland the Count:
"My lord, my dear nephew, of course you know
I will give you half my men, they are yours.   785
Let them serve you, it is your salvation."
"None of that!" said the Count. "May God strike me
if I discredit the history of my line.
I'll keep twenty thousand Franks—they are good men.
Go your way through the passes, you will be safe.   790
You must not fear any man while I live."

*   *   *

68

King Charles the Great cannot keep from weeping.
A hundred thousand Franks feel pity for him;
and for Roland, an amazing fear.
Ganelon the criminal has betrayed him;
got gifts for it from the pagan king,   845
gold and silver, cloths of silk, gold brocade,
mules and horses and camels and lions.
Marsilion sends for the barons of Spain,
counts and viscounts and dukes and almaçurs,
and the emirs,[5] and the sons of great lords: 850
four hundred thousand assembled in three days.
In Saragossa he has them beat the drums,

---

4. In this *laisse* a reviser tried to make the text more consistent by adding the reference to the staff.
5. All lords of high rank.

they raise Mahumet upon the highest tower:
no pagan now who does not worship him
and adore him. Then they ride, racing each other,   855
search through the land, the valleys, the mountains;
and then they saw the banners of the French.
The rear-guard of the Twelve Companions
will not fail now, they'll give the pagans battle.

*   *   *

80

Oliver climbs to the top of a hill,
looks to his right, across a grassy vale,
sees the pagan army on its way there;
and called down to Roland, his companion: 1020
"That way, toward Spain: the uproar I see coming!
All their hauberks, all blazing, helmets like flames!
It will be a bitter thing for our French.
Ganelon knew, that criminal, that traitor,
when he marked us out before the Emperor."   1025
"Be still, Oliver," Roland the Count replies.
"He is my stepfather—my stepfather.
  I won't have you speak one word against him."

*   *   *

82

Said Oliver: "I saw the Saracens,
no man on earth ever saw more of them—   1040
one hundred thousand, with their shields, up in front,
helmets laced on, hauberks blazing on them,
the shafts straight up, the iron heads like flames—
you'll get a battle, nothing like it before.
My lords, my French, may God give you the strength.   1045
Hold your ground now! Let them not defeat us!"
And the French say: "God hate the man who runs!
We may die here, but no man will fail you." AOI.

83

Said Oliver: "The pagan force is great;
from what I see, our French here are too few.   1050
Roland, my companion, sound your horn then,
Charles will hear it, the army will come back."
Roland replies: "I'd be a fool to do it.
I would lose my good name all through sweet France.
I will strike now, I'll strike with Durendal,   1055
"the blade will be bloody to the gold from striking!
These pagan traitors came to these passes doomed!
I promise you, they are marked men, they'll die." AOI.

*   *   *

86

Said Oliver: "I see no blame in it—
I watched the Saracens coming from Spain,
the valleys and mountains covered with them,
every hillside and every plain all covered, 1085
hosts and hosts everywhere of those strange men—
and here we have a little company."
Roland replies: "That whets my appetite.
May it not please God and his angels and saints
to let France lose its glory because of me— 1090
let me not end in shame, let me die first.
The Emperor loves us when we fight well."

87

Roland is good, and Oliver is wise,
both these vassals men of amazing courage:
once they are armed and mounted on their horses, 1095
they will not run, though they die for it, from battle.
Good men, these Counts, and their words full of spirit.
Traitor pagans are riding up in fury.
Said Oliver: "Roland, look—the first ones,
on top of us—and Charles is far away. 1100
You did not think it right to sound your olifant:
if the King were here, we'd come out without losses.
Now look up there, toward the passes of Aspre—
you can see the rear-guard: it will suffer.
No man in that detail will be in another." 1105
Roland replies: "Don't speak such foolishness—
shame on the heart gone coward in the chest.
We'll hold our ground, we'll stand firm—we're the ones!
We'll fight with spears, we'll fight them hand to hand!" AOI.

88

When Roland sees that there will be a battle, 1110
it makes him fiercer than a lion or leopard;
shouts to the French, calls out to Oliver:
"Lord, companion: friend, do not say such things.
The Emperor, who left us these good French,
had set apart these twenty thousand men: 1115
he knew there was no coward in their ranks.
A man must meet great troubles for his lord,
stand up to the great heat and the great cold,
give up some flesh and blood—it is his duty.
Strike with the lance, I'll strike with Durendal— 1120
it was the King who gave me this good sword!
If I die here, the man who gets it can say:
it was a noble's, a vassal's, a good man's sword."

89

And now there comes the Archbishop Turpin.
He spurs his horse, goes up into a mountain,   1125
summons the French; and he preached them a sermon:
"Barons, my lords, Charles left us in this place.
We know our duty: to die like good men for our King.
Fight to defend the holy Christian faith.
Now you will have a battle, you know it now,   1130
you see the Saracens with your own eyes.
Confess your sins, pray to the Lord for mercy.
I will absolve you all, to save your souls.
If you die here, you will stand up holy martyrs,
you will have seats in highest Paradise."   1135
The French dismount, cast themselves on the ground;
the Archbishop blesses them in God's name.
He commands them to do one penance: strike.

90

The French arise, stand on their feet again;
they are absolved, released from all their sins: 1140
the Archbishop has blessed them in God's name.
Now they are mounted on their swift battle horses,
bearing their arms like faithful warriors;
and every man stands ready for the battle.
Roland the Count calls out to Oliver: 1145
"Lord, Companion, you knew it, you were right,
Ganelon watched for his chance to betray us,
got gold for it, got goods for it, and money.
The Emperor will have to avenge us now.
King Marsilion made a bargain for our lives,   1150
but still must pay, and that must be with swords." AOI.

*   *   *

92

Said Oliver: "I will waste no more words.   1170
You did not think it right to sound your olifant,
there'll be no Charles coming to your aid now.
He knows nothing, brave man, he's done no wrong;
those men down there—they have no blame in this.
Well, then, ride now, and ride with all your might!   1175
Lords, you brave men, stand your ground, hold the field!
Make up your minds, I beg you in God's name,
to strike some blows, take them and give them back!
Here we must not forget Charlemagne's war cry."
And with that word the men of France cried out.   1180
A man who heard that shout: Munjoie![6] Munjoie!

---

6. According to Littré, a mountjoy (or montjoie) was a mound or cairn of stones set up to mark the site of a victory. The old French war cry "Montjoie St.-Denis!" (or, briefly, "Montjoie!") derived from the cairn set up at St.-Denis on the site of the saint's martyrdom (his spiritual victory). Others derive the word from the Hill of Rama, called "Mons Gaudii," from which pilgrims obtained their first view of Jerusalem.

would always remember what manhood is.
Then they ride, God! Look at their pride and spirit!
and they spur hard, to ride with all their speed,
come on to strike—what else would these men do?   1185
The Saracens kept coming, never fearing them.
Franks and pagans, here they are, at each other.

93

Marsilion's nephew is named Aëlroth.
He rides in front, at the head of the army,
comes on shouting insults against our French: 1190
"French criminals, today you fight our men.
One man should have saved you: he betrayed you.
A fool, your King, to leave you in these passes.
This is the day sweet France will lose its name,
and Charlemagne the right arm of his body."   1195
When he hears that—God!—Roland is outraged!
He spurs his horse, gives Veillantif its head.
The Count comes on to strike with all his might,
smashes his shield, breaks his hauberk apart,
and drives: rips through his chest, shatters the bones,   1200
knocks the whole backbone out of his back,
casts out the soul of Aëlroth with his lance;
which he thrusts deep, makes the whole body shake,
throws him down dead, lance straight out,[7] from his horse;
he has broken his neck; broken it in two.   1205
There is something, he says, he must tell him:
"Clown! Nobody! Now you know Charles is no fool,
he never was the man to love treason.
It took his valor to leave us in these passes!
France will not lose its name, sweet France! today.   1210
Brave men of France, strike hard! The first blow is ours!
We're in the right, and these swine in the wrong!" AOI.

94

A duke is there whose name is Falsaron,
he was the brother of King Marsilion,
held the wild land of Dathan and Abiram;[8]   1215
under heaven, no criminal more vile;
a tremendous forehead between his eyes—
a good half-foot long, if you had measured it.
His pain is bitter to see his nephew dead;
rides out alone, baits the foe with his body,   1220
and riding shouts the war cry of the pagans,

---

7. The lance is held, not thrown, and used to knock the enemy from his horse. To throw one's weapons is savage and ignoble. See *laisses* 154 and 160 and the outlandish names of the things the pagans throw at Roland, Gautier, and Turpin.   8. See Numbers 16.1–35.

full of hate and insults against the French:
"This is the day sweet France will lose its honor!"
Oliver hears, and it fills him with fury,
digs with his golden spurs into his horse,   1225
comes on to strike the blow a baron strikes,
smashes his shield, breaks his hauberk apart,
thrusts into him the long streamers of his gonfalon,
knocks him down, dead, lance straight out, from the saddle;
looks to the ground and sees the swine stretched out,   1230
and spoke these words—proud words, terrible words:
"You nobody, what are your threats to me!
Men of France, strike! Strike and we will beat them!"
Munjoie! he shouts—the war cry of King Charles. AOI.

* * *

104

The battle is fearful and wonderful   1320
and everywhere. Roland never spares himself,
strikes with his lance as long as the wood lasts:
the fifteenth blow he struck, it broke, was lost.
Then he draws Durendal, his good sword, bare,
and spurs his horse, comes on to strike Chernuble,   1325
smashes his helmet, carbuncles shed their light,
cuts through the coif, through the hair on his head,
cut through his eyes, through his face, through that look,
the bright, shining hauberk with its fine rings,
down through the trunk to the fork of his legs,   1330
through the saddle, adorned with beaten gold,
into the horse; and the sword came to rest:
cut through the spine, never felt for the joint;
knocks him down, dead, on the rich grass of the meadow;
then said to him: "You were doomed when you started,   1335
Clown! Nobody! Let Mahum help you now.
No pagan swine will win this field today."

105

Roland the Count comes riding through the field,
holds Durendal, that sword! it carves its way!
and brings terrible slaughter down on the pagans.   1340
To have seen him cast one man dead on another,
the bright red blood pouring out on the ground,
his hauberk, his two arms, running with blood,
his good horse—neck and shoulders running with blood!
And Oliver does not linger, he strikes!   1345
and the Twelve Peers, no man could reproach them;
and the brave French, they fight with lance and sword.
The pagans die, some simply faint away!
Said the Archbishop: "Bless our band of brave men!"
Munjoie! he shouts—the war cry of King Charles. AOI.   1350

and the great noise resounds across that country.   1455
Said Roland then: "Oliver, Companion, Brother,
that traitor Ganelon has sworn our deaths:
it is treason, it cannot stay hidden,
the Emperor will take his terrible revenge.
We have this battle now, it will be bitter,   1460
no man has ever seen the like of it.
I will fight here with Durendal, this sword,
and you, my companion, with Halteclere—
we've fought with them before, in many lands!
how many battles have we won with these two!   1465
Let no one sing a bad song of our swords." AOI.

* * *

125

Marsilion sees his people's martyrdom.
He commands them: sound his horns and trumpets;
and he rides now with the great host he has gathered.   1630
At their head rides the Saracen Abisme:
no worse criminal rides in that company,
stained with the marks of his crimes and great treasons,
lacking the faith in God, Saint Mary's son.
And he is black, as black as melted pitch,   1635
a man who loves murder and treason more
than all the gold of rich Galicia,
no living man ever saw him play or laugh;
a great fighter, a wild man, mad with pride,
and therefore dear to that criminal king;   1640
holds high his dragon,[1] where all his people gather.
The Archbishop will never love that man,
no sooner saw than wanted to strike him;
considered quietly, said to himself:
"That Saracen—a heretic, I'll wager.   1645
Now let me die if I do not kill him—
I never loved cowards or cowards' ways." AOI

126

Turpin the Archbishop begins the battle.
He rides the horse that he took from Grossaille,
who was a king this priest once killed in Denmark.   1650
Now this war horse is quick and spirited,
his hooves high-arched, the quick legs long and flat,
short in the thigh, wide in the rump, long in the flanks,
and the backbone so high, a battle horse!
and that white tail, the yellow mane on him,   1655
the little ears on him, the tawny head!
No beast on earth could ever run with him.

---

1. Banner.

The Archbishop—that valiant man!—spurs hard,
he will attack Abisme, he will not falter,
strikes on his shield, a miraculous blow: 1660
a shield of stones, of amethysts, topazes,
esterminals,[2] carbuncles all on fire—
a gift from a devil, in Val Metas,
sent on to him by the Amiral Galafre.
There Turpin strikes, he does not treat it gently—   1665
after that blow, I'd not give one cent for it;
cut through his body, from one side to the other,
and casts him down dead in a barren place.
And the French say: "A fighter, that Archbishop!
Look at him there, saving souls with that crozier!"   1670

127

Roland the Count calls out to Oliver:
"Lord, Companion, now you have to agree
the Archbishop is a good man on horse,
there's none better on earth or under heaven,
he knows his way with a lance and a spear."   1675
The Count replies: "Right! Let us help him then."
And with these words the Franks began anew,
the blows strike hard, and the fighting is bitter;
there is a painful loss of Christian men.
To have seen them, Roland and Oliver,   1680
these fighting men, striking down with their swords,
the Archbishop with them, striking with his lance!
One can recount the number these three killed:
it is written—in charters, in documents;
the Geste tells it: it was more than four thousand.   1685
Through four assaults all went well with our men;
then comes the fifth, and that one crushes them.
They are all killed, all these warriors of France,
all but sixty, whom the Lord God has spared:
they will die too, but first sell themselves dear. AOI.   1690

128

Count Roland sees the great loss of his men,
calls on his companion, on Oliver:
"Lord, Companion, in God's name, what would you do?
All these good men you see stretched on the ground.
We can mourn for sweet France, fair land of France!   1695
a desert now, stripped of such great vassals.
Oh King, and friend, if only you were here!
Oliver, Brother, how shall we manage it?
What shall we do to get word to the King?"
Said Oliver: "I don't see any way.   1700
I would rather die now than hear us shamed." AOI.

2. Precious ornaments.

129

And Roland said: "I'll sound the olifant,
Charles will hear it, drawing through the passes,
I promise you, the Franks will return at once."
Said Oliver: "That would be a great disgrace,   1705
a dishonor and reproach to all your kin,
the shame of it would last them all their lives.
When I urged it, you would not hear of it;
you will not do it now with my consent.
It is not acting bravely to sound it now—   1710
look at your arms, they are covered with blood."
The Count replies: "I've fought here like a lord."[3] AOI.

130

And Roland says: "We are in a rough battle.
I'll sound the olifant, Charles will hear it."
Said Oliver: "No good vassal would do it.   1715
When I urged it, friend, you did not think it right.
If Charles were here, we'd come out with no losses.
Those men down there—no blame can fall on them."
Oliver said: "Now by this beard of mine,
If I can see my noble sister, Aude,   1720
once more, you will never lie in her arms!"[4] AOI.

131

And Roland said: "Why are you angry at me?"
Oliver answers: "Companion, it is your doing.
I will tell you what makes a vassal good:
     it is judgment, it is never madness;
restraint is worth more than the raw nerve of a fool. 1725
Frenchmen are dead because of your wildness.
And what service will Charles ever have from us?
If you had trusted me, my lord would be here,
we would have fought this battle through to the end,
Marsilion would be dead, or our prisoner.   1730
Roland, your prowess mhad we never seen it!
     And now, dear friend, we've seen the last of it.
No more aid from us now for Charlemagne,
a man without equal till Judgment Day,
you will die here, and your death will shame France.
We kept faith, you and I, we were companions;
     and everything we were will end today.   1735
We part before evening, and it will be hard." AOI.

_____

3. Some have found lines 1710–12 difficult. Oliver means, "We have fought this far—look at the enemy's blood on your arms: It is too late, it would be a disgrace to summon help when there is no longer any chance of being saved." But Roland thinks that that is the one time when it is not a disgrace.   4. Aude had been betrothed to Roland.

132

Turpin the Archbishop hears their bitter words,
digs hard into his horse with golden spurs
and rides to them; begins to set them right:
"You, Lord Roland, and you, Lord Oliver, 1740
I beg you in God's name do not quarrel.
To sound the horn could not help us now, true,
but still it is far better that you do it:
let the King come, he can avenge us then—
these men of Spain must not go home exulting! 1745
Our French will come, they'll get down on their feet,
and find us here—we'll be dead, cut to pieces.
They will lift us into coffins on the backs of mules,
and weep for us, in rage and pain and grief,
and bury us in the courts of churches; 1750
and we will not be eaten by wolves or pigs or dogs."
Roland replies, "Lord, you have spoken well." AOI.

* * *

134

And now the mighty effort of Roland the Count:
he sounds his olifant; his pain is great,
and from his mouth the bright blood comes leaping out,
and the temple bursts in his forehead.
That horn, in Roland's hands, has a mighty voice: 1765
King Charles hears it drawing through the passes.
Naimon heard it, the Franks listen to it.
And the King said: "I hear Count Roland's horn;
he'd never sound it unless he had a battle."
Says Ganelon: "Now no more talk of battles! 1770
You are old now, your hair is white as snow,
the things you say make you sound like a child.
You know Roland and that wild pride of his—
what a wonder God has suffered it so long!
Remember? he took Noples without your command: 1775
the Saracens rode out, to break the siege;
they fought with him, the great vassal Roland.
Afterwards he used the streams to wash the blood
from the meadows: so that nothing would show.
He blasts his horn all day to catch a rabbit, 1780
he's strutting now before his peers and bragging—
who under heaven would dare meet him on the field?
So now: ride on! Why do you keep on stopping?
The Land of Fathers lies far ahead of us." AOI.

135

The blood leaping from Count Roland's mouth, 1785
the temple broken with effort in his forehead,

You'll feel the pain of it before we part,   1900
you will learn my sword's name by heart today";
comes on to strike—the image of a baron.
He has cut off Marsilion's right fist;
now takes the head of Jurfaleu the blond—
the head of Jurfaleu! Marsilion's son.   1905
The pagans cry: "Help, Mahumet! Help us!
Vengeance, our gods, on Charles! the man who set
these criminals on us in our own land,
they will not quit the field, they'll stand and die!"
And one said to the other: "Let *us* run then."   1910
And with that word, some hundred thousand flee.
Now try to call them back: they won't return. AOI.

143

What does it matter? If Marsilion has fled,
his uncle has remained: the Algalife,[6]
who holds Carthage, Alfrere, and Garmalie,   1915
and Ethiopia: a land accursed;
holds its immense black race under his power,
the huge noses, the enormous ears on them;
and they number more than fifty thousand.
These are the men who come riding in fury,   1920
and now they shout that pagan battle cry.
And Roland said: "Here comes our martyrdom;
I see it now: we have not long to live.
But let the world call any man a traitor
    who does not make them pay before he dies!
My lords, attack! Use those bright shining swords!   1925
Fight a good fight for your deaths and your lives,
let no shame touch sweet France because of us!
When Charles my lord comes to this battlefield
and sees how well we punished these Saracens,
finds fifteen of their dead for one of ours,   1930
I'll tell you what he will do: he will bless us." AOI.

*   *   *

145

The Saracens, when they saw these few French,   1940
looked at each other, took courage, and presumed,
telling themselves: "The Emperor is wrong!"
The Algalife rides a great sorrel horse,
digs into it with his spurs of fine gold,
strikes Oliver, from behind, in the back,   1945
shattered the white hauberk upon his flesh,
drove his spear through the middle of his chest;
and speaks to him: "Now you feel you've been struck!

6. The Caliph, Marsilion's uncle, whom Ganelon lied about to Charlemagne (see lines 680–91).

Your great Charles doomed you when he left you in this pass.
That man wronged us, he must not boast of it.   1950
I've avenged all our dead in you alone!"

146

Oliver feels: he has been struck to death;
grips Halteclere, that steel blade shining, strikes
on the gold-dressed pointed helm of the Algalife,
sends jewels and flowers crackling down to the earth,   1955
into the head, into the little teeth;
draws up his flashing sword, casts him down, dead,
and then he says: "Pagan, a curse on you!
If only I could say Charles has lost nothing—
but no woman, no lady you ever knew   1960
will hear you boast, in the land you came from,
that you could take one thing worth a cent from me,
or do me harm, or do any man harm";
then cries out to Roland to come to his aid. AOI.

147

Oliver feels he is wounded to death,   1965
will never have his fill of vengeance, strikes,
as a baron strikes, where they are thickest,
cuts through their lances, cuts through those buckled shields,
through feet, through fists, through saddles, and through flanks.
Had you seen him, cutting the pagans limb   1970
from limb, casting one corpse down on another,
you would remember a brave man keeping faith.
Never would he forget Charles' battle-cry,
Munjoie! he shouts, that mighty voice ringing;
calls to Roland, to his friend and his peer: 1975
"Lord, Companion, come stand beside me now.
We must part from each other in pain today." AOI.

148

Roland looks hard into Oliver's face,
it is ashen, all its color is gone,
the bright red blood streams down upon his body,   1980
Oliver's blood spattering on the earth.
"God!" said the Count, "I don't know what to do,
Lord, Companion, your fight is finished now.
There'll never be a man the like of you.
Sweet land of France, today you will be stripped   1985
of good vassals, laid low, a fallen land!
The Emperor will suffer the great loss";
faints with that word, mounted upon his horse. AOI.

149

Here is Roland, lords, fainted on his horse,
and Oliver the Count, wounded to death: 1990
he has lost so much blood, his eyes are darkened—
he cannot see, near or far, well enough
to recognize a friend or enemy:
struck when he came upon his companion,
strikes on his helm, adorned with gems in gold,   1995
cuts down straight through, from the point to the nasal,[7]
but never harmed him, he never touched his head.
Under this blow, Count Roland looked at him;
and gently, softly now, he asks of him:
"Lord, Companion, do you mean to do this?   2000
It is Roland, who always loved you greatly.
You never declared that we were enemies."
Said Oliver: "Now I hear it is you—
I don't see you, may the Lord God see you.
Was it you that I struck? Forgive me then."   2005
Roland replies: "I am not harmed, not harmed,
I forgive you, Friend, here and before God."
And with that word, each bowed to the other.
And this is the love, lords, in which they parted.

* * *

151

Roland the Count, when he sees his friend dead,
lying stretched out, his face against the earth,   2025
softly, gently, begins to speak the regret:[8]
"Lord, Companion, you were brave and died for it.
We have stood side by side through days and years,
you never caused me harm, I never wronged you;
when you are dead, to be alive pains me."   2030
And with that word the lord of marches faints
upon his horse, which he calls Veillantif.
He is held firm by his spurs of fine gold,
whichever way he leans, he cannot fall.

152

Before Roland could recover his senses   2035
and come out of his faint, and be aware,
a great disaster had come forth before him:
the French are dead, he has lost every man
except the Archbishop, and Gautier de l'Hum,
who has come back, down from that high mountain: 2040
he has fought well, he fought those men of Spain.
His men are dead, the pagans finished them;

---

7. The nosepiece protruding down from the cone-shaped helmet.   8. What follows is a formal and customary lament for the dead.

flees now down to these valleys, he has no choice,
and calls on Count Roland to come to his aid:
"My noble Count, my brave lord, where are you?   2045
I never feared whenever you were there.
It is Walter: I conquered Maëlgut,
my uncle is Droün, old and gray: your Walter
and always dear to you for the way I fought;
and I have fought this time: my lance is shattered,   2050
my good shield pierced, my hauberk's meshes broken;
and I am wounded, a lance struck through my body.
I will die soon, but I sold myself dear."
And with that word, Count Roland has heard him,
he spurs his horse, rides spurring to his man. AOI.   2055

153

Roland in pain, maddened with grief and rage:
rushes where they are thickest and strikes again,
strikes twenty men of Spain, strikes twenty dead,
and Walter six, and the Archbishop five.
The pagans say: "Look at those criminals!   2060
Now take care, Lords, they don't get out alive,
only a traitor will not attack them now!
Only a coward will let them save their skins!"
And then they raise their hue and cry once more,
rush in on them, once more, from every side. AOI.   2065

154

Count Roland was always a noble warrior,
Gautier de l'Hum is a fine mounted man,
the Archbishop, a good man tried and proved:
not one of them will ever leave the others;
strike, where they are thickest, at the pagans.   2070
A thousand Saracens get down on foot,
and forty thousand more are on their mounts:
and I tell you, not one will dare come close,
they throw, and from afar, lances and spears,
wigars and darts, mizraks, javelins, pikes.   2075
With the first blows they killed Gautier de l'Hum
and struck Turpin of Reims, pierced through his shield,
broke the helmet on him, wounded his head;
ripped his hauberk, shattered its rings of mail,
and pierced him with four spears in his body,   2080
the war horse killed under him; and now there comes
great pain and rage when the Archbishop falls. AOI.

155

Turpin of Reims, when he feels he is unhorsed,
struck to the earth with four spears in his body,
quickly, brave man, leaps to his feet again;   2085

his eyes find Roland now, he runs to him
and says one word: "See! I'm not finished yet!
What good vassal ever gives up alive!";
and draws Almace, his sword, that shining steel!
and strikes, where they are thickest, a thousand blows, and more.   2090
Later, Charles said: Turpin had spared no one;
he found four hundred men prostrate around him,
some of them wounded, some pierced from front to back,
some with their heads hacked off. So says the Geste,
and so says one who was there, on that field,   2095
the baron Saint Gilles,[9] for whom God performs miracles,
who made the charter setting forth these great things
    in the Church of Laon. Now any man
who does not know this much understands nothing.

156

Roland the Count fights well and with great skill,
but he is hot, his body soaked with sweat;   2100
has a great wound in his head, and much pain,
his temple broken because he blew the horn.
But he must know whether King Charles will come;
draws out the olifant, sounds it, so feebly.
The Emperor drew to a halt, listened.   2105
"Seigneurs," he said, "it goes badly for us—
My nephew Roland falls from our ranks today.
I hear it in the horn's voice: he hasn't long.
Let every man who wants to be with Roland
ride fast! Sound trumpets! Every trumpet in this host!"   2110
Sixty thousand, on these words, sound, so high
the mountains sound, and the valleys resound.
The pagans hear: it is no joke to them;
cry to each other: "We're getting Charles on us!"

157

The pagans say: "The Emperor is coming, AOI.   2115
listen to their trumpets—it is the French!
If Charles comes back, it's all over for us,
if Roland lives, this war begins again
and we have lost our land, we have lost Spain."
Some four hundred, helmets laced on, assemble,   2120
some of the best, as they think, on that field.
They storm Roland, in one fierce, bitter attack.
And now Count Roland has some work on his hands. AOI.

---

9. St. Gilles of Provence. These lines explain how the story of Rencesvals could be told after all who had
fought there died.

158

Roland the Count, when he sees them coming,
how strong and fierce and alert he becomes!   2125
He will not yield to them, not while he lives.
He rides the horse they call Veillantif, spurs,
digs into it with his spurs of fine gold,
and rushes at them all where they are thickest,
the Archbishop—that Turpin!—at his side.   2130
Said one man to the other: "Go at it, friend.
The horns we heard were the horns of the French,
King Charles is coming back with all his strength."[1]

159

Roland the Count never loved a coward,
a blusterer, an evil-natured man,   2135
a man on horse who was not a good vassal.
And now he called to Archbishop Turpin:
"You are on foot, Lord, and here I am mounted,
and so, here I take my stand: for love of you.
We'll take whatever comes, the good and bad,   2140
together, Lord: no one can make me leave you.
They will learn our swords' names today in battle,
the name of Almace, the name of Durendal!"
Said the Archbishop: "Let us strike or be shamed!
Charles is returning, and he brings our revenge."   2145

160

Say the pagans: "We were all born unlucky!
The evil day that dawned for us today!
We have lost our lords and peers, and now comes Charles—
that Charlemagne!—with his great host. Those trumpets!
that shrill sound on us—the trumpets of the French!   2150
And the loud roar of that Munjoie! This Roland
is a wild man, he is too great a fighter—
What man of flesh and blood can ever hope
to bring him down? Let us cast at him, and leave him there."
And so they did: arrows, wigars, darts,   2155
lances and spears, javelots dressed with feathers;
struck Roland's shield, pierced it, broke it to pieces,
ripped his hauberk, shattered its rings of mail,
but never touched his body, never his flesh.
They wounded Veillantif in thirty places,   2160
struck him dead, from afar, under the Count.
The pagans flee, they leave the field to him.
Roland the Count stood alone, on his feet. AOI.

---

1. The lines could be spoken either by Roland and the archbishop or by the pagans.

161

The pagans flee, in bitterness and rage,
strain every nerve running headlong toward Spain,   2165
and Count Roland has no way to chase them,
he has lost Veillantif, his battle horse,
he has no choice, left alone there on foot.
He went to the aid of Archbishop Turpin,
unlaced the gold-dressed helmet, raised it from his head,   2170
lifted away his bright, light coat of mail,
cut his under tunic into some lengths,
stilled his great wounds with thrusting on the strips;
then held him in his arms, against his chest,
and laid him down, gently, on the green grass;   2175
and softly now Roland entreated him:
"My noble lord, I beg you, give me leave:
our companions, whom we have loved so dearly,
are all dead now, we must not abandon them.
I want to look for them, know them once more,   2180
and set them in ranks, side by side, before you."
Said the Archbishop: "Go then, go and come back.
The field is ours, thanks be to God, yours and mine."

162

So Roland leaves him, walks the field all alone,
seeks in the valleys, and seeks in the mountains.   2185
He found Gerin, and Gerer his companion,
and then he found Berenger and Otun,
Anseïs and Sansun, and on that field
he found Gerard the old of Roussillon;
and carried them, brave man, all, one by one,   2190
came back to the Archbishop with these French dead,
and set them down in ranks before his knees.
The Archbishop cannot keep from weeping,
raises his hand and makes his benediction;
and said: "Lords, Lords, it was your terrible hour.   2195
May the Glorious God set all your souls
among the holy flowers of Paradise!
Here is my own death, Lords, pressing on me,
I shall not see our mighty Emperor."

163

And Roland leaves, seeks in the field again;   2200
he has found Oliver, his companion,
held him tight in his arms against his chest;
came back to the Archbishop, laid Oliver
down on a shield among the other dead.
The Archbishop absolved him, signed him with the Cross.   2205
And pity now and rage and grief increase;
and Roland says: "Oliver, dear companion,

you were the son of the great duke Renier,
who held the march of the vale of Runers.
Lord, for shattering lances, for breaking shields,   2210
for making men great with presumption weak with fright,
for giving life and counsel to good men,
for striking fear in that unbelieving race,
no warrior on earth surpasses you."

164

Roland the Count, when he sees his peers dead,   2215
and Oliver, whom he had good cause to love,
felt such grief and pity, he begins to weep;
and his face lost its color with what he felt:
a pain so great he cannot keep on standing,
he has no choice, falls fainting to the ground.   2220
Said the Archbishop: "Baron, what grief for you."

165

The Archbishop, when he saw Roland faint,
felt such pain then as he had never felt;
stretched out his hand and grasped the olifant.
At Rencesvals there is a running stream: 2225
he will go there and fetch some water for Roland;
and turns that way, with small steps, staggering;
he is too weak, he cannot go ahead,
he has no strength: all the blood he has lost.
In less time than a man takes to cross a little field   2230
that great heart fails, he falls forward, falls down;
and Turpin's death comes crushing down on him.

166

Roland the Count recovers from his faint,
gets to his feet, but stands with pain and grief;
looks down the valley, looks up the mountain, sees: 2235
on the green grass, beyond his companions,
that great and noble man down on the ground,
the Archbishop, whom God sent in His name;
who confesses his sins, lifts up his eyes,
holds up his hands joined together to heaven,   2240
and prays to God: grant him that Paradise.
Turpin is dead, King Charles' good warrior.
In great battles, in beautiful sermons
he was ever a champion against the pagans.
Now God grant Turpin's soul His holy blessing. AOI.   2245

167

Roland the Count sees the Archbishop down,
sees the bowels fallen out of his body,

and the brain boiling down from his forehead.
Turpin has crossed his hands upon his chest
beneath the collarbone, those fine white hands.
Roland speaks the lament, after the custom   2250
followed in his land: aloud, with all his heart:
"My noble lord, you great and well-born warrior,
I commend you today to the God of Glory,
whom none will ever serve with a sweeter will.
Since the Apostles no prophet the like of you[2]   2255
arose to keep the faith and draw men to it.
May your soul know no suffering or want,
and behold the gate open to Paradise."

168

Now Roland feels that death is very near.   2260
His brain comes spilling out through his two ears;
prays to God for his peers: let them be called;
and for himself, to the angel Gabriel;
took the olifant: there must be no reproach!
took Durendal his sword in his other hand,   2265
and farther than a crossbow's farthest shot
he walks toward Spain, into a fallow land,
and climbs a hill: there beneath two fine trees
stand four great blocks of stone, all are of marble;
and he fell back, to earth, on the green grass,   2270
has fainted there, for death is very near.

169

High are the hills, and high, high are the trees;
there stand four blocks of stone, gleaming of marble.
Count Roland falls fainting on the green grass,
and is watched, all this time, by a Saracen: 2275
who has feigned death and lies now with the others,
has smeared blood on his face and on his body;
and quickly now gets to his feet and runs—
a handsome man, strong, brave, and so crazed with pride
that he does something mad and dies for it: 2280
laid hands on Roland, and on the arms of Roland,
and cried: "Conquered! Charles's nephew conquered!
I'll carry this sword home to Arabia!"
As he draws it, the Count begins to come round.

170

Now Roland feels: *someone taking his sword!*   2285
opened his eyes, and had one word for him:
"I don't know you, you aren't one of ours";

---

2. Compare Deuteronomy 34.10, on the death of Moses: "And there arose not a prophet since in Israel like unto Moses, whom the Lord knew face to face."

grasps that olifant that he will never lose,
strikes on the helm beset with gems in gold,
shatters the steel, and the head, and the bones,   2290
sent his two eyes flying out of his head,
dumped him over stretched out at his feet dead;
and said: "You nobody! how could you dare
lay hands on me—rightly or wrongly: how?
Who'll hear of this and not call you a fool?   2295
Ah! the bell-mouth of the olifant is smashed,
the crystal and the gold fallen away."

171

Now Roland the Count feels: his sight is gone;
gets on his feet, draws on his final strength,
the color on his face lost now for good.   2300
Before him stands a rock; and on that dark rock
in rage and bitterness he strikes ten blows:
the steel blade grates, it will not break, it stands unmarked.
"Ah!" said the Count, "Blessed Mary, your help!
Ah Durendal, good sword, your unlucky day,   2305
for I am lost and cannot keep you in my care.
The battles I have won, fighting with you,
the mighty lands that holding you I conquered,
that Charles rules now, our King, whose beard is white!
Now you fall to another: it must not be
    a man who'd run before another man!   2310
For a long while a good vassal held you:
there'll never be the like in France's holy land."

172

Roland strikes down on that rock of Cerritania:
the steel blade grates, will not break, stands unmarked.
Now when he sees he can never break that sword,   2315
Roland speaks the lament, in his own presence:
"Ah Durendal, how beautiful and bright!
so full of light, all on fire in the sun!
King Charles was in the vales of Moriane
when God sent his angel and commanded him,   2320
from heaven, to give you to a captain count.
That great and noble King girded it on me.
And with this sword I won Anjou and Brittany,
I won Poitou, I won Le Maine for Charles,
and Normandy, that land where men are free,   2325
I won Provence and Aquitaine with this,
and Lombardy, and every field of Romagna,
I won Bavaria, and all of Flanders,
all of Poland, and Bulgaria, for Charles,
Constantinople, which pledged him loyalty,   2330
and Saxony, where he does as he wills;
and with this sword I won Scotland and Ireland,

and England, his chamber, his own domain—
the lands, the nations I conquered with this sword,
for Charles, who rules them now, whose beard is white!   2335
Now, for this sword, I am pained with grief and rage:
Let it not fall to pagans! Let me die first!
Our Father God, save France from that dishonor."

173

Roland the Count strikes down on a dark rock,
and the rock breaks, breaks more than I can tell,   2340
and the blade grates, but Durendal will not break,
the sword leaped up, rebounded toward the sky.
The Count, when he sees that sword will not be broken,
softly, in his own presence, speaks the lament:
"Ah Durendal, beautiful, and most sacred,   2345
the holy relics in this golden pommel!
Saint Peter's tooth and blood of Saint Basile,
a lock of hair of my lord Saint Denis,
and a fragment of blessed Mary's robe:
your power must not fall to the pagans,   2350
you must be served by Christian warriors.
May no coward ever come to hold you!
It was with you I conquered those great lands
that Charles has in his keeping, whose beard is white,
the Emperor's lands, that make him rich and strong."   2355

174

Now Roland feels: death coming over him,
death descending from his temples to his heart.
He came running underneath a pine tree
and there stretched out, face down, on the green grass,
lays beneath him his sword and the olifant.   2360
He turned his head toward the Saracen hosts,
and this is why: with all his heart he wants
King Charles the Great and all his men to say,
he died, that noble Count, a conqueror;
makes confession, beats his breast often, so feebly,   2365
offers his glove, for all his sins, to God. AOI.

175

Now Roland feels that his time has run out;
he lies on a steep hill, his face toward Spain;
and with one of his hands he beat his breast:
"Almighty God, *mea culpa* in thy sight,[3]   2370
forgive my sins, both the great and the small,

---

3. See Psalm 51.4: "Against thee, thee only, have I sinned, and done this evil in thy sight."

sins I committed from the hour I was born
until this day, in which I lie struck down."
And then he held his right glove out to God.
Angels descend from heaven and stand by him. AOI.   2375

176

Count Roland lay stretched out beneath a pine;
he turned his face toward the land of Spain,
began to remember many things now:
how many lands, brave man, he had conquered;
and he remembered: sweet France, the men of his line,   2380
remembered Charles, his lord, who fostered him:
cannot keep, remembering, from weeping, sighing;
but would not be unmindful of himself:
he confesses his sins, prays God for mercy:
"Loyal Father, you who never failed us,   2385
who resurrected Saint Lazarus from the dead,
and saved your servant Daniel from the lions:[4]
now save the soul of me from every peril
for the sins I committed while I still lived."
Then he held out his right glove to his Lord: 2390
Saint Gabriel took the glove from his hand.
He held his head bowed down upon his arm,
he is gone, his two hands joined, to his end.
Then God sent him his angel Cherubin;[5]
and Saint Michael, angel of the sea's Peril;   2395
and with these two there came Saint Gabriel:
they bear Count Roland's soul to Paradise.

* * *

4. See Daniel 6.12–13. For the raising of Lagaruss, see John 11.1–44.   5. The poet seems to have
regarded this as the name of a single angel.

MARIE DE FRANCE
twelfth century

The first woman writer in French (at least so far as we know), Marie de France created her work at a crucial time in the history of literature. In the twelfth century most of the major forms and themes that have shaped Western literature emerged in the vernacular languages of Europe. Primary among them were the works we now call romances, novelistic narratives that dealt with adventure and—above all—love. The most familiar of these narratives are the stories of King Arthur and his knights, tales as popular in the Middle Ages as today. The Arthurian legends were part of a vast mythology developed by the Celts of western Europe, peoples who were driven from their lands by the Germanic invaders of the fourth and fifth centuries and took refuge on the Atlantic fringe of the Continent in what are now Ireland, Wales, and Brittany. Yet if they were conquered as a people, the Celts triumphed through their stories. Much of medieval literature reveals the influence of Celtic mythology.

Less popular than the long Arthurian narratives but more finely crafted as works of art were the short narratives of love, adventure, and the supernatural, also of Celtic origin, known as *lais* or, in English, lays. As a form of literature, the lay first appears in a collection composed about 1165 by a woman who identifies herself only as "Marie." In another work she tells us that she is "from France," and ever since the Renaissance she has been given the designation "Marie de France." From the evidence of her writing, we know that she was a noblewoman; that she could read French, English, and Latin; and that she was familiar with a royal household, probably that of Henry II, king of England (reigned 1154–89). She may well have been a nun or even an abbess, since many noble daughters were placed in the elegant aristocratic convents of Europe. All of her work, including the twelve lays that survive, is written in octosyllabic verse in Anglo-Norman, a French dialect spoken by the nobility of postconquest England. The sources for her lays, she tells us, were stories that she heard, and while she provides us with several Breton terms—like the word *laüstic* for nightingale—we cannot know if she heard these stories in English, French, or Breton.

The two lays presented here deal with a topic that is central to the collection as a whole. These are stories in which love serves as an alternative—in one case successfully, in the other not—to an uncaring or unjust society. In both stories Marie combines an acute awareness of contemporary social conditions with sympathy for individuals who seek personal fulfillment. In the lay that bears his name, Lanval is a young foreigner who has come to the Arthurian court to seek his fortune. He is the son of a king, but his "inheritance"—by which Marie means his ancestral domain—is far away. The implication is that Lanval, like many noble young men in twelfth-century France and England, was a younger son excluded from inheriting the family land under the recently established system of primogeniture, by which only the eldest son inherited. Thus when at the beginning of the story Arthur hands out lands and wives to his knights but neglects the deserving Lanval, he is dooming Lanval to a life of continued obscurity and lonely service. Rescue comes to him in the form of the fairy lover, who is not merely beautiful and loving but—as Marie is careful to stress—rich. Now that Lanval can comport himself with the confidence and generosity that befits a nobleman, he becomes attractive to the queen (presumably Guinevere, although she is not named). And in rejecting her advances he asserts not simply the superior beauty of his lady but the superiority of her handmaiden, making it clear that he is attached to a court that surpasses in its grandeur that of Arthur himself. This is why Arthur so quickly supports his queen in her false accusation, and why Lanval is accused not just of a social gaffe but of felony and treason. For as Arthur's barons say, Lanval ought to honor his lord at all times, while he is acting (rightly, as it turns out) as if he is obligated to a different sovereign entirely. Yet the power of Marie's story derives from the fact that, despite this emphasis on social and material benefits, Lanval is primarily distressed because he has lost not the fairy queen's financial support but her love. And when the two pairs of damsels appear, he remains true to her by refusing to claim either of them as proof that his rash words to the queen were true. Perhaps because he passes this test his lover herself then appears and takes him away with her to Avalon, a world in which the petty jealousies of the Arthurian court can be forgotten. Here love seems to conquer all, but its triumph is possible only in the fantasy world of fiction.

Laüstic, on the other hand, is a story of unfulfilled love. In this case the social reality to which the story is addressed is the aristocratic custom of arranged marriages. In *Lanval* Arthur gives away wives, yet there is no indication that the women involved have any say in their marital fate. Yet at the same time as the European nobility was treating marriage as a financial and political matter, the church was teaching that marriage was above all a matter of free consent, that what made two people husband and wife was their agreement to enter into marriage with each other. Marie's lays are filled with unhappy wives—unhappy not only because they were forced into marriages against their will but because they know they deserve better (indeed, perhaps we should understand Guinevere's misbehavior in *Lanval* as caused by such knowledge). The young wife in *Laüstic* can only dream of escape as she gazes out her confining room at her would-be lover. The nightingale that she invokes to quiet her jealous husband becomes a symbol of this yearning to escape, and when her husband brutally kills it and throws its bleeding corpse at her, we can understand that the stain it leaves on the breast of her tunic is the outward sign of a broken heart. Yet this is not the end, for the golden casket in which her lover entombs the nightingale serves to celebrate a love that may not have found earthly fulfillment but has achieved another, higher permanence. In its exquisite concision, *Laüstic* is itself a literary version of that golden casket, a verbal equivalent to the jeweled reliquaries in which medieval people encased the bodies of their saints.

Lanval[1]

Just as it happened, I shall relate to you the story of another lay, which tells of a very noble young man whose name in Breton is Lanval.

Arthur, the worthy and courtly king, was at Carlisle on account of the Scots and the Picts who were ravaging the country, penetrating into the land of Logres[2] and frequently laying it waste.

The king was there during the summer, at Pentecost,[3] and he gave many rich gifts to counts and barons and to those of the Round Table: there was no such company in the whole world. He apportioned wives and lands to all, save to one who had served him: this was Lanval, whom he did not remember, and for whom no one put in a good word. Because of his valor, generosity, beauty and prowess, many were envious of him. There were those who pretended to hold him in esteem, but who would not have uttered a single regret if misfortune had befallen him. He was the son of a king of noble birth, but far from his inheritance, and although he belonged to Arthur's household he had spent all his wealth, for the king gave him nothing and Lanval asked for nothing. Now he was in a plight, very sad and forlorn. Lords, do not be surprised: a stranger bereft of advice can be very downcast in another land when he does not know where to seek help.

This knight whose tale I am telling you had served the king well. One day he mounted his horse and went to take his ease. He left the town and came alone to a meadow, dismounting by a stream; but there his horse trembled violently, so he loosened its saddlegirth and left it, allowing it to enter the meadow to roll over on its back. He folded his cloak, which he placed beneath his head, very disconsolate because of his troubles, and nothing could please him. Lying thus, he looked downriver and saw two damsels coming, more beautiful than any he had ever seen: they were richly dressed in closely fitting tunics of dark purple and their faces were very beautiful. The older one carried dishes of gold, well and finely made—I will not fail to tell you the truth—and the other carried a towel. They went straight to

1. Translated by Glyn S. Burgess and Keith Busby.   2. The Arthurian name for England. Carlisle is a city near the Scottish border.   3. A feast day celebrated on the seventh Sunday after Easter.

where the knight lay and Lanval, who was very well-mannered, stood up to meet them. They first greeted him and then delivered their message: "Sir Lanval, my damsel, who is very worthy, wise and fair, has sent us for you. Come with us, for we will conduct you safely. Look, her tent is near." The knight went with them, disregarding his horse which was grazing before him in the meadow. They led him to the tent, which was so beautiful and well-appointed that neither Queen Semiramis at the height of her wealth, power and knowledge, nor the Emperor Octavian,[4] could have afforded even the right-hand side of it. There was a golden eagle placed on the top, the value of which I cannot tell, nor of the ropes or the poles which supported the walls of the tent. There is no king under the sun who could afford it, however much he might give. Inside this tent was the maiden who surpassed in beauty the lily and the new rose when it appears in summer. She lay on a very beautiful bed—the coverlets cost as much as a castle— clad only in her shift. Her body was well formed and handsome, and in order to protect herself from the heat of the sun, she had cast about her a costly mantle of white ermine covered with Alexandrian purple. Her side, though, was uncovered, as well as her face, neck and breast; she was whiter than the hawthorn blossom.

The maiden called the knight, who came forward and sat before the bed. "Lanval," she said, "fair friend, for you I came from my country. I have come far in search of you and if you are worthy and courtly, no emperor, count or king will have felt as much joy or happiness as you, for I love you above all else." He looked at her and saw that she was beautiful. Love's spark pricked him so that his heart was set alight, and he replied to her in seemly manner: "Fair lady, if it were to please you to grant me the joy of wanting to love me, you could ask nothing that I would not do as best I could, be it foolish or wise. I shall do as you bid and abandon all others for you. I never want to leave you and this is what I most desire." When the girl heard these words from the man who loved her so, she granted him her love and her body. Now Lanval was on the right path! She gave him a boon, that henceforth he could wish for nothing which he would not have, and however generously he gave or spent, she would still find enough for him. Lanval was very well lodged, for the more he spent, the more gold and silver he would have. "Beloved," she said, "I admonish, order, and beg you not to reveal this secret to anyone! I shall tell you the long and the short of it: you would lose me forever if this love were to become known. You would never be able to see me or possess me." He replied that he would do what she commanded. He lay down beside her on the bed: now Lanval was well lodged. That afternoon he remained with her until evening and would have done so longer had he been able and had his love allowed him. "Beloved," she said, "arise! You can stay no longer. Go from here and I shall remain, but I shall tell you one thing: whenever you wish to speak with me, you will not be able to think of a place where a man may enjoy his love without reproach or wickedness, that I shall not be there with you to do your bidding. No man save you will see me or hear my voice." When he heard this, Lanval was well pleased and, kissing her, he arose. The damsels who had led him to the tent dressed him

---

4. Roman emperor Caesar Augustus (63 B.C.E.–14 C.E.). Semiramis was a legendary queen of Assyria.

in rich garments, and in his new clothes there was no more handsome young man on earth. He was neither foolish nor ill-mannered. The damsels gave him water to wash his hands and a towel to dry them and then brought him food. He took his supper, which was not to be disdained, with his beloved. He was very courteously served and dined joyfully. There was one dish in abundance that pleased the knight particularly, for he often kissed his beloved and embraced her closely.

When they had risen from table, his horse was brought to him, well saddled. Lanval was richly served there. He took his leave, mounted, and went towards the city, often looking behind him, for he was greatly disturbed, thinking of his adventure and uneasy in his heart. He was at a loss to know what to think, for he could not believe it was true. When he came to his lodgings, he found his men finely dressed. That night he offered lavish hospitality but no one knew how this came to be. There was no knight in the town in sore need of shelter whom he did not summon and serve richly and well. Lanval gave costly gifts, Lanval freed prisoners, Lanval clothed the jongleurs,[5] Lanval performed many honorable acts. There was no one, stranger or friend, to whom he would not have given gifts. He experienced great joy and pleasure, for day or night he could see his beloved often and she was entirely at his command.

In the same year, I believe, after St John's day,[6] as many as thirty knights had gone to relax in a garden beneath the tower where the queen was staying. Gawain was with them and his cousin, the fair Ywain. Gawain, the noble and the worthy, who endeared himself to all, said: "In God's name, lords, we treat our companion Lanval ill, for he is so generous and courtly, and his father is a rich king, yet we have not brought him with us." So they returned, went to his lodgings and persuaded him to come with them.

The queen, in the company of three ladies, was reclining by a window cut out of the stone when she caught sight of the king's household and recognized Lanval. She called one of her ladies to summon her most elegant and beautiful damsels to relax with her in the garden where the others were. She took more than thirty with her, and they went down the steps where the knights, glad of their coming, came to meet them. They took the girls by the hand and the conversation was not uncourtly. Lanval withdrew to one side, far from the others, for he was impatient to hold his beloved, to kiss, embrace and touch her. He cared little for other people's joy when he could not have his own pleasure. When the queen saw the knight alone, she approached him straightaway. Sitting down beside him, she spoke to him and opened her heart. "Lanval, I have honored, cherished and loved you much. You may have all my love: just tell me what you desire! I grant you my love and you should be glad to have me." "Lady," he said, "leave me be! I have no desire to love you, for I have long served the king and do not want to betray my faith. Neither you nor your love will ever lead me to wrong my lord!" The queen became angry and distressed, and spoke unwisely: "Lanval," she said, "I well believe that you do not like this kind of pleasure. I have been told often enough that you have no desire for women. You have well-trained young men and enjoy yourself with them. Base coward, wicked recreant, my lord is extremely unfortunate to have suffered you near him. I think he may have lost his salvation because of it!"

When he heard her, he was distressed, but not slow to reply. He said something in spite that he was often to regret. "Lady, I am not skilled in the profession you mention, but I love and am loved by a lady who should be prized above all others I know. And I will tell you one thing: you can be sure that one of her servants, even the very poorest girl, is worth more than you, my lady the Queen, in body, face and beauty, wisdom and goodness." Thereupon the queen left and went in tears to her chamber, very distressed and angry that he had humiliated her in this way. She took to her bed ill and said that she would never again get up, unless the king saw that justice was done her in respect of her complaint.

The king had returned from the woods after an extremely happy day. He entered the queen's apartments and when she saw him, she complained aloud, fell at his feet, cried for mercy and said that Lanval had shamed her. He had requested her love and because she had refused him, had insulted and deeply humiliated her. He had boasted of a beloved who was so well-bred, noble, and proud that her chambermaid, the poorest servant she had, was worthier than the queen. The king grew very angry and swore an oath that, if Lanval could not defend himself in court, he would have him burned or hanged. The king left the room, summoned three of his barons and sent them for Lanval, who was suffering great pain. He had returned to his lodgings, well aware of having lost his beloved by revealing their love. Alone in his chamber, distraught and anguished, he called his beloved repeatedly, but to no avail. He lamented and sighed, fainting from time to time; a hundred times he cried to her to have mercy, to come and speak with her beloved. He cursed his heart and his mouth and it was a wonder he did not kill himself. His cries and moans were not loud enough nor his agitation and torment such that she would have mercy on him, or even permit him to see her. Alas, what will he do?

The king's men arrived and told Lanval to go to court without delay: the king had summoned him through them, for the queen had accused him. Lanval went sorrowfully and would have been happy for them to kill him. He came before the king, sad, subdued and silent, betraying his great sorrow. The king said to him angrily: "Vassal, you have wronged me greatly! You were extremely ill-advised to shame and vilify me, and to slander the queen. You boasted out of folly, for your beloved must be very noble for her handmaiden to be more beautiful and more worthy than the queen."

Lanval denied point by point having offended and shamed his lord, and maintained that he had not sought the queen's love, but he acknowledged the truth of his words about the love of which he had boasted. He now regretted this, for as a result he had lost her. He told them he would do whatever the court decreed in this matter, but the king was very angry and sent for all his men to tell him exactly what he should do, so that his action would not be unfavorably interpreted. Whether they liked it or not, they obeyed his command and assembled to make a judgment, deciding that a day should be fixed for the trial, but that Lanval should provide his lord with pledges that he would await his judgment and return later to his presence. Then the court would be larger, for at that moment only the king's household itself was present. The barons returned to the king and explained their reasoning. The king asked for pledges, but Lanval was alone and forlorn, having no relation or friend there. Then Gawain approached and offered to stand bail, and all his companions did likewise. The king said to them: "I entrust him to you on surety of all that you hold from me, lands and fiefs, each man separately." When this had been pledged, there was no more to be done, and Lanval returned to his lodging with the knights escorting him. They chastised him and urged him strongly not to be so sorrowful, and cursed such foolish love. They went to see him every day, as they wished to know whether he was drinking and eating properly, being very much afraid that he might harm himself.

On the appointed day the barons assembled. The king and queen were there and the guarantors brought Lanval to court. They were all very sad on his account and I think there were a hundred who would have done all in their power to have him released without a trial because he had been wrongly accused. The king demanded the verdict according to the charge and the rebuttal, and now everything lay in the hands of the barons. They considered their judgment, very troubled and concerned on account of this noble man from abroad, who was in such a plight in their midst. Some of them wanted to harm him in conformity with their lord's will. Thus spoke the count of Cornwall: "There shall be no default on our part. Like it or not, right must prevail. The king accused his vassal, whom I heard you call Lanval, of a felony and charged him with a crime, about a love he boasted of which angered my lady. Only the king is accusing him, so by the faith I owe you, there ought, to tell the truth, to be no case to answer, were it not that one should honor one's lord in all things. An oath will bind Lanval and the king will put the matter in our hands. If he can provide proof and his beloved comes forward, and if what he said to incur the queen's displeasure is true, then he will be pardoned, since he did not say it to spite her. And if he cannot furnish proof, then we must inform him that he will lose the king's service and that the king must banish him." They sent word to the knight and informed him that he should send for his beloved to defend and protect him. He told them that this was not possible and that he would receive no help from her. The messengers returned to the judges, expecting no help to be forthcoming for Lanval. The king pressed them hard because the queen was waiting for them.

When they were about to give their verdict, they saw two maidens approaching on two fine ambling palfreys. They were extremely comely and dressed only in purple taffeta, next to their bare skin; the knights were pleased to see them. Gawain and three other knights went to Lanval, told him about this, and pointed the two maidens out to him. Gawain was very glad and strongly urged Lanval to tell him if this was his beloved, but he told them that he did not know who they were, whence they came or where they were going. The maidens continued to approach, still on horseback, and then dismounted before the dais where King Arthur was seated. They were of great beauty and spoke in courtly fashion: "King, make your chambers available and hang them with silken curtains so that my lady may stay here, for she wishes to lodge with you." This he granted them willingly and summoned two knights who led them to the upper chambers. For the moment they said no more.

The king asked his barons for the judgment and the responses, and said that they had greatly angered him by the long delay. "Lord," they said, "we are deliberating, but because of the ladies we saw, we have not reached a verdict. Let us continue with the trial." So they assembled in some anxiety, and there was a good deal of commotion and contention.

While they were in this troubled state, they saw two finely accoutred maidens coming along the street, dressed in garments of Phrygian[7] silk and riding on Spanish mules. The vassals were glad of this and they said to each other that Lanval, the worthy and brave, was now saved. Ywain went up to him with his companions, and said: "Lord, rejoice! For the love of God, speak to us! Two damsels are approaching, very comely and beautiful. It is surely your beloved." Lanval quickly replied that he did not recognize them, nor did he know or love them. When they had arrived, they dismounted before the king and many praised them highly for their bodies, faces, and complexions. They were both more worthy than the queen had ever been. The older of the two, who was courtly and wise, delivered her message fittingly: "King, place your chambers at our disposal for the purpose of lodging my lady. She is coming here to speak with you." He ordered them to be taken to the others who had arrived earlier. They paid no heed to their mules, and, as soon as they had left the king, he summoned all his barons so that they might deliver their verdict. This had taken up too much of the day and the queen, who had been waiting for them for such a long time, was getting angry.

Just as they were about to give their verdict, a maiden on horseback entered the town. There was none more beautiful in the whole world. She was riding a white palfrey which carried her well and gently; its neck and head were well-formed and there was no finer animal on earth. The palfrey was richly equipped, for no count or king on earth could have paid for it, save by selling or pledging his lands. The lady was dressed in a white tunic and shift, laced left and right so as to reveal her sides. Her body was comely, her lips low, her neck whiter than snow on a branch; her eyes were bright and her face white, her mouth fair and her nose well-placed; her eyebrows were brown and her brow fair, and her hair curly and rather blond. A golden thread does not shine as brightly as the rays reflected in the light from her hair. Her cloak was of dark silk and she had wrapped its skirts about her. She held a sparrowhawk on her wrist and behind her there followed a dog. There was no one in the town, humble or powerful, old or young, who did not watch her arrival, and no one jested about her beauty. She approached slowly and the judges who saw her thought it was a great wonder. No one who had looked at her could have failed to be inspired with real joy. Those who loved the knight went and told him about the maiden who was coming and who, please God, would deliver him. "Lord and friend, here comes a lady whose hair is neither tawny nor brown. She is the most beautiful of all women in the world." Lanval heard this and raised his head, for he knew her well, and sighed. His blood rushed to his face and he was quick to speak: "In faith," he said, "it is my beloved! If she shows me no mercy, I hardly care if anyone should kill me, for my cure is in seeing her." The lady entered the palace, where no one so

7. Phrygia is in modern Turkey, but here designates more generally the East.

beautiful had ever before been seen. She dismounted before the king, and in the sight of all, let her cloak fall so that they could see her better. The king, who was well-mannered, rose to meet her, and all the others honored her and offered themselves as her servants. When they had looked at her and praised her beauty greatly, she spoke thus, for she had no wish to remain: "King, I have loved one of your vassals, Lanval, whom you see there. Because of what he said, he was accused in your court, and I do not wish him to come to any harm. You should know that the queen was wrong, as he never sought her love. As regards the boast he made, if he can be acquitted by me, let your barons release him!" The king granted that it should be as the judges recommended, in accordance with justice. There was not one who did not consider that Lanval had successfully defended himself, and so he was freed by their decision. The maiden, who had many servants, then left, for the king could not retain her. Outside the hall there was a large block of dark marble on to which heavily armed men climbed when they left the king's court. Lanval mounted it and when the maiden came through the door, he leapt in a single bound on to the palfrey behind her. He went with her to Avalon,[8] so the Bretons tell us, to a very beautiful island. Thither the young man was borne and no one has heard any more about him, nor can I relate any more.

Laüstic[1]

I shall relate an adventure to you from which the Bretons composed a lay. *Laüstic* is its name, I believe, and that is what the Bretons call it in their land. In French the title is *Rossignol*, and Nightingale is the correct English word.

In the region of St Malo[2] was a famous town and two knights dwelt there, each with a fortified house. Because of the fine qualities of the two men the town acquired a good reputation. One of the knights had taken a wise, courtly and elegant wife who conducted herself, as custom dictated, with admirable propriety. The other knight was a young man who was well known amongst his peers for his prowess and great valor. He performed honorable deeds gladly and attended many tournaments, spending freely and giving generously whatever he had. He loved his neighbor's wife and so persistently did he request her love, so frequent were his entreaties and so many qualities did he possess that she loved him above all things, both for the good she had heard about him and because he lived close by. They loved each other prudently and well, concealing their love carefully to ensure that they were not seen, disturbed or suspected. This they could do because their dwellings were adjoining. Their houses, halls and keeps were close by each other and there was no barrier or division, apart from a high wall of dark-hued stone. When she stood at her bedroom window, the lady could talk to her beloved in the other house and he to her, and they could

8. The Celtic isle of the blessed.   1. Translated by Glyn S. Burgess and Keith Busby.   2. A town in Brittany.

toss gifts to each other. There was scarcely anything to displease them and they were both very content except for the fact that they could not meet and take their pleasure with each other, for the lady was closely guarded when her husband was in the region. But they were so resourceful that day or night they managed to speak to each other and no one could prevent their coming to the window and seeing each other there. For a long time they loved each other, until one summer when the copses and meadows were green and the gardens in full bloom. On the flower-tops the birds sang joyfully and sweetly. If love is on anyone's mind, no wonder he turns his attention towards it. I shall tell you the truth about the knight. Both he and the lady made the greatest possible effort with their words and with their eyes. At night, when the moon was shining and her husband was asleep, she often rose from beside him and put on her mantle. Knowing her beloved would be doing the same, she would go and stand at the window and stay awake most of the night. They took delight in seeing each other, since they were denied anything more. But so frequently did she stand there and so frequently leave her bed that her husband became angry and asked her repeatedly why she got up and where she went. "Lord," replied the lady, "anyone who does not hear the song of the nightingale knows none of the joys of this world. This is why I come and stand here. So sweet is the song I hear by night that it brings me great pleasure. I take such delight in it and desire it so much that I can get no sleep at all." When the lord heard what she said, he gave a spiteful, angry laugh and devised a plan to ensnare the nightingale. Every single servant in his household constructed some trap, net or snare and then arranged them throughout the garden. There was no hazel tree or chestnut tree on which they did not place a snare or bird-lime, until they had captured and retained it. When they had taken the nightingale, it was handed over, still alive, to the lord, who was overjoyed to hold it in his hands. He entered the lady's chamber. "Lady," he said, "where are you? Come forward and speak to us. With bird-lime I have trapped the nightingale which has kept you awake so much. Now you can sleep in peace, for it will never awaken you again." When the lady heard him she was grief-stricken and distressed. She asked her husband for the bird, but he killed it out of spite, breaking its neck wickedly with his two hands. He threw the body at the lady, so that the front of her tunic was bespattered with blood, just on her breast. Thereupon he left the chamber. The lady took the tiny corpse, wept profusely and cursed those who had betrayed the nightingale by constructing the traps and snares, for they had taken so much joy from her. "Alas," she said, "misfortune is upon me. Never again can I get up at night or go to stand at the window where I used to see my beloved. I know one thing for certain. He will think I am faint-hearted, so I must take action. I shall send him the nightingale and let him know what has happened." She wrapped the little bird in a piece of samite, embroidered in gold and covered in designs. She called one of her servants, entrusted him with her message and sent him to her beloved. He went to the knight, greeted him on behalf of his lady, related the whole message to him and presented him with the nightingale. When the messenger had finished speaking, the knight, who had listened attentively, was distressed by what had happened. But he was not uncourtly or tardy. He had a small vessel prepared, not of iron or steel, but of pure gold with fine stones, very precious and valuable. On it he carefully placed a lid and put the nightingale in it. Then he had the casket sealed and carried it with him at all times.

This adventure was related and could not long be concealed. The Bretons composed a lay about it which is called *Laüstic*.

DANTE ALIGHIERI
1265–1321

Called by its author a comedy, and named by later ages—in recognition of both its subject matter and its achievement—*The Divine Comedy*, Dante's poem is one of the indisputably great works of world literature. It combines into a coherent whole a wide range of disparate literary elements. It is organized with the precision and harmony of the great philosophical systems and the vast Gothic cathedrals of its time; and yet it attends with extraordinary care to the tiniest detail. It celebrates with unqualified enthusiasm and at times even dogmatism the central doctrines of medieval Christianity; and yet it remains persistently alert to the sympathies of the human heart. It is epic in its scope and its central themes; and yet it sings with an exquisite lyricism. It is a poem that declares everywhere its commitment to the culture of medieval Christendom; and yet it celebrates the achievements of the classical world and extends its admiration even to Islamic philosophy. It is one of the most deeply serious works in world literature, concerned with nothing less than the relation of the creator to his creatures and the ultimate destiny of the human soul; and yet it has room for not just grim irony but scenes of generous good humor and even vulgar horseplay. It does not shy away from episodes that the German writer Goethe accurately called "repulsive and often disgusting"; and yet it also includes moments of sublime beauty that have been rarely matched and never surpassed. Perhaps above all, it showed that a great work of literary art, equal to the great works of antiquity, can be created in the vernacular, providing the declaration of independence that made possible the various national traditions of post-medieval literature. In this sense *The Divine Comedy* is the foundational text for the European literary imagination.

Dante was born in Florence in the spring of 1265. In his early years he wrote some ninety lyrics, thirty-one of which he collected and provided with a narrative commentary in a work he called the *Vita nuova* or *New Life* (completed between 1292 and 1295). This work recounted his love for a young woman he named Beatrice ("blessed" in Italian), who died in 1290. More than a love story, it described how Beatrice led him from a merely human love to something transcendental, almost divine. Dante realized that this transformation also required a new form of poetry, and it is from the *New Life* that *The Divine Comedy* was to spring as both a fulfillment and an alternative.

Meanwhile, however, political conflicts had decisively altered Dante's life. The Florentine political class, like that of much of northern Italy, was divided into two factions. The Guelphs, generally members of the urban elite and artisans, supported Florentine independence and resisted the claims of the Holy Roman empire to sovereignty over the city or indeed any part of Italy, often by soliciting the support of the military power of the papacy. The Ghibellines, on the other hand, were drawn from the ancient feudal aristocracy and saw the empire as a

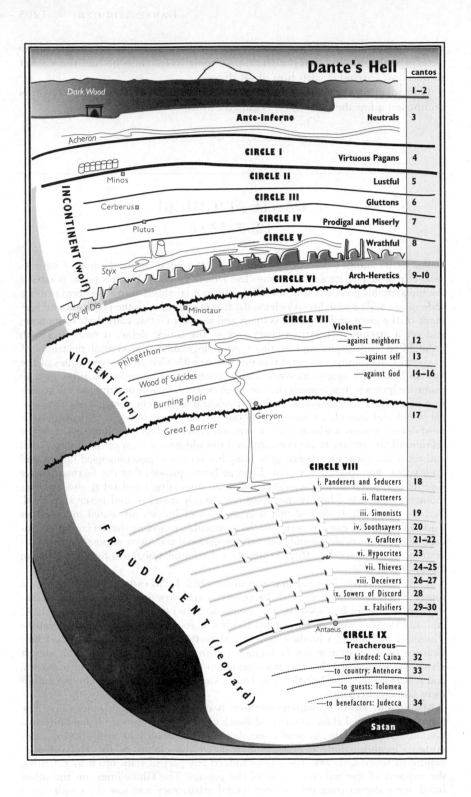

Dante's Hell

	cantos
Dark Wood	1–2
Ante-Inferno — Neutrals	3
Acheron	
CIRCLE I — Virtuous Pagans	4
Minos	
CIRCLE II — Lustful	5
CIRCLE III — Gluttons	6
Cerberus	
CIRCLE IV — Prodigal and Miserly	7
Plutus	
CIRCLE V — Wrathful	8
Styx	
CIRCLE VI — Arch-Heretics	9–10
City of Dis	
Minotaur	
CIRCLE VII Violent—	
—against neighbors	12
Phlegethon	
—against self	13
Wood of Suicides	
—against God	14–16
Burning Plain	
Geryon	
Great Barrier	17
CIRCLE VIII	
i. Panderers and Seducers	18
ii. flatterers	
iii. Simonists	19
iv. Soothsayers	20
v. Grafters	21–22
vi. Hypocrites	23
vii. Thieves	24–25
viii. Deceivers	26–27
ix. Sowers of Discord	28
x. Falsifiers	29–30
Antaeus	
CIRCLE IX Treacherous—	
—to kindred: Caina	32
—to country: Antenora	33
—to guests: Tolomea	
—to benefactors: Judecca	34
Satan	

INCONTINENT (wolf)

VIOLENT (lion)

FRAUDULENT (leopard)

means of furthering their own interests. After a series of bitter struggles, the Florentine Guelphs—of which Dante was a member—were triumphant. Around 1300, however, the Guelphs themselves broke into two parties, the Blacks and the Whites, and civil strife was renewed. The Whites, with Dante as a member, became associated with the Ghibellines in their resistance to the power of the pope. In 1301, while Dante was on a diplomatic mission for the city, the Blacks staged a coup with the help of Pope Boniface VII and his ally, the Frenchman Charles of Anjou. The next year Dante was condemned to exile, and he never returned to Florence. This experience of exile is central to *The Divine Comedy*, which on the most literal level recounts the journey of a lost traveler back to his ultimate homeland, Heaven. Also central is Dante's outrage at the internecine strife that tore northern Italy apart throughout his lifetime. Soon he came to believe that only the Holy Roman emperor could bring order out of chaos, and he condemned the interference of the church, and especially the pope, in political affairs, just as he condemned the Ghibellines' misuse of the empire's prestige for their own, self-seeking purposes. Dante's politics in *The Divine Comedy* are also religious and prophetic: he is concerned with restoring the conditions in which Christ first came—when Caesar Augustus presided over the "Roman peace" or *pax Romana*—so that He can come again and usher in the Final Judgment. Thus for Dante the Roman empire is divinely ordained: it first provided the earthly unity and order appropriate to the birth of Christ, and only when it is restored will His second coming be possible.

As a sign of the availability of the divine, this unity and order are everywhere present in Dante's poem. The three parts or canticles—the *Inferno, Purgatorio,* and *Paradiso*—are of equal length. Each of the latter two has thirty-three cantos; the first, the *Inferno*, has thirty-four, but the first canto is a prologue to the whole. This threefold pattern serves to embody the Trinity within the very structure of the poem, as does the verse form. Dante created a verse known as *terza rima*, which rhymes in the Italian original according to the scheme *aba bcb cdc* and so on. The lines thus form groups of three (known in Italian as *terzine*, or tercets) interlocked by a repeated rhyme word—a verbal equivalent to the three-in-one of the Trinity. Moreover, because each line contains eleven syllables, the total number of syllables in each tercet is thirty-three, the same as the number of cantos in each canticle (again, if we take *Inferno* 1 as a prologue). Each canticle even ends with the same word, *stelle* (stars), objects that are for Dante the visible signs of God's providential oversight. Nine, the square of three, figures centrally in the interior structure of each canticle. In Hell, the lost souls are arranged in three main groups and occupy nine circles; Purgatory is divided into an Ante-Purgatory, seven terraces, and the Earthly Paradise, for a total of nine locations; and Heaven consists of nine embedded spheres beyond which lies the infinite Empyrean of the Trinity.

In addition to these structures, the poem is organized according to an ethical pattern. For Dante, as for medieval philosophy generally, the natural inclination of every human being is love, a movement toward something outside the self. The natural and proper object of love is God, either directly or as mediated through the created world. Sin occurs when love is immoderately directed to the wrong object, when the creature (including the self) is loved not *for* but *instead of* the creator. In Hell, perverse love is represented in three forms, as incontinence, violence, and fraudulence. In Purgatory, it is also represented in three forms, as misdirected (pride, envy, and wrath), as defective (sloth), and as excessive (avarice, gluttony, and lust). In Paradise, the blessed are distinguished by the extent to which they enjoy the vision of God, and are again divided into three categories: those whose vision is limited by incomplete love, those who have fulfilled the four cardinal virtues (wisdom, fortitude, justice, and temperance), and finally those—like the angels—whose love comes nearest to perfection. Finally, Dante's geography is equally symmetrical.

The globe is divided into a northern and a southern hemisphere, but only the northern is inhabited. Its central point is Jerusalem, while to the east lies the Ganges and to the west the Strait of Gibraltar. Hell is a huge funnel extending into the center of the Earth that was created when Lucifer fell from Heaven. The earth displaced by his fall rose into the southern hemisphere—which had previously been covered entirely with water—and formed Mount Purgatory. This mountain, organized into its three parts as described above, has at its top the Earthly Paradise, or Eden, the original home of the human race. After descending into Hell, climbing up through the Earth, and then mounting to the Earthly Paradise, Dante is transported through the nine spheres described by medieval astronomy—those of the moon, Mercury, Venus, the sun, Mars, Jupiter, Saturn, the fixed stars, and the *primum mobile*, or outermost sphere, which moves the others—until he reaches the Empyrean, which exists beyond time and space. This final vision is presented in our selection from the *Paradiso.*

There is, finally, one other organizing principle that governs the form of the poem as a whole. When Dante is told that he is to journey through Hell, Purgatory, and Paradise, he protests that he is not worthy by comparing himself to two previous otherworldly travelers: "I am not Aeneas, I am not Paul" (*Inferno* 2.32). Aeneas visits the underworld in book 6 of Virgil's *Aeneid,* and Virgil plays a large role as both a literary influence and a character in Dante's poem. The reference to Paul is to a passage in 2 Corinthians 12.2: "I knew a man in Christ above fourteen years ago (whether in the body, I cannot tell; whether out of the body, I cannot tell: God knoweth;) such a one caught up to the third heaven." Medieval readers understood Paul to be talking about himself, but their problem was to understand what he meant by the third heaven, since there is presumably only one kingdom of God. The solution was provided by Augustine in one of his commentaries on Genesis, in which he argued that the three Pauline "heavens" were really metaphors for three ways in which human beings can know. These three are, in ascending order of clarity, "corporeal vision," or knowledge by means of the senses; "spiritual" or "imaginative vision," or knowledge through images that have corporeal shape without corporeal substance, as in dreams; and finally "intellectual vision," which is the direct knowledge of God and other realities, such as love, that have neither corporeal shape nor corporeal substance. God can be known in all three ways, which Augustine illustrated by passages from the Bible. He is known corporeally by Moses and the burning bush (Exodus 3–4); spiritually or imaginatively in the symbolic images of the Book of Revelation; and intellectually by Paul's vision, which he himself describes in 1 Corinthians 13.12: "For now we see through a glass, darkly but then face to face: now I know in part; but then shall I know even as also I am known."

The important point for us is that the three canticles of *The Divine Comedy* are each constructed according to one of these modes of vision. The *Purgatorio,* for example, is a place of images that have corporeal shape but not corporeal substance. In *Purgatorio* 2 we have a vivid illustration of this in a scene that appears in both Homer's and Virgil's underworlds: Dante tries three times to embrace his old friend Casella and three times he fails. With the form of a human being but not the substance, Casella is not merely *seen* by the imagination; he *exists* as an image rather than a thing. He is dematerialized, which shows that he is on his way up to Paradise. For in the *Paradiso* we find that its inhabitants are neither bodies nor images but simply lights. Furthermore, Dante himself, as he ascends the paradisal ladder, becomes "enlightened" or "illuminated." But because he is still in this life rather than a pure spirit this happens to him not literally but metaphorically, as he is instructed by various people in the nature of ultimate truth. This is the reason why the *Paradiso* is so didactic, with characters talking little about themselves and instead explaining what are to us often abstruse points of theological or scholastic teaching. In the *Paradiso* Dante is "enlightened" or "illuminated" by this teaching.

So what do we find in the *Inferno*? Not only are the inhabitants of Hell known corporeally but they *are* corporeal, and indeed become all the more so as Dante descends deeper into the pit. At the beginning of the journey, while Dante is in the upper levels, the characters flit about like the shades we expect them to be (as in canto 5), but very soon they become more and more substantial, so that—for example—Virgil and Dante can actually touch them, as in canto 8, where Virgil hurls Filippo Argenti back into the mud. Appropriately, the most corporeal place in Hell is the bottom circle, which is the most materialistic place in the universe. Dante calls it "the center / of the universe, where all weights must converge" (*Inferno* 32.73–74), because it is furthest from the pure spirituality and immateriality of Paradise (the Empyrean). At the bottom of Hell we find the heaviest thing in the universe, Satan: although originally Lucifer, the Angel of Light, he is now the being with the least amount of spirit, a speechless creature from whose mouths—he has three heads, an infernal parody of the Trinity, to prove that God is present even here in the pit of Hell—flows a bloody drool, what Dante calls in Italian *bava*, a word that refers to infantile slaver.

If the least sinful people are spun round with wind, then, the worst are frozen into ice and utterly immobile. This is Dante's way of showing us that the perfect order of the universe includes the moral law that one's punishment is not merely appropriate to the crime but *is* the crime: these are the sinners who most fully denied the spirit, and so their spirit, which was created eternal by God, has come as close to pure matter as is possible. This moral law is called by one of the sinners a "counter-penalty," or *contrapasso*. It is clear from discussions by philosophers known to Dante—such as Thomas Aquinas—that the Latin term *contrapassum* meant "retribution" according to the law of retribution as defined in the Old Testament: an eye for an eye, a tooth for a tooth (see Exodus 21.23–24). But this is not really the principle that governs the distribution of punishment in Hell: this is what the sinners think, but they are oversimplifying. On the contrary, the moral economy of Hell is explained in a single sentence by another of the sinners (Capaneus): "What I once was, alive, I still am, dead" (*Inferno* 14.51). The punishment of sin is the sin itself, as Augustine taught in the *Confessions*: "So You [God] have ordained and so it is: that every disorder of the soul is its own punishment." In the *Inferno* every sinner commits his sin forever, for all of eternity, and that is his punishment.

Before exploring in more detail the workings of divine justice in the *Inferno*, we need to understand the role of Virgil, and of the *Aeneid*, in the poem. When Dante protests in *Inferno* 2 that he is neither Aeneas nor Paul, he is indicating that his poem will bring together, in a combination that will find its ultimate fulfillment in Milton's *Paradise Lost*, both the classical and the Christian traditions. This is a bold and largely unprecedented ambition in Western literature. In the *Confessions* Augustine struggles with and finally rejects the *Aeneid*: he describes how as a student he was seduced by the beauty of Virgil's poetry into weeping for the death of Dido while ignoring the spiritual death of his own soul. For Augustine the poem's poetic power was irresistible, but its meaning was worse than useless to the Christian; as another of the church fathers put it, the *Aeneid* was "a beautiful vase filled with vipers." For Virgil's poem celebrated the founding of an earthly empire and, worse, one that Jupiter prophesied would continue "without end." In the *City of God*, written in part to defend Christians from the charge that it was their rejection of Rome's traditional deities that had caused the sack of Rome by the Goths in 410, Augustine poured scorn on these words, "without end." For him there was only one city, the heavenly Jerusalem, which was not a physical place at all but a condition of the soul—a vision of peace—available both in this life and in the life to come to those who have faith. The "eternal city" was not Rome but the City of God, populated by citizens faithful not to the emperor or the Roman deities but to the gospel of Jesus Christ.

But for Dante, as we have seen, Rome had a different meaning. For him, the establishment of the empire by Augustus, and the extension of Roman peace over the Western world, were the necessary preconditions for the birth of Christ. It was not just one city among many but the source of an imperial order that was divinely sanctioned. For Dante, since Virgil was the prophet and celebrant of this empire, he was—although he could not know it—inspired in writing the *Aeneid* not by Jupiter but by the Christian God. This notion of Virgilian inspiration was furthered by a Christian interpretation of one of Virgil's early poems, the Fourth Eclogue. The poem begins:

> Now comes the last age [prophesied] by the song of the Cumaean sybil; the great order of the ages is born anew; now the Virgin returns, now the reign of Saturn comes again; now a new child is sent down from heaven above.

It's easy enough to see how a devout reader could see in these words a prophecy of the birth of Christ, although Virgil was probably thinking of a son born to some prominent Roman, perhaps even to Augustus. Dante believed that the second coming of Christ, and the fulfillment of history, depended on the reestablishment of the imperial authority whose initial establishment Virgil had described in the *Aeneid*. This is why it is Virgil who in *Inferno* 1 provides an obscure prophecy of a savior who will bring peace to the war-torn cities of Italy. In sum, for Dante, Rome and its empire played a crucial role in history.

So part of the reason Virgil is chosen as the guide is that he is a poet who was divinely inspired to make known the meaning of history, a role that Dante assumes for himself as well—hence the political prophecies scattered throughout the poem. But Virgil is also chosen because he taught Dante what in *Inferno* 1 Dante calls "the noble style." What he means by this is that reading Virgil allowed him to move beyond the lyric love poetry that had characterized the early part of his career. This poetry was a necessary precondition to the writing of the *Comedy*. But it was Virgil who showed him that poetry might aspire to a vision of experience that dealt with the ultimate issues of life and death, and with a vision of the meaning of history. It was Virgil, in other words, who persuaded him that poetry could be a vehicle for moral and philosophical truth, and a means of self-fulfillment.

Yet despite the fact that Virgil is Dante's "master and author," there are important differences between them. Indeed, a central theme in both the *Inferno* and the *Purgatorio* is the fluctuation in the relationship between Dante and Virgil. Dante is usually submissive before Virgil, but there are moments when Virgil appears baffled and even inept. One of these occurs in canto 9 of the *Inferno*, when the devils in the City of Dis refuse Virgil entrance and he has to call upon a divine messenger sent from Heaven. In that canto the Furies threaten to bring Medusa in order to turn Dante to stone; Virgil makes Dante turn around and then covers up his eyes with both Dante's and his own hands. As soon as Virgil does this, Dante speaks—in the present tense— to the reader:

> O all of you whose intellects are sound,
> look now and see the meaning that is hidden
> beneath the veil that covers my strange verses. (9.61–63)

While Virgil the non-Christian covers up, Christian readers must *uncover*: they must interpret this action and this scene as a whole in order to understand the nature of the spiritual—not literal—threat posed by the Furies and Medusa. The answer has to do with the meaning of *petrification*, which in Christian terms means turning the heart to stone, being hard-hearted or *impenitent*; and the greatest source of impenitence is *despair*, which is the belief that you have committed sins so grave that they cannot be forgiven. The Furies are, for the Middle Ages, symbols of this despair, and despair is the condition of everyone in Hell, including Virgil: they have abandoned all hope of being saved. That is why in this very canto Dante mentions "that first circle / whose pain is all in having hope cut off" (9.17–18) and Virgil mentions "the pit of Judas," (9.27) Judas representing the New Testament type of despair. As a pagan, Virgil can *experience* this condition but cannot *understand* it: the despair or absence of hope at work here is Virgil's—he doesn't think they will get into the city of Dis—not Dante's; and the heavenly messenger who arrives is "filled with scorn" (9.88) not only because of the useless resistance of the inhabitants of Dis but also because of Virgil's incapacity. To appreciate something of the subtlety of Dante's poetry, we should notice that this messenger opens the gate with a touch of his wand, or *verghetta*. In the Middle Ages the power of Virgil's poetry was such that there developed a tradition that he was a magician, perhaps even a soothsayer: we meet this tradition in canto 20, where Dante will have Virgil revise his own poem so as to distance himself from this accusation. But one of the effects of this connection between Virgil and magic was that the spelling of his name was revised from Vergil—in Latin his name is *Vergilius Maro*—to Virgil by assimilation with the Latin word for a magician's wand, which is *virga*. In other words, Virgil wields a *virga*. But here Virgil's powers fail him, and it is an angel of God—the God whom Virgil did not know—who wields the *verghetta*.

There are many examples of the way in which Dante marks the difference between Virgil's pre-Christian understanding and his own confident Christianity. The reader might want to compare, for instance, the description in *Aeneid* 6 of the souls awaiting their trip across the river Acheron with its rewriting in *Inferno* 3, or any of the other passages—indicated in the notes—where Dante draws directly on the *Aeneid*. In addition to this indication of cultural and (for Dante) spiritual difference, Dante's relation to Virgil is not just literary but deeply emotional. Virgil may be a figure of authority, but he is also one of pathos, and nowhere more so than in the *Purgatorio*. There, in cantos 21 and 22, he meets his disciple Statius, the author of an epic poem that was, as Statius says, inspired by the *Aeneid*. More important is that Dante, quite unhistorically, presents Statius as having converted to Christianity by reading the lines from Virgil's Fourth Eclogue cited earlier. Statius says to Virgil,

> You were the lonely traveler in the dark
> who holds his lamp behind him, shedding light
> not for himself but to make others wise. (*Purgatorio* 22.67–69)

Dante is here, even more anachronistically, having Statius apply to Virgil a description that in one of his treatises Augustine applied to the Jews: "O Jews, you carried in your hands the lamp of the law in order to show the way to others while you remained in the darkness." The point is twofold: Virgil is a classical version of Moses, who saw the promised land but could not himself enter; and Virgil is to Statius (and to Dante) as Moses is to Christ: he is the prefiguration, and they are the fulfillment. This sense of Virgil's exclusion from the ultimate reward of the righteous life is expressed with great poignancy in *Purgatorio* 30, where Virgil disappears from the poem to be replaced by Beatrice.

A further distinction between Dante and Virgil is generic: in *Inferno* 20, Virgil refers to his poem as "my high tragedy"; in the next canto, Dante calls his poem "my Comedy." What are the differences between tragedy and comedy? In the Middle Ages, there are essentially four. First, *narrative structure*: a tragedy begins in happiness and ends in misery, while a comedy works in reverse, so that Dante begins in Hell and ends in Paradise. Second, *style*: tragedy is exalted in style, while comedy can indulge in a range of styles, and we see this in the *Inferno*, for example, where canto 21 provides a wonderful scene of a group of naughty devils who tease Virgil by pretending to be Roman soldiers but then, as they set off on their march, signal their departure with an obscene gesture. Third, *character*: a tragedy deals with important historical figures, while a comedy deals with all sorts of people, the common as well as the high-born—and certainly this is true of Dante's poem. And fourth, *subject matter*: tragedy deals with events of grand historical importance while comedy deals with people's private or inward lives.

We can understand this last, most important difference in the way Dante manipulates the word *pity* (*pietà* in the Italian). This is the Italian version of the key Virgilian term *pietas*: for Virgil piety means essentially a dutiful or obedient compliance to a larger responsibility—one that in fact entails the abandonment of one's own personal or inner self. But for Dante *pietà* means pity or compassion. In Virgil *pietas* is always good; but in Dante pity is not. In *Inferno* 2, for instance, Virgil explains that Beatrice feels compassion or *pietà* for Dante, but that the sufferings of those in Hell, including Virgil himself, do not touch her. It would have been wrong for her to feel pity for Virgil: everyone in Hell is there as an effect not just of God's justice but of his love as well, as the inscription over the gate in canto 3 tells us. As Virgil says to Dante in a line where the translator makes clear the distinction between the two words, "In this place piety lives when pity is dead" (20. 28). In a larger sense, one of the central concerns of the poem is precisely what the protagonist feels and the shifts of his personality—the turmoil within his inner self—throughout the course of the journey he undertakes. This is clearly not true, for example, of Aeneas, who is denied any but the most obvious emotions—and often not many of them. Indeed, Aeneas's piety is fully accomplished precisely when he has sacrificed his personality in the interest of founding Rome, whereas *The Divine Comedy* is concerned throughout with the spiritual development of its protagonist.

The Divine Comedy is concerned as well with the spiritual development of its readers. As Augustine's *Confessions* make clear, for the medieval Christian reading was itself a spiritual action with serious moral consequences. One of the greatest impediments to Augustine's conversion was his inability to understand how the Hebrew Bible—with what he thought was its unsophisticated language and outlandish narratives—could compete with either the wisdom available in Greek philosophy or the beautiful style of Latin poetry, or how it could be reconciled to Christian doctrine. But he learned, with the help of Bishop Ambrose of Milan, to read the Bible not literally but, as he calls it, spiritually. He means by this what we would call allegorical reading. For example, throughout the Middle Ages the Song of Songs in the Hebrew Bible was read not as a love poem but as an allegory about the love of God for the individual soul, or of Christ for the church, or of the Holy Spirit for the Virgin Mary. Moses, Isaac, Noah, and the other patriarchs were seen not just as leaders of Israel but as prefigurations of Christ. And so on: virtually every passage in the Hebrew Bible was interpreted so as to render it consistent with both the New Testament and Christian doctrine as defined by the church. In 2 Corinthians 3.6 Paul says that "the letter killeth, but the spirit giveth life." To read the Bible only literally, simply as a series of historical narratives, is not merely to miss its deeper significance but to place oneself in spiritual danger, to risk one's very soul. As Augustine argues, to read literally is to read carnally or corporeally, with the eye of the flesh; but to interpret is to read spiritually, with the eye of the heart.

We have already seen how at a crucial moment in the *Inferno* (canto 9) Virgil seeks to cover Dante's eyes while Dante himself urges the reader to uncover the meaning of the events being portrayed. Throughout the *Comedy,* and especially in the *Inferno*, the most corporeal of the three canticles, both Dante the pilgrim and the reader are tempted to read carnally or corporeally, to be distracted from the need for interpretation by the visually powerful scenes presented to them. An example is the account in canto 5 of Paolo and Francesca, who are located in the third circle, where the lustful are punished. These young lovers are here because they committed adultery, and the winds that blow them about are an infernal version of the gusts of desire that drove them in life. But if we stop here we will make the same mistake as does the pilgrim Dante, who feels for them exactly the wrong sort of pity. For Francesca's punishment is not to whirl about endlessly, locked in the arms of her beloved: after all, is that really a punishment? No, her punishment is to repeat throughout eternity the act of seduction that brought about her damnation; and Paolo's punishment is to watch her as she works her wiles. It is no accident that in the conversation with Dante and Virgil Paolo says not a word but only sobs; indeed, Francesca refers to him only once, with the contemptuous demonstrative pronoun *questi,* "*this one* who never shall leave my side." And whom does Francesca seduce? After listening to her tell her carefully crafted tale of love—one that incorporates within it lines from the kind of lyric poetry that Dante himself had written as a youth—Dante falls to the ground with pity. Indeed, his description is painfully apt: he "fell to Hell's floor as a body, dead, falls"—an act all too appropriate for a man in Hell. Nor does Francesca's power stop at Dante, for it has worked its magic on generations of readers. The challenge of this scene is to remember its deep significance—that this woman is in Hell, that she is currently repeating the very sin that put her there—while she does everything in her power to make you forget.

The interpretive drama acted out in this scene is repeated throughout the *Inferno.* The poem is peopled with brilliantly realized personalities who engage in rhetorical subtleties that simultaneously conceal and yet reveal their moral corruption. Farinata and Cavalcanti, Pier delle Vigne, Brunetto Latini, Vanni Fucci, Ulysses, Guido da Montefeltro, Bertran de Born, Geri del Bello, Ugolino—these and more provide a human drama that is unsurpassed in Western literature. Yet we are simultaneously never allowed to forget that they are all damned by a divine justice that is, for Dante, infallible. We are simultaneously intrigued and wary, powerfully drawn toward these men and women whose personalities have here, in eternity, achieved their full and at times glorious potential and yet also on the alert for the full meaning of their words. Of all the accomplishments of this great poem, perhaps its most enduring achievement is its capacity to provide the reader with a virtually limitless sense of the deep meaningfulness that literature can provide. For Dante this meaningfulness derived from God, but whatever its source, we can still agree with those readers who thought the poem divine.

PRONOUNCING GLOSSARY

The following list uses common English syllables to provide rough equivalents of selected words whose pronunciation may be unfamiliar to the general reader.

Abbagliato: *ah-bahl-lee-ah'-toh*

Aghinolfo: *ah-gee-nol'-foh*

Alichino: *a-lee-kee'-noh*

Bacchiglione: *bahk-eel-lee-oh'-nay*

Barbariccia: *bar-bar-eetch'-yah*

Caccia: *cah'-chyah*

Capocchio: *ka-pawk'-yoh*

Ciacco: *chyah'-koh*

Draghignazzo: *drah-gee-nyah'-zoh*

Focaccia: *foh-cah'-chyah*

Gianfigliazzi: *jyahn'-feel-yah-tzee*

Gianni Schicchi: *jyahn'-ee skee'-kee*

Hypsipyle: *hip-sip'-il-ay*

Maghinardo: *mah-ghee-nard'-oh*

Malebolge: *mahl-uh-bowl'-jay*

Malebranche: *mahl-uh-branck'-eh*

Paolo: *powl'-oh*

Peschiera: *pes-kee-ehr'-ah*

Puccio: *poo'-chyoh*

Rinier: *ree-nyay'*

Romagna: *row-mah'-nyah*

Ruggieri: *roo-jyehr'-ee*

Tagliacozzo: *tah-lyah-cot'-soh*

Tegghiaio: *teh-gyai'-oh*

Uguiccione: *oo-gwee-chyoh'-nay*

Verrucchio: *vehr-oo'-kyoh*

From The Divine Comedy[1]

Inferno

CANTO I

Halfway through his life, Dante the Pilgrim wakes to find himself lost in a dark wood. Terrified at being alone in so dismal a valley, he wanders until he comes to a hill bathed in sunlight, and his fear begins to leave him. But when he starts to climb the hill his path is blocked by three fierce beasts: first a Leopard, then a Lion, and finally a She-Wolf. They fill him with fear and drive him back down to the sunless wood. At that moment the figure of a man appears before him; it is the shade of Virgil, and the Pilgrim begs for help. Virgil tells him that he cannot overcome the beasts which obstruct his path; they must remain until a "Greyhound" comes who will drive them back to Hell. Rather by another path will the Pilgrim reach the sunlight, and Virgil promises to guide him on that path through Hell and Purgatory, after which another spirit, more fit than Virgil, will lead him to Paradise. The Pilgrim begs Virgil to lead on, and the Guide starts ahead. The Pilgrim follows.

Midway along the journey of our life[2]
  I woke to find myself in a dark wood,
  for I had wandered off from the straight path.[3]   3
How hard it is to tell what it was like,
  this wood of wilderness, savage and stubborn
  (the thought of it brings back all my old fears),   6
a bitter place! Death could scarce be bitterer.
  But if I would show the good that came of it
  I must talk about things other than the good.   9
How I entered there I cannot truly say,
  I had become so sleepy[4] at the moment
  when I first strayed, leaving the path of truth;[5]   12
but when I found myself at the foot of a hill,
  at the edge of the wood's beginning, down in the valley,
  where I first felt my heart plunged deep in fear,   15
I raised my head and saw the hilltop shawled
  in morning rays of light sent from the planet
  that leads men straight ahead on every road.[6]   18
And then only did terror start subsiding,
  in my heart's lake,[7] which rose to heights of fear
  that night I spent in deepest desperation.   21
Just as a swimmer, still with panting breath,
  now safe upon the shore, out of the deep,
  might turn for one last look at the dangerous waters,   24
so I, although my mind was turned to flee,
  turned round to gaze once more upon the pass
  that never let a living soul escape.[8]   27

1. Translated by Mark Musa. The notes are by Lee Patterson.   2. Born in 1265, Dante was thirty-five in 1300, the fictional date of the poem. The biblical span of human life is seventy (see Psalms 90.10 and Isaiah 38.10).   3. See Proverbs 2.13–14 and 4.18–19, and also 2 Peter 2.15.   4. See Romans 13.11–12. 5. See Psalms 23.3.   6. The sun, which in the astronomical system of Dante's time was a planet thought to revolve around the Earth.   7. This phrase refers to the inner chamber of the heart, a cavity that in the physiology of Dante's time was the location of fear. Not coincidentally, Dante's last stop in the *Inferno* ends at the lake of Cocytus (see 31.123).   8. This simile of Dante as the survivor of a passage through the sea invokes the story of the escape of the Israelites from Egypt through the Red Sea, a central metaphor throughout the *Comedy* (see *Purgatorio* 24.46): see Exodus 14. There is also probably an allusion to the opening of the *Aeneid*, where Aeneas and his men survive a storm.

I rested my tired body there awhile
   and then began to climb the barren slope
   (I dragged my stronger foot and limped along).[9]   30
Beyond the point the slope begins to rise
   sprang up a leopard, trim and very swift!
   It was covered by a pelt of many spots.   33
And, everywhere I looked, the beast was there
   blocking my way, so time and time again
   I was about to turn and go back down.   36
The hour was early in the morning then,
   the sun was climbing up with those same stars
   that had accompanied it on the world's first day,   39
the day Divine Love set their beauty turning;[1]
   so the hour and sweet season of creation
   encouraged me to think I could get past   42
that gaudy beast, wild in its spotted pelt,
   but then good hope gave way and fear returned
   when the figure of a lion loomed up before me,   45
and he was coming straight toward me, it seemed,
   with head raised high, and furious with hunger—
   the air around him seemed to fear his presence.   48
And now a she-wolf came, that in her leanness
   seemed racked with every kind of greediness
   (how many people she has brought to grief!).   51
This last beast brought my spirit down so low
   with fear that seized me at the sight of her,
   I lost all hope of going up the hill.[2]   54
As a man who, rejoicing in his gains,
   suddenly seeing his gain turn into loss,
   will grieve as he compares his then and now,   57
so she made me do, that relentless beast;
   coming toward me, slowly, step by step,
   she forced me back to where the sun is mute.   60
While I was rushing down to that low place,
   my eyes made out a figure coming toward me
   of one grown faint, perhaps from too much silence.[3]   63
And when I saw him standing in this wasteland,
   "Have pity on my soul," I cried to him,
   "whichever you are, shade or living man!"   66
"No longer living man, though once I was,"
   he said, "and my parents were from Lombardy,
   both of them were Mantuans by birth.[4]   69
I was born, though somewhat late, *sub Julio*,[5]

9. The pilgrim is limping because he suffers from the injury of original sin.   **1.** In the Middle Ages it was thought that the world was created in spring, when the sun is in the constellation Aries.   **2.** The meaning of the leopard, lion, and she-wolf is open to a number of interpretations, the most plausible being that they represent the three major forms of sin found in Hell, respectively fraud, violence, and incontinence or immoderation (see 11.78 ff.). The structure of Hell indicates that the last is the least serious morally, but its role in this canto shows that it is the most difficult to overcome psychologically. Dante probably took the identities of these three beasts from a passage in Jeremiah 5.6.   **3.** The Roman poet Virgil's voice has not been heard since he died in 19 B.C.E.   **4.** Lombardy is the most northern area of Italy; Mantua is located to the east of Milan.   **5.** Virgil (70–19 B.C.E.) was born *sub Julio*, during the reign of Julius Caesar (assassinated in 44 B.C.E), who was regarded by Dante as the founder of the Roman Empire.

and lived in Rome when good Augustus reigned,
    when still the false and lying gods were worshipped.   72
I was a poet and sang of that just man,
    son of Anchises, who sailed off from Troy
    after the burning of proud Ilium.[6]   75
But why retreat to so much misery?
    Why not climb up this blissful mountain here,
    the beginning and the source of all man's joy?"   78
"Are you then Virgil, are you then that fount
    from which pours forth so rich a stream of words?"
    I said to him, bowing my head modestly.   81
"O light and honor of the other poets,
    may my long years of study, and that deep love
    that made me search your verses, help me now!   84
You are my teacher, the first of all my authors,
    and you alone the one from whom I took
    the noble style that was to bring me honor.   87
You see the beast that forced me to retreat;
    save me from her, I beg you, famous sage,
    she makes me tremble, the blood throbs in my veins."   90
"But you must journey down another road,"
    he answered, when he saw me lost in tears,
    "if ever you hope to leave this wilderness;   93
this beast, the one you cry about in fear,
    allows no soul to succeed along her path,
    she blocks his way and puts an end to him.   96
She is by nature so perverse and vicious,
    her craving belly is never satisfied,
    still hungering for food the more she eats.   99
She mates with many creatures, and will go on
    mating with more until the greyhound comes
    and tracks her down to make her die in anguish.[7]   102
He will not feed on either land or money:
    his wisdom, love, and virtue shall sustain him;
    he will be born between Feltro and Feltro.[8]   105
He comes to save that fallen Italy
    for which the maid Camilla gave her life
    and Turnus, Nisus, Euryalus died of wounds.[9]   108
And he will hunt for her through every city
    until he drives her back to Hell once more,
    whence Envy first unleashed her on mankind.   111
And so, I think it best you follow me
    for your own good, and I shall be your guide
    and lead you out through an eternal place   114
where you will hear desperate cries, and see
    tormented shades, some old as Hell itself,

---

6. Aeneas, the hero of Virgil's *Aeneid*.   7. Dante's prediction of a modern political redeemer is so enigmatic that there can be no certainty of his identity. Most commentators think it is Cangrande (i.e., the great dog) della Scala of Verona, Dante's benefactor after his exile from Florence.   8. Feltre and Montefeltro are towns that roughly mark the limits of Cangrande's domains. But other interpretations are possible.   9. Characters in the *Aeneid* who die during Aeneas's conquest of Italy.   1. The second death is damnation; see Revelation 21.8.

and know what second death is, from their screams.[1] 117
And later you will see those who rejoice
   while they are burning, for they have hope of coming,
   whenever it may be, to join the blessèd[2]— 120
to whom, if you too wish to make the climb,
   a spirit, worthier than I, must take you;[3]
   I shall go back, leaving you in her care, 123
because that Emperor dwelling on high
   will not let me lead any to His city,
   since I in life rebelled against His law.[4] 126
Everywhere He reigns, and there He rules;
   there is His city, there is His high throne.
   Oh, happy the one He makes His citizen!" 129
And I to him: "Poet, I beg of you,
   in the name of God, that God you never knew,
   save me from this evil place and worse, 132
lead me there to the place you spoke about
   that I may see the gate Saint Peter guards
   and those whose anguish you have told me of." 135
Then he moved on, and I moved close behind him.

CANTO II

But the pilgrim begins to waver; he expresses to Virgil his misgivings about his ability to undertake the journey proposed by Virgil. His predecessors have been Aeneas and Saint Paul, and he feels unworthy to take his place in their company. But Virgil rebukes his cowardice, and relates the chain of events that led him to come to Dante. The Virgin Mary took pity on the Pilgrim in his despair and instructed Saint Lucia to aid him. The Saint turned to Beatrice because of Dante's great love for her, and Beatrice in turn went down to Hell, into Limbo, and asked Virgil to guide her friend until that time when she herself would become his guide. The Pilgrim takes heart at Virgil's explanation and agrees to follow him.

The day was fading and the darkening air
   was releasing all the creatures on our earth
   from their daily tasks, and I, one man alone, 3
was making ready to endure the battle
   of the journey, and of the pity it involved,
   which my memory, unerring, shall now retrace. 6
O Muses! O high genius! Help me now!
   O memory that wrote down what I saw,
   here your true excellence shall be revealed! 9
Then I began: "O poet come to guide me,
   tell me if you think my worth sufficient
   before you trust me to this arduous road. 12
You wrote about young Sylvius's father,[5]
   who went beyond, with flesh corruptible,
   with all his senses, to the immortal realm; 15
but if the Adversary of all evil
   was kind to him, considering who he was,

---

2. The souls in Purgatory; the blessèd are the saved in Paradise. 3. Beatrice. 4. Virgil "rebelled" against God because he was not a Christian. 5. Aeneas, who visited the underworld in *Aeneid* 6.

and the consequence that was to come from him,   18
this cannot seem, to thoughtful men, unfitting,
    for in the highest heaven he was chosen
    father of glorious Rome and of her empire,   21
and both the city and her lands, in truth,
    were established as the place of holiness
    where the successors of great Peter sit.[6]   24
And from this journey you celebrate in verse,
    Aeneas learned those things that were to bring
    victory for him, and for Rome, the Papal seat;   27
then later the Chosen Vessel, Paul, ascended
    to ring back confirmation of that faith
    which is the first step on salvation's road.[7]   30
But why am I to go? Who allows me to?
    I am not Aeneas, I am not Paul,
    neither I nor any man would think me worthy;   33
and so, if I should undertake the journey,
    I fear it might turn out an act of folly—
    you are wise, you see more than my words express."   36
As one who unwills what he willed, will change
    his purpose with some new second thought,
    completely quitting what he first had started,   39
so I did, standing there on that dark slope,
    thinking, ending the beginning of that venture
    I was so quick to take up at the start.   42
"If I have truly understood your words,"
    that shade of magnanimity replied,
    "your soul is burdened with that cowardice   45
which often weighs so heavily on man,
    it turns him from a noble enterprise
    like a frightened beast that shies at its own shadow.   48
To free you from this fear, let me explain
    the reason I came here, the words I heard
    that first time I felt pity for your soul: 51
I was among those dead who are suspended,[8]
    when a lady summoned me. She was so blessed
    and beautiful, I implored her to command me:[9]   54
With eyes of light more bright than any star,
    in low, soft tones she started to address me
    in her own language, with an angel's voice: 57
'O noble soul, courteous Mantuan,
    whose fame the world continues to preserve
    and will preserve as long as world there is,   60
my friend, who is no friend of Fortune's, strays
    on a desert slope; so many obstacles
    have crossed his path, his fright has turned him back   63
I fear he may have gone so far astray,
    from what report has come to me in Heaven,

6. The apostle Peter is considered by the Catholic Church to be the first pope.   7. St. Paul; see
2 Corinthians 12.2–4.   8. In Limbo, where the souls experience "neither joy nor sorrow" (4.84).
9. As we soon learn, the lady is Beatrice.

that I may have started to his aid too late.   66
Now go, and with your elegance of speech,
    with whatever may be needed for his freedom,
    give him your help, and thereby bring me solace.   69
I am Beatrice, who urges you to go;
    I come from the place I am longing to return to;[1]
    love moved me, as it moves me now to speak.   72
When I return to stand before my Lord,
    often I shall sing your praises to Him.'
    And then she spoke no more. And I began,   75
'O Lady of Grace, through whom alone mankind
    may go beyond all worldy things contained
    within the sphere that makes the smallest round,[2]   78
your plea fills me with happy eagerness—
    to have obeyed already would still seem late!
    You needed only to express your wish.   81
But tell me how you dared to make this journey
    all the way down to this point of spacelessness,
    away from your spacious home that calls you back.'   84
'Because your question searches for deep meaning,
    I shall explain in simple words,' she said,
    'just why I have no fear of coming here.   87
A man must stand in fear of just those things
    that truly have the power to do us harm,
    of nothing else, for nothing else is fearsome.   90
God gave me such a nature through His Grace,
    the torments you must bear cannot affect me,
    nor are the fires of Hell a threat to me.   93
A gracious lady[3] sits in Heaven grieving
    for what happened to the one I send you to,
    and her compassion breaks Heaven's stern decree.   96
She called Lucia[4] and making her request,
    she said, "Your faithful one is now in need
    of you, and to you I now commend his soul."   99
Lucia, the enemy of cruelty,
    hastened to make her way to where I was,
    sitting by the side of ancient Rachel,[5]   102
and said to me: "Beatrice, God's true praise,
    will you not help the one whose love was such
    it made him leave the vulgar crowd for you?   105
Do you not hear the pity of his weeping,
    do you not see what death it is that threatens him
    along that river the sea shall never conquer?"[6]   108
There never was a wordly person living
    more anxious to promote his selfish gains
    than I was at the sound of words like these—   111
to leave my holy seat and come down here
    and place my trust in you, in your noble speech

---

1. Paradise.   2. The sphere of the moon.   3. The Virgin Mary.   4. St. Lucy, a 3rd-century martyr
and the patron saint of those afflicted with poor or damaged sight.   5. Rachel signifies the contemplative life: see Genesis 29.16–17.   6. These are the metaphoric waters of 1.22–24.

that honors you and all those who have heard it!' 114
When she had finished reasoning, she turned
  her shining eyes away, and there were tears
  How eager then I was to come to you! 117
And I have come to you just as she wished,
  and I have freed you from the beast that stood
  blocking the quick way up the mount of bliss. 120
So what is wrong? Why, why do you delay?
  Why are you such a coward in your heart,
  why aren't you bold and free of all your fear, 123
when three such gracious ladies, who are blessed,
  watch out for you up there in Heaven's court,
  and my words, too, bring promise of such good?" 126
As little flowers from the frosty night
  are closed and limp, and when the sun shines down
  on them, they rise to open on their stem, 129
my wilted strength began to bloom within me,
  and such warm courage flowed into my heart
  that I spoke like a man set free of fear. 132
"O she, compassionate, who moved to help me!
  And you, all kindness, in obeying quick
  those words of truth she brought with her for you— 135
you and the words you spoke have moved my heart
  with such desire to continue onward
  that now I have returned to my first purpose. 138
Let us start, for both our wills, joined now, are one.
  You are my guide, you are my lord and teacher."
  These were my words to him and, when he moved, 141
I entered on that deep and rugged road.

CANTO III

*As the two poets enter the vestibule that leads to Hell itself, Dante sees the inscription
above the gate, and he hears the screams of anguish from the damned souls. Rejected
by God and not accepted by the powers of Hell, the first group of souls are "nowhere,"
because of their cowardly refusal to make a choice in life. Their punishment is to follow a banner at a furious pace forever, and to be tormented by flies and hornets. The
Pilgrim recognizes several of these shades but mentions none by name. Next they come
to the River Acheron, where they are greeted by the infernal boatman, Charon. Among
those doomed souls who are to be ferried across the river, Charon sees the living man
and challenges him, but Virgil lets it be known that his companion must pass. Then
across the landscape rushes a howling wind, which blasts the Pilgrim out of his senses,
and he falls to the ground.*

I AM THE WAY INTO THE DOLEFUL CITY,
  I AM THE WAY INTO ETERNAL GRIEF,
    I AM THE WAY TO A FORSAKEN RACE. 3
JUSTICE IT WAS THAT MOVED MY GREAT CREATOR;
  DIVINE OMNIPOTENCE CREATED ME,
    AND HIGHEST WISDOM JOINED WITH PRIMAL LOVE.[7] 6
BEFORE ME NOTHING BUT ETERNAL THINGS

---

7. God as Father, Son, and Holy Ghost.

WERE MADE, AND I SHALL LAST ETERNALLY.
ABANDON EVERY HOPE, ALL YOU WHO ENTER.   9
I saw these words spelled out in somber colors
   inscribed along the ledge above a gate;
   "Master," I said, "these words I see are cruel."   12
He answered me, speaking with experience:
   "Now here you must leave all distrust behind;
   let all your cowardice die on this spot.   15
We are at the place where earlier I said
   you could expect to see the suffering race
   of souls who lost the good of intellect."[8]   18
Placing his hand on mine, smiling at me
   in such a way that I was reassured,
   he led me in, into those mysteries.   21
Here sighs and cries and shrieks of lamentation
   echoed throughout the starless air of Hell;
   at first these sounds resounding made me weep: 24
tongues confused, a language strained in anguish
   with cadences of anger, shrill outcries
   and raucous groans that joined with sounds of hands,   27
raising a whirling storm that turns itself
   forever through that air of endless black,
   like grains of sand swirling when a whirlwind blows.   30
And I, in the midst of all this circling horror,
   began, "Teacher, what are these sounds I hear?
   What souls are these so overwhelmed by grief?"   33
And he to me: "This wretched state of being
   is the fate of those sad souls who lived a life
   but lived it with no blame and with no praise.   36
They are mixed with that repulsive choir of angels
   neither faithful nor unfaithful to their God,
   who undecided stood but for themselves.[9]   39
Heaven, to keep its beauty, cast them out,
   but even Hell itself would not receive them,
   to fear the damned might glory over them."   42
And I. "Master, what torments do they suffer
   that force them to lament so bitterly?"
   He answered: "I will tell you in few words: 45
these wretches have no hope of truly dying,
   and this blind life they lead is so abject
   it makes them envy every other fate.   48
The world will not record their having been there;
   Heaven's mercy and its justice turn from them.
   Let's not discuss them; look and pass them by."   51
And so I looked and saw a kind of banner
   rushing ahead, whirling with aimless speed
   as though it would not ever take a stand;   54
behind it an interminable train

8. *The good of intellect*: i.e., God.　9. The "neutral angels," not mentioned in the Bible but discussed by theologians throughout the Middle Ages, were those who declined to choose either side when Satan rebelled against God.

of souls pressed on, so many that I wondered
   how death could have undone so great a number.
When I had recognized a few of them,
   I saw the shade of the one who must have been
   the coward who had made the great refusal.[1]   60
At once I understood, and I was sure
   this was that sect of evil souls who were
   hateful to God and to His enemies.   63
These wretches, who had never truly lived,
   went naked, and were stung and stung again
   by the hornets and the wasps that circled them   66
and made their faces run with blood in streaks;
   their blood, mixed with their tears, dripped to their feet,
   and disgusting maggots collected in the pus.   69
And when I looked beyond this crowd I saw
   a throng upon the shore of a wide river,
   which made me ask, "Master, I would like to know: 72
who are these people, and what law is this
   that makes those souls so eager for the crossing—
   as I can see, even in this dim light?"   75
And he: "All this will be made plain to you
   as soon as we shall come to stop awhile
   upon the sorrowful shore of Acheron."[2]   78
And I, with eyes cast down in shame, for fear
   that I perhaps had spoken out of turn,
   said nothing more until we reached the river.   81
And suddenly, coming toward us in a boat,
   a man of years[3] whose ancient hair was white
   shouted at us, "Woe to you, perverted souls!   84
Give up all hope of ever seeing Heaven:
   I come to lead you to the other shore,
   into eternal darkness, ice, and fire.   87
And you, the living soul, you over there,
   get away from all these people who are dead."
   But when he saw I did not move aside,   90
he said, "Another way, by other ports,
   not here, shall you pass to reach the other shore;
   a lighter skiff than this must carry you."[4]   93
And my guide, "Charon, this is no time for anger!
   It is so willed, there where the power is
   for what is willed; that's all you need to know."   96
These words brought silence to the woolly cheeks
   of the ancient steersman of the livid marsh,
   whose eyes were set in glowing wheels of fire.   99
But all those souls there, naked, in despair,
   changed color and their teeth began to chatter
   at the sound of his announcement of their doom.   102

---

1. This is Pope Celestine V, who was elected in July 1294 but resigned five months later.   2. The first of
the four rivers of Hell.   3. Charon; see *Aeneid* 6.   4. Charon knows that after death Dante will be
taken not to Hell but to Purgatory in a "swift and light" vessel piloted by an angel; the arrival of the souls
in Purgatory is described in *Purgatorio* 2.22–48. This is the first of several places in the *Commedia* where
Dante predicts his own salvation.

They were cursing God, cursing their own parents,
   the human race, the time, the place, the seed
   of their beginning, and their day of birth.   105
Then all together, weeping bitterly,
   they packed themselves along the wicked shore
   that waits for every man who fears not God.   108
The devil, Charon, with eyes of glowing coals,
   summons them all together with a signal,
   and with an oar he strikes the laggard sinner.   111
As in autumn when the leaves begin to fall,
   one after the other (until the branch
   is witness to the spoils spread on the ground),   114
so did the evil seed of Adam's Fall
   drop from that shore to the boat, one at a time,
   at the signal, like the falcon to its lure.[5]   117
Away they go across the darkened waters,
   and before they reach the other side to land,
   a new throng starts collecting on this side.   120
"My son," the gentle master said to me,
   "all those who perish in the wrath of God
   assemble here from all parts of the earth;   123
they want to cross the river, they are eager;
   it is Divine Justice that spurs them on,
   turning the fear they have into desire.   126
A good soul never comes to make this crossing,
   so, if Charon grumbles at the sight of you,
   you see now what his words are really saying."   129
He finished speaking, and the grim terrain
   shook violently; and the fright it gave me
   even now in recollection makes me sweat.   132
Out of the tear-drenched land a wind arose
   which blasted forth into a reddish light,
   knocking my senses out of me completely,   135
and I fell as one falls tired into sleep.[6]

CANTO IV

Waking from his swoon, the Pilgrim is led by Virgil to the First Circle of Hell, known as Limbo, where the sad shades of the virtuous non-Christians dwell. The souls here, including Virgil, suffer no physical torment, but they must live, in desire, without hope of seeing God. Virgil tells about Christ's descent into Hell and His salvation of several Old Testament figures. The poets see a light glowing in the darkness, and as they proceed toward it, they are met by the four greatest (other than Virgil) pagan poets: Homer, Horace, Ovid, and Lucan, who take the Pilgrim into their group. As they come closer to the light, the Pilgrim perceives a splendid castle, where the greatest non-Christian thinkers dwell together with other famous historical figures. Once within the castle, the Pilgrim sees, among others, Electra, Aeneas, Caesar, Saladin, Aristotle, Plato, Orpheus, Cicero, Avicenna, and Averroës. But soon they must leave; and the poets move from the radiance of the castle toward the fearful encompassing darkness.

5. These similes are drawn from *Aeneid* 6.56–60   6. Dante is describing an earthquake, which medieval science understood as the escape of vapors from within the earth; it is while he is unconscious that he crosses Acheron into Hell proper.

A heavy clap of thunder! I awoke
    from the deep sleep that drugged my mind—startled,
    the way one is when shaken out of sleep.   3
I turned my rested eyes from side to side,
    already on my feet and, staring hard,
    I tried my best to find out where I was,   6
and this is what I saw: I found myself
    upon the brink of grief's abysmal valley
    that collects the thunderings of endless cries.   9
So dark and deep and nebulous it was,
    try as I might to force my sight below,
    I could not see the shape of anything.   12
"Let us descend into the sightless world,"
    began the poet (his face was deathly pale):
    "I will go first, and you will follow me."   15
And I, aware of his changed color, said:
    "But how can I go on if you are frightened?
    You are my constant strength when I lose heart."   18
And he to me: "The anguish of the souls
    that are down here paints my face with pity—
    which you have wrongly taken to be fear.   21
Let us go, the long road urges us."
    He entered then, leading the way for me
    down to the first circle of the abyss.   24
Down there, to judge only by what I heard,
    there were no wails but just the sounds of sighs
    rising and trembling through the timeless air,   27
the sounds of sighs of untormented grief
    burdening these groups, diverse and teeming,
    made up of men and women and of infants.   30
Then the good master said, "You do not ask
    what sort of souls are these you see around you.
    Now you should know before we go on farther,   33
they have not sinned. But their great worth alone
    was not enough, for they did not know Baptism,
    which is the gateway to the faith you follow,   36
and if they came before the birth of Christ,
    they did not worship God the way one should;
    I myself am a member of this group.   39
For this defect, and for no other guilt,
    we here are lost. In this alone we suffer:
    cut off from hope, we live on in desire."   42
The words I heard weighed heavy on my heart;
    to think that souls as virtuous as these
    were suspended in that limbo, and forever!   45
"Tell me, my teacher, tell me, O my master,"
    I began (wishing to have confirmed by him
    the teachings of unerring Christian doctrine),   48
"did any ever leave here, through his merit
    or with another's help, and go to bliss?"

And he, who understood my hidden question,[7]   51
answered: "I was a novice in this place
   when I saw a mighty lord descend to us
   who wore the sign of victory as his crown.   54
He took from us the shade of our first parent,[8]
   of Abel, his good son, of Noah, too,
   and of obedient Moses, who made the laws;   57
Abram, the Patriarch, David the King,
   Israel with his father and his children,
   with Rachel, whom he worked so hard to win;   60
and many more he chose for blessedness;
   and you should know, before these souls were taken,
   no human soul had ever reached salvation."   63
We did not stop our journey while he spoke,
   but continued on our way along the woods—
   I say the woods, for souls were thick as trees.   66
We had not gone too far from where I woke
   when I made out a fire up ahead,
   a hemisphere of light that lit the dark.   69
We were still at some distance from that place,
   but close enough for me vaguely to see
   that honorable souls possessed that spot.   72
"O glory of the sciences and arts,
   who are these souls enjoying special honor,
   dwelling apart from all the others here?"   75
And he to me: "The honored name they bear
   that still resounds above in your own world
   wins Heaven's favor for them in this place."[9]   78
And as he spoke I heard a voice announce:
   "Now let us honor our illustrious poet,
   his shade that left is now returned to us."   81
And when the voice was silent and all was quiet
   I saw four mighty shades approaching us,
   their faces showing neither joy nor sorrow.   84
Then my good master started to explain:
   "Observe the one who comes with sword in hand,
   leading the three as if he were their master.   87
It is the shade of Homer, sovereign poet,
   and coming second, Horace, the satirist;
   Ovid is the third, and last comes Lucan.[1]   90
Since they all share one name with me, the name
   you heard resounding in that single voice,
   they honor me and do well doing so."   93
So I saw gathered there the noble school
   of the master singer of sublimest verse,
   who soars above all others like the eagle.   96
And after they had talked awhile together,
   they turned and with a gesture welcomed me,
   and at that sign I saw my master smile.   99

7. Dante's question is about the Harrowing of Hell, when according to Christian doctrine, Christ descended into Hell after the crucifixion and rescued the souls of the righteous of Israel; see also 12.44.
8. Adam.   9. The "honored name" is "poet."   1. Horace, Ovid, and Lucan are famous Roman poets.

Greater honor still they deigned to grant me:
  they welcomed me as one of their own group,
  so that I numbered sixth among such minds.   102
We walked together toward the shining light,
  discussing things that here are best kept silent,
  as there they were most fitting for discussion.   105
We reached the boundaries of a splendid castle
  that seven times was circled by high walls
  defended by a sweetly flowing stream.[2]   108
We walked right over it as on hard ground;
  through seven gates I passed with those wise spirits,
  and then we reached a meadow fresh in bloom.[3]   111
There people were whose eyes were calm and grave,
  whose bearing told of great authority;
  seldom they spoke and always quietly.   114
Then moving to one side we reached a place
  spread out and luminous, higher than before,
  allowing us to view all who were there.   117
And right before us on the lustrous green
  the mighty shades were pointed out to me
  (my heart felt glory when I looked at them).   120
There was Electra standing with a group,
  among whom I saw Hector and Aeneas,
  and Caesar, falcon-eyed and fully armed.[4]   123
I saw Camilla and Penthesilea;
  across the way I saw the Latian King,
  with Lavinia, his daughter, by his side.[5]   126
I saw the Brutus who drove out the Tarquin;
  Lucretia, Julia, Marcia, and Cornelia;
  off, by himself, I noticed Saladin,[6]   129
and when I raised my eyes a little higher
  I saw the master sage of those who know,[7]
  sitting with his philosophic family.   132
All gaze at him, all pay their homage to him;
  and there I saw both Socrates and Plato,
  each closer to his side than any other;   135
Democritus, who said the world was chance,
  Diogenes, Thales, Anaxagoras,
  Empedocles, Zeno, and Heraclitus;   138
I saw the one who classified our herbs:
  Dioscorides I mean. And I saw Orpheus,

2. Commentators have suggested that this is a Castle of Fame, its seven walls symbolizing the seven liberal arts, a system of knowledge developed in the classical period.   3. A locale reminiscent of the classical Elysian fields as described in *Aeneid* 6.468–73.   4. Julius Caesar (d. 44 B.C.E.). *Electra:* the mother of Dardanus, the founder of Troy. *Hector:* the leading warrior of the Trojans in the *Iliad. Aeneas:* the hero of the *Aeneid.*   5. Heiress to King Latinus who ruled the area of Italy where Rome was later located and who married Aeneas. *Camilla:* a female warrior in the *Aeneid,* where she is compared to *Penthesilea,* who fought for the Trojans against the Greeks.   6. Admired for his chivalry in fighting against the crusaders, he was sultan of Egypt and Syria and died in 1193. *Brutus:* not the Brutus who killed Julius Caesar, but an earlier Roman who drove out the tyrant Tarquin. All four of the women mentioned were virtuous Roman matrons.   7. Aristotle (384–322 B.C.E.), Greek philosopher. The men mentioned in lines 132–38 are Greek philosophers of the 7th through the 4th centuries B.C.E.

Tully, Linus, Seneca the moralist,[8]   141
Euclid the geometer, and Ptolemy,
    Hippocrates, Galen, Avicenna,
    and Averroës, who made the Commentary.[9]   144
I cannot tell about them all in full;
    my theme is long and urges me ahead,
    often I must omit things I have seen.   147
The company of six becomes just two;
    my wise guide leads me by another way
    out of the quiet into tempestuous air.   150
I come into a place where no light is.

CANTO V

From Limbo Virgil leads his ward down to the threshold of the Second Circle of Hell,
where for the first time he will see the damned in Hell being punished for their sins.
There, barring their way, is the hideous figure of Minòs, the bestial judge of Dante's
underworld; but after strong words from Virgil, the poets are allowed to pass into the
dark space of this circle, where can be heard the wailing voices of the Lustful, whose
punishment consists in being forever whirled about in a dark, stormy wind. After seeing
a thousand or more famous lovers—including Semiramis, Dido, Helen, Achilles, and
Paris—the Pilgrim asks to speak to two figures he sees together. They are Francesca da
Rimini and her lover, Paolo, and the scene in which they appear is probably the most
famous episode of the Inferno. At the end of the scene, the Pilgrim, who has been over-
come by pity for the lovers, faints to the ground.

This way I went, descending from the first
    into the second round, that holds less space
    but much more pain—stinging the soul to wailing.   3
There stands Minòs grotesquely, and he snarls,
    examining the guilty at the entrance;
    he judges and dispatches, tail in coils.[1]   6
By this I mean that when the evil soul
    appears before him, it confesses all,
    and he, who is the expert judge of sins,   9
knows to what place in Hell the soul belongs;
    the times he wraps his tail around himself
    tell just how far the sinner must go down.   12
The damned keep crowding up in front of him:
    they pass along to judgment one by one;
    they speak, they hear, and then are hurled below.   15
"O you who come to the place where pain is host,"
    Minòs spoke out when he caught sight of me,
    putting aside the duties of his office,   18
"be careful how you enter and whom you trust

---

8. Roman philosopher and dramatist, killed by Nero in 65 C.E. *Dioscorides:* Greek physician (1st century
C.E.) *Orpheus:* mythical Greek poet. *Tully:* Cicero (d. 43 B.C.E.), Roman orator.   9. Avicenna (d. 1037)
and Averroës (d. 1198) were Islamic philosophers who wrote commentaries on Aristotle's works that were
highly influential in Christian Europe. *Euclid:* Greek mathematician (4th century B.C.E.). *Ptolemy:* Greek
astronomer and geographer (1st century C.E.) credited with devising the cosmological system that was
accepted until the time of Copernicus in the 16th century (hence the term *Ptolomaic universe*). *Hippocrates and Galen:* Greek physicians (4th and 2nd centuries B.C.E., respectively).   1. In *Aeneid*
6.207–11 Minos is described as judge of the underworld.

it's easy to get in, but don't be fooled!"
And my guide said to him: "Why keep on shouting? 21
Do not attempt to stop his fated journey;
    it is so willed there where the power is
    for what is willed,[2] that's all you need to know." 24
And now the notes of anguish start to play
    upon my ears; and now I find myself
    where sounds on sounds of weeping pound at me. 27
I came to a place where no light shone at all,
    bellowing like the sea racked by a tempest,
    when warring winds attack it from both sides. 30
The infernal storm, eternal in its rage,
    sweeps and drives the spirits with its blast:
    it whirls them, lashing them with punishment. 33
When they are swept back past their place of judgment,
    then come the shrieks, laments, and anguished cries;
    there they blaspheme God's almighty power. 36
I learned that to this place of punishment
    all those who sin in lust have been condemned,
    those who make reason slave to appetite; 39
and as the wings of starlings in the winter
    bear them along in wide-spread, crowded flocks,
    so does that wind propel the evil spirits: 42
now here, then there, and up and down, it drives them
    with never any hope to comfort them—
    hope not of rest but even of suffering less. 45
And just like cranes in flight, chanting their lays,
    stretching an endless line in their formation,
    I saw approaching, crying their laments, 48
spirits carried along by the battling winds,
    And so I asked, "Teacher, tell me, what souls
    are these punished in the sweep of the black wind?" 51
"The first of those whose story you should know,"
    my master wasted no time answering,
    "was empress over lands of many tongues; 54
her vicious tastes had so corrupted her
    she licensed every form of lust with laws
    to cleanse the stain of scandal she had spread; 57
she is Semiramis,[3] who, legend says,
    was Ninus' wife as well as his successor;
    she governed all the land the Sultan rules. 60
The next is she who killed herself for love
    and broke faith with the ashes of Sichaeus;[4]
    and there is Cleopatra, who loved men's lusting. 63
See Helen there, the root of evil woe
    lasting long years, and see the great Achilles,

2. It is willed in Heaven by God, who has the power to accomplish whatever He wills.   3. Renowned for licentiousness, a mythical queen of Assyria and wife of Ninus, the legendary founder of Ninevah. Because both the capital of Assyria and Old Cairo were known as Babylon, her land is here confused with that ruled by the sultan of Egypt.   4. Dido, whose suicide for love of Aeneas is described in *Aeneid* 4.542–942, was the widow of Sichaeus. Cleopatra killed herself after the death of her lover, Marc Antony, in 30 B.C.E.

who lost his life to love, in final combat;[5]   66
see Paris, Tristan[6]—then, more than a thousand
   he pointed out to me, and named them all,
   those shades whom love cut off from life on earth.   69
After I heard my teacher call the names
   of all these knights and ladies of ancient times,
   pity confused my senses, and I was dazed.   72
I began: "Poet, I would like, with all my heart,
   to speak to those two there who move together
   and seem to be so light upon the winds."[7]   75
And he: "You'll see when they are closer to us;
   if you entreat them by that love of theirs
   that carries them along, they'll come to you."   78
When the winds bent their course in our direction
   I raised my voice to them, "O wearied souls,
   come speak with us if it be not forbidden."   81
As doves, called by desire to return
   to their sweet nest, with wings raised high and poised,
   float downward through the air, guided by will,   84
so these two left the flock where Dido is
   and came toward us through the malignant air,
   such was the tender power of my call.   87
"O living creature, gracious and so kind,
   who makes your way here through this dingy air
   to visit us who stained the world with blood,   90
if we could claim as friend the King of Kings,
   we would beseech him that he grant you peace,
   you who show pity for our atrocious plight.   93
Whatever pleases you to hear or speak
   we will hear and we will speak about with you
   as long as the wind, here where we are, is silent.   96
The place where I was born lies on the shore
   where the river Po with its attendant streams
   descends to seek its final resting place.[8]   99
Love, quick to kindle in the gentle heart,
   seized this one for the beauty of my body,
   torn from me, (How it happened still offends me!)   102
Love, that excuses no one loved from loving,
   seized me so strongly with delight in him
   that, as you see, he never leaves my side.   105
Love led us straight to sudden death together.[9]
   Caïna awaits the one who quenched our lives."[1]
   These were the words that came from them to us.   108
When those offended souls had told their story,
   I bowed my head and kept it bowed until

5. The medieval version of the Troy story described Achilles as enamored of a Trojan princess, Polyxena, and killed in an ambush set by Paris when he went to meet her. Helen's seduction by Paris (see line 67) was the cause of the Trojan War.   6. The lover of Iseult, wife of his lord King Mark.   7. Francesca da Rimini and her brother-in-law Paolo Malatesta.   8. The *Po* is a river in northern Italy that empties into the Adriatic sea at Ravenna.   9. These seven lines (100–6) should be compared to the love sonnets by Guido Guinizzelli and Dante included in *Medieval Lyrics: A Selection* (pp. 1411 and 1414).   1. *Caïna* is the circle of Cain (described in canto 32), where those who killed their kin are punished; the lovers were killed by Gianciotto Malatesta, Francesca's husband and Paolo's brother.

the poet said, "What are you thinking of?" 111
When finally I spoke, I sighed, "Alas,
    all those sweet thoughts, and oh, how much desiring
    brought these two down into this agony." 114
And then I turned to them and tried to speak;
    I said, "Francesca, the torment that you suffer
    brings painful tears of pity to my eyes. 117
But tell me, in that time of your sweet sighing
    how, and by what signs, did love allow you
    to recognize your dubious desires?" 120
And she to me: "There is no greater pain
    than to remember, in our present grief,
    past happiness (as well your teacher knows)! 123
But if your great desire is to learn
    the very root of such a love as ours,
    I shall tell you, but in words of flowing tears. 126
One day we read, to pass the time away,
    of Lancelot,[2] of how he fell in love;
    we were alone, innocent of suspicion. 129
Time and again our eyes were brought together
    by the book we read; our faces flushed and paled.
    To the moment of one line alone we yielded: 132
it was when we read about those longed-for lips
    now being kissed by such a famous lover,
    that this one (who shall never leave my side) 135
then kissed my mouth, and trembled as he did.
    Our Galehot[3] was that book and he who wrote it.
    That day we read no further."[4] And all the while 138
the one of the two spirits spoke these words,
    the other wept, in such a way that pity
    blurred my senses; I swooned as though to die, 141
and fell to Hell's floor as a body, dead, falls.

CANTO VI

On recovering consciousness the Pilgrim finds himself with Virgil in the Third Circle, where the Gluttons are punished. These shades are mired in filthy muck and are eternally battered by cold and dirty hail, rain, and snow. Soon the travelers come upon Cerberus, the three-headed, doglike beast who guards the Gluttons, but Virgil pacifies him with fistfuls of slime and the two poets pass on. One of the shades recognizes Dante the Pilgrim and hails him. It is Ciacco, a Florentine who, before they leave, makes a prophecy concerning the political future of Florence. As the poets move away, the Pilgrim questions Virgil about the Last Judgment and other matters until the two arrive at the next circle.

Regaining now my senses, which had fainted
    at the sight of these two who were kinsmen lovers,
    a piteous sight confusing me to tears, 3
new suffering and new sinners suffering

---

2. In Arthurian legend, the lover of Arthur's wife, Guinevere.   3. The knight who, in the French romance being read by the lovers, acted as a go-between for Lancelot and Guinevere.   4. Compare this line to Augustine's account of his conversion by reading a passage in Paul's Epistle to the Romans.

appeared to me, no matter where I moved
   or turned my eyes, no matter where I gazed.   6
I am in the third circle, in the round of rain
   eternal, cursed, cold, and falling heavy,
   unchanging beat, unchanging quality.   9
Thick hail and dirty water mixed with snow
   come down in torrents through the murky air,
   and the earth is stinking from this soaking rain.   12
Cerberus,[5] a ruthless and fantastic beast,
   with all three throats howls out his doglike sounds
   above the drowning sinners of this place.   15
His eyes are red, his beard is slobbered black,
   his belly swollen, and he has claws for hands;
   he rips the spirits, flays and mangles them.   18
Under the rain they howl like dogs, lying
   now on one side with the other as a screen,
   now on the other turning, these wretched sinners.   21
When the slimy Cerberus caught sight of us,
   he opened up his mouths and showed his fangs;
   his body was one mass of twitching muscles.   24
My master stooped and, spreading wide his fingers,
   he grabbed up heaping fistfuls of the mud
   and flung it down into those greedy gullets.   27
As a howling cur, hungering to get fed,
   quiets down with the first mouthful of his food,
   busy with eating, wrestling with that alone,   30
so it was with all three filthy heads
   of the demon Cerberus, used to barking thunder
   on these dead souls, who wished that they were deaf.   33
We walked across this marsh of shades beaten
   down by the heavy rain, our feet pressing
   on their emptiness that looked like human form.   36
Each sinner there was stretched out on the ground
   except for one[6] who quickly sat up straight,
   the moment that he saw us pass him by.   39
"O you there being led through this inferno,"
   he said, "try to remember who I am,
   for you had life before I gave up mine."[7]   42
I said: "The pain you suffer here perhaps
   disfigures you beyond all recognition:
   I can't remember seeing you before.   45
But tell me who you are, assigned to grieve
   in this sad place, afflicted by such torture
   that—worse there well may be, but none more foul."   48
"Your own city," he said, "so filled with envy
   its cup already overflows the brim,
   once held me in the brighter life above.   51
You citizens gave me the name of Ciacco;
   and for my sin of gluttony I am damned,

---

5. For this creature as one of the guardians of Hell, see *Aeneid* 6.190–97.   6. A Florentine named Ciacco, known only through his appearance here.   7. "You were born before I died."

as you can see, to rain that beats me weak.   54
And my sad sunken soul is not alone,
     for all these sinners here share in my pain
     and in my sin." And that was his last word.   57
"Ciacco," I said to him, "your grievous state
     weighs down on me, it makes me want to weep;
     but tell me what will happen, if you know,   60
to the citizens of that divided state?
     And are there any honest men among them?
     And tell me, why is it so plagued with strife?"   63
And he replied:[8] "After much contention
     they will come to bloodshed; the rustic party
     will drive the other out by brutal means.   66
Then it will come to pass, this side will fall
     within three suns, and the other rise to power
     with the help of one now listing toward both sides.   69
For a long time they will keep their heads raised high,
     holding the others down with crushing weight,
     no matter how these weep or squirm for shame.   72
Two just men there are,[9] but no one listens,
     for pride, envy, avarice are the three sparks
     that kindle in men's hearts and set them burning."   75
With this his mournful words came to an end.
     But I spoke back: "There's more I want to know;
     I beg you to provide me with more facts: 78
Farinata and Tegghiaio, who were so worthy,
     Jacopo Rusticucci, Arrigo, Mosca,
     and all the rest so bent on doing good,[1]   81
where are they? Tell me what's become of them;
     one great desire tortures me: to know
     whether they taste Heaven's sweetness or Hell's gall."   84
"They lie below with blacker souls," he said,
     "by different sins pushed down to different depths;
     if you keep going you may see them all.   87
But when you are once more in the sweet world
     I beg you to remind our friends of me.
     I speak no more; no more I answer you."   90
He twisted his straight gaze into a squint
     and stared awhile at me, then bent his head,
     falling to join his other sightless peers   93
My guide then said to me: "He'll wake no more
     until the day the angel's trumpet blows,
     when the unfriendly Judge shall come down here;   96
each soul shall find again his wretched tomb,
     assume his flesh and take his human shape,
     and hear his fate resound eternally."[2]   99

8. The enigmatic "prophecy" that follows refers first to the triumph of the Whites, or "the rustic party" (to which Dante was allied), in 1300 and then their defeat by the Blacks, aided by Pope Boniface ("one now listing toward both sides"), in 1302, at which time Dante was exiled.   9. The identity of these two is unknown.   1. Dante asks about famous Florentines; he will find Farinata in canto 10, Tegghiaio and Rusticucci in canto 16, and Mosca in canto 28. Arrigo does not appear.   2. Virgil refers to the Last Judgment, when the dead will regain their bodies.

And so we made our way through the filthy mess
　　of muddy shades and slush, moving slowly,
　　talking a little about the afterlife.　　　　　　　　　　102
I said, "Master, will these torments be increased,
　　or lessened, on the final Judgment Day,
　　or will the pain be just the same as now?"　　　　　　105
And he: "Remember your philosophy:
　　the closer a thing comes to its perfection,
　　more keen will be its pleasure or its pain.　　　　　　108
Although this cursèd race of punished souls
　　shall never know the joy of true perfection,
　　more perfect will their pain be then than now."[3]　　111
We circled round that curving road while talking
　　of more than I shall mention at this time,
　　and came to where the ledge begins descending;　　　114
there we found Plutus, mankind's arch-enemy.[4]

CANTO VII

*At the boundary of the Fourth Circle the two travelers confront clucking Plutus, the
god of wealth, who collapses into emptiness at a word from Virgil. Descending farther,
the Pilgrim sees two groups of angry, shouting souls who clash huge rolling weights
against each other with their chests. They are the Prodigal and the Miserly. Their
earthly concern with material goods prompts the Pilgrim to question Virgil about Fortune and her distribution of the worldly goods of men. After Virgil's explanation, they
descend to the banks of the swamplike river Styx, which serves as the Fifth Circle.
Mired in the bog are the Wrathful, who constantly tear and mangle each other.
Beneath the slime of the Styx, Virgil explains, are the Slothful; the bubbles on the
muddy surface indicate their presence beneath. The poets walk around the swampy
area and soon come to the foot of a high tower.*

"Pape Satàn, pape Satàn aleppe!"[5]
　　the voice of Plutus clucked these words at us,
　　and that kind sage, to whom all things were known,　　3
said reassuringly: "Do not let fear
　　defeat you, for whatever be his power,
　　he cannot stop our journey down this rock."　　　　　6
Then he turned toward that swollen face of rage,
　　crying, "Be quiet, cursèd wolf of Hell:
　　feed on the burning bile that rots your guts.　　　　9
This journey to the depths does have a reason,
　　for it is willed on high, where Michael wrought
　　a just revenge for the bold assault on God."[6]　　　12
As sails swollen by wind, when the ship's mast breaks,
　　collapse, deflated, tangled in a heap,
　　just so the savage beast fell to the ground.　　　　15
And then we started down a fourth abyss,

---

3. They will be more perfect because body and soul will be reunited (a principle derived from Aristotelian
science), which will only increase their pain.　　**4.** Dante combines Pluto, the classical god of the underworld, with Plutus, the classical god of wealth.　　**5.** Virgil apparently understands this mysterious outburst regarding Satan, but commentators have remained baffled.　　**6.** A reference to the battle in heaven
between the Archangel Michael and Satan in the form of a dragon: see Revelation 12.7–9.

making our way along the dismal slope
   where all the evil of the world is dumped.   18
Ah, God's avenging justice! Who could heap up
   suffering and pain as strange as I saw here?
   How can we let our guilt bring us to this?   21
As every wave Charybdis[7] whirls to sea
   comes crashing against its counter-current wave,
   so these folks here must dance their roundelay.   24
More shades were here than anywhere above,
   and from both sides, to the sound of their own screams,
   straining their chests, they rolled enormous weights.   27
And when they met and clashed against each other
   they turned to push the other way, one side
   screaming, "Why hoard?," the other side, "Why waste?"   30
And so they moved back round the gloomy circle,
   returning on both sides to opposite poles
   to scream their shameful tune another time;   33
again they came to clash and turn and roll
   forever in their semicircle joust.
   And I, my heart pierced through by such a sight,   36
spoke out, "My Master, please explain to me
   who are these people here? Were they all priests,
   these tonsured[8] souls I see there to our left?"   39
He said, "In their first life all you see here
   had such myopic minds they could not judge
   with moderation when it came to spending;   42
their barking voices make this clear enough,
   when they arrive at the two points on the circle
   where opposing guilts divide them into two.   45
The ones who have the bald spot on their heads
   were priests and popes and cardinals, in whom
   avarice is most likely to prevail."   48
And I: "Master, in such a group as this
   I should be able to recognize a few
   who dirtied themselves by such crimes as these."   51
And he replied, "Yours is an empty hope:
   their undistinguished life that made them foul
   now makes it harder to distinguish them.   54
Eternally the two will come to blows;
   then from the tomb they will be resurrected:
   these with tight fists, those without any hair.   57
It was squandering and hoarding that have robbed them
   of the lovely world, and got them in this brawl:
   I will not waste choice words describing it!   60
You see, my son, the short-lived mockery
   of all the wealth that is in Fortune's keep,
   over which the human race is bickering;   63
for all the gold that is or ever was
   beneath the moon won't buy a moment's rest

---

7. A famous whirlpool in the Straits of Messina, between Sicily and Italy, described in *Aeneid* 3.   8. The tonsure—a shaving of part of the head—was a mark of clerical status.

for even one among these weary souls." 66
"Master, now tell me what this Fortune is
   you touched upon before. What is she like
   who holds all worldly wealth within her fists?" 69
And he to me, "O foolish race of man,
   how overwhelming is your ignorance!
   Now listen while I tell you what she means:[9] 72
that One, whose wisdom knows infinity,
   made all the heavens and gave each one a guide,
   and each sphere shining shines on all the others, 75
so light is spread with equal distribution:
   for worldly splendors He decreed the same
   and ordained a guide and general ministress 78
who would at her discretion shift the world's
   vain wealth from nation to nation, house to house,
   with no chance of interference from mankind; 81
so while one nation rules, another falls,
   according to whatever she decrees
   (her sentence hidden like a snake in grass). 84
Your knowledge has no influence on her;
   for she foresees, she judges, and she rules
   her kingdom as the other gods do theirs. 87
Her changing changes never take a rest;
   necessity keeps her in constant motion,
   as men come and go to take their turn with her. 90
And this is she so crucified and cursed;
   even those in luck, who should be praising her,
   instead revile her and condemn her acts. 93
But she is blest and in her bliss hears nothing;
   with all God's joyful first-created creatures
   she turns her sphere and, blest, turns it with joy. 96
Now let's move down to greater wretchedness;
   the stars that rose when I set out for you
   are going down—we cannot stay too long."[1] 99
We crossed the circle to its other bank,
   passing a spring that boils and overflows
   into a ditch the spring itself cut out. 102
The water was a deeper dark than perse,
   and we, with its gray waves for company,
   made our way down along a rough, strange path. 105
This dingy little stream, when it has reached
   the bottom of the gray malignant slopes,
   becomes a swamp that has the name of Styx.[2] 108
And I, intent on looking as we passed,
   saw muddy people moving in that marsh,
   all naked, with their faces scarred by rage. 111
They fought each other, not with hands alone,

9. Virgil now explains that each area of life is presided over by a *guide*, a kind of angel, under the ultimate authority of God. The classical goddess Fortune—the "ministress" of line 78—who was thought to distribute the world's goods capriciously is here described as acting according to God's supervision. 1. The stars that were rising at the start of the journey (1.37–40) are now setting: Good Friday has passed, and the time is now the early hours of Holy Saturday. 2. The second river of Hell.

but struck with head and chest and feet as well,
  with teeth they tore each other limb from limb.   114
And the good teacher said: "My son, now see
  the souls of those that anger overcame;
  and I ask you to believe me when I say,   117
beneath the slimy top are sighing souls
  who make these waters bubble at the surface;
  your eyes will tell you this—just look around.   120
Bogged in this slime they say, 'Sluggish we were
  in the sweet air made happy by the sun,
  and the smoke of sloth was smoldering in our hearts;   123
now we lie sluggish here in this black muck!'
  This is the hymn they gurgle in their throats
  but cannot sing in words that truly sound."   126
Then making a wide arc, we walked around
  the pond between the dry bank and the slime,
  our eyes still fixed on those who gobbled mud.   129
We came, in time, to the foot of a high tower.[3]

CANTO VIII

But before they had reached the foot of the tower, the Pilgrim had noticed two signal flames at the tower's top, and another flame answering from a distance; soon he realizes that the flames are signals to and from Phlegyas, the boatman of the Styx, who suddenly appears in a small boat speeding across the river. Wrathful and irritated though he is, the steersman must grant the poets passage, but during the crossing an angry shade rises from the slime to question the Pilgrim. After a brief exchange of words, scornful on the part of the Pilgrim, who has recognized this sinner, the spirit grabs hold of the boat. Virgil pushes him away, praising his ward for his just scorn, while a group of the wrathful attack the wretched soul, whose name is Filippo Argenti. At the far shore the poets debark and find themselves before the gates of the infernal City of Dis, where howling figures threaten them from the walls. Virgil speaks with them privately, but they slam the gate shut in his face. His ward is terrified, and Virgil too is shaken, but he insists that help from Heaven is already on the way.

I must explain, however, that before
  we finally reached the foot of that high tower,
  our eyes had been attracted to its summit   3
by two small flames we saw flare up just there;
  and, so far off the eye could hardly see,
  another burning torch flashed back a sign.   6
I turned to that vast sea of human knowledge:
  "What signal is this? And the other flame,
  what does it answer? And who's doing this?"   9
And he replied: "You should already see
  across the filthy waves what has been summoned,
  unless the marsh's vapors hide it from you."   12
A bowstring never shot an arrow off
  that cut the thin air any faster than

---

3. This watchtower guards the entrance to lower Hell or the city of Dis—another name for Pluto, the classical god of the underworld, that is throughout the *Inferno* applied to Satan (see 11.65 and 34.20).

a little boat I saw that very second 15
skimming along the water in our direction,
    with a solitary steersman, who was shouting,
    "Aha, I've got you now, you wretched soul!" 18
"Phlegyas, Phlegyas,[4] this time you shout in vain,"
    my lord responded, "you will have us with you
    no longer than it takes to cross the muck." 21
As one who learns of some incredible trick
    just played on him flares up resentfully—
    so, Phlegyas there was seething in his anger. 24
My leader calmly stepped into the skiff
    and when he was inside, he had me enter,
    and only then it seemed to carry weight. 27
Soon as my guide and I were in the boat
    the ancient prow began to plough the water,
    more deeply, now, than any time before.[5] 30
And as we sailed the course of this dead channel,
    before me there rose up a slimy shape
    that said: "Who are you, who come before your time?" 33
And I spoke back, "Though I come, I do not stay;
    but who are you, in all your ugliness?"
    "You see that I am one who weeps," he answered. 36
And then I said to him: "May you weep and wail,
    stuck here in this place forever, you damned soul,
    for, filthy as you are, I recognize you." 39
With that he stretched both hands out toward the boat
    but, on his guard, my teacher pushed him back:
    "Away, get down there with the other curs!" 42
And then he put his arms around my neck
    and kissed my face and said, "Indignant soul,
    blessèd is she in whose womb you were conceived.[6] 45
In the world this man was filled with arrogance,
    and nothing good about him decks his memory;
    for this, his shade is filled with fury here. 48
Many in life esteem themselves great men
    who then will wallow here like pigs in mud,
    leaving behind them their repulsive fame." 51
"Master, it certainly would make me happy
    to see him dunked deep in this slop just once
    before we leave this lake—it truly would." 54
And he to me, "Before the other shore
    comes into sight, you will be satisfied:
    a wish like that is worthy of fulfillment." 57
Soon afterward, I saw the wretch so mangled
    by a gang of muddy souls that, to this day,
    I thank my Lord and praise Him for that sight: 60
"Get Filippo Argenti!"[7] they all cried.

4. A mythological figure condemned to Hell for setting fire to the temple of Apollo in revenge for the god's seduction of his daughter; Dante found him in *Aeneid* 6.444–47.   5. Because of the weight of the living Dante.   6. See Luke 11.27, where these words are applied to Jesus.   7. A Florentine contemporary of Dante.

And at those shouts the Florentine, gone mad,
　turned on himself and bit his body fiercely.　　　　　　　63
We left him there, I'll say no more about him.
　A wailing noise began to pound my ears
　and made me strain my eyes to see ahead.　　　　　　66
"And now, my son," the gentle teacher said,
　"coming closer is the city we call Dis,
　with its great walls and its fierce citizens."　　　　　69
And I, "Master, already I can see
　the clear glow of its mosques above the valley,
　burning bright red, as though just forged, and left　　72
to smolder." And he to me: "Eternal fire
　burns within, giving off the reddish glow
　you see diffused throughout this lower Hell."　　　　75
And then at last we entered those deep moats
　the circled all of this unhappy city
　whose walls, it seemed to me, were made of iron.　　78
For quite a while we sailed around, until
　we reached a place and heard our boatsman shout
　with all his might, "Get out! Here is the entrance."　81
I saw more than a thousand fiendish angels[8]
　perching above the gates enraged, screaming:
　"Who is the one approaching? Who, without death,　84
dares walk into the kingdom of the dead?"
　And my wise teacher made some kind of signal
　announcing he would speak to them in secret.　　　87
They managed to suppress their great resentment
　enough to say: "You come, but he must go
　who thought to walk so boldly through this realm.　90
Let him retrace his foolish way alone,
　just let him try. And you who led him here
　through this dark land, you'll stay right where you are."　93
And now, my reader, consider how I felt
　when those foreboding words came to my ears!
　I thought I'd never see our world again!　　　　　　96
"O my dear guide, who more than seven times
　restored my confidence, and rescued me
　from the many dangers that blocked my going on,　99
don't leave me, please," I cried in my distress,
　"and if the journey onward is denied us
　let's turn our footsteps back together quickly."　　102
Then that lord who had brought me all this way
　said, "Do not fear, the journey we are making
　none can prevent: such power did decree it.　　　105
Wait here for me and feed your weary spirit
　with comfort and good hope; you can be sure
　I will not leave you in this underworld."　　　　　108
With this he walks away. He leaves me here,
　that gentle father, and I stay, doubting,
　and battling with my thoughts of "yes"—but "no."　111

---

8. The rebel angels, cast out of Heaven; see Luke 10.18 and Revelation 12.9.

I could not hear what he proposed to them,
   but they did not remain with him for long;
   I saw them race each other back for home.   114
Our adversaries slammed the heavy gates
   in my lord's face, and he stood there outside,
   then turned toward me and walked back very slowly   117
with eyes downcast, all self-assurance now
   erased from his forehead—sighing, "Who are these
   to forbid my entrance to the halls of grief!"   120
He spoke to me: "You need not be disturbed
   by my vexation, for I shall win the contest,
   no matter how they plot to keep us out!   123
This insolence of theirs is nothing new;
   they used it once at a less secret gate,[9]
   which is, and will forever be, unlocked;   126
you saw the deadly words inscribed above it;
   and now, already past it, and descending,
   across the circles, down the slope, alone,   129
comes one by whom the city will be opened."

CANTO IX

*The help from Heaven has not yet arrived; the Pilgrim is afraid and Virgil is obviously
worried. He reassures his ward by telling him that, soon after his own death, he was
forced by the Sorceress Erichtho to resume mortal shape and go to the very bottom of
Hell in order to bring up the soul of a traitor; thus Virgil knows the way well. But no
sooner is the Pilgrim comforted than the Three Furies appear before him, on top of the
tower, shrieking and tearing their breasts with their nails. They call for Medusa, whose
horrible face has the power of turning anyone who looks on her to stone. Virgil turns
his ward around and covers his eyes. After an "address to the reader" calling attention
to the coming allegory, a strident blast splits the air, and the poets perceive an Angel
coming through the murky darkness to open the gates of the City for them. Then the
angel returns on the path whence he had come, and the two travelers enter the gate.
Within are great open burning sarcophagi, from which groans of torment issue. Virgil
explains that these are Arch-Heretics and their lesser counterparts.*

The color of the coward on my face,
   when I realized my guide was turning back,
   made him quickly change the color of his own.   3
He stood alert, like one who strains to hear;
   his eyes could not see far enough ahead
   to cut the heavy fog of that black air.   6
"But surely we were meant to win this fight,"
   he said, "or else . . . but no, such help was promised!
   Oh, how much time it's taking him to come!"   9
I saw too well how quickly he amended
   his opening words with what he added on!
   They were different from the ones he first pronounced;   12
but nonetheless his words made me afraid,
   perhaps because the phrase he left unfinished

---

9. A reference to Christ's descent into Hell after the crucifixion for the "harrowing": see above, Canto
4.52.

I finished with worse meaning than he meant.   15
"Has anyone before ever descended
   to this sad hollow's depths from that first circle
   whose pain is all in having hope cut off?"[1]   18
I put this question to him. He replied,
   "It is not usual for one of us
   to make the journey I am making now.   21
But it happens I was down here once before,
   conjured by that heartless witch, Erichtho[2]
   (who could recall the spirit to its body).   24
Soon after I had left my flesh in death
   she sent me through these walls, and down as far
   as the pit of Judas to bring a spirit out;   27
and that place is the lowest and the darkest
   and the farthest from the sphere that circles all;[3]
   I know the road, and well, you can be sure.   30
This swamp that breathes with a prodigious stink
   lies in a circle round the doleful city
   that now we cannot enter without strife."   33
And he said other things, but I forget them,
   for suddenly my eyes were drawn above,
   up to the fiery top of that high tower   36
where in no time at all and all at once
   sprang up three hellish Furies[4] stained with blood,
   their bodies and their gestures those of females;   39
their waists were bound in cords of wild green hydras,
   horned snakes and little serpents grew as hair,
   and twined themselves around the savage temples.   42
And he who had occasion to know well
   the handmaids of the queen of timeless woe[5]
   cried out to me "Look there! The fierce Erinyes!   45
That is Megaera, the one there to the left,
   and that one raving on the right, Alecto,
   Tisiphone, in the middle." He said no more.   48
With flailing palms the three would beat their breasts,
   then tear them with their nails, shrieking so loud,
   I drew close to the poet, confused with fear.   51
"Medusa,[6] come, we'll turn him into stone,"
   they shouted all together glaring down,
   "how wrong we were to let off Theseus[7] lightly!"   54
"Now turn your back and cover up your eyes,
   for if the Gorgon comes and you should see her,
   there would be no returning to the world!"   57

---

1. "Has anyone from Limbo ever descended into lower Hell before?"   **2.** A legendary sorceress. The story of Virgil's prior descent into Hell is apparently Dante's own invention, although in the Middle Ages Virgil had the reputation of being a magician.   **3.** Judecca, the last subdivision of the last circle of Hell, where Judas is punished.   **4.** Three mythological monsters who represent the spirit of vengeance, known in Greek as the Erinyes (see below, line 45, and lines 46–48 for their individual names); they figure prominently in the *Aeneid* and other Latin poetry.   **5.** In classical mythology the queen of Hell is Hecate, or Proserpina, the wife of Pluto.   **6.** A mythological figure known as a Gorgon (line 56), so frightful in appearance that she turned those who gazed on her into stone.   **7.** *Theseus*, a legendary Athenian hero, descended into the underworld in order to try to rescue Proserpina, whom Pluto had abducted, and was rescued by Hercules.

These were my master's words. He turned me round
  and did not trust my hands to hide my eyes
  but placed his own on mine and kept them covered.   60
O all of you whose intellects are sound,
  look now and see the meaning that is hidden
  beneath the veil that covers my strange verses:[8]   63
and then, above the filthy swell, approaching,
  a blast of sound, shot through with fear, exploded,
  making both shores of Hell begin to tremble;   66
it sounded like one of those violent winds,
  born from the clash of counter-temperatures,
  that tear through forests; raging on unchecked,   69
it splits and rips and carries off the branches
  and proudly whips the dust up in its path
  and makes the beasts and shepherds flee its course!   72
He freed my eyes and said, "Now turn around
  and set your sight along the ancient scum,
  there where the marsh's mist is hovering thickest."   75
As frogs before their enemy, the snake,
  all scatter through the pond and then dive down
  until each one is squatting on the bottom,   78
so I saw more than a thousand fear-shocked souls
  in flight, clearing the path of one who came
  walking the Styx, his feet dry on the water.[9]   81
From time to time with his left hand he fanned
  his face to push the putrid air away,
  and this was all that seemed to weary him.   84
I was certain now that he was sent from Heaven.
  I turned to my guide, but he made me a sign
  to keep my silence and bow low to this one.   87
Ah, the scorn that filled his holy presence!
  He reached the gate and touched it with a wand;
  it opened without resistance from inside.   90
"O Heaven's outcasts, despicable souls,"
  he started, standing on the dreadful threshold,
  "what insolence is this that breeds in you?   93
Why do you stubbornly resist that will
  whose end can never be denied and which,
  more than one time, increased your suffering?   96
What do you gain by locking horns with fate?
  If you remember well, your Cerberus
  still bears his chin and throat peeled clean for that!"[1]   99
He turned then and retraced the squalid path,
  without one word to us, and on his face
  the look of one concerned and spurred by things   102
that were not those he found surrounding him.
  And then we started moving toward the city

---

8. Dante here reminds us of the need to interpret his poetry, although the lesson of this particular episode
is far from self-evident.   9. This is an angel, although described in a way reminiscent of Mercury, the
classical messenger of the gods.   1. According to classical mythology, Hercules dragged Cerberus into
the daylight.

in the safety of the holy words pronounced.   105
We entered there, and with no opposition.
    And I, so anxious to investigate
    the state of souls locked up in such a fortress,   108
once in the place, allowed my eyes to wander,
    and saw, in all directions spreading out,
    a countryside of pain and ugly anguish.   111
As at Arles where the Rhône turns to stagnant waters
    or as at Pola near Quarnero's Gulf
    that closes Italy and bathes her confines,   114
the sepulchers make all the land uneven,
    so they did here, strewn in all directions,
    except the graves here served a crueler purpose:[2]   117
for scattered everywhere among the tombs
    were flames that kept them glowing far more hot
    than any iron an artisan might use.   120
Each tomb had its lid loose, pushed to one side,
    and from within came forth such fierce laments
    that I was sure inside were tortured souls.   123
I asked, "Master, what kind of shades are these
    lying down here, buried in the graves of stone,
    speaking their presence in such dolorous sighs?"   126
And he replied: "There lie arch-heretics
    of every sect, with all of their disciples;
    more than you think are packed within these tombs.   129
Like heretics lie buried with their like
    and the graves burn more, or less, accordingly."
    Then turning to the right, we moved ahead   132
between the torments there and those high walls.

CANTO X

*They come to the tombs containing the Epicurean heretics, and as they are walking
by them, a shade suddenly rises to full height in one tomb, having recognized the
Pilgrim's Tuscan dialect. It is the proud Farinata, who, in life, opposed Dante's
party; while he and the Pilgrim are conversing, another figure suddenly rises out of
the same tomb. It is the shade of Cavalcante de Cavalcanti, who interrupts the conversation with questions about his son Guido. Misinterpreting the Pilgrim's confused silence as evidence of his son's death, Cavalcante falls back into his sepulcher
and Farinata resumes the conversation exactly where it had been broken off. He
defends his political actions in regard to Florence and prophesies that Dante, like
himself, will soon know the pain of exile. But the Pilgrim is also interested to know
how it is that the damned can see the future but not the present. When his curiosity
is satisfied, he asks Farinata to tell Cavalcante that his son is still alive, and that his
silence was caused only by his confusion about the shade's inability to know the
present.*

Now onward down a narrow path, between
    the city's ramparts and the suffering,
    my master walks, I following close behind.   3

---

2. *Arles,* located on the Rhone River in southern France, and *Pola,* located on the bay of Quarnero in what
is now Yugoslavia, were sites of Roman cemeteries.

"O lofty power who through these impious gyres[3]
   lead me around as you see fit," I said,
     "I want to know, I want to understand: 6
the people buried there in sepulchers,
   can they be seen? I mean, since all the lids
     are off the tombs and no one stands on guard."   9
And he: "They will forever be locked up,
   when they return here from Jehoshaphat
     with the bodies that they left up in the world.[4]   12
The private cemetery on this side
   serves Epicurus[5] and his followers,
     who make the soul die when the body dies.   15
As for the question you just put to me,
   it will be answered soon, while we are here;
     and the wish you are keeping from me will be granted."[6]   18
And I: "O my good guide, I do not hide
   my heart; I'm trying not to talk too much,
     as you have told me more than once to do."   21
"O Tuscan walking through our flaming city,
   alive, and speaking with such elegance,
     be kind enough to stop here for a while.   24
Your mode of speech identifies you clearly
   as one whose birthplace is that noble city
     with which in my time, perhaps, I was too harsh."   27
One of the vaults resounded suddenly
   with these clear words, and I, intimidated,
     drew up a little closer to my guide,   30
who said, "What are you doing? Turn around
   and look at Farinata,[7] who has risen,
     you will see him from the waist up standing straight."   33
I already had my eyes fixed on his face,
   and there he stood out tall, with his chest and brow
     proclaiming his disdain for all this Hell.   36
My guide, with a gentle push, encouraged me
   to move among the sepulchers toward him:
     "Be sure you choose your words with care," he said.   39
And when I reached the margin of his tomb
   he looked at me, and half-contemptuously
     he asked, "And *who* would *your* ancestors be?"   42
And I who wanted only to oblige him
   held nothing back but told him everything
     At this he lifted up his brows a little,   45
then said, "Bitter enemies of mine they were
   and of my ancestors and of my party;
     I had to scatter them not once but twice."[8]   48
"They were expelled, but only to return

3. *Gyres*: circular turns.   4. According to the Bible, the Last Judgment when the dead will again receive their bodies will take place in the Valley of Jehoshaphat: see Joel 3.2 and 3.12, and Matthew 25.31–32. 5. Greek philosopher (d. 270 B.C.E.) who rejected the idea of the immortality of the soul.   6. Presumably Dante's desire to see the Florentines who inhabit this circle.   7. Farinata degli Uberti (d. 1264), a leader of the Ghibelline faction in Florence.   8. Dante's family were Guelphs, who were driven out of Florence twice, in 1248 and 1260.

from everywhere," I said, "not once but twice—
   an art your men, however, never mastered!"[9]   51
Just then along that same tomb's open ledge
   a shade appeared, but just down to his chin,
   beside this other; I think he got up kneeling.[1]   54
He looked around as though he hoped to see
   if someone else, perhaps, had come with me
   and, when his expectation was deceived,   57
he started weeping: "If it be great genius
   that carries you along through this blind jail,
   where is my son? Why is he not with you?"   60
"I do not come alone," I said to him,
   "that one waiting over there guides me through here,
   the one, perhaps, your Guido held in scorn."[2]   63
(The place of pain assigned him, and what he asked,
   already had revealed his name to me
   and made my pointed answer possible.)   66
Instantly, he sprang to his full height and cried,
   "What did you say? He *held*? Is he not living?
   The day's sweet light no longer strikes his eyes?"[3]   69
And when he heard the silence of my delay
   responding to his question, he collapsed
   into his tomb, not to be seen again.   72
That other stately shade, at whose request
   I had first stopped to talk, showed no concern
   nor moved his head nor turned to see what happened;   75
he merely picked up where we had left off:
   "If that art they did not master," he went on,
   "that gives me greater pain than does this bed.   78
But the face of the queen who reigns down here[4] will glow
   not more than fifty times before you learn
   how hard it is to master such an art;[5]   81
and as I hope that you may once more know
   the sweet world, tell me, why should your party be
   so harsh to my clan in every law they make?"   84
I answered: "The massacre and butchery
   that stained the waters of the Arbia red[6]
   now cause such laws to issue from our councils."   87
He sighed, shaking his head. "It was not I
   alone took part," he said, "not certainly
   would I have joined the rest without good cause.   90

---

9. The Ghibellines were exiled in 1280, never to return.   1. This is Cavalcante de Cavalcanti, father of Dante's friend and fellow poet Guido; a Guelph, Guido married the daughter of Farinata in an unsuccessful attempt to heal the feud. In June 1300—after the fictional date of this conversation—Guido was exiled to a part of Italy where he caught the malaria from which he died in August. Dante was at that time a member of the governing body that made the decision to exile Guido.   2. The passage is ambiguous in the original Italian: as translated here, the "one" refers to Virgil; but the Italian word can also be translated to refer to Beatrice, so that these two lines would then read: "that one waiting over there guides me through here, / to her whom your Guido perhaps held in scorn."   3. In line 61 Dante used a verbal form known in Italian as the remote past, which leads Cavalcante to believe, wrongly, that now, in April 1300, Guido is dead—although, ironically, in about four months he will indeed die, as Dante knew when he was writing this canto.   4. Proserpina, who is also the goddess of the moon.   5. Farinata here predicts Dante's own exile.   6. A stream near the hill of Montaperti, where the Ghibellines defeated the Guelphs in 1260.

But I alone stood up when all of them
  were ready to have Florence razed. It was *I*
  who openly stood up in her defense."   93
"And now, as I would have your seed find peace,"
  I said, "I beg you to resolve a problem
  that has kept my reason tangled in a knot: 96
if I have heard correctly, all of you
  can see ahead to what the future holds
  but your knowledge of the present is not clear."   99
"Down here we see like those with faulty vision
  who only see," he said, "what's at a distance;
  this much the sovereign lord grants us here.   102
When events are close to us, or when they happen,
  our mind is blank, and were it not for others
  we would know nothing of your living state.   105
Thus you can understand how all our knowledge
  will be completely dead at that time when
  the door to future things is closed forever."[7]   108
Then I, moved by regret for what I'd done[8]
  said, "Now, will you please tell the fallen one
  his son is still on earth among the living;   111
and if, when he asked, silence was my answer,
  tell him: while he was speaking, all my thoughts
  were struggling with that point you solved for me." 114
My teacher had begun to call me back,
  so I quickly asked that spirit to reveal
  the names of those who shared the tomb with him.   117
He said, "More than a thousand lie with me,
  the Second Frederick[9] is here and the Cardinal[1]
  is with us. And the rest I shall not mention."   120
His figure disappeared. I made my way
  to the ancient poet, reflecting on those words
  those words which were prophetic enemies.[2]   123
He moved, and as we went along he said,
  "What troubles you? Why are you so distraught?"
  And I told him all the thoughts that filled my mind. 126
"Be sure your mind retains," the sage commanded,
  "those words you heard pronounced against yourself,
  and listen carefully now." He raised a finger: 129
"When at last you stand in the glow of her sweet ray,[3]
  the one whose splendid eyes see everything,
  from her you'll learn your life's itinerary."   132
Then to the left he turned. Leaving the walls,
  he headed toward the center by a path
  that strikes into a vale, whose stench arose,   135
disgusting us as high up as we were.

---

7. The damned can see the future but not the present; after the Last Judgment, when human time is abolished, they will know nothing.   8. See note 3, p. 1244.   9. Frederick II, Holy Roman emperor from 1215 until his death in 1250; he reputedly denied that there was life after death.   1. Ottaviano degli Ubaldini (d. 1273), who is reputed to have said, "If I have a soul, I have lost it for the Ghibellines." 2. That is, Farinata's prediction of his exile.   3. Beatrice's.

CANTO XI

Continuing their way within the Sixth Circle, where the heretics are punished, the poets are assailed by a stench rising from the abyss ahead of them which is so strong that they must stop in order to accustom themselves to the odor. They pause beside a tomb whose inscription declares that within is Pope Anastasius. When the Pilgrim expresses his desire to pass the time of waiting profitably, Virgil proceeds to instruct him about the plan of punishments in Hell. Then, seeing that dawn is only two hours away, he urges the Pilgrim on.

We reached the curving brink of a steep bank
   constructed of enormous broken rocks;
   below us was a crueler den of pain.   3
And the disgusting overflow of stench
   the deep abyss was vomiting forced us
   back from the edge. Crouched underneath the lid   6
of some great tomb, I saw it was inscribed:
   "Within lies Anastasius, the pope
   Photinus lured away from the straight path."[4]   9
"Our descent will have to be delayed somewhat
   so that our sense of smell may grow accustomed
   to these vile fumes; then we will not mind them,"   12
my master said. And I: "You will have to find
   some way to keep our time from being wasted."
   "That is precisely what I had in mind,"   15
he said, and then began the lesson:[5] "My son,
   within these boulders' bounds are three more circles,
   concentrically arranged like those above,   18
all tightly packed with souls; and so that, later,
   the sight of them alone will be enough,
   I'll tell you how and why they are imprisoned.   21
All malice has injustice as its end,
   an end achieved by violence or by fraud;
   while both are sins that earn the hate of Heaven,   24
since fraud belongs exclusively to man,
   God hates it more and, therefore, far below,
   the fraudulent are placed and suffer most.   27
In the first of the circles below are all the violent;
   since violence can be used against three persons,
   into three concentric rounds it is divided: 30
violence can be done to God, to self,
   or to one's neighbor—to him or to his goods,
   as my reasoned explanation will make clear.   33
By violent means a man can kill his neighbor
   or wound him grievously; his goods may suffer
   violence by arson, theft, and devastation;   36
so, homicides and those who strike with malice,
   those who destroy and plunder, are all punished

---

4. Pope Anastasius (d. 498) was thought, wrongly, to have accepted a heresy promoted by the 5th-century theologian Photinus that Christ was not divine but only human.   5. Virgil now describes the three remaining circles of Hell, the seventh, eighth, and ninth. The seventh is for the violent and is divided into three parts; the eighth and ninth are for the fraudulent, the eighth for those who deceive generally, the ninth for those who betray those who love them. For the scheme of Hell as a whole, see the diagram on p. 1206.

in the first round, but all in different groups.   39
Man can raise violent hands against himself
    and his own goods; so in the second round,
    paying the debt that never can be paid,   42
are suicides, self-robbers of your world,
    or those who gamble all their wealth away
    and weep up there when they should have rejoiced.   45
One can use violence against the deity
    by heartfelt disbelief and cursing Him,
    or by despising Nature and God's bounty;   48
therefore, the smallest round stamps with its seal
    both Sodom and Cahors[6] and all those souls
    who hate God in their hearts and curse His name.   51
Fraud, that gnaws the conscience of its servants,
    can be used on one who puts his trust in you
    or else on one who has no trust invested.   54
This latter sort seems only to destroy
    the bond of love that Nature gives to man;
    so in the second circle there are nests   57
of hypocrites, flatterers, dabblers in sorcery,
    falsifiers, thieves, and simonists,[7]
    panders, seducers, grafters, and like filth.   60
The former kind of fraud both disregards
    the love Nature enjoys and that extra bond
    between men which creates a special trust;   63
thus, it is in the smallest of the circles,
    at the earth's center, around the throne of Dis,[8]
    that traitors suffer their eternal pain."   66
And I, "Master, your reasoning runs smooth,
    and your explanation certainly makes clear
    the nature of this pit and of its inmates,   69
but what about those in the slimy swamp,
    those driven by the wind, those beat by rain,
    and those who come to blows with harsh refrains?   72
Why are they, too, not punished here inside
    the city of flame, if they have earned God's wrath?
    If they have not, why are they suffering?"   75
And he to me, "Why do you let your thoughts
    stray from the path they are accustomed to?
    Or have I missed the point you have in mind?   78
Have you forgotten how your *Ethics*[9] reads,
    those terms it explicates in such detail:
    the three conditions that the heavens hate,   81
incontinence, malice, and bestiality?
    Do you not remember how incontinence
    offends God least, and merits the least blame?   84

6. In the Middle Ages the names of Sodom (see Genesis 18.20–19.26) and Cahors, a city in southern France, became synonymous with sodomites and userers respectively. Usury, forbidden by the medieval church, is charging interest on loans; the logic of this prohibition—based on the argument that usury, like sodomy, is unnatural—is explained in lines 97–111 below.   7. Simony is the sin of selling a spiritual good, such as a church office or a sacrament like confession, for material gain. It is named after Simon Magus, a magician who sought to buy from the Apostles the power of baptism in Acts 8.9–24.   8. *Dis* is Satan, who is found at the bottom of Hell (see canto 34).   9. Aristotle's *Nicomachean Ethics*.

If you will reconsider well this doctrine
    and then recall to mind who those souls were   87
    suffering pain above, outside the walls,
you will clearly see why they are separated
    from these malicious ones, and why God's vengeance
    beats down upon their souls less heavily."   90
"O sun that shines to clear a misty vision,
    such joy is mine when you resolve my doubts
    that doubting pleases me no less than knowing!   93
Go back a little bit once more," I said
    "to where you say that usury offends
    God's goodness, and untie that knot for me."   96
"Philosophy," he said, "and more than once,
    points out to one who reads with understanding
    how Nature takes her course from the Divine   99
Intellect, from its artistic workmanship,[1]
    and if you have your *Physics*[2] well in mind
    you will find, not many pages from the start,   102
how your art too, as best it can, imitates
    Nature, the way an apprentice does his master;
    so your art may be said to be God's grandchild.   105
From Art and Nature man was meant to take
    his daily bread to live—if you recall
    the book of Genesis near the beginning,[3]   108
but the usurer, adopting other means,
    scorns Nature in herself and in her pupil,
    Art—he invests his hope in something else[4]   111
Now follow me, we should be getting on;
    the Fish are shimmering over the horizon,
    the Wain is now exactly over Caurus,[5]   114
and the passage down the bank is farther on."

CANTO XII

They descend the steep slope into the Seventh Circle by means of a great landslide, which was caused when Christ descended into Hell. At the edge of the abyss is the Minotaur, who presides over the circle of the Violent and whose own bestial rage sends him into such a paroxysm of violence that the two travelers are able to run past him without his interference. At the base of the precipice, they see a river of boiling blood, which contains those who have inflicted violence upon others. But before they can reach the river they are intercepted by three fierce Centaurs, whose task it is to keep those who are in the river at their proper depth by shooting arrows at them if they attempt to rise. Virgil explains to one of the centaurs (Chiron) that this journey of the Pilgrim and himself is ordained by God; and he requests him to assign some-one to guide the two of them to the ford in the river and carry the Pilgrim across it to the other bank. Chiron gives the task to Nessus, one of the centaurs, who, as he leads them to the river's ford, points out many of the sinners there in the boiling blood.

1. The laws of nature are determined by God.   2. Aristotle's *Physics*, which argues that human art should follow natural laws.   3. In Genesis 3.17–19, God decrees that because of the Fall people must toil, supporting themselves by the sweat of their brows.   4. The usurer makes money not from labor but from money itself, which is an unnatural and therefore illicit art.   5. The position of stars shows that it is now about 4 A.M. on Holy Saturday.

Not only was that place, where we had come
  to descend, craggy, but there was something there
    that made the scene appalling to the eye.   3
Like the ruins this side of Trent left by the landslide
  (an earthquake or erosion must have caused it)
    that hit the Adige on its left bank,[6]   6
when, from the mountain's top where the slide began
  to the plain below, the shattered rocks slipped down,
    shaping a path for a difficult descent—   9
so was the slope of our ravine's formation.
  And at the edge, along the shattered chasm,
    there lay stretched out the infamy of Crete:[7]   12
the son conceived in the pretended cow.
  When he saw us he bit into his flesh,
    gone crazy with the fever of his rage.   15
My wise guide cried to him: "Perhaps you think
  you see the Duke of Athens come again,
    who came once in the world to bring your death?[8]   18
Begone, you beast, for this one is not led
  down here by means of clues your sister[9] gave him;
    he comes here only to observe your torments."   21
The way a bull breaks loose the very moment
  he knows he has been dealt the mortal blow,
    and cannot run but jumps and twists and turns,   24
just so I saw the Minotaur perform,
  and my guide, alert, cried out: "Run to the pass!
    While he still writhes with rage, get started down."   27
And so we made our way down through the ruins
  of rocks, which often I felt shift and tilt
    beneath my feet from weight they were not used to.   30
I was deep in thought when he began: "Are you,
  perhaps, thinking about these ruins protected
    by the furious beast I quenched in its own rage?   33
Now let me tell you that the other time
  I came down to the lower part of Hell,
    this rock had not then fallen into ruins;   36
but certainly, if I remember well,
  it was just before the coming of that One
    who took from Hell's first circle the great spoil,   39
that this abyss of stench, from top to bottom
  began to shake,[1] so I thought the universe
    felt love—whereby, some have maintained, the world   42
has more than once renewed itself in chaos.[2]

---

6. A famous landslide on a mountain on the Adige River near Trent, a city in northern Italy.   **7.** The Minotaur, half man and half bull, was conceived when Pasiphaë, the wife of King Minos of Crete, had a wooden cow built within which she placed herself so as to have intercourse with a bull. The story of the Minotaur is told by Ovid, *Metamorphoses* 8.   **8.** Virgil is referring to Theseus, who killed the Minotaur in the labyrinth in which it was imprisoned.   **9.** Ariadne, daughter of Minos and Pasiphaë, who taught Theseus how to escape from the labyrinth within which the Minotaur was imprisoned.   **1.** Because of the earthquake that accompanied Christ's death, which occurred just before his descent to Hell and the "harrowing," Christ's rescue from the First Circle of the virtuous Israelites (see above, canto 4.52–63). **2.** A reference to a theory of the Greek philosopher Empedocles that the universe is held together by alternating forces of love and hate, and that if either one predominates the result is chaos. This classical theory is not consistent with the Christian belief that the universe is created and organized by God's love.

That was the moment when this ancient rock
   was split this way—here, and in other places.
But now look down the valley. Coming closer   45
   you will see the river of blood that boils the souls
   of those who through their violence injured others."   48
(Oh, blind cupidity[3] and insane wrath,
   spurring us on through our short life on earth
   to steep us then forever in such misery!)   51
I saw a river—wide, curved like a bow—
   that stretched embracing all the flatland there,
   just as my guide had told me to expect.   54
Between the river and the steep came centaurs,[4]
   galloping in single file, equipped with arrows,
   off hunting as they used to in the world;   57
then, seeing us descend, they all stopped short
   and three of them departed from the ranks
   with bows and arrows ready from their quivers.   60
One of them cried from his distant post: "You there,
   on your way down here, what torture are you seeking?
   Speak where you stand, if not, I draw my bow."   63
And then my master shouted back: "Our answer
   we will give to Chiron[5] when we're at his side;
   as for you, I see you are as rash as ever!"   66
He nudged me, saying: "That one there is Nessus,[6]
   who died from loving lovely Dejanira,
   and made of himself, of his blood, his own revenge.   69
The middle one, who contemplates his chest,
   is great Chiron, who reared and taught Achilles;
   the last is Pholus,[7] known for his drunken wrath.   72
They gallop by the thousands round the ditch,
   shooting at any daring soul emerging
   above the bloody level of his guilt."   75
When we came closer to those agile beasts,
   Chiron drew an arrow, and with its notch
   he parted his beard to both sides of his jaws,   78
and when he had uncovered his great mouth
   he spoke to his companions: "Have you noticed,
   how the one behind moves everything he touches?   81
This is not what a dead man's feet would do!"
   And my good guide, now standing by the torso
   at the point the beast's two natures joined,[8] replied: 84
"He is indeed alive, and so alone
   that I must show him through this dismal valley;
   he travels by necessity, not pleasure.   87
A spirit[9] came, from singing Alleluia,
   to give me this extraordinary mission;

---

3. Desire for wealth.   4. Mythological creatures that are half man and half horse.   5. A centaur
renowned for wisdom who educated many legendary Greek heroes, including Achilles.   6. Nessus fell in
love with Dejanira, wife of Hercules, who killed him; while dying, Nessus poisoned with his own blood a
robe that killed Hercules when he put it on.   7. Another centaur, killed by Hercules, whose rage is typical of the race.   8. When standing, Virgil reaches to the centaur's chest where his human and animal
natures join.   9. Beatrice.

he is no rogue nor I a criminal spirit.[1]   90
Now, in the name of that power by which I move
    my steps along so difficult a road,
    give us one of your troop to be our guide: 93
to lead us to the ford and, once we are there,
    to carry this one over on his back,
    for he is not a spirit who can fly."   96
Chiron looked over his right breast and said
    to Nessus, "You go, guide them as they ask,
    and if another troop protests, disperse them!"   99
So with this trusted escort we moved on
    along the boiling crimson river's bank,[2]
    where piercing shrieks rose from the boiling souls.   102
There I saw people sunken to their eyelids,
    and the huge centaur explained, "These are the tyrants
    who dealt in bloodshed and plundered wealth.   105
Their tears are paying for their heartless crimes:
    here stand Alexander and fierce Dionysius,
    who weighed down Sicily with years of pain;[3]   108
and there, that forehead smeared with coal-black hair,
    is Azzolino;[4] the other one, the blond,
    Opizzo d'Esti, who, and this is true,   111
was killed by his own stepson in your world."[5]
    With that I looked to Virgil, but he said
    "Let him instruct you now, don't look to me."   114
A little farther on, the centaur stopped
    above some people peering from the blood
    that came up to their throats. He pointed out   117
a shade off to one side, alone, and said:
    "There stands the one who, in God's keep, murdered
    the heart still dripping blood above the Thames."[6]   120
Then I saw other souls stuck in the river
    who had their heads and chests above the blood,
    and I knew the names of many who were there.   123
The river's blood began decreasing slowly
    until it cooked the feet and nothing more,
    and here we found the ford where we could cross.   126
"Just as you see the boiling river here
    on this side getting shallow gradually,"
    the centaur said, "I would also have you know   129
that on the other side the riverbed
    sinks deeper more and more until it reaches
    the deepest meeting place where tyrants moan: 132
it is there that Heaven's justice strikes its blow

---

1. Virgil is answering the question of lines 61–62, which assumes that they are condemned spirits.
2. A river of blood, which we later learn is named Phlegethon (see 14.116).   3. Alexander the Great (d.
323 B.C.E.) and Dionysius of Syracuse in Sicily (d. 367 B.C.E.).   4. Azzolino III (d. 1259), a brutal ruler
in northern Italy.   5. Opizzo II d'Este (d. 1293), another cruel northern Italian tyrant, reputedly murdered by his son; he is called "stepson" either because of the unnaturalness of the crime or because Opizzo
suspected his wife of adultery.   6. Guy de Montfort (d. 1298), who killed his cousin Prince Henry of
Cornwall during a church service ("in God's keep") in the Italian city of Viterbo. Nessus's image of the
blood dripping from the victim's heart indicates his focus on the fact that the murder is still unavenged.

against Attila,[7] known as the scourge of earth,
against Pyrrhus and Sextus,[8] and forever
extracts the tears the scalding blood produces,   135
from Rinier da Corneto and Rinier Pazzo,[9]
whose battlefields were highways where they robbed."   138
Then he turned round and crossed the ford again.

CANTO XIII

No sooner are the poets across the Phlegethon than they encounter a dense forest, from which come wails and moans, and which is presided over by the hideous harpies—half-woman, half-beast, bird-like creatures. Virgil tells his ward to break off a branch of one of the trees; when he does, the tree weeps blood and speaks. In life he was Pier Delle Vigne, chief counselor of Frederick II of Sicily; but he fell out of favor, was accused unjustly of treachery, and was imprisoned, whereupon he killed himself. The Pilgrim is overwhelmed by pity. The sinner also explains how the souls of the suicides come to this punishment and what will happen to them after the Last Judgment. Suddenly they are interrupted by the wild sounds of the hunt, and two naked figures, Lano of Siena and Giacomo da Sant' Andrea, dash across the landscape, shouting at each other, until one of them hides himself in a thorny bush; immediately a pack of fierce, black dogs rush in, pounce on the hidden sinner, and rip his body, carrying away mouthfuls of flesh. The bush, which has been torn in the process, begins to lament. The two learn that the cries are those of a Florentine who had hanged himself in his own home.

Not yet had Nessus reached the other side
    when we were on our way into a forest
    that was not marked by any path at all.   3
No green leaves, but rather black in color,
    no smooth branches, but twisted and entangled,
    no fruit, but thorns of poison bloomed instead.   6
No thick, rough, scrubby home like this exists—
    not even between Cecina and Corneto[1]—
    for those wild beasts that hate the run of farmlands.   9
Here the repulsive Harpies[2] twine their nests,
    who drove the Trojans from the Strophades
    with filthy forecasts of their close disaster.   12
Wide-winged they are, with human necks and faces,
    their feet are clawed, their bellies fat and feathered;
    perched in the trees they shriek their strange laments.   15
"Before we go on farther," my guide began,
    "remember, you are in the second round
    and shall be till we reach the dreadful sand,[3]   18
now look around you carefully and see
    with your own eyes what I will not describe,
    for if I did, you wouldn't believe my words."   21

---

7. Attila the Hun (d. 453).   8. Sextus, the son of the Roman consul Pompey, became a pirate (1st century B.C.E.); Pyrrhus, Achilles' son, killed the aged Priam at the fall of Troy, as described in *Aeneid* 2.595–704.   9. Both Riniers were bandits of Dante's day; they are now weeping from pain, whereas in life they never wept for their sins.   1. Two towns that mark the limits of the Maremma, a desolate area in Tuscany.   2. Birds with the faces of women and clawed hands; in *Aeneid* 3 they drive the wandering Trojans from their refuge in the Strophades Islands and predict their future suffering.   3. The *dreadful sand* is in the third ring or "round" of the seventh circle, described in the next canto.

Around me wails of grief were echoing,
    and I saw no one there to make those sounds;
    bewildered by all this, I had to stop.   24
I think perhaps he thought I might be thinking
    that all the voices coming from those stumps
    belonged to people hiding there from us,   27
and so my teacher said, "If you break off
    a little branch of any of these plants,
    what you are thinking now will break off too."[4]   30
Then slowly raising up my hand a bit
    I snapped the tiny branch of a great thornbush,
    and its trunk cried: "Why are you tearing me?"[5]   33
And when its blood turned dark around the wound,
    it started saying more: "Why do you rip me?
    Have you no sense of pity whatsoever?   36
Men were we once, now we are changed to scrub;
    but even if we had been souls of serpents,
    your hand should have shown more pity than it did."   39
Like a green log burning at one end only,
    sputtering at the other, oozing sap,
    and hissing with the air it forces out,   42
so from that splintered trunk a mixture poured
    of words and blood. I let the branch I held
    fall from my hand and stood there stiff with fear.   45
"O wounded soul," my sage replied to him,
    "if he had only let himself believe
    what he had read in verses I once wrote,[6]   48
he never would have raised his hand against you,
    but the truth itself was so incredible,
    I urged him on to do the thing that grieves me.   51
But tell him who you were; he can make amends,
    and will, by making bloom again your fame
    in the world above, where his return is sure."   54
And the trunk: "So appealing are your lovely words,
    I must reply. Be not displeased if I
    am lured into a little conversation.[7]   57
I am that one who held both of the keys
    that fitted Frederick's heart; I turned them both,
    locking and unlocking, with such finesse   60
that I let few into his confidence.
    I was so faithful to my glorious office,
    I lost not only sleep but life itself.   63
That courtesan who constantly surveyed
    Caesar's household with her adulterous eyes,

4. Your thoughts that the moans come from people concealed among the trees will cease or "break off."
5. This episode derives from *Aeneid* 3, where Aeneas and his Trojan companions, stopping in their search for a new home, discover Polydorus transformed into a bush. Sent out by Priam during the war to solicit aid from the Thracians, Polydorus had been murdered by his hosts, and the javelins with which his body had been pierced had grown into the bush from which Aeneas breaks off a branch that bleeds. See also Ovid, *Metamorphoses* 2.   6. Had Dante been able to believe the story of Polydorus recounted in the *Aeneid*.
7. This is the soul of Pier della Vigna (ca. 1190–1249), who had risen to become minister to the Emperor Frederick II (on whom see n. 9, p. 1245.); Frederick is referred to here as "Caesar" and "Augustus" because he sought to imitate the imperial court of Rome. Pier's name means Peter of the Vine, probably because his father had been a simple worker in a vineyard.

mankind's undoing, the special vice of courts,[8]   66
inflamed the hearts of everyone against me,
    and these, inflamed, inflamed in turn Augustus,
    and my happy honors turned to sad laments.   69
My mind, moved by scornful satisfaction,
    believing death would free me from all scorn,
    made me unjust to me, who was all just.[9]   72
By these strange roots of my own tree I swear
    to you that never once did I break faith
    with my lord, who was so worthy of all honor.   75
If one of you should go back to the world,
    restore the memory of me, who here
    remain cut down by the blow that Envy gave."   78
My poet paused awhile, then said to me,
    "Since he is silent now, don't lose your chance,
    ask him, if there is more you wish to know."   81
"Why don't you keep on questioning," I said,
    "and ask him, for my part, what I would ask,
    for I cannot, such pity chokes my heart."   84
He began again: "That this man may fulfill
    generously what your words cry out for,
    imprisoned soul, may it please you to continue   87
by telling us just how a soul gets bound
    into these knots, and tell us, if you know,
    whether any soul might someday leave his branches."   90
At that the trunk breathed heavily, and then
    the breath changed to a voice that spoke these words:
    "Your question will be answered very briefly.   93
The moment that the violent soul departs
    the body it has torn itself away from,
    Minòs sends it down to the seventh hole;   96
it drops to the wood, not in a place allotted,
    but anywhere that fortune tosses it.
    There, like a grain of spelt,[1] it germinates,   99
soon springs into a sapling, then a wild tree;
    at last the Harpies, feasting on its leaves,
    create its pain, and for the pain an outlet.   102
Like the rest, we shall return to claim our bodies,[2]
    but never again to wear them—wrong it is
    for a man to have again what he once cast off.   105
We shall drag them here and, all along the mournful
    forest, our bodies shall hang forever more,
    each one on a thorn of its own alien shade."   108
We were standing still attentive to the trunk,
    thinking perhaps it might have more to say,
    when we were startled by a rushing sound,   111
such as the hunter hears from where he stands:
    first the boar, then all the chase approaching,
    the crash of hunting dogs and branches smashing,   114

8. Pier means Envy, on whom he blames his fall from favor.   9. I unjustly committed suicide even though I was innocent of the accusations brought against me.   1. Wheat.   2. At the Last Judgment.

then, to the left of us appeared two shapes[3]
   naked and gashed, fleeing with such rough speed
   they tore away with them the bushes' branches.   117
The one ahead: "Come on, come quickly, Death!"
   The other, who could not keep up the pace,
   screamed, "Lano, your legs were not so nimble   120
when you jousted in the tournament of Toppo!"[4]
   And then, from lack of breath perhaps, he slipped
   into a bush and wrapped himself in thorns.   123
Behind these two the wood was overrun
   by packs of black bitches ravenous and ready,
   like hunting dogs just broken from their chains;   126
they sank their fangs in that poor wretch who hid,
   they ripped him open piece by piece, and then
   ran off with mouthfuls of his wretched limbs.   129
Quickly my escort took me by the hand
   and led me over to the bush that wept
   its vain laments from every bleeding sore.[5]   132
"O Giacomo da Sant' Andrea," it said,
   "what good was it for you to hide in me?
   What fault have I if you led an evil life?"   135
My master, standing over it, inquired:
   "Who were you once that now through many wounds
   breathes a grieving sermon with your blood?"   138
He answered us: "O souls who have just come
   in time to see this unjust mutilation
   that has separated me from all my leaves,   141
gather them round the foot of this sad bush.
   I was from the city that took the Baptist
   in exchange for her first patron,[6] who, for this,   144
swears by his art she will have endless sorrow;
   and were it not that on the Arno's[7] bridge
   some vestige of his image still remains,   147
those citizens who built anew the city
   on the ashes that Attila left behind
   would have accomplished such a task in vain;[8]   150
I turned my home into my hanging place."

CANTO XIV

*They come to the edge of the Wood of the Suicides, where they see before them a
stretch of burning sand upon which flames rain enternally and through which a stream
of boiling blood is carried in a raised channel formed of rock. There, many groups of
tortured souls are on the burning sand; Virgil explains that those lying supine on the
ground are the Blasphemers, those crouching are the Usurers, and those wandering
aimlessly, never stopping, are the Sodomites. Representative of the blasphemers is
Capaneus, who died cursing his god. The Pilgrim questions his guide about the source*

---

3. Lano of Siena and Giacomo da Sant' Andrea of Padua, two Italians of a generation earlier than
Dante's; both were reputed to be spendthrifts.   4. Lano was killed at a battle on the river Toppo in 1287.
5. Nothing is known about this suicide, who hanged himself from his own house.   6. Florence; when
the Florentines converted to Christianity, John the Baptist replaced Mars as patron of the city, and therefore Mars will forever persecute the city with civil war.   7. The river that runs through Florence.
8. According to legend, Attila the Hun destroyed Florence when he invaded Italy in the 5th century.

of the river of boiling blood; Virgil's reply contains the most elaborate symbol in the
Inferno, that of the Old Man of Crete, whose tears are the source of all the rivers in
Hell.

The love we both shared for our native city
   moved me to gather up the scattered leaves
   and give them back to the voice that now had faded.   3
We reached the confines of the woods that separate
   the second from the third round.[9] There I saw
   God's justice in its dreadful operation.   6
Now to picture clearly these unheard-of things:
   we arrived to face an open stretch of flatland
   whose soil refused the roots of any plant;   9
the grieving forest made a wreath around it,
   as the sad river of blood enclosed the woods.
   We stopped right here, right at the border line.   12
This wasteland was a dry expanse of sand,
   thick, burning sand, no different from the kind
   that Cato's[1] feet packed down in other times.   15
O just revenge of God! how awesomely
   you should be feared by everyone who reads
   these truths that were revealed to my own eyes!   18
Many separate herds of naked souls I saw,
   all weeping desperately; it seemed each group
   had been assigned a different penalty: 21
some souls were stretched out flat upon their backs,
   others were crouching there all tightly hunched,
   some wandered, never stopping, round and round.   24
Far more there were of those who roamed the sand
   and fewer were the souls stretched out to suffer,
   but their tongues were looser, for the pain was greater.   27
And over all that sandland, a fall of slowly
   raining broad flakes of fire showered steadily
   (a mountain snowstorm on a windless day),   30
like those that Alexander saw descending
   on his troops while crossing India's torrid lands:
   flames falling, floating solid to the ground,   33
and he with all his men began to tread
   the sand so that the burning flames might be
   extinguished one by one before they joined.[2]   36
Here too a never-ending blaze descended,
   kindling the sand like tinder under flint-sparks,
   and in this way the torment there was doubled.   39
Without a moment's rest the rhythmic dance
   of wretched hands went on, this side, that side,
   brushing away the freshly fallen flames.   42
And I: "My master, you who overcome

---

9. The third ring of the seventh circle is surrounded by the second ring of the woods through which Dante
has just passed and the first ring of the river of blood described in canto 12.   1. Roman general (1st century B.C.E.) who campaigned in Libya.   2. Dante is here following an account by the philosopher Alber-
tus Magnus (d. 1280) of a legendary adventure that befell Alexander the Great in his conquest of India.

all opposition (except for those tough demons
  who came to meet us at the gate of Dis),   45
who is that mighty one that seems unbothered
  by burning, stretched sullen and disdainful there,
  looking as if the rainfall could not tame him?"[3]   48
And that very one, who was quick to notice me
  inquiring of my guide about him, answered:
  "What I was once, alive, I still am, dead!   51
Let Jupiter wear out his smith,[4] from whom
  he seized in anger that sharp thunderbolt
  he hurled, to strike me down, my final day;   54
let him wear out those others, one by one,
  who work the soot-black forge of Mongibello[5]
  (as he shouts, 'Help me, good Vulcan, I need your help,' 57
the way he cried that time at Phlegra's battle),[6]
  and with all his force let him hurl his bolts at me,
  no joy of satisfaction would I give him!"   60
My guide spoke back at him with cutting force,
  (I never heard his voice so strong before):
  "O Capaneus, since your blustering pride   63
will not be stilled, you are made to suffer more:
  no torment other than your rage itself
  could punish your gnawing pride more perfectly." 66
And then he turned a calmer face to me,
  saying, "That was a king, one of the seven
  besieging Thebes; he scorned, and would seem still 69
to go on scorning God and treat him lightly,
  but, as I said to him, he decks his chest
  with ornaments of lavish words that prick him. 72
Now follow me and also pay attention
  not to put your feet upon the burning sand,
  but to keep them well within the wooded line." 75
Without exchanging words we reached a place
  where a narrow stream came gushing from the woods
  (its reddish water still runs fear through me!); 78
like the one that issues from the Bulicame,[7]
  whose waters are shared by prostitutes downstream,
  it wore its way across the desert sand.   81
This river's bed and banks were made of stone,
  so were the tops on both its sides; and then
  I understood this was our way across.   84
"Among the other marvels I have shown you,
  from the time we made our entrance through the gate
  whose threshold welcomes every evil soul,   87
your eyes have not discovered anything
  as remarkable as this stream you see here

---

3. Capaneus, one of the seven legendary kings who besieged Thebes as described in the *Thebaid* by Statius (d. 95 C.E.). He was struck with a thunderbolt when he boasted that not even Jupiter could stop him.
4. Vulcan.   5. The Sicilian name for Mt. Etna, thought to be Vulcan's furnace. *Those others* are the Cyclopes, Vulcan's helpers.   6. Jove defeated the rebellious Titans at the battle of Phlegra (see 31.43).
7. A hot sulphurous spring that supplied water to brothels in an area of northern Italy.

extinguishing the flames above its path."   90
These were my master's words, and I at once
  implored him to provide me with the food
  for which he had given me the appetite.   93
"In the middle of the sea there lies a wasteland,"
  he immediately began, "that is known as Crete,
  under whose king the world knew innocence.[8]   96
There is a mountain there that was called Ida;
  then happy in its verdure and its streams,
  now deserted like an old, discarded thing;   99
Rhea chose it once as a safe cradle
  for her son, and, to conceal his presence better,
  she had her servants scream loud when he cried.[9]   102
In the mountain's core an ancient man stands tall;
  he has his shoulders turned toward Damietta[1]
  and faces Rome as though it were his mirror.   105
His head is fashioned of the finest gold;
  pure silver are his arms and hands and chest;
  from there to where his legs spread, he is brass;   108
the rest of him is all of chosen iron,
  except his right foot which is terra cotta;
  he puts more weight on this foot than the other.[2]   111
Every part of him, except the gold, is broken
  by a fissure dripping tears down to his feet,
  where they collect to erode the cavern's rock;   114
from stone to stone they drain down here, becoming
  rivers: the Acheron, Styx, and Phlegethon,
  then overflow down through this tight canal   117
until they fall to where all falling ends:
  they form Cocytus.[3] What that pool is like
  I need not tell you. You will see, yourself."   120
And I to him: "If this small stream beside us
  has its source, as you have told me, in our world,
  why have we seen it only on this ledge?"   123
And he to me: "You know this place is round,
  and though your journey has been long, circling
  toward the bottom, turning only to the left,   126
you still have not completed a full circle;
  so you should never look surprised, as now,
  if you see something you have not seen before."   129
And I again: "Where, Master, shall we find
  Lethe and Phlegethon? You omit the first
  and say the other forms from the rain of tears."   132
"I am very happy when you question me,"
  he said, "but that the blood-red water boiled

---

8. Saturn, mythical king of Crete during the golden age.   9. Jupiter was hidden by his mother, Rhea, from his father, Saturn, who tried to devour all his children to thwart a prophecy that he would be dethroned by one of them. So that Saturn would not hear the infant's cries, Rhea had her servants cry out and beat their shields with their swords.   1. A city in Egypt. The Old Man has been interpreted as an emblem of the decline of human history.   2. The four metals and the clay represent the degeneration of history; Dante took them from Daniel 2.31–35.   3. The frozen lake at the bottom of Hell: see 32.22–30 and 34.52.

should answer certainly one of your questions.[4]   135
And Lethe you shall see, but beyond this valley,
   at a place where souls collect to wash themselves
   when penitence has freed them of their guilt.[5]   138
Now it is time to leave this edge of woods,"
   he added. "Be sure you follow close behind me:
   the margins are our road, they do not burn,   141
and all the flames above them are extinguished."

CANTO XV

They move out across the plain of burning sand, walking along the ditchlike edge of the conduit through which the Phlegethon flows, and after they have come some distance from the wood they see a group of souls running toward them. One, Brunetto Latini, a famous Florentine intellectual and Dante's former teacher, recognizes the Pilgrim and leaves his band to walk and talk with him. Brunetto learns the reason for the Pilgrim's journey and offers him a prophecy of the troubles lying in wait for him—an echo of Ciacco's words in Canto VI. Brunetto names some of the others being punished with him (Priscian, Francesco D'Accorso, Andrea de' Mozzi); but soon, in the distance, he sees a cloud of smoke approaching, which presages a new group, and because he must not associate with them, like a foot-racer Brunetto speeds away to catch up with his own band.

Now one of those stone margins bears us on
   and the river's vapors hover like a shade,
   sheltering the banks and the water from the flames.   3
As the Flemings, living with the constant threat
   of flood tides rushing in between Wissant
   and Bruges,[6] build their dikes to force the sea back;   6
as the Paduans build theirs on the shores of Brenta[7]
   to protect their town and homes before warm weather
   turns Chiarentana's snow to rushing water—   9
so were these walls we walked upon constructed,
   though the engineer, whoever he may have been,
   did not make them as high or thick as those.   12
We had left the wood behind (so far behind,
   by now, that if I had stopped to turn around,
   I am sure it could no longer have been seen)   15
when we saw a troop of souls come hurrying
   toward us beside the bank, and each of them
   looked us up and down, as some men look   18
at other men, at night, when the moon is new.
   They strained their eyebrows, squinting hard at us,
   as an old tailor might at his needle's eye.   21
Eyed in such a way by this strange crew,
   I was recognized by one of them, who grabbed
   my garment's hem and shouted: "How marvelous!"   24
And I, when he reached out his arm toward me,

---

4. See n. 2, p. 1251.   5. Lethe is crossed when Dante passes into the Earthly Paradise on the top of Mount Purgatory.   6. Cities that, for Dante, mark the two ends of the dike that protects Flanders from the sea.   7. A river that flows through Padua, fed by the melting snows in the mountains of the province of Chiarentana (modern Carinthia in Austria).

straining my eyes, saw through his face's crust,
    through his burned features that could not prevent   27
my memory from bringing back his name;
    and bending my face down to meet with his,
    I said: "Is this really you, here, Ser Brunetto?"[8]   30
And he: "O my son, may it not displease you
    if Brunetto Latini lets his troop file on
    while he walks at your side for a little while."   33
And I: "With all my heart I beg you to,
    and if you wish me to sit here with you,
    I will, if my companion does not mind."   36
"My son," he said, "a member of this herd
    who stops one moment lies one hundred years
    unable to brush off the wounding flames,   39
so, move on; I shall follow at your hem
    and then rejoin my family that moves
    along, lamenting their eternal pain."   42
I did not dare step off the margin-path
    to walk at his own level but, with head
    bent low in reverence, I moved along.   45
He began: "What fortune or what destiny
    leads you down here before your final hour?
    And who is this one showing you the way?"   48
"Up there above in the bright living life
    before I reached the end of all my years,
    I lost myself in a valley," I replied;   51
"just yesterday at dawn I turned from it.
    This spirit here appeared as I turned back,
    and by this road he guides me home again."   54
He said to me: "Follow your constellation
    and you cannot fail to reach your port of glory,
    not if I saw clearly in the happy life;   57
and if I had not died just when I did,
    I would have cheered you on in all your work,
    seeing how favorable Heaven was to you.   60
But that ungrateful and malignant race
    which descended from the Fiesole[9] of old,
    and still have rock and mountain in their blood,   63
will become, for your good deeds, your enemy—
    and right they are: among the bitter berries
    there's no fit place for the sweet fig to bloom.[1]   66
They have always had the fame of being blind,
    an envious race, proud and avaricious;
    you must not let their ways contaminate you,   69
Your destiny reserves such honors for you:
    both parties shall be hungry to devour you,

---

8. Brunetto Latini (ca. 1220–1294), active in Florentine politics and the author of—among other works—two books: a prose encyclopedia in French called the *Tresor*, which emphasizes the qualities needed for civic duty, and a shorter allegorical poem in Italian called the *Tesoretto*, which combines autobiography with philosophy.   9. A hill town north of Florence whose rustic inhabitants were supposed to have joined with noble Romans in the founding of Florence, creating an unstable mixture.   1. The *bitter berries* are the Florentines descended from Fiesole; the *sweet fig* is Brunetto's term for the aristocratic Dante.

but the grass will not be growing where the goat is.[2]   72
Let the wild beasts of Fiesole make fodder
   of each other, and let them leave the plant untouched
   (so rare it is that one grows in their dung-heap)   75
in which there lives again the holy seed
   of those remaining Romans who survived there
   when this new nest of malice was constructed."   78
"Oh, if all I wished for had been granted,"
   I answered him, "you certainly would not,
   not yet, be banished from our life on earth;   81
my mind is etched (and now my heart is pierced)
   with your kind image, loving and paternal,
   when, living in the world, hour after hour   84
you taught me how man makes himself eternal.[3]
   And while I live my tongue shall always speak
   of my debt to you, and of my gratitude.   87
I will write down what you tell me of my future
   and save it, with another text, to show
   a lady who can interpret, if I can reach her.[4]   90
This much, at least, let me make clear to you:
   if my conscience continues not to blame me,
   I am ready for whatever Fortune wants.   93
This prophecy is not new to my ears,
   and so let Fortune turn her wheel, spinning it
   as she pleases, and the peasant turn his spade."[5]   96
My master, hearing this, looked to the right,
   then, turning round and facing me, he said:
   "He listens well who notes well what he hears."   99
But I did not answer him; I went on talking,
   walking with Ser Brunetto, asking him
   who of his company were most distinguished.   102
And he: "It might be good to know who some are,
   about the rest I feel I should be silent,
   for the time would be too short, there are so many.   105
In brief, let me tell you, all here were clerics
   and respected men of letters of great fame,
   all befouled in the world by one same sin:[6]   108
Priscian is traveling with that wretched crowd
   and Franceso d'Accorso too,[7] and also there,
   if you could have stomached such repugnancy,   111
you might have seen the one the Servant of Servants
   transferred to the Bacchiglione from the Arno
   where his sinfully erected nerves were buried.[8]   114
I would say more, but my walk and conversation

2. Either both parties will ask you to join them or both parties will want to devour you—but keep yourself apart.   3. In the *Tresor* Brunetto says that earthly glory gives man a second life through an enduring reputation.   4. Beatrice.   5. The traditional image of Fortune and her wheel is here compared to the rustic image of the peasant turning the soil with his hoe.   6. Sodomy, condemned in the Middle Ages as unnatural.   7. *Priscian* was a Greek grammarian (6th century c.e.), *Francesco d'Accorso* a Florentine law professor (d. 1293).   8. Andrea de' Mozzi, bishop of Florence (1287–95), transferred by Pope Boniface (designated here by an official title for the pope, *the Servant of* [Christ's] *Servants*) from Florence to Vicenza: the Arno runs through Florence, the Bacchiglione through Vicenza.

with you cannot go on, for over there
   I see a new smoke rising from the sand: 117
people approach with whom I must not mingle.
   Remember my *Trésor*, where I live on,
   this is the only thing I ask of you."   120
Then he turned back, and he seemed like one of those
   who run Verona's race across its fields
   to win the green cloth prize;[9] and he was like   123
the winner of the group, not the last one in.

CANTO XVI

Continuing through the third round of the Circle of Violence, the Pilgrim hears the distant roar of a waterfall, which grows louder as he and his guide proceed. Suddenly three shades, having recognized him as a Florentine, break from their company and converse with him, all the while circling like a turning wheel. Their spokesman, Jacopo Rusticucci, identifies himself and his companions (Guido Guerra and Tegghiaio Aldobrandini) as well-known and honored citizens of Florence, and begs for news of their native city. The three ask to be remembered in the world and then rush off. By this time the sound of the waterfall is so deafening that it almost drowns out speech, and when the poets reach the edge of the precipice, Virgil takes a cord which had been bound around his pupil's waist and tosses it into the abyss. It is a signal, and in response a monstrous form looms up from below, swimming through the air. On this note of suspense, the canto ends.

Already we were where I could hear the rumbling
   of the water plunging down to the next circle,
   something like the sound of beehives humming,   3
when three shades with one impulse broke away,
   running, from a group of spirits passing us
   beneath the rain of bitter suffering.   6
They were coming toward us shouting with one voice:
   "O you there, stop! From the clothes you wear, you seem
   to be a man from our perverted city."[1]   9
Ah, the wounds I saw covering their limbs,
   some old, some freshly branded by the flames!
   Even now, when I think back to them, I grieve.   12
Their shouts caught the attention of my guide,
   and then he turned to face me, saying, "Wait,
   for these are shades that merit your respect.   15
And were it not the nature of this place
   to rain with piercing flames, I would suggest
   you run toward *them*, for it would be more fitting."[2]   18
When we stopped, they resumed their normal pace
   and when they reached us, then they started circling;
   the three together formed a turning wheel,   21
just like professional wrestlers stripped and oiled,
   eyeing one another for the first, best grip

---

9. A footrace run at Verona on the first Sunday in Lent, the prize being a piece of green cloth. For the race to be run by the Christian, see 1 Corinthians 9.24–25.   1. Florence.   2. To hurry was considered undignified.

before the actual blows and thrusts begin.[3] 24
And circling in this way each kept his face
  pointed up at me, so that their necks and feet
  moved constantly in opposite directions. 27
"And if the misery along these sterile sands,"
  one of them said, "and our charred and peeling flesh
  make us, and what we ask, repulsive to you, 30
let our great wordly fame persuade your heart
  to tell us who you are, how you can walk
  safely with living feet through Hell itself. 33
This one in front, whose footsteps I am treading,
  even though he runs his round naked and skinned,
  was of noble station, more than you may think: 36
he was the grandson of the good Gualdrada;
  his name was Guido Guerra,[4] and in his life
  he accomplished much with counsel and with sword. 39
This other one, who pounds the sand behind me,
  is Tegghiaio Aldobrandi,[5] whose wise voice
  the world would have done well to listen to. 42
And I, who share this post of pain with them,
  was Jacopo Rusticucci[6] and for sure
  my reluctant wife first drove me to my sin." 45
If I could have been sheltered from the fire,
  I would have thrown myself below with them,
  and I think my guide would have allowed me to; 48
but, as I knew I would be burned and seared,
  my fear won over my first good intention
  that made me want to put my arms around them. 51
And then I spoke: "Repulsion, no, but grief
  for your condition spread throughout my heart
  (and years will pass before it fades away), 54
as soon as my lord here began to speak
  in terms that led me to believe a group
  of such men as yourselves might be approaching. 57
I am from your city, and your honored names
  and your accomplishments I have always heard
  rehearsed, and have rehearsed, myself, with fondness. 60
I leave the bitter gall, and journey toward
  those sweet fruits promised me by my true guide,[7]
  but first I must go down to the very center." 63
"So may your soul remain to guide your body
  for years to come," that same one spoke again,
  "and your fame's light shine after you are gone, 66
tell us if courtesy and valor dwell
  within our city as they used to do,
  or have they both been banished from the place? 69
Guglielmo Borsiere,[8] who joined our painful ranks

---

3. The three naked Florentines form a circle and are compared to oiled wrestlers (a sport practiced in Dante's time).   4. A leading participant in the civil strife in Florence (d. 1272).   5. An ally of Guido (see 6.79).   6. An ally of Tegghiaio who blames his wife for his sodomy (see 6.80).   7. Leave Hell and head for Paradise.   8. An elegant member of Florentine society.

of late, and travels there with our companions,
    has given us reports that make us grieve."[9]   72
"A new breed of people with their sudden wealth
    have stimulated pride and unrestraint
    in you, O Florence, made to weep so soon."   75
These words I shouted with my head strained high,
    and the three below took this to be my answer
    and looked, as if on truth, at one another.   78
"If you always answer questions with such ease,"
    they all spoke up at once, "O happy you,
    to have this gift of ready, open speech;   81
therefore, if you survive these unlit regions
    and return to gaze upon the lovely stars,
    when it pleases you to say 'I was down there,'   84
do not fail to speak of us to living men."
    They broke their man-made wheel and ran away,
    their nimble legs were more like wings in flight.   87
"Amen" could not have been pronounced as quick
    as they were off, and vanished from our sight;
    and then my teacher thought it time to leave.   90
I followed him, and we had not gone far
    before the sound of water was so close
    that if we spoke we hardly heard each other.   93
As that river on the Apennines' left slope,[1]
    first springing from its source at Monte Veso,
    then flowing eastward holding its own course   96
(called Acquacheta at its start above
    before descending to its lower bed
    where, at Forli, it has another name),   99
reverberates there near San Benedetto
    dell'Alpe (plunging in a single bound),
    where at least a thousand vassals could be housed,   102
so down a single rocky precipice
    we found the tainted waters falling, roaring
    sound loud enough to deafen us in seconds.   105
I wore a cord that fastened round my waist,[2]
    with which I once had thought I might be able
    to catch the leopard with the gaudy skin.[3]   108
As soon as I removed it from my body
    just as my guide commanded me to do,
    I gave it to him looped into a coil.   111
Then taking it and turning to the right,
    he flung it quite a distance past the bank
    and down into the deepness of the pit.   114
"Now surely something strange is going to happen,"

---

9. An account of the recent dissension within the city, to which Dante himself was soon to fall victim.
1. Dante compares the roar of Phlegethon to the Montone River in northern Italy, whose course he traces in the next nine lines.   2. While commentators disagree, it seems likely that this cord is a reference both to Job 41.1, where God says He can draw Leviathan up with a hook and bind his tongue with a cord, and to Francis of Assisi, who wore a cord as a sign of humility and obedience. As a layman, Dante may have had a connection with the Franciscan friars, a common circumstance at the time.   3. The leopard of canto 1, representing fraud.

I thought to myself, "to answer the strange signal
   whose course my master follows with his eyes."
How cautious a man must be in company   117
   with one who can not only see his actions
   but read his mind and understand his thoughts!⁴   120
He spoke: "Soon will rise up what I expect;
   and what you are trying to imagine now
   soon must reveal itself before your eyes."   123
It is always better to hold one's tongue than speak
   a truth that seems a bold-faced lie when uttered,
   since to tell this truth could be embarrassing;   126
but I shall not keep quiet; and by the verses
   of my *Comedy*—so may they be received
   with lasting favor, Reader—I swear to you   129
I saw a figure coming, it was swimming
   through the thick and murky air, up to the top
   (a thing to startle even stalwart hearts),   132
like one returning who has swum below
   to free the anchor that has caught its hooks
   on a reef or something else the sea conceals,   135
spreading out his arms, and doubling up his legs.

CANTO XVII

*The beast that had been seen approaching at the end of the last canto is the horrible
monster Geryon; his face is appealing like that of an honest man, but his body ends in
a scorpionlike stinger. He perches on the edge of the abyss and Virgil advises his ward,
who has noticed new groups of sinners squatting on the fiery sand, to learn who they
are, while he makes arrangements with Geryon for the descent. The sinners are the
Usurers, unrecognizable except by the crests on the moneybags hanging about their
necks, which identify them as members of the Gianfigliazzi, Ubriachi, and Scrovegni
families. The Pilgrim listens to one of them briefly but soon returns to find his master
sitting on Geryon's back. After he conquers his fear and mounts, too, the monster
begins the slow, spiraling descent into the Eighth Circle.*

"And now, behold the beast with pointed tail
   that passes mountains, annulling walls and weapons,
   behold the one that makes the whole world stink!"⁵   3
These were the words I heard my master say
   as he signaled for the beast to come ashore,
   up close to where the rocky levee ends.   6
And that repulsive spectacle of fraud
   floated close, maneuvering head and chest
   on to the shore, but his tail he let hang free.   9
His face was the face of any honest man,
   it shone with such a look of benediction;
   and all the rest of him was serpentine;   12
his two clawed paws were hairy to the armpits,

---

4. Dante now realizes that Virgil can read his thoughts.   **5.** Geryon, the embodiment of fraud. For this
figure Dante drew upon classical literature, where he had not three natures—human, reptilian, and
bestial—combined into one, as here, but three bodies and three heads.

his back and all his belly and both flanks
  were painted arabesques and curlicues: 15
the Turks and Tartars never made a fabric
  with richer colors intricately woven,
  nor were such complex webs spun by Arachne.[6]   18
As sometimes fishing boats are seen ashore,
  part fixed in sand, and part still in the water;
  and as the beaver,[7] living in the land   21
of drunken Germans,[8] squats to catch his prey,
  just so that beast, the worst of beasts, hung waiting
  on the bank that bounds the stretch of sand in stone.   24
In the void beyond he exercised his tail,
  twitching and twisting-up the venomed fork
  that armed its tip just like a scorpion's stinger.   27
My leader said: "Now we must turn aside
  a little from our path, in the direction
  of that malignant beast that lies in wait."   30
Then we stepped off our path down to the right
  and moved ten paces straight across the brink
  to keep the sand and flames at a safe distance.   33
And when we stood by Geryon's side, I noticed,
  a little farther on, some people crouched
  in the sand quite close to the edge of emptiness.   36
Just then my master spoke: "So you may have
  a knowledge of this round that is complete,"
  he said, "go and see their torment for yourself.   39
But let your conversation there be brief;
  while you are gone I shall speak to this one
  and ask him for the loan of his strong back."   42
So I continued walking, all alone,
  along the seventh circle's outer edge
  to where the group of sufferers were sitting.   45
The pain was bursting from their eyes; their hands
  went scurrying up and down to give protection
  here from the flames, there from the burning sands.   48
They were, in fact, like a dog in summertime
  busy, now with his paw, now with his snout,
  tormented by the fleas and flies that bite him.   51
I carefully examined several faces
  among this group caught in the raining flames
  and did not know a soul, but I observed   54
that around each sinner's neck a pouch was hung,
  each of a different color, with a coat of arms,
  and fixed on these they seemed to feast their eyes.[9]   57
And while I looked about among the crowd,
  I saw something in blue on a yellow purse
  that had the face and bearing of a lion;   60

6. A woman in classical literature famous for weaving, turned into a spider: see Ovid, *Metamorphoses* 6.
7. Which was thought to catch fish by putting its tail into the water.   8. A tradition going back to the
Romans accused the Germans of drunkenness.   9. These are usurers, men who lent money for interest,
which was forbidden by the Church in the Middle Ages (although often practiced). Each has a coat of arms
on his purse by which he can be identified; all are Italians.

and while my eyes continued their inspection
   I saw another purse as red as blood
   exhibiting a goose more white than butter.   63
And one who had a blue sow, pregnant-looking,
   stamped on the whiteness of his moneybag
   asked me: "What are you doing in this pit?   66
Get out of here! And since you're still alive,
   I'll tell you that my neighbor Vitaliano
   will come to take his seat on my left side.[1]   69
Among these Florentines I sit, one Paduan:
   time after time they fill my ears with blasts
   of shouting: 'Send us down the sovereign knight[2]   72
who will come bearing three goats on his pouch.'"
   As final comment he stuck out his tongue—
   as far out as an ox licking its nose.   75
And I, afraid my staying there much longer
   might anger the one who warned me to be brief,
   turned my back on these frustrated sinners.   78
I found my guide already sitting high
   upon the back of that fierce animal;
   he said: "And now, take courage and be strong.   81
From now on we descend by stairs like these.
   Get on up front. I want to ride behind,
   to be between you and the dangerous tail."[3]   84
A man who feels the shivers of a fever
   coming on, his nails already dead of color,
   will tremble at the mere sight of cool shade;   87
I was that man when I had heard his words.
   But then I felt those stabs of shame that make
   a servant brave before his valorous master.   90
As I squirmed around on those enormous shoulders,
   I wanted to cry out, "Hold on to me,"
   but I had no voice to second my desire.   93
Then he who once before had helped me out
   when I was threatened put his arms around me
   as soon as I was settled, and held me tight;   96
and then he cried: "Now Geryon, start moving,
   descend with gentle motion, circling wide:
   remember you are carrying living weight."   99
Just as a boat slips back away from shore,
   back slowly, more and more, he left that pier;
   and when he felt himself all clear in space,   102
to where his breast had been he swung his tail
   and stretched it undulating like an eel,
   as with his paws he gathered in the air.   105
I doubt if Phaëthon[4] feared more—that time
   he dropped the sun-reins of his father's chariot
   and burned the streak of sky we see today—   108

1. The speaker is from Padua and here maliciously identifies another Paduan who will soon be joining him.
2. A prominent Florentine banker.   3. Virgil protects Dante from Geryon's scorpion's tail.   4. Son of Apollo, *Phaëthon* tried to drive the chariot of the sun, but when it got out of control it scorched both Earth and the heavens, creating the Milky Way (Ovid, *Metamorphoses* 2).

or if poor Icarus[5] did—feeling his sides
   unfeathering as the wax began to melt,
   his father shouting: "Wrong, your course is wrong"—   111
than I had when I felt myself in air
   and saw on every side nothing but air;
   only the beast I sat upon was there.   114
He moves along slowly, and swimming slowly,
   descends a spiral path—but I know this
   only from a breeze ahead and one below;   117
I hear now on my right the whirlpool roar
   with hideous sound beneath us on the ground;
   at this I stretch my neck to look below,   120
but leaning out soon made me more afraid,
   for I heard moaning there and saw the flames;
   trembling, I cowered back, tightening my legs,   123
and I saw then what I had not before:
   the spiral path of our descent to torment
   closing in on us, it seemed, from every side.   126
As the falcon on the wing for many hours,
   having found no prey, and having seen no signal
   (so that his falconer sighs: "Oh, he falls already"),   129
descends, worn out, circling a hundred times
   (instead of swooping down), settling at some distance
   from his master, perched in anger and disdain,[6]   132
so Geryon brought us down to the bottom
   at the foot of the jagged cliff, almost against it,
   and once he got our bodies off his back,   135
he shot off like a shaft shot from a bowstring.

CANTO XVIII

The Pilgrim describes the view he had of the Eighth Circle of Hell while descending through the air on Geryon's back. It consists of ten stone ravines called Malebolge *(Evil Pockets), and across each* bolgia *is an arching bridge. When the poets find themselves on the edge of the first ravine they see two lines of naked sinners, walking in opposite directions. In one are the Pimps or Panderers, and among them the Pilgrim recognizes Venedico Caccianemico; in the other are the Seducers, among whom Virgil points out Jason. As the two move toward the next* bolgia, *they are assailed by a terrible stench; for here the Flatterers are immersed in excrement. Among them are Alessio Interminei and Thaïs the whore.*

There is a place in Hell called Malebolge,
   cut out of stone the color of iron ore,
   just like the circling cliff that walls it in.   3
Right at the center of this evil plain
   there yawns a very wide, deep well, whose structure
   I will talk of when the place itself is reached.[7]   6
That belt of land remaining, then, runs round

---

5. Flying with wings made of wax and feathers, *Icarus* went too near the sun and fell (Ovid, *Metamorphoses* 8).   6. Unless it sights prey or is called back with a lure by its master, a trained falcon will continue flying until exhaustion compels it to descend.   7. The last, or ninth, circle of Hell, described in cantos 21–34.

between the well and cliff, and all this space
   is divided into ten descending valleys,   9
just like a ground-plan for successive moats
   that in concentric circles bind their center
   and serve to protect the ramparts of the castle.   12
This was the surface image they presented;
   and as bridges from a castle's portal stretch
   from moat to moat to reach the farthest bank,   15
so, from the great cliff's base, just spokes of rock,
   crossing from bank to bank, intersecting ditches
   until the pit's hub cuts them off from meeting.   18
This is the place in which we found ourselves,
   once shaken from the back of Geryon.
   The poet turned to the left, I walked behind him.   21
There, on our right, I saw new suffering souls,
   new means of torture, and new torturers,
   crammed into the depths of the first ditch.   24
Two files of naked souls walked on the bottom,
   the ones on our side faced us as they passed,
   the others moved as we did but more quickly.   27
The Romans, too, in the year of the Jubilee[8]
   took measures to accommodate the throngs
   that had to come and go across their bridge: 30
they fixed it so on one side all were looking
   at the castle, and were walking to St. Peter's;
   on the other, they were moving toward the mount.   33
On both sides, up along the deadly rock,
   I saw horned devils with enormous whips
   lashing the backs of shades with cruel delight.   36
Ah, how they made them skip and lift their heels
   at the very first crack of the whip! Not one of them
   dared pause to take a second or a third!   39
As I walked on my eyes met with the glance
   of one down there; I murmured to myself:
   "I know this face from somewhere, I am sure."[9]   42
And so I stopped to study him more closely;
   my leader also stopped, and was so kind
   as to allow me to retrace my steps;   45
and that whipped soul thought he would hide from me
   by lowering his face—which did no good.
   I said, "O you, there, with your head bent low,   48
if the features of your shade do not deceive me,
   you are Venedico Caccianemico, I'm sure.
   How did you get yourself in such a pickle?"   51
"I'm not so keen on answering," he said,
   "but I feel I must; your plain talk is compelling,
   it makes me think of old times in the world.   54
I was the one who coaxed Ghisolabella

---

8. The year 1300 was a Jubilee Year, and Dante here describes the crowd control on the bridge that ran between the Castle of St. Angelo and St. Peter's. 9. This is Venedico Caccianemico, a man from Bologna who was reputed to have turned his sister Ghisolabella over to the Marquis of Este.

to serve the lusty wishes of the Marquis,
   no matter how the sordid tale is told;   57
I'm not the only Bolognese who weeps here—
   hardly! This place is packed with us; in fact,
   there are more of us here than there are living tongues,   60
between Savena and Reno, saying 'Sipa';[1]
   I call on your own memory as witness:
   remember we have avaricious hearts."   63
Just at that point a devil let him have
   the feel of his tailed whip and cried: "Move on,
   you pimp, you can't cash in on women here!"   66
I turned and hurried to rejoin my guide;
   we walked a few more steps and then we reached
   the rocky bridge that juts out from the bank.   69
We had no difficulty climbing up,
   and turning right, along the jagged ridge,
   we left those shades to their eternal circlings.   72
When we were where the ditch yawned wide below
   the ridge, to make a passage for the scourged,
   my guide said: "Stop and stand where you can see   75
these other misbegotten souls, whose faces
   you could not see before, for they were moving
   in the same direction we were, over there."   78
So from the ancient bridge we viewed the train
   that hurried toward us along the other tract—
   kept moving, like the first, by stinging whips.   81
And the good master, without my asking him,
   said, "Look at that imposing one approaching,
   who does not shed a single tear of pain: 84
what majesty he still maintains down there!
   He is Jason,[2] who by courage and sharp wits,
   fleeced the Colchians of their golden ram.   87
He later journeyed through the isle of Lemnos,
   whose bold and heartless females, earlier,
   had slaughtered every male upon the island;   90
there with his words of love, and loving looks,
   he succeeded in deceiving young Hypsipyle,
   who had in turn deceived the other women.   93
He left her there, with child, and all alone:
   such sin condemns him to such punishment,
   and Medea, too, gets her revenge on him.   96
With him go all deceivers of this type,
   and let this be enough to know concerning
   the first valley and the souls locked in its jaws."   99
We were already where the narrow ridge
   begins to cross the second bank, to make it
   an abutment for another ditch's arch.   102

---

1. *Sipa* is a word for "yes" in the dialect spoken in the territory between the rivers Savena and Reno, which comprise the boundaries of Bologna.   2. *Jason* led the Argonauts on the voyage to the island of Colchis, where they stole the golden fleece. He seduced and abandoned Hypsipyle, who had hidden her father when the other women of Lemnos were killing all the males. He also abandoned Medea, the daughter of the king of Colchis. For his story, see Ovid, *Metamorphoses* 7.

Now we could hear the shades in the next pouch
  whimpering, making snorting grunting sounds
  and sounds of blows, slapping with open palms.   105
From a steaming stench below, the banks were coated
  with a slimy mold that stuck to them like glue,
  disgusting to behold and worse to smell.   108
The bottom was so hollowed out of sight,
  we saw it only when we climbed the arch
  and looked down from the bridge's highest point: 111
there we were, and from where I stood I saw
  souls in the ditch plunged into excrement
  that might well have been flushed from our latrines;   114
my eyes were searching hard along the bottom,
  and I saw somebody's head so smirched with shit,
  you could not tell if he were priest or layman.   117
He shouted up: "Why do you feast your eyes
  on me more than these other dirty beasts?"
  And I replied: "Because, remembering well,   120
I've seen you with your hair dry once or twice.
  You are Alessio Interminei from Lucca,[3]
  that's why I stare at you more than the rest."   123
He beat his slimy forehead as he answered:
  "I am stuck down here by all those flatteries
  that rolled unceasing off my tongue up there."   126
He finished speaking, and my guide began:
  "Lean out a little more, look hard down there
  so you can get a good look at the face   129
of that repulsive and disheveled tramp
  scratching herself with shitty fingernails,
  spreading her legs while squatting up and down: 132
it is Thaïs the whore,[4] who gave this answer
  to her lover when he asked: 'Am I very worthy
  of your thanks?': 'Very? Nay, incredibly so!'   135
I think our eyes have had their fill of this."

CANTO XIX

From the bridge above the Third Bolgia *can be seen a rocky landscape below filled with holes, from each of which protrude a sinner's legs and feet; flames dance across their soles. When the Pilgrim expresses curiosity about a particular pair of twitching legs, Virgil carries him down into the* bolgia *so that the Pilgrim himself may question the sinner. The legs belong to Pope Nicholas III, who astounds the Pilgrim by mistaking him for Boniface VIII, the next pope, who, as soon as he dies, will fall to the same hole, thereby pushing Nicholas farther down. He predicts that soon after Boniface, Pope Clement V will come, stuffing both himself and Boniface still deeper. To Nicholas's rather rhetoric-filled speech the Pilgrim responds with equally high language, inveighing against the Simonists, the evil churchmen who are punished here. Virgil is much pleased with his pupil and, lifting him in an affectionate embrace, he carries him to the top of the arch above the next* bolgia.

3. A prominent citizen of Lucca, in northern Italy.   4. A character in a play by the Roman writer Terence (186 or 185–159? B.C.E.).

O Simon Magus![5] O scum that followed him!
   Those things of God that rightly should be wed
   to holiness, you, rapacious creatures,   3
for the price of gold and silver, prostitute.
   Now, in your honor, I must sound my trumpet
   for here in the third pouch is where you dwell.   6
We had already climbed to see this tomb,
   and were standing high above it on the bridge,
   exactly at the mid-point of the ditch.   9
O Highest Wisdom, how you demonstrate
   your art in Heaven, on earth, and here in Hell!
   How justly does your power make awards![6]   12
I saw along the sides and on the bottom
   the livid-colored rock all full of holes;
   all were the same in size, and each was round.   15
To me they seemed no wider and no deeper
   than those inside my lovely San Giovanni,[7]
   in which the priest would stand or baptize from;   18
and one of these, not many years ago,
   I smashed for someone who was drowning in it:
   let this be mankind's picture of the truth!   21
From the mouth of every hole were sticking out
   a single sinner's feet, and then the legs
   up to the calf—the rest was stuffed inside.   24
The soles of every sinner's feet were flaming;
   their naked legs were twitching frenziedly—
   they would have broken any chain or rope.   27
Just as a flame will only move along
   an object's oily outer peel, so here
   the fire slid from heel to toe and back.   30
"Who is that one, Master, that angry wretch,
   who is writhing more than any of his comrades,"
   I asked, "the one licked by a redder flame?"[8]   33
And he to me, "If you want to be carried down
   along that lower bank to where he is,
   you can ask him who he is and why he's here."   36
And I, "My pleasure is what pleases you:
   you are my lord, you know that from your will
   I would not swerve. You even know my thoughts."   39
When we reached the fourth bank, we began to turn
   and, keeping to the left, made our way down
   to the bottom of the holed and narrow ditch.   42
The good guide did not drop me from his side
   until he brought me to the broken rock

---

5. Because in the Bible *Simon Magus* tried to buy spiritual power from the apostles (Acts 8.9–24), the selling of any spiritual good for material gain was known in the Middle Ages as simony. The most common form of simony was the selling of Church offices.   **6.** Dante is here applauding the artfulness of divine justice because the simoniacs, who cared most for their purses, are here stuffed into fiery purses hewn into the rock; see line 72 below.   **7.** The baptistery in Florence where Dante was baptized. The subsequent personal reference has never been satisfactorily explained.   **8.** Pope Nicholas III (pope 1277–80). He mistakenly believes that one of his successors, Boniface VIII, has come to be squeezed into the hole (line 53). Like all damned souls, Nicholas has foreknowledge, and because Boniface did not die until 1303 Nicholas is surprised at what he thinks is his appearance in 1300.

of that one who was fretting with his shanks.   45
"Whatever you are, holding your upside down,
   O wretched soul, stuck like a stake in ground,
   make a sound or something," I said, "if you can."   48
I stood there like a priest who is confessing
   some vile assassin who, fixed in his ditch,
   has called him back again to put off dying.[9]   51
He cried: "Is that *you*, here, already, upright?
   Is that you here already upright, Boniface?
   By many years the book has lied to me!   54
Are you fed up so soon with all that wealth
   for which you did not fear to take by guile
   the Lovely Lady,[1] then tear her asunder?"   57
I stood there like a person just made fun of,
   dumbfounded by a question for an answer,
   not knowing how to answer the reply.   60
Then Virgil said: "Quick, hurry up and tell him:
   'I'm not the one, I'm not the one you think!'"
   And I answered just the way he told me to.   63
The spirit heard, and twisted both his feet,
   then, sighing with a grieving, tearful voice,
   he said: "Well then, what do you want of me?   66
If it concerns you so to learn my name
   that for this reason you came down the bank,
   know that I once was dressed in the great mantle.   69
But actually I was the she-bear's son,[2]
   so greedy to advance my cubs, that wealth
   I pocketed in life, and here, myself.   72
Beneath my head are pushed down all the others
   who came, sinning in simony, before me,
   squeezed tightly in the fissures of the rock.   75
I, in my turn, shall join the rest below
   as soon as *he* comes, the one I thought you were
   when, all too quick, I put my question to you.   78
But already my feet have baked a longer time
   (and I have been stuck upside-down like this)
   than he will stay here planted with feet aflame: 81
soon after him shall come one from the West,[3]
   a lawless shepherd, one whose fouler deeds
   make him a fitting cover for us both.   84
He shall be another Jason,[4] like the one
   in Maccabees: just as his king was pliant,
   so France's king shall soften to this priest."   87
I do not know, perhaps I was too bold here,
   but I answered him in tune with his own words:
   "Well, tell me now: what was the sum of money   90
that holy Peter had to pay our Lord

---

9. Hired murderers were occasionally executed by being placed head-down in a ditch and then buried alive.
1. The church.   2. The arms of Nicholas's family (the Orsini) included a *she-bear*.   3. Clement V, who became pope in 1305 after agreeing with the French king to remove the papacy to Avignon in France. He is *from the West* because he was born in western France.   4. Jason became high priest of the Jews by bribing the king: see 2 Maccabees 4.7–9.

before He gave the keys into his keeping?
  Certainly He asked no more than 'Follow me.'[5] 93
Nor did Peter or the rest extort gold coins
  or silver from Matthias when he was picked
  to fill the place the evil one had lost.[6] 96
So stay stuck there, for you are rightly punished,
  and guard with care the money wrongly gained
  that made you stand courageous against Charles.[7] 99
And were it not for the reverence I have
  for those highest of all keys that you once held
  in the happy life—if this did not restrain me, 102
I would use even harsher words than these,
  for your avarice brings grief upon the world,
  crushing the good, exalting the depraved. 105
You shepherds it was the Evangelist[8] had in mind
  when the vision came to him of her who sits
  upon the waters playing whore with kings: 108
that one who with the seven heads was born
  and from her ten horns managed to draw strength
  so long as virtue was her bridegroom's joy. 111
You have built yourselves a God of gold and silver!
  How do you differ from the idolator,
  except he worships one, you worship hundreds? 114
O Constantine,[9] what evil did you sire,
  not by your conversion, but by the dower
  that the first wealthy Father got from you!" 117
And while I sang these very notes to him,
  his big flat feet kicked fiercely out of anger,
  —or perhaps it was his conscience gnawing him. 120
I think my master liked what I was saying,
  for all the while he smiled and was intent
  on hearing the ring of truly spoken words. 123
Then he took hold of me with both his arms,
  and when he had me firm against his breast,
  he climbed back up the path he had come down. 126
He did not tire of the weight clasped tight to him,
  but brought me to the top of the bridge's arch,
  the one that joins the fourth bank to the fifth. 129
And here he gently set his burden down—
  gently, for the ridge, so steep and rugged,
  would have been hard even for goats to cross. 132
From there another valley opened to me.

---

5. See Matthew 16.18–19: the keys are the church's power to bind (condemn) and to loose (absolve). For *follow me*, see Matthew 4.18–19.   6. *Matthias* was chosen by lot to fill the place of Judas (Acts 1.23–26).   7. Nicholas was supposed to be involved in a plot against Charles of Anjou (1226–1285), ruler of Naples and Sicily.   8. John, author of Revelation, who in the Middle Ages was identified with the author of the Gospel according to John: for this passage, which was originally interpreted as referring to pagan Rome but which Dante applies to the corrupt Church, see Revelation 17.1–18. The *seven heads* are the seven Sacraments; the *ten horns*, the Ten Commandments; the *bridegroom*, God.   9. Roman Emperor (d. 337) who was the supposed author of a document—known as the Donation of Constantine—in which he granted temporal power and the right to acquire wealth to Pope Sylvester I, *the first wealthy Father* of this passage. The document was proved to be a forgery in the 15th century.

CANTO XX

In the Fourth Bolgia they see a group of shades weeping as they walk slowly along the valley; they are the Soothsayers and their heads are twisted completely around so that their hair flows down their fronts and their tears flow down to their buttocks. Virgil points out many of them, including Amphiaraus, Tiresias, Aruns, and Manto. It was Manto who first inhabited the site of Virgil's home city of Mantua, and the poet gives a long description of the city's founding, after which he names more of the condemned soothsayers: Eurypylus, Michael Scot, Guido Bonatti, and Asdente.

Now I must turn strange torments into verse
   to form the matter of the twentieth canto
   of the first chant, the one about the damned.   3
Already I was where I could look down
   into the depths of the ditch: I saw its floor
   was wet with anguished tears shed by the sinners,   6
and I saw people in the valley's circle,
   silent, weeping, walking at a litany pace
   the way processions push along in our world.[1]   9
And when my gaze moved down below their faces,
   I saw all were incredibly distorted,
   the chin was not above the chest, the neck   12
was twisted—their faces looked down on their backs;
   they had to move ahead by moving backward,
   for they never saw what was ahead of them.   15
Perhaps there was a case of someone once
   in a palsy fit becoming so distorted,
   but none that *I* know of! I doubt there could be!   18
So may God grant you, Reader, benefit
   from reading of my poem, just ask yourself
   how I could keep my eyes dry when, close by,   21
I saw the image of our human form
   so twisted—the tears their eyes were shedding
   streamed down to wet their buttocks at the cleft.   24
Indeed I did weep, as I leaned my body
   against a jut of rugged rock. My guide:
   "So you are still like all the other fools?   27
In this place piety lives when pity is dead,
   for who could be more wicked than that man
   who tries to bend divine will to his own![2]   30
Lift your head up, lift it, see him for whom
   the earth split wide before the Thebans's eyes,
   while they all shouted, 'Where are you rushing off to,   33
Amphiaraus?[3] Why do you quit the war?'
   He kept on rushing downward through the gap
   until Minòs, who gets them all, got him.   36
You see how he has made his back his chest:
   because he wished to see too far ahead,
   he sees behind and walks a backward track.   39

---

1. A *litany* is a form of public prayer, often recited during stately *processions* in the church.   2. This is a rebuke to Dante, who errs by showing sympathy for the damned.   3. A priest swallowed up by the Earth in a battle against the Thebans as described in Statius's *Thebaid* (see n. 3, p. 1257). For Minos, see 5.4.

Behold Tiresias,[4] who changed his looks:
    from a man he turned himself into a woman,
    transforming all his body, part for part;   42
then later on he had to take the wand
    and strike once more those two snakes making love
    before he could get back his virile parts.   45
Backing up to this one's chest comes Aruns,[5]
    who, in the hills of Luni, worked by peasants
    of Carrara dwelling in the valley's plain,   48
lived in white marble cut into a cave,
    and from this site, where nothing blocked his view,
    he could observe the sea and stars with ease.   51
And that one, with her hair loose, flowing back
    to cover both her breasts you cannot see,
    and with her hairy parts in front behind her,   54
was Manto,[6] who had searched through many lands
    before she came to dwell where I was born;
    now let me tell you something of her story.   57
When her father had departed from the living,
    and Bacchus' sacred city[7] fell enslaved,
    she wandered through the world for many years.   60
High in fair Italy there spreads a lake,
    beneath the mountains bounding Germany
    beyond the Tyrol, known as Lake Benaco;[8]   63
by a thousand streams and more, I think, the Alps
    are bathed from Garda to the Val Camonica[9]
    with the waters flowing down into that lake;   66
at its center is a place where all three bishops
    of Trent and Brescia and Verona could,
    if they would ever visit there, say Mass;   69
Peschiera[1] sits, a handsome well-built fortress,
    to ward off Brescians and the Bergamese,
    along the lowest point of that lake's shore,   72
where all the water that Benaco's basin
    cannot hold must overflow to make a stream
    that winds its way through countrysides of green;   75
but when the water starts to flow, its name
    is not Benaco, but Mencio, all the way
    to Governol,[2] where it falls into the Po;   78
but before its course is run it strikes a lowland,
    on which it spreads and turns into a marsh
    that can become unbearable in summer.   81
Passing this place one day the savage virgin
    saw land that lay in the center of the mire,

---

4. A soothsayer of Thebes, he struck two coupling serpents with his rod and was transformed into a woman. Seven years later he repeated the action and was changed back into a man. See Ovid, *Metamorphoses* 3.   5. An Etruscan soothsayer from the city of Luni, in the area of Carrera where marble is quarried, is described by the Roman poet Lucan (d. 65 C.E.) in his *Pharsalia*.   6. Another Theban soothsayer described by Roman poets.   7. Thebes.   8. The present-day Lake Garda in northern Italy, located in terms of an island where the boundaries of the three dioceses of Trent, Brescia, and Verona meet. 9. *Garda* is a town by the lake and *Val Camonica* a valley below it.   1. *Peschiera* is a town on the south shore of the lake; the *Brescians* and the *Bergamese* are inhabitants of two towns to the northwest of Peschiera.   2. A town some thirty miles south of Peschiera. Presumably Virgil provides this detailed geography to illustrate that he is a native of this region.

untilled and empty of inhabitants. 84
There, to escape all human intercourse,
  she stopped to practice magic with her servants;
  there she lived, and there she left her corpse. 87
Later on, the men who lived around there gathered
  on that very spot, for it was well protected
  by the bog that girded it on every side. 90
They built a city over her dead bones,
  and for her, the first to choose that place, they named it
  Mantua,³ without recourse to sorcery. 93
Once, there were far more people living there,
  before the foolish Casalodi listened
  to the fraudulent advice of Pinamonte.⁴ 96
And so, I warn you, should you ever hear
  my city's origin told otherwise,
  let no false tales adulterate the truth."⁵ 99
And I replied: "Master, your explanations
  are truth for me, winning my faith entirely;
  any others would be just like burned-out coals. 102
But speak to me of these shades passing by,
  if you see anyone that is worth noting;
  for now my mind is set on only that." 105
He said: "That one, whose beard flows from his cheeks
  and settles on his back and makes it dark,
  was (when the war stripped Greece of all its males, 108
so that the few there were still rocked in cradles)
  an augur who, with Calchas,⁶ called the moment
  to cut the first ship's cable free at Aulis: 111
he is Eurypylus. I sang his story
  this way, somewhere in my high tragedy:
  you should know where—you know it, every line. 114
That other one, whose thighs are scarcely fleshed,
  was Michael Scot,⁷ who most assuredly
  knew every trick of magic fraudulence. 117
See there Guido Bonatti; see Asdente,⁸
  who wishes now he had been more devoted
  to making shoes—too late now for repentance. 120
And see those wretched hags⁹ who traded in
  needle, spindle, shuttle, for fortune-telling,
  and cast their spells with image-dolls and potions. 123
Now come along. Cain¹ with his thorn-bush straddles

3. Virgil's native city.   4. A reference to the internal intrigues of the rulers of Mantua in the 13th century.   5. Oddly enough, in book 10 of the *Aeneid* Virgil says that Mantua was named by Manto's son Ocnus, not by *the men who lived around there* (see line 88, above). It is not clear why Dante has Virgil contradict his own poem unless he is trying to clear Virgil of any taint of himself being a magician (see n. 2, p. 1240).   6. *Calchas* and *Eurypylus* were prophets (or augurs) involved in the Trojan War; here Virgil says that they determined when the Greeks were to set out for the war from the island of Aulis, although *Aeneid* 2 gives a different account.   7. A famous scientist, philosopher, and astrologer from Scotland, Scot spent many years at the court of Frederick II (10. 119) in Palermo and died in 1235.   8. A shoemaker famous as a soothsayer in 13th-century Italy. *Guido Bonatti*: an astrologer at the court of Guido da Montefeltro (see canto 32).   9. Common soothsayers and potion makers.   1. Popular belief held that God placed Cain in the moon after the murder of Abel; *Cain with his thorn-bush* means the moon with its spots, which is now setting at the western edge of the Northern Hemisphere. Overhead, in Jerusalem, it is the dawn of Holy Saturday.

the confines of both hemispheres already
   and dips into the waves below Seville;   126
and the moon last night already was at full;
   and you should well remember that at times
   when you were lost in the dark wood she helped you."   129
And we were moving all the time he spoke.

CANTO XXI

*When the two reach the summit of the arch over the Fifth Bolgia, they see in the ditch
below the bubbling of boiling pitch. Virgil's sudden warning of danger frightens the
Pilgrim even before he sees a black devil rushing toward them, with a sinner slung over
his shoulder. From the bridge the devil flings the sinner into the pitch, where he is
poked at and tormented by the family of Malebranche devils. Virgil, advising his ward
to hide behind a rock, crosses the bridge to face the devils alone. They threaten him
with their pitchforks, but when he announces to their leader, Malacoda, that Heaven
has willed that he lead another through Hell, the devil's arrogance collapses. Virgil
calls the Pilgrim back to him. Scarmiglione, who tries to take a poke at him, is rebuked
by his leader, who tells the travelers that the sixth arch is broken here but farther on
they will find another bridge to cross. He chooses a squad of his devils to escort them
there: Alichino, Calcabrina, Cagnazzo, Barbariccia, Libicocco, Draghignazzo, Ciriatto, Graffiacane, Farfarello, and Rubicante. The Pilgrim's suspicion about their unsavory escorts is brushed aside by his guide, and the squad starts off, giving an obscene
salute to their captain, who returns their salute with a fart.*

From this bridge to the next we walked and talked
   of things my Comedy does not care to tell;
   and when we reached the summit of the arch,   3
we stopped to see the next fosse² of Malebolge
   and to hear more lamentation voiced in vain:
   I saw that it was very strangely dark!   6
In the vast and busy shipyard of the Venetians³
   there boils all winter long a tough, thick pitch
   that is used to caulk the ribs of unsound ships.   9
Since winter will not let them sail, they toil:
   some build new ships, others repair the old ones,
   plugging the planks come loose from many sailings;   12
some hammer at the bow, some at the stern,
   one carves the oars while others twine the ropes,
   one mends the jib, one patches up the mainsail;   15
here, too, but heated by God's art, not fire,
   a sticky tar was boiling in the ditch
   that smeared the banks with viscous residue.   18
I saw it there, but I saw nothing in it,
   except the rising of the boiling bubbles
   breathing in air to burst and sink again.   21
I stood intently gazing there below,
   my guide, shouting to me: "Watch out, watch out!"
   took hold of me and drew me to his side.   24
I turned my head like one who can't resist

---

2. Ditch or pouch.   3. The huge shipyard at Venice was called the Arsenal.

looking to see what makes him run away
 (his body's strength draining with sudden fear),   27
but, looking back, does not delay his flight;
 and I saw coming right behind our backs,
 rushing along the ridge, a devil, black!   30
His face, his look, how frightening it was!
 With outstretched wings he skimmed along the rock,
 and every single move he made was cruel;   33
on one of his high-hunched and pointed shoulders
 he had a sinner slung by both his thighs,
 held tightly clawed at the tendons of his heels.   36
He shouted from our bridge: "Hey, Malebranche,[4]
 here's one of Santa Zita's elders for you!
 You stick him under—I'll go back for more;   39
I've got that city stocked with the likes of him,
 they're all a bunch of grafters, save Bonturo![5]
 You can change a 'no' to 'yes' for cash in Lucca."   42
He flung him in, then from the flinty cliff
 sprang off. No hound unleashed to chase a thief
 could have taken off with greater speed than he.   45
That sinner plunged, then floated up stretched out,
 and the devils underneath the bridge all shouted:
 "You shouldn't imitate the Holy Face!   48
The swimming's different here from in the Serchio![6]
 We have our grappling-hooks along with us—
 don't show yourself above the pitch, or else!"   51
With a hundred prongs or more they pricked him, shrieking:
 "You've got to do your squirming under cover,
 try learning how to cheat beneath the surface."   54
They were like cooks who make their scullery boys
 poke down into the caldron with their forks
 to keep the meat from floating to the top.   57
My master said: "We'd best not let them know
 that you are here with me; crouch down behind
 some jutting rock so that they cannot see you;   60
whatever insults they may hurl at me,
 you must not fear, I know how things are run here;
 I have been caught in as bad a fix before."[7]   63
He crossed the bridge and walked on past the end;
 as soon as he set foot on the sixth bank
 he forced himself to look as bold as possible.   66
With all the sound and fury that breaks loose
 when dogs rush out at some poor begging tramp,
 making him stop and beg from where he stands,   69
the ones who hid beneath the bridge sprang out

---

4. *Malebranche* (Evil-claws) is the generic name for the devils in this ditch, and each has a proper name as well (lines 76, 105, 118–26). The elders of *Saint Zita* in Lucca (a town near Florence) were ten citizens who ran the government. 5. A current official in Lucca, Bonturo Dati was in fact known as the most corrupt of all; the devil is being ironic. 6. The *Serchio* is a river near Lucca. The *Holy Face* of Lucca was a venerated icon. 7. Virgil may be referring to his difficulties with the devils in 8. 82–130, when he and Dante tried to enter the city of Dis.

and blocked him with a flourish of their pitchforks,
    but he shouted: "All of you behave yourselves! 72
Before you start to jab me with your forks,
    let one of you step forth to hear me out,
    and then decide if you still care to grapple." 75
They all cried out: "Let Malacoda[8] go!"
    One stepped forward—the others stood their ground—
    and moving, said, "What good will this do him?" 78
"Do you think, Malacoda," said my master,
    "that you would see me here, come all this way,
    against all opposition, and still safe, 81
without propitious fate and God's permission?
    Now let us pass, for it is willed in Heaven
    that I lead another by this savage path." 84
With this the devil's arrogance collapsed,
    his pitchfork, too, dropped right down to his feet,
    as he announced to all: "Don't touch this man!" 87
"You, hiding over there," my guide called me,
    "behind the bridge's rocks, curled up and quiet,
    come back to me, you may return in safety." 90
At his words I rose and then I ran to him
    and all the devils made a movement forward;
    I feared they would not really keep their pact. 93
(I remember seeing soldiers under truce,
    as they left the castle of Caprona, frightened
    to be passing in the midst of such an enemy.)[9] 96
I drew up close to him, as close as possible,
    and did not take my eyes from all those faces
    that certainly had nothing good about them. 99
Their prongs were aimed at me, and one was saying:
    "Now do I let him have it in the rump?"
    They answered all for one: "Sure, stick him good!" 102
But the devil who had spoken with my guide
    was quick to spin around and scream an order:
    "At ease there, take it easy, Scarmiglione!" 105
Then he said to us: "You cannot travel straight
    across this string of bridges, for the sixth arch
    lies broken at the bottom of its ditch;[1] 108
if you have made your mind up to proceed,
    you must continue on along this ridge;
    not far, you'll find a bridge that crosses it.[2] 111
Five hours more and it will be one thousand,
    two hundred sixty-six years and a day
    since the bridge-way here fell crumbling to the ground.[3] 114
I plan to send a squad of mine that way
    to see that no one airs himself down there;

---

8. Evil-tail.   9. A battle outside Florence in 1289, in which Dante may have taken part.   1. The bridge across the fifth ditch was smashed, as Malacoda explains, by the earthquake that occurred at the time of the Crucifixion.   2. As the travelers discover, this is a lie.   3. According to medieval tradition, Christ's death on the cross occurred on Good Friday at noon, in his thirty-third year, which would be 34 C.E.; the time at which Dante and Vigil are in this fifth ditch of Malebolge is 7 A.M. of Holy Saturday, 1300, which is 1266 years plus one day, less five hours later.

go along with them, they will not misbehave.   117
Front and center, Alichino, Calcabrina,"
    he shouted his commands, "you too, Cagnazzo;
    Barbariccia, you be captain of the squad.   120
Take Libicocco with you and Draghignazzo,
    toothy Ciriatto and Graffiacane,
    Farfarello and our crazy Rubicante.[4]   123
Now tour the ditch, inspect the boiling tar;
    these two shall have safe passage to the bridge
    connecting den to den without a break."   126
"O master, I don't like the looks of this,"
    I said, "let's go, just you and me, no escort,
    you know the way. I want no part of them!   129
If you're observant, as you usually are,
    why is it you don't see them grind their teeth
    and wink at one another?—we're in danger!"   132
And he to me: "I will not have you frightened;
    let them do all the grinding that they want,
    they do it for the boiling souls, not us."   135
Before they turned left-face along the bank
    each one gave their good captain a salute
    with farting tongue pressed tightly to his teeth,   138
and he blew back with his bugle of an ass-hole.

CANTO XXII

The note of grotesque comedy in the bolgia of the Malebranche continues, with a comparison between Malacoda's salute to his soldiers and different kinds of military signals the Pilgrim has witnessed in his lifetime. He sees many Grafters squatting in the pitch, but as soon as the Malebranche draw near, they dive below the surface. One unidentified Navarrese, however, fails to escape and is hoisted up on Graffiacane's hooks; Rubicante and the other Malebranche start to tear into him, but Virgil, at his ward's request, manages to question him between torments. The sinner briefly tells his story, and then relates that he has left below in the pitch an Italian, Fra Gomita, a particularly adept grafter, who spends his time talking to Michel Zanche.

The Navarrese sinner promises to lure some of his colleagues to the surface for the devils' amusement, if the tormentors will hide themselves for a moment. Cagnazzo is skeptical but Alichino agrees, and no sooner do the Malebranche turn away than the crafty grafter dives below the pitch. Alichino flies after him, but too late; now Calcabrina rushes after Alichino and both struggle above the boiling pitch, and then fall in. Barbariccia directs the rescue operation as the two poets steal away.

I have seen troops of horsemen breaking camp,
    opening the attack, or passing in review,
    I have even seen them fleeing for their lives;   3
I have seen scouts ride, exploring your terrain,
    O Aretines,[5] and I have seen raiding-parties
    and the clash of tournaments, the run of jousts—   6
to the tune of trumpets, to the ring of clanging bells,

---

4. These names—like Scarmiglione in line 105—imply raffish irreverence in general, although some do have specific if ignoble meanings: Cagnazzo = "Big Dog," Barbariccia = "Curly Beard," Graffiacane = "Dog-Scratcher."   5. The people of Arezzo, a city south of Florence.

to the roll of drums, to the flash of flares on ramparts,
    to the accompaniment of every known device;   9
but I never saw cavalry or infantry
    or ships that sail by landmarks or by stars
    signaled to set off by such strange bugling!   12
So, on our way we went with those ten fiends.
    What savage company! But—in church, with saints—
    with rowdy good-for-nothings, in the tavern!⁶   15
My attention now was fixed upon the pitch
    to see the operations of this *bolgia*,
    and how the cooking souls got on down there.   18
Much like the dolphins that are said to surface
    with their backs arched to warn all men at sea
    to rig their ships for stormy seas ahead,⁷   21
so now and then a sinner's back would surface
    in order to alleviate his pain,
    then dive to hide as quick as lightning strikes.   24
Like squatting frogs along the ditch's edge,
    with just their muzzles sticking out of water,
    their legs and all the rest concealed below,   27
these sinners squatted all around their pond;
    but as soon as Barbariccia would approach
    they quickly ducked beneath the boiling pitch.   30
I saw (my heart still shudders at the thought)
    one lingering behind⁸—as it sometimes happens
    one frog remains while all the rest dive down—   33
and Graffiacan, standing in front of him,
    hooked and twirled him by his pitchy hair
    and hoisted him. He looked just like an otter!   36
By then I knew the names of all the fiends:
    I had listened carefully when they were chosen,
    each of them stepping forth to match his name.   39
"Hey, Rubicante, dig your claws down deep
    into his back and peel the skin off him,"
    this fiendish chorus egged him on with screams.   42
I said: "Master, will you, if you can, find out
    the name of that poor wretch who has just fallen
    into the cruel hands of his adversaries?"   45
My guide walked right up to the sinner's side
    and asked where he was from, and he replied:
    "I was born and bred in the kingdom of Navarre;   48
my mother gave me to a lord to serve,
    for she had me by some dishonest spendthrift
    who ran through all he owned and killed himself.   51
Then I became a servant in the household
    of good King Thibault. There I learned my graft,
    and now I pay my bill by boiling here."   54
Ciriatto, who had two tusks sticking out

---

6. A popular proverb.   7. A common medieval belief.   8. The identity of this sinner is not known, but
he was employed in the household of Thibaut II of Champagne, a man renowned for his honesty who was
also king of Navarre, the area of Spain that is now Basque country.

on both sides of his mouth, just like a boar's,
    let him feel how just one tusk could rip him open.   57
The mouse had fallen prey to evil cats,
    but Barbariccia locked him with his arms,
    shouting: "Get back while I've got hold of him!"   60
Then toward my guide he turned his face and said:
    "If you want more from him, keep questioning
    before he's torn to pieces by the others."   63
My guide went on: "Then tell me, do you know
    of some Italian stuck among these sinners
    beneath the pitch?" And he, "A second ago   66
I was with one who lived around those parts.
    Oh, I wish I were undercover with him now!
    I wouldn't have these hooks or claws to fear."   69
Libicocco cried: "We've waited long enough,"
    then with his fork he hooked the sinner's arm
    and, tearing at it, he pulled out a piece.   72
Draghignazzo, too, was anxious for some fun;
    he tried the wretch's leg, but their captain quickly
    spun around and gave them all a dirty look.   75
As soon as they calmed down a bit, my master
    began again to interrogate the wretch,
    who still was contemplating his new wound: 78
"Who was it, you were saying, that unluckily
    you left behind you when you came ashore?"
    "Gomita," he said, "the friar from Gallura,[9]   81
receptacle for every kind of fraud:
    when his lord's enemies were in his hands,
    the treatment they received delighted them: 84
he took their cash, and as he says, hushed up
    the case and let them off; none of his acts
    was petty grafting, all were of sovereign order.   87
He spends his time with don Michele Zanche
    of Logodoro, talking on and on
    about Sardinia—their tongues no worse for wear![1]   90
Oh, but look how that one grins and grinds his teeth;
    I could tell you so much more, but I am afraid
    he is going to grate my scabby hide for me."   93
But their master-sergeant turned to Farfarello,
    whose wild eyes warned he was about to strike,
    shouting, "Get away, you filthy bird of prey."   96
"If you would like to see Tuscans or Lombards,"
    the frightened shade took up where he left off,
    "and have a talk with them, I'll bring some here;   99
but the Malebranche must back up a bit,
    or else those shades won't risk a surfacing;
    I, by myself, will bring you up a catch   102
of seven, without moving from this spot,

---

9. A friar who was chancellor of the Gallura district on the island of Sardinia. He was hanged by his master, a lord of Pisa, when it was discovered that he had sold prisoners their freedom.   1. Little is known of this sinner, except that he too was a Sardinian.

just by whistling—that's our signal to the rest
   when one peers out and sees the coast is clear." 105
Cagnazzo raised his snout at such a story,
   then shook his head and said: "Listen to the trick
   he's cooked up to get off the hook by jumping!" 108
And he, full of the tricks his trade had taught him,
   said: "Tricky, I surely am, especially
   when it comes to getting friends into worse trouble." 111
But Alichin could not resist the challenge,
   and in spite of what the others thought, cried out:
   "If you jump, I won't come galloping for you, 114
I've got my wings to beat you to the pitch.
   We'll clear this ledge and wait behind that slope.
   Let's see if one of you can outmatch us!" 117
Now listen, Reader, here's a game that's strange:
   they all turned toward the slope, and first to turn
   was the fiend who from the start opposed the game. 120
The Navarrese had perfect sense of timing:
   feet planted on the ground, in a flash he jumped,
   the devil's plan was foiled, and he was free. 123
The squad was stung with shame but most of all
   the one who brought this blunder to perfection;[2]
   he swooped down, howling, "Now I've got you caught!" 126
Little good it did, for wings could not outstrip
   the flight of terror: down the sinner dived
   and up the fiend was forced to strain his chest 129
like a falcon swooping down on a wild duck:
   the duck dives quickly out of sight, the falcon
   must fly back up dejected and defeated. 132
In the meantime, Calcabrina, furious,
   also took off, hoping the shade would make it,
   so he could pick a fight with his companion. 135
And when he saw the grafter hit the pitch,
   he turned his claws to grapple with his brother,
   and they tangled in mid-air above the ditch; 138
but the other was a full-fledged hawk as well
   and used his claws on him, and both of them
   went plunging straight into the boiling pond. 141
The heat was quick to make them separate,
   but there seemed no way of getting out of there;
   their wings were clogged and could not lift them up. 144
Barbariccia, no less peeved than all his men,
   sent four fiends flying to the other shore
   with their equipment at top speed; instantly, 147
some here, some there, they took the posts assigned them.
   They stretched their hooks to reach the pitch-dipped pair,
   who were by now deep-fried within their crusts. 150
And there we left them, all messed up that way.

2. Alichin.

CANTO XXIII

The antics of Ciampolo, the Navarrese, and the Malebranche *bring to the Pilgrim's mind the fable of the frog, the mouse, and the hawk—and that in turn reminds him of the immediate danger he and Virgil are in from the angry* Malebranche. *Virgil senses the danger too, and grabbing his ward as a mother would her child, he dashes to the edge of the bank and slides down the rocky slope into the Sixth* Bolgia—*not a moment too soon, for at the top of the slope they see the angry* Malebranche. *When the Pilgrim looks around him he sees weeping shades slowly marching in single file, each one covered from head to foot with a golden cloak lined with lead, which weights them down. These are the Hypocrites. Two in this group identify themselves as Catalano de' Malavolti and Loderingo degli Andalò, two Jovial Friars. The Pilgrim is about to address them when he sees the shade of Caiaphas (the evil counselor who advised Pontius Pilate to crucify Christ), crucified and transfixed by three stakes to the ground. Virgil discovers from the two friars that in order to leave this bolgia they must climb up a rockslide; he also learns that this is the only bolgia over which the bridge is broken. Virgil is angry with himself for having believed Malacoda's lie about the bridge over the Sixth* Bolgia (*canto XXI, iii*).

In silence, all alone, without an escort,
   we moved along, one behind the other,
   like minor friars[3] bent upon a journey. 3
I was thinking over one of Aesop's fables[4]
   that this recent skirmish had brought back to mind,
   where he tells the story of the frog and mouse; 6
for "yon" and "there" could not be more alike
   than the fable and the fact, if one compares
   the start and finish of both incidents. 9
As from one thought another often rises,
   so this thought gave quick birth to still another,
   and then the fear I first had felt was doubled. 12
I was thinking: "Since these fiends, on our account,
   were tricked and mortified by mockery,
   they certainly will be more than resentful; 15
with rage now added to their evil instincts,
   they will hunt us down with all the savagery
   of dogs about to pounce upon the hare." 18
I felt my body's skin begin to tighten—
   I was so frightened!—and I kept looking back:
   "O master," I said, "if you do not hide 21
both of us, and very quick, I am afraid
   of the Malebranche—right now they're on our trail—
   I feel they're there, I think I hear them now." 24
And he replied: "Even if I were a mirror
   I could not reflect your outward image faster
   than your inner thoughts transmit themselves to me. 27
In fact, just now they joined themselves with mine,

---

3. Franciscan friars, who were known as "minor" or "lesser" friars because Francis of Assisi, the founder of the order, insisted upon humility.   **4.** The fable that Dante seems to be referring to tells how a frog offers to ferry a mouse across a river, then halfway over tries to drown him, only to be seized by a kite (a hawklike bird) while the mouse escapes.

and since they were alike in birth and form,
   I decided to unite them toward one goal: 30
if the right-hand bank should slope in such a way
   as to allow us to descend to the next *bolgia,*
   we could escape that chase we have imagined."   33
He had hardly finished telling me his plan
   when I saw them coming with their wings wide open
   not too far off, and now they meant to get us!   36
My guide instinctively caught hold of me,
   like a mother waking to some warning sound,
   who sees the rising flames are getting close   39
and grabs her son and runs—she does not wait
   the short time it would take to put on something;
   she cares not for herself, only for him.   42
And over the edge, then down the stony bank
   he slid, on his back, along the sloping rock
   that walls the higher side of the next *bolgia.*   45
Water that turns a mill wheel never ran
   the narrow sluice at greater speed, not even
   at the point before it hits the paddle-blades,[5]   48
than down that sloping border my guide slid,
   bearing me with him, clasping me to his chest
   as though I were his child, not his companion.   51
His feet had hardly touched rock bottom, when
   there they were, the ten of them, above us
   on the height; but now there was no need to fear: 54
High Providence that willed for them to be
   the ministers in charge of the fifth ditch
   also willed them powerless to leave their realm.   57
And now, down there, we found a painted people,
   slow-motioned; step by step, they walked their round
   in tears, and seeming wasted by fatigue.   60
All were wearing cloaks with hoods pulled low
   covering the eyes (the style was much the same
   as those the Benedictines wear at Cluny),[6]   63
dazzling, gilded cloaks outside, but inside
   they were lined with lead, so heavy that the capes
   King Frederick used, compared to these, were straw.[7] 66
O cloak of everlasting weariness!
   We turned again, as usual, to the left
   and moved with them, those souls lost in their mourning; 69
but with their weight that tired-out race of shades
   paced on so slowly that we found ourselves
   in new company with every step we took;   72
and so I asked my guide: "Please look around
   and see, as we keep walking, if you find
   someone whose name or deeds are known to me." 75
And one who overheard me speaking Tuscan

---

5. A mill built on the land while the water of the river turns its wheel.   6. One of the largest monasteries in Europe, located in Burgundy in France; the *Benedictines* are monks who follow the Rule of St. Benedict (d. 587), one of the founders of monasticism.   7. Frederick II (see n. 9, p. 1245) was reported to have punished traitors by encasing them in lead and throwing them into heated cauldrons.

cried out somewhere behind us: "Not so fast,
   you there, rushing ahead through this heavy air,   78
perhaps from me you can obtain an answer."
   At this my guide turned toward me saying, "Stop,
   and wait for him, then match your pace with his."   81
I paused and saw two shades with straining faces
   revealing their mind's haste to join my side,
   but the weight they bore and the crowded road delayed them.   84
When they arrived, they looked at me sideways
   and for some time, without exchanging words;
   then they turned to one another and were saying: 87
"He seems alive, the way his throat is moving,
   and if both are dead, what privilege allows them
   to walk uncovered by the heavy cloak?"   90
Then they spoke to me: "O Tuscan who has come
   to visit the college of the sullen hypocrites,
   do not disdain to tell us who you are."   93
I answered them: "I was born and I grew up
   in the great city on the lovely Arno's shore,
   and I have the body I have always had.   96
But who are you, distilling tears of grief,
   so many I see running down your cheeks?
   And what kind of pain is this that it can glitter?"   99
One of them answered: "The orange-gilded cloaks
   are thick with lead so heavy that it makes us,
   who are the scales it hangs on, creak as we walk.   102
Jovial Friars we were, both from Bologna.
   My name was Catalano, his, Loderingo,
   and both of us were chosen by your city,   105
that usually would choose one man alone,
   to keep the peace. Evidence of what we were
   may still be seen around Gardingo's parts."[8]   108
I began: "O Friars, all your wretchedness . . ."
   but said no more; I couldn't, for I saw
   one crucified with three stakes on the ground.[9]   111
And when he saw me all his body writhed,
   and through his beard he heaved out sighs of pain;
   then Friar Catalano, who watched the scene,   114
remarked: "That impaled figure you see there
   advised the Pharisees it was expedient
   to sacrifice one man for all the people.   117
Naked he lies stretched out across the road,
   as you can see, and he must feel the load
   of every weight that steps on him to cross.   120
His father-in-law[1] and the other council members,
   who were the seed of evil for all Jews,

---

8. *Gardingo*: a district in Florence, was destroyed by a civil war incited by their meddling in Florentine affairs. *Jovial Friars*: a military and religious order in Bologna called the Knights of the Blessed Virgin Mary, or popularly the Jovial Friars because of the laxity of its rules. The members were meant to fight only in order to protect the weak and enforce peace. *Catalano* and *Loderingo* were two citizens of Bologna who were involved in founding the Jovial Friars in 1261.   9. This is Caiaphas, the high priest under Pontius Pilate who advised that Christ be crucified (John 11. 45–52).   1. Annas; see John 18. 13.

are racked the same way all along this ditch."   123
And I saw Virgil staring down amazed
   at this body stretching out in crucifixion,
   so vilely punished in the eternal exile.   126
Then he looked up and asked one of the friars:
   "Could you please tell us, if your rule permits:
   is there a passage-way on the right, somewhere,   129
by which the two of us may leave this place
   without summoning one of those black angels
   to come down here and raise us from this pit?"   132
He answered: "Closer than you might expect,
   a ridge jutting out from the base of the great circle
   extends, and bridges every hideous ditch   135
except this one, whose arch is totally smashed
   and crosses nowhere; but you can climb up
   its massive ruins that slope against this bank."   138
My guide stood there awhile, his head bent low,
   then said: "He told a lie about this business,
   that one who hooks the sinners over there."[2]   141
And the friar: "Once, in Bologna, I heard discussed
   the devil's many vices; one of them is
   that he tells lies and is father of all lies."[3]   144
In haste, taking great strides, my guide walked off,
   his face revealing traces of his anger.
   I turned and left the heavy-weighted souls   147
to make my way behind those cherished footprints.

CANTO XXIV

After an elaborate simile describing Virgil's anger and the return of his composure, the two begin the difficult, steep ascent up the rocks of the fallen bridge. The Pilgrim can barely make it to the top even with Virgil's help, and after the climb he sits down to catch his breath; but his guide urges him on, and they make their way back to the bridge over the Seventh Bolgia. From the bridge confused sounds can be heard rising from the darkness below. Virgil agrees to take his pupil down to the edge of the eighth encircling bank, and once they are there, the scene reveals a terrible confusion of serpents, and Thieves madly running.

Suddenly a snake darts out and strikes a sinner's neck, whereupon he flares up, turning into a heap of crumbling ashes; then the ashes gather together into the shape of a man. The metamorphosed sinner reveals himself to be Vanni Fucci, a Pistoiese condemned for stealing the treasure of the sacristy of the church of San Zeno at Pistoia. He makes a prophecy about the coming strife in Florence.

In the season of the newborn year, when the sun
   renews its rays beneath Aquarius[4]
   and nights begin to last as long as days,   3
at the time the hoarfrost paints upon the ground
   the outward semblance of his snow-white sister[5]
   (but the color from his brush soon fades away),   6
the peasant wakes, gets up, goes out and sees

2. See 21.111.   3. For this description of the devil, see John 8.44.   4. January 21–February 21.
5. That is, snow.

the fields all white. No fodder for his sheep!
He smites his thighs in anger and goes back   9
into his shack and, pacing up and down,
    complains, poor wretch, not knowing what to do;
    once more he goes outdoors, and hope fills him   12
again when he sees the world has changed its face
    in so little time, and he picks up his crook
    and out to pasture drives his sheep to graze—   15
just so I felt myself lose heart to see
    my master's face wearing a troubled look,
    and as quickly came the salve to heal my sore: 18
for when we reached the shattered heap of bridge,
    my leader turned to me with that sweet look
    of warmth I first saw at the mountain's foot.   21
He opened up his arms (but not before
    he had carefully studied how the ruins lay
    and found some sort of plan) to pick me up.   24
Like one who works and thinks things out ahead,
    always ready for the next move he will make,
    so, while he raised me up toward one great rock,   27
he had already singled out another,
    saying, "Now get a grip on that rock there,
    but test it first to see it holds your weight."   30
It was no road for one who wore a cloak!
    Even though I had his help and he weighed nothing,
    we could hardly lift ourselves from crag to crag.   33
And had it not been that the bank we climbed
    was lower than the one we had slid down[6]—
    I cannot speak for him—but I for one   36
surely would have quit. But since the Evil Pits
    slope toward the yawning well that is the lowest,
    each valley is laid out in such a way   39
that one bank rises higher than the next.
    We somehow finally reached the point above
    where the last of all that rock was shaken loose.   42
My lungs were so pumped out of breath by the time
    I reached the top, I could not go on farther,
    and instantly I sat down where I was.   45
"Come on, shake off the covers of this sloth,"
    the master said, "for sitting softly cushioned,
    or tucked in bed, is no way to win fame;   48
and without it man must waste his life away,
    leaving such traces of what he was on earth
    as smoke in wind and foam upon the water.   51
Stand up! Dominate this weariness of yours
    with the strength of soul that wins in every battle
    if it does not sink beneath the body's weight.   54
Much steeper stairs than these we'll have to climb;[7]

6. Because the whole of the eighth circle is tilted downward, the downside wall of each ditch is lower than that on the upside.   7. Both the climb from the pit of Hell back to Earth and the climb up Mount Purgatory.

we have not seen enough of sinners yet!
    If you understand me, act, learn from my words." 57
At this I stood up straight and made it seem
    I had more breath than I began to breathe,
    and said: "Move on, for I am strong and ready." 60
We climbed and made our way along the bridge,
    which was jagged, tight and difficult to cross,
    and steep—far more than any we had climbed. 63
Not to seem faint, I spoke while I was climbing;
    then came a voice from the depths of the next chasm,
    a voice unable to articulate. 66
I don't know what it said, even though I stood
    at the very top of the arch that crosses there;
    to me it seemed whoever spoke, spoke running. 69
I was bending over, but no living eyes
    could penetrate the bottom of that darkness;
    therefore I said: "Master, why not go down 72
this bridge onto the next encircling bank,[8]
    for I hear sounds I cannot understand,
    and I look down but cannot see a thing." 75
"No other answer," he replied, "I give you
    than doing what you ask, for a fit request
    is answered best in silence and in deed." 78
From the bridge's height we came down to the point
    where it ends and joins the edge of the eighth bank,
    and then the *bolgia* opened up to me:[9] 81
down there I saw a terrible confusion
    of serpents, all of such a monstrous kind
    the thought of them still makes my blood run cold.[1] 84
Let all the sands of Libya boast no longer,
    for though she breeds chelydri and jaculi,
    phareans, cenchres, and head-tailed amphisbenes, 87
she never bred so great a plague of venom,
    not even if combined with Ethiopia
    or all the sands that lie by the Red Sea. 90
Within this cruel and bitterest abundance
    people ran terrified and naked, hopeless
    of finding hiding-holes or heliotrope.[2] 93
Their hands were tied behind their backs with serpents,
    which pushed their tails and heads around the loins
    and coiled themselves in knots around the front. 96
And then—at a sinner running by our bank
    a snake shot out and, striking, hit his mark:
    right where the neck attaches to the shoulder. 99
No *o* or *i* was ever quicker put
    by pen to paper than he flared up and burned,

---

8. Of the seventh ditch.   9. They cross the bridge over the seventh ditch and then climb down the wall between the seventh and eighth ditches.   1. The following list of exotic serpents derives from a description by the Roman poet Lucan (39–65 C.E.) of the plagues of Libya.   2. A fictitious stone that was supposed to make the bearer invisible.

and turned into a heap of crumbled ash;   102
and then, these ashes scattered on the ground
   began to come together on their own
   and quickly take the form they had before: 105
precisely so, philosophers declare,
   the phoenix dies to be reborn again
   as she approaches her five-hundredth year;[3]   108
alive, she does not feed on herbs or grain,
   but on teardrops of frankincense and balm,
   and wraps herself to die in nard and myrrh.   111
As a man in a fit will fall, not knowing why
   (perhaps some hidden demon pulls him down,
   or some oppilation chokes his vital spirits),   114
then, struggling to his feet, will look around,
   confused and overwhelmed by the great anguish
   he has suffered, moaning as he stares about—   117
so did this sinner when he finally rose.
   Oh, how harsh the power of the Lord can be,
   raining in its vengeance blows like these!   120
My guide asked him to tell us who he was,
   and he replied: "It's not too long ago
   I rained from Tuscany to this fierce gullet.   123
I loved the bestial life more than the human,
   like the bastard that I was; I'm Vanni Fucci,
   the beast! Pistoia was my fitting den."[4]   126
I told my guide: "Tell him not to run away;
   ask him what sin has driven him down here,
   for I knew him as a man of bloody rage."   129
The sinner heard and did not try to feign;
   directing straight at me his mind and face,
   he reddened with a look of ugly shame,   132
and said: "That you have caught me by surprise
   here in this wretched *bolgia*, makes me grieve
   more than the day I lost my other life.   135
Now I am forced to answer what you ask:
   I am stuck so far down here because of theft:
   I stole the treasure of the sacristy—   138
a crime falsely attributed to another.
   I don't want you to rejoice at having seen me,
   if ever you escape from these dark pits,   141
so open your ears and hear my prophecy:[5]
   Pistoia first shall be stripped of all its Blacks,
   and Florence then shall change its men and laws;   144
from Valdimagra Mars shall thrust a bolt

---

3. The *phoenix* is a mythical bird that is supposed to burn to death in its own nest every five hundred years, after which either itself or its son is reborn from the ashes; for these details, including its diet of exotic herbs and its funeral preparations (lines 110–11), see Ovid, *Metamorphoses* 15. In medieval mythography the phoenix was often taken as a symbol of Christ.   **4.** The illegitimate son of a noble father of *Pistoia*, a town just north of Florence; known as "the beast" because of the extravagance of his misbehavior. He reputedly robbed a church in Pistoia, a crime for which a similarly named man was wrongly hanged. **5.** Vanni Fucci now prophesies, in the enigmatic terms appropriate to the genre, that the party of the Blacks (of which he was a member) will first be expelled from Pistoia by the Whites, but that then the Whites of Florence (Dante's party) will be defeated. The prophecy refers to events that occurred in either 1302 or 1306.

of lightning wrapped in thick, foreboding clouds,
    then bolt and clouds will battle bitterly   147
in a violent storm above Piceno's fields,
    where rapidly the bolt will burst the cloud,
    and no White will escape without his wounds.   150
And I have told you this so you will suffer!"

CANTO XXV

*The wrathful Vanni Fucci directs an obscene gesture to God, whereupon he is attacked
by several snakes, which coil about him, tying him so tight that he cannot move a muscle. As soon as he flees, the centaur Cacus gallops by with a fire-breathing dragon on his
back, and following close behind are three shades, concerned because they cannot find
Cianfa—who soon appears as a snake and attacks Agnèl; the two merge into one
hideous monster, which then steals off. Next, Guercio, in the form of a snake, strikes
Buoso, and the two exchange shapes. Only Puccio Sciancato is left unchanged.*

When he had finished saying this, the thief
    shaped his fists into figs[6] and raised them high
    and cried: "Here, God, I've shaped them just for you!"   3
From then on all those snakes became my friends,
    for one of them at once coiled round his neck
    as if to say, "That's all you're going to say,"   6
while another twisted round his arms in front;
    it tied itself into so tight a knot,
    between the two he could not move a muscle.   9
Pistoia, ah, Pistoia! why not resolve
    to burn yourself to ashes, ending all,
    since you have done more evil than your founders?[7]   12
Throughout the circles of this dark inferno
    I saw no shade so haughty toward his God,
    not even he who fell from Thebes' high walls.[8]   15
Without another word he fled, and then
    I saw a raging centaur gallop up
    roaring: "Where is he, where is that untamed beast?"   18
I think that all Maremma[9] does not have
    as many snakes as he had on his back,
    right up to where his human form begins.   21
Upon his shoulders, just behind the nape,
    a dragon with its wings spread wide was crouching
    and spitting fire at whoever came its way.   24
My master said to me: "That one is Cacus,[1]
    who more than once in the grotto far beneath
    Mount Aventine spilled blood to fill a lake.   27
He does not go the same road as his brothers
    because of the cunning way he committed theft
    when he stole his neighbor's famous cattle-herd;   30

6. An obscene gesture made by thrusting a protruding thumb between the first and second fingers of a
closed fist.   7. The most important founder of Pistoia was Catiline, who was a traitor against the Roman
republic in the 1st century B.C.E.   8. Capaneus (see 14.46–75).   9. A region infested with snakes; see
13.8.   1. A monster who lived in a cave on Mount Aventine in Rome and was killed by Hercules, from
whom he stole cattle; see *Aeneid* 8.

and then his evil deeds came to an end
    beneath the club of Hercules, who struck
    a hundred blows, and he, perhaps, felt ten."   33
While he was speaking Cacus galloped off;
    at the same time three shades appeared below us;
    my guide and I would not have seen them there   36
if they had not cried out: "Who are you two?"
    At this we cut our conversation short
    to give our full attention to these three.   39
I didn't know who they were, but then it happened,
    as often it will happen just by chance,
    that one of them was forced to name another: 42
"Where did Cianfa[2] go off to?" he asked. And then,
    to keep my guide from saying anything,
    I put my finger tight against my lips.   45
Now if, my reader, you should hesitate
    to believe what I shall say, there's little wonder,
    for I, the witness, scarcely can believe it.   48
While I was watching them, all of a sudden
    a serpent—and it had six feet—shot up
    and hooked one of these wretches with all six.   51
With the middle feet it hugged the sinner's stomach
    and, with the front ones, grabbed him by the arms,
    and bit him first through one cheek, then the other;   54
the serpent spread its hind feet round both thighs,
    then stuck its tail between the sinner's legs,
    and up against his back the tail slid stiff.   57
No ivy ever grew to any tree
    so tight entwined, as the way that hideous beast
    had woven in and out its limbs with his;   60
and then both started melting like hot wax
    and, fusing, they began to mix their colors
    (so neither one seemed what he was before),   63
just as a brownish tint, ahead of flame,
    creeps up a burning page that is not black
    completely, even though the white is dying.   66
The other two who watched began to shout:
    "O Agnèl![3] If you could see how you are changing!
    You're not yourself, and you're not both of you!"   69
The two heads had already fused to one
    and features from each flowed and blended into
    one face where two were lost in one another;   72
two arms of each were four blurred strips of flesh;
    and thighs with legs, then stomach and the chest
    sprouted limbs that human eyes have never seen.   75
Each former likeness now was blotted out:
    both, and neither one it seemed—this picture
    of deformity. And then it sneaked off slowly.   78
Just as a lizard darting from hedge to hedge,
    under the stinging lash of the dog-days' heat,

2. A noble Florentine, reputedly a thief.   3. Another noble Florentine thief.

zips across the road, like a flash of lightning,   81
so, rushing toward the two remaining thieves,
   aiming at their guts, a little serpent,
   fiery with rage and black as pepper-corn,   84
shot up and sank its teeth in one of them,
   right where the embryo receives its food,
   then back it fell and lay stretched out before him.   87
The wounded thief stared speechless at the beast,
   and standing motionless began to yawn
   as though he needed sleep, or had a fever.   90
The snake and he were staring at each other;
   one from his wound, the other from its mouth
   fumed violently, and smoke with smoke was mingling.   93
Let Lucan from this moment on be silent,
   who tells of poor Nasidius and Sabellus,[4]
   and wait to hear what I still have in store;   96
and Ovid, too, with his Cadmus and Arethusa—[5]
   though he metamorphosed one into a snake,
   the other to a fountain, I feel no envy,   99
for never did he interchange two beings
   face to face so that both forms were ready
   to exchange their substance, each one for the other's,   102
an interchange of perfect symmetry:
   the serpent split its tail into a fork,
   and the wounded sinner drew his feet together;   105
the legs, with both the thighs, closed in to join
   and in a short time fused, so that the juncture
   didn't show signs of ever having been there,   108
the while the cloven tail assumed the features
   that the other one was losing, and its skin
   was growing soft, the other's getting scaly;   111
I saw his arms retreating to the armpits,
   and the reptile's two front feet, that had been short,
   began to stretch the length the man's had shortened;   114
the beast's hind feet then twisted round each other
   and turned into the member man conceals,
   while from the wretch's member grew two legs.   117
The smoke from each was swirling round the other,
   exchanging colors, bringing out the hair
   where there was none, and stripping off the other's.   120
The one rose up, the other sank, but neither
   dissolved the bond between their evil stares,
   fixed eye to eye, exchanging face for face;   123
the standing creature's face began receding
   toward the temples; from the excess stuff pulled back,
   the ears were growing out of flattened cheeks,   126
while from the excess flesh that did not flee
   the front, a nose was fashioned for the face,
   and lips puffed out to just the normal size.   129
The prostrate creature strains his face out long

---

4. Two soldiers bitten by serpents in Lucan's *Pharsalia*.   5. See *Metamorphoses* 4.

and makes his ears withdraw into his head,
 the way a snail pulls in its horns. The tongue,   132
that once had been one piece and capable
 of forming words, divides into a fork,
 while the other's fork heals up. The smoke subsides.   135
The soul that had been changed into a beast
 went hissing off along the valley's floor,
 the other close behind him, spitting words.   138
Then he turned his new-formed back on him and said
 to the shade left standing there: "Let Buoso run
 the valley on all fours, the way I did."⁶   141
Thus I saw the cargo of the seventh hold
 exchange and interchange; and let the strangeness
 of it all excuse me, if my pen has failed.   144
And though this spectacle confused my eyes
 and stunned my mind, the two thieves could not flee
 so secretly I did not recognize   147
that one was certainly Puccio Sciancato⁷
 (and he alone, of that company of three
 that first appeared, did not change to something else),   150
the other, he who made you mourn, Gaville.⁸

CANTO XXVI

From the ridge high above the Eighth Bolgia can be perceived a myriad of flames flickering far below, and Virgil explains that within each flame is the suffering soul of a Deceiver. One flame, divided at the top, catches the Pilgrim's eye and he is told that within it are jointly punished Ulysses and Diomed. Virgil questions the pair for the benefit of the Pilgrim. Ulysses responds with the famous narrative of his last voyage, during which he passed the Pillars of Hercules and sailed the forbidden sea until he saw a mountain shape, from which came suddenly a whirlwind that spun his ship around three times and sank it.

Be joyful, Florence, since you are so great
 that your outstretched wings beat over land and sea,
 and your name is spread throughout the realm of Hell!   3
I was ashamed to find among the thieves
 five of your most eminent citizens,⁹
 a fact which does you very little honor   6
But if early morning dreams have any truth,
 you will have the fate, in not too long a time,
 that Prato and the others crave for you.¹   9
And were this the day, it would not be too soon!
 Would it had come to pass, since pass it must!
 The longer the delay, the more my grief.   12
We started climbing up the stairs of boulders

6. The identity of this *Buoso* is uncertain.   7. This third thief is also a noble Florentine.   8. The *little serpent* of line 83 above is now identified as Francesco de Cavalcanti, a Florentine nobleman who lived in *Gaville*, a town south of Florence. When he was murdered by his townsmen, his kinsmen took brutal revenge.   9. Cianfa (25.43), Agnello (25.68), Francesco (25.82, 149), Buoso (25.140), and Puccio (25.148) are all Florentines.   1. A town just north of Florence, on the way to Pistoia. The reason for this threat is unclear.

that had brought us to the place from where we watched;
   my guide went first and pulled me up behind him.   15
We went along our solitary way
   among the rocks, among the ridge's crags,
   where the foot could not advance without the hand.   18
I know that I grieved then, and now again
   I grieve when I remember what I saw,
   and more than ever I restrain my talent   21
lest it run a course that virtue has not set;
   for if a lucky star or something better
   has given me this good, I must not misuse it.   24
As many fireflies (in the season when
   the one who lights the world hides his face least,
   in the hour when the flies yield to mosquitoes)   27
as the peasant on the hillside at his ease
   sees, flickering in the valley down below,
   where perhaps he gathers grapes or tills the soil—   30
with just so many flames all the eighth *bolgia*
   shone brilliantly, as I became aware
   when at last I stood where the depths were visible.   33
As he[2] who was avenged by bears beheld
   Elijah's chariot at its departure,
   when the rearing horses took to flight toward Heaven,   36
and though he tried to follow with his eyes,
   he could not see more than the flame alone
   like a small cloud once it had risen high—   39
so each flame moves itself along the throat
   of the abyss, none showing what it steals
   but each one stealing nonetheless a sinner.   42
I was on the bridge, leaning far over—so far
   that if I had not grabbed some jut of rock
   I could easily have fallen to the bottom.   45
And my guide, who saw me so absorbed, explained:
   "There are souls concealed within these moving fires,
   each one swathed in his burning punishment."   48
"O master," I replied, "from what you say
   I know now I was right; I had guessed already
   it might be so, and I was about to ask you: 51
Who's in that flame with its tip split in two,
   like that one which once sprang up from the pyre
   where Eteocles was placed beside his brother?"[3]   54
He said: "Within, Ulysses and Diomed[4]
   are suffering in anger with each other,
   just vengeance makes them march together now.   57
And they lament inside one flame the ambush

---

2. Elisha, an Old Testament prophet, was mocked by children, who were then attacked by bears. He saw the ascent to heaven of the prophet Elijah in his chariot and continued Elijah's mission: 2 Kings 2.1–25. **3.** *Eteocles* and his brother, Polynices, were the sons of Oedipus; cursed by their father for their imprisonment of him, they engaged in a civil war over Thebes, killed each other, and were cremated on the same pyre, the flame of which divided into two as a sign of their enmity.   **4.** Two of the Greek leaders in the Trojan War. They devised the trick of the Trojan horse and stole the Palladium, a statue of Pallas Athena that protected the city. Their villainy is described by Aeneas in *Aeneid* 2.

of the horse become the gateway that allowed
   the Romans' noble seed[5] to issue forth.   60
Therein they mourn the trick that caused the grief
   of Deïdamia,[6] who still weeps for Achilles;
   and there they pay for the Palladium."   63
"If it is possible for them to speak
   from within those flames," I said, "master, I pray
   and repray you—let my prayer be like a thousand—   66
that you do not forbid me to remain
   until the two-horned flame comes close to us;
   you see how I bend toward it with desire!"   69
"Your prayer indeed is worthy of highest praise,"
   he said to me, "and therefore I shall grant it;
   but see to it your tongue refrains from speaking.   72
Leave it to me to speak, for I know well
   what you would ask; perhaps, since they were Greeks,
   they might not pay attention to your words."[7]   75
So when the flame had reached us, and my guide
   decided that the time and place were right,
   he addressed them and I listened to him speaking: 78
"O you who are two souls within one fire,
   if I have deserved from you when I was living,
   if I have deserved from you much praise or little,   81
when in the world I wrote my lofty verses,
   do not move on; let one of you tell where
   he lost himself through his own fault, and died."   84
The greater of the ancient flame's two horns
   began to sway and quiver, murmuring
   just like a flame that strains against the wind;   87
then, while its tip was moving back and forth,
   as if it were the tongue itself that spoke,
   the flame took on a voice and said: "When I   90
set sail from Circe,[8] who, more than a year,
   had kept me occupied close to Gaëta
   (before Aeneas called it by that name),[9]   93
not sweetness of a son, not reverence
   for an aging father, not the debt of love
   I owed Penelope[1] to make her happy,   96
could quench deep in myself the burning wish
   to know the world and have experience
   of all man's vices, of all human worth.   99
So I set out on the deep and open sea
   with just one ship and with that group of men,
   not many, who had not deserted me.   102
I saw as far as Spain, far as Morocco,
   both shores; I had left behind Sardinia,

---

5. The Trojan survivors, who founded Rome.   6. Achilles' lover, who tried to prevent him from going to
the Trojan War but was thwarted by Ulysses.   7. Virgil may assume that Greeks would disdain anyone
who, like Dante, did not know Greek (and was therefore a "barbarian"); or that because he derives from the
classical world he is the more appropriate interlocutor.   8. Dante places Circe's home near *Gaëta*, on the
coast of Italy north of Naples; she was a sorceress who transformed men into beasts   9. Aeneas named it
after his nurse Caieta, who died there: *Aeneid* 7.   1. Ulysses' faithful wife.

and the other islands which that sea encloses.   105
I and my mates were old and tired men.
   Then finally we reached the narrow neck
   where Hercules put up his signal-pillars   108
to warn men not to go beyond that point.[2]
   On my right I saw Seville, and passed beyond;
   on my left, Ceüta had already sunk behind me.   111
'Brothers,' I said, 'who through a hundred thousand
   perils have made your way to reach the West,
   during this so brief vigil of our senses   114
that is still reserved for us, do not deny
   yourself experience of what there is beyond,
   behind the sun, in the world they call unpeopled.[3]   117
Consider what you came from: you are Greeks!
   You were not born to live like mindless brutes
   but to follow paths of excellence and knowledge.'   120
With this brief exhortation I made my crew
   so anxious for the way that lay ahead,
   that then I hardly could have held them back;   123
and with our stern turned toward the morning light,
   we made our oars our wings for that mad flight,
   gaining distance, always sailing to the left.   126
The night already had surveyed the stars
   the other pole contains; it saw ours so low
   it did not show above the ocean floor.[4]   129
Five times we saw the splendor of the moon
   grow full and five times wane away again
   since we had entered through the narrow pass—   132
when there appeared a mountain shape, darkened
   by distance, that arose to endless heights.
   I had never seen another mountain like it.[5]   135
Our celebrations soon turned into grief:
   from the new land there rose a whirling wind
   that beat against the forepart of the ship   138
and whirled us round three times in churning waters;
   the fourth blast raised the stern up high, and sent
   the bow down deep, as pleased Another's will.   141
And then the sea was closed again, above us."

CANTO XXVII

*As soon as Ulysses has finished his narrative, another flame—its soul within having rec-
ognized Virgil's Lombard accent—comes forward asking the travelers to pause and
answer questions about the state of affairs in the region of Italy from which he came.
The Pilgrim responds by outlining the strife in Romagna and ends by asking the flame
who he is. The flame, although he insists he does not want his story to be known among
the living, answers because he is supposedly convinced that the Pilgrim will never*

2. The straits of Gibraltar, with Seville on the European side and Ceüta on the African. According to
myth, Hercules separated a single mountain into two to mark the point beyond which human beings
should not venture.   3. According to the geography of Dante's day, the southern hemisphere was made
up entirely of water, with the only land being Mount Purgatory. To go *behind the sun* means to follow a
westward course.   4. They had crossed the equator and could see only the stars of the Southern Hemisphere.   5. This is Mount Purgatory.

return to earth. He is another famous deceiver, Guido da Montefeltro, a soldier who became a friar in his old age; but he was untrue to his vows when, at the urging of Pope Boniface VIII, he counseled the use of fraud in the pope's campaign against the Colonna family. He was damned to Hell because he failed to repent his sins, trusting instead in the pope's fraudulent absolution.

By now the flame was standing straight and still,
    it said no more and had already turned
    from us, with sanction of the gentle poet,   3
when another, coming right behind it,
    attracted our attention to its tip,
    where a roaring of confusing sounds had started.   6
As the Sicilian bull—that bellowed first
    with cries of that one (and it served him right)
    who with his file had fashioned such a beast[6]—   9
would bellow with the victim's voice inside,
    so that, although the bull was only brass,
    the effigy itself seemed pierced with pain: 12
so, lacking any outlet to escape
    from the burning soul that was inside the flame,
    the suffering words became the fire's language.   15
But after they had made their journey upward
    to reach the tip, giving it that same quiver
    the sinner's tongue inside had given them,   18
we heard the words:[7] "O you to whom I point
    my voice, who spoke just now in Lombard,[8] saying:
    'you may move on, I won't ask more of you.'   21
although I have been slow in coming to you,
    be willing, please, to pause and speak with me.
    You see how willing I am—and I burn!   24
If you have just now fallen to this world
    of blindness, from that sweet Italian land
    where I took on the burden of my guilt,   27
tell me, are the Romagnols[9] at war or peace?
    For I come from the hills between Urbino
    and the mountain chain that lets the Tiber loose."   30
I was still bending forward listening
    when my master touched my side and said to me:
    "*You* speak to him; *this* one is Italian."   33
And I, who was prepared to answer him,
    began without delaying my response:
    "O soul who stands concealed from me down there,   36
your Romagna is not now and never was
    without war in her tyrants' hearts, although

6. According to classical legend, Phalaris, the tyrant of Agrigentum in Sicily, had an artisan build a brazen bull in which he roasted his victims alive, their shrieks emerging as the sounds of a bull's bellowing. His first victim was the artisan himself, Perillus.   7. The speaker is Guido da Montefeltro (d. 1298), a nobleman deeply involved in the constant warfare of thirteenth-century Italy but who became a friar two years before his death (see line 67).   8. The dialect of northern Italy. Dante believed that since Virgil came from Mantua, his spoken language would be not Latin but this dialect.   9. The people of Romagna, an area northeast of Florence and bordering the Adriatic Sea; the city of Urbino marks its southern limit, the Apennine mountains its northern. The subsequent passage describes the political conditions in the cities of Romagna.

there was no open warfare when I came here.   39
Ravenna's[1] situation has not changed:
  the eagle of Polenta broods up there,
  covering all of Cervia with its pinions;   42
the land[2] that stood the test of long endurance
  and left the French piled in a bloody heap
  is once again beneath the verdant claws.   45
Verrucchio's Old Mastiff and its New One,[3]
  who both were bad custodians of Montagna,
  still sink their fangs into their people's flesh;   48
the cities by Lamone and Santerno[4]
  are governed by the Lion of the White Lair,
  who changes parties every change of season.   51
As for the town[5] whose side the Savio bathes:
  just as it lies between the hills and plains,
  it lives between freedom and tyranny.   54
And now I beg you tell us who you are—
  grant me my wish as yours was granted you—
  so that your fame may hold its own on earth."   57
And when the fire, in its own way, had roared
  awhile, the flame's sharp tip began to sway
  to and fro, then released a blow of words: 60
"If I thought that I were speaking to a soul
  who someday might return to see the world,
  most certainly this flame would cease to flicker;   63
but since no one, if I have heard the truth,
  ever returns alive from this deep pit,
  with no fear of dishonor I answer you: 66
I was a man of arms and then a friar,
  believing with the cord to make amends;
  and surely my belief would have come true   69
were it not for that High Priest[6] (his soul be damned!)
  who put me back among my early sins;
  I want to tell you why and how it happened.   72
While I still had the form of the bones and flesh
  my mother gave me, all my actions were
  not those of a lion, but those of a fox;   75
the wiles and covert paths, I knew them all,
  and so employed my art that rumor of me
  spread to the farthest limits of the earth.   78
When I saw that the time of life had come
  for me, as it must come for every man,
  to lower the sails and gather in the lines,   81
things I once found pleasure in then grieved me;
  repentant and confessed, I took the vows

---

1. The major city of Romagna, ruled at the time by the Polenta family, who also controlled the small city of Cervia.   2. Forlì, which defeated French invaders but then fell under the control of the tyrannical Ordelaffi family, which had green paws on its coat of arms.   3. Malatesta de Verrucchio and his son Malatestino were tyrants of Rimini who killed their enemy *Montagna*.   4. The cities of Faenza and Imola, on the Lamone and Santerno Rivers respectively, governed by an unreliable ruler who had a lion on a white ground on his coat of arms.   5. Cesena, located on the Savio River, was a free municipality although its politics were dominated by a single family.   6. Pope Boniface VIII.

a monk takes. And, oh, to think it could have worked!   84
And then the Prince of the New Pharisees
    chose to wage war upon the Lateran
    instead of fighting Saracens or Jews,[7]   87
for all his enemies were Christian souls
    (none among the ones who conquered Acri,[8]
    none a trader in the Sultan's kingdom).   90
His lofty papal seat, his sacred vows
    were no concern to him, nor was the cord
    I wore (that once made those it girded leaner).[9]   93
As Constantine once had Silvestro brought
    from Mount Soracte to cure his leprosy,[1]
    so this one sought me out as his physician   96
to cure his burning fever caused by pride.
    He asked me to advise him. I was silent,
    for his words were drunken. Then he spoke again: 99
'Fear not, I tell you: the sin you will commit,
    it is forgiven. Now you will teach me how
    I can level Palestrina[2] to the ground.   102
Mine is the power, as you cannot deny,
    to lock and unlock Heaven. Two keys I have,
    those keys my predecessor did not cherish."[3]   105
And when his weighty arguments had forced me
    to the point that silence seemed the poorer choice,
    I said: 'Father, since you grant me absolution   108
for the sin I find I must fall into now:
    ample promise with a scant fulfillment
    will bring you triumph on your lofty throne.'   111
Saint Francis[4] came to get me when I died,
    but one of the black Cherubim cried out:
    'Don't touch him, don't cheat me of what is mine!   114
He must come down to join my other servants
    for the false counsel he gave. From then to now
    I have been ready at his hair, because   117
one cannot be absolved unless repentant,
    nor can one both repent and will a thing
    at once—the one is canceled by the other!"[5]   120
O wretched me! How I shook when he took me,
    saying: 'Perhaps you never stopped to think
    that I might be somewhat of a logician!'[6]   123
He took me down to Minòs,[7] who eight times
    twisted his tail around his hardened back,

7. Boniface was struggling to retain the papacy against the challenge of another Roman family, the Colonnas.   8. City in the Holy Land, captured by the crusaders and then recaptured by the Saracens.
9. Guido refers to the rough cord worn as a belt by Franciscan friars, a symbol of both obedience and poverty (hence it would make the wearer *leaner*); for another reference to this cord, see 16.106.
1. According to legend, the Emperor Constantine (d. 337) was cured of his leprosy by Pope Sylvester, who was hiding on Mount Soracte, some twenty miles north of Rome; see 19.115.   2. The fortress of the Colonnas.   3. The keys are those of damnation and absolution, given by Christ to Peter; see 19.92. Boniface's *predecessor* was Celestine V, who resigned after five months; see 3.59–60.   4. Francis of Assisi (1181/82–1226), founder of the order of friars joined by Guido.   5. Guido wanted forgiveness for his sin of guile at the same time as he was committing it; in willing the sin he showed that he was not truly repentant, the precondition for forgiveness.   6. The devil is referring to the logical law of noncontradiction.
7. For Minos, see 5.4.

then in his rage he bit it, and announced:⁣   126
'He goes with those the thievish fire burns.'
  And here you see me now, lost, wrapped this way,
  moving, as I do, with my resentment."⁣   129
When he had brought his story to a close,
  the flame, in grievous pain, departed from us
  gnarling and flickering its pointed horn.⁣   132
My guide and I moved farther on; we climbed
  the ridge until we stood on the next arch
  that spans the fosse where penalties are paid⁣   135
by those who, sowing discord, earned Hell's wages.

CANTO XXVIII

In the Ninth Bolgia the Pilgrim is overwhelmed by the sight of mutilated, bloody shades, many of whom are ripped open, with entrails spilling out. They are the Sowers of Scandal and Schism, and among them are Mahomet, Ali, Pier da Medicina, Gaius Scribonius Curio, Mosca de' Lamberti, and Bertran de Born. All bemoan their painful lot, and Mahomet and Pier da Medicina relay warnings through the Pilgrim to certain living Italians who are soon to meet terrible ends. Bertran de Born, who comes carrying his head in his hand like a lantern, is a particularly arresting example of a Dantean contrapasso.

Who could, even in the simplest kind of prose
  describe in full the scene of blood and wounds
  that I saw now—no matter how he tried!⁣   3
Certainly any tongue would have to fail:
  man's memory and man's vocabulary
  are not enough to comprehend such pain.⁣   6
If one could bring together all the wounded
  who once upon the fateful soil of Puglia
  grieved for their life's blood spilled by the Romans,[8]⁣   9
and spilled again in the long years of the war
  that ended in great spoils of golden rings
  (as Livy's history tells, that does not err),[9]⁣   12
and pile them with the ones who felt the blows
  when they stood up against great Robert Guiscard,[1]
  and with those others whose bones are still in heaps⁣   15
at Ceprano[2] (there where every Puglian
  turned traitor), and add those from Tagliacozzo,[3]
  where old Alardo conquered, weaponless—⁣   18
if all these maimed with limbs lopped off or pierced
  were brought together, the scene would be nothing
  to compare with the foul ninth *bolgia*'s bloody sight.⁣   21
No wine cask with its stave or cant-bar sprung

---

8. *Puglia* is in southern Italy, and Dante refers here to those killed when the Trojans conquered it in the *Aeneid* 7–12.   9. *Livy* is a Roman historian (d. 17 C.E.) and the *war* he chronicled is the Second Punic War (218–201 B.C.E.) between Rome and Carthage under Hannibal. After the Battle of Cannae (216) the victorious Carthaginians displayed rings taken from fallen Romans.   1. A Norman conqueror (1015–1085) who fought the Greeks and Saracens for control of Sicily and southern Italy in the 11th century.   2. A town that the barons of Puglia were pledged to defend for Manfred, the natural son of Frederick II (10.119), but whom they betrayed; he was then killed at the battle of Benevento in 1266.   3. A town where in 1268 Manfred's nephew Conradin was defeated by the strategy rather than the brute force of Alardo de Valery.

was ever split the way I saw someone
   ripped open from his chin to where we fart.   24
Between his legs his guts spilled out, with the heart
   and other vital parts, and the dirty sack
   that turns to shit whatever the mouth gulps down.   27
While I stood staring into his misery,
   he looked at me and with both hands he opened
   his chest and said: "See how I tear myself!   30
See how Mahomet[4] is deformed and torn!
   In front of me, and weeping, Ali walks,
   his face cleft from his chin up to the crown.   33
The souls that you see passing in this ditch
   were all sowers of scandal and schism in life,
   and so in death you see them torn asunder.   36
A devil stands back there who trims us all
   in this cruel way, and each one of this mob
   receives anew the blade of the devil's sword   39
each time we make one round of this sad road,
   because the wounds have all healed up again
   by the time each one presents himself once more.   42
But who are you there, gawking from the bridge
   and trying to put off, perhaps, fulfillment
   of the sentence passed on you when you confessed?"   45
"Death does not have him yet, he is not here
   to suffer for his guilt," my master answered;
   "but that he may have full experience,   48
I, who am dead, must lead him through this Hell
   from round to round, down to the very bottom,
   and this is as true as my presence speaking here."   51
More than a hundred in that ditch stopped short
   to look at me when they had heard his words,
   forgetting in their stupor what they suffered.   54
"And you, who will behold the sun, perhaps
   quite soon, tell Fra Dolcino[5] that unless
   he wants to follow me here quick, he'd better   57
stock up on food, or else the binding snows
   will give the Novarese their victory,
   a conquest not won easily otherwise."   60
With the heel of one foot raised to take a step,
   Mahomet said these words to me, and then
   stretched out and down his foot and moved away.   63
Another, with his throat slit, and his nose
   cut off as far as where the eyebrows start
   (and he only had a single ear to show),   66
who had stopped like all the rest to stare in wonder,
   stepped out from the group and opened up his throat,

4. Founder of Islam (570–632), regarded by some medieval Christians as a renegade Christian and a creator of religious disunity. Ali was his nephew and son-in-law, and his disputed claim to the rulership (or
caliphate) divided Islam into Suni and Shia sects.   5. In 1300 *Fra Dolcino* was head of a reformist order
known as the Apostolic Brothers that was condemned as heretical by the pope. He and his followers
escaped to the hills near the town of Novara, but starvation forced them out and many were executed.

which ran with red from all sides of his wound,   69
and spoke: "O you whom guilt does not condemn,
    whom I have seen in Italy up there,
    unless I am deceived by similarity,   72
recall to mind Pier da Medicina,[6]
    should you return to see the gentle plain
    declining from Vercelli to Marcabò,   75
and inform the two best citizens of Fano[7]—
    tell Messer Guido and tell Angiolello—
    that, if our foresight here is no deception,   78
from their ship they shall be hurled bound in a sack
    to drown in the water near Cattolica,
    the victims of a tyrant's treachery;   81
between the isles of Cyprus and Mallorca
    so great a crime Neptune never witnessed
    among the deeds of pirates or the Argives.[8]   84
That traitor, who sees only with one eye
    and rules the land that someone with me here
    wishes he'd never fed his eyes upon,[9]   87
will have them come to join him in a parley,
    then see to it they do not waste their breath
    on vows or prayers to escape Focara's wind."   90
And I to him: "If you want me to bring back
    to those on earth your message—who is the one
    sated with the bitter sight? Show him to me."   93
At once he grabbed the jaws of a companion[1]
    standing near by, and squeezed his mouth half open,
    announcing, "Here he is, and he is mute.   96
This man, in exile, drowned all Caesar's doubts
    and helped him cast the die, when he insisted:
    'A man prepared, who hesitates, is lost.'"   99
How helpless and bewildered he appeared,
    his tongue hacked off as far down as the throat,
    this Curio, once so bold and quick to speak!   102
And one[2] who had both arms but had no hands,
    raising the gory stumps in the filthy air
    so that the blood dripped down and smeared his face,   105
cried: "You, no doubt, also remember Mosca,
    who said, alas, 'What's done is over with,'
    and sowed the seed of discord for the Tuscans."   108
"And of death for all your clan," I quickly said,
    and he, this fresh wound added to his wound,
    turned and went off like one gone mad from pain.   111

6. The town of *Medicina* lies in the Po Valley between Vercelli and Marcabò. Nothing certain is known of Pier de Medicina.   7. A town on the Adriatic coast of Italy; its two leaders—named in the next line— were drowned in 1312 by the one-eyed tyrant Malatestino of Rimini (27.46) near the promontory of Focara (see line 90) after he had invited them to the town of La Cattolica for a parley.   8. *Cyprus and Majorca* are islands at the western and eastern ends of the Mediterranean. *Neptune* is the classical god of the sea and *Argives* is another name for Greeks.   9. This *someone* is Caius Curio, whose story is told in lines 94–102.   1. Caius Curio, a Roman of the 1st century B.C.E., was bribed by Julius Caesar to betray his friends; he urged Caesar to cross the Rubicon and invade the Roman republic, starting a civil war. 2. A Florentine noble, who in 1215 started the civil strife that tore the city apart by advising a father to avenge the slight to his daughter by killing the man who had broken his engagement to her. Mosca's own family was a victim of the strife some sixty years later.

But I remained to watch the multitude,
   and saw a thing that I would be afraid
   to tell about without more evidence,   114
were I not reassured by my own conscience—
   that good companion enheartening a man
   beneath the breastplate of its purity.   117
I saw it, I'm sure, and I seem to see it still:
   a body with no head that moved along,
   moving no differently from all the rest;   120
he held his severed head up by its hair,
   swinging it in one hand just like a lantern,
   and as it looked at us it said: "Alas!"   123
Of his own self he made himself a light
   and they were two in one and one in two.
   How could this be? He who ordained it knows.   126
And when he had arrived below our bridge,
   he raised the arm that held the head up high
   to let it speak to us at closer range.   129
It spoke:[3] "Now see the monstrous punishment,
   you there still breathing, looking at the dead,
   see if you find suffering to equal mine!   132
And that you may report on me up there,
   know that I am Bertran de Born, the one
   who evilly encouraged the young king.   135
Father and son I set against each other:
   Achitophel with his wicked instigations
   did not do more with Absalom and David.   138
Because I cut the bonds of those so joined,
   I bear my head cut off from its life-source,
   which is back there, alas, within its trunk.   141
In me you see the perfect *contrapasso!*"[4]

CANTO XXIX

*When the Pilgrim is rebuked by his mentor for his inappropriate interest in these
wretched shades, he replies that he was looking for someone. Virgil tells the Pilgrim
that he saw the person he was looking for, Geri del Bello, pointing a finger at him. They
discuss Geri until they reach the edge of the next bolgia, where all types of Falsifiers are
punished. There miserable, shrieking shades are afflicted with diseases of various kinds
and are arranged in various positions. Sitting back to back, madly scratching their lep-
rous sores, are the shades of Griffolino da Arezzo and one Capocchio, who talk to the
Pilgrim, the latter shade making wisecracks about the Sienese.*

The crowds, the countless, different mutilations,
   had stunned my eyes and left them so confused
   they wanted to keep looking and to weep,   3
but Virgil said: "What are you staring at?
   Why do your eyes insist on drowning there

---

3. This is Bertran de Born, a Provençal nobleman and poet, who reputedly advised the son of Henry II of
England to rebel against his father. For Achitophel's similar scheming between David and his son Absalom,
see 2 Samuel 15–17.   **4.** For *contrapasso*, see the headnote on p. 1209.

below, among those wretched, broken shades?   6
You did not act this way in other *bolge*.
   If you hope to count them one by one, remember
   the valley winds some twenty-two miles around;[5]   9
and already the moon is underneath our feet;
   the time remaining to us now is short[6]—
   and there is more to see than you see here."   12
"If you had taken time to find out what
   I was looking for," I started telling him,
   "perhaps you would have let me stay there longer."   15
My guide was moving on, with me behind him,
   answering as I did while we went on,
   and adding: "Somewhere down along this ditch   18
that I was staring at a while ago,
   I think there is a spirit of my family
   mourning the guilt that's paid so dear down there."   21
And then my master said: "From this time on
   you should not waste another thought on him;
   think on ahead, and let him stay behind,   24
for I saw him standing underneath the bridge
   pointing at you, and threatening with his gesture,
   and I heard his name called out: Geri del Bello.[7]   27
That was the moment you were so absorbed
   with him who was the lord of Altaforte[8]
   that you did not look his way before he left."   30
"Alas, my guide," I answered him, "his death
   by violence, which has not yet been avenged
   by anyone who shares in his disgrace,   33
made him resentful, and I suppose for this
   he went away without a word to me,
   and because he did I feel great piety."   36
We spoke of this until we reached the start
   of the bridge across the next *bolgia*, from which
   the bottom, with more light, might have been seen.   39
Having come to stand above the final cloister
   of Malebolge, we saw it spreading out,
   revealing to our eyes its congregation.   42
Weird shrieks of lamentation pierced through me
   like arrow-shafts whose tips are barbed with pity,
   so that my hands were covering my ears.   45
Imagine all the sick in the hospitals
   of Maremma, Valdichiana, and Sardinia
   between the months of July and September,[9]   48
crammed all together rotting in one ditch—
   such was the misery here; and such a stench

---

5. The reason for this exact measurement is not known. At 30.86 we are told that the circumference of the ninth circle is eleven miles, showing that Hell is shaped like a funnel.   6. This means that the sun (which they cannot see) is over their heads, and the time is about 2 P.M. The journey to the center of Hell lasts twenty-four hours, so only four hours are left.   7. First cousin to Dante's father; his death at the hands of a member of another Florentine family initiated a feud between the two families that lasted some fifty years.   8. Bertran de Born (see 28.134).   9. The region of *Maremma*, the river valley of *Val di Chiana*, and the island of *Sardinia* were all plagued by malaria.

was pouring out as comes from flesh decaying.   51
Still keeping to our left, we made our way
   down the long bridge onto the final bank,
   and now my sight was clear enough to find   54
the bottom where the High Lord's ministress,
   Justice infallible, metes out her punishment
   to falsifiers she registers on earth.   57
I doubt if all those dying in Aegina[1]
   when the air was blowing sick with pestilence
   and the animals, down to the smallest worm,   60
all perished (later on this ancient race,
   according to what the poets tell as true,
   was born again from families of ants)   63
offered a scene of greater agony
   than was the sight spread out in that dark valley
   of heaped-up spirits languishing in clumps.   66
Some sprawled out on others' bellies, some
   on others' backs, and some, on hands and knees,
   dragged themselves along that squalid alley.   69
Slowly, in silence, slowly we moved along,
   looking, listening to the words of all those sick,
   who had no strength to raise their bodies up.   72
I saw two sitting, leaning against each other
   like pans propped back to back against a fire,[2]
   and they were blotched from head to foot with scabs. 75
I never saw a curry-comb[3] applied
   by a stable-boy who is harried by his master,
   or simply wants to finish and go to bed,   78
the way those two applied their nails and dug
   and dug into their flesh, crazy to ease
   the itching that can never find relief.   81
They worked their nails down, scraping off the scabs
   the way one works a knife to scale a bream[4]
   or some other fish with larger, tougher scales.   84
"O you there scraping off your scabs of mail
   and even making pincers of your fingers,"
   my guide began to speak to one of them,   87
"so may your fingernails eternally
   suffice their task, tell us: among the many
   packed in this place is anyone Italian?"   90
"Both of us whom you see disfigured here,"
   one answered through his tears, "we are Italians.
   But you, who ask about us, who are you?"   93
"I am one accompanying this living man
   descending bank from bank," my leader said,
   "and I intend to show him all of Hell."   96
With that each lost the other back's support

1. A mythical island that was infected by Juno with a pestilence that killed all its inhabitants and was then repopulated when Jupiter turned ants into men: see Ovid, *Metamorphoses* 7. 2. The image is of pans leaned against one another before a kitchen fireplace. 3. A *curry-comb* is a bristled brush used to groom horses. 4. A *bream* is a large fish like a carp.

and each one, shaky, turned to look at me,
  as others did who overheard these words.   99
My gentle master came up close to me
  and said: "Now ask them what you want to know,"
  and since he wanted me to speak, I started: 102
"So may the memory of you not fade
  from the minds of men up there in the first world,
  but rather live on under many suns,   105
tell me your names and where it was you lived;
  do not let your dreadful, loathsome punishment
  discourage you from speaking openly."   108
"I'm from Arezzo," one of them replied,
  "and Albert of Siena had me burned,
  but I'm not here for what I died for there;[5]   111
it's true I told him, jokingly, of course:
  'I know the trick of flying through the air,'
  and he, eager to learn and not too bright,   114
asked me to demonstrate my art; and only
  just because I didn't make him Daedalus,
  he had me burned by one whose child he was.   117
But here, to the last *bolgia* of the ten,
  for the alchemy[6] I practiced in the world
  I was condemned by Minòs, who cannot err."   120
I said to my poet: "Have you ever known
  people as silly as the Sienese?
  Even the French cannot compare with them!"   123
With that the other leper[7] who was listening
  feigned exception to my quip: "Excluding,
  of course, Stricca, who lived so frugally,   126
and Niccolo, the first to introduce
  the luxury of the clove for condiment
  into that choice garden where the seed took root,   129
and surely not that fashionable club
  where Caccia squandered all his woods and vineyards
  and Abbagliato flaunted his great wit!   132
That you may know who this is backing you
  against the Sienese, look sharply at me
  so that my face will give you its own answer,   135
and you will recognize Capocchio's shade,
  betrayer of metals with his alchemy;
  you'll surely recall—if you're the one I think—   138
how fine an ape of nature[8] I once was."

---

5. Griffolino of Arezzo cheated Albero of Siena by promising to teach him the art of Daedalus—flying. The bishop of Siena, father of the illegitimate Albero, had Griffolino burned as a heretic.   6. A practice that sought to turn base metals like lead into gold.   7. The speaker is Capocchio, a Florentine burned in 1293 for alchemy, which he here admits was mere counterfeiting. The people he lists were rich young noblemen of Siena who joined a "Spendthrifts' Club"—the *fashionable club* of line 130—and sought to outdo each other in profligacy. For another member of this club, Lano of Siena, see 13.115.   8. By *ape of nature* Capocchio means that he merely imitated change in his alchemical displays rather than actually accomplishing it.

CANTO XXX

Capocchio's remarks are interrupted by two mad, naked shades who dash up, and one of them sinks his teeth into Capocchio's neck and drags him off; he is Gianni Schicchi and the other is Myrrha of Cyprus. When they have gone, the Pilgrim sees the ill-proportioned and immobile shade of Master Adamo, a counterfeiter, who explains how members of the Guidi family had persuaded him to practice his evil art in Romena. He points out the fever-stricken shades of two infamous liars, Potiphar's Wife and Sinon the Greek, whereupon the latter engages Master Adamo in a verbal battle. Virgil rebukes the Pilgrim for his absorption in such futile wrangling, but his immediate shame wins Virgil's immediate forgiveness.

In ancient times when Juno was enraged
   against the Thebans because of Semele[9]
   (she showed her wrath on more than one occasion),   3
she made King Athamas go raving mad:
   so mad that one day when he saw his wife
   coming with his two sons in either arm,   6
he cried: "Let's spread the nets, so I can catch
   the lioness with her lion cubs at the pass!"
Then he spread out his insane hands, like talons,   9
and, seizing one of his two sons, Learchus,
   he whirled him round and smashed him on a rock.
   She drowned herself with the other in her arms.   12
And when the wheel of Fortune brought down low
   the immeasurable haughtiness of Trojans,[1]
   destroying in their downfall king and kingdom,   15
Hecuba sad, in misery, a slave
   (after she saw Polyxena lie slain,
   after this grieving mother found her son   18
Polydorus left unburied on the shore),
   now gone quite mad, went barking like a dog—
   it was the weight of grief that snapped her mind.   21
But never in Thebes or Troy were madmen seen
   driven to acts of such ferocity
   against their victims, animal or human,   24
as two shades I saw, white with rage and naked,
   running, snapping crazily at things in sight,
   like pigs, directionless, broken from their pen.   27
One, landing on Capocchio, sank his teeth
   into his neck, and started dragging him
   along, scraping his belly on the rocky ground.   30
The Aretine[2] spoke, shaking where he sat:
   "You see that batty shade? He's Gianni Schicchi![3]
   He's rabid and he treats us all that way."   33

9. Daughter of the king of Thebes, *Semele* was loved by Jupiter and therefore incited the wrath of Juno, who drove her brother-in-law Athamas insane. While mad, Athamas thought his wife, Ino, and his two sons, Learchus and Melicertes, were a lioness and two cubs; he killed Learchus, and Ino drowned herself and Melicertes. See Ovid, *Metamorphoses* 4.   1. Parallel to the fate of Thebes is that of Troy, which is here represented by the madness into which Queen Hecuba fell when she saw her daughter Polyxena sacrificed on Achilles' tomb and the unburied body of her betrayed son Polydorus. See Ovid, *Metamorphoses* 13. 2. Griffolino (see 29.111).   3. A Florentine who impersonated Buoso Donati (line 44), who had just died, and dictated a new will that gave him Buoso's best beast (*the 'queen of studs'* of line 43).

"Oh," I answered, "so may that other shade
    never sink its teeth in you—if you don't mind,
    please tell me who it is before it's gone."   36
And he to me: "That is the ancient shade
    of Myrrha,[4] the depraved one, who became,
    against love's laws, too much her father's friend.   39
She went to him, and there she sinned in love,
    pretending that her body was another's—
    just as the other there fleeing in the distance,   42
contrived to make his own the 'queen of studs,'
    pretending that he was Buoso Donati,
    making his will and giving it due form."   45
Now that the rabid pair had come and gone
    (from whom I never took my eyes away),
    I turned to watch the other evil shades.   48
And there I saw a soul shaped like a lute,
    if only he'd been cut off from his legs
    below the belly, where they divide in two.   51
The bloating dropsy,[5] disproportioning
    the body's parts with unconverted humors,
    so that the face, matched with the paunch, was puny,   54
forced him to keep his parched lips wide apart,
    as a man who suffers thirst from raging fever
    has one lip curling up, the other sagging.   57
"O you who bear no punishment at all
    (I can't think why) within this world of sorrow,"
    he said to us, "pause here and look upon   60
the misery of one Master Adamo:[6]
    in life I had all that I could desire,
    and now, alas, I crave a drop of water.   63
The little streams that flow from the green hills
    of Casentino, descending to the Arno,
    keeping their banks so cool and soft with moisture,   66
forever flow before me, haunting me;
    and the image of them leaves me far more parched
    than the sickness that has dried my shriveled face.   69
Relentless Justice, tantalizing me,
    exploits the countryside that knew my sin,
    to draw from me ever new sighs of pain: 72
I still can see Romena, where I learned
    to falsify the coin stamped with the Baptist,
    for which I paid with my burned body there;   75
but if I could see down here the wretched souls
    of Guido or Alexander or their brother,
    I would not exchange the sight for Branda's fountain.[7]   78
One is here already, if those maniacs

4. *Myrrha* impersonated another woman in order to sleep with her father: see Ovid, *Metamorphoses* 10.
5. A disease in which fluid (*humors* of line 53) gathers in the cells and the affected part becomes grotesquely swollen. 6. A counterfeiter, burned in 1281, who made coins stamped with the image of John the Baptist, the patron saint of Florence, that contained twenty-one rather than twenty-four carets of gold (see line 90); he worked for a noble family of Romena (individual members are mentioned in line 77), a town in the Florentine district of Casentino. 7. A fountain near Romena.

running around this place have told the truth,
   but what good is it, with my useless legs?   81
If only I were lighter, just enough
   to move one inch in every hundred years,
   I would have started on my way by now   84
to find him somewhere in this gruesome lot,
   although this ditch winds round eleven miles
   and is at least a half a mile across.   87
It's their fault I am here with this choice family:
   they encouraged me to turn out florins
   whose gold contained three carats' worth of alloy."   90
And I to him: "Who are those two poor souls
   lying to the right, close to your body's boundary,
   steaming like wet hands in wintertime?"   93
"When I poured into this ditch, I found them here,"
   he answered, "and they haven't budged since then,
   and I doubt they'll move through all eternity.   96
One is the false accuser of young Joseph;
   the other is false Sinon, the Greek in Troy:[8]
   it's their burning fever makes them smell so bad."   99
And one of them, perhaps somewhat offended
   at the kind of introduction he received,
   with his fist struck out at the distended belly,   102
which responded like a drum reverberating;
   and Master Adam struck him in the face
   with an arm as strong as the fist he had received,   105
and he said to him: "Although I am not free
   to move around, with swollen legs like these,
   I have a ready arm for such occasions."   108
"*But* it was *not* as free and ready, was it,"
   the other answered, "when you went to the stake?
   Of course, when you were coining, it was readier!"   111
And he with the dropsy: "*Now* you tell the truth,
   but you were not as full of truth that time
   when you were asked to tell the truth at Troy!"   114
"My words were false—so were the coins you made,"
   said Sinon, "and *I* am here for one false act
   but *you* for more than any fiend in hell!"   117
"The horse, recall the horse, you falsifier,"
   the bloated paunch was quick to answer back,
   "may it burn your guts that all the world remembers!"   120
"May your guts burn with thirst that cracks your tongue,"
   the Greek said, "may they burn with rotting humors
   that swell your hedge of a paunch to block your eyes!"   123
And then the money-man: "So there you go,
   your evil mouth pours out its filth as usual;
   for if *I* thirst, and humors swell me up,   126
you burn more, and your head is fit to split,
   and it wouldn't take much coaxing to convince you

---

8. The *false accuser* is Potiphar's wife, who falsely accused Joseph of trying to lie with her (Genesis 39.6–20); *Sinon* is the Greek priest who persuaded the Trojans to accept the wooden horse (*Aeneid* 2).

to lap the mirror of Narcissus dry!"[9]   129
I was listening, all absorbed in this debate,
    when the master said to me: "Keep right on looking,
    a little more, and I shall lose my patience."   132
I heard the note of anger in his voice
    and turned to him; I was so full of shame
    that it still haunts my memory today.   135
Like one asleep who dreams himself in trouble
    and in his dream he wishes he were dreaming,
    longing for that which is, as if it were not,   138
just so I found myself: unable to speak,
    longing to beg for pardon and already
    begging for pardon, not knowing that I did.   141
"Less shame than yours would wash away a fault
    greater than yours has been," my master said,
    "and so forget about it, do not be sad.   144
If ever again you should meet up with men
    engaging in this kind of futile wrangling,
    remember I am always at your side;   147
to have a taste for talk like this is vulgar!"

CANTO XXXI

Through the murky air they move, up across the bank that separates the Malebolge
from the pit of Hell, the Ninth (and last) Circle of the Inferno. *From a distance is
heard the blast of a mighty horn, which turns out to have been that of the giant Nimrod. He and other giants, including Ephialtes, are fixed eternally in the pit of Hell; all
are chained except Antaeus, who, at Virgil's request, lifts the two poets in his monstrous
hand and deposits them below him, on the lake of ice known as Cocytus.*

The very tongue that first spoke—stinging me,
    making the blood rush up to both my cheeks—
    then gave the remedy to ease the pain,   3
just as, so I have heard, Achilles' lance,
    belonging to his father, was the source
    of pain, and then of balm, to him it struck.[1]   6
Turning our backs on that trench of misery
    gaining the bank again that walls it in,
    we cut across, walking in dead silence.   9
Here it was less than night and less than day,
    so that my eyes could not see far ahead;
    but then I heard the blast of some high horn   12
which would have made a thunder-clap sound dim;
    it drew my eyes directly to one place,
    as they retraced the sound's path to its source.   15
After the tragic rout when Charlemagne[2]
    lost all his faithful, holy paladins,
    the sound of Roland's horn was not as ominous.   18

---

9. Narcissus saw his reflection in a pool of water, referred to here as a *mirror* (Ovid, *Metamorphoses* 3).
1. Achilles' father, Peleus, gave him a lance that would heal any wound it inflicted.   2. In *The Song of
Roland*. Roland blows his horn to alert Charlemagne to the fact that the rear guard Roland commands has
been slaughtered. *Paladins* are the twelve peers or great warriors of Charlemagne's court.

Keeping my eyes still turned that way, I soon
  made out what seemed to be high, clustered towers.
  "Master," I said, "what city lies ahead?"   21
"Because you try to penetrate the shadows,"
  he said to me, "from much too far away,
  you confuse the truth with your imagination.   24
You will see clearly when you reach that place
  how much the eyes may be deceived by distance,
  and so, just push ahead a little more."   27
Then lovingly he took me by the hand
  and said: "But now, before we go on farther,
  to prepare you for the truth that could seem strange,   30
I'll tell you these aren't towers, they are giants;
  they're standing in the well around the bank—
  all of them hidden from their navels down."   33
As, when the fog begins to thin and clear,
  the sight can slowly make out more and more
  what is hidden in the mist that clogs the air,   36
so, as I pierced the thick and murky air,
  approaching slowly, closer to the well,
  confusion cleared and my fear took on more shape.   39
For just as Montereggion³ is crowned with towers
  soaring high above its curving ramparts,
  so, on the bank that runs around the well,   42
towering with only half their bodies out,
  stood the terrible giants,⁴ forever threatened
  by Jupiter in the heavens when he thunders.   45
And now I could make out one of the faces,
  the shoulders, the chest and a good part of the belly
  and, down along the sides, the two great arms.⁵   48
Nature, when she cast away the mold
  for shaping beasts like these, without a doubt
  did well, depriving Mars of more such agents.   51
And if she never did repent of whales
  and elephants, we must consider her,
  on sober thought, all the more just and wary: 54
for when the faculty of intellect
  is joined with brute force and with evil will,
  no man can win against such an alliance.   57
His face, it seemed to me, was about as long
  and just as wide as St. Peter's cone in Rome,⁶
  and all his body's bones were in proportion,   60
so that the bank which served to cover him
  from his waist down showed so much height above
  that three tall Frisians⁷ on each other's shoulders   63
could never boast of stretching to his hair,

---

3. A castle surrounded by towers, built to protect Siena from attack by Florence.   **4.** These *giants* are the mythological Titans, monsters born of the Earth who assaulted Olympus and were defeated and imprisoned by Jupiter.   **5.** This is Nimrod, described in Genesis as "the first on earth to be a mighty man" (10.8) and understood by medieval commentators to be a giant. He ruled over Babylon, where the tower of Babel was built (11.1–9).   **6.** This bronze pine cone, over twelve feet high, stood outside St. Peter's Cathedral in Dante's time; today it can be seen in the papal gardens in the Vatican.   **7.** Inhabitants of the northernmost province of what is now the Netherlands, considered the tallest men of the time.

for downward from the place men clasp their cloaks
   I saw a generous thirty hand-spans of him.[8]   66
"Raphel may amech zabi almi!"[9]
   He played these sputtering notes with prideful lips
   for which no sweeter psalm was suitable.   69
My guide called up to him: "Blathering idiot,
   stick to your horn[1] and take it out on that
   when you feel a fit of anger coming on;   72
search round your neck and you will find the strap
   it's tied to, you poor muddle-headed soul,
   and there's the horn so pretty on your chest."   75
And then he turned to me: "His words accuse him.
   He is Nimrod, through whose infamous device
   the world no longer speaks a common language.   78
But let's leave him alone and not waste breath,
   for he can no more understand our words
   than anyone can understand his language."   81
We had to walk still farther than before,
   continuing to the left, a full bow's-shot,
   to find another giant,[2] huger and more fierce.   84
What engineer it took to bind this brute
   I cannot say, but there he was, one arm
   pinned to his back, the other locked in front,   87
with a giant chain winding around him tight,
   which, starting from his neck, made five great coils—
   and that was counting only to his waist.   90
"This beast of pride decided he would try
   to pit his strength against almighty Jove,"
   my leader said, "and he has won this prize.   93
He's Ephialtes, who made his great attempt
   when the giants arose to fill the Gods with panic;
   the arms he lifted then, he moves no more."   96
And I to him: "If it were possible,
   I would really like to have the chance to see
   the fantastic figure of Briareus."[3]   99
His answer was: "Not far from here you'll see
   Antaeus,[4] who can speak and is not chained;
   he will set us down in the very pit of sin.   102
The one you want to see is farther off;
   he too is bound and looks just like this one,
   except for his expression, which is fiercer."   105
No earthquake of the most outrageous force
   ever shook a tower with such violence
   as, suddenly, Ephialtes shook himself.   108
I never feared to die as much as then,
   and my fear might have been enough to kill me,
   if I had not already seen those chains.   111

---

8. About fifteen feet.   9. Appropriately for the builder of Babel, he speaks an incomprehensible language.   1. Nimrod has a *horn* because in the Bible he is described as a hunter (Genesis 10.9). 2. This is Ephialtes, a Titan who with his twin brother Otus tried to attack Olympus by piling Mount Ossa on Mount Pelion; see Virgil, *Aeneid* 6.   3. Another Titan.   4. A Titan born too late to participate in the rebellion against Jupiter and therefore not chained; he was known for eating lions (line 118) and was defeated by Hercules in a wrestling match (line 132).

We left him and continued moving on
  and came to where Antaeus stood, extending
  from the well a good five ells up to his head.[5]   114
"O you who in the celebrated valley[6]
  (that saw Scipio become the heir of glory,
  when Hannibal with all his men retreated)   117
once captured a thousand lions as your quarry
  (and with whose aid, had you chosen to take part
  in the great war with your brothers, the sons of earth   120
would, as many still think, have been the victors),
  do not disdain this modest wish: take us,
  and put us down where ice locks in Cocytus.[7]   123
Don't make us go to Tityus or Typhon;[8]
  this man can give you what all long for here,
  and so bend down, and do not scowl at us.   126
He still can spread your legend in the world,
  for he yet lives, and long life lies before him,
  unless Grace summons him before his time."   129
Thus spoke my master, and the giant in haste
  stretched out the hands whose formidable grip
  great Hercules once felt, and took my guide.   132
And Virgil, when he felt the grasping hands,
  called out: "Now come and I'll take hold of you."
  Clasped together, we made a single burden.   135
As the Garisenda[9] looks from underneath
  its leaning side, at the moment when a cloud
  comes drifting over against the tower's slant,   138
just so the bending giant Antaeus seemed
  as I looked up, expecting him to topple.
  I wished then I had gone another way.   141
But he, most carefully, handed us down
  to the pit that swallows Lucifer with Judas.[1]
  And then, the leaning giant immediately   144
drew himself up as tall as a ship's mast.

CANTO XXXII

They descend farther down into the darkness of the immense plain of ice in which shades of Traitors are frozen. In the outer region of the ice-lake, Caïna, are those who betrayed their kin in murder; among them, locked in a frozen embrace, are Napoleone and Alessandro of Mangona, and others are Mordred, Focaccia, Sassol Mascheroni, and Camicion de'Pazzi. Then the two travelers enter the area of ice called Antenora, and suddenly the Pilgrim kicks one of the faces sticking out of the ice. He tries to force the sinner to reveal his name by pulling out his hair, and when another shade identifies him as Bocca Degli Abati, the Pilgrim's fury mounts still higher. Bocca, himself furious, names several other sinners in Antenora, including Buoso da Duera, Tesauro dei Beccheria, Gianni de' Soldanier, Ganelon, and Tibbald. Going farther on, the Pilgrim sees two heads frozen in one hole, the mouth of one gnawing at the brain of the other.

5. About fifteen feet.   6. The *valley* of the Bagradas River in Tunisia, where the Roman Scipio defeated the Carthaginian Hannibal in 202 b.c.e.   7. The frozen lake of *Cocytus* is in the ninth and last circle of Hell.   8. Two more Titans.   9. A leaning tower of Bologna; when a cloud passes over it, moving opposite to the tower's slant, it appears to be falling away from the sky.   1. Two of the inhabitants of Cocytus.

If I had words grating and crude enough
   that really could describe this horrid hole
   supporting the converging weight of Hell,   3
I could squeeze out the juice of my memories
   to the last drop. But I don't have these words,
   and so I am reluctant to begin.   6
To talk about the bottom of the universe
   the way it truly is, is no child's play,
   no task for tongues that gurgle baby-talk.   9
But may those heavenly ladies[2] aid my verse
   who aided Amphion to wall-in Thebes,
   that my words may tell exactly what I saw.   12
O misbegotten rabble of all rabble,
   who crowd this realm, hard even to describe,
   it were better you had lived as sheep or goats!   15
When we reached a point of darkness in the well
   below the giant's feet, farther down the slope,
   and I was gazing still at the high wall,   18
I heard somebody say: "Watch where you step!
   Be careful that you do not kick the heads
   of this brotherhood of miserable souls."   21
At that I turned around and saw before me
   a lake of ice stretching beneath my feet,
   more like a sheet of glass than frozen water.[3]   24
In the depths of Austria's wintertime, the Danube
   never in all its course showed ice so thick,
   nor did the Don beneath its frigid sky,   27
as this crust here; for if Mount Tambernic[4]
   or Pietrapana would crash down upon it,
   not even at its edges would a crack creak.   30
The way the frogs (in the season when the harvest
   will often haunt the dreams of the peasant girl)
   sit croaking with their muzzles out of water,   33
so these frigid, livid shades were stuck in ice
   up to where a person's shame appears;
   their teeth clicked notes like storks' beaks snapping shut.[5]   36
And each one kept his face bowed toward the ice:
   the mouth bore testimony to the cold,
   the eyes, to sadness welling in the heart.   39
I gazed around awhile and then looked down,
   and by my feet I saw two figures clasped
   so tight that one's hair could have been the other's.   42
"Tell me, you two, pressing your chests together,"
   I asked them, "who are you?"[6] Both stretched their necks
   and when they had their faces raised toward me,   45
their eyes, which had before been only glazed,
   dripped tears down to their lips, and the cold froze

---

2. The Muses who helped the legendary musician Amphion raise the walls of Thebes with the music of his lyre.   3. The water for this lake derives from the crack in the Old Man of Crete (14.103).   4. Probably Mount Tambura, close to Mount Pietrapana in the Italian Alps.   5. A harsh, clacking sound. *Where a person's shame appears* is the face because of blushing.   6. These are the two sons of Count Alberto degli Alberti of Florence; when he died (ca. 1280), they killed each other over politics and their inheritance.

the tears between them, locking the pair more tightly.   48
Wood to wood with iron was never clamped
    so firm! And the two of them like billy-goats
    were butting at each other, mad with anger.   51
Another one with both ears frozen off,
    and head still bowed over his icy mirror,
    cried out: "What makes you look at us so hard?   54
If you're interested to know who these two are:
    the valley where Bisenzio's waters[7] flow
    belonged to them and to their father, Albert;   57
the same womb bore them both, and if you scour
    all of Caïna,[8] you will not turn up one
    who's more deserving of this frozen aspic—   60
not him who had his breast and shadow pierced
    with one thrust of the lance from Arthur's hand;[9]
    not Focaccia, not even this one here,   63
whose head gets in my way and blocks my view,
    known in the world as Sassol Mascheroni,[1]
    and if you're Tuscan you must know who he was.   66
To save me from your asking for more news:
    I was Camicion de' Pazzi,[2] and I await
    Carlin,[3] whose guilt will make my own seem less."   69
Farther on I saw a thousand doglike faces,
    purple from the cold. That's why I shudder,
    and always will, when I see a frozen pond.   72
While we were getting closer to the center
    of the universe,[4] where all weights must converge,
    and I was shivering in the eternal chill—   75
by fate or chance or willfully perhaps,
    I do not know—but stepping among the heads,
    my foot kicked hard against one of those faces.   78
Weeping, he screamed: "Why are you kicking me?[5]
    You have not come to take revenge on me
    for Montaperti, have you? Why bother me?"   81
And I: "My master, please wait here for me,
    let me clear up a doubt concerning this one,
    then I shall be as rapid as you wish."   84
My leader stopped, and to that wretch, who still
    had not let up in his barrage of curses,
    I said: "Who are you, insulting other people?"   87
"And you, who are *you* who march through Antenora[6]

7. *Bisenzio* is a river north of Florence.   8. Named after Cain: this first of the four subdivisions of Cocytus is where those who betrayed their kin are imprisoned.   9. *Not him . . . hand:* This is Mordred, Arthur's nephew and son; when Arthur pierced him with a sword, he created a wound so large that the sun shone through, thus creating a hole in Mordred's shadow. *Focaccia* in the next line is a nobleman of Pistoia who killed his cousin.   1. A Florentine nobleman who murdered a relative.   2. A Florentine who killed his kinsman.   3. A Florentine who betrayed a castle belonging to his party. When he dies he will therefore be sent to the next subdivision, Antenora, for those who committed treachery against their country, city, or party—a harsher punishment, which Camicion says *will make my own [guilt] seem less.*   4. The *center of the universe* is where gravity is most strong and to which all material things are drawn.   5. Bocca degli Abati (his name is betrayed by one of the fellow damned in line 106); Bocca betrayed his party at the battle of Montaperti in 1260.   6. Dante and Virgil have moved into the second subdivision of Caïna, which is named after Antenor, a Trojan who betrayed the city to the Greeks; it is the location of those who betrayed their country.

kicking other people in their faces?
No living man could kick as hard!" he answered.   90
"I am a living man," was my reply,
    "and it might serve you well, if you seek fame,
    for me to put your name down in my notes."   93
And he said: "That's the last thing I would want!
    That's not the way to flatter in these lowlands!
    Stop pestering me like this—get out of here!"   96
At that I grabbed him by his hair in back[7]
    and said: "You'd better tell me who you are
    or else I'll not leave one hair on your head."   99
And he to me: "Go on and strip me bald
    and pound and stamp my head a thousand times,
    you'll never hear my name or see my face."   102
I had my fingers twisted in his hair
    and already I'd pulled out more than one fistful,
    while he yelped like a cur with eyes shut tight,   105
when someone else[8] yelled: "What's the matter, Bocca?
    It's bad enough to hear your shivering teeth;
    now you bark! What the devil's wrong with you?"   108
"There's no need now for you to speak," I said,
    "you vicious traitor! Now I know your name
    and I'll bring back the shameful truth about you."   111
"Go away!" he answered. "Tell them what you want;
    but if you do get out of here, be sure
    you also tell about that blabbermouth,   114
who's paying here what the French silver cost him:
    'I saw,' you can tell the world, 'the one from Duera
    stuck in with all the sinners keeping cool,'   117
And if you should be asked: 'Who else was there?'
    Right by your side is the one from Beccheria[9]
    whose head was chopped off by the Florentines.   120
As for Gianni Soldanier,[1] I think you'll find him
    farther along with Ganelon and Tibbald,
    who opened up Faenza while it slept."   123
Soon after leaving him I saw two souls
    frozen together in a single hole,
    so that one head used the other for a cap.   126
As a man with hungry teeth tears into bread,
    the soul with capping head had sunk his teeth
    into the other's neck, just beneath the skull.   129
Tydeus[2] in his fury did not gnaw
    the head of Menalippus with more relish
    than this one chewed that head of meat and bones.   132
"O you who show with every bestial bite

---

7. The hair at the nape of the neck.   8. This is Buoso da Duera, who betrayed Manfred, the ruler of
Naples, to his enemy Charles of Anjou in 1265.   9. Tesauro de' Beccheria, a churchman executed for
treason in Florence in 1258.   1. *Gianni Soldanier* was a Florentine nobleman who switched political
parties; *Ganelon* (line 122) is the betrayer of Roland in *The Song of Roland*; *Tibbald* (line 122) was the citizen of Faenza (a town east of Florence) who betrayed it to its enemies.   2. In the war against Thebes,
Tydeus was mortally wounded by Menalippus, whom he killed and whose skull he gnawed in fury while
dying.

your hatred for the head you are devouring,"
 I said, "tell me your reason, and I promise,   135
if you are justified in your revenge,
 once I know who you are and this one's sin,
 I'll repay your confidence in the world above   138
unless my tongue dry up before I die."

CANTO XXXIII

Count Ugolino is the shade gnawing at the brain of his one-time associate Archbishop Ruggieri, and Ugolino interrupts his gruesome meal long enough to tell the story of his imprisonment and cruel death, which his innocent offspring shared with him. Moving farther into the area of Cocytus known as Tolomea, where those who betrayed their guests and associates are condemned, the Pilgrim sees sinners with their faces raised high above the ice, whose tears freeze and lock their eyes. One of the shades agrees to identify himself on condition that the ice be removed from his eyes. The Pilgrim agrees, and learns that this sinner is Friar Alberigo and that his soul is dead and damned even though his body is still alive on earth, inhabited by a devil. Alberigo also names a fellow sinner with him in the ice, Branca d'Oria, whose body is still functioning up on earth. But the Pilgrim does not honor his promise to break the ice from Alberigo's eyes.

Lifting his mouth from his horrendous meal,
 this sinner[3] first wiped off his messy lips
 in the hair remaining on the chewed-up skull,   3
then spoke: "You want me to renew a grief
 so desperate that just the thought of it,
 much less the telling, grips my heart with pain;   6
but if my words can be the seed to bear
 the fruit of infamy for this betrayer,
 who feeds my hunger, then I shall speak—in tears. 9
I do not know your name, nor do I know
 how you have come down here, but Florentine
 you surely seem to be, to hear you speak.   12
First you should know I was Count Ugolino
 and my neighbor here, Ruggieri the Archbishop;
 now I'll tell you why I'm so unneighborly.   15
That I, trusting in him, was put in prison
 through his evil machinations, where I died,
 this much I surely do not have to tell you.   18
What you could not have known, however, is
 the inhuman circumstances of my death.
 Now listen, then decide if he has wronged me! 21
Through a narrow slit of window high in that mew[4]
 (which is called the tower of hunger, after me,
 and I'll not be the last to know that place)   24
I had watched moon after moon after moon go by,
 when finally I dreamed the evil dream
 which ripped away the veil that hid my future. 27
I dreamed of this one here as lord and huntsman,

---

3. Ugolino, a governor of Pisa who was betrayed by his enemy Archbishop Ruggieri in 1288. His own crime is obliquely explained by his narrative. 4. A cage for birds; the prison in Pisa where Ugolino and his relatives were confined became known as the Torre de Fame or Tower of Hunger.

pursuing the wolf and the wolf cubs up the mountain[5]
(which blocks the sight of Lucca from the Pisans)   30
with skinny bitches, well trained and obedient;
he had out front as leaders of the pack
Gualandi with Sismondi and Lanfranchi.[6]   33
A short run, and the father with his sons
seemed to grow tired, and then I thought I saw
long fangs sunk deep into their sides, ripped open.   36
When I awoke before the light of dawn,
I heard my children sobbing in their sleep
(you see they, too, were there), asking for bread.   39
If the thought of what my heart was telling me
does not fill you with grief, how cruel you are!
If you are not weeping now—do you ever weep?   42
And then they awoke. It was around the time
they usually brought our food to us. But now
each one of us was full of dread from dreaming;   45
then from below I heard them driving nails
into the dreadful tower's door; with that,
I stared in silence at my flesh and blood.   48
I did not weep, I turned to stone inside;
they wept, and my little Anselmuccio spoke:
'What is it, father? Why do you look that way?'   51
For them I held my tears back, saying nothing,
all of that day, and then all of that night,
until another sun shone on the world.   54
A meager ray of sunlight found its way
to the misery of our cell, and I could see
myself reflected four times in their faces;   57
I bit my hands in anguish. And my children,
who thought that hunger made me bite my hands,
were quick to draw up closer to me, saying: 60
'O father, you would make us suffer less,
if you would feed on us: you were the one
who gave us this sad flesh; you take it from us!'[7]   63
I calmed myself to make them less unhappy.
That day we sat in silence, and the next day.
O pitiless earth! You should have swallowed us!   66
The fourth day came, and it was on that day
my Gaddo fell prostrate before my feet,
crying: 'Why don't you help me? Why, my father?'[8]   69
There he died. Just as you see me here,
I saw the other three fall one by one,
as the fifth day and the sixth day passed. And I,   72
by then gone blind, groped over their dead bodies.
Though they were dead, two days I called their names.

---

5. Mount San Giuliano lies between Pisa and Lucca. *The Wolf and the wolf cubs*: Ugolino and his four sons, each of whom are named in subsequent lines (50, 68, 89). In fact, Ugolino was imprisoned with two sons (who were grown men) and two adolescent grandsons.   6. Pisan families of the political party opposed to that of Ugolino.   7. See Job 1.21.   8. See Matthew 27.46.

Then hunger proved more powerful than grief."   75
He spoke these words; then, glaring down in rage,
   attacked again the wretched skull with his teeth
   sharp as a dog's, and as fit for grinding bones.   78
O Pisa, blot of shame upon the people
   of that fair land where the sound of "sì" is heard![9]
   Since your neighbors hesitate to punish you,   81
let Capraia and Gorgona[1] move and join,
   damming up the River Arno at its mouth,
   and let every Pisan perish in its flood!   84
For if Count Ugolino was accused
   of turning traitor, trading-in your castles,[2]
   you had no right to make his children suffer.   87
Their newborn years (O newborn Thebes!)[3] made them
   all innocents: Brigata, Uguiccione,
   and the other two soft names my canto sings.   90
We moved ahead to where the frozen water
   wraps in harsh wrinkles another sinful race,
   with faces not turned down but looking up.[4]   93
Here, the weeping puts an end to weeping,
   and the grief that finds no outlet from the eyes
   turns inward to intensify the anguish: 96
for the tears they first wept knotted in a cluster
   and like a visor made for them in crystal,
   filled all the hollow part around their eyes.   99
Although the bitter coldness of the dark
   had driven all sensation from my face,
   as though it were not tender skin but callous,   102
I thought I felt the air begin to blow,
   and I: "What causes such a wind, my master?
   I thought no heat could reach into these depths."[5]   105
And he to me: "Before long you will be
   where your own eyes can answer for themselves,
   when they will see what keeps this wind in motion."   108
And one of the wretches with the frozen crust
   screamed out at us: "O wicked souls, so wicked
   that you have been assigned the ultimate post,   111
break off these hard veils covering my eyes
   and give relief from the pain that swells my heart—
   at least until the new tears freeze again."   114
I answered him: "If this is what you want,
   tell me your name; and if I do not help you,
   may I be forced to drop beneath this ice!"   117

9. That is, Italy, where *sì* means "yes."   1. Islands belonging to Pisa that lie close to the mouth of the Arno, which flows through Pisa.   2. In 1285 Ugolino conveyed three Pisan castles to Lucca and Florence. 3. In classical mythology, *Thebes* was notorious for its internecine violence, such as the story of Oedipus, his father, Laius, and his sons, Eteocles and Polynices (see 26.54).   4. Virgil and Dante pass into the third subdivision of Cocytus, called Tolomea (line 124) after Ptolemy, governor of Jericho, who killed his father-in-law, Simon, and two of his sons while they were dining with him (1 Maccabees 16.11–17). In Tolomea those who have betrayed their guests are punished.   5. Since the sun's heat was thought to cause wind, Dante wonders why he feels wind in this cold place. The answer will be given in 34.46–52.

He answered then: "I am Friar Alberigo,[6]
   I am he who offered fruit from the evil orchard:
   here dates are served me for the figs I gave."   120
"Oh, then!" I said. "Are you already dead?"
   And he to me: "Just how my body is
   in the world above, I have no way of knowing.   123
This zone of Tolomea is very special,
   for it often happens that a soul falls here
   before the time that Atropos[7] should send it.   126
And that you may more willingly scrape off
   my cluster of glass tears, let me tell you:
   whenever a soul betrays the way I did,   129
a demon takes possession of the body,
   controlling its maneuvers from then on,
   for all the years it has to live up there,   132
while the soul falls straight into this cistern here;
   and the shade in winter quarters just behind me
   may well have left his body up on earth.   135
But you should know, if you've just come from there:
   he is Ser Branca D'Oria;[8] and many years
   have passed since he first joined us here, icebound."   138
"I think you're telling me a lie," I said,
   "for Branca D'Oria is not dead at all;
   he eats and drinks, he sleeps and wears out clothes."   141
"The ditch the Malebranche watch above,"
   he said, "the ditch of clinging, boiling pitch,
   had not yet caught the soul of Michel Zanche,   144
when Branca left a devil in his body
   to take his place, and so did his close kinsman,
   his accomplice in this act of treachery.   147
But now, at last, give me the hand you promised.
   Open my eyes." I did not open them.
   To be mean to him was a generous reward.   150
O all you Genovese, you men estranged
   from every good, at home with every vice,
   why can't the world be wiped clean of your race?   153
For in company with Romagna's rankest soul[9]
   I found one of your men, whose deeds were such
   that his soul bathes already in Cocytus   156
but his body seems alive and walks among you.

CANTO XXXIV

Far across the frozen ice can be seen the gigantic figure of Lucifer, who appears from this distance like a windmill seen through fog; and as the two travelers walk on toward that terrifying sight, they see the shades of sinners totally buried in the frozen water. At

---

6. A member of the Jovial Friars (see 23.103), he killed two of his relatives during a banquet at his house, signaling the assassins with an order to bring the fruit. In saying that he is now being served dates instead of figs, he is ironically complimenting God for His generosity, since a date would be more valuable than a fig.   7. One of the mythological figures known as the Fates; she is the one who cuts the thread of life. 8. A nobleman of Genoa (a *Genovese* in line 151), who with a *close kinsman* (line 146) killed his father-in-law, *Michel Zanche* (line 144) at a banquet in 1275 or 1290.   9. That is, Friar Alberigo (line 118); *Romagna* is the part of Italy from which he and Branca come.

the center of the earth Lucifer stands frozen from the chest downward, and his horrible ugliness (he has three faces) is made more fearful by the fact that in each of his three mouths he chews on one of the three worst sinners of all mankind, the worst of those who betrayed their benefactors: Judas Iscariot, Brutus, and Cassius. Virgil, with the Pilgrim on his back, begins the descent down the shaggy body of Lucifer. They climb down through a crack in the ice, and when they reach the Evil One's thighs, Virgil turns and begins to struggle upward (because they have passed the center of the earth), still holding on to the hairy body of Lucifer, until they reach a cavern, where they stop for a short rest. Then a winding path brings them eventually to the earth's surface, where they see the stars.

"*Vexilla regis prodeunt Inferni,*"[1]
    my master said, "closer to us, so now
    look ahead and see if you can make him out."   3
A far-off windmill turning its huge sails
    when a thick fog begins to settle in,
    or when the light of day begins to fade,   6
that is what I thought I saw appearing.
    And the gusts of wind it stirred made me shrink back
    behind my guide, my only means of cover.   9
Down here,[2] I stood on souls fixed under ice
    (I tremble as I put this into verse);
    to me they looked like straws worked into glass.   12
Some lying flat, some perpendicular,
    either with their heads up or their feet,
    and some bent head to foot, shaped like a bow.   15
When we had moved far enough along the way
    that my master thought the time had come to show me
    the creature who was once so beautiful,[3]   18
he stepped aside, and stopping me, announced:
    "This is he, this is Dis;[4] this is the place
    that calls for all the courage you have in you."   21
How chilled and nerveless, Reader, I felt then;
    do not ask me—I cannot write about it—
    there are no words to tell you how I felt.   24
I did not die—I was not living either!
    Try to imagine, if you can imagine,
    me there, deprived of life and death at once.   27
The king of the vast kingdom of all grief
    stuck out with half his chest above the ice;
    my height is closer to the height of giants   30
than theirs is to the length of his great arms;
    consider now how large all of him was:
    this body in proportion to his arms.   33
If once he was as fair as now he's foul

---

1. The first three words—"the banners of the king advance"—are the opening lines of a sixth-century Latin hymn traditionally sung during Holy Week to celebrate Christ's Passion. Dante has added the last word, *Inferni*—"the banners of the king of Hell advance"—in order to apply the words to Satan. 2. This is the last and lowest subdivision of Caïna, known as Judecca after Judas; the sinners here are those who betrayed their benefactors. 3. Lucifer, the "light-bearer," was the most beautiful of angels before he rebelled and was renamed Satan. 4. A classical name for Pluto, here applied to Satan (see also 11.65 and 12.39).

and dared to raise his brows against his Maker,
    it is fitting that all grief should spring from him.   36
Oh, how amazed I was when I looked up
    and saw a head—one head wearing three faces![5]
    One was in front (and that was a bright red),   39
the other two attached themselves to this one
    just above the middle of each shoulder,
    and at the crown all three were joined in one: 42
The right face was a blend of white and yellow,
    the left the color of those people's skin
    who live along the river Nile's descent.[6]   45
Beneath each face two mighty wings stretched out,
    the size you might expect of this huge bird
    (I never saw a ship with larger sails):   48
not feathered wings but rather like the ones
    a bat would have. He flapped them constantly,
    keeping three winds continuously in motion   51
to lock Cocytus eternally in ice.
    He wept from his six eyes, and down three chins
    were dripping tears all mixed with bloody slaver.   54
In each of his three mouths he crunched a sinner,
    with teeth like those that rake the hemp and flax,
    keeping three sinners constantly in pain;   57
the one in front—the biting he endured
    was nothing like the clawing that he took:
    sometimes his back was raked clean of its skin.   60
"That soul up there who suffers most of all,"
    my guide explained, "is Judas Iscariot:
    the one with head inside and legs out kicking.   63
As for the other two whose heads stick out,
    the one who hangs from that black face is Brutus[7]—
    see how he squirms in silent desperation;   66
the other one is Cassius,[8] he still looks sturdy.
    But soon it will be night. Now is the time
    to leave this place, for we have seen it all."   69
I held on to his neck, as he told me to,
    while he watched and waited for the time and place,
    and when the wings were stretched out just enough,   72
he grabbed on to the shaggy sides of Satan;
    then downward, tuft by tuft, he made his way
    between the tangled hair and frozen crust.   75
When we had reached the point exactly where
    the thigh begins, right at the haunch's curve,
    my guide, with strain and force of every muscle,   78
turned his head toward the shaggy shanks of Dis
    and grabbed the hair as if about to climb—

---

5. Satan's three faces (and much else) make him an infernal parody of the Trinity.   6. I.e., Ethiopians. The significance of these three colors is not certain; it has been suggested that they represent hatred, impotence, and ignorance as the opposites of the Divine attributes of love, omnipotence, and wisdom (see 3.5–6).   7. The murderer of Julius Caesar in 44 B.C.E. and thus for Dante a betrayer of the empire. 8. The other murderer of Caesar.

I thought that we were heading back to Hell.[9]   81
"Hold tight, there is no other way," he said,
  panting, exhausted, "only by these stairs
  can we leave behind the evil we have seen."   84
When he had got me through the rocky crevice,
  he raised me to its edge and set me down,
  then carefully he climbed and joined me there.   87
I raised my eyes, expecting I would see
  the half of Lucifer I saw before.
  Instead I saw his two legs stretching upward.   90
If at that sight I found myself confused,
  so will those simple-minded folk who still
  don't see what point it was I must have passed.   93
"Get up," my master said, "get to your feet,
  the way is long, the road a rough climb up,
  already the sun approaches middle tierce!"[1]   96
It was no palace promenade we came to,
  but rather like some dungeon Nature built:
  it was paved with broken stone and poorly lit.   99
"Before we start to struggle out of here,
  O master," I said when I was on my feet,
  "I wish you would explain some things to me.   102
Where is the ice? And how can he be lodged
  upside-down? And how, in so little time,
  could the sun go all the way from night to day?"   105
"You think you're still on the center's other side,"
  he said, "where I first grabbed the hairy worm
  of rottenness that pierces the earth's core;   108
and you *were* there as long as I moved downward
  but, when I turned myself, you passed the point
  to which all weight from every part is drawn.[2]   111
Now you are standing beneath the hemisphere[3]
  which is opposite the side covered by land,
  where at the central point was sacrificed   114
the Man whose birth and life were free of sin.
  You have both feet upon a little sphere
  whose other side Judecca occupies;   117
when it is morning here, there it is evening.[4]
  And he whose hairs were stairs for our descent
  has not changed his position since his fall.   120

9. Virgil's reversal marks the point at which the two travelers pass from the northern to the southern hemisphere. They began by climbing down Satan's body, but now reverse directions and climb up from the Earth's center (hence when they have passed through the center Dante sees Satan's legs sticking up (line 90). Note that the travelers pass through the glassy ice, a passage that probably echoes 1 Corinthians 13.12: "We see now through a glass in a dark manner; but then face to face."   1. About 7:30 A.M. on Holy Saturday. Dante has added twelve hours to his scheme so that the travelers will emerge from the Earth and arrive at the shore of Mount Purgatory just before sunrise on the next day, Easter Sunday. **2.** The center of the earth, which is for Dante the center of the universe, and therefore the place where gravity is the strongest. Being furthest from Heaven, it is also the place which is most material and least spiritual.   **3.** I.e., under the Southern Hemisphere, exactly opposite Jerusalem where Christ (the Man whose birth and life were free of sin) was crucified. Jerusalem is the center of the Northern Hemisphere (see Ezekiel 5.5) and is located directly over the cavity of Hell.   **4.** The little sphere upon which they stand is the other side of Judecca, which is a hollow. The sun is now over the Southern Hemisphere, and therefore it is night in the Northern, where Hell is located.

When he fell from the heavens on this side,[5]
   all of the land that once was spread out here,
   alarmed by his plunge, took cover beneath the sea   123
and moved to our hemisphere; with equal fear
   the mountain-land, piled up on this side, fled
   and made this cavern here when it rushed upward.   126
Below somewhere there is a space, as far
   from Beelzebub[6] as the limit of his tomb,
   known not by sight but only by the sound   129
of a little stream[7] that makes its way down here
   through the hollow of a rock that it has worn,
   gently winding in gradual descent."   132
My guide and I entered that hidden road
   to make our way back up to the bright world.
   We never thought of resting while we climbed.   135
We climbed, he first and I behind, until,
   through a small round opening ahead of us
   I saw the lovely things the heavens hold,   138
and we came out to see once more the stars.[8]

5. The land that was in the Southern Hemisphere before Satan fell fled to the Northern to avoid him; hence the Southern Hemisphere is composed of water. The exception is that when Satan plunged into the center of the world, the earth close to his body in the Northern Hemisphere moved *with equal fear* (line 124) to the Southern Hemisphere and became *mountain-land* (line 125), which is Mount Purgatory. *This cavern* (line 126) refers to Hell; Mount Purgatory is thus comprised of the land displaced by Satan in his fall. This elaborate explanation for medieval geography is Dante's own poetic scheme.   6. Satan. 7. This stream must flow down from Purgatory, perhaps from Lethe. It finds its source in *a space* (line 127) on Mount Purgatory; thus it is *as far from Beelzebub as the limit of his tomb*—that is, it is located on the surface of the Southern Hemisphere, which since Satan is at the center of the earth is the same distance from him as Hell (his *tomb*) is deep. When Dante has Virgil say that it is *below* (line 127) he must be writing from the perspective of the Northern Hemisphere, since Mount Purgatory is at this moment above the travelers.   8. Each of the three parts of the *Divine Comedy* ends with the word *stars* as an affirmation of God's benevolent order.

GIOVANNI BOCCACCIO
1313–1375

The *Decameron* by Giovanni Boccaccio has a reputation as a ribald classic, and certainly many of its stories—including some selected here—deal with sexual misadventures. But it also gathers into its hundred stories the diversity and energy that made fourteenth-century Italy one of the great cultural resources of medieval Europe. With his predecessor Dante and his slightly older contemporary Petrarch, Boccaccio established Italy and specifically Florence as a center of literary production that influenced European writing for centuries.

Boccaccio was born in Tuscany, probably in Florence, to a merchant and banker who did not marry the child's mother until some five years later. At fourteen he was taken to Naples, where his father made him spend six years studying arithmetic and then, when it became clear that Boccaccio would not make a successful merchant, another six years preparing for a career as a lawyer. But this enterprise also failed, for Boccaccio was drawn to the sophisticated circle of writers and scholars that the ruler of southern Italy, Robert of Anjou, had assembled into a court that was the most advanced cultural center of its time. Although known to modern readers almost exclusively through the *Decameron*, Boccaccio wrote primarily either courtly tales of love in Italian verse or learned treatises on subjects such as history, classical mythology, and geography in Latin prose. Along with Petrarch, Boccaccio was one of the many medieval writers who worked to revive the literary heritage of the classical world. In a poem called the *Teseida* he produced the first vernacular version of a classical epic, initiating a tradition that was to culminate in Milton's *Paradise Lost*, and he sponsored the first translation of Homer from Greek (in this case into Latin). The humanism that was to come to fruition in the Renaissance finds one of its most important medieval inspirations in the work of Boccaccio.

The *Decameron* represents another aspect of Boccaccio's literary personality. Locating the collection, written between 1350 and 1353, in a specific historical context, Boccaccio first describes the devastating effects of the bubonic plague (or Black Death) of 1348–50 on Florence. Indeed, while the plague killed at least one third of the European population (as well as millions elsewhere in the world), in Florence the death rate was as high as 70 percent. Despite the vividness of Boccaccio's description, his account is not in fact based on experience. On the contrary, he borrowed historians' descriptions of earlier plagues. He emphasizes the destruction of both the social fabric of the city and the moral restraints on individual behavior, in effect the disappearance of civilization itself: "all respect for the laws of God and man had virtually broken down and been extinguished in our city." Partly in response to this collapse, but also partly as an effect of it, Boccaccio imagines an alternative society. He describes how seven young ladies of good family are joined by three young men and retreat from the ravaged city to a beautiful country estate. Here they restore themselves with pleasure, but a pleasure that is carefully regulated: as their leader, Pampinea, says, they will enjoy themselves in the country "without in any way overstepping the bounds of what is reasonable." Among their recreations is a tale-telling game: for ten days each member of the group tells a story, creating the hundred stories that make up the *Decameron*.

But if Boccaccio presents these tales as an alternative to the social and moral collapse of plague-stricken Florence, he also insists that pleasure is itself healthful. In this he sets his work in opposition to that of one of his own literary heroes, Dante. Much of Boccaccio's work is heavily influenced by Dante, and near the end of his life he both wrote a treatise celebrating Dante and delivered a set of lectures commenting in detail on the first twenty-eight cantos of the *Inferno*. Yet the *Decameron* is an implicitly anti-Dantean work. Its division into one hundred tales echoes Dante's division of his *Comedy* into one hundred cantos, and Boccaccio gives his work an alternative title—"Prince Galahalt"—that refers to a crucial moment in the *Inferno*. In canto 5 of the *Inferno* Francesca explains to Dante that she and her brother-in-law Paolo fell in love while reading the story of Lancelot and Guinevere. She blames the book for their fall, calling it a Galahalt: she is referring to the knight in the Arthurian court who served as a go-between for the lovers. Dante is implying here that reading, and especially reading for pleasure, can be morally dangerous. Yet Boccaccio insists by his subtitle, by the Prologue that defines his book as a consolation and distraction for lovesick ladies, and by the very occasion for the story-telling, that literature can provide a pleasure that is not merely legitimate but restorative.

Many different kinds of pleasure are both described in and made available by the *Decameron*. While the members of the company are flirtatious but always decorous, many of the stories told, especially by the men, celebrate sexual pleasure with a frank good humor. On the whole, the *Decameron* celebrates a pragmatic and relativistic value system, refusing to endow any single set of values with ultimate authority. If one story teaches one lesson, then the next will teach a contradictory one, and readers are allowed to decide for themselves where true value is to be found.

In this relativism Boccaccio's *Decameron* is very different from Dante's *Divine Comedy*. Dante is an absolutist: he insists throughout his great work that there *is* a single truth, and the many details of the poem are controlled by Christian doctrine.

But without being in any sense unmindful of the claims of religion—Boccaccio was certainly a fully devout Christian—the *Decameron* describes a much more multifarious, much less easily judged world than does *The Divine Comedy*. The first story tells of a thoroughgoing rogue, Ser Cepperello, who provides an outrageously false deathbed confession to a credulous and self-seeking friar. But while Cepperello seems to damn himself by his impenitent mockery of the salvation offered by the church, we are aware that he is acting out of charitable motives in trying to protect his Florentine friends. So it becomes difficult to know if the townspeople are entirely wrong in thinking he is a saint. And we are also aware that the good deed performed is itself an act of tale-telling, and a tale that is both an outrageous lie and a pleasure to read. On the other side, the story of Nastagio and the hunt of love (the eighth story of the fifth day) presents a scene straight out of the *Inferno*: a scornful lady is eternally hunted down and eviscerated by her suicidal lover. Are we to think that here divine justice is being done? The context in which the scene is placed might give us pause. Used by Nastagio to persuade his lady to accept him as a lover, this scene reveals both the obsessions of the courtly lover but also its cruelty and violence. Finally, these complexities are brought together in the story of Griselda (the tenth story of the tenth day), which proved to be one of the most popular stories of the later Middle Ages (both Petrarch and Chaucer produced versions). Is Griselda a saint of patience who is finally rewarded for her virtue? Or is she an unreasonably passive creature who solicits her own victimization? Is Walter a monster, a tyrant both politically and domestically, and the story a psychological study of despotism? Or is he an agent of God who makes possible the revelation of Griselda's superhuman virtue, or perhaps even God himself? In this fascinating puzzle of a story, Boccaccio poses questions without providing any obvious answer, showing us that perhaps the deepest pleasure that literature can offer is the pleasure of interpretation.

PRONOUNCING GLOSSARY

The following list uses common English syllables to provide rough equivalents of selected words whose pronunciation may be unfamiliar to the general reader.

Cepperello Dietaiuti: *chep-er-el-lo dee-ay-tie-yu'-tee*

Giannùcole: *gee-an-ooh'-co-lay*

Gualtieri: *gwal-tee-ay'-ree*

Guido degli Anastagi: *gwee'-do day'-lee an-as-ta'-jee*

Guillaume de Cabestanh: *gee-ohm' de cab-e s-stan'*

Guillaume de Roussillon: *gee-ohm' de roo-see-yonh*

Musciatto: *mus-chee-at'-to*

Nastagio degli Onesti: *nas-taj'-io day'-lee on-es'-tee*

Paolo Traversari: *pow'-lo tra-ver-sa'-ree*

Pinuccio: *pin-ooch'-ee-o*

From The Decameron[1]

Here begins the book called Decameron,[2] *otherwise known as Prince Galahalt, wherein are contained a hundred stories told in ten days by seven ladies and three young men.*

---

1. Translated by G. H. McWilliam.　2. The title is a pseudo-Greek word meaning "Ten Days"; it also ironically refers to a medieval devotional text called the Hexaemeron (Six Days) about the six days of creation described in Genesis.

[The Prologue]

To take pity on people in distress is a human quality which every man and woman should possess, but it is especially requisite in those who have once needed comfort, and found it in others. I number myself as one of these, because if ever anyone required or appreciated comfort, or indeed derived pleasure therefrom, I was that person. For from my earliest youth until the present day, I have been inflamed beyond measure with a most lofty and noble love, far loftier and nobler than might perhaps be thought proper, were I to describe it, in a person of my humble condition.[3] And although people of good judgment, to whose notice it had come, praised me for it and rated me much higher in their esteem, nevertheless it was exceedingly diffi-cult for me to endure. The reason, I hasten to add, was not the cruelty of my lady-love, but the immoderate passion engendered within my mind by a craving that was ill-restrained. This, since it would allow me no proper respite, often caused me an inordinate amount of distress. But in my anguish I have on occasion derived much relief from the agreeable conversation and the admirable expressions of sympathy offered by friends, without which I am firmly convinced that I should have perished. However, the One who is infinite decreed by immutable law that all earthly things should come to an end. And it pleased Him that this love of mine, whose warmth exceeded all others, and which had stood firm and unyielding against all the pressures of good intention, helpful advice, and the risk of danger and open scandal, should in the course of time diminish of its own accord. So that now, all that is left of it in my mind is the delectable feeling which Love habitually reserves for those who refrain from venturing too far upon its deepest waters. And thus what was once a source of pain has now become, having shed all discomfort, an abiding sensation of pleasure.

But though the pain has ceased, I still preserve a clear recollection of the kindnesses I received in the past from people who, prompted by feelings of goodwill towards me, showed a concern for my sufferings. This memory will never, I think, fade for as long as I live. And since it is my conviction that gratitude, of all the virtues, is most highly to be commended and its opposite condemned. I have resolved, in order not to appear ungrateful, to employ what modest talents I possess in making restitution for what I have received. Thus, now that I can claim to have achieved my freedom, I intend to offer some solace, if not to those who assisted me (since their good sense or good fortune will perhaps render such a gift superfluous), at least to those who stand in need of it. And even though my support, or if you prefer, my encour-agement, may seem very slight (as indeed it is) to the people concerned, I feel none the less that it should for preference be directed where it seems to be most needed, because that is the quarter in which it will be more effec-tive and, at the same time, more readily welcomed.

And who will deny that such encouragement, however small, should much rather be offered to the charming ladies than to the men? For the ladies, out of fear or shame, conceal the flames of passion within their fragile breasts, and a hidden love is far more potent than one which is worn on the sleeve, as everyone knows who has had experience of these matters. Moreover they

---

3. This claim to love a noble lady is conventional in medieval literature.

are forced to follow the whims, fancies and dictates of their fathers, mothers, brothers and husbands, so that they spend most of their time cooped up within the narrow confines of their rooms, where they sit in apparent idleness, wishing one thing and at the same time wishing its opposite, and reflecting on various matters, which cannot possibly always be pleasant to contemplate. And if, in the course of their meditations, their minds should be invaded by melancholy arising out of the flames of longing, it will inevitably take root there and make them suffer greatly, unless it be dislodged by new interests. Besides which, their powers of endurance are considerably weaker than those that men possess.

When men are in love, they are not affected in this way, as we can see quite plainly. They, whenever they are weighed down by melancholy or ponderous thoughts, have many ways of relieving or expelling them. For if they wish, they can always walk abroad, see and hear many things, go fowling, hunting, fishing, riding and gambling, or attend to their business affairs. Each of these pursuits has the power of engaging men's minds, either wholly or in part, and diverting them from their gloomy meditations, at least for a certain period: after which, some form of consolation will ensue, or the affliction will grow less intense.

So in order that I may to some extent repair the omissions of Fortune, which (as we may see in the case of the more delicate sex) was always more sparing of support wherever natural strength was more deficient, I intend to provide succor and diversion for the ladies, but only for those who are in love, since the others can make do with their needles, their reels and their spindles. I shall narrate a hundred stories or fables or parables or histories or whatever you choose to call them, recited in ten days by a worthy band of seven ladies and three young men, who assembled together during the plague which recently took such heavy toll of life. And I shall also include some songs, which these seven ladies sang for their mutual amusement.

In these tales will be found a variety of love adventures, bitter as well as pleasing, and other exciting incidents, which took place in both ancient and modern times. In reading them, the aforesaid ladies will be able to derive, not only pleasure from the entertaining matters therein set forth, but also some useful advice. For they will learn to recognize what should be avoided and likewise what should be pursued, and these things can only lead, in my opinion, to the removal of their affliction. If this should happen (and may God grant that it should), let them give thanks to Love, which, in freeing me from its bonds, has granted me the power of making provision for their pleasures.

First Day

Here begins the First Day of the Decameron, *wherein first of all the author explains the circumstances in which certain persons, who presently make their appearance, were induced to meet for the purpose of conversing together, after which, under the rule of* Pampinea, *each of them speaks on the subject they find most congenial.*

Whenever, fairest ladies, I pause to consider how compassionate you all are by nature, I invariably become aware that the present work will seem to you to possess an irksome and ponderous opening. For it carries at its head the painful memory of the deadly havoc wrought by the recent plague, which brought so much heartache and misery to those who witnessed, or had experience of it. But I do not want you to be deterred, for this reason, from reading any further, on the assumption that you are to be subjected, as you read, to an endless torrent of tears and sobbing. You will be affected no differently by this grim beginning than walkers confronted by a steep and rugged hill, beyond which there lies a beautiful and delectable plain. The degree of pleasure they derive from the latter will correspond directly to the difficulty of the climb and the descent. And just as the end of mirth is heaviness, so sorrows are dispersed by the advent of joy.

This brief unpleasantness (I call it brief, inasmuch as it is contained within few words) is quickly followed by the sweetness and the pleasure which I have already promised you, and which, unless you were told in advance, you would not perhaps be expecting to find after such a beginning as this. Believe me, if I could decently have taken you whither I desire by some other route, rather than along a path so difficult as this, I would gladly have done so. But since it is impossible without this memoir to show the origin of the events you will read about later, I really have no alternative but to address myself to its composition.

I say, then, that the sum of thirteen hundred and forty-eight years had elapsed since the fruitful Incarnation of the Son of God, when the noble city of Florence, which for its great beauty excels all others in Italy, was visited by the deadly pestilence. Some say that it descended upon the human race through the influence of the heavenly bodies, others that it was a punishment signifying God's righteous anger at our iniquitous way of life. But whatever its cause, it had originated some years earlier in the East, where it had claimed countless lives before it unhappily spread westward, growing in strength as it swept relentlessly on from one place to the next.[4]

In the face of its onrush, all the wisdom and ingenuity of man were unavailing. Large quantities of refuse were cleared out of the city by officials specially appointed for the purpose, all sick persons were forbidden entry, and numerous instructions were issued for safeguarding the people's health, but all to no avail. Nor were the countless petitions humbly directed to God by the pious, whether by means of formal processions or in all other ways, any less ineffectual. For in the early spring of the year we have mentioned, the plague began, in a terrifying and extraordinary manner, to make its disastrous effects apparent. It did not take the form it had assumed in the East, where if anyone bled from the nose it was an obvious portent of certain death. On the contrary, its earliest symptom, in men and women alike, was the appearance of certain swellings in the groin or the armpit, some of which were egg-shaped whilst others were roughly the size of the common apple. Sometimes the swellings were large, sometimes not so large, and they were referred to by the populace as gavòccioli.[5] From the two areas already mentioned, this deadly gavòcciolo would begin to spread, and within a short time it would appear at random all over the body. Later on, the symptoms of the disease changed, and many people began to find dark blotches and bruises on their arms, thighs, and other parts of the body, sometimes large

4. The bubonic plague originated on the steppes of central Asia and was carried to Europe by fleas that infested rats on the ships of European traders.   5. The medical name for these swellings is *buboes* (from Greek), whence the name bubonic plague.

and few in number, at other times tiny and closely spaced. These, to anyone unfortunate enough to contract them, were just as infallible a sign that he would die as the *gavòcciolo* had been earlier, and as indeed it still was.

Against these maladies, it seemed that all the advice of physicians and all the power of medicine were profitless and unavailing. Perhaps the nature of the illness was such that it allowed no remedy or perhaps those people who were treating the illness (whose numbers had increased enormously because the ranks of the qualified were invaded by people, both men and women, who had never received any training in medicine), being ignorant of its causes, were not prescribing the appropriate cure. At all events, few of those who caught it ever recovered, and in most cases death occurred within three days from the appearance of the symptoms we have described, some people dying more rapidly than others, the majority without any fever or other complications.

But what made this pestilence even more severe was that whenever those suffering from it mixed with people who were still unaffected, it would rush upon these with the speed of a fire racing through dry or oily substances that happened to come within its reach. Nor was this the full extent of its evil, for not only did it infect healthy persons who conversed or had any dealings with the sick, making them ill or visiting an equally horrible death upon them, but it also seemed to transfer the sickness to anyone touching the clothes or other objects which had been handled or used by its victims.

It is a remarkable story that I have to relate. And were it not for the fact that I am one of many people who saw it with their own eyes, I would scarcely dare to believe it, let alone commit it to paper, even though I had heard it from a person whose word I could trust. The plague I have been describing was of so contagious a nature that very often it visibly did more than simply pass from one person to another. In other words, whenever an animal other than a human being touched anything belonging to a person who had been stricken or exterminated by the disease, it not only caught the sickness, but died from it almost at once. To all of this, as I have just said, my own eyes bore witness on more than one occasion. One day, for instance, the rags of a pauper who had died from the disease were thrown into the street, where they attracted the attention of two pigs. In their wonted fashion, the pigs first of all gave the rags a thorough mauling with their snouts, after which they took them between their teeth and shook them against their cheeks. And within a short time they began to writhe as though they had been poisoned, then they both dropped dead to the ground, spread-eagled upon the rags that had brought about their undoing.

These things, and many others of a similar or even worse nature, caused various fears and fantasies to take root in the minds of those who were still alive and well. And almost without exception, they took a single and very inhuman precaution, namely to avoid or run away from the sick and their belongings, by which means they all thought that their own health would be preserved.

Some people were of the opinion that a sober and abstemious mode of living considerably reduced the risk of infection. They therefore formed themselves into groups and lived in isolation from everyone else. Having withdrawn to a comfortable abode where there were no sick persons, they locked themselves in and settled down to a peaceable existence, consuming modest quantities of delicate foods and precious wines and avoiding all excesses. They refrained from speaking to outsiders, refused to receive news of the dead or the sick, and entertained themselves with music and whatever other amusements they were able to devise.

Others took the opposite view, and maintained that an infallible way of warding off this appalling evil was to drink heavily, enjoy life to the full, go round singing and merrymaking, gratify all of one's cravings whenever the opportunity offered, and shrug the whole thing off as one enormous joke. Moreover, they practised what they preached to the best of their ability, for they would visit one tavern after another, drinking all day and night to immoderate excess; or alternatively (and this was their more frequent custom), they would do their drinking in various private houses, but only in the ones where the conversation was restricted to subjects that were pleasant or entertaining. Such places were easy to find, for people behaved as though their days were numbered, and treated their belongings and their own persons with equal abandon. Hence most houses had become common property, and any passing stranger could make himself at home as naturally as though he were the rightful owner. But for all their riotous manner of living, these people always took good care to avoid any contact with the sick.

In the face of so much affliction and misery, all respect for the laws of God and man had virtually broken down and been extinguished in our city. For like everybody else, those ministers and executors of the laws who were not either dead or ill were left with so few subordinates that they were unable to discharge any of their duties. Hence everyone was free to behave as he pleased.

There were many other people who steered a middle course between the two already mentioned, neither restricting their diet to the same degree as the first group, nor indulging so freely as the second in drinking and other forms of wantonness, but simply doing no more than satisfy their appetite. Instead of incarcerating themselves, these people moved about freely, holding in their hands a posy of flowers, or fragrant herbs, or one of a wide range of spices, which they applied at frequent intervals to their nostrils, thinking it an excellent idea to fortify the brain with smells of that particular sort; for the stench of dead bodies, sickness, and medicines seemed to fill and pollute the whole of the atmosphere.

Some people, pursuing what was possibly the safer alternative, callously maintained that there was no better or more efficacious remedy against a plague than to run away from it. Swayed by this argument, and sparing no thought for anyone but themselves, large numbers of men and women abandoned their city, their homes, their relatives, their estates and their belongings, and headed for the countryside, either in Florentine territory or, better still, abroad. It was as though they imagined that the wrath of God would not unleash this plague against men for their iniquities irrespective of where they happened to be, but would only be aroused against those who found themselves within the city walls; or possibly they assumed that the whole of the population would be exterminated and that the city's last hour had come.

Of the people who held these various opinions, not all of them died. Nor, however, did they all survive. On the contrary, many of each different persuasion fell ill here, there, and everywhere, and having themselves, when they were fit and well, set an example to those who were as yet unaffected, they languished away with virtually no one to nurse them. It was not merely a question of one citizen avoiding another, and of people almost invariably neglecting their neighbors and rarely or never visiting their relatives, addressing them only from a distance; this scourge had implanted so great a terror in the hearts of men and women that brothers abandoned brothers, uncles their nephews, sisters their brothers, and in many cases wives deserted their husbands. But even worse, and almost incredible, was the fact that fathers and mothers refused to nurse and assist their own children, as though they did not belong to them.

Hence the countless numbers of people who fell ill, both male and female, were entirely dependent upon either the charity of friends (who were few and far between) or the greed of servants, who remained in short supply despite the attraction of high wages out of all proportion to the services they performed. Furthermore, these latter were men and women of coarse intellect and the majority were unused to such duties, and they did little more than hand things to the invalid when asked to do so and watch over him when he was dying. And in performing this kind of service, they frequently lost their lives as well as their earnings.

As a result of this wholesale desertion of the sick by neighbors, relatives and friends, and in view of the scarcity of servants, there grew up a practice almost never previously heard of, whereby when a woman fell ill, no matter how gracious or beautiful or gently bred she might be, she raised no objection to being attended by a male servant, whether he was young or not. Nor did she have any scruples about showing him every part of her body as freely as she would have displayed it to a woman, provided that the nature of her infirmity required her to do so; and this explains why those women who recovered were possibly less chaste in the period that followed.

Moreover a great many people died who would perhaps have survived had they received some assistance. And hence, what with the lack of appropriate means for tending the sick, and the virulence of the plague, the number of deaths reported in the city whether by day or by night was so enormous that it astonished all who heard tell of it, to say nothing of the people who actually witnessed the carnage. And it was perhaps inevitable that among the citizens who survived there arose certain customs that were quite contrary to established tradition.

It had once been customary, as it is again nowadays, for the women relatives and neighbors of a dead man to assemble in his house in order to mourn in the company of the women who had been closest to him; moreover his kinsfolk would forgather in front of his house along with his neighbors and various other citizens, and there would be a contingent of priests, whose numbers varied according to the quality of the deceased; his body would be taken thence to the church in which he had wanted to be buried, being borne on the shoulders of his peers amidst the funeral pomp of candles and dirges. But as the ferocity of the plague began to mount, this practice all but disappeared entirely and was replaced by different customs. For not only did people die without having many women about them, but a great number departed this life without anyone at all to witness their going. Few indeed were those to whom the lamentations and bitter tears of their relatives were accorded; on the contrary, more often than not bereavement was the signal for laughter and witticisms and general jollification—the art of which the women, having for the most part suppressed their feminine concern for the salvation of the souls of the dead, had learned to perfection. Moreover it was rare for the bodies of the dead to be accompanied by more than ten or twelve neighbors to the church, nor were they borne on the shoulders of worthy and honest citizens, but by a kind of gravedigging fraternity, newly come into being and drawn from the lower orders of society. These people assumed the title of sexton, and demanded a fat fee for their services, which consisted in taking up the coffin and hauling it swiftly away, not to the church specified by the dead man in his will, but usually to the nearest at hand. They would be preceded by a group of four or six clerics, who between them carried one or two candles at most, and sometimes none at all. Nor did the priests go to the trouble of pronouncing solemn and lengthy funeral rites, but, with the aid of these so-called sextons, they hastily lowered the body into the nearest empty grave they could find.

As for the common people and a large proportion of the bourgeoisie, they presented a much more pathetic spectacle, for the majority of them were constrained, either by their poverty or the hope of survival, to remain in their houses. Being confined to their own parts of the city, they fell ill daily in their thousands, and since they had no one to assist them or attend to their needs, they inevitably perished almost without exception. Many dropped dead in the open streets, both by day and by night, whilst a great many others, though dying in their own houses, drew their neighbors' attention to the fact more by the smell of their rotting corpses than by any other means. And what with these, and the others who were dying all over the city, bodies were here, there and everywhere.

Whenever people died, their neighbors nearly always followed a single, set routine, prompted as much by their fear of being contaminated by the decaying corpse as by any charitable feelings they may have entertained towards the deceased. Either on their own, or with the assistance of bearers whenever these were to be had, they extracted the bodies of the dead from their houses and left them lying outside their front doors, where anyone going about the streets, especially in the early morning, could have observed countless numbers of them. Funeral biers would then be sent for, upon which the dead were taken away, though there were some who, for lack of biers, were carried off on plain boards. It was by no means rare for more than one of these biers to be seen with two or three bodies upon it at a time; on the contrary, many were seen to contain a husband and wife, two or three brothers and sisters, a father and son, or some other pair of close relatives. And times without number it happened that two priests would be on their way to bury someone, holding a cross before them, only to find that bearers carrying three or four additional biers would fall in behind them; so that whereas the priests had thought they had only one burial to attend to, they in fact had six or seven, and sometimes more. Even in these circumstances, however, there were no tears or candles or mourners to honor the dead; in fact, no more respect was accorded to dead people than would nowadays be shown towards dead goats. For it was quite apparent that the one thing which, in normal times, no wise man had ever learned to accept with patient resignation (even though it struck so seldom and unobtrusively), had now been brought home to the feeble-minded as well, but the scale of the calamity caused them to regard it with indifference.

Such was the multitude of corpses (of which further consignments were arriving every day and almost by the hour at each of the churches), that there was not sufficient consecrated ground for them to be buried in, especially if each was to have its own plot in accordance with long-established custom. So when all the graves were full, huge trenches were excavated in the churchyards, into which new arrivals were placed in their hundreds, stowed tier upon tier like ships' cargo, each layer of corpses being covered over with a thin layer of soil till the trench was filled to the top.

But rather than describe in elaborate detail the calamities we experienced in the city at that time, I must mention that, whilst an ill wind was blowing through Florence itself, the surrounding region was no less badly affected. In the fortified towns, conditions were similar to those in the city itself on a minor scale; but in the scattered hamlets and the countryside proper, the poor unfortunate peasants and their families had no physicians or servants whatever to assist them, and collapsed by the wayside, in their fields, and in their cottages at all hours of the day and night, dying more like animals than human beings. Like the townspeople, they too grew apathetic in their ways, disregarded their affairs, and neglected their possessions. Moreover they all behaved as though each day was to be their last, and far from making provision for the future by tilling their lands, tending their flocks, and adding to their previous labors, they tried in every way they could think of to squander the assets already in their possession. Thus it came about that oxen, asses, sheep, goats, pigs, chickens, and even dogs (for all their deep fidelity to man) were driven away and allowed to roam freely through the fields, where the crops lay abandoned and had not even been reaped, let alone gathered in. And after a whole day's feasting, many of these animals, as though possessing the power of reason, would return glutted in the evening to their own quarters, without any shepherd to guide them.

But let us leave the countryside and return to the city. What more remains to be said, except that the cruelty of heaven (and possibly, in some measure, also that of man) was so immense and so devastating that between March and July of the year in question, what with the fury of the pestilence and the fact that so many of the sick were inadequately cared for or abandoned in their hour of need because the healthy were too terrified to approach them, it is reliably thought that over a hundred thousand human lives were extinguished within the walls of the city of Florence? Yet before this lethal catastrophe fell upon the city, it is doubtful whether anyone would have guessed it contained so many inhabitants.

Ah, how great a number of splendid palaces, fine houses, and noble dwellings, once filled with retainers, with lords and with ladies, were bereft of all who had lived there, down to the tiniest child! How numerous were the famous families, the vast estates, the notable fortunes, that were seen to be left without a rightful successor! How many gallant gentlemen, fair ladies, and sprightly youths, who would have been judged hale and hearty by Galen, Hippocrates, and Aesculapius[6] (to say nothing of others), having breakfasted in

---

6. Classical god of medicine. Galen (died 199 C.E.) was a famous Greek medical authority. Hippocrates (died ca. 377 B.C.E.) is regarded as the founder of medicine.

the morning with their kinsfolk, acquaintances, and friends, supped that same evening with their ancestors in the next world!

The more I reflect upon all this misery, the deeper my sense of personal sorrow; hence I shall refrain from describing those aspects which can suitably be omitted, and proceed to inform you that these were the conditions prevailing in our city, which was by now almost emptied of its inhabitants, when one Tuesday morning (or so I was told by a person whose word can be trusted) seven young ladies were to be found in the venerable church of Santa Maria Novella,[7] which was otherwise almost deserted. They had been attending divine service, and were dressed in mournful attire appropriate to the times. Each was a friend, a neighbor, or a relative of the other six, none was older than twenty-seven or younger than eighteen, and all were intelligent, gently bred, fair to look upon, graceful in bearing, and charmingly unaffected. I could tell you their actual names, but refrain from doing so for a good reason, namely that I would not want any of them to feel embarrassed, at any time in the future, on account of the ensuing stories, all of which they either listened to or narrated themselves. For nowadays, laws relating to pleasure are somewhat restrictive, whereas at that time, for the reasons indicated above, they were exceptionally lax, not only for ladies of their own age but also for much older women. Besides, I have no wish to supply envious tongues, ever ready to censure a laudable way of life, with a chance to besmirch the good name of these worthy ladies with their lewd and filthy gossip. And therefore, so that we may perceive distinctly what each of them had to say, I propose to refer to them by names which are either wholly or partially appropriate to the qualities of each. The first of them, who was also the eldest, we shall call Pampinea, the second Fiammetta, Filomena the third, and the fourth Emilia, then we shall name the fifth Lauretta, and the sixth Neifile, whilst to the last, not without reason, we shall give the name of Elissa.[8]

Without prior agreement but simply by chance, these seven ladies found themselves sitting, more or less in a circle, in one part of the church, reciting their paternosters. Eventually, they left off and heaved a great many sighs, after which they began to talk among themselves on various different aspects of the times through which they were passing. But after a little while, they all fell silent except for Pampinea, who said:

"Dear ladies, you will often have heard it affirmed, as I have, that no man does injury to another in exercising his lawful rights. Every person born into this world has a natural right to sustain, preserve, and defend his own life to the best of his ability—a right so freely acknowledged that men have sometimes killed others in self-defence, and no blame whatever has attached to their actions. Now, if this is permitted by the laws, upon whose prompt application all mortal creatures depend for their well-being, how can it possibly be wrong, seeing that it harms no one, for us or anyone else to do all in our power to preserve our lives? If I pause to consider what we have been

---

7. An important church in Florence, perhaps chosen as the origin of the frame-story because its name *novella* can mean both "new" (which is why it was attached to this church) and "story." The present church has a facade added in the 15th century.   8. The first four names derive from earlier works by Boccaccio himself; the last three refer, respectively, to the poetry of Petrarch, Dante, and Virgil, the three poets whom Boccaccio most admired.

doing this morning, and what we have done on several mornings in the past, if I reflect on the nature and subject of our conversation, I realize, just as you also must realize, that each of us is apprehensive on her own account. This does not surprise me in the least, but what does greatly surprise me (seeing that each of us has the natural feelings of a woman) is that we do nothing to requite ourselves against the thing of which we are all so justly afraid.

"Here we linger for no other purpose, or so it seems to me, than to count the number of corpses being taken to burial, or to hear whether the friars of the church, very few of whom are left, chant their offices at the appropriate hours, or to exhibit the quality and quantity of our sorrows, by means of the clothes we are wearing, to all those whom we meet in this place. And if we go outside, we shall see the dead and the sick being carried hither and thither, or we shall see people, once condemned to exile by the courts for their misdeeds, careering wildly about the streets in open defiance of the law, well knowing that those appointed to enforce it are either dead or dying; or else we shall find ourselves at the mercy of the scum of our city who, having scented our blood, call themselves sextons and go prancing and bustling all over the place, singing bawdy songs that add insult to our injuries. Moreover, all we ever hear is 'So-and-so's dead' and 'So-and-so's dying'; and if there were anyone left to mourn, the whole place would be filled with sounds of weeping and wailing.

"And if we return to our homes, what happens? I know not whether your own experience is similar to mine, but my house was once full of servants, and now that there is no one left apart from my maid and myself, I am filled with foreboding and feel as if every hair of my head is standing on end. Wherever I go in the house, wherever I pause to rest, I seem to be haunted by the shades of the departed, whose faces no longer appear as I remember them but with strange and horribly twisted expressions that frighten me out of my senses.

"Accordingly, whether I am here in church or out in the streets or sitting at home, I always feel ill at ease, the more so because it seems to me that no one possessing private means and a place to retreat to is left here apart from ourselves. But even if such people are still to be found, they draw no distinction, as I have frequently heard and seen for myself, between what is honest and what is dishonest; and provided only that they are prompted by their appetites, they will do whatever affords them the greatest pleasure, whether by day or by night, alone or in company. It is not only of lay people that I speak, but also of those enclosed in monasteries, who, having convinced themselves that such behavior is suitable for them and is only unbecoming in others, have broken the rules of obedience and given themselves over to carnal pleasures, thereby thinking to escape, and have turned lascivious and dissolute.

"If this be so (and we plainly perceive that it is), what are we doing here? What are we waiting for? What are we dreaming about? Why do we lag so far behind all the rest of the citizens in providing for our safety? Do we rate ourselves lower than all other women? Or do we suppose that our own lives, unlike those of others, are bound to our bodies by such strong chains that we may ignore all those things which have the power to harm them? In that case we are deluded and mistaken. We have only to recall the names and the condition of the young men and women who have fallen victim to this cruel pestilence, in order to realize clearly the foolishness of such notions.

"And so, lest by pretending to be above such things or by becoming complacent we should succumb to that which we might possibly avoid if we so desired, I would think it an excellent idea (though I do not know whether you would agree with me) for us all to get away from this city, just as many others have done before us, and as indeed they are doing still. We could go and stay together on one of our various country estates, shunning at all costs the lewd practices of our fellow citizens and feasting and merrymaking as best we may without in any way overstepping the bounds of what is reasonable.

"There we shall hear the birds singing, we shall see fresh green hills and plains, fields of corn undulating like the sea, and trees of at least a thousand different species; and we shall have a clearer view of the heavens, which, troubled though they are, do not however deny us their eternal beauties, so much more fair to look upon than the desolate walls of our city. Moreover the country air is much more refreshing, the necessities of life in such a time as this are more abundant, and there are fewer obstacles to contend with. For although the farmworkers are dying there in the same way as the townspeople here in Florence, the spectacle is less harrowing inasmuch as the houses and people are more widely scattered. Besides, unless I am mistaken we shall not be abandoning anyone by going away from here; on the contrary, we may fairly claim that we are the ones who have been abandoned, for our kinsfolk are either dead or fled, and have left us to fend for ourselves in the midst of all this affliction, as though disowning us completely.

"Hence no one can reproach us for taking the course I have advocated, whereas if we do nothing we shall inevitably be confronted with distress and mourning, and possibly forfeit our lives into the bargain. Let us therefore do as I suggest, taking our maidservants with us and seeing to the dispatch of all the things we shall need. We can move from place to place, spending one day here and another there, pursuing whatever pleasures and entertainments the present times will afford. In this way of life we shall continue until such time as we discover (provided we are spared from early death) the end decreed by Heaven for these terrible events. You must remember, after all, that it is no more unseemly for us to go away and thus preserve our own honor than it is for most other women to remain here and forfeit theirs."

Having listened to Pampinea's suggestion, the other ladies not only applauded it but were so eager to carry it into effect that they had already begun to work out the details amongst themselves, as though they wanted to rise from their pews and set off without further ado. But Filomena, being more prudent than the others, said:

"Pampinea's arguments, ladies, are most convincing, but we should not follow her advice as hastily as you appear to wish. You must remember that we are all women, and every one of us is sufficiently adult to acknowledge that women, when left to themselves, are not the most rational of creatures, and that without the supervision of some man or other their capacity for getting things done is somewhat restricted. We are fickle, quarrelsome, suspicious, cowardly, and easily frightened; and hence I greatly fear that if we have none but ourselves to guide us, our little band will break up much more swiftly, and with far less credit to ourselves, than would otherwise be the case. We would be well advised to resolve this problem before we depart."

Then Elissa said:

"It is certainly true that man is the head of woman,[9] and that without a man to guide us it rarely happens that any enterprise of ours is brought to a worthy conclusion. But where are we to find these men? As we all know, most of our own menfolk are dead, and those few that are still alive are fleeing in scattered little groups from that which we too are intent upon avoiding. Yet we cannot very well go away with total strangers, for if self-preservation is our aim, we must so arrange our affairs that wherever we go for our pleasure and repose, no trouble or scandal should come of it."

Whilst the talk of the ladies was proceeding along these lines there came into the church three young men, in whom neither the horrors of the times nor the loss of friends or relatives nor concern for their own safety had dampened the flames of love, much less extinguished them completely. I have called them young, but none in fact was less than twenty-five years of age, and the first was called Panfilo, the second Filostrato, and the last Dioneo.[1] Each of them was most agreeable and gently bred, and by way of sweetest solace amid all this turmoil they were seeking to catch a glimpse of their lady-loves, all three of whom, as it happened, were among the seven we have mentioned, whilst some of the remaining four were closely related to one or other of the three. No sooner did they espy they young ladies than they too were espied, whereupon Pampinea smiled and said:

"See how Fortune favors us right from the beginning, in setting before us three young men of courage and intelligence, who will readily act as our guides and servants if we are not too proud to accept them for such duties."

Then Neifile, whose face had turned all scarlet with confusion since she was the object of one of the youth's affections, said:

"For goodness' sake do take care, Pampinea, of what you are saying! To my certain knowledge, nothing but good can be said of any one of them, and I consider them more than competent to fulfil the office of which we were speaking. I also think they would be good, honest company, not only for us, but for ladies much finer and fairer than ourselves. But since it is perfectly obvious that they are in love with certain of the ladies here present, I am apprehensive lest, by taking them with us, through no fault either of theirs or of our own, we should bring disgrace and censure on ourselves."

"That is quite beside the point," said Filomena. "If I live honestly, and my conscience is clear, then people may say whatever they like. God and Truth will take up arms in my defence. Now, if only they were prepared to accompany us, we should truly be able to claim as Pampinea has said, that Fortune favors our enterprise."

Filomena's words reassured the other ladies, who not only withdrew their objections but unanimously agreed to call the young men over, explain their intentions, and inquire whether they would be willing to join their expedition. And so, without any further discussion, Pampinea, who was a blood relation to one of the young men, got up and walked towards them. They

9. Here Elissa (whose name is also one given by Virgil to Dido in book 4 of the *Aeneid*) is quoting St. Paul (Ephesians 5.23). It is difficult to decide if Boccaccio is being ironic.   1. Associated with Aphrodite, the classical goddess of love. The first two names derive from Boccaccio's earlier work.

were standing there gazing at the young ladies, and Pampinea, having offered them a cheerful greeting, told them what they were planning to do, and asked them on behalf of all her companions whether they would be prepared to join them in a spirit of chaste and brotherly affection.

The young men thought at first that she was making mock of them, but when they realized she was speaking in earnest, they gladly agreed to place themselves at the young ladies' disposal. So that there should be no delay in putting the plan into effect, they made provision there and then for the various matters that would have to be attended to before their departure. Meticulous care was taken to see that all necessary preparations were put in hand, supplies were sent on in advance to the place at which they intended to stay, and as dawn was breaking on the morning of the next day, which was a Wednesday, the ladies and the three young men, accompanied by one or two of the maids and all three manservants, set out from the city. And scarcely had they travelled two miles from Florence before they reached the place at which they had agreed to stay.

The spot in question was some distance away from any road, on a small hill that was agreeable to behold for its abundance of shrubs and trees, all bedecked in green leaves. Perched on its summit was a palace, built round a fine, spacious courtyard, and containing loggias, halls, and sleeping apartments, which were not only excellently proportioned but richly embellished with paintings depicting scenes of gaiety. Delectable gardens and meadows lay all around, and there were wells of cool, refreshing water. The cellars were stocked with precious wines, more suited to the palates of connoisseurs than to sedate and respectable ladies. And on their arrival the company discovered, to their no small pleasure, that the place had been cleaned from top to bottom, the beds in the rooms were made up, the whole house was adorned with seasonable flowers of every description, and the floors had been carpeted with rushes.

Soon after reaching the palace, they all sat down, and Dioneo, a youth of matchless charm and readiness of wit, said:

"It is not our foresight, ladies, but rather your own good sense, that has led us to this spot. I know not what you intend to do with your troubles; my own I left inside the city gates when I departed thence a short while ago in your company. Hence you may either prepare to join with me in as much laughter, song and merriment as your sense of decorum will allow, or else you may give me leave to go back for my troubles and live in the afflicted city."

Pampinea, as though she too had driven away all her troubles, answered him in the same carefree vein.

"There is much sense in what you say, Dioneo," she replied. "A merry life should be our aim, since it was for no other reason that we were prompted to run away from the sorrows of the city. However, nothing will last for very long unless it possesses a definite form. And since it was I who led the discussions from which this fair company has come into being, I have given some thought to the continuance of our happiness, and consider it necessary for us to choose a leader, drawn from our own ranks, whom we would honor and obey as our superior, and whose sole concern will be that of devising the means whereby we may pass our time agreeably. But so that none of us will complain that he or she has had no opportunity to experience the burden of responsibility and the pleasure of command associated with sovereign power, I propose that the burden and the honor should be assigned to each of us in turn for a single day. It will be for all of us to decide who is to be our first ruler, after which it will be up to each ruler, when the hour of vespers[2] approaches, to elect his or her successor from among the ladies and gentlemen present. The person chosen to govern will be at liberty to make whatever arrangements he likes for the period covered by his rule, and to prescribe the place and the manner in which we are to live."

Pampinea's proposal was greatly to everyone's liking, and they unanimously elected her as their queen for the first day, whereupon Filomena quickly ran over to a laurel bush, for she had frequently heard it said that laurel leaves were especially worthy of veneration and that they conferred great honor upon those people of merit who were crowned with them.[3] Having plucked a few of its shoots, she fashioned them into a splendid and venerable garland, which she set upon Pampinea's brow, and which thenceforth became the outward symbol of sovereign power and authority to all the members of the company, for as long as they remained together.

Upon her election as their queen, Pampinea summoned the servants of the three young men to appear before her together with their own maidservants, who were four in number. And having called upon everyone to be silent, she said:

"So that I may begin by setting you all a good example, through which, proceeding from good to better, our company will be enabled to live an ordered and agreeable existence for as long as we choose to remain together, I first of all appoint Dioneo's manservant, Parmeno,[4] as my steward, and to him I commit the management and care of our household, together with all that appertains to the service of the hall. I desire that Panfilo's servant, Sirisco, should act as our buyer and treasurer, and carry out the instructions of Parmeno. As well as attending to the needs of Filostrato, Tindaro will look after the other two gentlemen in their rooms whenever their own manservants are prevented by their offices from performing such duties. My own maidservant, Misia, will be employed full-time in the kitchen along with Filomena's maidservant, Licisca, and they will prepare with diligence whatever dishes are prescribed by Parmeno. Chimera and Stratilia, the servants of Lauretta and Fiammetta, are required to act as chambermaids to all the ladies, as well as seeing that the places we frequent are neatly and tidily maintained. And unless they wish to incur our royal displeasure, we desire and command that each and every one of the servants should take good care, no matter what they should hear or observe in their comings and goings, to bring us no tidings of the world outside these walls unless they are tidings of happiness."

Her orders thus summarily given, and commended by all her companions, she rose gaily to her feet, and said:

"There are gardens here, and meadows, and other places of great charm and beauty, through which we may now wander in search of our amusement, each of us being free to do whatever he pleases. But on the stroke of tierce,[5] let us all return to this spot, so that we may breakfast together in the shade."

---

2. The hour at which evening prayer would be said, usually at sunset.   3. Crowning with laurel leaves was a form of accolade common in the classical world; here there may also be an allusion to the Laura who was celebrated by Petrarch in his lyric poetry.   4. The names of the servants are taken from comic characters in classical drama.   5. An hour at which prayer was said, about 9 A.M.

The merry company having thus been dismissed by their newly elected queen, the young men and their fair companions sauntered slowly through a garden, conversing on pleasant topics, weaving fair garlands for each other from the leaves of various trees, and singing songs of love.

After spending as much time there as the queen had allotted them, they returned to the house to find that Parmeno had made a zealous beginning to his duties, for as they entered the hall on the ground floor, they saw the tables ready laid, with pure white tablecloths and with goblets shining bright as silver, whilst the whole room was decorated with broom blossom. At the queen's behest, they rinsed their hands in water, then seated themselves in the places to which Parmeno had assigned them.

Dishes, daintily prepared, were brought in, excellent wines were at hand, and without a sound the three manservants promptly began to wait upon them. Everyone was delighted that these things had been so charmingly and efficiently arranged, and during the meal there was pleasant talk and merry laughter from all sides. Afterwards, the tables were cleared, and the queen sent for musical instruments so that one or two of their number, well versed in music, could play and sing, whilst the rest, ladies and gentlemen alike, could dance a *carole*.[6] At the queen's request, Dioneo took a lute and Fiammetta a viol, and they struck up a melodious tune, whereupon the queen, having sent the servants off to eat, formed a ring with the other ladies and the two young men, and sedately began to dance. And when the dance was over, they sang a number of gay and charming little songs.

In this fashion they continued until the queen decided that the time had come for them to retire to rest, whereupon she dismissed the whole company. The young men went away to their rooms which were separated from those of the ladies, and found that, like the hall, they too were full of flowers, and that their beds were neatly made. The ladies made a similar discovery in theirs, and having undressed, they lay down to rest.

The queen rose shortly after nones,[7] and caused the other ladies to be roused, as also the young men, declaring it was harmful to sleep too much during the day. They therefore betook themselves to a meadow, where the grass, being protected from the heat of the sun, grew thick and green, and where, perceiving that a gentle breeze was stirring, the queen suggested that they should all sit on the green grass in a circle. And when they were seated, she addressed them as follows:

"As you can see, the sun is high in the sky, it is very hot, and all is silent except for the cicadas in the olive-trees. For the moment, it would surely be foolish of us to venture abroad, this being such a cool and pleasant spot in which to linger. Besides, as you will observe, there are chessboards and other games here, and so we are free to amuse ourselves in whatever way we please. But if you were to follow my advice, this hotter part of the day would be spent, not in playing games (which inevitably bring anxiety to one of the players, without offering very much pleasure either to his opponent or to the spectators), but in telling stories—an activity that may afford some amusement both to the narrator and to the company at large.

6. A round dance.   7. About 3 P.M.

By the time each one of you has narrated a little tale of his own or her own, the sun will be setting, the heat will have abated, and we shall be able to go and amuse ourselves wherever you choose. Let us, then, if the idea appeals to you, carry this proposal of mine into effect. But I am willing to follow your own wishes in this matter, and if you disagree with my suggestion, let us all go and occupy our time in whatever way we please until the hour of vespers."

The whole company, ladies and gentlemen alike, were in favor of telling stories.

"Then if it is agreeable to you," said the queen, "I desire that on this first day each of us should be free to speak upon whatever topic he prefers."

And turning to Panfilo, who was seated on her right, she graciously asked him to introduce the proceedings with one of his stories. No sooner did he receive this invitation than Panfilo began as follows, with everyone listening intently:

[The First Story of the First Day]

Ser Cepperello deceives a holy friar with a false confession, then he dies; and although in life he was a most wicked man, in death he is reputed to be a Saint, and is called Saint Ciappelletto.

It is proper, dearest ladies, that everything made by man should begin with the sacred and admirable name of Him that was maker of all things. And therefore, since I am the first and must make a beginning to our story-telling, I propose to begin by telling you of one of His marvellous works, so that, when we have heard it out, our hopes will rest in Him as in something immutable, and we shall forever praise His name. It is obvious that since all temporal things are transient and mortal, so they are filled and surrounded by troubles, trials and tribulations, and fraught with infinite dangers which we, who live with them and are part of them, could without a shadow of a doubt neither endure, nor defend ourselves against, if God's special grace did not lend us strength and discernment. Nor should we suppose that His grace descends upon and within us through any merit of our own, for it is set in motion by His own loving-kindness, and is obtained by the pleas of people who like ourselves were mortal, and who, by firmly doing His pleasure whilst they were in this life, have now joined Him in eternal blessedness. To these, as to advocates made aware, through experience, of our frailty (perhaps because we have not the courage to submit our pleas personally in the presence of so great a judge) we present whatever we think is relevant to our cause. And our regard for Him, who is so compassionate and generous towards us, is all the greater when, the human eye being quite unable to penetrate the secrets of divine intelligence, common opinion deceives us and perhaps we appoint as our advocate in His majestic presence one who has been cast by Him into eternal exile. Yet He from whom nothing is hidden, paying more attention to the purity of the supplicant's motives than to his ignorance or to the banishment of the intercessor, answers those who pray to Him exactly as if the advocate were blessed in His sight. All of which can clearly be seen in the tale I propose to relate; and I say clearly because it is concerned, not with the judgment of God, but with that of men.

It is said, then, that Musciatto Franzesi,[8] having become a fine gentleman after acquiring enormous wealth and fame as a merchant in France, was obliged to come to Tuscany with the brother of the French king, the Lord Charles Lackland,[9] who had been urged and encouraged to come by Pope Boniface. But finding that his affairs, as is usually the case with merchants, were entangled here, there, and everywhere, and being unable quickly or easily to unravel them, he decided to place them in the hands of a number of different people. All this he succeeded in arranging, except that he was left with the problem of finding someone capable of recovering certain loans which he had made to various people in Burgundy.[1] The reason for his dilemma was that he had been told the Burgundians were a quarrelsome, thoroughly bad and unprincipled set of people; and he was quite unable to think of anyone he could trust, who was at the same time sufficiently villainous to match the villainy of the Burgundians. After devoting much thought to this problem, he suddenly recalled a man known as Ser Cepperello, of Prato,[2] who had been a frequent visitor to his house in Paris. This man was short in stature and used to dress very neatly, and the French, who did not know the meaning of the word Cepperello, thinking that it signified *chapel,* which in their language means "garland," and because as we have said he was a little man, used to call him, not Ciappello, but Ciappelletto: and everywhere in that part of the world, where few people knew him as Ser Cepperello, he was known as Ciappelletto.[3]

This Ciappelletto was a man of the following sort: a notary by profession, he would have taken it as a slight upon his honor if one of his legal deeds (and he drew up very few of them) were discovered to be other than false. In fact, he would have drawn up free of charge as many false documents as were requested of him, and done it more willingly than one who was highly paid for his services. He would take great delight in giving false testimony, whether asked for it or not. In those days, great reliance was placed in France upon sworn declarations, and since he had no scruples about swearing falsely, he used to win, by these nefarious means, every case in which he was required to swear upon his faith to tell the truth. He would take particular pleasure, and a great amount of trouble, in stirring up enmity, discord and bad blood between friends, relatives and anybody else; and the more calamities that ensued, the greater would be his rapture. If he were invited to witness a murder or any other criminal act, he would never refuse, but willingly go along; and he often found himself cheerfully assaulting or killing people with his own hands. He was a mighty blasphemer of God and His Saints, losing his temper on the tiniest pretext, as if he were the most hot-blooded man alive. He never went to church, and he would use foul language to pour scorn on all of her sacraments, declaring them repugnant. On the other hand, he would make a point of visiting taverns and other places of ill repute, and supplying them with his custom. Of women he was as fond as dogs are fond of a good stout stick; in their opposite, he took greater pleasure than the most depraved man on earth. He would rob and pilfer as conscientiously as

8. Like many other characters in the *Decameron,* those appearing in this first story are based on actual people. Musciatto was a Florentine financier who made a huge fortune in France by dubious means; 9. Brother of King Philip of France, who invaded Italy in 1301.   1. A region of northeastern France. 2. A city just to the north of Florence. Cepperello Dietaiuti was one of Franzesi's associates.   3. This nickname assumes that Ciapello's name derives from the Italian word *Ceppo* ("log" or tree-stump"), and the suffix *-etto* is a diminutive. Hence the name means "little stump," which may have an obscene connotation.

if he were a saintly man making an offering. He was such a prize glutton and heavy drinker, that he would occasionally suffer for his over-indulgence in a manner that was most unseemly. He was a gambler and a card-sharper of the first order. But why do I lavish so many words upon him? He was perhaps the worst man ever born. Yet for all his villainy, he had long been protected by the power and influence of Messer Musciatto, on whose account he was many a time treated with respect, both by private individuals, whom he frequently abused, and by the courts of law, which he was forever abusing.

So that when Musciatto, who was well acquainted with his way of living, called this Ser Ciappelletto to mind, he judged him to be the very man that the perverseness of the Burgundians required. He therefore sent for him and addressed him as follows:

"Ser Ciappelletto, as you know, I am about to go away from here altogether, but I have some business to settle, among others with the Burgundians. These people are full of tricks, and I know of no one better fitted than yourself to recover what they owe me. And so, since you are not otherwise engaged at present, if you will attend to this matter I propose to obtain favors for you at court, and allow you a reasonable portion of the money you recover."

Ser Ciappelletto, who was out of a job at the time and ill-supplied with worldly goods, seeing that the man who had long been his prop and stay was about to depart, made up his mind without delay and said (for he really had no alternative) that he would do it willingly. So that when they had agreed on terms, Ser Ciappelletto received powers of attorney from Musciatto and letters of introduction from the King, and after Musciatto's departure he went to Burgundy, where scarcely anybody knew him. And there, in a gentle and amiable fashion that ran contrary to his nature, as though he were holding his anger in reserve as a last resort, he issued his first demands and began to do what he had gone there to do. Before long, however, while lodging in the house of two Florentine brothers who ran a money-lending business there and did him great honor out of their respect for Musciatto, he happened to fall ill; whereupon the two brothers promptly summoned doctors and servants to attend him, and provided him with everything he needed to recover his health. But all their assistance was unavailing, because the good man, who was already advanced in years and had lived a disordered existence, was reported by his doctors to be going each day from bad to worse, like one who was suffering from a fatal illness. The two brothers were filled with alarm, and one day, alongside the room in which Ser Ciappelletto was lying, they began talking together.

"What are we to do about the fellow?" said one to the other. "We've landed ourselves in a fine mess on his account, because to turn him away from our house in his present condition would arouse a lot of adverse comment and show us to be seriously lacking in common sense. What would people say if they suddenly saw us evicting a dying man after giving him hospitality in the first place, and taking so much trouble to have him nursed and waited upon, when he couldn't possibly have done anything to offend us? On the other hand, he has led such a wicked life that he will never be willing to make his confession or receive the sacraments of the Church; and if he dies unconfessed, no church will want to accept his body and he'll be flung into the moat like a dog. But even if he makes his confession, his sins are so many and so appalling that the same thing will happen, because there will be neither friar nor priest who is either willing or able to give him absolution; in which case, since he will not have been absolved, he will be flung into the moat just the same. And when the townspeople see what has happened, they'll create a commotion, not only because of our profession which they consider iniquitous and never cease to condemn, but also because they long to get their hands on our money, and they will go about shouting: 'Away with these Lombard dogs[4] that the Church refuses to accept'; and they'll come running to our lodgings and perhaps, not content with stealing our goods, they'll take away our lives into the bargain. So we shall be in a pretty fix either way, if this fellow dies."

Ser Ciappelletto, who as we have said was lying near the place where they were talking, heard everything they were saying about him, for he was sharp of hearing, as invalids invariably are. So he called them in to him, and said:

"I don't want you to worry in the slightest on my account, nor to fear that I will cause you to suffer any harm. I heard what you were saying about me and I agree entirely that what you predict will actually come to pass, if matters take the course you anticipate; but they will do nothing of the kind. I have done our good Lord so many injuries whilst I lived, that to do Him another now that I am dying will be neither here nor there. So go and bring me the holiest and ablest friar you can find, if there is such a one, and leave everything to me, for I shall set your affairs and my own neatly in order, so that all will be well and you'll have nothing to complain of."

Whilst deriving little comfort from all this, the two brothers nevertheless went off to a friary and asked for a wise and holy man to come and hear the confession of a Lombard who was lying ill in their house. They were given an ancient friar of good and holy ways who was an expert in the Scriptures and a most venerable man, towards whom all the townspeople were greatly and specially devoted, and they conducted him to their house.

On reaching the room where Ser Ciappelletto was lying, he sat down at his bedside, and first he began to comfort him with kindly words, then he asked him how long it was since he had last been to confession. Whereupon Ser Ciappelletto, who had never been to confession in his life, replied:

"Father, it has always been my custom to go to confession at least once every week, except that there are many weeks in which I go more often. But to tell the truth, since I fell ill, nearly a week ago, my illness has caused me so much discomfort that I haven't been to confession at all."

"My son," said the friar, "you have done well, and you should persevere in this habit of yours. Since you go so often to confession, I can see that there will be little for me to hear or to ask."

"Master friar," said Ser Ciappelletto, "do not speak thus, for however frequently or regularly I confess, it is always my wish that I should make a general confession of all the sins I can remember committing from the day I was born till the day of my confession. I therefore beg you, good father, to question me about everything, just as closely as if I had never been confessed. Do not spare me because I happen to be ill, for I would much rather

---

4. Outside Italy, Italian bankers were known as Lombards, even if they came from a different province.

mortify this flesh of mine than that, by treating it with lenience, I should do anything that could lead to the perdition of my soul, which my Savior redeemed with His precious blood."

These words were greatly pleasing to the holy friar, and seemed to him proof of a well-disposed mind. Having warmly commended Ser Ciappelletto for this practice of his, he began by asking him whether he had ever committed the sin of lust with any woman. To which, heaving a sigh, Ser Ciappelletto replied:

"Father, I am loath to tell you the truth on this matter, in case I should sin by way of vainglory."

To which the holy friar replied:

"Speak out freely, for no man ever sinned by telling the truth, either in confession or otherwise."

"Since you assure me that this is so," said Ser Ciappelletto, "I will tell you. I am a virgin as pure as on the day I came forth from my mother's womb."

"Oh, may God give you His blessing!" said the friar. "How nobly you have lived! And your restraint is all the more deserving of praise in that, had you wished, you would have had greater liberty to do the opposite than those who, like ourselves, are expressly forbidden by rule."

Next he asked him whether he had displeased God by committing the sin of gluttony; to which, fetching a deep sigh, Ser Ciappelletto replied that he had, and on many occasions. For although, apart from the periods of fasting normally observed in the course of the year by the devout, he was accustomed to fasting on bread and water for at least three days every week, he had drunk the water as pleasurably and avidly (especially when he had been fatigued from praying or going on a pilgrimage) as any great bibber of wine; he had often experienced a craving for those dainty little wild herb salads that women eat when they go away to the country; and sometimes the thought of food had been more attractive to him than he considered proper in one who, like himself, was fasting out of piety. Whereupon the friar said:

"My son, these sins are natural and they are very trivial, and therefore I would not have you burden your conscience with them more than necessary. No matter how holy a man may be, he will be attracted by the thought of food after a long spell of fasting, and by the thought of drink when he is fatigued."

"Oh!" said Ser Ciappelletto. "Do not tell me this to console me, father. As you are aware, I know that things done in the service of God must all be done honestly and without any grudge; and if anyone should do otherwise, he is committing a sin."

The friar, delighted, said to him:

"I am contented to see you taking such a view, and it pleases me greatly that you should have such a good and pure conscience in this matter. But tell me, have you ever been guilty of avarice, by desiring to have more than was proper, or keeping what you should not have kept?"

To which Ser Ciappelletto replied:

"Father, I would not wish you to judge me ill because I am in the house of these money-lenders. I have nothing to do with their business; indeed I had come here with the express intention of warning and reproaching them, and dissuading them from this abominable form of money-making; and I think I would have succeeded, if God had not stricken me in this manner. However,

I would have you know that my father left me a wealthy man, and when he was dead, I gave the greater part of his fortune to charity. Since then, in order to support myself and enable me to assist the Christian poor, I have done a small amount of trading, in the course of which I have desired to gain, and I have always shared what I have gained with the poor, allocating one half to my own needs and giving the other half to them. And in this I have had so much help from my Creator that I have continually gone from strength to strength in the management of my affairs."

"You have done well," said the friar, "but tell me, how often have you lost your temper?"

"Oh!" said Ser Ciappelletto, "I can assure you I have done that very often. But who is there who could restrain himself, when the whole day long he sees men doing disgusting things, and failing to observe God's commandments, or to fear His terrible wrath? There have been many times in the space of a single day when I would rather have been dead than alive, looking about me and seeing young people frittering away their time, telling lies, going drinking in taverns, failing to go to church, and following the ways of the world rather than those of God."

"My son," said the friar, "this kind of anger is justified, and for my part I could not require you to do penance for it. But has it ever happened that your anger has led you to commit murder or to pour abuse on anyone or do them any other form of injury?"

To which Ser Ciappelletto replied:

"Oh, sir, however could you, that appear to be a man of God, say such a thing? If I had thought for a single moment of doing any of the things you mention, do you suppose I imagine that God would have treated me so generously? Those things are the business of cut-throats and evildoers, and whenever I have chanced upon one of their number, I have always sent him packing, and offered up a prayer for his conversion!"

"May God give you His blessing," said the friar, "but now, tell me, my son: have you ever borne false witness against any man, or spoken ill of people, or taken what belonged to others without seeking their permission?"

"Never, sir, except on one occasion," replied Ser Ciappelletto, "when I spoke ill of someone. For I once had a neighbor who, without the slightest cause, was forever beating his wife, so that on this one occasion I spoke ill of him to his wife's kinsfolk, for I felt extremely sorry for that unfortunate woman. Whenever the fellow had had too much to drink, God alone could tell you how he battered her."

Then the friar said:

"Let me see now, you tell me you were a merchant. Did you ever deceive anyone, as merchants do?"

"Faith, sir, I did," said Ser Ciappelletto. "But all I know about him is that he was a man who brought me some money that he owed me for a length of cloth I had sold him. I put the money away in a box without counting it, and a whole month passed before I discovered there were four pennies more than there should have been. I kept them for a year with the intention of giving them back, but I never saw him again, so I gave them away to a beggar."

"That was a trivial matter," said the friar, "and you did well to dispose of the money as you did."

The holy friar questioned him on many other matters, but always he answered in similar vein, and hence the friar was ready to proceed without further ado to give him absolution. But Ser Ciappelletto said:

"Sir, I still have one or two sins I have not yet told you about."

The friar asked him what they were, and he said:

"I recall that I once failed to show a proper respect for the Holy Sabbath, by making one of my servants sweep the house after nones[5] on a Saturday."

"Oh!" said the friar. "This, my son, is a trifling matter."

"No, father," said Ser Ciappelletto, "you must not call it trifling, for the Sabbath has to be greatly honored, seeing that this was the day on which our Lord rose from the dead."

Then the friar said:

"Have you done anything else?"

"Yes, sir," replied Ser Ciappelletto, "for I once, without thinking what I was doing, spat in the house of God."

The friar began to smile, and said:

"My son, this is not a thing to worry about. We members of religious orders spit there continually."

"That is very wicked of you," said Ser Ciappelletto, "for nothing should be kept more clean than the holy temple in which sacrifice is offered up to God."

In brief, he told the friar many things of this sort, and finally he began to sigh, and then to wail loudly, as he was well able to do whenever he pleased.

"My son," said the holy friar. "What is the matter?"

"Oh alas, sir," replied Ser Ciappelletto, "I have one sin left to which I have never confessed, so great is my shame in having to reveal it; and whenever I remember it, I cry as you see me doing now, and feel quite certain that God will never have mercy on me for this terrible sin."

"Come now, my son," said the holy friar, "what are you saying? If all the sins that were ever committed by the whole of mankind, together with those that men will yet commit till the end of the world, were concentrated in one single man, and he was as truly repentant and contrite as I see you to be, God is so benign and merciful that He would freely remit them on their being confessed to Him; and therefore you may safely reveal it."

Then Ser Ciappelletto said, still weeping loudly:

"Alas, father, my sin is too great, and I can scarcely believe that God will ever forgive me for it, unless you intercede with your prayers."

To which the friar replied:

"You may safely reveal it, for I promise that I will pray to God on your behalf."

Ser Ciappelletto went on weeping, without saying anything, and the friar kept encouraging him to speak. But after Ser Ciappelletto, by weeping in this manner, had kept the friar for a very long time on tenterhooks, he heaved a great sigh, and said:

"Father, since you promise that you will pray to God for me, I will tell you. You are to know then that once, when I was a little boy, I cursed my mother." And having said this, he began to weep loudly all over again.

"There now, my son," said the friar, "does this seem so great a sin to you? Why, people curse God the whole day long, and yet He willingly forgives

5. A church service held about 3 P.M.

those who repent for having cursed Him. Why then should you suppose He will not forgive you for this? Take heart and do not weep, for even if you had been one of those who set Him on the cross, I can see that you have so much contrition that He would certainly forgive you."

"Oh alas, father," said Ser Ciappelletto, "what are you saying? My dear, sweet mother, who carried me day and night for nine months in her body, and held me more than a hundred times in her arms! It was too wicked of me to curse her, and the sin is too great; and if you do not pray to God for me, it will never be forgiven me."

Perceiving that Ser Ciappelletto had nothing more to say, the friar absolved him and gave him his blessing. He took him for a very saintly man indeed, being fully convinced that what Ser Ciappelletto had said was true; but then, who is there who would not have been convinced, on hearing a dying man talk in this fashion? Finally, when all this was done, he said to him:

"Ser Ciappelletto, with God's help you will soon be well again. But in case it were to happen that God should summon your blessed and well-disposed soul to His presence, are you willing for your body to be buried in our convent?"

To which Ser Ciappelletto replied:

"Yes, father. In fact, I would not wish to be elsewhere, since you have promised that you will pray to God for me. Besides, I have always been especially devoted to your Order. So when you return to your convent, I beg you to see that I am sent that true body of Christ which you consecrate every morning on the altar. For although I am unworthy of it, I intend with your permission to take it, and afterwards to receive the holy Extreme Unction,[6] so that, having lived as a sinner, I shall at least die as a Christian."

The holy man said that he was greatly pleased, that the words were well spoken, and that he would see it was brought to him at once; and so it was.

The two brothers, who strongly suspected that Ser Ciappelletto was going to deceive them, had posted themselves behind a wooden partition which separated the room where Ser Ciappelletto was lying from another, and as they stood there listening they could easily follow what Ser Ciappelletto was saying to the friar. When they heard the things he confessed to having done, they were so amused that every so often they nearly exploded with mirth, and they said to each other:

"What manner of man is this, whom neither old age nor illness, nor fear of the death which he sees so close at hand, nor even the fear of God, before whose judgment he knows he must shortly appear, have managed to turn from his evil ways, or persuade to die any differently from the way he has lived?"

Seeing, however, that he had said all the right things to be received for burial in a church, they cared nothing for the rest.

Shortly thereafter Ser Ciappelletto made his communion, and, failing rapidly, he received Extreme Unction. Soon after vespers on the very day that he had made his fine confession, he died. Whereupon the two brothers made all necessary arrangements, using his own money to see that he had

---

6. The sacrament in which a dying person is anointed by a priest.

an honorable funeral, and sending news of his death to the friars and asking them to come that evening to observe the customary vigil, and the following morning to take away the body.

On hearing that he had passed away, the holy friar who had received his confession arranged with the prior for the chapterhouse bell to be rung, and to the assembled friars he showed that Ser Ciappelletto had been a saintly man, as his confession had amply proved. He expressed the hope that through him the Lord God would work many miracles, and persuaded them that his body should be received with the utmost reverence and loving care. Credulous to a man, the prior and the other friars agreed to do so, and that evening they went to the place where Ser Ciappelletto's body lay, and celebrated a great and solemn vigil over it; and in the morning, dressed in albs and copes,[7] carrying books in their hands and bearing crosses before them, singing as they went, they all came for the body, which they then carried back to their church with tremendous pomp and ceremony, followed by nearly all the people of the town, men and women alike. And when it had been set down in the church, the holy friar who had confessed him climbed into the pulpit and began to preach marvelous things about Ser Ciappelletto's life, his fasts, his virginity, his simplicity and innocence and saintliness, relating among other things what he had tearfully confessed to him as his greatest sin, and describing how he had barely been able to convince him that God would forgive him, at which point he turned to reprimand his audience, saying:

"And yet you miserable sinners have only to catch your feet in a wisp of straw for you to curse God and the Virgin and all the Saints in heaven."

Apart from this, he said much else about his loyalty and his purity of heart. And in brief, with a torrent of words that the people of the town believed implicitly, he fixed Ser Ciappelletto so firmly in the minds and affections of all those present that when the service was over, everyone thronged round the body to kiss his feet and his hands, all the clothes were torn from his back, and those who succeeded in grabbing so much as a tiny fragment felt they were in Paradise itself. He had to be kept lying there all day, so that everyone could come and gaze upon him, and on that same night he was buried with honor in a marble tomb in one of the chapels. From the next day forth, people began to go there to light candles and pray to him, and later they began to make votive offerings and to decorate the chapel with figures made of wax, in fulfilment of promises they had given.

The fame of his saintliness, and of the veneration in which he was held, grew to such proportions that there was hardly anyone who did not pray for his assistance in time of trouble, and they called him, and call him still, Saint Ciappelletto. Moreover it is claimed that through him God has wrought many miracles, and that He continues to work them on behalf of whoever commends himself devoutly to this particular Saint.

It was thus, then, that Ser Cepperello of Prato lived and died, becoming a Saint in the way you have heard. Nor would I wish to deny that perhaps God has blessed and admitted him to His presence. For albeit he led a wicked, sinful life, it is possible that at the eleventh hour he was so sincerely repentant that God had mercy upon him and received him into His kingdom. But

---

7. Religious vestments worn by priests while performing a religious ritual.

since this is hidden from us, I speak only with regard to the outward appearance, and I say that the fellow should rather be in Hell, in the hands of the devil, than in Paradise. And if this is the case, we may recognize how very great is God's loving-kindness towards us, in that it takes account, not of our error, but of the purity of our faith, and grants our prayers even when we appoint as our emissary one who is His enemy, thinking him to be His friend, as though we were appealing to one who was truly holy as our intercessor for His favor. And therefore, so that we, the members of this joyful company, may be guided safely and securely by His grace through these present adversities, let us praise the name of Him with whom we began our storytelling, let us hold Him in reverence, and let us commend ourselves to Him in the hour of our need, in the certain knowledge that we shall be heard.

And there the narrator fell silent.

[The Eighth Story of the Fifth Day][8]

In his love for a young lady of the Traversari family, Nastagio degli Onesti squanders his wealth without being loved in return. He is entreated by his friends to leave the city, and goes away to Classe, where he sees a girl being hunted down and killed by a horseman, and devoured by a brace of hounds. He then invites his kinsfolk and the lady he loves to a banquet, where this same girl is torn to pieces before the eyes of his beloved, who, fearing a similar fate, accepts Nastagio as her husband.

In Ravenna,[9] a city of great antiquity in Romagna, there once used to live a great many nobles and men of property, among them a young man called Nastagio degli Onesti, who had inherited an incredibly large fortune on the deaths of his father and one of his uncles. Being as yet unmarried, he fell in love, as is the way with young men, with a daughter of Messer Paolo Traversari, a girl of far more noble lineage than his own, whose love he hoped to win by dint of his accomplishments. But though these were very considerable, and splendid, and laudable, far from promoting his cause they appeared to damage it, inasmuch as the girl he loved was persistently cruel, harsh and unfriendly toward him. And on account possibly of her singular beauty, or perhaps because of her exalted rank, she became so haughty and contemptuous of him that she positively loathed him and everything he stood for.

All of this was so difficult for Nastagio to bear that he was frequently seized, after much weeping and gnashing of teeth, with the longing to kill himself out of sheer despair. But, having stayed his hand, he would then decide that he must give her up altogether, or learn if possible to hate her as she hated him. All such resolutions were unavailing, however, for the more his hopes dwindled, the greater his love seemed to grow.

As the young man persisted in wooing the girl and spending money like water, certain of his friends and relatives began to feel that he was in danger of exhausting both himself and his inheritance. They therefore implored and advised him to leave Ravenna and go to live for a while in some other place, with the object of curtailing both his wooing and his spending. Nastagio

8. The teller is Filomena, one of the young ladies.   9. On the west coast of Italy.

rejected this advice as often as it was offered, but they eventually pressed him so hard that he could not refuse them any longer, and agreed to do as they suggested. Having mustered an enormous baggage-train, as though he were intending to go to France or Spain or some other remote part of the world, he mounted his horse, rode forth from Ravenna with several of his friends, and repaired to a place which is known as Classe, some three miles distant from the city. Having sent for a number of tents and pavilions, he told his companions that this was where he intended to stay, and that they could all go back to Ravenna. So Nastagio pitched his camp in this place, and began to live in as fine and lordly a fashion as any man ever born, from time to time inviting various groups of friends to dine or breakfast with him, as had always been his custom.

Now, it so happened that one Friday morning toward the beginning of May, the weather being very fine, Nastagio fell to thinking about his cruel mistress. Having ordered his servants to leave him to his own devices so that he could meditate at greater leisure, he sauntered off, lost in thought, and his steps led him straight into the pinewoods. The fifth hour of the day was already spent, and he had advanced at least half a mile into the woods, oblivious of food and everything else, when suddenly he seemed to hear a woman giving vent to dreadful wailing and ear-splitting screams. His pleasant reverie being thus interrupted, he raised his head to investigate the cause, and discovered to his surprise that he was in the pinewoods. Furthermore, on looking straight ahead he caught sight of a naked woman, young and very beautiful, who was running through a dense thicket of shrubs and briars towards the very spot where he was standing. The woman's hair was dishevelled, her flesh was all torn by the briars and brambles, and she was sobbing and screaming for mercy. Nor was this all, for a pair of big, fierce mastiffs were running at the girl's heels, one on either side, and every so often they caught up with her and savaged her. Finally, bringing up the rear he saw a swarthy-looking knight, his face contorted with anger, who was riding a jet-black steed and brandishing a rapier, and who, in terms no less abusive than terrifying, was threatening to kill her.[1]

This spectacle struck both terror and amazement into Nastagio's breast, to say nothing of compassion for the hapless woman, a sentiment that in its turn engendered the desire to rescue her from such agony and save her life, if this were possible. But on finding that he was unarmed, he hastily took up a branch of a tree to serve as a cudgel, and prepared to ward off the dogs and do battle with the knight. When the latter saw what he was doing, he shouted to him from a distance:

"Keep out of this, Nastagio! Leave me and the dogs to give this wicked sinner her deserts!"

He had no sooner spoken than the dogs seized the girl firmly by the haunches and brought her to a halt. When the knight reached the spot he dismounted from his horse, and Nastagio went up to him saying:

"I do not know who you are, or how you come to know my name; but I can tell you that it is a gross outrage for an armed knight to try and kill a naked woman, and to set dogs upon her as though she were a savage beast. I shall do all in my power to defend her, of that you may be sure."

---

1. Compare the account of the punishment of the spendthrifts in Dante's *Inferno*. canto 13.

Whereupon the knight said:

"I was a fellow citizen of yours, Nastagio, my name was Guido degli Anastagi, and you were still a little child when I fell in love with this woman. I loved her far more deeply than you love that Traversari girl of yours, but her pride and cruelty led me to such a pass that, one day, I killed myself in sheer despair with this rapier that you see in my hand, and thus I am condemned to eternal punishment. My death pleased her beyond measure, but shortly thereafter she too died, and because she had sinned by her cruelty and by gloating over my sufferings, and was quite unrepentant, being convinced that she was more of a saint than a sinner, she too was condemned to the pains of Hell. No sooner was she cast into Hell than we were both given a special punishment, which consisted in her case of fleeing before me, and in my own of pursuing her as though she were my mortal enemy rather than the woman with whom I was once so deeply in love. Every time I catch up with her, I kill her with this same rapier by which I took my own life; then I slit her back open, and (as you will now observe for yourself) I tear from her body that hard, cold heart to which neither love nor pity could ever gain access, and together with the rest of her entrails I cast it to these dogs to feed upon.

"Within a short space of time, as ordained by the power and justice of God, she springs to her feet as though she had not been dead at all, and her agonizing flight begins all over again, with the dogs and myself in pursuit. Every Friday at this hour I overtake her in this part of the woods, and slaughter her in the manner you are about to observe; but you must not imagine that we are idle for the rest of the week, because on the remaining days I hunt her down in other places where she was cruel to me in thought and deed. As you can see for yourself, I am no longer her lover but her enemy, and in this guise I am obliged to pursue her for the same number of years as the months of her cruelty towards me. Stand aside, therefore, and let me carry out the judgment of God. Do not try to oppose what you cannot prevent."

On hearing these words, Nastagio was shaken to the core, there was scarcely a single hair on his head that was not standing on end, and he stepped back to fix his gaze on the unfortunate girl, waiting in fear and trembling to see what the knight would do to her. This latter, having finished speaking, pounced like a mad dog, rapier in hand, upon the girl, who was kneeling before him, held by the two mastiffs, and screaming for mercy at the top of her voice. Applying all his strength, the knight plunged his rapier into the middle of her breast and out again at the other side, whereupon the girl fell on her face, still sobbing and screaming, whilst the knight, having laid hold of a dagger, slashed open her back, extracted her heart and everything else around it, and hurled it to the two mastiffs, who devoured it greedily on the instant. But before very long the girl rose suddenly to her feet as though none of these things had happened, and sped off in the direction of the sea, being pursued by the dogs, who kept tearing away at her flesh as she ran. Remounting his horse, and seizing his rapier, the knight too began to give chase, and within a short space of time they were so far away that Nastagio could no longer see them.

For some time after bearing witness to these events, Nastagio stood rooted to the spot out of fear and compassion, but after a while it occurred to him that since this scene was enacted every Friday, it ought to prove very useful to him. So he marked the place and returned to his servants; and when the time seemed ripe, he sent for his friends and kinsfolk, and said to them:

"For some little time you have been urging me to desist from wooing this hostile mistress of mine and place a curb on my extravagance, and I am willing to do so on condition that you obtain for me a single favor, which is this: that on Friday next you arrange for Messer Paolo Traversari and his wife and daughter and all their womenfolk, together with any other lady you care to invite, to join me in this place for breakfast. My reason for wanting this will become apparent to you on the day itself."

They thought this a very trifling commission for them to undertake, and promised him they would do it. On their return to Ravenna, they invited all the people he had specified. And although they had a hard job, when the time came, in persuading Nastagio's beloved to go, she nevertheless went there along with the others.

Nastagio saw to it that a magnificent banquet was prepared, and had the tables placed beneath the pine-trees in such a way as to surround the place where he had witnessed the massacre of the cruel lady. Moreover, in seating the ladies and gentlemen at table, he so arranged matters that the girl he loved sat directly facing the spot where the scene would be enacted.

The last course had already been served, when they all began to hear the agonized yells of the fugitive girl. Everyone was greatly astonished and wanted to know what it was, but nobody was able to say. So they all stood up to see if they could find out what was going on, and caught sight of the wailing girl, together with the knight and the dogs. And shortly thereafter they came into the very midst of the company.

Everyone began shouting and bawling at the dogs and the knight, and several people rushed forward to the girl's assistance; but the knight, by repeating to them the story he had related to Nastagio, not only caused them to retreat but filled them all with terror and amazement. And when he dealt with the girl in the same way as before, all the ladies present (many of whom, being related either to the suffering girl or to the knight, still remembered his great love and the manner of his death) wept as plaintively as though what they had witnessed had been done to themselves.

When the spectacle was at an end, and the knight and the lady had gone, they all began to talk about what they had seen. But none was stricken with so much terror as the cruel maiden loved by Nastagio, for she had heard and seen everything distinctly and realized that these matters had more to do with herself than with any of the other guests, in view of the harshness she had always displayed towards Nastagio; consequently, she already had the sensation of fleeing before her enraged suitor, with the mastiffs tearing away at her haunches.

So great was the fear engendered within her by this episode, that in order to avoid a similar fate she converted her enmity into love; and, seizing the earliest opportunity (which came to her that very evening), she privily sent a trusted maidservant to Nastagio, requesting him to be good enough to call upon her, as she was ready to do anything he desired. Nastagio was overjoyed, and told her so in his reply, but added that if she had no objection he preferred to combine his pleasure with the preservation of her good name, by making her his lawful wedded wife.

Knowing that she alone was to blame for the fact that she and Nastagio were not already married, the girl readily sent him her consent. And so, acting as her own intermediary, she announced to her father and mother, to their enormous satisfaction, that she would be pleased to become Nastagio's wife. On the following Sunday Nastagio married her, and after celebrating their nuptials they settled down to a long and happy life together.

Their marriage was by no means the only good effect to be produced by this horrible apparition, for from that day forth the ladies of Ravenna in general were so frightened by it that they became much more tractable to men's pleasures than they had ever been in the past.

[The Tenth Story of the Tenth Day][2]

The Marquis of Saluzzo, obliged by the entreaties of his subjects to take a wife, follows his personal whims and marries the daughter of a peasant. She bears him two children, and he gives her the impression that he has put them to death. Later on, pretending that she has incurred his displeasure and that he has remarried, he arranges for his own daughter to return home and passes her off as his bride, having meanwhile turned his wife out of doors in no more than the shift she is wearing. But on finding that she endures it all with patience, he cherishes her all the more deeply, brings her back to his house, shows her their children, who have now grown up, and honors her as the Marchioness, causing others to honor her likewise.

A very long time ago, there succeeded to the marquisate of Saluzzo[3] a young man called Gualtieri, who, having neither wife nor children, spent the whole of his time hunting and hawking, and never even thought about marrying or raising a family, which says a great deal for his intelligence. His followers, however, disapproved of this, and repeatedly begged him to marry so that he should not be left without an heir nor they without a lord. Moreover, they offered to find him a wife whose parentage would be such as to strengthen their expectations and who would make him exceedingly happy.

So Gualtieri answered them as follows:

"My friends, you are pressing me to do something that I had always set my mind firmly against, seeing how difficult it is to find a person who will easily adapt to one's own way of living, how many thousands there are who will do precisely the opposite, and what a miserable life is in store for the man who stumbles upon a woman ill-suited to his own temperament. Moreover it is foolish of you to believe that you can judge the character of daughters from the ways of their fathers and mothers, hence claiming to provide me with a wife who will please me. For I cannot see how you are to know the fathers, or to discover the secrets of the mothers; and even if this were possible, daughters are very often different from either of their parents. Since, however, you are so determined to bind me in chains of this sort, I am ready to do as you ask; but so that I have only myself to blame if it should turn out badly, I must insist on marrying a wife of my own choosing. And I hereby declare that no matter who she may be, if you fail to honor her as your lady you will learn to your great cost how serious a matter it is for you to have urged me to marry against my will."

2. The teller is Dioneo, the young man who tells the last story of each day.   3. A town at the foot of the Alps about thirty miles south of Turin.

To this the gentlemen replied that if only he would bring himself to take a wife, they would be satisfied.

Now, for some little time, Gualtieri had been casting an appreciative eye on the manners of a poor girl from a neighboring village, and thinking her very beautiful, he considered that a life with her would have much to commend it. So without looking further afield, he resolved to marry the girl; and having summoned her father, who was very poor indeed, he arranged with him that he should take her as his wife.

This done, Gualtieri brought together all his friends from the various parts of his domain, and said to them:

"My friends, since you still persist in wanting me to take a wife, I am prepared to do it, not because I have any desire to marry, but rather in order to gratify your wishes. You will recall the promise you gave me, that no matter whom I should choose, you would rest content and honor her as your lady. The time has now come when I want you to keep that promise, and for me to honor the promise I gave to you. I have found a girl after my own heart, in this very district, and a few days hence I intend to marry her and convey her to my house. See to it, therefore, that the wedding-feast lacks nothing in splendor, and consider how you may honorably receive her, so that all of us may call ourselves contented—I with you for keeping your promise, and you with me for keeping mine."

As of one voice, the good folk joyously gave him their blessing, and said that whoever she happened to be, they would accept her as their lady and honor her as such in all respects. Then they all prepared to celebrate the wedding in a suitably grand and sumptuous manner, and Gualtieri did the same. A rich and splendid nuptial feast was arranged, to which he invited many of his friends, his kinsfolk, great nobles and other people of the locality; moreover he caused a quantity of fine, rich robes to be tailored to fit a girl whose figure appeared to match that of the young woman he intended to marry; and lastly he laid in a number of rings and ornamental belts, along with a precious and beautiful crown, and everything else that a bride could possibly need.

Early on the morning of the day he had fixed for the nuptials, Gualtieri, his preparations now complete, mounted his horse together with all the people who had come to do him honor, and said:

"Gentlemen, it is time for us to go and fetch the bride."

He then set forth with the whole of the company in train, and eventually they came to the village and made their way to the house of the girl's father, where they met her as she was returning with water from the fountain, making great haste so that she could go with other women to see Gualtieri's bride arriving. As soon as Gualtieri caught sight of her, he called to her by her name, which was Griselda, and asked her where her father was, to which she blushingly replied:

"My lord, he is at home."

So Gualtieri dismounted, and having ordered everyone to wait for him outside, he went alone into the humble dwelling, where he found the girl's father, whose name was Giannùcole, and said to him:

"I have come to marry Griselda, but first I want to ask her certain questions in your presence." He then asked her whether, if he were to marry her, she would always try to please him and never be upset by anything he said or did, whether she would obey him, and many other questions of this sort, to all of which she answered that she would.

Whereupon Gualtieri, having taken her by the hand, led her out of the house, and in the presence of his whole company and of all the other people there he caused her to be stripped naked. Then he called for the clothes and shoes which he had had specially made, and quickly got her to put them on, after which he caused a crown to be placed upon the dishevelled hair of her head. And just as everyone was wondering what this might signify, he said:

"Gentlemen, this is the woman I intend to marry, provided she will have me as her husband." Then, turning to Griselda, who was so embarrassed that she hardly knew where to look, he said: "Griselda, will you have me as your wedded husband?"

To which she replied:

"I will, my lord."

"And I will have you as my wedded wife," said Gualtieri, and he married her then and there before all the people present. He then helped her mount a palfrey, and led her back, honorably attended, to his house, where the nuptials were as splendid and as sumptuous, and the rejoicing as unrestrained, as if he had married the King of France's daughter.

Along with her new clothes, the young bride appeared to take on a new lease of life, and she seemed a different woman entirely. She was endowed, as we have said, with a fine figure and beautiful features, and lovely as she already was, she now acquired so confident, graceful and decorous a manner that she could have been taken for the daughter, not of the shepherd Gian-nùcole, but of some great nobleman, and consequently everyone who had known her before her marriage was filled with astonishment. But apart from this, she was so obedient to her husband, and so compliant to his wishes, that he thought himself the happiest and most contented man on earth. At the same time she was so gracious and benign towards her husband's subjects, that each and every one of them was glad to honor her, and accorded her his unselfish devotion, praying for her happiness, prosperity, and greater glory. And whereas they had been wont to say that Gualtieri had shown some lack of discretion in taking this woman as his wife, they now regarded him as the wisest and most discerning man on earth. For no one apart from Gualtieri could ever have perceived the noble qualities that lay concealed beneath her ragged and rustic attire.

In short, she comported herself in such a manner that she quickly earned widespread acclaim for her virtuous deeds and excellent character not only in her husband's domain but also in the world at large; and those who had formerly censured Gualtieri for choosing to marry her were now compelled to reverse their opinion.

Not long after she had gone to live with Gualtieri she conceived a child, and in the fullness of time, to her husband's enormous joy, she bore him a daughter. But shortly thereafter Gualtieri was seized with the strange desire to test Griselda's patience, by subjecting her to constant provocation and making her life unbearable.

At first he lashed her with his tongue, feigning to be angry and claiming that his subjects were thoroughly disgruntled with her on account of her lowly condition, especially now that they saw her bearing children; and he said they were greatly distressed about this infant daughter of theirs, of whom they did nothing but grumble.

The lady betrayed no sign of bitterness on hearing these words, and without changing her expression she said to him:

"My lord, deal with me as you think best[4] for your own good name and peace of mind, for I shall rest content whatever you decide, knowing myself to be their inferior and that I was unworthy of the honor which you so generously bestowed upon me."

This reply was much to Gualtieri's liking, for it showed him that she had not been puffed with pride by any honor that he or others had paid her.

A little while later, having told his wife in general terms that his subjects could not abide the daughter she had borne him, he gave certain instructions to one of his attendants, whom he sent to Griselda. The man looked very sorrowful, and said:

"My lady, if I do not wish to die, I must do as my lord commands me. He has ordered me to take this daughter of yours, and to . . ." And his voice trailed off into silence.

On hearing these words and perceiving the man's expression, Griselda, recalling what she had been told, concluded that he had been instructed to murder her child. So she quickly picked it up from its cradle, kissed it, gave it her blessing, and albeit she felt that her heart was about to break, placed the child in the arms of the servant without any trace of emotion, saying:

"There: do exactly as your lord, who is my lord too, has instructed you. But do not leave her to be devoured by the beasts and the birds, unless that is what he has ordered you to do."

The servant took away the little girl and reported Griselda's words to Gualtieri, who, marvelling at her constancy, sent him with the child to a kinswoman of his in Bologna,[5] requesting her to rear and educate her carefully, but without ever making it known whose daughter she was.

Then it came about that his wife once more became pregnant, and in due course she gave birth to a son, which pleased Gualtieri enormously. But not being content with the mischief he had done already, he abused her more viciously than ever, and one day he glowered at her angrily and said:

"Woman, from the day you produced this infant son, the people have made my life a complete misery, so bitterly do they resent the thought of a grandson of Giannùcole succeeding me as their lord. So unless I want to be deposed, I'm afraid I shall be forced to do as I did before, and eventually to leave you and marry someone else."

His wife listened patiently, and all she replied was:

"My lord, look to your own comfort, see that you fulfil your wishes, and spare no thought for me, since nothing brings me pleasure unless it pleases you also."

Before many days had elapsed, Gualtieri sent for his son in the same way that he had sent for his daughter, and having likewise pretended to have had the child put to death, he sent him, like the little girl, to Bologna. To all of this his wife reacted no differently, either in her speech or in her looks, than

---

4. See Luke 1.38, where the Virgin Mary replies to the Angel Gabriel, "Be it unto me according to thy word."   5. A city in northern Italy, not far from Florence.

she had on the previous occasion, much to the astonishment of Gualtieri, who told himself that no other woman could have remained so impassive. But for the fact that he had observed her doting upon the children for as long as he allowed her to do so, he would have assumed that she was glad to be rid of them, whereas he knew that she was too judicious to behave in any other way.

His subjects, thinking he had caused the children to be murdered, roundly condemned him and judged him a cruel tyrant, whilst his wife became the object of their deepest compassion. But to the women who offered her their sympathy in the loss of her children, all she ever said was that the decision of their father was good enough for her.

Many years after the birth of his daughter, Gualtieri decided that the time had come to put Griselda's patience to the final test. So he told a number of his men that in no circumstances could he put up with Griselda as his wife any longer, having now come to realize that his marriage was an aberration of his youth. He would therefore do everything in his power to obtain a dispensation from the Pope, enabling him to divorce Griselda and marry someone else. For this he was chided severely by many worthy men, but his only reply was that it had to be done.

On learning of her husband's intentions, from which it appeared she would have to return to her father's house, in order perhaps to look after the sheep as she had in the past, meanwhile seeing the man she adored being cherished by some other woman, Griselda was secretly filled with despair. But she prepared herself to endure this final blow as stoically as she had borne Fortune's earlier assaults.

Shortly thereafter, Gualtieri arranged for some counterfeit letters of his to arrive from Rome, and led his subjects to believe that in these, the Pope had granted him permission to abandon Griselda and remarry.

He accordingly sent for Griselda, and before a large number of people he said to her:

"Woman, I have had a dispensation from the Pope, allowing me to leave you and take another wife. Since my ancestors were great noblemen and rulers of these lands, whereas yours have always been peasants, I intend that you shall no longer be my wife, but return to Giannùcole's house with the dowry you brought me, after which I shall bring another lady here. I have already chosen her and she is far better suited to a man of my condition."

On hearing these words, the lady, with an effort beyond the power of any normal woman's nature, suppressed her tears and replied:

"My lord, I have always known that my lowly condition was totally at odds with your nobility, and that it is to God and to yourself that I owe whatever standing I possess. Nor have I ever regarded this as a gift that I might keep and cherish as my own, but rather as something I have borrowed; and now that you want me to return it, I must give it back to you with good grace. Here is the ring with which you married me: take it. As to your ordering me to take away the dowry that I brought, you will require no accountant, nor will I need a purse or a pack-horse, for this to be done. For it has not escaped my memory that you took me naked as on the day I was born.[6] If you think

---

6. See Job 1.21: "Naked came I out of my mother's womb, and naked shall I return thither: the Lord gave, and the Lord hath taken away."

it proper that the body in which I have borne your children should be seen by all the people, I shall go away naked. But in return for my virginity, which I brought to you and cannot retrieve, I trust you will at least allow me, in addition to my dowry, to take one shift away with me."

Gualtieri wanted above all else to burst into tears, but maintaining a stern expression he said:

"Very well, you may take a shift."

All the people present implored Gualtieri to let her have a dress, so that she who had been his wife for thirteen years and more would not have to suffer the indignity of leaving his house in a shift, like a pauper; but their pleas were unavailing. And so Griselda, wearing a shift, barefoot, and with nothing to cover her head, having bidden them farewell, set forth from Gualtieri's house and returned to her father amid the weeping and the wailing of all who set eyes upon her.

Giannùcole, who had never thought it possible that Gualtieri would keep his daughter as his wife, and was daily expecting this to happen, had preserved the clothes she discarded on the morning Gualtieri had married her. So he brought them to her, and Griselda, having put them on, applied herself as before to the menial chores in her father's house, bravely enduring the cruel assault of hostile Fortune.

No sooner did Gualtieri drive Griselda away, than he gave his subjects to understand that he was betrothed to a daughter of one of the Counts of Panago.[7] And having ordered that grandiose preparations were to be made for the nuptials, he sent for Griselda and said to her:

"I am about to fetch home this new bride of mine, and from the moment she sets foot inside the house, I intend to accord her an honorable welcome. As you know, I have no women here who can set the rooms in order for me, or attend to many of the things that a festive occasion of this sort requires. No one knows better than you how to handle these household affairs, so I want you to make all the necessary arrangements. Invite all the ladies you need, and receive them as though you were mistress of the house. And when the nuptials are over, you can go back home to your father."

Since Griselda was unable to lay aside her love for Gualtieri as readily as she had dispensed with her good fortune, his words pierced her heart like so many knives. But she replied:

"My lord, I am ready to do as you ask."[8]

And so, in her coarse, thick, woollen garments, Griselda returned to the house she had quitted shortly before in her shift, and started to sweep and tidy the various chambers. On her instructions, the beds were draped with hangings, the benches in the halls were suitably adorned, the kitchen was made ready; and she set her hand, as though she were a petty serving wench, to every conceivable household task, never stopping to draw breath until she had everything prepared and arranged as befitted the occasion.

Having done all this, she caused invitations to be sent, in Gualtieri's name, to all the ladies living in those parts, and began to await the event. And when at last the nuptial day arrived, heedless of her beggarly attire, she bade a cheerful welcome to each of the lady guests, displaying all the warmth and courtesy of a lady of the manor.

---

7. An area near Bologna.   8. See a Luke 1.38: "Behold the handmaid of the Lord."

Gualtieri's children having meanwhile been carefully reared by his kinswoman in Bologna, who had married into the family of the Courts of Panago, the girl was now twelve years old, the loveliest creature ever seen, whilst the boy had reached the age of six. Gualtieri had sent word to his kinswoman's husband, asking him to do him the kindness of bringing this daughter of his to Saluzzo along with her little brother, to see that she was nobly and honorably escorted, and to tell everyone he met that he was taking her to marry Gualtieri, without revealing who she really was to a living soul.

In accordance with the Marquis's request, the gentleman set forth with the girl and her brother and a noble company, and a few days later, shortly before the hour of breakfast, he arrived at Saluzzo, where he found that all the folk thereabouts, and numerous others from neighboring parts, were waiting for Gualtieri's latest bride.

After being welcomed by the ladies, she made her way to the hall where the tables were set, and Griselda, just as we have described her, went cordially up to meet her, saying:

"My lady, you are welcome."

The ladies, who in vain had implored Gualtieri to see that Griselda remained in another room, or to lend her one of the dresses that had once been hers, so that she would not cut such a sorry figure in front of his guests, took their seats at table and addressed themselves to the meal. All eyes were fixed upon the girl, and everyone said that Gualtieri had made a good exchange. But Griselda praised her as warmly as anyone present, speaking no less admiringly of her little brother.

Gualtieri felt that he had now seen all he wished to see of the patience of his lady, for he perceived that no event, however singular, produced the slightest change in her demeanor, and he was certain that this was not because of her obtuseness, as he knew her to be very intelligent. He therefore considered that the time had come for him to free her from the rancor that he judged her to be hiding beneath her tranquil outward expression. And having summoned her to his table, before all the people present he smiled at her and said:

"What do you think of our new bride?"

"My lord," replied Griselda, "I think very well of her. And if, as I believe, her wisdom matches her beauty, I have no doubt whatever that your life with her will bring you greater happiness than any gentleman on earth has ever known. But with all my heart I beg you not to inflict those same wounds upon her that you imposed upon her predecessor, for I doubt whether she could withstand them, not only because she is younger, but also because she has had a refined upbringing, whereas the other had to face continual hardship from her infancy."

On observing that Griselda was firmly convinced that the young lady was to be his wife, and that even so she allowed no hint of resentment to escape her lips, Gualtieri got her to sit down beside him, and said:

"Griselda, the time has come for you to reap the reward of your unfailing patience, and for those who considered me a cruel and bestial tyrant, to know that whatever I have done was done of set purpose, for I wished to show you how to be a wife, to teach these people how to choose and keep a wife, and to guarantee my own peace and quiet for as long as we were living beneath the same roof. When I came to take a wife, I was greatly afraid that this peace would be denied me, and in order to prove otherwise I tormented and provoked you in the ways you have seen. But as I have never known you to oppose my wishes, I now intend, being persuaded that you can offer me all the happiness I desired, to restore to you in a single instant that which I took from you little by little, and delectably assuage the pains I have inflicted upon you. Receive with gladsome heart, then, this girl whom you believe to be my bride, and also her brother. These are our children, whom you and many others have long supposed that I caused to be cruelly murdered; and I am your husband, who loves you above all else, for I think I can boast that there is no other man on earth whose contentment in his wife exceeds my own."

Having spoken these words, he embraced and kissed Griselda, who by now was weeping with joy; then they both got up from table and made their way to the place where their daughter sat listening in utter amazement to these tidings. And after they had fondly embraced the girl and her brother, the mystery was unravelled to her, as well as to many of the others who were present.

The ladies rose from table in transports of joy, and escorted Griselda to a chamber, where, with greater assurance of her future happiness, they divested her of her tattered garments and clothed her anew in one of her stately robes. And as their lady and their mistress, a rôle which even in her rags had seemed to be hers, they led her back to the hall, where she and Gualtieri rejoiced with the children in a manner marvelous to behold.

Everyone being delighted with the turn that events had taken, the feasting and the merrymaking were redoubled, and continued unabated for the next few days. Gualtieri was acknowledged to be very wise, though the trials to which he had subjected his lady were regarded as harsh and intolerable, whilst Griselda was accounted the wisest of all.

The Count of Panago returned a few days later to Bologna, and Gualtieri, having removed Giannùcole from his drudgery, set him up in a style befitting his father-in-law, so that he lived in great comfort and honor for the rest of his days. As for Gualtieri himself, having married off his daughter to a gentleman of renown, he lived long and contentedly with Griselda, never failing to honor her to the best of his ability.

What more needs to be said, except that celestial spirits may sometimes descend even into the houses of the poor, whilst there are those in royal palaces who would be better employed as swineherds than as rulers of men? Who else but Griselda could have endured so cheerfully the cruel and unheard of trials that Gualtieri imposed upon her without shedding a tear? For perhaps it would have served him right if he had chanced upon a wife, who, being driven from the house in her shift, had found some other man to shake her skin-coat for her, earning herself a fine new dress in the process.

GEOFFREY CHAUCER
1340?–1400

Chaucer is not only one of the earliest poets in the English literary tradition but also one of the greatest. Apart from the poetic virtuosity, psychological subtlety, and humane good humor of his writing, he is worthy of his place here because he is the poet who endowed English literature with a status equal to that of the other European vernaculars—who in effect showed that it could become a world literature. Ironically, the earliest important body of vernacular writing in the medieval period was that of Anglo-Saxon England (represented in this anthology by *Beowulf* and by the lyric poem "The Ruin"). With the Norman conquest of England in 1066 this rich tradition was soon extinguished, and cultural leadership was assumed by literature written in the languages of France—French, Provençal (the dialect of southern France), and Anglo-Norman (the dialect of Normandy and England)—and, to a lesser extent, Italy. Having undergone the break in cultural continuity caused by the Norman conquest, and hindered by the internal struggle for cultural dominance between French and English, English speakers did not develop their own national literature in their own language until the last third of the fourteenth century. This was when *Sir Gawain and the Green Knight* was written, and when other significant writers emerged, especially William Langland, the author of a brilliantly difficult long poem called *Piers Plowman*, and John Gower, who wrote in French and Latin but also composed a major English poem, the *Confessio amantis* (or *Lover's Confession*). Both Langland and Gower lived and worked in London, which was also Chaucer's home. But unlike these contemporaries, Chaucer was very much aware of the European literary traditions not just as collections of texts but as *traditions*, as ongoing cultural projects. This awareness gave to his poetry an artistic subtlety and cultural sophistication that has ensured his position in world literature. But just as important, it also allowed Chaucer to conceive of—and to accomplish—the establishment of an English literary tradition. For it was to his poetry that later English poets, including Shakespeare, Spenser, and Milton, turned to find the foundations of an English literary tradition upon which they could then build.

Chaucer was the son of a wealthy London merchant, and like many children in his position he was sent at an early age to serve as a page in a noble household, in his case that of the countess of Ulster, who was married to one of the sons of King Edward III. Although from a bourgeois background, Chaucer would there have been educated in the values of the aristocratic culture of the time, including its literary tastes, which were for the most part formed on French models. In 1359–60 Chaucer participated in one of the king's military expeditions against the French, was captured, and as was usual at the time, was ransomed by the king. By 1367 Chaucer was a squire in the king's household. This meant not that he resided with the king (although he may have), but that he was called on to perform a number of services, primarily traveling abroad on the king's business. Chaucer undertook diplomatic journeys to Spain, to France, and—first in 1372–73, then again in 1378—to Italy. These last trips are particularly important because they suggest that Chaucer knew Italian (which he could have learned in London from dealings with the many Italian merchants and bankers who lived there). His poetry—virtually alone among his contemporaries—shows the strong influence of Dante, Petrarch, and Boccaccio, and it is in part their example that provided him with the model for a national literature. In 1374 Chaucer became the controller of the customs in London, and he leased a house there (he had already been married for some eight years). He kept this job until 1386, when—probably under political pressure—he resigned. By this time the king was the young Richard II, who had ascended the throne in 1377 at the age of ten. Richard was throughout his reign involved in dangerous struggles for power with the leading members of the aristocracy, and in 1386 he seemed on the verge of being deposed. Chaucer was probably a member of the king's party, and his resignation reflects the decline of Richard's power. By 1389 Richard had regained command, and Chaucer was given other posts and gifts, but ten years later Richard was first deposed and then murdered by Henry Bolingbroke, who became Henry IV. This made little financial difference to Chaucer, who had long maintained a relationship with Henry's father, John of Gaunt, and with Henry himself: his annuity was quickly renewed.

As even this brief account suggests, Chaucer lived in turbulent times. In addition to the struggles for power among the royal family, England was throughout this time at war with France and with the Scots, wars that went progressively badly. It was also during this time—in 1381—that England experienced the shock of the Peasants' Revolt, a violent rebellion that accomplished little substantively but made disturbingly clear the intense animosity that existed between the classes. Finally, this was a period of religious turmoil, when John Wyclif and his supporters were challenging the church in terms of both its doctrine and its immense economic power—a challenge that would finally culminate in the Protestant Reformation of the sixteenth century. Oddly enough, most of these events find only the barest mention in Chaucer's poetry. Unlike Dante, he seems not to have held strong political convictions, and his religious commitments seem both generally orthodox and lacking in any special intensity. Finally, although Chaucer was generously rewarded by the great men of his day, there is no clear evidence that these rewards were given to him because he wrote poetry. He seems to have followed a career path much like that of other men of his background, and we do not know to what extent, if any, his extraordinary talent was appreciated in his own day. Indeed, two of the characteristics that make Chaucer such an appealing writer are a tolerant inquisitiveness toward all sorts of people and opinions and a self-effacing if sometimes disingenuous modesty. While he lacks Dante's learning, for example, and his intensity, he is a far more agreeable poet: one can hardly imagine Dante appreciating either the Miller's hilarious bawdy or the witty self-promotions of the Wife of Bath.

Chaucer's career as a poet can be usefully divided into three stages. The first stage comprises the poetry he wrote primarily under the influence of the fashionable French court poetry of the time. When Chaucer was a young man the literary language of the king's household was probably French, yet Chaucer seems to have written only in English. The earliest poem we can date with any certainty is an elegy, in English, for Blanche, duchess of Lancaster and the wife of John of Gaunt, who died in 1368. But while written in English, much of this poem is derived from the work of contemporary French court poets: Chaucer here gratifies the tastes of an elegant society hypersensitive to French fashions. This interest continues in all the poetry Chaucer wrote before *The Canterbury Tales,* even when his work begins to show the powerful influence of the Italian poets. This second phase begins as early as the late 1370s, when in a poem called the *House of Fame* Chaucer struggles to locate himself in relation to Dante, whose work he seems to have found both intimidating and pretentious. In the 1380s he wrote *Troilus and Criseyde,* a very beautiful narrative love poem based on a poem by Boccaccio, which explores the psychological depths and the ethical questions that are now treated by the novel. The third part of Chaucer's career is called the English period and comprises *The Canterbury Tales,* a work begun about 1386 and left incomplete. The twenty-four tales that Chaucer completed in fact draw on a wide variety of sources, almost all of them continental: Chaucer was never very interested in what native tradition of English writing there was. But *The Canterbury Tales* is still a very English work. It begins with a *General Prologue* that describes a group of about thirty pilgrims who meet by chance at an inn in a suburb of London before the trip to the shrine of St. Thomas à Becket at Canterbury cathedral. These pilgrims are drawn from almost every rank of fourteenth-century English society, with a decided emphasis on the middle strata, and the reader is left in no doubt that one of the purposes of the work as a whole is to provide a kind of portrait of the nation as a whole. Here Chaucer moves beyond the aristocratic circles to which all of his previous work had been addressed and writes for a larger, national audience. Whether he found such an audience in his own lifetime is very doubtful, but certainly his ambition has been amply rewarded by posterity.

The Canterbury Tales, like the Decameron and The Thousand and One Nights, is a collection of tales located within a frame. At the urging of their host, Harry Bailly, the pilgrims who have gathered at the Tabard Inn agree to tell two tales each, one while going to and one while returning from Canterbury. It seems doubtful that Chaucer himself meant to compose 120 tales, and there are clear indications that the tale-telling game is meant to end before the pilgrims reach Canterbury. Whether Chaucer decided that the twenty-four tales he did include were sufficient is not known, but he certainly did not complete all the links between the tales, and as a result the order in which many of the tales should be read is unclear. Yet this is not a serious impediment to understanding the individual tales, which together provide a brilliant anthology of virtually every medieval kind of writing. Chaucer offers us fabliaux, a mini-epic, romances, saints' lives, exempla, a lay, an animal fable, anecdotes, and even two prose treatises dealing with political and spiritual behavior. If he wants to show us almost every kind of person to be found in late medieval England, he also wants to survey almost the full range of medieval writing. Even the "General Prologue," which describes with an air of casual spontaneity the pilgrims who gather at the Tabard Inn, is a recognizable kind of medieval writing. Medieval social theory held that society was divided into three estates, or classes: the nobility, who ruled; the clergy, who prayed; and the laborers, who worked. Much social criticism of the time was offered in the form of a critical commentary on the members of each of these estates. These works are known as estates satires, and the "General Prologue" fits the pattern. Chaucer begins with portraits of the knightly estate (the Knight, the Squire, and their servant, the Yeoman), then moves to the clergy (the Prioress, Monk, and Friar), and then to the largest group of all, the estate of those who work for a living. And if he doesn't keep strictly to this scheme—the Clerk, the Parson, the Summoner, and the Pardoner are all technically members of the clergy—he nonetheless includes two "ideal" portraits of each estate: the Knight and the Squire, the Clerk and the Parson, and the Yeoman and the Plowman. Yet, as is usual with Chaucer, he adopts a conventional form only to revise it in a new direction. The estates satire is a social form: its focus is on the ills of society and how they can be cured. But Chaucer's focus in the "General Prologue" is primarily on individuals and their psychological makeup. We are much less interested in the degree to which the Prioress fulfills her spiritual duties than we are in the needs she seeks to fulfill with her elegant dress, her love of pets, and her refined but avid dining. We know that the Friar violates his vows, but our attention is drawn to the sort of person he is. Striking in this regard is the fact that not until the final portraits does Chaucer pay much attention to the social effects of his characters' misbehavior: until we come to the out-and-out rogues (the Manciple, Miller, Reeve, Summoner and Pardoner—a group in which the narrator places himself!), there is remarkably little sense of anyone being seriously victimized by the pilgrims' foibles. This is not to say that Chaucer is uninterested in morality, but that the moralist's responsibility to judge seems often to conflict with the artist's desire to understand and to appreciate. This conflict corresponds to one within the "General Prologue" itself, between the duty of pilgrimage and the pleasure of tale-telling. In reading this vivid gallery of portraits, then, we do well to try to balance moral judgment with psychological analysis, and to seek to understand the many motivations and needs of these characters and the differing attitudes that the enthusiastic narrator—who is not to be identified with the historical Chaucer—takes toward them.

When the tale-telling game begins, the Knight—the highest representative of the aristocratic estate—is asked to tell the first story. He responds with a medievalized version of a classical epic: it deals with the fervent love of two knights for a fair maiden, and the inconclusive efforts of a wise ruler to bring order out of the chaos their passion creates. The Host then begins to call on the highest representative of the clergy, the Monk, but is rudely interrupted by one of the lowest ranking members of the third estate, the Miller. The Miller says he will "pay off" the Knight, which means that he will both reward him and retaliate against him. But the social tensions of the time that for a moment burst into the tale-telling game are immediately displaced into "The Miller's Tale," which is itself about reward and retaliation. Like the Knight, the Miller tells of two young men (Nicholas and Absalom) who desire a beautiful woman (Alison), and of an older man (John) who tries unsuccessfully to control events. But rather than the Knight's high seriousness the Miller presents ribald comedy; and rather than the courtly love the Knight celebrates the Miller presents sexual desire in much less exalted terms. "The Miller's Tale" is a fabliau—indeed, it is two fabliaux brought brilliantly together. One deals with the triangle of Nicholas, Alison, and John and ends with Nicholas's triumph and John's humiliation; the other is the triangle of Nicholas, Absalom and Alison and ends with both men humiliated and Alison cheerfully unscathed. Both these plots are brought together with a single word—"Water!"—that creates an almost metaphysical sense of harmonious resolution. Two stories have unfolded in apparently random ways, and yet suddenly we see that they are in fact one beautifully complex story. One is tempted to say that each story "pays off"—rewards and retaliates against—the other. But does the harmony of the plot extend to the theme as well? Is there moral as well as narrative order? To answer this question the reader must realize that what is being punished is not transgression against social or religious conventions but a presumptuous desire to over-control. All three men want to control Alison, but she not only has a mind of her own but also knows when a joke has gone far enough. It is this combination of frank self-gratification with prudent self-restraint that the Miller seems to admire, and that the three men lack.

The Pardoner's subject is not love but religion. His function is to raise money for a charitable institution—in this case, a hospital—by selling papal indulgences. These were documents by which the church remitted some of the punishment that awaited sinners in purgatory by virtue of their charitable gifts. On no account, despite what this Pardoner says, did indulgences remit the guilt of sin: only Christ could do that. In his Prologue the Pardoner admits that he is a thorough rogue—indeed, he trumpets his viciousness, and his impenitent lack of concern for his own spiritual future, so loudly and so brazenly that we may think he protests too much. Even in the Prologue we get hints that the Pardoner harbors somewhere in his tortured soul the thought that he is, despite himself, doing God's work. And in fact the story he tells is one of the most brilliantly effective religious stories in all medieval literature. Generically it is an exemplum, one of those tales with which preachers would enliven their sermons. It demonstrates with an almost mathematical efficiency that the wages of sin are death, and it also provides us with a startling insight into the Pardoner himself. For he too is seeking the spiritual death of damnation, and in the figure of the eerie old man he expresses with painful vividness the common medieval understanding of damnation as a condition of perpetual dying, a dying that never finds death. In this complex character, Chaucer allows us to see the deep suffering endured by a man who mocks religious truths while simultaneously yearning for them.

The Canterbury Tales[1]

General Prologue

As soon as April pierces to the root
The drought of March, and bathes each bud and shoot
Through every vein of sap with gentle showers
From whose engendering liquor spring the flowers;
When zephyrs[2] have breathed softly all about   5
Inspiring every wood and field to sprout,
And in the zodiac the youthful sun
His journey halfway through the Ram[3] has run;
When little birds are busy with their song
Who sleep with open eyes the whole night long   10
Life stirs their hearts and tingles in them so,
Then off as pilgrims people long to go,
And palmers[4] to set out for distant strands
And foreign shrines renowned in many lands.
And specially in England people ride   15
To Canterbury from every countryside
To visit there the blessed martyred saint[5]
Who gave them strength when they were sick and faint.
    In Southwark at the Tabard[6] one spring day
It happened, as I stopped there on my way,   20
Myself a pilgrim with a heart devout
Ready for Canterbury to set out,
At night came all of twenty-nine assorted
Travelers, and to that same inn resorted,
Who by a turn of fortune chanced to fall   25
In fellowship together, and they were all
Pilgrims who had it in their minds to ride
Toward Canterbury. The stable doors were wide,
The rooms were large, and we enjoyed the best,
And shortly, when the sun had gone to rest,   30
I had so talked with each that presently
I was a member of their company
And promised to rise early the next day
To start, as I shall show, upon our way.
    But none the less, while I have time and space,   35
Before this tale has gone a further pace,
I should in reason tell you the condition
Of each of them, his rank and his position,
And also what array they all were in;
And so then, with a knight I will begin.   40
    A Knight was with us, and an excellent man,
Who from the earliest moment he began
To follow his career loved chivalry,
Truth, openhandedness, and courtesy.

---

1. Translated and edited by Theodore Morrison.   2. The west wind.   3. A sign of the zodiac (Aries).
The sun is in the Ram from March 12 to April 11.   4. Pilgrims, who, originally, brought back palm leaves
from the Holy Land.   5. St. Thomas à Becket, slain in Canterbury Cathedral in 1170.   6. An inn at
Southwark, across the river Thames from London.

He was a stout man in the king's campaigns   45
And in that cause had gripped his horse's reins
In Christian lands and pagan through the earth,
None farther, and always honored for his worth.
He was on hand at Alexandria's[7] fall.
He had often sat in precedence to all   50
The nations at the banquet board in Prussia.
He had fought in Lithuania and in Russia,
No Christian knight more often; he had been
In Moorish Africa at Benmarin,
At the siege of Algeciras in Granada,   55
And sailed in many a glorious armada
In the Mediterranean, and fought as well
At Ayas and Attalia when they fell
In Armenia and on Asia Minor's coast.
Of fifteen deadly battles he could boast,   60
And in Algeria, at Tremessen,
Fought for the faith and killed three separate men
In single combat. He had done good work
Joining against another pagan Turk
With the king of Palathia. And he was wise,   65
Despite his prowess, honored in men's eyes,
Meek as a girl and gentle in his ways.
He had never spoken ignobly all his days
To any man by even a rude inflection.
He was a knight in all things to perfection.   70
He rode a good horse, but his gear was plain,
For he had lately served on a campaign.
His tunic was still spattered by the rust
Left by his coat of mail, for he had just
Returned and set out on his pilgrimage.   75
    His son was with him, a young Squire, in age
Some twenty years as near as I could guess.
His hair curled as if taken from a press.
He was a lover and would become a knight.
In stature he was of a moderate height   80
But powerful and wonderfully quick.
He had been in Flanders, riding in the thick
Of forays in Artois and Picardy,
And bore up well for one so young as he,
Still hoping by his exploits in such places   85
To stand the better in his lady's graces.
He wore embroidered flowers, red and white,
And blazed like a spring meadow to the sight.
He sang or played his flute the livelong day.
He was as lusty as the month of May.   90
His coat was short, its sleeves were long and wide.
He sat his horse well, and knew how to ride,
And how to make a song and use his lance,
And he could write and draw well, too, and dance.

7. In Egypt, captured in 1365 by King Peter of Cyprus.

So hot his love that when the moon rose pale 95
He got no more sleep than a nightingale.
He was modest, and helped whomever he was able,
And carved as his father's squire at the table.

But one more servant had the Knight beside,
Choosing thus simply for the time to ride: 100
A Yeoman, in a coat and hood of green.
His peacock-feathered arrows, bright and keen,
He carried under his belt in tidy fashion.
For well-kept gear he had a yeoman's passion,
No draggled feather might his arrows show, 105
And in his hand he held a mighty bow.
He kept his hair close-cropped, his face was brown.
He knew the lore of woodcraft up and down.
His arm was guarded from the bowstring's whip
By a bracer, gaily trimmed. He had at hip 110
A sword and buckler, and at his other side
A dagger whose fine mounting was his pride,
Sharp-pointed as a spear. His horn he bore
In a sling of green, and on his chest he wore
A silver image of St. Christopher, 115
His patron, since he was a forester.

There was also a Nun, a Prioress,
Whose smile was gentle and full of guilelessness.
"By St. Loy!"[8] was the worst oath she would say.
She sang mass well, in a becoming way, 120
Intoning through her nose the words divine,
And she was known as Madame Eglantine.
She spoke good French, as taught at Stratford-Bow[9]
For the Parisian French she did not know.
She was schooled to eat so primly and so well 125
That from her lips no morsel ever fell.
She wet her fingers lightly in the dish
Of sauce, for courtesy was her first wish.
With every bite she did her skillful best
To see that no drop fell upon her breast. 130
She always wiped her upper lip so clean
That in her cup was never to be seen
A hint of grease when she had drunk her share.
She reached out for her meat with comely air.
She was a great delight, and always tried 135
To imitate court ways, and had her pride,
Both amiable and gracious in her dealings.
As for her charity and tender feelings,
She melted at whatever was piteous.
She would weep if she but came upon a mouse 140
Caught in a trap, if it were dead or bleeding.
Some little dogs that she took pleasure feeding
On roasted meat or milk or good wheat bread

8. Perhaps St. Eligius, apparently a popular saint at this time.   9. In Middlesex, near London, where
there was a nunnery.

She had, but how she wept to find one dead
Or yelping from a blow that made it smart,   145
And all was sympathy and loving heart.
Neat was her wimple in its every plait,
Her nose well formed, her eyes as gray as slate.
Her mouth was very small and soft and red.
She had so wide a brow I think her head   150
Was nearly a span broad, for certainly
She was not undergrown, as all could see.
She wore her cloak with dignity and charm,
And had her rosary about her arm,
The small beads coral and the larger green,   155
And from them hung a brooch of golden sheen,
On it a large A and a crown above;
Beneath, "All things are subject unto love."
      A Priest accompanied her toward Canterbury,
And an attendant Nun, her secretary.   160
      There was a Monk, and nowhere was his peer,
A hunter, and a roving overseer.
He was a manly man, and fully able
To be an abbot. He kept a hunting stable,
And when he rode the neighborhood could hear   165
His bridle jingling in the wind as clear
And loud as if it were a chapel bell.
Wherever he was master of a cell
The principles of good St. Benedict,[1]
For being a little old and somewhat strict,   170
Were honored in the breach, as past their prime.
He lived by the fashion of a newer time.
He would have swapped that text for a plucked hen
Which says that hunters are not holy men,
Or a monk outside his discipline and rule   175
Is too much like a fish outside his pool;
That is to say, a monk outside his cloister.
But such a text he deemed not worth an oyster.
I told him his opinion made me glad.
Why should he study always and go mad,   180
Mewed in his cell with only a book for neighbor?
Or why, as Augustine commanded, labor
And sweat his hands? How shall the world be served?
To Augustine be all such toil reserved!
And so he hunted, as was only right.   185
He had greyhounds as swift as birds in flight.
His taste was all for tracking down the hare,
And what his sport might cost he did not care.
His sleeves I noticed, where they met his hand,
Trimmed with gray fur, the finest in the land.   190
His hood was fastened with a curious pin
Made of wrought gold and clasped beneath his chin,
A love knot at the tip. His head might pass,

---

1. Monastic rules, authored by St. Maurus and St. Benedict in the 6th century.

Bald as it was, for a lump of shining glass,
And his face was glistening as if anointed.   195
Fat as a lord he was, and well appointed.
His eyes were large, and rolled inside his head
As if they gleamed from a furnace of hot lead.
His boots were supple, his horse superbly kept.
He was a prelate to dream of while you slept.   200
He was not pale nor peaked like a ghost.
He relished a plump swan as his favorite roast.
He rode a palfrey brown as a ripe berry.
    A Friar was with us, a gay dog and a merry,
Who begged his district with a jolly air.   205
No friar in all four orders could compare
With him for gallantry; his tongue was wooing.
Many a girl was married by his doing,
And at his own cost it was often done.
He was a pillar, and a noble one,   210
To his whole order. In his neighborhood
Rich franklins[2] knew him well, who served good food,
And worthy women welcomed him to town;
For the license that his order handed down,
He said himself, conferred on him possession   215
Of more than a curate's power of confession.
Sweetly the list of frailties he heard,
Assigning penance with a pleasant word.
He was an easy man for absolution
Where he looked forward to a contribution,   220
For if to a poor order a man has given
It signifies that he has been well shriven,
And if a sinner let his purse be dented
The Friar would stake his oath he had repented.
For many men become so hard of heart   225
They cannot weep, though conscience makes them smart.
Instead of tears and prayers, then, let the sinner
Supply the poor friars with the price of dinner.
For pretty women he had more than shrift.
His cape was stuffed with many a little gift,   230
As knives and pins and suchlike. He could sing
A merry note, and pluck a tender string,
And had no rival at all in balladry.
His neck was whiter than a fleur-de-lis,[3]
And yet he could have knocked a strong man down.   235
He knew the taverns well in every town.
The barmaids and innkeepers pleased his mind
Better than beggars and lepers and their kind.
In his position it was unbecoming
Among the wretched lepers to go slumming.   240
It mocks all decency, it sews no stitch
To deal with such riffraff, but with the rich,
With sellers of victuals, that's another thing.

2. Landowners or country squires, not belonging to the nobility.   3. Lily.

Wherever he saw some hope of profiting,
None so polite, so humble. He was good,   245
The champion beggar of his brotherhood.
Should a woman have no shoes against the snow,
So pleasant was his *"In principio"*[4]
He would have her widow's mite before he went.
He took in far more than he paid in rent   250
For his right of begging within certain bounds.
None of his brethren trespassed on his grounds!
He loved as freely as a half-grown whelp.
On arbitration-days[5] he gave great help,
For his cloak was never shiny nor threadbare   255
Like a poor cloistered scholar's. He had an air
As if he were a doctor or a pope.
It took stout wool to make his semicope[6]
That plumped out like a bell for portliness.
He lisped a little in his rakishness   260
To make his English sweeter on his tongue,
And twanging his harp to end some song he'd sung
His eyes would twinkle in his head as bright
As the stars twinkle on a frosty night.
Hubert this gallant Friar was by name.   265
   Among the rest a Merchant also came.
He wore a forked beard and a beaver hat
From Flanders. High up in the saddle he sat,
In figured cloth, his boots clasped handsomely,
Delivering his opinions pompously,   270
Always on how his gains might be increased.
At all costs he desired the sea policed[7]
From Middleburg in Holland to Orwell.[8]
He knew the exchange rates, and the time to sell
French currency, and there was never yet   275
A man who could have told he was in debt
So grave he seemed and hid so well his feelings
With all his shrewd engagements and close dealings.
You'd find no better man at any turn;
But what his name was I could never learn.   280
   There was an Oxford Student too, it chanced,
Already in his logic well advanced.
He rode a mount as skinny as a rake,
And he was hardly fat. For learning's sake
He let himself look hollow and sober enough.   285
He wore an outer coat of threadbare stuff,
For he had no benefice for his enjoyment
And was too unworldly for some lay employment.
He much preferred to have beside his bed
His twenty volumes bound in black or red   290
All packed with Aristotle from end to middle

---

4. In the beginning (Latin); the opening phrase of a famous passage in the New Testament (John 1.1–16), which the friar recites in Latin as a devotional exercise to awe the ignorant and extract their alms.   **5.** Days appointed for the adjustment of disputes.   **6.** A short cape.   **7.** For protection from piracy.   **8.** An English port near Harwich.

Than a sumptuous wardrobe or a merry fiddle.
For though he knew what learning had to offer
There was little coin to jingle in his coffer.
Whatever he got by touching up a friend   295
On books and learning he would promptly spend
And busily pray for the soul of anybody
Who furnished him the wherewithal for study.
His scholarship was what he truly heeded.
He never spoke a word more than was needed,   300
And that was said with dignity and force,
And quick and brief. He was of grave discourse
Giving new weight to virtue by his speech,
And gladly would he learn and gladly teach.

    There was a Lawyer, cunning and discreet,   305
Who had often been to St. Paul's porch[9] to meet
His clients. He was a Sergeant of the Law,
A man deserving to be held in awe,
Or so he seemed, his manner was so wise.
He had often served as Justice of Assize   310
By the king's appointment, with a broad commission,
For his knowledge and his eminent position.
He had many a handsome gift by way of fee.
There was no buyer of land as shrewd as he.
All ownership to him became fee simple.[1]   315
His titles were never faulty by a pimple.
None was so busy as he with case and cause,
And yet he seemed much busier than he was.
In all cases and decisions he was schooled
That were of record since King William[2] ruled.   320
No one could pick a loophole or a flaw
In any lease or contract he might draw.
Each statute on the books he knew by rote.
He traveled in a plain, silk-belted coat.

    A Franklin traveled in his company.   325
Whiter could never daisy petal[3] be
Than was his beard. His ruddy face gave sign
He liked his morning sop of toast in wine.
He lived in comfort, as he would assure us,
For he was a true son of Epicurus[4]   330
Who held the opinion that the only measure
Of perfect happiness was simply pleasure.
Such hospitality did he provide,
He was St. Julian[5] to his countryside.
His bread and ale were always up to scratch.   335
He had a cellar none on earth could match.
There was no lack of pasties in his house,
Both fish and flesh, and that so plenteous

---

9. A meeting place for lawyers and their clients in the porch of St. Paul's Cathedral, London. 1. Owned outright without legal impediments. 2. The Conqueror (reigned 1066–87). 3. The English daisy, a small white flower; not the same as the American. 4. Greek philosopher whose teaching (presented here in a somewhat debased form) is believed to make pleasure the goal of life. 5. Patron saint of hospitality.

That where he lived it snowed of meat and drink.
With every dish of which a man can think,   340
After the various seasons of the year,
He changed his diet for his better cheer.
He had coops of partridges as fat as cream,
He had a fishpond stocked with pike and bream.
Woe to his cook for an unready pot   345
Or a sauce that wasn't seasoned and spiced hot!
A table in his hall stood on display
Prepared and covered through the livelong day.
He presided at court sessions for his bounty
And sat in Parliament often for his county.   350
A well-wrought dagger and a purse of silk
Hung at his belt, as white as morning milk.
He had been a sheriff and county auditor.
On earth was no such rich proprietor!
    There were five Guildsmen, in the livery   355
Of one august and great fraternity,
A Weaver, a Dyer, and a Carpenter,
A Tapestry-maker and a Haberdasher.
Their gear was furbished new and clean as glass.
The mountings of their knives were not of brass   360
But silver. Their pouches were well made and neat,
And each of them, it seemed, deserved a seat
On the platform at the Guildhall, for each one
Was likely timber to make an alderman.
They had goods enough, and money to be spent,   365
Also their wives would willingly consent
And would have been at fault if they had not.
For to be "Madamed" is a pleasant lot,
And to march in first at feasts for being well married,
And royally to have their mantles carried.   370
    For the pilgrimage these Guildsmen brought their own
Cook to boil their chicken and marrow bone
With seasoning powder and capers and sharp spice.
In judging London ale his taste was nice.
He well knew how to roast and broil and fry,   375
To mix a stew, and bake a good meat pie,
Or capon creamed with almond, rice, and egg.
Pity he had an ulcer on his leg!
    A Skipper was with us, his home far in the west.
He came from the port of Dartmouth, as I guessed.   380
He sat his carthorse pretty much at sea
In a coarse smock that joggled on his knee.
From his neck a dagger on a string hung down
Under his arm. His face was burnished brown
By the summer sun. He was a true good fellow.   385
Many a time he had tapped a wine cask mellow
Sailing from Bordeaux while the owner slept.
Too nice a point of honor he never kept.
In a sea fight, if he got the upper hand,
Drowned prisoners floated home to every land.   390

But in navigation, whether reckoning tides,
Currents, or what might threaten him besides,
Harborage, pilotage, or the moon's demeanor,
None was his like from Hull to Cartagena.[6]
He knew each harbor and the anchorage there   395
From Gotland to the Cape of Finisterre[7]
And every creek in Brittany and Spain,
And he had called his ship the *Madeleine*.
      With us came also an astute Physician.
There was none like him for a disquisition   400
On the art of medicine or surgery,
For he was grounded in astrology.
He kept his patient long in observation,
Choosing the proper hour for application
Of charms and images by intuition   405
Of magic, and the planets' best position.
For he was one who understood the laws
That rule the humors, and could tell the cause
That brought on every human malady,
Whether of hot or cold, or moist or dry.   410
He was a perfect medico, for sure.
The cause once known, he would prescribe the cure
For he had his druggists ready at a motion
To provide the sick man with some pill or potion—
A game of mutual aid, with each one winning.   415
Their partnership was hardly just beginning!
He was well versed in his authorities,
Old Aesculapius, Dioscorides,
Rufus, and old Hippocrates, and Galen,
Haly, and Rhazes, and Serapion,   420
Averroës, Bernard, Johannes Damascenus,
Avicenna, Gilbert, Gaddesden, Constantinus.[8]
He urged a moderate fare on principle,
But rich in nourishment, digestible;
Of nothing in excess would he admit.   425
He gave but little heed to Holy Writ.
His clothes were lined with taffeta; their hue
Was all of blood red and of Persian blue,
Yet he was far from careless of expense.
He saved his fees from times of pestilence,   430
For gold is a cordial, as physicians hold,
And so he had a special love for gold.
      A worthy woman there was from near the city
Of Bath,[9] but somewhat deaf, and more's the pity.
For weaving she possessed so great a bent   435
She outdid the people of Ypres and of Ghent.[1]
No other woman dreamed of such a thing
As to precede her at the offering,

---

6. A Spanish port. Hull is an English port.   7. On the Spanish coast. Gotland is a Swedish island.
8. Eminent medical authorities from ancient Greece, ancient and medieval Arabic civilization, and England
in the 13th and 14th centuries.   9. A town in southwest England.   1. Towns in Flanders famous for
their cloth.

Or if any did, she fell in such a wrath
She dried up all the charity in Bath. 440
She wore fine kerchiefs of old-fashioned air,
And on a Sunday morning, I could swear,
She had ten pounds of linen on her head.
Her stockings were of finest scarlet-red,
Laced tightly, and her shoes were soft and new. 445
Bold was her face, and fair, and red in hue.
She had been an excellent woman all her life
Five men in turn had taken her to wife,
Omitting other youthful company—
But let that pass for now! Over the sea 450
She had traveled freely; many a distant stream
She crossed, and visited Jerusalem
Three times. She had been at Rome and at Boulogne,
At the shrine of Compostella, and at Cologne.[2]
She had wandered by the way through many a scene. 455
Her teeth were set with little gaps between.[3]
Easily on her ambling horse she sat.
She was well wimpled, and she wore a hat
As wide in circuit as a shield or targe.[4]
A skirt swathed up her hips, and they were large. 460
Upon her feet she wore sharp-roweled spurs.
She was a good fellow; a ready tongue was hers.
All remedies of love she knew by name,[5]
For she had all the tricks of that old game.

    There was a good man of the priests' vocation, 465
A poor town Parson of true consecration,
But he was rich in holy thought and work.
Learned he was, in the truest sense a clerk
Who meant Christ's gospel faithfully to preach
And truly his parishioners to teach. 470
He was a kind man, full of industry,
Many times tested by adversity
And always patient. If tithes[6] were in arrears,
He was loth to threaten any man with fears
Of excommunication; past a doubt 475
He would rather spread his offering about
To his poor flock, or spend his property.
To him a little meant sufficiency.
Wide was his parish, with houses far asunder,
But he would not be kept by rain or thunder, 480
If any had suffered a sickness or a blow,
From visiting the farthest, high or low
Plodding his way on foot, his staff in hand.
He was a model his flock could understand,
For first he did and afterward he taught. 485
That precept from the Gospel he had caught,

---

2. Sites of shrines much visited by pilgrims.   3. That is, gap-toothed; in a woman, considered a sign of
sexual prowess.   4. A small shield.   5. Chaucer has Ovid's *Love Cures* (*Remedia Amoris*) in mind.
6. Payments due to the priest, usually a tenth of annual income.

And he added as a metaphor thereto,
"If the gold rusts, what will the iron do?"
For if a priest is foul, in whom we trust,
No wonder a layman shows a little rust. 490
A priest should take to heart the shameful scene
Of shepherds filthy while the sheep are clean.
By his own purity a priest should give
The example to his sheep, how they should live.
He did not rent his benefice for hire,[7] 495
Leaving his flock to flounder in the mire,
And run to London, happiest of goals,
To sing paid masses in St. Paul's for souls,
Or as chaplain from some rich guild take his keep,
But dwelt at home and guarded well his sheep 500
So that no wolf should make his flock miscarry.
He was a shepherd, and not a mercenary.
And though himself a man of strict vocation
He was not harsh to weak souls in temptation,
Not overbearing nor haughty in his speech, 505
But wise and kind in all he tried to teach.
By good example and just words to turn
Sinners to heaven was his whole concern.
But should a man in truth prove obstinate,
Whoever he was, of rich or mean estate, 510
The Parson would give him a snub to meet the case.
I doubt there was a priest in any place
His better. He did not stand on dignity
Nor affect in conscience too much nicety,
But Christ's and his disciples' words he sought 515
To teach, and first he followed what he taught.
    There was a Plowman with him on the road,
His brother, who had forked up many a load
Of good manure. A hearty worker he,
Living in peace and perfect charity. 520
Whether his fortune made him smart or smile,
He loved God with his whole heart all the while
And his neighbor as himself. He would undertake,
For every luckless poor man, for the sake
Of Christ to thresh and ditch and dig by the hour 525
And with no wage, if it was in his power.
His tithes on goods and earnings he paid fair.
He wore a coarse, rough coat and rode a mare.
    There also were a Manciple, a Miller,
A Reeve, a Summoner, and a Pardoner,[8] 530
And I—this makes our company complete.
    As tough a yokel as you care to meet
The Miller was. His big-beefed arms and thighs
Took many a ram put up as wrestling prize.

---

7. Rent out his appointment to a substitute.   8. Dispenser of papal pardons. "Manciple": an officer in charge of supplies. "Reeve": farm overseer. "Summoner": one who summoned people to appear before the church court (presided over by the archdeacon) and in general acted as a kind of deputy sheriff of the court.

He was a thick, squat-shouldered lump of sins.   535
No door but he could heave it off its pins
Or break it running at it with his head.
His beard was broader than a shovel, and red
As a fat sow or fox. A wart stood clear
Atop his nose, and red as a pig's ear   540
A tuft of bristles on it. Black and wide
His nostrils were. He carried at his side
A sword and buckler. His mouth would open out
Like a great furnace, and he would sing and shout
His ballads and jokes of harlotries and crimes.   545
He could steal corn and charge for it three times,
And yet was honest enough, as millers come,
For a miller, as they say, has a golden thumb.
In white coat and blue hood this lusty clown,
Blowing his bagpipes, brought us out of town.   550
    The Manciple was of a lawyers' college,
And other buyers might have used his knowledge
How to be shrewd provisioners, for whether
He bought on cash or credit, altogether
He managed that the end should be the same: 555
He came out more than even with the game.
Now isn't it an instance of God's grace
How a man of little knowledge can keep pace
In wit with a whole school of learned men?
He had masters to the number of three times ten   560
Who knew each twist of equity and tort;
A dozen in that very Inn of Court
Were worthy to be steward of the estate
To any of England's lords, however great,
And keep him to his income well confined   565
And free from debt, unless he lost his mind,
Or let him scrimp, if he were mean in bounty;
They could have given help to a whole county
In any sort of case that might befall;
And yet this Manciple could cheat them all!   570
    The Reeve was a slender, fiery-tempered man.
He shaved as closely as a razor can.
His hair was cropped about his ears, and shorn
Above his forehead as a priest's is worn.
His legs were very long and very lean.   575
No calf on his lank spindles could be seen.
But he knew how to keep a barn or bin,
He could play the game with auditors and win.
He knew well how to judge by drought and rain
The harvest of his seed and of his grain.   580
His master's cattle, swine, and poultry flock,
Horses and sheep and dairy, all his stock,
Were altogether in this Reeve's control.
And by agreement, he had given the sole
Accounting since his lord reached twenty years.   585
No man could ever catch him in arrears.

There wasn't a bailiff, shepherd, or farmer working
But the Reeve knew all his tricks of cheating and shirking.
He would not let him draw an easy breath.
They feared him as they feared the very death. 590
He lived in a good house on an open space,
Well shaded by green trees, a pleasant place.
He was shrewder in acquisition than his lord.
With private riches he was amply stored.
He had learned a good trade young by work and will. 595
He was a carpenter of first-rate skill.
On a fine mount, a stallion, dappled gray.
Whose name was Scot, he rode along the way.
He wore a long blue coat hitched up and tied
As if it were a friar's, and at his side 600
A sword with rusty blade was hanging down.
He came from Norfolk, from nearby the town
That men call Bawdswell. As we rode the while,
The Reeve kept always hindmost in our file.
    A Summoner in our company had his place. 605
Red as the fiery cherubim[9] his face.
He was pocked and pimpled, and his eyes were narrow.
He was lecherous and hot as a cock sparrow.
His brows were scabby and black, and thin his beard.
His was a face that little children feared. 610
Brimstone or litharge bought in any quarter,
Quicksilver, ceruse, borax, oil of tartar,
No salve nor ointment that will cleanse or bite
Could cure him of his blotches, livid white,
Or the nobs and nubbins sitting on his cheeks. 615
He loved his garlic, his onions, and his leeks.
He loved to drink the strong wine down blood-red.
Then would he bellow as if he had lost his head.
And when he had drunk enough to parch his drouth,
Nothing but Latin issued from his mouth. 620
He had smattered up a few terms, two or three,
That he had gathered out of some decree—
No wonder; he heard law Latin all the day,
And everyone knows a parrot or a jay
Can cry out "Wat" or "Poll" as well as the pope; 625
But give him a strange term, he began to grope.
His little store of learning was paid out,
So *"Questio quod juris"*[1] he would shout.
He was a goodhearted bastard and a kind one.
If there were better, it was hard to find one. 630
He would let a good fellow, for a quart of wine,
The whole year round enjoy his concubine
Scot-free from summons, hearing, fine, or bail,
And on the sly he too could flush a quail.
If he liked a scoundrel, no matter for church law. 635

9. An order of angels; represented with red faces in medieval art.   1. The question is, what (part) of the law [applies] (Latin).

He would teach him that he need not stand in awe
If the archdeacon threatened with his curse—
That is, unless his soul was in his purse,
For in his purse he would be punished well.
"The purse," he said, "is the archdeacon's hell."   640
Of course I know he lied in what he said.
There is nothing a guilty man should so much dread
As the curse that damns his soul, when, without fail,
The church can save him, or send him off to jail.[2]
He had the young men and girls in his control   645
Throughout the diocese; he knew the soul
Of youth, and heard their every last design.
A garland big enough to be the sign
Above an alehouse balanced on his head,
And he made a shield of a great round loaf of bread.   650
    There was a Pardoner of Rouncivalle[3]
With him, of the blessed Mary's hospital,
But now come straight from Rome (or so said he).
Loudly he sang, "Come hither, love, to me,"
While the Summoner's counterbass trolled out profound—   655
No trumpet blew with half so vast a sound.
This Pardoner had hair as yellow as wax,
But it hung as smoothly as a hank of flax.
His locks trailed down in bunches from his head,
And he let the ends about his shoulders spread,   660
But in thin clusters, lying one by one.
Of hood, for rakishness, he would have none,
For in his wallet he kept it safely stowed.
He traveled, as he thought, in the latest mode,
Disheveled. Save for his cap, his head was bare,   665
And in his eyes he glittered like a hare.
A Veronica[4] was stitched upon his cap
His wallet lay before him in his lap
Brimful of pardons from the very seat
In Rome. He had a voice like a goat's bleat.   670
He was beardless and would never have a beard.
His cheek was always smooth as if just sheared.
I think he was a gelding or a mare;
But in this trade, from Berwick down to Ware,
No pardoner could beat him in the race,   675
For in his wallet he had a pillow case
Which he represented as Our Lady's veil;
He said he had a piece of the very sail
St. Peter, when he fished in Galilee
Before Christ caught him, used upon the sea.   680
He had a latten[5] cross embossed with stones

2. Lines 643–44 attempt to render the sense and tone of a passage in which Chaucer says literally that a guilty man should be in dread "because a curse will slay just as absolution saves, and he should also beware of a Significavit." This word, according to Robinson, was the first word of a writ remanding an excommunicated person to prison [translator's note].   3. A religious house near Charing Cross, now part of London: 4. A reproduction of the handkerchief bearing the miraculous impression of Christ's face, said to have been impressed on the handkerchief that St. Veronica gave him to wipe his face with on the way to his crucifixion.   5. An alloy of copper and zinc made to resemble brass.

And in a glass he carried some pig's bones,
And with these holy relics, when he found
Some village parson grubbing his poor ground,
He would get more money in a single day 685
Than in two months would come the parson's way.
Thus with his flattery and his trumped-up stock
He made dupes of the parson and his flock.
But though his conscience was a little plastic
He was in church a noble ecclesiastic. 690
Well could he read the Scripture or saint's story,
But best of all he sang the offertory,
For he understood that when this song was sung,
Then he must preach, and sharpen up his tongue
To rake in cash, as well he knew the art, 695
And so he sang out gaily, with full heart.
Now I have set down briefly, as it was,
Our rank, our dress, our number, and the cause
That many our sundry fellowship begin
In Southwark, at this hospitable inn 700
Known as the Tabard, nor far from the Bell.
But what we did that night I ought to tell,
And after that our journey, stage by stage,
And the whole story of our pilgrimage.
But first, in justice, do not look askance 705
I plead, nor lay it to my ignorance
If in this matter I should use plain speech
And tell you just the words and style of each,
Reporting all their language faithfully.
For it must be known to you as well as me 710
That whoever tells a story after a man
Must follow him as closely as he can.
If he takes the tale in charge, he must be true
To every word, unless he would find new
Or else invent a thing or falsify. 715
Better some breadth of language than a lie!
He may not spare the truth to save his brother.
He might as well use one word as another.
In Holy Writ Christ spoke in a broad sense
And surely his word is without offense. 720
Plato, if his pages you can read,
Says let the word be cousin to the deed.
So I petition your indulgence for it
If I have cut the cloth just as men wore it,
Here in this tale, and shown its very weave. 725
My wits are none too sharp, you must believe.
  Our Host gave each of us a cheerful greeting
And promptly of our supper had us eating.
The victuals that he served us were his best.
The wine was potent, and we drank with zest. 730
Our Host cut such a figure, all in all,
He might have been a marshal in a hall.
He was a big man, and his eyes bulged wide.

No sturdier citizen lived in all Cheapside,[6]
Lacking no trace of manhood, bold in speech,   735
Prudent, and well versed in what life can teach,
And with all this he was a jovial man.
And so when supper ended he began
To jolly us, when all our debts were clear.
"Welcome," he said. "I have not seen this year   740
So merry a company in this tavern as now,
And I would give you pleasure if I knew how.
And just this very minute a plan has crossed
My mind that might amuse you at no cost.
    "You go to Canterbury—may the Lord   745
Speed you, and may the martyred saint reward
Your journey! And to while the time away
You mean to talk and pass the time of day,
For you would be as cheerful all alone
As riding on your journey dumb as stone.   750
Therefore, if you'll abide by what I say,
Tomorrow, when you ride off on your way,
Now, by my father's soul, and he is dead,
If you don't enjoy yourselves, cut off my head!
Hold up your hands, if you accept my speech."   755
    Our counsel did not take us long to reach.
We bade him give his orders at his will.
"Well, sirs," he said, "then do not take it ill,
But hear me in good part, and for your sport.
Each one of you, to make our journey short,   760
Shall tell two stories, as we ride, I mean,
Toward Canterbury; and coming home again
Shall tell two other tales he may have heard
Of happenings that some time have occurred.
And the one of you whose stories please us most,   765
Here in this tavern, sitting by this post
Shall sup at our expense while we make merry
When we come riding home from Canterbury.
And to cheer you still the more, I too will ride
With you at my own cost, and be your guide.   770
And if anyone my judgment shall gainsay
He must pay for all we spend along the way.
If you agree, no need to stand and reason.
Tell me, and I'll be stirring in good season."
    This thing was granted, and we swore our pledge   775
To take his judgment on our pilgrimage,
His verdict on our tales, and his advice.
He was to plan a supper at a price
Agreed upon; and so we all assented
To his command, and we were well contented.   780
The wine was fetched; we drank, and went to rest.
    Next morning, when the dawn was in the east,

6. A London street.

Up spring our Host, who acted as our cock,
And gathered us together in a flock,
And off we rode, till presently our pace 785
Had brought us to St. Thomas' watering place.
And there our Host began to check his horse.
"Good sirs," he said, "you know your promise, of course.
Shall I remind you what it was about?
If evensong and matins don't fall out, 790
We'll soon find who shall tell us the first tale.
But as I hope to drink my wine and ale,
Whoever won't accept what I decide
Pays everything we spend along the ride.
Draw lots, before we're farther from the Inn. 795
Whoever draws the shortest shall begin.
Sir Knight," said he, "my master, choose your straw.
Come here, my lady Prioress, and draw,
And you, Sir Scholar, don't look thoughtful, man!
Pitch in now, everyone!" So all began 800
To draw the lots, and as the luck would fall
The draw went to the Knight, which pleased us all.
And when this excellent man saw how it stood,
Ready to keep his promise, he said, "Good!
Since it appears that I must start the game, 805
Why then, the draw is welcome, in God's name.
Now let's ride on, and listen, what I say."
And with that word we rode forth on our way,
And he, with his courteous manner and good cheer,
Began to tell his tale, as you shall hear. 810

The Miller's Prologue and Tale

The Prologue

When the Knight had finished,[1] no one, young or old,
In the whole company, but said he had told
A noble story, one that ought to be
Preserved and kept alive in memory,
Especially the gentlefolk, each one. 5
Our good Host laughed, and swore, "The game's begun,
The ball is rolling! This is going well.
Let's see who has another tale to tell.
Come, match the Knight's tale if you can, Sir Monk!"
    The Miller, who by this time was so drunk 10
He looked quite bloodless, and who hardly sat
His horse, he was never one to doff his hat
Or stand on courtesy for any man.
Like Pilate in the Church plays[2] he began

1. "The Knight's Tale" is the first told, immediately following the "General Prologue."   2. Miracle plays represented Pilate as a braggart and loudmouth. His lines were marked by frequent alliteration.

To bellow. "Arms and blood and bones," he swore,   15
"I know a yarn that will even up the score,
A noble one, I'll pay off the Knight's tale!"
    Our Host could see that he was drunk on ale.
"Robin," he said, "hold on a minute, brother.
Some better man shall come first with another.   20
Let's do this right. You tell yours by and by."
    "God's soul," the Miller told him, "that won't I!
Either I'll speak, or go on my own way."
    "The devil with you! Say what you have to say,"
Answered our Host. "You are a fool. Your head   25
Is overpowered."
                "Now," the Miller said,
"Everyone listen! But first I will propound
That I am drunk, I know it by my sound.
If I can't get my words out, put the blame
On Southwark ale, I ask you, in God's name!   30
For I'll tell a golden legend and a life
Both of a carpenter and of his wife,
How a student put horns on the fellow's head."
    "Shut up and stop your racket," the Reeve said.
"Forget your ignorant drunken bawdiness.   35
It is a sin and a great foolishness
To injure any man by defamation
And to give women such a reputation.
Tell us of other things; you'll find no lack."
    Promptly this drunken Miller answered back: 40
"Oswald, my brother, true as babes are suckled,
The man who has no wife, he is no cuckold.
I don't say for this reason that you are.
There are plenty of faithful wives, both near and far,
Always a thousand good for every bad,   45
And you know this yourself, unless you're mad.
I see you are angry with my tale, but why?
You have a wife; no less, by God, do I.
But I wouldn't, for the oxen in my plow,
Shoulder more than I need by thinking how   50
I may myself, for aught I know, be one.
I'll certainly believe that I am none.
A husband mustn't be curious, for his life,
About God's secrets or about his wife.
If she gives him plenty and he's in the clover,   55
No need to worry about what's left over."
    The Miller, to make the best of it I can,
Refused to hold his tongue for any man,
But told his tale like any low-born clown.
I am sorry that I have to set it down,   60
And all you people, for God's love, I pray,
Whose taste is higher, do not think I say
A word with evil purpose; I must rehearse
Their stories one and all, both better and worse,
Or play false with my matter, that is clear.   65

Whoever, therefore, may not wish to hear,
Turn over the page and choose another tale;
For small and great, he'll find enough, no fail,
Of things from history, touching courtliness,
And virtue too, and also holiness.   70
If you choose wrong, don't lay it on my head.
You know the Miller couldn't be called well bred.
So with the Reeve, and many more as well,
And both of them had bawdy tales to tell.
Reflect a little, and don't hold me to blame.   75
There's no sense making earnest out of game.

The Tale

There used to be a rich old oaf who made
His home at Oxford, a carpenter by trade,
And took in boarders. With him used to dwell
A student who had done his studies well,
But he was poor; for all that he had learned,   5
It was toward astrology his fancy turned.
He knew a number of figures and constructions
By which he could supply men with deductions
If they should ask him at a given hour
Whether to look for sunshine or for shower,   10
Or want to know whatever might befall,
Events of all sorts, I can't count them all.
   He was known as handy Nicholas,[3] this student.
Well versed in love, he knew how to be prudent,
Going about unnoticed, sly, and sure.   15
In looks no girl was ever more demure.
Lodged at this carpenter's, he lived alone;
He had a room there that he made his own,
Festooned with herbs, and he was sweet himself
As licorice or ginger. On a shelf   20
Above his bed's head, neatly stowed apart,
He kept the trappings that went with his art,
His astrolabe, his books—among the rest,
Thick ones and thin ones, lay his *Almagest*[4]—
And the counters for his abacus as well.   25
Over his cupboard a red curtain fell
And up above a pretty zither lay
On which at night so sweetly would he play
That with the music the whole room would ring.
"Angelus to the Virgin" he would sing   30
And then the song that's known as "The King's Note."
Blessings were called down on his merry throat!
So this sweet scholar passed his time, his end
Being to eat and live upon his friend.

---

3. Chaucer's word is hendë, implying, I take it, both *ready to hand* and *ingratiating*. Nicholas was a Johnny-on-the-spot and also had a way with him [translator's note].   4. A 2nd-century treatise by Ptolemy, an astronomy textbook.

This carpenter had newly wed a wife   35
And loved her better than he loved his life.
He was jealous, for she was eighteen in age;
He tried to keep her close as in a cage,
For she was wild and young, and old was he
And guessed that he might smack of cuckoldry.   40
His ignorant wits had never chanced to strike
On Cato's[5] word, that man should wed his like;
Men ought to wed where their conditions point,
For youth and age are often out of joint.
But now, since he had fallen in the snare,   45
He must, like other men, endure his care.
    Fair this young woman was, her body trim
As any mink, so graceful and so slim.
She wore a striped belt that was all of silk;
A piece-work apron, white as morning milk,   50
About her loins and down her lap she wore.
White was her smock, her collar both before
And on the back embroidered all about
In coal-black silk, inside as well as out.
And like her collar, her white-laundered bonnet   55
Had ribbons of the same embroidery on it.
Wide was her silken fillet, worn up high,
And for a fact she had a willing eye.
She plucked each brow into a little bow,
And each one was as black as any sloe.   60
She was a prettier sight to see by far
Than the blossoms of the early pear tree are,
And softer than the wool of an old wether.
Down from her belt there hung a purse of leather
With silken tassels and with studs of brass.   65
No man so wise, wherever people pass,
Who could imagine in this world at all
A wench like her, the pretty little doll!
Far brighter was the dazzle of her hue
Than a coin struck in the Tower,[6] fresh and new.   70
As for her song, it twittered from her head
Sharp as a swallow perching on a shed.
And she could skip and sport as a young ram
Or calf will gambol, following his dam.
Her mouth was sweet as honey-ale or mead   75
Or apples in the hay, stored up for need.
She was as skittish as an untrained colt,
Slim as a mast and straighter than a bolt.
On her simple collar she wore a big brooch-pin
Wide as a shield's boss underneath her chin.   80
High up along her legs she laced her shoes.
She was a pigsney, she was a primrose
For any lord to tumble in his bed
Or a good yeoman honestly to wed.

5. Dionysius Cato, the supposed author of a book of maxims employed in elementary education.
6. That is, minted in the Tower of London.

Now sir, and again sir, this is how it was: 85
A day came round when handy Nicholas,
While her husband was at Oseney,⁷ well away,
Began to fool with this young wife, and play.
These students always have a wily head.
He caught her in between the legs, and said, 90
"Sweetheart, unless I have my will with you
I'll die for stifled love, by all that's true,"
And held her by the haunches, hard. "I vow
I'll die unless you love me here and now,
Sure as my soul," he said, "is God's to save." 95
She shied just as a colt does in the trave,⁸
And turned her head hard from him, this young wife,
And said, "I will not kiss you, on my life.
Why, stop it now," she said, "stop, Nicholas,
Or I will cry out 'Help, help,' and 'Alas!' 100
Be good enough to take your hands away."
    "Mercy," this Nicholas began to pray,
And spoke so well and poured it on so fast
She promised she would be his love at last,
And swore by Thomas à Becket, saint of Kent, 105
That she would serve him when she could invent
Or spy out some good opportunity.
"My husband is so full of jealousy
You must be watchful and take care," she said,
"Or well I know I'll be as good as dead. 110
You must go secretly about this business."
    "Don't give a thought to that," said Nicholas.
"A student has been wasting time at school
If he can't make a carpenter a fool."
And so they were agreed, these two, and swore 115
To watch their chance, as I have said before.
When Nicholas had spanked her haunches neatly
And done all I have spoken of, he sweetly
Gave her a kiss, and then he took his zither
And loudly played, and sang his music with her. 120
    Now in her Christian duty, one saint's day,
To the parish church this good wife made her way,
And as she went her forehead cast a glow
As bright as noon, for she had washed it so
It glistened when she finished with her work. 125
    Serving this church there was a parish clerk
Whose name was Absolom, a ruddy man
With goose-gray eyes and curls like a great fan
That shone like gold on his neatly parted head.
His tunic was light blue and his nose red, 130
And he had patterns that had been cut through
Like the windows of St. Paul's in either shoe.
He wore above his tunic, fresh and gay,
A surplice white as a blossom on a spray.

7. A town near Oxford.   8. A wooden frame confining a horse being shod.

A merry devil, as true as God can save,   135
He knew how to let blood, trim hair, and shave,
Or write a deed of land in proper phrase,
And he could dance in twenty different ways
In the Oxford fashion, and sometimes he would sing
A loud falsetto to his fiddle string   140
Or his guitar. No tavern anywhere
But he had furnished entertainment there.
Yet his speech was delicate, and for his part
He was a little squeamish toward a fart.
    This Absolom, so jolly and so gay,   145
With a censer went about on the saint's day
Censing the parish women one and all.
Many the doting look that he let fall,
And specially on this carpenter's young wife.
To look at her, he thought, was a good life,   150
She was so trim, so sweetly lecherous.
I dare say that if she had been a mouse
And he a cat, he would have made short work
Of catching her. This jolly parish clerk
Had such a heartful of love-hankerings   155
He would not take the women's offerings;
No, no, he said, it would not be polite.
    The moon, when darkness fell, shone full and bright
And Absolom was ready for love's sake
With his guitar to be up and awake,   160
And toward the carpenter's, brisk and amorous,
He made his way until he reached the house
A little after the cocks began to crow.
Under a casement he sang sweet and low,
"Dear lady, by your will, be kind to me,"   165
And strummed on his guitar in harmony.
This lovelorn singing woke the carpenter
Who said to his wife, "What, Alison, don't you hear
Absolom singing under our bedroom wall?"
    "Yes, God knows, John," she answered, "I hear it all." 170
    What would you like? In this way things went on
Till jolly Absolom was woebegone
For wooing her, awake all night and day.
He combed his curls and made himself look gay.
He swore to be her slave and used all means   175
To court her with his gifts and go-betweens.
He sang and quavered like a nightingale.
He sent her sweet spiced wine and seasoned ale,
Cakes that were piping hot, mead sweet with honey,
And since she was town-bred, he proffered money.   180
For some are won by wealth, and some no less
By blows, and others yet by gentleness.
    Sometimes, to keep his talents in her gaze,
He acted Herod⁹ in the mystery plays

---

9. A role traditionally played as a bully in the Miracle plays.

High on the stage. But what can help his case? 185
For she so loves this handy Nicholas
That Absolom is living in a bubble.
He has nothing but a laugh for all his trouble.
She leaves his earnestness for scorn to cool
And makes this Absolom her proper fool. 190
For this is a true proverb, and no lie;
"It always happens that the nigh and sly
Will let the absent suffer." So 'tis said,
And Absolom may rage or lose his head
But just because he was farther from her sight 195
This nearby Nicholas got in his light.
　　Now hold your chin up, handy Nicholas,
For Absolom may wail and sing "Alas!"
One Saturday when the carpenter had gone
To Oseney, Nicholas and Alison 200
Agreed that he should use his wit and guile
This simple jealous husband to beguile.
And if it happened that the game went right
She would sleep in his arms the livelong night,
For this was his desire and hers as well. 205
At once, with no more words, this Nicholas fell
To working out his plan. He would not tarry,
But quietly to his room began to carry
Both food and drink to last him out a day,
Or more than one, and told her what to say 210
If her husband asked her about Nicholas.
She must say she had no notion where he was;
She hadn't laid eyes on him all day long;
He must be sick, or something must be wrong;
No matter how her maid had called and cried 215
He wouldn't answer, whatever might betide.
　　This was the plan, and Nicholas kept away,
Shut in his room, for that whole Saturday.
He ate and slept or did as he thought best
Till Sunday, when the sun was going to rest, 220
This carpenter began to wonder greatly
Where Nicholas was and what might ail him lately,
"Now, by St. Thomas, I begin to dread
All isn't right with Nicholas," he said.
"He hasn't, God forbid, died suddenly! 225
The world is ticklish these days, certainly.
Today I saw a corpse to church go past,
A man that I saw working Monday last!
Go up," he told his chore-boy, "call and shout,
Knock with a stone, find what it's all about 230
And let me know."
　　　　　　　　The boy went up and pounded
And yelled as if his wits had been confounded.
"What, how, what's doing, Master Nicholas?
How can you sleep all day?" But all his fuss
Was wasted, for he could not hear a word. 235

He noticed at the bottom of a board
A hole the cat used when she wished to creep
Into the room, and through it looked in deep
And finally of Nicholas caught sight.
This Nicholas sat gaping there upright   240
As though his wits were addled by the moon
When it was new. The boy went down, and soon
Had told his master how he had seen the man.
    The carpenter, when he heard this news, began
To cross himself. "Help us, St. Frideswide!   245
Little can we foresee what may betide!
The man's astronomy has turned his wit,
Or else he's in some agonizing fit.
I always knew that it would turn out so.
What God has hidden is not for men to know.   250
Aye, blessed is the ignorant man indeed,
Blessed is he that only knows his creed!
So fared another scholar of the sky,
For walking in the meadows once to spy
Upon the stars and what they might foretell,   255
Down in a clay-pit suddenly he fell!
He overlooked that! By St. Thomas, though,
I'm sorry for handy Nicholas. I'll go
And scold him roundly for his studying
If so I may, by Jesus, heaven's king!   260
Give me a staff, I'll pry up from the floor
While you, Robin, are heaving at the door.
He'll quit his books, I think."
                            He took his stand
Outside the room. The boy had a strong hand
And by the hasp he heaved it off at once.   265
The door fell flat. With gaping countenance
This Nicholas sat studying the air
As still as stone. He was in black despair,
The carpenter believed, and hard about
The shoulders caught and shook him, and cried out   270
Rudely, "What, how! What is it? Look down at us!
Wake up, think of Christ's passion, Nicholas!
I'll sign you with the cross to keep away
These elves and things!" And he began to say,
Facing the quarters of the house, each side,   275
And on the threshold of the door outside,
The night-spell: "Jesu and St. Benedict
From every wicked thing this house protect . . ."
    Choosing his time, this handy Nicholas
Produced a dreadful sigh, and said, "Alas,   280
This world, must it be all destroyed straightway?"
    "What," asked the carpenter, "what's that you say?
Do as we do, we working men, and think
Of God."
            Nicholas answered, "Get me a drink,
And afterwards I'll tell you privately   285

Of something that concerns us, you and me.
I'll tell you only, you among all men."
   This carpenter went down and came again
With a draught of mighty ale, a generous quart.
As soon as each of them had drunk his part   290
Nicholas shut the door and made it fast
And sat down by the carpenter at last
And spoke to him. "My host," he said, "John dear,
You must swear by all that you hold sacred here
That not to any man will you betray   295
My confidence. What I'm about to say
Is Christ's own secret. If you tell a soul
You are undone, and this will be the toll:
If you betray me, you shall go stark mad."
   "Now Christ forbid it, by His holy blood,"   300
Answered this simple man. "I don't go blabbing.
If I say it myself, I have no taste for gabbing.
Speak up just as you like, I'll never tell,
Not wife nor child, by Him that harrowed hell."[1]
   "Now, John," said Nicholas, "this is no lie.   305
I have discovered through astrology,
And studying the moon that shines so bright
That Monday next, a quarter through the night,
A rain will fall, and such a mad, wild spate
That Noah's flood was never half so great.   310
This world," he said, "in less time than an hour
Shall drown entirely in that hideous shower.
Yes, every man shall drown and lose his life."
   "Alas," the carpenter answered, "for my wife!
Alas, my Alison! And shall she drown?"   315
For grief at this he nearly tumbled down,
And said, "But is there nothing to be done?"
   "Why, happily there is, for anyone
Who will take advice," this handy Nicholas said.
"You mustn't expect to follow your own head.   320
For what said Solomon, whose words were true?
'Proceed by counsel, and you'll never rue.'
If you will act on good advice, no fail,
I'll promise, and without a mast or sail,
To see that she's preserved, and you and I.   325
Haven't you heard how Noah was kept dry
When, warned by Christ beforehand, he discovered
That the whole earth with water should be covered?"
   "Yes," said the carpenter, "long, long ago."
   "And then again," said Nicholas, "don't you know   330
The grief they all had trying to embark
Till Noah could get his wife into the Ark?[2]

---

1. That is, Christ, who descended into hell and led away Adam, Eve, the patriarchs, John the Baptist, and others, redeeming and releasing them. It was the subject of a number of Miracle plays. The original story comes from the Apocryphal New Testament.   2. A stock comedy scene in the mystery plays, of which the carpenter would have been an avid spectator [translator's note].

That was a time when Noah, I dare say,
Would gladly have given his best black wethers away
If she could have had a ship herself alone.   335
And therefore do you know what must be done?
This demands haste, and with a hasty thing
People can't stop for talk and tarrying.
    "Start out and get into the house right off
For each of us a tub or kneading-trough,   340
Above all making sure that they are large,
In which we'll float away as in a barge.
And put in food enough to last a day.
Beyond won't matter; the flood will fall away
Early next morning. Take care not to spill   345
A word to your boy Robin, nor to Jill
Your maid. I cannot save her, don't ask why.
I will not tell God's secrets, no, not I.
Let it be enough, unless your wits are mad,
To have as good a grace as Noah had.   350
I'll save your wife for certain, never doubt it.
Now go along, and make good time about it.
    "But when you have, for her and you and me,
Brought to the house these kneading-tubs, all three,
Then you must hang them under the roof, up high,   355
To keep our plans from any watchful eye.
When you have done exactly as I've said,
And put in snug our victuals and our bread,
Also an ax to cut the ropes apart
So when the rain comes we can make our start,   360
And when you've broken a hole high in the gable
Facing the garden plot, above the stable,
To give us a free passage out, each one,
Then, soon as the great fall of rain is done,
You'll swim as merrily, I undertake,   365
As the white duck paddles along behind her drake.
Then I shall call, 'How, Alison! How, John!
Be cheerful, for the flood will soon be gone.'
And 'Master Nicholas, what ho!' you'll say.
'Good morning, I see you clearly, for it's day.'   370
Then we shall lord it for the rest of life
Over the world, like Noah and his wife.
    "But one thing I must warn you of downright.
Use every care that on that selfsame night
When we have taken ship and climbed aboard,   375
No one of us must speak a single word,
Nor call, nor cry, but pray with all his heart.
It is God's will. You must hang far apart,
You and your wife, for there must be no sin
Between you, no more in a look than in   380
The very deed. Go now, the plans are drawn.
Go, set to work, and may God spur you on!
Tomorrow night when all men are asleep

Into our kneading-troughs we three shall creep
And sit there waiting, and abide God's grace.   385
Go along now, this isn't the time or place
For me to talk at length or sermonize.
The proverb says, 'Don't waste words on the wise.'
You are so wise there is no need to teach you.
Go, save our lives—that's all that I beseech you!"   390
   This simple carpenter went on his way.
Many a time he said, "Alack the day,"
And to his wife he laid the secret bare.
She knew it better than he; she was aware
What this quaint bargain was designed to buy.   395
She carried on as if about to die,
And said, "Alas, go get this business done.
Help us escape, or we are dead, each one.
I am your true, your faithful wedded wife.
Go, my dear husband, save us, limb and life!"   400
   Great things, in all truth, can the emotions be!
A man can perish through credulity
So deep the print imagination makes.
This simple carpenter, he quails and quakes.
He really sees, according to his notion,   405
Noah's flood come wallowing like an ocean
To drown his Alison, his pet, his dear.
He weeps and wails, and gone is his good cheer,
And wretchedly he sighs. But he goes off
And gets himself a tub, a kneading-trough,   410
Another tub, and has them on the sly
Sent home, and there in secret hangs them high
Beneath the roof. He made three ladders, these
With his own hands, and stowed in bread and cheese
And a jug of good ale, plenty for a day.   415
Before all this was done, he sent away
His chore-boy Robin and his wench likewise
To London on some trumped-up enterprise,
And so on Monday, when it drew toward night,
He shut the door without a candlelight   420
And saw that all was just as it should be,
And shortly they went clambering up, all three.
They sat there still, and let a moment pass.
   "Now then, 'Our Father,' mum!" said Nicholas,
And "Mum!" said John, and "Mum!" said Alison,   425
And piously this carpenter went on
Saying his prayers. He sat there still and straining,
Trying to make out whether he heard it raining.
   The dead of sleep, for very weariness,
Fell on this carpenter, as I should guess,   430
At about curfew time, or little more.
His head was twisted, and that made him snore.
His spirit groaned in its uneasiness.
Down from his ladder slipped this Nicholas,

And Alison too, downward she softly sped   435
And without further word they went to bed
Where the carpenter himself slept other nights.
There were the revels, there were the delights!
And so this Alison and Nicholas lay
Busy about their solace and their play   440
Until the bell for lauds began to ring
And in the chancel friars began to sing.
   Now on this Monday, woebegone and glum
For love, this parish clerk, this Absolom
Was with some friends at Oseney, and while there   445
Inquired after John the carpenter.
A member of the cloister drew him away
Out of the church, and told him, "I can't say.
I haven't seen him working hereabout
Since Saturday. The abbot sent him out   450
For timber, I suppose. He'll often go
And stay at the granary a day or so.
Or else he's at his own house, possibly.
I can't for certain say where he may be."
   Absolom at once felt jolly and light,   455
And thought, "Time now to be awake all night,
For certainly I haven't seen him making
A stir about his door since day was breaking.
Don't call me a man if when I hear the cock
Begin to crow I don't slip up and knock   460
On the low window by his bedroom wall.
To Alison at last I'll pour out all
My love-pangs, for at this point I can't miss,
Whatever happens, at the least a kiss.
Some comfort, by my word, will come my way.   465
I've felt my mouth itch the whole livelong day,
And that's a sign of kissing at the least.
I dreamed all night that I was at a feast.
So now I'll go and sleep an hour or two,
And then I'll wake and play the whole night through."   470
   When the first cockcrow through the dark had come
Up rose this jolly lover Absolom
And dressed up smartly. He was not remiss
About the least point. He chewed licorice
And cardamom to smell sweet, even before   475
He combed his hair. Beneath his tongue he bore
A sprig of Paris[3] like a truelove knot.
He strolled off to the carpenter's house, and got
Beneath the window. It came so near the ground
It reached his chest. Softly, with half a sound,   480
He coughed, "My honeycomb, sweet Alison,
What are you doing, my sweet cinnamon?
Awake, my sweetheart and my pretty bird,
Awake, and give me from your lips a word!

---

3. A cloverlike plant.

Little enough you care for all my woe,   485
How for your love I sweat wherever I go!
No wonder I sweat and faint and cannot eat
More than a girl; as a lamb does for the teat
I pine. Yes, truly, I so long for love
I mourn as if I were a turtledove."   490
    Said she, "You jack-fool, get away from here!
So help me God, I won't sing 'Kiss me, dear!'
I love another more than you. Get on,
For Christ's sake, Absolom, or I'll throw a stone.
The devil with you! Go and let me sleep."   495
    "Ah, that true love should ever have to reap
So evil a fortune," Absolom said. "A kiss,
At least, if it can be no more than this,
Give me, for love of Jesus and of me."
    "And will you go away for that?" said she.   500
    "Yes, truly, sweetheart," answered Absolom.
    "Get ready then," she said, "for here I come,"
And softly said to Nicholas, "Keep still,
And in a minute you can laugh your fill."
This Absolom got down upon his knee   505
And said, "I am a lord of pure degree,
For after this, I hope, comes more to savor.
Sweetheart, your grace, and pretty bird, your favor!"
    She undid the window quickly. "That will do,"
She said. "Be quick about it, and get through,   510
For fear the neighbors will look out and spy."
    Absolom wiped his mouth to make it dry.
The night was pitch dark, coal-black all about.
Her rear end through the window she thrust out.
He got no better or worse, did Absolom,   515
Than to kiss her with his mouth on the bare bum
Before he had caught on, a smacking kiss.
    He jumped back, thinking something was amiss.
A woman had no beard, he was well aware,
But what he felt was rough and had long hair.   520
    "Alas," he cried, "what have you made me do?"
    "Te-hee!" she said, and banged the window to.
    Absolom backed away a sorry pace.
    "You've bearded him!" said handy Nicholas.
"God's body, this is going fair and fit!"   525
    This luckless Absolom heard every bit,
And gnawed his mouth, so angry he became.
He said to himself, "I'll square you, all the same."
    But who now scrubs and rubs, who chafes his lips
With dust, with sand, with straw, with cloth and chips   530
If not this Absolom? "The devil," says he,
"Welcome my soul if I wouldn't rather be
Revenged than have the whole town in a sack!
Alas," he cries, "if only I'd held back!"
His hot love had become all cold and ashen.   535
He didn't have a curse to spare for passion

From the moment when he kissed her on the ass.
That was the cure to make his sickness pass!
He cried as a child does after being whipped;
He railed at love. Then quietly he slipped   540
Across the street to a smith who was forging out
Parts that the farmers needed round about.
He was busy sharpening colter[4] and plowshare
When Absolom knocked as though without a care.
    "Undo the door, Jervice, and let me come."   545
    "What? Who are you?"
                            "It is I, Absolom."
    "Absolom, is it! By Christ's precious tree,
Why are you up so early? Lord bless me,
What's ailing you? Some gay girl has the power
To bring you out, God knows, at such an hour!   550
Yes, by St. Neot, you know well what I mean!"
    Absolom thought his jokes not worth a bean.
Without a word he let them all go by.
He had another kind of fish to fry
Than Jervice guessed. "Lend me this colter here   555
That's hot in the chimney, friend," he said. "Don't fear,
I'll bring it back right off when I am through.
I need it for a job I have to do."
    "Of course," said Jervice. "Why, if it were gold
Or coins in a sack, uncounted and untold,   560
As I'm a rightful smith, I wouldn't refuse it.
But, Christ's foot! how on earth do you mean to use it?"
    "Let that," said Absolom, "be as it may.
I'll let you know tomorrow or next day,"
And took the colter where the steel was cold   565
And slipped out with it safely in his hold
And softly over to the carpenter's wall.
He coughed and then he rapped the window, all
As he had done before.
                        "Who's knocking there?"
Said Alison. "It is a thief, I swear."   570
    "No, no," said he. "God knows, my sugarplum,
My bird, my darling, it's your Absolom.
I've brought a golden ring my mother gave me,
Fine and well cut, as I hope that God will save me.
It's yours, if you will let me have a kiss."   575
    Nicholas had got up to take a piss
And thought he would improve the whole affair.
This clerk, before he got away from there,
Should give *his* ass a smack; and hastily
He opened the window, and thrust out quietly,   580
Buttocks and haunches, all the way, his bum.
Up spoke this clerk, this jolly Absolom:
"Speak, for I don't know where you are, sweetheart."
    Nicholas promptly let fly with a fart

---

4. A turf cutter on a plow.

As loud as if a clap of thunder broke,   585
So great he was nearly blinded by the stroke,
And ready with his hot iron to make a pass,
Absolom caught him fairly on the ass.
 Off flew the skin, a good handbreadth of fat
Lay bare, the iron so scorched him where he sat.   590
As for the pain, he thought that he would die,
And like a madman he began to cry.
"Help! Water! Water! Help, for God's own heart!"
 At this the carpenter came to with a start.
He heard a man cry "Water!" as if mad.   595
"It's coming now," was the first thought he had.
"It's Noah's flood, alas, God be our hope!"
He sat up with his ax and chopped the rope
And down at once the whole contraption fell.
He didn't take time out to buy or sell   600
Till he hit the floor and lay there in a swoon.
 Then up jumped Nicholas and Alison
And in the street began to cry, "Help, ho!"
The neighbors all came running, high and low,
And poured into the house to see the sight.   605
The man still lay there, passed out cold and white,
For in his tumble he had broken an arm.
But he himself brought on his greatest harm,
For when he spoke he was at once outdone
By handy Nicholas and Alison   610
Who told them one and all that he was mad.
So great a fear of Noah's flood he had,
By some delusion, that in his vanity
He had bought himself these kneading-troughs, all three.
And hung them from the roof there, up above,   615
And he had pleaded with them, for God's love,
To sit there in the loft for company.
 The neighbors laughed at such a fantasy,
And round the loft began to pry and poke
And turned his whole disaster to a joke.   620
He found it was no use to say a word.
Whatever reason he offered, no one heard.
With oaths and curses people swore him down
Until he passed for mad in the whole town.
Wit, clerk, and student all stood by each other.   625
They said, "It's clear the man is crazy, brother."
Everyone had his laugh about this feud.
So Alison, the carpenter's wife, got screwed
For all the jealous watching he could try,
And Absolom, he kissed her nether eye,   630
And Nicholas got his bottom roasted well.
God save this troop! That's all I have to tell.

The Pardoner's Prologue and Tale

The Prologue

"In churches," said the Pardoner, "when I preach,
I use, milords, a lofty style of speech
And ring it out as roundly as a bell,
Knowing by rote all that I have to tell.
My text is ever the same, and ever was: 5
Radix malorum est cupiditas.[1]
   "First I inform them whence I come; that done,
I then display my papal bulls, each one.
I show my license first, my body's warrant,
Sealed by the bishop, for it would be abhorrent   10
If any man made bold, though priest or clerk,
To interrupt me in Christ's holy work.
And after that I give myself full scope.
Bulls in the name of cardinal and pope,
Of bishops and of patriarchs I show.   15
I say in Latin some few words or so
To spice my sermon; it flavors my appeal
And stirs my listeners to greater zeal.
Then I display my cases made of glass
Crammed to the top with rags and bones. They pass   20
For relics with all the people in the place.
I have a shoulder bone in a metal case,
Part of a sheep owned by a holy Jew.
'Good men,' I say, 'heed what I'm telling you:
Just let this bone be dipped in any well   25
And if cow, calf, or sheep, or ox should swell
From eating a worm, or by a worm be stung,
Take water from this well and wash its tongue
And it is healed at once. And furthermore
Of scab and ulcers and of every sore   30
Shall every sheep be cured, and that straightway,
That drinks from the same well. Heed what I say:
If the good man who owns the beasts will go,
Fasting, each week, and drink before cockcrow
Out of this well, his cattle shall be brought   35
To multiply—that holy Jew so taught
Our elders—and his property increase.
   "'Moreover, sirs, this bone cures jealousies.
Though into a jealous madness a man fell,
Let him cook his soup in water from this well,   40
He'll never, though for truth he knew her sin,
Suspect his wife again, though she took in
A priest, or even two of them or three.
   "'Now here's a mitten that you all can see.
Whoever puts his hand in it shall gain,   45
When he sows his land, increasing crops of grain,

---

1. The root of evil is greed (Latin).

Be it wheat or oats, provided that he bring
His penny or so to make his offering.
   " 'There is one word of warning I must say,
Good men and women. If any here today   50
Has done a sin so horrible to name
He daren't be shriven of it for the shame,
Or if any woman, young or old, is here
Who has cuckolded her husband, be it clear
They may not make an offering in that case   55
To these my relics; they have no power nor grace.
But any who is free of such dire blame,
Let him come up and offer in God's name
And I'll absolve him through the authority
That by the pope's bull has been granted me.'   60
   "By such hornswoggling I've won, year by year,
A hundred marks[2] since being a pardoner.
I stand in my pulpit like a true divine,
And when the people sit I preach my line
To ignorant souls, as you have heard before,   65
And tell skullduggeries by the hundred more.
Then I take care to stretch my neck well out
And over the people I nod and peer about
Just like a dove perching on a shed.
My hands fly and my tongue wags in my head   70
So busily that to watch me is a joy.
Avarice is the theme that I employ
In all my sermons, to make the people free
In giving pennies—especially to me.
My mind is fixed on what I stand to win   75
And not at all upon correcting sin.
I do not care, when they are in the grave,
If souls go berry-picking that I could save.
Truth is that evil purposes determine,
And many a time, the origin of a sermon: 80
Some to please people and by flattery
To gain advancement through hypocrisy,
Some for vainglory, some again for hate.
For when I daren't fight otherwise, I wait
And give him a tongue-lashing when I preach.   85
No man escapes or gets beyond the reach
Of my defaming tongue, supposing he
Has done a wrong to my brethren or to me.
For though I do not tell his proper name,
People will recognize him all the same.   90
By sign and circumstance I let them learn.
Thus I serve those who have done us an ill turn.
Thus I spit out my venom under hue
Of sanctity, and seem devout and true!
   "But to put my purpose briefly, I confess   95
I preach for nothing but for covetousness.

---

2. Probably the equivalent of several thousand dollars.

That's why my text is still and ever was
Radix malorum est cupiditas.
For by this text I can denounce, indeed,
The very vice I practice, which is greed.   100
But though that sin is lodged in my own heart,
I am able to make other people part
From avarice, and sorely to repent,
Though that is not my principal intent.
    "Then I bring in examples, many a one,   105
And tell them many a tale of days long done.
Plain folk love tales that come down from of old.
Such things their minds can well report and hold.
Do you think that while I have the power to preach
And take in silver and gold for what I teach   110
I shall ever live in willful poverty?
No, no, that never was my thought, certainly.
I mean to preach and beg in sundry lands.
I won't do any labor with my hands,
Nor live by making baskets. I don't intend   115
To beg for nothing; that is not my end.
I won't ape the apostles; I must eat,
I must have money, wool, and cheese, and wheat,
Though I took it from the meanest wretch's tillage
Or from the poorest widow in a village,   120
Yes, though her children starved for want. In fine,
I mean to drink the liquor of the vine
And have a jolly wench in every town.
But, in conclusion, lords, I will get down
To business: you would have me tell a tale.   125
Now that I've had a drink of corny ale,
By God, I hope the thing I'm going to tell
Is one that you'll have reason to like well.
For though myself a very sinful man,
I can tell a moral tale, indeed I can,   130
One that I use to bring the profits in
While preaching. Now be still, and I'll begin."

The Tale

There was a company of young folk living
One time in Flanders, who were bent on giving
Their lives to follies and extravagances,
Brothels and taverns, where they held their dances
With lutes, harps, and guitars, diced at all hours,   5
And also ate and drank beyond their powers,
Through which they paid the devil sacrifice
In the devil's temple with their drink and dice,
Their abominable excess and dissipation.
They swore oaths that were worthy of damnation;   10
It was grisly to be listening when they swore.
The blessed body of our Lord they tore—
The Jews, it seemed to them, had failed to rend

His body enough—and each laughed at his friend
And fellow in sin. To encourage their pursuits   15
Came comely dancing girls, peddlers of fruits,
Singers with harps, bawds and confectioners
Who are the very devil's officers
To kindle and blow the fire of lechery
That is the follower of gluttony.   20
   Witness the Bible, if licentiousness
Does not reside in wine and drunkenness!
Recall how drunken Lot, unnaturally,
With his two daughters lay unwittingly,
So drunk he had no notion what he did.[3]   25
   Herod, the stories tell us, God forbid,
When full of liquor at his banquet board
Right at his very table gave the word
To kill the Baptist, John, though guiltless he.[4]
   Seneca says a good word, certainly.   30
He says there is no difference he can find
Between a man who has gone out of his mind
And one who carries drinking to excess,
Only that madness outlasts drunkenness.[5]
O gluttony, first cause of mankind's fall,[6]   35
Of our damnation the cursed original
Until Christ bought us with his blood again!
How dearly paid for by the race of men
Was this detestable iniquity!
This whole world was destroyed through gluttony.   40
   Adam our father and his wife also
From paradise to labor and to woe
Were driven for that selfsame vice, indeed.
As long as Adam fasted—so I read—
He was in heaven; but as soon as he   45
Devoured the fruit of that forbidden tree
Then he was driven out in sorrow and pain.
Of gluttony well ought we to complain!
Could a man know how many maladies
Follow indulgences and gluttonies   50
He would keep his diet under stricter measure
And sit at table with more temperate pleasure.
The throat is short and tender is the mouth,
And hence men toil east, west, and north, and south,
In earth, and air, and water—alas to think—   55
Fetching a glutton dainty meat and drink.
   This is a theme, O Paul, that you well treat:
"Meat unto belly, and belly unto meat,
God shall destroy them both," as Paul has said.[7]
When a man drinks the white wine and the red—   60
This is a foul word, by my soul, to say,
And fouler is the deed in every way—
He makes his throat his privy through excess.

3. Genesis 19.33–35.   4. Matthew 14.1–11; Mark 6.14–28.   5. Seneca's *Epistles* 83.   6. Because
the fall was caused by eating the forbidden fruit.   7. I Corinthians 6.13.

The Apostle says, weeping for piteousness,
"There are many of whom I told you—at a loss   65
I say it, weeping—enemies of Christ's cross,
Whose belly is their god; their end is death."[8]
O cursed belly! Sack of stinking breath
In which corruption lodges, dung abounds!
At either end of you come forth foul sounds.   70
Great cost it is to fill you, and great pain!
These cooks, how they must grind and pound and strain
And transform substance into accident[9]
To please your cravings, though exorbitant!
From the hard bones they knock the marrow out.   75
They'll find a use for everything, past doubt,
That down the gullet sweet and soft will glide.
The spiceries of leaf and root provide
Sauces that are concocted for delight,
To give a man a second appetite.   80
But truly, he whom gluttonies entice
Is dead, while he continues in that vice.
    O drunken man, disfigured is your face,
Sour is your breath, foul are you to embrace!
You seem to mutter through your drunken nose   85
The sound of "Samson, Samson," yet God knows
That Samson never indulged himself in wine.[1]
Your tongue is lost, you fall like a stuck swine,
And all the self-respect that you possess
Is gone, for of man's judgment, drunkenness   90
Is the very sepulcher and annihilation.
A man whom drink has under domination
Can never keep a secret in his head.
Now steer away from both the white and red,
And most of all from that white wine keep wide   95
That comes from Lepe.[2] They sell it in Cheapside
And Fish Street. It's a Spanish wine, and sly
To creep in other wines that grow nearby,
And such a vapor it has that with three drinks
It takes a man to Spain; although he thinks   100
He is home in Cheapside, he is far away
At Lepe. Then "Samson, Samson" will he say!
    By God himself, who is omnipotent,
All the great exploits in the Old Testament
Were done in abstinence, I say, and prayer.   105
Look in the Bible, you may learn it there.
    Attila,[3] conqueror of many a place,
Died in his sleep in shame and in disgrace
Bleeding out of his nose in drunkenness.
A captain ought to live in temperateness!   110
And more than this, I say, remember well

---

8. Philippians 3.18–19.   9. A distinction was made in philosophy between "substance," the real nature of a thing, and "accident," its merely sensory qualities, such as flavor (see also Dante's *Paradiso* 33.88 ff.)
1. Judges 13.4.   2. A town in Spain noted for strong wines.   3. Leader of the Hun invasion of Europe, 5th century.

The injunction that was laid on Lemuel[4]—
Not Samuel, but Lemuel, I say!
Read in the Bible; in the plainest way
Wine is forbidden to judges and to kings.   115
This will suffice; no more upon these things.
    Now that I've shown what gluttony will do,
Now I will warn you against gambling, too;
Gambling, the very mother of low scheming,
Of lying and forswearing and blaspheming   120
Against Christ's name, of murder and waste as well
Alike of goods and time; and, truth to tell,
With honor and renown it cannot suit
To be held a common gambler by repute.
The higher a gambler stands in power and place,   125
The more his name is lowered in disgrace.
If a prince gambles, whatever his kingdom be,
In his whole government and policy
He is, in all the general estimation,
Considered so much less in reputation.   130
    Stilbon, who was a wise ambassador,
From Lacedaemon once to Corinth bore
A mission of alliance. When he came
It happened that he found there at a game
Of hazard all the great ones of the land,   135
And so, as quickly as it could be planned,
He stole back, saying, "I will not lose my name
Nor have my reputation put to shame
Allying you with gamblers. You may send
Other wise emissaries to gain your end,   140
For by my honor, rather than ally
My countrymen to gamblers, I will die.
For you that are so gloriously renowned
Shall never with this gambling race be bound
By will of mine or treaty I prepare."   145
Thus did this wise philosopher declare.
    Remember also how the Parthians' lord
Sent King Demetrius, as the books record,
A pair of golden dice, by this proclaiming
His scorn, because that king was known for gaming,   150
And the king of Parthia therefore held his crown
Devoid of glory, value, or renown.
Lords can discover other means of play
More suitable to while the time away.
    Now about oaths I'll say a word or two,   155
Great oaths and false oaths, as the old books do.
Great swearing is a thing abominable,
And false oaths yet more reprehensible.
Almighty God forbade swearing at all,
Matthew be witness;[5] but specially I call   160
The holy Jeremiah on this head.

4. Proverbs 31.4–7.   5. Matthew 5.34.

"Swear thine oaths truly, do not lie," he said.
"Swear under judgment, and in righteousness."[6]
But idle swearing is a great wickedness.
Consult and see, and he that understands   165
In the first table of the Lord's commands
Will find the second of his commandments this:
"Take not the Lord's name idly or amiss."
If a man's oaths and curses are extreme,
Vengeance shall find his house, both roof and beam.   170
"By the precious heart of God," and "By his nails"—
"My chance is seven, by Christ's blood at Hailes,[7]
Yours five and three." "Cheat me, and if you do,
By God's arms, with this knife I'll run you through!"—
Such fruit comes from the bones,[8] that pair of bitches: 175
Oaths broken, treachery, murder. For the riches
Of Christ's love, give up curses, without fail,
Both great and small!—Now, sirs, I'll tell my tale.
      These three young roisterers of whom I tell
Long before prime had rung from any bell   180
Were seated in a tavern at their drinking,
And as they sat, they heard a bell go clinking
Before a corpse being carried to his grave.
One of these roisterers, when he heard it, gave
An order to his boy: "Go out and try   185
To learn whose corpse is being carried by.
Get me his name, and get it right. Take heed."
      "Sir," said the boy, "there isn't any need.
I learned before you came here, by two hours.
He was, it happens, an old friend of yours,   190
And all at once, there on his bench upright
As he was sitting drunk, he was killed last night.
A sly thief, Death men call him, who deprives
All the people in this country of their lives,
Came with his spear and smiting his heart in two   195
Went on his business with no more ado.
A thousand have been slaughtered by his hand
During this plague. And, sir, before you stand
Within his presence, it should be necessary,
It seems to me, to know your adversary.   200
Be evermore prepared to meet this foe.
My mother taught me thus; that's all I know."
      "Now by St. Mary," said the innkeeper,
"This child speaks truth. Man, woman, laborer,
Servant, and child the thief has slain this year   205
In a big village a mile or more from here.
I think it is his place of habitation.
It would be wise to make some preparation
Before he brought a man into disgrace."

---

6. Jeremiah 4.2   7. An abbey in Gloucestershire, where some of Christ's blood was believed to be preserved. "Chance": lucky number.   8. Dice.

"God's arms!" this roisterer said. "So that's the case! 210
Is it so dangerous with this thief to meet?
I'll look for him by every path and street,
I vow it, by God's holy bones! Hear me,
Fellows of mine, we are all one, we three.
Let each of us hold up his hand to the other 215
And each of us become his fellow's brother.
We'll slay this Death, who slaughters and betrays.
He shall be slain whose hand so many slays,
By the dignity of God, before tonight!"
    The three together set about to plight 220
Their oaths to live and die each for the other
Just as though each had been to each born brother,
And in their drunken frenzy up they get
And toward the village off at once they set
Which the innkeeper had spoken of before, 225
And many were the grisly oaths they swore.
They rent Christ's precious body limb from limb—
Death shall be dead, if they lay hands on him!
    When they had hardly gone the first half mile,
Just as they were about to cross a stile, 230
An old man, poor and humble, met them there.
The old man greeted them with a meek air
And said, "God bless you, lords, and be your guide."
    "What's this?" the proudest of the three replied.
"Old beggar, I hope you meet with evil grace! 235
Why are you all wrapped up except your face?
What are you doing alive so many a year?"
    The old man at these words began to peer
Into this gambler's face. "Because I can,
Though I should walk to India, find no man," 240
He said, "in any village or any town,
Who for my age is willing to lay down
His youth. So I must keep my old age still
For as long a time as it may be God's will.
Nor will Death take my life from me, alas! 245
Thus like a restless prisoner I pass
And on the ground, which is my mother's gate,
I walk and with my staff both early and late
I knock and say, 'Dear mother, let me in!
See how I vanish, flesh, and blood, and skin! 250
Alas, when shall my bones be laid to rest?
I would exchange with you my clothing chest,
Mother, that in my chamber long has been
For an old haircloth rag to wrap me in.'
And yet she still refuses me that grace. 255
All white, therefore, and withered is my face.
    "But, sirs, you do yourselves no courtesy
To speak to an old man so churlishly
Unless he had wronged you either in word or deed.
As you yourselves in Holy Writ may read, 260
'Before an aged man whose head is hoar

Men ought to rise."[9] I counsel you, therefore,
No harm nor wrong here to an old man do,
No more than you would have men do to you
In your old age, if you so long abide.   265
And God be with you, whether you walk or ride!
I must go yonder where I have to go."
    "No, you old beggar, by St. John, not so,"
Said another of these gamblers. "As for me,
By God, you won't get off so easily!   270
You spoke just now of that false traitor, Death,
Who in this land robs all our friends of breath.
Tell where he is, since you must be his spy,
Or you will suffer for it, so say I
By God and by the holy sacrament.   275
You are in league with him, false thief, and bent
On killing us young folk, that's clear to my mind."
    "If you are so impatient, sirs, to find
Death," he replied, "turn up this crooked way,
For in that grove I left him, truth to say,   280
Beneath a tree, and there he will abide.
No boast of yours will make him run and hide.
Do you see that oak tree? Just there you will find
This Death, and God, who bought again mankind,
Save and amend you!" So said this old man;   285
And promptly each of these three gamblers ran
Until he reached the tree, and there they found
Florins of fine gold, minted bright and round,
Nearly eight bushels of them, as they thought.
And after Death no longer then they sought.   290
Each of them was so ravished at the sight,
So fair the florins glittered and so bright,
That down they sat beside the precious hoard.
The worst of them, he uttered the first word.
    "Brothers," he told them, "listen to what I say.   295
My head is sharp, for all I joke and play.
Fortune has given us this pile of treasure
To set us up in lives of ease and pleasure.
Lightly it comes, lightly we'll make it go.
God's precious dignity! Who was to know   300
We'd ever tumble on such luck today?
If we could only carry this gold away,
Home to my house, or either one of yours—
For well you know that all this gold is ours—
We'd touch the summit of felicity.   305
But still, by daylight that can hardly be.
People would call us thieves, too bold for stealth,
And they would have us hanged for our own wealth.
It must be done by night, that's our best plan,
As prudently and slyly as we can.   310
Hence my proposal is that we should all

9. Leviticus 19.32.

Draw lots, and let's see where the lot will fall,
And the one of us who draws the shortest stick
Shall run back to the town, and make it quick,
And bring us bread and wine here on the sly,   315
And two of us will keep a watchful eye
Over this gold; and if he doesn't stay
Too long in town, we'll carry this gold away
By night, wherever we all agree it's best."
    One of them held the cut out in his fist   320
And had them draw to see where it would fall,
And the cut fell on the youngest of them all.
At once he set off on his way to town,
And the very moment after he was gone
The one who urged this plan said to the other: 325
"You know that by sworn oath you are my brother.
I'll tell you something you can profit by.
Our friend has gone, that's clear to any eye,
And here is gold, abundant as can be,
That we propose to share alike, we three.   330
But if I worked it out, as I could do,
So that it could be shared between us two,
Wouldn't that be a favor, a friendly one?"
    The other answered, "How that can be done,
I don't quite see. He knows we have the gold.   335
What shall we do, or what shall he be told?"
    "Will you keep the secret tucked inside your head?
And in a few words," the first scoundrel said,
"I'll tell you how to bring this end about."
    "Granted," the other told him. "Never doubt,   340
I won't betray you, that you can believe."
    "Now," said the first, "we are two, as you perceive,
And two of us must have more strength than one.
When he sits down, get up as if in fun
And wrestle with him. While you play this game   345
I'll run him through the ribs. You do the same
With your dagger there, and then this gold shall be
Divided, dear friend, between you and me.
Then all that we desire we can fulfill,
And both of us can roll the dice at will."   350
Thus in agreement these two scoundrels fell
To slay the third, as you have heard me tell.
    The youngest, who had started off to town,
Within his heart kept rolling up and down
The beauty of those florins, new and bright.   355
"O Lord," he thought, "were there some way I might
Have all this treasure to myself alone,
There isn't a man who dwells beneath God's throne
Could live a life as merry as mine should be!"
And so at last the fiend, our enemy,   360
Put in his head that he could gain his ends
If he bought poison to kill off his friends.
Finding his life in such a sinful state,

The devil was allowed to seal his fate.
For it was altogether his intent   365
To kill his friends, and never to repent.
So off he set, no longer would he tarry,
Into the town, to an apothecary,
And begged for poison; he wanted it because
He meant to kill his rats; besides, there was   370
A polecat living in his hedge, he said,
Who killed his capons; and when he went to bed
He wanted to take vengeance, if he might,
On vermin that devoured him by night.
　　The apothecary answered, "You shall have   375
A drug that as I hope the Lord will save
My soul, no living thing in all creation,
Eating or drinking of this preparation
A dose no bigger than a grain of wheat,
But promptly with his death-stroke he shall meet. 380
Die, that he will, and in a briefer while
Than you can walk the distance of a mile,
This poison is so strong and virulent."
　　Taking the poison, off the scoundrel went,
Holding it in a box, and next he ran   385
To the neighboring street, and borrowed from a man
Three generous flagons. He emptied out his drug
In two of them, and kept the other jug
For his own drink; he let no poison lurk
In that! And so all night he meant to work   390
Carrying off the gold. Such was his plan,
And when he had filled them, this accursed man
Retraced his path, still following his design,
Back to his friends with his three jugs of wine.
　　But why dilate upon it any more?   395
For just as they had planned his death before,
Just so they killed him, and with no delay.
When it was finished, one spoke up to say:
"Now let's sit down and drink, and we can bury
His body later on. First we'll be merry,"   400
And as he said the words, he took the jug
That, as it happened, held the poisonous drug,
And drank, and gave his friend a drink as well,
And promptly they both died. But truth to tell,
In all that Avicenna[1] ever wrote   405
He never described in chapter, rule, or note
More marvelous signs of poisoning, I suppose,
Than appeared in these two wretches at the close.
Thus they both perished for their homicide,
And thus the traitorous poisoner also died.   410
　　O sin accursed above all cursedness,
O treacherous murder, O foul wickedness,
O gambling, lustfulness, and gluttony,

---

1. An Arab physician.

Traducer of Christ's name by blasphemy
And monstrous oaths, through habit and through pride!   415
Alas, mankind! Ah, how may it betide
That you to your Creator, he that wrought you
And even with his precious heart's blood bought you,
So falsely and ungratefully can live?
    And now, good men, your sins may God forgive   420
And keep you specially from avarice!
My holy pardon will avail in this,
For it can heal each one of you that brings
His pennies, silver brooches, spoons, or rings.
Come, bow your head under this holy bull!   425
You wives, come offer up your cloth or wool!
I write your names here in my roll, just so.
Into the bliss of heaven you shall go!
I will absolve you here by my high power,
You that will offer, as clean as in the hour   430
When you were born.—Sirs, thus I preach. And now
Christ Jesus, our souls' healer, show you how
Within his pardon evermore to rest,
For that, I will not lie to you, is best.
    But in my tale, sirs, I forgot one thing.   435
The relics and the pardons that I bring
Here in my pouch, no man in the whole land
Has finer, given me by the pope's own hand.
If any of you devoutly wants to offer
And have my absolution, come and proffer   440
Whatever you have to give. Kneel down right here,
Humbly, and take my pardon, full and clear,
Or have a new, fresh pardon if you like
At the end of every mile of road we strike,
As long as you keep offering ever newly   445
Good coins, not counterfeit, but minted truly.
Indeed it is an honor I confer
On each of you, an authentic pardoner
Going along to absolve you as you ride.
For in the country mishaps may betide—   450
One or another of you in due course
May break his neck by falling from his horse.
Think what security it gives you all
That in this company I chanced to fall
Who can absolve you each, both low and high,   455
When the soul, alas, shall from the body fly!
By my advice, our Host here shall begin,
For he's the man enveloped most by sin.
Come, offer first, Sir Host, and once that's done,
Then you shall kiss the relics, every one,   460
Yes, for a penny! Come, undo your purse!
    "No, no," said he. "Then I should have Christ's curse!
I'll do nothing of the sort, for love or riches!
You'd make me kiss a piece of your old britches
And for a saintly relic make it pass   465

Although it had the tincture of your ass.
By the cross St. Helen[2] found in the Holy Land,
I wish I had your balls here in my hand
For relics! Cut 'em off, and I'll be bound
If I don't help you carry them around.   470
I'll have the things enshrined in a hog's turd!"
    The Pardoner did not answer; not a word,
He was so angry, could he find to say.
    "Now," said our Host, "I will not try to play
With you, nor any other angry man."   475
    Immediately the worthy Knight began,
When he saw that all the people laughed, "No more,
This has gone far enough. Now as before,
Sir Pardoner, be gay, look cheerfully,
And you, Sir Host, who are so dear to me,   480
Come, kiss the Pardoner, I beg of you,
And Pardoner, draw near, and let us do
As we've been doing, let us laugh and play."
And so they kissed, and rode along their way.

---

2. Mother of Constantine the Great; believed to have found the true cross.

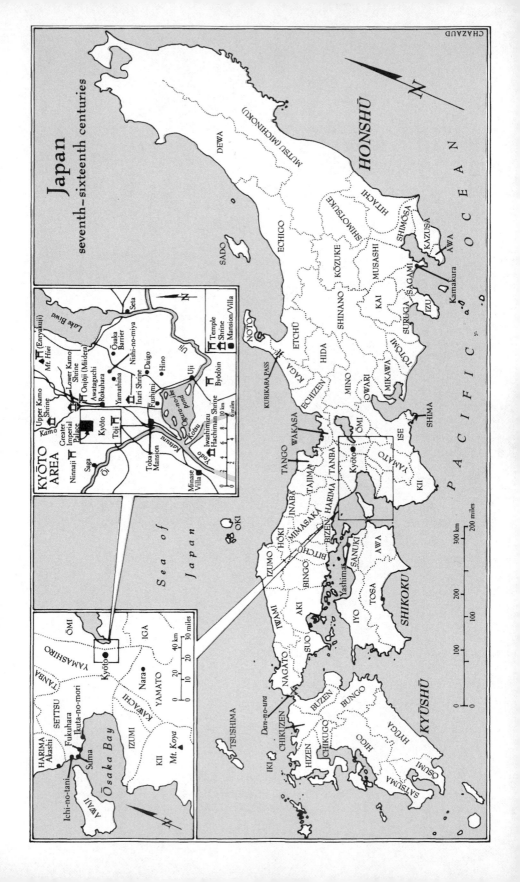

The Golden Age of Japanese Culture

Japan's economy, though weakened considerably in recent years, is one of the miracles of modern times. The material fortunes and technological output of Japan impinge so forcefully on our lives today, however, that they tend to crowd out all other considerations of Japan. Due in part to the barrier of language and, for much of history, a degree of geographical isolation, it is less well known that Japan has also produced one of the world's richest cultures. The first novel was written in Japan almost a thousand years ago. *The Tale of Genji* is a work that can still stand beside the finest accomplishments in fiction. One of poetry's most evocative and influential forms, *haiku*—a flash of insight expressed in a sliver of verse—is also a Japanese creation. Japanese woodblock prints had a profound influence on the French Impressionists, and the design of the traditional Japanese house, when discovered by Le Corbusier, Frank Lloyd Wright, and others in the twentieth century, helped determine the course of modern architecture.

Yet despite Japan's cultural achievements and their worldwide impact, two clichés haunt Western attitudes toward Japan. The first is that Japan is a small country with a homogeneous population. Japan is small only in one sense. The total land mass of the Japanese archipelago, which consists of four principal islands plus some thousand smaller ones, altogether would not fill the state of California. The gross domestic product, on the other hand, is the third largest in the world, and Japan has the tenth highest population—127 million people—in the world. A common myth about these 127 million people (and a myth to which the Japanese themselves subscribe) is that they constitute a singularly homogeneous group, one "tribe" moving in lockstep. Although Japan may lack the racial and ethnic diversity of a country like the United States, by no means are its citizens all cast from the same mold. As the selections printed here demonstrate, the Japanese speak with many voices, and the weight of their cultural output down through the centuries makes their voices anything but small.

The second stereotype is that Japan is a nation of imitators. This commonplace derives from the fact that it has been Japan's peculiar destiny to have lived at the edge of two great and contrasting traditions—Chinese civilization from the sixth century until the mid-nineteenth and Western modernity thereafter—always managing to accommodate influence while retaining the stamp of its own identity. Far from being a cultural parasite, Japan has demonstrated a genius for knowing when and what to learn from others. Furthermore, the Japanese have always been too vigorous a people to sit back and let someone else invent their culture for them. The same streak of perfectionism that defined Japanese quality control in business seems to have compelled Japan to improve perpetually on the original, whether it be Confucian theories of government or Henry Ford's assembly line. Nor should we let this agility as a cultural transformer obscure Japan's own creativity. The tea ceremony, the multicolor woodblock print, *kabuki*, *haiku*, and *sumo* all spring from native soil.

Yet in the sweep of history this is a newcomer, and twice in its existence Japan has found itself having to catch up. While the empires of Mesopotamia and ancient Egypt rose and fell and the civilizations of Greece, India, and China came to flower, the inhabitants of the Japanese islands remained hunters and gatherers. Their ancestors probably migrated to Japan in several waves, some from the Asian continent and others from the islands to the south. In the third century B.C.E. a new influx brought rice cultivation, and the Japanese exchanged a nomadic way of life for an agricultural one; they settled villages in the miniature plains nestled between the mountains and the sea. But the wanderers' past left its mark on Japanese civilization: an ingrained sense of the impermanence of things; an acute awareness of the changes brought by the seasons; a taste for the spare, the unrefined, the natural—even when prodigious artifice would sometimes be required to produce something "natural."

The new techniques of cultivating wet rice, one of the world's most labor-intensive crops, taught the Japanese people economy in the use of space and the advantages of cooperation. The latter, in turn, gave rise to the long-standing ideal in Japan that it is best to submit individual will to the greater needs of the group—the origin, perhaps, of the notion that the Japanese form a homogeneous and harmonious whole. This was no more true in 300 B.C.E. than it is today, for along with agriculture came bronze and iron; along with metallurgy came weapons; and with weapons, war. In other words, very early on another trait of Japanese culture surfaced: rule by warrior elites, precursors of the *samurai*. A class of martial aristocrats competed for power over the thickly settled countryside of the southern and central islands, until one clan succeeded in asserting its predominance, thereby establishing the imperial line.

The new governors quickly imported the superior fruits of Chinese civilization, which, by the seventh and eighth centuries, represented the most powerful, most advanced, and best administered country in the world. Having consolidated their hold over rival clans, the fledgling rulers claimed authority by absorbing Chinese theories of sovereignty and a centralized state, along with the economic and political apparatus—land surveys, districting, taxation, law codes, and bureaucratic management—to make their bold ambition work.

In many ways, the Japanese succeeded, though the political history of premodern Japan is ultimately the story of how the Chinese model proved a poor fit. It was a system that has been described by historians as a form of agricultural communism, with land divided equally among the population (and taxed uniformly) to ensure maximum returns. China's theory of government was profoundly egalitarian. The emperor reigned as an absolute sovereign, but his administrators were chosen on the basis of ability through an examination system that not only emphasized learning but fostered a true meritocracy. The emperor's bureaucrats thus provided the talent and diversity to help him rule impartially.

But the temperament and earliest traditions of the Japanese inclined them in a very different direction. Kinship ties from tribal times persisted in the emphasis of family and lineage, so that when Japan decided to adapt the Chinese model of bureaucracy, administrative positions went as a matter of course to those of good pedigree. There was no examination or open competition, because government was the right of the aristocracy. A system based on family connections rather than ability may strike us as unfair; it is also inherently unstable. Family fortunes wax and wane, and therein lies not only the formula for the political, economic, and military vicissitudes of premodern Japanese history but also the subject for much of Japan's best literature.

Life in premodern Japan, indeed the earthly realm, was seen as transitory, almost a dream. This was a central teaching of Buddhism, which Japan committed to memory during its Chinese tutelage. Buddhism had an exorbitant impact on Japanese civilization and is the best example of how much more enduring were some of the intellectual, artistic, and material influences that crossed the China Sea along with statecraft. The new religion was obviously congenial to the Japanese mind. While it is true that the native faith, Shinto, was little more than an amorphous and naive belief in the protective or baneful effect of supernatural powers—local divinities and the mythical creators of Japan—completely lacking in creed, scripture, or a developed metaphysic, these deficiencies alone do not account for the success of Buddhism among the Japanese. In a country where earthquakes and typhoons are common occurrences and where people lived close to nature in all its changing aspects, the doctrine of universal impermanence spoke to Japanese experience. More important, Buddhism brought meaning to that discordant experience. Precisely because human existence is fleeting and illusory, life is but dissatisfaction. So long as one clings to the things of this world, one is bound to suffer. Buddhism offered hope of escape, however, because it taught that we all hold the possibility of Buddhahood within us. To realize this Buddha nature and end the painful cycle of rebirth into worlds of continued suffering, we have only to stop our grasping.

Here is the kernel of a great literature. It would sprout in Japan as luxuriantly as anywhere Buddhism ever touched: a literature that takes as its main ambition to plumb the depths of longing. If the Japanese have not quite been the world's metaphysicians, they have been thinkers of another kind. Like the ancient Romans, the Japanese have always been a profoundly practical people. While they may never have distinguished themselves in abstract speculation, through art and literature rather than philosophy they have addressed, albeit more obliquely, the large questions of life: the nature of emotional attachment, the human need for affection, the clash between passion and reason, the curse of worldly ambition, the demon of the self, what courage means, what beauty is, where wisdom lies, the weight of the past, the true meaning of time.

PRONOUNCING GLOSSARY

The following list uses common English syllables to provide rough equivalents of selected words whose pronunciation may be unfamiliar to the general reader.

Genji: *gen-jee*   kabuki: *kah-boo-kee*

haiku: *hai-koo*   samurai: *sah-moo-rai*

Heike: *hay-ke*   sumō: *soo-moh*

TIME LINE

TEXTS	CONTEXTS
	4th–6th centuries Clans ally to form Yamato, precursor of Japanese state
	552 Buddhism introduced into Japan
	600 Chinese and Korean artisans settle in Japan
	645 Taika Reforms redistribute land and place imperial house in control of Japan
712 *A Record of Ancient Matters*, a mythic history legitimizing early Japanese rulers who commissioned it	**710–784** Nara period: capital established at Nara in time of first great intellectual and cultural achievement
ca. 759 *The Man'yōshū*, an anthology of over forty-five hundred poems	
	794–1185 Heian period: cultural life continues to flourish as capital moves to Heian (present-day Kyoto)
	800 Charlemagne crowned, inaugurating Holy Roman empire
ca. 890 *The Tale of the Bamboo Cutter*, first extant work of Japanese fiction	**9th century** Japanese syllabary is developed from Chinese characters
ca. 905 *The Kokinshū*, first imperially commissioned poetry anthology	
mid-10th century *Tales of Ise*, 125 brief lyrical episodes giving fictional context to one or more poems; influenced *The Tale of Genji*	
early 11th century *The Tale of Genji* (Murasaki Shikibu), considered world's first novel • *The Pillow Book* (Sei Shōnagon), collection of random observations on love, life at court, and human nature	**1180–85** Gempei Wars end aristocratic monopoly of power, inspiring *The Tale of the Heike*
	1185–1333 Kamakura period: political center moves east to Kamakura with rise of warrior elite known as *samurai*

Boldface titles indicate works in the anthology.

TIME LINE

TEXTS	CONTEXTS
ca. 1206 *The New Kokinshū*, the eighth imperial anthology of poetry	
	1215 Magna Carta grants rights to "free men" of England
	1271–95 Marco Polo journeys to China, opening trade routes and cultural ties between Europe and east Asia
13th–14th centuries *The Tale of the Heike*, an account of the Gempei Wars, which led to aristocracy's loss of wealth and political power	
1330s *Essays in Idleness* (Yoshida Kenkō), discursive observations revolving around aesthetic issues	**1338–1573** Muromachi period: culture flourishes despite social upheaval, reflected in austere, introspective character of the arts
14th–6th centuries *Nō* drama flourishes: Zeami Motokiyo's *Atsumori* and **Haku Rakuten,** and *Dōjōji* by Kanze Kojirō Nobumitsu	
15th century Linked poetry, composed by several poets, develops from entertainment into favored literary form	**15th century** Rise of Zen Buddhism
1463 *Murmured Conversations* (Shinkei), a treatise on principles of linked poetry	
1488 *Three Poets at Minase,* a hundred-verse sequence by Sōgi, Shōhaku, and Sōchō, epitomizes linked-poetry tradition	
	1519 Magellan circumnavigates globe, proving earth is round and revealing the Americas as a new world
	1543 Portuguese land in Japan, bringing firearms and Christianity
	1573–1600 Momoyama period: civil war leads to unification of Japan
	1597 Japanese build printing press with wooden movable type after Korean model in cast metal

THE MAN'YŌSHŪ
eighth century

The first monument of Japanese literature, and some would say its greatest, is a large collection of poetry whose range, complexity, and force still speak to us, more than one thousand years later, of the exuberance of a people experiencing literacy and cultural animation for the first time. Known as *The Man'yōshū* (The Collection of Ten thousand leaves), this earliest extant collection of Japanese poetry appears to have been intended as an anthology of anthologies. The compilers repeatedly refer to older anthologies, no longer existing, from which they have culled their selections. Furthermore, the "leaves" of the title refer not only to the poems but to future generations of readers, because, by tradition, the character for *leaf* also meant "age," or "generation." The anthologizers were proclaiming, then, that this "collection of ten thousand poems" (4,516 to be precise) was to serve as a "collection for ten thousand ages."

Such a claim might seem the height of audacity, given the circumstances. At the time that the last specifically dated poem in the collection was completed in 759, Japan had only recently emerged from a primitive preliterate past. A loose confederation of competing clans, who drew their wealth from the cultivation of rice and whose principal cultural accomplishment was the erection of enormous burial mounds equipped with clay statuary, had remade itself into a society with a national identity, a ruling imperial family, an elaborate government administration, a complex system of religious beliefs, a command of letters, and the other accouterments of civilization.

All this had been realized within the span of a mere century or two, as Japan worked frenetically to catch up with the world's exemplar of cultural sophistication: China. Once the Japanese comprehended the chasm separating them from this much older civilization, which by every standard—economic, political, and philosophical—threw their unseasoned situation into bold relief, national ambition and competitive pride propelled a stunning process of assimiliation. Where before there had been paddy fields and simple thatched-roof shrines intended to placate spirits residing in the rivers and mountains of the vicinity, now there were vast road networks, irrigation works, ports, and courier service and, in the capital, a hierarchy of court ranks, fine silks and brocades, and lacquered pagodas whose rooftops soared like the wings of a great bird gliding in mid-flight. These were all visible signs of the material progress Japan had accomplished as the diligent student of China.

But perhaps the most fateful decision that the Japanese made in their importation of Chinese culture was the bending of the Chinese writing system to the needs of their own very different language. The Chinese script, known as characters, had originated as a system of pictograms, evolving over time to incorporate pictographic, ideographic, and phonetic elements. Because it was designed solely to record the Chinese language and lacked the pliancy of a phonetic writing system—an alphabet or syllabary—the Chinese script required cumbersome manipulation before it could serve to record another language.

That the Japanese chose to borrow rather than invent a writing system makes them no different from most other peoples. The Greek alphabet, for example, is but a mutation of the Phoenician script, and the Roman alphabet merely the Greek slightly modified. What may set the Japanese apart, however (and would later become a cliché), is the ingenuity of their adaptation. The poems of *The Man'yōshū* were recorded using Chinese characters in three different ways: for meaning, for sound when read in Chinese, and for sound when read in Japanese. The character denoting "person," for instance, could naturally be used for its semantic value when the poet wanted to write the word *person*. But it could also be used to approximate the sound of its original Chinese pronunciation, *jen*, which Japanese phonology rendered *jin*, or *nin*. Or it could be used in an altogether different way. Because the Japanese word for "person" is *hito*, the character could represent that native sound in another word. For example, Hitomaro, the name of the first of the poets in the selections printed here, came to be written with the "person" character signifying the "Hito" element. The sheer perversity of this system (for there were thousands of Chinese characters to be mastered and the number had then to be multiplied by three) is a testament to the overwhelming desire of the Japanese people of the seventh and eighth centuries to express their new experiences through the written word.

Indeed the range of experience the early poets chronicled is one of the qualities that later generations of Japanese would prize in *The Man'yōshū*. Other qualities are its passion and sincerity, together with an innocence, vigor, and seeming artlessness that stand in marked contrast to the controlled, more self-conscious polish that would define Japanese poetry throughout the subsequent classical era. In the age of *The Man'yōshū*, the aristocratic customs of the court had yet to solidify into the weight of convention. And the cultural situation in Japan was still fluid enough that the aristocracy did not yet dominate.

In fact, one finds a surprising number of poems in *The Man'yōshū* by people completely outside court circles, whose literacy itself is surprising. The anonymous poems in the collection, nearly two thousand, far outnumber those by any of the known poets. There are rustic poems that tell of life in the wilderness of the eastern frontier, poems purportedly by fishers, poems recording local dialects, farewell poems by military conscripts, and even poems by travelers to Korea. Of course, one must allow for the possibility that aristocrats chose to romanticize rustic life, and no doubt some of the poems in a common voice are a reworking of folk elements. Nonetheless, in many cases sufficient internal evidence remains to convince scholars that a substantial number of the anonymous poems are the product of the ordinary citizen.

Authorship, however, is only one indication of the breadth of *The Man'yōshū*. Those poets who came from the privileged class and whose names we do know also ranged widely in their chosen topics. Kakinomoto Hitomaro* (flourished ca. 680–700), the undisputed master of the collection, captures the profound sadness of parting, the warrior's bravery, the shock of sudden death, the pageantry of the imperial institution, the burdens of travel, and the mysteries of the human fate. The three sets of poems included here by Hitomaro are representative of his genius. In the first he broods on the passing of time and the evanescence of worldly glory as he views the ruins of the ancient capital. In the second he laments the loneliness of parting from his wife. He depicts their union through the sensual imagery of stems of "sleek seaweed" that once "swayed toward" each other and intertwined but after too few nights have been sundered; the seaweed now grows alone "on the desolate shore."

Like so many of his best poems, it is a highly visual presentation. When the poet describes looking back through the falling leaves for a final glimpse of his wife, not only do we clearly see the sad autumn scene but we can picture the poet's wife disappearing before his (and our) eyes:

> And so I look back,
> still thinking of her . . .
> but in the storm
> of fallen scarlet leaves
> on Mount Watari,

---

* Names are given in the Japanese order, with surname first.

                    crossed as on
                        a great ship,
                I cannot make out the sleeves
                she waves in farewell.
                For she, alas,
                    is slowly hidden
                like the moon
                    in its crossing
                        between the clouds.

The same visual force is apparent in the third set of poems by Hitomaro, perhaps his most famous, inspired by the sight of a dead man lying amid the rocks on the forsaken shore of a distant island. Having traveled there through a storm that nearly cost him his own life, Hitomaro understandably identifies with the fate of the dead man. Through his rich use of imagistic language deployed in the lyric equivalent of narration, he makes us identify as well. In poems like these, Hitomaro perfected the techniques of the earliest Japanese poetry, still marked by the formulaic style of an oral tradition, and raised them to a poetry of high artistry.

What constituted that artistry is deceptively simple. Because the sound system of Japanese employs no stress accent, each syllable is pronounced with virtually equal emphasis, and the forms of meter based on stress that we associate with English poetry do not occur. Nor does rhyme figure in Japanese prosody. Most syllables consist of a single vowel or a consonant (or consonant cluster) followed by a vowel. With only five vowel sounds, given Japanese word structure, a poetry based on rhyme would be akin, as Robert Frost once said of free verse, to playing tennis without a net. Instead, Japanese poetry depended from its inception on the rhythm created by alternating phrases of long and short syllable counts. Japan's most archaic songs employ this pattern of alternation, which originally varied from combinations of phrases with four syllables paired with those of six to alternations of phrases of five syllables with those of three. Eventually, by the mid-seventh century the accepted pattern became an alternation of five and seven syllables, establishing a rhythm that would reign until the modern day.

The poets of *The Man'yōshū* compose in two principal forms. The *chōka*, or long poem, consists of an indeterminate number of lines of alternating five- and seven-syllable phrases, culminating in a couplet of two seven-syllable phrases. The *tanka*, or short poem, is identical in form to the last five lines of a *chōka*—that is, it is a thirty-one-syllable poem arranged in lines whose syllable counts are 5, 7, 5, 7, 7.

The long poems in *The Man'yōshū* are by far the rarest, and in fact the *chōka* disappears as a viable poetic form after *The Man'yōshū*. Approximately 4,200 of the 4,516 poems in the collection are *tanka*. Even most of the *chōka* have satellite *tanka* known as "envoys" that serve as a summing up or expand an imagistic or emotive theme from the original *chōka* to a fuller, still more lyrical realization.

Despite their numerical inferiority within the *The Man'yōshū* the longer poems by Hitomaro and others are what many readers remember best. No doubt their very scarcity makes them stand out against the subsequent history of a more confined form of poetry. At the same time, this mingling of *chōka* and *tanka* is yet another indication of the anthology's unusual range.

Among the finest *tanka* in the collection are the ironic poems in praise of wine by Ōtomo Tabito (665–731). Unlike Hitomaro, of whose extraliterary life we unfortunately know nothing, Tabito is a political figure with a well-documented government career. His affection for Chinese literature also sets him apart from Hitomaro, and his bibulous poems printed here are an excellent example of his expert handling of Chinese themes.

Like his friend Tabito, Yamanoue Okura (660–ca. 733), author of the last two sets of poems included here, was a devotee of Chinese culture. But the stances the two poets assume are completely different. If Tabito speaks as the Taoist epicure detached from the stress of life, Okura is the old Confucian gentleman, moralistic, with a strong sense of outrage at the ills of society. His poems on the impermanence of life treat a theme that had already become familiar in Japanese literature, but his poems on poverty depart radically from the norm. They become somewhat less radical, it is true, when we compare them with Chinese treatments of social injustice. Still, Okura's humble, earthy style, the vigor of his language, his genuine compassion, and the humorous, loving voice that breaks through his austere pose are all distinctive.

Owing to its amazing variety, *The Man'yōshū* has been all things to all readers. To some, it is proof that the earliest Japanese literature is derivative. For others, it is the repository of the essential Japanese identity: wholehearted, sincere, robust, and unaffected. It is important, however, to keep perspective. Susceptibility to influence does not preclude creative invention, and the Chinese example can best be viewed as a fertilizing one. Furthermore, a careful reading of *The Man'yōshū* reveals a work of considerable complexity, in which confidence in the artistic effect that language creates has overshadowed preliterate belief in the sheer incantatory power of words. Finally, it is one of the ironies of literary history that in the later generations invoked in the very title of the collection—for whom the poetic art was intended to endure—poetry was appropriated as the exclusive property of one group, the aristocracy. Compared with the later poetry of Japan's classical age, *The Man'yōshū*, in its diverse forms and multiplicity of voices, can rightly be viewed as the mirror of an entire nation.

PRONOUNCING GLOSSARY

The following list uses common English syllables to provide rough equivalents of selected words whose pronunciation may be unfamiliar to the general reader.

chōka: *choh-kah*

Dazaifu: *dah-zai-foo*

Iwami: *ee-wah-mee*

Izanagi: *ee-zah-nah-gee*

Izanami: *ee-zah-nah-mee*

Jinmu: *jeen-moo*

Kakinomoto Hitomaro: *kah-kee-noh-moh-toh hee-toh-mah-roh*

Kashiwara: *kah-shee-wah-rah*

Kyūshū: *kyoo-shoo*

Man'yōshū: *mahn-yoh-shoo*

Ōmi: *oh-mee*

Ōtomo Tabito: *oh-toh-moh tah-bee-toh*

Ōtsu: *oh-tsoo*

Samine: *sah-mee-ne*

Sanuki: *sah-noo-kee*

Sasanami: *sah-sah-nah-mee*

Shikoku: *shee-koh-ku*

tanka: *tahn-kah*

Unebi: *oo-ne-bee*

Watari: *wah-tah-ree*

Yamanoue Okura: *yah-mah-noh-oo-e oh-koo-rah*

Yamato: *yah-mah-toh*

FROM THE MAN'YŌSHŪ[1]

29–31

*Poem written by Kakinomoto Hitomaro when he passed the ruined
capital at Ōmi[2]*

Since the reign of the Master of the Sun[3]
at Kashiwara by Unebi Mountain,
    where the maidens
        wear strands of jewels,
all gods who have been born   5
have ruled the realm under heaven,
    each following each
    like generations of the spruce,
        in Yamato[4]
that spreads to the sky.   10

What was in his mind
that he would leave it
and cross beyond the hills of Nara,
    beautiful in blue earth?
Though a barbarous place   15
at the far reach of the heavens,
here in the land of Ōmi
where the waters race on stone,
at the Ōtsu Palace
in Sasanami   20
    by the rippling waves,
the Emperor, divine Prince,
ruled the realm under heaven.

Though I hear
this was the great palace,   25
though they tell me
here were the mighty halls,
now it is rank with spring grasses.
Mist rises, and the spring sun is dimmed.
Gazing on the ruins of the great palace,   30
its walls once thick with wood and stone,
I am filled with sorrow.

ENVOYS

Cape Kara in Shiga
at Sasanami
    by the rippling waves,   35

---

1. All selections translated by and with notes adapted from Ian Hideo Levy.   2. Because of the ancient Japanese belief that death polluted a dwelling, when the sovereign died it was customary for his successor to take up residence in a new palace. The capital shifted from place to place among the central provinces, until an edict in 646 called for the establishment of a permanent center of government.   3. Emperor Jinmu, in legend the founding sovereign of Japan, credited with subduing rival chieftains to create the first Japanese state.   4. An archaic name for Japan, which originally referred to the area around present-day Nara.

you are as before, but I
wait for courtiers' boats in vain.

Waters, you are quiet
in deep bends of Shiga's lake
at Sasanami   40
   by the rippling waves,
but never again may I
meet the men of ancient times.

135–137

*Poem written by Kakinomoto Hitomaro when he parted from his wife in
the land of Iwami and came up to the capital*

At Cape Kara
on the Sea of Iwami,
where the vines
   crawl on the rocks,
rockweed of the deep   5
grows on the reefs
and sleek seaweed
grows on the desolate shore.
As deeply do I
think of my wife   10
who swayed toward me in sleep
   like the lithe seaweed.
Yet few were the nights
we had slept together
before we were parted   15
like crawling vines uncurled.
And so I look back,
still thinking of her
with painful heart,
this clench of inner flesh,   20
but in the storm
of fallen scarlet leaves
on Mount Watari,[1]
crossed as on
   a great ship,   25
I cannot make out the sleeves
she waves in farewell.
For she, alas,
is slowly hidden
like the moon   30
   in its crossing
      between the clouds

---

1. Watari means "crossing"; thus the leaves fall at the very spot where the poet might have caught one last
glimpse of his wife.

over Yagami Mountain
just as the evening sun
coursing through the heavens 35
has begun to glow,
        and even I
who thought I was a brave man
find the sleeves
of my well-woven robe 40
drenched with tears.

ENVOYS

The quick gallop
of my dapple-blue steed
races me to the clouds,
passing far away 45
from where my wife dwells.

O scarlet leaves
falling on the autumn mountainside:
stop, for a while, the storm
your strewing makes, that I might glimpse 50
the place where my wife dwells.

220–222

*Poem written by Kakinomoto Hitomaro upon seeing a dead man lying
among the rocks on the island of Samine in Sanuki*

The land of Sanuki,[1]
    fine in sleek seaweed:
is it for the beauty of the land
that we do not tire
        to gaze upon it? 5
Is it for its divinity
that we deem it most noble?
Eternally flourishing,
    with the heavens
        and the earth, 10
    with the sun
        and the moon,
the very face of a god—
so it has come down
        through the ages. 15

Casting off
from Naka harbor,
we came rowing.
Then tide winds

---

1. In Japan's creation myth Sanuki (part of the island now called Shikoku) was one of the first places to be
formed by the union of the gods Izanagi and Izanami.

blew through the clouds;   20
on the offing
we saw the rustled waves,
on the strand
we saw the roaring crests.
Fearing the whale-hunted seas,   25
our ship plunged through—
we bent those oars!
Many were the islands
near and far,
but we beached on Samine—   30
        beautiful its name—
and built a shelter
        on the rugged shore.

Looking around,
                we saw you   35
lying there
on a jagged bed of stones,
the beach
        for your finely woven pillow,
by the breakers' roar.   40
        If I knew your home,
I would go and tell them.
If your wife knew,
she would come and seek you out.
But she does not even know the road,   45
        straight as a jade spear.
Does she not wait for you,
        worrying and longing,
your beloved wife?

ENVOYS

    If your wife were here,   50
        she would gather and feed you
        the starwort that grows
    on the Sami hillsides,
    but is its season not past?

    Making a finely woven pillow   55
    of the rocky shore
            where waves from the offing
                    draw near,
    you, who sleep there!

338–350

*Thirteen poems in praise of wine by Lord Ōtomo Tabito, the Commander
of the Dazaifu[1]*

Rather than engaging
in useless worries,
it's better to down a cup
of raw wine.

Great sages of the past
gave the name of "sage"[2] to wine.
How well they spoke!

What the Seven Wise Men[3]
        of ancient times
wanted, it seems,
        was wine.

Rather than making pronouncements
        with an air of wisdom,
it's better to down the wine
and sob drunken tears.

What is most noble,
    beyond all words
    and beyond all deeds,
is wine.

Rather than be half-heartedly human,
I wish I could be a jug of wine
and be soaked in it!

How ugly!
    those men who,
        with airs of wisdom,
            refuse to drink wine.
Take a good look,
and they resemble apes.

How could even
a priceless treasure
be better than a cup
    of raw wine?

How could even a gem
that glitters in the night
be as good as drinking wine
and cleansing the heart?

5

---

1. Government headquarters in Kyūshū, southernmost of the four main islands of Japan, an important
outpost for regulating contacts with China and Korea. In Tabito's time the flourishing city was nicknamed
"the distant captial."   **2.** So called by those who drank it secretly during the brief time in ancient China
when wine was prohibited by the emperor.   **3.** The Seven Sages of the Bamboo Grove of 3rd-century
China, a Taoist coterie of wealthy dissidents who expressed their social and political disaffection by withdrawing into a kind of intellectual hedonism, given over to tippling, poetastering, and philosophical debate.
One of the sages set the style for the group by employing an attendant who carried a wine jug in one hand
to quench his mater's thirst and a spade in the other to bury him if he fell dead.

Here in this life,
on these roads of pleasure,
it is fun to sob drunken tears.

As long as I have fun
    in this life,
let me be an insect or a bird
    in the next.[4]

Since all who live
must finally die,
let's have fun
while we're still alive.

Smug and silent airs of wisdom
are still not as good
as downing a cup of wine
and sobbing drunken tears.

804–805[1]

Poem sorrowing on the impermanence of life in this world

PREFACE

Easy to gather and difficult to dispel are the eight great hardships.[2] Difficult to fully enjoy and easy to expend are the pleasures of life's century span. So the ancients lamented, and so today our grief finds the same cause. Therefore I have composed a poem, and with it hope to dispel the sorrow of my black hair marked with white. My poem:

Our helplessness in this life
is like the streaming away
of the months and years.
Again and again
misfortune tracks us down   5
and assaults us with a hundred ills.
We cannot hold time
    in its blossoming:
        when young girls,
to be maidenly,   10
wrapped Chinese jewels
around their wrists
and, hand in hand
with companions of their age,
must once have played.   15
When has frost fallen
on hair as black

---

4. The poet adheres to the Buddhist belief in reincarnation, in which present deeds determine one's future life.   1. By Yamanoue Okura.   2. In Buddhism, birth, old age, sickness, death, separation, anger, coveting, and the so-called pain of five passions—the suffering derived from one's attachment to the five elemental aggregates of which the body, mind, and environment are formed (perception, conception, volition, consciousness, and form).

as the guts of river snails?
From where do wrinkles come
to crease those crimson faces?   20
We have let time go.
          Once strong young men,
to be manly,
girt their waists
with great swords   25
and, tossing saddles
with cloth embroidered
          in Yamato patterns
on their red-maned steeds,
mounted and rode for sport—   30
how could it last forever?
Few were the nights
I pushed apart the wooden doors
that young girls creak open and shut
and, groping to their side,   35
slept arm in jewelled arm,
arm in truly jewelled arm!
But now I walk
with a cane gripped in my hand
and propped against my waist.   40
Going this way,
          I am despised.
Going that way,
          I am hated.
Such, it seems,   45
is the fate of old men.
Though I regret the passing
of my life,
          that swelled with spirit,
there is nothing I can do.   50

ENVOY

Like the unchanging cliffs,
I would remain just as I am.
But I am living in this world
and cannot hold time back.

892–893[1]

Dialog of the Destitute

"On nights when rain falls,
          mixed with wind,
on nights when snow falls,
          mixed with rain,

---

1. By Yamanoue Okura.

I am cold   5
And the cold.
         leaves me helpless:
I lick black lumps of salt
and suck up melted dregs of *sake*.[2]
Coughing and sniffling,   10
I smooth my uncertain wisps
                    of beard.
I am proud—
         I know no man
               is better than me.   15
But I am cold.
I pull up my hempen nightclothes
and throw on every scrap
of cloth shirt that I own.
But the night is cold.   20
And I wonder how a man like you,
               even poorer than myself,
with his father and mother
starving and freezing,
with his wife and children   25
begging and begging
               through their tears,
can get through the world alive
               at times like this."

"Wide, they say,   30
               are heaven and earth—
but have they shrunk for me?
Bright, they say,
               are the sun and moon—
but do they refuse to shine for me?   35
Is it thus for all men,
               or for me alone?
Above all, I was born human,[3]
I too toil for my keep—
as much as the next man—   40
yet on my shoulders hangs
a cloth shirt
not even lined with cotton,
these tattered rags
thin as strips of seaweed.   45
In my groveling hut,
    my tilting hut,
sleeping on straw
cut and spread right on the ground,
with my father and mother   50
         huddled at my pillow
and my wife and children

---

2. A brewed alcoholic beverage made from fermented rice. 3. In the Buddhist doctrine of reincarnation one could not achieve enlightenment, thereby escaping the cyclical chain of rebirth, without first attaining the human level. In this, at least, he is fortunate.

> huddled at my feet,
> I grieve and lament.
> Not a spark rises in the stove,   55
> and in the pot
> a spider has drawn its web.
> I have forgotten
> what it is to cook rice!
> As I lie here,   60
> a thin cry tearing from my throat—
>   a   tiger   thrush's
> moan—
> then, as they say,
> to slice the ends   65
> of a thing already too short,
> to our rough bed
> comes the scream of the villman
>   with   his tax   collecting
> whip.   70
> Is it so helpless and desperate,
> the way of life in this world?"

> ENVOY

> I find this world
> a hard and shameful place.
> But I cannot fly away—   75
> I am not a bird.

MURASAKI SHIKIBU
ca. 973–1016

The Tale of Genji is the undisputed masterpiece of Japanese prose and the first great novel in the history of world literature. It was written in the early eleventh century by Murasaki Shikibu, a woman of the lower reaches of the aristocracy. Murasaki was the daughter of a provincial governor, but her service as lady-in-waiting to the empress allowed her the most intimate glimpse of the social and political doings of the imperial court. Unlike the fanciful romances that preceded it, *The Tale of Genji* (ca. 1001–13) is revered for its psychological insight, capturing a world that, however remote it might eventually become in time, has always retained the sharp authenticity of real life.

Vast in scale and peopled by hundreds of characters, this thousand-page novel has a plot of supreme simplicity. It depicts the lives and loves of a former prince and, following his death, the lives and loves of his descendants. But in a novel in which everything is finely calibrated, things are seldom really simple. To begin with, why is the hero a *former* prince? Though he is cherished by his father, the emperor, political exigencies force his removal from the imperial line. The family name *Genji* is bestowed on him, along with the sobriquet "the shining one" and generous emoluments. Nonetheless, before the first chapter is even over, the young hero has already lost the most important attribute of a man of his rank: the chance to rule someday as emperor.

Because political concerns were of little interest to the author except implicitly, she is not about to dissect the career of a favorite son as he rises through the ranks of the government. She is interested instead in how one compensates, substitutes, and replaces and in larger issues than worldly success: fate, retribution, sexual attraction, and the emotional depth of human experience.

What begins as the story of a glittering existence darkens with time. The sensitive aristocrat discovers more of life, including failure. Yet this is no ordinary story of age bringing wisdom or of the past repeating itself. As Murasaki augments her tale (which seems to have grown more by accretion than by blueprint), she questions, attenuates, and sometimes undermines the fundamental presumptions of its earlier portions.

By the time Genji dies two thirds of the way through the book, a deep pessimism has taken over. We have entered a world diminished, not only because Genji is gone but because his survivors are somehow smaller people, flawed fragments of their forebears. Murasaki now follows the hapless lives of Genji's two descendants, but here again things are not as simple as they appear. One of the two possesses the ultimate flaw of inauthenticity. He is only passing as Genji's son, being in fact, the issue of an illicit union between Genji's wife and the son of Genji's best friend. In their different ways, the two scions represent a sad falling off. The real grandson is frivolous and inconsequential, and the putative son is so wracked by neurotic indecision that he has been dubbed world literature's first antihero.

Though the armature supporting this long story lies in the lives of three men, it is fundamentally a work of women's literature. To a degree that would have been the envy of European women writers as recently as Virginia Woolf, Murasaki thrived in a culture where women had the leisure, financial security, and intellectual freedom to become writers of significance. "A woman must have money and a room of her own if she wants to write fiction," Virginia Woolf said in 1929. She was lamenting the fact that until the late eighteenth century such favorable conditions were usually wanting and Western literature was the poorer for its slender pantheon of women writers.

The situation in Murasaki's day, courtly Japan of nearly a thousand years earlier, could not have been more different. True, women led a circumscribed existence. The role of a lady was to marry and bear children, and if she came of a suitably good family, she was apt to find herself a pawn in the marriage politics of the imperial court. The most influential family of the time, the Fujiwara, had attained its influence by marrying daughters to emperors, who produced new emperors who could be dominated by their maternal grandfathers. (Murasaki was herself a member of a subsidiary branch of the Fujiwara family.) A noblewoman's days were spent behind curtains and screens, hidden from the world (or from the male world). The verb *to see* constituted an act of possession and was synonymous with having sexual relations. Proper ladies were not seen casually. Nor did they enjoy the same mobility as men or have careers, except as ladies-in-waiting.

They did, however, have the requisite leisure that Virginia Woolf specified. And they had the income. Although at this time Japan was a polygamous society, women of the aristocracy retained a degree of independence, thanks to a system of matrilineal inheritance, so that a well-born woman was not solely dependent on her husband for financial support.

Most important of all, the women of Murasaki's circle had the intellectual attainments to produce literature. Theirs was an education by default, but it was an education all the same. As is so often the case in early Japanese literature, the issue of language becomes crucial. Despite the new native writing system (described in the headnote "The Kokinshū," p. 2161) and the birth of an indigenous Japanese literature, both Chinese script and the Chinese language retained tremendous authority in eleventh-century Japan. Chinese, not Japanese, was the official language of the government, whose organization and institutions were themselves based on the model of China. The bureaucracy, the legal codes, political theory, even the calendar were of Chinese origin. To prepare for a career in the administration of the government—the only career for a male aristocrat—required a thorough education in the Chinese classics which made Chinese both the language of the practical, workaday world of men and the medium of intellection, like Latin in medieval Europe.

A command of Chinese was considered irrelevant to a woman's life, and if she happened to pick it up, this "mannish" attainment was best concealed. In her diary, Murasaki tells us this:

> When my brother, Secretary at the Ministry of Ceremonial, was a young boy learning the Chinese classics, I was in the habit of listening to him and I became unusually proficient at understanding those passages which he found too difficult to grasp. Father, a most learned man, was always regretting the fact: "Just my luck!" he would say. "What a pity she was not born a man!"*

After that, Murasaki feigned ignorance and turned her attention to the native language.

Left to their own devices and with plenty of time on their hands, Murasaki and her female contemporaries explored the potential of their own language and discovered it to be a supple instrument for a literature of introspection. One of the remarkable aspects of *The Tale of Genji* and other great works by women writers of Murasaki's time is that they appeared so early in the development of the native literature. Or put another way, it is astonishing that the prestige of the Chinese classics, which permeated every official element of Japanese life, should have proved a less formidable obstacle than the Greek and Latin precedent did in Europe to the rise of a vernacular literature. All evidence suggests that this was mainly thanks to women like Murasaki, whose talent and passion for expression were indomitable.

And what was it Murasaki wanted to express in writing *The Tale of Genji*? This is a question the Japanese have spent nearly a millennium answering, not because the novel is opaque but because it is so various. Perhaps the most obvious reading of the tale is to see it as a sexual poetics, a study of the distinctive features of love—its language, forms, and conventions. This is not to suggest that *Genji* is in any way an erotic novel. In the customs of the time, men took principal wives and secondary wives, akin to concubines, as well as the occasional lover. Men moved about with a great degree of sexual freedom. Women did not; they waited. It was not only attention and affection they sat waiting for behind their screens but a definition of themselves, which depended entirely on male recognition.

The whole process was fraught with uncertainty. If a man came, would he come again? A woman's position depended more on the frequency of the man's visits than on any formal arrangements. And even marriage, that is to say as the principal wife, was no guarantee of domestic security. A man's first wife usually remained with her parents, and he visited. Secondary wives also tended to live separately from their husbands. The man, then, was often elsewhere, and the tension that this produced on the woman's part in the form of longing, loneliness, insecurity, jealousy, resentment, and other vulnerabilities was balanced on the man's part by the unhappy fate of being forever on the outside looking in (or trying to), the endless traveler, the incessant aggressor. Both sides were condemned to a world of physical separation, with all its attendant agonies. And this is what Murasaki is really interested in: the dynamics of love at the emotional and psychological level, not the physical.

---

*Richard Bowring, *Murasaki Shikibu: Her Diary and Poetic Memoirs* (1982), p. 139.

Courtship and seduction might seem to form the central theme of the novel, but the real theme is the longing to connect with another person.

That is why Genji's life and the lives of his successors are presented as a search for the ideal woman. Like a symphony unfolding with its themes and variations, the novel announces early on its main motif. In the second chapter, "The Broom Tree" (the first of the selections printed here), the seventeen-year-old Genji and his friends while away a rainy night in his quarters at the palace debating what makes the perfect woman. In the process, the young men trade stories of their experiences with women, which, to their credit, involve fewer conquests than failures. But they remain undeterred to a man, and the rest of the long novel continues the quest for fulfilment in love.

Thus, in the manner of music, this early chapter anticipates episodes to follow, which in turn generate other episodes and further repercussions. The characters are unaware of it, but when Genji's best friend, Tō no Chūjō, mentions his most memorable affair, he describes the very woman with whom Genji will soon fall in love and whose death will be caused by the jealousy it inspires in a rival. These events appear in Chapter 4, "Evening Faces." And they too have repercussions later in the novel (see "Fireflies"), when Genji, now thirty-six, pursues the daughter of this same woman. In a twist of fate emblematic of the novel's pattern, the young lady, Tamakazura, is the child of Tō no Chūjō, and the product of the affair he recounted some twenty years before when the young courtiers spent their rainy night trying to define perfect love.

Gradually, through age and experience, the once-charmed Genji begins to comprehend that there is no such thing. The tale of his life may be read as a progress from youthful idealism (involving its share of insensitivity) to disillusion and then on to the edges of insight. It may further be read, in the lives of Genji's incomplete descendants, as an ironic comment on the novel's own earlier ideals—a parable about the process of maturing and the realization that all human bonds are by nature defective.

If the lives of the heroes represent a fruitless quest for the perfect woman, Murasaki's chronicle seems also a quest, ultimately abandoned, for the perfect man. One can easily imagine Murasaki in the tedium of slow-moving days at court, or perhaps on her own long rainy night, amusing herself and her empress by conjuring up a man who would not disappoint them. In the early pages of the novel, Genji possesses every manly virtue. "He had grown into a lad of such beauty," we are told, "that he hardly seemed meant for this world—and indeed one almost feared that he might only briefly be a part of it." He is witty, artistic, amusing, sophisticated, influential, generous, and more than any of his peers, understanding of women—in short, irresistible. Even his learning takes the breath away: "When he was seven he went through the ceremonial reading of the Chinese classics, and never before had there been so fine a performance. Again a tremor of apprehension passed over the emperor—might it be that such a prodigy was not to be long for this world?"

In fact, Genji endures into his early fifties (a ripe enough age for the era), and there is ample time to see him fall short of perfection. Very quickly Murasaki forsook romance, the tale's antecedent, in favor of realism. At the start, it is a cheerful sort of realism, but it darkens as the novel progresses, and we can detect this already in *Suma* and *Akashi*. The twin chapters are numbers twelve and thirteen of the novel, relatively early in a work of fifty-four chapters. Even so, the idealization of Genji that we saw in "The Broom Tree" has been muted by now. Genji has transgressed, and he is exiled. His expansive appetite for life has finally got him into real trouble.

The proximate cause of exile is an unwise affair with the daughter of a rival family, which Genji's enemies use as a pretext to remove him from the capital. But the actual, or moral, cause is a serious misstep. Genji has also had an affair with his father's consort, Fujitsubo, and the secret liaison has produced a child. While, strictly speaking, he has not violated the taboo on sexual relations between close family members, since Fujitsubo is his stepmother, Genji has come perilously close, and he has disturbed the imperial succession. His transgression is rooted in a central theme of the novel: repetition and substitution. Things that happen once have an uncanny tendency to recur under a slightly different guise. In Buddhist belief life is a wheel; as it spins we confront situations that echo our past, or the fates of those before us. But this sense of repetition is also partly an illusion. Nothing is exactly the same, much as we sometimes want it to be. And this is Genji's problem. His desire for a mother he lost when still a child has led him to seek substitutions. His father's consort is the closest substitute of all, since the grief-stricken emperor had originally selected the woman precisely because of her resemblance to Genji's mother.

Murasaki understands not only the sheer recklessness of her protagonist but also Genji's complex psychological makeup. When Genji trifles with the incest taboo, it is not only lust that drives him. It is the lure of the forbidden, intertwined with the persistent need for a symbolic repossession of his mother and perhaps even an unconscious will to disrupt the political order. It could well be that Genji's "theft" of the emperor's wife is the subliminal revenge of a fallen prince who lost paradise too young to recall it with equanimity. In any case, Murasaki fully appreciates how seductive prohibition can be. And she continually observes in her novel the multifarious ways that obsession demands to be reincarnated.

In exile, Genji has time to ruminate on his failings, but also to seek new substitutes for the women he has left behind in the capital. The wheel of life keeps turning. Genji pursues women to replace other women. In time, he himself sees the pattern. Eventually, his own wife is unfaithful. He cannot help remembering his father and wondering if, though the emperor remained silent, he knew. Genji's youthful misdeeds have come back to haunt him. By the end of his life he comprehends what unhappiness he has caused others.

Charming and handsome, gifted and ardent, rakish but faithful in his own way (unlike other men, he never abandons any woman he has loved), Genji is a charismatic figure. Yet he is also one of the most problematic of literary characters. All the world loves a lover perhaps, but even when he brings pain and suffering to so many of his loves? Genji may intend only the best for these women—he is inherently kind and noble—but his generous intentions are clouded by an impetuous, self-centered streak that lingers long after youth might have excused it. A man of taste he may be, gregarious and totally alive; Genji is also a past master of lechery, hypocrisy, and self-deceit. His sexual connoisseurship can seem positively arrogant, though not so different from the reported behavior of some of our own heroes in the twentieth century. Readers may hate Genji or adore him or fall somewhere in between, but we can hardly deny that his creator has fashioned a character both larger than life and believably human.

In a certain way, one ends up feeling sorry for Genji. The eleventh-century Japanese version of machismo was as emotionally confining for a man of his delicate sentiment as court conventions were physically restricting for women. Both sexes paid the price of membership in a beautiful, exclusive little world. Even the aristocrat's privileged myopia cannot obscure, finally, the ways actions have consequences— which are, if anything, magnified by the tight compass of their closed circle. Murasaki understands, as her characters do not, that narrow horizons bring their own penalties.

Loss, substitution, repetition. Transgression and retribution. In a work as oceanic as the Bible, here too the sins of the father are visited on the children. If Genji is flawed, his descendants are imperfection intensified. Time is succession, and life itself substitution. Just as youth will not return, neither will youthful assumptions. The full measure of the story's profundity is not merely its extraordinary insights into human nature, but its subversion of its own earlier suppositions. For many people *The Tale of Genji* has been a discovery. The novel's continually expanding reflection and self-scrutiny have shown them a way to look at themselves. For such readers, *Genji* is more than a book, it is an experience of life.

PRONOUNCING GLOSSARY

The following list uses common English syllables to provide rough equivalents of selected words whose pronunciation may be unfamiliar to the general reader.

Akashi: *ah-kah-shee*

Akikonomu: *ah-kee-koh-noh-moo*

AOI: *ah-oy*

Asagao: *ah-sah-gah-oh*

Atemiya: *ah-te-mee-yah*

aware: *ah-wah-re*

Chūjō: *choo-joh*

Chūnagon: *choo-nah-gohn*

Fujitsubo: *foo-jee-tsoo-boh*

Fujiwara: *foo-jee-wah-rah*

Genji: *gen-jee*

Gojō: *goh-joh*

Gosechi: *goh-se-chee*

Hiei: *hee-ay*

Higekuro: *hee-ge-koo-roh*

Hirohito: *hee-roh-hee-toh*

Hitachi: *hee-tah-chee*

Hotaru: *hoh-tah-roo*

hototogisu: *hoh-toh-toh-gee-soo*

Kamo: *kah-moh*

Kaoru: *kah-oh-roo*

Kashiwagi: *kah-shee-wah-gee*

Kasugano: *kah-soo-gah-noh*

Katano: *kah-tah-noh*

Kii: *kee-ee*

Kokiden: *koh-kee-den*

Koremitsu: *koh-ray-mee-tsoo*

Kumano: *koo-mah-noh*

Kumoinokari: *koo-moy-noh-kah-ree*

Matsushima: *mah-tsoo-shee-mah*

Matsuyama: *mah-tsoo-yah-mah*

Mitake: *mee-tah-ke*

Murasaki Shikibu: *moo-rah-sah-kee shee-kee-boo*

Nakatsukasa: *nah-kah-tsoo-kah-sah*

Nijō: *nee-joh*

Niou: *nee-oh*

Oborozukiyo: *oh-boh-roh-zoo-kee-yoh*

Oe: *oh-ay*

Omyōbu: *oh-myoh-boo*

Reikeiden: *ray-kay-den*

Reizei: *ray-zay*

Rokujō: *roh-koo-joh*

Saishō: *sai-shoh*

Sanjō: *sahn-joh*

Shōnagon: *shoh-nah-gohn*

Shōwa: *shoh-wah*

Sumiyoshi: *soo-mee-yoh-shee*

Tamakazura: *tah-mah-kah-zoo-rah*

Tanabata: *tah-nah-bah-tah*

Tatsuta: *tah-tsoo-tah*

Tō no Chūjō: *toh no choo-joh*

Uji: *oo-jee*

Ukifune: *oo-kee-foo-ne*

Ukon: *oo-kohn*

warekara: *wah-re-kah-rah*

wasuregusa: *wah-soo-re-goo-sah*

Yoshikiyo: *yoh-shee-kee-yoh*

Yūgiri: *yoo-gee-ree*

Yukihira: *yoo-kee-hee-rah*

From The Tale of Genji[1]

Summary   *The Tale of Genji* opens with the flavor of an old romance, in which the adventure is set in the distant past and the idealized characters dwell in an almost enchanted setting:

> In a certain reign there was a lady not of the first rank whom the emperor loved more than any of the others. The grand ladies with high ambitions thought her a presumptuous upstart, and lesser ladies were still more resentful. Everything she did offended someone. Probably aware of what was happening, she fell seriously ill and came to spend more time at home than at court. The emperor's pity and affection quite passed bounds. No longer caring what his ladies and courtiers might say, he behaved as if intent upon stirring gossip.

In time, a child is born to the woman, which makes the emperor even more devoted, but which also stirs the wrath of her rival, Kokiden, a powerful senior wife. The poor woman is persecuted, and, weakened from the strain, she dies. The emperor is devastated by her death. As solace, he takes some delight in his beautiful and brilliant son. As further solace, he installs in the palace a woman who he has heard bears a striking resemblance to his beloved. This proves true, and the new lady, Fujitsubo, wins the emperor's affections.

Meanwhile, his young son continues to dazzle almost everyone. The emperor would like to designate the boy crown prince, but he lacks political support. Furthermore, a Korean soothsayer warns that disaster will befall the country if the boy becomes emperor. Reluctantly, the emperor decides to reduce his son to the status of a mere subject, albeit a nobleman, ensuring that at least the boy will have an official career. He confers the name *Genji* on his son.

At the age of twelve, Genji undergoes the initiation into manhood. On the night of the initiation ceremonies Genji is married to Aoi, the daughter of a powerful minister of state. She is four years older than Genji, however, and they do not take a fancy to each other. Instead Genji finds himself drawn to Fujitsubo, his father's consort. "He could not remember his own mother," the narrator tells us, "and it moved him deeply to learn, from the lady who had first told the emperor of Fujitsubo, that the resemblance was striking. He wanted to be near her always."

With Genji's marriage off to a rocky start, he occupies the palace apartments that had belonged to his mother. As the handsome young man moves through the court, he becomes known as "the shining Genji."

CHAPTER 2

The Broom Tree

"The shining Genji": it was almost too grand a name. Yet he did not escape criticism for numerous little adventures. It seemed indeed that his indiscretions might give him a name for frivolity, and he did what he could to hide them. But his most secret affairs (such is the malicious work of the gossips) became common talk. If, on the other hand, he were to go through life concerned only for his name and avoid all these interesting and amusing little affairs, then he would be laughed to shame by the likes of the lieutenant of Katano.[2]

---

1. Translated by and with notes adapted from Edward G. Seidensticker.   2. Evidently the hero of a romance now lost.

Still a guards captain, Genji spent most of his time at the palace, going infrequently to the Sanjō mansion of his father-in-law. The people there feared that he might have been stained by the lavender of Kasugano.[3] Though in fact he had an instinctive dislike for the promiscuity he saw all around him, he had a way of sometimes turning against his own better inclinations and causing unhappiness.

The summer rains came, the court was in retreat, and an even longer interval than usual had passed since his last visit to Sanjō. Though the minister and his family were much put out, they spared no effort to make him feel welcome. The minister's sons were more attentive than to the emperor himself. Genji was on particularly good terms with Tō no Chūjō.[4] They enjoyed music together and more frivolous diversions as well. Tō no Chūjō was of an amorous nature and not at all comfortable in the apartments which his father-in-law, the Minister of the Right,[5] had at great expense provided for him. At Sanjō with his own family, on the other hand, he took very good care of his rooms, and when Genji came and went the two of them were always together. They were a good match for each other in study and at play. Reserve quite disappeared between them.

It had been raining all day. There were fewer courtiers than usual in the royal presence. Back in his own palace quarters, also unusually quiet, Genji pulled a lamp near and sought to while away the time with his books. He had Tō no Chūjō with him. Numerous pieces of colored paper, obviously letters, lay on a shelf. Tō no Chūjō made no attempt to hide his curiosity.

"Well," said Genji, "there are some I might let you see. But there are some I think it better not to."

"You miss the point. The ones I want to see are precisely the ones you want to hide. The ordinary ones—I'm not much of a hand at the game, you know, but even I am up to the ordinary give and take. But the ones from ladies who think you are not doing right by them, who sit alone through an evening and wait for you to come—those are the ones I want to see."

It was not likely that really delicate letters would be left scattered on a shelf, and it may be assumed that the papers treated so carelessly were the less important ones.

"You do have a variety of them," said Tō no Chūjō, reading the correspondence through piece by piece. This will be from her, and this will be from *her,* he would say. Sometimes he guessed correctly and sometimes he was far afield, to Genji's great amusement. Genji was brief with his replies and let out no secrets.

"It is I who should be asking to see *your* collection. No doubt it is huge. When I have seen it I shall be happy to throw my files open to you."

3. Alludes to a poem from another tale: "Kasugano lavender stains my robe, / In deep disorder, like my secret loves." (Lavender suggests a romantic affinity.) Note that throughout this translation of *The Tale of Genji* Seidensticker renders the *tanka,* or classical Japanese poem, as an unrhymed couplet. However, these thirty-one-syllable compositions in metric patterns of 5, 7, 5, 7, 7 are conventionally viewed as making up five lines and are usually so translated.   4. Brother of Genji's wife Aoi; he becomes Genji's closest friend.   5. One of the highest officials in the government. In rank, only the emperor, regent, chancellor, and minister of the left stood above him. The minister of the left was the legal head of government, responsible for the operation of the emperor's cabinet, known as the council of state. When he was absent, the minister of the right assumed his duties. Tō no Chūjō's father-in-law is, therefore, a powerful figure.

"I fear there is nothing that would interest you." Tō no Chūjō was in a contemplative mood. "It is with women as it is with everything else: the flawless ones are very few indeed. This is a sad fact which I have learned over the years. All manner of women seem presentable enough at first. Little notes, replies to this and that, they all suggest sensibility and cultivation. But when you begin sorting out the really superior ones you find that there are not many who have to be on your list. Each has her little tricks and she makes the most of them, getting in her slights at rivals, so broad sometimes that you almost have to blush. Hidden away by loving parents who build brilliant futures for them, they let word get out of this little talent and that little accomplishment and you are all in a stir. They are young and pretty and amiable and carefree, and in their boredom they begin to pick up a little from their elders, and in the natural course of things they begin to concentrate on one particular hobby and make something of it. A woman tells you all about it and hides the weak points and brings out the strong ones as if they were everything, and you can't very well call her a liar. So you begin keeping company, and it is always the same. The fact is not up to the advance notices."

Tō no Chūjō sighed, a sigh clearly based on experience. Some of what he had said, though not all, accorded with Genji's own experience. "And have you come upon any," said Genji, smiling, "who would seem to have nothing at all to recommend them?"

"Who would be fool enough to notice such a woman? And in any case, I should imagine that women with no merits are as rare as women with no faults. If a woman is of good family and well taken care of, then the things she is less than proud of are hidden and she gets by well enough. When you come to the middle ranks, each woman has her own little inclinations and there are thousands of ways to separate one from another. And when you come to the lowest—well, who really pays much attention?"

He appeared to know everything. Genji was by now deeply interested.

"You speak of three ranks," he said, "but is it so easy to make the division? There are well-born ladies who fall in the world and there are people of no background who rise to the higher ranks and build themselves fine houses as if intended for them all along. How would you fit such people into your system?"

At this point two young courtiers, a guards officer and a functionary in the ministry of rites, appeared on the scene, to attend the emperor in his retreat. Both were devotees of the way of love and both were good talkers. Tō no Chūjō, as if he had been waiting for them, invited their views on the question that had just been asked. The discussion progressed, and included a number of rather unconvincing points.

"Those who have just arrived at high position," said one of the newcomers, "do not attract the same sort of notice as those who were born to it. And those who were born to the highest rank but somehow do not have the right backing—in spirit they may be as proud and noble as ever, but they cannot hide their deficiencies. And so I think that they should both be put in your middle rank.

"There are those whose families are not quite of the highest rank but who go off and work hard in the provinces. They have their place in the world, though there are all sorts of little differences among them. Some of them would belong on anyone's list. So it is these days. Myself, I would take a woman from a middling family over one who has rank and nothing else. Let us say someone whose father is almost but not quite a councillor. Someone who has a decent enough reputation and comes from a decent enough family and can live in some luxury. Such people can be very pleasant. There is nothing wrong with the household arrangements, and indeed a daughter can sometimes be set out in a way that dazzles you. I can think of several such women it would be hard to find fault with. When they go into court service, they are the ones the unexpected favors have a way of falling on. I have seen cases enough of it, I can tell you."

Genji smiled. "And so a person should limit himself to girls with money?"

"That does not sound like you," said Tō no Chūjō.

"When a woman has the highest rank and a spotless reputation," continued the other, "but something has gone wrong with her upbringing, something is wrong in the way she puts herself forward, you wonder how it can possibly have been allowed to happen. But when all the conditions are right and the girl herself is pretty enough, she is taken for granted. There is no cause for the least surprise. Such ladies are beyond the likes of me, and so I leave them where they are, the highest of the high. There are surprisingly pretty ladies wasting away behind tangles of weeds, and hardly anyone even knows of their existence. The first surprise is hard to forget. There she is, a girl with a fat, sloppy old father and boorish brothers and a house that seems common at best. Off in the women's rooms is a proud lady who has acquired bits and snatches of this and that. You get wind of them, however small the accomplishments may be, and they take hold of your imagination. She is not the equal of the one who has everything, of course, but she has her charm. She is not easy to pass by."

He looked at his companion, the young man from the ministry of rites. The latter was silent, wondering if the reference might be to his sisters, just then coming into their own as subjects for conversation. Genji, it would seem, was thinking that on the highest levels there were sadly few ladies to bestow much thought upon. He was wearing several soft white singlets with an informal court robe thrown loosely over them. As he sat in the lamplight leaning against an armrest, his companions almost wished that he were a woman. Even the "highest of the high" might seem an inadequate match for him.

They talked on, of the varieties of women.

"A man sees women, all manner of them, who seem beyond reproach," said the guards officer, "but when it comes to picking the wife who must be everything, matters are not simple. The emperor has trouble, after all, finding the minister who has all the qualifications. A man may be very wise, but no man can govern by himself. Superior is helped by subordinate, subordinate defers to superior, and so affairs proceed by agreement and concession. But when it comes to choosing the woman who is to be in charge of your house, the qualifications are altogether too many. A merit is balanced by a defect, there is this good point and that bad point, and even women who though not perfect can be made to do are not easy to find. I would not like to have you think me a profligate who has to try them all. But it is a question of the woman who must be everything, and it seems best, other things being equal, to find someone who does not require shaping and training, someone who has most of the qualifications from the start. The man who begins his search with all this in mind must be reconciled to searching for a very long time.

"He comes upon a woman not completely and in every way to his liking but he makes certain promises and finds her hard to give up. The world praises him for his honest heart and begins to note good points in the woman too; and why not? But I have seen them all, and I doubt that there are any genuinely superior specimens among them. What about you gentlemen so far above us? How is it with you when you set out to choose your ladies?

"There are those who are young enough and pretty enough and who take care of themselves as if no particle of dust were allowed to fall upon them. When they write letters they choose the most inoffensive words, and the ink is so faint a man can scarcely read them. He goes to visit, hoping for a real answer. She keeps him waiting and finally lets him have a word or two in an almost inaudible whisper. They are clever, I can tell you, at hiding their defects.

"The soft, feminine ones are likely to assume a great deal. The man seeks to please, and the result is that the woman is presently looking elsewhere. That is the first difficulty in a woman.

"In the most important matter, the matter of running his household, a man can find that his wife has too much sensibility, an elegant word and device for every occasion. But what of the too domestic sort, the wife who bustles around the house the whole day long, her hair tucked up behind her ears, no attention to her appearance, making sure that everything is in order? There are things on his mind, things he has seen and heard in his comings and goings, the private and public demeanor of his colleagues, happy things and sad things. Is he to talk of them to an outsider? Of course not. He would much prefer someone near at hand, someone who will immediately understand. A smile passes over his face, tears well up. Or some event at court has angered him, things are too much for him. What good is it to talk to such a woman? He turns his back on her, and smiles, and sighs, and murmurs something to himself. 'I beg your pardon?' she says, finally noticing. Her blank expression is hardly what he is looking for.

"When a man picks a gentle, childlike wife, he of course must see to training her and making up for her inadequacies. Even if at times she seems a bit unsteady, he may feel that his efforts have not been wasted. When she is there beside him her gentle charm makes him forget her defects. But when he is away and sends asking her to perform various services, it becomes clear, however small the service, that she has no thoughts of her own in the matter. Her uselessness can be trying.

"I wonder if a woman who is a bit chilly and unfeeling cannot at times seem preferable."

His manner said that he had known them all; and he sighed at his inability to hand down a firm decision.

"No, let us not worry too much about rank and beauty. Let us be satisfied if a woman is not too demanding and eccentric. It is best to settle on a quiet, steady girl. If she proves to have unusual talent and discrimination—well, count them an unexpected premium. Do not, on the other hand, worry too much about remedying her defects. If she seems steady and not given to tantrums, then the charms will emerge of their own accord.

"There are those who display a womanly reticence to the world, as if they had never heard of complaining. They seem utterly calm. And then when their thoughts are too much for them they leave behind the most horrendous notes, the most flamboyant poems, the sort of keepsakes certain to call up dreadful memories, and off they go into the mountains or to some remote seashore. When I was a child I would hear the women reading romantic stories, and I would join them in their sniffling and think it all very sad, all very profound and moving. Now I am afraid that it suggests certain pretenses.

"It is very stupid really, to run off and leave a perfectly kind and sympathetic man. He may have been guilty of some minor dereliction, but to run off with no understanding at all of his true feelings, with no purpose other than to attract attention and hope to upset him—it is an unpleasant sort of memory to have to live with. She gets drunk with admiration for herself and there she is, a nun. When she enters her convent she is sure that she has found enlightenment and has no regrets for the vulgar world.

"Her women come to see her. 'How very touching,' they say. 'How brave of you.'

"But she no longer feels quite as pleased with herself. The man, who has not lost his affection for her, hears of what has happened and weeps, and certain of her old attendants pass this intelligence on to her. 'He is a man of great feeling, you see. What a pity that it should have come to this.' The woman can only brush aside her newly cropped hair to reveal a face on the edge of tears. She tries to hold them back and cannot, such are her regrets for the life she has left behind; and the Buddha is not likely to think her one who has cleansed her heart of passion. Probably she is in more danger of brimstone now in this fragile vocation than if she had stayed with us in our sullied world.

"The bond between husband and wife is a strong one. Suppose the man had hunted her out and brought her back. The memory of her acts would still be there, and inevitably, sooner or later, it would be cause for rancor. When there are crises, incidents, a woman should try to overlook them, for better or for worse, and make the bond into something durable. The wounds will remain, with the woman and with the man, when there are crises such as I have described. It is very foolish for a woman to let a little dalliance upset her so much that she shows her resentment openly. He has his adventures—but if he has fond memories of their early days together, his and hers, she may be sure that she matters. A commotion means the end of everything. She should be quiet and generous, and when something comes up that quite properly arouses her resentment she should make it known by delicate hints. The man will feel guilty and with tactful guidance he will mend his ways. Too much lenience can make a woman seem charmingly docile and trusting, but it can also make her seem somewhat wanting in substance. We have had instances enough of boats abandoned to the winds and waves. Do you not agree?"

Tō no Chūjō nodded. "It may be difficult when someone you are especially fond of, someone beautiful and charming, has been guilty of an indiscretion, but magnanimity produces wonders. They may not always work, but generosity and reasonableness and patience do on the whole seem best."

His own sister was a case in point, he was thinking, and he was somewhat annoyed to note that Genji was silent because he had fallen asleep. Meanwhile the young guards officer talked on, a dedicated student of his subject. Tō no Chūjō was determined to hear him out.

"Let us make some comparisons," said the guardsman. "Let us think of the cabinetmaker. He shapes pieces as he feels like shaping them. They may be only playthings, with no real plan or pattern. They may all the same have a certain style for what they are—they may take on a certain novelty as times change and be very interesting. But when it comes to the genuine object, something of such undeniable value that a man wants to have it always with him—the perfection of the form announces that it is from the hand of a master.

"Or let us look at painting. There are any number of masters in the academy. It is not easy to separate the good from the bad among those who work on the basic sketches. But let color be added. The painter of things no one ever sees, of paradises, of fish in angry seas, raging beasts in foreign lands, devils and demons—the painter abandons himself to his fancies and paints to terrify and astonish. What does it matter if the results seem somewhat remote from real life? It is not so with the things we know, mountains, streams, houses near and like our own. The soft, unspoiled, wooded hills must be painted layer on layer, the details added gently, quietly, to give a sense of affectionate familiarity. And the foreground too, the garden inside the walls, the arrangement of the stones and grasses and waters. It is here that the master has his own power. There are details a lesser painter cannot imitate.

"Or let us look at calligraphy. A man without any great skill can stretch out this line and that in the cursive style and give an appearance of boldness and distinction. The man who has mastered the principles and writes with concentration may, on the other hand, have none of the eyecatching tricks; but when you take the trouble to compare the two the real thing is the real thing.

"So it is with trivialities like painting and calligraphy. How much more so with matters of the heart! I put no trust in the showy sort of affection that is quick to come forth when a suitable occasion presents itself. Let me tell you of something that happened to me a long time ago. You may find the story a touch wanton, but hear me through all the same."

He drew close to Genji, who awoke from his slumber. Tō no Chūjō, chin in hand, sat opposite, listening with the greatest admiration and attention. There was in the young man's manner something slightly comical, as if he were a sage expostulating upon the deepest truths of the universe, but at such times a young man is not inclined to conceal his most intimate secrets.

"It happened when I was very young, hardly more than a page. I was attracted to a woman. She was of a sort I have mentioned before, not the most beautiful in the world. In my youthful frivolity, I did not at first think of making her my wife. She was someone to visit, not someone who deserved my full attention. Other places interested me more. She was violently jealous. If only she could be a little more understanding, I thought, wanting to be away from the interminable quarreling. And on the other hand it sometimes struck me as a little sad that she should be so worried about a man of so little account as myself. In the course of time I began to mend my ways.

"For my sake, she would try to do things for which her talent and nature did not suit her, and she was determined not to seem inferior even in matters for which she had no great aptitude. She served me diligently in everything. She did not want to be guilty of the smallest thing that might go against my wishes. I had at first thought her rather strong-willed, but she proved to be docile and pliant. She thought constantly about hiding her less favorable qualities, afraid that they might put me off, and she did what she could to avoid displaying herself and causing me embarrassment. She was a model of devotion. In a word, there was nothing wrong with her—save the one thing I found so trying.

"I told myself that she was devoted to the point of fear, and that if I led her to think I might be giving her up she might be a little less suspicious and given to nagging. I had had almost all I could stand. If she really wanted to be with me and I suggested that a break was near, then she might reform. I behaved with studied coldness, and when, as always, her resentment exploded, I said to her: 'Not even the strongest bond between husband and wife can stand an unlimited amount of this sort of thing. It will eventually break, and he will not see her again. If you want to bring matters to such a pass, then go on doubting me as you have. If you would like to be with me for the years that lie ahead of us, then bear the trials as they come, difficult though they may be, and think them the way of the world. If you manage to overcome your jealousy, my affection is certain to grow. It seems likely that I will move ahead into an office of some distinction, and you will go with me and have no one you need think of as a rival.' I was very pleased with myself. I had performed brilliantly as a preceptor.

"But she only smiled. 'Oh, it won't be all that much trouble to put up with your want of consequence and wait till you are important. It will be much harder to pass the months and the years in the barely discernible hope that you will settle down and mend your fickle ways. Maybe you are right. Maybe this is the time to part.'

"I was furious, and I said so, and she answered in kind. Then, suddenly, she took my hand and bit my finger.

"I reproved her somewhat extravagantly. 'You insult me, and now you have wounded me. Do you think I can go to court like this? I am, as you say, a person of no consequence, and now, mutilated as I am, what is to help me get ahead in the world? There is nothing left for me but to become a monk.' That meeting must be our last, I said, and departed, flexing my wounded finger.

"'I count them over, the many things between us.
    One finger does not, alas, count the sum of your failures.'

"I left the verse behind, adding that now she had nothing to complain about.

"She had a verse of her own. There were tears in her eyes.

"'I have counted them up myself, be assured, my failures.
    For one bitten finger must all be bitten away?'

"I did not really mean to leave her, but my days were occupied in wanderings here and there, and I sent her no message. Then, late one evening toward the end of the year—it was an evening of rehearsals for the Kamo festival—a sleet was falling as we all started for home. Home. It came to me that I really had nowhere to go but her house. It would be no pleasure to sleep alone at the palace, and if I visited a woman of sensibility I would be kept freezing while she admired the snow. I would go look in upon *her,* and see what sort of mood she might be in. And so, brushing away the sleet, I made my way to her house. I felt just a little shy, but told myself that the sleet melting from my coat should melt her resentment. There was a dim light turned toward the wall, and a comfortable old robe of thick silk lay spread out to warm. The curtains were raised, everything suggested that she was waiting for me. I felt that I had done rather well.

"But she was nowhere in sight. She had gone that evening to stay with her parents, said the women who had been left behind. I had been feeling somewhat unhappy that she had maintained such a chilly silence, sending no amorous poems or queries. I wondered, though not very seriously, whether her shrillness and her jealousy might not have been intended for the precise purpose of disposing of me; but now I found clothes laid out with more attention to color and pattern than usual, exactly as she knew I liked them. She was seeing to my needs even now that I had apparently discarded her.

"And so, despite this strange state of affairs, I was convinced that she did not mean to do without me. I continued to send messages, and she neither protested nor gave an impression of wanting to annoy me by staying out of sight, and in her answers she was always careful not to anger or hurt me. Yet she went on saying that she could not forgive the behavior I had been guilty of in the past. If I would settle down she would be very happy to keep company with me. Sure that we would not part, I thought I would give her another lesson or two. I told her I had no intention of reforming, and made a great show of independence. She was sad, I gathered, and then without warning she died. And the game I had been playing came to seem rather inappropriate.

"She was a woman of such accomplishments that I could leave everything to her. I continue to regret what I had done. I could discuss trivial things with her and important things. For her skills in dyeing she might have been compared to Princess Tatsuta and the comparison would not have seemed ridiculous, and in sewing she could have held her own with Princess Tanabata."[6]

The young man sighed and sighed again.

Tō no Chūjō nodded. "Leaving her accomplishments as a seamstress aside, I should imagine you were looking for someone as faithful as Princess Tanabata.[7] And if she could embroider like Princess Tatsuta, well, it does not seem likely that you will come on her equal again. When the colors of a robe do not match the seasons, the flowers of spring and the autumn tints, when they are somehow vague and muddy, then the whole effort is as futile as the dew. So it is with women. It is not easy in this world to find a perfect wife. We are all pursuing the ideal and failing to find it."

The guards officer talked on. "There was another one. I was seeing her at about the same time. She was more amiable than the one I have just described to you. Everything about her told of refinement. Her poems, her

---

6. A goddess and the patron of sewing and weaving. Tatsuta was the patron of autumn and, therefore, of dyeing.   7. Tanabata and her lover the Herdsman (the stars Altair and Vega) met annually on the seventh night of the Seventh Month.

handwriting when she dashed off a letter, the koto[8] she plucked a note on—
everything seemed right. She was clever with her hands and clever with
words. And her looks were adequate. The jealous woman's house had come
to seem the place I could really call mine, and I went in secret to the other
woman from time to time and became very fond of her. The jealous one
died, I wondered what to do next. I was sad, of course, but a man cannot go
on being sad forever. I visited the other more often. But there was something
a little too aggressive, a little too sensuous about her. As I came to know her
well and to think her a not very dependable sort, I called less often. And I
learned that I was not her only secret visitor.

"One bright moonlit autumn night I chanced to leave court with a friend.
He got in with me as I started for my father's. He was much concerned, he
said, about a house where he was sure someone would be waiting. It happened to be on my way.

"Through gaps in a neglected wall I could see the moon shining on a pond.
It seemed a pity not to linger a moment at a spot where the moon seemed so
much at home, and so I climbed out after my friend. It would appear that
this was not his first visit. He proceeded briskly to the veranda and took a
seat near the gate and looked up at the moon for a time. The chrysanthemums were at their best, very slightly touched by the frost, and the red
leaves were beautiful in the autumn wind. He took out a flute and played a
tune on it, and sang 'The Well of Asuka'[9] and several other songs. Blending
nicely with the flute came the mellow tones of a Japanese koto. It had been
tuned in advance, apparently, and was waiting. The *ritsu* scale[1] had a pleasant modern sound to it, right for a soft, womanly touch from behind blinds,
and right for the clear moonlight too. I can assure you that the effect was
not at all unpleasant.

"Delighted, my friend went up to the blinds.

"'I see that no one has yet broken a path through your fallen leaves,' he
said, somewhat sarcastically. He broke off a chrysanthemum and pushed it
under the blinds.

> "'Uncommonly fine this house, for moon, for koto.
> Does it bring to itself indifferent callers as well?

"'Excuse me for asking. You must not be parsimonious with your music.
You have a by no means indifferent listener.'

"He was very playful indeed. The woman's voice, when she offered a verse
of her own, was suggestive and equally playful.

> "'No match the leaves for the angry winter winds.
> Am I to detain the flute that joins those winds?'

"Naturally unaware of resentment so near at hand, she changed to a Chinese koto in an elegant *banjiki*.[2] Though I had to admit that she had talent, I
was very annoyed. It is amusing enough, if you let things go no further, to
exchange jokes from time to time with fickle and frivolous ladies; but as a
place to take seriously, even for an occasional visit, matters here seemed to
have gone too far. I made the events of that evening my excuse for leaving her.

---

8. A thirteen-stringed zither.   9. A folk song.   1. A pentatonic scale (that is, having five tones to an octave), resembling the Western minor without its half steps.   2. The note B in ancient Japanese music.

"I see, as I look back on the two affairs, that young though I was the second of the two women did not seem the kind to put my trust in. I have no doubt that the wariness will grow as the years go by. The dear, uncertain ones—the dew that will fall when the *hagi*[3] branch is bent, the speck of frost that will melt when it is lifted from the bamboo leaf—no doubt they can be interesting for a time. You have seven years to go before you are my age," he said to Genji. "Just wait and you will understand. Perhaps you can take the advice of a person of no importance, and avoid the uncertain ones. They stumble sooner or later, and do a man's name no good when they do."

Tō no Chūjō nodded, as always. Genji, though he only smiled, seemed to agree.

"Neither of the tales you have given us has been a very happy one," he said.

"Let me tell you a story about a foolish woman I once knew," said Tō no Chūjō. "I was seeing her in secret, and I did not think that the affair was likely to last very long. But she was very beautiful, and as time passed I came to think that I must go on seeing her, if only infrequently. I sensed that she had come to depend on me. I expected signs of jealousy. There were none. She did not seem to feel the resentment a man expects from a woman he visits so seldom. She waited quietly, morning and night. My affection grew, and I let it be known that she did indeed have a man she could depend on. There was something very appealing about her (she was an orphan), letting me know that I was all she had.

"She seemed content. Untroubled, I stayed away for rather a long time. Then—I heard of it only later—my wife found a roundabout way to be objectionable. I did not know that I had become a cause of pain. I had not forgotten, but I let a long time pass without writing. The woman was desperately lonely and worried for the child she had borne. One day she sent me a letter attached to a wild carnation." His voice trembled.

"And what did it say?" Genji urged him on.

"Nothing very remarkable. I do remember her poem, though:

> " 'The fence of the mountain rustic may fall to the ground.
> Rest gently, O dew, upon the wild carnation.'

"I went to see her again. The talk was open and easy, as always, but she seemed pensive as she looked out at the dewy garden from the neglected house. She seemed to be weeping, joining her laments to the songs of the autumn insects. It could have been a scene from an old romance. I whispered a verse:

> " 'No bloom in this wild array would I wish to slight.
> But dearest of all to me is the wild carnation.'

"Her carnation had been the child. I made it clear that my own was the lady herself, the wild carnation no dust falls upon.[4]

"She answered:

> " 'Dew wets the sleeve that brushes the wild carnation.
> The tempest rages. Now comes autumn too.'

3. Japanese bush clover.   4. Alludes to a poem in *The Kokinshū*: "Let no dust fall upon the wild carnation, / Upon the couch where lie my love and I." For the pink, or wild, carnation, she has used a word that can also mean "child." He has shifted to a synonym, the first two syllables of which mean "bed."

"She spoke quietly all the same, and she did not seem really angry. She did shed a tear from time to time, but she seemed ashamed of herself, and anxious to avoid difficult moments. I went away feeling much relieved. It was clear that she did not want to show any sign of anger at my neglect. And so once more I stayed away for rather a long time.

"And when I looked in on her again she had disappeared.

"If she is still living, it must be in very unhappy circumstances. She need not have suffered so if she had asserted herself a little more in the days when we were together. She need not have put up with my absences, and I would have seen to her needs over the years. The child was a very pretty little girl. I was fond of her, and I have not been able to find any trace of her.

"She must be listed among your reticent ones, I suppose? She let me have no hint of jealousy. Unaware of what was going on, I had no intention of giving her up. But the result was hopeless yearning, quite as if I had given her up. I am beginning to forget; and how is it with her? She must remember me sometimes, I should think, with regret, because she must remember too that it was not I who abandoned her. She was, I fear, not the sort of woman one finds it possible to keep for very long.

"Your jealous woman must be interesting enough to remember, but she must have been a bit wearying. And the other one, all her skill on the koto cannot have been much compensation for the undependability. And the one I have described to you—her very lack of jealousy might have brought a suspicion that there was another man in her life. Well, such is the way with the world—you cannot give your unqualified approval to any of them. Where are you to go for the woman who has no defects and who combines the virtues of all three? You might choose Our Lady of Felicity[5]—and find yourself married to unspeakable holiness."

The others laughed.

Tō no Chūjō turned to the young man from the ministry of rites. "You must have interesting stories too."

"Oh, please. How could the lowest of the low hope to hold your attention?"

"You must not keep us waiting."

"Let me think a minute." He seemed to be sorting out memories. "When I was still a student I knew a remarkably wise woman. She was the sort worth consulting about public affairs, and she had a good mind too for the little tangles that come into your private life. Her erudition would have put any ordinary sage to shame. In a word, I was awed into silence.

"I was studying under a learned scholar. I had heard that he had many daughters, and on some occasion or other I had made the acquaintance of this one. The father learned of the affair. Taking out wedding cups, he made reference, among other things, to a Chinese poem about the merits of an impoverished wife.[6] Although not exactly enamored of the woman, I had developed a certain fondness for her, and felt somewhat deferential toward the father. She was most attentive to my needs. I learned many estimable things from her, to add to my store of erudition and help me with my work. Her letters were lucidity itself, in the purest Chinese. None of this Japanese

5. A Buddhist deity who confers happiness and virtue.   6. *On Marriage*, a poem by Po Chü-i (772–846), the first of *Ten Poems Composed at Ch'ang-an*.

nonsense for her. I found it hard to think of giving her up, and under her tutelage I managed to turn out a few things in passable Chinese myself. And yet—though I would not wish to seem wanting in gratitude, it is undeniable that a man of no learning is somewhat daunted at the thought of being forever his wife's inferior. So it is in any case with an ignorant one like me; and what possible use could you gentlemen have for so formidable a wife? A stupid, senseless affair, a man tells himself, and yet he is dragged on against his will, as if there might have been a bond in some other life."

"She seems a most unusual woman." Genji and Tō no Chūjō were eager to hear more.

Quite aware that the great gentlemen were amusing themselves at his expense, he smiled somewhat impishly. "One day when I had not seen her for rather a long time I had some reason or other for calling. She was not in the room where we had been in the habit of meeting. She insisted on talking to me through a very obtrusive screen. I thought she might be sulking, and it all seemed very silly. And then again—if she was going to be so petty, I might have my excuse for leaving her. But no. She was not a person to let her jealousy show. She knew too much of the world. Her explanation of what was happening poured forth at great length, all of it very well reasoned.

"'I have been indisposed with a malady known as coryza.[7] Discommoded to an uncommon degree, I have been imbibing of a steeped potion made from bulbaceous herbs. Because of the noisome odor, I will not find it possible to admit of greater propinquity. If you have certain random matters for my attention, perhaps you can deposit the relevant materials where you are.'

"'Is that so?' I said. I could think of nothing else to say.

"I started to leave. Perhaps feeling a little lonely, she called after me, somewhat shrilly. "When I have disencumbered myself of this aroma, we can meet once more.'

"It seemed cruel to rush off, but the time was not right for a quiet visit. And it was as she said: her odor was rather high. Again I started out, pausing long enough to compose a verse:

"'The spider[8] must have told you I would come.
　　Then why am I asked to keep company with garlic?'

"I did not take time to accuse her of deliberately putting me off.
"She was quicker than I. She chased after me with an answer.

"'Were we two who kept company every night,
　　What would be wrong with garlic in the daytime?'[9]

"You must admit she was quick with her answers." He had quietly finished his story.

The two gentlemen, Genji and his friend, would have none of it. "A complete fabrication, from start to finish. Where could you find such a woman? Better to have a quiet evening with a witch." They thought it an outrageous story, and asked if he could come up with nothing more acceptable.

"Surely you would not wish for a more unusual sort of story?"

7. That is, the common cold, which she would have said if she were not flaunting her superior knowledge.
8. It was believed that a busy spider foretold a visit from one's lover.　9. The word for *daytime* is homophonous with a word for numbers of strongly scented roots.

The guards officer took up again. "In women as in men, there is no one worse than the one who tries to display her scanty knowledge in full. It is among the least endearing of accomplishments for a woman to have delved into the Three Histories and the Five Classics;[1] and who, on the other hand, can go through life without absorbing something of public affairs and private? A reasonably alert woman does not need to be a scholar to see and hear a great many things. The very worst are the ones who scribble off Chinese characters at such a rate that they fill a good half of letters where they are most out of place, letters to other women. 'What a bore,' you say. 'If only she had mastered a few of the feminine things.' She cannot of course intend it to be so, but the words read aloud seem muscular and unyielding, and in the end hopelessly mannered. I fear that even our highest of the high are too often guilty of the fault.

"Then there is the one who fancies herself a poetess. She immerses herself in the anthologies, and brings antique references into her very first line, interesting enough in themselves but inappropriate. A man has had enough with that first line, but he is called heartless if he does not answer, and cannot claim the honors if he does not answer in a similar vein. On the Day of the Iris he is frantic to get off to court and has no eye for irises, and there she is with subtle references to iris roots. On the Day of the Chrysanthemum,[2] his mind has no room for anything but the Chinese poem he must come up with in the course of the day, and there she is with something about the dew upon the chrysanthemum. A poem that might have been amusing and even moving on a less frantic day has been badly timed and must therefore be rejected. A woman who dashes off a poem at an unpoetic moment cannot be called a woman of taste.

"For someone who is not alive to the particular quality of each moment and each occasion, it is safer not to make a great show of taste and elegance; and from someone who is alive to it all, a man wants restraint. She should feign a certain ignorance, she should keep back a little of what she is prepared to say."

Through all the talk Genji's thoughts were on a single lady. His heart was filled with her. She answered every requirement, he thought. She had none of the defects, was guilty of none of the excesses, that had emerged from the discussion.

The talk went on and came to no conclusion, and as the rainy night gave way to dawn the stories became more and more improbable.

It appeared that the weather would be fine. Fearing that his father-in-law might resent his secluding himself in the palace, Genji set off for Sanjō. The mansion itself, his wife—every detail was admirable and in the best of taste. Nowhere did he find a trace of disorder. Here was a lady whom his friends must count among the truly dependable ones, the indispensable ones. And yet—she was too finished in her perfection, she was so cool and self-possessed that she made him uncomfortable. He turned to playful conversation with Chūnagon and Nakatsukasa and other pretty young women among

---

1. Ancient Chinese histories and the canonical works of early Chinese thought: *The Book of Poetry, The Book of History, The Book of Divination (I Ching), Spring and Autumn Annals,* and *The Book of Rites.* 2. The Day of the Chrysanthemum fell on the ninth of the Ninth Month. The Day of the Iris fell on the fifth of the Fifth Month.

her attendants. Because it was very warm, he loosened his dress, and they thought him even handsomer.

The minister came to pay his respects. Seeing Genji thus in dishabille, he made his greetings from behind a conveniently placed curtain. Though somewhat annoyed at having to receive such a distinguished visitor on such a warm day, Genji made it clear to the women that they were not to smile at his discomfort. He was a very calm, self-possessed young gentleman.

As evening approached, the women reminded him that his route from the palace had transgressed upon the domain of the Lord of the Center.[3] He must not spend the night here.

"To be sure. But my own house lies in the same direction. And I am very tired." He lay down as if he meant in spite of everything to stay the night.

"It simply will not do, my lord."

"The governor of Kii here," said one of Genji's men, pointing to another. "He has dammed the Inner River[4] and brought it into his garden, and the waters are very cool, very pleasant."

"An excellent idea. I really am very tired, and perhaps we can send ahead to see whether we might drive into the garden."

There were no doubt all sorts of secret places to which he could have gone to avoid the taboo. He had come to Sanjō, and after a considerable absence. The minister might suspect that he had purposely chosen a night on which he must leave early.

The governor of Kii was cordial enough with his invitation, but when he withdrew he mentioned certain misgivings to Genji's men. Ritual purification,[5] he said, had required all the women to be away from his father's house, and unfortunately they were all crowded into his own, a cramped enough place at best. He feared that Genji would be inconvenienced.

"Nothing of the sort," said Genji, who had overheard. "It is good to have people around. There is nothing worse than a night away from home with no ladies about. Just let me have a little corner behind their curtains."

"If that is what you want," said his men, "then the governor's place should be perfect."

And so they sent runners ahead. Genji set off immediately, though in secret, thinking that no great ceremony was called for. He did not tell the minister where he was going, and took only his nearest retainers. The governor grumbled that they were in rather too much of a hurry. No one listened.

The east rooms of the main hall had been cleaned and made presentable. The waters were as they had been described, a most pleasing arrangement. A fence of wattles, of a deliberately rustic appearance, enclosed the garden, and much care had gone into the plantings. The wind was cool. Insects were humming, one scarcely knew where, fireflies drew innumerable lines of

3. A god who changed his abode periodically and did not permit trespassers. Superstition influenced many aspects of Japanese life in the 11th century, with directional taboos among the most important. There were three main types of directional taboo. The northeast was regarded as a perpetually unlucky direction. Other directions were unfavorable during certain periods of one's life, so that at sixteen, for example, one might have to avoid the northwest. Still other directions were universally but temporarily inauspicious, caused by the transit of deities, whose descent from the heavens could close a sector to human traffic. A taboo of the third category is what affects Genji on this evening. 4. Marks the eastern limits of the capital. 5. Various purification rituals were conducted to ward off bad luck and to remove the polluting effects of sickness or a death in the family.

light, and all in all the time and the place could not have been more to his liking. His men were already tippling, out where they could admire a brook flowing under a gallery. The governor seemed to have "hurried off for viands."[6] Gazing calmly about him, Genji concluded that the house would be of the young guardsman's favored in-between category. Having heard that his host's stepmother, who would be in residence, was a high-spirited lady, he listened for signs of her presence. There were signs of someone's presence immediately to the west. He heard a swishing of silk and young voices that were not at all displeasing. Young ladies seemed to be giggling self-consciously and trying to contain themselves. The shutters were raised, it seemed, but upon a word from the governor they were lowered. There was a faint light over the sliding doors. Genji went for a look, but could find no opening large enough to see through. Listening for a time, he concluded that the women had gathered in the main room, next to his.

The whispered discussion seemed to be about Genji himself.

"He is dreadfully serious, they say, and has made a fine match for himself. And still so young. Don't you imagine he might be a little lonely? But they say he finds time for a quiet little adventure now and then."

Genji was startled. There was but one lady on his mind, day after day. So this was what the gossips were saying; and what if, in it all, there was evidence that rumors of his real love had spread abroad? But the talk seemed harmless enough, and after a time he wearied of it. Someone misquoted a poem he had sent to his cousin Asagao,[7] attached to a morning glory. Their standards seemed not of the most rigorous. A misquoted poem for every occasion. He feared he might be disappointed when he saw the woman.

The governor had more lights set out at the eaves, and turned up those in the room. He had refreshments brought.

"And are the curtains all hung?"[8] asked Genji. "You hardly qualify as a host if they are not."

"And what will you feast upon?" rejoined the governor, somewhat stiffly. "Nothing so very elaborate, I fear."

Genji found a cool place out near the veranda and lay down. His men were quiet. Several young boys were present, all very sprucely dressed, sons of the host and of his father, the governor of Iyo.[9] There was one particularly attractive lad of perhaps twelve or thirteen. Asking who were the sons of whom, Genji learned that the boy was the younger brother of the host's stepmother, son of a guards officer no longer living. His father had had great hopes for the boy and had died while he was still very young. He had come to this house upon his sister's marriage to the governor of Iyo. He seemed to have some aptitude for the classics, said the host, and was of a quiet, pleasant disposition; but he was young and without backing, and his prospects at court were not good.

"A pity. The sister, then, is your stepmother?"

"Yes."

6. Reference to a folk song: "The jeweled flask is here. / But where is our host, what of our host? / He has hurried off for viands, / Off to the beach for viands, / To Koyurugi for seaweed." 7. The word for various morning flowers, including the morning glory. 8. Reference to a folk song: "The curtains all are hung. / Come and be my bridegroom. / And what will you feast upon? / Abalone, turbo, / And sea urchins too." 9. He is sometimes called the governor and sometimes the vice governor.

"A very young stepmother. My father had thought of inviting her to court. He was asking just the other day what might have happened to her. Life," he added with a solemnity rather beyond his years, "is uncertain."

"It happened almost by accident. Yes, you are right: it is a very uncertain world, and it always has been, particularly for women. They are like bits of driftwood."

"Your father is no doubt very alert to her needs. Perhaps, indeed, one has trouble knowing who is the master?"

"He quite worships her. The rest of us are not entirely happy with the arrangements he has made."

"But you cannot expect him to let you young gallants have everything. He has a name in that regard himself, you know. And where might the lady be?"

"They have all been told to spend the night in the porter's lodge, but they don't seem in a hurry to go."

The wine was having its effect, and his men were falling asleep on the veranda.

Genji lay wide awake, not pleased at the prospect of sleeping alone. He sensed that there was someone in the room to the north. It would be the lady of whom they had spoken. Holding his breath, he went to the door and listened.

"Where are you?" The pleasantly husky voice was that of the boy who had caught his eye.

"Over here." It would be the sister. The two voices, very sleepy, resembled each other. "And where is our guest? I had thought he might be somewhere near, but he seems to have gone away."

"He's in the east room." The boy's voice was low. "I saw him. He is every bit as handsome as everyone says."

"If it were daylight I might have a look at him myself." The sister yawned, and seemed to draw the bedclothes over her face.

Genji was a little annoyed. She might have questioned her brother more energetically.

"I'll sleep out toward the veranda. But we should have more light." The boy turned up the lamp. The lady apparently lay at a diagonal remove from Genji. "And where is Chūjō? I don't like being left alone."

"She went to have a bath. She said she'd be right back." He spoke from out near the veranda.

All was quiet again. Genji slipped the latch open and tried the doors. They had not been bolted. A curtain had been set up just inside, and in the dim light he could make out Chinese chests and other furniture scattered in some disorder. He made his way through to her side. She lay by herself, a slight little figure. Though vaguely annoyed at being disturbed, she evidently took him for the woman Chūjō until he pulled back the covers.

"I heard you summoning a captain," he said, "and I thought my prayers over the months had been answered."[1]

She gave a little gasp. It was muffled by the bedclothes and no one else heard.

---

1. *Chūjō* means "captain," the rank Genji holds. Women's names were often derived from the titles of their fathers; hence the lady's companion is called Chūjō.

"You are perfectly correct if you think me unable to control myself. But I wish you to know that I have been thinking of you for a very long time. And the fact that I have finally found my opportunity and am taking advantage of it should show that my feelings are by no means shallow."

His manner was so gently persuasive that devils and demons could not have gainsaid him. The lady would have liked to announce to the world that a strange man had invaded her boudoir.

"I think you have mistaken me for someone else," she said, outraged, though the remark was under her breath.

The little figure, pathetically fragile and as if on the point of expiring from the shock, seemed to him very beautiful.

"I am driven by thoughts so powerful that a mistake is completely out of the question. It is cruel of you to pretend otherwise. I promise you that I will do nothing unseemly. I must ask you to listen to a little of what is on my mind."

She was so small that he lifted her easily. As he passed through the doors to his own room, he came upon the Chūjō who had been summoned earlier. He called out in surprise. Surprised in turn, Chūjō peered into the darkness. The perfume that came from his robes like a cloud of smoke told her who he was. She stood in confusion, unable to speak. Had he been a more ordinary intruder she might have ripped her mistress away by main force. But she would not have wished to raise an alarm all through the house.

She followed after, but Genji was quite unmoved by her pleas.

"Come for her in the morning," he said, sliding the doors closed.

The lady was bathed in perspiration and quite beside herself at the thought of what Chūjō, and the others too, would be thinking. Genji had to feel sorry for her. Yet the sweet words poured forth, the whole gamut of pretty devices for making a woman surrender.

She was not to be placated. "Can it be true? Can I be asked to believe that you are not making fun of me? Women of low estate should have husbands of low estate."

He was sorry for her and somewhat ashamed of himself, but his answer was careful and sober. "You take me for one of the young profligates you see around? I must protest. I am very young and know nothing of the estates which concern you so. You have heard of me, surely, and you must know that I do not go in for adventures. I must ask what unhappy entanglement imposes this upon me. You are making a fool of me, and nothing should surprise me, not even the tumultuous emotions that do in fact surprise me."

But now his very splendor made her resist. He might think her obstinate and insensitive, but her unfriendliness must make him dismiss her from further consideration. Naturally soft and pliant, she was suddenly firm. It was as with the young bamboo: she bent but was not to be broken. She was weeping. He had his hands full but would not for the world have missed the experience.

"Why must you so dislike me?" he asked with a sigh, unable to stop the weeping. "Don't you know that the unexpected encounters are the ones we were fated for? Really, my dear, you do seem to know altogether too little of the world."

"If I had met you before I came to this," she replied, and he had to admit the truth of it, "then I might have consoled myself with the thought—it might have been no more than self-deception, of course—that you would someday come to think fondly of me. But this is hopeless, worse than I can tell you. Well, it has happened. Say no to those who ask if you have seen me."[2]

One may imagine that he found many kind promises with which to comfort her.

The first cock was crowing and Genji's men were awake.

"Did you sleep well? I certainly did."

"Let's get the carriage ready."

Some of the women were heard asking whether people who were avoiding taboos were expected to leave again in the middle of the night.

Genji was very unhappy. He feared he could not find an excuse for another meeting. He did not see how he could visit her, and he did not see how they could write. Chūjō came out, also very unhappy. He let the lady go and then took her back again.

"How shall I write to you? Your feelings and my own—they are not shallow, and we may expect deep memories. Has anything ever been so strange?" He was in tears, which made him yet handsomer. The cocks were now crowing insistently. He was feeling somewhat harried as he composed his farewell verse:

> "Why must they startle with their dawn alarums
> When hours are yet required to thaw the ice?"

The lady was ashamed of herself that she had caught the eye of a man so far above her. His kind words had little effect. She was thinking of her husband, whom for the most part she considered a clown and a dolt. She trembled to think that a dream might have told him of the night's happenings.

This was the verse with which she replied:

> "Day has broken without an end to my tears.
> To my cries of sorrow are added the calls of the cocks."

It was lighter by the moment. He saw her to her door, for the house was coming to life. A barrier had fallen between them. In casual court dress, he leaned for a time against the south railing and looked out at the garden. Shutters were being raised along the west side of the house. Women seemed to be looking out at him, beyond a low screen at the veranda. He no doubt brought shivers of delight. The moon still bright in the dawn sky added to the beauty of the morning. The sky, without heart itself, can at these times be friendly or sad, as the beholder sees it. Genji was in anguish. He knew that there would be no way even to exchange notes. He cast many a glance backward as he left.

At Sanjō once more, he was unable to sleep. If the thought that they would not meet again so pained him, what must it do to the lady? She was no beauty, but she had seemed pretty and cultivated. Of the middling rank, he said to himself. The guards officer who had seen them all knew what he was talking about.

Spending most of his time now at Sanjō, he thought sadly of the unapproachable lady. At last he summoned her stepson, the governor of Kii.

---

2. An allusion to a poem in *The Kokinshū*: "As one small mark of your love, if such there be, / Say no to those who ask if you have seen me."

"The boy I saw the other night, your foster uncle. He seemed a promising lad. I think I might have a place for him. I might even introduce him to my father."

"Your gracious words quite overpower me. Perhaps I should take the matter up with his sister."

Genji's heart leaped at the mention of the lady. "Does she have children?"

"No. She and my father have been married for two years now, but I gather that she is not happy. Her father meant to send her to court."

"How sad for her. Rumor has it that she is a beauty. Might rumor be correct?"

"Mistaken, I fear. But of course stepsons do not see a great deal of stepmothers."

Several days later he brought the boy to Genji. Examined in detail the boy was not perfect, but he had considerable charm and grace. Genji addressed him in a most friendly manner, which both confused and pleased him. Questioning him about his sister, Genji did not learn a great deal. The answers were ready enough while they were on safe ground, but the boy's self-possession was a little disconcerting. Genji hinted rather broadly at what had taken place. The boy was startled. He guessed the truth but was not old enough to pursue the matter.

Genji gave him a letter for his sister. Tears came to her eyes. How much had her brother been told? she wondered, spreading the letter to hide her flushed cheeks.

It was very long, and concluded with a poem:

> "I yearn to dream again the dream of that night.
> The nights go by in lonely wakefulness.

"There are no nights of sleep."[3]

The hand was splendid, but she could only weep at the yet stranger turn her life had taken.

The next day Genji sent for the boy.

Where was her answer? the boy asked his sister.

"Tell him you found no one to give his letter to."

"Oh, please." The boy smiled knowingly. "How can I tell him that? I have learned enough to be sure there is no mistake."

She was horrified. It was clear that Genji had told everything.

"I don't know why you must always be so clever. Perhaps it would be better if you didn't go at all."

"But he sent for me." And the boy departed.

The governor of Kii was beginning to take an interest in his pretty young stepmother, and paying insistent court. His attention turned to the brother, who became his frequent companion.

"I waited for you all day yesterday," said Genji. "Clearly I am not as much on your mind as you are on mine."

The boy flushed.

"Where is her answer?" And when the boy told him: "A fine messenger. I had hoped for something better."

---

3. Alludes to a classical poem, "Where shall I find comfort in my longing? / There are no dreams, for there are no nights of sleep."

There were other letters.

"But didn't you know?" he said to the boy. "I knew her before that old man she married. She thought me feeble and useless, it seems, and looked for a stouter support. Well, she may spurn me, but you needn't. You will be my son. The gentleman you are looking to for help won't be with us long."

The boy seemed to be thinking what a nuisance his sister's husband was. Genji was amused.

He treated the boy like a son, making him a constant companion, giving him clothes from his own wardrobe, taking him to court. He continued to write to the lady. She feared that with so inexperienced a messenger the secret might leak out and add suspicions of promiscuity to her other worries. These were very grand messages, but something more in keeping with her station seemed called for. Her answers were stiff and formal when she answered at all. She could not forget his extraordinary good looks and elegance, so dimly seen that night. But she belonged to another, and nothing was to be gained by trying to interest him. His longing was undiminished. He could not forget how touchingly fragile and confused she had been. With so many people around, another invasion of her boudoir was not likely to go unnoticed, and the results would be sad.

One evening after he had been at court for some days he found an excuse: his mansion again lay in a forbidden direction. Pretending to set off for Sanjō, he went instead to the house of the governor of Kii. The governor was delighted, thinking that those well-designed brooks and lakes had made an impression. Genji had consulted with the boy, always in earnest attendance. The lady had been informed of the visit. She must admit that they seemed powerful, the urges that forced him to such machinations. But if she were to receive him and display herself openly, what could she expect save the anguish of the other night, a repetition of that nightmare? No, the shame would be too much.

The brother having gone off upon a summons from Genji, she called several of her women. "I think it might be in bad taste to stay too near. I am not feeling at all well, and perhaps a massage might help, somewhere far enough away that we won't disturb him."

The woman Chūjō had rooms on a secluded gallery. They would be her refuge.

It was as she had feared. Genji sent his men to bed early and dispatched his messenger. The boy could not find her. He looked everywhere and finally, at the end of his wits, came upon her in the gallery.

He was almost in tears. "But he will think me completely useless."

"And what do you propose to be doing? You are a child, and it is quite improper for you to be carrying such messages. Tell him I have not been feeling well and have kept some of my women to massage me. You should not be here. They will think it very odd."

She spoke with great firmness, but her thoughts were far from firm. How happy she might have been if she had not made this unfortunate marriage, and were still in the house filled with memories of her dead parents. Then she could have awaited his visits, however infrequent. And the coldness she must force herself to display—he must think her quite unaware of her place in the world. She had done what she thought best, and she was in anguish.

Well, it all was hard fact, about which she had no choice. She must continue to play the cold and insensitive woman.

Genji lay wondering what blandishments the boy might be using. He was not sanguine, for the boy was very young. Presently he came back to report his mission a failure. What an uncommonly strong woman! Genji feared he must seem a bit feckless beside her. He heaved a deep sigh. This evidence of despondency had the boy on the point of tears.

Genji sent the lady a poem:

> "I wander lost in the Sonohara moorlands,
> For I did not know the deceiving ways of the broom tree.[4]

"How am I to describe my sorrow?"

She too lay sleepless. This was her answer:

> "Here and not here, I lie in my shabby hut.
> Would that I might like the broom tree vanish away."

The boy traveled back and forth with messages, a wish to be helpful driving sleep from his thoughts. His sister beseeched him to consider what the others might think.

Genji's men were snoring away. He lay alone with his discontent. This unique stubbornness was no broom tree. It refused to vanish away. The stubbornness was what interested him. But he had had enough. Let her do as she wished. And yet—not even this simple decision was easy.

"At least take me to her."

"She is shut up in a very dirty room and there are all sorts of women with her. I do not think it would be wise." The boy would have liked to be more helpful.

"Well, you at least must not abandon me." Genji pulled the boy down beside him.

The boy was delighted, such were Genji's youthful charms. Genji, for his part, or so one is informed, found the boy more attractive than his chilly sister.

Summary   Genji continues to yearn for the woman he met in the last chapter, the wife of the governor of Iyo. He pays another visit to the house where she is staying and steals into the lady's quarters. She eludes him by slipping out of the room, and, unaware of this, Genji makes love to her stepdaughter, whom she has left behind. The governor's wife will reappear in future episodes, where she is called the lady of the locust shell, a reference to the light summer singlet she discards, like a locust shedding its shell, when she avoids Genji in this chapter.

CHAPTER 4

Evening Faces

On his way from court to pay one of his calls at Rokujō, Genji stopped to inquire after his old nurse, Koremitsu's[5] mother, at her house in Gojō. Gravely ill, she had become a nun. The carriage entrance was closed. He

---

4. Alludes to a poem: "O broom tree of Fuseya in Sonohara, / You seem to be there, and yet I cannot find you." The broom tree of Sonohara was said to disappear or change shape when one approached. *Fuseya* means "hut," which the lady employs in her response to Genji.   5. Genji's servant and confidant. Rokujō is the sixth ward. One of Genji's loves lives there and thus her name, the Rokujō lady. Daughter of an influential minister and widow of a crown prince, she is one of Genji's most demanding women. Although the reader does not learn much about her until chapter 9, she begins to make her presence felt here.

sent for Koremitsu and while he was waiting looked up and down the dirty, cluttered street. Beside the nurse's house was a new fence of plaited cypress. The four or five narrow shutters above had been raised, and new blinds, white and clean, hung in the apertures. He caught outlines of pretty foreheads beyond. He would have judged, as they moved about, that they belonged to rather tall women. What sort of women might they be? His carriage was simple and unadorned and he had no outrunners. Quite certain that he would not be recognized, he leaned out for a closer look. The hanging gate, of something like trelliswork, was propped on a pole, and he could see that the house was tiny and flimsy. He felt a little sorry for the occupants of such a place—and then asked himself who in this world had more than a temporary shelter.[6] A hut, a jeweled pavilion, they were the same. A pleasantly green vine was climbing a board wall. The white flowers, he thought, had a rather self-satisfied look about them.

"'I needs must ask the lady far off yonder,'"[7] he said, as if to himself.

An attendant came up, bowing deeply. "The white flowers far off yonder are known as 'evening faces.'" he said. "A very human sort of name—and what a shabby place they have picked to bloom in."

It was as the man said. The neighborhood was a poor one, chiefly of small houses. Some were leaning precariously, and there were "evening faces" at the sagging eaves.

"A hapless sort of flower. Pick one off for me, would you?"

The man went inside the raised gate and broke off a flower. A pretty little girl in long, unlined yellow trousers of raw silk came out through a sliding door that seemed too good for the surroundings. Beckoning to the man, she handed him a heavily scented white fan.

"Put it on this. It isn't much of a fan, but then it isn't much of a flower either."

Koremitsu, coming out of the gate, passed it on to Genji.

"They lost the key, and I have had to keep you waiting. You aren't likely to be recognized in such a neighborhood, but it's not a very nice neighborhood to keep you waiting in."

Genji's carriage was pulled in and he dismounted. Besides Koremitsu, a son and a daughter, the former an eminent cleric, and the daughter's husband, the governor of Mikawa, were in attendance upon the old woman. They thanked him profusely for his visit.

The old woman got up to receive him. "I did not at all mind leaving the world, except for the thought that I would no longer be able to see you as I am seeing you now. My vows seem to have given me a new lease on life, and this visit makes me certain that I shall receive the radiance of Lord Amitābha[8] with a serene and tranquil heart." And she collapsed in tears.

Genji was near tears himself. "It has worried me enormously that you should be taking so long to recover, and I was very sad to learn that you have withdrawn from the world. You must live a long life and see the career I make for myself. I am sure that if you do you will be reborn upon the high-

---

6. Alludes to a poem in *The Kokinshū*: "Where in all this world shall I call home? / A temporary shelter is my home." 7. Another allusion to *The Kokinshū*: "I needs must ask the lady far off yonder / What flower is off there that blooms so white." 8. The Buddha of Infinite Light, into whose paradise, the Pure Land, the faithful are reborn.

est summits of the Pure Land. I am told that it is important to rid oneself of the smallest regret for this world."

Fond of the child she has reared, a nurse tends to look upon him as a paragon even if he is a half-wit. How much prouder was the old woman, who somehow gained stature, who thought of herself as eminent in her own right for having been permitted to serve him. The tears flowed on.

Her children were ashamed for her. They exchanged glances. It would not do to have these contortions taken as signs of a lingering affection for the world.

Genji was deeply touched. "The people who were fond of me left me when I was very young. Others have come along, it is true, to take care of me, but you are the only one I am really attached to. In recent years there have been restrictions upon my movements, and I have not been able to look in upon you morning and evening as I would have wished, or indeed to have a good visit with you. Yet I become very depressed when the days go by and I do not see you. 'Would that there were on this earth no final partings.'"[9] He spoke with great solemnity, and the scent of his sleeve, as he brushed away a tear, quite flooded the room.

Yes, thought the children, who had been silently reproaching their mother for her want of control, the fates had been kind to her. They too were now in tears.

Genji left orders that prayers and services be resumed. As he went out he asked for a torch, and in its light examined the fan on which the "evening face" had rested. It was permeated with a lady's perfume, elegant and alluring. On it was a poem in a disguised cursive hand that suggested breeding and taste. He was interested.

> "I think I need not ask whose face it is,
> So bright, this evening face, in the shining dew."

"Who is living in the house to the west?" he asked Koremitsu. "Have you perhaps had occasion to inquire?"

At it again, thought Koremitsu. He spoke somewhat tartly. "I must confess that these last few days I have been too busy with my mother to think about her neighbors."

"You are annoyed with me. But this fan has the appearance of something it might be interesting to look into. Make inquiries, if you will, please, of someone who knows the neighborhood."

Koremitsu went in to ask his mother's steward, and emerged with the information that the house belonged to a certain honorary vice-governor. "The husband is away in the country, and the wife seems to be a young woman of taste. Her sisters are out in service here and there. They often come visiting. I suspect the fellow is too poorly placed to know the details."

His poetess would be one of the sisters, thought Genji. A rather practiced and forward young person, and, were he to meet her, perhaps vulgar as well—but the easy familiarity of the poem had not been at all unpleasant, not something to be pushed away in disdain. His amative propensities, it will be seen, were having their way once more.

---

9. Alludes to a poem by Ariwara Narihira in *The Kokinshū:* "Would that my mother might live a thousand years. / Would there were on this earth no final partings"

Carefully disguising his hand, he jotted down a reply on a piece of notepaper and sent it in by the attendant who had earlier been of service.

"Come a bit nearer, please. Then might you know
Whose was the evening face so dim in the twilight."

Thinking it a familiar profile, the lady had not lost the opportunity to surprise him with a letter, and when time passed and there was no answer she was left feeling somewhat embarrassed and disconsolate. Now came a poem by special messenger. Her women became quite giddy as they turned their minds to the problem of replying. Rather bored with it all, the messenger returned empty-handed. Genji made a quiet departure, lighted by very few torches. The shutters next door had been lowered. There was something sad about the light, dimmer than fireflies, that came through the cracks.

At the Rokujō house, the trees and the plantings had a quiet dignity. The lady herself was strangely cold and withdrawn. Thoughts of the "evening faces" quite left him. He overslept, and the sun was rising when he took his leave. He presented such a fine figure in the morning light that the women of the place understood well enough why he should be so universally admired. On his way he again passed those shutters, as he had no doubt done many times before. Because of that small incident he now looked at the house carefully, wondering who might be within.

"My mother is not doing at all well, and I have been with her," said Koremitsu some days later. And, coming nearer: "Because you seemed so interested, I called someone who knows about the house next door and had him questioned. His story was not completely clear. He said that in the Fifth Month or so someone came very quietly to live in the house, but that not even the domestics had been told who she might be. I have looked through the fence from time to time myself and had glimpses through blinds of several young women. Something about their dress suggests that they are in the service of someone of higher rank. Yesterday, when the evening light was coming directly through, I saw the lady herself writing a letter. She is very beautiful. She seemed lost in thought, and the women around her were weeping."

Genji had suspected something of the sort. He must find out more.

Koremitsu's view was that while Genji was undeniably someone the whole world took seriously, his youth and the fact that women found him attractive meant that to refrain from these little affairs would be less than human. It was not realistic to hold that certain people were beyond temptation.

"Looking for a chance to do a bit of exploring, I found a small pretext for writing to her. She answered immediately, in a good, practiced hand. Some of her women do not seem at all beneath contempt."

"Explore very thoroughly, if you will. I will not be satisfied until you do."

The house was what the guardsman would have described as the lowest of the low, but Genji was interested. What hidden charms might he not come upon!

He had thought the coldness of the governor's wife, the lady of "the locust shell," quite unique. Yet if she had proved amenable to his persuasions the affair would no doubt have been dropped as a sad mistake after that one encounter. As matters were, the resentment and the distinct possibility of final defeat never left his mind. The discussion that rainy night would seem to have made him curious about the several ranks. There had been a time when such a lady would not have been worth his notice. Yes, it had been broadening, that discussion! He had not found the willing and available one, the governor of Iyo's daughter, entirely uninteresting, but the thought that the stepmother must have been listening coolly to the interview was excruciating. He must await some sign of her real intentions.

The governor of Iyo returned to the city. He came immediately to Genji's mansion. Somewhat sunburned, his travel robes rumpled from the sea voyage, he was a rather heavy and displeasing sort of person. He was of good lineage, however, and, though aging, he still had good manners. As they spoke of his province, Genji wanted to ask the full count of those hot springs,[1] but he was somewhat confused to find memories chasing one another through his head. How foolish that he should be so uncomfortable before the honest old man! He remembered the guardsman's warning that such affairs are unwise, and he felt sorry for the governor. Though he resented the wife's coldness, he could see that from the husband's point of view it was admirable. He was upset to learn that the governor meant to find a suitable husband for his daughter and take his wife to the provinces. He consulted the lady's young brother upon the possibility of another meeting. It would have been difficult even with the lady's cooperation, however, and she was of the view that to receive a gentleman so far above her would be extremely unwise.

Yet she did not want him to forget her entirely. Her answers to his notes on this and that occasion were pleasant enough, and contained casual little touches that made him pause in admiration. He resented her chilliness, but she interested him. As for the stepdaughter, he was certain that she would receive him hospitably enough however formidable a husband she might acquire. Reports upon her arrangements disturbed him not at all.

Autumn came. He was kept busy and unhappy by affairs of his own making, and he visited Sanjō infrequently. There was resentment.

As for the affair at Rokujō, he had overcome the lady's resistance and had his way, and, alas, he had cooled toward her. People thought it worthy of comment that his passions should seem so much more governable than before he had made her his. She was subject to fits of despondency, more intense on sleepless nights when she awaited him in vain. She feared that if rumors were to spread the gossips would make much of the difference in their ages.

On a morning of heavy mists, insistently roused by the lady, who was determined that he be on his way, Genji emerged yawning and sighing and looking very sleepy. Chūjō, one of her women, raised a shutter and pulled a curtain aside as if urging her lady to come forward and see him off. The lady lifted her head from her pillow. He was an incomparably handsome figure as he paused to admire the profusion of flowers below the veranda. Chūjō followed him down a gallery. In an aster robe that matched the season pleasantly and a gossamer train worn with clean elegance, she was a pretty, graceful woman. Glancing back, he asked her to sit with him for a time at the corner railing. The ceremonious precision of the seated figure and the hair flowing over her robes were very fine.

He took her hand.

1. The province was noted for its hot springs.

"Though loath to be taxed with seeking fresher blooms,
I feel impelled to pluck this morning glory.

"Why should it be?"

She answered with practiced alacrity, making it seem that she was speaking not for herself but for her lady:

"In haste to plunge into the morning mists,
You seem to have no heart for the blossoms here."

A pretty little page boy, especially decked out for the occasion, it would seem, walked out among the flowers. His trousers wet with dew, he broke off a morning glory for Genji. He made a picture that called out to be painted.

Even persons to whom Genji was nothing were drawn to him. No doubt even rough mountain men wanted to pause for a time in the shade of the flowering tree, and those who had basked even briefly in his radiance had thought, each in accordance with his rank, of a daughter who might be taken into his service, a not ill-formed sister who might perform some humble service for him. One need not be surprised, then, that people with a measure of sensibility among those who had on some occasion received a little poem from him or been treated to some little kindness found him much on their minds. No doubt it distressed them not to be always with him.

I had forgotten: Koremitsu gave a good account of the fence peeping to which he had been assigned. "I am unable to identify her. She seems determined to hide herself from the world. In their boredom her women and girls go out to the long gallery at the street, the one with the shutters, and watch for carriages. Sometimes the lady who seems to be their mistress comes quietly out to join them. I've not had a good look at her, but she seems very pretty indeed. One day a carriage with outrunners went by. The little girls shouted to a person named Ukon that she must come in a hurry. The captain[2] was going by, they said. An older woman came out and motioned to them to be quiet. How did they know? she asked, coming out toward the gallery. The passage from the main house is by a sort of makeshift bridge. She was hurrying and her skirt caught on something, and she stumbled and almost fell off. 'The sort of thing the god of Katsuragi[3] might do,' she said, and seems to have lost interest in sightseeing. They told her that the man in the carriage was wearing casual court dress and that he had a retinue. They mentioned several names, and all of them were undeniably Lord Tō no Chūjō's guards and pages."

"I wish you had made positive identification." Might she be the lady of whom Tō no Chūjō had spoken so regretfully that rainy night?

Koremitsu went on, smiling at this open curiosity. "I have as a matter of fact made the proper overtures and learned all about the place. I come and go as if I did not know that they are not all equals. They think they are hiding the truth and try to insist that there is no one there but themselves when one of the little girls makes a slip."

"Let me have a peep for myself when I call on your mother."

---

2. Tō no Chūjō.　　3. Tradition held that he was very ugly and built a bridge that he used only at night. Katsuragi is south of Nara.

Even if she was only in temporary lodgings, the woman would seem to be of the lower class for which his friend had indicated such contempt that rainy evening. Yet something might come of it all. Determined not to go against his master's wishes in the smallest detail and himself driven by very considerable excitement, Koremitsu searched diligently for a chance to let Genji into the house. But the details are tiresome, and I shall not go into them.

Genji did not know who the lady was and he did not want her to know who he was. In very shabby disguise, he set out to visit her on foot. He must be taking her very seriously, thought Koremitsu, who offered his horse and himself went on foot.

"Though I do not think that our gentleman will look very good with tramps for servants."

To make quite certain that the expedition remained secret, Genji took with him only the man who had been his intermediary in the matter of the "evening faces" and a page whom no one was likely to recognize. Lest he be found out even so, he did not stop to see his nurse.

The lady had his messengers followed to see how he made his way home and tried by every means to learn where he lived; but her efforts came to nothing. For all his secretiveness, Genji had grown fond of her and felt that he must go on seeing her. They were of such different ranks, he tried to tell himself, and it was altogether too frivolous. Yet his visits were frequent. In affairs of this sort, which can muddle the senses of the most serious and honest of men, he had always kept himself under tight control and avoided any occasion for censure. Now, to a most astonishing degree, he would be asking himself as he returned in the morning from a visit how he could wait through the day for the next. And then he would rebuke himself. It was madness, it was not an affair he should let disturb him. She was of an extraordinarily gentle and quiet nature. Though there was a certain vagueness about her, and indeed an almost childlike quality, it was clear that she knew something about men. She did not appear to be of very good family. What was there about her, he asked himself over and over again, that so drew him to her?

He took great pains to hide his rank and always wore travel dress, and he did not allow her to see his face. He came late at night when everyone was asleep. She was frightened, as if he were an apparition from an old story. She did not need to see his face to know that he was a fine gentleman. But who might he be? Her suspicions turned to Koremitsu. It was that young gallant, surely, who had brought the strange visitor. But Koremitsu pursued his own little affairs unremittingly, careful to feign indifference to and ignorance of this other affair. What could it all mean? The lady was lost in unfamiliar speculations.

Genji had his own worries. If, having lowered his guard with an appearance of complete unreserve, she were to slip away and hide, where would he seek her? This seemed to be but a temporary residence, and he could not be sure when she would choose to change it, and for what other. He hoped that he might reconcile himself to what must be and forget the affair as just another dalliance; but he was not confident.

On days when, to avoid attracting notice, he refrained from visiting her, his fretfulness came near anguish. Suppose he were to move her in secret to

Nijō. If troublesome rumors were to arise, well, he could say that they had been fated from the start. He wondered what bond in a former life might have produced an infatuation such as he had not known before.

"Let's have a good talk," he said to her, "where we can be quite at our ease."

"It's all so strange. What you say is reasonable enough, but what you do is so strange. And rather frightening."

Yes, she might well be frightened. Something childlike in her fright brought a smile to his lips. "Which of us is the mischievous fox spirit?[4] I wonder. Just be quiet and give yourself up to its persuasions."

Won over by his gentle warmth, she was indeed inclined to let him have his way. She seemed such a pliant little creature, likely to submit absolutely to the most outrageous demands. He thought again of Tō no Chūjō's "wild carnation," of the equable nature his friend had described that rainy night. Fearing that it would be useless, he did not try very hard to question her. She did not seem likely to indulge in dramatics and suddenly run off and hide herself, and so the fault must have been Tō no Chūjō's. Genji himself would not be guilty of such negligence—though it did occur to him that a bit of infidelity might make her more interesting.

The bright full moon of the Eighth Month came flooding in through chinks in the roof. It was not the sort of dwelling he was used to, and he was fascinated. Toward dawn he was awakened by plebeian voices in the shabby houses down the street.

"Freezing, that's what it is, freezing. There's not much business this year, and when you can't get out into the country you feel like giving up. Do you hear me, neighbor?"

He could make out every word. It embarrassed the woman that, so near at hand, there should be this clamor of preparation as people set forth on their sad little enterprises. Had she been one of the stylish ladies of the world, she would have wanted to shrivel up and disappear. She was a placid sort, however, and she seemed to take nothing, painful or embarrassing or unpleasant, too seriously. Her manner elegant and yet girlish, she did not seem to know what the rather awful clamor up and down the street might mean. He much preferred this easygoing bewilderment to a show of consternation, a face scarlet with embarrassment. As if at his very pillow, there came the booming of a foot pestle, more fearsome than the stamping of the thunder god, genuinely earsplitting. He did not know what device the sound came from, but he did know that it was enough to awaken the dead. From this direction and that there came the faint thump of fulling hammers against coarse cloth; and mingled with it—these were sounds to call forth the deepest emotions—were the calls of geese flying overhead. He slid a door open and they looked out. They had been lying near the veranda. There were tasteful clumps of black bamboo just outside and the dew shone as in more familiar places. Autumn insects sang busily, as if only inches from an ear used to wall crickets at considerable distances. It was all very clamorous, and also rather wonderful. Countless details could be overlooked in the singleness of his affection for the girl. She was pretty and fragile in a soft, mod-

---

4. According to popular superstition, foxes played havoc with people by taking human form and deceiving them.

est cloak of lavender and a lined white robe. She had no single feature that struck him as especially beautiful, and yet, slender and fragile, she seemed so delicately beautiful that he was almost afraid to hear her voice. He might have wished her to be a little more assertive, but he wanted only to be near her, and yet nearer.

"Let's go off somewhere and enjoy the rest of the night. This is too much."

"But how is that possible?" She spoke very quietly. "You keep taking me by surprise."

There was a newly confiding response to his offer of his services as guardian in this world and the next. She was a strange little thing. He found it hard to believe that she had had much experience of men. He no longer cared what people might think. He asked Ukon to summon his man, who got the carriage ready. The women of the house, though uneasy, sensed the depth of his feelings and were inclined to put their trust in him.

Dawn approached. No cocks were crowing. There was only the voice of an old man making deep obeisance to a Buddha, in preparation, it would seem, for a pilgrimage to Mitake. He seemed to be prostrating himself repeatedly and with much difficulty. All very sad. In a life itself like the morning dew, what could he desire so earnestly?

"Praise to the Messiah to come," intoned the voice.

"Listen," said Genji. "He is thinking of another world.

"This pious one shall lead us on our way
As we plight our troth for all the lives to come."

The vow exchanged by the Chinese emperor and Yang Kuei-fei[5] seemed to bode ill, and so he preferred to invoke Lord Maitreya, the Buddha of the Future; but such promises are rash.

"So heavy the burden I bring with me from the past,
I doubt that I should make these vows for the future."

It was a reply that suggested doubts about his "lives to come."

The moon was low over the western hills. She was reluctant to go with him. As he sought to persuade her, the moon suddenly disappeared behind clouds in a lovely dawn sky. Always in a hurry to be off before daylight exposed him, he lifted her easily into his carriage and took her to a nearby villa. Ukon was with them. Waiting for the caretaker to be summoned, Genji looked up at the rotting gate and the ferns that trailed thickly down over it. The groves beyond were still dark, and the mist and the dews were heavy. Genji's sleeve was soaking, for he had raised the blinds of the carriage.

"This is a novel adventure, and I must say that it seems like a lot of trouble.

"And did it confuse them too, the men of old,
This road through the dawn, for me so new and strange?"

"How does it seem to you?"

She turned shyly away.

"And is the moon, unsure of the hills it approaches,
Foredoomed to lose its way in the empty skies?"

5. The emperor's concubine, whose execution during a rebellion in 756 drove the heartbroken emperor to abdicate.

"I am afraid."

She did seem frightened, and bewildered. She was so used to all those swarms of people, he thought with a smile.

The carriage was brought in and its traces propped against the veranda while a room was made ready in the west wing. Much excited, Ukon was thinking about earlier adventures. The furious energy with which the caretaker saw to preparations made her suspect who Genji was. It was almost daylight when they alighted from the carriage. The room was clean and pleasant, for all the haste with which it had been readied.

"There are unfortunately no women here to wait upon His Lordship." The man, who addressed him through Ukon, was a lesser steward who had served in the Sanjō mansion of Genji's father-in-law. "Shall I send for someone?"

"The last thing I want. I came here because I wanted to be in complete solitude, away from all possible visitors. You are not to tell a soul."

The man put together a hurried breakfast, but he was, as he had said, without serving women to help him.

Genji told the girl that he meant to show her a love as dependable as "the patient river of the loons."[6] He could do little else in these strange lodgings.

The sun was high when he arose. He opened the shutters. All through the badly neglected grounds not a person was to be seen. The groves were rank and overgrown. The flowers and grasses in the foreground were a drab monotone, an autumn moor. The pond was choked with weeds, and all in all it was a forbidding place. An outbuilding seemed to be fitted with rooms for the caretaker, but it was some distance away.

"It is a forbidding place," said Genji. "But I am sure that whatever devils emerge will pass me by."

He was still in disguise. She thought it unkind of him to be so secretive, and he had to agree that their relationship had gone beyond such furtiveness.

"Because of one chance meeting by the wayside
The flower now opens in the evening dew.

"And how does it look to you?"

"The face seemed quite to shine in the evening dew,
But I was dazzled by the evening light."

Her eyes turned away. She spoke in a whisper.

To him it may have seemed an interesting poem.

As a matter of fact, she found him handsomer than her poem suggested, indeed frighteningly handsome, given the setting.

"I hid my name from you because I thought it altogether too unkind of you to be keeping your name from me. Do please tell me now. This silence makes me feel that something awful might be coming."

"Call me the fisherman's daughter."[7] Still hiding her name, she was like a little child.

---

6. An allusion to a poem in *The Man'yōshū*: "The patient river of the patient loons / Will not run dry. My love will still outlast it."   7. Alludes to a poem: "A fisherman's daughter, I spend my life by the waves, / The waves that tell us nothing. I have no home."

"I see. I brought it all on myself? A case of *warekara?*"[8]

And so, sometimes affectionately, sometimes reproachfully, they talked the hours away.

Koremitsu had found them out and brought provisions. Feeling a little guilty about the way he had treated Ukon, he did not come near. He thought it amusing that Genji should thus be wandering the streets, and concluded that the girl must provide sufficient cause. And he could have had her himself, had he not been so generous.

Genji and the girl looked out at an evening sky of the utmost calm. Because she found the darkness in the recesses of the house frightening, he raised the blinds at the veranda and they lay side by side. As they gazed at each other in the gathering dusk, it all seemed very strange to her, unbelievably strange. Memories of past wrongs quite left her. She was more at ease with him now, and he thought her charming. Beside him all through the day, starting up in fright at each little noise, she seemed delightfully childlike. He lowered the shutters early and had lights brought.

"You seem comfortable enough with me, and yet you raise difficulties."

At court everyone would be frantic. Where would the search be directed? He thought what a strange love it was, and he thought of the turmoil the Rokujō lady was certain to be in. She had every right to be resentful, and yet her jealous ways were not pleasant. It was that sad lady to whom his thoughts first turned. Here was the girl beside him, so simple and undemanding; and the other was so impossibly forceful in her demands. How he wished he might in some measure have his freedom.

It was past midnight. He had been asleep for a time when an exceedingly beautiful woman appeared by his pillow.

"You do not even think of visiting me, when you are so much on my mind. Instead you go running off with someone who has nothing to recommend her, and raise a great stir over her. It is cruel, intolerable." She seemed about to shake the girl from her sleep. He awoke, feeling as if he were in the power of some malign being. The light had gone out. In great alarm, he pulled his sword to his pillow and awakened Ukon. She too seemed frightened.

"Go out to the gallery and wake the guard. Have him bring a light."

"It's much too dark."

He forced a smile. "You're behaving like a child."

He clapped his hands and a hollow echo answered. No one seemed to hear. The girl was trembling violently. She was bathed in sweat and as if in a trance, quite bereft of her senses.

"She is such a timid little thing," said Ukon, "frightened when there is nothing at all to be frightened of. This must be dreadful for her."

Yes, poor thing, thought Genji. She did seem so fragile, and she had spent the whole day gazing up at the sky.

"I'll go get someone. What a frightful echo. You stay here with her." He pulled Ukon to the girl's side.

The lights in the west gallery had gone out. There was a gentle wind. He had few people with him, and they were asleep. They were three in number:

---

8. Alludes to a poem in *The Kokinshū:* "The grass the fishermen take, the *warekara:* / 'I did it myself.' I shall weep but I shall not hate you." *Warekara* is both the fishermen's catch (skeleton shrimp) and a homonym meaning "I did it myself."

a young man who was one of his intimates and who was the son of the steward here, a court page, and the man who had been his intermediary in the matter of the "evening faces." He called out. Someone answered and came up to him.

"Bring a light. Wake the other, and shout and twang your bowstrings. What do you mean, going to sleep in a deserted house? I believe Lord Koremitsu was here."

"He was. But he said he had no orders and would come again at dawn."

An elite guardsman, the man was very adept at bow twanging. He went off with a shouting as of a fire watch. At court, thought Genji, the courtiers on night duty would have announced themselves, and the guard would be changing. It was not so very late.

He felt his way back inside. The girl was as before, and Ukon lay face down at her side.

"What is this? You're a fool to let yourself be so frightened. Are you worried about the fox spirits that come out and play tricks in deserted houses? But you needn't worry. They won't come near me." He pulled her to her knees.

"I'm not feeling at all well. That's why I was lying down. My poor lady must be terrified."

"She is indeed. And I can't think why."

He reached for the girl. She was not breathing. He lifted her and she was limp in his arms. There was no sign of life. She had seemed as defenseless as a child, and no doubt some evil power had taken possession of her. He could think of nothing to do. A man came with a torch. Ukon was not prepared to move, and Genji himself pulled up curtain frames to hide the girl.

"Bring the light closer."

It was a most unusual order. Not ordinarily permitted at Genji's side, the man hesitated to cross the threshold.

"Come, come, bring it here! There is a time and place for ceremony."

In the torchlight he had a fleeting glimpse of a figure by the girl's pillow. It was the woman in his dream. It faded away like an apparition in an old romance. In all the fright and horror, his confused thoughts centered upon the girl. There was no room for thoughts of himself.

He knelt over her and called out to her, but she was cold and had stopped breathing. It was too horrible. He had no confidant to whom he could turn for advice. It was the clergy one thought of first on such occasions. He had been so brave and confident, but he was young, and this was too much for him. He clung to the lifeless body.

"Come back, my dear, my dear. Don't do this awful thing to me." But she was cold and no longer seemed human.

The first paralyzing terror had left Ukon. Now she was writhing and wailing. Genji remembered a devil a certain minister had encountered in the Grand Hall.

"She can't possibly be dead." He found the strength to speak sharply. "All this noise in the middle of the night—you must try to be a little quieter." But it had been too sudden.

He turned again to the torchbearer. "There is someone here who seems to have had a very strange seizure. Tell your friend to find out where Lord Koremitsu is spending the night and have him come immediately. If the holy man is still at his mother's house, give him word, very quietly, that he is to come too. His mother and the people with her are not to hear. She does not approve of this sort of adventure."

He spoke calmly enough, but his mind was in a turmoil. Added to grief at the loss of the girl was horror, quite beyond describing, at this desolate place. It would be past midnight. The wind was higher and whistled more dolefully in the pines. There came a strange, hollow call of a bird. Might it be an owl? All was silence, terrifying solitude. He should not have chosen such a place—but it was too late now. Trembling violently, Ukon clung to him. He held her in his arms, wondering if she might be about to follow her lady. He was the only rational one present, and he could think of nothing to do. The flickering light wandered here and there. The upper parts of the screens behind them were in darkness, the lower parts fitfully in the light. There was a persistent creaking, as of someone coming up behind them. If only Koremitsu would come. But Koremitsu was a nocturnal wanderer without a fixed abode, and the man had to search for him in numerous places. The wait for dawn was like the passage of a thousand nights. Finally he heard a distant crowing. What legacy from a former life could have brought him to this mortal peril? He was being punished for a guilty love, his fault and no one else's, and his story would be remembered in infamy through all the ages to come. There were no secrets, strive though one might to have them. Soon everyone would know, from his royal father down, and the lowest court pages would be talking; and he would gain immortality as the model of the complete fool.

Finally Lord Koremitsu came. He was the perfect servant who did not go against his master's wishes in anything at any time; and Genji was angry that on this night of all nights he should have been away, and slow in answering the summons. Calling him inside even so, he could not immediately find the strength to say what must be said. Ukon burst into tears, the full horror of it all coming back to her at the sight of Koremitsu. Genji too lost control of himself. The only sane and rational one present, he had held Ukon in his arms, but now he gave himself up to his grief.

"Something very strange has happened," he said after a time. "Strange—'unbelievable' would not be too strong a word. I wanted a priest— one does when these things happen—and asked your reverend brother to come."

"He went back up the mountain yesterday. Yes, it is very strange indeed. Had there been anything wrong with her?"

"Nothing."

He was so handsome in his grief that Koremitsu wanted to weep. An older man who has had everything happen to him and knows what to expect can be depended upon in a crisis; but they were both young, and neither had anything to suggest.

Koremitsu finally spoke. "We must not let the caretaker know. He may be dependable enough himself, but he is sure to have relatives who will talk. We must get away from this place."

"You aren't suggesting that we could find a place where we would be less likely to be seen?"

"No, I suppose not. And the women at her house will scream and wail when they hear about it, and they live in a crowded neighborhood, and all the mob around will hear, and that will be that. But mountain temples are used to this sort of thing.[9] There would not be much danger of attracting attention." He reflected on the problem for a time. "There is a woman I used to know. She has gone into a nunnery up in the eastern hills. She is very old, my father's nurse, as a matter of fact. The district seems to be rather heavily populated, but the nunnery is off by itself."

It was not yet full daylight. Koremitsu had the carriage brought up. Since Genji seemed incapable of the task, he wrapped the body in a covering and lifted it into the carriage. It was very tiny and very pretty, and not at all repellent. The wrapping was loose and the hair streamed forth, as if to darken the world before Genji's eyes.

He wanted to see the last rites through to the end, but Koremitsu would not hear of it. "Take my horse and go back to Nijō, now while the streets are still quiet."

He helped Ukon into the carriage and himself proceeded on foot, the skirts of his robe hitched up. It was a strange, bedraggled sort of funeral procession, he thought, but in the face of such anguish he was prepared to risk his life. Barely conscious, Genji made his way back to Nijō.

"Where have you been?" asked the women. "You are not looking at all well."

He did not answer. Alone in his room, he pressed a hand to his heart. Why had he not gone with the others? What would she think if she were to come back to life? She would think that he had abandoned her. Self-reproach filled his heart to breaking. He had a headache and feared he had a fever. Might he too be dying? The sun was high and still he did not emerge. Thinking it all very strange, the women pressed breakfast upon him. He could not eat. A messenger reported that the emperor had been troubled by his failure to appear the day before.

His brothers-in-law came calling.

"Come in, please, just for a moment." He received only Tō no Chūjō and kept a blind between them. "My old nurse fell seriously ill and took her vows in the Fifth Month or so. Perhaps because of them, she seemed to recover. But recently she had a relapse. Someone came to ask if I would not call on her at least once more. I thought I really must go and see an old and dear servant who was on her deathbed, and so I went. One of her servants was ailing, and quite suddenly, before he had time to leave, he died. Out of deference to me they waited until night to take the body away. All this I learned later. It would be very improper of me to go to court with all these festivities coming up,[1] I thought, and so I stayed away. I have had a headache since early this morning—perhaps I have caught cold. I must apologize."

"I see. I shall so inform your father. He sent out a search party during the concert last night, and really seemed very upset." Tō no Chūjō turned to go, and abruptly turned back. "Come now. What sort of brush did you really have? I don't believe a word of it."

Genji was startled, but managed a show of nonchalance. "You needn't go into the details. Just say that I suffered an unexpected defilement. Very unexpected, really."

9. Corpses were brought to temples for burial.   1. There were many Shinto rites during the Ninth Month.

Despite his cool manner, he was not up to facing people. He asked a younger brother-in-law to explain in detail his reasons for not going to court. He got off a note to Sanjō with a similar explanation.

Koremitsu came in the evening. Having announced that he had suffered a defilement, Genji had callers remain outside, and there were few people in the house. He received Koremitsu immediately.

"Are you sure she is dead?" He pressed a sleeve to his eyes.

Koremitsu too was in tears. "Yes, I fear she is most certainly dead. I could not stay shut up in a temple indefinitely, and so I have made arrangements with a venerable priest whom I happen to know rather well. Tomorrow is a good day for funerals."

"And the other woman?"

"She has seemed on the point of death herself. She does not want to be left behind by her lady. I was afraid this morning that she might throw herself over a cliff. She wanted to tell the people at Gojō, but I persuaded her to let us have a little more time."

"I am feeling rather awful myself and almost fear the worst."

"Come, now. There is nothing to be done and no point in torturing yourself. You must tell yourself that what must be must be. I shall let absolutely no one know, and I am personally taking care of everything."

"Yes, to be sure. Everything is fated. So I tell myself. But it is terrible to think that I have sent a lady to her death. You are not to tell your sister, and you must be very sure that your mother does not hear. I would not survive the scolding I would get from her."

"And the priests too: I have told them a plausible story." Koremitsu exuded confidence.

The women had caught a hint of what was going on and were more puzzled than ever. He had said that he had suffered a defilement, and he was staying away from court; but why these muffled lamentations?

Genji gave instructions for the funeral. "You must make sure that nothing goes wrong."

"Of course. No great ceremony seems called for."

Koremitsu turned to leave.

"I know you won't approve," said Genji, a fresh wave of grief sweeping over him, "but I will regret it forever if I don't see her again. I'll go on horseback."

"Very well, if you must." In fact Koremitsu thought the proposal very ill advised. "Go immediately and be back while it is still early."

Genji set out in the travel robes he had kept ready for his recent amorous excursions. He was in the bleakest despair. He was on a strange mission and the terrors of the night before made him consider turning back. Grief urged him on. If he did not see her once more, when, in another world, might he hope to see her as she had been? He had with him only Koremitsu and the attendant of that first encounter. The road seemed a long one.

The moon came out, two nights past full. They reached the river. In the dim torchlight, the darkness off towards Mount Toribe was ominous and forbidding; but Genji was too dazed with grief to be frightened. And so they reached the temple.

It was a harsh, unfriendly region at best. The board hut and chapel where the nun pursued her austerities were lonely beyond description. The light at the altar came dimly through cracks. Inside the hut a woman was weeping.

In the outer chamber two or three priests were conversing and invoking the holy name in low voices. Vespers seemed to have ended in several temples nearby. Everything was quiet. There were lights and there seemed to be clusters of people in the direction of Kiyomizu. The grand tones in which the worthy monk, the son of the nun, was reading a sutra brought on what Genji thought must be the full flood tide of his tears.

He went inside. The light was turned away from the corpse. Ukon lay behind a screen. It must be very terrible for her, thought Genji. The girl's face was unchanged and very pretty.

"Won't you let me hear your voice again?" He took her hand. "What was it that made me give you all my love, for so short a time, and then made you leave me to this misery?" He was weeping uncontrollably.

The priests did not know who he was. They sensed something remarkable, however, and felt their eyes mist over.

"Come with me to Nijō," he said to Ukon.

"We have been together since I was very young. I never left her side, not for a single moment. Where am I to go now? I will have to tell the others what has happened. As if this weren't enough, I will have to put up with their accusations." She was sobbing. "I want to go with her."

"That is only natural. But it is the way of the world. Parting is always sad. Our lives must end, early or late. Try to put your trust in me." He comforted her with the usual homilies, but presently his real feelings came out. "Put your trust in me—when I fear I have not long to live myself." He did not after all seem likely to be much help.

"It will soon be light," said Koremitsu. "We must be on our way."

Looking back and looking back again, his heart near breaking, Genji went out. The way was heavy with dew and the morning mists were thick. He scarcely knew where he was. The girl was exactly as she had been that night. They had exchanged robes and she had on a red singlet of his. What might it have been in other lives that had brought them together? He managed only with great difficulty to stay in his saddle. Koremitsu was at the reins. As they came to the river Genji fell from his horse and was unable to remount.

"So I am to die by the wayside? I doubt that I can go on."

Koremitsu was in a panic. He should not have permitted this expedition, however strong Genji's wishes. Dipping his hands in the river, he turned and made supplication to Kiyomizu. Genji somehow pulled himself together. Silently invoking the holy name, he was seen back to Nijō.

The women were much upset by these untimely wanderings. "Very bad, very bad. He has been so restless lately. And why should he have gone out again when he was not feeling well?"

Now genuinely ill, he took to his bed. Two or three days passed and he was visibly thinner. The emperor heard of the illness and was much alarmed. Continuous prayers were ordered in this shrine and that temple. The varied rites, Shinto and Confucian and Buddhist, were beyond counting. Genji's good looks had been such as to arouse forebodings. All through the court it was feared that he would not live much longer. Despite his illness, he summoned Ukon to Nijō and assigned her rooms near his own. Koremitsu composed himself sufficiently to be of service to her, for he could see that she had no one else to turn to. Choosing times when he was feeling better, Genji would summon her for a talk, and she soon was accustomed to life at Nijō.

Dressed in deep mourning, she was a somewhat stern and forbidding young woman, but not without her good points.

"It lasted such a very little while. I fear that I will be taken too. It must be dreadful for you, losing your only support. I had thought that as long as I lived I would see to all your needs, and it seems sad and ironical that I should be on the point of following her." He spoke softly and there were tears in his eyes. For Ukon the old grief had been hard enough to bear, and now she feared that a new grief might be added to it.

All through the Nijō mansion there was a sense of helplessness. Emissaries from court were thicker than raindrops. Not wanting to worry his father, Genji fought to control himself. His father-in-law was extremely solicitous and came to Nijō every day. Perhaps because of all the prayers and rites the crisis passed—it had lasted some twenty days—and left no ill effects. Genji's full recovery coincided with the final cleansing of the defilement. With the unhappiness he had caused his father much on his mind, he set off for his apartments at court. For a time he felt out of things, as if he had come back to a strange new world.

By the end of the Ninth Month he was his old self once more. He had lost weight, but emaciation only made him handsomer. He spent a great deal of time gazing into space, and sometimes he would weep aloud. He must be in the clutches of some malign spirit, thought the women. It was all most peculiar.

He would summon Ukon on quiet evenings. "I don't understand it at all. Why did she so insist on keeping her name from me? Even if she *was* a fisherman's daughter it was cruel of her to be so uncommunicative. It was as if she did not know how much I loved her."

"There was no reason for keeping it secret. But why should she tell you about her insignificant self? Your attitude seemed so strange from the beginning. She used to say that she hardly knew whether she was waking or dreaming. Your refusal to identify yourself, you know, helped her guess who you were. It hurt her that you should belittle her by keeping your name from her."

"An unfortunate contest of wills. I did not want anything to stand between us; but I must always be worrying about what people will say. I must refrain from things my father and all the rest of them might take me to task for. I am not permitted the smallest indiscretion. Everything is exaggerated so. The little incident of the 'evening faces' affected me strangely and I went to very great trouble to see her. There must have been a bond between us. A love doomed from the start to be fleeting—why should it have taken such complete possession of me and made me find her so precious? You must tell me everything. What point is there in keeping secrets now? I mean to make offerings every week, and I want to know in whose name I am making them."

"Yes, of course—why have secrets now? It is only that I do not want to slight what she made so much of. Her parents are dead. Her father was a guards captain. She was his special pet, but his career did not go well and his life came to an early and disappointing end. She somehow got to know Lord Tō no Chūjō—it was when he was still a lieutenant. He was very attentive for three years or so, and then about last autumn there was a rather awful threat from his father-in-law's house. She was ridiculously timid and it frightened her beyond all reason. She ran off and hid herself at her nurse's in the western part of the city. It was a wretched little hovel of a place. She wanted to go off into the hills, but the direction she had in mind has been taboo since New Year's. So she moved to the odd place where she was so upset to have you find her. She was more reserved and withdrawn than most people, and I fear that her unwillingness to show her emotions may have seemed cold."

So it was true. Affection and pity welled up yet more strongly.

"He once told me of a lost child. Was there such a one?"

"Yes, a very pretty little girl, born two years ago last spring."

"Where is she? Bring her to me without letting anyone know. It would be such a comfort. I should tell my friend Tō no Chūjō, I suppose, but why invite criticism? I doubt that anyone could reprove me for taking in the child. You must think up a way to get around the nurse."

"It would make me very happy if you were to take the child. I would hate to have her left where she is. She is there because we had no competent nurses in the house where you found us."

The evening sky was serenely beautiful. The flowers below the veranda were withered, the songs of the insects were dying too, and autumn tints were coming over the maples. Looking out upon the scene, which might have been a painting, Ukon thought what a lovely asylum she had found herself. She wanted to avert her eyes at the thought of the house of the "evening faces." A pigeon called, somewhat discordantly, from a bamboo thicket. Remembering how the same call had frightened the girl in that deserted villa, Genji could see the little figure as if an apparition were there before him.

"How old was she? She seemed so delicate, because she was not long for this world, I suppose?"

"Nineteen, perhaps? My mother, who was her nurse, died and left me behind. Her father took a fancy to me, and so we grew up together, and I never once left her side. I wonder how I can go on without her. I am almost sorry that we were so close. She seemed so weak, but I can see now that she was a source of strength."

"The weak ones do have a power over us. The clear, forceful ones I can do without. I am weak and indecisive by nature myself, and a woman who is quiet and withdrawn and follows the wishes of a man even to the point of letting herself be used has much the greater appeal. A man can shape and mold her as he wishes, and becomes fonder of her all the while."

"She was exactly what you would have wished, sir." Ukon was in tears. "That thought makes the loss seem greater."

The sky had clouded over and a chilly wind had come up. Gazing off into the distance, Genji said softly:

"One sees the clouds as smoke that rose from the pyre,
And suddenly the evening sky seems nearer."

Ukon was unable to answer. If only her lady were here! For Genji even the memory of those fulling blocks was sweet.

"In the Eighth Month, the Ninth Month, the nights are long,"[2] he whispered, and lay down.

2. Alludes to the Chinese poem "The Fulling Blocks at Night," by Po Chü-i.

The young page, brother of the lady of the locust shell, came to Nijō from time to time, but Genji no longer sent messages for his sister. She was sorry that he seemed angry with her and sorry to hear of his illness. The prospect of accompanying her husband to his distant province was a dreary one. She sent off a note to see whether Genji had forgotten her.

"They tell me you have not been well.

> "Time goes by, you ask not why I ask not.
> Think if you will how lonely a life is mine.

"I might make reference to Masuda Pond."[3]

This was a surprise; and indeed he had not forgotten her. The uncertain hand in which he set down his reply had its own beauty.

"Who, I wonder, lives the more aimless life.

> "Hollow though it was, the shell of the locust
> Gave me strength to face a gloomy world.

"But only precariously."

So he still remembered "the shell of the locust." She was sad and at the same time amused. It was good that they could correspond without rancor. She wished no further intimacy, and she did not want him to despise her.

As for the other, her stepdaughter, Genji heard that she had married a guards lieutenant. He thought it a strange marriage and he felt a certain pity for the lieutenant. Curious to know something of her feelings, he sent a note by his young messenger.

"Did you know that thoughts of you had brought me to the point of expiring?

> "I bound them loosely, the reeds beneath the eaves,[4]
> And reprove them now for having come undone."

He attached it to a long reed.

The boy was to deliver it in secret, he said. But he thought that the lieutenant would be forgiving if he were to see it, for he would guess who the sender was. One may detect here a note of self-satisfaction.

Her husband was away. She was confused, but delighted that he should have remembered her. She sent off in reply a poem the only excuse for which was the alacrity with which it was composed:

> "The wind brings words, all softly, to the reed,
> And the under leaves are nipped again by the frost."

It might have been cleverer and in better taste not to have disguised the clumsy handwriting. He thought of the face he had seen by lamplight. He could forget neither of them, the governor's wife, seated so primly before him, or the younger woman, chattering on so contentedly, without the smallest suggestion of reserve. The stirrings of a susceptible heart suggested that he still had important lessons to learn.

Quietly, forty-ninth-day services[5] were held for the dead lady in the Lotus Hall on Mount Hiei. There was careful attention to all the details, the

---

3. Alludes to a poem: "Long the roots of the Masuda waters shield, / Longer still the aimless, sleepless nights." **4.** The girl is traditionally called Nokiba-no-ogi, The Reeds Beneath the Eaves. **5.** Held to pray for the woman's successful rebirth. Buddhist doctrine maintains that the spirit of the dead leads an indeterminate existence for forty-nine days, after which it begins a new incarnation.

priestly robes and the scrolls and the altar decorations. Koremitsu's older brother was a priest of considerable renown, and his conduct of the services was beyond reproach. Genji summoned a doctor of letters with whom he was friendly and who was his tutor in Chinese poetry and asked him to prepare a final version of the memorial petition. Genji had prepared a draft. In moving language he committed the one he had loved and lost, though he did not mention her name, to the mercy of Amitābha.

"It is perfect, just as it is. Not a word needs to be changed." Noting the tears that refused to be held back, the doctor wondered who might be the subject of these prayers. That Genji should not reveal the name, and that he should be in such open grief—someone, no doubt, who had brought a very large bounty of grace from earlier lives.

Genji attached a poem to a pair of lady's trousers which were among his secret offerings:

> "I weep and weep as today I tie this cord.
> It will be untied in an unknown world to come."

He invoked the holy name with great feeling. Her spirit had wandered uncertainly these last weeks. Today it would set off down one of the ways of the future.

His heart raced each time he saw Tō no Chūjō. He longed to tell his friend that "the wild carnation" was alive and well; but there was no point in calling forth reproaches.

In the house of the "evening faces," the women were at a loss to know what had happened to their lady. They had no way of inquiring. And Ukon too had disappeared. They whispered among themselves that they had been right about that gentleman, and they hinted at their suspicions to Koremitsu. He feigned complete ignorance, however, and continued to pursue his little affairs. For the poor women it was all like a nightmare. Perhaps the wanton son of some governor, fearing Tō no Chūjō, had spirited her off to the country? The owner of the house was her nurse's daughter. She was one of three children and related to Ukon. She could only long for her lady and lament that Ukon had not chosen to enlighten them. Ukon for her part was loath to raise a stir, and Genji did not want gossip at this late date. Ukon could not even inquire after the child. And so the days went by bringing no light on the terrible mystery.

Genji longed for a glimpse of the dead girl, if only in a dream. On the day after the services he did have a fleeting dream of the woman who had appeared that fatal night. He concluded, and the thought filled him with horror, that he had attracted the attention of an evil spirit haunting the neglected villa.

Early in the Tenth Month the governor of Iyo left for his post, taking the lady of the locust shell with him. Genji chose his farewell presents with great care. For the lady there were numerous fans, and combs of beautiful workmanship, and pieces of cloth (she could see that he had had them dyed specially) for the wayside gods. He also returned her robe, "the shell of the locust."

> "A keepsake till we meet again, I had hoped,
> And see, my tears have rotted the sleeves away."

There were other things too, but it would be tedious to describe them. His messenger returned empty-handed. It was through her brother that she answered his poem.

> "Autumn comes, the wings of the locust are shed.
> A summer robe returns, and I weep aloud."

She had remarkable singleness of purpose, whatever else she might have. It was the first day of winter. There were chilly showers, as if to mark the occasion, and the skies were dark. He spent the day lost in thought.

> "The one has gone, to the other I saw farewell.
> They go their unknown ways. The end of autumn."

He knew how painful a secret love can be.

I had hoped, out of deference to him, to conceal these difficult matters; but I have been accused of romancing, of pretending that because he was the son of an emperor he had no faults. Now, perhaps, I shall be accused of having revealed too much.

Summary Nine years elapse in the chapters between *Evening Faces* and *Suma*, and many things happen. Genji meets Murasaki, a ten-year-old child, whom he grooms as his future wife, and in due course they marry. Of all the women he will know, throughout his life Genji remains supremely devoted to this one.

Although relations have been chilly with his first wife, Aoi, she bears him a son, Yūgiri, only to die soon after. It is following the period of mourning for Aoi that Genji consummates his union with Murasaki.

Despite his new love, Genji's eye continues to wander. Unwisely, he allows his obsession with Fujitsubo to run away with him. She becomes pregnant as a result, and although the emperor is delighted with the thought of an heir, Genji and Fujitsubo are greatly troubled. A son is born, a future emperor, and Fujitsubo is elevated to the rank of empress.

In the meantime, Genji has also become enamored of Oborozukiyo, the sister of his greatest enemy, his mother's old rival, Kokiden. When Kokiden discovers her sister's affair, in her fury she vows to drive Genji from the court. The death of his father abruptly alters the climate for Genji. Kokiden, with her son on the throne, is now in control. And Fujitsubo, remorseful over her actions, which have violated both her husband's trust and the sanctity of the imperial institution, renounces the world and becomes a nun. Everything has changed. It would seem that for Genji the palmy days are over.

CHAPTER 12

Suma[6]

For Genji life had become an unbroken succession of reverses and afflictions. He must consider what to do next. If he went on pretending that nothing was amiss, then even worse things might lie ahead. He thought of the Suma coast. People of worth had once lived there, he was told, but now it was deserted save for the huts of fishermen, and even they were few. The alternative was worse, to go on living this public life, so to speak, with people streaming in and out of his house. Yet he would hate to leave, and affairs

---

6. The village on the Inland Sea, southwest of the capital, where Genji goes into exile.

at court would continue to be much on his mind if he did leave. This irreso-lution was making life difficult for his people.

Unsettling thoughts of the past and the future chased one another through his mind. The thought of leaving the city aroused a train of regrets, led by the image of a grieving Murasaki. It was very well to tell himself that somehow, someday, by some route they would come together again. Even when they were separated for a day or two Genji was beside himself with worry and Murasaki's gloom was beyond describing. It was not as if they would be parting for a fixed span of years; and if they had only the possibil-ity of a reunion on some unnamed day with which to comfort themselves, well, life is uncertain, and they might be parting forever. He thought of con-sulting no one and taking her with him, but the inappropriateness of sub-jecting such a fragile lady to the rigors of life on that harsh coast, where the only callers would be the wind and the waves, was too obvious. Having her with him would only add to his worries. She guessed his thoughts and was unhappy. She let it be known that she did not want to be left behind, how-ever forbidding the journey and life at the end of it.

Then there was the lady of the orange blossoms.[7] He did not visit her often, it is true, but he was her only support and comfort, and she would have every right to feel lonely and insecure. And there were women who, after the most fleeting affairs with him, went on nursing their various secret sorrows.

Fujitsubo, though always worried about rumors, wrote frequently. It struck him as bitterly ironical that she had not returned his affection earlier, but he told himself that a fate which they had shared from other lives must require that they know the full range of sorrows.

He left the city late in the Third Month. He made no announcement of his departure, which was very inconspicuous, and had only seven or eight trusted retainers with him. He did write to certain people who should know of the event. I have no doubt that there were many fine passages in the let-ters with which he saddened the lives of his many ladies, but, grief-stricken myself, I did not listen as carefully as I might have.

Two or three days before his departure he visited his father-in-law. It was sad, indeed rather eerie, to see the care he took not to attract notice. His car-riage, a humble one covered with cypress basketwork, might have been mis-taken for a woman's. The apartments of his late wife wore a lonely, neglected aspect. At the arrival of this wondrous and unexpected guest, the little boy's nurse and all the other women who had not taken positions elsewhere gath-ered for a last look. Even the shallowest of the younger women were moved to tears at the awareness he brought of transience and mutability. Yūgiri, the lit-tle boy, was very pretty indeed, and indefatigably noisy.

"It has been so long. I am touched that he has not forgotten me." He took the boy on his knee and seemed about to weep.

The minister, his father-in-law, came in. "I know that you are shut up at home with little to occupy you, and I had been thinking I would like to call on you and have a good talk. I talk on and on when once I let myself get started. But I have told them I am ill and have been staying away from court, and I have even resigned my offices; and I know what they would say if I

---

7. One of Genji's lesser loves.

were to stretch my twisted old legs for my own pleasure. I hardly need to worry about such things any more, of course, but I am still capable of being upset by false accusations. When I see how things are with you, I know all too painfully what a sad day I have come on at the end of too long a life. I would have expected the world to end before this was allowed to happen, and I see not a ray of light in it all."

"Dear sir, we must accept the disabilities we bring from other lives. Everything that has happened to me is a result of my own inadequacy. I have heard that in other lands as well as our own an offense which does not, like mine, call for dismissal from office is thought to become far graver if the culprit goes on happily living his old life. And when exile is considered, as I believe it is in my case, the offense must have been thought more serious. Though I know I am innocent, I know too what insults I may look forward to if I stay, and so I think that I will forestall them by leaving."

Brushing away tears, the minister talked of old times, of Genji's father, and all he had said and thought. Genji too was weeping. The little boy scrambled and rolled about the room, now pouncing upon his father and now making demands upon his grandfather.

"I have gone on grieving for my daughter. And then I think what agony all this would have been to her, and am grateful that she lived such a short life and was spared the nightmare. So I try to tell myself, in any event. My chief sorrows and worries are for our little man here. He must grow up among us dotards, and the days and months will go by without the advantage of your company. It used to be that even people who were guilty of serious crimes escaped this sort of punishment; and I suppose we must call it fate, in our land and other lands too, that punishment should come all the same. But one does want to know what the charges are. In your case they quite defy the imagination."

Tō no Chūjō came in. They drank until very late, and Genji was induced to stay the night. He summoned Aoi's various women. Chūnagon was the one whom he had most admired, albeit in secret. He went on talking to her after everything was quiet, and it would seem to have been because of her that he was prevailed upon to spend the night. Dawn was at hand when he got up to leave. The moon in the first suggestions of daylight was very beautiful. The cherry blossoms were past their prime, and the light through the few that remained flooded the garden silver. Everything faded together into a gentle mist, sadder and more moving than on a night in autumn. He sat for a time leaning against the railing at a corner of the veranda. Chūnagon was waiting at the door as if to see him off.

"I wonder when we will be permitted to meet again." He paused, choking with tears. "Never did I dream that this would happen, and I neglected you in the days when it would have been so easy to see you."

Saishō, Yūgiri's nurse, came with a message from Princess Omiya.[8] "I would have liked to say goodbye in person, but I have waited in hope that the turmoil of my thoughts might quiet a little. And now I hear that you are leaving, and it is still so early. Everything seems changed, completely wrong. It is a pity that you cannot at least wait until our little sleepyhead is up and about."

---

8. Mother of Aoi and Tō no Chūjō.

Weeping softly, Genji whispered to himself, not precisely by way of reply:

"There on the shore, the salt burners' fires await me.
Will their smoke be as the smoke over Toribe Moor?

Is this the parting at dawn we are always hearing of? No doubt there are those who know.

"I have always hated the word 'farewell,'" said Saishō, whose grief seemed quite unfeigned. "And our farewells today are unlike any others."

"Over and over again," he sent back to Princess Omiya, "I have thought of all the things I would have liked to say to you; and I hope you will understand and forgive my muteness. As for our little sleepyhead, I fear that if I were to see him I would wish to stay on even in this hostile city, and so I shall collect myself and be on my way."

All the women were there to see him go. He looked more elegant and handsome than ever in the light of the setting moon, and his dejection would have reduced tigers and wolves to tears. These were women who had served him since he was very young. It was a sad day for them.

There was a poem from Princess Omiya:

"Farther retreats the day when we bade her goodbye,
For now you depart the skies that received the smoke."[9]

Sorrow was added to sorrow, and the tears almost seemed to invite further misfortunes.

He returned to Nijō. The women, awake the whole night through, it seemed, were gathered in sad clusters. There was no one in the guardroom. The men closest to him, reconciled to going with him, were making their own personal farewells. As for other court functionaries, there had been ominous hints of sanctions were they to come calling, and so the grounds, once crowded with horses and carriages, were empty and silent. He knew again what a hostile world it had become. There was dust on the tables, cushions had been put away. And what would be the extremes of waste and the neglect when he was gone?

He went to Murasaki's wing of the house. She had been up all night, not even lowering the shutters. Out near the verandas little girls[1] were noisily bestirring themselves. They were so pretty in their night dress—and presently, no doubt, they would find the loneliness too much, and go their various ways. Such thoughts had not before been a part of his life.

He told Murasaki what had kept him at Sanjō. "And I suppose you are filled with the usual odd suspicions. I have wanted to be with you every moment I am still in the city, but there are things that force me to go out. Life is uncertain enough at best, and I would not want to seem cold and unfeeling."

"And what should be 'odd' now except that you are going away?"

That she should feel these sad events more cruelly than any of the others was not surprising. From her childhood she had been closer to Genji than to her own father, who now bowed to public opinion and had not offered a word of sympathy. His coldness had caused talk among her women. She was beginning to wish that they had kept him in ignorance of her whereabouts.

---

9. Refers to Aoi's cremation.   1. Murasaki's companions in Genji's absence.

Someone reported what her stepmother was saying: "She had a sudden stroke of good luck, and now just as suddenly everything goes wrong. It makes a person shiver. One after another, each in his own way, they all run out on her."

This was too much. There was nothing more she wished to say to them. Henceforth she would have only Genji.

"If the years go by and I am still an outcast," he continued, "I will come for you and bring you to my 'cave among the rocks.'[2] But we must not be hasty. A man who is out of favor at court is not permitted the light of the sun and the moon, and it is thought a great crime, I am told, for him to go on being happy. The cause of it all is a great mystery to me, but I must accept it as fate. There seems to be no precedent for sharing exile with a lady, and I am sure that to suggest it would be to invite worse insanity from an insane world."

He slept until almost noon.

Tō no Chūjō and Genji's brother, Prince Hotaru, came calling. Since he was now without rank and office, he changed to informal dress of unfigured silk, more elegant, and even somehow grand, for its simplicity. As he combed his hair he could not help noticing that loss of weight had made him even handsomer.

"I am skin and bones," he said to Murasaki, who sat gazing at him, tears in her eyes. "Can I really be as emaciated as this mirror makes me? I am a little sorry for myself.

"I now must go into exile. In this mirror
An image of me will yet remain beside you."

Huddling against a pillar to hide her tears, she replied as if to herself:

"If when we part an image yet remains,
Then will I find some comfort in my sorrow."

Yes, she was unique—a new awareness of that fact stabbed at his heart.

Prince Hotaru kept him affectionate company through the day and left in the evening.

It was not hard to imagine the loneliness that brought frequent notes from the house of the falling orange blossoms. Fearing that he would seem unkind if he did not visit the ladies again, he resigned himself to spending yet another night away from home. It was very late before he gathered himself for the effort.

"We are honored that you should consider us worth a visit," said Lady Reikeiden—and it would be difficult to record the rest of the interview.

They lived precarious lives, completely dependent on Genji. So lonely indeed was their mansion that he could imagine the desolation awaiting it once he himself was gone; and the heavily wooded hill rising dimly beyond the wide pond in misty moonlight made him wonder whether the "cave among the rocks" at Suma would be such a place.

He went to the younger sister's room, at the west side of the house. She had been in deep despondency, almost certain that he would not find time for a visit. Then, in the soft, sad lights of the moon, his robes giving off an

2. Alludes to a poem in *The Kokinshū*: "Where shall I go, to what cave among the rocks, / To be free of tidings of this gloomy world?"

indescribable fragrance, he made his way in. She came to the veranda and looked up at the moon. They talked until dawn.

"What a short night it has been. I think how difficult it will be for us to meet again, and I am filled with regrets for the days I wasted. I fear I worried too much about the precedents I might be setting."

A cock was crowing busily as he talked on about the past. He made a hasty departure, fearful of attracting notice. The setting moon is always sad, and he was prompted to think its situation rather like his own. Catching the deep purple of the lady's robe, the moon itself seemed to be weeping.[3]

> "Narrow these sleeves, now lodging for the moonlight.
> Would they might keep a light which I do not tire of."

Sad himself, Genji sought to comfort her.

> "The moon will shine upon this house once more.
> Do not look at the clouds which now conceal it.

"I wish I were really sure it is so, and find the unknown future clouding my heart."

He left as dawn was coming over the sky.

His affairs were in order. He assigned all the greater and lesser affairs of the Nijō mansion to trusted retainers who had not been swept up in the currents of the times, and he selected others to go with him to Suma. He would take only the simplest essentials for a rustic life, among them a book chest, selected writings of Po Chü-i and other poets, and a seven-stringed Chinese koto. He carefully refrained from anything which in its ostentation might not become a nameless rustic.

Assigning all the women to Murasaki's west wing, he left behind deeds to pastures and manors and the like and made provision for all his various warehouses and storerooms. Confident of Shōnagon's perspicacity he gave her careful instructions and put stewards at her disposal. He had been somewhat brisk and businesslike toward his own serving women, but they had had security—and now what was to become of them?

"I shall be back, I know, if I live long enough. Do what you can in the west wing, please, those of you who are prepared to wait."

And so they all began a new life.

To Yūgiri's nurse and maids and to the lady of the orange blossoms he sent elegant parting gifts and plain, useful everyday provisions as well.

He even wrote to Oborozukiyo. "I know that I have no right to expect a letter from you; but I am not up to describing the gloom and the bitterness of leaving this life behind.

> "Snagged upon the shoals of this river of tears,
> I cannot see you. Deeper waters await me.

"Remembering is the crime to which I cannot plead innocent."

He wrote nothing more, for there was a danger that his letter would be intercepted.

Though she fought to maintain her composure, there was nothing she could do about the tears that wet her sleeves.

---

3. Alludes to a poem by Lady Ise in *The Kokinshū:* "Catching the drops on my sleeves as I lay in thought, / The moonlight seemed to be shedding tears of its own."

"The foam on the river of tears will disappear
Short of the shoals of meeting that wait downstream."

There was something very fine about the hand disordered by grief.

He longed to see her again, but she had too many relatives who wished him ill. Discretion forbade further correspondence.

On the night before his departure he visited his father's grave in the northern hills. Since the moon would be coming up shortly before dawn, he went first to take leave of Fujitsubo. Receiving him in person, she spoke of her worries for the crown prince. It cannot have been, so complicated were matters between them, a less than deeply felt interview. Her dignity and beauty were as always. He would have liked to hint at old resentments; but why, at this late date, invite further unpleasantness, and risk adding to his own agitation?

He only said, and it was reasonable enough: "I can think of a single offense for which I must undergo this strange, sad punishment, and because of it I tremble before the heavens. Though I would not care in the least if my own unworthy self were to vanish away, I only hope that the crown prince's reign is without unhappy event."

She knew too well what he meant, and was unable to reply. He was almost too handsome as at last he succumbed to tears.

"I am going to pay my respects at His Majesty's grave. Do you have a message?"

She was silent for a time, seeking to control herself.

"The one whom I served is gone, the other must go.
Farewell to the world was no farewell to its sorrows."

But for both of them the sorrow was beyond words.
He replied:

"The worst of grief for him should long have passed.
And now I must leave the world where dwells the child."

The moon had risen and he set out. He was on horseback and had only five or six attendants, all of them trusted friends. I need scarcely say that it was a far different procession from those of old. Among his men was that guards officer who had been his special attendant at the Kamo lustration services.[4] The promotion he might have expected had long since passed him by, and now his right of access to the royal presence and his offices had been taken away. Remembering that day as they came in sight of the Lower Kamo Shrine, he dismounted and took Genji's bridle.

"There was heartvine[5] in our caps. I led your horse.
And now at this jeweled fence I berate the gods."

Yes, the memory must be painful, for the young man had been the most resplendent in Genji's retinue. Dismounting, Genji bowed toward the shrine and said as if by way of farewell:

---

4. Held to inaugurate the shrines' new high priestess. The Kamo shrines were two of the most important Shinto shrines. In the novel, the entire imperial court turns out to observe the ceremonial procession. During the procession the retainers of Genji's wife Aoi tangle with those of the Rokujō lady, who is humiliated.   5. A pun that suggests Genji's wife Aoi, whose name can be translated as "heartvine," or "hollyhock."

> "I leave this world of gloom. I leave my name
> To the offices of the god who rectifies."[6]

The guards officer, an impressionable young man, gazed at him in wonder and admiration.

Coming to the grave, Genji almost thought he could see his father before him. Power and position were nothing once a man was gone. He wept and silently told his story, but there came no answer, no judgment upon it. And all those careful instructions and admonitions had served no purpose at all?

Grasses overgrew the path to the grave, the dew seemed to gather weight as he made his way through. The moon had gone behind a cloud and the groves were dark and somehow terrible. It was as if he might lose his way upon turning back. As he bowed in farewell, a chill came over him, for he seemed to see his father as he once had been.

> "And how does he look upon me? I raise my eyes,
> And the moon now vanishes behind the clouds."

Back at Nijō at daybreak, he sent a last message to the crown prince. Tying it to a cherry branch from which the blossoms had fallen, he addressed it to Omyōbu, whom Fujitsubo had put in charge of her son's affairs. "Today I must leave. I regret more than anything that I cannot see you again. Imagine my feelings, if you will, and pass them on to the prince.

> "When shall I, a ragged, rustic outcast,
> See again the blossoms of the city?"

She explained everything to the crown prince. He gazed at her solemnly. "How shall I answer?" Omyōbu asked.

"I am sad when he is away for a little, and he is going so far, and how—tell him that, please."

A sad little answer, thought Omyōbu.[7]

All the details of that unhappy love came back to her. The two of them should have led placid, tranquil lives, and she felt as if she and she alone had been the cause of all the troubles.

"I can think of nothing to say." It was clear to him that her answer had indeed been composed with great difficulty. "I passed your message on to the prince, and was sadder than ever to see how sad it made him.

> "Quickly the blossoms fall. Though spring departs,
> You will come again, I know, to a city of flowers."

There was sad talk all through the crown prince's apartments in the wake of the letter, and there were sounds of weeping. Even people who scarcely knew him were caught up in the sorrow. As for people in his regular service, even scullery maids of whose existence he can hardly have been aware were sad at the thought that they must for a time do without his presence.

So it was all through the court. Deep sorrow prevailed. He had been with his father day and night from his seventh year, and, since nothing he had said to his father had failed to have an effect, almost everyone was in his debt. A cheerful sense of gratitude should have been common in the upper

---

6. Tadasu no Kami, who has his abode in the Lower Kamo Shrine.   7. The crown prince's answer breaks into seven-syllable lines, as if he were trying to compose a poem.

ranks of the court and the ministries, and omnipresent in the lower ranks. It was there, no doubt; but the world had become a place of quick punishments. A pity, people said, silently reproving the great ones whose power was now absolute; but what was to be accomplished by playing the martyr? Not that everyone was satisfied with passive acceptance. If he had not known before, Genji knew now that the human race is not perfect.

He spent a quiet day with Murasaki and late in the night set out in rough travel dress.

"The moon is coming up. Do please come out and see me off. I know that later I will think of any number of things I wanted to say to you. My gloom strikes me as ridiculous when I am away from you for even a day or two."

He raised the blinds and urged her to come forward. Trying not to weep, she at length obeyed. She was very beautiful in the moonlight. What sort of home would this unkind, inconstant city be for her now? But she was sad enough already, and these thoughts were best kept to himself.

He said with forced lightness:

"At least for this life we might make our vows, we thought.
And so we vowed that nothing would ever part us.

How silly we were!"

This was her answer:

"I would give a life for which I have no regrets
If it might postpone for a little the time of parting."

They were not empty words, he knew; but he must be off, for he did not want the city to see him in broad daylight.

Her face was with him the whole of the journey. In great sorrow he boarded the boat that would take him to Suma. It was a long spring day and there was a tail wind, and by late afternoon he had reached the strand where he was to live. He had never before been on such a journey, however short. All the sad, exotic things along the way were new to him. The Oe station[8] was in ruins, with only a grove of pines to show where it had stood.

"More remote, I fear, my place of exile
Than storied ones in lands beyond the seas."

The surf came in and went out again. "I envy the waves," he whispered to himself.[9] It was a familiar poem, but it seemed new to those who heard him, and sad as never before. Looking back toward the city, he saw that the mountains were enshrouded in mist. It was as though he had indeed come "three thousand leagues."[1] The spray from the oars brought thoughts scarcely to be borne.

"Mountain mists cut off that ancient village.
Is the sky I see the sky that shelters it?"

8. In the heart of present-day Osaka; it was used by high priestesses on their way to and from the Ise Shrine.   9. Alludes to a poem by Ariwara Narihira: "Strong my yearning for what I have left behind. / I envy the waves that go back whence they came."   1. Alludes to Po Chü-i's poem "Lines Written on the Winter Solstice, in the Arbutus Hall."

Not far away Yukihira had lived in exile, "dripping brine from the sea grass."[2] Genji's new house was some distance from the coast, in mountains utterly lonely and desolate. The fences and everything within were new and strange. The grass-roofed cottages, the reed-roofed galleries—or so they seemed—were interesting enough in their way. It was a dwelling proper to a remote littoral, and different from any he had known. Having once had a taste for out-of-the-way places, he might have enjoyed this Suma had the occasion been different.

Yoshikiyo had appointed himself a sort of confidential steward. He summoned the overseers of Genji's several manors in the region and assigned them to necessary tasks. Genji watched admiringly. In very quick order he had a rather charming new house. A deep brook flowed through the garden with a pleasing murmur, new plantings were set out; and when finally he was beginning to feel a little at home he could scarcely believe that it all was real. The governor of the province, an old retainer, discreetly performed numerous services. All in all it was a brighter and livelier place than he had a right to expect, although the fact that there was no one whom he could really talk to kept him from forgetting that it was a house of exile, strange and alien. How was he to get through the months and years ahead?

The rainy season came. His thoughts traveled back to the distant city. There were people whom he longed to see, chief among them the lady at Nijō, whose forlorn figure was still before him. He thought too of the crown prince, and of little Yūgiri, running so happily, that last day, from father to grandfather and back again. He sent off letters to the city. Some of them, especially those to Murasaki and to Fujitsubo, took a great deal of time, for his eyes clouded over repeatedly.

This is what he wrote to Fujitsubo:

"Briny our sleeves on the Suma strand; and yours
In the fisher cots of thatch at Matsushima?[3]

"My eyes are dark as I think of what is gone and what is to come, and 'the waters rise.'"[4]

His letter to Oborozukiyo he sent as always to Chūnagon, as if it were a private matter between the two of them. "With nothing else to occupy me, I find memories of the past coming back.

"At Suma, unchastened, one longs for the deep-lying sea pine.
And she, the fisher lady burning salt?"

I shall leave the others, among them letters to his father-in-law and Yūgiri's nurse, to the reader's imagination. They reached their several destinations and gave rise to many sad and troubled thoughts.

Murasaki had taken to her bed. Her women, doing everything they could think of to comfort her, feared that in her grief and longing she might fall into a fatal decline. Brooding over the familiar things he had left behind, the koto, the perfumed robes, she almost seemed on the point of departing the world. Her women were beside themselves. Shōnagon sent asking that

---

2. From a poem by Ariwara Yukihira in The Kokinshū: "If someone should inquire for me, reply: / 'He idles at Suma, dripping brine from the sea grass.'" Yukihira was himself exiled at Suma. **3.** A very common pun makes *Matsushima* "The isle of one who waits." **4.** Another poetic allusion: "The sorrow of parting brings such flood of tears / That the waters of this river must surely rise."

the bishop, her uncle, pray for her. He did so, and to double purpose, that she be relieved of her present sorrows and that she one day be permitted a tranquil life with Genji.

She sent bedding and other supplies to Suma. The robes and trousers of stiff, unfigured white silk brought new pangs of sorrow, for they were unlike anything he had worn before. She kept always with her the mirror to which he had addressed his farewell poem, though it was not acquitting itself of the duty he had assigned to it. The door through which he had come and gone, the cypress pillar at his favorite seat—everything brought sad memories. So it is even for people hardened and seasoned by trials, and how much more for her, to whom he had been father and mother! "Grasses of forgetfulness"[5] might have sprung up had he quite vanished from the earth; but he was at Suma, not so very far away, she had heard. She could not know when he would return.

For Fujitsubo, sorrow was added to uncertainty about her son. And how, at the thought of the fate that had joined them, could her feelings for Genji be of a bland and ordinary kind? Fearful of gossips, she had coldly turned away each small show of affection, she had become more and more cautious and secretive, and she had given him little sign that she sensed the depth of his affection. He had been uncommonly careful himself. Gossips are cruelly attentive people (it was a fact she knew too well), but they seemed to have caught no suspicion of the affair. He had kept himself under tight control and preserved the most careful appearances. How then could she not, in this extremity, have fond thoughts for him?

Her reply was more affectionate than usual.

> "The nun of Matsushima burns the brine
> And fuels the fires with the logs of her lamenting,

now more than ever."

Enclosed with Chūnagon's letter was a brief reply from Oborozukiyo:

> "The fisherwife burns salt and hides her fires
> And strangles, for the smoke has no escape.

"I shall not write of things which at this late date need no saying."

Chūnagon wrote in detail of her lady's sorrows. There were tears in his eyes as he read her letter.

And Murasaki's reply was of course deeply moving. There was this poem:

> "Taking brine on that strand, let him compare
> His dripping sleeves with these night sleeves of mine."

The robes that came with it were beautifully dyed and tailored. She did everything so well. At Suma there were no silly and frivolous distractions, and it seemed a pity that they could not enjoy the quiet life together. Thoughts of her, day and night, became next to unbearable. Should he send for her in secret? But no: his task in this gloomy situation must be to make amends for past misdoings. He began a fast and spent his days in prayer and meditation.

5. The literal translation of *wasuregusa*, "day lilies."

There were also messages about his little boy, Yūgiri. They of course filled him with longing; but he would see the boy again one day, and in the meantime he was in good hands. Yet a father must, however he tries, "wander lost in thoughts upon his child."[6]

In the confusion I had forgotten: he had sent off a message to the Rokujō lady, and she on her own initiative had sent a messenger to seek out his place of exile. Her letter was replete with statements of the deepest affection. The style and the calligraphy, superior to those of anyone else he knew, showed unique breeding and cultivation.

"Having been told of the unthinkable place in which you find yourself, I feel as if I were wandering in an endless nightmare. I should imagine that you will be returning to the city before long, but it will be a very long time before I, so lost in sin, will be permitted to see you.

"Imagine, at Suma of the dripping brine,
The woman of Ise,[7] gathering briny sea grass.

"And what is to become of one, in a world where everything conspires to bring new sorrow?" It was a long letter.

"The tide recedes along the coast of Ise.
No hope, no promise in the empty shells."

Laying down her brush as emotion overcame her and then beginning again, she finally sent off some four or five sheets of white Chinese paper. The gradations of ink were marvelous. He had been fond of her, and it had been wrong to make so much of that one incident.[8] She had turned against him and presently left him. It all seemed such a waste. The letter itself and the occasion for it so moved him that he even felt a certain affection for the messenger, an intelligent young man in her daughter's service. Detaining him for several days, he heard about life at Ise. The house being rather small, the messenger was able to observe Genji at close range. He was moved to tears of admiration by what he saw.

The reader may be left to imagine Genji's reply. He said among other things: "Had I known I was destined to leave the city, it would have been better, I tell myself in the tedium and loneliness here, to go off with you to Ise.

"With the lady of Ise I might have ridden small boats
That row the waves, and avoided dark sea tangles.[9]

"How long, dripping brine on driftwood logs,
On logs of lament, must I gaze at this Suma coast?

"I cannot know when I will see you again."

But at least his letters brought the comfort of knowing that he was well.

There came letters, sad and yet comforting, from the lady of the orange blossoms and her sister.

---

6. Alludes to a poem: "The heart of a parent is not darkness, and yet / He wanders lost in thoughts upon his child." 7. She has gone to Ise, where her daughter serves as high priestess. 8. It was the Rokujō lady's jealousy, in the form of a vengeful spirit, that killed the lady in chapter 4. 9. From the folk song "Men of Ise": "Oh, the men of Ise are strange ones. / How so? How are they strange? / They ride small boats that row the waves, / That row the waves, they do."

"Ferns of remembrance weigh our eaves ever more,
And heavily falls the dew upon our sleeves."

There was no one, he feared, whom they might now ask to clear away the rank growth. Hearing that the long rains had damaged their garden walls, he sent off orders to the city that people from nearby manors see to repairs.

Oborozukiyo had delighted the scandalmongers, and she was now in very deep gloom. Her father, the minister, for she was his favorite daughter, sought to intercede on her behalf with the emperor and Kokiden. The emperor was moved to forgive her. She had been severely punished, it was true, for her grave offense, but not as severely as if she had been one of the companions of the royal bedchamber. In the Seventh Month she was permitted to return to court. She continued to long for Genji. Much of the emperor's old love remained, and he chose to ignore criticism and keep her near him, now berating her and now making impassioned vows. He was a handsome man and he groomed himself well, and it was something of an affront that old memories should be so much with her.

"Things do not seem right now that he is gone," he said one evening when they were at music together. "I am sure that there are many who feel the loss even more strongly than I do. I cannot put away the fear that I have gone against Father's last wishes and that it is a dereliction for which I must one day suffer." There were tears in his eyes and she too was weeping. "I have awakened to the stupidity of the world and I do not feel that I wish to remain in it much longer. And how would you feel if I were to die? I hate to think that you would grieve less for me gone forever than for him gone so briefly such a short distance away. The poet[1] who said that we love while we live did not know a great deal about love." Tears were streaming from Oborozukiyo's eyes. "And whom might you be weeping for? It is sad that we have no children. I would like to follow Father's instructions and adopt the crown prince, but people will raise innumerable objections. It all seems very sad."

There were some whose ideas of government did not accord with his own, but he was too young to impose his will. He passed his days in helpless anger and sorrow.

At Suma, melancholy autumn winds were blowing. Genji's house was some distance from the sea, but at night the wind that blew over the barriers, now as in Yukihira's day, seemed to bring the surf to his bedside. Autumn was hushed and lonely at a place of exile. He had few companions. One night when they were all asleep he raised his head from his pillow and listened to the roar of the wind and of the waves, as if at his ears. Though he was unaware that he wept, his tears were enough to set his pillow afloat. He plucked a few notes on his koto, but the sound only made him sadder.

"The waves on the strand, like moans of helpless longing.
The winds—like messengers from those who grieve?"

He had awakened the others. They sat up, and one by one they were in tears.

1. Unidentified.

This would not do. Because of him they had been swept into exile, leaving families from whom they had never before been parted. It must be very difficult for them, and his own gloom could scarcely be making things easier. So he set about cheering them. During the day he would invent games and make jokes, and set down this and that poem on multicolored patchwork, and paint pictures on fine specimens of figured Chinese silk. Some of his larger paintings were masterpieces. He had long ago been told of this Suma coast and these hills and had formed a picture of them in his mind, and he found now that his imagination had fallen short of the actuality. What a pity, said his men, that they could not summon Tsunenori and Chieda and other famous painters of the day to add colors to Genji's monochromes. This resolute cheerfulness had the proper effect. His men, four or five of whom were always with him, would not have dreamed of leaving him.

There was a profusion of flowers in the garden. Genji came out, when the evening colors were at their best, to a gallery from which he had a good view of the coast. His men felt chills of apprehension as they watched him, for the loneliness of the setting made him seem like a visitor from another world. In a dark robe tied loosely over singlets of figured white and aster-colored trousers, he announced himself as "a disciple of the Buddha" and slowly intoned a sutra, and his men thought that they had never heard a finer voice. From offshore came the voices of fishermen raised in song. The barely visible boats were like little seafowl on an utterly lonely sea, and as he brushed away a tear induced by the splashing of oars and the calls of wild geese overhead, the white of his hand against the jet black of his rosary was enough to bring comfort to men who had left their families behind.

> "Might they be companions of those I long for?
> Their cries ring sadly through the sky of their journey."

This was Yoshikiyo's reply:

> "I know not why they bring these thoughts of old,
> These wandering geese. They were not then my comrades."

And Koremitsu's:

> "No colleagues of mine, these geese beyond the clouds.
> They chose to leave their homes, and I did not."

And that of the guards officer who had cut such a proud figure on the day of the Kamo lustration:

> "Sad are their cries as they wing their way from home.
> They still find solace, for they still have comrades.

It is cruel to lose one's comrades."

His father had been posted to Hitachi, but he himself had come with Genji. He contrived, for all that must have been on his mind, to seem cheerful.

A radiant moon had come out. They were reminded that it was the harvest full moon. Genji could not take his eyes from it. On other such nights there had been concerts at court, and perhaps they of whom he was thinking would be gazing at this same moon and thinking of him.

"My thoughts are of you, old friend," he sang, "two thousand leagues away."[2] His men were in tears.

His longing was intense at the memory of Fujitsubo's farewell poem, and as other memories came back, one after another, he had to turn away to hide his tears. It was very late, said his men, but still he did not come inside.

> "So long as I look upon it I find comfort,
> The moon which comes again to the distant city."

He thought of the emperor and how much he had resembled their father, that last night when they had talked so fondly of old times. "I still have with me the robe which my lord gave me,"[3] he whispered, going inside. He did in fact have a robe that was a gift from the emperor, and he kept it always beside him.

> "Not bitter thoughts alone does this singlet bring.
> Its sleeves are damp with tears of affection too."

The assistant viceroy of Kyushu was returning to the capital. He had a large family and was especially well provided with daughters, and since progress by land would have been difficult he had sent his wife and the daughters by boat. They proceeded by easy stages, putting in here and there along the coast. The scenery at Suma was especially pleasing, and the news that Genji was in residence produced blushes and sighs far out at sea. The Gosechi dancer[4] would have liked to cut the tow rope and drift ashore. The sound of a koto came faint from the distance, the sadness of it joined to a sad setting and sad memories. The more sensitive members of the party were in tears.

The assistant viceroy sent a message. "I had hoped to call on you immediately upon returning to the city from my distant post, and when, to my surprise, I found myself passing your house, I was filled with the most intense feelings of sorrow and regret. Various acquaintances who might have been expected to come from the city have done so, and our party has become so numerous that it would be out of the question to call on you. I shall hope to do so soon."

His son, the governor of Chikuzen, brought the message. Genji had taken notice of the youth and obtained an appointment for him in the imperial secretariat. He was sad to see his patron in such straits, but people were watching and had a way of talking, and he stayed only briefly.

"It was kind of you to come," said Genji. "I do not often see old friends these days."

His reply to the assistant viceroy was in a similar vein. Everyone in the Kyushu party and in the party newly arrived from the city as well was deeply moved by the governor's description of what he had seen. The tears of sympathy almost seemed to invite worse misfortunes.

The Gosechi dancer contrived to send him a note.

> "Now taut, now slack, like my unruly heart,
> The tow rope is suddenly still at the sound of a koto.

---

2. From Po Chü-i's poem "On the Evening of the Full Moon of the Eighth Month."   3. From a poem by Sugawara Michizane (9th century), scholar, poet, and bureaucrat; he was in exile.   4. Gosechi dances were part of a festival held in the Eleventh Month, usually performed by the young daughters of noble families. The appearance of the Gosechi dancer here is abrupt and puzzling. See n. 1, p. 1516.

"Scolding will not improve me."[5]
He smiled, so handsome a smile that his men felt rather inadequate.

> "Why, if indeed your heart is like the tow rope,
> Unheeding must you pass this strand of Suma?

"I had not expected to leave you for these wilds."[6]

There once was a man who, passing Akashi on his way into exile,[7] brought pleasure into an innkeeper's life with an impromptu Chinese poem. For the Gosechi dancer the pleasure was such that she would have liked to make Suma her home.

As time passed, the people back in the city, and even the emperor himself, found that Genji was more and more in their thoughts. The crown prince was the saddest of all. His nurse and Omyōbu would find him weeping in a corner and search helplessly for ways to comfort him. Once so fearful of rumors and their possible effect on this child of hers and Genji's, Fujitsubo now grieved that Genji must be away.

In the early days of his exile he corresponded with his brothers and with important friends at court. Some of his Chinese poems were widely praised.

Kokiden flew into a rage. "A man out of favor with His Majesty is expected to have trouble feeding himself. And here he is living in a fine stylish house and saying awful things about all of us. No doubt the grovelers around him are assuring him that a deer is a horse."[8]

And so writing to Genji came to be rather too much to ask of people, and letters stopped coming.

The months went by, and Murasaki was never really happy. All the women from the other wings of the house were now in her service. They had been of the view that she was beneath their notice, but as they came to observe her gentleness, her magnanimity in household matters, her thoughtfulness, they changed their minds, and not one of them departed her service. Among them were women of good family. A glimpse of her was enough to make them admit that she deserved Genji's altogether remarkable affection.

And as time went by at Suma, Genji began to feel that he could bear to be away from her no longer. But he dismissed the thought of sending for her: this cruel punishment was for himself alone. He was seeing a little of plebeian life, and he thought it very odd and, he must say, rather dirty. The smoke near at hand would, he supposed, be the smoke of the salt burners' fires. In fact, someone was trying to light wet kindling just behind the house.

> "Over and over the rural ones light fires.
> Not so unflagging the urban ones with their visits."

It was winter, and the snowy skies were wild. He beguiled the tedium with music, playing the koto himself and setting Koremitsu to the flute, with Yoshikiyo to sing for them. When he lost himself in a particularly moving strain the others would fall silent, tears in their eyes.

---

5. Alludes to a poem in *The Kokinshū*: "My heart is like a ship upon the seas. / I am easily moved. Scolding will not improve me." 6. An allusion to *The Kokinshū*: "I had not expected to leave you for these wilds. / A fisherman's net is mine, an angler's line." 7. Sugawara Michizane. 8. It is recorded in the *Shih chi* (historical records) of ancient China that a eunuch planning a rebellion showed the high courtiers a deer and required them to call it a horse, ensuring that they feared him.

He thought of the lady the Chinese emperor sent off to the Huns.[9] How must the emperor have felt, how would Genji himself feel, in so disposing of a beautiful lady? He shuddered, as if some such task might be approaching, "at the end of a frosty night's dream."[1]

A bright moon flooded in, lighting the shallow-eaved cottage to the farthest corners. He was able to imitate the poet's feat of looking up at the night sky without going to the veranda.[2] There was a weird sadness in the setting moon. "The moon goes always to the west,"[3] he whispered.

> "All aimless is my journey through the clouds.
> It shames me that the unswerving moon should see me."

He recited it silently to himself. Sleepless as always, he heard the sad calls of the plovers in the dawn and (the others were not yet awake) repeated several times to himself:

> "Cries of plovers in the dawn bring comfort
> To one who awakens in a lonely bed."

His practice of going through his prayers and ablutions in the deep of night seemed strange and wonderful to his men. Far from being tempted to leave him, they did not return even for brief visits to their families.

The Akashi coast was a very short distance away. Yoshikiyo remembered the daughter of the former governor, now a monk, and wrote to her. She did not answer.

"I would like to see you for a few moments sometime at your convenience," came a note from her father. "There is something I want to ask you."

Yoshikiyo was not encouraged. He would look very silly if he went to Akashi only to be turned away. He did not go.

The former governor was an extremely proud and intractable man. The incumbent governor was all-powerful in the province, but the eccentric old man had no wish to marry his daughter to such an upstart. He learned of Genji's presence at Suma.

"I hear that the shining Genji is out of favor," he said to his wife, "and that he has come to Suma. What a rare stroke of luck—the chance we have been waiting for. We must offer our girl."

"Completely out of the question. People from the city tell me that he has any number of fine ladies of his own and that he has reached out for one of the emperor's. That is why the scandal. What interest can he possibly take in a country lump like her?"

"You don't understand the first thing about it. My own views couldn't be more different. We must make our plans. We must watch for a chance to bring him here." His mind was quite made up, and he had the look of someone whose plans were not easily changed. The finery which he had lavished upon house and daughter quite dazzled the eye.

"He may be ever so grand a grand gentleman," persisted the mother, "but it hardly seems the right and sensible thing to choose of all people a man

---

9. Wang Chao-chün was dispatched to the Huns from the harem of the Han emperor Yüan-ti because she had failed to bribe the artists who did portraits of court ladies, and the emperor therefore thought her ill-favored. 1. From a poem about the unlucky Wang Chao-chün. 2. Alludes to a poem written in Chinese, in which the poet describes a view of the night sky from within a ruined palace. 3. From "To the Moon," a poem by Sugawara Michizane.

who has been sent into exile for a serious crime. It might just possibly be different if he were likely to look at her—but no. You must be joking."

"A serious crime! Why in China too exactly this sort of thing happens to every single person who has remarkable talents and stands out from the crowd. And who do you think he is? His late mother was the daughter of my uncle, the Lord Inspector. She had talent and made a name for herself, and when there wasn't enough of the royal love to go around, the others were jealous, and finally they killed her. But she left behind a son who was a royal joy and comfort. Ladies should have pride and high ambitions. I may be a bumpkin myself, but I doubt that he will think her entirely beneath contempt."

Though the girl was no great beauty, she was intelligent and sensitive and had a gentle grace of which someone of far higher rank would have been proud. She was reconciled to her sad lot. No one among the great persons of the land was likely to think her worth a glance. The prospect of marrying someone nearer her station in life revolted her. If she was left behind by those on whom she depended, she would become a nun, or perhaps throw herself into the sea.

Her father had done everything for her. He sent her twice a year to the Sumiyoshi Shrine, hoping that the god might be persuaded to notice her.

The New Year came to Suma, the days were longer, and time went by slowly. The sapling cherry Genji had planted the year before sent out a scattering of blossoms, the air was soft and warm, and memories flooded back, bringing him often to tears. He thought longingly of the ladies for whom he had wept when, toward the end of the Second Month the year before, he had prepared to depart the city. The cherries would now be in bloom before the Grand Hall. He thought of that memorable cherry-blossom festival, and his father, and the extraordinarily handsome figure his brother, now the emperor, had presented, and he remembered how his brother had favored him by reciting his Chinese poem.

A Japanese poem[4] formed in his mind:

> "Fond thoughts I have of the noble ones on high,
> And the day of the flowered caps has come again."

Tō no Chūjō was now a councillor. He was a man of such fine character that everyone wished him well, but he was not happy. Everything made him think of Genji. Finally he decided that he did not care what rumors might arise and what misdeeds he might be accused of and hurried off to Suma. The sight of Genji brought tears of joy and sadness. Genji's house seemed very strange and exotic. The surroundings were such that he would have liked to paint them. The fence was of plaited bamboo and the pillars were of pine and the stairs of stone.[5] It was a rustic, provincial sort of dwelling, and very interesting.

Genji's dress too was somewhat rustic. Over a singlet dyed lightly in a yellowish color denoting no rank or office he wore a hunting robe and trousers of greenish gray. It was plain garb and intentionally countrified, but it so became the wearer as to bring an immediate smile of pleasure to his friend's lips. Genji's personal utensils and accessories were of a makeshift nature,

---

4. The poem he remembers was written in Chinese. The poem he composes is in Japanese.   5. Giving the house a Chinese aspect.

and his room was open to anyone who wished to look in. The gaming boards and stones were also of rustic make. The religious objects that lay about told of earnest devotion. The food was very palatable and very much in the local taste. For his friend's amusement, Genji had fishermen bring fish and shells. Tō no Chūjō had them questioned about their maritime life, and learned of perils and tribulations. Their speech was as incomprehensible as the chirping of birds, but no doubt their feelings were like his own. He brightened their lives with clothes and other gifts. The stables being nearby, fodder was brought from a granary or something of the sort beyond, and the feeding process was as novel and interesting as everything else. Tō no Chūjō hummed the passage from "The Well of Asuka"[6] about the well-fed horses.

Weeping and laughing, they talked of all that had happened over the months.

"Yūgiri quite rips the house to pieces, and Father worries and worries about him."

Genji was of course sorry to hear it; but since I am not capable of recording the whole of the long conversation, I should perhaps refrain from recording any part of it. They composed Chinese poetry all through the night. Tō no Chūjō had come in defiance of the gossips and slanderers, but they intimidated him all the same. His stay was a brief one.

Wine was brought in, and their toast was from Po Chü-i:

"Sad topers we. Our springtime cups flow with tears."

The tears were general, for it had been too brief a meeting.
A line of geese flew over in the dawn sky.

"In what spring tide will I see again my old village?
I envy the geese, returning whence they came."

Sorrier than ever that he must go, Tō no Chūjō replied:

"Sad are the geese to leave their winter's lodging.
Dark my way of return to the flowery city."

He had brought gifts from the city, both elegant and practical. Genji gave him in return a black pony, a proper gift for a traveler.

"Considering its origins, you may fear that it will bring bad luck; but you will find that it neighs into the northern winds."[7]

It was a fine beast.

"To remember me by," said Tō no Chūjō, giving in return what was recognized to be a very fine flute. The situation demanded a certain reticence in the giving of gifts.

The sun was high, and Tō no Chūjō's men were becoming restive. He looked back and looked back, and Genji almost felt that no visit at all would have been better than such a brief one.

"And when will we meet again? It is impossible to believe that you will be here forever."

"Look down upon me, cranes who skim the clouds,
And see me unsullied as this cloudless day.

___
6. A folk song popular with the nobility.   7. Alludes to a Chinese poem: "The Tartar pony faces towards the north. / The Annamese bird nests on the southern branch."

"Yes, I do hope to go back, someday. But when I think how difficult it has been for even the most remarkable men to pick up their old lives, I am no longer sure that I want to see the city again."

> "Lonely the voice of the crane among the clouds.
> Gone the comrade that once flew at its side.

"I have been closer to you than ever I have deserved. My regrets for what has happened are bitter."

They scarcely felt that they had had time to renew their friendship. For Genji the loneliness was unrelieved after his friend's departure.

It was the day of the serpent, the first such day in the Third Month.

"The day when a man who has worries goes down and washes them away," said one of his men, admirably informed, it would seem, in all the annual observances.

Wishing to have a look at the seashore, Genji set forth. Plain, rough curtains were strung up among the trees, and a soothsayer who was doing the circuit of the province was summoned to perform the lustration.

Genji thought he could see something of himself in the rather large doll being cast off to sea, bearing away sins and tribulations.

> "Cast away to drift on an alien vastness,
> I grieve for more than a doll cast out to sea."

The bright, open seashore showed him to wonderful advantage. The sea stretched placid into measureless distances. He thought of all that had happened to him, and all that was still to come.

> "You eight hundred myriad gods must surely help me,
> For well you know that blameless I stand before you."

Suddenly a wind came up and even before the services were finished the sky was black. Genji's men rushed about in confusion. Rain came pouring down, completely without warning. Though the obvious course would have been to return straightway to the house, there had been no time to send for umbrellas. The wind was now a howling tempest, everything that had not been tied down was scuttling off across the beach. The surf was biting at their feet. The sea was white, as if spread over with white linen. Fearful every moment of being struck down, they finally made their way back to the house.

"I've never seen anything like it," said one of the men. "Winds do come up from time to time, but not without warning. It is all very strange and very terrible."

The lightning and thunder seemed to announce the end of the world, and the rain to beat its way into the ground; and Genji sat calmly reading a sutra. The thunder subsided in the evening, but the wind went on through the night.

"Our prayers seem to have been answered. A little more and we would have been carried off. I've heard that tidal waves do carry people off before they know what is happening to them, but I've not seen anything like this."

Towards dawn sleep was at length possible. A man whom he did not recognize came to Genji in a dream.

"The court summons you." He seemed to be reaching for Genji. "Why do you not go?"

It would be the king of the sea, who was known to have a partiality for handsome men. Genji decided that he could stay no longer at Suma.

CHAPTER 13

Akashi[8]

The days went by and the thunder and rain continued. What was Genji to do? People would laugh if, in this extremity, out of favor at court, he were to return to the city. Should he then seek a mountain retreat? But if it were to be noised about that a storm had driven him away, then he would cut a ridiculous figure in history.

His dreams were haunted by that same apparition. Messages from the city almost entirely ceased coming as the days went by without a break in the storms. Might he end his days at Suma? No one was likely to come calling in these tempests.

A messenger did come from Murasaki, a sad, sodden creature. Had they passed in the street, Genji would scarcely have known whether he was man or beast, and of course would not have thought of inviting him to come near. Now the man brought a surge of pleasure and affection—though Genji could not help asking himself whether the storm had weakened his moorings.

Murasaki's letter, long and melancholy, said in part: "The terrifying deluge goes on without a break, day after day. Even the skies are closed off, and I am denied the comfort of gazing in your direction.

"What do they work, the sea winds down at Suma?
At home, my sleeves are assaulted by wave after wave."

Tears so darkened his eyes that it was as if they were inviting the waters to rise higher.

The man said that the storms had been fierce in the city too, and that a special reading of the Prajñāpāramitā Sutra[9] had been ordered. "The streets are all closed and the great gentlemen can't get to court, and everything has closed down."

The man spoke clumsily and haltingly, but he did bring news. Genji summoned him near and had him questioned.

"It's not the way it usually is. You don't usually have rain going on for days without a break and the wind howling on and on. Everyone is terrified. But it's worse here. They haven't had this hail beating right through the ground and thunder going on and on and not letting a body think." The terror written so plainly on his face did nothing to improve the spirits of the people at Suma.

Might it be the end of the world? From dawn the next day the wind was so fierce and the tide so high and the surf so loud that it was as if the crags and the mountains must fall. The horror of the thunder and lightning was beyond description. Panic spread at each new flash. For what sins, Genji's

---

8. A coastal village on the Inland Sea, approximately six miles west of Suma.   9. "The Wisdom Sutra," which sets forth the Buddhist doctrine of Śūnyātā ("void" or "nothingness" or "relativity"): there is no such thing as static existence, since life is flux, causal factors change by the moment and all phenomena are relative and interdependent.

men asked, were they being punished? Were they to perish without another glimpse of their mothers and fathers, their dear wives and children?

Genji tried to tell himself that he had been guilty of no misdeed for which he must perish here on the seashore. Such were the panic and confusion around him, however, that he bolstered his confidence with special offerings to the god of Sumiyoshi.[1]

"O you of Sumiyoshi who protect the lands about: if indeed you are an avatar of the Blessed One, then you must save us."

His men were of course fearful for their lives; but the thought that so fine a gentleman (and in these deplorable circumstances) might be swept beneath the waters seemed altogether too tragic. The less distraught among them prayed in loud voices to this and that favored deity, Buddhist and Shinto, that their own lives be taken if it meant that his might be spared.

They faced Sumiyoshi and prayed and made vows: "Our lord was reared deep in the fastnesses of the palace, and all blessings were his. You who, in the abundance of your mercy, have brought strength through these lands to all who have sunk beneath the weight of their troubles: in punishment for what crimes do you call forth these howling waves? Judge his case if you will, you gods of heaven and earth. Guiltless, he is accused of a crime, stripped of his offices, driven from his house and city, left as you see him with no relief from the torture and the lamentation. And now these horrors, and even his life seems threatened. Why? we must ask. Because of sins in some other life, because of crimes in this one? If your vision is clear, O you gods, then take all this away."

Genji offered prayers to the king of the sea and countless other gods as well. The thunder was increasingly more terrible, and finally the gallery adjoining his rooms was struck by lightning. Flames sprang up and the gallery was destroyed. The confusion was immense; the whole world seemed to have gone mad. Genji was moved to a building out in back, a kitchen or something of the sort it seemed to be. It was crowded with people of every station and rank. The clamor was almost enough to drown out the lightning and thunder. Night descended over a sky already as black as ink.

Presently the wind and rain subsided and stars began to come out. The kitchen being altogether too mean a place, a move back to the main hall was suggested. The charred remains of the gallery were an ugly sight, however, and the hall had been badly muddied and all the blinds and curtains blown away. Perhaps, Genji's men suggested somewhat tentatively, it might be better to wait until dawn. Genji sought to concentrate upon the holy name, but his agitation continued to be very great.

He opened a wattled door and looked out. The moon had come up. The line left by the waves was white and dangerously near, and the surf was still high. There was no one here whom he could turn to, no student of the deeper truths who could discourse upon past and present and perhaps explain these wild events. All the fisherfolk had gathered at what they had heard was the house of a great gentleman from the city. They were as noisy and impossible to communicate with as a flock of birds, but no one thought of telling them to leave.

---

1. Deity venerated at a Shinto shrine in the Sumiyoshi ward of Osaka, a kind of patron saint of mariners and fishermen.

"If the wind had kept up just a little longer," someone said, "absolutely everything would have been swept under. The gods did well by us."

There are no words—"lonely" and "forlorn" seem much too weak—to describe his feelings.

"Without the staying hand of the king of the sea
The roar of the eight hundred waves would have taken us under."

Genji was as exhausted as if all the buffets and fires of the tempest had been aimed at him personally. He dozed off, his head against some nondescript piece of furniture.

The old emperor came to him, quite as when he had lived. "And why are you in this wretched place?" He took Genji's hand and pulled him to his feet. "You must do as the god of Sumiyoshi tells you. You must put out to sea immediately. You must leave this shore behind."

"Since I last saw you, sir," said Genji, overjoyed, "I have suffered an unbroken series of misfortunes. I had thought of throwing myself into the sea."

"That you must not do. You are undergoing brief punishment for certain sins. I myself did not commit any conscious crimes while I reigned, but a person is guilty of transgressions and oversights without his being aware of them. I am doing penance and have no time to look back towards this world. But an echo of your troubles came to me and I could not stand idle. I fought my way through the sea and up to this shore and I am very tired; but now that I am here I must see to a matter in the city." And he disappeared.

Genji called after him, begging to be taken along. He looked around him. There was only the bright face of the moon. His father's presence had been too real for a dream, so real that he must still be here. Clouds traced sad lines across the sky. It had been clear and palpable, the figure he had so longed to see even in a dream, so clear that he could almost catch an afterimage. His father had come through the skies to help him in what had seemed the last extremity of his sufferings. He was deeply grateful, even to the tempests; and in the aftermath of the dream he was happy.

Quite different emotions now ruffled his serenity. He forgot his immediate troubles and only regretted that his father had not stayed longer. Perhaps he would come again. Genji would have liked to go back to sleep, but he lay wakeful until daylight.

A little boat had pulled in at the shore and two or three men came up.

"The revered monk who was once governor of Harima has come from Akashi. If the former Minamoto councillor, Lord Yoshikiyo, is here, we wonder if we might trouble him to come down and hear the details of our mission."

Yoshikiyo pretended to be surprised and puzzled. "He was once among my closer acquaintances here in Harima, but we had a falling out and it has been some time since we last exchanged letters. What can have brought him through such seas in that little boat?"

Genji's dream had given intimations. He sent Yoshikiyo down to the boat immediately. Yoshikiyo marveled that it could even have been launched upon such a sea.

These were the details of the mission, from the mouth of the old governor: "Early this month a strange figure came to me in a dream. I listened, though somewhat incredulously, and was told that on the thirteenth there would be a clear and present sign. I was to ready a boat and make for this shore when the waves subsided. I did ready a boat, and then came this savage wind and lightning. I thought of numerous foreign sovereigns who have received instructions in dreams on how to save their lands, and I concluded that even at the risk of incurring his ridicule I must on the day appointed inform your lord of the import of the dream. And so I did indeed put out to sea. A strange jet blew all the way and brought us to this shore. I cannot think of it except as divine intervention. And might I ask whether there have been corresponding manifestations here? I do hate to trouble you, but might I ask you to communicate all of this to your lord?"

Yoshikiyo quietly relayed the message, which brought new considerations. There had been these various unsettling signs conveyed to Genji dreaming and waking. The possibility of being laughed at for having departed these shores under threat now seemed the lesser risk. To turn his back on what might be a real offer of help from the gods would be to ask for still worse misfortunes. It was not easy to reject ordinary advice, and personal reservations counted for little when the advice came from great eminences. "Defer to them; they will cause you no reproaches," a wise man of old once said. He could scarcely face worse misfortunes by deferring than by not deferring, and he did not seem likely to gain great merit and profit by hesitating out of concern for his brave name. Had not his own father come to him? What room was there for doubts?

He sent back his answer: "I have been through a great deal in this strange place, and I hear nothing at all from the city. I but gaze upon a sun and moon going I know not where as comrades from my old home; and now comes this angler's boat, happy tidings on an angry wind.[2] Might there be a place along your Akashi coast where I can hide myself?"

The old man was delighted. Genji's men pressed him to set out even before sunrise. Taking along only four or five of his closest attendants, he boarded the boat. That strange wind came up again and they were at Akashi as if they had flown. It was very near, within crawling distance, so to speak; but still the workings of the wind were strange and marvelous.

The Akashi coast was every bit as beautiful as he had been told it was. He would have preferred fewer people, but on the whole he was pleased. Along the coast and in the hills the old monk had put up numerous buildings with which to take advantage of the four seasons: a reed-roofed beach cottage with fine seasonal vistas; beside a mountain stream a chapel of some grandeur and dignity, suitable for rites and meditation and invocation of the holy name; and rows of storehouses where the harvest was put away and a bountiful life assured for the years that remained. Fearful of the high tides, the old monk had sent his daughter and her women off to the hills. The house on the beach was at Genji's disposal.

The sun was rising as Genji left the boat and got into a carriage. This first look by daylight at his new guest brought a happy smile to the old man's lips. He felt as if the accumulated years were falling away and as if new years had been granted him. He gave silent thanks to the god of Sumiyoshi. He might have seemed ridiculous as he bustled around seeing to Genji's needs, as if

---

2. Alludes to a poem by Ki no Tsurayuki: "An angler's boat upon the waves that pound us, / Happy tidings on an angry wind."

the radiance of the sun and the moon had become his private property; but no one laughed at him.

I need not describe the beauty of the Akashi coast. The careful attention that had gone into the house and the rocks and plantings of the garden, the graceful line of the coast—it was infinitely pleasanter than Suma, and one would not have wished to ask a less than profoundly sensitive painter to paint it. The house was in quiet good taste. The old man's way of life was as Genji had heard it described, hardly more rustic than that of the grandees at court. In sheer luxury, indeed, he rather outdid them.

When Genji had rested for a time he got off messages to the city. He summoned Murasaki's messenger, who was still at Suma recovering from the horrors of his journey. Loaded with rewards for his services, he now set out again for the city. It would seem that Genji sent off a description of his perils to priests and others of whose services he regularly made use, but he told only Fujitsubo how narrow his escape had in fact been. He repeatedly laid down his brush as he sought to answer that very affectionate letter from Murasaki.

"I feel that I have run the whole gamut of horrors and then run it again, and more than ever I would like to renounce the world; but though everything else has fled away, the image which you entrusted to the mirror has not for an instant left me. I think that I might not see you again.

"Yet farther away, upon the beach at Akashi,
My thoughts of a distant city, and of you.

"I am still half dazed, which fact will I fear be too apparent in the confusion and disorder of this letter."

Though it was true that his letter was somewhat disordered, his men thought it splendid. How very fond he must be of their lady! It would seem that they sent off descriptions of their own perils.

The apparently interminable rains had at last stopped and the sky was bright far into the distance. The fishermen radiated good spirits. Suma had been a lonely place with only a few huts scattered among the rocks. It was true that the crowds here at Akashi were not entirely to Genji's liking, but it was a pleasant spot with much to interest him and take his mind from his troubles.

The old man's devotion to the religious life was rather wonderful. Only one matter interfered with it: worry about his daughter. He told Genji a little of his concern for the girl. Genji was sympathetic. He had heard that she was very handsome and wondered if there might not be some bond between them,[3] that he should have come upon her in this strange place. But no; here he was in the remote provinces, and he must think of nothing but his own prayers. He would be unable to face Murasaki if he were to depart from the promises he had made her. Yet he continued to be interested in the girl. Everything suggested that her nature and appearance were very far from ordinary.

Reluctant to intrude himself, the old man had moved to an outbuilding. He was restless and unhappy when away from Genji, however, and he prayed more fervently than ever to the gods and Buddhas that his unlikely

---

3. Essentially a Buddhist conception, that their fates might be linked from former lives.

hope might be realized. Though in his sixties he had taken good care of himself and was young for his age. The religious life and the fact that he was of proud lineage may have had something to do with the matter. He was stubborn and intractable, as old people often are, but he was well versed in antiquities and not without a certain subtlety. His stories of old times did a great deal to dispel Genji's boredom. Genji had been too busy himself for the sort of erudition, the lore about customs and precedents, which he now had in bits and installments, and he told himself that it would have been a great loss if he had not known Akashi and its venerable master.

In a sense they were friends, but Genji rather overawed the old man. Though he had seemed so confident when he told his wife of his hopes, he hesitated, unable to broach the matter, now that the time for action had come, and seemed capable only of bemoaning his weakness and inadequacy. As for the daughter, she rarely saw a passable man here in the country among people of her own rank; and now she had had a glimpse of a man the like of whom she had not suspected to exist. She was a shy, modest girl, and she thought him quite beyond her reach. She had had hints of her father's ambitions and thought them wildly inappropriate, and her discomfort was greater for having Genji near.

It was the Fourth Month. The old man had all the curtains and fixtures of Genji's rooms changed for fresh summery ones. Genji was touched and a little embarrassed, feeling that the old man's attentions were perhaps a bit overdone; but he would not have wished for the world to offend so proud a nature.

A great many messages now came from the city inquiring after his safety. On a quiet moonlit night when the sea stretched off into the distance under a cloudless sky, he almost felt that he was looking at the familiar waters of his own garden. Overcome with longing, he was like a solitary, nameless wanderer. "Awaji, distant foam,"[4] he whispered to himself.

"Awaji: in your name is all my sadness,
And clear you stand in the light of the moon tonight."

He took out the seven-stringed koto, long neglected, which he had brought from the city and spread a train of sad thoughts through the house as he plucked out a few tentative notes. He exhausted all his skills on "The Wide Barrow,"[5] and the sound reached the house in the hills on a sighing of wind and waves. Sensitive young ladies heard it and were moved. Lowly rustics, though they could not have identified the music, were lured out into the sea winds, there to catch cold.

The old man could not sit still. Casting aside his beads, he came running over to the main house.

"I feel as if a world I had thrown away were coming back," he said, breathless and tearful. "It is a night such as to make one feel that the blessed world for which one longs must be even so."

Genji played on in a reverie, a flood of memories of concerts over the years, of this gentleman and that lady on flute and koto, of voices raised in

4. Alludes to a poem: "Awaji in the moonlight, like distant foam: / From these cloudy sovereign heights it seems so near." The place name *Awaji* contains the word *awa*, "foam," and also suggests the Japanese word *aware*, an exclamation of vague and undefined sadness.   5. A Chinese composition, apparently, which does not survive.

song, of times when he and they had been the center of attention, recipients of praise and favors from the emperor himself. Sending to the house on the hill for a lute and a thirteen-stringed koto, the old man now seemed to change roles and become one of these priestly mendicants who make their living by the lute. He played a most interesting and affecting strain. Genji played a few notes on the thirteen-stringed koto which the old man pressed on him and was thought an uncommonly impressive performer on both sorts of koto. Even the most ordinary music can seem remarkable if the time and place are right; and here on the wide seacoast, open far into the distance, the groves seemed to come alive in colors richer than the bloom of spring or the change of autumn, and the calls of the water rails were as if they were pounding on the door and demanding to be admitted.

The old man had a delicate style to which the instruments were beautifully suited and which delighted Genji. "One likes to see a gentle lady quite at her ease with a koto," said Genji, as if with nothing specific in mind.

The old man smiled. "And where, sir, is one likely to find a gentler, more refined musician than yourself? On the koto I am in the third generation from the emperor Daigo. I have left the great world for the rustic surroundings in which you have found me, and sometimes when I have been more gloomy than usual I have taken out a koto and picked away at it; and, curiously, there has been someone who has imitated me. Her playing has come quite naturally to resemble my master's. Or perhaps it has only seemed so to the degenerate ear of the mountain monk who has only the pine winds for company. I wonder if it might be possible to let you hear a strain, in the greatest secrecy of course." He brushed away a tear.

"I have been rash and impertinent. My playing must have sounded like no playing at all." Genji turned away from the koto. "I do not know why, but it has always been the case that ladies have taken especially well to the koto. One hears that with her father to teach her the fifth daughter of the emperor Saga was a great master of the instrument, but it would seem that she had no successors. The people who set themselves up as masters these days are quite ordinary performers with no real grounding at all. How fascinating that someone who still holds to the grand style should be hidden away on this coast. Do let me hear her."

"No difficulty at all, if that is what you wish. If you really wish it, I can summon her. There was once a poet,[6] you will remember, who was much pleased at the lute of a tradesman's wife. While we are on the subject of lutes, there were not many even in the old days who could bring out the best in the instrument. Yet it would seem that the person of whom I speak plays with a certain sureness and manages to affect a rather pleasing delicacy. I have no idea where she might have acquired these skills. It seems wrong that she should be asked to compete with the wild waves, but sometimes in my gloom I do have her strike up a tune."

He spoke with such spirit that Genji, much interested, pushed the lute toward him.

He did indeed play beautifully, adding decorations that have gone out of fashion. There was a Chinese elegance in his touch, and he was able to induce a particularly solemn tremolo from the instrument. Though it might

6. Po Chü-i's "The Lutist."

have been argued that the setting was wrong, an adept among his retainers was persuaded to sing for them about the clean shore of Ise.[7] Tapping out the rhythm, Genji would join in from time to time, and the old man would pause to offer a word of praise. Refreshments were brought in, very prettily arranged. The old man was most assiduous in seeing that the cups were kept full, and it became the sort of evening when troubles are forgotten.

Late in the night the sea breezes were cool and the moon seemed brighter and clearer as it sank towards the west. All was quiet. In pieces and fragments the old man told about himself, from his feelings upon taking up residence on this Akashi coast to his hopes for the future life and the prospects which his devotions seemed to be opening. He added, unsolicited, an account of his daughter. Genji listened with interest and sympathy.

"It is not easy for me to say it, sir, but the fact that you are here even briefly in what must be for you strange and quite unexpected surroundings, and the fact that you are being asked to undergo trials new to your experience—I wonder if it might not be that the powers to whom an aged monk has so fervently prayed for so many years have taken pity on him. It is now eighteen years since I first prayed and made vows to the god of Sumiyoshi. I have had certain hopes for my daughter since she was very young, and every spring and autumn I have taken her to Sumiyoshi. At each of my six daily services, three of them in the daytime and three at night, I have put aside my own wishes for salvation and ventured a suggestion that my hopes for the girl be noticed. I have sunk to this provincial obscurity because I brought an unhappy destiny with me into this life. My father was a minister, and you see what I have become. If my family is to follow the same road in the future, I ask myself, then where will it end? But I have had high hopes for her since she was born. I have been determined that she go to some noble gentleman in the city. I have been accused of arrogance and unworthy ambitions and subjected to some rather unpleasant treatment. I have not let it worry me. I have said to her that while I live I will do what I can for her, limited though my resources may be; and that if I die before my hopes are realized she is to throw herself into the sea." He was weeping. It had taken great resolve for him to speak so openly.

Genji wept easily these days. "I had been feeling put upon, bundled off to this strange place because of crimes I was not aware of having committed. Your story makes me feel that there is a bond between us. Why did you not tell me earlier? Nothing has seemed quite real since I came here, and I have given myself up to prayers to the exclusion of everything else, and so I fear that I will have struck you as spiritless. Though reports had reached me of the lady of whom you have spoken, I had feared that she would want to have nothing to do with an outcast like myself. You will be my guide and intermediary? May I look forward to company these lonely evenings?"

The old man was thoroughly delighted.

> "Do you too know the sadness of the nights
> On the shore of Akashi with only thoughts for companions?

---

7. Refers to the folk song "The Sea of Ise": "On the clean shore of Ise, / Let us gather shells in the tide. / Let us gather shells and jewels."

"Imagine, if you will, how it has been for us through the long months and years." He faltered, though with no loss of dignity, and his voice was trembling.

"But you, sir, are used to this seacoast.

"The traveler passes fretful nights at Akashi.
The grass which he reaps for his pillow reaps no dreams."

His openness delighted the old man, who talked on and on—and became rather tiresome, I fear. In my impatience I may have allowed inaccuracies to creep in, and exaggerated his eccentricities.

In any event, he felt a clean happiness sweep over him. A beginning had been made.

At about noon the next day Genji got off a note to the house on the hill. A real treasure might lie buried in this unlikely spot. He took a great deal of trouble with his note, which was on a fine saffron-colored Korean paper.

"Do I catch, as I gaze into unresponsive skies,
A glimpse of a grove of which I have had certain tidings?

"My resolve has been quite dissipated."[8]
And was that all? one wonders.

The old man had been waiting. Genji's messenger came staggering back down the hill, for he had been hospitably received.

But the girl was taking time with her reply. The old man rushed to her rooms and urged haste, but to no avail. She thought her hand quite unequal to the task, and awareness of the difference in their stations dismayed her. She was not feeling well, she said, and lay down.

Though he would certainly have wished it otherwise, the old man finally answered in her place. "Her rustic sleeves are too narrow to encompass such awesome tidings, it would seem, and indeed she seems to have found herself incapable of even reading your letter.

"She gazes into the skies into which you gaze.
May they bring your thoughts and hers into some accord.

"But I fear that I will seem impertinent and forward."

It was in a most uncompromisingly old-fashioned hand, on sturdy Michinoku paper; but there was something spruce and dashing about it too. Yes, "forward" was the proper word. Indeed, Genji was rather startled. He gave the messenger a "bejeweled apron," an appropriate gift, he thought, from a beach cottage.[9]

He got off another message the next day, beautifully written on soft, delicate paper. "I am not accustomed to receiving letters from ladies' secretaries.

"Unwillingly reticent about my sorrows
I still must be—for no one makes inquiry.

"Though it is difficult to say just what I mean."

There would have been something unnatural about a girl who refused to be interested in such a letter. She thought it splendid, but she also thought

---

8. Alludes to a poem in *The Kokinshū:* "Resolve that I would keep them to myself, / These thoughts of you, has been quite dissipated."   9. There is a pun on *tamamo,* "jeweled apron" (an elegant word for "apron") and a kind of seaweed.

it impossibly out of her reach. Notice from such supreme heights had the perverse effect of reducing her to tears and inaction.

She was finally badgered into setting something down. She chose delicately perfumed lavender paper and took great care with the gradations of her ink.

> "Unwillingly reticent—how can it be so?
> How can you sorrow for someone you have not met?"

The diction and the handwriting would have done credit to any of the fine ladies at court. He fell into a deep reverie, for he was reminded of days back in the city. But he did not want to attract attention, and presently shook it off.

Every other day or so, choosing times when he was not likely to be noticed, and when he imagined that her thoughts might be similar to his—a quiet, uneventful evening, a lonely dawn—he would get off a note to her. There was a proud reserve in her answers which made him want more than ever to meet her. But there was Yoshikiyo to think of. He had spoken of the lady as if he thought her his property, and Genji did not wish to contravene these long-standing claims. If her parents persisted in offering her to him, he would make that fact his excuse, and seek to pursue the affair as quietly as possible. Not that she was making things easy for him. She seemed prouder and more aloof than the proudest lady at court; and so the days went by in a contest of wills.

The city was more than ever on his mind now that he had moved beyond the Suma barrier. He feared that not even in jest[1] could he do without Murasaki. Again he was asking himself if he might not bring her quietly to Akashi, and he was on the point of doing just that. But he did not expect to be here very much longer, and nothing was to be gained by inviting criticism at this late date.

In the city it had been a year of omens and disturbances. On the thirteenth day of the Third Month, as the thunder and winds mounted to new fury, the emperor had a dream. His father stood glowering at the stairs to the royal bedchamber and had a great deal to say, all of it, apparently, about Genji. Deeply troubled, the emperor described the dream to his mother.

"On stormy nights a person has a way of dreaming about the things that are on his mind," she said. "If I were you I would not give it a second thought."

Perhaps because his eyes had met the angry eyes of his father, he came down with a very painful eye ailment. Retreat and fasting were ordered for the whole court, even Kokiden's household. Then the minister, her father, died. He was of such years that his death need have surprised no one, but Kokiden too was unwell, and worse as the days went by; and the emperor had a great deal to worry about. So long as an innocent Genji was off in the wilderness, he feared, he must suffer. He ventured from time to time a suggestion that Genji be restored to his old rank and offices.

His mother sternly advised against it. "People will tax you with shallowness and indecision. Can you really think of having a man go into exile and then bringing him back before the minimum three years have gone by?"

---

1. Alludes to a poem in *The Kokinshū:* "I wondered if even in jest I could do without you. / I gave it a try, to which I proved unequal."

And so he hesitated, and he and his mother were in increasingly poor health.

At Akashi it was the season when cold winds blow from the sea to make a lonely bed even lonelier.

Genji sometimes spoke to the old man. "If you were perhaps to bring her here when no one is looking?"

He thought that he could hardly be expected to visit her. She had her own ideas. She knew that rustic maidens should come running at a word from a city gentleman who happened to be briefly in the vicinity. No, she did not belong to his world, and she would only be inviting grief if she pretended that she did. Her parents had impossible hopes, it seemed, and were asking the unthinkable and building a future on nothing. What they were really doing was inviting endless trouble. It was good fortune enough to exchange notes with him for so long as he stayed on this shore. Her own prayers had been modest: that she be permitted a glimpse of the gentleman of whom she had heard so much. She had had her glimpse, from a distance, to be sure, and, brought in on the wind, she had also caught hints of his unmatched skill (of this too she had heard) on the koto. She had learned rather a great deal about him these past days, and she was satisfied. Indeed a nameless woman lost among the fishermen's huts had no right to expect even this. She was acutely embarrassed at any suggestion that he be invited nearer.

Her father too was uneasy. Now that his prayers were being answered he began to have thoughts of failure. It would be very sad for the girl, offered heedlessly to Genji, to learn that he did not want her. Rejection was painful at the hands of the finest gentleman. His unquestioning faith in all the invisible gods had perhaps led him to overlook human inclinations and probabilities.

"How pleasant," Genji kept saying, "if I could hear that koto to the singing of the waves. It is the season for such things. We should not let it pass."

Dismissing his wife's reservations and saying nothing to his disciples, the old man selected an auspicious day. He bustled around making preparations, the results of which were dazzling. The moon was near full. He sent off a note which said only: "This night that should not be wasted."[2] It seemed a bit arch, but Genji changed to informal court dress and set forth late in the night. He had a carriage decked out most resplendently, and then, deciding that it might seem ostentatious, went on horseback instead. The lady's house was some distance back in the hills. The coast lay in full view below, the bay silver in the moonlight. He would have liked to show it to Murasaki. The temptation was strong to turn his horse's head and gallop on to the city.

"Race on through the moonlit sky, O roan-colored horse,
    And let me be briefly with her for whom I long."[3]

The house was a fine one, set in a grove of trees. Careful attention had gone into all the details. In contrast to the solid dignity of the house on the

---

2. Alludes to a poem: "If only I could show them to someone who knows, / This moon, these flowers, this night that should not be wasted." 3. A play on words gives a roan horse a special affinity with moonlight.

beach, this house in the hills had a certain fragility about it, and he could imagine the melancholy thoughts that must come to one who lived here. There was sadness in the sound of the temple bells borne in on pine breezes from a hall of meditation nearby. Even the pines seemed to be asking for something as they sent their roots out over the crags. All manner of autumn insects were singing in the garden. He looked about him and saw a pavilion finer than the others. The cypress door upon which the moonlight seemed to focus was slightly open.

He hesitated and then spoke. There was no answer. She had resolved to admit him no nearer. All very aristocratic, thought Genji. Even ladies so wellborn that they were sheltered from sudden visitors usually tried to make conversation when the visitor was Genji. Perhaps she was letting him know that he was under a cloud. He was annoyed and thought of leaving. It would run against the mood of things to force himself upon her, and on the other hand he would look rather silly if it were to seem that she had bested him at this contest of wills. One would indeed have wished to show him, the picture of dejection, "to someone who knows."[4]

A curtain string brushed against a koto, to tell him that she had been passing a quiet evening at her music.

"And will you not play for me on the koto of which I have heard so much?
"Would there were someone with whom I might share my thoughts
And so dispel some part of these sad dreams."

"You speak to one for whom the night has no end.
How can she tell the dreaming from the waking?"

The almost inaudible whisper reminded him strongly of the Rokujō lady.

This lady had not been prepared for an incursion and could not cope with it. She fled to an inner room. How she could have contrived to bar it he could not tell, but it was very firmly barred indeed. Though he did not exactly force his way through, it is not to be imagined that he left matters as they were. Delicate, slender—she was almost too beautiful. Pleasure was mingled with pity at the thought that he was imposing himself upon her. She was even more pleasing than reports from afar had had her. The autumn night, usually so long, was over in a trice. Not wishing to be seen, he hurried out, leaving affectionate assurances behind.

He got off an unobtrusive note later in the morning. Perhaps he was feeling twinges of conscience. The old monk was equally intent upon secrecy, and sorry that he was impelled to treat the messenger rather coolly.

Genji called in secret from time to time. The two houses being some distance apart, he feared being seen by fishermen, who were known to relish a good rumor, and sometimes several days would elapse between his visits. Exactly as she had expected, thought the girl. Her father, forgetting that enlightenment was his goal, quite gave his prayers over to silent queries as to when Genji might be expected to come again; and so (and it seems a pity) a tranquillity very laboriously attained was disturbed at a very late date.

Genji dreaded having Murasaki learn of the affair. He still loved her more than anyone, and he did not want her to make even joking reference to it.

4. See n. 2, p. 1509.

She was a quiet, docile lady, but she had more than once been unhappy with him. Why, for the sake of brief pleasure, had he caused her pain? He wished it were all his to do over again. The sight of the Akashi lady only brought new longing for the other lady.

He got off a more earnest and affectionate letter than usual, at the end of which he said: "I am in anguish at the thought that, because of foolish occurrences for which I have been responsible but have had little heart, might appear in a guise distasteful to you. There has been a strange, fleeting encounter. That I should volunteer this story will make you see, I hope, how little I wish to have secrets from you. Let the gods be my judges.

> "It was but the fisherman's brush with the salty sea pine
> Followed by a tide of tears of longing."

Her reply was gentle and unreproachful, and at the end of it she said: "That you should have deigned to tell me a dreamlike story which you could not keep to yourself calls to mind numbers of earlier instances.

> "Naïve of me, perhaps; yet we did make our vows.
> And now see the waves that wash the Mountain of Waiting!"[5]

It was the one note of reproach in a quiet, undemanding letter. He found it hard to put down, and for some nights he stayed away from the house in the hills.

The Akashi lady was convinced once more that her fears had become actuality. Now seemed the time to throw herself into the sea. She had only her parents to turn to and they were very old. She had had no ambitions for herself, no thought of making a respectable marriage. Yet the years had gone by happily enough, without storms or tears. Now she saw that the world can be very cruel. She managed to conceal her worries, however, and to do nothing that might annoy Genji. He was more and more pleased with her as time went by.

But there was the other, the lady in the city, waiting and waiting for his return. He did not want to do anything that would make her unhappy, and he spent his nights alone. He sent sketchbooks off to her, adding poems calculated to provoke replies. No doubt her women were delighted with them; and when the sorrow was too much for her (and as if by thought transference) she too would make sketches and set down notes which came to resemble a journal.

And what did the future have in store for the two of them?

The New Year came, the emperor was ill, and a pall settled over court life. There was a son, by Lady Shōkyōden, daughter of the Minister of the Right, but the child was only two, far too young for the throne. The obvious course was to abdicate in favor of the crown prince. As the emperor turned over in his mind the problem of advice and counsel for his successor, he thought it more than ever a pity that Genji should be off in the provinces. Finally he went against Kokiden's injunctions and issued an amnesty. Kokiden had been ill from the previous year, the victim of a malign spirit, it seemed, and numerous other dire omens had disturbed the court. Though the emperor's

---

5. Alludes to a poem in *The Kokinshū*: "On the day that I am unfaithful to my vows, / May the waves break over the Mountain of Waiting of Sué." A very common pun makes *Matsuyama,* "Mount of Pines," also "Mountain of Waiting."

eye ailment had for a time improved, perhaps because of strict fasting, it was worse again. Late in the Seventh Month, in deep despondency, he issued a second order, summoning Genji back to the city.

Genji had been sure that a pardon would presently come, but he also knew that life is uncertain. That it should come so soon was of course pleasing. At the same time the thought of leaving this Akashi coast filled him with regret. The old monk, though granting that it was most proper and just, was upset at the news. He managed all the same to tell himself that Genji's prosperity was in his own best interest. Genji visited the lady every night and sought to console her. From about the Sixth Month she had shown symptoms such as to make their relations more complex. A sad, ironical affair seemed at the same time to come to a climax and to disintegrate. He wondered at the perverseness of fates that seemed always to be bringing new surprises. The lady, and one could scarcely have blamed her, was sunk in the deepest gloom. Genji had set forth on a strange, dark journey with a comforting certainty that he would one day return to the city; and he now lamented that he would not see this Akashi again.

His men, in their several ways, were delighted. An escort came from the city, there was a joyous stir of preparation, and the master of the house was lost in tears. So the month came to an end. It was a season for sadness in any case, and sad thoughts accosted Genji. Why, now and long ago, had he abandoned himself, heedlessly but of his own accord, to random, profitless affairs of the heart?

"What a great deal of trouble he does cause," said those who knew the secret. "The same thing all over again. For almost a year he didn't tell anyone and he didn't seem to care the first thing about her. And now just when he ought to be letting well enough alone he makes things worse."

Yoshikiyo was the uncomfortable one. He knew what his fellows were saying: that he had talked too much and started it all.

Two days before his departure Genji visited his lady, setting out earlier than usual. This first really careful look at her revealed an astonishingly proud beauty. He comforted her with promises that he would choose an opportune time to bring her to the city. I shall not comment again upon his own good looks. He was thinner from fasting, and emaciation seemed to add the final touches to the picture. He made tearful vows. The lady replied in her heart that this small measure of affection was all she wanted and deserved, and that his radiance only emphasized her own dullness. The waves moaned in the autumn winds, and smoke from the salt burners' fires drew faint lines across the sky, and all the symbols of loneliness seemed to gather together.

"Even though we now must part for a time,
The smoke from these briny fires will follow me."

"Smoldering thoughts like the sea grass burned on these shores.
And what good now to ask for anything more?"

She fell silent, weeping softly, and a rather conventional poem seemed to say a great deal.

She had not, through it all, played for him on the koto of which he had heard so much.

"Do let me hear it. Let it be a memento."

Sending for the seven-stringed koto he had brought from the city, he played an unusual strain, quiet but wonderfully clear on the midnight air. Unable to restrain himself, the old man pushed a thirteen-stringed koto toward his daughter. She was apparently in a mood for music. Softly she tuned the instrument, and her touch suggested very great polish and elegance. He had thought Fujitsubo's playing quite incomparable. It was in the modern style, and enough to bring cries of wonder from anyone who knew a little about music. For him it was like Fujitsubo herself, the essence of all her delicate awareness. The koto of the lady before him was quiet and calm, and so rich in overtones as almost to arouse envy. She left off playing just as the connoisseur who was her listener had passed the first stages of surprise and become eager attention. Disappointment and regret succeeded pleasure. He had been here for nearly a year. Why had he not insisted that she play for him, time after time? All he could do now was repeat the old vows.

"Take this koto," he said, "to remember me by. Someday we will play together."

Her reply was soft and almost casual:

> "One heedless word, one koto, to set me at rest.
> In the sound of it the sound of my weeping, forever."

He could not let it pass.

> "Do not change the middle string[6] of this koto.
> Unchanging I shall be till we meet again."

"And we will meet again before it has slipped out of tune."

Yet it was not unnatural that the parting should seem more real than the reunion.

On the last morning Genji was up and ready before daybreak. Though he had little time to himself in all the stir, he contrived to write to her:

> "Sad the retreating waves at leaving this shore.
> Sad I am for you, remaining after."

> "You leave, my reed-roofed hut will fall to ruin.
> Would that I might go out with these waves."

It was an honest poem, and in spite of himself he was weeping. One could, after all, become fond of a hostile place, said those who did not know the secret. Those who did, Yoshikiyo and others, were a little jealous, concluding that it must have been a rather successful affair.

There were tears, for all the joy; but I shall not dwell upon them.

The old man had arranged the grandest of farewell ceremonies. He had splendid travel robes for everyone, even the lowliest footmen. One marveled that he had found time to collect them all. The gifts for Genji himself were of course the finest, chests and chests of them, borne by a retinue which he attached to Genji's. Some of them would make very suitable gifts in the city. He had overlooked nothing.

The lady had pinned a poem to a travel robe:

---

6. There are various theories about what this expression means. The most plausible is that the middle string remains unaltered during tuning, although the translator does not follow this interpretation.

"I made it for you, but the surging brine has wet it.
And might you find it unpleasant and cast it off?"

Despite the confusion, he sent one of his own robes in return, and with it a note:
"It was very thoughtful of you.

"Take it, this middle robe, let it be the symbol
Of days uncounted but few between now and then."

Something else, no doubt, to put in her chest of memories. It was a fine robe and it bore a most remarkable fragrance. How could it fail to move her?

The old monk, his face like one of the twisted shells on the beach, was meanwhile making some of the younger people smile. "I have quite renounced the world," he said, "but the thought that I may not see you back to the city—

"Though weary of life, seasoned by salty winds,
I am not able to leave this shore behind,

and I wander lost in thoughts upon my child.[7] Do let me see you at least as far as the border. It may seem forward of me, but if something should from time to time call up thoughts of her, do please let her hear from you."

"It is an impossibility, sir, for very particular reasons, that I can ever forget her. You will very quickly be made to see my real intentions. If I seem dispirited, it is only because I am sad to leave all this behind.

"I wept upon leaving the city in the spring.
I weep in the autumn on leaving this home by the sea.

"What else can I do?" And he brushed away a tear.

The old man seemed on the point of expiring.

The lady did not want anyone to guess the intensity of her grief, but it was there, and with it sorrow at the lowly rank (she knew that she could not complain) that had made this parting inevitable. His image remained before her, and she seemed capable only of weeping.

Her mother tried everything to console her. "What could we have been thinking of? You have such odd ideas," she said to her husband, "and I should have been more careful."

"Enough, enough. There are reasons why he cannot abandon her. I have no doubt that he has already made his plans. Stop worrying, mix yourself a dose of something or other. This wailing will do no good." But he was sitting disconsolate in a corner.

The women of the house, the mother and the nurse and the rest, went on charging him with unreasonable methods. "We had hoped and prayed over the years that she might have the sort of life any girl wants, and things finally seemed to be going well—and now see what has happened."

It was true. Old age suddenly advanced and subdued him, and he spent his days in bed. But when night came he was up and alert.

"What can have happened to my beads?"

Unable to find them, he brought empty hands together in supplication. His disciples giggled. They giggled again when he set forth on a moonlight

7. See n. 6, p. 1490.

peregrination and managed to fall into the brook and bruise his hip on one of the garden stones he had chosen so carefully. For a time pain drove away, or at least obscured, his worries.

Genji went through lustration ceremonies at Naniwa and sent a messenger to Sumiyoshi with thanks that he had come thus far and a promise to visit at a later date in fulfillment of his vows. His retinue had grown to an army and did not permit side excursions. He made his way directly back to the city. At Nijō the reunion was like a dream. Tears of joy flowed so freely as almost to seem inauspicious. Murasaki, for whom life had come to seem of as little value as her farewell poem had suggested it to be, shared in the joy. She had matured and was more beautiful than ever. Her hair had been almost too rich and thick. Worry and sorrow had thinned it somewhat and thereby improved it. And now, thought Genji, a deep peace coming over him, they would be together. And in that instant there came to him the image of the one whom he had not been ready to leave. It seemed that his life must go on being complicated.

He told Murasaki about the other lady. A pensive, dreamy look passed over his face, and she whispered, as if to dismiss the matter: "For myself I do not worry."[8]

He smiled. It was a charmingly gentle reproof. Unable to take his eyes from her now that he had her before him, he could not think how he had survived so many months and years without her. All the old bitterness came back. He was restored to his former rank and made a supernumerary councillor. All his followers were similarly rehabilitated. It was as if spring had come to a withered tree.

The emperor summoned him and as they made their formal greetings thought how exile had improved him. Courtiers looked on with curiosity, wondering what the years in the provinces would have done to him. For the elderly women who had been in service since the reign of his late father, regret gave way to noisy rejoicing. The emperor had felt rather shy at the prospect of receiving Genji and had taken great pains with his dress. He seemed pale and sickly, though he had felt somewhat better these last few days. They talked fondly of this and that, and presently it was night. A full moon flooded the tranquil scene. There were tears in the emperor's eyes.

"We have not had music here of late," he said, "and it has been a very long time since I last heard any of the old songs."

Genji replied:

"Cast out upon the sea, I passed the years
As useless as the leech child of the gods."[9]

The emperor was touched and embarrassed.

"The leech child's parents met beyond the pillar.
We meet again to forget the spring of parting."

He was a man of delicate grace and charm.

---

8. Alludes to a poem, "For myself, who am forgotten, I do not worry, / But for him who vowed fidelity while he lived."   9. Refers to the native creation myth, in which the leech child, among the Sun Goddess's siblings, lives approximately the period of Genji's exile before being cast out to sea. It is at a pillar (see the emperor's answering poem) that both the leech and the Sun Goddess are conceived.

Genji's first task was to commission a grand reading of the Lotus Sutra in his father's memory. He called on the crown prince, who had grown in his absence, and was touched that the boy should be so pleased to see him. He had done so well with his studies that there need be no misgivings about his competence to rule. It would seem that Genji also called on Fujitsubo, and managed to control himself sufficiently for a quiet and affectionate conversation.

I had forgotten: he sent a note with the retinue which, like a returning wave, returned to Akashi. Very tender, it had been composed when no one was watching.

"And how is it with you these nights when the waves roll in?

> "I wonder, do the morning mists yet rise,
> There at Akashi of the lonely nights?"

The Kyushu Gosechi dancer[1] had had fond thoughts of the exiled Genji, and she was vaguely disappointed to learn that he was back in the city and once more in the emperor's good graces. She sent a note, with instructions that the messenger was to say nothing of its origin:

> "There once came tidings from a boat at Suma,
> From one who now might show you sodden sleeves."

Her hand had improved, though not enough to keep him from guessing whose it was.

> "It is I, not you, from whom the complaints should come.
> My sleeves have refused to dry since last you wrote."

He had not seen enough of her, and her letter brought fond memories. But he was not going to embark upon new adventures.

To the lady of the orange blossoms he sent only a note, cause more for disappointment than for pleasure.

Summary   Eight years pass in the novel before we come to Chapter 25, *Fireflies*. When Genji returns to the capital, he is quickly restored to his former glory. And when his son by Fujitsubo assumes the throne as Emperor Reizei (although neither the emperor himself nor the world at large knows his true parentage), Genji's position could hardly be more secure. Genji is promoted to minister, his father-in-law is made prime minister, and his supporters reign supreme.

In his personal life, things are as eventful as ever. The Akashi lady gives birth to a baby girl. Though jealous at first, Murasaki is persuaded by Genji to adopt the child, an act to which the Akashi lady accedes in the interests of her daughter's future. Now in his early thirties, however, Genji loses a woman on whom he had always been fixated and with whom he shares a terrible secret. After a grave illness, Fujitsubo succumbs, and Genji is plunged into mourning.

Even worse, once the funeral observances end, a meddling priest informs the emperor who his real father is. Shocked and feeling somehow guilty himself, Emperor Reizei considers abdicating, though Genji argues against it.

In the meantime, Genji's other son, by Aoi, is rising nicely in the world. Yūgiri completes his education and is named chamberlain, a prestigious post, if not in the very upper reaches of administration.

---

1. See n. 4, p. 1493. The translator asserts that this is not the dancer mentioned in chapter 12, but the "charming girl, the daughter of the assistant viceroy of Kyushu" (mentioned in an earlier chapter), with whom Genji had a dalliance.

In his mid-thirties, Genji turns his attention to constructing a proper mansion for his various ladies—a kind of surrogate palace for the man who will never be emperor and the women who will never be his imperial consorts. It is a splendid building, particularly the gardens, which are organized in seasonal progression. Pride of place, the spring compound, naturally goes to Murasaki.

But in the summer wing Genji establishes a newcomer, Tamakazura, the twenty-year-old daughter of the woman he once loved briefly (told in Chapter 4). Genji has just discovered her, and with parental interest that quickly raises the suspicions of both Tamakazura and Murasaki, he installs her in his new palace. She is so much like her mother that Genji cannot bear it. When he confesses his feelings, however, Tamakazura rebuffs him, and for once, Genji appears abashed. "He knew that this impetuous behavior did not become his age and eminence. Collecting himself, he withdrew before the lateness of the hour brought her women to mistaken conclusions." Many a courtier would like to woo the lovely Tamakazura, but Genji, who still nurses his own unrequited affection, will allow only three contenders: Kashiwagi, the son of his old friend Tō no Chūjō; a nobleman named Higekuro; and his own brother, Prince Hotaru, whose name—literally Fireflies—makes up the title of the next chapter.

CHAPTER 25

Fireflies

Genji was famous and life was secure and peaceful. His ladies had in their several ways made their own lives and were happy. There was an exception, Tamakazura, who faced a new crisis and was wondering what to do next. She was not as genuinely frightened of him, of course, as she had been of the Higo man;[2] but since few people could possibly know what had happened, she must keep her disquiet to herself, and her growing sense of isolation. Old enough to know a little of the world, she saw more than ever what a handicap it was not to have a mother.

Genji had made his confession. The result was that his longing increased. Fearful of being overheard, however, he found the subject a difficult one to approach, even gingerly. His visits were very frequent. Choosing times when she was likely to have few people with her, he would hint at his feelings, and she would be in an agony of embarrassment. Since she was not in a position to turn him away, she could only pretend that she did not know what was happening.

She was of a cheerful, affectionate disposition. Though she was also of a cautious and conservative nature, the chief impression she gave was of a delicate, winsome girlishness.

Prince Hotaru continued to pay energetic court. His labors had not yet gone on for very long when he had the early-summer rains to be resentful of.

"Admit me a little nearer, please," he wrote. "I will feel better if I can unburden myself of even part of what is in my heart."

Genji saw the letter. "Princes," he said, "should be listened to. Aloofness is not permitted. You must let him have an occasional answer." He even told her what to say.

---

2. An uncouth suitor of the past. After her mother's death (in chapter 4) Tamakazura is taken by her nurse to the distant southern province of Higo, where the nurse's husband has been appointed an official. She grows up there, and in due course a rustic official ("the Higo man") pursues her. He is powerful and persistent, but a little crude. Finally, under cover of darkness, Tamakazura and her nurse flee, setting sail for the capital.

But he only made things worse. She said that she was not feeling well and did not answer.

There were few really highborn women in her household. She did have a cousin called Saishō, daughter of a maternal uncle who had held a seat on the council. Genji had heard that she had been having a difficult time since her father's death, and had put her in Tamakazura's service. She wrote a passable hand and seemed generally capable and well informed. He assigned her the task of composing replies to gentlemen who deserved them. It was she whom he summoned today. One may imagine that he was curious to see all of his brother's letters. Tamakazura herself had been reading them with more interest since that shocking evening. It must not be thought that she had fallen in love with Hotaru, but he did seem to offer a way of evading Genji. She was learning rapidly.

Unaware that Genji himself was eagerly awaiting him, Hotaru was delighted at what seemed a positive invitation and quietly came calling. A seat was put out for him near the corner doors, where she received him with only a curtain between them. Genji had given close attention to the incense, which was mysterious and seductive—rather more attention, indeed, than a guardian might have felt that his duty demanded. One had to admire the results, whatever the motive. Saishō was at a loss to reply to Hotaru's overtures. Genji pinched her gently to remind her that her mistress must not behave like an unfeeling lump, and only added to her discomfiture. The dark nights of the new moon were over and there was a bland quarter-moon in the cloudy sky. Calm and dignified, the prince was very handsome indeed. Genji's own very special perfume mixed with the incense that drifted through the room as people moved about. More interesting than he would have expected, thought the prince. In calm control of himself all the while (and in pleasant contrast to certain other people), he made his avowals.

Tamakazura withdrew to the east penthouse and lay down. Genji followed Saishō as she brought a new message from the prince.

"You are not being kind," he said to Tamakazura. "A person should behave as the occasion demands. You are unnecessarily coy. You should not be sending a messenger back and forth over such distances. If you do not wish him to hear your voice, very well, but at least you should move a little nearer."

She was in despair. She suspected that his real motive was to impose himself upon her, and each course open to her seemed worse than all the others. She slipped away and lay down at a curtain between the penthouse and the main hall.

She was sunk in thought, unable to answer the prince's outpourings. Genji came up beside her and lifted the curtain back over its frame. There was a flash of light. She looked up startled. Had someone lighted a torch? No— Genji had earlier in the evening put a large number of fireflies in a cloth bag. Now, letting no one guess what he was about, he released them. Tamakazura brought a fan to her face. Her profile was very beautiful.

Genji had worked everything out very carefully. Prince Hotaru[3] was certain to look in her direction. He was making a show of passion, Genji suspected, because he thought her Genji's daughter, and not because he had

---

3. It is from this episode that the prince obtains his name, Hotaru (Firefly).

guessed what a beauty she was. Now he would see, and be genuinely excited. Genji would not have gone to such trouble if she had in fact been his daughter. It all seems rather perverse of him.

He slipped out through another door and returned to his part of the house.

The prince had guessed where the lady would be. Now he sensed that she was perhaps a little nearer. His heart racing, he looked through an opening in the rich gossamer curtains. Suddenly, some six or seven feet away, there was a flash of light—and such beauty as was revealed in it! Darkness was quickly restored, but for the brief glimpse he had had was the sort of thing that makes for romance. The figure at the curtains may have been indistinct but it most certainly was slim and tall and graceful. Genji would not have been disappointed at the interest it had inspired.

> "You put out this silent fire to no avail.
> Can you extinguish the fire in the human heart?

"I hope I make myself understood."
Speed was the important thing in answering such a poem.

> "The firefly but burns and makes no comment.
> Silence sometimes tells of deeper thoughts."

It was a brisk sort of reply, and having made it, she was gone. His lament about this chilly treatment was rather wordy, but he would not have wished to overdo it by staying the night. It was late when he braved the dripping eaves (and tears as well) and went out. I have no doubt that a cuckoo sent him on his way,[4] but did not trouble myself to learn all the details.

So handsome, so poised, said the women—so very much like Genji. Not knowing their lady's secret, they were filled with gratitude for Genji's attentions. Why, not even her mother could have done more for her.

Unwelcome attentions, the lady was thinking. If she had been recognized by her father and her situation were nearer the ordinary, then they need not be entirely unwelcome. She had had wretched luck, and she lived in dread of rumors.

Genji too was determined to avoid rumors. Yet he continued to have his ways. Can one really be sure, for instance, that he no longer had designs upon Akikonomu?[5] There was something different about his manner when he was with her, something especially charming and seductive. But she was beyond the reach of direct overtures. Tamakazura was a modern sort of girl, and approachable. Sometimes dangerously near losing control of himself, he would do things which, had they been noticed, might have aroused suspicions. It was a difficult and complicated relationship indeed, and he must be given credit for the fact that he held back from the final line.

On the fifth day of the Fifth Month, the Day of the Iris, he stopped by her apartments on his way to the equestrian grounds.

"What happened? Did he stay late? You must be careful with him. He is not to be trusted—not that there are very many men these days a girl really can trust."

4. The narrator slips into the mode of pathetic fallacy, attributing feelings of sympathy for Genji to the cuckoo (*hototogisu*), a bird whose poetic overtones are lost in translation; nightingale would be closer to the mood. 5. Like Tamakazura, the daughter of a former love (the Rokujō lady). Genji has also posed as her father and been erotically attracted. She is now married to the current emperor, Genji's illegitimate son with Fujitsubo, and is thus empress.

He praised his brother and blamed him. He seemed very young and was very handsome as he offered this word of caution. As for his clothes, the singlets and the robe thrown casually over them glowed in such rich and pleasing colors that they seemed to brim over and seek more space. One wondered whether a supernatural hand might not have had some part in the dyeing. The colors themselves were familiar enough, but the woven patterns were as if everything had pointed to this day of flowers.[6] The lady was sure she would have been quite intoxicated with the perfumes burned into them had she not had these worries.

A letter came from Prince Hotaru, on white tissue paper in a fine, aristocratic hand. At first sight the contents seemed very interesting, but somehow they became ordinary upon repeating.

"Even today the iris is neglected.
Its roots, my cries, are lost among the waters."[7]

It was attached to an iris root certain to be much talked of.

"You must get off an answer," said Genji, preparing to leave.

Her women argued that she had no choice.

Whatever she may have meant to suggest by it, this was her answer, a simple one set down in a faint, delicate hand:

"It might have flourished better in concealment,
The iris root washed purposelessly away."

"Exposure seems rather unwise."

A connoisseur, the prince thought that the hand could just possibly be improved.

Gifts of medicinal herbs[8] in decorative packets came from this and that well-wisher. The festive brightness did much to make her forget earlier unhappiness and hope that she might come uninjured through this new trial.

Genji also called on the lady of the orange blossoms, in the east wing of the same northeast quarter.

"Yūgiri is to bring some friends around after the archery meet. I should imagine it will still be daylight. I have never understood why our efforts to avoid attention always end in failure. The princes and the rest of them hear that something is up and come around to see, and so we have a much noisier party than we had planned on. We must in any event be ready."

The equestrian stands were very near the galleries of the northeast quarter.

"Come, girls," he said. "Open all the doors and enjoy yourselves. Have a look at all the handsome officers. The ones in the Left Guards are especially handsome, several cuts above the common run at court."

They had a delightful time. Tamakazura joined them. There were fresh green blinds all along the galleries, and new curtains too, the rich colors at the hems fading, as is the fashion these days, to white above. Women and little girls clustered at all the doors. The girls in green robes and trains of purple gossamer seemed to be from Tamakazura's wing. There were four of

6. *Ayame* means both "iris" and "patterns." The pun is repeated several times in the following passage, as for instance in Hotaru's poem, in which *ayame* suggests something like "discernment." 7. There is a pun on *ne*, which means both "root" and "cry" or "sob." 8. Conventional on the Day of the Iris.

them, all very pretty and well behaved. Her women too were in festive dress, trains blending from lavender at the waist down to deeper purple and formal jackets the color of carnation shoots.

The lady of the orange blossoms had her little girls in very dignified dress, singlets of deep pink and trains of red lined with green. It was very amusing to see all the women striking new poses as they draped their finery about them. The young courtiers noticed and seemed to be striking poses of their own.

Genji went out to the stands toward midafternoon. All the princes were there, as he had predicted. The equestrian archery was freer and more varied than at the palace. The officers of the guard joined in, and everyone sat entranced through the afternoon. The women may not have understood all the finer points, but the uniforms of even the common guardsmen were magnificent and the horsemanship was complicated and exciting. The grounds were very wide, fronting also on Murasaki's southeast quarter, where young women were watching. There was music and dancing, Chinese polo music and the Korean dragon dance. As night came on, the triumphal music rang out high and wild. The guardsmen were richly rewarded according to their several ranks. It was very late when the assembly dispersed.

Genji spent the night with the lady of the orange blossoms.

"Prince Hotaru is a man of parts," he said. "He may not be the handsomest man in the world, but everything about him tells of breeding and cultivation, and he is excellent company. Did you chance to catch a glimpse of him? He has many good points, as I have said, but it may be that in the final analysis there is something just a bit lacking in him."

"He is younger than you but I thought he looked older. I have heard that he never misses a chance to come calling. I saw him once long ago at court and had not really seen him again until today. He has improved. Prince Sochi[9] is a very fine gentleman too, but somehow he does not quite look like royalty."

Genji smiled. Her judgment was quick and sure. But he kept his own counsel. This sort of open appraisal of people still living was not to his taste. He could not understand why the world had such a high opinion of Higekuro and would not have been pleased to receive him into the family, but these views too he kept to himself.

They were good friends, he and she, and no more, and they went to separate beds. Genji wondered when they had begun to drift apart. She never let fall the tiniest hint of jealousy. It had been the usual thing over the years for reports of such festivities to come to her through others. The events of the day seemed to bring new recognition to her and her household.

She said softly:

> "You honor the iris on the bank to which
> No pony comes to taste of withered grasses?"[1]

9. One of Genji's brothers.   1. Alludes to a poem in *The Kokinshū:* "Withered is the grass of Oaraki, / No pony comes for it, no harvester."

One could scarcely have called it a masterpiece, but he was touched:

> "This pony, like the love grebe, wants a comrade.
> Shall it forget the iris on the bank?"

Nor was his a very exciting poem.

"I do not see as much of you as I would wish, but I do enjoy you." There was a certain irony in the words, from his bed to hers, but also affection. She was a dear, gentle lady. She had let him have her bed and spread quilts for herself outside the curtains. She had in the course of time come to accept such arrangements as proper, and he did not suggest changing them.

The rains of early summer continued without a break, even gloomier than in most years. The ladies at Rokujō amused themselves with illustrated romances. The Akashi lady, a talented painter, sent pictures to her daughter.

Tamakazura was the most avid reader of all. She quite lost herself in pictures and stories and would spend whole days with them. Several of her young women were well informed in literary matters. She came upon all sorts of interesting and shocking incidents (she could not be sure whether they were true or not), but she found little that resembled her own unfortunate career. There was *The Tale of Sumiyoshi*,[2] popular in its day, of course, and still well thought of. She compared the plight of the heroine, within a hairbreadth of being taken by the chief accountant, with her own escape from the Higo person.

Genji could not help noticing the clutter of pictures and manuscripts. "What a nuisance this all is," he said one day. "Women seem to have been born to be cheerfully deceived. They know perfectly well that in all these old stories there is scarcely a shred of truth, and yet they are captured and made sport of by the whole range of trivialities and go on scribbling them down, quite unaware that in these warm rains their hair is all dank and knotted."

He smiled. "What would we do if there were not these old romances to relieve our boredom? But amid all the fabrication I must admit that I do find real emotions and plausible chains of events. We can be quite aware of the frivolity and the idleness and still be moved. We have to feel a little sorry for a charming princess in the depths of gloom. Sometimes a series of absurd and grotesque incidents which we know to be quite improbable holds our interest, and afterwards we must blush that it was so. Yet even then we can see what it was that held us. Sometimes I stand and listen to the stories they read to my daughter, and I think to myself that there certainly are good talkers in the world. I think that these yarns must come from people much practiced in lying. But perhaps that is not the whole of the story?"

She pushed away her inkstone. "I can see that that would be the view of someone much given to lying himself. For my part, I am convinced of their truthfulness."

He laughed. "I have been rude and unfair to your romances, haven't I. They have set down and preserved happenings from the age of the gods to our own. *The Chronicles of Japan*[3] and the rest are a mere fragment of the whole truth. It is your romances that fill in the details.

---

2. Does not survive except in a 13th-century revision, which is a Japanese equivalent of the Cinderella story. If the revision is faithful to the original tale, Tamakazura might well have identified with the heroine, whose stepmother plots to have her kidnapped by a man not at all to her liking, and so she runs away with her nurse (as Tamakazura fled Higo) to hide in Sumiyoshi, now part of Osaka.   3. One of the early histories.

"We are not told of things that happened to specific people exactly as they happened; but the beginning is when there are good things and bad things, things that happen in this life which one never tires of seeing and hearing about, things which one cannot bear not to tell of and must pass on for all generations. If the storyteller wishes to speak well, then he chooses the good things; and if he wishes to hold the reader's attention he chooses bad things, extraordinarily bad things. Good things and bad things alike, they are things of this world and no other.

"Writers in other countries approach the matter differently. Old stories in our own are different from new. There are differences in the degree of seriousness. But to dismiss them as lies is itself to depart from the truth. Even in the writ which the Buddha drew from his noble heart are parables, devices for pointing obliquely at the truth. To the ignorant they may seem to operate at cross purposes. The Greater Vehicle[4] is full of them, but the general burden is always the same. The difference between enlightenment and confusion is of about the same order as the difference between the good and the bad in a romance. If one takes the generous view, then nothing is empty and useless."

He now seemed bent on establishing the uses of fiction.

"But tell me: is there in any of your old stories a proper, upright fool like myself?" He came closer. "I doubt that even among the most unworldly of your heroines there is one who manages to be as distant and unnoticing as you are. Suppose the two of us set down our story and give the world a really interesting one."

"I think it very likely that the world will take notice of our curious story even if we do not go to the trouble." She hid her face in her sleeves.

"Our curious story? Yes, incomparably curious, I should think." Smiling and playful, he pressed nearer.

> "Beside myself, I search through all the books,
> And come upon no daughter so unfilial.

"You are breaking one of the commandments."

He stroked her hair as he spoke, but she refused to look up. Presently, however, she managed a reply:

> "So too it is with me. I too have searched,
> And found no cases quite so unparental."

Somewhat chastened, he pursued the matter no further. Yet one worried. What was to become of her?

Murasaki too had become addicted to romances. Her excuse was that Genji's little daughter[5] insisted on being read to.

"Just see what a fine one this is," she said, showing Genji an illustration for *The Tale of Kumano*.[6] The young girl in tranquil and confident slumber made her think of her own younger self. "How precocious even very little children seem to have been. I suppose I might have set myself up as a specimen of the slow, plodding variety. I would have won that competition easily."

---

4. Mahayana Buddhism, the later form of the religion that prevailed in Tibet, China, and Japan.   5. Genji's daughter by the Akashi lady, whom Murasaki has been raising.   6. Or *The Tale of Komano*. It does not survive.

Genji might have been the hero of some rather more eccentric stories.

"You must not read love stories to her. I doubt that clandestine affairs would arouse her unduly, but we would not want her to think them commonplace."

What would Tamakazura have made of the difference between his remarks to her and these remarks to Murasaki?

"I would not of course offer the wanton ones as a model," replied Murasaki, "but I would have doubts too about the other sort. Lady Atemiya in *The Tale of the Hollow Tree*,[7] for instance. She is always very brisk and efficient and in control of things, and she never makes mistakes; but there is something unwomanly about her cool manner and clipped speech."

"I should imagine that it is in real life as in fiction. We are all human and we all have our ways. It is not easy to be unerringly right. Proper, well-educated parents go to great trouble over a daughter's education and tell themselves that they have done well if something quiet and demure emerges. It seems a pity when defects come to light one after another and people start asking what her good parents can possibly have been up to. Yet the rewards are very great when a girl's manner and behavior seem just right for her station. Even then empty praise is not satisfying. One knows that the girl is not perfect and looks at her more critically than before. I would not wish my own daughter to be praised by people who have no standards."

He was genuinely concerned that she acquit herself well in the tests that lay before her.

Wicked stepmothers are of course standard fare for the romancers, and he did not want them poisoning relations between Murasaki and the child. He spent a great deal of time selecting romances he thought suitable, and ordered them copied and illustrated.

He kept Yūgiri from Murasaki but encouraged him to be friends with the girl. While he himself was alive it might not matter a great deal one way or the other, but if they were good friends now their affection was likely to deepen after he was dead. He permitted Yūgiri inside the front room, though the inner rooms were forbidden. Having so few children, he had ample time for Yūgiri, who was a sober lad and seemed completely dependable. The girl was still devoted to her dolls. They made Yūgiri think of his own childhood games with Kumoinokari.[8] Sometimes as he waited in earnest attendance upon a doll princess, tears would come to his eyes. He sometimes joked with ladies of a certain standing, but he was careful not to lead them too far. Even those who might have expected more had to make do with a joke. The thing that really concerned him and never left his mind was getting back at the nurse who had sneered at his blue sleeves. He was fairly sure that he could better Tō no Chūjō at a contest of wills, but sometimes the old anger and chagrin came back and he wanted more.[9] He wanted to make Tō no Chūjō genuinely regretful for what he had done. He revealed these feelings only to Kumoinokari. Before everyone else he was a model of cool composure.

---

7. A late-10th-century work of fiction. The tale describes, among other things, the efforts of several suitors to win the hand of the beautiful Atemiya, their disappointment when she marries the crown prince, and the ensuing power struggle over imperial succession.   8. Tō no Chūjō's daughter; she is Yūgiri's childhood playmate and eventually his wife.   9. Tō no Chūjō has so far thwarted Yūgiri's desire to wed Kumoinokari.

Her brothers sometimes thought him rather conceited. Kashiwagi, the oldest, was greatly interested these days in Tamakazura. Lacking a better intermediary, he came sighing to Yūgiri. The friendship of the first generation was being repeated in the second.

"One does not undertake to plead another's case," replied Yūgiri quietly.

Tō no Chūjō was a very important man, and his many sons were embarked upon promising careers, as became their several pedigrees and inclinations. He had only two daughters. The one who had gone to court had been a disappointment. The prospect of having the other do poorly did not of course please him. He had not forgotten the lady of the evening faces. He often spoke of her, and he went on wondering what had happened to the child. The lady had put him off guard with her gentleness and appearance of helplessness, and so he had lost a daughter. A man must not under any circumstances let a woman out of his sight. Suppose the girl were to turn up now in some outlandish guise and stridently announce herself as his daughter—well, he would take her in.

"Do not dismiss anyone who says she is my daughter," he told his sons. "In my younger days I did many things I ought not to have done. There was a lady of not entirely contemptible birth who lost patience with me over some triviality or other, and so I lost a daughter, and I have so few."

There had been a time when he had almost forgotten the lady. Then he began to see what great things his friends were doing for their daughters, and to feel resentful that he had been granted so few.

One night he had a dream. He called in a famous seer and asked for an interpretation.

"Might it be that you will hear of a long-lost child who has been taken in by someone else?"

This was very puzzling. He could think of no daughters whom he had put out for adoption. He began to wonder about Tamakazura.

Summary   Twenty-nine chapters follow chapter 25. Eventually Tamakazura marries Higekuro, and Genji, for political reasons, agrees to marry the favorite daughter of a retired emperor. Murasaki worries that Genji's new wife will supplant her in Genji's affections, but what happens is something else altogether. The new wife is unfaithful. After a liaison with Tō no Chūjō's son, she gives birth to the boy Kaoru. Genji learns the truth and remains indifferent to mother and child. The incident reminds Genji of his own transgression. He has no choice but to suffer in silence, mindful of the wrong he did his father.

In the meantime, Murasaki becomes ill. Before long she dies, and Genji is inconsolable. His grief is made worse when he realizes how his recent marriage had distressed Murasaki. Late in life, once again Genji confronts the unhappiness he has caused others. Sensing that his own end is near, the fifty-two-year-old Genji begins to put his affairs in order. And then, suddenly, we are told that he is dead:

> The shining Genji was dead, and there was no one quite like him. . . . Niou [his grandson], the third son of the present emperor, and Kaoru, the young son of Genji's [wife, the] Third Princess, had grown up in the same house and were both thought by the world to be uncommonly handsome, but somehow they did not shine with the same radiance. They were but sensitive, cultivated young men, and the fact that they were rather more loudly acclaimed than Genji had been at their age was very probably because they had been so close to him.

They will never equal him, however, and the rest of the novel, the account of their rivalry for the affections of three sisters, is the story of their failure to do so. Niou is a brash, carefree sort, inclined to take his pleasure where he finds it. One cannot avoid the conclusion that he is a coarser version of his grandfather. Kaoru, while not in fact descended from Genji, seems to represent the extreme form of one of Genji's most admirable traits: sensitivity gone pathological. Both men are exaggerations of qualities that in Genji were "shining," like two halves—Kaoru's deference and Niou's impetuousness—that, if fused, might approximate the whole of Genji.

Instead we have their misadventures, which take place for the most part in a world removed from the capital, a forsaken spot called Uji. The very name means gloom or melancholy, and this is the tone for the balance of the tale. In search of love off the beaten path, the two men pursue an ideal first articulated at the beginning of the novel (chapter 2): the affair of the heart unsullied by court intrigue. Unfortunately, intrigue and discontent are what Niou and Kaoru bring to the three women in the hinterlands. One dies of anxiousness, the second languishes in an unhappy marriage to Niou, and the third tries to kill herself; when she fails, she vows to have nothing more to do with men.

Not knowing whether she is dead or alive, Kaoru keeps searching for the third sister. The novel ends enigmatically, when he thinks he may have located her. His messenger is rebuffed, however, and the last, inconclusive lines of *The Tale of Genji* leave our antihero wondering, his life more unresolved than ever:

> It would seem that, as he examined the several possibilities, a suspicion crossed his mind: the memory of how he himself had behaved in earlier days made him ask whether someone might be hiding her from the world.

Nō Drama

Nō, the classical theater of Japan, is the world's oldest extant professional theater. It is also among the world's gravest and most stylized. Performed on an austere, undecorated stage of polished cypress, with no scenery and virtually no props, the ritual-like poetic dance-dramas of the *nō* have been described as a theater free of the artifice of stagecraft. But it would be more accurate to characterize the *nō* as a theater elevating stagecraft to the *n*th power. The absence of illusory scrims, revolving sets, or cyclorama floodlights is only the absence of the most obvious artifice. The word *nō* may be translated as "talent," "skill," or "accomplishment." And the ways that "accomplishment" has been cultivated by *nō* actors (all *nō* performers are male) demonstrate how fundamental, in fact, artifice, or stratagem, has always been to the tradition of the *nō*.

In Japan's medieval period, when *nō* coalesced from disparate origins—mystery plays, rice-planting rituals, classical poetry, carnival tricks, myth, and Buddhist liturgy—Zeami Motokiyo, master actor, playwright, and critic of the *nō*, analyzed the actor's art in a series of treatises as rigorous and self-conscious as the pronouncements of Stanislavsky, progenitor of the twentieth-century school of "method acting." Zeami's dissection of acting technique reveals both a practical and philosophical command of his craft. It also demonstrates the indissoluble link between *nō* and Zen Buddhism.

Let's begin first with the practical. Because *nō* shunned the trappings of representational theater, the actor's own talent or accomplishment (that is, his *nō*) became paramount. While over time the practice developed of incorporating a chorus and musical instruments to assist the actor, he had nonetheless little but his own artistry to convey the reality of his performance. The stately pace of nō drama and its highly conventionalized formal and thematic patterns may distance some audiences today, but the nō actor's subtle if stylized stage business can express an astonishing artistry. This artistry rejects theatricality. It also avoids both improvisation and the actor's deployment of personal experience to flesh out or give psychological depth to his characterization. (In fact, as we will see, the Western concept of "characterization" has little utility in the realm of nō.)

Instead, in Zeami's conception, the ideal nō actor combines a commonsense approach to performing ("If an actor thinks he has attained a higher level of skill than he has reached . . . he will lose even the level he has achieved") with a less-is-more view of art that today sounds curiously modern. "The expression 'when you feel ten in your heart, express seven in your movements,'" he tells us, refers to the necessity of underplaying. "When a beginner . . . learns to gesture . . . he will use all his energies to perform. . . . Later he will learn to move less. . . . No matter how slight a bodily action, if the motion is more restrained than the emotion behind it, the emotion will become the Substance and the movement of the body its Function, thus moving his audience."*

To these technical concerns of the impresario Zeami weds some of the more abstruse values of medieval Japanese aesthetics. *Yūgen* is the key criterion, a complex term with a web of meanings: mystery, depth, darkness, but also beauty and elegance, all tinged with the sadness of the ephemeral. The word *yūgen* originated in China (*yu hsüan*), where it described an object concealed from view, something that lay hidden too deep to be either seen or comprehended. *Yūgen* developed in Japan as a poetic principle denoting the profound. Poetry capturing the spirit of *yūgen* expressed emotions so delicate or subtle that they could only be implied. This taste for implication embodied in *yūgen* influenced all the major arts of medieval Japan, not only poetry and drama but also painting, calligraphy, ceramics, and even architecture. In the visual arts, the *yūgen* aesthetic preferred monochrome to color, and the evocative ink landscapes of the fourteenth century—in which a still mountain ridge appears and disappears within the mist, creating from the illusion of vast space a sense of infinity—testify to the fact that a monochromatic work can suggest more than the richest palette. In defining too well, color proves oddly restrictive. But with monochrome, there are no limits to what can be evoked through suggestion.

A famous anecdote about the sixteenth-century warlord Hideyoshi will demonstrate how central the suggestive component of *yūgen* has been to Japanese cultural identity. Hideyoshi was a brute foot soldier who, having risen to unify Japan through prowess and cunning, sought culture under the tutelage of a man of superior taste, Rikyū the tea master. The two men met often to perform the tea ceremony. One afternoon Hideyoshi asked Rikyū to show him his garden, which was famous for its morning glories. Rikyū demurred, but when Hideyoshi persisted Rikyū invited him to return the following morning. Hideyoshi arrived at the appointed hour, only to find that all the morning glories had been removed from the garden. A man with a hot temper who was accustomed to having his way, Hideyoshi stormed over to the tea hut, where he knew Rikyū would be waiting. He slid back the little door to the hut and entered. Before he could demand an explanation, however, he saw that the tea master had placed a single morning glory in the alcove. The one blossom was the essence of all morning glories. To Hideyoshi it was a revelation.

In the same manner, *yūgen*'s powers of suggestion were for Zeami the apex of the theatrical art of nō, what he calls "the art of the flower of mystery." This can by symbolized, he says, by the paradoxical phrase "In Silla† at midnight the sun is bright." Zeami elaborates:

---

* Zeami Motokiyo, *On the Art of Nō Drama*, trans. J. Thomas Rimer and Yamazaki Masakazu (1984), 7, 75.
† A kingdom in ancient Korea, founded in 57 B.C.E.

It is impossible to express in words or even to grasp in the mind the mystery of this art. When one speaks of the sun rising at midnight, the words themselves do not explain anything; thus too, in the art of *nō*, the *yūgen* of a supreme actor defies our attempts to praise it. We are so deeply impressed that we do not know what to single out as being of special excellence, and, if we attempt to assign it a rank, we discover that it is peerless artistry which transcends any degrees. This kind of artistic expression, which is invisible to ordinary eyes, may be what is termed the Art of the Flower of Mystery."*

The profundity of *nō*, according to Zeami, is ineffable. *Nō* must pierce the brittle surface of everyday reality and reach for the truth that lies hidden underneath. Distilled to its essence, *yūgen* is truth, and *nō*'s quest for the truth marks this theater as the literary progeny of Zen. Both see outward reality as illusory and ultimate reality as beyond words, beyond the senses. Both adhere to the doctrine of karma and the transmigration of souls. All human beings are born into an endless cycle of reincarnation. In this life we sow the seeds for the next. But flawed by our appetite for worldly things, each successive existence is steeped in delusion, suffering, and discontent. There is only one escape: *satori*, or enlightenment, the realization that material phenomena are fancies, not facts. This discovery frees us to let go of illusory attachments, whether love, passion, hatred, ambition, or greed. It is a discovery to be made in our own backyard, as it were. In Zen, enlightenment has nothing to do with cerebration, and everything to do with uncovering the meaning hidden in the particulars of daily experience. Illumination is apt to be sudden, mystical, even accidental.

At the same time, paradoxically, great discipline is demanded of the Zen aspirant, and considerable effort goes into achieving effortlessness. The initiate must submit to the grueling practice of *zazen*, or "meditation sitting," assuming a tortuous yogic position and contemplating an intractable riddle assigned by the Zen master. These riddles vary from seemingly unanswerable questions (What is the sound of one hand clapping?) to gnomic conundrums (A flag waved in the air. Two monks disputed whether the flag was moving or the wind was moving. A third monk retorted, "It is not the wind that is moving; it is not the flag that is moving; it is your mind that is moving!"). Whether such mental exercises strike one as intriguing or exasperating, the persistent meditation of Zen puzzles, when it succeeds, is thought to enable the aspirant to break free of the constraints of logic, to cast off the conceptualization we learn to superimpose on the flow of life's encounters, and thus to experience intuitive insight: enlightenment.

A further refinement of Zen, with important implications for the *nō* theater, was the belief that enlightenment did not occur in a vacuum, that the profane world at all times intrudes on Zen. The secular arts—archery, *nō*, calligraphy, swordsmanship, and the tea ceremony—were seen as a means of spiritual training. This endeared Zen to the ruling *samurai* class, who were the patrons of the *nō*. Because there was no distinction, or antagonism, between enlightenment and empirical existence and because the anti-intellectual strain in Zen held that an aspirant does not so much ignore the everyday, or the material, as work through it, it was possible for a *samurai* to live the illuminated life within his secular station. Discipline and dedication were required, to be sure, but in the discourse of the times these were already the defining attributes of the *samurai*.

The warrior schooled in the austerities of military training and Zen meditation found the severe aspects of *nō* to his liking. The bare stage, the ritualistic disregard for verisimilitude, the harsh musical accompaniment—hardly melodic and more like a dolorous Gregorian chant, in which the shrill flute and irregular drumbeats seem to puncture the performance more than they accompany it—all were the perfect correlates to the theatrical paring away that is *nō*.

* Donald Keene, *Nō: The Classical Theatre of Japan* (1973), 23.

Considering the many dramatic elements that *nō* does not possess, at least from a Eurocentric perspective, one might be forgiven the punning thought that perhaps this is the reason it is called *nō* theater. Where, one might ask, is the conflict that drives a Western play, the touchstone of dramaturgy since Aeschylus? *Nō* plays seldom offer a confrontation between dramatic equals. Instead one figure, the *shite* (literally, the "doer"), dominates the stage. If this is the protagonist, the *shite* lacks any foil with enough dramatic heft to weigh in as a viable antagonist. The other actors, the *waki* ("sideman") and the *tsure* ("companion"), are mere observers. And what they observe can hardly be called the action. That took place a long time ago—in what Hollywood would call the "backstory." To continue in the current idiom, one might characterize present time on stage as the depiction of an obsession precisely about "the action" of the past. The play portrays an emotion, and the *shite* is nothing other than the embodiment of that emotion. Just as the tea master needed only one morning glory to convey the essence of all morning glories, the *nō* play needs only the present moment—stripped of the impedimenta of theatrical realism—to capture the essence of an emotion. At first glance *nō* may appear an abbreviation, but in fact it is a concentration.

The typical play opens with the entrance of the *waki,* often in the role of a priest. He proceeds down the bridge, or runway, at the audience's left, which connects the stage to the greenroom, and announces the circumstances of the play: the season, the place, and the central theme. The statement of the theme is repeated in a poem or chant by the chorus of six or eight men, who, together with the "orchestra" of flute player and one or two drummers, have preceded the *waki* on stage. (The musicians sit along the back of the stage under the lone pine tree painted on the wall, the single and unvarying decoration for all *nō* plays. The chorus sits on a veranda at the side of the stage, to the audience's right.) The *waki* moves onto the stage proper and states his name and his intentions. "I am Kumagai no Naozane," declaims the *waki* in *Atsumori,* the first of the *nō* plays printed here, "a man of the country of Musashi. I have left my home and call myself the priest Rensei; this I have done because of my grief at the death of Atsumori, who fell in battle by my hand. Hence it comes that I am dressed in priestly guise. And now I am going down to Ichi-no-Tani to pray for the salvation of Atsumori's soul." As he trails across the stage, intoning a travel song, his slow progress represents his journey. When he reaches the opposite side of the stage, he announces his arrival at his destination, "I have come so fast that here I am already at Ichi-no-Tani, in the country of Tsu." With this, the first, or introductory, movement of the play concludes.

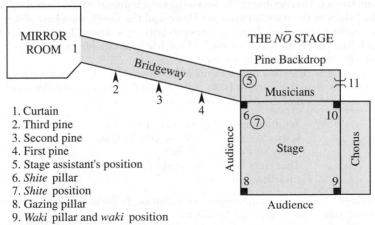

MIRROR ROOM 1

THE *NŌ* STAGE

Pine Backdrop

Bridgeway

2

3

4

5 Musicians

11

6 7

10

Audience

Stage

Chorus

8

9

Audience

1. Curtain
2. Third pine
3. Second pine
4. First pine
5. Stage assistant's position
6. *Shite* pillar
7. *Shite* position
8. Gazing pillar
9. *Waki* pillar and *waki* position
10. Flute pillar
11. Slit door

The second, expository, movement opens with the appearance of the *shite,* the principal actor, who is usually followed by his companion, the *tsure.* Advancing down the bridge in slow-motion and making his way onto the stage, the *shite* sings an entrance song that describes his current situation without revealing who he really is. The *shite* in *Atsumori* first appears as a young reaper. He and his companion enter chanting,

> To the music of the reaper's flute
> No song is sung
> But the sighing of wind in the fields.

And the *shite* adds,

> They that were reaping,
> Reaping on that hill,
> Walk now through the fields
> Homeward, for it is dusk.

Soon the *shite* encounters the *waki,* who, being a stranger to the region, asks various questions, first about the locality and then about the identity of the *shite.* The chorus elaborates this dialogue in a song of poetic allusion. By now the *waki* begins to realize that there is something odd about the *shite,* and the *shite* tries to evade him. Agitated, the *shite* begins to dance, which in the *nō* is always a sign of emotional excitement. The *shite* implores the priest to pray for him. As the chorus reiterates his plea for help, the *shite* moves onto the bridge and departs, concluding the second movement.

An interlude precedes the third and final movement of the play. An actor identified as a "man of the place" appears to recount the "backstory," which, in this play, would make up the events of Atsumori's death on the battlefield. Note, however, that the translator does not include the entr'acte because, as he explains, "These interludes are subject to variation and are not considered part of the literary text." Audiences today regard this portion of the play as an intermission, during which they are free to whisper, or rustle through their programs, or slip out for a cup of tea.

After the interlude comes the climax, or *kyū,* a "rushing to the end," which begins with the *waki*'s "waiting song," an admission of willingness to pray for the deliverance of the *shite.* Soon the *shite* reappears, but in a different guise. He has changed his costume and mask to reveal his true self. "Would you know who I am?" asks the *shite.* "Listen, Rensei. I am Atsumori," he says—the very Atsumori whom Rensei, or Kumagai, had slain in the wars between the Heike and the Genji, the ghost of a restless spirit unable to free itself from an obsession with past defeat, bound to this world through fixation on the last moments of final battle, incapable of letting go, and so perpetually deprived of enlightenment.

Atsumori now rehearses the elements of his obsession. He recounts the disasters that befell his clan, the Taira, or Heike, whereupon the chorus assists him, as though it were an extension of Atsumori's anxious mind:

> Yet their prosperity lasted but for a day;
> It was like the flower of the convolvulus.
> There was none to tell them
> That glory flashes like sparks from flint-stone,
> And after,—darkness.

But perhaps Atsumori is on the verge of a breakthrough, for he begins to comprehend the darker side of the Taira clan. He admits,

> When they were on high they afflicted the humble;
> When they were rich they were reckless in pride.

Pride led inevitably to war, and war to the trauma that haunts him. As Atsumori revisits the ordeals of war, he works himself into a frenzy, until frenzy bursts into dance. In this final dance, he relives his mortal struggle with Kumagai, narrated by the chorus:

> He looks behind him and sees
> That Kumagai pursues him;
> He cannot escape.
> Then Atsumori turns his horse
> Knee-deep in the lashing waves,
> And draws his sword.
> Twice, three times he strikes; then, still saddled,
> In close fight they twine; roll headlong together
> Among the surf of the shore.
> So Atsumori fell. . . .

But fate seems to have given Atsumori a second chance. He comes out of his dance as from a seizure. The enemy stands before him; revenge is his. Atsumori lifts his sword. Suddenly, however, something strange happens. What he sees is neither a foe nor a warrior, but a priest intoning the name of Buddha. "No," Atsumori understands, "Rensei is not my enemy." The play ends as he asks the priest to pray for him. The audience sits riveted. Slowly, Atsumori makes his final exit. The *shite* glides along the bridge like an apparition fading from sight or a soul on the way to salvation.

Given the subject of *nō*, it should not come as a surprise that many of the plays are peopled by ghosts, for, in the world of *nō*, ghosts represent emotion unreconciled, the mind caught in the spiral of material illusion. Technically, there are five categories of *nō* plays in a repertoire of some 240 dramas: (1) celebratory "god plays," in which the *shite* appears first in human form and later as the deity it really is, performed at New Year's and on other felicitous occasions (the second play included here is an example); (2) plays like *Atsumori*, about the ghosts of warriors doomed to eternal battle, unless a priest will pray to release them from their suffering; (3) "wig plays," in which the *shite* portrays the spirit of an angry woman, often obsessed with unhappy love; (4) "mundane plays" (assuming ghosts are mundane), which make up almost half the repertoire and tend to focus on derangement, a woman driven mad by the loss of a lover or child, or a husband distraught over the death of his wife; and (5) "demon plays," depicting supernatural creatures, devils in particular, who threaten to overwhelm the forces of good.

Clearly, in the majority of plays, the *shite* embodies the human mind, and this psychological dimension is one of the things that has given *nō* a new lease on life in the present century. While the protagonist of a *nō* play is never a fully wrought character, endowed with a complex temperament or granted realistic substance through individualistic detail, the dramatization of an obsession takes on fresh, contemporary relevance in the wake of Freud and Jung. The psychology of *nō*, combined with its Zen astringency, sloughing off both the decorative and the mimetic, appealed to Yeats, Pound, and other writers of an experimental bent, for whom realism was an outdated bourgeois convention. The very things *nō* lacked were seen by the modernists as its strong suit. Its bold simplicity was a near relation to the new calligraphic line in abstract painting. Its nuanced precision was preferable to traditional Western theater, in which, in the opinion of Pound, "subtlety must give way; where every fineness of word or of word-cadence is sacrificed to the 'broad effect'; where the paint must be put on with a broom." Pound, more than any other, idealized the *nō*, but under his tutorship *nō*'s rich fusion of poetry and prose, creating a compact collage of fragmentary images and complex allusions, helped revivify twentieth-century British and American poetry. We see this particularly in the poetry of Yeats, who drew inspiration from *nō*'s reliance on a single symbol (in *Atsumori*, for example, the flute) to strive for a similar metaphoric unity. Yeats's encounter with the *nō* even led him to write his own brand of *nō* plays, in which he attempted to mine the legends and layered literary traditions of Western culture as Zeami had done with those of Japan.

The two plays offered here are excellent examples of the *nō*. *Atsumori* demonstrates as well as any play *nō*'s debt to classical Japanese literature, in this case *The Death of Atsumori* from chapter 9 of *The Tale of the Heike*. The second play, *Haku Rakuten*, is a curious piece, in which the "obsession" would seem to be Japan's collective national fear of that old bugbear, Chinese influence. *Haku Rakuten* is the Japanese pronunciation of Po Chü-i (772–846), one of the greatest of Chinese poets, whose influence in classical Japan extended even to *The Tale of Genji*. Chinese influence reasserted itself in the fourteenth century, the age of *nō*, and in one of Japan's periodic pendulum swings of reaction, *Haku Rakuten* is a dramatization of cultural, or literary, peril. In the play, Po Chü-i, or Haku Rakuten, is sent by the Chinese emperor to subdue Japan with his superior art. In fact, Po Chü-i never set foot in Japan. But the Japanese have at times been extremely sensitive about their receptivity to foreign example, and the danger must have seemed real enough at the time. It is interesting that, in the play, Haku Rakuten is repulsed by the god of Japanese poetry, who in legend was a reincarnation of the historical figure Sugawara Michizane—one of Po Chü-i's most slavish imitators. A further irony is that Zeami himself was addicted to the poetry of Po Chü-i, if we are to judge by the number of times he quotes Po Chü-i's poems in his plays.

Where are we as readers when we are left only with the text and none of the stagecraft? Something is definitely lost. *Nō* may be spare, but it is highly visual: the rich brocade costumes; the shrinelike atmosphere of the stage; the mad, climactic dances of ghostly characters; the evocative masks worn by the *shite*. And no flute will sound, unless you use your imagination, though, of course, imagination has always been an important part of *nō*. Perhaps this is the key to appreciating *nō* as literature. Imagine yourself as a Zen master. The actors are gone. The chorus is gone. The musicians are gone. The stage is gone. The audience is gone. The words remain—diminishment or essence?

PRONOUNCING GLOSSARY

The following list uses common English syllables to provide rough equivalents of selected words whose pronunciation may be unfamiliar to the general reader.

Ariso: *ah-ree-soh*

Atsumori: *ah-tsoo-moh-ree*

Awaji: *ah-wah-jee*

eito: *ay-toh*

eiya: *ay-yah*

Etsu: *e-tsoo*

Haku Rakuten: *hah-koo rah-koo-ten*

Hideyoshi: *hee-de-yoh-shee*

Ichi-no-Tani: *ee-chee–noh–tah-nee*

Juyei: *joo-ay*

Kanze Kojirō Nobumitsu: *kahn-ze koh-jee-roh noh-boo-mee-tsoo*

kotsuzumi: *koh-tsoo-zoo-mee*

Kumagai no Naozane: *koo-mah-gai noh nah-oh-zah-ne*

Matsura: *mah-tsoo-rah*

Michinari: *mee-chee-nah-ree*

Musashi: *moo-sah-shee*

Nihon: *nee-hohn*

nō: *noh*

rambyōshi: *rahm-byoh-shee*

Rensei: *ren-say*

Rikyū: *ree-kyoo*

shite: *shee-te*

Sugawara Michizane: *soo-gah-wah-rahmee-chee-zah-ne*

Sumiyoshi: *soo-mee-yoo-shee*

Tsu: *tsoo*

Tsukushi: *tsoo-koo-shee*

Tsunemori: *tsoo-ne-moh-ree*

tsure: *tsoo-re*

Yamabushi: *yah-mah-boo-shee*

yūgen: *yoo-gen*

zazen: *zah-zen*

Zeami Motokiyo: *ze-ah-mee moh-toh-kee-yoh*

ZEAMI MOTOKIYO
1364–1443

Atsumori[1]

PERSONS

The PRIEST RENSEI (formerly the warrior Kumagai)
A YOUNG REAPER, who turns out to be the ghost of ATSUMORI
His Companion, another REAPER
CHORUS

PRIEST

> Life is a lying dream, he only wakes
> Who casts the World aside.

I am Kumagai no Naozane, a man of the country of Musashi.[2] I have left my home and call myself the priest Rensei; this I have done because of my grief at the death of Atsumori, who fell in battle by   5
my hand. Hence it comes that I am dressed in priestly guise.
And now I am going down to Ichi-no-Tani to pray for the salvation of Atsumori's soul.
[*He walks slowly across the stage, singing a song descriptive of his journey.*]
I have come so fast that here I am already at Ichi-no-Tani, in the country of Tsu.   10
Truly the past returns to my mind as though it were a thing of to-day.
But listen! I hear the sound of a flute coming from a knoll of rising ground. I will wait here till the flute-player passes, and ask him to tell me the story of this place.
REAPERS [*Together.*]

> To the music of the reaper's flute   15
> No song is sung
> But the sighing of wind in the fields.

---

1. Translated by and with notes adapted from Arthur Waley.   2. A province in eastern Japan under Minamoto/Genji control at the time of the war between the Heike and the Genji (1180–1185). Note that Waley translates the word for *province* as "country" and spells *Kumagai* differently from the translator of *The Tale of the Heike.*

YOUNG REAPER

They that were reaping,
Reaping on that hill,
Walk now through the fields   20
Homeward, for it is dusk.

REAPERS [*Together.*]

Short is the way that leads
From the sea of Suma[3] back to my home.
This little journey, up to the hill
And down to the shore again, and up to the hill,—   25
This is my life, and the sum of hateful tasks.
If one should ask me
I too[4] would answer
That on the shore of Suma
I live in sadness.   30
Yet if any guessed my name,
Then might I too have friends.
But now from my deep misery
Even those that were dearest
Are grown estranged. Here must I dwell abandoned   35
To one thought's anguish:
That I must dwell here.

PRIEST   Hey, you reapers! I have a question to ask you.

YOUNG REAPER   Is it to us you are speaking? What do you wish to know?

PRIEST   Was it one of you who was playing on the flute just now?   40

YOUNG REAPER   Yes, it was we who were playing.

PRIEST   It was a pleasant sound, and all the pleasanter because one does not look for such music from men of your condition.[5]

YOUNG REAPER   Unlooked for from men of our condition, you say!
Have you not read:—   45
"Do not envy what is above you
Nor despise what is below you"?
Moreover the songs of woodmen and the flute-playing of herdsmen,
Flute-playing even of reapers and songs of wood-fellers
Through poets' verses are known to all the world.   50
Wonder not to hear among us
The sound of a bamboo-flute.

PRIEST   You are right. Indeed it is as you have told me.
     Songs of woodmen and flute-playing of herdsmen . . .

REAPER   Flute-playing of reapers . . .   55

PRIEST   Songs of wood-fellers . . .

REAPER   Guide us on our passage through this sad world.

PRIEST   Song . . .

---

3. A coastal town, rich in literary associations. *Kokinshū* poet Ariwara Yukihara spent time there, Genji is exiled there (in chapter 12 of *The Tale of Genji*), and the decisive battle of Ichi-no-Tani, where Atsumori dies, is fought nearby (told in *The Tale of the Heike*). This layering of levels of literary association is an essential feature of *nō* plays. Suma was also known for its production of salt.   4. Like the literary exiles to Suma.   5. Because the flute was a courtly instrument.

REAPER   And dance . . .

PRIEST   And the flute . . .   60

REAPER   And music of many instruments . . .

CHORUS

> These are the pastimes that each chooses to his taste.
> Of floating bamboo-wood
> Many are the famous flutes that have been made;
> Little-Branch and Cicada-Cage,[6]   65
> And as for the reaper's flute,
> Its name is Green-leaf;
> On the shore of Sumiyoshi
> The Korean flute[7] they play.
> And here on the shore of Suma   70
> On Stick[8] of the Salt-kilns
> The fishers blow their tune.

PRIEST   How strange it is! The other reapers have all gone home, but you alone stay loitering here. How is that?

REAPER   How is it, you ask? I am seeking for a prayer in the voice of   75
the evening waves. Perhaps *you* will pray the Ten Prayers[9] for me?

PRIEST   I can easily pray the Ten Prayers for you, if you will tell me who you are.

REAPER   To tell you the truth—I am one of the family of Lord Atsumori.   80

PRIEST   One of Atsumori's family? How glad I am!

> [*Then the* PRIEST *joined his hands (he kneels down) and prayed:*—]

> Praise to Amida Buddha!
> "If I attain to Buddhahood,
> In the whole world and its ten spheres
> Of all that dwell here none shall call on my name   85
> And be rejected or cast aside."

CHORUS[1]

> "Oh, reject me not!
> One cry suffices for salvation,
> Yet day and night
> Your prayers will rise for me.   90
> Happy am I, for though you know not my name,
> Yet for my soul's deliverance
> At dawn and dusk henceforward I know that you will pray."

So he spoke. Then vanished and was seen no more.

> [*Here follows the Interlude between the two Acts, in which a recitation concerning* ATSUMORI's *death takes place. These interludes are subject to variation and are not considered part of the literary text of the play.*]

---

6. The names of two famous flutes in *the Tale of the Heike*. Little-Branch is the name of a flute of imperial provenance that Atsumori carried until he died. Cicada-Cage belonged to the son of retired Emperor Go-Shirakawa (Prince Mochihito), whose revolt against the Heike precipitated the war between the Heike and the Genji.   7. Because Sumiyoshi was where Korean ships docked.   8. That is, wood for the salt maker's fires.   9. Repeat Amida Buddha's name ten times. By invoking the name of Amida (Amitābha in Sanskrit), the buddha of infinite light, one could achieve rebirth in his paradise, known as the Pure Land.
1. Speaking for the young reaper, or Atsumori.

PRIEST   Since this is so, I will perform all night the rites of prayer for   95
the dead, and calling upon Amida's name will pray again for the salvation of Atsumori.

[*The ghost of* ATSUMORI *appears, dressed as a young warrior.*]

ATSUMORI

> Would you know who I am
> That like the watchmen at Suma Pass
> Have wakened at the cry of sea-birds roaming   100
> Upon Awaji shore?
> Listen, Rensei. I am Atsumori.

PRIEST   How strange! All this while I have never stopped beating my
gong and performing the rites of the Law. I cannot for a moment have
dozed, yet I thought that Atsumori was standing before me. Surely   105
it was a dream.

ATSUMORI   Why need it be a dream? It is to clear the karma of my waking life that I am come here in visible form before you.

PRIEST   It is not written that one prayer will wipe away ten thousand
sins? Ceaselessly I have performed the ritual of the Holy Name that   110
clears all sin away. After such prayers, what evil can be left? Though
you should be sunk in sin as deep . . .

ATSUMORI

> As the sea by a rocky shore,
> Yet should I be salved[2] by prayer.

PRIEST   And that my prayers should save you . . .   115

ATSUMORI

> This too must spring
> From kindness of a former life.[3]

PRIEST   Once enemies . . .

ATSUMORI   But now . . .

PRIEST   In truth may we be named . . .   120

ATSUMORI   Friends in Buddha's Law.

CHORUS   There is a saying, "Put away from you a wicked friend; summon to your side a virtuous enemy." For you it was said, and you
have proven it true.

And now come tell with us the tale of your confession, while the night   125
is still dark.

CHORUS

> He[4] bids the flowers of Spring
> Mount the tree-top that men may raise their eyes
> And walk on upward paths;
> He bids the moon in autumn waves be drowned   130
> In token that he visits laggard men
> And leads them out from valleys of despair.

---

2. Saved.   3. Atsumori must have done Kumagai some kindness in a former incarnation to account for
Kumagai's remorse.   4. Buddha.

ATSUMORI

> Now the clan of Taira, building wall to wall,
> Spread over the earth like the leafy branches of a great tree.

CHORUS

> Yet their prosperity lasted but for a day;   135
> It was like the flower of the convolvulus.
> There was none to tell them
> That glory flashes like sparks from flint-stone,
> And after,—darkness.
> Oh wretched, the life of men!   140

ATSUMORI

> When they were on high they afflicted the humble;
> When they were rich they were reckless in pride.
> And so for twenty years and more
> They ruled this land.

But truly a generation passes like the space of a dream.   145
The leaves of the autumn of Juyei[5]
Were tossed by the four winds;
Scattered, scattered (like leaves too) floated their ships.
And they, asleep on the heaving sea, not even in dreams
Went back to home.   150
Caged birds longing for the clouds,—
Wild geese were they rather, whose ranks are broken
As they fly to southward on their doubtful journey.
So days and months went by; Spring came again.
And for a little while   155
Here dwelt they on the shore of Suma
At the first valley.[6]
From the mountain behind us the winds blew down
Till the fields grew wintry again.
Our ships lay by the shore, where night and day   160
The sea-gulls cried and salt waves washed on our sleeves.
We slept with fishers in their huts
On pillows of sand.
We knew none but the people of Suma.
And when among the pine-trees   165
The evening smoke was rising,
Brushwood, as they called it,[7]
Brushwood we gathered
And spread for carpet.
Sorrowful we lived   170
On the wild shore of Suma,
Till the clan Taira and all its princes
Were but villagers of Suma.

---

5. Or Juei, the year 1183, when the Taira (Heike) evacuated the capital.   6. Literal translation of Ichi-no-Tani.   7. The name of so humble a thing was unfamiliar to nobles like Atsumori.

ATSUMORI

       But on the night of the sixth day of the second month
My father Tsunemori gathered us together.   175
"To-morrow," he said, "we shall fight our last fight.
To-night is all that is left us."
We sang songs together, and danced.

PRIEST

           Yes, I remember; we in our siege-camp
           Heard the sound of music   180
           Echoing from your tents that night;
           There was the music of a flute . . .

ATSUMORI   The bamboo-flute! I wore it when I died.
PRIEST   We heard the singing . . .
ATSUMORI   Songs and ballads . . .   185
PRIEST   Many voices
ATSUMORI

           Singing to one measure.

   [ATSUMORI *dances*.]

           First comes the Royal Boat.[8]
CHORUS

           The whole clan has put its boats to sea.
           He[9] will not be left behind;   190
           He runs to the shore.
           But the Royal Boat and the soldiers' boats
           Have sailed far away.

ATSUMORI

           What can he do?
           He spurs his horse into the waves.   195
           He is full of perplexity.
           And then

CHORUS

       He looks behind him and sees
       That Kumagai pursues him;
       He cannot escape.   200
       Then Atsumori turns his horse
       Knee-deep in the lashing waves,
       And draws his sword.
       Twice, three times he strikes; then, still saddled,
       In close fight they twine; roll headlong together   205
       Among the surf of the shore.
       So Atsumori fell and was slain, but now the Wheel of Fate
       Has turned and brought him back.
   [ATSUMORI *rises from the ground and advances towards the* PRIEST
   with uplifted sword.]

---

8. Bearing the child emperor Antoku, fleeing after the rout at Ichi-no-Tani.   9. Atsumori. This passage
is mimed throughout.

"There is my enemy," he cries, and would strike,
But the other is grown gentle   210
And calling on Buddha's name
Has obtained salvation for his foe;
So that they shall be re-born together
On one lotus-seat.[1]
"No, Rensei is not my enemy.   215
Pray for me again, oh pray for me again."

Haku Rakuten[1]

PERSONS

HAKU RAKUTEN (a Chinese poet)   Another FISHERMAN
An OLD FISHERMAN, Sumiyoshi no   CHORUS of fishermen
  Kami, who in Act II becomes the
  god of Japanese poetry

Act I

HAKU   I am Haku Rakuten, a courtier of the Prince of China. There is
a land in the East called Nippon.[2] Now, at my master's bidding, I am
sent to that land to make proof of the wisdom of its people. I must
travel over the paths of the sea.

  I will row my boat towards the setting sun,   5
    The setting sun;
  And seek the country that lies to the far side
  Over the wave-paths of the Eastern Sea.
    Far my boat shall go,
    My boat shall go,—   10
  With the light of the setting sun in the waves of its wake
  And a cloud like a banner shaking the void of the sky.
  Now the moon rises, and on the margin of the sea
    A mountain I discern.
  I am come to the land of Nippon,   15
    The land of Nippon.

So swiftly have I passed over the ways of the ocean that I am come
already to the shores of Nippon. I will cast anchor here a little while.
I would know what manner of land this may be.

THE TWO FISHERMEN   [Together.]

  Dawn over the Sea of Tsukushi,[3]   20
    Place of the Unknown Fire.
  Only the moonlight—nothing else left!

---

1. In Amida Buddha's paradise.   1. Translated by and with notes adapted from Arthur Waley.
2. Japan, which is written with two characters that mean "source of the sun." The fact that Haku Rakuten
is a foreigner is conventionally emphasized by his use of *Nippon*, considered an archaic pronunciation.
Note that the Japanese fishermen say *Nihon*.   3. Ancient name for Kyūshū, one of the four main Japanese islands, lying to the southwest and closest to China.

THE OLD FISHERMAN

> The great waters toss and toss;
> The grey waves soak the sky.

THE TWO FISHERMEN

> So was it when Han Rei[4] left the land of Etsu   25
> And rowed in a little boat
> Over the misty waves of the Five Lakes.
>
> How pleasant the sea looks!
> From the beach of Matsura[5]
> Westward we watch the hill-less dawn.   30
> A cloud, where the moon is setting,
> Floats like a boat at sea,
>   A boat at sea
> That would anchor near us in the dawn.
> Over the sea from the far side,   35
> From China the journey of a ship's travel
> Is a single night's sailing, they say.
> And lo! the moon has vanished!

HAKU   I have borne with the billows of a thousand miles of sea and come at last to the land of Nippon. Here is a little ship anchored 40 near me. An old fisherman is in it. Can this be indeed an inhabitant of Nippon?

OLD FISHERMAN   Aye, so it is. I am an old fisher of Nihon. And your Honour, I think, is Haku Rakuten of China.

HAKU   How strange! No sooner am I come to this land than they call 45 me by my name! How can this be?

SECOND FISHERMAN   Although your Honour is a man of China, your name and fame have come before you.

HAKU   Even though my name be known, yet that you should know my face is strange surely! 50

THE TWO FISHERMEN   It was said everywhere in the Land of Sunrise that your Honour, Rakuten, would come to make trial of the wisdom of Nihon. And when, as we gazed westwards, we saw a boat coming in from the open sea, the hearts of us all thought in a twinkling, "This is he." 55

CHORUS

> "He has come, he has come."
> So we cried when the boat came in
> To the shore of Matsura,
> The shore of Matsura.
> Sailing in from the sea   60
> Openly before us—
> A Chinese ship
> And a man from China,—

---

4. In Chinese, Fan Li. Having rendered important services to the state of Yüeh ("Etsu") in ancient China, Fan Li (Han Rei) went off with his mistress in a skiff, knowing that if he remained in public life his popularity was bound to decline. The fishermen are groping toward the concept of a visitor from China and the appearance of his boat. They are not yet consciously aware of the arrival of Po Chü-i (Haku Rakuten).
5. In Kyūshū, located on a bay off the Japan Sea; a likely mooring for boats arriving from Korea or China.

How could we fail to know you,
    Haku Rakuten?   65
But your halting words tire us.
Listen as we will, we cannot understand
    Your foreign talk.
Come, our fishing-time is precious.
    Let us cast our hooks,   70
    Let us cast our hooks!

HAKU   Stay! Answer me one question.[6] Bring your boat closer and tell me, Fisherman, what is your pastime now in Nippon?

OLD FISHERMAN   And in the land of China, pray how do your Honours disport themselves?   75

HAKU   In China we play at making poetry.

OLD FISHERMAN   And in Nihon, may it please you, we venture on the sport of making "uta."[7]

HAKU   And what are "uta"?

OLD FISHERMAN   You in China make your poems and odes out of the   80
Scriptures of India; and we have made our "uta" out of the poems and odes of China. Since then our poetry is a blend of three lands, we have named it Yamato,[8] the great Blend, and all our songs "Yamato Uta." But I think you question me only to mock an old man's simplicity.   85

HAKU   No, truly; that was not my purpose. But come, I will sing a Chinese poem about the scene before us.

    "Green moss donned like a cloak
    Lies on the shoulders of the rocks;
    White clouds drawn like a belt   90
    Surround the flanks of the mountains."

How does that song please you?

OLD FISHERMAN   It is indeed a pleasant verse. In our tongue we would say the poem thus:

    Koke-goromo   95
    Kitaru iwao wa
    Samonakute,
    Kinu kinu yama no
    Obi wo suru kana!

HAKU   How strange that a poor fisherman should put my verse into   100
a sweet native measure! Who can he be?

OLD FISHERMAN   A poor man and unknown. But as for the making of "uta," it is not only men that make them. "For among things that live there is none that has not the gift of song."[9]

HAKU   [*Taking up the other's words as if hypnotized.*][1] "Among things   105
that have life,—yes, and birds and insects—"

---

6. Throughout, Haku Rakuten omits the honorific turns of speech that civility demands. The fishermen, being proper Japanese, speak in elaborately deferential language. Zeami wishes to portray the visitor as an ill-bred foreigner.   7. The traditional thirty-one syllable poem.   8. An archaic name for Japan.   9. A quotation from the preface to *The Kokinshū*.   1. The fact that Haku Rakuten continues the quotation shows that he is under a sort of spell and makes it clear for the first time that his interlocutor is not an ordinary mortal. From this point onward, the fisherman gradually becomes a god.

OLD FISHERMAN   They have sung Yamato songs.
HAKU   In the land of Yamato . . .
OLD FISHERMAN   . . . many such have been sung.
CHORUS

> "The nightingale singing on the bush,   110
> Even the frog that dwells in the pond——"
> I know not if it be in your Honour's land,
> But in Nihon they sing the stanzas of the "uta."
> And so it comes that an old man
> Can sing the song you have heard,   115
> A song of great Yamato.

CHORUS [*Changing the chant.*]

> And as for the nightingale and the poem it made,—
> They say that in the royal reign
> Of the Emperor Kōren
> In the land of Yamato, in the temple of High Heaven   120
> A priest was dwelling
> Each year at the season of Spring
> There came a nightingale[2]
> To the plum-tree at his window.
> And when he listened to its song   125
> He heard it singing a verse:
>   "*Sho-yō mei-chō rai*
>   *Fu-sō gem-bon sei.*"[3]
> And when he wrote down the characters,
> Behold, it was an "uta"-song   130
> Of thirty letters and one.
> And the words of the song—

OLD FISHERMAN

> Of Spring's beginning
> At each dawn
> Though I come,   135

CHORUS

> Unmet I return
> To my old nest.
> Thus first the nightingale,
> And many birds and beasts thereto,
> Sing "uta," like the songs of men.   140
> And instances are many;
> Many as the myriad pebbles that lie
> On the shore of the sea of Ariso.[4]

---

2. The priest's acolyte had died, and the nightingale was the boy's soul.   3. Each sound in the nightingale's song is represented in the original text with a Chinese character, and the meaning of the song, when rearranged in Japanese syntax, is as recited below by the Fisherman and Chorus.   4. A place name conventionally linked in Japanese poetry with the words *shore, beach, sand,* and so forth, probably because a pun on the *ari* element in Ariso suggested the verb "have," and thus "having many grains of sand." The wordplay occurred particularly in metaphors depicting love beyond reckoning, usually along the lines of "love as inexhaustible as the grains of sand on a beach."

"For among things that live
There is none that has not the gift of song."   145

Truly the fisherman has the ways of Yamato in his heart. Truly, this
custom is excellent.

OLD FISHERMAN   If we speak of the sports of Yamato and sing its songs,
we should show too what dances we use; for there are many kinds.

CHORUS   Yes, there are the dances; but there is no one to dance.   150

OLD FISHERMAN   Though there be no dancer, yet even I—

CHORUS

For drums—the beating of the waves.
For flutes—the song of the sea-dragon.
For dancer—this ancient man
Despite his furrowed brow   155
Standing on the furrowed sea
Floating on the green waves
Shall dance the Sea Green Dance.

OLD FISHERMAN   And the land of Reeds and Rushes . . .

CHORUS   The thousand years our land inviolate!   160

Act II[5]

OLD FISHERMAN [*Transformed into Sumiyoshi no Kami,*[6] THE GOD *of poetry.*]

Sea that is green with the shadow of the hills in the water!
Sea Green Dance, danced to the beating of the waves.
[*He dances the Sea Green Dance.*[7]]

Out of the wave-lands,
Out of the fields of the Western Sea

CHORUS

He rises before us,   5
The God of Sumiyoshi,
The God of Sumiyoshi!

THE GOD

I rise before you
The god—

CHORUS

The God of Sumiyoshi whose strength is such   10
That he will not let you subdue us, O Rakuten!

5. The remainder of the play is dance, the words a kind of poetic commentary.   **6.** The god of poetry, or as the Chorus calls him, "the god of Sumiyoshi," the historical person Sugawara Michizane (845–903), a leading political figure and court scholar of his day. He became enbroiled in intrigue that led to his exile; and after his death, when a series of misfortunes in the capital were interpreted as the work of his angry spirit, he was deified as the god of scholarship, including poetry. Sumiyoshi is the name of a shrine in Osaka with which the deified Michizane is traditionally associated.   **7.** Obscure. Recent commentaries identify "Green Sea Music" (here, *Sea Green Dance*) as a piece in the repertory of *gagaku*, the traditional music of the Japanese court, but it is without an accompanying dance.

So we bid you return to your home,
Swiftly over the waves of the shore!
First the God of Sumiyoshi came.
Now other gods[8] have come—   15
    Of Isé and Iwa-shimizu,
    Of Kamo and Kasuga,
    Of Ka-shima and Mi-shima,
    Of Suwa and Atsu-ta.[9]
And the goddess of the Beautiful Island,   20
The daughter of Shakāra[1]
King of the Dragons of the Sea—
Skimming the face of the waves
They have danced the Sea Green Dance.
And the King of the Eight Dragons[2]—   25
With his Symphony of Eight Musics.
As they hovered over the void of the sea,
Moved in the dance, the sleeves of their dancing-dress
Stirred up a wind, a magic wind
That blew on the Chinese boat   30
And filled its sails
And sent it back again to the land of Han.[3]
Truly, the God is wondrous;
The God is wondrous, and thou, our Prince,
Mayest thou rule for many, many years   35
    Our Land Inviolate!

---

8. They do not appear on stage.   9. These places are all associated with Shinto shrines and, therefore, with native deities.   1. One of the eight great dragon kings: Buddhist deities in dragon form who live in the sea; control wind, rain, and thunder; and protect the Buddhist faith. Although the following line names Shakāra king of the dragons, he is but one among eight.   2. *Hachidairyūō*, usually translated "eight great dragon kings," referring to all of them.   3. The Chinese dynasty (206 B.C.E.–220 C.E.), used as an archaism for China.

Western Africa
1350–1600

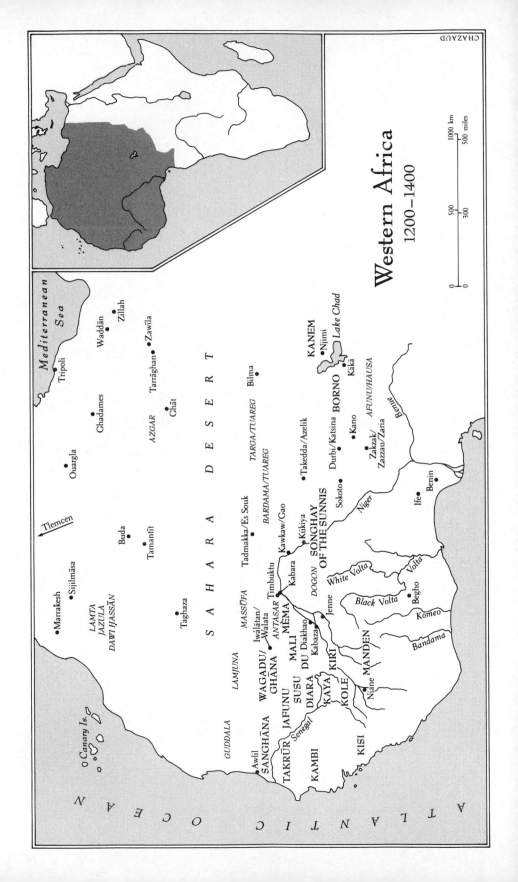

Western Africa
1200–1400

Africa: The Mali Epic of *Son-Jara*

late thirteenth–early fourteenth century

The epic of *Son-Jara* is the national epic of the Manding people, who inhabit what may be called the heartland of West Africa. The greater part of this area is in the savanna belt, in present-day Mali, but it also embraces, to the west and southwest, considerable parts of the coastal region bordering the Atlantic, in the modern states of Senegal, the Gambia, and Guinea. The people of this extensive area, which cuts across the boundaries established since the late nineteenth century by French and British colonial administrations, share a common history and culture deriving from a continuing sense of affiliation to the ancient, precolonial empire of Mali.

The founding of the Mali empire in the mid-thirteenth century is attributed to Son-Jara Keita, whose life and exploits are celebrated in the epic and whose hold on the feelings and imagination of the Manding people it has helped in no small measure to sustain to this day. In its oral form (as it is still performed all over the Manding area) the epic is considered to be not only the record of great events that led to the formation of the empire in the distant past—a factual recollection of its auspicious beginnings—but also a repository of the values of the society itself, even in its present circumstance. The epic thus functions for the Manding as a significant cultural reference, similar in this respect to the *Iliad* in ancient Greece and the *Rāmāyaṇa* in India.

The personality of Son-Jara (also known as Sundiata) is shrouded in mystery. All we know about him has had to be reconstructed from the oral tradition of the Manding—the epic itself forming the principal element of this tradition—and various Arab historical records concerning ancient Mali, which refer to its founder as "Mari Jata." Some of these records date from the very beginnings of the empire, but the most important historical account is the work of Ibn Khaldoun, whose fifteenth-century descriptions of the imperial court and the political and social life of the empire include a dynastic list of the rulers, traced back in every case to Son-Jara. Thus, although he has been transformed in the oral tradition into a figure of myth and legend, like the warriors of the Greek expedition to Troy, there seems no doubt about his historical existence. Nor is there doubt about his determining role in the establishment of Mali, initially as a centralized monarchical state and subsequently as a powerful empire that welded the various ethnic groups in the West African savanna into a distinctive national community.

The rise of ancient Mali in the thirteenth century represents an important stage in the process of state formation in West Africa, a process closely associated with the spread of Islam into the region, which began as early as the seventh century. The literacy Islam introduced enabled the formation (during the period that corresponds to the European Middle Ages) of an elite educated in Arabic, whose services to the early rulers made possible the establishment of their rule over ever-widening territories and fostered the emergence of the three best-known West African medieval empires: Songhai, Ghana, and Mali.

To understand the association of these early West African states with Islam, it is important to observe that in the oral tradition Son-Jara Keita is held to be the descendant of Bilal, a companion of Muhammad and a religious leader. Bilal's family is said to have migrated from the Near East and settled in the region, founding a religious community in the Manden, which proved to be the nucleus of ancient Mali. The version of the Son-Jara epic printed here begins with an invocation in which the hero is assimilated to Adam, the first man in both the Bible and the Koran, and thus underlines their common status as founding figures. Moreover, despite the fact that the epic's outlook on the world is essentially pagan, the invocation, which incorporates an allusion to Bilal as a close associate of Muhammad, and the many other references to Islam throughout the epic lend the sanction of an established world religion to the commemoration of the hero. The invocation thus intimates and prefigures the subsequent interaction between the practices and tenets of Islam and local Manding beliefs and customs. This cultural fusion within the poem mirrors the way in which a literate culture bound to Islam and the Arabic language was appropriated and integrated into the forms of an indigenous African orality.

Although the epic of Son-Jara has been recorded and transcribed by literary scholars in recent times, and thus carried one more stage into the realm of writing, it remains an integral part of the oral tradition in Africa. This tradition comprises various expressive forms—folk tales, legends, myths, and poetry—through which the imaginative impulse of preliterate societies takes shape. A conscious elaboration of language in these forms, managed through imagery and structural devices, distinguishes them from ordinary speech and gives them an aesthetic function above and beyond any referential content. Moreover, it is often the case that over the years oral cultures evolve a consecrated body of texts, a term that in oral literature applies to any extensive expression of experience in a *settled* art form. The generation, performance, and oral transmission of such texts endow them with a life of their own, so that they come to represent the literary monuments of the culture. In this respect, they function for oral societies in the same way that written literature does for literate societies.

The principal custodians of the oral tradition among the Manding are professional bards, known variously as *dyeli, belein-tigui,* or more commonly by the French term *griot.* They are specially trained oral performers who in former times were attached to the imperial court (and to its local replications across the Mali empire) as well as to members of the aristocracy. Their role was to recite from memory, on great occasions of state, the oral chronicles and family history of their patrons. In this capacity, they were expected not merely to recall the bare historical narrative as handed down by tradition but also, as poets and wordsmiths, to endow their recitations with all the power of language they could command, thus creating an ever-developing imaginative expression of the community's historical consciousness. It is to these "masters of the word" that we owe the persistence of the oral tradition and especially, among the Manding, the continued existence of the epic of Son-Jara.

The epic probably originated in a series of praise poems addressed to Son-Jara during his reign; their allusions to his virtues and exploits were developed later into an extended narrative of his life and heroic achievement. This development by accretion, together with the oral transmission of the resulting narrative, may explain why the epic exists not as a fixed text but rather as a fusion of three distinct generic layers.

Most important is the narrative framework. This is the overarching "master text" in which the movement of the epic is broadly formulated. This framework is composed of structural episodes, and it is the narrator's immediate task to recall these in appropriate sequence. He is, however, at liberty to expand on them in whatever way best suits the context of performance and the character of the audience, employing in the process a number of formulaic devices not only as props to memory but as building blocks in his re-creation of the epic story. The interplay between core elements of the text, which are relatively fixed (for example, genealogies of families and clans), and the performer's free improvisations (often involving digressions and general reflections as well as anachronistic references and topical allusions), generates a profound sense that the story, though established by tradition, is at the same time constantly renewed in performance. Thus if orality implies limitations, it also implies creative possibilities, apparent in the many differing versions of the epic recorded by individual *griots*.

The other two generic layers derive from the conditions of oral performance outlined earlier. The many passages of praise poetry with which the epic is interspersed stand in a close formal relationship to the formulaic plan of the narrative. Their shape attests to their independent existence before they were integrated into the epic we have today, and they are still on occasion recited outside its narrative framework. As generally with praise poems in oral literature, they are composed of strings of epithets, often hyperbolic, emphasizing the uncommon attributes—the heroic essence as it were—of their subject. Finally, in the third layer are the songs. These function as interludes within the epic narrative but, like the praise poems, are often performed as autonomous pieces to the accompaniment of the *kora*, an elaborate stringed instrument with tonal qualities comparable to those of the harp.

Performance of the epic is highly rhythmic, with breath stops, often accentuated by tonal patterns, rather than meter or rhyme, determining the verse lines. This basic register frequently intensifies into a chanting mode, notably for the praise poems. The song mode, in which musical instruments intervene, is another resource available to performers of the epic. To these effects must be added movement and gesture, with which the narrator dramatizes action or provides a visual delineation of character. Such extraliterary aspects of epic performance represent crucial factors and subtly evoke that direct relationship of the *griot* to his audience without which it would have been difficult, if not impossible, to sustain the cultural vitality of the epic. In short, the *griot*'s task consists far less in reproducing an exact text of the epic from one performance to the other—a text with which the audience is usually familiar—than in bringing to life the master text: the epic narrative prescribed by tradition, as actualized, through his living agency, in a dramatic reenactment.

The epic of *Son-Jara* is primarily a political poem, centered on the rivalry of two brothers for succession to their father's throne, a theme exemplified by the conflict between Cain and Abel and Jacob and Esau in the Bible and that between Poly[chnices and Eteocles in Sophocles' *Antigone*. This rivalry develops later into a wider contest between two rival chieftains for territorial control. Its ideological function as a myth to legitimize the ruling dynasty of ancient Mali is apparent not only from the heroic glorification of its historical founder but also from the motifs that structure the epic narrative. As in many early epics, psychological interest is limited and the hero's character is simply sketched; it is, however, endowed with symbolic significance. The story is essentially a relation of Son-Jara's trials, which he overcomes through his personal qualities—his piety, his filial devotion to his mother, his courage and tenacity. His final victory is also presented in moral terms as a triumph of good over evil. Fa-Koli's disaffection from the Susu Sumamuru (his uncle and Son-Jara's rival), which leads to his defection to Son-Jara—an act that proves decisive for the outcome of the struggle between Sumamuru and Son-Jara—is prompted by his sense of wrong. The moral implication of this episode, identifying Son-Jara's cause with that of universal justice, confirms the political and ideological thrust of the epic on a note that is distinctly personal and human.

The ideological function of the epic needs, however, to be placed in a broader perspective, that of the construction of a Manding collective identity around the figure of their founding hero. In its relation to the process of state formation in the West African savanna region, the epic of *Son-Jara* serves as the essential medium of the collective memory of the Manding people, keeping alive not only a sense of their historical continuities but also of the integrity of their communal values. The epic is thus the repository not merely of the achievements of an outstanding individual but of the growth of a national consciousness.

Although a singular work in many respects, the epic of *Son-Jara* is representative of the heritage of oral poetry in Africa. Scholarly research has made it increasingly evident that this heritage is more diversified than was thought; that it goes beyond

folktales; and especially, that it includes extended forms, of which the epic genre—
exemplified by the Son-Jara epic and other African narratives such as *Kabili, Da
Monzon of Segou*, the *Mwindo* epic, and the *Ozidi* saga—forms an integral part.
Beyond their intrinsic interest as outstanding forms of imaginative expression, these
products of the African oral tradition point to a universal heritage—that literature
seems almost everywhere (with few exceptions, notably China and Japan) to have
had its beginnings in heroic song.

  The epic of *Son-Jara* represents a communal resource, whose various versions are
associated with individual *griots*. The earliest published version is the prose adaptation brought out in French in 1968 by the Malian historian, Djibril Tamsir Niane,
Sundiata, an Epic of Old Mali (1989). This adaptation, undertaken as part of the
nationalist reclamation of the African past, brought the work into the limelight and
has remained its best-known version. While it presents a faithful rendering of the
action, it fails to capture the epic's heroic movement and the atmosphere of performance essential to its character. Three further versions have been collected by Gordon Innes in *Sunjata: Three Madinka Versions* (1974), a work of interest mainly for
comparative purposes. More recent is a prose adaptation by the Guinean novelist
Camara Laye, *The Guardian of the Word* (1980), a controversial version in its highly
personal reinterpretation as well as, in the view of many scholars, its distortion of the
material. The version printed here was transcribed from a recital performed by the
griot Fa-Digi Sisoko and translated by John William Johnson. More than any published version, this version conveys a sense of the epic's tone and movement as well
as of the dynamics of its performance.

PRONOUNCING GLOSSARY

The following list uses common English syllables to provide rough equivalents of selected
words whose pronunciation may be unfamiliar to the general reader.

belein-tigui: *bay-len–tee-ghee*

Bintanyan Kamalan: *been-tah-yarn
kah-mah-lan*

Bugu Turu: *boo-goo too-roo*

Dankaran Tuman: *dahn-kah-ran too-
man*

Dan Mansa Wulandin: *dahn man-sah
woo-lahn-deen*

Dan Mansa Wulanba: *dahn man-sah
woo-lahn-bah*

Dòka: *doh-kah*

Du Kamisa: *do kah-mee-sah*

Dun Fayiri: *doon fah-yee-ree*

dyeli: *jay-lee*

Fa-Digi Sisoko: *fah–dee-gee see-soh-
koh*

Fata Magan: *fah-tah mah-gahn*

Genu: *gay-noo*

griot: *gree-oh*

Kamasiga: *kah-mah-see-gah*

Kanu Simbon: *kah-noo seem-bon*

Kukuba: *koo-koo-bah*

Kulu-Kòrò: *koo-loo–koh-roh*

Kuyatè: *koo-yah-tay*

Magan Jata Kòndè: *mah-gahn jah-ta
kon-day*

Mane: *ma-nay*

Nakana Tiliba: *nah-kah-nah tee-lee-
bah*

Nare Magan Kònatè: *nah-ray mah-gan
koh-nah-tay*

Nyani (Niane): *neer-nee*

Saman Berete: *sah-mahn bay-ray-tay*

Sane: *sah-nay*

Sasagalò: *sah-sag-gah-loh*

Son-Jara Keita: *sawn–jah-rah kay-ee-
tah*

Sugulun Kòndè: *soo-goo-loon kon-day*

Sundiata: *soon-jah-tah*

Tanimunari: *tah-nee-moo-nah-ree*

Tarawere: *tah-rah-way-ray*

Tura Magan: *too-rah mah-gahn*

TIME LINE

TEXTS	CONTEXTS
ca. 300 C.E. Development of the Geez Script	
	200–350 C.E. Introduction and spread of Christianity in North Africa
397 Augustine begins *Confessions*	
	500–1495 Rise of the West African savanna empires: Ghana in the northwest (ca. 500), Kanem around Lake Chad (ca. 900), Mali (ca. 1200), and Songhay in the Middle Niger (ca. 1495)
	600–1000 Introduction and spread of Islam in East and west Africa
13th–14th centuries *Epic of Son-Jara*	
	1300–1500 Rise of the Kongo kingdom on the lower Zaire (Congo) River, including present-day Angola, in central Africa; rise of Benin in west African forest belt, in the hinterland of the Niger Delta (ca. 1400); and rise of Monomotapa ("Great Zimbabwe") in southern Africa, north of the Limpopo River (ca. 1500)
1352 *Arab Chronicles:* Ibn Battuta on ancient Mali	
	1450–1600 Portuguese explorers on the west and central African coasts
ca. 1513 Leo Africanus, *History and Description of Africa*	
	late 16th–mid 19th century The Atlantic slave trade

Boldface titles indicate works in the anthology.

From The Epic of Son-Jara[1]

FROM EPISODE I

Prologue in Paradise

Nare Magan Kònatè[2]	
Sorcerer-Seizing-Sorcerer![3]	
A man of power is hard to find.	
And four mastersingers.	(Indeed)
5 O Kala Jula Sangoyi[4]	
Sorcerer-Seizing-Sorcerer!	(Mmm)
It is of Adam that I sing.	
Of Adam,	
Ben Adam.[5]	('Tis true)
10 As you succeeded some,	
So shall you have successors![6]	
It is of Adam that I sing, of Adam.	(Indeed)
I sing of Biribiriba![7]	(Indeed)
Of Nare Magan Kònatè!	
15 Sorcerer-Seizing Sorcerer!	(True)
From Fatiyataligara	
All the way to Sokoto,[8]	(Indeed)
Belonged to Magan Son-Jara.	(Indeed)
Africans call that, my father,[9]	
20 The Republic of Mali,[1]	(Indeed)
The Maninka[2] realm:	(Mmm, 'tis true)
That's the meaning of Mali.	
Magan Son-Jara,	
He slayed Bambara-of-the-Border;[3]	
25 Settling on the border[4] does not suit the weak.	(Indeed)
And slayed Bambara-the-Lizard;[5]	

1. Text by Fa-Digi Sisoko; translated by John William Johnson. The words in parentheses at the right are interjections made by members of the audience, principally by Bèmba.   2. Son-Jara. This praise name combines a reference to his place of origin (*Nare*) with his royal title (*Magan,*] "king" or "lord"; the title of the emperor of ancient Ghana was *Kaya Magan*). *Kònatè* is Son-Jara's clan.   3. This praise name refers to Son-Jara's superior magical powers.   4. A bard reputed to be the originator of the epic; he can thus be considered the equivalent of Homer with respect to the *Iliad*. He is invoked here in homage to the artistic ancestor of Fa-Digi Sisoko, the bard who is re-creating the epic on this occasion. The exact reference of line 4 is obscure, but its allusion to the bard's professional status is clearly related to the invocation of Kala Jula Sangoyi.   5. The Adam of Genesis.   6. A formulaic device employed by the bard at various points in the epic; here it stresses the unbroken continuity of Son-Jara's dynastic line.   7. This praise name for Son-Jara conveys his immense physical prowess.   8. An ancient city in northern Nigeria, several hundred miles east of the Manding area. The city was the capital of the Fulani empire, which by the early 19th century had embraced most of the area in the Niger-Benue basin and was conquered by the British in the early years of this century. Fayitaligara can no longer be identified. The bard means the extent of the old Mali empire from west to east.   9. A term of reverence; here an aside addressed to the older members of the audience.   1. That is, present-day Mali; the name of the ancient empire was revived in 1960, when the modern republic achieved independence from France.   2. Manding or Mandenka; the term covers many more ethnic groups than are found in the present Republic of Mali.   3. That is, Sumamuru, Son-Jara's principal antagonist, who was a Susu, an ethnic group related to the Bambara of present-day Mali. 4. All areas beyond the safe limits of human settlement. The implication is that it requires an intrepid character, such as that associated with the professional hunter, to venture beyond these limits and confront the dangers of the wilderness.   5. A derogatory term, which alludes to the fact that young boys start to practice hunting with lizards; hence the reptile is associated with the weak and uninitiated.

No weak one should call himself lizard. (Indeed)
And slayed Bambara-of-the-Backwoods;
Settling the backwoods does not suit the weak. (Indeed)
30 All this by the hand of Nare Magan Kònaè.
Sorcerer-Seizing-Sorcerer!
Simbon, Lion-Born-of-the-Cat.[6] ('Tis true)

Summary Fa-Digi Sisoko follows this opening invocation with a lengthy account of the Genesis story, in a version that incorporates a cosmological myth and the origin of the races of the world. This provides a background to the epic recall, in the next section, of the original migration of Bilal from the Middle East with his band of followers, and their settlement among and interaction with the indigenous peoples in the West African savannah. This reconstruction of the early history of the region is directly linked to Son-Jara's genealogy, traced from Bilal right down to Son-Jara's father, Fata Magan the Handsome, who settles in a place called Kamalen, destined to be the center of the Manding kingdom. The bard recounts Fata Magan's marriage to Saman Berete, who will later bear him a son, in the confused circumstances that will pit this son against Son-Jara, his half brother, in a struggle for succession to the thone.

Having thus established Son-Jara's paternal line of descent, the bard next traces the origins of his maternal clan, the Kòndès. He recounts the quarrel between the leader of the clan and his aunt, Du Kamisa, over her exclusion from a family ritual. Du Kamisa is enraged and transforms herself into a wild buffalo who ravages the countryside and kills many of the hunters sent after her. At this point, two brothers, Dan Mansa Wulandin and Dan Mansa Wulanba, hunters from another clan, the Tarawere, enter the story. As much by sheer skill and courage as by supernatural help, the younger brother Dan Wulandin succeeds in killing the buffalo, and is rewarded for this exploit with the gift of a maiden of the clan, Sugulun Kòndè. The Tarawere brothers continue on their journey, seeking further adventures, and finally arrive at the town founded by Fata Magan the Handsome. Dan Mansa Wulanba attempts to consumate his marriage with Sugulun Kòndè who repulses him, saying, "My husband is in the Manden." Thus, her virginity is preserved for her future husband, Fata Magan the Handsome, for whom she will bear her first child, Son-Jara. The episode that follows recounts the circumstances in which Sugulun Kòndè enters Fata Magan's household, and the events that ensue.

FROM EPISODE 4

The Manden

Now, Fata Magan, the Handsome was about to leave that
town.
He was leaving to trade in a far market. (Mmm)
1000 But a jinn came and laid a hand on him:[7] (Mmm)
"Stay right here! (Indeed)
"Two youths have come amongst us, (Mmm)
"Two youths with an ugly young maid. (Mmm)
"Should you come by that ugly maid, (Mmm)
1005 "She will bear you a son. (Indeed)
"The Manden will belong to him." (Indeed)

6. Compare with "Lion Heart," which became attached to the name of the medieval king of England, Richard. "Simbon": hunter; the ideal of manhood in traditional African societies.   7. Implying that the jinn is an agent of providence.

O! Bèmba!	(Indeed)
I sing of the Sorcerer's future;	(Mmm, that's true)
Of the life ahead of Son-Jara!	

1010	There were two ways to greet in the Manden of Old	(Mmm)
	Brave young men said, "Ilu tuntun!"	(That's true)
	To which the reply, "Tuntun bèrè!"	
	The women said, "Ilu kònkòn!"	
	To which the reply, "Kònkòn lògòsò!"	(Indeed)
1015	The Taraweres came forward:	(True)
	"I tuntun!"	
	He answered them, "Tuntun bèrè!	(Mmm)
	"Where do you come from?	
	"Where are you going?"	
1020	"We have come from the land of Du.	
	"We go to Bintanya Kamalen."	
	"Whose people are you?"	(Mmm)
	"We are Taraweres."	
	"O Taraweres,	
1025	"Were this young prince to find the right wife,	(Mmm)
	"She would be the reward of a Tarawere struggle.	(True)

	"My flesh-and-blood sister is here,	(Indeed)
	"Nakana Tiliba.	(Indeed)
	"I will give her to you.	
1030	"You must give me your ugly maid.	(Mmm)
	"My forefather Bilal,	(Indeed)
	"When he departed from the Messenger of God,	(True)
	"He designed a certain token,	(Mmm)
	"Saying that his ninth descendant,	(Indeed)
1035	"Having taken his first wife,	(True)
	"When he takes his second wife,	(Indeed)
	"Must add that token to that marriage.	(Mmm)
	"I am adding that token	
	"Together with Nakana Tiliba,	(Mmm)
1040	"And giving them to you,[8]	
	"You must give me your ugly little maid."	
	That token was added to Nakana Tiliba,	
	Exchanging her for Sugulun Kòndè.	(Indeed)
	It is said that Fata Magan, the Handsome	
1045	Took the Kòndè maiden to bed.	(Mmm)
	His Berete wife became pregnant.	(Indeed)
	His Kòndè wife became pregnant.	(Indeed)

	One day as dawn was breaking,	(Indeed)
	The Berete woman give birth to a son.	(Indeed)
1050	She cried out, "Ha! Old Women!	(Indeed)
	"That which causes co-wife conflict	
	"Is nothing but the co-wife's child.[9]	(True)
	"Go forth and tell my husband	(Indeed)

---

8. Fata Magan's readiness to part with the token inherited from his ancestor Bilal emphasizes the importance to him of securing Sugulun Kòndè for a wife.   9. Rivalry between co-wives and their offspring in polygamous households is a common theme in African folktales.

"His first wife has borne him a son." (Indeed)

1055 The old women came up running. (Indeed)
"Alu kònkòn!" (Mmm)
They replied to them, "Kònkòn dògòsò!
"Come let us eat." (Mmm)
They fixed their eyes on one another:
1060 "Ah! Man must swallow his saliva!"[1] (True)
They sat down around the food. (Indeed)
The Kòndòe woman then bore a son. (Indeed)
They sent the Kuyatè matriarch, Tumu Maniya: (Indeed)
"Tumu Maniya, go tell it, (True)
1065 "Tell Fata Magan, the Handsome,
"Say, 'the Tarawere trip to Du was good.' (True)
"Say, 'the ugly maid they brought with them,'
"Say, 'that woman has just borne a son.'" (True)

The Kuyatè matriarch came forward: (True)
1070 "Alu kònkòn!" (Mmm)
They replied to her, "Kònkòn dògòsò! (Indeed)
"Come and let us eat."

The female bard Tumu Maniya goes to find the king and, like the old women who pre-ceded her, is also invited to eat, but she rejects the food until her message is delivered. The announcing of the birth of Son-Jara first, though he was actually born second, causes the father to designate him as first-born. The old women then burst out their message of the Berete woman's child, but alas, they are too late. The reversal of announcements is viewed as theft of birthright, and the Berete woman is under-standably furious at the old women, who flop their hands about nervously.][2]

Some just flopped their hands about:
"I will not hear of this from anyone!
1075 "I spent a sleepless night.
"The lids of my eyes are dried out,
bèrè-bèrè-bèrè.[3] (That's true)
"But I will not hear of this from anyone!"
Some just clasped their hands together.
What travail it had become!
1080 Ha! The old woman had forgotten her message
And abandoned it for a meal.
Those-Caught-by-their-Craws![4]
That was the first day of battle in the Manden.
Pandemonium broke loose! bòkòlen![5]

* * *

Both women were confined in one hut.
Pandemonium broke loose! bòkòlen! (Indeed)
Saman Berete,

___

1. To placate their hunger. The food the women are offered is presumably too tempting to be ignored, hence their delay in announcing the birth of the Berete woman's child; this leads to the confusion about the order of precedence between him and Son-Jara and to dissension in the family.   2. Johnson's sum-mary. He noted that Fa-Digi Sisoko broke off his performance at this point to answer the call of nature and that he resumed the narration at a point further along in the story.   3. Ideophone for the distraught state of the women.   4. Derogatory term for the women.   5. Ideophone summing up the pandemonium.

1100	The daughter of Tall Magan Berete-of-the Ruins,	
	Saman Berete,	(Indeed)
	Still bloodstained, she came out.	(Indeed)
	"What happened then!	
	"O Messengers, what happened?	(Indeed)
1105	"O Messengers, what became of the message?"	(Indeed)

The Kuyatè matriarch spoke out:
"Nothing happened at all. (Indeed)
"I was the first to pronounce myself. (Indeed)
"Your husband said the first name heard,
1110 "Said, he would be the elder, (Indeed)
"And thus yours became the younger." (Indeed)
She[6] cried out, "Old women, (Indeed)
"Now you have really reached the limit! (True)
"I was the first to marry my husband,
1115 "And the first to bear him a son. (Indeed)
"Now you have made him the younger. (Indeed)
"You have really reached your limit!"
She spoke then to her younger co-wife, (Indeed)
"Oh Lucky Karunga,[7] (Indeed)
1120 "For you marriage has turned sweet. (Indeed)
"A first son birth is the work of old,
"And yours has become the elder."[8] (That's the truth)

The infants were bathed.
Both were laid beneath a cloth. (Indeed)
1125 The grandmother[9] had gone to fetch firewood. (Indeed)
The old mother had gone to fe . . . , to
  fetch firewood. (Indeed)
She then quit the firewood-fetching place,
And came and left her load of wood. (Indeed)
She came into the hut. (Indeed)
1130 She cast her eye on the Berete woman, (Indeed)
And cast her eye on the Kòndè woman, (Indeed)
And looked the Berete woman over,
And looked the Kòndè woman over. (Indeed)

She lifted the edge of the cloth.
1135 And examined the child of the Berete woman,
And lifted again the edge of the cloth,
And examined the child of the Kòndè woman. (Indeed)
From the very top of Son-Jara's head, (Indeed)
To the very tip of his toes, all hair![1] (Indeed)

1140 The old mother went outside. (Indeed)
She laughed out: "Ha! Birth-givers! Hurrah!
"The little mother has borne a lion thief." (That's true)
Thus gave the old mother Son-Jara his name. (Indeed)

---

6. Saman Berete.   7. Sugulun Kòndè.   8. A bitter comment on what Saman Berete perceives as an ironic reversal of situations.   9. Son-Jara's paternal grandmother.   1. An extraordinary circumstance that earns him his praise name of Lion-Born-of-the-Cat.

"Givers of birth, Hurrah!

1145 "The little mother has borne a lion thief.   (That's true)

"Hurrah! The mother has given birth to a lion thief."

Biribiriba!   (Indeed)

And thus they say of him,

Son-Jara. Nare Magan Kònatè.   (Indeed)

1150 Simbon. Lion-Born-of-the-Cat.   (Indeed)

The Berete woman,

She summoned to her a holy-man,

Charging him to pray to God,   (Indeed)

So Son-Jara would not walk.   (Indeed)

1155 And summoned to her an Omen Master,   (Indeed)

For him to read the signs in sand,   (Indeed)

So Son-Jara would not walk.   (Indeed)

For nine years, Son-Jara crawled upon the ground.   (Indeed)

Magan Kònatè could not rise.   (Indeed)

1160 The benefactor of the Kòndè woman's child,

It was a jinn Magan Son-Jara had.   (Indeed)

His name was Tanimunari.

Tanimunari,   (Indeed)

He took the lame Son-Jara   (Indeed)

1165 And made the hājj[2]   (Indeed)

To the gates of the Kaabah.[3]   (Indeed)

Have you never heard this warrant of his hājj?   (Indeed)

"Ah! God!   (Indeed)

"I am the man for the morrow.   (Indeed)

1170 "I am the man for the day to follow.   (Indeed)

"I will rule over the bards,   (Indeed)

"And the three and thirty warrior clans.

"I will rule over all these people.   (Indeed)

"The Manden shall be mine!"[4]   (Indeed)

1175 That is how he made the hājj.

He[5] took him up still lame,

And brought him back to Bintanya Kamalen.   (Indeed)

In the month before Dònba,   (Indeed)

On the twenty-fifth day,

1180 The Berete woman's Omen Master emerged from

retreat:[6]   (Indeed)

"Damn! My fingers are worn out!   (Indeed)

"My buttocks are worn out!   (Indeed)

"A tragic thing will come to pass in the Manden.   (Indeed)

"There is no remedy to stop it.

1185 "There is no sacrifice to halt it.

"Its cause cannot be ascertained,   (Indeed)

"Until two rams be sacrificed.   (Indeed)

---

2. The pilgrimage to Mecca that Muslims are obliged by the tenets of their religion to undertake at least once in their lifetime.   3. The mosque in Mecca that contains the sacred stone, draped in black, around which a special ceremony takes place during the month of the pilgrimage.   4. An ambition attributed by the bard to Son-Jara even in his youth.   5. Tanimunari.   6. His place of seclusion, where he has been preparing magical charms for Saman Berete.

"The one for Son-Jara, a black-headed ram. (True)
"Dankaran Tuma, an all white ram.[7] (Indeed)
1190 "Have them do battle this very day." (Indeed)
By the time of the midday meal,
Son-Jara's ram had won. (Indeed)
They slaughtered both the rams. (Indeed)
And cast them down a well,
1195 So the deed would not be known. (Indeed)
But known it did become. (Indeed)
Knowing never fails its time,
Except its day not come. (That's true, eh,
Fa-Digi, that's true)

In the month before Dònba (That's true)
1200 On the twenty-seventh day, (Indeed)
The holy-man emerged from his retreat! (Indeed)
"Hey! A tragic thing will come to pass in the
Manden. (Indeed)
"There is no remedy to stop it.
"There is no sacrifice to halt it. (Indeed)
1205 "Its cause cannot be ascertained,
"Until a toothless dog be sacrificed."[8]
Now whoever saw a toothless dog in the Manden? (Indeed)
They went forth to Kong,[9] (Indeed)
And bought a snub-nosed dog, (Indeed)
1210 A little spotted dog,
And pulled its teeth with pliers,
And mixed a potion for its mouth, (Indeed)
And brought it back to the Manden,
Saying, with this toothless dog, (Indeed)
1215 Saying, Magan Kònatè should not walk. (Indeed)
Son-Jara should not rise!

                *   *   *

Ah! Bèmba! (Indeed)
They made a sacrifice of the spotted dog (Indeed)
So that the Wizard would not walk. (Indeed)
1255 In the month of Dòmba, (Indeed)
The very, very, very first day, (Indeed)
Son-Jara's Muslim jinn came forward: (Indeed)
"That which God has said to me, (Indeed)
"To me Tanimunari, (Indeed)
1260 "That which God has said to me, (Indeed)
"So it will be done. (Indeed)
"When the month of Dòmba is ten days old, (Indeed)
"Son-Jara will rise and walk." (Indeed)
In the month of Dòmba, (Indeed)
1265 On its twelfth day, (Indeed)
The Messenger of God was born. (Indeed)
On the thirteenth day, (Indeed)

---

7. The contrasting colors of the two animals represent the sharp opposition between the brothers. Dankaran Tuma is Saman Berete's son. 8. The bizarre and desperate nature of this stipulation is brought out in the lines that follow. 9. A town in present-day Ivory Coast.

Jòn Bilal was born. (Indeed)
On its tenth day, (Indeed)
1270 Was the day for Son-Jara to walk.[1]

O Nare Magan Kònatè! (That's true)

. . .

Master and Warrior Master!
O Nare Magan Kònatè!
1275 O Sorcerer-Seizing-Sorcerer!
A man of power is hard to find. (Mmm)
All people with their empty words,
They all seek to be men of power. (That's true)
Ministers, deputies and presidents, (Indeed)
1280 All of them seek after power,
But there is no easy way to power. (That's true)

Here in our Mali,
We have found our freedom. (Indeed)
Though a person find no gold,
1285 Though he find no silver, (Indeed)
Should he find his freedom,
Then noble will he be. (That's the truth)
A man of power is hard to find. (Mmm)
Ah! Bèmba!

1290 On the tenth day of Dòmba, (Indeed)
The Wizard's mother cooked some couscous,[2] (Indeed)
Sacrificial couscous for Son-Jara.
Whatever woman's door she went to, (Indeed)
The Wizard's mother would cry: (Indeed)
1295 "Give me some sauce of baobab leaf."[3] (Indeed)
The woman would retort,
"I have some sauce of baobab leaf,
"But it is not to give to you.
"Go tell that cripple child of yours
1300 "That he should harvest some for you. (Mmm)
" 'Twas my son harvested these for me." (True)

And bitterly did she weep: bilika bilika.[4]
She went to another woman's door; (Mmm)
That one too did say: (Mmm)
1305 "I have some sauce of baobab leaf,
"But it is not to give to you.
"Go tell that cripple child of yours
"That he should harvest some for you.
" 'Twas my son harvested these for me." (True)

1310 With bitter tears, the Kòndè woman
came back, bilika bilika.
"King of Nyani, King of Nyani,[5]

---

1. The bard makes an explicit connection between the hero's rising to his feet and the sense of origins that underlies the epic.　2. Here a meal, similar in texture to the North African couscous, made from millet grain; it is brownish red in color.　3. A huge tree that grows in the semidesert conditions of the West African savanna; its leaves are eaten as a vegetable. The tree is associated with nobility.　4. Ideophone for the weeping.　5. Her ambition for her son.

"Will you never rise?   (Mmm)
1315   "King of Nyani, King of Nyani,
"Will you never rise?   (Mmm)
"King of Nyani with helm of mail,
"He says he fears no man.
"Will you never rise?
"Rise up, O King of Nyani!   (That's true)

"King of Nyani, King of Nyani,
1320   "Will you never rise?
"King of Nyani with shirt of mail,
"He says he fears no man,
"Will you never rise?
"Rise up, O King of Nyani!   (True)

1325   "O Wizard, I have failed!"   (True)
"Ah, my mother,
"There is a thickener, I hear, called black *lele*.[6]   (True)
"Why not put some in my sauce?
" 'Tis the thickener grown in gravel."

1330   She put black *lele* in the couscous.
The Wizard ate of it.
Ma'an[7] Kònatè ate his fill: (True)
"My mother,   (Indeed)
"Go to the home of the blacksmith patriarchs,   (Indeed)
1335   "To Dun Fayiri and Nun Fayiri.   (Indeed)
"Have them shape a staff, seven-fold forged,
"So that Magan Kònatè may rise up."   (Indeed)
The blacksmith patriarchs shaped a staff, seven-fold
    forged.   (Indeed)
The Wizard came forward.   (Indeed)
1340   He put his right hand o'er his left,
And upwards drew himself,   (Indeed)
And upwards drew himself.
He had but reached the halfway point.   (Indeed)
"Take this staff away from me!"
1345   Magan Kònatè did not rise.   (True)

In misery his mother wept: bilika bilika: (Indeed)
"Giving birth has made me suffer!"   (Mmm)
"Ah, my mother,   (Mmm)
"Return to the blacksmith patriarchs.   (Indeed)
1350   "Ask that they forge that staff anew,   (Indeed)
"And shape it twice again in size.   (Mmm)
"Today I arise, my holy-man said."   (Mmm)

The patriarchs of the smiths forged the staff,
Shaping it twice again in size.   (True)
1355   They forged that staff,
And gave it to Ma'an Kònatè.   (Indeed)
He put his right hand o'er his left,   (Indeed)

---

6. A seasoning.   7. Short for Magan (Son-Jara's name).

	And upwards Son-Jara drew himself.	(Indeed)
	Upwards Nare Magan Kònatè drew himself.	(Indeed)
1360	Again he reached the halfway point:	(Mmm)
	"Take this staff away from me!"	
	Ma'an Kònatè did not rise.	
	He sat back down again.	(Indeed)
	His mother wrung her hands atop her head,	
1365	And wailed: "dèndèlen!	
	"Giving birth has made me suffer!"	(True)
	"Ah, my mother,	(Mmm)
	"Whate'er has come twixt you and God,	(Indeed)
	"Go and speak to God about it now!"[8]	(Indeed)

1370	On that, his mother left,	
	And went to the east of Bintanya,	(Indeed)
	To seek a custard apple tree.	(Indeed)

	Ah! Bèmba!	(Indeed)
	And found some custard apple trees,[9]	(Indeed)
1375	And cut one down,	(Indeed)
	And trimmed it level to her breast,	(Indeed)
	And stood as if in prayer:	(Indeed)
	"O God!	
	"For Son-Jara I have made this staff.	(Indeed)
1380	"If he be the man for the morrow,	(Indeed)
	"If he be the man for the day to follow,	(Indeed)
	"If he is to rule the bards,	(Indeed)
	"If he is to rule the smiths,	(Indeed)
	"The three and thirty warrior clans,	(Indeed)
1385	"If he is to rule all those,	(Indeed)
	"When this staff I give to Nare Magan Kònatè,	(Indeed)
	"Let Magan Kònatè arise.	(True)
	"If he be not the man for the morrow,	(Indeed)
	"If he be not the man for the day to follow,	(Indeed)
1390	"If he is not to rule the bards,	(Indeed)
	"If he is not to rule the smiths,	(Indeed)
	"When this staff I give to the King of Nyani,	
	"Let Son-Jara not arise.	
	"O God, from the day of my creation,	(Indeed)
1395	"If I have known another man,	
	"Save Fata Magan, the Handsome alone,	
	"When this staff I give to the King of Nyani,	
	"Let Son-Jara arise.	(Indeed)
	"From the day of my creation,	(True)
1400	"If I have known a second man,	
	"And not just Fata Magan, the Handsome,	(Indeed)
	"Let Ma'an Kònatè not arise!"	(True)

	She cut down that staff,	
	Going to give it to Nare Magan Kònatè,	
1405	To the Kòndè woman's child, the Answerer-of Needs!	(True)

8. Son-Jara insinuates that his inability to walk may be God's punishment for some act of infidelity on his mother's part. This is made clear in Sugulun Kònde's prayer a few lines below.   9. Trees that bear a fruit with fleshy white pulp that is believed to have magical potency.

The Wizard took the staff,	(Mmm)
And put his right hand o'er his left,	(Indeed)
And upwards drew himself,	(Indeed)
And upwards drew himself.	
1410 Magan Kònatè rose up!	(Mmm)
Running, his mother came forward,	
And clasped his legs	
And squeezed them,	(Indeed)
And squeezed them:	(True)
1415 *"This home of ours,*	
"The home of happiness.	(Indeed)
"Happiness did not pass us by.	
"Magan Kònatè has risen!"	(Indeed)
"Oh! Today!	(Indeed)
1420 *"Today is sweet!*	(Indeed)
"God the King ne'er made today's equal!	*(Indeed)*
"Ma'an Kònatè has risen!"	(Indeed)
"There is no way of standing without worth.	
"Behold his way of standing: danka![1]	
1425 *"O Kapok Tree and Flame Tree!"*[2]	(Fa-Digi, that's true)
"My mother,	(Mmm)
"That baobab there in Manden country,	
"That baobab from which the best sauce comes,	(Indeed)
"Where is that baobab, my mother?"	(Indeed)
1430 "Ah, my lame one,	(Indeed)
"You have yet to walk."	(Indeed)
The Wizard took his right foot,	
And put it before his left.	(Indeed)
His mother followed behind him,	
1435 And sang these songs for him:	(Indeed)
"Tunyu Tanya![3]	(Indeed)
"Brave men fit well among warriors!	(Indeed)
"Tunyu tanya!	(Indeed)
"Brave men fit well among warriors!	(Indeed)
1440 *"Ma'an Kònatè, you have risen!"*	(Indeed)
"Muddy water,	(Indeed)
"Do not compare yourself to water among the stones.	(Indeed)
"That among the stones is pure, wasili![4]	(Indeed)
". . .	(Indeed)
". . .	(Indeed)
1445 *"And a good reputation.*	(Indeed)
"Khalif Magan Kònatè has risen.	(True)
"Great snake, O great snake,	(Indeed)
"I will tolerate you.	(Indeed)
"Should you confront me, toleration.	(Indeed)
1450 *"O great snake upon the path,*	(Indeed)

---

1. Ideophone to emphasize the words said.   2. Both trees rise tall and straight and hence provide an image of the hero.   3. Ideophones, depicting the unsteady movement of the child learning to walk. 4. A somewhat onomatopoeic ideophone for movement of water; the three lines of this part of Sugulun Kòndè's song convey the idea that her son is superior to other children.

	"Whatever confronts me, I will tolerate."[5]	(Indeed)
	"Arrow-shaft of happiness.	(Indeed)
	"It is in one hundred.	(Indeed)
	"The one hundred dead,	
1455	"All but Son-Jara.	(True)
	"The higher stones get crushed![6]	(Indeed)
	"Who can mistake the Destroyer-of-Origins!	
	"And this by the hand of Nare Magan Kònatè!"	

	Hey! Biribiriba came forward.	(Indeed)
1460	He shook the baobab tree.	(Indeed)
	A young boy fell out.	
	His leg was broken.	
	The bards thus sing, "Leg-Crushing-Ruler!	
	"Magan Kònatè has risen!"	(Indeed)
1465	He shook the baobab again.	(Indeed)
	Another young boy fell out.	
	His arm was broken.	(Indeed)
	The bards thus sing, "Arm-Breaking-Ruler!	
	"Magan Kònatè has risen!"	(Indeed)
1470	He shook the baobab again.	(Indeed)
	Another young boy fell out.	(Indeed)
	His neck was broken.	(Indeed)
	And thus the bards sing, "Neck-Breaking-Ruler!	
	"Magan Kònatè has risen!"	(Indeed)
1475	The Wizard uprooted the baobab tree,	
	And laid it across his shoulder.	(Mmm)
	Nare Magan Kònatè rose up.[7]	(Indeed)

* * *

	Biribiriba came forward.	(Mmm)
	He planted the baobab behind his mother's house:	
	"In and about the Manden,	(Mmm)
	"From my mother they must seek these leaves!"	(Mmm)
1520	To which his mother said, "I do not think I heard."	(Mmm)
	"Ah, my mother,	(Indeed)
	"Now all the Manden baobabs are yours."	
	"I do not think I heard."	
	"Ah, my mother,	(Indeed)
1525	"All those women who refused you leaves,	
	"They all must seek those leaves from you."	(Indeed)
	His mother fell upon her knees, gejebu![8]	
	On both her knees,	
	And laid her head aside the baobab.	(Indeed)
1530	"For years and years,	
	"My ear was deaf.	(Indeed)
	"Only this year	
	"Has my ear heard news.	
	"Khalif Magan Kònatè has risen!"	(That's true)

5. She will brave any danger for her son's sake.   6. An image of Son-Jara storming the heights of power and overcoming them.   7. The series of mishaps caused by the hero in these lines prefigures his later prowess in war and explains the praise names he thus earns.   8. An exclamation.

1535	Biribiriba!	(Indeed)
	Since he began to walk,	(Indeed)
	Whenever he went into the bush,	(Mmm)
	Were he to kill some game,	(Indeed)
	He would give his elder the tail.[9]	
1540	And think no more of it.	
	. . .	(Indeed)

> Took up the bow!
> Simbon, Master-of-the-Bush!
> Took up the bow!

1545	Took up the bow!	(Indeed)

> Ruler of bards and smiths
> Took up the bow!
> Took up the bow!
> The Kòndè woman's child,

1550		

> Answerer-of-Needs,
> He took up the bow.
> Sugulun's Ma'an took up the bow!

> The Wizard has risen!

1555		

> King of Nyani, Nare Magan Kònatè!
> The Wizard has risen!

	The Wizard has risen!	(Indeed)
	Ah! Bèmba!	(Indeed)
	Whenever he went to the bush,	(Indeed)
	Were he to kill some game,	(Indeed)
1560	He would give to his elder the tail,	
	And think no more of it.	
	. . .	(Indeed)
	As Biribiriba walked forth one day,	(That's true)
	A jinn came upon him,	
1565	And laid his hand on Son-Jara's shoulder:	
	"O Son-Jara!	(Mmm)
	"In the Manden, there's a plot against you.	(Mmm)
	"That spotted dog you see before you,[1]	(Indeed)
	"Is an offering made against you,	(Indeed)
1570	"So that you not rule the bards,	(Indeed)
	"So that you not rule the smiths,	
	"So, the three and thirty warrior clans,	
	"That you rule over none of them.	(Mmm)
	"When you go forth today,	(Mmm)
1575	"Make an offering of a safo-dog,[2]	(Indeed)
	"Should God will it,	
	"The Manden will be yours!"	(Indeed)
	Ah! Bèmba!	
	On that, Biribiriba went forth, my father,	
1580	And made an offering of a safo-dog,	
	And hung a weight around its neck,[3]	
	And fastened an iron chain about it.	(Indeed)
	Even tomorrow morning,	

9. Considered a delicacy. This detail emphasizes Son-Jara's generous disposition toward his brother, despite the conflict between them.   1. The toothless dog (line 1206).   2. A dog consecrated for ritual sacrifice.   3. To restrain the dog's ferocity.

The Europeans will imitate him.
1585   Whenever the Europeans leave a dog,   (Mmm)
Its neck weight,
They fasten that dog with an iron chain, Manden!   (Indeed)

O! Bèmba!
He hung a weight around the dog's neck,
1590   And fastened it with a chain.   (Mmm)
That done, whatever home he passed before,   (Indeed)
The people stood gaping at him:
"Causer-of-Loss![4]   (Indeed)
"A cow with its neckweight,
1595   "But a dog with a neckweight?"   (Indeed)
To which the Wizard did retort:
"Leave me be!   (True)
"Cast your eyes on the dog of the prince.[5]
"There's not a tooth in that dog's mouth!
1600   "But there are teeth in my dog's mouth,
"My commoner's[6] dog. Leave me be!   (Indeed)
"My dog's name is Tomorrow's Affair."

Son-Jara's sacrificial dog,
That dog was called Tomorrow's Affair.[7]

1605   From his neckwright he broke loose,
And also from his chain,   (Indeed)
And charged the dog of Dankaran Tuman,   (Indeed)
And ripped him into shreds, fèsè fèsè fèsè![8]   (Indeed)
And stacked one piece atop the other.   (Indeed)
1610   The mother of Dankaran Tuman, she wrung her
      hands atop her head,
And gave a piercing cry: "dèndèlen!   (Indeed)
"That a dog would bite a dog,   (Indeed)
"A natural thing in the Manden.   (Indeed)
"That a dog would kill a dog.
1615   "The natural thing in the Manden.
"That a dog shred another like an old cloth,
"My mother, there must be something with his master!"[9]
Dankaran Tuman replied, "Ah! my mother,   (Mmm)
"I called my dog Younger-Leave-Me-Be.   (Mmm)
1620   "Ah! My mother, do not sever the bonds of family.[1]   (True)
"My mother!   (Indeed)
"That is the dog that stalked the bush
"To go and kill some game,
"Bringing it back to me, my mother.   (True)
1625   "Do not sever the bonds of family, my mother!"   (True)
The mother of Dankaran Tuman had no answer:[2]   (Indeed)

---

4. That is, to his enemies; the praise name anticipates Son-Jara's later deeds. 5. That is, Dankaran Tuman, considered the heir apparent. 6. By referring to himself as a commoner, Son-Jara seems here to concede his half-brother's birthright. 7. Compare Du Kamisa's *A thing for tomorrow* (line 343). The implication is that he counts on the future to bring a change to his fortunes. 8. Ideophone evocative of the action described. 9. That is, Son-Jara must have superior magical power. The words carry a note of deep apprehension. 1. It is apparent from these words and from Son-Jara's attitude toward his half brother (see n. 9, p. 1564) that the primary source of the conflict between the princes is the rivalry between their mothers. 2. She remains insensitive to her son's entreaty.

"One afternoon, the time will come for Son-Jara to
    depart. (Mmm)
"Indeed what the wise men have said, (Mmm)
"His time is for the morrow.³ (Mmm)
1630   "The one that I have borne, (Mmm)
"He is being left behind without explanation. (Mmm)
"Son-Jara, (Mmm)
"The Kòndè woman's offspring, (Mmm)
"He will take the Manden tribute, (Mmm)
1635   "And he will rule the bards, (Mmm)
"And he will rule the smiths, (Indeed)
"And rule the funès⁴ and the cordwainers. (Indeed)
"The Manden will be his.
"That time will yet arrive, (Indeed)
1640   "And that by the hand of Nare Magan Kònatè.
"Nothing leaves its time behind."
    O Biribiriba!
    Kirikisa, Spear-of-Access, Spear-of-Service!
    People of Kaya, Son-Jara entered Kaya.
1645   All this by the hand of Nare Magan Kònatè.
    Gaining power is not easy! (Indeed)
Ah! Bèmba! (Indeed)
The mother of King Dankaran Tuman, (Indeed)
When the Wizard had left the bush, (Indeed)
1650   And offered his flesh-and-blood-brother the tail, (Indeed)
And when he said, "Here take the tail,"⁵
She retorted: "Your mother, Sugulun Kòndè, will
    take the tail! (Indeed)
"And your younger sister, Sugulun Kulukan, (Indeed)
"And your younger brother, Manden Bukari. (Indeed)
1655   "Go and seek a place to die, (Indeed)
"If not, I will chop through your necks,
"Cutting a handspan down into the ground.
"Be it so; you'll never return to the Manden again." (Indeed)
Son-Jara bitterly wept, bilika bilika! (Indeed)
1660   And went to tell his mother. (Indeed)
His mother said, (Indeed)
"Ah! My child, (Indeed)
"Be calm. Salute your brother. (Indeed)
"Had he banished you as a cripple,
1665   "Where would you have gone?
"Let us at least agree on that.
"Let us depart.
"What sitting will not solve,
"Travel will resolve." (That's true)

---

3. Saman Berete woman is credited with a foresight that contradicts her deepest sentiment. This is, however, only a narrative effect, the result of the bard's identification with Son-Jara and his anticipation of
events.   4. A subclass of *griots* who only recite and do not play musical instruments.   5. There is a
play on words in the original text, so that the phrase is interpreted by Saman Berete as an injunction to
leave.

FROM EPISODE 5

MÈMA

1670	They rose up	(Mmm)
	The Kuyatè matriarch took up the iron rasp.[6]	(Mmm)
	She sang a hunter's song for Nare Magan Kònatè:	
	"Took up the bow!	(Indeed)
	"Simbon, Master-of-the-Bush!	
1675	"Took up the bow!	
	"Took up the bow!	(Indeed)
	"Simbon, Master-of-Wild-Beasts!	
	"Took up the bow!	(Indeed)
	"Took up the bow!	(Indeed)
1680	"Warrior and Master-of-Slaves!	
	"Took up the bow!	(Indeed)
	"The Kòndè woman's child,	
	"Answerer-of-Needs,	(Indeed)
	"Took up the bow.	(Indeed)
1685	"Sugulan's Ma'an took up the bow.	(Indeed)
	You seized him, O Lion!	(Indeed)
	"And the Wizard killed him!	
	"O Simbon, that, the sound of your chords."	(True)

	He fled from suffering	(Mmm)
1690	To seek refuge with the blacksmith patriarch,[7]	(Indeed)
	Because of the hardships of rivalry.	(Mmm)
	But they counted out one measure of gold,[8]	(Mmm)
	And gave it to the blacksmith patriarch,	(Indeed)
	Saying, were he not to cast the Wizard out,	(Indeed)
1695	Saying, he would jeopardize the land,	(Indeed)
	Saying, the Manden would be the Wizard's,	(Indeed)
	Because of the hardships of rivalry.	(Indeed)
	The Wizard fled anew from suffering.	(Mmm)
	He went to seek refute with the Karanga patriarch.	(Indeed)
1700	Do you not know that person's name?	(Mmm)
	Jobi, the Seer.	(Indeed)
	The Karanga patriarch was Jobi, the Seer.	(I did not know that until you told me)

Because of the hardships of rivalry,
He cast the Wizard out.

[Son-Jara and his mother wander from town to town seeking refuge and are cast out in the same manner everywhere. In desperation, they turn for help to a company of women who represent the forces of evil. Meanwhile, Son-Jara's half brother succeeds to the throne, but the Manden is now threatened by a powerful neighbor, the Susu king Sumamuru.]

---

6. A musical instrument. The Kuyatè matriarch is Tumu Maniya, the female bard who announced Son-Jara's birth to his father.   7. His profession indicates that he is of lowly station. By seeking refuge with him, Son-Jara thus accepts a humiliated condition.   8. To reward the blacksmith for casting out Son-Jara and his mother. The reward is paid by Dankaran Tuman's people ("they").

Biribiriba went on to seek refuge
With the nine Queens-of-Darkness.[9]
1770   "What brought you here?" they asked of him.   (Mmm)
"Have you not heard that none come here?   (Indeed)
"What brought you here?"   (Indeed)
The Sorcerer spoke out.
"Ah! Those who are feared by all,
1775   "If you join them, you are spared.
"It is that which made me come here."
He sat down.   (Indeed)
His flesh-and-blood elder, King Dankaran Tuman,   (Indeed)
He took his first-born daughter,   (Indeed)
1780   Caress-of-Hot-Fire,[1]   (Indeed)
And gave her to the Kuyatè patriarch, Dòka the Cat,[2]   (Indeed)
Saying, "Give her to Susu Mountain Sumamuru,"[3]   (Indeed)
Saying, "Should he not slay the King of Nyani,"
Saying, "He's gone to seek refuge with the nine
     Queens-of-Darkness,"
1785   Saying, "The folk have lost their faith in him."   (True)

At that time, the bards did not have balaphones,[4]   (True)
Nor had the smiths a balaphone,
Nor had the funès a balaphone,
Nor did the cordwainers have one,   (Indeed)
1790   None but Susu Mountain Sumamuru.   (Indeed)
    Sori Kantè the Tall,   (Indeed)
    Who begat Bala Kantè of Susu,   (Indeed)
    And who begat Kabani Kantè,   (True)
    And who begat Kankuba Kantè,
1795   And who begat Susu Mountain Sumamuru Kantè.[5]
The village where Sumamuru was,
That village was called Dark Forest.[6]   (True)

It was there he came forth, my father,   (Indeed)
Ah! Bèmba!   (Indeed)
1800   He came in Sumamuru's absence,   (Indeed)
Dòka the Cat,   (Indeed)
He asked for Sumamuru.[7]   (Indeed)
They said, "If you seek Sumamuru,
"Ask of the hawk!"   (Mmm)
1805   The balaphone of seven keys,   (Mmm)
After Sumamuru had played that balaphone,   (Indeed)
The mallets of the balaphone he would take,
And give them to the hawk.   (Indeed)
It would fly up high in a Flame Tree,

9. Probably a cult of women devoted to the practice of magic.   1. So named because of her sexual prowess. By giving his daughter to Sumamuru in marriage, Dankaran Tuman hopes to placate the Susu king and to enlist his aid in eliminating Son-Jara, who remains a threat even in exile.   2. Son-Jara's personal bard, whom he had to leave behind in the Manden, has been appropriated by Dankaran Tuman. 3. Son-Jara's principal antagonist is introduced here for the first time. His massive physical aspect is denoted in the sobriquet "Mountain" that has become attached to his name.   4. Musical instruments, akin to the xylophone, with boards of varying length laid out for the different notes.   5. These lines are a rapid summary of Sumamuru's genealogy.   6. The name of the village identifies Sumamuru with paganism, as opposed to the Muslim affiliations of Son-Jara.   7. Dòka the Cat's motive in seeking out Sumamuru, who is ravaging the Manden, is not made clear, for it soon becomes apparent he has no intention of entering his service.

1810	And there in the depths of Susu Forest sit.	(Indeed)
	Dòka the Cat called to the hawk.	(Indeed)
	The balaphone mallets it delivered to him.	(Indeed)
	"Dun Fayiri, Nun Fayiri!	(Indeed)
	"Manda Kantè and Sama Kantè!	(Indeed)
1815	"Sori Kantè, the Tall![8]	(Mmm)
	"Susu Mountain Sumamuru Kantè!	(Indeed)
	"Salute Sumamuru!	(Indeed)
	"Sumamuru came amongst us,	
	"His pants of human skin.[9]	(Indeed)
1820	"Sumamuru came amongst us,	
	"His coat of human skin.	(Indeed)
	"Sumamuru came amongst us,	
	"His helm of human skin.	(Indeed)
	"The first and ancient king,	
1825	"The King of yesteryear.[1]	(Indeed)
	"So, respite does not end resolve.	
	"Sumamuru, I found you gone.	
	"Oh! Glorious Janjon!"[2]	

	Sumamuru was off doing battle,	
1830	With pants of human skin,	
	And coat of human skin.	
	Whenever he would mount a hill,	
	Down another he would go.	
	Up one and down another.	
1835	Was it God or man?[3]	
	He approached the Kuyatè patriarch, Dòka the Cat:	(Mmm)
	"God or man?"	(Indeed)
	"I am a man," the reply.	
	"Where do you hail from?"	(Mmm)
1840	"I come," he said, "from the Manden.	(Indeed)
	"I am from Nyani."	(Indeed)

	"Play something for me to hear," he said.	(Indeed)
	He took up the balaphone:	(Indeed)
	"Kukuba and Bantanba!	
1845	"Nyani-nyani and Kamasiga![4]	
	"Brave child of the warrior!	
	"And Deliverer-of-the-Benign.	
	"Sumamuru came amongst us	
	"With pants of human skin.	
1850	"Sumamuru came amongst us,	
	"With coat of human skin.	
	"Sumamuru came amongst us	
	"With helm of human skin.	
	"The first and ancient king,	
1855	"The king of yesteryear.	

8. These are the names of Sumamuru's ancestors, invoked in his praise song.   9. Symbolic of his savage ferocity.   1. As addressed by Dòka the Cat to Sumamuru, this praise epithet is shot through with ambivalence. It may refer to the sanction bestowed by the years on Sumamuru's ancestry and reign, but it also suggests that the addressee belongs to a past age that is to be superseded by a new one, that of Son-Jara.   2. War song, a genre of oral poetry in the Manding.   3. As the notes of his balaphone reach his ears, Sumamuru wonders who is playing the instrument.   4. These are place names in the Manden.

> "So, respite does not end resolve!
> "Sumamuru, I found you gone.
> "Oh! Glorious Janjon!"

He[5] said, "Ah! What is your name?"

1860 "My name is Dòka, the Cat." (Mmm)

"Will you not remain with me?"

"Not I! Two kings I cannot praise.

"I am Son-Jara's bard.

"From the Manden I have come,

1865 "And to the Manden I must return." (True)

He laid hold of the Kuyatè patriarch,

And severed both Achilles tendons,[6]

And by the Susu balaphone set him. (Indeed)

"Now what is your name?" (Indeed)

1870 "Dòka, the Cat is still my name." (Indeed)

"Dòka, the Cat will no longer do." (Indeed)

He drew water and poured it over his head, (Indeed)

And shaved it clean,[7] (Indeed)

And gave him the name Bala Faseke Kuyatè.

1875 That Bala Faseke Kuyatè, (Indeed)

He fathered three children, (Indeed)

Musa and Mansa Magan, (Indeed)

Making Baturu, the Holy his last-born son in the
    Manden. (Indeed)

Those were the Kuyatès.

1880 And this by the hand of Sumamuru.

He sent forth a messenger,

Saying, "Go tell King Dankaran Tuman," (Indeed)

Saying, "If you kill your own vicious dog,"

Saying, "Another man's will surely bite you."[8] (Indeed, that's the
    truth)

1885 With this he declared war, my father,

And went forth from Susu.

Going to fall on King Dankaran Tuman, (Indeed)

Breaking the Manden like an old pot, (Indeed)

Breaking the Manden like an old gourd, (Indeed)

1890 Slaying the nine and ninety Masters-of-Shadow,[9]

Slaying the nine and ninety royal princes,

And ousting King Dankaran Tuman.

He fled to Nsèrè-kòrò,[1]

Saying, "I was spared. (Indeed)

1895 "From your torment, I was spared. (True)

From death, I have been spared." (Indeed)

And thus he settled there.

---

5. Sumamuru.   **6.** In other versions of the epic, this violation of his bard is presented as Son-Jara's principal grievance against Sumamuru.   **7.** As with a newborn child at its naming ceremony. The shaving of the bard's hair and his new name signify his rededication to a new service.   **8.** The meaning is that Dankaran Tuman can expect to suffer the same fate he inflicted on Son-Jara.   **9.** Diviners in the royal household.   **1.** In present-day Guinea.

	The sons he there begat, my father,	(Indeed)
	They became the Kisi[2] people.	
1900	They are all in Masanta.[3]	
	They had come from the Manden.	
	Their family name, it is Gindo.	(Indeed)
	Ah! Bèmba!	(Indeed)
1905	O Biribiriba!	
	He put gourds in the mouths[4]	
	of the poor and the powerful.	
	This by the hand of Susu Mountain Sumamuru,	(Indeed)
	Saying each must speak into his gourd,	
	Saying there is no pleasure in weakness,[5]	
	Saying the Manden was now his.	
1910	He summoned Kankira-of-Silver	(Indeed)
	And Kankira-of-Gold,[6]	(Indeed)
	The latter, the Saginugu patriarch,	(Indeed)
	And one red[7] bull did give to them,	(Indeed)
	Saying they should offer it	
1915	To the nine Queens-of-Darkness,	(Indeed)
	Asking them to slay Son-Jara,	(Mmm)
	That he not enter the Manden again,	
	To say that the Manden be his,	
	Saying they have slain the nine and	
	ninety Masters-of-Shadow,	
1920	Saying they have slain the nine and	
	ninety royal princes,	
	And put gourds o'er the mouths	
	of the poor and the powerful,	(Indeed)
	Saying that they should slay him,	(Indeed)
	So he not enter the Manden again	(Mmm)
	To say that the Manden be his.	(Indeed)
1925	Those messengers arrived.	(Indeed)
	They came upon the witches there:	(Indeed)
	"Ilu tuntun!"	(Indeed)
	The witches did not speak.	(Mmm)
	"Peace be unto you."	(Mmm)
1930	The witches did not speak.	
	"Alu tuntun!"	
	The witches did not speak.	
	"Peace be with you!"	
	The witches did not speak.	(That's true)
1935	"The slaughtered bull,	(Indeed)
	"Lay it out in nine piles."	(Indeed)
	Nakana Tiliba[8] then said to the witches,	

2. An ethnic group spread along the coast from Guinea to Senegal.   3. An area farther inland, to the north.   4. Metaphor to denote Sumamuru's repressive rule.   5. Expressive of the arrogance of power. 6. Silversmith and Goldsmith; they belong to a special caste of craftsmen.   7. In many African societies, the red symbolizes the supernatural world.   8. Son-Jara's paternal aunt, previously given by Fata Magan the Handsome to the Tarawere brothers in exchange for Sugulun Kòndè (see line 1028). She is now the principal queen of darkness.

	"Each must either take her own,	(Indeed)
	"Questions without end looking for trouble,[9]	(That's true)
1940	"Then take the meat and be off,	(Indeed)
	"Or," Nakana Tiliba continued,	(Indeed)
	"You must not take the meat.	
	"O Son-Jara,	(Indeed)
	"A message has come from the Manden,	(Indeed)
1945	"From Susu Mountain Sumamuru,	(Indeed)
	"Saying to come and tell us,	(Indeed)
	"Saying we should slay you,	(Indeed)
	"So that you not enter the Manden again,	
	"Saying, the folk have lost their faith in you.	(Indeed)
1950	"Saying, he has slain the nine and ninety	
	Masters-of-the-Shadow,	(Indeed)
	"Saying, he has slain the nine and ninety royal	
	princes.	(Indeed)
	"Nine were the times he razed the Manden,	
	"And nine were the times he rebuilt it,	(Indeed)
	Saying, he put gourds on the mouths of the poor and	
	the powerful,	(Indeed)
1955	"Saying, all must speak into their gourds,	
	"Saying, there is no pleasure in weakness,	
	Saying, he has ousted King Dankaran Tuman,	
	Saying, who has fled to Nsèrè-kòrò,	
	"Saying, we should slay you,	
1960	"So that you not enter the Manden again,	
	"And that is the reason for this meat."	
	"Then kill me," his reply.	
	"A person flees to be spared,	
	"But should one not be spared, then kill me!"[1]	(True)
1965	Biribiriba!	(Mmm)
	He went to the back of the house.	
	Into a lion he transformed himself,	(Mmm)
	A lion seizing no one,[2]	
	Before he had sounded a roar.	(Mmm)
1970	He went and seized a buffalo,	
	And came back and laid it down,	
	And went and seized another,	
	And came and laid it down,	
	And went and seized another,	
1975	And came and laid it down.	
	"Nine water buffalos, nine witches!	(Mmm)
	"Each take your own!"	(True)
	The witches then replied to him,	
	"Let us hold a council.	
1980	"The town where people hold no council,	
	"There will living not be good."	
	They went to hold their council,	
	"From the Manden and its neighbors,	(Indeed)

9. That is, each must take her part without argument.   1. Note the equanimity with which Son-Jara receives Nakana Tiliba's words.   2. That is, one that does not bother any human being, because he is only after game.

"All of it together, and only one red bull! (Indeed)
1985 "Son-Jara, you alone, nine buffalos!
"It is to him the Manden must belong!
"Let us then release him!" (True)
They trimmed a branch of the custard apple tree: (Indeed)
"When you leave the land of the nine
    Queens-of-Darkness, (Indeed)
1990 "You will see no village, (Mmm)
"Until you see Jula Fundu, (Mmm)
"The original town of the Mossi[3] patriarch, (Indeed)
"Jula Fundu and Wagadugu, (Indeed)
"In Mèma Farin Tunkara's land of Mèma."
1995 They stacked the bull meat in one pile, (Mmm)
And upon it laid its skin,
And upon this placed its head. (Mmm)
"All of you witches, say your verses! (Indeed)

"All of you witches, read your signs!" (Indeed)
2000 Nakana Tiliba,
From her head she took her scarf,
And tied three knots[4] into it,
And laid it o'er the meat,
Saying, "Rise up!
2005 "Kitibili Kintin![5] (Indeed)
" 'Twas a man that puts us in conflict.
"A matter of truth is not to be feared."[6]
The bull rose up and stretched. (Mmm)
It bellowed to Muhammad.[7] (Mmm)
2010 The Messenger of God was thus evoked. (That's true)

That bull rose up and stretched. (Indeed)
Ah! Bèmba! (Indeed)
Son-Jara came forth: (Indeed)
"O Kankira-of-Silver and Kankira-of-Gold, (Indeed)
2015 "A messenger is not to be whipped. (Indeed)
"A messenger is not to be defiled.[8] (Indeed)
"When you go forth from here,
"You should go tell Susu Mountain Sumamuru, (Indeed)
"When you go forth from here, (Indeed)
2020 "You should go tell Susu Mountain Sumamuru: (Indeed)
" 'The cowherd offers naught of the cow,'
" 'But the milk of Friday past.'
" 'No matter how loving the wet nurse,'
" 'The child will never be hers.'
2025 "Say, 'A child may be first-born, but that does not always
    make him the elder.'
"Say, 'Today may belong to some,'
" 'Tomorrow will belong to another.'

---

3. An ethnic group in Burkina Faso. Nothing more is known about Jula Fundu (founder of the Mossi).
4. To give it magical potency.   5. An incantation.   6. Or telling the truth is a moral obligation, even if
it means offending the powerful.   7. An example of the mix of religions that occasionally surfaces in the
epic. It is obvious, however, that invocation of Muhammad is out of keeping with the atmosphere of the
scene described here.   8. By tradition, a messenger enjoys absolute immunity, even if sent by an enemy.

"Say, 'As you succeeded some,'
"'So shall you have successors.'
2030 "Say, 'I am off to seek refuge with Mèma's Prince Tunkara,'
"'In the land of Mèma.'"[9]

He took the shape of a hawk.
You took it, Nare Magan Kònatè.
Biribiriba and Bow-of-the-Bush . . . ,
2035 . . . fled because of suffering.
Gaining power is not easy.

Ah! Bèmba!
Son-Jara went to seek refuge in Mèma,
In a town of the Tunkaras, my father, in Mèma. (Indeed)

[There follows a long account of a ritual ordeal Son-Jara must undergo before he is allowed by Prince Burama, the ruler of Mèma, to settle in the town. Mèma Sira, Prince Burama's eldest daughter, who has fallen in love with Son-Jara, reveals the secret of the ordeal to him so that he passes it without difficulty. With his mother, brother, and sister, Son-Jara settles in Mèma, practicing his profession as a hunter, while waiting for a chance to return to the Manden, which is meanwhile being devastated by Sumamuru.]

2410 Son-Jara had a certain fetish (Indeed)
Accepting no sacrifice save shea butter. (Indeed)
There were no shea trees there in Mèma. (Indeed)
O Mansa Magan! (Indeed)
Wherever you sacrifice to the shea tree, (Indeed)
2415 That town must be in Mandenland. (Indeed)

All of them are in the Manden. (Indeed)
No shea trees were there in Mèma. (Indeed)
Save one old dry Shea tree in Mèma. (Indeed)
Son-Jara's mother came forward:[1] (Indeed)
2420 "Ah! God! (Indeed)
"Let Son-Jara go to the Manden. (Indeed)
"He is the man for the morrow. (Indeed)
"He is the man for the day to follow. (Indeed)
"He is to rule o'er the bards, (Indeed)
2425 "He is to rule o'er the smiths, (Indeed)
"And the three and thirty warrior clans. (Indeed)
"He will rule o'er all those people. (Indeed)
"Ah, God! (Indeed)
"Before the break of day, (Indeed)
2430 "That dried up shea tree here, (Indeed)
"Let it bear leaf and fruit. (Indeed)
"Let the fruit fall down to earth, (Indeed)
"So that Son-Jara may gather the fruit,
"From it to make shea butter, (Indeed)
2435 "To offer his fetish. (Indeed, yes, Fa-Digi)

9. Thus Son-Jara and his mother chose to seek refuge in Mèma.   1. Because they were running out of the oil they had brought with them from the Manden, Sugulun Kòndè prays for the rejuvenation of this lone shea tree.

	"Ah, God!	(Indeed)
	"Let Son-Jara go to the Manden.	(Indeed)
	"He is the man for the morrow.	
	"He is the man for the day to follow.	(Indeed)
2440	"He will rule the bards and smiths.	(Indeed)
	"The Manden belongs to the Wizard.	(Indeed)
	"Before the break of day,	(Indeed)
	"Let me change my dwelling,[2]	(Indeed)
	"Old am I and cannot travel.	(Indeed)
2445	"Let Nare Magan Kònatè go home."	(Indeed)
	When the day was dawning,	(Indeed)
	The dried up shea tree did bear leaf.	(Indeed)
	Its fruit did fall to earth.	(Indeed)
	Son-Jara looked in on the Kòndè woman,	(Indeed)
2450	But the Kòndè woman had abandoned the world.	(Indeed)
	He washed his mother's body,	(Indeed)
	And then he dug her grave,	(Indeed)
	And wrapped her in a shroud,	(Indeed)
	And laid his mother in the earth,	(Indeed)
2455	And then chopped down a kapok tree,	(Indeed)
	And wrapped it in a shroud,	(Indeed)
	And laid it in the house,	(Indeed)
	And laid a blanket over it.	(Indeed)
	And sent a messenger to Prince Birama,	
2460	Asking of him a grant of land,	(Indeed)
	In order to bury his mother in Mèma,	
	So that he could return to the Manden.	(Indeed)
	This answer they did give to him	
	That no land could he have,	
2465	Unless he were to pay its price.	(Indeed)
	Prince Birama decreed,	(Indeed)
	Saying he could have no land,	(Indeed)
	Unless he were to pay its price.	(Indeed)
	He[3] took feathers of Guinea fowl and partridge,	(Indeed)
2470	And took some leaves of arrow-shaft plant,	(Indeed)
	And took some leaves of wild grass reed,	(Indeed)
	And took some red fanda-vines,	(Indeed)
	And took one measure of shot,	(Indeed)
	And took a haftless knife,	(Indeed)
2475	And added a cornerstone fetish[4] to that,	(Indeed)
	And put it all in a leather pouch,	(Indeed)
	Saying go give it to Prince Birama,	(Indeed)
	Saying it was the price of his land.	(Indeed, ha, Fa-Digi)
	That person gave it to Prince Birama.	(Indeed)
2480	Prince Birama summoned his three sages,[5]	(Indeed)
	All-Knowing Sage,	(Indeed)
	All-Seeing-Sage,	(Indeed)
	All-Saying-Sage.	(Indeed)

---

2. That is, depart this world for the next.   3. Son-Jara.   4. The allusion is obscure, but this is probably a fetish object.   5. To explain the meaning of Son-Jara's gesture.

	The three sages counseled Prince Birama.	(Indeed)
2485	He said, "O Sages!	(Indeed)
	"The forest by the river is never empty.[6]	(Indeed)
	"You also should take this.[7]	(Indeed)
	"That which came first,	(Indeed)
	"I will not take it.	(Indeed)
2490	"Tis yours."[8]	(Indeed)
	O Garan!	(Indeed)
	All-Seeing-Sage,	
	All-Saying-Sage,	
	All-Knowing-Sage,	(Indeed)
2495	They untied the mouth of the pouch,	
	And shook its contents out.	(Indeed)
	The All-Seeing Sage exclaimed,	(Indeed)
	"Anyone can see that!	(Indeed)
	"I am going home!"[9]	(Indeed)
2500	The All-Knowing-Sage exclaimed,	(Indeed)
	"Everybody knows that!	(Indeed)
	"I am going home."	(Indeed)
	All-Saying-Sage exclaimed,	(Indeed)
	"Everyone knows that?	(Indeed)
2505	"That is a lie!	(Indeed)
	"Everyone sees that?	(Indeed)
	"That is a lie!	(Indeed)
	"There may be something one may see,	
	"Be it ne'er explained to him,	
2510	"He will never know it.	(Indeed)
	"Prince Birama,	(Indeed)
	"Did you not see feathers of Guinea fowl and partridge?	
	"They are the things of ruins.[1]	(Indeed)
	"Did you not see the leaf of arrow-shaft plant?	
2515	"That is a thing of ruins.	(Indeed)
	"Was not your eye on the wild grass reed?	(Indeed)
	"That is a thing of ruins.	(Indeed)
	"Did you not see those broken shards?	(Indeed)
	"They are the things of ruins.	(Indeed)
2520	"Did you not see that measure of shot?[2]	(Indeed)
	"The annihilator of Mèma![3]	(Indeed)
	"Did you not see that haftless knife?	(Indeed)
	"The warrior-head-severing blade!	(Indeed)
	"Was not your eye on the red fanda-vine?[4]	(Indeed)
2525	"The warrior-head-severing blood!	(Indeed)
	"If you do not give the land to him,	(Indeed)
	"That cornerstone fetish your eye beheld,	
	"It is the warrior's thunder shot!	(Indeed)
	"If you do not give the land to him,	
2530	"To Nare Magan Kònatè,	

6. There is more to this than meets the eye.   7. Look into this for me.   8. Within your domain as seers.   9. The matter is too trivial to detain him. It is an ironic comment on the self-importance of seers. 1. In other words, a threat of destruction.   2. An anachronism.   3. Son-Jara, if his request is not granted.   4. An unidentified creeping plant.

"The Wizard will reduce the town to ruin. (Indeed)
"Son-Jara is to return to the Manden!" (That's the truth)

They gave the land to the Sorcerer, (Indeed)
He buried his mother in Mèma's earth.
2535 He rose up.
That which sitting will not solve,
Travel will resolve. (Indeed)

FROM EPISODE 6

Kulu-Kòrò

* * *

2575   O Biribiriba! (Indeed)
When he and his mother were going to Mèma, (Indeed)
She took her silver bracelet off,
And gave it to the Boatman patriarch,
To Sasagalò, the Tall. (Indeed)
2580 The ancestor of the boatman was Sasagalò, the Tall.
She took her silver bracelet off: (Indeed)
"When one digs a distant-day well,
"Should a distant-day thirst descend, then drink!"[5] (Indeed)

A partridge was sent to deliver the message[6] (Indeed)
2585 To Susu Mountain Sumamuru: (Indeed)
     "Manda and Sama Kantè! (Indeed)
     "Susu Bala Kantè!
     "Kukuba and Bantanba!
     "Nyani-nyani and Kamasiga! (Indeed)
2590   *"Brave child of the warrior!*
     "And Deliverer-of-the-Benign!
     "Sumamuru came among us
     "With pants of human skin! (Indeed)
     "Sumamuru came among us
2595   *"With coat of human skin.* (Indeed)
     "Applaud him! (Indeed)
     "Susu Mountain Sumamuru!
"The Sorcerer with his army has left Mèma. (Indeed)
"He has entered the Manden!"[7] (Indeed)

2600 Susu Mountain Sumamuru, (Indeed)
He took four measures of gold, (Indeed)
To the Boatman patriarch,
Sasagalò, the Tall, did give them, (Indeed)
Saying, "That army coming from Mèma, (Indeed)
2605 "That army must not cross!" (Indeed)

---

5. A proverb counseling foresight.   6. It is not clear whether Son-Jara sends this message to challenge
Sumumuru or whether it is a general report by the latter's retainers and spies. "Partridge": birds were often
used to carry messages over long distances in earlier societies and in Europe even as late as the 19th century. The partridge, however, was never used for this purpose; thus it is not clear whether the reference
here is intended as a realistic detail or is merely symbolic.   7. This announcement marks the point at
which Son-Jara's campaign for recovery of his kingdom begins.

	For one entire month,	(Indeed)
	Son-Jara and his army by the riverbank sat.	(Indeed)
	He wandered up and down.	(Indeed)
	One day Son-Jara rose up	
2610	And followed up the river:	(Indeed)
	"Being good, a bane.	(Indeed)
	"Not being good, a bane.	(Indeed)
	"When my mother and I were going to Mèma,	(Indeed)
	"She took her silver bracelet off,	(Indeed)
2615	"And gave it to a person here,	(Indeed)
	Saying when you dig a distant-day well,	
	"When a distant-day thirst descends, then drink.	(Indeed)
	"Thus have I come with my army,	(Indeed)
	"And we have not yet made a crossing."[8]	(Indeed)
2620	The Boatman patriarch responded:	(Indeed)
	"Ah! Is it you who are Son-Jara?"	(Indeed)
	The reply, "It is I who am Son-Jara."	(Indeed)
	"You are Son-Jara?"	(Indeed)
	"Indeed I am Son-Jara!"	(Indeed)
2625	"It is you who are Nare Magan Kònatè?	(Indeed)
	"If God wills,	
	"With the break of day,	
	"Tomorrow will the army cross."	(Indeed)

	At the break of day,	(Indeed)
2630	The Boatman patriarch, Sasagalò the Tall,	(Indeed)
	He brought Son-Jara across.	(Indeed)
	The Wizard advanced with his army.	(Indeed)
	They fell upon Sumamuru at Dark Forest.	(Indeed)
	But he drove them off.	(Indeed)
2635	Susu Mountain Sumamuru drove Son-Jara off.	(Indeed)
	He went and founded a town called Anguish.[9]	(Indeed)
	Of which the bards did sing:	
	"We will not move to Anguish.	(Indeed)
	"Should one go to Anguish.	
2640	"Should not anguish he endure.	(Indeed)
	"Then nothing would he reap.	(Indeed)
	"We will not move to Anguish."	(Indeed)

	That Anguish,	(Indeed)
	The Maninka sing this of it, my father:	
2645	"There is no joy in you."	(Indeed)
	Our name for that town is Anguish (Nyani).	(Indeed)

	The Wizard advanced with his army.	(Indeed)
	They went to fall on Susu Mountain Sumamuru.	(Indeed)
	He drove Son-Jara off again.	(Indeed)
2650	He went to found the town called Resolve.	(Indeed)

8. Son-Jara reproaches Sasagalò the Tall for not keeping his part of the bargain with his mother. 9. A metaphor for Son-Jara's mental condition as a result of his setback. The names of the other locations he founds have a more general moral significance.

The bards thus sing of it:
"We will not move to Resolve.
"Should one move to Resolve,
"Should not resolve he entertain,
2655 "Then nothing would he reap. (Indeed)
"We will not move to Resolve." (Indeed)
The Wizard advanced again. (Indeed)
He with his bards advanced. (Indeed)
They went to fall on Susu Mountain Sumamuru. (Indeed)
2660 Sumamuru drove him off with his bards. (Indeed)
They went to found the town called Sharing.[1] (Indeed)
And they sang:
Let us move to the Wizard's town, my father.
"To Sharing, (Indeed)
2665 "The town where sharing is not done,
"Founding that town is not easy." (Indeed)
They went to found the town called Sharing. (Indeed)

Son-Jara's flesh-and-blood-sister, Sugulun
Kulunkan, (Indeed)
She said, "O Magan Son-Jara, (Indeed)
2670 "One person cannot fight this war.[2] (Indeed)
"Let me go seek Sumamuru. (Indeed)
"Were I then to reach him,
"To you I will deliver him, (Indeed)
"So that the folk of the Manden be yours, (Indeed)
2675 "And all the Mandenland you shield." (Indeed)
Sugulun Kulunkan arose, (Indeed)
And went up to the gates of Sumamuru's fortress: (Indeed)
"Manda and Sama Kantè! (Indeed)
"Kukuba and Bantamba
2680 *"Nyani-nyani and Kamasiga!* (Indeed)
"Brave child of the Warrior,
"And Deliverer-of-the Benign. (Indeed)
"Sumamuru came amongst us
"With pants of human skin. (Indeed)
"Sumamuru came amongst us
"With shirt of human skin. (Indeed)
2685 *"Sumamuru came amongst us*
"With helm of human skin. (Indeed)
"Come open the gates, Susu Mountain
Sumamuru! (Indeed)

2690 "Come make me your bed companion!" (Indeed)
Sumamuru came to the gates: (Indeed)
"What manner of person are you?" (Indeed)
"It is I Sugulun Kulunkan!" (Indeed)
"Well, now, Sugulun Kulunkan, (Indeed)
2695 "If you have come to trap me, (Indeed)
"To turn me over to some person, (Indeed)

---

1. That is, partial success.   2. It cannot be won by arms alone. Like Judith and Dalila in the Bible, Son-Jara's sister intends to employ her feminine charms in the struggle against her brother's enemy.

       "Know that none can ever vanquish me.   (Indeed)
       "I have found the Manden secret,   (Indeed)
       "And made the Manden sacrifice,   (Indeed)
2700   "And in five score millet stalks placed it,   (Indeed)
       "And buried them here in the earth.   (Indeed)
       " 'Tis I who found the Manden secret,   (Indeed)
       "And made the Manden sacrifice,   (Indeed)
       "And in a red piebald bull did place it,   (Indeed)
2705   "And buried it here in the earth.   (Indeed)
       "Know that none can vanquish me.   (Indeed)
       " 'Tis I who found the Manden secret   (Indeed)
       "And made a sacrifice to it.   (Indeed)
       "And in a pure white cock did place it.   (Indeed)
2710   "Were you to kill it,   (Indeed)
       "And uproot some barren groundnut plants, (Indeed)
       "And strip them of their leaves,
       "And spread them round the fortress,   (Indeed)
       "And uproot more barren peanut plants,   (Indeed)
2715   "And fling them into the fortress,   (Indeed)
       "Only then can I be vanquished,"[3]   (Indeed)
       His mother sprang forward at that: (Indeed)
       "Heh! Susu Mountain Sumamuru!   (Indeed)
       "Never tell all to a woman,
2720   "To a one-night woman!   (Indeed)
       "The woman is not safe, Sumamuru."   (Indeed)
       Sumamuru sprang towards his mother,   (Indeed)
       And came and seized his mother,   (Indeed)
       And slashed off her breast with a knife, magasi![4] (Indeed)
2725   She went and got the old menstrual cloth.   (Indeed)
       "Ah! Sumamuru!" she swore.   (Indeed)
       "If your birth was ever a fact,
       "I have cut your old menstrual cloth!"[5]

       O Kalajula Sangoyi Mamunaka!   (Indeed)
2730   He lay Sugulun Kulunkan down on the bed. (Indeed)
       After one week had gone by,
       Sugulun Kulunkan spoke up: (Indeed)
       "Ah, my husband,   (Indeed)
       "Will you not let me go to the Manden,   (Indeed)
2735   "That I may get my bowls and spoons,[6]
       "For me to build my household here?   (Indeed)
       From that day to this,
       Should you marry a woman in Mandenland, (Indeed)
       When the first week has passed,
2740   She will take a backward glance,   (Indeed)
       And this is what that custom means.   (Yes, Fa-Digi, that's
                                 the truth)

---

3. Sumamuru's bravado here is in keeping with his vaingloriousness as it comes through in the narrative.
4. The same words used for Jata Magan Kòndè's treatment of his sister, Du Kamisa. **5.** The cloth in which he was wrapped at his birth, stained with the blood of parturition. By tearing it up, she disowns her son. **6.** It is customary among the Manding for a new bride to return to her home a last time to collect her belongings before settling into her new life. The passage traces the custom to the incident recounted here.

Sugulun returned to reveal those secrets
To her flesh-and-blood-brother, Son-Jara.   (Indeed)
The sacrifices did Son-Jara thus discover.   (Indeed)
2745   The sacrifices did he thus discover.[7]   (Indeed)
Now five score wives had Susu Mountain Sumamuru,   (Indeed)
One hundred wives had he.   (Indeed)
His nephew, Fa-Koli, had but one,[8]   (Indeed)

        . . .   (Mmm)
2750   And Sumamuru, five score!   (Indeed)
When a hundred bowls they would cook
To make the warriors' meal,   (Indeed)
Fa-Koli's wife alone would one hundred cook
To make the warriors' meal,   (That's the truth, eh,
                                                      Fa-Digi, indeed,
                                                              indeed)

2755   "Let the fonio[9] increase!   (Indeed)
"Let the rice increase!   (Indeed)
"Let the groundnuts increase!   (Indeed)
"Let the groundpeas increase!   (Indeed)
"Let the beans increase!"[1]   (Indeed)
2760   She took them all one by one,   (Indeed)
And put them all in one pot,   (Indeed)
And in that pot they all were cooked,   (Indeed)
And served it all in her calabash,   (Indeed)
And all of this for Fa-Koli.   (Indeed)

[Sumamuru takes Fa-Koli's wife, causing a rift between him and his nephew, who
defects to Son-Jara.]

        Hero-of-the-Original-Clans and Magan
2770   Sukudana![2]   (Indeed)
Son-Jara called out,   (Indeed)
"Who in the Manden will make this sacrifice?"[3]   (Indeed)
"I shall!" Fa-Koli's reply.   (Indeed)
"The thing that drove me away,   (Indeed)
"And took my only wife from me,
2775   "So that not even a weak wife have I now,   (Indeed)
"I shall make the whole sacrifice!"   (Indeed)
Fa-Koli thus made the whole sacrifice.   (Indeed)
He came and reported to the Wizard.
Son-Jara then called out: (Indeed)
2780   "Who will bring us face to face,
"That we may join in battle?"   (Indeed)
"I shall," Fa-Koli's reply.   (Indeed)
On that Fa-Koli rose up.   (Indeed)
He arrived in Dark Forest.   (Indeed)

---

7. To be acted on later.   8. In contrast to Sumamuru's "five score," which emphasizes his sexual desire.
9. A cereal.   1. Fa-Koli's wife's incantations over the food she has prepared.   2. Praise name of Fa-
Koli.   3. Revealed by Son-Jara's sister (see line 2742).

2785 As he espied the rooftops of Sumamuru's city, Dark
          Forest,   (Indeed)
      With every single step he took,   (Indeed)
      He thrust a dart[4] into the earth,   (Indeed)
      And in a tree fork laid another.   (Indeed, yes, Fa-Digi)
      With every single step he took,   (Indeed)
2790 He thrust a dart into the earth,   (Indeed)
      And in a tree fork laid another,[5]   (That's the truth)
      Until he entered the very gates,
      Until he entered the city.   (Indeed)
      O, Garan!   (Indeed)
2795 The daughter given by King Dankaran Tuman,[6]   (Indeed)
      Given to Susu Mountain Sumamuru,   (Indeed)
      That he should go and kill Son-Jara,   (Indeed)
      Fa-Koli went and seized that maiden,   (Indeed)
2800 "Come! Your uncle has left Mèma!   (Indeed)
      "Your uncle has summoned you.   (Indeed)
      "Your uncle has now come. He has left Mèma!"   (Indeed)
      The people of Susu pursued them: biri biri biri.   (Indeed)
      They came attacking after them: yrrrrrrr!   (Indeed)
2805 With every single step he took,   (Indeed)
      He drew a war dart from the earth,
      And hurled it at the Susu,   (Indeed)
      And from a tree fork grabbed another,   (Indeed)
      And hurled it at the Susu,   (Indeed)
2810 "Heh! Come to my aid!   (Indeed)
      "Heaven and Earth, come aid me!
      "Susu Mountain Sumamuru is after
          me!"   (Indeed, yes, father)
      He retreated on and on.[7]
      He drew a war dart from the earth,
2815 And hurled it at the Susu,   (Indeed)
      And from a tree fork grabbed another,   (Indeed)
      And fired it at the Susu.   (Indeed)
      "Heh! Come to my aid!   (Indeed)
      "Heaven and Earth, come to my aid!
2820 "Susu Mountain Sumamuru is after me!"   (That's the truth)

      At that, the Susu said, my father,   (Indeed)
      "If we do not fall back from Fa-Koli,   (Indeed)
      "Fa-Koli will bring all our folk to an end![8]   (Indeed)
      "Let us fall back from Fa-Koli!   (Indeed)
2825   Hero-of-the-Original-Clans and Magan Sukudana.
          . . .   (That's the truth)
      And thus they fell back from Fa-Koli.   (Indeed)
      They readied themselves for battle.   (Indeed)
      Susu Mountain Sumamuru came forward.   (Indeed)
2830 And taking his favorite wife,
      On the saddle's cantle sat her,   (Indeed)

---

4. It will soon be clear that this is a magic dart.   5. The motif here is a heroicized variant of the Hansel and Gretel story.   6. Caress-of-Hot-Fire.   7. Clearly as a diversionary tactic to draw out the enemy lines.   8. He is single-handedly destroying the enemy ranks with his magic dart.

	With golden ladle and silver ladle.	(Indeed)
	Son-Jara attacked and encircled the walls.	(Indeed)
	He had split the enemy army,[9]	(Indeed)
2835	And taken the fortress gates.	(Indeed)
	Susu Mountain Sumamuru charged out at a gallop.[1]	(Indeed)
	Fa-Koli,	(Indeed)
	With Tura-Magan-and-Kanke-jan,	(Indeed)
	And Bee-King-of-the-Wilderness,	(Indeed)
2840	And Fa-Kanda Tunandi,	(Indeed)
	And Sura, the Jawara patriarch,	(Indeed)
	And Son-Jara,	(Indeed)
	They all chased after Sumamuru.	(True)
	They arrived at Kukuba.	(Indeed)
2845	He told them, "I am not ready!"	(Indeed)
	They let him go:[2]	(Indeed)
	"Prepare yourself!"	(Indeed)
	They arrived at Kamasiga,[3]	(Indeed)
	"I am not ready."	(Indeed)
2850	They let him go:	(Indeed)
	"Prepare yourself!"	(Indeed)
	They arrived at Nyani-Nyani.	(Indeed)
	Said, "I am not ready."	(Indeed)
	They let him go again:	
2855	"Prepare yourself!"	(Indeed)
	They arrived at Bantanba,	(Indeed)
	"I am not ready."	(Indeed)
	And again they let him go:	
	"Prepare yourself!"	(Indeed)
2860	And still they attacked him from behind,	
	Behind Susu Mountain Sumamuru.	(That's the truth, yes, Fa-Digi)

	Sumamuru crossed the river at Kulu-Kòrò,[4]	(Indeed)
	And had his favored wife dismount,	(Indeed)
	And gave her the ladle of gold,	
2865	Saying that he would drink,	(Indeed)
	Saying else the thirst would kill him.	(That's the truth)
	The favored wife took the ladle of gold,	(Indeed)
	And filled it up with water,	(Indeed)
	And to Sumamuru stretched her hand,	
2870	And passed the water to him.	(Indeed)
	Fa-Koli with his darts charged up:	
	"O Colossus,	(Indeed)
	"We have taken you!	(That's the truth)
	"We have taken you, Colossus!	
2875	"We have taken you, Colossus!	
	"We have taken you!"	(Indeed)
	Tura Magan held him at bladepoint.	(Indeed)

9. Thanks to Fa-Koli.   1. Forcefully breaking out of the siege laid to his fortress.   2. This can only mean that Sumamuru escaped their clutches.   3. The places named are the scenes of the successive engagements between the two armies.   4. A village near Bamako, on the river Niger. In some versions of the epic, Sumamuru disappears into the hillside on a site near this village.

Sura, the Jawara patriarch held him at bladepoint.   (Indeed)
Fa-Koli came up and held him at bladepoint.
2880   Son-Jara held him at bladepoint:[5]   (Indeed)
    "We have taken you, Colossus!   (That's the truth)
    "We have taken you!"   (Indeed)
Sumamuru dried up on the spot: nyònyòwu![6]   (Indeed)
He has become the sacred fetish of Kulu-Kòrò.   (Indeed)
2885   The Bambara worship that now,[7] my father.
Susu Mountain Sumamuru,
He became that sacred fetish.   (That's the truth,
                        indeed, father, yes,
                              yes, yes, yes)

FROM EPISODE 7

Kanbi

Biribiriba turned back, Son-Jara!   (Indeed)
    Stranger-in-the-Morning, Chief-in-the Afternoon![8]   (Indeed)
2890   Great-Host-Slaying-Stranger!
Stump-in-the-Dark-of-Night!   (Indeed)
Should you bump against it,
It will bump against you!   (That's the truth)
The Granary Guard Dog.   (Indeed)
2895   The thing discerning not the stranger,
Nor the familiar.
Should it come upon any person,
He will be bitten.   (That's the truth)
Kirikara Watita!   (Indeed)
2900   Adversity's true place!
Man's reason and woman's are not the same.
Pretty words and truth are not the same.   (That's the truth)
No matter how long the road,
It always comes out at someone's home.[9]   (Indeed)
2905   The Nyani king with his army came forward,   (Indeed)
Saying the Manden belonged to him,   (That's the truth)
Saying no more was he rival to any,   (That's the truth)
Saying the Manden belonged to him.   (That's the truth)

He found the Kuyatè patriarch[1] with tendons cut,   (Indeed)
2910   And beckoned him to rise, "Let us go!   (Indeed)
"Bala Faseke Kuyatè, arise. Let us go!"   (Indeed)
He lurched forward.   (Indeed)
Saying he would rise.
He fell back to the ground again,   (Indeed)
2915   His two Achilles tendons cut: (Indeed)
"O Nare Magan Kònatè!"   (Indeed)
"Arise and let us go!   (Indeed)

---

5. We must imagine the warriors crowding in on Sumamuru from various directions. Note too that they are all given credit for his final defeat.   6. Ideophone for the drying up.   7. Sumamuru is still revered among his people, who have kept his memory alive in a counterepic devoted to him as well as in various forms of ritual.   8. With his victory, Son-Jara is suddenly transformed from a homeless vagrant into a powerful ruler.   9. A proverb: everything has a beginning and an end.   1. Bala Faseke.

I have no rival in Mandenland now!	(That's the truth)
"The Manden is mine alone."	(Indeed)
2920 He lurched forward,	(Indeed)
Saying that he would rise.	(Indeed)
He fell back to the ground again.	(Indeed)
"Had Sumamuru no child?" they queried.	(Indeed)
"Here is his first born son," the reply.	(Indeed)
2925 "What is his name?"	(Indeed)
"His name is Mansa Saman."	(Indeed)
They summoned Mansa Saman	(Indeed)
And brought forth Dòka the Cat,	
And placed him on Mansa Saman's shoulders,[2]	(Indeed)
2930 Laying the balaphone on his head, serew!	(Indeed)
He followed after the Wizard:	(Indeed)
"Biribiriba!	(Indeed)
"O Nare Magan Kònatè!	(Indeed)
"*Entered Kaya,*	
"*Son-Jara entered Kaya.*	(That's the truth)
2935 "*Entered Kaya,*	
"*Sugulun's Ma'an entered Kaya.*[3]	(Yes, Fa-Digi)
"If they took no gold,	(Indeed)
"If they took no measure of gold for the Wizard,	(Indeed)
"The reason for Son-Jara's coming to the Manden,	
2940 "To stabilize the Manden,	
"To improve the people's lot:[4] jon jon!	(That's the truth)
"O Sorcerer, you have come for the Manden people!	(Indeed)
"O Nare Magan Kònatè,	(Indeed)
"O Khalif Magan Kònatè!"	(That's the truth)
2945 They arrived back in the Manden.	(Indeed)
The Sorcerer ruled over everyone.	(Indeed)
He continued on at that.[5]	(Indeed)

[Although he has regained his homeland, Son-Jara still must establish his authority over the neighboring territories. A quarrel with the Jolof king provides him with a pretext for a new campaign for the expansion of his domain. The Jolof king has seized a large herd of horses Son-Jara has sent his retainers to collect within Jolof territory and sends him instead a pack of dogs, with the message that he knows Son-Jara not as king but only as a mere hunter ("a runner of dogs"). This challenge angers Son-Jara, who summons his generals to a council of war.]

In turn, the warriors swore their fealty:[6]	(Indeed)
"Let me the battle-master be!"	(Indeed)
Fa-Koli and Tura Magan swore their fealty.	(Indeed)
"Let me lead the army!" Fa-Koli adjured.	(That's the truth)
"Let me lead the army!" Tura Magan adjured.	(Indeed)
3000 Son-Jara finally spoke,	(Indeed)
"'Tis I who will lead the army,	(Indeed)
"And go to Dark Jòlòf land."	(Indeed)

2. As a sign of his humiliation.   3. The refrain of a song celebrating Son-Jara's triumphal return to the Manden.   4. The ideological function of the epic becomes fully evident here.   5. That is, until the end of his reign.   6. Made necessary by the defiance of the Jolof king.

	O Nare Magan Kònatè!	(Indeed)
	Tura Magan plunged into grief,	(Indeed)
3005	And went to the graveyard to dig his grave,	(Indeed)
	And laid himself down in his grave.[7]	(Indeed)
	The bards came forth: "O Nare Magan Kònatè,	(Indeed)
	"If you don't go see Tura Magan,	(Indeed)
	"Your army will not succeed!"	(Indeed)
3010	He sent the bards forth	
	That they should summon Tura Magan.	
	And so the bards went forth.	(Indeed)
	But Tura Magan they could not find.	(That's the truth)
	Son-Jara came and stood in the graveyard:	(Indeed)
3015	*"Bugu Turu and Bugu Bò!*	(Indeed)
	"Muke Musa and Muke Dantuman!	(Indeed)
	"Juru Kèta and Juru Moriba!	(Indeed)
	"Tunbila the Manden Slave!	(Indeed)
3020	*"Kalabila, the Manden Slave!*	(Indeed)
	"Sana Fa-Buren, Danka Fa-Buren!	(Indeed)
	"Dark-Pilgrim and Light-Pilgrim![8]	(Indeed)
	"Ah! Bards,	(Indeed)
	"Let us give the army to Tura Magan,	(Indeed)
3025	"To the Slave-of-the-Tomb,[9] Tura Magan,	(Indeed)
	"O Tura Magan-and-Kanke-jan!"	(That's the truth)
	Tura Magan spoke out,	(Indeed)
	"That is the best of all things to my ear!"	(Indeed)
	To Tura Magan they gave quiver and bow.	(Indeed)
3030	Tura Magan advanced to cross the river here,	(Indeed)
	At the Passage-of-Tura-Magan.[1]	(Indeed)
	A member of the troop cried out,	(Indeed)
	"Hey! The war to which we go,	(Indeed)
	"That war will not be easy!	(Indeed)
3035	"Ninety iron drums has the Dark Jòlòf King.	(Indeed)
	"No drum like this has the Manden.	(Indeed)
	"Nor balaphone has the Manden.	(Indeed)
	"There is no such thing in the Manden,	(Indeed)
	"Save the Jawara patriarch, Sita Fata,	(Indeed)
3040	"Save when he puffs out his cheeks,	(Indeed)
	"Making with them like drum and balaphone,[2]	
	"To go awaken the Nyani King.	(Indeed)
	"This battle will not be easy!"	(Indeed)
	But they drove this agitator off.	(Indeed)
3045	Saying better in the bush a frightened brave	
	Than a loudmouthed agitator.	(That's the truth)
	He went back across the river,	(Indeed)
	At the place they call Salakan,[3]	(Indeed)
	And Ford-of-the-Frightened.	(Indeed)
3050	The Ford-of-the-Frightened-Braves.	(Indeed)

7. A sign of his disappointment. 8. This passage is a reference to the pilgrimage he is reputed to have made to Mecca, from which he is also said to have brought magical powers. The names are of Tura Magan's ancestors, invoked by Son-Jara in appealing to him. 9. This is the "Manden Slave" mentioned in line 3020. 1. A ford across the Senegal River. 2. The inspirational role of bards is once again affirmed. 3. A ford whose name and significance are explained in lines 3049–50.

Tura Magan with battle met.	(Indeed)
He slayed that dog-giving king,[4]	(Indeed)
Saying he was but running the dogs.[5]	(That's the truth)
Tura Magan with army marched on,	(Indeed)
3055 He went to slay Nyani Mansa,	
Saying he was but running the dogs.	(That's the truth)
Tura Magan with the army marched on,	(Indeed)
He slayed the Sanumu King,	
Saying that he was but running the dogs,	(Indeed)
3060 He slayed Ba-dugu King	(Indeed)
Saying he was but running the dogs,	(Indeed)
And marched on thus through Jòlòf land.[6]	(Indeed)
Their name for stone is Jòlòf.	(Indeed)
Once there was this king . . . ,	(Indeed)
3065 The stone there that is red,	(Indeed)
The Wòlòf call it Jòlòf.	(Indeed)
There once was a king in that country, my father,	
Called King of Dark Jòlòfland.	(Indeed)
3070 And that is the meaning of this.	(That's the truth)
He slayed that Dark Jòlòf King,	(Indeed)
Severing his great head at his shoulders,	(Indeed)
From whence comes the Wòlòf name, Njòp![7]	(Indeed)
They are Taraweres.	(Indeed)
Sane and Mane,[8]	(Indeed)
3075 They are Taraweres.	(Indeed)
Mayga, they are Taraweres.	(Indeed)
Magaraga, they are Taraweres.	(Indeed)
Tura Magan-and-Kanke-jan,	
He with the army marched on,	
3080 To destroy the golden sword and the tall throne.[9]	(That's the truth)
This by the hand of Tura Magan-and-Kanke-jan.	
Kirikisa, Spear-of-Access, Spear-of Service!	(Indeed)
Ah! Garan!	(Indeed)
Let us leave the words[1] right here.	(That's the truth, indeed, it's over now!)

---

4. A reference to the Jolof king's insult.   5. That is, out hunting with his dogs. A pun on the previous line, expressing Tura Magan's pleasure in waging war.   6. In present-day Senegal, to the west of the original Manden homeland. Note the way the repetitions give a terse economy to the narration.
7. A common Wòlòf surname. This is an example of folk etymology. *Njòp* can also be spelled "Diop" and "Dyob," and in Gambia, "Job."   8. Two important clans in Senegal and in Gambia; the names often serve as surnames.   9. Emblems of the Jolof king.   1. In many African languages the word *word* refers not only to ordinary speech but also to reflective thought in general, especially as conveyed in a proverb or a story.

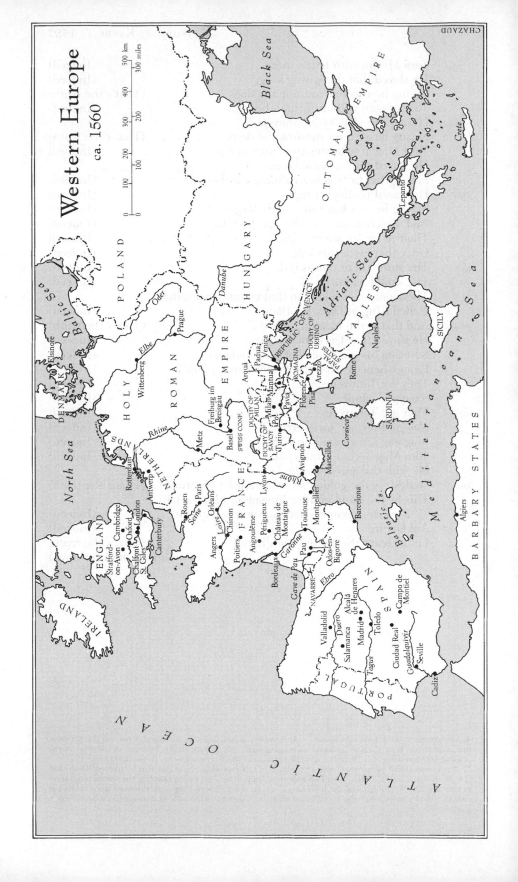

Western Europe
ca. 1560

0 100 200 300 400 500 km
0 100 200 300 miles

CHAZAUD

Baltic Sea

North Sea

POLAND

DENMARK

Elsinore

Elbe

Wittenberg

Prague

Oder

Danube

HOLY   ROMAN   EMPIRE

HUNGARY

Freiburg im
Breisgau

Arquà

Rhine

Metz

Basel

SWISS CONF.

Padua

Mantua

Venice

REPUBLIC OF VENICE

DUCHY OF
MILAN

Milan

Pavia

DUCHY OF
SAVOY

Turin

Adriatic Sea

ROMAGNA

Florence

Arezzo

DUCHY OF
URBINO

PAPAL
STATES

Pisa

Rome

NAPLES

Naples

Lepanto

OTTOMAN   EMPIRE

Black Sea

Crete

NETHERLANDS

Rotterdam

Antwerp

Avignon

Marseilles

Corsica

SARDINIA

SICILY

Mediterranean   Sea

Algiers

BARBARY   STATES

IRELAND

ENGLAND

Stratford-
on-Avon   Cambridge

Oxford

Chalfont   London
St. Giles

Canterbury

Rouen

Paris

Seine

Orléans

Loire

Angers

Chinon

FRANCE

Lyons

Rhône

Poitiers

Angoulême

Périgueux

Château de
Montaigne

Toulouse

Montpellier

Barcelona

Bordeaux

Garonne

Gave de Pau

Pau

Odos-en-
Bigorre

NAVARRE

Ebro

Balearic Is.

SPAIN

Valladolid

Duero

Salamanca

Alcalá
de Henares

Madrid

Toledo

Tagus

Ciudad Real

Campo de
Montiel

Guadalquivir

Seville

Cadiz

PORTUGAL

ATLANTIC   OCEAN

The Renaissance
in Europe

"All the world's a stage, / And all the men and women merely players": Shakespeare's famous comparison of human beings to actors playing their various roles in the great theater of the world conjures up the exhilarating liberty and mobility we associate with the memorable characters of Renaissance literature. Because "merely" meant, in Shakespeare's day, "wholly" and "entirely," the line evokes a lively sense of the men and women of that world performing their roles with the gusto of actors. Their social roles as princes, clowns, thieves, or housewives appear, from one angle, exciting opportunities for the characters to explore. Yet such roles are also clearly confining: Renaissance men and women were born into societies that strictly regulated their actions and even their clothing—only actors had the right to vary their garb and dress above their station. Whether Renaissance subjects relished the pleasures of playing or resented the constraints of their social roles is a subject often taken up in the literature of the day.

When Renaissance writers explore the relationship of their characters to the social roles the characters play, they partly follow in the tradition exemplified in the Middle Ages by Chaucer's *Canterbury Tales*. Yet the most memorable characters of Renaissance literature enjoy greater autonomy and more fully realized personalities than Chaucer's pilgrims. Characters like Cervantes's idealistic but mad Don Quixote or Shakespeare's brooding Hamlet are presented in acts of thought, fantasy, planning, doubt, and internal debate. Deliberating with others and themselves about what to do seems at least as important to these characters as putting their plans into action.

One reason for this shift toward internal, mental, and psychological portraiture is that Renaissance authors, like the characters they invented, inhabited a world of such widespread revolutionary change that they could not passively receive the traditional wisdom of previous ages. When Nicolaus Copernicus (1473–1543) discovered that the earth moves around the sun and when Galileo Galilei (1564–1642) turned his telescope up to the heavens, the Renaissance mind had to reconceive the nature of the universe and creation. When Christopher Columbus (1451–1506) sailed to what he thought were the Indies, he proved that the earth was not flat and introduced a new world to Europe, which began for the first time to think of itself as the Old World. Around the time that Columbus was sailing to America, humanist scholars in Italy began to use new scholarly methods that gave them fuller access to the cultural legacy of the ancient world of Greece and Rome and a new sense of their own place in history. On scientific, geographical, and scholarly fronts, the world of Renaissance Europe was undergoing revolutionary change.

The new discoveries' challenge to European and human centrality in the world and in creation met with fervent, if varied, responses. In 1633 the Inquisition forced Galileo to repudiate the Copernican theory that the earth rotates around the sun. In his dialogue *The City of the Sun* (1602) Galileo's friend and supporter Tommasso Campanella (1568–1639) optimistically asserted that the three great inventions of his day—the compass, the printing press, and the gun—were "signs of the union of the entire world." François Rabelais, less sanguine about the idea of world union enforced by the gun and artillery, placed his hopes for peace only on the printing press, an instrument for intellectual deliberation and the dissemination of ideas. In *The First Anniversary*, John Donne (1572–1631), on the other hand, focused on the psychological threat of the new discoveries and theories to individuals unable to cope with so much uncertainty:

> The new philosophy calls all in doubt,
> The element of fire is quite put out;
> The sun is lost and the earth, and no man's wit
> Can well direct him where to look for it.
> And freely men confess that this world's spent,
> When in the planets and the firmament
> They seek so many new; they see that this
> Is crumbled out again to his atomies . . .

In Donne's poem, the new discoveries amount to a second creation, so radical is the new theory of the world's construction. For Renaissance intellectuals and for the literary characters they created, there was almost literally no firm ground to stand on as they moved through life in an increasingly complex and uncertain world. Although received wisdom appeared from one angle like an anchor in a sea of change, from another it seemed like a shackle to error: it is no wonder, then, that the reasoning and choices of the characters in Renaissance poetry and prose began to matter enormously.

As with other terms that have currency in cultural history (for instance, *Romanticism*), the usefulness of the term *Renaissance* depends on its keeping a certain degree of elasticity. The literal meaning of the word—"rebirth"—suggests that one impulse toward the great intellectual and artistic achievements of the period came from the example of ancient culture or, even better, from a certain vision that the artists and intellectuals of the Renaissance possessed of the world of antiquity, which was "reborn" through their work. Especially in the more mature phase of the Renaissance, these individuals were aware of having brought about a vigorous renewal, which they openly associated with the cult of antiquity. The restoration of ancient canons was regarded as a glorious achievement to be set beside the thrilling discoveries of their own age. "For now," Rabelais writes through his Gargantua,

> all courses of study have been restored, and the acquisition of languages has become supremely honorable: Greek, without which it is shameful for any man to be called a scholar; Hebrew; Chaldean; and Latin. And in my time we have learned how to produce wonderfully elegant and accurate printed books, just as, on the other hand, we have also learned (by diabolic suggestion) how to make cannon and other such fearful weapons.

Machiavelli, whose infatuation with antiquity is as typical a trait as his better-advertised political realism, suggests in the opening of his *Discourses on the First Ten Books of Livy* (1513–21) that rulers should be as keen on the imitation of ancient "virtues" as are artists, lawyers, and the scientists: "The civil laws are nothing but decisions given by the ancient jurisconsults. . . . And what is the science of medicine, but the experience of ancient physicians, which their successors have taken for their guide?"

Elasticity should likewise be maintained in regard to the chronological span of the Renaissance as a "movement" extending through varying periods of years and as including phases and traits of the epoch that is otherwise known as the Middle Ages (and vice versa). The peak of the Renaissance can be shown to have occurred at different times in different countries, the "movement" having had its inception in Italy, where its impact was at first most remarkable in the visual arts, while in England, for instance, it developed later and its main achievements were in literature, particularly the drama. The meaning of the term has also, in the course of time, widened considerably. Nowadays it conveys, to say the least, a general notion of artistic creativity, of extraordinary zest for life and knowledge, of sensory delight in opulence and magnificence, of spectacular individual achievement, thus extending far beyond the literal meaning of rebirth and the strict idea of a revival and imitation of antiquity.

Even in its stricter sense, however, the term continues to have its function. The degree to which European intellectuals of the period possessed and were possessed by the writings of the ancient world is difficult for the average modern reader to realize. For these writers references to classical mythology, philosophy, and literature are not ornaments or affectations. Along with references to the Scriptures they are part, and a major part, of their mental equipment and way of thinking. When Machiavelli writes to a friend: "I get up before daylight, prepare my birdlime, and go out with a bundle of cages on my back, so that I look like Geta when he came back from the harbor with the books of Amphitryo" the words have by no means the sound of erudite self-gratification that they might have nowadays. Within Machiavelli's intellectual circle, they are wholly natural, familiar, unassuming.

When we are overcome by sudden emotion, our first exclamations are likely to be in the language most familiar to us—our dialect, if we happen to have one. Montaigne relates of himself that when once his father unexpectedly fell back in his arms in a swoon, the first words he uttered under the emotion of that experience were in Latin. Similarly Benvenuto Cellini, the Italian sculptor, goldsmith, and autobiographer, talking to his patron and expressing admiration of a Greek statue, establishes with the ancient artist an immediate contact, a proud familiarity:

> I cried to the Duke: "My lord, this is a statue in Greek marble, and it is a miracle of beauty. . . . If your Excellency permits, I should like to restore it—head and arms and feet. . . . It is certainly not my business to patch up statues, that being the trade of botchers, who do it in all conscience villainously ill; yet the art displayed by this great master of antiquity cries out to me to help him."

The people who, starting at about the middle of the fourteenth century, gave new impulse to this emulation of the classics are often referred to as humanists. The word in that sense is related to what we call the humanities, and the humanities at that time were Latin and Greek. Every cultivated person wrote and spoke Latin, with the result that a Western community of intellectuals could exist, a spiritual "republic of letters" above individual nations. There was also a considerable amount of individual contact among humanists. In glancing at the biographies of the authors included in this section, the extensiveness of their travels may strike us as a remarkable or even surprising fact, considering the hardships and slowness of traveling during those centuries.

The archetype of literature as a vocation is often said to be Petrarch—the first author in this section—who anticipated certain ideals of the high Renaissance: a lofty conception of the literary art, a taste for the good life, a basic pacifism, and a strong sense of the memories and glories of antiquity. In this last respect, what should be emphasized is the imaginative quality, the visionary impulse with which the writers of the period looked at those memories—the same vision and imagination with which they regarded such contemporary heroes as the great navigators and astronomers. The Renaissance view of the cultural monuments of antiquity was far from being that of the philologist and the antiquarian; indeed, familiarity was facilitated by the very lack of a scientific sense of history. We find the visionary and imaginative element not only in the creations of poets and dramatists but also in the works of political writers: as when Machiavelli describes himself entering, through his reading, the

> ancient courts of ancient men, where, being lovingly received, I feed on that food which alone is mine, and which I was born for; I am not ashamed to speak with

them and to ask the reasons for their actions, and they courteously answer me. For . . . hours I feel no boredom and forget every worry; I do not fear poverty, and death does not terrify me. I give myself completely over to the ancients.

Imitation of antiquity acquires, in Machiavelli and many others, a special quality; whereas "academic" imitations transcribe, Machiavelli plunges into vital and reciprocal communication—even communion—with the ancients.

The vision of an ancient age of glorious intellectual achievement that is "now" brought to life again implies, of course, however roughly, the idea of an intervening "middle" time, by comparison ignorant and dark. The hackneyed, vastly inaccurate notion that the "light" of the Renaissance broke through a long "night" of the Middle Ages was not devised by subsequent "enlightened" centuries; it was held by the humanist scholars of the Renaissance themselves. In his genealogy of giants from Grangousier to Gargantua to Pantagruel, Rabelais conveniently represents the generations of modern learning with their varying degrees of enlightenment. Thus Gargantua writes to his son:

> Though my late father of worthy memory, Grandgousier, devoted all his energy to those things of which I might take the fullest advantage, and from which I might acquire the most sensible knowledge, and though my own effort matched his—or even surpassed it—still, as you know very well, it was neither so fit nor so right a time for learning as exists today, nor was there an abundance of such teachers as you have had. It was still a murky, dark time, oppressed by the misery, unhappiness, and disasters of the Goths, who destroyed all worthwhile literature of every sort. But divine goodness has let me live to see light and dignity returned to humanistic studies, and to see such an improvement, indeed, that it would be hard for me to qualify for the very first class of little schoolboys—I who, in my prime, had the reputation (and not in error) of the most learned man of my day.

The combination of self-deprecation, aspiration, and arrogance aptly characterizes the period's sense of its own achievements and its standing in relation to antiquity and the Middle Ages.

Definitions of the Renaissance must also take account of the period's preoccupation with this life rather than with the life beyond. The contrast of an ideal medieval man or woman, whose mode of action is basically oriented toward the thought of the afterlife (and who therefore conceives of life on earth as transient and preparatory) with an ideal Renaissance man or woman, possessing and cherishing earthly interests so concrete and self-sufficient that the very realization of the ephemeral quality of life is to him or her nothing but an added spur to its immediate enjoyment—this is a useful contrast even though it represents an enormous oversimplification of the facts.

The same emphasis on the immediate and tangible is reflected in the earthly, amoral, and aesthetic character of what we may call the Renaissance code of behavior. According to this "code," human action is judged not in terms of right and wrong, of good and evil (as it is judged when life is viewed as a moral "test," with reward or punishment in the afterlife), but in terms of its present concrete validity and effectiveness, of the delight it affords, of its memorability and its beauty. In that sense a good deal that is typical of the Renaissance, from architecture to poetry, from sculpture to rhetoric, may be related to a taste for the harmonious and the memorable, for the spectacular effect, for the successful striking of a pose. Individual human action, seeking as it were in itself its own reward, finds justification in its formal appropriateness; in its being a well-rounded achievement, perfect of its kind; in the zest and gusto with which it is, here and now, performed; and, finally, in its proving worthy of remaining as a testimony to the performer's power on earth.

A convenient way to illustrate this emphasis is to consider certain words especially expressive of the interests of the period—*virtue, fame, glory. Virtue,* particularly in its Italian form, *virtù*, is to be understood in a wide sense. As we may see even now in some relics of its older meanings, the word (from the Latin *vir*, "man") connotes active power—the intrinsic force and ability of a person or thing (the "virtue" of a law or of a medicine)—and hence, also, technical skill (the capacity of the "virtuoso"). The Machiavellian prince's "virtues," therefore, are not necessarily goodness, temperance, clemency, and the like; they are whatever forces and skills may help him in the efficient management and preservation of his princely powers. The idealistic, intangible part of the prince's success is consigned to such concepts as "fame" and "glory," but even in this case the dimension within which human action is considered is still an earthly one. These concepts connote the hero's success and reputation with his contemporaries, or look forward to splendid recognition from posterity, on earth.

In this sense (though completely pure examples of such an attitude are rare) the purpose of life is the unrestrained and self-sufficient practice of one's "virtue," the competent and delighted exercise of one's skill. At the same time, there is no reason to forget that such virtues and skills are God's gift. The worldview of even some of the most clearly earthbound Renaissance writers was hardly godless; Machiavelli, Rabelais, Cellini take for granted the presence of God in their own and in their heroes' lives:

> . . . we have before our eyes extraordinary and unexampled means prepared by God. The sea has been divided. A cloud has guided you on your way. The rock has given forth water. Manna has fallen. Everything has united to make you great. The rest is for you to do. God does not intend to do everything, lest he deprive us of our free will and the share of glory that belongs to us. (Machiavelli)

> And then Gargantua and Powerbrain would briefly recapitulate, according to the Pythagorean fashion, everything Gargantua had read and seen and understood, everything he had done and heard, all day long.
> They would both pray to God their Creator, worshiping, reaffirming their faith, glorifying Him for His immense goodness and thanking Him for all they had been given, and forever placing themselves in His hands.
> And then they would go to sleep. (Rabelais)

> I found that all the bronze my furnace contained had been exhausted in the head of this figure [of the statue of Perseus]. It was a miracle to observe that not one fragment remained in the orifice of the channel, and that nothing was wanting to the statue. In my great astonishment I seemed to see in this the hand of God arranging and controlling all. (Cellini)

Yet if we compare the attitudes of these authors with the view of the world and of the value of human action that emerges from the major literary work of the Middle Ages, *The Divine Comedy*, and with the manner in which human action is there seen within a grand extratemporal design, we see that the presence of God in the Renaissance writers just cited is conspicuously less dominating.

Renaissance intellectuals, artists, aristocrats, and princes did not lack in abiding religious faith or fervor. The most powerful lords of opulent Renaissance courts would unhesitatingly affirm John Calvin's starkly religious assessment of earthly life and gain:

> For if heaven is our country, what is earth but a place of exile! If the departure out of the world is an entrance into life, what is the world but a sepulchre? What is a continuance in it but an absorption in death? If deliverance from the body is an introduction into complete liberty, what is the body but a prison? Therefore, if the terrestrial life be compared with the celestial, it should undoubtedly be despised and accounted of no value.

These princes, however, sharply felt the conflict between the values of worldly goods and spiritual renunciation. The religious conviction in the transitory nature of earthly possessions, moreover, did not prevent princes and lords from seeking to expand their kingdoms. An anonymous Spanish writer was inspired to celebrate Spain's growing empire as "the greatest event since the making of the world, apart from the incarnation and death of him who created it," a phrase that today rings with more patriotism than piety. At the time it was written, however, church and state seemed inextricably bound together. The papacy was a political and military power as well as a spiritual one; Charles V of Spain united most of Europe under his rule and declared himself the Holy Roman emperor; and Henry VIII of England broke with the Catholic Church and declared himself head of the Church of England. Even movements originally intended to reform the Catholic Church—such as the Reformist movements associated with Martin Luther (1483–1546), Ulrich Zwingli (1484–1531), and John Calvin (1509–1564)—were rapidly adopted by Renaissance princes bridling under papal authority. Given the political force of the Catholic Church and the Protestant Reformation, it is no wonder that the Renaissance often appears to be more preoccupied with earthly princes and empires than with the heavenly king.

Much about the religious temper of the age is expressed in its art, particularly in Italian painting, where Renaissance Madonnas often make it difficult, as the saying goes, to recite a properly devout Hail Mary—serving as celebrations of earthly beauty rather than exhortations to contrite thoughts and mystical hopes of salvation. Baldesar Castiglione in the first pages of the *Book of the Courtier* pays homage to the memory of the late lord of Montefeltro, in whose palace at Urbino the book's personages hold their lofty debate on the idea of a perfect gentleman (an earlier Montefeltro appears in Dante's Hell, another in Dante's Purgatory); but Castiglione praises him only for his achievements as a man of arms and a promoter of the arts. There is no thought of either the salvation or the damnation of his soul (though the general tone of the work would seem to imply his salvation); he is exalted instead for military victories, and even more warmly, for having built a splendid palace:

> He built on the rugged site of Urbino a palace thought by many the most beautiful to be found anywhere in all Italy and he furnished it so well with every suitable thing that it seemed not a palace but a city in the form of a palace; and furnished it not only with what is customary, such as silver vases, wall hangings of the richest cloth of gold, silk, and other like things, but for ornament he added countless ancient statues of marble and bronze, rare paintings, and musical instruments of every sort; nor did he wish to have anything there that was not most rare and excellent. Then, at great expense, he collected many very excellent and rare books in Greek, Latin, and Hebrew, all of which he adorned with gold and silver, deeming these to be the supreme excellence of his great palace.

The almost legendary Duke Federico defines, through his life's history, the ideal prince as a heroic empire builder, able to tame "rugged" terrain by force, amass luxurious wealth, and, best of all, collect fine arts. The supreme testimony to his heroic virtue is his library of costly and sumptuous volumes, all collected to conserve the wisdom of antiquity and to promote the exchange of ideas at Urbino.

Thus the popular view that associates the idea of the Renaissance especially with the flourishing of the arts is correct. The leaders of the period saw in a work of art the clearest instance of beautiful, harmonious, and self-justified performance. To create such a work became the valuable occupation par excellence, the most satisfactory display of *virtù*. The Renaissance view of antiquity exemplifies this attitude. The artists and intellectuals of the period not only drew on antiquity for certain practices and forms but also found there a recognition of the place of the arts among outstanding modes of human action. In this way, the concepts of "fame" and "glory" became particularly associated with the art of poetry because the Renaissance drew from antiquity the idea of the poet as celebrator of high deeds, the "dispenser of glory."

There is, then, an important part of the Renaissance mind that sees terrestrial life as positive fulfillment. This is especially clear when there is a close association between the practical and the intellectual, as in the exercise of political power, the act of scientific discovery, the creation of works of art. The Renaissance assumption is that there are things highly worth doing, within a strictly temporal pattern. By doing them, humanity proves its privileged position in creation and therefore incidentally follows God's intent. The often cited phrase "the dignity of man" describes this positive, strongly affirmed awareness of the intellectual and physical "virtues" of the human being, and of the individual's place in creation.

It is important, however, to see this fact about the Renaissance in the light of another phenomenon. Where there is a singularly high capacity for feeling the delight of earthly achievement, there is a possibility that its ultimate worth will also be questioned profoundly. What (the Renaissance mind usually seems to ask at some point) is the purpose of all this activity? What meaningful relation does it bear to any all-inclusive, cosmic pattern? The Renaissance coincided with, and perhaps to some extent occasioned, a loss of firm belief in the final unity and the final intelligibility of the universe, such belief as underlies, for example, *The Divine Comedy*, enabling Dante to say in Paradise:

> I saw within Its depth how It conceives
>   all things in a single volume bound by Love,
>   of which the universe is the scattered leaves;
> substance, accident, and their relation
>   so fused that all I say could do no more
>   than yield a glimpse of that bright revelation.

Once the notion of this grand unity of design has lost its authority, certainty about the final value of human actions is no longer to be found. For some minds, indeed, the sense of void becomes so strong as to paralyze all aspiration to power or thirst for knowledge or delight in beauty; the resulting attitude we may call Renaissance melancholy, whether it be openly shown (as by some characters in Elizabethan drama) or provide an undercurrent of sadness, or incite to ironical forms of compromise, to some sort of wise adjustment (as in Montaigne.) Thus while on one, and perhaps the better-known, side of the picture human intellect in Renaissance literature enthusiastically expatiates over the realms of knowledge and unveils the mysteries of the universe, on the other it is beset by puzzling doubts and a profound mistrust of its own powers.

Doubts about the value of human action within the scheme of eternity did not, however, diminish the outpouring of ideas about the ideal ordering of this world. Renaissance poets and intellectuals turned to the printing press as the means to disseminate and test ideas about the ideal prince, courtier, councilor, and humble subject as well as the ideal court and society. In all the works of imaginative scope and supreme artistic skill produced during the Renaissance, writers can be seen tirelessly examining the nature of their own world, the problem of power, and the vexed relations between the absolute authority of the prince and the rights and liberties of the people. Its zeal for defining the social contract partly explains why the Renaissance is often viewed as the "early modern" period; the "rebirth" and flourishing of antiquity also heralded ideas that we associate with the modern political world.

The joining of philosophical and imaginative thinking in literary expression is characteristic of the Renaissance, which cultivated the idea of "serious play." Throughout the literature of the period, we see the creative and restless mind of the Renaissance intellectual "freely ranging," as Sir Philip Sidney put it, "only in the zodiac of his own wit," creating fictional characters and worlds that might, if the poet is sufficiently persuasive, be put into practice and change the nature of the real world.

TIME LINE

TEXTS	CONTEXTS
1335 Petrarch's poems to Laura, including *Sonnets,* under way (published 1360)	
	1338–1453 Hundred Years' War
	1348–50 The Black Death: Petrarch's Laura dies in the plague
1349–53 Boccaccio's *Decameron* in progress	
1387–1399 Chaucer's *The Canterbury Tales* in progress; he dies in 1400	
	1428 Joan of Arc liberates Orléans from the British; she is burned at the stake for heresy in 1431
	1453 Constantinople falls to the Turks, increasing dissemination of Greek culture in western Europe
	1473 Printing comes to Spain
	1474 William Caxton prints the first book in English
	1492 Columbus discovers America • Expulsion of the Jews from Spain • Spanish reconquest of Granada • Expedition of Charles VIII of France
1494 Sebastian Brandt's *Ship of Fools*	
	1502 The "Nuremberg Egg," first portable timepiece
	1503 Leonardo da Vinci paints the *Mona Lisa*
1511 Erasmus's *The Praise of Folly* published	
	1512 Michelangelo completes the Sistine Chapel ceiling
1516 Erasmus's edition of the New Testament of the Bible • First publication of Ariosto's *Orlando Furioso*	
	1517 Luther's Ninety-five Theses denouncing abuses of the Roman Church
	1519 Charles I of Spain becomes Holy Roman emperor, Charles V
1521 Second edition of *Orlando Furioso*	**1521** Luther is excommunicated
	1524 Francis I is captured in battle against the armies of Charles V

Boldface titles indicate works in the anthology.

TIME LINE

TEXTS	CONTEXTS
	1527 Rome sacked by the French • Castiglione, now bishop of Ávila, is accused of treachery • Marguerite marries Henri d'Albret, king of Navarre
1528 Castiglione's *Book of the Courtier* published; he dies the following year	
1531 Erasmus publishes first complete edition of Aristotle's works	
1532 Rabelais's *Pantagruel* • Machiavelli's *The Prince* • Final publication of *Orlando Furioso*; Ariosto dies the following year	
	1533 Sorbonne accuses Marguerite's chaplain of heresy
1534 Rabelais's *Gargantua*	**1534** Henry VIII breaks with Rome and becomes head of the Church of England
1536 John Calvin's *Institutes of the Christian Religion*	
1546 Rabelais's *Third Book*	
	1547 Francis I dies; Henry II accedes to the French throne
1549 Rabelais's *Fourth Book*	**1549** England declares war on France
1551 First English translation of More's *Utopia*; More had been executed for high treason by Henry VIII in 1535	
	1555 Tobacco brought to Spain from America for the first time
1558 Marguerite de Navarre's *Heptameron* published	
	1559 Spain's most severe index of banned books
	1563 Council of Trent concludes
1571? Montaigne's *Essays* in progress; books 1 and 2 published in 1580; complete publication in 1588	**1571** Spain's battle of Lepanto against the Turks
1581 Tasso's *Jerusalem Delivered*	
	1586 El Greco paints the *Burial of Count Orgaz*
	1588 Spain's Invincible Armada defeated by England

TIME LINE

TEXTS	CONTEXTS
1590 Sir Philip Sidney's revised *Arcadia*	
1596 Edmund Spenser's *The Faerie Queene* 1–6 plus the *Mutabilitie Cantos*	
1597 Tasso's revised *Jerusalem Conquered*	
1597–1604 Cervantes's ***Don Quixote*** in progress; part 1 was published in 1605, part 2 in 1615	
	1598 Philip II of Spain dies; Philip III crowned • Literary quarrel between Lope de Vega and Luis de Góngora
1603–4 Shakespeare's *Othello* appears	
	1608 Dutch scientist Johann Lippershey invents the telescope
1611 King James version of the Bible published	
	1620 Colony founded by Pilgrims at Plymouth, Massachusetts
	1633 Galileo forced by the Inquisition to repudiate Copernican theory that earth rotates around the sun
1641 René Descartes publishes his *Meditations on First Philosophy*	
	1643–1715 Reign of Louis XIV of France, "the Sun King"
	1645–49 England's Charles I surrenders to antimonarchical forces of Oliver Cromwell and is executed; monarchy is abolished
1655? Milton's *Paradise Lost* in progress; published 1667	**1655** Velázquez paints *Las Meninas*
	1660 Charles II restores the English monarchy

FRANCIS PETRARCH
1304–1374

Although Petrarch, a contemporary of Dante and Boccaccio, lived and died in the Middle Ages, he did everything in his power to distinguish himself and his scholarship from the period he dismissed as the "Dark Ages." Frustrated with the corruption of scholarly Latin, Petrarch dedicated himself to the recovery of classical learning in a spirit commonly associated with a later period. If Petrarch can be called a precursor of the Renaissance, it is not for his scholarly output in Latin or his reforms to Latin prose style. The credit is instead due to an aspect of Petrarch's work that neither he nor his contemporaries regarded as a lasting contribution to letters: Petrarch's 366 lyric poems in the vernacular, mostly dedicated to his frustrated desire for an elusive woman named Laura. Petrarch's art; experience of love; and sense of his own fragmented, fluid, and metamorphic self set the standard for the lyric expression of subjective and erotic experience in the Renaissance. His efforts to scrutinize himself intently and at times unflatteringly and to capture his own elusive inner workings in verse inspired a poetic tradition that has influenced lyric sequences from Shakespeare's sonnets to Walt Whitman's *Leaves of Grass* and to modern pop lyrics.

Francesco Petrarca was born in Arezzo on July 20, 1304, three years after his father (along with Dante) was exiled from Florence. In 1314, Petrarch's father moved his family to Avignon, the new seat of the papacy (1309–77), where he became prosperous in the legal profession. Petrarch himself trained as a law student for ten years, but chose to pursue the study of classical culture and literature. He soon came to the attention of the powerful Colonna family, whose patronage launched his career as a diplomat-scholar and allowed him to travel widely and move in the intimate circles of European princes and scholars. He conducted diplomatic missions for popes and princes but refused the offices of bishop and papal secretary, preferring instead to ground his growing prestige in his humanistic scholarship. He did not always manage to protect his scholarly independence from the manipulations of the powerful, such as the tyrannical Visconti family in Milan (as his usually admiring friend Boccaccio remarked). His politics are not easy to decipher: although he served as diplomat for the Visconti at one time, at another he supported the republican dream of the Roman tribune, Cola di Rienzo. Petrarch bequeathed to later humanists the hope that scholar-poets might one day be recognized as shaping forces of the nation-state; in practice, however, he established the humanist scholar's ambiguous position as councillor and exploited servant of powerful princes.

Petrarch expected that he would secure enduring fame through *Africa*, his unfinished epic poem in Latin hexameters on the life of Scipio Africanus, who embodied the valiant and pious virtues that Petrarch admired in Roman heroism. Of greater importance were Petrarch's manuscript discoveries of Cicero's *Pro Archia* (For Archias), a Roman "defense of poetry," in 1333 and letters to Atticus in 1345. The discovery of Cicero's personal correspondence inspired Petrarch to compose his own familiar letters, learned, intellectually exploratory, often moving, and profoundly dialogical. Addressed to his many friends and even to the ancients themselves, these letters illustrate how essential the dialogue was to Petrarch as a literary form and as a way of thinking about the past. Imaginative conversation with the ancients, like imitation of their poetry, brought him into volatile contact with the past: his research into classical history and arts profoundly influenced his sense of himself and his own cultural moment. He had discovered how faulty the medieval transmission of classical culture was, with a paradoxical result: he was convinced that he was at the cusp of a classical revival and tragically aware that the classical world was irretrievably lost. By learning that the past was like a foreign world, Petrarch discovered a modern sense of alienation. He understood, too, that the dislocations of history affect cultural and individual identity. This awareness ties Petrarch's thought and work to the aspects of the Renaissance that most anticipate modernity. In 1370, Petrarch retired to the Euganean hills at Arquà near Padua, where he lived with his daughter, Francesca (his estranged son, Giovanni, died of the plague in 1361). When Petrarch died on the night of July 18, 1374, his head was resting on an open volume of his beloved Virgil.

Petrarch's most famous work, the *Rime Sparse* (Scattered rhymes) or *Rerum Fragmenta Vulgarium* (Fragments in the vernacular), is a collection of 366 songs and sonnets (based on the calendar year associated with the liturgy) of extraordinary technical virtuosity and variety. Written in Italian and woven into a highly introspective narrative, the lyric collection takes the poet himself as its object of study; the poems painstakingly record how his thoughts and identity are scattered and transformed by the experience of love for a beautiful, unattainable woman named Laura. Even some of his friends suspected that Laura was merely the theme and emblem of his lyric poetry and not a historical woman; she appears to have been both. On the flyleaf of his magnificent copy of Virgil, Petrarch inscribed a note on her life:

> Laura, illustrious through her own virtues, and long famed through my verses, first appeared to my eyes in my youth, in the year of our Lord 1327, on the sixth day of April, in the church of St. Clare in Avignon, at matins; and in the same city, also on the sixth day of April, at the same first hour, but in the year 1348, the light of her life was withdrawn from the light of day, while I, as it chanced, was in Verona, unaware of my fate.* * * Her chaste and lovely form was laid to rest at vesper time.* * * I am persuaded that her soul returned to the heaven from which it came, as Seneca says of Africanus. I have thought to write this, in bitter memory, yet with a certain bitter sweetness, here in this place that is often before my eyes, so that I may be admonished, by the sight of these words and by the consideration of the swift flight of time, that there is nothing in this life in which I should find pleasure; and that it is time, now that the strongest tie is broken, to flee from Babylon; and this, by the prevenient grace of God, should be easy for me, if I meditate deeply and manfully on the futile cares, the empty hopes, and the unforeseen events of my past years. (Translated by E. H. Wilkins.)

Petrarch's note illuminates the powerful role that Laura plays in his personal struggles between spiritual aspirations and earthly attachments. His thoughts of Laura habitually turn his mind to the problem of his own will, torn between spiritual and sensual desires, always delaying worldly renunciation. Even when he expresses disgust with earthly rewards and pleasures, his habitual ambivalence makes a last-minute entrance in the conditional "if" upon which his renunciation depends: he will choose the right course of action, Petrarch writes, *if* he meditates "deeply and manfully" on the disappointments and failures of his past and denies memory's seductively bittersweet pleasures.

In the *Rime Sparse*, Laura's ambiguous position between divine guide and earthly temptress contrasts sharply with the role that Beatrice played in Dante's spiritual pilgrimage. Whereas Dante's love finally leads him to paradise, it is never clear to Petrarch whether he is pursuing heavenly or earthly delights and whether his amorous and philosophical wanderings will lead him to any destination or "port" (in the nautical image of sonnet 189) at all. When Dante looks into Beatrice's eyes on Mt. Purgatory, he sees a reflection of the heavens; when Petrarch gazes into Laura's eyes, he sees himself. Not even his use of the liturgical year (especially the anniversaries of Christ's death and resurrection) to structure his account of their relationship guarantees that a spiritual conversion will follow Petrarch's self-analysis or "confession" of his life. It might instead represent a trap, as it does in sonnet 211, written on the eleventh anniversary of his first glimpse of Laura: "One thousand three hundred twenty seven, exactly at the first hour of the sixth day of April, I entered the labyrinth, nor do I see where I may get out of it." The image of the labyrinth evokes Petrarch's tortuous experience of love and mental wandering: apparently fresh paths turn into dead ends and avenues already traced in frustration. An allusion to the maze that the mythical Greek artist Daedalus created to contain the Minotaur, Petrarch's labyrinth also suggests that a threat lies at the center of the ingeniously crafted lyric collection. The metaphor of the self-enclosed and secretive labyrinth hints that love of the very classical figures that prompt philosophical discoveries may bar the poet from the less sensually appealing knowledge of Christian truths. For this reason, Dante must finally move beyond the guidance of his beloved Virgil. Petrarch is less confident: in a contrary and skeptical mood at the end of one of his most philosophical poems (song 264), Petrarch asserts, "I see the better, but choose the worse."

In terms of literary and moral authorities, the "better" models that Petrarch employs in his poetry are Dante and St. Augustine, both of whom famously described their lives in narratives of conversion (Dante's *The New Life* and St. Augustine's *Confessions*). The "worse" model—the one Petrarch repeatedly chooses to represent his own wayward mind—is Ovid. Of particular importance is the *Metamorphoses*, the classical counterepic that artfully uses fragmentation, fluid change, and scattering as principles of narrative composition and as motifs describing the effects of power—divine, political, or erotic—on bodies and on minds. Petrarch refers to a variety of Ovidian figures in the *Rime Sparse*, including Narcissus and Echo, Actaeon and Diana, Medusa, and Pygmalion. His chief Ovidian model, however, is the story of Apollo, the god who "invents" the genre of lyric during his amorous chase of the nymph Daphne. While running, Apollo describes her various beauties—eyes, figure, and hair—and imaginatively embellishes what he sees. When Daphne eludes him through her transformation into the laurel, Apollo claims her as his tree, if not his lover, and declares that the laurel will be the sign of triumph in letters and warfare.

Like Ovid's Apollo, Petrarch uses language to possess as well as describe his lady. Her name interweaves key attributes of Petrarch's poetic imagination: *lauro* and *alloro* ("laurel"), *oro* ("gold," for her tresses and value), *l'aura* ("breeze" and "inspiration," which etymologically relates to "breath"), *laus* or *lauda* ("praise"). Such play on words suggests the selective, even obsessive character of Petrarch's poetic style. Like Apollo, Petrarch also "translates" his beloved's elusive body into the more tangible "figures" of rhetoric: her physical attributes reflect the style of his poetry and proclaim his triumphant glory. The Ovidian model poses the threat of the labyrinth, the trap of the artist's own making: the most significant and evocative words limit the poet to ranging within his well-defined obsessions. The Ovidian lover in Petrarch can expect no transcendence, only repeated and uncontrollable metamorphoses of the mind (e.g., despair, hope, ecstasy).

Petrarch's great legacy to Renaissance European literature is the *Rime Sparse*'s language of self-description. He absorbed the conventional use of hyperbole, antithesis, and oxymoron (rhetorical exaggeration and opposition) from troubadour songs, provençal lyric, and classical love elegy: *I freeze and burn, love is bitter and sweet, my sighs are tempests and my tears are floods, I am in ecstasy and agony, I am possessed by memories of her and I am in exile from myself*. Petrarch forged such rhetorical figures or tropes of love into a powerful language of introspection and self-fashioning that swept through European literature. Although it was often faddish and stylized, it had quite serious dimensions that helped articulate growing questions about the self: is it determined by God or flexible and in the shaping hands of men? Do culture, history, and force of will compose and transform it? The beloved does not fare as well: the eloquent expression of the male poet-lover's complex *interior* life depends, as Petrarchan successors noticed, on a correspondingly detailed description of the beloved's *exterior*. In the Petrarchan inventory of the beloved's adorable parts, from eyes to hair, cheeks, and hand, the poet converts her living body to ornaments, metal, and minerals, such as gold, topaz, and pearls. Although any one of her beauties is capable of scattering the poet's thoughts, the beloved herself has little independent coherence. Some of her parts, as critics have noticed, are greater than their sum.

SONNETS

1[1]

O you who hear within these scattered verses[2]
the sound of sighs with which I fed my heart
in my first errant youthful days when I
in part was not the man I am today;

for all the ways in which I weep and speak   5
between vain hopes, between vain suffering,
in anyone who knows love through its trials,
in them, may I find pity and forgiveness.

But now I see how I've become the talk
so long a time of people all around   10
(it often makes me feel so full of shame),

and from my vanities there comes shame's fruit,
and my repentance, and the clear awareness
that worldly joy is just a fleeting dream.

3[1]

It was the day the sun's ray had turned pale
with pity for the suffering of his Maker[2]
when I was caught (and I put up no fight),
my lady, for your lovely eyes had bound me.

It seemed no time to be on guard against   5
Love's blows; therefore, I went my way
secure and fearless—so, all my misfortunes
began in midst of universal woe.[3]

Love found me all disarmed and saw the way
was clear to reach my heart down through the eyes,   10
which have become the halls and doors of tears.

---

1. Translated by Mark Musa.   2. Reference to the sonnet collection's title: *Rime Sparse*.   1. Translated by Mark Musa.   2. The anniversary of Christ's crucifixion. Elsewhere (sonnet 211 and a note in Petrarch's copy of Virgil) given as April 6, 1327.   3. The communal Christian grief that contrasts with Petrarch's private woes.

It seems to me it did him little honor
to wound me with his arrow in my state[4]
and to you, armed, not show his bow at all.

61[1]

Blest be the day, and blest the month and year,
Season and hour[2] and very moment blest,
The lovely land and place[3] where first possessed
By two pure eyes I found me prisoner;

And blest the first sweet pain, the first most dear,   5
Which burnt my heart when Love came in as guest;
And blest the bow, the shafts which shook my breast,
And even the wounds which Love delivered there.

Blest be the words and voices which filled grove
And glen with echoes of my lady's name;   10
The sighs, the tears, the fierce despair of love;

And blest the sonnet-sources of my fame;
And blest that thought of thoughts which is her own,
Of her, her only, of herself alone!

62[1]

Father in heaven, after each lost day,
Each night spent raving with that fierce desire
Which in my heart has kindled into fire
Seeing your acts adorned for my dismay;

Grant henceforth that I turn, within your light[2]   5
To another life and deeds more truly fair,
So having spread to no avail the snare
My bitter foe[3] might hold it in despite.

The eleventh year,[4] my Lord, has now come round
Since I was yoked beneath the heavy trace   10
That on the meekest weighs most cruelly.

Pity the abject plight where I am found;
Return my straying thoughts to a nobler place;
Show them this day you were on Calvary.

---

4. State of grief over the crucifixion.   **1.** Translated by Joseph Auslander.   **2.** That is, April 6, 1327, in the spring, at sunrise.   **3.** The Church of Saint Clare at Avignon.   **1.** Translated by Bernard Bergonzi. **2.** Of grace.   **3.** Satan.   **4.** That is, 1338.

78[1]

When Simon[2] first received that high idea
which for my sake he used his drawing pen,
had he then given to his gracious work
a voice and intellect as well as form,

he would have freed my breast of many sighs   5
that make what others cherish vile to me,
for she appears so humble in her image
and her expression promises me peace.

And then when I begin to speak to her,
most kindly she appears to hear me speak—   10
if only she could answer what I say!

Pygmalion,[3] how happy you should be
with your creation, since a thousand times
you have received what I yearn for just once!

90[1]

She used to let her golden hair fly free
For the wind to toy and tangle and molest;
Her eyes were brighter than the radiant west.
(Seldom they shine so now.) I used to see

Pity look out of those deep eyes on me.   5
("It was false pity," you would now protest.)
I had love's tinder heaped within my breast;
What wonder that the flame burned furiously?

She did not walk in any mortal way,[2]
But with angelic progress; when she spoke,   10
Unearthly voices sang in unison.

She seemed divine among the dreary folk
Of earth. You say she is not so today?
Well, though the bow's unbent, the wound bleeds on.

---

1. Translated by Mark Musa.   2. Simone Martini (active 1315–1344), a Sienese painter. His painting of Laura is the occasion of the poem.   3. Sculptor, from Ovid's *Metamorphoses* 10.243–97, who fell in love with his own ivory statue, which Venus brought to life. Whereas Ovid's Pygmalion enjoys a thousand physical embraces, Petrarch yearns only for a reply to his words, or poem.   1. Translated by Morris Bishop.   2. Like Venus in book 1 of Virgil's *Aeneid*, when the goddess of love appears to Aeneas in the guise of a Spartan huntress. In the Renaissance, the image of Venus armed conjured up an ideal synthesis of eroticism and chastity.

126[1]

Clear, fresh, sweet waters,[2] where she who alone seems lady to me
rested her lovely body,
   gentle branch where it pleased her (with sighing I remember) to make a
column for her lovely side,
   grass and flowers that her rich garment covered along with   5
her angelic breast, sacred bright air where Love opened my heart
with her lovely eyes: listen all together to my sorrowful dying
words.

   If it is indeed my destiny and Heaven exerts itself that Love
close these eyes while they are still weeping,   10
   let some grace bury my poor body among you and let my soul return
naked to this its own dwelling;
   death will be less harsh if I bear this hope to the fearful pass, for my
weary spirit could never in a more restful port or a more tranquil grave flee
my laboring flesh and my bones.   15

   There will come a time perhaps when to her accustomed sojourn the
lovely, gentle wild one will return
   and, seeking me, turn her desirous and happy eyes toward where she saw
me on that blessed day,
   and oh the pity! seeing me already dust amid the stones, Love will   20
inspire her to sigh so sweetly that she will win mercy for me and
force Heaven, drying her eyes with her lovely veil.

   From the lovely branches was descending (sweet in memory) a rain of
flowers over her bosom,
   and she was sitting humble in such a glory,[3] already covered with the 25
loving cloud;
   this flower was falling on her skirt, this one on her blond braids,
which were burnished gold and pearls to see that day; this one was coming
to rest on the ground, this one on the water, this one, with a lovely
wandering, turning about seemed to say: "Here reigns Love."[4]   30

   How many times did I say to myself then, full of awe: "She was surely
born in Paradise!"
   Her divine bearing and her face and her words and her sweet smile had
so laden me with forgetfulness   35
   and so divided me from the true image, that I was sighing: "How did I
come here and when?" thinking I was in Heaven, not there where I was.
From then on this grass has pleased me so that elsewhere I have no peace.

   If you had as many beauties as you have desire, you could boldly leave   40
the wood and go among people.[5]

---

1. Translated by Robert M. Durling.   2. Of the river Sorgue.   3. An image associated with the Virgin
Mary.   4. Amor (Cupid) or Christ. The floral and bejeweled images associate Laura's body with the
bride of the Song of Songs, whose erotic chastity is celebrated as an "enclosed garden," and "fountain sealed."
5. The last two lines are addressed to the poem.

189[1]

My ship full of forgetful cargo[2] sails
through rough seas at the midnight of a winter
between Charybdis and the Scylla reef,[3]
my master, no, my foe,[4] is at the helm;

at each oar sits a quick and insane thought   5
that seems to scorn the storm and what it brings;
the sail, by wet eternal winds of sighs,
of hopes and of desires blowing, breaks;

a rain of tears, a mist of my disdain
washes and frees those all too weary ropes   10
made up of wrong entwined with ignorance.

Hidden are those two trusty signs of mine;[5]
dead in the waves is reason as is skill,
and I despair of ever reaching port.

190[1]

A doe of purest white upon green grass
wearing two horns of gold appeared to me
between two streams beneath a laurel's shade
at sunrise in that season not yet ripe.

The sight of her was so sweetly austere   5
that I left all my work to follow her,
just like a miser who in search of treasure
with pleasure makes his effort bitterless.

"No one touch me,"[2] around her lovely neck
was written out in diamonds, and in topaz: 10
"It pleased my Caesar to create me free."

The sun by now had climbed the sky midway,
my eyes were tired but not full from looking
when I fell in the water and she vanished.

1. Translated by Mark Musa.   2. Forgetfulness of oneself and of God is sinful in Augustinian terms.
The ship, captained by Reason, is a traditional figure for the embodied soul.   3. The twinned oceanic
dangers through which Odysseus, in Homer's *Odyssey*, and Aeneas, in Virgil's *Aeneid*, must chart a middle
course.   4. Love.   5. Laura's eyes.   1. Translated by Mark Musa.   2. These are Christ's words to
Mary Magdalene at the resurrection.

333[1]

Go, grieving rimes of mine, to that hard stone
Whereunder lies my darling, lies my dear,
And cry to her to speak from heaven's sphere.
Her mortal part with grass is overgrown.

Tell her, I'm sick of living; that I'm blown   5
By winds of grief from the course I ought to steer,
That praise of her is all my purpose here
And all my business; that of her alone

Do I go telling, that how she lived and died
And lives again in immortality,   10
All men may know, and love my Laura's grace.

Oh, may she deign to stand at my bedside
When I come to die; and may she call to me
And draw me to her in the blessèd place!

1. Translated by Morris Bishop.

NICCOLÒ MACHIAVELLI
1469–1527

The most famous and controversial political writer and theorist of his time—indeed, possibly of all time—Niccolò Machiavelli was born in Florence on May 3, 1469. Little is known of his schooling, but it is obvious from his works that he knew the Latin and Italian writers well. He entered public life in 1494 as a clerk and from 1498 to 1512 was secretary to the second chancery of the commune of Florence, whose magistrates were in charge of internal and war affairs. During the conflict between Florence and Pisa, he dealt with military problems firsthand. Thus he had a direct experience of war as well as of diplomacy; he was entrusted with many missions—among others, to King Louis XII of France in 1500 and in 1502 to Cesare Borgia, duke of Valentinois or "il duca Valentino," the favorite son of Pope Alexander VI. Machiavelli described the duke's ruthless methods in crushing a conspiracy during his conquest of the Romagna region in a terse booklet *Of the Method followed by Duke Valentino in Killing Vitellozzo Vitelli*, which already shows direct insight into the type of the amoral and technically efficient "prince." In 1506 Machiavelli went on a mission to Pope Julius II, whose expedition into Romagna (an old name for north-central Italy) he followed closely. From this and other missions—to Emperor Maximilian (1508) and again to the king of France (1509)—Machiavelli drew his two books of observations or *Portraits* of the affairs of those territories, written in 1508 and 1510.

Preeminently a student of politics and an acute observer of historical events, Machiavelli endeavored to apply his experience of other states to the strengthening of his own, the Florentine republic, and busied himself in 1507 with the establishment of a Florentine militia, encountering great difficulties. When the republican regime came to an end, he lost his post and was exiled from the city proper, though forbidden to leave Florentine territory. The new regime of the Medici accused him unjustly of conspiracy, and he was released only after a period of imprisonment and torture. To the period of his exile (spent near San Casciano, a few miles from Florence, where he retired with his wife, Marietta Corsini, and his five children), we owe his major works: the *Discourses on the First Ten Books of Livy* (1513–21) and *The Prince*, written in 1513 with the hope of obtaining public office from the Medici. In 1520 Machiavelli was commissioned to write a history of Florence, which he presented in 1525 to Pope Clement VII (Giulio de' Medici). The following year, conscious of imminent dangers, he took part in the work to improve the military fortifications of Florence. The fate of the city at that point depended on the outcome of the larger struggle between Francis I of France and the Holy Roman Emperor, Charles V. Pope Clement's siding with the king of France led to the disastrous "Sack of Rome" by Charles V in 1527, and the result for Florence was the collapse of Medici domination. Machiavelli's hopes, briefly raised by the reestablishment of the republic, came to naught, because he was now regarded as a Medici sympathizer. This last disappointment may have accelerated his end. He died on June 22, 1527, and was buried in the church of Santa Croce.

Though Machiavelli has a place in literary history for a short novel and two plays—one of which, *La mandragola* (The mandrake), first performed in the early 1520s, belongs in the upper rank of Italian comedies of intrigue—his world reputation is based on *The Prince*. This "handbook" on how to obtain and keep political power consists of twenty-six chapters. The first eleven deal with different types of dominions and the ways in which they are acquired and preserved—the early title of the whole book, in Latin, was *De principatibus* (Of princedoms)—and the twelfth to fourteenth chapters focus particularly on problems of military power. The book's astounding fame, however, is based on the final part (from chapter fifteen to the end), which deals primarily with the attributes and "virtues" of the prince himself. In other words, despite its reputation for cool, precise realism, the work presents a hypothetical type, the idealized portrait of a certain kind of person.

Manuals of this sort may be classified, in one sense, as pedagogical literature. Because of their merits of form and of vivid, if stylized, characterization they can be considered works of art, but their overt purpose is to codify a certain set of manners and rules of conduct; the authors, therefore, present themselves as especially wise, experts in the field, "minds" offering advice to the executive "arm." Machiavelli is a clear example of this approach. His fervor, the dramatic, oratorical way he confronts his reader, the wealth and pertinence of his illustrations are all essential qualities of his pedagogical *persona*. The implied tone of *I know, I have seen such things myself* adds a special immediacy to Machiavelli's prose. His view of the practical world may have been an especially startling one, but the sensation caused by his work would have been far less without the rhetorical power, the drama of argumentation, that makes *The Prince* a unique example of "the art of persuasion."

The view of humanity in Machiavelli is not at all cheerful. Indeed, the pessimistic notion that humanity is evil is not so much Machiavelli's conclusion about human nature as his premise; it is the point of departure of all subsequent reasoning on the course for a ruler to follow. The very fact of its being given as a premise, however, tends to qualify it; it is not a firm philosophical judgment but a stratagem, dictated by the facts as they are seen by a lucid observer of the here and now. The author is committed to his view of the human being not as a philosopher or as a religious man but as a practical politician. He indicates the rules of the game as his experience shows it must, under the circumstances, be played.

A basic question in the study of Machiavelli, therefore, is, How much of a realist is he? His picture of the perfectly efficient ruler has something of the quality of an abstraction; it shows the well-known Renaissance tendency toward "perfected" form. Machiavelli's abandonment of complex actualities in favor of an ideal vision is shown most clearly at the conclusion of the book, particularly in the last chapter. This is where he offers what amounts to the greatest of his illustrations as the prince's preceptor and counselor: the ideal ruler, now technically equipped by his pedagogue, is to undertake a mission—the liberation of Machiavelli's Italy. If we regard the last chapter of *The Prince* as a culmination of Machiavelli's discussion rather than as a dissonant addition to it, we are likely to feel at that point not only that Machiavelli's realistic method is ultimately directed toward an ideal task but also that his conception of that task, far from being based on immediate realities, is founded on cultural and poetic myths. Machiavelli's method here becomes imaginative rather than scientific. His exhortation to liberate Italy, and his final prophecy, belong to the tradition of poetic visions in which a present state of decay is lamented and a hope of future redemption is expressed.

As in Hamlet's Denmark, something is rotten in Machiavelli's Italy. And we become more and more detached even from the particular example, Italy, as we recognize in the situation a pattern frequently exemplified in tragedy: the desire for communal regeneration, for the cleansing of the city-state, the *polis*. Of this cleansing, Italy on the one side and the imaginary prince on the other may be taken as symbols. The envisaged redemption is identified with antiquity and Roman virtue, while the realism of the political observer is here drowned out by the cry of the humanist dreaming of ancient glories.

PRONOUNCING GLOSSARY

The following list uses common English syllables and stress accents to provide rough equivalents of selected words whose pronunciation may be unfamiliar to the general reader.

Borgia: *bor'-juh*

Chiron: *kai'-ron*

de' Medici: *day may'-dee-chee*

Machiavelli: *ma-kee-ah-vel'-lee*

Pistoia: *pees-toh'-yah*

San Casciano: *san ka-shah'-noh*

Santa Croce: *san'-tuh croh'-chay*

From The Prince[1]

XV

ON THE REASONS WHY MEN ARE PRAISED OR BLAMED—ESPECIALLY PRINCES

It remains now to be seen what style and principles a prince ought to adopt in dealing with his subjects and friends. I know the subject has been treated frequently before, and I fear people will think me rash for trying to do so again, especially since I intend to differ in this discussion from what others have said. But since I intend to write something useful to an understanding reader, it seemed better to go after the real truth of the matter than to repeat what people have imagined. A great many men have imagined states and princedoms such as nobody ever saw or knew in the real world, and there's such a difference between the way we really live and the way we ought to live that the man who neglects the real to study the ideal will learn how to accomplish his ruin, not his salvation. Any man who tries to be good all the time is bound to come to ruin among the great number who are not

1. Translated by Robert M. Adams.

good. Hence a prince who wants to keep his authority must learn how not to be good, and use that knowledge, or refrain from using it, as necessity requires.

Putting aside, then, all the imaginary things that are said about princes, and getting down to the truth, let me say that whenever men are discussed (and especially princes because they are prominent), there are certain qualities that bring them either praise or blame. Thus some are considered generous, others stingy (I use a Tuscan term, since "greedy" in our speech means a man who wants to take other people's goods; we call a man "stingy" who clings to his own); some are givers, others grabbers; some cruel, others humane; one man is treacherous, another faithful; one is feeble and effeminate, another fierce and spirited; one modest, another proud; one lustful, another chaste; one straightforward, another sly; one harsh, another gentle; one serious, another playful; one religious, another skeptical, and so on. I know everyone will agree that among these many qualities a prince certainly ought to have all those that are considered good. But since it is impossible to have and exercise them all, because the conditions of human life simply do not allow it, a prince must be shrewd enough to avoid the public disgrace of those vices that would lose him his state. If he possibly can, he should also guard against vices that will not lose him his state; but if he cannot prevent them, he should not be too worried about indulging them. And furthermore, he should not be too worried about incurring blame for any vice without which he would find it hard to save his state. For if you look at matters carefully, you will see that something resembling virtue, if you follow it, may be your ruin, while something else resembling vice will lead, if you follow it, to your security and well-being.

XVI

ON LIBERALITY AND STINGINESS

Let me begin, then, with the first of the qualities mentioned above, by saying that a reputation for liberality is doubtless very fine; but the generosity that earns you that reputation can do you great harm. For if you exercise your generosity in a really virtuous way as you should, nobody will know of it, and you cannot escape the odium of the opposite vice. Hence if you wish to be widely known as a generous man, you must seize every opportunity to make a big display of your giving. A prince of this character is bound to use up his entire revenue in works of ostentation. In the end, if he wants to keep a name for generosity, he will have to load his people with exorbitant taxes and squeeze money out of them in every way he can. This is the first step in making him odious to his subjects; for when he is poor, nobody will respect him. Then, when his generosity has angered many and brought rewards to a few, the slightest difficulty will trouble him, and at the first approach of danger, down he goes. If by chance he foresees this, and tries to change his ways, he will immediately be labelled a miser.

Since a prince cannot use this virtue [virtù] of liberality in such a way as to become known for it unless he harms his own security, he will not mind, if he judges prudently of things, being known as a miser. In due course he will be thought the more liberal man, when people see that his parsimony enables him to live on his income, to defend himself against his enemies, and to undertake major projects without burdening his people with taxes. Thus he will be acting liberally toward all those people from whom he takes nothing (and there are an immense number of them), and in a stingy way toward those people on whom he bestows nothing (and they are very few). In our times, we have seen great things being accomplished only by men who have had the name of misers; all the others have gone under. Pope Julius II, though he used his reputation as a generous man to gain the papacy, sacrificed it in order to be able to make war; the present king of France[2] has waged many wars without levying a single extra tax on his people, simply because he could take care of the extra expenses out of the savings from his long parsimony. If the present king of Spain[3] had a reputation for generosity, he would never have been able to undertake so many campaigns, or win so many of them.

Hence a prince who prefers not to rob his subjects, who wants to be able to defend himself, who wants to avoid poverty and contempt, and who has no desire to become a plunderer, should not mind in the least if people consider him a miser; this is simply one of the vices that enable him to reign. Someone may object that Caesar used a reputation for generosity to become emperor, and many other people have also risen in the world, because they were generous or were supposed to be so. Well, I answer, either you are a prince already, or you are in the process of becoming one; in the first case, this reputation for generosity is harmful to you, in the second case it is very necessary. Caesar was one of those who wanted to become ruler in Rome; but after he had reached his goal, if he had lived, and had not cut down on his expenses, he would have ruined the empire itself. Someone may say: there have been plenty of princes, very successful in warfare, who have had a reputation for generosity. But I answer: either the prince is spending his own money and that of his subjects, or he is spending someone else's. In the first case, he ought to be sparing; in the second case, he ought to spend money like water. Any prince at the head of his army, which lives on loot, extortion, and plunder, disposes of other people's property, and is bound to be very generous; otherwise, his soldiers would desert him. You can always be a more generous giver when what you give is not yours or your subjects'; Cyrus, Caesar, and Alexander were generous in this way. Spending what belongs to other people does no harm to your reputation, rather it enhances it; only spending your own substance harms you. And there is nothing that wears out faster than generosity; even as you practice it, you lose the means of practicing it, and you become either poor and contemptible or (in the course of escaping poverty) rapacious and hateful. The thing above all against which a prince must protect himself is being contemptible and hateful; generosity leads to both. Thus, it is much wiser to put up with the reputation of being a miser, which brings you shame without hate, than to be forced—just because you want to appear generous—into a reputation for rapacity, whch brings shame on you and hate along with it.

---

2. Louis XII (1462–1515). Julius II was Giuliano della Rovere (1443–1513), elected to the papacy in 1503 at the death of Pius III, who had been successor to Alexander VI (Rodrigo Borgia).   3. Ferdinand II, "the Catholic" (1452–1516).

XVII

ON CRUELTY AND CLEMENCY: WHETHER IT IS BETTER TO BE LOVED OR FEARED

Continuing now with our list of qualities, let me say that every prince should prefer to be considered merciful rather than cruel, yet he should be careful not to mismanage this clemency of his. People thought Cesare Borgia[4] was cruel, but that cruelty of his reorganized the Romagna, united it, and established it in peace and loyalty. Anyone who views the matter realistically will see that this prince was much more merciful than the people of Florence, who, to avoid the reputation of cruelty, allowed Pistoia to be destroyed.[5] Thus, no prince should mind being called cruel for what he does to keep his subjects united and loyal; he may make examples of a very few, but he will be more merciful in reality than those who, in their tenderheartedness, allow disorders to occur, with their attendant murders and lootings. Such turbulence brings harm to an entire community, while the executions ordered by a prince affect only one individual at a time. A new prince, above all others, cannot possibly avoid a name for cruelty, since new states are always in danger. And Virgil, speaking through the mouth of Dido, says: "Harsh pressures and the newness of my reign / Compel me to these steps; I must maintain / My borders against foreign foes."[6] Yet a prince should be slow to believe rumors and to commit himself to action on the basis of them. He should not be afraid of his own thoughts; he ought to proceed cautiously, moderating his conduct with prudence and humanity, allowing neither overconfidence to make him careless, nor excess suspicion to make him intolerable.

Here the question arises: is it better to be loved than feared, or vice versa? I don't doubt that every prince would like to be both; but since it is hard to accommodate these qualities, if you have to make a choice, to be feared is much safer than to be loved. For it is a good general rule about men, that they are ungrateful, fickle, liars and deceivers, fearful of danger and greedy for gain. While you serve their welfare, they are all yours, offering their blood, their belongings, their lives, and their children's lives, as we noted above—so long as the danger is remote. But when the danger is close at hand, they turn against you. Then, any prince who has relied on their words and has made no other preparations will come to grief; because friendships that are bought at a price, and not with greatness and nobility of soul, may be paid for but they are not acquired, and they cannot be used in time of need. People are less concerned with offending a man who makes himself loved than one who makes himself feared: the reason is that love is a link of obligation which men, because they are rotten, will break any time they think doing so serves their advantage; but fear involves dread of punishment, from which they can never escape.

Still, a prince should make himself feared in such a way that, even if he gets no love, he gets no hate either; because it is perfectly possible to be feared and not hated, and this will be the result if only the prince will keep his hands off the property of his subjects or citizens, and off their women. When he does have to shed blood, he should be sure to have a strong justification and manifest cause; but above all, he should not confiscate people's

---

4. Duke of Vlentinois and Romagna and son of Alexander VI. His skillful and merciless subjugation of the local lords of Romagna occurred between 1499 and 1502.   5. By internal dissensions, because the Florentines, Machiavelli contends, failed to treat the leaders of the dissenting parties with an iron hand.
6. *Aeneid* 1.563–64.

property, because men are quicker to forget the death of a father than the loss of a patrimony. Besides, pretexts for confiscation are always plentiful; it never fails that a prince who starts to live by plunder can find reasons to rob someone else. Excuses for proceeding against someone's life are much rarer and more quickly exhausted.

But a prince at the head of his armies and commanding a multitude of soldiers should not care a bit if he is considered cruel; without such a reputation, he could never hold his army together and ready for action. Among the marvelous deeds of Hannibal, this was prime: that, having an immense army, which included men of many different races and nations, and which he led to battle in distant countries, he never allowed them to fight among themselves or to rise against him, whether his fortune was good or bad. The reason for this could only be his inhuman cruelty, which, along with his countless other talents [*virtù*], made him an object of awe and terror to his soldiers; and without the cruelty, his other qualities [*le altre sua virtù*] would never have sufficed. The historians who pass snap judgments on these matters admire his accomplishments and at the same time condemn the cruelty which was their main cause.

When I say, "His other qualities would never have sufficed," we can see that this is true from the example of Scipio, an outstanding man not only among those of his own time, but in all recorded history; yet his armies revolted in Spain,[7] for no other reason than his excessive leniency in allowing his soldiers more freedom than military discipline permits. Fabius Maximus rebuked him in the senate for this failing, calling him the corrupter of the Roman armies. When a lieutenant of Scipio's plundered the Locrians,[8] he took no action in behalf of the people, and did nothing to discipline that insolent lieutenant; again, this was the result of his easygoing nature. Indeed, when someone in the senate wanted to excuse him on this occasion, he said there are many men who know better how to avoid error themselves than how to correct error in others. Such a soft temper would in time have tarnished the fame and glory of Scipio, had he brought it to the office of emperor; but as he lived under the control of the senate, this harmful quality of his not only remained hidden but was considered creditable.

Returning to the question of being feared or loved, I conclude that since men love at their own inclination but can be made to fear at the inclination of the prince, a shrewd prince will lay his foundations on what is under his own control, not on what is controlled by others. He should simply take pains not to be hated, as I said.

XVIII

THE WAY PRINCES SHOULD KEEP THEIR WORD

How praiseworthy it is for a prince to keep his word and live with integrity rather than by craftiness, everyone understands; yet we see from recent experience that those princes have accomplished most who paid little heed to keeping their promises, but who knew how to manipulate the minds of men craftily. In the end, they won out over those who tried to act honestly.

7. The mutiny occurred in 206 B.C.E. Publius Cornelious Scipio Africanus the Elder (235–183 B.C.E.).
8. Citizens of Locri, in Sicily.

You should consider then, that there are two ways of fighting, one with laws and the other with force. The first is properly a human method, the second belongs to beasts. But as the first method does not always suffice, you sometimes have to turn to the second. Thus a prince must know how to make good use of both the beast and man. Ancient writers made subtle note of this fact when they wrote that Achilles and many other princes of antiquity[9] were sent to be reared by Chiron the centaur, who trained them in his discipline. Having a teacher who is half man and half beast can only mean that a prince must know how to use both these two natures, and that one without the other has no lasting effect.

Since a prince must know how to use the character of beasts, he should pick for imitation the fox and the lion. As the lion cannot protect himself from traps, and the fox cannot defend himself from wolves, you have to be a fox in order to be wary of traps, and a lion to overawe the wolves. Those who try to live by the lion alone are badly mistaken. Thus a prudent prince cannot and should not keep his word when to do so would go against his interest, or when the reasons that made him pledge it no longer apply. Doubtless if all men were good, this rule would be bad; but since they are a sad lot, and keep no faith with you, you in your turn are under no obligation to keep it with them.

Besides, a prince will never lack for legitimate excuses to explain away his breaches of faith. Modern history will furnish innumerable examples of this behavior, showing how many treaties and promises have been made null and void by the faithlessness of princes, and how the man succeeded best who knew best how to play the fox. But it is necessary in playing this part that you conceal it carefully; you must be a great liar and hypocrite. Men are so simple of mind, and so much dominated by their immediate needs, that a deceitful man will always find plenty who are ready to be deceived. One of many recent examples calls for mention. Alexander VI[1] never did anything else, never had another thought, except to deceive men, and he always found fresh material to work on. Never was there a man more convincing in his assertions, who sealed his promises with more solemn oaths, and who observed them less. Yet his deceptions were always successful, because he knew exactly how to manage this sort of business.

In actual fact, a prince may not have all the admirable qualities listed above, but it is very necessary that he should seem to have them. Indeed, I will venture to say that when you have them and exercise them all the time, they are harmful to you; when you just seem to have them, they are useful. It is good to appear merciful, truthful, humane, sincere, and religious; it is good to be so in reality. But you must keep your mind so disposed that, in case of need, you can turn to the exact contrary. This has to be understood: a prince, and especially a new prince, cannot possibly exercise all those virtues for which men are called "good." To preserve the state, he often has to do things against his word, against charity, against humanity, against religion. Thus he has to have a mind ready to shift as the winds of fortune and the varying circumstances of life may dictate. And as I said above, he should not depart from the good if he can hold to it, but he should be ready to enter on evil if he has to.

Hence a prince should take great care never to drop a word that does not seem imbued with the five good qualities noted above; to anyone who sees or

---

9. For example, Theseus, Jason, and Hercules.   1. Pope from 1492 to 1503; father of Cesare Borgia.

hears him, he should appear all compassion, all honor, all humanity, all integrity, all religion. Nothing is more necessary than to seem to have this last virtue. Men in general judge more by the sense of sight than by the sense of touch, because everyone can see but only a few can test by feeling. Everyone sees what you seem to be, few know what you really are; and those few do not dare take a stand against the general opinion, supported by the majesty of the government. In the actions of all men, and especially of princes who are not subject to a court of appeal, we must always look to the end. Let a prince, therefore, win victories and uphold his state; his methods will always be considered worthy, and everyone will praise them, because the masses are always impressed by the superficial appearance of things, and by the outcome of an enterprise. And the world consists of nothing but the masses; the few have no influence when the many feel secure. A certain prince of our own time, whom it is just as well not to name,[2] preaches nothing but peace and mutual trust, yet he is the determined enemy of both; and if on several different occasions he had observed either, he would have lost both his reputation and his throne.

XXV

THE INFLUENCE OF LUCK ON HUMAN AFFAIRS AND THE WAYS TO COUNTER IT

I realize that many people have thought, and still do think, that events are so governed in this world that the wisdom of men cannot possibly avail against them, indeed is altogether useless. On this basis, you might say that there is no point in sweating over anything, we should simply leave all matters to fate. This opinion has been popular in our own times because of the tremendous change in public affairs during our lifetime, that actually is still going on today, beyond what anyone could have imagined. Indeed, sometimes when I think of it, I incline toward this opinion myself. Still, rather than give up on our free will altogether, I think it may be true that Fortune governs half of our actions, but that even so she leaves the other half more or less in our power to control. I would compare her to one of those torrential streams which, when they overflow, flood the plains, rip up trees and tear down buildings, wash the land away here and deposit it there; everyone flees before them, everyone yields to their onslaught, unable to stand up to them in any way. This is how they are; yet this does not mean that men cannot take countermeasures while the weather is still fine, shoring up dikes and dams, so that when the waters rise again, they are either carried off in a channel or confined where they do no harm. So with Fortune, who exerts all her power where there is no strength [*virtù*] prepared to oppose her, and turns to smashing things up wherever there are no dikes and restraining dams. And if you look at Italy, which is the seat of all these tremendous changes, where they all began, you will see that she is an open country without any dikes or ditches. If she were protected by forces of proper valor [*virtù*], as are Germany, Spain, and France, either this flood would never have wrought such destruction as it has, or it might not even have occurred at all. And let this much suffice on the general topic of opposing Fortune.

2. That is, Ferdinand II. In refraining from mentioning him, Machiavelli apparently had in mind the good relations existing between Spain and the house of Medici.

But coming now to the particulars, let me observe that we see a prince flourishing today and ruined tomorrow, and yet no change has taken place in his nature or any of his qualities. I think this happens, primarily, for the reasons discussed at length above, that is, that a prince who depends entirely on Fortune comes to grief immediately she changes. I believe further that a prince will be fortunate who adjusts his behavior to the temper of the times, and on the other hand will be unfortunate when his behavior is not well attuned to the times. Anyone can see that men take different paths in their search for the common goals of glory and riches; one goes cautiously, another boldly; one by violence, another by stealth; one by patience, another in the contrary way; yet any one of these different methods may be successful. Of two cautious men, one will succeed in his design the other not; so too, a rash man and a cautious man may both succeed, though their approaches are so different. And this stems from nothing but the temper of the times, which does or does not accord with their method of operating. Hence two men proceeding in different ways may, as I have said, produce the same effect; while two men proceeding in the same way will vary in their effectiveness, one failing, one succeeding. This too explains the variation in what is good; for if a prince conducts himself with patience and caution, and the times and circumstances are favorable to those qualities, he will flourish; but if times and circumstances change, he will come to ruin unless he changes his method of proceeding. No man, however prudent, can adjust to such radical changes, not only because we cannot go against the inclination of nature, but also because when one has always prospered by following a particular course, he cannot be persuaded to leave it. Thus the cautious man, when it is time to act boldly, does not know how, and comes to grief; if he could only change his nature with times and circumstances, his fortune would not change.

In everything he undertook, Pope Julius proceeded boldly; and he found the times and circumstances of his life so favorable to this sort of procedure, that he always came off well. Consider his first campaign against Bologna, when Messer Giovanni Bentivogli[3] was still alive. The Venetians were unhappy with it, and so was the king of Spain; he held conversations about it with the French; but Julius, with his usual assurance and energy, directed the expedition in person. His activity kept the Spanish and the Venetians uneasy and inactive; the former were afraid, and the latter thought they saw a chance to recover the entire kingdom of Naples. Finally, the pope drew the king of France into his enterprise, because when the king saw what he was doing, and realized that he needed the pope's friendship to put down the Venetians, he judged that he could not deny the support of his troops without openly offending him. Thus Julius carried off, in his rash and adventurous way, an enterprise that no other pope, even one who exercised the greatest human prudence, could successfully have performed. If he had waited before leaving Rome till all the diplomatic formalities were concluded, as any other pope would have done, he would never have succeeded. The king of France would have found a thousand excuses, and the other powers would have given him a thousand reasons to be afraid. His other actions can be omitted, as they were all like this one, and all turned out well. The shortness of his life prevented him from having the opposite experience; but in fact if circumstances had

---

3. The pope undertook to dislodge him from Bologna in 1506. "Messer": my lord.

ever required him to act cautiously, he would have been ruined at once; he could never have varied from the style to which nature inclined him.

I conclude, then, that so long as Fortune varies and men stand still, they will prosper while they suit the times, and fail when they do not. But I do feel this: that it is better to be rash than timid, for Fortune is a woman, and the man who wants to hold her down must beat and bully her. We see that she yields more often to men of this stripe than to those who come coldly toward her. Like a woman, too, she is always a friend of the young, because they are less timid, more brutal, and take charge of her more recklessly.

XXVI

AN EXHORTATION TO RESTORE ITALY TO LIBERTY AND FREE HER FROM THE BARBARIANS

Considering, therefore, the matters discussed above, I ask myself whether at present the hour is ripe to hail a new prince in Italy, if there is material here that a careful, able [*virtuoso*] leader could mold into a new form which might bring honor to him and benefits to all men; and I answer that all things now appear favorable to a new prince, so much so that I cannot think of any time more suitable than the present. And if, as I said above, it was necessary, to bring out the power [*virtù*] of Moses, that the children of Israel should be slaves in Egypt; and if, to know the magnanimity of Cyrus, it was necessary that the Persians be oppressed by the Medes; and for Theseus's merit to be known, that the Athenians should be scattered; then, at the present time, if the power [*virtù*] of an Italian spirit is to be manifested, it was necessary that Italy be reduced to her present state; and that she be more enslaved than the Hebrews, more abject than the Persians, more widely dispersed than the Athenians; headless, orderless, beaten, stripped, scarred, overrun, and plagued by every sort of disaster.

And though one man[4] recently showed certain gleams, such as made us think he was ordained by God for our salvation, still we saw how, at the very zenith of his career, he was deserted by Fortune. Thus Italy, left almost lifeless, waits for a leader who will heal her wounds, stop the ravaging of Lombardy, end the looting of the Kingdom and of Tuscany, and minister to those sores of hers that have been festering so long. Behold how she implores God to send someone to free her from the cruel insolence of the barbarians; see how ready and eager she is to follow a banner joyously, if only someone will raise it up. There is no figure presently in sight in whom she can better place her trust than your illustrious house,[5] which, with its fortune and its merits [*virtù*] favored by God and the Church of which it is now the head, can take the lead in this process of redemption.

The task will not be too hard if you keep your eye on the actions and lives of those leaders described above. Men of this sort are rare and wonderful, indeed, but they were nothing more than men, and each of them faced circumstances less promising than those of the present. Their cause was no

---

4. Possibly Cesare Borgia, who was discussed earlier in the book.   5. That is, the Medicis. Pope Leo X (1475–1521) was a Medici (Giovanni de' Medici). *The Prince* was first meant for Giuliano de' Medici. After Giuliano's death it was dedicated to his nephew Lorenzo, later Duke of Urbino.

more just than the present one, nor any easier, and God was no more favorable to them than to you. Your cause *is* just: "for war is justified when it is necessary, and arms are pious when without them there would be no hope at all."[6] Everyone is eager, and where there is such eagerness there can be no great difficulty, if you imitate the methods of those I have proposed as examples. Apart from this, we have experienced extraordinary, unexampled leadings from God in this matter; the sea has divided, a cloud has shown the way, a stone has yielded water, manna has rained from heaven.[7] All things point toward your greatness. The rest is up to you. God will not do everything, lest he deprive us of our free will and a part of that glory which belongs to us.

There is nothing surprising in the fact that none of the Italians whom I have named[8] was able to do what we hope for from your illustrious house; no reason even for wonder if, after so many revolutions in Italy and so many military campaigns, it seems as if military manhood [*virtù*] is quite extinct. The reason is simply that the old methods of warfare were not good, and no one has been able to find new ones. Nothing does so much honor to a man newly risen to power, as the new laws and rules that he discovers. When they are well-grounded and have in them the seeds of greatness, these institutions make him the object of awe and admiration. In Italy there is no lack of material to be given new forms; the limbs of the nation have great strength [*virtù*], so long as the heads are not deficient. Only look at the duels and tourneys where a few men are involved, and you will find that the Italians excel in strength, in dexterity, in mental agility; but when it is a matter of armies, they don't stand the comparison. This all comes from the weakness of the heads; because those who know what they are doing cannot enforce obedience. Each one thinks he knows best, and there has not been anyone hitherto who has raised himself, by strength [*virtù*] or fortune to a point where the others would yield to him. This is the reason why for a long time, in all the wars waged over the last twenty years, whenever an army composed of Italians took the field, it showed up badly. Among the examples of this are, first, the Taro, then Alexandria, Capua, Genoa, Vailà, Bologna, and Mestre.[9]

If, then, your illustrious house is to follow the example of those excellent men who redeemed their native lands, you must first of all, before anything else, provide yourself with your own armies; that is the foundation stone of any enterprise, and you cannot possibly have more faithful, more reliable, or better soldiers than your own. And though each may be a good man individually, they will be even better as a group, when they see themselves united behind a prince of their own, who will support and reward them. It is necessary to build up an army of this sort, if you are to defend yourself with Italian valor [*virtù*] against foreigners. Doubtless the Swiss and Spanish infantry have fearful reputations, yet they are both deficient in ways that will allow a third force not only to withstand them, but to feel confident of overcoming them. The Spaniards cannot stand up against horsemen; and the Swiss are bound to crumble when they meet in battle enemies who are as stubborn as they are. We have seen this, and know by experience that the Spaniards could not hold up against French cavalrymen, and the Swiss were cut up by Spanish infantry. This last theory has not been completely tested,

6. Livy's *History* 9.1, para. 10.   7. An allusion to Moses.   8. Perhaps another reference to Borgia and Sforza.   9. Sites of battles occurring between the end of the century and 1513.

but we had a sample at the battle of Ravenna,[1] where the Spanish infantry came up against battalions of Germans, who are organized in the same way as the Swiss. The agile Spaniards, with the help of their spiked shields, got under the pikes of the Germans, or between them, and were able to stab at them without being in any danger themselves. If it had not been for the cavalry that charged them, the Spaniards would have eaten them all up. When you know the faults of these two infantries, you can set up a third sort, which will stand up to cavalry and not be afraid of infantry; this can be done by raising new armies and changing their formations. Such new inventions as these give a new prince the reputation of a great man.[2]

The occasion must not be allowed to slip away; Italy has been waiting too long for a glimpse of her redeemer. I cannot describe the joy with which he will be greeted in all those districts which have suffered from the flood of foreigners; nor the thirst for vengeance, the deep devotion, the dedication, the tears, that will greet him. What doors would be closed to him? what people would deny him obedience? what envy could oppose him? what Italian would refuse allegiance? This barbarian occupation stinks in all our nostrils! Let your illustrious house, then, take up this task with that courage and with that hope which suit a just enterprise; so that, under your banner, our country may become noble again, and the verses of Petrarch may come true:

> Then virtue[3] boldly shall engage
> And swiftly vanquish barbarous rage,
> Proving that ancient and heroic pride
> In true Italian hearts has never died.[4]

---

1. Between Spain and France in April 1512.   2. Machiavelli was subsequently the author of the treatise *Art of War* (1521).   3. An etymological translation of the original *virtù* (from the Latin *vir,* "man"). 4. From the canzone "My Italy."

MICHEL DE MONTAIGNE
1533–1592

The stylistically rich and thematically varied essays of Michel Eyquem de Montaigne offer an unparalleled view into a single Renaissance mind exploring its own workings. The first writer to ask "Who am I?" and pursue the question with extraordinary honesty and rigor, Montaigne presents himself, in his essays, as an explorer of existential dilemmas and of cultural and psychological identity crises. If at times he appears surprisingly modern in his outlook, his habits of thought, and his theories of selfhood, he is, in fact, best viewed as at once a precursor of modernity, a representative of his time, and an avid student of the classical past. The ease with which his thought turns from classical antiquity to the emerging modern world underscores Montaigne's awareness of his own position in history: he knew that the world he inhabited was undergoing dramatic cultural and geopolitical changes, and he understood that the idea of the self was being transformed along with it.

Montaigne was born on February 28, 1533, in the castle of Montaigne, to a Catholic father and a Protestant mother of Spanish-Jewish descent. His father, Pierre Eyquem, was for two terms mayor of Bordeaux and had fought in Italy under

Francis I. Though no man of learning, Pierre had unconventional ideas of upbringing: Michel was awakened in the morning by the sound of music and had Latin taught him as his mother tongue. At six Michel went to the famous Collège de Guienne at Bordeaux; later he studied law, probably at Toulouse; and in 1557 he became a member of the Bordeaux parliament. In 1565 he married Françoise de la Chassaigne, daughter of a man who, as one of Montaigne's colleagues in the Bordeaux parliament, was a member of the new legal nobility (*noblesse de robe*). Perhaps because of disappointed political ambitions, Montaigne retired from politics in 1570 at the age of thirty-eight: he sold his post as magistrate and retreated to his castle of Montaigne, which he had inherited two years earlier. There in his country estate, he devoted himself to meditation and writing. His famous *Essays*, which began as a collection of interesting quotations, observations, and recordings of remarkable events, slowly developed into its final form of three large books. Although Montaigne spent, as he put it, "most of his days, and most hours of the day" in his library on the third floor of a round tower, the demands of his health and France's tumultuous politics often drew him out of retirement. For the sake of his health (he suffered from gallstones), in 1580 he took a journey through Switzerland, Germany, and Italy. While in Italy he received news that he had been appointed mayor of Bordeaux, an office that he held for two terms (1581–85).

His greatest political distractions, however, concerned the Catholic and Protestant factions that violently divided the court and France itself. French politics profoundly influenced the attitudes toward warfare, political resistance, and clemency expressed in Montaigne's *Essays*. When Henry II died in a jousting accident in 1559 and left the fifteen-year-old Francis II to succeed him, the Huguenots (French Reformers in the tradition of John Calvin), recognized the opportunity to influence the weakened royal government. Catherine de Médicis, the queen mother, seized power when Francis II died in 1560 (his successor, Charles IX, was only ten years old). Her policy of limited religious toleration satisfied neither the Catholic nor the Huguenot factions, and from 1562 to 1568 France fell into civil war three times. Struggles among France, Spain, and England over territorial rights in the Netherlands led to the dangerous possibility of a French war with Spain, which Catherine tried to avoid by planning the assassination of its most influential supporter, the Huguenot Coligny. When her plot failed, she persuaded the young Charles IX that the Huguenots were planning a coup. He is said to have shouted "Then kill them all," sanctioning the St. Bartholomew's Day Massacre of August 24, 1572: noblemen, municipal authorities, and the Parisian mobs indiscriminately slaughtered the Protestants in Paris. The slaughter was imitated in other French cities, and the civil wars once again broke out, with the house of Guise leading the Catholic party and the Bourbons leading the Huguenots.

A third party of *politiques*, including Montaigne, the political theorist Jean Bodin, and the Duke of Alençon (Catherine's youngest son), arose. This party favored religious tolerance and sought a compromise to the old saying that had facilitated so much carnage in France on religious grounds: "one faith, one law, one king." Throughout his country's political struggles, Montaigne sympathized with the unfanatical Henry of Navarre, leader of the Protestants, but his attitude was neutral and conservative. He expressed his joy when Henry of Navarre became King Henry IV and turned Catholic to do so: "Paris," Henry memorably observed, "is well worth a Mass." Montaigne, who died on September 13, 1592, did not live to see Henry's triumphal entrance into Paris.

Montaigne's essays are at once highly personal and outward looking; they present a curious mind in acts of investigating history, the complex and changing sociopolitical world, and the mind's own slightly mysterious workings. "I am a man," he says, quoting the Roman playwright Terence, and "I consider nothing human to be alien to me." As an ethnographer and historian, he studies the characteristics of geographically and historically distant cultures and insists that cultural norms are relative and should be free from judgment by sixteenth-century European standards. As a psychologist, he is drawn to the "alien" or disowned thoughts and experiences of himself and his countrymen. His method is not didactic, and his criticism, which he reserves for fellow Europeans, emerges largely through subtle ironies that he leaves readers to detect. He moves suddenly, for example, from introspection to an ethical challenge. "Authors communicate themselves to the world by some special and extrinsic mark," he comments in the essay *Of Repentance,* but "I am the first to do so by my general being, as Michel de Montaigne, not as a grammarian or a poet or a lawyer. If the world finds fault with me for speaking too much of myself, I find fault with the world for not even thinking of itself."

When Montaigne thinks of himself, he does not aggrandize or justify himself but seeks to enlarge knowledge of how the mind works. Far from prizing his capacity for reason and judgment, for example, he neutrally observes, "My judgment floats, it wanders." Montaigne is, in fact, disarmingly modest: "Reader, I am myself the subject of my book; it is not reasonable to expect you to waste your leisure on a matter so frivolous and empty." Although massively learned, he emphasizes not what he knows but rather, like Plato's Socrates, the ways that knowledge reveals how little he truly knows. Ultimately, his essays lead readers away from character study toward philosophical questions about the grounds for knowledge itself (the branch of philosophy called *epistemology*).

Montaigne's assertions of doubt and consciousness of human vanity have little to do with gloomy despair: his stance is skeptical, not cynical. Thus if he "essays" or probes the human capacity to act purposefully and coherently—as he does in the essay *Of the Inconsistency of Our Actions*—his implicit verdict is not that our action is absolutely futile. Instead, he refuses to attribute to the human mind a coherence it does not possess; to Montaigne, if a man were able to achieve the Stoic ideal of the "constant man," unmoved by circumstance or emotion, the result would be impoverishing. "Our actions are nothing but a patchwork," he remarks, and the insight into the fragmentary, inconsistent pattern of our personal lives leads him to a dramatic perception of the strangeness and instability of the self: "There is as much difference between us and ourselves as between us and others." This idea became highly influential in Renaissance thinking and shaped such haunting insights as John Donne's observation that "ourselves are what we know not." For Renaissance thinkers who embraced Montaigne's perception of psychological mysteriousness, the difficult philosophical imperative of Socrates, "know thyself," seemed endlessly intriguing but doomed.

Montaigne pursues his arguments about the elusive and unstable character of the "self" by considering a wide range of anecdotes, both contemporary and classical. A slippery or undefinable historical character intrigues him far more than a monolithic or single-minded one. Alexander the Great—the legendary warrior who also haunts the pages of Castiglione's *Courtier*—is rendered frighteningly transparent by his obsession with power and conquest: he wants nothing less than to be a god. Emperor Augustus, on the other hand, rewards study precisely because his character has "escaped" the willful reductions of historians bent on "fashioning a consistent and solid fabric" of his character. As Montaigne admiringly puts it in *Of the Inconsistency of Our Actions,* there is in the life of Augustus "such an obvious, abrupt, and continual variety of actions that even the boldest judges have had to let him go, intact and unsolved."

Why was Montaigne so unusually able to suspend the self-interest and bias he considered ingrained in human nature in order to analyze himself, his culture, and the place of humankind in the cosmos? As his life in politics indicates, the violent instability of French history taught him tolerance, skepticism about human self-interest, and hatred of dogmatic positions:

> It demands a great deal of self-love and presumption, to take one's own opinions so seriously as to disrupt the peace in order to establish them, introducing so many inevitable evils, and so terrible a corruption of manners as civil wars and political revolutions with them.

His hatred of political radicalism influenced much of what he saw in ancient history and in contemporary accounts of New World discovery and conquest. This alienation from his own political context suggests one cause of his celebrated doubleness of perspective, which is at once ethnographic (outward looking and impartial) and self-critical (introspective and moral). As he reflects on the ancient and new worlds, he pays special attention to how human beings respond to adversity, oppression, and physical torture. If we keep in mind his impatience with the political and religious ideologues of his own country, we may understand why the heroic self-assertions of Alexander the Great or Hernán Cortés hold no sway over his imagination and sympathies. Violent repression and implacable resistance alike repel Montaigne, who keenly scrutinizes displays of courage that camouflage lessthan-noble motives.

In the most famous essay, *Of Cannibals,* Montaigne compares the behavioral codes of Brazilian cannibals and those of "ourselves" (Europeans) and concludes that "each man calls barbarism whatever is not his own practice." Once he has asserted the relativity of customs, Montaigne is able to praise elements of the savages' culture that he regards as superior to Europe's. He admires the savages' courage, for instance, in which "the honor of valor consists in combating, not in beating." Moreover, he finds in the positive example of the Brazilian cannibals an implicit criticism of violence by Europeans both at home and in the New World. Montaigne remarks, "I am not sorry that we notice the barbarous horror" of cannibal culture, and then continues,

> but I am heartily sorry that judging their faults rightly, we should be so blind to our own. I think there is more barbarity in eating a man alive than in eating him dead; and in tearing by tortures and the rack a body still full of feeling, in roasting a man bit by bit, in having him bitten and mangled by dogs and swine (as we have not only read but seen within fresh memory, not among ancient enemies, but among neighbors and fellow citizens and what is worse, on the pretext of piety and religion), than in roasting and eating him after he is dead.

As an ethnographer, Montaigne is able to grapple with the distinct and alien culture of the savages without passing judgment; but when he reflects on France, he becomes a moralist. Central to the entire essay is the invocation of the Catholics' torture and burning of fellow citizens (Huguenots) that Montaigne ironically tucks in parentheses. Montaigne here juxtaposes two kinds of savagery: that which appears foreign (cannibalism) and that which has grown too familiar (religious persecution).

Montaigne shows as much interest in the behavior of Brazilian and European victims as he does in their torturers. Montaigne writes of paintings that show a Brazilian prisoner of war "spitting in the face of his slayers and scowling at them. Indeed, to the last gasp they never stop braving and defying their enemies by word and look." He continues, "Truly, here are real savages by our standards; for either they must be thoroughly so, or we must be; there is an amazing distance between their character and ours." What Montaigne's example suggests is an unnerving *identity* between the defiant Brazilian natives and the Huguenots of France, who have become inured to the ideas of violent resistance and martyrdom. Like the Brazilian victims of cannibalism, the Huguenots are unwilling, even in the face of death, to moderate their dealings with their torturers, the Catholics who dominate French politics. Montaigne's cannibals, then, help make the entrenched behavior of France's religious factions seem foreign, strange, and savage: both sides are guilty (if not equally so) of "so terrible a corruption of manners as civil wars and political revolutions." His own country's civil strife inspires in Montaigne an unusual ability to transcend smug cultural bias, making him a powerful critic of European culture and an ethnographer able to imagine and study communities other than his own. Like the world of antiquity, which also riveted his imagination, the idea of America allowed Montaigne to explore alternate worlds for their own sake and for their illumination of his own.

FROM Essays[1]

To the Reader

This book was written in good faith, reader. It warns you from the outset that in it I have set myself no goal but a domestic and private one. I have had no thought of serving either you or my own glory. My powers are inadequate for such a purpose. I have dedicated it to the private convenience of my relatives and friends, so that when they have lost me (as soon they must), they may recover here some features of my habits and temperament, and by this means keep the knowledge they have had of me more complete and alive.

If I had written to seek the world's favor, I should have bedecked myself better, and should present myself in a studied posture. I want to be seen here in my simple, natural, ordinary fashion, without straining or artifice; for it is myself that I portray. My defects will here be read to the life, and also my natural form, as far as respect for the public has allowed. Had I been placed among those nations which are said to live still in the sweet freedom of nature's first laws, I assure you I should very gladly have portrayed myself here entire and wholly naked.

Thus, reader, I am myself the matter of my book; you would be unreasonable to spend your leisure on so frivolous and vain a subject.

So farewell. Montaigne, this first day of March, fifteen hundred and eighty.

Of the Power of the Imagination

A strong imagination creates the event, say the scholars. I am one of those who are very much influenced by the imagination. Everyone feels its impact, but some are overthrown by it. Its impression on me is piercing. And my art is to escape it, not to resist it. I would live solely in the presence of gay, healthy people. The sight of other people's anguish causes very real anguish to me, and my feelings have often usurped the feelings of others. A continual

1. Translated by Donald Frame.

cougher irritates my lungs and throat. I visit less willingly the sick toward whom duty directs me than those toward whom I am less attentive and concerned. I catch the disease that I study, and lodge it in me. I do not find it strange that imagination brings fevers and death to those who give it a free hand and encourage it.

Simon Thomas was a great doctor in his time. I remember that one day, when he met me at the house of a rich old consumptive with whom he was discussing ways to cure his illness, he told him that one of these would be to give me occasion to enjoy his company; and that by fixing his eyes on the freshness of my face and his thoughts on the blitheness and overflowing vigor of my youth, and filling all his senses with my flourishing condition, he might improve his constitution. But he forgot to say that mine might get worse at the same time.

Gallus Vibius[1] strained his mind so hard to understand the essence and impulses of insanity that he dragged his judgment off its seat and never could get it back again; and he could boast of having become mad through wisdom. There are some who through fear anticipate the hand of the executioner. And one man who was being unbound to have his pardon read him dropped stone dead on the scaffold, struck down by his mere imagination. We drip with sweat, we tremble, we turn pale and turn red at the blows of our imagination; reclining in our feather beds we feel our bodies agitated by their impact, sometimes to the point of expiring. And boiling youth, fast asleep, grows so hot in the harness that in dreams it satisfies its amorous desires:

> So that as though it were an actual affair,
> They pour out mighty streams, and stain the clothes they wear.
> LUCRETIUS[2]

And although it is nothing new to see horns grow overnight on someone who did not have them when he went to bed, nevertheless what happened to Cippus,[3] king of Italy, is memorable; having been in the daytime a very excited spectator at a bullfight and having all night in his dreams had horns on his head, he grew actual horns on his forehead by the power of his imagination. Passion gave the son of Croesus[4] the voice that nature had refused him. And Antiochus[5] took fever from the beauty of Stratonice too vividly imprinted in his soul. Pliny says he saw Lucius Cossitius changed from a woman into a man on his wedding day. Pontanus[6] and others report similar metamorphoses as having happened in Italy in these later ages. And through his and his mother's vehement desire,

> Iphis the man fulfilled vows made when he was a girl.[7]
> OVID

Passing through Vitry-le-François, I might have seen a man whom the bishop of Soissons had named Germain at confirmation, but whom all the

---

1. Roman orator. Montaigne illustrates his points with many examples from both antiquity and contemporary Europe; it is less important to know who these historical persons were than to follow Montaigne's presentation of telling moments of their lives.   2. Titus Lucretius Caro (94–55 B.C.E.), Roman poet and Epicurean philosopher. From *On the Nature of Things* 4.1035–36.   3. The story of Cippus is told by Pliny (23/24–79 C.E.).   4. Last king of Lydia (reigned ca. 560–46 B.C.E.)   5. Antiochus I (324–261 B.C.E.), who ruled the eastern Seleucide territories from 293/2 B.C.E., took Seleucus's wife, Stratonice. 6. Johannes Pontanus (1426–1503), Renaissance scholar and philosopher.   7. *Metamorphoses* 9.793.

inhabitants of that place had seen and known as a girl named Marie until the age of twenty-two. He was now heavily bearded, and old, and not married. Straining himself in some way in jumping, he says, his masculine organs came forth; and among the girls there a song is still current by which they warn each other not to take big strides for fear of becoming boys, like Marie Germain. It is not so great a marvel that this sort of accident is frequently met with. For if the imagination has power in such things, it is so continually and vigorously fixed on this subject that in order not to have to relapse so often into the same thought and sharpness of desire, it is better off if once and for all it incorporates this masculine member in girls.

Some attribute to the power of imagination the scars of King Dagobert and of Saint Francis. It is said that thereby bodies are sometimes removed from their places. And Celsus tells of a priest who used to fly with his soul into such ecstasy that his body would remain a long time without breath and without sensation. Saint Augustine[8] names another who whenever he heard lamentable and plaintive cries would suddenly go into a trance and get so carried away that it was no use to shake him and shout at him, to pinch him and burn him, until he had come to; then he would say that he had heard voices, but as if coming from afar, and he would notice his burns and bruises. And that this was no feigned resistance to his senses was shown by the fact that while in this state he had neither pulse nor breath.

It is probable that the principal credit of miracles, visions, enchantments, and such extraordinary occurrences comes from the power of imagination, acting principally upon the minds of the common people, which are softer. Their belief has been so strongly seized that they think they see what they do not see.

I am still of this opinion, that those comical inhibitions by which our society is so fettered that people talk of nothing else are for the most part the effects of apprehension and fear. For I know by experience that one man,[9] whom I can answer for as for myself, on whom there could fall no suspicion whatever of impotence and just as little of being enchanted, having heard a friend of his tell the story of an extraordinary impotence into which he had fallen at the moment when he needed it least, and finding himself in a similar situation, was all at once so struck in his imagination by the horror of this story that he incurred the same fate. And from then on he was subject to relapse, for the ugly memory of his mishap checked him and tyrannized him. He found some remedy for this fancy by another fancy: which was that by admitting this weakness and speaking about it in advance, he relieved the tension of his soul, for when the trouble had been presented as one to be expected, his sense of responsibility diminished and weighed upon him less. When he had a chance of his own choosing, with his mind unembroiled and relaxed and his body in good shape, to have his bodily powers first tested, then seized and taken by surprise, with the other party's full knowledge of his problem, he was completely cured in this respect. A man is never after incapable, unless from genuine impotence, with a woman with whom he has once been capable.

This mishap is to be feared only in enterprises where our soul is immoderately tense with desire and respect, and especially if the opportunity is

8. Early Christian church father (354–430 C.E.).   9. Possibly Montaigne himself.

unexpected and pressing; there is no way of recovering from this trouble. I know one man who found it helpful to bring to it a body that had already begun to be sated elsewhere, so as to lull his frenzied ardor, and who with age finds himself less impotent through being less potent. And I know another who was helped when a friend assured him that he was supplied with a counterbattery of enchantments that were certain to save him. I had better tell how this happened.

A count, a member of a very distinguished family, with whom I was quite intimate, upon getting married to a beautiful lady who had been courted by a man who was present at the wedding feast, had his friends very worried and especially an old lady, a relative of his, who was presiding at the wedding and holding it at her house. She was fearful of these sorceries, and gave me to understand this. I asked her to rely on me. I had by chance in my coffers a certain little flat piece of gold on which were engraved some celestial figures, to protect against sunstroke and take away a headache by placing it precisely on the suture of the skull; and, to keep it there, it was sewed to a ribbon intended to be tied under the chin: a kindred fancy to the one we are speaking of. Jacques Peletier[1] had given me this singular present. I thought of making some use of it, and said to the count that he might incur the same fate as others, there being men present who would like to bring this about; but that he should boldly go to bed and I would do him a friendly turn and would not, if he needed it, spare a miracle which was in my power, provided that he promised me on his honor to keep it most faithfully secret; he was only to make a given signal to me, when they came to bring him the midnight meal, if things had gone badly with him. He had had his soul and his ears so battered that he did find himself fettered by the trouble of his imagination, and gave me his signal. I told him then that he should get up on the pretext of chasing us out, and playfully take the bathrobe that I had on (we were very close in height) and put it on him until he had carried out my prescription, which was this: when we had left, he should withdraw to pass water, say certain prayers three times and go through certain motions; each of these three times he should tie the ribbon I was putting in his hand around him and very carefully lay the medal that was attached to it on his kidneys, with the figure in such and such a position; this done, having tied this ribbon firmly so that it could neither come untied nor slip from its place, he should return to his business with complete assurance and not forget to spread my robe over his bed so that it should cover them both. These monkey tricks are the main part of the business, our mind being unable to get free of the idea that such strange means must come from some abstruse science. Their inanity gives them weight and reverence. All in all, it is certain that the characters on my medal proved themselves more venereal than solar, more useful for action than for prevention. It was a sudden and curious whim that led me to do such a thing, which was alien to my nature. I am an enemy of subtle and dissimulated acts and hate trickery in myself, not only for sport but also for someone's profit. If the action is not vicious, the road to it is.

Amasis,[2] king of Egypt, married Laodice, a very beautiful Greek girl; and he, who showed himself a gay companion everywhere else, fell short when it

1. Renaissance mathematician (1517–1582). 2. Pharaoh ca. 569 B.C.E., known for his great public works and unconventional life.

came to enjoying her, and threatened to kill her, thinking it was some sort of sorcery. As is usual in matters of fancy, she referred him to religion; and having made his vows and promises to Venus, he found himself divinely restored from the first night after his oblations and sacrifices.

Now women are wrong to greet us with those threatening, quarrelsome, and coy countenances, which put out our fires even as they light them. The daughter-in-law of Pythagoras used to say that the woman who goes to bed with a man should put off her modesty with her skirt and put it on again with her petticoat. The soul of the assailant, when troubled with many various alarms, is easily discouraged; and when imagination has once made a man suffer this shame—and it does so only at the first encounters, inasmuch as these are more boiling and violent, and also because in this first intimacy a man is much more afraid of failing—having begun badly, he gets from this accident a feverishness and vexation which lasts into subsequent occasions.

Married people, whose time is all their own, should neither press their undertaking nor even attempt it if they are not ready; it is better to fail unbecomingly to handsel the nuptial couch, which is full of agitation and feverishness, and wait for some other more private and less tense opportunity, than to fall into perpetual misery for having been stunned and made desperate by a first refusal. Before taking possession, the patient should try himself out and offer himself, lightly, by sallies at different times, without priding himself and obstinately insisting on convincing himself definitively. Those who know that their members are naturally obedient, let them take care only to counteract the tricks of their fancies.

People are right to notice the unruly liberty of this member, obtruding so importunately when we have no use for it, and failing so importunately when we have the most use for it, and struggling for mastery so imperiously with our will, refusing with so much pride and obstinacy our solicitations, both mental and manual.

If, however, in the matter of his rebellion being blamed and used as proof to condemn him, he had paid me to plead his cause, I should perhaps place our other members, his fellows, under suspicion of having framed this trumped-up charge out of sheer envy of the importance and pleasure of the use of him, and of having armed everyone against him by a conspiracy, malignantly charging him alone with their common fault. For I ask you to think whether there is a single one of the parts of our body that does not often refuse its function to our will and exercise it against our will. They each have passions of their own which rouse them and put them to sleep without our leave. How many times do the forced movements of our face bear witness to the thoughts that we were holding secret, and betray us to those present. The same cause that animates this member also animates, without our knowledge, the heart, the lungs, and the pulse; the sight of a pleasing object spreading in us imperceptibly the flame of a feverish emotion. Are there only these muscles and these veins that stand up and lie down without the consent, not only of our will, but even of our thoughts? We do not command our hair to stand on end or our skin to shiver with desire or fear. The hand often moves itself to where we do not send it. The tongue is paralyzed, and the voice congealed, at their own time. Even when, having nothing to put in to fry, we should like to forbid it, the appetite for eating and drinking does not fail to stir the parts that are subject to it, no more nor less than that other appetite; and it likewise abandons us inopportunely when it sees fit. The organs that serve to discharge the stomach have their own dilatations and compressions, beyond and against our plans, just like those that are destined to discharge the kidneys. To vindicate the omnipotence of our will, Saint Augustine alleges that he knew a man who commanded his behind to produce as many farts as he wanted, and his commentator Vives[3] goes him one better with another example of his own time, of farts arranged to suit the tone of verses pronounced to their accompaniment; but all this does not really argue any pure obedience in this organ; for is there any that is ordinarily more indiscreet or tumultuous? Besides, I know one so turbulent and unruly, that for forty years it has kept its master farting with a constant and unremitting wind and compulsion, and is thus taking him to his death.

But as for our will, on behalf of whose rights we set forth this complaint, how much more plausibly may we charge it with rebellion and sedition for its disorderliness and disobedience! Does it always will what we would will it to will? Doesn't it often will what we forbid it to will, and that to our evident disadvantage? Is it any more amenable than our other parts to the decisions of our reason?

To conclude, I would say this in defense of the honorable member whom I represent: May it please the court to take into consideration that in this matter, although my client's case is inseparably and indistinguishably linked with that of an accessory, nevertheless he alone has been brought to trial; and that the arguments and charges against him are such as cannot—in view of the status of the parties—be in any manner pertinent or relevant to the aforesaid accessory. Whereby is revealed his accusers' manifest animosity and disrespect for law. However that may be, Nature will meanwhile go her way, protesting that the lawyers and judges quarrel and pass sentence in vain. Indeed, she would have done no more than is right if she had endowed with some particular privilege this member, author of the sole immortal work of mortals. Wherefore to Socrates generation is a divine act; and love, a desire for immortality and itself an immortal daemon.[4]

Perhaps it is by this effect of the imagination that one man here gets rid of the scrofula which his companion carries back to Spain.[5] This effect is the reason why, in such matters, it is customary to demand that the mind be prepared. Why do the doctors work on the credulity of their patient beforehand with so many false promises of a cure, if not so that the effect of the imagination may make up for the imposture of their decoction? They know that one of the masters of the trade left them this in writing, that there have been men for whom the mere sight of medicine did the job.

And this whole caprice[6] has just come to hand apropos of the story that an apothecary, a servant of my late father, used to tell me, a simple man and Swiss, of a nation little addicted to vanity and lying. He had long known a merchant at Toulouse,[7] sickly and subject to the stone, who often needed enemas, and ordered various kinds from his doctors according to the circum-

3. Juan Luis Vives (1492–1540), Renaissance philosopher and scholar. 4. Socrates (ca. 470–399 B.C.E.) describes love as a "daemon" in Plato's *Symposium*. 5. Scrofula, or king's evil, was supposed to be curable by the touch of the kings of France. In Montaigne's time great numbers of Spaniards came to France for this purpose [Translator's note]. 6. Montaigne's "cure" for his impotent friend. 7. City in southwestern France.

stances of his illness. Once they were brought to him, nothing was omitted of the accustomed formalities; often he tested them by hand to make sure they were not too hot. There he was, lying on his stomach, and all the motions were gone through—except that no injection was made. After this ceremony, the apothecary having retired and the patient being accommodated as if he had really taken the enema, he felt the same effect from it as those who do take them. And if the doctor did not find its operation sufficient, he would give him two or three more, of the same sort. My witness swears that when to save the expense (for he paid for them as if he had taken them) this sick man's wife sometimes tried to have just warm water used, the effect revealed the fraud; and having found that kind useless, they were obliged to return to the first method.

A woman, thinking she had swallowed a pin with her bread, was screaming in agony as though she had an unbearable pain in her throat, where she thought she felt it stuck; but because externally there was neither swelling nor alteration, a smart man, judging that it was only a fancy and notion derived from some bit of bread that had scratched her as it went down, made her vomit, and, on the sly, tossed a crooked pin into what she threw up. The woman, thinking she had thrown it up, felt herself suddenly relieved of her pain. I know that one gentleman, having entertained a goodly company at his house, three or four days later boasted, as a sort of joke (for there was nothing in it), that he had made them eat cat in a pie; at which one lady in the party was so horrified that she fell into a violent stomach disorder and fever, and it was impossible to save her. Even animals are subject like ourselves to the power of imagination. Witness dogs, who let themselves die out of grief for the loss of their masters. We also see them yap and twitch in their dreams, and horses whinny and writhe.

But all this may be attributed to the narrow seam between the soul and body, through which the experience of the one is communicated to the other. Sometimes, however, one's imagination acts not only against one's own body, but against someone else's. And just as a body passes on its sickness to its neighbor, as is seen in the plague, the pox, and soreness of the eyes, which are transmitted from one body to the other—

> By looking at sore eyes, eyes become sore:
> From body into body ills pass o'er[8]
>
> OVID

—likewise the imagination, when vehemently stirred, launches darts that can injure an external object. The ancients maintained that certain women of Scythia,[9] when animated and enraged against anyone, would kill him with their mere glance. Tortoises and ostriches hatch their eggs just by looking at them, a sign that their sight has some ejaculative virtue. And as for sorcerers, they are said to have baleful and harmful eyes:

> some evil eye bewitched my tender lambs.[1]
>
> VIRGIL

To me, magicians are poor authorities. Nevertheless, we know by experience that women transmit marks of their fancies to the bodies of the children they

8. *The Cure for Love*, lines 615–16.   9. Scythians, the Greek name for Asian tribes who lived in what are now parts of Iran and Turkey, were legendary in the Renaissance for their "barbarity."   1. *Eclogue* 3.103.

carry in their womb; witness the one who gave birth to the Moor.[2] And there was presented to Charles, king of Bohemia and Emperor, a girl from near Pisa, all hairy and bristly, who her mother said had been thus conceived because of a picture of Saint John the Baptist hanging by her bed.

With animals it is the same: witness Jacob's sheep,[3] and the partridges and hares that the snow turns white in the mountains. Recently at my house a cat was seen watching a bird on a treetop, and, after they had locked gazes for some time, the bird let itself fall as if dead between the cat's paws, either intoxicated by its own imagination or drawn by some attracting power of the cat. Those who like falconry have heard the story of the falconer who, setting his gaze obstinately upon a kite in the air, wagered that by the sole power of his gaze he would bring it down, and did. At least, so they say—for I refer the stories that I borrow to the conscience of those from whom I take them. The reflections are my own, and depend on the proofs of reason, not of experience; everyone can add his own examples to them; and he who has none, let him not fail to believe that there are plenty, in view of the number and variety of occurrences. If I do not apply them well, let another apply them for me.

So in the study that I am making of our behavior and motives, fabulous testimonies, provided they are possible, serve like true ones. Whether they have happened or no, in Paris or Rome, to John or Peter, they exemplify, at all events, some human potentiality, and thus their telling imparts useful information to me. I see it and profit from it just as well in shadow as in substance. And of the different readings that histories often give, I take for my use the one that is most rare and memorable. There are authors whose end is to tell what has happened. Mine, if I could attain it, would be to talk about what can happen. The schools are justly permitted to suppose similitudes when they have none at hand. I do not do so, however, and in that respect I surpass all historical fidelity, being scrupulous to the point of superstition. In the examples that I bring in here of what I have heard, done, or said, I have forbidden myself to dare to alter even the slightest and most inconsequential circumstances. My conscience does not falsify one iota; my knowledge, I don't know.

In this connection, I sometimes fall to thinking whether it befits a theologian, a philosopher, and such people of exquisite and exact conscience and prudence, to write history. How can they stake their fidelity on the fidelity of an ordinary person? How be responsible for the thoughts of persons unknown and give their conjectures as coin of the realm? Of complicated actions that happen in their presence they would refuse to give testimony if placed under oath by a judge; and they know no man so intimately that they would undertake to answer fully for his intentions. I consider it less hazardous to write of things past than present, inasmuch as the writer has only to give an account of a borrowed truth.

Some urge me to write the events of my time, believing that I see them with a view less distorted by passion than another man's, and from closer,

2. Saint Jerome tells of a woman who, accused of adultery for giving birth to a black child, was absolved when Hippocrates explained that she had a picture of a dark man hanging in her room by her bed [Translator's note].   3. Genesis 30.37–42. After Laban agreed to give Jacob the striped sheep from his flocks, Jacob bred the sheep in front of rods (the visual stimulation was thought to cause the females to produce striped offspring).

because of the access that fortune has given me to the heads of different parties.[4] What they forget is that even for all the glory of Sallust,[5] I would not take the trouble, being a sworn enemy of obligation, assiduity, perseverance; and that there is nothing so contrary to my style as an extended narration. I cut myself off so often for lack of breath; I have neither composition nor development that is worth anything; I am more ignorant than a child of the phrases and terms that serve for the commonest things. And so I have chosen to say what I know how to say, accommodating the matter to my power. If I took a subject that would lead me along, I might not be able to measure up to it; and with my freedom being so very free, I might publish judgments which, even according to my own opinion and to reason, would be illegitimate and punishable. Plutarch[6] might well say to us, concerning his accomplishments in this line, that the credit belongs to others if his examples are wholly and everywhere true; but that their being useful to posterity, and presented with a luster which lights our way to virtue, that is his work. There is no danger—as there is in a medicinal drug—in an old story being this way or that.

Of Cannibals

When King Pyrrhus[1] passed over into Italy, after he had reconnoitered the formation of the army that the Romans were sending to meet him, he said: "I do not know what barbarians these are" (for so the Greeks called all foreign nations), "but the formation of this army that I see is not at all barbarous." The Greeks said as much of the army that Flaminius brought into their country, and so did Philip, seeing from a knoll the order and distribution of the Roman camp, in his kingdom, under Publius Sulpicius Galba.[2] Thus we should beware of clinging to vulgar opinions, and judge things by reason's way, not by popular say.

I had with me for a long time a man who had lived for ten or twelve years in that other world which has been discovered in our century, in the place where Villegaignon landed, and which he called Antarctic France.[3] This discovery of a boundless country seems worthy of consideration. I don't know if I can guarantee that some other such discovery will not be made in the future, so many personages greater than ourselves having been mistaken about this one. I am afraid we have eyes bigger than our stomachs, and more curiosity than capacity. We embrace everything, but we clasp only wind.

Plato brings in Solon,[4] telling how he had learned from the priests of the city of Saïs in Egypt that in days of old, before the Flood, there was a great island named Atlantis, right at the mouth of the Strait of Gibraltar, which contained more land than Africa and Asia put together, and that the kings of that country, who not only possessed that island but had stretched out so far on the mainland that they held the breadth of Africa as far as Egypt, and the

---

4. A centrist, Montaigne knew leaders of the rivaling factions in France.   5. Roman historian (probably 86–35 B.C.E.).   6. Philosopher and biographer (ca. 50–120 C.E.).   1. King of Epirus (in Greece) who fought the Romans in Italy in 280 B.C.E.   2. Both Titus Quinctius Flaminius and Publius Sulpicius Galba were Roman statesmen and generals who fought Philip V of Macedon in the early years of the 2nd century B.C.E.   3. In Brazil. Villegaignon landed there in 1557.   4. In his *Timaeus*.

length of Europe as far as Tuscany, undertook to step over into Asia and sub-
jugate all the nations that border on the Mediterranean, as far as the Black
Sea; and for this purpose crossed the Spains, Gaul, Italy, as far as Greece,
where the Athenians checked them; but that some time after, both the Athenians and themselves and their island were swallowed up by the Flood.

It is quite likely that that extreme devastation of waters made amazing
changes in the habitations of the earth, as people maintain that the sea cut
off Sicily from Italy—

> 'Tis said an earthquake once asunder tore
> These lands with dreadful havoc, which before
> Formed but one land, one coast[5]
>
> VIRGIL

—Cyprus from Syria, the island of Euboea from the mainland of Boeotia;
and elsewhere joined lands that were divided, filling the channels between
them with sand and mud:

> A sterile marsh, long fit for rowing, now
> Feeds neighbor towns, and feels the heavy plow.
>
> HORACE[6]

But there is no great likelihood that that island was the new world which we
have just discovered; for it almost touched Spain, and it would be an incredible result of a flood to have forced it away as far as it is, more than twelve
hundred leagues; besides, the travels of the moderns have already almost
revealed that it is not an island, but a mainland connected with the East
Indies on one side, and elsewhere with the lands under the two poles; or, if
it is separated from them, it is by so narrow a strait and interval that it does
not deserve to be called an island on that account.

It seems that there are movements, some natural, others feverish, in these
great bodies, just as in our own. When I consider the inroads that my river,
the Dordogne, is making in my lifetime into the right bank in its descent, and
that in twenty years it has gained so much ground and stolen away the foundations of several buildings, I clearly see that this is an extraordinary disturbance; for if it had always gone at this rate, or was to do so in the future, the
face of the world would be turned topsy-turvy. But rivers are subject to
changes: now they overflow in one direction, now in another, now they keep
to their course. I am not speaking of the sudden inundations whose causes
are manifest. In Médoc, along the seashore, my brother, the sieur d'Arsac,
can see an estate of his buried under the sands that the sea spews forth; the
tops of some buildings are still visible; his farms and domains have changed
into very thin pasturage. The inhabitants say that for some time the sea has
been pushing toward them so hard that they have lost four leagues of land.
These sands are its harbingers; and we see great dunes of moving sand that
march half a league ahead of it and keep conquering land.

The other testimony of antiquity with which some would connect this discovery is in Aristotle, at least if that little book Of Unheard-of Wonders is by
him. He there relates that certain Carthaginians, after setting out upon the
Atlantic Ocean from the Strait of Gibraltar and sailing a long time, at last

5. Aeneid 3.414–15.   6. Horatius Flaccus (65–8 B.C.E.), great poet of Augustan Rome. From Art of
Poetry, lines 65–66.

discovered a great fertile island, all clothed in woods and watered by great deep rivers, far remote from any mainland; and that they, and others since, attracted by the goodness and fertility of the soil, went there with their wives and children, and began to settle there. The lords of Carthage, seeing that their country was gradually becoming depopulated, expressly forbade anyone to go there any more, on pain of death, and drove out these new inhabitants, fearing, it is said, that in course of time they might come to multiply so greatly as to supplant their former masters and ruin their state. This story of Aristotle does not fit our new lands any better than the other.

This man I had was a simple, crude fellow—a character fit to bear true witness; for clever people observe more things and more curiously, but they interpret them; and to lend weight and conviction to their interpretation, they cannot help altering history a little. They never show you things as they are, but bend and disguise them according to the way they have seen them; and to give credence to their judgment and attract you to it, they are prone to add something to their matter, to stretch it out and amplify it. We need a man either very honest, or so simple that he has not the stuff to build up false inventions and give them plausibility; and wedded to no theory. Such was my man; and besides this, he at various times brought sailors and merchants, whom he had known on that trip, to see me. So I content myself with his information, without inquiring what the cosmographers say about it.

We ought to have topographers who would give us an exact account of the places where they have been. But because they have over us the advantage of having seen Palestine, they want to enjoy the privilege of telling us news about all the rest of the world. I would like everyone to write what he knows, and as much as he knows, not only in this, but in all other subjects; for a man may have some special knowledge and experience of the nature of a river or a fountain, who in other matters knows only what everybody knows. However, to circulate this little scrap of knowledge, he will undertake to write the whole of physics. From this vice spring many great abuses.

Now, to return to my subject, I think there is nothing barbarous and savage in that nation, from what I have been told, except that each man calls barbarism whatever is not his own practice; for indeed it seems we have no other test of truth and reason than the example and pattern of the opinions and customs of the country we live in. *There* is always the perfect religion, the perfect government, the perfect and accomplished manners in all things. Those people are wild, just as we call wild the fruits that Nature has produced by herself and in her normal course; whereas really it is those that we have changed artificially and led astray from the common order, that we should rather call wild. The former retain alive and vigorous their genuine, their most useful and natural, virtues and properties, which we have debased in the latter in adapting them to gratify our corrupted taste. And yet for all that, the savor and delicacy of some uncultivated fruits of those countries is quite as excellent, even to our taste, as that of our own. It is not reasonable that art should win the place of honor over our great and powerful mother Nature. We have so overloaded the beauty and richness of her works by our inventions that we have quite smothered her. Yet wherever her purity shines forth, she wonderfully puts to shame our vain and frivolous attempts:

> Ivy comes readier without our care;
> In lonely caves the arbutus grows more fair;
> No art with artless bird song can compare.[7]
>
> PROPERTIS

All our efforts cannot even succeed in reproducing the nest of the tiniest little bird, its contexture, its beauty and convenience; or even the web of the puny spider. All things, says Plato,[8] are produced by nature, by fortune, or by art; the greatest and most beautiful by one or the other of the first two, the least and most imperfect by the last.

These nations, then, seem to me barbarous in this sense, that they have been fashioned very little by the human mind, and are still very close to their original naturalness. The laws of nature still rule them, very little corrupted by ours; and they are in such a state of purity that I am sometimes vexed that they were unknown earlier, in the days when there were men able to judge them better than we. I am sorry that Lycurgus[9] and Plato did not know of them; for it seems to me that what we actually see in these nations surpasses not only all the pictures in which poets have idealized the golden age and all their inventions in imagining a happy state of man, but also the conceptions and the very desire of philosophy. They could not imagine a naturalness so pure and simple as we see by experience; nor could they believe that our society could be maintained with so little artifice and human solder. This is a nation, I should say to Plato, in which there is no sort of traffic, no knowledge of letters, no science of numbers, no name for a magistrate or for political superiority, no custom of servitude, no riches or poverty, no contracts, no successions, no partitions, no occupations but leisure ones, no care for any but common kinship, no clothes, no agriculture, no metal, no use of wine or wheat.[1] The very words that signify lying, treachery, dissimulation, avarice, envy, belittling, pardon—unheard of. How far from this perfection would he find the republic that he imagined: *Men fresh sprung from the gods* [Seneca].[2]

> These manners nature first ordained.[3]
>
> VIRGIL

For the rest, they live in a country with a very pleasant and temperate climate, so that according to my witnesses it is rare to see a sick man there; and they have assured me that they never saw one palsied, bleary-eyed, toothless, or bent with age. They are settled along the sea and shut in on the land side by great high mountains, with a stretch about a hundred leagues wide in between. They have a great abundance of fish and flesh which bear no resemblance to ours, and they eat them with no other artifice than cooking. The first man who rode a horse there, though he had had dealings with them on several other trips, so horrified them in this posture that they shot him dead with arrows before they could recognize him.

Their buildings are very long, with a capacity of two or three hundred souls; they are covered with the bark of great trees, the strips reaching to the ground at one end and supporting and leaning on one another at the top, in

---

7. *Elegies* 1.2.10–12.   8. See his *Laws.*   9. The half-legendary Spartan lawgiver (9th century B.C.E.).
1. This passage is always compared with Shakespeare's *The Tempest* 2.1.147 ff.   2. Roman tragedian (4? B.C.E.–65 C.E.), philosopher, and political leader. The quotation is from *Epistles* 90.   3. *Georgics* 2.20.

the manner of some of our barns, whose covering hangs down to the ground and acts as a side. They have wood so hard that they cut with it and make of it their swords and grills to cook their food. Their beds are of a cotton weave, hung from the roof like those in our ships, each man having his own; for the wives sleep apart from their husbands.

They get up with the sun, and eat immediately upon rising, to last them through the day; for they take no other meal than that one. Like some other Eastern peoples, of whom Suidas[4] tells us, who drank apart from meals, they do not drink then; but they drink several times a day, and to capacity. Their drink is made of some root, and is of the color of our claret wines. They drink it only lukewarm. This beverage keeps only two or three days; it has a slightly sharp taste, is not at all heady, is good for the stomach, and has a lax-ative effect upon those who are not used to it; it is a very pleasant drink for anyone who is accustomed to it. In place of bread they use a certain white substance like preserved coriander. I have tried it; it tastes sweet and a little flat.

The whole day is spent in dancing. The younger men go to hunt animals with bows. Some of the women busy themselves meanwhile with warming their drink, which is their chief duty. Some one of the old men, in the morn-ing before they begin to eat, preaches to the whole barnful in common, walking from one end to the other, and repeating one single sentence several times until he has completed the circuit (for the buildings are fully a hun-dred paces long). He recommends to them only two things: valor against the enemy and love for their wives. And they never fail to point out this obliga-tion, as their refrain, that it is their wives who keep their drink warm and seasoned.

There may be seen in several places, including my own house, specimens of their beds, of their ropes, of their wooden swords and the bracelets with which they cover their wrists in combats, and of the big canes, open at one end, by whose sound they keep time in their dances. They are close shaven all over, and shave themselves much more cleanly than we, with nothing but a wooden or stone razor. They believe that souls are immortal, and that those who have deserved well of the gods are lodged in that part of heaven where the sun rises, and the damned in the west.

They have some sort of priests and prophets, but they rarely appear before the people, having their home in the mountains. On their arrival there is a great feast and solemn assembly of several villages—each barn, as I have described it, makes up a village, and they are about one French league[5] from each other. The prophet speaks to them in public, exhorting them to virtue and their duty; but their whole ethical science contains only these two arti-cles: resoluteness in war and affection for their wives. He prophesies to them things to come and the results they are to expect from their undertak-ings, and urges them to war or holds them back from it; but this is on the condition that when he fails to prophesy correctly, and if things turn out otherwise than he has predicted, he is cut into a thousand pieces if they catch him, and condemned as a false prophet. For this reason, the prophet who has once been mistaken is never seen again.

4. A Byzantine lexicographer.   5. About 2.49 miles.

Divination is a gift of God; that is why its abuse should be punished as imposture. Among the Scythians, when the soothsayers failed to hit the mark, they were laid, chained hand and foot, on carts full of heather and drawn by oxen, on which they were burned. Those who handle matters subject to the control of human capacity are excusable if they do the best they can. But these others who come and trick us with assurances of an extraordinary faculty that is beyond our ken, should they not be punished for not making good their promise, and for the temerity of their imposture?

They have their wars with the nations beyond the mountains, further inland, to which they go quite naked, with no other arms than bows or wooden swords ending in a sharp point, in the manner of the tongues of our boar spears. It is astonishing what firmness they show in their combats, which never end but in slaughter and bloodshed; for as to routs and terror, they know nothing of either.

Each man brings back his trophy the head of the enemy he has killed, and sets it up at the entrance to his dwelling. After they have treated their prisoners well for a long time with all the hospitality they can think of, each man who has a prisoner calls a great assembly of his acquaintances. He ties a rope to one of the prisoner's arms, by the end of which he holds him, a few steps away, for fear of being hurt, and gives his dearest friend the other arm to hold in the same way; and these two, in the presence of the whole assembly, kill him with their swords. This done, they roast him and eat him in common and send some pieces to their absent friends. This is not, as people think, for nourishment, as of old the Scythians used to do; it is to betoken an extreme revenge. And the proof of this came when they saw the Portuguese, who had joined forces with their adversaries, inflict a different kind of death on them when they took them prisoner, which was to bury them up to the waist, shoot the rest of their body full of arrows, and afterward hang them. They thought that these people from the other world, being men who had sown the knowledge of many vices among their neighbors and were much greater masters than themselves in every sort of wickedness, did not adopt this sort of vengeance without some reason, and that it must be more painful than their own; so they began to give up their old method and to follow this one.

I am not sorry that we notice the barbarous horror of such acts, but I am heartily sorry that, judging their faults rightly, we should be so blind to our own. I think there is more barbarity in eating a man alive than in eating him dead; and in tearing by tortures and the rack a body still full of feeling, in roasting a man bit by bit, in having him bitten and mangled by dogs and swine (as we have not only read but seen within fresh memory, not among ancient enemies, but among neighbors and fellow citizens, and what is worse, on the pretext of piety and religion),[6] than in roasting and eating him after he is dead.

Indeed, Chrysippus and Zeno, heads of the Stoic sect, thought there was nothing wrong in using our carcasses for any purpose in case of need, and getting nourishment from them; just as our ancestors,[7] when besieged by Caesar in the city of Alésia, resolved to relieve their famine by eating old men, women, and other people useless for fighting.

---

6. The allusion is to the spectacles of religious warfare that Montaigne himself had witnessed in his time and country.   7. The Gauls.

> The Gascons once, 'tis said, their life renewed
> By eating of such food.
>
> JUVENAL[8]

And physicians do not fear to use human flesh in all sorts of ways for our health, applying it either inwardly or outwardly. But there never was any opinion so disordered as to excuse treachery, disloyalty, tyranny, and cruelty, which are our ordinary vices.

So we may well call these people barbarians, in respect to the rules of reason, but not in respect to ourselves, who surpass them in every kind of barbarity.

Their warfare is wholly noble and generous, and as excusable and beautiful as this human disease can be; its only basis among them is their rivalry in valor. They are not fighting for the conquest of new lands, for they still enjoy that natural abundance that provides them without toil and trouble with all necessary things in such profusion that they have no wish to enlarge their boundaries. They are still in that happy state of desiring only as much as their natural needs demand; anything beyond that is superfluous to them.

They generally call those of the same age, brothers; those who are younger, children; and the old men are fathers to all the others. These leave to their heirs in common the full possession of their property, without division or any other title at all than just the one that Nature gives to her creatures in bringing them into the world.

If their neighbors cross the mountains to attack them and win a victory, the gain of the victor is glory, and the advantage of having proved the master in valor and virtue; for apart from this they have no use for the goods of the vanquished, and they return to their own country, where they lack neither anything necessary nor that great thing, the knowledge of how to enjoy their condition happily and be content with it. These men of ours do the same in their turn. They demand of their prisoners no other ransom than that they confess and acknowledge their defeat. But there is not one in a whole century who does not choose to die rather than to relax a single bit, by word or look, from the grandeur of an invincible courage; not one who would not rather be killed and eaten than so much as ask not to be. They treat them very freely, so that life may be all the dearer to them, and usually entertain them with threats of their coming death, of the torments they will have to suffer, the preparations that are being made for the purpose, the cutting up of their limbs, and the feast that will be made at their expense. All this is done for the sole purpose of extorting from their lips some weak or base word, or making them want to flee, so as to gain the advantage of having terrified them and broken down their firmness. For indeed, if you take it the right way, it is in this point alone that true victory lies:

> It is no victory
> Unless the vanquished foe admits your mastery.[9]
>
> CLAUDIAN

The Hungarians, very bellicose fighters, did not in olden times pursue their advantage beyond putting the enemy at their mercy. For having wrung

---

8. Decimus Junius Juvenal (flourished early 2nd century C.E.), last great Roman satirist. From *Satires* 15.93–94.   9. *Of the Sixth Consulate of Honorius*, lines 248–49.

a confession from him to this effect, they let him go unharmed and unransomed, except, at most, for exacting his promise never again to take up arms against them.

We win enough advantages over our enemies that are borrowed advantages, not really our own. It is the quality of a porter, not of valor, to have sturdier arms and legs; agility is a dead and corporeal quality; it is a stroke of luck to make our enemy stumble, or dazzle his eyes by the sunlight; it is a trick of art and technique, which may be found in a worthless coward, to be an able fencer. The worth and value of a man is in his heart and his will; there lies his real honor. Valor is the strength, not of legs and arms, but of heart and soul; it consists not in the worth of our horse or our weapons, but in our own. He who falls obstinate in his courage, *if he has fallen, he fights on his knees*[1] [Seneca]. He who relaxes none of his assurance, no matter how great the danger of imminent death; who, giving up his soul, still looks firmly and scornfully at his enemy—he is beaten not by us, but by fortune; he is killed, not conquered.

The most valiant are sometimes the most unfortunate. Thus there are triumphant defeats that rival victories. Nor did those four sister victories, the fairest that the sun ever set eyes on—Salamis, Plataea, Mycale, and Sicily—ever dare match all their combined glory against the glory of the annihilation of King Leonidas and his men at the pass of Thermopylae.[2]

Who ever hastened with more glorious and ambitious desire to win a battle than Captain Ischolas to lose one? Who ever secured his safety more ingeniously and painstakingly than he did his destruction? He was charged to defend a certain pass in the Peloponnesus against the Arcadians. Finding himself wholly incapable of doing this, in view of the nature of the place and the inequality of the forces, he made up his mind that all who confronted the enemy would necessarily have to remain on the field. On the other hand, deeming it unworthy both of his own virtue and magnanimity and of the Lacedaemonian name to fail in his charge, he took a middle course between these two extremes, in this way. The youngest and fittest of his band he preserved for the defense and service of their country, and sent them home; and with those whose loss was less important, he determined to hold this pass, and by their death to make the enemy buy their entry as dearly as he could. And so it turned out. For he was presently surrounded on all sides by the Arcadians, and after slaughtering a large number of them, he and his men were all put to the sword. Is there a trophy dedicated to victors that would not be more due to these vanquished? The role of true victory is in fighting, not in coming off safely; and the honor of valor consists in combating, not in beating.

To return to our story. These prisoners are so far from giving in, in spite of all that is done to them, that on the contrary, during the two or three months that they are kept, they wear a gay expression; they urge their captors to hurry and put them to the test; they defy them, insult them, reproach them with their cowardice and the number of battles they have lost to the prisoners' own people.

---

1. *Of Providence* 2.   2. The Spartan king Leonidas's defense here took place in 480 B.C.E., during the war against the Persians. "Victories": famous Greek victories against the Persians and (at Himera, Sicily) against the Carthaginians in or about 480 B.C.E.

I have a song composed by a prisoner which contains this challenge, that they should all come boldly and gather to dine off him, for they will be eating at the same time their own fathers and grandfathers, who have served to feed and nourish his body. "These muscles," he says, "this flesh and these veins are your own, poor fools that you are. You do not recognize that the substance of your ancestors' limbs is still contained in them. Savor them well; you will find in them the taste of your own flesh." An idea that certainly does not smack of barbarity. Those that paint these people dying, and who show the execution, portray the prisoner spitting in the face of his slayers and scowling at them. Indeed, to the last gasp they never stop braving and defying their enemies by word and look. Truly here are real savages by our standards; for either they must be thoroughly so, or we must be; there is an amazing distance between their character and ours.

The men there have several wives, and the higher their reputation for valor the more wives they have. It is a remarkably beautiful thing about their marriages that the same jealousy our wives have to keep us from the affection and kindness of other women, theirs have to win this for them. Being more concerned for their husbands' honor than for anything else, they strive and scheme to have as many companions as they can, since that is a sign of their husbands' valor.

Our wives will cry "Miracle!" but it is no miracle. It is a properly matrimonial virtue, but one of the highest order. In the Bible, Leah, Rachel, Sarah, and Jacob's wives gave their beautiful handmaids to their husbands; and Livia seconded the appetites of Augustus to her own disadvantage; and Stratonice, the wife of King Deiotarus,[3] not only lent her husband for his use a very beautiful young chambermaid in her service, but carefully brought up her children, and backed them up to succeed to their father's estates.

And lest it be thought that all this is done through a simple and servile bondage to usage and through the pressure of the authority of their ancient customs, without reasoning or judgment, and because their minds are so stupid that they cannot take any other course, I must cite some examples of their capacity. Besides the warlike song I have just quoted, I have another, a love song, which begins in this vein: "Adder, stay; stay, adder, that from the pattern of your coloring my sister may draw the fashion and the workmanship of a rich girdle that I may give to my love; so may your beauty and your pattern be forever preferred to all other serpents." This first couplet is the refrain of the song. Now I am familiar enough with poetry to be a judge of this: not only is there nothing barbarous in this fancy, but it is altogether Anacreontic.[4] Their language, moreover, is a soft language, with an agreeable sound, somewhat like Greek in its endings.

Three of these men, ignorant of the price they will pay some day, in loss of repose and happiness, for gaining knowledge of the corruptions of this side of the ocean; ignorant also of the fact that of this intercourse will come their ruin (which I suppose is already well advanced: poor wretches, to let themselves be tricked by the desire for new things, and to have left the serenity of their own sky to come and see ours!)—three of these men were at Rouen, at

---

3. Tetrarch of Galatia, in Asia Minor.   **4.** Worthy of Anacreon (572?–488? B.C.E.), major Greek writer of amatory lyrics.

the time the late King Charles IX was there. The king talked to them for a long time; they were shown our ways, our splendor, the aspect of a fine city. After that, someone asked their opinion, and wanted to know what they had found most amazing. They mentioned three things, of which I have forgotten the third, and I am very sorry for it; but I still remember two of them. They said that in the first place they thought it very strange that so many grown men, bearded, strong, and armed, who were around the king (it is likely that they were talking about the Swiss of his guard) should submit to obey a child, and that one of them was not chosen to command instead. Second (they have a way in their language of speaking of men as halves of one another), they had noticed that there were among us men full and gorged with all sorts of good things, and that their other halves were beggars at their doors, emaciated with hunger and poverty; and they thought it strange that these needy halves could endure such an injustice, and did not take the others by the throat, or set fire to their houses.

I had a very long talk with one of them; but I had an interpreter who followed my meaning so badly, and who was so hindered by his stupidity in taking in my ideas, that I could get hardly any satisfaction from the man. When I asked him what profit he gained from his superior position among his people (for he was a captain, and our sailors called him king), he told me that it was to march foremost in war. How many men followed him? He pointed to a piece of ground, to signify as many as such a space could hold; it might have been four or five thousand men. Did all this authority expire with the war? He said that this much remained, that when he visited the villages dependent on him, they made paths for him through the underbrush by which he might pass quite comfortably.

All this is not too bad—but what's the use? They don't wear breeches.

Of the Inconsistency of Our Actions

Those who make a practice of comparing human actions are never so perplexed as when they try to see them as a whole and in the same light; for they commonly contradict each other so strangely that it seems impossible that they have come from the same shop. One moment young Marius is a son of Mars, another moment a son of Venus.[1] Pope Boniface VIII, they say, entered office like a fox, behaved in it like a lion, and died like a dog. And who would believe that it was Nero, that living image of cruelty, who said, when they brought him in customary fashion the sentence of a condemned criminal to sign: "Would to God I had never learned to write!" So much his heart was wrung at condemning a man to death!

Everything is so full of such examples—each man, in fact, can supply himself with so many—that I find it strange to see intelligent men sometimes going to great pains to match these pieces; seeing that irresolution seems to me the most common and apparent defect of our nature, as witness that famous line of Publilius, the farce writer:

---

1. Goddess of love. Marius was the nephew of the older and better-known Marius. Montaigne's source is Plutarch's *Life of Marius*. Mars was the god of war.

Bad is the plan that never can be changed.[2]
PUBLILIUS SYRUS

There is some justification for basing a judgment of a man on the most ordinary acts of his life; but in view of the natural instability of our conduct and opinions, it has often seemed to me that even good authors are wrong to insist on fashioning a consistent and solid fabric out of us. They choose one general characteristic, and go and arrange and interpret all a man's actions to fit their picture; and if they cannot twist them enough, they go and set them down to dissimulation. Augustus has escaped them; for there is in this man throughout the course of his life such an obvious, abrupt, and continual variety of actions that even the boldest judges have had to let him go, intact and unsolved. Nothing is harder for me than to believe in men's consistency, nothing easier than to believe in their inconsistency. He who would judge them in detail and distinctly, bit by bit, would more often hit upon the truth.

In all antiquity it is hard to pick out a dozen men who set their lives to a certain and constant course, which is the principal goal of wisdom. For, to comprise all wisdom in a word, says an ancient [Seneca], and to embrace all the rules of our life in one, it is "always to will the same things, and always to oppose the same things."[3] I would not deign, he says, to add "provided the will is just"; for if it is not just, it cannot always be whole.

In truth, I once learned that vice is only unruliness and lack of moderation, and that consequently consistency cannot be attributed to it. It is a maxim of Demosthenes, they say, that the beginning of all virtue is consultation and deliberation; and the end and perfection, consistency. If it were by reasoning that we settled on a particular course of action, we would choose the fairest course—but no one has thought of that:

> He spurns the thing he sought, and seeks anew
> What he just spurned; he seethes, his life's askew.[4]
> **HORACE**

Our ordinary practice is to follow the inclinations of our appetite, to the left, to the right, uphill and down, as the wind of circumstance carries us. We think of what we want only at the moment we want it, and we change like that animal which takes the color of the place you set it on. What we have just now planned, we presently change, and presently again we retrace our steps: nothing but oscillation and inconsistency:

> Like puppets we are moved by outside strings.[5]
> **HORACE**

We do not go; we are carried away, like floating objects, now gently, now violently, according as the water is angry or calm:

> Do we not see all humans unaware
> Of what they want, and always searching everywhere,
> And changing place, as if to drop the load they bear?[6]
> **LUCRETIUS**

---

2. *Apothegms (Sententiae)*, line 362.   3. *Epistles* 20.   4. *Epistles* 1.1.98–99.   5. *Satires* 2.7.82.
6. *On the Nature of Things* 3.1057–59.

Every day a new fancy, and our humors shift with the shifts in the weather:

> Such are the minds of men, as is the fertile light
> That Father Jove himself sends down to make earth bright.[7]
>
> HOMER

We float between different states of mind; we wish nothing freely, nothing absolutely, nothing constantly. If any man could prescribe and establish definite laws and a definite organization in his head, we should see shining throughout his life an evenness of habits, an order, and an infallible relation between his principles and his practice.

Empedocles noticed this inconsistency in the Agrigentines, that they abandoned themselves to pleasures as if they were to die on the morrow, and built as if they were never to die.[8]

This man would be easy to understand, as is shown by the example of the younger Cato:[9] he who has touched one chord of him has touched all; he is a harmony of perfectly concordant sounds, which cannot conflict. With us, it is the opposite: for so many actions, we need so many individual judgments. The surest thing, in my opinion, would be to trace our actions to the neighboring circumstances, without getting into any further research and without drawing from them any other conclusions.

During the disorders of our poor country,[1] I was told that a girl, living near where I then was, had thrown herself out of a high window to avoid the violence of a knavish soldier quartered in her house. Not killed by the fall, she reasserted her purpose by trying to cut her throat with a knife. From this she was prevented, but only after wounding herself gravely. She herself confessed that the soldier had as yet pressed her only with requests, solicitations, and gifts; but she had been afraid, she said, that he would finally resort to force. And all this with such words, such expressions, not to mention the blood that testified to her virtue, as would have become another Lucrece.[2] Now, I learned that as a matter of fact, both before and since, she was a wench not so hard to come to terms with. As the story[3] says: Handsome and gentlemanly as you may be, when you have had no luck, do not promptly conclude that your mistress is inviolably chaste; for all you know, the mule driver may get his will with her.

Antigonus,[4] having taken a liking to one of his soldiers for his virtue and valor, ordered his physicians to treat the man for a persistent internal malady that had long tormented him. After his cure, his master noticed that he was going about his business much less warmly, and asked him what had changed him so and made him such a coward. "You yourself, Sire," he answered, "by delivering me from the ills that made my life indifferent to me." A soldier of Lucullus[5] who had been robbed of everything by the enemy made a bold attack on them to get revenge. When he had retrieved his loss, Lucullus, having formed a good opinion of him, urged him to some dangerous exploit with all the fine expostulations he could think of,

---

7. *Odyssey* XVIII.135–36, 152–53 in the Fitzgerald translation.   8. From Diogenes Laertius's life of the Greek philosopher Empedocles (5th century).   9. Cato Uticensis (1st century B.C.E.), a philosopher. He is traditionally considered the epitome of moral and intellectual integrity.   1. Montaigne had witnessed spectacles of religious warfare in his homeland.   2. The legendary virtuous Roman who stabbed herself after being raped by King Tarquinius Superbus's son.   3. A common folktale.   4. Macedonian king (382–301 B.C.E.).   5. Roman general (1st century B.C.E.).

> With words that might have stirred a coward's heart.[6]
>
> HORACE

"Urge some poor soldier who has been robbed to do it," he replied;

> Though but a rustic lout,
> "That man will go who's lost his money," he called out;[7]
>
> HORACE

and resolutely refused to go.

We read that Sultan Mohammed outrageously berated Hassan, leader of his Janissaries, because he saw his troops giving way to the Hungarians and Hassan himself behaving like a coward in the fight. Hassan's only reply was to go and hurl himself furiously—alone, just as he was, arms in hand—into the first body of enemies that he met, by whom he was promptly swallowed up; this was perhaps not so much self-justification as a change of mood, nor so much his natural valor as fresh spite.

That man whom you saw so adventurous yesterday, do not think it strange to find him just as cowardly today: either anger, or necessity, or company, or wine, or the sound of a trumpet, had put his heart in his belly. His was a courage formed not by reason, but by one of these circumstances; it is no wonder if he has now been made different by other, contrary circumstances.

These supple variations and contradictions that are seen in us have made some imagine that we have two souls, and others that two powers accompany us and drive us, each in its own way, one toward good, the other toward evil; for such sudden diversity cannot well be reconciled with a simple subject.

Not only does the wind of accident move me at will, but, besides, I am moved and disturbed as a result merely of my own unstable posture; and anyone who observes carefully can hardly find himself twice in the same state. I give my soul now one face, now another, according to which direction I turn it. If I speak of myself in different ways, that is because I look at myself in different ways. All contradictions may be found in me by some twist and in some fashion. Bashful, insolent; chaste, lascivious; talkative, taciturn; tough, delicate; clever, stupid; surly, affable; lying, truthful; learned, ignorant; liberal, miserly, and prodigal: all this I see in myself to some extent according to how I turn; and whoever studies himself really attentively finds in himself, yes, even in his judgment, this gyration and discord. I have nothing to say about myself absolutely, simply, and solidly, without confusion and without mixture, or in one word. *Distinguo*[8] is the most universal member of my logic.

Although I am always minded to say good of what is good, and inclined to interpret favorably anything that can be so interpreted, still it is true that the strangeness of our condition makes it happen that we are often driven to do good by vice itself—were it not that doing good is judged by intention alone.

Therefore one courageous deed must not be taken to prove a man valiant; a man who was really valiant would be so always and on all occasions. If valor were a habit of virtue, and not a sally, it would make a man equally resolute in any contingency, the same alone as in company, the same in single

---

6. *Epistles* 2.2.36.   7. *Epistles* 2.2.39–40.   8. I distinguish (Latin)—that is, I separate into its components.

combat as in battle; for, whatever they say, there is not one valor for the pavement and another for the camp. As bravely would he bear an illness in his bed as a wound in camp, and he would fear death no more in his home than in an assault. We would not see the same man charging into the breach with brave assurance, and later tormenting himself, like a woman, over the loss of a lawsuit or a son. When, though a coward against infamy, he is firm against poverty; when, though weak against the surgeons' knives, he is steadfast against the enemy's swords, the action is praiseworthy, not the man.

Many Greeks, says Cicero, cannot look at the enemy, and are brave in sickness; the Cimbrians and Celtiberians, just the opposite; *for nothing can be uniform that does not spring from a firm principle* [Cicero].[9]

There is no more extreme valor of its kind than Alexander's; but it is only of one kind, and not complete and universal enough. Incomparable though it is, it still has its blemishes; which is why we see him worry so frantically when he conceives the slightest suspicion that his men are plotting against his life, and why he behaves in such matters with such violent and indiscriminate injustice and with a fear that subverts his natural reason. Also superstition, with which he was so strongly tainted, bears some stamp of pusillanimity. And the excessiveness of the penance he did for the murder of Clytus[1] is also evidence of the unevenness of his temper.

Our actions are nothing but a patchwork—*they despise pleasure, but are too cowardly in pain; they are indifferent to glory, but infamy breaks their spirit*[2] [Cicero]—and we want to gain honor under false colors. Virtue will not be followed except for her own sake; and if we sometimes borrow her mask for some other purpose, she promptly snatches it from our face. It is a strong and vivid dye, once the soul is steeped in it, and will not go without taking the fabric with it. That is why, to judge a man, we must follow his traces long and carefully. If he does not maintain consistency for its own sake, *with a way of life that has been well considered and preconcerted*[3] [Cicero]; if changing circumstances makes him change his pace (I mean his path, for his pace may be hastened or slowed), let him go: that man goes before the wind, as the motto of our Talbot[4] says.

It is no wonder, says an ancient [Seneca], that chance has so much power over us, since we live by chance.[5] A man who has not directed his life as a whole toward a definite goal cannot possibly set his particular actions in order. A man who does not have a picture of the whole in his head cannot possibly arrange the pieces. What good does it do a man to lay in a supply of paints if he does not know what he is to paint? No one makes a definite plan of his life; we think about it only piecemeal. The archer must first know what he is aiming at, and then set his hand, his bow, his string, his arrow, and his movements for that goal. Our plans go astray because they have no direction and no aim. No wind works for the man who has no port of destination.

I do not agree with the judgment given in favor of Sophocles, on the strength of seeing one of his tragedies, that it proved him competent to manage his

---

9. Marcus Tullius Cicero (106–43 B.C.E.), Roman orator. The quotation is from *Tusculan Disputations* 2.27.   1. A commander in Alexander's army who was killed by him during an argument, an act Alexander immediately and bitterly regretted, as related by Plutarch in his *Life of Alexander*, chaps. 50–52. 2. *On Duties (De officiis)* 1.21.   3. *Paradoxes* 5.   4. An English captain who fought in France and died there in 1453.   5. *Epistles* 71.

domestic affairs, against the accusation of his son. Nor do I think that the conjecture of the Parians sent to reform the Milesians was sufficient ground for the conclusion they drew. Visiting the island, they noticed the best-cultivated lands and the best-run country houses, and noted down the names of their owners. Then they assembled the citizens in the town and appointed these owners the new governors and magistrates, judging that they, who were careful of their private affairs, would be careful of those of the public.

We are all patchwork, and so shapeless and diverse in composition that each bit, each moment, plays its own game. And there is as much difference between us and ourselves as between us and others. *Consider it a great thing to play the part of one single man*[6] [Seneca]. Ambition can teach men valor, and temperance, and liberality, and even justice. Greed can implant in the heart of a shop apprentice, brought up in obscurity and idleness, the confidence to cast himself far from hearth and home, in a frail boat at the mercy of the waves and angry Neptune; it also teaches discretion and wisdom. Venus herself supplies resolution and boldness to boys still subject to discipline and the rod, and arms the tender hearts of virgins who are still in their mothers' laps:

> Furtively passing sleeping guards, with Love as guide,
> Alone by night the girl comes to the young man's side.[7]
> TIBULLUS

In view of this, a sound intellect will refuse to judge men simply by their outward actions; we must probe the inside and discover what springs set men in motion. But since this is an arduous and hazardous undertaking, I wish fewer people would meddle with it.

6. *Epistles* 120.   7. *Elegies* 2.1.75–76.

MIGUEL DE CERVANTES
1547–1616

The author of Don Quixote's extravagant adventures himself had a most unusual and adventurous life. The son of an apothecary, Miguel de Cervantes Saavedra was born in Alcalá de Henares, a university town near Madrid. Almost nothing is known of his childhood and early education. Only in 1569 is he mentioned as a favorite pupil by a Madrid humanist, Juan López. Records indicate that by the end of that year he had left Spain and was living in Rome, for a time in the service of Giulio Acquaviva, who later became a cardinal. We know that he enlisted in the Spanish fleet under the command of Don John of Austria and that he took part in the struggle of the allied forces of Christendom against the Turks. He was at the crucial Battle of Lepanto (1571), where in spite of fever he fought valiantly and received three gunshot wounds, one of which permanently impaired the use of his left hand, "for the greater glory of the right." After further military action and garrison duty at Palermo and Naples, he and his brother Rodrigo, bearing testimonials from Don John and from the viceroy of Sicily, began the journey back to Spain, where Miguel hoped to obtain a captaincy. In September 1575 their ship was captured near the Marseille coast by

Barbary pirates, and the two brothers were taken as prisoners to Algiers. Cervantes' captors, considering him a person of some consequence, held him as a slave for a high ransom. He repeatedly attempted to escape, and his daring and fortitude excited the admiration of Hassan Pasha, the viceroy of Algiers, who bought him for five hundred crowns after five years of captivity.

Cervantes was freed on September 15, 1580, and reached Madrid in December of that year. There his literary career began rather inauspiciously; he wrote twenty to thirty plays, with little success, and in 1585 published a pastoral romance, *Galatea*. At about this time he had a daughter with Ana Franca de Rojas, and during the same period married Catalina de Salazar, who was eighteen years his junior. Seeking non-literary employment, he obtained a position in the navy, requisitioning and collecting supplies for the "Invincible Armada." Irregularities in his administration, for which he was held responsible if not directly guilty, caused him to spend more time in prison. In 1590 he tried unsuccessfully to obtain colonial employment in the New World. Later he served as tax collector in the province of Granada but was dismissed from government service in 1597.

The following years of Cervantes' life are the most obscure; there is a legend that *Don Quixote* was first conceived and planned while its author was in prison in Seville. In 1604 he was in Valladolid, then the temporary capital of Spain, living in sordid surroundings with the numerous women of his family (his wife, daughter, niece, and two sisters). It was in Valladolid, in late 1604, that he obtained the official license for the publication of *Don Quixote* (Part I). The book appeared in 1605 and was a popular success. Cervantes followed the Spanish court when it returned to Madrid, where he continued to live poorly in spite of a popularity with readers that quickly made proverbial figures of his heroes. A false sequel to his book appeared, prompting him to write his own continuation, *Don Quixote*, Part II, published in 1615. His *Exemplary Tales* had appeared in 1613. He died on April 23, 1616, and was buried in the convent of the Barefooted Trinitarian nuns. *Persiles and Sigismunda*, his last novel, was published posthumously in 1617.

Although, as we have indicated, *The Ingenious Gentleman Don Quixote de la Mancha* was a popular success from the time Part I was published in 1605, it was only later recognized as an important work of literature. This delay was due partly to the fact that in a period of established and well-defined literary genres such as the epic, the tragedy, and the pastoral romance (Cervantes himself had tried his hand at some of these forms), the unconventional combination of elements in *Don Quixote* resulted in a work of considerable novelty, with the serious aspects hidden under a mocking surface.

The initial and overt purpose of the book was to satirize the romances of chivalry. In those long yarns—which had to do with the Carolingian and Arthurian legends and which were full of supernatural deeds of valor, implausible and complicated adventures, duels, and enchantments—the literature that had expressed the medieval spirit of chivalry and romance had degenerated to the same extent to which, in our day, certain conventions of romantic literature have degenerated in "pulp" fiction and film melodrama. Up to a point, then, what Cervantes set out to do was to produce a parody, a caricature of a literary type. But neither the nature of his genius nor the particular method he chose allowed him to limit himself to such a relatively simple and direct undertaking. The actual method he followed to expose the silliness of the romances of chivalry was to show to what extraordinary consequences they would lead a man insanely infatuated with them, once this man set out to live "now" according to their patterns of action and belief.

So what we have is not mere parody or caricature; for there is a great deal of difference between presenting a remote and more or less imaginary world and presenting an individual deciding to live by the standards of that world in a modern and realistic context. The first consequence is a mingling of genres. On the one hand much of the book has the color and intonation of the world of medieval chivalry as its poets had portrayed it. The fact that that vision and that tone depend for their existence in the book on the self-deception of the hero makes them no less operative artistically and adds, in fact, an important element of idealization. On the other hand the chivalric world is continuously jostled by elements of contemporary life evoked by the narrator—the realities of landscape and speech, peasants and nobles, inns and highways. So the author can draw on two sources, roughly the realistic and the romantic, truth and vision, practical facts and lofty values. In this respect—having found a way to bring together concrete actuality and highly ideal values—Cervantes can be said to have created the modern novel.

The consequences of Cervantes' invention are more apparent when we begin to analyze a little more closely the nature of these worlds, romantic and realistic, and the kind of impact the first exerts on the second. The hero embodying the world of the romances is not, as we know, a cavalier; he is an impoverished country gentleman who embraces that code in the "modern" world. Chivalry is not directly satirized; it is simply placed in a context different from its native one. The result of that new association is a new whole, a new unity. The "code" is renovated; it is put into a different perspective, given another chance.

We should remember at this point that in the process of deterioration that the romances of chivalry had undergone, certain basically attractive ideals had become empty conventions—for instance, the ideal of love as devoted "service." In this connection, it may be especially interesting to observe that the treatment of love and Don Quixote's conception of it are not limited to his well-known admiration for his purely fantastic lady Dulcinea but are also dealt with from a feminine point of view. See, as illustration, Marcela's elaborate, logical, and poetic speech (Part I, chapter 14, printed here) that Don Quixote warmly admires; in it the noble shepherdess defends herself against the accusation of being "a wild beast and a basilisk" for having caused Grisóstomo's death and proclaims her right to choose her particular kind of freedom in nature, where "these mountain trees are my company, the clear running waters in these brooks are my mirror."

No less relevant are Quixote's ideals of adventurousness, of loyalty to high concepts of valor and generosity. In the new context those values are reexamined. Cervantes may well have gained a practical sense of them in his own life while still a youth, for instance at the Battle of Lepanto (the great victory of the European coalition against the "infidels") and as a pirate's captive. Because he began writing *Don Quixote* in his late fifties, a vantage point from which the adventures of his youth must have appeared impossibly remote, a factor of nostalgia—which could hardly have been present in a pure satire—may well have entered into his work. Furthermore, had he undertaken a direct caricature of the romance genre, the serious and noble values of chivalry could not have been made apparent except negatively, whereas in the context devised by him in *Don Quixote* they find a way to assert themselves positively as well.

The book in its development is, to a considerable extent, the story of that assertion—of the impact that Don Quixote's revitalization of the chivalric code has on a contemporary world. We must remember, of course, that there is ambiguity in the way the assertion is made; it works slowly on the reader, as his or her own discovery rather than as the narrator's overt suggestion. Actually, whatever attraction the chivalric world of his hero's vision may have had for Cervantes, he does not openly support Don Quixote at all. He even seems at times to go further in repudiating him than he needs to, for the hero is officially insane, and the narrator never tires of reminding us of this. One critic has described the attitude Cervantes affects toward his creature as "animosity." Nevertheless, by the very magniloquence and, often, the extraordinary coherence and beauty that the narrator allows his hero to display in his speeches in defense of his vision and his code, we are gradually led to discover for ourselves the serious and important elements these contain. For instance, Don Quixote's speech evoking the lost Golden Age and justifying the institution of knight-errantry (in Part I, chapter 11, printed here) is described by the narrator—after Don Quixote has delivered it—as a "futile harangue" that "might very well have been dispensed with"; but there it is, in all of its fervor and effectiveness. Thus the narrator's so-called animosity ultimately does nothing but intensify our interest in Don Quixote and our sympathy for him. And in that process we are, as audience, simply repeating the experience many characters have on the "stage" of the book, in their relationships with him.

Generally speaking, the encounters between the ordinary world and Don Quixote are encounters between the world of reality and that of illusion, between reason and imagination, and ultimately between the world in which action is prompted by material considerations and interests and a world in which action is prompted by ideal motives. The selections printed here illustrate these aspects of the experience. Among the first adventures are some that have most contributed to the popularity of the Don Quixote legend: he sees windmills and decides they are giants, country inns become castles, and flocks of sheep become armies. Though the conclusions of such episodes often have the ludicrousness of slapstick comedy, there is a powerfully imposing quality about Don Quixote's insanity; his madness always has method, a commanding persistence and coherence. And there is perhaps an inevitable sense of moral grandeur in the spectacle of anyone remaining so unflinchingly faithful to his or her own vision. The world of "reason" may win in point of fact, but we come to wonder whether from a moral point of view Quixote is not the victor.

Furthermore, we increasingly realize that Quixote's own manner of action has greatness in itself, and not only the greatness of persistence: his purpose is to redress wrongs, to come to the aid of the afflicted, to offer generous help, to challenge danger, and to practice valor. And we finally feel the impact of the arguments that sustain his action—for example, in the episode of the lions in which he expounds "the meaning of valor." The ridiculousness of the situation is counterbalanced by the basic seriousness of Quixote's motives; his notion of courage for its own sake appears, and is recognized, as singularly noble, a sort of generous display of integrity in a world usually ruled by lower standards. Thus the distinction between reason and madness, truth and illusion, becomes, to say the least, ambiguous. The hero's delusions are indeed exposed when they come up against hard facts, but the authority of such facts is seen to be morally questionable.

The effectiveness of Don Quixote's conduct and vision is seen most clearly in his relationship with his "squire," Sancho Panza. It would be a crude oversimplification to say that Don Quixote and Sancho represent illusion and reality, the insane code of knight-errantry versus down-to-earth practicalities. Actually Sancho—though his nature is strongly defined by such elements as his common sense, his earthy speech, his simple phrases studded with proverbs set against the hero's magniloquence—is mainly characterized in his development by the degree to which he believes in his master. He is caught in the snare of Don Quixote's vision; the seeds of the imaginative life are successfully implanted in him.

The impact of Quixote's view of life on Sancho serves, therefore, to illustrate one of the important qualities of the protagonist and, we may finally say, one of the important aspects of Renaissance literature: the attempt, ultimately frustrated but extremely attractive as long as it lasts, of the individual mind to produce a vision and a system of its own in a world that often seems to have lost a universal frame of reference and a fully satisfactory sense of the value and meaning of action. What Don Quixote presents is a vision of a world that, for all its aberrant qualities, appears generally to be more colorful and more thrilling and also, incidentally, to be inspired by more honorable rules of conduct than the world of ordinary people, "realism," current affairs, private interests, easy jibes, and petty pranks. It is a world in which actions are performed out of a sense of their beauty and excitement, not for the sake of their usefulness. It is, again, the world as stage, animated by "folly"; in this case the lights go out at the end, an end that is "reasonable" and, therefore, gloomy. Sancho provides the main example of one who is exposed to that vision and absorbs that light while it lasts. How successfully he has done so is seen during Don Quixote's death scene, in which Sancho begs his master not to die but to continue the play, as has been suggested, in a new costume—that of shepherds in an Arcadian setting. But at that final point the hero is "cured" and killed, and Sancho is restored to the petty interests of the world as he can see it by his own lights, after the cord connecting him to his imaginative master is cut by the latter's "repentance" and death.

PRONOUNCING GLOSSARY

The following list uses common English syllables and stress accents to provide rough equivalents of selected words whose pronunciation may be unfamiliar to the general reader.

Acquaviva: *ahk-wah-vee'-vah*

Benengeli: *ben-en-hel'-ee*

Boiardo: *boy-ar'-doh*

Eugenio: *yoo-hen'-yoh*

Fonseca: *fon-say'-kah*

Mondoñedo: *mon-don-yay'-thoh*

Orbaneja: *or-bah-nay'-hah*

Periquillo: *pehr-i-kee'-yoh*

Quejana: *kay-hah'-nah*

Quesada: *kay-sah'-dah*

Quijada: *kee-hah'-dah*

Quintanar: *kin-ta-nar'*

real: *ray-al'*

Requesenses: *re-ke-sen'-ses*

Roque: *ro'-kay*

Tordesillas: *tor-thay-see'-yas*

FROM DON QUIXOTE[1]

From Part I

Prologue

Idling reader, you may believe me when I tell you that I should have liked this book, which is the child of my brain, to be the fairest, the sprightliest, and the cleverest that could be imagined; but I have not been able to contravene the law of nature which would have it that like begets like. And so, what was to be expected of a sterile and uncultivated wit such as that which I possess if not an offspring that was dried up, shriveled, and eccentric: a story filled with thoughts that never occurred to anyone else, of a sort that might be engendered in a prison where every annoyance has its home and every mournful sound its habitation?[2] Peace and tranquility, the pleasures of the countryside, the serenity of the heavens, the murmur of fountains, and ease of mind can do much toward causing the most unproductive of muses to become fecund and bring forth progeny that will be the marvel and delight of mankind.

It sometimes happens that a father has an ugly son with no redeeming grace whatever, yet love will draw a veil over the parental eyes which then behold only cleverness and beauty in place of defects, and in speaking to his friends he will make those defects out to be the signs of comeliness and intellect. I, however, who am but Don Quixote's stepfather, have no desire to go with the current of custom, nor would I, dearest reader, beseech you with

---

1. Translated by Samuel Putnam. 2. Cervantes was imprisoned in Seville in 1597 and 1602.

tears in my eyes as others do to pardon or overlook the faults you discover in this book; you are neither relative nor friend but may call your soul your own and exercise your free judgment. You are in your own house where you are master as the king is of his taxes, for you are familiar with the saying, "Under my cloak I kill the king."[3] All of which exempts and frees you from any kind of respect or obligation; you may say of this story whatever you choose without fear of being slandered for an ill opinion any more than you will be rewarded for a good one.

I should like to bring you the tale unadulterated and unadorned, stripped of the usual prologue and the endless string of sonnets, epigrams, and eulogies such as are commonly found at the beginning of books. For I may tell you that, although I expended no little labor upon the work itself, I have found no task more difficult than the composition of this preface which you are now reading. Many times I took up my pen and many times I laid it down again, not knowing what to write. On one occasion when I was thus in suspense, paper before me, pen over my ear, elbow on the table, and chin in hand, a very clever friend of mine came in. Seeing me lost in thought, he inquired as to the reason, and I made no effort to conceal from him the fact that my mind was on the preface which I had to write for the story of Don Quixote, and that it was giving me so much trouble that I had about decided not to write any at all and to abandon entirely the idea of publishing the exploits of so noble a knight.

"How," I said to him, "can you expect me not to be concerned over what that venerable legislator, the Public, will say when it sees me, at my age, after all these years of silent slumber, coming out with a tale that is as dried as a rush, a stranger to invention, paltry in style, impoverished in content, and wholly lacking in learning and wisdom, without marginal citations or notes at the end of the book when other works of this sort, even though they be fabulous and profane, are so packed with maxims from Aristotle and Plato and the whole crowd of philosophers as to fill the reader with admiration and lead him to regard the author as a well read, learned, and eloquent individual? Not to speak of the citations from Holy Writ! You would think they were at the very least so many St. Thomases[4] and other doctors of the Church; for they are so adroit at maintaining a solemn face that, having portrayed in one line a distracted lover, in the next they will give you a nice little Christian sermon that is a joy and a privilege to hear and read.

"All this my book will lack, for I have no citations for the margins, no notes for the end. To tell the truth, I do not even know who the authors are to whom I am indebted, and so am unable to follow the example of all the others by listing them alphabetically at the beginning, starting with Aristotle and closing with Xenophon, or, perhaps, with Zoilus or Zeuxis, notwithstanding the fact that the former was a snarling critic, the latter a painter. This work will also be found lacking in prefatory sonnets by dukes, marquises, counts, bishops, ladies, and poets of great renown; although if I were to ask two or three colleagues of mine, they would supply the deficiency by furnishing me with productions that could not be equaled by the authors of most repute in all Spain.

---

3. That is, the king does not own your body.   4. Thomas Aquinas (1225–1274), Italian philosopher and theologian.

"In short, my friend," I went on, "I am resolved that Señor Don Quixote shall remain buried in the archives of La Mancha until Heaven shall provide him with someone to deck him out with all the ornaments that he lacks; for I find myself incapable of remedying the situation, being possessed of little learning or aptitude, and I am, moreover, extremely lazy when it comes to hunting up authors who will say for me what I am unable to say for myself. And if I am in a state of suspense and my thoughts are woolgathering, you will find a sufficient explanation in what I have just told you."

Hearing this, my friend struck his forehead with the palm of his hand and burst into a loud laugh.

"In the name of God, brother," he said, "you have just deprived me of an illusion. I have known you for a long time, and I have always taken you to be clever and prudent in all your actions; but I now perceive that you are as far from all that as Heaven from the earth. How is it that things of so little moment and so easily remedied can worry and perplex a mind as mature as yours and ordinarily so well adapted to break down and trample underfoot far greater obstacles? I give you my word, this does not come from any lack of cleverness on your part, but rather from excessive indolence and a lack of experience. Do you ask for proof of what I say? Then pay attention closely and in the blink of an eye you shall see how I am going to solve all your difficulties and supply all those things the want of which, so you tell me, is keeping you in suspense, as a result of which you hesitate to publish the history of that famous Don Quixote of yours, the light and mirror of all knight-errantry."

"Tell me, then," I replied, "how you propose to go about curing my diffidence and bringing clarity out of the chaos and confusion of my mind?"

"Take that first matter," he continued, "of the sonnets, epigrams, or eulogies, which should bear the names of grave and titled personages: you can remedy that by taking a little trouble and composing the pieces yourself, and afterward you can baptize them with any name you see fit, fathering them on Prester John of the Indies or the Emperor of Trebizond, for I have heard tell that they were famous poets; and supposing they were not and that a few pedants and bachelors of arts should go around muttering behind your back that it is not so, you should not give so much as a pair of maravedis[5] for all their carping, since even though they make you out to be a liar, they are not going to cut off the hand that put these things on paper.

"As for marginal citations and authors in whom you may find maxims and sayings that you may put in your story, you have but to make use of those scraps of Latin that you know by heart or can look up without too much bother. Thus, when you come to treat of liberty and slavery, jot down:

Non bene pro toto libertas venditur auro.[6]

And then in the margin you will cite Horace or whoever it was that said it. If the subject is death, come up with:

Pallida mors aequo pulsat pede pauperum tabernas
Regumque turres.[7]

---

5. Coin worth one thirty-fourth of a *real;* that is, even two *maravedis* were worth very little.   6. Freedom is not bought by gold (Latin); from the anonymous *Aesopian Fables* 3.14.   7. Pale death knocks at the cottages of the poor and the palaces of kings with equal foot (Latin); Horace, *Odes* 1.4.13–14.

If it is friendship or the love that God commands us to show our enemies, then is the time to fall back on the Scriptures, which you can do by putting yourself out very little; you have but to quote the words of God himself:

Ego autem dico vobis: diligite inimicos vestros.[8]

If it is evil thoughts, lose no time in turning to the Gospels:

De corde exeunt cogitationes malae.[9]

If it is the instability of friends, here is Cato for you with a distich:

Donec eris felix multos numerabis amicos;
Tempora si fuerint nubila, solus eris.[1]

With these odds and ends of Latin and others of the same sort, you can cause yourself to be taken for a grammarian, although I must say that is no great honor or advantage these days.

"So far as notes at the end of the book are concerned, you may safely go about it in this manner: let us suppose that you mentioned some giant, Goliath let us say; with this one allusion which costs you little or nothing, you have a fine note which you may set down as follows: *The giant Golias or Goliath. This was a Philistine whom the shepherd David slew with a mighty cast from his slingshot in the valley of Terebinth,*[2] according to what we read in the Book of Kings, chapter so-and-so where you find it written.

"In addition to this, by way of showing that you are a learned humanist and a cosmographer, contrive to bring into your story the name of the River Tagus, and there you are with another great little note: *The River Tagus was so called after a king of Spain; it rises in such and such a place and empties into the ocean, washing the walls of the famous city of Lisbon; it is supposed to have golden sands,* etc. If it is robbers, I will let you have the story of Cacus,[3] which I know by heart. If it is loose women, there is the Bishop of Mondoñedo,[4] who will lend you Lamia, Laïs, and Flora, an allusion that will do you great credit. If the subject is cruelty, Ovid will supply you with Medea; or if it is enchantresses and witches, Homer has Calypso and Vergil Circe. If it is valorous captains, Julius Caesar will lend you himself, in his *Commentaries,* and Plutarch will furnish a thousand Alexanders. If it is loves, with the ounce or two of Tuscan that you know you may make the acquaintance of Leon the Hebrew,[5] who will satisfy you to your heart's content. And in case you do not care to go abroad, here in your own house you have Fonseca's *Of the Love of God,*[6] where you will encounter in condensed form all that the most imaginative person could wish upon this subject. The short of the matter is, you have but to allude to these names or touch upon those stories that I have mentioned and leave to me the business of the notes and citations; I will guarantee you enough to fill the margins and four whole sheets at the back.

"And now we come to the list of authors cited, such as other works contain but in which your own is lacking. Here again the remedy is an easy one; you have but to look up some book that has them all, from A to Z as you were saying, and transfer the entire list as it stands. What if the imposition is

---

8. But I say unto you, love your enemies (Latin); Matthew 5.44. 9. For out of the heart proceed evil thoughts (Latin); Matthew 15.19. 1. As long as you are happy, you will count many friends, but if times become clouded, you will be alone (Latin); Ovid, *Sorrows* 1.9.5–6. 2. 1 Samuel 17.48–49. 3. Gigantic thief in *Aeneid* 8, defeated by Hercules. 4. Father Anthony of Guevara. 5. Leone Ebreo, Neoplatonic author of the *Dialogues of Love* (1535). 6. Cristóbal de Fonseca, *Treatise of the Love of God* (1592).

plain for all to see? You have little need to refer to them, and so it does not matter; and some may be so simple-minded as to believe that you have drawn upon them all in your simple unpretentious little story. If it serves no other purpose, this imposing list of authors will at least give your book an unlooked-for air of authority. What is more, no one is going to put himself to the trouble of verifying your references to see whether or not you have followed all these authors, since it will not be worth his pains to do so.

"This is especially true in view of the fact that your book stands in no need of all these things whose absence you lament; for the entire work is an attack upon the books of chivalry of which Aristotle never dreamed, of which St. Basil has nothing to say, and of which Cicero had no knowledge; nor do the fine points of truth or the observations of astrology have anything to do with its fanciful absurdities; geometrical measurements, likewise, and rhetorical argumentations serve for nothing here; you have no sermon to preach to anyone by mingling the human with the divine, a kind of motley in which no Christian intellect should be willing to clothe itself.

"All that you have to do is to make proper use of imitation in what you write, and the more perfect the imitation the better will your writing be. Inasmuch as you have no other object in view than that of overthrowing the authority and prestige which books of chivalry enjoy in the world at large and among the vulgar, there is no reason why you should go begging maxims of the philosophers, counsels of Holy Writ, fables of the poets, orations of the rhetoricians, or miracles of the saints; see to it, rather, that your style flows along smoothly, pleasingly, and sonorously, and that your words are the proper ones, meaningful and well placed, expressive of your intention in setting them down and of what you wish to say, without any intricacy or obscurity.

"Let it be your aim that, by reading your story, the melancholy may be moved to laughter and the cheerful man made merrier still; let the simple not be bored, but may the clever admire your originality; let the grave ones not despise you, but let the prudent praise you. And keep in mind, above all, your purpose, which is that of undermining the ill-founded edifice that is constituted by those books of chivalry, so abhorred by many but admired by many more; if you succeed in attaining it, you will have accomplished no little."

Listening in profound silence to what my friend had to say, I was so impressed by his reasoning that, with no thought of questioning them, I decided to make use of his arguments in composing this prologue. Here, gentle reader, you will perceive my friend's cleverness, my own good fortune in coming upon such a counselor at a time when I needed him so badly, and the profit which you yourselves are to have in finding so sincere and straightforward an account of the famous Don Quixote de la Mancha, who is held by the inhabitants of the Campo de Montiel region to have been the most chaste lover and the most valiant knight that had been seen in those parts for many a year. I have no desire to enlarge upon the service I am rendering you in bringing you the story of so notable and honored a gentleman; I merely would have you thank me for having made you acquainted with the famous Sancho Panza, his squire, in whom, to my mind, is to be found an epitome of all the squires and their drolleries scattered here and there throughout the pages of those vain and empty books of chivalry. And with this, may God give you health, and may He be not unmindful of me as well. VALE.[7]

7. Farewell (Latin).

["I Know Who I Am, and Who I May Be, If I Choose"]

CHAPTER 1

Which treats of the station in life and the pursuits of the famous gentleman,
Don Quixote de la Mancha.

In a village of La Mancha[8] the name of which I have no desire to recall,
there lived not so long ago one of those gentlemen who always have a lance
in the rack, an ancient buckler, a skinny nag, and a greyhound for the chase.
A stew with more beef than mutton in it, chopped meat for his evening meal,
scraps for a Saturday, lentils on Friday, and a young pigeon as a special delicacy for Sunday, went to account for three-quarters of his income. The rest
of it he laid out on a broadcloth greatcoat and velvet stockings for feast days,
with slippers to match, while the other days of the week he cut a figure in a
suit of the finest homespun. Living with him were a housekeeper in her for-
ties, a niece who was not yet twenty, and a lad of the field and market place
who saddled his horse for him and wielded the pruning knife.

This gentleman of ours was close on to fifty, of a robust constitution but
with little flesh on his bones and a face that was lean and gaunt. He was
noted for his early rising, being very fond of the hunt. They will try to tell
you that his surname was Quijada or Quesada—there is some difference of
opinion among those who have written on the subject—but according to the
most likely conjectures we are to understand that it was really Quejana. But
all this means very little so far as our story is concerned, providing that in
the telling of it we do not depart one iota from the truth.

You may know, then, that the aforesaid gentleman, on those occasions
when he was at leisure, which was most of the year around, was in the
habit of reading books of chivalry with such pleasure and devotion as to
lead him almost wholly to forget the life of a hunter and even the administration of his estate. So great was his curiosity and infatuation in this
regard that he even sold many acres of tillable land in order to be able to
buy and read the books that he loved, and he would carry home with him as
many of them as he could obtain.

Of all those that he thus devoured none pleased him so well as the ones
that had been composed by the famous Feliciano de Silva,[9] whose lucid
prose style and involved conceits were as precious to him as pearls; especially when he came to read those tales of love and amorous challenges that
are to be met with in many places, such a passage as the following, for
example: "The reason of the unreason that afflicts my reason, in such a
manner weakens my reason that I with reason lament me of your comeliness." And he was similarly affected when his eyes fell upon such lines as
these: ". . . the high Heaven of your divinity divinely fortifies you with the
stars and renders you deserving of that desert your greatness doth deserve."

The poor fellow used to lie awake nights in an effort to disentangle the
meaning and make sense out of passages such as these, although Aristotle
himself would not have been able to understand them, even if he had been
resurrected for that sole purpose. He was not at ease in his mind over those

---

8. Efforts at identifying the village have proved inconclusive. La Mancha is a section of Spain south of
Madrid.   9. Author of romances (16th century); the lines that follow are from his *Don Florisel de*
Niguea.

wounds that Don Belianís[1] gave and received; for no matter how great the surgeons who treated him, the poor fellow must have been left with his face and his entire body covered with marks and scars. Nevertheless, he was grateful to the author for closing the book with the promise of an interminable adventure to come; many a time he was tempted to take up his pen and literally finish the tale as had been promised, and he undoubtedly would have done so, and would have succeeded at it very well, if his thoughts had not been constantly occupied with other things of greater moment.

He often talked it over with the village curate, who was a learned man, a graduate of Sigüenza,[2] and they would hold long discussions as to who had been the better knight, Palmerin of England or Amadis of Gaul; but Master Nicholas, the barber of the same village, was in the habit of saying that no one could come up to the Knight of Phoebus,[3] and that if anyone *could* compare with him it was Don Galaor, brother of Amadis of Gaul, for Galaor was ready for anything—he was none of your finical knights, who went around whimpering as his brother did, and in point of valor he did not lag behind him.

In short, our gentleman became so immersed in his reading that he spent whole nights from sundown to sunup and his days from dawn to dusk in poring over his books, until, finally, from so little sleeping and so much reading, his brain dried up and he went completely out of his mind. He had filled his imagination with everything that he had read, with enchantments, knightly encounters, battles, challenges, wounds, with tales of love and its torments, and all sorts of impossible things, and as a result had come to believe that all these fictitious happenings were true; they were more real to him than anything else in the world. He would remark that the Cid Ruy Díaz had been a very good knight, but there was no comparison between him and the Knight of the Flaming Sword, who with a single backward stroke had cut in half two fierce and monstrous giants. He preferred Bernardo del Carpio, who at Roncesvalles had slain Roland despite the charm the latter bore, availing himself of the stratagem which Hercules employed when he strangled Antaeus,[4] the son of Earth, in his arms.

He had much good to say for Morgante;[5] who, though he belonged to the haughty, overbearing race of giants, was of an affable disposition and well brought up. But, above all, he cherished an admiration for Rinaldo of Montalbán,[6] especially as he beheld him sallying forth from his castle to rob all those that crossed his path, or when he thought of him overseas stealing the image of Mohammed which, so the story has it, was all of gold. And he would have liked very well to have had his fill of kicking that traitor Galalón,[7] a privilege for which he would have given his housekeeper with his niece thrown into the bargain.

At last, when his wits were gone beyond repair, he came to conceive the strangest idea that ever occurred to any madman in this world. It now

---

1. The allusion is to a romance by Jerónimo Fernández.   2. Ironical, for Sigüenza was the seat of a minor and discredited university.   3. Or Knight of Sun. Heroes of romances customarily adopted emblematic names and also changed them according to circumstances. Palmerin and Amadis were each a hero of a very famous romance of chivalry.   4. In mythology, he was invulnerable as long as he maintained contact with his mother, Earth. Hercules killed him while holding him raised in his arms. "Charm": the magic gift of invulnerability.   5. In Pulci's *Morgante maggiore*, a comic-epic poem of the Italian Renaissance.   6. Roland's cousin. In Boiardo's *Roland in Love* (*Orlando Innamorato*) and Ariosto's *Roland Mad* (*Orlando Furioso*), romantic and comic-epic poems of the Italian Renaissance.   7. Ganelón, the villain in the Charlemagne legend who betrayed the French at Roncesvalles.

appeared to him fitting and necessary, in order to win a greater amount of honor for himself and serve his country at the same time, to become a knight-errant and roam the world on horseback, in a suit of armor; he would go in quest of adventures, by way of putting into practice all that he had read in his books; he would right every manner of wrong, placing himself in situations of the greatest peril such as would redound to the eternal glory of his name. As a reward for his valor and the might of his arm, the poor fellow could already see himself crowned Emperor of Trebizond at the very least; and so, carried away by the strange pleasure that he found in such thoughts as these, he at once set about putting his plan into effect.

The first thing he did was to burnish up some old pieces of armor, left him by his great-grandfather, which for ages had lain in a corner, moldering and forgotten. He polished and adjusted them as best he could, and then he noticed that one very important thing was lacking: there was no closed helmet, but only a morion, or visorless headpiece, with turned up brim of the kind foot soldiers wore. His ingenuity, however, enabled him to remedy this, and he proceeded to fashion out of cardboard a kind of half-helmet, which, when attached to the morion, gave the appearance of a whole one. True, when he went to see if it was strong enough to withstand a good slashing blow, he was somewhat disappointed; for when he drew his sword and gave it a couple of thrusts, he succeeded only in undoing a whole week's labor. The ease with which he had hewed it to bits disturbed him no little, and he decided to make it over. This time he placed a few strips of iron on the inside, and then, convinced that it was strong enough, refrained from putting it to any further test; instead, he adopted it then and there as the finest helmet ever made.

After this, he went out to have a look at his nag; and although the animal had more *cuartos*, or cracks, in its hoof than there are quarters in a real,[8] and more blemishes than Gonela's steed which *tantum pellis et ossa fuit*,[9] it nonetheless looked to its master like a far better horse than Alexander's Bucephalus or the Babieca of the Cid.[1] He spent all of four days in trying to think up a name for his mount; for—so he told himself—seeing that it belonged to so famous and worthy a knight, there was no reason why it should not have a name of equal renown. The kind of name he wanted was one that would at once indicate what the nag had been before it came to belong to a knight-errant and what its present status was; for it stood to reason that, when the master's worldly condition changed, his horse also ought to have a famous, high-sounding appellation, one suited to the new order of things and the new profession that it was to follow.

After he in his memory and imagination had made up, struck out, and discarded many names, now adding to and now subtracting from the list, he finally hit upon "Rocinante," a name that impressed him as being sonorous and at the same time indicative of what the steed had been when it was but a hack, whereas now it was nothing other than the first and foremost of all the hacks[2] in the world.

Having found a name for his horse that pleased his fancy, he then desired to do as much for himself, and this required another week, and by the end of

8. A coin (about five cents). "Cuartos": coins worth one eighth of a *real*. 9. Was so much skin and bones (Latin). 1. The chief (Spanish); that is, Ruy Díaz, celebrated hero of *Poema del Cid* (12th century). 2. In Spanish, *rocín*.

that period he had made up his mind that he was henceforth to be known as Don Quixote, which, as has been stated, has led the authors of this veracious history to assume that his real name must undoubtedly have been Quijada, and not Quesada as others would have it. But remembering that the valiant Amadis was not content to call himself that and nothing more, but added the name of his kingdom and fatherland that he might make it famous also, and thus came to take the name Amadis of Gaul, so our good knight chose to add his place of origin and become "Don Quixote de la Mancha"; for by this means, as he saw it, he was making very plain his lineage and was conferring honor upon his country by taking its name as his own.

And so, having polished up his armor and made the morion over into a closed helmet, and having given himself and his horse a name, he naturally found but one thing lacking still: he must seek out a lady of whom he could become enamored; for a knight-errant without a lady-love was like a tree without leaves or fruit, a body without a soul.

"If," he said to himself, "as a punishment for my sins or by a stroke of fortune I should come upon some giant hereabouts, a thing that very commonly happens to knights-errant, and if I should slay him in a hand-to-hand encounter or perhaps cut him in two, or, finally, if I should vanquish and subdue him, would it not be well to have someone to whom I may send him as a present, in order that he, if he is living, may come in, fall upon his knees in front of my sweet lady, and say in a humble and submissive tone of voice, 'I, lady, am the giant Caraculiambro, lord of the island Malindrania, who has been overcome in single combat by that knight who never can be praised enough, Don Quixote de la Mancha, the same who sent me to present myself before your Grace that your Highness may dispose of me as you see fit'?"

Oh, how our good knight reveled in this speech, and more than ever when he came to think of the name that he should give his lady! As the story goes, there was a very good-looking farm girl who lived near by, with whom he had once been smitten, although it is generally believed that she never knew or suspected it. Her name was Aldonza Lorenzo, and it seemed to him that she was the one upon whom he should bestow the title of mistress of his thoughts. For her he wished a name that should not be incongruous with his own and that would convey the suggestion of a princess or a great lady; and, accordingly, he resolved to call her "Dulcinea del Toboso," she being a native of that place. A musical name to his ears, out of the ordinary and significant, like the others he had chosen for himself and his appurtenances.

CHAPTER 2

Which treats of the first sally that the ingenious Don Quixote made from his native heath.

Having, then, made all these preparations, he did not wish to lose any time in putting his plan into effect, for he could not but blame himself for what the world was losing by his delay, so many were the wrongs that were to be righted, the grievances to be redressed, the abuses to be done away with, and the duties to be performed. Accordingly, without informing anyone of his intention and without letting anyone see him, he set out one morning before daybreak on one of those very hot days in July. Donning all his armor, mounting Rocinante, adjusting his ill-contrived helmet, bracing his shield on his arm, and taking up his lance, he sallied forth by the back gate of his stable yard into the open countryside. It was with great contentment and joy that he saw how easily he had made a beginning toward the fulfillment of his desire.

No sooner was he out on the plain, however, than a terrible thought assailed him, one that all but caused him to abandon the enterprise he had undertaken. This occurred when he suddenly remembered that he had never formally been dubbed a knight, and so, in accordance with the law of knighthood, was not permitted to bear arms against one who had a right to that title. And even if he had been, as a novice knight he would have had to wear white armor, without any device on his shield, until he should have earned one by his exploits. These thoughts led him to waver in his purpose, but, madness prevailing over reason, he resolved to have himself knighted by the first person he met, as many others had done if what he had read in those books that he had at home was true. And so far as white armor was concerned, he would scour his own the first chance that offered until it shone whiter than any ermine. With this he became more tranquil and continued on his way, letting his horse take whatever path it chose, for he believed that therein lay the very essence of adventures.

And so we find our newly fledged adventurer jogging along and talking to himself. "Undoubtedly," he is saying, "in the days to come, when the true history of my famous deeds is published, the learned chronicler who records them, when he comes to describe my first sally so early in the morning, will put down something like this: 'No sooner had the rubicund Apollo spread over the face of the broad and spacious earth the gilded filaments of his beauteous locks, and no sooner had the little singing birds of painted plumage greeted with their sweet and mellifluous harmony the coming of the Dawn, who, leaving the soft couch of her jealous spouse, now showed herself to mortals at all the doors and balconies of the horizon that bounds La Mancha—no sooner had this happened than the famous knight, Don Quixote de la Mancha, forsaking his own downy bed and mounting his famous steed, Rocinante, fared forth and began riding over the ancient and famous Campo de Montiel.'"[3]

And this was the truth, for he was indeed riding over that stretch of plain.

"O happy age and happy century," he went on, "in which my famous exploits shall be published, exploits worthy of being engraved in bronze, sculptured in marble, and depicted in paintings for the benefit of posterity. O wise magician, whoever you be, to whom shall fall the task of chronicling this extraordinary history of mine! I beg of you not to forget my good Rocinante, eternal companion of my wayfarings and my wanderings."

Then, as though he really had been in love: "O Princess Dulcinea, lady of this captive heart! Much wrong have you done me in thus sending me forth with your reproaches and sternly commanding me not to appear in your beauteous presence. O lady, deign to be mindful of this your subject who endures so many woes for the love of you."

And so he went on, stringing together absurdities, all of a kind that his books had taught him, imitating insofar as he was able the language of their authors. He rode slowly, and the sun came up so swiftly and with so much heat that it would have been sufficient to melt his brains if he had had any.

3. The scene of a battle in 1369.

He had been on the road almost the entire day without anything happening that is worthy of being set down here; and he was on the verge of despair, for he wished to meet someone at once with whom he might try the valor of his good right arm. Certain authors say that his first adventure was that of Puerto Lápice, while others state that it was that of the windmills; but in this particular instance I am in a position to affirm what I have read in the annals of La Mancha; and that is to the effect that he went all that day until nightfall, when he and his hack found themselves tired to death and famished. Gazing all around him to see if he could discover some castle or shepherd's hut where he might take shelter and attend to his pressing needs, he caught sight of an inn not far off the road along which they were traveling, and this to him was like a star guiding him not merely to the gates, but rather, let us say, to the palace of redemption. Quickening his pace, he came up to it just as night was falling.

By chance there stood in the doorway two lasses of the sort known as "of the district"; they were on their way to Seville in the company of some mule drivers who were spending the night in the inn. Now, everything that this adventurer of ours thought, saw, or imagined seemed to him to be directly out of one of the storybooks he had read, and so, when he caught sight of the inn, it at once became a castle with its four turrets and its pinnacles of gleaming silver, not to speak of the drawbridge and moat and all the other things that are commonly supposed to go with a castle. As he rode up to it, he accordingly reined in Rocinante and sat there waiting for a dwarf to appear upon the battlements and blow his trumpet by way of announcing the arrival of a knight. The dwarf, however, was slow in coming, and as Rocinante was anxious to reach the stable, Don Quixote drew up to the door of the hostelry and surveyed the two merry maidens, who to him were a pair of beauteous damsels or gracious ladies taking their ease at the castle gate.

And then a swineherd came along, engaged in rounding up his drove of hogs—for, without any apology, that is what they were. He gave a blast on his horn to bring them together, and this at once became for Don Quixote just what he wished it to be: some dwarf who was heralding his coming; and so it was with a vast deal of satisfaction that he presented himself before the ladies in question, who, upon beholding a man in full armor like this, with lance and buckler, were filled with fright and made as if to flee indoors. Realizing that they were afraid, Don Quixote raised his pasteboard visor and revealed his withered, dust-covered face.

"Do not flee, your Ladyships," he said to them in a courteous manner and gentle voice. "You need not fear that any wrong will be done you, for it is not in accordance with the order of knighthood which I profess to wrong anyone, much less such highborn damsels as your appearance shows you to be."

The girls looked at him, endeavoring to scan his face, which was half hidden by his ill-made visor. Never having heard women of their profession called damsels before, they were unable to restrain their laughter, at which Don Quixote took offense.

"Modesty," he observed, "well becomes those with the dower of beauty, and, moreover, laughter that has not good cause is a very foolish thing. But I do not say this to be discourteous or to hurt your feelings; my only desire is to serve you."

The ladies did not understand what he was talking about, but felt more than ever like laughing at our knight's unprepossessing figure. This increased his annoyance, and there is no telling what would have happened if at that moment the innkeeper had not come out. He was very fat and very peaceably inclined; but upon sighting this grotesque personage clad in bits of armor that were quite as oddly matched as were his bridle, lance, buckler, and corselet, mine host was not at all indisposed to join the lasses in their merriment. He was suspicious, however, of all this paraphernalia and decided that it would be better to keep a civil tongue in his head.

"If, Sir Knight," he said, "your Grace desires a lodging, aside from a bed— for there is none to be had in this inn—you will find all else that you may want in great abundance."

When Don Quixote saw how humble the governor of the castle was—for he took the innkeeper and his inn to be no less than that—he replied, "For me, Sir Castellan,[4] anything will do, since

> Arms are my only ornament,
> My only rest the fight, etc."

The landlord thought that the knight had called him a castellan because he took him for one of those worthies of Castile, whereas the truth was, he was an Andalusian from the beach of Sanlúcar, no less a thief than Cacus[5] himself, and as full of tricks as a student or a page boy.

"In that case," he said,

> "Your bed will be the solid rock,
> Your sleep: to watch all night.

This being so, you may be assured of finding beneath this roof enough to keep you awake for a whole year, to say nothing of a single night."

With this, he went up to hold the stirrup for Don Quixote, who encountered much difficulty in dismounting, not having broken his fast all day long. The knight then directed his host to take good care of his steed, as it was the best piece of horseflesh in all the world. The innkeeper looked it over, and it did not impress him as being half as good as Don Quixote had said it was. Having stabled the animal, he came back to see what his guest would have and found the latter being relieved of his armor by the damsels, who by now had made their peace with the new arrival. They had already removed his breastplate and backpiece but had no idea how they were going to open his gorget or get his improvised helmet off. That piece of armor had been tied on with green ribbons which it would be necessary to cut, since the knots could not be undone, but he would not hear of this, and so spent all the rest of that night with his headpiece in place, which gave him the weirdest, most laughable appearance that could be imagined.

Don Quixote fancied that these wenches who were assisting him must surely be the chatelaine and other ladies of the castle, and so proceeded to address them very gracefully and with much wit:

---

4. The Spanish, *castellano*, means both "castellan" and "Castilian."   **5.** In Roman mythology he stole some of Hercules' cattle, concealing the theft by having them walk backward into his cave; Cacus was finally discovered and slain.

Never was knight so served
By any noble dame
As was Don Quixote
When from his village he came,
With damsels to wait on his every need
While princesses cared for his hack . . .

"By hack," he explained, "is meant my steed Rocinante, for that is his name, and mine is Don Quixote de la Mancha. I had no intention of revealing my identity until my exploits done in your service should have made me known to you; but the necessity of adapting to present circumstances that old ballad of Lancelot has led to your becoming acquainted with it prematurely. However, the time will come when your Ladyships shall command and I will obey and with the valor of my good right arm show you how eager I am to serve you."

The young women were not used to listening to speeches like this and had not a word to say, but merely asked him if he desired to eat anything.

"I could eat a bite of something, yes," replied Don Quixote. "Indeed, I feel that a little food would go very nicely just now."

He thereupon learned that, since it was Friday, there was nothing to be had in all the inn except a few portions of codfish, which in Castile is called *abadejo,* in Andalusia *bacalao,* in some places *curadillo,* and elsewhere *truchuella* or small trout. Would his Grace, then, have some small trout, seeing that was all there was that they could offer him?

"If there are enough of them," said Don Quixote, "they will take the place of a trout, for it is all one to me whether I am given in change eight reales or one piece of eight. What is more, those small trout may be like veal, which is better than beef, or like kid, which is better than goat. But however that may be, bring them on at once, for the weight and burden of arms is not to be borne without inner sustenance."

Placing the table at the door of the hostelry, in the open air, they brought the guest a portion of badly soaked and worse cooked codfish and a piece of bread as black and moldy as the suit of armor that he wore. It was a mirth-provoking sight to see him eat, for he still had his helmet on with his visor fastened, which made it impossible for him to put anything into his mouth with his hands, and so it was necessary for one of the girls to feed him. As for giving him anything to drink, that would have been out of the question if the innkeeper had not hollowed out a reed, placing one end in Don Quixote's mouth while through the other end he poured the wine. All this the knight bore very patiently rather than have them cut the ribbons of his helmet.

At this point a gelder of pigs approached the inn, announcing his arrival with four or five blasts on his horn, all of which confirmed Don Quixote in the belief that this was indeed a famous castle, for what was this if not music that they were playing for him? The fish was trout, the bread was the finest, the wenches were ladies, and the innkeeper was the castellan. He was convinced that he had been right in his resolve to sally forth and roam the world at large, but there was one thing that still distressed him greatly, and that was the fact that he had not as yet been dubbed a knight; as he saw it, he could not legitimately engage in any adventure until he had received the order of knighthood.

CHAPTER 3

Of the amusing manner in which Don Quixote had himself dubbed a knight.

Wearied of his thoughts, Don Quixote lost no time over the scanty repast which the inn afforded him. When he had finished, he summoned the landlord and, taking him out to the stable, closed the doors and fell on his knees in front of him.

"Never, valiant knight," he said, "shall I arise from here until you have courteously granted me the boon I seek, one which will redound to your praise and to the good of the human race."

Seeing his guest at his feet and hearing him utter such words as these, the innkeeper could only stare at him in bewilderment, not knowing what to say or do. It was in vain that he entreated him to rise, for Don Quixote refused to do so until his request had been granted.

"I expected nothing less of your great magnificence, my lord," the latter then continued, "and so I may tell you that the boon I asked and which you have so generously conceded me is that tomorrow morning you dub me a knight. Until that time, in the chapel of this your castle, I will watch over my armor, and when morning comes, as I have said, that which I so desire shall then be done, in order that I may lawfully go to the four corners of the earth in quest of adventures and to succor the needy, which is the chivalrous duty of all knights-errant such as I who long to engage in deeds of high emprise."

The innkeeper, as we have said, was a sharp fellow. He already had a suspicion that his guest was not quite right in the head, and he was now convinced of it as he listened to such remarks as these. However, just for the sport of it, he determined to humor him; and so he went on to assure Don Quixote that he was fully justified in his request and that such a desire and purpose was only natural on the part of so distinguished a knight as his gallant bearing plainly showed him to be.

He himself, the landlord added, when he was a young man, had followed the same honorable calling. He had gone through various parts of the world seeking adventures, among the places he had visited being the Percheles of Málaga, the Isles of Riarán, the District of Seville, the Little Market Place of Segovia, the Olivera of Valencia, the Rondilla of Granada, the beach of Sanlúcar, the Horse Fountain of Cordova, the Small Taverns of Toledo,[6] and numerous other localities where his nimble feet and light fingers had found much exercise. He had done many wrongs, cheated many widows, ruined many maidens, and swindled not a few minors until he had finally come to be known in almost all the courts and tribunals that are to be found in the whole of Spain.

At last he had retired to his castle here, where he lived upon his own income and the property of others; and here it was that he received all knights-errant of whatever quality and condition, simply out of the great affection that he bore them and that they might share with him their possessions in payment of his good will. Unfortunately, in this castle there was no chapel where Don Quixote might keep watch over his arms, for the old chapel had been torn down to make way for a new one; but in case of neces-

---

6. All reputed to be haunts of robbers and rogues.

sity, he felt quite sure that such a vigil could be maintained anywhere, and for the present occasion the courtyard of the castle would do; and then in the morning, please God, the requisite ceremony could be performed and his guest be duly dubbed a knight, as much a knight as anyone ever was.

He then inquired if Don Quixote had any money on his person, and the latter replied that he had not a cent, for in all the storybooks he had never read of knights-errant carrying any. But the innkeeper told him he was mistaken on this point: supposing the authors of those stories had not set down the fact in black and white, that was because they did not deem it necessary to speak of things as indispensable as money and a clean shirt, and one was not to assume for that reason that those knights-errant of whom the books were so full did not have any. He looked upon it as an absolute certainty that they all had well-stuffed purses, that they might be prepared for any emergency; and they also carried shirts and a little box of ointment for healing the wounds that they received.

For when they had been wounded in combat on the plains and in desert places, there was not always someone at hand to treat them, unless they had some skilled enchanter for a friend who then would succor them, bringing to them through the air, upon a cloud, some damsel or dwarf bearing a vial of water of such virtue that one had but to taste a drop of it and at once his wounds were healed and he was as sound as if he had never received any.

But even if this was not the case, knights in times past saw to it that their squires were well provided with money and other necessities, such as lint and ointment for healing purposes; and if they had no squires—which happened very rarely—they themselves carried these objects in a pair of saddlebags very cleverly attached to their horses' croups in such a manner as to be scarcely noticeable, as if they held something of greater importance than that, for among the knights-errant saddlebags as a rule were not favored. Accordingly, he would advise the novice before him, and inasmuch as the latter was soon to be his godson, he might even command him, that henceforth he should not go without money and a supply of those things that have been mentioned, as he would find that they came in useful at a time when he least expected it.

Don Quixote promised to follow his host's advice punctiliously; and so it was arranged that he should watch his armor in a large barnyard at one side of the inn. He gathered up all the pieces, placed them in a horse trough that stood near the well, and, bracing his shield on his arm, took up his lance and with stately demeanor began pacing up and down in front of the trough even as night was closing in.

The innkeeper informed his other guests of what was going on, of Don Quixote's vigil and his expectation of being dubbed a knight; and, marveling greatly at so extraordinary a variety of madness, they all went out to see for themselves and stood there watching from a distance. For a while the knight-to-be, with tranquil mien, would merely walk up and down; then, leaning on his lance, he would pause to survey his armor, gazing fixedly at it for a considerable length of time. As has been said, it was night now, but the brightness of the moon, which well might rival that of Him who lent it, was such that everything the novice knight did was plainly visible to all.

At this point one of the mule drivers who were stopping at the inn came out to water his drove, and in order to do this it was necessary to remove the armor from the trough.

As he saw the man approaching, Don Quixote cried out to him, "O bold knight, whoever you may be, who thus would dare to lay hands upon the accouterments of the most valiant man of arms that ever girded on a sword, look well what you do and desist if you do not wish to pay with your life for your insolence!"

The muleteer gave no heed to these words—it would have been better for his own sake had he done so—but, taking it up by the straps, tossed the armor some distance from him. When he beheld this, Don Quixote rolled his eyes heavenward and with his thoughts apparently upon his Dulcinea exclaimed, "Succor, O lady mine, this vassal heart in this my first encounter; let not your favor and protection fail me in the peril in which for the first time I now find myself."

With these and other similar words, he loosed his buckler, grasped his lance in both his hands, and let the mule driver have such a blow on the head that the man fell to the ground stunned; and had it been followed by another one, he would have had no need of a surgeon to treat him. Having done this, Don Quixote gathered up his armor and resumed his pacing up and down with the same calm manner as before. Not long afterward, without knowing what had happened—for the first muleteer was still lying there unconscious—another came out with the same intention of watering his mules, and he too was about to remove the armor from the trough when the knight, without saying a word or asking favor of anyone, once more adjusted his buckler and raised his lance, and if he did not break the second mule driver's head to bits, he made more than three pieces of it by dividing it into quarters. At the sound of the fracas everybody in the inn came running out, among them the innkeeper; whereupon Don Quixote again lifted his buckler and laid his hand on his sword.

"O lady of beauty," he said, "strength and vigor of this fainting heart of mine! Now is the time to turn the eyes of your greatness upon this captive knight of yours who must face so formidable an adventure."

By this time he had worked himself up to such a pitch of anger that if all the mule drivers in the world had attacked him he would not have taken one step backward. The comrades of the wounded men, seeing the plight those two were in, now began showering stones on Don Quixote, who shielded himself as best he could with his buckler, although he did not dare stir from the trough for fear of leaving his armor unprotected. The landlord, meanwhile, kept calling for them to stop, for he had told them that this was a madman who would be sure to go free even though he killed them all. The knight was shouting louder than ever, calling them knaves and traitors. As for the lord of the castle, who allowed knights-errant to be treated in this fashion, he was a lowborn villain, and if he, Don Quixote, had but received the order of knighthood, he would make him pay for his treachery.

"As for you others, vile and filthy rabble, I take no account of you; you may stone me or come forward and attack me all you like; you shall see what the reward of your folly and insolence will be."

He spoke so vigorously and was so undaunted in bearing as to strike terror in those who would assail him; and for this reason, and owing also to the persuasions of the innkeeper, they ceased stoning him. He then permitted them to carry away the wounded, and went back to watching his armor with the same tranquil, unconcerned air that he had previously displayed.

The landlord was none too well pleased with these mad pranks on the part of his guest and determined to confer upon him that accursed order of knighthood before something else happened. Going up to him, he begged Don Quixote's pardon for the insolence which, without his knowledge, had been shown the knight by those of low degree. They, however, had been well punished for their impudence. As he had said, there was no chapel in this castle, but for that which remained to be done there was no need of any. According to what he had read of the ceremonial of the order, there was nothing to this business of being dubbed a knight except a slap on the neck and one across the shoulder, and that could be performed in the middle of a field as well as anywhere else. All that was required was for the knight-to-be to keep watch over his armor for a couple of hours, and Don Quixote had been at it more than four. The latter believed all this and announced that he was ready to obey and get the matter over with as speedily as possible. Once dubbed a knight, if he were attacked one more time, he did not think that he would leave a single person in the castle alive, save such as he might command be spared, at the bidding of his host and out of respect to him.

Thus warned, and fearful that it might occur, the castellan brought out the book in which he had jotted down the hay and barley for which the mule drivers owed him, and, accompanied by a lad bearing the butt of a candle and the two aforesaid damsels, he came up to where Don Quixote stood and commanded him to kneel. Reading from the account book—as if he had been saying a prayer—he raised his hand and, with the knight's own sword, gave him a good thwack upon the neck and another lusty one upon the shoulder, muttering all the while between his teeth. He then directed one of the ladies to gird on Don Quixote's sword, which she did with much gravity and composure; for it was all they could do to keep from laughing at every point of the ceremony, but the thought of the knight's prowess which they had already witnessed was sufficient to restrain their mirth.

"May God give your Grace much good fortune," said the worthy lady as she attached the blade, "and prosper you in battle."

Don Quixote thereupon inquired her name, for he desired to know to whom it was he was indebted for the favor he had just received, that he might share with her some of the honor which his strong right arm was sure to bring him. She replied very humbly that her name was Tolosa and that she was the daughter of a shoemaker, a native of Toledo who lived in the stalls of Sancho Bicnaya.[7] To this the knight replied that she would do him a very great favor if from then on she would call herself Doña Tolosa, and she promised to do so. The other girl then helped him on with his spurs, and practically the same conversation was repeated. When asked her name, she stated that it was La Molinera and added that she was the daughter of a respectable miller of Antequera. Don Quixote likewise requested her to assume the "don" and become Doña Molinera and offered to render her further services and favors.

These unheard-of ceremonies having been dispatched in great haste, Don Quixote could scarcely wait to be astride his horse and sally forth on his quest for adventures. Saddling and mounting Rocinante, he embraced his

7. An old square in Toledo.

host, thanking him for the favor of having dubbed him a knight and saying such strange things that it would be quite impossible to record them here. The innkeeper, who was only too glad to be rid of him, answered with a speech that was no less flowery, though somewhat shorter, and he did not so much as ask him for the price of a lodging, so glad was he to see him go.

CHAPTER 4

Of what happened to our knight when he sallied forth from the inn.

Day was dawning when Don Quixote left the inn, so well satisfied with himself, so gay, so exhilarated, that the very girths of his steed all but burst with joy. But remembering the advice which his host had given him concerning the stock of necessary provisions that he should carry with him, especially money and shirts, he decided to turn back home and supply himself with whatever he needed, and with a squire as well; he had in mind a farmer who was a neighbor of his, a poor man and the father of a family but very well suited to fulfill the duties of squire to a man of arms. With this thought in mind he guided Rocinante toward the village once more, and that animal, realizing that he was homeward bound, began stepping out at so lively a gait that it seemed as if his feet barely touched the ground.

The knight had not gone far when from a hedge on his right hand he heard the sound of faint moans as of someone in distress.

"Thanks be to Heaven," he at once exclaimed, "for the favor it has shown me by providing me so soon with an opportunity to fulfill the obligations that I owe to my profession, a chance to pluck the fruit of my worthy desires. Those, undoubtedly, are the cries of someone in distress, who stands in need of my favor and assistance."

Turning Rocinante's head, he rode back to the place from which the cries appeared to be coming. Entering the wood, he had gone but a few paces when he saw a mare attached to an oak, while bound to another tree was a lad of fifteen or thereabouts, naked from the waist up. It was he who was uttering the cries, and not without reason, for there in front of him was a lusty farmer with a girdle who was giving him many lashes, each one accompanied by a reproof and a command, "Hold your tongue and keep your eyes open"; and the lad was saying, "I won't do it again, sir; by God's Passion, I won't do it again. I promise you that after this I'll take better care of the flock."

When he saw what was going on, Don Quixote was very angry. "Discourteous knight," he said, "it ill becomes you to strike one who is powerless to defend himself. Mount your steed and take your lance in hand"—for there was a lance leaning against the oak to which the mare was tied—"and I will show you what a coward you are."

The farmer, seeing before him this figure all clad in armor and brandishing a lance, decided that he was as good as done for. "Sir Knight," he said, speaking very mildly, "this lad that I am punishing here is my servant; he tends a flock of sheep which I have in these parts and he is so careless that every day one of them shows up missing. And when I punish him for his carelessness or his roguery, he says it is just because I am a miser and do not want to pay him the wages that I owe him, but I swear to God and upon my soul that he lies."

"It is you who lie, base lout," said Don Quixote, "and in my presence; and by the sun that gives us light, I am minded to run you through with this lance. Pay him and say no more about it, or else, by the God who rules us, I will make an end of you and annihilate you here and now. Release him at once."

The farmer hung his head and without a word untied his servant. Don Quixote then asked the boy how much has master owed him. For nine months' work, the lad told him, at seven reales the month. The knight did a little reckoning and found that this came to sixty-three reales; whereupon he ordered the farmer to pay over the money immediately, as he valued his life. The cowardly bumpkin replied that, facing death as he was and by the oath that he had sworn—he had not sworn any oath as yet—it did not amount to as much as that; for there were three pairs of shoes which he had given the lad that were to be deducted and taken into account, and a real for two blood-lettings when his servant was ill.

"That," said Don Quixote, "is all very well; but let the shoes and the blood-lettings go for the undeserved lashings which you have given him; if he has worn out the leather of the shoes that you paid for, you have taken the hide off his body, and if the barber let a little blood for him when he was sick,[8] you have done the same when he was well; and so far as that goes, he owes you nothing."

"But the trouble is, Sir Knight, that I have no money with me. Come along home with me, Andrés, and I will pay you real for real."

"I go home with him!" cried the lad. "Never in the world! No, sir, I would not even think of it; for once he has me alone he'll flay me like a St. Bartholomew."

"He will do nothing of the sort," said Don Quixote. "It is sufficient for me to command, and he out of respect will obey. Since he has sworn to me by the order of knighthood which he has received, I shall let him go free and I will guarantee that you will be paid."

"But look, your Grace," the lad remonstrated, "my master is no knight; he has never received any order of knighthood whatsoever. He is Juan Haldudo, a rich man and a resident of Quintanar."

"That makes little difference," declared Don Quixote, "for there may well be knights among the Haldudos, all the more so in view of the fact that every man is the son of his works."

"That is true enough," said Andrés, "but this master of mine—of what works is he the son, seeing that he refuses me the pay for my sweat and labor?"

"I do not refuse you, brother Andrés," said the farmer. "Do me the favor of coming with me, and I swear to you by all the orders of knighthood that there are in this world to pay you, as I have said, real for real, and perfumed at that."

"You can dispense with the perfume," said Don Quixote; "just give him the reales and I shall be satisfied. And see to it that you keep your oath, or by the one that I myself have sworn I shall return to seek you out and chastise you, and I shall find you though you be as well hidden as a lizard. In case you would like to know who it is that is giving you this command in order that you may feel the more obliged to comply with it, I may tell you that I am the

8. Barbers were also surgeons.

valorous Don Quixote de la Mancha, righter of wrongs and injustices; and so, God be with you, and do not fail to do as you have promised, under that penalty that I have pronounced."

As he said this, he put spurs to Rocinante and was off. The farmer watched him go, and when he saw that Don Quixote was out of the wood and out of sight, he turned to his servant, Andrés.

"Come here, my son," he said. "I want to pay you what I owe you as that righter of wrongs has commanded me."

"Take my word for it," replied Andrés, "your Grace would do well to observe the command of that good knight—may he live a thousand years; for as he is valorous and a righteous judge, if you don't pay me then, by Rocque,[9] he will come back and do just what he said!"

"And I will give you my word as well," said the farmer; "but seeing that I am so fond of you, I wish to increase the debt, that I may owe you all the more." And with this he seized the lad's arm and bound him to the tree again and flogged him within an inch of his life. "There, Master Andrés, you may call on that righter of wrongs if you like and you will see whether or not he rights this one. I do not think I have quite finished with you yet, for I have a good mind to flay you alive as you feared."

Finally, however, he unbound him and told him he might go look for that judge of his to carry out the sentence that had been pronounced. Andrés left, rather down in the mouth, swearing that he would indeed go look for the brave Don Quixote de la Mancha; he would relate to him everything that had happened, point by point, and the farmer would have to pay for it seven times over. But for all that, he went away weeping, and his master stood laughing at him.

Such was the manner in which the valorous knight righted this particular wrong. Don Quixote was quite content with the way everything had turned out; it seemed to him that he had made a very fortunate and noble beginning with his deeds of chivalry, and he was very well satisfied with himself as he jogged along in the direction of his native village, talking to himself in a low voice all the while.

"Well may'st thou call thyself fortunate today, above all other women on earth, O fairest of the fair, Dulcinea del Toboso! Seeing that it has fallen to thy lot to hold subject and submissive to thine every wish and pleasure so valiant and renowned a knight as Don Quixote de la Mancha is and shall be, who, as everyone knows, yesterday received the order of knighthood and this day has righted the greatest wrong and grievance that injustice ever conceived or cruelty ever perpetrated, by snatching the lash from the hand of the merciless foeman who was so unreasonably flogging that tender child."

At this point he came to a road that forked off in four directions, and at once he thought of those crossroads where knights-errant would pause to consider which path they should take. By way of imitating them, he halted there for a while; and when he had given the subject much thought, he slackened Rocinante's rein and let the hack follow its inclination. The animal's first impulse was to make straight for its own stable. After they had gone a couple of miles or so Don Quixote caught sight of what appeared to be a great throng of people, who, as was afterward learned, were certain

9. The origin of this oath is unknown.

merchants of Toledo on their way to purchase silk at Murcia. There were six of them altogether with their sunshades, accompanied by four attendants on horseback and three mule drivers on foot.

No sooner had he sighted them than Don Quixote imagined that he was on the brink of some fresh adventure. He was eager to imitate those passages at arms of which he had read in his books, and here, so it seemed to him, was one made to order. And so, with bold and knightly bearing, he settled himself firmly in the stirrups, couched his lance, covered himself with his shield, and took up a position in the middle of the road, where he paused to wait for those other knights-errant (for such he took them to be) to come up to him. When they were near enough to see and hear plainly, Don Quixote raised his voice and made a haughty gesture.

"Let everyone," he cried, "stand where he is, unless everyone will confess that there is not in all the world a more beauteous damsel than the Empress of La Mancha, the peerless Dulcinea del Toboso."

Upon hearing these words and beholding the weird figure who uttered them, the merchants stopped short. From the knight's appearance and his speech they knew at once that they had to deal with a madman; but they were curious to know what was meant by that confession that was demanded of them, and one of their number who was somewhat of a jester and a very clever fellow raised his voice.

"Sir Knight," he said, "we do not know who this beauteous lady is of whom you speak. Show her to us, and if she is as beautiful as you say, then we will right willingly and without any compulsion confess the truth as you have asked of us."

"If I were to show her to you," replied Don Quixote, "what merit would there be in your confessing a truth so self-evident? The important thing is for you, without seeing her, to believe, confess, affirm, swear, and defend that truth. Otherwise, monstrous and arrogant creatures that you are, you shall do battle with me. Come on, then, one by one, as the order of knighthood prescribes; or all of you together, if you will have it so, as is the sorry custom of those of your breed. Come on, and I will await you here, for I am confident that my cause is just."

"Sir Knight," responded the merchant, "I beg your Grace, in the name of all the princes here present, in order that we may not have upon our consciences the burden of confessing a thing which we have never seen nor heard, and one, moreover, so prejudicial to the empresses and queens of Alcarria and Estremadura,[1] that your Grace will show us some portrait of this lady, even though it be no larger than a grain of wheat, for by the thread one comes to the ball of yarn; and with this we shall remain satisfied and assured, and your Grace will likewise be content and satisfied. The truth is, I believe that we are already so much of your way of thinking that though it should show her to be blind of one eye and distilling vermilion and brimstone from the other, nevertheless, to please your Grace, we would say in her behalf all that you desire.'

"She distills nothing of the sort, infamous rabble!" shouted Don Quixote, for his wrath was kindling now. "I tell you, she does not distill what you say at all, but amber and civet[2] wrapped in cotton; and she is neither one-eyed

---

1. Ironical, because both were known as particularly backward regions.   2. A musky substance used in perfume, imported from Africa in cotton packings.

nor hunchbacked but straighter than a spindle that comes from Guadarrama. You shall pay for the great blasphemy which you have uttered against such a beauty as is my lady!"

Saying this, he came on with lowered lance against the one who had spoken, charging with such wrath and fury that if fortune had not caused Rocinante to stumble and fall in mid-career, things would have gone badly with the merchant and he would have paid for his insolent gibe. As it was, Don Quixote went rolling over the plain for some little distance, and when he tried to get to his feet, found that he was unable to do so, being too encumbered with his lance, shield, spurs, helmet, and the weight of that ancient suit of armor.

"Do not flee, cowardly ones," he cried even as he struggled to rise. "Stay, cravens, for it is not my fault but that of my steed that I am stretched out here."

One of the muleteers, who must have been an ill-natured lad, upon hearing the poor fallen knight speak so arrogantly, could not refrain from giving him an answer in the ribs. Going up to him, he took the knight's lance and broke it into bits, and then with a companion proceeded to belabor him so mercilessly that in spite of his armor they milled him like a hopper[3] of wheat. The merchants called to them not to lay on so hard, saying that was enough and they should desist, but the mule driver by this time had warmed up to the sport and would not stop until he had vented his wrath, and, snatching up the broken pieces of the lance, he began hurling them at the wretched victim as he lay there on the ground. And through all this tempest of sticks that rained upon him Don Quixote never once closed his mouth nor ceased threatening Heaven and earth and these ruffians, for such he took them to be, who were thus mishandling him.

Finally the lad grew tired, and the merchants went their way with a good story to tell about the poor fellow who had had such a cudgeling. Finding himself alone, the knight endeavored to see if he could rise; but if this was a feat that he could not accomplish when he was sound and whole, how was he to achieve it when he had been thrashed and pounded to a pulp? Yet nonetheless he considered himself fortunate; for as he saw it, misfortunes such as this were common to knights-errant, and he put all the blame upon his horse; and if he was unable to rise, that was because his body was so bruised and battered all over.

CHAPTER 5

In which is continued the narrative of the misfortune that befell our knight.

Seeing, then, that he was indeed unable to stir, he decided to fall back upon a favorite remedy of his, which was to think of some passage or other in his books; and as it happened, the one that he in his madness now recalled was the story of Baldwin and the Marquis of Mantua, when Carloto left the former wounded upon the mountainside,[4] a tale that is known to children, not unknown to young men, celebrated and believed in by the old, and, for all of that, not any truer than the miracles of Mohammed. Moreover,

---

3. Funnel-shaped container for grain.   4. The allusion is to an old ballad about Charlemagne's son Charlot (Carloto) wounding Baldwin, nephew of the Marquis of Mantua.

it impressed him as being especially suited to the straits in which he found himself; and, accordingly, with a great show of feeling, he began rolling and tossing on the ground as he feebly gasped out the lines which the wounded knight of the wood is supposed to have uttered:

> "Where art thou, lady mine,
> That thou dost not grieve for my woe?
> Either thou art disloyal,
> Or my grief thou dost not know."

He went on reciting the old ballad until he came to the following verses:

> "O noble Marquis of Mantua,
> My uncle and liege lord true!"

He had reached this point when down the road came a farmer of the same village, a neighbor of his, who had been to the mill with a load of wheat. Seeing a man lying there stretched out like that, he went up to him and inquired who he was and what was the trouble that caused him to utter such mournful complaints. Thinking that this must undoubtedly be his uncle, the Marquis of Mantua, Don Quixote did not answer but went on with his recitation of the ballad, giving an account of the Marquis' misfortunes and the amours of his wife and the emperor's son, exactly as the ballad has it.

The farmer was astounded at hearing all these absurdities, and after removing the knight's visor which had been battered to pieces by the blows it had received, the good man bathed the victim's face, only to discover, once the dust was off, that he knew him very well.

"Señor Quejana," he said (for such must have been Don Quixote's real name when he was in his right senses and before he had given up the life of a quiet country gentleman to become a knight-errant), "who is responsible for your Grace's being in such a plight as this?"

But the knight merely went on with his ballad in response to all the questions asked of him. Perceiving that it was impossible to obtain any information from him, the farmer as best he could relieved him of his breastplate and backpiece to see if he had any wounds, but there was no blood and no mark of any sort. He then tried to lift him from the ground, and with a great deal of effort finally managed to get him astride the ass, which appeared to be the easier mount for him. Gathering up the armor, including even the splinters from the lance, he made a bundle and tied it on Rocinante's back, and, taking the horse by the reins and the ass by the halter, he started out for the village. He was worried in his mind at hearing all the foolish things that Don Quixote said, and that individual himself was far from being at ease. Unable by reason of his bruises and his soreness to sit upright on the donkey, our knight-errant kept sighing to Heaven, which led the farmer to ask him once more what it was that ailed him.

It must have been the devil himself who caused him to remember those tales that seemed to fit his own case; for at this point he forgot all about Baldwin and recalled Abindarráez, and how the governor of Antequera, Rodrigo de Narváez, had taken him prisoner and carried him off captive to his castle. Accordingly, when the countryman turned to inquire how he was and what was troubling him, Don Quixote replied with the very same words and phrases that the captive Abindarráez used in answering Rodrigo, just as he had read in the story *Diana* of Jorge de Montemayor,[5] where it is all written down, applying them very aptly to the present circumstances as the farmer went along cursing his luck for having to listen to such a lot of nonsense. Realizing that his neighbor was quite mad, he made haste to reach the village that he might not have to be annoyed any longer by Don Quixote's tiresome harangue.

"Señor Don Rodrigo de Narváez," the knight was saying, "I may inform your Grace that this beautiful Jarifa of whom I speak is not the lovely Dulcinea del Toboso, in whose behalf I have done, am doing, and shall do the most famous deeds of chivalry that ever have been or will be seen in all the world."

"But, sir," replied the farmer, "sinner that I am, cannot your Grace see that I am not Don Rodrigo de Narváez nor the Marquis of Mantua, but Pedro Alonso, your neighbor? And your Grace is neither Baldwin nor Abindarráez but a respectable gentleman by the name of Señor Quijana."

"I know who I am," said Don Quixote, "and who I may be, if I choose: not only those I have mentioned but all the Twelve Peers of France and the Nine Worthies[6] as well; for the exploits of all of them together, or separately, cannot compare with mine."

With such talk as this they reached their destination just as night was falling; but the farmer decided to wait until it was a little darker in order that the badly battered gentleman might not be seen arriving in such a condition and mounted on an ass. When he thought the proper time had come, they entered the village and proceeded to Don Quixote's house, where they found everything in confusion. The curate and the barber were there, for they were great friends of the knight, and the housekeeper was speaking to them.

"Señor Licentiate Pero Pérez," she was saying, for that was the manner in which she addressed the curate, "what does your Grace think could have happened to my master? Three days now, and not a word of him, nor the hack, nor the buckler, nor the lance, nor the suit of armor. Ah, poor me! I am as certain as I am that I was born to die that it is those cursed books of chivalry he is always reading that have turned his head; for now that I recall, I have often heard him muttering to himself that he must become a knighterrant and go through the world in search of adventures. May such books as those be consigned to Satan and Barabbas,[7] for they have sent to perdition the finest mind in all La Mancha."

The niece was of the same opinion. "I may tell you, Señor Master Nicholas," she said, for that was the barber's name, "that many times my uncle would sit reading those impious tales of misadventure for two whole days and nights at a stretch; and when he was through, he would toss the book aside, lay his hand on his sword, and begin slashing at the walls. When

---

5. The reference is to the tale of the love of Abindarráez, a captive Moor, for the beautiful Jarifa, included in the second edition of Jorge de Montemayor's *Diana*, a pastoral romance.   6. In a tradition originating in France, the Nine Worthies consisted of three biblical, three classical, and three Christian figures (David, Hector, Alexander, Charlemagne, and so on). In French medieval epics, the Twelve Peers (Roland, Oliver, and so on) were warriors equal in rank, forming a kind of guard of honor around Charlemagne.   7. The thief whose release, rather than that of Jesus, the crowd requested when Pilate, conforming to Passover custom, was ready to have one prisoner set free.

he was completely exhausted, he would tell us that he had just killed four giants as big as castle towers, while the sweat that poured off him was blood from the wounds that he had received in battle. He would then drink a big jug of cold water, after which he would be very calm and peaceful, saying that the water was the most precious liquid which the wise Esquife, a great magician and his friend, had brought to him. But I blame myself for everything. I should have advised your Worships of my uncle's nonsensical actions so that you could have done something about it by burning those damnable books of his before things came to such a pass; for he has many that ought to be burned as if they were heretics."

"I agree with you," said the curate, "and before tomorrow's sun has set there shall be a public *auto da fé,* and those works shall be condemned to the flames that they may not lead some other who reads them to follow the example of my good friend."

Don Quixote and the farmer overheard all this, and it was then that the latter came to understand the nature of his neighbor's affliction.

"Open the door, your Worships," the good man cried. "Open for Sir Baldwin and the Marquis of Mantua, who comes badly wounded, and for Señor Abindarráez the Moor whom the valiant Rodrigo de Narváez, governor of Antequera, brings captive."

At the sound of his voice they all ran out, recognizing at once friend, master, and uncle, who as yet was unable to get down off the donkey's back. They all ran up to embrace him.

"Wait, all of you," said Don Quixote, "for I am sorely wounded through fault of my steed. Bear me to my couch and summon, if it be possible, the wise Urganda to treat and care for my wounds."

"There!" exclaimed the housekeeper. "Plague take it! Did not my heart tell me right as to which foot my master limped on? To bed with your Grace at once, and we will take care of you without sending for that Urganda of yours. A curse, I say, and a hundred other curses, on those books of chivalry that have brought your Grace to this."

And so they carried him off to bed, but when they went to look for his wounds, they found none at all. He told them it was all the result of a great fall he had taken with Rocinante, his horse, while engaged in combating ten giants, the hugest and most insolent that were ever heard of in all the world.

"Tut, tut," said the curate. "So there are giants in the dance now, are there? Then, by the sign of the cross, I'll have them burned before nightfall tomorrow."

They had a thousand questions to put to Don Quixote, but his only answer was that they should give him something to eat and let him sleep, for that was the most important thing of all; so they humored him in this. The curate then interrogated the farmer at great length concerning the conversation he had had with his neighbor. The peasant told him everything, all the absurd things their friend had said when he found him lying there and afterward on the way home, all of which made the licentiate more anxious than ever to do what he did the following day,[8] when he summoned Master Nicholas and went with him to Don Quixote's house.

---

8. He and the barber burned most of Don Quixote's library.

[Fighting the Windmills and a Choleric Biscayan]

CHAPTER 7

Of the second sally of our good knight, Don Quixote de la Mancha.

* * * After that he remained at home very tranquilly for a couple of weeks, without giving sign of any desire to repeat his former madness. During that time he had the most pleasant conversations with his two old friends, the curate and the barber, on the point he had raised to the effect that what the world needed most was knights-errant and a revival of chivalry. The curate would occasionally contradict him and again would give in, for it was only by means of this artifice that he could carry on a conversation with him at all.

In the meanwhile Don Quixote was bringing his powers of persuasion to bear upon a farmer who lived near by, a good man—if this title may be applied to one who is poor—but with very few wits in his head. The short of it is, by pleas and promises, he got the hapless rustic to agree to ride forth with him and serve him as his squire. Among other things, Don Quixote told him that he ought to be more than willing to go, because no telling what adventure might occur which would win them an island, and then he (the farmer) would be left to be the governor of it. As a result of these and other similar assurances, Sancho Panza forsook his wife and children and consented to take upon himself the duties of squire to his neighbor.

Next, Don Quixote set out to raise some money, and by selling this thing and pawning that and getting the worst of the bargain always, he finally scraped together a reasonable amount. He also asked a friend of his for the loan of a buckler and patched up his broken helmet as well as he could. He advised his squire, Sancho, of the day and hour when they were to take to the road and told him to see to laying in a supply of those things that were most necessary, and, above all, not to forget the saddlebags. Sancho replied that he would see to all this and added that he was also thinking of taking along with him a very good ass that he had, as he was not much used to going on foot.

With regard to the ass, Don Quixote had to do a little thinking, trying to recall if any knight-errant had ever had a squire thus asininely mounted. He could not think of any, but nevertheless he decided to take Sancho with the intention of providing him with a nobler steed as soon as occasion offered; he had but to appropriate the horse of the first discourteous knight he met. Having furnished himself with shirts and all the other things that the innkeeper had recommended, he and Panza rode forth one night unseen by anyone and without taking leave of wife and children, housekeeper or niece. They went so far that by the time morning came they were safe from discovery had a hunt been started for them.

Mounted on his ass, Sancho Panza rode along like a patriarch, with saddlebags and flask, his mind set upon becoming governor of that island that his master had promised him. Don Quixote determined to take the same route and road over the Campo de Montiel that he had followed on his first journey; but he was not so uncomfortable this time, for it was early morning and the sun's rays fell upon them slantingly and accordingly did not tire them too much.

"Look, Sir Knight-errant," said Sancho, "your Grace should not forget that island you promised me; for no matter how big it is, I'll be able to govern it right enough."

"I would have you know, friend Sancho Panza," replied Don Quixote, "that among the knights-errant of old it was a very common custom to make their squires governors of the islands or the kingdoms that they won, and I am resolved that in my case so pleasing a usage shall not fall into desuetude. I even mean to go them one better; for they very often, perhaps most of the time, waited until their squires were old men who had had their fill of serving their masters during bad days and worse nights, whereupon they would give them the title of count, or marquis at most, of some valley or province more or less. But if you live and I live, it well may be that within a week I shall win some kingdom with others dependent upon it, and it will be the easiest thing in the world to crown you king of one of them. You need not marvel at this, for all sorts of unforeseen things happen to knights like me, and I may readily be able to give you even more than I have promised."

"In that case," said Sancho Panza, "if by one of those miracles of which your Grace was speaking I should become king, I would certainly send for Juana Gutiérrez, my old lady, to come and be my queen, and the young ones could be infantes."

"There is no doubt about it," Don Quixote assured him.

"Well, I doubt it," said Sancho, "for I think that even if God were to rain kingdoms upon the earth, no crown would sit well on the head of Mari Gutiérrez,[9] for I am telling you, sir, as a queen she is not worth two maravedis. She would do better as a countess, God help her."

"Leave everything to God, Sancho," said Don Quixote, "and he will give you whatever is most fitting; but I trust you will not be so pusillanimous as to be content with anything less than the title of viceroy."

"That I will not," said Sancho Panza, "especially seeing that I have in your Grace so illustrious a master who can give me all that is suitable to me and all that I can manage."

CHAPTER 8

Of the good fortune which the valorous Don Quixote had in the terrifying and never-before-imagined adventure of the windmills, along with other events that deserve to be suitably recorded.

At this point they caught sight of thirty or forty windmills which were standing on the plain there, and no sooner had Don Quixote laid eyes upon them than he turned to his squire and said, "Fortune is guiding our affairs better than we could have wished; for you see there before you, friend Sancho Panza, some thirty or more lawless giants with whom I mean to do battle. I shall deprive them of their lives, and with the spoils from this encounter we shall begin to enrich ourselves; for this is righteous warfare, and it is a great service to God to remove so accursed a breed from the face of the earth."

"What giants?" said Sancho Panza.

"Those that you see there," replied his master, "those with the long arms some of which are as much as two leagues in length."

9. Sancho's wife, Juana Gutiérrez.

"But look, your Grace, those are not giants but windmills, and what appear to be arms are their wings which, when whirled in the breeze, cause the millstone to go."

"It is plain to be seen," said Don Quixote, "that you have had little experience in this matter of adventures. If you are afraid, go off to one side and say your prayers while I am engaging them in fierce, unequal combat."

Saying this, he gave spurs to his steed Rocinante, without paying any heed to Sancho's warning that these were truly windmills and not giants that he was riding forth to attack. Nor even when he was close upon them did he perceive what they really were, but shouted at the top of his lungs, "Do not seek to flee, cowards and vile creatures that you are, for it is but a single knight with whom you have to deal!"

At that moment a little wind came up and the big wings began turning.

"Though you flourish as many arms as did the giant Briareus,"[1] said Don Quixote when he perceived this, "you still shall have to answer to me."

He thereupon commended himself with all his heart to his lady Dulcinea, beseeching her to succor him in this peril; and, being well covered with his shield and with his lance at rest, he bore down upon them at a full gallop and fell upon the first mill that stood in his way, giving a thrust at the wing, which was whirling at such a speed that his lance was broken into bits and both horse and horseman went rolling over the plain, very much battered indeed. Sancho upon his donkey came hurrying to his master's assistance as fast as he could, but when he reached the spot, the knight was unable to move, so great was the shock with which he and Rocinante had hit the ground.

"God help us!" exclaimed Sancho, "did I not tell your Grace to look well, that those were nothing but windmills, a fact which no one could fail to see unless he had other mills of the same sort in his head?"

"Be quiet, friend Sancho," said Don Quixote. "Such are the fortunes of war, which more than any other are subject to constant change. What is more, when I come to think of it, I am sure that this must be the work of that magician Frestón, the one who robbed me of my study and my books,[2] and who has thus changed the giants into windmills in order to deprive me of the glory of overcoming them, so great is the enmity that he bears me; but in the end his evil arts shall not prevail against this trusty sword of mine."

"May God's will be done," was Sancho Panza's response. And with the aid of his squire the knight was once more mounted on Rocinante, who stood there with one shoulder half out of joint. And so, speaking of the adventure that had just befallen them, they continued along the Puerto Lápice highway; for there, Don Quixote said, they could not fail to find many and varied adventures, this being a much traveled thoroughfare. The only thing was, the knight was exceedingly downcast over the loss of his lance.

"I remember," he said to his squire, "having read of a Spanish knight by the name of Diego Pérez de Vargas, who, having broken his sword in battle, tore from an oak a heavy bough or branch and with it did such feats of valor that day, and pounded so many Moors, that he came to be known as Machuca,[3] and he and his descendants from that day forth have been called

---

1. Mythological giant with a hundred arms.   2. Don Quixote had promptly attributed the ruin of his library to magical intervention (see n. 8, p. 87).   3. "The Crusher," the hero of a folk ballad.

Vargas y Machuca. I tell you this because I too intend to provide myself with just such a bough as the one he wielded, and with it I propose to do such exploits that you shall deem yourself fortunate to have been found worthy to come with me and behold and witness things that are almost beyond belief."

"God's will be done," said Sancho. "I believe everything that your Grace says; but straighten yourself up in the saddle a little, for you seem to be slipping down on one side, owing, no doubt, to the shaking-up that you received in your fall."

"Ah, that is the truth," replied Don Quixote, "and if I do not speak of my sufferings, it is for the reason that it is not permitted knights-errant to complain of any wound whatsoever, even though their bowels may be dropping out."

"If that is the way it is," said Sancho, "I have nothing more to say; but, God knows, it would suit me better if your Grace did complain when something hurts him. I can assure you that I mean to do so, over the least little thing that ails me—that is, unless the same rule applies to squires as well."

Don Quixote laughed long and heartily over Sancho's simplicity, telling him that he might complain as much as he liked and where and when he liked, whether he had good cause or not; for he had read nothing to the contrary in the ordinances of chivalry. Sancho then called his master's attention to the fact that it was time to eat. The knight replied that he himself had no need of food at the moment, but his squire might eat whenever he chose. Having been granted this permission, Sancho seated himself as best he could upon his beast, and, taking out from his saddlebags the provisions that he had stored there, he rode along leisurely behind his master, munching his victuals and taking a good, hearty swig now and then at the leather flask in a manner that might well have caused the biggest-bellied tavern-keeper of Málaga to envy him. Between draughts he gave not so much as a thought to any promise that his master might have made him, nor did he look upon it as any hardship, but rather as good sport, to go in quest of adventures however hazardous they might be.

The short of the matter is, they spent the night under some trees, from one of which Don Quixote tore off a withered bough to serve him as a lance, placing it in the lance head from which he had removed the broken one. He did not sleep all night long for thinking of his lady Dulcinea; for this was in accordance with what he had read in his books, of men of arms in the forest or desert places who kept a wakeful vigil, sustained by the memory of their ladies fair. Not so with Sancho, whose stomach was full, and not with chicory water. He fell into a dreamless slumber, and had not his master called him, he would not have been awakened either by the rays of the sun in his face or by the many birds who greeted the coming of the new day with their merry song.

Upon arising, he had another go at the flask, finding it somewhat more flaccid then it had been the night before, a circumstance which grieved his heart, for he could not see that they were on the way to remedying the deficiency within any very short space of time. Don Quixote did not wish any breakfast; for, as has been said, he was in the habit of nourishing himself on savorous memories. They then set out once more along the road to Puerto Lápice, and around three in the afternoon they came in sight of the pass that bears that name.

"There," said Don Quixote as his eyes fell upon it, "we may plunge our arms up to the elbow in what are known as adventures. But I must warn you that even though you see me in the greatest peril in the world, you are not to lay hand upon your sword to defend me, unless it be that those who attack me are rabble and men of low degree, in which case you may very well come to my aid; but if they be gentlemen, it is in no wise permitted by the laws of chivalry that you should assist me until you yourself shall have been dubbed a knight."

"Most certainly, sir," replied Sancho, "your Grace shall be very well obeyed in this; all the more so for the reason that I myself am of a peaceful disposition and not fond of meddling in the quarrels and feuds of others. However, when it comes to protecting my own person, I shall not take account of those laws of which you speak, seeing that all laws, human and divine, permit each one to defend himself whenever he is attacked."

"I am willing to grant you that," assented Don Quixote, "but in this matter of defending me against gentlemen you must restrain your natural impulses."

"I promise you I shall do so," said Sancho. "I will observe this precept as I would the Sabbath day."

As they were conversing in this manner, there appeared in the road in front of them two friars of the Order of St. Benedict, mounted upon dromedaries—for the she-mules they rode were certainly no smaller than that. The friars wore travelers' spectacles and carried sunshades, and behind them came a coach accompanied by four or five men on horseback and a couple of muleteers on foot. In the coach, as was afterwards learned, was a lady of Biscay, on her way to Seville to bid farewell to her husband, who had been appointed to some high post in the Indies. The religious were not of her company although they were going by the same road.

The instant Don Quixote laid eyes upon them he turned to his squire. "Either I am mistaken or this is going to be the most famous adventure that ever was seen; for those black-clad figures that you behold must be, and without any doubt are, certain enchanters who are bearing with them a captive princess in that coach, and I must do all I can to right this wrong."

"It will be worse than the windmills," declared Sancho. "Look you, sir, those are Benedictine friars and the coach must be that of some travelers. Mark well what I say and what you do, lest the devil lead you astray."

"I have already told you, Sancho," replied Don Quixote, "that you know little where the subject of adventures is concerned. What I am saying to you is the truth, as you shall now see."

With this, he rode forward and took up a position in the middle of the road along which the friars were coming, and as soon as they appeared to be within earshot he cried out to them in a loud voice, "O devilish and monstrous beings, set free at once the highborn princesses whom you bear captive in that coach, or else prepare at once to meet your death as the just punishment of your evil deeds."

The friars drew rein and sat there in astonishment, marveling as much at Don Quixote's appearance as at the words he spoke. "Sir Knight," they answered him, "we are neither devilish nor monstrous but religious of the Order of St. Benedict who are merely going our way. We know nothing of those who are in that coach, nor of any captive princesses either."

"Soft words," said Don Quixote, "have no effect on me. I know you for what you are, lying rabble!" And without waiting for any further parley he gave spur to Rocinante and, with lowered lance, bore down upon the first friar with such fury and intrepidity that, had not the fellow tumbled from his mule of his own accord, he would have been hurled to the ground and either killed or badly wounded. The second religious, seeing how his companion had been treated, dug his legs into his she-mule's flanks and scurried away over the countryside faster than the wind.

Seeing the friar upon the ground, Sancho Panza slipped lightly from his mount and, falling upon him, began stripping him of his habit. The two mule drivers accompanying the religious thereupon came running up and asked Sancho why he was doing this. The latter replied that the friar's garments belonged to him as legitimate spoils of the battle that his master Don Quixote had just won. The muleteers, however, were lads with no sense of humor, nor did they know what all this talk of spoils and battles was about; but, perceiving that Don Quixote had ridden off to one side to converse with those inside the coach, they pounced upon Sancho, threw him to the ground, and proceeded to pull out the hair of his beard and kick him to a pulp, after which they went off and left him stretched out there, bereft at once of breath and sense.

Without losing any time, they then assisted the friar to remount. The good brother was trembling all over from fright, and there was not a speck of color in his face, but when he found himself in the saddle once more, he quickly spurred his beast to where his companion, at some little distance, sat watching and waiting to see what the result of the encounter would be. Having no curiosity as to the final outcome of the fray, the two of them now resumed their journey, making more signs of the cross than the devil would be able to carry upon his back.

Meanwhile Don Quixote, as we have said, was speaking to the lady in the coach.

"Your beauty, my lady, may now dispose of your person as best may please you, for the arrogance of your abductors lies upon the ground, overthrown by this good arm of mine; and in order that you may not pine to know the name of your liberator, I may inform you that I am Don Quixote de la Mancha, knight-errant and adventurer and captive of the peerless and beauteous Doña Dulcinea del Toboso. In payment of the favor which you have received from me, I ask nothing other than that you return to El Toboso and on my behalf pay your respects to this lady, telling her that it was I who set you free."

One of the squires accompanying those in the coach, a Biscayan,[4] was listening to Don Quixote's words, and when he saw that the knight did not propose to let the coach proceed upon its way but was bent upon having it turn back to El Toboso, he promptly went up to him, seized his lance, and said to him in bad Castilian and worse Biscayan, "Go, *caballero,* and bad luck go with you; for by the God that created me, if you do not let this coach pass, me kill you or me no Biscayan."

Don Quixote heard him attentively enough and answered him very mildly, "If you were a *caballero,*[5] which you are not, I should already have chastised you, wretched creature, for your foolhardiness and your impudence."

4. From the Basque region.   5. Knight, gentleman (Spanish).

"Me no *caballero*." cried the Biscayan. "Me swear to God, you lie like a Christian. If you will but lay aside your lance and unsheath your sword, you will soon see that you are carrying water to the cat![6] Biscayan on land, gentleman at sea, but a gentleman in spite of the devil, and you lie if you say otherwise."

"'You shall see as to that presently,' said Agrajes,"[7] Don Quixote quoted. He cast his lance to the earth, drew his sword, and, taking his buckler on his arm, attacked the Biscayan with intent to slay him. The latter, when he saw his adversary approaching, would have liked to dismount from his mule, for she was one of the worthless sort that are let for hire and he had no confidence in her; but there was no time for this, and so he had no choice but to draw his own sword in turn and make the best of it. However, he was near enough to the coach to be able to snatch a cushion from it to serve him as a shield; and then they fell upon each other as though they were mortal enemies. The rest of those present sought to make peace between them but did not succeed, for the Biscayan with his disjointed phrases kept muttering that if they did not let him finish the battle then he himself would have to kill his mistress and anyone else who tried to stop him.

The lady inside the carriage, amazed by it all and trembling at what she saw, directed her coachman to drive on a little way; and there from a distance she watched the deadly combat, in the course of which the Biscayan came down with a great blow on Don Quixote's shoulder, over the top of the latter's shield, and had not the knight been clad in armor, it would have split him to the waist.

Feeling the weight of this blow, Don Quixote cried out, "O lady of my soul, Dulcinea, flower of beauty, succor this your champion who out of gratitude for your many favors finds himself in so perilous a plight!" To utter these words, lay hold of his sword, cover himself with his buckler, and attack the Biscayan was but the work of a moment; for he was now resolved to risk everything upon a single stroke.

As he saw Don Quixote approaching with so dauntless a bearing, the Biscayan was well aware of his adversary's courage and forthwith determined to imitate the example thus set him. He kept himself protected with his cushion, but he was unable to get his she-mule to budge to one side or the other, for the beast, out of sheer exhaustion and being, moreover, unused to such childish play, was incapable of taking a single step. And so, then, as has been stated, Don Quixote was approaching the wary Biscayan, his sword raised on high and with the firm resolve of cleaving his enemy in two; and the Biscayan was awaiting the knight in the same posture, cushion in front of him and with uplifted sword. All the bystanders were trembling with suspense at what would happen as a result of the terrible blows that were threatened, and the lady in the coach and her maids were making a thousand vows and offerings to all the images and shrines in Spain, praying that God would save them all and the lady's squire from this great peril that confronted them.

But the unfortunate part of the matter is that at this very point the author of the history breaks off and leaves the battle pending, excusing himself upon the ground that he has been unable to find anything else in writing

---

6. An inversion of a proverbial phrase: "carrying the cat to the water."   7. A violent character in the romance *Amadis de Gaul*. His challenging phrase is the conventional opener of a fight.

concerning the exploits of Don Quixote beyond those already set forth. It is true, on the other hand, that the second author[8] of this work could not bring himself to believe that so unusual a chronicle would have been consigned to oblivion, nor that the learned ones of La Mancha were possessed of so little curiosity as not to be able to discover in their archives or registry offices certain papers that have to do with this famous knight. Being convinced of this, he did not despair of coming upon the end of this pleasing story. * * *

CHAPTER 9

In which is concluded and brought to an end the stupendous battle between the gallant Biscayan and the valiant Knight of La Mancha.

* * * We left the valorous Biscayan and the famous Don Quixote with swords unsheathed and raised aloft, about to let fall furious slashing blows which, had they been delivered fairly and squarely, would at the very least have split them in two and laid them wide open from top to bottom like a pomegranate; and it was at this doubtful point that the pleasing chronicle came to a halt and broke off, without the author's informing us as to where the rest of it might be found.

I was deeply grieved by such a circumstance, and the pleasure I had had in reading so slight a portion was turned into annoyance as I thought of how difficult it would be to come upon the greater part which it seemed to me must still be missing. It appeared impossible and contrary to all good precedent that so worthy a knight should not have had some scribe to take upon himself the task of writing an account of these unheard-of exploits; for that was something that had happened to none of the knights-errant who, as the saying has it, had gone forth in quest of adventures, seeing that each of them had one or two chroniclers, as if ready at hand, who not only had set down their deeds, but had depicted their most trivial thoughts and amiable weaknesses, however well concealed they might be. The good knight of La Mancha surely could not have been so unfortunate as to have lacked what Platir and others like him had in abundance. And so I could not bring myself to believe that this gallant history could have remained thus lopped off and mutilated, and I could not but lay the blame upon the malignity of time, that devourer and consumer of all things, which must either have consumed it or kept it hidden.

On the other hand, I reflected that inasmuch as among the knight's books had been found such modern works as *The Disenchantments of Jealousy* and *The Nymphs and Shepherds of Henares,* his story likewise must be modern, and that even though it might not have been written down, it must remain in the memory of the good folk of his village and the surrounding ones. This thought left me somewhat confused and more than ever desirous of knowing the real and true story, the whole story, of the life and wondrous deeds of our famous Spaniard, Don Quixote, light and mirror of the chivalry of La Mancha, the first in our age and in these calamitous times to devote himself to the hardships and exercises of knight-errantry and to go about righting wrongs, succoring widows, and protecting damsels—damsels such as those

8. Cervantes himself, adopting here—with tongue in cheek—a device used in the romances of chivalry to create suspense.

who, mounted upon their palfreys and with riding-whip in hand, in full possession of their virginity, were in the habit of going from mountain to mountain and from valley to valley; for unless there were some villain, some rustic with an ax and hood, or some monstrous giant to force them, there were in times past maiden ladies who at the end of eighty years, during all which time they had not slept for a single day beneath a roof, would go to their graves as virginal as when their mothers had borne them.

If I speak of these things, it is for the reason that in this and in all other respects our gallant Quixote is deserving of constant memory and praise, and even I am not to be denied my share of it for my diligence and the labor to which I put myself in searching out the conclusion of this agreeable narrative; although if heaven, luck, and circumstance had not aided me, the world would have had to do without the pleasure and the pastime which anyone may enjoy who will read this work attentively for an hour or two. The manner in which it came about was as follows:

I was standing one day in the Alcaná, or market place, of Toledo when a lad came up to sell some old notebooks and other papers to a silk weaver who was there. As I am extremely fond of reading anything, even though it be but the scraps of paper in the streets, I followed my natural inclination and took one of the books, whereupon I at once perceived that it was written in characters which I recognized as Arabic. I recognized them, but reading them was another thing; and so I began looking around to see if there was any Spanish-speaking Moor near by who would be able to read them for me. It was not very hard to find such an interpreter, nor would it have been even if the tongue in question had been an older and a better one.[9] To make a long story short, chance brought a fellow my way; and when I told him what it was I wished and placed the book in his hands, he opened it in the middle and began reading and at once fell to laughing. When I asked him what the cause of his laughter was, he replied that it was a note which had been written in the margin.

I besought him to tell me the content of the note, and he, laughing still, went on, "As I told you, it is something in the margin here: 'This Dulcinea del Toboso, so often referred to, is said to have been the best hand at salting pigs of any woman in all La Mancha.'"

No sooner had I heard the name Dulcinea del Toboso than I was astonished and held in suspense, for at once the thought occurred to me that those notebooks must contain the history of Don Quixote. With this in mind I urged him to read me the title, and he proceeded to do so, turning the Arabic into Castilian upon the spot: *History of Don Quixote de la Mancha, Written by Cid Hamete Benengeli*[1] Arabic Historian. It was all I could do to conceal my satisfaction and, snatching them from the silk weaver, I bought from the lad all the papers and notebooks that he had for half a real; but if he had known or suspected how very much I wanted them, he might well have had more than six reales for them.

The Moor and I then betook ourselves to the cathedral cloister, where I requested him to translate for me into the Castilian tongue all the books that had to do with Don Quixote, adding nothing and subtracting nothing;

9. That is, Hebrew.   1. Eggplant (Arabic). Citing some ancient chronicle as the author's source and authority is very much in the tradition of the romances.

and I offered him whatever payment he desired. He was content with two arrobas of raisins and two fanegas[2] of wheat and promised to translate them well and faithfully and with all dispatch. However, in order to facilitate matters, and also because I did not wish to let such a find as this out of my hands, I took the fellow home with me, where in a little more than a month and a half he translated the whole of the work just as you will find it set down here.

In the first of the books there was a very lifelike picture of the battle between Don Quixote and the Biscayan, the two being in precisely the same posture as described in the history, their swords upraised, the one covered by his buckler, the other with his cushion. As for the Biscayan's mule, you could see at the distance of a crossbow shot that it was one for hire. Beneath the Biscayan there was a rubric which read: "Don Sancho de Azpeitia," which must undoubtedly have been his name; while beneath the feet of Rocinante was another inscription: "Don Quixote." Rocinante was marvelously portrayed: so long and lank, so lean and flabby, so extremely consumptive-looking that one could well understand the justness and propriety with which the name of "hack" had been bestowed upon him.

Alongside Rocinante stood Sancho Panza, holding the halter of his ass, and below was the legend: "Sancho Zancas." The picture showed him with a big belly, a short body and long shanks, and that must have been where he got the names of Panza y Zancas[3] by which he is a number of times called in the course of the history. There are other small details that might be mentioned, but they are of little importance and have nothing to do with the truth of the story—and no story is bad so long as it is true.

If there is any objection to be raised against the veracity of the present one, it can be only that the author was an Arab, and that nation is known for its lying propensities; but even though they be our enemies, it may readily be understood that they would more likely have detracted from, rather than added to, the chronicle. So it seems to me, at any rate; for whenever he might and should deploy the resources of his pen in praise of so worthy a knight, the author appears to take pains to pass over the matter in silence; all of which in my opinion is ill done and ill conceived, for it should be the duty of historians to be exact, truthful, and dispassionate, and neither interest nor fear nor rancor nor affection should swerve them from the path of truth, whose mother is history, rival of time, depository of deeds, witness of the past, exemplar and adviser to the present, and the future's councilor. In this work, I am sure, will be found all that could be desired in the way of pleasant reading; and if it is lacking in any way, I maintain that this is the fault of that hound of an author rather than of the subject.

But to come to the point, the second part, according to the translation, began as follows:

As the two valorous and enraged combatants stood there, swords upraised and poised on high, it seemed from their bold mien as if they must surely be threatening heaven, earth, and hell itself. The first to let fall a blow was the choleric Biscayan, and he came down with such force and fury that, had not his sword been deflected in mid-air, that single stroke would have sufficed to put an end to this fearful combat and to all our knight's adventures at the

2. About fifty pounds. "Two arrobas": three bushels.   3. Paunch and Shanks (Spanish).

same time; but fortune, which was reserving him for greater things, turned aside his adversary's blade in such a manner that, even though it fell upon his left shoulder, it did him no other damage than to strip him completely of his armor on that side, carrying with it a good part of his helmet along with half an ear, the headpiece clattering to the ground with a dreadful din, leaving its wearer in a sorry state.

Heaven help me! Who could properly describe the rage that now entered the heart of our hero of La Mancha as he saw himself treated in this fashion? It may merely be said that he once more reared himself in the stirrups, laid hold of his sword with both hands, and dealt the Biscayan such a blow, over the cushion and upon the head, that, even so good a defense proving useless, it was as if a mountain had fallen upon his enemy. The latter now began bleeding through the mouth, nose, and ears; he seemed about to fall from his mule, and would have fallen, no doubt, if he had not grasped the beast about the neck, but at that moment his feet slipped from the stirrups and his arms let go, and the mule, frightened by the terrible blow, began running across the plain, hurling its rider to the earth with a few quick plunges.

Don Quixote stood watching all this very calmly. When he saw his enemy fall, he leaped from his horse, ran over very nimbly, and thrust the point of his sword into the Biscayan's eyes, calling upon him at the same time to surrender or otherwise he would cut off his head. The Biscayan was so bewildered that he was unable to utter a single word in reply, and things would have gone badly with him, so blind was Don Quixote in his rage, if the ladies of the coach, who up to then had watched the struggle in dismay, had not come up to him at this point and begged him with many blandishments to do them the very great favor of sparing their squire's life.

To which Don Quixote replied with much haughtiness and dignity, "Most certainly, lovely ladies, I shall be very happy to do that which you ask of me, but upon one condition and understanding, and that is that this knight promise me that he will go to El Toboso and present himself in my behalf before Doña Dulcinea, in order that she may do with him as she may see fit."

Trembling and disconsolate, the ladies did not pause to discuss Don Quixote's request, but without so much as inquiring who Dulcinea might be they promised him that the squire would fulfill that which was commanded of him.

"Very well, then, trusting in your word, I will do him no further harm, even though he has well deserved it."

CHAPTER 10

Of the pleasing conversation that took place between Don Quixote and Sancho Panza, his squire.

By this time Sancho Panza had got to his feet, somewhat the worse for wear as the result of the treatment he had received from the friars' lads. He had been watching the battle attentively and praying God in his heart to give the victory to his master, Don Quixote, in order that he, Sancho, might gain some island where he could go to be governor as had been promised him. Seeing now that the combat was over and the knight was returning to mount

Rocinante once more, he went up to hold the stirrup for him; but first he fell on his knees in front of him and, taking his hand, kissed it and said, "May your Grace be pleased, Señor Don Quixote, to grant me the governorship of that island which you have won in this deadly affray; for however large it may be, I feel that I am indeed capable of governing it as well as any man in this world has ever done."

To which Don Quixote replied, "Be advised, brother Sancho, that this adventure and other similar ones have nothing to do with islands; they are affairs of the crossroads in which one gains nothing more than a broken head or an ear the less. Be patient, for there will be others which will not only make you a governor, but more than that."

Sancho thanked him very much and, kissing his hand again and the skirt of his cuirass, he assisted him up on Rocinante's back, after which the squire bestraddled his own mount and started jogging along behind his master, who was now going at a good clip. Without pausing for any further converse with those in the coach, the knight made for a near-by wood, with Sancho following as fast as his beast could trot; but Rocinante was making such speed that the ass and its rider were left behind, and it was necessary to call out to Don Quixote to pull up and wait for them. He did so, reining in Rocinante until the weary Sancho had drawn abreast of him.

"It strikes me, sir," said the squire as he reached his master's side, "that it would be better for us to take refuge in some church; for in view of the way you have treated that one with whom you were fighting, it would be small wonder if they did not lay the matter before the Holy Brotherhood[4] and have us arrested; and faith, if they do that, we shall have to sweat a-plenty before we come out of jail."

"Be quiet," said Don Quixote. "And where have you ever seen, or read of, a knight being brought to justice no matter how many homicides he might have committed?"

"I know nothing about omecils,"[5] replied Sancho, "nor ever in my life did I bear one to anybody; all I know is that the Holy Brotherhood has something to say about those who go around fighting on the highway, and I want nothing of it."

"Do not let it worry you," said Don Quixote, "for I will rescue you from the hands of the Chaldeans, not to speak of the Brotherhood. But answer me upon your life: have you ever seen a more valorous knight than I on all the known face of the earth? Have you ever read in the histories of any other who had more mettle in the attack, more perseverance in sustaining it, more dexterity in wounding his enemy, or more skill in overthrowing him?"

"The truth is," said Sancho, "I have never read any history whatsoever, for I do not know how to read or write; but what I would wager is that in all the days of my life I have never served a more courageous master than your Grace; I only hope your courage is not paid for in the place that I have mentioned. What I would suggest is that your Grace allow me to do something for that ear, for there is much blood coming from it, and I have here in my saddlebags some lint and a little white ointment."

---

4. A tribunal instituted by Ferdinand and Isabella at the end of the 15th century to punish highway robbers.   5. In Spanish a wordplay on *homecidio-omecillo*. Not to bear an *omecillo* to anybody means not to bear a grudge, and good-natured Sancho does not.

"We could well dispense with all that," said Don Quixote, "if only I had remembered to bring along a vial of Fierabrás's[6] balm, a single drop of which saves time and medicines."

"What vial and what balm is that?" inquired Sancho Panza.

"It is a balm the receipt[7] for which I know by heart; with it one need have no fear of death nor think of dying from any wound. I shall make some of it and give it to you; and thereafter, whenever in any battle you see my body cut in two—as very often happens—all that is necessary is for you to take the part that lies on the ground, before the blood has congealed, and fit it very neatly and with great nicety upon the other part that remains in the saddle, taking care to adjust it evenly and exactly. Then you will give me but a couple of swallows of the balm of which I have told you, and you will see me sounder than an apple in no time at all."

"If that is so," said Panza, "I herewith renounce the governorship of the island you promised me and ask nothing other in payment of my many and faithful services than that your Grace give me the receipt for this wonderful potion, for I am sure that it would be worth more than two reales the ounce anywhere, and that is all I need for a life of ease and honor. But may I be so bold as to ask how much it costs to make it?"

"For less than three reales you can make something like six quarts," Don Quixote told him.

"Sinner that I am!" exclaimed Sancho. "Then why does your Grace not make some at once and teach me also?"

"Hush, my friend," said the knight, "I mean to teach you greater secrets than that and do you greater favors; but, for the present, let us look after this ear of mine, for it is hurting me more than I like."

Sancho thereupon took the lint and the ointment from his saddlebags; but when Don Quixote caught a glimpse of his helmet, he almost went out of his mind and, laying his hand upon his sword and lifting his eyes heavenward, he cried, "I make a vow to the Creator of all things and to the four holy Gospels in all their fullness of meaning that I will lead from now on the life that the great Marquis of Mantua did after he had sworn to avenge the death of his nephew Baldwin: not to eat bread of a tablecloth, not to embrace his wife, and other things which, although I am unable to recall them, we will look upon as understood—all this until I shall have wreaked an utter vengeance upon the one who has perpetrated such an outrage upon me."

"But let me remind your Grace," said Sancho when he heard these words, "that if the knight fulfills that which was commanded of him, by going to present himself before my lady Dulcinea del Toboso, then he will have paid his debt to you and merits no further punishment at your hands, unless it be for some fresh offense."

"You have spoken very well and to the point," said Don Quixote, "and so I annul the vow I have just made insofar as it has to do with any further vengeance, but I make it and confirm it anew so far as leading the life of which I have spoken is concerned, until such time as I shall have obtained by force of arms from some other knight another headpiece as good as this. And do not think, Sancho, that I am making smoke out of straw; there is one

6. A giant Saracen healer in the medieval epics of the Twelve Peers (see n. 6, p. 86).　7. Recipe.

whom I well may imitate in this matter, for the same thing happened in all literalness in the case of Mambrino's helmet[8] which cost Sacripante so dear."

"I wish," said Sancho, "that your Grace would send all such oaths to the devil, for they are very bad for the health and harmful for the conscience as well. Tell me, please; supposing that for many days to come we meet no man wearing a helmet, then what are we to do? Must you still keep your vow in spite of all the inconveniences and discomforts, such as sleeping with your clothes on, not sleeping in any town, and a thousand other penances contained in the oath of that old madman of a Marquis of Mantua, an oath which you would now revive? Mark you, sir, along all these roads you meet no men of arms but only muleteers and carters, who not only do not wear helmets but quite likely have never heard tell of them in all their livelong days."

"In that you are wrong," said Don Quixote, "for we shall not be at these crossroads for the space of two hours before we shall see more men of arms than came to Albraca to win the fair Angélica."[9] "Very well, then," said Sancho, "so be it, and pray God that all turns out for the best so that I may at last win that island that is costing me so dearly, and then let me die."

"I have already told you, Sancho, that you are to give no thought to that; should the island fail, there is the kingdom of Denmark or that of Sobradisa, which would fit you like a ring on your finger, and you ought, moreover, to be happy to be on *terra firma*.[1] But let us leave all this for some other time, while you look and see if you have something in those saddlebags for us to eat, after which we will go in search of some castle where we may lodge for the night and prepare that balm of which I was telling you, for I swear to God that my ear is paining me greatly."

"I have here an onion, a little cheese, and a few crusts of bread," said Sancho, "but they are not victuals fit for a valiant knight like your grace."

"How little you know about it!" replied Don Quixote. "I would inform you, Sancho, that it is a point of honor with knights-errant to go for a month at a time without eating, and when they do eat, it is whatever may be at hand. You would certainly know that if you had read the histories as I have. There are many of them, and in none have I found any mention of knights eating unless it was by chance or at some sumptuous banquet that was tendered them; on other days they fasted. And even though it is well understood that, being men like us, they could not go without food entirely, any more than they could fail to satisfy the other necessities of nature, nevertheless, since they spent the greater part of their lives in forest and desert places without any cook to prepare their meals, their diet ordinarily consisted of rustic viands such as those that you now offer me. And so, Sancho my friend, do not be grieved at that which pleases me, nor seek to make the world over, nor to unhinge the institution of knight-errantry."

"Pardon me, your Grace," said Sancho, "but seeing that, as I have told you I do not know how to read or write, I am consequently not familiar with the rules of the knightly calling. Hereafter, I will stuff my saddlebags with all

---

8. The enchanted helmet of Mambrino, a Moorish king, is stolen by Rinaldo in Boiardo's *Roland in Love*.
9. Another allusion to *Roland in Love*.   1. Solid earth (Latin, literal trans.); here Firm Island, an imaginary final destination for the squires of knights-errant. Sobradisa is an imaginary realm.

manner of dried fruit for your Grace, but inasmuch as I am not a knight, I shall lay in for myself a stock of fowls and other more substantial fare."

"I am not saying, Sancho, that it is incumbent upon knights-errant to eat only those fruits of which you speak; what I am saying is that their ordinary sustenance should consist of fruit and a few herbs such as are to be found in the fields and with which they are well acquainted, as am I myself."

"It is a good thing," said Sancho, "to know those herbs, for, so far as I can see, we are going to have need of that knowledge one of these days."

With this, he brought out the articles he had mentioned, and the two of them ate in peace, and most companionably. Being desirous, however, of seeking a lodging for the night, they did not tarry long over their humble and unsavory repast. They then mounted and made what haste they could that they might arrive at a shelter before nightfall but the sun failed them, and with it went the hope of attaining their wish. As the day ended they found themselves beside some goatherds' huts, and they accordingly decided to spend the night there. Sancho was as much disappointed at their not having reached a town as his master was content with sleeping under the open sky; for it seemed to Don Quixote that every time this happened it merely provided him with yet another opportunity to establish his claim to the title of knight-errant.

[Of Goatherds, Roaming Shepherdesses, and Unrequited Loves]

CHAPTER 11

Of what happened to Don Quixote in the company of certain goatherds.

He was received by the herders with good grace, and Sancho having looked after Rocinante and the ass to the best of his ability, the knight, drawn by the aroma, went up to where some pieces of goat's meat were simmering in a pot over the fire. He would have liked then and there to see if they were done well enough to be transferred from pot to stomach, but he refrained in view of the fact that his hosts were already taking them off the fire. Spreading a few sheepskins on the ground, they hastily laid their rustic board and invited the strangers to share what there was of it. There were six of them altogether who belonged to that fold, and after they had urged Don Quixote, with rude politeness, to seat himself upon a small trough which they had turned upside down for the purpose, they took their own places upon the sheep hides round about. While his master sat there, Sancho remained standing to serve him the cup, which was made of horn. When the knight perceived this, he addressed his squire as follows.

"In order, Sancho, that you may see the good that there is in knight-errantry and how speedily those who follow the profession, no matter what the nature of their service may be, come to be honored and esteemed in the eyes of the world, I would have you here in the company of these good folk seat yourself at my side, that you may be even as I who am your master and natural lord, and eat from my plate and drink from where I drink; for of knight-errantry one may say the same as of love that it makes all things equal."

"Many thanks!" said Sancho, "but if it is all the same to your Grace, providing there is enough to go around, I can eat just as well, or better, standing up and alone as I can seated beside an emperor. And if the truth must be

told, I enjoy much more that which I eat in my own corner without any bow-
ings and scrapings, even though it be only bread and onions, that I do a meal
of roast turkey where I have to chew slowly, drink little, be always wiping my
mouth, and can neither sneeze nor cough if I feel like it, nor do any of those
other things that you can when you are free and alone.

"And so, my master," he went on, "these honors that your Grace would
confer upon me as your servant and a follower of knight-errantry—which I
am, being your Grace's squire—I would have you convert, if you will, into
other things that will be of more profit and advantage to me; for though I
hereby acknowledge them as duly received, I renounce them from this time
forth to the end of the world."

"But for all that," said Don Quixote, "you must sit down, for whosoever
humbleth himself, him God will exalt." And, laying hold of his squire's arm,
he compelled him to take a seat beside him.

The goatherds did not understand all this jargon about squires and
knights-errant; they did nothing but eat, keep silent, and study their guests,
who very dexterously and with much appetite were stowing away chunks of
meat as big as your fist. When the meat course was finished, they laid out
upon the sheepskins a great quantity of dried acorns and half a cheese,
which was harder than if it had been made of mortar. The drinking horn all
this while was not idle but went the rounds so often—now full, now empty,
like the bucket of a water wheel—that they soon drained one of the two
wine bags that were on hand. After Don Quixote had well satisfied his stomach, he took up a handful of acorns and, gazing at them attentively, fell into
a soliloquy.

"Happy the age and happy those centuries to which the ancients gave the
name of golden, and not because gold, which is so esteemed in this iron age
of ours, was then to be had without toil, but because those who lived in that
time did not know the meaning of the words 'thine' and 'mine.' In that
blessed year all things were held in common, and to gain his daily sustenance no labor was required of any man save to reach forth his hand and
take it from the sturdy oaks that stood liberally inviting him with their sweet
and seasoned fruit. The clear-running fountains and rivers in magnificent
abundance offered him palatable and transparent water for his thirst; while
in the clefts of the rocks and the hollows of the trees the wise and busy
honey-makers set up their republic so that any hand whatever might avail
itself, fully and freely, of the fertile harvest which their fragrant toil had produced. The vigorous cork trees of their own free will and grace, without the
asking, shed their broad, light bark with which men began to cover their
dwellings, erected upon rude stakes merely as a protection against the
inclemency of the heavens.

"All then was peace, all was concord and friendship; the crooked plowshare had not as yet grievously laid open and pried into the merciful bowels
of our first mother, who without any forcing on man's part yielded her spacious fertile bosom on every hand for the satisfaction, sustenance, and delight
of her first sons. Then it was that lovely and unspoiled young shepherdesses,
with locks that were sometimes braided, sometimes flowing, went roaming
from valley to valley and hillock to hillock with no more garments than were
needed to cover decently that which modesty requires and always had
required should remain covered. Nor were their adornments such as those in

usc today—of Tyrian purple and silk worked up in tortured patterns; a few green leaves of burdock or of ivy, and they were as splendidly and as becomingly clad as our ladies of the court with all the rare and exotic tricks of fashion that idle curiosity has taught them.

"Thoughts of love, also, in those days were set forth as simply as the simple hearts that conceived them, without any roundabout and artificial play of words by way of ornament. Fraud, deceit, and malice had not yet come to mingle with truth and plain-speaking. Justice kept its own domain, where favor and self-interest dared not trespass, dared not impair her rights, becloud, and persecute her as they now do. There was no such thing then as arbitrary judgments, for the reason that there was no one to judge or be judged. Maidens in all their modesty, as I have said, went where they would and unattended; whereas in this hateful age of ours none is safe, even though she go to hide and shut herself up in some new labyrinth like that of Crete; for in spite of all her seclusion, through chinks and crevices or borne upon the air, the amorous plague with all its cursed importunities will find her out and lead her to her ruin.

"It was for the safety of such as these, as time went on and depravity increased, that the order of knights-errant was instituted, for the protection of damsels, the aid of widows and orphans, and the succoring of the needy. It is to this order that I belong, my brothers, and I thank you for the welcome and the kindly treatment that you have accorded to me and my squire. By natural law, all living men are obliged to show favor to knights-errant, yet without being aware of this you have received and entertained me; and so it is with all possible good will that I acknowledge your own good will to me."

This long harangue on the part of our knight—it might very well have been dispensed with—was all due to the acorns they had given him, which had brought back to memory the age of gold; whereupon the whim had seized him to indulge in this futile harangue with the goatherds as his auditors. They listened in open-mouthed wonderment, saying not a word, and Sancho himself kept quiet and went on munching acorns, taking occasion very frequently to pay a visit to the second wine bag, which they had suspended from a cork tree to keep it cool.

It took Don Quixote much longer to finish his speech than it did to put away his supper; and when he was through, one of the goatherds addressed him.

"In order that your Grace may say with more truth that we have received you with readiness and good will, we desire to give you solace and contentment by having one of our comrades, who will be here soon, sing for you. He is a very bright young fellow and deeply in love, and what is more, you could not ask for anything better than to hear him play the three-stringed lute."

Scarcely had he done saying this when the sound of a rebec was heard, and shortly afterward the one who played it appeared. He was a goodlooking youth, around twenty-two years of age. His companions asked him if he had had his supper, and when he replied that he had, the one who had spoken to Don Quixote said to him, "Well, then, Antonio, you can give us the pleasure of hearing you sing, in order that this gentleman whom we have as our guest may see that we of the woods and mountains also know something about music. We have been telling him how clever you are, and now we want you to show him that we were speaking the truth. And so I beg you by all means to sit down and sing us that lovesong of yours that your uncle the prebendary composed for you and which the villagers liked so well."

"With great pleasure," the lad replied, and without any urging he seated himself on the stump of an oak that had been felled and, tuning up his rebec, soon began singing, very prettily, the following ballad:

The Ballad That Antonio Sang

I know well that thou dost love me,
My Olalla, even though
Eyes of thine have never spoken—
Love's mute tongues—to tell me so.
   Since I know thou knowest my passion,   5
Of thy love I am more sure:
No love ever was unhappy
When it was both frank and pure.
   True it is, Olalla, sometimes
Thou a heart of bronze hast shown,   10
And it seemed to me that bosom,
White and fair, was made of stone.
   Yet in spite of all repulses
And a chastity so cold,
It appeared that I Hope's garment   15
By the hem did clutch and hold.
   For my faith I ever cherished;
It would rise to meet the bait;
Spurned, it never did diminish;
Favorefd, it preferred to wait.   20
   Love, they say, hath gentle manners:
Thus it is it shows its face;
Then may I take hope, Olalla,
Trust to win a longed for grace.
   If devotion hath the power   25
Hearts to move and make them kind,
Let the loyalty I've shown thee
Plead my cause, be kept in mind.
   For if thou didst note my costume,
More than once thou must have seen,   30
Worn upon a simple Monday
Sunday's garb so bright and clean.
   Love and brightness go together.
Dost thou ask the reason why
I thus deck myself on Monday?   35
It is but to catch thine eye.
   I say nothing of the dances
I have danced for thy sweet sake;
Nor the serenades I've sung thee
Till the first cock did awake.   40
   Nor will I repeat my praises
Of that beauty all can see;
True my words but oft unwelcome—
Certain lasses hated me.

> One girl there is, I well remember—   45
> She's Teresa on the hill—
> Said, "You think you love an angel,
> But she is a monkey still.
>   "Thanks to all her many trinkets
> And her artificial hair   50
> And her many aids to beauty,
> Love's own self she would ensnare."
>   She was lying, I was angry,
> And her cousin, very bold,
> Challenged me upon my honor;   55
> What ensued need not be told.
>   Highflown words do not become me;
> I'm a plain and simple man.
> Pure the love that I would offer,
> Serving thee as best I can.   60
>   Silken are the bonds of marriage,
> When two hearts do intertwine;
> Mother Church the yoke will fasten;
> Bow your neck and I'll bow mine.
>   Or if not, my word I'll give thee,   65
> From these mountains I'll come down—
> Saint most holy be my witness—
> Wearing a Capuchin gown.

With this the goatherd brought his song to a close, and although Don Quixote begged him to sing some more, Sancho Panza would not hear of this as he was too sleepy for any more ballads.

"Your Grace," he said to his master, "would do well to find out at once where his bed is to be, for the labor that these good men have to perform all day long does not permit them to stay up all night singing."

"I understand, Sancho," replied Don Quixote. "I perceive that those visits to the wine bag call for sleep rather than music as a recompense."

"It tastes well enough to all of us, God be praised," said Sancho.

"I am not denying that," said his master; "but go ahead and settle yourself down wherever you like. As for men of my profession, they prefer to keep vigil. But all the same, Sancho, perhaps you had better look after this ear, for it is paining me more than I like."

Sancho started to do as he was commanded, but one of the goatherds, when he saw the wound, told him not to bother, that he would place a remedy upon it that would heal it in no time. Taking a few leaves of rosemary, of which there was a great deal growing thereabouts, he mashed them in his mouth and, mixing them with a little salt, laid them on the ear, with the assurance that no other medicine was needed; and this proved to be the truth.

CHAPTER 12

Of the story that one of the goatherds told to Don Quixote and the others.

Just then, another lad came up, one of those who brought the goatherds their provisions from the village.

"Do you know what's happening down there, my friends?" he said.

"How should we know?" one of the men answered him.

"In that case," the lad went on, "I must tell you that the famous student and shepherd known as Grisóstomo died this morning, muttering that the cause of his death was the love he had for that bewitched lass of a Marcela, daughter of the wealthy Guillermo—you know, the one who's been going around in these parts dressed like a shepherdess."

"For love of Marcela, you say?" one of the herders spoke up.

"That is what I'm telling you," replied the other lad. "And the best part of it is that he left directions in his will that he was to be buried in the field, as if he were a Moor, and that his grave was to be at the foot of the cliff where the Cork Tree Spring is; for, according to report, and he is supposed to have said so himself, that is the place where he saw her for the first time. There were other provisions, which the clergy of the village say cannot be carried out, nor would it be proper to fulfill them, seeing that they savor of heathen practices. But Grisóstomo's good friend, the student Ambrosio, who also dresses like a shepherd, insists that everything must be done to the letter, and as a result there is great excitement in the village.

"Nevertheless, from all I can hear, they will end by doing as Ambrosio and Grisóstomo's other friends desire, and tomorrow they will bury him with great ceremony in the place that I have mentioned. I believe it is going to be something worth seeing; at any rate, I mean to see it, even though it is too far for me to be able to return to the village before nightfall."

"We will all do the same," said the other goatherds. "We will cast lots to see who stays to watch the goats."

"That is right, Pedro," said one of their number, "but it will not be necessary to go to the trouble of casting lots. I will take care of the flocks for all of us; and do not think that I am being generous or that I am not as curious as the rest of you; it is simply that I cannot walk on account of the splinter I picked up in this foot the other day."

"Well, we thank you just the same," said Pedro.

Don Quixote then asked Pedro to tell him more about the dead man and the shepherd lass; to which the latter replied that all he knew was that Grisóstomo was a rich gentleman who had lived in a near-by village. He had been a student for many years at Salamanca and then had returned to his birthplace with the reputation of being very learned and well read; he was especially noted for his knowledge of the science of the stars and what the sun and moon were doing up there in the heavens, "for he would promptly tell us when their clips was to come."

"*Eclipse*, my friend, not *clips*," said Don Quixote, "is the name applied to the darkening-over of those major luminaries."

But Pedro, not pausing for any trifles, went on with his story. "He could also tell when the year was going to be plentiful or estil—"

"*Sterile*, you mean to say, friend—"

"*Sterile* or *estil*," said Pedro, "it all comes out the same in the end. But I can tell you one thing, that his father and his friends, who believed in him, did just as he advised them and they became rich; for he would say to them, 'This year, sow barley and not wheat'; and again, 'Sow chickpeas and not barley'; or, 'This season there will be a good crop of oil[2] but the three following ones you will not get a drop.'"

2. Olive oil.

"That science," Don Quixote explained, "is known as astrology."

"I don't know what it's called," said Pedro, "but he knew all this and more yet. Finally, not many months after he returned from Salamanca, he appeared one day dressed like a shepherd with crook and sheepskin jacket; for he had resolved to lay aside the long gown that he wore as a scholar, and in this he was joined by Ambrosio, a dear friend of his and the companion of his studies. I forgot to tell you that Grisóstomo was a great one for composing verses; he even wrote the carols for Christmas Eve and the plays that were performed at Corpus Christi by the lads of our village, and everyone said that they were the best ever.

"When the villagers saw the two scholars coming out dressed like shepherds, they were amazed and could not imagine what was the reason for such strange conduct on their part. It was about that time that Grisóstomo's father died and left him the heir to a large fortune, consisting of land and chattels, no small quantity of cattle, and a considerable sum of money, of all of which the young man was absolute master; and, to tell the truth, he deserved it, for he was very sociable and charitably inclined, a friend to all worthy folk, and he had a face that was like a benediction. Afterward it was learned that if he had changed his garments like this, it was only that he might be able to wander over the wastelands on the trail of that shepherdess Marcela of whom our friend was speaking, for the poor fellow had fallen in love with her. And now I should like to tell you, for it is well that you should know, just who this lass is; for it may be—indeed, there is no maybe about it—you will never hear the like in all the days of your life, though you live to be older than Sarna."

"You should say *Sarah*," Don Quixote corrected him; for he could not bear hearing the goatherd using the wrong words all the time.[3]

"The itch," said Pedro, "lives long enough; and if, sir, you go on interrupting me at every word, we'll never be through in a year."

"Pardon me, friend," said Don Quixote, "it was only because there is so great a difference between Sarna and Sarah that I pointed it out to you; but you have given me a very good answer, for the itch does live longer than Sarah; and so go on with your story, and I will not contradict you any more."

"I was about to say, then, my dear sir," the goatherd went on, "that in our village there was a farmer who was richer still than Grisóstomo's father. His name was Guillermo, and, over and above his great wealth, God gave him a daughter whose mother, the most highly respected woman in these parts, died in bearing her. It seems to me I can see the good lady now, with that face that rivaled the sun and moon; and I remember, above all, what a friend she was to the poor, for which reason I believe that her soul at this very moment must be enjoying God's presence in the other world.

"Grieving for the loss of so excellent a wife, Guillermo himself died, leaving his daughter Marcela, now a rich young woman, in the custody of one of her uncles, a priest who holds a benefice in our village. The girl grew up with such beauty as to remind us of her mother, beautiful as that lady had been. By the time she was fourteen or fifteen no one looked at her without giving thanks to God who had created such comeliness, and almost all were hope-

---

3. Actually in this case the goatherd is not really wrong, for *sama* means "itch" and "older than the itch" was a proverbial expression.

lessly in love with her. Her uncle kept her very closely shut up, but, for all of that, word of her great beauty spread to such an extent that by reason of it, as much as on account of the girl's wealth, her uncle found himself besought and importuned not only by the young men of our village, but by those for leagues around who desired to have her for a wife.

"But he, an upright Christian, although he wished to marry her off as soon as she was of age, had no desire to do so without her consent, not that he had any eye to the gain and profit which the custody of his niece's property brought him while her marriage was deferred. Indeed, this much was said in praise of the good priest in more than one circle of the village; for I would have you know, Sir Knight, that in these little places everything is discussed and becomes a subject of gossip; and you may rest assured, as I am for my part, that a priest must be more than ordinarily good if his parishioners feel bound to speak well of him, especially in the small towns."

"That is true," said Don Quixote, "but go on. I like your story very much, and you, good Pedro, tell it with very good grace."

"May the Lord's grace never fail me, for that is what counts. But to go on: Although the uncle set forth to his niece the qualities of each one in particular of the many who sought her hand, begging her to choose and marry whichever one she pleased, she never gave him any answer other than this: that she did not wish to marry at all, since being but a young girl she did not feel that she was equal to bearing the burdens of matrimony. As her reasons appeared to be proper and just, the uncle did not insist but thought he would wait until she was a little older, when she would be capable of selecting someone to her taste. For, he said, and quite right he was, parents ought not to impose a way of life upon their children against the latters' will. And then, one fine day, lo and behold, there was the finical Marcela turned shepherdess; and without paying any attention to her uncle or all those of the village who advised against it, she set out to wander through the fields with the other lasses, guarding flocks as they did.

"Well, the moment she appeared in public and her beauty was uncovered for all to see, I really cannot tell you how many rich young bachelors, gentlemen, and farmers proceeded to don a shepherd's garb and go to make love to her in the meadows. One of her suitors, as I have told you, was our deceased friend, and it is said that he did not love but adored her. But you must not think that because Marcela chose so free and easy a life, and one that offers little or no privacy, that she was thereby giving the faintest semblance of encouragement to those who would disparage her modesty and prudence; rather, so great was the vigilance with which she looked after her honor that of all those who waited upon her and solicited her favors, none could truly say that she had given him the slightest hope of attaining his desire.

"For although she does not flee nor shun the company and conversation of the shepherds, treating them in courteous and friendly fashion, the moment she discovers any intentions on their part, even though it be the just and holy one of matrimony, she hurls them from her like a catapult. As a result, she is doing more damage in this land than if a plague had fallen upon it; for her beauty and graciousness win the hearts of all who would serve her, but her disdain and the disillusionment it brings lead them in the end to despair, and then they can only call her cruel and ungrateful, along with other similar epithets that reveal all too plainly the state of mind that prompts them. If

you were to stay here some time, sir, you would hear these uplands and valleys echo with the laments of those who have followed her only to be
deceived.

"Not far from here is a place where there are a couple of dozen tall
beeches, and there is not a one of them on whose smooth bark Marcela's
name has not been engraved; and above some of these inscriptions you will
find a crown, as if by this her lover meant to indicate that she deserved to
wear the garland of beauty above all the women on the earth. Here a shepherd sighs and there another voices his lament. Now are to be heard
amorous ballads, and again despairing ditties. One will spend all the hours
of the night seated at the foot of some oak or rock without once closing his
tearful eyes, and the morning sun will find him there, stupefied and lost in
thought. Another, without giving truce or respite to his sights, will lie
stretched upon the burning sands in the full heat of the most exhausting
summer noontide, sending up his complaint to merciful Heaven.

"And, meanwhile, over this one and that one, over one and all, the beauteous Marcela triumphs and goes her own way, free and unconcerned. All
those of us who know her are waiting to see how far her pride will carry her,
and who will be the fortunate man who will succeed in taming this terrible
creature and thus come into possession of a beauty so matchless as hers.
Knowing all this that I have told you to be undoubtedly true, I can readily
believe this lad's story about the cause of Grisóstomo's death. And so I advise
you, sir, not to fail to be present tomorrow at his burial; it will be well worth
seeing, for he has many friends, and the place is not half a league from here."

"I will make a point of it," said Don Quixote, "and I thank you for the pleasure you have given me by telling me so delightful a tale."

"Oh," said the goatherd, "I do not know the half of the things that have
happened to Marcela's lovers; but it is possible that tomorrow we may meet
along the way some shepherd who will tell us more. And now it would be
well for you to go and sleep under cover, for the night air may not be good
for your wound, though with the remedy that has been put on it there is not
much to fear."

Sancho Panza, who had been sending the goatherd to the devil for talking
so much, now put in a word with his master, urging him to come and sleep
in Pedro's hut. Don Quixote did so; and all the rest of the night was spent by
him in thinking of his lady Dulcinea, in imitation of Marcela's lovers. As for
Sancho, he made himself comfortable between Rocinante and the ass and at
once dropped off to sleep, not like a lovelorn swain but, rather, like a man
who has had a sound kicking that day.

CHAPTER 13

In which is brought to a close the story of the shepherdess Marcela,
along with other events.

Day had barely begun to appear upon the balconies of the east when five or
six goatherds arose and went to awaken Don Quixote and tell him that if he
was still of a mind to go see Grisóstomo's famous burial they would keep him
company. The knight, desiring nothing better, ordered Sancho to saddle at
once, which was done with much dispatch, and then they all set out forthwith.

They had not gone more than a quarter of a league when, upon crossing a footpath, they saw coming toward them six shepherds clad in black sheepskins and with garlands of cypress and bitter rosebay on their heads. Each of them carried a thick staff made of the wood of the holly, and with them came two gentlemen on horseback in handsome traveling attire, accompanied by three lads on foot. As the two parties met they greeted each other courteously, each inquiring as to the other's destination, where upon they learned that they were all going to the burial, and so continued to ride along together.

Speaking to his companion, one of them said, "I think, Señor Vivaldo, that we are going to be well repaid for the delay it will cost us to see this famous funeral; for famous it must surely be, judging by the strange things that these shepherds have told us of the dead man and the homicidal shepherdess."

"I think so too," agreed Vivaldo. "I should be willing to delay our journey not one day, but four, for the sake of seeing it."

Don Quixote then asked them what it was they had heard of Marcela and Grisóstomo. The traveler replied that on that very morning they had fallen in with those shepherds and, seeing them so mournfully trigged out, had asked them what the occasion for it was. One of the fellows had then told them of the beauty and strange demeanor of a shepherdess by the name of Marcela, her many suitors, and the death of this Grisóstomo, to whose funeral they were bound. He related, in short, the entire story as Don Quixote had heard it from Pedro.

Changing the subject, the gentleman called Vivaldo inquired of Don Quixote what it was that led him to go armed in that manner in a land that was so peaceful.

"The calling that I profess," replied Don Quixote, "does not permit me to do otherwise. An easy pace, pleasure, and repose—those things were invented for delicate courtiers; but toil, anxiety, and arms—they are for those whom the world knows as knights-errant, of whom I, though unworthy, am the very least."

No sooner had they heard this than all of them immediately took him for a madman. By way of assuring himself further and seeing what kind of madness it was of which Don Quixote was possessed, Vivaldo now asked him what was meant by the term knights-errant.

"Have not your Worships read the annals and the histories of England that treat of the famous exploits of King Arthur, who in our Castilian balladry is always called King Artús? According to a very old tradition that is common throughout the entire realm of Great Britain, this king did not die, but by an act of enchantment was changed into a raven; and in due course of time he is to return and reign once more, recovering his kingdom and his scepter; for which reason, from that day to this, no Englishman is known to have killed one of those birds. It was, moreover, in the time of that good king that the famous order of the Knights of the Round Table was instituted; and as for the love of Sir Lancelot of the Lake and Queen Guinevere, everything took place exactly as the story has it, their confidante and go-between being the honored matron Quintañona; whence comes that charming ballad that is such a favorite with us Spaniards:

Never was there a knight
So served by maid and dame
As the one they call Sir Lancelot
When from Britain he came—

to carry on the gentle, pleasing course of his loves and noble deeds.

"From that time forth, the order of chivalry was passed on and propagated from one individual to another until it had spread through many and various parts of the world. Among those famed for their exploits was the valiant Amadis of Gaul, with all his sons and grandsons to the fifth generation; and there was also the brave Felixmarte of Hircania, and the never sufficiently praised Tirant lo Blanch; and in view of the fact that he lived in our own day, almost, we came near to seeing, hearing, and conversing with that other courageous knight, Don Belianís of Greece.

"And that, gentlemen, is what it means to be a knight-errant, and what I have been telling you of is the order of chivalry which such a knight professes, an order to which, as I have already informed you, I, although a sinner, have the honor of belonging; for I have made the same profession as have those other knights. That is why it is you find me in these wild and lonely places, riding in quest of adventure, being resolved to offer my arm and my person in the most dangerous undertaking fate may have in store for me, that I may be of aid to the weak and needy."

Listening to this speech, the travelers had some while since come to the conclusion that Don Quixote was out of his mind, and were likewise able to perceive the peculiar nature of his madness, and they wondered at it quite as much as did all those who encountered it for the first time. Being endowed with a ready wit and a merry disposition and thinking to pass the time until they reached the end of the short journey which, so he was told, awaited them before they should arrive at the mountain where the burial was to take place, Vivaldo decided to give him a further opportunity of displaying his absurdities.

"It strikes me, Sir Knight-errant," he said, "that your Grace has espoused one of the most austere professions to be found anywhere on earth—even more austere, if I am not mistaken, than that of the Carthusian monks."

"Theirs may be as austere as ours," Don Quixote replied, "but that it is as necessary I am very much inclined to doubt. For if the truth be told, the soldier who carries out his captain's order does no less than the captain who gives the order. By that I mean to say that the religious, in all peace and tranquility, pray to Heaven for earth's good, but we soldiers and knights put their prayers into execution by defending with the might of our good right arms and at the edge of the sword those things for which they pray; and we do this not under cover of a roof but under the open sky, beneath the insufferable rays of the summer sun and the biting cold of winter. Thus we become the ministers of God on earth, and our arms the means by which He executes His decrees. And just as war and all the things that have to do with it are impossible without toil, sweat, and anxiety, it follows that those who have taken upon themselves such a profession must unquestionably labor harder than do those who in peace and tranquility and at their ease pray God to favor the ones who can do little in their own behalf.

"I do not mean to say—I should not think of saying—that the state of knight-errant is as holy as that of the cloistered monk; I merely would imply, from what I myself endure, that ours is beyond a doubt the more laborious and arduous calling, more beset by hunger and thirst, more wretched, ragged, and ridden with lice. It is an absolute certainty that the knights-errant of old experienced much misfortune in the course of their lives; and if some by their might and valor came to be emperors, you may take my word for it, it cost them dearly in blood and sweat, and if those who rose to such a rank had lacked enchanters and magicians to aid them, they surely would have been cheated of their desires, deceived in their hopes and expectations."

"I agree with you on that," said the traveler, "but there is one thing among others that gives me a very bad impression of the knights-errant, and that is the fact that when they are about to enter upon some great and perilous adventure in which they are in danger of losing their lives, they never at that moment think of commending themselves to God as every good Christian is obliged to do under similar circumstances, but, rather, commend themselves to their ladies with as much fervor and devotion as if their mistresses were God himself; all of which to me smacks somewhat of paganism."

"Sir," Don Quixote answered him, "it could not by any means be otherwise; the knight-errant who did not do so would fall into disgrace, for it is the usage and custom of chivalry that the knight, before engaging in some great feat of arms, shall behold his lady in front of him and shall turn his eyes toward her, gently and lovingly, as if beseeching her favor and protection in the hazardous encounter that awaits him, and even though no one hears him, he is obliged to utter certain words between his teeth, commending himself to her with all his heart; and of this we have numerous examples in the histories. Nor is it to be assumed that he does not commend himself to God also, but the time and place for that is in the course of the undertaking."

"All the same," said the traveler, "I am not wholly clear in this matter; for I have often read of two knights-errant exchanging words until, one word leading to another, their wrath is kindled; whereupon, turning their steeds and taking a good run up the field, they whirl about and bear down upon each other at full speed, commending themselves to their ladies in the midst of it all. What commonly happens then is that one of the two topples from his horse's flanks and is run through and through with the other's lance; and his adversary would also fall to the ground if he did not cling to his horse's mane. What I do not understand is how the dead man would have had time to commend himself to God in the course of this accelerated combat. It would be better if the words he wasted in calling upon his lady as he ran toward the other knight had been spent in paying the debt that he owed as a Christian. Moreover, it is my personal opinion that not all knights-errant have ladies to whom to commend themselves, for not all of them are in love."

"That" said Don Quixote, "is impossible. I assert there can be no knight-errant without a lady; for it is as natural and proper for them to be in love as it is for the heavens to have stars, and I am quite sure that no one ever read a story in which a loveless man of arms was to be met with, for the simple reason that such a one would not be looked upon as a legitimate knight but as a bastard one who had entered the fortress of chivalry not by the main gate, but over the walls, like a robber and a thief."

"Nevertheless," said the traveler, "if my memory serves me right, I have read that Don Galaor, brother of the valorous Amadis of Gaul, never had a special lady to whom he prayed, yet he was not held in any the less esteem for that but was a very brave and famous knight."

Once again, our Don Quixote had an answer. "Sir, one swallow does not make a summer. And in any event, I happen to know that this knight was secretly very much in love. As for his habit of paying court to all the ladies that caught his fancy, that was a natural propensity on his part and one that he was unable to resist. There was, however, one particular lady whom he had made the mistress of his will and to whom he did commend himself very frequently and privately; for he prided himself upon being a reticent knight."

"Well, then," said the traveler, "if it is essential that every knight-errant be in love, it is to be presumed that your Grace is also, since you are of the profession. And unless it be that you pride yourself upon your reticence as much as did Don Galaor, then I truly, on my own behalf and in the name of all this company, beseech your Grace to tell us your lady's name, the name of the country where she resides, what her rank is, and something of the beauty of her person, that she may esteem herself fortunate in having all the world know that she is loved and served by such a knight as your Grace appears to me to be."

At this, Don Quixote heaved a deep sigh. "I cannot say," he began, "as to whether or not my sweet enemy would be pleased that all the world should know I serve her. I can only tell you, in response to the question which you have so politely put to me, that her name is Dulcinea, her place of residence El Toboso, a village of La Mancha. As to her rank, she should be at the very least a princess, seeing that she is my lady and my queen. Her beauty is superhuman, for in it are realized all the impossible and chimerical attributes that poets are accustomed to give their fair ones. Her locks are golden, her brow the Elysian Fields, her eyebrows rainbows, her eyes suns, her cheeks roses, her lips coral, her teeth pearls, her neck alabaster, her bosom marble, her hands ivory, her complexion snow-white. As for those parts which modesty keeps covered from the human sight, it is my opinion that, discreetly considered, they are only to be extolled and not compared to any other."

"We should like," said Vivaldo, "to know something as well of her lineage, her race and ancestry."

"She is not," said Don Quixote, "of the ancient Roman Curtii, Caii, or Scipios, nor of the modern Colonnas and Orsini, nor of the Moncades and Requesenses of Catalonia, nor is she of the Rebellas and Villanovas of Valencia, or the Palafoxes, Nuzas, Rocabertis, Corellas, Lunas, Alagones, Urreas, or Gurreas of Aragon, the Cerdas, Manriques, Mendozas, or Guzmanes of Castile, the Alencastros, Pallas, or Menezes of Portugal; but she is of the Tobosos of La Mancha, and although the line is a modern one, it well may give rise to the most illustrious families of the centuries to come. And let none dispute this with me, unless it be under the conditions which Zerbino has set forth in the inscription beneath Orlando's arms:

These let none move
Who dares not with Orlando his valor prove."[4]

4. From Ludovico Ariosto's *Orlando Furioso*, canto XXIV, stanza 57.

"Although my own line," replied the traveler, "is that of the Gachupins of Laredo, I should not venture to compare it with the Tobosos of La Mancha, in view of the fact that, to tell you the truth, I have never heard the name before."

"How does it come that you have never heard it!" exclaimed Don Quixote.

The others were listening most attentively to the conversation of these two, and even the goatherds and shepherds were by now aware that our knight of La Mancha was more than a little insane. Sancho Panza alone thought that all his master said was the truth, for he was well acquainted with him, having known him since birth. The only doubt in his mind had to do with the beauteous Dulcinea del Toboso, for he knew of no such princess and the name was strange to his ears, although he lived not far from that place.

They were continuing on their way, conversing in this manner, when they caught sight of some twenty shepherds coming through the gap between two high mountains, all of them clad in black woolen garments and with wreaths on their heads, some of the garlands, as was afterward learned, being of cypress, others of yew. Six of them were carrying a bier covered with a great variety of flowers and boughs.

"There they come with Grisóstomo's body," said one of the goatherds, "and the foot of the mountain yonder is where he wished to be buried."

They accordingly quickened their pace and arrived just as those carrying the bier had set it down on the ground. Four of the shepherds with sharpened picks were engaged in digging a grave alongside the barren rock. After a courteous exchange of greetings, Don Quixote and his companions turned to look at the bier. Upon it lay a corpse covered with flowers, the body of a man dressed like a shepherd and around thirty years of age. Even in death it could be seen that he had had a handsome face and had been of a jovial disposition. Round about him upon the bier were a number of books and many papers, open and folded.

Meanwhile, those who stood gazing at the dead man and those who were digging the grave—everyone present, in fact—preserved an awed silence, until one of the pallbearers said to another, "Look well, Ambrosio, and make sure that this is the place that Grisóstomo had in mind, since you are bent upon carrying out to the letter the provisions of his will."

"This is it," replied Ambrosio; "for many times my unfortunate friend told me the story of his misadventure. He told me that it was here that he first laid eyes upon that mortal enemy of the human race, and it was here, also, that he first revealed to her his passion, for he was as honorable as he was lovelorn; and it was here, finally, at their last meeting, that she shattered his illusions and showed him her disdain, thus bringing to an end the tragedy of his wretched life. And here, in memory of his great misfortune, he wished to be laid in the bowels of eternal oblivion."

Then, turning to Don Quixote and the travelers, he went on, "This body, gentlemen, on which you now look with pitying eyes was the depository of a soul which heaven had endowed with a vast share of its riches. This is the body of Grisóstomo, who was unrivaled in wit, unequaled in courtesy, supreme in gentleness of bearing, a model of friendship, generous without stint, grave without conceit, merry without being vulgar—in short, first in all that is good and second to none in the matter of misfortunes. He loved well and was hated, he adored and was disdained; he wooed a wild beast, importuned a piece of marble, ran after the wind, cried out to loneliness, waited upon ingratitude, and his reward was to be the spoils of death midway in his life's course—a life that was brought to an end by a shepherdess whom he sought to immortalize that she might live on in the memory of mankind, as those papers that you see there would very plainly show if he had not commanded me to consign them to the flames even as his body is given to the earth."

"You," said Vivaldo, "would treat them with greater harshness and cruelty than their owner himself, for it is neither just nor fitting to carry out the will of one who commands what is contrary to all reason. It would not have been a good thing for Augustus Caesar to consent to have them execute the behests of the divine Mantuan in his last testament.[5] And so, Señor Ambrosio, while you may give the body of your friend to the earth, you ought not to give his writings to oblivion. If out of bitterness he left such an order, that does not mean that you are to obey it without using your own discretion. Rather, by granting life to these papers, you permit Marcela's cruelheartedness to live forever and serve as an example to the others in the days that are to come in order that they may flee and avoid such pitfalls as these.

"I and those that have come with me know the story of this lovesick and despairing friend of yours; we know the affection that was between you, and what the occasion of his death was, and the things that he commanded be done as his life drew to a close. And from this lamentable tale anyone may see how great was Marcela's cruelty; they may behold Grisóstomo's love, the loyalty that lay in your friendship, and the end that awaits those who run headlong, with unbridled passion, down the path that doting love opens before their gaze. Last night we heard of your friend's death and learned that he was to be buried here, and out of pity and curiosity we turned aside from our journey and resolved to come see with our own eyes that which had aroused so much compassion when it was told to us. And in requital of that compassion, and the desire that has been born in us to prevent if we can a recurrence of such tragic circumstances, we beg you, O prudent Ambrosio!—or, at least, I for my part implore you—to give up your intention of burning these papers and let me carry some of them away with me."

Without waiting for the shepherd to reply he put out his hand and took a few of those that were nearest him.

"Out of courtesy, sir," said Ambrosio when he saw this, "I will consent for you to keep those that you have taken; but it is vain to think that I will refrain from burning the others."

Vivaldo, who was anxious to find out what was in the papers, opened one of them and perceived that it bore the title "Song of Despair."

Hearing this, Ambrosio said, "That is the last thing the poor fellow wrote; and in order, sir, that you may see the end to which his misfortunes brought him, read it aloud if you will, for we shall have time for it while they are digging the grave."

"That I will very willingly do," said Vivaldo.

And since all the bystanders had the same desire, they gathered around as he in a loud clear voice read the following poem.

---

5. Virgil (born near Mantua) had left instructions that his Roman epic the *Aeneid* should be burned.

CHAPTER 14

*In which are set down the despairing verses of the deceased shepherd,
with other unlooked-for happenings.*

Grisóstomo's Song

Since thou desirest that thy cruelty
Be spread from tongue to tongue and land to land,
The unrelenting sternness of thy heart
Shall turn my bosom's hell to minstrelsy
That all men everywhere may understand   5
The nature of my grief and what thou art.
And as I seek my sorrows to impart,
Telling of all the things that thou hast done,
My very entrails shall speak out to brand
Thy heartlessness, thy soul to reprimand,   10
Where no compassion ever have I won.
Then listen well, lend an attentive ear;
This ballad that thou art about to hear
Is not contrived by art; 'tis a simple song
Such as shepherds sing each day throughout the year—   15
Surcease of pain for me, for thee a prong.
    Then let the roar of lion, fierce wolf's cry,
The horrid hissing of the scaly snake,
The terrifying sound of monsters strange,
Ill-omened call of crow against the sky,   20
The howling of the wind as it doth shake
The tossing sea where all is constant change,
Bellow of vanquished bull that cannot range
As it was wont to do, the piteous sob
Of the widowed dove as if its heart would break,   25
Hoot of the envied owl,[6] ever awake,
From hell's own choir the deep and mournful throb—
Let all these sounds come forth and mingle now.
For if I'm to tell my woes, why then, I vow,
I must new measures find, new modes invent,   30
With sound confusing sense, I may somehow
Portray the inferno where my days are spent.
    The mournful echoes of my murmurous plaint
Father Tagus[7] shall not hear as he rolls his sand,
Nor olive-bordered Betis;[8] my lament shall be   35
To the tall and barren rock as I acquaint
The caves with my sorrow; the far and lonely strand
No human foot has trod shall hear from me
The story of thine inhumanity
As told with lifeless tongue but living word.   40
I'll tell it to the valleys near at hand
Where never shines the sun upon the land;
By venomous serpents shall my tale be heard
On the low-lying, marshy river plain.

6. Envied by other birds as the only one that witnessed the crucifixion.   **7.** The river Tagus.
8. The Guadalquivir.

And yet, the telling will not be in vain;   45
For the reverberations of my plight,
Thy matchless austerity and this my pain,
Through the wide world shall go, thee to indict.
    Didsain may kill; suspicion false or true
May slay all patience; deadliest of all   50
Is jealousy; while absence renders life
Worse than a void; Hope lends no roseate hue
Against forgetfulness or the dread call
Of death inevitable, the end of strife.
Yet—unheard miracle!—with sorrows rife,   55
My own existence somehow still goes on;
The flame of life with me doth rise and fall.
Jealous I am, disdained; I know the gall
Of those suspicions that will not be gone,
Which leave me not the shadow of a hope,   60
And, desperate, I will not even grope
But rather will endure until the end,
And with despair eternally I'll cope,
Knowing that things for me will never mend.
    Can one both hope and fear at the same season?   65
Would it be well to do so in any case,
Seeing that fear, by far, hath the better excuse?
Confronting jealousy, is there any reason
For me to close my eyes to its stern face,
Pretend to see it not? What is the use,   70
When its dread presence I can still deduce
From countless gaping wounds deep in my heart?
When suspicion—bitter change!—to truth gives place,
And truth itself, losing its virgin grace,
Becomes a lie, is it not wisdom's part   75
To open wide the door to frank mistrust?
When disdain's unveiled, to doubt is only just.
O ye fierce tyrants of Love's empery!
Shackle these hands with stout cord, if ye must.
My pain shall drown your triumph—woe is me!   80
    I die, in short, and since nor life nor death
Yields any hope, to my fancy will I cling.
That man is freest who is Love's bond slave:
I'll say this with my living-dying breath,
And the ancient tyrant's praises I will sing.   85
Love is the greatest blessing Heaven e'er gave.
What greater beauty could a lover crave
Than that which my fair enemy doth show
In soul and body and in everything?
E'en her forgetfulness of me doth spring   90
From my own lack of grace, that I well know.
In spite of all the wrongs that he has wrought,
Love rules his empire justly as he ought.
Throw all to the winds and speed life's wretched span
By feeding on his self-deluding thought.   95
No blessing holds the future that I scan.

Thou whose unreasonableness reason doth give
For putting an end to this tired life of mine,
From the deep heart wounds which thou mayest plainly see,
Judge if the better course be to die or live.   100
Gladly did I surrender my will to thine,
Gladly I suffered all thou didst to me;
And now that I'm dying, should it seem to thee
My death is worth a tear from thy bright eyes,
Pray hold it back, fair one, do not repine,   105
For I would have from thee no faintest sign
Of penitence, e'en though my soul thy prize.
Rather, I'd have thee laugh, be very gay,
And let my funeral be a festive day—
But I am very simple! knowing full well   110
That thou art bound to go thy blithesome way,
And my untimely end thy fame shall swell.
    Come, thirsting Tantalus from out Hell's pit;
Come, Sisyphus with the terrifying weight
Of that stone thou rollest; Tityus, bring   115
Thy vulture and thine anguish infinite;
Ixion[9] with thy wheel, be thou not late;
Come, too, ye sisters ever laboring;[1]
Come all, your griefs into my bosom fling,
And then, with lowered voices, intone a dirge,   120
If dirge be fitting for one so desperate,
A body without a shroud, unhappy fate!
And Hell's three-headed gateman,[2] do thou emerge
With a myriad other phantoms, monstrous swarm,
Beings infernal of fantastic form,   125
Raising their voices for the uncomforted
In a counterpoint of grief, harmonious storm.
What better burial for a lover dead?
    Despairing song of mine, do not complain,
Nor let our parting cause thee any pain,   130
For my misfortune is not wholly bad,
Seeing her fortune's bettered by my demise.
Then, even in the grave, be thou not sad.

Those who had listened to Grisóstomo's poem liked it well enough, but the one who read it remarked that it did not appear to him to conform to what had been told him of Marcela's modesty and virtue, seeing that in it the author complains of jealousy, suspicion, and absence, all to the prejudice of her good name. To this Ambrosio, as one who had known his friend's most deeply hidden thoughts, replied as follows:

"By way of satisfying, sir, the doubt that you entertain, it is well for you to know that when the unfortunate man wrote that poem, he was by his own volition absent from Marcela, to see if this would work a cure; but when the

---

9. In Greek myth, all four are proverbial images of mortals punished by the Gods with different forms of torture. Tantalus craves water and fruit, which he always fails to reach. Sisyphus forever vainly tries to roll a stone upward to the top of a hill. Tityus has his liver devoured by a vulture. Ixion is bound to a revolving wheel.   1. In classical mythology the three Fates (Moerae to the Greeks, Parcae to the Romans), spinners of man's destiny.   2. Cerberus, a dog-like three-headed monster, the mythological guardian of Hell.

enamored one is away from his love, there is nothing that does not inspire in him fear and torment, and such was the case with Grisóstomo, for whom jealous imaginings, fears, and suspicions became a seeming reality. And so, in this respect, Marcela's reputation for virtue remains unimpaired; beyond being cruel and somewhat arrogant, and exceedingly disdainful, she could not be accused by the most envious of any other fault."

"Yes, that is so," said Vivaldo.

He was about to read another of the papers he had saved from the fire when he was stopped by a marvelous vision—for such it appeared—that suddenly met his sight; for there atop the rock beside which the grave was being hollowed out stood the shepherdess Marcela herself, more beautiful even than she was reputed to be. Those who up to then had never seen her looked on in silent admiration, while those who were accustomed to beholding her were held in as great a suspense as the ones who were gazing upon her for the first time.

No sooner had Ambrosio glimpsed her than, with a show of indignation, he called out to her, "So, fierce basilisk of these mountains, have you perchance come to see if in your presence blood will flow from the wounds of this poor wretch whom you by your cruelty have deprived of life?[3] Have you come to gloat over your inhuman exploits, or would you from that height look down like another pitiless Nero upon your Rome in flames and ashes?[4] Or perhaps you would arrogantly tread under foot this poor corpse, as an ungrateful daughter did that of her father Tarquinius?[5] Tell us quickly why you have come and what it is that you want most; for I know that Grisóstomo thoughts never failed to obey you in life, and though he is dead now, I will see that all those who call themselves his friends obey you likewise."

"I do not come, O Ambrosio, for any of the reasons that you have mentioned," replied Marcela. "I come to defend myself and to demonstrate how unreasonable all those persons are who blame me for their sufferings and for Grisóstomo's death. I therefore ask all present to hear me attentively. It will not take long and I shall not have to spend many words in persuading those of you who are sensible that I speak the truth.

"Heaven made me beautiful, you say, so beautiful that you are compelled to love me whether you will or no; and in return for the love that you show me, you would have it that I am obliged to love you in return. I know, with that natural understanding that God has given me, that everything beautiful is lovable; but I cannot see that it follows that the object that is loved for its beauty must love the one who loves it. Let us suppose that the lover of the beautiful were ugly and, being ugly, deserved to be shunned; it would then be highly absurd for him to say, 'I love you because you are beautiful; you must love me because I am ugly.'

"But assuming that two individuals are equally beautiful, it does not mean that their desires are the same; for not all beauty inspires love, but may sometimes merely delight the eye and leave the will intact. If it were other-

3. According to folklore, the corpse of a murdered person was supposed to bleed in the presence of the murderer. "Basilisk": a mythical lizard-like creature whose look and breath were supposed to be lethal. 4. The Roman emperor Nero is supposed, in tale and proverb, to have been singing while from a tower he observed the burning of Rome in 64 C.E. 5. The inaccurate allusion is to Tullia, actually the wife of the last of the legendary kings of early Rome, Tarquinius; she let the wheel of her carriage trample over the body of her father—the previous king Servius Tullius—whom her husband, Tarquinius, had liquidated.

wise, no one would know what he wanted, but all would wander vaguely and aimlessly with nothing upon which to settle their affections; for the number of beautiful objects being infinite, desires similarly would be boundless. I have heard it said that true love knows no division and must be voluntary and not forced. This being so, as I believe it is, then why would you compel me to surrender my will for no other reason than that you say you love me? But tell me: supposing that Heaven which made me beautiful had made me ugly instead, should I have any right to complain because you did not love me? You must remember, moreover, that I did not choose this beauty that is mine; such as it is, Heaven gave it to me of its grace, without any choice or asking on my part. As the viper is not to be blamed for the deadly poison that it bears, since that is a gift of nature, so I do not deserve to be reprehended for my comeliness of form.

"Beauty in a modest woman is like a distant fire or a sharp-edged sword: the one does not burn, the other does not cut, those who do not come near it. Honor and virtue are the adornments of the soul, without which the body is not beautiful though it may appear to be. If modesty is one of the virtues that most adorn and beautiful body and soul, why should she who is loved for her beauty part with that virtue merely to satisfy the whim of one who solely for his own pleasure strives with all his force and energy to cause her to lose it? I was born a free being, and in order to live freely I chose the solitude of the fields; these mountain trees are my company, the clear-running waters in these brooks are my mirror, and to the trees and waters I communicate my thoughts and lend them of my beauty.

"In short, I am that distant fire, that sharp-edged sword, that does not burn or cut. Those who have been enamored by the sight of me I have disillusioned with my words; and if desire is sustained by hope, I gave none to Grisóstomo or any other, and of none of them can it be said that I killed them with my cruelty, for it was rather their own obstinacy that was to blame. And if you reproach me with the fact that his intentions were honorable and that I ought for that reason to have complied with them, I will tell you that when, on this very spot where his grave is now being dug, he revealed them to me, I replied that it was my own intention to live in perpetual solitude and that only the earth should enjoy the fruit of my retirement and the spoils of my beauty; and if he with all this plain-speaking was still stubbornly bent upon hoping against hope and sailing against the wind, is it to be wondered at if he drowned in the gulf of his own folly?

"Had I led him on, it would have been falsely; had I gratified his passion, it would have been against my own best judgment and intentions; but, though I had disillusioned him, he persisted, and though I did not hate him, he was driven to despair. Ask yourselves, then, if it is reasonable to blame me for his woes! Let him who has been truly deceived complain; let him despair who has been cheated of his promised hopes; if I have enticed any, let him speak up; if I have accepted the attentions of any, let him boast of it; but let not him to whom I have promised nothing, whom I have neither enticed nor accepted, apply to me such terms as cruel and homicidal. It has not as yet been Heaven's will to destine me to love any man, and there is no use expecting me to love of my own free choice.

"Let what I am saying now apply to each and every one of those who would have me for their own, and let it be understood from now on that if any die on account of me, he is not to be regarded as an unfortunate victim of jealousy, since she that cares for none can give to none the occasion for being jealous; nor is my plain-speaking to be taken as disdain. He who calls me a wild beast and a basilisk, let him leave me alone as something that is evil and harmful; let him who calls me ungrateful cease to wait upon me; let him who finds me strange shun my acquaintance; if I am cruel, do not run after me; in which case this wild beast, this basilisk, this strange, cruel, ungrateful creature will not run after them, seek them, out, wait upon them, nor endeavor to know them in any way.

"The thing that killed Grisóstomo was his impatience and the impetuosity of his desire; so why blame my modest conduct and retiring life? If I choose to preserve my purity here in the company of the trees, how can he complain of my unwillingness to lose it who would have me keep it with other men? I, as you know, have a worldly fortune of my own and do not covet that of others. My life is a free one, and I do not wish to be subject to another in any way. I neither love nor hate anyone; I do not repel this one and allure that one; I do not play fast and loose with any. The modest conversation of these village lasses and the care of my goats is sufficient to occupy me. Those mountains there represent the bounds of my desire, and should my wishes go beyond them, it is but to contemplate the beauty of the heavens, that pathway by which the soul travels to its first dwelling place."

Saying this and without waiting for any reply, she turned her back and entered the thickest part of a near-by wood, leaving all present lost in admiration of her wit as well as her beauty. A few—those who had felt the powerful dart of her glances and bore the wounds inflicted by her lovely eyes—were of a mind to follow her, taking no heed of the plainly worded warning they had just had from her lips; whereupon Don Quixote, seeing this and thinking to himself that here was an opportunity to display his chivalry by succoring a damsel in distress, laid his hand upon the hilt of his sword and cried out, loudly and distinctly, "Let no person of whatever state or condition he may be dare to follow the beauteous Marcela under pain of incurring my furious wrath. She has shown with clear and sufficient reasons that little or no blame for Grisóstomo's death is to be attached to her; she has likewise shown how far she is from acceding to the desires of any of her suitors, and it is accordingly only just that in place of being hounded and persecuted she should be honored and esteemed by all good people in this world as the only woman in it who lives with such modesty and good intentions."

Whether it was due to Don Quixote's threats or because Ambrosio now told them that they should finish doing the things which his good friend had desired should be done, no one stirred from the spot until the burial was over and Grisóstomo's papers had been burned. As the body was laid in the grave, many tears were shed by the bystanders. Then they placed a heavy stone upon it until the slab which Ambrosio was thinking of having made should be ready, with an epitaph that was to read:

> Here lies a shepherd by love betrayed,
> His body cold in death,
> Who with his last and faltering breath
> Spoke of a faithless maid.
> He died by the cruel, heartless hand   5
> Of a coy and lovely lass,

Who by bringing men to so sorry a pass
Love's tyranny doth expand.

They then scattered many flowers and boughs over the top of the grave, and, expressing their condolences to the dead man's friend, Ambrosio, they all took their leave, including Vivaldo and his companions. Don Quixote now said good-by to the travelers as well, although they urged him to come with them to Seville, assuring him that he would find in every street and at every corner of that city more adventures than are to be met with anywhere else. He thanked them for the invitation and the courtesy they had shown him in offering it, but added that for the present he had no desire to visit Seville, not until he should have rid these mountains of the robbers and bandits of which they were said to be full.

Seeing that his mind was made up, the travelers did not urge him further but, bidding him another farewell, left him and continued on their way; and the reader may be sure that in the course of their journey they did not fail to discuss the story of Marcela and Grisóstomo as well as Don Quixote's madness. As for the good knight himself, he was resolved to go seek the shepherdess and offer her any service that lay in his power; but things did not turn out the way he expected. . . .

[Fighting the Sheep]

CHAPTER 18

In which is set forth the conversation that Sancho Panza had with his master, Don Quixote, along with other adventures deserving of record.

* * * Don Quixote caught sight down the road of a large cloud of dust that was drawing nearer.

"This, O Sancho," he said, turning to his squire, "is the day when you shall see the boon that fate has in store for me; this, I repeat, is the day when, as well as on any other, shall be displayed the valor of my good right arm. On this day I shall perform deeds that will be written down in the book of fame for all centuries to come. Do you see that dust cloud rising there, Sancho? That is the dust stirred up by a vast army marching in this direction and composed of many nations."

"At that rate," said Sancho, "there must be two of them, for there is another one just like it on the other side."

Don Quixote turned to look and saw that this was so. He was overjoyed by the thought that these were indeed two armies about to meet and clash in the middle of the broad plain; for at every hour and every moment his imagination was filled with battles, enchantments, nonsensical adventures, tales of love, amorous challenges, and the like, such as he had read of in the books of chivalry, and every word he uttered, every thought that crossed his mind, every act he performed, had to do with such things as these. The dust clouds he had sighted were raised by two large droves of sheep coming along the road in opposite directions, which by reason of the dust were not visible until they were close at hand, but Don Quixote insisted so earnestly that they were armies that Sancho came to believe it.

"Sir," he said, "what are we to do?"

"What are we to do?" echoed his master. "Favor and aid the weak and needy. I would inform you, Sancho, that the one coming toward us is led and commanded by the great emperor Alifanfarón, lord of the great isle of Trapobana. This other one at my back is that of his enemy, the king of the Garamantas, Pentapolín of the Rolled-up Sleeve, for he always goes into battle with his right arm bare."

"But why are they such enemies?" Sancho asked.

"Because," said Don Quixote, "this Alifanfarón is a terrible pagan and in love with Pentapolín's daughter, who is a very beautiful and gracious lady and a Christian, for which reason her father does not wish to give her to the pagan king unless the latter first abjures the law of the false prophet, Mohammed, and adopts the faith that is Pentapolín's own."

"Then, by my beard," said Sancho, "if Pentapolín isn't right, and I am going to aid him all I can."

"In that," said Don Quixote, "you will only be doing your duty; for to engage in battles of this sort you need not have been dubbed a knight."

"I can understand that," said Sancho, "but where are we going to put this ass so that we will be certain of finding him after the fray is over? As for going into battle on such a mount, I do not think that has been done up to now."

"That is true enough," said Don Quixote. "What you had best do with him is to turn him loose and run the risk of losing him; for after we emerge the victors we shall have so many horses that even Rocinante will be in danger of being exchanged for another. But listen closely to what I am about to tell you, for I wish to give you an account of the principal knights that are accompanying these two armies; and in order that you may be the better able to see and take note of them, let us retire to that hillock over there which will afford us a very good view."

They then stationed themselves upon a slight elevation from which they would have been able to see very well the two droves of sheep that Don Quixote took to be armies if it had not been for the blinding clouds of dust. In spite of this, however, the worthy gentleman contrived to behold in his imagination what he did not see and what did not exist in reality.

Raising his voice, he went on to explain, "That knight in the gilded armor that you see there, bearing upon his shield a crowned lion crouched at the feet of a damsel, is the valiant Laurcalco, lord of the Silver Bridge; the other with the golden flowers on his armor, and on his shield three crowns argent on an azure field, is the dread Micocolembo, grand duke of Quirocia. And that one on Micocolembo's right hand, with the limbs of a giant, is the ever undaunted Brandabarbarán de Boliche, lord of the three Arabias. He goes armored in a serpent's skin and has for shield a door which, so report has it, is one of those from the temple that Samson pulled down, that time when he avenged himself on his enemies with his own death.

"But turn your eyes in this direction, and you will behold at the head of the other army the ever victorious, never vanquished Timonel de Carcajona, prince of New Biscay, who comes with quartered arms—azure, vert, argent, and or—and who has upon his shield a cat or on a field tawny, with the inscription *Miau*, which is the beginning of his lady's name; for she, so it is said, is the peerless Miulina, daughter of Alfeñquén, duke of Algarve. And that one over there, who weights down and presses the loins of that power-ful charger, in a suit of snow-white armor with a white shield that bears no device whatever—he is a novice knight of the French nation, called Pierres Papin, lord of the baronies of Utrique. As for him you see digging his iron spurs into the flanks of that fleet-footed zebra courser and whose arms are vairs azure, he is the mighty duke of Nervia, Espartafilardo of the Wood, who has for device upon his shield an asparagus plant with a motto in Castilian that says '*Rastrea mi suerte.*'"[6]

In this manner he went on naming any number of imaginary knights on either side, describing on the spur of the moment their arms, colors, devices, and mottoes; for he was completely carried away by his imagination and by this unheard-of madness that had laid hold of him.

Without pausing, he went on, "This squadron in front of us is composed of men of various nations. There are those who drink the sweet waters of the famous Xanthus; woodsmen who tread the Massilian plain; those that sift the fine gold nuggets of Arabia Felix; those that are so fortunate as to dwell on the banks of the clear-running Thermodon, famed for their coolness; those who in many and diverse ways drain the golden Pactolus; Numidians, whose word is never to be trusted; Persians, with their famous bows and arrows; Medes and Parthians, who fight as they flee; Scythians, as cruel as they are fair of skin; Ethiopians, with their pierced lips; and an infinite number of other nationalities whose visages I see and recognize although I cannot recall their names.

"In this other squadron come those that drink from the crystal currents of the olive-bearing Betis; those that smooth and polish their faces with the liquid of the ever rich and gilded Tagus; those that enjoy the beneficial waters of the divine Genil; those that roam the Tartessian plains with their abundant pasturage; those that disport themselves in the Elysian meadows of Jerez; the men of La Mancha, rich and crowned with golden ears of corn; others clad in iron garments, ancient relics of the Gothic race; those that bathe in the Pisuerga, noted for the mildness of its current; those that feed their herds in the wide-spreading pasture lands along the banks of the winding Guadiana, celebrated for its underground course;[7] those that shiver from the cold of the wooded Pyrenees or dwell amid the white peaks of the lofty Apennines—in short, all those whom Europe holds within its girth."

So help me God! How many provinces, how many nations did he not mention by name, giving to each one with marvelous readiness its proper attributes; for he was wholly absorbed and filled to the brim with what he had read in those lying books of his! Sancho Panza hung on his words, saying nothing, merely turning his head from time to time to have a look at those knights and giants that his master was pointing out to him; but he was unable to discover any of them.

"Sir," he said, "may I go to the devil if I see a single man, giant, or knight of all those that your Grace is talking about. Who knows? Maybe it is another spell, like last night."[8]

"How can you say that?" replied Don Quixote. "Can you not hear the neighing of the horses, the sound of trumpets, the roll of drums?"

"I hear nothing," said Sancho, "except the bleating of sheep."

And this, of course, was the truth; for the flocks were drawing near.

6. Probably a pun on *rastrear.* The meaning of the motto may be either "On Fortune's track" or "My Fortune creeps." 7. The Guadiana does run underground part of the way through La Mancha. 8. The inn where they had spent the previous night had been pronounced by Don Quixote to be an enchanted castle.

"The trouble is, Sancho," said Don Quixote, "you are so afraid that you cannot see or hear properly; for one of the effects of fear is to disturb the senses and cause things to appear other than what they are. If you are so craven as all that, go off to one side and leave me alone, and I without your help will assure the victory to that side to which I lend my aid."

Saying this, he put spurs to Rocinante and, with his lance at rest, darted down the hillside like a flash of lightning.

As he did so, Sancho called after him, "Come back, your Grace, Señor Don Quixote; I vow to God those are sheep that you are charging. Come back! O wretched father that bore me! What madness is this? Look you, there are no giants, nor knights, nor cats, nor shields either quartered or whole, nor vairs azure or bedeviled. What is this you are doing, O sinner that I am in God's sight?"

But all this did not cause Don Quixote to turn back. Instead, he rode on, crying out at the top of his voice, "Ho, knights, those of you who follow and fight under the banners of the valiant Pentapolín of the Rolled-up Sleeve; follow me, all of you, and you shall see how easily I give you revenge on your enemy, Alifanfarón of Trapobana."

With these words he charged into the middle of the flock of sheep and began spearing at them with as much courage and boldness as if they had been his mortal enemies. The shepherds and herdsmen who were with the animals called to him to stop; but seeing it was no use, they unloosed their slings and saluted his ears with stones as big as your fist.

Don Quixote paid no attention to the missiles and, dashing about here and there, kept crying, "Where are you, haughty Alifanfarón? Come out to me; for here is a solitary knight who desires in single combat to test your strength and deprive you of your life, as a punishment for that which you have done to the valorous Pentapolín Garamanta."

At that instant a pebble from the brook struck him in the side and buried a couple of ribs in his body. Believing himself dead or badly wounded, and remembering his potion, he took out his vial, placed it to his mouth, and began to swallow the balm; but before he had had what he thought was enough, there came another almond, which struck him in the hand, crushing the tin vial and carrying away with it a couple of grinders from his mouth, as well as badly mashing two of his fingers. As a result of these blows the poor knight tumbled from his horse. Believing that they had killed him, the shepherds hastily collected their flock and, picking up the dead beasts, of which there were more than seven, they went off down the road without more ado.

Sancho all this time was standing on the slope observing the insane things that his master was doing; and as he plucked savagely at his beard he cursed the hour and minute when luck had brought them together. But when he saw him lying there on the ground and perceived that the shepherds were gone, he went down the hill and came up to him, finding him in very bad shape though not unconscious.

"Didn't I tell you, Señor Don Quixote," he said, "that you should come back, that those were not armies you were charging but flocks of sheep?"

"This," said Don Quixote, "is the work of that thieving magician, my enemy, who thus counterfeits things and causes them to disappear. You must know, Sancho, that it is very easy for them to make us assume any appearance that they choose; and so it is that malign one who persecutes me, envious of the glory he saw me about to achieve in this battle, changed the squadrons of the foe into flocks of sheep. If you do not believe me, I beseech you on my life to do one thing for me, that you may be undeceived and discover for yourself that what I say is true. Mount your ass and follow them quietly, and when you have gone a short way from here, you will see them become their former selves once more; they will no longer be sheep but men exactly as I described them to you in the first place. But do not go now, for I need your kind assistance; come over here and have a look and tell me how many grinders are missing, for it feels as if I did not have a single one left."

["To Right Wrongs and Come to the Aid of the Wretched"]

CHAPTER 22

Of how Don Quixote freed many unfortunate ones who, much against their will, were being taken where they did not wish to go.

Cid Hamete Benengeli, the Arabic and Manchegan;[9] author, in the course of this most grave, high-sounding, minute, delightful, and imaginative history, informs us that, following the remarks that were exchanged between Don Quixote de la Mancha and Sancho Panza, his squire, . . . the knight looked up and saw coming toward them down the road which they were following a dozen or so men on foot, strung together by their necks like beads on an iron chain and all of them wearing handcuffs. They were accompanied by two men on horseback and two on foot, the former carrying wheel-lock muskets while the other two were armed with swords and javelins.

"That," said Sancho as soon as he saw them, "is a chain of galley slaves, people on their way to the galleys where by order of the king they are forced to labor."

"What do you mean by 'forced'?" asked Don Quixote. "Is it possible that the king uses force on anyone?"

"I did not say that," replied Sancho. "What I did say was that these are folks who have been condemned for their crimes to forced labor in the galleys for his Majesty the King."

"The short of it is," said the knight, "whichever way you put it, these people are being taken there by force and not of their own free will."

"That is the way it is," said Sancho.

"Well, in that case," said his master, "now is the time for me to fulfill the duties of my calling, which is to right wrongs and come to the aid of the wretched."

"But take note, your Grace," said Sancho, "that justice, that is to say, the king himself, is not using any force upon, or doing any wrong to, people like these, but is merely punishing them for the crimes they have committed."

The chain of galley slaves had come up to them by this time, whereupon Don Quixote very courteously requested the guards to inform him of the reason or reasons why they were conducting these people in such a manner as this. One of the men on horseback then replied that the men were prisoners who had been condemned by his Majesty to serve in the galleys,

9. Of La Mancha.

whither they were bound, and that was all there was to be said about it and all that he, Don Quixote, need know.

"Nevertheless," said the latter, "I should like to inquire of each one of them, individually, the cause of his misfortune." And he went on speaking so very politely in an effort to persuade them to tell him what he wanted to know that the other mounted guard finally said, "Although we have here the record and certificate of sentence of each one of these wretches, we have not the time to get them out and read them to you; and so your Grace may come over and ask the prisoners themselves, and they will tell you if they choose, and you may be sure that they will, for these fellows take a delight in their knavish exploits and in boasting of them afterward."

With this permission, even though he would have done so if it had not been granted him, Don Quixote went up to the chain of prisoners and asked the first whom he encountered what sins had brought him to so sorry a plight. The man replied that it was for being a lover that he found himself in that line.

"For that and nothing more?" said Don Quixote. "And do they, then, send lovers to the galleys? If so, I should have been rowing there long ago."

"But it was not the kind of love that your Grace has in mind," the prisoner went on. "I loved a wash basket full of white linen so well and hugged it so tightly that, if they had not taken it away from me by force, I would never of my own choice have let go of it to this very minute. I was caught in the act, there was no need to torture me, the case was soon disposed of, and they supplied me with a hundred lashes across the shoulders and, in addition, a three-year stretch in the *gurapas,* and that's all there is to tell."

"What are *gurapas?*" asked Don Quixote.

"*Gurapas* are the galleys," replied the prisoner. He was a lad of around twenty-four and stated that he was a native of Piedrahita.

The knight then put the same question to a second man, who appeared to be very downcast and melancholy and did not have a word to say. The first man answered for him.

"This one, sir," he said, "is going as a canary—I mean, as a musician and singer."

"How is that?" Don Quixote wanted to know. "Do musicians and singers go to the galleys too?"

"Yes, sir; and there is nothing worse than singing when you're in trouble."

"On the contrary," said Don Quixote, "I have heard it said that he who sings frightens away his sorrows."

"It is just the opposite," said the prisoner; "for he who sings once weeps all his life long."

"I do not understand," said the knight.

One of the guards then explained. "Sir Knight, with this *non sancta*[1] tribe, to sing when you're in trouble means to confess under torture. This singer was put to the torture and confessed his crime, which was that of being a *cuatrero,* or cattle thief, and as a result of his confession he was condemned to six years in the galleys in addition to two hundred lashes which he took on his shoulders; and so it is he is always downcast and moody, for the other thieves, those back where he came from and the ones here, mistreat, snub, ridicule, and despise him for having confessed and for not having had the

1. Unholy (Latin).

courage to deny his guilt. They are in the habit of saying that the word *no* has the same number of letters as the word *sí,* and that a culprit is in luck when his life or death depends on his own tongue and not that of witnesses or upon evidence; and, in my opinion, they are not very far wrong."

"And I," said Don Quixote, "feel the same way about it." He then went on to a third prisoner and repeated his question.

The fellow answered at once, quite unconcernedly. "I'm going to my ladies, the *gurapas,* for five years, for the lack of five ducats."

"I would gladly give twenty," said Don Quixote, "to get you out of this."

"That," said the prisoner, "reminds me of the man in the middle of the ocean who has money and is dying of hunger because there is no place to buy what he needs. I say this for the reason that if I had had, at the right time, those twenty ducats your Grace is now offering me, I'd have greased the notary's quill and freshened up the attorney's wit with them, and I'd now be living in the middle of Zocodover Square in Toledo instead of being here on this highway coupled like a greyhound. But God is great; patience, and that's enough of it."

Don Quixote went on to a fourth prisoner, a venerable-looking old fellow with a white beard that fell over his bosom. When asked how he came to be there, this one began weeping and made no reply, but a fifth comrade spoke up in his behalf.

"This worthy man," he said, "is on his way to the galleys after having made the usual rounds clad in a robe of state and on horseback."[2]

"That means, I take it," said Sancho, "that he has been put to shame in public."

"That is it," said the prisoner, "and the offense for which he is being punished is that of having been an ear broker, or, better, a body broker. By that I mean to say, in short, that the gentleman is a pimp, and besides, he has his points as a sorcerer."

"If that point had not been thrown in," said Don Quixote, "he would not deserve, for merely being a pimp, to have to row in the galleys, but rather should be the general and give orders there. For the office of pimp is not an indifferent one; it is a function to be performed by persons of discretion and is most necessary in a well-ordered state; it is a profession that should be followed only by the wellborn, and there should, moreover, be a supervisor or examiner as in the case of other offices, and the number of practitioners should be fixed by law as is done with brokers on the exchange. In that way many evils would be averted that arise when this office is filled and this calling practiced by stupid folk and those with little sense, such as silly women and pages or mountebanks with few years and less experience to their credit, who, on the most pressing occasions, when it is necessary to use one's wits, let the crumbs freeze between their hand and their mouth and do not know which is their right hand and which is the left.

"I would go on and give reasons why it is fitting to choose carefully those who are to fulfill so necessary a state function, but this is not the place for it. One of these days I will speak of the matter to someone who is able to do something about it. I will say here only that the pain I felt at seeing those white hairs and this venerable countenance in such a plight, and all for his

---

2. After having been flogged in public, with all the ceremony that accompanied that punishment.

having been a pimp, has been offset for me by the additional information you have given me, to the effect that he is a sorcerer as well; for I am convinced that there are no sorcerers in the world who can move and compel the will, as some simple-minded persons think, but that our will is free and no herb or charm can force it.[3] All that certain foolish women and cunning tricksters do is to compound a few mixtures and poisons with which they deprive men of their senses while pretending that they have the power to make them loved, although, as I have just said, one cannot affect another's will in that manner."

"That is so," said the worthy old man; "but the truth is, sir, I am not guilty on the sorcery charge. As for being a pimp, that is something I cannot deny. I never thought there was any harm in it, however, my only desire being that everyone should enjoy himself and live in peace and quiet, without any quarrels or troubles. But these good intentions on my part cannot prevent me from going where I do not want to go, to a place from which I do not expect to return; for my years are heavy upon me and an affection of the urine that I have will not give me a moment's rest."

With this, he began weeping once more, and Sancho was so touched by it that he took a four-real piece from his bosom and gave it to him as an act of charity.

Don Quixote then went on and asked another what his offense was. The fellow answered him, not with less, but with much more, briskness than the preceding one had shown.

"I am here," he said, "for the reason that I carried a joke too far with a couple of cousins-german of mine and a couple of others who were not mine, and I ended by jesting with all of them to such an extent that the devil himself would never be able to straighten out the relationship. They proved everything on me, there was no one to show me favor, I had no money, I came near swinging for it, they sentenced me to the galleys for six years, and I accepted the sentence as the punishment that was due me. I am young yet, and if I live long enough, everything will come out all right. If, Sir Knight, your Grace has anything with which to aid these poor creatures that you see before you, God will reward you in Heaven, and we here on earth will make it a point to ask God in our prayers to grant you long life and good health, as long and as good as your amiable presence deserves."

This man was dressed as a student, and one of the guards told Don Quixote that he was a great talker and a very fine Latinist.

Back of these came a man around thirty years of age and of very good appearance, except that when he looked at you his eyes were seen to be a little crossed. He was shackled in a different manner from the others, for he dragged behind a chain so huge that it was wrapped all around his body, with two rings at the throat, one of which was attached to the chain while the other was fastened to what is known as a keep-friend or friend's foot, from which two irons hung down to his waist, ending in handcuffs secured by a heavy padlock in such a manner that he could neither raise his hands to his mouth nor lower his head to reach his hands.

---

3. Here Don Quixote despises charms and love potions, although often elsewhere, in his own vision of himself as a knight-errant, he accepts enchantments and spells as part of his world of fantasy.

When Don Quixote asked why this man was so much more heavily chained than the others, the guard replied that it was because he had more crimes against him than all the others put together, and he was so bold and cunning that, even though they had him chained like this, they were by no means sure of him but feared that he might escape from them.

"What crimes could he have committed," asked the knight, "if he has merited a punishment no greater than that of being sent to the galleys?"

"He is being sent there for ten years," replied the guard, "and that is equivalent to civil death. I need tell you no more than that this good man is the famous Ginés de Pasamonte, otherwise known as Ginesillo de Parapilla."

"Señor Commissary," spoke up the prisoner at this point, "go easy there and let us not be so free with names and surnames. My just name is Ginés and not Ginesillo; and Pasamonte, not Parapilla as you make it out to be, is my family name. Let each one mind his own affairs and he will have his hands full."

"Speak a little more respectfully, you big thief, you," said the commissary, "unless you want me to make you be quiet in a way you won't like."

"Man goes as God pleases, that is plain to be seen," replied the galley slave, "but someday someone will know whether my name is Ginesillo de Parapilla or not."

"But, you liar, isn't that what they call you?"

"Yes," said Ginés, "they do call me that; but I'll put a stop to it, or else I'll skin their you-know-what. And you, sir, if you have anything to give us, give it and may God go with you, for I am tired of all this prying into other people's lives. If you want to know anything about my life, know that I am Ginés de Pasamonte whose life story has been written down by these fingers that you see here."

"He speaks the truth," said the commissary, "for he has himself written his story, as big as you please, and has left the book in the prison, having pawned it for two hundred reales."

"And I mean to redeem it," said Ginés, "even if it costs me two hundred ducats."

"Is it as good as that?" inquired Don Quixote.

"It is so good," replied Ginés, "that it will cast into the shade *Lazarillo de Tormes*[4] and all others of that sort that have been or will be written. What I would tell you is that it deals with facts, and facts so interesting and amusing that no lies could equal them."

"And what is the title of the book?" asked Don Quixote.

"The Life of Ginés de Pasamonte."

"Is it finished?"

"How could it be finished," said Ginés, "when my life is not finished as yet? What I have written thus far is an account of what happened to me from the time I was born up to the last time that they sent me to the galleys."

"Then you have been there before?"

"In the service of God and the king I was there four years, and I know what the biscuit and the cowhide are like. I don't mind going very much, for there I will have a chance to finish my book. I still have many things to say,

---

4. A picaresque or rogue novel, published anonymously about the middle of the 15th century.

and in the Spanish galleys I shall have all the leisure that I need, though I don't need much, since I know by heart what it is I want to write."

"You seem to be a clever fellow," said Don Quixote.

"And an unfortunate one," said Ginés; "for misfortunes always pursue men of genius."

"They pursue rogues," said the commissary.

"I have told you to go easy, Señor Commissary," said Pasamonte, "for their Lordships did not give you that staff in order that you might mistreat us poor devils with it, but they intended that you should guide and conduct us in accordance with his Majesty's command. Otherwise, by the life of— But enough. It may be that someday the stains made in the inn will come out in the wash. Meanwhile, let everyone hold his tongue, behave well, and speak better, and let us be on our way. We've had enough of this foolishness."

At this point the commissary raised his staff as if to let Pasamonte have it in answer to his threats, but Don Quixote placed himself between them and begged the officer not to abuse the man; for it was not to be wondered at if one who had his hands so bound should be a trifle free with his tongue. With this, he turned and addressed them all.

"From all that you have told me, my dearest brothers," he said, "one thing stands out clearly for me, and that is the fact that, even though it is a punishment for offenses which you have committed, the penalty you are about to pay is not greatly to your liking and you are going to the galleys very much against your own will and desire. It may be that the lack of spirit which one of you displayed under torture, the lack of money on the part of another, the lack of influential friends, or, finally, warped judgment on the part of the magistrate, was the thing that led to your downfall; and, as a result, justice was not done you. All of which presents itself to my mind in such a fashion that I am at this moment engaged in trying to persuade and even force myself to show you what the purpose was for which Heaven sent me into this world, why it was it led me to adopt the calling of knighthood which I profess and take the knightly vow to favor the needy and aid those who are oppressed by the powerful.

"However, knowing as I do that it is not the part of prudence to do by foul means what can be accomplished by fair ones, I propose to ask these gentlemen, your guards, and the commissary to be so good as to unshackle you and permit you to go in peace. There will be no dearth of others to serve his Majesty under more propitious circumstances; and it does not appear to me to be just to make slaves of those whom God created as free men. What is more, gentlemen of the guard, these poor fellows have committed no offense against you. Up there, each of us will have to answer for his own sins; for God in Heaven will not fail to punish the evil and reward the good; and it is not good for self-respecting men to be executioners of their fellow-men in something that does not concern them. And so, I ask this of you, gently and quietly, in order that, if you comply with my request, I shall have reason to thank you; and if you do not do so of your own accord, then this lance and this sword and the valor of my arm shall compel you to do it by force."

"A fine lot of foolishness!" exclaimed the commissary. "So he comes out at last with this nonsense! He would have us let the prisoners of the king go free, as if we had any authority to do so or he any right to command it! Be on your way, sir, at once; straighten that basin that you have on your head, and do not go looking for three feet on a cat."[5]

"You," replied Don Quixote, "are the cat and the rat and the rascal!" And, saying this, he charged the commissary so quickly that the latter had no chance to defend himself but fell to the ground badly wounded by the lance blow. The other guards were astounded by this unexpected occurrence; but, recovering their self-possession, those on horseback drew their swords, those on foot leveled their javelins, and all bore down on Don Quixote, who stood waiting for them very calmly. Things undoubtedly would have gone badly for him if the galley slaves, seeing an opportunity to gain their freedom, had not succeeded in breaking the chain that linked them together. Such was the confusion that the guards, now running to fall upon the prisoners and now attacking Don Quixote, who in turn was attacking them, accomplished nothing that was of any use.

Sancho for his part aided Ginés de Pasamonte to free himself, and that individual was the first to drop his chains and leap out onto the field, where, attacking the fallen commissary, he took away that officer's sword and musket; and as he stood there, aiming first at one and then at another, though without firing, the plain was soon cleared of guards, for they had taken to their heels, fleeing at once Pasamonte's weapon and the stones which the galley slaves, freed now, were hurling at them. Sancho, meanwhile, was very much disturbed over this unfortunate event, as he felt sure that the fugitives would report the matter to the Holy Brotherhood, which, to the ringing of the alarm bell, would come out to search for the guilty parties. He said as much to his master, telling him that they should leave at once and go into hiding in the near-by mountains.

"That is all very well," said Don Quixote, "but I know what had best be done now." He then summoned all the prisoners, who, running riot, had by this time despoiled the commissary of everything that he had, down to his skin, and as they gathered around to hear what he had to say, he addressed them as follows:

"It is fitting that those who are wellborn should give thanks for the benefits they have received, and one of the sins with which God is most offended is that of ingratitude. I say this, gentlemen, for the reason that you have seen and had manifest proof of what you owe to me; and now that you are free of the yoke which I have removed from about your necks, it is my will and desire that you should set out and proceed to the city of El Toboso and there present yourselves before the lady Dulcinea del Toboso and say to her that her champion, the Knight of the Mournful Countenance, has sent you; and then you will relate to her, point by point, the whole of this famous adventure which has won you your longed-for freedom. Having done that, you may go where you like, and may good luck go with you."

To this Ginés de Pasamonte replied in behalf of all of them, "It is absolutely impossible, your Grace, our liberator, for us to do what you have commanded. We cannot go down the highway all together but must

5. Looking for the impossible ("five feet" is the more usual form of the proverb).

separate and go singly, each in his own direction, endeavoring to hide ourselves in the bowels of the earth in order not to be found by the Holy
Brotherhood, which undoubtedly will come out to search for us. What
your Grace can do, and it is right that you should do so, is to change this
service and toll that you require of us in connection with the lady Dulcinea del Toboso into a certain number of Credos and Hail Marys which
we will say for your Grace's intention, as this is something that can be
accomplished by day or night, fleeing or resting, in peace or in war. To
imagine, on the other hand, that we are going to return to the fleshpots of
Egypt, by which I mean, take up our chains again by setting out along the
highway for El Toboso, is to believe that it is night now instead of ten
o'clock in the morning and is to ask of us something that is the same as
asking pears of the elm tree."

"Then by all that's holy!" exclaimed Don Quixote, whose wrath was now
aroused, "you, Don Son of a Whore, Don Ginesillo de Parapilla, or whatever
your name is, you shall go alone, your tail between your legs and the whole
chain on your back."

Pasamonte, who was by no means a long-suffering individual, was by this
time convinced that Don Quixote was not quite right in the head, seeing
that he had been guilty of such a folly as that of desiring to free them; and
so, when he heard himself insulted in this manner, he merely gave the wink
to his companions and, going off to one side, began raining so many stones
upon the knight that the latter was wholly unable to protect himself with his
buckler, while poor Rocinante paid no more attention to the spur than if he
had been made of brass. As for Sancho, he took refuge behind his donkey as
a protection against the cloud and shower of rocks that was falling on both
of them, but Don Quixote was not able to shield himself so well, and there
is no telling how many struck his body, with such force as to unhorse and
bring him to the ground.

No sooner had he fallen than the student was upon him. Seizing the basin
from the knight's head, he struck him three or four blows with it across the
shoulders and banged it against the ground an equal number of times until
it was fairly shattered to bits. They then stripped Don Quixote of the doublet
which he wore over his armor, and would have taken his hose as well, if his
greaves had not prevented them from doing so, and made off with Sancho's
greatcoat, leaving him naked; after which, dividing the rest of the battle
spoils amongst themselves, each of them went his own way, being a good
deal more concerned with eluding the dreaded Holy Brotherhood than they
were with burdening themselves with a chain or going to present themselves
before the lady Dulcinea del Toboso.

They were left alone now—the ass and Rocinante, Sancho and Don
Quixote: the ass, crestfallen and pensive, wagging its ears now and then,
being under the impression that the hurricane of stones that had raged
about them was not yet over; Rocinante, stretched alongside his master, for
the hack also had been felled by a stone; Sancho, naked and fearful of the
Holy Brotherhood; and Don Quixote, making wry faces at seeing himself so
mishandled by those to whom he had done so much good.

["Set Free at Once That Lovely Lady"]

CHAPTER 52

Of the quarrel that Don Quixote had with the goatherd, together with the rare adventure of the penitents, which the knight by the sweat of his brow brought to a happy conclusion.[6]

All those who had listened to it were greatly pleased with the goatherd's story, especially the canon,[7] who was more than usually interested in noting the manner in which it had been told. Far from being a mere rustic herdsman, the narrator seemed rather a cultured city dweller; and the canon accordingly remarked that the curate had been quite right in saying that the mountain groves bred men of learning. They all now offered their services to Eugenio, and Don Quixote was the most generous of any in this regard.

"Most assuredly, brother goatherd," he said, "if it were possible for me to undertake any adventure just now, I would set out at once to aid you and would take Leandra out of that convent, where she is undoubtedly being held against her will, in spite of the abbess and all the others who might try to prevent me, after which I would place her in your hands to do with as you liked, with due respect, however, for the laws of chivalry, which command that no violence be offered to any damsel. But I trust in God, Our Lord, that the power of one malicious enchanter is not so great that another magician may not prove still more powerful, and then I promise you my favor and my aid, as my calling obliges me to do, since it is none other than that of succoring the weak and those who are in distress."

The goatherd stared at him, observing in some astonishment the knight's unprepossessing appearance.

"Sir," he said, turning to the barber who sat beside him, "who is this man who looks so strange and talks in this way?"

"Who should it be," the barber replied, "if not the famous Don Quixote de la Mancha, righter of wrongs, avenger of injustices, protector of damsels, terror of giants, and champion of battles?"

"That," said the goatherd, "sounds to me like the sort of thing you read of in books of chivalry, where they do all those things that your Grace has mentioned in connection with this man. But if you ask me, either your Grace is joking or this worthy gentleman must have a number of rooms to let inside his head."

"You are the greatest villain that ever was!" cried Don Quixote when he heard this. "It is you who are the empty one; I am fuller than the bitch that bore you ever was." Saying this, he snatched up a loaf of bread that was lying beside him and hurled it straight in the goatherd's face with such force as to flatten the man's nose. Upon finding himself thus mistreated in earnest, Eugenio, who did not understand this kind of joke, forgot all about the carpet, the tablecloth, and the other diners and leaped upon Don Quixote. Seizing

---

6. Last chapter of Part I. Through various devices, including the use of Don Quixote's own belief in enchantments and spells, the curate and the barber have persuaded the knight to let himself be taken home in an ox cart.   7. A canon from Toledo who has joined Don Quixote and his guardians on the way; conversing about chivalry with the knight, he has had cause to be "astonished at Don Quixote's well-reasoned nonsense." Eugenio, a very literate goatherd met on the way, has just told them the story of his unhappy love for Leandra. The girl, instead of choosing one of her local suitors, had eloped with a flashy and crooked soldier; robbed and abandoned by him, she had been put by her father in a convent.

him by the throat with both hands, he would no doubt have strangled him if Sancho Panza, who now came running up, had not grasped him by the shoulders and flung him backward over the table, smashing plates and cups and spilling and scattering all the food and drink that was there. Thus freed of his assailant, Don Quixote then threw himself upon the shepherd, who, with bleeding face and very much battered by Sancho's feet, was creeping about on his hands and knees in search of a table knife with which to exact a sanguinary vengeance, a purpose which the canon and the curate prevented him from carrying out. The barber, however, so contrived it that the goatherd came down on top of his opponent, upon whom he now showered so many blows that the poor knight's countenance was soon as bloody as his own.

As all this went on, the canon and the curate were laughing fit to burst, the troopers[8] were dancing with glee, and they all hissed on the pair as men do at a dog fight. Sancho Panza alone was in despair, being unable to free himself of one of the canon's servants who held him back from going to his master's aid. And then, just as they were all enjoying themselves hugely, with the exception of the two who were mauling each other, the note of a trumpet fell upon their ears, a sound so mournful that it caused them all to turn their heads in the direction from which it came. The one who was most excited by it was Don Quixote; who, very much against his will and more than a little bruised, was lying pinned beneath the goatherd.

"Brother Demon," he now said to the shepherd, "for you could not possibly be anything but a demon, seeing that you have shown a strength and valor greater than mine, I request you to call a truce for no more than an hour; for the doleful sound of that trumpet that we hear seems to me to be some new adventure that is calling me."

Tired of mauling and being mauled, the goatherd let him up at once. As he rose to his feet and turned his head in the direction of the sound, Don Quixote then saw, coming down the slope of a hill, a large number of persons clad in white after the fashion of penitents; for, as it happened, the clouds that year had denied their moisture to the earth, and in all the villages of that district processions for prayer and penance were being organized with the purpose of beseeching God to have mercy and send rain. With this object in view, the good folk from a near-by town were making a pilgrimage to a devout hermit who dwelt on these slopes. Upon beholding the strange costumes that the penitents wore, without pausing to think how many times he had seen them before, Don Quixote imagined that this must be some adventure or other, and that it was for him alone as a knight-errant to undertake it. He was strengthened in this belief by the sight of a covered image that they bore, as it seemed to him this must be some highborn lady whom these scoundrelly and discourteous brigands were forcibly carrying off; and no sooner did this idea occur to him than he made for Rocinante, who was grazing not far away.

Taking the bridle and his bucker from off the saddletree, he had the bridle adjusted in notime, and then, asking Sancho for his sword, he climbed into the saddle, braced his shield upon his arm, and cried out to those present, "And now, valorous company, you shall see how important it is to have in the

8. Law officers from the Holy Brotherhood. They had wanted to arrest Don Quixote for his attempt to liberate the galley slaves, but had been persuaded not to do so because of the knight's insanity.

world those who follow the profession of knight-errantry. You have but to watch how I shall set at liberty that worthy lady who there goes captive, and then you may tell me whether or not such knights are to be esteemed."

As he said this, he dug his legs into Rocinante's flanks, since he had no spurs, and at a fast trot (for nowhere in this veracious history are we ever told that the hack ran full speed) he bore down on the penitents in spite of all that the canon, the curate, and the barber could do to restrain him— their efforts were as vain as were the pleadings of his squire.

"Where are you bound for, Señor Don Quixote?" Sancho called after him. "What evil spirits in your bosom spur you on to go against our Catholic faith? Plague take me, can't you see that's a procession of penitents and that lady they're carrying on the litter is the most blessed image of the Immaculate Virgin? Look well what you're doing, my master, for this time it may be said that you really do not know."

His exertions were in vain, however, for his master was so bent upon having it out with the sheeted figures and freeing the lady clad in mourning that he did not hear a word, nor would he have turned back if he had, though the king himself might have commanded it. Having reached the procession, he reined in Rocinante, who by this time was wanting a little rest, and in a hoarse, excited voice he shouted, "You who go there with your faces covered, out of shame, it may be, listen well to what I have to say to you."

The first to come to a halt were those who carried the image; and then one of the four clerics who were intoning the litanies, upon beholding Don Quixote's weird figure, his bony nag, and other amusing appurtenances, spoke up in reply.

"Brother, if you have something to say to us, say it quickly, for these brethren are engaged in macerating their flesh, and we cannot stop to hear any thing, nor is it fitting that we should, unless it is capable of being said in a couple of words."

"I will say it to you in one word," Don Quixote answered, "and that word is the following: 'Set free at once that lovely lady whose tears and mournful countenance show plainly that you are carrying her away against her will and that you have done her some shameful wrong. I will not consent to your going one step farther until you shall have given her the freedom that should be hers.'"

Hearing these words, they all thought that Don Quixote must be some madman or other and began laughing heartily; but their laughter proved to be gunpowder to his wrath, and without saying another word he drew his sword and fell upon the litter. One of those who bore the image, leaving his share of the burden to his companions, then sallied forth to meet the knight, flourishing a forked stick that he used to support the Virgin while he was resting; and upon this stick he now received a mighty slash that Don Quixote dealt him, one that shattered it in two, but with the piece about a third long that remained in his hand he came down on the shoulder of his opponent's sword arm, left unprotected by the buckler, with so much force that the poor fellow sank to the ground sorely battered and bruised.

Sancho Panza, who was puffing along close behind his master, upon seeing him fall cried out to the attacker not to deal another blow, as this was an unfortunate knight who was under a magic spell but who had never in all the days of his life done any harm to anyone. But the thing that stopped the rustic was not Sancho's words; it was, rather, the sight of Don Quixote lying there without moving hand or foot. And so, thinking that he had killed him, he hastily girded up his tunic and took to his heels across the countryside like a deer.

By this time all of Don Quixote's companions had come running up to where he lay; and the penitents, when they observed this, and especially when they caught sight of the officers of the Brotherhood with their crossbows, at once rallied around the image, where they raised their hoods and grasped their whips as the priests raised their tapers aloft in expectations of an assault; for they were resolved to defend themselves and even, if possible, to take the offensive against their assailants, but, as luck would have it, things turned out better than they had hoped. Sancho, meanwhile, believing Don Quixote to be dead, had flung himself across his master's body and was weeping and wailing in the most lugubrious and, at the same time, the most laughable fashion that could be imagined; and the curate had discovered among those who marched in the procession another curate whom he knew, their recognition of each other serving to allay the fears of all parties concerned. The first curate then gave the second a very brief account of who Don Quixote was, whereupon all the penitents came up to see if the poor knight was dead. And as they did do, they heard Sancho Panza speaking with tears in his eyes.

"O flower of chivalry,"[9] he was saying, "the course of whose well-spent years has been brought to an end by a single blow of a club! O honor of your line, honor and glory of all La Mancha and of all the world, which, with you absent from it, will be full of evil-doers who will not fear being punished for their deeds! O master more generous than all the Alexanders, who after only eight months of service presented me with the best island that the sea washes and surrounds! Humble with the proud, haughty with the humble, brave in facing dangers, long-suffering under outrages, in love without reason, imitator of the good, scourge of the wicked, enemy of the mean—in a word, a knight-errant, which is all there is to say."

At the sound of Sancho's cries and moans, Don Quixote revived, and the first thing he said was, "He who lives apart from thee, O fairest Dulcinea, is subject to greater woes than those I now endure. Friend Sancho, help me onto that enchanted cart, as I am in no condition to sit in Rocinante's saddle with this shoulder of mine knocked to pieces the way it is."

"That I will gladly do, my master," replied Sancho, "and we will go back to my village in the company of these gentlemen who are concerned for your welfare, and there we will arrange for another sally and one, let us hope, that will bring us more profit and fame than this one has."

"Well spoken, Sancho," said Don Quixote, "for it will be an act of great prudence to wait until the present evil influence of the stars has passed."

The canon, the curate, and the barber all assured him that he would be wise in doing this; and so, much amused by Sancho Panza's simplicity, they placed Don Quixote upon the cart as before, while the procession of penitents re-formed and continued on its way. The goatherd took leave of all of them, and the curate paid the troopers what was coming to them, since they did not wish to go any farther. The canon requested the priest to inform him of the outcome of Don Quixote's madness, as to whether it yielded to

---

9. Note how Sancho has absorbed some of his master's speech mannerisms.

treatment or not; and with this he begged permission to resume his journey. In short, the party broke up and separated, leaving only the curate and the barber, Don Quixote and Panza, and the good Rocinante, who looked upon everything that he had seen with the same resignation as his master. Yoking his oxen, the carter made the knight comfortable upon a bale of hay, and then at his customary slow pace proceeded to follow the road that the curate directed him to take. At the end of the six days they reached Don Quixote's village, making their entrance at noon of a Sunday, when the square was filled with a crowd of people through which the cart had to pass.

They all came running to see who it was, and when they recognized their townsman, they were vastly astonished. One lad sped to bring the news to the knight's housekeeper and his niece, telling them that their master had returned lean and jaundiced and lying stretched out upon a bale of hay on an ox-cart. It was pitiful to hear the good ladies' screams, to behold the way in which they beat their breasts, and to listen to the curses which they once more heaped upon those damnable books of chivalry, and this demonstration increased as they saw Don Quixote coming through the doorway.

At news of the knight's return, Sancho Panza's wife had hurried to the scene, for she had some while since learned that her husband had accompanied him as his squire; and now, as soon as she laid eyes upon her man, the first question she asked was if all was well with the ass, to which Sancho replied that the beast was better off than his master.

"Thank God," she exclaimed, "for all his blessings! But tell me now, my dear, what have you brought me from all your squirings? A new cloak to wear? Or shoes for the young ones?"

"I've brought you nothing of the sort, good wife," said Sancho, "but other things of greater value and importance."

"I'm glad to hear that," she replied. "Show me those things of greater value and importance, my dear. I'd like a sight of them just to cheer this heart of mine which has been so sad and unhappy all the centuries that you've been gone."

"I will show them to you at home, wife," said Sancho. "For the present be satisfied that if, God willing, we set out on another journey in search of adventures, you will see me in no time a count or the governor of an island, and not one of those around here, but the best that is to be had."

"I hope to Heaven it's true, my husband, for we certainly need it. But tell me, what is all this about islands? I don't understand."

"Honey," replied Sancho, "is not for the mouth of an ass. You will find out in good time, woman; and you're going to be surprised to hear yourself called 'my Ladyship' by all your vassals."

"What's this you are saying, Sancho, about ladyships, islands, and vassals?" Juana Panza insisted on knowing—for such was the name of Sancho's wife, although they were not blood relatives, it being the custom in La Mancha for wives to take their husbands' surnames.

"Do not be in such a hurry to know all this, Juana," he said. "It is enough that I am telling you the truth. Sew up your mouth, then; for all I will say, in passing, is that there is nothing in the world that is more pleasant than being a respected man, squire to a knight-errant who goes in search of adventures. It is true that most of the adventures you meet with do not come out the way you'd like them to, for ninety-nine out of a hundred will prove to be all twisted and crosswise. I know that from experience, for I've come out of some of them blanketed and out of others beaten to a pulp. But, all the same, it's a fine thing to go along waiting for what will happen next, crossing mountains, making your way through woods, climbing over cliffs, visiting castles, and putting up at inns free of charge, and the devil take the maravedi that is to pay."

Such was the conversation that took place between Sancho Panza and Juana Panza, his wife, as Don Quixote's housekeeper and niece were taking him in, stripping him, and stretching him out on his old-time bed. He gazed at them blankly, being unable to make out where he was. The curate charged the niece to take great care to see that her uncle was comfortable and to keep close watch over him so that he would not slip away from them another time. He then told them of what it had been necessary to do in order to get him home, at which they once more screamed to Heaven and began cursing the books of chivalry all over again, praying God to plunge the authors of such lying nonsense into the center of the bottomless pit. In short, they scarcely knew what to do, for they were very much afraid that their master and uncle would give them the slip once more, the moment he was a little better, and it turned out just the way they feared it might.

From Part II

Prologue

TO THE READER

God bless me, gentle or, it may be, plebeian reader, how eagerly you must be awaiting this prologue, thinking to find in it vengeful scoldings and vituperations directed against the author of the second Don Quixote—I mean the one who, so it is said, was begotten in Tordesillas and born in Tarragona.[1] The truth is, however, that I am not going to be able to satisfy you in this regard; for granting that injuries are capable of awakening wrath in the humblest of bosoms, my own must be an exception to the rule. You would, perhaps, have me call him an ass, a crackbrain, and an upstart, but it is not my intention so to chastise him for his sin. Let him eat it with his bread and have done with it.

What I cannot but resent is the fact that he describes me as being old and one-handed, as if it were in my power to make time stand still for me, or as if I had lost my hand in some tavern instead of upon the greatest occasion that the past or present has ever known or the future may ever hope to see.[2] If my wounds are not resplendent in the eyes of the chance beholder, they are at least highly thought of by those who know where they were received. The soldier who lies dead in battle has a more impressive mien than the one who by flight attains his liberty. So strongly do I feel about this that even if it were possible to work a miracle in my case, I still would rather have taken part in that prodigious battle than be today free of my wounds without hav-

---

1. A continuation of *Don Quixote* was published by a writer who gave himself the name of Avellaneda and claimed to come from Tordesillas. The mood of the second prologue is grim in comparison to the optimistic and witty prologue to Part I.   2. The Battle of Lepanto in 1571.

ing been there. The scars that the soldier has to show on face and breast are stars that guide others to the Heaven of honor, inspiring them with a longing for well-merited praise. What is more, it may be noted that one does not write with gray hairs but with his understanding, which usually grows better with the years.

I likewise resent his calling me envious; and as though I were some ignorant person, he goes on to explain to me what is meant by envy; when the truth of the matter is that of the two kinds, I am acquainted only with that which is holy, noble, and right-intentioned.[3] And this being so, as indeed it is, it is not likely that I should attack any priest, above all, one that is a familiar of the Holy Office.[4] If he made this statement, as it appears that he did, on behalf of a certain person, then he is utterly mistaken; for the person in question is one whose genius I hold in veneration and whose works I admire, as well as his constant industry and powers of application. But when all is said, I wish to thank this gentlemanly author for observing that my *Novels*[5] are more satirical than exemplary, while admitting at the same time that they are good; for they could not be good unless they had in them a little of everything.

You will likely tell me that I am being too restrained and overmodest, but it is my belief that affliction is not to be heaped upon the afflicted, and this gentleman must be suffering greatly, seeing that he does not dare to come out into the open and show himself by the light of day, but must conceal his name and dissemble his place of origin, as if he had been guilty of some treason or act of lese majesty. If you by chance should come to know him, tell him on my behalf that I do not hold it against him; for I know what temptations the devil has to offer, one of the greatest of which consists in putting it into a man's head that he can write a book and have it printed and thereby achieve as much fame as he does money and acquire as much money as he does fame; in confirmation of which I would have you, in your own witty and charming manner, tell him this tale.

There was in Seville a certain madman whose madness assumed one of the drollest forms that ever was seen in this world. Taking a hollow reed sharpened at one end, he would catch a dog in the street or somewhere else; and, holding one of the animal's legs with his foot and raising the other with his hand, he would fix his reed as best he could in a certain part, after which he would blow the dog up, round as a ball. When he had it in this condition he would give it a couple of slaps on the belly and let it go, remarking to the bystanders, of whom there were always plenty, "Do your Worships think, then, that it is so easy a thing to inflate a dog?" So you might ask, "Does your Grace think that it is so easy a thing to write a book?" And if this story does not set well with him, here is another one, dear reader, that you may tell him. This one, also, is about a madman and a dog.

The madman in this instance lived in Cordova. He was in the habit of carrying on his head a marble slab or stone of considerable weight, and when he met some stray cur he would go up alongside it and drop the weight full upon it, and the dog in a rage, barking and howling, would then scurry off down three whole streets without stopping. Now, it happened that

---

3. *Jealousy* and *zealousness* are etymologically related.   4. An allusion to the Spanish playwright Lope de Vega, who had been made a priest and appointed an official of the Spanish Inquisition. Avellaneda accused Cervantes of envying Lope's enormous popularity.   5. *Exemplary Tales.*

among the dogs that he treated in this fashion was one belonging to a cap-maker, who was very fond of the beast. Going up to it as usual, the madman let the stone fall on its head, whereupon the animal set up a great yowling, and its owner, hearing its moans and seeing what had been done to it, promptly snatched up a measuring rod and fell upon the dog's assailant, flaying him until there was not a sound bone left in the fellow's body; and with each blow that he gave him he cried, "You dog! You thief! Treat my greyhound like that, would you? You brute, couldn't you see it was a grey-hound?" And repeating the word "greyhound" over and over, he sent the madman away beaten to a pulp.

Profiting by the lesson that had been taught him, the fellow disappeared and was not seen in public for more than a month, at the end of which time he returned, up to his old tricks and with a heavier stone than ever on his head. He would go up to a dog and stare at it, long and hard, and without daring to drop his stone, would say, "This is a greyhound; beware." And so with all the dogs that he encountered: whether they were mastiffs or curs, he would assert that they were greyhounds and let them go unharmed.

The same thing possibly may happen to our historian; it may be that he will not again venture to let fall the weight of his wit in the form of books which, being bad ones, are harder than rocks.

As for the threat he has made to the effect that through his book he will deprive me of the profits on my own,[6] you may tell him that I do not give a rap. Quoting from the famous interlude, *La Perendenga*,[7] I will say to him in reply, "Long live my master, the Four-and-twenty,[8] and Christ be with us all." Long live the great Count of Lemos, whose Christian spirit and well-known liberality have kept me on my feet despite all the blows an unkind fate has dealt me. Long life to his Eminence of Toledo, the supremely charitable Don Bernardo de Sandoval y Rojas.[9] Even though there were no printing presses in all the world, or such as there are should print more books directed against me than there are letters in the verses of *Mingo Revulgo*,[1] what would it matter to me? These two princes, without any cringing flattery or adulation on my part but solely out of their own goodness of heart, have taken it upon themselves to grant me their favor and protection, in which respect I consider myself richer and more fortunate than if by ordinary means I had attained the peak of prosperity. The poor man may keep his honor, but not the vicious one. Poverty may cast a cloud over nobility but cannot wholly obscure it. Virtue of itself gives off a certain light, even though it be through the chinks and crevices and despite the obstacles of adversity, and so comes to be esteemed and as a consequence favored by high and noble minds.

Tell him no more than this, nor do I have anything more to say to you, except to ask you to bear in mind that this *Second Part of Don Quixote*, which I herewith present to you, is cut from the same cloth and by the same craftsman as Part I. In this book I give you Don Quixote continued and, finally, dead and buried, in order that no one may dare testify any further concerning him, for there has been quite enough evidence as it is. It is suffi-

---

6. Avellaneda asserted that his second part would earn the profits Cervantes might have expected from a continuation of his own.   7. No interlude by this name has survived.   8. Council of the town hall at Andalucía.   9. Archbishop of Toledo, uncle of the Duke of Lerma, and patron of Cervantes.   1. Long verse satire.

cient that a reputable individual should have chronicled these ingenious acts of madness once and for all, without going into the matter again; for an abundance even of good things causes them to be little esteemed, while scarcity may lend a certain worth to those that are bad.

I almost forgot to tell you that you may look forward to the *Persiles*, on which I am now putting the finishing touches, as well as Part Second of the *Galatea*.[2]

["Put into a Book"]

CHAPTER 3

*Of the laughable conversation that took place between Don Quixote,
Sancho Panza, and the bachelor Sansón Carrasco.*

Don Quixote remained in a thoughtful mood as he waited for the bachelor Carrasco,[3] from whom he hoped to hear the news as to how he had been put into a book, as Sancho had said. He could not bring himself to believe that any such history existed, since the blood of the enemies he had slain was not yet dry on the blade of his sword; and here they were trying to tell him that his high deeds of chivalry were already circulating in printed form. But, for that matter, he imagined that some sage, either friend or enemy, must have seen to the printing of them through the art of magic. If the chronicler was a friend, he must have undertaken the task in order to magnify and exalt Don Quixote's exploits above the most notable ones achieved by knights-errant of old. If an enemy, his purpose would have been to make them out as nothing at all, by debasing them below the meanest acts ever recorded of any mean squire. The only thing was, the knight reflected, the exploits of squires never were set down in writing. If it was true that such a history existed, being about a knight-errant, then it must be eloquent and lofty in tone, a splendid and distinguished piece of work and veracious in its details.

This consoled him somewhat, although he was a bit put out at the thought that the author was a Moor, if the appellation "Cid" was to be taken as an indication,[4] and from the Moors you could never hope for any word of truth, seeing that they are all of them cheats, forgers, and schemers. He feared lest his love should not have been treated with becoming modesty but rather in a way that would reflect upon the virtue of his lady Dulcinea del Toboso. He hoped that his fidelity had been made clear, and the respect he had always shown her, and that something had been said as to how he had spurned queens, empresses, and damsels of every rank while keeping a rein upon those impulses that are natural to a man. He was still wrapped up in these and many other similar thoughts when Sancho returned with Carrasco.

Don Quixote received the bachelor very amiably. The latter, although his name was Sansón, or Samson, was not very big so far as bodily size went, but he was a great joker, with a sallow complexion and a ready wit. He was going on twenty-four and had a round face, a snub nose, and a large mouth, all of which showed him to be of a mischievous disposition and fond of jests

---

2. Never published.   3. The bachelor of arts Sansón Carrasco, an important new character who appears at the beginning of Part II and will play a considerable role in the story with his attempts at "curing" Don Quixote. Just now he has been telling Sancho about a book relating the adventures of Don Quixote and his squire, by which the two have been made famous; the book is, of course, *Don Quixote*, Part I.   4. The allusion is to Cid Hamete Benengeli (see n. 1, p. 96). The word *cid* is of Arabic derivation.

and witticisms. This became apparent when, as soon as he saw Don Quixote, he fell upon his knees and addressed the knight as follows:

"O mighty Don Quixote de la Mancha, give me your hands; for by the habit of St. Peter that I wear[5]—though I have received but the first four orders—your Grace is one of the most famous knights-errant that ever have been or ever will be anywhere on this earth. Blessings upon Cid Hamete Benengeli who wrote down the history of your great achievements, and upon that curious-minded one who was at pains to have it translated from the Arabic into our Castilian vulgate for the universal entertainment of the people."

Don Quixote bade him rise. "Is it true, then," he asked, "that there is a book about me and that it was some Moorish sage who composed it?"

"By way of showing you how true it is," replied Sansón, "I may tell you that it is my belief that there are in existence today more than twelve thousand copies of that history. If you do not believe me, you have but to make inquiries in Portugal, Barcelona, and Valencia, where editions have been brought out, and there is even a report to the effect that one edition was printed at Antwerp. In short, I feel certain that there will soon not be a nation that does not know it or a language into which it has not been translated."

"One of the things," remarked Don Quixote, "that should give most satisfaction to a virtuous and eminent man is to see his good name spread abroad during his own lifetime, by means of the printing press, through translations into the languages of the various peoples. I have said 'good name,' for if he has any other kind, his fate is worse than death."

"If it is a matter of good name and good reputation," said the bachelor, "your Grace bears off the palm from all the knights-errant in the world; for the Moor in his tongue and the Christian in his have most vividly depicted your Grace's gallantry, your courage in facing dangers, your patience in adversity and suffering, whether the suffering be due to wounds or to misfortunes of another sort, and your virtue and continence in love, in connection with that platonic relationship that exists between your Grace and my lady Doña Dulcinea del Toboso."

At this point Sancho spoke up. "Never in my life," he said, "have I heard my lady Dulcinea called 'Doña,' but only 'la Señora Dulcinea del Toboso'; so on that point, already, the history is wrong."

"That is not important," said Carrasco.

"No, certainly not," Don Quixote agreed. "But tell me, Señor Bachelor, what adventures of mine as set down in this book have made the deepest impression?"

"As to that," the bachelor answered, "opinions differ, for it is a matter of individual taste. There are some who are very fond of the adventure of the windmills—those windmills which to your Grace appeared to be so many Briareuses and giants. Others like the episode at the fulling mill. One relishes the story of the two armies which took on the appearance of droves of sheep, while another fancies the tale of the dead man whom they were taking to Segovia for burial. One will assert that the freeing of the galley slaves is the best of all, and yet another will maintain that nothing can come up to the Benedictine giants and the encounter with the valiant Biscayan."

Again Sancho interrupted him. "Tell me, Señor Bachelor," he said, "does

---

5. The dress of one of the minor clerical orders.

the book say anything about the adventure with the Yanguesans, that time our good Rocinante took it into his head to go looking for tidbits in the sea?"

"The sage," replied Sansón, "has left nothing in the inkwell. He has told everything and to the point, even to the capers which the worthy Sancho cut as they tossed him in the blanket."

"I cut no capers in the blanket," objected Sancho, "but I did in the air, and more than I liked."

"I imagine," said Don Quixote, "that there is no history in the world, dealing with humankind, that does not have its ups and downs, and this is particularly true of those that have to do with deeds of chivalry, for they can never be filled with happy incidents alone."

"Nevertheless," the bachelor went on, "there are some who have read the book who say that they would have been glad if the authors had forgotten a few of the innumerable cudgelings which Señor Don Quixote received in the course of his various encounters."

"But that is where the truth of the story comes in," Sancho protested.

"For all of that," observed Don Quixote, "they might well have said nothing about them; for there is no need of recording those events that do not alter the veracity of the chronicle, when they tend only to lessen the reader's respect for the hero. You may be sure that Aeneas was not as pious as Vergil would have us believe, nor was Ulysses as wise as Homer depicts him."

"That is true enough," replied Sansón, "but it is one thing to write as a poet and another as a historian. The former may narrate or sing of things not as they were but as they should have been; the latter must describe them not as they should have been but as they were, without adding to or detracting from the truth in any degree whatsoever."

"Well," said Sancho, "if this Moorish gentleman is bent upon telling the truth, I have no doubt that among my master's thrashings my own will be found; for they never took the measure of his Grace's shoulders without measuring my whole body. But I don't wonder at that; for as my master himself says, when there's an ache in the head the members have to share it."

"You are a sly fox, Sancho," said Don Quixote. "My word, but you can remember things well enough when you choose to do so!"

"Even if I wanted to forget the whacks they gave me," Sancho answered him, "the welts on my ribs wouldn't let me, for they are still fresh."

"Be quiet, Sancho," his master admonished him, "and do not interrupt the bachelor. I beg him to go on and tell me what is said of me in this book."

"And what it says about me, too," put in Sancho, "for I have heard that I am one of the main presonages in it—"

"*Personages,* not *presonages,* Sancho my friend," said Sansón.

"So we have another one who catches you up on everything you say," was Sancho's retort. "If we go on at this rate, we'll never be through in a lifetime."

"May God put a curse on *my* life," the bachelor told him, "if you are not the second most important person in the story; and there are some who would rather listen to you talk than to anyone else in the book. It is true, there are those who say that you are too gullible in believing it to be the truth that you could become the governor of that island that was offered you by Señor Don Quixote, here present."

"There is still sun on the top of the wall," said Don Quixote, "and when

Sancho is a little older, with the experience that the years bring, he will be wiser and better fitted to be a governor than he is at the present time."

"By God, master," said Sancho, "the island that I couldn't govern right now I'd never be able to govern if I lived to be as old as Methuselah. The trouble is, I don't know where that island we are talking about is located; it is not due to any lack of noddle on my part."

"Leave it to God, Sancho," was Don Quixote's advice, "and everything will come out all right, perhaps even better than you think; for not a leaf on the tree stirs except by His will."

"Yes," said Sansón, "if it be God's will, Sancho will not lack a thousand islands to govern, not to speak of one island alone."

"I have seen governors around here," said Sancho, "that are not to be compared to the sole of my shoe, and yet they call them 'your Lordship' and serve them on silver plate."

"Those are not the same kind of governors," Sansón informed him. "Their task is a good deal easier. The ones that govern islands must at least know grammar."

"I could make out well enough with the *gram*," replied Sancho, "but with the *mar* I want nothing to do, for I don't understand it at all. But leaving this business of the governorship in God's hands—for He will send me wherever I can best serve Him—I will tell you, Señor Bachelor Sansón Carrasco, that I am very much pleased that the author of the history should have spoken of me in such a way as does not offend me; for, upon the word of a faithful squire, if he had said anything about me that was not becoming to an old Christian, the deaf would have heard of it."

"That would be to work miracles," said Sansón.

"Miracles or no miracles," was the answer, "let everyone take care as to what he says or writes about people and not be setting down the first thing that pops into his head."

"One of the faults that is found with the book," continued the bachelor, "is that the author has inserted in it a story entitled *The One Who Was Too Curious for His Own Good*. It is not that the story in itself is a bad one or badly written; it is simply that it is out of place there, having nothing to do with the story of his Grace, Señor Don Quixote."[6]

"I will bet you," said Sancho, "that the son of a dog has mixed the cabbages with the baskets."[7]

"And I will say right now," declared Don Quixote, "that the author of this book was not a sage but some ignorant prattler who at haphazard and without any method set about the writing of it, being content to let things turn out as they might. In the same manner, Orbaneja,[8] the painter of Ubeda, when asked what he was painting would reply, 'Whatever it turns out to be.' Sometimes it would be a cock, in which case he would have to write alongside it, in Gothic letters, 'This is a cock.' And so it must be with my story, which will need a commentary to make it understandable."

"No," replied Sansón, "that it will not; for it is so clearly written that none can fail to understand it. Little children leaf through it, young people read it, adults appreciate it, and the aged sing its praises. In short, it is so

6. The story, a tragic tale about a jealousy-ridden husband, occupies several chapters of Part I. Here, as elsewhere in this chapter, Cervantes echoes criticism currently aimed at his book.   7. Has jumbled together things of different kinds.   8. Unidentified.

thumbed and read and so well known to persons of every walk in life that no sooner do folks see some skinny nag than they at once cry, 'There goes Rocinante!' Those that like it best of all are the pages; for there is no lord's antechamber where a *Don Quixote* is not to be found. If one lays it down, another will pick it up; one will pounce upon it, and another will beg for it. It affords the pleasantest and least harmful reading of any book that has been published up to now. In the whole of it there is not to be found an indecent word or a thought that is other than Catholic."

"To write in any other manner," observed Don Quixote, "would be to write lies and not the truth. Those historians who make use of falsehoods ought to be burned like the makers of counterfeit money. I do not know what could have led the author to introduce stories and episodes that are foreign to the subject matter when he had so much to write about in describing my adventures. He must, undoubtedly, have been inspired by the old saying, 'With straw or with hay[9] . . .' For, in truth, all he had to do was to record my thoughts, my sighs, my tears, my lofty purposes, and my undertakings, and he would have had a volume bigger or at least as big as that which the works of El Tostado[1] would make. To sum the matter up, Señor Bachelor, it is my opinion that, in composing histories or books of any sort, a great deal of judgment and ripe understanding is called for. To say and write witty and amusing things is the mark of great genius. The cleverest character in a comedy is the clown, since he who would make himself out to be a simpleton cannot be one. History is a near-sacred thing, for it must be true, and where the truth is, there is God. And yet there are those who compose books and toss them out into the world as if they were no more than fritters."

"There is no book so bad," opined the bachelor, "that there is not some good in it."

"Doubtless that is so," replied Don Quixote, "but it very often happens that those who have won in advance a great and well-deserved reputation for their writings, lose it in whole or in part when they give their works to the printer."

"The reason for it," said Sansón, "is that, printed works being read at leisure, their faults are the more readily apparent, and the greater the reputation of the author the more closely are they scrutinized. Men famous for their genius, great poets, illustrious historians, are almost always envied by those who take a special delight in criticizing the writings of others without having produced anything of their own."

"That is not to be wondered at," said Don Quixote, "for there are many theologians who are not good enough for the pulpit but who are very good indeed when it comes to detecting the faults or excesses of those who preach."

"All of this is very true, Señor Don Quixote," replied Carrasco, "but, all the same, I could wish that these self-appointed censors were a bit more forbearing and less hypercritical; I wish they would pay a little less attention to the spots on the bright sun of the work that occasions their faultfinding. For if *aliquando bonus dormitat Homerus*,[2] let them consider how

---

9. The proverb concludes either "the mattress is filled" or "I fill my belly."   1. Alonso de Madrigal, bishop of Ávila, a prolific author of devotional works.   2. Good Homer sometimes nods too (Latin); Horace, *Art of Poetry*, line 359.

much of his time he spent awake, shedding the light of his genius with a minimum of shade. It well may be that what to them seems a flaw is but one of those moles which sometimes add to the beauty of a face. In any event, I insist that he who has a book printed runs a very great risk, inasmuch as it is an utter impossibility to write it in such a manner that it will please all who read it."

"This book about me must have pleased very few," remarked Don Quixote.

"Quite the contrary," said Sansón, "for just as *stultorum infinitus est numerus*,[3] so the number of those who have enjoyed this history is likewise infinite. Some, to be sure, have complained of the author's forgetfulness, seeing that he neglected to make it plain who the thief was who stole Sancho's gray;[4] for it is not stated there, but merely implied, that the ass was stolen; and, a little further on, we find the knight mounted on the same beast, although it has not made its reappearance in the story. They also say that the author forgot to tell us what Sancho did with those hundred crowns that he found in the valise on the Sierra Morena, as nothing more is said of them and there are many who would like to know how he disposed of the money or how he spent it. This is one of the serious omissions to be found in the work."

To this Sancho replied, "I, Señor Sansón, do not feel like giving any account or accounting just now; for I feel a little weak in my stomach, and if I don't do something about it by taking a few swigs of the old stuff, I'll be sitting on St. Lucy's thorn.[5] I have some of it at home, and my old woman is waiting for me. After I've had my dinner, I'll come back and answer any questions your Grace or anybody else wants to ask me, whether it's about the loss of the ass or the spending of the hundred crowns."

And without waiting for a reply or saying another word, he went on home. Don Quixote urged the bachelor to stay and take potluck with him, and Sansón accepted the invitation and remained. In addition to the knight's ordinary fare, they had a couple of pigeons, and at table their talk was of chivalry and feats of arms.

[A Victorious Duel]

CHAPTER 12

Of the strange adventure that befell the valiant Don Quixote with the fearless Knight of the Mirrors.[6]

The night following the encounter with Death was spent by Don Quixote and his squire beneath some tall and shady trees,[7] the knight having been persuaded to eat a little from the stock of provisions carried by the gray.

"Sir," said Sancho, in the course of their repast, "how foolish I'd have been if I had chosen the spoils from your Grace's first adventure rather than the

---

3. Infinite is the number of fools (Latin). 4. In Part I, chap. 23. 5. I shall be weak and exhausted.
6. Until he earns this title (in chap. 15), he will be referred to as the Knight of the Wood. 7. Don Quixote and his squire are now in the woody region around El Toboso, Dulcinea's town. Sancho has been sent to look for his knight's lady and has saved the day by pretending to see the beautiful damsel in a "village wench, and not a pretty one at that, for she was round-faced and snub-nosed." But by his imaginative lie he has succeeded, as he had planned, in setting in motion Don Quixote's belief in spells and enchantments: enemy magicians, envious of him, have hidden his lady's splendor only from his sight. While the knight was still under the shock of this experience, farther along their way he and his squire have met a group of itinerant players dressed in their proper costumes for a religious play, *The Parliament of Death.*

foals from the three mares.[8] Truly, truly, a sparrow in the hand is worth more than a vulture on the wing."[9]

"And yet, Sancho," replied Don Quixote, "if you had but let me attack them as I wished to do, you would at least have had as spoils the Empress's gold crown and Cupid's[1] painted wings; for I should have taken them whether or no and placed them in your hands."

"The crowns and scepters of stage emperors," remarked Sancho, "were never known to be of pure gold; they are always of tinsel or tinplate."

"That is the truth," said Don Quixote, "for it is only right that the accessories of a drama should be fictitious and not real, like the play itself. Speaking of that, Sancho, I would have you look kindly upon the art of the theater and, as a consequence, upon those who write the pieces and perform in them, for they all render a service of great value to the State by holding up a mirror for us at each step that we take, wherein we may observe, vividly depicted, all the varied aspects of human life; and I may add that there is nothing that shows us more clearly, by similitude, what we are and what we ought to be than do plays and players.

"Tell me, have you not seen some comedy in which kings, emperors, pontiffs, knights, ladies, and numerous other characters are introduced? One plays the ruffian, another the cheat, this one a merchant and that one a soldier, while yet another is the fool who is not so foolish as he appears, and still another the one of whom love has made a fool. Yet when the play is over and they have taken off their players' garments, all the actors are once more equal."

"Yes," replied Sancho, "I have seen all that."

"Well," continued Don Quixote, "the same thing happens in the comedy that we call life, where some play the part of emperors, others that of pontiffs—in short, all the characters that a drama may have—but when it is all over, that is to say, when life is done, death takes from each the garb that differentiates him, and all at last are equal in the grave."

"It is a fine comparison," Sancho admitted, "though not so new but that I have heard it many times before. It reminds me of that other one, about the game of chess. So long as the game lasts, each piece has its special qualities, but when it is over they are all mixed and jumbled together and put into a bag, which is to the chess pieces what the grave is to life."

"Every day, Sancho," said Don Quixote, "you are becoming less stupid and more sensible."

"It must be that some of your Grace's good sense is sticking to me," was Sancho's answer. "I am like a piece of land that of itself is dry and barren, but if you scatter manure over it and cultivate it, it will bear good fruit. By this I mean to say that your Grace's conversation is the manure that has been cast upon the barren land of my dry wit; the time that I spend in your service, associating with you, does the cultivating; and as a result of it all, I hope to bring forth blessed fruits by not departing, slipping, or sliding, from those paths of good breeding which your Grace has marked out for me in my parched understanding."

8. Don Quixote has promised them to Sancho as a reward for bringing news of Dulcinea.   9. That is, a bird in the hand is worth two in the bush.   1. Characters in *The Parliament of Death*.

Don Quixote had to laugh at this affected speech of Sancho's, but he could not help perceiving that what the squire had said about his improvement was true enough; for every now and then the servant would speak in a manner that astonished his master. It must be admitted, however, that most of the time when he tried to use fine language, he would tumble from the mountain of his simple-mindedness into the abyss of his ignorance. It was when he was quoting old saws and sayings, whether or not they had anything to do with the subject under discussion, that he was at his best, displaying upon such occasions a prodigious memory, as will already have been seen and noted in the course of this history.

With such talk as this they spent a good part of the night. Then Sancho felt a desire to draw down the curtains of his eyes, as he was in the habit of saying when he wished to sleep, and, unsaddling his mount, he turned him loose to graze at will on the abundant grass. If he did not remove Rocinante's saddle, this was due to his master's express command; for when they had taken the field and were not sleeping under a roof, the hack was under no circumstances to be stripped. This was in accordance with an old and established custom which knights-errant faithfully observed: the bridle and saddlebow might be removed, but beware of touching the saddle itself! Guided by this precept, Sancho now gave Rocinante the same freedom that the ass enjoyed.

The close friendship that existed between the two animals was a most unusual one, so remarkable indeed that it has become a tradition handed down from father to son, and the author of this veracious chronicle even wrote a number of special chapters on the subject, although, in order to preserve the decency and decorum that are fitting in so heroic an account, he chose to omit them in the final version. But he forgets himself once in a while and goes on to tell us how the two beasts when they were together would hasten to scratch each other, and how, when they were tired and their bellies were full, Rocinante would lay his long neck over that of the ass—it extended more than a half a yard on the other side—and the pair would then stand there gazing pensively at the ground for as much as three whole days at a time, or at least until someone came for them or hunger compelled them to seek nourishment.

I may tell you that I have heard it said that the author of this history, in one of his writings, has compared the friendship of Rocinante and the gray to that of Nisus and Euryalus and that of Pylades and Orestes;[2] and if this be true, it shows for the edification of all what great friends these two peace-loving animals were, and should be enough to make men ashamed, who are so inept at preserving friendship with one another. For this reason it has been said:

> There is no friend for friend,
> Reeds to lances turn[3] . . .

And there was the other poet who sang:

> Between friend and friend the bug[4] . . .

---

2. Famous examples of friendship in Virgil's *Aeneid* and in Greek tradition and drama.   3. From a popular ballad.   4. The Spanish "a bug in the eye" implies keeping a watchful eye on somebody.

Let no one think that the author has gone out of his way in comparing the friendship of animals with that of men; for human beings have received valuable lessons from the beasts and have learned many important things from them. From the stork they have learned the use of clysters; the dog has taught them the salutary effects of vomiting as well as a lesson in gratitude; the cranes have taught them vigilance, the ants foresight, the elephants modesty, and the horse loyalty.[5]

Sancho had at last fallen asleep at the foot of a cork tree, while Don Quixote was slumbering beneath a sturdy oak. Very little time had passed when the knight was awakened by a noise behind him, and, starting up, he began looking about him and listening to see if he could make out where it came from. Then he caught sight of two men on horseback, one of whom, slipping down from the saddle, said to the other, "Dismount, my friend, and unbridle the horses; for there seems to be plenty of grass around here for them and sufficient silence and solitude for my amorous thoughts."

Saying this, he stretched himself out on the ground, and as he flung himself down the armor that he wore made such a noise that Don Quixote knew at once, for a certainty, that he must be a knight-errant. Going over to Sancho, who was still sleeping, he shook him by the arm and with no little effort managed to get him awake.

"Brother Sancho," he said to him in a low voice, "we have an adventure on our hands."

"God give us a good one," said Sancho. "And where, my master, may her Ladyship, Mistress Adventure, be?"

"Where, Sancho?" replied Don Quixote. "Turn your eyes and look, and you will see stretched out over there a knight-errant who, so far as I can make out, is not any too happy; for I saw him fling himself from his horse to the ground with a certain show of despondency, and as he fell his armor rattled."

"Well," said Sancho, "and how does your Grace make this out to be an adventure?"

"I would not say," the knight answered him, "that this is an adventure in itself, but rather the beginning of one, for that is the way they start. But listen; he seems to be tuning a lute or guitar, and from the way he is spitting and clearing his throat he must be getting ready to sing something."

"Faith, so he is," said Sancho. "He must be some lovesick knight."

"There are no knights-errant that are not lovesick," Don Quixote informed him. "Let us listen to him, and the thread of his song will lead us to the yarn-ball of his thoughts; for out of the abundance of the heart the mouth speaketh."

Sancho would have liked to reply to his master, but the voice of the Knight of the Wood, which was neither very good nor very bad, kept him from it; and as the two of them listened attentively, they heard the following:

5. All folkloristic beliefs about the virtues of animals.

Sonnet

Show me, O lady, the pattern of thy will,
That mine may take that very form and shape;
For my will in thine own I fain would drape,
Each slightest wish of thine I would fulfill.
If thou wouldst have me silence this dead ill   5
Of which I'm dying now, prepare the crape!
Or if I must another manner ape,
Then let Love's self display his rhyming skill.
Of opposites I am made, that's manifest:
In part soft wax, in part hard-diamond fire;   10
Yet to Love's laws my heart I do adjust,
And, hard or soft, I offer thee this breast:
Print or engrave there what thou may'st desire,
And I'll preserve it in eternal trust.[6]

With an *Ay!* that appeared to be wrung from the very depths of his heart, the Knight of the Wood brought his song to a close, and then after a brief pause began speaking in a grief-stricken voice that was piteous to hear.

"O most beautiful and most ungrateful woman in all the world!" he cried, "how is it possible, O most serene Casildea de Vandalia,[7] for you to permit this captive knight of yours to waste away and perish in constant wanderings, amid rude toils and bitter hardships? Is it not enough that I have compelled all the knights of Navarre, all those of León, all the Tartessians and Castilians, and, finally, all those of La Mancha, to confess that there is no beauty anywhere that can rival yours?"

"That is not so!" cried Don Quixote at this point. "I am of La Mancha, and I have never confessed, I never could nor would confess a thing so prejudicial to the beauty of my lady. The knight whom you see there, Sancho, is raving; but let us listen and perhaps he will tell us more."

"That he will," replied Sancho, "for at the rate he is carrying on, he is good for a month at a stretch."

This did not prove to be the case, however; for when the Knight of the Wood heard voices near him, he cut short his lamentations and rose to his feet.

"Who goes there?" he called in a loud but courteous tone. "What kind of people are you? Are you, perchance, numbered among the happy or among the afflicted?"

"Among the afflicted," was Don Quixote's response.

"Then come to me," said the one of the Wood, "and, in doing so, know that you come to sorrow's self and the very essence of affliction."

Upon receiving so gentle and courteous an answer, Don Quixote and Sancho as well went over to him, whereupon the sorrowing one took the Manchegan's arm.

"Sit down here, Sir Knight," he continued, "for in order to know that you are one of those who follow the profession of knight-errantry, it is enough for me to have found you in this place where solitude and serenity keep you company, such a spot being the natural bed and proper dwelling of wandering men of arms."

---

6. The poem intentionally follows affected conventions of the time.   7. The Knight of the Wood's counterpart to Don Quixote's Dulcinea del Toboso.

"A knight I am," replied Don Quixote, "and of the profession that you mention; and though sorrows, troubles, and misfortunes have made my heart their abode, this does not mean that compassion for the woes of others has been banished from it. From your song a while ago I gather that your misfortunes are due to love—the love you bear that ungrateful fair one whom you named in your lamentations."

As they conversed in this manner, they sat together upon the hard earth, very peaceably and companionably, as if at daybreak they were not going to break each other's heads.

"Sir Knight," inquired the one of the Wood, "are you by any chance in love?"

"By mischance I am," said Don Quixote, "although the ills that come from well-placed affection should be looked upon as favors rather than as misfortunes."

"That is the truth," the Knight of the Wood agreed, "if it were not that the loved one's scorn disturbs our reason and understanding; for when it is excessive scorn appears as vengeance."

"I was never scorned by my lady," said Don Quixote.

"No, certainly not," said Sancho, who was standing near by, "for my lady is gentle as a ewe lamb and soft as butter."

"Is he your squire?" asked the one of the Wood.

"He is," replied Don Quixote.

"I never saw a squire," said the one of the Wood, "who dared to speak while his master was talking. At least, there is mine over there; he is as big as your father, and it cannot be proved that he has ever opened his lips while I was conversing."

"Well, upon my word," said Sancho, "I have spoken, and I will speak in front of any other as good—but never mind; it only makes it worse to stir it."

The Knight of the Wood's squire now seized Sancho's arm. "Come along," he said, "let the two of us go where we can talk all we like, squire fashion, and leave these gentlemen our masters to come to lance blows as they tell each other the story of their loves; for you may rest assured, daybreak will find them still at it."

"Let us, by all means," said Sancho, "and I will tell your Grace who I am, so that you may be able to see for yourself whether or not I am to be numbered among the dozen most talkative squires."

With this, the pair went off to one side, and there then took place between them a conversation that was as droll as the one between their masters was solemn.

CHAPTER 13

In which is continued the adventure of the Knight of the Wood, together with the shrewd, highly original, and amicable conversation that took place between the two squires.

The knights and the squires had now separated, the latter to tell their life stories, the former to talk of their loves; but the history first relates the conversation of the servants and then goes on to report that of the masters. We are told that, after they had gone some little distance from where the others were, the one who served the Knight of the Wood began speaking to Sancho as follows:

"It is a hard life that we lead and live, *Señor mio,* those of us who are squires to knights-errant. It is certainly true that we eat our bread in the sweat of our faces, which is one of the curses that God put upon our first parents."[8]

"It might also be said," added Sancho, "that we eat it in the chill of our bodies, for who endures more heat and cold than we wretched ones who wait upon these wandering men of arms? It would not be so bad if we did eat once in a while, for troubles are less where there is bread; but as it is, we sometimes go for a day or two without breaking our fast, unless we feed on the wind that blows."

"But all this," said the other, "may very well be put up with, by reason of the hope we have of being rewarded; for if a knight is not too unlucky, his squire after a little while will find himself the governor of some fine island or prosperous earldom."

"I," replied Sancho, "have told my master that I would be satisfied with the governorship of an island, and he is so noble and so generous that he has promised it to me on many different occasions."

"In return for my services," said the Squire of the Wood, "I'd be content with a canonry. My master has already appointed me to one—and what a canonry!"

"Then he must be a churchly knight," said Sancho, "and in a position to grant favors of that sort to his faithful squire; but mine is a layman, pure and simple, although, as I recall, certain shrewd and, as I see it, scheming persons did advise him to try to become an archbishop. However, he did not want to be anything but an emperor. And there I was, all the time trembling for fear he would take it into his head to enter the Church, since I was not educated enough to hold any benefices. For I may as well tell your Grace that, though I look like a man, I am no more than a beast where holy orders are concerned."

"That is where you are making a mistake," the Squire of the Wood assured him. "Not all island governments are desirable. Some of them are misshapen bits of land, some are poor, others are gloomy, and, in short, the best of them lays a heavy burden of care and trouble upon the shoulders of the unfortunate one to whose lot it falls. It would be far better if we who follow this cursed trade were to go back to our homes and there engage in pleasanter occupations, such as hunting or fishing, for example; for where is there in this world a squire so poor that he does not have a hack, a couple of greyhounds, and a fishing rod to provide him with sport in his own village?"

"I don't lack any of those," replied Sancho. "It is true, I have no hack, but I do have an ass that is worth twice as much as my master's horse. God send me a bad Easter, and let it be the next one that comes, if I would make a trade, even though he gave me four fanegas[9] of barley to boot. Your Grace will laugh at the price I put on my gray—for that is the color of the beast. As to greyhounds, I shan't want for them, as there are plenty and to spare in my village. And, anyway, there is more pleasure in hunting when someone else pays for it."

8. Compare Genesis 3.19: "In the sweat of thy face shalt thou eat bread, till thou return unto the ground."
9. About 1.6 bushels.

"Really and truly, Sir Squire," said the one of the Wood, "I have made up my mind and resolved to have no more to do with the mad whims of these knights; I intend to retire to my village and bring up my little ones—I have three of them, and they are like oriental pearls."

"I have two of them," said Sancho, "that might be presented to the Pope in person, especially one of my girls that I am bringing up to be a countess, God willing, in spite of what her mother says."

"And how old is this young lady that is destined to be a countess?"

"Fifteen," replied Sancho, "or a couple of years more or less. But she is tall as a lance, fresh as an April morning, and strong as a porter."

"Those," remarked the one of the Wood, "are qualifications that fit her to be not merely a countess but a nymph of the verdant wildwood. O whore's daughter of a whore! What strength the she-rogue must have!"

Sancho was a bit put out by this. "She is not a whore," he said, "nor was her mother before her, nor will either of them ever be, please God, so long as I live. And you might speak more courteously. For one who has been brought up among knights-errant, who are the soul of courtesy, those words are not very becoming."

"Oh, how little your Grace knows about compliments, Sir Squire!" the one of the Wood exclaimed. "Are you not aware that when some knight gives a good lance thrust to the bull in the plaza, or when a person does anything remarkably well, it is the custom for the crowd to cry out, 'Well done, whore-son rascal!' and that what appears to be vituperation in such a case is in reality high praise? Sir, I would bid you disown those sons or daughters who do nothing to cause such praise to be bestowed upon their parents."

"I would indeed disown them if they didn't," replied Sancho, "and so your Grace may go ahead and call me, my children, and my wife all the whores in the world if you like, for everything that they say and do deserves the very highest praise. And in order that I may see them all again, I pray God to deliver me from mortal sin, or, what amounts to the same thing, from this dangerous calling of squire, seeing that I have fallen into it a second time, decoyed and deceived by a purse of a hundred ducats that I found one day in the heart of the Sierra Morena.[1] The devil is always holding up a bag full of doubloons in front of my eyes, here, there—no, not here, but there— everywhere, until it seems to me at every step I take that I am touching it with my hand, hugging it, carrying it off home with me, investing it, drawing an income from it, and living on it like a prince. And while I am thinking such thoughts, all the hardships I have to put up with serving this crack-brained master of mine, who is more of a madman than a knight, seem to me light and easy to bear."

"That," observed the Squire of the Wood, "is why it is they say that avarice bursts the bag. But, speaking of madmen, there is no greater one in all this world than my master; for he is one of those of whom it is said, 'The cares of others kill the ass.' Because another knight has lost his senses, he has to play mad too[2] and go hunting for that which, when he finds it, may fly up in his snout."

---

1. When Don Quixote retired there in Part I, chap. 23.   2. In the Sierra Morena, Don Quixote had decided to imitate Amadis de Gaul and Ariosto's Roland "by playing the part of a desperate and raving madman" as a consequence of love.

"Is he in love, maybe?"

"Yes, with a certain Casildea de Vandalia, the rawest[3] and best-roasted lady to be found anywhere on earth; but her rawness is not the foot he limps on, for he has other and greater schemes rumbling in his bowels, as you will hear tell before many hours have gone by."

"There is no road so smooth," said Sancho, "that it does not have some hole or rut to make you stumble. In other houses they cook horse beans, in mine they boil them by the kettleful.[4] Madness has more companions and attendants than good sense does. But if it is true what they say, that company in trouble brings relief, I may take comfort from your Grace, since you serve a master as foolish as my own."

"Foolish but brave," the one of the Wood corrected him, "and more of a rogue than anything else."

"That is not true of my master," replied Sancho. "I can assure you there is nothing of the rogue about him; he is as open and aboveboard as a wine pitcher and would not harm anyone but does good to all. There is no malice in his make-up, and a child could make him believe it was night at midday. For that very reason I love him with all my heart and cannot bring myself to leave him, no matter how many foolish things he does."

"But, nevertheless, good sir and brother," said the Squire of the Wood, "with the blind leading the blind, both are in danger of falling into the pit. It would be better for us to get out of all this as quickly as we can and return to our old haunts; for those that go seeking adventures do not always find good ones."

Sancho kept clearing his throat from time to time, and his saliva seemed rather viscous and dry; seeing which, the woodland squire said to him, "It looks to me as if we have been talking so much that our tongues are cleaving to our palates, but I have a loosener over there, hanging from the bow of my saddle, and a pretty good one it is." With this, he got up and went over to his horse and came back a moment later with a big flask of wine and a meat pie half a yard in diameter. This is no exaggeration, for the pasty in question was made of a hutch-rabbit of such a size that Sancho took it to be a goat, or at the very least a kid.

"And are you in the habit of carrying this with you, Señor?" he asked.

"What do you think?" replied the other. "Am I by any chance one of your wood-and-water[5] squires? I carry better rations on the flanks of my horse than a general does when he takes the field."

Sancho ate without any urging, gulping down mouthfuls that were like the knots on a tether, as they sat there in the dark.

"You are a squire of the right sort," he said, "loyal and true, and you live in grand style as shown by this feast, which I would almost say was produced by magic. You are not like me, poor wretch, who have in my saddle-bags only a morsel of cheese so hard you could crack a giant's skull with it, three or four dozen carob beans, and a few nuts. For this I have my master to thank, who believes in observing the rule that knights-errant should nourish and sustain themselves on nothing but dried fruits and the herbs of the field."

---

3. The Spanish has a pun on *crudo*, meaning both "raw" and "cruel."   4. Meaning that his misfortunes always come in large quantities.   5. Of low quality.

"Upon my word, brother," said the other squire, "my stomach was not made for thistles, wild pears, and woodland herbs. Let our masters observe those knightly laws and traditions and eat what their rules prescribe; I carry a hamper of food and a flask on my saddlebow, whether they like it or not. And speaking of that flask, how I love it! There is scarcely a minute in the day that I'm not hugging and kissing it, over and over again."

As he said this, he placed the wine bag in Sancho's hands, who put it to his mouth, threw his head back, and sat there gazing up at the stars for a quarter of an hour. Then, when he had finished drinking, he let his head loll on one side and heaved a deep sigh.

"The whoreson rascal!" he exclaimed, "that's a fine vintage for you!"

"There!" cried the Squire of the Wood, as he heard the epithet Sancho had used, "do you see how you have praised this wine by calling it 'whoreson'?"

"I grant you," replied Sancho, "that it is no insult to call anyone a son of a whore so long as you really do mean to praise him. But tell me, sir, in the name of what you love most, is this the wine of Ciudad Real?"[6]

"What a winetaster you are! It comes from nowhere else, and it's a few years old, at that."

"Leave it to me," said Sancho, "and never fear, I'll show you how much I know about it. Would you believe me, Sir Squire, I have such a great natural instinct in this matter of wines that I have but to smell a vintage and I will tell you the country where it was grown, from what kind of grapes, what it tastes like, and how good it is, and everything that has to do with it. There is nothing so unusual about this, however, seeing that on my father's side were two of the best winetasters La Mancha has known in many a year, in proof of which, listen to the story of what happened to them.

"The two were given a sample of wine from a certain vat and asked to state its condition and quality and determine whether it was good or bad. One of them tasted it with the tip of his tongue while the other merely brought it up to his nose. The first man said that it tasted of iron, the second that it smelled of Cordovan leather. The owner insisted that the vat was clean and that there could be nothing in the wine to give it a flavor of leather or of iron, but, nevertheless, the two famous winetasters stood their ground. Time went by, and when they came to clean out the vat they found in it a small key attached to a leather strap. And so your Grace may see for yourself whether or not one who comes of that kind of stock has a right to give his opinion in such cases."

"And for that very reason," said the Squire of the Wood, "I maintain that we ought to stop going about in search of adventures. Seeing that we have loaves, let us not go looking for cakes, but return to our cottages, for God will find us there if He so wills."

"I mean to stay with my master," Sancho replied, "until he reaches Saragossa, but after that we will come to an understanding."

The short of the matter is, the two worthy squires talked so much and drank so much that sleep had to tie their tongues and moderate their thirst, since to quench the latter was impossible. Clinging to the wine flask, which was almost empty by now, and with half-chewed morsels of food in their

6. The main town in La Mancha and the center of a wine region.

mouths, they both slept peacefully; and we shall leave them there as we go on to relate what took place between the Knight of the Wood and the Knight of the Mournful Countenance.

CHAPTER 14

Wherein is continued the adventure of the Knight of the Wood.

In the course of the long conversation that took place between Don Quixote and the Knight of the Wood, the history informs us that the latter addressed the following remarks to the Manchegan:

"In short, Sir Knight, I would have you know that my destiny, or, more properly speaking, my own free choice, has led me to fall in love with the peerless Casildea de Vandalia. I call her peerless for the reason that she has no equal as regards either her bodily proportions or her very great beauty. This Casildea, then, of whom I am telling you, repaid my worthy affections and honorable intentions by forcing me, as Hercules[7] was forced by his stepmother, to incur many and diverse perils; and each time as I overcame one of them she would promise me that with the next one I should have that which I desired; but instead my labors have continued, forming a chain whose links I am no longer able to count, nor can I say which will be the last one, that shall mark the beginning of the realization of my hopes.

"One time she sent me forth to challenge that famous giantess of Seville, known as La Giralda,[8] who is as strong and brave as if made of brass, and who without moving from the spot where she stands is the most changeable and fickle woman in the world. I came, I saw, I conquered her, I made her stand still and point in one direction only, and for more than a week nothing but north winds blew. Then, there was that other time when Casildea sent me to lift those ancient stones, the mighty Bulls of Guisando,[9] an enterprise that had better have been entrusted to porters than to knights. On another occasion she commanded me to hurl myself down into the Cabra chasm[1]— an unheard-of and terribly dangerous undertaking—and bring her back a detailed account of what lay concealed in that deep and gloomy pit. I rendered La Giralda motionless, I lifted the Bulls of Guisando, and I threw myself into the abyss and brought to light what was hidden in its depths; yet my hopes are dead—how dead!—while her commands and her scorn are as lively as can be.

"Finally, she commanded me to ride through all the provinces of Spain and compel all the knights-errant whom I met with to confess that she is the most beautiful woman now living and that I am the most enamored man of arms that is to be found anywhere in the world. In fulfillment of this behest I have already traveled over the greater part of these realms and have vanquished many knights who have dared to contradict me. But the one whom I am proudest to have overcome in single combat is that famous gentleman, Don Quixote de la Mancha; for I made him confess that my Casildea is more beautiful than his Dulcinea, and by achieving such a conquest I reckon that I have conquered all the others on the face of the earth, seeing

---

7. Son of Zeus and Alcmena; he was persecuted by Zeus's wife, Hera.   8. Actually a statue on the Moorish belfry of the cathedral at Seville.   9. Statues representing animals and supposedly marking a place where Caesar defeated Pompey.   1. Possibly an ancient mine in the Sierra de Cabra near Cordova.

that this same Don Quixote had himself routed them. Accordingly, when I vanquished him, his fame, glory, and honor passed over and were transferred to my person.

> The brighter is the conquered one's lost crown,
> The greater is the conqueror's renown.[2]

Thus, the innumerable exploits of the said Don Quixote are now set down to my account and are indeed my own."

Don Quixote was astounded as he listened to the Knight of the Wood, and was about to tell him any number of times that he lied; the words were on the tip of his tongue, but he held them back as best he could, thinking that he would bring the other to confess with his own lips that what he had said was a lie. And so it was quite calmly that he now replied to him.

"Sir Knight," he began, "as to the assertion that your Grace has conquered most of the knights-errant in Spain and even in all the world, I have nothing to say, but that you have vanquished Don Quixote de la Mancha, I am inclined to doubt. It may be that it was someone else who resembled him, although there are very few that do."

"What do you mean?" replied the one of the Wood. "I swear by the heavens above that I did fight with Don Quixote and that I overcame him and forced him to yield. He is a tall man, with a dried-up face, long, lean legs, graying hair, an eagle-like nose somewhat hooked, and a big, black, drooping mustache. He takes the field under the name of the Knight of the Mournful Countenance, he has for squire a peasant named Sancho Panza, and he rides a famous steed called Rocinante. Lastly, the lady of his heart is a certain Dulcinea del Toboso, once upon a time known as Aldonza Lorenzo, just as my own lady, whose name is Casildea and who is an Andalusian by birth, is called by me Casildea de Vandalia. If all this is not sufficient to show that I speak the truth, here is my sword which shall make incredulity itself believe."

"Calm yourself, Sir Knight," replied Don Quixote, "and listen to what I have to say to you. You must know that this Don Quixote of whom you speak is the best friend that I have in the world, so great a friend that I may say that I feel toward him as I do toward my own self; and from all that you have told me, the very definite and accurate details that you have given me, I cannot doubt that he is the one whom you have conquered. On the other hand, the sight of my eyes and the touch of my hands assure me that he could not possibly be the one, unless some enchanter who is his enemy—for he has many, and one in particular who delights in persecuting him—may have assumed the knight's form and then permitted himself to be routed, by way of defrauding Don Quixote of the fame which his high deeds of chivalry have earned for him throughout the known world. To show you how true this may be, I will inform you that not more than a couple of days ago those same enemy magicians transformed the figure and person of the beauteous Dulcinea del Toboso into a low and mean village lass, and it is possible that they have done something of the same sort to the knight who is her lover. And if all this does not suffice to convince you of the truth of what I say, here is

---

2. From Alonso de Ercilla y Zúñiga's *Araucana*, a poem about the Spanish struggle against the Araucanian Indians of Chile.

Don Quixote himself who will maintain it by force of arms, on foot or on horseback, or in any way you like."

Saying this, he rose and laid hold of his sword, and waited to see what the Knight of the Wood's decision would be. That worthy now replied in a voice as calm as the one Don Quixote had used.

"Pledges," he said, "do not distress one who is sure of his ability to pay. He who was able to overcome you when you were transformed, Señor Don Quixote, may hope to bring you to your knees when you are your own proper self. But inasmuch as it is not fitting that knights should perform their feats of arms in the darkness, like ruffians and highwaymen, let us wait until it is day in order that the sun may behold what we do. And the condition governing our encounter shall be that the one who is vanquished must submit to the will of his conqueror and perform all those things that are commanded of him, provided they are such as are in keeping with the state of knighthood."

"With that condition and understanding," said Don Quixote, "I shall be satisfied."

With this, they went off to where their squires were, only to find them snoring away as hard as when sleep had first overtaken them. Awakening the pair, they ordered them to look to the horses; for as soon as the sun was up the two knights meant to stage an arduous and bloody single-handed combat. At this news Sancho was astonished and terrified, since, as a result of what the other squire had told him of the Knight of the Wood's prowess, he was led to fear for his master's safety. Nevertheless, he and his friend now went to seek the mounts without saying a word, and they found the animals all together, for by this time the two horses and the ass had smelled one another out. On the way the Squire of the Wood turned to Sancho and addressed him as follows:

"I must inform you, brother, that it is the custom of the fighters of Andalusia, when they are godfathers in any combat, not to remain idly by, with folded hands, while their godsons fight it out. I tell you this by way of warning you that while our masters are settling matters, we, too, shall have to come to blows and hack each other to bits."

"The custom, Sir Squire," replied Sancho, "may be all very well among the fighters and ruffians that you mention, but with the squires of knights-errant it is not to be thought of. At least, I have never heard my master speak of any such custom, and he knows all the laws of chivalry by heart. But granting that it is true and that there is a law which states in so many words that squires must fight while their masters do, I have no intention of obeying it but rather will pay whatever penalty is laid on peaceable-minded ones like myself, for I am sure it cannot be more than a couple of pounds of wax,[3] and that would be less expensive than the lint which it would take to heal my head—I can already see it split in two. What's more, it's out of the question for me to fight since I have no sword nor did I ever in my life carry one."

"That," said the one of the Wood, "is something that is easily remedied. I have here two linen bags of the same size. You take one and I'll take the other and we will fight that way, on equal terms."

3. In some confraternities, penalties were paid in wax, presumably to make church candles.

"So be it, by all means," said Sancho, "for that will simply knock the dust out of us without wounding us."

"But that's not the way it's to be,' said the other squire. "Inside the bags, to keep the wind from blowing them away, we will put a half-dozen nice smooth pebbles of the same weight, and so we'll be able to give each other a good pounding without doing ourselves any real harm or damage."

"Body of my father!" cried Sancho, "just look, will you, at the marten and sable and wads of carded cotton that he's stuffing into those bags so that we won't get our heads cracked or our bones crushed to a pulp. But I am telling you, *Señor mio,* that even though you fill them with silken pellets, I don't mean to fight. Let our masters fight and make the best of it, but as for us, let us drink and live; for time will see to ending our lives without any help on our part by way of bringing them to a close before they have reached their proper season and fall from ripeness."

"Nevertheless," replied the Squire of the Wood, "fight we must, if only for half an hour."

"No," Sancho insisted, "that I will not do. I will not be so impolite or so ungrateful as to pick any quarrel however slight with one whose food and drink I've shared. And, moreover, who in the devil could bring himself to fight in cold blood, when he's not angry or vexed in any way?"

"I can take care of that, right enough," said the one of the Wood. "Before we begin, I will come up to your Grace as nicely as you please and give you three or four punches that will stretch you out at my feet; and that will surely be enough to awaken your anger, even though it's sleeping sounder than a dormouse."

"And I," said Sancho, "have another idea that's every bit as good as yours. I will take a big club, and before your Grace has had a chance to awaken my anger I will put yours to sleep with such mighty whacks that if it wakes at all it will be in the other world; for it is known there that I am not the man to let my face be mussed by anyone, and let each look out for the arrow.[4] But the best thing to do would be to leave one's anger to its slumbers, for no one knows the heart of any other, he who comes for wool may go back shorn, and God bless peace and curse all strife. If a hunted cat when surrounded and cornered turns into a lion, God knows what I who am a man might not become. And so from this time forth I am warning you, Sir Squire, that all the harm and damage that may result from our quarrel will be upon your head."

"Very well," the one of the Wood replied, "God will send the dawn and we shall make out somehow."

At that moment gay-colored birds of all sorts began warbling in the trees and with their merry and varied songs appeared to be greeting and welcoming the fresh-dawning day, which already at the gates and on the balconies of the east was revealing its beautiful face as it shook out from its hair an infinite number of liquid pearls. Bathed in this gentle moisture, the grass seemed to shed a pearly spray, the willows distilled a savory manna, the fountains laughed, the brooks murmured, the woods were glad, and the meadows put on their finest raiment. The first thing that Sancho Panza beheld, as soon as it was light enough to tell one object from another, was

---

4. A proverbial expression from archery: let each one take care of his or her own arrow. Other obviously proverbial expressions follow, as is typical of Sancho's speech.

the Squire of the Wood's nose, which was so big as to cast into the shade all the rest of his body. In addition to being of enormous size, it is said to have been hooked in the middle and all covered with warts of a mulberry hue, like eggplant; it hung down for a couple of inches below his mouth, and the size, color, warts, and shape of this organ gave his face so ugly an appearance that Sancho began trembling hand and foot like a child with convulsions and made up his mind then and there that he would take a couple of hundred punches before he would let his anger be awakened to a point where he would fight with this monster.

Don Quixote in the meanwhile was surveying his opponent, who had already adjusted and closed his helmet so that it was impossible to make out what he looked like. It was apparent, however, that he was not very tall and was stockily built. Over his armor he wore a coat of some kind or other made of what appeared to be the finest cloth of gold, all bespangled with glittering mirrors that resembled little moons and that gave him a most gallant and festive air, while above his helmet were a large number of waving plumes, green, white, and yellow in color. His lance, which was leaning against a tree, was very long and stout and had a steel point of more than a palm in length. Don Quixote took all this in, and from what he observed concluded that his opponent must be of tremendous strength, but he was not for this reason filled with fear as Sancho Panza was. Rather, he proceeded to address the Knight of the Mirrors, quite boldly and in a highbred manner.

"Sir Knight," he said, "if in your eagerness to fight you have not lost your courtesy, I would beg you to be so good as to raise your visor a little in order that I may see if your face is as handsome as your trappings."

"Whether you come out of this emprise the victor or the vanquished, Sir Knight," he of the Mirrors replied, "there will be ample time and opportunity for you to have a sight of me. If I do not now gratify your desire, it is because it seems to me that I should be doing a very great wrong to the beauteous Casildea de Vandalia by wasting the time it would take me to raise my visor before having forced you to confess that I am right in my contention, with which you are well acquainted."

"Well, then," said Don Quixote, "while we are mounting our steeds you might at least inform me if I am that knight of La Mancha whom you say you conquered."

"To that our[5] answer," said he of the Mirrors, "is that you are as like the knight I overcame as one egg is like another; but since you assert that you are persecuted by enchanters, I should not venture to state positively that you are the one in question."

"All of which," said Don Quixote, "is sufficient to convince me that you are laboring under a misapprehension; but in order to relieve you of it once and for all, let them bring our steeds, and in less time than you would spend in lifting your visor, if God, my lady, and my arm give me strength, I will see your face and you shall see that I am not the vanquished knight you take me to be."

With this, they cut short their conversation and mounted, and, turning Rocinante around, Don Quixote began measuring off the proper length of

5. Note the dignified, "majestic" plural form.

field for a run against his opponent as he of the Mirrors did the same. But the Knight of La Mancha had not gone twenty paces when he heard his adversary calling to him, whereupon each of them turned halfway and he of the Mirrors spoke.

"I must remind you, Sir Knight," he said, "of the condition under which we fight, which is that the vanquished, as I have said before, shall place himself wholly at the disposition of the victor."

"I am aware of that," replied Don Quixote, "not forgetting the provision that the behest laid upon the vanquished shall not exceed the bounds of chivalry."

"Agreed," said the Knight of the Mirrors.

At that moment Don Quixote caught sight of the other squire's weird nose and was as greatly astonished by it as Sancho had been. Indeed, he took the fellow for some monster, or some new kind of human being wholly unlike those that people this world. As he saw his master riding away down the field preparatory to the tilt, Sancho was alarmed; for he did not like to be left alone with the big-nosed individual, fearing that one powerful swipe of that protuberance against his own nose would end the battle so far as he was concerned and he would be lying stretched out on the ground, from fear if not from the force of the blow.

He accordingly ran after the knight, clinging to one of Rocinante's stirrup straps, and when he thought it was time for Don Quixote to whirl about and bear down upon his opponent, he called to him and said, "Señor mio, I beg your Grace, before you turn for the charge, to help me up into that cork tree yonder where I can watch the encounter which your Grace is going to have with this knight better than I can from the ground and in a way that is much more to my liking."

"I rather think, Sancho," said Don Quixote, "that what you wish to do is to mount a platform where you can see the bulls without any danger to yourself."

"The truth of the matter is," Sancho admitted, "the monstrous nose on that squire has given me such a fright that I don't dare stay near him."

"It is indeed of such a sort," his master assured him, "that if I were not the person I am, I myself should be frightened. And so, come, I will help you up."

While Don Quixote tarried to see Sancho ensconced in the cork tree, the Knight of the Mirrors measured as much ground as seemed to him necessary and then, assuming that his adversary had done the same, without waiting for sound of trumpet or any other signal, he wheeled his horse, which was no swifter nor any more impressive-looking than Rocinante, and bore down upon his enemy at a mild trot; but when he saw that the Manchegan was busy helping his squire, he reined in his mount and came to a stop midway in his course, for which his horse was extremely grateful, being no longer able to stir a single step. To Don Quixote, on the other hand, it seemed as if his enemy was flying, and digging his spurs with all his might into Rocinante's lean flanks he caused that animal to run a bit for the first and only time, according to the history, for on all other occasions a simple trot had represented his utmost speed. And so it was that, with an unheard-of-fury, the Knight of the Mournful Countenance came down upon the Knight of the Mirrors as the latter sat there sinking his spurs all the way up to the buttons without being able to persuade his horse to budge a single inch from the spot where he had come to a sudden standstill.

It was at this fortunate moment, while his adversary was in such a predicament, that Don Quixote fell upon him, quite unmindful of the fact that the other knight was having trouble with his mount and either was unable or did not have time to put his lance at rest. The upshot of it was, he encountered him with such force that, much against his will, the Knight of the Mirrors went rolling over his horse's flanks and tumbled to the ground, where as a result of his terrific fall he lay as if dead, without moving hand or foot.

No sooner did Sancho perceive what had happened than he slipped down from the cork tree and ran up as fast as he could to where his master was. Dismounting from Rocinante, Don Quixote now stood over the Knight of the Mirrors, and undoing the helmet straps to see if the man was dead, or to give him air in case he was alive, he beheld—who can say what he beheld without creating astonishment, wonder, and amazement in those who hear the tale? The history tells us that it was the very countenance, form, aspect, physiognomy, effigy, and image of the bachelor Sansón Carrasco!

"Come, Sancho," he cried in a loud voice, "and see what is to be seen but is not to be believed. Hasten, my son, and learn what magic can do and how great is the power of wizards and enchanters."

Sancho came, and the moment his eyes fell on the bachelor Carrasco's face he began crossing and blessing himself a countless number of times. Meanwhile, the overthrown knight gave no signs of life.

"If you ask me, master," said Sancho, "I would say that the best thing for your Grace to do is to run his sword down the mouth of this one who appears to be the bachelor Carrasco; maybe by so doing you would be killing one of your enemies, the enchanters."

"That is not a bad idea," replied Don Quixote, "for the fewer enemies the better." And, drawing his sword, he was about to act upon Sancho's advice and counsel when the Knight of the Mirrors' squire came up to them, now minus the nose which had made him so ugly.

"Look well what you are doing, Don Quixote!" he cried. "The one who lies there at your feet is your Grace's friend, the bachelor Sansón Carrasco, and I am his squire."

"And where is your nose?" inquired Sancho, who was surprised to see him without that deformity.

"Here in my pocket," was the reply. And, thrusting his hand into his coat, he drew out a nose of varnished pasteboard of the make that has been described. Studying him more and more closely, Sancho finally exclaimed, in a voice that was filled with amazement, "Holy Mary preserve me! And is this not my neighbor and crony, Tomé Cecial?"

"That is who I am!" replied the de-nosed squire, "your good friend Tomé Cecial, Sancho Panza. I will tell you presently of the means and snares and falsehoods that brought me here. But, for the present, I beg and entreat your master not to lay hands on, mistreat, wound, or slay the Knight of the Mirrors whom he now has at his feet; for without any doubt it is the rash and ill-advised bachelor Sansón Carrasco, our fellow villager."

The Knight of the Mirrors now recovered consciousness, and, seeing this, Don Quixote at once placed the naked point of his sword above the face of the vanquished one.

"Dead you are, knight," he said, "unless you confess that the peerless Dulcinea del Toboso is more beautiful than your Casildea de Vandalia. And what is more, you will have to promise that, should you survive this encounter and the fall you have had, you will go to the city of El Toboso and present yourself to her in my behalf, that she may do with you as she may see fit. And in case she leaves you free to follow your own will, you are to return to seek me out—the trail of my exploits will serve as a guide to bring you wherever I may be—and tell me all that has taken place between you and her. These conditions are in conformity with those that we arranged before our combat and they do not go beyond the bounds of knight-errantry."

"I confess," said the fallen knight, "that the tattered and filthy shoe of the lady Dulcinea del Toboso is of greater worth than the badly combed if clean beard of Casildea, and I promise to go to her presence and return to yours and to give you a complete and detailed account concerning anything you may wish to know."

"Another thing," added Don Quixote, "that you will have to confess and believe is that the knight you conquered was not and could not have been Don Quixote de la Mancha, but was some other that resembled him, just as I am convinced that you, though you appear to be the bachelor Sansón Carrasco, are another person in his form and likeness who has been put here by my enemies to induce me to restrain and moderate the impetuosity of my wrath and make a gentle use of my glorious victory."

"I confess, think, and feel as you feel, think, and believe," replied the lamed knight. "Permit me to rise, I beg of you, if the jolt I received in my fall will let me do so, for I am in very bad shape."

Don Quixote and Tomé Cecial the squire now helped him to his feet. As for Sancho, he could not take his eyes off Tomé but kept asking him one question after another, and although the answers he received afforded clear enough proof that the man was really his fellow townsman, the fear that had been aroused in him by his master's words—about the enchanters' having transformed the Knight of the Mirrors into the bachelor Sansón Carrasco—prevented him from believing the truth that was apparent to his eyes. The short of it is, both master and servant were left with this delusion as the other ill-errant knight and his squire, in no pleasant state of mind, took their departure with the object of looking for some village where they might be able to apply poultices and splints to the bachelor's battered ribs.

Don Quixote and Sancho then resumed their journey along the road to Saragossa, and here for the time being the history leaves them in order to give an account of who the Knight of the Mirrors and his long-nosed squire really were.

CHAPTER 15

*Wherein is told and revealed who the Knight of the Mirrors
and his squire were.*

Don Quixote went off very happy, self-satisfied, and vainglorious at having achieved a victory over so valiant a knight as he imagined the one of the Mirrors to be, from whose knightly word he hoped to learn whether or not the spell which had been put upon his lady was still in effect; for, unless he chose to forfeit his honor, the vanquished contender must of necessity return and give an account of what had happened in the course of his inter-view with her. But Don Quixote was of one mind, the Knight of the Mirrors of another, for, as has been stated, the latter's only thought at the moment was to find some village where plasters were available.

The history goes on to state that when the bachelor Sansón Carrasco advised Don Quixote to resume his feats of chivalry, after having desisted from them for a while, this action was taken as the result of a conference which he had held with the curate and the barber as to the means to be adopted in persuading the knight to remain quietly at home and cease agi-tating himself over his unfortunate adventures. It had been Carrasco's suggestion, to which they had unanimously agreed, that they let Don Quixote sally forth, since it appeared to be impossible to prevent his doing so, and that Sansón should then take to the road as a knight-errant and pick a quarrel and do battle with him. There would be no difficulty about finding a pretext, and then the bachelor knight would overcome him (which was looked upon as easy of accomplishment), having first entered into a pact to the effect that the vanquished should remain at the mercy and bidding of his conqueror. The behest in this case was to be that the fallen one should return to his village and home and not leave it for the space of two years or until further orders were given him, it being a cer-tainty that, once having been overcome, Don Quixote would fulfill the agreement, in order not to contravene or fail to obey the laws of chivalry. And it was possible that in the course of his seclusion he would forget his fancies, or they would at least have an opportunity to seek some suitable cure for his madness.

Sansón agreed to undertake this, and Tomé Cecial, Sancho's friend and neighbor, a merry but featherbrained chap, offered to go along as squire. Sansón then proceeded to arm himself in the manner that has been described, while Tomé disguised his nose with the aforementioned mask so that his crony would not recognize him when they met. Thus equipped, they followed the same route as Don Quixote and had almost caught up with him by the time he had the adventure with the Cart of Death. They finally over-took him in the wood, where those events occurred with which the attentive reader is already familiar; and if it had not been for the knight's extraordi-nary fancies, which led him to believe that the bachelor was not the bache-lor, the said bachelor might have been prevented from ever attaining his degree of licentiate, as a result of having found no nests where he thought to find birds.

Seeing how ill they had succeeded in their undertaking and what an end they had reached, Tomé Cecial now addressed his master.

"Surely, Señor Sansón Carrasco," he said, "we have had our deserts. It is easy enough to plan and embark upon an enterprise, but most of the time it's hard to get out of it. Don Quixote is a madman and we are sane, yet he goes away sound and laughing while your Grace is left here, battered and sorrowful. I wish you would tell me now who is the crazier: the one who is so because he cannot help it, or he who turns crazy of his own free will?"

"The difference between the two," replied Sansón, "lies in this: that the one who cannot help being crazy will be so always, whereas the one who is a madman by choice can leave off being one whenever he so desires."

"Well," said Tomé Cecial, "since that is the way it is, and since I chose to be crazy when I became your Grace's squire, by the same reasoning I now choose to stop being insane and to return to my home."

"That is your affair," said Sansón, "but to imagine that I am going back before I have given Don Quixote a good thrashing is senseless; and what will urge me on now is not any desire to see him recover his wits, but rather a thirst for vengeance; for with the terrible pain that I have in my ribs, you can't expect me to feel very charitable."

Conversing in this manner they kept on until they reached a village where it was their luck to find a bonesetter to take care of poor Sansón. Tomé Cecial then left him and returned home, while the bachelor meditated plans for revenge. The history has more to say of him in due time, but for the present it goes on to make merry with Don Quixote.

CHAPTER 16

Of what happened to Don Quixote upon his meeting with a
prudent gentleman of La Mancha.

With that feeling of happiness and vainglorious self-satisfaction that has been mentioned, Don Quixote continued on his way, imagining himself to be, as a result of the victory he had just achieved, the most valiant knight-errant of the age. Whatever adventures might befall him from then on he regarded as already accomplished and brought to a fortunate conclusion. He thought little now of enchanters and enchantments and was unmindful of the innumerable beatings he had received in the course of his knightly wanderings, of the volley of pebbles that had knocked out half his teeth, of the ungratefulness of the galley slaves and the audacity of the Yanguesans whose poles had fallen upon his body like rain. In short, he told himself, if he could but find the means, manner, or way of freeing his lady Dulcinea of the spell that had been put upon her, he would not envy the greatest good fortune that the most fortunate of knights-errant in ages past had ever by any possibility attained.

He was still wholly wrapped up in these thoughts when Sancho spoke to him.

"Isn't it strange, sir, that I can still see in front of my eyes the huge and monstrous nose of my old crony, Tomé Cecial?"

"And do you by any chance believe, Sancho, that the Knight of the Mirrors was the bachelor Sansón Carrasco and that his squire was your friend Tomé?"

"I don't know what to say to that," replied Sancho. "All I know is that the things he told me about my home, my wife and young ones, could not have come from anybody else; and the face, too, once you took the nose away, was the same as Tomé Cecial's, which I have seen many times in our village, right next door to my own house, and the tone of voice was the same also."

"Let us reason the matter out, Sancho," said Don Quixote. "Look at it this way: how can it be thought that the bachelor Sansón Carrasco would come as a knight-errant, equipped with offensive and defensive armor, to contend with me? Am I, perchance, his enemy? Have I given him any occasion to cherish a grudge against me? Am I a rival of his? Or can it be jealousy of the fame I have acquired that has led him to take up the profession of arms?"

"Well, then, sir," Sancho answered him, "how are we to explain the fact that the knight was so like the bachelor and his squire like my friend? And if this was a magic spell, as your Grace has said, was there no other pair in the world whose likeness they might have taken?"

"It is all a scheme and a plot," replied Don Quixote, "on the part of those wicked magicians who are persecuting me and who, foreseeing that I would be the victor in the combat, saw to it that the conquered knight should display the face of my friend the bachelor, so that the affection which I bear him would come between my fallen enemy and the edge of my sword and might of my arm, to temper the righteous indignation of my heart. In that way, he who had sought by falsehood and deceits to take my life, would be left to go on living. As proof of all this, Sancho, experience, which neither lies nor deceives, has already taught you how easy it is for enchanters to change one countenance into another, making the beautiful ugly and the ugly beautiful. It was not two days ago that you beheld the peerless Dulcinea's beauty and elegance in its entirety and natural form, while I saw only the repulsive features of a low and ignorant peasant girl with cataracts over her eyes and a foul smell in her mouth. And if the perverse enchanter was bold enough to effect so vile a transformation as this, there is certainly no cause for wonderment at what he has done in the case of Sansón Carrasco and your friend, all by way of snatching my glorious victory out of my hands. But in spite of it all, I find consolation in the fact that, whatever the shape he may have chosen to assume, I have laid my enemy low."

"God knows what the truth of it all may be," was Sancho's comment. Knowing as he did that Dulcinea's transformation had been due to his own scheming and plotting, he was not taken in by his master's delusions. He was at a loss for a reply, however, lest he say something that would reveal his own trickery.

As they were carrying on this conversation, they were overtaken by a man who, following the same road, was coming along behind them. He was mounted on a handsome flea-bitten mare and wore a hooded greatcoat of fine green cloth trimmed in tawny velvet and a cap of the same material, while the trappings of his steed, which was accoutered for the field, were green and mulberry in hue, his saddle being of the *jineta*[6] mode. From his broad green and gold shoulder strap there dangled a Moorish cutlass, and his half-boots were of the same make as the baldric. His spurs were not gilded but were covered with highly polished green lacquer, so that harmonizing as they did with the rest of his apparel, they seemed more appropriate than if they had been of purest gold. As he came up, he greeted the pair courteously and, spurring his mare, was about to ride on past when Don Quixote called to him.

"Gallant sir," he said, "If your Grace is going our way and is not in a hurry, it would be a favor to us if we might travel together."

"The truth is," replied the stranger, "I should not have ridden past you if I had not been afraid that the company of my mare would excite your horse."

"In that case, sir," Sancho spoke up, "you may as well rein in, for this horse of ours is the most virtuous and well mannered of any that there is. Never on such an occasion has he done anything that was not right—the only time he

6. It has a high pommel and short stirrups.

did misbehave, my master and I suffered for it aplenty. And so, I say again, your Grace may slow up if you like; for even if you offered him your mare on a couple of platters, he'd never try to mount her."

With this, the other traveler drew rein, being greatly astonished at Don Quixote's face and figure. For the knight was now riding along without his helmet, which was carried by Sancho like a piece of luggage on the back of his gray, in front of the packsaddle. If the green-clad gentleman stared hard at his new-found companion, the latter returned his gaze with an even greater intensity. He impressed Don Quixote as being a man of good judgment, around fifty years of age, with hair that was slightly graying and an aquiline nose, while the expression of his countenance was half humorous, half serious. In short, both his person and his accouterments indicated that he was an individual of some worth.

As for the man in green's impression of Don Quixote de la Mancha, he was thinking that he had never before seen any human being that resembled this one. He could not but marvel at the knight's long neck, his tall frame, and the leanness and the sallowness of his face, as well as his armor and his grave bearing, the whole constituting a sight such as had not been seen for many a day in those parts. Don Quixote in turn was quite conscious of the attentiveness with which the traveler was studying him and could tell from the man's astonished look how curious he was; and so, being very courteous and fond of pleasing everyone, he proceeded to anticipate any questions that might be asked him.

"I am aware," he said, "that my appearance must strike your Grace as being very strange and out of the ordinary, and for that reason I am not surprised at your wonderment. But your Grace will cease to wonder when I tell you, as I am telling you now, that I am a knight, one of those

> Of whom it is folks say,
> They to adventures go.

I have left my native health, mortgaged my estate, given up my comfortable life, and cast myself into fortune's arms for her to do with me what she will. It has been my desire to revive a knight-errantry that is now dead, and for some time past, stumbling here and falling there, now throwing myself down headlong and then rising up once more, I have been able in good part to carry out my design by succoring widows, protecting damsels, and aiding the fallen, the orphans, and the young, all of which is the proper and natural duty of knights-errant. As a result, owing to my many valiant and Christian exploits, I have been deemed worthy of visiting in printed form nearly all the nations of the world. Thirty thousand copies of my history have been published, and, unless Heaven forbid, they will print thirty million of them.

"In short, to put it all into a few words, or even one, I will tell you that I am Don Quixote de la Mancha, otherwise known as the Knight of the Mournful Countenance. Granted that self-praise is degrading, there still are times when I must praise myself, that is to say, when there is no one else present to speak in my behalf. And so, good sir, neither this steed nor this lance nor this buckler nor this squire of mine, nor all the armor that I wear and arms I carry, nor the sallowness of my complexion, nor my leanness and gauntness, should any longer astonish you, now that you know who I am and what the profession is that I follow."

Having thus spoken, Don Quixote fell silent, and the man in green was so slow in replying that it seemed as if he was at a loss for words. Finally, however, after a considerable while, he brought himself to the point of speaking.

"You were correct, Sir Knight," he said, "about my astonishment and my curiosity, but you have not succeeded in removing the wonderment that the sight of you has aroused in me. You say that, knowing who you are, I should not wonder any more, but such is not the case, for I am now more amazed than ever. How can it be that there are knights-errant in the world today and that histories of them are actually printed? I find it hard to convince myself that at the present time there is anyone on earth who goes about aiding widows, protecting damsels, defending the honor of wives, and succoring orphans, and I should never have believed it had I not beheld your Grace with my own eyes. Thank Heaven for that book that your Grace tells me has been published concerning your true and exalted deeds of chivalry, as it should cast into oblivion all the innumerable stories of fictitious knights-errant with which the world is filled, greatly to the detriment of good morals and the prejudice and discredit of legitimate histories."

"As to whether the stories of knights-errant are fictitious or not," observed Don Quixote, "there is much that remains to be said."

"Why," replied the gentleman in green, "is there anyone who can doubt that such tales are false?"

"I doubt it," was the knight's answer, "but let the matter rest there. If our journey lasts long enough, I trust with God's help to be able to show your Grace that you are wrong in going along with those who hold it to be a certainty that they are not true."

From this last remark the traveler was led to suspect that Don Quixote must be some kind of crackbrain, and he was waiting for him to confirm the impression by further observations of the same sort; but before they could get off on another subject, the knight, seeing that he had given an account of his own station in life, turned to the stranger and politely inquired who his companion might be.

"I, Sir Knight of the Mournful Countenance," replied the one in the green-colored greatcoat, "am a gentleman, and a native of the village where, please God, we are going to dine today. I am more than moderately rich, and my name is Don Diego de Miranda. I spend my life with my wife and children and with my friends. My occupations are hunting and fishing, though I keep neither falcon nor hounds but only a tame partridge[7] and a bold ferret or two. I am the owner of about six dozen books, some of them in Spanish, others in Latin, including both histories and devotional works. As for books of chivalry, they have not as yet crossed the threshold of my door. My own preference is for profane rather than devotional writings, such as afford an innocent amusement, charming us by their style and arousing and holding our interest by their inventiveness, although I must say there are very few of that sort to be found in Spain.

"Sometimes," the man in green continued, "I dine with my friends and neighbors, and I often invite them to my house. My meals are wholesome and well prepared and there is always plenty to eat. I do not care for gossip,

7. Used as a decoy.

nor will I permit it in my presence. I am not lynx-eyed and do not pry into the lives and doings of others. I hear mass every day and share my substance with the poor, but make no parade of my good works lest hypocrisy and vainglory, those enemies that so imperceptibly take possession of the most modest heart, should find their way into mine. I try to make peace between those who are at strife. I am the devoted servant of Our Lady, and my trust is in the infinite mercy of God Our Savior."

Sancho had listened most attentively to the gentleman's account of his mode of life, and inasmuch as it seemed to him that this was a good and holy way to live and that the one who followed such a pattern ought to be able to work miracles, he now jumped down from his gray's back and, running over to seize the stranger's right stirrup, began kissing the feet of the man in green with a show of devotion that bordered on tears.

"Why are you doing that, brother?" the gentleman asked him. "What is the meaning of these kisses?"

"Let me kiss your feet," Sancho insisted, "for if I am not mistaken, your Grace is the first saint riding *jineta* fashion that I have seen in all the days of my life."

"I am not a saint," the gentleman assured him, "but a great sinner. It is you, brother, who are the saint; for you must be a good man, judging by the simplicity of heart that you show."

Sancho then went back to his packsaddle, having evoked a laugh from the depths of his master's melancholy and given Don Diego fresh cause for astonishment.

Don Quixote thereupon inquired of the newcomer how many children he had, remarking as he did so that the ancient philosophers, who were without a true knowledge of God, believed that mankind's greatest good lay in the gifts of nature, in those of fortune, and in having many friends and many and worthy sons.

"I, Señor Don Quixote," replied the gentleman, "have a son without whom I should, perhaps, be happier than I am. It is not that he is bad, but rather that he is not as good as I should like him to be. He is eighteen years old, and for six of those years he has been at Salamanca studying the Greek and Latin languages. When I desired him to pass on to other branches of learning, I found him so immersed in the science of Poetry (if it can be called such) that it was not possible to interest him in the Law, which I wanted him to study, nor in Theology, the queen of them all. My wish was that he might be an honor to his family; for in this age in which we are living our monarchs are in the habit of highly rewarding those forms of learning that are good and virtuous, since learning without virtue is like pearls on a dunghill. But he spends the whole day trying to decide whether such and such a verse of Homer's *Iliad* is well conceived or not, whether or not Martial is immodest in a certain epigram, whether certain lines of Vergil are to be understood in this way or in that. In short, he spends all of his time with the books written by those poets whom I have mentioned and with those of Horace, Persius, Juvenal, and Tibullus. As for our own moderns, he sets little store by them, and yet, for all his disdain of Spanish poetry, he is at this moment racking his brains in an effort to compose a gloss on a quatrain that was sent him from Salamanca and which, I fancy, is for some literary tournament."

To all this Don Quixote made the following answer:

"Children, sir, are out of their parents' bowels and so are to be loved whether they be good or bad, just as we love those that gave us life. It is for parents to bring up their offspring, from the time they are infants, in the paths of virtue, good breeding, proper conduct, and Christian morality, in order that, when they are grown, they may be a staff to the old age of the ones that bore them and an honor to their own posterity. As to compelling them to study a particular branch of learning, I am not so sure as to that, though there may be no harm in trying to persuade them to do so. But where there is no need to study *pane lucrando*[8]—where Heaven has provided them with parents that can supply their daily bread—I should be in favor of permitting them to follow that course to which they are most inclined; and although poetry may be more pleasurable than useful, it is not one of those pursuits that bring dishonor upon those who engage in them.

"Poetry in my opinion, my dear sir," he went on, "is a young and tender maid of surpassing beauty, who has many other damsels (that is to say, the other disciplines) whose duty it is to bedeck, embellish, and adorn her. She may call upon all of them for service, and all of them in turn depend upon her nod. She is not one to be rudely handled, nor dragged through the streets, nor exposed at street corners, in the market place, or in the private nooks of palaces. She is fashioned through an alchemy of such power that he who knows how to make use of it will be able to convert her into the purest gold of inestimable price. Possessing her, he must keep her within bounds and not permit her to run wild in bawdy satires or soulless sonnets. She is not to be put up for sale in any manner, unless it be in the form of heroic poems, pity-inspiring tragedies, or pleasing and ingenious comedies. Let mountebanks keep hands off her, and the ignorant mob as well, which is incapable of recognizing or appreciating the treasures that are locked within her. And do not think, sir, that I apply that term 'mob' solely to plebeians and those of low estate; for anyone who is ignorant, whether he be lord or prince, may, and should, be included in the vulgar herd.

"But," Don Quixote continued, "he who possesses the gift of poetry and who makes the use of it that I have indicated, shall become famous and his name shall be honored among all the civilized nations of the world. You have stated, sir, that your son does not greatly care for poetry written in our Spanish tongue, and in that I am inclined to think he is somewhat mistaken. My reason for saying so is this: the great Homer did not write in Latin, for the reason that he was a Greek, and Vergil did not write in Greek since he was a Latin. In a word, all the poets of antiquity wrote in the language which they had imbibed with their mother's milk and did not go searching after foreign ones to express their loftiest conceptions. This being so, it would be well if the same custom were to be adopted by all nations, the German poet being no longer looked down upon because he writes in German, nor the Castilian or the Basque for employing his native speech.

"As for your son, I fancy, sir, that his quarrel is not so much with Spanish poetry as with those poets who have no other tongue or discipline at their command such as would help to awaken their natural gift; and yet, here, too, he may be wrong. There is an opinion, and a true one, to the effect that

8. Earning one's bread (Latin).

'the poet is born,' that is to say, it is as a poet that he comes forth from his mother's womb, and with the propensity that has been bestowed upon him by Heaven, without study or artifice, he produces those compositions that attest the truth of the line: '*Est deus in nobis,*'[9] etc. I further maintain that the born poet who is aided by art will have a great advantage over the one who by art alone would become a poet, the reason being that art does not go beyond, but merely perfects, nature; and so it is that, by combining nature with art and art with nature, the finished poet is produced.

"In conclusion, then, my dear sir, my advice to you would be to let your son go where his star beckons him; for being a good student as he must be, and having already successfully mounted the first step on the stairway of learning, which is that of languages, he will be able to continue of his own accord to the very peak of humane letters, an accomplishment that is altogether becoming in a gentleman, one that adorns, honors, and distinguishes him as much as the miter does the bishop or his flowing robe the learned jurisconsult. Your Grace well may reprove your son, should he compose satires that reflect upon the honor of other persons; in that case, punish him and tear them up. But should he compose discourses in the manner of Horace, in which he reprehends vice in general as that poet so elegantly does, then praise him by all means; for it is permitted the poet to write verses in which he inveighs against envy and the other vices as well, and to lash out at the vicious without, however, designating any particular individual. On the other hand, there are poets who for the sake of uttering something malicious would run the risk of being banished to the shores of Pontus.[1]

"If the poet be chaste where his own manners are concerned, he would likewise be modest in his verses, for the pen is the tongue of the mind, and whatever thoughts are engendered there are bound to appear in his writings. When kings and princes behold the marvelous art of poetry as practiced by prudent, virtuous, and serious-minded subjects of their realm, they honor, esteem, and reward those persons and crown them with the leaves of the tree that is never struck by lightning[2]—as if to show that those who are crowned and adorned with such wreaths are not to be assailed by anyone."

The gentleman in the green-colored greatcoat was vastly astonished by this speech of Don Quixote's and was rapidly altering the opinion he had previously held, to the effect that his companion was but a crackbrain. In the middle of the long discourse, which was not greatly to his liking, Sancho had left the highway to go seek a little milk from some shepherds who were draining the udders of their ewes near by. Extremely well pleased with the knight's sound sense and excellent reasoning, the gentleman was about to resume the conversation when, raising his head, Don Quixote caught sight of a cart flying royal flags that was coming toward them down the road and, thinking it must be a fresh adventure, began calling to Sancho in a loud voice to bring him his helmet. Whereupon Sancho hastily left the shepherds and spurred his gray until he was once more alongside his master, who was now about to encounter a dreadful and bewildering ordeal.

---

9. There is a god in us (Latin); Ovid's *Fasti* 6.5.   1. As Ovid was by Augustus in 8 C.E.   2. The laurel.

["For Well I Know the Meaning of Valor"]

CHAPTER 17

Wherein Don Quixote's unimaginable courage reaches its highest point, together with the adventure of the lions and its happy ending.

The history relates that, when Don Quixote called to Sancho to bring him his helmet, the squire was busy buying some curds from the shepherds and, flustered by his master's great haste, did not know what to do with them or how to carry them. Having already paid for the curds, he did not care to lose them, and so he decided to put them into the headpiece, and, acting upon this happy inspiration, he returned to see what was wanted of him.

"Give me that helmet," said the knight; "for either I know little about adventures or here is one where I am going to need my armor."

Upon hearing this, the gentleman in the green-colored greatcoat looked around in all directions but could see nothing except the cart that was approaching them, decked out with two or three flags which indicated that the vehicle in question must be conveying his Majesty's property. He remarked as much to Don Quixote, but the latter paid no attention, for he was always convinced that whatever happened to him meant adventures and more adventures.

"Forewarned is forearmed," he said. "I lose nothing by being prepared, knowing as I do that I have enemies both visible and invisible and cannot tell when or where or in what form they will attack me."

Turning to Sancho, he asked for his helmet again, and as there was no time to shake out the curds, the squire had to hand it to him as it was. Don Quixote took it and, without noticing what was in it, hastily clapped it on his head; and forthwith, as a result of the pressure on the curds, the whey began running down all over his face and beard, at which he was very much startled.

"What is this, Sancho?" he cried. "I think my head must be softening or my brains melting, or else I am sweating from head to foot. If sweat it be, I assure you it is not from fear, though I can well believe that the adventure which now awaits me is a terrible one indeed. Give me something with which to wipe my face, if you have anything, for this perspiration is so abundant that it blinds me."

Sancho said nothing but gave him a cloth and at the same time gave thanks to God that his master had not discovered what the trouble was. Don Quixote wiped his face and then took off his helmet to see what it was that made his head feel so cool. Catching sight of that watery white mass, he lifted it to his nose and smelled it.

"By the life of my lady Dulcinea del Toboso!" he exclaimed. "Those are curds that you have put there, you treacherous, brazen, ill-mannered squire!"

To this Sancho replied, very calmly and with a straight face, "If they are curds, give them to me, your Grace, so that I can eat them. But no, let the devil eat them, for he must be the one who did it. Do you think I would be so bold as to soil your Grace's helmet? Upon my word, master, by the understanding that God has given me, I, too, must have enchanters who are persecuting me as your Grace's creature and one of his members, and they are the ones who put that filthy mess there to make you lose your patience and your temper and cause you to whack my ribs as you are in the habit of doing. Well, this time, I must say, they have missed the mark; for I trust my master's good sense to tell him that I have neither curds nor milk nor anything of the kind, and if I did have, I'd put it in my stomach and not in that helmet."

"That may very well be," said Don Quixote.

Don Diego was observing all this and was more astonished than ever, especially when, after he had wiped his head, face, beard, and helmet, Don Quixote once more donned the piece of armor and, settling himself in the stirrups, proceeded to adjust his sword and fix his lance.

"Come what may, here I stand, ready to take on Satan himself in person!" shouted the knight.

The cart with the flags had come up to them by this time, accompanied only by a driver riding one of the mules and a man seated up in front.

"Where are you going, brothers?" Don Quixote called out as he placed himself in the path of the cart. "What conveyance is this, what do you carry in it, and what is the meaning of those flags?"

"The cart is mine," replied the driver, "and in it are two fierce lions in cages which the governor of Oran is sending to court as a present for his Majesty. The flags are those of our lord the King, as a sign that his property goes here."

"And are the lions large?" inquired Don Quixote.

It was the man sitting at the door of the cage who answered him. "The largest," he said, "that ever were sent from Africa to Spain. I am the lion-keeper and I have brought back others, but never any like these. They are male and female. The male is in this first cage, the female in the one behind. They are hungry right now, for they have had nothing to eat today; and so we'd be obliged if your Grace would get out of the way, for we must hasten on to the place where we are to feed them."

"Lion whelps against me?" said Don Quixote with a slight smile. "Lion whelps against me? And at such an hour? Then, by God, those gentlemen who sent them shall see whether I am the man to be frightened by lions. Get down, my good fellow, and since you are the lionkeeper, open the cages and turn those beasts out for me; and in the middle of this plain I will teach them who Don Quixote de la Mancha is, notwithstanding and in spite of the enchanters who are responsible for their being here."

"So," said the gentleman to himself as he heard this, "our worthy knight has revealed himself. It must indeed be true that the curds have softened his skull and mellowed his brains."

At this point Sancho approached him. "For God's sake, sir," he said, "do something to keep my master from fighting those lions. For if he does, they're going to tear us all to bits."

"Is your master, then, so insane," the gentleman asked, "that you fear and believe he means to tackle those fierce animals?"

"It is not that he is insane," replied Sancho, "but, rather, foolhardy."

"Very well," said the gentleman, "I will put a stop to it." And going up to Don Quixote, who was still urging the lionkeeper to open the cages, he said, "Sir Knight, knights-errant should undertake only those adventures that afford some hope of a successful outcome, not those that are utterly hopeless to begin with; for valor when it turns to temerity has in it more of madness than of bravery. Moreover, these lions have no thought of attacking your Grace but are a present to his Majesty, and it would not be well to detain them or interfere with their journey."

"My dear sir," answered Don Quixote, "you had best go mind your tame partridge and that bold ferret of yours and let each one attend to his own business. This is my affair, and I know whether these gentlemen, the lions, have come to attack me or not." He then turned to the lionkeeper. "I swear, Sir Rascal, if you do not open those cages at once, I'll pin you to the cart with this lance!"

Perceiving how determined the armed phantom was, the driver now spoke up. "Good sir," he said, "will your Grace please be so kind as to let me unhitch the mules and take them to a safe place before you turn those lions loose? For if they kill them for me, I am ruined for life, since the mules and cart are all the property I own."

"O man of little faith!" said Don Quixote. "Get down and unhitch your mules if you like, but you will soon see that it was quite unnecessary and that you might have spared yourself the trouble."

The driver did so, in great haste, as the lionkeeper began shouting, "I want you all to witness that I am being compelled against my will to open the cages and turn the lions out, and I further warn this gentleman that he will be responsible for all the harm and damage the beasts may do, plus my wages and my fees. You other gentlemen take cover before I open the doors; I am sure they will not do any harm to me."

Once more Don Diego sought to persuade his companion not to commit such an act of madness, as it was tempting God to undertake anything so foolish as that; but Don Quixote's only answer was that he knew what he was doing. And when the gentleman in green insisted that he was sure the knight was laboring under a delusion and ought to consider the matter well, the latter cut him short.

"Well, then, sir," he said, "if your Grace does not care to be a spectator at what you believe is going to turn out to be a tragedy, all you have to do is to spur your flea-bitten mare and seek safety."

Hearing this, Sancho with tears in his eyes again begged him to give up the undertaking, in comparison with which the adventure of the windmills and the dreadful one at the fulling mills—indeed, all the exploits his master had ever in the course of his life undertaken—were but bread and cakes.

"Look, sir," Sancho went on, "there is no enchantment here nor anything of the sort. Through the bars and chinks of that cage I have seen a real lion's claw, and judging by the size of it, the lion that it belongs to is bigger than a mountain."

"Fear, at any rate," said Don Quixote, "will make him look bigger to you than half the world. Retire, Sancho, and leave me, and if I die here, you know our ancient pact: you are to repair to Dulcinea—I say no more."

To this he added other remarks that took away any hope they had that he might not go through with his insane plan. The gentleman in the green-colored greatcoat was of a mind to resist him but saw that he was no match for the knight in the matter of arms. Then, too, it did not seem to him the part of wisdom to fight it out with a madman; for Don Quixote now impressed him as being quite mad in every way. Accordingly, while the knight was repeating his threats to the lionkeeper, Don Diego spurred his mare, Sancho his gray, and the driver his mules, all of them seeking to put as great a distance as possible between themselves and the cart before the lions broke loose.

Sancho already was bewailing his master's death, which he was convinced was bound to come from the lions' claws, and at the same time he cursed his fate and called it an unlucky hour in which he had taken it into his head to serve such a one. But despite his tears and lamentations, he did not leave off thrashing his gray in an effort to leave the cart behind them. When the lionkeeper saw that those who had fled were a good distance away, he once more entreated and warned Don Quixote as he had warned and entreated him before, but the answer he received was that he might save his breath as it would do him no good and he had best hurry and obey. In the space of time that it took the keeper to open the first cage, Don Quixote considered the question as to whether it would be well to give battle on foot or on horseback. He finally decided that he would do better on foot, as he feared that Rocinante would become frightened at sight of the lions; and so, leaping down from his horse, he fixed his lance, braced his buckler, and drew his sword, and then advanced with marvelous daring and great resoluteness until he stood directly in front of the cart, meanwhile commending himself to God with all his heart and then to his lady Dulcinea.

Upon reaching this point, the reader should know, the author of our veracious history indulges in the following exclamatory passage:

"O great-souled Don Quixote de la Mancha, thou whose courage is beyond all praise, mirror wherein all the valiant of the world may behold themselves, a new and second Don Manuel de León,[3] once the glory and the honor of Spanish knighthood! With what words shall I relate thy terrifying exploit, how render it credible to the ages that are to come? What eulogies do not belong to thee of right, even though they consist of hyperbole piled upon hyperbole? On foot and singlehanded, intrepid and with greathearted valor, armed but with a sword, and not one of the keen-edged Little Dog[4] make, and with a shield that was not of gleaming and polished steel, thou didst stand and wait for the two fiercest lions that ever the African forests bred! Thy deeds shall be thy praise, O valorous Manchegan; I leave them to speak for thee, since words fail me with which to extol them."

Here the author leaves off his exclamations and resumes the thread of the story.

Seeing Don Quixote posed there before him and perceiving that, unless he wished to incur the bold knight's indignation there was nothing for him to do but release the male lion, the keeper now opened the first cage, and it could be seen at once how extraordinarily big and horribly ugly the beast was. The first thing the recumbent animal did was to turn round, put out a claw, and stretch himself all over. Then he opened his mouth and yawned very slowly, after which he put out a tongue that was nearly two palms in length and with it licked the dust out of his eyes and washed his face. Having

---

3. Don Manuel Ponce de León, a paragon of gallantry and courtesy, from the time of Ferdinand and Isabella.   4. The trademark of a famous armorer of Toledo and Saragossa.

done this, he stuck his head outside the cage and gazed about him in all directions. His eyes were now like live coals and his appearance and demeanor were such as to strike terror in temerity itself. But Don Quixote merely stared at him attentively, waiting for him to descend from the cart so that they could come to grips, for the knight was determined to hack the brute to pieces, such was the extent of his unheard-of madness.

The lion, however, proved to be courteous rather than arrogant and was in no mood for childish bravado. After having gazed first in one direction and then in another, as has been said, he turned his back and presented his hind parts to Don Quixote and then very calmly and peaceably lay down and stretched himself out once more in his cage. At this, Don Quixote ordered the keeper to stir him up with a stick in order to irritate him and drive him out.

"That I will not do," the keeper replied, "for if I stir him, I will be the first one he will tear to bits. Be satisfied with what you have already accomplished, Sir Knight, which leaves nothing more to be said on the score of valor, and do not go tempting your fortune a second time. The door was open and the lion could have gone out if he had chosen; since he has not done so up to now, that means he will stay where he is all day long. Your Grace's stoutheartedness has been well established; for no brave fighter, as I see it, is obliged to do more than challenge his enemy and wait for him in the field; his adversary, if he does not come, is the one who is disgraced and the one who awaits him gains the crown of victory."

"That is the truth," said Don Quixote. "Shut the door, my friend, and bear me witness as best you can with regard to what you have seen me do here. I would have you certify: that you opened the door for the lion, that I waited for him and he did not come out, that I continued to wait and still he stayed there, and finally went back and lay down. I am under no further obligation. Away with enchantments, and God uphold the right, the truth, and true chivalry! So close the door, as I have told you, while I signal to the fugitives in order that they who were not present may hear of this exploit from your lips."

The keeper did as he was commanded, and Don Quixote, taking the cloth with which he had dried his face after the rain of curds, fastened it to the point of his lance and began summoning the runaways, who, all in a body with the gentleman in green bringing up the rear, were still fleeing and turning around to look back at every step. Sancho was the first to see the white cloth.

"May they slay me," he said, "if my master hasn't conquered those fierce beasts, for he's calling to us."

They all stopped and made sure that the one who was doing the signaling was indeed Don Quixote, and then, losing some of their fear, they little by little made their way back to a point where they could distinctly hear what the knight was saying. At last they returned to the cart, and as they drew near Don Quixote spoke to the driver.

"You may come back, brother, hitch your mules, and continue your journey. And you, Sancho, may give each of them two gold crowns to recompense them for the delay they have suffered on my account."

"That I will, right enough," said Sancho. "But what has become of the lions? Are they dead or alive?"

The keeper thereupon, in leisurely fashion and in full detail, proceeded to tell them how the encounter had ended, taking pains to stress to the best of his ability the valor displayed by Don Quixote, at sight of whom the lion had been so cowed that he was unwilling to leave his cage, though the door had been left open quite a while. The fellow went on to state that the knight had wanted him to stir the lion up and force him out, but had finally been convinced that this would be tempting God and so, much to his displeasure and against his will, had permitted the door to be closed.

"What do you think of that, Sancho?" asked Don Quixote. "Are there any spells that can withstand true gallantry? The enchanters may take my luck away, but to deprive me of my strength and courage is an impossibility."

Sancho then bestowed the crowns, the driver hitched his mules, and the lionkeeper kissed Don Quixote's hands for the favor received, promising that, when he reached the court, he would relate this brave exploit to the king himself.

"In that case," replied Don Quixote, "if his Majesty by any chance should inquire who it was that performed it, you are to say that it was the Knight of the Lions; for that is the name by which I wish to be known from now on, thus changing, exchanging, altering, and converting the one I have previously borne, that of Knight of the Mournful Countenance; in which respect I am but following the old custom of knights-errant, who changed their names whenever they liked or found it convenient to do so."

With this, the cart continued on its way, and Don Quixote, Sancho, and the gentleman in the green-colored greatcoat likewise resumed their journey. During all this time Don Diego de Miranda had not uttered a word but was wholly taken up with observing what Don Quixote did and listening to what he had to say. The knight impressed him as being a crazy sane man and an insane one on the verge of sanity. The gentleman did not happen to be familiar with the first part of our history, but if he had read it he would have ceased to wonder at such talk and conduct, for he would then have known what kind of madness this was. Remaining as he did in ignorance of his companion's malady, he took him now for a sensible individual and now for a madman, since what Don Quixote said was coherent, elegantly phrased, and to the point, whereas his actions were nonsensical, foolhardy, and downright silly. What greater madness could there be, Don Diego asked himself, than to don a helmet filled with curds and then persuade oneself that enchanters were softening one's cranium? What could be more rashly absurd than to wish to fight lions by sheer strength alone? He was roused from these thoughts, this inward soliloquy, by the sound of Don Quixote's voice.

"Undoubtedly, Señor Don Diego de Miranda, your Grace must take me for a fool and a madman, am I not right? And it would be small wonder if such were the case, seeing that my deeds give evidence of nothing else. But, nevertheless, I would advise your Grace that I am neither so mad nor so lacking in wit as I must appear to you to be. A gaily caparisoned knight giving a fortunate lance thrust to a fierce bull in the middle of a great square makes a pleasing appearance in the eyes of his king. The same is true of a knight clad in shining armor as he paces the lists in front of the ladies in some joyous tournament. It is true of all those knights who, by means of military exercises or what appear to be such, divert and entertain and, if one may say so, honor the courts of princes. But the best showing of all is made by a knight-errant who, traversing deserts and solitudes, crossroads, forests, and mountains, goes seeking dangerous adventures with the intention of bringing them to a happy and successful conclusion, and solely for the purpose of winning a glorious and enduring renown.

"More impressive, I repeat, is the knight-errant succoring a widow in some unpopulated place than a courtly man of arms making love to a damsel in the city. All knights have their special callings: let the courtier wait upon the ladies and lend luster by his liveries to his sovereign's palace; let him nourish impoverished gentlemen with the splendid fare of his table; let him give tourneys and show himself truly great, generous, and magnificent and a good Christian above all, thus fulfilling his particular obligations. But the knight-errant's case is different.

"Let the latter seek out the nooks and corners of the world; let him enter into the most intricate of labyrinths; let him attempt the impossible at every step; let him endure on desolate highlands the burning rays of the midsummer sun and in winter the harsh inclemencies of wind and frost; let no lions inspire him with fear, no monsters frighten him, no dragons terrify him, for to seek them out, attack them, and conquer them all is his chief and legitimate occupation. Accordingly, I whose lot it is to be numbered among the knights-errant cannot fail to attempt anything that appears to me to fall within the scope of my duties, just as I attacked those lions a while ago even though I knew it to be an exceedingly rash thing to do, for that was a matter that directly concerned me.

"For I well know the meaning of valor: namely, a virtue that lies between the two extremes of cowardice on the one hand and temerity on the other. It is, nonetheless, better for the brave man to carry his bravery to the point of rashness than for him to sink into cowardice. Even as it is easier for the prodigal to become a generous man than it is for the miser, so is it easier for the foolhardy to become truly brave than it is for the coward to attain valor. And in this matter of adventures, you may believe me, Señor Don Diego, it is better to lose by a card too many than a card too few, and 'Such and such a knight is temerarious and overbold' sounds better to the ear than 'That knight is timid and a coward.'"

"I must assure you, Señor Don Quixote," replied Don Diego, "that everything your Grace has said and done will stand the test of reason; and it is my opinion that if the laws and ordinances of knight-errantry were to be lost, they would be found again in your Grace's bosom, which is their depository and storehouse. But it is growing late; let us hasten to my village and my home, where your Grace shall rest from your recent exertions; for if the body is not tired the spirit may be, and that sometimes results in bodily fatigue."

"I accept your offer as a great favor and an honor, Señor Don Diego," was the knight's reply. And, by spurring their mounts more than they had up to then, they arrived at the village around two in the afternoon and came to the house that was occupied by Don Diego, whom Don Quixote had dubbed the Knight of the Green-colored Greatcoat.

[*Last Duel*]

CHAPTER 64

Which treats of the adventure that caused Don Quixote the most sorrow of all those that have thus far befallen him.

* * * One morning, as Don Quixote went for a ride along the beach,[5] clad in full armor—for, as he was fond of saying, that was his only ornament, his only rest the fight, and, accordingly, he was never without it for a moment—he saw approaching him a horseman similarly arrayed from head to foot and with a brightly shining moon blazoned upon his shield.

As soon as he had come within earshot the stranger cried out to Don Quixote in a loud voice. "O illustrious knight, the never to be sufficiently praised Don Quixote de la Mancha, I am the Knight of the White Moon whose incomparable exploits you will perhaps recall. I come to contend with you and try the might of my arm, with the purpose of having you acknowledge and confess that my lady, whoever she may be, is beyond comparison more beautiful than your own Dulcinea del Toboso. If you will admit the truth of this fully and freely, you will escape death and I shall be spared the trouble of inflicting it upon you. On the other hand, if you choose to fight and I should overcome you, I ask no other satisfaction than that, laying down your arms and seeking no further adventures, you retire to your own village for the space of a year, during which time you are not to lay hand to sword but are to dwell peacefully and tranquilly, enjoying a beneficial rest that shall redound to the betterment of your worldly fortunes and the salvation of your soul. But if you are the victor, then my head shall be at your disposal, my arms and steed shall be the spoils, and the fame of my exploits shall go to increase your own renown. Consider well which is the better course and let me have your answer at once, for today is all the time I have for the dispatching of this business."

Don Quixote was amazed at the knight's arrogance as well as at the nature of the challenge, but it was with a calm and stern demeanor that he replied to him.

"Knight of the White Moon," he said, "of whose exploits up to now I have never heard, I will venture to take an oath that you have not once laid eyes upon the illustrious Dulcinea; for I am quite certain that if you had beheld her you would not be staking your all upon such an issue, since the sight of her would have convinced you that there never has been, and never can be, any beauty to compare with hers. I do not say that you lie, I simply say that you are mistaken; and so I accept your challenge with the conditions you have laid down, and at once, before this day you have fixed upon shall have ended. The only exception I make is with regard to the fame of your deeds being added to my renown, since I do not know what the character of your exploits has been and am quite content with my own, such as they are. Take, then, whichever side of the field you like, and I will take up my position, and may St. Peter bless what God may give."

---

5. Don Quixote and Sancho, after numberless encounters and experiences (of which the most prominent have been Don Quixote's descent into the cave of Montesinos and their residence at the castle of the playful ducal couple who give Sancho the "governorship of an island" for ten days), are now in Barcelona. Famous as they are, they meet the viceroy and the nobles; their host is Don Antonio Moreno, "a gentleman of wealth and discernment who was fond of amusing himself in an innocent and kindly way."

Now, as it happened, the Knight of the White Moon was seen by some of the townspeople, who informed the viceroy that he was there, talking to Don Quixote de la Mancha. Believing this to be a new adventure arranged by Don Antonio Moreno or some other gentleman of the place, the viceroy at once hastened down to the beach, accompanied by a large retinue, including Don Antonio, and they arrived just as Don Quixote was wheeling Rocinante to measure off the necessary stretch of field. When the viceroy perceived that they were about to engage in combat, he at once interposed and inquired of them what it was that impelled them thus to do battle all of a sudden.

The Knight of the White Moon replied that it was a matter of beauty and precedence and briefly repeated what he had said to Don Quixote, explaining the terms to which both parties had agreed. The viceroy then went up to Don Antonio and asked him if he knew any such knight as this or if it was some joke that they were playing, but the answer that he received left him more puzzled than ever; for Don Antonio did not know who the knight was, nor could he say as to whether this was a real encounter or not. The viceroy, accordingly, was doubtful about letting them proceed, but inasmuch as he could not bring himself to believe that it was anything more than a jest, he withdrew to one side, saying, "Sir Knights, if there is nothing for it but to confess or die, and if Señor Don Quixote's mind is made up and your Grace, the Knight of the White Moon, is even more firmly resolved, then fall to it in the name of God and may He bestow the victory."

The Knight of the White Moon thanked the viceroy most courteously and in well-chosen words for the permission which had been granted them, and Don Quixote did the same, whereupon the latter, commending himself with all his heart to Heaven and to his lady Dulcinea, as was his custom at the beginning of a fray, fell back a little farther down the field as he saw his adversary doing the same. And then, without blare of trumpet or other war-like instrument to give them the signal for the attack, both at the same instant wheeled their steeds about and returned for the charge. Being mounted upon the swifter horse, the Knight of the White Moon met Don Quixote two-thirds of the way and with such tremendous force that, without touching his opponent with his lance (which, it seemed, he deliberately held aloft) he brought both Rocinante and his rider to the ground in an exceedingly perilous fall. At once the victor leaped down and placed his lance at Don Quixote's visor.

"You are vanquished, O knight! Nay, more, you are dead unless you make confession in accordance with the conditions governing our encounter."

Stunned and battered, Don Quixote did not so much as raise his visor but in a faint, wan voice, as if speaking from the grave, he said, "Dulcinea del Toboso is the most beautiful woman in the world and I the most unhappy knight upon the face of this earth. It is not right that my weakness should serve to defraud the truth. Drive home your lance, O knight, and take my life since you already have deprived me of my honor."

"That I most certainly shall not do," said the one of the White Moon. "Let the fame of my lady Dulcinea del Toboso's beauty live on undiminished. As for me, I shall be content if the great Don Quixote will retire to his village for a year or until such a time as I may specify, as was agreed upon between us before joining battle."

The viceroy, Don Antonio, and all the many others who were present heard this, and they also heard Don Quixote's response, which was to the effect that, seeing nothing was asked of him that was prejudicial to Dulcinea, he would fulfill all the other conditions like a true and punctilious knight. The one of the White Moon thereupon turned and with a bow to the viceroy rode back to the city at a mild canter. The viceroy promptly dispatched Don Antonio to follow him and make every effort to find out who he was; and, in the meanwhile, they lifted Don Quixote up and uncovered his face, which held no sign of color and was bathed in perspiration. Rocinante, however, was in so sorry a state that he was unable to stir for the present.

Brokenhearted over the turn that events had taken, Sancho did not know what to say or do. It seemed to him that all this was something that was happening in a dream and that everything was the result of magic. He saw his master surrender, heard him consent not to take up arms again for a year to come as the light of his glorious exploits faded into darkness. At the same time his own hopes, based upon the fresh promises that had been made him, were whirled away like smoke before the wind. He feared that Rocinante was maimed for life, his master's bones permanently dislocated—it would have been a bit of luck if his madness also had been jolted out of him.[6]

Finally, in a hand litter which the viceroy had them bring, they bore the knight back to town. The viceroy himself then returned, for he was very anxious to ascertain who the Knight of the White Moon was who had left Don Quixote in so lamentable a condition.

CHAPTER 65

Wherein is revealed who the Knight of the White Moon was.

The Knight of the White Moon was followed not only by Don Antonio Moreno, but by a throng of small boys as well, who kept after him until the doors of one of the city's hostelries had closed behind him. A squire came out to meet him and remove his armor, for which purpose the victor proceeded to shut himself up in a lower room, in the company of Don Antonio, who had also entered the inn and whose bread would not bake until he had learned the knight's identity. Perceiving that the gentleman had no intention of leaving him, he of the White Moon then spoke.

"Sir," he said, "I am well aware that you have come to find out who I am; and, seeing that there is no denying you the information that you seek, while my servant here is removing my armor I will tell you the exact truth of the matter. I would have you know, sir, that I am the bachelor Sansón Carrasco from the same village as Don Quixote de la Mancha, whose madness and absurdities inspire pity in all of us who know him and in none more than me. And so, being convinced that his salvation lay in his returning home for a period of rest in his own house, I formed a plan for bringing him back.

"It was three months ago that I took to the road as a knight-errant, calling myself the Knight of the Mirrors, with the object of fighting and overcoming him without doing him any harm, intending first to lay down the condition that the vanquished was to yield to the victor's will. What I meant to ask of him—for I looked upon him as conquered from the start—was that he

---

6. The Spanish has an untranslatable pun on *deslocado*, which means "out of joint" ("dislocated") and also "cured of madness" (from loco, "mad").

should return to his village and not leave it for a whole year, in the course of which time he might be cured. Fate, however, ordained things otherwise; for he was the one who conquered me and overthrew me from my horse, and thus my plan came to naught. He continued on his wanderings, and I went home, defeated, humiliated, and bruised from my fall, which was quite a dangerous one. But I did not for this reason give up the idea of hunting him up once more and vanquishing him as you have seen me do today.

"Since he is the soul of honor when it comes to observing the ordinances of knight-errantry, there is not the slightest doubt that he will keep the promise he has given me and fulfill his obligations. And that, sir, is all that I need to tell you concerning what has happened. I beg you not to disclose my secret or reveal my identity to Don Quixote, in order that my well-intentioned scheme may be carried out and a man of excellent judgment be brought back to his senses—for a sensible man he would be, once rid of the follies of chivalry."

"My dear sir," exclaimed Don Antonio, "may God forgive you for the wrong you have done the world by seeking to deprive it of its most charming madman! Do you not see that the benefit accomplished by restoring Don Quixote to his senses can never equal the pleasure which others derive from his vagaries? But it is my opinion that all the trouble to which the Señor Bachelor has put himself will not suffice to cure a man who is so hopelessly insane; and if it were not uncharitable, I would say let Don Quixote never be cured, since with his return to health we lose not only his own drolleries but also those of his squire, Sancho Panza, for either of the two is capable of turning melancholy itself into joy and merriment. Nevertheless, I will keep silent and tell him nothing, that I may see whether or not I am right in my suspicion that Señor Carrasco's efforts will prove to have been of no avail."

The bachelor replied that, all in all, things looked very favorable and he hoped for a fortunate outcome. With this, he took his leave of Don Antonio, after offering to render him any service that he could; and, having had his armor tied up and placed upon a mule's back, he rode out of the city that same day on the same horse on which he had gone into battle, returning to his native province without anything happening to him that is worthy of being set down in this veracious chronicle.

[Homecoming and Death]

CHAPTER 73

Of the omens that Don Quixote encountered upon entering his village, with other incidents that embellish and lend credence to this great history.

As they entered the village, Cid Hamete informs us, Don Quixote caught sight of two lads on the communal threshing floor who were engaged in a dispute.

"Don't let it worry you, Periquillo," one of them was saying to the other; "you'll never lay eyes on it again as long as you live."

Hearing this, Don Quixote turned to Sancho. "Did you mark what that boy said, my friend?" he asked. " 'You'll never lay eyes on it[7] again . . . ' "

---

7. The same as *her* in the Spanish, because the reference is to a cricket cage, which is a feminine noun. Hence Don Quixote's inference concerning Dulcinea.

"Well," replied Sancho, "what difference does it make what he said?"

"What difference?" said Don Quixote. "Don't you see that, applied to the one I love, it means I shall never again see Dulcinea."

Sancho was about to answer him when his attention was distracted by a hare that came flying across the fields pursued by a large number of hunters with their greyhounds. The frightened animal took refuge by huddling down beneath the donkey, whereupon Sancho reached out his hand and caught it and presented it to his master.

"*Malum signum, malum signum*,"[8] the knight was muttering to himself. "A hare flees, the hounds pursue it, Dulcinea appears not."

"It is very strange to hear your Grace talk like that," said Sancho. "Let us suppose that this hare is Dulcinea del Toboso and the hounds pursuing it are those wicked enchanters that transformed her into a peasant lass; she flees, I catch her and turn her over to your Grace, you hold her in your arms and caress her. Is that a bad sign? What ill omen can you find in it?"

The two lads who had been quarreling now came up to have a look at the hare, and Sancho asked them what their dispute was about. To this the one who had uttered the words "You'll never lay eyes on it again as long as you live," replied that he had taken a cricket cage from the other boy and had no intention of returning it ever. Sancho then brought out from his pocket four cuartos and gave them to the lad in exchange for the cage, which he placed in Don Quixote's hands.

"There, master," he said, "these omens are broken and destroyed, and to my way of thinking, even though I may be a dunce, they have no more to do with what is going to happen to us than the clouds of yesteryear. If I am not mistaken, I have heard our curate say that sensible persons of the Christian faith should pay no heed to such foolish things, and you yourself in the past have given me to understand that all those Christians who are guided by omens are fools. But there is no need to waste a lot of words on the subject; come, let us go on and enter our village."

The hunters at this point came up and asked for the hare, and Don Quixote gave it to them. Continuing on their way, the returning pair encountered the curate and the bachelor Carrrasco, who were strolling in a small meadow on the outskirts of the town as they read their breviaries. And here it should be mentioned that Sancho Panza, by way of sumpter cloth, had thrown over his gray and the bundle of armor it bore the flame-covered buckram robe in which they had dressed the squire at the duke's castle, on the night that witnessed Altisidora's[9] resurrection; and he had also fitted the miter over the donkey's head, the result being the weirdest transformation and the most bizarrely appareled ass that ever were seen in this world. The curate and the bachelor recognized the pair at once and came forward to receive them with open arms. Don Quixote dismounted and gave them both a warm embrace; meanwhile, the small boys (boys are like lynxes in that nothing escapes them), having spied the ass's miter, ran up for a closer view.

"Come, lads," they cried, "and see Sancho Panza's ass trigged out finer than Mingo,[1] and Don Quixote's beast is skinnier than ever!"

8. Meeting a hare is considered an ill omen (Latin); that is, a bad sign.   9. A girl in the duke's castle, where Don Quixote and Sancho were guests for a time. She dramatically pretended to be in love with Don Quixote.   1. The allusion is to the opening lines of *Mingo Revulgo* (15th century), a satire.

Finally, surrounded by the urchins and accompanied by the curate and the bachelor, they entered the village and made their way to Don Quixote's house, where they found the housekeeper and the niece standing in the doorway, for the news of their return had preceded them. Teresa Panza, Sancho's wife, had also heard of it, and, half naked and disheveled, dragging her daughter Sanchica by the hand, she hastened to greet her husband and was disappointed when she saw him, for he did not look to her as well fitted out as a governor ought to be.

"How does it come, my husband," she said, "that you return like this, tramping and footsore? You look more like a vagabond than you do like a governor."

"Be quiet, Teresa," Sancho admonished her, "for very often there are stakes where there is no bacon. Come on home with me and you will hear marvels. I am bringing money with me, which is the thing that matters, money earned by my own efforts and without harm to anyone."

"You just bring along the money, my good husband," said Teresa, "and whether you got it here or there, or by whatever means, you will not be introducing any new custom into the world."

Sanchica then embraced her father and asked him if he had brought her anything, for she had been looking forward to his coming as to the showers in May. And so, with his wife holding him by the hand while his daughter kept one arm about his waist and at the same time led the gray, Sancho went home, leaving Don Quixote under his own roof in the company of niece and housekeeper, the curate and the barber.

Without regard to time or season, the knight at once drew his guests to one side and in a few words informed them of how he had been overcome in battle and had given his promise not to leave his village for a year, a promise that he meant to observe most scrupulously, without violating it in the slightest degree, as every knight-errant was obliged to do by the laws of chivalry. He accordingly meant to spend that year as a shepherd,[2] he said, amid the solitude of the fields, where he might give free rein to his amorous fancies as he practiced the virtues of the pastoral life; and he further begged them, if they were not too greatly occupied and more urgent matters did not prevent their doing so, to consent to be his companions. He would purchase a flock sufficiently large to justify their calling themselves shepherds; and, moreover, he would have them know, the most important thing of all had been taken care of, for he had hit upon names that would suit them marvelously well. When the curate asked him what these names were, Don Quixote replied that he himself would be known as "the shepherd Quixotiz," the bachelor as "the shepherd Carrascón," the curate as "the shepherd Curiambro," and Sancho Panza as "the shepherd Pancino."

Both his listeners were dismayed at the new form which his madness had assumed. However, in order that he might not go faring forth from the village on another of his expeditions (for they hoped that in the course of the year he would be cured), they decided to fall in with his new plan and approve it as being a wise one, and they even agreed to be his companions in the calling he proposed to adopt.

---

2. Because the knight-errant's life has been forbidden him by his defeat, Don Quixote for a time plans to live according to another and no less "literary" code, that of the pastoral. The following paragraphs, especially through the bachelor Carrasco, refer humorously to some of the conventions of pastoral literature.

"What's more," remarked Sansón Carrasco, "I am a very famous poet, as everyone knows, and at every turn I will be composing pastoral or courtly verses or whatever may come to mind, by way of a diversion for us as we wander in those lonely places; but what is most necessary of all, my dear sirs, is that each one of us should choose the name of the shepherd lass to whom he means to dedicate his songs, so that we may not leave a tree, however hard its bark may be, where their names are not inscribed and engraved as is the custom with lovelorn shepherds."

"That is exactly what we should do," replied Don Quixote, "although, for my part, I am relieved of the necessity of looking for an imaginary shepherdess, seeing that I have the peerless Dulcinea del Toboso, glory of these brookside regions, adornment of these meadows, beauty's mainstay, cream of the Graces—in short, one to whom all praise is well becoming however hyperbolical it may be."

"That is right," said the curate, "but we will seek out some shepherd maids that are easily handled, who if they do not square with us will fit in the corners."

"And," added Sansón Carrasco, "if we run out of names we will give them those that we find printed in books the world over: such as Fílida, Amarilis, Diana, Flérida, Galatea, and Belisarda; for since these are for sale in the market place, we can buy them and make them our own. If my lady, or, rather, my shepherdess, should be chance be called Ana, I will celebrate her charms under the name of Anarda; if she is Francisca, she will become Francenia; if Lucía, Luscinda; for it all amounts to the same thing. And Sancho Panza, if he enters this confraternity, may compose verses to his wife, Teresa Panza, under the name of Teresaina."

Don Quixote had to laugh at this, and the curate then went on to heap extravagant praise upon him for his noble resolution which did him so much credit, and once again he offered to keep the knight company whenever he could spare the time from the duties of his office. With this, they took their leave of him, advising and beseeching him to take care of his health and to eat plentifully of the proper food.

As fate would have it, the niece and the housekeeper had overheard the conversation of the three men, and as soon as the visitors had left they both descended upon Don Quixote.

"What is the meaning of this, my uncle? Here we were thinking your Grace had come home to lead a quiet and respectable life, and do you mean to tell us you are going to get yourself involved in fresh complications—

> Young shepherd, thou who comest here,
> Young shepherd, thou who goest there[3] . . .

For, to tell the truth, the barley is too hard now to make shepherds' pipes of it."[4]

"And how," said the housekeeper, "is your Grace going to stand the midday heat in summer, the winter cold, the howling of the wolves out there in the fields? You certainly cannot endure it. That is an occupation for robust men, cut out and bred for such a calling almost from their swaddling clothes. Setting one evil over against another, it is better to be a knight-

---

3. From a ballad.   4. A proverb.

errant than a shepherd. Look, sir, take my advice, for I am not stuffed with bread and wine when I give it to you but am fasting and am going on fifty years of age: stay at home, attend to your affairs, go often to confession, be charitable to the poor, and let it be upon my soul if any harm comes to you as a result of it."

"Be quiet, daughters," said Don Quixote. "I know very well what I must do. Take me up to bed, for I do not feel very well; and you may be sure of one thing: whether I am a knight-errant now or a shepherd to be, I never will fail to look after your needs as you will see when the time comes."

And good daughters that they unquestionably were, the housekeeper and the niece helped him up to bed, where they gave him something to eat and made him as comfortable as they could.

CHAPTER 74

Of how Don Quixote fell sick, of the will that he made, and of the manner of his death.

Inasmuch as nothing that is human is eternal but is ever declining from its beginning to its close, this being especially true of the lives of men, and since Don Quixote was not endowed by Heaven with the privilege of staying the downward course of things, his own end came when he was least expecting it. Whether it was owing to melancholy occasioned by the defeat he had suffered, or was, simply, the will of Heaven which had so ordained it, he was taken with a fever that kept him in bed for a week, during which time his friends, the curate, the bachelor, and the barber, visited him frequently, while Sancho Panza, his faithful squire, never left his bedside.

Believing that the knight's condition was due to sorrow over his downfall and disappointment at not having been able to accomplish the disenchantment and liberation of Dulcinea, Sancho and the others endeavored to cheer him up in every possible way. The bachelor urged him to take heart and get up from bed that he might begin his pastoral life, adding that he himself had already composed an eclogue that would cast in the shade all that Sannazaro[5] had ever written, and had purchased with his own money from a herdsman of Quintanar two fine dogs to guard the flock, one of them named Barcino and the other Butrón. All this, however, did not serve to relieve Don Quixote's sadness; whereupon his friends called in the doctor, who took his pulse and was not very well satisfied with it. In any case, the physician told them, they should attend to the health of his soul as that of his body was in grave danger.

Don Quixote received this news calmly enough, but not so his housekeeper, niece, and squire, who began weeping bitterly, as if he were already lying dead in front of them. It was the doctor's opinion that melancholy and depression were putting an end to his patient's life. The knight then requested them to leave him alone as he wished to sleep a little, and they complied. He slept for more than six hours at a stretch, as the saying is, and so soundly that the housekeeper and niece thought he would never wake.

---

5. Jacopo Sannazaro (1456–1530), Italian poet, whose *Arcadia* is one of the milestones in the pastoral tradition.

At last he did, however, and at once cried out in a loud voice, "Blessed be Almighty God who has given me so many blessings! Truly His mercy is boundless and is not limited or restrained by the sins of men."

The niece listened carefully to what her uncle said, and it seemed to her that he was speaking more rationally than was his wont, at least during his illness.

"Sir," she said to him, "what does your Grace mean? Has something occurred that we know nothing about? What is this talk of mercy and sins?"

"The mercy that I speak of," replied Don Quixote, "is that which God is showing me at this moment—in spite of my sins, as I have said. My mind now is clear, unencumbered by those misty shadows of ignorance that were cast over it by my bitter and continual reading of those hateful books of chivalry. I see through all the nonsense and fraud contained in them, and my only regret is that my disillusionment has come so late, leaving me no time to make any sort of amends by reading those that are the light of the soul. I find myself, niece, at the point of death, and I would die in such a way as not to leave the impression of a life so bad that I shall be remembered as a madman; for even though I have been one, I do not wish to confirm it on my deathbed. And so, my dear, call in my good friends: the curate, the bachelor Sansón Carrasco, and Master Nicholas the barber; for I want to confess my sins and make my last will and testament."

The niece, however, was relieved of this errand, for the three of them came in just then.

"I have good news for you, kind sirs," said Don Quixote the moment he saw them. "I am no longer Don Quixote de la Mancha but Alonso Quijano, whose mode of life won for him the name of 'Good.' I am the enemy of Amadis of Gaul and all his innumerable progeny; for those profane stories dealing with knight-errantry are odious to me, and I realize how foolish I was and the danger I courted in reading them; but I am in my right senses now and I abominate them."

Hearing this, they all three were convinced that some new kind of madness must have laid hold of him.

"Why, Señor Don Quixote!" exclaimed Sansón. "What makes you talk like that, just when we have received news that my lady Dulcinea is disenchanted? And just when we are on the verge of becoming shepherds so that we may spend the rest of our lives in singing like a lot of princes, why does your Grace choose to turn hermit? Say no more, in Heaven's name, but be sensible and forget these idle tales."

"Tales of that kind," said Don Quixote, "have been the truth for me in the past, and to my detriment, but with Heaven's aid I trust to turn them to my profit now that I am dying. For I feel, gentlemen, that death is very near; so, leave all jesting aside and bring me a confessor for my sins and a notary to draw up my will. In such straits as these a man cannot trifle with his soul. Accordingly, while the Señor Curate is hearing my confession, let the notary be summoned."

Amazed at his words, they gazed at one another in some perplexity, yet they could not but believe him. One of the signs that led them to think he was dying was this quick return from madness to sanity and all the additional things he had to say, so well reasoned and well put and so becoming in a Christian that none of them could any longer doubt that he was in full possession of his faculties. Sending the others out of the room, the curate stayed behind to confess him, and before long the bachelor returned with the notary and Sancho Panza, who had been informed of his master's condition, and who, finding the housekeeper and the niece in tears, began weeping with them. When the confession was over, the curate came out.

"It is true enough," he said, "that Alonso Quijano the Good is dying, and it is also true that he is a sane man. It would be well for us to go in now while he makes his will."

At this news the housekeeper, niece, and the good squire Sancho Panza were so overcome with emotion that the tears burst forth from their eyes and their bosoms heaved with sobs; for, as has been stated more than once, whether Don Quixote was plain Alonso Quijano the Good or Don Quixote de la Mancha, he was always of a kindly and pleasant disposition and for this reason was beloved not only by the members of his household but by all who knew him.

The notary had entered along with the others, and as soon as the preamble had been attended to and the dying man had commended his soul to his Maker with all those Christian formalities that are called for in such a case, they came to the matter of bequests, with Don Quixote dictating as follows:

"ITEM. With regard to Sancho Panza, whom, in my madness, I appointed to be my squire, and who has in his possession a certain sum of money belonging to me: inasmuch as there has been a standing account between us, of debits and credits, it is my will that he shall not be asked to give any accounting whatsoever of this sum, but if any be left over after he has had payment for what I owe him, the balance, which will amount to very little, shall be his, and much good may it do him. If when I was mad I was responsible for his being given the governorship of an island, now that I am of sound mind I would present him with a kingdom if it were in my power, for his simplicity of mind and loyal conduct merit no less."

At this point he turned to Sancho. "Forgive me, my friend," he said, "for having caused you to appear as mad as I by leading you to fall into the same error, that of believing that there are still knights-errant in the world."

"Ah, master," cried Sancho through his tears, "don't die, your Grace, but take my advice and go on living for many years to come; for the greatest madness that a man can be guilty of in this life is to die without good reason, without anyone's killing him, slain only by the hands of melancholy. Look you, don't be lazy but get up from this bed and let us go out into the fields clad as shepherds as we agreed to do. Who knows but behind some bush we may come upon the lady Dulcinea, as disenchanted as you could wish. If it is because of worry over your defeat that you are dying, put the blame on me by saying that the reason for your being overthrown was that I had not properly fastened Rocinante's girth. For the matter of that, your Grace knows from reading your books of chivalry that it is a common thing for certain knights to overthrow others, and he who is vanquished today will be the victor tomorrow."

"That is right," said Sansón, "the worthy Sancho speaks the truth."

"Not so fast, gentlemen," said Don Quixote. "In last year's nests there are no birds this year. I was mad and now I am sane; I was Don Quixote de la Mancha, and now I am, as I have said, Alonso Quijano the Good. May my repentance and the truth I now speak restore to me the place I once held in your esteem. And now, let the notary proceed:

"ITEM. I bequeath my entire estate, without reservation, to my niece Antonia Quijana, here present, after the necessary deductions shall have been made from the most available portion of it to satisfy the bequests that I have stipulated. The first payment shall be to my housekeeper for the wages due her, with twenty ducats over to buy her a dress. And I hereby appoint the Señor Curate and the Señor Bachelor Sansón Carrasco to be my executors.

"ITEM. It is my will that if my niece Antonia Quijana should see fit to marry, it shall be to a man who does not know what books of chivalry are; and if it shall be established that he is acquainted with such books and my niece still insists on marrying him, then she shall lose all that I have bequeathed her and my executors shall apply her portion to works of charity as they may see fit.

"ITEM. I entreat the aforementioned gentlemen, my executors, if by good fortune they should come to know the author who is said to have composed a history now going the rounds under the title of *Second Part of the Exploits of Don Quixote de la Mancha*, to beg his forgiveness in my behalf, as earnestly as they can, since it was I who unthinkingly led him to set down so many and such great absurdities as are to be found in it; for I leave this life with a feeling of remorse at having provided him with the occasion for putting them into writing."

The will ended here, and Don Quixote, stretching himself at length in the bed, fainted away. They all were alarmed at this and hastened to aid him. The same thing happened very frequently in the course of the three days of life that remained to him after he had made his will. The household was in a state of excitement, but with it all the niece continued to eat her meals, the housekeeper had her drink, and Sancho Panza was in good spirits; for this business of inheriting property effaces or mitigates the sorrow which the heir ought to feel and causes him to forget.

Death came at last for Don Quixote, after he had received all the sacraments and once more, with many forceful arguments, had expressed his abomination of books of chivalry. The notary who was present remarked that in none of those books had he read of any knight-errant dying in his own bed so peacefully and in so Christian a manner. And thus, amid the tears and lamentations of those present, he gave up the ghost; that is to say, he died. Perceiving that their friend was no more, the curate asked the notary to be a witness to the fact that Alonso Quijano the Good, commonly known as Don Quixote, was truly dead, this being necessary in order that some author other than Cid Hamete Benengeli might not have the opportunity of falsely resurrecting him and writing endless histories of his exploits.

Such was the end of the Ingenious Gentleman of La Mancha, whose birthplace Cid Hamete was unwilling to designate exactly in order that all the towns and villages of La Mancha might contend among themselves for the right to adopt him and claim him as their own, just as the seven cities of Greece did in the case of Homer. The lamentations of Sancho and those of Don Quixote's niece and his housekeeper, as well as the original epitaphs that were composed for his tomb, will not be recorded here, but mention may be made of the verses by Sansón Carrasco:

Here lies a gentleman bold
Who was so very brave
He went to lengths untold,
And on the brink of the grave
Death had on him no hold.   5
By the world he set small store—
He frightened it to the core—
Yet somehow, by Fate's plan,
Though he'd lived a crazy man,
When he died he was sane once more.   10

WILLIAM SHAKESPEARE
1564–1616

William Shakespeare was born in the rural community of Stratford-upon-Avon in Warwickshire. His father, John Shakespeare, was a glover and, when William was born, prominent in the town's government. Little is known of Shakespeare's early life, although it is likely that he received an education at the good local grammar school and is certain that he married Anne Hathaway, about seven years his senior, when he was eighteen. The couple had three children, Susanna (1583) and the twins Judith and Hamnet (1585). By 1592 Shakespeare was in London, rapidly becoming the "greatest shake-scene" around, in the irritated words of a rival who envied Shakespeare's ability to impress audiences despite his lack of a university education. Shakespeare soon became a shareholder in a prominent players' company that claimed the Lord Chamberlain as patron and the tragic actor Richard Burbage and the comedian Will Kempe as members. Composing dramas that drew on the strengths of his repertory company, Shakespeare brought to the English stage such famous characters as Falstaff and Prince Hal, Hamlet and Ophelia, Othello and Desdemona, and King Lear.

The company originally performed at the Theatre, north of the city of London, where its actor-owner, James Burbage, faced steady opposition from the puritanical city officials who sought to close the theaters, which they considered to be hotbeds of immorality. Burbage conceived of a means to escape civic legislation against theatrical performances, and secretly moved the boards of his playhouse across the river Thames to the south bank; with these planks he constructed the Globe, the theater most often associated with Shakespeare's name. The Globe was open to all social classes: anyone who wished could enter the theater by paying a penny, and at the cost of another, get a bench, cushion, and protection (in the boxes) from bad weather. Shakespeare, who began his career as a player, found his calling as a playwright and his fortune as a shareholder in his company. His financial successes enabled him to purchase the title of gentleman for his father, a purchase that made Shakespeare himself officially a "gentleman born."

The influence of Shakespeare's plays on the course of English literature is matched only by the King James translation of the Bible. In his time, Shakespeare gained the interest of two British monarchs (Elizabeth I and James I), the love of popular audiences, and the respect of such tough critics as the poet and playwright Ben Jonson. After Shakespeare's death in 1616, when his friends and colleagues John Heminges and Henry Condell collected his plays into one volume (the First Folio), Ben Jonson wrote a magnificent verse memorial to the rival whose wit had seemed almost too fertile for the good of his art. In a poem that introduces the collected plays, Jonson praises Shakespeare as a poet who was "the Soule of the Age" and "Not of an age, but for all time!" Jonson's insistence that Shakespeare transcended the age he simultaneously embodied is paradoxical. For Jonson, however, great artists immortalize their nations and eras. In his view, the publication of Shakespeare's plays in the form of a book meant that the entire age of "Eliza, and our James" would enter triumphantly into world history: "triumph, my Britain, thou hast one to show, / To whom all scenes of Europe homage owe." Shakespeare himself may have suspected that his dramatic works would one day count as cultural arts, but he also kept his eye on more humble and material successes. When he retired to Stratford-upon-Avon in 1612, he lived a quiet life in the house he had built (New House) from the savings he had accumulated while working in London's premiere playhouse.

Shakespeare's plays constitute the most important body of dramatic work in the modern world, and no character in literature is more familiar to audiences around the globe than Hamlet. The unparalleled reputation of the work may also have certain nonliterary causes. For instance, it is a play whose central role is singularly cherished by actors in all languages as the test of their skill, and conversely, audiences sometimes content themselves with a rather vague notion of the work as a whole and concentrate on the attractively problematical and eloquent hero and on the actor impersonating him, waiting for his performance of his famous soliloquies rather than following the action and interpretation of the play. But along with the impact of the protagonist, there are other and deeper reasons why Hamlet has commanded a leading place in our literary heritage. Though it is a drama that concerns persons of superior station and the conflicts and problems associated with men and women of high degree, it reveals these problems in terms of a particular family, presenting an individual and domestic dimension along with a public one—the pattern of family conflict within the larger pattern of the polis—like the plays of antiquity that deal with the Theban myth, such as Oedipus and Antigone.

This public dimension of Hamlet helps us see it, for our present purposes, in relation to the literature of the Renaissance—for the framework within which the characters are presented and come into conflict is a court. In spite of the Danish locale and the relatively remote period of the action, it is plainly a Renaissance court exhibiting the structure of interests to which Machiavelli's Prince has potently drawn our attention. There is a ruler holding power, and much of the action is related to questions concerning the nature of that power—the way in which he had acquired it and the ways in which it can be preserved. Moreover, there is a courtly structure: the king has several courtiers around him, among whom Hamlet, the heir apparent, is only the most prominent.

We have seen some of the forms of the Renaissance court pattern in earlier selections in this anthology—in Castiglione, Rabelais, and Machiavelli. The court, the ruling nucleus of the community, was also an arena for conflicts of interest and of wit, a setting for the cultivation and codification of aristocratic virtues (valor, physical and intellectual brilliance, "courtesy"). The positive view of human achievement on earth, so prominent in the Renaissance, was given in courtly life its characteristic setting and testing ground. And as we have observed, the negative view (melancholy, sense of void and purposelessness) also emerged there.

Examining Hamlet, we soon realize that its temper belongs more to the negative than to the positive Renaissance outlook. Certain outstanding forms of human endeavor (the establishment of earthly power, the display of gallantry, the confident attempt of the mind to acquire knowledge and to inspire purposeful action), which elsewhere are presented as highly worthwhile, or are at least soberly discussed in terms of their value and limits, seem to be caught here in a condition of disorder and imbued with a sense of vanity and emptiness.

The way in which the state and the court of Denmark are presented in *Hamlet* is significant: they are shown in images of disease and rottenness. And here again, excessive stress on the protagonist himself must be avoided. His position as denouncer of the prevailing decadence, and the major basis for his denunciation—the murder of his father, which leads to his desire to obtain revenge and purify the court by destroying the present king—are central elements in the play, but they are not the *whole* play. The public situation is indicated, and Marcellus has pronounced his famous "Something is rotten" before Hamlet has talked to the Ghost and learned the Ghost's version of events. Moreover, the sense of outside dangers and internal disruption everywhere transcends the personal story of Hamlet, of his revenge, of Claudius's crime; these are rather the signs of the breakdown, portents of a general situation. In this sense, we may tentatively say that the general theme of the play has to do with a kingdom, a society, a *polis,* going to pieces—or even more, with its realization that it has already gone to pieces. Concomitant with this is a sense of the vanity of those forms of human endeavor and power of which the kingdom and the court are symbols.

The tone Shakespeare wants to establish is evident from the opening scenes: the night air is full of dread premonitions; sentinels turn their eyes toward the threatening outside world; meanwhile, the Ghost has already made his appearance, a sinister omen. The kingdom, as we proceed, is presented in terms that are an almost point by point reversal of the ideal. Claudius, the *pater patriae* and *pater familias,* whether we believe the Ghost's indictment or not (Hamlet does not necessarily, and some of his famous indecision has been attributed to his seeking evidence of the Ghost's truthfulness before acting), has by marrying the queen committed an act that by Elizabethan standards is incestuous. There is an overwhelming sense of disintegration in the body of the state, evident in the first court assembly and in all subsequent ones. In their various ways the two courtiers, Hamlet and Laertes, are strangers, contemplating departure; they offer, around their king, a picture quite unlike that of the conventional paladins, supports of the throne, in a well-manned and well-mannered court. (In Rabelais's "kingdom," when Grangousier is ruler, the pattern is also a courtly and knightly one, but the young heir, Gargantua, who is like Hamlet a university student, readily abandons his studies to answer the fatherland's call; here the direction is reversed.)

On the other hand, as in all late and decadent phases of a social or artistic structure (the court in a sense is both), we have semblance instead of substance, ornate and empty facades, of which the more enlightened members of the group are mockingly aware. Thus Polonius, who after Hamlet is the major figure in the king's retinue, is presented satirically in his empty formalities of speech and conventional patterns of behavior. And there are numerous instances (for example, Osric) of manners being replaced by mannerisms. Hence the way courtly life is depicted in the play suggests always the hollow, the fractured, and the crooked. The traditional forms and institutions of gentle living and all the pomp and solemnity are marred by corruption and distortion. Courtship and love are reduced to Hamlet's mockery of a "civil conversation" in the play scene, his phrases presenting not Castiglione's Platonic loftiness and the repartee of "gentilesse" but punning undercurrents of bawdiness. The theater, a traditional institution of court life, is "politically" used by the hero as a device to expose the king's crime. There are elements of macabre caricature in Shakespeare's treatment of the solemn theme of death (see, for instance, the manner of Polonius's death, which is a sort of sarcastic version of a cloak-and-dagger scene, or the effect of the clownish gravediggers' talk). Finally, the arms tournament, the typical occasion for the display of courtiers' gallantry in front of their king, is here turned by the scheming of the king himself into the play's conclusive scene of carnage. And the person who, on the king's behalf, invites Hamlet to that feast is Osric, the "waterfly," the caricature of the hollow courtier.

This sense of corruption and decadence dominates the temper of the play and obviously qualifies the character of Hamlet, his indecision, and his sense of vanity and disenchantment with the world in which he lives. In Hamlet the relation between thought and deed, intent and realization, is confused in the same way the norms and institutions that would regulate the life of a well-ordered court have been deprived of their original purpose and beauty. He and the king are "mighty opposites," and it can be argued that against Hamlet's indecision and negativism the king presents a more positive scheme of action, at least in the purely Machiavellian sense, at the level of practical power politics. But even this conclusion will prove only partly true. There are indeed moments in which all that the king seems to wish for himself is to forget the past and rule honorably. He advises Hamlet not to mourn his father excessively, for melancholy is not in accord with "nature." On various occasions the king shows a high and competent conception of his office: a culminating instance is the courageous and cunning way in which he confronts and handles Laertes's wrath. The point can be made that since his life is obviously threatened by Hamlet (who was seeking to kill him when by mistake he killed Polonius instead), the king acts within a legitimate pattern of politics in wanting to have Hamlet liquidated. But this argument cannot be carried so far as to demonstrate that he represents a fully positive attitude toward life and the world, even in the strictly amoral terms of political technique. For in fact his action is corroded by an element alien to that technique—the vexations of his own conscience. Despite his energy and his extrovert qualities, he too becomes part of the negative picture of disruption and lacks concentration of purpose. The images of decay and putrescence that characterize his court extend to his own speech: his "offense," in his own words, "smells to heaven."

Hamlet as a Renaissance tragedy presents a world particularly "out of joint," a world that, having long ago lost the sense of a grand extratemporal design that was so important in medieval times (to Hamlet the thought of the afterlife is even more puzzling and dark than that of this life), looks with an even greater sense of disenchantment at the circle of temporal action symbolized by the kingdom and the court. These structures could have offered certain codes of conduct and objects of allegiance that would have given individual action a purposeful meaning. But now their order has been destroyed. Ideals that once had power and freshness have lost their vigor under the impact of satiety, doubt, and melancholy.

Because communal values are so degraded, it is natural to ask in the end whether some alternative attempt at a settlement could be imagined, with Hamlet—like other Renaissance heroes—adopting an individual code of conduct, however extravagant. On the whole, Hamlet seems too steeped in his own hopelessness and in the courtly mechanism to which he inevitably belongs to be able to find personal intellectual and moral compromise or his own version of total escape or total dream; for his "antic disposition" is a strategy, his "folly" is politically motivated. Still, the tone of his brooding and often moralizing speech, his melancholy and dissatisfaction, his very desire for revenge imply a nostalgia for a world—associated with his father—of loyal allegiances and ideals of honor. Yet in *Hamlet* the political world turns out to offer no protection for the values—friendship, loyalty, and honesty—that Hamlet himself most cherishes. These virtues belong only to intimate relationships, such as that between Hamlet and Horatio, and to the world of story, such as the one Horatio will tell of Hamlet after his death.

Hamlet, Prince of Denmark

CHARACTERS

CLAUDIUS, *king of Denmark*
HAMLET, *son to the late, and nephew*
    to the present king
POLONIUS, *lord chamberlain*
HORATIO, *friend to Hamlet*
LAERTES, *son of Polonius*
PRIEST
MARCELLUS, ⎫
BERNARDO, ⎬ *officers*
FRANCISCO, *a soldier*
REYNALDO, *servant to Polonius*
PLAYERS
TWO CLOWNS, *grave-diggers*
FORTINBRAS, *prince of Norway*
CAPTAIN

VOLTIMAND, ⎫
CORNELIUS, ⎪
ROSENCRANTZ, ⎬ *courtiers*
GUILDENSTERN, ⎪
OSRIC, ⎪
GENTLEMAN, ⎭
ENGLISH AMBASSADORS
GERTRUDE, *queen of Denmark, and*
    mother to Hamlet
OPHELIA, *daughter of Polonius*
LORDS, LADIES, OFFICERS, SOLDIERS,
    SAILORS, MESSENGERS, *and*
    OTHER ATTENDANTS
GHOST OF HAMLET'S FATHER

[SCENE: *Denmark.*]

Act I

SCENE 1

[SCENE: *Elsinore. A platform before the castle.*]

[FRANCISCO *at his post. Enter to him* BERNARDO.]

BERNARDO   Who's there?
FRANCISCO   Nay, answer me: stand, and unfold yourself.
BERNARDO   Long live the king!
FRANCISCO   Bernardo?
BERNARDO   He.   5
FRANCISCO   You come most carefully upon your hour.
BERNARDO   'Tis now struck twelve; get thee to bed, Francisco.
FRANCISCO   For this relief much thanks: 'tis bitter cold,
    And I am sick at heart.
BERNARDO   Have you had quiet guard?
FRANCISCO   Not a mouse stirring.   10
BERNARDO   Well, good night.
    If you do meet Horatio and Marcellus,
    The rivals[1] of my watch, bid them make haste.
FRANCISCO   I think I hear them. Stand, ho! Who is there?
        [*Enter* HORATIO *and* MARCELLUS.]
HORATIO   Friends to this ground.
MARCELLUS   And liegemen to the Dane.[2]   15
FRANCISCO   Give you good night.
MARCELLUS   O, farewell, honest soldier:
    Who hath relieved you?

1. Partners.   2. The king of Denmark.

FRANCISCO   Bernardo hath my place.
  Give you good night.
    [*Exit.*]
MARCELLUS   Holla! Bernardo!
BERNARDO   Say,
  What, is Horatio there?
HORATIO   A piece of him.
BERNARDO   Welcome, Horatio; welcome, good Marcellus.   20
MARCELLUS   What, has this thing appeared again to-night?
BERNARDO   I have seen nothing.
MARCELLUS   Horatio says 'tis but our fantasy,
  And will not let belief take hold of him
  Touching this dreaded sight, twice seen of us: 25
  Therefore I have entreated him along
  With us to watch the minutes of this night,
  That if again this apparition come,
  He may approve our eyes[3] and speak to it.
HORATIO   Tush, tush, 'twill not appear.
BERNARDO   Sit down a while;   30
  And let us once again assail your ears,
  That are so fortified against our story,
  What we have two nights seen.
HORATIO   Well, sit we down,
  And let us hear Bernardo speak of this.
BERNARDO   Last night of all,   35
  When yond same star that's westward from the pole
  Had made his course to illume that part of heaven
  Where now it burns, Marcellus and myself,
  The bell then beating one,—
    [*Enter* GHOST.]
MARCELLUS   Peace, break thee off; look, where it comes again!   40
BERNARDO   In the same figure, like the king that's dead.
MARCELLUS   Thou art a scholar; speak to it, Horatio.
BERNARDO   Looks it not like the king? mark it, Horatio.
HORATIO   Most like it: it harrows me with fear and wonder.
BERNARDO   It would be spoke to.
MARCELLUS   Question it, Horatio.   45
HORATIO   What art thou, that usurp'st this time of night,
  Together with that fair and warlike form
  In which the majesty of buried Denmark
  Did sometimes[4] march? by heaven I charge thee, speak!
MARCELLUS   It is offended.
BERNARDO   See, it stalks away!   50
HORATIO   Stay! speak, speak! I charge thee, speak!
    [*Exit* GHOST.]
MARCELLUS   'Tis gone, and will not answer.
BERNARDO   How now, Horatio! you tremble and look pale:
  Is not this something more than fantasy?

3. Confirm what we saw.   4. Formerly. "Denmark": the king of Denmark.

What think you on't?   55

HORATIO   Before my God, I might not this believe
Without the sensible and true avouch
Of mine own eyes.

MARCELLUS   Is it not like the king?

HORATIO   As thou art to thyself:
Such was the very armor he had on   60
When he the ambitious Norway[5] combated;
So frown'd he once, when, in an angry parle,
He smote the sledded[6] Polacks on the ice.
'Tis strange.

MARCELLUS   Thus twice before, and jump[7] at this dead hour,   65
With martial stalk hath he gone by our watch.

HORATIO   In what particular thought to work I know not;
But, in the gross and scope of my opinion,[8]
This bodes some strange eruption to our state.

MARCELLUS   Good now, sit down, and tell me, he that knows,   70
Why this same strict and most observant watch
So nightly toils the subject[9] of the land,
And why such daily cast of brazen cannon,
And foreign mart for implements of war;
Why such impress of shipwrights,[1] whose sore task   75
Does not divide the Sunday from the week;
What might be toward,[2] that this sweaty haste
Doth make the night joint-laborer with the day:
Who is't that can inform me?

HORATIO   That can I;
At least the whisper goes so. Our last king,   80
Whose image even but now appear'd to us,
Was, as you know, by Fortinbras of Norway,
Thereto pricked on by a most emulate pride,
Dared to the combat; in which our valiant Hamlet—
For so this side of our known world esteem'd him—   85
Did slay this Fortinbras; who by a seal'd compact
Well ratified by law and heraldry,[3]
Did forfeit, with his life, all those his lands
Which he stood seized[4] of, to the conqueror:
Against the which, a moiety competent   90
Was gagèd[5] by our king; which had returned
To the inheritance of Fortinbras,
Had he been vanquisher; as, by the same covenant
And carriage[6] of the article design'd,
His fell to Hamlet. Now, sir, young Fortinbras,   95
Of unimprovèd metal hot and full,
Hath in the skirts[7] of Norway here and there

5. The king of Norway (the elder Fortinbras).   6. They travel in sledges. "Parle": parley.   7. Just.
8. Taking a general view.   9. The people.   1. Ship carpenters. "Mart": trading. "Impress": pressing
into service.   2. Impending.   3. Duly ratified and proclaimed through heralds.   4. Possessed.
5. Pledged. "Moiety competent": equal share.   6. Purport.   7. Outskirts, border regions. "Unimprovèd": untested.

Shark'd up a list of lawless resolutes,
For food and diet, to some enterprise
That hath a stomach in't:[8] which is no other—   100
As it doth well appear unto our state—
But to recover of us, by strong hand
And terms compulsatory, those foresaid lands
So by his father lost: and this, I take it,
Is the main motive of our preparations,   105
The source of this our watch and the chief head
Of this post-haste and romage[9] in the land.

BERNARDO   I think it be no other but e'en so:
Well may it sort,[1] that this portentous figure
Comes armèd through our watch, so like the king   110
That was and is the question of these wars.

HORATIO   A mote it is to trouble the mind's eye.
In the most high and palmy state of Rome,
A little ere the mightiest Julius fell,
The graves stood tenantless, and the sheeted dead   115
Did squeak and gibber in the Roman streets:
As stars with trains of fire and dews of blood,
Disasters in the sun; and the moist star,
Upon whose influence Neptune's empire stands,[2]
Was sick almost to doomsday with eclipse: 120
And even the like precurse[3] of fierce events,
As harbingers preceding still the fates
And prologue to the omen coming on,
Have heaven and earth together demonstrated
Unto our climatures[4] and countrymen.   125
        [Re-enter GHOST.]
But soft, behold! lo, where it comes again!
I'll cross it, though it blast me. Stay, illusion!
If thou hast any sound, or use of voice,
Speak to me:
If there be any good thing to be done,   130
That may to thee do ease and grace to me,
Speak to me:
If thou art privy to thy country's fate,
Which, happily, foreknowing may avoid,
O, speak!   135
Or if thou hast uphoarded in thy life
Extorted treasure in the womb of earth,
For which, they say, you spirits oft walk in death,
Speak of it: stay, and speak! [The cock crows.] Stop it, Marcellus.

MARCELLUS   Shall I strike at it with my partisan?   140

HORATIO   Do, if it will not stand.

BERNARDO   'Tis here!

HORATIO   'Tis here!

8. Calls for courage.   9. Bustle. "Head": origin, cause.   1. Fit with the other signs of war.   2. The
moon ("moist star") regulates the sea's tides. "Disasters": ill omens.   3. Foreboding.   4. Regions.

[*Exit* GHOST.]

MARCELLUS 'Tis gone!
    We do it wrong, being so majestical,
    To offer it the show of violence;
    For it is, as the air, invulnerable,   145
    And our vain blows malicious mockery.
BERNARDO It was about to speak, when the cock crew.
HORATIO And then it started like a guilty thing
    Upon a fearful summons. I have heard
    The cock, that is the trumpet to the morn,   150
    Doth with his lofty and shrill-sounding throat
    Awake the god of day, and at his warning,
    Whether in sea or fire, in earth or air,
    The extravagant[5] and erring spirit hies
    To his confine: and of the truth herein   155
    This present object made probation.[6]
MARCELLUS It faded on the crowing of the cock.
    Some say that ever 'gainst[7] that season comes
    Wherein our Saviour's birth is celebrated,
    The bird of dawning singeth all night long: 160
    And then, they say, no spirit dare stir abroad,
    The nights are wholesome, then no planets strike,[8]
    No fairy takes nor witch hath power to charm,
    So hallowed and so gracious[9] is the time.
HORATIO So have I heard and do in part believe it.   165
    But look, the morn, in russet mantle clad,
    Walks o'er the dew of yon high eastward hill:
    Break we our watch up; and by my advice,
    Let us impart what we have seen to-night
    Unto young Hamlet; for, upon my life,   170
    This spirit, dumb to us, will speak to him:
    Do you consent we shall acquaint him with it,
    As needful in our loves, fitting our duty?
MARCELLUS Let's do't, I pray; and I this morning know
    Where we shall find him most conveniently.   175
        [*Exeunt.*]

SCENE 2

[SCENE: *A room of state in the castle.*]

[*Flourish. Enter the* KING, QUEEN, HAMLET, POLONIUS, LAERTES,
    VOLTIMAND, CORNELIUS, LORDS, *and* ATTENDANTS.]
KING Though yet of Hamlet our dear brother's death
    The memory be green, and that it us befitted
    To bear our hearts in grief and our whole kingdom
    To be contracted in one brow of woe,
    Yet so far hath discretion[1] fought with nature   5

5. Wandering out of its confines.   6. Gave proof.   7. Just before.   8. Exercise evil influence (compare "moonstruck").   9. Full of blessing. "Fairy takes": bewitches.   1. Restraint (on grief).

That we with wisest sorrow think on him,
Together with remembrance of ourselves.
Therefore our sometime sister, now our queen,
The imperial jointress to this warlike state,
Have we, as 'twere with a defeated joy,— 10
With an auspicious and a dropping eye,
With mirth in funeral and with dirge in marriage,
In equal scale weighing delight and dole,—
Taken to wife: nor have we herein barr'd[2]
Your better wisdoms, which have freely gone 15
With this affair along. For all, our thanks.
Now follows, that[3] you know, young Fortinbras,
Holding a weak supposal of our worth,
Or thinking by our late dear brother's death
Our state to be disjoint and out of frame, 20
Colleaguèd with this dream[4] of his advantage,
He hath not failed to pester us with message,
Importing the surrender of those lands
Lost by his father, with all bonds of law,
To our most valiant brother. So much for him. 25
Now for ourself, and for this time of meeting:
Thus much the business is: we have here writ
To Norway, uncle of young Fortinbras,—
Who, impotent and bed-rid, scarcely hears
Of this his nephew's purpose,—to suppress 30
His further gait herein; in that the levies,
The lists and full proportions,[5] are all made
Out of his subject: and we here dispatch
You, good Cornelius, and you, Voltimand,
For bearers of this greeting to old Norway, 35
Giving to you no further personal power
To business with the king more than the scope
Of these delated[6] articles allow.
Farewell, and let your haste commend your duty.

CORNELIUS ⎫
VOLTIMAND ⎭ In that and all things will we show our duty. 40

KING   We doubt it nothing: heartily farewell.
        [*Exeunt* VOLTIMAND *and* CORNELIUS.]
And now, Laertes, what's the news with you?
You told us of some suit; what is't, Laertes?
You cannot speak of reason to the Dane,
And lose your voice: what wouldst thou beg, Laertes, 45
That shall not be my offer, not thy asking?
The head is not more native to[7] the heart,
The hand more instrumental to the mouth,
Than is the throne of Denmark to thy father.
What wouldst thou have, Laertes?

2. Ignored. "Dole": grief.   3. What.   4. Combined with this fantastic notion.   5. Amounts of forces and supplies. "Gait": proceeding.   6. Detailed.   7. Naturally bound to.

LAERTES   My dread lord,   50
　Your leave and favor to return to France,
　From whence though willingly I came to Denmark,
　To show my duty in your coronation,
　Yet now, I must confess, that duty done,
　My thoughts and wishes bend again toward France   55
　And bow them to your gracious leave and pardon.
KING   Have you your father's leave? What says Polonius?
POLONIUS   He hath, my lord, wrung from me my slow leave
　By laborsome petition, and at last
　Upon his will I sealed my hard consent: 60
　I do beseech you, give him leave to go.
KING   Take thy fair hour, Laertes; time be thine,
　And thy best graces spend it at thy will!
　But now, my cousin Hamlet, and my son,—
HAMLET [*Aside.*]   A little more than kin, and less than kind.   65
KING   How is it that the clouds still hang on you?
HAMLET   Not so, my lord; I am too much i' the sun.[8]
QUEEN   Good Hamlet, cast thy nighted color off,
　And let thine eye look like a friend on Denmark.
　Do not for ever with thy vailèd[9] lids   70
　Seek for thy noble father in the dust:
　Thou know'st 'tis common; all that lives must die,
　Passing through nature to eternity.
HAMLET   Aye, madam, it is common.
QUEEN   If it be,
　Why seems it so particular with thee?   75
HAMLET   Seems, madam! nay, it is; I know not "seems."
　'Tis not alone my inky cloak, good mother,
　Nor customary suits of solemn black,
　Nor windy suspiration of forced breath,
　No, nor the fruitful river in the eye,   80
　Nor the dejected havior of the visage,
　Together with all forms, moods, shapes of grief,
　That can denote me truly: these indeed seem,
　For they are actions that a man might play:
　But I have that within which passeth show;   85
　These but the trappings and the suits of woe.
KING   'Tis sweet and cómmendàble in your nature, Hamlet,
　To give these mourning duties to your father:
　But, you must know, your father lost a father,
　That father lost, lost his, and the survivor bound   90
　In filial obligation for some term
　To do obsequious[1] sorrow: but to persevere
　In obstinate condolement is a course
　Of impious stubborness; 'tis unmanly grief:
　It shows a will most incorrect[2] to heaven,   95

---

8. The cue to Hamlet's irony is given by the king's "my cousin . . . my son" (line 64). Hamlet is punning on *son*.   9. Downcast.   1. Dutiful, especially concerning funeral rites (obsequies).   2. Not subdued.

A heart unfortified, a mind impatient,
An understanding simple and unschool'd:
For what we know must be and is as common
As any the most vulgar thing to sense,
Why should we in our peevish opposition   100
Take it to heart? Fie! 'tis a fault to heaven,
A fault against the dead, a fault to nature,
To reason most absurd, whose common theme
Is death of fathers, and who still hath cried,
From the first corse till he that died to-day,   105
"this must be so." We pray you, throw to earth
This unprevailing[3] woe, and think of us
As of a father: for let the world take note,
You are the most immediate to our throne,
And with no less nobility of love   110
Than that which dearest father bears his son
Do I impart toward you. For your intent
In going back to school in Wittenberg,
It is most retrograde[4] to our desire:
And we beseech you, bend you to remain   115
Here in the cheer and comfort of our eye,
Our chiefest courtier, cousin and our son.
QUEEN   Let not thy mother lose her prayers, Hamlet:
I pray thee, stay with us; go not to Wittenberg.
HAMLET   I shall in all my best obey you, madam.   120
KING   Why, 'tis a loving and a fair reply:
Be as ourself in Denmark. Madam, come;
This gentle and unforced accord of Hamlet
Sits smiling to my heart: in grace whereof,
No jocund health that Denmark drinks to-day,   125
But the great cannon to the clouds shall tell,
And the king's rouse the heaven shall bruit[5]again,
Re-speaking earthly thunder. Come away.
     [*Flourish. Exeunt all but* HAMLET.]
HAMLET   O, that this too too sullied flesh would melt,
Thaw and resolve itself into a dew!   130
Or that the Everlasting had not fixed
His canon[6] 'gainst self-slaughter! O God! God!
How weary, stale, flat and unprofitable
Seem to me all the uses of this world!
Fie on't! ah fie! 'tis an unweeded garden,   135
That grows to seed; things rank and gross in nature
Possess it merely. That it should come to this!
But two months dead! nay, not so much, not two:
So excellent a king; that was, to this,
Hyperion to a satyr: so loving to my mother,   140

---

3. Useless.   4. Opposed. Wittenberg is the seat of a university; at the peak of fame in Shakespeare's time because of its connection with Martin Luther.   5. Proclaim, echo. "Rouse": carousal, revel.   6. Law.

That he might not beteem[7] the winds of heaven
Visit her face too roughly. Heaven and earth!
Must I remember? why, she would hang on him,
As if increase of appetite had grown
By what it fed on: and yet, within a month—   145
Let me not think on't—Frailty, thy name is woman!—
A little month, or ere those shoes were old
With which she followed my poor father's body,
Like Niobe,[8] all tears:—why she, even she,—
O God! a beast that wants discourse[9] of reason   150
Would have mourned longer,—married with my uncle,
My father's brother, but no more like my father
Than I to Hercules: within a month;
Ere yet the salt of most unrighteous tears
Had left the flushing in her gallèd[1] eyes,   155
She married. O, most wicked speed, to post
With such dexterity to incestuous sheets![2]
It is not, nor it cannot come to good:
But break, my heart, for I must hold my tongue!
       [Enter horatio, marcellus, and bernardo.]
HORATIO   Hail to your lordship!
HAMLET   I am glad to see you well: 160
    Horatio,—or I do forget myself.
HORATIO   The same, my lord, and your poor servant ever.
HAMLET   Sir, my good friend; I'll change[3] that name with you:
    And what make you from Wittenberg, Horatio?
    Marcellus?
MARCELLUS   My good lord?   165
HAMLET   I am very glad to see you. [To BERNARDO.] Good even, sir.
    But what, in faith, make you from Wittenberg?
HORATIO   A truant disposition, good my lord.
HAMLET   I would not hear your enemy say so,
    Nor shall you do my ear that violence,   170
    To make it truster of your own report
    Against yourself: I know you are no truant.
    But what is your affair in Elsinore?
    We'll teach you to drink deep ere you depart.
HORATIO   My lord, I came to see your father's funeral.   175
HAMLET   I pray thee, do not mock me, fellow-student;
    I think it was to see my mother's wedding.
HORATIO   Indeed, my lord, it followed hard upon.
HAMLET   Thrift, thrift, Horatio! the funeral baked-meats
    Did coldly furnish forth the marriage tables.   180
    Would I had met my dearest[4] foe in heaven
    Or ever I had seen that day, Horatio!

7. Allow. Hyperion is the sun god.   8. A proud mother who boasted of having more children than Leto;
her seven sons and seven daughters were slain by Apollo and Artemis, children of Leto. The grieving Niobe
was changed by Zeus into a continually weeping stone.   9. Lacks the faculty.   1. Inflamed.
2. According to principles that Hamlet accepts, marrying one's brother's widow is incest.   3. Exchange.
4. Bitterest.

My father!—methinks I see my father.

HORATIO   O where, my lord?

HAMLET   In my mind's eye, Horatio.

HORATIO   I saw him once; he was a goodly king.   185

HAMLET   He was a man, take him for all in all,
I shall not look upon his like again.

HORATIO   My lord, I think I saw him yesternight.

HAMLET   Saw? who?

HORATIO   My lord, the king your father.

HAMLET   The king my father!   190

HORATIO   Season your admiration[5] for a while
With an attent ear, till I may deliver,
Upon the witness of these gentlemen,
This marvel to you.

HAMLET   For God's love, let me hear.

HORATIO   Two nights together had these gentlemen,   195
Marcellus and Bernardo, on their watch,
In the dead vast and middle of the night,
Been thus encountered. A figure like your father,
Armed at point exactly, cap-a-pe,[6]
Appears before them, and with solemn march   200
Goes slow and stately by them: thrice he walked
By their oppressed and fear-surprisèd eyes,
Within his truncheon's length; whilst they, distilled
Almost to jelly with the act of fear,
Stand dumb, and speak not to him. This to me   205
In dreadful secrecy impart they did;
And I with them the third night kept the watch:
Where, as they had delivered, both in time,
Form of the thing, each word made true and good,
The apparition comes: I knew your father;   210
These hands were not more like.

HAMLET   But where was this?

MARCELLUS   My lord, upon the platform where we watched.

HAMLET   Did you not speak to it?

HORATIO   My lord, I did.
But answer made it none: yet once methought
It lifted up its head and did address   215
Itself to motion, like as it would speak:
But even then the morning cock crew loud,
And at the sound it shrunk in haste away
And vanished from our sight.

HAMLET   'Tis very strange.

HORATIO   As I do live, my honored lord, 'tis true,   220
And we did think it writ down in our duty
To let you know of it.

HAMLET   Indeed, indeed, sirs, but this troubles me.
Hold you the watch to-night?

---

5. Restrain your astonishment.   6. From head to foot. "At point": completely.

MARCELLUS }   We do, my lord.
BERNARDO }

HAMLET   Armed, say you?

MARCELLUS }   Armed, my lord.   225
BERNARDO }

HAMLET   From top to toe?

MARCELLUS }   My lord, from head to foot.
BERNARDO }

HAMLET   Then saw you not his face?

HORATIO   O, yes, my lord; he wore his beaver[7] up.

HAMLET   What, looked he frowningly?

HORATIO   A countenance more in sorrow than in anger.   230

HAMLET   Pale, or red?

HORATIO   Nay, very pale.

HAMLET   And fixed his eyes upon you?

HORATIO   Most constantly.

HAMLET   I would I had been there.

HORATIO   It would have much amazed you.

HAMLET   Very like, very like. Stayed it long?   235

HORATIO   While one with moderate haste might tell[8] a hundred.

MARCELLUS }   Longer, longer.
BERNARDO }

HORATIO   Not when I saw't.

HAMLET   His beard was grizzled?[9] no?

HORATIO   It was, as I have seen it in his life,
A sable silvered.[1]

HAMLET   I will watch to-night;   240
Perchance 'twill walk again.

HORATIO   I warrant it will.

HAMLET   If it assume my noble father's person,
I'll speak to it, though hell itself should gape
And bid me hold my peace. I pray you all,
If you have hitherto concealed this sight,   245
Let it be tenable in your silence still,[2]
And whatsoever else shall hap to-night,
Give it an understanding, but no tongue:
I will requite your loves. So fare you well:
Upon the platform, 'twixt eleven and twelve,   250
I'll visit you.

ALL   Our duty to your honor.

HAMLET   Your loves, as mine to you: farewell.
     [*Exeunt all but* HAMLET.]
My father's spirit in arms! all is not well;
I doubt[3] some foul play: would the night were come!
Till then sit still, my soul: foul deeds will rise,   255
Though all the earth o'erwhelm them, to men's eyes.
     [*Exit.*]

---

7. Visor.   8. Count.   9. Gray.   1. Black and white.   2. Consider it still a secret.   3. Suspect.

SCENE 3

[SCENE: *A room in Polonius's house.*]

[*Enter* LAERTES *and* OPHELIA.]

LAERTES   My necessaries are embarked: farewell:
And, sister, as the winds give benefit
And convoy[4] is assistant, do not sleep,
But let me hear from you.

OPHELIA   Do you doubt that?

LAERTES   For Hamlet, and the trifling of his favor,   5
Hold it a fashion,[5] and a toy in blood,
A violet in the youth of primy nature,
Forward,[6] not permanent, sweet, not lasting,
The perfume and suppliance of a minute;
No more.   10

OPHELIA   No more but so?

LAERTES   Think it no more:
For nature crescent does not grow alone
In thews and bulk; but, as this temple[7] waxes,
The inward service of the mind and soul   15
Grows wide withal. Perhaps he loves you now;
And now no soil nor cautel[8] doth besmirch
The virtue of his will: but you must fear,
His greatness weighed,[9] his will is not his own;
For he himself is subject to his birth: 20
He may not, as unvalued persons do,
Carve for himself, for on his choice depends
The safety and health of this whole state,
And therefore must his choice be circumscribed
Unto the voice and yielding[1] of that body   25
Whereof he is the head. Then if he says he loves you,
It fits your wisdom so far to believe it
As he in his particular act and place
May give his saying deed; which is no further
Than the main voice of Denmark goes withal.[2]   30
Then weigh what loss your honor may sustain,
If with too credent ear you list his songs,
Or lose your heart, or your chaste treasure open
To his unmastered importunity.
Fear it, Ophelia, fear it, my dear sister,   35
And keep you in the rear of your affection,
Out of the shot and danger of desire.
The chariest maid is prodigal enough
If she unmask her beauty to the moon:
Virtue itself 'scapes not calumnious strokes: 40
The canker galls the infants of the spring

4. Conveyance, means of transport.   5. Passing mood.   6. Early. "Primy": early, young.   7. The body.
"Crescent": growing.   8. No foul or deceitful thoughts.   9. When you consider his rank. "Will":
desire.   1. Assent.   2. Goes along with, agrees. "Main": powerful.

Too oft before their buttons be disclosed,
And in the morn and liquid dew of youth
Contagious blastments[3] are most imminent.
Be wary then; best safety lies in fear: 45
Youth to itself[4] rebels, though none else near.

OPHELIA   I shall the effect of this good lesson keep,
As watchman to my heart. But, good my brother,
Do not, as some ungracious pastors do,
Show me the steep and thorny way to heaven,   50
Whilst, like a puffed and reckless libertine,
Himself the primrose path of dalliance treads
And recks not his own rede.[5]

LAERTES   O, fear me not.
I stay too long; but here my father comes.
        [Enter POLONIUS.]
A double blessing is a double grace;   55
Occasion smiles upon a second leave.

POLONIUS   Yet here, Laertes! Aboard, aboard, for shame!
The wind sits in the shoulder of your sail,
And you are stayed for. There; my blessing with thee!
And these few precepts in thy memory   60
See thou chárácter.[6] Give thy thoughts no tongue,
Nor any unproportioned[7] thought his act.
Be thou familiar, but by no means vulgar.
Those friends thou hast, and their adoption tried,
Grapple them to thy soul with hoops of steel,   65
But do not dull thy palm[8] with entertainment
Of each new-hatched unfledged comrade. Beware
Of entrance to a quarrel; but being in,
Bear't, that the opposèd may beware of thee.
Give every man thy ear, but few thy voice: 70
Take each man's censure,[9] but reserve thy judgment.
Costly thy habit as thy purse can buy,
But not expressed in fancy; rich, not gaudy:
For the apparel oft proclaims the man;
And they in France of the best rank and station   75
Are of a most select and generous chief[1] in that.
Neither a borrower nor a lender be:
For loan oft loses both itself and friend,
And borrowing dulls the edge of husbandry.[2]
This above all: to thine own self be true,   80
And it must follow, as the night the day,
Thou canst not then be false to any man.
Farewell: my blessing season[3] this in thee!

LAERTES   Most humbly do I take my leave, my lord.

POLONIUS   The time invites you; go, your servants tend.[4]   85

---

3. Blights.   4. Against its better self.   5. Does not follow his own advice.   6. Engrave in your memory.   7. Unsuitable.   8. Make the palm of your hand callous (by the indiscriminate shaking of hands).
9. Opinion.   1. Preeminence.   2. Thriftiness.   3. Ripen.   4. Wait.

LAERTES   Farewell, Ophelia, and remember well
    What I have said to you.
OPHELIA   'Tis in my memory locked,
    And you yourself shall keep the key of it.
LAERTES   Farewell.
        [*Exit.*]
POLONIUS   What is't, Ophelia, he hath said to you?
OPHELIA   So please you, something touching the Lord Hamlet.   90
POLONIUS   Marry, well bethought:
    'Tis told me, he hath very oft of late
    Given private time to you, and you yourself
    Have of your audience been most free and bounteous:
    If it be so—as so 'tis put on me,   95
    And that in way of caution—I must tell you,
    You do not understand yourself so clearly
    As it behoves my daughter and your honor.
    What is between you? give me up the truth.
OPHELIA   He hath, my lord, of late made many tenders   100
    Of his affection to me.
POLONIUS   Affection! pooh! you speak like a green girl,
    Unsifted[5] in such perilous circumstance.
    Do you believe his tenders, as you call them?
OPHELIA   I do not know, my lord, what I should think.   105
POLONIUS   Marry, I'll teach you: think yourself a baby,
    That you have ta'en these tenders for true pay,
    Which are not sterling. Tender[6] yourself more dearly;
    Or—not to crack the wind of the poor phrase,
    Running it thus—you'll tender me a fool.[7]   110
OPHELIA   My lord, he hath importuned me with love
    In honorable fashion.
POLONIUS   Aye, fashion you may call it; go to, go to.
OPHELIA   And hath given countenance[8] to his speech, my lord,
    With almost all the holy vows of heaven.   115
POLONIUS   Aye, springes to catch woodcocks. I do know,
    When the blood burns, how prodigal the soul
    Lends the tongue vows: these blazes, daughter,
    Giving more light than heat, extinct in both,
    Even in their promise, as it is a-making,   120
    You must not take for fire. From this time
    Be something scanter of your maiden presence;
    Set your entreatments[9] at a higher rate
    Than a command to parley. For Lord Hamlet,
    Believe so much in him, that he is young,   125
    And with a larger tether may he walk
    Than may be given you: in few, Ophelia,
    Do not believe his vows; for they are brokers,
    Not of that dye which their investments[1] show,

5. Untested.   6. Regard.   7. You'll furnish me with a fool (a foolish daughter).   8. Authority.
9. Conversation, company.   1. Clothes. "Brokers": procurers, panders.

But mere implorators of unholy suits,   130
Breathing like sanctified and pious bawds,
The better to beguile. This is for all:
I would not, in plain terms, from this time forth,
Have you so slander any moment[2] leisure,
As to give words or talk with the Lord Hamlet.   135
Look to't, I charge you: come your ways.

OPHELIA   I shall obey, my lord.
    [*Exeunt.*]

SCENE 4

[SCENE: *The platform.*]

[*Enter* HAMLET, HORATIO, *and* MARCELLUS.]

HAMLET   The air bites shrewdly; it is very cold.

HORATIO   It is a nipping and an eager[3] air.

HAMLET   What hour now?

HORATIO   I think it lacks of twelve.

MARCELLUS   No, it is struck.

HORATIO   Indeed? I heard it not: it then draws near the season   5
Wherein the spirit held his wont to walk.
    [*A flourish of trumpets, and ordnance shot off within.*]
What doth this mean, my lord?

HAMLET   The king doth wake to-night, and takes his rouse,
Keeps wassail, and the swaggering up-spring reels;
And as he drains his draughts of Rhenish[4] down,   10
The kettle-drum and trumpet thus bray out
The triumph of his pledge.[5]

HORATIO   Is it a custom?

HAMLET   Aye, marry, is't:
But to my mind, though I am native here
And to the manner born, it is a custom   15
More honored[6] in the breach than the observance.
This heavy-headed revel east and west
Makes us traduced and taxed[7]of other nations:
They clepe us drunkards, and with swinish phrase
Soil our addition;[8] and indeed it takes   20
From our achievements, though performed at height,[9]
The pith and marrow of our attribute.[1]
So, oft it chances in particular men,
That for some vicious mole of nature in them,
As, in their birth,—wherein they are not guilty,   25
Since nature cannot choose his origin,—
By the o'ergrowth of some complexion,[2]
Oft breaking down the pales and forts of reason,

---

2. Use badly any momentary.   3. Sharp.   4. Rhine wine. "Up-spring reels": wild dances.   5. In downing the cup in one draught.   6. Honorable.   7. Blamed.   8. Reputation. "Clepe": call. 9. Done in the best possible manner.   1. Reputation.   2. Excess in one side of their temperament.

Or by some habit that too much o'er-leavens[3]
The form of plausive[4] manners, that these men,—   30
Carrying, I say, the stamp of one defect,
Being nature's livery, or fortune's star,—
Their virtues else[5]—be they as pure as grace,
As infinite as man may undergo—
Shall in the general censure take corruption   35
From that particular fault: the dram of evil
Doth all the noble substance often dout
To his own scandal.[6]
            [*Enter* GHOST.]
HORATIO   Look, my lord it comes!
HAMLET   Angels and ministers of grace defend us!
Be thou a spirit of health or goblin damned,   40
Bring with thee airs from heaven or blasts from hell,
Be thy intents wicked or charitable,
Thou comest in such a questionable shape
That I will speak to thee: I'll call thee Hamlet,
King, father, royal Dane: O, answer me!   45
Let me not burst in ignorance; but tell
Why thy canónized bones, hearsèd in death,
Have burst their cerements; why the sepulchre,
Wherein we saw thee quietly inurned,
Hath oped his ponderous and marble jaws,   50
To cast thee up again. What may this mean,
That thou, dead corse, again, in complete steel,
Revisit'st thus the glimpses of the moon,
Making night hideous; and we fools of nature
So horridly to shake our disposition   55
With thoughts beyond the reaches of our souls?
Say, why is this? Wherefore? what should we do?
            [GHOST *beckons* HAMLET.]
HORATIO   It beckons you to go away with it,
As if it some impartment did desire
To you alone.   60
MARCELLUS   Look, with what courteous action
It waves you to a more removèd ground:
But do not go with it.
HORATIO   No, by no means.
HAMLET   It will not speak; then I will follow it.
HORATIO   Do not, my lord.
HAMLET   Why, what should be the fear?   65
I do not set my life at a pin's fee;
And for my soul, what can it do to that,
Being a thing immortal as itself?
It waves me forth again: I'll follow it.

---

3. Modifies, as yeast changes dough.   4. Agreeable.   5. The rest of their qualities.   6. To its own
harm. "Dout": extinguish, nullify.

HORATIO   What if it tempt you toward the flood, my lord,   70
   Or to the dreadful summit of the cliff
   That beetles o'er[7] his base into the sea,
   And there assume some other horrible form,
   Which might deprive your sovereignty of reason
   And draw you into madness? think of it: 75
   The very place puts toys[8] of desperation,
   Without more motive, into every brain
   That looks so many fathoms to the sea
   And hears it roar beneath.
HAMLET   It waves me still.
   Go on; I'll follow thee.   80
MARCELLUS   You shall not go, my lord.
HAMLET   Hold off your hands.
HORATIO   Be ruled; you shall not go.
HAMLET   My fate cries out,
   And makes each petty artery in this body
   As hardy as the Nemean lion's nerve.[9]
   Still am I called, unhand me, gentlemen;   85
   By heaven, I'll make a ghost of him that lets[1] me:
   I say, away! Go on; I'll follow thee.
     [*Exeunt* GHOST *and* HAMLET.]
HORATIO   He waxes desperate with imagination.
MARCELLUS   Let's follow; 'tis not fit thus to obey him.
HORATIO   Have after. To what issue will this come?   90
MARCELLUS   Something is rotten in the state of Denmark.
HORATIO   Heaven will direct it.
MARCELLUS   Nay, let's follow him.
     [*Exeunt.*]

SCENE 5

[SCENE: *Another part of the platform.*]

   [*Enter* GHOST *and* HAMLET.]
HAMLET   Whither wilt thou lead me? speak; I'll go no further.
GHOST   Mark me.
HAMLET   I will.
GHOST   My hour is almost come,
   When I to sulphurous and tormenting flames[2]
   Must render up myself.
HAMLET   Alas, poor ghost!
GHOST   Pity me not, but lend thy serious hearing   5
   To what I shall unfold.
HAMLET   Speak; I am bound to hear.
GHOST   So art thou to revenge, when thou shalt hear.
HAMLET   What?
GHOST   I am thy father's spirit;

---

7. Juts over.   8. Fancies.   9. Sinew, muscle. The Nemean lion was slain by Hercules as one of his
twelve labors.   1. Hinders.   2. Of purgatory.

Doomed for a certain term to walk the night,   10
And for the day confined to fast in fires,
Till the foul crimes done in my days of nature
Are burnt and purged away. But that I am forbid
To tell the secrets of my prison-house,
I could a tale unfold whose lightest word   15
Would harrow up thy soul, freeze thy young blood,
Make thy two eyes, like stars, start from their spheres,[3]
Thy knotted and combinèd locks to part
And each particular hair to stand on end,
Like quills upon the fretful porpentine: 20
But this eternal blazon[4] must not be
To ears of flesh and blood. List, list, O, list!
If thou didst ever thy dear father love—
HAMLET   O God!
GHOST   Revenge his foul and most unnatural murder.   25
HAMLET   Murder!
GHOST   Murder most foul, as in the best it is,
But this most foul, strange, and unnatural.
HAMLET   Haste me to know't, that I, with wings as swift
As meditation or the thoughts of love,   30
May sweep to my revenge.
GHOST   I find thee apt;
And duller shouldst thou be than the fat weed
That roots itself in ease on Lethe[5] wharf,
Wouldst thou not stir in this. Now, Hamlet, hear:
'Tis given out that, sleeping in my orchard,   35
A serpent stung me; so the whole ear of Denmark
Is by a forgèd process of my death
Rankly abused: but know, thou noble youth,
The serpent that did sting thy father's life
Now wears his crown.
HAMLET   O my prophetic soul!   40
My uncle!
GHOST   Aye, that incestuous, that adulterate beast,
With witchcraft of his wit, with traitorous gifts,—
O wicked wit and gifts, that have the power
So to seduce!—won to his shameful lust   45
The will of my most seeming-virtuous queen:
O Hamlet, what a falling-off was there!
From me, whose love was of that dignity
That it went hand in hand even with the vow
I made to her in marriage; and to decline   50
Upon a wretch, whose natural gifts were poor
To those of mine!
But virtue, as it never will be moved,

---

3. Transparent revolving shells in each of which, according to Ptolemaic astronomy, a planet or other heavenly body was placed.   4. Publication of the secrets of the other world (of eternity). "Porpentine": porcupine.   5. The river of forgetfulness in Hades.

Though lewdness court it in a shape of heaven,[6]
So lust, though to a radiant angel linked,   55
Will sate itself in a celestial bed
And prey on garbage.
But, soft! methinks I scent the morning air;
Brief let me be. Sleeping within my orchard,
My custom always of the afternoon,   60
Upon my secure hour thy uncle stole,
With juice of cursed hebenon[7] in a vial,
And in the porches of my ears did pour
The leperous distilment; whose effect
Holds such an enmity with blood of man   65
That swift as quicksilver it courses through
The natural gates and alleys of the body;
And with a sudden vigor it doth posset
And curd, like eager[8] droppings into milk,
The thin and wholesome blood: so did it mine;   70
And a most instant tetter barked about,[9]
Most lazar-like,[1] with vile and loathsome crust,
All my smooth body.
Thus was I, sleeping, by a brother's hand
Of life, of crown, of queen, at once dispatched: 75
Cut off even in the blossoms of my sin,
Unhouseled, disappointed, unaneled;[2]
No reckoning made, but sent to my account
With all my imperfections on my head:
O, horrible! O, horrible! most horrible!   80
If thou hast nature in thee, bear it not;
Let not the royal bed of Denmark be
A couch for luxury and damned incest.
But, howsoever thou pursuest this act,
Taint not thy mind, nor let thy soul contrive   85
Against thy mother aught: leave her to heaven,
And to those thorns that in her bosom lodge,
To prick and sting her. Fare thee well at once!
The glow-worm shows the matin to be near,
And 'gins to pale his uneffectual fire: 90
Adieu, adieu, adieu! remember me.
        [Exit.]
HAMLET   O all you host of heaven! O earth! what else?
And shall I couple hell? O, fie! Hold, hold, my heart;
And you, my sinews, grow not instant old,
But bear me stiffly up. Remember thee!   95
Aye, thou poor ghost, while memory holds a seat
In this distracted globe. Remember thee!
Yea, from the table[3] of my memory

6. A heavenly, angelic form.   7. Henbane, a poisonous herb.   8. Sour. "Posset": coagulate.   9. The skin immediately became thick like the bark of a tree.   1. Leper-like (from the beggar Lazarus, "full of sores," in Luke 16.20).   2. Without sacrament, unprepared, without extreme unction.   3. Writing tablet; used in the same sense in line 107. "Globe": head.

I'll wipe away all trivial fond records,
All saws of books, all forms, all pressures past,   100
That youth and observation copied there:
And thy commandment all alone shall live
Within the book and volume of my brain,
Unmixed with baser matter: yes, by heaven!
O most pernicious woman!   105
O villain, villain, smiling, damnèd villain!
My tables,—meet it is I set it down,
That one may smile, and smile, and be a villain;
At least I'm sure it may be so in Denmark.
            [Writing.]
So, uncle, there you are. Now to my word;   110
It is "Adieu, adieu! remember me."
I have sworn't.

HORATIO   ⎫
MARCELLUS ⎭ [Within.]
            My lord, my lord!
        [Enter HORATIO and MARCELLUS.]
MARCELLUS   Lord Hamlet!
HORATIO   Heaven
                                            secure him!
HAMLET   So be it!
MARCELLUS   Illo,[4] ho, ho, my lord!   115
HAMLET   Hillo, ho, ho, boy! come, bird, come.
MARCELLUS   How is't, my noble lord?
HORATIO   What news, my lord?
HAMLET   O, wonderful!
HORATIO   Good my lord, tell it.
HAMLET   No; you will reveal it.
HORATIO   Not I, my lord, by heaven.
MARCELLUS   Nor I, my lord.   120
HAMLET   How say you, then; would heart of man once think it?
    But you'll be secret?
HORATIO   ⎫
MARCELLUS ⎭ Aye, by heaven, my lord.
HAMLET   There's ne'er a villain dwelling in all Denmark
    But he's an arrant knave.
HORATIO   There needs no ghost, my lord, come from the grave   125
    To tell us this.
HAMLET   Why, right; you are i' the right;
And so, without more circumstance[5] at all,
I hold it fit that we shake hands and part:
You, as your business and desire shall point you;
For every man hath business and desire,
Such as it is; and for my own poor part,   130
Look you, I'll go pray.

4. A falconer's call.   5. Ceremony.

HORATIO   These are but wild and whirling words, my lord.
HAMLET   I'm sorry they offend you, heartily;
   Yes, faith, heartily.
HORATIO   There's no offense, my lord.   135
HAMLET   Yes, by Saint Patrick, but there is, Horatio,
   And much offense too. Touching this vision here,
   It is an honest[6] ghost, that let me tell you:
   For your desire to know what is between us,
   O'ermaster't as you may. And now, good friends,   140
   As you are friends, scholars and soldiers,
   Give me one poor request.
HORATIO   What is't, my lord? we will.
HAMLET   Never make known what you have seen tonight.
MARCELLUS ⎫ My lord, we will not.
HORATIO   ⎭
HAMLET   Nay, but swear't.
HORATIO   In faith,
   My lord, not I.
MARCELLUS   Nor I, my lord, in faith.   145
HAMLET   Upon my sword.
MARCELLUS   We have sworn, my lord, already.
HAMLET   Indeed, upon my sword, indeed.
GHOST [Beneath.]   Swear.
HAMLET   Ah, ha, boy! say'st thou so? art thou there, true-penny?[7]
   Come on: you hear this fellow in the cellarage:
   Consent to swear.
HORATIO   Propose the oath, my lord.   150
HAMLET   Never to speak of this that you have seen,
   Swear by my sword.
GHOST [Beneath.]   Swear.
HAMLET   Hic et ubique?[8] then we'll shift our ground.
   Come hither, gentlemen,   155
   And lay your hands again upon my sword:
   Never to speak of this that you have heard,
   Swear by my sword.
GHOST [Beneath.]   Swear.
HAMLET   Well said, old mole! canst work i' the earth so fast? 160
   A worthy pioner![9] Once more remove, good friends.
HORATIO   O day and night, but this is wondrous strange!
HAMLET   And therefore as a stranger give it welcome.
   There are more things in heaven and earth, Horatio,
   Than are dreamt of in your philosophy.   165
   But come;
   Here, as before, never, so help you mercy,
   How strange or odd soe'er I bear myself,
   As I perchance hereafter shall think meet
   To put an antic[1] disposition on,   170

6. Genuine.   7. Honest fellow.   8. Here and everywhere (Latin).   9. Miner.   1. Odd, fantastic.

That you, at such times seeing me, never shall,
With arms encumbered[2] thus, or this head-shake,
Or by pronouncing of some doubtful phrase,
As "Well, well, we know," or "We could, an if we would,"
Or "If we list to speak," or "There be, an if they might,"   175
Or such ambiguous giving out, to note
That you know aught of me: this not to do,
So grace and mercy at your most need help you,
Swear.
GHOST [*Beneath.*]   Swear.
HAMLET   Rest, rest, perturbèd spirit!   180
    [*They swear.*]
So, gentlemen,
With all my love I do commend[3] me to you:
And what so poor a man as Hamlet is
May do, to express his love and friending to you,   185
God willing, shall not lack. Let us go in together;
And still your fingers on your lips, I pray.
The time is out of joint: O cursèd spite,
That ever I was born to set it right!
Nay, come, let's go together.   190
    [*Exeunt.*]

Act II

SCENE 1

[SCENE: *A room in Polonius's house.*]

[*Enter* POLONIUS *and* REYNALDO.]
POLONIUS   Give him this money and these notes, Reynaldo.
REYNALDO   I will, my lord.
POLONIUS   You shall do marvelous wisely, good Reynaldo,
  Before you visit him, to make inquire
  Of his behavior.
REYNALDO   My lord, I did intend it.   5
POLONIUS   Marry, well said, very well said. Look you, sir,
  Inquire me first what Danskers are in Paris,
  And how, and who, what means, and where they keep,[4]
  What company, at what expense, and finding
  By this encompassment[5] and drift of question   10
  That they do know my son, come you more nearer
  Than your particular demands will touch it:
  Take you, as 'twere, some distant knowledge of him,
  As thus, "I know his father and his friends,
  And in part him": do you mark this, Reynaldo?   15
REYNALDO   Aye, very well, my lord.
POLONIUS   "And in part him; but," you may say, "not well:

---

2. Folded.   3. Entrust.   4. Dwell. "Danskers": Danes.   5. Roundabout way.

But if 't be he I mean, he's very wild,
Addicted so and so"; and there put on him
What forgeries you please; marry, none so rank   20
As may dishonor him; take heed of that;
But, sir, such wanton, wild and usual slips
As are companions noted and most known
To youth and liberty.
REYNALDO   As gaming, my lord.
POLONIUS   Aye, or drinking, fencing, swearing, quarreling,   25
Drabbing:[6] you may go so far.
REYNALDO   My lord, that would dishonor him.
POLONIUS   Faith, no; as you may season it in the charge.[7]
You must not put another scandal on him,
That he is open to incontinency;[7]   30
That's not my meaning: but breathe his faults so quaintly[8]
That they may seem the taints of liberty,
The flash and outbreak of a fiery mind,
A savageness in unreclaimèd blood,
Of general assault.[9]
REYNALDO   But, my good lord,—   35
POLONIUS   Wherefore should you do this?
REYNALDO   Aye, my lord,
I would know that.
POLONIUS   Marry, sir, here's my drift,
And I believe it is a fetch of warrant:[1]
You laying these slight sullies on my son,
As 'twere a thing a little soiled i' the working,   40
Mark you,
Your party in converse, him you would sound,
Having ever seen in the prenominate[2] crimes
The youth you breathe of guilty, be assured
He closes with you in this consequence;[3]   45
"Good sir," or so, or "friend," or "gentleman,"
According to the phrase or the addition[4]
Of man and country.
REYNALDO   Very good, my lord.
POLONIUS   And then, sir, does he this—he does—what was I about to
say? By the mass, I was about to say something: where did I leave?   50
REYNALDO   At "closes in the consequence," at "friend or so," and "gen-
tleman."
POLONIUS   At "closes in the consequence," aye, marry;
He closes with you thus: "I know the gentleman;
I saw him yesterday, or t' other day,   55
Or then, or then, with such, or such, and, as you say,
There was a' gaming, there o'ertook in 's rouse,[5]

6. Whoring.   7. Qualify it in making the accusation.   8. Delicately, skillfully. "Incontinency":
extreme sensuality.   9. Assailing all. "Unreclaimèd": untamed.   1. Allowable stratagem.   2. Aforementioned. "Having ever": if he has ever.   3. You may be sure he will agree in this conclusion.
4. Title.   5. Intoxicated in his reveling.

There falling out at tennis": or perchance,
"I saw him enter such a house of sale,"
Videlicet,[6] a brothel, or so forth.   60
See you now;
Your bait of falsehood takes this carp of truth:
And thus do we of wisdom and of reach,[7]
With windlasses and with assays of bias,[8]
By indirections find directions out: 65
So, by my former lecture and advice,
Shall you my son. You have me, have you not?

REYNALDO   My lord, I have.

POLONIUS   God be wi' ye; fare ye well.

REYNALDO   Good my lord!

POLONIUS   Observe his inclination in yourself.[9]   70

REYNALDO   I shall, my lord.

POLONIUS   And let him ply his music.

REYNALDO   Well, my lord.

POLONIUS   Farewell!

          [Exit REYNALDO.—Enter OPHELIA.]
How now, Ophelia! what's the matter?

OPHELIA   O, my lord, I have been so affrighted!   75

POLONIUS   With what, i' the name of God?

OPHELIA   My lord, as I was sewing in my closet,
Lord Hamlet, with his doublet[1] all unbraced,
No hat upon his head, his stockings fouled,
Ungartered and down-gyvèd[2] to his ankle;   80
Pale as his shirt, his knees knocking each other,
And with a look so piteous in purport
As if he had been loosèd out of hell
To speak of horrors, he comes before me.

POLONIUS   Mad for thy love?

OPHELIA   My lord, I do not know,   85
But truly I do fear it.

POLONIUS   What said he?

OPHELIA   He took me by the wrist and held me hard;
Then goes he to the length of all his arm,
And with his other hand thus o'er his brow,
He falls to such perusal of my face   90
As he would draw it. Long stayed he so;
At last, a little shaking of mine arm,
And thrice his head thus waving up and down,
He raised a sigh so piteous and profound
As it did seem to shatter all his bulk   95
And end his being: that done, he lets me go:
And with his head over his shoulder turned,
He seemed to find his way without his eyes;

6. Namely.   7. Wise and farsighted.   8. Sending the ball indirectly (in bowling), devious attacks.
"Windlasses": winding ways, roundabout courses.   9. Ways of procedure by yourself.   1. Jacket.
"Closet": private room.   2. Pulled down like fetters on a prisoner's leg.

For out o' doors he went without their help,
And to the last bended their light on me. 100
POLONIUS   Come, go with me: I will go seek the king.
This is the very ecstasy of love;
Whose violent property fordoes itself[3]
And leads the will to desperate undertakings
As oft as any passion under heaven 105
That does afflict our natures. I am sorry.
What, have you given him any hard words of late?
OPHELIA   No, my good lord, but, as you did command,
I did repel his letters and denied
His access to me.
POLONIUS   That hath made him mad. 110
I am sorry that with better heed and judgment
I had not quoted him: I fear'd he did but trifle
And meant to wreck thee; but beshrew my jealousy![4]
By heaven, it is as proper to our age
To cast beyond ourselves[5] in our opinions 115
As it is common for the younger sort
To lack discretion. Come, go we to the king:
This must be known; which, being kept close, might move
More grief to hide than hate to utter love.[6]
Come. 120
   [Exeunt.]

SCENE 2

[SCENE: A room in the castle.]

[Flourish. Enter KING, QUEEN, ROSENCRANTZ, GUILDENSTERN,
   and ATTENDANTS.]
KING   Welcome, dear Rosencrantz and Guildenstern!
Moreover that we much did long to see you,
The need we have to use you did provoke
Our hasty sending. Something have you heard
Of Hamlet's transformation; so call it, 5
Sith[7] nor the exterior nor the inward man
Resembles that it was. What it should be,
More than his father's death, that thus hath put him
So much from the understanding of himself,
I cannot dream of: I entreat you both, 10
That, being of so young days brought up with him
And sith so neighbored to his youth and behavior,
That you vouchsafe your rest[8] here in our court
Some little time: so by your companies
To draw him on to pleasures, and to gather 15
So much as from occasion you may glean,

---

3. Which, when violent, destroys itself. "Ecstasy": madness.   4. Curse my suspicion. "Quoted": noted.
5. Overshoot, go too far.   6. If Hamlet's love is revealed. "To hide": if kept hidden.   7. Since.
8. Consent to stay.

Whether aught to us unknown afflicts him thus,
That opened[9] lies within our remedy.
QUEEN   Good gentlemen, he hath much talked of you,
And sure I am two men there are not living   20
To whom he more adheres.[1] If it will please you
To show us so much gentry[2] and good will
As to expend your time with us awhile
For the supply and profit of our hope,
Your visitation shall receive such thanks   25
As fits a king's remembrance.
ROSENCRANTZ   Both your majesties
Might, by the sovereign power you have of us,
Put your dread pleasures more into[3] command
Than to entreaty.
GUILDENSTERN   But we both obey,
And here give up ourselves, in the full bent[4]   30
To lay our service freely at your feet,
To be commanded.
KING   Thanks, Rosencrantz and gentle Guildenstern.
QUEEN   Thanks, Guildenstern and gentle Rosencrantz:
And I beseech you instantly to visit   35
My too much changéd son. Go, some of you,
And bring these gentlemen where Hamlet is.
GUILDENSTERN   Heavens make our presence and our practices
Pleasant and helpful to him!
QUEEN   Aye, amen!
     [*Exeunt* ROSENCRANTZ, GUILDENSTERN, *and some* ATTENDANTS.—*Enter*
     POLONIUS.]
POLONIUS   The ambassadors from Norway, my good lord,   40
Are joyfully returned.
KING   Thou still[5] hast been the father of good news.
POLONIUS   Have I, my lord? I assure my good liege,
I hold my duty as I hold my soul,
Both to my God and to my gracious king: 45
And I do think, or else this brain of mine
Hunts not the trail of policy so sure
As it hath used to do, that I have found
The very cause of Hamlet's lunacy.
KING   O, speak of that; that do I long to hear.   50
POLONIUS   Give first admittance to the ambassadors;
My news shall be the fruit to that great feast.
KING   Thyself do grace[6] to them, and bring them in.
     [*Exit* POLONIUS.]
He tells me, my dear Gertrude, he hath found
The head and source of all your son's distemper.   55
QUEEN   I doubt it is no other but the main;
His father's death and our o'erhasty marriage.

---

9. Once revealed.   1. Is more attached.   2. Courtesy.   3. Give your sovereign wishes the form of.
4. Bent (as a bow) to the limit.   5. Always.   6. Honor. "Fruit": dessert.

KING   Well, we shall sift him.
    [*Re-enter* POLONIUS, *with* VOLTIMAND *and* CORNELIUS.]
                   Welcome, my good friends!
  Say, Voltimand, what from our brother Norway?
VOLTIMAND   Most fair return of greetings and desires.   60
  Upon our first,[7] he sent out to suppress
  His nephew's levies, which to him appeared
  To be a preparation 'gainst the Polack,
  But better looked into, he truly found
  It was against your highness: whereat grieved,   65
  That so his sickness, age and impotence
  Was falsely borne in hand,[8] sends out arrests
  On Fortinbras; which he, in brief, obeys,
  Receives rebuke from Norway, and in fine[9]
  Makes vow before his uncle never more   70
  To give the assay[1] of arms against your majesty.
  Whereon old Norway, overcome with joy,
  Gives him three thousand crowns in annual fee
  And his commission to employ those soldiers,
  So levied as before, against the Polack: 75
  With an entreaty, herein further shown,
      [*Giving a paper.*]
  That it might please you to give quiet pass
  Through your dominions for this enterprise,
  On such regards of safety and allowance
  As therein are set down.
KING   It likes us well,   80
  And at our more considered time we'll read,
  Answer, and think upon this business.
  Meantime we thank you for your well-took labor:
  Go to your rest; at night we'll feast together:
  Most welcome home!
      [*Exeunt* VOLTIMAND *and* CORNELIUS.]
POLONIUS   This business is well ended.   85
  My liege, and madam, to expostulate
  What majesty should be, what duty is,
  Why day is day, night night, and time is time,
  Were nothing but to waste night, day and time.
  Therefore, since brevity is the soul of wit   90
  And tediousness the limbs and outward flourishes,
  I will be brief. Your noble son is mad:
  Mad call I it; for, to define true madness,
  What is 't but to be nothing else but mad?
  But let that go.
QUEEN   More matter, with less art.   95
POLONIUS   Madam, I swear I use no art at all.
  That he is mad, 'tis true: 'tis true 'tis pity,
  And pity 'tis 'tis true: a foolish figure;[2]

---

7. As soon as we made the request.   8. Deceived, deluded.   9. Finally.   1. Test.   2. Of speech.

But farewell it, for I will use no art.
Mad let us grant him then: and now remains   100
That we find out the cause of this effect,
Or rather say, the cause of this defect,
For this effect defective comes by cause:
Thus it remains and the remainder thus.
Perpend.[3]   105
I have a daughter,—have while she is mine,—
Who in her duty and obedience, mark,
Hath given me this: now gather and surmise.
[*Reads.*] "To the celestial, and my soul's idol, the most beautified
Ophelia,"—That's an ill phrase, a vile phrase; "beautified" is a vile   110
phrase; but you shall hear. Thus:
    [*Reads.*] "In her excellent white bosom, these," &c.
QUEEN   Came this from Hamlet to her?
POLONIUS   Good madam, stay awhile; I will be faithful.
    [*Reads.*]   "Doubt thou the stars are fire;   115
          Doubt that the sun doth move;
          Doubt truth to be a liar;
          But never doubt I love.
"O dear Ophelia, I am ill at these numbers;[4] I have not art to reckon
my groans: but that I love thee best, O most best, believe it. Adieu.   120
       "Thine evermore, most dear lady, whilst this
          machine is to him,[5] HAMLET."
This in obedience hath my daughter shown me;
And more above,[6] hath his solicitings,
As they fell out by time, by means and place,   125
All given to mine ear.
KING   But how hath she
  Received his love?
POLONIUS   What do you think of me?
KING   As of a man faithful and honorable.
POLONIUS   I would fain prove so. But what might you think,
When I had seen this hot love on the wing,—   130
As I perceived it, I must tell you that,
Before my daughter told me,—what might you,
Or my dear majesty your queen here, think,
If I had played the desk or table-book,[7]
Or given my heart a winking,[8] mute and dumb,   135
Or looked upon this love with idle sight;
What might you think? No, I went round[9] to work,
And my young mistress thus I did bespeak:
"Lord Hamlet is a prince, out of thy star;[1]
This must not be:" and then I prescripts gave her,   140
That she should lock herself from his resort,
Admit no messengers, receive no tokens.
Which done, she took the fruits of my advice;

---

3. Consider.   4. Verses.   5. Body is attached.   6. Moreover.   7. If I had acted as a desk or note-
book (in keeping the matter secret).   8. Shut my heart's eye.   9. Straight.   1. Sphere.

And he repulsed, a short tale to make,
Fell into a sadness, then into a fast,   145
Thence to a watch, thence into a weakness,
Thence to a lightness,[2] and by this declension
Into the madness wherein now he raves
And all we mourn for.
KING   Do you think this?
QUEEN   It may be, very like.   150
POLONIUS   Hath there been such a time, I'd fain know that,
That I have positively said "'tis so,"
When it proved otherwise?
KING   Not that I know.
POLONIUS [*Pointing to his head and shoulder.*]   Take this, from this,
if this be otherwise: 155
If circumstances lead me, I will find
Where truth is hid, though it were hid indeed
Within the center.[3]
KING   How may we try it further?
POLONIUS   You know, sometimes he walks for hours together
Here in the lobby.
QUEEN   So he does, indeed.   160
POLONIUS   At such a time I'll loose my daughter to him:
Be you and I behind an arras then;
Mark the encounter: if he love her not,
And be not from his reason fall'n thereon,[4]
Let me be no assistant for a state,   165
But keep a farm and carters.
KING   We will try it.
QUEEN   But look where sadly the poor wretch comes reading.
POLONIUS   Away, I do beseech you, both away:
I'll board him presently.[5]
          [*Exeunt* KING, QUEEN, *and* ATTENDANTS.—*Enter* HAMLET, *reading.*]
O, give me leave: how does my good Lord Hamlet?   170
HAMLET   Well, God-a-mercy.
POLONIUS   Do you know me, my lord?
HAMLET   Excellent well; you are a fishmonger.[6]
POLONIUS   Not I, my lord.
HAMLET   Then I would you were so honest a man.   175
POLONIUS: Honest, my lord!
HAMLET   Aye, sir; to be honest, as this world goes, is to be one man
picked out of ten thousand.
POLONIUS   That's very true, my lord.
HAMLET   For if the sun breed maggots in a dead dog, being a good   180
kissing carrion[7]—Have you a daughter?
POLONIUS   I have, my lord.
HAMLET   Let her not walk i' the sun: conception is a blessing; but as
your daughter may conceive,—friend, look to 't.

---

2. Light-headedness. "Watch": insomnia.   3. Of the earth.   4. For that reason.   5. Approach him
at once.   6. Fish seller but also slang for procurer.   7. Good bit of flesh for kissing.

POLONIUS [*Aside.*] How say you by that? Still harping on my daughter: 185
yet he knew me not at first; he said I was a fishmonger: he is far
gone: and truly in my youth I suffered much extremity for love; very
near this. I'll speak to him again.—What do you read, my lord?

HAMLET Words, words, words.

POLONIUS What is the matter,[8] my lord?   190

HAMLET Between who?

POLONIUS I mean, the matter that you read, my lord.

HAMLET Slanders, sir: for the satirical rogue says here that old men
have gray beards, that their faces are wrinkled, their eyes purging
thick amber and plum-tree gum, and that they have a plentiful lack   195
of wit, together with most weak hams: all which, sir, though I most
powerfully and potently believe, yet I hold it not honesty to have it
thus set down; for yourself, sir, shall grow old as I am, if like a crab
you could go backward.

POLONIUS [*Aside.*] Though this be madness, yet there is method in   200
't.—Will you walk out of the air, my lord?

HAMLET Into my grave.

POLONIUS Indeed, that's out of the air.
     [*Aside.*]
How pregnant sometimes his replies are! a happiness[9] that often
madness hits on, which reason and sanity could not so prosperously   205
be delivered of. I will leave him, and suddenly contrive the means of
meeting between him and my daughter.—My honorable lord, I will
most humbly take my leave of you.

HAMLET You cannot, sir, take from me any thing that I will more
willingly part withal: except my life, except my life, except my life.   210

POLONIUS Fare you well, my lord.

HAMLET These tedious old fools.
     [*Re-enter* ROSENCRANTZ *and* GUILDENSTERN.]

POLONIUS You go to seek the Lord Hamlet; there he is.

ROSENCRANTZ [*To* POLONIUS.] God save you, sir!
     [*Exit* POLONIUS.]

GUILDENSTERN My honored lord!   215

ROSENCRANTZ My most dear lord!

HAMLET My excellent good friends! How dost thou, Guildenstern? Ah,
Rosencrantz! Good lads, how do you both?

ROSENCRANTZ As the indifferent[1] children of the earth.

GUILDENSTERN Happy, in that we are not over-happy;   220
On Fortune's cap we are not the very button.[2]

HAMLET Nor the soles of her shoe?

ROSENCRANTZ Neither, my lord.

HAMLET Then you live about her waist, or in the middle of her favors?

GUILDENSTERN Faith, her privates[3] we.   225

HAMLET In the secret parts of Fortune? O, most true; she is a strumpet. What's the news?

---

8. The subject matter of the book. Hamlet responds as if he referred to the subject of a quarrel.
9. Aptness of expression.   1. Average.   2. Top.   3. Ordinary men (with obvious play on the sexual
term *private parts*).

ROSENCRANTZ None, my lord, but that the world's grown honest.

HAMLET Then is doomsday near: but your news is not true. Let me question more in particular: what have you, my good friends, deserved at the hands of Fortune, that she sends you to prison hither? 230

GUILDENSTERN Prison, my lord!

HAMLET Denmark's a prison.

ROSENCRANTZ Then is the world one. 235

HAMLET A goodly one; in which there are many confines, wards[4] and dungeons, Denmark being one o' the worst.

ROSENCRANTZ We think not so, my lord.

HAMLET Why, then, 'tis none to you; for there is nothing either good or bad, but thinking makes it so: to me it is a prison. 240

ROSENCRANTZ Why, then your ambition makes it one; 'tis too narrow for your mind.

HAMLET O God, I could be bounded in a nut-shell and count myself a king of infinite space, were it not that I have bad dreams.

GUILDENSTERN Which dreams indeed are ambition; for the very sub- 245 stance of the ambitious is merely the shadow of a dream.

HAMLET A dream itself is but a shadow.

ROSENCRANTZ Truly, and I hold ambition of so airy and light a quality that it is but a shadow's shadow.

HAMLET Then are our beggars bodies, and our monarchs and out- 250 stretched heroes the beggars' shadows. Shall we to the court? for, by my fay, I cannot reason.

ROSENCRANTZ ⎫
GUILDENSTERN ⎬ We'll wait upon you.

HAMLET No such matter: I will not sort you[5] with the rest of my ser- vants; for, to speak to you like an honest man, I am most dreadfully 255 attended. But, in the beaten way of friendship, what make you at Elsinore?

ROSENCRANTZ To visit you, my lord; no other occasion.

HAMLET Beggar that I am, I am even poor in thanks; but I thank you: and sure, dear friends, my thanks are too dear a halfpenny.[6] Were 260 you not sent for? Is it your own inclining? Is it a free visitation? Come, deal justly[7] with me: come, come; nay, speak.

GUILDENSTERN What should we say, my lord?

HAMLET Why, any thing, but to the purpose. You were sent for; and there is a kind of confession in your looks, which your modesties 265 have not craft enough to color: I know the good king and queen have sent for you.

ROSENCRANTZ To what end, my lord?

HAMLET That you must teach me. But let me conjure you, by the rights of our fellowship, by the consonancy of our youth, by the obli- 270 gation of our ever-preserved love, and by what more dear a better proposer[8] could charge you withal, be even and direct with me, whether you were sent for, or no.

---

4. Cells. "Confines": places of confinement. 5. Put you together. 6. If priced at a halfpenny.
7. Honestly. 8. Speaker.

ROSENCRANTZ [*Aside to* GUILDENSTERN.]   What say you?

HAMLET [*Aside.*]   Nay then, I have an eye of[9] you.—If you love me,   275
hold not off.

GUILDENSTERN   My lord, we were sent for.

HAMLET   I will tell you why; so shall my anticipation prevent your discovery,[1] and your secrecy to the king and queen moult no feather. I
have of late—but wherefore I know not—lost all my mirth, forgone   280
all custom of exercises; and indeed it goes so heavily with my disposition that this goodly frame, the earth, seems to me a sterile promontory; this most excellent canopy, the air, look you, this brave
o'erhanging firmament, this majestical roof fretted[2] with golden fire,
why, it appears no other thing to me than a foul and pestilent con-   285
gregation of vapors. What a piece of work is a man! how noble in
reason! how infinite in faculty! in form and moving how express[3] and
admirable! in action how like an angel! in apprehension how like a
god! the beauty of the world! the paragon of animals! And yet, to me,
what is this quintessence of dust? man delights not me; no, nor   290
woman neither, though by your smiling you seem to say so.

ROSENCRANTZ   My lord, there was no such stuff in my thoughts.

HAMLET   Why did you laugh then, when I said "man delights not me"?

ROSENCRANTZ   To think, my lord, if you delight not in man, what
lenten entertainment the players shall receive from you: we coted[4]   295
them on the way; and hither are they coming, to offer you service.

HAMLET   He that plays the king shall be welcome; his majesty shall
have tribute of me; the adventurous knight shall use his foil and
target; the lover shall not sigh gratis; the humorous[5] man shall end
his part in peace; the clown shall make those laugh whose lungs are   300
tickle o' the sere,[6] and the lady shall say her mind freely, or the blank
verse shall halt for 't. What players are they?

ROSENCRANTZ   Even those you were wont to take such delight in, the
tragedians of the city.

HAMLET   How chances it they travel? their residence, both in reputa-   305
tion and profit, was better both ways.

ROSENCRANTZ   I think their inhibition comes by means of the late
innovation.[7]

HAMLET   Do they hold the same estimation they did when I was in the
city? are they so followed?   310

ROSENCRANTZ   No, indeed, are they not.

HAMLET   How comes it? do they grow rusty?

ROSENCRANTZ   Nay, their endeavor keeps in the wonted pace: but
there is, sir, an eyrie of children, little eyases, that cry out on the
top of question[8] and are most tyrannically clapped for 't: these are   315
now the fashion, and so berattle the common stages—so they call
them—that many wearing rapiers are afraid of goose-quills,[9] and
dare scarce come thither.

9. On.   1. Precede your disclosure.   2. Adorned.   3. Precise.   4. Overtook.   5. Eccentric, whimsical.   6. Ready to shoot off at a touch.   7. The introduction of the children (line 314), as Rosencrantz explains in his subsequent replies to Hamlet. "Inhibition": prohibition.   8. Above others on matter of dispute. "Eyrie": nest. "Eyases": nestling hawks.   9. Gentlemen are afraid of pens (that is, of poets satirizing the "common stages").

HAMLET   What, are they children? who maintains 'em? how are they
    escoted?[1] Will they pursue the quality[2] no longer than they can sing?   320
    will they not say afterwards, if they should grow themselves to com-
    mon players—as it is most like, if their means are no better,—their
    writers do them wrong, to make them exclaim against their own
    succession?[3]

ROSENCRANTZ   Faith, there has been much to-do on both sides, and   325
    the nation holds it no sin to tarre them to controversy: there was
    for a while no money bid for argument unless the poet and the player
    went to cuffs in the question.[4]

HAMLET   Is 't possible?

GUILDENSTERN   O, there has been much throwing about of brains.   330

HAMLET   Do the boys carry it away?[5]

ROSENCRANTZ   Aye, that they do, my lord; Hercules and his load too.[6]

HAMLET   It is not very strange; for my uncle is king of Denmark, and
    those that would make mows[7] at him while my father lived, give
    twenty, forty, fifty, a hundred ducats a-piece, for his picture in little.   335
    'Sblood, there is something in this more than natural, if philosophy
    could find it out.
        [Flourish of trumpets within.]

GUILDENSTERN   There are the players.

HAMLET   Gentlemen, you are welcome to Elsinore. Your hands, come
    then: the appurtenance of welcome is fashion and ceremony: let me   340
    comply with you in this garb, lest my extent to the players, which,
    I tell you, must show fairly outwards, should more appear like enter-
    tainment[8] than yours. You are welcome: but my uncle-father and
    aunt-mother are deceived.

GUILDENSTERN   In what, my dear lord?   345

HAMLET   I am but mad north-north-west: when the wind is southerly
    I know a hawk from a handsaw.[9]
        [Re-enter POLONIUS.]

POLONIUS   Well be with you, gentlemen!

HAMLET   Hark you, Guildenstern; and you too: at each ear a hearer:
    that great baby you see there is not yet out of his swaddling clouts.[1]   350

ROSENCRANTZ   Happily he's the second time come to them; for they
    say an old man is twice a child.

HAMLET   I will prophesy he comes to tell me of the players; mark it.
    You say right, sir: o' Monday morning; 'twas so, indeed.[2]

POLONIUS   My lord, I have news to tell you.   355

HAMLET   My lord, I have news to tell you. When Roscius[3] was an actor
    in Rome,—

POLONIUS   The actors are come hither, my lord.

HAMLET   Buz, buz![4]

---

1. Financially supported.   2. Profession of acting. "Berattle": berate.   3. Recite satiric pieces against
what they are themselves likely to become, common players.   4. No offer to buy a plot for a play if it did
not contain a quarrel between poet and player on that subject. "Tarre": incite.   5. Win out.   6. The sign
in front of the Globe theater showed Hercules bearing the world on his shoulders.   7. Faces, grimaces.
8. Welcome. "Garb": style. "Extent": welcoming behavior.   9. A hawk from a heron as well as a kind of ax
from a handsaw.   1. Clothes.   2. Hamlet, for Polonius's sake, pretends he is deep in talk with Rosencrantz.   3. A famous Roman comic actor (126?–62? B.C.E.).   4. An expression used to stop the teller of a
stale story.

POLONIUS   Upon my honor,—   360
HAMLET   Then came each actor on his ass,—
POLONIUS   The best actors in the world, either for tragedy, comedy,
history, pastoral, pastoral-comical, historical-pastoral, tragical-
historical, tragical-comical-historical-pastoral, scene individable, or
poem unlimited:[5] Seneca cannot be too heavy, nor Plautus[6] too light.   365
For the law of writ and the liberty,[7] these are the only men.
HAMLET   O Jephthah,[8] judge of Israel, what a treasure hadst thou!
POLONIUS   What a treasure had he, my lord?
HAMLET   Why,
         "One fair daughter, and no more,   370
            The which he lovèd passing well."[9]
POLONIUS   [Aside.]   Still on my daughter.
HAMLET   Am I not i' the right, old Jephthah?
POLONIUS   If you call me Jephthah, my lord, I have a daughter that I
love passing well.   375
HAMLET   Nay, that follows not.
POLONIUS   What follows, then, my lord?
HAMLET   Why,
         "As by lot, God wot."
and then you know,
         "It came to pass, as most like it was,"—   380
the first row of the pious chanson will show you more; for look, where
my abridgment[1] comes.
         [Enter four or five PLAYERS.]
You are welcome, masters; welcome, all. I am glad to see thee well.
Welcome, good friends. O, my old friend! Why thy face is valanced[2]
since I saw thee last; comest thou to beard me in Denmark? What,   385
my young lady and mistress! By'r lady, your ladyship is nearer to
heaven than when I saw you last, by the altitude of a chopine.[3] Pray
God, your voice, like a piece of uncurrent gold, be not cracked within
the ring.[4] Masters, you are all welcome. We'll e'en to 't like French
falconers, fly at any thing we see: we'll have a speech straight: come,   390
give us a taste of your quality; come, a passionate speech.
FIRST PLAYER   What speech, my good lord?
HAMLET   I heard thee speak me a speech once, but it was never acted;
or, if it was, not above once; for the play, I remember, pleased not
the million; 'twas caviare to the general:[5] but it was—as I received 395
it, and others, whose judgments in such matters cried in the top of
mine[6]—an excellent play, well digested in the scenes, set down with
as much modesty as cunning. I remember, one said there were no
sallets in the lines to make the matter savory, nor no matter in the
phrase that might indict the author of affection;[7] but called it an   400

5. For plays governed and those not governed by classical rules.   6. A Roman who wrote comedies
(254?–184? B.C.E.). Seneca (after 4 B.C.E.–65 C.E.) was a Roman who wrote tragedies.   7. Possibly, for
both written and extemporized plays.   8. He was compelled to sacrifice a dearly beloved daughter
(Judges 11).   9. From an old ballad about Jephthah.   1. That is, the players interrupting him. "Row":
stanza. "Chanson": song.   2. Draped (with a beard).   3. A thick-soled shoe.   4. A pun on the *ring*
of the voice and the *ring* around the king's head on a coin. "Uncurrent": unfit for currency.   5. A delicacy wasted on the general public.   6. Were louder (more authoritative than) mine.   7. Affectation.
"Sallets": salads (that is, relish, spicy passages).

honest method, as wholesome as sweet, and by very much more
handsome than fine.[9] One speech in it I chiefly loved: 'twas Æneas'
tale to Dido; and thereabout of it especially, where he speaks of
Priam's slaughter:[1] it live in your memory, begin at this line; let me
see, let me see;   405
"The rugged Pyrrhus, like th' Hyrcanian beast,"[2]—
It is not so: it begins with "Pyrrhus."
"the rugged Pyrrhus, he whose sable arms,
Black as his purpose, did the night resemble
When he lay couchèd in the ominous horse,[3]   410
Hath now this dread and black complexion smeared
With heraldry more dismal: head to foot
Now is he total gules; horridly tricked[4]
With the blood of fathers, mothers, daughters, sons,
Baked and impasted with the parching streets,   415
That lend a tyrannous[5] and a damnèd light
To their lord's murder: roasted in wrath and fire,
And thus o'er-sizèd[6] with coagulate gore,
With eyes like carbuncles, the hellish Pyrrhus
Old grandsire Priam seeks."   420
So, proceed you.
POLONIUS   'Fore God, my lord, well spoken, with good accent and good
  discretion.
FIRST PLAYER   'Anon he finds him
  Striking too short at Greeks; his antique sword,   425
  Rebellious to his arm, lies where it falls,
  Repugnant to command: unequal matched,
  Pyrrhus at Priam drives; in rage strikes wide;
  But with the whiff and wind of his fell sword
  The unnervèd father falls. Then senseless Ilium,[7]   430
  Seeming to feel this blow, with flaming top
  Stoops to his base, and with a hideous crash
  Takes prisoner Pyrrhus's ear: for, lo! his sword,
  Which was declining on the milky [8] head
  Of reverend Priam seemed i' the air to stick: 435
  So, as a painted tyrant, Pyrrhus stood,
  And like a neutral to his will and matter,
  Did nothing.
  But as we often see, against some storm,
  A silence in the heavens, the rack[9] stand still,   440
  The bold winds speechless and the orb below
  As hush as death, anon the dreadful thunder
  Doth rend the region, so after Pyrrhus's pause
  Aroused vengeance sets him new a-work;
  And never did the Cyclops'[1] hammers fall   445

9. More elegant than showy.   1. The story of the fall of Troy, told by Aeneas to Queen Dido. Priam was
the king of Troy.   2. Tiger. Pyrrhus was Achilles' son (also called Neoptolemus).   3. The wooden
horse in which Greek warriors were smuggled into Troy.   4. Adorned. "Gules": heraldic term for *red*.
5. Savage.   6. Glued over.   7. Troy's citadel.   8. White-haired.   9. Clouds. "Against": just
before.   1. The gigantic workmen of Hephaestus (Vulcan), god of blacksmiths and fire.

On Mars's armor, forged for proof [2] eterne,
With less remorse than Pyrrhus's bleeding sword
Now falls on Priam.
Out, thou strumpet, Fortune! All you gods,
In general synod take away her power,   450
Break all the spokes and fellies from her wheel,
And bowl the round nave[3] down the hill of heaven
As low as to the fiends!

POLONIUS   This is too long.

HAMLET   It shall to the barber's, with your beard. Prithee, say on: he's   455
for a jig[4] or a tale of bawdry, or he sleeps: say on: come to Hecuba.

FIRST PLAYER   "But who, O, who had seen the mobled[5] queen—"

HAMLET   "the mobled queen?"

POLONIUS   That's good; "mobled queen" is good.

FIRST PLAYER   "Run barefoot up and down, threatening the flames   460
With bisson rheum; a clout[6] upon that head
Where late the diadem stood; and for a robe,
About her lank and all o'er-teemèd loins,[7]
A blanket, in the alarm of fear caught up:
Who this had seen, with tongue in venom steeped   465
'Gainst Fortune's state[8] would treason have pronounced:
But if the gods themselves did see her then,
When she saw Pyrrhus make malicious sport
In mincing with his sword her husband's limbs,
The instant burst of clamor that she made,   470
Unless things mortal move them[9] not at all,
Would have made milch the burning eyes of heaven[1]
And passion in the gods."

POLONIUS   Look, whether he has not turned his color and has tears in
's eyes. Prithee, no more.   475

HAMLET   'Tis well; I'll have thee speak out the rest of this soon. Good
my lord, will you see the players well bestowed?[2] Do you hear, let
them be well used, for they are the abstracts and brief chronicles of
the time: after your death you were better have a bad epitaph than
their ill report while you live.   480

POLONIUS   My lord, I will use them according to their desert.

HAMLET   God's bodykins,[3] man, much better: use every man after his
desert, and who shall 'scape whipping? Use them after your own
honor and dignity: the less they deserve, the more merit is in your
bounty. Take them in.   485

POLONIUS   Come, sirs.

HAMLET   Follow him, friends: we'll hear a play to-morrow. [*Exit*
POLONIUS *with all the* PLAYERS *but the first.*] Dost thou hear me, old
friend; can you play the Murder of Gonzago?

FIRST PLAYER   Aye, my lord.   490

---

2. Protection.   3. Hub. "Fellies": rims.   4. Ludicrous sung dialogue, short farce.   5. Muffled.
6. Cloth. "Bisson rheum": blinding moisture, tears.   7. Worn out by childbearing.   8. Government.
9. The gods.   1. The stars. "Milch": moist (milk-giving).   2. Taken care of, lodged.   3. By God's
little body.

HAMLET   We'll ha 't to-morrow night. You could, for a need, study a
  speech of some dozen or sixteen lines, which I would set down and
  insert in 't, could you not?
FIRST PLAYER   Aye, my lord.
HAMLET   Very well. Follow that lord; and look you mock him not.   495
  [*Exit* FIRST PLAYER] My good friends, I'll leave you till night: you are
  welcome to Elsinore.
ROSENCRANTZ   Good my lord!
HAMLET   Aye, so, God be wi' ye! [*Exeunt* ROSENCRANTZ *and* GUILDEN-
  STERN.] Now I am alone.   500
  O, what a rogue and peasant slave am I!
  Is it not monstrous that this player here,
  But in a fiction, in a dream of passion,
  Could force his soul so to his own conceit
  That from her[4] working all his visage wanned;   505
  Tears in his eyes, distraction in 's aspect,
  A broken voice, and his whole function[5] suiting
  With forms to his conceit? and all for nothing!
  For Hecuba![6]
  What's Hecuba to him, or he to Hecuba,   510
  That he should weep for her? What would he do,
  Had he the motive and the cue for passion
  That I have? He would drown the stage with tears
  And cleave the general air with horrid speech,
  Make mad the guilty and appal the free,   515
  Confound the ignorant, and amaze indeed
  The very faculties of eyes and ears.
  Yet I,
  A dull and muddy-mettled rascal, peak,[7]
  Like John-a-dreams, unpregnant of my cause,[8]   520
  And can say nothing; no, not for a king,
  Upon whose property and most dear life
  A damn'd defeat was made. Am I a coward?
  Who calls me villain? breaks my pate across?
  Plucks off my beard, and blows it in my face?   525
  Tweaks me by the nose? gives me the lie i' the throat,
  As deep as to the lungs? who does me this?
  Ha!
  'Swounds, I should take it: for it cannot be
  But I am pigeon-livered and lack gall   530
  To make oppression bitter, or ere this
  I should have fatted all the region kites[9]
  With this slave's offal: bloody, bawdy villain!
  Remorseless, treacherous, lecherous, kindless[1] villain!
  O, vengeance!   535
  Why, what an ass am I! This is most brave,

---

4. His soul's.   5. Bodily action.   6. Queen of Troy, Priam's wife. "Conceit": imagination, conception
of the role played.   7. Mope. "Muddy-mettled": of poor metal (spirit, temper), dull-spirited.   8. Not
really conscious of my cause, unquickened by it. "John-a-dreams": a dreamy, absentminded character.
9. Hawks of the air.   1. Unnatural.

That I, the son of a dear father murdered,
Prompted to my revenge by heaven and hell,
Must, like a whore, unpack my heart with words,
And fall a-cursing, like a very drab,   540
A scullion!
Fie upon 't! About,² my brain! Hum, I have heard
That guilty creatures, sitting at a play,
Have by the very cunning of the scene
Been struck so to the soul that presently   545
They have proclaimed their malefactions;
For murder, though it have no tongue, will speak
With most miraculous organ. I'll have these players
Play something like the murder of my father
Before mine uncle: I'll observe his looks;   550
I'll tent him to the quick: if he but blench,³
I know my course. The spirit that I have seen
May be the devil; and the devil hath power
To assume a pleasing shape; yea, and perhaps
Out of my weakness and my melancholy,   555
As he is very potent with such spirits,
Abuses me to damn me. I'll have grounds
More relative⁴ than this. The play's the thing
Wherein I'll catch the conscience of the king.   560
    [*Exit.*]

Act III

SCENE 1

[SCENE: *A room in the castle.*]

[*Enter* KING, QUEEN, POLONIUS, OPHELIA, ROSENCRANTZ, *and*
    GUILDENSTERN.]
KING   And can you, by no drift of circumstance,⁵
  Get from him why he puts on this confusion,
  Grating so harshly all his days of quiet
  With turbulent and dangerous lunacy?
ROSENCRANTZ   He does confess he feels himself distracted,   5
  But from what cause he will by no means speak.
GUILDENSTERN   Nor do we find him forward to be sounded;
  But, with a crafty madness, keeps aloof,
  When we would bring him on to some confession
  Of his true state.
QUEEN   Did he receive you well?   10
ROSENCRANTZ   Most like a gentleman.
GUILDENSTERN   But with much forcing of his disposition.
ROSENCRANTZ   Niggard of question, but of our demands
  Most free in his reply.

---

2. To work!   3. Flinch. "Tent": probe.   4. Relevant.   5. Turn of talk, or roundabout way.

QUEEN   Did you assay[6] him
  To any pastime?   15
ROSENCRANTZ Madam, it so fell out that certain players
  We o'er-raught[7] on the way: of these we told him,
  And there did seem in him a kind of joy
  To hear of it: they are about the court,
  And, as I think, they have already order   20
  This night to play before him.
POLONIUS   'Tis most true:
  And he beseeched me to entreat your majesties
  To hear and see the matter.
KING   With all my heart; and it doth much content me
  To hear him so inclined.   25
  Good gentlemen, give him a further edge,[8]
  And drive his purpose on to these delights.
ROSENCRANTZ We shall, my lord.
        [Exeunt ROSENCRANTZ and GUILDENSTERN.]
KING   Sweet Gertrude, leave us too;
  For we have closely[9] sent for Hamlet hither,
  That he, as 'twere by accident, may here   30
  Affront[1] Ophelia:
  Her father and myself, lawful espials,
  Will so bestow[2] ourselves that, seeing unseen,
  We may of their encounter frankly judge,
  And gather by him, as he is behaved,   35
  If 't be the affliction of his love or no
  That thus he suffers for.
QUEEN   I shall obey you:
  And for your part, Ophelia, I do wish
  That your good beauties be the happy cause
  Of hamlet's wildness: so shall I hope your virtues   40
  Will bring him to his wonted way again,
  To both your honors.
OPHELIA   Madam, I wish it may.
        [Exit QUEEN.]
POLONIUS   Ophelia, walk you here. Gracious, so please you,
  We will bestow ourselves. [To OPHELIA.] Read on this book;
  That show of such an exercise may color[3]   45
  Your loneliness. We are oft to blame in this,—
  'Tis too much proved—that with devotion's visage
  And pious action we do sugar o'er
  The devil himself.
KING [Aside.]   O, 'tis too true!
  How smart a lash that speech doth give my conscience!   50
  The harlot's cheek, beautied with plastering art,
  Is not more ugly to the thing that helps it

---

6. Try to attract him.   7. Overtook.   8. Incitement.   9. Privately.   1. Confront.   2. Place.
"Espials": spies.   3. Excuse.

Than is my deed to my most painted word:
O heavy burthen!
POLONIUS   I hear him coming: let's withdraw, my lord.   55
     [*Exeunt* KING *and* POLONIUS.—*Enter* HAMLET.]
HAMLET   To be, or not to be: that is the question:
  Whether 'tis nobler in the mind to suffer
  The slings and arrows of outrageous fortune,
  Or to take arms against a sea of troubles,
  And by opposing end them. To die: to sleep;   60
  No more; and by a sleep to say we end
  The heart-ache, and the thousand natural shocks
  That flesh is heir to, 'tis a consummation[4]
  Devoutly to be wished. To die, to sleep;
  To sleep: perchance to dream: aye, there's the rub;[5]   65
  For in that sleep of death what dreams may come,
  When we have shuffled off this mortal coil,[6]
  Must give us pause: there's the respect
  That makes calamity of so long life;[7]
  For who would bear the whips and scorns of time,   70
  The oppressor's wrong, the proud man's contumely,
  The pangs of despisèd love, the law's delay,
  The insolence of office, and the spurns
  That patient merit of the unworthy takes,
  When he himself might his quietus make   75
  With a bare bodkin? who would fardels[8] bear,
  To grunt and sweat under a weary life,
  But that the dread of something after death,
  The undiscovered country from whose bourn[9]
  No traveler returns, puzzles the will,   80
  And makes us rather bear those ills we have
  Than fly to others that we know not of ?
  Thus conscience does make cowards of us all,
  And thus the native hue of resolution
  Is sicklied o'er with the pale cast of thought,   85
  And enterprises of great pitch[1] and moment
  With this regard their currents turn awry
  And lose the name of action. Soft you now!
  The fair Ophelia! Nymph, in thy orisons[2]
  Be all my sins remembered.
OPHELIA   Good my lord,   90
  How does your honor for this many a day?
HAMLET   I humbly thank you: well, well, well.
OPHELIA   My lord, I have remembrances of yours,
  That I have longed to re-deliver;
  I pray you, now receive them.
HAMLET   No, not I;   95

---

4. Final settlement.   5. The impediment (a bowling term).   6. Have rid ourselves of the turmoil of
mortal life.   7. So long-lived. "Respect": consideration.   8. Burdens. "Bodkin": poniard, dagger.
9. Boundary.   1. Height.   2. Prayers.

I never gave you aught.

OPHELIA   My honored lord, you know right well you did;
And with them words of so sweet breath composed
As made the things more rich: their perfume lost,
Take these again; for to the noble mind   100
Rich gifts wax poor when givers prove unkind.
There, my lord.

HAMLET   Ha, ha! are you honest?

OPHELIA   My lord?   105

HAMLET   Are you fair?

OPHELIA   What means your lordship?

HAMLET   That if you be honest and fair, your honesty should admit no
discourse to your beauty.

OPHELIA   Could beauty, my lord, have better commerce[3] than with
honesty?   110

HAMLET   Aye, truly; for the power of beauty will sooner transform honesty from what it is to a bawd than the force of honesty can translate
beauty into his likeness: this was sometime a paradox, but now the
time gives it proof.[4] I did love you once.

OPHELIA   Indeed, my lord, you made me believe so.   115

HAMLET   You should not have believed me; for virtue cannot so inoculate our old stock, but we shall relish[5] of it: I loved you not.

OPHELIA   I was the more deceived.

HAMLET   Get thee to a nunnery: why wouldst thou be a breeder of
sinners? I am myself indifferent honest; but yet I could accuse me   120
of such things that it were better my mother had not borne me: I am
very proud, revengeful, ambitious; with more offenses at my beck
than I have thoughts to put them in, imagination to give them shape,
or time to act them in. What should such fellows as I do crawling
between heaven and earth! We are arrant knaves all; believe none   125
of us. Go thy ways to a nunnery. Where's your father?

OPHELIA   At home, my lord.

HAMLET   Let the doors be shut upon him, that he may play the fool
no where but in 's own house. Farewell.

OPHELIA   O, help him, you sweet heavens!   130

HAMLET   If thou dost marry, I'll give thee this plague for thy dowry: be
thou as chaste as ice, as pure as snow, thou shalt not escape cal-
umny. Get thee to a nunnery, go: farewell. Or, if thou wilt needs
marry, marry a fool; for wise men know well enough what monsters[6]
you make of them. To a nunnery, go; and quickly too. Farewell.   135

OPHELIA   O heavenly powers, restore him!

HAMLET   I have heard of your paintings too, well enough; God hath
given you one face, and you make yourselves another: you jig, you
amble, and you lisp, and nick-name God's creatures, and make your
wantonness your ignorance.[7] Go to, I'll no more on 't; it hath made   140

---

3. Intercourse.   4. In his mother's adultery. "His": its.   5. Retain the flavor of. "Inoculate": graft
itself onto.   6. Cuckolds bear imaginary horns and "a horned man's a monster" (*Othello* 4.1).
7. Misname (out of affectation) the most natural things, and pretend that this is due to ignorance instead
of affectation.

me mad. I say, we will have no more marriages: those that are mar
ried already, all but one, shall live; the rest shall keep as they are.
To a nunnery, go.
    [Exit.]
OPHELIA   O, what a noble mind is here o'erthrown!
  The courtier's, soldier's, scholar's, eye, tongue, sword: 145
  The expectancy and rose of the fair state,
  The glass of fashion and the mould of form.[8]
  The observed of all observers, quite, quite down!
  And I, of ladies most deject and wretched,
  That sucked the honey of his music vows,   150
  Now see that noble and most sovereign reason,
  Like sweet bells jangled, out of tune and harsh;
  That unmatched form and feature of blown[9] youth
  Blasted with ecstasy: O, woe is me,
  To have seen what I have seen, see what I see!   155
    [Re-enter KING and POLONIUS.]
KING   Love! his affections do not that way tend;
  Nor what he spake, though it lacked form a little,
  Was not like madness. There's something in his soul
  O'er which his melancholy sits on brood,
  And I do doubt[1] the hatch and the disclose   160
  Will be some danger: which for to prevent,
  I have in quick determination
  Thus set it down:—he shall with speed to England,
  For the demand of our neglected tribute:
  Haply the seas and countries different   165
  With variable objects shall expel
  This something-settled matter in his heart,
  Whereon his brains still beating puts him thus
  From fashion of himself.[2] What think you on 't?
POLONIUS   It shall do well: but yet do I believe   170
  The origin and commencement of his grief
  Sprung from neglected love. How now, Ophelia!
  You need not tell us what Lord hamlet said;
  We heard it all. My lord, do as you please;
  But, if you hold it fit, after the play,   175
  Let his queen mother all alone entreat him
  To show his grief: let her be round[3] with him;
  And I'll be placed, so please you, in the ear
  Of all their conference. If she find him not,
  To England send him, or confine him where   180
  Your wisdom best shall think.
KING   It shall be so:
  Madness in great ones must not unwatched go.
    [Exeunt.]

---

8. The mirror of fashion and the model of behavior.   9. In full bloom.   1. Fear.   2. Makes him
behave unusually.   3. Direct.

SCENE 2

[SCENE: *A hall in the castle.*]

[*Enter* HAMLET *and* PLAYERS.]

HAMLET   Speak the speech, I pray you, as I pronounced it to you,
trippingly on the tongue: but if you mouth it, as many of your players do, I had as lief the town-crier spoke my lines. Nor do not saw
the air too much with your hand, thus; but use all gently: for in the
very torrent, tempest, and, as I may say, whirlwind of your passion,   5
you must acquire and beget a temperance that may give it smooth-
ness. O, it offends me to the soul to hear a robustious periwig-pated
fellow tear a passion to tatters, to very rags, to split the ears of the
groundlings,[4] who, for the most part, are capable of nothing but
inexplicable dumb-shows and noise: I would have such a fellow   10
whipped for o'er doing Termagant;[5] it out-herods Herod: pray you,
avoid it.

FIRST PLAYER   I warrant your honor.

HAMLET   Be not too tame neither, but let your own discretion be your
tutor: suit the action to the word, the word to the action; with this   15
special observance, that you o'erstep not the modesty[6] of nature: for
anything so overdone is from the purpose of playing, whose end, both
at the first and now, was and is, to hold, as 'twere, the mirror up to
nature; to show virtue her own feature, scorn her own image, and
the very age and body of the time his form and pressure.[7] Now this   20
overdone or come tardy off, though it make the unskillful laugh,
cannot but make the judicious grieve; the censure of the which one
must in your allowance o'erweigh a whole theater of others. O, there
be players that I have seen play, and heard others praise, and that
highly, not to speak it profanely,[8] that neither having the accent of   25
Christians nor the gait of Christian, pagan, nor man, have so strutted
and bellowed, that I have thought some of nature's journeymen had
made men, and not made them well, they imitated humanity so
abominably.

FIRST PLAYER   I hope we have reformed that indifferently[9] with us, sir.   30

HAMLET   O, reform it altogether. And let those that play your clowns
speak no more than is set down for them: for there be of them that
will themselves laugh, to set on some quantity of barren[1] spectators
to laugh too, though in the mean time some necessary question of
the play be then to be considered: that's villainous, and shows a most   35
pitiful ambition in the fool that uses it. Go, make you ready.

[*Exeunt* PLAYERS. —*Enter* POLONIUS, ROSENCRANTZ, *and* GUILDEN-
STERN.]

How now, my lord! will the king hear this piece of work?

POLONIUS   And the queen too, and that presently.

HAMLET   Bid the players make haste.

[*Exit* POLONIUS.]

---

4. Spectators in the pit, where admission was cheapest.   5. Muslim god in old romances and morality
plays; he was portrayed as being noisy and excitable.   6. Moderation.   7. Impress, shape. "Feature":
form. "His": its.   8. Hamlet apologizes for the profane implication that there could be men not of God's
making.   9. Pretty well.   1. Silly.

Will you two help to hasten them? 40

ROSENCRANTZ
GUILDENSTERN } We will, my lord.

[*Exeunt* ROSENCRANTZ *and* GUILDENSTERN.]

HAMLET   What ho! Horatio!

[*Enter* HORATIO.]

HORATIO   Here, sweet lord, at your service.

HAMLET   Horatio, thou art e'en as just a man
As e'er my conversation coped withal.[2] 45

HORATIO   O, my dear lord,—

HAMLET   Nay, do not think I flatter;
For what advancement may I hope from thee,
That no revenue hast but thy good spirits,
To feed and clothe thee? Why should the poor be flattered?
No, let the candied tongue lick absurd pomp, 50
And crook the pregnant hinges of the knee
Where thrift may follow fawning.[3] Dost thou hear?
Since my dear soul was mistress of her choice,
And could of men distinguish, her election
Hath sealed thee for herself: for thou hast been 55
As one, in suffering all, that suffers nothing;
A man that fortune's buffets and rewards
Hast ta'en with equal thanks: and blest are those
Whose blood and judgment[4] are so well commingled
That they are not a pipe for fortune's finger 60
To sound what stop she please.[5] Give me that man
That is not passion's slave, and I will wear him
In my heart's core, ay, in my heart of heart,
As I do thee. Something too much of this.
There is a play to-night before the king; 65
One scene of it comes near the circumstance
Which I have told thee of my father's death:
I prithee, when thou sees that act a-foot,
Even with the very comment of thy soul[6]
Observe my uncle: if his occulted guilt 70
Do not itself unkennel in one speech
It is a damned ghost that we have seen,
And my imaginations are as foul
As Vulcan's stithy.[7] Give him heedful note;
For I mine eyes will rivet to his face, 75
And after we will both our judgments join
In censure of his seeming.[8]

HORATIO   Well, my lord:
If he steal aught the whilst this play is playing,
And 'scape detecting, I will pay the theft.

HAMLET   They are coming to the play: I must be idle:[9] 80

---

2. As I ever associated with.   3. Material profit may be derived from cringing. "Pregnant hinges": supple joints.   4. Passion and reason.   5. For Fortune to put her finger on any windhole of the pipe she wants.   6. With all your powers of observation.   7. Smithy.   8. To judge his behavior.   9. Crazy.

Get you a place.

[*Danish march. A flourish. Enter* KING, QUEEN, POLONIUS, OPHELIA, ROSENCRANTZ, GUILDENSTERN, *and other* LORDS *attendant, with the* GUARD *carrying torches.*]

KING   How fares our cousin Hamlet?

HAMLET   Excellent, i' faith; of the chameleon's dish: I eat the air,[1] promise-crammed: you cannot feed capons so.

KING   I have nothing with this answer, Hamlet; these words are not   85
mine.[2]

HAMLET   No, nor mine now. [*To* POLONIUS.] My lord, you played once i' the university, you say?

POLONIUS   That did I, my lord, and was accounted a good actor.

HAMLET   What did you enact?   90

POLONIUS   I did enact Julius Caesar: I was killed i' the Capitol; Brutus killed me.

HAMLET   It was a brute part of him to kill so capital a calf there. Be the players ready?

ROSENCRANTZ   Aye, my lord; they stay upon your patience.   95

QUEEN   Come hither, my dear Hamlet, sit by me.

HAMLET   No, good mother, here's metal more attractive.

POLONIUS [*To the* KING.]   O, ho! do you mark that?

HAMLET   Lady, shall I lie in your lap? [*Lying down at* OPHELIA*'s feet.*]

OPHELIA   No, my lord.   100

HAMLET   I mean, my head upon your lap?

OPHELIA   Aye, my lord.

HAMLET   Do you think I meant country matters?

OPHELIA   I think nothing, my lord.

HAMLET   That's a fair thought to lie between maids' legs.   105

OPHELIA   What is, my lord?

HAMLET   Nothing.[3]

OPHELIA   You are merry, my lord.

HAMLET   Who, I?

OPHELIA   Aye, my lord.   110

HAMLET   O God, your only jig-maker.[4] What should a man do but be merry? for, look you, how cheerfully my mother looks, and my father died within 's two hours.

OPHELIA   Nay, 'tis twice two months, my lord.

HAMLET   So long? Nay then, let the devil wear black, for I'll have a   115
suit of sables.[5] O heavens! die two months ago, and not forgotten yet? Then there's hope a great man's memory may outlive his life half a year: but, by 'r lady, he must build churches then; or else shall he suffer not thinking on, with the hobby-horse,[6] whose epitaph is, "For, O, for, O, the hobby-horse is forgot."   120

[*Hautboys play. The dumb-show enters. —Enter a King and a Queen very lovingly; the Queen embracing him and he her. She kneels, and makes show of protestation unto him. He takes her up, and declines his*

---

1. The chameleon was supposed to feed on air.   2. Have nothing to do with my question.   3. A sexual pun: no thing.   4. Maker of comic songs.   5. Hamlet notes sarcastically the lack of mourning for his father in the fancy dress of court and king.   6. A figure in the old May Day games and Morris dances.

head upon her neck; lays him down upon a bank of flowers: she, seeing him asleep, leaves him. Anon comes in a fellow, takes off his crown, kisses it, and pours poison in the King's ears, and exits. The Queen returns; finds the King dead, and makes passionate action. The Poisoner, with some two or three Mutes comes in again, seeming to lament with her. The dead body is carried away. The Poisoner woos the Queen with gifts: she seems loath and unwilling awhile, but in the end accepts his love. —Exeunt.]

OPHELIA   What means this, my lord?

HAMLET   Marry, this is miching mallecho;[7] it means mischief.

OPHELIA   Belike this show imports the argument of the play.

    [*Enter* PROLOGUE.]

HAMLET   We shall know by this fellow: the players cannot keep counsel;[8] they'll tell all.   125

OPHELIA   Will he tell us what this show meant?

HAMLET   Aye, or any show that you'll show him: be not you ashamed to show, he'll not shame to tell you what it means.

OPHELIA   You are naught,[9] you are naught: I'll mark the play.

PROLOGUE   For us, and for our tragedy,   130
       Here stooping to your clemency,
       We beg your hearing patiently.

HAMLET   Is this a prologue, or the posy[1] of a ring?

OPHELIA   'Tis brief, my lord.

HAMLET   As woman's love.   135

    [*Enter two* PLAYERS, KING *and* QUEEN.]

PLAYER KING   Full thirty times hath Phœbus's cart[2] gone round
  Neptune's salt wash and Tellus's orbed ground,
  And thirty dozen moons with borrowed sheen
  About the world have times twelve thirties been,
  Since love our hearts and Hymen did our hands   140
  Unite commutual in most sacred bands.

PLAYER QUEEN   So many journeys may the sun and moon
  Make us again count o'er ere love be done!
  But, woe is me, you are so sick of late,
  So far from cheer and from your former state,   145
  That I distrust you.[3] Yet, though I distrust,
  Discomfort you, my lord, it nothing must:
  For women's fear and love holds quantity,[4]
  In neither aught, or in extremity.
  Now, what my love is, proof hath made you know,   150
  And as my love is sized, my fear is so:
  Where love is great, the littlest doubts are fear,
  Where little fears grow great, great love grows there.

PLAYER KING   Faith, I must leave thee, love, and shortly too;
  My operant powers their functions leave[5] to do: 155
  And thou shalt live in this fair world behind,
  Honored, beloved; and haply one as kind

---

7. Sneaking misdeed.   8. A secret.   9. Naughty, improper.   1. Motto, inscription.   2. The chariot of the sun.   3. I am worried about you.   4. Maintain mutual balance.   5. Cease.

For husband shalt thou—
PLAYER QUEEN   O, confound the rest!
  Such love must needs be treason in my breast:
  In second husband let me be accurst!   160
  None wed the second but who killed the first.
HAMLET [*Aside.*]   Wormwood, wormwood.
PLAYER QUEEN   The instances that second marriage move
  Are base respects of thrift,[6] but none of love:
  A second time I kill my husband dead,   165
  When second husband kisses me in bed.
PLAYER KING   I do believe you think what now you speak,
  But what we do determine oft we break.
  Purpose is but the slave to memory,
  Of violent birth but poor validity: 170
  Which now, like fruit unripe, sticks on the tree,
  But fall unshaken when they mellow be.
  Most necessary 'tis that we forget
  To pay ourselves what to ourselves is debt:
  What to ourselves in passion we propose,   175
  The passion ending, both the purpose lose.
  The violence of either grief or joy
  Their own enactures[7] with themselves destroy:
  Where joy most revels, grief doth most lament;
  Grief joys, joy grieves, on slender accident.   180
  This world is not for aye, nor 'tis not strange
  That even our loves should with our fortunes change,
  For 'tis a question left us yet to prove,
  Whether love lead fortune or else fortune love.
  The great man down, you mark his favorite flies;   185
  The poor advanced makes friends of enemies:
  And hitherto doth love on fortune tend;
  For who not needs shall never lack a friend,
  And who in want a hollow friend doth try
  Directly seasons[8] him his enemy.   190
  But, orderly to end where I begun,
  Our wills and fates do so contrary run,
  That our devices still are overthrown,
  Our thoughts are ours, their ends none of our own:
  So think thou wilt no second husband wed,   195
  But die thy thoughts when thy first lord is dead.
PLAYER QUEEN   Nor earth to me give food nor heaven light!
  Sport and repose lock from me day and night!
  To desperation turn my trust and hope!
  An anchor's cheer in prison be my scope!   200
  Each opposite, that blanks[9] the face of joy,
  Meet what I would have well and it destroy!
  Both here and hence pursue me lasting strife,

---

6. Considerations of material profit. "Instances": motives.   7. Their own fulfillment in action.
8. Matures.   9. Makes pale. "Anchor's cheer": hermit's, or anchorite's, fare.

If, once a widow, ever I be wife!

HAMLET   If she should break it now!   205

PLAYER KING   'Tis deeply sworn. Sweet, leave me here a while;
My spirits grow dull, and fain I would beguile
The tedious day with sleep.
    [*Sleeps.*]

PLAYER QUEEN   Sleep rock thy brain;
And never come mischance between us twain!
    [*Exit.*]

HAMLET   Madam, how like you this play?   210

QUEEN   The lady doth protest[1] too much, methinks.

HAMLET   O, but she'll keep her word.

KING   Have you heard the argument?[2] Is there no offense in 't?

HAMLET   No, no, they do but jest, poison in jest; no offense i' the
world.   215

KING   What do you call the play?

HAMLET   The Mouse-Trap. Marry, how? Tropically.[3] This play is the
image of a murder done in Vienna: Gonzago is the duke's name; his
wife, Baptista: you shall see anon; 'tis a knavish piece of work; but
what o' that? your majesty, and we that have free souls, it touches   220
us not: let the galled jade wince, our withers are unwrung.[4]
    [*Enter* LUCIANUS.]
This is one Lucianus, nephew to the king.

OPHELIA   You are as good as a chorus, my lord.

HAMLET   I could interpret[5] between you and your love, if I could see
the puppets dallying.   225

OPHELIA   You are keen,[6] my lord, you are keen.

HAMLET   It would cost you a groaning to take off my edge.

OPHELIA   Still better and worse.

HAMLET   So you must take[7] your husbands. Begin, murderer; pox,
leave thy damnable faces, and begin. Come: the croaking raven doth   230
bellow for revenge.

LUCIANUS   Thoughts black, hands apt, drugs fit, and time agreeing;
Confederate[8] season, else no creature seeing;
Thou mixture rank, of midnight weeds collected,
With Hecate's ban[9] thrice blasted, thrice infected,   235
Thy natural magic and dire property,
On wholesome life usurp immediately.
    [*Pours the poison into the sleeper's ear.*]

HAMLET   He poisons him i' the garden for his estate. His name's Gonzago: the story is extant, and written in very choice Italian: you shall
see anon how the murderer gets the love of Gonzago's wife.   240

OPHELIA   The king rises.

HAMLET   What, frighted with false fire![1]

QUEEN   How fares my lord?

1. Promise.   2. Plot of the play in outline.   3. By a trope, figuratively.   4. Not wrenched. "Galled
jade": injured horse. "Withers": the area between a horse's shoulders.   5. Act as interpreter (regular feature in puppet shows).   6. Bitter, but Hamlet chooses to take the word sexually.   7. That is, for better
or for worse, as in the marriage service—but in fact you "mis-take," deceive them.   8. Favorable.
9. Goddess of witchcraft's curse.   1. Blank shot.

POLONIUS   Give o'er the play.

KING   Give me some light. Away!   245

POLONIUS   Lights, lights, lights!

    [*Exeunt all but* HAMLET *and* HORATIO.]

HAMLET   Why, let the stricken deer go weep,
        The hart ungallèd play;
          For some must watch, while some must sleep:
            Thus runs the world away.   250
Would not this, sir, and a forest of feathers—if the rest of my fortunes turn Turk with me—with two Provincial roses on my razed
shoes, get me a fellowship in a cry[2] of players, sir?

HORATIO   Half a share.

HAMLET   A whole one, I.   255
      For thou dost know, O Damon dear,
        This realm dismantled was
      Of Jove himself; and now reigns here
        A very, very—pajock.[3]

HORATIO   You might have rhymed.[4]   260

HAMLET   O good Horatio, I'll take the ghost's word for a thousand
pound. Didst perceive?

HORATIO   Very well, my lord.

HAMLET   Upon the talk of the poisoning?

HORATIO   I did very well note him.   265

HAMLET   Ah, ha! Come, some music! come, the recorders!
      For if the king like not the comedy,
      Why then, belike, he likes it not, perdy.[5]
    Come, some music!

    [*Re-enter* ROSENCRANTZ *and* GUILDENSTERN.]

GUILDENSTERN   Good my lord, vouchsafe me a word with you.   270

HAMLET   Sir, a whole history.

GUILDENSTERN   The king, sir—

HAMLET   Aye, sir, what of him?

GUILDENSTERN   Is in his retirement marvelous distempered.

HAMLET   With drink, sir?   275

GUILDENSTERN   No, my lord, rather with choler.[6]

HAMLET   Your wisdom should show itself more richer to signify this to
the doctor; for, for me to put him to his purgation would perhaps
plunge him into far more choler.

GUILDENSTERN   Good my lord, put your discourse into some frame,   280
and start not so wildly from my affair.

HAMLET   I am tame, sir: pronounce.

GUILDENSTERN   The queen, your mother, in most great affliction of
spirit, hath sent me to you.

HAMLET   You are welcome.   285

GUILDENSTERN   Nay, good my lord, this courtesy is not of the right
breed. If it shall please you to make me a wholesome[7] answer, I will

---

2. Company; a term generally used with hounds. "Turk with": betray. "Razed shoes": sometimes worn
by actors.   3. Peacock.   4. *Ass* would have rhymed.   5. By God (*per Dieu*).   6. Bile, anger.
7. Sensible.

do your mother's commandment: if not, your pardon and my return shall be the end of my business.

HAMLET   Sir, I cannot.   290

GUILDENSTERN   What, my lord?

HAMLET   Make you a wholesome answer; my wit's diseased: but, sir, such answer as I can make, you shall command; or rather, as you say, my mother: therefore no more, but to the matter: my mother, you say,—   295

ROSENCRANTZ   Then thus she says; your behavior hath struck her into amazement and admiration.[8]

HAMLET   O wonderful son, that can so astonish a mother! But is there no sequel at the heels of this mother's admiration? Impart.

ROSENCRANTZ   She desires to speak with you in her closet, ere you go   300
to bed.

HAMLET   We shall obey, were she ten times our mother. Have you any further trade with us?

ROSENCRANTZ   My lord, you once did love me.

HAMLET   So I do still, by these pickers and stealers.[9]   305

ROSENCRANTZ   Good my lord, what is your cause of distemper? you do surely bar the door upon your own liberty, if you deny your griefs to your friend.

HAMLET   Sir, I lack advancement.[1]

ROSENCRANTZ   How can that be, when you have the voice of the king   310
himself for your succession in Denmark?

HAMLET   Aye, sir, but "while the grass grows,"[2]—the proverb is some-thing musty.

   [*Re-enter* PLAYERS *with recorders.*]

O, the recorders! let me see one. To withdraw with you:—why do you go about to recover the wind of me, as if you would drive me   315
into a toil?[3]

GUILDENSTERN   O, my lord, if my duty be too bold, my love is too unmannerly.

HAMLET   I do not well understand that. Will you play upon this pipe?

GUILDENSTERN   My lord, I cannot.   320

HAMLET   I pray you.

GUILDENSTERN   Believe me, I cannot.

HAMLET   I do beseech you.

GUILDENSTERN   I know no touch of it, my lord.

HAMLET   It is as easy as lying: govern these ventages[4] with your fingers   325
and thumb, give it breath with your mouth, and it will discourse most eloquent music. Look you, these are the stops.

GUILDENSTERN   But these cannot I command to any utterance of har-mony; I have not the skill.

HAMLET   Why, look you now, how unworthy a thing you make of me!   330
You would play upon me; you would seem to know my stops; you would pluck out the heart of my mystery; you would sound me from

---

8. Confusion and surprise.   9. The hands.   1. Hamlet pretends that the cause of his "distemper" is frustrated ambition.   2. The proverb ends: "oft starves the silly steed."   3. Snare. "Withdraw": retire, talk in private. "Recover the wind of": get to the windward.   4. Windholes.

my lowest note to the top of my compass: and there is much music,
excellent voice, in this little organ; yet cannot you make it speak.
'Sblood, do you think I am easier to be played on than a pipe? Call   335
me what instrument you will, though you can fret[5] me, yet you cannot play upon me.

    [*Re-enter* POLONIUS.]

God bless you, sir!

POLONIUS   My lord, the queen would speak with you, and presently.

HAMLET   Do you see yonder cloud that's almost in shape of a camel?   340

POLONIUS   By the mass, and 'tis like a camel, indeed.

HAMLET   Methinks it is like a weasel.

POLONIUS   It is backed like a weasel.

HAMLET   Or like a whale?

POLONIUS   Very like a whale.   345

HAMLET   Then I will come to my mother by and by. They fool me to
the top of my bent. I will come by and by.

POLONIUS   I will say so.

    [*Exit* POLONIUS.]

HAMLET   "By and by" is easily said. Leave me, friends.

    [*Exeunt all but* HAMLET.]

'Tis now the very witching time of night,   350
When churchyards yawn, and hell itself breathes out
Contagion to this world: now could I drink hot blood,
And do such bitter business as the day
Would quake to look on. Soft! now to my mother.
O heart, lose not thy nature; let not ever   355
The soul of Nero[6] enter this firm bosom:
Let me be cruel, not unnatural:
I will speak daggers to her, but use none;
My tongue and soul in this be hypocrites;
How in my words soever she be shent,   360
To give them seals[7] never, my soul, consent!

    [*Exit.*]

SCENE 3

[SCENE: *A room in the castle.*]

[*Enter* KING, ROSENCRANTZ, *and* GUILDENSTERN.]

KING   I like him not, nor stands it safe with us
To let his madness range. Therefore prepare you;
I your commission will forthwith dispatch,
And he to England shall along with you:
The terms of our estate[8] may not endure   5
Hazard so near us as doth hourly grow
Out of his lunacies.

---

5. Vex, with a pun on *frets*, meaning the ridges placed across the finger board of a guitar to regulate the fin-
gering.   6. Roman emperor (37–68 C.E.), who murdered his mother.   7. Ratify them by action.
"Shent": reproached.   8. My position as king.

GUILDENSTERN   We will ourselves provide:
  Most holy and religious fear it is
  To keep those many many bodies safe
  That live and feed upon your majesty.   10
ROSENCRANTZ   The single and peculiar[9] life is bound
  With all the strength and armor of the mind
  To keep itself from noyance; but much more
  That spirit upon whose weal depends and rests
  The lives of many. The cease[1] of majesty   15
  Dies not alone, but like a gulf doth draw
  What 's near it with it; it is a massy wheel,
  Fixed on the summit of the highest mount,
  To whose huge spokes ten thousand lesser things
  Are mortised[2] and adjoined; which, when it falls,   20
  Each small annexment, petty consequence,
  Attends the boisterous ruin. Never alone
  Did the king sigh, but with a general groan.
KING   Arm you, I pray you, to this speedy voyage,
  For we will fetters put about this fear,   25
  Which now goes too free-footed.
ROSENCRANTZ
GUILDENSTERN   } We will haste us.
    [*Exeunt* ROSENCRANTZ *and* GUILDENSTERN.—*Enter* POLONIUS.]
POLONIUS   My lord, he's going to his mother's closet:
  Behind the arras I'll convey myself,
  To hear the process: I'll warrant she'll tax him home:[3]   30
  And, as you said, and wisely was it said
  'Tis meet that some more audience than a mother,
  Since nature makes them partial, should o'erhear
  The speech, of vantage.[4] Fare you well, my liege:
  I'll call upon you ere you go to bed,   35
  And tell you what I know.
KING   Thanks, dear my lord.
    [*Exit* POLONIUS.]
  O, my offense is rank, it smells to heaven;
  It hath the primal eldest curse[5] upon 't,
  A brother's murder. Pray can I not,
  Though inclination be as sharp as will: 40
  My stronger guilt defeats my strong intent,
  And like a man to double business bound,
  I stand in pause where I shall first begin,
  And both neglect. What if this cursed hand
  Were thicker than itself with brother's blood,   45
  Is there not rain enough in the sweet heavens
  To wash it white as snow? Whereto serves mercy
  But to confront the visage of offense?[6]
  And what's in prayer but this twofold force,

9. Individual.   1. Decease, extinction.   2. Fastened.   3. Take him to task thoroughly.   4. From a vantage point.   5. The curse of Cain.   6. Guilt.

To be forestalled ere we come to fall,   50
Or pardoned being down? Then I'll look up;
My fault is past. But O, what form of prayer
Can serve my turn? "Forgive me my foul murder?"
That cannot be, since I am still possessed
Of those effects for which I did the murder,   55
My crown, mine own ambition and my queen.
May one be pardoned and retain the offense?[7]
In the corrupted currents of this world
Offense's gilded hand may shove by justice,
And oft 'tis seen the wicked prize itself   60
Buys out the law:[8] but 'tis not so above;
There is no shuffling, there the action lies
In his[9] true nature, and we ourselves compelled
Even to the teeth and forehead of our faults
To give in evidence. What then? what rests?[1]   65
Try what repentance can: what can it not?
Yet what can it when one can not repent?
O wretched state! O bosom black as death!
O limèd soul, that struggling to be free
Art more engaged! Help, angels! make assay![2]   70
Bow, stubborn knees, and, heart with strings of steel,
Be soft as sinews of the new-born babe!
All may be well.
        [Retires and kneels.—Enter HAMLET.]
HAMLET   Now might I do it pat,[3] now he is praying
And now I'll do 't: and so he goes to heaven: 75
And so am I revenged. That would be scanned:[4]
A villain kills my father; and for that,
I, his sole son, do this same villain send
To heaven.
O, this is hire and salary, not revenge.   80
He took my father grossly, full of bread,
With all his crimes broad blown, as flush as May;
And how his audit[5] stands who knows save heaven?
But in our circumstance and course of thought,
'Tis heavy with him: and am I then revenged,   85
To take him in the purging of his soul,
When he is fit and seasoned[6] for his passage?
No.
Up, sword, and know thou a more horrid hent:[7]
When he is drunk asleep, or in his rage,   90
Or, in the incestuous pleasure of his bed;
At game, a-swearing, or about some act
That has no relish of salvation in 't;

---

7. The things obtained through the offense.   8. The wealth unduly acquired is used for bribery.   9. Its.
1. What remains?   2. Make the attempt! "Limèd": caught as with birdlime.   3. Conveniently.
4. Would have to be considered carefully.   5. Account. "Broad blown": in full bloom.   6. Ripe, ready.
7. Grip.

Then trip him, that his heels may kick at heaven
And that his soul may be as damned and black   95
As hell, whereto it goes. My mother stays:
This physic but prolongs thy sickly days.
    [*Exit.*]
KING [*Rising.*]   My words fly up, my thoughts remain below:
  Words without thoughts never to heaven go.
    [*Exit.*]

SCENE 4

[SCENE: *The Queen's closet.*]

[*Enter* QUEEN *and* POLONIUS.]
POLONIUS He will come straight. Look you lay home to him:
  Tell him his pranks have been too broad[8] to bear with,
  And that your grace hath screen'd and stood between
  Much heat and him. I'll sconce me even here.
  Pray you, be round[9] with him.
HAMLET [*Within.*]   Mother, mother, mother!   5
QUEEN I'll warrant you; fear me not. Withdraw,
  I hear him coming.
    [POLONIUS *hides behind the arras.—Enter* HAMLET.]
HAMLET Now, mother, what's the matter?
QUEEN Hamlet, thou hast thy father much offended.
HAMLET Mother, you have my father much offended.   10
QUEEN Come, come, you answer with an idle tongue.
HAMLET Go, go, you question with a wicked tongue.
QUEEN Why, how now, Hamlet!
HAMLET   What's the matter now?
QUEEN Have you forgot me?
HAMLET   No, by the rood,[1] not so:
  You are the queen, your husband's brother's wife;   15
  And—would it were not so!—you are my mother.
QUEEN Nay, then, I'll set those to you that can speak.
HAMLET Come, come, and sit you down; you shall not budge:
  You go not till I set you up a glass[2]
  Where you may see the inmost part of you.   20
QUEEN What wilt thou do? thou wilt not murder me?
  Help, help, ho!
POLONIUS [*Behind.*] What, ho! help, help, help!
HAMLET [*Drawing.*] How now! a rat? Dead, for a ducat, dead!
    [*Makes a pass through the arras.*]
POLONIUS [*Behind.*] O, I am slain!
    [*Falls and dies.*]
QUEEN   O me, what hast thou done?   25
HAMLET Nay, I know not: is it the king?
QUEEN O, what a rash and bloody deed is this!

---

8. Unrestrained. "Lay home": give him a stern lesson.   9. Straightforward.   1. Cross.   2. Mirror.

HAMLET A bloody deed! almost as bad, good mother,
 As kill a king, and marry with his brother.
QUEEN As kill a king!
HAMLET   Aye, lady, 'twas my word.   30
  [*Lifts up the arras and discovers* POLONIUS.]
  Thou wretched, rash, intruding fool, farewell!
  I took thee for thy better: take thy fortune;
  Thou find'st to be too busy[3] is some danger.
  Leave wringing of your hands: peace! sit you down,
  And let me wring your heart: for so I shall,   35
  If it be made of penetrable stuff;
  If damned custom have not brassed it so,
  That it be proof and bulwark against sense.[4]
QUEEN What have I done, that thou darest wag thy tongue
  In noise so rude against me?
HAMLET   Such an act   40
  That blurs the grace and blush of modesty,
  Calls virtue hypocrite, takes off the rose
  From the fair forehead of an innocent love,
  And sets a blister there; makes marriage vows
  As false as dicers' oaths: O, such a deed   45
  As from the body of contraction[5] plucks
  The very soul, and sweet religion makes
  A rhapsody of words: heaven's face doth glow;[6]
  Yea, this solidity and compound mass,
  With tristful visage, as against the doom,[7]   50
  Is thought-sick at the act.
QUEEN   Aye me, what act,
  That roars so loud and thunders in the index?[8]
HAMLET Look here, upon this picture, and on this,
  The counterfeit presentment[9] of two brothers.   55
  See what a grace was seated on this brow;
  Hyperion's curls, the front of Jove himself,
  An eye like Mars, to threaten and command;
  A station[1] like the herald Mercury
  New-lighted on a heaven-kissing hill;   60
  A combination and a form indeed,
  Where every god did seem to set his seal
  To give the world assurance of a man:
  This was your husband. Look you now, what follows:
  Here is your husband; like a mildewed ear,[2]   65
  Blasting his wholesome brother. Have you eyes?
  Could you on this fair mountain leave to feed,
  And batten[3] on this moor? Ha! have you eyes?
  You cannot call it love, for at your age
  The hey-day in the blood is tame, it's humble,   70

---

3. Too much of a busybody.   4. Feeling.   5. Duty to the marriage contract.   6. Blush with shame.
7. Doomsday. "Tristful": sad.   8. Prologue, table of contents.   9. Portrait.   1. Posture.   2. Of
corn.   3. Gorge, fatten. "Leave": cease.

And waits upon[4] the judgment: and what judgment
Would step from this to this? Sense sure you have,
Else could you not have motion: but sure that sense
Is apoplexed: for madness would not err,
Nor sense to ecstasy was ne'er so thralled   75
But it reserved some quantity of choice,
To serve in such a difference. What devil was 't
That thus hath cozened you at hoodman-blind?[5]
Eyes without feeling, feeling without sight,
Ears without hands or eyes, smelling sans[6] all,   80
Or but a sickly part of one true sense
Could not so mope.[7]
O shame! where is thy blush? Rebellious hell,
If thou canst mutine in a matron's bones,
To flaming youth let virtue be as wax   85
And melt in her own fire: proclaim no shame
When the compulsive ardor gives the charge,[8]
Since frost itself as actively doth burn,
And reason panders[9] will.

QUEEN   O Hamlet, speak no more:
Thou turn'st mine eyes into my very soul,   90
And there I see such black and grained spots
As will not leave their tinct.[1]

HAMLET   Nay, but to live
In the rank sweat of an enseamèd[2] bed,
Stew'd in corruption, honeying and making love
Over the nasty sty,—

QUEEN   O, speak to me no more;   95
These words like daggers enter in my ears;
No more, sweet HAMLET!

HAMLET   A murderer and a villain;
A slave that is not twentieth part the tithe[3]
Of your precédent lord; a vice of kings;
A cutpurse[4] of the empire and the rule,   100
That from a shelf the precious diadem stole
And put it in his pocket!

QUEEN   No more!

HAMLET   A king of shreds and patches—
[Enter GHOST.]
Save me, and hover o'er me with your wings,
You heavenly guards! What would your gracious figure?   105

QUEEN   Alas, he's mad!

HAMLET   Do you not come your tardy son to chide,
That, lapsed in time and passion, lets go by
The important acting of your dread command?
O, say!

---

4. Is subordinated to.   5. Blindman's buff. "Cozened": tricked.   6. Without.   7. Be stupid.
8. Attack.   9. Becomes subservient to.   1. Lose their color. "Grained": dyed in.   2. Greasy.
3. Tenth.   4. Pickpocket. "Vice": clown, from the custom in the old morality plays of having a buffoon take the part of Vice or of a particular vice.

GHOST   Do not forget: this visitation   110

   Is but to whet thy almost blunted purpose.
   But look, amazement on thy mother sits:
   O, step between her and her fighting soul:
   Conceit[5] in weakest bodies strongest works:
   Speak to her, hamlet.

HAMLET   How is it with you, lady?   115

QUEEN   Alas, how is 't with you,
   That you do bend your eye on vacancy
   And with the incorporal air do hold discourse?
   Forth at your eyes your spirits wildly peep;
   And, as the sleeping soldiers in the alarm,   120

   Your bedded hairs, like life in excrements,[6]
   Start up and stand on end. O gentle son,
   Upon the heat and flame of thy distemper
   Sprinkle cool patience. Whereon do you look?

HAMLET   On him, on him! Look you how pale he glares!   125

   His form and cause conjoined, preaching to stones,
   Would make them capable.[7] Do not look upon me,
   Lest with this piteous action you convert
   My stern effects:[8] then what I have to do
   Will want true color; tears perchance for[9] blood.   130

QUEEN   To whom do you speak this?

HAMLET   Do you see nothing there?

QUEEN   Nothing at all; yet all that is I see.

HAMLET   Nor did you nothing hear?

QUEEN   No, nothing but ourselves.

HAMLET   Why, look you there! look, how it steals away!

   My father, in his habit as he lived!   135

   Look, where he goes, even now, out at the portal!
       [Exit GHOST.]

QUEEN   This is the very coinage of your brain:
   This bodiless creation ecstasy
   Is very cunning in.

HAMLET   Ecstasy!
   My pulse, as yours, doth temperately keep time,   140

   And makes as healthful music: it is not madness
   That I have uttered: bring me to the test,
   And I the matter will re-word, which madness
   Would gambol from. Mother, for love of grace,
   Lay not that flattering unction to your soul,   145

   That not your trespass but my madness speaks:
   It will but skin and film the ulcerous place,
   Whiles rank corruption, mining all within,
   Infects unseen. Confess yourself to heaven;
   Repent what's past, avoid what is to come,   150

   And do not spread the compost on the weeds,

---

5. Imagination.   6. Outgrowths. "Alarm": call to arms.   7. Of feeling.   8. You make me change my purpose.   9. Instead of.

To make them ranker. Forgive me this my virtue,
For in the fatness of these pursy[1] times
Virtue itself of vice must pardon beg.
Yea, curb[2] and woo for leave to do him good.   155
QUEEN   O hamlet, thou hast cleft my heart in twain.
HAMLET   O, throw away the worser part of it,
And live the purer with the other half.
Good night: but go not to my uncle's bed;
Assume a virtue, if you have it not.   160
That monster, custom, who all sense doth eat,
Of habits devil, is angel yet in this,
That to the use of actions fair and good
He likewise gives a frock or livery,
That aptly is put on.[3] Refrain to-night,   165
And that shall lend a kind of easiness
To the next abstinence; the next more easy;
For use almost can change the stamp[4] of nature,
And either curb the devil, or throw him out
With wondrous potency. Once more, good night: 170
And when you are desirous to be blest,
I'll blessing beg of you. For this same lord,
     [*Pointing to* POLONIUS.]
I do repent: but heaven hath pleased it so,
To punish me with this, and this with me,
That I must be their scourge and minister.   175
I will bestow[5] him, and will answer well
The death I gave him. So, again, good night.
I must be cruel, only to be kind:
Thus bad begins, and worse remains behind.
One word more, good lady.
QUEEN   What shall I do?   180
HAMLET   Not this, by no means, that I bid you do:
Let the bloat[6] king tempt you again to bed;
Pinch wanton on your cheek, call you his mouse;
And let him, for a pair of reechy[7] kisses,
Or paddling in your neck with his damned fingers,   185
Make you to ravel all this matter out,
That I essentially am not in madness,
But mad in craft.[8] 'Twere good you let him know;
For who, that's but a queen, fair, sober, wise,
Would from a paddock, from a bat, a gib,   190
Such dear concernings[9] hide? who would do so?
No, in despite of sense and secrecy,
Unpeg the basket on the house's top,
Let the birds fly, and like the famous ape,[1]

---

1. Swollen from pampering.   2. Bow.   3. That is, habit, although like a devil in establishing evil ways in us, is like an angel in doing the same for virtues. "Aptly": easily.   4. Cast, form. "Use": habit.   5. Stow away. "Minister": agent of punishment.   6. Bloated with drink.   7. Fetid.   8. Simulation.   9. Matters with which one is closely concerned. "Paddock": toad. "Gib": tomcat.   1. The ape in the unidentified animal fable to which Hamlet alludes; apparently the animal saw birds fly out of a basket and drew the conclusion that by placing himself in a basket he too could fly.

To try conclusions, in the basket creep   195
And break your own neck down.
QUEEN   Be thou assured, if words be made of breath
And breath of life, I have no life to breathe
What thou hast said to me.
HAMLET   I must to England; you know that?
QUEEN   Alack,   200
I had forgot: 'tis so concluded on.
HAMLET   There's letters sealed: and my two schoolfellows,
Whom I will trust as I will adders fanged,
They bear the mandate; they must sweep my way,
And marshal me to knavery. Let it work;   205
For 'tis the sport to have the enginer[2]
Hoist with his own petard:[3] and 't shall go hard
But I will delve one yard below their mines,
And blow them at the moon: I, 'tis most sweet
When in one line two crafts directly meet.   210
This man shall set me packing:
I'll lug the guts into the neighbor room.
Mother, good night. Indeed this councillor
Is now most still, most secret and most grave,[4]
Who was in life a foolish prating knave.   215
Come, sir, to draw toward an end with you.
Good night, mother.
          [*Exeunt severally;* HAMLET *dragging in* POLONIUS.]

Act IV

SCENE 1

[SCENE: *A room in the castle.*]

          [*Enter* KING, QUEEN, ROSENCRANTZ, *and* GUILDENSTERN.]
KING   There's matter in these sighs, these profound heaves:
You must translate: 'tis fit we understand them.
Where is your son?
QUEEN   Bestow this place on us[5] a little while.
          [*Exeunt* ROSENCRANTZ *and* GUILDENSTERN.]
Ah, mine own lord, what have I seen to-night!   5
KING   What, Gertrude? How does Hamlet?
QUEEN   Mad as the sea and wind, when both contend
Which is the mightier: in his lawless fit,
Behind the arras hearing something stir,
Whips out his rapier, cries "A rat, a rat!"   10
And in this brainish apprehension[6] kills
The unseen good old man.
KING   O heavy deed!

----

2. Military engineer. "Marshal": lead.   3. A variety of bomb. "Hoist": blow up.   4. Hamlet is punning
on the word.   5. Leave us alone.   6. Imaginary notion.

It had been so with us, had we been there:
His liberty is full of threats to all,
To you yourself, to us, to every one. 15
Alas, how shall this bloody deed be answered?
It will be laid to us, whose providence
Should have kept short,[7] restrained and out of haunt,
This mad young man: but so much was our love,
We would not understand what was most fit, 20
But, like the owner of a foul disease,
To keep it from divulging, let it feed
Even on the pith of life. Where is he gone?
QUEEN   To draw apart the body he hath killed:
O'er whom his very madness, like some ore 25
Among a mineral[8] of metals base,
Shows itself pure; he weeps for what is done.
KING   O Gertrude, come away!
The sun no sooner shall the mountains touch,
But we will ship him hence: and this vile deed 30
We must, with all our majesty and skill,
Both countenance[9] and excuse. Ho, guildenstern!
[Re-enter ROSENCRANTZ and GUILDENSTERN.]
Friends both, go join you with some further aid:
Hamlet in madness hath Polonius slain,
And from his mother's closet hath he dragged him: 35
Go seek him out; speak fair, and bring the body
Into the chapel. I pray you, haste in this.
[Exeunt ROSENCRANTZ and GUILDENSTERN.]
Come, Gertrude, we'll call up our wisest friends;
And let them know, both what we mean to do,
And what's untimely done. . . . [1] 40
Whose whisper o'er the world's diameter
As level as the cannon to his blank[2]
Transports his poisoned shot, may miss our name
And hit the woundless air. O, come away!
My soul is full of discord and dismay. 45
[Exeunt.]

SCENE 2

[SCENE: *Another room in the castle.*]

[*Enter* HAMLET.]
HAMLET   Safely stowed.
ROSENCRANTZ   } [*Within.*] Hamlet! Lord Hamlet!
GUILDENSTERN }
HAMLET   But soft, what noise? who calls on Hamlet?
O, here they come.
[*Enter* ROSENCRANTZ *and* GUILDENSTERN.]

7. Under close watch.   8. Mine. "Ore": gold.   9. Recognize.   1. This gap in the text has been guessingly filled in with "So envious slander."   2. His target.

ROSENCRANTZ   What have you done, my lord, with the dead body?   5

HAMLET   Compounded[3] it with dust, whereto 'tis kin.

ROSENCRANTZ   Tell us where 'tis, that we may take it thence
 And bear it to the chapel.

HAMLET   Do not believe it.

ROSENCRANTZ   Believe what?   10

HAMLET   That I can keep your counsel and not mine own. Besides, to
 be demanded[4] of a sponge![5] what replication should be made by the
 son of a king?

ROSENCRANTZ   Take you me for a sponge, my lord?

HAMLET   Aye, sir; that soaks up the king's countenance,[6] his rewards,   15
 his authorities. But such officers do the king best service in the end:
 he keeps them, like an ape, in the corner of his jaw; first mouthed, to
 be last swallowed: when he needs what you have gleaned, it is but
 squeezing you, and sponge, you shall be dry again.

ROSENCRANTZ   I understand you not, my lord.   20

HAMLET   I am glad of it: a knavish speech sleeps in a foolish ear.

ROSENCRANTZ   My lord, you must tell us where the body is, and go
 with us to the king.

HAMLET   The body is with the king, but the king is not with the body.
 The king is a thing—   25

GUILDENSTERN   A thing, my lord?

HAMLET   Of nothing: bring me to him. Hide fox, and all after.[7]
    [*Exeunt.*]

SCENE 3

[Scene: *Another room in the castle.*]

[*Enter* KING, *attended.*]

KING   I have sent to seek him, and to find the body.
 How dangerous is it that this man goes loose!
 Yet must not we put the strong law on him:
 He's loved of the distracted multitude,
 Who like not in their judgment, but their eyes;   5
 And where 'tis so, the offender's scourge is weighed,
 But never the offense. To bear[8] all smooth and even,
 This sudden sending away must seem
 Deliberate pause: diseases desperate grown
 By desperate appliance[9] are relieved,   10
 Or not at all.
    [*Enter* ROSENCRANTZ.]
       How now! what hath befall'n?

ROSENCRANTZ   Where the dead body is bestowed, my lord,
 We cannot get from him.

KING   But where is he?

ROSENCRANTZ   Without, my lord; guarded, to know your pleasure.

---

3. Mixed.   4. Questioned by.   5. Formal reply.   6. Favor.   7. A children's game.   8. Conduct. "Scourge": punishment.   9. Treatment. "Deliberate pause": the result of careful argument.

KING   Bring him before us.   15
ROSENCRANTZ   Ho, Guildenstern! bring in my lord.
          [*Enter* HAMLET *and* GUILDENSTERN.]
KING   Now, Hamlet, where's Polonius?
HAMLET   At supper.
KING   At supper! where?
HAMLET   Not where he eats, but where he is eaten: a certain convo-   20
    cation of public worms are e'en at him. Your worm is your only
    emperor for diet:[1] we fat all creatures else to fat us, and we fat our-
    selves for maggots: your fat king   and your lean beggar is but variable
    service,[2] two dishes, but to one table: that's the end.
KING   Alas, alas!   25
HAMLET   A man may fish with the worm that hath eat of a king, and
    eat of the fish that hath fed of that worm.
KING   What dost thou mean by this?
HAMLET   Nothing but to show you how a king may go a progress[3]
    through the guts of a beggar.   30
KING   Where is Polonius?
HAMLET   In heaven; send thither to see: if your messenger find him
    not there, seek him i' the other place yourself. But indeed, if you
    find him not within this month, you shall nose[4] him as you go up
    the stairs into the lobby.   35
KING   [*To some* ATTENDANTS.] Go seek him there.
HAMLET   He will stay till you come.
          [*Exeunt* ATTENDANTS.]
KING   Hamlet this deed, for thine especial safety,
    Which we do tender,[5] as we dearly grieve
    For that which thou hast done, must send thee hence   40
    With fiery quickness: therefore prepare thyself;
    The bark is ready and the wind at help,
    The associates tend, and every thing is bent
    For England.
HAMLET   For England?
KING   Aye, Hamlet
HAMLET   Good.
KING   So is it, if thou knew'st our purposes.   45
HAMLET   I see a cherub that sees them. But, come; for England!
    Farewell, dear mother.
KING   Thy loving father, Hamlet.
HAMLET   My mother: father and mother is man and wife; man and
    wife is one flesh, and so, my mother. Come, for England!   50
          [*Exit.*]
KING   Follow him at foot;[6] tempt him with speed aboard;
    Delay it not; I'll have him hence to-night:
    Away! for every thing is sealed and done
    That else leans on[7] the affair: pray you, make haste.

---

1. Possibly a punning reference to the Diet (assembly) of the Holy Roman empire at Worms.   2. That is, the service varies, not the food.   3. Royal state journey.   4. Smell.   5. Care for.   6. At his heels.   7. Pertains to.

[*Exeunt* ROSENCRANTZ *and* GUILDENSTERN.]
And, England,[8] if my love thou hold'st at aught—   55
As my great power thereof may give thee sense,
Since yet thy cicatrice looks raw and red
After the Danish sword, and thy free awe
Pays homage to us—thou mayst not coldly set[9]
Our sovereign process; which imports at full,   60
By letters conjuring[1] to that effect,
The present death of Hamlet. Do it, England;
For like the hectic[2] in my blood he rages,
And thou must cure me; till I know 'tis done,
Howe'er my haps, my joys were ne'er begun.   65
          [*Exit.*]

SCENE 4

[SCENE: *A plain in Denmark.*]

[*Enter* FORTINBRAS, *a* CAPTAIN *and* SOLDIERS, *marching.*]

FORTINBRAS   Go, captain, from me greet the Danish king;
   Tell him that by his license Fortinbras
   Craves the conveyance[3] of a promised march
   Over his kingdom. You know the rendezvous.
   If that his majesty would aught with us,   5
   We shall express our duty in his eye;[4]
   And let him know so.
CAPTAIN   I will do 't, my lord.
FORTINBRAS   Go softly on.
          [*Exeunt* FORTINBRAS *and* SOLDIERS.—*Enter* HAMLET, ROSENCRANTZ,
          GUILDENSTERN, *and others.*]
HAMLET   Good sir, whose powers[5] are these?
CAPTAIN   They are of Norway, sir.   10
HAMLET   How purposed, sir, I pray you?
CAPTAIN   Against some part of Poland.
HAMLET   Who commands them, sir?
CAPTAIN   The nephew to Old Norway, Fortinbras.
HAMLET   Goes it against the main[6] of Poland, sir,   15
   Or for some frontier?
CAPTAIN   Truly to speak, and with no addition,
   We go to gain a little patch of ground
   That hath in it no profit but the name.
   To pay five ducats, five, I would not farm it;   20
   Nor will it yield to Norway or the Pole
   A ranker rate, should it be sold in fee.[7]
HAMLET   Why, then the Polack never will defend it.
CAPTAIN   Yes, it is already garrisoned.
HAMLET   Two thousand souls and twenty thousand ducats   25

8. The king of England.   9. Regard with indifference.   1. Enjoining.   2. Fever.   3. Convoy.
4. Presence.   5. Armed forces.   6. The whole of.   7. For absolute possession. "Ranker": higher.

Will not debate the question of this straw!
This is the imposthume[8] of much wealth and peace,
That inward breaks, and shows no cause without
Why the man dies. I humbly thank you, sir.
CAPTAIN   God be wi' you, sir.
          [Exit.]
ROSENCRANTZ   Will 't please you go, my lord?   30
HAMLET   I'll be with you straight. Go a little before.
          [Exeunt all but HAMLET.]
How all occasions do inform against[9] me,
And spur my dull revenge! What is a man,
If his chief good and market[1] of his time
Be but to sleep and feed? a beast, no more.   35
Sure, he that made us with such large discourse,[2]
Looking before and after, gave us not
That capability and god-like reason
To fust[3] in us unused. Now, whether it be
Bestial oblivion, or some craven scruple   40
Of thinking too precisely on the event,[4]—
A thought which, quartered, hath but one part wisdom
And ever three parts coward,—I do not know
Why yet I live to say "this thing's to do,"
Sith I have cause, and will, and strength, and means,   45
To do 't. Examples gross as earth exhort me:
Witness this army, of such mass and charge,[5]
Led by a delicate and tender prince,
Whose spirit with divine ambition puffed
Makes mouths[6] at the invisible event,   50
Exposing what is mortal and unsure
To all that fortune, death, and danger dare,
Even for an egg-shell. Rightly to be great
Is not to stir without great argument,
But greatly to find quarrel in a straw   55
When honor's at the stake. How stand I then,
That have a father killed, a mother stained,
Excitements of my reason and my blood,
And let all sleep, while to my shame I see
The imminent death of twenty thousand men,   60
That for a fantasy and trick[7] of fame
Go to their graves like beds, fight for a plot
Whereon the numbers cannot try the cause,[8]
Which is not tomb enough and continent[9]
To hide the slain? O, from this time forth,   65
My thoughts be bloody, or be nothing worth!
          [Exit.]

---

8. Ulcer.   9. Denounce.   1. Payment for, reward.   2. Reasoning power.   3. Become moldy,
taste of the cask.   4. Outcome.   5. Cost.   6. Laughs at.   7. Trifle.   8. So small that it cannot
hold the men who fight for it.   9. Container.

SCENE 5

[SCENE: *Elsinore. A room in the castle.*]

[*Enter* QUEEN, HORATIO, *and a* GENTLEMAN.]

QUEEN   I will not speak with her.

GENTLEMAN   She is importunate, indeed distract:
Her mood will needs be pitied.

QUEEN   What would she have?

GENTLEMAN   She speaks much of her father, says she hears
There's tricks i' the world, and hems and beats her heart,   5
Spurns enviously at straws;[1] speaks things in doubt,
That carry but half sense: her speech is nothing,
Yet the unshapèd use of it doth move
The hearers to collection; they aim[2] at it,
And botch[3] the words up fit to their own thoughts;   10
Which, as her winks and nods and gestures yield them,
Indeed would make one think there might be thought,
Though nothing sure, yet much unhappily.

HORATIO   'Twere good she were spoken with, for she may strew
Dangerous conjectures in ill-breeding minds.[4]   15

QUEEN   Let her come in.
          [*Exit* GENTLEMAN.]
[*Aside.*] To my sick soul, as sin's true nature is,
Each toy seems prologue to some great amiss:
So full of artless jealousy[5] is guilt,
It spills itself in fearing to be spilt.   20
          [*Re-enter* GENTLEMAN, *with* OPHELIA.]

OPHELIA   Where is the beauteous majesty of Denmark?

QUEEN   How now, Ophelia!

OPHELIA [*Sings.*]   How should I your true love know
                          From another one?
                          By his cockle hat and staff   25
                          And his sandal shoon.[6]

QUEEN   Alas, sweet lady, what imports this song?

OPHELIA   Say you? nay, pray you, mark.
     [*Sings.*]   He is dead and gone, lady,
                          He is dead and gone;   30
                          At his head a grass-green turf,
                          At his heels a stone.
     Oh, oh!

QUEEN   Nay, but Ophelia,—

OPHELIA   Pray you, mark.
     [*Sings.*]   White his shroud as the mountain snow,—
          [*Enter* KING.]

QUEEN   Alas, look here, my lord.   35

---

1. Gets angry at trifles.   2. Guess. "Collection": gathering up her words and trying to make sense of them.   3. Patch.   4. Minds breeding evil thoughts.   5. Uncontrolled suspicion. "Toy": trifle. "Amiss": misfortune.   6. Shoes. These are all typical signs of pilgrims traveling to places of devotion.

OPHELIA [*Sings.*]   Larded[7] with sweet flowers;
        Which bewept to the grave did—not—go
        With true-love showers.

KING   How do you, pretty lady?

OPHELIA   Well, God 'ild[8] you! They say the owl was a baker's daughter.   40
Lord, we know what we are, but know not what we may be.[9] God be
at your table!

KING   Conceit upon her father.

OPHELIA   Pray you, let's have no words of this; but when they ask
you what it means, say you this: 45
   [*Sings.*]   To-morrow is Saint Valentine's day
        All in the morning betime,
    And I a maid at your window,
        To be your Valentine.
    Then up he rose, and donned his clothes,   50
        And dupped[1] the chamber-door;
    Let in the maid, that out a maid
        Never departed more.

KING   Pretty Ophelia!

OPHELIA   Indeed, la, without an oath, I'll make an end on 't: 55
   [*Sings.*]   By Gis[2] and by Saint Charity,
        Alack, and fie for shame!
    Young men will do 't, if they come to 't;
        By Cock,[3] they are to blame.
    Quoth she, before you tumbled me,   60
        You promised me to wed.
  He answers:
    So would I ha' done, by yonder sun,
        An thou hadst not come to my bed.

KING   How long hath she been thus?   65

OPHELIA   I hope all will be well. We must be patient: but I cannot
choose but weep, to think they should lay him i' the cold ground.
My brother shall know of it: and so I thank you for your good counsel. Come, my coach! Good night, ladies; good night, sweet ladies;
good night, good night.   70
   [*Exit.*]

KING   Follow her close; give her good watch, I pray you.
   [*Exit* HORATIO.]
O, this is the poison of deep grief; it springs
All from her father's death. O Gertrude, Gertrude,
When sorrows come, they come not single spies,
But in battalions! First, her father slain: 75
Next, your son gone; and he most violent author
Of his own just remove: the people muddied,[4]
Thick and unwholesome in their thoughts and whispers,
For good Polonius' death; and we have done but greenly

---

7. Garnished.   8. Yield; that is, repay.   9. An allusion to a folk tale about a baker's daughter changed into an owl for having shown no charity to those in need.   1. Opened.   2. By Jesus.   3. Corruption of *God*, but with a sexual undermeaning.   4. Confused, their thoughts made turbid (as water by mud).

In hugger-mugger[5] to inter him: poor Ophelia 80
Divided from herself and her fair judgment,
Without the which we are pictures, or mere beasts:
Last, and as much containing as all these,
Her brother is in secret come from France,
Feeds on his wonder,[6] keeps himself in clouds, 85
And wants not buzzers[7] to infect his ear
With pestilent speeches of his father's death;
Wherein necessity, of matter beggared,[8]
Will nothing stick our person to arraign[9]
In ear and ear. O my dear Gertrude, this, 90
Like to a murdering-piece,[1] in many places
Gives me superfluous death.
    [A noise within.]
QUEEN   Alack, what noise is this?
KING   Where are my Switzers?[2] Let them guard the door.
    [Enter another GENTLEMAN.]
    What is the matter?
GENTLEMAN   Save yourself, my lord:
    The ocean, overpeering of his list,[3] 95
    Eats not the flats with more impetuous haste
    Than young Laertes, in a riotous head,[4]
    O'erbears your officers. The rabble call him lord;
    And, as the world were now but to begin,
    Antiquity forgot, custom not known, 100
    The ratifiers and props of every word,
    They cry "Choose we; Laertes shall be king!"
    Caps, hands and tongues applaud it to the clouds,
    "Laertes shall be king, Laertes king!"
QUEEN   How cheerfully on the false trail they cry! 105
    O, this is counter,[5] you false Danish dogs!
    [Noise within.]
KING   The doors are broke.
    [Enter LAERTES, armed; DANES following.]
LAERTES   Where is this king? Sirs, stand you all without.
DANES   No, let's come in.
LAERTES   I pray you, give me leave.
DANES   We will, we will. 110
    [They retire without the door.]
LAERTES   I thank you: keep the door. O thou vile king,
    Give me my father!
QUEEN   Calmly, good Laertes.
LAERTES   That drop of blood that's calm proclaims me bastard;
    Cries cuckold to my father; brands the harlot
    Even here, between the chaste unsmirchèd brows 115

---

5. Hasty secrecy. "Greenly": foolishly.   6. Broods, keeps wondering.   7. Lacks not tale bearers.
8. The necessity to build up a story without the materials for doing so.   9. Will not hesitate to accuse me.
1. A variety of cannon that scattered its shot in many directions.   2. Swiss guards.   3. Overflowing
above the high-water mark.   4. Group of rebels.   5. Following the scent in the wrong direction.

Of my true mother.

KING   What is the cause, Laertes,
  That thy rebellion looks so giant-like?
  Let him go, Gertrude; do not fear[6] our person
  There's such divinity doth hedge a king,
  That treason can but peep to what it would,[7]   120
  Acts little of his[8] will. Tell me, Laertes,
  Why thou art thus incensed: let him go, Gertrude
  Speak, man.

LAERTES   Where is my father?

KING   Dead.

QUEEN   But not by him.

KING   Let him demand his fill.   125

LAERTES   How came he dead? I'll not be juggled with
  To hell, allegiance! vows, to the blackest devil!
  Conscience and grace, to the profoundest pit
  I dare damnation: to this point I stand,
  That both the worlds I give to negligence,[9]   130
  Let come what comes; only I'll be revenged
  Most thoroughly for my father.

KING   Who shall stay you?

LAERTES   My will, not all the world
  And for my means, I'll husband them so well,
  They shall go far with little.

KING   Good Laertes,   135
  If you desire to know the certainty
  Of your dear father's death, is 't writ in your revenge
  That, swoopstake,[1] you will draw both friend and foe,
  Winner and loser?

LAERTES   None but his enemies.

KING   Will you know them then?   140

LAERTES   To his good friends thus wide I'll ope my arms;
  And, like the kind life-rendering pelican,[2]
  Repast them with my blood.

KING   Why, now you speak
  Like a good child and a true gentleman.
  That I am guiltless of your father's death,   145
  And am most sensibly in grief for it,
  It shall as level to your judgment pierce
  As day does to your eye.

DANES [*Within.*]   Let her come in.

LAERTES   How now! what noise is that?
     [*Re-enter* OPHELIA.]
  O heat, dry up my brains! tears seven times salt,   150
  Burn out the sense and virtue[3] of mine eye!

---

6. Fear for.   7. Look from a distance at what it desires.   8. Its.   9. I don't care what may happen to me in either this world or the next.   1. Without making any distinction, as the winner takes the whole stake in a card game.   2. In myth, the pelican is supposed to feed its young with its own blood. 3. Power, faculty.

By heaven, thy madness shall be paid with weight,
Till our scale turn the beam. O rose of May!
Dear maid, kind sister, sweet Ophelia!
O heavens! is 't possible a young maid's wits   155
Should be as mortal as an old man's life?
Nature is fine in love, and where 'tis fine
It sends some precious instance[4] of itself
After the thing it loves.

OPHELIA [*Sings.*]   They bore him barefaced on the bier   160
      Hey non nonny, nonny, hey nonny
      And in his grave rained many a tear,—
Fare you well, my dove!

LAERTES   Hadst thou thy wits, and didst persuade revenge,
It could not move thus.   165

OPHELIA [*Sings.*]   You must sing down a-down,
      An you call him a-down-a.
O, how the wheel becomes it![5] It is the false steward,[6] that stole his
master's daughter.

LAERTES   This nothing's more than matter.[7]   170

OPHELIA   There's rosemary, that's for remembrance: pray you, love,
remember: and there is pansies, that's for thoughts.

LAERTES   A document[8] in madness; thoughts and remembrance fitted.

OPHELIA   There's fennel for you, and columbines: there's rue for you:
and here's some for me: we may call it herbs of grace o' Sundays: O,   175
you must wear your rue with a difference. There's a daisy: I would
give you some violets,[9] but they withered all when my father died:
they say he made a good end,—
[*Sings.*]   For bonnie sweet Robin is all my joy.

LAERTES   Thought and affliction, passion, hell itself,   180
She turns to favor[1] and to prettiness.

OPHELIA [*Sings.*]   And will he not come again?
      And will he not come again?
       No, no, he is dead,
       Go to thy death-bed,   185
      He never will come again.
      His beard was as white as snow,
      All flaxen was his poll
       He is gone, he is gone,
       And we cast away moan   190
      God ha' mercy on his soul!
And of all Christian souls, I pray God. God be wi' you.
  [*Exit.*]

LAERTES   Do you see this, O God?

KING   Laertes, I must commune with your grief,

---

4. Sample, token. "Fine": refined.   5. That is, how well the refrain fits.   6. An allusion (probably to a lost ballad) further expressing Ophelia's preoccupation with betrayal, lost love, and death.   7. This nonsense is more indicative than sane speech.   8. Lesson. Traditionally, flowers and herbs have symbolic meanings. Here rosemary is the symbol for remembrance and pansies symbolize thoughts.   9. Violets symbolize faithfulness. Fennel stands for flattery, columbines for cuckoldom, and rue for sorrow and repentance (compare the verb *rue*).   1. Charm.

Or you deny me right. Go but apart, 195
Make choice of whom your wisest friends you will.
And they shall hear and judge 'twixt you and me:
If by direct or by collateral hand
They find us touched,[2] we will our kingdom give,
Our crown, our life, and all that we call ours, 200
To you in satisfaction; but if not,
Be you content to lend your patience to us,
And we shall jointly labor with your soul
To give it due content.

LAERTES   Let this be so;
His means of death, his obscure funeral, 205
No trophy, sword, nor hatchment[3] o'er his bones,
No noble rite nor formal ostentation,
Cry to be heard, as 'twere from heaven to earth,
That I must call 't in question.

KING   So you shall;
And where the offense is let the great axe fall. 210
I pray you, go with me.
          [Exeunt.]

SCENE 6

[SCENE: Another room in the castle.]

          [Enter HORATIO and a SERVANT.]
HORATIO   What are they that would speak with me?
SERVANT   Sea-faring men, sir: they say they have letters for you.
HORATIO   Let them come in.
          [Exit SERVANT.]
I do not know from what part of the world
I should be greeted, if not from Lord Hamlet. 5
          [Enter SAILORS.]
FIRST SAILOR   God bless you, sir.
HORATIO   Let him bless thee too.
FIRST SAILOR   He shall, sir, an 't please him.
There's a letter for you, sir; it comes from the ambassador that was
bound for England; if your name be Horatio, as I am let to know 10
it is.
HORATIO [Reads.] "Horatio, when thou shalt have overlooked[4] this,
give these fellows some means to the king: they have letters for him.
Ere we were two days old at sea, a pirate of very warlike appointment
gave us chase. Finding ourselves too slow of sail, we put on a com- 15
pelled valor, and in the grapple I boarded them: on the instant they
got clear of our ship; so I alone became their prisoner. They have
dealt with me like thieves of mercy:[5] but they knew what they did; I
am to do a good turn for them. Let the king have the letters I have
sent; and repair thou to me with as much speed as thou wouldst fly 20

2. Involved (in the murder). "Collateral": indirect.   3. Coat of arms.   4. Read over.   5. Merciful.

death. I have words to speak in thine ear will make thee dumb; yet
are they much too light for the bore[6] of the matter. These good
fellows will bring thee where I am. Rosencrantz and Guildenstern
hold their course for England: of them I have much to tell thee.
Farewell.   25

        "He that thou knowest thine, HAMLET."

Come, I will make you way for these your letters;
And do 't the speedier, that you may direct me
To him from whom you brought them.
      [*Exeunt.*]

SCENE 7

[SCENE: *Another room in the castle.*]

[*Enter* KING *and* LAERTES.]

KING   Now must your conscience my acquittance seal,
  And you must put me in your heart for friend,
  Sith you have heard, and with a knowing ear,
  That he which hath your noble father slain
  Pursued my life.

LAERTES   It well appears: but tell me   5
  Why you proceeded not against these feats,
  So crimeful and so capital in nature,
  As by your safety, wisdom, all things else,
  You mainly[7] were stirred up.

KING   O, for two special reasons,
  Which may to you perhaps seem much unsinewed,[8]   10
  But yet to me they're strong. The queen his mother
  Lives almost by his looks; and for myself—
  My virtue or my plague, be it either which—
  She's so conjunctive[9] to my life and soul,
  That, as the star moves not but in his sphere,   15
  I could not but by her. The other motive,
  Why to a public count I might not go,
  Is the great love the general gender[1] bear him;
  Who, dipping all his faults in their affection,
  Would, like the spring that turneth wood to stone,   20
  Convert his gyves[2] to graces; so that my arrows,
  Too slightly timber'd for so loud a wind,
  Would have reverted to my bow again
  And not where I had aim'd them.

LAERTES And so have I a noble father lost;   25
  A sister driven into desperate terms,
  Whose worth, if praises may go back again,
  Stood challenger on mount of[3] all the age
  For her perfections: but my revenge will come.

---

6. Caliber; that is, importance.   **7.** Powerfully.   **8.** Weak.   **9.** Closely joined.   **1.** Common people. "Count": accounting, trial.   **2.** Leg irons (shames).   **3.** Above. "Go back": to what she was before
her madness.

KING   Break not your sleeps for that: you must not think   30
  That we are made of stuff so flat and dull
  That we can let our beard be shook with danger
  And think it pastime. You shortly shall hear more:
  I loved your father, and we love ourself;
  And that, I hope, will teach you to imagine—   35
       [*Enter a* MESSENGER, *with letters.*]
  How now! what news?
MESSENGER   Letters, my lord, from Hamlet:
  This to your majesty; this to the queen.
KING   From Hamlet! who brought them?
MESSENGER   Sailors, my lord, they say; I saw them not:
  They were given me by Claudio; he received them   40
  Of him that brought them.
KING   Laertes, you shall hear them.
  Leave us.
      [*Exit* MESSENGER.]
  [*Reads.*] "High and mighty, you shall know I am set naked on your
  kingdom. To-morrow shall I beg leave to see your kingly eyes: when
  I shall, first asking your pardon thereunto, recount the occasion of   45
  my sudden and more strange return. *Hamlet.*"
  What should this mean? Are all the rest come back?
  Or is it some abuse, and no such thing?[4]
LAERTES   Know you the hand?
KING   'Tis Hamlet's character.[5] "Naked!"   50
  And in a postscript here, he says "alone."
  Can you advise me?
LAERTES   I'm lost in it, my lord. But let him come;
  It warms the very sickness in my heart,
  That I shall live and tell him to his teeth,   55
  "thus diddest thou."
KING   If it be so, Laertes,—
  As how should it be so? how otherwise?—
  Will you be ruled by me?
LAERTES   Aye, my lord;
  So you will not o'errule me to a peace.
KING   To thine own peace. If he be now returned,   60
  As checking[6] at his voyage, and that he means
  No more to undertake it, I will work him
  To an exploit now ripe in my device,
  Under the which he shall not choose but fall:
  And for his death no wind of blame shall breathe;   65
  But even his mother shall uncharge the practice,[7]
  call it accident.
LAERTES   My lord, I will be ruled;
  The rather, if you could devise it so
  That I might be the organ.[8]

---

4. A delusion, not a reality.   5. Handwriting.   6. Changing the course of, refusing to continue.
7. Not recognize it as a plot.   8. Instrument.

KING   It falls right.
You have been talked of since your travel much,   70
And that in Hamlet's hearing, for a quality
Wherein, they say, you shine; your sum of parts⁹
Did not together pluck such envy from him,
As did that one, and that in my regard
Of the unworthiest siege.¹
LAERTES   What part is that, my lord?   75
KING   A very riband in the cap of youth,
Yet needful too; for youth no less becomes²
The light and careless livery that it wears
Than settled age his sables and his weeds,³
Importing health and graveness. Two months since   80
Here was a gentleman of Normandy:—
I've seen myself, and served against, the French,
And they can well on horseback: but this gallant
Had witchcraft in 't; he grew unto his seat,
And to such wondrous doing brought his horse   85
As had he been incorpsed and demi-natured⁴
With the brave beast: so far he topped my thought
That I, in forgery of shapes and tricks,⁵
Come short of what he did.
LAERTES   A Norman was 't?
KING   A Norman.   90
LAERTES   Upon my life, Lamord.
KING   The very same.
LAERTES   I know him well: he is the brooch⁶ indeed
And gem of all the nation.
KING   He made confession of you,
And gave you such a masterly report,   95
For art and exercise in your defense,⁷
And for your rapier most especial,
That he cried out, 'twould be a sight indeed
If one could match you: the scrimers⁸ of their nation,
He swore, had neither motion, guard, nor eye,   100
If you opposed them. Sir, this report of his
Did Hamlet so envenom with his envy
That he could nothing do but wish and beg
Your sudden coming o'er, to play with him.
Now, out of this—
LAERTES   What out of this, my lord?   105
KING   Laertes, was your father dear to you?
Or are you like the painting of a sorrow,
A face without a heart?
LAERTES   Why ask you this?
KING   Not that I think you did not love your father,
But that I know love is begun by time,   110

---

9. The sum of your gifts.   1. Seat; that is, rank.   2. Is the appropriate age for. "Riband": ribbon,
ornament.   3. Furs (also meaning "blacks," dark colors) and robes.   4. Incorporated and split his
nature in two.   5. In imagining methods and skills of horsemanship.   6. Ornament.   7. Report of
your mastery in the theory and practice of fencing.   8. Fencers.

And that I see, in passages of proof,[9]
Time qualifies[1] the spark and fire of it.
There lives within the very flame of love
A kind of wick or snuff[2] that will abate it;
And nothing is at a like goodness still,   115
For goodness, growing to a plurisy,[3]
Dies in his own too much: that we would do
We should do when we would; for this "would" changes
And hath abatements and delays as many
As there are tongues, are hands, are accidents,   120
And then this "should" is like a spendthrift sigh,
That hurts by easing.[4] But, to the quick o' the ulcer:
Hamlet comes back: what would you undertake,
To show yourself your father's son in deed
More than in words?

LAERTES   To cut his throat i' the church.   125

KING   No place indeed should murder sanctuarize;
Revenge should have no bounds. But, good Laertes,
Will you do this, keep close within your chamber.
Hamlet returned shall know you are come home:
We'll put on[5] those shall praise your excellence   130
And set a double varnish on the fame
The Frenchman gave you; bring you in fine together
And wager on your heads: he, being remiss,[6]
Most generous and free from all contriving,
Will not peruse[7] the foils, so that with ease,   135
Or with a little shuffling, you may choose
A sword unbated, and in a pass of practice[8]
Requite him for your father.

LAERTES   I will do 't;
And for that purpose I'll anoint my sword.
I bought an unction of a mountebank,[9]   140
So mortal that but dip a knife in it,
Where it draws blood no cataplasm so rare,
Collected from all simples[1] that have virtue
Under the moon, can save the thing from death
That is but scratched withal: I'll touch my point   145
With this contagion, that, if I gall[2] him slightly,
It may be death.

KING   Let's further think of this;
Weigh what convenience both of time and means
May fit us to our shape: if this should fail,
And that our drift look through[3] our bad performance,   150
'Twere better not assayed: therefore this project
Should have a back or second, that might hold
If this did blast in proof.[4] Soft! let me see:

9. Instances that prove it.   1. Weakens.   2. Charred part of the wick.   3. Excess. "Still": constantly.   4. A sigh that gives relief but is harmful (according to an old notion that it draws blood from
the heart).   5. Instigate.   6. Careless. "In fine": finally.   7. Examine closely.   8. Treacherous
thrust. "Unbated": not blunted (as a rapier for exercise ordinarily would be).   9. Ointment of a peddler
of quack medicines.   1. Healing herbs. "Cataplasm": plaster.   2. Scratch.   3. Our design should
show through. "Shape": plan.   4. Burst (like a new firearm) once it is put to the test.

We'll make a solemn wager on your cunnings:
I ha 't: 155
When in your motion you are hot and dry—
As make your bouts more violent to that end—
And that he calls for drink, I'll have prepared him
A chalice for the nonce;[5] whereon but sipping,
If he by chance escape your venomed stuck,[6]   160
Our purpose may hold there. But stay, what noise?
         [*Enter* QUEEN.]
    How now, sweet queen!
QUEEN   One woe doth tread upon another's heel,
    So fast they follow: your sister's drowned, Laertes.
LAERTES   Drowned! O, where?   165
QUEEN   There is a willow grows aslant[7] a brook,
    That shows his hoar leaves in the glassy stream;
    There with fantastic garlands did she come
    Of crow-flowers, nettles, daisies, and long purples,
    That liberal shepherds give a grosser name,   170
    But our cold maids do dead men's fingers call them:
    There, on the pendent boughs her coronet weeds
    Clambering to hang, an envious sliver[8] broke;
    When down her weedy trophies and herself
    Fell in the weeping brook. Her clothes spread wide,   175
    And mermaid-like a while they bore her up:
    Which time she chanted snatches of old tunes,
    As one incapable of[9] her own distress,
    Or like a creature native and indued[1]
    Unto that element: but long it could not be   180
    Till that her garments, heavy with their drink,
    Pulled the poor wretch from her melodious lay
    To muddy death.
LAERTES   Alas, then she is drowned!
QUEEN   Drowned, drowned.
LAERTES   Too much of water hast thou, poor Ophelia,   185
    And therefore I forbid my tears: but yet
    It is our trick;[2] nature her custom holds,
    Let shame say what it will: when these are gone,
    The woman[3] will be out. Adieu, my lord:
    I have a speech of fire that fain would blaze,   190
    But that this folly douts[4] it.
         [*Exit.*]
KING   Let's follow, Gertrude:
    How much I had to do to calm his rage!
    Now fear I this will give it start again;
    Therefore let's follow.
         [*Exeunt.*]

---

5. For that particular occasion.   6. Thrust.   7. Across.   8. Malicious bough.   9. Insensitive to.
1. Adapted, in harmony with.   2. Peculiar trait.   3. The softer qualities, the woman in me.
4. Extinguishes.

Act V

SCENE 1

[SCENE: *A churchyard.*]

[*Enter two* CLOWNS, *with spades, etc.*]

FIRST CLOWN   Is she to be buried in Christian burial that willfully seeks her own salvation?

SECOND CLOWN   I tell thee she is; and therefore make her grave straight: the crowner[5] hath sat on her, and finds it Christian burial.

FIRST CLOWN   How can that be, unless she drowned herself in her own   5
defense?

SECOND CLOWN   Why, 'tis found so.

FIRST CLOWN   It must be "se offendendo";[6] it cannot be else. For here lies the point: if I drown myself wittingly, it argues an act: and an act hath three branches; it is, to act, to do, to perform: argal,[7] she   10
drowned herself wittingly.

SECOND CLOWN   Nay, but hear you, goodman delver.

FIRST CLOWN   Give me leave. Here lies the water; good: here stands the man; good: if the man go to this water and drown himself, it is, will he, nill he,[8] he goes; mark you that; but if the water come to   15
him and drown him, he drowns not himself: argal, he that is not guilty of his own death shortens not his own life.

SECOND CLOWN   But is this law?

FIRST CLOWN   Aye, marry, is 't; crowner's quest[9] law.

SECOND CLOWN   Will you ha' the truth on 't? If this had not been a   20
gentlewoman, she should have been buried out o' Christian burial.

FIRST CLOWN   Why, there thou say'st: and the more pity that great folk should have countenance in this world to drown or hang themselves, more than their even[1] Christian. Come, my spade. There is no ancient gentlemen but gardeners, ditchers and gravemakers: they   25
hold up Adam's profession.

SECOND CLOWN   Was he a gentleman?

FIRST CLOWN   A' was the first that ever bore arms.

SECOND CLOWN   Why, he had none.

FIRST CLOWN   What, art a heathen? How dost thou understand the   30
Scripture? The Scripture says Adam digged: could he dig without arms? I'll put another question to thee: if thou answerest me not to the purpose, confess thyself—

SECOND CLOWN   Go to.

FIRST CLOWN   What is he that builds stronger than either the mason,   35
the shipwright, or the carpenter?

SECOND CLOWN   The gallows-maker; for that frame outlives a thousand tenants.

FIRST CLOWN   I like thy wit well, in good faith: the gallows does well; but how does it well? it does well to those that do ill: now, thou dost   40

---

5. Coroner. "Straight": right away.   6. The Clown's blunder for *se defendendo*: "in self-defense" (Latin).
7. Blunder for *ergo*: "therefore" (Latin).   8. Willy-nilly.   9. Inquest.   1. Fellow. "Countenance":
sanction.

ill to say the gallows is built stronger than the church: argal, the gallows may do well to thee. To 't again, come.

SECOND CLOWN   "Who builds stronger than a mason, a shipwright, or a carpenter?"

FIRST CLOWN   Aye, tell me that, and unyoke.[2]   45

SECOND CLOWN   Marry, now I can tell.

FIRST CLOWN   To 't.

SECOND CLOWN   Mass, I cannot tell.

[*Enter* HAMLET *and* HORATIO, *afar off.*]

FIRST CLOWN   Cudgel thy brains no more about it, for your dull ass will not mend his pace with beating, and when you are asked this   50 question next, say "a grave-maker": the houses that he makes last till doomsday. Go, get thee to Yaughan; fetch me a stoup[3] of liquor.

[*Exit* SECOND CLOWN.—FIRST CLOWN *digs and sings.*]

> In youth, when I did love, did love,
>   Methought it was very sweet,
> To contract, O, the time, for-a my behove,   55
>   O, methought, there-a was nothing-a meet.[4]

HAMLET   Has this fellow no feeling of his business that he sings at grave-making?

HORATIO   Custom hath made it in him a property of easiness.[5]

HAMLET   'Tis e'en so: the hand of little employment hath the daintier[6]   60 sense.

FIRST CLOWN [*Sings.*]   But age, with his stealing steps,
>   Hath clawed me in his clutch,
>   And hath shipped me intil[7] the land,
>   As if I had never been such.   65

[*Throws up a skull.*]

HAMLET   That skull had a tongue in it, and could sing once: how the knave jowls it to the ground, as if it were Cain's jaw-bone, that did the first murder![8] It might be the pate of a politician,[9] which this ass now o'er-reaches;[1] one that would circumvent God, might it not?

HORATIO   It might, my lord.   70

HAMLET   Or of a courtier, which could say, "Good morrow, sweet lord! How dost thou, sweet lord?" This might be my lord such-a-one, that praised my lord such-a-one's horse, when he meant to beg it; might it not?

HORATIO   Aye, my lord.   75

HAMLET   Why, e'en so: and now my Lady Worm's; chapless, and knocked about the mazzard[2] with a sexton's spade: here's fine revolution, an we had the trick to see 't. Did these bones cost no more the breeding, but to play at loggats[3] with 'em? mine ache to think on 't.   80

FIRST CLOWN [*Sings.*]   A pick-axe, and a spade, a spade,
>   For a shrouding sheet:

---

2. Call it a day.   **3.** Mug. "Yaughan": apparently a tavern keeper's name.   **4.** Fitting. "Contract": shorten. "Behove": profit.   **5.** Has made it a matter of indifference to him.   **6.** Finer sensitivity. "Of little employment": that does little labor.   **7.** Into.   **8.** Possibly an allusion to the legend that Cain slew Abel with an ass's jawbone. "Jowls": knocks.   **9.** In a pejorative sense.   **1.** Outwits.   **2.** Pate. "Chapless": the lower jawbone missing.   **3.** A game resembling bowls. "Trick": faculty.

O, a pit of clay for to be made
For such a guest is meet.
[*Throws up another skull.*]

HAMLET   There's another: why may not that be the skull of a lawyer?   85
Where be his quiddities now, his quillets, his cases, his tenures,[4] and
his tricks? why does he suffer this rude knave now to knock him
about the sconce with a dirty shovel, and will not tell him of his
action of battery?[5] Hum! This fellow might be in 's time a great buyer
of land, with his statutes, his recognizances, his fines, his double   90
vouchers, his recoveries: is this the fine[6] of his fines and the recovery
of his recoveries, to have his fine pate full of fine dirt? will his vouchers vouch him no more of his purchases, and double ones too, than
the length and breadth of a pair of indentures?[7] The very convey-
ances[8] of his lands will hardly lie in this box; and must the inheritor   95
himself have no more, ha?

HORATIO   Not a jot more, my lord.

HAMLET   Is not parchment made of sheep-skins?

HORATIO   Aye, my lord, and of calf-skins too.

HAMLET   They are sheep and calves which seek out assurance[9] in that.   100
I will speak to this fellow. Whose grave's this, sirrah?

FIRST CLOWN   Mine, sir.
[*Sings.*]   O, a pit of clay for to be made
For such a guest is meet.

HAMLET   I think it be thine indeed, for thou liest in 't.   105

FIRST CLOWN   You lie out on 't, sir, and therefore 'tis not yours: for my
part, I do not lie in 't, and yet it is mine.

HAMLET   Thou dost lie in 't, to be in 't and say it is thine: 'tis for the
dead, not for the quick;[1] therefore thou liest.

FIRST CLOWN   'Tis a quick lie, sir; 'twill away again, from me to you.   110

HAMLET   What man dost thou dig it for?

FIRST CLOWN   For no man, sir.

HAMLET   What woman then?

FIRST CLOWN   For none neither.

HAMLET   Who is to be buried in 't?   115

FIRST CLOWN   One that was a woman, sir; but, rest her soul, she's dead.

HAMLET   How absolute the knave is! we must speak by the card,[2] or
equivocation will undo us. By the Lord, Horatio, these three years I
have taken note of it; the age is grown so picked that the toe of the
peasant comes so near the heel of the courtier, he galls his kibe.[3]   120
How long hast thou been a grave-maker?

FIRST CLOWN   Of all the days i' the year, I came to 't that day that our
last King Hamlet o'ercame Fortinbras.

HAMLET   How long is that since?

FIRST CLOWN   Cannot you tell that? every fool can tell that: it was that   125

---

4. Real estate holdings. "Quiddities": subtle definitions. "Quillets": quibbles.   **5.** Assault. "Sconce":
head.   **6.** End. Hamlet is punning on the legal and nonlegal meanings of the word.   **7.** Contracts
drawn in duplicate on the same piece of parchment; the two copies were separated by an indented line.
8. Deeds.   **9.** Security; another pun, because the word is also a legal term.   **1.** Living.   **2.** By
the chart, that is, exactness. "Absolute": positive.   **3.** Hurts the chilblain on the courtier's heel.
"Picked": choice, fastidious.

very day that young Hamlet was born: he that is mad, and sent into
England.

HAMLET   Aye, marry, why was he sent into England?

FIRST CLOWN   Why, because a' was mad; a' shall recover his wits there:
or, if a' do not, 'tis no great matter there.   130

HAMLET   Why?

FIRST CLOWN   'Twill not be seen in him there; there the men are as
mad as he.

HAMLET   How came he mad?

FIRST CLOWN   Very strangely, they say.   135

HAMLET   How "strangely?"

FIRST CLOWN   Faith, e'en with losing his wits.

HAMLET   Upon what ground?

FIRST CLOWN   Why, here in Denmark: I have been sexton here, man
and boy, thirty years.   140

HAMLET   How long will a man lie i' the earth ere he rot?

FIRST CLOWN   I' faith, if a' be not rotten before a' die—as we have
many pocky corses now-a-days, that will scarce hold the laying in[4]—
a' will last you some eight year or nine year: a tanner will last you
nine year.   145

HAMLET   Why he more than another?

FIRST CLOWN   Why, sir, his hide is so tanned with his trade that a' will
keep out water a great while; and your water is a sore decayer of
your whoreson dead body. Here's a skull now: this skull has lain in
the earth three and twenty years.   150

HAMLET   Whose was it?

FIRST CLOWN   A whoreson mad fellow's it was: whose do you think it
was?

HAMLET   Nay, I know not.

FIRST CLOWN   A pestilence on him for a mad rogue! a' poured a flagon   155
of Rhenish on my head once. This same skull, sir, was Yorick's skull,
the king's jester.

HAMLET   This?

FIRST CLOWN   E'en that.

HAMLET   Let me see. [*Takes the skull.*] Alas, poor Yorick! I knew him,   160
Horatio: a fellow of infinite jest, of most excellent fancy: he hath
borne me on his back a thousand times; and now how abhorred in
my imagination it is! my gorge rises at it. Here hung those lips that
I have kissed I know not how oft. Where be your gibes now? your
gambols? your songs? your flashes of merriment, that were wont to   165
set the table on a roar? Not one now, to mock your own grinning?
quite chop-fallen?[5] Now get you to my lady's chamber, and tell her,
let her paint an inch thick, to this favor[6] she must come; make her
laugh at that. Prithee, Horatio, tell me one thing.

HORATIO   What's that, my lord?   170

HAMLET   Dost thou think Alexander looked o' this fashion i' the earth?

HORATIO   E'en so.

HAMLET   And smelt so? pah!

4. Hold together till they are buried. "Pocky": with marks of disease (from "pox").   5. The lower jaw
fallen down, hence dejected.   6. Appearance.

[*Puts down the skull.*]

HORATIO E'en so, my lord.

HAMLET To what base uses we may return, Horatio! Why may not 175
imagination trace the noble dust of Alexander, till he find it stopping
a bung-hole?

HORATIO 'Twere to consider too curiously, to consider so.

HAMLET No, faith, not a jot; but to follow him thither with modesty
enough[7] and likelihood to lead it: as thus: Alexander died, Alexander 180
was buried, Alexander returneth into dust; the dust is earth; of earth
we make loam; and why of that loam, whereto he was converted,
might they not stop a beer-barrel?

> Imperious Caesar, dead and turned to clay,
> Might stop a hole to keep the wind away: 185
> O, that that earth, which kept the world in awe,
> Should patch a wall to expel the winter's flaw!

But soft! but soft! aside: here comes the king.

[*Enter* PRIESTS *etc., in procession; the Corpse of Ophelia,* LAERTES *and*
MOURNERS *following;* KING, QUEEN, *their trains, etc.*]

The queen, the courtiers: who is this they follow?
And with such maimèd rites?[8] This doth betoken 190
The corse they follow did with desperate hand
Fordo its own life: 'twas of some estate.[9]
Couch we awhile, and mark.

[*Retiring with* HORATIO.]

LAERTES What ceremony else?

HAMLET That is Laertes, a very noble youth: mark. 195

LAERTES What ceremony else?

FIRST PRIEST Her obsequies have been as far enlarged
As we have warranty: her death was doubtful;
And, but that great command o'ersways the order[1]
She should in ground unsanctified have lodged 200
Till the last trumpet; for[2] charitable prayers,
Shards, flints and pebbles should be thrown on her:
Yet here she is allowed her virgin crants,
Her maiden strewments and the bringing home[3]
Of bell and burial. 205

LAERTES Must there no more be done?

FIRST PRIEST   No more be done:
We should profane the service of the dead
To sing a requiem and such rest to her
As to peace-parted souls.

LAERTES   Lay her i' the earth:
And from her fair and unpolluted flesh 210
May violets spring! I tell thee, churlish priest,
A ministering angel shall my sister be,
When thou liest howling.

HAMLET   What, the fair Ophelia!

---

7. Without exaggeration.   8. Incomplete, mutilated ritual.   9. Rank. "Fordo": destroy.   1. The king's
command prevails against ordinary rules. "Doubtful": of uncertain cause (that is, accident or suicide).
2. Instead of.   3. Laying to rest. "Crants": garlands. "Strewments": strews the grave with flowers.

QUEEN [*Scattering flowers.*]   Sweets to the sweet: farewell!
    I hoped thou shouldst have been my Hamlet's wife;   215
    I thought thy bride-bed to have decked, sweet maid,
    And not have strewed thy grave.
LAERTES   O, treble woe
    Fall ten times treble on that cursed head
    Whose wicked deed thy most ingenious sense
    Deprived thee of! Hold off the earth a while,   220
    Till I have caught her once more in mine arms.
        [*Leaps into the grave.*]
    Now pile your dust upon the quick and dead,
    Till of this flat a mountain you have made
    To o'ertop old Pelion[4] or the skyish head
    Of blue Olympus.   225
HAMLET [*Advancing.*]   What is he whose grief
    Bears such an emphasis? whose phrase of sorrow
    Conjures the wandering stars and makes them stand
    Like wonder-wounded hearers? This is I,
    Hamlet the Dane.   230
        [*Leaps into the grave.*]
LAERTES   The devil take thy soul!
        [*Grappling with him.*]
HAMLET   Thou pray'st not well.
    I prithee, take thy fingers from my throat;
    For, though I am not splenitive[5] and rash,
    Yet have I in me something dangerous,
    Which let thy wisdom fear. Hold off thy hand.   235
KING   Pluck them asunder.
QUEEN   Hamlet, Hamlet!
ALL   Gentlemen,—
HORATIO   Good my lord, be quiet.
    [*The* ATTENDANTS *part them, and they come out of the grave.*]
HAMLET   Why, I will fight with him upon this theme
    Until my eyelids will no longer wag.
QUEEN   O my son, what theme?   240
HAMLET   I loved Ophelia: forty thousand brothers
    Could not, with all their quantity of love,
    Make up my sum. What wilt thou do for her?
KING   O, he is mad, Laertes.
QUEEN   For love of God, forbear him.   245
HAMLET   'Swounds, show me what thou 'lt do:
    Woo't weep? woo't fight? woo't fast? woo't tear thyself ?
    Woo't drink up eisel?[6] eat a crocodile?
    I'll do't. Dost thou come here to whine?
    To outface me with leaping in her grave?   250
    Be buried quick with her, and so will I:
    And, if thou prate of mountains, let them throw
    Millions of acres on us, till our ground,

---

4. The mountain on which the Aloadae, two rebellious giants in Greek mythology, piled up Mount Ossa in their attempt to reach Olympus.   5. Easily moved to anger.   6. Vinegar (the bitter drink given to Christ). "Woo't": wilt thou.

Singeing his pate against the burning zone,
Make Ossa like a wart! Nay, an thou 'lt mouth, 255
I'll rant as well as thou.
QUEEN   This is mere madness:
And thus a while the fit will work on him;
Anon, as patient as the female dove
When that her golden couplets are disclosed,[7]
His silence will sit drooping.
HAMLET   Hear you, sir; 260
What is the reason that you use me thus?
I loved you ever: but it is no matter;
Let Hercules himself do what he may,
The cat will mew, and dog will have his day.
     [*Exit.*]
KING   I pray thee, good Horatio, wait upon him. 265
     [*Exit* HORATIO.]
[*To* LAERTES.] Strengthen your patience in our last night's speech;
We'll put the matter to the present push.[8]
Good Gertrude, set some watch over your son.
This grave shall have a living monument:
An hour of quiet shortly shall we see; 270
Till then, in patience our proceeding be.
     [*Exeunt.*]

SCENE 2

[SCENE: *A hall in the castle.*]

[*Enter* HAMLET *and* HORATIO.]
HAMLET   So much for this, sir: now shall you see the other;
You do remember all the circumstance?
HORATIO   Remember it, my lord?
HAMLET   Sir, in my heart there was a kind of fighting,
That would not let me sleep: methought I lay 5
Worse than the mutines in the bilboes.[9] Rashly,
And praised be rashness for it, let us know,
Our indiscretion sometime serves us well
When our deep plots do pall;[1] and that should learn us
There's a divinity that shapes our ends, 10
Rough-hew them how we will.
HORATIO   That is most certain.
HAMLET   Up from my cabin,
My sea-gown scarfed about me, in the dark
Groped I to find out them; had my desire,
Fingered their packet, and in fine withdrew 15
To mine own room again; making so bold,
My fears forgetting manners, to unseal
Their grand commission; where I found, Horatio,—

7. Twins are hatched.   8. We'll push the matter on immediately.   9. Mutineers in iron fetters.
1. Become useless.

O royal knavery!—an exact command,
Larded with many several sorts of reasons,   20
Importing² Denmark's health and England's too,
With, ho! such bugs and goblins in my life,
That, on the supervise, no leisure bated,³
No, not to stay the grinding of the axe,
My head should be struck off.
HORATIO   Is't possible?   25
HAMLET   Here's the commission: read it at more leisure.
But wilt thou hear now how I did proceed?
HORATIO   I beseech you.
HAMLET   Being thus be-netted round with villainies,—
Ere I could make a prologue to my brains,   30
They had begun the play,—I sat me down;
Devised a new commission; wrote it fair:
I once did hold it, as our statists⁴ do,
A baseness to write fair, and labored much
How to forget that learning; but, sir, now   35
It did me yeoman's service:⁵ wilt thou know
The effect of what I wrote?
HORATIO   Aye, good my lord.
HAMLET   An earnest conjuration from the king,
As England was his faithful tributary,
As love between them like the palm might flourish,   40
As peace should still her wheaten garland wear
And stand a comma⁶ 'tween their amities,
And many such-like "As"es of great charge,⁷
That, on the view and knowing of these contents,
Without debatement further, more or less,   45
He should the bearers put to sudden death,
Not shriving-time⁸ allowed.
HORATIO   How was this sealed?
HAMLET   Why, even in that was heaven ordinant.⁹
I had my father's signet in my purse,
Which was the model of that Danish seal: 50
Folded the writ up in the form of the other;
Subscribed it; gave 't the impression;¹ placed it safely,
The changeling never known. Now, the next day
Was our sea-fight; and what to this was sequent
Thou know'st already.   55
HORATIO   So Guildenstern and Rosencrantz go to 't.
HAMLET   Why, man, they did make love to this employment;
They are not near my conscience; their defeat
Does by their own insinuation² grow:
'Tis dangerous when the baser nature comes   60
Between the pass and fell³-incensèd points

---

2. Concerning.   3. As soon as the message was read, with no time subtracted for leisure. "Bugs": imaginary horrors to be expected if I lived.   4. Statesmen.   5. Excellent service.   6. Connecting element.   7. "'As'es" is a pun on *as* and *ass*, which extends to "of great charge," signifying both "moral weight" and "ass's burden."   8. Time for confession and absolution.   9. Ordaining.   1. Of the seal.
2. Meddling. "Defeat": destruction.   3. Fiercely. "Baser": lower in rank than the king and Prince Hamlet. "Pass": thrust.

Of mighty opposites.

HORATIO   Why, what a king is this!

HAMLET   Does it not, think'st thee, stand me now upon[4]—
He that hath killed my king, and whored my mother;
Popped in between the election and my hopes;   65
Thrown out his angle for my proper life,[5]
And with such cozenage—is't not perfect conscience,
To quit[6] him with this arm? and is't not to be damned,
To let this canker of our nature come
In further evil?   70

HORATIO   It must be shortly known to him from England
What is the issue of the business there.

HAMLET   It will be short: the interim is mine;
And a man's life's no more than to say "One."
But I am very sorry, good Horatio,   75
That to Laertes I forgot myself;
For, by the image of my cause, I see
The portraiture of his: I'll court his favors:
But, sure, the bravery[7] of his grief did put me
Into a towering passion.

HORATIO   Peace! who comes here?   80

    [Enter OSRIC.]

OSRIC   Your lordship is right welcome back to Denmark.

HAMLET   I humbly thank you, sir. Dost know this waterfly?

HORATIO   No, my good lord.

HAMLET   Thy state is the more gracious, for 'tis a vice to know him.
He hath much land, and fertile: let a beast be lord of beasts, and his   85
crib shall stand at the king's mess: 'tis a chough,[8] but, as I say, spacious in the possession of dirt.

OSRIC   Sweet lord, if your lordship were at leisure, I should impart a
thing to you from his majesty.

HAMLET   I will receive it, sir, with all diligence of spirit. Put your   90
bonnet to his right use; 'tis for the head.

OSRIC   I thank your lordship, it is very hot.

HAMLET   No, believe me, 'tis very cold; the wind is northerly.

OSRIC   It is indifferent[9] cold, my lord, indeed.

HAMLET   But yet methinks it is very sultry and hot, or my complex-   95
ion—

OSRIC   Exceedingly, my lord; it is very sultry, as 'twere,—I cannot tell
how. But, my lord, his majesty bade me signify to you that he has
laid a great wager on your head: sir, this is the matter—

HAMLET   I beseech you, remember—   100

    [HAMLET moves him to put on his hat.]

OSRIC   Nay, good my lord; for mine ease, in good faith. Sir, here is
newly come to court Laertes; believe me, an absolute gentleman, full
of most excellent differences, of very soft society and great showing:[1]
indeed, to speak feelingly of him, he is the card or calendar of gen-

---

4. Is it not my duty now?   5. An angling line for my own life.   6. Pay back.   7. Ostentation,
bravado.   8. Jackdaw. "Mess": table.   9. Fairly.   1. Agreeable company, handsome in appearance.
"Differences": distinctions.

try,[2] for you shall find in him the continent of what part[3] a gentleman   105
would see.

HAMLET   Sir, his definement suffers no perdition in you; though, I
know, to divide him inventorially would dizzy the arithmetic of
memory, and yet but yaw neither, in respect of his quick sail.[4] But
in the verity of extolment, I take him to be a soul of great article,   110
and his infusion of such dearth and rareness, as, to make true diction of him, his semblable is his mirror, and who else would trace
him, his umbrage,[5] nothing more.

OSRIC   Your lordship speaks most infallibly of him.

HAMLET   The concernancy,[6] sir? why do we wrap the gentleman[7] in   115
our more rawer breath?

OSRIC   Sir?

HORATIO   Is 't not possible to understand in another tongue?[8] You will
do 't, sir, really.

HAMLET   What imports the nomination of this gentleman?   120

OSRIC   Of Laertes?

HORATIO   His purse is empty already; all's golden words are spent.

HAMLET   Of him, sir.

OSRIC   I know you are not ignorant—

HAMLET   I would you did, sir; yet, in faith, if you did, it would not   125
much approve me.[9] Well, sir?

OSRIC   You are not ignorant of what excellence Laertes is—

HAMLET   I dare not confess that, lest I should compare with him in
excellence; but, to know a man well, were to know himself.[1]

OSRIC   I mean, sir, for his weapon; but in the imputation laid on him   130
by them, in his meed he's unfellowed.[2]

HAMLET   What's his weapon?

OSRIC   Rapier and dagger.

HAMLET   That's two of his weapons: but, well.

OSRIC   The king, sir, hath wagered with him six Barbary horses: 135
against the which he has imponed, as I take it, six French rapiers and
poniards, with their assigns,[3] as girdle, hanger, and so: three of the
carriages, in faith, are very dear to fancy, very responsive[4] to the hilts,
most delicate carriages, and of very liberal conceit.[5]

HAMLET   What call you the carriages?   140

HORATIO   I knew you must be edified by the margent[6] ere you had
done.

OSRIC   The carriages, sir, are the hangers.

HAMLET   The phrase would be more germane to the matter if we could
carry a cannon by our sides:[7] I would it might be hangers till then.   145
But, on: six Barbary horses against six French swords, their assigns,

---

2. Chart and model of gentlemanly manners.   3. Whatever quality. "Continent": container.   4. And yet would only be able to steer unsteadily (unable to catch up with the *sail* of Laertes' virtues). "Perdition": loss. "Inventorially": make an inventory of his virtues. "Arithmetic": arithmetical power.   5. Keep pace with him, his shadow. "His infusion": the virtues infused into him. "Verify of extolment": to prize Laertes truthfully. "Article": importance.   6. Meaning.   7. Laertes.   8. In a less affected jargon or in the same jargon when spoken by another (that is, Hamlet's) tongue.   9. Be to my credit.   1. To know others one has to know oneself.   2. In the reputation given him by his weapons, his merit is unparalleled. 3. Appendages. "Imponed": wagered.   4. Closely matched. "Carriages": ornamented straps by which the rapiers hung from the belt. "Very dear to fancy": agreeable to the taste.   5. Elegant design. 6. Instructed by the marginal note.   7. Hamlet is playfully criticizing Osric's affected application of the term *carriage*, more properly used to mean "gun carriage."

and three liberal-conceited carriages; that's the French bet against the Danish. Why is this "imponed," as you call it?

OSRIC   The king, sir, hath laid, sir, that in a dozen passes between yourself and him, he shall not exceed you three hits: he hath laid   150
on twelve for nine; and it would come to immediate trial, if your lordship would vouchsafe the answer.[8]

HAMLET   How if I answer "no"?

OSRIC   I mean, my lord, the opposition of your person in trial.

HAMLET   Sir, I will walk here in the hall: if it please his majesty, it is   155
the breathing time[9] of day with me; let the foils be brought, the gentleman willing, and the king hold his purpose, I will win for him an I can; if not, I will gain nothing but my shame and the odd hits.

OSRIC   Shall I redeliver you e'en so?[1]

HAMLET   To this effect, sir, after what flourish your nature will.   160

OSRIC   I commend my duty to your lordship.

HAMLET   Yours, yours. [Exit OSRIC] He does well to commend it himself; there are no tongues else for's turn.

HORATIO   This lapwing[2] runs away with the shell on his head.

HAMLET   He did comply[3] with his dug before he sucked it. Thus has   165
he—and many more of the same breed that I know the drossy[4] age dotes on—only got the tune of the time and outward habit of encounter; a kind of yesty collection, which carries them through and through the most fond and winnowed opinions;[5] and do but blow them to their trial, the bubbles are out.   170

   [Enter a LORD.]

LORD   My lord, his majesty commended him[6] to you by young Osric, who brings back to him, that you attend him in the hall: he sends to know if your pleasure hold to play with Laertes, or that you will take longer time.

HAMLET   I am constant to my purposes; they follow the king's pleasure: 175
if his fitness speaks, mine is ready; now or whensoever, provided I be so able as now.

LORD   The king and queen and all are coming down.

HAMLET   In happy time.

LORD   The queen desires you to use some gentle entertainment[7] to   180
Laertes before you fall to play.

HAMLET   She well instructs me.

   [Exit LORD.]

HORATIO   You will lose this wager, my lord.

HAMLET   I do not think so; since he went into France, I have been in continual practice; I shall win at the odds. But thou wouldst not   185
think how ill all's here about my heart: but it is no matter.

HORATIO   Nay, good my lord,—

HAMLET   It is but foolery; but it is such a kind of gaingiving[8] as would perhaps trouble a woman.

HORATIO   If your mind dislike anything, obey it. I will forestall their   190
repair[9] hither, and say you are not fit.

8. The terms of this wager have never been satisfactorily clarified.   9. Time for exercise.   1. Is that the reply you want me to carry back?   2. A bird supposedly able to run as soon as it is out of its shell. 3. Use ceremony.   4. Degenerate.   5. Makes them pass the test of the most refined judgment. "Yesty": frothy.   6. Sent his regards.   7. Kind word of greeting.   8. Misgiving.   9. Coming.

HAMLET Not a whit; we defy augury: there is special providence in
the fall of a sparrow. If it be now, 'tis not to come; if it be not to
come, it will be now; if it be not now, yet it will come: the readiness
is all; since no man has aught of what he leaves, what is't to leave   195
betimes?[1] Let be.

[*Enter* KING, QUEEN, LAERTES, *and* LORDS, OSRIC *and other* ATTENDANTS
with foils and gauntlets; a table and flagons of wine on it.]

KING   Come, Hamlet, come, and take this hand from me.

[*The* KING *puts* LAERTES's *hand into* HAMLET's.]

HAMLET   Give me your pardon, sir: I've done you wrong;
But pardon't, as you are a gentleman.
This presence[2] knows,   200
And you must needs have heard, how I am punished
With sore distraction. What I have done,
That might your nature, honor and exception[3]
Roughly awake, I here proclaim was madness.
Was't Hamlet wronged Laertes? Never Hamlet: 205
If Hamlet from himself be ta'en away,
And when he's not himself does wrong Laertes,
Then Hamlet does it not, Hamlet denies it.
Who does it then? His madness: if't be so,
Hamlet is of the faction that is wronged;   210
His madness is poor Hamlet's enemy.
Sir, in this audience,
Let my disclaiming from a purposed evil
Free me so far in your most generous thoughts,
That I have shot mine arrow o'er the house,   215
And hurt my brother.

LAERTES   I am satisfied in nature,
Whose motive, in this case, should stir me most
To my revenge: but in my terms of honor[4]
I stand aloof, and will no reconcilement,
Till by some elder masters of known honor   220
I have a voice and precedent of peace,
To keep my name ungored.[5] But till that time
I do receive your offered love like love
And will not wrong it.

HAMLET   I embrace it freely,
And will this brother's wager frankly play.   225
Give us the foils. Come on.

LAERTES   Come, one for me.

HAMLET   I'll be your foil,[6] Laertes: in mine ignorance
Your skill shall, like a star i' the darkest night,
Stick fiery off[7] indeed.

LAERTES   You mock me, sir.

HAMLET   No, by this hand.   230

---

1. What is wrong with dying early (leaving "betimes"), because man knows nothing of life ("what he
leaves")?   2. Audience.   3. Objection.   4. Laertes answers separately each of the two points
brought up by Hamlet in line 86. "Nature": Laertes' natural feeling toward his father. "Honor": the code
of honor with its conventional rules.   5. Unwounded. "A voice and": an opinion based on.   6. A pun,
because *foil* means both "rapier" and "a thing that sets off another to advantage" (as gold leaf under a jewel).
7. Stand out brilliantly.

KING Give them the foils, young Osric. Cousin Hamlet,
   You know the wager?
HAMLET   Very well, my lord;
   Your grace has laid the odds o' the weaker side.
KING I do not fear it; I have seen you both:
   But since he is bettered, we have therefore odds.   235
LAERTES This is too heavy; let me see another.
HAMLET This likes me well. These foils have all a length?
    [*They prepare to play.*]
OSRIC Aye, my good lord.
KING Set me the stoups[8] of wine upon that table.
   If Hamlet give the first or second hit,   240
   Or quit in answer of the third exchange,[9]
   Let all the battlements their ordnance fire;
   The king shall drink to Hamlet's better breath;
   And in the cup an union[1] shall he throw,
   Richer than that which four successive kings   245
   In Denmark's crown have worn. Give me the cups;
   And let the kettle[2] to the trumpet speak,
   The trumpet to the cannoneer without,
   The cannons to the heavens, the heaven to earth,
   "Now the king drinks to Hamlet." Come, begin;   250
   And you, the judges, bear a wary eye.
HAMLET Come on, sir.
LAERTES   Come, my lord.
    [*They play.*]
HAMLET   One.
LAERTES   No.
HAMLET   Judgment.
OSRIC A hit, a very palpable hit.
LAERTES   Well; again.
KING Stay; give me drink. Hamlet, this pearl is thine;
   Here's to thy health.
    [*Trumpets sound, and cannon shot off within.*]
                Give him the cup.   255
HAMLET I'll play this bout first; set it by awhile.
   Come. [*They play.*] Another hit; what say you?
LAERTES A touch, a touch, I do confess.
KING Our son shall win.
QUEEN   He's fat and scant of breath.
   Here, Hamlet, take my napkin,[3] rub thy brows: 260
   The queen carouses to thy fortune, Hamlet.
HAMLET Good madam!
KING   Gertrude, do not drink.
QUEEN I will, my lord; I pray you, pardon me.
KING [*Aside.*] is the poisoned cup; it is too late.
QUEEN Come, let me wipe thy face.   265
LAERTES My lord, I'll hit him now.

---

8. Cups.   9. Requite, or repay (by scoring a hit) on the third bout.   1. A large pearl.   2. Kettledrum.
3. Handkerchief. "Fat": sweaty, or soft, because out of training.

L

KING   I do not think't.
LAERTES [*Aside.*]   And yet it is almost against my conscience.
HAMLET   Come, for the third, Laertes: you but dally;
  I pray you, pass with your best violence;
  I am afeard you make a wanton[4] of me.   270
LAERTES   Say you so? come on.
        [*They play.*]
OSRIC   Nothing, neither way.
LAERTES   Have at you now!
        [LAERTES *wounds* HAMLET; *then, in scuffling, they change rapiers, and*
        HAMLET *wounds* LAERTES.]
KING   Part them; they are incensed.
HAMLET   Nay, come, again.
        [*The* QUEEN *falls.*]
OSRIC   Look to the queen there, ho!
HORATIO   They bleed on both sides. How is it, my lord?
OSRIC   How is't, Laertes?   275
LAERTES   Why, as a woodcock to mine own springe,[5] Osric;
  I am justly killed with mine own treachery.
HAMLET   How does the queen?
KING   She swounds to see them bleed.
QUEEN   No, no, the drink, the drink,—O my dear Hamlet,—   280
  The drink, the drink! I am poisoned.
        [*Dies.*]
HAMLET   O villainy! Ho! let the door be locked:
  Treachery! seek it out.
        [LAERTES *falls.*]
LAERTES   It is here, Hamlet: Hamlet, thou art slain;
  No medicine in the world can do thee good,   285
  In thee there is not half an hour of life;
  The treacherous instrument is in thy hand,
  Unbated and envenomed: the foul practice[6]
  Hath turned itself on me; lo, here I lie,
  Never to rise again: thy mother's poisoned: 290
  I can no more: the king, the king's to blame.
HAMLET   The point envenomed too!
  Then, venom, to thy work.
        [*Stabs the* KING.]
ALL   Treason! treason!
KING   O, yet defend me, friends; I am but hurt.   295
HAMLET   Here, thou incestuous, murderous, damnèd Dane,
  Drink off this potion: is thy union here?
  Follow my mother.
        [KING *dies.*]
LAERTES   He is justly served;
  It is a poison tempered[7] by himself.
  Exchange forgiveness with me, noble Hamlet: 300
  Mine and my father's death come not upon thee,

---

4. Weakling, spoiled child.   5. Snare.   6. Plot.   7. Compounded.

    Nor thine on me!
      [Dies.]
HAMLET   Heaven make thee free of it! I follow thee.
    I am dead, Horatio. Wretched queen, adieu!
    You that look pale and tremble at this chance,   305
    That are but mutes or audience to this act,
    Had I but time—as this fell sergeant, death,
    Is strict in his arrest—O, I could tell you—
    But let it be. Horatio, I am dead;
    Thou livest; report me and my cause aright   310
    To the unsatisfied.
HORATIO   Never believe it:
    I am more an antique Roman than a Dane:
    Here's yet some liquor left.
HAMLET   As thou'rt a man,
    Give me the cup: let go; by heaven, I'll have 't.
    O good Horatio, what a wounded name,   315
    Things standing thus unknown, shall live behind me!
    If thou didst ever hold me in thy heart,
    Absent thee from felicity a while,
    And in this harsh world draw thy breath in pain,
    To tell my story.
      [March afar off, and shot within.]
                What warlike noise is this?   320
OSRIC   Young Fortinbras, with conquest come from Poland,
    To the ambassadors of England gives
    This warlike volley.
HAMLET   O, I die, Horatio;
    The potent poison quite o'er-crows[8] my spirit:
    I cannot live to hear the news from England;   325
    But I do prophesy the election lights
    On Fortinbras: he has my dying voice;
    So tell him, with the occurrents, more and less,
    Which have solicited.[9] The rest is silence.
      [Dies.]
HORATIO   Now cracks a noble heart. Good night sweet prince,   330
    And flights of angels sing thee to thy rest;
      [March within.]
    Why does the drum come hither?
      [Enter FORTINBRAS, *and the* ENGLISH AMBASSADORS, *with drum, colors,*
      and ATTENDANTS.*]*
FORTINBRAS   Where is this sight?
HORATIO   What is it you would see?
    If aught of woe or wonder, cease your search.
FORTINBRAS   This quarry cries on havoc.[1] O proud death,   335
    What feast is toward[2] in thine eternal cell,
    That thou so many princes at a shot

---

8. Overcomes.   9. Which have brought all this about. "Occurrents": occurrences.   1. This heap of corpses proclaims a carnage.   2. Imminent.

So bloodily hast struck?

FIRST AMBASSADOR   The sight is dismal;
And our affairs from England come too late:
The ears are senseless that should give us hearing,   340
To tell him his commandment is fulfilled,
That Rosencrantz and Guildenstern are dead:
Where should we have our thanks?

HORATIO   Not from his mouth
Had it the ability of life to thank you:
He never gave commandment for their death.   345
But since, so jump upon[3] this bloody question,
You from the Polack wars, and you from England
Are here arrived, give order that these bodies
High on a stage be placèd to the view;
And let me speak to the yet unknowing world   350
How these things came about; so shall you hear
Of carnal, bloody and unnatural acts,
Of accidental judgments, casual slaughters,
Of deaths put on[4] by cunning and forced cause,
And, in this upshot, purposes mistook   355
Fall'n on the inventors' heads: all this can I
Truly deliver.

FORTINBRAS   Let us haste to hear it,
And call the noblest to the audience.
For me, with sorrow I embrace my fortune:
I have some rights of memory[5] in this kingdom,   360
Which now to claim my vantage[6] doth invite me.

HORATIO   Of that I shall have also cause to speak,
And from his mouth whose voice will draw on more:[7]
But let this same be presently performed,
Even while men's minds are wild; lest more mischance   365
On[8] plots and errors happen.

FORTINBRAS   Let four captains
Bear Hamlet, like a soldier, to the stage;
For he was likely, had he been put on,[9]
To have proved most royal: and, for his passage,[1]
The soldiers' music and the rites of war   370
Speak loudly for him.
Take up the bodies: such a sight as this
Becomes the field, but here shows much amiss.
Go, bid the soldiers shoot.

> [A dead march. Exeunt, bearing off the bodies: after which a peal of ordnance is shot off.]

---

3. So immediately on.   4. Prompted. "Casual": chance.   5. Am still remembered.   6. Advantageous position, opportunity.   7. More voices.   8. Following on.   9. Tried (as a king).   1. Death.

Selected Bibliography

THE INVENTION OF WRITING AND THE EARLIEST LITERATURES

Henri Frankfort et al., *Before Philosophy: The Intellectual Adventure of Ancient Man* (1949), is a brilliant evocation of the intellectual life of ancient cultures. For concise, informative, and up-to-date articles on three ancient literatures, see Miguel Civil, "Sumerian Poetry"; John L. Foster, "Egyptian Poetry"; and Erica Reiner, "Assyro-Babylonian Poetry," in *The New Princeton Encyclopedia of Poetry and Poetics* (1993).

Ancient Egyptian Poetry
John L. Foster, *Echoes of Egyptian Voices* (1992), contains an extensive bibliography of works on ancient Egyptian culture in English. Among more general studies of ancient Egyptian culture, Cyril Aldred, *The Egyptians* (1984), is a useful general history by an art historian. B. G. Trigger et al., *Ancient Egypt: A Social History* (1983), is, as its title promises, a work that gives more attention to Egyptian society.

Gilgamesh
Andrew George's two-volume *The Babylonian Gilgamesh Epic: Introduction, Critical Edition, and Cuneiform Texts* (2003) is an authoritative new edition and discussion of ancient texts. Jeffrey Tigay, *The Evolution of the Gilgamesh Epic* (1982), examines differences among successive versions of the epic. Benjamin Foster's critical edition, *The Epic of Gilgamesh* (2001), includes a helpful brief introduction, translations of analogous Sumerian and Hittite *Gilgamesh* texts and a Mesopotamian parody of Tablet VIII, four valuable critical essays, and a glossary. The introduction to the translation by N. K. Sandars, *The Epic of Gilgamesh* (1972), contains much useful information. Two scholarly translations—Stephanie Delany, *Myths from Mesopotamia: Creation, the Flood, Gilgamesh, and Others* (1998), and Maureen Kovacs, *The Epic of Gilgamesh* (1989)—are quite readable and provide abundant and useful supplementary material. A. Leo Oppenheim gives a comprehensive interpretation of Mesopotamian civilization in *Ancient Mesopotamia* (1977). More essays and a large bibliography are available in John Maier, ed., *Gilgamesh: A Reader* (1997). Alexander Heidel addresses the importance of *Gilgamesh* for biblical studies in *The Gilgamesh Epic and Old Testament Parallels* (1963); and Malcolm C. Lyons, *The Arabian Epic: Heroic and Oral Story-Telling* (1995), includes references to *Gilgamesh* in his copious notes on shared epic motifs. Useful studies of ancient Near Eastern civilization include Amélie Kuhrt, *The Ancient Near East, c. 3000–330 BC* (1995); Thorkild Jacobsen, *The Treasures of Darkness: A History of Mesopotamian Religion* (1976); and Rivkah Harris, *Gender and Aging in Mesopotamia: The Gilgamesh Epic and Other Ancient Literature* (2000).

The Hebrew Bible
The student will find good background in R. R. Ackroyd and C. F. Evans, eds., *The Cambridge History of the Bible* (1970), vol. 1. The various volumes of *The Anchor Bible* contain modern translations and informative introductions and notes. The volume on the Song of Songs by Marvin Pope (1977) is especially helpful. Full and helpful articles on a great variety of topics can be found in Bruce M. Metzger and Michael D. Coogan, eds., *The Oxford Companion to the Bible* (1993). For Job, see P. Sanders, ed., *Twentieth-Century Interpretations of the Book of Job* (1968), and Harold Bloom, ed., *Modern Critical Interpretations: The Book of Job* (1988). See also Robert Alter and Frank Kermode, eds., *The Literary Guide to the Bible* (1987), and Leland Ryken and Tremper Longman III, eds., *A Complete Literary Guide to the Bible* (1993).

ANCIENT GREECE AND THE FORMATION
OF THE WESTERN WORLD

H. M. Orlinsky, *Ancient Israel,* 2nd ed. (1960), is a short but clearly written outline of the history of Israel up to the return from Babylonian exile. John Boardman, Jasper Griffin, and Oswyn Murray, eds., *The Oxford History of the Classical World* (1986), is a handsomely illustrated survey, by many different specialists, of the whole sweep of classical culture—social, political, literary, artistic, and religious. For the history of Greece, see J. B. Bury, *A History of Greece to the Death of Alexander the Great* (1975), 4th ed., rev. Russell Meiggs, and Thomas R. Martin, *Ancient Greece* (1996)—the latter clearly written especially for the nonspecialist reader. Michael Grant, *History of Rome* (1978), presents a well-illustrated, eminently readable survey. For surveys of Greek and Roman civilization organized according to different types of people and their social experiences, see Jean-Pierre Vernant, ed., *The Greeks* (1995), and Andrea Giardina, ed., *The Romans* (1993). A rich and beautifully illustrated survey of women in Greece and Rome is Elaine Fantham, Helene Foley, Natalie Kampen, Sarah Pomeroy, and Alan Shapiro, eds., *Women in the Classical World* (1994).

Aristotle
Kenneth McLeish, *Poetics/Aristotle* (1999), is a succinct guide to the argument and its implications. Stephen Halliwell, *The Poetics of Aristotle* (1987), gives a translation and detailed commentary.

Euripides
For a short, general survey of Euripidean drama, see B. M. W. Knox in *The Cambridge History of Classical Literature* (1985), pp. 316–39. Perceptive analyses of *Medea* can be found in Emily A. McDermott, *Euripides' Medea: The Incarnation of Disorder* (1989); and E. Segal, ed., *Euripides: A Collection of Critical Essays* (1968). William Allen, *Euripides: Medea* (2001), is a helpful short guide to the context of the play and to such issues as gender, the relation between Greek and non-Greek in the play, and revenge. Knox, "The *Medea* of Euripides," and P. E. Easterling, "The Infanticide in Euripides' *Medea,*" both in *Yale Classical Studies* 24 (1977), will also be helpful to students, as will the introduction to Donald Mastronarde's edition of the Greek text, *Euripides/Medea* (2002). Helene Foley, *Female Acts in Greek Tragedy* (2001), contains her essay "Tragic Wives: Medea's Divided Self." For essays on Medea in ancient myth, literature, and art and on the modern stage, see James J. Clauss and Sarah Iles Johnston, eds., *Medea* (1997).

Homer
A sensitive exploration of Homer's vision of human life and the nature of the gods is Jasper Griffin, *Homer on Life and Death* (1980). Mark W. Edwards, *Homer: Poet of the Iliad* (1987), discusses the oral style and gives a detailed commentary on selected books of the poem, including all of those printed here. Martin Mueller, *The Iliad* (1984), is a highly readable discussion of almost every aspect of the poem, and Seth Schein, *The Mortal Hero: An Introduction to Homer's Iliad* (1987), is an eloquent reading. The psychiatrist Jonathan Shay, in *Achilles in Vietnam: Combat Trauma and the Undoing of Character* (1994), gives a highly interesting discussion of violence and its effects in Homer and in modern warfare, drawing on his work with Vietnam veterans. Basic introductions to the *Odyssey* are Jasper Griffin, *Homer: The Odyssey* (1987); and W. G. Thalmann, *The Odyssey: An Epic of Return* (1992). An excellent companion to the poem is Ralph Hexter, *A Guide to the Odyssey: A Companion to the Translation by Robert Fitzgerald* (1993). Essays covering various aspects of the poem may be found in Charles Segal, *Singers, Heroes, and Gods in the Odyssey* (1994); Seth Schein, *Reading the Odyssey: Selected Interpretive Essays* (1996); and (on women) Beth Cohen, *The Distaff Side: Representing the Female in Homer's Odyssey* (1995). An excellent discussion of gender in the poem is Nancy Felson, *Regarding Penelope: From Character to Poetics* (1994), with further bibliography.

Plato
A. E. Taylor, *Plato, the Man and His Work* (1927), is a detailed analysis of the whole corpus of Platonic dialogues. Excellent succinct discussions of various aspects of Plato's writings and thought may be found in Bernard Williams, *Plato* (1999), and Julia Annas, *Plato: A Very Short Introduction* (2003). For an introduction to Socrates' life and thought, see W. K. C. Guthrie, *Socrates* (1971). C. D. C. Reeve, *Socrates in the Apology* (1989), offers a detailed interpretation of the *Apology* and an assessment of Socrates as he is presented there. Thomas G. West, in *Plato's Apology of Socrates* (1979), accompanies his translations with detailed interpretive essays. On Socrates' condemnation and death, see I. F. Stone, *The Trial of Socrates* (1989).

Sappho of Lesbos
Another translation of Sappho's poetry, with excellent introduction and notes, is given in Diane Rayor, *Sappho's Lyre: Archaic Lyric and Women Poets of Ancient Greece* (1991). Margaret Williamson, *Sappho's Immortal Daughters* (1995), is a comprehensive introduction to various aspects of the poetry. Accessible surveys from varying points of view may be found in Jane M. Snyder, *The Woman and the Lyre: Women Writers in Classical Greece and Rome* (1989),

Richard Jenkyns, *Three Classical Poets: Sappho, Catullus, and Juvenal* (1982), and Anne Burnett, *Three Archaic Poets: Archilochus, Alcaeus, Sappho* (1983). An outstanding assessment of Sappho's position as a woman in Greek society is John J. Winkler, "Double Consciousness in Sappho's Lyrics," in his *The Constraints of Desire: The Anthropology of Sex and Gender in Ancient Greece* (1990). Page duBois, *Sappho Is Burning* (1995), is a challenging discussion of Sappho's poetry as resisting the categories of Western thought. Two collections of essays edited by Ellen Greene, *Reading Sappho: Contemporary Approaches* (1996) and *Re-reading Sappho: Reception and Transmission* (1996), offer a generous sampling of approaches to Sappho's poetry and its later reception.

Sophocles
For a short, general survey of Sophoclean drama, see P. E. Easterling in *The Cambridge History of Classical Literature* (1985), pp. 295–316. B. M. W. Knox, *Oedipus at Thebes* (1957), is a detailed examination of the play in the context of its age; Knox, *The Heroic Temper* (1964), concentrates on the characters of Oedipus, Antigone, Electra, and Philoctetes. Harold Bloom, *Sophocles's Oedipus Rex* (1988), is a well-chosen collection of

essays on the play, and Charles Segal, *Oedipus Tyrannus: Tragic Heroism and the Limits of Knowledge* (1993; 2nd, expanded ed., 2001), is an outstanding full-length treatment. Helene Foley, *Female Acts in Greek Tragedy* (2001), contains an essay on Antigone as a moral agent. Jean-Pierre Vernant and Pierre Vidal-Naquet, *Myth and Tragedy in Ancient Greece* (1972; English trans. 1988) contains Vernant's influential essays "Oedipus without the Complex," a critical engagement with Freudian readings, and "Ambiguity and Reversal: On the Enigmatic Structure of *Oedipus Rex*." Mark Griffith, *Antigone/Sophocles* (1999), although an edition meant to guide a reading of the Greek text, contains an excellent and accessible introduction, including a survey of various critical approaches to the play. See also R. P. Winnington-Ingram, *Sophocles: An Interpretation* (1980), pp. 91–149 (*Antigone*) and 150–204 (*Oedipus the King*); and Charles Segal, *Tragedy and Civilization: An Interpretation of Sophocles* (1981), pp. 152–206 (*Antigone*) and 207–48 (*Oedipus the King*). David Seale, *Vision and Stagecraft in Sophocles* (1982), is a stimulating discussion of the themes of sight, blindness, and knowledge in relation to the experience of watching a play.

POETRY AND THOUGHT IN EARLY CHINA

A good general introduction to writing in this period can be found in Burton Watson, *Early Chinese Literature* (1962). Henri Maspero, *China in Antiquity* (first published 1927, English trans. 1978), is an older, but still useful survey of early Chinese history and culture. Wang Ching-hsien, *From Ritual to Allegory: Seven Essays in Early Chinese Poetry* (1988), is a study of the *Book of Songs* (that is, *Classic of Poetry*) and the *Chu-tz'u*. The best study of early Chinese philosophers is A. C. Graham, *Disputers of the Tao: Philosophical Argument in Ancient China* (1989). Early Chinese reflection on and interpretation of the ancient classics, using the case of the *Book of Songs*, are studied in Steven Van Zoeren, *Poetry and Personality* (1991).

Chuang Chou
For another translation of the *Chuang Tzu* by one of the most distinguished scholars of Chinese philosophy, see A. C. Graham's *Chuang Tzu: The Inner Chapters* (1981). Graham also

includes an excellent discussion of the *Chuang Tzu* in the context of other early thinkers in *Disputers of the Tao: Philosophical Argument in Ancient China* (1989).

Classic of Poetry
A basic introduction to the *Classic of Poetry* can be found in Wang Ching-hsien, *From Ritual to Allegory: Seven Essays in Early Chinese Poetry* (1988). Pauline Yu, *The Reading of Imagery in the Chinese Tradition* (1987), has an excellent chapter on the traditional understanding of imagery in the *Classic of Poetry*.

Confucius
D. C. Lau's translation of the *Analects* (1979) has a long introduction that offers a lucid exposition of key concepts used in the work. The philosopher Herbert Fingarette, *Confucius— The Secular as Sacred* (1972), remains one of the most persuasive accounts of the appeal of the *Analects*.

INDIA'S HEROIC AGE

Arthur Llewellyn Basham, *The Wonder That Was India* (1954), is the best general introduction to Indian civilization up to 1565. William Theodore De Bary, ed., *Sources of Indian Tradition* (1958), is a comprehensive volume of the textual sources of Indian thought from the beginnings to the present, with concise, accessible introductory notes. Thomas J. Hopkin, *The Hindu Religious Tradition* (1971), and R. C. Zaehner, *Hinduism* (1900), are more detailed introductions to Hinduism, while similar treatments of Buddhism may be found in Edward Conze, *Buddhism: Its Essence and Development* (1900), and Richard Robinson and Willard Johnson, *The Buddhist Religion* (1900). Edward C. Dimock et al., eds., *The Literatures of India: An Introduction* (1974), is an excellent introduction to Indian literature. For Indian mythology and the Hindu gods, consult Veronica Ions, *Indian Mythology* (1967), and A. K. Coomaraswamy and Sister Nivedita, *Myths of the Hindus and Buddhists* (1967).

The Bhagavad-Gītā

Among the scriptures of the world, the *Bhagavad-Gītā* is second only to the Bible in the number of times it has been translated. Barbara Stoler Miller, *The Bhagavad-Gītā: Krishna's Counsel in Time of War* (1986), the translation reprinted in this anthology, is enhanced by a lucid introductory essay and a glossary of key words. Among older translations and interpretations, readers might find it useful to consult Eliot Deutsch for a good explanation of key philosophical ideas, and S. Radhakrishnan for the parallel Sanskrit text (in transliteration), accompanied by a commentary from the point of view of an eminent modern Indian philosopher. On Indian interpreters of the *Gītā*, see Robert Minor, *Modern Interpreters of the Bhagavadgītā* (1986). For the *Gītā*'s career in the West, consult Eric Sharpe, *The Universal Gītā: Western Images of the Bhagavad Gītā, A Bicentennial Survey* (1985).

The Rāmāyaṇa of Vālmīki

Swami Venkatasananda's condensed prose translation in *The Concise Rāmāyaṇa* (1988) conveys the narrative power of Vālmīki's epic. Noteworthy among the many popular retellings of the main story of Vālmīki's *Rāmāyaṇa* are A. K. Coomaraswamy and Sister Nivedita's version in *Myths of the Hindus and Buddhists* (1967) and C. Rajagopalachari's in *Rāmāyaṇa* (1951). Older translations of the entire epic text, such as Hari Prasad Shastri's prose translation in three volumes (*The Rāmāyaṇa of Vālmīki*, 1957), and N. Raghunathan, *Srīmad Vālmīki Rāmāyaṇa* (1981–82), 3 vols, will soon be superseded by the excellent, readable, liberally annotated Princeton translation, with good introductory essays, by a number of scholars headed by Robert Goldman, *The Rāmāyaṇa of Vālmīki: An Epic of Ancient India* (1984), when all seven volumes are complete (five have appeared so far). In addition to the books and articles on the epic listed under "India's Heroic Age," readers interested in the social background of Vālmīki's epic should refer to J. L. Brockington, *Righteous Rāma: The Evolution of an Epic* (1984). For later versions of the Rāma story in relation to Vālmīki, see Paula Richman, ed., *Many Rāmāyaṇas: The Diversity of a Narrative Tradition in South Asia* (1991).

THE ROMAN EMPIRE

John Boardman, Jasper Griffin, and Oswyn Murray, eds., *The Oxford History of the Classical World* (1986), is a handsomely illustrated survey, by many different specialists, of the whole sweep of classical culture—social, political, literary, artistic, and religious. Michael Grant, *History of Rome* (1978), presents a well-illustrated, eminently readable survey. For a survey of Roman civilization organized according to different types of people and their social experiences, see Andrea Giardina, ed., *The Romans* (1993). For a detailed survey of Roman literature, see E. J. Kenney and W. V. Clausen, eds., *The Cambridge History of Classical Literature*, vol. 2: *Latin Literature* (1982). A rich and beautifully illustrated survey of women in Greece and Rome is Elaine Fantham, Helene Foley, Natalie Kampen, Sarah Pomeroy, and Alan Shapiro, eds., *Women in the Classical World* (1994).

Catullus

The best general introduction to Catullus, with essential background and perceptive discussion of the poetry, is Charles Martin, *Catullus* (1992). For more detailed but highly readable discussions of contemporary culture and society, Clodia and her circle, and the poems' relation to this context, T. P. Wiseman, *Catullus and His World: A Reappraisal* (1985), is excellent. Two older books are still valuable: A. L. Wheeler, *Catullus and the Traditions of Ancient Poetry* (1934), and E. A. Havelock, *The Lyric Genius of Catullus* (1964). The first puts Catullus in his cultural and literary context; the second translates selected poems and offers a sensitive appreciation of them. Kenneth Quinn, *Catullus: An Interpretation* (1973), gives an interesting if idiosyncratic view of the poetry. An excellent newer discussion is William Fitzgerald, *Catullan Provo-*

cations: *Lyric Poetry and the Drama of Position* (1995). For a depiction of Catullus as well as Lesbia/Clodia and her circle in a carefully researched historical detective novel, see Steven Saylor, *The Venus Throw* (1995).

Ovid
Sara Mack, *Ovid* (1988), provides an excellent introduction to all of Ovid's poems for the general reader, with a long chapter on the *Metamorphoses*. A classic treatment of this poem is Brooks Otis, *Ovid as an Epic Poet* (1966; 2nd ed. 1970). G. K. Galinsky, *Ovid's Metamorphoses: An Introduction to the Basic Aspects,* is also a useful guide. L. P. Wilkinson, *Ovid Recalled* (1955), abridged as *Ovid Surveyed* (1962), gives a comprehensive overview of various aspects of Ovid's poetry. See also Niklas Holzberg, *Ovid: The Poet and His Work* (1997; trans. 2002). For later poets and artists' uses of Ovid, see the essays collected in Charles Martindale, *Ovid Renewed: Ovidian Influences on Literature and Art from the Middle Ages to the Twentieth Century* (1988). An excellent collection of essays on Ovid's poetry, its historical context, and its reception is Philip Hardie, ed., *The Cambridge Companion to Ovid* (2002).

Virgil
Useful and accessible discussions of basic aspects of the *Aeneid* and of its historical and literary context are W. A. Camps, *An Introduc-tion to Virgil's Aeneid* (1969); Jasper Griffin, *Virgil* (1986); and K. W. Gransden, *Virgil, the Aeneid* (1990; 2nd ed., 2004). R. D. Williams, *The Aeneid of Virgil: A Companion to the Translation of C. Day Lewis* (1985), gives a summary and outline of the poem, with brief notes on specific passages. Articles on individual books of the poem, and on general topics, may be found in Christine Perkell, ed., *Reading Vergil's Aeneid: An Interpretive Guide* (1999). Peter Levi, *Virgil: His Life and Times* (1998), surveys all of Virgil's poetry with particular attention to contemporary historical events and the poems' relation to Italy (chapters 5–8 are on the *Aeneid*). W. S. Anderson, *The Art of the Aeneid* (1969), is a sensible book-by-book reading of the poem. Brooks Otis, *Virgil: A Study in Civilized Poetry* (1963), and R. O. A. M. Lyne, *Further Voices in Virgil's Aeneid* (1987), are more detailed but readable and influential works of criticism. Valuable collections of essays by various authors are Steele Commager, ed., *Virgil: A Collection of Critical Essays* (1966); Harold Bloom, ed., *Virgil* (1986); and Harold Bloom, ed., *Virgil's Aeneid* (1987). Charles Martindale, ed., *The Cambridge Companion to Virgil* (1997), contains essays on various aspects of Virgil's life and works, including the later reception of the poetry. Useful commentary on the *Aeneid* and on various aspects of Virgil's work may be found in Nicholas Horsfall, ed., *A Companion to the Study of Virgil* (2000).

FROM ROMAN EMPIRE TO CHRISTIAN EUROPE

Jaroslav Pelikan, *The Excellent Empire: The Fall of Rome and the Triumph of the Church* (1987), is a collection of brilliant essays by a famous historian of the Christian church on Gibbon's *Decline and Fall,* the early centuries of the church, and St. Augustine. For a critical assessment of Constantine by a noted historian of Rome, see Ramsay MacMullen, *Constantine* (1969); Michael Grant, *Constantine the Great* (1994), is also recommended. Averil Cameron, *The Later Roman Empire* (1993), is a basic source for the study of "late antiquity" (Diocletian to Constantine) by a well-known specialist on the period. F. W. Walbank, *The Awful Revolution: The Decline of the Roman Empire in the West* (1969), provides a detailed but lucid analysis of the crisis and collapse of Roman imperial power—Gibbon's "awful Revolution."

Augustine
Peter Brown, *Augustine of Hippo* (1967), is an authoritative and engrossing account of Augustine's career and major works. Warren Thomas Smith, *Augustine, His Life and Thought* (1980), gives a brief and readable overview of his biography, his times, and his intellectual development.

Another introduction to Augustine's life and thought, with a substantial discussion of the *Confessions,* is James J. O'Donnell, *Augustine* (1985). Gillian Clark, *Augustine, the Confessions* (1993), is an excellent short guide to this work, with discussions of various literary and intellectual issues that it raises and particular attention to the historical context. See also Colin Stearnes, *Augustine's Conversion: A Guide to the Argument of Confessions I–IX* (1990); Garry Wills, *Saint Augustine* (1999); and Eleanor Stump and Norman Kretzmann, eds., *The Cambridge Companion to Augustine* (2001).

The Christian Bible
Recommended reading is Bruce M. Metzger, *The New Testament: Its Background, Growth, and Content* (1965), and the relevant chapters in Robert Alter and Frank Kermode, eds., *The Literary Guide to the Bible* (1987). For a translation with commentary, see *The New Oxford Annotated Bible* (1975), ed. Herbert E. May and Bruce Metzger. *The Oxford Companion to the Bible* (1993), ed. Bruce Metzger and Michael Coogan, is a mine of information on almost any biblical topic.

INDIA'S CLASSICAL AGE

The Literatures of India (1974), ed. Edward C. Dimock and co-workers, contains good introductions to the various genres of classical Sanskrit literature, and Daniel H. H. Ingalls, *Sanskrit Poetry from Vidyākara's Treasury* (1968), offers an outstanding introduction to *kāvya* poetry and its aesthetic. A. L. Basham, *The Wonder That Was India* (1956), is the best study of India's classical civilization. For a history of Sanskrit literature, see A. B. Keith, *History of Classical Sanskrit Literature* (1928). The *Kāmasūtra* may be consulted in Richard Burton's translation, *The Kama Sutra of Vatsyayana* (1923). On women in classical civilization, see A. S. Altekar, *The Position of Women in Hindu Civilization* (1938), and J. J. Meyer, *Sexual Life in Ancient India* (1930).

Amaru
Daniel H. H. Ingalls's general introduction to *Sanskrit Poetry from Vidyākara's Treasury* (1968) is the best introduction to the aesthetics of the Sanskrit short lyric. In addition to translations of a number of love poems by Amaru and other authors, this volume also contains excellent sectional introductions that treat the conventions and classificatory schemes relating to love poetry. For Amaru in (rhymed) English verse, see John Brough, *Poems from the Sanskrit* (1968). In *Fires of Love, Waters of Peace* (1983) Lee Siegel offers lively translations and a comparison of Amaru and the philosopher poet

Śaṃkara. Selected translations of Amaru may also be found in J. Moussaieff Masson and W. S. Merwin, *The Peacock's Egg* (1981).

Bhartṛhari
For translations of a judicious selection of Bhartṛhari's poems, with an excellent introduction, see Barbara Stoler Miller, *The Hermit and the Love-Thief* (1978).

Somadeva
A complete translation of the *Kathāsaritsāgara*, with extensive notes bearing on comparative folklore is available in C. H. Tawney and N. M. Penzer, *The Kathāsaritsāgara or Ocean of the Streams of Story* (1880). For a thoughtful introduction to the Sanskrit story literature, and for excellent translations of selections from the *Kathāsaritsāgara* and two other Sanskrit narrative texts, see J. A. B. van Buitenen, *Tales of Ancient India* (1959).

Viṣṇuśarman
For the history of the *Pañcatantra* and its transmission to the Middle East and Europe, see Maurice Winternitz, *A History of Indian Literature* (1963), and Joseph Jacobs, *History of the Aesopic Fable* (1889). Francis Hutchins offers a fine translation of the *Hitopadeśa*, with many illustrations, in *Animal Fables from India; Nārāyaṇa's Hitopadesha or Friendly Counsel* (1985).

CHINA'S "MIDDLE PERIOD"

A general study of Chinese poetry from the Han Dynasty through the T'ang can be found in Burton Watson, *Chinese Lyricism* (1971). For a general introduction to the forms of Chinese poetry there is James J. Y. Liu, *The Art of Chinese Poetry* (1962). A somewhat different approach can be found in Stephen Owen, *Traditional Chinese Poetry and Poetics: Omen of the World* (1985). A general study of poetry before the T'ang is Kang-i Sun Chang, *Six Dynasties Poetry* (1986); the eighth century is covered in Stephen Owen, *The Great Age of Chinese Poetry: The High T'ang* (1980). The Sung period is studied in Burton Watson's translation of Yoshikawa Kojiro, *An Introduction to Sung Poetry* (1967).

Li Ch'ing-Chao
A discussion of the "Afterword" can be found in Stephen Owen, *Remembrances: The Experience of the Past in Classical Chinese Literature* (1986). For a discussion of the development of the song lyric, see Kang-i (Sun) Chang, *The*

Evolution of Chinese Tz'u Poetry: From Late T'ang to Northern Sung (1980). For a complete and very free translation of Li Ch'ing-chao's song lyrics, see Kenneth Rexroth and Ling Chung, *Li Ch'ing-chao: Complete Poems* (1979).

Li Po
Arthur Waley, *The Genius of Li Po* (1950), is an excellent biography. There is a long chapter on Li Po's poetry in Stephen Owen, *The Great Age of Chinese Poetry: The High T'ang* (1980).

T'ang Poetry
A general survey of the poetry of the eighth century can be found in Stephen Owen, *The Great Age of Chinese Poetry: The High T'ang* (1980). A more general introduction to Chinese poetry can be found in James Liu, *The Art of Chinese Poetry* (1962), and in Stephen Owen, *Traditional Chinese Poetry and Poetics: An Omen of the World* (1985).

T'ao Ch'ien

There are two complete English translations of T'ao Ch'ien's poetry (and much of his prose), *The Poetry of T'ao Ch'ien* (1970), by James Robert Hightower, and *T'ao Yüan-ming* (1984), by A. R. Davis.

Tu Fu

David Hawkes, *A Little Primer of Tu Fu* (1967), gives the Chinese text and a word-by-word explanation of a small group of Tu Fu's poems. Another study is A. R. Davis, *Tu Fu* (1971).

THE RISE OF ISLAM AND ISLAMIC LITERATURE

The best brief introduction to Arabic literature is still H. A. R. Gibb, *Arabic Literature* (1926). The articles "Arabic Poetics and Arabic Poetry" and "Arabic Prosody" by Roger M. A. Allen and David Semah, respectively, in *The New Princeton Encyclopedia of Poetry and Poetics* (1993) provide brief introductions to these topics as well as extensive bibliographies. For the Persian tradition, see Ehsan Yarshater, ed., *Persian Literature* (1988), and Julie Scott Meisami, *Medieval Persian Court Poetry* (1987). There are few good introductory studies of Ottoman poetry, but Walter G. Andrews, *An Introduction to Ottoman Poetry* (1976), is by far the best of these, and his study of the Ottoman lyric poetry, *Poetry's Voice, Society's Song* (1985), gives clear and illuminating insight into the relation of poetic production to the larger dynamics of an Islamic society. Marshall G. S. Hodgson, *The Venture of Islam: Volumes One to Three* (1974), is the best general history of the Islamic world and contains sections on the literary tradition. There are a number of anthologies of Arabic poetry. Charles Greville Tuetey, *Classical Arabic Poetry: 162 Poems from Imrulkais to Ma'arri* (1985), has the advantage of being comprehensive and highly readable. Tuetey also provides good historical and critical introductions to each poem.

The Koran

The most informative general introduction to the Koran is the revised edition of *Bell's Introduction to the Qur'ân* (1970). Michael Cook, *Muhammad* (1983), is an excellent brief biography of the Prophet of Islam. Fazlur Rahman, *Major Themes of the Qur'ân* (1980), is a lucid presentation by a Muslim scholar who has taught in the United States for many years of the principal beliefs of Islam as they appear in the Koran. Marilyn R. Waldman, "New Approaches to 'Biblical' Materials in the Qur'ân," *The Muslim World* 75.1 (January 1985): 1–16, gives a good comparison of Joseph in the Koran and the Bible.

Jalâloddin Rumi

Translations of Rumi are legion but few convey any sense of the poetic fabric of the original. The *Spiritual Couplets* has been translated into En-

glish only once, by R. A. Nicholson, and printed together with an edition of the texts and extended notes and commentary, *The Mathnawi of Jalaluddin Rumi* (1982). Nicholson's translation is prosaic, literal, and explanatory rather than poetic. He has also published a volume of *ghazals* with Persian text and literal Persian translation on facing pages, *The Divani Shamsi Tabrizi* (1977). A. J. Arberry has produced two collections of Rumi's *ghazals*, *The Mystical Poems of Rumi* (1968), and *The Mystical Poems of Rumi: Second Selection* (1979), that are, like Nicholson's, literal and prosaic. American poets who know no Persian—most notably Robert Bly, Coleman Barks, and W. S. Merwin—have translated Rumi into modern verse with the help of Nicholson and Arberry or some other literal rendering. The most successful of these poets is Barks. Though less literally accurate than Nicholson's or Arberry's versions, Barks's are both better poetry and truer to the spirit of Rumi. He has published extensive translations, or retranslations, from both the *Spiritual Couplets* and the *Divân-e Shams-e Tabrizi*, among them *Open Secret* (1984), *Unseen Rain* (1986), *This Longing: Forty Odes by Rumi* (1986), *Feeling the Shoulder of the Lion* (1991), *We Are Three* (1987), *Delicious Laughter* (1991), and *The Essential Rumi* (1995).

Rumi is mentioned in many studies of mysticism and mystical poetry. Annemarie Schimmel, *The Triumphal Sun* (1980), is a scholarly survey of Rumi's life and work. The best study of his lyric poetry is F. Keshavarz, *Reading Mystical Lyric: The Case of Jalal al-Din Rumi* (1998). There are also chapters on Rumi in virtually every literary history of Iran, including E. Yarshater, *Persian Literature* (1987). J. Spencer Trimingham, *The Sufi Orders of Islam* (1971), provides a comprehensive introduction to sufism as a spiritual community and social force within Islam.

The Thousand and One Nights

Husain Haddawy, *The Arabian Nights* (1990), is a complete translation of the text of Muhsin Mahdi's critical edition of the Syrian manuscript (1984), and his *Arabian Nights II: Sindbad and Other Popular Stories* (1995) is a selection of tales that were added to it by later authors. The earliest English version of the *Nights*, made from the French of Antoine Galland by an anonymous English translator, has been published in paperback by R. L. Mack as *Arabian Nights' Entertainments* (1995). The nineteenth-century translations by Edward William Lane (1838–42) and Richard Burton (1885–88) were made directly from Arabic but were based on late, heterogeneous manuscripts. Burton's is the better known, but Lane's is closer to the original although it bowdlerizes the erotic scenes. Muhsin Mahdi has published an introduction to his edition titled simply *The Thousand and One Nights* (1995). Mia Gerhardt, *The Art of Storytelling: A Literary Study of the Thousand and One Nights* (1963), is virtually the only interpretive study of the whole of the *Thousand and One Nights* in English. It contains an excellent discussion of European interest in the work but is less satisfactory for individual stories. Ferial Jabouri Ghazoul, *The Arabian Nights: A Structural Analysis* (1980), focuses on several stories and groups of stories, among them the "Prologue." She also argues the central importance of the feminine in the *Nights*. Bruno Bettelheim, *The Uses of Enchantment: The Meaning and Importance of Fairy Tales* (1976), includes a brief discussion of Shahrazad in his study of the therapeutic role of fairy tales. Jerome W. Clinton gives a more detailed discussion of this same question in "Madness and Cure in the 1001 Nights," in *Fairy Tales and Society: Illusion, Allusion, Paradigm* (1986), ed. Ruth B. Bottigheimer.

THE FORMATION OF A WESTERN LITERATURE

An excellent reference work that contains articles on virtually all medieval topics, with bibliographies, is *The Dictionary of the Middle Ages* (1987), 13 vols. Specific questions about medieval Christian doctrines can be answered by consulting Jaroslav Pelikan, *The Christian Tradition: A History of the Development of Doctrine* (1971–84), vols. 1–4. C. W. Previté-Orton, *Shorter Cambridge Medieval History* (1952), 2 vols., provides useful information on the relevant historical context of each literary work. An authoritative and readable introduction to social and economic conditions is M. M. Postan, *The Medieval Economy and Society* (1975). Two classic accounts well worth reading are R. W. Southern, *The Making of the Middle Ages* (1953), and J. W. Huizinga, *The Autumn of the Middle Ages* (first published in 1919, more recently translated in 1996).

Beowulf
A good introduction to the Anglo-Saxon period, and to the techniques of Anglo-Saxon poetry, can be found in the essays collected by Malcolm Godden and Michael Lapidge, eds., *The Cambridge Companion to Old English Literature* (1991). *A Beowulf Handbook* (1997), ed. Robert E. Bjork and John D. Niles, provides useful essays about the poem, its context, and its criticism. Other useful collections of essays are R. D. Fulk, ed., *Interpretations of Beowulf* (1991), and Peter S. Baker, ed., *Beowulf: Basic Readings* (1995). An excellent account of the relation of pagan to Christian in the poem is Fred C. Robinson, *Beowulf and the Appositive Style* (1985), and a good treatment of other issues is Edward B. Irving, *Rereading Beowulf* (1989).

Giovanni Boccaccio
Vittore Branca, *Boccaccio: The Man and His Works* (1975), is the standard biography with useful literary commentary. For guides to the *Decameron*, see Giuseppe Mazzotta, *The World at Play in Boccaccio's Decameron* (1986), and David Wallace, *Giovanni Boccaccio: Decameron* (1991).

Geoffrey Chaucer
The standard edition of Chaucer's works is Larry Benson, ed., *The Riverside Chaucer* (1987), 3rd ed., which provides a fully annotated text in Middle English with a glossary and full introductions and notes. Useful guides to *The Canterbury Tales* are provided in accessible books by Derek A. Pearsall (1985) and Winthrop Wetherbee (1989). More detailed analyses of the three tales selected here may be found in Lee Patterson, *Chaucer and the Subject of History* (1991).

Dante Alighieri
Of the many excellent commentaries in English, one of the most complete is in the edition and translation by Charles S. Singleton (1970–75). An excellent commentary on the *Inferno* can be found in the edition and translation by Robert M. Durling and Ronald L. Martinez (1996), who are preparing similar volumes for the rest of the poem. Useful commentaries on individual cantos can also be found in Ricardo Quinones, *Dante* (1979). A rightly celebrated essay on *Inferno* 10, with important comments on the *Comedy* as a whole, is by Erich Auerbach in his *Mimesis*, and illuminating and learned essays by one of the leading English-speaking Dantists are in John Freccero, *Dante: The Poetics of Conversion* (1986). *Dante Studies* is published annually and includes an annotated bibliography.

Marie de France
A complete translation of the *Lais*, with a helpful introduction and full bibliography, can be found in Glyn S. Burgess and Keith Busby, trans., *The Lais of Marie de France* (1986). A verse translation with commentary is provided by Robert Hanning and Joan Ferrante, *The Lais of Marie de France* (1978).

The Song of Roland
A scholarly edition, with translation and commentary, is Gerald S. Brault, *The Song of Roland: An Analytical Edition* (1978), 2 vols. Useful critical discussions are Eugene Vance, *Reading the Song of Roland* (1970), and Robert Francis Cook, *The Sense of the Song of Roland* (1987).

THE GOLDEN AGE OF JAPANESE CULTURE

The Man'yōshū
Two good partial translations of *The Man'yōshū* exist in English: Nippon Gakujutsu Shinkōkai, *The Manyōshū* (1965), and Ian Hideo Levy, *The Ten Thousand Leaves* (1981). Both have informative introductions. Levy has also produced a detailed study of one poet, *Hitomaro and the Birth of Japanese Lyricism* (1984). The best overall study of *The Man'yōshū* is contained in Robert H. Brower and Earl Miner, *Japanese Court Poetry* (1961). For a concise history of Japan see John Whitney Hall, *Japan: From Prehistory to Modern Times* (1991), and for a short, general introduction to Japanese literature see Donald Keene, *The Pleasures of Japanese Literature* (1988).

Nō Drama
The most accessible introduction to the *nō* is by Donald Keene, *Nō: The Classical Theatre of Japan* (1973), which is also valuable for its photographs. Zeami's theories of drama are available in English in J. Thomas Rimer and Yamazaki Masakazu, *On the Art of Nō Drama: The Major Treatises of Zeami* (1894); they are discussed by Makoto Ueda in "Zeami and the Art of the Nō Drama: Imitation, Yugen and Sublimity," in *Japanese Aesthetics and Culture: A Reader* (1998), ed. Nancy G. Hulme, and Benito Ortolani and

Samuel L. Leiter, eds., *Zeami and the Nō Theatre in the World* (1998). Two excellent technical works are P. G. O'Neill, *Early Nō Drama* (1974), and Thomas Blenman Hare, *Zeami's Style: The Noh Plays of Zeami Motokiyo* (1986). Appraisals of the *nō* by Pound and Yeats are found in a collection of translated plays: Ezra Pound and Ernest Fenollosa, *The Classic Noh Theatre of Japan* (1959). Other collections of translations include Arthur Waley, *The Nō Plays of Japan* (1921); Donald Keene, ed., *Twenty Plays of the Nō Theatre* (1970); Nippon Gakujutsu Shinkōkai, *The Noh Drama* (1973); Kenneth Yasuda, *Masterworks of the Nō Theatre* (1989); and Royall Tyler, *Japanese Nō Dramas* (1992).

Murasaki Shikibu
The best brief introduction is Richard Bowring, *The Tale of Genji* (1988). Two excellent longer studies are Norma Field, *The Splendor of Longing in the "Tale of Genji"* (1987), and Haruo Shirane, *The Bridge of Dreams: A Poetics of "The Tale of Genji"* (1987). A collection of essays on the last part of the novel representative of recent American scholarship is Andrew Pekarik, ed., *Ukifune: Love in "The Tale of Genji"* (1982). For a glimpse into the life of the author see Richard Bowring, *Murasaki Shikibu: Her Diary and Poetic Memoirs* (1982).

AFRICA: THE MALI EPIC OF SON-JARA

For a comprehensive discussion, from a cross-cultural perspective, of the epic genre in Africa, see Isidore Okpewho, *The Epic in Africa* (1979). The translation printed here is John William Johnson, *The Epic of Son-Jara: A West African Tradition* (1992), which contains a valuable introduction. Adu Boahen, *Topics in West African History* (1990), provides in a succinct and readable form the general historical background. On the specific role of Islam as a historical and cultural factor in West Africa, see J. Spencer Trimingham, *A History of Islam in West Africa* (1970).

THE RENAISSANCE IN EUROPE

Richard L. DeMolen, ed., *The Meaning of Renaissance and Reformation* (1974), is a collection of essays by experts on the Renaissance and Reformation, with maps and illustrations. Eugene Rice with Anthony Grafton, *The Foundations of Early Modern Europe*, 2nd ed. (1994), is the finest introduction to the contexts in which Renaissance or early modern literature was produced. Theodore K. Rabb,

Renaissance Lives: Portrait of an Age (2000), offers an illuminating perspective on key figures in the period. William Bouwsma, *A Usable Past: Essays in European Cultural History* (1990), especially the chapter "Anxiety and the Formation of Early Modern Culture," also offers illuminating perspectives on the intellectual character of the period. Constance Jordan, *Renaissance Feminism: Literary Texts and Political*

Models (1990), is a recommended study of the place of women in history and political thought. William Kerrigan and Gordon Braden, *The Idea of the Renaissance* (1989), offers a helpful and direct analysis of the critical construction of the Renaissance as a concept. Harry Berger Jr., *Second World and Green World: Studies in Renaissance Fiction-Making* (1988), especially the title essay, is a dense but recommended study of the aims of fiction making.

Miguel de Cervantes

William Byron, *Cervantes: A Biography* (1978), is thorough, Anthony J. Cascard, *The Cambridge Companion to Cervantes* (2002), is an indispensable guide to Cervantes and his works. Ruth El Saffar, ed., *Critical Essays on Cervantes* (1986), offers interesting essays by eminent scholars. Vladimir Nabokov, *Lectures on Don Quixote* (1983), presents an elegant engagement with Cervantes's fiction. More-technical studies can be found in Henry Higuera, *Eros and Empire: Politics and Christianity in Don Quijote* (1995); Thomas R. Hart, *Cervantes and Ariosto: Renewing Fiction* (1989); Howard Mancing, *The Chivalric World of Don Quijote: Style, Structure, and Narrative Techniques* (1982); Stephen Gilman, *The Novel According to Cervantes* (1980); and Ruth El Saffar, *Distance and Control: A Study in Narrative Technique* (1975).

Niccolò Machiavelli

Peter E. Bondanella focuses on the literary aspects of Machiavelli's works in *Machiavelli and the Art of Renaissance History* (1973). Sebastian De Grazia, *Machiavelli in Hell* (1989), on politics in *The Prince*, contains indexes and a bibliography. J. R. Hale's biography, *Machiavelli and Renaissance Italy* (1972), places Machiavelli in a historical perspective. A political analysis is provided by Anthony Parel, *The Political Calculus: Essays on Machiavelli's Political Philosophy* (1972). Roberto Ridolfi, *The Life of Niccolò Machiavelli* (1963), is still considered the best and most accurate biography. Silvia Ruffo-Fiore, *Niccolò Machiavelli* (1982), is a useful comprehensive guide for the beginning student. Victoria Kahn, *Machiavellian Rhetoric: From the Counter-Reformation to Milton* (1994); and Wayne A. Rebhorn, *Foxes and Lions: Machiavelli's Confidence Men* (1988), are recommended.

Michel de Montaigne

Hugo Friedrich, *Montaigne* (1991), is a careful historical study of the author. David Quint, *Montaigne and the Quality of Mercy* (1999), analyzes the rhetorical structure and political implications of Montaigne's famous essay on the Cannibals. Judith Shklar, *Ordinary Vices* (1984), and Edwin Duval, "Lessons of the New World: Design and Meaning in Montaigne's 'Des Cannibales' (1:31) and 'Des coches' (III:6)," in *Montaigne: Essays in Reading* (1983), ed. Gerard Defaux, *Yale French Studies* 64, provide excellent studies of Montaigne that include, but are not limited to, his New World contexts. Marcel Tetel, *Montaigne*, updated ed. (1990), and Richard Sayce, *The Essays of Montaigne: A Critical Exploration* (1972), are excellent introductions designed for the general reader.

Francis Petrarch

Ernest Hatch Wilkins's biography, *Life of Petrarch* (1961), is informative, but tends to take Petrarch's autobiographical writings at face value. In *The Poet as Philosopher* and *In Our Image and Likeness* (1970), Charles Trinkaus provides general studies of Petrarch and humanism. Robert Durling's introduction to *Petrarch's Lyric Poems* (1976) and Leonard Forster's essays in *The Icy Fire: Five Studies in European Petrarchism* (1969) are outstanding introductions to Petrarch's lyric poetry. Indispensable, if specialized, are Giuseppe Mazzotta, *The Worlds of Petrarch* (1993); Leonard Barkan, *The Gods Made Flesh: Metamorphosis and the Pursuit of Paganism* (1986); Thomas M. Greene, *The Light in Troy: Imitation and Discovery in Renaissance Poetry* (1982); Nancy Vickers, "Diana Described: Scattered Woman and Scattered Rhyme," in *Writing and Sexual Difference* (1982), ed. Elizabeth Abel; and John Freccero, "The Fig Tree and the Laurel: Petrarch's Poetics," *Literary Theory / Renaissance Text* (1986), ed. Patricia Parker and David Quint.

William Shakespeare

Anthony Burgess, *Shakespeare* (1970), is an informed and imaginative biography. William Schoenbaum. *William Shakespeare: A Compact Documentary Life* (1977), is the standard reference. On the theatrical companies and players, Muriel Bradbrook, *The Rise of the Common Player* (1964), and Andrew Gurr, *The Shakespearean Stage, 1574–1642*, 3rd ed. (1992), are recommended. *William Shakespeare's "Hamlet"* (1986), ed. Harold Bloom, contains some unconventional critical approaches. A biography placing Shakespeare in his social context is M. C. Bradbrook, *Shakespeare the Poet in His World* (1978), while E. K. Chambers, *William Shakespeare, A Study of Facts and Problems*, 2 vols. (1930), is considered the most fully documented biography. Paul Arthur Cantor, *Shakespeare, "Hamlet"* (1989), is an in-depth study of the tragedy. Arthur F. Kinney, *Hamlet: New Critical Essays* (2002), offers a useful guide. Valuable studies are to be found in Maynard Mack, "The World of *Hamlet*," *Yale Review* 41 (1952); Harry Levin, *The Question of "Hamlet"* (1959); and Janet Adelman, *Suffocating Mothers* (1992).

A Note on Translation

Reading literature in translation is a pleasure on which it is fruitless to frown. The purist may insist that we ought always read in the original languages, and we know ideally that this is true. But it is a counsel of perfection, quite impractical even for the purist, since no one in a lifetime can master all the languages whose literatures it would be a joy to explore. Master languages as fast as we may, we shall always have to read to some extent in translation, and this means we must be alert to what we are about: if in reading a work of literature in translation we are not reading the "original," what precisely are we reading? This is a question of great complexity, to which justice cannot be done in a brief note, but the following sketch of some of the considerations may be helpful.

One of the memorable scenes of ancient literature is the meeting of Hector and Andromache in book 6 of Homer's *Iliad*. Hector, leader and mainstay of the armies defending Troy, is implored by his wife, Andromache, to withdraw within the city walls and carry on the defense from there, where his life will not be constantly at hazard. In Homer's text her opening words to him are these: δαιμόνιε, φθίσει σε τὸ σὸν μένος (daimonie, phthisei se to son menos). How should they be translated into English?

Here is how they have actually been translated into English by capable translators, at various periods, in verse and prose:

1. George Chapman, 1598:

    O noblest in desire,
    Thy mind, inflamed with others' good, will set thy self on fire.

2. John Dryden, 1693:

    Thy dauntless heart (which I foresee too late),
    Too daring man, will urge thee to thy fate.

3. Alexander Pope, 1715:

    Too daring Prince! . . .
    For sure such courage length of life denies,
    And thou must fall, thy virtue's sacrifice.

4. William Cowper, 1791:

    Thy own great courage will cut short thy days,
    My noble Hector . . .

5. Lang, Leaf, and Myers, 1883 (prose):

    Dear my lord, this thy hardihood will undo thee. . . .

6. A. T. Murray, 1924 (prose):

    Ah, my husband, this prowess of thine will be thy doom. . . .

7. E. V. Rieu, 1950 (prose):

    "Hector," she said, "you are possessed. This bravery of yours will be your end."

8. I. A. Richards, 1950 (prose):

"Strange man," she said, "your courage will be your destruction."

9. Richmond Lattimore, 1951:

> Dearest,
> Your own great strength will be your death. . . .

10. Robert Fitzgerald, 1979:

> O my wild one, your bravery will be
> Your own undoing!

11. Robert Fagles, 1990:

> reckless one,
> Your own fiery courage will destroy you!

From these strikingly different renderings of the same six words, certain facts about the nature of translation begin to emerge. We notice, for one thing, that Homer's word μένος (menos) is diversified by the translators into "mind," "dauntless heart," "such courage," "great courage," "hardihood," "prowess," "bravery," "courage," "great strength," "bravery," and "fiery courage." The word has in fact all these possibilities. Used of things, it normally means "force"; of animals, "fierceness" or "brute strength" or (in the case of horses) "mettle"; of men and women, "passion" or "spirit" or even "purpose." Homer's application of it in the present case points our attention equally— whatever particular sense we may imagine Andromache to have uppermost—to Hector's force, strength, fierceness in battle, spirited heart and mind. But since English has no matching term of like inclusiveness, the passage as the translators give it to us reflects this lack and we find one attribute singled out to the exclusion of the rest.

Here then is the first and most crucial fact about any work of literature read in translation. It cannot escape the linguistic characteristics of the language into which it is turned: the grammatical, syntactical, lexical, and phonetic boundaries that constitute collectively the individuality or "genius" of that language. A Greek play or a Russian novel in English will be governed first of all by the resources of the English language, resources that are certain to be in every instance very different, as the efforts with μένος show, from those of the original.

Turning from μένος to δαιμόνιε (daimonie) in Homer's clause, we encounter a second crucial fact about translations. Nobody knows exactly what shade of meaning δαιμονιε had for Homer. In later writers the word normally suggests divinity, something miraculous, wondrous; but in Homer it appears as a vocative of address for both chieftain and commoner, man and wife. The coloring one gives it must, therefore, be determined either by the way one thinks a Greek wife of Homer's era might actually address her husband (a subject on which we have no information whatever) or in the way one thinks it suitable for a hero's wife to address her husband in an epic poem, that is to say, a highly stylized and formal work. In general, the translators of our century have abandoned formality to stress the intimacy; the wifeliness; and, especially in Lattimore's case, a certain chiding tenderness, in Andromache's appeal: (6) "Ah, my husband," (7) "Hector" (with perhaps a hint, in "you are possessed," of the alarmed distaste with which wives have so often viewed their husbands' bellicose moods), (8) "Strange man," (9) "Dearest," (10) "O my wild one" (mixing an almost motherly admiration with reproach and concern), and (11) "reckless one." On the other hand, the older translators have obviously removed Andromache to an epic or heroic distance from her beloved, whence she sees and kindles to his selfless courage, acknowledging, even in the moment of pleading with him to be otherwise, his moral grandeur and the tragic destiny this too certainly implies: (1) "O noblest in desire, . . . inflamed by others' good"; (2) "Thy dauntless heart (which I foresee too late), / Too daring man"; (3) "Too daring Prince! . . . / And thou must fall, thy virtue's sacrifice"; (4) "My noble Hector." Even the less specific "Dear my lord" of Lang, Leaf, and Myers looks in the same direction because of its echo of the speech of countless Shakespearean men and women who have shared this powerful moral sense: "Dear my lord, make me acquainted with your cause of grief"; "Perseverance, dear my lord, keeps honor bright"; etc.

The fact about translation that emerges from all this is that just as the translated work reflects the individuality of the language it is turned into, so it reflects the individuality of the age in which it is made, and the age will permeate it everywhere like yeast in dough. We think of one kind of permeation when we think of the governing verse forms and attitudes toward verse at a given epoch. In Chapman's time, experiments seeking an "heroic" verse form for English were widespread, and accordingly he tries a "fourteener" couplet (two rhymed lines of seven stresses each) in his *Iliad* and a pentameter couplet in his *Odyssey.* When Dryden and Pope wrote, a closed pentameter couplet had become established as the heroic form par excellence. By Cowper's day, thanks largely to the prestige of *Paradise Lost,* the couplet had gone out of fashion for narrative poetry in favor of blank verse. Our age, inclining to prose and in verse to proselike informalities and relaxations, has, predictably, produced half a dozen excellent prose translations of the *Iliad* but only three in verse (by Fagles, Lattimore, and Fitzgerald), all relying on rhythms that are much of the time closer to the verse of William Carlos Williams and some of the prose of novelists like Faulkner than to the swift firm tread of Homer's Greek. For if it is true that what we translate from a given work is what, wearing the spectacles of our time, we see in it, it is also true that we see in it what we have the power to translate.

Of course, there are other effects of the translator's epoch on a translation besides those exercised by contemporary taste in verse and verse forms. Chapman writes in a great age of poetic metaphor and, therefore, almost instinctively translates his understanding of Homer's verb φθίσει (phthisei, "to cause to wane, consume, waste, pine") into metaphorical terms of flame, presenting his Hector to us as a man of burning generosity who will be consumed by his very ardor. This is a conception rooted in large part in the psychology of the Elizabethans, who had the habit of speaking of the soul as "fire," of one of the four temperaments as "fiery," of even the more material bodily processes, like digestion, as if they were carried on by the heat of fire ("concoction," "decoction"). It is rooted too in that characteristic Renaissance élan so unforgettably expressed in characters such as Tamburlaine and Dr. Faustus, the former of whom exclaims to the stars above:

> . . . I, the chiefest lamp of all the earth,
> First rising in the East with mild aspect,
> But fixèd now in the meridian line,
> Will send up fire to your turning spheres,
> And cause the sun to borrow light of you. . . .

Pope and Dryden, by contrast, write to audiences for whom strong metaphor has become suspect. They, therefore, reject the fire image (which we must recall is not present in the Greek) in favor of a form of speech more congenial to their age, the *sententia* or aphorism, and give it extra vitality by making it the scene of a miniature drama: in Dryden's case, the hero's dauntless heart "urges" him (in the double sense of physical as well as moral pressure) to his fate; in Pope's, the hero's courage, like a judge, "denies" continuance of life, with the consequence that he "falls"—and here Pope's second line suggests analogy to the sacrificial animal—the victim of his own essential nature, of what he is.

To pose even more graphically the pressures that a translator's period brings, consider the following lines from Hector's reply to Andromache's appeal that he withdraw, first in Chapman's Elizabethan version, then in Lattimore's twentieth-century one:

Chapman, 1598:

> The spirit I did first breathe
> Did never teach me that—much less since the contempt of death
> Was settled in me, and my mind knew what a Worthy was,
> Whose office is to lead in fight and give no danger pass
> Without improvement. In this fire must Hector's trial shine.
> Here must his country, father, friends be in him made divine.

Lattimore, 1951:

> and the spirit will not let me, since I have learned to be valiant
> and to fight always among the foremost ranks of the Trojans,
> winning for my own self great glory, and for my father.

If one may exaggerate to make a necessary point, the world of Henry V and Othello suddenly gives way here to our own, a world whose discomfort with any form of heroic self-assertion is remarkably mirrored in the burial of Homer's key terms (*spirit, valiant, fight, foremost, glory*)—five out of twenty-two words in the original, five out of thirty-six in the translation—in a cushioning huddle of harmless sounds.

Besides the two factors so far mentioned (language and period) as affecting the character of a translation, there is inevitably a third—the translator, with a particular degree of talent; a personal way of regarding the work to be translated; a special hierarchy of values, moral, aesthetic, metaphysical (which may or may not be summed up in a "worldview"); and a unique style or lack of it. But this influence all readers are likely to bear in mind, and it needs no laboring here. That, for example, two translators of Hamlet, one a Freudian, the other a Jungian, will produce impressively different translations is obvious from the fact that when Freudian and Jungian argue about the play in English they often seem to have different plays in mind.

We can now return to the question from which we started. After all allowances have been made for language, age, and individual translator, is anything of the original left? What, in short, does the reader of translations read? Let it be said at once that in utility prose—prose whose function is mainly referential—the reader who reads a translation reads everything that matters. "Nicht Rauchen," "Défense de Fumer," and "No Smoking," posted in a railway car, make their point, and the differences between them in sound and form have no significance for us in that context. Since the prose of a treatise and of most fiction is preponderantly referential, we rightly feel, when we have paid close attention to Cervantes or Montaigne or Machiavelli or Tolstoy in a good English translation, that we have had roughly the same experience as a native Spaniard, Frenchman, Italian, or Russian. But *roughly* is the correct word; for good prose points iconically *to* itself as well as referentially beyond itself, and everything that it points to in itself in the original (rhythms, sounds, idioms, wordplay, etc.) must alter radically in being translated. The best analogy is to imagine a van Gogh painting reproduced in the medium of tempera, etching, or engraving: the "picture" remains, but the intricate interanimation of volumes with colorings with brushstrokes has disappeared.

When we move on to poetry, even in its longer narrative and dramatic forms—plays like *Oedipus,* poems like the *Iliad* or *The Divine Comedy*—our situation as English readers worsens appreciably, as the many unlike versions of Andromache's appeal to Hector make very clear. But, again, only appreciably. True, this is the point at which the fact that a translation is *always* an interpretation explodes irresistibly on our attention; but if it is the best translation of its time, like Robert Fagles's translation of the *Odyssey* for our time, the result will be not only a sensitive interpretation but also a work with intrinsic interest in its own right—at very best, a true work of art, a new poem. In these longer works, moreover, even if the translation is uninspired, many distinctive structural features—plot, setting, characters, meetings, partings, confrontations, and specific episodes generally—survive virtually unchanged. It is only when

the shorter, primarily lyrical forms of poetry are presented that the reader of translations faces insuperable disadvantage. In these forms, the referential aspect of language has a tendency to disappear into, or, more often, draw its real meaning and
accreditation from, the iconic aspect. Let us look for just a moment at a brief poem by
Federico García Lorca and its English translation (by Stephen Spender and J. L. Gili):

> ¡Alto pinar!
> Cuatro palomas por el aire van.
>
> Cuatro palomas
> vuelan y tornan.
> Llevan heridas
> sus cuatro sombras.
>
> ¡Bajo pinar!
> Cuatro palomas en la tierra están.
>
> the pine trees:
> Four pigeons go through the air.
>
> Four pigeons
> fly and turn round.
> They carry wounded
> their four shadows.
>
> Below the pine trees:
> Four pigeons lie on the earth.

In this translation the referential sense of the English words follows with remarkable exactness the referential sense of the Spanish words they replace. But the life of
Lorca's poem does not lie in that sense. It lies in such matters as the abruptness, like
an intake of breath at a sudden revelation, of the two exclamatory lines (1 and 7),
which then exhale musically in images of flight and death; or as the echoings of *palo-
mas* in *heridas* and *sombras*, bringing together (as in fact the hunter's gun has done)
these unrelated nouns and the unrelated experiences they stand for in a sequence
that seems, momentarily, to have all the logic of a tragic action, in which *doves*
become *wounds* become *shadows,* or as the external and internal rhyming among the
five verbs, as though all motion must (as in fact it must) end with *están.*

Since none of this can be brought over into another tongue (least of all Lorca's
rhythms), the translator must decide between leaving a reader to wonder why Lorca
is a poet to be bothered about at all and making a new but true poem, whose merit
will almost certainly be in inverse ratio to its likeness to the original. Samuel Johnson
made such a poem in translating Horace's famous *Diffugere nives,* and so did A. E.
Housman. If we juxtapose the last two stanzas of each translation, and the corresponding Latin, we can see at a glance that each has the consistency and inner life of
a genuine poem and that neither of them (even if we consider only what is obvious to
the eye, the line-lengths) is very close to Horace:

> Cum semel occideris, et de te splendida Minos
>   fecerit arbitria,
> non, Torquate, genus, non te facundia, non te
>   restituet pietas.
> Infernis neque enim tenebris Diana pudicum
>   liberat Hippolytum
> nec Lethaea valet Theseus abrumpere caro
>   vincula Pirithoo.

Johnson:

> Not you, Torquatus, boast of Rome,
> When Minos once has fixed your doom,
> Or eloquence, or splendid birth,
> Or virtue, shall restore to earth.
> Hippolytus, unjustly slain,
> Diana calls to life in vain;
> Nor can the might of Theseus rend
> The chains of hell that hold his friend.

Housman:

> When thou descendest once the shades among,
>   The stern assize and equal judgment o'er,
> Not thy long lineage nor thy golden tongue,
>   No, nor thy righteousness, shall friend thee more.
>
> Night holds Hippolytus the pure of stain,
>   Diana steads him nothing, he must stay;
> And Theseus leaves Pirithous in the chain
>   The love of comrades cannot take away.

The truth of the matter is that when the translator of short poems chooses to be literal, most or all of the poetry is lost; and when the translator succeeds in forging a new poetry, most or all of the original author is lost.

The best practical advice for those of us who must read poems in English translations is to focus intently on the images and dramatic scenes these poems evoke and ask ourselves what there is in them or in their effect on each other that produces each poem's particular electricity. To that extent, we can compensate for a part of our losses, learn something positive about the immense explosive powers of imagery, and rest easy in the secure knowledge that translation even in the mode of the short poem brings us (despite losses) closer to the work itself than not reading it at all. "To a thousand cavils," said Samuel Johnson, "one answer is sufficient; the purpose of a writer is to be read, and the criticism which would destroy the power of pleasing must be blown aside." Johnson was defending Pope's Homer for those marks of its own time and place that make it the great interpretation it is, but Johnson's exhilarating common sense applies equally to the problem we are considering here. Literature is to be read, and the criticism that would destroy the reader's power to make some form of contact with much of the world's great writing must indeed be blown aside.

MAYNARD MACK

Sophocles: *Oedipus the King* from THREE THEBAN PLAYS by Sophocles, trans. by Robert Fagles, copyright © 1982 by Robert Fagles. Used by permission of Viking Penguin, a division of Penguin Group (USA), Inc.

T'ao Ch'ien: "Biography of the Master Five Willows" is reprinted by permission of the publisher from REMEMBRANCES: THE EXPERIENCE OF THE PAST IN CLASSICAL CHINESE LITERATURE by Stephen Owen, pp. 84–85, Cambridge, Mass.: Harvard University Press, copyright © 1986 by the President and Fellows of Harvard College. From THE POETRY OF TAO CH'IEN (1970), ed. by James Hightower (trans.). By permission of Oxford University Press.

The Thousand and One Nights: From THE ARABIAN NIGHTS: THE THOUSAND AND ONE NIGHTS, trans. by Husain Haddawy. Copyright © 1990 by W. W. Norton & Company, Inc. Used by permission of W. W. Norton & Company, Inc. "The Third Old Man's Tale," trans. by Jerome M. Clinton. We have made diligent efforts to contact the copyright holder to obtain permission to reprint this selection. If you have information that would help us, please write to W. W. Norton & Company, Inc., 500 Fifth Ave., New York, NY 10110.

Tu Fu: From THE GREAT AGE OF CHINESE POETRY: THE HIGH TANG, trans. by Stephen Owen. Copyright © 1981 by Yale University Press. Reprinted by permission of Yale University Press. From AN ANTHOLOGY OF CHINESE LITERATURE: BEGINNINGS TO 1911, ed. and trans. by Stephen Owen. Copyright © 1996 by Stephen Owen and The Council for Cultural Planning and Development of the Executive Yuan of the Republic of China. Used by permission of W. W. Norton & Company, Inc.

Virgil: From THE AENEID, trans. by Robert Fitzgerald, translation copyright © 1980, 1982, 1983 by Robert Fitzgerald. Used by permission of Random House, Inc.

Visnusarman: From THE PANCATANTRA, ed. and trans. by Arthur W. Ryder. Copyright 1925 by University of Chicago, copyright renewed 1953 by Mary E. and Winifred Ryder. Reprinted by permission of University of Chicago Press.

Yuan Chen: "The Story of Ying-ying," trans. by James R. Hightower, from TRADITIONAL CHINESE STORIES: THEMES AND VARIATIONS, edited by Y. W. Ma and Joseph S. M. Lau, copyright © 1978 by Columbia University Press, is reprinted by permission of Joseph S. M. Lau.

Zeami Motokiyo: From THE NŌ PLAYS OF JAPAN, trans. by Arthur Waley (London: George Allen and Unwin, 1921). Copyright © by permission of The Arthur Waley Estate.

COLOR PLATES

Ajanta Cave temples, third–sixth century. Gupta period. Maharashtra, India. Photo: SEF / Art Resource, NY.

Anonymous. Babylonian epic of *Gilgamesh*, fifteenth century B.C., Israel Museum (IDAM), Jerusalem, Israel. Photo: Erich Lessing / Art Resource, NY.

Anonymous. *Canterbury Tales: Wife of Bath.* Ellesmere Manuscript (Facsimile Edition). Private Collection. Photo: Art Resource, NY.

Anonymous. *Dante, Virgil, and The Plague Stricken,* fourteenth century. Manuscript illumination from Dante's *Divine Comedy.* Venetian school. Biblioteca Marciana, Venice, Italy. Photo: Giraudon / Art Resource, NY.

Anonymous. *Iris Germanica (fleur-de-lis or bearded lily),* 987–990. Islamic, from Samarkand. Oriental Collection, State University Library, Leiden, The Netherlands. Photo: Werner Forman / Art Resource, NY.

Anonymous. A leaf from a Koran written in kufic script, ninth century, Abbasid dynasty. Iraq. Collection of Mrs. Bashir Mohamed, London. Photo: Werner Forman / Art Resource, NY.

Anonymous. Mask of Agamemnon, 1500 B.C., National Archaeological Museum, Athens, Greece. Photo: Nimatallah / Art Resource, NY.

Anonymous. Overhead view of terra-cotta soldiers, 259–210 B.C. Photo: Bettmann / Corbis.

Anonymous. *Portrait of Paquio Proculo and His wife (The Baker and His Wife),* 27 B.C.–A.D. 396. Museo Archeologico Nazionale. Photo: Scala / Art Resource, NY.

Cave number one of Ajanta Caves, wall painting of Vajrapani, 600–650, Gupta period. Maharashtra, India. Photo: Benoy K. Behl.

Clasp from the Sutton Hoo Ship Burial, 625–30. British Museum, London, UK. Photo: Bridgeman Art Library.

El Greco. *The nobleman, probably Don Juan de Silva, with his hand on his chest,* 1577–84. Museo del Prado, Madrid, Spain. Photo: Erich Lessing / Art Resource, NY.

Exterior view of Ajanta Cave Temples, third–sixth century. Gupta period. Maharashtra, India. Photo: Scala / Art Resource, NY.

Exterior view of the Dome of the Rock. Completed in 691. Islamic, Umayyad Caliphate. Jerusalem, Israel. Photo: Scala / Art Resource, NY.

Great Buddha, Todai-ji temple, 745–752. Nara, Japan. Photo: Werner Forman / Art Resource, NY.

Helmet from the Sutton Hoo Ship Burial, 625–30. British Museum, London, UK. Photo: Bridgeman Art Library.

Hans Holbein (the Younger). *The French Ambassadors of King Henry II at the Court of the English King Henry VIII*, 1533. National Gallery, London, Great Britain. Photo: Erich Lessing / Art Resource, NY.

Interior view of the Dome of the Rock. Built in 691 and restored in 810 and 913. Jerusalem, Israel. Photo: David Lees / Corbis.

Adrian Meyer. Detail of the East Torana at the Great Stupa at Sanchi. Sanchi, Madhya Pradesh, India. Photo: Edifice / Corbis.

Adrian Meyer. View from the Southwest of the Great Stupa at Sanchi, first century B.C.–first century A.D. Sanchi, India. Photo: Edifice / Corbis.

Jean Pragen. The Theatre of the Sanctuary of Asklepios at Epidaurus. Photo: Getty Images.

Terra-cotta figure of a man excavated in the Djenne / Mopti area, ca. thirteenth–fourteenth century. Mali. Entwistle Gallery, London, Great Britain. Photo: Werner Forman / Art Resource, NY.

Index